TABLE OF CONTENTS

PREFACE

The goal of the New International Version (NIV) is to enable English-speaking people from around the world to read and hear God's eternal Word in their own language. Our work as translators is motivated by our conviction that the Bible is God's Word in written form. We believe that the Bible contains the divine answer to the deepest needs of humanity, sheds unique light on our path in a dark world and sets forth the way to our eternal well-being. Out of these deep convictions, we have sought to recreate as far as possible the experience of the original audience — blending transparency to the original text with accessibility for the millions of English speakers around the world. We have prioritized accuracy, clarity and literary quality with the goal of creating a translation suitable for public and private reading, evangelism, teaching, preaching, memorizing and liturgical use. We have also sought to preserve a measure of continuity with the long tradition of translating the Scriptures into English.

The complete NIV Bible was first published in 1978. It was a completely new translation made by over a hundred scholars working directly from the best available Hebrew, Aramaic and Greek texts. The translators came from the United States, Great Britain, Canada, Australia and New Zealand, giving the translation an international scope. They were from many denominations and churches — including Anglican, Assemblies of God, Baptist, Brethren, Christian Reformed, Church of Christ, Evangelical Covenant, Evangelical Free, Lutheran, Mennonite, Methodist, Nazarene, Presbyterian, Wesleyan and others. This breadth of denominational and theological perspective helped to safeguard the translation from sectarian bias. For these reasons, and by the grace of God, the NIV has gained a wide readership in all parts of the English-speaking world.

The work of translating the Bible is never finished. As good as they are, English translations must be regularly updated so that they will continue to communicate accurately the meaning of God's Word. Updates are needed in order to reflect the latest developments in our understanding of the biblical world and its languages and to keep pace with changes in English usage. Recognizing, then, that the NIV would retain its ability to communicate God's Word accurately only if it were regularly updated, the original translators established the Committee on Bible Translation (CBT). The Committee is a self-perpetuating group of biblical scholars charged with keeping abreast of advances in biblical scholarship and changes in English and issuing periodic updates to the NIV. The CBT is an independent, self-governing body and has sole responsibility for the NIV text. The Committee mirrors the original group of translators in its diverse international and denominational makeup and in its unifying commitment to the Bible as God's inspired Word.

In obedience to its mandate, the Committee has issued periodic updates to the NIV. An initial revision was released in 1984. A more thorough revision process was completed in 2005, resulting in the separately published TNIV. The updated NIV you now have in your hands builds on both the original NIV and the TNIV and represents the latest effort of the Committee to articulate God's unchanging Word in the way the original authors might have said it had they been speaking in English to the global English-speaking audience today.

Translation Philosophy

The Committee's translating work has been governed by three widely accepted principles about the way people use words and about the way we understand them.

First, the meaning of words is determined by the way that users of the language actually use them at any given time. For the biblical languages, therefore, the Committee utilizes the best and most recent scholarship on the way Hebrew, Aramaic and Greek words were being used in biblical times. At the same time, the Committee carefully studies the state of modern English. Good translation is like good communication: one must know the target audience so that the appropriate choices can be made about which English words to use to represent the original words of Scripture. From its inception, the NIV has had as its target the general English-speaking population all over the world, the "International" in its title reflecting this concern. The aim of the Committee is to put the Scriptures into natural English that will communicate effectively with the broadest possible audience of English speakers.

Modern technology has enhanced the Committee's ability to choose the right English words to convey the meaning of the original text. The field of computational linguistics harnesses the power of computers to provide broadly applicable and current data about the state of the language. Translators can now access huge databases of modern English to better understand the current meaning and usage of key words. The Committee utilized this resource in preparing the 2011 edition of the NIV. An area of especially rapid and significant change in English is the way certain nouns and pronouns are used to refer to human beings. The Committee therefore requested experts in computational linguistics at Collins Dictionaries to pose some key questions about this usage to its database of English — the largest in the world, with over 4.4 billion words, gathered from several English-speaking countries and including both spoken and written English. (The Collins Study, called "The Development and Use of Gender Language in Contemporary English," can be accessed at *http://www.thenivbible.com/about-the-niv/about-the-2011-edition/.*) The study revealed that the most popular words to describe the human race in modern U.S. English were "humanity," "man" and "mankind." The Committee then used this data in the updated NIV, choosing from among these three words (and occasionally others also) depending on the context.

A related issue creates a larger problem for modern translations: the move away from using the third-person masculine singular pronouns — "he/him/his" — to refer to men and women equally. This usage does persist in some forms of English, and this revision therefore occasionally uses these pronouns in a generic sense. But the tendency, recognized in day-to-day usage and confirmed by the Collins study, is away from the generic use of "he," "him" and "his." In recognition of this shift in language and in an effort to translate into the natural English that people are actually using, this revision of the NIV generally uses other constructions when the biblical text is plainly addressed to men and women equally. The reader will encounter especially frequently a "they," "their" or "them" to express a generic singular idea. Thus, for instance, Mark 8:36 reads: "What good is it for someone to gain the whole world, yet forfeit their soul?" This generic use of the "distributive" or "singular" "they/them/their" has been used for many centuries by respected writers of English and has now become established as standard English, spoken and written, all over the world.

A second linguistic principle that feeds into the Committee's translation work is that meaning is found not in individual words, as vital as they are, but in larger clusters: phrases, clauses, sentences, discourses. Translation is not, as many people think, a matter of word substitution: English word *x* in place of Hebrew word *y*. Translators must first determine the meaning of the words of the biblical languages in the context of the passage and then select English words that accurately communicate that meaning to modern listeners and readers. This means that accurate translation will not always reflect the exact structure of the original language. To be sure, there is debate over the degree to which translators should try to preserve the "form" of the original text in English. From the beginning, the NIV has taken a mediating position on this issue. The manual produced when the translation that became the NIV was first being planned states: "If the Greek or Hebrew syntax has a good parallel in modern English, it should be used. But if there is no good parallel, the English syntax appropriate to the meaning of the original is to be chosen." It is fine, in other words, to carry over the form of the biblical languages into English — but not at the expense of natural expression. The principle that meaning resides in larger clusters of words means that the Committee has not insisted on a "word-for-word" approach to translation. We certainly believe that every word of Scripture is inspired by God and therefore to be carefully studied to determine what God is saying to us. It is for this reason that the Committee labors over every single word of the original texts, working hard to determine how each of those words contributes to what the text is saying. Ultimately, however, it is how these individual words function in combination with other words that determines meaning.

A third linguistic principle guiding the Committee in its translation work is the recognition that words have a spectrum of meaning. It is popular to define a word by using another word, or "gloss," to substitute for it. This substitute word is then sometimes called the "literal" meaning of a word. In fact, however, words have a range of possible meanings. Those meanings will vary depending on the context, and words in one language will usually not occupy the same semantic range as words in another language. The Committee therefore studies each original word of Scripture in its context to identify its meaning in a particular verse and then chooses an appropriate English word (or phrase) to represent it. It is impossible, then, to translate any given Hebrew, Aramaic or Greek word with the same English word all the time. The Committee does try to translate related occurrences of a word in the original languages with the same English word in order to preserve the connection for the English reader. But the Committee generally privileges clear natural meaning over a concern with consistency in rendering particular words.

Textual Basis

For the Old Testament the standard Hebrew text, the Masoretic Text as published in the latest edition of *Biblia Hebraica*, has been used throughout. The Masoretic Text tradition contains marginal notations that offer variant readings. These have sometimes been followed instead of the text itself. Because such instances involve variants within the Masoretic tradition, they have not been indicated in the textual notes. In a few cases, words in the basic consonantal text have been divided differently than in the Masoretic Text. Such cases are usually indicated in the textual footnotes. The Dead Sea Scrolls contain biblical texts that represent an earlier stage of the transmission of the Hebrew text. They have been consulted, as have been the Samaritan Pentateuch and the ancient scribal traditions concerning deliberate textual changes. The translators also consulted the more important early versions. Readings from these versions, the Dead Sea Scrolls and the scribal traditions were occasionally followed where the Masoretic Text seemed doubtful and where accepted principles of textual criticism showed that one or more of these textual witnesses appeared to provide the correct reading. In rare cases, the translators have emended the Hebrew text where it appears to have become corrupted at an even earlier stage of its transmission. These departures from the Masoretic Text are also indicated in the textual footnotes. Sometimes the vowel indicators (which are later additions to the basic consonantal text) found in the Masoretic Text did not, in the judgment of the translators, represent the correct vowels for the original text. Accordingly, some words have been read with a different set of vowels. These instances are usually not indicated in the footnotes.

The Greek text used in translating the New Testament has been an eclectic one, based on the latest editions of the Nestle-Aland/United Bible Societies' Greek New Testament.

The translators have made their choices among the variant readings in accordance with widely accepted principles of New Testament textual criticism. Footnotes call attention to places where uncertainty remains.

The New Testament authors, writing in Greek, often quote the Old Testament from its ancient Greek version, the Septuagint. This is one reason why some of the Old Testament quotations in the NIV New Testament are not identical to the corresponding passages in the NIV Old Testament. Such quotations in the New Testament are indicated with the footnote "(see Septuagint)."

Footnotes and Formatting

Footnotes in this version are of several kinds, most of which need no explanation. Those giving alternative translations begin with "Or" and generally introduce the alternative with the last word preceding it in the text, except when it is a single-word alternative. When poetry is quoted in a footnote a slash mark indicates a line division.

It should be noted that references to diseases, minerals, flora and fauna, architectural details, clothing, jewelry, musical instruments and other articles cannot always be identified with precision. Also, linear measurements and measures of capacity can only be approximated (see the Table of Weights and Measures). Although *Selah*, used mainly in the Psalms, is probably a musical term, its meaning is uncertain. Since it may interrupt reading and distract the reader, this word has not been kept in the English text, but every occurrence has been signaled by a footnote.

As an aid to the reader, sectional headings have been inserted. They are not to be regarded as part of the biblical text and are not intended for oral reading. It is the Committee's hope that these headings may prove more helpful to the reader than the traditional chapter divisions, which were introduced long after the Bible was written.

Sometimes the chapter and/or verse numbering in English translations of the Old Testament differs from that found in published Hebrew texts. This is particularly the case in the Psalms, where the traditional titles are included in the Hebrew verse numbering. Such differences are indicated in the footnotes at the bottom of the page. In the New Testament, verse numbers that marked off portions of the traditional English text not supported by the best Greek manuscripts now appear in brackets, with a footnote indicating the text that has been omitted (see, for example, Matthew 17:[21]).

Mark 16:9–20 and John 7:53 — 8:11, although long accorded virtually equal status with the rest of the Gospels in which they stand, have a questionable standing in the textual history of the New Testament, as noted in the bracketed annotations with which they are set off. A different typeface has been chosen for these passages to indicate their uncertain status.

Basic formatting of the text, such as lining the poetry, paragraphing (both prose and poetry), setting up of (administrative-like) lists, indenting letters and lengthy prayers within narratives and the insertion of sectional headings, has been the work of the Committee. However, the choice between single-column and double-column formats has been left to the publishers. Also the issuing of "red-letter" editions is a publisher's choice — one that the Committee does not endorse.

The Committee has again been reminded that every human effort is flawed — including this revision of the NIV. We trust, however, that many will find in it an improved representation of the Word of God, through which they hear his call to faith in our Lord Jesus Christ and to service in his kingdom. We offer this version of the Bible to him in whose name and for whose glory it has been made.

The Committee on Bible Translation

PRESENTED

TO

BY

ON

BUILDING FAITH, WISDOM AND STRENGTH

NEW INTERNATIONAL VERSION

NIV BIBLE FOR TEEN GUYS

BUILDING FAITH, WISDOM AND STRENGTH

ZONDERVAN®

Library of Congress Catalog Card Number 2016935577

16 17 18 19 20 21 22 23 24 25 26 27 28 29 30/DSC/15 14 13 12 11 10 9 8 7 6 5 4 3 2 1

A portion of the purchase price of your NIV® Bible is provided to Biblica so together we support the mission of *transforming lives through God's Word.*

Biblica provides God's Word to people through translation, publishing and Bible engagement in Africa, Asia Pacific, Europe, Latin America, Middle East and North America. Through its worldwide reach, Biblica engages people with God's Word so that their lives are transformed through a relationship with Jesus Christ.

TABLE OF CONTENTS

PREFACE

The goal of the New International Version (NIV) is to enable English-speaking people from around the world to read and hear God's eternal Word in their own language. Our work as translators is motivated by our conviction that the Bible is God's Word in written form. We believe that the Bible contains the divine answer to the deepest needs of humanity, sheds unique light on our path in a dark world and sets forth the way to our eternal well-being. Out of these deep convictions, we have sought to recreate as far as possible the experience of the original audience — blending transparency to the original text with accessibility for the millions of English speakers around the world. We have prioritized accuracy, clarity and literary quality with the goal of creating a translation suitable for public and private reading, evangelism, teaching, preaching, memorizing and liturgical use. We have also sought to preserve a measure of continuity with the long tradition of translating the Scriptures into English.

The complete NIV Bible was first published in 1978. It was a completely new translation made by over a hundred scholars working directly from the best available Hebrew, Aramaic and Greek texts. The translators came from the United States, Great Britain, Canada, Australia and New Zealand, giving the translation an international scope. They were from many denominations and churches — including Anglican, Assemblies of God, Baptist, Brethren, Christian Reformed, Church of Christ, Evangelical Covenant, Evangelical Free, Lutheran, Mennonite, Methodist, Nazarene, Presbyterian, Wesleyan and others. This breadth of denominational and theological perspective helped to safeguard the translation from sectarian bias. For these reasons, and by the grace of God, the NIV has gained a wide readership in all parts of the English-speaking world.

The work of translating the Bible is never finished. As good as they are, English translations must be regularly updated so that they will continue to communicate accurately the meaning of God's Word. Updates are needed in order to reflect the latest developments in our understanding of the biblical world and its languages and to keep pace with changes in English usage. Recognizing, then, that the NIV would retain its ability to communicate God's Word accurately only if it were regularly updated, the original translators established the Committee on Bible Translation (CBT). The Committee is a self-perpetuating group of biblical scholars charged with keeping abreast of advances in biblical scholarship and changes in English and issuing periodic updates to the NIV. The CBT is an independent, self-governing body and has sole responsibility for the NIV text. The Committee mirrors the original group of translators in its diverse international and denominational makeup and in its unifying commitment to the Bible as God's inspired Word.

In obedience to its mandate, the Committee has issued periodic updates to the NIV. An initial revision was released in 1984. A more thorough revision process was completed in 2005, resulting in the separately published TNIV. The updated NIV you now have in your hands builds on both the original NIV and the TNIV and represents the latest effort of the Committee to articulate God's unchanging Word in the way the original authors might have said it had they been speaking in English to the global English-speaking audience today.

Translation Philosophy

The Committee's translating work has been governed by three widely accepted principles about the way people use words and about the way we understand them.

First, the meaning of words is determined by the way that users of the language actually use them at any given time. For the biblical languages, therefore, the Committee utilizes the best and most recent scholarship on the way Hebrew, Aramaic and Greek words were being used in biblical times. At the same time, the Committee carefully studies the state of modern English. Good translation is like good communication: one must know the target audience so that the appropriate choices can be made about which English words to use to represent the original words of Scripture. From its inception, the NIV has had as its target the general English-speaking population all over the world, the "International" in its title reflecting this concern. The aim of the Committee is to put the Scriptures into natural English that will communicate effectively with the broadest possible audience of English speakers.

Modern technology has enhanced the Committee's ability to choose the right English words to convey the meaning of the original text. The field of computational linguistics harnesses the power of computers to provide broadly applicable and current data about the state of the language. Translators can now access huge databases of modern English to better understand the current meaning and usage of key words. The Committee utilized this resource in preparing the 2011 edition of the NIV. An area of especially rapid and significant change in English is the way certain nouns and pronouns are used to refer to human beings. The Committee therefore requested experts in computational linguistics at Collins Dictionaries to pose some key questions about this usage to its database of English — the largest in the world, with over 4.4 billion words, gathered from several English-speaking countries and including both spoken and written English. (The Collins Study, called "The Development and Use of Gender Language in Contemporary English," can be accessed at *http://www.thenivbible.com/about-the-niv/about-the-2011-edition/*.) The study revealed that the most popular words to describe the human race in modern U.S. English were "humanity," "man" and "mankind." The Committee then used this data in the updated NIV, choosing from among these three words (and occasionally others also) depending on the context.

A related issue creates a larger problem for modern translations: the move away from using the third-person masculine singular pronouns — "he/him/his" — to refer to men and women equally. This usage does persist in some forms of English, and this revision therefore occasionally uses these pronouns in a generic sense. But the tendency, recognized in day-to-day usage and confirmed by the Collins study, is away from the generic use of "he," "him" and "his." In recognition of this shift in language and in an effort to translate into the natural English that people are actually using, this revision of the NIV generally uses other constructions when the biblical text is plainly addressed to men and women equally. The reader will encounter especially frequently a "they," "their" or "them" to express a generic singular idea. Thus, for instance, Mark 8:36 reads: "What good is it for someone to gain the whole world, yet forfeit their soul?" This generic use of the "distributive" or "singular" "they/them/their" has been used for many centuries by respected writers of English and has now become established as standard English, spoken and written, all over the world.

A second linguistic principle that feeds into the Committee's translation work is that meaning is found not in individual words, as vital as they are, but in larger clusters: phrases, clauses, sentences, discourses. Translation is not, as many people think, a matter of word substitution: English word *x* in place of Hebrew word *y*. Translators must first determine the meaning of the words of the biblical languages in the context of the passage and then select English words that accurately communicate that meaning to modern listeners and readers. This means that accurate translation will not always reflect the exact structure of the original language. To be sure, there is debate over the degree to which translators should try to preserve the "form" of the original text in English. From the beginning, the NIV has taken a mediating position on this issue. The manual produced when the translation that became the NIV was first being planned states: "If the Greek or Hebrew syntax has a good parallel in modern English, it should be used. But if there is no good parallel, the English syntax appropriate to the meaning of the original is to be chosen." It is fine, in other words, to carry over the form of the biblical languages into English — but not at the expense of natural expression. The principle that meaning resides in larger clusters of words means that the Committee has not insisted on a "word-for-word" approach to translation. We certainly believe that every word of Scripture is inspired by God and therefore to be carefully studied to determine what God is saying to us. It is for this reason that the Committee labors over every single word of the original texts, working hard to determine how each of those words contributes to what the text is saying. Ultimately, however, it is how these individual words function in combination with other words that determines meaning.

A third linguistic principle guiding the Committee in its translation work is the recognition that words have a spectrum of meaning. It is popular to define a word by using another word, or "gloss," to substitute for it. This substitute word is then sometimes called the "literal" meaning of a word. In fact, however, words have a range of possible meanings. Those meanings will vary depending on the context, and words in one language will usually not occupy the same semantic range as words in another language. The Committee therefore studies each original word of Scripture in its context to identify its meaning in a particular verse and then chooses an appropriate English word (or phrase) to represent it. It is impossible, then, to translate any given Hebrew, Aramaic or Greek word with the same English word all the time. The Committee does try to translate related occurrences of a word in the original languages with the same English word in order to preserve the connection for the English reader. But the Committee generally privileges clear natural meaning over a concern with consistency in rendering particular words.

Textual Basis

For the Old Testament the standard Hebrew text, the Masoretic Text as published in the latest edition of *Biblia Hebraica*, has been used throughout. The Masoretic Text tradition contains marginal notations that offer variant readings. These have sometimes been followed instead of the text itself. Because such instances involve variants within the Masoretic tradition, they have not been indicated in the textual notes. In a few cases, words in the basic consonantal text have been divided differently than in the Masoretic Text. Such cases are usually indicated in the textual footnotes. The Dead Sea Scrolls contain biblical texts that represent an earlier stage of the transmission of the Hebrew text. They have been consulted, as have been the Samaritan Pentateuch and the ancient scribal traditions concerning deliberate textual changes. The translators also consulted the more important early versions. Readings from these versions, the Dead Sea Scrolls and the scribal traditions were occasionally followed where the Masoretic Text seemed doubtful and where accepted principles of textual criticism showed that one or more of these textual witnesses appeared to provide the correct reading. In rare cases, the translators have emended the Hebrew text where it appears to have become corrupted at an even earlier stage of its transmission. These departures from the Masoretic Text are also indicated in the textual footnotes. Sometimes the vowel indicators (which are later additions to the basic consonantal text) found in the Masoretic Text did not, in the judgment of the translators, represent the correct vowels for the original text. Accordingly, some words have been read with a different set of vowels. These instances are usually not indicated in the footnotes.

The Greek text used in translating the New Testament has been an eclectic one, based on the latest editions of the Nestle-Aland/United Bible Societies' Greek New Testament.

The translators have made their choices among the variant readings in accordance with widely accepted principles of New Testament textual criticism. Footnotes call attention to places where uncertainty remains.

The New Testament authors, writing in Greek, often quote the Old Testament from its ancient Greek version, the Septuagint. This is one reason why some of the Old Testament quotations in the NIV New Testament are not identical to the corresponding passages in the NIV Old Testament. Such quotations in the New Testament are indicated with the footnote "(see Septuagint)."

Footnotes and Formatting

Footnotes in this version are of several kinds, most of which need no explanation. Those giving alternative translations begin with "Or" and generally introduce the alternative with the last word preceding it in the text, except when it is a single-word alternative. When poetry is quoted in a footnote a slash mark indicates a line division.

It should be noted that references to diseases, minerals, flora and fauna, architectural details, clothing, jewelry, musical instruments and other articles cannot always be identified with precision. Also, linear measurements and measures of capacity can only be approximated (see the Table of Weights and Measures). Although *Selah*, used mainly in the Psalms, is probably a musical term, its meaning is uncertain. Since it may interrupt reading and distract the reader, this word has not been kept in the English text, but every occurrence has been signaled by a footnote.

As an aid to the reader, sectional headings have been inserted. They are not to be regarded as part of the biblical text and are not intended for oral reading. It is the Committee's hope that these headings may prove more helpful to the reader than the traditional chapter divisions, which were introduced long after the Bible was written.

Sometimes the chapter and/or verse numbering in English translations of the Old Testament differs from that found in published Hebrew texts. This is particularly the case in the Psalms, where the traditional titles are included in the Hebrew verse numbering. Such differences are indicated in the footnotes at the bottom of the page. In the New Testament, verse numbers that marked off portions of the traditional English text not supported by the best Greek manuscripts now appear in brackets, with a footnote indicating the text that has been omitted (see, for example, Matthew 17:[21]).

Mark 16:9-20 and John 7:53 — 8:11, although long accorded virtually equal status with the rest of the Gospels in which they stand, have a questionable standing in the textual history of the New Testament, as noted in the bracketed annotations with which they are set off. A different typeface has been chosen for these passages to indicate their uncertain status.

Basic formatting of the text, such as lining the poetry, paragraphing (both prose and poetry), setting up of (administrative-like) lists, indenting letters and lengthy prayers within narratives and the insertion of sectional headings, has been the work of the Committee. However, the choice between single-column and double-column formats has been left to the publishers. Also the issuing of "red-letter" editions is a publisher's choice — one that the Committee does not endorse.

The Committee has again been reminded that every human effort is flawed — including this revision of the NIV. We trust, however, that many will find in it an improved representation of the Word of God, through which they hear his call to faith in our Lord Jesus Christ and to service in his kingdom. We offer this version of the Bible to him in whose name and for whose glory it has been made.

The Committee on Bible Translation

THE

OLD

TESTAMENT

GENESIS

WHEN DID THIS HAPPEN?
About 2166–1406 B.C.

WHO IS IN THIS BOOK?

Adam and Eve
Cain and Abel
Noah
Abraham
Sarah
Ishmael
Lot
Isaac
Rebekah
Esau
Jacob
Rachel
Laban
Joseph

VERSES YOU MIGHT RECOGNIZE

GENESIS 1:1
"In the beginning God created the heavens and the earth."

GENESIS 12:2
"I will make you into a great nation, and I will bless you; I will make your name great, and you will be a blessing."

WHAT'S IT ABOUT?

enesis means "beginning," so it's a fitting title for the first book of the Bible. This book recounts how God created the world and began a relationship with the very first people—Adam and Eve. At first the world was perfect, just like its Creator, and humans, who were created in God's image, shared a special relationship with him. When Adam and Eve chose to disobey God, sin separated them from him and warped their perspective.

In order to restore a relationship with humanity, God made a covenant with Abraham, whose descendants would become his chosen people—Israel. He promised Abraham that through his children all nations everywhere would be blessed. You'll find many familiar stories in Genesis, including that of the creation of the world, the fall of humanity through sin, and the flood. In this book, you will begin to see God's great story unfold. When the first people sin, God already has a plan to save them from their sin through the sacrifice of his Son.

GENESIS

The Beginning

1 In the beginning God created the heavens and the earth. ²Now the earth was formless and empty, darkness was over the surface of the deep, and the Spirit of God was hovering over the waters.

³And God said, "Let there be light," and there was light. ⁴God saw that the light was good, and he separated the light from the darkness. ⁵God called the light "day," and the darkness he called "night." And there was evening, and there was morning—the first day.

⁶And God said, "Let there be a vault between the waters to separate water from water." ⁷So God made the vault and separated the water under the vault from the water above it. And it was so. ⁸God called the vault "sky." And there was evening, and there was morning—the second day.

⁹And God said, "Let the water under the sky be gathered to one place, and let dry ground appear." And it was so. ¹⁰God called the dry ground "land," and the gathered waters he called "seas." And God saw that it was good.

¹¹Then God said, "Let the land produce vegetation: seed-bearing plants and trees on the land that bear fruit with seed in it, according to their various kinds." And it was so. ¹²The land produced vegetation: plants bearing seed according to their kinds and trees bearing fruit with seed in it according to their kinds. And God saw that it was good. ¹³And there was evening, and there was morning—the third day.

¹⁴And God said, "Let there be lights in the vault of the sky to separate the day from the night, and let them serve as signs to mark sacred times, and days and years, ¹⁵and let them be lights in the vault of the sky to give light on the earth." And it was so. ¹⁶God made two great lights—the greater light to govern the day and the lesser light to govern the night. He also made the stars. ¹⁷God set them in the vault of the sky to give light on the earth, ¹⁸to govern the day and the night, and to separate light from darkness. And God saw that it was good. ¹⁹And there was evening, and there was morning—the fourth day.

²⁰And God said, "Let the water teem with living creatures, and let birds fly above the earth across the vault of the sky." ²¹So God created the great creatures of the sea and every living thing with which the water teems and that moves about in it, according to their kinds, and every winged bird according to its kind. And God saw that it was good. ²²God blessed them and said, "Be fruitful and increase in number and fill the water in the seas, and let the birds increase on the earth." ²³And there was evening, and there was morning—the fifth day.

²⁴And God said, "Let the land produce living creatures according to their kinds: the livestock, the creatures that move along the ground, and the wild animals, each according to its kind." And it was so. ²⁵God made the wild animals according to their kinds, the livestock according to their kinds, and all the creatures that move along the ground according to their kinds. And God saw that it was good.

²⁶Then God said, "Let us make mankind in our image, in our likeness, so that they may rule over the fish in the sea and the birds in the sky, over the livestock and all the wild animals,ᵃ and over all the creatures that move along the ground."

ᵃ 26 Probable reading of the original Hebrew text (see Syriac); Masoretic Text *the earth*

PERFECT SCULPTURE

READ: GENESIS 1:1

I t's tough to wrap your head around the start of everything. But the Genesis account of the world's beginnings is more than a tale of distant history. It's more than a reason to debate with modern scientific theory. The first chapters of the Bible tell why you exist.

Suppose you make a clay sculpture in art class. Suddenly you hold in your hands an object that belongs uniquely to you. Because you made it, you own it. When God created the world, he instantly became master of all his handiwork. Psalm 24:1-2 says, "The earth is the LORD's, and everything in it, the world, and all who live in it; for he founded it on the seas and established it on the waters." The world belongs completely to God.

You might never be satisfied with what you shape from a lump of clay. But God was incredibly pleased when he made people. First he dreamed up our design. He determined our purpose. He thought of everything humans need for a happy existence. Then he went to work. He put us in the most perfect place ever. He made us partners with each other and gave us solid work to do. Because we belong to him, he expects us to follow his commands.

So why did God make you? He created you to enjoy life close to him—and to people.

BUILDING FAITH WISDOM STRENGTH

²⁷So God created mankind in his own
image,
in the image of God he created them;
male and female he created them.

²⁸God blessed them and said to
them, "Be fruitful and increase in number; fill the earth and subdue it. Rule
over the fish in the sea and the birds in
the sky and over every living creature
that moves on the ground."

²⁹Then God said, "I give you every seed-bearing plant on the face of
the whole earth and every tree that
has fruit with seed in it. They will be
yours for food. ³⁰And to all the beasts
of the earth and all the birds in the sky
and all the creatures that move along
the ground—everything that has the
breath of life in it—I give every green
plant for food." And it was so.

³¹God saw all that he had made, and
it was very good. And there was evening, and there was morning—the
sixth day.

2   Thus the heavens and the earth were
completed in all their vast array.

²By the seventh day God had finished the
work he had been doing; so on the seventh day he rested from all his work.
³Then God blessed the seventh day
and made it holy, because on it he rested from all the work of creating that he
had done.

Adam and Eve

⁴This is the account of the heavens and
the earth when they were created, when the
Lord God made the earth and the heavens.

⁵Now no shrub had yet appeared on the
earthᵃ and no plant had yet sprung up, for
the Lord God had not sent rain on the earth
and there was no one to work the ground,
⁶but streamsᵇ came up from the earth and
watered the whole surface of the ground.
⁷Then the Lord God formed a manᶜ from
the dust of the ground and breathed into his
nostrils the breath of life, and the man became a living being.

⁸Now the Lord God had planted a garden in the east, in Eden; and there he put the
man he had formed. ⁹The Lord God made
all kinds of trees grow out of the ground—
trees that were pleasing to the eye and good
for food. In the middle of the garden were the
tree of life and the tree of the knowledge of
good and evil.

¹⁰A river watering the garden flowed from
Eden; from there it was separated into four
headwaters. ¹¹The name of the first is the
Pishon; it winds through the entire land of
Havilah, where there is gold. ¹²(The gold of
that land is good; aromatic resinᵈ and onyx
are also there.) ¹³The name of the second river is the Gihon; it winds through the entire
land of Cush.ᵉ ¹⁴The name of the third river is the Tigris; it runs along the east side of
Ashur. And the fourth river is the Euphrates.

¹⁵The Lord God took the man and put
him in the Garden of Eden to work it and take
care of it. ¹⁶And the Lord God commanded
the man, "You are free to eat from any tree in
the garden; ¹⁷but you must not eat from the
tree of the knowledge of good and evil, for
when you eat from it you will certainly die."

¹⁸The Lord God said, "It is not good for
the man to be alone. I will make a helper
suitable for him."

¹⁹Now the Lord God had formed out of
the ground all the wild animals and all the
birds in the sky. He brought them to the man
to see what he would name them; and whatever the man called each living creature,
that was its name. ²⁰So the man gave names
to all the livestock, the birds in the sky and
all the wild animals.

But for Adamᶠ no suitable helper was
found. ²¹So the Lord God caused the man
to fall into a deep sleep; and while he was
sleeping, he took one of the man's ribsᵍ and
then closed up the place with flesh. ²²Then
the Lord God made a woman from the ribʰ
he had taken out of the man, and he brought
her to the man.

²³The man said,

"This is now bone of my bones
and flesh of my flesh;
she shall be called 'woman,'
for she was taken out of man."

ᵃ 5 Or *land*; also in verse 6   ᵇ 6 Or *mist*   ᶜ 7 The Hebrew for *man (adam)* sounds like and may be
related to the Hebrew for *ground (adamah)*; it is also the name *Adam* (see verse 20).   ᵈ 12 Or *good;
pearls*   ᵉ 13 Possibly southeast Mesopotamia   ᶠ 20 Or *the man*   ᵍ 21 Or *took part of the man's side*
ʰ 22 Or *part*

6 | GENESIS 2:24

ADAM

The Lᴏʀᴅ God formed a man from the dust of the ground and breathed into his nostrils the breath of life, and the man became a living being. GENESIS 2:7

HIS NAME MEANS: "of the ground," "taken out of the red earth"

READ HIS STORY: *Genesis 1:26–3:24*

OF THE BIBLE

I magine being the first man on earth. You're walking through a beautiful garden when a golden beast catches your eye. The great cat sleeps in the sun. "Look at that thing lyin' around," you say to yourself. And the name sticks!

After God breathed life into Adam, the Lord brought all the animals to him to name (Genesis 2:19). Human beings were the crowning achievement of creation. While God saw everything he made as *good*, after creating humankind, "God saw all that he had made, and it was very good" (Genesis 1:31).

God put Adam in the Garden of Eden and gave him clear instructions: "You are free to eat from any tree in the garden; but you must not eat from the tree of the knowledge of good and evil" (Genesis 2:16–17). Most of us know what happened next: God saw that man shouldn't be alone, so he created Eve; Eve encountered a smooth-talking serpent; Eve ate the forbidden fruit.

Illustrations of this tragic scene normally show Eve alone being tempted by Satan. But here's the truth—Adam was right there with her. Genesis 3:6 says, "She took some and ate it. She also gave some to her husband, who was with her, and he ate it." Adam wasn't out naming animals or hunting down dinner. He could've taken the fruit away from Eve before it touched her lips. Even better, he could've grabbed a stick and stabbed the serpent until its forked tongue lay limp. Instead, Adam did nothing and said nothing as sin entered the world.

²⁴That is why a man leaves his father and mother and is united to his wife, and they become one flesh.

²⁵Adam and his wife were both naked, and they felt no shame.

The Fall

3 Now the serpent was more crafty than any of the wild animals the LORD God had made. He said to the woman, "Did God really say, 'You must not eat from any tree in the garden'?"

²The woman said to the serpent, "We may eat fruit from the trees in the garden, ³but God did say, 'You must not eat fruit from the tree that is in the middle of the garden, and you must not touch it, or you will die.'"

⁴"You will not certainly die," the serpent said to the woman. ⁵"For God knows that when you eat from it your eyes will be opened, and you will be like God, knowing good and evil."

⁶When the woman saw that the fruit of the tree was good for food and pleasing to the eye, and also desirable for gaining wisdom, she took some and ate it. She also gave some to her husband, who was with her, and he ate it. ⁷Then the eyes of both of them were opened, and they realized they were naked; so they sewed fig leaves together and made coverings for themselves.

⁸Then the man and his wife heard the sound of the LORD God as he was walking in the garden in the cool of the day, and they hid from the LORD God among the trees of the garden. ⁹But the LORD God called to the man, "Where are you?"

¹⁰He answered, "I heard you in the garden, and I was afraid because I was naked; so I hid."

¹¹And he said, "Who told you that you were naked? Have you eaten from the tree that I commanded you not to eat from?"

¹²The man said, "The woman you put here with me — she gave me some fruit from the tree, and I ate it."

¹³Then the LORD God said to the woman, "What is this you have done?"

The woman said, "The serpent deceived me, and I ate."

¹⁴So the LORD God said to the serpent, "Because you have done this,

"Cursed are you above all livestock
  and all wild animals!
You will crawl on your belly
  and you will eat dust
  all the days of your life.
¹⁵And I will put enmity
  between you and the woman,
  and between your offspring[a] and hers;
he will crush[b] your head,
  and you will strike his heel."

¹⁶To the woman he said,

"I will make your pains in childbearing
    very severe;
  with painful labor you will give birth
    to children.
Your desire will be for your husband,
  and he will rule over you."

¹⁷To Adam he said, "Because you listened to your wife and ate fruit from the tree about which I commanded you, 'You must not eat from it,'

"Cursed is the ground because of you;
    through painful toil you will eat food
      from it
    all the days of your life.
¹⁸It will produce thorns and thistles for you,
    and you will eat the plants of the field.
¹⁹By the sweat of your brow
    you will eat your food
until you return to the ground,
    since from it you were taken;
for dust you are
    and to dust you will return."

²⁰Adam[c] named his wife Eve,[d] because she would become the mother of all the living.

²¹The LORD God made garments of skin for Adam and his wife and clothed them. ²²And the LORD God said, "The man has now become like one of us, knowing good and evil. He must not be allowed to reach out his hand and take also from the tree of life and eat, and live forever." ²³So the LORD God banished him from the Garden of Eden to work the ground from which he had been taken. ²⁴After he drove the man out, he placed on the east side[e] of the Garden of Eden cherubim and a flaming sword flashing back and forth to guard the way to the tree of life.

ᵃ 15 Or seed ᵇ 15 Or strike ᶜ 20 Or The man ᵈ 20 Eve probably means living. ᵉ 24 Or placed in front

Cain and Abel

4 Adam[a] made love to his wife Eve, and she became pregnant and gave birth to Cain.[b] She said, "With the help of the LORD I have brought forth[c] a man." [2]Later she gave birth to his brother Abel.

Now Abel kept flocks, and Cain worked the soil. [3]In the course of time Cain brought some of the fruits of the soil as an offering to the LORD. [4]And Abel also brought an offering—fat portions from some of the firstborn of his flock. The LORD looked with favor on Abel and his offering, [5]but on Cain and his offering he did not look with favor. So Cain was very angry, and his face was downcast.

[6]Then the LORD said to Cain, "Why are you angry? Why is your face downcast? [7]If you do what is right, will you not be accepted? But if you do not do what is right, sin is crouching at your door; it desires to have you, but you must rule over it."

[8]Now Cain said to his brother Abel, "Let's go out to the field."[d] While they were in the field, Cain attacked his brother Abel and killed him.

[9]Then the LORD said to Cain, "Where is your brother Abel?"

"I don't know," he replied. "Am I my brother's keeper?"

[10]The LORD said, "What have you done? Listen! Your brother's blood cries out to me from the ground. [11]Now you are under a curse and driven from the ground, which opened its mouth to receive your brother's blood from your hand. [12]When you work the ground, it will no longer yield its crops for you. You will be a restless wanderer on the earth."

[13]Cain said to the LORD, "My punishment is more than I can bear. [14]Today you are driving me from the land, and I will be hidden from your presence; I will be a restless wanderer on the earth, and whoever finds me will kill me."

[15]But the LORD said to him, "Not so[e]; anyone who kills Cain will suffer vengeance seven times over." Then the LORD put a mark on Cain so that no one who found him would kill him. [16]So Cain went out from the LORD's presence and lived in the land of Nod,[f] east of Eden.

[17]Cain made love to his wife, and she became pregnant and gave birth to Enoch. Cain was then building a city, and he named it after his son Enoch. [18]To Enoch was born Irad, and Irad was the father of Mehujael, and Mehujael was the father of Methushael, and Methushael was the father of Lamech.

[19]Lamech married two women, one named Adah and the other Zillah. [20]Adah gave birth to Jabal; he was the father of those who live in tents and raise livestock. [21]His brother's name was Jubal; he was the father of all who play stringed instruments and pipes. [22]Zillah also had a son, Tubal-Cain, who forged all kinds of tools out of[g] bronze and iron. Tubal-Cain's sister was Naamah.

[23]Lamech said to his wives,

"Adah and Zillah, listen to me;
      wives of Lamech, hear my words.
I have killed a man for wounding me,
      a young man for injuring me.
[24]If Cain is avenged seven times,
      then Lamech seventy-seven times."

[25]Adam made love to his wife again, and she gave birth to a son and named him Seth,[h] saying, "God has granted me another child in place of Abel, since Cain killed him." [26]Seth also had a son, and he named him Enosh.

At that time people began to call on[i] the name of the LORD.

From Adam to Noah

5 This is the written account of Adam's family line.

When God created mankind, he made them in the likeness of God. [2]He created them male and female and blessed them. And he named them "Mankind"[j] when they were created.

[3]When Adam had lived 130 years, he had a son in his own likeness, in his own image; and he named him Seth. [4]After Seth was born, Adam lived 800 years and had other sons and daughters. [5]Altogether, Adam lived a total of 930 years, and then he died.

---

[a] 1 Or *The man*   [b] 1 *Cain* sounds like the Hebrew for *brought forth* or *acquired*.   [c] 1 Or *have acquired*
[d] 8 Samaritan Pentateuch, Septuagint, Vulgate and Syriac; Masoretic Text does not have *"Let's go out to the field."*   [e] 15 Septuagint, Vulgate and Syriac; Hebrew *Very well*   [f] 16 *Nod* means *wandering* (see verses 12 and 14).   [g] 22 Or *who instructed all who work in*   [h] 25 *Seth* probably means *granted*.
[i] 26 Or *to proclaim*   [j] 2 Hebrew *adam*

SLOW FADE

READ: GENESIS 4:6-7

Any Christian can fall. I've seen families that everyone admires crumble. I've seen teenagers with a love for God and a passion for reaching people give it all away for a little more popularity.

It's not uncommon to find yourself in church one day, zoned-out and thinking, *What in the world happened to me? Why am I so numb and incapable of caring? I know I'm far away, but why don't I want to get closer? How did I get here?*

It's not as if you enjoy an awesome you-and-God time, go to bed, wake up in the morning, and—bam!—crash and burn. It never happens that way. It's a slow process, a series of compromises by which you descend from delighting in God to sitting with the scoffers and mocking your former faith (Psalm 1).

Remember that you're not the first person Satan has ever messed with. He went to war against God, so launching an attack on you isn't going to give him any pause. He finds out where your buttons are and starts punching. One little compromise leads to another until you find yourself at a place you never thought you'd be, doing things you never thought you'd do.

Our counsel is our foundation. Who and what am I allowing to influence me? Am I delighting in the Lord? Am I sowing to the Spirit, or am I sowing to the flesh? (See Galatians 6:8.)

BUILDING FAITH WISDOM STRENGTH

⁶When Seth had lived 105 years, he became the father*ᵃ* of Enosh. ⁷After he became the father of Enosh, Seth lived 807 years and had other sons and daughters. ⁸Altogether, Seth lived a total of 912 years, and then he died.

⁹When Enosh had lived 90 years, he became the father of Kenan. ¹⁰After he became the father of Kenan, Enosh lived 815 years and had other sons and daughters. ¹¹Altogether, Enosh lived a total of 905 years, and then he died.

¹²When Kenan had lived 70 years, he became the father of Mahalalel. ¹³After he became the father of Mahalalel, Kenan lived 840 years and had other sons and daughters. ¹⁴Altogether, Kenan lived a total of 910 years, and then he died.

¹⁵When Mahalalel had lived 65 years, he became the father of Jared. ¹⁶After he became the father of Jared, Mahalalel lived 830 years and had other sons and daughters. ¹⁷Altogether, Mahalalel lived a total of 895 years, and then he died.

¹⁸When Jared had lived 162 years, he became the father of Enoch. ¹⁹After he became the father of Enoch, Jared lived 800 years and had other sons and daughters. ²⁰Altogether, Jared lived a total of 962 years, and then he died.

²¹When Enoch had lived 65 years, he became the father of Methuselah. ²²After he became the father of Methuselah, Enoch walked faithfully with God 300 years and had other sons and daughters. ²³Altogether, Enoch lived a total of 365 years. ²⁴Enoch walked faithfully with God; then he was no more, because God took him away.

²⁵When Methuselah had lived 187 years, he became the father of Lamech. ²⁶After he became the father of Lamech, Methuselah lived 782 years and had other sons and daughters. ²⁷Altogether, Methuselah lived a total of 969 years, and then he died.

²⁸When Lamech had lived 182 years, he had a son. ²⁹He named him Noah*ᵇ* and said, "He will comfort us in the labor and painful toil of our hands caused by the ground the LORD has cursed." ³⁰After Noah was born, Lamech lived 595 years and had other sons and daughters. ³¹Altogether, Lamech lived a total of 777 years, and then he died.

³²After Noah was 500 years old, he became the father of Shem, Ham and Japheth.

Wickedness in the World

6 When human beings began to increase in number on the earth and daughters were born to them, ²the sons of God saw that the daughters of humans were beautiful, and they married any of them they chose. ³Then the LORD said, "My Spirit will not contend with*ᶜ* humans forever, for they are mortal*ᵈ*; their days will be a hundred and twenty years."

⁴The Nephilim were on the earth in those days — and also afterward — when the sons of God went to the daughters of humans and had children by them. They were the heroes of old, men of renown.

⁵The LORD saw how great the wickedness of the human race had become on the earth, and that every inclination of the thoughts of the human heart was only evil all the time. ⁶The LORD regretted that he had made human beings on the earth, and his heart was deeply troubled. ⁷So the LORD said, "I will wipe from the face of the earth the human race I have created — and with them the animals, the birds and the creatures that move along the ground — for I regret that I have made them." ⁸But Noah found favor in the eyes of the LORD.

Noah and the Flood

⁹This is the account of Noah and his family.

Noah was a righteous man, blameless among the people of his time, and he walked faithfully with God. ¹⁰Noah had three sons: Shem, Ham and Japheth.

¹¹Now the earth was corrupt in God's sight and was full of violence. ¹²God saw how corrupt the earth had become, for all the people on earth had corrupted their ways. ¹³So God said to Noah, "I am going to put an end to all people, for the earth is filled with violence because of them. I am surely going to destroy both them and the earth. ¹⁴So make yourself an ark of cypress*ᵉ* wood; make rooms in it and coat it with pitch inside and out. ¹⁵This is how you are to build it: The ark is to be three hundred cubits long, fifty

---

ᵃ 6 *Father* may mean *ancestor*; also in verses 7-26.
ᶜ 3 Or *My spirit will not remain in*   *ᵈ* 3 Or *corrupt* uncertain.

ᵇ 29 *Noah* sounds like the Hebrew for *comfort*.
ᵉ 14 The meaning of the Hebrew for this word is

IT TAKES AWHILE

READ: GENESIS 6:9-22

Noah's ark project ranks as one of history's largest and longest construction projects. I think we fail to appreciate it for what it is—a really big boat built a really long time ago! And they didn't have power tools back then like we do today.

The internal volume of the ark was 1,518,750 cubit feet—the equivalent of 569 boxcars. If the average animal was the size of a sheep, it had capacity for 125,000 animals. To put that into perspective, there are only 2,000 animals from 400 different species at the National Zoo in Washington, DC. That means you could fit 60 National Zoos on board Noah's ark!

It's not like it came with an instruction manual. It was also backbreaking work. It took buckets of blood, sweat, and tears. But even more than brains and brawn, it took some insane faith to build this beast.

Who builds a boat in the desert? Who hammers away for 120 years at something they might not even need? He based his entire future on something that had never happened before.

BUILDING FAITH WISDOM STRENGTH

That's going all out for God. Noah obviously wasn't after fifteen minutes of fame, he was after eternal glory.

Noah built the ark because God commanded it. It's what he was supposed to do. When everything was said and done, it was the longest act of obedience recorded in the entire Bible. From start to finish, Noah's one act of obedience took 43,800 days.

Taken from *All In Student Edition* by Mark Batterson and Parker Batterson, copyright © 2014 by Mark Batterson, published by Zondervan.

cubits wide and thirty cubits high.[a] [16]Make a roof for it, leaving below the roof an opening one cubit[b] high all around.[c] Put a door in the side of the ark and make lower, middle and upper decks. [17]I am going to bring floodwaters on the earth to destroy all life under the heavens, every creature that has the breath of life in it. Everything on earth will perish. [18]But I will establish my covenant with you, and you will enter the ark—you and your sons and your wife and your sons' wives with you. [19]You are to bring into the ark two of all living creatures, male and female, to keep them alive with you. [20]Two of every kind of bird, of every kind of animal and of every kind of creature that moves along the ground will come to you to be kept alive. [21]You are to take every kind of food that is to be eaten and store it away as food for you and for them."

[22]Noah did everything just as God commanded him.

7 The LORD then said to Noah, "Go into the ark, you and your whole family, because I have found you righteous in this generation. [2]Take with you seven pairs of every kind of clean animal, a male and its mate, and one pair of every kind of unclean animal, a male and its mate, [3]and also seven pairs of every kind of bird, male and female, to keep their various kinds alive throughout the earth. [4]Seven days from now I will send rain on the earth for forty days and forty nights, and I will wipe from the face of the earth every living creature I have made."

[5]And Noah did all that the LORD commanded him.

[6]Noah was six hundred years old when the floodwaters came on the earth. [7]And Noah and his sons and his wife and his sons' wives entered the ark to escape the waters of the flood. [8]Pairs of clean and unclean animals, of birds and of all creatures that move along the ground, [9]male and female, came to Noah and entered the ark, as God had commanded Noah. [10]And after the seven days the floodwaters came on the earth.

[11]In the six hundredth year of Noah's life, on the seventeenth day of the second month—on that day all the springs of the great deep burst forth, and the floodgates of the heavens were opened. [12]And rain fell on the earth forty days and forty nights.

[13]On that very day Noah and his sons, Shem, Ham and Japheth, together with his wife and the wives of his three sons, entered the ark. [14]They had with them every wild animal according to its kind, all livestock according to their kinds, every creature that moves along the ground according to its kind and every bird according to its kind, everything with wings. [15]Pairs of all creatures that have the breath of life in them came to Noah and entered the ark. [16]The animals going in were male and female of every living thing, as God had commanded Noah. Then the LORD shut him in.

[17]For forty days the flood kept coming on the earth, and as the waters increased they lifted the ark high above the earth. [18]The waters rose and increased greatly on the earth, and the ark floated on the surface of the water. [19]They rose greatly on the earth, and all the high mountains under the entire heavens were covered. [20]The waters rose and covered the mountains to a depth of more than fifteen cubits.[d,e] [21]Every living thing that moved on land perished—birds, livestock, wild animals, all the creatures that swarm over the earth, and all mankind. [22]Everything on dry land that had the breath of life in its nostrils died. [23]Every living thing on the face of the earth was wiped out; people and animals and the creatures that move along the ground and the birds were wiped from the earth. Only Noah was left, and those with him in the ark.

[24]The waters flooded the earth for a hundred and fifty days.

8 But God remembered Noah and all the wild animals and the livestock that were with him in the ark, and he sent a wind over the earth, and the waters receded. [2]Now the springs of the deep and the floodgates of the heavens had been closed, and the rain had stopped falling from the sky. [3]The water receded steadily from the earth. At the end of the hundred and fifty days the water had gone down, [4]and on the seventeenth day of the seventh month the ark came to rest on

---

[a] 15 That is, about 450 feet long, 75 feet wide and 45 feet high or about 135 meters long, 23 meters wide and 14 meters high   [b] 16 That is, about 18 inches or about 45 centimeters   [c] 16 The meaning of the Hebrew for this clause is uncertain.   [d] 20 That is, about 23 feet or about 6.8 meters   [e] 20 Or *rose more than fifteen cubits, and the mountains were covered*

the mountains of Ararat. ⁵The waters continued to recede until the tenth month, and on the first day of the tenth month the tops of the mountains became visible.

⁶After forty days Noah opened a window he had made in the ark ⁷and sent out a raven, and it kept flying back and forth until the water had dried up from the earth. ⁸Then he sent out a dove to see if the water had receded from the surface of the ground. ⁹But the dove could find nowhere to perch because there was water over all the surface of the earth; so it returned to Noah in the ark. He reached out his hand and took the dove and brought it back to himself in the ark. ¹⁰He waited seven more days and again sent out the dove from the ark. ¹¹When the dove returned to him in the evening, there in its beak was a freshly plucked olive leaf! Then Noah knew that the water had receded from the earth. ¹²He waited seven more days and sent the dove out again, but this time it did not return to him.

¹³By the first day of the first month of Noah's six hundred and first year, the water had dried up from the earth. Noah then removed the covering from the ark and saw that the surface of the ground was dry. ¹⁴By the twenty-seventh day of the second month the earth was completely dry.

¹⁵Then God said to Noah, ¹⁶"Come out of the ark, you and your wife and your sons and their wives. ¹⁷Bring out every kind of living creature that is with you—the birds, the animals, and all the creatures that move along the ground—so they can multiply on the earth and be fruitful and increase in number on it."

¹⁸So Noah came out, together with his sons and his wife and his sons' wives. ¹⁹All the animals and all the creatures that move along the ground and all the birds—everything that moves on land—came out of the ark, one kind after another.

²⁰Then Noah built an altar to the Lᴏʀᴅ and, taking some of all the clean animals and clean birds, he sacrificed burnt offerings on it. ²¹The Lᴏʀᴅ smelled the pleasing aroma and said in his heart: "Never again will I curse the ground because of humans, even though*ᵃ* every inclination of the human heart is evil from childhood. And never

again will I destroy all living creatures, as I have done.

²²"As long as the earth endures,
   seedtime and harvest,
   cold and heat,
   summer and winter,
   day and night
   will never cease."

God's Covenant With Noah

9 Then God blessed Noah and his sons, saying to them, "Be fruitful and increase in number and fill the earth. ²The fear and dread of you will fall on all the beasts of the earth, and on all the birds in the sky, on every creature that moves along the ground, and on all the fish in the sea; they are given into your hands. ³Everything that lives and moves about will be food for you. Just as I gave you the green plants, I now give you everything.

⁴"But you must not eat meat that has its lifeblood still in it. ⁵And for your lifeblood I will surely demand an accounting. I will demand an accounting from every animal. And from each human being, too, I will demand an accounting for the life of another human being.

⁶"Whoever sheds human blood,
   by humans shall their blood be shed;
   for in the image of God
   has God made mankind.

⁷As for you, be fruitful and increase in number; multiply on the earth and increase upon it."

⁸Then God said to Noah and to his sons with him: ⁹"I now establish my covenant with you and with your descendants after you ¹⁰and with every living creature that was with you—the birds, the livestock and all the wild animals, all those that came out of the ark with you—every living creature on earth. ¹¹I establish my covenant with you: Never again will all life be destroyed by the waters of a flood; never again will there be a flood to destroy the earth."

¹²And God said, "This is the sign of the covenant I am making between me and you and every living creature with you, a covenant for all generations to come: ¹³I have set my rainbow in the clouds, and it will be

---

ᵃ 21 Or *humans, for*

the sign of the covenant between me and the earth. [14]Whenever I bring clouds over the earth and the rainbow appears in the clouds, [15]I will remember my covenant between me and you and all living creatures of every kind. Never again will the waters become a flood to destroy all life. [16]Whenever the rainbow appears in the clouds, I will see it and remember the everlasting covenant between God and all living creatures of every kind on the earth." [17]So God said to Noah, "This is the sign of the covenant I have established between me and all life on the earth."

The Sons of Noah

[18]The sons of Noah who came out of the ark were Shem, Ham and Japheth. (Ham was the father of Canaan.) [19]These were the three sons of Noah, and from them came the people who were scattered over the whole earth.

[20]Noah, a man of the soil, proceeded[a] to plant a vineyard. [21]When he drank some of its wine, he became drunk and lay uncovered inside his tent. [22]Ham, the father of Canaan, saw his father naked and told his two brothers outside. [23]But Shem and Japheth took a garment and laid it across their shoulders; then they walked in backward and covered their father's naked body. Their faces were turned the other way so that they would not see their father naked.

[24]When Noah awoke from his wine and found out what his youngest son had done to him, [25]he said,

"Cursed be Canaan!
    The lowest of slaves
    will he be to his brothers."

[26]He also said,

"Praise be to the LORD, the God of Shem!
    May Canaan be the slave of Shem.
[27]May God extend Japheth's[b] territory;
    may Japheth live in the tents of Shem,
    and may Canaan be the slave of
        Japheth."

[28]After the flood Noah lived 350 years. [29]Noah lived a total of 950 years, and then he died.

The Table of Nations

10 This is the account of Shem, Ham and Japheth, Noah's sons, who themselves had sons after the flood.

The Japhethites

[2]The sons[c] of Japheth:
    Gomer, Magog, Madai, Javan, Tubal,
    Meshek and Tiras.
[3]The sons of Gomer:
    Ashkenaz, Riphath and Togarmah.
[4]The sons of Javan:
    Elishah, Tarshish, the Kittites and the Rodanites.[d] [5](From these the maritime peoples spread out into their territories by their clans within their nations, each with its own language.)

The Hamites

[6]The sons of Ham:
    Cush, Egypt, Put and Canaan.
[7]The sons of Cush:
    Seba, Havilah, Sabtah, Raamah and Sabteka.
    The sons of Raamah:
        Sheba and Dedan.

[8]Cush was the father[e] of Nimrod, who became a mighty warrior on the earth. [9]He was a mighty hunter before the LORD; that is why it is said, "Like Nimrod, a mighty hunter before the LORD." [10]The first centers of his kingdom were Babylon, Uruk, Akkad and Kalneh, in[f] Shinar.[g] [11]From that land he went to Assyria, where he built Nineveh, Rehoboth Ir,[h] Calah [12]and Resen, which is between Nineveh and Calah—which is the great city.

[13]Egypt was the father of
    the Ludites, Anamites, Lehabites, Naphtuhites, [14]Pathrusites, Kasluhites (from whom the Philistines came) and Caphtorites.
[15]Canaan was the father of
    Sidon his firstborn,[i] and of the Hittites, [16]Jebusites, Amorites, Girga-

shites, [17]Hivites, Arkites, Sinites, [18]Arvadites, Zemarites and Hamathites.

Later the Canaanite clans scattered [19]and the borders of Canaan reached from Sidon toward Gerar as far as Gaza, and then toward Sodom, Gomorrah, Admah and Zeboyim, as far as Lasha. [20]These are the sons of Ham by their clans and languages, in their territories and nations.

The Semites

[21]Sons were also born to Shem, whose older brother was[a] Japheth; Shem was the ancestor of all the sons of Eber.

[22]The sons of Shem:

Elam, Ashur, Arphaxad, Lud and Aram.

[23]The sons of Aram:

Uz, Hul, Gether and Meshek.[b]

[24]Arphaxad was the father of[c] Shelah, and Shelah the father of Eber.

[25]Two sons were born to Eber:

One was named Peleg,[d] because in his time the earth was divided; his brother was named Joktan.

[26]Joktan was the father of

Almodad, Sheleph, Hazarmaveth, Jerah, [27]Hadoram, Uzal, Diklah, [28]Obal, Abimael, Sheba, [29]Ophir, Havilah and Jobab. All these were sons of Joktan.

[30]The region where they lived stretched from Mesha toward Sephar, in the eastern hill country.

[31]These are the sons of Shem by their clans and languages, in their territories and nations.

[32]These are the clans of Noah's sons, according to their lines of descent, within their nations. From these the nations spread out over the earth after the flood.

The Tower of Babel

11 Now the whole world had one language and a common speech. [2]As people moved eastward,[e] they found a plain in Shinar[f] and settled there.

[3]They said to each other, "Come, let's make bricks and bake them thoroughly." They used brick instead of stone, and tar for mortar. [4]Then they said, "Come, let us build ourselves a city, with a tower that reaches to the heavens, so that we may make a name for ourselves; otherwise we will be scattered over the face of the whole earth."

[5]But the LORD came down to see the city and the tower the people were building. [6]The LORD said, "If as one people speaking the same language they have begun to do this, then nothing they plan to do will be impossible for them. [7]Come, let us go down and confuse their language so they will not understand each other."

[8]So the LORD scattered them from there over all the earth, and they stopped building the city. [9]That is why it was called Babel[g] — because there the LORD confused the language of the whole world. From there the LORD scattered them over the face of the whole earth.

From Shem to Abram

[10]This is the account of Shem's family line.

Two years after the flood, when Shem was 100 years old, he became the father[h] of Arphaxad. [11]And after he became the father of Arphaxad, Shem lived 500 years and had other sons and daughters.

[12]When Arphaxad had lived 35 years, he became the father of Shelah. [13]And after he became the father of Shelah, Arphaxad lived 403 years and had other sons and daughters.[i]

[14]When Shelah had lived 30 years, he became the father of Eber. [15]And after he became the father of Eber, Shelah lived 403 years and had other sons and daughters.

---

[a] 21 Or *Shem, the older brother of*   [b] 23 See Septuagint and 1 Chron. 1:17; Hebrew *Mash.*   [c] 24 Hebrew; Septuagint *father of Cainan, and Cainan was the father of*   [d] 25 *Peleg* means *division.*   [e] 2 Or *from the east*; or *in the east*   [f] 2 That is, Babylonia   [g] 9 That is, Babylon; *Babel* sounds like the Hebrew for *confused.*   [h] 10 *Father* may mean *ancestor*; also in verses 11-25.   [i] 12,13 Hebrew; Septuagint (see also Luke 3:35, 36 and note at Gen. 10:24) *35 years, he became the father of Cainan.* [13]*And after he became the father of Cainan, Arphaxad lived 430 years and had other sons and daughters, and then he died. When Cainan had lived 130 years, he became the father of Shelah. And after he became the father of Shelah, Cainan lived 330 years and had other sons and daughters*

[16]When Eber had lived 34 years, he became the father of Peleg. [17]And after he became the father of Peleg, Eber lived 430 years and had other sons and daughters.

[18]When Peleg had lived 30 years, he became the father of Reu. [19]And after he became the father of Reu, Peleg lived 209 years and had other sons and daughters.

[20]When Reu had lived 32 years, he became the father of Serug. [21]And after he became the father of Serug, Reu lived 207 years and had other sons and daughters.

[22]When Serug had lived 30 years, he became the father of Nahor. [23]And after he became the father of Nahor, Serug lived 200 years and had other sons and daughters.

[24]When Nahor had lived 29 years, he became the father of Terah. [25]And after he became the father of Terah, Nahor lived 119 years and had other sons and daughters.

[26]After Terah had lived 70 years, he became the father of Abram, Nahor and Haran.

Abram's Family

[27]This is the account of Terah's family line.

Terah became the father of Abram, Nahor and Haran. And Haran became the father of Lot. [28]While his father Terah was still alive, Haran died in Ur of the Chaldeans, in the land of his birth. [29]Abram and Nahor both married. The name of Abram's wife was Sarai, and the name of Nahor's wife was Milkah; she was the daughter of Haran, the father of both Milkah and Iskah. [30]Now Sarai was childless because she was not able to conceive.

[31]Terah took his son Abram, his grandson Lot son of Haran, and his daughter-in-law Sarai, the wife of his son Abram, and together they set out from Ur of the Chaldeans to go to Canaan. But when they came to Harran, they settled there.

[32]Terah lived 205 years, and he died in Harran.

The Call of Abram

12 The LORD had said to Abram, "Go from your country, your people and your father's household to the land I will show you.

[2]"I will make you into a great nation,
and I will bless you;

I will make your name great,
and you will be a blessing.[a]
[3]I will bless those who bless you,
and whoever curses you I will curse;
and all peoples on earth
will be blessed through you."[b]

[4]So Abram went, as the LORD had told him; and Lot went with him. Abram was seventy-five years old when he set out from Harran. [5]He took his wife Sarai, his nephew Lot, all the possessions they had accumulated and the people they had acquired in Harran, and they set out for the land of Canaan, and they arrived there.

[6]Abram traveled through the land as far as the site of the great tree of Moreh at Shechem. At that time the Canaanites were in the land. [7]The LORD appeared to Abram and said, "To your offspring[c] I will give this land." So he built an altar there to the LORD, who had appeared to him.

[8]From there he went on toward the hills east of Bethel and pitched his tent, with Bethel on the west and Ai on the east. There he built an altar to the LORD and called on the name of the LORD.

[9]Then Abram set out and continued toward the Negev.

Abram in Egypt

[10]Now there was a famine in the land, and Abram went down to Egypt to live there for a while because the famine was severe. [11]As he was about to enter Egypt, he said to his wife Sarai, "I know what a beautiful woman you are. [12]When the Egyptians see you, they will say, 'This is his wife.' Then they will kill me but will let you live. [13]Say you are my sister, so that I will be treated well for your sake and my life will be spared because of you."

[14]When Abram came to Egypt, the Egyptians saw that Sarai was a very beautiful woman. [15]And when Pharaoh's officials saw her, they praised her to Pharaoh, and she was taken into his palace. [16]He treated Abram well for her sake, and Abram acquired sheep and cattle, male and female donkeys, male and female servants, and camels.

[17]But the LORD inflicted serious diseases on Pharaoh and his household because of Abram's wife Sarai. [18]So Pharaoh summoned Abram. "What have you done to me?"

---

[a] 2 Or *be seen as blessed*   [b] 3 Or *earth / will use your name in blessings* (see 48:20)   [c] 7 Or *seed*

YOU ARE PART OF THE PLAN

READ: GENESIS 12:1-2

You know how it feels to have a plan where nothing turns out? When problems seem impossible, no one faults you for giving up. Not long after Adam and Eve sinned back in the garden of Eden, God looked at the human race and concluded, "Every inclination of the thoughts of the human heart was only evil all the time" (Genesis 6:5). Even after the Lord started over with Noah—the one good person he could find—everyone slid back into sin. God had every reason to be done with the human race. Instead he picked Abram as the beginning of a new plan. When he told Abram to go to a distant, unnamed land, this faith-filled man heeded God's command. He immediately obeyed, packing up and moving his entire household without any idea where he was going.

BUILDING

FAITH

WISDOM

STRENGTH

God had an extraordinary future in store for Abram, but this blessing wouldn't stop with one man. The Lord would make him a powerful nation and use him to bless everyone on earth. Abram was the start of the plan that comes to completion in Christ. Abram—later known as Abraham—is your spiritual ancestor (Romans 4:16).

When God blessed that ancient nomad, he had you in mind. The Lord wanted so much for you to know him that he refused to give up. He dreamed up a plan to lead you to him.

he said. "Why didn't you tell me she was your wife? ¹⁹Why did you say, 'She is my sister,' so that I took her to be my wife? Now then, here is your wife. Take her and go!" ²⁰Then Pharaoh gave orders about Abram to his men, and they sent him on his way, with his wife and everything he had.

Abram and Lot Separate

13 So Abram went up from Egypt to the Negev, with his wife and everything he had, and Lot went with him. ²Abram had become very wealthy in livestock and in silver and gold.

³From the Negev he went from place to place until he came to Bethel, to the place between Bethel and Ai where his tent had been earlier ⁴and where he had first built an altar. There Abram called on the name of the LORD.

⁵Now Lot, who was moving about with Abram, also had flocks and herds and tents. ⁶But the land could not support them while they stayed together, for their possessions were so great that they were not able to stay together. ⁷And quarreling arose between Abram's herders and Lot's. The Canaanites and Perizzites were also living in the land at that time.

⁸So Abram said to Lot, "Let's not have any quarreling between you and me, or between your herders and mine, for we are close relatives. ⁹Is not the whole land before you? Let's part company. If you go to the left, I'll go to the right; if you go to the right, I'll go to the left."

¹⁰Lot looked around and saw that the whole plain of the Jordan toward Zoar was well watered, like the garden of the LORD, like the land of Egypt. (This was before the LORD destroyed Sodom and Gomorrah.) ¹¹So Lot chose for himself the whole plain of the Jordan and set out toward the east. The two men parted company: ¹²Abram lived in the land of Canaan, while Lot lived among the cities of the plain and pitched his tents near Sodom. ¹³Now the people of Sodom were wicked and were sinning greatly against the LORD.

¹⁴The LORD said to Abram after Lot had parted from him, "Look around from where you are, to the north and south, to the east and west. ¹⁵All the land that you see I will give to you and your offspring*ᵃ* forever. ¹⁶I will make your offspring like the dust of the earth, so that if anyone could count the dust, then your offspring could be counted. ¹⁷Go, walk through the length and breadth of the land, for I am giving it to you."

¹⁸So Abram went to live near the great trees of Mamre at Hebron, where he pitched his tents. There he built an altar to the LORD.

Abram Rescues Lot

14 At the time when Amraphel was king of Shinar,ᵇ Arioch king of Ellasar, Kedorlaomer king of Elam and Tidal king of Goyim, ²these kings went to war against Bera king of Sodom, Birsha king of Gomorrah, Shinab king of Admah, Shemeber king of Zeboyim, and the king of Bela (that is, Zoar). ³All these latter kings joined forces in the Valley of Siddim (that is, the Dead Sea Valley). ⁴For twelve years they had been subject to Kedorlaomer, but in the thirteenth year they rebelled.

⁵In the fourteenth year, Kedorlaomer and the kings allied with him went out and defeated the Rephaites in Ashteroth Karnaim, the Zuzites in Ham, the Emites in Shaveh Kiriathaim ⁶and the Horites in the hill country of Seir, as far as El Paran near the desert. ⁷Then they turned back and went to En Mishpat (that is, Kadesh), and they conquered the whole territory of the Amalekites, as well as the Amorites who were living in Hazezon Tamar.

⁸Then the king of Sodom, the king of Gomorrah, the king of Admah, the king of Zeboyim and the king of Bela (that is, Zoar) marched out and drew up their battle lines in the Valley of Siddim ⁹against Kedorlaomer king of Elam, Tidal king of Goyim, Amraphel king of Shinar and Arioch king of Ellasar—four kings against five. ¹⁰Now the Valley of Siddim was full of tar pits, and when the kings of Sodom and Gomorrah fled, some of the men fell into them and the rest fled to the hills. ¹¹The four kings seized all the goods of Sodom and Gomorrah and all their food; then they went away. ¹²They also carried off Abram's nephew Lot and his possessions, since he was living in Sodom.

¹³A man who had escaped came and reported this to Abram the Hebrew. Now

---

ᵃ *15* Or *seed*; also in verse 16   ᵇ *1* That is, Babylonia; also in verse 9

Abram was living near the great trees of Mamre the Amorite, a brother[a] of Eshkol and Aner, all of whom were allied with Abram. [14]When Abram heard that his relative had been taken captive, he called out the 318 trained men born in his household and went in pursuit as far as Dan. [15]During the night Abram divided his men to attack them and he routed them, pursuing them as far as Hobah, north of Damascus. [16]He recovered all the goods and brought back his relative Lot and his possessions, together with the women and the other people.

[17]After Abram returned from defeating Kedorlaomer and the kings allied with him, the king of Sodom came out to meet him in the Valley of Shaveh (that is, the King's Valley).

[18]Then Melchizedek king of Salem brought out bread and wine. He was priest of God Most High, [19]and he blessed Abram, saying,

"Blessed be Abram by God Most High,
Creator of heaven and earth.
[20]And praise be to God Most High,
who delivered your enemies into your hand."

Then Abram gave him a tenth of everything.

[21]The king of Sodom said to Abram, "Give me the people and keep the goods for yourself."

[22]But Abram said to the king of Sodom, "With raised hand I have sworn an oath to the LORD, God Most High, Creator of heaven and earth, [23]that I will accept nothing belonging to you, not even a thread or the strap of a sandal, so that you will never be able to say, 'I made Abram rich.' [24]I will accept nothing but what my men have eaten and the share that belongs to the men who went with me — to Aner, Eshkol and Mamre. Let them have their share."

The LORD's Covenant With Abram

15 After this, the word of the LORD came to Abram in a vision:

"Do not be afraid, Abram.
I am your shield,[b]
your very great reward.[c]"

[2]But Abram said, "Sovereign LORD, what can you give me since I remain childless and the one who will inherit[d] my estate is Eliezer of Damascus?" [3]And Abram said, "You have given me no children; so a servant in my household will be my heir."

[4]Then the word of the LORD came to him: "This man will not be your heir, but a son who is your own flesh and blood will be your heir." [5]He took him outside and said, "Look up at the sky and count the stars — if indeed you can count them." Then he said to him, "So shall your offspring[e] be."

[6]Abram believed the LORD, and he credited it to him as righteousness.

[7]He also said to him, "I am the LORD, who brought you out of Ur of the Chaldeans to give you this land to take possession of it."

[8]But Abram said, "Sovereign LORD, how can I know that I will gain possession of it?"

[9]So the LORD said to him, "Bring me a heifer, a goat and a ram, each three years old, along with a dove and a young pigeon."

[10]Abram brought all these to him, cut them in two and arranged the halves opposite each other; the birds, however, he did not cut in half. [11]Then birds of prey came down on the carcasses, but Abram drove them away.

[12]As the sun was setting, Abram fell into a deep sleep, and a thick and dreadful darkness came over him. [13]Then the LORD said to him, "Know for certain that for four hundred years your descendants will be strangers in a country not their own and that they will be enslaved and mistreated there. [14]But I will punish the nation they serve as slaves, and afterward they will come out with great possessions. [15]You, however, will go to your ancestors in peace and be buried at a good old age. [16]In the fourth generation your descendants will come back here, for the sin of the Amorites has not yet reached its full measure."

[17]When the sun had set and darkness had fallen, a smoking firepot with a blazing torch appeared and passed between the pieces. [18]On that day the LORD made a covenant with Abram and said, "To your descendants I give this land, from the Wadi[f] of Egypt to the great river, the Euphrates — [19]the land of the Kenites, Kenizzites, Kadmonites, [20]Hittites, Perizzites, Rephaites, [21]Amorites, Canaanites, Girgashites and Jebusites."

---

[a] 13 Or *a relative*; or *an ally*   [b] 1 Or *sovereign*   [c] 1 Or *shield; / your reward will be very great*
[d] 2 The meaning of the Hebrew for this phrase is uncertain.   [e] 5 Or *seed*   [f] 18 Or *river*

ABRAHAM

"Look up at the sky and count the stars—if indeed you can count them." Then he said to him, "So shall your offspring be." Abram believed the LORD. GENESIS 15:5-6

HIS NAME MEANS: "father of a multitude"
READ HIS STORY: *Genesis 12-18, 20-23, 25:1-12*

MEN

OF THE BIBLE

At first glance, Abraham doesn't appear very special. He was born in the sprawling city of Ur. He tended sheep. If he got in a sticky situation, he was willing to be deceitful. He told foreign leaders—twice—the half truth that his wife was his sister. (Abraham and his wife had the same father, so she was his half sister.) But God considered him a friend (read James 2:23) and made him the father of the nation Israel. A deeper look into Abraham's life may reveal why God chose him for such an honor. He was ordinary, but he possessed extraordinary patience and faith.

When Abram (the Lord doesn't change his name to Abraham until Genesis 17:5) still lived in Ur, God told him to leave his country and promised to make him into a great nation (Genesis 12:1-2). First Abram went with his father, his wife Sarai, and his nephew Lot to the city of Harran. After his father died, Abram—at age seventy-five—left for Canaan. At first, things didn't go as Abram might have anticipated. A famine forced him to Egypt. He and Lot parted ways. Sarai didn't have any children. Twenty-five years passed before Sarah (her name changed too) had their son, Isaac. But that was after Sarai told Abram to start building a family with her maidservant, Hagar, who gave birth to Ishmael.

Through it all, Abraham trusted God to deliver on his covenant. God ultimately made Abraham into a great nation. The God of Abraham still follows through on his promises, but we must have faith and patience too.

Hagar and Ishmael

16 Now Sarai, Abram's wife, had borne him no children. But she had an Egyptian slave named Hagar; ²so she said to Abram, "The LORD has kept me from having children. Go, sleep with my slave; perhaps I can build a family through her."

Abram agreed to what Sarai said. ³So after Abram had been living in Canaan ten years, Sarai his wife took her Egyptian slave Hagar and gave her to her husband to be his wife. ⁴He slept with Hagar, and she conceived.

When she knew she was pregnant, she began to despise her mistress. ⁵Then Sarai said to Abram, "You are responsible for the wrong I am suffering. I put my slave in your arms, and now that she knows she is pregnant, she despises me. May the LORD judge between you and me."

⁶"Your slave is in your hands," Abram said. "Do with her whatever you think best." Then Sarai mistreated Hagar; so she fled from her.

⁷The angel of the LORD found Hagar near a spring in the desert; it was the spring that is beside the road to Shur. ⁸And he said, "Hagar, slave of Sarai, where have you come from, and where are you going?"

"I'm running away from my mistress Sarai," she answered.

⁹Then the angel of the LORD told her, "Go back to your mistress and submit to her." ¹⁰The angel added, "I will increase your descendants so much that they will be too numerous to count."

¹¹The angel of the LORD also said to her:

"You are now pregnant
    and you will give birth to a son.
You shall name him Ishmael,ᵃ
    for the LORD has heard of your misery.
¹²He will be a wild donkey of a man;
    his hand will be against everyone
    and everyone's hand against him,
and he will live in hostility
    towardᵇ all his brothers."

¹³She gave this name to the LORD who spoke to her: "You are the God who sees me," for she said, "I have now seenᶜ the One who sees me." ¹⁴That is why the well was called Beer Lahai Roiᵈ; it is still there, between Kadesh and Bered.

¹⁵So Hagar bore Abram a son, and Abram gave the name Ishmael to the son she had borne. ¹⁶Abram was eighty-six years old when Hagar bore him Ishmael.

The Covenant of Circumcision

17 When Abram was ninety-nine years old, the LORD appeared to him and said, "I am God Almightyᵉ; walk before me faithfully and be blameless. ²Then I will make my covenant between me and you and will greatly increase your numbers."

³Abram fell facedown, and God said to him, ⁴"As for me, this is my covenant with you: You will be the father of many nations. ⁵No longer will you be called Abramᶠ; your name will be Abraham,ᵍ for I have made you a father of many nations. ⁶I will make you very fruitful; I will make nations of you, and kings will come from you. ⁷I will establish my covenant as an everlasting covenant between me and you and your descendants after you for the generations to come, to be your God and the God of your descendants after you. ⁸The whole land of Canaan, where you now reside as a foreigner, I will give as an everlasting possession to you and your descendants after you; and I will be their God."

⁹Then God said to Abraham, "As for you, you must keep my covenant, you and your descendants after you for the generations to come. ¹⁰This is my covenant with you and your descendants after you, the covenant you are to keep: Every male among you shall be circumcised. ¹¹You are to undergo circumcision, and it will be the sign of the covenant between me and you. ¹²For the generations to come every male among you who is eight days old must be circumcised, including those born in your household or bought with money from a foreigner — those who are not your offspring. ¹³Whether born in your household or bought with your money, they must be circumcised. My covenant in your flesh is to be an everlasting covenant. ¹⁴Any uncircumcised male, who has not been circumcised in the flesh, will be cut

---

ᵃ 11 *Ishmael* means *God hears.*   ᵇ 12 Or *live to the east / of*   ᶜ 13 Or *seen the back of*   ᵈ 14 *Beer Lahai Roi* means *well of the Living One who sees me.*   ᵉ 1 Hebrew *El-Shaddai*   ᶠ 5 *Abram* means *exalted father.*   ᵍ 5 *Abraham* probably means *father of many.*

off from his people; he has broken my covenant."

[15] God also said to Abraham, "As for Sarai your wife, you are no longer to call her Sarai; her name will be Sarah. [16] I will bless her and will surely give you a son by her. I will bless her so that she will be the mother of nations; kings of peoples will come from her."

[17] Abraham fell facedown; he laughed and said to himself, "Will a son be born to a man a hundred years old? Will Sarah bear a child at the age of ninety?" [18] And Abraham said to God, "If only Ishmael might live under your blessing!"

[19] Then God said, "Yes, but your wife Sarah will bear you a son, and you will call him Isaac.[a] I will establish my covenant with him as an everlasting covenant for his descendants after him. [20] And as for Ishmael, I have heard you: I will surely bless him; I will make him fruitful and will greatly increase his numbers. He will be the father of twelve rulers, and I will make him into a great nation. [21] But my covenant I will establish with Isaac, whom Sarah will bear to you by this time next year." [22] When he had finished speaking with Abraham, God went up from him.

[23] On that very day Abraham took his son Ishmael and all those born in his household or bought with his money, every male in his household, and circumcised them, as God told him. [24] Abraham was ninety-nine years old when he was circumcised, [25] and his son Ishmael was thirteen; [26] Abraham and his son Ishmael were both circumcised on that very day. [27] And every male in Abraham's household, including those born in his household or bought from a foreigner, was circumcised with him.

The Three Visitors

18 The LORD appeared to Abraham near the great trees of Mamre while he was sitting at the entrance to his tent in the heat of the day. [2] Abraham looked up and saw three men standing nearby. When he saw them, he hurried from the entrance of his tent to meet them and bowed low to the ground.

[3] He said, "If I have found favor in your eyes, my lord,[b] do not pass your servant by. [4] Let a little water be brought, and then you may all wash your feet and rest under this tree. [5] Let me get you something to eat, so you can be refreshed and then go on your way—now that you have come to your servant."

"Very well," they answered, "do as you say."

[6] So Abraham hurried into the tent to Sarah. "Quick," he said, "get three seahs[c] of the finest flour and knead it and bake some bread."

[7] Then he ran to the herd and selected a choice, tender calf and gave it to a servant, who hurried to prepare it. [8] He then brought some curds and milk and the calf that had been prepared, and set these before them. While they ate, he stood near them under a tree.

[9] "Where is your wife Sarah?" they asked him.

"There, in the tent," he said.

[10] Then one of them said, "I will surely return to you about this time next year, and Sarah your wife will have a son."

Now Sarah was listening at the entrance to the tent, which was behind him. [11] Abraham and Sarah were already very old, and Sarah was past the age of childbearing. [12] So Sarah laughed to herself as she thought, "After I am worn out and my lord is old, will I now have this pleasure?"

[13] Then the LORD said to Abraham, "Why did Sarah laugh and say, 'Will I really have a child, now that I am old?' [14] Is anything too hard for the LORD? I will return to you at the appointed time next year, and Sarah will have a son."

[15] Sarah was afraid, so she lied and said, "I did not laugh."

But he said, "Yes, you did laugh."

Abraham Pleads for Sodom

[16] When the men got up to leave, they looked down toward Sodom, and Abraham walked along with them to see them on their way. [17] Then the LORD said, "Shall I hide from Abraham what I am about to do? [18] Abraham will surely become a great and powerful nation, and all nations on earth will be blessed through him.[d] [19] For I have chosen him, so that he will direct his children and his household after him to keep the way of the LORD by doing what is right and just, so that

---

[a] 19 *Isaac* means *he laughs*.   [b] 3 Or *eyes, Lord*   [c] 6 That is, probably about 36 pounds or about 16 kilograms   [d] 18 Or *will use his name in blessings* (see 48:20)

the LORD will bring about for Abraham what he has promised him."

²⁰Then the LORD said, "The outcry against Sodom and Gomorrah is so great and their sin so grievous ²¹that I will go down and see if what they have done is as bad as the outcry that has reached me. If not, I will know."

²²The men turned away and went toward Sodom, but Abraham remained standing before the LORD.ᵃ ²³Then Abraham approached him and said: "Will you sweep away the righteous with the wicked? ²⁴What if there are fifty righteous people in the city? Will you really sweep it away and not spareᵇ the place for the sake of the fifty righteous people in it? ²⁵Far be it from you to do such a thing—to kill the righteous with the wicked, treating the righteous and the wicked alike. Far be it from you! Will not the Judge of all the earth do right?"

²⁶The LORD said, "If I find fifty righteous people in the city of Sodom, I will spare the whole place for their sake."

²⁷Then Abraham spoke up again: "Now that I have been so bold as to speak to the Lord, though I am nothing but dust and ashes, ²⁸what if the number of the righteous is five less than fifty? Will you destroy the whole city for lack of five people?"

"If I find forty-five there," he said, "I will not destroy it."

²⁹Once again he spoke to him, "What if only forty are found there?"

He said, "For the sake of forty, I will not do it."

³⁰Then he said, "May the Lord not be angry, but let me speak. What if only thirty can be found there?"

He answered, "I will not do it if I find thirty there."

³¹Abraham said, "Now that I have been so bold as to speak to the Lord, what if only twenty can be found there?"

He said, "For the sake of twenty, I will not destroy it."

³²Then he said, "May the Lord not be angry, but let me speak just once more. What if only ten can be found there?"

He answered, "For the sake of ten, I will not destroy it."

³³When the LORD had finished speaking with Abraham, he left, and Abraham returned home.

Sodom and Gomorrah Destroyed

19 The two angels arrived at Sodom in the evening, and Lot was sitting in the gateway of the city. When he saw them, he got up to meet them and bowed down with his face to the ground. ²"My lords," he said, "please turn aside to your servant's house. You can wash your feet and spend the night and then go on your way early in the morning."

"No," they answered, "we will spend the night in the square."

³But he insisted so strongly that they did go with him and entered his house. He prepared a meal for them, baking bread without yeast, and they ate. ⁴Before they had gone to bed, all the men from every part of the city of Sodom—both young and old—surrounded the house. ⁵They called to Lot, "Where are the men who came to you tonight? Bring them out to us so that we can have sex with them."

⁶Lot went outside to meet them and shut the door behind him ⁷and said, "No, my friends. Don't do this wicked thing. ⁸Look, I have two daughters who have never slept with a man. Let me bring them out to you, and you can do what you like with them. But don't do anything to these men, for they have come under the protection of my roof."

⁹"Get out of our way," they replied. "This fellow came here as a foreigner, and now he wants to play the judge! We'll treat you worse than them." They kept bringing pressure on Lot and moved forward to break down the door.

¹⁰But the men inside reached out and pulled Lot back into the house and shut the door. ¹¹Then they struck the men who were at the door of the house, young and old, with blindness so that they could not find the door.

¹²The two men said to Lot, "Do you have anyone else here—sons-in-law, sons or daughters, or anyone else in the city who belongs to you? Get them out of here, ¹³because we are going to destroy this place. The outcry to the LORD against its people is so great that he has sent us to destroy it."

¹⁴So Lot went out and spoke to his sons-in-law, who were pledged to marryᶜ his daughters. He said, "Hurry and get out of this place, because the LORD is about to destroy the city!" But his sons-in-law thought he was joking.

ᵃ 22 Masoretic Text; an ancient Hebrew scribal tradition *but the LORD remained standing before Abraham*
ᵇ 24 Or *forgive*; also in verse 26   ᶜ 14 Or *were married to*

¹⁵With the coming of dawn, the angels urged Lot, saying, "Hurry! Take your wife and your two daughters who are here, or you will be swept away when the city is punished."

¹⁶When he hesitated, the men grasped his hand and the hands of his wife and of his two daughters and led them safely out of the city, for the LORD was merciful to them. ¹⁷As soon as they had brought them out, one of them said, "Flee for your lives! Don't look back, and don't stop anywhere in the plain! Flee to the mountains or you will be swept away!"

¹⁸But Lot said to them, "No, my lords,ᵃ please! ¹⁹Yourᵇ servant has found favor in yourᵇ eyes, and youᵇ have shown great kindness to me in sparing my life. But I can't flee to the mountains; this disaster will overtake me, and I'll die. ²⁰Look, here is a town near enough to run to, and it is small. Let me flee to it — it is very small, isn't it? Then my life will be spared."

²¹He said to him, "Very well, I will grant this request too; I will not overthrow the town you speak of. ²²But flee there quickly, because I cannot do anything until you reach it." (That is why the town was called Zoar.ᶜ)

²³By the time Lot reached Zoar, the sun had risen over the land. ²⁴Then the LORD rained down burning sulfur on Sodom and Gomorrah — from the LORD out of the heavens. ²⁵Thus he overthrew those cities and the entire plain, destroying all those living in the cities — and also the vegetation in the land. ²⁶But Lot's wife looked back, and she became a pillar of salt.

²⁷Early the next morning Abraham got up and returned to the place where he had stood before the LORD. ²⁸He looked down toward Sodom and Gomorrah, toward all the land of the plain, and he saw dense smoke rising from the land, like smoke from a furnace.

²⁹So when God destroyed the cities of the plain, he remembered Abraham, and he brought Lot out of the catastrophe that overthrew the cities where Lot had lived.

Lot and His Daughters

³⁰Lot and his two daughters left Zoar and settled in the mountains, for he was afraid to stay in Zoar. He and his two daughters lived in a cave. ³¹One day the older daughter said to the younger, "Our father is old, and there is no man around here to give us children — as is the custom all over the earth. ³²Let's get our father to drink wine and then sleep with him and preserve our family line through our father."

³³That night they got their father to drink wine, and the older daughter went in and slept with him. He was not aware of it when she lay down or when she got up.

³⁴The next day the older daughter said to the younger, "Last night I slept with my father. Let's get him to drink wine again tonight, and you go in and sleep with him so we can preserve our family line through our father." ³⁵So they got their father to drink wine that night also, and the younger daughter went in and slept with him. Again he was not aware of it when she lay down or when she got up.

³⁶So both of Lot's daughters became pregnant by their father. ³⁷The older daughter had a son, and she named him Moabᵈ; he is the father of the Moabites of today. ³⁸The younger daughter also had a son, and she named him Ben-Ammiᵉ; he is the father of the Ammonitesᶠ of today.

Abraham and Abimelek

20 Now Abraham moved on from there into the region of the Negev and lived between Kadesh and Shur. For a while he stayed in Gerar, ²and there Abraham said of his wife Sarah, "She is my sister." Then Abimelek king of Gerar sent for Sarah and took her.

³But God came to Abimelek in a dream one night and said to him, "You are as good as dead because of the woman you have taken; she is a married woman."

⁴Now Abimelek had not gone near her, so he said, "Lord, will you destroy an innocent nation? ⁵Did he not say to me, 'She is my sister,' and didn't she also say, 'He is my brother'? I have done this with a clear conscience and clean hands."

⁶Then God said to him in the dream, "Yes, I know you did this with a clear conscience, and so I have kept you from sinning against me. That is why I did not let you touch her.

ᵃ 18 Or No, Lord; or No, my lord   ᵇ 19 The Hebrew is singular.   ᶜ 22 Zoar means small.   ᵈ 37 Moab sounds like the Hebrew for from father.   ᵉ 38 Ben-Ammi means son of my father's people.   ᶠ 38 Hebrew Bene-Ammon

[7] Now return the man's wife, for he is a prophet, and he will pray for you and you will live. But if you do not return her, you may be sure that you and all who belong to you will die."

[8] Early the next morning Abimelek summoned all his officials, and when he told them all that had happened, they were very much afraid. [9] Then Abimelek called Abraham in and said, "What have you done to us? How have I wronged you that you have brought such great guilt upon me and my kingdom? You have done things to me that should never be done." [10] And Abimelek asked Abraham, "What was your reason for doing this?"

[11] Abraham replied, "I said to myself, 'There is surely no fear of God in this place, and they will kill me because of my wife.' [12] Besides, she really is my sister, the daughter of my father though not of my mother; and she became my wife. [13] And when God had me wander from my father's household, I said to her, 'This is how you can show your love to me: Everywhere we go, say of me, "He is my brother." ' "

[14] Then Abimelek brought sheep and cattle and male and female slaves and gave them to Abraham, and he returned Sarah his wife to him. [15] And Abimelek said, "My land is before you; live wherever you like."

[16] To Sarah he said, "I am giving your brother a thousand shekels[a] of silver. This is to cover the offense against you before all who are with you; you are completely vindicated."

[17] Then Abraham prayed to God, and God healed Abimelek, his wife and his female slaves so they could have children again, [18] for the LORD had kept all the women in Abimelek's household from conceiving because of Abraham's wife Sarah.

The Birth of Isaac

21 Now the LORD was gracious to Sarah as he had said, and the LORD did for Sarah what he had promised. [2] Sarah became pregnant and bore a son to Abraham in his old age, at the very time God had promised him. [3] Abraham gave the name Isaac[b] to the son Sarah bore him. [4] When his son Isaac was eight days old, Abraham circumcised him, as God commanded him.

[5] Abraham was a hundred years old when his son Isaac was born to him.

[6] Sarah said, "God has brought me laughter, and everyone who hears about this will laugh with me." [7] And she added, "Who would have said to Abraham that Sarah would nurse children? Yet I have borne him a son in his old age."

Hagar and Ishmael Sent Away

[8] The child grew and was weaned, and on the day Isaac was weaned Abraham held a great feast. [9] But Sarah saw that the son whom Hagar the Egyptian had borne to Abraham was mocking, [10] and she said to Abraham, "Get rid of that slave woman and her son, for that woman's son will never share in the inheritance with my son Isaac."

[11] The matter distressed Abraham greatly because it concerned his son. [12] But God said to him, "Do not be so distressed about the boy and your slave woman. Listen to whatever Sarah tells you, because it is through Isaac that your offspring[c] will be reckoned. [13] I will make the son of the slave into a nation also, because he is your offspring."

[14] Early the next morning Abraham took some food and a skin of water and gave them to Hagar. He set them on her shoulders and then sent her off with the boy. She went on her way and wandered in the Desert of Beersheba.

[15] When the water in the skin was gone, she put the boy under one of the bushes. [16] Then she went off and sat down about a bowshot away, for she thought, "I cannot watch the boy die." And as she sat there, she[d] began to sob.

[17] God heard the boy crying, and the angel of God called to Hagar from heaven and said to her, "What is the matter, Hagar? Do not be afraid; God has heard the boy crying as he lies there. [18] Lift the boy up and take him by the hand, for I will make him into a great nation."

[19] Then God opened her eyes and she saw a well of water. So she went and filled the skin with water and gave the boy a drink.

[20] God was with the boy as he grew up. He lived in the desert and became an archer. [21] While he was living in the Desert of Paran, his mother got a wife for him from Egypt.

---

[a] 16 That is, about 25 pounds or about 12 kilograms
[d] 16 Hebrew; Septuagint *the child*
[b] 3 *Isaac* means *he laughs*.   [c] 12 Or *seed*

The Treaty at Beersheba

²²At that time Abimelek and Phicol the commander of his forces said to Abraham, "God is with you in everything you do. ²³Now swear to me here before God that you will not deal falsely with me or my children or my descendants. Show to me and the country where you now reside as a foreigner the same kindness I have shown to you."

²⁴Abraham said, "I swear it."

²⁵Then Abraham complained to Abimelek about a well of water that Abimelek's servants had seized. ²⁶But Abimelek said, "I don't know who has done this. You did not tell me, and I heard about it only today."

²⁷So Abraham brought sheep and cattle and gave them to Abimelek, and the two men made a treaty. ²⁸Abraham set apart seven ewe lambs from the flock, ²⁹and Abimelek asked Abraham, "What is the meaning of these seven ewe lambs you have set apart by themselves?"

³⁰He replied, "Accept these seven lambs from my hand as a witness that I dug this well."

³¹So that place was called Beersheba,ᵃ because the two men swore an oath there.

³²After the treaty had been made at Beersheba, Abimelek and Phicol the commander of his forces returned to the land of the Philistines. ³³Abraham planted a tamarisk tree in Beersheba, and there he called on the name of the Lord, the Eternal God. ³⁴And Abraham stayed in the land of the Philistines for a long time.

Abraham Tested

22 Some time later God tested Abraham. He said to him, "Abraham!"

"Here I am," he replied.

²Then God said, "Take your son, your only son, whom you love—Isaac—and go to the region of Moriah. Sacrifice him there as a burnt offering on a mountain I will show you."

³Early the next morning Abraham got up and loaded his donkey. He took with him two of his servants and his son Isaac. When he had cut enough wood for the burnt offering, he set out for the place God had told him about. ⁴On the third day Abraham looked up and saw the place in the distance. ⁵He said to his servants, "Stay here with the donkey while I and the boy go over there. We will worship and then we will come back to you."

⁶Abraham took the wood for the burnt offering and placed it on his son Isaac, and he himself carried the fire and the knife. As the two of them went on together, ⁷Isaac spoke up and said to his father Abraham, "Father?"

"Yes, my son?" Abraham replied.

"The fire and wood are here," Isaac said, "but where is the lamb for the burnt offering?"

⁸Abraham answered, "God himself will provide the lamb for the burnt offering, my son." And the two of them went on together.

⁹When they reached the place God had told him about, Abraham built an altar there and arranged the wood on it. He bound his son Isaac and laid him on the altar, on top of the wood. ¹⁰Then he reached out his hand and took the knife to slay his son. ¹¹But the angel of the Lord called out to him from heaven, "Abraham! Abraham!"

"Here I am," he replied.

¹²"Do not lay a hand on the boy," he said. "Do not do anything to him. Now I know that you fear God, because you have not withheld from me your son, your only son."

¹³Abraham looked up and there in a thicket he saw a ramᵇ caught by its horns. He went over and took the ram and sacrificed it as a burnt offering instead of his son. ¹⁴So Abraham called that place The Lord Will Provide. And to this day it is said, "On the mountain of the Lord it will be provided."

¹⁵The angel of the Lord called to Abraham from heaven a second time ¹⁶and said, "I swear by myself, declares the Lord, that because you have done this and have not withheld your son, your only son, ¹⁷I will surely bless you and make your descendants as numerous as the stars in the sky and as the sand on the seashore. Your descendants will take possession of the cities of their enemies, ¹⁸and through your offspringᶜ all nations on earth will be blessed,ᵈ because you have obeyed me."

¹⁹Then Abraham returned to his servants, and they set off together for Beersheba. And Abraham stayed in Beersheba.

ᵃ 31 *Beersheba* can mean *well of seven* and *well of the oath.*   ᵇ 13 Many manuscripts of the Masoretic Text, Samaritan Pentateuch, Septuagint and Syriac; most manuscripts of the Masoretic Text *a ram behind him*   ᶜ 18 Or *seed*   ᵈ 18 Or *and all nations on earth will use the name of your offspring in blessings* (see 48:20)

PASS OR FAIL

READ: GENESIS 22:1-2

How could a loving heavenly Father even suggest something like this? But honestly, it's the biblical stories that cause the most discomfort to our logical minds that usually have the best revelations. We like to read stories like this one as if God's on trial, but it's not his character that is in question, it's ours. And that's precisely why God tests us.

God never planned on letting Abraham actually sacrifice his son. It was only a test. He wanted see if Abe was willing to obey the most absurd command imaginable. God tested Abraham. And Abraham passed with flying colors. That's how you get a testimony; you have to pass the test.

No test = No testimony

I didn't get a testimony in seminary or church. You don't get a testimony by listening to a lecture or sermon or speech in the comfortable confines of a classroom, church, or conference. You get a testimony in the wilderness like Moses, on the Sea of Galilee like Peter, or on the mountain like Abraham.

BUILDING FAITH WISDOM STRENGTH

According to Jewish tradition, God gave Abraham ten different tests. This one is the final exam. It was specifically designed to test whether Abraham was all in.

God tests us for two primary reasons. First, it's an opportunity for God to prove himself to us. Second, it's an opportunity for us to prove ourselves to God. Tests are the proving grounds.

Nahor's Sons

²⁰Some time later Abraham was told, "Milkah is also a mother; she has borne sons to your brother Nahor: ²¹Uz the firstborn, Buz his brother, Kemuel (the father of Aram), ²²Kesed, Hazo, Pildash, Jidlaph and Bethuel." ²³Bethuel became the father of Rebekah. Milkah bore these eight sons to Abraham's brother Nahor. ²⁴His concubine, whose name was Reumah, also had sons: Tebah, Gaham, Tahash and Maakah.

The Death of Sarah

23 Sarah lived to be a hundred and twenty-seven years old. ²She died at Kiriath Arba (that is, Hebron) in the land of Canaan, and Abraham went to mourn for Sarah and to weep over her.

³Then Abraham rose from beside his dead wife and spoke to the Hittites.ᵃ He said, ⁴"I am a foreigner and stranger among you. Sell me some property for a burial site here so I can bury my dead."

⁵The Hittites replied to Abraham, ⁶"Sir, listen to us. You are a mighty prince among us. Bury your dead in the choicest of our tombs. None of us will refuse you his tomb for burying your dead."

⁷Then Abraham rose and bowed down before the people of the land, the Hittites. ⁸He said to them, "If you are willing to let me bury my dead, then listen to me and intercede with Ephron son of Zohar on my behalf ⁹so he will sell me the cave of Machpelah, which belongs to him and is at the end of his field. Ask him to sell it to me for the full price as a burial site among you."

¹⁰Ephron the Hittite was sitting among his people and he replied to Abraham in the hearing of all the Hittites who had come to the gate of his city. ¹¹"No, my lord," he said. "Listen to me; I giveᵇ you the field, and I giveᵇ you the cave that is in it. I giveᵇ it to you in the presence of my people. Bury your dead."

¹²Again Abraham bowed down before the people of the land ¹³and he said to Ephron in their hearing, "Listen to me, if you will. I will pay the price of the field. Accept it from me so I can bury my dead there."

¹⁴Ephron answered Abraham, ¹⁵"Listen to me, my lord; the land is worth four hundred shekelsᶜ of silver, but what is that between you and me? Bury your dead."

¹⁶Abraham agreed to Ephron's terms and weighed out for him the price he had named in the hearing of the Hittites: four hundred shekels of silver, according to the weight current among the merchants.

¹⁷So Ephron's field in Machpelah near Mamre — both the field and the cave in it, and all the trees within the borders of the field — was deeded ¹⁸to Abraham as his property in the presence of all the Hittites who had come to the gate of the city. ¹⁹Afterward Abraham buried his wife Sarah in the cave in the field of Machpelah near Mamre (which is at Hebron) in the land of Canaan. ²⁰So the field and the cave in it were deeded to Abraham by the Hittites as a burial site.

Isaac and Rebekah

24 Abraham was now very old, and the LORD had blessed him in every way. ²He said to the senior servant in his household, the one in charge of all that he had, "Put your hand under my thigh. ³I want you to swear by the LORD, the God of heaven and the God of earth, that you will not get a wife for my son from the daughters of the Canaanites, among whom I am living, ⁴but will go to my country and my own relatives and get a wife for my son Isaac."

⁵The servant asked him, "What if the woman is unwilling to come back with me to this land? Shall I then take your son back to the country you came from?"

⁶"Make sure that you do not take my son back there," Abraham said. ⁷"The LORD, the God of heaven, who brought me out of my father's household and my native land and who spoke to me and promised me on oath, saying, 'To your offspringᵈ I will give this land' — he will send his angel before you so that you can get a wife for my son from there. ⁸If the woman is unwilling to come back with you, then you will be released from this oath of mine. Only do not take my son back there." ⁹So the servant put his hand under the thigh of his master Abraham and swore an oath to him concerning this matter.

¹⁰Then the servant left, taking with him ten of his master's camels loaded with all kinds of good things from his master. He set

---

ᵃ 3 Or *the descendants of Heth*; also in verses 5, 7, 10, 16, 18 and 20   ᵇ 11 Or *sell*   ᶜ 15 That is, about 10 pounds or about 4.6 kilograms   ᵈ 7 Or *seed* out for Aram Naharaim[a] and made his way to the town of Nahor. [11]He had the camels kneel down near the well outside the town; it was toward evening, the time the women go out to draw water.

[12]Then he prayed, "LORD, God of my master Abraham, make me successful today, and show kindness to my master Abraham. [13]See, I am standing beside this spring, and the daughters of the townspeople are coming out to draw water. [14]May it be that when I say to a young woman, 'Please let down your jar that I may have a drink,' and she says, 'Drink, and I'll water your camels too' — let her be the one you have chosen for your servant Isaac. By this I will know that you have shown kindness to my master."

[15]Before he had finished praying, Rebekah came out with her jar on her shoulder. She was the daughter of Bethuel son of Milkah, who was the wife of Abraham's brother Nahor. [16]The woman was very beautiful, a virgin; no man had ever slept with her. She went down to the spring, filled her jar and came up again.

[17]The servant hurried to meet her and said, "Please give me a little water from your jar."

[18]"Drink, my lord," she said, and quickly lowered the jar to her hands and gave him a drink.

[19]After she had given him a drink, she said, "I'll draw water for your camels too, until they have had enough to drink." [20]So she quickly emptied her jar into the trough, ran back to the well to draw more water, and drew enough for all his camels. [21]Without saying a word, the man watched her closely to learn whether or not the LORD had made his journey successful.

[22]When the camels had finished drinking, the man took out a gold nose ring weighing a beka[b] and two gold bracelets weighing ten shekels.[c] [23]Then he asked, "Whose daughter are you? Please tell me, is there room in your father's house for us to spend the night?"

[24]She answered him, "I am the daughter of Bethuel, the son that Milkah bore to Nahor." [25]And she added, "We have plenty of straw and fodder, as well as room for you to spend the night."

[26]Then the man bowed down and worshiped the LORD, [27]saying, "Praise be to the LORD, the God of my master Abraham, who has not abandoned his kindness and faithfulness to my master. As for me, the LORD has led me on the journey to the house of my master's relatives."

[28]The young woman ran and told her mother's household about these things. [29]Now Rebekah had a brother named Laban, and he hurried out to the man at the spring. [30]As soon as he had seen the nose ring, and the bracelets on his sister's arms, and had heard Rebekah tell what the man said to her, he went out to the man and found him standing by the camels near the spring. [31]"Come, you who are blessed by the LORD," he said. "Why are you standing out here? I have prepared the house and a place for the camels."

[32]So the man went to the house, and the camels were unloaded. Straw and fodder were brought for the camels, and water for him and his men to wash their feet. [33]Then food was set before him, but he said, "I will not eat until I have told you what I have to say."

"Then tell us," Laban said.

[34]So he said, "I am Abraham's servant. [35]The LORD has blessed my master abundantly, and he has become wealthy. He has given him sheep and cattle, silver and gold, male and female servants, and camels and donkeys. [36]My master's wife Sarah has borne him a son in her old age, and he has given him everything he owns. [37]And my master made me swear an oath, and said, 'You must not get a wife for my son from the daughters of the Canaanites, in whose land I live, [38]but go to my father's family and to my own clan, and get a wife for my son.'

[39]"Then I asked my master, 'What if the woman will not come back with me?'

[40]"He replied, 'The LORD, before whom I have walked faithfully, will send his angel with you and make your journey a success, so that you can get a wife for my son from my own clan and from my father's family. [41]You will be released from my oath if, when you go to my clan, they refuse to give her to you — then you will be released from my oath.'

[42]"When I came to the spring today, I said, 'LORD, God of my master Abraham, if you will, please grant success to the journey on which I have come. [43]See, I am standing beside this spring. If a young woman comes

---

[a] 10 That is, Northwest Mesopotamia about 4 ounces or about 115 grams   [b] 22 That is, about 1/5 ounce or about 5.7 grams   [c] 22 That is,

out to draw water and I say to her, "Please let me drink a little water from your jar," [44] and if she says to me, "Drink, and I'll draw water for your camels too," let her be the one the LORD has chosen for my master's son.'

[45] "Before I finished praying in my heart, Rebekah came out, with her jar on her shoulder. She went down to the spring and drew water, and I said to her, 'Please give me a drink.'

[46] "She quickly lowered her jar from her shoulder and said, 'Drink, and I'll water your camels too.' So I drank, and she watered the camels also.

[47] "I asked her, 'Whose daughter are you?'

"She said, 'The daughter of Bethuel son of Nahor, whom Milkah bore to him.'

"Then I put the ring in her nose and the bracelets on her arms, [48] and I bowed down and worshiped the LORD. I praised the LORD, the God of my master Abraham, who had led me on the right road to get the granddaughter of my master's brother for his son. [49] Now if you will show kindness and faithfulness to my master, tell me; and if not, tell me, so I may know which way to turn."

[50] Laban and Bethuel answered, "This is from the LORD; we can say nothing to you one way or the other. [51] Here is Rebekah; take her and go, and let her become the wife of your master's son, as the LORD has directed."

[52] When Abraham's servant heard what they said, he bowed down to the ground before the LORD. [53] Then the servant brought out gold and silver jewelry and articles of clothing and gave them to Rebekah; he also gave costly gifts to her brother and to her mother. [54] Then he and the men who were with him ate and drank and spent the night there.

When they got up the next morning, he said, "Send me on my way to my master."

[55] But her brother and her mother replied, "Let the young woman remain with us ten days or so; then you[a] may go."

[56] But he said to them, "Do not detain me, now that the LORD has granted success to my journey. Send me on my way so I may go to my master."

[57] Then they said, "Let's call the young woman and ask her about it." [58] So they called Rebekah and asked her, "Will you go with this man?"

"I will go," she said.

[59] So they sent their sister Rebekah on her way, along with her nurse and Abraham's servant and his men. [60] And they blessed Rebekah and said to her,

"Our sister, may you increase
    to thousands upon thousands;
may your offspring possess
    the cities of their enemies."

[61] Then Rebekah and her attendants got ready and mounted the camels and went back with the man. So the servant took Rebekah and left.

[62] Now Isaac had come from Beer Lahai Roi, for he was living in the Negev. [63] He went out to the field one evening to meditate,[b] and as he looked up, he saw camels approaching. [64] Rebekah also looked up and saw Isaac. She got down from her camel [65] and asked the servant, "Who is that man in the field coming to meet us?"

"He is my master," the servant answered. So she took her veil and covered herself.

[66] Then the servant told Isaac all he had done. [67] Isaac brought her into the tent of his mother Sarah, and he married Rebekah. So she became his wife, and he loved her; and Isaac was comforted after his mother's death.

The Death of Abraham

25 Abraham had taken another wife, whose name was Keturah. [2] She bore him Zimran, Jokshan, Medan, Midian, Ishbak and Shuah. [3] Jokshan was the father of Sheba and Dedan; the descendants of Dedan were the Ashurites, the Letushites and the Leummites. [4] The sons of Midian were Ephah, Epher, Hanok, Abida and Eldaah. All these were descendants of Keturah.

[5] Abraham left everything he owned to Isaac. [6] But while he was still living, he gave gifts to the sons of his concubines and sent them away from his son Isaac to the land of the east.

[7] Abraham lived a hundred and seventy-five years. [8] Then Abraham breathed his last and died at a good old age, an old man and full of years; and he was gathered to his people. [9] His sons Isaac and Ishmael buried him in the cave of Machpelah near Mamre, in the

---

[a] 55 Or she   [b] 63 The meaning of the Hebrew for this word is uncertain.

field of Ephron son of Zohar the Hittite, [10] the field Abraham had bought from the Hittites.[a] There Abraham was buried with his wife Sarah. [11] After Abraham's death, God blessed his son Isaac, who then lived near Beer Lahai Roi.

Ishmael's Sons

[12] This is the account of the family line of Abraham's son Ishmael, whom Sarah's slave, Hagar the Egyptian, bore to Abraham.

[13] These are the names of the sons of Ishmael, listed in the order of their birth: Nebaioth the firstborn of Ishmael, Kedar, Adbeel, Mibsam, [14] Mishma, Dumah, Massa, [15] Hadad, Tema, Jetur, Naphish and Kedemah. [16] These were the sons of Ishmael, and these are the names of the twelve tribal rulers according to their settlements and camps. [17] Ishmael lived a hundred and thirty-seven years. He breathed his last and died, and he was gathered to his people. [18] His descendants settled in the area from Havilah to Shur, near the eastern border of Egypt, as you go toward Ashur. And they lived in hostility toward[b] all the tribes related to them.

Jacob and Esau

[19] This is the account of the family line of Abraham's son Isaac.

Abraham became the father of Isaac, [20] and Isaac was forty years old when he married Rebekah daughter of Bethuel the Aramean from Paddan Aram[c] and sister of Laban the Aramean.

[21] Isaac prayed to the LORD on behalf of his wife, because she was childless. The LORD answered his prayer, and his wife Rebekah became pregnant. [22] The babies jostled each other within her, and she said, "Why is this happening to me?" So she went to inquire of the LORD.

[23] The LORD said to her,

"Two nations are in your womb,
    and two peoples from within you will
        be separated;
one people will be stronger than the
        other,
    and the older will serve the younger."

[24] When the time came for her to give birth, there were twin boys in her womb. [25] The first to come out was red, and his whole body was like a hairy garment; so they named him Esau.[d] [26] After this, his brother came out, with his hand grasping Esau's heel; so he was named Jacob.[e] Isaac was sixty years old when Rebekah gave birth to them.

[27] The boys grew up, and Esau became a skillful hunter, a man of the open country, while Jacob was content to stay at home among the tents. [28] Isaac, who had a taste for wild game, loved Esau, but Rebekah loved Jacob.

[29] Once when Jacob was cooking some stew, Esau came in from the open country, famished. [30] He said to Jacob, "Quick, let me have some of that red stew! I'm famished!" (That is why he was also called Edom.[f])

[31] Jacob replied, "First sell me your birthright."

[32] "Look, I am about to die," Esau said. "What good is the birthright to me?"

[33] But Jacob said, "Swear to me first." So he swore an oath to him, selling his birthright to Jacob.

[34] Then Jacob gave Esau some bread and some lentil stew. He ate and drank, and then got up and left.

So Esau despised his birthright.

Isaac and Abimelek

26 Now there was a famine in the land — besides the previous famine in Abraham's time — and Isaac went to Abimelek king of the Philistines in Gerar. [2] The LORD appeared to Isaac and said, "Do not go down to Egypt; live in the land where I tell you to live. [3] Stay in this land for a while, and I will be with you and will bless you. For to you and your descendants I will give all these lands and will confirm the oath I swore to your father Abraham. [4] I will make your descendants as numerous as the stars in the sky and will give them all these lands, and through your offspring[g] all nations on earth will be blessed,[h] [5] because Abraham obeyed me and did everything I required of him, keeping my commands, my decrees and my instructions." [6] So Isaac stayed in Gerar.

---

[a] 10 Or *the descendants of Heth*   [b] 18 Or *lived to the east of*   [c] 20 That is, Northwest Mesopotamia
[d] 25 *Esau* may mean *hairy*.   [e] 26 *Jacob* means *he grasps the heel*, a Hebrew idiom for *he deceives*.
[f] 30 *Edom* means *red*.   [g] 4 Or *seed*   [h] 4 Or *and all nations on earth will use the name of your offspring in blessings* (see 48:20)

7When the men of that place asked him about his wife, he said, "She is my sister," because he was afraid to say, "She is my wife." He thought, "The men of this place might kill me on account of Rebekah, because she is beautiful."

8When Isaac had been there a long time, Abimelek king of the Philistines looked down from a window and saw Isaac caressing his wife Rebekah. 9So Abimelek summoned Isaac and said, "She is really your wife! Why did you say, 'She is my sister'?"

Isaac answered him, "Because I thought I might lose my life on account of her."

10Then Abimelek said, "What is this you have done to us? One of the men might well have slept with your wife, and you would have brought guilt upon us."

11So Abimelek gave orders to all the people: "Anyone who harms this man or his wife shall surely be put to death."

12Isaac planted crops in that land and the same year reaped a hundredfold, because the LORD blessed him. 13The man became rich, and his wealth continued to grow until he became very wealthy. 14He had so many flocks and herds and servants that the Philistines envied him. 15So all the wells that his father's servants had dug in the time of his father Abraham, the Philistines stopped up, filling them with earth.

16Then Abimelek said to Isaac, "Move away from us; you have become too powerful for us."

17So Isaac moved away from there and encamped in the Valley of Gerar, where he settled. 18Isaac reopened the wells that had been dug in the time of his father Abraham, which the Philistines had stopped up after Abraham died, and he gave them the same names his father had given them.

19Isaac's servants dug in the valley and discovered a well of fresh water there. 20But the herders of Gerar quarreled with those of Isaac and said, "The water is ours!" So he named the well Esek,ᵃ because they disputed with him. 21Then they dug another well, but they quarreled over that one also; so he named it Sitnah.ᵇ 22He moved on from there and dug another well, and no one quarreled over it. He named it Rehoboth,ᶜ saying, "Now

the LORD has given us room and we will flourish in the land."

23From there he went up to Beersheba. 24That night the LORD appeared to him and said, "I am the God of your father Abraham. Do not be afraid, for I am with you; I will bless you and will increase the number of your descendants for the sake of my servant Abraham."

25Isaac built an altar there and called on the name of the LORD. There he pitched his tent, and there his servants dug a well.

26Meanwhile, Abimelek had come to him from Gerar, with Ahuzzath his personal adviser and Phicol the commander of his forces. 27Isaac asked them, "Why have you come to me, since you were hostile to me and sent me away?"

28They answered, "We saw clearly that the LORD was with you; so we said, 'There ought to be a sworn agreement between us' — between us and you. Let us make a treaty with you 29that you will do us no harm, just as we did not harm you but always treated you well and sent you away peacefully. And now you are blessed by the LORD."

30Isaac then made a feast for them, and they ate and drank. 31Early the next morning the men swore an oath to each other. Then Isaac sent them on their way, and they went away peacefully.

32That day Isaac's servants came and told him about the well they had dug. They said, "We've found water!" 33He called it Shibah,ᵈ and to this day the name of the town has been Beersheba.ᵉ

Jacob Takes Esau's Blessing

34When Esau was forty years old, he married Judith daughter of Beeri the Hittite, and also Basemath daughter of Elon the Hittite. 35They were a source of grief to Isaac and Rebekah.

27 When Isaac was old and his eyes were so weak that he could no longer see, he called for Esau his older son and said to him, "My son."

"Here I am," he answered.

2Isaac said, "I am now an old man and don't know the day of my death. 3Now then, get your equipment — your quiver and bow —

ᵃ 20 *Esek* means *dispute.*   ᵇ 21 *Sitnah* means *opposition.*   ᶜ 22 *Rehoboth* means *room.*   ᵈ 33 *Shibah* can mean *oath* or *seven.*   ᵉ 33 *Beersheba* can mean *well of the oath* and *well of seven.*

and go out to the open country to hunt some wild game for me. [4]Prepare me the kind of tasty food I like and bring it to me to eat, so that I may give you my blessing before I die."

[5]Now Rebekah was listening as Isaac spoke to his son Esau. When Esau left for the open country to hunt game and bring it back, [6]Rebekah said to her son Jacob, "Look, I overheard your father say to your brother Esau, [7]'Bring me some game and prepare me some tasty food to eat, so that I may give you my blessing in the presence of the LORD before I die.' [8]Now, my son, listen carefully and do what I tell you: [9]Go out to the flock and bring me two choice young goats, so I can prepare some tasty food for your father, just the way he likes it. [10]Then take it to your father to eat, so that he may give you his blessing before he dies."

[11]Jacob said to Rebekah his mother, "But my brother Esau is a hairy man while I have smooth skin. [12]What if my father touches me? I would appear to be tricking him and would bring down a curse on myself rather than a blessing."

[13]His mother said to him, "My son, let the curse fall on me. Just do what I say; go and get them for me."

[14]So he went and got them and brought them to his mother, and she prepared some tasty food, just the way his father liked it. [15]Then Rebekah took the best clothes of Esau her older son, which she had in the house, and put them on her younger son Jacob. [16]She also covered his hands and the smooth part of his neck with the goatskins. [17]Then she handed to her son Jacob the tasty food and the bread she had made.

[18]He went to his father and said, "My father."

"Yes, my son," he answered. "Who is it?"

[19]Jacob said to his father, "I am Esau your firstborn. I have done as you told me. Please sit up and eat some of my game, so that you may give me your blessing."

[20]Isaac asked his son, "How did you find it so quickly, my son?"

"The LORD your God gave me success," he replied.

[21]Then Isaac said to Jacob, "Come near so I can touch you, my son, to know whether you really are my son Esau or not."

[22]Jacob went close to his father Isaac, who touched him and said, "The voice is the voice of Jacob, but the hands are the hands of Esau." [23]He did not recognize him, for his hands were hairy like those of his brother Esau; so he proceeded to bless him. [24]"Are you really my son Esau?" he asked.

"I am," he replied.

[25]Then he said, "My son, bring me some of your game to eat, so that I may give you my blessing."

Jacob brought it to him and he ate; and he brought some wine and he drank. [26]Then his father Isaac said to him, "Come here, my son, and kiss me."

[27]So he went to him and kissed him. When Isaac caught the smell of his clothes, he blessed him and said,

"Ah, the smell of my son
    is like the smell of a field
    that the LORD has blessed.
[28]May God give you heaven's dew
    and earth's richness—
    an abundance of grain and new wine.
[29]May nations serve you
    and peoples bow down to you.
Be lord over your brothers,
    and may the sons of your mother bow
        down to you.
May those who curse you be cursed
    and those who bless you be blessed."

[30]After Isaac finished blessing him, and Jacob had scarcely left his father's presence, his brother Esau came in from hunting. [31]He too prepared some tasty food and brought it to his father. Then he said to him, "My father, please sit up and eat some of my game, so that you may give me your blessing."

[32]His father Isaac asked him, "Who are you?"

"I am your son," he answered, "your firstborn, Esau."

[33]Isaac trembled violently and said, "Who was it, then, that hunted game and brought it to me? I ate it just before you came and I blessed him—and indeed he will be blessed!"

[34]When Esau heard his father's words, he burst out with a loud and bitter cry and said to his father, "Bless me—me too, my father!"

[35]But he said, "Your brother came deceitfully and took your blessing."

[36]Esau said, "Isn't he rightly named Jacob[a]? This is the second time he has taken

---

[a] 36 *Jacob* means *he grasps the heel*, a Hebrew idiom for *he takes advantage of* or *he deceives*.

advantage of me: He took my birthright, and now he's taken my blessing!" Then he asked, "Haven't you reserved any blessing for me?"

[37] Isaac answered Esau, "I have made him lord over you and have made all his relatives his servants, and I have sustained him with grain and new wine. So what can I possibly do for you, my son?"

[38] Esau said to his father, "Do you have only one blessing, my father? Bless me too, my father!" Then Esau wept aloud.

[39] His father Isaac answered him,

"Your dwelling will be
  away from the earth's richness,
  away from the dew of heaven above.
[40] You will live by the sword
  and you will serve your brother.
But when you grow restless,
  you will throw his yoke
  from off your neck."

[41] Esau held a grudge against Jacob because of the blessing his father had given him. He said to himself, "The days of mourning for my father are near; then I will kill my brother Jacob."

[42] When Rebekah was told what her older son Esau had said, she sent for her younger son Jacob and said to him, "Your brother Esau is planning to avenge himself by killing you. [43] Now then, my son, do what I say: Flee at once to my brother Laban in Harran. [44] Stay with him for a while until your brother's fury subsides. [45] When your brother is no longer angry with you and forgets what you did to him, I'll send word for you to come back from there. Why should I lose both of you in one day?"

[46] Then Rebekah said to Isaac, "I'm disgusted with living because of these Hittite women. If Jacob takes a wife from among the women of this land, from Hittite women like these, my life will not be worth living."

28 So Isaac called for Jacob and blessed him. Then he commanded him: "Do not marry a Canaanite woman. [2] Go at once to Paddan Aram,[a] to the house of your mother's father Bethuel. Take a wife for yourself there, from among the daughters of Laban, your mother's brother. [3] May God Almighty[b] bless you and make you fruitful and increase your numbers until you become a community of peoples. [4] May he give you and your descendants the blessing given to Abraham, so that you may take possession of the land where you now reside as a foreigner, the land God gave to Abraham." [5] Then Isaac sent Jacob on his way, and he went to Paddan Aram, to Laban son of Bethuel the Aramean, the brother of Rebekah, who was the mother of Jacob and Esau.

[6] Now Esau learned that Isaac had blessed Jacob and had sent him to Paddan Aram to take a wife from there, and that when he blessed him he commanded him, "Do not marry a Canaanite woman," [7] and that Jacob had obeyed his father and mother and had gone to Paddan Aram. [8] Esau then realized how displeasing the Canaanite women were to his father Isaac; [9] so he went to Ishmael and married Mahalath, the sister of Nebaioth and daughter of Ishmael son of Abraham, in addition to the wives he already had.

Jacob's Dream at Bethel

[10] Jacob left Beersheba and set out for Harran. [11] When he reached a certain place, he stopped for the night because the sun had set. Taking one of the stones there, he put it under his head and lay down to sleep. [12] He had a dream in which he saw a stairway resting on the earth, with its top reaching to heaven, and the angels of God were ascending and descending on it. [13] There above it[c] stood the LORD, and he said: "I am the LORD, the God of your father Abraham and the God of Isaac. I will give you and your descendants the land on which you are lying. [14] Your descendants will be like the dust of the earth, and you will spread out to the west and to the east, to the north and to the south. All peoples on earth will be blessed through you and your offspring.[d] [15] I am with you and will watch over you wherever you go, and I will bring you back to this land. I will not leave you until I have done what I have promised you."

[16] When Jacob awoke from his sleep, he thought, "Surely the LORD is in this place, and I was not aware of it." [17] He was afraid and said, "How awesome is this place! This is none other than the house of God; this is the gate of heaven."

---

[a] 2 That is, Northwest Mesopotamia; also in verses 5, 6 and 7   [b] 3 Hebrew *El-Shaddai*   [c] 13 Or *There beside him*   [d] 14 Or *will use your name and the name of your offspring in blessings* (see 48:20)

SIBLING RIVALRY

READ: **GENESIS 27:41**

Siblings fight. They might clash more with each other than anyone else they ever meet. In fact, the feud between Isaac's sons Jacob and Esau grew so intense that people still tell the story thousands of years later. These twin boys start fighting back in Genesis 25, where they elbow inside their mother's womb. Esau is born first, and Jacob comes out grabbing his brother's heel. They grow up into complete opposites, and their parents do little to help the situation. Old Isaac favors Esau, while Rebekah likes Jacob better.

At the end of Genesis 25, Esau comes back famished from hunting. Jacob convinces Esau to swap all the benefits that belong to him as the oldest son for a pot of red stew. The scheming repeats when Jacob deceitfully steals his father's blessing. When Esau's anger grows into a murderous rage, Jacob has to flee for his life. It takes many years for the two grown brothers to call a truce and live at peace (Genesis 32–33). Even though they had their differences, they were still family. They had to find a way to get along.

If you have siblings at your house, you're setting patterns of getting along that will last a lifetime. So start by letting God be the Lord of your family. When you choose to live his way, there's far less to fight about.

BUILDING

FAITH

WISDOM

STRENGTH

[18]Early the next morning Jacob took the stone he had placed under his head and set it up as a pillar and poured oil on top of it. [19]He called that place Bethel,[a] though the city used to be called Luz.

[20]Then Jacob made a vow, saying, "If God will be with me and will watch over me on this journey I am taking and will give me food to eat and clothes to wear [21]so that I return safely to my father's household, then the Lord[b] will be my God [22]and[c] this stone that I have set up as a pillar will be God's house, and of all that you give me I will give you a tenth."

Jacob Arrives in Paddan Aram

29 Then Jacob continued on his journey and came to the land of the eastern peoples. [2]There he saw a well in the open country, with three flocks of sheep lying near it because the flocks were watered from that well. The stone over the mouth of the well was large. [3]When all the flocks were gathered there, the shepherds would roll the stone away from the well's mouth and water the sheep. Then they would return the stone to its place over the mouth of the well.

[4]Jacob asked the shepherds, "My brothers, where are you from?"

"We're from Harran," they replied.

[5]He said to them, "Do you know Laban, Nahor's grandson?"

"Yes, we know him," they answered.

[6]Then Jacob asked them, "Is he well?"

"Yes, he is," they said, "and here comes his daughter Rachel with the sheep."

[7]"Look," he said, "the sun is still high; it is not time for the flocks to be gathered. Water the sheep and take them back to pasture."

[8]"We can't," they replied, "until all the flocks are gathered and the stone has been rolled away from the mouth of the well. Then we will water the sheep."

[9]While he was still talking with them, Rachel came with her father's sheep, for she was a shepherd. [10]When Jacob saw Rachel daughter of his uncle Laban, and Laban's sheep, he went over and rolled the stone away from the mouth of the well and watered his uncle's sheep. [11]Then Jacob kissed Rachel and began to weep aloud. [12]He had told Rachel that he was a relative of her father and a son of Rebekah. So she ran and told her father.

[13]As soon as Laban heard the news about Jacob, his sister's son, he hurried to meet him. He embraced him and kissed him and brought him to his home, and there Jacob told him all these things. [14]Then Laban said to him, "You are my own flesh and blood."

Jacob Marries Leah and Rachel

After Jacob had stayed with him for a whole month, [15]Laban said to him, "Just because you are a relative of mine, should you work for me for nothing? Tell me what your wages should be."

[16]Now Laban had two daughters; the name of the older was Leah, and the name of the younger was Rachel. [17]Leah had weak[d] eyes, but Rachel had a lovely figure and was beautiful. [18]Jacob was in love with Rachel and said, "I'll work for you seven years in return for your younger daughter Rachel."

[19]Laban said, "It's better that I give her to you than to some other man. Stay here with me." [20]So Jacob served seven years to get Rachel, but they seemed like only a few days to him because of his love for her.

[21]Then Jacob said to Laban, "Give me my wife. My time is completed, and I want to make love to her."

[22]So Laban brought together all the people of the place and gave a feast. [23]But when evening came, he took his daughter Leah and brought her to Jacob, and Jacob made love to her. [24]And Laban gave his servant Zilpah to his daughter as her attendant.

[25]When morning came, there was Leah! So Jacob said to Laban, "What is this you have done to me? I served you for Rachel, didn't I? Why have you deceived me?"

[26]Laban replied, "It is not our custom here to give the younger daughter in marriage before the older one. [27]Finish this daughter's bridal week; then we will give you the younger one also, in return for another seven years of work."

[28]And Jacob did so. He finished the week with Leah, and then Laban gave him his daughter Rachel to be his wife. [29]Laban gave his servant Bilhah to his daughter Rachel as her attendant. [30]Jacob made love to Rachel also, and his love for Rachel was greater than

---

[a] 19 *Bethel* means *house of God.*   [b] 20,21 Or *Since God . . . father's household, the* Lord   [c] 21,22 Or *household, and the* Lord *will be my God,* [22]*then*   [d] 17 Or *delicate*

DREAM ON

READ: GENESIS 28:10-22

It's impossible to dream with an "it can't be done" attitude. Dreaming demands an "anything is possible" attitude. It doesn't matter if your dream needs seven things invented before you can ever do it. It doesn't matter if you need to meet several high-powered people before your eighteenth birthday. If your dream is to use Mars as a space station, who cares if no human has been to Mars yet?

Dreamers are people who notice possibility. They understand potential. They fully realize that ideas can change the world. And before you say it, let me say it for you; there are realities. We are all limited. We can't all get elected president, star in movies, write bestsellers, pitch in the World Series, build a log cabin, start a restaurant, and save the whales. But you know, even as I say that, I feel kind of conflicted. Of course there are limits, but who says what those limits are? Who sets the boundaries on possibility?

BUILDING

FAITH

WISDOM

STRENGTH

The best thing about dreaming is that as we move toward accomplishing the great thing we've set out to do, God uses that momentum and guides us to where he needs us. Sometimes, he takes us to the exact place we'd dreamed. Other times he reshapes that dream and takes us down another road. But the whole time, we're moving, and God is using that.

his love for Leah. And he worked for Laban another seven years.

Jacob's Children

[31] When the LORD saw that Leah was not loved, he enabled her to conceive, but Rachel remained childless. [32] Leah became pregnant and gave birth to a son. She named him Reuben,[a] for she said, "It is because the LORD has seen my misery. Surely my husband will love me now."

[33] She conceived again, and when she gave birth to a son she said, "Because the LORD heard that I am not loved, he gave me this one too." So she named him Simeon.[b]

[34] Again she conceived, and when she gave birth to a son she said, "Now at last my husband will become attached to me, because I have borne him three sons." So he was named Levi.[c]

[35] She conceived again, and when she gave birth to a son she said, "This time I will praise the LORD." So she named him Judah.[d] Then she stopped having children.

30 When Rachel saw that she was not bearing Jacob any children, she became jealous of her sister. So she said to Jacob, "Give me children, or I'll die!"

[2] Jacob became angry with her and said, "Am I in the place of God, who has kept you from having children?"

[3] Then she said, "Here is Bilhah, my servant. Sleep with her so that she can bear children for me and I too can build a family through her."

[4] So she gave him her servant Bilhah as a wife. Jacob slept with her, [5] and she became pregnant and bore him a son. [6] Then Rachel said, "God has vindicated me; he has listened to my plea and given me a son." Because of this she named him Dan.[e]

[7] Rachel's servant Bilhah conceived again and bore Jacob a second son. [8] Then Rachel said, "I have had a great struggle with my sister, and I have won." So she named him Naphtali.[f]

[9] When Leah saw that she had stopped having children, she took her servant Zilpah

and gave her to Jacob as a wife. [10] Leah's servant Zilpah bore Jacob a son. [11] Then Leah said, "What good fortune!"[g] So she named him Gad.[h]

[12] Leah's servant Zilpah bore Jacob a second son. [13] Then Leah said, "How happy I am! The women will call me happy." So she named him Asher.[i]

[14] During wheat harvest, Reuben went out into the fields and found some mandrake plants, which he brought to his mother Leah. Rachel said to Leah, "Please give me some of your son's mandrakes."

[15] But she said to her, "Wasn't it enough that you took away my husband? Will you take my son's mandrakes too?"

"Very well," Rachel said, "he can sleep with you tonight in return for your son's mandrakes."

[16] So when Jacob came in from the fields that evening, Leah went out to meet him. "You must sleep with me," she said. "I have hired you with my son's mandrakes." So he slept with her that night.

[17] God listened to Leah, and she became pregnant and bore Jacob a fifth son. [18] Then Leah said, "God has rewarded me for giving my servant to my husband." So she named him Issachar.[j]

[19] Leah conceived again and bore Jacob a sixth son. [20] Then Leah said, "God has presented me with a precious gift. This time my husband will treat me with honor, because I have borne him six sons." So she named him Zebulun.[k]

[21] Some time later she gave birth to a daughter and named her Dinah.

[22] Then God remembered Rachel; he listened to her and enabled her to conceive. [23] She became pregnant and gave birth to a son and said, "God has taken away my disgrace." [24] She named him Joseph,[l] and said, "May the LORD add to me another son."

Jacob's Flocks Increase

[25] After Rachel gave birth to Joseph, Jacob said to Laban, "Send me on my way so I can go back to my own homeland. [26] Give me my

---

[a] 32 *Reuben* sounds like the Hebrew for *he has seen my misery*; the name means *see, a son*.   [b] 33 *Simeon* probably means *one who hears*.   [c] 34 *Levi* sounds like and may be derived from the Hebrew for *attached*.   [d] 35 *Judah* sounds like and may be derived from the Hebrew for *praise*.   [e] 6 *Dan* here means *he has vindicated*.   [f] 8 *Naphtali* means *my struggle*.   [g] 11 Or *"A troop is coming!"*   [h] 11 *Gad* can mean *good fortune* or *a troop*.   [i] 13 *Asher* means *happy*.   [j] 18 *Issachar* sounds like the Hebrew for *reward*.   [k] 20 *Zebulun* probably means *honor*.   [l] 24 *Joseph* means *may he add*.

wives and children, for whom I have served you, and I will be on my way. You know how much work I've done for you."

²⁷But Laban said to him, "If I have found favor in your eyes, please stay. I have learned by divination that the LORD has blessed me because of you." ²⁸He added, "Name your wages, and I will pay them."

²⁹Jacob said to him, "You know how I have worked for you and how your livestock has fared under my care. ³⁰The little you had before I came has increased greatly, and the LORD has blessed you wherever I have been. But now, when may I do something for my own household?"

³¹"What shall I give you?" he asked.

"Don't give me anything," Jacob replied. "But if you will do this one thing for me, I will go on tending your flocks and watching over them: ³²Let me go through all your flocks today and remove from them every speckled or spotted sheep, every dark-colored lamb and every spotted or speckled goat. They will be my wages. ³³And my honesty will testify for me in the future, whenever you check on the wages you have paid me. Any goat in my possession that is not speckled or spotted, or any lamb that is not dark-colored, will be considered stolen."

³⁴"Agreed," said Laban. "Let it be as you have said." ³⁵That same day he removed all the male goats that were streaked or spotted, and all the speckled or spotted female goats (all that had white on them) and all the dark-colored lambs, and he placed them in the care of his sons. ³⁶Then he put a three-day journey between himself and Jacob, while Jacob continued to tend the rest of Laban's flocks.

³⁷Jacob, however, took fresh-cut branches from poplar, almond and plane trees and made white stripes on them by peeling the bark and exposing the white inner wood of the branches. ³⁸Then he placed the peeled branches in all the watering troughs, so that they would be directly in front of the flocks when they came to drink. When the flocks were in heat and came to drink, ³⁹they mated in front of the branches. And they bore young that were streaked or speckled or spotted. ⁴⁰Jacob set apart the young of the flock by themselves, but made the rest face the streaked and dark-colored animals that belonged to Laban. Thus he made separate flocks for himself and did not put them with Laban's animals. ⁴¹Whenever the stronger females were in heat, Jacob would place the branches in the troughs in front of the animals so they would mate near the branches, ⁴²but if the animals were weak, he would not place them there. So the weak animals went to Laban and the strong ones to Jacob. ⁴³In this way the man grew exceedingly prosperous and came to own large flocks, and female and male servants, and camels and donkeys.

Jacob Flees From Laban

31 Jacob heard that Laban's sons were saying, "Jacob has taken everything our father owned and has gained all this wealth from what belonged to our father." ²And Jacob noticed that Laban's attitude toward him was not what it had been.

³Then the LORD said to Jacob, "Go back to the land of your fathers and to your relatives, and I will be with you."

⁴So Jacob sent word to Rachel and Leah to come out to the fields where his flocks were. ⁵He said to them, "I see that your father's attitude toward me is not what it was before, but the God of my father has been with me. ⁶You know that I've worked for your father with all my strength, ⁷yet your father has cheated me by changing my wages ten times. However, God has not allowed him to harm me. ⁸If he said, 'The speckled ones will be your wages,' then all the flocks gave birth to speckled young; and if he said, 'The streaked ones will be your wages,' then all the flocks bore streaked young. ⁹So God has taken away your father's livestock and has given them to me.

¹⁰"In breeding season I once had a dream in which I looked up and saw that the male goats mating with the flock were streaked, speckled or spotted. ¹¹The angel of God said to me in the dream, 'Jacob.' I answered, 'Here I am.' ¹²And he said, 'Look up and see that all the male goats mating with the flock are streaked, speckled or spotted, for I have seen all that Laban has been doing to you. ¹³I am the God of Bethel, where you anointed a pillar and where you made a vow to me. Now leave this land at once and go back to your native land.'"

¹⁴Then Rachel and Leah replied, "Do we still have any share in the inheritance of our

father's estate? **15**Does he not regard us as foreigners? Not only has he sold us, but he has used up what was paid for us. **16**Surely all the wealth that God took away from our father belongs to us and our children. So do whatever God has told you."

17Then Jacob put his children and his wives on camels, **18**and he drove all his livestock ahead of him, along with all the goods he had accumulated in Paddan Aram,*a* to go to his father Isaac in the land of Canaan.

19When Laban had gone to shear his sheep, Rachel stole her father's household gods. **20**Moreover, Jacob deceived Laban the Aramean by not telling him he was running away. **21**So he fled with all he had, crossed the Euphrates River, and headed for the hill country of Gilead.

Laban Pursues Jacob

22On the third day Laban was told that Jacob had fled. **23**Taking his relatives with him, he pursued Jacob for seven days and caught up with him in the hill country of Gilead. **24**Then God came to Laban the Aramean in a dream at night and said to him, "Be careful not to say anything to Jacob, either good or bad."

25Jacob had pitched his tent in the hill country of Gilead when Laban overtook him, and Laban and his relatives camped there too. **26**Then Laban said to Jacob, "What have you done? You've deceived me, and you've carried off my daughters like captives in war. **27**Why did you run off secretly and deceive me? Why didn't you tell me, so I could send you away with joy and singing to the music of timbrels and harps? **28**You didn't even let me kiss my grandchildren and my daughters goodbye. You have done a foolish thing. **29**I have the power to harm you; but last night the God of your father said to me, 'Be careful not to say anything to Jacob, either good or bad.' **30**Now you have gone off because you longed to return to your father's household. But why did you steal my gods?"

31Jacob answered Laban, "I was afraid, because I thought you would take your daughters away from me by force. **32**But if you find anyone who has your gods, that person shall not live. In the presence of our relatives, see for yourself whether there is anything of yours here with me; and if so, take it." Now Jacob did not know that Rachel had stolen the gods.

33So Laban went into Jacob's tent and into Leah's tent and into the tent of the two female servants, but he found nothing. After he came out of Leah's tent, he entered Rachel's tent. **34**Now Rachel had taken the household gods and put them inside her camel's saddle and was sitting on them. Laban searched through everything in the tent but found nothing.

35Rachel said to her father, "Don't be angry, my lord, that I cannot stand up in your presence; I'm having my period." So he searched but could not find the household gods.

36Jacob was angry and took Laban to task. "What is my crime?" he asked Laban. "How have I wronged you that you hunt me down? **37**Now that you have searched through all my goods, what have you found that belongs to your household? Put it here in front of your relatives and mine, and let them judge between the two of us.

38"I have been with you for twenty years now. Your sheep and goats have not miscarried, nor have I eaten rams from your flocks. **39**I did not bring you animals torn by wild beasts; I bore the loss myself. And you demanded payment from me for whatever was stolen by day or night. **40**This was my situation: The heat consumed me in the daytime and the cold at night, and sleep fled from my eyes. **41**It was like this for the twenty years I was in your household. I worked for you fourteen years for your two daughters and six years for your flocks, and you changed my wages ten times. **42**If the God of my father, the God of Abraham and the Fear of Isaac, had not been with me, you would surely have sent me away empty-handed. But God has seen my hardship and the toil of my hands, and last night he rebuked you."

43Laban answered Jacob, "The women are my daughters, the children are my children, and the flocks are my flocks. All you see is mine. Yet what can I do today about these daughters of mine, or about the children they have borne? **44**Come now, let's make a covenant, you and I, and let it serve as a witness between us."

a 18 That is, Northwest Mesopotamia

⁴⁵So Jacob took a stone and set it up as a pillar. ⁴⁶He said to his relatives, "Gather some stones." So they took stones and piled them in a heap, and they ate there by the heap. ⁴⁷Laban called it Jegar Sahadutha, and Jacob called it Galeed.ᵃ

⁴⁸Laban said, "This heap is a witness between you and me today." That is why it was called Galeed. ⁴⁹It was also called Mizpah,ᵇ because he said, "May the LORD keep watch between you and me when we are away from each other. ⁵⁰If you mistreat my daughters or if you take any wives besides my daughters, even though no one is with us, remember that God is a witness between you and me."

⁵¹Laban also said to Jacob, "Here is this heap, and here is this pillar I have set up between you and me. ⁵²This heap is a witness, and this pillar is a witness, that I will not go past this heap to your side to harm you and that you will not go past this heap and pillar to my side to harm me. ⁵³May the God of Abraham and the God of Nahor, the God of their father, judge between us."

So Jacob took an oath in the name of the Fear of his father Isaac. ⁵⁴He offered a sacrifice there in the hill country and invited his relatives to a meal. After they had eaten, they spent the night there.

⁵⁵Early the next morning Laban kissed his grandchildren and his daughters and blessed them. Then he left and returned home.ᶜ

Jacob Prepares to Meet Esau

32ᵈ Jacob also went on his way, and the angels of God met him. ²When Jacob saw them, he said, "This is the camp of God!" So he named that place Mahanaim.ᵉ

³Jacob sent messengers ahead of him to his brother Esau in the land of Seir, the country of Edom. ⁴He instructed them: "This is what you are to say to my lord Esau: 'Your servant Jacob says, I have been staying with Laban and have remained there till now. ⁵I have cattle and donkeys, sheep and goats, male and female servants. Now I am sending this message to my lord, that I may find favor in your eyes.'"

⁶When the messengers returned to Jacob, they said, "We went to your brother Esau, and now he is coming to meet you, and four hundred men are with him."

⁷In great fear and distress Jacob divided the people who were with him into two groups,ᶠ and the flocks and herds and camels as well. ⁸He thought, "If Esau comes and attacks one group,ᵍ the groupᵍ that is left may escape."

⁹Then Jacob prayed, "O God of my father Abraham, God of my father Isaac, LORD, you who said to me, 'Go back to your country and your relatives, and I will make you prosper,' ¹⁰I am unworthy of all the kindness and faithfulness you have shown your servant. I had only my staff when I crossed this Jordan, but now I have become two camps. ¹¹Save me, I pray, from the hand of my brother Esau, for I am afraid he will come and attack me, and also the mothers with their children. ¹²But you have said, 'I will surely make you prosper and will make your descendants like the sand of the sea, which cannot be counted.'"

¹³He spent the night there, and from what he had with him he selected a gift for his brother Esau: ¹⁴two hundred female goats and twenty male goats, two hundred ewes and twenty rams, ¹⁵thirty female camels with their young, forty cows and ten bulls, and twenty female donkeys and ten male donkeys. ¹⁶He put them in the care of his servants, each herd by itself, and said to his servants, "Go ahead of me, and keep some space between the herds."

¹⁷He instructed the one in the lead: "When my brother Esau meets you and asks, 'Who do you belong to, and where are you going, and who owns all these animals in front of you?' ¹⁸then you are to say, 'They belong to your servant Jacob. They are a gift sent to my lord Esau, and he is coming behind us.'"

¹⁹He also instructed the second, the third and all the others who followed the herds: "You are to say the same thing to Esau when you meet him. ²⁰And be sure to say, 'Your servant Jacob is coming behind us.'" For he thought, "I will pacify him with these gifts I am sending on ahead; later, when I see him, perhaps he will receive me." ²¹So Jacob's gifts went on ahead of him, but he himself spent the night in the camp.

ᵃ 47 The Aramaic *Jegar Sahadutha* and the Hebrew *Galeed* both mean *witness heap.*   ᵇ 49 *Mizpah* means *watchtower.*   ᶜ 55 In Hebrew texts this verse (31:55) is numbered 32:1.   ᵈ In Hebrew texts 32:1-32 is numbered 32:2-33.   ᵉ 2 *Mahanaim* means *two camps.*   ᶠ 7 Or *camps*   ᵍ 8 Or *camp*

Jacob Wrestles With God

²²That night Jacob got up and took his two wives, his two female servants and his eleven sons and crossed the ford of the Jabbok. ²³After he had sent them across the stream, he sent over all his possessions. ²⁴So Jacob was left alone, and a man wrestled with him till daybreak. ²⁵When the man saw that he could not overpower him, he touched the socket of Jacob's hip so that his hip was wrenched as he wrestled with the man. ²⁶Then the man said, "Let me go, for it is daybreak."

But Jacob replied, "I will not let you go unless you bless me."

²⁷The man asked him, "What is your name?"

"Jacob," he answered.

²⁸Then the man said, "Your name will no longer be Jacob, but Israel,ᵃ because you have struggled with God and with humans and have overcome."

²⁹Jacob said, "Please tell me your name."

But he replied, "Why do you ask my name?" Then he blessed him there.

³⁰So Jacob called the place Peniel,ᵇ saying, "It is because I saw God face to face, and yet my life was spared."

³¹The sun rose above him as he passed Peniel,ᶜ and he was limping because of his hip. ³²Therefore to this day the Israelites do not eat the tendon attached to the socket of the hip, because the socket of Jacob's hip was touched near the tendon.

Jacob Meets Esau

33 Jacob looked up and there was Esau, coming with his four hundred men; so he divided the children among Leah, Rachel and the two female servants. ²He put the female servants and their children in front, Leah and her children next, and Rachel and Joseph in the rear. ³He himself went on ahead and bowed down to the ground seven times as he approached his brother.

⁴But Esau ran to meet Jacob and embraced him; he threw his arms around his neck and kissed him. And they wept. ⁵Then Esau looked up and saw the women and children. "Who are these with you?" he asked.

Jacob answered, "They are the children God has graciously given your servant."

⁶Then the female servants and their children approached and bowed down. ⁷Next, Leah and her children came and bowed down. Last of all came Joseph and Rachel, and they too bowed down.

⁸Esau asked, "What's the meaning of all these flocks and herds I met?"

"To find favor in your eyes, my lord," he said.

⁹But Esau said, "I already have plenty, my brother. Keep what you have for yourself."

¹⁰"No, please!" said Jacob. "If I have found favor in your eyes, accept this gift from me. For to see your face is like seeing the face of God, now that you have received me favorably. ¹¹Please accept the present that was brought to you, for God has been gracious to me and I have all I need." And because Jacob insisted, Esau accepted it.

¹²Then Esau said, "Let us be on our way; I'll accompany you."

¹³But Jacob said to him, "My lord knows that the children are tender and that I must care for the ewes and cows that are nursing their young. If they are driven hard just one day, all the animals will die. ¹⁴So let my lord go on ahead of his servant, while I move along slowly at the pace of the flocks and herds before me and the pace of the children, until I come to my lord in Seir."

¹⁵Esau said, "Then let me leave some of my men with you."

"But why do that?" Jacob asked. "Just let me find favor in the eyes of my lord."

¹⁶So that day Esau started on his way back to Seir. ¹⁷Jacob, however, went to Sukkoth, where he built a place for himself and made shelters for his livestock. That is why the place is called Sukkoth.ᵈ

¹⁸After Jacob came from Paddan Aram,ᵉ he arrived safely at the city of Shechem in Canaan and camped within sight of the city. ¹⁹For a hundred pieces of silver,ᶠ he bought from the sons of Hamor, the father of Shechem, the plot of ground where he pitched his tent. ²⁰There he set up an altar and called it El Elohe Israel.ᵍ

ᵃ 28 Israel probably means he struggles with God.   ᵇ 30 Peniel means face of God.   ᶜ 31 Hebrew Penuel, a variant of Peniel   ᵈ 17 Sukkoth means shelters.   ᵉ 18 That is, Northwest Mesopotamia   ᶠ 19 Hebrew hundred kesitahs; a kesitah was a unit of money of unknown weight and value.   ᵍ 20 El Elohe Israel can mean El is the God of Israel or mighty is the God of Israel.

Dinah and the Shechemites

34 Now Dinah, the daughter Leah had borne to Jacob, went out to visit the women of the land. ²When Shechem son of Hamor the Hivite, the ruler of that area, saw her, he took her and raped her. ³His heart was drawn to Dinah daughter of Jacob; he loved the young woman and spoke tenderly to her. ⁴And Shechem said to his father Hamor, "Get me this girl as my wife."

⁵When Jacob heard that his daughter Dinah had been defiled, his sons were in the fields with his livestock; so he did nothing about it until they came home.

⁶Then Shechem's father Hamor went out to talk with Jacob. ⁷Meanwhile, Jacob's sons had come in from the fields as soon as they heard what had happened. They were shocked and furious, because Shechem had done an outrageous thing in*a* Israel by sleeping with Jacob's daughter—a thing that should not be done.

⁸But Hamor said to them, "My son Shechem has his heart set on your daughter. Please give her to him as his wife. ⁹Intermarry with us; give us your daughters and take our daughters for yourselves. ¹⁰You can settle among us; the land is open to you. Live in it, trade*b* in it, and acquire property in it."

¹¹Then Shechem said to Dinah's father and brothers, "Let me find favor in your eyes, and I will give you whatever you ask. ¹²Make the price for the bride and the gift I am to bring as great as you like, and I'll pay whatever you ask me. Only give me the young woman as my wife."

¹³Because their sister Dinah had been defiled, Jacob's sons replied deceitfully as they spoke to Shechem and his father Hamor. ¹⁴They said to them, "We can't do such a thing; we can't give our sister to a man who is not circumcised. That would be a disgrace to us. ¹⁵We will enter into an agreement with you on one condition only: that you become like us by circumcising all your males. ¹⁶Then we will give you our daughters and take your daughters for ourselves. We'll settle among you and become one people with you. ¹⁷But if you will not agree to be circumcised, we'll take our sister and go."

¹⁸Their proposal seemed good to Hamor and his son Shechem. ¹⁹The young man, who was the most honored of all his father's family, lost no time in doing what they said, because he was delighted with Jacob's daughter. ²⁰So Hamor and his son Shechem went to the gate of their city to speak to the men of their city. ²¹"These men are friendly toward us," they said. "Let them live in our land and trade in it; the land has plenty of room for them. We can marry their daughters and they can marry ours. ²²But the men will agree to live with us as one people only on the condition that our males be circumcised, as they themselves are. ²³Won't their livestock, their property and all their other animals become ours? So let us agree to their terms, and they will settle among us."

²⁴All the men who went out of the city gate agreed with Hamor and his son Shechem, and every male in the city was circumcised.

²⁵Three days later, while all of them were still in pain, two of Jacob's sons, Simeon and Levi, Dinah's brothers, took their swords and attacked the unsuspecting city, killing every male. ²⁶They put Hamor and his son Shechem to the sword and took Dinah from Shechem's house and left. ²⁷The sons of Jacob came upon the dead bodies and looted the city where*c* their sister had been defiled. ²⁸They seized their flocks and herds and donkeys and everything else of theirs in the city and out in the fields. ²⁹They carried off all their wealth and all their women and children, taking as plunder everything in the houses.

³⁰Then Jacob said to Simeon and Levi, "You have brought trouble on me by making me obnoxious to the Canaanites and Perizzites, the people living in this land. We are few in number, and if they join forces against me and attack me, I and my household will be destroyed."

³¹But they replied, "Should he have treated our sister like a prostitute?"

Jacob Returns to Bethel

35 Then God said to Jacob, "Go up to Bethel and settle there, and build an altar there to God, who appeared to you when you were fleeing from your brother Esau."

²So Jacob said to his household and to all who were with him, "Get rid of the foreign

---

a 7 Or *against*   *b* 10 Or *move about freely*; also in verse 21   *c* 27 Or *because*

JACOB

"Let us go up to Bethel, where I will build an altar to God, who answered me in the day of my distress and who has been with me wherever I have gone." GENESIS 35:3

HIS NAME MEANS: "he grasps the heel," "he deceives"
READ HIS STORY: *Genesis 25:19–34; 27–33, 35*

Jacob's grandfather was Abraham, the father of faith for the entire nation of Israel. Jacob's father was Isaac, God's promise of faith fulfilled for Abraham. Yet Jacob did not always follow the faith of his father or his grandfather. Just because Jacob grew up in a home of faith didn't automatically make him a man of faith. Jacob had to meet God himself.

At first, life seemed easy for Jacob. He learned how to make things happen the way he wanted them to. He was his mother's favorite. Although his twin brother, Esau, was born first, Jacob the schemer was able to grab both the birthright (double inheritance) and the father's blessing that belonged to the firstborn. Fearing for his life and running away from the mess he made, however, Jacob finally called out to God in his distress (Genesis 28:10–22).

From that day forward, Jacob knew God for himself. Even when his father-in-law, Laban, tricked Jacob on his wedding day, even when Jacob worked long hours caring for Laban's sheep, and even when Jacob thought his beloved son Joseph had died, Jacob knew God was with him through it all.

There's no need to wait for a day of distress as Jacob did. Call out to God today with all your heart. He will be your God. He promises to be with you wherever you go. God will be *your* God, and not just the God of your fathers.

gods you have with you, and purify yourselves and change your clothes. ³Then come, let us go up to Bethel, where I will build an altar to God, who answered me in the day of my distress and who has been with me wherever I have gone." ⁴So they gave Jacob all the foreign gods they had and the rings in their ears, and Jacob buried them under the oak at Shechem. ⁵Then they set out, and the terror of God fell on the towns all around them so that no one pursued them.

⁶Jacob and all the people with him came to Luz (that is, Bethel) in the land of Canaan. ⁷There he built an altar, and he called the place El Bethel,ᵃ because it was there that God revealed himself to him when he was fleeing from his brother.

⁸Now Deborah, Rebekah's nurse, died and was buried under the oak outside Bethel. So it was named Allon Bakuth.ᵇ

⁹After Jacob returned from Paddan Aram,ᶜ God appeared to him again and blessed him. ¹⁰God said to him, "Your name is Jacob,ᵈ but you will no longer be called Jacob; your name will be Israel.ᵉ" So he named him Israel.

¹¹And God said to him, "I am God Almighty;ᶠ be fruitful and increase in number. A nation and a community of nations will come from you, and kings will be among your descendants. ¹²The land I gave to Abraham and Isaac I also give to you, and I will give this land to your descendants after you." ¹³Then God went up from him at the place where he had talked with him.

¹⁴Jacob set up a stone pillar at the place where God had talked with him, and he poured out a drink offering on it; he also poured oil on it. ¹⁵Jacob called the place where God had talked with him Bethel.ᵍ

The Deaths of Rachel and Isaac

¹⁶Then they moved on from Bethel. While they were still some distance from Ephrath, Rachel began to give birth and had great difficulty. ¹⁷And as she was having great difficulty in childbirth, the midwife said to her, "Don't despair, for you have another son." ¹⁸As she breathed her last—for she was dying—she named her son Ben-Oni.ʰ But his father named him Benjamin.ⁱ

¹⁹So Rachel died and was buried on the way to Ephrath (that is, Bethlehem). ²⁰Over her tomb Jacob set up a pillar, and to this day that pillar marks Rachel's tomb.

²¹Israel moved on again and pitched his tent beyond Migdal Eder. ²²While Israel was living in that region, Reuben went in and slept with his father's concubine Bilhah, and Israel heard of it.

Jacob had twelve sons:

²³The sons of Leah:
Reuben the firstborn of Jacob,
Simeon, Levi, Judah, Issachar and
Zebulun.
²⁴The sons of Rachel:
Joseph and Benjamin.
²⁵The sons of Rachel's servant Bilhah:
Dan and Naphtali.
²⁶The sons of Leah's servant Zilpah:
Gad and Asher.
These were the sons of Jacob, who were born to him in Paddan Aram.

²⁷Jacob came home to his father Isaac in Mamre, near Kiriath Arba (that is, Hebron), where Abraham and Isaac had stayed. ²⁸Isaac lived a hundred and eighty years. ²⁹Then he breathed his last and died and was gathered to his people, old and full of years. And his sons Esau and Jacob buried him.

Esau's Descendants

36 This is the account of the family line of Esau (that is, Edom).

²Esau took his wives from the women of Canaan: Adah daughter of Elon the Hittite, and Oholibamah daughter of Anah and granddaughter of Zibeon the Hivite— ³also Basemath daughter of Ishmael and sister of Nebaioth.

⁴Adah bore Eliphaz to Esau, Basemath bore Reuel, ⁵and Oholibamah bore Jeush, Jalam and Korah. These were the sons of Esau, who were born to him in Canaan.

⁶Esau took his wives and sons and daughters and all the members of his household, as well as his livestock and all his other animals and all the goods he had acquired in Canaan, and moved

---

ᵃ 7 *El Bethel* means *God of Bethel.*   ᵇ 8 *Allon Bakuth* means *oak of weeping.*   ᶜ 9 That is, Northwest Mesopotamia; also in verse 26   ᵈ 10 *Jacob* means *he grasps the heel,* a Hebrew idiom for *he deceives.*   ᵉ 10 *Israel* probably means *he struggles with God.*   ᶠ 11 Hebrew *El-Shaddai*   ᵍ 15 *Bethel* means *house of God.*   ʰ 18 *Ben-Oni* means *son of my trouble.*   ⁱ 18 *Benjamin* means *son of my right hand.*

to a land some distance from his brother Jacob. [7] Their possessions were too great for them to remain together; the land where they were staying could not support them both because of their livestock. [8] So Esau (that is, Edom) settled in the hill country of Seir.

[9] This is the account of the family line of Esau the father of the Edomites in the hill country of Seir.

[10] These are the names of Esau's sons:

Eliphaz, the son of Esau's wife Adah, and Reuel, the son of Esau's wife Basemath.

[11] The sons of Eliphaz:

Teman, Omar, Zepho, Gatam and Kenaz.

[12] Esau's son Eliphaz also had a concubine named Timna, who bore him Amalek. These were grandsons of Esau's wife Adah.

[13] The sons of Reuel:

Nahath, Zerah, Shammah and Mizzah. These were grandsons of Esau's wife Basemath.

[14] The sons of Esau's wife Oholibamah daughter of Anah and granddaughter of Zibeon, whom she bore to Esau:

Jeush, Jalam and Korah.

[15] These were the chiefs among Esau's descendants:

The sons of Eliphaz the firstborn of Esau:

Chiefs Teman, Omar, Zepho, Kenaz, [16]Korah,[a] Gatam and Amalek. These were the chiefs descended from Eliphaz in Edom; they were grandsons of Adah.

[17] The sons of Esau's son Reuel:

Chiefs Nahath, Zerah, Shammah and Mizzah. These were the chiefs descended from Reuel in Edom; they were grandsons of Esau's wife Basemath.

[18] The sons of Esau's wife Oholibamah:

Chiefs Jeush, Jalam and Korah. These were the chiefs descended from Esau's wife Oholibamah daughter of Anah.

[19] These were the sons of Esau (that is, Edom), and these were their chiefs.

[20] These were the sons of Seir the Horite, who were living in the region:

Lotan, Shobal, Zibeon, Anah, [21]Dishon, Ezer and Dishan. These sons of Seir in Edom were Horite chiefs.

[22] The sons of Lotan:

Hori and Homam.[b] Timna was Lotan's sister.

[23] The sons of Shobal:

Alvan, Manahath, Ebal, Shepho and Onam.

[24] The sons of Zibeon:

Aiah and Anah. This is the Anah who discovered the hot springs[c] in the desert while he was grazing the donkeys of his father Zibeon.

[25] The children of Anah:

Dishon and Oholibamah daughter of Anah.

[26] The sons of Dishon[d]:

Hemdan, Eshban, Ithran and Keran.

[27] The sons of Ezer:

Bilhan, Zaavan and Akan.

[28] The sons of Dishan:

Uz and Aran.

[29] These were the Horite chiefs:

Lotan, Shobal, Zibeon, Anah, [30]Dishon, Ezer and Dishan. These were the Horite chiefs, according to their divisions, in the land of Seir.

The Rulers of Edom

[31] These were the kings who reigned in Edom before any Israelite king reigned:

[32] Bela son of Beor became king of Edom. His city was named Dinhabah.

[33] When Bela died, Jobab son of Zerah from Bozrah succeeded him as king.

[34] When Jobab died, Husham from the land of the Temanites succeeded him as king.

[35] When Husham died, Hadad son of Bedad, who defeated Midian in the country of Moab, succeeded him as king. His city was named Avith.

[36] When Hadad died, Samlah from Masrekah succeeded him as king.

[37] When Samlah died, Shaul from Reho-

---

[a] 16 Masoretic Text; Samaritan Pentateuch (also verse 11 and 1 Chron. 1:36) does not have *Korah*.
[b] 22 Hebrew *Hemam*, a variant of *Homam* (see 1 Chron. 1:39)   [c] 24 Vulgate; Syriac *discovered water*; the meaning of the Hebrew for this word is uncertain.   [d] 26 Hebrew *Dishan*, a variant of *Dishon*

both on the river succeeded him as king.

³⁸When Shaul died, Baal-Hanan son of Akbor succeeded him as king.

³⁹When Baal-Hanan son of Akbor died, Hadad*ᵃ* succeeded him as king. His city was named Pau, and his wife's name was Mehetabel daughter of Matred, the daughter of Me-Zahab.

⁴⁰These were the chiefs descended from Esau, by name, according to their clans and regions:

Timna, Alvah, Jetheth, ⁴¹Oholibamah, Elah, Pinon, ⁴²Kenaz, Teman, Mibzar, ⁴³Magdiel and Iram. These were the chiefs of Edom, according to their settlements in the land they occupied.

This is the family line of Esau, the father of the Edomites.

Joseph's Dreams

37 Jacob lived in the land where his father had stayed, the land of Canaan.

²This is the account of Jacob's family line.

Joseph, a young man of seventeen, was tending the flocks with his brothers, the sons of Bilhah and the sons of Zilpah, his father's wives, and he brought their father a bad report about them.

³Now Israel loved Joseph more than any of his other sons, because he had been born to him in his old age; and he made an ornate*ᵇ* robe for him. ⁴When his brothers saw that their father loved him more than any of them, they hated him and could not speak a kind word to him.

⁵Joseph had a dream, and when he told it to his brothers, they hated him all the more. ⁶He said to them, "Listen to this dream I had: ⁷We were binding sheaves of grain out in the field when suddenly my sheaf rose and stood upright, while your sheaves gathered around mine and bowed down to it."

⁸His brothers said to him, "Do you intend to reign over us? Will you actually rule us?" And they hated him all the more because of his dream and what he had said.

⁹Then he had another dream, and he told it to his brothers. "Listen," he said, "I had another dream, and this time the sun and moon and eleven stars were bowing down to me."

¹⁰When he told his father as well as his brothers, his father rebuked him and said, "What is this dream you had? Will your mother and I and your brothers actually come and bow down to the ground before you?" ¹¹His brothers were jealous of him, but his father kept the matter in mind.

Joseph Sold by His Brothers

¹²Now his brothers had gone to graze their father's flocks near Shechem, ¹³and Israel said to Joseph, "As you know, your brothers are grazing the flocks near Shechem. Come, I am going to send you to them."

"Very well," he replied.

¹⁴So he said to him, "Go and see if all is well with your brothers and with the flocks, and bring word back to me." Then he sent him off from the Valley of Hebron.

When Joseph arrived at Shechem, ¹⁵a man found him wandering around in the fields and asked him, "What are you looking for?"

¹⁶He replied, "I'm looking for my brothers. Can you tell me where they are grazing their flocks?"

¹⁷"They have moved on from here," the man answered. "I heard them say, 'Let's go to Dothan.'"

So Joseph went after his brothers and found them near Dothan. ¹⁸But they saw him in the distance, and before he reached them, they plotted to kill him.

¹⁹"Here comes that dreamer!" they said to each other. ²⁰"Come now, let's kill him and throw him into one of these cisterns and say that a ferocious animal devoured him. Then we'll see what comes of his dreams."

²¹When Reuben heard this, he tried to rescue him from their hands. "Let's not take his life," he said. ²²"Don't shed any blood. Throw him into this cistern here in the wilderness, but don't lay a hand on him." Reuben said this to rescue him from them and take him back to his father.

²³So when Joseph came to his brothers, they stripped him of his robe—the ornate robe he was wearing—²⁴and they took him

---

ᵃ 39 Many manuscripts of the Masoretic Text, Samaritan Pentateuch and Syriac (see also 1 Chron. 1:50); most manuscripts of the Masoretic Text *Hadar*   *ᵇ 3* The meaning of the Hebrew for this word is uncertain; also in verses 23 and 32.

WHAT A MESS

READ: GENESIS 37:5

Like the story of Jacob and Esau back in Genesis 25–33, the account of Joseph that spans from Genesis 37–47 shows off an ugly tale of violent sibling rivalry. This isn't a band of brothers whose relationships you want to imitate, but God had a plan bigger than any of them.

Joseph was exactly seventeen when he tattled about his older brothers' bad behavior. The brothers boiled with hatred as their father dressed Joseph in an ornate robe (made famous in the Broadway musical *Joseph and the Amazing Technicolor Dreamcoat*). And Joseph had an unhelpful habit of sharing dreams that elevated him at his brothers' expense. None of this helped Joseph get along at home, and it wasn't a surprise when his brothers plotted to kill him. When the opportunity arose, they spared his life and sold him as a slave. Then they told Jacob that his favorite son was dead.

The saddest part of this story is watching it go from bad to worse. Jacob (who should have known better, having grown up in a family where his father preferred his brother) didn't treat his sons fairly. Joseph wouldn't shut his arrogant mouth. And ten adult brothers don't bother to find a better way to deal with their upstart sibling.

While God used Joseph's dire situation for his own purposes later, that doesn't excuse everyone's bad behavior. You might be able to slide by with mediocre relationships in your family, but the Lord wants you to aim higher than that.

BUILDING
FAITH
WISDOM
STRENGTH

and threw him into the cistern. The cistern was empty; there was no water in it.

²⁵ As they sat down to eat their meal, they looked up and saw a caravan of Ishmaelites coming from Gilead. Their camels were loaded with spices, balm and myrrh, and they were on their way to take them down to Egypt.

²⁶ Judah said to his brothers, "What will we gain if we kill our brother and cover up his blood? ²⁷ Come, let's sell him to the Ishmaelites and not lay our hands on him; after all, he is our brother, our own flesh and blood." His brothers agreed.

²⁸ So when the Midianite merchants came by, his brothers pulled Joseph up out of the cistern and sold him for twenty shekels*ᵃ* of silver to the Ishmaelites, who took him to Egypt.

²⁹ When Reuben returned to the cistern and saw that Joseph was not there, he tore his clothes. ³⁰ He went back to his brothers and said, "The boy isn't there! Where can I turn now?"

³¹ Then they got Joseph's robe, slaughtered a goat and dipped the robe in the blood. ³² They took the ornate robe back to their father and said, "We found this. Examine it to see whether it is your son's robe."

³³ He recognized it and said, "It is my son's robe! Some ferocious animal has devoured him. Joseph has surely been torn to pieces."

³⁴ Then Jacob tore his clothes, put on sackcloth and mourned for his son many days. ³⁵ All his sons and daughters came to comfort him, but he refused to be comforted. "No," he said, "I will continue to mourn until I join my son in the grave." So his father wept for him.

³⁶ Meanwhile, the Midianites*ᵇ* sold Joseph in Egypt to Potiphar, one of Pharaoh's officials, the captain of the guard.

Judah and Tamar

38 At that time, Judah left his brothers and went down to stay with a man of Adullam named Hirah. ² There Judah met the daughter of a Canaanite man named Shua. He married her and made love to her; ³ she became pregnant and gave birth to a son, who was named Er. ⁴ She conceived again and gave birth to a son and named him Onan. ⁵ She gave birth to still another son and named him Shelah. It was at Kezib that she gave birth to him.

⁶ Judah got a wife for Er, his firstborn, and her name was Tamar. ⁷ But Er, Judah's firstborn, was wicked in the LORD's sight; so the LORD put him to death.

⁸ Then Judah said to Onan, "Sleep with your brother's wife and fulfill your duty to her as a brother-in-law to raise up offspring for your brother." ⁹ But Onan knew that the child would not be his; so whenever he slept with his brother's wife, he spilled his semen on the ground to keep from providing offspring for his brother. ¹⁰ What he did was wicked in the LORD's sight; so the LORD put him to death also.

¹¹ Judah then said to his daughter-in-law Tamar, "Live as a widow in your father's household until my son Shelah grows up." For he thought, "He may die too, just like his brothers." So Tamar went to live in her father's household.

¹² After a long time Judah's wife, the daughter of Shua, died. When Judah had recovered from his grief, he went up to Timnah, to the men who were shearing his sheep, and his friend Hirah the Adullamite went with him.

¹³ When Tamar was told, "Your father-in-law is on his way to Timnah to shear his sheep," ¹⁴ she took off her widow's clothes, covered herself with a veil to disguise herself, and then sat down at the entrance to Enaim, which is on the road to Timnah. For she saw that, though Shelah had now grown up, she had not been given to him as his wife.

¹⁵ When Judah saw her, he thought she was a prostitute, for she had covered her face. ¹⁶ Not realizing that she was his daughter-in-law, he went over to her by the roadside and said, "Come now, let me sleep with you."

"And what will you give me to sleep with you?" she asked.

¹⁷ "I'll send you a young goat from my flock," he said.

"Will you give me something as a pledge until you send it?" she asked.

¹⁸ He said, "What pledge should I give you?"

"Your seal and its cord, and the staff in your hand," she answered. So he gave them

---

ᵃ 28 That is, about 8 ounces or about 230 grams   *ᵇ 36* Samaritan Pentateuch, Septuagint, Vulgate and Syriac (see also verse 28); Masoretic Text *Medanites* to her and slept with her, and she became pregnant by him. ¹⁹After she left, she took off her veil and put on her widow's clothes again.

²⁰Meanwhile Judah sent the young goat by his friend the Adullamite in order to get his pledge back from the woman, but he did not find her. ²¹He asked the men who lived there, "Where is the shrine prostitute who was beside the road at Enaim?"

"There hasn't been any shrine prostitute here," they said.

²²So he went back to Judah and said, "I didn't find her. Besides, the men who lived there said, 'There hasn't been any shrine prostitute here.'"

²³Then Judah said, "Let her keep what she has, or we will become a laughingstock. After all, I did send her this young goat, but you didn't find her."

²⁴About three months later Judah was told, "Your daughter-in-law Tamar is guilty of prostitution, and as a result she is now pregnant."

Judah said, "Bring her out and have her burned to death!"

²⁵As she was being brought out, she sent a message to her father-in-law. "I am pregnant by the man who owns these," she said. And she added, "See if you recognize whose seal and cord and staff these are."

²⁶Judah recognized them and said, "She is more righteous than I, since I wouldn't give her to my son Shelah." And he did not sleep with her again.

²⁷When the time came for her to give birth, there were twin boys in her womb. ²⁸As she was giving birth, one of them put out his hand; so the midwife took a scarlet thread and tied it on his wrist and said, "This one came out first." ²⁹But when he drew back his hand, his brother came out, and she said, "So this is how you have broken out!" And he was named Perez.ᵃ ³⁰Then his brother, who had the scarlet thread on his wrist, came out. And he was named Zerah.ᵇ

Joseph and Potiphar's Wife

39 Now Joseph had been taken down to Egypt. Potiphar, an Egyptian who was one of Pharaoh's officials, the captain of the guard, bought him from the Ishmaelites who had taken him there.

²The LORD was with Joseph so that he prospered, and he lived in the house of his Egyptian master. ³When his master saw that the LORD was with him and that the LORD gave him success in everything he did, ⁴Joseph found favor in his eyes and became his attendant. Potiphar put him in charge of his household, and he entrusted to his care everything he owned. ⁵From the time he put him in charge of his household and of all that he owned, the LORD blessed the household of the Egyptian because of Joseph. The blessing of the LORD was on everything Potiphar had, both in the house and in the field. ⁶So Potiphar left everything he had in Joseph's care; with Joseph in charge, he did not concern himself with anything except the food he ate.

Now Joseph was well-built and handsome, ⁷and after a while his master's wife took notice of Joseph and said, "Come to bed with me!"

⁸But he refused. "With me in charge," he told her, "my master does not concern himself with anything in the house; everything he owns he has entrusted to my care. ⁹No one is greater in this house than I am. My master has withheld nothing from me except you, because you are his wife. How then could I do such a wicked thing and sin against God?" ¹⁰And though she spoke to Joseph day after day, he refused to go to bed with her or even be with her.

¹¹One day he went into the house to attend to his duties, and none of the household servants was inside. ¹²She caught him by his cloak and said, "Come to bed with me!" But he left his cloak in her hand and ran out of the house.

¹³When she saw that he had left his cloak in her hand and had run out of the house, ¹⁴she called her household servants. "Look," she said to them, "this Hebrew has been brought to us to make sport of us! He came in here to sleep with me, but I screamed. ¹⁵When he heard me scream for help, he left his cloak beside me and ran out of the house."

¹⁶She kept his cloak beside her until his master came home. ¹⁷Then she told him this story: "That Hebrew slave you brought us came to me to make sport of me. ¹⁸But as

---

ᵃ 29 Perez means breaking out.   ᵇ 30 Zerah can mean scarlet or brightness.

soon as I screamed for help, he left his cloak beside me and ran out of the house."

[19]When his master heard the story his wife told him, saying, "This is how your slave treated me," he burned with anger. [20]Joseph's master took him and put him in prison, the place where the king's prisoners were confined.

But while Joseph was there in the prison, [21]the LORD was with him; he showed him kindness and granted him favor in the eyes of the prison warden. [22]So the warden put Joseph in charge of all those held in the prison, and he was made responsible for all that was done there. [23]The warden paid no attention to anything under Joseph's care, because the LORD was with Joseph and gave him success in whatever he did.

The Cupbearer and the Baker

40 Some time later, the cupbearer and the baker of the king of Egypt offended their master, the king of Egypt. [2]Pharaoh was angry with his two officials, the chief cupbearer and the chief baker, [3]and put them in custody in the house of the captain of the guard, in the same prison where Joseph was confined. [4]The captain of the guard assigned them to Joseph, and he attended them.

After they had been in custody for some time, [5]each of the two men—the cupbearer and the baker of the king of Egypt, who were being held in prison—had a dream the same night, and each dream had a meaning of its own.

[6]When Joseph came to them the next morning, he saw that they were dejected. [7]So he asked Pharaoh's officials who were in custody with him in his master's house, "Why do you look so sad today?"

[8]"We both had dreams," they answered, "but there is no one to interpret them."

Then Joseph said to them, "Do not interpretations belong to God? Tell me your dreams."

[9]So the chief cupbearer told Joseph his dream. He said to him, "In my dream I saw a vine in front of me, [10]and on the vine were three branches. As soon as it budded, it blossomed, and its clusters ripened into grapes. [11]Pharaoh's cup was in my hand, and I took the grapes, squeezed them into Pharaoh's cup and put the cup in his hand."

[12]"This is what it means," Joseph said to him. "The three branches are three days. [13]Within three days Pharaoh will lift up your head and restore you to your position, and you will put Pharaoh's cup in his hand, just as you used to do when you were his cupbearer. [14]But when all goes well with you, remember me and show me kindness; mention me to Pharaoh and get me out of this prison. [15]I was forcibly carried off from the land of the Hebrews, and even here I have done nothing to deserve being put in a dungeon."

[16]When the chief baker saw that Joseph had given a favorable interpretation, he said to Joseph, "I too had a dream: On my head were three baskets of bread.[a] [17]In the top basket were all kinds of baked goods for Pharaoh, but the birds were eating them out of the basket on my head."

[18]"This is what it means," Joseph said. "The three baskets are three days. [19]Within three days Pharaoh will lift off your head and impale your body on a pole. And the birds will eat away your flesh."

[20]Now the third day was Pharaoh's birthday, and he gave a feast for all his officials. He lifted up the heads of the chief cupbearer and the chief baker in the presence of his officials: [21]He restored the chief cupbearer to his position, so that he once again put the cup into Pharaoh's hand— [22]but he impaled the chief baker, just as Joseph had said to them in his interpretation.

[23]The chief cupbearer, however, did not remember Joseph; he forgot him.

Pharaoh's Dreams

41 When two full years had passed, Pharaoh had a dream: He was standing by the Nile, [2]when out of the river there came up seven cows, sleek and fat, and they grazed among the reeds. [3]After them, seven other cows, ugly and gaunt, came up out of the Nile and stood beside those on the riverbank. [4]And the cows that were ugly and gaunt ate up the seven sleek, fat cows. Then Pharaoh woke up.

[5]He fell asleep again and had a second dream: Seven heads of grain, healthy and good, were growing on a single stalk. [6]After them, seven other heads of grain sprouted—

---

a 16 Or *three wicker baskets*

thin and scorched by the east wind. ⁷The thin heads of grain swallowed up the seven healthy, full heads. Then Pharaoh woke up; it had been a dream.

⁸In the morning his mind was troubled, so he sent for all the magicians and wise men of Egypt. Pharaoh told them his dreams, but no one could interpret them for him.

⁹Then the chief cupbearer said to Pharaoh, "Today I am reminded of my shortcomings. ¹⁰Pharaoh was once angry with his servants, and he imprisoned me and the chief baker in the house of the captain of the guard. ¹¹Each of us had a dream the same night, and each dream had a meaning of its own. ¹²Now a young Hebrew was there with us, a servant of the captain of the guard. We told him our dreams, and he interpreted them for us, giving each man the interpretation of his dream. ¹³And things turned out exactly as he interpreted them to us: I was restored to my position, and the other man was impaled."

¹⁴So Pharaoh sent for Joseph, and he was quickly brought from the dungeon. When he had shaved and changed his clothes, he came before Pharaoh.

¹⁵Pharaoh said to Joseph, "I had a dream, and no one can interpret it. But I have heard it said of you that when you hear a dream you can interpret it."

¹⁶"I cannot do it," Joseph replied to Pharaoh, "but God will give Pharaoh the answer he desires."

¹⁷Then Pharaoh said to Joseph, "In my dream I was standing on the bank of the Nile, ¹⁸when out of the river there came up seven cows, fat and sleek, and they grazed among the reeds. ¹⁹After them, seven other cows came up—scrawny and very ugly and lean. I had never seen such ugly cows in all the land of Egypt. ²⁰The lean, ugly cows ate up the seven fat cows that came up first. ²¹But even after they ate them, no one could tell that they had done so; they looked just as ugly as before. Then I woke up.

²²"In my dream I saw seven heads of grain, full and good, growing on a single stalk. ²³After them, seven other heads sprouted—withered and thin and scorched by the east wind. ²⁴The thin heads of grain swallowed up the seven good heads. I told this to the magicians, but none of them could explain it to me."

²⁵Then Joseph said to Pharaoh, "The dreams of Pharaoh are one and the same. God has revealed to Pharaoh what he is about to do. ²⁶The seven good cows are seven years, and the seven good heads of grain are seven years; it is one and the same dream. ²⁷The seven lean, ugly cows that came up afterward are seven years, and so are the seven worthless heads of grain scorched by the east wind: They are seven years of famine.

²⁸"It is just as I said to Pharaoh: God has shown Pharaoh what he is about to do. ²⁹Seven years of great abundance are coming throughout the land of Egypt, ³⁰but seven years of famine will follow them. Then all the abundance in Egypt will be forgotten, and the famine will ravage the land. ³¹The abundance in the land will not be remembered, because the famine that follows it will be so severe. ³²The reason the dream was given to Pharaoh in two forms is that the matter has been firmly decided by God, and God will do it soon.

³³"And now let Pharaoh look for a discerning and wise man and put him in charge of the land of Egypt. ³⁴Let Pharaoh appoint commissioners over the land to take a fifth of the harvest of Egypt during the seven years of abundance. ³⁵They should collect all the food of these good years that are coming and store up the grain under the authority of Pharaoh, to be kept in the cities for food. ³⁶This food should be held in reserve for the country, to be used during the seven years of famine that will come upon Egypt, so that the country may not be ruined by the famine."

³⁷The plan seemed good to Pharaoh and to all his officials. ³⁸So Pharaoh asked them, "Can we find anyone like this man, one in whom is the spirit of God[a]?"

³⁹Then Pharaoh said to Joseph, "Since God has made all this known to you, there is no one so discerning and wise as you. ⁴⁰You shall be in charge of my palace, and all my people are to submit to your orders. Only with respect to the throne will I be greater than you."

Joseph in Charge of Egypt

⁴¹So Pharaoh said to Joseph, "I hereby put you in charge of the whole land of Egypt." ⁴²Then Pharaoh took his signet ring from his finger and put it on Joseph's finger.

[a] 38 Or *of the gods*

REDEFINING SUCCESS

READ: GENESIS 41:15-40

You never know what relationship, skill, experience, or attribute God will use in you! He used a beauty pageant to strategically make Esther queen of Persia and stop the genocide of the Jews. He used Nehemiah's cupbearer skills to position him for a royal favor that would end up rebuilding the wall of Jerusalem. He used David's musical chops to open the palace door and give him access to the king of Israel. He used Joseph's imprisonment and his ability to interpret dreams to save two nations from a famine. And he used the intensity of a mass murderer named Saul to spread the gospel, while writing half of the New Testament in the process.

BUILDING

FAITH

WISDOM

STRENGTH

If God used them, he can use you. He's cultivating talents within you right now that will serve his kingdom in ways that you had no idea were possible. It could be athletic abilities or musical skills that God uses to give you a platform. It may be your creative genius. It may be something you don't even like about yourself! No matter what it is, just make sure he gets the praise for your excellence (which he gave you)!

Do the best you can with what you have where you are. That's my definition of success. It's not based on past experience or future potential. It's maximizing every opportunity in every way, every second of time, every ounce of talent, and every penny of money.

He dressed him in robes of fine linen and put a gold chain around his neck. ⁴³He had him ride in a chariot as his second-in-command,ᵃ and people shouted before him, "Make wayᵇ!" Thus he put him in charge of the whole land of Egypt.

⁴⁴Then Pharaoh said to Joseph, "I am Pharaoh, but without your word no one will lift hand or foot in all Egypt." ⁴⁵Pharaoh gave Joseph the name Zaphenath-Paneah and gave him Asenath daughter of Potiphera, priest of On,ᶜ to be his wife. And Joseph went throughout the land of Egypt.

⁴⁶Joseph was thirty years old when he entered the service of Pharaoh king of Egypt. And Joseph went out from Pharaoh's presence and traveled throughout Egypt. ⁴⁷During the seven years of abundance the land produced plentifully. ⁴⁸Joseph collected all the food produced in those seven years of abundance in Egypt and stored it in the cities. In each city he put the food grown in the fields surrounding it. ⁴⁹Joseph stored up huge quantities of grain, like the sand of the sea; it was so much that he stopped keeping records because it was beyond measure.

⁵⁰Before the years of famine came, two sons were born to Joseph by Asenath daughter of Potiphera, priest of On. ⁵¹Joseph named his firstborn Manassehᵈ and said, "It is because God has made me forget all my trouble and all my father's household." ⁵²The second son he named Ephraimᵉ and said, "It is because God has made me fruitful in the land of my suffering."

⁵³The seven years of abundance in Egypt came to an end, ⁵⁴and the seven years of famine began, just as Joseph had said. There was famine in all the other lands, but in the whole land of Egypt there was food. ⁵⁵When all Egypt began to feel the famine, the people cried to Pharaoh for food. Then Pharaoh told all the Egyptians, "Go to Joseph and do what he tells you."

⁵⁶When the famine had spread over the whole country, Joseph opened all the storehouses and sold grain to the Egyptians, for the famine was severe throughout Egypt. ⁵⁷And all the world came to Egypt to buy grain from Joseph, because the famine was severe everywhere.

Joseph's Brothers Go to Egypt

42 When Jacob learned that there was grain in Egypt, he said to his sons, "Why do you just keep looking at each other?" ²He continued, "I have heard that there is grain in Egypt. Go down there and buy some for us, so that we may live and not die."

³Then ten of Joseph's brothers went down to buy grain from Egypt. ⁴But Jacob did not send Benjamin, Joseph's brother, with the others, because he was afraid that harm might come to him. ⁵So Israel's sons were among those who went to buy grain, for there was famine in the land of Canaan also.

⁶Now Joseph was the governor of the land, the person who sold grain to all its people. So when Joseph's brothers arrived, they bowed down to him with their faces to the ground. ⁷As soon as Joseph saw his brothers, he recognized them, but he pretended to be a stranger and spoke harshly to them. "Where do you come from?" he asked.

"From the land of Canaan," they replied, "to buy food."

⁸Although Joseph recognized his brothers, they did not recognize him. ⁹Then he remembered his dreams about them and said to them, "You are spies! You have come to see where our land is unprotected."

¹⁰"No, my lord," they answered. "Your servants have come to buy food. ¹¹We are all the sons of one man. Your servants are honest men, not spies."

¹²"No!" he said to them. "You have come to see where our land is unprotected."

¹³But they replied, "Your servants were twelve brothers, the sons of one man, who lives in the land of Canaan. The youngest is now with our father, and one is no more."

¹⁴Joseph said to them, "It is just as I told you: You are spies! ¹⁵And this is how you will be tested: As surely as Pharaoh lives, you will not leave this place unless your youngest brother comes here. ¹⁶Send one of your number to get your brother; the rest of you will be kept in prison, so that your words may be tested to see if you are telling the truth. If you are not, then as surely as Pharaoh lives, you are spies!" ¹⁷And he put them all in custody for three days.

¹⁸On the third day, Joseph said to them,

ᵃ 43 Or *in the chariot of his second-in-command*; or *in his second chariot*   ᵇ 43 Or *Bow down*
ᶜ 45 That is, Heliopolis; also in verse 50   ᵈ 51 *Manasseh* sounds like and may be derived from the Hebrew for *forget.*   ᵉ 52 *Ephraim* sounds like the Hebrew for *twice fruitful.*

"Do this and you will live, for I fear God: ¹⁹If you are honest men, let one of your brothers stay here in prison, while the rest of you go and take grain back for your starving households. ²⁰But you must bring your youngest brother to me, so that your words may be verified and that you may not die." This they proceeded to do.

²¹They said to one another, "Surely we are being punished because of our brother. We saw how distressed he was when he pleaded with us for his life, but we would not listen; that's why this distress has come on us."

²²Reuben replied, "Didn't I tell you not to sin against the boy? But you wouldn't listen! Now we must give an accounting for his blood." ²³They did not realize that Joseph could understand them, since he was using an interpreter.

²⁴He turned away from them and began to weep, but then came back and spoke to them again. He had Simeon taken from them and bound before their eyes.

²⁵Joseph gave orders to fill their bags with grain, to put each man's silver back in his sack, and to give them provisions for their journey. After this was done for them, ²⁶they loaded their grain on their donkeys and left.

²⁷At the place where they stopped for the night one of them opened his sack to get feed for his donkey, and he saw his silver in the mouth of his sack. ²⁸"My silver has been returned," he said to his brothers. "Here it is in my sack."

Their hearts sank and they turned to each other trembling and said, "What is this that God has done to us?"

²⁹When they came to their father Jacob in the land of Canaan, they told him all that had happened to them. They said, ³⁰"The man who is lord over the land spoke harshly to us and treated us as though we were spying on the land. ³¹But we said to him, 'We are honest men; we are not spies. ³²We were twelve brothers, sons of one father. One is no more, and the youngest is now with our father in Canaan.'

³³"Then the man who is lord over the land said to us, 'This is how I will know whether you are honest men: Leave one of your brothers here with me, and take food for your starving households and go. ³⁴But bring your youngest brother to me so I will know that you are not spies but honest men. Then I will give your brother back to you, and you can trade*a* in the land.' "

³⁵As they were emptying their sacks, there in each man's sack was his pouch of silver! When they and their father saw the money pouches, they were frightened. ³⁶Their father Jacob said to them, "You have deprived me of my children. Joseph is no more and Simeon is no more, and now you want to take Benjamin. Everything is against me!"

³⁷Then Reuben said to his father, "You may put both of my sons to death if I do not bring him back to you. Entrust him to my care, and I will bring him back."

³⁸But Jacob said, "My son will not go down there with you; his brother is dead and he is the only one left. If harm comes to him on the journey you are taking, you will bring my gray head down to the grave in sorrow."

The Second Journey to Egypt

43 Now the famine was still severe in the land. ²So when they had eaten all the grain they had brought from Egypt, their father said to them, "Go back and buy us a little more food."

³But Judah said to him, "The man warned us solemnly, 'You will not see my face again unless your brother is with you.' ⁴If you will send our brother along with us, we will go down and buy food for you. ⁵But if you will not send him, we will not go down, because the man said to us, 'You will not see my face again unless your brother is with you.' "

⁶Israel asked, "Why did you bring this trouble on me by telling the man you had another brother?"

⁷They replied, "The man questioned us closely about ourselves and our family. 'Is your father still living?' he asked us. 'Do you have another brother?' We simply answered his questions. How were we to know he would say, 'Bring your brother down here'?"

⁸Then Judah said to Israel his father, "Send the boy along with me and we will go at once, so that we and you and our children may live and not die. ⁹I myself will guarantee his safety; you can hold me personally responsible for him. If I do not bring him back to you and set him here before you, I will bear the blame before you all my life. ¹⁰As it

---

a 34 Or *move about freely*

is, if we had not delayed, we could have gone and returned twice."

¹¹ Then their father Israel said to them, "If it must be, then do this: Put some of the best products of the land in your bags and take them down to the man as a gift — a little balm and a little honey, some spices and myrrh, some pistachio nuts and almonds. ¹² Take double the amount of silver with you, for you must return the silver that was put back into the mouths of your sacks. Perhaps it was a mistake. ¹³ Take your brother also and go back to the man at once. ¹⁴ And may God Almighty*a* grant you mercy before the man so that he will let your other brother and Benjamin come back with you. As for me, if I am bereaved, I am bereaved."

¹⁵ So the men took the gifts and double the amount of silver, and Benjamin also. They hurried down to Egypt and presented themselves to Joseph. ¹⁶ When Joseph saw Benjamin with them, he said to the steward of his house, "Take these men to my house, slaughter an animal and prepare a meal; they are to eat with me at noon."

¹⁷ The man did as Joseph told him and took the men to Joseph's house. ¹⁸ Now the men were frightened when they were taken to his house. They thought, "We were brought here because of the silver that was put back into our sacks the first time. He wants to attack us and overpower us and seize us as slaves and take our donkeys."

¹⁹ So they went up to Joseph's steward and spoke to him at the entrance to the house. ²⁰ "We beg your pardon, our lord," they said, "we came down here the first time to buy food. ²¹ But at the place where we stopped for the night we opened our sacks and each of us found his silver — the exact weight — in the mouth of his sack. So we have brought it back with us. ²² We have also brought additional silver with us to buy food. We don't know who put our silver in our sacks."

²³ "It's all right," he said. "Don't be afraid. Your God, the God of your father, has given you treasure in your sacks; I received your silver." Then he brought Simeon out to them.

²⁴ The steward took the men into Joseph's house, gave them water to wash their feet and provided fodder for their donkeys. ²⁵ They prepared their gifts for Joseph's ar-

rival at noon, because they had heard that they were to eat there.

²⁶ When Joseph came home, they presented to him the gifts they had brought into the house, and they bowed down before him to the ground. ²⁷ He asked them how they were, and then he said, "How is your aged father you told me about? Is he still living?" ²⁸ They replied, "Your servant our father is still alive and well." And they bowed down, prostrating themselves before him.

²⁹ As he looked about and saw his brother Benjamin, his own mother's son, he asked, "Is this your youngest brother, the one you told me about?" And he said, "God be gracious to you, my son." ³⁰ Deeply moved at the sight of his brother, Joseph hurried out and looked for a place to weep. He went into his private room and wept there.

³¹ After he had washed his face, he came out and, controlling himself, said, "Serve the food."

³² They served him by himself, the brothers by themselves, and the Egyptians who ate with him by themselves, because Egyptians could not eat with Hebrews, for that is detestable to Egyptians. ³³ The men had been seated before him in the order of their ages, from the firstborn to the youngest; and they looked at each other in astonishment. ³⁴ When portions were served to them from Joseph's table, Benjamin's portion was five times as much as anyone else's. So they feasted and drank freely with him.

A Silver Cup in a Sack

44 Now Joseph gave these instructions to the steward of his house: "Fill the men's sacks with as much food as they can carry, and put each man's silver in the mouth of his sack. ² Then put my cup, the silver one, in the mouth of the youngest one's sack, along with the silver for his grain." And he did as Joseph said.

³ As morning dawned, the men were sent on their way with their donkeys. ⁴ They had not gone far from the city when Joseph said to his steward, "Go after those men at once, and when you catch up with them, say to them, 'Why have you repaid good with evil? ⁵ Isn't this the cup my master drinks from and also uses for divination? This is a wicked thing you have done.'"

a 14 Hebrew *El-Shaddai*

⁶When he caught up with them, he repeated these words to them. ⁷But they said to him, "Why does my lord say such things? Far be it from your servants to do anything like that! ⁸We even brought back to you from the land of Canaan the silver we found inside the mouths of our sacks. So why would we steal silver or gold from your master's house? ⁹If any of your servants is found to have it, he will die; and the rest of us will become my lord's slaves."

¹⁰"Very well, then," he said, "let it be as you say. Whoever is found to have it will become my slave; the rest of you will be free from blame."

¹¹Each of them quickly lowered his sack to the ground and opened it. ¹²Then the steward proceeded to search, beginning with the oldest and ending with the youngest. And the cup was found in Benjamin's sack. ¹³At this, they tore their clothes. Then they all loaded their donkeys and returned to the city.

¹⁴Joseph was still in the house when Judah and his brothers came in, and they threw themselves to the ground before him. ¹⁵Joseph said to them, "What is this you have done? Don't you know that a man like me can find things out by divination?"

¹⁶"What can we say to my lord?" Judah replied. "What can we say? How can we prove our innocence? God has uncovered your servants' guilt. We are now my lord's slaves—we ourselves and the one who was found to have the cup."

¹⁷But Joseph said, "Far be it from me to do such a thing! Only the man who was found to have the cup will become my slave. The rest of you, go back to your father in peace."

¹⁸Then Judah went up to him and said: "Pardon your servant, my lord, let me speak a word to my lord. Do not be angry with your servant, though you are equal to Pharaoh himself. ¹⁹My lord asked his servants, 'Do you have a father or a brother?' ²⁰And we answered, 'We have an aged father, and there is a young son born to him in his old age. His brother is dead, and he is the only one of his mother's sons left, and his father loves him.'

²¹"Then you said to your servants, 'Bring him down to me so I can see him for myself.' ²²And we said to my lord, 'The boy cannot leave his father; if he leaves his father, his father will die.' ²³But you told your servants, 'Unless your youngest brother comes down with you, you will not see my face again.' ²⁴When we went back to your servant my father, we told him what my lord had said.

²⁵"Then our father said, 'Go back and buy a little more food.' ²⁶But we said, 'We cannot go down. Only if our youngest brother is with us will we go. We cannot see the man's face unless our youngest brother is with us.'

²⁷"Your servant my father said to us, 'You know that my wife bore me two sons. ²⁸One of them went away from me, and I said, "He has surely been torn to pieces." And I have not seen him since. ²⁹If you take this one from me too and harm comes to him, you will bring my gray head down to the grave in misery.'

³⁰"So now, if the boy is not with us when I go back to your servant my father, and if my father, whose life is closely bound up with the boy's life, ³¹sees that the boy isn't there, he will die. Your servants will bring the gray head of our father down to the grave in sorrow. ³²Your servant guaranteed the boy's safety to my father. I said, 'If I do not bring him back to you, I will bear the blame before you, my father, all my life!'

³³"Now then, please let your servant remain here as my lord's slave in place of the boy, and let the boy return with his brothers. ³⁴How can I go back to my father if the boy is not with me? No! Do not let me see the misery that would come on my father."

Joseph Makes Himself Known

45 Then Joseph could no longer control himself before all his attendants, and he cried out, "Have everyone leave my presence!" So there was no one with Joseph when he made himself known to his brothers. ²And he wept so loudly that the Egyptians heard him, and Pharaoh's household heard about it.

³Joseph said to his brothers, "I am Joseph! Is my father still living?" But his brothers were not able to answer him, because they were terrified at his presence.

⁴Then Joseph said to his brothers, "Come close to me." When they had done so, he said, "I am your brother Joseph, the one you sold into Egypt! ⁵And now, do not be distressed and do not be angry with yourselves for selling me here, because it was to save lives that God sent me ahead of you. ⁶For

two years now there has been famine in the land, and for the next five years there will be no plowing and reaping. ⁷But God sent me ahead of you to preserve for you a remnant on earth and to save your lives by a great deliverance.ᵃ

⁸"So then, it was not you who sent me here, but God. He made me father to Pharaoh, lord of his entire household and ruler of all Egypt. ⁹Now hurry back to my father and say to him, 'This is what your son Joseph says: God has made me lord of all Egypt. Come down to me; don't delay. ¹⁰You shall live in the region of Goshen and be near me—you, your children and grandchildren, your flocks and herds, and all you have. ¹¹I will provide for you there, because five years of famine are still to come. Otherwise you and your household and all who belong to you will become destitute.'

¹²"You can see for yourselves, and so can my brother Benjamin, that it is really I who am speaking to you. ¹³Tell my father about all the honor accorded me in Egypt and about everything you have seen. And bring my father down here quickly."

¹⁴Then he threw his arms around his brother Benjamin and wept, and Benjamin embraced him, weeping. ¹⁵And he kissed all his brothers and wept over them. Afterward his brothers talked with him.

¹⁶When the news reached Pharaoh's palace that Joseph's brothers had come, Pharaoh and all his officials were pleased. ¹⁷Pharaoh said to Joseph, "Tell your brothers, 'Do this: Load your animals and return to the land of Canaan, ¹⁸and bring your father and your families back to me. I will give you the best of the land of Egypt and you can enjoy the fat of the land.'

¹⁹"You are also directed to tell them, 'Do this: Take some carts from Egypt for your children and your wives, and get your father and come. ²⁰Never mind about your belongings, because the best of all Egypt will be yours.'"

²¹So the sons of Israel did this. Joseph gave them carts, as Pharaoh had commanded, and he also gave them provisions for their journey. ²²To each of them he gave new clothing, but to Benjamin he gave three hundred shekelsᵇ of silver and five sets of clothes. ²³And this is what he sent to his father: ten donkeys loaded with the best things of Egypt, and ten female donkeys loaded with grain and bread and other provisions for his journey. ²⁴Then he sent his brothers away, and as they were leaving he said to them, "Don't quarrel on the way!"

²⁵So they went up out of Egypt and came to their father Jacob in the land of Canaan. ²⁶They told him, "Joseph is still alive! In fact, he is ruler of all Egypt." Jacob was stunned; he did not believe them. ²⁷But when they told him everything Joseph had said to them, and when he saw the carts Joseph had sent to carry him back, the spirit of their father Jacob revived. ²⁸And Israel said, "I'm convinced! My son Joseph is still alive. I will go and see him before I die."

Jacob Goes to Egypt

46 So Israel set out with all that was his, and when he reached Beersheba, he offered sacrifices to the God of his father Isaac.

²And God spoke to Israel in a vision at night and said, "Jacob! Jacob!"

"Here I am," he replied.

³"I am God, the God of your father," he said. "Do not be afraid to go down to Egypt, for I will make you into a great nation there. ⁴I will go down to Egypt with you, and I will surely bring you back again. And Joseph's own hand will close your eyes."

⁵Then Jacob left Beersheba, and Israel's sons took their father Jacob and their children and their wives in the carts that Pharaoh had sent to transport him. ⁶So Jacob and all his offspring went to Egypt, taking with them their livestock and the possessions they had acquired in Canaan. ⁷Jacob brought with him to Egypt his sons and grandsons and his daughters and granddaughters—all his offspring.

⁸These are the names of the sons of Israel (Jacob and his descendants) who went to Egypt:

Reuben the firstborn of Jacob.
⁹The sons of Reuben:
Hanok, Pallu, Hezron and Karmi.
¹⁰The sons of Simeon:
Jemuel, Jamin, Ohad, Jakin, Zohar

and Shaul the son of a Canaanite woman.

[11] The sons of Levi:

Gershon, Kohath and Merari.

[12] The sons of Judah:

Er, Onan, Shelah, Perez and Zerah (but Er and Onan had died in the land of Canaan).

The sons of Perez:

Hezron and Hamul.

[13] The sons of Issachar:

Tola, Puah,[a] Jashub[b] and Shimron.

[14] The sons of Zebulun:

Sered, Elon and Jahleel.

[15] These were the sons Leah bore to Jacob in Paddan Aram,[c] besides his daughter Dinah. These sons and daughters of his were thirty-three in all.

[16] The sons of Gad:

Zephon,[d] Haggi, Shuni, Ezbon, Eri, Arodi and Areli.

[17] The sons of Asher:

Imnah, Ishvah, Ishvi and Beriah.

Their sister was Serah.

The sons of Beriah:

Heber and Malkiel.

[18] These were the children born to Jacob by Zilpah, whom Laban had given to his daughter Leah — sixteen in all.

[19] The sons of Jacob's wife Rachel:

Joseph and Benjamin. [20] In Egypt, Manasseh and Ephraim were born to Joseph by Asenath daughter of Potiphera, priest of On.[e]

[21] The sons of Benjamin:

Bela, Beker, Ashbel, Gera, Naaman, Ehi, Rosh, Muppim, Huppim and Ard.

[22] These were the sons of Rachel who were born to Jacob — fourteen in all.

[23] The son of Dan:

Hushim.

[24] The sons of Naphtali:

Jahziel, Guni, Jezer and Shillem.

[25] These were the sons born to Jacob by Bilhah, whom Laban had given to his daughter Rachel — seven in all.

[26] All those who went to Egypt with Jacob — those who were his direct descendants, not counting his sons' wives — numbered sixty-six persons. [27] With the two sons[f] who had been born to Joseph in Egypt, the members of Jacob's family, which went to Egypt, were seventy[g] in all.

[28] Now Jacob sent Judah ahead of him to Joseph to get directions to Goshen. When they arrived in the region of Goshen, [29] Joseph had his chariot made ready and went to Goshen to meet his father Israel. As soon as Joseph appeared before him, he threw his arms around his father[h] and wept for a long time.

[30] Israel said to Joseph, "Now I am ready to die, since I have seen for myself that you are still alive."

[31] Then Joseph said to his brothers and to his father's household, "I will go up and speak to Pharaoh and will say to him, 'My brothers and my father's household, who were living in the land of Canaan, have come to me. [32] The men are shepherds; they tend livestock, and they have brought along their flocks and herds and everything they own.' [33] When Pharaoh calls you in and asks, 'What is your occupation?' [34] you should answer, 'Your servants have tended livestock from our boyhood on, just as our fathers did.' Then you will be allowed to settle in the region of Goshen, for all shepherds are detestable to the Egyptians."

47 Joseph went and told Pharaoh, "My father and brothers, with their flocks and herds and everything they own, have come from the land of Canaan and are now in Goshen." [2] He chose five of his brothers and presented them before Pharaoh.

[3] Pharaoh asked the brothers, "What is your occupation?"

"Your servants are shepherds," they replied to Pharaoh, "just as our fathers were." [4] They also said to him, "We have come to live here for a while, because the famine is severe in Canaan and your servants' flocks have no pasture. So now, please let your servants settle in Goshen."

---

a 13 Samaritan Pentateuch and Syriac (see also 1 Chron. 7:1); Masoretic Text *Puvah*   *b 13* Samaritan Pentateuch and some Septuagint manuscripts (see also Num. 26:24 and 1 Chron. 7:1); Masoretic Text *Iob*   *c 15* That is, Northwest Mesopotamia   *d 16* Samaritan Pentateuch and Septuagint (see also Num. 26:15); Masoretic Text *Ziphion*   *e 20* That is, Heliopolis   *f 27* Hebrew; Septuagint *the nine children*   *g 27* Hebrew (see also Exodus 1:5 and note); Septuagint (see also Acts 7:14) *seventy-five*   *h 29* Hebrew *around him*

⁵Pharaoh said to Joseph, "Your father and your brothers have come to you, ⁶and the land of Egypt is before you; settle your father and your brothers in the best part of the land. Let them live in Goshen. And if you know of any among them with special ability, put them in charge of my own livestock."

⁷Then Joseph brought his father Jacob in and presented him before Pharaoh. After Jacob blessed[a] Pharaoh, ⁸Pharaoh asked him, "How old are you?"

⁹And Jacob said to Pharaoh, "The years of my pilgrimage are a hundred and thirty. My years have been few and difficult, and they do not equal the years of the pilgrimage of my fathers." ¹⁰Then Jacob blessed[b] Pharaoh and went out from his presence.

¹¹So Joseph settled his father and his brothers in Egypt and gave them property in the best part of the land, the district of Rameses, as Pharaoh directed. ¹²Joseph also provided his father and his brothers and all his father's household with food, according to the number of their children.

Joseph and the Famine

¹³There was no food, however, in the whole region because the famine was severe; both Egypt and Canaan wasted away because of the famine. ¹⁴Joseph collected all the money that was to be found in Egypt and Canaan in payment for the grain they were buying, and he brought it to Pharaoh's palace. ¹⁵When the money of the people of Egypt and Canaan was gone, all Egypt came to Joseph and said, "Give us food. Why should we die before your eyes? Our money is all gone."

¹⁶"Then bring your livestock," said Joseph. "I will sell you food in exchange for your livestock, since your money is gone." ¹⁷So they brought their livestock to Joseph, and he gave them food in exchange for their horses, their sheep and goats, their cattle and donkeys. And he brought them through that year with food in exchange for all their livestock.

¹⁸When that year was over, they came to him the following year and said, "We cannot hide from our lord the fact that since our money is gone and our livestock belongs to you, there is nothing left for our lord except our bodies and our land. ¹⁹Why should we perish before your eyes — we and our land as well? Buy us and our land in exchange for food, and we with our land will be in bondage to Pharaoh. Give us seed so that we may live and not die, and that the land may not become desolate."

²⁰So Joseph bought all the land in Egypt for Pharaoh. The Egyptians, one and all, sold their fields, because the famine was too severe for them. The land became Pharaoh's, ²¹and Joseph reduced the people to servitude,[c] from one end of Egypt to the other. ²²However, he did not buy the land of the priests, because they received a regular allotment from Pharaoh and had food enough from the allotment Pharaoh gave them. That is why they did not sell their land.

²³Joseph said to the people, "Now that I have bought you and your land today for Pharaoh, here is seed for you so you can plant the ground. ²⁴But when the crop comes in, give a fifth of it to Pharaoh. The other four-fifths you may keep as seed for the fields and as food for yourselves and your households and your children."

²⁵"You have saved our lives," they said. "May we find favor in the eyes of our lord; we will be in bondage to Pharaoh."

²⁶So Joseph established it as a law concerning land in Egypt — still in force today — that a fifth of the produce belongs to Pharaoh. It was only the land of the priests that did not become Pharaoh's.

²⁷Now the Israelites settled in Egypt in the region of Goshen. They acquired property there and were fruitful and increased greatly in number.

²⁸Jacob lived in Egypt seventeen years, and the years of his life were a hundred and forty-seven. ²⁹When the time drew near for Israel to die, he called for his son Joseph and said to him, "If I have found favor in your eyes, put your hand under my thigh and promise that you will show me kindness and faithfulness. Do not bury me in Egypt, ³⁰but when I rest with my fathers, carry me out of Egypt and bury me where they are buried."

"I will do as you say," he said.

³¹"Swear to me," he said. Then Joseph swore to him, and Israel worshiped as he leaned on the top of his staff.[d]

---

[a] 7 Or *greeted*   [b] 10 Or *said farewell to*   [c] 21 Samaritan Pentateuch and Septuagint (see also Vulgate); Masoretic Text *and he moved the people into the cities*   [d] 31 Or *Israel bowed down at the head of his bed*

Manasseh and Ephraim

48 Some time later Joseph was told, "Your father is ill." So he took his two sons Manasseh and Ephraim along with him. ²When Jacob was told, "Your son Joseph has come to you," Israel rallied his strength and sat up on the bed.

³Jacob said to Joseph, "God Almighty*ᵃ* appeared to me at Luz in the land of Canaan, and there he blessed me ⁴and said to me, 'I am going to make you fruitful and increase your numbers. I will make you a community of peoples, and I will give this land as an everlasting possession to your descendants after you.'

⁵"Now then, your two sons born to you in Egypt before I came to you here will be reckoned as mine; Ephraim and Manasseh will be mine, just as Reuben and Simeon are mine. ⁶Any children born to you after them will be yours; in the territory they inherit they will be reckoned under the names of their brothers. ⁷As I was returning from Paddan,*ᵇ* to my sorrow Rachel died in the land of Canaan while we were still on the way, a little distance from Ephrath. So I buried her there beside the road to Ephrath" (that is, Bethlehem).

⁸When Israel saw the sons of Joseph, he asked, "Who are these?"

⁹"They are the sons God has given me here," Joseph said to his father.

Then Israel said, "Bring them to me so I may bless them."

¹⁰Now Israel's eyes were failing because of old age, and he could hardly see. So Joseph brought his sons close to him, and his father kissed them and embraced them.

¹¹Israel said to Joseph, "I never expected to see your face again, and now God has allowed me to see your children too."

¹²Then Joseph removed them from Israel's knees and bowed down with his face to the ground. ¹³And Joseph took both of them, Ephraim on his right toward Israel's left hand and Manasseh on his left toward Israel's right hand, and brought them close to him. ¹⁴But Israel reached out his right hand and put it on Ephraim's head, though he was the younger, and crossing his arms, he put his left hand on Manasseh's head, even though Manasseh was the firstborn.

¹⁵Then he blessed Joseph and said,

"May the God before whom my fathers
    Abraham and Isaac walked faithfully,
the God who has been my shepherd
    all my life to this day,
¹⁶the Angel who has delivered me from all
        harm
    —may he bless these boys.
May they be called by my name
    and the names of my fathers Abraham
        and Isaac,
and may they increase greatly
    on the earth."

¹⁷When Joseph saw his father placing his right hand on Ephraim's head he was displeased; so he took hold of his father's hand to move it from Ephraim's head to Manasseh's head. ¹⁸Joseph said to him, "No, my father, this one is the firstborn; put your right hand on his head."

¹⁹But his father refused and said, "I know, my son, I know. He too will become a people, and he too will become great. Nevertheless, his younger brother will be greater than he, and his descendants will become a group of nations." ²⁰He blessed them that day and said,

"In your*ᶜ* name will Israel pronounce this
        blessing:
    'May God make you like Ephraim and
        Manasseh.'"

So he put Ephraim ahead of Manasseh.

²¹Then Israel said to Joseph, "I am about to die, but God will be with you*ᵈ* and take you*ᵈ* back to the land of your*ᵈ* fathers. ²²And to you I give one more ridge of land*ᵉ* than to your brothers, the ridge I took from the Amorites with my sword and my bow."

Jacob Blesses His Sons

49 Then Jacob called for his sons and said: "Gather around so I can tell you what will happen to you in days to come.

²"Assemble and listen, sons of Jacob;
    listen to your father Israel.

³"Reuben, you are my firstborn,
    my might, the first sign of my strength,
    excelling in honor, excelling in power.

ᵃ 3 Hebrew *El-Shaddai*   *ᵇ 7* That is, Northwest Mesopotamia   *ᶜ 20* The Hebrew is singular.
ᵈ 21 The Hebrew is plural.   *ᵉ 22* The Hebrew for *ridge of land* is identical with the place name Shechem.

HEADED FOR DISASTER?

READ: GENESIS 48:11

Sometimes you know you're headed for disaster. You're convinced you're going to flunk a test. Or hit a car. Or lose your spot on the team. Or face raging conflict with your parents. You're smart enough to read the signs and know what comes next, and it isn't good.

Joseph surely must have wondered where his life was headed when his brothers tossed him in a pit and then sold him into slavery. Life looked better when he rose to power within his master's household, but then he was wrongly jailed, where he was left to rot for years. But after many years God raised him to enormous responsibility, putting him in charge of one nation's critical food supplies. By the time he revealed his identity to his stunned brothers, and after his father died, Joseph has fresh insight into how the Lord works. He tells his brothers, "You intended to harm me, but God intended it for good to accomplish what is now being done, the saving of many lives" (Genesis 50:20).

BUILDING FAITH WISDOM STRENGTH

You might feel like you're sure to crash and burn. Yet whether you can see it or not, the Lord has a different plan going on. Even when bad things happen, he works for your good and strives to fulfill his purposes (Romans 8:28). Like Joseph found out, with God on your side, the worst situations aren't as dire as they seem.

⁴Turbulent as the waters, you will no
longer excel,
for you went up onto your father's bed,
onto my couch and defiled it.

⁵"Simeon and Levi are brothers—
their swords*a* are weapons of violence.
⁶Let me not enter their council,
let me not join their assembly,
for they have killed men in their anger
and hamstrung oxen as they pleased.
⁷Cursed be their anger, so fierce,
and their fury, so cruel!
I will scatter them in Jacob
and disperse them in Israel.

⁸"Judah,*b* your brothers will praise you;
your hand will be on the neck of your
enemies;
your father's sons will bow down to you.
⁹You are a lion's cub, Judah;
you return from the prey, my son.
Like a lion he crouches and lies down,
like a lioness—who dares to rouse him?
¹⁰The scepter will not depart from Judah,
nor the ruler's staff from between his
feet,*c*
until he to whom it belongs*d* shall come
and the obedience of the nations shall
be his.
¹¹He will tether his donkey to a vine,
his colt to the choicest branch;
he will wash his garments in wine,
his robes in the blood of grapes.
¹²His eyes will be darker than wine,
his teeth whiter than milk.*e*

¹³"Zebulun will live by the seashore
and become a haven for ships;
his border will extend toward Sidon.

¹⁴"Issachar is a rawboned*f* donkey
lying down among the sheep pens.*g*
¹⁵When he sees how good is his resting
place
and how pleasant is his land,
he will bend his shoulder to the burden
and submit to forced labor.

¹⁶"Dan*h* will provide justice for his people
as one of the tribes of Israel.
¹⁷Dan will be a snake by the roadside,
a viper along the path,
that bites the horse's heels
so that its rider tumbles backward.

¹⁸"I look for your deliverance, LORD.

¹⁹"Gad*i* will be attacked by a band of
raiders,
but he will attack them at their heels.

²⁰"Asher's food will be rich;
he will provide delicacies fit for a king.

²¹"Naphtali is a doe set free
that bears beautiful fawns.*j*

²²"Joseph is a fruitful vine,
a fruitful vine near a spring,
whose branches climb over a wall.*k*
²³With bitterness archers attacked him;
they shot at him with hostility.
²⁴But his bow remained steady,
his strong arms stayed*l* limber,
because of the hand of the Mighty One of
Jacob,
because of the Shepherd, the Rock of
Israel,
²⁵because of your father's God, who helps
you,
because of the Almighty,*m* who blesses
you
with blessings of the skies above,
blessings of the deep springs below,
blessings of the breast and womb.
²⁶Your father's blessings are greater
than the blessings of the ancient
mountains,
than*n* the bounty of the age-old hills.
Let all these rest on the head of Joseph,
on the brow of the prince among*o* his
brothers.

²⁷"Benjamin is a ravenous wolf;
in the morning he devours the prey,
in the evening he divides the
plunder."

a 5 The meaning of the Hebrew for this word is uncertain.   *b 8 Judah* sounds like and may be derived
from the Hebrew for *praise.*   *c 10* Or *from his descendants*   *d 10* Or *to whom tribute belongs;* the
meaning of the Hebrew for this phrase is uncertain.   *e 12* Or *will be dull from wine, / his teeth white from
milk*   *f 14* Or *strong*   *g 14* Or *the campfires;* or *the saddlebags*   *h 16 Dan* here means *he provides
justice.*   *i 19 Gad* sounds like the Hebrew for *attack* and also for *band of raiders.*   *j 21* Or *free; / he
utters beautiful words*   *k 22* Or *Joseph is a wild colt, / a wild colt near a spring, / a wild donkey on a
terraced hill*   *l 23,24* Or *archers will attack . . . will shoot . . . will remain . . . will stay*   *m 25* Hebrew
Shaddai   *n 26* Or *of my progenitors, / as great as*   *o 26* Or *of the one separated from*

²⁸All these are the twelve tribes of Israel, and this is what their father said to them when he blessed them, giving each the blessing appropriate to him.

The Death of Jacob

²⁹Then he gave them these instructions: "I am about to be gathered to my people. Bury me with my fathers in the cave in the field of Ephron the Hittite, ³⁰the cave in the field of Machpelah, near Mamre in Canaan, which Abraham bought along with the field as a burial place from Ephron the Hittite. ³¹There Abraham and his wife Sarah were buried, there Isaac and his wife Rebekah were buried, and there I buried Leah. ³²The field and the cave in it were bought from the Hittites.ᵃ"

³³When Jacob had finished giving instructions to his sons, he drew his feet up into the bed, breathed his last and was gathered to his people.

50 Joseph threw himself on his father and wept over him and kissed him. ²Then Joseph directed the physicians in his service to embalm his father Israel. So the physicians embalmed him, ³taking a full forty days, for that was the time required for embalming. And the Egyptians mourned for him seventy days.

⁴When the days of mourning had passed, Joseph said to Pharaoh's court, "If I have found favor in your eyes, speak to Pharaoh for me. Tell him, ⁵'My father made me swear an oath and said, "I am about to die; bury me in the tomb I dug for myself in the land of Canaan." Now let me go up and bury my father; then I will return.'"

⁶Pharaoh said, "Go up and bury your father, as he made you swear to do."

⁷So Joseph went up to bury his father. All Pharaoh's officials accompanied him — the dignitaries of his court and all the dignitaries of Egypt — ⁸besides all the members of Joseph's household and his brothers and those belonging to his father's household. Only their children and their flocks and herds were left in Goshen. ⁹Chariots and horsemenᵇ also went up with him. It was a very large company.

¹⁰When they reached the threshing floor of Atad, near the Jordan, they lamented loudly and bitterly; and there Joseph observed a seven-day period of mourning for his father. ¹¹When the Canaanites who lived there saw the mourning at the threshing floor of Atad, they said, "The Egyptians are holding a solemn ceremony of mourning." That is why that place near the Jordan is called Abel Mizraim.ᶜ

¹²So Jacob's sons did as he had commanded them: ¹³They carried him to the land of Canaan and buried him in the cave in the field of Machpelah, near Mamre, which Abraham had bought along with the field as a burial place from Ephron the Hittite. ¹⁴After burying his father, Joseph returned to Egypt, together with his brothers and all the others who had gone with him to bury his father.

Joseph Reassures His Brothers

¹⁵When Joseph's brothers saw that their father was dead, they said, "What if Joseph holds a grudge against us and pays us back for all the wrongs we did to him?" ¹⁶So they sent word to Joseph, saying, "Your father left these instructions before he died: ¹⁷'This is what you are to say to Joseph: I ask you to forgive your brothers the sins and the wrongs they committed in treating you so badly.' Now please forgive the sins of the servants of the God of your father." When their message came to him, Joseph wept.

¹⁸His brothers then came and threw themselves down before him. "We are your slaves," they said.

¹⁹But Joseph said to them, "Don't be afraid. Am I in the place of God? ²⁰You intended to harm me, but God intended it for good to accomplish what is now being done, the saving of many lives. ²¹So then, don't be afraid. I will provide for you and your children." And he reassured them and spoke kindly to them.

The Death of Joseph

²²Joseph stayed in Egypt, along with all his father's family. He lived a hundred and ten years ²³and saw the third generation of Ephraim's children. Also the children of Makir son of Manasseh were placed at birth on Joseph's knees.ᵈ

²⁴Then Joseph said to his brothers, "I am

ᵃ 32 Or *the descendants of Heth*   ᵇ 9 Or *charioteers*
Egyptians.   ᵈ 23 That is, were counted as his   ᶜ 11 *Abel Mizraim* means *mourning of the*

about to die. But God will surely come to your aid and take you up out of this land to the land he promised on oath to Abraham, Isaac and Jacob." 25 And Joseph made the Israelites swear an oath and said, "God will surely come to your aid, and then you must carry my bones up from this place."

26 So Joseph died at the age of a hundred and ten. And after they embalmed him, he was placed in a coffin in Egypt.

EXODUS

WHEN DID THIS HAPPEN?

During the 1400s B.C. while the Israelites were traveling in the desert

WHO IS IN THIS BOOK?

Moses
Aaron
Miriam
Pharaoh's daughter
Zipporah
Jethro
Pharaoh
Jochebed

VERSES YOU MIGHT RECOGNIZE

EXODUS 8:1

"Then the LORD said to Moses, 'Go to Pharaoh and say to him, "This is what the LORD says: Let my people go, so that they may worship me."'"

EXODUS 20:8

"Remember the Sabbath day by keeping it holy."

WHAT'S IT ABOUT?

Exodus recounts what happened to the descendants of Joseph after they moved to Egypt from Canaan. After Joseph died, the Israelites had grown so great in number that Pharaoh, the king of Egypt, was afraid they might outnumber the Egyptians. He made them slaves, forcing them to do hard labor under harsh masters. To keep the Israelite population under control, Pharaoh ordered that all Hebrew infant boys be thrown into the Nile River. One brave mother saved her baby by setting him afloat in a basket, where the pharaoh's daughter discovered him. That baby was Moses.

Exodus tells the story of Moses and the Israelites. Moses grew up in the palace, murdered an Egyptian, fled to the desert, conversed with a burning bush and ultimately freed the Israelites and led them to the promised land. God didn't forget the Israelites in their troubles and oppression. He saw their suffering and provided a miraculous way of escape. Life didn't get easier for the people immediately after they left Egypt. While in the desert, they had to learn to trust God for their basic needs, and they learned some difficult and painful lessons before they reached the promised land forty years later.

In the book of Exodus, God continues his plan to save all people. Just as the Israelites painted their doorframes with the blood of a perfect lamb (see Exodus 12:13) to be saved from a deadly plague, Jesus, the perfect Lamb of God, would one day shed his blood for the sin of the world.

EXODUS

The Israelites Oppressed

1 These are the names of the sons of Israel who went to Egypt with Jacob, each with his family: ²Reuben, Simeon, Levi and Judah; ³Issachar, Zebulun and Benjamin; ⁴Dan and Naphtali; Gad and Asher. ⁵The descendants of Jacob numbered seventy[a] in all; Joseph was already in Egypt.

⁶Now Joseph and all his brothers and all that generation died, ⁷but the Israelites were exceedingly fruitful; they multiplied greatly, increased in numbers and became so numerous that the land was filled with them.

⁸Then a new king, to whom Joseph meant nothing, came to power in Egypt. ⁹"Look," he said to his people, "the Israelites have become far too numerous for us. ¹⁰Come, we must deal shrewdly with them or they will become even more numerous and, if war breaks out, will join our enemies, fight against us and leave the country."

¹¹So they put slave masters over them to oppress them with forced labor, and they built Pithom and Rameses as store cities for Pharaoh. ¹²But the more they were oppressed, the more they multiplied and spread; so the Egyptians came to dread the Israelites ¹³and worked them ruthlessly. ¹⁴They made their lives bitter with harsh labor in brick and mortar and with all kinds of work in the fields; in all their harsh labor the Egyptians worked them ruthlessly.

¹⁵The king of Egypt said to the Hebrew midwives, whose names were Shiphrah and Puah, ¹⁶"When you are helping the Hebrew women during childbirth on the delivery stool, if you see that the baby is a boy, kill him; but if it is a girl, let her live." ¹⁷The midwives, however, feared God and did not do what the king of Egypt had told them to do; they let the boys live. ¹⁸Then the king of Egypt summoned the midwives and asked them, "Why have you done this? Why have you let the boys live?"

¹⁹The midwives answered Pharaoh, "Hebrew women are not like Egyptian women; they are vigorous and give birth before the midwives arrive."

²⁰So God was kind to the midwives and the people increased and became even more numerous. ²¹And because the midwives feared God, he gave them families of their own.

²²Then Pharaoh gave this order to all his people: "Every Hebrew boy that is born you must throw into the Nile, but let every girl live."

The Birth of Moses

2 Now a man of the tribe of Levi married a Levite woman, ²and she became pregnant and gave birth to a son. When she saw that he was a fine child, she hid him for three months. ³But when she could hide him no longer, she got a papyrus basket[b] for him and coated it with tar and pitch. Then she placed the child in it and put it among the reeds along the bank of the Nile. ⁴His sister stood at a distance to see what would happen to him.

⁵Then Pharaoh's daughter went down to the Nile to bathe, and her attendants were walking along the riverbank. She saw the basket among the reeds and sent her female slave to get it. ⁶She opened it and saw the baby. He was crying, and she felt sorry for him. "This is one of the Hebrew babies," she said.

⁷Then his sister asked Pharaoh's daughter, "Shall I go and get one of the Hebrew women to nurse the baby for you?"

⁸"Yes, go," she answered. So the girl went and got the baby's mother. ⁹Pharaoh's daughter said to her, "Take this baby and nurse him for me, and I will pay you." So the woman took the baby and nursed him. ¹⁰When the child grew older, she took him to Pharaoh's daughter and he became her son.

---

[a] 5 Masoretic Text (see also Gen. 46:27); Dead Sea Scrolls and Septuagint (see also Acts 7:14 and note at Gen. 46:27) *seventy-five*   [b] 3 The Hebrew can also mean *ark*, as in Gen. 6:14.

She named him Moses,[a] saying, "I drew him out of the water."

Moses Flees to Midian

[11] One day, after Moses had grown up, he went out to where his own people were and watched them at their hard labor. He saw an Egyptian beating a Hebrew, one of his own people. [12] Looking this way and that and seeing no one, he killed the Egyptian and hid him in the sand. [13] The next day he went out and saw two Hebrews fighting. He asked the one in the wrong, "Why are you hitting your fellow Hebrew?"

[14] The man said, "Who made you ruler and judge over us? Are you thinking of killing me as you killed the Egyptian?" Then Moses was afraid and thought, "What I did must have become known."

[15] When Pharaoh heard of this, he tried to kill Moses, but Moses fled from Pharaoh and went to live in Midian, where he sat down by a well. [16] Now a priest of Midian had seven daughters, and they came to draw water and fill the troughs to water their father's flock. [17] Some shepherds came along and drove them away, but Moses got up and came to their rescue and watered their flock.

[18] When the girls returned to Reuel their father, he asked them, "Why have you returned so early today?"

[19] They answered, "An Egyptian rescued us from the shepherds. He even drew water for us and watered the flock."

[20] "And where is he?" Reuel asked his daughters. "Why did you leave him? Invite him to have something to eat."

[21] Moses agreed to stay with the man, who gave his daughter Zipporah to Moses in marriage. [22] Zipporah gave birth to a son, and Moses named him Gershom,[b] saying, "I have become a foreigner in a foreign land."

[23] During that long period, the king of Egypt died. The Israelites groaned in their slavery and cried out, and their cry for help because of their slavery went up to God. [24] God heard their groaning and he remembered his covenant with Abraham, with Isaac and with Jacob. [25] So God looked on the Israelites and was concerned about them.

Moses and the Burning Bush

3 Now Moses was tending the flock of Jethro his father-in-law, the priest of Midian, and he led the flock to the far side of the wilderness and came to Horeb, the mountain of God. [2] There the angel of the LORD appeared to him in flames of fire from within a bush. Moses saw that though the bush was on fire it did not burn up. [3] So Moses thought, "I will go over and see this strange sight — why the bush does not burn up."

[4] When the LORD saw that he had gone over to look, God called to him from within the bush, "Moses! Moses!"

And Moses said, "Here I am."

[5] "Do not come any closer," God said. "Take off your sandals, for the place where you are standing is holy ground." [6] Then he said, "I am the God of your father,[c] the God of Abraham, the God of Isaac and the God of Jacob." At this, Moses hid his face, because he was afraid to look at God.

[7] The LORD said, "I have indeed seen the misery of my people in Egypt. I have heard them crying out because of their slave drivers, and I am concerned about their suffering. [8] So I have come down to rescue them from the hand of the Egyptians and to bring them up out of that land into a good and spacious land, a land flowing with milk and honey — the home of the Canaanites, Hittites, Amorites, Perizzites, Hivites and Jebusites. [9] And now the cry of the Israelites has reached me, and I have seen the way the Egyptians are oppressing them. [10] So now, go. I am sending you to Pharaoh to bring my people the Israelites out of Egypt."

[11] But Moses said to God, "Who am I that I should go to Pharaoh and bring the Israelites out of Egypt?"

[12] And God said, "I will be with you. And this will be the sign to you that it is I who have sent you: When you have brought the people out of Egypt, you[d] will worship God on this mountain."

[13] Moses said to God, "Suppose I go to the Israelites and say to them, 'The God of your fathers has sent me to you,' and they ask me, 'What is his name?' Then what shall I tell them?"

[14] God said to Moses, "I AM WHO I AM.[e] This

---

[a] 10 *Moses* sounds like the Hebrew for *draw out.*   [b] 22 *Gershom* sounds like the Hebrew for *a foreigner there.*   [c] 6 Masoretic Text; Samaritan Pentateuch (see Acts 7:32) *fathers*   [d] 12 The Hebrew is plural.
[e] 14 Or *I WILL BE WHAT I WILL BE*

ANY OLD BUSH WILL DO

READ: EXODUS 3:1-6

Roger Glidewell of Global Youth Ministries often taught at our summer camps. He told our students the story of Moses and the burning bush. "Any old bush would do," he said. "Why was it a bush? Why wasn't it a tree? When something is on fire and not burning up, it doesn't really matter what it is."

It hit me that the bush was still just being a bush. It didn't have anything extra in it. There wasn't an extra chemical. It was just a bush and nothing more, and it brought all it had to the table.

All David had was his sling and his rocks. He brought them to the table and God used him. God will use whatever you bring to the table, but he also will add something only he can add. We limit God because we can't figure out the X factor—the ingredient he adds. All we see is what we can do, and we think that's too insignificant.

But God says, "Hey, any old bush will do here. You just be ready, because if you follow me, I'm going to throw in the fire. That's nowhere in your backpack. Nowhere."

Listen to that inner tug. See the hole you're supposed to fill. Learn the lessons God sends to mold you. Most of all, expect the X factor.

BUILDING FAITH WISDOM STRENGTH

Taken from *Thrive Student Edition* by Mark Hall with Tim Luke, copyright © 2014 by Mark Hall, published by Zondervan.

is what you are to say to the Israelites: 'I AM has sent me to you.'"

¹⁵God also said to Moses, "Say to the Israelites, 'The LORD,ᵃ the God of your fathers — the God of Abraham, the God of Isaac and the God of Jacob — has sent me to you.'

"This is my name forever,
the name you shall call me
from generation to generation.

¹⁶"Go, assemble the elders of Israel and say to them, 'The LORD, the God of your fathers — the God of Abraham, Isaac and Jacob — appeared to me and said: I have watched over you and have seen what has been done to you in Egypt. ¹⁷And I have promised to bring you up out of your misery in Egypt into the land of the Canaanites, Hittites, Amorites, Perizzites, Hivites and Jebusites — a land flowing with milk and honey.'

¹⁸"The elders of Israel will listen to you. Then you and the elders are to go to the king of Egypt and say to him, 'The LORD, the God of the Hebrews, has met with us. Let us take a three-day journey into the wilderness to offer sacrifices to the LORD our God.' ¹⁹But I know that the king of Egypt will not let you go unless a mighty hand compels him. ²⁰So I will stretch out my hand and strike the Egyptians with all the wonders that I will perform among them. After that, he will let you go.

²¹"And I will make the Egyptians favorably disposed toward this people, so that when you leave you will not go empty-handed. ²²Every woman is to ask her neighbor and any woman living in her house for articles of silver and gold and for clothing, which you will put on your sons and daughters. And so you will plunder the Egyptians."

Signs for Moses

4 Moses answered, "What if they do not believe me or listen to me and say, 'The LORD did not appear to you'?"

²Then the LORD said to him, "What is that in your hand?"

"A staff," he replied.

³The LORD said, "Throw it on the ground." Moses threw it on the ground and it became a snake, and he ran from it. ⁴Then the LORD said to him, "Reach out your hand and take it by the tail." So Moses reached out and took hold of the snake and it turned back into a staff in his hand. ⁵"This," said the LORD, "is so that they may believe that the LORD, the God of their fathers — the God of Abraham, the God of Isaac and the God of Jacob — has appeared to you."

⁶Then the LORD said, "Put your hand inside your cloak." So Moses put his hand into his cloak, and when he took it out, the skin was leprousᵇ — it had become as white as snow.

⁷"Now put it back into your cloak," he said. So Moses put his hand back into his cloak, and when he took it out, it was restored, like the rest of his flesh.

⁸Then the LORD said, "If they do not believe you or pay attention to the first sign, they may believe the second. ⁹But if they do not believe these two signs or listen to you, take some water from the Nile and pour it on the dry ground. The water you take from the river will become blood on the ground."

¹⁰Moses said to the LORD, "Pardon your servant, Lord. I have never been eloquent, neither in the past nor since you have spoken to your servant. I am slow of speech and tongue."

¹¹The LORD said to him, "Who gave human beings their mouths? Who makes them deaf or mute? Who gives them sight or makes them blind? Is it not I, the LORD? ¹²Now go; I will help you speak and will teach you what to say."

¹³But Moses said, "Pardon your servant, Lord. Please send someone else."

¹⁴Then the LORD's anger burned against Moses and he said, "What about your brother, Aaron the Levite? I know he can speak well. He is already on his way to meet you, and he will be glad to see you. ¹⁵You shall speak to him and put words in his mouth; I will help both of you speak and will teach you what to do. ¹⁶He will speak to the people for you, and it will be as if he were your mouth and as if you were God to him. ¹⁷But take this staff in your hand so you can perform the signs with it."

Moses Returns to Egypt

¹⁸Then Moses went back to Jethro his father-in-law and said to him, "Let me return to my own people in Egypt to see if any of them are still alive."

ᵃ 15 The Hebrew for LORD sounds like and may be related to the Hebrew for *I AM* in verse 14.
ᵇ 6 The Hebrew word for *leprous* was used for various diseases affecting the skin.

LET GO AND THROW DOWN

READ: EXODUS 4:2-3

Throwing down your staff is letting go and letting God. As in letting God do his thing. This is for all of the control freaks of the world (me included)! One of our pastors, Joel Schmidgall, likes to say, "You can have faith or you can have control, but you can't have both." If you want God to do something cool, you have to take your hands off the controls.

You have to loosen your grip on your staff. The staff represented Moses' identity and security as a shepherd. It was the way Moses made a living. It was also the way he protected himself and his flock. So when God told Moses to throw it down, he was essentially asking Moses to let go of who he was. It was like God asking you to throw down your car, girlfriend, your smartphone, whatever! Whatever defines you and whatever you find your security in.

BUILDING

FAITH

WISDOM

STRENGTH

What are you holding on to? Or maybe I should ask, what are you not willing to let go of? If you aren't willing to let go, then it's pretty obvious that you're not in control of that thing, that thing controls you. And if you don't throw it down, your staff will forever remain a staff. Lame. It will always be what it currently is. Still lame. But if you have the courage to throw down your staff . . . well, you probably know how the story goes.

Jethro said, "Go, and I wish you well."

[19] Now the LORD had said to Moses in Midian, "Go back to Egypt, for all those who wanted to kill you are dead." [20] So Moses took his wife and sons, put them on a donkey and started back to Egypt. And he took the staff of God in his hand.

[21] The LORD said to Moses, "When you return to Egypt, see that you perform before Pharaoh all the wonders I have given you the power to do. But I will harden his heart so that he will not let the people go. [22] Then say to Pharaoh, 'This is what the LORD says: Israel is my firstborn son, [23] and I told you, "Let my son go, so he may worship me." But you refused to let him go; so I will kill your firstborn son.'"

[24] At a lodging place on the way, the LORD met Moses[a] and was about to kill him. [25] But Zipporah took a flint knife, cut off her son's foreskin and touched Moses' feet with it.[b] "Surely you are a bridegroom of blood to me," she said. [26] So the LORD let him alone. (At that time she said "bridegroom of blood," referring to circumcision.)

[27] The LORD said to Aaron, "Go into the wilderness to meet Moses." So he met Moses at the mountain of God and kissed him. [28] Then Moses told Aaron everything the LORD had sent him to say, and also about all the signs he had commanded him to perform.

[29] Moses and Aaron brought together all the elders of the Israelites, [30] and Aaron told them everything the LORD had said to Moses. He also performed the signs before the people, [31] and they believed. And when they heard that the LORD was concerned about them and had seen their misery, they bowed down and worshiped.

Bricks Without Straw

5 Afterward Moses and Aaron went to Pharaoh and said, "This is what the LORD, the God of Israel, says: 'Let my people go, so that they may hold a festival to me in the wilderness.'"

[2] Pharaoh said, "Who is the LORD, that I should obey him and let Israel go? I do not know the LORD and I will not let Israel go."

[3] Then they said, "The God of the Hebrews has met with us. Now let us take a three-day journey into the wilderness to offer sacrifices to the LORD our God, or he may strike us with plagues or with the sword."

[4] But the king of Egypt said, "Moses and Aaron, why are you taking the people away from their labor? Get back to your work!" [5] Then Pharaoh said, "Look, the people of the land are now numerous, and you are stopping them from working."

[6] That same day Pharaoh gave this order to the slave drivers and overseers in charge of the people: [7] "You are no longer to supply the people with straw for making bricks; let them go and gather their own straw. [8] But require them to make the same number of bricks as before; don't reduce the quota. They are lazy; that is why they are crying out, 'Let us go and sacrifice to our God.' [9] Make the work harder for the people so that they keep working and pay no attention to lies."

[10] Then the slave drivers and the overseers went out and said to the people, "This is what Pharaoh says: 'I will not give you any more straw. [11] Go and get your own straw wherever you can find it, but your work will not be reduced at all.'" [12] So the people scattered all over Egypt to gather stubble to use for straw. [13] The slave drivers kept pressing them, saying, "Complete the work required of you for each day, just as when you had straw." [14] And Pharaoh's slave drivers beat the Israelite overseers they had appointed, demanding, "Why haven't you met your quota of bricks yesterday or today, as before?"

[15] Then the Israelite overseers went and appealed to Pharaoh: "Why have you treated your servants this way? [16] Your servants are given no straw, yet we are told, 'Make bricks!' Your servants are being beaten, but the fault is with your own people."

[17] Pharaoh said, "Lazy, that's what you are — lazy! That is why you keep saying, 'Let us go and sacrifice to the LORD.' [18] Now get to work. You will not be given any straw, yet you must produce your full quota of bricks."

[19] The Israelite overseers realized they were in trouble when they were told, "You are not to reduce the number of bricks required of you for each day." [20] When they left Pharaoh, they found Moses and Aaron waiting to meet them, [21] and they said, "May the LORD look on you and judge you! You have

---

[a] 24 Hebrew *him*   [b] 25 The meaning of the Hebrew for this clause is uncertain.

made us obnoxious to Pharaoh and his officials and have put a sword in their hand to kill us."

God Promises Deliverance

[22] Moses returned to the LORD and said, "Why, Lord, why have you brought trouble on this people? Is this why you sent me? [23] Ever since I went to Pharaoh to speak in your name, he has brought trouble on this people, and you have not rescued your people at all."

6 Then the LORD said to Moses, "Now you will see what I will do to Pharaoh: Because of my mighty hand he will let them go; because of my mighty hand he will drive them out of his country."

[2] God also said to Moses, "I am the LORD. [3] I appeared to Abraham, to Isaac and to Jacob as God Almighty,[a] but by my name the LORD[b] I did not make myself fully known to them. [4] I also established my covenant with them to give them the land of Canaan, where they resided as foreigners. [5] Moreover, I have heard the groaning of the Israelites, whom the Egyptians are enslaving, and I have remembered my covenant.

[6] "Therefore, say to the Israelites: 'I am the LORD, and I will bring you out from under the yoke of the Egyptians. I will free you from being slaves to them, and I will redeem you with an outstretched arm and with mighty acts of judgment. [7] I will take you as my own people, and I will be your God. Then you will know that I am the LORD your God, who brought you out from under the yoke of the Egyptians. [8] And I will bring you to the land I swore with uplifted hand to give to Abraham, to Isaac and to Jacob. I will give it to you as a possession. I am the LORD.'"

[9] Moses reported this to the Israelites, but they did not listen to him because of their discouragement and harsh labor.

[10] Then the LORD said to Moses, [11] "Go, tell Pharaoh king of Egypt to let the Israelites go out of his country."

[12] But Moses said to the LORD, "If the Israelites will not listen to me, why would Pharaoh listen to me, since I speak with faltering lips[c]?"

Family Record of Moses and Aaron

[13] Now the LORD spoke to Moses and Aaron about the Israelites and Pharaoh king of Egypt, and he commanded them to bring the Israelites out of Egypt.

[14] These were the heads of their families[d]:

The sons of Reuben the firstborn son of Israel were Hanok and Pallu, Hezron and Karmi. These were the clans of Reuben.

[15] The sons of Simeon were Jemuel, Jamin, Ohad, Jakin, Zohar and Shaul the son of a Canaanite woman. These were the clans of Simeon.

[16] These were the names of the sons of Levi according to their records: Gershon, Kohath and Merari. Levi lived 137 years.

[17] The sons of Gershon, by clans, were Libni and Shimei.

[18] The sons of Kohath were Amram, Izhar, Hebron and Uzziel. Kohath lived 133 years.

[19] The sons of Merari were Mahli and Mushi.

These were the clans of Levi according to their records.

[20] Amram married his father's sister Jochebed, who bore him Aaron and Moses. Amram lived 137 years.

[21] The sons of Izhar were Korah, Nepheg and Zikri.

[22] The sons of Uzziel were Mishael, Elzaphan and Sithri.

[23] Aaron married Elisheba, daughter of Amminadab and sister of Nahshon, and she bore him Nadab and Abihu, Eleazar and Ithamar.

[24] The sons of Korah were Assir, Elkanah and Abiasaph. These were the Korahite clans.

[25] Eleazar son of Aaron married one of the daughters of Putiel, and she bore him Phinehas.

These were the heads of the Levite families, clan by clan.

[26] It was this Aaron and Moses to whom the LORD said, "Bring the Israelites out of

---

[a] 3 Hebrew *El-Shaddai*   [b] 3 See note at 3:15.   [c] 12 Hebrew *I am uncircumcised of lips*; also in verse 30
[d] 14 The Hebrew for *families* here and in verse 25 refers to units larger than clans.

Egypt by their divisions." 27They were the ones who spoke to Pharaoh king of Egypt about bringing the Israelites out of Egypt—this same Moses and Aaron.

Aaron to Speak for Moses

28Now when the LORD spoke to Moses in Egypt, 29he said to him, "I am the LORD. Tell Pharaoh king of Egypt everything I tell you."

30But Moses said to the LORD, "Since I speak with faltering lips, why would Pharaoh listen to me?"

7 Then the LORD said to Moses, "See, I have made you like God to Pharaoh, and your brother Aaron will be your prophet. 2You are to say everything I command you, and your brother Aaron is to tell Pharaoh to let the Israelites go out of his country. 3But I will harden Pharaoh's heart, and though I multiply my signs and wonders in Egypt, 4he will not listen to you. Then I will lay my hand on Egypt and with mighty acts of judgment I will bring out my divisions, my people the Israelites. 5And the Egyptians will know that I am the LORD when I stretch out my hand against Egypt and bring the Israelites out of it."

6Moses and Aaron did just as the LORD commanded them. 7Moses was eighty years old and Aaron eighty-three when they spoke to Pharaoh.

Aaron's Staff Becomes a Snake

8The LORD said to Moses and Aaron, 9"When Pharaoh says to you, 'Perform a miracle,' then say to Aaron, 'Take your staff and throw it down before Pharaoh,' and it will become a snake."

10So Moses and Aaron went to Pharaoh and did just as the LORD commanded. Aaron threw his staff down in front of Pharaoh and his officials, and it became a snake. 11Pharaoh then summoned wise men and sorcerers, and the Egyptian magicians also did the same things by their secret arts: 12Each one threw down his staff and it became a snake. But Aaron's staff swallowed up their staffs. 13Yet Pharaoh's heart became hard and he would not listen to them, just as the LORD had said.

The Plague of Blood

14Then the LORD said to Moses, "Pharaoh's heart is unyielding; he refuses to let the people go. 15Go to Pharaoh in the morning as he goes out to the river. Confront him on the bank of the Nile, and take in your hand the staff that was changed into a snake. 16Then say to him, 'The LORD, the God of the Hebrews, has sent me to say to you: Let my people go, so that they may worship me in the wilderness. But until now you have not listened. 17This is what the LORD says: By this you will know that I am the LORD: With the staff that is in my hand I will strike the water of the Nile, and it will be changed into blood. 18The fish in the Nile will die, and the river will stink; the Egyptians will not be able to drink its water.'"

19The LORD said to Moses, "Tell Aaron, 'Take your staff and stretch out your hand over the waters of Egypt—over the streams and canals, over the ponds and all the reservoirs—and they will turn to blood.' Blood will be everywhere in Egypt, even in vessels*a* of wood and stone."

20Moses and Aaron did just as the LORD had commanded. He raised his staff in the presence of Pharaoh and his officials and struck the water of the Nile, and all the water was changed into blood. 21The fish in the Nile died, and the river smelled so bad that the Egyptians could not drink its water. Blood was everywhere in Egypt.

22But the Egyptian magicians did the same things by their secret arts, and Pharaoh's heart became hard; he would not listen to Moses and Aaron, just as the LORD had said. 23Instead, he turned and went into his palace, and did not take even this to heart. 24And all the Egyptians dug along the Nile to get drinking water, because they could not drink the water of the river.

The Plague of Frogs

25Seven days passed after the LORD struck the Nile. 8*b* 1Then the LORD said to Moses, "Go to Pharaoh and say to him, 'This is what the LORD says: Let my people go, so that they may worship me. 2If you refuse to let them go, I will send a plague of frogs on your whole country. 3The Nile will teem with frogs. They will come up into your palace and your bedroom and onto your bed, into the houses of your officials and on your people, and into your ovens and kneading

---

a 19 Or *even on their idols*　　*b* In Hebrew texts 8:1-4 is numbered 7:26-29, and 8:5-32 is numbered 8:1-28.

SMART FOOL

READ: **EXODUS 7:1-7**

Faith is the willingness to look foolish. Foolishness is a feeling that Moses was very familiar with. He had to feel foolish going before Pharaoh and demanding that he let God's people go. He probably felt pretty foolish raising his staff over the Red Sea. And you bet he felt foolish promising meat to eat for the entire nation of Israel in the middle of a desert. Brilliant. But his willingness to look foolish resulted in epic miracles—the exodus of Israel out of Egypt, the parting of the Red Sea, and the quail miracle.

But if you aren't willing to step out of the boat, you'll never walk on water. If you aren't willing to circle the city, the wall will never fall. And if you aren't willing to follow the star, you'll miss out on the greatest adventure of your life!

In order to experience a miracle, you have to take a risk. And one of the most difficult types of risks to take is risking your reputation. Someone once said that youth wasn't made for fun, it was made for heroism. And heroism always involves risk. In fact, the greatest chapters in history always begin with a risk, and the same is true with the chapters of your life. There comes a moment when you need to make a call, make a decision, or make the move.

Moses had learned this lesson well: If you don't take the risk, you forfeit the miracle.

BUILDING

FAITH

WISDOM

STRENGTH

Taken from *The Circle Maker Student Edition* by Mark Batterson with Parker Batterson, copyright © 2012 by Mark Batterson, published by Zondervan.

troughs. [4]The frogs will come up on you and your people and all your officials.'"

[5]Then the LORD said to Moses, "Tell Aaron, 'Stretch out your hand with your staff over the streams and canals and ponds, and make frogs come up on the land of Egypt.'"

[6]So Aaron stretched out his hand over the waters of Egypt, and the frogs came up and covered the land. [7]But the magicians did the same things by their secret arts; they also made frogs come up on the land of Egypt.

[8]Pharaoh summoned Moses and Aaron and said, "Pray to the LORD to take the frogs away from me and my people, and I will let your people go to offer sacrifices to the LORD."

[9]Moses said to Pharaoh, "I leave to you the honor of setting the time for me to pray for you and your officials and your people that you and your houses may be rid of the frogs, except for those that remain in the Nile."

[10]"Tomorrow," Pharaoh said.

Moses replied, "It will be as you say, so that you may know there is no one like the LORD our God. [11]The frogs will leave you and your houses, your officials and your people; they will remain only in the Nile."

[12]After Moses and Aaron left Pharaoh, Moses cried out to the LORD about the frogs he had brought on Pharaoh. [13]And the LORD did what Moses asked. The frogs died in the houses, in the courtyards and in the fields. [14]They were piled into heaps, and the land reeked of them. [15]But when Pharaoh saw that there was relief, he hardened his heart and would not listen to Moses and Aaron, just as the LORD had said.

The Plague of Gnats

[16]Then the LORD said to Moses, "Tell Aaron, 'Stretch out your staff and strike the dust of the ground,' and throughout the land of Egypt the dust will become gnats." [17]They did this, and when Aaron stretched out his hand with the staff and struck the dust of the ground, gnats came on people and animals. All the dust throughout the land of Egypt became gnats. [18]But when the magicians tried to produce gnats by their secret arts, they could not.

Since the gnats were on people and animals everywhere, [19]the magicians said to

Pharaoh, "This is the finger of God." But Pharaoh's heart was hard and he would not listen, just as the LORD had said.

The Plague of Flies

[20]Then the LORD said to Moses, "Get up early in the morning and confront Pharaoh as he goes to the river and say to him, 'This is what the LORD says: Let my people go, so that they may worship me. [21]If you do not let my people go, I will send swarms of flies on you and your officials, on your people and into your houses. The houses of the Egyptians will be full of flies; even the ground will be covered with them.

[22]"'But on that day I will deal differently with the land of Goshen, where my people live; no swarms of flies will be there, so that you will know that I, the LORD, am in this land. [23]I will make a distinction[a] between my people and your people. This sign will occur tomorrow.'"

[24]And the LORD did this. Dense swarms of flies poured into Pharaoh's palace and into the houses of his officials; throughout Egypt the land was ruined by the flies.

[25]Then Pharaoh summoned Moses and Aaron and said, "Go, sacrifice to your God here in the land."

[26]But Moses said, "That would not be right. The sacrifices we offer the LORD our God would be detestable to the Egyptians. And if we offer sacrifices that are detestable in their eyes, will they not stone us? [27]We must take a three-day journey into the wilderness to offer sacrifices to the LORD our God, as he commands us."

[28]Pharaoh said, "I will let you go to offer sacrifices to the LORD your God in the wilderness, but you must not go very far. Now pray for me."

[29]Moses answered, "As soon as I leave you, I will pray to the LORD, and tomorrow the flies will leave Pharaoh and his officials and his people. Only let Pharaoh be sure that he does not act deceitfully again by not letting the people go to offer sacrifices to the LORD."

[30]Then Moses left Pharaoh and prayed to the LORD, [31]and the LORD did what Moses asked. The flies left Pharaoh and his officials and his people; not a fly remained. [32]But this

---

[a] 23 Septuagint and Vulgate; Hebrew *will put a deliverance*

time also Pharaoh hardened his heart and would not let the people go.

The Plague on Livestock

9 Then the LORD said to Moses, "Go to Pharaoh and say to him, 'This is what the LORD, the God of the Hebrews, says: "Let my people go, so that they may worship me." ²If you refuse to let them go and continue to hold them back, ³the hand of the LORD will bring a terrible plague on your livestock in the field—on your horses, donkeys and camels and on your cattle, sheep and goats. ⁴But the LORD will make a distinction between the livestock of Israel and that of Egypt, so that no animal belonging to the Israelites will die.'"

⁵The LORD set a time and said, "Tomorrow the LORD will do this in the land." ⁶And the next day the LORD did it: All the livestock of the Egyptians died, but not one animal belonging to the Israelites died. ⁷Pharaoh investigated and found that not even one of the animals of the Israelites had died. Yet his heart was unyielding and he would not let the people go.

The Plague of Boils

⁸Then the LORD said to Moses and Aaron, "Take handfuls of soot from a furnace and have Moses toss it into the air in the presence of Pharaoh. ⁹It will become fine dust over the whole land of Egypt, and festering boils will break out on people and animals throughout the land."

¹⁰So they took soot from a furnace and stood before Pharaoh. Moses tossed it into the air, and festering boils broke out on people and animals. ¹¹The magicians could not stand before Moses because of the boils that were on them and on all the Egyptians. ¹²But the LORD hardened Pharaoh's heart and he would not listen to Moses and Aaron, just as the LORD had said to Moses.

The Plague of Hail

¹³Then the LORD said to Moses, "Get up early in the morning, confront Pharaoh and say to him, 'This is what the LORD, the God of the Hebrews, says: Let my people go, so that they may worship me, ¹⁴or this time I will send the full force of my plagues against you and against your officials and your people, so you may know that there is no one like me in all the earth. ¹⁵For by now I could have stretched out my hand and struck you and your people with a plague that would have wiped you off the earth. ¹⁶But I have raised you up[a] for this very purpose, that I might show you my power and that my name might be proclaimed in all the earth. ¹⁷You still set yourself against my people and will not let them go. ¹⁸Therefore, at this time tomorrow I will send the worst hailstorm that has ever fallen on Egypt, from the day it was founded till now. ¹⁹Give an order now to bring your livestock and everything you have in the field to a place of shelter, because the hail will fall on every person and animal that has not been brought in and is still out in the field, and they will die.'"

²⁰Those officials of Pharaoh who feared the word of the LORD hurried to bring their slaves and their livestock inside. ²¹But those who ignored the word of the LORD left their slaves and livestock in the field.

²²Then the LORD said to Moses, "Stretch out your hand toward the sky so that hail will fall all over Egypt—on people and animals and on everything growing in the fields of Egypt." ²³When Moses stretched out his staff toward the sky, the LORD sent thunder and hail, and lightning flashed down to the ground. So the LORD rained hail on the land of Egypt; ²⁴hail fell and lightning flashed back and forth. It was the worst storm in all the land of Egypt since it had become a nation. ²⁵Throughout Egypt hail struck everything in the fields—both people and animals; it beat down everything growing in the fields and stripped every tree. ²⁶The only place it did not hail was the land of Goshen, where the Israelites were.

²⁷Then Pharaoh summoned Moses and Aaron. "This time I have sinned," he said to them. "The LORD is in the right, and I and my people are in the wrong. ²⁸Pray to the LORD, for we have had enough thunder and hail. I will let you go; you don't have to stay any longer."

²⁹Moses replied, "When I have gone out of the city, I will spread out my hands in prayer to the LORD. The thunder will stop and there will be no more hail, so you may know that

---

the earth is the LORD's. [30] But I know that you and your officials still do not fear the LORD God."

[31] (The flax and barley were destroyed, since the barley had headed and the flax was in bloom. [32] The wheat and spelt, however, were not destroyed, because they ripen later.)

[33] Then Moses left Pharaoh and went out of the city. He spread out his hands toward the LORD; the thunder and hail stopped, and the rain no longer poured down on the land. [34] When Pharaoh saw that the rain and hail and thunder had stopped, he sinned again: He and his officials hardened their hearts. [35] So Pharaoh's heart was hard and he would not let the Israelites go, just as the LORD had said through Moses.

The Plague of Locusts

10 Then the LORD said to Moses, "Go to Pharaoh, for I have hardened his heart and the hearts of his officials so that I may perform these signs of mine among them [2] that you may tell your children and grandchildren how I dealt harshly with the Egyptians and how I performed my signs among them, and that you may know that I am the LORD."

[3] So Moses and Aaron went to Pharaoh and said to him, "This is what the LORD, the God of the Hebrews, says: 'How long will you refuse to humble yourself before me? Let my people go, so that they may worship me. [4] If you refuse to let them go, I will bring locusts into your country tomorrow. [5] They will cover the face of the ground so that it cannot be seen. They will devour what little you have left after the hail, including every tree that is growing in your fields. [6] They will fill your houses and those of all your officials and all the Egyptians—something neither your parents nor your ancestors have ever seen from the day they settled in this land till now.'" Then Moses turned and left Pharaoh.

[7] Pharaoh's officials said to him, "How long will this man be a snare to us? Let the people go, so that they may worship the LORD their God. Do you not yet realize that Egypt is ruined?"

[8] Then Moses and Aaron were brought back to Pharaoh. "Go, worship the LORD your God," he said. "But tell me who will be going."

[9] Moses answered, "We will go with our young and our old, with our sons and our daughters, and with our flocks and herds, because we are to celebrate a festival to the LORD."

[10] Pharaoh said, "The LORD be with you—if I let you go, along with your women and children! Clearly you are bent on evil.[a] [11] No! Have only the men go and worship the LORD, since that's what you have been asking for." Then Moses and Aaron were driven out of Pharaoh's presence.

[12] And the LORD said to Moses, "Stretch out your hand over Egypt so that locusts swarm over the land and devour everything growing in the fields, everything left by the hail."

[13] So Moses stretched out his staff over Egypt, and the LORD made an east wind blow across the land all that day and all that night. By morning the wind had brought the locusts; [14] they invaded all Egypt and settled down in every area of the country in great numbers. Never before had there been such a plague of locusts, nor will there ever be again. [15] They covered all the ground until it was black. They devoured all that was left after the hail—everything growing in the fields and the fruit on the trees. Nothing green remained on tree or plant in all the land of Egypt.

[16] Pharaoh quickly summoned Moses and Aaron and said, "I have sinned against the LORD your God and against you. [17] Now forgive my sin once more and pray to the LORD your God to take this deadly plague away from me."

[18] Moses then left Pharaoh and prayed to the LORD. [19] And the LORD changed the wind to a very strong west wind, which caught up the locusts and carried them into the Red Sea.[b] Not a locust was left anywhere in Egypt. [20] But the LORD hardened Pharaoh's heart, and he would not let the Israelites go.

The Plague of Darkness

[21] Then the LORD said to Moses, "Stretch out your hand toward the sky so that darkness spreads over Egypt—darkness that can be felt." [22] So Moses stretched out his hand toward the sky, and total darkness covered all Egypt for three days. [23] No one could see

---

[a] 10 Or *Be careful, trouble is in store for you!*   [b] 19 Or *the Sea of Reeds*

anyone else or move about for three days. Yet all the Israelites had light in the places where they lived.

²⁴Then Pharaoh summoned Moses and said, "Go, worship the LORD. Even your women and children may go with you; only leave your flocks and herds behind."

²⁵But Moses said, "You must allow us to have sacrifices and burnt offerings to present to the LORD our God. ²⁶Our livestock too must go with us; not a hoof is to be left behind. We have to use some of them in worshiping the LORD our God, and until we get there we will not know what we are to use to worship the LORD."

²⁷But the LORD hardened Pharaoh's heart, and he was not willing to let them go. ²⁸Pharaoh said to Moses, "Get out of my sight! Make sure you do not appear before me again! The day you see my face you will die."

²⁹"Just as you say," Moses replied. "I will never appear before you again."

The Plague on the Firstborn

11 Now the LORD had said to Moses, "I will bring one more plague on Pharaoh and on Egypt. After that, he will let you go from here, and when he does, he will drive you out completely. ²Tell the people that men and women alike are to ask their neighbors for articles of silver and gold." ³(The LORD made the Egyptians favorably disposed toward the people, and Moses himself was highly regarded in Egypt by Pharaoh's officials and by the people.)

⁴So Moses said, "This is what the LORD says: 'About midnight I will go throughout Egypt. ⁵Every firstborn son in Egypt will die, from the firstborn son of Pharaoh, who sits on the throne, to the firstborn son of the female slave, who is at her hand mill, and all the firstborn of the cattle as well. ⁶There will be loud wailing throughout Egypt—worse than there has ever been or ever will be again. ⁷But among the Israelites not a dog will bark at any person or animal.' Then you will know that the LORD makes a distinction between Egypt and Israel. ⁸All these officials of yours will come to me, bowing down before me and saying, 'Go, you and all the people who follow you!' After that I will leave." Then Moses, hot with anger, left Pharaoh.

⁹The LORD had said to Moses, "Pharaoh will refuse to listen to you—so that my wonders may be multiplied in Egypt." ¹⁰Moses and Aaron performed all these wonders before Pharaoh, but the LORD hardened Pharaoh's heart, and he would not let the Israelites go out of his country.

The Passover and the Festival of Unleavened Bread

12 The LORD said to Moses and Aaron in Egypt, ²"This month is to be for you the first month, the first month of your year. ³Tell the whole community of Israel that on the tenth day of this month each man is to take a lamb*ᵃ* for his family, one for each household. ⁴If any household is too small for a whole lamb, they must share one with their nearest neighbor, having taken into account the number of people there are. You are to determine the amount of lamb needed in accordance with what each person will eat. ⁵The animals you choose must be year-old males without defect, and you may take them from the sheep or the goats. ⁶Take care of them until the fourteenth day of the month, when all the members of the community of Israel must slaughter them at twilight. ⁷Then they are to take some of the blood and put it on the sides and tops of the doorframes of the houses where they eat the lambs. ⁸That same night they are to eat the meat roasted over the fire, along with bitter herbs, and bread made without yeast. ⁹Do not eat the meat raw or boiled in water, but roast it over a fire—with the head, legs and internal organs. ¹⁰Do not leave any of it till morning; if some is left till morning, you must burn it. ¹¹This is how you are to eat it: with your cloak tucked into your belt, your sandals on your feet and your staff in your hand. Eat it in haste; it is the LORD's Passover.

¹²"On that same night I will pass through Egypt and strike down every firstborn of both people and animals, and I will bring judgment on all the gods of Egypt. I am the LORD. ¹³The blood will be a sign for you on the houses where you are, and when I see the blood, I will pass over you. No destructive plague will touch you when I strike Egypt.

¹⁴"This is a day you are to commemorate; for the generations to come you shall cele-

---

ᵃ 3 The Hebrew word can mean *lamb* or *kid*; also in verse 4.

brate it as a festival to the LORD — a lasting ordinance. [15]For seven days you are to eat bread made without yeast. On the first day remove the yeast from your houses, for whoever eats anything with yeast in it from the first day through the seventh must be cut off from Israel. [16]On the first day hold a sacred assembly, and another one on the seventh day. Do no work at all on these days, except to prepare food for everyone to eat; that is all you may do.

[17]"Celebrate the Festival of Unleavened Bread, because it was on this very day that I brought your divisions out of Egypt. Celebrate this day as a lasting ordinance for the generations to come. [18]In the first month you are to eat bread made without yeast, from the evening of the fourteenth day until the evening of the twenty-first day. [19]For seven days no yeast is to be found in your houses. And anyone, whether foreigner or native-born, who eats anything with yeast in it must be cut off from the community of Israel. [20]Eat nothing made with yeast. Wherever you live, you must eat unleavened bread."

[21]Then Moses summoned all the elders of Israel and said to them, "Go at once and select the animals for your families and slaughter the Passover lamb. [22]Take a bunch of hyssop, dip it into the blood in the basin and put some of the blood on the top and on both sides of the doorframe. None of you shall go out of the door of your house until morning. [23]When the LORD goes through the land to strike down the Egyptians, he will see the blood on the top and sides of the doorframe and will pass over that doorway, and he will not permit the destroyer to enter your houses and strike you down.

[24]"Obey these instructions as a lasting ordinance for you and your descendants. [25]When you enter the land that the LORD will give you as he promised, observe this ceremony. [26]And when your children ask you, 'What does this ceremony mean to you?' [27]then tell them, 'It is the Passover sacrifice to the LORD, who passed over the houses of the Israelites in Egypt and spared our homes when he struck down the Egyptians.'" Then the people bowed down and worshiped. [28]The Israelites did just what the LORD commanded Moses and Aaron.

[29]At midnight the LORD struck down all the firstborn in Egypt, from the firstborn of Pharaoh, who sat on the throne, to the firstborn of the prisoner, who was in the dungeon, and the firstborn of all the livestock as well. [30]Pharaoh and all his officials and all the Egyptians got up during the night, and there was loud wailing in Egypt, for there was not a house without someone dead.

The Exodus

[31]During the night Pharaoh summoned Moses and Aaron and said, "Up! Leave my people, you and the Israelites! Go, worship the LORD as you have requested. [32]Take your flocks and herds, as you have said, and go. And also bless me."

[33]The Egyptians urged the people to hurry and leave the country. "For otherwise," they said, "we will all die!" [34]So the people took their dough before the yeast was added, and carried it on their shoulders in kneading troughs wrapped in clothing. [35]The Israelites did as Moses instructed and asked the Egyptians for articles of silver and gold and for clothing. [36]The LORD had made the Egyptians favorably disposed toward the people, and they gave them what they asked for; so they plundered the Egyptians.

[37]The Israelites journeyed from Rameses to Sukkoth. There were about six hundred thousand men on foot, besides women and children. [38]Many other people went up with them, and also large droves of livestock, both flocks and herds. [39]With the dough the Israelites had brought from Egypt, they baked loaves of unleavened bread. The dough was without yeast because they had been driven out of Egypt and did not have time to prepare food for themselves.

[40]Now the length of time the Israelite people lived in Egypt[a] was 430 years. [41]At the end of the 430 years, to the very day, all the LORD's divisions left Egypt. [42]Because the LORD kept vigil that night to bring them out of Egypt, on this night all the Israelites are to keep vigil to honor the LORD for the generations to come.

Passover Restrictions

[43]The LORD said to Moses and Aaron, "These are the regulations for the Passover meal:

---

[a] 40 Masoretic Text; Samaritan Pentateuch and Septuagint *Egypt and Canaan*

"No foreigner may eat it. ⁴⁴Any slave you have bought may eat it after you have circumcised him, ⁴⁵but a temporary resident or a hired worker may not eat it.

⁴⁶"It must be eaten inside the house; take none of the meat outside the house. Do not break any of the bones. ⁴⁷The whole community of Israel must celebrate it.

⁴⁸"A foreigner residing among you who wants to celebrate the LORD's Passover must have all the males in his household circumcised; then he may take part like one born in the land. No uncircumcised male may eat it. ⁴⁹The same law applies both to the native-born and to the foreigner residing among you."

⁵⁰All the Israelites did just what the LORD had commanded Moses and Aaron. ⁵¹And on that very day the LORD brought the Israelites out of Egypt by their divisions.

Consecration of the Firstborn

13 The LORD said to Moses, ²"Consecrate to me every firstborn male. The first offspring of every womb among the Israelites belongs to me, whether human or animal."

³Then Moses said to the people, "Commemorate this day, the day you came out of Egypt, out of the land of slavery, because the LORD brought you out of it with a mighty hand. Eat nothing containing yeast. ⁴Today, in the month of Aviv, you are leaving. ⁵When the LORD brings you into the land of the Canaanites, Hittites, Amorites, Hivites and Jebusites — the land he swore to your ancestors to give you, a land flowing with milk and honey — you are to observe this ceremony in this month: ⁶For seven days eat bread made without yeast and on the seventh day hold a festival to the LORD. ⁷Eat unleavened bread during those seven days; nothing with yeast in it is to be seen among you, nor shall any yeast be seen anywhere within your borders. ⁸On that day tell your son, 'I do this because of what the LORD did for me when I came out of Egypt.' ⁹This observance will be for you like a sign on your hand and a reminder on your forehead that this law of the LORD is to be on your lips. For the LORD brought you out of Egypt with his mighty hand. ¹⁰You must keep this ordinance at the appointed time year after year.

¹¹"After the LORD brings you into the land of the Canaanites and gives it to you, as he promised on oath to you and your ancestors, ¹²you are to give over to the LORD the first offspring of every womb. All the firstborn males of your livestock belong to the LORD. ¹³Redeem with a lamb every firstborn donkey, but if you do not redeem it, break its neck. Redeem every firstborn among your sons.

¹⁴"In days to come, when your son asks you, 'What does this mean?' say to him, 'With a mighty hand the LORD brought us out of Egypt, out of the land of slavery. ¹⁵When Pharaoh stubbornly refused to let us go, the LORD killed the firstborn of both people and animals in Egypt. This is why I sacrifice to the LORD the first male offspring of every womb and redeem each of my firstborn sons.' ¹⁶And it will be like a sign on your hand and a symbol on your forehead that the LORD brought us out of Egypt with his mighty hand."

Crossing the Sea

¹⁷When Pharaoh let the people go, God did not lead them on the road through the Philistine country, though that was shorter. For God said, "If they face war, they might change their minds and return to Egypt." ¹⁸So God led the people around by the desert road toward the Red Sea.ᵃ The Israelites went up out of Egypt ready for battle.

¹⁹Moses took the bones of Joseph with him because Joseph had made the Israelites swear an oath. He had said, "God will surely come to your aid, and then you must carry my bones up with you from this place."ᵇ

²⁰After leaving Sukkoth they camped at Etham on the edge of the desert. ²¹By day the LORD went ahead of them in a pillar of cloud to guide them on their way and by night in a pillar of fire to give them light, so that they could travel by day or night. ²²Neither the pillar of cloud by day nor the pillar of fire by night left its place in front of the people.

14 Then the LORD said to Moses, ²"Tell the Israelites to turn back and encamp near Pi Hahiroth, between Migdol and the sea. They are to encamp by the sea, directly opposite Baal Zephon. ³Pharaoh will think, 'The Israelites are wandering around the land in confusion, hemmed in by the

---

ᵃ 18 Or *the Sea of Reeds*   ᵇ 19 See Gen. 50:25.

desert.' [4]And I will harden Pharaoh's heart, and he will pursue them. But I will gain glory for myself through Pharaoh and all his army, and the Egyptians will know that I am the LORD." So the Israelites did this.

[5]When the king of Egypt was told that the people had fled, Pharaoh and his officials changed their minds about them and said, "What have we done? We have let the Israelites go and have lost their services!" [6]So he had his chariot made ready and took his army with him. [7]He took six hundred of the best chariots, along with all the other chariots of Egypt, with officers over all of them. [8]The LORD hardened the heart of Pharaoh king of Egypt, so that he pursued the Israelites, who were marching out boldly. [9]The Egyptians—all Pharaoh's horses and chariots, horsemen[a] and troops—pursued the Israelites and overtook them as they camped by the sea near Pi Hahiroth, opposite Baal Zephon.

[10]As Pharaoh approached, the Israelites looked up, and there were the Egyptians, marching after them. They were terrified and cried out to the LORD. [11]They said to Moses, "Was it because there were no graves in Egypt that you brought us to the desert to die? What have you done to us by bringing us out of Egypt? [12]Didn't we say to you in Egypt, 'Leave us alone; let us serve the Egyptians'? It would have been better for us to serve the Egyptians than to die in the desert!"

[13]Moses answered the people, "Do not be afraid. Stand firm and you will see the deliverance the LORD will bring you today. The Egyptians you see today you will never see again. [14]The LORD will fight for you; you need only to be still."

[15]Then the LORD said to Moses, "Why are you crying out to me? Tell the Israelites to move on. [16]Raise your staff and stretch out your hand over the sea to divide the water so that the Israelites can go through the sea on dry ground. [17]I will harden the hearts of the Egyptians so that they will go in after them. And I will gain glory through Pharaoh and all his army, through his chariots and his horsemen. [18]The Egyptians will know that I am the LORD when I gain glory through Pharaoh, his chariots and his horsemen."

[19]Then the angel of God, who had been traveling in front of Israel's army, withdrew and went behind them. The pillar of cloud also moved from in front and stood behind them, [20]coming between the armies of Egypt and Israel. Throughout the night the cloud brought darkness to the one side and light to the other side; so neither went near the other all night long.

[21]Then Moses stretched out his hand over the sea, and all that night the LORD drove the sea back with a strong east wind and turned it into dry land. The waters were divided, [22]and the Israelites went through the sea on dry ground, with a wall of water on their right and on their left.

[23]The Egyptians pursued them, and all Pharaoh's horses and chariots and horsemen followed them into the sea. [24]During the last watch of the night the LORD looked down from the pillar of fire and cloud at the Egyptian army and threw it into confusion. [25]He jammed[b] the wheels of their chariots so that they had difficulty driving. And the Egyptians said, "Let's get away from the Israelites! The LORD is fighting for them against Egypt."

[26]Then the LORD said to Moses, "Stretch out your hand over the sea so that the waters may flow back over the Egyptians and their chariots and horsemen." [27]Moses stretched out his hand over the sea, and at daybreak the sea went back to its place. The Egyptians were fleeing toward[c] it, and the LORD swept them into the sea. [28]The water flowed back and covered the chariots and horsemen—the entire army of Pharaoh that had followed the Israelites into the sea. Not one of them survived.

[29]But the Israelites went through the sea on dry ground, with a wall of water on their right and on their left. [30]That day the LORD saved Israel from the hands of the Egyptians, and Israel saw the Egyptians lying dead on the shore. [31]And when the Israelites saw the mighty hand of the LORD displayed against the Egyptians, the people feared the LORD and put their trust in him and in Moses his servant.

The Song of Moses and Miriam

15 Then Moses and the Israelites sang this song to the LORD:

"I will sing to the LORD,
for he is highly exalted.

---

[a] 9 Or *charioteers*; also in verses 17, 18, 23, 26 and 28   [b] 25 See Samaritan Pentateuch, Septuagint and Syriac; Masoretic Text *removed*   [c] 27 Or *from*

JUST IN TIME

READ: **EXODUS 14:10-31**

We love miracles. We just don't like being in a situation that demands one. We hate finding ourselves between an Egyptian army and a Red Sea, but that's how God reveals his glory. We want God to part the Red Sea when the Egyptian army is still in Egypt. We want God to provide before we even need it. But sometimes God waits. And then he waits longer.

At first, the Israelites can see a dust cloud in the distance. Then they can hear the hooves of their horses and the wheels on their chariots. Then they can recognize the faces of their former taskmasters ready to kill them.

Put yourself in their shoes. The Israelites are sitting ducks, and God is the one who led them to this place. It seems like a tactical error, doesn't it? Yet God sets up camp where there is no means of retreat. I think it reveals something about his strange and mysterious ways. Sometimes God leads us to a place where we have nowhere to turn but to him.

BUILDING

FAITH

WISDOM

STRENGTH

So why does God let the Egyptian army get that close? Because you could make a movie about that someday! And we love those kinds of movies—unless, of course, we're in the middle of them.

Praying hard is trusting that God will fight our battles for us. It's the way we take our hands off the challenges we face and put them into the hands of God Almighty. And he can handle them. The hard thing is keeping our hands off.

Taken from *The Circle Maker Student Edition* by Mark Batterson with Parker Batterson, copyright © 2012 by Mark Batterson, published by Zondervan.

Both horse and driver
    he has hurled into the sea.

2 "The LORD is my strength and my
       defense*a*;
    he has become my salvation.
He is my God, and I will praise him,
    my father's God, and I will exalt him.
3 The LORD is a warrior;
    the LORD is his name.
4 Pharaoh's chariots and his army
    he has hurled into the sea.
The best of Pharaoh's officers
    are drowned in the Red Sea.*b*
5 The deep waters have covered them;
    they sank to the depths like a stone.
6 Your right hand, LORD,
    was majestic in power.
Your right hand, LORD,
    shattered the enemy.

7 "In the greatness of your majesty
    you threw down those who opposed
       you.
You unleashed your burning anger;
    it consumed them like stubble.
8 By the blast of your nostrils
    the waters piled up.
The surging waters stood up like a wall;
    the deep waters congealed in the heart
       of the sea.
9 The enemy boasted,
    'I will pursue, I will overtake them.
I will divide the spoils;
    I will gorge myself on them.
I will draw my sword
    and my hand will destroy them.'
10 But you blew with your breath,
    and the sea covered them.
They sank like lead
    in the mighty waters.
11 Who among the gods
    is like you, LORD?
Who is like you—
    majestic in holiness,
awesome in glory,
    working wonders?

12 "You stretch out your right hand,
    and the earth swallows your enemies.
13 In your unfailing love you will lead
    the people you have redeemed.
In your strength you will guide them

to your holy dwelling.
14 The nations will hear and tremble;
    anguish will grip the people of
       Philistia.
15 The chiefs of Edom will be terrified,
    the leaders of Moab will be seized with
       trembling,
the people*c* of Canaan will melt away;
16   terror and dread will fall on them.
By the power of your arm
    they will be as still as a stone—
until your people pass by, LORD,
    until the people you bought*d* pass by.
17 You will bring them in and plant them
    on the mountain of your inheritance—
the place, LORD, you made for your
       dwelling,
the sanctuary, Lord, your hands
       established.
18 "The LORD reigns
    for ever and ever."

19 When Pharaoh's horses, chariots and horsemen*e* went into the sea, the LORD brought the waters of the sea back over them, but the Israelites walked through the sea on dry ground. 20 Then Miriam the prophet, Aaron's sister, took a timbrel in her hand, and all the women followed her, with timbrels and dancing. 21 Miriam sang to them:

    "Sing to the LORD,
       for he is highly exalted.
    Both horse and driver
       he has hurled into the sea."

The Waters of Marah and Elim

22 Then Moses led Israel from the Red Sea and they went into the Desert of Shur. For three days they traveled in the desert without finding water. 23 When they came to Marah, they could not drink its water because it was bitter. (That is why the place is called Marah.*f*) 24 So the people grumbled against Moses, saying, "What are we to drink?"

25 Then Moses cried out to the LORD, and the LORD showed him a piece of wood. He threw it into the water, and the water became fit to drink.

There the LORD issued a ruling and instruction for them and put them to the test. 26 He said, "If you listen carefully to the LORD

---

a 2 Or *song*   *b* 4 Or *the Sea of Reeds*; also in verse 22   *c* 15 Or *rulers*   *d* 16 Or *created*
e 19 Or *charioteers*   *f* 23 *Marah* means *bitter*.

your God and do what is right in his eyes, if you pay attention to his commands and keep all his decrees, I will not bring on you any of the diseases I brought on the Egyptians, for I am the LORD, who heals you."

²⁷Then they came to Elim, where there were twelve springs and seventy palm trees, and they camped there near the water.

Manna and Quail

16 The whole Israelite community set out from Elim and came to the Desert of Sin, which is between Elim and Sinai, on the fifteenth day of the second month after they had come out of Egypt. ²In the desert the whole community grumbled against Moses and Aaron. ³The Israelites said to them, "If only we had died by the LORD's hand in Egypt! There we sat around pots of meat and ate all the food we wanted, but you have brought us out into this desert to starve this entire assembly to death."

⁴Then the LORD said to Moses, "I will rain down bread from heaven for you. The people are to go out each day and gather enough for that day. In this way I will test them and see whether they will follow my instructions. ⁵On the sixth day they are to prepare what they bring in, and that is to be twice as much as they gather on the other days."

⁶So Moses and Aaron said to all the Israelites, "In the evening you will know that it was the LORD who brought you out of Egypt, ⁷and in the morning you will see the glory of the LORD, because he has heard your grumbling against him. Who are we, that you should grumble against us?" ⁸Moses also said, "You will know that it was the LORD when he gives you meat to eat in the evening and all the bread you want in the morning, because he has heard your grumbling against him. Who are we? You are not grumbling against us, but against the LORD."

⁹Then Moses told Aaron, "Say to the entire Israelite community, 'Come before the LORD, for he has heard your grumbling.'"

¹⁰While Aaron was speaking to the whole Israelite community, they looked toward the desert, and there was the glory of the LORD appearing in the cloud.

¹¹The LORD said to Moses, ¹²"I have heard the grumbling of the Israelites. Tell them, 'At twilight you will eat meat, and in the morning you will be filled with bread. Then you will know that I am the LORD your God.'"

¹³That evening quail came and covered the camp, and in the morning there was a layer of dew around the camp. ¹⁴When the dew was gone, thin flakes like frost on the ground appeared on the desert floor. ¹⁵When the Israelites saw it, they said to each other, "What is it?" For they did not know what it was.

Moses said to them, "It is the bread the LORD has given you to eat. ¹⁶This is what the LORD has commanded: 'Everyone is to gather as much as they need. Take an omer*ᵃ* for each person you have in your tent.'"

¹⁷The Israelites did as they were told; some gathered much, some little. ¹⁸And when they measured it by the omer, the one who gathered much did not have too much, and the one who gathered little did not have too little. Everyone had gathered just as much as they needed.

¹⁹Then Moses said to them, "No one is to keep any of it until morning."

²⁰However, some of them paid no attention to Moses; they kept part of it until morning, but it was full of maggots and began to smell. So Moses was angry with them.

²¹Each morning everyone gathered as much as they needed, and when the sun grew hot, it melted away. ²²On the sixth day, they gathered twice as much — two omers*ᵇ* for each person — and the leaders of the community came and reported this to Moses. ²³He said to them, "This is what the LORD commanded: 'Tomorrow is to be a day of sabbath rest, a holy sabbath to the LORD. So bake what you want to bake and boil what you want to boil. Save whatever is left and keep it until morning.'"

²⁴So they saved it until morning, as Moses commanded, and it did not stink or get maggots in it. ²⁵"Eat it today," Moses said, "because today is a sabbath to the LORD. You will not find any of it on the ground today. ²⁶Six days you are to gather it, but on the seventh day, the Sabbath, there will not be any."

²⁷Nevertheless, some of the people went out on the seventh day to gather it, but they found none. ²⁸Then the LORD said to Moses, "How long will you*ᶜ* refuse to keep my

---

ᵃ 16 That is, possibly about 3 pounds or about 1.4 kilograms; also in verses 18, 32, 33 and 36   *ᵇ 22* That is, possibly about 6 pounds or about 2.8 kilograms   *ᶜ 28* The Hebrew is plural.

WHAT A BUNCH OF WHINERS

READ: EXODUS 16:1-3

The Israelites were complaining. I know, shocking! Instead of manna, they want meat to eat. And as a hardcore carnivore, I understand that. If you haven't eaten at an all-you-can-eat Brazilian steakhouse, you aren't ready to die yet.

But talk about selective memory! They can only remember the free fish they ate in Egypt, and forget the little fact that the food was free because they weren't. The Israelites weren't just slaves; they had been the victims of genocide. Yet they missed the meat on the menu? And isn't it just a little ironic that the Israelites were complaining about one miracle while asking for another one?

But don't we do the same thing? Just listen to the words of those in your school hallway or read the posts on your friend's wall venting about their utterly disastrous life.

There are miracles all around us all the time, yet it's so easy to find something to complain about in the middle of those miracles. The simple act of reading involves millions of impulses firing across billions of synapses. While you're reading, your heart goes about its business circulating five quarts of blood through a hundred thousand miles of veins, arteries, and capillaries. And it's amazing you can even concentrate, given the fact that you're on a planet that is traveling 67,000 miles per hour through space while spinning around its axis at about 1,000 miles per hour. But we take those manna miracles, the miracles that happen day in, day out, for granted.

BUILDING
FAITH
WISDOM
STRENGTH

Taken from *The Circle Maker Student Edition* by Mark Batterson with Parker Batterson, copyright © 2012 by Mark Batterson, published by Zondervan.

commands and my instructions? [29] Bear in mind that the LORD has given you the Sabbath; that is why on the sixth day he gives you bread for two days. Everyone is to stay where they are on the seventh day; no one is to go out." [30] So the people rested on the seventh day.

[31] The people of Israel called the bread manna.[a] It was white like coriander seed and tasted like wafers made with honey. [32] Moses said, "This is what the LORD has commanded: 'Take an omer of manna and keep it for the generations to come, so they can see the bread I gave you to eat in the wilderness when I brought you out of Egypt.'"

[33] So Moses said to Aaron, "Take a jar and put an omer of manna in it. Then place it before the LORD to be kept for the generations to come."

[34] As the LORD commanded Moses, Aaron put the manna with the tablets of the covenant law, so that it might be preserved. [35] The Israelites ate manna forty years, until they came to a land that was settled; they ate manna until they reached the border of Canaan.

[36] (An omer is one-tenth of an ephah.)

Water From the Rock

17 The whole Israelite community set out from the Desert of Sin, traveling from place to place as the LORD commanded. They camped at Rephidim, but there was no water for the people to drink. [2] So they quarreled with Moses and said, "Give us water to drink."

Moses replied, "Why do you quarrel with me? Why do you put the LORD to the test?"

[3] But the people were thirsty for water there, and they grumbled against Moses. They said, "Why did you bring us up out of Egypt to make us and our children and livestock die of thirst?"

[4] Then Moses cried out to the LORD, "What am I to do with these people? They are almost ready to stone me."

[5] The LORD answered Moses, "Go out in front of the people. Take with you some of the elders of Israel and take in your hand the staff with which you struck the Nile, and go. [6] I will stand there before you by the rock at Horeb. Strike the rock, and water will come out of it for the people to drink." So Moses did this in the sight of the elders of Israel. [7] And he called the place Massah[b] and Meribah[c] because the Israelites quarreled and because they tested the LORD saying, "Is the LORD among us or not?"

The Amalekites Defeated

[8] The Amalekites came and attacked the Israelites at Rephidim. [9] Moses said to Joshua, "Choose some of our men and go out to fight the Amalekites. Tomorrow I will stand on top of the hill with the staff of God in my hands."

[10] So Joshua fought the Amalekites as Moses had ordered, and Moses, Aaron and Hur went to the top of the hill. [11] As long as Moses held up his hands, the Israelites were winning, but whenever he lowered his hands, the Amalekites were winning. [12] When Moses' hands grew tired, they took a stone and put it under him and he sat on it. Aaron and Hur held his hands up — one on one side, one on the other — so that his hands remained steady till sunset. [13] So Joshua overcame the Amalekite army with the sword.

[14] Then the LORD said to Moses, "Write this on a scroll as something to be remembered and make sure that Joshua hears it, because I will completely blot out the name of Amalek from under heaven."

[15] Moses built an altar and called it The LORD is my Banner. [16] He said, "Because hands were lifted up against[d] the throne of the LORD,[e] the LORD will be at war against the Amalekites from generation to generation."

Jethro Visits Moses

18 Now Jethro, the priest of Midian and father-in-law of Moses, heard of everything God had done for Moses and for his people Israel, and how the LORD had brought Israel out of Egypt.

[2] After Moses had sent away his wife Zipporah, his father-in-law Jethro received her [3] and her two sons. One son was named Gershom,[f] for Moses said, "I have become a foreigner in a foreign land"; [4] and the other was named Eliezer,[g] for he said, "My father's God

---

[a] 31 *Manna* sounds like the Hebrew for *What is it?* (see verse 15).   [b] 7 *Massah* means *testing.*
[c] 7 *Meribah* means *quarreling.*   [d] 16 Or *to*   [e] 16 The meaning of the Hebrew for this clause is uncertain.
[f] 3 *Gershom* sounds like the Hebrew for *a foreigner there.*   [g] 4 *Eliezer* means *my God is helper.*

JETHRO

Moses listened to his father-in-law and did everything he said. EXODUS 18:24

HIS NAME MEANS: "excellence"
READ HIS STORY: *Exodus 2:15–3:1; 4:18; 18*

MEN

OF THE BIBLE

Jethro (also known by the name of Reuel) was the father-in-law of Moses. Moses met Jethro when he fled from Egypt. Though not an Israelite, Jethro came to realize that "the LORD is greater than all other gods" (Exodus 18:11), and he gave Moses wise and godly counsel.

After Moses led the Israelites out of Egypt and headed toward the promised land, Jethro went to visit Moses. Jethro heard about the miracles God had done to set his people free, and saw how Moses was leading the people. He then offered Moses advice on becoming a better leader. Moses listened to his father-in-law's words of wisdom, accepted what he had to say and followed his guidance.

The relationship between Moses and Jethro is a perfect picture of the fifth of the Ten Commandments. Deuteronomy 5:16 says, "Honor your father and your mother, as the LORD your God has commanded you, so that you may live long and that it may go well with you in the land the LORD your God is giving you."

Often, in your teen years, there is temptation to rebel against or disrespect your parents. But God has a better path for you to take. You can choose to honor your parents as Moses honored his father-in-law. When your parents offer you advice, set guidelines, or put family rules in place, listen respectfully and honor them by doing what they say. If you have parents who aren't Christians, ask God to show you how to honor and respect them as well.

When you do, God's Word says that it will go well with you. That's a promise!

was my helper; he saved me from the sword of Pharaoh."

⁵ Jethro, Moses' father-in-law, together with Moses' sons and wife, came to him in the wilderness, where he was camped near the mountain of God. ⁶ Jethro had sent word to him, "I, your father-in-law Jethro, am coming to you with your wife and her two sons."

⁷ So Moses went out to meet his father-in-law and bowed down and kissed him. They greeted each other and then went into the tent. ⁸ Moses told his father-in-law about everything the LORD had done to Pharaoh and the Egyptians for Israel's sake and about all the hardships they had met along the way and how the LORD had saved them.

⁹ Jethro was delighted to hear about all the good things the LORD had done for Israel in rescuing them from the hand of the Egyptians. ¹⁰ He said, "Praise be to the LORD, who rescued you from the hand of the Egyptians and of Pharaoh, and who rescued the people from the hand of the Egyptians. ¹¹ Now I know that the LORD is greater than all other gods, for he did this to those who had treated Israel arrogantly." ¹² Then Jethro, Moses' father-in-law, brought a burnt offering and other sacrifices to God, and Aaron came with all the elders of Israel to eat a meal with Moses' father-in-law in the presence of God.

¹³ The next day Moses took his seat to serve as judge for the people, and they stood around him from morning till evening. ¹⁴ When his father-in-law saw all that Moses was doing for the people, he said, "What is this you are doing for the people? Why do you alone sit as judge, while all these people stand around you from morning till evening?"

¹⁵ Moses answered him, "Because the people come to me to seek God's will. ¹⁶ Whenever they have a dispute, it is brought to me, and I decide between the parties and inform them of God's decrees and instructions."

¹⁷ Moses' father-in-law replied, "What you are doing is not good. ¹⁸ You and these people who come to you will only wear yourselves out. The work is too heavy for you; you cannot handle it alone. ¹⁹ Listen now to me and I will give you some advice, and may God be with you. You must be the people's representative before God and bring their disputes to him. ²⁰ Teach them his decrees and instructions, and show them the way they are to live and how they are to behave. ²¹ But select capable men from all the people—men who fear God, trustworthy men who hate dishonest gain—and appoint them as officials over thousands, hundreds, fifties and tens. ²² Have them serve as judges for the people at all times, but have them bring every difficult case to you; the simple cases they can decide themselves. That will make your load lighter, because they will share it with you. ²³ If you do this and God so commands, you will be able to stand the strain, and all these people will go home satisfied."

²⁴ Moses listened to his father-in-law and did everything he said. ²⁵ He chose capable men from all Israel and made them leaders of the people, officials over thousands, hundreds, fifties and tens. ²⁶ They served as judges for the people at all times. The difficult cases they brought to Moses, but the simple ones they decided themselves.

²⁷ Then Moses sent his father-in-law on his way, and Jethro returned to his own country.

At Mount Sinai

19 On the first day of the third month after the Israelites left Egypt—on that very day—they came to the Desert of Sinai. ² After they set out from Rephidim, they entered the Desert of Sinai, and Israel camped there in the desert in front of the mountain.

³ Then Moses went up to God, and the LORD called to him from the mountain and said, "This is what you are to say to the descendants of Jacob and what you are to tell the people of Israel: ⁴ 'You yourselves have seen what I did to Egypt, and how I carried you on eagles' wings and brought you to myself. ⁵ Now if you obey me fully and keep my covenant, then out of all nations you will be my treasured possession. Although the whole earth is mine, ⁶ you*ᵃ* will be for me a kingdom of priests and a holy nation.' These are the words you are to speak to the Israelites."

⁷ So Moses went back and summoned the elders of the people and set before them all the words the LORD had commanded him to speak. ⁸ The people all responded together, "We will do everything the LORD has said."

ᵃ 5,6 Or possession, for the whole earth is mine. ⁶You

So Moses brought their answer back to the LORD.

⁹The LORD said to Moses, "I am going to come to you in a dense cloud, so that the people will hear me speaking with you and will always put their trust in you." Then Moses told the LORD what the people had said.

¹⁰And the LORD said to Moses, "Go to the people and consecrate them today and tomorrow. Have them wash their clothes ¹¹and be ready by the third day, because on that day the LORD will come down on Mount Sinai in the sight of all the people. ¹²Put limits for the people around the mountain and tell them, 'Be careful that you do not approach the mountain or touch the foot of it. Whoever touches the mountain is to be put to death. ¹³They are to be stoned or shot with arrows; not a hand is to be laid on them. No person or animal shall be permitted to live.' Only when the ram's horn sounds a long blast may they approach the mountain."

¹⁴After Moses had gone down the mountain to the people, he consecrated them, and they washed their clothes. ¹⁵Then he said to the people, "Prepare yourselves for the third day. Abstain from sexual relations."

¹⁶On the morning of the third day there was thunder and lightning, with a thick cloud over the mountain, and a very loud trumpet blast. Everyone in the camp trembled. ¹⁷Then Moses led the people out of the camp to meet with God, and they stood at the foot of the mountain. ¹⁸Mount Sinai was covered with smoke, because the LORD descended on it in fire. The smoke billowed up from it like smoke from a furnace, and the whole mountain*ᵃ* trembled violently. ¹⁹As the sound of the trumpet grew louder and louder, Moses spoke and the voice of God answered him.*ᵇ*

²⁰The LORD descended to the top of Mount Sinai and called Moses to the top of the mountain. So Moses went up ²¹and the LORD said to him, "Go down and warn the people so they do not force their way through to see the LORD and many of them perish. ²²Even the priests, who approach the LORD, must consecrate themselves, or the LORD will break out against them."

²³Moses said to the LORD, "The people cannot come up Mount Sinai, because you yourself warned us, 'Put limits around the mountain and set it apart as holy.'"

²⁴The LORD replied, "Go down and bring Aaron up with you. But the priests and the people must not force their way through to come up to the LORD, or he will break out against them."

²⁵So Moses went down to the people and told them.

The Ten Commandments

20 And God spoke all these words:

²"I am the LORD your God, who brought you out of Egypt, out of the land of slavery.

³"You shall have no other gods before*ᶜ* me.

⁴"You shall not make for yourself an image in the form of anything in heaven above or on the earth beneath or in the waters below. ⁵You shall not bow down to them or worship them; for I, the LORD your God, am a jealous God, punishing the children for the sin of the parents to the third and fourth generation of those who hate me, ⁶but showing love to a thousand generations of those who love me and keep my commandments.

⁷"You shall not misuse the name of the LORD your God, for the LORD will not hold anyone guiltless who misuses his name.

⁸"Remember the Sabbath day by keeping it holy. ⁹Six days you shall labor and do all your work, ¹⁰but the seventh day is a sabbath to the LORD your God. On it you shall not do any work, neither you, nor your son or daughter, nor your male or female servant, nor your animals, nor any foreigner residing in your towns. ¹¹For in six days the LORD made the heavens and the earth, the sea, and all that is in them, but he rested on the seventh day. Therefore the LORD blessed the Sabbath day and made it holy.

ᵃ 18 Most Hebrew manuscripts; a few Hebrew manuscripts and Septuagint *and all the people*
ᵇ 19 Or *and God answered him with thunder*   *ᶜ 3* Or *besides*

NO HIERARCHY

READ: **EXODUS 20:4, 22-23**

When God issued this command during the time of Moses, the people were familiar with a lot of other gods. God's people had spent more than 400 years in Egypt as slaves. Egypt was crowded with gods. They had taken over the neighborhood—literally. The Egyptians had local gods for every district. Egypt was the Baskin-Robbins of gods. You could pick and choose the flavors you wanted.

The Bible has a different standard. When we hear God say, "You will have no other gods before me," we think of it as a hierarchy: God is always in first place. But there are no places. God isn't interested in competing against others or being first among many. God will not be part of any hierarchy. A better understanding of the Hebrew word translated "before me" is "in my presence."

God declines to step inside the octagon; he is the ultimate fighting champion. He is not interested in competing in a reality TV show; he is the ultimate reality. Life doesn't work properly until every other "contestant" sitting around the boardroom of your heart is fired.

There are no partial gods, no honorary gods, no interim gods, no assistants to the regional gods.

God isn't saying this because he is insecure, but because it's the way of truth in this universe. Only one God created it. Only one God designed it, and only one God knows how it works. He is the only God who can help us, direct us, satisfy us, save us.

BUILDING
FAITH
WISDOM
STRENGTH

Taken from *Gods at War Student Edition* by Kyle Idleman, copyright © 2014 by City on a Hill Studio, LLC, published by Zondervan.

¹² "Honor your father and your mother, so that you may live long in the land the LORD your God is giving you.

¹³ "You shall not murder.

¹⁴ "You shall not commit adultery.

¹⁵ "You shall not steal.

¹⁶ "You shall not give false testimony against your neighbor.

¹⁷ "You shall not covet your neighbor's house. You shall not covet your neighbor's wife, or his male or female servant, his ox or donkey, or anything that belongs to your neighbor."

¹⁸ When the people saw the thunder and lightning and heard the trumpet and saw the mountain in smoke, they trembled with fear. They stayed at a distance ¹⁹ and said to Moses, "Speak to us yourself and we will listen. But do not have God speak to us or we will die."

²⁰ Moses said to the people, "Do not be afraid. God has come to test you, so that the fear of God will be with you to keep you from sinning."

²¹ The people remained at a distance, while Moses approached the thick darkness where God was.

Idols and Altars

²² Then the LORD said to Moses, "Tell the Israelites this: 'You have seen for yourselves that I have spoken to you from heaven: ²³ Do not make any gods to be alongside me; do not make for yourselves gods of silver or gods of gold.

²⁴ "'Make an altar of earth for me and sacrifice on it your burnt offerings and fellowship offerings, your sheep and goats and your cattle. Wherever I cause my name to be honored, I will come to you and bless you. ²⁵ If you make an altar of stones for me, do not build it with dressed stones, for you will defile it if you use a tool on it. ²⁶ And do not go up to my altar on steps, or your private parts may be exposed.'

21 "These are the laws you are to set before them:

Hebrew Servants

² "If you buy a Hebrew servant, he is to serve you for six years. But in the seventh year, he shall go free, without paying anything. ³ If he comes alone, he is to go free alone; but if he has a wife when he comes, she is to go with him. ⁴ If his master gives him a wife and she bears him sons or daughters, the woman and her children shall belong to her master, and only the man shall go free.

⁵ "But if the servant declares, 'I love my master and my wife and children and do not want to go free,' ⁶ then his master must take him before the judges.^a He shall take him to the door or the doorpost and pierce his ear with an awl. Then he will be his servant for life.

⁷ "If a man sells his daughter as a servant, she is not to go free as male servants do. ⁸ If she does not please the master who has selected her for himself,^b he must let her be redeemed. He has no right to sell her to foreigners, because he has broken faith with her. ⁹ If he selects her for his son, he must grant her the rights of a daughter. ¹⁰ If he marries another woman, he must not deprive the first one of her food, clothing and marital rights. ¹¹ If he does not provide her with these three things, she is to go free, without any payment of money.

Personal Injuries

¹² "Anyone who strikes a person with a fatal blow is to be put to death. ¹³ However, if it is not done intentionally, but God lets it happen, they are to flee to a place I will designate. ¹⁴ But if anyone schemes and kills someone deliberately, that person is to be taken from my altar and put to death.

¹⁵ "Anyone who attacks^c their father or mother is to be put to death.

¹⁶ "Anyone who kidnaps someone is to be put to death, whether the victim has been sold or is still in the kidnapper's possession.

¹⁷ "Anyone who curses their father or mother is to be put to death.

¹⁸ "If people quarrel and one person hits another with a stone or with their fist^d and the victim does not die but is confined to bed, ¹⁹ the one who struck the blow will not be held liable if the other can get up and walk around outside with a staff; however, the guilty party must pay the injured person for any loss of time and see that the victim is completely healed.

^a 6 Or *before God*   ^b 8 Or *master so that he does not choose her*   ^c 15 Or *kills*   ^d 18 Or *with a tool*

²⁰"Anyone who beats their male or female slave with a rod must be punished if the slave dies as a direct result, ²¹but they are not to be punished if the slave recovers after a day or two, since the slave is their property.

²²"If people are fighting and hit a pregnant woman and she gives birth prematurely*a* but there is no serious injury, the offender must be fined whatever the woman's husband demands and the court allows. ²³But if there is serious injury, you are to take life for life, ²⁴eye for eye, tooth for tooth, hand for hand, foot for foot, ²⁵burn for burn, wound for wound, bruise for bruise.

²⁶"An owner who hits a male or female slave in the eye and destroys it must let the slave go free to compensate for the eye. ²⁷And an owner who knocks out the tooth of a male or female slave must let the slave go free to compensate for the tooth.

²⁸"If a bull gores a man or woman to death, the bull is to be stoned to death, and its meat must not be eaten. But the owner of the bull will not be held responsible. ²⁹If, however, the bull has had the habit of goring and the owner has been warned but has not kept it penned up and it kills a man or woman, the bull is to be stoned and its owner also is to be put to death. ³⁰However, if payment is demanded, the owner may redeem his life by the payment of whatever is demanded. ³¹This law also applies if the bull gores a son or daughter. ³²If the bull gores a male or female slave, the owner must pay thirty shekels*b* of silver to the master of the slave, and the bull is to be stoned to death.

³³"If anyone uncovers a pit or digs one and fails to cover it and an ox or a donkey falls into it, ³⁴the one who opened the pit must pay the owner for the loss and take the dead animal in exchange.

³⁵"If anyone's bull injures someone else's bull and it dies, the two parties are to sell the live one and divide both the money and the dead animal equally. ³⁶However, if it was known that the bull had the habit of goring, yet the owner did not keep it penned up, the owner must pay, animal for animal, and take the dead animal in exchange.

Protection of Property

22^c "Whoever steals an ox or a sheep and slaughters it or sells it must pay back five head of cattle for the ox and four sheep for the sheep.

²"If a thief is caught breaking in at night and is struck a fatal blow, the defender is not guilty of bloodshed; ³but if it happens after sunrise, the defender is guilty of bloodshed.

"Anyone who steals must certainly make restitution, but if they have nothing, they must be sold to pay for their theft. ⁴If the stolen animal is found alive in their possession—whether ox or donkey or sheep—they must pay back double.

⁵"If anyone grazes their livestock in a field or vineyard and lets them stray and they graze in someone else's field, the offender must make restitution from the best of their own field or vineyard.

⁶"If a fire breaks out and spreads into thornbushes so that it burns shocks of grain or standing grain or the whole field, the one who started the fire must make restitution.

⁷"If anyone gives a neighbor silver or goods for safekeeping and they are stolen from the neighbor's house, the thief, if caught, must pay back double. ⁸But if the thief is not found, the owner of the house must appear before the judges, and they must*d* determine whether the owner of the house has laid hands on the other person's property. ⁹In all cases of illegal possession of an ox, a donkey, a sheep, a garment, or any other lost property about which somebody says, 'This is mine,' both parties are to bring their cases before the judges.*e* The one whom the judges declare*f* guilty must pay back double to the other.

¹⁰"If anyone gives a donkey, an ox, a sheep or any other animal to their neighbor for safekeeping and it dies or is injured or is taken away while no one is looking, ¹¹the issue between them will be settled by the taking of an oath before the LORD that the neighbor did not lay hands on the other person's property. The owner is to accept this, and no restitution is required. ¹²But if the animal was stolen from the neighbor, restitution must be made to the owner. ¹³If it was torn to pieces

---

a 22 Or *she has a miscarriage*   *b* 32 That is, about 12 ounces or about 345 grams   *c* In Hebrew texts 22:1 is numbered 21:37, and 22:2-31 is numbered 22:1-30.   *d* 8 Or *before God, and he will*   *e* 9 Or *before God*   *f* 9 Or *whom God declares* by a wild animal, the neighbor shall bring in the remains as evidence and shall not be required to pay for the torn animal.

¹⁴ "If anyone borrows an animal from their neighbor and it is injured or dies while the owner is not present, they must make restitution. ¹⁵ But if the owner is with the animal, the borrower will not have to pay. If the animal was hired, the money paid for the hire covers the loss.

Social Responsibility

¹⁶ "If a man seduces a virgin who is not pledged to be married and sleeps with her, he must pay the bride-price, and she shall be his wife. ¹⁷ If her father absolutely refuses to give her to him, he must still pay the bride-price for virgins.

¹⁸ "Do not allow a sorceress to live.

¹⁹ "Anyone who has sexual relations with an animal is to be put to death.

²⁰ "Whoever sacrifices to any god other than the LORD must be destroyed.ᵃ

²¹ "Do not mistreat or oppress a foreigner, for you were foreigners in Egypt.

²² "Do not take advantage of the widow or the fatherless. ²³ If you do and they cry out to me, I will certainly hear their cry. ²⁴ My anger will be aroused, and I will kill you with the sword; your wives will become widows and your children fatherless.

²⁵ "If you lend money to one of my people among you who is needy, do not treat it like a business deal; charge no interest. ²⁶ If you take your neighbor's cloak as a pledge, return it by sunset, ²⁷ because that cloak is the only covering your neighbor has. What else can they sleep in? When they cry out to me, I will hear, for I am compassionate.

²⁸ "Do not blaspheme Godᵇ or curse the ruler of your people.

²⁹ "Do not hold back offerings from your granaries or your vats.ᶜ

"You must give me the firstborn of your sons. ³⁰ Do the same with your cattle and your sheep. Let them stay with their mothers for seven days, but give them to me on the eighth day.

³¹ "You are to be my holy people. So do not eat the meat of an animal torn by wild beasts; throw it to the dogs.

Laws of Justice and Mercy

23 "Do not spread false reports. Do not help a guilty person by being a malicious witness.

² "Do not follow the crowd in doing wrong. When you give testimony in a lawsuit, do not pervert justice by siding with the crowd, ³ and do not show favoritism to a poor person in a lawsuit.

⁴ "If you come across your enemy's ox or donkey wandering off, be sure to return it. ⁵ If you see the donkey of someone who hates you fallen down under its load, do not leave it there; be sure you help them with it.

⁶ "Do not deny justice to your poor people in their lawsuits. ⁷ Have nothing to do with a false charge and do not put an innocent or honest person to death, for I will not acquit the guilty.

⁸ "Do not accept a bribe, for a bribe blinds those who see and twists the words of the innocent.

⁹ "Do not oppress a foreigner; you yourselves know how it feels to be foreigners, because you were foreigners in Egypt.

Sabbath Laws

¹⁰ "For six years you are to sow your fields and harvest the crops, ¹¹ but during the seventh year let the land lie unplowed and unused. Then the poor among your people may get food from it, and the wild animals may eat what is left. Do the same with your vineyard and your olive grove.

¹² "Six days do your work, but on the seventh day do not work, so that your ox and your donkey may rest, and so that the slave born in your household and the foreigner living among you may be refreshed.

¹³ "Be careful to do everything I have said to you. Do not invoke the names of other gods; do not let them be heard on your lips.

The Three Annual Festivals

¹⁴ "Three times a year you are to celebrate a festival to me.

¹⁵ "Celebrate the Festival of Unleavened Bread; for seven days eat bread made without yeast, as I commanded you. Do this at the appointed time in the month of Aviv, for in that month you came out of Egypt.

ᵃ 20 The Hebrew term refers to the irrevocable giving over of things or persons to the LORD, often by totally destroying them.   ᵇ 28 Or *Do not revile the judges*   ᶜ 29 The meaning of the Hebrew for this phrase is uncertain.

"No one is to appear before me empty-handed.

¹⁶"Celebrate the Festival of Harvest with the firstfruits of the crops you sow in your field.

"Celebrate the Festival of Ingathering at the end of the year, when you gather in your crops from the field.

¹⁷"Three times a year all the men are to appear before the Sovereign LORD.

¹⁸"Do not offer the blood of a sacrifice to me along with anything containing yeast.

"The fat of my festival offerings must not be kept until morning.

¹⁹"Bring the best of the firstfruits of your soil to the house of the LORD your God.

"Do not cook a young goat in its mother's milk.

God's Angel to Prepare the Way

²⁰"See, I am sending an angel ahead of you to guard you along the way and to bring you to the place I have prepared. ²¹Pay attention to him and listen to what he says. Do not rebel against him; he will not forgive your rebellion, since my Name is in him. ²²If you listen carefully to what he says and do all that I say, I will be an enemy to your enemies and will oppose those who oppose you. ²³My angel will go ahead of you and bring you into the land of the Amorites, Hittites, Perizzites, Canaanites, Hivites and Jebusites, and I will wipe them out. ²⁴Do not bow down before their gods or worship them or follow their practices. You must demolish them and break their sacred stones to pieces. ²⁵Worship the LORD your God, and his blessing will be on your food and water. I will take away sickness from among you, ²⁶and none will miscarry or be barren in your land. I will give you a full life span.

²⁷"I will send my terror ahead of you and throw into confusion every nation you encounter. I will make all your enemies turn their backs and run. ²⁸I will send the hornet ahead of you to drive the Hivites, Canaanites and Hittites out of your way. ²⁹But I will not drive them out in a single year, because the land would become desolate and the wild animals too numerous for you. ³⁰Little by little I will drive them out before you, until you have increased enough to take possession of the land.

³¹"I will establish your borders from the Red Sea*ᵃ* to the Mediterranean Sea,*ᵇ* and from the desert to the Euphrates River. I will give into your hands the people who live in the land, and you will drive them out before you. ³²Do not make a covenant with them or with their gods. ³³Do not let them live in your land or they will cause you to sin against me, because the worship of their gods will certainly be a snare to you."

The Covenant Confirmed

24 Then the LORD said to Moses, "Come up to the LORD, you and Aaron, Nadab and Abihu, and seventy of the elders of Israel. You are to worship at a distance, ²but Moses alone is to approach the LORD; the others must not come near. And the people may not come up with him."

³When Moses went and told the people all the LORD's words and laws, they responded with one voice, "Everything the LORD has said we will do." ⁴Moses then wrote down everything the LORD had said.

He got up early the next morning and built an altar at the foot of the mountain and set up twelve stone pillars representing the twelve tribes of Israel. ⁵Then he sent young Israelite men, and they offered burnt offerings and sacrificed young bulls as fellowship offerings to the LORD. ⁶Moses took half of the blood and put it in bowls, and the other half he splashed against the altar. ⁷Then he took the Book of the Covenant and read it to the people. They responded, "We will do everything the LORD has said; we will obey."

⁸Moses then took the blood, sprinkled it on the people and said, "This is the blood of the covenant that the LORD has made with you in accordance with all these words."

⁹Moses and Aaron, Nadab and Abihu, and the seventy elders of Israel went up ¹⁰and saw the God of Israel. Under his feet was something like a pavement made of lapis lazuli, as bright blue as the sky. ¹¹But God did not raise his hand against these leaders of the Israelites; they saw God, and they ate and drank.

¹²The LORD said to Moses, "Come up to me on the mountain and stay here, and I will give you the tablets of stone with the law and commandments I have written for their instruction."

ᵃ 31 Or *the Sea of Reeds*   ᵇ 31 Hebrew *to the Sea of the Philistines*

¹³Then Moses set out with Joshua his aide, and Moses went up on the mountain of God. ¹⁴He said to the elders, "Wait here for us until we come back to you. Aaron and Hur are with you, and anyone involved in a dispute can go to them."

¹⁵When Moses went up on the mountain, the cloud covered it, ¹⁶and the glory of the Lord settled on Mount Sinai. For six days the cloud covered the mountain, and on the seventh day the Lord called to Moses from within the cloud. ¹⁷To the Israelites the glory of the Lord looked like a consuming fire on top of the mountain. ¹⁸Then Moses entered the cloud as he went on up the mountain. And he stayed on the mountain forty days and forty nights.

Offerings for the Tabernacle

25 The Lord said to Moses, ²"Tell the Israelites to bring me an offering. You are to receive the offering for me from everyone whose heart prompts them to give. ³These are the offerings you are to receive from them: gold, silver and bronze; ⁴blue, purple and scarlet yarn and fine linen; goat hair; ⁵ram skins dyed red and another type of durable leather*a*; acacia wood; ⁶olive oil for the light; spices for the anointing oil and for the fragrant incense; ⁷and onyx stones and other gems to be mounted on the ephod and breastpiece.

⁸Then have them make a sanctuary for me, and I will dwell among them. ⁹Make this tabernacle and all its furnishings exactly like the pattern I will show you.

The Ark

¹⁰"Have them make an ark*b* of acacia wood—two and a half cubits long, a cubit and a half wide, and a cubit and a half high.*c* ¹¹Overlay it with pure gold, both inside and out, and make a gold molding around it. ¹²Cast four gold rings for it and fasten them to its four feet, with two rings on one side and two rings on the other. ¹³Then make poles of acacia wood and overlay them with gold. ¹⁴Insert the poles into the rings on the sides of the ark to carry it. ¹⁵The poles are to remain in the rings of this ark; they are not to

be removed. ¹⁶Then put in the ark the tablets of the covenant law, which I will give you.

¹⁷"Make an atonement cover of pure gold—two and a half cubits long and a cubit and a half wide. ¹⁸And make two cherubim out of hammered gold at the ends of the cover. ¹⁹Make one cherub on one end and the second cherub on the other; make the cherubim of one piece with the cover, at the two ends. ²⁰The cherubim are to have their wings spread upward, overshadowing the cover with them. The cherubim are to face each other, looking toward the cover. ²¹Place the cover on top of the ark and put in the ark the tablets of the covenant law that I will give you. ²²There, above the cover between the two cherubim that are over the ark of the covenant law, I will meet with you and give you all my commands for the Israelites.

The Table

²³"Make a table of acacia wood—two cubits long, a cubit wide and a cubit and a half high.*d* ²⁴Overlay it with pure gold and make a gold molding around it. ²⁵Also make around it a rim a handbreadth*e* wide and put a gold molding on the rim. ²⁶Make four gold rings for the table and fasten them to the four corners, where the four legs are. ²⁷The rings are to be close to the rim to hold the poles used in carrying the table. ²⁸Make the poles of acacia wood, overlay them with gold and carry the table with them. ²⁹And make its plates and dishes of pure gold, as well as its pitchers and bowls for the pouring out of offerings. ³⁰Put the bread of the Presence on this table to be before me at all times.

The Lampstand

³¹"Make a lampstand of pure gold. Hammer out its base and shaft, and make its flowerlike cups, buds and blossoms of one piece with them. ³²Six branches are to extend from the sides of the lampstand—three on one side and three on the other. ³³Three cups shaped like almond flowers with buds and blossoms are to be on one branch, three on the next branch, and the same for all six branches extending from the lampstand. ³⁴And on the lampstand there are to be four

---

a 5 Possibly the hides of large aquatic mammals   *b 10* That is, a chest   *c 10* That is, about 3 3/4 feet long and 2 1/4 feet wide and high or about 1.1 meters long and 68 centimeters wide and high; similarly in verse 17   *d 23* That is, about 3 feet long, 1 1/2 feet wide and 2 1/4 feet high or about 90 centimeters long, 45 centimeters wide and 68 centimeters high   *e 25* That is, about 3 inches or about 7.5 centimeters cups shaped like almond flowers with buds and blossoms. [35] One bud shall be under the first pair of branches extending from the lampstand, a second bud under the second pair, and a third bud under the third pair— six branches in all. [36] The buds and branches shall all be of one piece with the lampstand, hammered out of pure gold.

[37] "Then make its seven lamps and set them up on it so that they light the space in front of it. [38] Its wick trimmers and trays are to be of pure gold. [39] A talent[a] of pure gold is to be used for the lampstand and all these accessories. [40] See that you make them according to the pattern shown you on the mountain.

The Tabernacle

26 "Make the tabernacle with ten curtains of finely twisted linen and blue, purple and scarlet yarn, with cherubim woven into them by a skilled worker. [2] All the curtains are to be the same size—twenty-eight cubits long and four cubits wide.[b] [3] Join five of the curtains together, and do the same with the other five. [4] Make loops of blue material along the edge of the end curtain in one set, and do the same with the end curtain in the other set. [5] Make fifty loops on one curtain and fifty loops on the end curtain of the other set, with the loops opposite each other. [6] Then make fifty gold clasps and use them to fasten the curtains together so that the tabernacle is a unit.

[7] "Make curtains of goat hair for the tent over the tabernacle—eleven altogether. [8] All eleven curtains are to be the same size— thirty cubits long and four cubits wide.[c] [9] Join five of the curtains together into one set and the other six into another set. Fold the sixth curtain double at the front of the tent. [10] Make fifty loops along the edge of the end curtain in one set and also along the edge of the end curtain in the other set. [11] Then make fifty bronze clasps and put them in the loops to fasten the tent together as a unit. [12] As for the additional length of the tent curtains, the half curtain that is left over is to hang down at the rear of the tab-

ernacle. [13] The tent curtains will be a cubit[d] longer on both sides; what is left will hang over the sides of the tabernacle so as to cover it. [14] Make for the tent a covering of ram skins dyed red, and over that a covering of the other durable leather.[e]

[15] "Make upright frames of acacia wood for the tabernacle. [16] Each frame is to be ten cubits long and a cubit and a half wide,[f] [17] with two projections set parallel to each other. Make all the frames of the tabernacle in this way. [18] Make twenty frames for the south side of the tabernacle [19] and make forty silver bases to go under them—two bases for each frame, one under each projection. [20] For the other side, the north side of the tabernacle, make twenty frames [21] and forty silver bases—two under each frame. [22] Make six frames for the far end, that is, the west end of the tabernacle, [23] and make two frames for the corners at the far end. [24] At these two corners they must be double from the bottom all the way to the top and fitted into a single ring; both shall be like that. [25] So there will be eight frames and sixteen silver bases— two under each frame.

[26] "Also make crossbars of acacia wood: five for the frames on one side of the tabernacle, [27] five for those on the other side, and five for the frames on the west, at the far end of the tabernacle. [28] The center crossbar is to extend from end to end at the middle of the frames. [29] Overlay the frames with gold and make gold rings to hold the crossbars. Also overlay the crossbars with gold.

[30] "Set up the tabernacle according to the plan shown you on the mountain.

[31] "Make a curtain of blue, purple and scarlet yarn and finely twisted linen, with cherubim woven into it by a skilled worker. [32] Hang it with gold hooks on four posts of acacia wood overlaid with gold and standing on four silver bases. [33] Hang the curtain from the clasps and place the ark of the covenant law behind the curtain. The curtain will separate the Holy Place from the Most Holy Place. [34] Put the atonement cover on the ark of the covenant law in the Most Holy Place. [35] Place the table outside the curtain

---

[a] 39 That is, about 75 pounds or about 34 kilograms   [b] 2 That is, about 42 feet long and 6 feet wide or about 13 meters long and 1.8 meters wide   [c] 8 That is, about 45 feet long and 6 feet wide or about 13.5 meters long and 1.8 meters wide   [d] 13 That is, about 18 inches or about 45 centimeters   [e] 14 Possibly the hides of large aquatic mammals (see 25:5)   [f] 16 That is, about 15 feet long and 2 1/4 feet wide or about 4.5 meters long and 68 centimeters wide

on the north side of the tabernacle and put the lampstand opposite it on the south side.

36 "For the entrance to the tent make a curtain of blue, purple and scarlet yarn and finely twisted linen — the work of an embroiderer. 37 Make gold hooks for this curtain and five posts of acacia wood overlaid with gold. And cast five bronze bases for them.

The Altar of Burnt Offering

27 "Build an altar of acacia wood, three cubits[a] high; it is to be square, five cubits long and five cubits wide.[b] 2 Make a horn at each of the four corners, so that the horns and the altar are of one piece, and overlay the altar with bronze. 3 Make all its utensils of bronze — its pots to remove the ashes, and its shovels, sprinkling bowls, meat forks and firepans. 4 Make a grating for it, a bronze network, and make a bronze ring at each of the four corners of the network. 5 Put it under the ledge of the altar so that it is halfway up the altar. 6 Make poles of acacia wood for the altar and overlay them with bronze. 7 The poles are to be inserted into the rings so they will be on two sides of the altar when it is carried. 8 Make the altar hollow, out of boards. It is to be made just as you were shown on the mountain.

The Courtyard

9 "Make a courtyard for the tabernacle. The south side shall be a hundred cubits[c] long and is to have curtains of finely twisted linen, 10 with twenty posts and twenty bronze bases and with silver hooks and bands on the posts. 11 The north side shall also be a hundred cubits long and is to have curtains, with twenty posts and twenty bronze bases and with silver hooks and bands on the posts.

12 "The west end of the courtyard shall be fifty cubits[d] wide and have curtains, with ten posts and ten bases. 13 On the east end, toward the sunrise, the courtyard shall also be fifty cubits wide. 14 Curtains fifteen cubits[e] long are to be on one side of the entrance, with three posts and three bases, 15 and curtains fifteen cubits long are to be on the other side, with three posts and three bases.

16 "For the entrance to the courtyard, provide a curtain twenty cubits[f] long, of blue, purple and scarlet yarn and finely twisted linen — the work of an embroiderer — with four posts and four bases. 17 All the posts around the courtyard are to have silver bands and hooks, and bronze bases. 18 The courtyard shall be a hundred cubits long and fifty cubits wide,[g] with curtains of finely twisted linen five cubits[h] high, and with bronze bases. 19 All the other articles used in the service of the tabernacle, whatever their function, including all the tent pegs for it and those for the courtyard, are to be of bronze.

Oil for the Lampstand

20 "Command the Israelites to bring you clear oil of pressed olives for the light so that the lamps may be kept burning. 21 In the tent of meeting, outside the curtain that shields the ark of the covenant law, Aaron and his sons are to keep the lamps burning before the LORD from evening till morning. This is to be a lasting ordinance among the Israelites for the generations to come.

The Priestly Garments

28 "Have Aaron your brother brought to you from among the Israelites, along with his sons Nadab and Abihu, Eleazar and Ithamar, so they may serve me as priests. 2 Make sacred garments for your brother Aaron to give him dignity and honor. 3 Tell all the skilled workers to whom I have given wisdom in such matters that they are to make garments for Aaron, for his consecration, so he may serve me as priest. 4 These are the garments they are to make: a breastpiece, an ephod, a robe, a woven tunic, a turban and a sash. They are to make these sacred garments for your brother Aaron and his sons, so they may serve me as priests. 5 Have them use gold, and blue, purple and scarlet yarn, and fine linen.

The Ephod

6 "Make the ephod of gold, and of blue, purple and scarlet yarn, and of finely twisted linen — the work of skilled hands. 7 It is to

---

a 1 That is, about 4 1/2 feet or about 1.4 meters   b 1 That is, about 7 1/2 feet or about 2.3 meters long and wide   c 9 That is, about 150 feet or about 45 meters; also in verse 11   d 12 That is, about 75 feet or about 23 meters; also in verse 13   e 14 That is, about 23 feet or about 6.8 meters; also in verse 15   f 16 That is, about 30 feet or about 9 meters   g 18 That is, about 150 feet long and 75 feet wide or about 45 meters long and 23 meters wide   h 18 That is, about 7 1/2 feet or about 2.3 meters have two shoulder pieces attached to two of its corners, so it can be fastened. [8]Its skillfully woven waistband is to be like it—of one piece with the ephod and made with gold, and with blue, purple and scarlet yarn, and with finely twisted linen.

[9]"Take two onyx stones and engrave on them the names of the sons of Israel [10]in the order of their birth—six names on one stone and the remaining six on the other. [11]Engrave the names of the sons of Israel on the two stones the way a gem cutter engraves a seal. Then mount the stones in gold filigree settings [12]and fasten them on the shoulder pieces of the ephod as memorial stones for the sons of Israel. Aaron is to bear the names on his shoulders as a memorial before the LORD. [13]Make gold filigree settings [14]and two braided chains of pure gold, like a rope, and attach the chains to the settings.

The Breastpiece

[15]"Fashion a breastpiece for making decisions—the work of skilled hands. Make it like the ephod: of gold, and of blue, purple and scarlet yarn, and of finely twisted linen. [16]It is to be square—a span[a] long and a span wide—and folded double. [17]Then mount four rows of precious stones on it. The first row shall be carnelian, chrysolite and beryl; [18]the second row shall be turquoise, lapis lazuli and emerald; [19]the third row shall be jacinth, agate and amethyst; [20]the fourth row shall be topaz, onyx and jasper.[b] Mount them in gold filigree settings. [21]There are to be twelve stones, one for each of the names of the sons of Israel, each engraved like a seal with the name of one of the twelve tribes.

[22]"For the breastpiece make braided chains of pure gold, like a rope. [23]Make two gold rings for it and fasten them to two corners of the breastpiece. [24]Fasten the two gold chains to the rings at the corners of the breastpiece, [25]and the other ends of the chains to the two settings, attaching them to the shoulder pieces of the ephod at the front. [26]Make two gold rings and attach them to the other two corners of the breastpiece on the inside edge next to the ephod. [27]Make two more gold rings and attach them to the bottom of the shoulder pieces on the front of the ephod, close to the seam just above the waist-band of the ephod. [28]The rings of the breastpiece are to be tied to the rings of the ephod with blue cord, connecting it to the waist-band, so that the breastpiece will not swing out from the ephod.

[29]"Whenever Aaron enters the Holy Place, he will bear the names of the sons of Israel over his heart on the breastpiece of decision as a continuing memorial before the LORD. [30]Also put the Urim and the Thummim in the breastpiece, so they may be over Aaron's heart whenever he enters the presence of the LORD. Thus Aaron will always bear the means of making decisions for the Israelites over his heart before the LORD.

Other Priestly Garments

[31]"Make the robe of the ephod entirely of blue cloth, [32]with an opening for the head in its center. There shall be a woven edge like a collar[c] around this opening, so that it will not tear. [33]Make pomegranates of blue, purple and scarlet yarn around the hem of the robe, with gold bells between them. [34]The gold bells and the pomegranates are to alternate around the hem of the robe. [35]Aaron must wear it when he ministers. The sound of the bells will be heard when he enters the Holy Place before the LORD and when he comes out, so that he will not die.

[36]"Make a plate of pure gold and engrave on it as on a seal: HOLY TO THE LORD. [37]Fasten a blue cord to it to attach it to the turban; it is to be on the front of the turban. [38]It will be on Aaron's forehead, and he will bear the guilt involved in the sacred gifts the Israelites consecrate, whatever their gifts may be. It will be on Aaron's forehead continually so that they will be acceptable to the LORD.

[39]"Weave the tunic of fine linen and make the turban of fine linen. The sash is to be the work of an embroiderer. [40]Make tunics, sashes and caps for Aaron's sons to give them dignity and honor. [41]After you put these clothes on your brother Aaron and his sons, anoint and ordain them. Consecrate them so they may serve me as priests.

[42]"Make linen undergarments as a covering for the body, reaching from the waist to the thigh. [43]Aaron and his sons must wear them whenever they enter the tent of meeting or approach the altar to minister in the

---

[a] 16 That is, about 9 inches or about 23 centimeters   [b] 20 The precise identification of some of these precious stones is uncertain.   [c] 32 The meaning of the Hebrew for this word is uncertain.

AARON

After you put these clothes on your brother Aaron and his sons, anoint and ordain them. Consecrate them so they may serve me as priests. EXODUS 28:41

HIS NAME MEANS: "enlightened," "mountain of strength"
READ HIS STORY: *Exodus 4–7, 17:8–16; Numbers 12*

OF THE BIBLE

How would you feel if your younger brother got picked for a great honor? Would you be jealous or wish it were you? As far as we know, the only time Aaron gave in to those kind of feelings was when he joined their sister Miriam in speaking against their little brother, Moses (Numbers 12). And he had plenty of other opportunities for envy. God chose Moses to free the Hebrew people. Moses even grew up in Pharaoh's palace, while Aaron lived as a slave. But Aaron supported Moses and served God any way he could.

Sometimes that support was literal, like when Aaron helped hold Moses' arms in the air so the Israelites could defeat the Amalekites in a battle (Exodus 17:8-16). Other times, Aaron supported Moses in areas where his brother lacked, such as when Aaron spoke powerfully to Pharaoh. Moses had a ton of ability, but he was "slow of speech and tongue" (Exodus 4:10), so Aaron did a lot of the speaking.

After leaving Egypt, Aaron had the privilege of becoming Israel's first high priest. From then on, all of Israel's priests came from Aaron's family. They helped the people follow God's laws and encouraged them to worship the one true God.

Aaron witnessed a dizzying array of miracles: rivers turned to blood, a total frog takeover, water pouring from rocks, God's commandments written in stone, the ground swallowing people. He would've missed it all had he said, "Beat it, little bro, I'm not helping you." But more importantly, Aaron would've missed God's reward for a lifetime of support.

Holy Place, so that they will not incur guilt and die.

"This is to be a lasting ordinance for Aaron and his descendants.

Consecration of the Priests

29 "This is what you are to do to consecrate them, so they may serve me as priests: Take a young bull and two rams without defect. ²And from the finest wheat flour make round loaves without yeast, thick loaves without yeast and with olive oil mixed in, and thin loaves without yeast and brushed with olive oil. ³Put them in a basket and present them along with the bull and the two rams. ⁴Then bring Aaron and his sons to the entrance to the tent of meeting and wash them with water. ⁵Take the garments and dress Aaron with the tunic, the robe of the ephod, the ephod itself and the breastpiece. Fasten the ephod on him by its skillfully woven waistband. ⁶Put the turban on his head and attach the sacred emblem to the turban. ⁷Take the anointing oil and anoint him by pouring it on his head. ⁸Bring his sons and dress them in tunics ⁹and fasten caps on them. Then tie sashes on Aaron and his sons.ᵃ The priesthood is theirs by a lasting ordinance.

"Then you shall ordain Aaron and his sons.

¹⁰"Bring the bull to the front of the tent of meeting, and Aaron and his sons shall lay their hands on its head. ¹¹Slaughter it in the LORD's presence at the entrance to the tent of meeting. ¹²Take some of the bull's blood and put it on the horns of the altar with your finger, and pour out the rest of it at the base of the altar. ¹³Then take all the fat on the internal organs, the long lobe of the liver, and both kidneys with the fat on them, and burn them on the altar. ¹⁴But burn the bull's flesh and its hide and its intestines outside the camp. It is a sin offering.ᵇ

¹⁵"Take one of the rams, and Aaron and his sons shall lay their hands on its head. ¹⁶Slaughter it and take the blood and splash it against the sides of the altar. ¹⁷Cut the ram into pieces and wash the internal organs and the legs, putting them with the head and the other pieces. ¹⁸Then burn the entire ram on the altar. It is a burnt offering to the LORD, a

pleasing aroma, a food offering presented to the LORD.

¹⁹"Take the other ram, and Aaron and his sons shall lay their hands on its head. ²⁰Slaughter it, take some of its blood and put it on the lobes of the right ears of Aaron and his sons, on the thumbs of their right hands, and on the big toes of their right feet. Then splash blood against the sides of the altar. ²¹And take some blood from the altar and some of the anointing oil and sprinkle it on Aaron and his garments and on his sons and their garments. Then he and his sons and their garments will be consecrated.

²²"Take from this ram the fat, the fat tail, the fat on the internal organs, the long lobe of the liver, both kidneys with the fat on them, and the right thigh. (This is the ram for the ordination.) ²³From the basket of bread made without yeast, which is before the LORD, take one round loaf, one thick loaf with olive oil mixed in, and one thin loaf. ²⁴Put all these in the hands of Aaron and his sons and have them wave them before the LORD as a wave offering. ²⁵Then take them from their hands and burn them on the altar along with the burnt offering for a pleasing aroma to the LORD, a food offering presented to the LORD. ²⁶After you take the breast of the ram for Aaron's ordination, wave it before the LORD as a wave offering, and it will be your share.

²⁷"Consecrate those parts of the ordination ram that belong to Aaron and his sons: the breast that was waved and the thigh that was presented. ²⁸This is always to be the perpetual share from the Israelites for Aaron and his sons. It is the contribution the Israelites are to make to the LORD from their fellowship offerings.

²⁹"Aaron's sacred garments will belong to his descendants so that they can be anointed and ordained in them. ³⁰The son who succeeds him as priest and comes to the tent of meeting to minister in the Holy Place is to wear them seven days.

³¹"Take the ram for the ordination and cook the meat in a sacred place. ³²At the entrance to the tent of meeting, Aaron and his sons are to eat the meat of the ram and the bread that is in the basket. ³³They are to eat these offerings by which atonement was

---

ᵃ 9 Hebrew; Septuagint *on them*   ᵇ 14 Or *purification offering*; also in verse 36 made for their ordination and consecration. But no one else may eat them, because they are sacred. ³⁴And if any of the meat of the ordination ram or any bread is left over till morning, burn it up. It must not be eaten, because it is sacred.

³⁵"Do for Aaron and his sons everything I have commanded you, taking seven days to ordain them. ³⁶Sacrifice a bull each day as a sin offering to make atonement. Purify the altar by making atonement for it, and anoint it to consecrate it. ³⁷For seven days make atonement for the altar and consecrate it. Then the altar will be most holy, and whatever touches it will be holy.

³⁸"This is what you are to offer on the altar regularly each day: two lambs a year old. ³⁹Offer one in the morning and the other at twilight. ⁴⁰With the first lamb offer a tenth of an ephah*ᵃ* of the finest flour mixed with a quarter of a hin*ᵇ* of oil from pressed olives, and a quarter of a hin of wine as a drink offering. ⁴¹Sacrifice the other lamb at twilight with the same grain offering and its drink offering as in the morning — a pleasing aroma, a food offering presented to the LORD.

⁴²"For the generations to come this burnt offering is to be made regularly at the entrance to the tent of meeting, before the LORD. There I will meet you and speak to you; ⁴³there also I will meet with the Israelites, and the place will be consecrated by my glory.

⁴⁴"So I will consecrate the tent of meeting and the altar and will consecrate Aaron and his sons to serve me as priests. ⁴⁵Then I will dwell among the Israelites and be their God. ⁴⁶They will know that I am the LORD their God, who brought them out of Egypt so that I might dwell among them. I am the LORD their God.

The Altar of Incense

30 "Make an altar of acacia wood for burning incense. ²It is to be square, a cubit long and a cubit wide, and two cubits high*ᶜ* — its horns of one piece with it. ³Overlay the top and all the sides and the horns with pure gold, and make a gold molding around it. ⁴Make two gold rings for the al-

tar below the molding — two on each of the opposite sides — to hold the poles used to carry it. ⁵Make the poles of acacia wood and overlay them with gold. ⁶Put the altar in front of the curtain that shields the ark of the covenant law — before the atonement cover that is over the tablets of the covenant law — where I will meet with you.

⁷"Aaron must burn fragrant incense on the altar every morning when he tends the lamps. ⁸He must burn incense again when he lights the lamps at twilight so incense will burn regularly before the LORD for the generations to come. ⁹Do not offer on this altar any other incense or any burnt offering or grain offering, and do not pour a drink offering on it. ¹⁰Once a year Aaron shall make atonement on its horns. This annual atonement must be made with the blood of the atoning sin offering*ᵈ* for the generations to come. It is most holy to the LORD."

Atonement Money

¹¹Then the LORD said to Moses, ¹²"When you take a census of the Israelites to count them, each one must pay the LORD a ransom for his life at the time he is counted. Then no plague will come on them when you number them. ¹³Each one who crosses over to those already counted is to give a half shekel,*ᵉ* according to the sanctuary shekel, which weighs twenty gerahs. This half shekel is an offering to the LORD. ¹⁴All who cross over, those twenty years old or more, are to give an offering to the LORD. ¹⁵The rich are not to give more than a half shekel and the poor are not to give less when you make the offering to the LORD to atone for your lives. ¹⁶Receive the atonement money from the Israelites and use it for the service of the tent of meeting. It will be a memorial for the Israelites before the LORD, making atonement for your lives."

Basin for Washing

¹⁷Then the LORD said to Moses, ¹⁸"Make a bronze basin, with its bronze stand, for washing. Place it between the tent of meeting and the altar, and put water in it. ¹⁹Aaron and his sons are to wash their hands and feet with

---

ᵃ 40 That is, probably about 3 1/2 pounds or about 1.6 kilograms   *ᵇ 40* That is, probably about 1 quart or about 1 liter   *ᶜ 2* That is, about 1 1/2 feet long and wide and 3 feet high or about 45 centimeters long and wide and 90 centimeters high   *ᵈ 10* Or *purification offering*   *ᵉ 13* That is, about 1/5 ounce or about 5.8 grams; also in verse 15 water from it. ²⁰Whenever they enter the tent of meeting, they shall wash with water so that they will not die. Also, when they approach the altar to minister by presenting a food offering to the LORD, ²¹they shall wash their hands and feet so that they will not die. This is to be a lasting ordinance for Aaron and his descendants for the generations to come."

Anointing Oil

²²Then the LORD said to Moses, ²³"Take the following fine spices: 500 shekels^a of liquid myrrh, half as much (that is, 250 shekels) of fragrant cinnamon, 250 shekels^b of fragrant calamus, ²⁴500 shekels of cassia—all according to the sanctuary shekel—and a hin^c of olive oil. ²⁵Make these into a sacred anointing oil, a fragrant blend, the work of a perfumer. It will be the sacred anointing oil. ²⁶Then use it to anoint the tent of meeting, the ark of the covenant law, ²⁷the table and all its articles, the lampstand and its accessories, the altar of incense, ²⁸the altar of burnt offering and all its utensils, and the basin with its stand. ²⁹You shall consecrate them so they will be most holy, and whatever touches them will be holy.

³⁰"Anoint Aaron and his sons and consecrate them so they may serve me as priests. ³¹Say to the Israelites, 'This is to be my sacred anointing oil for the generations to come. ³²Do not pour it on anyone else's body and do not make any other oil using the same formula. It is sacred, and you are to consider it sacred. ³³Whoever makes perfume like it and puts it on anyone other than a priest must be cut off from their people.'"

Incense

³⁴Then the LORD said to Moses, "Take fragrant spices—gum resin, onycha and galbanum—and pure frankincense, all in equal amounts, ³⁵and make a fragrant blend of incense, the work of a perfumer. It is to be salted and pure and sacred. ³⁶Grind some of it to powder and place it in front of the ark of the covenant law in the tent of meeting, where I will meet with you. It shall be most holy to you. ³⁷Do not make any incense with this formula for yourselves; consider it holy to the LORD. ³⁸Whoever makes incense like it to enjoy its fragrance must be cut off from their people."

Bezalel and Oholiab

31 Then the LORD said to Moses, ²"See, I have chosen Bezalel son of Uri, the son of Hur, of the tribe of Judah, ³and I have filled him with the Spirit of God, with wisdom, with understanding, with knowledge and with all kinds of skills— ⁴to make artistic designs for work in gold, silver and bronze, ⁵to cut and set stones, to work in wood, and to engage in all kinds of crafts. ⁶Moreover, I have appointed Oholiab son of Ahisamak, of the tribe of Dan, to help him. Also I have given ability to all the skilled workers to make everything I have commanded you: ⁷the tent of meeting, the ark of the covenant law with the atonement cover on it, and all the other furnishings of the tent— ⁸the table and its articles, the pure gold lampstand and all its accessories, the altar of incense, ⁹the altar of burnt offering and all its utensils, the basin with its stand— ¹⁰and also the woven garments, both the sacred garments for Aaron the priest and the garments for his sons when they serve as priests, ¹¹and the anointing oil and fragrant incense for the Holy Place. They are to make them just as I commanded you."

The Sabbath

¹²Then the LORD said to Moses, ¹³"Say to the Israelites, 'You must observe my Sabbaths. This will be a sign between me and you for the generations to come, so you may know that I am the LORD, who makes you holy.

¹⁴"'Observe the Sabbath, because it is holy to you. Anyone who desecrates it is to be put to death; those who do any work on that day must be cut off from their people. ¹⁵For six days work is to be done, but the seventh day is a day of sabbath rest, holy to the LORD. Whoever does any work on the Sabbath day is to be put to death. ¹⁶The Israelites are to observe the Sabbath, celebrating it for the generations to come as a lasting covenant. ¹⁷It will be a sign between me and the Israelites forever, for in six days the LORD made the heavens and the earth, and on the seventh day he rested and was refreshed.'"

¹⁸When the LORD finished speaking to Moses on Mount Sinai, he gave him the two tablets of the covenant law, the tablets of stone inscribed by the finger of God.

---

^a 23 That is, about 12 1/2 pounds or about 5.8 kilograms; also in verse 24   ^b 23 That is, about 6 1/4 pounds or about 2.9 kilograms   ^c 24 That is, probably about 1 gallon or about 3.8 liters

SUPPOSED TO

READ: EXODUS 31:6

I know what I'm supposed to do: write books. I actually scored below average on an aptitude exam for writing when I was in graduate school, but I knew I was called to write. And my lack of "aptitude" just means I have to rely on God even more when I write. For thirteen years, I was a frustrated writer. I couldn't complete even one manuscript. When I finally published my first book, *In a Pit with a Lion on a Snowy Day*, I felt more relief than joy. I knew I had finally done exactly what I was supposed to do.

Writing is a lot more than combinations of words and sentences and paragraphs and chapters. For me, writing a book is an act of obedience that takes like six months of early mornings and late nights.

BUILDING FAITH WISDOM STRENGTH

I don't write with a keyboard. I pray with it. Setting my alarm for early in the morning and sitting down at my keyboard are acts of obedience. It's what I'm supposed to do. The harder it is and the longer it takes, the more God is glorified! The more he's pleased.

No matter what tool your tool is—a football, some sheet music, a hammer, a keyboard, a mop, a microphone, or an espresso machine—using it is an act of obedience! It's the mechanism whereby you worship God. It's the way you do what you're supposed to do.

Taken from *All In Student Edition* by Mark Batterson and Parker Batterson, copyright © 2014 by Mark Batterson, published by Zondervan.

The Golden Calf

32 When the people saw that Moses was so long in coming down from the mountain, they gathered around Aaron and said, "Come, make us gods*a* who will go before us. As for this fellow Moses who brought us up out of Egypt, we don't know what has happened to him."

²Aaron answered them, "Take off the gold earrings that your wives, your sons and your daughters are wearing, and bring them to me." ³So all the people took off their earrings and brought them to Aaron. ⁴He took what they handed him and made it into an idol cast in the shape of a calf, fashioning it with a tool. Then they said, "These are your gods,*b* Israel, who brought you up out of Egypt."

⁵When Aaron saw this, he built an altar in front of the calf and announced, "Tomorrow there will be a festival to the Lord." ⁶So the next day the people rose early and sacrificed burnt offerings and presented fellowship offerings. Afterward they sat down to eat and drink and got up to indulge in revelry.

⁷Then the Lord said to Moses, "Go down, because your people, whom you brought up out of Egypt, have become corrupt. ⁸They have been quick to turn away from what I commanded them and have made themselves an idol cast in the shape of a calf. They have bowed down to it and sacrificed to it and have said, 'These are your gods, Israel, who brought you up out of Egypt.'

⁹"I have seen these people," the Lord said to Moses, "and they are a stiff-necked people. ¹⁰Now leave me alone so that my anger may burn against them and that I may destroy them. Then I will make you into a great nation."

¹¹But Moses sought the favor of the Lord his God. "Lord," he said, "why should your anger burn against your people, whom you brought out of Egypt with great power and a mighty hand? ¹²Why should the Egyptians say, 'It was with evil intent that he brought them out, to kill them in the mountains and to wipe them off the face of the earth'? Turn from your fierce anger; relent and do not bring disaster on your people. ¹³Remember your servants Abraham, Isaac and Israel, to whom you swore by your own self: 'I will make your descendants as numerous as the stars in the sky and I will give your descendants all this land I promised them, and it will be their inheritance forever.'" ¹⁴Then the Lord relented and did not bring on his people the disaster he had threatened.

¹⁵Moses turned and went down the mountain with the two tablets of the covenant law in his hands. They were inscribed on both sides, front and back. ¹⁶The tablets were the work of God; the writing was the writing of God, engraved on the tablets.

¹⁷When Joshua heard the noise of the people shouting, he said to Moses, "There is the sound of war in the camp."

¹⁸Moses replied:

"It is not the sound of victory,
    it is not the sound of defeat;
    it is the sound of singing that I hear."

¹⁹When Moses approached the camp and saw the calf and the dancing, his anger burned and he threw the tablets out of his hands, breaking them to pieces at the foot of the mountain. ²⁰And he took the calf the people had made and burned it in the fire; then he ground it to powder, scattered it on the water and made the Israelites drink it.

²¹He said to Aaron, "What did these people do to you, that you led them into such great sin?"

²²"Do not be angry, my lord," Aaron answered. "You know how prone these people are to evil. ²³They said to me, 'Make us gods who will go before us. As for this fellow Moses who brought us up out of Egypt, we don't know what has happened to him.' ²⁴So I told them, 'Whoever has any gold jewelry, take it off.' Then they gave me the gold, and I threw it into the fire, and out came this calf!"

²⁵Moses saw that the people were running wild and that Aaron had let them get out of control and so become a laughingstock to their enemies. ²⁶So he stood at the entrance to the camp and said, "Whoever is for the Lord, come to me." And all the Levites rallied to him.

²⁷Then he said to them, "This is what the Lord, the God of Israel, says: 'Each man strap a sword to his side. Go back and forth through the camp from one end to the other, each killing his brother and friend and neighbor.'" ²⁸The Levites did as Moses com-

---

a 1 Or *a god*; also in verses 23 and 31   *b* 4 Or *This is your god*; also in verse 8

MOSES

The LORD would speak to Moses face to face, as one speaks to a friend. EXODUS 33:11

HIS NAME MEANS: "drawn forth," "taken out of the water"
READ HIS STORY: *Exodus 2–4, 12–14; Deuteronomy 34; Acts 7:20–38; Hebrews 11:23–29*

More stories exist about Moses than nearly any other man in the Bible. That makes sense, considering he wrote the first five books of the Old Testament.

We have heard how Moses was rescued from the Nile River by Pharaoh's daughter, killed an Egyptian who was beating a Hebrew slave, escaped into the wilderness, heard God talk through a burning bush, led the Israelites out of Egypt, parted the Red Sea and received the Ten Commandments.

Sure, Moses served God mightily, but he never set foot in the promised land. For all his faithful service and all the wonders he witnessed, he made a mistake that cost him this one honor. In Numbers 20, God's people were thirsty. The Lord told Moses to take his staff, gather the people, and speak to a rock. Then God would make water flow out of the rock. But Moses didn't talk to the rock; he hit it—twice! Because he didn't follow God's instructions and honor the Lord, Moses wasn't allowed to lead Israel into the promised land.

Wasn't Moses God's friend? we might think. *Why would God be so harsh?*

God demanded obedience. By hitting the rock, Moses drew attention to himself and away from God. Moses' frustration with the Israelites led to a poor decision. He understood what it meant to sin against a holy God.

Moses saw the promised land; he climbed Mount Nebo and looked out on the wall of Jericho across the Jordan River. So Moses died knowing God's promises always come true.

manded, and that day about three thousand of the people died. ²⁹Then Moses said, "You have been set apart to the LORD today, for you were against your own sons and brothers, and he has blessed you this day."

³⁰The next day Moses said to the people, "You have committed a great sin. But now I will go up to the LORD; perhaps I can make atonement for your sin."

³¹So Moses went back to the LORD and said, "Oh, what a great sin these people have committed! They have made themselves gods of gold. ³²But now, please forgive their sin—but if not, then blot me out of the book you have written."

³³The LORD replied to Moses, "Whoever has sinned against me I will blot out of my book. ³⁴Now go, lead the people to the place I spoke of, and my angel will go before you. However, when the time comes for me to punish, I will punish them for their sin."

³⁵And the LORD struck the people with a plague because of what they did with the calf Aaron had made.

33 Then the LORD said to Moses, "Leave this place, you and the people you brought up out of Egypt, and go up to the land I promised on oath to Abraham, Isaac and Jacob, saying, 'I will give it to your descendants.' ²I will send an angel before you and drive out the Canaanites, Amorites, Hittites, Perizzites, Hivites and Jebusites. ³Go up to the land flowing with milk and honey. But I will not go with you, because you are a stiff-necked people and I might destroy you on the way."

⁴When the people heard these distressing words, they began to mourn and no one put on any ornaments. ⁵For the LORD had said to Moses, "Tell the Israelites, 'You are a stiff-necked people. If I were to go with you even for a moment, I might destroy you. Now take off your ornaments and I will decide what to do with you.'" ⁶So the Israelites stripped off their ornaments at Mount Horeb.

The Tent of Meeting

⁷Now Moses used to take a tent and pitch it outside the camp some distance away, calling it the "tent of meeting." Anyone inquiring of the LORD would go to the tent of meeting outside the camp. ⁸And whenever Moses went out to the tent, all the people rose and stood at the entrances to their tents, watch-

ing Moses until he entered the tent. ⁹As Moses went into the tent, the pillar of cloud would come down and stay at the entrance, while the LORD spoke with Moses. ¹⁰Whenever the people saw the pillar of cloud standing at the entrance to the tent, they all stood and worshiped, each at the entrance to their tent. ¹¹The LORD would speak to Moses face to face, as one speaks to a friend. Then Moses would return to the camp, but his young aide Joshua son of Nun did not leave the tent.

Moses and the Glory of the LORD

¹²Moses said to the LORD, "You have been telling me, 'Lead these people,' but you have not let me know whom you will send with me. You have said, 'I know you by name and you have found favor with me.' ¹³If you are pleased with me, teach me your ways so I may know you and continue to find favor with you. Remember that this nation is your people."

¹⁴The LORD replied, "My Presence will go with you, and I will give you rest."

¹⁵Then Moses said to him, "If your Presence does not go with us, do not send us up from here. ¹⁶How will anyone know that you are pleased with me and with your people unless you go with us? What else will distinguish me and your people from all the other people on the face of the earth?"

¹⁷And the LORD said to Moses, "I will do the very thing you have asked, because I am pleased with you and I know you by name."

¹⁸Then Moses said, "Now show me your glory."

¹⁹And the LORD said, "I will cause all my goodness to pass in front of you, and I will proclaim my name, the LORD, in your presence. I will have mercy on whom I will have mercy, and I will have compassion on whom I will have compassion. ²⁰But," he said, "you cannot see my face, for no one may see me and live."

²¹Then the LORD said, "There is a place near me where you may stand on a rock. ²²When my glory passes by, I will put you in a cleft in the rock and cover you with my hand until I have passed by. ²³Then I will remove my hand and you will see my back; but my face must not be seen."

The New Stone Tablets

34 The LORD said to Moses, "Chisel out two stone tablets like the first ones,

LIMITS OF LANGUAGE

READ: EXODUS 33:12-23

It's interesting that we never hear Moses try to describe what he saw that day when he saw God's glory. Come to think of it, Moses never describes any of his one-on-one encounters with God. I wonder if that's because Moses felt the limitations of language. Why try and describe the presence of the Creator when your words will never do justice to what you've seen and felt?

It's impossible to explain the Almighty. And finding words for our own pursuit of God falls in the same category. How do we put words around the on-and-off passion we feel?

We may say passion, but the word can't really express our desire for God. We might talk about God's love, but that doesn't begin to express all God has done for us. Our passion for God will constantly push us upward and outward toward him.

If our souls truly crave to know God, it will come out in all kinds of expressions. In tears. In silence. In words we make up. In movements we make with our hands and body. In drawings and other expressions of creativity.

BUILDING
FAITH
WISDOM
STRENGTH

Words are useful for part of my expression, but they don't even begin to express the agony or the joy of my walk with God—because the moment I use finite words to express my infinite journey I have reduced the immeasurable to something measurable.

Taken from *Jesus Is for Liars: A Hypocrite's Guide to Authenticity* by Tim Baker, copyright © 2009 by Tim Baker, published by Zondervan.

and I will write on them the words that were on the first tablets, which you broke. ²Be ready in the morning, and then come up on Mount Sinai. Present yourself to me there on top of the mountain. ³No one is to come with you or be seen anywhere on the mountain; not even the flocks and herds may graze in front of the mountain."

⁴So Moses chiseled out two stone tablets like the first ones and went up Mount Sinai early in the morning, as the LORD had commanded him; and he carried the two stone tablets in his hands. ⁵Then the LORD came down in the cloud and stood there with him and proclaimed his name, the LORD. ⁶And he passed in front of Moses, proclaiming, "The LORD, the LORD, the compassionate and gracious God, slow to anger, abounding in love and faithfulness, ⁷maintaining love to thousands, and forgiving wickedness, rebellion and sin. Yet he does not leave the guilty unpunished; he punishes the children and their children for the sin of the parents to the third and fourth generation."

⁸Moses bowed to the ground at once and worshiped. ⁹"Lord," he said, "if I have found favor in your eyes, then let the Lord go with us. Although this is a stiff-necked people, forgive our wickedness and our sin, and take us as your inheritance."

¹⁰Then the LORD said: "I am making a covenant with you. Before all your people I will do wonders never before done in any nation in all the world. The people you live among will see how awesome is the work that I, the LORD, will do for you. ¹¹Obey what I command you today. I will drive out before you the Amorites, Canaanites, Hittites, Perizzites, Hivites and Jebusites. ¹²Be careful not to make a treaty with those who live in the land where you are going, or they will be a snare among you. ¹³Break down their altars, smash their sacred stones and cut down their Asherah poles.ᵃ ¹⁴Do not worship any other god, for the LORD, whose name is Jealous, is a jealous God.

¹⁵"Be careful not to make a treaty with those who live in the land; for when they prostitute themselves to their gods and sacrifice to them, they will invite you and you will eat their sacrifices. ¹⁶And when you choose some of their daughters as wives for your sons and those daughters prostitute themselves to their gods, they will lead your sons to do the same.

¹⁷"Do not make any idols.

¹⁸"Celebrate the Festival of Unleavened Bread. For seven days eat bread made without yeast, as I commanded you. Do this at the appointed time in the month of Aviv, for in that month you came out of Egypt.

¹⁹"The first offspring of every womb belongs to me, including all the firstborn males of your livestock, whether from herd or flock. ²⁰Redeem the firstborn donkey with a lamb, but if you do not redeem it, break its neck. Redeem all your firstborn sons.

"No one is to appear before me empty-handed.

²¹"Six days you shall labor, but on the seventh day you shall rest; even during the plowing season and harvest you must rest.

²²"Celebrate the Festival of Weeks with the firstfruits of the wheat harvest, and the Festival of Ingathering at the turn of the year.ᵇ ²³Three times a year all your men are to appear before the Sovereign LORD, the God of Israel. ²⁴I will drive out nations before you and enlarge your territory, and no one will covet your land when you go up three times each year to appear before the LORD your God.

²⁵"Do not offer the blood of a sacrifice to me along with anything containing yeast, and do not let any of the sacrifice from the Passover Festival remain until morning.

²⁶"Bring the best of the firstfruits of your soil to the house of the LORD your God.

"Do not cook a young goat in its mother's milk."

²⁷Then the LORD said to Moses, "Write down these words, for in accordance with these words I have made a covenant with you and with Israel." ²⁸Moses was there with the LORD forty days and forty nights without eating bread or drinking water. And he wrote on the tablets the words of the covenant—the Ten Commandments.

The Radiant Face of Moses

²⁹When Moses came down from Mount Sinai with the two tablets of the covenant law in his hands, he was not aware that his face was radiant because he had spoken

---

ᵃ 13 That is, wooden symbols of the goddess Asherah   ᵇ 22 That is, in the autumn

THE WHYS

READ: EXODUS 34:27-28

A word picture of sin I appreciate for its frankness is this: Sin is lifting your middle finger to God and saying, "Buzz off!" I believe that's the overarching idea of sin in the whole Bible. Sin isn't merely a matter of "disobeying" or "doing something wrong" or "breaking the law." Sin is missing the mark foremost by breaking relationships.

In the Old Testament, God gives the Israelites laws on how to conduct their society as image bearers of him. People often refer to these as the Ten Commandments. But the book of Deuteronomy adds a few more to the list—more than 600! God gave his people these laws because they didn't naturally do what was right and just.

The Israelites didn't view God's laws as arbitrary dos and don'ts that God created just to make them miserable. They were intended, in part, to create order for their society. They were also intended, in part, to let the Israelites know what the character of God is like. The law was a signpost for free travelers. People were supposed to check out the Israelites and get a picture of God.

They'd seen what God is like in terms of power and deliverance when they crossed the Red Sea. But at Mount Sinai they see God's heart. They see God's character. They see what kind of souls they were created to have—large souls, ordered and free. That's the spirit behind the Law of God.

BUILDING

FAITH

WISDOM

STRENGTH

with the LORD. ³⁰When Aaron and all the Israelites saw Moses, his face was radiant, and they were afraid to come near him. ³¹But Moses called to them; so Aaron and all the leaders of the community came back to him, and he spoke to them. ³²Afterward all the Israelites came near him, and he gave them all the commands the LORD had given him on Mount Sinai.

³³When Moses finished speaking to them, he put a veil over his face. ³⁴But whenever he entered the LORD's presence to speak with him, he removed the veil until he came out. And when he came out and told the Israelites what he had been commanded, ³⁵they saw that his face was radiant. Then Moses would put the veil back over his face until he went in to speak with the LORD.

Sabbath Regulations

35 Moses assembled the whole Israelite community and said to them, "These are the things the LORD has commanded you to do: ²For six days, work is to be done, but the seventh day shall be your holy day, a day of sabbath rest to the LORD. Whoever does any work on it is to be put to death. ³Do not light a fire in any of your dwellings on the Sabbath day."

Materials for the Tabernacle

⁴Moses said to the whole Israelite community, "This is what the LORD has commanded: ⁵From what you have, take an offering for the LORD. Everyone who is willing is to bring to the LORD an offering of gold, silver and bronze; ⁶blue, purple and scarlet yarn and fine linen; goat hair; ⁷ram skins dyed red and another type of durable leather[a]; acacia wood; ⁸olive oil for the light; spices for the anointing oil and for the fragrant incense; ⁹and onyx stones and other gems to be mounted on the ephod and breastpiece.

¹⁰"All who are skilled among you are to come and make everything the LORD has commanded: ¹¹the tabernacle with its tent and its covering, clasps, frames, crossbars, posts and bases; ¹²the ark with its poles and the atonement cover and the curtain that shields it; ¹³the table with its poles and all its articles and the bread of the Presence; ¹⁴the lampstand that is for light with its ac-

cessories, lamps and oil for the light; ¹⁵the altar of incense with its poles, the anointing oil and the fragrant incense; the curtain for the doorway at the entrance to the tabernacle; ¹⁶the altar of burnt offering with its bronze grating, its poles and all its utensils; the bronze basin with its stand; ¹⁷the curtains of the courtyard with its posts and bases, and the curtain for the entrance to the courtyard; ¹⁸the tent pegs for the tabernacle and for the courtyard, and their ropes; ¹⁹the woven garments worn for ministering in the sanctuary—both the sacred garments for Aaron the priest and the garments for his sons when they serve as priests."

²⁰Then the whole Israelite community withdrew from Moses' presence, ²¹and everyone who was willing and whose heart moved them came and brought an offering to the LORD for the work on the tent of meeting, for all its service, and for the sacred garments. ²²All who were willing, men and women alike, came and brought gold jewelry of all kinds: brooches, earrings, rings and ornaments. They all presented their gold as a wave offering to the LORD. ²³Everyone who had blue, purple or scarlet yarn or fine linen, or goat hair, ram skins dyed red or the other durable leather brought them. ²⁴Those presenting an offering of silver or bronze brought it as an offering to the LORD, and everyone who had acacia wood for any part of the work brought it. ²⁵Every skilled woman spun with her hands and brought what she had spun—blue, purple or scarlet yarn or fine linen. ²⁶And all the women who were willing and had the skill spun the goat hair. ²⁷The leaders brought onyx stones and other gems to be mounted on the ephod and breastpiece. ²⁸They also brought spices and olive oil for the light and for the anointing oil and for the fragrant incense. ²⁹All the Israelite men and women who were willing brought to the LORD freewill offerings for all the work the LORD through Moses had commanded them to do.

Bezalel and Oholiab

³⁰Then Moses said to the Israelites, "See, the LORD has chosen Bezalel son of Uri, the son of Hur, of the tribe of Judah, ³¹and he has filled him with the Spirit of God, with wis-

---

[a] 7 Possibly the hides of large aquatic mammals; also in verse 23

dom, with understanding, with knowledge and with all kinds of skills— [32]to make artistic designs for work in gold, silver and bronze, [33]to cut and set stones, to work in wood and to engage in all kinds of artistic crafts. [34]And he has given both him and Oholiab son of Ahisamak, of the tribe of Dan, the ability to teach others. [35]He has filled them with skill to do all kinds of work as engravers, designers, embroiderers in blue, purple and scarlet yarn and fine linen, and weavers— all of them skilled workers and designers. [1]So Bezalel, Oholiab and every skilled person to whom the LORD has given skill and ability to know how to carry out all the work of constructing the sanctuary are to do the work just as the LORD has commanded."

36

[2]Then Moses summoned Bezalel and Oholiab and every skilled person to whom the LORD had given ability and who was willing to come and do the work. [3]They received from Moses all the offerings the Israelites had brought to carry out the work of constructing the sanctuary. And the people continued to bring freewill offerings morning after morning. [4]So all the skilled workers who were doing all the work on the sanctuary left what they were doing [5]and said to Moses, "The people are bringing more than enough for doing the work the LORD commanded to be done."

[6]Then Moses gave an order and they sent this word throughout the camp: "No man or woman is to make anything else as an offering for the sanctuary." And so the people were restrained from bringing more, [7]because what they already had was more than enough to do all the work.

The Tabernacle

[8]All those who were skilled among the workers made the tabernacle with ten curtains of finely twisted linen and blue, purple and scarlet yarn, with cherubim woven into them by expert hands. [9]All the curtains were the same size— twenty-eight cubits long and four cubits wide.[a] [10]They joined five of the curtains together and did the same with the other five. [11]Then they made loops of blue material along the edge of the end

curtain in one set, and the same was done with the end curtain in the other set. [12]They also made fifty loops on one curtain and fifty loops on the end curtain of the other set, with the loops opposite each other. [13]Then they made fifty gold clasps and used them to fasten the two sets of curtains together so that the tabernacle was a unit.

[14]They made curtains of goat hair for the tent over the tabernacle— eleven altogether. [15]All eleven curtains were the same size— thirty cubits long and four cubits wide.[b] [16]They joined five of the curtains into one set and the other six into another set. [17]Then they made fifty loops along the edge of the end curtain in one set and also along the edge of the end curtain in the other set. [18]They made fifty bronze clasps to fasten the tent together as a unit. [19]Then they made for the tent a covering of ram skins dyed red, and over that a covering of the other durable leather.[c]

[20]They made upright frames of acacia wood for the tabernacle. [21]Each frame was ten cubits long and a cubit and a half wide,[d] [22]with two projections set parallel to each other. They made all the frames of the tabernacle in this way. [23]They made twenty frames for the south side of the tabernacle [24]and made forty silver bases to go under them— two bases for each frame, one under each projection. [25]For the other side, the north side of the tabernacle, they made twenty frames [26]and forty silver bases— two under each frame. [27]They made six frames for the far end, that is, the west end of the tabernacle, [28]and two frames were made for the corners of the tabernacle at the far end. [29]At these two corners the frames were double from the bottom all the way to the top and fitted into a single ring; both were made alike. [30]So there were eight frames and sixteen silver bases— two under each frame.

[31]They also made crossbars of acacia wood: five for the frames on one side of the tabernacle, [32]five for those on the other side, and five for the frames on the west, at the far end of the tabernacle. [33]They made the center crossbar so that it extended from end to end at the middle of the frames. [34]They

---

[a] 9 That is, about 42 feet long and 6 feet wide or about 13 meters long and 1.8 meters wide   [b] 15 That is, about 45 feet long and 6 feet wide or about 14 meters long and 1.8 meters wide   [c] 19 Possibly the hides of large aquatic mammals (see 35:7)   [d] 21 That is, about 15 feet long and 2 1/4 feet wide or about 4.5 meters long and 68 centimeters wide

TRAINING YOUR TALENTS

READ: EXODUS 36:1-7

Your artwork might hang on the refrigerator at home or in a showcase at school.

The more you practice your craft, the more likely your art will land in a contest or exhibition. A handful of gifted artists even show up in the pages of Scripture.

Moses and the Israelites set out to build an elaborate tent according to God's design, a place set aside for worshiping God. Detailed instructions for this "tabernacle" or "dwelling" fill the book of Exodus. The tent was a special place of God's presence, and at the end of Exodus his shining glory moves into the tent (Exodus 40:34).

God gave artists like Bezalel every gift they needed to fill his tent with beautiful designs. The Spirit gave them wisdom, knowledge, and every kind of skill "to make artistic designs for work in gold, silver and bronze, to cut and set stones, to work in wood and to engage in all kinds of artistic crafts" (35:32-33).

BUILDING
FAITH
WISDOM
STRENGTH

The Lord has loaded you up with a unique mix of gifts (1 Corinthians 12:7). You can't choose what you're good at—that's up to God—but you can choose to practice the skills he builds into you. Whatever your skill, he intends for you to put it to use for your growth, others' good, and his glory.

overlaid the frames with gold and made gold rings to hold the crossbars. They also overlaid the crossbars with gold.

³⁵They made the curtain of blue, purple and scarlet yarn and finely twisted linen, with cherubim woven into it by a skilled worker. ³⁶They made four posts of acacia wood for it and overlaid them with gold. They made gold hooks for them and cast their four silver bases. ³⁷For the entrance to the tent they made a curtain of blue, purple and scarlet yarn and finely twisted linen — the work of an embroiderer; ³⁸and they made five posts with hooks for them. They overlaid the tops of the posts and their bands with gold and made their five bases of bronze.

The Ark

37 Bezalel made the ark of acacia wood — two and a half cubits long, a cubit and a half wide, and a cubit and a half high.[a] ²He overlaid it with pure gold, both inside and out, and made a gold molding around it. ³He cast four gold rings for it and fastened them to its four feet, with two rings on one side and two rings on the other. ⁴Then he made poles of acacia wood and overlaid them with gold. ⁵And he inserted the poles into the rings on the sides of the ark to carry it.

⁶He made the atonement cover of pure gold — two and a half cubits long and a cubit and a half wide. ⁷Then he made two cherubim out of hammered gold at the ends of the cover. ⁸He made one cherub on one end and the second cherub on the other; at the two ends he made them of one piece with the cover. ⁹The cherubim had their wings spread upward, overshadowing the cover with them. The cherubim faced each other, looking toward the cover.

The Table

¹⁰They[b] made the table of acacia wood — two cubits long, a cubit wide and a cubit and a half high.[c] ¹¹Then they overlaid it with pure gold and made a gold molding around it. ¹²They also made around it a rim a handbreadth[d] wide and put a gold molding on the rim. ¹³They cast four gold rings for the table and fastened them to the four corners, where the four legs were. ¹⁴The rings were put close to the rim to hold the poles used in carrying the table. ¹⁵The poles for carrying the table were made of acacia wood and were overlaid with gold. ¹⁶And they made from pure gold the articles for the table — its plates and dishes and bowls and its pitchers for the pouring out of drink offerings.

The Lampstand

¹⁷They made the lampstand of pure gold. They hammered out its base and shaft, and made its flowerlike cups, buds and blossoms of one piece with them. ¹⁸Six branches extended from the sides of the lampstand — three on one side and three on the other. ¹⁹Three cups shaped like almond flowers with buds and blossoms were on one branch, three on the next branch and the same for all six branches extending from the lampstand. ²⁰And on the lampstand were four cups shaped like almond flowers with buds and blossoms. ²¹One bud was under the first pair of branches extending from the lampstand, a second bud under the second pair, and a third bud under the third pair — six branches in all. ²²The buds and the branches were all of one piece with the lampstand, hammered out of pure gold.

²³They made its seven lamps, as well as its wick trimmers and trays, of pure gold. ²⁴They made the lampstand and all its accessories from one talent[e] of pure gold.

The Altar of Incense

²⁵They made the altar of incense out of acacia wood. It was square, a cubit long and a cubit wide and two cubits high[f] — its horns of one piece with it. ²⁶They overlaid the top and all the sides and the horns with pure gold, and made a gold molding around it. ²⁷They made two gold rings below the molding — two on each of the opposite sides — to hold the poles used to carry it. ²⁸They made the poles of acacia wood and overlaid them with gold.

---

[a] 1 That is, about 3 3/4 feet long and 2 1/4 feet wide and high or about 1.1 meters long and 68 centimeters wide and high; similarly in verse 6   [b] 10 Or *He*; also in verses 11-29   [c] 10 That is, about 3 feet long, 1 1/2 feet wide and 2 1/4 feet high or about 90 centimeters long, 45 centimeters wide and 68 centimeters high   [d] 12 That is, about 3 inches or about 7.5 centimeters   [e] 24 That is, about 75 pounds or about 34 kilograms   [f] 25 That is, about 1 1/2 feet long and wide and 3 feet high or about 45 centimeters long and wide and 90 centimeters high

29They also made the sacred anointing oil and the pure, fragrant incense — the work of a perfumer.

The Altar of Burnt Offering

38 They[a] built the altar of burnt offering of acacia wood, three cubits[b] high; it was square, five cubits long and five cubits wide.[c] 2They made a horn at each of the four corners, so that the horns and the altar were of one piece, and they overlaid the altar with bronze. 3They made all its utensils of bronze — its pots, shovels, sprinkling bowls, meat forks and firepans. 4They made a grating for the altar, a bronze network, to be under its ledge, halfway up the altar. 5They cast bronze rings to hold the poles for the four corners of the bronze grating. 6They made the poles of acacia wood and overlaid them with bronze. 7They inserted the poles into the rings so they would be on the sides of the altar for carrying it. They made it hollow, out of boards.

The Basin for Washing

8They made the bronze basin and its bronze stand from the mirrors of the women who served at the entrance to the tent of meeting.

The Courtyard

9Next they made the courtyard. The south side was a hundred cubits[d] long and had curtains of finely twisted linen, 10with twenty posts and twenty bronze bases, and with silver hooks and bands on the posts. 11The north side was also a hundred cubits long and had twenty posts and twenty bronze bases, with silver hooks and bands on the posts.

12The west end was fifty cubits[e] wide and had curtains, with ten posts and ten bases, with silver hooks and bands on the posts. 13The east end, toward the sunrise, was also fifty cubits wide. 14Curtains fifteen cubits[f] long were on one side of the entrance, with three posts and three bases, 15and curtains fifteen cubits long were on the other side of the entrance to the courtyard, with three posts and three bases. 16All the curtains around the courtyard were of finely twisted linen. 17The bases for the posts were bronze. The hooks and bands on the posts were silver, and their tops were overlaid with silver; so all the posts of the courtyard had silver bands.

18The curtain for the entrance to the courtyard was made of blue, purple and scarlet yarn and finely twisted linen — the work of an embroiderer. It was twenty cubits[g] long and, like the curtains of the courtyard, five cubits[h] high, 19with four posts and four bronze bases. Their hooks and bands were silver, and their tops were overlaid with silver. 20All the tent pegs of the tabernacle and of the surrounding courtyard were bronze.

The Materials Used

21These are the amounts of the materials used for the tabernacle, the tabernacle of the covenant law, which were recorded at Moses' command by the Levites under the direction of Ithamar son of Aaron, the priest. 22(Bezalel son of Uri, the son of Hur, of the tribe of Judah, made everything the LORD commanded Moses; 23with him was Oholiab son of Ahisamak, of the tribe of Dan — an engraver and designer, and an embroiderer in blue, purple and scarlet yarn and fine linen.) 24The total amount of the gold from the wave offering used for all the work on the sanctuary was 29 talents and 730 shekels,[i] according to the sanctuary shekel.

25The silver obtained from those of the community who were counted in the census was 100 talents[j] and 1,775 shekels,[k] according to the sanctuary shekel — 26one beka per person, that is, half a shekel,[l] according to the sanctuary shekel, from everyone who had crossed over to those counted, twenty years old or more, a total of 603,550 men. 27The 100 talents of silver were used to cast the bases for the sanctuary and for the curtain — 100 bases from the 100 talents, one

---

a 1 Or *He*; also in verses 2-9   *b 1* That is, about 4 1/2 feet or about 1.4 meters   *c 1* That is, about 7 1/2 feet or about 2.3 meters long and wide   *d 9* That is, about 150 feet or about 45 meters   *e 12* That is, about 75 feet or about 23 meters   *f 14* That is, about 22 feet or about 6.8 meters   *g 18* That is, about 30 feet or about 9 meters   *h 18* That is, about 7 1/2 feet or about 2.3 meters   *i 24* The weight of the gold was a little over a ton or about 1 metric ton.   *j 25* That is, about 3 3/4 tons or about 3.4 metric tons; also in verse 27   *k 25* That is, about 44 pounds or about 20 kilograms; also in verse 28   *l 26* That is, about 1/5 ounce or about 5.7 grams talent for each base. [28] They used the 1,775 shekels to make the hooks for the posts, to overlay the tops of the posts, and to make their bands.

[29] The bronze from the wave offering was 70 talents and 2,400 shekels.[a] [30] They used it to make the bases for the entrance to the tent of meeting, the bronze altar with its bronze grating and all its utensils, [31] the bases for the surrounding courtyard and those for its entrance and all the tent pegs for the tabernacle and those for the surrounding courtyard.

The Priestly Garments

39 From the blue, purple and scarlet yarn they made woven garments for ministering in the sanctuary. They also made sacred garments for Aaron, as the LORD commanded Moses.

The Ephod

[2] They[b] made the ephod of gold, and of blue, purple and scarlet yarn, and of finely twisted linen. [3] They hammered out thin sheets of gold and cut strands to be worked into the blue, purple and scarlet yarn and fine linen — the work of skilled hands. [4] They made shoulder pieces for the ephod, which were attached to two of its corners, so it could be fastened. [5] Its skillfully woven waistband was like it — of one piece with the ephod and made with gold, and with blue, purple and scarlet yarn, and with finely twisted linen, as the LORD commanded Moses.

[6] They mounted the onyx stones in gold filigree settings and engraved them like a seal with the names of the sons of Israel. [7] Then they fastened them on the shoulder pieces of the ephod as memorial stones for the sons of Israel, as the LORD commanded Moses.

The Breastpiece

[8] They fashioned the breastpiece — the work of a skilled craftsman. They made it like the ephod: of gold, and of blue, purple and scarlet yarn, and of finely twisted linen. [9] It was square — a span[c] long and a span wide — and folded double. [10] Then they mounted four rows of precious stones on it. The first row was carnelian, chrysolite and beryl; [11] the second row was turquoise, lapis lazuli

and emerald; [12] the third row was jacinth, agate and amethyst; [13] the fourth row was topaz, onyx and jasper.[d] They were mounted in gold filigree settings. [14] There were twelve stones, one for each of the names of the sons of Israel, each engraved like a seal with the name of one of the twelve tribes.

[15] For the breastpiece they made braided chains of pure gold, like a rope. [16] They made two gold filigree settings and two gold rings, and fastened the rings to two of the corners of the breastpiece. [17] They fastened the two gold chains to the rings at the corners of the breastpiece, [18] and the other ends of the chains to the two settings, attaching them to the shoulder pieces of the ephod at the front. [19] They made two gold rings and attached them to the other two corners of the breastpiece on the inside edge next to the ephod. [20] Then they made two more gold rings and attached them to the bottom of the shoulder pieces on the front of the ephod, close to the seam just above the waistband of the ephod. [21] They tied the rings of the breastpiece to the rings of the ephod with blue cord, connecting it to the waistband so that the breastpiece would not swing out from the ephod — as the LORD commanded Moses.

Other Priestly Garments

[22] They made the robe of the ephod entirely of blue cloth — the work of a weaver — [23] with an opening in the center of the robe like the opening of a collar,[e] and a band around this opening, so that it would not tear. [24] They made pomegranates of blue, purple and scarlet yarn and finely twisted linen around the hem of the robe. [25] And they made bells of pure gold and attached them around the hem between the pomegranates. [26] The bells and pomegranates alternated around the hem of the robe to be worn for ministering, as the LORD commanded Moses.

[27] For Aaron and his sons, they made tunics of fine linen — the work of a weaver — [28] and the turban of fine linen, the linen caps and the undergarments of finely twisted linen. [29] The sash was made of finely twisted linen and blue, purple and scarlet yarn — the work of an embroiderer — as the LORD commanded Moses.

---

[a] 29 The weight of the bronze was about 2 1/2 tons or about 2.4 metric tons.   [b] 2 Or He; also in verses 7, 8 and 22   [c] 9 That is, about 9 inches or about 23 centimeters   [d] 13 The precise identification of some of these precious stones is uncertain.   [e] 23 The meaning of the Hebrew for this word is uncertain.

[30]They made the plate, the sacred emblem, out of pure gold and engraved on it, like an inscription on a seal: HOLY TO THE LORD. [31]Then they fastened a blue cord to it to attach it to the turban, as the LORD commanded Moses.

Moses Inspects the Tabernacle

[32]So all the work on the tabernacle, the tent of meeting, was completed. The Israelites did everything just as the LORD commanded Moses. [33]Then they brought the tabernacle to Moses: the tent and all its furnishings, its clasps, frames, crossbars, posts and bases; [34]the covering of ram skins dyed red and the covering of another durable leather[a] and the shielding curtain; [35]the ark of the covenant law with its poles and the atonement cover; [36]the table with all its articles and the bread of the Presence; [37]the pure gold lampstand with its row of lamps and all its accessories, and the olive oil for the light; [38]the gold altar, the anointing oil, the fragrant incense, and the curtain for the entrance to the tent; [39]the bronze altar with its bronze grating, its poles and all its utensils; the basin with its stand; [40]the curtains of the courtyard with its posts and bases, and the curtain for the entrance to the courtyard; the ropes and tent pegs for the courtyard; all the furnishings for the tabernacle, the tent of meeting; [41]and the woven garments worn for ministering in the sanctuary, both the sacred garments for Aaron the priest and the garments for his sons when serving as priests.

[42]The Israelites had done all the work just as the LORD had commanded Moses. [43]Moses inspected the work and saw that they had done it just as the LORD had commanded. So Moses blessed them.

Setting Up the Tabernacle

40 Then the LORD said to Moses: [2]"Set up the tabernacle, the tent of meeting, on the first day of the first month. [3]Place the ark of the covenant law in it and shield the ark with the curtain. [4]Bring in the table and set out what belongs on it. Then bring in the lampstand and set up its lamps. [5]Place the gold altar of incense in front of the ark of the covenant law and put the curtain at the entrance to the tabernacle.

[6]"Place the altar of burnt offering in front of the entrance to the tabernacle, the tent of meeting; [7]place the basin between the tent of meeting and the altar and put water in it. [8]Set up the courtyard around it and put the curtain at the entrance to the courtyard.

[9]"Take the anointing oil and anoint the tabernacle and everything in it; consecrate it and all its furnishings, and it will be holy. [10]Then anoint the altar of burnt offering and all its utensils; consecrate the altar, and it will be most holy. [11]Anoint the basin and its stand and consecrate them.

[12]"Bring Aaron and his sons to the entrance to the tent of meeting and wash them with water. [13]Then dress Aaron in the sacred garments, anoint him and consecrate him so he may serve me as priest. [14]Bring his sons and dress them in tunics. [15]Anoint them just as you anointed their father, so they may serve me as priests. Their anointing will be to a priesthood that will continue throughout their generations." [16]Moses did everything just as the LORD commanded him.

[17]So the tabernacle was set up on the first day of the first month in the second year. [18]When Moses set up the tabernacle, he put the bases in place, erected the frames, inserted the crossbars and set up the posts. [19]Then he spread the tent over the tabernacle and put the covering over the tent, as the LORD commanded him.

[20]He took the tablets of the covenant law and placed them in the ark, attached the poles to the ark and put the atonement cover over it. [21]Then he brought the ark into the tabernacle and hung the shielding curtain and shielded the ark of the covenant law, as the LORD commanded him.

[22]Moses placed the table in the tent of meeting on the north side of the tabernacle outside the curtain [23]and set out the bread on it before the LORD, as the LORD commanded him.

[24]He placed the lampstand in the tent of meeting opposite the table on the south side of the tabernacle [25]and set up the lamps before the LORD, as the LORD commanded him.

[26]Moses placed the gold altar in the tent of meeting in front of the curtain [27]and burned fragrant incense on it, as the LORD commanded him.

[28]Then he put up the curtain at the en-

---

[a] 34 Possibly the hides of large aquatic mammals

trance to the tabernacle. [29] He set the altar of burnt offering near the entrance to the tabernacle, the tent of meeting, and offered on it burnt offerings and grain offerings, as the LORD commanded him.

[30] He placed the basin between the tent of meeting and the altar and put water in it for washing, [31] and Moses and Aaron and his sons used it to wash their hands and feet. [32] They washed whenever they entered the tent of meeting or approached the altar, as the LORD commanded Moses.

[33] Then Moses set up the courtyard around the tabernacle and altar and put up the curtain at the entrance to the courtyard. And so Moses finished the work.

The Glory of the LORD

[34] Then the cloud covered the tent of meeting, and the glory of the LORD filled the tabernacle. [35] Moses could not enter the tent of meeting because the cloud had settled on it, and the glory of the LORD filled the tabernacle.

[36] In all the travels of the Israelites, whenever the cloud lifted from above the tabernacle, they would set out; [37] but if the cloud did not lift, they did not set out — until the day it lifted. [38] So the cloud of the LORD was over the tabernacle by day, and fire was in the cloud by night, in the sight of all the Israelites during all their travels.

LEVITICUS

➤ **WHEN DID THIS HAPPEN?**

During the 1400s B.C. while the Israelites were traveling in the desert

➤ **WHO IS IN THIS BOOK?**

Moses
Aaron
Nadab
Abihu

➤ **VERSES YOU MIGHT RECOGNIZE**

LEVITICUS 11:45

"I am the LORD, who brought you up out of Egypt to be your God; therefore be holy, because I am holy."

LEVITICUS 19:37

"Keep all my decrees and all my laws and follow them. I am the LORD."

WHAT'S IT ABOUT?

If you're trying to read through the Bible, you might find yourself getting a little bogged down when you reach Leviticus. Offerings. Clean and unclean foods. Purification after childbirth. Skin diseases. What is the point of all of these strange rules and regulations? When Moses led the Israelites out of Egypt, they were a brand-new nation. They needed to learn to live in a way that would set them apart from the nations around them who didn't believe in the one true God. Through Moses, God gave the Israelites a new set of rules that would allow them to live in a way that reflected him and also keep them healthy and safe.

These rules, also called "the law," would highlight how people must work hard to obey God and to live up to his standard of holiness. When Jesus came, he kept the law perfectly, and his sacrifice paid the price for every sin ever committed.

In Leviticus, God also appointed Aaron and his sons to serve in the tent of meeting and mediate for the people as priests. Aaron's sons, Nadab and Abihu, didn't follow God's instructions for serving and died for their disobedience. This shows that God was serious about the people honoring him and obeying his commands.

The Burnt Offering

1 The Lord called to Moses and spoke to him from the tent of meeting. He said, [2] "Speak to the Israelites and say to them: 'When anyone among you brings an offering to the Lord, bring as your offering an animal from either the herd or the flock.

[3] "'If the offering is a burnt offering from the herd, you are to offer a male without defect. You must present it at the entrance to the tent of meeting so that it will be acceptable to the Lord. [4] You are to lay your hand on the head of the burnt offering, and it will be accepted on your behalf to make atonement for you. [5] You are to slaughter the young bull before the Lord, and then Aaron's sons the priests shall bring the blood and splash it against the sides of the altar at the entrance to the tent of meeting. [6] You are to skin the burnt offering and cut it into pieces. [7] The sons of Aaron the priest are to put fire on the altar and arrange wood on the fire. [8] Then Aaron's sons the priests shall arrange the pieces, including the head and the fat, on the wood that is burning on the altar. [9] You are to wash the internal organs and the legs with water, and the priest is to burn all of it on the altar. It is a burnt offering, a food offering, an aroma pleasing to the Lord.

[10] "'If the offering is a burnt offering from the flock, from either the sheep or the goats, you are to offer a male without defect. [11] You are to slaughter it at the north side of the altar before the Lord, and Aaron's sons the priests shall splash its blood against the sides of the altar. [12] You are to cut it into pieces, and the priest shall arrange them, including the head and the fat, on the wood that is burning on the altar. [13] You are to wash the internal organs and the legs with water, and the priest is to bring all of them and burn them on the altar. It is a burnt offering, a food offering, an aroma pleasing to the Lord.

[14] "'If the offering to the Lord is a burnt offering of birds, you are to offer a dove or a young pigeon. [15] The priest shall bring it to the altar, wring off the head and burn it on the altar; its blood shall be drained out on the side of the altar. [16] He is to remove the crop and the feathers[a] and throw them down east of the altar where the ashes are. [17] He shall tear it open by the wings, not dividing it completely, and then the priest shall burn it on the wood that is burning on the altar. It is a burnt offering, a food offering, an aroma pleasing to the Lord.

The Grain Offering

2 "'When anyone brings a grain offering to the Lord, their offering is to be of the finest flour. They are to pour olive oil on it, put incense on it [2] and take it to Aaron's sons the priests. The priest shall take a handful of the flour and oil, together with all the incense, and burn this as a memorial[b] portion on the altar, a food offering, an aroma pleasing to the Lord. [3] The rest of the grain offering belongs to Aaron and his sons; it is a most holy part of the food offerings presented to the Lord.

[4] "'If you bring a grain offering baked in an oven, it is to consist of the finest flour: either thick loaves made without yeast and with olive oil mixed in or thin loaves made without yeast and brushed with olive oil. [5] If your grain offering is prepared on a griddle, it is to be made of the finest flour mixed with oil, and without yeast. [6] Crumble it and pour oil on it; it is a grain offering. [7] If your grain offering is cooked in a pan, it is to be made of the finest flour and some olive oil. [8] Bring the grain offering made of these things to the Lord; present it to the priest, who shall take it to the altar. [9] He shall take out the memorial portion from the grain offering and burn it on the altar as a food offering, an aroma pleasing to the Lord. [10] The rest of the grain offering belongs to Aaron and his sons; it is a

[a] 16 Or *crop with its contents*; the meaning of the Hebrew for this word is uncertain.
[b] 2 Or *representative*; also in verses 9 and 16

most holy part of the food offerings presented to the LORD.

¹¹ "'Every grain offering you bring to the LORD must be made without yeast, for you are not to burn any yeast or honey in a food offering presented to the LORD. ¹²You may bring them to the LORD as an offering of the firstfruits, but they are not to be offered on the altar as a pleasing aroma. ¹³Season all your grain offerings with salt. Do not leave the salt of the covenant of your God out of your grain offerings; add salt to all your offerings.

¹⁴ "'If you bring a grain offering of firstfruits to the LORD, offer crushed heads of new grain roasted in the fire. ¹⁵Put oil and incense on it; it is a grain offering. ¹⁶The priest shall burn the memorial portion of the crushed grain and the oil, together with all the incense, as a food offering presented to the LORD.

The Fellowship Offering

3 "'If your offering is a fellowship offering, and you offer an animal from the herd, whether male or female, you are to present before the LORD an animal without defect. ²You are to lay your hand on the head of your offering and slaughter it at the entrance to the tent of meeting. Then Aaron's sons the priests shall splash the blood against the sides of the altar. ³From the fellowship offering you are to bring a food offering to the LORD: the internal organs and all the fat that is connected to them, ⁴both kidneys with the fat on them near the loins, and the long lobe of the liver, which you will remove with the kidneys. ⁵Then Aaron's sons are to burn it on the altar on top of the burnt offering that is lying on the burning wood; it is a food offering, an aroma pleasing to the LORD.

⁶ "'If you offer an animal from the flock as a fellowship offering to the LORD, you are to offer a male or female without defect. ⁷If you offer a lamb, you are to present it before the LORD, ⁸lay your hand on its head and slaughter it in front of the tent of meeting. Then Aaron's sons shall splash its blood against the sides of the altar. ⁹From the fellowship offering you are to bring a food offering to the LORD: its fat, the entire fat tail cut off close to the backbone, the internal organs and all the fat that is connected to them, ¹⁰both kidneys with the fat on them near the loins, and the long lobe of the liver, which you will remove with the kidneys. ¹¹The priest shall burn them on the altar as a food offering presented to the LORD.

¹² "'If your offering is a goat, you are to present it before the LORD, ¹³lay your hand on its head and slaughter it in front of the tent of meeting. Then Aaron's sons shall splash its blood against the sides of the altar. ¹⁴From what you offer you are to present this food offering to the LORD: the internal organs and all the fat that is connected to them, ¹⁵both kidneys with the fat on them near the loins, and the long lobe of the liver, which you will remove with the kidneys. ¹⁶The priest shall burn them on the altar as a food offering, a pleasing aroma. All the fat is the LORD's.

¹⁷ "'This is a lasting ordinance for the generations to come, wherever you live: You must not eat any fat or any blood.'"

The Sin Offering

4 The LORD said to Moses, ²"Say to the Israelites: 'When anyone sins unintentionally and does what is forbidden in any of the LORD's commands—

³ "'If the anointed priest sins, bringing guilt on the people, he must bring to the LORD a young bull without defect as a sin offering[a] for the sin he has committed. ⁴He is to present the bull at the entrance to the tent of meeting before the LORD. He is to lay his hand on its head and slaughter it there before the LORD. ⁵Then the anointed priest shall take some of the bull's blood and carry it into the tent of meeting. ⁶He is to dip his finger into the blood and sprinkle some of it seven times before the LORD, in front of the curtain of the sanctuary. ⁷The priest shall then put some of the blood on the horns of the altar of fragrant incense that is before the LORD in the tent of meeting. The rest of the bull's blood he shall pour out at the base of the altar of burnt offering at the entrance to the tent of meeting. ⁸He shall remove all the fat from the bull of the sin offering—all the fat that is connected to the internal organs, ⁹both kidneys with the fat on them near the loins, and the long lobe of the liver, which he will remove with the kidneys—¹⁰just as

---

ᵃ 3 Or *purification offering*; here and throughout this chapter

SALTY GRAIN REQUIRED

READ: LEVITICUS 2:11-13

When a friend lifts a law from Leviticus to prove how outdated the Bible appears, the best way to answer is to share why these laws are in the Bible in the first place. Laws reveal God's interaction with broken humans, helping us understand how God wanted a fallen, nomadic people to live in a fallen world thousands of years ago. Laws tell us about God's character, but his laws to the Hebrews are neither comprehensive nor universal. These laws are literal commands to the Jewish people, but God did not intend every human to cut and paste every Hebrew law into their lives. Perhaps we misunderstand that we should, because of our exposure to and appreciation of laws such as the Ten Commandments. But the laws in Scripture are not automatic commands for non-Jews.

BUILDING FAITH WISDOM STRENGTH

To determine what applies to non-Jews today, we need a little background to discover the categories of laws. Biblical law books combine laws for an entire nation about morality, health, civil orderliness, and ceremony. Compare what it might be like if a law book in America today listed laws against murder and against jaywalking in one section. We know the difference between them in our culture, but people 2,000 years from now may not. If we can cultivate the same awareness when looking at the early Jewish culture, we can share these distinctions when we talk with friends.

the fat is removed from the ox[a] sacrificed as a fellowship offering. Then the priest shall burn them on the altar of burnt offering. [11]But the hide of the bull and all its flesh, as well as the head and legs, the internal organs and the intestines— [12]that is, all the rest of the bull—he must take outside the camp to a place ceremonially clean, where the ashes are thrown, and burn it there in a wood fire on the ash heap.

[13]" 'If the whole Israelite community sins unintentionally and does what is forbidden in any of the LORD's commands, even though the community is unaware of the matter, when they realize their guilt [14]and the sin they committed becomes known, the assembly must bring a young bull as a sin offering and present it before the tent of meeting. [15]The elders of the community are to lay their hands on the bull's head before the LORD, and the bull shall be slaughtered before the LORD. [16]Then the anointed priest is to take some of the bull's blood into the tent of meeting. [17]He shall dip his finger into the blood and sprinkle it before the LORD seven times in front of the curtain. [18]He is to put some of the blood on the horns of the altar that is before the LORD in the tent of meeting. The rest of the blood he shall pour out at the base of the altar of burnt offering at the entrance to the tent of meeting. [19]He shall remove all the fat from it and burn it on the altar, [20]and do with this bull just as he did with the bull for the sin offering. In this way the priest will make atonement for the community, and they will be forgiven. [21]Then he shall take the bull outside the camp and burn it as he burned the first bull. This is the sin offering for the community.

[22]" 'When a leader sins unintentionally and does what is forbidden in any of the commands of the LORD his God, when he realizes his guilt [23]and the sin he has committed becomes known, he must bring as his offering a male goat without defect. [24]He is to lay his hand on the goat's head and slaughter it at the place where the burnt offering is slaughtered before the LORD. It is a sin offering. [25]Then the priest shall take some of the blood of the sin offering with his finger and put it on the horns of the altar of burnt offer-

ing and pour out the rest of the blood at the base of the altar. [26]He shall burn all the fat on the altar as he burned the fat of the fellowship offering. In this way the priest will make atonement for the leader's sin, and he will be forgiven.

[27]" 'If any member of the community sins unintentionally and does what is forbidden in any of the LORD's commands, when they realize their guilt [28]and the sin they have committed becomes known, they must bring as their offering for the sin they committed a female goat without defect. [29]They are to lay their hand on the head of the sin offering and slaughter it at the place of the burnt offering. [30]Then the priest is to take some of the blood with his finger and put it on the horns of the altar of burnt offering and pour out the rest of the blood at the base of the altar. [31]They shall remove all the fat, just as the fat is removed from the fellowship offering, and the priest shall burn it on the altar as an aroma pleasing to the LORD. In this way the priest will make atonement for them, and they will be forgiven.

[32]" 'If someone brings a lamb as their sin offering, they are to bring a female without defect. [33]They are to lay their hand on its head and slaughter it for a sin offering at the place where the burnt offering is slaughtered. [34]Then the priest shall take some of the blood of the sin offering with his finger and put it on the horns of the altar of burnt offering and pour out the rest of the blood at the base of the altar. [35]They shall remove all the fat, just as the fat is removed from the lamb of the fellowship offering, and the priest shall burn it on the altar on top of the food offerings presented to the LORD. In this way the priest will make atonement for them for the sin they have committed, and they will be forgiven.

5 " 'If anyone sins because they do not speak up when they hear a public charge to testify regarding something they have seen or learned about, they will be held responsible.

[2]" 'If anyone becomes aware that they are guilty—if they unwittingly touch anything ceremonially unclean (whether the carcass of an unclean animal, wild or domestic, or of

---

[a] 10 The Hebrew word can refer to either male or female.

any unclean creature that moves along the ground) and they are unaware that they have become unclean, but then they come to realize their guilt; [3]or if they touch human uncleanness (anything that would make them unclean) even though they are unaware of it, but then they learn of it and realize their guilt; [4]or if anyone thoughtlessly takes an oath to do anything, whether good or evil (in any matter one might carelessly swear about) even though they are unaware of it, but then they learn of it and realize their guilt — [5]when anyone becomes aware that they are guilty in any of these matters, they must confess in what way they have sinned. [6]As a penalty for the sin they have committed, they must bring to the LORD a female lamb or goat from the flock as a sin offering[a]; and the priest shall make atonement for them for their sin.

[7]"'Anyone who cannot afford a lamb is to bring two doves or two young pigeons to the LORD as a penalty for their sin — one for a sin offering and the other for a burnt offering. [8]They are to bring them to the priest, who shall first offer the one for the sin offering. He is to wring its head from its neck, not dividing it completely, [9]and is to splash some of the blood of the sin offering against the side of the altar; the rest of the blood must be drained out at the base of the altar. It is a sin offering. [10]The priest shall then offer the other as a burnt offering in the prescribed way and make atonement for them for the sin they have committed, and they will be forgiven.

[11]"'If, however, they cannot afford two doves or two young pigeons, they are to bring as an offering for their sin a tenth of an ephah[b] of the finest flour for a sin offering. They must not put olive oil or incense on it, because it is a sin offering. [12]They are to bring it to the priest, who shall take a handful of it as a memorial[c] portion and burn it on the altar on top of the food offerings presented to the LORD. It is a sin offering. [13]In this way the priest will make atonement for them for any of these sins they have committed, and they will be forgiven. The rest of the offering will belong to the priest, as in the case of the grain offering.'"

The Guilt Offering

[14]The LORD said to Moses: [15]"When anyone is unfaithful to the LORD by sinning unintentionally in regard to any of the LORD's holy things, they are to bring to the LORD as a penalty a ram from the flock, one without defect and of the proper value in silver, according to the sanctuary shekel.[d] It is a guilt offering. [16]They must make restitution for what they have failed to do in regard to the holy things, pay an additional penalty of a fifth of its value and give it all to the priest. The priest will make atonement for them with the ram as a guilt offering, and they will be forgiven.

[17]"If anyone sins and does what is forbidden in any of the LORD's commands, even though they do not know it, they are guilty and will be held responsible. [18]They are to bring to the priest as a guilt offering a ram from the flock, one without defect and of the proper value. In this way the priest will make atonement for them for the wrong they have committed unintentionally, and they will be forgiven. [19]It is a guilt offering; they have been guilty of[e] wrongdoing against the LORD."

6[f] The LORD said to Moses: [2]"If anyone sins and is unfaithful to the LORD by deceiving a neighbor about something entrusted to them or left in their care or about something stolen, or if they cheat their neighbor, [3]or if they find lost property and lie about it, or if they swear falsely about any such sin that people may commit — [4]when they sin in any of these ways and realize their guilt, they must return what they have stolen or taken by extortion, or what was entrusted to them, or the lost property they found, [5]or whatever it was they swore falsely about. They must make restitution in full, add a fifth of the value to it and give it all to the owner on the day they present their guilt offering. [6]And as a penalty they must bring to the priest, that is, to the LORD, their guilt offering, a ram from the flock, one without defect and of the proper value. [7]In this way the priest will make atonement for them before the LORD, and they will be forgiven for any of the things they did that made them guilty."

WEIGHT OF SIN

READ: LEVITICUS 5:13

The New Testament clarifies a fact you may have already figured out. All the Old Testament animal sacrifices you read about in Leviticus couldn't fix the problem of human sin. Hebrews 10:4 says, "It is impossible for the blood of bulls and goats to take away sins." So what was God thinking when he gave his people these detailed instructions about animal sacrifice?

The New Testament explains that the blood of those animals made people "outwardly clean" (Hebrews 9:13), offering a temporary solution to humankind's long-term problem of sin. They also taught God's people the high price of wrongdoing, serving as an "annual reminder of sins" (10:3). Every time an animal bled and died, people saw with their own eyes the horrors of evil.

And those sacrifices were a foreshadowing of what lay ahead. At God's right time, Jesus came and offered himself as a complete and permanent payment for every human sin. Hebrews 9:26 says, "He has appeared once for all at the culmination of the ages to do away with sin by the sacrifice of himself."

It's easy to think sin can't possibly be as bad as the Bible says. But the only real way to understand the true awfulness of evil is to measure it the way God does. Sin is so bad Jesus had to die for it.

BUILDING

FAITH

WISDOM

STRENGTH

The Burnt Offering

[8]The LORD said to Moses: [9]"Give Aaron and his sons this command: 'These are the regulations for the burnt offering: The burnt offering is to remain on the altar hearth throughout the night, till morning, and the fire must be kept burning on the altar. [10]The priest shall then put on his linen clothes, with linen undergarments next to his body, and shall remove the ashes of the burnt offering that the fire has consumed on the altar and place them beside the altar. [11]Then he is to take off these clothes and put on others, and carry the ashes outside the camp to a place that is ceremonially clean. [12]The fire on the altar must be kept burning; it must not go out. Every morning the priest is to add firewood and arrange the burnt offering on the fire and burn the fat of the fellowship offerings on it. [13]The fire must be kept burning on the altar continuously; it must not go out.

The Grain Offering

[14]"'These are the regulations for the grain offering: Aaron's sons are to bring it before the LORD, in front of the altar. [15]The priest is to take a handful of the finest flour and some olive oil, together with all the incense on the grain offering, and burn the memorial[a] portion on the altar as an aroma pleasing to the LORD. [16]Aaron and his sons shall eat the rest of it, but it is to be eaten without yeast in the sanctuary area; they are to eat it in the courtyard of the tent of meeting. [17]It must not be baked with yeast; I have given it as their share of the food offerings presented to me. Like the sin offering[b] and the guilt offering, it is most holy. [18]Any male descendant of Aaron may eat it. For all generations to come it is his perpetual share of the food offerings presented to the LORD. Whatever touches them will become holy.[c]'"

[19]The LORD also said to Moses, [20]"This is the offering Aaron and his sons are to bring to the LORD on the day he[d] is anointed: a tenth of an ephah[e] of the finest flour as a regular grain offering, half of it in the morning and half in the evening. [21]It must be prepared with oil on a griddle; bring it well-mixed and present the grain offering broken[f] in pieces as an aroma pleasing to the LORD. [22]The son who is to succeed him as anointed priest shall prepare it. It is the LORD's perpetual share and is to be burned completely. [23]Every grain offering of a priest shall be burned completely; it must not be eaten."

The Sin Offering

[24]The LORD said to Moses, [25]"Say to Aaron and his sons: 'These are the regulations for the sin offering: The sin offering is to be slaughtered before the LORD in the place the burnt offering is slaughtered; it is most holy. [26]The priest who offers it shall eat it; it is to be eaten in the sanctuary area, in the courtyard of the tent of meeting. [27]Whatever touches any of the flesh will become holy, and if any of the blood is spattered on a garment, you must wash it in the sanctuary area. [28]The clay pot the meat is cooked in must be broken; but if it is cooked in a bronze pot, the pot is to be scoured and rinsed with water. [29]Any male in a priest's family may eat it; it is most holy. [30]But any sin offering whose blood is brought into the tent of meeting to make atonement in the Holy Place must not be eaten; it must be burned up.

The Guilt Offering

7 "'These are the regulations for the guilt offering, which is most holy: [2]The guilt offering is to be slaughtered in the place where the burnt offering is slaughtered, and its blood is to be splashed against the sides of the altar. [3]All its fat shall be offered: the fat tail and the fat that covers the internal organs, [4]both kidneys with the fat on them near the loins, and the long lobe of the liver, which is to be removed with the kidneys. [5]The priest shall burn them on the altar as a food offering presented to the LORD. It is a guilt offering. [6]Any male in a priest's family may eat it, but it must be eaten in the sanctuary area; it is most holy.

[7]"'The same law applies to both the sin offering[g] and the guilt offering: They belong to the priest who makes atonement with them. [8]The priest who offers a burnt offering for

---

[a] 15 Or representative   [b] 17 Or purification offering; also in verses 25 and 30   [c] 18 Or Whoever touches them must be holy; similarly in verse 27   [d] 20 Or each   [e] 20 That is, probably about 3 1/2 pounds or about 1.6 kilograms   [f] 21 The meaning of the Hebrew for this word is uncertain.   [g] 7 Or purification offering; also in verse 37

anyone may keep its hide for himself. [9]Every grain offering baked in an oven or cooked in a pan or on a griddle belongs to the priest who offers it, [10]and every grain offering, whether mixed with olive oil or dry, belongs equally to all the sons of Aaron.

The Fellowship Offering

[11]"'These are the regulations for the fellowship offering anyone may present to the LORD:

[12]"'If they offer it as an expression of thankfulness, then along with this thank offering they are to offer thick loaves made without yeast and with olive oil mixed in, thin loaves made without yeast and brushed with oil, and thick loaves of the finest flour well-kneaded and with oil mixed in. [13]Along with their fellowship offering of thanksgiving they are to present an offering with thick loaves of bread made with yeast. [14]They are to bring one of each kind as an offering, a contribution to the LORD; it belongs to the priest who splashes the blood of the fellowship offering against the altar. [15]The meat of their fellowship offering of thanksgiving must be eaten on the day it is offered; they must leave none of it till morning.

[16]"'If, however, their offering is the result of a vow or is a freewill offering, the sacrifice shall be eaten on the day they offer it, but anything left over may be eaten on the next day. [17]Any meat of the sacrifice left over till the third day must be burned up. [18]If any meat of the fellowship offering is eaten on the third day, the one who offered it will not be accepted. It will not be reckoned to their credit, for it has become impure; the person who eats any of it will be held responsible.

[19]"'Meat that touches anything ceremonially unclean must not be eaten; it must be burned up. As for other meat, anyone ceremonially clean may eat it. [20]But if anyone who is unclean eats any meat of the fellowship offering belonging to the LORD, they must be cut off from their people. [21]Anyone who touches something unclean—whether human uncleanness or an unclean animal or any unclean creature that moves along the ground[a]—and then eats any of the meat of the fellowship offering belonging to the LORD must be cut off from their people.'"

Eating Fat and Blood Forbidden

[22]The LORD said to Moses, [23]"Say to the Israelites: 'Do not eat any of the fat of cattle, sheep or goats. [24]The fat of an animal found dead or torn by wild animals may be used for any other purpose, but you must not eat it. [25]Anyone who eats the fat of an animal from which a food offering may be[b] presented to the LORD must be cut off from their people. [26]And wherever you live, you must not eat the blood of any bird or animal. [27]Anyone who eats blood must be cut off from their people.'"

The Priests' Share

[28]The LORD said to Moses, [29]"Say to the Israelites: 'Anyone who brings a fellowship offering to the LORD is to bring part of it as their sacrifice to the LORD. [30]With their own hands they are to present the food offering to the LORD; they are to bring the fat, together with the breast, and wave the breast before the LORD as a wave offering. [31]The priest shall burn the fat on the altar, but the breast belongs to Aaron and his sons. [32]You are to give the right thigh of your fellowship offerings to the priest as a contribution. [33]The son of Aaron who offers the blood and the fat of the fellowship offering shall have the right thigh as his share. [34]From the fellowship offerings of the Israelites, I have taken the breast that is waved and the thigh that is presented and have given them to Aaron the priest and his sons as their perpetual share from the Israelites.'"

[35]This is the portion of the food offerings presented to the LORD that were allotted to Aaron and his sons on the day they were presented to serve the LORD as priests. [36]On the day they were anointed, the LORD commanded that the Israelites give this to them as their perpetual share for the generations to come.

[37]These, then, are the regulations for the burnt offering, the grain offering, the sin offering, the guilt offering, the ordination offering and the fellowship offering, [38]which the LORD gave Moses at Mount Sinai in the Desert of Sinai on the day he commanded the Israelites to bring their offerings to the LORD.

---

[a] 21 A few Hebrew manuscripts, Samaritan Pentateuch, Syriac and Targum (see 5:2); most Hebrew manuscripts *any unclean, detestable thing*   [b] 25 Or *offering is*

The Ordination of Aaron and His Sons

8 The LORD said to Moses, [2]"Bring Aaron and his sons, their garments, the anointing oil, the bull for the sin offering,[a] the two rams and the basket containing bread made without yeast, [3]and gather the entire assembly at the entrance to the tent of meeting." [4]Moses did as the LORD commanded him, and the assembly gathered at the entrance to the tent of meeting.

[5]Moses said to the assembly, "This is what the LORD has commanded to be done." [6]Then Moses brought Aaron and his sons forward and washed them with water. [7]He put the tunic on Aaron, tied the sash around him, clothed him with the robe and put the ephod on him. He also fastened the ephod with a decorative waistband, which he tied around him. [8]He placed the breastpiece on him and put the Urim and Thummim in the breastpiece. [9]Then he placed the turban on Aaron's head and set the gold plate, the sacred emblem, on the front of it, as the LORD commanded Moses.

[10]Then Moses took the anointing oil and anointed the tabernacle and everything in it, and so consecrated them. [11]He sprinkled some of the oil on the altar seven times, anointing the altar and all its utensils and the basin with its stand, to consecrate them. [12]He poured some of the anointing oil on Aaron's head and anointed him to consecrate him. [13]Then he brought Aaron's sons forward, put tunics on them, tied sashes around them and fastened caps on them, as the LORD commanded Moses.

[14]He then presented the bull for the sin offering, and Aaron and his sons laid their hands on its head. [15]Moses slaughtered the bull and took some of the blood, and with his finger he put it on all the horns of the altar to purify the altar. He poured out the rest of the blood at the base of the altar. So he consecrated it to make atonement for it. [16]Moses also took all the fat around the internal organs, the long lobe of the liver, and both kidneys and their fat, and burned it on the altar. [17]But the bull with its hide and its flesh and its intestines he burned up outside the camp, as the LORD commanded Moses.

[18]He then presented the ram for the burnt offering, and Aaron and his sons laid their hands on its head. [19]Then Moses slaughtered the ram and splashed the blood against the sides of the altar. [20]He cut the ram into pieces and burned the head, the pieces and the fat. [21]He washed the internal organs and the legs with water and burned the whole ram on the altar. It was a burnt offering, a pleasing aroma, a food offering presented to the LORD, as the LORD commanded Moses.

[22]He then presented the other ram, the ram for the ordination, and Aaron and his sons laid their hands on its head. [23]Moses slaughtered the ram and took some of its blood and put it on the lobe of Aaron's right ear, on the thumb of his right hand and on the big toe of his right foot. [24]Moses also brought Aaron's sons forward and put some of the blood on the lobes of their right ears, on the thumbs of their right hands and on the big toes of their right feet. Then he splashed blood against the sides of the altar. [25]After that, he took the fat, the fat tail, all the fat around the internal organs, the long lobe of the liver, both kidneys and their fat and the right thigh. [26]And from the basket of bread made without yeast, which was before the LORD, he took one thick loaf, one thick loaf with olive oil mixed in, and one thin loaf, and he put these on the fat portions and on the right thigh. [27]He put all these in the hands of Aaron and his sons, and they waved them before the LORD as a wave offering. [28]Then Moses took them from their hands and burned them on the altar on top of the burnt offering as an ordination offering, a pleasing aroma, a food offering presented to the LORD. [29]Moses also took the breast, which was his share of the ordination ram, and waved it before the LORD as a wave offering, as the LORD commanded Moses.

[30]Then Moses took some of the anointing oil and some of the blood from the altar and sprinkled them on Aaron and his garments and on his sons and their garments. So he consecrated Aaron and his garments and his sons and their garments.

[31]Moses then said to Aaron and his sons, "Cook the meat at the entrance to the tent of meeting and eat it there with the bread from the basket of ordination offerings, as I was commanded: 'Aaron and his sons are to eat it.' [32]Then burn up the rest of the meat and the bread. [33]Do not leave the entrance to the

---

[a] 2 Or *purification offering*; also in verse 14

tent of meeting for seven days, until the days of your ordination are completed, for your ordination will last seven days. ³⁴What has been done today was commanded by the LORD to make atonement for you. ³⁵You must stay at the entrance to the tent of meeting day and night for seven days and do what the LORD requires, so you will not die; for that is what I have been commanded."

³⁶So Aaron and his sons did everything the LORD commanded through Moses.

The Priests Begin Their Ministry

9 On the eighth day Moses summoned Aaron and his sons and the elders of Israel. ²He said to Aaron, "Take a bull calf for your sin offering*a* and a ram for your burnt offering, both without defect, and present them before the LORD. ³Then say to the Israelites: 'Take a male goat for a sin offering, a calf and a lamb—both a year old and without defect—for a burnt offering, ⁴and an ox*b* and a ram for a fellowship offering to sacrifice before the LORD, together with a grain offering mixed with olive oil. For today the LORD will appear to you.'"

⁵They took the things Moses commanded to the front of the tent of meeting, and the entire assembly came near and stood before the LORD. ⁶Then Moses said, "This is what the LORD has commanded you to do, so that the glory of the LORD may appear to you."

⁷Moses said to Aaron, "Come to the altar and sacrifice your sin offering and your burnt offering and make atonement for yourself and the people; sacrifice the offering that is for the people and make atonement for them, as the LORD has commanded."

⁸So Aaron came to the altar and slaughtered the calf as a sin offering for himself. ⁹His sons brought the blood to him, and he dipped his finger into the blood and put it on the horns of the altar; the rest of the blood he poured out at the base of the altar. ¹⁰On the altar he burned the fat, the kidneys and the long lobe of the liver from the sin offering, as the LORD commanded Moses; ¹¹the flesh and the hide he burned up outside the camp.

¹²Then he slaughtered the burnt offering. His sons handed him the blood, and he splashed it against the sides of the altar. ¹³They handed him the burnt offering piece by piece, including the head, and he burned them on the altar. ¹⁴He washed the internal organs and the legs and burned them on top of the burnt offering on the altar.

¹⁵Aaron then brought the offering that was for the people. He took the goat for the people's sin offering and slaughtered it and offered it for a sin offering as he did with the first one.

¹⁶He brought the burnt offering and offered it in the prescribed way. ¹⁷He also brought the grain offering, took a handful of it and burned it on the altar in addition to the morning's burnt offering.

¹⁸He slaughtered the ox and the ram as the fellowship offering for the people. His sons handed him the blood, and he splashed it against the sides of the altar. ¹⁹But the fat portions of the ox and the ram—the fat tail, the layer of fat, the kidneys and the long lobe of the liver— ²⁰these they laid on the breasts, and then Aaron burned the fat on the altar. ²¹Aaron waved the breasts and the right thigh before the LORD as a wave offering, as Moses commanded.

²²Then Aaron lifted his hands toward the people and blessed them. And having sacrificed the sin offering, the burnt offering and the fellowship offering, he stepped down.

²³Moses and Aaron then went into the tent of meeting. When they came out, they blessed the people; and the glory of the LORD appeared to all the people. ²⁴Fire came out from the presence of the LORD and consumed the burnt offering and the fat portions on the altar. And when all the people saw it, they shouted for joy and fell facedown.

The Death of Nadab and Abihu

10 Aaron's sons Nadab and Abihu took their censers, put fire in them and added incense; and they offered unauthorized fire before the LORD, contrary to his command. ²So fire came out from the presence of the LORD and consumed them, and they died before the LORD. ³Moses then said to Aaron, "This is what the LORD spoke of when he said:

" 'Among those who approach me
    I will be proved holy;
in the sight of all the people
    I will be honored.' "

Aaron remained silent.

---

a 2 Or *purification offering*; here and throughout this chapter male or female; also in verses 18 and 19.   *b 4* The Hebrew word can refer to either

REAL REVERENCE

READ: LEVITICUS 10:1-2

The book of Leviticus needs only two sentences to recount the story of Nadab and Abihu. They took shovels made for carrying hot coals, scooped them full of fire and incense, and offered it all to God. Fire licked at them from the Lord's presence, and they died.

The Bible doesn't say precisely what the men did wrong, except that their fire was "strange," unauthorized by God. The fire might have come from a source other than the altar, or it might have been offered to false gods. Either way, you get the same point. God demands to be treated as holy, honored with reverent obedience.

BUILDING FAITH WISDOM STRENGTH

You also see here that God holds leaders to high standards. Nadab and Abihu weren't random individuals but rather sons of Aaron, high priest and second only to Moses in leading Israel. The Lord didn't let these boys off easy because they were born to a notable family. Thankfully, we don't have to have a fear of being instantly burned for disobeying God's rules today—Jesus' death on the cross gave us the gift of grace. But the idea of worshiping God with respect still holds true. Even if you've been going to church since you were a baby, God still expects reverence.

In addition, God gives you everything you need to be a leader—some time, some way, in the venue he designs for you. Whatever he has planned, take the advice the apostle Paul offered his friend Timothy: "Don't let anyone look down on you because you are young, but set an example for the believers in speech, in conduct, in love, in faith and in purity" (1 Timothy 4:12). Show others the way to follow God with their whole heart.

[4] Moses summoned Mishael and Elzaphan, sons of Aaron's uncle Uzziel, and said to them, "Come here; carry your cousins outside the camp, away from the front of the sanctuary." [5] So they came and carried them, still in their tunics, outside the camp, as Moses ordered.

[6] Then Moses said to Aaron and his sons Eleazar and Ithamar, "Do not let your hair become unkempt[a] and do not tear your clothes, or you will die and the LORD will be angry with the whole community. But your relatives, all the Israelites, may mourn for those the LORD has destroyed by fire. [7] Do not leave the entrance to the tent of meeting or you will die, because the LORD's anointing oil is on you." So they did as Moses said.

[8] Then the LORD said to Aaron, [9] "You and your sons are not to drink wine or other fermented drink whenever you go into the tent of meeting, or you will die. This is a lasting ordinance for the generations to come, [10] so that you can distinguish between the holy and the common, between the unclean and the clean, [11] and so you can teach the Israelites all the decrees the LORD has given them through Moses."

[12] Moses said to Aaron and his remaining sons, Eleazar and Ithamar, "Take the grain offering left over from the food offerings prepared without yeast and presented to the LORD and eat it beside the altar, for it is most holy. [13] Eat it in the sanctuary area, because it is your share and your sons' share of the food offerings presented to the LORD; for so I have been commanded. [14] But you and your sons and your daughters may eat the breast that was waved and the thigh that was presented. Eat them in a ceremonially clean place; they have been given to you and your children as your share of the Israelites' fellowship offerings. [15] The thigh that was presented and the breast that was waved must be brought with the fat portions of the food offerings, to be waved before the LORD as a wave offering. This will be the perpetual share for you and your children, as the LORD has commanded."

[16] When Moses inquired about the goat of the sin offering[b] and found that it had been burned up, he was angry with Eleazar and Ithamar, Aaron's remaining sons, and asked, [17] "Why didn't you eat the sin offering in the sanctuary area? It is most holy; it was given to you to take away the guilt of the community by making atonement for them before the LORD. [18] Since its blood was not taken into the Holy Place, you should have eaten the goat in the sanctuary area, as I commanded."

[19] Aaron replied to Moses, "Today they sacrificed their sin offering and their burnt offering before the LORD, but such things as this have happened to me. Would the LORD have been pleased if I had eaten the sin offering today?" [20] When Moses heard this, he was satisfied.

Clean and Unclean Food

11 The LORD said to Moses and Aaron, [2] "Say to the Israelites: 'Of all the animals that live on land, these are the ones you may eat: [3] You may eat any animal that has a divided hoof and that chews the cud.

[4] "'There are some that only chew the cud or only have a divided hoof, but you must not eat them. The camel, though it chews the cud, does not have a divided hoof; it is ceremonially unclean for you. [5] The hyrax, though it chews the cud, does not have a divided hoof; it is unclean for you. [6] The rabbit, though it chews the cud, does not have a divided hoof; it is unclean for you. [7] And the pig, though it has a divided hoof, does not chew the cud; it is unclean for you. [8] You must not eat their meat or touch their carcasses; they are unclean for you.

[9] "'Of all the creatures living in the water of the seas and the streams you may eat any that have fins and scales. [10] But all creatures in the seas or streams that do not have fins and scales—whether among all the swarming things or among all the other living creatures in the water—you are to regard as unclean. [11] And since you are to regard them as unclean, you must not eat their meat; you must regard their carcasses as unclean. [12] Anything living in the water that does not have fins and scales is to be regarded as unclean by you.

[13] "'These are the birds you are to regard as unclean and not eat because they are unclean: the eagle,[c] the vulture, the black vulture, [14] the red kite, any kind of black kite, [15] any kind of raven, [16] the horned owl,

---

[a] 6 Or *Do not uncover your heads*   [b] 16 Or *purification offering*; also in verses 17 and 19   [c] 13 The precise identification of some of the birds, insects and animals in this chapter is uncertain.

the screech owl, the gull, any kind of hawk, [17]the little owl, the cormorant, the great owl, [18]the white owl, the desert owl, the osprey, [19]the stork, any kind of heron, the hoopoe and the bat.

[20] " 'All flying insects that walk on all fours are to be regarded as unclean by you. [21]There are, however, some flying insects that walk on all fours that you may eat: those that have jointed legs for hopping on the ground. [22]Of these you may eat any kind of locust, katydid, cricket or grasshopper. [23]But all other flying insects that have four legs you are to regard as unclean.

[24] " 'You will make yourselves unclean by these; whoever touches their carcasses will be unclean till evening. [25]Whoever picks up one of their carcasses must wash their clothes, and they will be unclean till evening.

[26] " 'Every animal that does not have a divided hoof or that does not chew the cud is unclean for you; whoever touches the carcass of any of them will be unclean. [27]Of all the animals that walk on all fours, those that walk on their paws are unclean for you; whoever touches their carcasses will be unclean till evening. [28]Anyone who picks up their carcasses must wash their clothes, and they will be unclean till evening. These animals are unclean for you.

[29] " 'Of the animals that move along the ground, these are unclean for you: the weasel, the rat, any kind of great lizard, [30]the gecko, the monitor lizard, the wall lizard, the skink and the chameleon. [31]Of all those that move along the ground, these are unclean for you. Whoever touches them when they are dead will be unclean till evening. [32]When one of them dies and falls on something, that article, whatever its use, will be unclean, whether it is made of wood, cloth, hide or sackcloth. Put it in water; it will be unclean till evening, and then it will be clean. [33]If one of them falls into a clay pot, everything in it will be unclean, and you must break the pot. [34]Any food you are allowed to eat that has come into contact with water from any such pot is unclean, and any liquid that is drunk from such a pot is unclean. [35]Anything that one of their carcasses falls on becomes unclean; an oven or cooking pot must be broken up. They are unclean, and you are to regard them as unclean. [36]A spring, however, or a cistern for collecting water remains clean, but anyone who touches one of these carcasses is unclean. [37]If a carcass falls on any seeds that are to be planted, they remain clean. [38]But if water has been put on the seed and a carcass falls on it, it is unclean for you.

[39] " 'If an animal that you are allowed to eat dies, anyone who touches its carcass will be unclean till evening. [40]Anyone who eats some of its carcass must wash their clothes, and they will be unclean till evening. Anyone who picks up the carcass must wash their clothes, and they will be unclean till evening.

[41] " 'Every creature that moves along the ground is to be regarded as unclean; it is not to be eaten. [42]You are not to eat any creature that moves along the ground, whether it moves on its belly or walks on all fours or on many feet; it is unclean. [43]Do not defile yourselves by any of these creatures. Do not make yourselves unclean by means of them or be made unclean by them. [44]I am the LORD your God; consecrate yourselves and be holy, because I am holy. Do not make yourselves unclean by any creature that moves along the ground. [45]I am the LORD, who brought you up out of Egypt to be your God; therefore be holy, because I am holy.

[46] " 'These are the regulations concerning animals, birds, every living thing that moves about in the water and every creature that moves along the ground. [47]You must distinguish between the unclean and the clean, between living creatures that may be eaten and those that may not be eaten.' "

Purification After Childbirth

12 The LORD said to Moses, [2] "Say to the Israelites: 'A woman who becomes pregnant and gives birth to a son will be ceremonially unclean for seven days, just as she is unclean during her monthly period. [3]On the eighth day the boy is to be circumcised. [4]Then the woman must wait thirty-three days to be purified from her bleeding. She must not touch anything sacred or go to the sanctuary until the days of her purification are over. [5]If she gives birth to a daughter, for two weeks the woman will be unclean, as during her period. Then she must wait sixty-six days to be purified from her bleeding. [6] " 'When the days of her purification for a son or daughter are over, she is to bring to the priest at the entrance to the tent of meeting a year-old lamb for a burnt offering and a young pigeon or a dove for a sin offering.[a] [7] He shall offer them before the LORD to make atonement for her, and then she will be ceremonially clean from her flow of blood.

" 'These are the regulations for the woman who gives birth to a boy or a girl. [8] But if she cannot afford a lamb, she is to bring two doves or two young pigeons, one for a burnt offering and the other for a sin offering. In this way the priest will make atonement for her, and she will be clean.' "

Regulations About Defiling Skin Diseases

13 The LORD said to Moses and Aaron, [2] "When anyone has a swelling or a rash or a shiny spot on their skin that may be a defiling skin disease,[b] they must be brought to Aaron the priest or to one of his sons[c] who is a priest. [3] The priest is to examine the sore on the skin, and if the hair in the sore has turned white and the sore appears to be more than skin deep, it is a defiling skin disease. When the priest examines that person, he shall pronounce them ceremonially unclean. [4] If the shiny spot on the skin is white but does not appear to be more than skin deep and the hair in it has not turned white, the priest is to isolate the affected person for seven days. [5] On the seventh day the priest is to examine them, and if he sees that the sore is unchanged and has not spread in the skin, he is to isolate them for another seven days. [6] On the seventh day the priest is to examine them again, and if the sore has faded and has not spread in the skin, the priest shall pronounce them clean; it is only a rash. They must wash their clothes, and they will be clean. [7] But if the rash does spread in their skin after they have shown themselves to the priest to be pronounced clean, they must appear before the priest again. [8] The priest is to examine that person, and if the rash has spread in the skin, he shall pronounce them unclean; it is a defiling skin disease.

[9] "When anyone has a defiling skin disease, they must be brought to the priest. [10] The priest is to examine them, and if there is a white swelling in the skin that has turned

the hair white and if there is raw flesh in the swelling, [11] it is a chronic skin disease and the priest shall pronounce them unclean. He is not to isolate them, because they are already unclean.

[12] "If the disease breaks out all over their skin and, so far as the priest can see, it covers all the skin of the affected person from head to foot, [13] the priest is to examine them, and if the disease has covered their whole body, he shall pronounce them clean. Since it has all turned white, they are clean. [14] But whenever raw flesh appears on them, they will be unclean. [15] When the priest sees the raw flesh, he shall pronounce them unclean. The raw flesh is unclean; they have a defiling disease. [16] If the raw flesh changes and turns white, they must go to the priest. [17] The priest is to examine them, and if the sores have turned white, the priest shall pronounce the affected person clean; then they will be clean.

[18] "When someone has a boil on their skin and it heals, [19] and in the place where the boil was, a white swelling or reddish-white spot appears, they must present themselves to the priest. [20] The priest is to examine it, and if it appears to be more than skin deep and the hair in it has turned white, the priest shall pronounce that person unclean. It is a defiling skin disease that has broken out where the boil was. [21] But if, when the priest examines it, there is no white hair in it and it is not more than skin deep and has faded, then the priest is to isolate them for seven days. [22] If it is spreading in the skin, the priest shall pronounce them unclean; it is a defiling disease. [23] But if the spot is unchanged and has not spread, it is only a scar from the boil, and the priest shall pronounce them clean.

[24] "When someone has a burn on their skin and a reddish-white or white spot appears in the raw flesh of the burn, [25] the priest is to examine the spot, and if the hair in it has turned white, and it appears to be more than skin deep, it is a defiling disease that has broken out in the burn. The priest shall pronounce them unclean; it is a defiling skin disease. [26] But if the priest examines it and there is no white hair in the spot and if it is not more than skin deep and has faded, then the priest is to isolate them for

---

[a] 6 Or *purification offering*; also in verse 8   [b] 2 The Hebrew word for *defiling skin disease*, traditionally translated "leprosy," was used for various diseases affecting the skin; here and throughout verses 3-46.
[c] 2 Or *descendants*

seven days. [27] On the seventh day the priest is to examine that person, and if it is spreading in the skin, the priest shall pronounce them unclean; it is a defiling skin disease. [28] If, however, the spot is unchanged and has not spread in the skin but has faded, it is a swelling from the burn, and the priest shall pronounce them clean; it is only a scar from the burn.

[29] "If a man or woman has a sore on their head or chin, [30] the priest is to examine the sore, and if it appears to be more than skin deep and the hair in it is yellow and thin, the priest shall pronounce them unclean; it is a defiling skin disease on the head or chin. [31] But if, when the priest examines the sore, it does not seem to be more than skin deep and there is no black hair in it, then the priest is to isolate the affected person for seven days. [32] On the seventh day the priest is to examine the sore, and if it has not spread and there is no yellow hair in it and it does not appear to be more than skin deep, [33] then the man or woman must shave themselves, except for the affected area, and the priest is to keep them isolated another seven days. [34] On the seventh day the priest is to examine the sore, and if it has not spread in the skin and appears to be no more than skin deep, the priest shall pronounce them clean. They must wash their clothes, and they will be clean. [35] But if the sore does spread in the skin after they are pronounced clean, [36] the priest is to examine them, and if he finds that the sore has spread in the skin, he does not need to look for yellow hair; they are unclean. [37] If, however, the sore is unchanged so far as the priest can see, and if black hair has grown in it, the affected person is healed. They are clean, and the priest shall pronounce them clean.

[38] "When a man or woman has white spots on the skin, [39] the priest is to examine them, and if the spots are dull white, it is a harmless rash that has broken out on the skin; they are clean.

[40] "A man who has lost his hair and is bald is clean. [41] If he has lost his hair from the front of his scalp and has a bald forehead, he is clean. [42] But if he has a reddish-white sore on his bald head or forehead, it is a defiling disease breaking out on his head or forehead. [43] The priest is to examine him, and if the swollen sore on his head or forehead is reddish-white like a defiling skin disease, [44] the man is diseased and is unclean. The priest shall pronounce him unclean because of the sore on his head.

[45] "Anyone with such a defiling disease must wear torn clothes, let their hair be unkempt,[a] cover the lower part of their face and cry out, 'Unclean! Unclean!' [46] As long as they have the disease they remain unclean. They must live alone; they must live outside the camp.

Regulations About Defiling Molds

[47] "As for any fabric that is spoiled with a defiling mold — any woolen or linen clothing, [48] any woven or knitted material of linen or wool, any leather or anything made of leather — [49] if the affected area in the fabric, the leather, the woven or knitted material, or any leather article, is greenish or reddish, it is a defiling mold and must be shown to the priest. [50] The priest is to examine the affected area and isolate the article for seven days. [51] On the seventh day he is to examine it, and if the mold has spread in the fabric, the woven or knitted material, or the leather, whatever its use, it is a persistent defiling mold; the article is unclean. [52] He must burn the fabric, the woven or knitted material of wool or linen, or any leather article that has been spoiled; because the defiling mold is persistent, the article must be burned.

[53] "But if, when the priest examines it, the mold has not spread in the fabric, the woven or knitted material, or the leather article, [54] he shall order that the spoiled article be washed. Then he is to isolate it for another seven days. [55] After the article has been washed, the priest is to examine it again, and if the mold has not changed its appearance, even though it has not spread, it is unclean. Burn it, no matter which side of the fabric has been spoiled. [56] If, when the priest examines it, the mold has faded after the article has been washed, he is to tear the spoiled part out of the fabric, the leather, or the woven or knitted material. [57] But if it reappears in the fabric, in the woven or knitted material, or in the leather article, it is a spreading mold; whatever has the mold must be burned. [58] Any fabric, woven or knitted material, or any leather article that has

been washed and is rid of the mold, must be washed again. Then it will be clean."

⁵⁹These are the regulations concerning defiling molds in woolen or linen clothing, woven or knitted material, or any leather article, for pronouncing them clean or unclean.

Cleansing From Defiling Skin Diseases

14 The Lᴏʀᴅ said to Moses, ²"These are the regulations for any diseased person at the time of their ceremonial cleansing, when they are brought to the priest: ³The priest is to go outside the camp and examine them. If they have been healed of their defiling skin disease,ᵃ ⁴the priest shall order that two live clean birds and some cedar wood, scarlet yarn and hyssop be brought for the person to be cleansed. ⁵Then the priest shall order that one of the birds be killed over fresh water in a clay pot. ⁶He is then to take the live bird and dip it, together with the cedar wood, the scarlet yarn and the hyssop, into the blood of the bird that was killed over the fresh water. ⁷Seven times he shall sprinkle the one to be cleansed of the defiling disease, and then pronounce them clean. After that, he is to release the live bird in the open fields.

⁸"The person to be cleansed must wash their clothes, shave off all their hair and bathe with water; then they will be ceremonially clean. After this they may come into the camp, but they must stay outside their tent for seven days. ⁹On the seventh day they must shave off all their hair; they must shave their head, their beard, their eyebrows and the rest of their hair. They must wash their clothes and bathe themselves with water, and they will be clean.

¹⁰"On the eighth day they must bring two male lambs and one ewe lamb a year old, each without defect, along with three-tenths of an ephahᵇ of the finest flour mixed with olive oil for a grain offering, and one logᶜ of oil. ¹¹The priest who pronounces them clean shall present both the one to be cleansed and their offerings before the Lᴏʀᴅ at the entrance to the tent of meeting.

¹²"Then the priest is to take one of the male lambs and offer it as a guilt offering, along with the log of oil; he shall wave them before the Lᴏʀᴅ as a wave offering. ¹³He is to slaughter the lamb in the sanctuary area where the sin offeringᵈ and the burnt offering are slaughtered. Like the sin offering, the guilt offering belongs to the priest; it is most holy. ¹⁴The priest is to take some of the blood of the guilt offering and put it on the lobe of the right ear of the one to be cleansed, on the thumb of their right hand and on the big toe of their right foot. ¹⁵The priest shall then take some of the log of oil, pour it in the palm of his own left hand, ¹⁶dip his right forefinger into the oil in his palm, and with his finger sprinkle some of it before the Lᴏʀᴅ seven times. ¹⁷The priest is to put some of the oil remaining in his palm on the lobe of the right ear of the one to be cleansed, on the thumb of their right hand and on the big toe of their right foot, on top of the blood of the guilt offering. ¹⁸The rest of the oil in his palm the priest shall put on the head of the one to be cleansed and make atonement for them before the Lᴏʀᴅ.

¹⁹"Then the priest is to sacrifice the sin offering and make atonement for the one to be cleansed from their uncleanness. After that, the priest shall slaughter the burnt offering ²⁰and offer it on the altar, together with the grain offering, and make atonement for them, and they will be clean.

²¹"If, however, they are poor and cannot afford these, they must take one male lamb as a guilt offering to be waved to make atonement for them, together with a tenth of an ephahᵉ of the finest flour mixed with olive oil for a grain offering, a log of oil, ²²and two doves or two young pigeons, such as they can afford, one for a sin offering and the other for a burnt offering.

²³"On the eighth day they must bring them for their cleansing to the priest at the entrance to the tent of meeting, before the Lᴏʀᴅ. ²⁴The priest is to take the lamb for the guilt offering, together with the log of oil, and wave them before the Lᴏʀᴅ as a wave offering. ²⁵He shall slaughter the lamb for

---

ᵃ 3 The Hebrew word for *defiling skin disease*, traditionally translated "leprosy," was used for various diseases affecting the skin; also in verses 7, 32, 54 and 57.   ᵇ 10 That is, probably about 11 pounds or about 5 kilograms   ᶜ 10 That is, about 1/3 quart or about 0.3 liter; also in verses 12, 15, 21 and 24   ᵈ 13 Or *purification offering*; also in verses 19, 22 and 31   ᵉ 21 That is, probably about 3 1/2 pounds or about 1.6 kilograms the guilt offering and take some of its blood and put it on the lobe of the right ear of the one to be cleansed, on the thumb of their right hand and on the big toe of their right foot. ²⁶The priest is to pour some of the oil into the palm of his own left hand, ²⁷and with his right forefinger sprinkle some of the oil from his palm seven times before the LORD. ²⁸Some of the oil in his palm he is to put on the same places he put the blood of the guilt offering—on the lobe of the right ear of the one to be cleansed, on the thumb of their right hand and on the big toe of their right foot. ²⁹The rest of the oil in his palm the priest shall put on the head of the one to be cleansed, to make atonement for them before the LORD. ³⁰Then he shall sacrifice the doves or the young pigeons, such as the person can afford, ³¹one as a sin offering and the other as a burnt offering, together with the grain offering. In this way the priest will make atonement before the LORD on behalf of the one to be cleansed."

³²These are the regulations for anyone who has a defiling skin disease and who cannot afford the regular offerings for their cleansing.

Cleansing From Defiling Molds

³³The LORD said to Moses and Aaron, ³⁴"When you enter the land of Canaan, which I am giving you as your possession, and I put a spreading mold in a house in that land, ³⁵the owner of the house must go and tell the priest, 'I have seen something that looks like a defiling mold in my house.' ³⁶The priest is to order the house to be emptied before he goes in to examine the mold, so that nothing in the house will be pronounced unclean. After this the priest is to go in and inspect the house. ³⁷He is to examine the mold on the walls, and if it has greenish or reddish depressions that appear to be deeper than the surface of the wall, ³⁸the priest shall go out the doorway of the house and close it up for seven days. ³⁹On the seventh day the priest shall return to inspect the house. If the mold has spread on the walls, ⁴⁰he is to order that the contaminated stones be torn out and thrown into an unclean place outside the town. ⁴¹He must have all the inside walls of the house scraped and the material that is scraped off dumped into an unclean place outside the town. ⁴²Then they are to

take other stones to replace these and take new clay and plaster the house.

⁴³"If the defiling mold reappears in the house after the stones have been torn out and the house scraped and plastered, ⁴⁴the priest is to go and examine it and, if the mold has spread in the house, it is a persistent defiling mold; the house is unclean. ⁴⁵It must be torn down—its stones, timbers and all the plaster—and taken out of the town to an unclean place.

⁴⁶"Anyone who goes into the house while it is closed up will be unclean till evening. ⁴⁷Anyone who sleeps or eats in the house must wash their clothes.

⁴⁸"But if the priest comes to examine it and the mold has not spread after the house has been plastered, he shall pronounce the house clean, because the defiling mold is gone. ⁴⁹To purify the house he is to take two birds and some cedar wood, scarlet yarn and hyssop. ⁵⁰He shall kill one of the birds over fresh water in a clay pot. ⁵¹Then he is to take the cedar wood, the hyssop, the scarlet yarn and the live bird, dip them into the blood of the dead bird and the fresh water, and sprinkle the house seven times. ⁵²He shall purify the house with the bird's blood, the fresh water, the live bird, the cedar wood, the hyssop and the scarlet yarn. ⁵³Then he is to release the live bird in the open fields outside the town. In this way he will make atonement for the house, and it will be clean."

⁵⁴These are the regulations for any defiling skin disease, for a sore, ⁵⁵for defiling molds in fabric or in a house, ⁵⁶and for a swelling, a rash or a shiny spot, ⁵⁷to determine when something is clean or unclean.

These are the regulations for defiling skin diseases and defiling molds.

Discharges Causing Uncleanness

15 The LORD said to Moses and Aaron, ²"Speak to the Israelites and say to them: 'When any man has an unusual bodily discharge, such a discharge is unclean. ³Whether it continues flowing from his body or is blocked, it will make him unclean. This is how his discharge will bring about uncleanness:

⁴"'Any bed the man with a discharge lies on will be unclean, and anything he sits on will be unclean. ⁵Anyone who touches his bed must wash their clothes and bathe with

water, and they will be unclean till evening. ⁶Whoever sits on anything that the man with a discharge sat on must wash their clothes and bathe with water, and they will be unclean till evening.

⁷"'Whoever touches the man who has a discharge must wash their clothes and bathe with water, and they will be unclean till evening.

⁸"'If the man with the discharge spits on anyone who is clean, they must wash their clothes and bathe with water, and they will be unclean till evening.

⁹"'Everything the man sits on when riding will be unclean, ¹⁰and whoever touches any of the things that were under him will be unclean till evening; whoever picks up those things must wash their clothes and bathe with water, and they will be unclean till evening.

¹¹"'Anyone the man with a discharge touches without rinsing his hands with water must wash their clothes and bathe with water, and they will be unclean till evening.

¹²"'A clay pot that the man touches must be broken, and any wooden article is to be rinsed with water.

¹³"'When a man is cleansed from his discharge, he is to count off seven days for his ceremonial cleansing; he must wash his clothes and bathe himself with fresh water, and he will be clean. ¹⁴On the eighth day he must take two doves or two young pigeons and come before the Lord to the entrance to the tent of meeting and give them to the priest. ¹⁵The priest is to sacrifice them, the one for a sin offering[a] and the other for a burnt offering. In this way he will make atonement before the Lord for the man because of his discharge.

¹⁶"'When a man has an emission of semen, he must bathe his whole body with water, and he will be unclean till evening. ¹⁷Any clothing or leather that has semen on it must be washed with water, and it will be unclean till evening. ¹⁸When a man has sexual relations with a woman and there is an emission of semen, both of them must bathe with water, and they will be unclean till evening.

¹⁹"'When a woman has her regular flow of blood, the impurity of her monthly period will last seven days, and anyone who touches her will be unclean till evening.

²⁰"'Anything she lies on during her period will be unclean, and anything she sits on will be unclean. ²¹Anyone who touches her bed will be unclean; they must wash their clothes and bathe with water, and they will be unclean till evening. ²²Anyone who touches anything she sits on will be unclean; they must wash their clothes and bathe with water, and they will be unclean till evening. ²³Whether it is the bed or anything she was sitting on, when anyone touches it, they will be unclean till evening.

²⁴"'If a man has sexual relations with her and her monthly flow touches him, he will be unclean for seven days; any bed he lies on will be unclean.

²⁵"'When a woman has a discharge of blood for many days at a time other than her monthly period or has a discharge that continues beyond her period, she will be unclean as long as she has the discharge, just as in the days of her period. ²⁶Any bed she lies on while her discharge continues will be unclean, as is her bed during her monthly period, and anything she sits on will be unclean, as during her period. ²⁷Anyone who touches them will be unclean; they must wash their clothes and bathe with water, and they will be unclean till evening.

²⁸"'When she is cleansed from her discharge, she must count off seven days, and after that she will be ceremonially clean. ²⁹On the eighth day she must take two doves or two young pigeons and bring them to the priest at the entrance to the tent of meeting. ³⁰The priest is to sacrifice one for a sin offering and the other for a burnt offering. In this way he will make atonement for her before the Lord for the uncleanness of her discharge.

³¹"'You must keep the Israelites separate from things that make them unclean, so they will not die in their uncleanness for defiling my dwelling place,[b] which is among them.'"

³²These are the regulations for a man with a discharge, for anyone made unclean by an emission of semen, ³³for a woman in her monthly period, for a man or a woman with a discharge, and for a man who has sexual relations with a woman who is ceremonially unclean.

---

[a] 15 Or *purification offering*; also in verse 30   [b] 31 Or *my tabernacle*

The Day of Atonement

16 The LORD spoke to Moses after the death of the two sons of Aaron who died when they approached the LORD. ²The LORD said to Moses: "Tell your brother Aaron that he is not to come whenever he chooses into the Most Holy Place behind the curtain in front of the atonement cover on the ark, or else he will die. For I will appear in the cloud over the atonement cover.

³"This is how Aaron is to enter the Most Holy Place: He must first bring a young bull for a sin offering*a* and a ram for a burnt offering. ⁴He is to put on the sacred linen tunic, with linen undergarments next to his body; he is to tie the linen sash around him and put on the linen turban. These are sacred garments; so he must bathe himself with water before he puts them on. ⁵From the Israelite community he is to take two male goats for a sin offering and a ram for a burnt offering.

⁶"Aaron is to offer the bull for his own sin offering to make atonement for himself and his household. ⁷Then he is to take the two goats and present them before the LORD at the entrance to the tent of meeting. ⁸He is to cast lots for the two goats — one lot for the LORD and the other for the scapegoat.*b* ⁹Aaron shall bring the goat whose lot falls to the LORD and sacrifice it for a sin offering. ¹⁰But the goat chosen by lot as the scapegoat shall be presented alive before the LORD to be used for making atonement by sending it into the wilderness as a scapegoat.

¹¹"Aaron shall bring the bull for his own sin offering to make atonement for himself and his household, and he is to slaughter the bull for his own sin offering. ¹²He is to take a censer full of burning coals from the altar before the LORD and two handfuls of finely ground fragrant incense and take them behind the curtain. ¹³He is to put the incense on the fire before the LORD, and the smoke of the incense will conceal the atonement cover above the tablets of the covenant law, so that he will not die. ¹⁴He is to take some of the bull's blood and with his finger sprinkle it on the front of the atonement cover; then he shall sprinkle some of it with his finger seven times before the atonement cover.

¹⁵"He shall then slaughter the goat for the sin offering for the people and take its blood behind the curtain and do with it as he did with the bull's blood: He shall sprinkle it on the atonement cover and in front of it. ¹⁶In this way he will make atonement for the Most Holy Place because of the uncleanness and rebellion of the Israelites, whatever their sins have been. He is to do the same for the tent of meeting, which is among them in the midst of their uncleanness. ¹⁷No one is to be in the tent of meeting from the time Aaron goes in to make atonement in the Most Holy Place until he comes out, having made atonement for himself, his household and the whole community of Israel.

¹⁸"Then he shall come out to the altar that is before the LORD and make atonement for it. He shall take some of the bull's blood and some of the goat's blood and put it on all the horns of the altar. ¹⁹He shall sprinkle some of the blood on it with his finger seven times to cleanse it and to consecrate it from the uncleanness of the Israelites.

²⁰"When Aaron has finished making atonement for the Most Holy Place, the tent of meeting and the altar, he shall bring forward the live goat. ²¹He is to lay both hands on the head of the live goat and confess over it all the wickedness and rebellion of the Israelites — all their sins — and put them on the goat's head. He shall send the goat away into the wilderness in the care of someone appointed for the task. ²²The goat will carry on itself all their sins to a remote place; and the man shall release it in the wilderness.

²³"Then Aaron is to go into the tent of meeting and take off the linen garments he put on before he entered the Most Holy Place, and he is to leave them there. ²⁴He shall bathe himself with water in the sanctuary area and put on his regular garments. Then he shall come out and sacrifice the burnt offering for himself and the burnt offering for the people, to make atonement for himself and for the people. ²⁵He shall also burn the fat of the sin offering on the altar.

²⁶"The man who releases the goat as a scapegoat must wash his clothes and bathe himself with water; afterward he may come into the camp. ²⁷The bull and the goat for the sin offerings, whose blood was brought into the Most Holy Place to make atonement, must be taken outside the camp; their hides,

---

a 3 Or *purification offering*; here and throughout this chapter   *b 8* The meaning of the Hebrew for this word is uncertain; also in verses 10 and 26.

flesh and intestines are to be burned up. [28]The man who burns them must wash his clothes and bathe himself with water; afterward he may come into the camp.

[29]"This is to be a lasting ordinance for you: On the tenth day of the seventh month you must deny yourselves[a] and not do any work — whether native-born or a foreigner residing among you — [30]because on this day atonement will be made for you, to cleanse you. Then, before the LORD, you will be clean from all your sins. [31]It is a day of sabbath rest, and you must deny yourselves; it is a lasting ordinance. [32]The priest who is anointed and ordained to succeed his father as high priest is to make atonement. He is to put on the sacred linen garments [33]and make atonement for the Most Holy Place, for the tent of meeting and the altar, and for the priests and all the members of the community.

[34]"This is to be a lasting ordinance for you: Atonement is to be made once a year for all the sins of the Israelites."

And it was done, as the LORD commanded Moses.

Eating Blood Forbidden

17 The LORD said to Moses, [2]"Speak to Aaron and his sons and to all the Israelites and say to them: 'This is what the LORD has commanded: [3]Any Israelite who sacrifices an ox,[b] a lamb or a goat in the camp or outside of it [4]instead of bringing it to the entrance to the tent of meeting to present it as an offering to the LORD in front of the tabernacle of the LORD — that person shall be considered guilty of bloodshed; they have shed blood and must be cut off from their people. [5]This is so the Israelites will bring to the LORD the sacrifices they are now making in the open fields. They must bring them to the priest, that is, to the LORD, at the entrance to the tent of meeting and sacrifice them as fellowship offerings. [6]The priest is to splash the blood against the altar of the LORD at the entrance to the tent of meeting and burn the fat as an aroma pleasing to the LORD. [7]They must no longer offer any of their sacrifices to the goat idols[c] to whom they prostitute themselves. This is to be a lasting ordinance for them and for the generations to come.'

[8]"Say to them: 'Any Israelite or any foreigner residing among them who offers a burnt offering or sacrifice [9]and does not bring it to the entrance to the tent of meeting to sacrifice it to the LORD must be cut off from the people of Israel.

[10]"'I will set my face against any Israelite or any foreigner residing among them who eats blood, and I will cut them off from the people. [11]For the life of a creature is in the blood, and I have given it to you to make atonement for yourselves on the altar; it is the blood that makes atonement for one's life.[d] [12]Therefore I say to the Israelites, "None of you may eat blood, nor may any foreigner residing among you eat blood."

[13]"'Any Israelite or any foreigner residing among you who hunts any animal or bird that may be eaten must drain out the blood and cover it with earth, [14]because the life of every creature is its blood. That is why I have said to the Israelites, "You must not eat the blood of any creature, because the life of every creature is its blood; anyone who eats it must be cut off."

[15]"'Anyone, whether native-born or foreigner, who eats anything found dead or torn by wild animals must wash their clothes and bathe with water, and they will be ceremonially unclean till evening; then they will be clean. [16]But if they do not wash their clothes and bathe themselves, they will be held responsible.'"

Unlawful Sexual Relations

18 The LORD said to Moses, [2]"Speak to the Israelites and say to them: 'I am the LORD your God. [3]You must not do as they do in Egypt, where you used to live, and you must not do as they do in the land of Canaan, where I am bringing you. Do not follow their practices. [4]You must obey my laws and be careful to follow my decrees. I am the LORD your God. [5]Keep my decrees and laws, for the person who obeys them will live by them. I am the LORD.

[6]"'No one is to approach any close relative to have sexual relations. I am the LORD.

[7]"'Do not dishonor your father by having sexual relations with your mother. She is your mother; do not have relations with her.

---

[a] 29 Or *must fast*; also in verse 31   [b] 3 The Hebrew word can refer to either male or female.   [c] 7 Or *the demons*   [d] 11 Or *atonement by the life in the blood*

AT ONE WITH GOD

READ: LEVITICUS 16:30

O f all the sacrifices detailed in Leviticus, the Day of Atonement is the most profound. This once-a-year ceremony foreshadowed Jesus' sacrificial death on the cross, illustrating his payment for sin and the removal of sin.

The Bible says that "without the shedding of blood there is no forgiveness" (Hebrews 9:22). God instituted Old Testament sacrifices to show the awfulness of sin and temporarily cleanse the people.

The Day of Atonement was Israel's most sacred moment. On that day, the head priest chose two goats. He sacrificed the first as an offering for sins, sprinkling the blood in the Most Holy Place, a small room of the Lord's strong presence entered only by the high priest once a year on this day. The priest then placed his hands on the second goat's head, symbolically transferring the nation's sins to the goat. This "scapegoat" was led into the desert, taking the people's sins far away as a sign of the removal of sin.

BUILDING

FAITH

WISDOM

STRENGTH

Jesus fulfilled this divine drama. Because of his death on the cross, God welcomes you into his presence. Hebrews 10:19–20 says, "We have confidence to enter the Most Holy Place by the blood of Jesus, by a new and living way opened for us through the curtain, that is, his body." Because of Jesus, you can boldly get close to God wherever and whenever you want.

⁸ "'Do not have sexual relations with your father's wife; that would dishonor your father.

⁹ "'Do not have sexual relations with your sister, either your father's daughter or your mother's daughter, whether she was born in the same home or elsewhere.

¹⁰ "'Do not have sexual relations with your son's daughter or your daughter's daughter; that would dishonor you.

¹¹ "'Do not have sexual relations with the daughter of your father's wife, born to your father; she is your sister.

¹² "'Do not have sexual relations with your father's sister; she is your father's close relative.

¹³ "'Do not have sexual relations with your mother's sister, because she is your mother's close relative.

¹⁴ "'Do not dishonor your father's brother by approaching his wife to have sexual relations; she is your aunt.

¹⁵ "'Do not have sexual relations with your daughter-in-law. She is your son's wife; do not have relations with her.

¹⁶ "'Do not have sexual relations with your brother's wife; that would dishonor your brother.

¹⁷ "'Do not have sexual relations with both a woman and her daughter. Do not have sexual relations with either her son's daughter or her daughter's daughter; they are her close relatives. That is wickedness.

¹⁸ "'Do not take your wife's sister as a rival wife and have sexual relations with her while your wife is living.

¹⁹ "'Do not approach a woman to have sexual relations during the uncleanness of her monthly period.

²⁰ "'Do not have sexual relations with your neighbor's wife and defile yourself with her.

²¹ "'Do not give any of your children to be sacrificed to Molek, for you must not profane the name of your God. I am the LORD.

²² "'Do not have sexual relations with a man as one does with a woman; that is detestable.

²³ "'Do not have sexual relations with an animal and defile yourself with it. A woman must not present herself to an animal to have sexual relations with it; that is a perversion.

²⁴ "'Do not defile yourselves in any of these ways, because this is how the nations that I am going to drive out before you be-

came defiled. ²⁵ Even the land was defiled; so I punished it for its sin, and the land vomited out its inhabitants. ²⁶ But you must keep my decrees and my laws. The native-born and the foreigners residing among you must not do any of these detestable things, ²⁷ for all these things were done by the people who lived in the land before you, and the land became defiled. ²⁸ And if you defile the land, it will vomit you out as it vomited out the nations that were before you.

²⁹ "'Everyone who does any of these detestable things—such persons must be cut off from their people. ³⁰ Keep my requirements and do not follow any of the detestable customs that were practiced before you came and do not defile yourselves with them. I am the LORD your God.'"

Various Laws

19 The LORD said to Moses, ² "Speak to the entire assembly of Israel and say to them: 'Be holy because I, the LORD your God, am holy.

³ "'Each of you must respect your mother and father, and you must observe my Sabbaths. I am the LORD your God.

⁴ "'Do not turn to idols or make metal gods for yourselves. I am the LORD your God.

⁵ "'When you sacrifice a fellowship offering to the LORD, sacrifice it in such a way that it will be accepted on your behalf. ⁶ It shall be eaten on the day you sacrifice it or on the next day; anything left over until the third day must be burned up. ⁷ If any of it is eaten on the third day, it is impure and will not be accepted. ⁸ Whoever eats it will be held responsible because they have desecrated what is holy to the LORD; they must be cut off from their people.

⁹ "'When you reap the harvest of your land, do not reap to the very edges of your field or gather the gleanings of your harvest. ¹⁰ Do not go over your vineyard a second time or pick up the grapes that have fallen. Leave them for the poor and the foreigner. I am the LORD your God.

¹¹ "'Do not steal.

"'Do not lie.

"'Do not deceive one another.

¹² "'Do not swear falsely by my name and so profane the name of your God. I am the LORD.

¹³ "'Do not defraud or rob your neighbor.

THE SEARCH FOR HOLINESS

READ: **LEVITICUS 19:2**

As you press on through the Old Testament, you might find yourself feeling like an ancient Israelite, forever wandering through the desert on the hunt for a cool drink. Suddenly Leviticus 19:2 rises on the horizon. It's like an oasis, a refreshing spot of green in the midst of endless hot sand.

That verse repeats a statement God first made in Leviticus 11:44. He intends for you and the rest of his people to be just like him, and the quality he chooses for you to imitate is his holiness. That awesome trait is the heart of who God is. The root of the Hebrew word for "holy" wraps together "separation" and "brightness," and it adds up to the Lord's one-of-a-kind distinctiveness and glory. To be holy is to be completely pure and without fault.

Being like God is impossible, at least if you try to be good without the Lord's help. But later in Scripture the apostle Peter explains how holiness happens. He quotes this passage, then reminds you how Jesus rescued you from an empty way of life. He bought your life with his own precious blood. Because he came back from the dead, you have faith and hope in God. His Word causes you to be born again (1 Peter 1:14–2:3).

And the result? Now you can grow up and rid your life of every kind of evil.

"'Do not hold back the wages of a hired worker overnight.

14 "'Do not curse the deaf or put a stumbling block in front of the blind, but fear your God. I am the LORD.

15 "'Do not pervert justice; do not show partiality to the poor or favoritism to the great, but judge your neighbor fairly.

16 "'Do not go about spreading slander among your people.

"'Do not do anything that endangers your neighbor's life. I am the LORD.

17 "'Do not hate a fellow Israelite in your heart. Rebuke your neighbor frankly so you will not share in their guilt.

18 "'Do not seek revenge or bear a grudge against anyone among your people, but love your neighbor as yourself. I am the LORD.

19 "'Keep my decrees.

"'Do not mate different kinds of animals.

"'Do not plant your field with two kinds of seed.

"'Do not wear clothing woven of two kinds of material.

20 "'If a man sleeps with a female slave who is promised to another man but who has not been ransomed or given her freedom, there must be due punishment.*a* Yet they are not to be put to death, because she had not been freed. 21 The man, however, must bring a ram to the entrance to the tent of meeting for a guilt offering to the LORD. 22 With the ram of the guilt offering the priest is to make atonement for him before the LORD for the sin he has committed, and his sin will be forgiven.

23 "'When you enter the land and plant any kind of fruit tree, regard its fruit as forbidden.*b* For three years you are to consider it forbidden*b*; it must not be eaten. 24 In the fourth year all its fruit will be holy, an offering of praise to the LORD. 25 But in the fifth year you may eat its fruit. In this way your harvest will be increased. I am the LORD your God.

26 "'Do not eat any meat with the blood still in it.

"'Do not practice divination or seek omens.

27 "'Do not cut the hair at the sides of your head or clip off the edges of your beard.

28 "'Do not cut your bodies for the dead or put tattoo marks on yourselves. I am the LORD.

29 "'Do not degrade your daughter by making her a prostitute, or the land will turn to prostitution and be filled with wickedness.

30 "'Observe my Sabbaths and have reverence for my sanctuary. I am the LORD.

31 "'Do not turn to mediums or seek out spiritists, for you will be defiled by them. I am the LORD your God.

32 "'Stand up in the presence of the aged, show respect for the elderly and revere your God. I am the LORD.

33 "'When a foreigner resides among you in your land, do not mistreat them. 34 The foreigner residing among you must be treated as your native-born. Love them as yourself, for you were foreigners in Egypt. I am the LORD your God.

35 "'Do not use dishonest standards when measuring length, weight or quantity. 36 Use honest scales and honest weights, an honest ephah*c* and an honest hin.*d* I am the LORD your God, who brought you out of Egypt.

37 "'Keep all my decrees and all my laws and follow them. I am the LORD.'"

Punishments for Sin

20 The LORD said to Moses, 2 "Say to the Israelites: 'Any Israelite or any foreigner residing in Israel who sacrifices any of his children to Molek is to be put to death. The members of the community are to stone him. 3 I myself will set my face against him and will cut him off from his people; for by sacrificing his children to Molek, he has defiled my sanctuary and profaned my holy name. 4 If the members of the community close their eyes when that man sacrifices one of his children to Molek and if they fail to put him to death, 5 I myself will set my face against him and his family and will cut them off from their people together with all who follow him in prostituting themselves to Molek.

6 "'I will set my face against anyone who turns to mediums and spiritists to prostitute themselves by following them, and I will cut them off from their people.

7 "'Consecrate yourselves and be holy, because I am the LORD your God. 8 Keep my

---

a 20 Or *be an inquiry*   *b 23* Hebrew *uncircumcised*   *c 36* An ephah was a dry measure having the
capacity of about 3/5 of a bushel or about 22 liters.   *d 36* A hin was a liquid measure having the capacity
of about 1 gallon or about 3.8 liters.

EVERY SECOND, EVERY OUNCE

READ: LEVITICUS 20:7

Before God does crazy miracles in people's lives, they usually consecrate themselves to God, which means they decide to be 100 percent dedicated to God.

Here's our problem: we try to do God's job for him. We want to do amazing things for God. And that seems cool and noble and all, but we've got it backward. God wants to do amazing things for us. That's his job, not ours. Our job is consecration. That's it. And if we do our job, God will definitely do his. Here's a taste of what consecration is NOT:

- Going to church once a week like good little boys.
- Daily devotions, done by waking up 4.7 minutes earlier than normal.
- Fasting during Lent. Not even eating chocolate.
- Keeping the Ten Commandments.
- Sharing your faith with friends who need "saving."
- Repeating the sinner's prayer. Not even twenty times.
- Raising your hands when you're singing.
- Going on a mission trip.

Those are fine things, but that isn't necessarily consecration. It's something deeper, and much truer.

I want to break that zing you feel when you hear "consecration." The actual word *consecrate* means to set yourself apart; consecration demands full devotion. It's taking your rear off Jesus' throne. It's giving God veto power. It's surrendering all of you to all of him. It's recognizing that every second of time, every last ounce of energy, and every penny of money is a gift from God and for God.

decrees and follow them. I am the Lord, who makes you holy.

9 " 'Anyone who curses their father or mother is to be put to death. Because they have cursed their father or mother, their blood will be on their own head.

10 " 'If a man commits adultery with another man's wife — with the wife of his neighbor — both the adulterer and the adulteress are to be put to death.

11 " 'If a man has sexual relations with his father's wife, he has dishonored his father. Both the man and the woman are to be put to death; their blood will be on their own heads.

12 " 'If a man has sexual relations with his daughter-in-law, both of them are to be put to death. What they have done is a perversion; their blood will be on their own heads.

13 " 'If a man has sexual relations with a man as one does with a woman, both of them have done what is detestable. They are to be put to death; their blood will be on their own heads.

14 " 'If a man marries both a woman and her mother, it is wicked. Both he and they must be burned in the fire, so that no wickedness will be among you.

15 " 'If a man has sexual relations with an animal, he is to be put to death, and you must kill the animal.

16 " 'If a woman approaches an animal to have sexual relations with it, kill both the woman and the animal. They are to be put to death; their blood will be on their own heads.

17 " 'If a man marries his sister, the daughter of either his father or his mother, and they have sexual relations, it is a disgrace. They are to be publicly removed from their people. He has dishonored his sister and will be held responsible.

18 " 'If a man has sexual relations with a woman during her monthly period, he has exposed the source of her flow, and she has also uncovered it. Both of them are to be cut off from their people.

19 " 'Do not have sexual relations with the sister of either your mother or your father, for that would dishonor a close relative; both of you would be held responsible.

20 " 'If a man has sexual relations with his aunt, he has dishonored his uncle. They will be held responsible; they will die childless.

21 " 'If a man marries his brother's wife, it is an act of impurity; he has dishonored his brother. They will be childless.

22 " 'Keep all my decrees and laws and follow them, so that the land where I am bringing you to live may not vomit you out. 23 You must not live according to the customs of the nations I am going to drive out before you. Because they did all these things, I abhorred them. 24 But I said to you, "You will possess their land; I will give it to you as an inheritance, a land flowing with milk and honey." I am the Lord your God, who has set you apart from the nations.

25 " 'You must therefore make a distinction between clean and unclean animals and between unclean and clean birds. Do not defile yourselves by any animal or bird or anything that moves along the ground — those that I have set apart as unclean for you. 26 You are to be holy to me because I, the Lord, am holy, and I have set you apart from the nations to be my own.

27 " 'A man or woman who is a medium or spiritist among you must be put to death. You are to stone them; their blood will be on their own heads.' "

Rules for Priests

21 The Lord said to Moses, "Speak to the priests, the sons of Aaron, and say to them: 'A priest must not make himself ceremonially unclean for any of his people who die, 2 except for a close relative, such as his mother or father, his son or daughter, his brother, 3 or an unmarried sister who is dependent on him since she has no husband — for her he may make himself unclean. 4 He must not make himself unclean for people related to him by marriage,[a] and so defile himself.

5 " 'Priests must not shave their heads or shave off the edges of their beards or cut their bodies. 6 They must be holy to their God and must not profane the name of their God. Because they present the food offerings to the Lord, the food of their God, they are to be holy.

7 " 'They must not marry women defiled by prostitution or divorced from their husbands, because priests are holy to their God. 8 Regard them as holy, because they offer up the food of your God. Consider them holy,

---

[a] 4 Or *unclean as a leader among his people*

because I the LORD am holy—I who make you holy.

9 " 'If a priest's daughter defiles herself by becoming a prostitute, she disgraces her father; she must be burned in the fire.

10 " 'The high priest, the one among his brothers who has had the anointing oil poured on his head and who has been ordained to wear the priestly garments, must not let his hair become unkempt[a] or tear his clothes. 11 He must not enter a place where there is a dead body. He must not make himself unclean, even for his father or mother, 12 nor leave the sanctuary of his God or desecrate it, because he has been dedicated by the anointing oil of his God. I am the LORD.

13 " 'The woman he marries must be a virgin. 14 He must not marry a widow, a divorced woman, or a woman defiled by prostitution, but only a virgin from his own people, 15 so that he will not defile his offspring among his people. I am the LORD, who makes him holy.' "

16 The LORD said to Moses, 17 "Say to Aaron: 'For the generations to come none of your descendants who has a defect may come near to offer the food of his God. 18 No man who has any defect may come near: no man who is blind or lame, disfigured or deformed; 19 no man with a crippled foot or hand, 20 or who is a hunchback or a dwarf, or who has any eye defect, or who has festering or running sores or damaged testicles. 21 No descendant of Aaron the priest who has any defect is to come near to present the food offerings to the LORD. He has a defect; he must not come near to offer the food of his God. 22 He may eat the most holy food of his God, as well as the holy food; 23 yet because of his defect, he must not go near the curtain or approach the altar, and so desecrate my sanctuary. I am the LORD, who makes them holy.' "

24 So Moses told this to Aaron and his sons and to all the Israelites.

22 The LORD said to Moses, 2 "Tell Aaron and his sons to treat with respect the sacred offerings the Israelites consecrate to me, so they will not profane my holy name. I am the LORD.

3 "Say to them: 'For the generations to come, if any of your descendants is ceremonially unclean and yet comes near the sacred offerings that the Israelites consecrate to the LORD, that person must be cut off from my presence. I am the LORD.

4 " 'If a descendant of Aaron has a defiling skin disease[b] or a bodily discharge, he may not eat the sacred offerings until he is cleansed. He will also be unclean if he touches something defiled by a corpse or by anyone who has an emission of semen, 5 or if he touches any crawling thing that makes him unclean, or any person who makes him unclean, whatever the uncleanness may be. 6 The one who touches any such thing will be unclean till evening. He must not eat any of the sacred offerings unless he has bathed himself with water. 7 When the sun goes down, he will be clean, and after that he may eat the sacred offerings, for they are his food. 8 He must not eat anything found dead or torn by wild animals, and so become unclean through it. I am the LORD.

9 " 'The priests are to perform my service in such a way that they do not become guilty and die for treating it with contempt. I am the LORD, who makes them holy.

10 " 'No one outside a priest's family may eat the sacred offering, nor may the guest of a priest or his hired worker eat it. 11 But if a priest buys a slave with money, or if slaves are born in his household, they may eat his food. 12 If a priest's daughter marries anyone other than a priest, she may not eat any of the sacred contributions. 13 But if a priest's daughter becomes a widow or is divorced, yet has no children, and she returns to live in her father's household as in her youth, she may eat her father's food. No unauthorized person, however, may eat it.

14 " 'Anyone who eats a sacred offering by mistake must make restitution to the priest for the offering and add a fifth of the value to it. 15 The priests must not desecrate the sacred offerings the Israelites present to the LORD 16 by allowing them to eat the sacred offerings and so bring upon them guilt requiring payment. I am the LORD, who makes them holy.' "

Unacceptable Sacrifices

17 The LORD said to Moses, 18 "Speak to Aaron and his sons and to all the Israelites and say to them: 'If any of you—whether an

---

[a] 10 Or *not uncover his head*   [b] 4 The Hebrew word for *defiling skin disease*, traditionally translated "leprosy," was used for various diseases affecting the skin.

Israelite or a foreigner residing in Israel—presents a gift for a burnt offering to the LORD, either to fulfill a vow or as a freewill offering, ¹⁹you must present a male without defect from the cattle, sheep or goats in order that it may be accepted on your behalf. ²⁰Do not bring anything with a defect, because it will not be accepted on your behalf. ²¹When anyone brings from the herd or flock a fellowship offering to the LORD to fulfill a special vow or as a freewill offering, it must be without defect or blemish to be acceptable. ²²Do not offer to the LORD the blind, the injured or the maimed, or anything with warts or festering or running sores. Do not place any of these on the altar as a food offering presented to the LORD. ²³You may, however, present as a freewill offering an ox^a or a sheep that is deformed or stunted, but it will not be accepted in fulfillment of a vow. ²⁴You must not offer to the LORD an animal whose testicles are bruised, crushed, torn or cut. You must not do this in your own land, ²⁵and you must not accept such animals from the hand of a foreigner and offer them as the food of your God. They will not be accepted on your behalf, because they are deformed and have defects.'"

²⁶The LORD said to Moses, ²⁷"When a calf, a lamb or a goat is born, it is to remain with its mother for seven days. From the eighth day on, it will be acceptable as a food offering presented to the LORD. ²⁸Do not slaughter a cow or a sheep and its young on the same day.

²⁹"When you sacrifice a thank offering to the LORD, sacrifice it in such a way that it will be accepted on your behalf. ³⁰It must be eaten that same day; leave none of it till morning. I am the LORD.

³¹"Keep my commands and follow them. I am the LORD. ³²Do not profane my holy name, for I must be acknowledged as holy by the Israelites. I am the LORD, who made you holy ³³and who brought you out of Egypt to be your God. I am the LORD."

The Appointed Festivals

23 The LORD said to Moses, ²"Speak to the Israelites and say to them: 'These are my appointed festivals, the appointed festivals of the LORD, which you are to proclaim as sacred assemblies.

The Sabbath

³"'There are six days when you may work, but the seventh day is a day of sabbath rest, a day of sacred assembly. You are not to do any work; wherever you live, it is a sabbath to the LORD.

The Passover and the Festival of Unleavened Bread

⁴"'These are the LORD's appointed festivals, the sacred assemblies you are to proclaim at their appointed times: ⁵The LORD's Passover begins at twilight on the fourteenth day of the first month. ⁶On the fifteenth day of that month the LORD's Festival of Unleavened Bread begins; for seven days you must eat bread made without yeast. ⁷On the first day hold a sacred assembly and do no regular work. ⁸For seven days present a food offering to the LORD. And on the seventh day hold a sacred assembly and do no regular work.'"

Offering the Firstfruits

⁹The LORD said to Moses, ¹⁰"Speak to the Israelites and say to them: 'When you enter the land I am going to give you and you reap its harvest, bring to the priest a sheaf of the first grain you harvest. ¹¹He is to wave the sheaf before the LORD so it will be accepted on your behalf; the priest is to wave it on the day after the Sabbath. ¹²On the day you wave the sheaf, you must sacrifice as a burnt offering to the LORD a lamb a year old without defect, ¹³together with its grain offering of two-tenths of an ephah^b of the finest flour mixed with olive oil—a food offering presented to the LORD, a pleasing aroma—and its drink offering of a quarter of a hin^c of wine. ¹⁴You must not eat any bread, or roasted or new grain, until the very day you bring this offering to your God. This is to be a lasting ordinance for the generations to come, wherever you live.

The Festival of Weeks

¹⁵"'From the day after the Sabbath, the day you brought the sheaf of the wave offering, count off seven full weeks. ¹⁶Count off fifty days up to the day after the seventh Sabbath, and then present an offering of new grain to the LORD. ¹⁷From wherever you

---

^a 23 The Hebrew word can refer to either male or female.   ^b 13 That is, probably about 7 pounds or about 3.2 kilograms; also in verse 17   ^c 13 That is, about 1 quart or about 1 liter

live, bring two loaves made of two-tenths of an ephah of the finest flour, baked with yeast, as a wave offering of firstfruits to the LORD. [18] Present with this bread seven male lambs, each a year old and without defect, one young bull and two rams. They will be a burnt offering to the LORD, together with their grain offerings and drink offerings — a food offering, an aroma pleasing to the LORD. [19] Then sacrifice one male goat for a sin offering[a] and two lambs, each a year old, for a fellowship offering. [20] The priest is to wave the two lambs before the LORD as a wave offering, together with the bread of the firstfruits. They are a sacred offering to the LORD for the priest. [21] On that same day you are to proclaim a sacred assembly and do no regular work. This is to be a lasting ordinance for the generations to come, wherever you live.

[22] "'When you reap the harvest of your land, do not reap to the very edges of your field or gather the gleanings of your harvest. Leave them for the poor and for the foreigner residing among you. I am the LORD your God.'"

The Festival of Trumpets

[23] The LORD said to Moses, [24] "Say to the Israelites: 'On the first day of the seventh month you are to have a day of sabbath rest, a sacred assembly commemorated with trumpet blasts. [25] Do no regular work, but present a food offering to the LORD.'"

The Day of Atonement

[26] The LORD said to Moses, [27] "The tenth day of this seventh month is the Day of Atonement. Hold a sacred assembly and deny yourselves,[b] and present a food offering to the LORD. [28] Do not do any work on that day, because it is the Day of Atonement, when atonement is made for you before the LORD your God. [29] Those who do not deny themselves on that day must be cut off from their people. [30] I will destroy from among their people anyone who does any work on that day. [31] You shall do no work at all. This is to be a lasting ordinance for the generations to come, wherever you live. [32] It is a day of sabbath rest for you, and you must deny yourselves. From the evening of the ninth day of the month until the following evening you are to observe your sabbath."

The Festival of Tabernacles

[33] The LORD said to Moses, [34] "Say to the Israelites: 'On the fifteenth day of the seventh month the LORD's Festival of Tabernacles begins, and it lasts for seven days. [35] The first day is a sacred assembly; do no regular work. [36] For seven days present food offerings to the LORD, and on the eighth day hold a sacred assembly and present a food offering to the LORD. It is the closing special assembly; do no regular work.

[37] ("'These are the LORD's appointed festivals, which you are to proclaim as sacred assemblies for bringing food offerings to the LORD — the burnt offerings and grain offerings, sacrifices and drink offerings required for each day. [38] These offerings are in addition to those for the LORD's Sabbaths and[c] in addition to your gifts and whatever you have vowed and all the freewill offerings you give to the LORD.)

[39] "'So beginning with the fifteenth day of the seventh month, after you have gathered the crops of the land, celebrate the festival to the LORD for seven days; the first day is a day of sabbath rest, and the eighth day also is a day of sabbath rest. [40] On the first day you are to take branches from luxuriant trees — from palms, willows and other leafy trees — and rejoice before the LORD your God for seven days. [41] Celebrate this as a festival to the LORD for seven days each year. This is to be a lasting ordinance for the generations to come; celebrate it in the seventh month. [42] Live in temporary shelters for seven days: All native-born Israelites are to live in such shelters [43] so your descendants will know that I had the Israelites live in temporary shelters when I brought them out of Egypt. I am the LORD your God.'"

[44] So Moses announced to the Israelites the appointed festivals of the LORD.

Olive Oil and Bread Set Before the LORD

24 The LORD said to Moses, [2] "Command the Israelites to bring you clear oil of pressed olives for the light so that the lamps may be kept burning continually. [3] Outside the curtain that shields the ark of

---

[a] 19 Or *purification offering*   [b] 27 Or *and fast*; similarly in verses 29 and 32   [c] 38 Or *These festivals are in addition to the LORD's Sabbaths, and these offerings are*

the covenant law in the tent of meeting, Aaron is to tend the lamps before the LORD from evening till morning, continually. This is to be a lasting ordinance for the generations to come. ⁴The lamps on the pure gold lampstand before the LORD must be tended continually.

⁵"Take the finest flour and bake twelve loaves of bread, using two-tenths of an ephah*ᵃ* for each loaf. ⁶Arrange them in two stacks, six in each stack, on the table of pure gold before the LORD. ⁷By each stack put some pure incense as a memorial*ᵇ* portion to represent the bread and to be a food offering presented to the LORD. ⁸This bread is to be set out before the LORD regularly, Sabbath after Sabbath, on behalf of the Israelites, as a lasting covenant. ⁹It belongs to Aaron and his sons, who are to eat it in the sanctuary area, because it is a most holy part of their perpetual share of the food offerings presented to the LORD."

A Blasphemer Put to Death

¹⁰Now the son of an Israelite mother and an Egyptian father went out among the Israelites, and a fight broke out in the camp between him and an Israelite. ¹¹The son of the Israelite woman blasphemed the Name with a curse; so they brought him to Moses. (His mother's name was Shelomith, the daughter of Dibri the Danite.) ¹²They put him in custody until the will of the LORD should be made clear to them.

¹³Then the LORD said to Moses: ¹⁴"Take the blasphemer outside the camp. All those who heard him are to lay their hands on his head, and the entire assembly is to stone him. ¹⁵Say to the Israelites: 'Anyone who curses their God will be held responsible; ¹⁶anyone who blasphemes the name of the LORD is to be put to death. The entire assembly must stone them. Whether foreigner or native-born, when they blaspheme the Name they are to be put to death.

¹⁷"'Anyone who takes the life of a human being is to be put to death. ¹⁸Anyone who takes the life of someone's animal must make restitution—life for life. ¹⁹Anyone who injures their neighbor is to be injured in the same manner: ²⁰fracture for fracture, eye for eye, tooth for tooth. The one who has inflicted the injury must suffer the same in-

jury. ²¹Whoever kills an animal must make restitution, but whoever kills a human being is to be put to death. ²²You are to have the same law for the foreigner and the native-born. I am the LORD your God.'"

²³Then Moses spoke to the Israelites, and they took the blasphemer outside the camp and stoned him. The Israelites did as the LORD commanded Moses.

The Sabbath Year

25 The LORD said to Moses at Mount Sinai, ²"Speak to the Israelites and say to them: 'When you enter the land I am going to give you, the land itself must observe a sabbath to the LORD. ³For six years sow your fields, and for six years prune your vineyards and gather their crops. ⁴But in the seventh year the land is to have a year of sabbath rest, a sabbath to the LORD. Do not sow your fields or prune your vineyards. ⁵Do not reap what grows of itself or harvest the grapes of your untended vines. The land is to have a year of rest. ⁶Whatever the land yields during the sabbath year will be food for you—for yourself, your male and female servants, and the hired worker and temporary resident who live among you, ⁷as well as for your livestock and the wild animals in your land. Whatever the land produces may be eaten.

The Year of Jubilee

⁸"'Count off seven sabbath years—seven times seven years—so that the seven sabbath years amount to a period of forty-nine years. ⁹Then have the trumpet sounded everywhere on the tenth day of the seventh month; on the Day of Atonement sound the trumpet throughout your land. ¹⁰Consecrate the fiftieth year and proclaim liberty throughout the land to all its inhabitants. It shall be a jubilee for you; each of you is to return to your family property and to your own clan. ¹¹The fiftieth year shall be a jubilee for you; do not sow and do not reap what grows of itself or harvest the untended vines. ¹²For it is a jubilee and is to be holy for you; eat only what is taken directly from the fields.

¹³"'In this Year of Jubilee everyone is to return to their own property.

¹⁴"'If you sell land to any of your own people or buy land from them, do not take advantage of each other. ¹⁵You are to buy from

---

ᵃ 5 That is, probably about 7 pounds or about 3.2 kilograms   *ᵇ* 7 Or *representative* your own people on the basis of the number of years since the Jubilee. And they are to sell to you on the basis of the number of years left for harvesting crops. ¹⁶When the years are many, you are to increase the price, and when the years are few, you are to decrease the price, because what is really being sold to you is the number of crops. ¹⁷Do not take advantage of each other, but fear your God. I am the LORD your God.

¹⁸ " 'Follow my decrees and be careful to obey my laws, and you will live safely in the land. ¹⁹Then the land will yield its fruit, and you will eat your fill and live there in safety. ²⁰You may ask, "What will we eat in the seventh year if we do not plant or harvest our crops?" ²¹I will send you such a blessing in the sixth year that the land will yield enough for three years. ²²While you plant during the eighth year, you will eat from the old crop and will continue to eat from it until the harvest of the ninth year comes in.

²³ " 'The land must not be sold permanently, because the land is mine and you reside in my land as foreigners and strangers. ²⁴Throughout the land that you hold as a possession, you must provide for the redemption of the land.

²⁵ " 'If one of your fellow Israelites becomes poor and sells some of their property, their nearest relative is to come and redeem what they have sold. ²⁶If, however, there is no one to redeem it for them but later on they prosper and acquire sufficient means to redeem it themselves, ²⁷they are to determine the value for the years since they sold it and refund the balance to the one to whom they sold it; they can then go back to their own property. ²⁸But if they do not acquire the means to repay, what was sold will remain in the possession of the buyer until the Year of Jubilee. It will be returned in the Jubilee, and they can then go back to their property.

²⁹ " 'Anyone who sells a house in a walled city retains the right of redemption a full year after its sale. During that time the seller may redeem it. ³⁰If it is not redeemed before a full year has passed, the house in the walled city shall belong permanently to the buyer and the buyer's descendants. It is not to be returned in the Jubilee. ³¹But houses in villages without walls around them are to be considered as belonging to the open country. They can be redeemed, and they are to be returned in the Jubilee.

³² " 'The Levites always have the right to redeem their houses in the Levitical towns, which they possess. ³³So the property of the Levites is redeemable — that is, a house sold in any town they hold — and is to be returned in the Jubilee, because the houses in the towns of the Levites are their property among the Israelites. ³⁴But the pastureland belonging to their towns must not be sold; it is their permanent possession.

³⁵ " 'If any of your fellow Israelites become poor and are unable to support themselves among you, help them as you would a foreigner and stranger, so they can continue to live among you. ³⁶Do not take interest or any profit from them, but fear your God, so that they may continue to live among you. ³⁷You must not lend them money at interest or sell them food at a profit. ³⁸I am the LORD your God, who brought you out of Egypt to give you the land of Canaan and to be your God.

³⁹ " 'If any of your fellow Israelites become poor and sell themselves to you, do not make them work as slaves. ⁴⁰They are to be treated as hired workers or temporary residents among you; they are to work for you until the Year of Jubilee. ⁴¹Then they and their children are to be released, and they will go back to their own clans and to the property of their ancestors. ⁴²Because the Israelites are my servants, whom I brought out of Egypt, they must not be sold as slaves. ⁴³Do not rule over them ruthlessly, but fear your God.

⁴⁴ " 'Your male and female slaves are to come from the nations around you; from them you may buy slaves. ⁴⁵You may also buy some of the temporary residents living among you and members of their clans born in your country, and they will become your property. ⁴⁶You can bequeath them to your children as inherited property and can make them slaves for life, but you must not rule over your fellow Israelites ruthlessly.

⁴⁷ " 'If a foreigner residing among you becomes rich and any of your fellow Israelites become poor and sell themselves to the foreigner or to a member of the foreigner's clan, ⁴⁸they retain the right of redemption after they have sold themselves. One of their relatives may redeem them: ⁴⁹An uncle or a cousin or any blood relative in their clan may redeem them. Or if they prosper, they may redeem themselves. ⁵⁰They and their buyer are to count the time from the year

they sold themselves up to the Year of Jubilee. The price for their release is to be based on the rate paid to a hired worker for that number of years. ⁵¹ If many years remain, they must pay for their redemption a larger share of the price paid for them. ⁵² If only a few years remain until the Year of Jubilee, they are to compute that and pay for their redemption accordingly. ⁵³ They are to be treated as workers hired from year to year; you must see to it that those to whom they owe service do not rule over them ruthlessly.

⁵⁴ " 'Even if someone is not redeemed in any of these ways, they and their children are to be released in the Year of Jubilee, ⁵⁵ for the Israelites belong to me as servants. They are my servants, whom I brought out of Egypt. I am the LORD your God.

Reward for Obedience

26 " 'Do not make idols or set up an image or a sacred stone for yourselves, and do not place a carved stone in your land to bow down before it. I am the LORD your God.

² " 'Observe my Sabbaths and have reverence for my sanctuary. I am the LORD.

³ " 'If you follow my decrees and are careful to obey my commands, ⁴ I will send you rain in its season, and the ground will yield its crops and the trees their fruit. ⁵ Your threshing will continue until grape harvest and the grape harvest will continue until planting, and you will eat all the food you want and live in safety in your land.

⁶ " 'I will grant peace in the land, and you will lie down and no one will make you afraid. I will remove wild beasts from the land, and the sword will not pass through your country. ⁷ You will pursue your enemies, and they will fall by the sword before you. ⁸ Five of you will chase a hundred, and a hundred of you will chase ten thousand, and your enemies will fall by the sword before you.

⁹ " 'I will look on you with favor and make you fruitful and increase your numbers, and I will keep my covenant with you. ¹⁰ You will still be eating last year's harvest when you will have to move it out to make room for the new. ¹¹ I will put my dwelling place*a* among you, and I will not abhor you. ¹² I will walk among you and be your God, and you will be my people. ¹³ I am the LORD your God, who brought you out of Egypt so that you would no longer be slaves to the Egyptians; I broke the bars of your yoke and enabled you to walk with heads held high.

Punishment for Disobedience

¹⁴ " 'But if you will not listen to me and carry out all these commands, ¹⁵ and if you reject my decrees and abhor my laws and fail to carry out all my commands and so violate my covenant, ¹⁶ then I will do this to you: I will bring on you sudden terror, wasting diseases and fever that will destroy your sight and sap your strength. You will plant seed in vain, because your enemies will eat it. ¹⁷ I will set my face against you so that you will be defeated by your enemies; those who hate you will rule over you, and you will flee even when no one is pursuing you.

¹⁸ " 'If after all this you will not listen to me, I will punish you for your sins seven times over. ¹⁹ I will break down your stubborn pride and make the sky above you like iron and the ground beneath you like bronze. ²⁰ Your strength will be spent in vain, because your soil will not yield its crops, nor will the trees of your land yield their fruit.

²¹ " 'If you remain hostile toward me and refuse to listen to me, I will multiply your afflictions seven times over, as your sins deserve. ²² I will send wild animals against you, and they will rob you of your children, destroy your cattle and make you so few in number that your roads will be deserted.

²³ " 'If in spite of these things you do not accept my correction but continue to be hostile toward me, ²⁴ I myself will be hostile toward you and will afflict you for your sins seven times over. ²⁵ And I will bring the sword on you to avenge the breaking of the covenant. When you withdraw into your cities, I will send a plague among you, and you will be given into enemy hands. ²⁶ When I cut off your supply of bread, ten women will be able to bake your bread in one oven, and they will dole out the bread by weight. You will eat, but you will not be satisfied.

²⁷ " 'If in spite of this you still do not listen to me but continue to be hostile toward me, ²⁸ then in my anger I will be hostile toward

---

a 11 Or *my tabernacle*

you, and I myself will punish you for your sins seven times over. ²⁹You will eat the flesh of your sons and the flesh of your daughters. ³⁰I will destroy your high places, cut down your incense altars and pile your dead bodies[a] on the lifeless forms of your idols, and I will abhor you. ³¹I will turn your cities into ruins and lay waste your sanctuaries, and I will take no delight in the pleasing aroma of your offerings. ³²I myself will lay waste the land, so that your enemies who live there will be appalled. ³³I will scatter you among the nations and will draw out my sword and pursue you. Your land will be laid waste, and your cities will lie in ruins. ³⁴Then the land will enjoy its sabbath years all the time that it lies desolate and you are in the country of your enemies; then the land will rest and enjoy its sabbaths. ³⁵All the time that it lies desolate, the land will have the rest it did not have during the sabbaths you lived in it.

³⁶ " 'As for those of you who are left, I will make their hearts so fearful in the lands of their enemies that the sound of a windblown leaf will put them to flight. They will run as though fleeing from the sword, and they will fall, even though no one is pursuing them. ³⁷They will stumble over one another as though fleeing from the sword, even though no one is pursuing them. So you will not be able to stand before your enemies. ³⁸You will perish among the nations; the land of your enemies will devour you. ³⁹Those of you who are left will waste away in the lands of their enemies because of their sins; also because of their ancestors' sins they will waste away.

⁴⁰ " 'But if they will confess their sins and the sins of their ancestors — their unfaithfulness and their hostility toward me, ⁴¹which made me hostile toward them so that I sent them into the land of their enemies — then when their uncircumcised hearts are humbled and they pay for their sin, ⁴²I will remember my covenant with Jacob and my covenant with Isaac and my covenant with Abraham, and I will remember the land. ⁴³For the land will be deserted by them and will enjoy its sabbaths while it lies desolate without them. They will pay for their sins because they rejected my laws and abhorred my decrees. ⁴⁴Yet in spite of this, when they are in the land of their enemies, I will not reject them or abhor them so as to destroy them completely, breaking my covenant with them. I am the LORD their God. ⁴⁵But for their sake I will remember the covenant with their ancestors whom I brought out of Egypt in the sight of the nations to be their God. I am the LORD.' "

⁴⁶These are the decrees, the laws and the regulations that the LORD established at Mount Sinai between himself and the Israelites through Moses.

Redeeming What Is the LORD's

27 The LORD said to Moses, ²"Speak to the Israelites and say to them: 'If anyone makes a special vow to dedicate a person to the LORD by giving the equivalent value, ³set the value of a male between the ages of twenty and sixty at fifty shekels[b] of silver, according to the sanctuary shekel[c]; ⁴for a female, set her value at thirty shekels[d]; ⁵for a person between the ages of five and twenty, set the value of a male at twenty shekels[e] and of a female at ten shekels[f]; ⁶for a person between one month and five years, set the value of a male at five shekels[g] of silver and that of a female at three shekels[h] of silver; ⁷for a person sixty years old or more, set the value of a male at fifteen shekels[i] and of a female at ten shekels. ⁸If anyone making the vow is too poor to pay the specified amount, the person being dedicated is to be presented to the priest, who will set the value according to what the one making the vow can afford.

⁹ " 'If what they vowed is an animal that is acceptable as an offering to the LORD, such an animal given to the LORD becomes holy. ¹⁰They must not exchange it or substitute a good one for a bad one, or a bad one for a good one; if they should substitute one animal for another, both it and the substitute become holy. ¹¹If what they vowed is a ceremonially unclean animal — one that is not acceptable as an offering to the LORD — the animal must be presented to the priest, ¹²who will judge its quality as good or bad.

---

[a] 30 Or *your funeral offerings*   [b] 3 That is, about 1 1/4 pounds or about 575 grams; also in verse 16   [c] 3 That is, about 2/5 ounce or about 12 grams; also in verse 25   [d] 4 That is, about 12 ounces or about 345 grams   [e] 5 That is, about 8 ounces or about 230 grams   [f] 5 That is, about 4 ounces or about 115 grams; also in verse 7   [g] 6 That is, about 2 ounces or about 58 grams   [h] 6 That is, about 1 1/4 ounces or about 35 grams   [i] 7 That is, about 6 ounces or about 175 grams

Whatever value the priest then sets, that is what it will be. [13] If the owner wishes to redeem the animal, a fifth must be added to its value.

[14] "'If anyone dedicates their house as something holy to the LORD, the priest will judge its quality as good or bad. Whatever value the priest then sets, so it will remain. [15] If the one who dedicates their house wishes to redeem it, they must add a fifth to its value, and the house will again become theirs.

[16] "'If anyone dedicates to the LORD part of their family land, its value is to be set according to the amount of seed required for it—fifty shekels of silver to a homer[a] of barley seed. [17] If they dedicate a field during the Year of Jubilee, the value that has been set remains. [18] But if they dedicate a field after the Jubilee, the priest will determine the value according to the number of years that remain until the next Year of Jubilee, and its set value will be reduced. [19] If the one who dedicates the field wishes to redeem it, they must add a fifth to its value, and the field will again become theirs. [20] If, however, they do not redeem the field, or if they have sold it to someone else, it can never be redeemed. [21] When the field is released in the Jubilee, it will become holy, like a field devoted to the LORD; it will become priestly property.

[22] "'If anyone dedicates to the LORD a field they have bought, which is not part of their family land, [23] the priest will determine its value up to the Year of Jubilee, and the owner must pay its value on that day as something holy to the LORD. [24] In the Year of Jubilee the field will revert to the person from whom it was bought, the one whose land it was. [25] Every value is to be set according to the sanctuary shekel, twenty gerahs to the shekel.

[26] "'No one, however, may dedicate the firstborn of an animal, since the firstborn already belongs to the LORD; whether an ox[b] or a sheep, it is the LORD's. [27] If it is one of the unclean animals, it may be bought back at its set value, adding a fifth of the value to it. If it is not redeemed, it is to be sold at its set value.

[28] "'But nothing that a person owns and devotes[c] to the LORD—whether a human being or an animal or family land—may be sold or redeemed; everything so devoted is most holy to the LORD.

[29] "'No person devoted to destruction[d] may be ransomed; they are to be put to death.

[30] "'A tithe of everything from the land, whether grain from the soil or fruit from the trees, belongs to the LORD; it is holy to the LORD. [31] Whoever would redeem any of their tithe must add a fifth of the value to it. [32] Every tithe of the herd and flock—every tenth animal that passes under the shepherd's rod—will be holy to the LORD. [33] No one may pick out the good from the bad or make any substitution. If anyone does make a substitution, both the animal and its substitute become holy and cannot be redeemed.'"

[34] These are the commands the LORD gave Moses at Mount Sinai for the Israelites.

---

[a] 16 That is, probably about 300 pounds or about 135 kilograms   [b] 26 The Hebrew word can refer to either male or female.   [c] 28 The Hebrew term refers to the irrevocable giving over of things or persons to the LORD.   [d] 29 The Hebrew term refers to the irrevocable giving over of things or persons to the LORD, often by totally destroying them.

NUMBERS

➡ WHEN DID THIS HAPPEN?

During the 1400s B.C. while the Israelites were traveling in the desert

➡ WHO IS IN THIS BOOK?

Moses
Aaron
Caleb
Joshua
Korah, the king of Edom
Balaam

➡ VERSES YOU MIGHT RECOGNIZE

NUMBERS 6:24-25
"The LORD bless you and keep you; the LORD make his face shine on you and be gracious to you."

NUMBERS 14:18
"The LORD is slow to anger, abounding in love and forgiving sin and rebellion."

WHAT'S IT ABOUT?

This book is probably called Numbers because it talks about the counting of two Israelite generations—more than two million people! One generation would die in the desert—including Moses—but God would keep his promise and bring the other generation into the promised land under a new leader: Joshua.

Like stubborn, disobedient children, the Israelites made a lot of mistakes in the desert as they learned to trust and honor God. But even when Israel messed up by disobeying the Lord's instructions and complaining about their circumstances, God still loved them and took care of them. In spite of their rebellion, God was patient, loving and forgiving.

The book of Numbers also gives more instructions to the priests and Levites who were to serve in the tabernacle, where people came to worship God. But if you're worried that Numbers might be a little boring, don't be. This book is filled with amazing stories about water gushing out of a rock, exciting battles, and even a talking donkey!

NUMBERS

The Census

1 The LORD spoke to Moses in the tent of meeting in the Desert of Sinai on the first day of the second month of the second year after the Israelites came out of Egypt. He said: ²"Take a census of the whole Israelite community by their clans and families, listing every man by name, one by one. ³You and Aaron are to count according to their divisions all the men in Israel who are twenty years old or more and able to serve in the army. ⁴One man from each tribe, each of them the head of his family, is to help you. ⁵These are the names of the men who are to assist you:

from Reuben, Elizur son of Shedeur;
⁶from Simeon, Shelumiel son of Zurishaddai;
⁷from Judah, Nahshon son of Amminadab;
⁸from Issachar, Nethanel son of Zuar;
⁹from Zebulun, Eliab son of Helon;
¹⁰from the sons of Joseph:
    from Ephraim, Elishama son of Ammihud;
    from Manasseh, Gamaliel son of Pedahzur;
¹¹from Benjamin, Abidan son of Gideoni;
¹²from Dan, Ahiezer son of Ammishaddai;
¹³from Asher, Pagiel son of Okran;
¹⁴from Gad, Eliasaph son of Deuel;
¹⁵from Naphtali, Ahira son of Enan."

¹⁶These were the men appointed from the community, the leaders of their ancestral tribes. They were the heads of the clans of Israel.

¹⁷Moses and Aaron took these men whose names had been specified, ¹⁸and they called the whole community together on the first day of the second month. The people registered their ancestry by their clans and families, and the men twenty years old or more were listed by name, one by one, ¹⁹as the LORD commanded Moses. And so he counted them in the Desert of Sinai:

²⁰From the descendants of Reuben the firstborn son of Israel:
All the men twenty years old or more who were able to serve in the army were listed by name, one by one, according to the records of their clans and families. ²¹The number from the tribe of Reuben was 46,500.

²²From the descendants of Simeon:
All the men twenty years old or more who were able to serve in the army were counted and listed by name, one by one, according to the records of their clans and families. ²³The number from the tribe of Simeon was 59,300.

²⁴From the descendants of Gad:
All the men twenty years old or more who were able to serve in the army were listed by name, according to the records of their clans and families. ²⁵The number from the tribe of Gad was 45,650.

²⁶From the descendants of Judah:
All the men twenty years old or more who were able to serve in the army were listed by name, according to the records of their clans and families. ²⁷The number from the tribe of Judah was 74,600.

²⁸From the descendants of Issachar:
All the men twenty years old or more who were able to serve in the army were listed by name, according to the records of their clans and families. ²⁹The number from the tribe of Issachar was 54,400.

³⁰From the descendants of Zebulun:
All the men twenty years old or more who were able to serve in the army were listed by name, according to the records of their clans and families. ³¹The number from the tribe of Zebulun was 57,400.

³² From the sons of Joseph:

From the descendants of Ephraim:

All the men twenty years old or more who were able to serve in the army were listed by name, according to the records of their clans and families. ³³ The number from the tribe of Ephraim was 40,500.

³⁴ From the descendants of Manasseh:

All the men twenty years old or more who were able to serve in the army were listed by name, according to the records of their clans and families. ³⁵ The number from the tribe of Manasseh was 32,200.

³⁶ From the descendants of Benjamin:

All the men twenty years old or more who were able to serve in the army were listed by name, according to the records of their clans and families. ³⁷ The number from the tribe of Benjamin was 35,400.

³⁸ From the descendants of Dan:

All the men twenty years old or more who were able to serve in the army were listed by name, according to the records of their clans and families. ³⁹ The number from the tribe of Dan was 62,700.

⁴⁰ From the descendants of Asher:

All the men twenty years old or more who were able to serve in the army were listed by name, according to the records of their clans and families. ⁴¹ The number from the tribe of Asher was 41,500.

⁴² From the descendants of Naphtali:

All the men twenty years old or more who were able to serve in the army were listed by name, according to the records of their clans and families. ⁴³ The number from the tribe of Naphtali was 53,400.

⁴⁴ These were the men counted by Moses and Aaron and the twelve leaders of Israel, each one representing his family. ⁴⁵ All the Israelites twenty years old or more who were able to serve in Israel's army were counted according to their families. ⁴⁶ The total number was 603,550.

⁴⁷ The ancestral tribe of the Levites, however, was not counted along with the others.

⁴⁸ The LORD had said to Moses: ⁴⁹ "You must not count the tribe of Levi or include them in the census of the other Israelites. ⁵⁰ Instead, appoint the Levites to be in charge of the tabernacle of the covenant law — over all its furnishings and everything belonging to it. They are to carry the tabernacle and all its furnishings; they are to take care of it and encamp around it. ⁵¹ Whenever the tabernacle is to move, the Levites are to take it down, and whenever the tabernacle is to be set up, the Levites shall do it. Anyone else who approaches it is to be put to death. ⁵² The Israelites are to set up their tents by divisions, each of them in their own camp under their standard. ⁵³ The Levites, however, are to set up their tents around the tabernacle of the covenant law so that my wrath will not fall on the Israelite community. The Levites are to be responsible for the care of the tabernacle of the covenant law."

⁵⁴ The Israelites did all this just as the LORD commanded Moses.

The Arrangement of the Tribal Camps

2 The LORD said to Moses and Aaron: ² "The Israelites are to camp around the tent of meeting some distance from it, each of them under their standard and holding the banners of their family."

³ On the east, toward the sunrise, the divisions of the camp of Judah are to encamp under their standard. The leader of the people of Judah is Nahshon son of Amminadab. ⁴ His division numbers 74,600.

⁵ The tribe of Issachar will camp next to them. The leader of the people of Issachar is Nethanel son of Zuar. ⁶ His division numbers 54,400.

⁷ The tribe of Zebulun will be next. The leader of the people of Zebulun is Eliab son of Helon. ⁸ His division numbers 57,400.

⁹ All the men assigned to the camp of Judah, according to their divisions, number 186,400. They will set out first.

¹⁰ On the south will be the divisions of the camp of Reuben under their standard. The leader of the people of Reuben is Elizur son of Shedeur. ¹¹ His division numbers 46,500.

¹² The tribe of Simeon will camp next

to them. The leader of the people of Simeon is Shelumiel son of Zurishaddai. [13] His division numbers 59,300.

[14] The tribe of Gad will be next. The leader of the people of Gad is Eliasaph son of Deuel.[a] [15] His division numbers 45,650.

[16] All the men assigned to the camp of Reuben, according to their divisions, number 151,450. They will set out second.

[17] Then the tent of meeting and the camp of the Levites will set out in the middle of the camps. They will set out in the same order as they encamp, each in their own place under their standard.

[18] On the west will be the divisions of the camp of Ephraim under their standard. The leader of the people of Ephraim is Elishama son of Ammihud. [19] His division numbers 40,500.

[20] The tribe of Manasseh will be next to them. The leader of the people of Manasseh is Gamaliel son of Pedahzur. [21] His division numbers 32,200.

[22] The tribe of Benjamin will be next. The leader of the people of Benjamin is Abidan son of Gideoni. [23] His division numbers 35,400.

[24] All the men assigned to the camp of Ephraim, according to their divisions, number 108,100. They will set out third.

[25] On the north will be the divisions of the camp of Dan under their standard. The leader of the people of Dan is Ahiezer son of Ammishaddai. [26] His division numbers 62,700.

[27] The tribe of Asher will camp next to them. The leader of the people of Asher is Pagiel son of Okran. [28] His division numbers 41,500.

[29] The tribe of Naphtali will be next. The leader of the people of Naphtali is Ahira son of Enan. [30] His division numbers 53,400.

[31] All the men assigned to the camp of Dan number 157,600. They will set out last, under their standards.

[32] These are the Israelites, counted according to their families. All the men in the camps, by their divisions, number 603,550. [33] The Levites, however, were not counted along with the other Israelites, as the LORD commanded Moses.

[34] So the Israelites did everything the LORD commanded Moses; that is the way they encamped under their standards, and that is the way they set out, each of them with their clan and family.

The Levites

3 This is the account of the family of Aaron and Moses at the time the LORD spoke to Moses at Mount Sinai.

[2] The names of the sons of Aaron were Nadab the firstborn and Abihu, Eleazar and Ithamar. [3] Those were the names of Aaron's sons, the anointed priests, who were ordained to serve as priests. [4] Nadab and Abihu, however, died before the LORD when they made an offering with unauthorized fire before him in the Desert of Sinai. They had no sons, so Eleazar and Ithamar served as priests during the lifetime of their father Aaron.

[5] The LORD said to Moses, [6] "Bring the tribe of Levi and present them to Aaron the priest to assist him. [7] They are to perform duties for him and for the whole community at the tent of meeting by doing the work of the tabernacle. [8] They are to take care of all the furnishings of the tent of meeting, fulfilling the obligations of the Israelites by doing the work of the tabernacle. [9] Give the Levites to Aaron and his sons; they are the Israelites who are to be given wholly to him.[b] [10] Appoint Aaron and his sons to serve as priests; anyone else who approaches the sanctuary is to be put to death."

[11] The LORD also said to Moses, [12] "I have taken the Levites from among the Israelites in place of the first male offspring of every Israelite woman. The Levites are mine, [13] for all the firstborn are mine. When I struck down all the firstborn in Egypt, I set apart for myself every firstborn in Israel, whether human or animal. They are to be mine. I am the LORD."

---

[a] 14 Many manuscripts of the Masoretic Text, Samaritan Pentateuch and Vulgate (see also 1:14); most manuscripts of the Masoretic Text *Reuel*   [b] 9 Most manuscripts of the Masoretic Text; some manuscripts of the Masoretic Text, Samaritan Pentateuch and Septuagint (see also 8:16) *to me*

RAW DATA

READ: NUMBERS 2:32, 3:39

I f you set out to write a blockbuster book meant to sell millions of copies and play on the big screen, you wouldn't fill your work with numbers and long family lists. But God had a different purpose when he included raw data in the pages of Scripture.

Numbers isn't all about numbers. Much of the book records the tragic failure of God's people to conquer the land promised to their ancestor Abraham. Instead of enjoying a land of plenty, most of the slaves who left Egypt died wandering in the desert.

The book gets its name from two censuses. The first one begins the book, a count of God's people after leaving Egypt. The second concludes the book, a numbering of the people as they again prepare to enter the promised land. If you do the math—or check Numbers 1:46—you learn there were 603,550 men of fighting age at the time of the first census, implying a total population of two or three million.

BUILDING

FAITH

WISDOM

STRENGTH

Learn a couple lessons as you ponder that overwhelming crowd. First, the Lord knew every one of the individuals he counted. To him, not a single one was just a number. Second, that enormous tally shows the Lord's amazing power. You serve a God who thinks big. He reached out to rescue a crowd we can hardly imagine.

[14]The LORD said to Moses in the Desert of Sinai, [15]"Count the Levites by their families and clans. Count every male a month old or more." [16]So Moses counted them, as he was commanded by the word of the LORD.

[17]These were the names of the sons of Levi:

Gershon, Kohath and Merari.

[18]These were the names of the Gershonite clans:

Libni and Shimei.

[19]The Kohathite clans:

Amram, Izhar, Hebron and Uzziel.

[20]The Merarite clans:

Mahli and Mushi.

These were the Levite clans, according to their families.

[21]To Gershon belonged the clans of the Libnites and Shimeites; these were the Gershonite clans. [22]The number of all the males a month old or more who were counted was 7,500. [23]The Gershonite clans were to camp on the west, behind the tabernacle. [24]The leader of the families of the Gershonites was Eliasaph son of Lael. [25]At the tent of meeting the Gershonites were responsible for the care of the tabernacle and tent, its coverings, the curtain at the entrance to the tent of meeting, [26]the curtains of the courtyard, the curtain at the entrance to the courtyard surrounding the tabernacle and altar, and the ropes—and everything related to their use.

[27]To Kohath belonged the clans of the Amramites, Izharites, Hebronites and Uzzielites; these were the Kohathite clans. [28]The number of all the males a month old or more was 8,600.[a] The Kohathites were responsible for the care of the sanctuary. [29]The Kohathite clans were to camp on the south side of the tabernacle. [30]The leader of the families of the Kohathite clans was Elizaphan son of Uzziel. [31]They were responsible for the care of the ark, the table, the lampstand, the altars, the articles of the sanctuary used in ministering, the curtain, and everything related to their use. [32]The chief leader of the Levites was Eleazar son of Aaron, the priest. He was appointed over those who were responsible for the care of the sanctuary.

[33]To Merari belonged the clans of the Mahlites and the Mushites; these were the Merarite clans. [34]The number of all the males a month old or more who were counted was 6,200. [35]The leader of the families of the Merarite clans was Zuriel son of Abihail; they were to camp on the north side of the tabernacle. [36]The Merarites were appointed to take care of the frames of the tabernacle, its crossbars, posts, bases, all its equipment, and everything related to their use, [37]as well as the posts of the surrounding courtyard with their bases, tent pegs and ropes.

[38]Moses and Aaron and his sons were to camp to the east of the tabernacle, toward the sunrise, in front of the tent of meeting. They were responsible for the care of the sanctuary on behalf of the Israelites. Anyone else who approached the sanctuary was to be put to death.

[39]The total number of Levites counted at the LORD's command by Moses and Aaron according to their clans, including every male a month old or more, was 22,000.

[40]The LORD said to Moses, "Count all the firstborn Israelite males who are a month old or more and make a list of their names. [41]Take the Levites for me in place of all the firstborn of the Israelites, and the livestock of the Levites in place of all the firstborn of the livestock of the Israelites. I am the LORD."

[42]So Moses counted all the firstborn of the Israelites, as the LORD commanded him. [43]The total number of firstborn males a month old or more, listed by name, was 22,273.

[44]The LORD also said to Moses, [45]"Take the Levites in place of all the firstborn of Israel, and the livestock of the Levites in place of their livestock. The Levites are to be mine. I am the LORD. [46]To redeem the 273 firstborn Israelites who exceed the number of the Levites, [47]collect five shekels[b] for each one, according to the sanctuary shekel, which weighs twenty gerahs. [48]Give the money for the redemption of the additional Israelites to Aaron and his sons."

[49]So Moses collected the redemption money from those who exceeded the number redeemed by the Levites. [50]From the

---

[a] 28 Hebrew; some Septuagint manuscripts 8,300   [b] 47 That is, about 2 ounces or about 58 grams

firstborn of the Israelites he collected silver weighing 1,365 shekels,[a] according to the sanctuary shekel. [51]Moses gave the redemption money to Aaron and his sons, as he was commanded by the word of the Lord.

The Kohathites

4 The Lord said to Moses and Aaron: [2]"Take a census of the Kohathite branch of the Levites by their clans and families. [3]Count all the men from thirty to fifty years of age who come to serve in the work at the tent of meeting.

[4]"This is the work of the Kohathites at the tent of meeting: the care of the most holy things. [5]When the camp is to move, Aaron and his sons are to go in and take down the shielding curtain and put it over the ark of the covenant law. [6]Then they are to cover the curtain with a durable leather,[b] spread a cloth of solid blue over that and put the poles in place.

[7]"Over the table of the Presence they are to spread a blue cloth and put on it the plates, dishes and bowls, and the jars for drink offerings; the bread that is continually there is to remain on it. [8]They are to spread a scarlet cloth over them, cover that with the durable leather and put the poles in place.

[9]"They are to take a blue cloth and cover the lampstand that is for light, together with its lamps, its wick trimmers and trays, and all its jars for the olive oil used to supply it. [10]Then they are to wrap it and all its accessories in a covering of the durable leather and put it on a carrying frame.

[11]"Over the gold altar they are to spread a blue cloth and cover that with the durable leather and put the poles in place.

[12]"They are to take all the articles used for ministering in the sanctuary, wrap them in a blue cloth, cover that with the durable leather and put them on a carrying frame.

[13]"They are to remove the ashes from the bronze altar and spread a purple cloth over it. [14]Then they are to place on it all the utensils used for ministering at the altar, including the firepans, meat forks, shovels and sprinkling bowls. Over it they are to spread a covering of the durable leather and put the poles in place.

[15]"After Aaron and his sons have finished covering the holy furnishings and all the holy articles, and when the camp is ready to move, only then are the Kohathites to come and do the carrying. But they must not touch the holy things or they will die. The Kohathites are to carry those things that are in the tent of meeting.

[16]"Eleazar son of Aaron, the priest, is to have charge of the oil for the light, the fragrant incense, the regular grain offering and the anointing oil. He is to be in charge of the entire tabernacle and everything in it, including its holy furnishings and articles."

[17]The Lord said to Moses and Aaron, [18]"See that the Kohathite tribal clans are not destroyed from among the Levites. [19]So that they may live and not die when they come near the most holy things, do this for them: Aaron and his sons are to go into the sanctuary and assign to each man his work and what he is to carry. [20]But the Kohathites must not go in to look at the holy things, even for a moment, or they will die."

The Gershonites

[21]The Lord said to Moses, [22]"Take a census also of the Gershonites by their families and clans. [23]Count all the men from thirty to fifty years of age who come to serve in the work at the tent of meeting.

[24]"This is the service of the Gershonite clans in their carrying and their other work: [25]They are to carry the curtains of the tabernacle, that is, the tent of meeting, its covering and its outer covering of durable leather, the curtains for the entrance to the tent of meeting, [26]the curtains of the courtyard surrounding the tabernacle and altar, the curtain for the entrance to the courtyard, the ropes and all the equipment used in the service of the tent. The Gershonites are to do all that needs to be done with these things. [27]All their service, whether carrying or doing other work, is to be done under the direction of Aaron and his sons. You shall assign to them as their responsibility all they are to carry. [28]This is the service of the Gershonite clans at the tent of meeting. Their duties are to be under the direction of Ithamar son of Aaron, the priest.

---

[a] 50 That is, about 35 pounds or about 16 kilograms also in verses 8, 10, 11, 12, 14 and 25   [b] 6 Possibly the hides of large aquatic mammals;

The Merarites

²⁹"Count the Merarites by their clans and families. ³⁰Count all the men from thirty to fifty years of age who come to serve in the work at the tent of meeting. ³¹As part of all their service at the tent, they are to carry the frames of the tabernacle, its crossbars, posts and bases, ³²as well as the posts of the surrounding courtyard with their bases, tent pegs, ropes, all their equipment and everything related to their use. Assign to each man the specific things he is to carry. ³³This is the service of the Merarite clans as they work at the tent of meeting under the direction of Ithamar son of Aaron, the priest."

The Numbering of the Levite Clans

³⁴Moses, Aaron and the leaders of the community counted the Kohathites by their clans and families. ³⁵All the men from thirty to fifty years of age who came to serve in the work at the tent of meeting, ³⁶counted by clans, were 2,750. ³⁷This was the total of all those in the Kohathite clans who served at the tent of meeting. Moses and Aaron counted them according to the LORD's command through Moses.

³⁸The Gershonites were counted by their clans and families. ³⁹All the men from thirty to fifty years of age who came to serve in the work at the tent of meeting, ⁴⁰counted by their clans and families, were 2,630. ⁴¹This was the total of those in the Gershonite clans who served at the tent of meeting. Moses and Aaron counted them according to the LORD's command.

⁴²The Merarites were counted by their clans and families. ⁴³All the men from thirty to fifty years of age who came to serve in the work at the tent of meeting, ⁴⁴counted by their clans, were 3,200. ⁴⁵This was the total of those in the Merarite clans. Moses and Aaron counted them according to the LORD's command through Moses.

⁴⁶So Moses, Aaron and the leaders of Israel counted all the Levites by their clans and families. ⁴⁷All the men from thirty to fifty years of age who came to do the work of serving and carrying the tent of meeting ⁴⁸numbered 8,580. ⁴⁹At the LORD's command through Moses, each was assigned his work and told what to carry.

Thus they were counted, as the LORD commanded Moses.

The Purity of the Camp

5 The LORD said to Moses, ²"Command the Israelites to send away from the camp anyone who has a defiling skin disease^a or a discharge of any kind, or who is ceremonially unclean because of a dead body. ³Send away male and female alike; send them outside the camp so they will not defile their camp, where I dwell among them." ⁴The Israelites did so; they sent them outside the camp. They did just as the LORD had instructed Moses.

Restitution for Wrongs

⁵The LORD said to Moses, ⁶"Say to the Israelites: 'Any man or woman who wrongs another in any way^b and so is unfaithful to the LORD is guilty ⁷and must confess the sin they have committed. They must make full restitution for the wrong they have done, add a fifth of the value to it and give it all to the person they have wronged. ⁸But if that person has no close relative to whom restitution can be made for the wrong, the restitution belongs to the LORD and must be given to the priest, along with the ram with which atonement is made for the wrongdoer. ⁹All the sacred contributions the Israelites bring to a priest will belong to him. ¹⁰Sacred things belong to their owners, but what they give to the priest will belong to the priest.'"

The Test for an Unfaithful Wife

¹¹Then the LORD said to Moses, ¹²"Speak to the Israelites and say to them: 'If a man's wife goes astray and is unfaithful to him ¹³so that another man has sexual relations with her, and this is hidden from her husband and her impurity is undetected (since there is no witness against her and she has not been caught in the act), ¹⁴and if feelings of jealousy come over her husband and he suspects his wife and she is impure — or if he is jealous and suspects her even though she is not impure — ¹⁵then he is to take his wife to the priest. He must also take an offering of a tenth of an ephah^c of barley flour on

---

^a 2 The Hebrew word for *defiling skin disease*, traditionally translated "leprosy," was used for various diseases affecting the skin.   ^b 6 Or *woman who commits any wrong common to mankind*   ^c 15 That is, probably about 3 1/2 pounds or about 1.6 kilograms

her behalf. He must not pour olive oil on it or put incense on it, because it is a grain offering for jealousy, a reminder-offering to draw attention to wrongdoing.

¹⁶ "'The priest shall bring her and have her stand before the LORD. ¹⁷ Then he shall take some holy water in a clay jar and put some dust from the tabernacle floor into the water. ¹⁸ After the priest has had the woman stand before the LORD, he shall loosen her hair and place in her hands the reminder-offering, the grain offering for jealousy, while he himself holds the bitter water that brings a curse. ¹⁹ Then the priest shall put the woman under oath and say to her, "If no other man has had sexual relations with you and you have not gone astray and become impure while married to your husband, may this bitter water that brings a curse not harm you. ²⁰ But if you have gone astray while married to your husband and you have made yourself impure by having sexual relations with a man other than your husband" — ²¹ here the priest is to put the woman under this curse — "may the LORD cause you to become a curse*a* among your people when he makes your womb miscarry and your abdomen swell. ²² May this water that brings a curse enter your body so that your abdomen swells or your womb miscarries."

"'Then the woman is to say, "Amen. So be it."

²³ "'The priest is to write these curses on a scroll and then wash them off into the bitter water. ²⁴ He shall make the woman drink the bitter water that brings a curse, and this water that brings a curse and causes bitter suffering will enter her. ²⁵ The priest is to take from her hands the grain offering for jealousy, wave it before the LORD and bring it to the altar. ²⁶ The priest is then to take a handful of the grain offering as a memorial*b* offering and burn it on the altar; after that, he is to have the woman drink the water. ²⁷ If she has made herself impure and been unfaithful to her husband, this will be the result: When she is made to drink the water that brings a curse and causes bitter suffering, it will enter her, her abdomen will swell and her womb will miscarry, and she will become a curse. ²⁸ If, however, the woman has not made herself impure, but is clean, she will

be cleared of guilt and will be able to have children.

²⁹ "'This, then, is the law of jealousy when a woman goes astray and makes herself impure while married to her husband, ³⁰ or when feelings of jealousy come over a man because he suspects his wife. The priest is to have her stand before the LORD and is to apply this entire law to her. ³¹ The husband will be innocent of any wrongdoing, but the woman will bear the consequences of her sin.'"

The Nazirite

6 The LORD said to Moses, ² "Speak to the Israelites and say to them: 'If a man or woman wants to make a special vow, a vow of dedication to the LORD as a Nazirite, ³ they must abstain from wine and other fermented drink and must not drink vinegar made from wine or other fermented drink. They must not drink grape juice or eat grapes or raisins. ⁴ As long as they remain under their Nazirite vow, they must not eat anything that comes from the grapevine, not even the seeds or skins.

⁵ "'During the entire period of their Nazirite vow, no razor may be used on their head. They must be holy until the period of their dedication to the LORD is over; they must let their hair grow long.

⁶ "'Throughout the period of their dedication to the LORD, the Nazirite must not go near a dead body. ⁷ Even if their own father or mother or brother or sister dies, they must not make themselves ceremonially unclean on account of them, because the symbol of their dedication to God is on their head. ⁸ Throughout the period of their dedication, they are consecrated to the LORD.

⁹ "'If someone dies suddenly in the Nazirite's presence, thus defiling the hair that symbolizes their dedication, they must shave their head on the seventh day — the day of their cleansing. ¹⁰ Then on the eighth day they must bring two doves or two young pigeons to the priest at the entrance to the tent of meeting. ¹¹ The priest is to offer one as a sin offering*c* and the other as a burnt offering to make atonement for the Nazirite because they sinned by being in the presence of the dead body. That same day they are to consecrate their head again. ¹² They must

---

a 21 That is, may he cause your name to be used in cursing (see Jer. 29:22); or, may others see that you are cursed; similarly in verse 27.   *b 26* Or *representative*   *c 11* Or *purification offering*; also in verses 14 and 16 rededicate themselves to the Lord for the same period of dedication and must bring a year-old male lamb as a guilt offering. The previous days do not count, because they became defiled during their period of dedication.

¹³ " 'Now this is the law of the Nazirite when the period of their dedication is over. They are to be brought to the entrance to the tent of meeting. ¹⁴ There they are to present their offerings to the Lord: a year-old male lamb without defect for a burnt offering, a year-old ewe lamb without defect for a sin offering, a ram without defect for a fellowship offering, ¹⁵ together with their grain offerings and drink offerings, and a basket of bread made with the finest flour and without yeast — thick loaves with olive oil mixed in, and thin loaves brushed with olive oil.

¹⁶ " 'The priest is to present all these before the Lord and make the sin offering and the burnt offering. ¹⁷ He is to present the basket of unleavened bread and is to sacrifice the ram as a fellowship offering to the Lord, together with its grain offering and drink offering.

¹⁸ " 'Then at the entrance to the tent of meeting, the Nazirite must shave off the hair that symbolizes their dedication. They are to take the hair and put it in the fire that is under the sacrifice of the fellowship offering.

¹⁹ " 'After the Nazirite has shaved off the hair that symbolizes their dedication, the priest is to place in their hands a boiled shoulder of the ram, and one thick loaf and one thin loaf from the basket, both made without yeast. ²⁰ The priest shall then wave these before the Lord as a wave offering; they are holy and belong to the priest, together with the breast that was waved and the thigh that was presented. After that, the Nazirite may drink wine.

²¹ " 'This is the law of the Nazirite who vows offerings to the Lord in accordance with their dedication, in addition to whatever else they can afford. They must fulfill the vows they have made, according to the law of the Nazirite.' "

The Priestly Blessing

²² The Lord said to Moses, ²³ "Tell Aaron and his sons, 'This is how you are to bless the Israelites. Say to them:

²⁴ " ' "The Lord bless you
    and keep you;
²⁵ the Lord make his face shine on you
    and be gracious to you;
²⁶ the Lord turn his face toward you
    and give you peace." '

²⁷ "So they will put my name on the Israelites, and I will bless them."

Offerings at the Dedication of the Tabernacle

7 When Moses finished setting up the tabernacle, he anointed and consecrated it and all its furnishings. He also anointed and consecrated the altar and all its utensils. ²Then the leaders of Israel, the heads of families who were the tribal leaders in charge of those who were counted, made offerings. ³They brought as their gifts before the Lord six covered carts and twelve oxen — an ox from each leader and a cart from every two. These they presented before the tabernacle.

⁴The Lord said to Moses, ⁵"Accept these from them, that they may be used in the work at the tent of meeting. Give them to the Levites as each man's work requires."

⁶So Moses took the carts and oxen and gave them to the Levites. ⁷He gave two carts and four oxen to the Gershonites, as their work required, ⁸and he gave four carts and eight oxen to the Merarites, as their work required. They were all under the direction of Ithamar son of Aaron, the priest. ⁹But Moses did not give any to the Kohathites, because they were to carry on their shoulders the holy things, for which they were responsible.

¹⁰When the altar was anointed, the leaders brought their offerings for its dedication and presented them before the altar. ¹¹For the Lord had said to Moses, "Each day one leader is to bring his offering for the dedication of the altar."

¹²The one who brought his offering on the first day was Nahshon son of Amminadab of the tribe of Judah.

¹³His offering was one silver plate weighing a hundred and thirty shekels ᵃ and one silver sprinkling bowl weighing seventy shekels, ᵇ both according to the sanctuary shekel, each filled with the finest flour mixed with olive oil as

---

ᵃ 13 That is, about 3 1/4 pounds or about 1.5 kilograms; also elsewhere in this chapter   ᵇ 13 That is, about 1 3/4 pounds or about 800 grams; also elsewhere in this chapter

IT'S EMOTIONAL

READ: NUMBERS 6:24-26

This section of Numbers might leave you flipping through emotions ranging from a wry smile to deep thoughtfulness to puzzled concern. Who knew a skin disease would make someone unfit to live with God's people? How can the principles of restitution be applied today? And what's up with that test of an unfaithful wife?

Not every portion of God's Word is easy to understand or apply. Every honest Bible reader needs a plan to deal with difficult parts.

You can start by coming to the Bible to learn. Some people read this book looking for points to correct instead of letting it alter how they think and act. Or when you can't understand the details, look for the main point. A puzzling passage like the test for unfaithful wives shows that God cares about sexual purity. Or keep digging for answers. Ask your pastor or look for Bible helps online that deal with everything from language to archaeology. Or admit you don't know everything. You don't need answers for every minor issue.

No matter where you read in the Bible, one truth comes through. The Lord has a plan to bless you. He will keep you safe and smile at you. He will grant you favor you don't deserve. He will look your way and fill you with peace.

BUILDING

FAITH

WISDOM

STRENGTH

a grain offering; ¹⁴one gold dish weighing ten shekels,^a filled with incense; ¹⁵one young bull, one ram and one male lamb a year old for a burnt offering; ¹⁶one male goat for a sin offering^b; ¹⁷and two oxen, five rams, five male goats and five male lambs a year old to be sacrificed as a fellowship offering. This was the offering of Nahshon son of Amminadab.

¹⁸On the second day Nethanel son of Zuar, the leader of Issachar, brought his offering.

¹⁹The offering he brought was one silver plate weighing a hundred and thirty shekels and one silver sprinkling bowl weighing seventy shekels, both according to the sanctuary shekel, each filled with the finest flour mixed with olive oil as a grain offering; ²⁰one gold dish weighing ten shekels, filled with incense; ²¹one young bull, one ram and one male lamb a year old for a burnt offering; ²²one male goat for a sin offering; ²³and two oxen, five rams, five male goats and five male lambs a year old to be sacrificed as a fellowship offering. This was the offering of Nethanel son of Zuar.

²⁴On the third day, Eliab son of Helon, the leader of the people of Zebulun, brought his offering.

²⁵His offering was one silver plate weighing a hundred and thirty shekels and one silver sprinkling bowl weighing seventy shekels, both according to the sanctuary shekel, each filled with the finest flour mixed with olive oil as a grain offering; ²⁶one gold dish weighing ten shekels, filled with incense; ²⁷one young bull, one ram and one male lamb a year old for a burnt offering; ²⁸one male goat for a sin offering; ²⁹and two oxen, five rams, five male goats and five male lambs a year old to be sacrificed as a fellowship offering. This was the offering of Eliab son of Helon.

³⁰On the fourth day Elizur son of Shedeur, the leader of the people of Reuben, brought his offering.

³¹His offering was one silver plate weighing a hundred and thirty shekels and one silver sprinkling bowl weighing seventy shekels, both according to the sanctuary shekel, each filled with the finest flour mixed with olive oil as a grain offering; ³²one gold dish weighing ten shekels, filled with incense; ³³one young bull, one ram and one male lamb a year old for a burnt offering; ³⁴one male goat for a sin offering; ³⁵and two oxen, five rams, five male goats and five male lambs a year old to be sacrificed as a fellowship offering. This was the offering of Elizur son of Shedeur.

³⁶On the fifth day Shelumiel son of Zurishaddai, the leader of the people of Simeon, brought his offering.

³⁷His offering was one silver plate weighing a hundred and thirty shekels and one silver sprinkling bowl weighing seventy shekels, both according to the sanctuary shekel, each filled with the finest flour mixed with olive oil as a grain offering; ³⁸one gold dish weighing ten shekels, filled with incense; ³⁹one young bull, one ram and one male lamb a year old for a burnt offering; ⁴⁰one male goat for a sin offering; ⁴¹and two oxen, five rams, five male goats and five male lambs a year old to be sacrificed as a fellowship offering. This was the offering of Shelumiel son of Zurishaddai.

⁴²On the sixth day Eliasaph son of Deuel, the leader of the people of Gad, brought his offering.

⁴³His offering was one silver plate weighing a hundred and thirty shekels and one silver sprinkling bowl weighing seventy shekels, both according to the sanctuary shekel, each filled with the finest flour mixed with olive oil as a grain offering; ⁴⁴one gold dish weighing ten shekels, filled with incense; ⁴⁵one young bull, one ram and one male lamb a year old for a burnt offering; ⁴⁶one male goat for a sin offering; ⁴⁷and two oxen, five rams, five male goats and five male lambs a year old to

---

^a *14* That is, about 4 ounces or about 115 grams; also elsewhere in this chapter   ^b *16* Or *purification offering*; also elsewhere in this chapter

be sacrificed as a fellowship offering. This was the offering of Eliasaph son of Deuel.

⁴⁸On the seventh day Elishama son of Ammihud, the leader of the people of Ephraim, brought his offering.

⁴⁹His offering was one silver plate weighing a hundred and thirty shekels and one silver sprinkling bowl weighing seventy shekels, both according to the sanctuary shekel, each filled with the finest flour mixed with olive oil as a grain offering; ⁵⁰one gold dish weighing ten shekels, filled with incense; ⁵¹one young bull, one ram and one male lamb a year old for a burnt offering; ⁵²one male goat for a sin offering; ⁵³and two oxen, five rams, five male goats and five male lambs a year old to be sacrificed as a fellowship offering. This was the offering of Elishama son of Ammihud.

⁵⁴On the eighth day Gamaliel son of Pedahzur, the leader of the people of Manasseh, brought his offering.

⁵⁵His offering was one silver plate weighing a hundred and thirty shekels and one silver sprinkling bowl weighing seventy shekels, both according to the sanctuary shekel, each filled with the finest flour mixed with olive oil as a grain offering; ⁵⁶one gold dish weighing ten shekels, filled with incense; ⁵⁷one young bull, one ram and one male lamb a year old for a burnt offering; ⁵⁸one male goat for a sin offering; ⁵⁹and two oxen, five rams, five male goats and five male lambs a year old to be sacrificed as a fellowship offering. This was the offering of Gamaliel son of Pedahzur.

⁶⁰On the ninth day Abidan son of Gideoni, the leader of the people of Benjamin, brought his offering.

⁶¹His offering was one silver plate weighing a hundred and thirty shekels and one silver sprinkling bowl weighing seventy shekels, both according to the sanctuary shekel, each filled with the finest flour mixed with olive oil as a grain offering; ⁶²one gold dish weighing ten shekels, filled with incense; ⁶³one young bull, one ram and one

male lamb a year old for a burnt offering; ⁶⁴one male goat for a sin offering; ⁶⁵and two oxen, five rams, five male goats and five male lambs a year old to be sacrificed as a fellowship offering. This was the offering of Abidan son of Gideoni.

⁶⁶On the tenth day Ahiezer son of Ammishaddai, the leader of the people of Dan, brought his offering.

⁶⁷His offering was one silver plate weighing a hundred and thirty shekels and one silver sprinkling bowl weighing seventy shekels, both according to the sanctuary shekel, each filled with the finest flour mixed with olive oil as a grain offering; ⁶⁸one gold dish weighing ten shekels, filled with incense; ⁶⁹one young bull, one ram and one male lamb a year old for a burnt offering; ⁷⁰one male goat for a sin offering; ⁷¹and two oxen, five rams, five male goats and five male lambs a year old to be sacrificed as a fellowship offering. This was the offering of Ahiezer son of Ammishaddai.

⁷²On the eleventh day Pagiel son of Okran, the leader of the people of Asher, brought his offering.

⁷³His offering was one silver plate weighing a hundred and thirty shekels and one silver sprinkling bowl weighing seventy shekels, both according to the sanctuary shekel, each filled with the finest flour mixed with olive oil as a grain offering; ⁷⁴one gold dish weighing ten shekels, filled with incense; ⁷⁵one young bull, one ram and one male lamb a year old for a burnt offering; ⁷⁶one male goat for a sin offering; ⁷⁷and two oxen, five rams, five male goats and five male lambs a year old to be sacrificed as a fellowship offering. This was the offering of Pagiel son of Okran.

⁷⁸On the twelfth day Ahira son of Enan, the leader of the people of Naphtali, brought his offering.

⁷⁹His offering was one silver plate weighing a hundred and thirty shekels and one silver sprinkling bowl weighing seventy shekels, both according to the sanctuary shekel, each filled with

the finest flour mixed with olive oil as a grain offering; [80] one gold dish weighing ten shekels, filled with incense; [81] one young bull, one ram and one male lamb a year old for a burnt offering; [82] one male goat for a sin offering; [83] and two oxen, five rams, five male goats and five male lambs a year old to be sacrificed as a fellowship offering. This was the offering of Ahira son of Enan.

[84] These were the offerings of the Israelite leaders for the dedication of the altar when it was anointed: twelve silver plates, twelve silver sprinkling bowls and twelve gold dishes. [85] Each silver plate weighed a hundred and thirty shekels, and each sprinkling bowl seventy shekels. Altogether, the silver dishes weighed two thousand four hundred shekels,[a] according to the sanctuary shekel. [86] The twelve gold dishes filled with incense weighed ten shekels each, according to the sanctuary shekel. Altogether, the gold dishes weighed a hundred and twenty shekels.[b] [87] The total number of animals for the burnt offering came to twelve young bulls, twelve rams and twelve male lambs a year old, together with their grain offering. Twelve male goats were used for the sin offering. [88] The total number of animals for the sacrifice of the fellowship offering came to twenty-four oxen, sixty rams, sixty male goats and sixty male lambs a year old. These were the offerings for the dedication of the altar after it was anointed.

[89] When Moses entered the tent of meeting to speak with the LORD, he heard the voice speaking to him from between the two cherubim above the atonement cover on the ark of the covenant law. In this way the LORD spoke to him.

Setting Up the Lamps

8 The LORD said to Moses, [2] "Speak to Aaron and say to him, 'When you set up the lamps, see that all seven light up the area in front of the lampstand.'"

[3] Aaron did so; he set up the lamps so that they faced forward on the lampstand, just as the LORD commanded Moses. [4] This is how the lampstand was made: It was made of hammered gold—from its base to its blossoms. The lampstand was made exactly like the pattern the LORD had shown Moses.

The Setting Apart of the Levites

[5] The LORD said to Moses: [6] "Take the Levites from among all the Israelites and make them ceremonially clean. [7] To purify them, do this: Sprinkle the water of cleansing on them; then have them shave their whole bodies and wash their clothes. And so they will purify themselves. [8] Have them take a young bull with its grain offering of the finest flour mixed with olive oil; then you are to take a second young bull for a sin offering.[c] [9] Bring the Levites to the front of the tent of meeting and assemble the whole Israelite community. [10] You are to bring the Levites before the LORD, and the Israelites are to lay their hands on them. [11] Aaron is to present the Levites before the LORD as a wave offering from the Israelites, so that they may be ready to do the work of the LORD.

[12] "Then the Levites are to lay their hands on the heads of the bulls, using one for a sin offering to the LORD and the other for a burnt offering, to make atonement for the Levites. [13] Have the Levites stand in front of Aaron and his sons and then present them as a wave offering to the LORD. [14] In this way you are to set the Levites apart from the other Israelites, and the Levites will be mine.

[15] "After you have purified the Levites and presented them as a wave offering, they are to come to do their work at the tent of meeting. [16] They are the Israelites who are to be given wholly to me. I have taken them as my own in place of the firstborn, the first male offspring from every Israelite woman. [17] Every firstborn male in Israel, whether human or animal, is mine. When I struck down all the firstborn in Egypt, I set them apart for myself. [18] And I have taken the Levites in place of all the firstborn sons in Israel. [19] From among all the Israelites, I have given the Levites as gifts to Aaron and his sons to do the work at the tent of meeting on behalf of the Israelites and to make atonement for them so that no plague will strike the Israelites when they go near the sanctuary."

[20] Moses, Aaron and the whole Israelite community did with the Levites just as the

---

[a] 85 That is, about 60 pounds or about 28 kilograms kilograms   [c] 8 Or *purification offering*; also in verse 12   [b] 86 That is, about 3 pounds or about 1.4

LORD commanded Moses. ²¹The Levites purified themselves and washed their clothes. Then Aaron presented them as a wave offering before the LORD and made atonement for them to purify them. ²²After that, the Levites came to do their work at the tent of meeting under the supervision of Aaron and his sons. They did with the Levites just as the LORD commanded Moses.

²³The LORD said to Moses, ²⁴"This applies to the Levites: Men twenty-five years old or more shall come to take part in the work at the tent of meeting, ²⁵but at the age of fifty, they must retire from their regular service and work no longer. ²⁶They may assist their brothers in performing their duties at the tent of meeting, but they themselves must not do the work. This, then, is how you are to assign the responsibilities of the Levites."

The Passover

9 The LORD spoke to Moses in the Desert of Sinai in the first month of the second year after they came out of Egypt. He said, ²"Have the Israelites celebrate the Passover at the appointed time. ³Celebrate it at the appointed time, at twilight on the fourteenth day of this month, in accordance with all its rules and regulations."

⁴So Moses told the Israelites to celebrate the Passover, ⁵and they did so in the Desert of Sinai at twilight on the fourteenth day of the first month. The Israelites did everything just as the LORD commanded Moses.

⁶But some of them could not celebrate the Passover on that day because they were ceremonially unclean on account of a dead body. So they came to Moses and Aaron that same day ⁷and said to Moses, "We have become unclean because of a dead body, but why should we be kept from presenting the LORD's offering with the other Israelites at the appointed time?"

⁸Moses answered them, "Wait until I find out what the LORD commands concerning you."

⁹Then the LORD said to Moses, ¹⁰"Tell the Israelites: 'When any of you or your descendants are unclean because of a dead body or are away on a journey, they are still to celebrate the LORD's Passover, ¹¹but they are to do it on the fourteenth day of the second month at twilight. They are to eat the lamb, together with unleavened bread and bitter herbs. ¹²They must not leave any of it till morning or break any of its bones. When they celebrate the Passover, they must follow all the regulations. ¹³But if anyone who is ceremonially clean and not on a journey fails to celebrate the Passover, they must be cut off from their people for not presenting the LORD's offering at the appointed time. They will bear the consequences of their sin.

¹⁴"'A foreigner residing among you is also to celebrate the LORD's Passover in accordance with its rules and regulations. You must have the same regulations for both the foreigner and the native-born.'"

The Cloud Above the Tabernacle

¹⁵On the day the tabernacle, the tent of the covenant law, was set up, the cloud covered it. From evening till morning the cloud above the tabernacle looked like fire. ¹⁶That is how it continued to be; the cloud covered it, and at night it looked like fire. ¹⁷Whenever the cloud lifted from above the tent, the Israelites set out; wherever the cloud settled, the Israelites encamped. ¹⁸At the LORD's command the Israelites set out, and at his command they encamped. As long as the cloud stayed over the tabernacle, they remained in camp. ¹⁹When the cloud remained over the tabernacle a long time, the Israelites obeyed the LORD's order and did not set out. ²⁰Sometimes the cloud was over the tabernacle only a few days; at the LORD's command they would encamp, and then at his command they would set out. ²¹Sometimes the cloud stayed only from evening till morning, and when it lifted in the morning, they set out. Whether by day or by night, whenever the cloud lifted, they set out. ²²Whether the cloud stayed over the tabernacle for two days or a month or a year, the Israelites would remain in camp and not set out; but when it lifted, they would set out. ²³At the LORD's command they encamped, and at the LORD's command they set out. They obeyed the LORD's order, in accordance with his command through Moses.

The Silver Trumpets

10 The LORD said to Moses: ²"Make two trumpets of hammered silver, and use them for calling the community together and for having the camps set out. ³When both are sounded, the whole community is to assemble before you at the entrance to the tent of meeting. ⁴If only one is sounded, the leaders — the heads of the clans of Israel — are to assemble before you. ⁵When a trumpet blast is sounded, the tribes camping on the east are to set out. ⁶At the sounding of a second blast, the camps on the south are to set out. The blast will be the signal for setting out. ⁷To gather the assembly, blow the trumpets, but not with the signal for setting out.

⁸"The sons of Aaron, the priests, are to blow the trumpets. This is to be a lasting ordinance for you and the generations to come. ⁹When you go into battle in your own land against an enemy who is oppressing you, sound a blast on the trumpets. Then you will be remembered by the LORD your God and rescued from your enemies. ¹⁰Also at your times of rejoicing — your appointed festivals and New Moon feasts — you are to sound the trumpets over your burnt offerings and fellowship offerings, and they will be a memorial for you before your God. I am the LORD your God."

The Israelites Leave Sinai

¹¹On the twentieth day of the second month of the second year, the cloud lifted from above the tabernacle of the covenant law. ¹²Then the Israelites set out from the Desert of Sinai and traveled from place to place until the cloud came to rest in the Desert of Paran. ¹³They set out, this first time, at the LORD's command through Moses.

¹⁴The divisions of the camp of Judah went first, under their standard. Nahshon son of Amminadab was in command. ¹⁵Nethanel son of Zuar was over the division of the tribe of Issachar, ¹⁶and Eliab son of Helon was over the division of the tribe of Zebulun. ¹⁷Then the tabernacle was taken down, and the Gershonites and Merarites, who carried it, set out.

¹⁸The divisions of the camp of Reuben went next, under their standard. Elizur son of Shedeur was in command. ¹⁹Shelumiel son of Zurishaddai was over the division of the tribe of Simeon, ²⁰and Eliasaph son of Deuel was over the division of the tribe of Gad. ²¹Then the Kohathites set out, carrying the holy things. The tabernacle was to be set up before they arrived.

²²The divisions of the camp of Ephraim went next, under their standard. Elishama son of Ammihud was in command. ²³Gamaliel son of Pedahzur was over the division of the tribe of Manasseh, ²⁴and Abidan son of Gideoni was over the division of the tribe of Benjamin.

²⁵Finally, as the rear guard for all the units, the divisions of the camp of Dan set out under their standard. Ahiezer son of Ammishaddai was in command. ²⁶Pagiel son of Okran was over the division of the tribe of Asher, ²⁷and Ahira son of Enan was over the division of the tribe of Naphtali. ²⁸This was the order of march for the Israelite divisions as they set out.

²⁹Now Moses said to Hobab son of Reuel the Midianite, Moses' father-in-law, "We are setting out for the place about which the LORD said, 'I will give it to you.' Come with us and we will treat you well, for the LORD has promised good things to Israel."

³⁰He answered, "No, I will not go; I am going back to my own land and my own people."

³¹But Moses said, "Please do not leave us. You know where we should camp in the wilderness, and you can be our eyes. ³²If you come with us, we will share with you whatever good things the LORD gives us."

³³So they set out from the mountain of the LORD and traveled for three days. The ark of the covenant of the LORD went before them during those three days to find them a place to rest. ³⁴The cloud of the LORD was over them by day when they set out from the camp.

³⁵Whenever the ark set out, Moses said,

"Rise up, LORD!
    May your enemies be scattered;
    may your foes flee before you."

³⁶Whenever it came to rest, he said,

"Return, LORD,
    to the countless thousands of Israel."

Fire From the LORD

11 Now the people complained about their hardships in the hearing of the LORD, and when he heard them his anger was aroused. Then fire from the LORD burned among them and consumed some of the outskirts of the camp. ²When the people cried out to Moses, he prayed to the LORD and the fire died down. ³So that place was called Taberah,[a] because fire from the LORD had burned among them.

Quail From the LORD

[4] The rabble with them began to crave other food, and again the Israelites started wailing and said, "If only we had meat to eat! [5] We remember the fish we ate in Egypt at no cost—also the cucumbers, melons, leeks, onions and garlic. [6] But now we have lost our appetite; we never see anything but this manna!"

[7] The manna was like coriander seed and looked like resin. [8] The people went around gathering it, and then ground it in a hand mill or crushed it in a mortar. They cooked it in a pot or made it into loaves. And it tasted like something made with olive oil. [9] When the dew settled on the camp at night, the manna also came down.

[10] Moses heard the people of every family wailing at the entrance to their tents. The LORD became exceedingly angry, and Moses was troubled. [11] He asked the LORD, "Why have you brought this trouble on your servant? What have I done to displease you that you put the burden of all these people on me? [12] Did I conceive all these people? Did I give them birth? Why do you tell me to carry them in my arms, as a nurse carries an infant, to the land you promised on oath to their ancestors? [13] Where can I get meat for all these people? They keep wailing to me, 'Give us meat to eat!' [14] I cannot carry all these people by myself; the burden is too heavy for me. [15] If this is how you are going to treat me, please go ahead and kill me—if I have found favor in your eyes—and do not let me face my own ruin."

[16] The LORD said to Moses: "Bring me seventy of Israel's elders who are known to you as leaders and officials among the people. Have them come to the tent of meeting, that they may stand there with you. [17] I will come down and speak with you there, and I will take some of the power of the Spirit that is on you and put it on them. They will share the burden of the people with you so that you will not have to carry it alone.

[18] "Tell the people: 'Consecrate yourselves in preparation for tomorrow, when you will eat meat. The LORD heard you when you wailed, "If only we had meat to eat! We were better off in Egypt!" Now the LORD will give you meat, and you will eat it. [19] You will not eat it for just one day, or two days, or five, ten or twenty days, [20] but for a whole month—until it comes out of your nostrils and you loathe it—because you have rejected the LORD, who is among you, and have wailed before him, saying, "Why did we ever leave Egypt?"'"

[21] But Moses said, "Here I am among six hundred thousand men on foot, and you say, 'I will give them meat to eat for a whole month!' [22] Would they have enough if flocks and herds were slaughtered for them? Would they have enough if all the fish in the sea were caught for them?"

[23] The LORD answered Moses, "Is the LORD's arm too short? Now you will see whether or not what I say will come true for you."

[24] So Moses went out and told the people what the LORD had said. He brought together seventy of their elders and had them stand around the tent. [25] Then the LORD came down in the cloud and spoke with him, and he took some of the power of the Spirit that was on him and put it on the seventy elders. When the Spirit rested on them, they prophesied—but did not do so again.

[26] However, two men, whose names were Eldad and Medad, had remained in the camp. They were listed among the elders, but did not go out to the tent. Yet the Spirit also rested on them, and they prophesied in the camp. [27] A young man ran and told Moses, "Eldad and Medad are prophesying in the camp."

[28] Joshua son of Nun, who had been Moses' aide since youth, spoke up and said, "Moses, my lord, stop them!"

[29] But Moses replied, "Are you jealous for my sake? I wish that all the LORD's people were prophets and that the LORD would put his Spirit on them!" [30] Then Moses and the elders of Israel returned to the camp.

[31] Now a wind went out from the LORD and drove quail in from the sea. It scattered them up to two cubits[b] deep all around the camp, as far as a day's walk in any direction. [32] All that day and night and all the next day the people went out and gathered quail. No

---

[a] 3 *Taberah* means *burning*.   [b] 31 That is, about 3 feet or about 90 centimeters

HOW MANY WHAT?

READ: **NUMBERS 11:4-32**

The Israelites were parked about fifty miles inland from the Mediterranean Sea and fifty miles southwest of the Dead Sea. The significance is this: Quail tend to live by the water; they don't fly long distances. If it hadn't been for a little supernatural wind, they would have never made it this far. So this is a meteorological miracle.

When quail get tired, they dive-bomb. We're not talking about a perfectly angled duck that makes a smooth landing on a watery runway; quail were falling from the sky like huge pieces of hail. There had to be more than one black eye as the Israelites looked up to see quail falling from the sky.

Can you imagine seeing that many birds fly into the camp? It was like a bird blizzard. Quailmageddon. The cloud of birds was so massive that it seemed like a solar eclipse. For the rest of their lives, when the eyewitnesses who were there that day closed their eyes at night, they counted quail.

BUILDING

FAITH

WISDOM

STRENGTH

Once the quail stopped falling, the Israelites started gathering. Each Israelite gathered no less than ten homers. Ten homers multiplied by 600,000 men equals 6 million homers at a minimum. A homer equated to roughly 200 liters, and assuming that the quail were of an average size, it rained somewhere in the neighborhood of 105 million quail. You read that right: 105 million quail. God doesn't just provide in dramatic fashion; God provides in dramatic proportion. You never know how God will provide, but it's always cloudy with a chance of quail.

Taken from *The Circle Maker Student Edition* by Mark Batterson with Parker Batterson, copyright © 2012 by Mark Batterson, published by Zondervan.

one gathered less than ten homers.*a* Then they spread them out all around the camp. ³³But while the meat was still between their teeth and before it could be consumed, the anger of the LORD burned against the people, and he struck them with a severe plague. ³⁴Therefore the place was named Kibroth Hattaavah,*b* because there they buried the people who had craved other food.

³⁵From Kibroth Hattaavah the people traveled to Hazeroth and stayed there.

Miriam and Aaron Oppose Moses

12 Miriam and Aaron began to talk against Moses because of his Cushite wife, for he had married a Cushite. ²"Has the LORD spoken only through Moses?" they asked. "Hasn't he also spoken through us?" And the LORD heard this.

³(Now Moses was a very humble man, more humble than anyone else on the face of the earth.)

⁴At once the LORD said to Moses, Aaron and Miriam, "Come out to the tent of meeting, all three of you." So the three of them went out. ⁵Then the LORD came down in a pillar of cloud; he stood at the entrance to the tent and summoned Aaron and Miriam. When the two of them stepped forward, ⁶he said, "Listen to my words:

"When there is a prophet among you,
    I, the LORD, reveal myself to them in
        visions,
    I speak to them in dreams.
⁷But this is not true of my servant Moses;
    he is faithful in all my house.
⁸With him I speak face to face,
    clearly and not in riddles;
    he sees the form of the LORD.
Why then were you not afraid
    to speak against my servant Moses?"

⁹The anger of the LORD burned against them, and he left them.

¹⁰When the cloud lifted from above the tent, Miriam's skin was leprous*c*—it became as white as snow. Aaron turned toward her and saw that she had a defiling skin disease, ¹¹and he said to Moses, "Please, my lord, I ask you not to hold against us the sin we have so foolishly committed. ¹²Do not let her be like a stillborn infant coming from its mother's womb with its flesh half eaten away."

¹³So Moses cried out to the LORD, "Please, God, heal her!"

¹⁴The LORD replied to Moses, "If her father had spit in her face, would she not have been in disgrace for seven days? Confine her outside the camp for seven days; after that she can be brought back." ¹⁵So Miriam was confined outside the camp for seven days, and the people did not move on till she was brought back.

¹⁶After that, the people left Hazeroth and encamped in the Desert of Paran.

Exploring Canaan

13 The LORD said to Moses, ²"Send some men to explore the land of Canaan, which I am giving to the Israelites. From each ancestral tribe send one of its leaders."

³So at the LORD's command Moses sent them out from the Desert of Paran. All of them were leaders of the Israelites. ⁴These are their names:

from the tribe of Reuben, Shammua son of Zakkur;
⁵from the tribe of Simeon, Shaphat son of Hori;
⁶from the tribe of Judah, Caleb son of Jephunneh;
⁷from the tribe of Issachar, Igal son of Joseph;
⁸from the tribe of Ephraim, Hoshea son of Nun;
⁹from the tribe of Benjamin, Palti son of Raphu;
¹⁰from the tribe of Zebulun, Gaddiel son of Sodi;
¹¹from the tribe of Manasseh (a tribe of Joseph), Gaddi son of Susi;
¹²from the tribe of Dan, Ammiel son of Gemalli;
¹³from the tribe of Asher, Sethur son of Michael;
¹⁴from the tribe of Naphtali, Nahbi son of Vophsi;
¹⁵from the tribe of Gad, Geuel son of Maki.

¹⁶These are the names of the men Moses sent to explore the land. (Moses gave Hoshea son of Nun the name Joshua.)

¹⁷When Moses sent them to explore Canaan, he said, "Go up through the Negev and

---

a 32 That is, possibly about 1 3/4 tons or about 1.6 metric tons   *b 34 Kibroth Hattaavah* means *graves of craving.*   *c 10* The Hebrew for *leprous* was used for various diseases affecting the skin.

on into the hill country. ¹⁸See what the land is like and whether the people who live there are strong or weak, few or many. ¹⁹What kind of land do they live in? Is it good or bad? What kind of towns do they live in? Are they unwalled or fortified? ²⁰How is the soil? Is it fertile or poor? Are there trees in it or not? Do your best to bring back some of the fruit of the land." (It was the season for the first ripe grapes.)

²¹So they went up and explored the land from the Desert of Zin as far as Rehob, toward Lebo Hamath. ²²They went up through the Negev and came to Hebron, where Ahiman, Sheshai and Talmai, the descendants of Anak, lived. (Hebron had been built seven years before Zoan in Egypt.) ²³When they reached the Valley of Eshkol,ᵃ they cut off a branch bearing a single cluster of grapes. Two of them carried it on a pole between them, along with some pomegranates and figs. ²⁴That place was called the Valley of Eshkol because of the cluster of grapes the Israelites cut off there. ²⁵At the end of forty days they returned from exploring the land.

Report on the Exploration

²⁶They came back to Moses and Aaron and the whole Israelite community at Kadesh in the Desert of Paran. There they reported to them and to the whole assembly and showed them the fruit of the land. ²⁷They gave Moses this account: "We went into the land to which you sent us, and it does flow with milk and honey! Here is its fruit. ²⁸But the people who live there are powerful, and the cities are fortified and very large. We even saw descendants of Anak there. ²⁹The Amalekites live in the Negev; the Hittites, Jebusites and Amorites live in the hill country; and the Canaanites live near the sea and along the Jordan."

³⁰Then Caleb silenced the people before Moses and said, "We should go up and take possession of the land, for we can certainly do it."

³¹But the men who had gone up with him said, "We can't attack those people; they are stronger than we are." ³²And they spread among the Israelites a bad report about the land they had explored. They said, "The land we explored devours those living in it. All the people we saw there are of great size. ³³We

saw the Nephilim there (the descendants of Anak come from the Nephilim). We seemed like grasshoppers in our own eyes, and we looked the same to them."

The People Rebel

14 That night all the members of the community raised their voices and wept aloud. ²All the Israelites grumbled against Moses and Aaron, and the whole assembly said to them, "If only we had died in Egypt! Or in this wilderness! ³Why is the LORD bringing us to this land only to let us fall by the sword? Our wives and children will be taken as plunder. Wouldn't it be better for us to go back to Egypt?" ⁴And they said to each other, "We should choose a leader and go back to Egypt."

⁵Then Moses and Aaron fell facedown in front of the whole Israelite assembly gathered there. ⁶Joshua son of Nun and Caleb son of Jephunneh, who were among those who had explored the land, tore their clothes ⁷and said to the entire Israelite assembly, "The land we passed through and explored is exceedingly good. ⁸If the LORD is pleased with us, he will lead us into that land, a land flowing with milk and honey, and will give it to us. ⁹Only do not rebel against the LORD. And do not be afraid of the people of the land, because we will devour them. Their protection is gone, but the LORD is with us. Do not be afraid of them."

¹⁰But the whole assembly talked about stoning them. Then the glory of the LORD appeared at the tent of meeting to all the Israelites. ¹¹The LORD said to Moses, "How long will these people treat me with contempt? How long will they refuse to believe in me, in spite of all the signs I have performed among them? ¹²I will strike them down with a plague and destroy them, but I will make you into a nation greater and stronger than they."

¹³Moses said to the LORD, "Then the Egyptians will hear about it! By your power you brought these people up from among them. ¹⁴And they will tell the inhabitants of this land about it. They have already heard that you, LORD, are with these people and that you, LORD, have been seen face to face, that your cloud stays over them, and that you go before them in a pillar of cloud by day and

---

ᵃ 23 *Eshkol* means *cluster*; also in verse 24.

MILK AND HONEY

READ: **NUMBERS 13:32**

The trip from Egypt to the promised land hadn't gone as smoothly as planned. There were peak moments, like when God's people bolted across the Red Sea (Exodus 13:17-14:31) and heard the Lord speak his Ten Commandments (20:1-21). But then the people bowed to a false god (32:1-35) and complained about the Lord's care (Numbers 11:4-35).

Now those escaped slaves had camped on the edge of the land the Lord had sworn to their ancestor Abraham. A series of battles loomed near, so Moses sent a dozen spies to scout the land. These men returned carrying a giant cluster of grapes and reported that the land was as full of milk and honey as the Lord had promised. But there was a catch: the land was also occupied by strong people and well-fortified cities. Only Caleb and Joshua believed the Lord was mighty enough to fulfill his promise to give the land to the Israelites. When the people rebelled and refused to enter, the Lord sent them to wander in the desert. None of the adults except Joshua and Caleb would survive to enter the land—not even Moses.

BUILDING FAITH WISDOM STRENGTH

The Lord expects you to take him at his word. His commands might seem unattainable and his promises unreal. But when you refuse to believe and act on his word, you risk missing out on his very best. Trust is the only way you can grab hold of his amazing promises.

a pillar of fire by night. ¹⁵If you put all these people to death, leaving none alive, the nations who have heard this report about you will say, ¹⁶'The Lord was not able to bring these people into the land he promised them on oath, so he slaughtered them in the wilderness.'

¹⁷"Now may the Lord's strength be displayed, just as you have declared: ¹⁸'The Lord is slow to anger, abounding in love and forgiving sin and rebellion. Yet he does not leave the guilty unpunished; he punishes the children for the sin of the parents to the third and fourth generation.' ¹⁹In accordance with your great love, forgive the sin of these people, just as you have pardoned them from the time they left Egypt until now."

²⁰The Lord replied, "I have forgiven them, as you asked. ²¹Nevertheless, as surely as I live and as surely as the glory of the Lord fills the whole earth, ²²not one of those who saw my glory and the signs I performed in Egypt and in the wilderness but who disobeyed me and tested me ten times— ²³not one of them will ever see the land I promised on oath to their ancestors. No one who has treated me with contempt will ever see it. ²⁴But because my servant Caleb has a different spirit and follows me wholeheartedly, I will bring him into the land he went to, and his descendants will inherit it. ²⁵Since the Amalekites and the Canaanites are living in the valleys, turn back tomorrow and set out toward the desert along the route to the Red Sea.^a"

²⁶The Lord said to Moses and Aaron: ²⁷"How long will this wicked community grumble against me? I have heard the complaints of these grumbling Israelites. ²⁸So tell them, 'As surely as I live, declares the Lord, I will do to you the very thing I heard you say: ²⁹In this wilderness your bodies will fall—every one of you twenty years old or more who was counted in the census and who has grumbled against me. ³⁰Not one of you will enter the land I swore with uplifted hand to make your home, except Caleb son of Jephunneh and Joshua son of Nun. ³¹As for your children that you said would be taken as plunder, I will bring them in to enjoy the land you have rejected. ³²But as

for you, your bodies will fall in this wilderness. ³³Your children will be shepherds here for forty years, suffering for your unfaithfulness, until the last of your bodies lies in the wilderness. ³⁴For forty years—one year for each of the forty days you explored the land—you will suffer for your sins and know what it is like to have me against you.' ³⁵I, the Lord, have spoken, and I will surely do these things to this whole wicked community, which has banded together against me. They will meet their end in this wilderness; here they will die."

³⁶So the men Moses had sent to explore the land, who returned and made the whole community grumble against him by spreading a bad report about it— ³⁷these men who were responsible for spreading the bad report about the land were struck down and died of a plague before the Lord. ³⁸Of the men who went to explore the land, only Joshua son of Nun and Caleb son of Jephunneh survived.

³⁹When Moses reported this to all the Israelites, they mourned bitterly. ⁴⁰Early the next morning they set out for the highest point in the hill country, saying, "Now we are ready to go up to the land the Lord promised. Surely we have sinned!"

⁴¹But Moses said, "Why are you disobeying the Lord's command? This will not succeed! ⁴²Do not go up, because the Lord is not with you. You will be defeated by your enemies, ⁴³for the Amalekites and the Canaanites will face you there. Because you have turned away from the Lord, he will not be with you and you will fall by the sword."

⁴⁴Nevertheless, in their presumption they went up toward the highest point in the hill country, though neither Moses nor the ark of the Lord's covenant moved from the camp. ⁴⁵Then the Amalekites and the Canaanites who lived in that hill country came down and attacked them and beat them down all the way to Hormah.

Supplementary Offerings

15 The Lord said to Moses, ²"Speak to the Israelites and say to them: 'After you enter the land I am giving you as a home ³and you present to the Lord food offerings from the herd or the flock, as an aroma

^a 25 Or the Sea of Reeds

pleasing to the LORD — whether burnt offerings or sacrifices, for special vows or freewill offerings or festival offerings — [4]then the person who brings an offering shall present to the LORD a grain offering of a tenth of an ephah[a] of the finest flour mixed with a quarter of a hin[b] of olive oil. [5]With each lamb for the burnt offering or the sacrifice, prepare a quarter of a hin of wine as a drink offering.

[6]"'With a ram prepare a grain offering of two-tenths of an ephah[c] of the finest flour mixed with a third of a hin[d] of olive oil, [7]and a third of a hin of wine as a drink offering. Offer it as an aroma pleasing to the LORD.

[8]"'When you prepare a young bull as a burnt offering or sacrifice, for a special vow or a fellowship offering to the LORD, [9]bring with the bull a grain offering of three-tenths of an ephah[e] of the finest flour mixed with half a hin[f] of olive oil, [10]and also bring half a hin of wine as a drink offering. This will be a food offering, an aroma pleasing to the LORD. [11]Each bull or ram, each lamb or young goat, is to be prepared in this manner. [12]Do this for each one, for as many as you prepare.

[13]"'Everyone who is native-born must do these things in this way when they present a food offering as an aroma pleasing to the LORD. [14]For the generations to come, whenever a foreigner or anyone else living among you presents a food offering as an aroma pleasing to the LORD, they must do exactly as you do. [15]The community is to have the same rules for you and for the foreigner residing among you; this is a lasting ordinance for the generations to come. You and the foreigner shall be the same before the LORD: [16]The same laws and regulations will apply both to you and to the foreigner residing among you.'"

[17]The LORD said to Moses, [18]"Speak to the Israelites and say to them: 'When you enter the land to which I am taking you [19]and you eat the food of the land, present a portion as an offering to the LORD. [20]Present a loaf from the first of your ground meal and present it as an offering from the threshing floor. [21]Throughout the generations to come you are to give this offering to the LORD from the first of your ground meal.

Offerings for Unintentional Sins

[22]"'Now if you as a community unintentionally fail to keep any of these commands the LORD gave Moses — [23]any of the LORD's commands to you through him, from the day the LORD gave them and continuing through the generations to come — [24]and if this is done unintentionally without the community being aware of it, then the whole community is to offer a young bull for a burnt offering as an aroma pleasing to the LORD, along with its prescribed grain offering and drink offering, and a male goat for a sin offering.[g] [25]The priest is to make atonement for the whole Israelite community, and they will be forgiven, for it was not intentional and they have presented to the LORD for their wrong a food offering and a sin offering. [26]The whole Israelite community and the foreigners residing among them will be forgiven, because all the people were involved in the unintentional wrong.

[27]"'But if just one person sins unintentionally, that person must bring a year-old female goat for a sin offering. [28]The priest is to make atonement before the LORD for the one who erred by sinning unintentionally, and when atonement has been made, that person will be forgiven. [29]One and the same law applies to everyone who sins unintentionally, whether a native-born Israelite or a foreigner residing among you.

[30]"'But anyone who sins defiantly, whether native-born or foreigner, blasphemes the LORD and must be cut off from the people of Israel. [31]Because they have despised the LORD's word and broken his commands, they must surely be cut off; their guilt remains on them.'"

The Sabbath-Breaker Put to Death

[32]While the Israelites were in the wilderness, a man was found gathering wood on the Sabbath day. [33]Those who found him gathering wood brought him to Moses and Aaron and the whole assembly, [34]and they kept him in custody, because it was not clear what should be done to him. [35]Then the LORD said to Moses, "The man must die. The whole assembly must stone him outside the

---

[a] *4 That is, probably about 3 1/2 pounds or about 1.6 kilograms*   [b] *4 That is, about 1 quart or about 1 liter; also in verse 5*   [c] *6 That is, probably about 7 pounds or about 3.2 kilograms*   [d] *6 That is, about 1 1/3 quarts or about 1.3 liters; also in verse 7*   [e] *9 That is, probably about 11 pounds or about 5 kilograms*   [f] *9 That is, about 2 quarts or about 1.9 liters; also in verse 10*   [g] *24 Or* purification offering; *also in verses 25 and 27*

camp." ³⁶So the assembly took him outside the camp and stoned him to death, as the LORD commanded Moses.

Tassels on Garments

³⁷The LORD said to Moses, ³⁸"Speak to the Israelites and say to them: 'Throughout the generations to come you are to make tassels on the corners of your garments, with a blue cord on each tassel. ³⁹You will have these tassels to look at and so you will remember all the commands of the LORD, that you may obey them and not prostitute yourselves by chasing after the lusts of your own hearts and eyes. ⁴⁰Then you will remember to obey all my commands and will be consecrated to your God. ⁴¹I am the LORD your God, who brought you out of Egypt to be your God. I am the LORD your God.' "

Korah, Dathan and Abiram

16 Korah son of Izhar, the son of Kohath, the son of Levi, and certain Reubenites—Dathan and Abiram, sons of Eliab, and On son of Peleth—became insolent^a ²and rose up against Moses. With them were 250 Israelite men, well-known community leaders who had been appointed members of the council. ³They came as a group to oppose Moses and Aaron and said to them, "You have gone too far! The whole community is holy, every one of them, and the LORD is with them. Why then do you set yourselves above the LORD's assembly?"

⁴When Moses heard this, he fell facedown. ⁵Then he said to Korah and all his followers: "In the morning the LORD will show who belongs to him and who is holy, and he will have that person come near him. The man he chooses he will cause to come near him. ⁶You, Korah, and all your followers are to do this: Take censers ⁷and tomorrow put burning coals and incense in them before the LORD. The man the LORD chooses will be the one who is holy. You Levites have gone too far!"

⁸Moses also said to Korah, "Now listen, you Levites! ⁹Isn't it enough for you that the God of Israel has separated you from the rest of the Israelite community and brought you near himself to do the work at the LORD's tabernacle and to stand before the community and minister to them? ¹⁰He has brought you and all your fellow Levites near himself, but now you are trying to get the priesthood too. ¹¹It is against the LORD that you and all your followers have banded together. Who is Aaron that you should grumble against him?"

¹²Then Moses summoned Dathan and Abiram, the sons of Eliab. But they said, "We will not come! ¹³Isn't it enough that you have brought us up out of a land flowing with milk and honey to kill us in the wilderness? And now you also want to lord it over us! ¹⁴Moreover, you haven't brought us into a land flowing with milk and honey or given us an inheritance of fields and vineyards. Do you want to treat these men like slaves^b? No, we will not come!"

¹⁵Then Moses became very angry and said to the LORD, "Do not accept their offering. I have not taken so much as a donkey from them, nor have I wronged any of them."

¹⁶Moses said to Korah, "You and all your followers are to appear before the LORD tomorrow—you and they and Aaron. ¹⁷Each man is to take his censer and put incense in it—250 censers in all—and present it before the LORD. You and Aaron are to present your censers also." ¹⁸So each of them took his censer, put burning coals and incense in it, and stood with Moses and Aaron at the entrance to the tent of meeting. ¹⁹When Korah had gathered all his followers in opposition to them at the entrance to the tent of meeting, the glory of the LORD appeared to the entire assembly. ²⁰The LORD said to Moses and Aaron, ²¹"Separate yourselves from this assembly so I can put an end to them at once."

²²But Moses and Aaron fell facedown and cried out, "O God, the God who gives breath to all living things, will you be angry with the entire assembly when only one man sins?"

²³Then the LORD said to Moses, ²⁴"Say to the assembly, 'Move away from the tents of Korah, Dathan and Abiram.' "

²⁵Moses got up and went to Dathan and Abiram, and the elders of Israel followed him. ²⁶He warned the assembly, "Move back from the tents of these wicked men! Do not touch anything belonging to them, or you will be swept away because of all their sins."

---

^a 1 Or Peleth—took men   ^b 14 Or to deceive these men; Hebrew Will you gouge out the eyes of these men

²⁷So they moved away from the tents of Korah, Dathan and Abiram. Dathan and Abiram had come out and were standing with their wives, children and little ones at the entrances to their tents.

²⁸Then Moses said, "This is how you will know that the LORD has sent me to do all these things and that it was not my idea: ²⁹If these men die a natural death and suffer the fate of all mankind, then the LORD has not sent me. ³⁰But if the LORD brings about something totally new, and the earth opens its mouth and swallows them, with everything that belongs to them, and they go down alive into the realm of the dead, then you will know that these men have treated the LORD with contempt."

³¹As soon as he finished saying all this, the ground under them split apart ³²and the earth opened its mouth and swallowed them and their households, and all those associated with Korah, together with their possessions. ³³They went down alive into the realm of the dead, with everything they owned; the earth closed over them, and they perished and were gone from the community. ³⁴At their cries, all the Israelites around them fled, shouting, "The earth is going to swallow us too!"

³⁵And fire came out from the LORD and consumed the 250 men who were offering the incense.

³⁶The LORD said to Moses, ³⁷"Tell Eleazar son of Aaron, the priest, to remove the censers from the charred remains and scatter the coals some distance away, for the censers are holy— ³⁸the censers of the men who sinned at the cost of their lives. Hammer the censers into sheets to overlay the altar, for they were presented before the LORD and have become holy. Let them be a sign to the Israelites."

³⁹So Eleazar the priest collected the bronze censers brought by those who had been burned to death, and he had them hammered out to overlay the altar, ⁴⁰as the LORD directed him through Moses. This was to remind the Israelites that no one except a descendant of Aaron should come to burn incense before the LORD, or he would become like Korah and his followers.

⁴¹The next day the whole Israelite community grumbled against Moses and Aaron.

"You have killed the LORD's people," they said.

⁴²But when the assembly gathered in opposition to Moses and Aaron and turned toward the tent of meeting, suddenly the cloud covered it and the glory of the LORD appeared. ⁴³Then Moses and Aaron went to the front of the tent of meeting, ⁴⁴and the LORD said to Moses, ⁴⁵"Get away from this assembly so I can put an end to them at once." And they fell facedown.

⁴⁶Then Moses said to Aaron, "Take your censer and put incense in it, along with burning coals from the altar, and hurry to the assembly to make atonement for them. Wrath has come out from the LORD; the plague has started." ⁴⁷So Aaron did as Moses said, and ran into the midst of the assembly. The plague had already started among the people, but Aaron offered the incense and made atonement for them. ⁴⁸He stood between the living and the dead, and the plague stopped. ⁴⁹But 14,700 people died from the plague, in addition to those who had died because of Korah. ⁵⁰Then Aaron returned to Moses at the entrance to the tent of meeting, for the plague had stopped.^a

The Budding of Aaron's Staff

17^b The LORD said to Moses, ²"Speak to the Israelites and get twelve staffs from them, one from the leader of each of their ancestral tribes. Write the name of each man on his staff. ³On the staff of Levi write Aaron's name, for there must be one staff for the head of each ancestral tribe. ⁴Place them in the tent of meeting in front of the ark of the covenant law, where I meet with you. ⁵The staff belonging to the man I choose will sprout, and I will rid myself of this constant grumbling against you by the Israelites."

⁶So Moses spoke to the Israelites, and their leaders gave him twelve staffs, one for the leader of each of their ancestral tribes, and Aaron's staff was among them. ⁷Moses placed the staffs before the LORD in the tent of the covenant law.

⁸The next day Moses entered the tent and saw that Aaron's staff, which represented the tribe of Levi, had not only sprouted but had budded, blossomed and produced almonds. ⁹Then Moses brought out all the staffs from

^a 50 In Hebrew texts 16:36-50 is numbered 17:1-15.   ^b In Hebrew texts 17:1-13 is numbered 17:16-28.

the LORD's presence to all the Israelites. They looked at them, and each of the leaders took his own staff.

¹⁰The LORD said to Moses, "Put back Aaron's staff in front of the ark of the covenant law, to be kept as a sign to the rebellious. This will put an end to their grumbling against me, so that they will not die." ¹¹Moses did just as the LORD commanded him.

¹²The Israelites said to Moses, "We will die! We are lost, we are all lost! ¹³Anyone who even comes near the tabernacle of the LORD will die. Are we all going to die?"

Duties of Priests and Levites

18 The LORD said to Aaron, "You, your sons and your family are to bear the responsibility for offenses connected with the sanctuary, and you and your sons alone are to bear the responsibility for offenses connected with the priesthood. ²Bring your fellow Levites from your ancestral tribe to join you and assist you when you and your sons minister before the tent of the covenant law. ³They are to be responsible to you and are to perform all the duties of the tent, but they must not go near the furnishings of the sanctuary or the altar. Otherwise both they and you will die. ⁴They are to join you and be responsible for the care of the tent of meeting—all the work at the tent—and no one else may come near where you are.

⁵"You are to be responsible for the care of the sanctuary and the altar, so that my wrath will not fall on the Israelites again. ⁶I myself have selected your fellow Levites from among the Israelites as a gift to you, dedicated to the LORD to do the work at the tent of meeting. ⁷But only you and your sons may serve as priests in connection with everything at the altar and inside the curtain. I am giving you the service of the priesthood as a gift. Anyone else who comes near the sanctuary is to be put to death."

Offerings for Priests and Levites

⁸Then the LORD said to Aaron, "I myself have put you in charge of the offerings presented to me; all the holy offerings the Israelites give me I give to you and your sons as your portion, your perpetual share. ⁹You are to have the part of the most holy offerings that is kept from the fire. From all the gifts they bring me as most holy offerings, whether grain or sin*ᵃ* or guilt offerings, that part belongs to you and your sons. ¹⁰Eat it as something most holy; every male shall eat it. You must regard it as holy.

¹¹"This also is yours: whatever is set aside from the gifts of all the wave offerings of the Israelites. I give this to you and your sons and daughters as your perpetual share. Everyone in your household who is ceremonially clean may eat it.

¹²"I give you all the finest olive oil and all the finest new wine and grain they give the LORD as the firstfruits of their harvest. ¹³All the land's firstfruits that they bring to the LORD will be yours. Everyone in your household who is ceremonially clean may eat it.

¹⁴"Everything in Israel that is devoted*ᵇ* to the LORD is yours. ¹⁵The first offspring of every womb, both human and animal, that is offered to the LORD is yours. But you must redeem every firstborn son and every firstborn male of unclean animals. ¹⁶When they are a month old, you must redeem them at the redemption price set at five shekels*ᶜ* of silver, according to the sanctuary shekel, which weighs twenty gerahs.

¹⁷"But you must not redeem the firstborn of a cow, a sheep or a goat; they are holy. Splash their blood against the altar and burn their fat as a food offering, an aroma pleasing to the LORD. ¹⁸Their meat is to be yours, just as the breast of the wave offering and the right thigh are yours. ¹⁹Whatever is set aside from the holy offerings the Israelites present to the LORD I give to you and your sons and daughters as your perpetual share. It is an everlasting covenant of salt before the LORD for both you and your offspring."

²⁰The LORD said to Aaron, "You will have no inheritance in their land, nor will you have any share among them; I am your share and your inheritance among the Israelites.

²¹"I give to the Levites all the tithes in Israel as their inheritance in return for the work they do while serving at the tent of meeting. ²²From now on the Israelites must not go near the tent of meeting, or they will bear the consequences of their sin and will die. ²³It is the Levites who are to do the work at the tent of meeting and bear the responsibility

---

ᵃ 9 Or *purification*   *ᵇ 14* The Hebrew term refers to the irrevocable giving over of things or persons to the LORD.   *ᶜ 16* That is, about 2 ounces or about 58 grams for any offenses they commit against it. This is a lasting ordinance for the generations to come. They will receive no inheritance among the Israelites. ²⁴Instead, I give to the Levites as their inheritance the tithes that the Israelites present as an offering to the LORD. That is why I said concerning them: 'They will have no inheritance among the Israelites.'"

²⁵The LORD said to Moses, ²⁶"Speak to the Levites and say to them: 'When you receive from the Israelites the tithe I give you as your inheritance, you must present a tenth of that tithe as the LORD's offering. ²⁷Your offering will be reckoned to you as grain from the threshing floor or juice from the winepress. ²⁸In this way you also will present an offering to the LORD from all the tithes you receive from the Israelites. From these tithes you must give the LORD's portion to Aaron the priest. ²⁹You must present as the LORD's portion the best and holiest part of everything given to you.'

³⁰"Say to the Levites: 'When you present the best part, it will be reckoned to you as the product of the threshing floor or the winepress. ³¹You and your households may eat the rest of it anywhere, for it is your wages for your work at the tent of meeting. ³²By presenting the best part of it you will not be guilty in this matter; then you will not defile the holy offerings of the Israelites, and you will not die.'"

The Water of Cleansing

19 The LORD said to Moses and Aaron: ²"This is a requirement of the law that the LORD has commanded: Tell the Israelites to bring you a red heifer without defect or blemish and that has never been under a yoke. ³Give it to Eleazar the priest; it is to be taken outside the camp and slaughtered in his presence. ⁴Then Eleazar the priest is to take some of its blood on his finger and sprinkle it seven times toward the front of the tent of meeting. ⁵While he watches, the heifer is to be burned—its hide, flesh, blood and intestines. ⁶The priest is to take some cedar wood, hyssop and scarlet wool and throw them onto the burning heifer. ⁷After that, the priest must wash his clothes and bathe himself with water. He may then come into the camp, but he will be ceremonially unclean till evening. ⁸The man who burns

it must also wash his clothes and bathe with water, and he too will be unclean till evening.

⁹"A man who is clean shall gather up the ashes of the heifer and put them in a ceremonially clean place outside the camp. They are to be kept by the Israelite community for use in the water of cleansing; it is for purification from sin. ¹⁰The man who gathers up the ashes of the heifer must also wash his clothes, and he too will be unclean till evening. This will be a lasting ordinance both for the Israelites and for the foreigners residing among them.

¹¹"Whoever touches a human corpse will be unclean for seven days. ¹²They must purify themselves with the water on the third day and on the seventh day; then they will be clean. But if they do not purify themselves on the third and seventh days, they will not be clean. ¹³If they fail to purify themselves after touching a human corpse, they defile the LORD's tabernacle. They must be cut off from Israel. Because the water of cleansing has not been sprinkled on them, they are unclean; their uncleanness remains on them.

¹⁴"This is the law that applies when a person dies in a tent: Anyone who enters the tent and anyone who is in it will be unclean for seven days, ¹⁵and every open container without a lid fastened on it will be unclean.

¹⁶"Anyone out in the open who touches someone who has been killed with a sword or someone who has died a natural death, or anyone who touches a human bone or a grave, will be unclean for seven days.

¹⁷"For the unclean person, put some ashes from the burned purification offering into a jar and pour fresh water over them. ¹⁸Then a man who is ceremonially clean is to take some hyssop, dip it in the water and sprinkle the tent and all the furnishings and the people who were there. He must also sprinkle anyone who has touched a human bone or a grave or anyone who has been killed or anyone who has died a natural death. ¹⁹The man who is clean is to sprinkle those who are unclean on the third and seventh days, and on the seventh day he is to purify them. Those who are being cleansed must wash their clothes and bathe with water, and that evening they will be clean. ²⁰But if those who are unclean do not purify themselves, they must be cut off from the community,

because they have defiled the sanctuary of the LORD. The water of cleansing has not been sprinkled on them, and they are unclean. ²¹ This is a lasting ordinance for them.

"The man who sprinkles the water of cleansing must also wash his clothes, and anyone who touches the water of cleansing will be unclean till evening. ²² Anything that an unclean person touches becomes unclean, and anyone who touches it becomes unclean till evening."

Water From the Rock

20 In the first month the whole Israelite community arrived at the Desert of Zin, and they stayed at Kadesh. There Miriam died and was buried.

² Now there was no water for the community, and the people gathered in opposition to Moses and Aaron. ³ They quarreled with Moses and said, "If only we had died when our brothers fell dead before the LORD! ⁴ Why did you bring the LORD's community into this wilderness, that we and our livestock should die here? ⁵ Why did you bring us up out of Egypt to this terrible place? It has no grain or figs, grapevines or pomegranates. And there is no water to drink!"

⁶ Moses and Aaron went from the assembly to the entrance to the tent of meeting and fell facedown, and the glory of the LORD appeared to them. ⁷ The LORD said to Moses, ⁸ "Take the staff, and you and your brother Aaron gather the assembly together. Speak to that rock before their eyes and it will pour out its water. You will bring water out of the rock for the community so they and their livestock can drink."

⁹ So Moses took the staff from the LORD's presence, just as he commanded him. ¹⁰ He and Aaron gathered the assembly together in front of the rock and Moses said to them, "Listen, you rebels, must we bring you water out of this rock?" ¹¹ Then Moses raised his arm and struck the rock twice with his staff. Water gushed out, and the community and their livestock drank.

¹² But the LORD said to Moses and Aaron, "Because you did not trust in me enough to honor me as holy in the sight of the Israelites, you will not bring this community into the land I give them."

¹³ These were the waters of Meribah,ᵃ where the Israelites quarreled with the LORD and where he was proved holy among them.

Edom Denies Israel Passage

¹⁴ Moses sent messengers from Kadesh to the king of Edom, saying:

"This is what your brother Israel says: You know about all the hardships that have come on us. ¹⁵ Our ancestors went down into Egypt, and we lived there many years. The Egyptians mistreated us and our ancestors, ¹⁶ but when we cried out to the LORD, he heard our cry and sent an angel and brought us out of Egypt.

"Now we are here at Kadesh, a town on the edge of your territory. ¹⁷ Please let us pass through your country. We will not go through any field or vineyard, or drink water from any well. We will travel along the King's Highway and not turn to the right or to the left until we have passed through your territory."

¹⁸ But Edom answered:

"You may not pass through here; if you try, we will march out and attack you with the sword."

¹⁹ The Israelites replied:

"We will go along the main road, and if we or our livestock drink any of your water, we will pay for it. We only want to pass through on foot — nothing else."

²⁰ Again they answered:

"You may not pass through."

Then Edom came out against them with a large and powerful army. ²¹ Since Edom refused to let them go through their territory, Israel turned away from them.

The Death of Aaron

²² The whole Israelite community set out from Kadesh and came to Mount Hor. ²³ At Mount Hor, near the border of Edom, the LORD said to Moses and Aaron, ²⁴ "Aaron will be gathered to his people. He will not enter the land I give the Israelites, because both

---

ᵃ 13 Meribah means quarreling.

of you rebelled against my command at the waters of Meribah. ²⁵Get Aaron and his son Eleazar and take them up Mount Hor. ²⁶Remove Aaron's garments and put them on his son Eleazar, for Aaron will be gathered to his people; he will die there."

²⁷Moses did as the LORD commanded: They went up Mount Hor in the sight of the whole community. ²⁸Moses removed Aaron's garments and put them on his son Eleazar. And Aaron died there on top of the mountain. Then Moses and Eleazar came down from the mountain, ²⁹and when the whole community learned that Aaron had died, all the Israelites mourned for him thirty days.

Arad Destroyed

21 When the Canaanite king of Arad, who lived in the Negev, heard that Israel was coming along the road to Atharim, he attacked the Israelites and captured some of them. ²Then Israel made this vow to the LORD: "If you will deliver these people into our hands, we will totally destroy^a their cities." ³The LORD listened to Israel's plea and gave the Canaanites over to them. They completely destroyed them and their towns; so the place was named Hormah.^b

The Bronze Snake

⁴They traveled from Mount Hor along the route to the Red Sea,^c to go around Edom. But the people grew impatient on the way; ⁵they spoke against God and against Moses, and said, "Why have you brought us up out of Egypt to die in the wilderness? There is no bread! There is no water! And we detest this miserable food!"

⁶Then the LORD sent venomous snakes among them; they bit the people and many Israelites died. ⁷The people came to Moses and said, "We sinned when we spoke against the LORD and against you. Pray that the LORD will take the snakes away from us." So Moses prayed for the people.

⁸The LORD said to Moses, "Make a snake and put it up on a pole; anyone who is bitten can look at it and live." ⁹So Moses made a bronze snake and put it up on a pole. Then when anyone was bitten by a snake and looked at the bronze snake, they lived.

The Journey to Moab

¹⁰The Israelites moved on and camped at Oboth. ¹¹Then they set out from Oboth and camped in Iye Abarim, in the wilderness that faces Moab toward the sunrise. ¹²From there they moved on and camped in the Zered Valley. ¹³They set out from there and camped alongside the Arnon, which is in the wilderness extending into Amorite territory. The Arnon is the border of Moab, between Moab and the Amorites. ¹⁴That is why the Book of the Wars of the LORD says:

> ". . . Zahab^d in Suphah and the ravines,
>   the Arnon ¹⁵and^e the slopes of the
>   ravines
> that lead to the settlement of Ar
> and lie along the border of Moab."

¹⁶From there they continued on to Beer, the well where the LORD said to Moses, "Gather the people together and I will give them water."

¹⁷Then Israel sang this song:

> "Spring up, O well!
>   Sing about it,
> ¹⁸about the well that the princes dug,
>   that the nobles of the people sank—
>   the nobles with scepters and staffs."

Then they went from the wilderness to Mattanah, ¹⁹from Mattanah to Nahaliel, from Nahaliel to Bamoth, ²⁰and from Bamoth to the valley in Moab where the top of Pisgah overlooks the wasteland.

Defeat of Sihon and Og

²¹Israel sent messengers to say to Sihon king of the Amorites:

> ²²"Let us pass through your country. We will not turn aside into any field or vineyard, or drink water from any well. We will travel along the King's Highway until we have passed through your territory."

²³But Sihon would not let Israel pass through his territory. He mustered his entire army and marched out into the wilderness against Israel. When he reached Jahaz, he fought with Israel. ²⁴Israel, however, put him to the sword and took over his land from

---

^a 2 The Hebrew term refers to the irrevocable giving over of things or persons to the LORD, often by totally destroying them; also in verse 3.   ^b 3 *Hormah* means *destruction.*   ^c 4 Or *the Sea of Reeds*
^d 14 Septuagint; Hebrew *Waheb*   ^e 14,15 Or *"I have been given from Suphah and the ravines / of the Arnon* ^15*to*

the Arnon to the Jabbok, but only as far as the Ammonites, because their border was fortified. ²⁵ Israel captured all the cities of the Amorites and occupied them, including Heshbon and all its surrounding settlements. ²⁶ Heshbon was the city of Sihon king of the Amorites, who had fought against the former king of Moab and had taken from him all his land as far as the Arnon.

²⁷ That is why the poets say:

"Come to Heshbon and let it be rebuilt;
   let Sihon's city be restored.

²⁸ "Fire went out from Heshbon,
      a blaze from the city of Sihon.
   It consumed Ar of Moab,
      the citizens of Arnon's heights.
²⁹ Woe to you, Moab!
      You are destroyed, people of Chemosh!
   He has given up his sons as fugitives
      and his daughters as captives
   to Sihon king of the Amorites.

³⁰ "But we have overthrown them;
      Heshbon's dominion has been
         destroyed all the way to Dibon.
   We have demolished them as far as
         Nophah,
      which extends to Medeba."

³¹ So Israel settled in the land of the Amorites.

³² After Moses had sent spies to Jazer, the Israelites captured its surrounding settlements and drove out the Amorites who were there. ³³ Then they turned and went up along the road toward Bashan, and Og king of Bashan and his whole army marched out to meet them in battle at Edrei.

³⁴ The LORD said to Moses, "Do not be afraid of him, for I have delivered him into your hands, along with his whole army and his land. Do to him what you did to Sihon king of the Amorites, who reigned in Heshbon."

³⁵ So they struck him down, together with his sons and his whole army, leaving them no survivors. And they took possession of his land.

Balak Summons Balaam

22 Then the Israelites traveled to the plains of Moab and camped along the Jordan across from Jericho.

² Now Balak son of Zippor saw all that Israel had done to the Amorites, ³ and Moab was terrified because there were so many people.

Indeed, Moab was filled with dread because of the Israelites.

⁴ The Moabites said to the elders of Midian, "This horde is going to lick up everything around us, as an ox licks up the grass of the field."

So Balak son of Zippor, who was king of Moab at that time, ⁵ sent messengers to summon Balaam son of Beor, who was at Pethor, near the Euphrates River, in his native land. Balak said:

"A people has come out of Egypt;
   they cover the face of the land and have
   settled next to me. ⁶ Now come and put
   a curse on these people, because they
   are too powerful for me. Perhaps then
   I will be able to defeat them and drive
   them out of the land. For I know that
   whoever you bless is blessed, and whoever you curse is cursed."

⁷ The elders of Moab and Midian left, taking with them the fee for divination. When they came to Balaam, they told him what Balak had said.

⁸ "Spend the night here," Balaam said to them, "and I will report back to you with the answer the LORD gives me." So the Moabite officials stayed with him.

⁹ God came to Balaam and asked, "Who are these men with you?"

¹⁰ Balaam said to God, "Balak son of Zippor, king of Moab, sent me this message: ¹¹ 'A people that has come out of Egypt covers the face of the land. Now come and put a curse on them for me. Perhaps then I will be able to fight them and drive them away.' "

¹² But God said to Balaam, "Do not go with them. You must not put a curse on those people, because they are blessed."

¹³ The next morning Balaam got up and said to Balak's officials, "Go back to your own country, for the LORD has refused to let me go with you."

¹⁴ So the Moabite officials returned to Balak and said, "Balaam refused to come with us."

¹⁵ Then Balak sent other officials, more numerous and more distinguished than the first. ¹⁶ They came to Balaam and said:

"This is what Balak son of Zippor says: Do not let anything keep you from coming to me, ¹⁷ because I will reward you handsomely and do whatever you

TALKING DONKEYS

READ: **NUMBERS 22**

In all fairness, I don't think any one of us knows how we would respond if one of our pets just started talking to us. But Balaam is so enraged that he's not thinking straight. Dude, if you have a talking donkey on your hands, the last thing you want to do is kill it. You don't even need that chunk of change anymore; you're going to make a fortune. You can take your talking donkey show on the road. Go to Vegas.

I love the donkey's rational response. And I can't help but wonder if he had a distinguished British accent to go along with his superior intellect.

The most respected prophet in the ancient world has zero comebacks. His only response to his cultured donkey is, "No." And he probably mumbled it.

Sometimes we get ticked off Balaam-style when we can't get to where we want to go. We hate detours! They're frustrating. They are confusing. But the divine detours often get us where God wants us to go. The real miracle in this story isn't the talking donkey; the real miracle is a God who loves us enough to get in the way when we're going the wrong way. These are the miracles we don't really prefer, but they are the miracles we need. And when I look back on my own life, I'm grateful for the moments God got in the way of my plans and rerouted me. What seems like an unanswered prayer means that God has a better answer.

BUILDING
FAITH
WISDOM
STRENGTH

say. Come and put a curse on these people for me."

[18] But Balaam answered them, "Even if Balak gave me all the silver and gold in his palace, I could not do anything great or small to go beyond the command of the LORD my God. [19] Now spend the night here so that I can find out what else the LORD will tell me."

[20] That night God came to Balaam and said, "Since these men have come to summon you, go with them, but do only what I tell you."

Balaam's Donkey

[21] Balaam got up in the morning, saddled his donkey and went with the Moabite officials. [22] But God was very angry when he went, and the angel of the LORD stood in the road to oppose him. Balaam was riding on his donkey, and his two servants were with him. [23] When the donkey saw the angel of the LORD standing in the road with a drawn sword in his hand, it turned off the road into a field. Balaam beat it to get it back on the road.

[24] Then the angel of the LORD stood in a narrow path through the vineyards, with walls on both sides. [25] When the donkey saw the angel of the LORD, it pressed close to the wall, crushing Balaam's foot against it. So he beat the donkey again.

[26] Then the angel of the LORD moved on ahead and stood in a narrow place where there was no room to turn, either to the right or to the left. [27] When the donkey saw the angel of the LORD, it lay down under Balaam, and he was angry and beat it with his staff. [28] Then the LORD opened the donkey's mouth, and it said to Balaam, "What have I done to you to make you beat me these three times?"

[29] Balaam answered the donkey, "You have made a fool of me! If only I had a sword in my hand, I would kill you right now."

[30] The donkey said to Balaam, "Am I not your own donkey, which you have always ridden, to this day? Have I been in the habit of doing this to you?"

"No," he said.

[31] Then the LORD opened Balaam's eyes, and he saw the angel of the LORD standing in the road with his sword drawn. So he bowed low and fell facedown.

[32] The angel of the LORD asked him, "Why have you beaten your donkey these three times? I have come here to oppose you because your path is a reckless one before me.[a] [33] The donkey saw me and turned away from me these three times. If it had not turned away, I would certainly have killed you by now, but I would have spared it."

[34] Balaam said to the angel of the LORD, "I have sinned. I did not realize you were standing in the road to oppose me. Now if you are displeased, I will go back."

[35] The angel of the LORD said to Balaam, "Go with the men, but speak only what I tell you." So Balaam went with Balak's officials.

[36] When Balak heard that Balaam was coming, he went out to meet him at the Moabite town on the Arnon border, at the edge of his territory. [37] Balak said to Balaam, "Did I not send you an urgent summons? Why didn't you come to me? Am I really not able to reward you?"

[38] "Well, I have come to you now," Balaam replied. "But I can't say whatever I please. I must speak only what God puts in my mouth."

[39] Then Balaam went with Balak to Kiriath Huzoth. [40] Balak sacrificed cattle and sheep, and gave some to Balaam and the officials who were with him. [41] The next morning Balak took Balaam up to Bamoth Baal, and from there he could see the outskirts of the Israelite camp.

Balaam's First Message

23 Balaam said, "Build me seven altars here, and prepare seven bulls and seven rams for me." [2] Balak did as Balaam said, and the two of them offered a bull and a ram on each altar.

[3] Then Balaam said to Balak, "Stay here beside your offering while I go aside. Perhaps the LORD will come to meet with me. Whatever he reveals to me I will tell you." Then he went off to a barren height.

[4] God met with him, and Balaam said, "I have prepared seven altars, and on each altar I have offered a bull and a ram."

[5] The LORD put a word in Balaam's mouth and said, "Go back to Balak and give him this word."

---

[a] 32 The meaning of the Hebrew for this clause is uncertain.

⁶So he went back to him and found him standing beside his offering, with all the Moabite officials. ⁷Then Balaam spoke his message:

"Balak brought me from Aram,
    the king of Moab from the eastern
      mountains.
'Come,' he said, 'curse Jacob for me;
    come, denounce Israel.'
⁸How can I curse
    those whom God has not cursed?
How can I denounce
    those whom the LORD has not
      denounced?
⁹From the rocky peaks I see them,
    from the heights I view them.
I see a people who live apart
    and do not consider themselves one of
      the nations.
¹⁰Who can count the dust of Jacob
    or number even a fourth of Israel?
Let me die the death of the righteous,
    and may my final end be like theirs!"

¹¹Balak said to Balaam, "What have you done to me? I brought you to curse my enemies, but you have done nothing but bless them!"

¹²He answered, "Must I not speak what the LORD puts in my mouth?"

Balaam's Second Message

¹³Then Balak said to him, "Come with me to another place where you can see them; you will not see them all but only the outskirts of their camp. And from there, curse them for me." ¹⁴So he took him to the field of Zophim on the top of Pisgah, and there he built seven altars and offered a bull and a ram on each altar.

¹⁵Balaam said to Balak, "Stay here beside your offering while I meet with him over there."

¹⁶The LORD met with Balaam and put a word in his mouth and said, "Go back to Balak and give him this word."

¹⁷So he went to him and found him standing beside his offering, with the Moabite officials. Balak asked him, "What did the LORD say?"

¹⁸Then he spoke his message:

"Arise, Balak, and listen;
    hear me, son of Zippor.
¹⁹God is not human, that he should lie,
    not a human being, that he should
      change his mind.
Does he speak and then not act?
    Does he promise and not fulfill?
²⁰I have received a command to bless;
    he has blessed, and I cannot
      change it.

²¹"No misfortune is seen in Jacob,
    no misery observed[a] in Israel.
The LORD their God is with them;
    the shout of the King is among them.
²²God brought them out of Egypt;
    they have the strength of a wild ox.
²³There is no divination against[b] Jacob,
    no evil omens against[b] Israel.
It will now be said of Jacob
    and of Israel, 'See what God has
      done!'
²⁴The people rise like a lioness;
    they rouse themselves like a lion
that does not rest till it devours its prey
    and drinks the blood of its victims."

²⁵Then Balak said to Balaam, "Neither curse them at all nor bless them at all!"

²⁶Balaam answered, "Did I not tell you I must do whatever the LORD says?"

Balaam's Third Message

²⁷Then Balak said to Balaam, "Come, let me take you to another place. Perhaps it will please God to let you curse them for me from there." ²⁸And Balak took Balaam to the top of Peor, overlooking the wasteland.

²⁹Balaam said, "Build me seven altars here, and prepare seven bulls and seven rams for me." ³⁰Balak did as Balaam had said, and offered a bull and a ram on each altar.

24 Now when Balaam saw that it pleased the LORD to bless Israel, he did not resort to divination as at other times, but turned his face toward the wilderness. ²When Balaam looked out and saw Israel encamped tribe by tribe, the Spirit of God came on him ³and he spoke his message:

"The prophecy of Balaam son of Beor,
    the prophecy of one whose eye sees
      clearly,
⁴the prophecy of one who hears the words
    of God,

[a] 21 Or *He has not looked on Jacob's offenses / or on the wrongs found*   [b] 23 Or *in*

who sees a vision from the Almighty,[a]
who falls prostrate, and whose eyes are
opened:

⁵ "How beautiful are your tents, Jacob,
your dwelling places, Israel!

⁶ "Like valleys they spread out,
like gardens beside a river,
like aloes planted by the LORD,
like cedars beside the waters.
⁷ Water will flow from their buckets;
their seed will have abundant water.

"Their king will be greater than Agag;
their kingdom will be exalted.

⁸ "God brought them out of Egypt;
they have the strength of a wild ox.
They devour hostile nations
and break their bones in pieces;
with their arrows they pierce them.
⁹ Like a lion they crouch and lie down,
like a lioness — who dares to rouse
them?

"May those who bless you be blessed
and those who curse you be cursed!"

¹⁰ Then Balak's anger burned against Balaam. He struck his hands together and said to him, "I summoned you to curse my enemies, but you have blessed them these three times. ¹¹ Now leave at once and go home! I said I would reward you handsomely, but the LORD has kept you from being rewarded."

¹² Balaam answered Balak, "Did I not tell the messengers you sent me, ¹³ 'Even if Balak gave me all the silver and gold in his palace, I could not do anything of my own accord, good or bad, to go beyond the command of the LORD — and I must say only what the LORD says'? ¹⁴ Now I am going back to my people, but come, let me warn you of what this people will do to your people in days to come."

Balaam's Fourth Message

¹⁵ Then he spoke his message:

"The prophecy of Balaam son of Beor,
the prophecy of one whose eye sees
clearly,

¹⁶ the prophecy of one who hears the words
of God,
who has knowledge from the Most
High,
who sees a vision from the Almighty,
who falls prostrate, and whose eyes are
opened:

¹⁷ "I see him, but not now;
I behold him, but not near.
A star will come out of Jacob;
a scepter will rise out of Israel.
He will crush the foreheads of Moab,
the skulls[b] of[c] all the people of Sheth.[d]
¹⁸ Edom will be conquered;
Seir, his enemy, will be conquered,
but Israel will grow strong.
¹⁹ A ruler will come out of Jacob
and destroy the survivors of the city."

Balaam's Fifth Message

²⁰ Then Balaam saw Amalek and spoke his message:

"Amalek was first among the nations,
but their end will be utter destruction."

Balaam's Sixth Message

²¹ Then he saw the Kenites and spoke his message:

"Your dwelling place is secure,
your nest is set in a rock;
²² yet you Kenites will be destroyed
when Ashur takes you captive."

Balaam's Seventh Message

²³ Then he spoke his message:

"Alas! Who can live when God does this?[e]
²⁴   Ships will come from the shores of
Cyprus;
they will subdue Ashur and Eber,
but they too will come to ruin."

²⁵ Then Balaam got up and returned home, and Balak went his own way.

Moab Seduces Israel

25 While Israel was staying in Shittim, the men began to indulge in sexual

---

[a] 4 Hebrew *Shaddai*; also in verse 16   [b] 17 Samaritan Pentateuch (see also Jer. 48:45); the meaning of the word in the Masoretic Text is uncertain.   [c] 17 Or possibly *Moab, / batter*   [d] 17 Or *all the noisy boasters*   [e] 23 Masoretic Text; with a different word division of the Hebrew *The people from the islands will gather from the north.*

immorality with Moabite women, [2]who invited them to the sacrifices to their gods. The people ate the sacrificial meal and bowed down before these gods. [3]So Israel yoked themselves to the Baal of Peor. And the LORD's anger burned against them.

[4]The LORD said to Moses, "Take all the leaders of these people, kill them and expose them in broad daylight before the LORD, so that the LORD's fierce anger may turn away from Israel."

[5]So Moses said to Israel's judges, "Each of you must put to death those of your people who have yoked themselves to the Baal of Peor."

[6]Then an Israelite man brought into the camp a Midianite woman right before the eyes of Moses and the whole assembly of Israel while they were weeping at the entrance to the tent of meeting. [7]When Phinehas son of Eleazar, the son of Aaron, the priest, saw this, he left the assembly, took a spear in his hand [8]and followed the Israelite into the tent. He drove the spear into both of them, right through the Israelite man and into the woman's stomach. Then the plague against the Israelites was stopped; [9]but those who died in the plague numbered 24,000.

[10]The LORD said to Moses, [11]"Phinehas son of Eleazar, the son of Aaron, the priest, has turned my anger away from the Israelites. Since he was as zealous for my honor among them as I am, I did not put an end to them in my zeal. [12]Therefore tell him I am making my covenant of peace with him. [13]He and his descendants will have a covenant of a lasting priesthood, because he was zealous for the honor of his God and made atonement for the Israelites."

[14]The name of the Israelite who was killed with the Midianite woman was Zimri son of Salu, the leader of a Simeonite family. [15]And the name of the Midianite woman who was put to death was Kozbi daughter of Zur, a tribal chief of a Midianite family.

[16]The LORD said to Moses, [17]"Treat the Midianites as enemies and kill them. [18]They treated you as enemies when they deceived you in the Peor incident involving their sister Kozbi, the daughter of a Midianite leader, the woman who was killed when the plague came as a result of that incident."

The Second Census

26 After the plague the LORD said to Moses and Eleazar son of Aaron, the priest, [2]"Take a census of the whole Israelite community by families — all those twenty years old or more who are able to serve in the army of Israel." [3]So on the plains of Moab by the Jordan across from Jericho, Moses and Eleazar the priest spoke with them and said, [4]"Take a census of the men twenty years old or more, as the LORD commanded Moses."

These were the Israelites who came out of Egypt:

[5]The descendants of Reuben, the firstborn son of Israel, were:

through Hanok, the Hanokite clan;
through Pallu, the Palluite clan;
[6]through Hezron, the Hezronite clan;
through Karmi, the Karmite clan.
[7]These were the clans of Reuben; those numbered were 43,730.

[8]The son of Pallu was Eliab, [9]and the sons of Eliab were Nemuel, Dathan and Abiram. The same Dathan and Abiram were the community officials who rebelled against Moses and Aaron and were among Korah's followers when they rebelled against the LORD. [10]The earth opened its mouth and swallowed them along with Korah, whose followers died when the fire devoured the 250 men. And they served as a warning sign. [11]The line of Korah, however, did not die out.

[12]The descendants of Simeon by their clans were:

through Nemuel, the Nemuelite clan;
through Jamin, the Jaminite clan;
through Jakin, the Jakinite clan;
[13]through Zerah, the Zerahite clan;
through Shaul, the Shaulite clan.
[14]These were the clans of Simeon; those numbered were 22,200.

[15]The descendants of Gad by their clans were:

through Zephon, the Zephonite clan;
through Haggi, the Haggite clan;
through Shuni, the Shunite clan;
[16]through Ozni, the Oznite clan;
through Eri, the Erite clan;
[17]through Arodi,[a] the Arodite clan;
through Areli, the Arelite clan.

---

[a] 17 Samaritan Pentateuch and Syriac (see also Gen. 46:16); Masoretic Text *Arod*

¹⁸These were the clans of Gad; those numbered were 40,500.

¹⁹Er and Onan were sons of Judah, but they died in Canaan.
²⁰The descendants of Judah by their clans were:

through Shelah, the Shelanite clan;
through Perez, the Perezite clan;
through Zerah, the Zerahite clan.
²¹The descendants of Perez were:
through Hezron, the Hezronite clan;
through Hamul, the Hamulite clan.
²²These were the clans of Judah; those numbered were 76,500.

²³The descendants of Issachar by their clans were:

through Tola, the Tolaite clan;
through Puah, the Puite^a clan;
²⁴through Jashub, the Jashubite clan;
through Shimron, the Shimronite clan.
²⁵These were the clans of Issachar; those numbered were 64,300.

²⁶The descendants of Zebulun by their clans were:

through Sered, the Seredite clan;
through Elon, the Elonite clan;
through Jahleel, the Jahleelite clan.
²⁷These were the clans of Zebulun; those numbered were 60,500.

²⁸The descendants of Joseph by their clans through Manasseh and Ephraim were:

²⁹The descendants of Manasseh:
through Makir, the Makirite clan (Makir was the father of Gilead);
through Gilead, the Gileadite clan.
³⁰These were the descendants of Gilead:
through Iezer, the Iezerite clan;
through Helek, the Helekite clan;
³¹through Asriel, the Asrielite clan;
through Shechem, the Shechemite clan;
³²through Shemida, the Shemidaite clan;
through Hepher, the Hepherite clan.
³³(Zelophehad son of Hepher had no sons; he had only daughters, whose names were Mahlah, Noah, Hoglah, Milkah and Tirzah.)

³⁴These were the clans of Manasseh; those numbered were 52,700.

³⁵These were the descendants of Ephraim by their clans:

through Shuthelah, the Shuthelahite clan;
through Beker, the Bekerite clan;
through Tahan, the Tahanite clan.
³⁶These were the descendants of Shuthelah:
through Eran, the Eranite clan.
³⁷These were the clans of Ephraim; those numbered were 32,500.

These were the descendants of Joseph by their clans.

³⁸The descendants of Benjamin by their clans were:

through Bela, the Belaite clan;
through Ashbel, the Ashbelite clan;
through Ahiram, the Ahiramite clan;
³⁹through Shupham,^b the Shuphamite clan;
through Hupham, the Huphamite clan.
⁴⁰The descendants of Bela through Ard and Naaman were:
through Ard,^c the Ardite clan;
through Naaman, the Naamite clan.
⁴¹These were the clans of Benjamin; those numbered were 45,600.

⁴²These were the descendants of Dan by their clans:

through Shuham, the Shuhamite clan.
These were the clans of Dan: ⁴³All of them were Shuhamite clans; and those numbered were 64,400.

⁴⁴The descendants of Asher by their clans were:

through Imnah, the Imnite clan;
through Ishvi, the Ishvite clan;
through Beriah, the Beriite clan;
⁴⁵and through the descendants of Beriah:
through Heber, the Heberite clan;
through Malkiel, the Malkielite clan.
⁴⁶(Asher had a daughter named Serah.)
⁴⁷These were the clans of Asher; those numbered were 53,400.

⁴⁸The descendants of Naphtali by their clans were:

---

^a 23 Samaritan Pentateuch, Septuagint, Vulgate and Syriac (see also 1 Chron. 7:1); Masoretic Text *through Puvah, the Punite*   ^b 39 A few manuscripts of the Masoretic Text, Samaritan Pentateuch, Vulgate and Syriac (see also Septuagint); most manuscripts of the Masoretic Text *Shephupham*   ^c 40 Samaritan Pentateuch and Vulgate (see also Septuagint); Masoretic Text does not have *through Ard*.

through Jahzeel, the Jahzeelite clan;
through Guni, the Gunite clan;
⁴⁹through Jezer, the Jezerite clan;
through Shillem, the Shillemite clan.
⁵⁰These were the clans of Naphtali; those numbered were 45,400.

⁵¹The total number of the men of Israel was 601,730.

⁵²The LORD said to Moses, ⁵³"The land is to be allotted to them as an inheritance based on the number of names. ⁵⁴To a larger group give a larger inheritance, and to a smaller group a smaller one; each is to receive its inheritance according to the number of those listed. ⁵⁵Be sure that the land is distributed by lot. What each group inherits will be according to the names for its ancestral tribe. ⁵⁶Each inheritance is to be distributed by lot among the larger and smaller groups."

⁵⁷These were the Levites who were counted by their clans:
through Gershon, the Gershonite clan;
through Kohath, the Kohathite clan;
through Merari, the Merarite clan.
⁵⁸These also were Levite clans:
the Libnite clan,
the Hebronite clan,
the Mahlite clan,
the Mushite clan,
the Korahite clan.
(Kohath was the forefather of Amram; ⁵⁹the name of Amram's wife was Jochebed, a descendant of Levi, who was born to the Levites[a] in Egypt. To Amram she bore Aaron, Moses and their sister Miriam. ⁶⁰Aaron was the father of Nadab and Abihu, Eleazar and Ithamar. ⁶¹But Nadab and Abihu died when they made an offering before the LORD with unauthorized fire.)

⁶²All the male Levites a month old or more numbered 23,000. They were not counted along with the other Israelites because they received no inheritance among them.

⁶³These are the ones counted by Moses and Eleazar the priest when they counted the Israelites on the plains of Moab by the Jordan across from Jericho. ⁶⁴Not one

of them was among those counted by Moses and Aaron the priest when they counted the Israelites in the Desert of Sinai. ⁶⁵For the LORD had told those Israelites they would surely die in the wilderness, and not one of them was left except Caleb son of Jephunneh and Joshua son of Nun.

Zelophehad's Daughters

27 The daughters of Zelophehad son of Hepher, the son of Gilead, the son of Makir, the son of Manasseh, belonged to the clans of Manasseh son of Joseph. The names of the daughters were Mahlah, Noah, Hoglah, Milkah and Tirzah. They came forward ²and stood before Moses, Eleazar the priest, the leaders and the whole assembly at the entrance to the tent of meeting and said, ³"Our father died in the wilderness. He was not among Korah's followers, who banded together against the LORD, but he died for his own sin and left no sons. ⁴Why should our father's name disappear from his clan because he had no son? Give us property among our father's relatives."

⁵So Moses brought their case before the LORD, ⁶and the LORD said to him, ⁷"What Zelophehad's daughters are saying is right. You must certainly give them property as an inheritance among their father's relatives and give their father's inheritance to them.

⁸"Say to the Israelites, 'If a man dies and leaves no son, give his inheritance to his daughter. ⁹If he has no daughter, give his inheritance to his brothers. ¹⁰If he has no brothers, give his inheritance to his father's brothers. ¹¹If his father had no brothers, give his inheritance to the nearest relative in his clan, that he may possess it. This is to have the force of law for the Israelites, as the LORD commanded Moses.'"

Joshua to Succeed Moses

¹²Then the LORD said to Moses, "Go up this mountain in the Abarim Range and see the land I have given the Israelites. ¹³After you have seen it, you too will be gathered to your people, as your brother Aaron was, ¹⁴for when the community rebelled at the waters in the Desert of Zin, both of you disobeyed my command to honor me as holy before their eyes." (These were the waters of Meribah Kadesh, in the Desert of Zin.)

---

[a] 59 Or *Jochebed, a daughter of Levi, who was born to Levi*

¹⁵Moses said to the LORD, ¹⁶"May the LORD, the God who gives breath to all living things, appoint someone over this community ¹⁷to go out and come in before them, one who will lead them out and bring them in, so the LORD's people will not be like sheep without a shepherd."

¹⁸So the LORD said to Moses, "Take Joshua son of Nun, a man in whom is the spirit of leadership,ᵃ and lay your hand on him. ¹⁹Have him stand before Eleazar the priest and the entire assembly and commission him in their presence. ²⁰Give him some of your authority so the whole Israelite community will obey him. ²¹He is to stand before Eleazar the priest, who will obtain decisions for him by inquiring of the Urim before the LORD. At his command he and the entire community of the Israelites will go out, and at his command they will come in."

²²Moses did as the LORD commanded him. He took Joshua and had him stand before Eleazar the priest and the whole assembly. ²³Then he laid his hands on him and commissioned him, as the LORD instructed through Moses.

Daily Offerings

28 The LORD said to Moses, ²"Give this command to the Israelites and say to them: 'Make sure that you present to me at the appointed time my food offerings, as an aroma pleasing to me.' ³Say to them: 'This is the food offering you are to present to the LORD: two lambs a year old without defect, as a regular burnt offering each day. ⁴Offer one lamb in the morning and the other at twilight, ⁵together with a grain offering of a tenth of an ephahᵇ of the finest flour mixed with a quarter of a hinᶜ of oil from pressed olives. ⁶This is the regular burnt offering instituted at Mount Sinai as a pleasing aroma, a food offering presented to the LORD. ⁷The accompanying drink offering is to be a quarter of a hin of fermented drink with each lamb. Pour out the drink offering to the LORD at the sanctuary. ⁸Offer the second lamb at twilight, along with the same kind of grain offering and drink offering that you

offer in the morning. This is a food offering, an aroma pleasing to the LORD.

Sabbath Offerings

⁹"'On the Sabbath day, make an offering of two lambs a year old without defect, together with its drink offering and a grain offering of two-tenths of an ephahᵈ of the finest flour mixed with olive oil. ¹⁰This is the burnt offering for every Sabbath, in addition to the regular burnt offering and its drink offering.

Monthly Offerings

¹¹"'On the first of every month, present to the LORD a burnt offering of two young bulls, one ram and seven male lambs a year old, all without defect. ¹²With each bull there is to be a grain offering of three-tenths of an ephahᵉ of the finest flour mixed with oil; with the ram, a grain offering of two-tenths of an ephah of the finest flour mixed with oil; ¹³and with each lamb, a grain offering of a tenth of an ephah of the finest flour mixed with oil. This is for a burnt offering, a pleasing aroma, a food offering presented to the LORD. ¹⁴With each bull there is to be a drink offering of half a hinᶠ of wine; with the ram, a third of a hinᵍ; and with each lamb, a quarter of a hin. This is the monthly burnt offering to be made at each new moon during the year. ¹⁵Besides the regular burnt offering with its drink offering, one male goat is to be presented to the LORD as a sin offering.ʰ

The Passover

¹⁶"'On the fourteenth day of the first month the LORD's Passover is to be held. ¹⁷On the fifteenth day of this month there is to be a festival; for seven days eat bread made without yeast. ¹⁸On the first day hold a sacred assembly and do no regular work. ¹⁹Present to the LORD a food offering consisting of a burnt offering of two young bulls, one ram and seven male lambs a year old, all without defect. ²⁰With each bull offer a grain offering of three-tenths of an ephah of the finest flour mixed with oil; with the ram, two-tenths; ²¹and with each of the seven lambs, one-tenth. ²²Include one male

---

ᵃ 18 Or the Spirit   ᵇ 5 That is, probably about 3 1/2 pounds or about 1.6 kilograms; also in verses 13, 21 and 29   ᶜ 5 That is, about 1 quart or about 1 liter; also in verses 7 and 14   ᵈ 9 That is, probably about 7 pounds or about 3.2 kilograms; also in verses 12, 20 and 28   ᵉ 12 That is, probably about 11 pounds or about 5 kilograms; also in verses 20 and 28   ᶠ 14 That is, about 2 quarts or about 1.9 liters   ᵍ 14 That is, about 1 1/3 quarts or about 1.3 liters   ʰ 15 Or purification offering; also in verse 22 goat as a sin offering to make atonement for you. ²³Offer these in addition to the regular morning burnt offering. ²⁴In this way present the food offering every day for seven days as an aroma pleasing to the LORD; it is to be offered in addition to the regular burnt offering and its drink offering. ²⁵On the seventh day hold a sacred assembly and do no regular work.

The Festival of Weeks

²⁶" 'On the day of firstfruits, when you present to the LORD an offering of new grain during the Festival of Weeks, hold a sacred assembly and do no regular work. ²⁷Present a burnt offering of two young bulls, one ram and seven male lambs a year old as an aroma pleasing to the LORD. ²⁸With each bull there is to be a grain offering of three-tenths of an ephah of the finest flour mixed with oil; with the ram, two-tenths; ²⁹and with each of the seven lambs, one-tenth. ³⁰Include one male goat to make atonement for you. ³¹Offer these together with their drink offerings, in addition to the regular burnt offering and its grain offering. Be sure the animals are without defect.

The Festival of Trumpets

29 " 'On the first day of the seventh month hold a sacred assembly and do no regular work. It is a day for you to sound the trumpets. ²As an aroma pleasing to the LORD, offer a burnt offering of one young bull, one ram and seven male lambs a year old, all without defect. ³With the bull offer a grain offering of three-tenths of an ephahᵃ of the finest flour mixed with olive oil; with the ram, two-tenthsᵇ; ⁴and with each of the seven lambs, one-tenth.ᶜ ⁵Include one male goat as a sin offeringᵈ to make atonement for you. ⁶These are in addition to the monthly and daily burnt offerings with their grain offerings and drink offerings as specified. They are food offerings presented to the LORD, a pleasing aroma.

The Day of Atonement

⁷" 'On the tenth day of this seventh month hold a sacred assembly. You must deny yourselvesᵉ and do no work. ⁸Present as an aroma pleasing to the LORD a burnt offering of one young bull, one ram and seven male lambs a year old, all without defect. ⁹With the bull offer a grain offering of three-tenths of an ephah of the finest flour mixed with oil; with the ram, two-tenths; ¹⁰and with each of the seven lambs, one-tenth. ¹¹Include one male goat as a sin offering, in addition to the sin offering for atonement and the regular burnt offering with its grain offering, and their drink offerings.

The Festival of Tabernacles

¹²" 'On the fifteenth day of the seventh month, hold a sacred assembly and do no regular work. Celebrate a festival to the LORD for seven days. ¹³Present as an aroma pleasing to the LORD a food offering consisting of a burnt offering of thirteen young bulls, two rams and fourteen male lambs a year old, all without defect. ¹⁴With each of the thirteen bulls offer a grain offering of three-tenths of an ephah of the finest flour mixed with oil; with each of the two rams, two-tenths; ¹⁵and with each of the fourteen lambs, one-tenth. ¹⁶Include one male goat as a sin offering, in addition to the regular burnt offering with its grain offering and drink offering.

¹⁷" 'On the second day offer twelve young bulls, two rams and fourteen male lambs a year old, all without defect. ¹⁸With the bulls, rams and lambs, offer their grain offerings and drink offerings according to the number specified. ¹⁹Include one male goat as a sin offering, in addition to the regular burnt offering with its grain offering, and their drink offerings.

²⁰" 'On the third day offer eleven bulls, two rams and fourteen male lambs a year old, all without defect. ²¹With the bulls, rams and lambs, offer their grain offerings and drink offerings according to the number specified. ²²Include one male goat as a sin offering, in addition to the regular burnt offering with its grain offering and drink offering.

²³" 'On the fourth day offer ten bulls, two rams and fourteen male lambs a year old, all without defect. ²⁴With the bulls, rams and lambs, offer their grain offerings and drink

---

ᵃ 3 That is, probably about 11 pounds or about 5 kilograms; also in verses 9 and 14   ᵇ 3 That is, probably about 7 pounds or about 3.2 kilograms; also in verses 9 and 14   ᶜ 4 That is, probably about 3 1/2 pounds or about 1.6 kilograms; also in verses 10 and 15   ᵈ 5 Or *purification offering*; also elsewhere in this chapter   ᵉ 7 Or *must fast* offerings according to the number specified. [25]Include one male goat as a sin offering, in addition to the regular burnt offering with its grain offering and drink offering.

[26]"'On the fifth day offer nine bulls, two rams and fourteen male lambs a year old, all without defect. [27]With the bulls, rams and lambs, offer their grain offerings and drink offerings according to the number specified. [28]Include one male goat as a sin offering, in addition to the regular burnt offering with its grain offering and drink offering.

[29]"'On the sixth day offer eight bulls, two rams and fourteen male lambs a year old, all without defect. [30]With the bulls, rams and lambs, offer their grain offerings and drink offerings according to the number specified. [31]Include one male goat as a sin offering, in addition to the regular burnt offering with its grain offering and drink offering.

[32]"'On the seventh day offer seven bulls, two rams and fourteen male lambs a year old, all without defect. [33]With the bulls, rams and lambs, offer their grain offerings and drink offerings according to the number specified. [34]Include one male goat as a sin offering, in addition to the regular burnt offering with its grain offering and drink offering.

[35]"'On the eighth day hold a closing special assembly and do no regular work. [36]Present as an aroma pleasing to the LORD a food offering consisting of a burnt offering of one bull, one ram and seven male lambs a year old, all without defect. [37]With the bull, the ram and the lambs, offer their grain offerings and drink offerings according to the number specified. [38]Include one male goat as a sin offering, in addition to the regular burnt offering with its grain offering and drink offering.

[39]"'In addition to what you vow and your freewill offerings, offer these to the LORD at your appointed festivals: your burnt offerings, grain offerings, drink offerings and fellowship offerings.'"

[40]Moses told the Israelites all that the LORD commanded him.[a]

Vows

30 [b] Moses said to the heads of the tribes of Israel: "This is what the LORD

commands: [2]When a man makes a vow to the LORD or takes an oath to obligate himself by a pledge, he must not break his word but must do everything he said.

[3]"When a young woman still living in her father's household makes a vow to the LORD or obligates herself by a pledge [4]and her father hears about her vow or pledge but says nothing to her, then all her vows and every pledge by which she obligated herself will stand. [5]But if her father forbids her when he hears about it, none of her vows or the pledges by which she obligated herself will stand; the LORD will release her because her father has forbidden her.

[6]"If she marries after she makes a vow or after her lips utter a rash promise by which she obligates herself [7]and her husband hears about it but says nothing to her, then her vows or the pledges by which she obligated herself will stand. [8]But if her husband forbids her when he hears about it, he nullifies the vow that obligates her or the rash promise by which she obligates herself, and the LORD will release her.

[9]"Any vow or obligation taken by a widow or divorced woman will be binding on her.

[10]"If a woman living with her husband makes a vow or obligates herself by a pledge under oath [11]and her husband hears about it but says nothing to her and does not forbid her, then all her vows or the pledges by which she obligated herself will stand. [12]But if her husband nullifies them when he hears about them, then none of the vows or pledges that came from her lips will stand. Her husband has nullified them, and the LORD will release her. [13]Her husband may confirm or nullify any vow she makes or any sworn pledge to deny herself.[c] [14]But if her husband says nothing to her about it from day to day, then he confirms all her vows or the pledges binding on her. He confirms them by saying nothing to her when he hears about them. [15]If, however, he nullifies them some time after he hears about them, then he must bear the consequences of her wrongdoing."

[16]These are the regulations the LORD gave Moses concerning relationships between a man and his wife, and between a father and his young daughter still living at home.

---

[a] 40 In Hebrew texts this verse (29:40) is numbered 30:1. [b] In Hebrew texts 30:1-16 is numbered 30:2-17.
[c] 13 Or to fast

Vengeance on the Midianites

31 The LORD said to Moses, ² "Take vengeance on the Midianites for the Israelites. After that, you will be gathered to your people."

³ So Moses said to the people, "Arm some of your men to go to war against the Midianites so that they may carry out the LORD's vengeance on them. ⁴ Send into battle a thousand men from each of the tribes of Israel." ⁵ So twelve thousand men armed for battle, a thousand from each tribe, were supplied from the clans of Israel. ⁶ Moses sent them into battle, a thousand from each tribe, along with Phinehas son of Eleazar, the priest, who took with him articles from the sanctuary and the trumpets for signaling.

⁷ They fought against Midian, as the LORD commanded Moses, and killed every man. ⁸ Among their victims were Evi, Rekem, Zur, Hur and Reba — the five kings of Midian. They also killed Balaam son of Beor with the sword. ⁹ The Israelites captured the Midianite women and children and took all the Midianite herds, flocks and goods as plunder. ¹⁰ They burned all the towns where the Midianites had settled, as well as all their camps. ¹¹ They took all the plunder and spoils, including the people and animals, ¹² and brought the captives, spoils and plunder to Moses and Eleazar the priest and the Israelite assembly at their camp on the plains of Moab, by the Jordan across from Jericho.

¹³ Moses, Eleazar the priest and all the leaders of the community went to meet them outside the camp. ¹⁴ Moses was angry with the officers of the army — the commanders of thousands and commanders of hundreds — who returned from the battle.

¹⁵ "Have you allowed all the women to live?" he asked them. ¹⁶ "They were the ones who followed Balaam's advice and enticed the Israelites to be unfaithful to the LORD in the Peor incident, so that a plague struck the LORD's people. ¹⁷ Now kill all the boys. And kill every woman who has slept with a man, ¹⁸ but save for yourselves every girl who has never slept with a man.

¹⁹ "Anyone who has killed someone or touched someone who was killed must stay outside the camp seven days. On the third and seventh days you must purify yourselves and your captives. ²⁰ Purify every garment as well as everything made of leather, goat hair or wood."

²¹ Then Eleazar the priest said to the soldiers who had gone into battle, "This is what is required by the law that the LORD gave Moses: ²² Gold, silver, bronze, iron, tin, lead ²³ and anything else that can withstand fire must be put through the fire, and then it will be clean. But it must also be purified with the water of cleansing. And whatever cannot withstand fire must be put through that water. ²⁴ On the seventh day wash your clothes and you will be clean. Then you may come into the camp."

Dividing the Spoils

²⁵ The LORD said to Moses, ²⁶ "You and Eleazar the priest and the family heads of the community are to count all the people and animals that were captured. ²⁷ Divide the spoils equally between the soldiers who took part in the battle and the rest of the community. ²⁸ From the soldiers who fought in the battle, set apart as tribute for the LORD one out of every five hundred, whether people, cattle, donkeys or sheep. ²⁹ Take this tribute from their half share and give it to Eleazar the priest as the LORD's part. ³⁰ From the Israelites' half, select one out of every fifty, whether people, cattle, donkeys, sheep or other animals. Give them to the Levites, who are responsible for the care of the LORD's tabernacle." ³¹ So Moses and Eleazar the priest did as the LORD commanded Moses.

³² The plunder remaining from the spoils that the soldiers took was 675,000 sheep, ³³ 72,000 cattle, ³⁴ 61,000 donkeys ³⁵ and 32,000 women who had never slept with a man.

³⁶ The half share of those who fought in the battle was:

337,500 sheep, ³⁷ of which the tribute for the LORD was 675;

³⁸ 36,000 cattle, of which the tribute for the LORD was 72;

³⁹ 30,500 donkeys, of which the tribute for the LORD was 61;

⁴⁰ 16,000 people, of whom the tribute for the LORD was 32.

⁴¹ Moses gave the tribute to Eleazar the priest as the LORD's part, as the LORD commanded Moses.

⁴² The half belonging to the Israelites,

which Moses set apart from that of the fighting men — ⁴³the community's half — was 337,500 sheep, ⁴⁴36,000 cattle, ⁴⁵30,500 donkeys ⁴⁶and 16,000 people. ⁴⁷From the Israelites' half, Moses selected one out of every fifty people and animals, as the LORD commanded him, and gave them to the Levites, who were responsible for the care of the LORD's tabernacle.

⁴⁸Then the officers who were over the units of the army — the commanders of thousands and commanders of hundreds — went to Moses ⁴⁹and said to him, "Your servants have counted the soldiers under our command, and not one is missing. ⁵⁰So we have brought as an offering to the LORD the gold articles each of us acquired — armlets, bracelets, signet rings, earrings and necklaces — to make atonement for ourselves before the LORD."

⁵¹Moses and Eleazar the priest accepted from them the gold — all the crafted articles. ⁵²All the gold from the commanders of thousands and commanders of hundreds that Moses and Eleazar presented as a gift to the LORD weighed 16,750 shekels.ᵃ ⁵³Each soldier had taken plunder for himself. ⁵⁴Moses and Eleazar the priest accepted the gold from the commanders of thousands and commanders of hundreds and brought it into the tent of meeting as a memorial for the Israelites before the LORD.

The Transjordan Tribes

32 The Reubenites and Gadites, who had very large herds and flocks, saw that the lands of Jazer and Gilead were suitable for livestock. ²So they came to Moses and Eleazar the priest and to the leaders of the community, and said, ³"Ataroth, Dibon, Jazer, Nimrah, Heshbon, Elealeh, Sebam, Nebo and Beon — ⁴the land the LORD subdued before the people of Israel — are suitable for livestock, and your servants have livestock. ⁵If we have found favor in your eyes," they said, "let this land be given to your servants as our possession. Do not make us cross the Jordan."

⁶Moses said to the Gadites and Reubenites, "Should your fellow Israelites go to war while you sit here? ⁷Why do you discourage the Israelites from crossing over into the land the LORD has given them? ⁸This is what your fathers did when I sent them from Kadesh Barnea to look over the land. ⁹After they went up to the Valley of Eshkol and viewed the land, they discouraged the Israelites from entering the land the LORD had given them. ¹⁰The LORD's anger was aroused that day and he swore this oath: ¹¹'Because they have not followed me wholeheartedly, not one of those who were twenty years old or more when they came up out of Egypt will see the land I promised on oath to Abraham, Isaac and Jacob — ¹²not one except Caleb son of Jephunneh the Kenizzite and Joshua son of Nun, for they followed the LORD wholeheartedly.' ¹³The LORD's anger burned against Israel and he made them wander in the wilderness forty years, until the whole generation of those who had done evil in his sight was gone.

¹⁴"And here you are, a brood of sinners, standing in the place of your fathers and making the LORD even more angry with Israel. ¹⁵If you turn away from following him, he will again leave all this people in the wilderness, and you will be the cause of their destruction."

¹⁶Then they came up to him and said, "We would like to build pens here for our livestock and cities for our women and children. ¹⁷But we will arm ourselves for battleᵇ and go ahead of the Israelites until we have brought them to their place. Meanwhile our women and children will live in fortified cities, for protection from the inhabitants of the land. ¹⁸We will not return to our homes until each of the Israelites has received their inheritance. ¹⁹We will not receive any inheritance with them on the other side of the Jordan, because our inheritance has come to us on the east side of the Jordan."

²⁰Then Moses said to them, "If you will do this — if you will arm yourselves before the LORD for battle ²¹and if all of you who are armed cross over the Jordan before the LORD until he has driven his enemies out before him — ²²then when the land is subdued before the LORD, you may return and be free from your obligation to the LORD and to Israel. And this land will be your possession before the LORD.

ᵃ 52 That is, about 420 pounds or about 190 kilograms

ᵇ 17 Septuagint; Hebrew *will be quick to arm ourselves*

²³ "But if you fail to do this, you will be sinning against the LORD; and you may be sure that your sin will find you out. ²⁴ Build cities for your women and children, and pens for your flocks, but do what you have promised."

²⁵ The Gadites and Reubenites said to Moses, "We your servants will do as our lord commands. ²⁶ Our children and wives, our flocks and herds will remain here in the cities of Gilead. ²⁷ But your servants, every man who is armed for battle, will cross over to fight before the LORD, just as our lord says."

²⁸ Then Moses gave orders about them to Eleazar the priest and Joshua son of Nun and to the family heads of the Israelite tribes. ²⁹ He said to them, "If the Gadites and Reubenites, every man armed for battle, cross over the Jordan with you before the LORD, then when the land is subdued before you, you must give them the land of Gilead as their possession. ³⁰ But if they do not cross over with you armed, they must accept their possession with you in Canaan."

³¹ The Gadites and Reubenites answered, "Your servants will do what the LORD has said. ³² We will cross over before the LORD into Canaan armed, but the property we inherit will be on this side of the Jordan."

³³ Then Moses gave to the Gadites, the Reubenites and the half-tribe of Manasseh son of Joseph the kingdom of Sihon king of the Amorites and the kingdom of Og king of Bashan — the whole land with its cities and the territory around them.

³⁴ The Gadites built up Dibon, Ataroth, Aroer, ³⁵ Atroth Shophan, Jazer, Jogbehah, ³⁶ Beth Nimrah and Beth Haran as fortified cities, and built pens for their flocks. ³⁷ And the Reubenites rebuilt Heshbon, Elealeh and Kiriathaim, ³⁸ as well as Nebo and Baal Meon (these names were changed) and Sibmah. They gave names to the cities they rebuilt.

³⁹ The descendants of Makir son of Manasseh went to Gilead, captured it and drove out the Amorites who were there. ⁴⁰ So Moses gave Gilead to the Makirites, the descendants of Manasseh, and they settled there. ⁴¹ Jair, a descendant of Manasseh, captured their settlements and called them Havvoth Jair.*ᵃ* ⁴² And Nobah captured Kenath and its surrounding settlements and called it Nobah after himself.

Stages in Israel's Journey

33 Here are the stages in the journey of the Israelites when they came out of Egypt by divisions under the leadership of Moses and Aaron. ² At the LORD's command Moses recorded the stages in their journey. This is their journey by stages:

³ The Israelites set out from Rameses on the fifteenth day of the first month, the day after the Passover. They marched out defiantly in full view of all the Egyptians, ⁴ who were burying all their firstborn, whom the LORD had struck down among them; for the LORD had brought judgment on their gods.

⁵ The Israelites left Rameses and camped at Sukkoth.

⁶ They left Sukkoth and camped at Etham, on the edge of the desert.

⁷ They left Etham, turned back to Pi Hahiroth, to the east of Baal Zephon, and camped near Migdol.

⁸ They left Pi Hahiroth*ᵇ* and passed through the sea into the desert, and when they had traveled for three days in the Desert of Etham, they camped at Marah.

⁹ They left Marah and went to Elim, where there were twelve springs and seventy palm trees, and they camped there.

¹⁰ They left Elim and camped by the Red Sea.*ᶜ*

¹¹ They left the Red Sea and camped in the Desert of Sin.

¹² They left the Desert of Sin and camped at Dophkah.

¹³ They left Dophkah and camped at Alush.

¹⁴ They left Alush and camped at Rephidim, where there was no water for the people to drink.

¹⁵ They left Rephidim and camped in the Desert of Sinai.

¹⁶ They left the Desert of Sinai and camped at Kibroth Hattaavah.

ᵃ 41 Or *them the settlements of Jair*   *ᵇ 8* Many manuscripts of the Masoretic Text, Samaritan Pentateuch and Vulgate; most manuscripts of the Masoretic Text *left from before Hahiroth*   *ᶜ 10* Or *the Sea of Reeds;* also in verse 11

TRAINING AND MERCY

READ: NUMBERS 33:1

Forty years spent wandering in the scorching desert. The Lord didn't intend for the time span between his people's escape from Egypt and their enjoyment of the promised land to last so long. Yet that's how it played out after God's people were too timid to enter the land he swore to their ancestor Abraham. Of all the adults who left Egypt, none except Joshua and Caleb survived to make a home in the Lord's amazing new place (Numbers 14:30).

Numbers 33 lists every step on the people's extended journey, from Rameses in Egypt to the plains of Moab just east of the Jordan River. While the sites of many of these temporary camps can't be pinpointed on the ground today, they were sites of the Lord's astonishing care. For forty years, God fed his people with manna (Exodus 16:35). During that time the people's clothes and sandals didn't wear out (Deuteronomy 29:5).

BUILDING FAITH WISDOM STRENGTH

Even though God's people had sinned terribly, he nevertheless showed them mercy. He used their years of walking to discipline them, teaching them to follow him without question. Like Moses described their experience, "Know then in your heart that as a man disciplines his son, so the LORD your God disciplines you" (Deuteronomy 8:5).

As God leads you step by step through life, he's training you to walk with him no matter where he sends you.

¹⁷They left Kibroth Hattaavah and camped at Hazeroth.

¹⁸They left Hazeroth and camped at Rithmah.

¹⁹They left Rithmah and camped at Rimmon Perez.

²⁰They left Rimmon Perez and camped at Libnah.

²¹They left Libnah and camped at Rissah.

²²They left Rissah and camped at Kehelathah.

²³They left Kehelathah and camped at Mount Shepher.

²⁴They left Mount Shepher and camped at Haradah.

²⁵They left Haradah and camped at Makheloth.

²⁶They left Makheloth and camped at Tahath.

²⁷They left Tahath and camped at Terah.

²⁸They left Terah and camped at Mithkah.

²⁹They left Mithkah and camped at Hashmonah.

³⁰They left Hashmonah and camped at Moseroth.

³¹They left Moseroth and camped at Bene Jaakan.

³²They left Bene Jaakan and camped at Hor Haggidgad.

³³They left Hor Haggidgad and camped at Jotbathah.

³⁴They left Jotbathah and camped at Abronah.

³⁵They left Abronah and camped at Ezion Geber.

³⁶They left Ezion Geber and camped at Kadesh, in the Desert of Zin.

³⁷They left Kadesh and camped at Mount Hor, on the border of Edom. ³⁸At the LORD's command Aaron the priest went up Mount Hor, where he died on the first day of the fifth month of the fortieth year after the Israelites came out of Egypt. ³⁹Aaron was a hundred and twenty-three years old when he died on Mount Hor.

⁴⁰The Canaanite king of Arad, who lived in the Negev of Canaan, heard that the Israelites were coming.

⁴¹They left Mount Hor and camped at Zalmonah.

⁴²They left Zalmonah and camped at Punon.

⁴³They left Punon and camped at Oboth.

⁴⁴They left Oboth and camped at Iye Abarim, on the border of Moab.

⁴⁵They left Iye Abarim and camped at Dibon Gad.

⁴⁶They left Dibon Gad and camped at Almon Diblathaim.

⁴⁷They left Almon Diblathaim and camped in the mountains of Abarim, near Nebo.

⁴⁸They left the mountains of Abarim and camped on the plains of Moab by the Jordan across from Jericho. ⁴⁹There on the plains of Moab they camped along the Jordan from Beth Jeshimoth to Abel Shittim.

⁵⁰On the plains of Moab by the Jordan across from Jericho the LORD said to Moses, ⁵¹"Speak to the Israelites and say to them: 'When you cross the Jordan into Canaan, ⁵²drive out all the inhabitants of the land before you. Destroy all their carved images and their cast idols, and demolish all their high places. ⁵³Take possession of the land and settle in it, for I have given you the land to possess. ⁵⁴Distribute the land by lot, according to your clans. To a larger group give a larger inheritance, and to a smaller group a smaller one. Whatever falls to them by lot will be theirs. Distribute it according to your ancestral tribes.

⁵⁵"'But if you do not drive out the inhabitants of the land, those you allow to remain will become barbs in your eyes and thorns in your sides. They will give you trouble in the land where you will live. ⁵⁶And then I will do to you what I plan to do to them.'"

Boundaries of Canaan

34 The LORD said to Moses, ²"Command the Israelites and say to them: 'When you enter Canaan, the land that will be allotted to you as an inheritance is to have these boundaries:

³"'Your southern side will include some of the Desert of Zin along the border of Edom. Your southern boundary will start in the east from the southern end of the Dead Sea, ⁴cross south of Scorpion Pass, continue on to Zin and go south of Kadesh Barnea. Then it

will go to Hazar Addar and over to Azmon, [5] where it will turn, join the Wadi of Egypt and end at the Mediterranean Sea.

[6] "'Your western boundary will be the coast of the Mediterranean Sea. This will be your boundary on the west.

[7] "'For your northern boundary, run a line from the Mediterranean Sea to Mount Hor [8] and from Mount Hor to Lebo Hamath. Then the boundary will go to Zedad, [9] continue to Ziphron and end at Hazar Enan. This will be your boundary on the north.

[10] "'For your eastern boundary, run a line from Hazar Enan to Shepham. [11] The boundary will go down from Shepham to Riblah on the east side of Ain and continue along the slopes east of the Sea of Galilee.[a] [12] Then the boundary will go down along the Jordan and end at the Dead Sea.

"'This will be your land, with its boundaries on every side.'"

[13] Moses commanded the Israelites: "Assign this land by lot as an inheritance. The LORD has ordered that it be given to the nine and a half tribes, [14] because the families of the tribe of Reuben, the tribe of Gad and the half-tribe of Manasseh have received their inheritance. [15] These two and a half tribes have received their inheritance east of the Jordan across from Jericho, toward the sunrise."

[16] The LORD said to Moses, [17] "These are the names of the men who are to assign the land for you as an inheritance: Eleazar the priest and Joshua son of Nun. [18] And appoint one leader from each tribe to help assign the land. [19] These are their names:

Caleb son of Jephunneh,
  from the tribe of Judah;
[20] Shemuel son of Ammihud,
  from the tribe of Simeon;
[21] Elidad son of Kislon,
  from the tribe of Benjamin;
[22] Bukki son of Jogli,
  the leader from the tribe of Dan;
[23] Hanniel son of Ephod,
  the leader from the tribe of Manasseh son of Joseph;
[24] Kemuel son of Shiphtan,
  the leader from the tribe of Ephraim son of Joseph;
[25] Elizaphan son of Parnak,
  the leader from the tribe of Zebulun;
[26] Paltiel son of Azzan,
  the leader from the tribe of Issachar;
[27] Ahihud son of Shelomi,
  the leader from the tribe of Asher;
[28] Pedahel son of Ammihud,
  the leader from the tribe of Naphtali."

[29] These are the men the LORD commanded to assign the inheritance to the Israelites in the land of Canaan.

Towns for the Levites

35 On the plains of Moab by the Jordan across from Jericho, the LORD said to Moses, [2] "Command the Israelites to give the Levites towns to live in from the inheritance the Israelites will possess. And give them pasturelands around the towns. [3] Then they will have towns to live in and pasturelands for the cattle they own and all their other animals.

[4] "The pasturelands around the towns that you give the Levites will extend a thousand cubits[b] from the town wall. [5] Outside the town, measure two thousand cubits[c] on the east side, two thousand on the south side, two thousand on the west and two thousand on the north, with the town in the center. They will have this area as pastureland for the towns.

Cities of Refuge

[6] "Six of the towns you give the Levites will be cities of refuge, to which a person who has killed someone may flee. In addition, give them forty-two other towns. [7] In all you must give the Levites forty-eight towns, together with their pasturelands. [8] The towns you give the Levites from the land the Israelites possess are to be given in proportion to the inheritance of each tribe: Take many towns from a tribe that has many, but few from one that has few."

[9] Then the LORD said to Moses: [10] "Speak to the Israelites and say to them: 'When you cross the Jordan into Canaan, [11] select some towns to be your cities of refuge, to which a person who has killed someone accidentally may flee. [12] They will be places of refuge

---

[a] 11 Hebrew *Kinnereth*   [b] 4 That is, about 1,500 feet or about 450 meters   [c] 5 That is, about 3,000 feet or about 900 meters

from the avenger, so that anyone accused of murder may not die before they stand trial before the assembly. ¹³These six towns you give will be your cities of refuge. ¹⁴Give three on this side of the Jordan and three in Canaan as cities of refuge. ¹⁵These six towns will be a place of refuge for Israelites and for foreigners residing among them, so that anyone who has killed another accidentally can flee there.

¹⁶ " 'If anyone strikes someone a fatal blow with an iron object, that person is a murderer; the murderer is to be put to death. ¹⁷Or if anyone is holding a stone and strikes someone a fatal blow with it, that person is a murderer; the murderer is to be put to death. ¹⁸Or if anyone is holding a wooden object and strikes someone a fatal blow with it, that person is a murderer; the murderer is to be put to death. ¹⁹The avenger of blood shall put the murderer to death; when the avenger comes upon the murderer, the avenger shall put the murderer to death. ²⁰If anyone with malice aforethought shoves another or throws something at them intentionally so that they die ²¹or if out of enmity one person hits another with their fist so that the other dies, that person is to be put to death; that person is a murderer. The avenger of blood shall put the murderer to death when they meet.

²² " 'But if without enmity someone suddenly pushes another or throws something at them unintentionally ²³or, without seeing them, drops on them a stone heavy enough to kill them, and they die, then since that other person was not an enemy and no harm was intended, ²⁴the assembly must judge between the accused and the avenger of blood according to these regulations. ²⁵The assembly must protect the one accused of murder from the avenger of blood and send the accused back to the city of refuge to which they fled. The accused must stay there until the death of the high priest, who was anointed with the holy oil.

²⁶ " 'But if the accused ever goes outside the limits of the city of refuge to which they fled ²⁷and the avenger of blood finds them outside the city, the avenger of blood may kill the accused without being guilty of murder. ²⁸The accused must stay in the city of refuge until the death of the high priest; only after the death of the high priest may they return to their own property.

²⁹ " 'This is to have the force of law for you throughout the generations to come, wherever you live.

³⁰ " 'Anyone who kills a person is to be put to death as a murderer only on the testimony of witnesses. But no one is to be put to death on the testimony of only one witness.

³¹ " 'Do not accept a ransom for the life of a murderer, who deserves to die. They are to be put to death.

³² " 'Do not accept a ransom for anyone who has fled to a city of refuge and so allow them to go back and live on their own land before the death of the high priest.

³³ " 'Do not pollute the land where you are. Bloodshed pollutes the land, and atonement cannot be made for the land on which blood has been shed, except by the blood of the one who shed it. ³⁴Do not defile the land where you live and where I dwell, for I, the LORD, dwell among the Israelites.' "

Inheritance of Zelophehad's Daughters

36 The family heads of the clan of Gilead son of Makir, the son of Manasseh, who were from the clans of the descendants of Joseph, came and spoke before Moses and the leaders, the heads of the Israelite families. ²They said, "When the LORD commanded my lord to give the land as an inheritance to the Israelites by lot, he ordered you to give the inheritance of our brother Zelophehad to his daughters. ³Now suppose they marry men from other Israelite tribes; then their inheritance will be taken from our ancestral inheritance and added to that of the tribe they marry into. And so part of the inheritance allotted to us will be taken away. ⁴When the Year of Jubilee for the Israelites comes, their inheritance will be added to that of the tribe into which they marry, and their property will be taken from the tribal inheritance of our ancestors."

⁵Then at the LORD's command Moses gave this order to the Israelites: "What the tribe of the descendants of Joseph is saying is right. ⁶This is what the LORD commands for Zelophehad's daughters: They may marry anyone they please as long as they marry within their father's tribal clan. ⁷No inheritance in Israel is to pass from one tribe to another, for every Israelite shall keep the tribal inheritance of their ancestors. ⁸Every daughter who inherits land in any Israelite

tribe must marry someone in her father's tribal clan, so that every Israelite will possess the inheritance of their ancestors. [9]No inheritance may pass from one tribe to another, for each Israelite tribe is to keep the land it inherits."

[10]So Zelophehad's daughters did as the LORD commanded Moses. [11]Zelophehad's daughters — Mahlah, Tirzah, Hoglah, Milkah and Noah — married their cousins on their father's side. [12]They married within the clans of the descendants of Manasseh son of Joseph, and their inheritance remained in their father's tribe and clan.

[13]These are the commands and regulations the LORD gave through Moses to the Israelites on the plains of Moab by the Jordan across from Jericho.

DEUTERONOMY

➡ **WHEN DID THIS HAPPEN?**

During the 1400s B.C. while the Israelites were traveling in the desert

➡ **WHO IS IN THIS BOOK?**

Moses
Joshua
Sihon, the king of the Amorites
Og, the king of Bashan

➡ **VERSES YOU MIGHT RECOGNIZE**

DEUTERONOMY 6:5

"Love the LORD your God with all your heart and with all your soul and with all your strength."

DEUTERONOMY 30:19B

"I have set before you life and death, blessings and curses. Now choose life, so that you and your children may live."

WHAT'S IT ABOUT?

After wandering in the desert for forty years, the Israelites were about to enter the promised land of Canaan. During their time in the desert, the people had made some big mistakes, but God was willing to let them start over. The Israelites heard all of the rules again, and as they were about to enter the promised land, they made a new commitment to follow God.

At the end of the book, Moses died. A new generation of Israelites would enter the promised land. In fact, Joshua and Caleb would be the only two men old enough to remember leaving Egypt and able to remind the new generation of what God had done for them. This book tells us that Moses was considered the greatest prophet to ever live. But in the New Testament, we discover that Jesus, God's Son, is the prophet who would surpass even Moses' greatness (see John 1:17–18 and Hebrews 3:3).

DEUTERONOMY

The Command to Leave Horeb

1 These are the words Moses spoke to all Israel in the wilderness east of the Jordan — that is, in the Arabah — opposite Suph, between Paran and Tophel, Laban, Hazeroth and Dizahab. ²(It takes eleven days to go from Horeb to Kadesh Barnea by the Mount Seir road.)

³In the fortieth year, on the first day of the eleventh month, Moses proclaimed to the Israelites all that the LORD had commanded him concerning them. ⁴This was after he had defeated Sihon king of the Amorites, who reigned in Heshbon, and at Edrei had defeated Og king of Bashan, who reigned in Ashtaroth.

⁵East of the Jordan in the territory of Moab, Moses began to expound this law, saying:

⁶The LORD our God said to us at Horeb, "You have stayed long enough at this mountain. ⁷Break camp and advance into the hill country of the Amorites; go to all the neighboring peoples in the Arabah, in the mountains, in the western foothills, in the Negev and along the coast, to the land of the Canaanites and to Lebanon, as far as the great river, the Euphrates. ⁸See, I have given you this land. Go in and take possession of the land the LORD swore he would give to your fathers — to Abraham, Isaac and Jacob — and to their descendants after them."

The Appointment of Leaders

⁹At that time I said to you, "You are too heavy a burden for me to carry alone. ¹⁰The LORD your God has increased your numbers so that today you are as numerous as the stars in the sky. ¹¹May the LORD, the God of your ancestors, increase you a thousand times and bless you as he has promised! ¹²But how can I bear your problems and your burdens and your disputes all by myself? ¹³Choose some wise, understanding and respected men from each of your tribes, and I will set them over you."

¹⁴You answered me, "What you propose to do is good."

¹⁵So I took the leading men of your tribes, wise and respected men, and appointed them to have authority over you — as commanders of thousands, of hundreds, of fifties and of tens and as tribal officials. ¹⁶And I charged your judges at that time, "Hear the disputes between your people and judge fairly, whether the case is between two Israelites or between an Israelite and a foreigner residing among you. ¹⁷Do not show partiality in judging; hear both small and great alike. Do not be afraid of anyone, for judgment belongs to God. Bring me any case too hard for you, and I will hear it." ¹⁸And at that time I told you everything you were to do.

Spies Sent Out

¹⁹Then, as the LORD our God commanded us, we set out from Horeb and went toward the hill country of the Amorites through all that vast and dreadful wilderness that you have seen, and so we reached Kadesh Barnea. ²⁰Then I said to you, "You have reached the hill country of the Amorites, which the LORD our God is giving us. ²¹See, the LORD your God has given you the land. Go up and take possession of it as the LORD, the God of your ancestors, told you. Do not be afraid; do not be discouraged."

²²Then all of you came to me and said, "Let us send men ahead to spy out the land for us and bring back a report about the route we are to take and the towns we will come to."

²³The idea seemed good to me; so I selected twelve of you, one man from each tribe. ²⁴They left and went up into the hill country, and came to the Valley of Eshkol and explored it. ²⁵Taking with them some of the fruit of the land, they brought it down to us and reported, "It is a good land that the LORD our God is giving us."

Rebellion Against the LORD

²⁶But you were unwilling to go up; you rebelled against the command of the LORD your God. ²⁷You grumbled in your tents and said, "The LORD hates us; so he brought us out of Egypt to deliver us into the hands of the Amorites to destroy us. ²⁸Where can we go? Our brothers have made our hearts melt in fear. They say, 'The people are stronger and taller than we are; the cities are large, with walls up to the sky. We even saw the Anakites there.'"

²⁹Then I said to you, "Do not be terrified; do not be afraid of them. ³⁰The LORD your God, who is going before you, will fight for you, as he did for you in Egypt, before your very eyes, ³¹and in the wilderness. There you saw how the LORD your God carried you, as a father carries his son, all the way you went until you reached this place."

³²In spite of this, you did not trust in the LORD your God, ³³who went ahead of you on your journey, in fire by night and in a cloud by day, to search out places for you to camp and to show you the way you should go.

³⁴When the LORD heard what you said, he was angry and solemnly swore: ³⁵"No one from this evil generation shall see the good land I swore to give your ancestors, ³⁶except Caleb son of Jephunneh. He will see it, and I will give him and his descendants the land he set his feet on, because he followed the LORD wholeheartedly."

³⁷Because of you the LORD became angry with me also and said, "You shall not enter it, either. ³⁸But your assistant, Joshua son of Nun, will enter it. Encourage him, because he will lead Israel to inherit it. ³⁹And the little ones that you said would be taken captive, your children who do not yet know good from bad — they will enter the land. I will give it to them and they will take possession of it. ⁴⁰But as for you, turn around and set out toward the desert along the route to the Red Sea.ᵃ"

⁴¹Then you replied, "We have sinned against the LORD. We will go up and fight, as the LORD our God commanded us." So every one of you put on his weapons, thinking it easy to go up into the hill country.

⁴²But the LORD said to me, "Tell them, 'Do not go up and fight, because I will not be with you. You will be defeated by your enemies.'"

⁴³So I told you, but you would not listen. You rebelled against the LORD's command and in your arrogance you marched up into the hill country. ⁴⁴The Amorites who lived in those hills came out against you; they chased you like a swarm of bees and beat you down from Seir all the way to Hormah. ⁴⁵You came back and wept before the LORD, but he paid no attention to your weeping and turned a deaf ear to you. ⁴⁶And so you stayed in Kadesh many days — all the time you spent there.

Wanderings in the Wilderness

2 Then we turned back and set out toward the wilderness along the route to the Red Sea,ᵃ as the LORD had directed me. For a long time we made our way around the hill country of Seir.

²Then the LORD said to me, ³"You have made your way around this hill country long enough; now turn north. ⁴Give the people these orders: 'You are about to pass through the territory of your relatives the descendants of Esau, who live in Seir. They will be afraid of you, but be very careful. ⁵Do not provoke them to war, for I will not give you any of their land, not even enough to put your foot on. I have given Esau the hill country of Seir as his own. ⁶You are to pay them in silver for the food you eat and the water you drink.'"

⁷The LORD your God has blessed you in all the work of your hands. He has watched over your journey through this vast wilderness. These forty years the LORD your God has been with you, and you have not lacked anything.

⁸So we went on past our relatives the descendants of Esau, who live in Seir. We turned from the Arabah road, which comes up from Elath and Ezion Geber, and traveled along the desert road of Moab.

⁹Then the LORD said to me, "Do not harass the Moabites or provoke them to war, for I will not give you any part of their land. I have given Ar to the descendants of Lot as a possession."

¹⁰(The Emites used to live there — a people strong and numerous, and as tall as the Anakites. ¹¹Like the Anakites, they too were considered Rephaites, but the Moabites called them Emites. ¹²Horites used to live in

Seir, but the descendants of Esau drove them out. They destroyed the Horites from before them and settled in their place, just as Israel did in the land the LORD gave them as their possession.)

[13] And the LORD said, "Now get up and cross the Zered Valley." So we crossed the valley.

[14] Thirty-eight years passed from the time we left Kadesh Barnea until we crossed the Zered Valley. By then, that entire generation of fighting men had perished from the camp, as the LORD had sworn to them. [15] The LORD's hand was against them until he had completely eliminated them from the camp.

[16] Now when the last of these fighting men among the people had died, [17] the LORD said to me, [18] "Today you are to pass by the region of Moab at Ar. [19] When you come to the Ammonites, do not harass them or provoke them to war, for I will not give you possession of any land belonging to the Ammonites. I have given it as a possession to the descendants of Lot."

[20] (That too was considered a land of the Rephaites, who used to live there; but the Ammonites called them Zamzummites. [21] They were a people strong and numerous, and as tall as the Anakites. The LORD destroyed them from before the Ammonites, who drove them out and settled in their place. [22] The LORD had done the same for the descendants of Esau, who lived in Seir, when he destroyed the Horites from before them. They drove them out and have lived in their place to this day. [23] And as for the Avvites who lived in villages as far as Gaza, the Caphtorites coming out from Caphtor[a] destroyed them and settled in their place.)

Defeat of Sihon King of Heshbon

[24] "Set out now and cross the Arnon Gorge. See, I have given into your hand Sihon the Amorite, king of Heshbon, and his country. Begin to take possession of it and engage him in battle. [25] This very day I will begin to put the terror and fear of you on all the nations under heaven. They will hear reports of you and will tremble and be in anguish because of you."

[26] From the Desert of Kedemoth I sent messengers to Sihon king of Heshbon offering peace and saying, [27] "Let us pass through your country. We will stay on the main road; we will not turn aside to the right or to the left. [28] Sell us food to eat and water to drink for their price in silver. Only let us pass through on foot— [29] as the descendants of Esau, who live in Seir, and the Moabites, who live in Ar, did for us—until we cross the Jordan into the land the LORD our God is giving us." [30] But Sihon king of Heshbon refused to let us pass through. For the LORD your God had made his spirit stubborn and his heart obstinate in order to give him into your hands, as he has now done.

[31] The LORD said to me, "See, I have begun to deliver Sihon and his country over to you. Now begin to conquer and possess his land."

[32] When Sihon and all his army came out to meet us in battle at Jahaz, [33] the LORD our God delivered him over to us and we struck him down, together with his sons and his whole army. [34] At that time we took all his towns and completely destroyed[b] them— men, women and children. We left no survivors. [35] But the livestock and the plunder from the towns we had captured we carried off for ourselves. [36] From Aroer on the rim of the Arnon Gorge, and from the town in the gorge, even as far as Gilead, not one town was too strong for us. The LORD our God gave us all of them. [37] But in accordance with the command of the LORD our God, you did not encroach on any of the land of the Ammonites, neither the land along the course of the Jabbok nor that around the towns in the hills.

Defeat of Og King of Bashan

3 Next we turned and went up along the road toward Bashan, and Og king of Bashan with his whole army marched out to meet us in battle at Edrei. [2] The LORD said to me, "Do not be afraid of him, for I have delivered him into your hands, along with his whole army and his land. Do to him what you did to Sihon king of the Amorites, who reigned in Heshbon."

[3] So the LORD our God also gave into our hands Og king of Bashan and all his army. We struck them down, leaving no survivors. [4] At that time we took all his cities. There was not one of the sixty cities that we did not take

---

[a] 23 That is, Crete   [b] 34 The Hebrew term refers to the irrevocable giving over of things or persons to the LORD, often by totally destroying them.

from them—the whole region of Argob, Og's kingdom in Bashan. [5]All these cities were fortified with high walls and with gates and bars, and there were also a great many unwalled villages. [6]We completely destroyed[a] them, as we had done with Sihon king of Heshbon, destroying[a] every city—men, women and children. [7]But all the livestock and the plunder from their cities we carried off for ourselves.

[8]So at that time we took from these two kings of the Amorites the territory east of the Jordan, from the Arnon Gorge as far as Mount Hermon. [9](Hermon is called Sirion by the Sidonians; the Amorites call it Senir.) [10]We took all the towns on the plateau, and all Gilead, and all Bashan as far as Salekah and Edrei, towns of Og's kingdom in Bashan. [11](Og king of Bashan was the last of the Rephaites. His bed was decorated with iron and was more than nine cubits long and four cubits wide.[b] It is still in Rabbah of the Ammonites.)

Division of the Land

[12]Of the land that we took over at that time, I gave the Reubenites and the Gadites the territory north of Aroer by the Arnon Gorge, including half the hill country of Gilead, together with its towns. [13]The rest of Gilead and also all of Bashan, the kingdom of Og, I gave to the half-tribe of Manasseh. (The whole region of Argob in Bashan used to be known as a land of the Rephaites. [14]Jair, a descendant of Manasseh, took the whole region of Argob as far as the border of the Geshurites and the Maakathites; it was named after him, so that to this day Bashan is called Havvoth Jair.[c]) [15]And I gave Gilead to Makir. [16]But to the Reubenites and the Gadites I gave the territory extending from Gilead down to the Arnon Gorge (the middle of the gorge being the border) and out to the Jabbok River, which is the border of the Ammonites. [17]Its western border was the Jordan in the Arabah, from Kinnereth to the Sea of the Arabah (that is, the Dead Sea), below the slopes of Pisgah.

[18]I commanded you at that time: "The LORD your God has given you this land to take possession of it. But all your able-bodied men, armed for battle, must cross over ahead of the other Israelites. [19]However, your wives, your children and your livestock (I know you have much livestock) may stay in the towns I have given you, [20]until the LORD gives rest to your fellow Israelites as he has to you, and they too have taken over the land that the LORD your God is giving them across the Jordan. After that, each of you may go back to the possession I have given you."

Moses Forbidden to Cross the Jordan

[21]At that time I commanded Joshua: "You have seen with your own eyes all that the LORD your God has done to these two kings. The LORD will do the same to all the kingdoms over there where you are going. [22]Do not be afraid of them; the LORD your God himself will fight for you."

[23]At that time I pleaded with the LORD: [24]"Sovereign LORD, you have begun to show to your servant your greatness and your strong hand. For what god is there in heaven or on earth who can do the deeds and mighty works you do? [25]Let me go over and see the good land beyond the Jordan—that fine hill country and Lebanon."

[26]But because of you the LORD was angry with me and would not listen to me. "That is enough," the LORD said. "Do not speak to me anymore about this matter. [27]Go up to the top of Pisgah and look west and north and south and east. Look at the land with your own eyes, since you are not going to cross this Jordan. [28]But commission Joshua, and encourage and strengthen him, for he will lead this people across and will cause them to inherit the land that you will see." [29]So we stayed in the valley near Beth Peor.

Obedience Commanded

4 Now, Israel, hear the decrees and laws I am about to teach you. Follow them so that you may live and may go in and take possession of the land the LORD, the God of your ancestors, is giving you. [2]Do not add to what I command you and do not subtract from it, but keep the commands of the LORD your God that I give you.

[3]You saw with your own eyes what the LORD did at Baal Peor. The LORD your God

---

[a] 6 The Hebrew term refers to the irrevocable giving over of things or persons to the LORD, often by totally destroying them.   [b] 11 That is, about 14 feet long and 6 feet wide or about 4 meters long and 1.8 meters wide   [c] 14 Or *called the settlements of Jair*

destroyed from among you everyone who followed the Baal of Peor, [4]but all of you who held fast to the LORD your God are still alive today.

[5]See, I have taught you decrees and laws as the LORD my God commanded me, so that you may follow them in the land you are entering to take possession of it. [6]Observe them carefully, for this will show your wisdom and understanding to the nations, who will hear about all these decrees and say, "Surely this great nation is a wise and understanding people." [7]What other nation is so great as to have their gods near them the way the LORD our God is near us whenever we pray to him? [8]And what other nation is so great as to have such righteous decrees and laws as this body of laws I am setting before you today?

[9]Only be careful, and watch yourselves closely so that you do not forget the things your eyes have seen or let them fade from your heart as long as you live. Teach them to your children and to their children after them. [10]Remember the day you stood before the LORD your God at Horeb, when he said to me, "Assemble the people before me to hear my words so that they may learn to revere me as long as they live in the land and may teach them to their children." [11]You came near and stood at the foot of the mountain while it blazed with fire to the very heavens, with black clouds and deep darkness. [12]Then the LORD spoke to you out of the fire. You heard the sound of words but saw no form; there was only a voice. [13]He declared to you his covenant, the Ten Commandments, which he commanded you to follow and then wrote them on two stone tablets. [14]And the LORD directed me at that time to teach you the decrees and laws you are to follow in the land that you are crossing the Jordan to possess.

Idolatry Forbidden

[15]You saw no form of any kind the day the LORD spoke to you at Horeb out of the fire. Therefore watch yourselves very carefully, [16]so that you do not become corrupt and make for yourselves an idol, an image of any shape, whether formed like a man or a woman, [17]or like any animal on earth or any bird that flies in the air, [18]or like any creature that moves along the ground or any fish in the waters below. [19]And when you look up to the sky and see the sun, the moon and the stars—all the heavenly array—do not be enticed into bowing down to them and worshiping things the LORD your God has apportioned to all the nations under heaven. [20]But as for you, the LORD took you and brought you out of the iron-smelting furnace, out of Egypt, to be the people of his inheritance, as you now are.

[21]The LORD was angry with me because of you, and he solemnly swore that I would not cross the Jordan and enter the good land the LORD your God is giving you as your inheritance. [22]I will die in this land; I will not cross the Jordan; but you are about to cross over and take possession of that good land. [23]Be careful not to forget the covenant of the LORD your God that he made with you; do not make for yourselves an idol in the form of anything the LORD your God has forbidden. [24]For the LORD your God is a consuming fire, a jealous God.

[25]After you have had children and grandchildren and have lived in the land a long time—if you then become corrupt and make any kind of idol, doing evil in the eyes of the LORD your God and arousing his anger, [26]I call the heavens and the earth as witnesses against you this day that you will quickly perish from the land that you are crossing the Jordan to possess. You will not live there long but will certainly be destroyed. [27]The LORD will scatter you among the peoples, and only a few of you will survive among the nations to which the LORD will drive you. [28]There you will worship man-made gods of wood and stone, which cannot see or hear or eat or smell. [29]But if from there you seek the LORD your God, you will find him if you seek him with all your heart and with all your soul. [30]When you are in distress and all these things have happened to you, then in later days you will return to the LORD your God and obey him. [31]For the LORD your God is a merciful God; he will not abandon or destroy you or forget the covenant with your ancestors, which he confirmed to them by oath.

The LORD Is God

[32]Ask now about the former days, long before your time, from the day God created human beings on the earth; ask from one end of the heavens to the other. Has anything so great as this ever happened, or has anything

AHEM . . .

READ: DEUTERONOMY 4:35

At the start of Deuteronomy, Moses sounds like a coach drilling his team with a motivating talk before a championship game. But the stakes here are higher than any sports contest. This wise leader is getting God's people ready to enter the land promised to them hundreds of years before.

Moses begins by recapping highlights of the forty years since the Lord freed his people from slavery from Egypt. Three chapters later, he finally gets around to the reason for his speech. He plans to outline everything God's people need to know to conquer the land and live well (Deuteronomy 4:1).

Moses reminds the people of a truth they can't afford to forget: "The LORD is God; besides him there is no other" (v. 35). Moses proves that fact from the people's own history. From the day of creation until then, no one has ever seen anything as great as the birth of that nation. No other people have heard God's voice and lived. No other god has ever done such awesome miracles as when the Lord's presence and strength brought the Israelites out of Egypt.

God accomplished all these things to prove he's the one-and-only God. He worked mighty wonders to demonstrate his love. When the Lord acts in your life, he wants you to know that his love for you will never stop. And when he does amazing deeds, he's reminding you that he alone is God.

BUILDING

FAITH

WISDOM

STRENGTH

like it ever been heard of? ³³Has any other people heard the voice of God[a] speaking out of fire, as you have, and lived? ³⁴Has any god ever tried to take for himself one nation out of another nation, by testings, by signs and wonders, by war, by a mighty hand and an outstretched arm, or by great and awesome deeds, like all the things the LORD your God did for you in Egypt before your very eyes?

³⁵You were shown these things so that you might know that the LORD is God; besides him there is no other. ³⁶From heaven he made you hear his voice to discipline you. On earth he showed you his great fire, and you heard his words from out of the fire. ³⁷Because he loved your ancestors and chose their descendants after them, he brought you out of Egypt by his Presence and his great strength, ³⁸to drive out before you nations greater and stronger than you and to bring you into their land to give it to you for your inheritance, as it is today.

³⁹Acknowledge and take to heart this day that the LORD is God in heaven above and on the earth below. There is no other. ⁴⁰Keep his decrees and commands, which I am giving you today, so that it may go well with you and your children after you and that you may live long in the land the LORD your God gives you for all time.

Cities of Refuge

⁴¹Then Moses set aside three cities east of the Jordan, ⁴²to which anyone who had killed a person could flee if they had unintentionally killed a neighbor without malice aforethought. They could flee into one of these cities and save their life. ⁴³The cities were these: Bezer in the wilderness plateau, for the Reubenites; Ramoth in Gilead, for the Gadites; and Golan in Bashan, for the Manassites.

Introduction to the Law

⁴⁴This is the law Moses set before the Israelites. ⁴⁵These are the stipulations, decrees and laws Moses gave them when they came out of Egypt ⁴⁶and were in the valley near Beth Peor east of the Jordan, in the land of Sihon king of the Amorites, who reigned in Heshbon and was defeated by Moses and the Israelites as they came out of Egypt. ⁴⁷They took possession of his land and the land of Og king of Bashan, the two Amorite kings east of the Jordan. ⁴⁸This land extended from Aroer on the rim of the Arnon Gorge to Mount Sirion[b] (that is, Hermon), ⁴⁹and included all the Arabah east of the Jordan, as far as the Dead Sea,[c] below the slopes of Pisgah.

The Ten Commandments

5 Moses summoned all Israel and said:
Hear, Israel, the decrees and laws I declare in your hearing today. Learn them and be sure to follow them. ²The LORD our God made a covenant with us at Horeb. ³It was not with our ancestors[d] that the LORD made this covenant, but with us, with all of us who are alive here today. ⁴The LORD spoke to you face to face out of the fire on the mountain. ⁵(At that time I stood between the LORD and you to declare to you the word of the LORD, because you were afraid of the fire and did not go up the mountain.) And he said:

⁶"I am the LORD your God, who brought you out of Egypt, out of the land of slavery.

⁷"You shall have no other gods before[e] me.

⁸"You shall not make for yourself an image in the form of anything in heaven above or on the earth beneath or in the waters below. ⁹You shall not bow down to them or worship them; for I, the LORD your God, am a jealous God, punishing the children for the sin of the parents to the third and fourth generation of those who hate me, ¹⁰but showing love to a thousand generations of those who love me and keep my commandments.

¹¹"You shall not misuse the name of the LORD your God, for the LORD will not hold anyone guiltless who misuses his name.

¹²"Observe the Sabbath day by keeping it holy, as the LORD your God has commanded you. ¹³Six days you shall labor and do all your work, ¹⁴but the seventh day is a sabbath

---

[a] 33 Or of a god   [b] 48 Syriac (see also 3:9); Hebrew Siyon   [c] 49 Hebrew the Sea of the Arabah
[d] 3 Or not only with our parents   [e] 7 Or besides

NOT INTERESTED IN SHARING

READ: DEUTERONOMY 5:9, 6:15

Jealous? That word doesn't seem very ... well, positive. It feels petty—like a couple of junior high girls who are both interested in the same boy; like a basketball player who avoids passing the ball to the teammate who keeps getting the high score; like a possessive high school boyfriend who becomes upset if his girlfriend makes eye contact with another guy.

Besides, what reason would God have to be jealous? Doesn't everything already belong to him? Is there anything that competes with his power or his greatness? Of course not— at least not in reality.

But what about in your heart?

God is jealous for your heart, not because he is petty or insecure, but because he loves you. He loves you too much to share you.

In the Bible, the words *jealous* and *zealous* are basically interchangeable—it's the same Hebrew word in the original texts. In English, we spell the two almost the same because they derive from the same Greek root. We think of zeal as intense enthusiasm. That idea captures why God is so possessive about us: He is, as he says, a consuming fire of passion for us.

BUILDING FAITH WISDOM STRENGTH

Have you ever seen someone who's fallen deeply in love—who is so consumed by those feelings that it's all he or she ever talks about? Well, that's only the barest shadow of God's love for you. Everything comes back to a passionate love that is so immense, so powerful, that it burns hotter than a billion suns.

to the LORD your God. On it you shall not do any work, neither you, nor your son or daughter, nor your male or female servant, nor your ox, your donkey or any of your animals, nor any foreigner residing in your towns, so that your male and female servants may rest, as you do. ¹⁵Remember that you were slaves in Egypt and that the LORD your God brought you out of there with a mighty hand and an outstretched arm. Therefore the LORD your God has commanded you to observe the Sabbath day.

¹⁶"Honor your father and your mother, as the LORD your God has commanded you, so that you may live long and that it may go well with you in the land the LORD your God is giving you.

¹⁷"You shall not murder.

¹⁸"You shall not commit adultery.

¹⁹"You shall not steal.

²⁰"You shall not give false testimony against your neighbor.

²¹"You shall not covet your neighbor's wife. You shall not set your desire on your neighbor's house or land, his male or female servant, his ox or donkey, or anything that belongs to your neighbor."

²²These are the commandments the LORD proclaimed in a loud voice to your whole assembly there on the mountain from out of the fire, the cloud and the deep darkness; and he added nothing more. Then he wrote them on two stone tablets and gave them to me.

²³When you heard the voice out of the darkness, while the mountain was ablaze with fire, all the leaders of your tribes and your elders came to me. ²⁴And you said, "The LORD our God has shown us his glory and his majesty, and we have heard his voice from the fire. Today we have seen that a person can live even if God speaks with them. ²⁵But now, why should we die? This great fire will consume us, and we will die if we hear the voice of the LORD our God any longer. ²⁶For what mortal has ever heard the voice of the living God speaking out of fire, as we have, and survived? ²⁷Go near and listen to all that the LORD our God says. Then tell us whatever the LORD our God tells you. We will listen and obey."

²⁸The LORD heard you when you spoke to me, and the LORD said to me, "I have heard what this people said to you. Everything they said was good. ²⁹Oh, that their hearts would be inclined to fear me and keep all my commands always, so that it might go well with them and their children forever!

³⁰"Go, tell them to return to their tents. ³¹But you stay here with me so that I may give you all the commands, decrees and laws you are to teach them to follow in the land I am giving them to possess."

³²So be careful to do what the LORD your God has commanded you; do not turn aside to the right or to the left. ³³Walk in obedience to all that the LORD your God has commanded you, so that you may live and prosper and prolong your days in the land that you will possess.

Love the LORD Your God

6 These are the commands, decrees and laws the LORD your God directed me to teach you to observe in the land that you are crossing the Jordan to possess, ²so that you, your children and their children after them may fear the LORD your God as long as you live by keeping all his decrees and commands that I give you, and so that you may enjoy long life. ³Hear, Israel, and be careful to obey so that it may go well with you and that you may increase greatly in a land flowing with milk and honey, just as the LORD, the God of your ancestors, promised you.

⁴Hear, O Israel: The LORD our God, the LORD is one.ᵃ ⁵Love the LORD your God with all your heart and with all your soul and with all your strength. ⁶These commandments that I give you today are to be on your hearts. ⁷Impress them on your children. Talk about them when you sit at home and when you walk along the road, when you lie down and when you get up. ⁸Tie them as symbols on your hands and bind them on your foreheads. ⁹Write them on the doorframes of your houses and on your gates.

¹⁰When the LORD your God brings you

ᵃ 4 Or *The LORD our God is one LORD*; or *The LORD is our God, the LORD is one*; or *The LORD is our God, the LORD alone* into the land he swore to your fathers, to Abraham, Isaac and Jacob, to give you—a land with large, flourishing cities you did not build, ¹¹ houses filled with all kinds of good things you did not provide, wells you did not dig, and vineyards and olive groves you did not plant—then when you eat and are satisfied, ¹² be careful that you do not forget the LORD, who brought you out of Egypt, out of the land of slavery.

¹³ Fear the LORD your God, serve him only and take your oaths in his name. ¹⁴ Do not follow other gods, the gods of the peoples around you; ¹⁵ for the LORD your God, who is among you, is a jealous God and his anger will burn against you, and he will destroy you from the face of the land. ¹⁶ Do not put the LORD your God to the test as you did at Massah. ¹⁷ Be sure to keep the commands of the LORD your God and the stipulations and decrees he has given you. ¹⁸ Do what is right and good in the LORD's sight, so that it may go well with you and you may go in and take over the good land the LORD promised on oath to your ancestors, ¹⁹ thrusting out all your enemies before you, as the LORD said.

²⁰ In the future, when your son asks you, "What is the meaning of the stipulations, decrees and laws the LORD our God has commanded you?" ²¹ tell him: "We were slaves of Pharaoh in Egypt, but the LORD brought us out of Egypt with a mighty hand. ²² Before our eyes the LORD sent signs and wonders—great and terrible—on Egypt and Pharaoh and his whole household. ²³ But he brought us out from there to bring us in and give us the land he promised on oath to our ancestors. ²⁴ The LORD commanded us to obey all these decrees and to fear the LORD our God, so that we might always prosper and be kept alive, as is the case today. ²⁵ And if we are careful to obey all this law before the LORD our God, as he has commanded us, that will be our righteousness."

Driving Out the Nations

7 When the LORD your God brings you into the land you are entering to possess and drives out before you many nations—the Hittites, Girgashites, Amorites, Canaanites, Perizzites, Hivites and Jebusites, seven nations larger and stronger than you— ² and when the LORD your God has delivered them over to you and you have defeated them, then you must destroy them totally.^a Make no treaty with them, and show them no mercy. ³ Do not intermarry with them. Do not give your daughters to their sons or take their daughters for your sons, ⁴ for they will turn your children away from following me to serve other gods, and the LORD's anger will burn against you and will quickly destroy you. ⁵ This is what you are to do to them: Break down their altars, smash their sacred stones, cut down their Asherah poles^b and burn their idols in the fire. ⁶ For you are a people holy to the LORD your God. The LORD your God has chosen you out of all the peoples on the face of the earth to be his people, his treasured possession.

⁷ The LORD did not set his affection on you and choose you because you were more numerous than other peoples, for you were the fewest of all peoples. ⁸ But it was because the LORD loved you and kept the oath he swore to your ancestors that he brought you out with a mighty hand and redeemed you from the land of slavery, from the power of Pharaoh king of Egypt. ⁹ Know therefore that the LORD your God is God; he is the faithful God, keeping his covenant of love to a thousand generations of those who love him and keep his commandments. ¹⁰ But

those who hate him he will repay to their face by destruction;
he will not be slow to repay to their face those who hate him.

¹¹ Therefore, take care to follow the commands, decrees and laws I give you today.

¹² If you pay attention to these laws and are careful to follow them, then the LORD your God will keep his covenant of love with you, as he swore to your ancestors. ¹³ He will love you and bless you and increase your numbers. He will bless the fruit of your womb, the crops of your land—your grain, new wine and olive oil—the calves of your herds and the lambs of your flocks in the land he swore to your ancestors to give you. ¹⁴ You will be blessed more than any other people; none of your men or women will

---

^a 2 The Hebrew term refers to the irrevocable giving over of things or persons to the LORD, often by totally destroying them; also in verse 26.   ^b 5 That is, wooden symbols of the goddess Asherah; here and elsewhere in Deuteronomy

MORE TO THE STORY

Your parents could promise you a new room, but the sibling you push out of that space wouldn't be happy. When God swore he would give a spectacular land to his people, there was one major problem. The land was already occupied by other people, and they weren't about to leave without a fight. Why would God eject one group from the land, and basically destroy them, simply to give that land to another?

Bible critics claim this predicament exposes the God of the Bible as completely unjust, yet Scripture offers a bigger picture. The inhabitants of Canaan were known for their blatant sin as far back as the days of Abraham. Leviticus offers ghastly details about their involvement in adultery, incest, homosexuality, and child sacrifice (Leviticus 18:3, 24). Rather than immediately drive these peoples from the land, God waited to judge them until their sins were so serious they deserved to be wiped out (Genesis 15:16). God warned that if these inhabitants were allowed to remain in the land, they would lure his people into the same terrible sins.

BUILDING FAITH WISDOM STRENGTH

The Lord's Old Testament command isn't an order for you to physically do battle with sinful people today. Jesus won the battle against sin for us. But it's still a warning against letting sin remain in your life after you come to believe in God. You're wise if you get rid of anything that pulls you away from the Lord.

be childless, nor will any of your livestock be without young. [15]The LORD will keep you free from every disease. He will not inflict on you the horrible diseases you knew in Egypt, but he will inflict them on all who hate you. [16]You must destroy all the peoples the LORD your God gives over to you. Do not look on them with pity and do not serve their gods, for that will be a snare to you.

[17]You may say to yourselves, "These nations are stronger than we are. How can we drive them out?" [18]But do not be afraid of them; remember well what the LORD your God did to Pharaoh and to all Egypt. [19]You saw with your own eyes the great trials, the signs and wonders, the mighty hand and outstretched arm, with which the LORD your God brought you out. The LORD your God will do the same to all the peoples you now fear. [20]Moreover, the LORD your God will send the hornet among them until even the survivors who hide from you have perished. [21]Do not be terrified by them, for the LORD your God, who is among you, is a great and awesome God. [22]The LORD your God will drive out those nations before you, little by little. You will not be allowed to eliminate them all at once, or the wild animals will multiply around you. [23]But the LORD your God will deliver them over to you, throwing them into great confusion until they are destroyed. [24]He will give their kings into your hand, and you will wipe out their names from under heaven. No one will be able to stand up against you; you will destroy them. [25]The images of their gods you are to burn in the fire. Do not covet the silver and gold on them, and do not take it for yourselves, or you will be ensnared by it, for it is detestable to the LORD your God. [26]Do not bring a detestable thing into your house or you, like it, will be set apart for destruction. Regard it as vile and utterly detest it, for it is set apart for destruction.

Do Not Forget the LORD

8 Be careful to follow every command I am giving you today, so that you may live and increase and may enter and possess the land the LORD promised on oath to your ancestors. [2]Remember how the LORD your God led you all the way in the wilderness these forty years, to humble and test you in order to know what was in your heart, whether or not you would keep his commands. [3]He humbled you, causing you to hunger and then feeding you with manna, which neither you nor your ancestors had known, to teach you that man does not live on bread alone but on every word that comes from the mouth of the LORD. [4]Your clothes did not wear out and your feet did not swell during these forty years. [5]Know then in your heart that as a man disciplines his son, so the LORD your God disciplines you.

[6]Observe the commands of the LORD your God, walking in obedience to him and revering him. [7]For the LORD your God is bringing you into a good land — a land with brooks, streams, and deep springs gushing out into the valleys and hills; [8]a land with wheat and barley, vines and fig trees, pomegranates, olive oil and honey; [9]a land where bread will not be scarce and you will lack nothing; a land where the rocks are iron and you can dig copper out of the hills.

[10]When you have eaten and are satisfied, praise the LORD your God for the good land he has given you. [11]Be careful that you do not forget the LORD your God, failing to observe his commands, his laws and his decrees that I am giving you this day. [12]Otherwise, when you eat and are satisfied, when you build fine houses and settle down, [13]and when your herds and flocks grow large and your silver and gold increase and all you have is multiplied, [14]then your heart will become proud and you will forget the LORD your God, who brought you out of Egypt, out of the land of slavery. [15]He led you through the vast and dreadful wilderness, that thirsty and waterless land, with its venomous snakes and scorpions. He brought you water out of hard rock. [16]He gave you manna to eat in the wilderness, something your ancestors had never known, to humble and test you so that in the end it might go well with you. [17]You may say to yourself, "My power and the strength of my hands have produced this wealth for me." [18]But remember the LORD your God, for it is he who gives you the ability to produce wealth, and so confirms his covenant, which he swore to your ancestors, as it is today.

[19]If you ever forget the LORD your God and follow other gods and worship and bow down to them, I testify against you today that you will surely be destroyed. [20]Like the nations the LORD destroyed before you,

THE WAY IT WORKS

READ: DEUTERONOMY 8:1-4

When God provided the miraculous manna, he provided just enough. The description's pretty precise. Those who gathered a lot had nothing left over, and those who gathered a little had enough. Then he gave them a curious command: "No one is to keep any of it until morning" (Exodus 16:19).

Why would God forbid leftovers? What's wrong with taking a little initiative and gathering enough manna for a couple days or weeks?

Here's my take on the manna miracle: The manna was a daily reminder of their daily dependence on God. God wanted to cultivate their daily dependence by providing for their needs on a daily basis.

Nothing's changed. We want a one-week or one-month or one-year supply of God's provision, but God wants us to drop to our knees every day in raw dependence on him. And God knows that if he provided too much too soon, we'd lose our spiritual hunger. He knows we'd stop trusting in our Provider and start trusting in the provision.

BUILDING FAITH WISDOM STRENGTH

Spiritual maturity is often confused with independence. It's the exact opposite. The goal is codependence on God. God didn't design us to "grow up" and be independent from him. Our desire for self-sufficiency is a subtle expression of our sinful nature. It's a desire to get to a place where we don't need God, don't need faith, don't need a local church home, and don't need to pray. We want God to provide more so we need him less. That's just not the way it's supposed to work.

so you will be destroyed for not obeying the LORD your God.

Not Because of Israel's Righteousness

9 Hear, Israel: You are now about to cross the Jordan to go in and dispossess nations greater and stronger than you, with large cities that have walls up to the sky. ²The people are strong and tall — Anakites! You know about them and have heard it said: "Who can stand up against the Anakites?" ³But be assured today that the LORD your God is the one who goes across ahead of you like a devouring fire. He will destroy them; he will subdue them before you. And you will drive them out and annihilate them quickly, as the LORD has promised you.

⁴After the LORD your God has driven them out before you, do not say to yourself, "The LORD has brought me here to take possession of this land because of my righteousness." No, it is on account of the wickedness of these nations that the LORD is going to drive them out before you. ⁵It is not because of your righteousness or your integrity that you are going in to take possession of their land; but on account of the wickedness of these nations, the LORD your God will drive them out before you, to accomplish what he swore to your fathers, to Abraham, Isaac and Jacob. ⁶Understand, then, that it is not because of your righteousness that the LORD your God is giving you this good land to possess, for you are a stiff-necked people.

The Golden Calf

⁷Remember this and never forget how you aroused the anger of the LORD your God in the wilderness. From the day you left Egypt until you arrived here, you have been rebellious against the LORD. ⁸At Horeb you aroused the LORD's wrath so that he was angry enough to destroy you. ⁹When I went up on the mountain to receive the tablets of stone, the tablets of the covenant that the LORD had made with you, I stayed on the mountain forty days and forty nights; I ate no bread and drank no water. ¹⁰The LORD gave me two stone tablets inscribed by the finger of God. On them were all the commandments the LORD proclaimed to you on the mountain out of the fire, on the day of the assembly.

¹¹At the end of the forty days and forty nights, the LORD gave me the two stone tablets, the tablets of the covenant. ¹²Then the LORD told me, "Go down from here at once, because your people whom you brought out of Egypt have become corrupt. They have turned away quickly from what I commanded them and have made an idol for themselves."

¹³And the LORD said to me, "I have seen this people, and they are a stiff-necked people indeed! ¹⁴Let me alone, so that I may destroy them and blot out their name from under heaven. And I will make you into a nation stronger and more numerous than they."

¹⁵So I turned and went down from the mountain while it was ablaze with fire. And the two tablets of the covenant were in my hands. ¹⁶When I looked, I saw that you had sinned against the LORD your God; you had made for yourselves an idol cast in the shape of a calf. You had turned aside quickly from the way that the LORD had commanded you. ¹⁷So I took the two tablets and threw them out of my hands, breaking them to pieces before your eyes.

¹⁸Then once again I fell prostrate before the LORD for forty days and forty nights; I ate no bread and drank no water, because of all the sin you had committed, doing what was evil in the LORD's sight and so arousing his anger. ¹⁹I feared the anger and wrath of the LORD, for he was angry enough with you to destroy you. But again the LORD listened to me. ²⁰And the LORD was angry enough with Aaron to destroy him, but at that time I prayed for Aaron too. ²¹Also I took that sinful thing of yours, the calf you had made, and burned it in the fire. Then I crushed it and ground it to powder as fine as dust and threw the dust into a stream that flowed down the mountain.

²²You also made the LORD angry at Taberah, at Massah and at Kibroth Hattaavah.

²³And when the LORD sent you out from Kadesh Barnea, he said, "Go up and take possession of the land I have given you." But you rebelled against the command of the LORD your God. You did not trust him or obey him. ²⁴You have been rebellious against the LORD ever since I have known you.

²⁵I lay prostrate before the LORD those forty days and forty nights because the LORD had said he would destroy you. ²⁶I prayed to

the LORD and said, "Sovereign LORD, do not destroy your people, your own inheritance that you redeemed by your great power and brought out of Egypt with a mighty hand. ²⁷Remember your servants Abraham, Isaac and Jacob. Overlook the stubbornness of this people, their wickedness and their sin. ²⁸Otherwise, the country from which you brought us will say, 'Because the LORD was not able to take them into the land he had promised them, and because he hated them, he brought them out to put them to death in the wilderness.' ²⁹But they are your people, your inheritance that you brought out by your great power and your outstretched arm."

Tablets Like the First Ones

10 At that time the LORD said to me, "Chisel out two stone tablets like the first ones and come up to me on the mountain. Also make a wooden ark.[a] ²I will write on the tablets the words that were on the first tablets, which you broke. Then you are to put them in the ark."

³So I made the ark out of acacia wood and chiseled out two stone tablets like the first ones, and I went up on the mountain with the two tablets in my hands. ⁴The LORD wrote on these tablets what he had written before, the Ten Commandments he had proclaimed to you on the mountain, out of the fire, on the day of the assembly. And the LORD gave them to me. ⁵Then I came back down the mountain and put the tablets in the ark I had made, as the LORD commanded me, and they are there now.

⁶(The Israelites traveled from the wells of Bene Jaakan to Moserah. There Aaron died and was buried, and Eleazar his son succeeded him as priest. ⁷From there they traveled to Gudgodah and on to Jotbathah, a land with streams of water. ⁸At that time the LORD set apart the tribe of Levi to carry the ark of the covenant of the LORD, to stand before the LORD to minister and to pronounce blessings in his name, as they still do today. ⁹That is why the Levites have no share or inheritance among their fellow Israelites; the LORD is their inheritance, as the LORD your God told them.)

¹⁰Now I had stayed on the mountain forty days and forty nights, as I did the first time,

and the LORD listened to me at this time also. It was not his will to destroy you. ¹¹"Go," the LORD said to me, "and lead the people on their way, so that they may enter and possess the land I swore to their ancestors to give them."

Fear the LORD

¹²And now, Israel, what does the LORD your God ask of you but to fear the LORD your God, to walk in obedience to him, to love him, to serve the LORD your God with all your heart and with all your soul, ¹³and to observe the LORD's commands and decrees that I am giving you today for your own good?

¹⁴To the LORD your God belong the heavens, even the highest heavens, the earth and everything in it. ¹⁵Yet the LORD set his affection on your ancestors and loved them, and he chose you, their descendants, above all the nations — as it is today. ¹⁶Circumcise your hearts, therefore, and do not be stiff-necked any longer. ¹⁷For the LORD your God is God of gods and Lord of lords, the great God, mighty and awesome, who shows no partiality and accepts no bribes. ¹⁸He defends the cause of the fatherless and the widow, and loves the foreigner residing among you, giving them food and clothing. ¹⁹And you are to love those who are foreigners, for you yourselves were foreigners in Egypt. ²⁰Fear the LORD your God and serve him. Hold fast to him and take your oaths in his name. ²¹He is the one you praise; he is your God, who performed for you those great and awesome wonders you saw with your own eyes. ²²Your ancestors who went down into Egypt were seventy in all, and now the LORD your God has made you as numerous as the stars in the sky.

Love and Obey the LORD

11 Love the LORD your God and keep his requirements, his decrees, his laws and his commands always. ²Remember today that your children were not the ones who saw and experienced the discipline of the LORD your God: his majesty, his mighty hand, his outstretched arm; ³the signs he performed and the things he did in the heart of Egypt, both to Pharaoh king of Egypt and

---

^a 1 That is, a chest

to his whole country; ⁴what he did to the Egyptian army, to its horses and chariots, how he overwhelmed them with the waters of the Red Sea*ᵃ* as they were pursuing you, and how the LORD brought lasting ruin on them. ⁵It was not your children who saw what he did for you in the wilderness until you arrived at this place, ⁶and what he did to Dathan and Abiram, sons of Eliab the Reubenite, when the earth opened its mouth right in the middle of all Israel and swallowed them up with their households, their tents and every living thing that belonged to them. ⁷But it was your own eyes that saw all these great things the LORD has done.

⁸Observe therefore all the commands I am giving you today, so that you may have the strength to go in and take over the land that you are crossing the Jordan to possess, ⁹and so that you may live long in the land the LORD swore to your ancestors to give to them and their descendants, a land flowing with milk and honey. ¹⁰The land you are entering to take over is not like the land of Egypt, from which you have come, where you planted your seed and irrigated it by foot as in a vegetable garden. ¹¹But the land you are crossing the Jordan to take possession of is a land of mountains and valleys that drinks rain from heaven. ¹²It is a land the LORD your God cares for; the eyes of the LORD your God are continually on it from the beginning of the year to its end.

¹³So if you faithfully obey the commands I am giving you today—to love the LORD your God and to serve him with all your heart and with all your soul— ¹⁴then I will send rain on your land in its season, both autumn and spring rains, so that you may gather in your grain, new wine and olive oil. ¹⁵I will provide grass in the fields for your cattle, and you will eat and be satisfied.

¹⁶Be careful, or you will be enticed to turn away and worship other gods and bow down to them. ¹⁷Then the LORD's anger will burn against you, and he will shut up the heavens so that it will not rain and the ground will yield no produce, and you will soon perish from the good land the LORD is giving you. ¹⁸Fix these words of mine in your hearts and minds; tie them as symbols on your hands and bind them on your foreheads. ¹⁹Teach them to your children, talking about them when you sit at home and when you walk along the road, when you lie down and when you get up. ²⁰Write them on the doorframes of your houses and on your gates, ²¹so that your days and the days of your children may be many in the land the LORD swore to give your ancestors, as many as the days that the heavens are above the earth.

²²If you carefully observe all these commands I am giving you to follow—to love the LORD your God, to walk in obedience to him and to hold fast to him— ²³then the LORD will drive out all these nations before you, and you will dispossess nations larger and stronger than you. ²⁴Every place where you set your foot will be yours: Your territory will extend from the desert to Lebanon, and from the Euphrates River to the Mediterranean Sea. ²⁵No one will be able to stand against you. The LORD your God, as he promised you, will put the terror and fear of you on the whole land, wherever you go.

²⁶See, I am setting before you today a blessing and a curse— ²⁷the blessing if you obey the commands of the LORD your God that I am giving you today; ²⁸the curse if you disobey the commands of the LORD your God and turn from the way that I command you today by following other gods, which you have not known. ²⁹When the LORD your God has brought you into the land you are entering to possess, you are to proclaim on Mount Gerizim the blessings, and on Mount Ebal the curses. ³⁰As you know, these mountains are across the Jordan, westward, toward the setting sun, near the great trees of Moreh, in the territory of those Canaanites living in the Arabah in the vicinity of Gilgal. ³¹You are about to cross the Jordan to enter and take possession of the land the LORD your God is giving you. When you have taken it over and are living there, ³²be sure that you obey all the decrees and laws I am setting before you today.

The One Place of Worship

12 These are the decrees and laws you must be careful to follow in the land that the LORD, the God of your ancestors, has given you to possess—as long as you live in the land. ²Destroy completely all the places on the high mountains, on the hills and under every spreading tree, where the nations

---

ᵃ 4 Or *the Sea of Reeds*

you are dispossessing worship their gods. ³Break down their altars, smash their sacred stones and burn their Asherah poles in the fire; cut down the idols of their gods and wipe out their names from those places.

⁴You must not worship the LORD your God in their way. ⁵But you are to seek the place the LORD your God will choose from among all your tribes to put his Name there for his dwelling. To that place you must go; ⁶there bring your burnt offerings and sacrifices, your tithes and special gifts, what you have vowed to give and your freewill offerings, and the firstborn of your herds and flocks. ⁷There, in the presence of the LORD your God, you and your families shall eat and shall rejoice in everything you have put your hand to, because the LORD your God has blessed you.

⁸You are not to do as we do here today, everyone doing as they see fit, ⁹since you have not yet reached the resting place and the inheritance the LORD your God is giving you. ¹⁰But you will cross the Jordan and settle in the land the LORD your God is giving you as an inheritance, and he will give you rest from all your enemies around you so that you will live in safety. ¹¹Then to the place the LORD your God will choose as a dwelling for his Name—there you are to bring everything I command you: your burnt offerings and sacrifices, your tithes and special gifts, and all the choice possessions you have vowed to the LORD. ¹²And there rejoice before the LORD your God—you, your sons and daughters, your male and female servants, and the Levites from your towns who have no allotment or inheritance of their own. ¹³Be careful not to sacrifice your burnt offerings anywhere you please. ¹⁴Offer them only at the place the LORD will choose in one of your tribes, and there observe everything I command you.

¹⁵Nevertheless, you may slaughter your animals in any of your towns and eat as much of the meat as you want, as if it were gazelle or deer, according to the blessing the LORD your God gives you. Both the ceremonially unclean and the clean may eat it. ¹⁶But you must not eat the blood; pour it out on the ground like water. ¹⁷You must not eat in your own towns the tithe of your grain and new wine and olive oil, or the firstborn of your herds and flocks, or whatever you have vowed to give, or your freewill offerings or special gifts. ¹⁸Instead, you are to eat them in the presence of the LORD your God at the place the LORD your God will choose—you, your sons and daughters, your male and female servants, and the Levites from your towns—and you are to rejoice before the LORD your God in everything you put your hand to. ¹⁹Be careful not to neglect the Levites as long as you live in your land.

²⁰When the LORD your God has enlarged your territory as he promised you, and you crave meat and say, "I would like some meat," then you may eat as much of it as you want. ²¹If the place where the LORD your God chooses to put his Name is too far away from you, you may slaughter animals from the herds and flocks the LORD has given you, as I have commanded you, and in your own towns you may eat as much of them as you want. ²²Eat them as you would gazelle or deer. Both the ceremonially unclean and the clean may eat. ²³But be sure you do not eat the blood, because the blood is the life, and you must not eat the life with the meat. ²⁴You must not eat the blood; pour it out on the ground like water. ²⁵Do not eat it, so that it may go well with you and your children after you, because you will be doing what is right in the eyes of the LORD.

²⁶But take your consecrated things and whatever you have vowed to give, and go to the place the LORD will choose. ²⁷Present your burnt offerings on the altar of the LORD your God, both the meat and the blood. The blood of your sacrifices must be poured beside the altar of the LORD your God, but you may eat the meat. ²⁸Be careful to obey all these regulations I am giving you, so that it may always go well with you and your children after you, because you will be doing what is good and right in the eyes of the LORD your God.

²⁹The LORD your God will cut off before you the nations you are about to invade and dispossess. But when you have driven them out and settled in their land, ³⁰and after they have been destroyed before you, be careful not to be ensnared by inquiring about their gods, saying, "How do these nations serve their gods? We will do the same." ³¹You must not worship the LORD your God in their way, because in worshiping their gods, they do all kinds of detestable things the LORD hates.

They even burn their sons and daughters in the fire as sacrifices to their gods.

³²See that you do all I command you; do not add to it or take away from it.ᵃ

Worshiping Other Gods

13ᵇ If a prophet, or one who foretells by dreams, appears among you and announces to you a sign or wonder, ²and if the sign or wonder spoken of takes place, and the prophet says, "Let us follow other gods" (gods you have not known) "and let us worship them," ³you must not listen to the words of that prophet or dreamer. The LORD your God is testing you to find out whether you love him with all your heart and with all your soul. ⁴It is the LORD your God you must follow, and him you must revere. Keep his commands and obey him; serve him and hold fast to him. ⁵That prophet or dreamer must be put to death for inciting rebellion against the LORD your God, who brought you out of Egypt and redeemed you from the land of slavery. That prophet or dreamer tried to turn you from the way the LORD your God commanded you to follow. You must purge the evil from among you.

⁶If your very own brother, or your son or daughter, or the wife you love, or your closest friend secretly entices you, saying, "Let us go and worship other gods" (gods that neither you nor your ancestors have known, ⁷gods of the peoples around you, whether near or far, from one end of the land to the other), ⁸do not yield to them or listen to them. Show them no pity. Do not spare them or shield them. ⁹You must certainly put them to death. Your hand must be the first in putting them to death, and then the hands of all the people. ¹⁰Stone them to death, because they tried to turn you away from the LORD your God, who brought you out of Egypt, out of the land of slavery. ¹¹Then all Israel will hear and be afraid, and no one among you will do such an evil thing again.

¹²If you hear it said about one of the towns the LORD your God is giving you to live in ¹³that troublemakers have arisen among you and have led the people of their town astray, saying, "Let us go and worship oth-

er gods" (gods you have not known), ¹⁴then you must inquire, probe and investigate it thoroughly. And if it is true and it has been proved that this detestable thing has been done among you, ¹⁵you must certainly put to the sword all who live in that town. You must destroy it completely,ᶜ both its people and its livestock. ¹⁶You are to gather all the plunder of the town into the middle of the public square and completely burn the town and all its plunder as a whole burnt offering to the LORD your God. That town is to remain a ruin forever, never to be rebuilt, ¹⁷and none of the condemned thingsᶜ are to be found in your hands. Then the LORD will turn from his fierce anger, will show you mercy, and will have compassion on you. He will increase your numbers, as he promised on oath to your ancestors — ¹⁸because you obey the LORD your God by keeping all his commands that I am giving you today and doing what is right in his eyes.

Clean and Unclean Food

14 You are the children of the LORD your God. Do not cut yourselves or shave the front of your heads for the dead, ²for you are a people holy to the LORD your God. Out of all the peoples on the face of the earth, the LORD has chosen you to be his treasured possession.

³Do not eat any detestable thing. ⁴These are the animals you may eat: the ox, the sheep, the goat, ⁵the deer, the gazelle, the roe deer, the wild goat, the ibex, the antelope and the mountain sheep.ᵈ ⁶You may eat any animal that has a divided hoof and that chews the cud. ⁷However, of those that chew the cud or that have a divided hoof you may not eat the camel, the rabbit or the hyrax. Although they chew the cud, they do not have a divided hoof; they are ceremonially unclean for you. ⁸The pig is also unclean; although it has a divided hoof, it does not chew the cud. You are not to eat their meat or touch their carcasses.

⁹Of all the creatures living in the water, you may eat any that has fins and scales. ¹⁰But anything that does not have fins and scales you may not eat; for you it is unclean.

¹¹You may eat any clean bird. ¹²But these

ᵃ 32 In Hebrew texts this verse (12:32) is numbered 13:1.   ᵇ In Hebrew texts 13:1-18 is numbered 13:2-19.
ᶜ 15,17 The Hebrew term refers to the irrevocable giving over of things or persons to the LORD, often by totally destroying them.   ᵈ 5 The precise identification of some of the birds and animals in this chapter is uncertain.

SOLID FRIENDSHIPS

READ: DEUTERONOMY 13:6,8

Make a mental list of the five or six people you hang out with most. Then answer this. Who pushes you closer to God? Who pulls you away?

You're wise if you think hard about what the Lord says in this passage about people who hurt your relationship with him. He describes a "prophet" or "dreamer" who offers persuasive reasons you should follow a different god. The Lord warns you to shut your ears to that person. He urges you to "purge the evil from among you" (Deuteronomy 13:5).

In the Old Testament laws of the nation of Israel, that meant the person should be put to death. The Lord's rule applied not just to strangers but to anyone who taught others to disobey God's commands or worship other gods, even family and close friends. Today, talking against God isn't a crime. It's not punishable by death or anything else. It isn't your job to silence followers of other religions. And if you never get close to unbelievers, you'll never have opportunities to tell others about Jesus.

Yet this scene shows how seriously God treats anything that tears you away from him. So watch out for relationships that encourage you to live against God (2 Corinthians 6:14). Search out friendships that help you flee evil and pursue the Lord (2 Timothy 2:22). God doesn't want anything coming between you and him.

BUILDING

FAITH

WISDOM

STRENGTH

you may not eat: the eagle, the vulture, the black vulture, [13] the red kite, the black kite, any kind of falcon, [14] any kind of raven, [15] the horned owl, the screech owl, the gull, any kind of hawk, [16] the little owl, the great owl, the white owl, [17] the desert owl, the osprey, the cormorant, [18] the stork, any kind of heron, the hoopoe and the bat.

[19] All flying insects are unclean to you; do not eat them. [20] But any winged creature that is clean you may eat.

[21] Do not eat anything you find already dead. You may give it to the foreigner residing in any of your towns, and they may eat it, or you may sell it to any other foreigner. But you are a people holy to the LORD your God.

Do not cook a young goat in its mother's milk.

Tithes

[22] Be sure to set aside a tenth of all that your fields produce each year. [23] Eat the tithe of your grain, new wine and olive oil, and the firstborn of your herds and flocks in the presence of the LORD your God at the place he will choose as a dwelling for his Name, so that you may learn to revere the LORD your God always. [24] But if that place is too distant and you have been blessed by the LORD your God and cannot carry your tithe (because the place where the LORD will choose to put his Name is so far away), [25] then exchange your tithe for silver, and take the silver with you and go to the place the LORD your God will choose. [26] Use the silver to buy whatever you like: cattle, sheep, wine or other fermented drink, or anything you wish. Then you and your household shall eat there in the presence of the LORD your God and rejoice. [27] And do not neglect the Levites living in your towns, for they have no allotment or inheritance of their own.

[28] At the end of every three years, bring all the tithes of that year's produce and store it in your towns, [29] so that the Levites (who have no allotment or inheritance of their own) and the foreigners, the fatherless and the widows who live in your towns may come and eat and be satisfied, and so that the LORD your God may bless you in all the work of your hands.

The Year for Canceling Debts

15 At the end of every seven years you must cancel debts. [2] This is how it is to be done: Every creditor shall cancel any loan they have made to a fellow Israelite. They shall not require payment from anyone among their own people, because the LORD's time for canceling debts has been proclaimed. [3] You may require payment from a foreigner, but you must cancel any debt your fellow Israelite owes you. [4] However, there need be no poor people among you, for in the land the LORD your God is giving you to possess as your inheritance, he will richly bless you, [5] if only you fully obey the LORD your God and are careful to follow all these commands I am giving you today. [6] For the LORD your God will bless you as he has promised, and you will lend to many nations but will borrow from none. You will rule over many nations but none will rule over you.

[7] If anyone is poor among your fellow Israelites in any of the towns of the land the LORD your God is giving you, do not be hardhearted or tightfisted toward them. [8] Rather, be openhanded and freely lend them whatever they need. [9] Be careful not to harbor this wicked thought: "The seventh year, the year for canceling debts, is near," so that you do not show ill will toward the needy among your fellow Israelites and give them nothing. They may then appeal to the LORD against you, and you will be found guilty of sin. [10] Give generously to them and do so without a grudging heart; then because of this the LORD your God will bless you in all your work and in everything you put your hand to. [11] There will always be poor people in the land. Therefore I command you to be openhanded toward your fellow Israelites who are poor and needy in your land.

Freeing Servants

[12] If any of your people — Hebrew men or women — sell themselves to you and serve you six years, in the seventh year you must let them go free. [13] And when you release them, do not send them away empty-handed. [14] Supply them liberally from your flock, your threshing floor and your winepress. Give to them as the LORD your God has blessed you. [15] Remember that you were slaves in Egypt and the LORD your God redeemed you. That is why I give you this command today.

[16] But if your servant says to you, "I do not want to leave you," because he loves you and

your family and is well off with you, [17] then take an awl and push it through his earlobe into the door, and he will become your servant for life. Do the same for your female servant.

[18] Do not consider it a hardship to set your servant free, because their service to you these six years has been worth twice as much as that of a hired hand. And the LORD your God will bless you in everything you do.

The Firstborn Animals

[19] Set apart for the LORD your God every firstborn male of your herds and flocks. Do not put the firstborn of your cows to work, and do not shear the firstborn of your sheep. [20] Each year you and your family are to eat them in the presence of the LORD your God at the place he will choose. [21] If an animal has a defect, is lame or blind, or has any serious flaw, you must not sacrifice it to the LORD your God. [22] You are to eat it in your own towns. Both the ceremonially unclean and the clean may eat it, as if it were gazelle or deer. [23] But you must not eat the blood; pour it out on the ground like water.

The Passover

16 Observe the month of Aviv and celebrate the Passover of the LORD your God, because in the month of Aviv he brought you out of Egypt by night. [2] Sacrifice as the Passover to the LORD your God an animal from your flock or herd at the place the LORD will choose as a dwelling for his Name. [3] Do not eat it with bread made with yeast, but for seven days eat unleavened bread, the bread of affliction, because you left Egypt in haste — so that all the days of your life you may remember the time of your departure from Egypt. [4] Let no yeast be found in your possession in all your land for seven days. Do not let any of the meat you sacrifice on the evening of the first day remain until morning.

[5] You must not sacrifice the Passover in any town the LORD your God gives you [6] except in the place he will choose as a dwelling for his Name. There you must sacrifice the Passover in the evening, when the sun goes down, on the anniversary[a] of your departure from Egypt. [7] Roast it and eat it at the place the LORD your God will choose. Then in the morning return to your tents. [8] For six days eat unleavened bread and on the seventh day hold an assembly to the LORD your God and do no work.

The Festival of Weeks

[9] Count off seven weeks from the time you begin to put the sickle to the standing grain. [10] Then celebrate the Festival of Weeks to the LORD your God by giving a freewill offering in proportion to the blessings the LORD your God has given you. [11] And rejoice before the LORD your God at the place he will choose as a dwelling for his Name — you, your sons and daughters, your male and female servants, the Levites in your towns, and the foreigners, the fatherless and the widows living among you. [12] Remember that you were slaves in Egypt, and follow carefully these decrees.

The Festival of Tabernacles

[13] Celebrate the Festival of Tabernacles for seven days after you have gathered the produce of your threshing floor and your winepress. [14] Be joyful at your festival — you, your sons and daughters, your male and female servants, and the Levites, the foreigners, the fatherless and the widows who live in your towns. [15] For seven days celebrate the festival to the LORD your God at the place the LORD will choose. For the LORD your God will bless you in all your harvest and in all the work of your hands, and your joy will be complete.

[16] Three times a year all your men must appear before the LORD your God at the place he will choose: at the Festival of Unleavened Bread, the Festival of Weeks and the Festival of Tabernacles. No one should appear before the LORD empty-handed: [17] Each of you must bring a gift in proportion to the way the LORD your God has blessed you.

Judges

[18] Appoint judges and officials for each of your tribes in every town the LORD your God is giving you, and they shall judge the people fairly. [19] Do not pervert justice or show partiality. Do not accept a bribe, for a bribe blinds the eyes of the wise and twists the words of the innocent. [20] Follow justice and justice alone, so that you may live and possess the land the LORD your God is giving you.

---

[a] 6 Or *down, at the time of day*

SIGNING UP FOR SLAVERY

READ: DEUTERONOMY 15:16-17

We think of slavery as something you're forced into, but Jesus invites us to deny ourselves and become his slaves. Why would anyone ever want to be a slave? Actually, it was rare, but in the Old Testament some people chose to be slaves. They were called *bondslaves*. These were people who were set free after being a slave for six years, but they decided they wanted to stay a slave. A bondslave is how many of the New Testament writers describe themselves. Luke 1 tells us that when Mary was told that she would be giving birth to the Messiah, her response was, "I am the Lord's servant." But the word is *bondslave*.

Choosing to become a bondslave was an act of complete self-denial. A bondslave gave up all their rights and possessions to the master. A slave couldn't pick and choose what was part of the deal. He couldn't say, "I'm going to be a slave but I want to keep the car, and I need every other weekend off. I need to have a room with a view."

BUILDING

FAITH

WISDOM

STRENGTH

Who signs up for that? Well, did you notice in Deuteronomy 15 what the motivation is for someone to choose slavery? A slave realizes that as crazy as it might seem to everyone else, he's going to choose a life of slavery. He loves his master and realizes that he's better off as a slave.

So out of love we become a slave to Jesus. It's only by becoming a slave to Jesus that you ever truly find freedom.

Taken from *Not a Fan Student Edition* by Kyle Idleman, copyright © 2012 by City on the Hill Studio, Inc., published by Zondervan.

Worshiping Other Gods

²¹ Do not set up any wooden Asherah pole beside the altar you build to the LORD your God, ²² and do not erect a sacred stone, for these the LORD your God hates.

17 Do not sacrifice to the LORD your God an ox or a sheep that has any defect or flaw in it, for that would be detestable to him.

² If a man or woman living among you in one of the towns the LORD gives you is found doing evil in the eyes of the LORD your God in violation of his covenant, ³ and contrary to my command has worshiped other gods, bowing down to them or to the sun or the moon or the stars in the sky, ⁴ and this has been brought to your attention, then you must investigate it thoroughly. If it is true and it has been proved that this detestable thing has been done in Israel, ⁵ take the man or woman who has done this evil deed to your city gate and stone that person to death. ⁶ On the testimony of two or three witnesses a person is to be put to death, but no one is to be put to death on the testimony of only one witness. ⁷ The hands of the witnesses must be the first in putting that person to death, and then the hands of all the people. You must purge the evil from among you.

Law Courts

⁸ If cases come before your courts that are too difficult for you to judge — whether bloodshed, lawsuits or assaults — take them to the place the LORD your God will choose. ⁹ Go to the Levitical priests and to the judge who is in office at that time. Inquire of them and they will give you the verdict. ¹⁰ You must act according to the decisions they give you at the place the LORD will choose. Be careful to do everything they instruct you to do. ¹¹ Act according to whatever they teach you and the decisions they give you. Do not turn aside from what they tell you, to the right or to the left. ¹² Anyone who shows contempt for the judge or for the priest who stands ministering there to the LORD your God is to be put to death. You must purge the evil from Israel. ¹³ All the people will hear and be afraid, and will not be contemptuous again.

The King

¹⁴ When you enter the land the LORD your God is giving you and have taken possession of it and settled in it, and you say, "Let us set a king over us like all the nations around us," ¹⁵ be sure to appoint over you a king the LORD your God chooses. He must be from among your fellow Israelites. Do not place a foreigner over you, one who is not an Israelite. ¹⁶ The king, moreover, must not acquire great numbers of horses for himself or make the people return to Egypt to get more of them, for the LORD has told you, "You are not to go back that way again." ¹⁷ He must not take many wives, or his heart will be led astray. He must not accumulate large amounts of silver and gold.

¹⁸ When he takes the throne of his kingdom, he is to write for himself on a scroll a copy of this law, taken from that of the Levitical priests. ¹⁹ It is to be with him, and he is to read it all the days of his life so that he may learn to revere the LORD his God and follow carefully all the words of this law and these decrees ²⁰ and not consider himself better than his fellow Israelites and turn from the law to the right or to the left. Then he and his descendants will reign a long time over his kingdom in Israel.

Offerings for Priests and Levites

18 The Levitical priests — indeed, the whole tribe of Levi — are to have no allotment or inheritance with Israel. They shall live on the food offerings presented to the LORD, for that is their inheritance. ² They shall have no inheritance among their fellow Israelites; the LORD is their inheritance, as he promised them.

³ This is the share due the priests from the people who sacrifice a bull or a sheep: the shoulder, the internal organs and the meat from the head. ⁴ You are to give them the firstfruits of your grain, new wine and olive oil, and the first wool from the shearing of your sheep, ⁵ for the LORD your God has chosen them and their descendants out of all your tribes to stand and minister in the LORD's name always.

⁶ If a Levite moves from one of your towns anywhere in Israel where he is living, and comes in all earnestness to the place the LORD will choose, ⁷ he may minister in the name of the LORD his God like all his fellow Levites who serve there in the presence of the LORD. ⁸ He is to share equally in their benefits, even though he has received money from the sale of family possessions.

Occult Practices

⁹When you enter the land the LORD your God is giving you, do not learn to imitate the detestable ways of the nations there. ¹⁰Let no one be found among you who sacrifices their son or daughter in the fire, who practices divination or sorcery, interprets omens, engages in witchcraft, ¹¹or casts spells, or who is a medium or spiritist or who consults the dead. ¹²Anyone who does these things is detestable to the LORD; because of these same detestable practices the LORD your God will drive out those nations before you. ¹³You must be blameless before the LORD your God.

The Prophet

¹⁴The nations you will dispossess listen to those who practice sorcery or divination. But as for you, the LORD your God has not permitted you to do so. ¹⁵The LORD your God will raise up for you a prophet like me from among you, from your fellow Israelites. You must listen to him. ¹⁶For this is what you asked of the LORD your God at Horeb on the day of the assembly when you said, "Let us not hear the voice of the LORD our God nor see this great fire anymore, or we will die."

¹⁷The LORD said to me: "What they say is good. ¹⁸I will raise up for them a prophet like you from among their fellow Israelites, and I will put my words in his mouth. He will tell them everything I command him. ¹⁹I myself will call to account anyone who does not listen to my words that the prophet speaks in my name. ²⁰But a prophet who presumes to speak in my name anything I have not commanded, or a prophet who speaks in the name of other gods, is to be put to death."

²¹You may say to yourselves, "How can we know when a message has not been spoken by the LORD?" ²²If what a prophet proclaims in the name of the LORD does not take place or come true, that is a message the LORD has not spoken. That prophet has spoken presumptuously, so do not be alarmed.

Cities of Refuge

19 When the LORD your God has destroyed the nations whose land he is giving you, and when you have driven them out and settled in their towns and houses, ²then set aside for yourselves three cities in the land the LORD your God is giving you to possess. ³Determine the distances involved and divide into three parts the land the LORD your God is giving you as an inheritance, so that a person who kills someone may flee for refuge to one of these cities.

⁴This is the rule concerning anyone who kills a person and flees there for safety — anyone who kills a neighbor unintentionally, without malice aforethought. ⁵For instance, a man may go into the forest with his neighbor to cut wood, and as he swings his ax to fell a tree, the head may fly off and hit his neighbor and kill him. That man may flee to one of these cities and save his life. ⁶Otherwise, the avenger of blood might pursue him in a rage, overtake him if the distance is too great, and kill him even though he is not deserving of death, since he did it to his neighbor without malice aforethought. ⁷This is why I command you to set aside for yourselves three cities.

⁸If the LORD your God enlarges your territory, as he promised on oath to your ancestors, and gives you the whole land he promised them, ⁹because you carefully follow all these laws I command you today — to love the LORD your God and to walk always in obedience to him — then you are to set aside three more cities. ¹⁰Do this so that innocent blood will not be shed in your land, which the LORD your God is giving you as your inheritance, and so that you will not be guilty of bloodshed.

¹¹But if out of hate someone lies in wait, assaults and kills a neighbor, and then flees to one of these cities, ¹²the killer shall be sent for by the town elders, be brought back from the city, and be handed over to the avenger of blood to die. ¹³Show no pity. You must purge from Israel the guilt of shedding innocent blood, so that it may go well with you.

¹⁴Do not move your neighbor's boundary stone set up by your predecessors in the inheritance you receive in the land the LORD your God is giving you to possess.

Witnesses

¹⁵One witness is not enough to convict anyone accused of any crime or offense they may have committed. A matter must be established by the testimony of two or three witnesses.

¹⁶If a malicious witness takes the stand to accuse someone of a crime, ¹⁷the two people involved in the dispute must stand in

DEFENSE AGAINST THE DARK ARTS

READ: DEUTERONOMY 18:10-11

Reckless people think it's safe to climb all over an electrical tower, but smart people hear the wires buzz with high voltage. That's how it is with dark arts. Others might think they're harmless, but wise people recognize their dangerous spiritual powers.

God warned his people about the occult ("hidden") practices of nations inhabiting the promised land. These people attempted to gain supernatural power and secret information from sources other than God. They cast spells. They sought to contact the dead. They interpreted omens. They even sacrificed their children to win favors from their pagan gods.

The Lord absolutely forbade these practices, promising to speak to his people through prophets whose truthfulness could be tested. New Testament believers confessed their involvement in the occult and publicly burned their magic scrolls.

BUILDING FAITH WISDOM STRENGTH

God's Word spread widely and grew in power as a result (Acts 19:17-20). Those forbidden arts haven't gone away. While some people dismiss dark arts as harmless, nothing about them is safe. If you look to horoscopes, tarot cards, and Ouija boards for guidance, you are attempting to tap into evil powers. If you engage in séances and spells, you tangle with dangerous forces. All of these dark arts take you far from God. Don't give them the smallest place in your life.

the presence of the LORD before the priests and the judges who are in office at the time. [18]The judges must make a thorough investigation, and if the witness proves to be a liar, giving false testimony against a fellow Israelite, [19]then do to the false witness as that witness intended to do to the other party. You must purge the evil from among you. [20]The rest of the people will hear of this and be afraid, and never again will such an evil thing be done among you. [21]Show no pity: life for life, eye for eye, tooth for tooth, hand for hand, foot for foot.

Going to War

20 When you go to war against your enemies and see horses and chariots and an army greater than yours, do not be afraid of them, because the LORD your God, who brought you up out of Egypt, will be with you. [2]When you are about to go into battle, the priest shall come forward and address the army. [3]He shall say: "Hear, Israel: Today you are going into battle against your enemies. Do not be fainthearted or afraid; do not panic or be terrified by them. [4]For the LORD your God is the one who goes with you to fight for you against your enemies to give you victory."

[5]The officers shall say to the army: "Has anyone built a new house and not yet begun to live in it? Let him go home, or he may die in battle and someone else may begin to live in it. [6]Has anyone planted a vineyard and not begun to enjoy it? Let him go home, or he may die in battle and someone else enjoy it. [7]Has anyone become pledged to a woman and not married her? Let him go home, or he may die in battle and someone else marry her." [8]Then the officers shall add, "Is anyone afraid or fainthearted? Let him go home so that his fellow soldiers will not become disheartened too." [9]When the officers have finished speaking to the army, they shall appoint commanders over it.

[10]When you march up to attack a city, make its people an offer of peace. [11]If they accept and open their gates, all the people in it shall be subject to forced labor and shall work for you. [12]If they refuse to make peace and they engage you in battle, lay siege to that city. [13]When the LORD your God delivers it into your hand, put to the sword all the men in it. [14]As for the women, the children, the livestock and everything else in the city, you may take these as plunder for yourselves. And you may use the plunder the LORD your God gives you from your enemies. [15]This is how you are to treat all the cities that are at a distance from you and do not belong to the nations nearby.

[16]However, in the cities of the nations the LORD your God is giving you as an inheritance, do not leave alive anything that breathes. [17]Completely destroy[a] them — the Hittites, Amorites, Canaanites, Perizzites, Hivites and Jebusites — as the LORD your God has commanded you. [18]Otherwise, they will teach you to follow all the detestable things they do in worshiping their gods, and you will sin against the LORD your God.

[19]When you lay siege to a city for a long time, fighting against it to capture it, do not destroy its trees by putting an ax to them, because you can eat their fruit. Do not cut them down. Are the trees people, that you should besiege them?[b] [20]However, you may cut down trees that you know are not fruit trees and use them to build siege works until the city at war with you falls.

Atonement for an Unsolved Murder

21 If someone is found slain, lying in a field in the land the LORD your God is giving you to possess, and it is not known who the killer was, [2]your elders and judges shall go out and measure the distance from the body to the neighboring towns. [3]Then the elders of the town nearest the body shall take a heifer that has never been worked and has never worn a yoke [4]and lead it down to a valley that has not been plowed or planted and where there is a flowing stream. There in the valley they are to break the heifer's neck. [5]The Levitical priests shall step forward, for the LORD your God has chosen them to minister and to pronounce blessings in the name of the LORD and to decide all cases of dispute and assault. [6]Then all the elders of the town nearest the body shall wash their hands over the heifer whose neck was broken in the valley, [7]and they shall declare: "Our hands did not shed this blood, nor did our eyes see it done. [8]Accept this

---

[a] 17 The Hebrew term refers to the irrevocable giving over of things or persons to the LORD, often by totally destroying them.   [b] 19 Or down to use in the siege, for the fruit trees are for the benefit of people.

atonement for your people Israel, whom you have redeemed, LORD, and do not hold your people guilty of the blood of an innocent person." Then the bloodshed will be atoned for, ⁹and you will have purged from yourselves the guilt of shedding innocent blood, since you have done what is right in the eyes of the LORD.

Marrying a Captive Woman

¹⁰When you go to war against your enemies and the LORD your God delivers them into your hands and you take captives, ¹¹if you notice among the captives a beautiful woman and are attracted to her, you may take her as your wife. ¹²Bring her into your home and have her shave her head, trim her nails ¹³and put aside the clothes she was wearing when captured. After she has lived in your house and mourned her father and mother for a full month, then you may go to her and be her husband and she shall be your wife. ¹⁴If you are not pleased with her, let her go wherever she wishes. You must not sell her or treat her as a slave, since you have dishonored her.

The Right of the Firstborn

¹⁵If a man has two wives, and he loves one but not the other, and both bear him sons but the firstborn is the son of the wife he does not love, ¹⁶when he wills his property to his sons, he must not give the rights of the firstborn to the son of the wife he loves in preference to his actual firstborn, the son of the wife he does not love. ¹⁷He must acknowledge the son of his unloved wife as the firstborn by giving him a double share of all he has. That son is the first sign of his father's strength. The right of the firstborn belongs to him.

A Rebellious Son

¹⁸If someone has a stubborn and rebellious son who does not obey his father and mother and will not listen to them when they discipline him, ¹⁹his father and mother shall take hold of him and bring him to the elders at the gate of his town. ²⁰They shall say to the elders, "This son of ours is stubborn and rebellious. He will not obey us. He is a glutton and a drunkard." ²¹Then all the men of his town are to stone him to death. You must

purge the evil from among you. All Israel will hear of it and be afraid.

Various Laws

²²If someone guilty of a capital offense is put to death and their body is exposed on a pole, ²³you must not leave the body hanging on the pole overnight. Be sure to bury it that same day, because anyone who is hung on a pole is under God's curse. You must not desecrate the land the LORD your God is giving you as an inheritance.

22 If you see your fellow Israelite's ox or sheep straying, do not ignore it but be sure to take it back to its owner. ²If they do not live near you or if you do not know who owns it, take it home with you and keep it until they come looking for it. Then give it back. ³Do the same if you find their donkey or cloak or anything else they have lost. Do not ignore it.

⁴If you see your fellow Israelite's donkey or ox fallen on the road, do not ignore it. Help the owner get it to its feet.

⁵A woman must not wear men's clothing, nor a man wear women's clothing, for the LORD your God detests anyone who does this.

⁶If you come across a bird's nest beside the road, either in a tree or on the ground, and the mother is sitting on the young or on the eggs, do not take the mother with the young. ⁷You may take the young, but be sure to let the mother go, so that it may go well with you and you may have a long life.

⁸When you build a new house, make a parapet around your roof so that you may not bring the guilt of bloodshed on your house if someone falls from the roof.

⁹Do not plant two kinds of seed in your vineyard; if you do, not only the crops you plant but also the fruit of the vineyard will be defiled.ᵃ

¹⁰Do not plow with an ox and a donkey yoked together.

¹¹Do not wear clothes of wool and linen woven together.

¹²Make tassels on the four corners of the cloak you wear.

Marriage Violations

¹³If a man takes a wife and, after sleeping with her, dislikes her ¹⁴and slanders her and gives her a bad name, saying, "I married

---

ᵃ 9 Or *be forfeited to the sanctuary*

this woman, but when I approached her, I did not find proof of her virginity," [15] then the young woman's father and mother shall bring to the town elders at the gate proof that she was a virgin. [16] Her father will say to the elders, "I gave my daughter in marriage to this man, but he dislikes her. [17] Now he has slandered her and said, 'I did not find your daughter to be a virgin.' But here is the proof of my daughter's virginity." Then her parents shall display the cloth before the elders of the town, [18] and the elders shall take the man and punish him. [19] They shall fine him a hundred shekels[a] of silver and give them to the young woman's father, because this man has given an Israelite virgin a bad name. She shall continue to be his wife; he must not divorce her as long as he lives.

[20] If, however, the charge is true and no proof of the young woman's virginity can be found, [21] she shall be brought to the door of her father's house and there the men of her town shall stone her to death. She has done an outrageous thing in Israel by being promiscuous while still in her father's house. You must purge the evil from among you.

[22] If a man is found sleeping with another man's wife, both the man who slept with her and the woman must die. You must purge the evil from Israel.

[23] If a man happens to meet in a town a virgin pledged to be married and he sleeps with her, [24] you shall take both of them to the gate of that town and stone them to death — the young woman because she was in a town and did not scream for help, and the man because he violated another man's wife. You must purge the evil from among you.

[25] But if out in the country a man happens to meet a young woman pledged to be married and rapes her, only the man who has done this shall die. [26] Do nothing to the woman; she has committed no sin deserving of death. This case is like that of someone who attacks and murders a neighbor, [27] for the man found the young woman out in the country, and though the betrothed woman screamed, there was no one to rescue her.

[28] If a man happens to meet a virgin who is not pledged to be married and rapes her and they are discovered, [29] he shall pay her father fifty shekels[b] of silver. He must marry the young woman, for he has violated her. He can never divorce her as long as he lives.

[30] A man is not to marry his father's wife; he must not dishonor his father's bed.[c]

Exclusion From the Assembly

23[d] No one who has been emasculated by crushing or cutting may enter the assembly of the LORD.

[2] No one born of a forbidden marriage[e] nor any of their descendants may enter the assembly of the LORD, not even in the tenth generation.

[3] No Ammonite or Moabite or any of their descendants may enter the assembly of the LORD, not even in the tenth generation. [4] For they did not come to meet you with bread and water on your way when you came out of Egypt, and they hired Balaam son of Beor from Pethor in Aram Naharaim[f] to pronounce a curse on you. [5] However, the LORD your God would not listen to Balaam but turned the curse into a blessing for you, because the LORD your God loves you. [6] Do not seek a treaty of friendship with them as long as you live.

[7] Do not despise an Edomite, for the Edomites are related to you. Do not despise an Egyptian, because you resided as foreigners in their country. [8] The third generation of children born to them may enter the assembly of the LORD.

Uncleanness in the Camp

[9] When you are encamped against your enemies, keep away from everything impure. [10] If one of your men is unclean because of a nocturnal emission, he is to go outside the camp and stay there. [11] But as evening approaches he is to wash himself, and at sunset he may return to the camp.

[12] Designate a place outside the camp where you can go to relieve yourself. [13] As part of your equipment have something to dig with, and when you relieve yourself, dig a hole and cover up your excrement. [14] For the LORD your God moves about in your camp to protect you and to deliver your enemies to you. Your camp must be holy, so that he will not see among you anything indecent and turn away from you.

---

[a] 19 That is, about 2 1/2 pounds or about 1.2 kilograms   [b] 29 That is, about 1 1/4 pounds or about 575 grams   [c] 30 In Hebrew texts this verse (22:30) is numbered 23:1.   [d] In Hebrew texts 23:1-25 is numbered 23:2-26.   [e] 2 Or one of illegitimate birth   [f] 4 That is, Northwest Mesopotamia

Miscellaneous Laws

[15] If a slave has taken refuge with you, do not hand them over to their master. [16] Let them live among you wherever they like and in whatever town they choose. Do not oppress them.

[17] No Israelite man or woman is to become a shrine prostitute. [18] You must not bring the earnings of a female prostitute or of a male prostitute[a] into the house of the LORD your God to pay any vow, because the LORD your God detests them both.

[19] Do not charge a fellow Israelite interest, whether on money or food or anything else that may earn interest. [20] You may charge a foreigner interest, but not a fellow Israelite, so that the LORD your God may bless you in everything you put your hand to in the land you are entering to possess.

[21] If you make a vow to the LORD your God, do not be slow to pay it, for the LORD your God will certainly demand it of you and you will be guilty of sin. [22] But if you refrain from making a vow, you will not be guilty. [23] Whatever your lips utter you must be sure to do, because you made your vow freely to the LORD your God with your own mouth.

[24] If you enter your neighbor's vineyard, you may eat all the grapes you want, but do not put any in your basket. [25] If you enter your neighbor's grainfield, you may pick kernels with your hands, but you must not put a sickle to their standing grain.

24 If a man marries a woman who becomes displeasing to him because he finds something indecent about her, and he writes her a certificate of divorce, gives it to her and sends her from his house, [2] and if after she leaves his house she becomes the wife of another man, [3] and her second husband dislikes her and writes her a certificate of divorce, gives it to her and sends her from his house, or if he dies, [4] then her first husband, who divorced her, is not allowed to marry her again after she has been defiled. That would be detestable in the eyes of the LORD. Do not bring sin upon the land the LORD your God is giving you as an inheritance.

[5] If a man has recently married, he must not be sent to war or have any other duty laid on him. For one year he is to be free to stay at home and bring happiness to the wife he has married.

[6] Do not take a pair of millstones — not even the upper one — as security for a debt, because that would be taking a person's livelihood as security.

[7] If someone is caught kidnapping a fellow Israelite and treating or selling them as a slave, the kidnapper must die. You must purge the evil from among you.

[8] In cases of defiling skin diseases,[b] be very careful to do exactly as the Levitical priests instruct you. You must follow carefully what I have commanded them. [9] Remember what the LORD your God did to Miriam along the way after you came out of Egypt.

[10] When you make a loan of any kind to your neighbor, do not go into their house to get what is offered to you as a pledge. [11] Stay outside and let the neighbor to whom you are making the loan bring the pledge out to you. [12] If the neighbor is poor, do not go to sleep with their pledge in your possession. [13] Return their cloak by sunset so that your neighbor may sleep in it. Then they will thank you, and it will be regarded as a righteous act in the sight of the LORD your God.

[14] Do not take advantage of a hired worker who is poor and needy, whether that worker is a fellow Israelite or a foreigner residing in one of your towns. [15] Pay them their wages each day before sunset, because they are poor and are counting on it. Otherwise they may cry to the LORD against you, and you will be guilty of sin.

[16] Parents are not to be put to death for their children, nor children put to death for their parents; each will die for their own sin.

[17] Do not deprive the foreigner or the fatherless of justice, or take the cloak of the widow as a pledge. [18] Remember that you were slaves in Egypt and the LORD your God redeemed you from there. That is why I command you to do this.

[19] When you are harvesting in your field and you overlook a sheaf, do not go back to get it. Leave it for the foreigner, the fatherless and the widow, so that the LORD your God may bless you in all the work of your hands. [20] When you beat the olives from your trees, do not go over the branches a second time.

---

a 18 Hebrew *of a dog*   *b* 8 The Hebrew word for *defiling skin diseases*, traditionally translated "leprosy," was used for various diseases affecting the skin.

Leave what remains for the foreigner, the fatherless and the widow. ²¹When you harvest the grapes in your vineyard, do not go over the vines again. Leave what remains for the foreigner, the fatherless and the widow. ²²Remember that you were slaves in Egypt. That is why I command you to do this.

25 When people have a dispute, they are to take it to court and the judges will decide the case, acquitting the innocent and condemning the guilty. ²If the guilty person deserves to be beaten, the judge shall make them lie down and have them flogged in his presence with the number of lashes the crime deserves, ³but the judge must not impose more than forty lashes. If the guilty party is flogged more than that, your fellow Israelite will be degraded in your eyes.

⁴Do not muzzle an ox while it is treading out the grain.

⁵If brothers are living together and one of them dies without a son, his widow must not marry outside the family. Her husband's brother shall take her and marry her and fulfill the duty of a brother-in-law to her. ⁶The first son she bears shall carry on the name of the dead brother so that his name will not be blotted out from Israel.

⁷However, if a man does not want to marry his brother's wife, she shall go to the elders at the town gate and say, "My husband's brother refuses to carry on his brother's name in Israel. He will not fulfill the duty of a brother-in-law to me." ⁸Then the elders of his town shall summon him and talk to him. If he persists in saying, "I do not want to marry her," ⁹his brother's widow shall go up to him in the presence of the elders, take off one of his sandals, spit in his face and say, "This is what is done to the man who will not build up his brother's family line." ¹⁰That man's line shall be known in Israel as The Family of the Unsandaled.

¹¹If two men are fighting and the wife of one of them comes to rescue her husband from his assailant, and she reaches out and seizes him by his private parts, ¹²you shall cut off her hand. Show her no pity.

¹³Do not have two differing weights in your bag — one heavy, one light. ¹⁴Do not have two differing measures in your house — one large, one small. ¹⁵You must have accurate and honest weights and measures, so that you may live long in the land the LORD your God is giving you. ¹⁶For the LORD your God detests anyone who does these things, anyone who deals dishonestly.

¹⁷Remember what the Amalekites did to you along the way when you came out of Egypt. ¹⁸When you were weary and worn out, they met you on your journey and attacked all who were lagging behind; they had no fear of God. ¹⁹When the LORD your God gives you rest from all the enemies around you in the land he is giving you to possess as an inheritance, you shall blot out the name of Amalek from under heaven. Do not forget!

Firstfruits and Tithes

26 When you have entered the land the LORD your God is giving you as an inheritance and have taken possession of it and settled in it, ²take some of the firstfruits of all that you produce from the soil of the land the LORD your God is giving you and put them in a basket. Then go to the place the LORD your God will choose as a dwelling for his Name ³and say to the priest in office at the time, "I declare today to the LORD your God that I have come to the land the LORD swore to our ancestors to give us." ⁴The priest shall take the basket from your hands and set it down in front of the altar of the LORD your God. ⁵Then you shall declare before the LORD your God: "My father was a wandering Aramean, and he went down into Egypt with a few people and lived there and became a great nation, powerful and numerous. ⁶But the Egyptians mistreated us and made us suffer, subjecting us to harsh labor. ⁷Then we cried out to the LORD, the God of our ancestors, and the LORD heard our voice and saw our misery, toil and oppression. ⁸So the LORD brought us out of Egypt with a mighty hand and an outstretched arm, with great terror and with signs and wonders. ⁹He brought us to this place and gave us this land, a land flowing with milk and honey; ¹⁰and now I bring the firstfruits of the soil that you, LORD, have given me." Place the basket before the LORD your God and bow down before him. ¹¹Then you and the Levites and the foreigners residing among you shall rejoice in all the good things the LORD your God has given to you and your household.

¹²When you have finished setting aside a tenth of all your produce in the third year, the

year of the tithe, you shall give it to the Levite, the foreigner, the fatherless and the widow, so that they may eat in your towns and be satisfied. ¹³Then say to the LORD your God: "I have removed from my house the sacred portion and have given it to the Levite, the foreigner, the fatherless and the widow, according to all you commanded. I have not turned aside from your commands nor have I forgotten any of them. ¹⁴I have not eaten any of the sacred portion while I was in mourning, nor have I removed any of it while I was unclean, nor have I offered any of it to the dead. I have obeyed the LORD my God; I have done everything you commanded me. ¹⁵Look down from heaven, your holy dwelling place, and bless your people Israel and the land you have given us as you promised on oath to our ancestors, a land flowing with milk and honey."

Follow the LORD's Commands

¹⁶The LORD your God commands you this day to follow these decrees and laws; carefully observe them with all your heart and with all your soul. ¹⁷You have declared this day that the LORD is your God and that you will walk in obedience to him, that you will keep his decrees, commands and laws—that you will listen to him. ¹⁸And the LORD has declared this day that you are his people, his treasured possession as he promised, and that you are to keep all his commands. ¹⁹He has declared that he will set you in praise, fame and honor high above all the nations he has made and that you will be a people holy to the LORD your God, as he promised.

The Altar on Mount Ebal

27 Moses and the elders of Israel commanded the people: "Keep all these commands that I give you today. ²When you have crossed the Jordan into the land the LORD your God is giving you, set up some large stones and coat them with plaster. ³Write on them all the words of this law when you have crossed over to enter the land the LORD your God is giving you, a land flowing with milk and honey, just as the LORD, the God of your ancestors, promised you. ⁴And when you have crossed the Jordan, set up these stones on Mount Ebal, as I command you today, and coat them with plaster. ⁵Build there an altar to the LORD your God, an altar of stones. Do not use any iron tool on them.

⁶Build the altar of the LORD your God with fieldstones and offer burnt offerings on it to the LORD your God. ⁷Sacrifice fellowship offerings there, eating them and rejoicing in the presence of the LORD your God. ⁸And you shall write very clearly all the words of this law on these stones you have set up."

Curses From Mount Ebal

⁹Then Moses and the Levitical priests said to all Israel, "Be silent, Israel, and listen! You have now become the people of the LORD your God. ¹⁰Obey the LORD your God and follow his commands and decrees that I give you today."

¹¹On the same day Moses commanded the people:

¹²When you have crossed the Jordan, these tribes shall stand on Mount Gerizim to bless the people: Simeon, Levi, Judah, Issachar, Joseph and Benjamin. ¹³And these tribes shall stand on Mount Ebal to pronounce curses: Reuben, Gad, Asher, Zebulun, Dan and Naphtali.

¹⁴The Levites shall recite to all the people of Israel in a loud voice:

¹⁵"Cursed is anyone who makes an idol—a thing detestable to the LORD, the work of skilled hands—and sets it up in secret."

Then all the people shall say, "Amen!"

¹⁶"Cursed is anyone who dishonors their father or mother."

Then all the people shall say, "Amen!"

¹⁷"Cursed is anyone who moves their neighbor's boundary stone."

Then all the people shall say, "Amen!"

¹⁸"Cursed is anyone who leads the blind astray on the road."

Then all the people shall say, "Amen!"

¹⁹"Cursed is anyone who withholds justice from the foreigner, the fatherless or the widow."

Then all the people shall say, "Amen!"

²⁰"Cursed is anyone who sleeps with his father's wife, for he dishonors his father's bed."

Then all the people shall say, "Amen!"

²¹ "Cursed is anyone who has sexual relations with any animal."

Then all the people shall say, "Amen!"

²² "Cursed is anyone who sleeps with his sister, the daughter of his father or the daughter of his mother."

Then all the people shall say, "Amen!"

²³ "Cursed is anyone who sleeps with his mother-in-law."

Then all the people shall say, "Amen!"

²⁴ "Cursed is anyone who kills their neighbor secretly."

Then all the people shall say, "Amen!"

²⁵ "Cursed is anyone who accepts a bribe to kill an innocent person."

Then all the people shall say, "Amen!"

²⁶ "Cursed is anyone who does not uphold the words of this law by carrying them out."

Then all the people shall say, "Amen!"

Blessings for Obedience

28 If you fully obey the LORD your God and carefully follow all his commands I give you today, the LORD your God will set you high above all the nations on earth. ² All these blessings will come on you and accompany you if you obey the LORD your God:

³ You will be blessed in the city and blessed in the country.

⁴ The fruit of your womb will be blessed, and the crops of your land and the young of your livestock — the calves of your herds and the lambs of your flocks.

⁵ Your basket and your kneading trough will be blessed.

⁶ You will be blessed when you come in and blessed when you go out.

⁷ The LORD will grant that the enemies who rise up against you will be defeated before you. They will come at you from one direction but flee from you in seven.

⁸ The LORD will send a blessing on your barns and on everything you put your hand to. The LORD your God will bless you in the land he is giving you.

⁹ The LORD will establish you as his holy people, as he promised you on oath, if you keep the commands of the LORD your God and walk in obedience to him. ¹⁰ Then all the peoples on earth will see that you are called by the name of the LORD, and they will fear you. ¹¹ The LORD will grant you abundant prosperity — in the fruit of your womb, the young of your livestock and the crops of your ground — in the land he swore to your ancestors to give you.

¹² The LORD will open the heavens, the storehouse of his bounty, to send rain on your land in season and to bless all the work of your hands. You will lend to many nations but will borrow from none. ¹³ The LORD will make you the head, not the tail. If you pay attention to the commands of the LORD your God that I give you this day and carefully follow them, you will always be at the top, never at the bottom. ¹⁴ Do not turn aside from any of the commands I give you today, to the right or to the left, following other gods and serving them.

Curses for Disobedience

¹⁵ However, if you do not obey the LORD your God and do not carefully follow all his commands and decrees I am giving you today, all these curses will come on you and overtake you:

¹⁶ You will be cursed in the city and cursed in the country.

¹⁷ Your basket and your kneading trough will be cursed.

¹⁸ The fruit of your womb will be cursed, and the crops of your land, and the calves of your herds and the lambs of your flocks.

¹⁹ You will be cursed when you come in and cursed when you go out.

²⁰ The LORD will send on you curses, confusion and rebuke in everything you put your hand to, until you are destroyed and come to sudden ruin because of the evil you have done in forsaking him.ᵃ ²¹ The LORD will plague you with diseases until he has destroyed you from the land you are entering

ᵃ 20 Hebrew *me*

to possess. ²²The LORD will strike you with wasting disease, with fever and inflammation, with scorching heat and drought, with blight and mildew, which will plague you until you perish. ²³The sky over your head will be bronze, the ground beneath you iron. ²⁴The LORD will turn the rain of your country into dust and powder; it will come down from the skies until you are destroyed.

²⁵The LORD will cause you to be defeated before your enemies. You will come at them from one direction but flee from them in seven, and you will become a thing of horror to all the kingdoms on earth. ²⁶Your carcasses will be food for all the birds and the wild animals, and there will be no one to frighten them away. ²⁷The LORD will afflict you with the boils of Egypt and with tumors, festering sores and the itch, from which you cannot be cured. ²⁸The LORD will afflict you with madness, blindness and confusion of mind. ²⁹At midday you will grope about like a blind person in the dark. You will be unsuccessful in everything you do; day after day you will be oppressed and robbed, with no one to rescue you.

³⁰You will be pledged to be married to a woman, but another will take her and rape her. You will build a house, but you will not live in it. You will plant a vineyard, but you will not even begin to enjoy its fruit. ³¹Your ox will be slaughtered before your eyes, but you will eat none of it. Your donkey will be forcibly taken from you and will not be returned. Your sheep will be given to your enemies, and no one will rescue them. ³²Your sons and daughters will be given to another nation, and you will wear out your eyes watching for them day after day, powerless to lift a hand. ³³A people that you do not know will eat what your land and labor produce, and you will have nothing but cruel oppression all your days. ³⁴The sights you see will drive you mad. ³⁵The LORD will afflict your knees and legs with painful boils that cannot be cured, spreading from the soles of your feet to the top of your head.

³⁶The LORD will drive you and the king you set over you to a nation unknown to you or your ancestors. There you will worship other gods, gods of wood and stone. ³⁷You will become a thing of horror, a byword and an object of ridicule among all the peoples where the LORD will drive you.

³⁸You will sow much seed in the field but you will harvest little, because locusts will devour it. ³⁹You will plant vineyards and cultivate them but you will not drink the wine or gather the grapes, because worms will eat them. ⁴⁰You will have olive trees throughout your country but you will not use the oil, because the olives will drop off. ⁴¹You will have sons and daughters but you will not keep them, because they will go into captivity. ⁴²Swarms of locusts will take over all your trees and the crops of your land.

⁴³The foreigners who reside among you will rise above you higher and higher, but you will sink lower and lower. ⁴⁴They will lend to you, but you will not lend to them. They will be the head, but you will be the tail.

⁴⁵All these curses will come on you. They will pursue you and overtake you until you are destroyed, because you did not obey the LORD your God and observe the commands and decrees he gave you. ⁴⁶They will be a sign and a wonder to you and your descendants forever. ⁴⁷Because you did not serve the LORD your God joyfully and gladly in the time of prosperity, ⁴⁸therefore in hunger and thirst, in nakedness and dire poverty, you will serve the enemies the LORD sends against you. He will put an iron yoke on your neck until he has destroyed you.

⁴⁹The LORD will bring a nation against you from far away, from the ends of the earth, like an eagle swooping down, a nation whose language you will not understand, ⁵⁰a fierce-looking nation without respect for the old or pity for the young. ⁵¹They will devour the young of your livestock and the crops of your land until you are destroyed. They will leave you no grain, new wine or olive oil, nor any calves of your herds or lambs of your flocks until you are ruined. ⁵²They will lay siege to all the cities throughout your land until the high fortified walls in which you trust fall down. They will besiege all the cities throughout the land the LORD your God is giving you.

⁵³Because of the suffering your enemy will inflict on you during the siege, you will eat the fruit of the womb, the flesh of the sons and daughters the LORD your God has given you. ⁵⁴Even the most gentle and sensitive man among you will have no compassion on his own brother or the wife he loves

or his surviving children, [55]and he will not give to one of them any of the flesh of his children that he is eating. It will be all he has left because of the suffering your enemy will inflict on you during the siege of all your cities. [56]The most gentle and sensitive woman among you — so sensitive and gentle that she would not venture to touch the ground with the sole of her foot — will begrudge the husband she loves and her own son or daughter [57]the afterbirth from her womb and the children she bears. For in her dire need she intends to eat them secretly because of the suffering your enemy will inflict on you during the siege of your cities.

[58]If you do not carefully follow all the words of this law, which are written in this book, and do not revere this glorious and awesome name — the LORD your God — [59]the LORD will send fearful plagues on you and your descendants, harsh and prolonged disasters, and severe and lingering illnesses. [60]He will bring on you all the diseases of Egypt that you dreaded, and they will cling to you. [61]The LORD will also bring on you every kind of sickness and disaster not recorded in this Book of the Law, until you are destroyed. [62]You who were as numerous as the stars in the sky will be left but few in number, because you did not obey the LORD your God. [63]Just as it pleased the LORD to make you prosper and increase in number, so it will please him to ruin and destroy you. You will be uprooted from the land you are entering to possess.

[64]Then the LORD will scatter you among all nations, from one end of the earth to the other. There you will worship other gods — gods of wood and stone, which neither you nor your ancestors have known. [65]Among those nations you will find no repose, no resting place for the sole of your foot. There the LORD will give you an anxious mind, eyes weary with longing, and a despairing heart. [66]You will live in constant suspense, filled with dread both night and day, never sure of your life. [67]In the morning you will say, "If only it were evening!" and in the evening, "If only it were morning!" — because of the terror that will fill your hearts and the sights that your eyes will see. [68]The LORD will send you back in ships to Egypt on a journey I said you should never make again.

There you will offer yourselves for sale to your enemies as male and female slaves, but no one will buy you.

Renewal of the Covenant

29[a] These are the terms of the covenant the LORD commanded Moses to make with the Israelites in Moab, in addition to the covenant he had made with them at Horeb.

[2]Moses summoned all the Israelites and said to them:

Your eyes have seen all that the LORD did in Egypt to Pharaoh, to all his officials and to all his land. [3]With your own eyes you saw those great trials, those signs and great wonders. [4]But to this day the LORD has not given you a mind that understands or eyes that see or ears that hear. [5]Yet the LORD says, "During the forty years that I led you through the wilderness, your clothes did not wear out, nor did the sandals on your feet. [6]You ate no bread and drank no wine or other fermented drink. I did this so that you might know that I am the LORD your God."

[7]When you reached this place, Sihon king of Heshbon and Og king of Bashan came out to fight against us, but we defeated them. [8]We took their land and gave it as an inheritance to the Reubenites, the Gadites and the half-tribe of Manasseh.

[9]Carefully follow the terms of this covenant, so that you may prosper in everything you do. [10]All of you are standing today in the presence of the LORD your God — your leaders and chief men, your elders and officials, and all the other men of Israel, [11]together with your children and your wives, and the foreigners living in your camps who chop your wood and carry your water. [12]You are standing here in order to enter into a covenant with the LORD your God, a covenant the LORD is making with you this day and sealing with an oath, [13]to confirm you this day as his people, that he may be your God as he promised you and as he swore to your fathers, Abraham, Isaac and Jacob. [14]I am making this covenant, with its oath, not only with you [15]who are standing here with us today in the presence of the LORD our God but also with those who are not here today.

[16]You yourselves know how we lived in

---

[a] In Hebrew texts 29:1 is numbered 28:69, and 29:2-29 is numbered 29:1-28.

NOT PLAYING FAVORITES

READ: DEUTERONOMY 28:64

Y ou might feel uneasy hearing God order the Israelites to storm the promised land and drive out the people who already live there (Deuteronomy 7:2). Yet the Lord's judgment was the result of the persistent sin of the Amorites and other nations (Genesis 15:16).

This section of Deuteronomy gives you more insight into God's justice. As the Lord prepares his people to enter the land, he utters amazing promises. If they obey him fully, he will bless them in every imaginable way. He will root them in the land as his holy people, causing all the nations to see and show them appropriate respect (Deuteronomy 28:1-14). Yet if the people ignore the Lord's commands, they will face all kinds of disasters as individuals and as a nation.

That's where you spot God's ultimate fairness. If the people fail to follow the Lord, he will remove them from the land he gave them, scattering them to distant nations for worshiping other gods. The Lord gave them a home as a free gift, but they won't get to stick around and enjoy the gift if they don't obey.

God has the same high expectations of everyone on earth. He alone deserves worship, and he wants everyone to quit sinning and turn to him. And the Lord is fair. When it comes to judgment, he doesn't play favorites.

BUILDING FAITH WISDOM STRENGTH

Egypt and how we passed through the countries on the way here. [17] You saw among them their detestable images and idols of wood and stone, of silver and gold. [18] Make sure there is no man or woman, clan or tribe among you today whose heart turns away from the LORD our God to go and worship the gods of those nations; make sure there is no root among you that produces such bitter poison.

[19] When such a person hears the words of this oath and they invoke a blessing on themselves, thinking, "I will be safe, even though I persist in going my own way," they will bring disaster on the watered land as well as the dry. [20] The LORD will never be willing to forgive them; his wrath and zeal will burn against them. All the curses written in this book will fall on them, and the LORD will blot out their names from under heaven. [21] The LORD will single them out from all the tribes of Israel for disaster, according to all the curses of the covenant written in this Book of the Law.

[22] Your children who follow you in later generations and foreigners who come from distant lands will see the calamities that have fallen on the land and the diseases with which the LORD has afflicted it. [23] The whole land will be a burning waste of salt and sulfur — nothing planted, nothing sprouting, no vegetation growing on it. It will be like the destruction of Sodom and Gomorrah, Admah and Zeboyim, which the LORD overthrew in fierce anger. [24] All the nations will ask: "Why has the LORD done this to this land? Why this fierce, burning anger?"

[25] And the answer will be: "It is because this people abandoned the covenant of the LORD, the God of their ancestors, the covenant he made with them when he brought them out of Egypt. [26] They went off and worshiped other gods and bowed down to them, gods they did not know, gods he had not given them. [27] Therefore the LORD's anger burned against this land, so that he brought on it all the curses written in this book. [28] In furious anger and in great wrath the LORD uprooted them from their land and thrust them into another land, as it is now."

[29] The secret things belong to the LORD our God, but the things revealed belong to us and to our children forever, that we may follow all the words of this law.

Prosperity After Turning to the LORD

30 When all these blessings and curses I have set before you come on you and you take them to heart wherever the LORD your God disperses you among the nations, [2] and when you and your children return to the LORD your God and obey him with all your heart and with all your soul according to everything I command you today, [3] then the LORD your God will restore your fortunes[a] and have compassion on you and gather you again from all the nations where he scattered you. [4] Even if you have been banished to the most distant land under the heavens, from there the LORD your God will gather you and bring you back. [5] He will bring you to the land that belonged to your ancestors, and you will take possession of it. He will make you more prosperous and numerous than your ancestors. [6] The LORD your God will circumcise your hearts and the hearts of your descendants, so that you may love him with all your heart and with all your soul, and live. [7] The LORD your God will put all these curses on your enemies who hate and persecute you. [8] You will again obey the LORD and follow all his commands I am giving you today. [9] Then the LORD your God will make you most prosperous in all the work of your hands and in the fruit of your womb, the young of your livestock and the crops of your land. The LORD will again delight in you and make you prosperous, just as he delighted in your ancestors, [10] if you obey the LORD your God and keep his commands and decrees that are written in this Book of the Law and turn to the LORD your God with all your heart and with all your soul.

The Offer of Life or Death

[11] Now what I am commanding you today is not too difficult for you or beyond your reach. [12] It is not up in heaven, so that you have to ask, "Who will ascend into heaven to get it and proclaim it to us so we may obey it?" [13] Nor is it beyond the sea, so that you have to ask, "Who will cross the sea to get it and proclaim it to us so we may obey it?" [14] No, the word is very near you; it is in your mouth and in your heart so you may obey it.

[15] See, I set before you today life and prosperity, death and destruction. [16] For I command you today to love the LORD your God,

---

[a] 3 Or *will bring you back from captivity*

to walk in obedience to him, and to keep his commands, decrees and laws; then you will live and increase, and the LORD your God will bless you in the land you are entering to possess.

17 But if your heart turns away and you are not obedient, and if you are drawn away to bow down to other gods and worship them, 18 I declare to you this day that you will certainly be destroyed. You will not live long in the land you are crossing the Jordan to enter and possess.

19 This day I call the heavens and the earth as witnesses against you that I have set before you life and death, blessings and curses. Now choose life, so that you and your children may live 20 and that you may love the LORD your God, listen to his voice, and hold fast to him. For the LORD is your life, and he will give you many years in the land he swore to give to your fathers, Abraham, Isaac and Jacob.

Joshua to Succeed Moses

31 Then Moses went out and spoke these words to all Israel: 2 "I am now a hundred and twenty years old and I am no longer able to lead you. The LORD has said to me, 'You shall not cross the Jordan.' 3 The LORD your God himself will cross over ahead of you. He will destroy these nations before you, and you will take possession of their land. Joshua also will cross over ahead of you, as the LORD said. 4 And the LORD will do to them what he did to Sihon and Og, the kings of the Amorites, whom he destroyed along with their land. 5 The LORD will deliver them to you, and you must do to them all that I have commanded you. 6 Be strong and courageous. Do not be afraid or terrified because of them, for the LORD your God goes with you; he will never leave you nor forsake you."

7 Then Moses summoned Joshua and said to him in the presence of all Israel, "Be strong and courageous, for you must go with this people into the land that the LORD swore to their ancestors to give them, and you must divide it among them as their inheritance. 8 The LORD himself goes before you and will be with you; he will never leave you nor forsake you. Do not be afraid; do not be discouraged."

Public Reading of the Law

9 So Moses wrote down this law and gave it to the Levitical priests, who carried the ark of the covenant of the LORD, and to all the elders of Israel. 10 Then Moses commanded them: "At the end of every seven years, in the year for canceling debts, during the Festival of Tabernacles, 11 when all Israel comes to appear before the LORD your God at the place he will choose, you shall read this law before them in their hearing. 12 Assemble the people — men, women and children, and the foreigners residing in your towns — so they can listen and learn to fear the LORD your God and follow carefully all the words of this law. 13 Their children, who do not know this law, must hear it and learn to fear the LORD your God as long as you live in the land you are crossing the Jordan to possess."

Israel's Rebellion Predicted

14 The LORD said to Moses, "Now the day of your death is near. Call Joshua and present yourselves at the tent of meeting, where I will commission him." So Moses and Joshua came and presented themselves at the tent of meeting.

15 Then the LORD appeared at the tent in a pillar of cloud, and the cloud stood over the entrance to the tent. 16 And the LORD said to Moses: "You are going to rest with your ancestors, and these people will soon prostitute themselves to the foreign gods of the land they are entering. They will forsake me and break the covenant I made with them. 17 And in that day I will become angry with them and forsake them; I will hide my face from them, and they will be destroyed. Many disasters and calamities will come on them, and in that day they will ask, 'Have not these disasters come on us because our God is not with us?' 18 And I will certainly hide my face in that day because of all their wickedness in turning to other gods.

19 "Now write down this song and teach it to the Israelites and have them sing it, so that it may be a witness for me against them. 20 When I have brought them into the land flowing with milk and honey, the land I promised on oath to their ancestors, and when they eat their fill and thrive, they will turn to other gods and worship them, rejecting me and breaking my covenant. 21 And when many disasters and calamities come on them, this song will testify against them, because it will not be forgotten by their descendants. I know what they are disposed to

ID THE GODS

READ: DEUTERONOMY 30:17-20

Our choices are a strong indication of what gods we are worshiping.

- How I choose to spend my money.
- What I choose to watch on TV.
- The people I choose to have as friends.
- The websites I choose to visit.
- The clothes I choose to wear.
- The way I choose to spend my free time.
- What I choose to think about.

All of these choices reveal my god of choice.

So instead of me asking you about what gods you are worshiping, let me ask you about what choices you are making.

Consider those things you will do or decide this week. What gods and goals have you inherited without really realizing it?

BUILDING FAITH WISDOM STRENGTH

What gods would you identify as the "gods of culture"? Perhaps this question demands reflection, because these gods are often such a part of our daily lives that we don't recognize them. But take a moment and look at the world around you through the lens of idolatry. Can you recognize the true American idols? How has following Christ impacted your choices? Have your priorities and pursuits changed since you started following Jesus? What continues to influence you? Is there something or someone from your past that takes the place of the Lord God in your life?

Stop for a moment and consider your options, and then choose carefully.

do, even before I bring them into the land I promised them on oath." ²²So Moses wrote down this song that day and taught it to the Israelites.

²³The LORD gave this command to Joshua son of Nun: "Be strong and courageous, for you will bring the Israelites into the land I promised them on oath, and I myself will be with you."

²⁴After Moses finished writing in a book the words of this law from beginning to end, ²⁵he gave this command to the Levites who carried the ark of the covenant of the LORD: ²⁶"Take this Book of the Law and place it beside the ark of the covenant of the LORD your God. There it will remain as a witness against you. ²⁷For I know how rebellious and stiff-necked you are. If you have been rebellious against the LORD while I am still alive and with you, how much more will you rebel after I die! ²⁸Assemble before me all the elders of your tribes and all your officials, so that I can speak these words in their hearing and call the heavens and the earth to testify against them. ²⁹For I know that after my death you are sure to become utterly corrupt and to turn from the way I have commanded you. In days to come, disaster will fall on you because you will do evil in the sight of the LORD and arouse his anger by what your hands have made."

The Song of Moses

³⁰And Moses recited the words of this song from beginning to end in the hearing of the whole assembly of Israel:

32 Listen, you heavens, and I will
        speak;
    hear, you earth, the words of my
        mouth.
²Let my teaching fall like rain
    and my words descend like dew,
  like showers on new grass,
    like abundant rain on tender plants.

³I will proclaim the name of the LORD.
    Oh, praise the greatness of our God!
⁴He is the Rock, his works are perfect,
    and all his ways are just.
  A faithful God who does no wrong,
    upright and just is he.

⁵They are corrupt and not his children;
    to their shame they are a warped and
        crooked generation.
⁶Is this the way you repay the LORD,
    you foolish and unwise people?
  Is he not your Father, your Creator,[a]
    who made you and formed you?

⁷Remember the days of old;
    consider the generations long past.
  Ask your father and he will tell you,
    your elders, and they will explain to
        you.
⁸When the Most High gave the nations
        their inheritance,
    when he divided all mankind,
  he set up boundaries for the peoples
    according to the number of the sons of
        Israel.[b]
⁹For the LORD's portion is his people,
    Jacob his allotted inheritance.

¹⁰In a desert land he found him,
    in a barren and howling waste.
  He shielded him and cared for him;
    he guarded him as the apple of his eye,
¹¹like an eagle that stirs up its nest
    and hovers over its young,
  that spreads its wings to catch them
    and carries them aloft.
¹²The LORD alone led him;
    no foreign god was with him.

¹³He made him ride on the heights of the
        land
    and fed him with the fruit of the fields.
  He nourished him with honey from the
        rock,
    and with oil from the flinty crag,
¹⁴with curds and milk from herd and flock
    and with fattened lambs and goats,
  with choice rams of Bashan
    and the finest kernels of wheat.
  You drank the foaming blood of the
        grape.

¹⁵Jeshurun[c] grew fat and kicked;
    filled with food, they became heavy
        and sleek.
  They abandoned the God who made
        them
    and rejected the Rock their Savior.
¹⁶They made him jealous with their
        foreign gods

---

[a] 6 Or *Father, who bought you*   [b] 8 Masoretic Text; Dead Sea Scrolls (see also Septuagint) *sons of God*
[c] 15 *Jeshurun* means *the upright one*, that is, Israel.

and angered him with their detestable
   idols.
¹⁷ They sacrificed to false gods, which are
   not God —
   gods they had not known,
   gods that recently appeared,
   gods your ancestors did not fear.
¹⁸ You deserted the Rock, who fathered you;
   you forgot the God who gave you birth.

¹⁹ The LORD saw this and rejected them
   because he was angered by his sons
   and daughters.
²⁰ "I will hide my face from them," he said,
   "and see what their end will be;
for they are a perverse generation,
   children who are unfaithful.
²¹ They made me jealous by what is no god
   and angered me with their worthless
   idols.
I will make them envious by those who
   are not a people;
   I will make them angry by a nation
   that has no understanding.
²² For a fire will be kindled by my wrath,
   one that burns down to the realm of
   the dead below.
It will devour the earth and its harvests
   and set afire the foundations of the
   mountains.

²³ "I will heap calamities on them
   and spend my arrows against them.
²⁴ I will send wasting famine against them,
   consuming pestilence and deadly
   plague;
I will send against them the fangs of wild
   beasts,
   the venom of vipers that glide in the
   dust.
²⁵ In the street the sword will make them
   childless;
   in their homes terror will reign.
The young men and young women will
   perish,
   the infants and those with gray hair.
²⁶ I said I would scatter them
   and erase their name from human
   memory,
²⁷ but I dreaded the taunt of the enemy,
   lest the adversary misunderstand
and say, 'Our hand has triumphed;
   the LORD has not done all this.' "

²⁸ They are a nation without sense,
   there is no discernment in them.
²⁹ If only they were wise and would
   understand this
   and discern what their end will be!
³⁰ How could one man chase a thousand,
   or two put ten thousand to flight,
unless their Rock had sold them,
   unless the LORD had given them up?
³¹ For their rock is not like our Rock,
   as even our enemies concede.
³² Their vine comes from the vine of Sodom
   and from the fields of Gomorrah.
Their grapes are filled with poison,
   and their clusters with bitterness.
³³ Their wine is the venom of serpents,
   the deadly poison of cobras.

³⁴ "Have I not kept this in reserve
   and sealed it in my vaults?
³⁵ It is mine to avenge; I will repay.
   In due time their foot will slip;
their day of disaster is near
   and their doom rushes upon them."

³⁶ The LORD will vindicate his people
   and relent concerning his servants
when he sees their strength is gone
   and no one is left, slave or free.^a
³⁷ He will say: "Now where are their gods,
   the rock they took refuge in,
³⁸ the gods who ate the fat of their sacrifices
   and drank the wine of their drink
   offerings?
Let them rise up to help you!
   Let them give you shelter!

³⁹ "See now that I myself am he!
   There is no god besides me.
I put to death and I bring to life,
   I have wounded and I will heal,
   and no one can deliver out of
   my hand.
⁴⁰ I lift my hand to heaven and solemnly
   swear:
   As surely as I live forever,
⁴¹ when I sharpen my flashing sword
   and my hand grasps it in judgment,
I will take vengeance on my adversaries
   and repay those who hate me.
⁴² I will make my arrows drunk with blood,
   while my sword devours flesh:
the blood of the slain and the captives,
   the heads of the enemy leaders."

---

^a 36 Or *and they are without a ruler or leader*

⁴³Rejoice, you nations, with his people,[a,b]
  for he will avenge the blood of his
      servants;
  he will take vengeance on his enemies
      and make atonement for his land and
      people.

⁴⁴Moses came with Joshua[c] son of Nun and spoke all the words of this song in the hearing of the people. ⁴⁵When Moses finished reciting all these words to all Israel, ⁴⁶he said to them, "Take to heart all the words I have solemnly declared to you this day, so that you may command your children to obey carefully all the words of this law. ⁴⁷They are not just idle words for you—they are your life. By them you will live long in the land you are crossing the Jordan to possess."

Moses to Die on Mount Nebo

⁴⁸On that same day the LORD told Moses, ⁴⁹"Go up into the Abarim Range to Mount Nebo in Moab, across from Jericho, and view Canaan, the land I am giving the Israelites as their own possession. ⁵⁰There on the mountain that you have climbed you will die and be gathered to your people, just as your brother Aaron died on Mount Hor and was gathered to his people. ⁵¹This is because both of you broke faith with me in the presence of the Israelites at the waters of Meribah Kadesh in the Desert of Zin and because you did not uphold my holiness among the Israelites. ⁵²Therefore, you will see the land only from a distance; you will not enter the land I am giving to the people of Israel."

Moses Blesses the Tribes

33 This is the blessing that Moses the man of God pronounced on the Israelites before his death. ²He said:

"The LORD came from Sinai
    and dawned over them from Seir;
  he shone forth from Mount Paran.
  He came with[d] myriads of holy ones
    from the south, from his mountain
      slopes.[e]
³Surely it is you who love the people;
  all the holy ones are in your hand.

At your feet they all bow down,
    and from you receive instruction,
⁴the law that Moses gave us,
    the possession of the assembly of
      Jacob.
⁵He was king over Jeshurun[f]
    when the leaders of the people
      assembled,
    along with the tribes of Israel.

⁶"Let Reuben live and not die,
    nor[g] his people be few."

⁷And this he said about Judah:

"Hear, LORD, the cry of Judah;
    bring him to his people.
With his own hands he defends his
    cause.
  Oh, be his help against his foes!"

⁸About Levi he said:

"Your Thummim and Urim belong
    to your faithful servant.
You tested him at Massah;
    you contended with him at the waters
      of Meribah.
⁹He said of his father and mother,
    'I have no regard for them.'
He did not recognize his brothers
    or acknowledge his own children,
but he watched over your word
    and guarded your covenant.
¹⁰He teaches your precepts to Jacob
    and your law to Israel.
He offers incense before you
    and whole burnt offerings on your
      altar.
¹¹Bless all his skills, LORD,
    and be pleased with the work of his
      hands.
Strike down those who rise against him,
    his foes till they rise no more."

¹²About Benjamin he said:

"Let the beloved of the LORD rest secure
    in him,
    for he shields him all day long,
    and the one the LORD loves rests
      between his shoulders."

¹³About Joseph he said:

---

[a] 43 Or *Make his people rejoice, you nations* / *and let all the angels worship him,* /   [b] 43 Masoretic Text; Dead Sea Scrolls (see also Septuagint)
people, / *and let all the angels worship him,* /   [c] 44 Hebrew *Hoshea*, a variant of *Joshua*   [d] 2 Or *from*
[e] 2 The meaning of the Hebrew for this phrase is uncertain.   [f] 5 *Jeshurun* means *the upright one,* that is,
Israel; also in verse 26.   [g] 6 Or *but let*

"May the LORD bless his land
  with the precious dew from heaven
    above
  and with the deep waters that lie
    below;
¹⁴with the best the sun brings forth
  and the finest the moon can yield;
¹⁵with the choicest gifts of the ancient
    mountains
  and the fruitfulness of the everlasting
    hills;
¹⁶with the best gifts of the earth and its
    fullness
  and the favor of him who dwelt in the
    burning bush.
Let all these rest on the head of Joseph,
  on the brow of the prince among*ᵃ* his
    brothers.
¹⁷In majesty he is like a firstborn bull;
  his horns are the horns of a wild ox.
With them he will gore the nations,
  even those at the ends of the earth.
Such are the ten thousands of Ephraim;
  such are the thousands of Manasseh."

¹⁸About Zebulun he said:

"Rejoice, Zebulun, in your going out,
  and you, Issachar, in your tents.
¹⁹They will summon peoples to the
    mountain
  and there offer the sacrifices of the
    righteous;
they will feast on the abundance of the
    seas,
  on the treasures hidden in the sand."

²⁰About Gad he said:

"Blessed is he who enlarges Gad's
    domain!
  Gad lives there like a lion,
    tearing at arm or head.
²¹He chose the best land for himself;
  the leader's portion was kept for him.
When the heads of the people assembled,
  he carried out the LORD's righteous
    will,
  and his judgments concerning Israel."

²²About Dan he said:

"Dan is a lion's cub,
  springing out of Bashan."

²³About Naphtali he said:

"Naphtali is abounding with the favor of
    the LORD
  and is full of his blessing;
  he will inherit southward to the lake."

²⁴About Asher he said:

"Most blessed of sons is Asher;
  let him be favored by his brothers,
  and let him bathe his feet in oil.
²⁵The bolts of your gates will be iron and
    bronze,
  and your strength will equal your
    days.

²⁶"There is no one like the God of
    Jeshurun,
  who rides across the heavens to
    help you
  and on the clouds in his majesty.
²⁷The eternal God is your refuge,
  and underneath are the everlasting
    arms.
He will drive out your enemies
    before you,
  saying, 'Destroy them!'
²⁸So Israel will live in safety;
  Jacob will dwell*ᵇ* secure
in a land of grain and new wine,
  where the heavens drop dew.
²⁹Blessed are you, Israel!
  Who is like you,
  a people saved by the LORD?
He is your shield and helper
  and your glorious sword.
Your enemies will cower before you,
  and you will tread on their heights."

The Death of Moses

34 Then Moses climbed Mount Nebo from the plains of Moab to the top of Pisgah, across from Jericho. There the LORD showed him the whole land—from Gilead to Dan, ²all of Naphtali, the territory of Ephraim and Manasseh, all the land of Judah as far as the Mediterranean Sea, ³the Negev and the whole region from the Valley of Jericho, the City of Palms, as far as Zoar. ⁴Then the LORD said to him, "This is the land I promised on oath to Abraham, Isaac and Jacob when I said, 'I will give it to your descendants.' I have let you see it with your eyes, but you will not cross over into it."

⁵And Moses the servant of the LORD died

ᵃ 16 Or *of the one separated from*   *ᵇ 28* Septuagint; Hebrew *Jacob's spring is* there in Moab, as the LORD had said. [6]He buried him[a] in Moab, in the valley opposite Beth Peor, but to this day no one knows where his grave is. [7]Moses was a hundred and twenty years old when he died, yet his eyes were not weak nor his strength gone. [8]The Israelites grieved for Moses in the plains of Moab thirty days, until the time of weeping and mourning was over.

[9]Now Joshua son of Nun was filled with the spirit[b] of wisdom because Moses had laid his hands on him. So the Israelites listened to him and did what the LORD had commanded Moses.

[10]Since then, no prophet has risen in Israel like Moses, whom the LORD knew face to face, [11]who did all those signs and wonders the LORD sent him to do in Egypt — to Pharaoh and to all his officials and to his whole land. [12]For no one has ever shown the mighty power or performed the awesome deeds that Moses did in the sight of all Israel.

---

[a] 6 Or *He was buried*   [b] 9 Or *Spirit*

JOSHUA

WHEN DID THIS HAPPEN?

Probably around 1390 B.C. in Canaan (the promised land), modern-day Israel

WHO IS IN THIS BOOK?

Joshua
Rahab
Achan

VERSES YOU MIGHT RECOGNIZE

JOSHUA 1:7

"Be strong and very courageous. Be careful to obey all the law my servant Moses gave you; do not turn from it to the right or to the left, that you may be successful wherever you go."

JOSHUA 24:15B

"As for me and my household, we will serve the LORD."

WHAT'S IT ABOUT?

At the beginning of this book, the Israelites are about to cross the Jordan River and enter the promised land of Canaan. You may remember that God promised the land to Abraham (in Genesis 15). For many years, Israel had been waiting to claim it. Moses led the people for 40 years, but before he died he put a new leader in charge: Joshua.

As Joshua prepared to lead the people into the land, God reminded the people that he would help them. He told them to be strong and courageous. It wasn't going to be easy, because other people were already living in the land and wouldn't want to leave. But we see God kept his promise to Abraham by helping the Israelites conquer the land. Later he would also keep his promise to send a Savior to free people from the bondage of their sin. Keep your eyes open for the story of Rahab, a woman in Jericho who believed in the one true God and hid two of Israel's spies. Later we learn that Rahab is an ancestor of Jesus (see Matthew 1:5)!

JOSHUA

Joshua Installed as Leader

1 After the death of Moses the servant of the LORD, the LORD said to Joshua son of Nun, Moses' aide: ²"Moses my servant is dead. Now then, you and all these people, get ready to cross the Jordan River into the land I am about to give to them — to the Israelites. ³I will give you every place where you set your foot, as I promised Moses. ⁴Your territory will extend from the desert to Lebanon, and from the great river, the Euphrates — all the Hittite country — to the Mediterranean Sea in the west. ⁵No one will be able to stand against you all the days of your life. As I was with Moses, so I will be with you; I will never leave you nor forsake you. ⁶Be strong and courageous, because you will lead these people to inherit the land I swore to their ancestors to give them.

⁷"Be strong and very courageous. Be careful to obey all the law my servant Moses gave you; do not turn from it to the right or to the left, that you may be successful wherever you go. ⁸Keep this Book of the Law always on your lips; meditate on it day and night, so that you may be careful to do everything written in it. Then you will be prosperous and successful. ⁹Have I not commanded you? Be strong and courageous. Do not be afraid; do not be discouraged, for the LORD your God will be with you wherever you go."

¹⁰So Joshua ordered the officers of the people: ¹¹"Go through the camp and tell the people, 'Get your provisions ready. Three days from now you will cross the Jordan here to go in and take possession of the land the LORD your God is giving you for your own.' "

¹²But to the Reubenites, the Gadites and the half-tribe of Manasseh, Joshua said, ¹³"Remember the command that Moses the servant of the LORD gave you after he said, 'The LORD your God will give you rest by giving you this land.' ¹⁴Your wives, your children and your livestock may stay in the land that Moses gave you east of the Jordan, but all your fighting men, ready for battle, must cross over ahead of your fellow Israelites. You are to help them ¹⁵until the LORD gives them rest, as he has done for you, and until they too have taken possession of the land the LORD your God is giving them. After that, you may go back and occupy your own land, which Moses the servant of the LORD gave you east of the Jordan toward the sunrise."

¹⁶Then they answered Joshua, "Whatever you have commanded us we will do, and wherever you send us we will go. ¹⁷Just as we fully obeyed Moses, so we will obey you. Only may the LORD your God be with you as he was with Moses. ¹⁸Whoever rebels against your word and does not obey it, whatever you may command them, will be put to death. Only be strong and courageous!"

Rahab and the Spies

2 Then Joshua son of Nun secretly sent two spies from Shittim. "Go, look over the land," he said, "especially Jericho." So they went and entered the house of a prostitute named Rahab and stayed there.

²The king of Jericho was told, "Look, some of the Israelites have come here tonight to spy out the land." ³So the king of Jericho sent this message to Rahab: "Bring out the men who came to you and entered your house, because they have come to spy out the whole land."

⁴But the woman had taken the two men and hidden them. She said, "Yes, the men came to me, but I did not know where they had come from. ⁵At dusk, when it was time to close the city gate, they left. I don't know which way they went. Go after them quickly. You may catch up with them." ⁶(But she had taken them up to the roof and hidden them under the stalks of flax she had laid out on the roof.) ⁷So the men set out in pursuit of the spies on the road that leads to the fords of the Jordan, and as soon as the pursuers had gone out, the gate was shut.

⁸Before the spies lay down for the night,

BOLD AND OUTNUMBERED

READ: JOSHUA 1:9

God's stunning plans were coming together. After forty years of wandering in the desert, his people were finally once again poised to enter the land promised to their ancestor Abraham (Genesis 12:6-7). The Lord mapped out property stretching from the southern desert to Lebanon in the north, from the Euphrates in the east to the Mediterranean Sea in the west.

Besides the passing of the old generation of escaped slaves who had refused to enter the land, there was another major shift for the new nation. Moses was gone, and Joshua now stood as the head of the people.

Joshua was one of only two men unafraid to storm the land forty years earlier, convinced the Lord was on their side. Along with his friend Caleb, he stood up to the entire Israelite nation (Numbers 14:1-9). Joshua obviously wasn't a coward, but as the people readied their military invasion, God gave him an extra boost of courage. The Lord had commanded this next step and would go with Joshua wherever he went. Joshua had no reason to feel discouraged or give in to fear.

BUILDING FAITH WISDOM STRENGTH

That's the secret to obtaining God's boldness. When you follow the Lord's command, you don't have to worry what lies ahead. When you do his will, you don't have to feel anxious. Be courageous and press on. You can be sure the Lord is with you.

JOSHUA

"Be strong and very courageous. Be careful to obey all the law my servant Moses gave you; do not turn from it to the right or to the left, that you may be successful wherever you go." JOSHUA 1:7

HIS NAME MEANS: "the LORD saves"

READ HIS STORY: *Exodus 17:8–16, 33:11; Numbers 13:1–14:38; Deuteronomy 31:1–8; Joshua 1, 24*

J oshua's life is a case study on how to become a leader. Joshua rose from being born a slave in Egypt to leading God's people into the promised land. Taking over for Moses wasn't easy, but God chose the right man to bring the Israelites through a turbulent time.

Joshua led through service. He was with Moses from the start of the exodus from Egypt. He witnessed Moses' leadership style and reliance on the Lord. Joshua served Moses until Moses died.

Joshua led by example. When Moses sent twelve spies into the promised land, ten came back saying, "The land is perfect, but there's no way we can defeat the people who live there." Joshua and Caleb stood strong. Joshua believed the Lord would give his people the land, saying "The LORD is with us. Do not be afraid of them" (Numbers 14:9). Whenever he saw the people straying from God, he called them to do the right thing. Just before he died at 110 years old, Joshua said, "Choose for yourselves this day whom you will serve... But as for me and my household, we will serve the LORD" (Joshua 24:15).

Joshua led with courage. He won numerous battles through sound military strategy. He also saw God bring him success—by knocking down the wall around Jericho (Joshua 6:20) and halting the sun in the sky (Joshua 10:12–14)—when he obediently stepped out with courage.

she went up on the roof [9] and said to them, "I know that the LORD has given you this land and that a great fear of you has fallen on us, so that all who live in this country are melting in fear because of you. [10] We have heard how the LORD dried up the water of the Red Sea[a] for you when you came out of Egypt, and what you did to Sihon and Og, the two kings of the Amorites east of the Jordan, whom you completely destroyed.[b] [11] When we heard of it, our hearts melted in fear and everyone's courage failed because of you, for the LORD your God is God in heaven above and on the earth below.

[12] "Now then, please swear to me by the LORD that you will show kindness to my family, because I have shown kindness to you. Give me a sure sign [13] that you will spare the lives of my father and mother, my brothers and sisters, and all who belong to them — and that you will save us from death."

[14] "Our lives for your lives!" the men assured her. "If you don't tell what we are doing, we will treat you kindly and faithfully when the LORD gives us the land."

[15] So she let them down by a rope through the window, for the house she lived in was part of the city wall. [16] She said to them, "Go to the hills so the pursuers will not find you. Hide yourselves there three days until they return, and then go on your way."

[17] Now the men had said to her, "This oath you made us swear will not be binding on us [18] unless, when we enter the land, you have tied this scarlet cord in the window through which you let us down, and unless you have brought your father and mother, your brothers and all your family into your house. [19] If any of them go outside your house into the street, their blood will be on their own heads; we will not be responsible. As for those who are in the house with you, their blood will be on our head if a hand is laid on them. [20] But if you tell what we are doing, we will be released from the oath you made us swear."

[21] "Agreed," she replied. "Let it be as you say."

So she sent them away, and they departed. And she tied the scarlet cord in the window.

[22] When they left, they went into the hills and stayed there three days, until the pursuers had searched all along the road and returned without finding them. [23] Then the two men started back. They went down out of the hills, forded the river and came to Joshua son of Nun and told him everything that had happened to them. [24] They said to Joshua, "The LORD has surely given the whole land into our hands; all the people are melting in fear because of us."

Crossing the Jordan

3 Early in the morning Joshua and all the Israelites set out from Shittim and went to the Jordan, where they camped before crossing over. [2] After three days the officers went throughout the camp, [3] giving orders to the people: "When you see the ark of the covenant of the LORD your God, and the Levitical priests carrying it, you are to move out from your positions and follow it. [4] Then you will know which way to go, since you have never been this way before. But keep a distance of about two thousand cubits[c] between you and the ark; do not go near it."

[5] Joshua told the people, "Consecrate yourselves, for tomorrow the LORD will do amazing things among you."

[6] Joshua said to the priests, "Take up the ark of the covenant and pass on ahead of the people." So they took it up and went ahead of them.

[7] And the LORD said to Joshua, "Today I will begin to exalt you in the eyes of all Israel, so they may know that I am with you as I was with Moses. [8] Tell the priests who carry the ark of the covenant: 'When you reach the edge of the Jordan's waters, go and stand in the river.'"

[9] Joshua said to the Israelites, "Come here and listen to the words of the LORD your God. [10] This is how you will know that the living God is among you and that he will certainly drive out before you the Canaanites, Hittites, Hivites, Perizzites, Girgashites, Amorites and Jebusites. [11] See, the ark of the covenant of the Lord of all the earth will go into the Jordan ahead of you. [12] Now then, choose twelve men from the tribes of Israel, one from each tribe. [13] And as soon as the priests who carry the ark of the LORD — the Lord of all the earth — set foot in the Jordan, its waters flowing downstream will be cut off and stand up in a heap."

---

[a] 10 Or *the Sea of Reeds*   [b] 10 The Hebrew term refers to the irrevocable giving over of things or persons to the LORD, often by totally destroying them.   [c] 4 That is, about 3,000 feet or about 900 meters

WET FEET

READ: JOSHUA 3:8-17

When the Israelites were on the verge of entering the promised land, God commanded the priests to not just look toward the sea but to step into the river. It's one of the most illogical commands in Scripture. I don't know about you, but I don't really like getting my feet wet all that much. I'd much rather have God part the river, and then I'll step into the miracle. We want God to go first. That way we don't have to get our feet wet. But it's often our unwillingness to take a step of faith and get a little uncomfortable that keeps us from experiencing a miracle. We'll spend our entire lives on the eastern shore of the Jordan waiting for God to part the river while God waits for us to get our feet wet. After you have prayed hard, you need to swallow hard and take a flying leap of faith.

But what if the priests hadn't stepped into the river? What if they had sat around waiting for God to do his parting thing? Sometimes we're so close to the dream, so close to the promise, so close to the miracle, but unless we risk stepping forward, we get stuck. We end up living our entire lives on the eastern banks of the Jordan River instead of crossing into the promised land.

Moral of the story: if you make a move, you'll see God move. And he can move heaven and earth.

BUILDING
FAITH
WISDOM
STRENGTH

Taken from *The Circle Maker Student Edition* by Mark Batterson with Parker Batterson, copyright © 2012 by Mark Batterson, published by Zondervan.

[14] So when the people broke camp to cross the Jordan, the priests carrying the ark of the covenant went ahead of them. [15] Now the Jordan is at flood stage all during harvest. Yet as soon as the priests who carried the ark reached the Jordan and their feet touched the water's edge, [16] the water from upstream stopped flowing. It piled up in a heap a great distance away, at a town called Adam in the vicinity of Zarethan, while the water flowing down to the Sea of the Arabah (that is, the Dead Sea) was completely cut off. So the people crossed over opposite Jericho. [17] The priests who carried the ark of the covenant of the LORD stopped in the middle of the Jordan and stood on dry ground, while all Israel passed by until the whole nation had completed the crossing on dry ground.

4 When the whole nation had finished crossing the Jordan, the LORD said to Joshua, [2] "Choose twelve men from among the people, one from each tribe, [3] and tell them to take up twelve stones from the middle of the Jordan, from right where the priests are standing, and carry them over with you and put them down at the place where you stay tonight."

[4] So Joshua called together the twelve men he had appointed from the Israelites, one from each tribe, [5] and said to them, "Go over before the ark of the LORD your God into the middle of the Jordan. Each of you is to take up a stone on his shoulder, according to the number of the tribes of the Israelites, [6] to serve as a sign among you. In the future, when your children ask you, 'What do these stones mean?' [7] tell them that the flow of the Jordan was cut off before the ark of the covenant of the LORD. When it crossed the Jordan, the waters of the Jordan were cut off. These stones are to be a memorial to the people of Israel forever."

[8] So the Israelites did as Joshua commanded them. They took twelve stones from the middle of the Jordan, according to the number of the tribes of the Israelites, as the LORD had told Joshua; and they carried them over with them to their camp, where they put them down. [9] Joshua set up the twelve stones that had been[a] in the middle of the Jordan at the spot where the priests who carried the ark of the covenant had stood. And they are there to this day.

[10] Now the priests who carried the ark remained standing in the middle of the Jordan until everything the LORD had commanded Joshua was done by the people, just as Moses had directed Joshua. The people hurried over, [11] and as soon as all of them had crossed, the ark of the LORD and the priests came to the other side while the people watched. [12] The men of Reuben, Gad and the half-tribe of Manasseh crossed over, ready for battle, in front of the Israelites, as Moses had directed them. [13] About forty thousand armed for battle crossed over before the LORD to the plains of Jericho for war.

[14] That day the LORD exalted Joshua in the sight of all Israel; and they stood in awe of him all the days of his life, just as they had stood in awe of Moses.

[15] Then the LORD said to Joshua, [16] "Command the priests carrying the ark of the covenant law to come up out of the Jordan."

[17] So Joshua commanded the priests, "Come up out of the Jordan."

[18] And the priests came up out of the river carrying the ark of the covenant of the LORD. No sooner had they set their feet on the dry ground than the waters of the Jordan returned to their place and ran at flood stage as before.

[19] On the tenth day of the first month the people went up from the Jordan and camped at Gilgal on the eastern border of Jericho. [20] And Joshua set up at Gilgal the twelve stones they had taken out of the Jordan. [21] He said to the Israelites, "In the future when your descendants ask their parents, 'What do these stones mean?' [22] tell them, 'Israel crossed the Jordan on dry ground.' [23] For the LORD your God dried up the Jordan before you until you had crossed over. The LORD your God did to the Jordan what he had done to the Red Sea[b] when he dried it up before us until we had crossed over. [24] He did this so that all the peoples of the earth might know that the hand of the LORD is powerful and so that you might always fear the LORD your God."

5 Now when all the Amorite kings west of the Jordan and all the Canaanite kings along the coast heard how the LORD had dried up the Jordan before the Israelites until they[c] had crossed over, their hearts melted

---

[a] 9 Or Joshua also set up twelve stones   [b] 23 Or the Sea of Reeds   [c] 1 Another textual tradition we

in fear and they no longer had the courage to face the Israelites.

Circumcision and Passover at Gilgal

[2] At that time the LORD said to Joshua, "Make flint knives and circumcise the Israelites again." [3] So Joshua made flint knives and circumcised the Israelites at Gibeath Haaraloth.[a]

[4] Now this is why he did so: All those who came out of Egypt — all the men of military age — died in the wilderness on the way after leaving Egypt. [5] All the people that came out had been circumcised, but all the people born in the wilderness during the journey from Egypt had not. [6] The Israelites had moved about in the wilderness forty years until all the men who were of military age when they left Egypt had died, since they had not obeyed the LORD. For the LORD had sworn to them that they would not see the land he had solemnly promised their ancestors to give us, a land flowing with milk and honey. [7] So he raised up their sons in their place, and these were the ones Joshua circumcised. They were still uncircumcised because they had not been circumcised on the way. [8] And after the whole nation had been circumcised, they remained where they were in camp until they were healed.

[9] Then the LORD said to Joshua, "Today I have rolled away the reproach of Egypt from you." So the place has been called Gilgal[b] to this day.

[10] On the evening of the fourteenth day of the month, while camped at Gilgal on the plains of Jericho, the Israelites celebrated the Passover. [11] The day after the Passover, that very day, they ate some of the produce of the land: unleavened bread and roasted grain. [12] The manna stopped the day after[c] they ate this food from the land; there was no longer any manna for the Israelites, but that year they ate the produce of Canaan.

The Fall of Jericho

[13] Now when Joshua was near Jericho, he looked up and saw a man standing in front of him with a drawn sword in his hand. Joshua went up to him and asked, "Are you for us or for our enemies?"

[14] "Neither," he replied, "but as command-er of the army of the LORD I have now come." Then Joshua fell facedown to the ground in reverence, and asked him, "What message does my Lord[d] have for his servant?"

[15] The commander of the LORD's army replied, "Take off your sandals, for the place where you are standing is holy." And Joshua did so.

6 Now the gates of Jericho were securely barred because of the Israelites. No one went out and no one came in.

[2] Then the LORD said to Joshua, "See, I have delivered Jericho into your hands, along with its king and its fighting men. [3] March around the city once with all the armed men. Do this for six days. [4] Have seven priests carry trumpets of rams' horns in front of the ark. On the seventh day, march around the city seven times, with the priests blowing the trumpets. [5] When you hear them sound a long blast on the trumpets, have the whole army give a loud shout; then the wall of the city will collapse and the army will go up, everyone straight in."

[6] So Joshua son of Nun called the priests and said to them, "Take up the ark of the covenant of the LORD and have seven priests carry trumpets in front of it." [7] And he ordered the army, "Advance! March around the city, with an armed guard going ahead of the ark of the LORD."

[8] When Joshua had spoken to the people, the seven priests carrying the seven trumpets before the LORD went forward, blowing their trumpets, and the ark of the LORD's covenant followed them. [9] The armed guard marched ahead of the priests who blew the trumpets, and the rear guard followed the ark. All this time the trumpets were sounding. [10] But Joshua had commanded the army, "Do not give a war cry, do not raise your voices, do not say a word until the day I tell you to shout. Then shout!" [11] So he had the ark of the LORD carried around the city, circling it once. Then the army returned to camp and spent the night there.

[12] Joshua got up early the next morning and the priests took up the ark of the LORD. [13] The seven priests carrying the seven trumpets went forward, marching before the ark of the LORD and blowing the trumpets. The armed men went ahead of them and the rear

---

[a] 3 Gibeath Haaraloth means *the hill of foreskins.*
[c] 12 Or *the day*   [d] 14 Or *lord*
[b] 9 Gilgal sounds like the Hebrew for *roll.*

MARCHING MADNESS

READ: JOSHUA 6

The first glimpse of Jericho was both awe-inspiring and frightening. While wandering in the wilderness for forty years, the Israelites had never seen anything like the skyline of Jericho. The closer they got, the smaller they felt. They finally understood why the generation before them felt so miniscule and failed to enter the promised land because of fear.

A six-foot-wide lower wall and fifty-foot-high upper wall encircled the ancient metropolis. The mud-brick walls were so thick and tall that the twelve-acre city appeared to be an impenetrable fortress. It seemed like God had promised something impossible, and his battle plan made zero sense.

BUILDING FAITH WISDOM STRENGTH

Every soldier in the army had to have wondered why. The first time around, the soldiers must have felt kind of dumb. But with each circle, their stride grew a little longer. With each circle, a holy confidence was building pressure inside their souls. By the seventh day, their faith was ready to pop. They got up before dawn and started circling at six o'clock in the morning. Let's pull out some algebra here: at three miles per hour, each mile-and-a-half march around the city took a half hour. (See? Algebra does apply to real life.) By nine o'clock, they began their final lap.

After seven days of circling Jericho, God delivered on a 400-year-old promise. He proved, once again, that his promises don't have expiration dates. And Jericho stands, and falls, as evidence to this simple truth: If you keep circling the promise, God will ultimately deliver on it.

Taken from *The Circle Maker Student Edition* by Mark Batterson with Parker Batterson, copyright © 2012 by Mark Batterson, published by Zondervan.

guard followed the ark of the LORD, while the trumpets kept sounding. ¹⁴So on the second day they marched around the city once and returned to the camp. They did this for six days.

¹⁵On the seventh day, they got up at daybreak and marched around the city seven times in the same manner, except that on that day they circled the city seven times. ¹⁶The seventh time around, when the priests sounded the trumpet blast, Joshua commanded the army, "Shout! For the LORD has given you the city! ¹⁷The city and all that is in it are to be devoted*ᵃ* to the LORD. Only Rahab the prostitute and all who are with her in her house shall be spared, because she hid the spies we sent. ¹⁸But keep away from the devoted things, so that you will not bring about your own destruction by taking any of them. Otherwise you will make the camp of Israel liable to destruction and bring trouble on it. ¹⁹All the silver and gold and the articles of bronze and iron are sacred to the LORD and must go into his treasury."

²⁰When the trumpets sounded, the army shouted, and at the sound of the trumpet, when the men gave a loud shout, the wall collapsed; so everyone charged straight in, and they took the city. ²¹They devoted the city to the LORD and destroyed with the sword every living thing in it—men and women, young and old, cattle, sheep and donkeys.

²²Joshua said to the two men who had spied out the land, "Go into the prostitute's house and bring her out and all who belong to her, in accordance with your oath to her." ²³So the young men who had done the spying went in and brought out Rahab, her father and mother, her brothers and sisters and all who belonged to her. They brought out her entire family and put them in a place outside the camp of Israel.

²⁴Then they burned the whole city and everything in it, but they put the silver and gold and the articles of bronze and iron into the treasury of the LORD's house. ²⁵But Joshua spared Rahab the prostitute, with her family and all who belonged to her, because she hid the men Joshua had sent as spies to Jericho—and she lives among the Israelites to this day.

²⁶At that time Joshua pronounced this solemn oath: "Cursed before the LORD is the one who undertakes to rebuild this city, Jericho:

"At the cost of his firstborn son
    he will lay its foundations;
at the cost of his youngest
    he will set up its gates."

²⁷So the LORD was with Joshua, and his fame spread throughout the land.

Achan's Sin

7 But the Israelites were unfaithful in regard to the devoted things*ᵇ*; Achan son of Karmi, the son of Zimri,*ᶜ* the son of Zerah, of the tribe of Judah, took some of them. So the LORD's anger burned against Israel.

²Now Joshua sent men from Jericho to Ai, which is near Beth Aven to the east of Bethel, and told them, "Go up and spy out the region." So the men went up and spied out Ai. ³When they returned to Joshua, they said, "Not all the army will have to go up against Ai. Send two or three thousand men to take it and do not weary the whole army, for only a few people live there." ⁴So about three thousand went up; but they were routed by the men of Ai, ⁵who killed about thirty-six of them. They chased the Israelites from the city gate as far as the stone quarries and struck them down on the slopes. At this the hearts of the people melted in fear and became like water.

⁶Then Joshua tore his clothes and fell facedown to the ground before the ark of the LORD, remaining there till evening. The elders of Israel did the same, and sprinkled dust on their heads. ⁷And Joshua said, "Alas, Sovereign LORD, why did you ever bring this people across the Jordan to deliver us into the hands of the Amorites to destroy us? If only we had been content to stay on the other side of the Jordan! ⁸Pardon your servant, Lord. What can I say, now that Israel has been routed by its enemies? ⁹The Canaanites and the other people of the country will hear about this and they will surround us

---

ᵃ 17 The Hebrew term refers to the irrevocable giving over of things or persons to the LORD, often by totally destroying them; also in verses 18 and 21.   *ᵇ 1* The Hebrew term refers to the irrevocable giving over of things or persons to the LORD, often by totally destroying them; also in verses 11, 12, 13 and 15.
ᶜ 1 See Septuagint and 1 Chron. 2:6; Hebrew *Zabdi*; also in verses 17 and 18.

and wipe out our name from the earth. What then will you do for your own great name?"

¹⁰The LORD said to Joshua, "Stand up! What are you doing down on your face? ¹¹Israel has sinned; they have violated my covenant, which I commanded them to keep. They have taken some of the devoted things; they have stolen, they have lied, they have put them with their own possessions. ¹²That is why the Israelites cannot stand against their enemies; they turn their backs and run because they have been made liable to destruction. I will not be with you anymore unless you destroy whatever among you is devoted to destruction.

¹³"Go, consecrate the people. Tell them, 'Consecrate yourselves in preparation for tomorrow; for this is what the LORD, the God of Israel, says: There are devoted things among you, Israel. You cannot stand against your enemies until you remove them.

¹⁴"'In the morning, present yourselves tribe by tribe. The tribe the LORD chooses shall come forward clan by clan; the clan the LORD chooses shall come forward family by family; and the family the LORD chooses shall come forward man by man. ¹⁵Whoever is caught with the devoted things shall be destroyed by fire, along with all that belongs to him. He has violated the covenant of the LORD and has done an outrageous thing in Israel!'"

¹⁶Early the next morning Joshua had Israel come forward by tribes, and Judah was chosen. ¹⁷The clans of Judah came forward, and the Zerahites were chosen. He had the clan of the Zerahites come forward by families, and Zimri was chosen. ¹⁸Joshua had his family come forward man by man, and Achan son of Karmi, the son of Zimri, the son of Zerah, of the tribe of Judah, was chosen.

¹⁹Then Joshua said to Achan, "My son, give glory to the LORD, the God of Israel, and honor him. Tell me what you have done; do not hide it from me."

²⁰Achan replied, "It is true! I have sinned against the LORD, the God of Israel. This is what I have done: ²¹When I saw in the plunder a beautiful robe from Babylonia,ᵃ two hundred shekelsᵇ of silver and a bar of gold weighing fifty shekels,ᶜ I coveted them and

took them. They are hidden in the ground inside my tent, with the silver underneath."

²²So Joshua sent messengers, and they ran to the tent, and there it was, hidden in his tent, with the silver underneath. ²³They took the things from the tent, brought them to Joshua and all the Israelites and spread them out before the LORD.

²⁴Then Joshua, together with all Israel, took Achan son of Zerah, the silver, the robe, the gold bar, his sons and daughters, his cattle, donkeys and sheep, his tent and all that he had, to the Valley of Achor. ²⁵Joshua said, "Why have you brought this trouble on us? The LORD will bring trouble on you today."

Then all Israel stoned him, and after they had stoned the rest, they burned them. ²⁶Over Achan they heaped up a large pile of rocks, which remains to this day. Then the LORD turned from his fierce anger. Therefore that place has been called the Valley of Achorᵈ ever since.

Ai Destroyed

8 Then the LORD said to Joshua, "Do not be afraid; do not be discouraged. Take the whole army with you, and go up and attack Ai. For I have delivered into your hands the king of Ai, his people, his city and his land. ²You shall do to Ai and its king as you did to Jericho and its king, except that you may carry off their plunder and livestock for yourselves. Set an ambush behind the city."

³So Joshua and the whole army moved out to attack Ai. He chose thirty thousand of his best fighting men and sent them out at night ⁴with these orders: "Listen carefully. You are to set an ambush behind the city. Don't go very far from it. All of you be on the alert. ⁵I and all those with me will advance on the city, and when the men come out against us, as they did before, we will flee from them. ⁶They will pursue us until we have lured them away from the city, for they will say, 'They are running away from us as they did before.' So when we flee from them, ⁷you are to rise up from ambush and take the city. The LORD your God will give it into your hand. ⁸When you have taken the city, set it on fire. Do what the LORD has commanded. See to it; you have my orders."

ᵃ 21 Hebrew *Shinar*   ᵇ 21 That is, about 5 pounds or about 2.3 kilograms   ᶜ 21 That is, about 1 1/4 pounds or about 575 grams   ᵈ 26 *Achor* means *trouble*.

⁹Then Joshua sent them off, and they went to the place of ambush and lay in wait between Bethel and Ai, to the west of Ai—but Joshua spent that night with the people.

¹⁰Early the next morning Joshua mustered his army, and he and the leaders of Israel marched before them to Ai. ¹¹The entire force that was with him marched up and approached the city and arrived in front of it. They set up camp north of Ai, with the valley between them and the city. ¹²Joshua had taken about five thousand men and set them in ambush between Bethel and Ai, to the west of the city. ¹³So the soldiers took up their positions—with the main camp to the north of the city and the ambush to the west of it. That night Joshua went into the valley.

¹⁴When the king of Ai saw this, he and all the men of the city hurried out early in the morning to meet Israel in battle at a certain place overlooking the Arabah. But he did not know that an ambush had been set against him behind the city. ¹⁵Joshua and all Israel let themselves be driven back before them, and they fled toward the wilderness. ¹⁶All the men of Ai were called to pursue them, and they pursued Joshua and were lured away from the city. ¹⁷Not a man remained in Ai or Bethel who did not go after Israel. They left the city open and went in pursuit of Israel.

¹⁸Then the LORD said to Joshua, "Hold out toward Ai the javelin that is in your hand, for into your hand I will deliver the city." So Joshua held out toward the city the javelin that was in his hand. ¹⁹As soon as he did this, the men in the ambush rose quickly from their position and rushed forward. They entered the city and captured it and quickly set it on fire.

²⁰The men of Ai looked back and saw the smoke of the city rising up into the sky, but they had no chance to escape in any direction; the Israelites who had been fleeing toward the wilderness had turned back against their pursuers. ²¹For when Joshua and all Israel saw that the ambush had taken the city and that smoke was going up from it, they turned around and attacked the men of Ai. ²²Those in the ambush also came out of the city against them, so that they were caught in the middle, with Israelites on both sides. Israel cut them down, leaving them neither survivors nor fugitives. ²³But they took the king of Ai alive and brought him to Joshua.

²⁴When Israel had finished killing all the men of Ai in the fields and in the wilderness where they had chased them, and when every one of them had been put to the sword, all the Israelites returned to Ai and killed those who were in it. ²⁵Twelve thousand men and women fell that day—all the people of Ai. ²⁶For Joshua did not draw back the hand that held out his javelin until he had destroyed[a] all who lived in Ai. ²⁷But Israel did carry off for themselves the livestock and plunder of this city, as the LORD had instructed Joshua.

²⁸So Joshua burned Ai[b] and made it a permanent heap of ruins, a desolate place to this day. ²⁹He impaled the body of the king of Ai on a pole and left it there until evening. At sunset, Joshua ordered them to take the body from the pole and throw it down at the entrance of the city gate. And they raised a large pile of rocks over it, which remains to this day.

The Covenant Renewed at Mount Ebal

³⁰Then Joshua built on Mount Ebal an altar to the LORD, the God of Israel, ³¹as Moses the servant of the LORD had commanded the Israelites. He built it according to what is written in the Book of the Law of Moses—an altar of uncut stones, on which no iron tool had been used. On it they offered to the LORD burnt offerings and sacrificed fellowship offerings. ³²There, in the presence of the Israelites, Joshua wrote on stones a copy of the law of Moses. ³³All the Israelites, with their elders, officials and judges, were standing on both sides of the ark of the covenant of the LORD, facing the Levitical priests who carried it. Both the foreigners living among them and the native-born were there. Half of the people stood in front of Mount Gerizim and half of them in front of Mount Ebal, as Moses the servant of the LORD had formerly commanded when he gave instructions to bless the people of Israel.

³⁴Afterward, Joshua read all the words of the law—the blessings and the curses—just as it is written in the Book of the Law. ³⁵There was not a word of all that Moses had commanded that Joshua did not read

---

[a] 26 The Hebrew term refers to the irrevocable giving over of things or persons to the LORD, often by totally destroying them.   [b] 28 Ai means the ruin.

to the whole assembly of Israel, including the women and children, and the foreigners who lived among them.

The Gibeonite Deception

9 Now when all the kings west of the Jordan heard about these things — the kings in the hill country, in the western foothills, and along the entire coast of the Mediterranean Sea as far as Lebanon (the kings of the Hittites, Amorites, Canaanites, Perizzites, Hivites and Jebusites) — ²they came together to wage war against Joshua and Israel.

³However, when the people of Gibeon heard what Joshua had done to Jericho and Ai, ⁴they resorted to a ruse: They went as a delegation whose donkeys were loaded[a] with worn-out sacks and old wineskins, cracked and mended. ⁵They put worn and patched sandals on their feet and wore old clothes. All the bread of their food supply was dry and moldy. ⁶Then they went to Joshua in the camp at Gilgal and said to him and the Israelites, "We have come from a distant country; make a treaty with us."

⁷The Israelites said to the Hivites, "But perhaps you live near us, so how can we make a treaty with you?"

⁸"We are your servants," they said to Joshua.

But Joshua asked, "Who are you and where do you come from?"

⁹They answered: "Your servants have come from a very distant country because of the fame of the LORD your God. For we have heard reports of him: all that he did in Egypt, ¹⁰and all that he did to the two kings of the Amorites east of the Jordan — Sihon king of Heshbon, and Og king of Bashan, who reigned in Ashtaroth. ¹¹And our elders and all those living in our country said to us, 'Take provisions for your journey; go and meet them and say to them, "We are your servants; make a treaty with us."' ¹²This bread of ours was warm when we packed it at home on the day we left to come to you. But now see how dry and moldy it is. ¹³And these wineskins that we filled were new, but see how cracked they are. And our clothes and sandals are worn out by the very long journey."

¹⁴The Israelites sampled their provisions but did not inquire of the LORD. ¹⁵Then Joshua made a treaty of peace with them to let them live, and the leaders of the assembly ratified it by oath.

¹⁶Three days after they made the treaty with the Gibeonites, the Israelites heard that they were neighbors, living near them. ¹⁷So the Israelites set out and on the third day came to their cities: Gibeon, Kephirah, Beeroth and Kiriath Jearim. ¹⁸But the Israelites did not attack them, because the leaders of the assembly had sworn an oath to them by the LORD, the God of Israel.

The whole assembly grumbled against the leaders, ¹⁹but all the leaders answered, "We have given them our oath by the LORD, the God of Israel, and we cannot touch them now. ²⁰This is what we will do to them: We will let them live, so that God's wrath will not fall on us for breaking the oath we swore to them." ²¹They continued, "Let them live, but let them be woodcutters and water carriers in the service of the whole assembly." So the leaders' promise to them was kept.

²²Then Joshua summoned the Gibeonites and said, "Why did you deceive us by saying, 'We live a long way from you,' while actually you live near us? ²³You are now under a curse: You will never be released from service as woodcutters and water carriers for the house of my God."

²⁴They answered Joshua, "Your servants were clearly told how the LORD your God had commanded his servant Moses to give you the whole land and to wipe out all its inhabitants from before you. So we feared for our lives because of you, and that is why we did this. ²⁵We are now in your hands. Do to us whatever seems good and right to you."

²⁶So Joshua saved them from the Israelites, and they did not kill them. ²⁷That day he made the Gibeonites woodcutters and water carriers for the assembly, to provide for the needs of the altar of the LORD at the place the LORD would choose. And that is what they are to this day.

The Sun Stands Still

10 Now Adoni-Zedek king of Jerusalem heard that Joshua had taken Ai and

---

[a] 4 Most Hebrew manuscripts; some Hebrew manuscripts, Vulgate and Syriac (see also Septuagint) *They prepared provisions and loaded their donkeys*

totally destroyed[a] it, doing to Ai and its king as he had done to Jericho and its king, and that the people of Gibeon had made a treaty of peace with Israel and had become their allies. [2]He and his people were very much alarmed at this, because Gibeon was an important city, like one of the royal cities; it was larger than Ai, and all its men were good fighters. [3]So Adoni-Zedek king of Jerusalem appealed to Hoham king of Hebron, Piram king of Jarmuth, Japhia king of Lachish and Debir king of Eglon. [4]"Come up and help me attack Gibeon," he said, "because it has made peace with Joshua and the Israelites."

[5]Then the five kings of the Amorites — the kings of Jerusalem, Hebron, Jarmuth, Lachish and Eglon — joined forces. They moved up with all their troops and took up positions against Gibeon and attacked it.

[6]The Gibeonites then sent word to Joshua in the camp at Gilgal: "Do not abandon your servants. Come up to us quickly and save us! Help us, because all the Amorite kings from the hill country have joined forces against us."

[7]So Joshua marched up from Gilgal with his entire army, including all the best fighting men. [8]The LORD said to Joshua, "Do not be afraid of them; I have given them into your hand. Not one of them will be able to withstand you."

[9]After an all-night march from Gilgal, Joshua took them by surprise. [10]The LORD threw them into confusion before Israel, so Joshua and the Israelites defeated them completely at Gibeon. Israel pursued them along the road going up to Beth Horon and cut them down all the way to Azekah and Makkedah. [11]As they fled before Israel on the road down from Beth Horon to Azekah, the LORD hurled large hailstones down on them, and more of them died from the hail than were killed by the swords of the Israelites.

[12]On the day the LORD gave the Amorites over to Israel, Joshua said to the LORD in the presence of Israel:

"Sun, stand still over Gibeon,
    and you, moon, over the Valley of
        Aijalon."
[13]So the sun stood still,
    and the moon stopped,

till the nation avenged itself on[b] its
    enemies,

as it is written in the Book of Jashar.

The sun stopped in the middle of the sky and delayed going down about a full day. [14]There has never been a day like it before or since, a day when the LORD listened to a human being. Surely the LORD was fighting for Israel!

[15]Then Joshua returned with all Israel to the camp at Gilgal.

Five Amorite Kings Killed

[16]Now the five kings had fled and hidden in the cave at Makkedah. [17]When Joshua was told that the five kings had been found hiding in the cave at Makkedah, [18]he said, "Roll large rocks up to the mouth of the cave, and post some men there to guard it. [19]But don't stop; pursue your enemies! Attack them from the rear and don't let them reach their cities, for the LORD your God has given them into your hand."

[20]So Joshua and the Israelites defeated them completely, but a few survivors managed to reach their fortified cities. [21]The whole army then returned safely to Joshua in the camp at Makkedah, and no one uttered a word against the Israelites.

[22]Joshua said, "Open the mouth of the cave and bring those five kings out to me." [23]So they brought the five kings out of the cave — the kings of Jerusalem, Hebron, Jarmuth, Lachish and Eglon. [24]When they had brought these kings to Joshua, he summoned all the men of Israel and said to the army commanders who had come with him, "Come here and put your feet on the necks of these kings." So they came forward and placed their feet on their necks.

[25]Joshua said to them, "Do not be afraid; do not be discouraged. Be strong and courageous. This is what the LORD will do to all the enemies you are going to fight." [26]Then Joshua put the kings to death and exposed their bodies on five poles, and they were left hanging on the poles until evening.

[27]At sunset Joshua gave the order and they took them down from the poles and threw them into the cave where they had been hiding. At the mouth of the cave they placed large rocks, which are there to this day.

[a] 1 The Hebrew term refers to the irrevocable giving over of things or persons to the LORD, often by totally destroying them; also in verses 28, 35, 37, 39 and 40.   [b] 13 Or *nation triumphed over*

Southern Cities Conquered

²⁸That day Joshua took Makkedah. He put the city and its king to the sword and totally destroyed everyone in it. He left no survivors. And he did to the king of Makkedah as he had done to the king of Jericho.

²⁹Then Joshua and all Israel with him moved on from Makkedah to Libnah and attacked it. ³⁰The LORD also gave that city and its king into Israel's hand. The city and everyone in it Joshua put to the sword. He left no survivors there. And he did to its king as he had done to the king of Jericho.

³¹Then Joshua and all Israel with him moved on from Libnah to Lachish; he took up positions against it and attacked it. ³²The LORD gave Lachish into Israel's hands, and Joshua took it on the second day. The city and everyone in it he put to the sword, just as he had done to Libnah. ³³Meanwhile, Horam king of Gezer had come up to help Lachish, but Joshua defeated him and his army — until no survivors were left.

³⁴Then Joshua and all Israel with him moved on from Lachish to Eglon; they took up positions against it and attacked it. ³⁵They captured it that same day and put it to the sword and totally destroyed everyone in it, just as they had done to Lachish.

³⁶Then Joshua and all Israel with him went up from Eglon to Hebron and attacked it. ³⁷They took the city and put it to the sword, together with its king, its villages and everyone in it. They left no survivors. Just as at Eglon, they totally destroyed it and everyone in it.

³⁸Then Joshua and all Israel with him turned around and attacked Debir. ³⁹They took the city, its king and its villages, and put them to the sword. Everyone in it they totally destroyed. They left no survivors. They did to Debir and its king as they had done to Libnah and its king and to Hebron.

⁴⁰So Joshua subdued the whole region, including the hill country, the Negev, the western foothills and the mountain slopes, together with all their kings. He left no survivors. He totally destroyed all who breathed, just as the LORD, the God of Israel, had commanded. ⁴¹Joshua subdued them from Kadesh Barnea to Gaza and from the whole region of Goshen to Gibeon. ⁴²All these kings and their lands Joshua conquered in one campaign, because the LORD, the God of Israel, fought for Israel.

⁴³Then Joshua returned with all Israel to the camp at Gilgal.

Northern Kings Defeated

11 When Jabin king of Hazor heard of this, he sent word to Jobab king of Madon, to the kings of Shimron and Akshaph, ²and to the northern kings who were in the mountains, in the Arabah south of Kinnereth, in the western foothills and in Naphoth Dor on the west; ³to the Canaanites in the east and west; to the Amorites, Hittites, Perizzites and Jebusites in the hill country; and to the Hivites below Hermon in the region of Mizpah. ⁴They came out with all their troops and a large number of horses and chariots — a huge army, as numerous as the sand on the seashore. ⁵All these kings joined forces and made camp together at the Waters of Merom to fight against Israel.

⁶The LORD said to Joshua, "Do not be afraid of them, because by this time tomorrow I will hand all of them, slain, over to Israel. You are to hamstring their horses and burn their chariots."

⁷So Joshua and his whole army came against them suddenly at the Waters of Merom and attacked them, ⁸and the LORD gave them into the hand of Israel. They defeated them and pursued them all the way to Greater Sidon, to Misrephoth Maim, and to the Valley of Mizpah on the east, until no survivors were left. ⁹Joshua did to them as the LORD had directed: He hamstrung their horses and burned their chariots.

¹⁰At that time Joshua turned back and captured Hazor and put its king to the sword. (Hazor had been the head of all these kingdoms.) ¹¹Everyone in it they put to the sword. They totally destroyed^a them, not sparing anyone that breathed, and he burned Hazor itself.

¹²Joshua took all these royal cities and their kings and put them to the sword. He totally destroyed them, as Moses the servant of the LORD had commanded. ¹³Yet Israel did not burn any of the cities built on their mounds — except Hazor, which Joshua burned. ¹⁴The Israelites carried off for

---

^a 11 The Hebrew term refers to the irrevocable giving over of things or persons to the LORD, often by totally destroying them; also in verses 12, 20 and 21.

themselves all the plunder and livestock of these cities, but all the people they put to the sword until they completely destroyed them, not sparing anyone that breathed. [15] As the LORD commanded his servant Moses, so Moses commanded Joshua, and Joshua did it; he left nothing undone of all that the LORD commanded Moses.

[16] So Joshua took this entire land: the hill country, all the Negev, the whole region of Goshen, the western foothills, the Arabah and the mountains of Israel with their foothills, [17] from Mount Halak, which rises toward Seir, to Baal Gad in the Valley of Lebanon below Mount Hermon. He captured all their kings and put them to death. [18] Joshua waged war against all these kings for a long time. [19] Except for the Hivites living in Gibeon, not one city made a treaty of peace with the Israelites, who took them all in battle. [20] For it was the LORD himself who hardened their hearts to wage war against Israel, so that he might destroy them totally, exterminating them without mercy, as the LORD had commanded Moses.

[21] At that time Joshua went and destroyed the Anakites from the hill country: from Hebron, Debir and Anab, from all the hill country of Judah, and from all the hill country of Israel. Joshua totally destroyed them and their towns. [22] No Anakites were left in Israelite territory; only in Gaza, Gath and Ashdod did any survive.

[23] So Joshua took the entire land, just as the LORD had directed Moses, and he gave it as an inheritance to Israel according to their tribal divisions. Then the land had rest from war.

List of Defeated Kings

12 These are the kings of the land whom the Israelites had defeated and whose territory they took over east of the Jordan, from the Arnon Gorge to Mount Hermon, including all the eastern side of the Arabah:

[2] Sihon king of the Amorites, who reigned in Heshbon.

He ruled from Aroer on the rim of the Arnon Gorge — from the middle of the gorge — to the Jabbok River, which is the border of the Ammonites. This included half of Gilead. [3] He also ruled over the eastern Arabah from the Sea of Galilee[a] to the Sea of the Arabah (that is, the Dead Sea), to Beth Jeshimoth, and then southward below the slopes of Pisgah.

[4] And the territory of Og king of Bashan, one of the last of the Rephaites, who reigned in Ashtaroth and Edrei.

[5] He ruled over Mount Hermon, Salekah, all of Bashan to the border of the people of Geshur and Maakah, and half of Gilead to the border of Sihon king of Heshbon.

[6] Moses, the servant of the LORD, and the Israelites conquered them. And Moses the servant of the LORD gave their land to the Reubenites, the Gadites and the half-tribe of Manasseh to be their possession.

[7] Here is a list of the kings of the land that Joshua and the Israelites conquered on the west side of the Jordan, from Baal Gad in the Valley of Lebanon to Mount Halak, which rises toward Seir. Joshua gave their lands as an inheritance to the tribes of Israel according to their tribal divisions. [8] The lands included the hill country, the western foothills, the Arabah, the mountain slopes, the wilderness and the Negev. These were the lands of the Hittites, Amorites, Canaanites, Perizzites, Hivites and Jebusites. These were the kings:

[9] the king of Jericho	one
the king of Ai (near Bethel)	one
[10] the king of Jerusalem	one
the king of Hebron	one
[11] the king of Jarmuth	one
the king of Lachish	one
[12] the king of Eglon	one
the king of Gezer	one
[13] the king of Debir	one
the king of Geder	one
[14] the king of Hormah	one
the king of Arad	one
[15] the king of Libnah	one
the king of Adullam	one
[16] the king of Makkedah	one
the king of Bethel	one
[17] the king of Tappuah	one
the king of Hepher	one
[18] the king of Aphek	one
the king of Lasharon	one

a 3 Hebrew *Kinnereth*

[19] the king of Madon	one
the king of Hazor	one
[20] the king of Shimron Meron	one
the king of Akshaph	one
[21] the king of Taanach	one
the king of Megiddo	one
[22] the king of Kedesh	one
the king of Jokneam in Carmel	one
[23] the king of Dor (in Naphoth Dor)	one
the king of Goyim in Gilgal	one
[24] the king of Tirzah	one
thirty-one kings in all.	

Land Still to Be Taken

13 When Joshua had grown old, the LORD said to him, "You are now very old, and there are still very large areas of land to be taken over.

[2] "This is the land that remains: all the regions of the Philistines and Geshurites, [3] from the Shihor River on the east of Egypt to the territory of Ekron on the north, all of it counted as Canaanite though held by the five Philistine rulers in Gaza, Ashdod, Ashkelon, Gath and Ekron; the territory of the Avvites [4] on the south; all the land of the Canaanites, from Arah of the Sidonians as far as Aphek and the border of the Amorites; [5] the area of Byblos; and all Lebanon to the east, from Baal Gad below Mount Hermon to Lebo Hamath.

[6] "As for all the inhabitants of the mountain regions from Lebanon to Misrephoth Maim, that is, all the Sidonians, I myself will drive them out before the Israelites. Be sure to allocate this land to Israel for an inheritance, as I have instructed you, [7] and divide it as an inheritance among the nine tribes and half of the tribe of Manasseh."

Division of the Land East of the Jordan

[8] The other half of Manasseh,[a] the Reubenites and the Gadites had received the inheritance that Moses had given them east of the Jordan, as he, the servant of the LORD, had assigned it to them.

[9] It extended from Aroer on the rim of the Arnon Gorge, and from the town in the middle of the gorge, and included the whole plateau of Medeba as far

as Dibon, [10] and all the towns of Sihon king of the Amorites, who ruled in Heshbon, out to the border of the Ammonites. [11] It also included Gilead, the territory of the people of Geshur and Maakah, all of Mount Hermon and all Bashan as far as Salekah— [12] that is, the whole kingdom of Og in Bashan, who had reigned in Ashtaroth and Edrei. (He was the last of the Rephaites.) Moses had defeated them and taken over their land. [13] But the Israelites did not drive out the people of Geshur and Maakah, so they continue to live among the Israelites to this day.

[14] But to the tribe of Levi he gave no inheritance, since the food offerings presented to the LORD, the God of Israel, are their inheritance, as he promised them.

[15] This is what Moses had given to the tribe of Reuben, according to its clans:

[16] The territory from Aroer on the rim of the Arnon Gorge, and from the town in the middle of the gorge, and the whole plateau past Medeba [17] to Heshbon and all its towns on the plateau, including Dibon, Bamoth Baal, Beth Baal Meon, [18] Jahaz, Kedemoth, Mephaath, [19] Kiriathaim, Sibmah, Zereth Shahar on the hill in the valley, [20] Beth Peor, the slopes of Pisgah, and Beth Jeshimoth— [21] all the towns on the plateau and the entire realm of Sihon king of the Amorites, who ruled at Heshbon. Moses had defeated him and the Midianite chiefs, Evi, Rekem, Zur, Hur and Reba—princes allied with Sihon—who lived in that country. [22] In addition to those slain in battle, the Israelites had put to the sword Balaam son of Beor, who practiced divination. [23] The boundary of the Reubenites was the bank of the Jordan. These towns and their villages were the inheritance of the Reubenites, according to their clans.

[24] This is what Moses had given to the tribe of Gad, according to its clans:

[25] The territory of Jazer, all the towns of Gilead and half the Ammonite country as far as Aroer, near Rabbah; [26] and

---

[a] 8 Hebrew *With it* (that is, with the other half of Manasseh)

CONQUER TEMPTATIONS

READ: JOSHUA 13:1

Unless you're a crazed fan of ancient maps, your eyes will glaze over when you read the geographic features marking the land boundaries between Israel's twelve tribes. But there's a story behind these lists.

Joshua 10–11 sounds as if every last corner of the land God promised has been conquered. Cities fell from north to south, and a total of thirty-one petty kings lost their thrones. But then the Lord speaks up in Joshua 13. He breaks the news to Joshua that he has grown too old to finish conquering the land. Yet there's an extended list of places the people haven't occupied.

While the Lord promises to continue driving out the inhabitants of the land, the people's commitment to his purposes begin to fade. They fail to destroy the worship sites dedicated to pagan gods, letting those unpleasant altars stand. And so the Lord lets their enemies live. By the start of the Bible's next book, he says, "I will not drive them out before you; they will become traps for you, and their gods will become snares to you" (Judges 2:3).

Once again you spot the big lesson of this section of the Bible. While today it's not your job to drive out worshipers of other religions, it's still your task to rid your life of anything that tempts you away from God. If you don't, you will end up snared.

BUILDING FAITH WISDOM STRENGTH

from Heshbon to Ramath Mizpah and Betonim, and from Mahanaim to the territory of Debir; ²⁷and in the valley, Beth Haram, Beth Nimrah, Sukkoth and Zaphon with the rest of the realm of Sihon king of Heshbon (the east side of the Jordan, the territory up to the end of the Sea of Galilee*ᵃ*). ²⁸These towns and their villages were the inheritance of the Gadites, according to their clans.

²⁹This is what Moses had given to the half-tribe of Manasseh, that is, to half the family of the descendants of Manasseh, according to its clans:

³⁰The territory extending from Maha-naim and including all of Bashan, the entire realm of Og king of Bashan — all the settlements of Jair in Bashan, sixty towns, ³¹half of Gilead, and Ashtaroth and Edrei (the royal cities of Og in Ba-shan). This was for the descendants of Makir son of Manasseh — for half of the sons of Makir, according to their clans.

³²This is the inheritance Moses had giv-en when he was in the plains of Moab across the Jordan east of Jericho. ³³But to the tribe of Levi, Moses had given no inheritance; the LORD, the God of Israel, is their inheritance, as he promised them.

Division of the Land West of the Jordan

14 Now these are the areas the Israel-ites received as an inheritance in the land of Canaan, which Eleazar the priest, Joshua son of Nun and the heads of the tribal clans of Israel allotted to them. ²Their inher-itances were assigned by lot to the nine and a half tribes, as the LORD had commanded through Moses. ³Moses had granted the two and a half tribes their inheritance east of the Jordan but had not granted the Levites an inheritance among the rest, ⁴for Joseph's descendants had become two tribes — Ma-nasseh and Ephraim. The Levites received no share of the land but only towns to live in, with pasturelands for their flocks and herds. ⁵So the Israelites divided the land, just as the LORD had commanded Moses.

Allotment for Caleb

⁶Now the people of Judah approached Joshua at Gilgal, and Caleb son of Jephun-neh the Kenizzite said to him, "You know what the LORD said to Moses the man of God at Kadesh Barnea about you and me. ⁷I was forty years old when Moses the servant of the LORD sent me from Kadesh Barnea to explore the land. And I brought him back a report according to my convictions, ⁸but my fellow Israelites who went up with me made the hearts of the people melt in fear. I, how-ever, followed the LORD my God wholeheart-edly. ⁹So on that day Moses swore to me, 'The land on which your feet have walked will be your inheritance and that of your children forever, because you have followed the LORD my God wholeheartedly.'ᵇ

¹⁰"Now then, just as the LORD promised, he has kept me alive for forty-five years since the time he said this to Moses, while Israel moved about in the wilderness. So here I am today, eighty-five years old! ¹¹I am still as strong today as the day Moses sent me out; I'm just as vigorous to go out to battle now as I was then. ¹²Now give me this hill coun-try that the LORD promised me that day. You yourself heard then that the Anakites were there and their cities were large and forti-fied, but, the LORD helping me, I will drive them out just as he said."

¹³Then Joshua blessed Caleb son of Je-phunneh and gave him Hebron as his inher-itance. ¹⁴So Hebron has belonged to Caleb son of Jephunneh the Kenizzite ever since, because he followed the LORD, the God of Israel, wholeheartedly. ¹⁵(Hebron used to be called Kiriath Arba after Arba, who was the greatest man among the Anakites.)

Then the land had rest from war.

Allotment for Judah

15 The allotment for the tribe of Ju-dah, according to its clans, extended down to the territory of Edom, to the Desert of Zin in the extreme south.

²Their southern boundary start-ed from the bay at the southern end of the Dead Sea, ³crossed south of Scorpion Pass, continued on to Zin and went over to the south of Kadesh Barnea. Then it ran past Hezron up to Addar and curved around to Karka. ⁴It then passed along to Azmon and joined the Wadi of Egypt, ending at the

Mediterranean Sea. This is their[a] southern boundary.

[5] The eastern boundary is the Dead Sea as far as the mouth of the Jordan.

The northern boundary started from the bay of the sea at the mouth of the Jordan, [6] went up to Beth Hoglah and continued north of Beth Arabah to the Stone of Bohan son of Reuben. [7] The boundary then went up to Debir from the Valley of Achor and turned north to Gilgal, which faces the Pass of Adummim south of the gorge. It continued along to the waters of En Shemesh and came out at En Rogel. [8] Then it ran up the Valley of Ben Hinnom along the southern slope of the Jebusite city (that is, Jerusalem). From there it climbed to the top of the hill west of the Hinnom Valley at the northern end of the Valley of Rephaim. [9] From the hilltop the boundary headed toward the spring of the waters of Nephtoah, came out at the towns of Mount Ephron and went down toward Baalah (that is, Kiriath Jearim). [10] Then it curved westward from Baalah to Mount Seir, ran along the northern slope of Mount Jearim (that is, Kesalon), continued down to Beth Shemesh and crossed to Timnah. [11] It went to the northern slope of Ekron, turned toward Shikkeron, passed along to Mount Baalah and reached Jabneel. The boundary ended at the sea.

[12] The western boundary is the coastline of the Mediterranean Sea.

These are the boundaries around the people of Judah by their clans.

[13] In accordance with the LORD's command to him, Joshua gave to Caleb son of Jephunneh a portion in Judah—Kiriath Arba, that is, Hebron. (Arba was the forefather of Anak.) [14] From Hebron Caleb drove out the three Anakites—Sheshai, Ahiman and Talmai, the sons of Anak. [15] From there he marched against the people living in Debir (formerly called Kiriath Sepher). [16] And Caleb said, "I will give my daughter Aksah in marriage to the man who attacks and captures Kiriath Sepher." [17] Othniel son of Kenaz, Caleb's brother, took it; so Caleb gave his daughter Aksah to him in marriage.

[18] One day when she came to Othniel, she urged him[b] to ask her father for a field. When she got off her donkey, Caleb asked her, "What can I do for you?"

[19] She replied, "Do me a special favor. Since you have given me land in the Negev, give me also springs of water." So Caleb gave her the upper and lower springs.

[20] This is the inheritance of the tribe of Judah, according to its clans:

[21] The southernmost towns of the tribe of Judah in the Negev toward the boundary of Edom were:

Kabzeel, Eder, Jagur, [22] Kinah, Dimonah, Adadah, [23] Kedesh, Hazor, Ithnan, [24] Ziph, Telem, Bealoth, [25] Hazor Hadattah, Kerioth Hezron (that is, Hazor), [26] Amam, Shema, Moladah, [27] Hazar Gaddah, Heshmon, Beth Pelet, [28] Hazar Shual, Beersheba, Biziothiah, [29] Baalah, Iyim, Ezem, [30] Eltolad, Kesil, Hormah, [31] Ziklag, Madmannah, Sansannah, [32] Lebaoth, Shilhim, Ain and Rimmon—a total of twenty-nine towns and their villages.

[33] In the western foothills:

Eshtaol, Zorah, Ashnah, [34] Zanoah, En Gannim, Tappuah, Enam, [35] Jarmuth, Adullam, Sokoh, Azekah, [36] Shaaraim, Adithaim and Gederah (or Gederothaim)[c]—fourteen towns and their villages.

[37] Zenan, Hadashah, Migdal Gad, [38] Dilean, Mizpah, Joktheel, [39] Lachish, Bozkath, Eglon, [40] Kabbon, Lahmas, Kitlish, [41] Gederoth, Beth Dagon, Naamah and Makkedah—sixteen towns and their villages.

[42] Libnah, Ether, Ashan, [43] Iphtah, Ashnah, Nezib, [44] Keilah, Akzib and Mareshah—nine towns and their villages.

[45] Ekron, with its surrounding settlements and villages; [46] west of Ekron, all that were in the vicinity of Ashdod, together with their villages; [47] Ashdod, its surrounding settlements and villages; and Gaza, its settlements and villages, as far as the Wadi of Egypt and the coastline of the Mediterranean Sea.

---

[a] 4 Septuagint; Hebrew *your*   [b] 18 Hebrew and some Septuagint manuscripts; other Septuagint manuscripts (see also note at Judges 1:14) *Othniel, he urged her*   [c] 36 Or *Gederah and Gederothaim*

48 In the hill country:

Shamir, Jattir, Sokoh, 49 Dannah, Kiriath Sannah (that is, Debir), 50 Anab, Eshtemoh, Anim, 51 Goshen, Holon and Giloh — eleven towns and their villages.

52 Arab, Dumah, Eshan, 53 Janim, Beth Tappuah, Aphekah, 54 Humtah, Kiriath Arba (that is, Hebron) and Zior — nine towns and their villages.

55 Maon, Carmel, Ziph, Juttah, 56 Jezreel, Jokdeam, Zanoah, 57 Kain, Gibeah and Timnah — ten towns and their villages.

58 Halhul, Beth Zur, Gedor, 59 Maarath, Beth Anoth and Eltekon — six towns and their villages.[a]

60 Kiriath Baal (that is, Kiriath Jearim) and Rabbah — two towns and their villages.

61 In the wilderness:

Beth Arabah, Middin, Sekakah, 62 Nibshan, the City of Salt and En Gedi — six towns and their villages.

63 Judah could not dislodge the Jebusites, who were living in Jerusalem; to this day the Jebusites live there with the people of Judah.

Allotment for Ephraim and Manasseh

16 The allotment for Joseph began at the Jordan, east of the springs of Jericho, and went up from there through the desert into the hill country of Bethel. 2 It went on from Bethel (that is, Luz),[b] crossed over to the territory of the Arkites in Ataroth, 3 descended westward to the territory of the Japhletites as far as the region of Lower Beth Horon and on to Gezer, ending at the Mediterranean Sea.

4 So Manasseh and Ephraim, the descendants of Joseph, received their inheritance.

5 This was the territory of Ephraim, according to its clans:

The boundary of their inheritance went from Ataroth Addar in the east to Upper Beth Horon 6 and continued to the Mediterranean Sea. From Mikmethath on the north it curved eastward to Taanath Shiloh, passing by it to Janoah on the east. 7 Then it went down from Janoah to Ataroth and Naarah, touched Jericho and came out at the Jordan. 8 From Tappuah the border went west to the Kanah Ravine and ended at the Mediterranean Sea. This was the inheritance of the tribe of the Ephraimites, according to its clans. 9 It also included all the towns and their villages that were set aside for the Ephraimites within the inheritance of the Manassites.

10 They did not dislodge the Canaanites living in Gezer; to this day the Canaanites live among the people of Ephraim but are required to do forced labor.

17 This was the allotment for the tribe of Manasseh as Joseph's firstborn, that is, for Makir, Manasseh's firstborn. Makir was the ancestor of the Gileadites, who had received Gilead and Bashan because the Makirites were great soldiers. 2 So this allotment was for the rest of the people of Manasseh — the clans of Abiezer, Helek, Asriel, Shechem, Hepher and Shemida. These are the other male descendants of Manasseh son of Joseph by their clans.

3 Now Zelophehad son of Hepher, the son of Gilead, the son of Makir, the son of Manasseh, had no sons but only daughters, whose names were Mahlah, Noah, Hoglah, Milkah and Tirzah. 4 They went to Eleazar the priest, Joshua son of Nun, and the leaders and said, "The Lord commanded Moses to give us an inheritance among our relatives." So Joshua gave them an inheritance along with the brothers of their father, according to the Lord's command. 5 Manasseh's share consisted of ten tracts of land besides Gilead and Bashan east of the Jordan, 6 because the daughters of the tribe of Manasseh received an inheritance among the sons. The land of Gilead belonged to the rest of the descendants of Manasseh.

7 The territory of Manasseh extended from Asher to Mikmethath east of Shechem. The boundary ran southward from there to include the people living at En Tappuah. 8 (Manasseh had the land of Tappuah, but Tappuah itself, on the boundary of Manasseh, belonged to the Ephraimites.) 9 Then the boundary continued south to the Kanah Ravine. There were towns belonging to

---

[a] 59 The Septuagint adds another district of eleven towns, including Tekoa and Ephrathah (Bethlehem).
[b] 2 Septuagint; Hebrew *Bethel to Luz*

Ephraim lying among the towns of Manasseh, but the boundary of Manasseh was the northern side of the ravine and ended at the Mediterranean Sea. [10]On the south the land belonged to Ephraim, on the north to Manasseh. The territory of Manasseh reached the Mediterranean Sea and bordered Asher on the north and Issachar on the east.

[11]Within Issachar and Asher, Manasseh also had Beth Shan, Ibleam and the people of Dor, Endor, Taanach and Megiddo, together with their surrounding settlements (the third in the list is Naphoth[a]).

[12]Yet the Manassites were not able to occupy these towns, for the Canaanites were determined to live in that region. [13]However, when the Israelites grew stronger, they subjected the Canaanites to forced labor but did not drive them out completely.

[14]The people of Joseph said to Joshua, "Why have you given us only one allotment and one portion for an inheritance? We are a numerous people, and the Lord has blessed us abundantly."

[15]"If you are so numerous," Joshua answered, "and if the hill country of Ephraim is too small for you, go up into the forest and clear land for yourselves there in the land of the Perizzites and Rephaites."

[16]The people of Joseph replied, "The hill country is not enough for us, and all the Canaanites who live in the plain have chariots fitted with iron, both those in Beth Shan and its settlements and those in the Valley of Jezreel."

[17]But Joshua said to the tribes of Joseph — to Ephraim and Manasseh — "You are numerous and very powerful. You will have not only one allotment [18]but the forested hill country as well. Clear it, and its farthest limits will be yours; though the Canaanites have chariots fitted with iron and though they are strong, you can drive them out."

Division of the Rest of the Land

18 The whole assembly of the Israelites gathered at Shiloh and set up the tent of meeting there. The country was brought under their control, [2]but there were still seven Israelite tribes who had not yet received their inheritance.

[3]So Joshua said to the Israelites: "How long will you wait before you begin to take possession of the land that the Lord, the God of your ancestors, has given you? [4]Appoint three men from each tribe. I will send them out to make a survey of the land and to write a description of it, according to the inheritance of each. Then they will return to me. [5]You are to divide the land into seven parts. Judah is to remain in its territory on the south and the tribes of Joseph in their territory on the north. [6]After you have written descriptions of the seven parts of the land, bring them here to me and I will cast lots for you in the presence of the Lord our God. [7]The Levites, however, do not get a portion among you, because the priestly service of the Lord is their inheritance. And Gad, Reuben and the half-tribe of Manasseh have already received their inheritance on the east side of the Jordan. Moses the servant of the Lord gave it to them."

[8]As the men started on their way to map out the land, Joshua instructed them, "Go and make a survey of the land and write a description of it. Then return to me, and I will cast lots for you here at Shiloh in the presence of the Lord." [9]So the men left and went through the land. They wrote its description on a scroll, town by town, in seven parts, and returned to Joshua in the camp at Shiloh. [10]Joshua then cast lots for them in Shiloh in the presence of the Lord, and there he distributed the land to the Israelites according to their tribal divisions.

Allotment for Benjamin

[11]The first lot came up for the tribe of Benjamin according to its clans. Their allotted territory lay between the tribes of Judah and Joseph:

[12]On the north side their boundary began at the Jordan, passed the northern slope of Jericho and headed west into the hill country, coming out at the wilderness of Beth Aven. [13]From there it crossed to the south slope of Luz (that is, Bethel) and went down to Ataroth Addar on the hill south of Lower Beth Horon.

[14]From the hill facing Beth Horon on the south the boundary turned south

---

[a] 11 That is, Naphoth Dor

along the western side and came out at Kiriath Baal (that is, Kiriath Jearim), a town of the people of Judah. This was the western side.

¹⁵ The southern side began at the outskirts of Kiriath Jearim on the west, and the boundary came out at the spring of the waters of Nephtoah. ¹⁶ The boundary went down to the foot of the hill facing the Valley of Ben Hinnom, north of the Valley of Rephaim. It continued down the Hinnom Valley along the southern slope of the Jebusite city and so to En Rogel. ¹⁷ It then curved north, went to En Shemesh, continued to Geliloth, which faces the Pass of Adummim, and ran down to the Stone of Bohan son of Reuben. ¹⁸ It continued to the northern slope of Beth Arabah[a] and on down into the Arabah. ¹⁹ It then went to the northern slope of Beth Hoglah and came out at the northern bay of the Dead Sea, at the mouth of the Jordan in the south. This was the southern boundary.

²⁰ The Jordan formed the boundary on the eastern side.

These were the boundaries that marked out the inheritance of the clans of Benjamin on all sides.

²¹ The tribe of Benjamin, according to its clans, had the following towns:

Jericho, Beth Hoglah, Emek Keziz, ²² Beth Arabah, Zemaraim, Bethel, ²³ Avvim, Parah, Ophrah, ²⁴ Kephar Ammoni, Ophni and Geba — twelve towns and their villages.

²⁵ Gibeon, Ramah, Beeroth, ²⁶ Mizpah, Kephirah, Mozah, ²⁷ Rekem, Irpeel, Taralah, ²⁸ Zelah, Haeleph, the Jebusite city (that is, Jerusalem), Gibeah and Kiriath — fourteen towns and their villages.

This was the inheritance of Benjamin for its clans.

Allotment for Simeon

19 The second lot came out for the tribe of Simeon according to its clans. Their inheritance lay within the territory of Judah. ² It included:

Beersheba (or Sheba),[b] Moladah, ³ Hazar Shual, Balah, Ezem, ⁴ Eltolad, Bethul, Hormah, ⁵ Ziklag, Beth Markaboth, Hazar Susah, ⁶ Beth Lebaoth and Sharuhen — thirteen towns and their villages;

⁷ Ain, Rimmon, Ether and Ashan — four towns and their villages — ⁸ and all the villages around these towns as far as Baalath Beer (Ramah in the Negev).

This was the inheritance of the tribe of the Simeonites, according to its clans. ⁹ The inheritance of the Simeonites was taken from the share of Judah, because Judah's portion was more than they needed. So the Simeonites received their inheritance within the territory of Judah.

Allotment for Zebulun

¹⁰ The third lot came up for Zebulun according to its clans:

The boundary of their inheritance went as far as Sarid. ¹¹ Going west it ran to Maralah, touched Dabbesheth, and extended to the ravine near Jokneam. ¹² It turned east from Sarid toward the sunrise to the territory of Kisloth Tabor and went on to Daberath and up to Japhia. ¹³ Then it continued eastward to Gath Hepher and Eth Kazin; it came out at Rimmon and turned toward Neah. ¹⁴ There the boundary went around on the north to Hannathon and ended at the Valley of Iphtah El. ¹⁵ Included were Kattath, Nahalal, Shimron, Idalah and Bethlehem. There were twelve towns and their villages.

¹⁶ These towns and their villages were the inheritance of Zebulun, according to its clans.

Allotment for Issachar

¹⁷ The fourth lot came out for Issachar according to its clans. ¹⁸ Their territory included:

Jezreel, Kesulloth, Shunem, ¹⁹ Hapharaim, Shion, Anaharath, ²⁰ Rabbith, Kishion, Ebez, ²¹ Remeth, En Gannim, En Haddah and Beth Pazzez. ²² The boundary touched Tabor, Shahazumah and Beth Shemesh, and ended at the Jordan. There were sixteen towns and their villages.

---

a 18 Septuagint; Hebrew *slope facing the Arabah* b 2 Or *Beersheba, Sheba*; 1 Chron. 4:28 does not have *Sheba*.

²³These towns and their villages were the inheritance of the tribe of Issachar, according to its clans.

Allotment for Asher

²⁴The fifth lot came out for the tribe of Asher according to its clans. ²⁵Their territory included:

Helkath, Hali, Beten, Akshaph, ²⁶Allammelek, Amad and Mishal. On the west the boundary touched Carmel and Shihor Libnath. ²⁷It then turned east toward Beth Dagon, touched Zebulun and the Valley of Iphtah El, and went north to Beth Emek and Neiel, passing Kabul on the left. ²⁸It went to Abdon,ᵃ Rehob, Hammon and Kanah, as far as Greater Sidon. ²⁹The boundary then turned back toward Ramah and went to the fortified city of Tyre, turned toward Hosah and came out at the Mediterranean Sea in the region of Akzib, ³⁰Ummah, Aphek and Rehob. There were twenty-two towns and their villages.

³¹These towns and their villages were the inheritance of the tribe of Asher, according to its clans.

Allotment for Naphtali

³²The sixth lot came out for Naphtali according to its clans:

³³Their boundary went from Heleph and the large tree in Zaanannim, passing Adami Nekeb and Jabneel to Lakkum and ending at the Jordan. ³⁴The boundary ran west through Aznoth Tabor and came out at Hukkok. It touched Zebulun on the south, Asher on the west and the Jordanᵇ on the east. ³⁵The fortified towns were Ziddim, Zer, Hammath, Rakkath, Kinnereth, ³⁶Adamah, Ramah, Hazor, ³⁷Kedesh, Edrei, En Hazor, ³⁸Iron, Migdal El, Horem, Beth Anath and Beth Shemesh. There were nineteen towns and their villages.

³⁹These towns and their villages were the inheritance of the tribe of Naphtali, according to its clans.

Allotment for Dan

⁴⁰The seventh lot came out for the tribe of Dan according to its clans. ⁴¹The territory of their inheritance included:

Zorah, Eshtaol, Ir Shemesh, ⁴²Shaalabbin, Aijalon, Ithlah, ⁴³Elon, Timnah, Ekron, ⁴⁴Eltekeh, Gibbethon, Baalath, ⁴⁵Jehud, Bene Berak, Gath Rimmon, ⁴⁶Me Jarkon and Rakkon, with the area facing Joppa.

⁴⁷(When the territory of the Danites was lost to them, they went up and attacked Leshem, took it, put it to the sword and occupied it. They settled in Leshem and named it Dan after their ancestor.) ⁴⁸These towns and their villages were the inheritance of the tribe of Dan, according to its clans.

Allotment for Joshua

⁴⁹When they had finished dividing the land into its allotted portions, the Israelites gave Joshua son of Nun an inheritance among them, ⁵⁰as the LORD had commanded. They gave him the town he asked for—Timnath Serahᶜ in the hill country of Ephraim. And he built up the town and settled there.

⁵¹These are the territories that Eleazar the priest, Joshua son of Nun and the heads of the tribal clans of Israel assigned by lot at Shiloh in the presence of the LORD at the entrance to the tent of meeting. And so they finished dividing the land.

Cities of Refuge

20 Then the LORD said to Joshua: ²"Tell the Israelites to designate the cities of refuge, as I instructed you through Moses, ³so that anyone who kills a person accidentally and unintentionally may flee there and find protection from the avenger of blood. ⁴When they flee to one of these cities, they are to stand in the entrance of the city gate and state their case before the elders of that city. Then the elders are to admit the fugitive into their city and provide a place to live among them. ⁵If the avenger of blood comes in pursuit, the elders must not surrender the fugitive, because the fugitive killed their neighbor unintentionally and without malice aforethought. ⁶They are to stay in that city until they have stood trial before the assembly and until the death of the high priest who is serving at that time. Then they may

---

ᵃ 28 Some Hebrew manuscripts (see also 21:30); most Hebrew manuscripts *Ebron*   ᵇ 34 Septuagint; Hebrew *west, and Judah, the Jordan,*   ᶜ 50 Also known as *Timnath Heres* (see Judges 2:9) go back to their own home in the town from which they fled."

[7] So they set apart Kedesh in Galilee in the hill country of Naphtali, Shechem in the hill country of Ephraim, and Kiriath Arba (that is, Hebron) in the hill country of Judah. [8] East of the Jordan (on the other side from Jericho) they designated Bezer in the wilderness on the plateau in the tribe of Reuben, Ramoth in Gilead in the tribe of Gad, and Golan in Bashan in the tribe of Manasseh. [9] Any of the Israelites or any foreigner residing among them who killed someone accidentally could flee to these designated cities and not be killed by the avenger of blood prior to standing trial before the assembly.

Towns for the Levites

21 Now the family heads of the Levites approached Eleazar the priest, Joshua son of Nun, and the heads of the other tribal families of Israel [2] at Shiloh in Canaan and said to them, "The LORD commanded through Moses that you give us towns to live in, with pasturelands for our livestock." [3] So, as the LORD had commanded, the Israelites gave the Levites the following towns and pasturelands out of their own inheritance:

[4] The first lot came out for the Kohathites, according to their clans. The Levites who were descendants of Aaron the priest were allotted thirteen towns from the tribes of Judah, Simeon and Benjamin. [5] The rest of Kohath's descendants were allotted ten towns from the clans of the tribes of Ephraim, Dan and half of Manasseh.

[6] The descendants of Gershon were allotted thirteen towns from the clans of the tribes of Issachar, Asher, Naphtali and the half-tribe of Manasseh in Bashan.

[7] The descendants of Merari, according to their clans, received twelve towns from the tribes of Reuben, Gad and Zebulun.

[8] So the Israelites allotted to the Levites these towns and their pasturelands, as the LORD had commanded through Moses.

[9] From the tribes of Judah and Simeon they allotted the following towns by name [10] (these towns were assigned to the descendants of Aaron who were from the Kohathite clans of the Levites, because the first lot fell to them):

[11] They gave them Kiriath Arba (that is, Hebron), with its surrounding pastureland, in the hill country of Judah. (Arba was the forefather of Anak.) [12] But the fields and villages around the city they had given to Caleb son of Jephunneh as his possession.

[13] So to the descendants of Aaron the priest they gave Hebron (a city of refuge for one accused of murder), Libnah, [14] Jattir, Eshtemoa, [15] Holon, Debir, [16] Ain, Juttah and Beth Shemesh, together with their pasturelands — nine towns from these two tribes.

[17] And from the tribe of Benjamin they gave them Gibeon, Geba, [18] Anathoth and Almon, together with their pasturelands — four towns.

[19] The total number of towns for the priests, the descendants of Aaron, came to thirteen, together with their pasturelands.

[20] The rest of the Kohathite clans of the Levites were allotted towns from the tribe of Ephraim:

[21] In the hill country of Ephraim they were given Shechem (a city of refuge for one accused of murder) and Gezer, [22] Kibzaim and Beth Horon, together with their pasturelands — four towns.

[23] Also from the tribe of Dan they received Eltekeh, Gibbethon, [24] Aijalon and Gath Rimmon, together with their pasturelands — four towns.

[25] From half the tribe of Manasseh they received Taanach and Gath Rimmon, together with their pasturelands — two towns.

[26] All these ten towns and their pasturelands were given to the rest of the Kohathite clans.

[27] The Levite clans of the Gershonites were given:

from the half-tribe of Manasseh,
Golan in Bashan (a city of refuge for one accused of murder) and Be Eshterah, together with their pasturelands — two towns;

[28] from the tribe of Issachar,
Kishion, Daberath, [29] Jarmuth and En Gannim, together with their pasturelands — four towns;

[30] from the tribe of Asher,
Mishal, Abdon, [31] Helkath and Rehob, together with their pasturelands — four towns;

[32] from the tribe of Naphtali,

Kedesh in Galilee (a city of refuge for one accused of murder), Hammoth Dor and Kartan, together with their pasturelands — three towns.

³³The total number of towns of the Gershonite clans came to thirteen, together with their pasturelands.

³⁴The Merarite clans (the rest of the Levites) were given:

from the tribe of Zebulun,

Jokneam, Kartah, ³⁵Dimnah and Nahalal, together with their pasturelands — four towns;

³⁶from the tribe of Reuben,

Bezer, Jahaz, ³⁷Kedemoth and Mephaath, together with their pasturelands — four towns;

³⁸from the tribe of Gad,

Ramoth in Gilead (a city of refuge for one accused of murder), Mahanaim, ³⁹Heshbon and Jazer, together with their pasturelands — four towns in all.

⁴⁰The total number of towns allotted to the Merarite clans, who were the rest of the Levites, came to twelve.

⁴¹The towns of the Levites in the territory held by the Israelites were forty-eight in all, together with their pasturelands. ⁴²Each of these towns had pasturelands surrounding it; this was true for all these towns.

⁴³So the LORD gave Israel all the land he had sworn to give their ancestors, and they took possession of it and settled there. ⁴⁴The LORD gave them rest on every side, just as he had sworn to their ancestors. Not one of their enemies withstood them; the LORD gave all their enemies into their hands. ⁴⁵Not one of all the LORD's good promises to Israel failed; every one was fulfilled.

Eastern Tribes Return Home

22 Then Joshua summoned the Reubenites, the Gadites and the half-tribe of Manasseh ²and said to them, "You have done all that Moses the servant of the LORD commanded, and you have obeyed me in everything I commanded. ³For a long time now — to this very day — you have not deserted your fellow Israelites but have carried out the mission the LORD your God gave you. ⁴Now that the LORD your God has given them rest as he promised, return to your homes in the land that Moses the servant of

the LORD gave you on the other side of the Jordan. ⁵But be very careful to keep the commandment and the law that Moses the servant of the LORD gave you: to love the LORD your God, to walk in obedience to him, to keep his commands, to hold fast to him and to serve him with all your heart and with all your soul."

⁶Then Joshua blessed them and sent them away, and they went to their homes. ⁷(To the half-tribe of Manasseh Moses had given land in Bashan, and to the other half of the tribe Joshua gave land on the west side of the Jordan along with their fellow Israelites.) When Joshua sent them home, he blessed them, ⁸saying, "Return to your homes with your great wealth — with large herds of livestock, with silver, gold, bronze and iron, and a great quantity of clothing — and divide the plunder from your enemies with your fellow Israelites."

⁹So the Reubenites, the Gadites and the half-tribe of Manasseh left the Israelites at Shiloh in Canaan to return to Gilead, their own land, which they had acquired in accordance with the command of the LORD through Moses.

¹⁰When they came to Geliloth near the Jordan in the land of Canaan, the Reubenites, the Gadites and the half-tribe of Manasseh built an imposing altar there by the Jordan. ¹¹And when the Israelites heard that they had built the altar on the border of Canaan at Geliloth near the Jordan on the Israelite side, ¹²the whole assembly of Israel gathered at Shiloh to go to war against them.

¹³So the Israelites sent Phinehas son of Eleazar, the priest, to the land of Gilead — to Reuben, Gad and the half-tribe of Manasseh. ¹⁴With him they sent ten of the chief men, one from each of the tribes of Israel, each the head of a family division among the Israelite clans.

¹⁵When they went to Gilead — to Reuben, Gad and the half-tribe of Manasseh — they said to them: ¹⁶"The whole assembly of the LORD says: 'How could you break faith with the God of Israel like this? How could you turn away from the LORD and build yourselves an altar in rebellion against him now? ¹⁷Was not the sin of Peor enough for us? Up to this very day we have not cleansed ourselves from that sin, even though a plague fell on the community of the LORD! ¹⁸And are you now turning away from the LORD?

JUST OK

READ: JOSHUA 22:4

It's like getting a B when you could have earned an A. Or jogging a twelve-minute mile when you know you can run an eight. Or giving five dollars to a good cause when you know you can afford ten dollars or more. There's something not quite right in this passage about two-and-a-half tribes wanting to live east of the Jordan River. Back when the Israelites were getting ready to enter the promised land, the tribes of Reuben, Gad, and half of Manasseh said they didn't want to cross the Jordan. They liked the land on the east of the river, and they persuaded Moses to let them live there (Numbers 32:1–5).

That area is called the "Transjordan," and Bible scholars argue whether it was right for tribes to settle there. Moses had commanded the tribes to help conquer the land west of the Jordan (vv. 20–23). When Joshua lets them go home after the battles have ended, he calls the Transjordan the land given them by "Moses the servant of the Lord," as if it didn't come from God.

BUILDING FAITH WISDOM STRENGTH

That territory might have been good, but it wasn't the best. It was almost the promised land, but not quite. That's a choice you face every day. You can try, or you can go all-out. You can be good, or you can be great. You can settle, or you can pursue God's very best. What will you choose?

GOD'S WILL, PLAIN AND SIMPLE

READ: JOSHUA 22:5-6

The more I read the Bible, and the more I listen to people talk about what they think God's will is, the more I'm convinced that we're imposing our ideas about God's will on God rather than building our understanding on what we find in God's Word. We want so badly for God to have an exact call and will for us that we create the idea that he has a specific will for us. Then, we create steps about finding God's will that don't exist in the Bible.

What if we understood God as the one who lovingly created us and continues to shape us into the people he longs for us to be? What if we understood God's desire was not that each of us would follow some pre-designed path like a rat in a maze, but instead that we would all lovingly live in response to the wonder and imagination with which we were created? If we did that, we'd discover the truth of God's will, that it isn't some blueprint we have to follow, but something we live in response to who God created us to be. We'd fall in love with God all over again, and instead of spending all our energy to figure out God's plan, we'd start living lives of meaning and passion in response to God's love.

BUILDING FAITH WISDOM STRENGTH

Taken from *Leave a Footprint—Change the World* by Tim Baker, copyright © 2009 by Tim Baker, published by Zondervan.

"'If you rebel against the LORD today, tomorrow he will be angry with the whole community of Israel. ¹⁹If the land you possess is defiled, come over to the LORD's land, where the LORD's tabernacle stands, and share the land with us. But do not rebel against the LORD or against us by building an altar for yourselves, other than the altar of the LORD our God. ²⁰When Achan son of Zerah was unfaithful in regard to the devoted things,ᵃ did not wrath come on the whole community of Israel? He was not the only one who died for his sin.'"

²¹Then Reuben, Gad and the half-tribe of Manasseh replied to the heads of the clans of Israel: ²²"The Mighty One, God, the LORD! The Mighty One, God, the LORD! He knows! And let Israel know! If this has been in rebellion or disobedience to the LORD, do not spare us this day. ²³If we have built our own altar to turn away from the LORD and to offer burnt offerings and grain offerings, or to sacrifice fellowship offerings on it, may the LORD himself call us to account.

²⁴"No! We did it for fear that some day your descendants might say to ours, 'What do you have to do with the LORD, the God of Israel? ²⁵The LORD has made the Jordan a boundary between us and you—you Reubenites and Gadites! You have no share in the LORD.' So your descendants might cause ours to stop fearing the LORD.

²⁶"That is why we said, 'Let us get ready and build an altar—but not for burnt offerings or sacrifices.' ²⁷On the contrary, it is to be a witness between us and you and the generations that follow, that we will worship the LORD at his sanctuary with our burnt offerings, sacrifices and fellowship offerings. Then in the future your descendants will not be able to say to ours, 'You have no share in the LORD.'

²⁸"And we said, 'If they ever say this to us, or to our descendants, we will answer: Look at the replica of the LORD's altar, which our ancestors built, not for burnt offerings and sacrifices, but as a witness between us and you.'

²⁹"Far be it from us to rebel against the LORD and turn away from him today by building an altar for burnt offerings, grain offerings and sacrifices, other than the altar of the LORD our God that stands before his tabernacle."

³⁰When Phinehas the priest and the leaders of the community—the heads of the clans of the Israelites—heard what Reuben, Gad and Manasseh had to say, they were pleased. ³¹And Phinehas son of Eleazar, the priest, said to Reuben, Gad and Manasseh, "Today we know that the LORD is with us, because you have not been unfaithful to the LORD in this matter. Now you have rescued the Israelites from the LORD's hand."

³²Then Phinehas son of Eleazar, the priest, and the leaders returned to Canaan from their meeting with the Reubenites and Gadites in Gilead and reported to the Israelites. ³³They were glad to hear the report and praised God. And they talked no more about going to war against them to devastate the country where the Reubenites and the Gadites lived.

³⁴And the Reubenites and the Gadites gave the altar this name: A Witness Between Us—that the LORD is God.

Joshua's Farewell to the Leaders

23 After a long time had passed and the LORD had given Israel rest from all their enemies around them, Joshua, by then a very old man, ²summoned all Israel—their elders, leaders, judges and officials—and said to them: "I am very old. ³You yourselves have seen everything the LORD your God has done to all these nations for your sake; it was the LORD your God who fought for you. ⁴Remember how I have allotted as an inheritance for your tribes all the land of the nations that remain—the nations I conquered—between the Jordan and the Mediterranean Sea in the west. ⁵The LORD your God himself will push them out for your sake. He will drive them out before you, and you will take possession of their land, as the LORD your God promised you.

⁶"Be very strong; be careful to obey all that is written in the Book of the Law of Moses, without turning aside to the right or to the left. ⁷Do not associate with these nations that remain among you; do not invoke the names of their gods or swear by them. You must not serve them or bow down to them. ⁸But you are to hold fast to the LORD your God, as you have until now.

ᵃ 20 The Hebrew term refers to the irrevocable giving over of things or persons to the LORD, often by totally destroying them.

⁹"The LORD has driven out before you great and powerful nations; to this day no one has been able to withstand you. ¹⁰One of you routs a thousand, because the LORD your God fights for you, just as he promised. ¹¹So be very careful to love the LORD your God.

¹²"But if you turn away and ally yourselves with the survivors of these nations that remain among you and if you intermarry with them and associate with them, ¹³then you may be sure that the LORD your God will no longer drive out these nations before you. Instead, they will become snares and traps for you, whips on your backs and thorns in your eyes, until you perish from this good land, which the LORD your God has given you.

¹⁴"Now I am about to go the way of all the earth. You know with all your heart and soul that not one of all the good promises the LORD your God gave you has failed. Every promise has been fulfilled; not one has failed. ¹⁵But just as all the good things the LORD your God has promised you have come to you, so he will bring on you all the evil things he has threatened, until the LORD your God has destroyed you from this good land he has given you. ¹⁶If you violate the covenant of the LORD your God, which he commanded you, and go and serve other gods and bow down to them, the LORD's anger will burn against you, and you will quickly perish from the good land he has given you."

The Covenant Renewed at Shechem

24 Then Joshua assembled all the tribes of Israel at Shechem. He summoned the elders, leaders, judges and officials of Israel, and they presented themselves before God.

²Joshua said to all the people, "This is what the LORD, the God of Israel, says: 'Long ago your ancestors, including Terah the father of Abraham and Nahor, lived beyond the Euphrates River and worshiped other gods. ³But I took your father Abraham from the land beyond the Euphrates and led him throughout Canaan and gave him many descendants. I gave him Isaac, ⁴and to Isaac I gave Jacob and Esau. I assigned the hill country of Seir to Esau, but Jacob and his family went down to Egypt.

⁵"'Then I sent Moses and Aaron, and I afflicted the Egyptians by what I did there, and I brought you out. ⁶When I brought your people out of Egypt, you came to the sea, and the Egyptians pursued them with chariots and horsemen[a] as far as the Red Sea.[b] ⁷But they cried to the LORD for help, and he put darkness between you and the Egyptians; he brought the sea over them and covered them. You saw with your own eyes what I did to the Egyptians. Then you lived in the wilderness for a long time.

⁸"'I brought you to the land of the Amorites who lived east of the Jordan. They fought against you, but I gave them into your hands. I destroyed them from before you, and you took possession of their land. ⁹When Balak son of Zippor, the king of Moab, prepared to fight against Israel, he sent for Balaam son of Beor to put a curse on you. ¹⁰But I would not listen to Balaam, so he blessed you again and again, and I delivered you out of his hand.

¹¹"'Then you crossed the Jordan and came to Jericho. The citizens of Jericho fought against you, as did also the Amorites, Perizzites, Canaanites, Hittites, Girgashites, Hivites and Jebusites, but I gave them into your hands. ¹²I sent the hornet ahead of you, which drove them out before you—also the two Amorite kings. You did not do it with your own sword and bow. ¹³So I gave you a land on which you did not toil and cities you did not build; and you live in them and eat from vineyards and olive groves that you did not plant.'

¹⁴"Now fear the LORD and serve him with all faithfulness. Throw away the gods your ancestors worshiped beyond the Euphrates River and in Egypt, and serve the LORD. ¹⁵But if serving the LORD seems undesirable to you, then choose for yourselves this day whom you will serve, whether the gods your ancestors served beyond the Euphrates, or the gods of the Amorites, in whose land you are living. But as for me and my household, we will serve the LORD."

¹⁶Then the people answered, "Far be it from us to forsake the LORD to serve other gods! ¹⁷It was the LORD our God himself who brought us and our parents up out of Egypt, from that land of slavery, and performed those great signs before our eyes. He protected us on our entire journey and among

---

[a] 6 Or *charioteers*   [b] 6 Or *the Sea of Reeds*

DOOR 1, 2 OR 3

READ: JOSHUA 24:14-15

By this time in his life, Joshua has been a general through many wars. He fought off hostile tribes who sought to destroy the Israelites. He saw the walls of Jericho come thundering down in miraculous fashion. He fought battles and bears the scars, as well as the wisdom and faith that grows and deepens with struggle. Joshua seems to know he doesn't have much time left in this world. He gathers the people of Israel together, clears his throat, and speaks with power.

Joshua doesn't tiptoe around what he wants to say. He gets right to the point and throws down a challenge: It's time for the people to make a choice. The people can follow the Lord God, the God of Abraham, Isaac, and Jacob, or they can choose a different god. It's time to accept a worldview and allow it to remake them. "It's up to you," Joshua is saying.

BUILDING FAITH WISDOM STRENGTH

I find it interesting that Joshua gives three options along with the one true God. When I offer an invitation to salvation in church, I don't make it multiple choice. But even though Joshua is a commander who's used to giving orders, he knows that a personal choice must be made. No one can be ordered into the kingdom of God. No one can be driven there or carried bodily over the threshold. It's a path that individuals must choose.

all the nations through which we traveled. [18] And the LORD drove out before us all the nations, including the Amorites, who lived in the land. We too will serve the LORD, because he is our God."

[19] Joshua said to the people, "You are not able to serve the LORD. He is a holy God; he is a jealous God. He will not forgive your rebellion and your sins. [20] If you forsake the LORD and serve foreign gods, he will turn and bring disaster on you and make an end of you, after he has been good to you."

[21] But the people said to Joshua, "No! We will serve the LORD."

[22] Then Joshua said, "You are witnesses against yourselves that you have chosen to serve the LORD."

"Yes, we are witnesses," they replied.

[23] "Now then," said Joshua, "throw away the foreign gods that are among you and yield your hearts to the LORD, the God of Israel."

[24] And the people said to Joshua, "We will serve the LORD our God and obey him."

[25] On that day Joshua made a covenant for the people, and there at Shechem he reaffirmed for them decrees and laws. [26] And Joshua recorded these things in the Book of the Law of God. Then he took a large stone and set it up there under the oak near the holy place of the LORD.

[27] "See!" he said to all the people. "This stone will be a witness against us. It has heard all the words the LORD has said to us. It will be a witness against you if you are untrue to your God."

[28] Then Joshua dismissed the people, each to their own inheritance.

Buried in the Promised Land

[29] After these things, Joshua son of Nun, the servant of the LORD, died at the age of a hundred and ten. [30] And they buried him in the land of his inheritance, at Timnath Serah[a] in the hill country of Ephraim, north of Mount Gaash.

[31] Israel served the LORD throughout the lifetime of Joshua and of the elders who outlived him and who had experienced everything the LORD had done for Israel.

[32] And Joseph's bones, which the Israelites had brought up from Egypt, were buried at Shechem in the tract of land that Jacob bought for a hundred pieces of silver[b] from the sons of Hamor, the father of Shechem. This became the inheritance of Joseph's descendants.

[33] And Eleazar son of Aaron died and was buried at Gibeah, which had been allotted to his son Phinehas in the hill country of Ephraim.

---

[a] 30 Also known as *Timnath Heres* (see Judges 2:9) of money of unknown weight and value.   [b] 32 Hebrew *hundred kesitahs*; a kesitah was a unit

JUDGES

WHEN DID THIS HAPPEN?

Between 1200 and 1000 B.C. in Canaan (the promised land), modern-day Israel

WHO IS IN THIS BOOK?

Deborah
Barak
Gideon
Samson
Delilah

VERSES YOU MIGHT RECOGNIZE

JUDGES 6:8

"This is what the LORD, the God of Israel, says: I brought you up out of Egypt, out of the land of slavery."

JUDGES 17:6

"In those days Israel had no king; everyone did as they saw fit."

WHAT'S IT ABOUT?

With Joshua as their leader, the Israelites had followed God's instructions and taken over the promised land. Unfortunately, their obedience didn't last long. After Joshua died, the people started to ignore some of God's commands. In fact, things got so bad that Judges tells us the people "did as they saw fit" instead of honoring the Lord. God wanted the people's full obedience, so he appointed judges to rule over them and remind them of his instructions.

In this book, you'll read about a strong and brave female judge (Deborah), a wimpy, weak judge (Gideon), and a hot-tempered judge with super-strength and long hair (Samson). When the Israelites obeyed God, he fought for them. But when they ignored his commands, they lost his blessing and protection. The judges gave the people a fresh chance to obey.

JUDGES

Israel Fights the Remaining Canaanites

1 After the death of Joshua, the Israelites asked the LORD, "Who of us is to go up first to fight against the Canaanites?"

²The LORD answered, "Judah shall go up; I have given the land into their hands."

³The men of Judah then said to the Simeonites their fellow Israelites, "Come up with us into the territory allotted to us, to fight against the Canaanites. We in turn will go with you into yours." So the Simeonites went with them.

⁴When Judah attacked, the LORD gave the Canaanites and Perizzites into their hands, and they struck down ten thousand men at Bezek. ⁵It was there that they found Adoni-Bezek and fought against him, putting to rout the Canaanites and Perizzites. ⁶Adoni-Bezek fled, but they chased him and caught him, and cut off his thumbs and big toes.

⁷Then Adoni-Bezek said, "Seventy kings with their thumbs and big toes cut off have picked up scraps under my table. Now God has paid me back for what I did to them." They brought him to Jerusalem, and he died there.

⁸The men of Judah attacked Jerusalem also and took it. They put the city to the sword and set it on fire.

⁹After that, Judah went down to fight against the Canaanites living in the hill country, the Negev and the western foothills. ¹⁰They advanced against the Canaanites living in Hebron (formerly called Kiriath Arba) and defeated Sheshai, Ahiman and Talmai. ¹¹From there they advanced against the people living in Debir (formerly called Kiriath Sepher).

¹²And Caleb said, "I will give my daughter Aksah in marriage to the man who attacks and captures Kiriath Sepher." ¹³Othniel son of Kenaz, Caleb's younger brother, took it; so Caleb gave his daughter Aksah to him in marriage.

¹⁴One day when she came to Othniel, she urged him*a* to ask her father for a field. When she got off her donkey, Caleb asked her, "What can I do for you?"

¹⁵She replied, "Do me a special favor. Since you have given me land in the Negev, give me also springs of water." So Caleb gave her the upper and lower springs.

¹⁶The descendants of Moses' father-in-law, the Kenite, went up from the City of Palms*b* with the people of Judah to live among the inhabitants of the Desert of Judah in the Negev near Arad.

¹⁷Then the men of Judah went with the Simeonites their fellow Israelites and attacked the Canaanites living in Zephath, and they totally destroyed*c* the city. Therefore it was called Hormah.*d* ¹⁸Judah also took*e* Gaza, Ashkelon and Ekron — each city with its territory.

¹⁹The LORD was with the men of Judah. They took possession of the hill country, but they were unable to drive the people from the plains, because they had chariots fitted with iron. ²⁰As Moses had promised, Hebron was given to Caleb, who drove from it the three sons of Anak. ²¹The Benjamites, however, did not drive out the Jebusites, who were living in Jerusalem; to this day the Jebusites live there with the Benjamites.

²²Now the tribes of Joseph attacked Bethel, and the LORD was with them. ²³When they sent men to spy out Bethel (formerly called Luz), ²⁴the spies saw a man coming out of the city and they said to him, "Show us how to get into the city and we will see that you are treated well." ²⁵So he showed them, and they put the city to the sword but spared the man and his whole family. ²⁶He then went to the land of the Hittites, where he built a city and called it Luz, which is its name to this day.

²⁷But Manasseh did not drive out the

---

a 14 Hebrew; Septuagint and Vulgate *Othniel, he urged her*   *b 16* That is, Jericho   *c 17* The Hebrew term refers to the irrevocable giving over of things or persons to the LORD, often by totally destroying them.   *d 17 Hormah* means *destruction.*   *e 18* Hebrew; Septuagint *Judah did not take* people of Beth Shan or Taanach or Dor or Ibleam or Megiddo and their surrounding settlements, for the Canaanites were determined to live in that land. [28]When Israel became strong, they pressed the Canaanites into forced labor but never drove them out completely. [29]Nor did Ephraim drive out the Canaanites living in Gezer, but the Canaanites continued to live there among them. [30]Neither did Zebulun drive out the Canaanites living in Kitron or Nahalol, so these Canaanites lived among them, but Zebulun did subject them to forced labor. [31]Nor did Asher drive out those living in Akko or Sidon or Ahlab or Akzib or Helbah or Aphek or Rehob. [32]The Asherites lived among the Canaanite inhabitants of the land because they did not drive them out. [33]Neither did Naphtali drive out those living in Beth Shemesh or Beth Anath; but the Naphtalites too lived among the Canaanite inhabitants of the land, and those living in Beth Shemesh and Beth Anath became forced laborers for them. [34]The Amorites confined the Danites to the hill country, not allowing them to come down into the plain. [35]And the Amorites were determined also to hold out in Mount Heres, Aijalon and Shaalbim, but when the power of the tribes of Joseph increased, they too were pressed into forced labor. [36]The boundary of the Amorites was from Scorpion Pass to Sela and beyond.

The Angel of the Lord at Bokim

2 The angel of the Lord went up from Gilgal to Bokim and said, "I brought you up out of Egypt and led you into the land I swore to give to your ancestors. I said, 'I will never break my covenant with you, [2]and you shall not make a covenant with the people of this land, but you shall break down their altars.' Yet you have disobeyed me. Why have you done this? [3]And I have also said, 'I will not drive them out before you; they will become traps for you, and their gods will become snares to you.'"

[4]When the angel of the Lord had spoken these things to all the Israelites, the people wept aloud, [5]and they called that place Bokim.[a] There they offered sacrifices to the Lord.

Disobedience and Defeat

[6]After Joshua had dismissed the Israelites, they went to take possession of the land, each to their own inheritance. [7]The people served the Lord throughout the lifetime of Joshua and of the elders who outlived him and who had seen all the great things the Lord had done for Israel.

[8]Joshua son of Nun, the servant of the Lord, died at the age of a hundred and ten. [9]And they buried him in the land of his inheritance, at Timnath Heres[b] in the hill country of Ephraim, north of Mount Gaash.

[10]After that whole generation had been gathered to their ancestors, another generation grew up who knew neither the Lord nor what he had done for Israel. [11]Then the Israelites did evil in the eyes of the Lord and served the Baals. [12]They forsook the Lord, the God of their ancestors, who had brought them out of Egypt. They followed and worshiped various gods of the peoples around them. They aroused the Lord's anger [13]because they forsook him and served Baal and the Ashtoreths. [14]In his anger against Israel the Lord gave them into the hands of raiders who plundered them. He sold them into the hands of their enemies all around, whom they were no longer able to resist. [15]Whenever Israel went out to fight, the hand of the Lord was against them to defeat them, just as he had sworn to them. They were in great distress.

[16]Then the Lord raised up judges,[c] who saved them out of the hands of these raiders. [17]Yet they would not listen to their judges but prostituted themselves to other gods and worshiped them. They quickly turned from the ways of their ancestors, who had been obedient to the Lord's commands. [18]Whenever the Lord raised up a judge for them, he was with the judge and saved them out of the hands of their enemies as long as the judge lived; for the Lord relented because of their groaning under those who oppressed and afflicted them. [19]But when the judge died, the people returned to ways even more corrupt than those of their ancestors, following other gods and serving and worshiping them. They refused to give up their evil practices and stubborn ways.

---

[a] 5 *Bokim* means *weepers*.   [b] 9 Also known as *Timnath Serah* (see Joshua 19:50 and 24:30)
[c] 16 Or *leaders*; similarly in verses 17-19

NO HANGING ON COATTAILS

READ: JUDGES 2:10-11

Maybe you're growing up in a Christian family, a group of people that trusts Jesus as the one-and-only Savior and that aims to follow him wholeheartedly. That's an unbeatable advantage as you build your own relationship with the Lord. But don't assume you get your family's faith automatically.

Judges reports that the generation that conquered the promised land served the Lord "throughout the lifetime of Joshua and of the elders who outlived him and who had seen all the great things the LORD had done for Israel" (Judges 2:7).

After those folks died, the next generation slid into evil. They worshiped Baal, the god of the Canaanites, and the Ashtoreths, pagan goddesses of the Philistines. These false gods were allegedly in charge of the fertility of people, herds, and crops. Instead of counting on the Lord for those good things, the Israelites looked to pagan gods to ensure them success.

It's no secret why the Israelites stopped trusting God. That next generation "knew neither the LORD nor what he had done for Israel" (Judges 2:10). Either their parents didn't tell them the stories of God's mighty power, or they weren't paying attention.

If you want to walk closely with the Lord, you have to meet him firsthand. You need to apply his promises and commands to your life. You have to make your own choice to live as his child, because God doesn't have grandchildren.

BUILDING FAITH WISDOM STRENGTH

²⁰Therefore the LORD was very angry with Israel and said, "Because this nation has violated the covenant I ordained for their ancestors and has not listened to me, ²¹I will no longer drive out before them any of the nations Joshua left when he died. ²²I will use them to test Israel and see whether they will keep the way of the LORD and walk in it as their ancestors did." ²³The LORD had allowed those nations to remain; he did not drive them out at once by giving them into the hands of Joshua.

3 These are the nations the LORD left to test all those Israelites who had not experienced any of the wars in Canaan ²(he did this only to teach warfare to the descendants of the Israelites who had not had previous battle experience): ³the five rulers of the Philistines, all the Canaanites, the Sidonians, and the Hivites living in the Lebanon mountains from Mount Baal Hermon to Lebo Hamath. ⁴They were left to test the Israelites to see whether they would obey the LORD's commands, which he had given their ancestors through Moses.

⁵The Israelites lived among the Canaanites, Hittites, Amorites, Perizzites, Hivites and Jebusites. ⁶They took their daughters in marriage and gave their own daughters to their sons, and served their gods.

Othniel

⁷The Israelites did evil in the eyes of the LORD; they forgot the LORD their God and served the Baals and the Asherahs. ⁸The anger of the LORD burned against Israel so that he sold them into the hands of Cushan-Rishathaim king of Aram Naharaim,^a to whom the Israelites were subject for eight years. ⁹But when they cried out to the LORD, he raised up for them a deliverer, Othniel son of Kenaz, Caleb's younger brother, who saved them. ¹⁰The Spirit of the LORD came on him, so that he became Israel's judge^b and went to war. The LORD gave Cushan-Rishathaim king of Aram into the hands of Othniel, who overpowered him. ¹¹So the land had peace for forty years, until Othniel son of Kenaz died.

Ehud

¹²Again the Israelites did evil in the eyes of the LORD, and because they did this evil the LORD gave Eglon king of Moab power over Israel. ¹³Getting the Ammonites and Amalekites to join him, Eglon came and attacked Israel, and they took possession of the City of Palms.^c ¹⁴The Israelites were subject to Eglon king of Moab for eighteen years.

¹⁵Again the Israelites cried out to the LORD, and he gave them a deliverer—Ehud, a left-handed man, the son of Gera the Benjamite. The Israelites sent him with tribute to Eglon king of Moab. ¹⁶Now Ehud had made a double-edged sword about a cubit^d long, which he strapped to his right thigh under his clothing. ¹⁷He presented the tribute to Eglon king of Moab, who was a very fat man. ¹⁸After Ehud had presented the tribute, he sent on their way those who had carried it. ¹⁹But on reaching the stone images near Gilgal he himself went back to Eglon and said, "Your Majesty, I have a secret message for you."

The king said to his attendants, "Leave us!" And they all left.

²⁰Ehud then approached him while he was sitting alone in the upper room of his palace^e and said, "I have a message from God for you." As the king rose from his seat, ²¹Ehud reached with his left hand, drew the sword from his right thigh and plunged it into the king's belly. ²²Even the handle sank in after the blade, and his bowels discharged. Ehud did not pull the sword out, and the fat closed in over it. ²³Then Ehud went out to the porch^f; he shut the doors of the upper room behind him and locked them.

²⁴After he had gone, the servants came and found the doors of the upper room locked. They said, "He must be relieving himself in the inner room of the palace." ²⁵They waited to the point of embarrassment, but when he did not open the doors of the room, they took a key and unlocked them. There they saw their lord fallen to the floor, dead.

²⁶While they waited, Ehud got away. He passed by the stone images and escaped to Seirah. ²⁷When he arrived there, he blew a trumpet in the hill country of Ephraim, and the Israelites went down with him from the hills, with him leading them.

---

^a 8 That is, Northwest Mesopotamia   ^b 10 Or *leader*   ^c 13 That is, Jericho   ^d 16 That is, about 18 inches or about 45 centimeters   ^e 20 The meaning of the Hebrew for this word is uncertain; also in verse 24.   ^f 23 The meaning of the Hebrew for this word is uncertain.

[28] "Follow me," he ordered, "for the LORD has given Moab, your enemy, into your hands." So they followed him down and took possession of the fords of the Jordan that led to Moab; they allowed no one to cross over. [29] At that time they struck down about ten thousand Moabites, all vigorous and strong; not one escaped. [30] That day Moab was made subject to Israel, and the land had peace for eighty years.

Shamgar

[31] After Ehud came Shamgar son of Anath, who struck down six hundred Philistines with an oxgoad. He too saved Israel.

Deborah

4 Again the Israelites did evil in the eyes of the LORD, now that Ehud was dead. [2] So the LORD sold them into the hands of Jabin king of Canaan, who reigned in Hazor. Sisera, the commander of his army, was based in Harosheth Haggoyim. [3] Because he had nine hundred chariots fitted with iron and had cruelly oppressed the Israelites for twenty years, they cried to the LORD for help.

[4] Now Deborah, a prophet, the wife of Lappidoth, was leading[a] Israel at that time. [5] She held court under the Palm of Deborah between Ramah and Bethel in the hill country of Ephraim, and the Israelites went up to her to have their disputes decided. [6] She sent for Barak son of Abinoam from Kedesh in Naphtali and said to him, "The LORD, the God of Israel, commands you: 'Go, take with you ten thousand men of Naphtali and Zebulun and lead them up to Mount Tabor. [7] I will lead Sisera, the commander of Jabin's army, with his chariots and his troops to the Kishon River and give him into your hands.'"

[8] Barak said to her, "If you go with me, I will go; but if you don't go with me, I won't go."

[9] "Certainly I will go with you," said Deborah. "But because of the course you are taking, the honor will not be yours, for the LORD will deliver Sisera into the hands of a woman." So Deborah went with Barak to Kedesh. [10] There Barak summoned Zebulun and Naphtali, and ten thousand men went up under his command. Deborah also went up with him.

[11] Now Heber the Kenite had left the other Kenites, the descendants of Hobab, Moses' brother-in-law,[b] and pitched his tent by the great tree in Zaanannim near Kedesh.

[12] When they told Sisera that Barak son of Abinoam had gone up to Mount Tabor, [13] Sisera summoned from Harosheth Haggoyim to the Kishon River all his men and his nine hundred chariots fitted with iron.

[14] Then Deborah said to Barak, "Go! This is the day the LORD has given Sisera into your hands. Has not the LORD gone ahead of you?" So Barak went down Mount Tabor, with ten thousand men following him. [15] At Barak's advance, the LORD routed Sisera and all his chariots and army by the sword, and Sisera got down from his chariot and fled on foot.

[16] Barak pursued the chariots and army as far as Harosheth Haggoyim, and all Sisera's troops fell by the sword; not a man was left. [17] Sisera, meanwhile, fled on foot to the tent of Jael, the wife of Heber the Kenite, because there was an alliance between Jabin king of Hazor and the family of Heber the Kenite.

[18] Jael went out to meet Sisera and said to him, "Come, my lord, come right in. Don't be afraid." So he entered her tent, and she covered him with a blanket.

[19] "I'm thirsty," he said. "Please give me some water." She opened a skin of milk, gave him a drink, and covered him up.

[20] "Stand in the doorway of the tent," he told her. "If someone comes by and asks you, 'Is anyone in there?' say 'No.'"

[21] But Jael, Heber's wife, picked up a tent peg and a hammer and went quietly to him while he lay fast asleep, exhausted. She drove the peg through his temple into the ground, and he died.

[22] Just then Barak came by in pursuit of Sisera, and Jael went out to meet him. "Come," she said, "I will show you the man you're looking for." So he went in with her, and there lay Sisera with the tent peg through his temple — dead.

[23] On that day God subdued Jabin king of Canaan before the Israelites. [24] And the hand of the Israelites pressed harder and harder against Jabin king of Canaan until they destroyed him.

The Song of Deborah

5 On that day Deborah and Barak son of Abinoam sang this song:

---

[a] 4 Traditionally *judging*   [b] 11 Or *father-in-law*

GRAB YOUR OXGOAD

READ: JUDGES 3:31

One sentence. That's the only attention Shamgar gets in Scripture. But look again—this one line tells me everything I need to know about him. One farm tool and one decision end up saving the entire nation of Israel. This one risk was a huge deal.

Israel was in spiritual anarchy and political tyranny. They did some straight-up evil and their punishment was enslavement to the Philistines, who ruled with intimidation and fear. But one man refused to be ruled by that fear. Next to David, Shamgar has to rank as one of history's most improbable heroes. And just like the shepherd-turned-king, this farmer-turned-warrior transformed this makeshift cattle prod into a weapon of war. I don't think Shamgar had a clue while he was driving oxen that God would turn his oxgoad into the instrument of Israel's deliverance.

BUILDING FAITH WISDOM STRENGTH

Shamgar was a one-man army. All he had was an oxgoad, which was basically a long stick. But he knew that if God was for him, no one could stand against him. So Shamgar grabbed his oxgoad and charged the enemy armies. He looked as dumb as David coming at Goliath with a dinky slingshot. But courage doesn't wait until the situation is in your favor. It doesn't wait until a plan is perfectly formed. Courage only waits for one thing: a green light from God.

Taken from *All In Student Edition* by Mark Batterson and Parker Batterson, copyright © 2014 by Mark Batterson, published by Zondervan.

2 "When the princes in Israel take the lead,
    when the people willingly offer
        themselves —
    praise the LORD!

3 "Hear this, you kings! Listen, you rulers!
    I, even I, will sing to^a the LORD;
    I will praise the LORD, the God of
        Israel, in song.

4 "When you, LORD, went out from Seir,
    when you marched from the land of
        Edom,
    the earth shook, the heavens poured,
        the clouds poured down water.
5 The mountains quaked before the LORD,
        the One of Sinai,
    before the LORD, the God of Israel.

6 "In the days of Shamgar son of Anath,
    in the days of Jael, the highways were
        abandoned;
    travelers took to winding paths.
7 Villagers in Israel would not fight;
    they held back until I, Deborah, arose,
    until I arose, a mother in Israel.
8 God chose new leaders
    when war came to the city gates,
    but not a shield or spear was seen
        among forty thousand in Israel.
9 My heart is with Israel's princes,
    with the willing volunteers among the
        people.
    Praise the LORD!

10 "You who ride on white donkeys,
    sitting on your saddle blankets,
    and you who walk along the road,
    consider 11 the voice of the singers^b at the
        watering places.
    They recite the victories of the LORD,
    the victories of his villagers in Israel.

"Then the people of the LORD
    went down to the city gates.
12 'Wake up, wake up, Deborah!
    Wake up, wake up, break out in song!
    Arise, Barak!
    Take captive your captives, son of
        Abinoam.'

13 "The remnant of the nobles came down;
    the people of the LORD came down to
        me against the mighty.

14 Some came from Ephraim, whose roots
        were in Amalek;
    Benjamin was with the people who
        followed you.
    From Makir captains came down,
    from Zebulun those who bear a
        commander's^b staff.
15 The princes of Issachar were with
        Deborah;
    yes, Issachar was with Barak,
    sent under his command into the
        valley.
    In the districts of Reuben
    there was much searching of heart.
16 Why did you stay among the sheep
        pens^c
    to hear the whistling for the flocks?
    In the districts of Reuben
    there was much searching of heart.
17 Gilead stayed beyond the Jordan.
    And Dan, why did he linger by the
        ships?
    Asher remained on the coast
    and stayed in his coves.
18 The people of Zebulun risked their very
        lives;
    so did Naphtali on the terraced fields.

19 "Kings came, they fought,
    the kings of Canaan fought.
    At Taanach, by the waters of Megiddo,
    they took no plunder of silver.
20 From the heavens the stars fought,
    from their courses they fought against
        Sisera.
21 The river Kishon swept them away,
    the age-old river, the river Kishon.
    March on, my soul; be strong!
22 Then thundered the horses' hooves —
    galloping, galloping go his mighty
        steeds.
23 'Curse Meroz,' said the angel of the LORD.
    'Curse its people bitterly,
    because they did not come to help the
        LORD,
    to help the LORD against the mighty.'

24 "Most blessed of women be Jael,
    the wife of Heber the Kenite,
    most blessed of tent-dwelling women.
25 He asked for water, and she gave him
        milk;

---

^{a} 3 Or of ^{b} 11,14 The meaning of the Hebrew for this word is uncertain. ^{c} 16 Or the campfires; or the
saddlebags

in a bowl fit for nobles she brought him
  curdled milk.
²⁶ Her hand reached for the tent peg,
  her right hand for the workman's
    hammer.
She struck Sisera, she crushed his head,
  she shattered and pierced his temple.
²⁷ At her feet he sank,
  he fell; there he lay.
At her feet he sank, he fell;
  where he sank, there he fell—dead.

²⁸ "Through the window peered Sisera's
    mother;
  behind the lattice she cried out,
  'Why is his chariot so long in coming?
  Why is the clatter of his chariots
    delayed?'
²⁹ The wisest of her ladies answer her;
  indeed, she keeps saying to herself,
³⁰ 'Are they not finding and dividing the
    spoils:
  a woman or two for each man,
  colorful garments as plunder for Sisera,
  colorful garments embroidered,
  highly embroidered garments for my
    neck—
  all this as plunder?'

³¹ "So may all your enemies perish, LORD!
  But may all who love you be like the
    sun
  when it rises in its strength."

Then the land had peace forty years.

Gideon

6 The Israelites did evil in the eyes of the
LORD, and for seven years he gave them
into the hands of the Midianites. ² Because
the power of Midian was so oppressive, the
Israelites prepared shelters for themselves
in mountain clefts, caves and strongholds.
³ Whenever the Israelites planted their
crops, the Midianites, Amalekites and other
eastern peoples invaded the country. ⁴ They
camped on the land and ruined the crops all
the way to Gaza and did not spare a living
thing for Israel, neither sheep nor cattle nor
donkeys. ⁵ They came up with their livestock
and their tents like swarms of locusts. It was
impossible to count them or their camels;
they invaded the land to ravage it. ⁶ Midi-

an so impoverished the Israelites that they
cried out to the LORD for help.

⁷ When the Israelites cried out to the LORD
because of Midian, ⁸ he sent them a prophet, who said, "This is what the LORD, the
God of Israel, says: I brought you up out of
Egypt, out of the land of slavery. ⁹ I rescued
you from the hand of the Egyptians. And I
delivered you from the hand of all your oppressors; I drove them out before you and
gave you their land. ¹⁰ I said to you, 'I am the
LORD your God; do not worship the gods of
the Amorites, in whose land you live.' But
you have not listened to me."

¹¹ The angel of the LORD came and sat
down under the oak in Ophrah that belonged to Joash the Abiezrite, where his son
Gideon was threshing wheat in a winepress
to keep it from the Midianites. ¹² When the
angel of the LORD appeared to Gideon, he
said, "The LORD is with you, mighty warrior."

¹³ "Pardon me, my lord," Gideon replied,
"but if the LORD is with us, why has all this
happened to us? Where are all his wonders
that our ancestors told us about when they
said, 'Did not the LORD bring us up out of
Egypt?' But now the LORD has abandoned us
and given us into the hand of Midian."

¹⁴ The LORD turned to him and said, "Go in
the strength you have and save Israel out of
Midian's hand. Am I not sending you?"

¹⁵ "Pardon me, my lord," Gideon replied,
"but how can I save Israel? My clan is the
weakest in Manasseh, and I am the least in
my family."

¹⁶ The LORD answered, "I will be with you,
and you will strike down all the Midianites,
leaving none alive."

¹⁷ Gideon replied, "If now I have found favor in your eyes, give me a sign that it is really you talking to me. ¹⁸ Please do not go away
until I come back and bring my offering and
set it before you."

And the LORD said, "I will wait until you
return."

¹⁹ Gideon went inside, prepared a young
goat, and from an ephah^a of flour he made
bread without yeast. Putting the meat in a
basket and its broth in a pot, he brought them
out and offered them to him under the oak.

²⁰ The angel of God said to him, "Take
the meat and the unleavened bread, place

---

^{a} 19 That is, probably about 36 pounds or about 16 kilograms

GIDEON

The LORD turned to him and said, "Go in the strength you have and save Israel out of Midian's hand. Am I not sending you?" "Pardon me, my lord," Gideon replied, "but how can I save Israel? My clan is the weakest in Manasseh, and I am the least in my family." JUDGES 6:14-15

HIS NAME MEANS: "he who bruises or breaks to pieces"
READ HIS STORY: *Judges 6-8; Hebrews 11:32*

MEN

OF THE BIBLE

Over time, the Israelites stopped following the God who had led them out of Egypt with miracles, and fell into idolatry and worshiping other gods. The neighboring countries attacked them without mercy until the Israelites were hiding in caves, just trying to survive.

During these days, the Israelites turned once again to God and cried out for help. God answered their prayers and chose a very unlikely person to lead them into battle and win the victory over their enemies.

When God called Gideon to this task, Gideon put himself down, saying he was too poor and puny. Although he was trying to duck personal responsibility, he was understandably scared. He was the farthest thing from being a warrior. Most likely, God chose Gideon *because* of his weaknesses. That's so Gideon wouldn't win the victory in his own strength—God gave Gideon the strength to be the "mighty warrior" God called him to be. Gideon would have to trust God, because he had nothing else to fall back on.

The real mighty men of God can face any situation with confidence—not because of their own strength but because they have the strength of the Almighty God. God transformed this weak, frightened guy into a bold fighter who led his people to freedom.

them on this rock, and pour out the broth." And Gideon did so. ²¹Then the angel of the LORD touched the meat and the unleavened bread with the tip of the staff that was in his hand. Fire flared from the rock, consuming the meat and the bread. And the angel of the LORD disappeared. ²²When Gideon realized that it was the angel of the LORD, he exclaimed, "Alas, Sovereign LORD! I have seen the angel of the LORD face to face!"

²³But the LORD said to him, "Peace! Do not be afraid. You are not going to die."

²⁴So Gideon built an altar to the LORD there and called it The LORD Is Peace. To this day it stands in Ophrah of the Abiezrites.

²⁵That same night the LORD said to him, "Take the second bull from your father's herd, the one seven years old.ᵃ Tear down your father's altar to Baal and cut down the Asherah poleᵇ beside it. ²⁶Then build a proper kind ofᶜ altar to the LORD your God on the top of this height. Using the wood of the Asherah pole that you cut down, offer the secondᵈ bull as a burnt offering."

²⁷So Gideon took ten of his servants and did as the LORD told him. But because he was afraid of his family and the townspeople, he did it at night rather than in the daytime.

²⁸In the morning when the people of the town got up, there was Baal's altar, demolished, with the Asherah pole beside it cut down and the second bull sacrificed on the newly built altar!

²⁹They asked each other, "Who did this?"

When they carefully investigated, they were told, "Gideon son of Joash did it."

³⁰The people of the town demanded of Joash, "Bring out your son. He must die, because he has broken down Baal's altar and cut down the Asherah pole beside it."

³¹But Joash replied to the hostile crowd around him, "Are you going to plead Baal's cause? Are you trying to save him? Whoever fights for him shall be put to death by morning! If Baal really is a god, he can defend himself when someone breaks down his altar." ³²So because Gideon broke down Baal's altar, they gave him the name Jerub-Baalᵉ that day, saying, "Let Baal contend with him."

³³Now all the Midianites, Amalekites and other eastern peoples joined forces and crossed over the Jordan and camped in the Valley of Jezreel. ³⁴Then the Spirit of the LORD came on Gideon, and he blew a trumpet, summoning the Abiezrites to follow him. ³⁵He sent messengers throughout Manasseh, calling them to arms, and also into Asher, Zebulun and Naphtali, so that they too went up to meet them.

³⁶Gideon said to God, "If you will save Israel by my hand as you have promised— ³⁷look, I will place a wool fleece on the threshing floor. If there is dew only on the fleece and all the ground is dry, then I will know that you will save Israel by my hand, as you said." ³⁸And that is what happened. Gideon rose early the next day; he squeezed the fleece and wrung out the dew—a bowlful of water.

³⁹Then Gideon said to God, "Do not be angry with me. Let me make just one more request. Allow me one more test with the fleece, but this time make the fleece dry and let the ground be covered with dew." ⁴⁰That night God did so. Only the fleece was dry; all the ground was covered with dew.

Gideon Defeats the Midianites

7 Early in the morning, Jerub-Baal (that is, Gideon) and all his men camped at the spring of Harod. The camp of Midian was north of them in the valley near the hill of Moreh. ²The LORD said to Gideon, "You have too many men. I cannot deliver Midian into their hands, or Israel would boast against me, 'My own strength has saved me.' ³Now announce to the army, 'Anyone who trembles with fear may turn back and leave Mount Gilead.'" So twenty-two thousand men left, while ten thousand remained.

⁴But the LORD said to Gideon, "There are still too many men. Take them down to the water, and I will thin them out for you there. If I say, 'This one shall go with you,' he shall go; but if I say, 'This one shall not go with you,' he shall not go."

⁵So Gideon took the men down to the water. There the LORD told him, "Separate those who lap the water with their tongues

---

ᵃ 25 Or *Take a full-grown, mature bull from your father's herd*   ᵇ 25 That is, a wooden symbol of the goddess Asherah; also in verses 26, 28 and 30   ᶜ 26 Or *build with layers of stone an*   ᵈ 26 Or *full-grown*; also in verse 28   ᵉ 32 *Jerub-Baal* probably means *let Baal contend*.

as a dog laps from those who kneel down to drink." ⁶Three hundred of them drank from cupped hands, lapping like dogs. All the rest got down on their knees to drink.

⁷The LORD said to Gideon, "With the three hundred men that lapped I will save you and give the Midianites into your hands. Let all the others go home." ⁸So Gideon sent the rest of the Israelites home but kept the three hundred, who took over the provisions and trumpets of the others.

Now the camp of Midian lay below him in the valley. ⁹During that night the LORD said to Gideon, "Get up, go down against the camp, because I am going to give it into your hands. ¹⁰If you are afraid to attack, go down to the camp with your servant Purah ¹¹and listen to what they are saying. Afterward, you will be encouraged to attack the camp." So he and Purah his servant went down to the outposts of the camp. ¹²The Midianites, the Amalekites and all the other eastern peoples had settled in the valley, thick as locusts. Their camels could no more be counted than the sand on the seashore.

¹³Gideon arrived just as a man was telling a friend his dream. "I had a dream," he was saying. "A round loaf of barley bread came tumbling into the Midianite camp. It struck the tent with such force that the tent overturned and collapsed."

¹⁴His friend responded, "This can be nothing other than the sword of Gideon son of Joash, the Israelite. God has given the Midianites and the whole camp into his hands."

¹⁵When Gideon heard the dream and its interpretation, he bowed down and worshiped. He returned to the camp of Israel and called out, "Get up! The LORD has given the Midianite camp into your hands." ¹⁶Dividing the three hundred men into three companies, he placed trumpets and empty jars in the hands of all of them, with torches inside.

¹⁷"Watch me," he told them. "Follow my lead. When I get to the edge of the camp, do exactly as I do. ¹⁸When I and all who are with me blow our trumpets, then from all around the camp blow yours and shout, 'For the LORD and for Gideon.'"

¹⁹Gideon and the hundred men with him reached the edge of the camp at the beginning of the middle watch, just after they had changed the guard. They blew their trumpets and broke the jars that were in their hands. ²⁰The three companies blew the trumpets and smashed the jars. Grasping the torches in their left hands and holding in their right hands the trumpets they were to blow, they shouted, "A sword for the LORD and for Gideon!" ²¹While each man held his position around the camp, all the Midianites ran, crying out as they fled.

²²When the three hundred trumpets sounded, the LORD caused the men throughout the camp to turn on each other with their swords. The army fled to Beth Shittah toward Zererah as far as the border of Abel Meholah near Tabbath. ²³Israelites from Naphtali, Asher and all Manasseh were called out, and they pursued the Midianites. ²⁴Gideon sent messengers throughout the hill country of Ephraim, saying, "Come down against the Midianites and seize the waters of the Jordan ahead of them as far as Beth Barah."

So all the men of Ephraim were called out and they seized the waters of the Jordan as far as Beth Barah. ²⁵They also captured two of the Midianite leaders, Oreb and Zeeb. They killed Oreb at the rock of Oreb, and Zeeb at the winepress of Zeeb. They pursued the Midianites and brought the heads of Oreb and Zeeb to Gideon, who was by the Jordan.

Zebah and Zalmunna

8 Now the Ephraimites asked Gideon, "Why have you treated us like this? Why didn't you call us when you went to fight Midian?" And they challenged him vigorously.

²But he answered them, "What have I accomplished compared to you? Aren't the gleanings of Ephraim's grapes better than the full grape harvest of Abiezer? ³God gave Oreb and Zeeb, the Midianite leaders, into your hands. What was I able to do compared to you?" At this, their resentment against him subsided.

⁴Gideon and his three hundred men, exhausted yet keeping up the pursuit, came to the Jordan and crossed it. ⁵He said to the men of Sukkoth, "Give my troops some bread; they are worn out, and I am still pursuing Zebah and Zalmunna, the kings of Midian."

⁶But the officials of Sukkoth said, "Do you

CRAZY-MAKING

READ: JUDGES 7

I f we had the transcript of Gideon's thoughts, I wonder if it would read, *This is crazy, this is crazy, this is crazy.*

I had one of those "this is crazy" moments last summer while traveling in Peru. After hiking the Inca Trail to Machu Picchu, my son and I checked a goal off our life goal lists by paragliding over the Sacred Valley. Paragliding is one of those experiences that sounds amazing when your feet are firmly planted on ground, but the closer you get to the cliff the more you wonder whether you should be running off it. I have a minor fear of heights, and that fear was not alleviated by the sixty-second orientation given in broken English by my Peruvian tandem partner, who was half my height. His instructions? Run as fast as you can toward the cliff. That's it.

As I sprinted toward the 10,000-foot drop-off, one thought kept going through my mind: *This is crazy, this is crazy, this is crazy!* But it was quickly followed by, *This is awesome, this is awesome, this is awesome!*

BUILDING

FAITH

WISDOM

STRENGTH

We ran off the cliff, and the next thing I knew we were sailing over the Sacred Valley at 14,000 feet. I learned that if you aren't willing to put yourself in "this is crazy" situations, you'll never experience "this is awesome" moments.

If you aren't willing to run off the cliff, you'll never fly.

Taken from *The Circle Maker Student Edition* by Mark Batterson with Parker Batterson, copyright © 2012 by Mark Batterson, published by Zondervan.

already have the hands of Zebah and Zalmunna in your possession? Why should we give bread to your troops?"

⁷Then Gideon replied, "Just for that, when the LORD has given Zebah and Zalmunna into my hand, I will tear your flesh with desert thorns and briers."

⁸From there he went up to Peniel[a] and made the same request of them, but they answered as the men of Sukkoth had. ⁹So he said to the men of Peniel, "When I return in triumph, I will tear down this tower."

¹⁰Now Zebah and Zalmunna were in Karkor with a force of about fifteen thousand men, all that were left of the armies of the eastern peoples; a hundred and twenty thousand swordsmen had fallen. ¹¹Gideon went up by the route of the nomads east of Nobah and Jogbehah and attacked the unsuspecting army. ¹²Zebah and Zalmunna, the two kings of Midian, fled, but he pursued them and captured them, routing their entire army.

¹³Gideon son of Joash then returned from the battle by the Pass of Heres. ¹⁴He caught a young man of Sukkoth and questioned him, and the young man wrote down for him the names of the seventy-seven officials of Sukkoth, the elders of the town. ¹⁵Then Gideon came and said to the men of Sukkoth, "Here are Zebah and Zalmunna, about whom you taunted me by saying, 'Do you already have the hands of Zebah and Zalmunna in your possession? Why should we give bread to your exhausted men?'" ¹⁶He took the elders of the town and taught the men of Sukkoth a lesson by punishing them with desert thorns and briers. ¹⁷He also pulled down the tower of Peniel and killed the men of the town.

¹⁸Then he asked Zebah and Zalmunna, "What kind of men did you kill at Tabor?"

"Men like you," they answered, "each one with the bearing of a prince."

¹⁹Gideon replied, "Those were my brothers, the sons of my own mother. As surely as the LORD lives, if you had spared their lives, I would not kill you." ²⁰Turning to Jether, his oldest son, he said, "Kill them!" But Jether did not draw his sword, because he was only a boy and was afraid.

²¹Zebah and Zalmunna said, "Come, do it yourself. 'As is the man, so is his strength.'"

So Gideon stepped forward and killed them, and took the ornaments off their camels' necks.

Gideon's Ephod

²²The Israelites said to Gideon, "Rule over us — you, your son and your grandson — because you have saved us from the hand of Midian."

²³But Gideon told them, "I will not rule over you, nor will my son rule over you. The LORD will rule over you." ²⁴And he said, "I do have one request, that each of you give me an earring from your share of the plunder." (It was the custom of the Ishmaelites to wear gold earrings.)

²⁵They answered, "We'll be glad to give them." So they spread out a garment, and each of them threw a ring from his plunder onto it. ²⁶The weight of the gold rings he asked for came to seventeen hundred shekels,[b] not counting the ornaments, the pendants and the purple garments worn by the kings of Midian or the chains that were on their camels' necks. ²⁷Gideon made the gold into an ephod, which he placed in Ophrah, his town. All Israel prostituted themselves by worshiping it there, and it became a snare to Gideon and his family.

Gideon's Death

²⁸Thus Midian was subdued before the Israelites and did not raise its head again. During Gideon's lifetime, the land had peace forty years.

²⁹Jerub-Baal son of Joash went back home to live. ³⁰He had seventy sons of his own, for he had many wives. ³¹His concubine, who lived in Shechem, also bore him a son, whom he named Abimelek. ³²Gideon son of Joash died at a good old age and was buried in the tomb of his father Joash in Ophrah of the Abiezrites.

³³No sooner had Gideon died than the Israelites again prostituted themselves to the Baals. They set up Baal-Berith as their god ³⁴and did not remember the LORD their God, who had rescued them from the hands of all their enemies on every side. ³⁵They also failed to show any loyalty to the family of Jerub-Baal (that is, Gideon) in spite of all the good things he had done for them.

---

[a] 8 Hebrew *Penuel*, a variant of *Peniel*; also in verses 9 and 17   [b] 26 That is, about 43 pounds or about 20 kilograms

Abimelek

9 Abimelek son of Jerub-Baal went to his mother's brothers in Shechem and said to them and to all his mother's clan, ²"Ask all the citizens of Shechem, 'Which is better for you: to have all seventy of Jerub-Baal's sons rule over you, or just one man?' Remember, I am your flesh and blood."

³When the brothers repeated all this to the citizens of Shechem, they were inclined to follow Abimelek, for they said, "He is related to us." ⁴They gave him seventy shekels*a* of silver from the temple of Baal-Berith, and Abimelek used it to hire reckless scoundrels, who became his followers. ⁵He went to his father's home in Ophrah and on one stone murdered his seventy brothers, the sons of Jerub-Baal. But Jotham, the youngest son of Jerub-Baal, escaped by hiding. ⁶Then all the citizens of Shechem and Beth Millo gathered beside the great tree at the pillar in Shechem to crown Abimelek king.

⁷When Jotham was told about this, he climbed up on the top of Mount Gerizim and shouted to them, "Listen to me, citizens of Shechem, so that God may listen to you. ⁸One day the trees went out to anoint a king for themselves. They said to the olive tree, 'Be our king.'

⁹"But the olive tree answered, 'Should I give up my oil, by which both gods and humans are honored, to hold sway over the trees?'

¹⁰"Next, the trees said to the fig tree, 'Come and be our king.'

¹¹"But the fig tree replied, 'Should I give up my fruit, so good and sweet, to hold sway over the trees?'

¹²"Then the trees said to the vine, 'Come and be our king.'

¹³"But the vine answered, 'Should I give up my wine, which cheers both gods and humans, to hold sway over the trees?'

¹⁴"Finally all the trees said to the thornbush, 'Come and be our king.'

¹⁵"The thornbush said to the trees, 'If you really want to anoint me king over you, come and take refuge in my shade; but if not, then let fire come out of the thornbush and consume the cedars of Lebanon!'

¹⁶"Have you acted honorably and in good faith by making Abimelek king? Have you been fair to Jerub-Baal and his family? Have you treated him as he deserves? ¹⁷Remember that my father fought for you and risked his life to rescue you from the hand of Midian. ¹⁸But today you have revolted against my father's family. You have murdered his seventy sons on a single stone and have made Abimelek, the son of his female slave, king over the citizens of Shechem because he is related to you. ¹⁹So have you acted honorably and in good faith toward Jerub-Baal and his family today? If you have, may Abimelek be your joy, and may you be his, too! ²⁰But if you have not, let fire come out from Abimelek and consume you, the citizens of Shechem and Beth Millo, and let fire come out from you, the citizens of Shechem and Beth Millo, and consume Abimelek!"

²¹Then Jotham fled, escaping to Beer, and he lived there because he was afraid of his brother Abimelek.

²²After Abimelek had governed Israel three years, ²³God stirred up animosity between Abimelek and the citizens of Shechem so that they acted treacherously against Abimelek. ²⁴God did this in order that the crime against Jerub-Baal's seventy sons, the shedding of their blood, might be avenged on their brother Abimelek and on the citizens of Shechem, who had helped him murder his brothers. ²⁵In opposition to him these citizens of Shechem set men on the hilltops to ambush and rob everyone who passed by, and this was reported to Abimelek.

²⁶Now Gaal son of Ebed moved with his clan into Shechem, and its citizens put their confidence in him. ²⁷After they had gone out into the fields and gathered the grapes and trodden them, they held a festival in the temple of their god. While they were eating and drinking, they cursed Abimelek. ²⁸Then Gaal son of Ebed said, "Who is Abimelek, and why should we Shechemites be subject to him? Isn't he Jerub-Baal's son, and isn't Zebul his deputy? Serve the family of Hamor, Shechem's father! Why should we serve Abimelek? ²⁹If only this people were under my command! Then I would get rid of him. I would say to Abimelek, 'Call out your whole army!'"*b*

³⁰When Zebul the governor of the city heard what Gaal son of Ebed said, he was

---

a 4 That is, about 1 3/4 pounds or about 800 grams   *b* 29 Septuagint; Hebrew *him." Then he said to Abimelek, "Call out your whole army!"*

very angry. ³¹Under cover he sent messengers to Abimelek, saying, "Gaal son of Ebed and his clan have come to Shechem and are stirring up the city against you. ³²Now then, during the night you and your men should come and lie in wait in the fields. ³³In the morning at sunrise, advance against the city. When Gaal and his men come out against you, seize the opportunity to attack them."

³⁴So Abimelek and all his troops set out by night and took up concealed positions near Shechem in four companies. ³⁵Now Gaal son of Ebed had gone out and was standing at the entrance of the city gate just as Abimelek and his troops came out from their hiding place.

³⁶When Gaal saw them, he said to Zebul, "Look, people are coming down from the tops of the mountains!"

Zebul replied, "You mistake the shadows of the mountains for men."

³⁷But Gaal spoke up again: "Look, people are coming down from the central hill,ᵃ and a company is coming from the direction of the diviners' tree."

³⁸Then Zebul said to him, "Where is your big talk now, you who said, 'Who is Abimelek that we should be subject to him?' Aren't these the men you ridiculed? Go out and fight them!"

³⁹So Gaal led outᵇ the citizens of Shechem and fought Abimelek. ⁴⁰Abimelek chased him all the way to the entrance of the gate, and many were killed as they fled. ⁴¹Then Abimelek stayed in Arumah, and Zebul drove Gaal and his clan out of Shechem.

⁴²The next day the people of Shechem went out to the fields, and this was reported to Abimelek. ⁴³So he took his men, divided them into three companies and set an ambush in the fields. When he saw the people coming out of the city, he rose to attack them. ⁴⁴Abimelek and the companies with him rushed forward to a position at the entrance of the city gate. Then two companies attacked those in the fields and struck them down. ⁴⁵All that day Abimelek pressed his attack against the city until he had captured it and killed its people. Then he destroyed the city and scattered salt over it.

⁴⁶On hearing this, the citizens in the tower of Shechem went into the stronghold of the temple of El-Berith. ⁴⁷When Abimelek heard that they had assembled there, ⁴⁸he and all his men went up Mount Zalmon. He took an ax and cut off some branches, which he lifted to his shoulders. He ordered the men with him, "Quick! Do what you have seen me do!" ⁴⁹So all the men cut branches and followed Abimelek. They piled them against the stronghold and set it on fire with the people still inside. So all the people in the tower of Shechem, about a thousand men and women, also died.

⁵⁰Next Abimelek went to Thebez and besieged it and captured it. ⁵¹Inside the city, however, was a strong tower, to which all the men and women — all the people of the city — had fled. They had locked themselves in and climbed up on the tower roof. ⁵²Abimelek went to the tower and attacked it. But as he approached the entrance to the tower to set it on fire, ⁵³a woman dropped an upper millstone on his head and cracked his skull.

⁵⁴Hurriedly he called to his armor-bearer, "Draw your sword and kill me, so that they can't say, 'A woman killed him.'" So his servant ran him through, and he died. ⁵⁵When the Israelites saw that Abimelek was dead, they went home.

⁵⁶Thus God repaid the wickedness that Abimelek had done to his father by murdering his seventy brothers. ⁵⁷God also made the people of Shechem pay for all their wickedness. The curse of Jotham son of Jerub-Baal came on them.

Tola

10 After the time of Abimelek, a man of Issachar named Tola son of Puah, the son of Dodo, rose to save Israel. He lived in Shamir, in the hill country of Ephraim. ²He ledᶜ Israel twenty-three years; then he died, and was buried in Shamir.

Jair

³He was followed by Jair of Gilead, who led Israel twenty-two years. ⁴He had thirty sons, who rode thirty donkeys. They controlled thirty towns in Gilead, which to this day are called Havvoth Jair.ᵈ ⁵When Jair died, he was buried in Kamon.

Jephthah

⁶Again the Israelites did evil in the eyes of the LORD. They served the Baals and the

---

ᵃ 37 The Hebrew for this phrase means *the navel of the earth.*   ᵇ 39 Or *Gaal went out in the sight of*
ᶜ 2 Traditionally *judged*; also in verse 3   ᵈ 4 Or *called the settlements of Jair*

Ashtoreths, and the gods of Aram, the gods of Sidon, the gods of Moab, the gods of the Ammonites and the gods of the Philistines. And because the Israelites forsook the LORD and no longer served him, [7] he became angry with them. He sold them into the hands of the Philistines and the Ammonites, [8] who that year shattered and crushed them. For eighteen years they oppressed all the Israelites on the east side of the Jordan in Gilead, the land of the Amorites. [9] The Ammonites also crossed the Jordan to fight against Judah, Benjamin and Ephraim; Israel was in great distress. [10] Then the Israelites cried out to the LORD, "We have sinned against you, forsaking our God and serving the Baals."

[11] The LORD replied, "When the Egyptians, the Amorites, the Ammonites, the Philistines, [12] the Sidonians, the Amalekites and the Maonites[a] oppressed you and you cried to me for help, did I not save you from their hands? [13] But you have forsaken me and served other gods, so I will no longer save you. [14] Go and cry out to the gods you have chosen. Let them save you when you are in trouble!"

[15] But the Israelites said to the LORD, "We have sinned. Do with us whatever you think best, but please rescue us now." [16] Then they got rid of the foreign gods among them and served the LORD. And he could bear Israel's misery no longer.

[17] When the Ammonites were called to arms and camped in Gilead, the Israelites assembled and camped at Mizpah. [18] The leaders of the people of Gilead said to each other, "Whoever will take the lead in attacking the Ammonites will be head over all who live in Gilead."

11 Jephthah the Gileadite was a mighty warrior. His father was Gilead; his mother was a prostitute. [2] Gilead's wife also bore him sons, and when they were grown up, they drove Jephthah away. "You are not going to get any inheritance in our family," they said, "because you are the son of another woman." [3] So Jephthah fled from his brothers and settled in the land of Tob, where a gang of scoundrels gathered around him and followed him.

[4] Some time later, when the Ammonites were fighting against Israel, [5] the elders of Gilead went to get Jephthah from the land of Tob. [6] "Come," they said, "be our commander, so we can fight the Ammonites."

[7] Jephthah said to them, "Didn't you hate me and drive me from my father's house? Why do you come to me now, when you're in trouble?"

[8] The elders of Gilead said to him, "Nevertheless, we are turning to you now; come with us to fight the Ammonites, and you will be head over all of us who live in Gilead."

[9] Jephthah answered, "Suppose you take me back to fight the Ammonites and the LORD gives them to me — will I really be your head?"

[10] The elders of Gilead replied, "The LORD is our witness; we will certainly do as you say." [11] So Jephthah went with the elders of Gilead, and the people made him head and commander over them. And he repeated all his words before the LORD in Mizpah.

[12] Then Jephthah sent messengers to the Ammonite king with the question: "What do you have against me that you have attacked my country?"

[13] The king of the Ammonites answered Jephthah's messengers, "When Israel came up out of Egypt, they took away my land from the Arnon to the Jabbok, all the way to the Jordan. Now give it back peaceably."

[14] Jephthah sent back messengers to the Ammonite king, [15] saying:

"This is what Jephthah says: Israel did not take the land of Moab or the land of the Ammonites. [16] But when they came up out of Egypt, Israel went through the wilderness to the Red Sea[b] and on to Kadesh. [17] Then Israel sent messengers to the king of Edom, saying, 'Give us permission to go through your country,' but the king of Edom would not listen. They sent also to the king of Moab, and he refused. So Israel stayed at Kadesh.

[18] "Next they traveled through the wilderness, skirted the lands of Edom and Moab, passed along the eastern side of the country of Moab, and camped on the other side of the Arnon. They did not enter the territory of Moab, for the Arnon was its border.

[19] "Then Israel sent messengers to

---

[a] 12 Hebrew; some Septuagint manuscripts *Midianites*   [b] 16 Or *the Sea of Reeds*

Sihon king of the Amorites, who ruled in Heshbon, and said to him, 'Let us pass through your country to our own place.' ²⁰Sihon, however, did not trust Israel*a* to pass through his territory. He mustered all his troops and encamped at Jahaz and fought with Israel.

²¹"Then the Lord, the God of Israel, gave Sihon and his whole army into Israel's hands, and they defeated them. Israel took over all the land of the Amorites who lived in that country, ²²capturing all of it from the Arnon to the Jabbok and from the desert to the Jordan.

²³"Now since the Lord, the God of Israel, has driven the Amorites out before his people Israel, what right have you to take it over? ²⁴Will you not take what your god Chemosh gives you? Likewise, whatever the Lord our God has given us, we will possess. ²⁵Are you any better than Balak son of Zippor, king of Moab? Did he ever quarrel with Israel or fight with them? ²⁶For three hundred years Israel occupied Heshbon, Aroer, the surrounding settlements and all the towns along the Arnon. Why didn't you retake them during that time? ²⁷I have not wronged you, but you are doing me wrong by waging war against me. Let the Lord, the Judge, decide the dispute this day between the Israelites and the Ammonites."

²⁸The king of Ammon, however, paid no attention to the message Jephthah sent him.

²⁹Then the Spirit of the Lord came on Jephthah. He crossed Gilead and Manasseh, passed through Mizpah of Gilead, and from there he advanced against the Ammonites. ³⁰And Jephthah made a vow to the Lord: "If you give the Ammonites into my hands, ³¹whatever comes out of the door of my house to meet me when I return in triumph from the Ammonites will be the Lord's, and I will sacrifice it as a burnt offering."

³²Then Jephthah went over to fight the Ammonites, and the Lord gave them into his hands. ³³He devastated twenty towns from Aroer to the vicinity of Minnith, as far as Abel Keramim. Thus Israel subdued Ammon.

³⁴When Jephthah returned to his home in Mizpah, who should come out to meet him but his daughter, dancing to the sound of timbrels! She was an only child. Except for her he had neither son nor daughter. ³⁵When he saw her, he tore his clothes and cried, "Oh no, my daughter! You have brought me down and I am devastated. I have made a vow to the Lord that I cannot break."

³⁶"My father," she replied, "you have given your word to the Lord. Do to me just as you promised, now that the Lord has avenged you of your enemies, the Ammonites. ³⁷But grant me this one request," she said. "Give me two months to roam the hills and weep with my friends, because I will never marry."

³⁸"You may go," he said. And he let her go for two months. She and her friends went into the hills and wept because she would never marry. ³⁹After the two months, she returned to her father, and he did to her as he had vowed. And she was a virgin.

From this comes the Israelite tradition ⁴⁰that each year the young women of Israel go out for four days to commemorate the daughter of Jephthah the Gileadite.

Jephthah and Ephraim

12 The Ephraimite forces were called out, and they crossed over to Zaphon. They said to Jephthah, "Why did you go to fight the Ammonites without calling us to go with you? We're going to burn down your house over your head."

²Jephthah answered, "I and my people were engaged in a great struggle with the Ammonites, and although I called, you didn't save me out of their hands. ³When I saw that you wouldn't help, I took my life in my hands and crossed over to fight the Ammonites, and the Lord gave me the victory over them. Now why have you come up today to fight me?"

⁴Jephthah then called together the men of Gilead and fought against Ephraim. The Gileadites struck them down because the Ephraimites had said, "You Gileadites are renegades from Ephraim and Manasseh. ⁵The Gileadites captured the fords of the Jordan leading to Ephraim, and whenever a survivor of Ephraim said, "Let me cross over,"

---

a 20 Or *however, would not make an agreement for Israel*

PARENT PATTERNS

READ: **JUDGES 11:31**

Parents aren't perfect. Their children get the brunt of their issues, and the scene of Jephthah and his daughter shows a family at its worst. The Israelites had fallen into another cycle of sin, doing evil by serving the false gods of all their neighbors. When the Israelites abandon the Lord, he hands them over to be crushed by their enemies. The people cry to God, but he tells them to beg their new gods for help.

After the Israelites get rid of their false gods, the Lord can't stand to watch their misery any longer and raises up Jephthah to save them. But the judge makes a reckless vow, promising to sacrifice to God the first thing that welcomes him home after his victory. Unfortunately, the first one out the door is not an animal, as he expected, but his daughter. It's not clear if Jephthah kills his daughter or if he sacrifices her by not letting her marry. Either way, the girl suffers horribly for her father's stupidity.

BUILDING
FAITH
WISDOM
STRENGTH

If you or a friend is caught in an intense home situation, get help from an adult you trust. If you suffer the brunt of your parents' bad choices, remember the Lord loves you even when parents seem like they don't (Isaiah 49:15). And if you see yourself falling into bad patterns you might see at home, ask God to show you how to break the cycle of sin.

the men of Gilead asked him, "Are you an Ephraimite?" If he replied, "No," ⁶they said, "All right, say 'Shibboleth.'" If he said, "Sibboleth," because he could not pronounce the word correctly, they seized him and killed him at the fords of the Jordan. Forty-two thousand Ephraimites were killed at that time.

⁷Jephthah led*a* Israel six years. Then Jephthah the Gileadite died and was buried in a town in Gilead.

Ibzan, Elon and Abdon

⁸After him, Ibzan of Bethlehem led Israel. ⁹He had thirty sons and thirty daughters. He gave his daughters away in marriage to those outside his clan, and for his sons he brought in thirty young women as wives from outside his clan. Ibzan led Israel seven years. ¹⁰Then Ibzan died and was buried in Bethlehem.

¹¹After him, Elon the Zebulunite led Israel ten years. ¹²Then Elon died and was buried in Aijalon in the land of Zebulun.

¹³After him, Abdon son of Hillel, from Pirathon, led Israel. ¹⁴He had forty sons and thirty grandsons, who rode on seventy donkeys. He led Israel eight years. ¹⁵Then Abdon son of Hillel died and was buried at Pirathon in Ephraim, in the hill country of the Amalekites.

The Birth of Samson

13 Again the Israelites did evil in the eyes of the LORD, so the LORD delivered them into the hands of the Philistines for forty years.

²A certain man of Zorah, named Manoah, from the clan of the Danites, had a wife who was childless, unable to give birth. ³The angel of the LORD appeared to her and said, "You are barren and childless, but you are going to become pregnant and give birth to a son. ⁴Now see to it that you drink no wine or other fermented drink and that you do not eat anything unclean. ⁵You will become pregnant and have a son whose head is never to be touched by a razor because the boy is to be a Nazirite, dedicated to God from the womb. He will take the lead in delivering Israel from the hands of the Philistines."

⁶Then the woman went to her husband and told him, "A man of God came to me. He looked like an angel of God, very awesome. I didn't ask him where he came from, and he didn't tell me his name. ⁷But he said to me, 'You will become pregnant and have a son. Now then, drink no wine or other fermented drink and do not eat anything unclean, because the boy will be a Nazirite of God from the womb until the day of his death.'"

⁸Then Manoah prayed to the LORD: "Pardon your servant, Lord. I beg you to let the man of God you sent to us come again to teach us how to bring up the boy who is to be born."

⁹God heard Manoah, and the angel of God came again to the woman while she was out in the field; but her husband Manoah was not with her. ¹⁰The woman hurried to tell her husband, "He's here! The man who appeared to me the other day!"

¹¹Manoah got up and followed his wife. When he came to the man, he said, "Are you the man who talked to my wife?"

"I am," he said.

¹²So Manoah asked him, "When your words are fulfilled, what is to be the rule that governs the boy's life and work?"

¹³The angel of the LORD answered, "Your wife must do all that I have told her. ¹⁴She must not eat anything that comes from the grapevine, nor drink any wine or other fermented drink nor eat anything unclean. She must do everything I have commanded her."

¹⁵Manoah said to the angel of the LORD, "We would like you to stay until we prepare a young goat for you."

¹⁶The angel of the LORD replied, "Even though you detain me, I will not eat any of your food. But if you prepare a burnt offering, offer it to the LORD." (Manoah did not realize that it was the angel of the LORD.)

¹⁷Then Manoah inquired of the angel of the LORD, "What is your name, so that we may honor you when your word comes true?"

¹⁸He replied, "Why do you ask my name? It is beyond understanding.*b*" ¹⁹Then Manoah took a young goat, together with the grain offering, and sacrificed it on a rock to the LORD. And the LORD did an amazing thing while Manoah and his wife watched: ²⁰As

---

a 7 Traditionally *judged*; also in verses 8-14   *b* 18 Or *is wonderful* the flame blazed up from the altar toward heaven, the angel of the LORD ascended in the flame. Seeing this, Manoah and his wife fell with their faces to the ground. ²¹When the angel of the LORD did not show himself again to Manoah and his wife, Manoah realized that it was the angel of the LORD.

²²"We are doomed to die!" he said to his wife. "We have seen God!"

²³But his wife answered, "If the LORD had meant to kill us, he would not have accepted a burnt offering and grain offering from our hands, nor shown us all these things or now told us this."

²⁴The woman gave birth to a boy and named him Samson. He grew and the LORD blessed him, ²⁵and the Spirit of the LORD began to stir him while he was in Mahaneh Dan, between Zorah and Eshtaol.

Samson's Marriage

14 Samson went down to Timnah and saw there a young Philistine woman. ²When he returned, he said to his father and mother, "I have seen a Philistine woman in Timnah; now get her for me as my wife."

³His father and mother replied, "Isn't there an acceptable woman among your relatives or among all our people? Must you go to the uncircumcised Philistines to get a wife?"

But Samson said to his father, "Get her for me. She's the right one for me." ⁴(His parents did not know that this was from the LORD, who was seeking an occasion to confront the Philistines; for at that time they were ruling over Israel.)

⁵Samson went down to Timnah together with his father and mother. As they approached the vineyards of Timnah, suddenly a young lion came roaring toward him. ⁶The Spirit of the LORD came powerfully upon him so that he tore the lion apart with his bare hands as he might have torn a young goat. But he told neither his father nor his mother what he had done. ⁷Then he went down and talked with the woman, and he liked her.

⁸Some time later, when he went back to marry her, he turned aside to look at the lion's carcass, and in it he saw a swarm of bees and some honey. ⁹He scooped out the honey with his hands and ate as he went along. When he rejoined his parents, he gave them some, and they too ate it. But he did not tell them that he had taken the honey from the lion's carcass.

¹⁰Now his father went down to see the woman. And there Samson held a feast, as was customary for young men. ¹¹When the people saw him, they chose thirty men to be his companions.

¹²"Let me tell you a riddle," Samson said to them. "If you can give me the answer within the seven days of the feast, I will give you thirty linen garments and thirty sets of clothes. ¹³If you can't tell me the answer, you must give me thirty linen garments and thirty sets of clothes."

"Tell us your riddle," they said. "Let's hear it."

¹⁴He replied,

"Out of the eater, something to eat;
    out of the strong, something sweet."

For three days they could not give the answer.

¹⁵On the fourth[a] day, they said to Samson's wife, "Coax your husband into explaining the riddle for us, or we will burn you and your father's household to death. Did you invite us here to steal our property?"

¹⁶Then Samson's wife threw herself on him, sobbing, "You hate me! You don't really love me. You've given my people a riddle, but you haven't told me the answer."

"I haven't even explained it to my father or mother," he replied, "so why should I explain it to you?" ¹⁷She cried the whole seven days of the feast. So on the seventh day he finally told her, because she continued to press him. She in turn explained the riddle to her people.

¹⁸Before sunset on the seventh day the men of the town said to him,

"What is sweeter than honey?
    What is stronger than a lion?"

Samson said to them,

"If you had not plowed with my heifer,
    you would not have solved my riddle."

¹⁹Then the Spirit of the LORD came powerfully upon him. He went down to Ashkelon,

---

[a] 15 Some Septuagint manuscripts and Syriac; Hebrew *seventh*

struck down thirty of their men, stripped them of everything and gave their clothes to those who had explained the riddle. Burning with anger, he returned to his father's home. 20 And Samson's wife was given to one of his companions who had attended him at the feast.

Samson's Vengeance on the Philistines

15 Later on, at the time of wheat harvest, Samson took a young goat and went to visit his wife. He said, "I'm going to my wife's room." But her father would not let him go in.

2 "I was so sure you hated her," he said, "that I gave her to your companion. Isn't her younger sister more attractive? Take her instead."

3 Samson said to them, "This time I have a right to get even with the Philistines; I will really harm them." 4 So he went out and caught three hundred foxes and tied them tail to tail in pairs. He then fastened a torch to every pair of tails, 5 lit the torches and let the foxes loose in the standing grain of the Philistines. He burned up the shocks and standing grain, together with the vineyards and olive groves.

6 When the Philistines asked, "Who did this?" they were told, "Samson, the Timnite's son-in-law, because his wife was given to his companion."

So the Philistines went up and burned her and her father to death. 7 Samson said to them, "Since you've acted like this, I swear that I won't stop until I get my revenge on you." 8 He attacked them viciously and slaughtered many of them. Then he went down and stayed in a cave in the rock of Etam.

9 The Philistines went up and camped in Judah, spreading out near Lehi. 10 The people of Judah asked, "Why have you come to fight us?"

"We have come to take Samson prisoner," they answered, "to do to him as he did to us."

11 Then three thousand men from Judah went down to the cave in the rock of Etam and said to Samson, "Don't you realize that the Philistines are rulers over us? What have you done to us?"

He answered, "I merely did to them what they did to me."

12 They said to him, "We've come to tie you up and hand you over to the Philistines."

Samson said, "Swear to me that you won't kill me yourselves."

13 "Agreed," they answered. "We will only tie you up and hand you over to them. We will not kill you." So they bound him with two new ropes and led him up from the rock. 14 As he approached Lehi, the Philistines came toward him shouting. The Spirit of the LORD came powerfully upon him. The ropes on his arms became like charred flax, and the bindings dropped from his hands. 15 Finding a fresh jawbone of a donkey, he grabbed it and struck down a thousand men.

16 Then Samson said,

"With a donkey's jawbone
    I have made donkeys of them.[a]
With a donkey's jawbone
    I have killed a thousand men."

17 When he finished speaking, he threw away the jawbone; and the place was called Ramath Lehi.[b]

18 Because he was very thirsty, he cried out to the LORD, "You have given your servant this great victory. Must I now die of thirst and fall into the hands of the uncircumcised?" 19 Then God opened up the hollow place in Lehi, and water came out of it. When Samson drank, his strength returned and he revived. So the spring was called En Hakkore,[c] and it is still there in Lehi.

20 Samson led[d] Israel for twenty years in the days of the Philistines.

Samson and Delilah

16 One day Samson went to Gaza, where he saw a prostitute. He went in to spend the night with her. 2 The people of Gaza were told, "Samson is here!" So they surrounded the place and lay in wait for him all night at the city gate. They made no move during the night, saying, "At dawn we'll kill him."

3 But Samson lay there only until the middle of the night. Then he got up and took hold of the doors of the city gate, together with the two posts, and tore them loose, bar

---

[a] 16 Or made a heap or two; the Hebrew for donkey sounds like the Hebrew for heap.   [b] 17 Ramath Lehi means jawbone hill.   [c] 19 En Hakkore means caller's spring.   [d] 20 Traditionally judged

SAMSON

Samson led Israel for twenty years in the days of the Philistines. JUDGES 15:20

HIS NAME MEANS: "little sun," "brightness"
READ HIS STORY: *Judges 13–16*

I f the Bible had a strongest man competition, Samson would definitely win. His feats of strength didn't include stacking boulders or pulling a train with his teeth. Instead, he yanked out the city gates at Gaza and carried them to the top of a hill perhaps thirty miles away (Judges 16:3). The gates may have weighed as much as 5,000 pounds, maybe more. That's impressive! But not nearly as impressive as his anger toward the Philistines. On one occasion, Samson slaughtered 1,000 Philistines with the jawbone of a donkey (Judges 15:15). Sounds gruesome—and it was. It was also part of God's plan.

After God's people entered the promised land, but before the first king was appointed, the Lord raised up fourteen judges to maintain order. The judges helped fight Israel's enemies and guided the people to repentance. Samson was one of those judges. Samson's role was to lead the Israelites against the Philistines.

Samson had superhuman strength, thanks to following God's law as a Nazirite. We don't know much about Samson's guidance of Israel. But we do know he slept with prostitutes and looked at women as objects. He chose his first wife simply because she looked good to him (Judges 14:3). Ultimately, women proved to be his downfall. Once he hooked up with Delilah and told her the secret to his strength, Samson was captured, blinded and put to forced labor in prison. In the end, he prayed to God for a chance to save Israel once again from the Philistines. God gave Samson the power to topple a Philistine temple, killing thousands of Philistines—and himself—in one last feat of strength.

and all. He lifted them to his shoulders and carried them to the top of the hill that faces Hebron.

⁴Some time later, he fell in love with a woman in the Valley of Sorek whose name was Delilah. ⁵The rulers of the Philistines went to her and said, "See if you can lure him into showing you the secret of his great strength and how we can overpower him so we may tie him up and subdue him. Each one of us will give you eleven hundred shekels*ᵃ* of silver."

⁶So Delilah said to Samson, "Tell me the secret of your great strength and how you can be tied up and subdued."

⁷Samson answered her, "If anyone ties me with seven fresh bowstrings that have not been dried, I'll become as weak as any other man."

⁸Then the rulers of the Philistines brought her seven fresh bowstrings that had not been dried, and she tied him with them. ⁹With men hidden in the room, she called to him, "Samson, the Philistines are upon you!" But he snapped the bowstrings as easily as a piece of string snaps when it comes close to a flame. So the secret of his strength was not discovered.

¹⁰Then Delilah said to Samson, "You have made a fool of me; you lied to me. Come now, tell me how you can be tied."

¹¹He said, "If anyone ties me securely with new ropes that have never been used, I'll become as weak as any other man."

¹²So Delilah took new ropes and tied him with them. Then, with men hidden in the room, she called to him, "Samson, the Philistines are upon you!" But he snapped the ropes off his arms as if they were threads.

¹³Delilah then said to Samson, "All this time you have been making a fool of me and lying to me. Tell me how you can be tied." He replied, "If you weave the seven braids of my head into the fabric on the loom and tighten it with the pin, I'll become as weak as any other man." So while he was sleeping, Delilah took the seven braids of his head, wove them into the fabric ¹⁴and*ᵇ* tightened it with the pin.

Again she called to him, "Samson, the Philistines are upon you!" He awoke from his sleep and pulled up the pin and the loom, with the fabric.

¹⁵Then she said to him, "How can you say, 'I love you,' when you won't confide in me? This is the third time you have made a fool of me and haven't told me the secret of your great strength." ¹⁶With such nagging she prodded him day after day until he was sick to death of it.

¹⁷So he told her everything. "No razor has ever been used on my head," he said, "because I have been a Nazirite dedicated to God from my mother's womb. If my head were shaved, my strength would leave me, and I would become as weak as any other man."

¹⁸When Delilah saw that he had told her everything, she sent word to the rulers of the Philistines, "Come back once more; he has told me everything." So the rulers of the Philistines returned with the silver in their hands. ¹⁹After putting him to sleep on her lap, she called for someone to shave off the seven braids of his hair, and so began to subdue him.*ᶜ* And his strength left him.

²⁰Then she called, "Samson, the Philistines are upon you!"

He awoke from his sleep and thought, "I'll go out as before and shake myself free." But he did not know that the Lᴏʀᴅ had left him.

²¹Then the Philistines seized him, gouged out his eyes and took him down to Gaza. Binding him with bronze shackles, they set him to grinding grain in the prison. ²²But the hair on his head began to grow again after it had been shaved.

The Death of Samson

²³Now the rulers of the Philistines assembled to offer a great sacrifice to Dagon their god and to celebrate, saying, "Our god has delivered Samson, our enemy, into our hands."

²⁴When the people saw him, they praised their god, saying,

"Our god has delivered our enemy
　　into our hands,
the one who laid waste our land
　　and multiplied our slain."

²⁵While they were in high spirits, they shouted, "Bring out Samson to entertain us."

ᵃ 5 That is, about 28 pounds or about 13 kilograms　　*ᵇ 13,14* Some Septuagint manuscripts; Hebrew *replied, "I can if you weave the seven braids of my head into the fabric on the loom."* *¹⁴So she*　　*ᶜ 19* Hebrew; some Septuagint manuscripts *and he began to weaken*

So they called Samson out of the prison, and he performed for them.

When they stood him among the pillars, ²⁶Samson said to the servant who held his hand, "Put me where I can feel the pillars that support the temple, so that I may lean against them." ²⁷Now the temple was crowded with men and women; all the rulers of the Philistines were there, and on the roof were about three thousand men and women watching Samson perform. ²⁸Then Samson prayed to the LORD, "Sovereign LORD, remember me. Please, God, strengthen me just once more, and let me with one blow get revenge on the Philistines for my two eyes." ²⁹Then Samson reached toward the two central pillars on which the temple stood. Bracing himself against them, his right hand on the one and his left hand on the other, ³⁰Samson said, "Let me die with the Philistines!" Then he pushed with all his might, and down came the temple on the rulers and all the people in it. Thus he killed many more when he died than while he lived.

³¹Then his brothers and his father's whole family went down to get him. They brought him back and buried him between Zorah and Eshtaol in the tomb of Manoah his father. He had led*a* Israel twenty years.

Micah's Idols

17 Now a man named Micah from the hill country of Ephraim ²said to his mother, "The eleven hundred shekels*b* of silver that were taken from you and about which I heard you utter a curse—I have that silver with me; I took it."

Then his mother said, "The LORD bless you, my son!"

³When he returned the eleven hundred shekels of silver to his mother, she said, "I solemnly consecrate my silver to the LORD for my son to make an image overlaid with silver. I will give it back to you."

⁴So after he returned the silver to his mother, she took two hundred shekels*c* of silver and gave them to a silversmith, who used them to make the idol. And it was put in Micah's house.

⁵Now this man Micah had a shrine, and he made an ephod and some household gods and installed one of his sons as his priest. ⁶In those days Israel had no king; everyone did as they saw fit.

⁷A young Levite from Bethlehem in Judah, who had been living within the clan of Judah, ⁸left that town in search of some other place to stay. On his way*d* he came to Micah's house in the hill country of Ephraim.

⁹Micah asked him, "Where are you from?"

"I'm a Levite from Bethlehem in Judah," he said, "and I'm looking for a place to stay."

¹⁰Then Micah said to him, "Live with me and be my father and priest, and I'll give you ten shekels*e* of silver a year, your clothes and your food." ¹¹So the Levite agreed to live with him, and the young man became like one of his sons to him. ¹²Then Micah installed the Levite, and the young man became his priest and lived in his house. ¹³And Micah said, "Now I know that the LORD will be good to me, since this Levite has become my priest."

The Danites Settle in Laish

18 In those days Israel had no king.

And in those days the tribe of the Danites was seeking a place of their own where they might settle, because they had not yet come into an inheritance among the tribes of Israel. ²So the Danites sent five of their leading men from Zorah and Eshtaol to spy out the land and explore it. These men represented all the Danites. They told them, "Go, explore the land."

So they entered the hill country of Ephraim and came to the house of Micah, where they spent the night. ³When they were near Micah's house, they recognized the voice of the young Levite; so they turned in there and asked him, "Who brought you here? What are you doing in this place? Why are you here?"

⁴He told them what Micah had done for him, and said, "He has hired me and I am his priest."

⁵Then they said to him, "Please inquire of God to learn whether our journey will be successful."

⁶The priest answered them, "Go in peace. Your journey has the LORD's approval."

---

a 31 Traditionally *judged*　*b 2* That is, about 28 pounds or about 13 kilograms　*c 4* That is, about 5 pounds or about 2.3 kilograms　*d 8* Or *To carry on his profession*　*e 10* That is, about 4 ounces or about 115 grams

⁷So the five men left and came to Laish, where they saw that the people were living in safety, like the Sidonians, at peace and secure. And since their land lacked nothing, they were prosperous.ᵃ Also, they lived a long way from the Sidonians and had no relationship with anyone else.ᵇ

⁸When they returned to Zorah and Eshtaol, their fellow Danites asked them, "How did you find things?"

⁹They answered, "Come on, let's attack them! We have seen the land, and it is very good. Aren't you going to do something? Don't hesitate to go there and take it over. ¹⁰When you get there, you will find an unsuspecting people and a spacious land that God has put into your hands, a land that lacks nothing whatever."

¹¹Then six hundred men of the Danites, armed for battle, set out from Zorah and Eshtaol. ¹²On their way they set up camp near Kiriath Jearim in Judah. This is why the place west of Kiriath Jearim is called Mahaneh Danᶜ to this day. ¹³From there they went on to the hill country of Ephraim and came to Micah's house.

¹⁴Then the five men who had spied out the land of Laish said to their fellow Danites, "Do you know that one of these houses has an ephod, some household gods and an image overlaid with silver? Now you know what to do." ¹⁵So they turned in there and went to the house of the young Levite at Micah's place and greeted him. ¹⁶The six hundred Danites, armed for battle, stood at the entrance of the gate. ¹⁷The five men who had spied out the land went inside and took the idol, the ephod and the household gods while the priest and the six hundred armed men stood at the entrance of the gate.

¹⁸When the five men went into Micah's house and took the idol, the ephod and the household gods, the priest said to them, "What are you doing?"

¹⁹They answered him, "Be quiet! Don't say a word. Come with us, and be our father and priest. Isn't it better that you serve a tribe and clan in Israel as priest rather than just one man's household?" ²⁰The priest was very pleased. He took the ephod, the household gods and the idol and went along with the people. ²¹Putting their little children, their livestock and their possessions in front of them, they turned away and left.

²²When they had gone some distance from Micah's house, the men who lived near Micah were called together and overtook the Danites. ²³As they shouted after them, the Danites turned and said to Micah, "What's the matter with you that you called out your men to fight?"

²⁴He replied, "You took the gods I made, and my priest, and went away. What else do I have? How can you ask, 'What's the matter with you?'"

²⁵The Danites answered, "Don't argue with us, or some of the men may get angry and attack you, and you and your family will lose your lives." ²⁶So the Danites went their way, and Micah, seeing that they were too strong for him, turned around and went back home.

²⁷Then they took what Micah had made, and his priest, and went on to Laish, against a people at peace and secure. They attacked them with the sword and burned down their city. ²⁸There was no one to rescue them because they lived a long way from Sidon and had no relationship with anyone else. The city was in a valley near Beth Rehob.

The Danites rebuilt the city and settled there. ²⁹They named it Dan after their ancestor Dan, who was born to Israel—though the city used to be called Laish. ³⁰There the Danites set up for themselves the idol, and Jonathan son of Gershom, the son of Moses,ᵈ and his sons were priests for the tribe of Dan until the time of the captivity of the land. ³¹They continued to use the idol Micah had made, all the time the house of God was in Shiloh.

A Levite and His Concubine

19 In those days Israel had no king.

Now a Levite who lived in a remote area in the hill country of Ephraim took a concubine from Bethlehem in Judah. ²But she was unfaithful to him. She left him and went back to her parents' home in Bethlehem, Judah. After she had been there four

---

ᵃ 7 The meaning of the Hebrew for this clause is uncertain.   ᵇ 7 Hebrew; some Septuagint manuscripts
with the Arameans   ᶜ 12 *Mahaneh Dan* means *Dan's camp.*   ᵈ 30 Many Hebrew manuscripts, some
Septuagint manuscripts and Vulgate; many other Hebrew manuscripts and some other Septuagint
manuscripts *Manasseh*

months, ³her husband went to her to persuade her to return. He had with him his servant and two donkeys. She took him into her parents' home, and when her father saw him, he gladly welcomed him. ⁴His father-in-law, the woman's father, prevailed on him to stay; so he remained with him three days, eating and drinking, and sleeping there.

⁵On the fourth day they got up early and he prepared to leave, but the woman's father said to his son-in-law, "Refresh yourself with something to eat; then you can go." ⁶So the two of them sat down to eat and drink together. Afterward the woman's father said, "Please stay tonight and enjoy yourself." ⁷And when the man got up to go, his father-in-law persuaded him, so he stayed there that night. ⁸On the morning of the fifth day, when he rose to go, the woman's father said, "Refresh yourself. Wait till afternoon!" So the two of them ate together.

⁹Then when the man, with his concubine and his servant, got up to leave, his father-in-law, the woman's father, said, "Now look, it's almost evening. Spend the night here; the day is nearly over. Stay and enjoy yourself. Early tomorrow morning you can get up and be on your way home." ¹⁰But, unwilling to stay another night, the man left and went toward Jebus (that is, Jerusalem), with his two saddled donkeys and his concubine.

¹¹When they were near Jebus and the day was almost gone, the servant said to his master, "Come, let's stop at this city of the Jebusites and spend the night."

¹²His master replied, "No. We won't go into any city whose people are not Israelites. We will go on to Gibeah." ¹³He added, "Come, let's try to reach Gibeah or Ramah and spend the night in one of those places." ¹⁴So they went on, and the sun set as they neared Gibeah in Benjamin. ¹⁵There they stopped to spend the night. They went and sat in the city square, but no one took them in for the night.

¹⁶That evening an old man from the hill country of Ephraim, who was living in Gibeah (the inhabitants of the place were Benjamites), came in from his work in the fields. ¹⁷When he looked and saw the traveler in the city square, the old man asked, "Where are you going? Where did you come from?"

¹⁸He answered, "We are on our way from Bethlehem in Judah to a remote area in the hill country of Ephraim where I live. I have been to Bethlehem in Judah and now I am going to the house of the LORD.ᵃ No one has taken me in for the night. ¹⁹We have both straw and fodder for our donkeys and bread and wine for ourselves your servants — me, the woman and the young man with us. We don't need anything."

²⁰"You are welcome at my house," the old man said. "Let me supply whatever you need. Only don't spend the night in the square." ²¹So he took him into his house and fed his donkeys. After they had washed their feet, they had something to eat and drink.

²²While they were enjoying themselves, some of the wicked men of the city surrounded the house. Pounding on the door, they shouted to the old man who owned the house, "Bring out the man who came to your house so we can have sex with him."

²³The owner of the house went outside and said to them, "No, my friends, don't be so vile. Since this man is my guest, don't do this outrageous thing. ²⁴Look, here is my virgin daughter, and his concubine. I will bring them out to you now, and you can use them and do to them whatever you wish. But as for this man, don't do such an outrageous thing."

²⁵But the men would not listen to him. So the man took his concubine and sent her outside to them, and they raped her and abused her throughout the night, and at dawn they let her go. ²⁶At daybreak the woman went back to the house where her master was staying, fell down at the door and lay there until daylight.

²⁷When her master got up in the morning and opened the door of the house and stepped out to continue on his way, there lay his concubine, fallen in the doorway of the house, with her hands on the threshold. ²⁸He said to her, "Get up; let's go." But there was no answer. Then the man put her on his donkey and set out for home.

²⁹When he reached home, he took a knife and cut up his concubine, limb by limb, into twelve parts and sent them into all the areas of Israel. ³⁰Everyone who saw it was saying to one another, "Such a thing has never been

<hr>

ᵃ 18 Hebrew, Vulgate, Syriac and Targum; Septuagint *going home* seen or done, not since the day the Israelites came up out of Egypt. Just imagine! We must do something! So speak up!"

The Israelites Punish the Benjamites

20 Then all Israel from Dan to Beersheba and from the land of Gilead came together as one and assembled before the LORD in Mizpah. ²The leaders of all the people of the tribes of Israel took their places in the assembly of God's people, four hundred thousand men armed with swords. ³(The Benjamites heard that the Israelites had gone up to Mizpah.) Then the Israelites said, "Tell us how this awful thing happened."

⁴So the Levite, the husband of the murdered woman, said, "I and my concubine came to Gibeah in Benjamin to spend the night. ⁵During the night the men of Gibeah came after me and surrounded the house, intending to kill me. They raped my concubine, and she died. ⁶I took my concubine, cut her into pieces and sent one piece to each region of Israel's inheritance, because they committed this lewd and outrageous act in Israel. ⁷Now, all you Israelites, speak up and tell me what you have decided to do."

⁸All the men rose up together as one, saying, "None of us will go home. No, not one of us will return to his house. ⁹But now this is what we'll do to Gibeah: We'll go up against it in the order decided by casting lots. ¹⁰We'll take ten men out of every hundred from all the tribes of Israel, and a hundred from a thousand, and a thousand from ten thousand, to get provisions for the army. Then, when the army arrives at Gibeah*a* in Benjamin, it can give them what they deserve for this outrageous act done in Israel." ¹¹So all the Israelites got together and united as one against the city.

¹²The tribes of Israel sent messengers throughout the tribe of Benjamin, saying, "What about this awful crime that was committed among you? ¹³Now turn those wicked men of Gibeah over to us so that we may put them to death and purge the evil from Israel."

But the Benjamites would not listen to their fellow Israelites. ¹⁴From their towns they came together at Gibeah to fight against the Israelites. ¹⁵At once the Benjamites mobilized twenty-six thousand swordsmen from their towns, in addition to seven hundred able young men from those living in Gibeah. ¹⁶Among all these soldiers there were seven hundred select troops who were left-handed, each of whom could sling a stone at a hair and not miss.

¹⁷Israel, apart from Benjamin, mustered four hundred thousand swordsmen, all of them fit for battle.

¹⁸The Israelites went up to Bethel*b* and inquired of God. They said, "Who of us is to go up first to fight against the Benjamites?"

The LORD replied, "Judah shall go first."

¹⁹The next morning the Israelites got up and pitched camp near Gibeah. ²⁰The Israelites went out to fight the Benjamites and took up battle positions against them at Gibeah. ²¹The Benjamites came out of Gibeah and cut down twenty-two thousand Israelites on the battlefield that day. ²²But the Israelites encouraged one another and again took up their positions where they had stationed themselves the first day. ²³The Israelites went up and wept before the LORD until evening, and they inquired of the LORD. They said, "Shall we go up again to fight against the Benjamites, our fellow Israelites?"

The LORD answered, "Go up against them."

²⁴Then the Israelites drew near to Benjamin the second day. ²⁵This time, when the Benjamites came out from Gibeah to oppose them, they cut down another eighteen thousand Israelites, all of them armed with swords.

²⁶Then all the Israelites, the whole army, went up to Bethel, and there they sat weeping before the LORD. They fasted that day until evening and presented burnt offerings and fellowship offerings to the LORD. ²⁷And the Israelites inquired of the LORD. (In those days the ark of the covenant of God was there, ²⁸with Phinehas son of Eleazar, the son of Aaron, ministering before it.) They asked, "Shall we go up again to fight against the Benjamites, our fellow Israelites, or not?"

The LORD responded, "Go, for tomorrow I will give them into your hands."

²⁹Then Israel set an ambush around

---

a 10 One Hebrew manuscript; most Hebrew manuscripts *Geba*, a variant of *Gibeah*   *b* 18 Or *to the house of God*; also in verse 26

Gibeah. ³⁰They went up against the Benjamites on the third day and took up positions against Gibeah as they had done before. ³¹The Benjamites came out to meet them and were drawn away from the city. They began to inflict casualties on the Israelites as before, so that about thirty men fell in the open field and on the roads — the one leading to Bethel and the other to Gibeah. ³²While the Benjamites were saying, "We are defeating them as before," the Israelites were saying, "Let's retreat and draw them away from the city to the roads."

³³All the men of Israel moved from their places and took up positions at Baal Tamar, and the Israelite ambush charged out of its place on the west*ᵃ* of Gibeah.*ᵇ* ³⁴Then ten thousand of Israel's able young men made a frontal attack on Gibeah. The fighting was so heavy that the Benjamites did not realize how near disaster was. ³⁵The LORD defeated Benjamin before Israel, and on that day the Israelites struck down 25,100 Benjamites, all armed with swords. ³⁶Then the Benjamites saw that they were beaten.

Now the men of Israel had given way before Benjamin, because they relied on the ambush they had set near Gibeah. ³⁷Those who had been in ambush made a sudden dash into Gibeah, spread out and put the whole city to the sword. ³⁸The Israelites had arranged with the ambush that they should send up a great cloud of smoke from the city, ³⁹and then the Israelites would counterattack.

The Benjamites had begun to inflict casualties on the Israelites (about thirty), and they said, "We are defeating them as in the first battle." ⁴⁰But when the column of smoke began to rise from the city, the Benjamites turned and saw the whole city going up in smoke. ⁴¹Then the Israelites counterattacked, and the Benjamites were terrified, because they realized that disaster had come on them. ⁴²So they fled before the Israelites in the direction of the wilderness, but they could not escape the battle. And the Israelites who came out of the towns cut them down there. ⁴³They surrounded the Benjamites, chased them and easily*ᶜ* overran them in the vicinity of Gibeah on the

east. ⁴⁴Eighteen thousand Benjamites fell, all of them valiant fighters. ⁴⁵As they turned and fled toward the wilderness to the rock of Rimmon, the Israelites cut down five thousand men along the roads. They kept pressing after the Benjamites as far as Gidom and struck down two thousand more.

⁴⁶On that day twenty-five thousand Benjamite swordsmen fell, all of them valiant fighters. ⁴⁷But six hundred of them turned and fled into the wilderness to the rock of Rimmon, where they stayed four months. ⁴⁸The men of Israel went back to Benjamin and put all the towns to the sword, including the animals and everything else they found. All the towns they came across they set on fire.

Wives for the Benjamites

21 The men of Israel had taken an oath at Mizpah: "Not one of us will give his daughter in marriage to a Benjamite."

²The people went to Bethel,*ᵈ* where they sat before God until evening, raising their voices and weeping bitterly. ³"LORD, God of Israel," they cried, "why has this happened to Israel? Why should one tribe be missing from Israel today?"

⁴Early the next day the people built an altar and presented burnt offerings and fellowship offerings.

⁵Then the Israelites asked, "Who from all the tribes of Israel has failed to assemble before the LORD?" For they had taken a solemn oath that anyone who failed to assemble before the LORD at Mizpah was to be put to death.

⁶Now the Israelites grieved for the tribe of Benjamin, their fellow Israelites. "Today one tribe is cut off from Israel," they said. ⁷"How can we provide wives for those who are left, since we have taken an oath by the LORD not to give them any of our daughters in marriage?" ⁸Then they asked, "Which one of the tribes of Israel failed to assemble before the LORD at Mizpah?" They discovered that no one from Jabesh Gilead had come to the camp for the assembly. ⁹For when they counted the people, they found that none of the people of Jabesh Gilead were there.

ᵃ 33 Some Septuagint manuscripts and Vulgate; the meaning of the Hebrew for this word is uncertain.
ᵇ 33 Hebrew *Geba*, a variant of *Gibeah*   *ᶜ 43* The meaning of the Hebrew for this word is uncertain.
ᵈ 2 Or *to the house of God*

[10]So the assembly sent twelve thousand fighting men with instructions to go to Jabesh Gilead and put to the sword those living there, including the women and children. [11]"This is what you are to do," they said. "Kill every male and every woman who is not a virgin." [12]They found among the people living in Jabesh Gilead four hundred young women who had never slept with a man, and they took them to the camp at Shiloh in Canaan.

[13]Then the whole assembly sent an offer of peace to the Benjamites at the rock of Rimmon. [14]So the Benjamites returned at that time and were given the women of Jabesh Gilead who had been spared. But there were not enough for all of them.

[15]The people grieved for Benjamin, because the LORD had made a gap in the tribes of Israel. [16]And the elders of the assembly said, "With the women of Benjamin destroyed, how shall we provide wives for the men who are left? [17]The Benjamite survivors must have heirs," they said, "so that a tribe of Israel will not be wiped out. [18]We can't give them our daughters as wives, since we Israelites have taken this oath: 'Cursed be anyone who gives a wife to a Benjamite.' [19]But look, there is the annual festival of the LORD in Shiloh, which lies north of Bethel, east of the road that goes from Bethel to Shechem, and south of Lebonah."

[20]So they instructed the Benjamites, saying, "Go and hide in the vineyards [21]and watch. When the young women of Shiloh come out to join in the dancing, rush from the vineyards and each of you seize one of them to be your wife. Then return to the land of Benjamin. [22]When their fathers or brothers complain to us, we will say to them, 'Do us the favor of helping them, because we did not get wives for them during the war. You will not be guilty of breaking your oath because you did not give your daughters to them.'"

[23]So that is what the Benjamites did. While the young women were dancing, each man caught one and carried her off to be his wife. Then they returned to their inheritance and rebuilt the towns and settled in them.

[24]At that time the Israelites left that place and went home to their tribes and clans, each to his own inheritance.

[25]In those days Israel had no king; everyone did as they saw fit.

RUTH

➡ **WHEN DID THIS HAPPEN?**

Around 1000 B.C. in Canaan (the promised land), modern-day Israel

➡ **WHO IS IN THIS BOOK?**

Elimelek
Mahlon
Kilion
Orpah
Naomi
Ruth
Boaz

➡ **VERSES YOU MIGHT RECOGNIZE**

RUTH 1:16
"Where you go I will go, and where you stay I will stay. Your people will be my people and your God my God."

RUTH 4:14
"Praise be to the LORD, who this day has not left you without a guardian-redeemer. May he become famous throughout Israel!"

WHAT'S IT ABOUT?

You might think that one of two books named after women in the Bible (the other is Esther) would be about an Israelite woman. But the story of Ruth is about an outsider—a Moabite. Ruth grew up in a culture that didn't believe in the one true God. At the beginning of the book, we find out that Ruth's husband had died. She set off with her mother-in-law, Naomi, also a widow, to return to Naomi's homeland, Judah.

The book of Ruth takes place during the time of the judges. While many of those in Israel were disobeying God, some people like Naomi and her family still followed God. This book tells the love story of Ruth and Boaz. God's faithfulness to this godly couple shows what happens when people do things God's way—and how God keeps his promises even during difficult times. Ruth would be the great-grandmother of King David, an ancestor of Jesus Christ.

RUTH

Naomi Loses Her Husband and Sons

1 In the days when the judges ruled,[a] there was a famine in the land. So a man from Bethlehem in Judah, together with his wife and two sons, went to live for a while in the country of Moab. ²The man's name was Elimelek, his wife's name was Naomi, and the names of his two sons were Mahlon and Kilion. They were Ephrathites from Bethlehem, Judah. And they went to Moab and lived there.

³Now Elimelek, Naomi's husband, died, and she was left with her two sons. ⁴They married Moabite women, one named Orpah and the other Ruth. After they had lived there about ten years, ⁵both Mahlon and Kilion also died, and Naomi was left without her two sons and her husband.

Naomi and Ruth Return to Bethlehem

⁶When Naomi heard in Moab that the LORD had come to the aid of his people by providing food for them, she and her daughters-in-law prepared to return home from there. ⁷With her two daughters-in-law she left the place where she had been living and set out on the road that would take them back to the land of Judah.

⁸Then Naomi said to her two daughters-in-law, "Go back, each of you, to your mother's home. May the LORD show you kindness, as you have shown kindness to your dead husbands and to me. ⁹May the LORD grant that each of you will find rest in the home of another husband."

Then she kissed them goodbye and they wept aloud ¹⁰and said to her, "We will go back with you to your people."

¹¹But Naomi said, "Return home, my daughters. Why would you come with me? Am I going to have any more sons, who could become your husbands? ¹²Return home, my daughters; I am too old to have another husband. Even if I thought there was still hope for me — even if I had a husband tonight and then gave birth to sons — ¹³would you wait until they grew up? Would you remain unmarried for them? No, my daughters. It is more bitter for me than for you, because the LORD's hand has turned against me!"

¹⁴At this they wept aloud again. Then Orpah kissed her mother-in-law goodbye, but Ruth clung to her.

¹⁵"Look," said Naomi, "your sister-in-law is going back to her people and her gods. Go back with her."

¹⁶But Ruth replied, "Don't urge me to leave you or to turn back from you. Where you go I will go, and where you stay I will stay. Your people will be my people and your God my God. ¹⁷Where you die I will die, and there I will be buried. May the LORD deal with me, be it ever so severely, if even death separates you and me." ¹⁸When Naomi realized that Ruth was determined to go with her, she stopped urging her.

¹⁹So the two women went on until they came to Bethlehem. When they arrived in Bethlehem, the whole town was stirred because of them, and the women exclaimed, "Can this be Naomi?"

²⁰"Don't call me Naomi,[b]" she told them. "Call me Mara,[c] because the Almighty[d] has made my life very bitter. ²¹I went away full, but the LORD has brought me back empty. Why call me Naomi? The LORD has afflicted[e] me; the Almighty has brought misfortune upon me."

²²So Naomi returned from Moab accompanied by Ruth the Moabite, her daughter-in-law, arriving in Bethlehem as the barley harvest was beginning.

Ruth Meets Boaz in the Grain Field

2 Now Naomi had a relative on her husband's side, a man of standing from the clan of Elimelek, whose name was Boaz.

²And Ruth the Moabite said to Naomi,

---

[a] 1 Traditionally *judged*   [b] 20 *Naomi* means *pleasant.*   [c] 20 *Mara* means *bitter.*   [d] 20 Hebrew
Shaddai; also in verse 21   [e] 21 Or *has testified against*

"Let me go to the fields and pick up the left-over grain behind anyone in whose eyes I find favor."

Naomi said to her, "Go ahead, my daughter." [3] So she went out, entered a field and began to glean behind the harvesters. As it turned out, she was working in a field belonging to Boaz, who was from the clan of Elimelek.

[4] Just then Boaz arrived from Bethlehem and greeted the harvesters, "The LORD be with you!"

"The LORD bless you!" they answered.

[5] Boaz asked the overseer of his harvesters, "Who does that young woman belong to?"

[6] The overseer replied, "She is the Moabite who came back from Moab with Naomi. [7] She said, 'Please let me glean and gather among the sheaves behind the harvesters.' She came into the field and has remained here from morning till now, except for a short rest in the shelter."

[8] So Boaz said to Ruth, "My daughter, listen to me. Don't go and glean in another field and don't go away from here. Stay here with the women who work for me. [9] Watch the field where the men are harvesting, and follow along after the women. I have told the men not to lay a hand on you. And whenever you are thirsty, go and get a drink from the water jars the men have filled."

[10] At this, she bowed down with her face to the ground. She asked him, "Why have I found such favor in your eyes that you notice me—a foreigner?"

[11] Boaz replied, "I've been told all about what you have done for your mother-in-law since the death of your husband—how you left your father and mother and your homeland and came to live with a people you did not know before. [12] May the LORD repay you for what you have done. May you be richly rewarded by the LORD, the God of Israel, under whose wings you have come to take refuge."

[13] "May I continue to find favor in your eyes, my lord," she said. "You have put me at ease by speaking kindly to your servant—though I do not have the standing of one of your servants."

[14] At mealtime Boaz said to her, "Come over here. Have some bread and dip it in the wine vinegar."

When she sat down with the harvesters, he offered her some roasted grain. She ate all she wanted and had some left over. [15] As she got up to glean, Boaz gave orders to his men, "Let her gather among the sheaves and don't reprimand her. [16] Even pull out some stalks for her from the bundles and leave them for her to pick up, and don't rebuke her."

[17] So Ruth gleaned in the field until evening. Then she threshed the barley she had gathered, and it amounted to about an ephah.[a] [18] She carried it back to town, and her mother-in-law saw how much she had gathered. Ruth also brought out and gave her what she had left over after she had eaten enough.

[19] Her mother-in-law asked her, "Where did you glean today? Where did you work? Blessed be the man who took notice of you!"

Then Ruth told her mother-in-law about the one at whose place she had been working. "The name of the man I worked with today is Boaz," she said.

[20] "The LORD bless him!" Naomi said to her daughter-in-law. "He has not stopped showing his kindness to the living and the dead." She added, "That man is our close relative; he is one of our guardian-redeemers.[b]"

[21] Then Ruth the Moabite said, "He even said to me, 'Stay with my workers until they finish harvesting all my grain.'"

[22] Naomi said to Ruth her daughter-in-law, "It will be good for you, my daughter, to go with the women who work for him, because in someone else's field you might be harmed."

[23] So Ruth stayed close to the women of Boaz to glean until the barley and wheat harvests were finished. And she lived with her mother-in-law.

Ruth and Boaz at the Threshing Floor

3 One day Ruth's mother-in-law Naomi said to her, "My daughter, I must find a home[c] for you, where you will be well provided for. [2] Now Boaz, with whose women you

---

[a] 17 That is, probably about 30 pounds or about 13 kilograms   [b] 20 The Hebrew word for *guardian-redeemer* is a legal term for one who has the obligation to redeem a relative in serious difficulty (see Lev. 25:25-55).   [c] 1 Hebrew *find rest* (see 1:9)

have worked, is a relative of ours. Tonight he will be winnowing barley on the threshing floor. ³Wash, put on perfume, and get dressed in your best clothes. Then go down to the threshing floor, but don't let him know you are there until he has finished eating and drinking. ⁴When he lies down, note the place where he is lying. Then go and uncover his feet and lie down. He will tell you what to do."

⁵"I will do whatever you say," Ruth answered. ⁶So she went down to the threshing floor and did everything her mother-in-law told her to do.

⁷When Boaz had finished eating and drinking and was in good spirits, he went over to lie down at the far end of the grain pile. Ruth approached quietly, uncovered his feet and lay down. ⁸In the middle of the night something startled the man; he turned— and there was a woman lying at his feet!

⁹"Who are you?" he asked.

"I am your servant Ruth," she said. "Spread the corner of your garment over me, since you are a guardian-redeemer^a of our family."

¹⁰"The Lᴏʀᴅ bless you, my daughter," he replied. "This kindness is greater than that which you showed earlier: You have not run after the younger men, whether rich or poor. ¹¹And now, my daughter, don't be afraid. I will do for you all you ask. All the people of my town know that you are a woman of noble character. ¹²Although it is true that I am a guardian-redeemer of our family, there is another who is more closely related than I. ¹³Stay here for the night, and in the morning if he wants to do his duty as your guardian-redeemer, good; let him redeem you. But if he is not willing, as surely as the Lᴏʀᴅ lives I will do it. Lie here until morning."

¹⁴So she lay at his feet until morning, but got up before anyone could be recognized; and he said, "No one must know that a woman came to the threshing floor."

¹⁵He also said, "Bring me the shawl you are wearing and hold it out." When she did

so, he poured into it six measures of barley and placed the bundle on her. Then he^b went back to town.

¹⁶When Ruth came to her mother-in-law, Naomi asked, "How did it go, my daughter?"

Then she told her everything Boaz had done for her ¹⁷and added, "He gave me these six measures of barley, saying, 'Don't go back to your mother-in-law empty-handed.' "

¹⁸Then Naomi said, "Wait, my daughter, until you find out what happens. For the man will not rest until the matter is settled today."

Boaz Marries Ruth

4 Meanwhile Boaz went up to the town gate and sat down there just as the guardian-redeemer^c he had mentioned came along. Boaz said, "Come over here, my friend, and sit down." So he went over and sat down.

²Boaz took ten of the elders of the town and said, "Sit here," and they did so. ³Then he said to the guardian-redeemer, "Naomi, who has come back from Moab, is selling the piece of land that belonged to our relative Elimelek. ⁴I thought I should bring the matter to your attention and suggest that you buy it in the presence of these seated here and in the presence of the elders of my people. If you will redeem it, do so. But if you^d will not, tell me, so I will know. For no one has the right to do it except you, and I am next in line."

"I will redeem it," he said.

⁵Then Boaz said, "On the day you buy the land from Naomi, you also acquire Ruth the Moabite, the^e dead man's widow, in order to maintain the name of the dead with his property."

⁶At this, the guardian-redeemer said, "Then I cannot redeem it because I might endanger my own estate. You redeem it yourself. I cannot do it."

⁷(Now in earlier times in Israel, for the redemption and transfer of property to become final, one party took off his sandal and gave it

---

^{a} 9 The Hebrew word for *guardian-redeemer* is a legal term for one who has the obligation to redeem a relative in serious difficulty (see Lev. 25:25-55); also in verses 12 and 13. ^{b} 15 Most Hebrew manuscripts; many Hebrew manuscripts, Vulgate and Syriac *she* ^{c} 1 The Hebrew word for *guardian-redeemer* is a legal term for one who has the obligation to redeem a relative in serious difficulty (see Lev. 25:25-55); also in verses 3, 6, 8 and 14. ^{d} 4 Many Hebrew manuscripts, Septuagint, Vulgate and Syriac; most Hebrew manuscripts *he* ^{e} 5 Vulgate and Syriac; Hebrew (see also Septuagint) *Naomi and from Ruth the Moabite, you acquire the*

OF THE BIBLE

BOAZ

Then Ruth told her mother-in-law about the one at whose place she had been working. "The name of the man I worked with today is Boaz," she said. "The LORD bless him!' Naomi said to her daughter-in-law. "He has not stopped showing his kindness to the living and the dead." She added, "That man is our close relative; he is one of our guardian-redeemers." RUTH 2:19-20

HIS NAME MEANS: "in him is strength"
READ HIS STORY: *Ruth 2-4*

A wealthy Israelite from Bethlehem, Boaz was in a position to be the redeemer of his relative's widowed wife Ruth, according to Old Testament law. Boaz obeyed the law, paid the price, and married Ruth.

The story we read about Boaz in the book of Ruth, however, isn't just the historical account of a man obeying the law. Instead, it is a tender love story between Boaz and Ruth.

What is so extraordinary about Boaz? He is an Old Testament example of the Messiah who was to come. According to the prophecies, God would send a Messiah to redeem his people.

When Jesus came to earth as our Redeemer, he died on the cross and paid the price for the punishment of our sins. He fulfilled the Old Testament laws. When we read the New Testament, however, we see that Jesus was not merely obeying the law. As in the story of Boaz and Ruth, we discover a tender love story between Jesus and the church.

The story of Boaz and Ruth teaches us that true faith is not about a religion, but a relationship with the One who loves you most of all.

to the other. This was the method of legalizing transactions in Israel.)

⁸So the guardian-redeemer said to Boaz, "Buy it yourself." And he removed his sandal.

⁹Then Boaz announced to the elders and all the people, "Today you are witnesses that I have bought from Naomi all the property of Elimelek, Kilion and Mahlon. ¹⁰I have also acquired Ruth the Moabite, Mahlon's widow, as my wife, in order to maintain the name of the dead with his property, so that his name will not disappear from among his family or from his hometown. Today you are witnesses!"

¹¹Then the elders and all the people at the gate said, "We are witnesses. May the Lord make the woman who is coming into your home like Rachel and Leah, who together built up the family of Israel. May you have standing in Ephrathah and be famous in Bethlehem. ¹²Through the offspring the Lord gives you by this young woman, may your family be like that of Perez, whom Tamar bore to Judah."

Naomi Gains a Son

¹³So Boaz took Ruth and she became his wife. When he made love to her, the Lord enabled her to conceive, and she gave birth to a son. ¹⁴The women said to Naomi: "Praise be to the Lord, who this day has not left you without a guardian-redeemer. May he become famous throughout Israel! ¹⁵He will renew your life and sustain you in your old age. For your daughter-in-law, who loves you and who is better to you than seven sons, has given him birth."

¹⁶Then Naomi took the child in her arms and cared for him. ¹⁷The women living there said, "Naomi has a son!" And they named him Obed. He was the father of Jesse, the father of David.

The Genealogy of David

¹⁸This, then, is the family line of Perez:

Perez was the father of Hezron,
¹⁹Hezron the father of Ram,
Ram the father of Amminadab,
²⁰Amminadab the father of Nahshon,
Nahshon the father of Salmon,ᵃ
²¹Salmon the father of Boaz,
Boaz the father of Obed,
²²Obed the father of Jesse,
and Jesse the father of David.

ᵃ 20 A few Hebrew manuscripts, some Septuagint manuscripts and Vulgate (see also verse 21 and Septuagint of 1 Chron. 2:11); most Hebrew manuscripts *Salma*

1 SAMUEL

WHEN DID THIS HAPPEN?

About 1100-1000 B.C. in the land of Israel

WHO IS IN THIS BOOK?

Hannah
Eli
Samuel
Saul
David
Jonathan
Abigail

VERSES YOU MIGHT RECOGNIZE

1 SAMUEL 15:22

"To obey is better than sacrifice, and to heed is better than the fat of rams."

1 SAMUEL 16:7B

"People look at the outward appearance, but the LORD looks at the heart."

WHAT'S IT ABOUT?

This book begins with the story of Samuel, the final judge of Israel. In the 1,000 years since God had made his promise to Abraham, he ruled his people directly, through leaders such as Moses, Joshua and the judges. But the Israelites noticed that the nations around them were ruled by human kings and told God they wanted one too. God granted them their request and Samuel appointed Saul to be Israel's first king.

Even though God gave the Israelites what they wanted, he told Samuel that the people had rejected him (God) as their king and they would face consequences for their choices. No human king could lead them and care for them the way God could. In the rest of the book, we learn more about Saul and his successor to the throne, David. Neither of these two kings ruled perfectly, but one day, the true King, Jesus, would be born into the line of David and would reign perfectly for eternity.

1 SAMUEL

The Birth of Samuel

1 There was a certain man from Ramathaim, a Zuphite[a] from the hill country
of Ephraim, whose name was Elkanah son of
Jeroham, the son of Elihu, the son of Tohu,
the son of Zuph, an Ephraimite. [2] He had two
wives; one was called Hannah and the other
Peninnah. Peninnah had children, but Hannah had none.

[3] Year after year this man went up from
his town to worship and sacrifice to the
LORD Almighty at Shiloh, where Hophni and
Phinehas, the two sons of Eli, were priests of
the LORD. [4] Whenever the day came for Elkanah to sacrifice, he would give portions
of the meat to his wife Peninnah and to all
her sons and daughters. [5] But to Hannah
he gave a double portion because he loved
her, and the LORD had closed her womb.
[6] Because the LORD had closed Hannah's
womb, her rival kept provoking her in order
to irritate her. [7] This went on year after year.
Whenever Hannah went up to the house
of the LORD, her rival provoked her till she
wept and would not eat. [8] Her husband Elkanah would say to her, "Hannah, why are you
weeping? Why don't you eat? Why are you
downhearted? Don't I mean more to you
than ten sons?"

[9] Once when they had finished eating and
drinking in Shiloh, Hannah stood up. Now
Eli the priest was sitting on his chair by the
doorpost of the LORD's house. [10] In her deep
anguish Hannah prayed to the LORD, weeping bitterly. [11] And she made a vow, saying,
"LORD Almighty, if you will only look on your
servant's misery and remember me, and not
forget your servant but give her a son, then
I will give him to the LORD for all the days
of his life, and no razor will ever be used on
his head."

[12] As she kept on praying to the LORD, Eli
observed her mouth. [13] Hannah was praying
in her heart, and her lips were moving but
her voice was not heard. Eli thought she was
drunk [14] and said to her, "How long are you
going to stay drunk? Put away your wine."

[15] "Not so, my lord," Hannah replied, "I am
a woman who is deeply troubled. I have not
been drinking wine or beer; I was pouring
out my soul to the LORD. [16] Do not take your
servant for a wicked woman; I have been
praying here out of my great anguish and
grief."

[17] Eli answered, "Go in peace, and may the
God of Israel grant you what you have asked
of him."

[18] She said, "May your servant find favor
in your eyes." Then she went her way and
ate something, and her face was no longer
downcast.

[19] Early the next morning they arose and
worshiped before the LORD and then went
back to their home at Ramah. Elkanah made
love to his wife Hannah, and the LORD remembered her. [20] So in the course of time
Hannah became pregnant and gave birth to
a son. She named him Samuel,[b] saying, "Because I asked the LORD for him."

Hannah Dedicates Samuel

[21] When her husband Elkanah went up
with all his family to offer the annual sacrifice to the LORD and to fulfill his vow, [22] Hannah did not go. She said to her husband,
"After the boy is weaned, I will take him and
present him before the LORD, and he will live
there always."[c]

[23] "Do what seems best to you," her husband Elkanah told her. "Stay here until you
have weaned him; only may the LORD make
good his[d] word." So the woman stayed at
home and nursed her son until she had
weaned him.

[24] After he was weaned, she took the boy
with her, young as he was, along with a

---

[a] 1 See Septuagint and 1 Chron. 6:26-27,33-35; or *from Ramathaim Zuphim.*   [b] 20 *Samuel* sounds like
the Hebrew for *heard by God.*   [c] 22 Masoretic Text; Dead Sea Scrolls *always. I have dedicated him as a
Nazirite—all the days of his life."*   [d] 23 Masoretic Text; Dead Sea Scrolls, Septuagint and Syriac *your*

AIM FOR THROUGH

READ: 1 SAMUEL 1:4-17

We desperately need to rediscover the difference between praying *for* and praying *through*. There are certainly circumstances where praying *for* something will get the job done. Trust me, I believe in short prayers before meals because, quite frankly, I believe in eating food while it's still hot. But there are also situations where you need to lock yourself in and refuse to disconnect from God until he answers. Simply put: intercede until God intervenes.

Praying *through* is all about consistency. It's like circling Jericho so many times it makes you dizzy. Like the story Jesus told about the persistent widow who drove the judge crazy with her relentless requests, praying through means not taking no for an answer. That's what makes prayer so unpredictable—and exciting.

Praying *through* is all about intensity. Ever heard someone make completely guttural noises while they pray or bawling with their hands tightly clenched? Drawing prayer circles involves more than words; it's literally about sweat and tears. That is what gets our heavenly Father's attention.

BUILDING FAITH WISDOM STRENGTH

When was the last time you found yourself flat on your face in prayer? When was the last time you got sore knees kneeling before the Lord? When was the last time you pulled an all-nighter in prayer? There will always be higher heights and deeper depths in prayer, and God wants to take you there.

Taken from *The Circle Maker Student Edition* by Mark Batterson with Parker Batterson, copyright © 2012 by Mark Batterson, published by Zondervan.

three-year-old bull,[a] an ephah[b] of flour and a skin of wine, and brought him to the house of the LORD at Shiloh. ²⁵When the bull had been sacrificed, they brought the boy to Eli, ²⁶and she said to him, "Pardon me, my lord. As surely as you live, I am the woman who stood here beside you praying to the LORD. ²⁷I prayed for this child, and the LORD has granted me what I asked of him. ²⁸So now I give him to the LORD. For his whole life he will be given over to the LORD." And he worshiped the LORD there.

Hannah's Prayer

2 Then Hannah prayed and said:

"My heart rejoices in the LORD;
in the LORD my horn[c] is lifted high.
My mouth boasts over my enemies,
for I delight in your deliverance.

²"There is no one holy like the LORD;
there is no one besides you;
there is no Rock like our God.

³"Do not keep talking so proudly
or let your mouth speak such
arrogance,
for the LORD is a God who knows,
and by him deeds are weighed.

⁴"The bows of the warriors are broken,
but those who stumbled are armed
with strength.
⁵Those who were full hire themselves out
for food,
but those who were hungry are hungry
no more.
She who was barren has borne seven
children,
but she who has had many sons
pines away.

⁶"The LORD brings death and makes alive;
he brings down to the grave and
raises up.
⁷The LORD sends poverty and wealth;
he humbles and he exalts.
⁸He raises the poor from the dust
and lifts the needy from the ash heap;
he seats them with princes
and has them inherit a throne of
honor.

"For the foundations of the earth are
the LORD's;
on them he has set the world.
⁹He will guard the feet of his faithful
servants,
but the wicked will be silenced in the
place of darkness.

"It is not by strength that one prevails;
¹⁰ those who oppose the LORD will be
broken.
The Most High will thunder from heaven;
the LORD will judge the ends of the
earth.

"He will give strength to his king
and exalt the horn of his anointed."

¹¹Then Elkanah went home to Ramah, but the boy ministered before the LORD under Eli the priest.

Eli's Wicked Sons

¹²Eli's sons were scoundrels; they had no regard for the LORD. ¹³Now it was the practice of the priests that, whenever any of the people offered a sacrifice, the priest's servant would come with a three-pronged fork in his hand while the meat was being boiled ¹⁴and would plunge the fork into the pan or kettle or caldron or pot. Whatever the fork brought up the priest would take for himself. This is how they treated all the Israelites who came to Shiloh. ¹⁵But even before the fat was burned, the priest's servant would come and say to the person who was sacrificing, "Give the priest some meat to roast; he won't accept boiled meat from you, but only raw."

¹⁶If the person said to him, "Let the fat be burned first, and then take whatever you want," the servant would answer, "No, hand it over now; if you don't, I'll take it by force."

¹⁷This sin of the young men was very great in the LORD's sight, for they[d] were treating the LORD's offering with contempt.

¹⁸But Samuel was ministering before the LORD—a boy wearing a linen ephod. ¹⁹Each year his mother made him a little robe and took it to him when she went up with her husband to offer the annual sacrifice. ²⁰Eli would bless Elkanah and his

---

[a] 24 Dead Sea Scrolls, Septuagint and Syriac; Masoretic Text *with three bulls*   [b] 24 That is, probably about 36 pounds or about 16 kilograms   [c] 1 *Horn* here symbolizes strength; also in verse 10.   [d] 17 Dead Sea Scrolls and Septuagint; Masoretic Text *people*

HOPHNI AND PHINEHAS

Eli's sons were scoundrels; they had no regard for the LORD. 1 SAMUEL 2:12

THEIR NAMES MEAN: Hophni—"strong," Phinehas—"mouth of brass"

READ THEIR STORY: *1 Samuel 2:12—4:26*

These infamous brothers were the sons of the high priest Eli. Eli served the Lord with a pure heart and honored God. His sons did not. They used their position as priests to serve themselves.

At that point in history, the people made animal sacrifices to the Lord to take away the guilt of their sins. (We don't have to do that anymore, because Jesus makes us holy when we believe in his sacrifice of dying on the cross. See Hebrews 10:10). God's law stated that a portion of the sacrificed animal meat should be boiled and given to the priests to eat. Hophni and Phinehas didn't want boiled meat. They ordered their servants to demand the best raw meat from the sacrificed animals so they could cook it themselves (1 Samuel 2:12-16). Because of their actions, the Bible calls these brothers wicked men who had no regard for the Lord. They disgraced God's tabernacle.

Sadly, some things don't change. Even now, wicked men disgrace Christ's church. Some steal money from the offering. Others take advantage of people and use their power to try to hide their evil actions. But the Lord sees everything and always brings the ultimate judgment. He did back in the Old Testament days, and he still does today.

Hophni and Phinehas were killed (1 Samuel 4:10-11). They were judged for their selfish actions that disgraced and disrespected God's law.

MEN

OF THE BIBLE

wife, saying, "May the LORD give you children by this woman to take the place of the one she prayed for and gave to[a] the LORD." Then they would go home. [21] And the LORD was gracious to Hannah; she gave birth to three sons and two daughters. Meanwhile, the boy Samuel grew up in the presence of the LORD.

[22] Now Eli, who was very old, heard about everything his sons were doing to all Israel and how they slept with the women who served at the entrance to the tent of meeting. [23] So he said to them, "Why do you do such things? I hear from all the people about these wicked deeds of yours. [24] No, my sons; the report I hear spreading among the LORD's people is not good. [25] If one person sins against another, God[b] may mediate for the offender; but if anyone sins against the LORD, who will intercede for them?" His sons, however, did not listen to their father's rebuke, for it was the LORD's will to put them to death.

[26] And the boy Samuel continued to grow in stature and in favor with the LORD and with people.

Prophecy Against the House of Eli

[27] Now a man of God came to Eli and said to him, "This is what the LORD says: 'Did I not clearly reveal myself to your ancestor's family when they were in Egypt under Pharaoh? [28] I chose your ancestor out of all the tribes of Israel to be my priest, to go up to my altar, to burn incense, and to wear an ephod in my presence. I also gave your ancestor's family all the food offerings presented by the Israelites. [29] Why do you[c] scorn my sacrifice and offering that I prescribed for my dwelling? Why do you honor your sons more than me by fattening yourselves on the choice parts of every offering made by my people Israel?'

[30] "Therefore the LORD, the God of Israel, declares: 'I promised that members of your family would minister before me forever.' But now the LORD declares: 'Far be it from me! Those who honor me I will honor, but those who despise me will be disdained. [31] The time is coming when I will cut short your strength and the strength of your priestly house, so that no one in it will reach old age, [32] and you will see distress in my dwelling. Although good will be done to Israel, no one in your family line will ever reach old age. [33] Every one of you that I do not cut off from serving at my altar I will spare only to destroy your sight and sap your strength, and all your descendants will die in the prime of life.

[34] "'And what happens to your two sons, Hophni and Phinehas, will be a sign to you—they will both die on the same day. [35] I will raise up for myself a faithful priest, who will do according to what is in my heart and mind. I will firmly establish his priestly house, and they will minister before my anointed one always. [36] Then everyone left in your family line will come and bow down before him for a piece of silver and a loaf of bread and plead, "Appoint me to some priestly office so I can have food to eat."' "

The LORD Calls Samuel

3 The boy Samuel ministered before the LORD under Eli. In those days the word of the LORD was rare; there were not many visions.

[2] One night Eli, whose eyes were becoming so weak that he could barely see, was lying down in his usual place. [3] The lamp of God had not yet gone out, and Samuel was lying down in the house of the LORD, where the ark of God was. [4] Then the LORD called Samuel.

Samuel answered, "Here I am." [5] And he ran to Eli and said, "Here I am; you called me."

But Eli said, "I did not call; go back and lie down." So he went and lay down.

[6] Again the LORD called, "Samuel!" And Samuel got up and went to Eli and said, "Here I am; you called me."

"My son," Eli said, "I did not call; go back and lie down."

[7] Now Samuel did not yet know the LORD: The word of the LORD had not yet been revealed to him.

[8] A third time the LORD called, "Samuel!" And Samuel got up and went to Eli and said, "Here I am; you called me."

Then Eli realized that the LORD was calling the boy. [9] So Eli told Samuel, "Go and lie down, and if he calls you, say, 'Speak, LORD,

---

[a] 20 Dead Sea Scrolls; Masoretic Text *and asked from*   [b] 25 Or *the judges*   [c] 29 The Hebrew is plural.

for your servant is listening.' " So Samuel went and lay down in his place.

[10]The LORD came and stood there, calling as at the other times, "Samuel! Samuel!"

Then Samuel said, "Speak, for your servant is listening."

[11]And the LORD said to Samuel: "See, I am about to do something in Israel that will make the ears of everyone who hears about it tingle. [12]At that time I will carry out against Eli everything I spoke against his family—from beginning to end. [13]For I told him that I would judge his family forever because of the sin he knew about; his sons blasphemed God,[a] and he failed to restrain them. [14]Therefore I swore to the house of Eli, 'The guilt of Eli's house will never be atoned for by sacrifice or offering.' "

[15]Samuel lay down until morning and then opened the doors of the house of the LORD. He was afraid to tell Eli the vision, [16]but Eli called him and said, "Samuel, my son."

Samuel answered, "Here I am."

[17]"What was it he said to you?" Eli asked. "Do not hide it from me. May God deal with you, be it ever so severely, if you hide from me anything he told you." [18]So Samuel told him everything, hiding nothing from him. Then Eli said, "He is the LORD; let him do what is good in his eyes."

[19]The LORD was with Samuel as he grew up, and he let none of Samuel's words fall to the ground. [20]And all Israel from Dan to Beersheba recognized that Samuel was attested as a prophet of the LORD. [21]The LORD continued to appear at Shiloh, and there he revealed himself to Samuel through his word.

4 And Samuel's word came to all Israel.

The Philistines Capture the Ark

Now the Israelites went out to fight against the Philistines. The Israelites camped at Ebenezer, and the Philistines at Aphek. [2]The Philistines deployed their forces to meet Israel, and as the battle spread, Israel was defeated by the Philistines, who killed about four thousand of them on the battlefield. [3]When the soldiers returned to camp, the elders of Israel asked, "Why did the LORD bring defeat on us today before

the Philistines? Let us bring the ark of the LORD's covenant from Shiloh, so that he may go with us and save us from the hand of our enemies."

[4]So the people sent men to Shiloh, and they brought back the ark of the covenant of the LORD Almighty, who is enthroned between the cherubim. And Eli's two sons, Hophni and Phinehas, were there with the ark of the covenant of God.

[5]When the ark of the LORD's covenant came into the camp, all Israel raised such a great shout that the ground shook. [6]Hearing the uproar, the Philistines asked, "What's all this shouting in the Hebrew camp?"

When they learned that the ark of the LORD had come into the camp, [7]the Philistines were afraid. "A god has[b] come into the camp," they said. "Oh no! Nothing like this has happened before. [8]We're doomed! Who will deliver us from the hand of these mighty gods? They are the gods who struck the Egyptians with all kinds of plagues in the wilderness. [9]Be strong, Philistines! Be men, or you will be subject to the Hebrews, as they have been to you. Be men, and fight!"

[10]So the Philistines fought, and the Israelites were defeated and every man fled to his tent. The slaughter was very great; Israel lost thirty thousand foot soldiers. [11]The ark of God was captured, and Eli's two sons, Hophni and Phinehas, died.

Death of Eli

[12]That same day a Benjamite ran from the battle line and went to Shiloh with his clothes torn and dust on his head. [13]When he arrived, there was Eli sitting on his chair by the side of the road, watching, because his heart feared for the ark of God. When the man entered the town and told what had happened, the whole town sent up a cry.

[14]Eli heard the outcry and asked, "What is the meaning of this uproar?"

The man hurried over to Eli, [15]who was ninety-eight years old and whose eyes had failed so that he could not see. [16]He told Eli, "I have just come from the battle line; I fled from it this very day."

Eli asked, "What happened, my son?"

[17]The man who brought the news replied,

[a] 13 An ancient Hebrew scribal tradition (see also Septuagint); Masoretic Text *sons made themselves contemptible*   [b] 7 Or *"Gods have* (see Septuagint)

"Israel fled before the Philistines, and the army has suffered heavy losses. Also your two sons, Hophni and Phinehas, are dead, and the ark of God has been captured."

¹⁸When he mentioned the ark of God, Eli fell backward off his chair by the side of the gate. His neck was broken and he died, for he was an old man, and he was heavy. He had led^a Israel forty years.

¹⁹His daughter-in-law, the wife of Phinehas, was pregnant and near the time of delivery. When she heard the news that the ark of God had been captured and that her father-in-law and her husband were dead, she went into labor and gave birth, but was overcome by her labor pains. ²⁰As she was dying, the women attending her said, "Don't despair; you have given birth to a son." But she did not respond or pay any attention.

²¹She named the boy Ichabod,^b saying, "The Glory has departed from Israel"—because of the capture of the ark of God and the deaths of her father-in-law and her husband. ²²She said, "The Glory has departed from Israel, for the ark of God has been captured."

The Ark in Ashdod and Ekron

5 After the Philistines had captured the ark of God, they took it from Ebenezer to Ashdod. ²Then they carried the ark into Dagon's temple and set it beside Dagon. ³When the people of Ashdod rose early the next day, there was Dagon, fallen on his face on the ground before the ark of the LORD! They took Dagon and put him back in his place. ⁴But the following morning when they rose, there was Dagon, fallen on his face on the ground before the ark of the LORD! His head and hands had been broken off and were lying on the threshold; only his body remained. ⁵That is why to this day neither the priests of Dagon nor any others who enter Dagon's temple at Ashdod step on the threshold.

⁶The LORD's hand was heavy on the people of Ashdod and its vicinity; he brought devastation on them and afflicted them with tumors.^c ⁷When the people of Ashdod saw what was happening, they said, "The ark of the god of Israel must not stay here with us, because his hand is heavy on us and on Dagon our god." ⁸So they called together all the rulers of the Philistines and asked them, "What shall we do with the ark of the god of Israel?"

They answered, "Have the ark of the god of Israel moved to Gath." So they moved the ark of the God of Israel.

⁹But after they had moved it, the LORD's hand was against that city, throwing it into a great panic. He afflicted the people of the city, both young and old, with an outbreak of tumors.^d ¹⁰So they sent the ark of God to Ekron.

As the ark of God was entering Ekron, the people of Ekron cried out, "They have brought the ark of the god of Israel around to us to kill us and our people." ¹¹So they called together all the rulers of the Philistines and said, "Send the ark of the god of Israel away; let it go back to its own place, or it^e will kill us and our people." For death had filled the city with panic; God's hand was very heavy on it. ¹²Those who did not die were afflicted with tumors, and the outcry of the city went up to heaven.

The Ark Returned to Israel

6 When the ark of the LORD had been in Philistine territory seven months, ²the Philistines called for the priests and the diviners and said, "What shall we do with the ark of the LORD? Tell us how we should send it back to its place."

³They answered, "If you return the ark of the god of Israel, do not send it back to him without a gift; by all means send a guilt offering to him. Then you will be healed, and you will know why his hand has not been lifted from you."

⁴The Philistines asked, "What guilt offering should we send to him?"

They replied, "Five gold tumors and five gold rats, according to the number of the Philistine rulers, because the same plague has struck both you and your rulers. ⁵Make models of the tumors and of the rats that are destroying the country, and give glory to Israel's god. Perhaps he will lift his hand from you and your gods and your land. ⁶Why do

---

^a 18 Traditionally *judged*   ^b 21 *Ichabod* means *no glory.*   ^c 6 Hebrew; Septuagint and Vulgate *tumors. And rats appeared in their land, and there was death and destruction throughout the city*   ^d 9 Or *with tumors in the groin* (see Septuagint)   ^e 11 Or *he*

GOD'S ARK

READ: 1 SAMUEL 5:4

The "ark of God" or "ark of the covenant" was the most sacred object in ancient Israel, because God's presence dwelt within it. Built according to a pattern God gave Moses (Exodus 25:10–22), this gold-covered wood chest measured four feet long and two feet deep and high. It contained two stone tablets listing the Ten Commandments (v. 16). Each year on the Day of Atonement, Israel's high priest sprinkled blood on the ark's gold cover to gain forgiveness of sin (vv. 17–22, Leviticus 16:15).

The ark was normally housed inside the tabernacle in the Most Holy Place, but when the Israelite's moved, the portable box was carried on poles. The ark made the Jordan River split so the Israelites could cross on dry ground (Joshua 3:6–4:18). It also went before the people during the march around Jericho (6:1–14).

BUILDING FAITH WISDOM STRENGTH

The Israelites ran into trouble when they began to think the ark had magic power of its own, like the ability to win battles (1 Samuel 4:1–11). But like the Philistines found out, the ark's true power came from God. When they put the ark in a temple to their pagan god, it knocked the Philistine's false god Dagon flat.

The Lord doesn't let you play with his power like magic. If you need his strength, just ask. You won't get hold of God's power without going directly to him.

you harden your hearts as the Egyptians and Pharaoh did? When Israel's god dealt harshly with them, did they not send the Israelites out so they could go on their way?

⁷ "Now then, get a new cart ready, with two cows that have calved and have never been yoked. Hitch the cows to the cart, but take their calves away and pen them up. ⁸ Take the ark of the LORD and put it on the cart, and in a chest beside it put the gold objects you are sending back to him as a guilt offering. Send it on its way, ⁹ but keep watching it. If it goes up to its own territory, toward Beth Shemesh, then the LORD has brought this great disaster on us. But if it does not, then we will know that it was not his hand that struck us but that it happened to us by chance."

¹⁰ So they did this. They took two such cows and hitched them to the cart and penned up their calves. ¹¹ They placed the ark of the LORD on the cart and along with it the chest containing the gold rats and the models of the tumors. ¹² Then the cows went straight up toward Beth Shemesh, keeping on the road and lowing all the way; they did not turn to the right or to the left. The rulers of the Philistines followed them as far as the border of Beth Shemesh.

¹³ Now the people of Beth Shemesh were harvesting their wheat in the valley, and when they looked up and saw the ark, they rejoiced at the sight. ¹⁴ The cart came to the field of Joshua of Beth Shemesh, and there it stopped beside a large rock. The people chopped up the wood of the cart and sacrificed the cows as a burnt offering to the LORD. ¹⁵ The Levites took down the ark of the LORD, together with the chest containing the gold objects, and placed them on the large rock. On that day the people of Beth Shemesh offered burnt offerings and made sacrifices to the LORD. ¹⁶ The five rulers of the Philistines saw all this and then returned that same day to Ekron.

¹⁷ These are the gold tumors the Philistines sent as a guilt offering to the LORD — one each for Ashdod, Gaza, Ashkelon, Gath and Ekron. ¹⁸ And the number of the gold rats was according to the number of Philistine towns belonging to the five rulers — the fortified towns with their country villages. The large rock on which the Levites set the ark of the LORD is a witness to this day in the field of Joshua of Beth Shemesh.

¹⁹ But God struck down some of the inhabitants of Beth Shemesh, putting seventy[a] of them to death because they looked into the ark of the LORD. The people mourned because of the heavy blow the LORD had dealt them. ²⁰ And the people of Beth Shemesh asked, "Who can stand in the presence of the LORD, this holy God? To whom will the ark go up from here?"

²¹ Then they sent messengers to the people of Kiriath Jearim, saying, "The Philistines have returned the ark of the LORD. Come down and take it up to your town." ⁷:¹ So the men of Kiriath Jearim came and took up the ark of the LORD. They brought it to Abinadab's house on the hill and consecrated Eleazar his son to guard the ark of the LORD. ² The ark remained at Kiriath Jearim a long time — twenty years in all.

Samuel Subdues the Philistines at Mizpah

Then all the people of Israel turned back to the LORD. ³ So Samuel said to all the Israelites, "If you are returning to the LORD with all your hearts, then rid yourselves of the foreign gods and the Ashtoreths and commit yourselves to the LORD and serve him only, and he will deliver you out of the hand of the Philistines." ⁴ So the Israelites put away their Baals and Ashtoreths, and served the LORD only.

⁵ Then Samuel said, "Assemble all Israel at Mizpah, and I will intercede with the LORD for you." ⁶ When they had assembled at Mizpah, they drew water and poured it out before the LORD. On that day they fasted and there they confessed, "We have sinned against the LORD." Now Samuel was serving as leader[b] of Israel at Mizpah.

⁷ When the Philistines heard that Israel had assembled at Mizpah, the rulers of the Philistines came up to attack them. When the Israelites heard of it, they were afraid because of the Philistines. ⁸ They said to Samuel, "Do not stop crying out to the LORD our God for us, that he may rescue us from the hand of the Philistines." ⁹ Then Samuel took a suckling lamb and sacrificed it as a whole burnt offering to the LORD. He cried out to

---

a 19 A few Hebrew manuscripts; most Hebrew manuscripts and Septuagint *50,070*   *b* 6 Traditionally *judge*; also in verse 15 the LORD on Israel's behalf, and the LORD answered him.

[10]While Samuel was sacrificing the burnt offering, the Philistines drew near to engage Israel in battle. But that day the LORD thundered with loud thunder against the Philistines and threw them into such a panic that they were routed before the Israelites. [11]The men of Israel rushed out of Mizpah and pursued the Philistines, slaughtering them along the way to a point below Beth Kar.

[12]Then Samuel took a stone and set it up between Mizpah and Shen. He named it Ebenezer,[a] saying, "Thus far the LORD has helped us."

[13]So the Philistines were subdued and they stopped invading Israel's territory. Throughout Samuel's lifetime, the hand of the LORD was against the Philistines. [14]The towns from Ekron to Gath that the Philistines had captured from Israel were restored to Israel, and Israel delivered the neighboring territory from the hands of the Philistines. And there was peace between Israel and the Amorites.

[15]Samuel continued as Israel's leader all the days of his life. [16]From year to year he went on a circuit from Bethel to Gilgal to Mizpah, judging Israel in all those places. [17]But he always went back to Ramah, where his home was, and there he also held court for Israel. And he built an altar there to the LORD.

Israel Asks for a King

8 When Samuel grew old, he appointed his sons as Israel's leaders.[b] [2]The name of his firstborn was Joel and the name of his second was Abijah, and they served at Beersheba. [3]But his sons did not follow his ways. They turned aside after dishonest gain and accepted bribes and perverted justice.

[4]So all the elders of Israel gathered together and came to Samuel at Ramah. [5]They said to him, "You are old, and your sons do not follow your ways; now appoint a king to lead[c] us, such as all the other nations have."

[6]But when they said, "Give us a king to lead us," this displeased Samuel; so he prayed to the LORD. [7]And the LORD told him: "Listen to all that the people are saying to you; it is not you they have rejected, but they have rejected me as their king. [8]As they have done from the day I brought them up out of Egypt until this day, forsaking me and serving other gods, so they are doing to you. [9]Now listen to them; but warn them solemnly and let them know what the king who will reign over them will claim as his rights."

[10]Samuel told all the words of the LORD to the people who were asking him for a king. [11]He said, "This is what the king who will reign over you will claim as his rights: He will take your sons and make them serve with his chariots and horses, and they will run in front of his chariots. [12]Some he will assign to be commanders of thousands and commanders of fifties, and others to plow his ground and reap his harvest, and still others to make weapons of war and equipment for his chariots. [13]He will take your daughters to be perfumers and cooks and bakers. [14]He will take the best of your fields and vineyards and olive groves and give them to his attendants. [15]He will take a tenth of your grain and of your vintage and give it to his officials and attendants. [16]Your male and female servants and the best of your cattle[d] and donkeys he will take for his own use. [17]He will take a tenth of your flocks, and you yourselves will become his slaves. [18]When that day comes, you will cry out for relief from the king you have chosen, but the LORD will not answer you in that day."

[19]But the people refused to listen to Samuel. "No!" they said. "We want a king over us. [20]Then we will be like all the other nations, with a king to lead us and to go out before us and fight our battles."

[21]When Samuel heard all that the people said, he repeated it before the LORD. [22]The LORD answered, "Listen to them and give them a king."

Then Samuel said to the Israelites, "Everyone go back to your own town."

Samuel Anoints Saul

9 There was a Benjamite, a man of standing, whose name was Kish son of Abiel, the son of Zeror, the son of Bekorath, the son of Aphiah of Benjamin. [2]Kish had a son named Saul, as handsome a young man as

---

a 12 Ebenezer means stone of help.   *b 1 Traditionally judges*   *c 5 Traditionally judge; also in verses 6 and 20*   *d 16 Septuagint; Hebrew young men* could be found anywhere in Israel, and he was a head taller than anyone else.

³Now the donkeys belonging to Saul's father Kish were lost, and Kish said to his son Saul, "Take one of the servants with you and go and look for the donkeys." ⁴So he passed through the hill country of Ephraim and through the area around Shalisha, but they did not find them. They went on into the district of Shaalim, but the donkeys were not there. Then he passed through the territory of Benjamin, but they did not find them.

⁵When they reached the district of Zuph, Saul said to the servant who was with him, "Come, let's go back, or my father will stop thinking about the donkeys and start worrying about us."

⁶But the servant replied, "Look, in this town there is a man of God; he is highly respected, and everything he says comes true. Let's go there now. Perhaps he will tell us what way to take."

⁷Saul said to his servant, "If we go, what can we give the man? The food in our sacks is gone. We have no gift to take to the man of God. What do we have?"

⁸The servant answered him again. "Look," he said, "I have a quarter of a shekel[a] of silver. I will give it to the man of God so that he will tell us what way to take." ⁹(Formerly in Israel, if someone went to inquire of God, they would say, "Come, let us go to the seer," because the prophet of today used to be called a seer.)

¹⁰"Good," Saul said to his servant. "Come, let's go." So they set out for the town where the man of God was.

¹¹As they were going up the hill to the town, they met some young women coming out to draw water, and they asked them, "Is the seer here?"

¹²"He is," they answered. "He's ahead of you. Hurry now; he has just come to our town today, for the people have a sacrifice at the high place. ¹³As soon as you enter the town, you will find him before he goes up to the high place to eat. The people will not begin eating until he comes, because he must bless the sacrifice; afterward, those who are invited will eat. Go up now; you should find him about this time."

¹⁴They went up to the town, and as they were entering it, there was Samuel, coming toward them on his way up to the high place.

¹⁵Now the day before Saul came, the LORD had revealed this to Samuel: ¹⁶"About this time tomorrow I will send you a man from the land of Benjamin. Anoint him ruler over my people Israel; he will deliver them from the hand of the Philistines. I have looked on my people, for their cry has reached me."

¹⁷When Samuel caught sight of Saul, the LORD said to him, "This is the man I spoke to you about; he will govern my people."

¹⁸Saul approached Samuel in the gateway and asked, "Would you please tell me where the seer's house is?"

¹⁹"I am the seer," Samuel replied. "Go up ahead of me to the high place, for today you are to eat with me, and in the morning I will send you on your way and will tell you all that is in your heart. ²⁰As for the donkeys you lost three days ago, do not worry about them; they have been found. And to whom is all the desire of Israel turned, if not to you and your whole family line?"

²¹Saul answered, "But am I not a Benjamite, from the smallest tribe of Israel, and is not my clan the least of all the clans of the tribe of Benjamin? Why do you say such a thing to me?"

²²Then Samuel brought Saul and his servant into the hall and seated them at the head of those who were invited — about thirty in number. ²³Samuel said to the cook, "Bring the piece of meat I gave you, the one I told you to lay aside."

²⁴So the cook took up the thigh with what was on it and set it in front of Saul. Samuel said, "Here is what has been kept for you. Eat, because it was set aside for you for this occasion from the time I said, 'I have invited guests.' " And Saul dined with Samuel that day.

²⁵After they came down from the high place to the town, Samuel talked with Saul on the roof of his house. ²⁶They rose about daybreak, and Samuel called to Saul on the roof, "Get ready, and I will send you on your way." When Saul got ready, he and Samuel went outside together. ²⁷As they were going down to the edge of the town, Samuel said to Saul, "Tell the servant to go on ahead of us" — and the servant did so — "but you stay

---

ᵃ 8 That is, about 1/10 ounce or about 3 grams

here for a while, so that I may give you a message from God."

10 Then Samuel took a flask of olive oil and poured it on Saul's head and kissed him, saying, "Has not the LORD anointed you ruler over his inheritance?*[a]* ²When you leave me today, you will meet two men near Rachel's tomb, at Zelzah on the border of Benjamin. They will say to you, 'The donkeys you set out to look for have been found. And now your father has stopped thinking about them and is worried about you. He is asking, "What shall I do about my son?"'

³"Then you will go on from there until you reach the great tree of Tabor. Three men going up to worship God at Bethel will meet you there. One will be carrying three young goats, another three loaves of bread, and another a skin of wine. ⁴They will greet you and offer you two loaves of bread, which you will accept from them.

⁵"After that you will go to Gibeah of God, where there is a Philistine outpost. As you approach the town, you will meet a procession of prophets coming down from the high place with lyres, timbrels, pipes and harps being played before them, and they will be prophesying. ⁶The Spirit of the LORD will come powerfully upon you, and you will prophesy with them; and you will be changed into a different person. ⁷Once these signs are fulfilled, do whatever your hand finds to do, for God is with you.

⁸"Go down ahead of me to Gilgal. I will surely come down to you to sacrifice burnt offerings and fellowship offerings, but you must wait seven days until I come to you and tell you what you are to do."

Saul Made King

⁹As Saul turned to leave Samuel, God changed Saul's heart, and all these signs were fulfilled that day. ¹⁰When he and his servant arrived at Gibeah, a procession of prophets met him; the Spirit of God came powerfully upon him, and he joined in their prophesying. ¹¹When all those who had formerly known him saw him prophesying with the prophets, they asked each other, "What is this that has happened to the son of Kish? Is Saul also among the prophets?"

¹²A man who lived there answered, "And who is their father?" So it became a saying: "Is Saul also among the prophets?" ¹³After Saul stopped prophesying, he went to the high place.

¹⁴Now Saul's uncle asked him and his servant, "Where have you been?"

"Looking for the donkeys," he said. "But when we saw they were not to be found, we went to Samuel."

¹⁵Saul's uncle said, "Tell me what Samuel said to you."

¹⁶Saul replied, "He assured us that the donkeys had been found." But he did not tell his uncle what Samuel had said about the kingship.

¹⁷Samuel summoned the people of Israel to the LORD at Mizpah ¹⁸and said to them, "This is what the LORD, the God of Israel, says: 'I brought Israel up out of Egypt, and I delivered you from the power of Egypt and all the kingdoms that oppressed you.' ¹⁹But you have now rejected your God, who saves you out of all your disasters and calamities. And you have said, 'No, appoint a king over us.' So now present yourselves before the LORD by your tribes and clans."

²⁰When Samuel had all Israel come forward by tribes, the tribe of Benjamin was taken by lot. ²¹Then he brought forward the tribe of Benjamin, clan by clan, and Matri's clan was taken. Finally Saul son of Kish was taken. But when they looked for him, he was not to be found. ²²So they inquired further of the LORD, "Has the man come here yet?"

And the LORD said, "Yes, he has hidden himself among the supplies."

²³They ran and brought him out, and as he stood among the people he was a head taller than any of the others. ²⁴Samuel said to all the people, "Do you see the man the LORD has chosen? There is no one like him among all the people."

Then the people shouted, "Long live the king!"

²⁵Samuel explained to the people the rights and duties of kingship. He wrote them down on a scroll and deposited it before the LORD. Then Samuel dismissed the people to go to their own homes.

²⁶Saul also went to his home in Gibeah,

---

[a] 1 Hebrew; Septuagint and Vulgate *over his people Israel? You will reign over the LORD's people and save them from the power of their enemies round about. And this will be a sign to you that the LORD has anointed you ruler over his inheritance:*

accompanied by valiant men whose hearts God had touched. ²⁷But some scoundrels said, "How can this fellow save us?" They despised him and brought him no gifts. But Saul kept silent.

Saul Rescues the City of Jabesh

11 Nahash*ᵃ* the Ammonite went up and besieged Jabesh Gilead. And all the men of Jabesh said to him, "Make a treaty with us, and we will be subject to you."

²But Nahash the Ammonite replied, "I will make a treaty with you only on the condition that I gouge out the right eye of every one of you and so bring disgrace on all Israel."

³The elders of Jabesh said to him, "Give us seven days so we can send messengers throughout Israel; if no one comes to rescue us, we will surrender to you."

⁴When the messengers came to Gibeah of Saul and reported these terms to the people, they all wept aloud. ⁵Just then Saul was returning from the fields, behind his oxen, and he asked, "What is wrong with everyone? Why are they weeping?" Then they repeated to him what the men of Jabesh had said.

⁶When Saul heard their words, the Spirit of God came powerfully upon him, and he burned with anger. ⁷He took a pair of oxen, cut them into pieces, and sent the pieces by messengers throughout Israel, proclaiming, "This is what will be done to the oxen of anyone who does not follow Saul and Samuel." Then the terror of the LORD fell on the people, and they came out together as one. ⁸When Saul mustered them at Bezek, the men of Israel numbered three hundred thousand and those of Judah thirty thousand.

⁹They told the messengers who had come, "Say to the men of Jabesh Gilead, 'By the time the sun is hot tomorrow, you will be rescued.'" When the messengers went and reported this to the men of Jabesh, they were elated. ¹⁰They said to the Ammonites, "Tomorrow we will surrender to you, and you can do to us whatever you like."

¹¹The next day Saul separated his men into three divisions; during the last watch of the night they broke into the camp of the Ammonites and slaughtered them until the heat of the day. Those who survived were scattered, so that no two of them were left together.

Saul Confirmed as King

¹²The people then said to Samuel, "Who was it that asked, 'Shall Saul reign over us?' Turn these men over to us so that we may put them to death."

¹³But Saul said, "No one will be put to death today, for this day the LORD has rescued Israel."

¹⁴Then Samuel said to the people, "Come, let us go to Gilgal and there renew the kingship." ¹⁵So all the people went to Gilgal and made Saul king in the presence of the LORD. There they sacrificed fellowship offerings before the LORD, and Saul and all the Israelites held a great celebration.

Samuel's Farewell Speech

12 Samuel said to all Israel, "I have listened to everything you said to me and have set a king over you. ²Now you have a king as your leader. As for me, I am old and gray, and my sons are here with you. I have been your leader from my youth until this day. ³Here I stand. Testify against me in the presence of the LORD and his anointed. Whose ox have I taken? Whose donkey have I taken? Whom have I cheated? Whom have I oppressed? From whose hand have I accepted a bribe to make me shut my eyes? If I have done any of these things, I will make it right."

⁴"You have not cheated or oppressed us," they replied. "You have not taken anything from anyone's hand."

⁵Samuel said to them, "The LORD is witness against you, and also his anointed is witness this day, that you have not found anything in my hand."

"He is witness," they said.

⁶Then Samuel said to the people, "It is the LORD who appointed Moses and Aaron and brought your ancestors up out of Egypt. ⁷Now then, stand here, because I am going

---

ᵃ 1 Masoretic Text; Dead Sea Scrolls *gifts. Now Nahash king of the Ammonites oppressed the Gadites and Reubenites severely. He gouged out all their right eyes and struck terror and dread in Israel. Not a man remained among the Israelites beyond the Jordan whose right eye was not gouged out by Nahash king of the Ammonites, except that seven thousand men fled from the Ammonites and entered Jabesh Gilead. About a month later,* ¹*Nahash* to confront you with evidence before the Lord as to all the righteous acts performed by the Lord for you and your ancestors.

⁸"After Jacob entered Egypt, they cried to the Lord for help, and the Lord sent Moses and Aaron, who brought your ancestors out of Egypt and settled them in this place.

⁹"But they forgot the Lord their God; so he sold them into the hand of Sisera, the commander of the army of Hazor, and into the hands of the Philistines and the king of Moab, who fought against them. ¹⁰They cried out to the Lord and said, 'We have sinned; we have forsaken the Lord and served the Baals and the Ashtoreths. But now deliver us from the hands of our enemies, and we will serve you.' ¹¹Then the Lord sent Jerub-Baal,ᵃ Barak,ᵇ Jephthah and Samuel,ᶜ and he delivered you from the hands of your enemies all around you, so that you lived in safety.

¹²"But when you saw that Nahash king of the Ammonites was moving against you, you said to me, 'No, we want a king to rule over us'—even though the Lord your God was your king. ¹³Now here is the king you have chosen, the one you asked for; see, the Lord has set a king over you. ¹⁴If you fear the Lord and serve and obey him and do not rebel against his commands, and if both you and the king who reigns over you follow the Lord your God—good! ¹⁵But if you do not obey the Lord, and if you rebel against his commands, his hand will be against you, as it was against your ancestors.

¹⁶"Now then, stand still and see this great thing the Lord is about to do before your eyes! ¹⁷Is it not wheat harvest now? I will call on the Lord to send thunder and rain. And you will realize what an evil thing you did in the eyes of the Lord when you asked for a king."

¹⁸Then Samuel called on the Lord, and that same day the Lord sent thunder and rain. So all the people stood in awe of the Lord and of Samuel.

¹⁹The people all said to Samuel, "Pray to the Lord your God for your servants so that we will not die, for we have added to all our other sins the evil of asking for a king."

²⁰"Do not be afraid," Samuel replied. "You have done all this evil; yet do not turn away from the Lord, but serve the Lord with all your heart. ²¹Do not turn away after useless idols. They can do you no good, nor can they rescue you, because they are useless. ²²For the sake of his great name the Lord will not reject his people, because the Lord was pleased to make you his own. ²³As for me, far be it from me that I should sin against the Lord by failing to pray for you. And I will teach you the way that is good and right. ²⁴But be sure to fear the Lord and serve him faithfully with all your heart; consider what great things he has done for you. ²⁵Yet if you persist in doing evil, both you and your king will perish."

Samuel Rebukes Saul

13 Saul was thirtyᵈ years old when he became king, and he reigned over Israel forty-ᵉtwo years.

²Saul chose three thousand men from Israel; two thousand were with him at Mikmash and in the hill country of Bethel, and a thousand were with Jonathan at Gibeah in Benjamin. The rest of the men he sent back to their homes.

³Jonathan attacked the Philistine outpost at Geba, and the Philistines heard about it. Then Saul had the trumpet blown throughout the land and said, "Let the Hebrews hear!" ⁴So all Israel heard the news: "Saul has attacked the Philistine outpost, and now Israel has become obnoxious to the Philistines." And the people were summoned to join Saul at Gilgal.

⁵The Philistines assembled to fight Israel, with three thousandᶠ chariots, six thousand charioteers, and soldiers as numerous as the sand on the seashore. They went up and camped at Mikmash, east of Beth Aven. ⁶When the Israelites saw that their situation was critical and that their army was hard pressed, they hid in caves and thickets, among the rocks, and in pits and cisterns. ⁷Some Hebrews even crossed the Jordan to the land of Gad and Gilead.

Saul remained at Gilgal, and all the troops with him were quaking with fear. ⁸He waited

---

ᵃ 11 Also called *Gideon*   ᵇ 11 Some Septuagint manuscripts and Syriac; Hebrew *Bedan*   ᶜ 11 Hebrew; some Septuagint manuscripts and Syriac *Samson*   ᵈ 1 A few late manuscripts of the Septuagint; Hebrew does not have *thirty*.   ᵉ 1 Probable reading of the original Hebrew text (see Acts 13:21); Masoretic Text does not have *forty-*.   ᶠ 5 Some Septuagint manuscripts and Syriac; Hebrew *thirty thousand*

OPEN-ENDED

READ: 1 SAMUEL 12:22-24

For me, prayer is like a long text conversation in which I never say good-bye. I always pray with very long pauses. Anyone who has ever texted me understands this concept. They'll ask me a question and I'll answer, "I think so."

Then they answer back. "Well, what are we going to do?"

Hours later, I finally respond. "OK, how about this?"

That's how I pray too. I never hang up. I do the same thing for all my friends in need because I believe God can help. It's not like I'm performing some giant missionary work. I just pray for my friend. But guess what I do the next time I hang out with him? I follow up.

I bring Jesus into my friendship. It takes the relationship to a different depth from the connection you have when you talk about football or homework. This is a little more intimate and a lot more meaningful. You don't have all the answers and you don't know all the Greek words of the New Testament, but you have something that lasts an eternity: "I'm praying for you, man."

BUILDING FAITH WISDOM STRENGTH

That builds a bridge to Jesus. Remember, Jesus built a bridge to God for us. We build a bridge to Jesus by loving people and meeting them where they are, praying for them, and sharing truth.

seven days, the time set by Samuel; but Samuel did not come to Gilgal, and Saul's men began to scatter. [9]So he said, "Bring me the burnt offering and the fellowship offerings." And Saul offered up the burnt offering. [10]Just as he finished making the offering, Samuel arrived, and Saul went out to greet him.

[11]"What have you done?" asked Samuel.

Saul replied, "When I saw that the men were scattering, and that you did not come at the set time, and that the Philistines were assembling at Mikmash, [12]I thought, 'Now the Philistines will come down against me at Gilgal, and I have not sought the LORD's favor.' So I felt compelled to offer the burnt offering."

[13]"You have done a foolish thing," Samuel said. "You have not kept the command the LORD your God gave you; if you had, he would have established your kingdom over Israel for all time. [14]But now your kingdom will not endure; the LORD has sought out a man after his own heart and appointed him ruler of his people, because you have not kept the LORD's command."

[15]Then Samuel left Gilgal[a] and went up to Gibeah in Benjamin, and Saul counted the men who were with him. They numbered about six hundred.

Israel Without Weapons

[16]Saul and his son Jonathan and the men with them were staying in Gibeah[b] in Benjamin, while the Philistines camped at Mikmash. [17]Raiding parties went out from the Philistine camp in three detachments. One turned toward Ophrah in the vicinity of Shual, [18]another toward Beth Horon, and the third toward the borderland overlooking the Valley of Zeboyim facing the wilderness.

[19]Not a blacksmith could be found in the whole land of Israel, because the Philistines had said, "Otherwise the Hebrews will make swords or spears!" [20]So all Israel went down to the Philistines to have their plow points, mattocks, axes and sickles[c] sharpened. [21]The price was two-thirds of a shekel[d] for sharpening plow points and mattocks, and

a third of a shekel[e] for sharpening forks and axes and for repointing goads.

[22]So on the day of the battle not a soldier with Saul and Jonathan had a sword or spear in his hand; only Saul and his son Jonathan had them.

Jonathan Attacks the Philistines

[23]Now a detachment of Philistines had gone out to the pass at Mikmash. [1]One day Jonathan son of Saul said to his young armor-bearer, "Come, let's go over to the Philistine outpost on the other side." But he did not tell his father.

[2]Saul was staying on the outskirts of Gibeah under a pomegranate tree in Migron. With him were about six hundred men, [3]among whom was Ahijah, who was wearing an ephod. He was a son of Ichabod's brother Ahitub son of Phinehas, the son of Eli, the LORD's priest in Shiloh. No one was aware that Jonathan had left.

[4]On each side of the pass that Jonathan intended to cross to reach the Philistine outpost was a cliff; one was called Bozez and the other Seneh. [5]One cliff stood to the north toward Mikmash, the other to the south toward Geba.

[6]Jonathan said to his young armor-bearer, "Come, let's go over to the outpost of those uncircumcised men. Perhaps the LORD will act in our behalf. Nothing can hinder the LORD from saving, whether by many or by few."

[7]"Do all that you have in mind," his armor-bearer said. "Go ahead; I am with you heart and soul."

[8]Jonathan said, "Come on, then; we will cross over toward them and let them see us. [9]If they say to us, 'Wait there until we come to you,' we will stay where we are and not go up to them. [10]But if they say, 'Come up to us,' we will climb up, because that will be our sign that the LORD has given them into our hands."

[11]So both of them showed themselves to the Philistine outpost. "Look!" said the Philistines. "The Hebrews are crawling out of the holes they were hiding in." [12]The men of

---

[a] 15 Hebrew; Septuagint *Gilgal and went his way; the rest of the people went after Saul to meet the army, and they went out of Gilgal*   [b] 16 Two Hebrew manuscripts; most Hebrew manuscripts *Geba*, a variant of *Gibeah*   [c] 20 Septuagint; Hebrew *plow points*   [d] 21 That is, about 1/4 ounce or about 8 grams   [e] 21 That is, about 1/8 ounce or about 4 grams

STANDING OUT FOR ALL THE WRONG REASONS

READ: 1 SAMUEL 13:14

When the Israelites assembled a yearbook for the class of 1026 B.C, Saul definitely got voted "Most Likely to Succeed." In the year the son of Kish ascended to the throne of Israel, he looked as if he was headed for outrageous success. "Headed" is the appropriate word, because Saul stood a head taller than anyone else in the nation, a detail Scripture notes twice (1 Samuel 9:2, 10:23).

This good-looking guy (9:2) was famed as a gifted military leader, but his dubious character was visible right from the start. On the day the Lord decided to appoint him king, the entire nation gathered before the prophet Samuel, but Saul was nowhere to be found. God had to speak up from heaven and reveal that the future king was hiding among the luggage (10:22).

BUILDING
FAITH
WISDOM
STRENGTH

Then Saul led an attack on a Philistine outpost. When the enemy fought back, the Israelites fled. Because Samuel was slow to show up and give advice from the Lord, Saul lit up a burnt offering. This grave offense against God's rules for worship cost him his throne.

God isn't looking for followers who necessarily stand out because of their looks, talents, or intelligence. The first quality he looks for is a heart that belongs to him. If you don't keep the Lord's commands, none of your other good qualities matter.

the outpost shouted to Jonathan and his armor-bearer, "Come up to us and we'll teach you a lesson."

So Jonathan said to his armor-bearer, "Climb up after me; the LORD has given them into the hand of Israel."

¹³Jonathan climbed up, using his hands and feet, with his armor-bearer right behind him. The Philistines fell before Jonathan, and his armor-bearer followed and killed behind him. ¹⁴In that first attack Jonathan and his armor-bearer killed some twenty men in an area of about half an acre.

Israel Routs the Philistines

¹⁵Then panic struck the whole army — those in the camp and field, and those in the outposts and raiding parties — and the ground shook. It was a panic sent by God.ᵃ

¹⁶Saul's lookouts at Gibeah in Benjamin saw the army melting away in all directions. ¹⁷Then Saul said to the men who were with him, "Muster the forces and see who has left us." When they did, it was Jonathan and his armor-bearer who were not there.

¹⁸Saul said to Ahijah, "Bring the ark of God." (At that time it was with the Israelites.)ᵇ ¹⁹While Saul was talking to the priest, the tumult in the Philistine camp increased more and more. So Saul said to the priest, "Withdraw your hand."

²⁰Then Saul and all his men assembled and went to the battle. They found the Philistines in total confusion, striking each other with their swords. ²¹Those Hebrews who had previously been with the Philistines and had gone up with them to their camp went over to the Israelites who were with Saul and Jonathan. ²²When all the Israelites who had hidden in the hill country of Ephraim heard that the Philistines were on the run, they joined the battle in hot pursuit. ²³So on that day the LORD saved Israel, and the battle moved on beyond Beth Aven.

Jonathan Eats Honey

²⁴Now the Israelites were in distress that day, because Saul had bound the people under an oath, saying, "Cursed be anyone who eats food before evening comes, before I have avenged myself on my enemies!" So none of the troops tasted food.

²⁵The entire army entered the woods, and there was honey on the ground. ²⁶When they went into the woods, they saw the honey oozing out; yet no one put his hand to his mouth, because they feared the oath. ²⁷But Jonathan had not heard that his father had bound the people with the oath, so he reached out the end of the staff that was in his hand and dipped it into the honeycomb. He raised his hand to his mouth, and his eyes brightened.ᶜ ²⁸Then one of the soldiers told him, "Your father bound the army under a strict oath, saying, 'Cursed be anyone who eats food today!' That is why the men are faint."

²⁹Jonathan said, "My father has made trouble for the country. See how my eyes brightened when I tasted a little of this honey. ³⁰How much better it would have been if the men had eaten today some of the plunder they took from their enemies. Would not the slaughter of the Philistines have been even greater?"

³¹That day, after the Israelites had struck down the Philistines from Mikmash to Aijalon, they were exhausted. ³²They pounced on the plunder and, taking sheep, cattle and calves, they butchered them on the ground and ate them, together with the blood. ³³Then someone said to Saul, "Look, the men are sinning against the LORD by eating meat that has blood in it."

"You have broken faith," he said. "Roll a large stone over here at once." ³⁴Then he said, "Go out among the men and tell them, 'Each of you bring me your cattle and sheep, and slaughter them here and eat them. Do not sin against the LORD by eating meat with blood still in it.'"

So everyone brought his ox that night and slaughtered it there. ³⁵Then Saul built an altar to the LORD; it was the first time he had done this.

³⁶Saul said, "Let us go down and pursue the Philistines by night and plunder them till dawn, and let us not leave one of them alive."

"Do whatever seems best to you," they replied.

But the priest said, "Let us inquire of God here."

³⁷So Saul asked God, "Shall I go down and

ᵃ 15 Or *a terrible panic*   ᵇ 18 Hebrew; Septuagint *"Bring the ephod." (At that time he wore the ephod before the Israelites.)*   ᶜ 27 Or *his strength was renewed*; similarly in verse 29

CLIMB THE CLIFF

READ: 1 SAMUEL 14:4-14

What triggered Jonathan's twenty seconds of insane courage? To be perfectly honest, it seems like a dumb plan. It has to rank as the worst military strategy ever. Jonathan exposes himself to the enemy in broad daylight and hands over the high ground. I'm not sure which was more dangerous—climbing the cliff or fighting the Philistines. There's no guarantee that Jonathan would even survive the climb. It's not like the Philistines dropped a rope. And even if he made it to the top, Jonathan and his armor-bearer were outnumbered like a hundred to one.

It's impossible to psychoanalyze someone who lived thousands of years ago, but one statement reveals Jonathan's MO. It's the key code in his operating system. And it's easily one of my favorite sentences in the whole Bible. It's even our philosophy of ministry at NCC. One statement reveals everything I need to know about Jonathan.

BUILDING FAITH WISDOM STRENGTH

"Perhaps the LORD will act in our behalf." I think most of the doubters of the world think the opposite: perhaps the Lord won't act in our behalf. They let fear make their decisions instead of faith!

Our lack of guts is really a lack of faith. Instead of playing to win, we play not to lose. But cliff climbers would rather make mistakes than miss opportunities. Cliff climbers know that one step of faith brings out the big guns: God! That's precisely what happened because of Jonathan's bold move.

All it took was one daring decision! That's really all it ever takes.

pursue the Philistines? Will you give them into Israel's hand?" But God did not answer him that day.

[38] Saul therefore said, "Come here, all you who are leaders of the army, and let us find out what sin has been committed today. [39] As surely as the LORD who rescues Israel lives, even if the guilt lies with my son Jonathan, he must die." But not one of them said a word.

[40] Saul then said to all the Israelites, "You stand over there; I and Jonathan my son will stand over here."

"Do what seems best to you," they replied.

[41] Then Saul prayed to the LORD, the God of Israel, "Why have you not answered your servant today? If the fault is in me or my son Jonathan, respond with Urim, but if the men of Israel are at fault,[a] respond with Thummim." Jonathan and Saul were taken by lot, and the men were cleared. [42] Saul said, "Cast the lot between me and Jonathan my son." And Jonathan was taken.

[43] Then Saul said to Jonathan, "Tell me what you have done."

So Jonathan told him, "I tasted a little honey with the end of my staff. And now I must die!"

[44] Saul said, "May God deal with me, be it ever so severely, if you do not die, Jonathan."

[45] But the men said to Saul, "Should Jonathan die — he who has brought about this great deliverance in Israel? Never! As surely as the LORD lives, not a hair of his head will fall to the ground, for he did this today with God's help." So the men rescued Jonathan, and he was not put to death.

[46] Then Saul stopped pursuing the Philistines, and they withdrew to their own land.

[47] After Saul had assumed rule over Israel, he fought against their enemies on every side: Moab, the Ammonites, Edom, the kings[b] of Zobah, and the Philistines. Wherever he turned, he inflicted punishment on them.[c] [48] He fought valiantly and defeated the Amalekites, delivering Israel from the hands of those who had plundered them.

Saul's Family

[49] Saul's sons were Jonathan, Ishvi and Malki-Shua. The name of his older daughter was Merab, and that of the younger was Michal. [50] His wife's name was Ahinoam daughter of Ahimaaz. The name of the commander of Saul's army was Abner son of Ner, and Ner was Saul's uncle. [51] Saul's father Kish and Abner's father Ner were sons of Abiel.

[52] All the days of Saul there was bitter war with the Philistines, and whenever Saul saw a mighty or brave man, he took him into his service.

The LORD Rejects Saul as King

15 Samuel said to Saul, "I am the one the LORD sent to anoint you king over his people Israel; so listen now to the message from the LORD. [2] This is what the LORD Almighty says: 'I will punish the Amalekites for what they did to Israel when they waylaid them as they came up from Egypt. [3] Now go, attack the Amalekites and totally destroy[d] all that belongs to them. Do not spare them; put to death men and women, children and infants, cattle and sheep, camels and donkeys.' "

[4] So Saul summoned the men and mustered them at Telaim — two hundred thousand foot soldiers and ten thousand from Judah. [5] Saul went to the city of Amalek and set an ambush in the ravine. [6] Then he said to the Kenites, "Go away, leave the Amalekites so that I do not destroy you along with them; for you showed kindness to all the Israelites when they came up out of Egypt." So the Kenites moved away from the Amalekites.

[7] Then Saul attacked the Amalekites all the way from Havilah to Shur, near the eastern border of Egypt. [8] He took Agag king of the Amalekites alive, and all his people he totally destroyed with the sword. [9] But Saul and the army spared Agag and the best of the sheep and cattle, the fat calves[e] and lambs — everything that was good. These they were unwilling to destroy completely, but everything that was despised and weak they totally destroyed.

[10] Then the word of the LORD came to Samuel: [11] "I regret that I have made Saul king, because he has turned away from me and has not carried out my instructions."

---

[a] 41 Septuagint; Hebrew does not have "Why... at fault.   [b] 47 Masoretic Text; Dead Sea Scrolls and Septuagint king   [c] 47 Hebrew; Septuagint he was victorious   [d] 3 The Hebrew term refers to the irrevocable giving over of things or persons to the LORD, often by totally destroying them; also in verses 8, 9, 15, 18, 20 and 21.   [e] 9 Or the grown bulls; the meaning of the Hebrew for this phrase is uncertain.

Samuel was angry, and he cried out to the LORD all that night.

¹²Early in the morning Samuel got up and went to meet Saul, but he was told, "Saul has gone to Carmel. There he has set up a monument in his own honor and has turned and gone on down to Gilgal."

¹³When Samuel reached him, Saul said, "The LORD bless you! I have carried out the LORD's instructions."

¹⁴But Samuel said, "What then is this bleating of sheep in my ears? What is this lowing of cattle that I hear?"

¹⁵Saul answered, "The soldiers brought them from the Amalekites; they spared the best of the sheep and cattle to sacrifice to the LORD your God, but we totally destroyed the rest."

¹⁶"Enough!" Samuel said to Saul. "Let me tell you what the LORD said to me last night."

"Tell me," Saul replied.

¹⁷Samuel said, "Although you were once small in your own eyes, did you not become the head of the tribes of Israel? The LORD anointed you king over Israel. ¹⁸And he sent you on a mission, saying, 'Go and completely destroy those wicked people, the Amalekites; wage war against them until you have wiped them out.' ¹⁹Why did you not obey the LORD? Why did you pounce on the plunder and do evil in the eyes of the LORD?"

²⁰"But I did obey the LORD," Saul said. "I went on the mission the LORD assigned me. I completely destroyed the Amalekites and brought back Agag their king. ²¹The soldiers took sheep and cattle from the plunder, the best of what was devoted to God, in order to sacrifice them to the LORD your God at Gilgal."

²²But Samuel replied:

"Does the LORD delight in burnt offerings
        and sacrifices
    as much as in obeying the LORD?
To obey is better than sacrifice,
    and to heed is better than the fat of
        rams.
²³For rebellion is like the sin of
        divination,
    and arrogance like the evil of idolatry.
Because you have rejected the word of
        the LORD,
    he has rejected you as king."

²⁴Then Saul said to Samuel, "I have sinned. I violated the LORD's command and your instructions. I was afraid of the men and so I gave in to them. ²⁵Now I beg you, forgive my sin and come back with me, so that I may worship the LORD."

²⁶But Samuel said to him, "I will not go back with you. You have rejected the word of the LORD, and the LORD has rejected you as king over Israel!"

²⁷As Samuel turned to leave, Saul caught hold of the hem of his robe, and it tore. ²⁸Samuel said to him, "The LORD has torn the kingdom of Israel from you today and has given it to one of your neighbors — to one better than you. ²⁹He who is the Glory of Israel does not lie or change his mind; for he is not a human being, that he should change his mind."

³⁰Saul replied, "I have sinned. But please honor me before the elders of my people and before Israel; come back with me, so that I may worship the LORD your God." ³¹So Samuel went back with Saul, and Saul worshiped the LORD.

³²Then Samuel said, "Bring me Agag king of the Amalekites."

Agag came to him in chains.ᵃ And he thought, "Surely the bitterness of death is past."

³³But Samuel said,

"As your sword has made women
        childless,
    so will your mother be childless
        among women."

And Samuel put Agag to death before the LORD at Gilgal.

³⁴Then Samuel left for Ramah, but Saul went up to his home in Gibeah of Saul. ³⁵Until the day Samuel died, he did not go to see Saul again, though Samuel mourned for him. And the LORD regretted that he had made Saul king over Israel.

Samuel Anoints David

16 The LORD said to Samuel, "How long will you mourn for Saul, since I have rejected him as king over Israel? Fill your horn with oil and be on your way; I am sending you to Jesse of Bethlehem. I have chosen one of his sons to be king."

ᵃ 32 The meaning of the Hebrew for this phrase is uncertain.

DREAM IT UP

READ: 1 SAMUEL 16:1-13

I'm sure David dreamed of bigger and better things than just tending his father's livestock. He didn't long to sit in a pasture his whole life and count sheep.

Can you imagine the downtime as he sat on a hill and watched his sheep feed? Any time a guy has downtime, he dreams. He's thinking, *One day, I'm going to be in a better place and have a cool job and people are going to respect me.*

Like all of us, David had dreams. Maybe one shepherd down the road was the talk of the town because he had three times more sheep, and David always had to hear about the guy and his awesome farm. He had to hear the stories of his older brothers' exploits. He got tired of the "Isn't he cute?" pat on the head, even when he was trying to say something serious.

BUILDING FAITH WISDOM STRENGTH

As I thought about David, a question popped into my mind. What do our dreams sound like to God? I imagined God listening to David's dreams, knowing that David loved him and had a heart for him. I could just hear God whispering to him in a breezy pasture: "I know you have dreams and plans, which is awesome. But my dream for you will not even fit in your head. In fact, I can't even tell you everything yet."

That's how God arranges our lives. He lets us chase our little sparks of inspiration until he's ready to move us in his perfect timing. All along, he orchestrates our lives and our circumstances to confirm what he wants.

[2] But Samuel said, "How can I go? If Saul hears about it, he will kill me."

The LORD said, "Take a heifer with you and say, 'I have come to sacrifice to the LORD.' [3] Invite Jesse to the sacrifice, and I will show you what to do. You are to anoint for me the one I indicate."

[4] Samuel did what the LORD said. When he arrived at Bethlehem, the elders of the town trembled when they met him. They asked, "Do you come in peace?"

[5] Samuel replied, "Yes, in peace; I have come to sacrifice to the LORD. Consecrate yourselves and come to the sacrifice with me." Then he consecrated Jesse and his sons and invited them to the sacrifice.

[6] When they arrived, Samuel saw Eliab and thought, "Surely the LORD's anointed stands here before the LORD."

[7] But the LORD said to Samuel, "Do not consider his appearance or his height, for I have rejected him. The LORD does not look at the things people look at. People look at the outward appearance, but the LORD looks at the heart."

[8] Then Jesse called Abinadab and had him pass in front of Samuel. But Samuel said, "The LORD has not chosen this one either." [9] Jesse then had Shammah pass by, but Samuel said, "Nor has the LORD chosen this one." [10] Jesse had seven of his sons pass before Samuel, but Samuel said to him, "The LORD has not chosen these." [11] So he asked Jesse, "Are these all the sons you have?"

"There is still the youngest," Jesse answered. "He is tending the sheep."

Samuel said, "Send for him; we will not sit down until he arrives."

[12] So he sent for him and had him brought in. He was glowing with health and had a fine appearance and handsome features.

Then the LORD said, "Rise and anoint him; this is the one."

[13] So Samuel took the horn of oil and anointed him in the presence of his brothers, and from that day on the Spirit of the LORD came powerfully upon David. Samuel then went to Ramah.

David in Saul's Service

[14] Now the Spirit of the LORD had departed from Saul, and an evil[a] spirit from the LORD tormented him.

[15] Saul's attendants said to him, "See, an evil spirit from God is tormenting you. [16] Let our lord command his servants here to search for someone who can play the lyre. He will play when the evil spirit from God comes on you, and you will feel better."

[17] So Saul said to his attendants, "Find someone who plays well and bring him to me."

[18] One of the servants answered, "I have seen a son of Jesse of Bethlehem who knows how to play the lyre. He is a brave man and a warrior. He speaks well and is a fine-looking man. And the LORD is with him."

[19] Then Saul sent messengers to Jesse and said, "Send me your son David, who is with the sheep." [20] So Jesse took a donkey loaded with bread, a skin of wine and a young goat and sent them with his son David to Saul.

[21] David came to Saul and entered his service. Saul liked him very much, and David became one of his armor-bearers. [22] Then Saul sent word to Jesse, saying, "Allow David to remain in my service, for I am pleased with him."

[23] Whenever the spirit from God came on Saul, David would take up his lyre and play. Then relief would come to Saul; he would feel better, and the evil spirit would leave him.

David and Goliath

17 Now the Philistines gathered their forces for war and assembled at Sokoh in Judah. They pitched camp at Ephes Dammim, between Sokoh and Azekah. [2] Saul and the Israelites assembled and camped in the Valley of Elah and drew up their battle line to meet the Philistines. [3] The Philistines occupied one hill and the Israelites another, with the valley between them.

[4] A champion named Goliath, who was from Gath, came out of the Philistine camp. His height was six cubits and a span.[b] [5] He had a bronze helmet on his head and wore a coat of scale armor of bronze weighing five thousand shekels[c]; [6] on his legs he wore bronze greaves, and a bronze javelin was slung on his back. [7] His spear shaft was like a weaver's rod, and its iron point weighed six hundred shekels.[d] His shield bearer went ahead of him.

---

[a] 14 Or *and a harmful*; similarly in verses 15, 16 and 23
[c] 5 That is, about 125 pounds or about 58 kilograms
[b] 4 That is, about 9 feet 9 inches or about 3 meters
[d] 7 That is, about 15 pounds or about 6.9 kilograms

DAVID

[God] made David their king. God testified concerning him: "I have found David son of Jesse, a man after my own heart; he will do everything I want him to do." ACTS 13:22

HIS NAME MEANS: "beloved"

READ HIS STORY: *Ruth 4:16–22; 1 Samuel 16–20; 2 Samuel 11–12; 1 Chronicles 11*

OF THE BIBLE

David was fearless. As a young teenager, he killed lions and bears that tried to attack his father's sheep (1 Samuel 17:34–35) and rocked the giant Goliath on the battlefield (1 Samuel 17:41–51). His exploits as a fighter and warrior were legendary.

David was also flawed. When he saw Bathsheba, he lusted after her and used his position as king to sleep with her. Then he ordered her husband, Uriah, to the frontlines in a battle, so he would be killed (2 Samuel 11). Adulterer and murderer aren't words that normally describe a Bible hero. But they are part of David's story. In spite of his faults, he remained focused on God.

Read David's heartfelt confession of sinning with Bathsheba in Psalm 51. He asked for mercy and to be cleansed from his sin. Then he said, "Create in me a pure heart, O God, and renew a steadfast spirit within me" (Psalm 51:10). When God chose David to be king, he looked at David's heart (1 Samuel 16:7). David's heart for God never wavered, even when he made bad choices.

The psalms David wrote show us a good picture of his heart. He called for God to destroy his enemies. He asked God for strength and protection. And he remained faithful in his desire to follow God.

⁸Goliath stood and shouted to the ranks of Israel, "Why do you come out and line up for battle? Am I not a Philistine, and are you not the servants of Saul? Choose a man and have him come down to me. ⁹If he is able to fight and kill me, we will become your subjects; but if I overcome him and kill him, you will become our subjects and serve us." ¹⁰Then the Philistine said, "This day I defy the armies of Israel! Give me a man and let us fight each other." ¹¹On hearing the Philistine's words, Saul and all the Israelites were dismayed and terrified.

¹²Now David was the son of an Ephrathite named Jesse, who was from Bethlehem in Judah. Jesse had eight sons, and in Saul's time he was very old. ¹³Jesse's three oldest sons had followed Saul to the war: The firstborn was Eliab; the second, Abinadab; and the third, Shammah. ¹⁴David was the youngest. The three oldest followed Saul, ¹⁵but David went back and forth from Saul to tend his father's sheep at Bethlehem.

¹⁶For forty days the Philistine came forward every morning and evening and took his stand.

¹⁷Now Jesse said to his son David, "Take this ephah*ᵃ* of roasted grain and these ten loaves of bread for your brothers and hurry to their camp. ¹⁸Take along these ten cheeses to the commander of their unit. See how your brothers are and bring back some assurance*ᵇ* from them. ¹⁹They are with Saul and all the men of Israel in the Valley of Elah, fighting against the Philistines."

²⁰Early in the morning David left the flock in the care of a shepherd, loaded up and set out, as Jesse had directed. He reached the camp as the army was going out to its battle positions, shouting the war cry. ²¹Israel and the Philistines were drawing up their lines facing each other. ²²David left his things with the keeper of supplies, ran to the battle lines and asked his brothers how they were. ²³As he was talking with them, Goliath, the Philistine champion from Gath, stepped out from his lines and shouted his usual defiance, and David heard it. ²⁴Whenever the Israelites saw the man, they all fled from him in great fear.

²⁵Now the Israelites had been saying, "Do you see how this man keeps coming out? He comes out to defy Israel. The king will give great wealth to the man who kills him. He will also give him his daughter in marriage and will exempt his family from taxes in Israel."

²⁶David asked the men standing near him, "What will be done for the man who kills this Philistine and removes this disgrace from Israel? Who is this uncircumcised Philistine that he should defy the armies of the living God?"

²⁷They repeated to him what they had been saying and told him, "This is what will be done for the man who kills him."

²⁸When Eliab, David's oldest brother, heard him speaking with the men, he burned with anger at him and asked, "Why have you come down here? And with whom did you leave those few sheep in the wilderness? I know how conceited you are and how wicked your heart is; you came down only to watch the battle."

²⁹"Now what have I done?" said David. "Can't I even speak?" ³⁰He then turned away to someone else and brought up the same matter, and the men answered him as before. ³¹What David said was overheard and reported to Saul, and Saul sent for him.

³²David said to Saul, "Let no one lose heart on account of this Philistine; your servant will go and fight him."

³³Saul replied, "You are not able to go out against this Philistine and fight him; you are only a young man, and he has been a warrior from his youth."

³⁴But David said to Saul, "Your servant has been keeping his father's sheep. When a lion or a bear came and carried off a sheep from the flock, ³⁵I went after it, struck it and rescued the sheep from its mouth. When it turned on me, I seized it by its hair, struck it and killed it. ³⁶Your servant has killed both the lion and the bear; this uncircumcised Philistine will be like one of them, because he has defied the armies of the living God. ³⁷The LORD who rescued me from the paw of the lion and the paw of the bear will rescue me from the hand of this Philistine."

Saul said to David, "Go, and the LORD be with you."

³⁸Then Saul dressed David in his own tunic. He put a coat of armor on him and

---

ᵃ 17 That is, probably about 36 pounds or about 16 kilograms   *ᵇ 18* Or *some token;* or *some pledge of spoils* a bronze helmet on his head. [39]David fastened on his sword over the tunic and tried walking around, because he was not used to them.

"I cannot go in these," he said to Saul, "because I am not used to them." So he took them off. [40]Then he took his staff in his hand, chose five smooth stones from the stream, put them in the pouch of his shepherd's bag and, with his sling in his hand, approached the Philistine.

[41]Meanwhile, the Philistine, with his shield bearer in front of him, kept coming closer to David. [42]He looked David over and saw that he was little more than a boy, glowing with health and handsome, and he despised him. [43]He said to David, "Am I a dog, that you come at me with sticks?" And the Philistine cursed David by his gods. [44]"Come here," he said, "and I'll give your flesh to the birds and the wild animals!"

[45]David said to the Philistine, "You come against me with sword and spear and javelin, but I come against you in the name of the LORD Almighty, the God of the armies of Israel, whom you have defied. [46]This day the LORD will deliver you into my hands, and I'll strike you down and cut off your head. This very day I will give the carcasses of the Philistine army to the birds and the wild animals, and the whole world will know that there is a God in Israel. [47]All those gathered here will know that it is not by sword or spear that the LORD saves; for the battle is the LORD's, and he will give all of you into our hands."

[48]As the Philistine moved closer to attack him, David ran quickly toward the battle line to meet him. [49]Reaching into his bag and taking out a stone, he slung it and struck the Philistine on the forehead. The stone sank into his forehead, and he fell facedown on the ground.

[50]So David triumphed over the Philistine with a sling and a stone; without a sword in his hand he struck down the Philistine and killed him.

[51]David ran and stood over him. He took hold of the Philistine's sword and drew it from the sheath. After he killed him, he cut off his head with the sword.

When the Philistines saw that their hero was dead, they turned and ran. [52]Then the men of Israel and Judah surged forward with a shout and pursued the Philistines to the entrance of Gath[a] and to the gates of Ekron. Their dead were strewn along the Shaaraim road to Gath and Ekron. [53]When the Israelites returned from chasing the Philistines, they plundered their camp.

[54]David took the Philistine's head and brought it to Jerusalem; he put the Philistine's weapons in his own tent.

[55]As Saul watched David going out to meet the Philistine, he said to Abner, commander of the army, "Abner, whose son is that young man?"

Abner replied, "As surely as you live, Your Majesty, I don't know."

[56]The king said, "Find out whose son this young man is."

[57]As soon as David returned from killing the Philistine, Abner took him and brought him before Saul, with David still holding the Philistine's head.

[58]"Whose son are you, young man?" Saul asked him.

David said, "I am the son of your servant Jesse of Bethlehem."

Saul's Growing Fear of David

18 After David had finished talking with Saul, Jonathan became one in spirit with David, and he loved him as himself. [2]From that day Saul kept David with him and did not let him return home to his family. [3]And Jonathan made a covenant with David because he loved him as himself. [4]Jonathan took off the robe he was wearing and gave it to David, along with his tunic, and even his sword, his bow and his belt.

[5]Whatever mission Saul sent him on, David was so successful that Saul gave him a high rank in the army. This pleased all the troops, and Saul's officers as well.

[6]When the men were returning home after David had killed the Philistine, the women came out from all the towns of Israel to meet King Saul with singing and dancing, with joyful songs and with timbrels and lyres. [7]As they danced, they sang:

"Saul has slain his thousands,
    and David his tens of thousands."

---

[a] 52 Some Septuagint manuscripts; Hebrew *of a valley*

⁸Saul was very angry; this refrain displeased him greatly. "They have credited David with tens of thousands," he thought, "but me with only thousands. What more can he get but the kingdom?" ⁹And from that time on Saul kept a close eye on David.

¹⁰The next day an evil*a* spirit from God came forcefully on Saul. He was prophesying in his house, while David was playing the lyre, as he usually did. Saul had a spear in his hand ¹¹and he hurled it, saying to himself, "I'll pin David to the wall." But David eluded him twice.

¹²Saul was afraid of David, because the LORD was with David but had departed from Saul. ¹³So he sent David away from him and gave him command over a thousand men, and David led the troops in their campaigns. ¹⁴In everything he did he had great success, because the LORD was with him. ¹⁵When Saul saw how successful he was, he was afraid of him. ¹⁶But all Israel and Judah loved David, because he led them in their campaigns.

¹⁷Saul said to David, "Here is my older daughter Merab. I will give her to you in marriage; only serve me bravely and fight the battles of the LORD." For Saul said to himself, "I will not raise a hand against him. Let the Philistines do that!"

¹⁸But David said to Saul, "Who am I, and what is my family or my clan in Israel, that I should become the king's son-in-law?" ¹⁹So*b* when the time came for Merab, Saul's daughter, to be given to David, she was given in marriage to Adriel of Meholah.

²⁰Now Saul's daughter Michal was in love with David, and when they told Saul about it, he was pleased. ²¹"I will give her to him," he thought, "so that she may be a snare to him and so that the hand of the Philistines may be against him." So Saul said to David, "Now you have a second opportunity to become my son-in-law."

²²Then Saul ordered his attendants: "Speak to David privately and say, 'Look, the king likes you, and his attendants all love you; now become his son-in-law.'"

²³They repeated these words to David. But David said, "Do you think it is a small matter to become the king's son-in-law? I'm only a poor man and little known."

²⁴When Saul's servants told him what David had said, ²⁵Saul replied, "Say to David, 'The king wants no other price for the bride than a hundred Philistine foreskins, to take revenge on his enemies.'" Saul's plan was to have David fall by the hands of the Philistines.

²⁶When the attendants told David these things, he was pleased to become the king's son-in-law. So before the allotted time elapsed, ²⁷David took his men with him and went out and killed two hundred Philistines and brought back their foreskins. They counted out the full number to the king so that David might become the king's son-in-law. Then Saul gave him his daughter Michal in marriage.

²⁸When Saul realized that the LORD was with David and that his daughter Michal loved David, ²⁹Saul became still more afraid of him, and he remained his enemy the rest of his days.

³⁰The Philistine commanders continued to go out to battle, and as often as they did, David met with more success than the rest of Saul's officers, and his name became well known.

Saul Tries to Kill David

19 Saul told his son Jonathan and all the attendants to kill David. But Jonathan had taken a great liking to David ²and warned him, "My father Saul is looking for a chance to kill you. Be on your guard tomorrow morning; go into hiding and stay there. ³I will go out and stand with my father in the field where you are. I'll speak to him about you and will tell you what I find out."

⁴Jonathan spoke well of David to Saul his father and said to him, "Let not the king do wrong to his servant David; he has not wronged you, and what he has done has benefited you greatly. ⁵He took his life in his hands when he killed the Philistine. The LORD won a great victory for all Israel, and you saw it and were glad. Why then would you do wrong to an innocent man like David by killing him for no reason?"

⁶Saul listened to Jonathan and took this oath: "As surely as the LORD lives, David will not be put to death."

⁷So Jonathan called David and told him

---

a 10 Or *a harmful*   *b 19* Or *However,*

the whole conversation. He brought him to Saul, and David was with Saul as before.

⁸Once more war broke out, and David went out and fought the Philistines. He struck them with such force that they fled before him.

⁹But an evil*a* spirit from the LORD came on Saul as he was sitting in his house with his spear in his hand. While David was playing the lyre, ¹⁰Saul tried to pin him to the wall with his spear, but David eluded him as Saul drove the spear into the wall. That night David made good his escape.

¹¹Saul sent men to David's house to watch it and to kill him in the morning. But Michal, David's wife, warned him, "If you don't run for your life tonight, tomorrow you'll be killed." ¹²So Michal let David down through a window, and he fled and escaped. ¹³Then Michal took an idol and laid it on the bed, covering it with a garment and putting some goats' hair at the head.

¹⁴When Saul sent the men to capture David, Michal said, "He is ill."

¹⁵Then Saul sent the men back to see David and told them, "Bring him up to me in his bed so that I may kill him." ¹⁶But when the men entered, there was the idol in the bed, and at the head was some goats' hair.

¹⁷Saul said to Michal, "Why did you deceive me like this and send my enemy away so that he escaped?"

Michal told him, "He said to me, 'Let me get away. Why should I kill you?'"

¹⁸When David had fled and made his escape, he went to Samuel at Ramah and told him all that Saul had done to him. Then he and Samuel went to Naioth and stayed there. ¹⁹Word came to Saul: "David is in Naioth at Ramah"; ²⁰so he sent men to capture him. But when they saw a group of prophets prophesying, with Samuel standing there as their leader, the Spirit of God came on Saul's men, and they also prophesied. ²¹Saul was told about it, and he sent more men, and they prophesied too. Saul sent men a third time, and they also prophesied. ²²Finally, he himself left for Ramah and went to the great cistern at Seku. And he asked, "Where are Samuel and David?"

"Over in Naioth at Ramah," they said.

²³So Saul went to Naioth at Ramah. But the Spirit of God came even on him, and he walked along prophesying until he came to Naioth. ²⁴He stripped off his garments, and he too prophesied in Samuel's presence. He lay naked all that day and all that night. This is why people say, "Is Saul also among the prophets?"

David and Jonathan

20 Then David fled from Naioth at Ramah and went to Jonathan and asked, "What have I done? What is my crime? How have I wronged your father, that he is trying to kill me?"

²"Never!" Jonathan replied. "You are not going to die! Look, my father doesn't do anything, great or small, without letting me know. Why would he hide this from me? It isn't so!"

³But David took an oath and said, "Your father knows very well that I have found favor in your eyes, and he has said to himself, 'Jonathan must not know this or he will be grieved.' Yet as surely as the LORD lives and as you live, there is only a step between me and death."

⁴Jonathan said to David, "Whatever you want me to do, I'll do for you."

⁵So David said, "Look, tomorrow is the New Moon feast, and I am supposed to dine with the king; but let me go and hide in the field until the evening of the day after tomorrow. ⁶If your father misses me at all, tell him, 'David earnestly asked my permission to hurry to Bethlehem, his hometown, because an annual sacrifice is being made there for his whole clan.' ⁷If he says, 'Very well,' then your servant is safe. But if he loses his temper, you can be sure that he is determined to harm me. ⁸As for you, show kindness to your servant, for you have brought him into a covenant with you before the LORD. If I am guilty, then kill me yourself! Why hand me over to your father?"

⁹"Never!" Jonathan said. "If I had the least inkling that my father was determined to harm you, wouldn't I tell you?"

¹⁰David asked, "Who will tell me if your father answers you harshly?"

¹¹"Come," Jonathan said, "let's go out into the field." So they went there together.

¹²Then Jonathan said to David, "I swear

---

a 9 Or *But a harmful*

by the Lord, the God of Israel, that I will surely sound out my father by this time the day after tomorrow! If he is favorably disposed toward you, will I not send you word and let you know? ¹³But if my father intends to harm you, may the Lord deal with Jonathan, be it ever so severely, if I do not let you know and send you away in peace. May the Lord be with you as he has been with my father. ¹⁴But show me unfailing kindness like the Lord's kindness as long as I live, so that I may not be killed, ¹⁵and do not ever cut off your kindness from my family — not even when the Lord has cut off every one of David's enemies from the face of the earth."

¹⁶So Jonathan made a covenant with the house of David, saying, "May the Lord call David's enemies to account." ¹⁷And Jonathan had David reaffirm his oath out of love for him, because he loved him as he loved himself.

¹⁸Then Jonathan said to David, "Tomorrow is the New Moon feast. You will be missed, because your seat will be empty. ¹⁹The day after tomorrow, toward evening, go to the place where you hid when this trouble began, and wait by the stone Ezel. ²⁰I will shoot three arrows to the side of it, as though I were shooting at a target. ²¹Then I will send a boy and say, 'Go, find the arrows.' If I say to him, 'Look, the arrows are on this side of you; bring them here,' then come, because, as surely as the Lord lives, you are safe; there is no danger. ²²But if I say to the boy, 'Look, the arrows are beyond you,' then you must go, because the Lord has sent you away. ²³And about the matter you and I discussed — remember, the Lord is witness between you and me forever."

²⁴So David hid in the field, and when the New Moon feast came, the king sat down to eat. ²⁵He sat in his customary place by the wall, opposite Jonathan,ᵃ and Abner sat next to Saul, but David's place was empty. ²⁶Saul said nothing that day, for he thought, "Something must have happened to David to make him ceremonially unclean — surely he is unclean." ²⁷But the next day, the second day of the month, David's place was empty again. Then Saul said to his son Jonathan, "Why hasn't the son of Jesse come to the meal, either yesterday or today?"

²⁸Jonathan answered, "David earnestly asked me for permission to go to Bethlehem. ²⁹He said, 'Let me go, because our family is observing a sacrifice in the town and my brother has ordered me to be there. If I have found favor in your eyes, let me get away to see my brothers.' That is why he has not come to the king's table."

³⁰Saul's anger flared up at Jonathan and he said to him, "You son of a perverse and rebellious woman! Don't I know that you have sided with the son of Jesse to your own shame and to the shame of the mother who bore you? ³¹As long as the son of Jesse lives on this earth, neither you nor your kingdom will be established. Now send someone to bring him to me, for he must die!"

³²"Why should he be put to death? What has he done?" Jonathan asked his father. ³³But Saul hurled his spear at him to kill him. Then Jonathan knew that his father intended to kill David.

³⁴Jonathan got up from the table in fierce anger; on that second day of the feast he did not eat, because he was grieved at his father's shameful treatment of David.

³⁵In the morning Jonathan went out to the field for his meeting with David. He had a small boy with him, ³⁶and he said to the boy, "Run and find the arrows I shoot." As the boy ran, he shot an arrow beyond him. ³⁷When the boy came to the place where Jonathan's arrow had fallen, Jonathan called out after him, "Isn't the arrow beyond you?" ³⁸Then he shouted, "Hurry! Go quickly! Don't stop!" The boy picked up the arrow and returned to his master. ³⁹(The boy knew nothing about all this; only Jonathan and David knew.) ⁴⁰Then Jonathan gave his weapons to the boy and said, "Go, carry them back to town."

⁴¹After the boy had gone, David got up from the south side of the stone and bowed down before Jonathan three times, with his face to the ground. Then they kissed each other and wept together — but David wept the most.

⁴²Jonathan said to David, "Go in peace, for we have sworn friendship with each other in the name of the Lord, saying, 'The Lord is witness between you and me, and between your descendants and my descendants

---

ᵃ 25 Septuagint; Hebrew *wall. Jonathan arose*

MALE BONDING

READ: 1 SAMUEL 20:41

Peter, James, and John were close friends with Jesus, but they dozed while he prayed in such awful agony that he sweat blood (Mark 14:37, Luke 22:39-46). The apostle Paul went on the road with Barnabas to spread the good news about Jesus, but they split after a sharp fight (Acts 15:36-41). So as you study this scene with David and Jonathan, know that it likely ranks as the Bible's ultimate example of male bonding.

Jonathan should have hated David. Any political advisor would have told him to exterminate David long before this scene. As the oldest son of King Saul, Jonathan might have assumed he would someday ascend to the throne. As David grew more and more popular, all the people and even Saul recognized that David threatened Jonathan's future role as king (1 Samuel 18:7).

BUILDING
FAITH
WISDOM
STRENGTH

As Saul tried harder to kill David, Jonathan went against his father and sided with the guy who had become his best friend. When David finally had to flee Saul, he and Jonathan wept together and swore that their godly friendship would never end. (That kissing, by the way, shows up almost three dozen times in the Bible as an ancient cultural greeting.)

You can't survive life on your own, and you can't get along without friends who have your back. So when you tick through the long list of qualities you look for in a friend, make sure loyalty comes somewhere near the top.

forever.'" Then David left, and Jonathan went back to the town.[a]

David at Nob

21 [b] David went to Nob, to Ahimelek the priest. Ahimelek trembled when he met him, and asked, "Why are you alone? Why is no one with you?"

[2] David answered Ahimelek the priest, "The king sent me on a mission and said to me, 'No one is to know anything about the mission I am sending you on.' As for my men, I have told them to meet me at a certain place. [3] Now then, what do you have on hand? Give me five loaves of bread, or whatever you can find."

[4] But the priest answered David, "I don't have any ordinary bread on hand; however, there is some consecrated bread here — provided the men have kept themselves from women."

[5] David replied, "Indeed women have been kept from us, as usual whenever[c] I set out. The men's bodies are holy even on missions that are not holy. How much more so today!" [6] So the priest gave him the consecrated bread, since there was no bread there except the bread of the Presence that had been removed from before the LORD and replaced by hot bread on the day it was taken away.

[7] Now one of Saul's servants was there that day, detained before the LORD; he was Doeg the Edomite, Saul's chief shepherd.

[8] David asked Ahimelek, "Don't you have a spear or a sword here? I haven't brought my sword or any other weapon, because the king's mission was urgent."

[9] The priest replied, "The sword of Goliath the Philistine, whom you killed in the Valley of Elah, is here; it is wrapped in a cloth behind the ephod. If you want it, take it; there is no sword here but that one."

David said, "There is none like it; give it to me."

David at Gath

[10] That day David fled from Saul and went to Achish king of Gath. [11] But the servants of Achish said to him, "Isn't this David, the king of the land? Isn't he the one they sing about in their dances:

"'Saul has slain his thousands,
    and David his tens of thousands'?"

[12] David took these words to heart and was very much afraid of Achish king of Gath. [13] So he pretended to be insane in their presence; and while he was in their hands he acted like a madman, making marks on the doors of the gate and letting saliva run down his beard.

[14] Achish said to his servants, "Look at the man! He is insane! Why bring him to me? [15] Am I so short of madmen that you have to bring this fellow here to carry on like this in front of me? Must this man come into my house?"

David at Adullam and Mizpah

22 David left Gath and escaped to the cave of Adullam. When his brothers and his father's household heard about it, they went down to him there. [2] All those who were in distress or in debt or discontented gathered around him, and he became their commander. About four hundred men were with him.

[3] From there David went to Mizpah in Moab and said to the king of Moab, "Would you let my father and mother come and stay with you until I learn what God will do for me?" [4] So he left them with the king of Moab, and they stayed with him as long as David was in the stronghold.

[5] But the prophet Gad said to David, "Do not stay in the stronghold. Go into the land of Judah." So David left and went to the forest of Hereth.

Saul Kills the Priests of Nob

[6] Now Saul heard that David and his men had been discovered. And Saul was seated, spear in hand, under the tamarisk tree on the hill at Gibeah, with all his officials standing at his side. [7] He said to them, "Listen, men of Benjamin! Will the son of Jesse give all of you fields and vineyards? Will he make all of you commanders of thousands and commanders of hundreds? [8] Is that why you have all conspired against me? No one tells me when my son makes a covenant with the son of Jesse. None of you is concerned about me or tells me that my son has

---

[a] 42 In Hebrew texts this sentence (20:42b) is numbered 21:1.   [b] In Hebrew texts 21:1-15 is numbered 21:2-16.   [c] 5 Or *from us in the past few days since*

incited my servant to lie in wait for me, as he does today."

⁹But Doeg the Edomite, who was standing with Saul's officials, said, "I saw the son of Jesse come to Ahimelek son of Ahitub at Nob. ¹⁰Ahimelek inquired of the LORD for him; he also gave him provisions and the sword of Goliath the Philistine."

¹¹Then the king sent for the priest Ahimelek son of Ahitub and all the men of his family, who were the priests at Nob, and they all came to the king. ¹²Saul said, "Listen now, son of Ahitub."

"Yes, my lord," he answered.

¹³Saul said to him, "Why have you conspired against me, you and the son of Jesse, giving him bread and a sword and inquiring of God for him, so that he has rebelled against me and lies in wait for me, as he does today?"

¹⁴Ahimelek answered the king, "Who of all your servants is as loyal as David, the king's son-in-law, captain of your bodyguard and highly respected in your household? ¹⁵Was that day the first time I inquired of God for him? Of course not! Let not the king accuse your servant or any of his father's family, for your servant knows nothing at all about this whole affair."

¹⁶But the king said, "You will surely die, Ahimelek, you and your whole family."

¹⁷Then the king ordered the guards at his side: "Turn and kill the priests of the LORD, because they too have sided with David. They knew he was fleeing, yet they did not tell me."

But the king's officials were unwilling to raise a hand to strike the priests of the LORD.

¹⁸The king then ordered Doeg, "You turn and strike down the priests." So Doeg the Edomite turned and struck them down. That day he killed eighty-five men who wore the linen ephod. ¹⁹He also put to the sword Nob, the town of the priests, with its men and women, its children and infants, and its cattle, donkeys and sheep.

²⁰But one son of Ahimelek son of Ahitub, named Abiathar, escaped and fled to join David. ²¹He told David that Saul had killed the priests of the LORD. ²²Then David said to Abiathar, "That day, when Doeg the Edomite was there, I knew he would be sure to tell Saul. I am responsible for the death of your whole family. ²³Stay with me; don't be afraid.

The man who wants to kill you is trying to kill me too. You will be safe with me."

David Saves Keilah

23 When David was told, "Look, the Philistines are fighting against Keilah and are looting the threshing floors," ²he inquired of the LORD, saying, "Shall I go and attack these Philistines?"

The LORD answered him, "Go, attack the Philistines and save Keilah."

³But David's men said to him, "Here in Judah we are afraid. How much more, then, if we go to Keilah against the Philistine forces!"

⁴Once again David inquired of the LORD, and the LORD answered him, "Go down to Keilah, for I am going to give the Philistines into your hand." ⁵So David and his men went to Keilah, fought the Philistines and carried off their livestock. He inflicted heavy losses on the Philistines and saved the people of Keilah. ⁶(Now Abiathar son of Ahimelek had brought the ephod down with him when he fled to David at Keilah.)

Saul Pursues David

⁷Saul was told that David had gone to Keilah, and he said, "God has delivered him into my hands, for David has imprisoned himself by entering a town with gates and bars." ⁸And Saul called up all his forces for battle, to go down to Keilah to besiege David and his men.

⁹When David learned that Saul was plotting against him, he said to Abiathar the priest, "Bring the ephod." ¹⁰David said, "LORD, God of Israel, your servant has heard definitely that Saul plans to come to Keilah and destroy the town on account of me. ¹¹Will the citizens of Keilah surrender me to him? Will Saul come down, as your servant has heard? LORD, God of Israel, tell your servant."

And the LORD said, "He will."

¹²Again David asked, "Will the citizens of Keilah surrender me and my men to Saul?"

And the LORD said, "They will."

¹³So David and his men, about six hundred in number, left Keilah and kept moving from place to place. When Saul was told that David had escaped from Keilah, he did not go there.

¹⁴David stayed in the wilderness strongholds and in the hills of the Desert of Ziph. Day after day Saul searched for him, but God did not give David into his hands.

¹⁵While David was at Horesh in the Desert of Ziph, he learned that[a] Saul had come out to take his life. ¹⁶And Saul's son Jonathan went to David at Horesh and helped him find strength in God. ¹⁷"Don't be afraid," he said. "My father Saul will not lay a hand on you. You will be king over Israel, and I will be second to you. Even my father Saul knows this." ¹⁸The two of them made a covenant before the LORD. Then Jonathan went home, but David remained at Horesh.

¹⁹The Ziphites went up to Saul at Gibeah and said, "Is not David hiding among us in the strongholds at Horesh, on the hill of Hakilah, south of Jeshimon? ²⁰Now, Your Majesty, come down whenever it pleases you to do so, and we will be responsible for giving him into your hands."

²¹Saul replied, "The LORD bless you for your concern for me. ²²Go and get more information. Find out where David usually goes and who has seen him there. They tell me he is very crafty. ²³Find out about all the hiding places he uses and come back to me with definite information. Then I will go with you; if he is in the area, I will track him down among all the clans of Judah."

²⁴So they set out and went to Ziph ahead of Saul. Now David and his men were in the Desert of Maon, in the Arabah south of Jeshimon. ²⁵Saul and his men began the search, and when David was told about it, he went down to the rock and stayed in the Desert of Maon. When Saul heard this, he went into the Desert of Maon in pursuit of David.

²⁶Saul was going along one side of the mountain, and David and his men were on the other side, hurrying to get away from Saul. As Saul and his forces were closing in on David and his men to capture them, ²⁷a messenger came to Saul, saying, "Come quickly! The Philistines are raiding the land." ²⁸Then Saul broke off his pursuit of David and went to meet the Philistines. That is why they call this place Sela Hammahlekoth.[b] ²⁹And David went up from there and lived in the strongholds of En Gedi.[c]

David Spares Saul's Life

24[d] After Saul returned from pursuing the Philistines, he was told, "David is in the Desert of En Gedi." ²So Saul took three thousand able young men from all Israel and set out to look for David and his men near the Crags of the Wild Goats.

³He came to the sheep pens along the way; a cave was there, and Saul went in to relieve himself. David and his men were far back in the cave. ⁴The men said, "This is the day the LORD spoke of when he said[e] to you, 'I will give your enemy into your hands for you to deal with as you wish.'" Then David crept up unnoticed and cut off a corner of Saul's robe.

⁵Afterward, David was conscience-stricken for having cut off a corner of his robe. ⁶He said to his men, "The LORD forbid that I should do such a thing to my master, the LORD's anointed, or lay my hand on him; for he is the anointed of the LORD." ⁷With these words David sharply rebuked his men and did not allow them to attack Saul. And Saul left the cave and went his way.

⁸Then David went out of the cave and called out to Saul, "My lord the king!" When Saul looked behind him, David bowed down and prostrated himself with his face to the ground. ⁹He said to Saul, "Why do you listen when men say, 'David is bent on harming you'? ¹⁰This day you have seen with your own eyes how the LORD delivered you into my hands in the cave. Some urged me to kill you, but I spared you; I said, 'I will not lay my hand on my lord, because he is the LORD's anointed.' ¹¹See, my father, look at this piece of your robe in my hand! I cut off the corner of your robe but did not kill you. See that there is nothing in my hand to indicate that I am guilty of wrongdoing or rebellion. I have not wronged you, but you are hunting me down to take my life. ¹²May the LORD judge between you and me. And may the LORD avenge the wrongs you have done to me, but my hand will not touch you. ¹³As the old saying goes, 'From evildoers come evil deeds,' so my hand will not touch you.

¹⁴"Against whom has the king of Israel come out? Who are you pursuing? A dead dog? A flea? ¹⁵May the LORD be our judge and decide between us. May he consider my cause and uphold it; may he vindicate me by delivering me from your hand."

---

[a] 15 Or *he was afraid because*   [b] 28 *Sela Hammahlekoth* means *rock of parting.*   [c] 29 In Hebrew texts this verse (23:29) is numbered 24:1.   [d] In Hebrew texts 24:1-22 is numbered 24:2-23.   [e] 4 Or *"Today the* LORD *is saying*

¹⁶When David finished saying this, Saul asked, "Is that your voice, David my son?" And he wept aloud. ¹⁷"You are more righteous than I," he said. "You have treated me well, but I have treated you badly. ¹⁸You have just now told me about the good you did to me; the LORD delivered me into your hands, but you did not kill me. ¹⁹When a man finds his enemy, does he let him get away unharmed? May the LORD reward you well for the way you treated me today. ²⁰I know that you will surely be king and that the kingdom of Israel will be established in your hands. ²¹Now swear to me by the LORD that you will not kill off my descendants or wipe out my name from my father's family."

²²So David gave his oath to Saul. Then Saul returned home, but David and his men went up to the stronghold.

David, Nabal and Abigail

25 Now Samuel died, and all Israel assembled and mourned for him; and they buried him at his home in Ramah. Then David moved down into the Desert of Paran.ᵃ

²A certain man in Maon, who had property there at Carmel, was very wealthy. He had a thousand goats and three thousand sheep, which he was shearing in Carmel. ³His name was Nabal and his wife's name was Abigail. She was an intelligent and beautiful woman, but her husband was surly and mean in his dealings—he was a Calebite.

⁴While David was in the wilderness, he heard that Nabal was shearing sheep. ⁵So he sent ten young men and said to them, "Go up to Nabal at Carmel and greet him in my name. ⁶Say to him: 'Long life to you! Good health to you and your household! And good health to all that is yours!

⁷"'Now I hear that it is sheep-shearing time. When your shepherds were with us, we did not mistreat them, and the whole time they were at Carmel nothing of theirs was missing. ⁸Ask your own servants and they will tell you. Therefore be favorable toward my men, since we come at a festive time. Please give your servants and your son David whatever you can find for them.'"

⁹When David's men arrived, they gave Nabal this message in David's name. Then they waited.

¹⁰Nabal answered David's servants, "Who is this David? Who is this son of Jesse? Many servants are breaking away from their masters these days. ¹¹Why should I take my bread and water, and the meat I have slaughtered for my shearers, and give it to men coming from who knows where?"

¹²David's men turned around and went back. When they arrived, they reported every word. ¹³David said to his men, "Each of you strap on your sword!" So they did, and David strapped his on as well. About four hundred men went up with David, while two hundred stayed with the supplies.

¹⁴One of the servants told Abigail, Nabal's wife, "David sent messengers from the wilderness to give our master his greetings, but he hurled insults at them. ¹⁵Yet these men were very good to us. They did not mistreat us, and the whole time we were out in the fields near them nothing was missing. ¹⁶Night and day they were a wall around us the whole time we were herding our sheep near them. ¹⁷Now think it over and see what you can do, because disaster is hanging over our master and his whole household. He is such a wicked man that no one can talk to him."

¹⁸Abigail acted quickly. She took two hundred loaves of bread, two skins of wine, five dressed sheep, five seahsᵇ of roasted grain, a hundred cakes of raisins and two hundred cakes of pressed figs, and loaded them on donkeys. ¹⁹Then she told her servants, "Go on ahead; I'll follow you." But she did not tell her husband Nabal.

²⁰As she came riding her donkey into a mountain ravine, there were David and his men descending toward her, and she met them. ²¹David had just said, "It's been useless—all my watching over this fellow's property in the wilderness so that nothing of his was missing. He has paid me back evil for good. ²²May God deal with David,ᶜ be it ever so severely, if by morning I leave alive one male of all who belong to him!"

²³When Abigail saw David, she quickly

ᵃ 1 Hebrew and some Septuagint manuscripts; other Septuagint manuscripts *Maon*   ᵇ 18 That is, probably about 60 pounds or about 27 kilograms   ᶜ 22 Some Septuagint manuscripts; Hebrew *with David's enemies* got off her donkey and bowed down before David with her face to the ground. ²⁴She fell at his feet and said: "Pardon your servant, my lord, and let me speak to you; hear what your servant has to say. ²⁵Please pay no attention, my lord, to that wicked man Nabal. He is just like his name—his name means Fool, and folly goes with him. And as for me, your servant, I did not see the men my lord sent. ²⁶And now, my lord, as surely as the LORD your God lives and as you live, since the LORD has kept you from bloodshed and from avenging yourself with your own hands, may your enemies and all who are intent on harming my lord be like Nabal. ²⁷And let this gift, which your servant has brought to my lord, be given to the men who follow you.

²⁸"Please forgive your servant's presumption. The LORD your God will certainly make a lasting dynasty for my lord, because you fight the LORD's battles, and no wrongdoing will be found in you as long as you live. ²⁹Even though someone is pursuing you to take your life, the life of my lord will be bound securely in the bundle of the living by the LORD your God, but the lives of your enemies he will hurl away as from the pocket of a sling. ³⁰When the LORD has fulfilled for my lord every good thing he promised concerning him and has appointed him ruler over Israel, ³¹my lord will not have on his conscience the staggering burden of needless bloodshed or of having avenged himself. And when the LORD your God has brought my lord success, remember your servant."

³²David said to Abigail, "Praise be to the LORD, the God of Israel, who has sent you today to meet me. ³³May you be blessed for your good judgment and for keeping me from bloodshed this day and from avenging myself with my own hands. ³⁴Otherwise, as surely as the LORD, the God of Israel, lives, who has kept me from harming you, if you had not come quickly to meet me, not one male belonging to Nabal would have been left alive by daybreak."

³⁵Then David accepted from her hand what she had brought him and said, "Go home in peace. I have heard your words and granted your request."

³⁶When Abigail went to Nabal, he was in the house holding a banquet like that of a king. He was in high spirits and very drunk. So she told him nothing at all until daybreak. ³⁷Then in the morning, when Nabal was sober, his wife told him all these things, and his heart failed him and he became like a stone. ³⁸About ten days later, the LORD struck Nabal and he died.

³⁹When David heard that Nabal was dead, he said, "Praise be to the LORD, who has upheld my cause against Nabal for treating me with contempt. He has kept his servant from doing wrong and has brought Nabal's wrongdoing down on his own head."

Then David sent word to Abigail, asking her to become his wife. ⁴⁰His servants went to Carmel and said to Abigail, "David has sent us to you to take you to become his wife."

⁴¹She bowed down with her face to the ground and said, "I am your servant and am ready to serve you and wash the feet of my lord's servants." ⁴²Abigail quickly got on a donkey and, attended by her five female servants, went with David's messengers and became his wife. ⁴³David had also married Ahinoam of Jezreel, and they both were his wives. ⁴⁴But Saul had given his daughter Michal, David's wife, to Paltiel[a] son of Laish, who was from Gallim.

David Again Spares Saul's Life

26 The Ziphites went to Saul at Gibeah and said, "Is not David hiding on the hill of Hakilah, which faces Jeshimon?"

²So Saul went down to the Desert of Ziph, with his three thousand select Israelite troops, to search there for David. ³Saul made his camp beside the road on the hill of Hakilah facing Jeshimon, but David stayed in the wilderness. When he saw that Saul had followed him there, ⁴he sent out scouts and learned that Saul had definitely arrived.

⁵Then David set out and went to the place where Saul had camped. He saw where Saul and Abner son of Ner, the commander of the army, had lain down. Saul was lying inside the camp, with the army encamped around him.

⁶David then asked Ahimelek the Hittite and Abishai son of Zeruiah, Joab's brother, "Who will go down into the camp with me to Saul?"

ª 44 Hebrew *Palti*, a variant of *Paltiel*

"I'll go with you," said Abishai.

[7] So David and Abishai went to the army by night, and there was Saul, lying asleep inside the camp with his spear stuck in the ground near his head. Abner and the soldiers were lying around him.

[8] Abishai said to David, "Today God has delivered your enemy into your hands. Now let me pin him to the ground with one thrust of the spear; I won't strike him twice."

[9] But David said to Abishai, "Don't destroy him! Who can lay a hand on the LORD's anointed and be guiltless? [10] As surely as the LORD lives," he said, "the LORD himself will strike him, or his time will come and he will die, or he will go into battle and perish. [11] But the LORD forbid that I should lay a hand on the LORD's anointed. Now get the spear and water jug that are near his head, and let's go."

[12] So David took the spear and water jug near Saul's head, and they left. No one saw or knew about it, nor did anyone wake up. They were all sleeping, because the LORD had put them into a deep sleep.

[13] Then David crossed over to the other side and stood on top of the hill some distance away; there was a wide space between them. [14] He called out to the army and to Abner son of Ner, "Aren't you going to answer me, Abner?"

Abner replied, "Who are you who calls to the king?"

[15] David said, "You're a man, aren't you? And who is like you in Israel? Why didn't you guard your lord the king? Someone came to destroy your lord the king. [16] What you have done is not good. As surely as the LORD lives, you and your men must die, because you did not guard your master, the LORD's anointed. Look around you. Where are the king's spear and water jug that were near his head?"

[17] Saul recognized David's voice and said, "Is that your voice, David my son?"

David replied, "Yes it is, my lord the king." [18] And he added, "Why is my lord pursuing his servant? What have I done, and what wrong am I guilty of? [19] Now let my lord the king listen to his servant's words. If the LORD has incited you against me, then may he accept an offering. If, however, people have done it, may they be cursed before the LORD! They have driven me today from my share in the LORD's inheritance and have said, 'Go, serve other gods.' [20] Now do not let my blood fall to the ground far from the presence of the LORD. The king of Israel has come out to look for a flea — as one hunts a partridge in the mountains."

[21] Then Saul said, "I have sinned. Come back, David my son. Because you considered my life precious today, I will not try to harm you again. Surely I have acted like a fool and have been terribly wrong."

[22] "Here is the king's spear," David answered. "Let one of your young men come over and get it. [23] The LORD rewards everyone for their righteousness and faithfulness. The LORD delivered you into my hands today, but I would not lay a hand on the LORD's anointed. [24] As surely as I valued your life today, so may the LORD value my life and deliver me from all trouble."

[25] Then Saul said to David, "May you be blessed, David my son; you will do great things and surely triumph."

So David went on his way, and Saul returned home.

David Among the Philistines

27 But David thought to himself, "One of these days I will be destroyed by the hand of Saul. The best thing I can do is to escape to the land of the Philistines. Then Saul will give up searching for me anywhere in Israel, and I will slip out of his hand."

[2] So David and the six hundred men with him left and went over to Achish son of Maok king of Gath. [3] David and his men settled in Gath with Achish. Each man had his family with him, and David had his two wives: Ahinoam of Jezreel and Abigail of Carmel, the widow of Nabal. [4] When Saul was told that David had fled to Gath, he no longer searched for him.

[5] Then David said to Achish, "If I have found favor in your eyes, let a place be assigned to me in one of the country towns, that I may live there. Why should your servant live in the royal city with you?"

[6] So on that day Achish gave him Ziklag, and it has belonged to the kings of Judah ever since. [7] David lived in Philistine territory a year and four months.

[8] Now David and his men went up and raided the Geshurites, the Girzites and the Amalekites. (From ancient times these peoples had lived in the land extending to Shur and Egypt.) [9] Whenever David attacked

an area, he did not leave a man or woman alive, but took sheep and cattle, donkeys and camels, and clothes. Then he returned to Achish.

¹⁰When Achish asked, "Where did you go raiding today?" David would say, "Against the Negev of Judah" or "Against the Negev of Jerahmeel" or "Against the Negev of the Kenites." ¹¹He did not leave a man or woman alive to be brought to Gath, for he thought, "They might inform on us and say, 'This is what David did.'" And such was his practice as long as he lived in Philistine territory. ¹²Achish trusted David and said to himself, "He has become so obnoxious to his people, the Israelites, that he will be my servant for life."

28 In those days the Philistines gathered their forces to fight against Israel. Achish said to David, "You must understand that you and your men will accompany me in the army."

²David said, "Then you will see for yourself what your servant can do."

Achish replied, "Very well, I will make you my bodyguard for life."

Saul and the Medium at Endor

³Now Samuel was dead, and all Israel had mourned for him and buried him in his own town of Ramah. Saul had expelled the mediums and spiritists from the land.

⁴The Philistines assembled and came and set up camp at Shunem, while Saul gathered all Israel and set up camp at Gilboa. ⁵When Saul saw the Philistine army, he was afraid; terror filled his heart. ⁶He inquired of the LORD, but the LORD did not answer him by dreams or Urim or prophets. ⁷Saul then said to his attendants, "Find me a woman who is a medium, so I may go and inquire of her."

"There is one in Endor," they said.

⁸So Saul disguised himself, putting on other clothes, and at night he and two men went to the woman. "Consult a spirit for me," he said, "and bring up for me the one I name."

⁹But the woman said to him, "Surely you know what Saul has done. He has cut off the mediums and spiritists from the land. Why have you set a trap for my life to bring about my death?"

¹⁰Saul swore to her by the LORD, "As surely as the LORD lives, you will not be punished for this."

¹¹Then the woman asked, "Whom shall I bring up for you?"

"Bring up Samuel," he said.

¹²When the woman saw Samuel, she cried out at the top of her voice and said to Saul, "Why have you deceived me? You are Saul!"

¹³The king said to her, "Don't be afraid. What do you see?"

The woman said, "I see a ghostly figure*ᵃ coming up out of the earth."

¹⁴"What does he look like?" he asked.

"An old man wearing a robe is coming up," she said.

Then Saul knew it was Samuel, and he bowed down and prostrated himself with his face to the ground.

¹⁵Samuel said to Saul, "Why have you disturbed me by bringing me up?"

"I am in great distress," Saul said. "The Philistines are fighting against me, and God has departed from me. He no longer answers me, either by prophets or by dreams. So I have called on you to tell me what to do."

¹⁶Samuel said, "Why do you consult me now that the LORD has departed from you and become your enemy? ¹⁷The LORD has done what he predicted through me. The LORD has torn the kingdom out of your hands and given it to one of your neighbors—to David. ¹⁸Because you did not obey the LORD or carry out his fierce wrath against the Amalekites, the LORD has done this to you today. ¹⁹The LORD will deliver both Israel and you into the hands of the Philistines, and tomorrow you and your sons will be with me. The LORD will also give the army of Israel into the hands of the Philistines."

²⁰Immediately Saul fell full length on the ground, filled with fear because of Samuel's words. His strength was gone, for he had eaten nothing all that day and all that night.

²¹When the woman came to Saul and saw that he was greatly shaken, she said, "Look, your servant has obeyed you. I took my life in my hands and did what you told me to do. ²²Now please listen to your servant and let me give you some food so you may eat and have the strength to go on your way."

²³He refused and said, "I will not eat."

ᵃ 13 Or *see spirits*; or *see gods*

But his men joined the woman in urging him, and he listened to them. He got up from the ground and sat on the couch.

²⁴ The woman had a fattened calf at the house, which she butchered at once. She took some flour, kneaded it and baked bread without yeast. ²⁵ Then she set it before Saul and his men, and they ate. That same night they got up and left.

Achish Sends David Back to Ziklag

29 The Philistines gathered all their forces at Aphek, and Israel camped by the spring in Jezreel. ² As the Philistine rulers marched with their units of hundreds and thousands, David and his men were marching at the rear with Achish. ³ The commanders of the Philistines asked, "What about these Hebrews?"

Achish replied, "Is this not David, who was an officer of Saul king of Israel? He has already been with me for over a year, and from the day he left Saul until now, I have found no fault in him."

⁴ But the Philistine commanders were angry with Achish and said, "Send the man back, that he may return to the place you assigned him. He must not go with us into battle, or he will turn against us during the fighting. How better could he regain his master's favor than by taking the heads of our own men? ⁵ Isn't this the David they sang about in their dances:

" 'Saul has slain his thousands,
  and David his tens of thousands'?"

⁶ So Achish called David and said to him, "As surely as the LORD lives, you have been reliable, and I would be pleased to have you serve with me in the army. From the day you came to me until today, I have found no fault in you, but the rulers don't approve of you. ⁷ Now turn back and go in peace; do nothing to displease the Philistine rulers."

⁸ "But what have I done?" asked David. "What have you found against your servant from the day I came to you until now? Why can't I go and fight against the enemies of my lord the king?"

⁹ Achish answered, "I know that you have been as pleasing in my eyes as an angel of God; nevertheless, the Philistine commanders have said, 'He must not go up with us into battle.' ¹⁰ Now get up early, along with your master's servants who have come with you, and leave in the morning as soon as it is light."

¹¹ So David and his men got up early in the morning to go back to the land of the Philistines, and the Philistines went up to Jezreel.

David Destroys the Amalekites

30 David and his men reached Ziklag on the third day. Now the Amalekites had raided the Negev and Ziklag. They had attacked Ziklag and burned it, ² and had taken captive the women and everyone else in it, both young and old. They killed none of them, but carried them off as they went on their way.

³ When David and his men reached Ziklag, they found it destroyed by fire and their wives and sons and daughters taken captive. ⁴ So David and his men wept aloud until they had no strength left to weep. ⁵ David's two wives had been captured—Ahinoam of Jezreel and Abigail, the widow of Nabal of Carmel. ⁶ David was greatly distressed because the men were talking of stoning him; each one was bitter in spirit because of his sons and daughters. But David found strength in the LORD his God.

⁷ Then David said to Abiathar the priest, the son of Ahimelek, "Bring me the ephod." Abiathar brought it to him, ⁸ and David inquired of the LORD, "Shall I pursue this raiding party? Will I overtake them?"

"Pursue them," he answered. "You will certainly overtake them and succeed in the rescue."

⁹ David and the six hundred men with him came to the Besor Valley, where some stayed behind. ¹⁰ Two hundred of them were too exhausted to cross the valley, but David and the other four hundred continued the pursuit.

¹¹ They found an Egyptian in a field and brought him to David. They gave him water to drink and food to eat— ¹² part of a cake of pressed figs and two cakes of raisins. He ate and was revived, for he had not eaten any food or drunk any water for three days and three nights.

¹³ David asked him, "Who do you belong to? Where do you come from?"

He said, "I am an Egyptian, the slave of an Amalekite. My master abandoned me when I became ill three days ago. ¹⁴ We raided the

Negev of the Kerethites, some territory belonging to Judah and the Negev of Caleb. And we burned Ziklag."

¹⁵David asked him, "Can you lead me down to this raiding party?"

He answered, "Swear to me before God that you will not kill me or hand me over to my master, and I will take you down to them."

¹⁶He led David down, and there they were, scattered over the countryside, eating, drinking and reveling because of the great amount of plunder they had taken from the land of the Philistines and from Judah. ¹⁷David fought them from dusk until the evening of the next day, and none of them got away, except four hundred young men who rode off on camels and fled. ¹⁸David recovered everything the Amalekites had taken, including his two wives. ¹⁹Nothing was missing: young or old, boy or girl, plunder or anything else they had taken. David brought everything back. ²⁰He took all the flocks and herds, and his men drove them ahead of the other livestock, saying, "This is David's plunder."

²¹Then David came to the two hundred men who had been too exhausted to follow him and who were left behind at the Besor Valley. They came out to meet David and the men with him. As David and his men approached, he asked them how they were. ²²But all the evil men and troublemakers among David's followers said, "Because they did not go out with us, we will not share with them the plunder we recovered. However, each man may take his wife and children and go."

²³David replied, "No, my brothers, you must not do that with what the LORD has given us. He has protected us and delivered into our hands the raiding party that came against us. ²⁴Who will listen to what you say? The share of the man who stayed with the supplies is to be the same as that of him who went down to the battle. All will share alike." ²⁵David made this a statute and ordinance for Israel from that day to this.

²⁶When David reached Ziklag, he sent some of the plunder to the elders of Judah, who were his friends, saying, "Here is a gift for you from the plunder of the LORD's enemies."

²⁷David sent it to those who were in Beth-el, Ramoth Negev and Jattir; ²⁸to those in Aroer, Siphmoth, Eshtemoa ²⁹and Rakal; to those in the towns of the Jerahmeelites and the Kenites; ³⁰to those in Hormah, Bor Ashan, Athak ³¹and Hebron; and to those in all the other places where he and his men had roamed.

Saul Takes His Life

31 Now the Philistines fought against Israel; the Israelites fled before them, and many fell dead on Mount Gilboa. ²The Philistines were in hot pursuit of Saul and his sons, and they killed his sons Jonathan, Abinadab and Malki-Shua. ³The fighting grew fierce around Saul, and when the archers overtook him, they wounded him critically.

⁴Saul said to his armor-bearer, "Draw your sword and run me through, or these uncircumcised fellows will come and run me through and abuse me."

But his armor-bearer was terrified and would not do it; so Saul took his own sword and fell on it. ⁵When the armor-bearer saw that Saul was dead, he too fell on his sword and died with him. ⁶So Saul and his three sons and his armor-bearer and all his men died together that same day.

⁷When the Israelites along the valley and those across the Jordan saw that the Israelite army had fled and that Saul and his sons had died, they abandoned their towns and fled. And the Philistines came and occupied them.

⁸The next day, when the Philistines came to strip the dead, they found Saul and his three sons fallen on Mount Gilboa. ⁹They cut off his head and stripped off his armor, and they sent messengers throughout the land of the Philistines to proclaim the news in the temple of their idols and among their people. ¹⁰They put his armor in the temple of the Ashtoreths and fastened his body to the wall of Beth Shan.

¹¹When the people of Jabesh Gilead heard what the Philistines had done to Saul, ¹²all their valiant men marched through the night to Beth Shan. They took down the bodies of Saul and his sons from the wall of Beth Shan and went to Jabesh, where they burned them. ¹³Then they took their bones and buried them under a tamarisk tree at Jabesh, and they fasted seven days.

2 SAMUEL

➡ **WHEN DID THIS HAPPEN?**

About 1100–960 B.C. in the land of Israel

➡ **WHO IS IN THIS BOOK?**

David
Mephibosheth
Bathsheba
Nathan
Absalom

➡ **VERSES YOU MIGHT RECOGNIZE**

2 SAMUEL 7:24

"You have established your people Israel as your very own forever, and you, LORD, have become their God."

2 SAMUEL 22:47

"The LORD lives! Praise be to my Rock! Exalted be my God, the Rock, my Savior!"

WHAT'S IT ABOUT?

David is known as one of Israel's greatest kings, and this book is all about how he led Israel. David was called a man after God's own heart (see 1 Samuel 13:14). Even though he honored God, David also made some big mistakes, such as committing adultery and murder. But he always repented and returned to God.

God established a covenant—a permanent promise—with David. God promised the ruler that his kingdom would last forever (see 2 Samuel 7:16). This meant the Messiah would be born into the line of David. Jesus was that Messiah whose rule would never end. God also told David that his son will build the temple.

2 SAMUEL

David Hears of Saul's Death

1 After the death of Saul, David returned from striking down the Amalekites and stayed in Ziklag two days. ²On the third day a man arrived from Saul's camp with his clothes torn and dust on his head. When he came to David, he fell to the ground to pay him honor.

³"Where have you come from?" David asked him.

He answered, "I have escaped from the Israelite camp."

⁴"What happened?" David asked. "Tell me."

"The men fled from the battle," he replied. "Many of them fell and died. And Saul and his son Jonathan are dead."

⁵Then David said to the young man who brought him the report, "How do you know that Saul and his son Jonathan are dead?"

⁶"I happened to be on Mount Gilboa," the young man said, "and there was Saul, leaning on his spear, with the chariots and their drivers in hot pursuit. ⁷When he turned around and saw me, he called out to me, and I said, 'What can I do?'

⁸"He asked me, 'Who are you?'

"'An Amalekite,' I answered.

⁹"Then he said to me, 'Stand here by me and kill me! I'm in the throes of death, but I'm still alive.'

¹⁰"So I stood beside him and killed him, because I knew that after he had fallen he could not survive. And I took the crown that was on his head and the band on his arm and have brought them here to my lord."

¹¹Then David and all the men with him took hold of their clothes and tore them. ¹²They mourned and wept and fasted till evening for Saul and his son Jonathan, and for the army of the LORD and for the nation of Israel, because they had fallen by the sword.

¹³David said to the young man who brought him the report, "Where are you from?"

"I am the son of a foreigner, an Amalekite," he answered.

¹⁴David asked him, "Why weren't you afraid to lift your hand to destroy the LORD's anointed?"

¹⁵Then David called one of his men and said, "Go, strike him down!" So he struck him down, and he died. ¹⁶For David had said to him, "Your blood be on your own head. Your own mouth testified against you when you said, 'I killed the LORD's anointed.'"

David's Lament for Saul and Jonathan

¹⁷David took up this lament concerning Saul and his son Jonathan, ¹⁸and he ordered that the people of Judah be taught this lament of the bow (it is written in the Book of Jashar):

¹⁹"A gazelle[a] lies slain on your heights, Israel.
How the mighty have fallen!

²⁰"Tell it not in Gath,
proclaim it not in the streets of Ashkelon,
lest the daughters of the Philistines be glad,
lest the daughters of the uncircumcised rejoice.

²¹"Mountains of Gilboa,
may you have neither dew nor rain,
may no showers fall on your terraced fields.[b]
For there the shield of the mighty was despised,
the shield of Saul — no longer rubbed with oil.

²²"From the blood of the slain,
from the flesh of the mighty,
the bow of Jonathan did not turn back,
the sword of Saul did not return unsatisfied.

²³Saul and Jonathan —
in life they were loved and admired,

---

[a] 19 *Gazelle* here symbolizes a human dignitary.   [b] 21 Or / *nor fields that yield grain for offerings*

and in death they were not
parted.
They were swifter than eagles,
they were stronger than lions.

24 "Daughters of Israel,
weep for Saul,
who clothed you in scarlet and finery,
who adorned your garments with
ornaments of gold.

25 "How the mighty have fallen in battle!
Jonathan lies slain on your heights.
26 I grieve for you, Jonathan my brother;
you were very dear to me.
Your love for me was wonderful,
more wonderful than that of women.

27 "How the mighty have fallen!
The weapons of war have perished!"

David Anointed King Over Judah

2 In the course of time, David inquired
of the LORD. "Shall I go up to one of the
towns of Judah?" he asked.

The LORD said, "Go up."

David asked, "Where shall I go?"

"To Hebron," the LORD answered.

2 So David went up there with his two
wives, Ahinoam of Jezreel and Abigail, the
widow of Nabal of Carmel. 3 David also took
the men who were with him, each with his
family, and they settled in Hebron and its
towns. 4 Then the men of Judah came to Hebron, and there they anointed David king
over the tribe of Judah.

When David was told that it was the men
from Jabesh Gilead who had buried Saul, 5 he
sent messengers to them to say to them, "The
LORD bless you for showing this kindness to
Saul your master by burying him. 6 May the
LORD now show you kindness and faithfulness, and I too will show you the same favor
because you have done this. 7 Now then, be
strong and brave, for Saul your master is
dead, and the people of Judah have anointed
me king over them."

War Between the Houses of David and Saul

8 Meanwhile, Abner son of Ner, the commander of Saul's army, had taken Ish-Bosheth son of Saul and brought him over to
Mahanaim. 9 He made him king over Gilead,

Ashuri and Jezreel, and also over Ephraim,
Benjamin and all Israel.

10 Ish-Bosheth son of Saul was forty years
old when he became king over Israel, and he
reigned two years. The tribe of Judah, however, remained loyal to David. 11 The length
of time David was king in Hebron over Judah
was seven years and six months.

12 Abner son of Ner, together with the men
of Ish-Bosheth son of Saul, left Mahanaim
and went to Gibeon. 13 Joab son of Zeruiah
and David's men went out and met them at
the pool of Gibeon. One group sat down on
one side of the pool and one group on the
other side.

14 Then Abner said to Joab, "Let's have
some of the young men get up and fight hand
to hand in front of us."

"All right, let them do it," Joab said.

15 So they stood up and were counted
off — twelve men for Benjamin and Ish-Bosheth son of Saul, and twelve for David.
16 Then each man grabbed his opponent by
the head and thrust his dagger into his opponent's side, and they fell down together.
So that place in Gibeon was called Helkath
Hazzurim.a

17 The battle that day was very fierce, and
Abner and the Israelites were defeated by
David's men.

18 The three sons of Zeruiah were there:
Joab, Abishai and Asahel. Now Asahel was
as fleet-footed as a wild gazelle. 19 He chased
Abner, turning neither to the right nor to the
left as he pursued him. 20 Abner looked behind him and asked, "Is that you, Asahel?"

"It is," he answered.

21 Then Abner said to him, "Turn aside
to the right or to the left; take on one of the
young men and strip him of his weapons."
But Asahel would not stop chasing him.

22 Again Abner warned Asahel, "Stop
chasing me! Why should I strike you down?
How could I look your brother Joab in the
face?"

23 But Asahel refused to give up the pursuit; so Abner thrust the butt of his spear
into Asahel's stomach, and the spear came
out through his back. He fell there and died
on the spot. And every man stopped when
he came to the place where Asahel had fall-
en and died.

---

a 16 *Helkath Hazzurim* means *field of daggers* or *field of hostilities.*

²⁴But Joab and Abishai pursued Abner, and as the sun was setting, they came to the hill of Ammah, near Giah on the way to the wasteland of Gibeon. ²⁵Then the men of Benjamin rallied behind Abner. They formed themselves into a group and took their stand on top of a hill.

²⁶Abner called out to Joab, "Must the sword devour forever? Don't you realize that this will end in bitterness? How long before you order your men to stop pursuing their fellow Israelites?"

²⁷Joab answered, "As surely as God lives, if you had not spoken, the men would have continued pursuing them until morning."

²⁸So Joab blew the trumpet, and all the troops came to a halt; they no longer pursued Israel, nor did they fight anymore.

²⁹All that night Abner and his men marched through the Arabah. They crossed the Jordan, continued through the morning hours[a] and came to Mahanaim.

³⁰Then Joab stopped pursuing Abner and assembled the whole army. Besides Asahel, nineteen of David's men were found missing. ³¹But David's men had killed three hundred and sixty Benjamites who were with Abner. ³²They took Asahel and buried him in his father's tomb at Bethlehem. Then Joab and his men marched all night and arrived at Hebron by daybreak.

3 The war between the house of Saul and the house of David lasted a long time. David grew stronger and stronger, while the house of Saul grew weaker and weaker.

²Sons were born to David in Hebron:

His firstborn was Amnon the son of Ahinoam of Jezreel;

³his second, Kileab the son of Abigail the widow of Nabal of Carmel;

the third, Absalom the son of Maakah daughter of Talmai king of Geshur;

⁴the fourth, Adonijah the son of Haggith;

the fifth, Shephatiah the son of Abital;

⁵and the sixth, Ithream the son of David's wife Eglah.

These were born to David in Hebron.

Abner Goes Over to David

⁶During the war between the house of Saul and the house of David, Abner had been strengthening his own position in the house of Saul. ⁷Now Saul had had a concubine named Rizpah daughter of Aiah. And Ish-Bosheth said to Abner, "Why did you sleep with my father's concubine?"

⁸Abner was very angry because of what Ish-Bosheth said. So he answered, "Am I a dog's head—on Judah's side? This very day I am loyal to the house of your father Saul and to his family and friends. I haven't handed you over to David. Yet now you accuse me of an offense involving this woman! ⁹May God deal with Abner, be it ever so severely, if I do not do for David what the LORD promised him on oath ¹⁰and transfer the kingdom from the house of Saul and establish David's throne over Israel and Judah from Dan to Beersheba." ¹¹Ish-Bosheth did not dare to say another word to Abner, because he was afraid of him.

¹²Then Abner sent messengers on his behalf to say to David, "Whose land is it? Make an agreement with me, and I will help you bring all Israel over to you."

¹³"Good," said David. "I will make an agreement with you. But I demand one thing of you: Do not come into my presence unless you bring Michal daughter of Saul when you come to see me." ¹⁴Then David sent messengers to Ish-Bosheth son of Saul, demanding, "Give me my wife Michal, whom I betrothed to myself for the price of a hundred Philistine foreskins."

¹⁵So Ish-Bosheth gave orders and had her taken away from her husband Paltiel son of Laish. ¹⁶Her husband, however, went with her, weeping behind her all the way to Bahurim. Then Abner said to him, "Go back home!" So he went back.

¹⁷Abner conferred with the elders of Israel and said, "For some time you have wanted to make David your king. ¹⁸Now do it! For the LORD promised David, 'By my servant David I will rescue my people Israel from the hand of the Philistines and from the hand of all their enemies.'"

¹⁹Abner also spoke to the Benjamites in person. Then he went to Hebron to tell David everything that Israel and the whole tribe of Benjamin wanted to do. ²⁰When Abner, who had twenty men with him, came to David at Hebron, David prepared a feast for him and

---

[a] 29 See Septuagint; the meaning of the Hebrew for this phrase is uncertain.

WARRING FAMILIES

READ: 2 SAMUEL 3:1

Long before this scene, Saul's disobedience made him unfit to be king (1 Samuel 13:14). The Lord picked David as the new ruler (16:13), and from that time forward, God's spirit left Saul (v. 14). Saul took his own life rather than be tormented by warring Philistines (31:4).

Saul's death seemed like it should end Israel's infighting, bringing God's pick to the throne. But the tragedy didn't settle anything. It ignited a struggle for the kingdom between David's army and Saul's remaining family and allies. Since David's beloved friend Jonathan had died in battle, Saul's next-eldest son, Ish-Bosheth, was crowned king of Israel, while David rules only his own tribe, Judah. But when Ish-Bosheth angered Abner, the head general went over to David's side.

You might not track all of those details. But words from Abner make sense of what's going on: "Must the sword devour forever? Don't you realize that this will end in bitterness?" (2 Samuel 2:26). When nations, tribes, and individuals turn against God, violence spreads and life turns bitter.

You can't control what happens in your larger world. But you can do everything in your power to get along with the people around you. Like the apostle Paul wrote, "If it is possible, as far as it depends on you, live at peace with everyone" (Romans 12:18).

BUILDING

FAITH

WISDOM

STRENGTH

his men. ²¹Then Abner said to David, "Let me go at once and assemble all Israel for my lord the king, so that they may make a covenant with you, and that you may rule over all that your heart desires." So David sent Abner away, and he went in peace.

Joab Murders Abner

²²Just then David's men and Joab returned from a raid and brought with them a great deal of plunder. But Abner was no longer with David in Hebron, because David had sent him away, and he had gone in peace. ²³When Joab and all the soldiers with him arrived, he was told that Abner son of Ner had come to the king and that the king had sent him away and that he had gone in peace.

²⁴So Joab went to the king and said, "What have you done? Look, Abner came to you. Why did you let him go? Now he is gone! ²⁵You know Abner son of Ner; he came to deceive you and observe your movements and find out everything you are doing."

²⁶Joab then left David and sent messengers after Abner, and they brought him back from the cistern at Sirah. But David did not know it. ²⁷Now when Abner returned to Hebron, Joab took him aside into an inner chamber, as if to speak with him privately. And there, to avenge the blood of his brother Asahel, Joab stabbed him in the stomach, and he died.

²⁸Later, when David heard about this, he said, "I and my kingdom are forever innocent before the LORD concerning the blood of Abner son of Ner. ²⁹May his blood fall on the head of Joab and on his whole family! May Joab's family never be without someone who has a running sore or leprosy^a or who leans on a crutch or who falls by the sword or who lacks food."

³⁰(Joab and his brother Abishai murdered Abner because he had killed their brother Asahel in the battle at Gibeon.)

³¹Then David said to Joab and all the people with him, "Tear your clothes and put on sackcloth and walk in mourning in front of Abner." King David himself walked behind the bier. ³²They buried Abner in Hebron, and the king wept aloud at Abner's tomb. All the people wept also.

³³The king sang this lament for Abner:

"Should Abner have died as the lawless die?
³⁴   Your hands were not bound,
      your feet were not fettered.
You fell as one falls before the wicked."

And all the people wept over him again. ³⁵Then they all came and urged David to eat something while it was still day; but David took an oath, saying, "May God deal with me, be it ever so severely, if I taste bread or anything else before the sun sets!"

³⁶All the people took note and were pleased; indeed, everything the king did pleased them. ³⁷So on that day all the people there and all Israel knew that the king had no part in the murder of Abner son of Ner.

³⁸Then the king said to his men, "Do you not realize that a commander and a great man has fallen in Israel this day? ³⁹And today, though I am the anointed king, I am weak, and these sons of Zeruiah are too strong for me. May the LORD repay the evildoer according to his evil deeds!"

Ish-Bosheth Murdered

4 When Ish-Bosheth son of Saul heard that Abner had died in Hebron, he lost courage, and all Israel became alarmed. ²Now Saul's son had two men who were leaders of raiding bands. One was named Baanah and the other Rekab; they were sons of Rimmon the Beerothite from the tribe of Benjamin—Beeroth is considered part of Benjamin, ³because the people of Beeroth fled to Gittaim and have resided there as foreigners to this day.

⁴(Jonathan son of Saul had a son who was lame in both feet. He was five years old when the news about Saul and Jonathan came from Jezreel. His nurse picked him up and fled, but as she hurried to leave, he fell and became disabled. His name was Mephibosheth.)

⁵Now Rekab and Baanah, the sons of Rimmon the Beerothite, set out for the house of Ish-Bosheth, and they arrived there in the heat of the day while he was taking his noonday rest. ⁶They went into the inner part of the house as if to get some wheat, and they stabbed him in the stomach. Then Rekab and his brother Baanah slipped away.

⁷They had gone into the house while he

---

^a 29 The Hebrew for *leprosy* was used for various diseases affecting the skin.

was lying on the bed in his bedroom. After they stabbed and killed him, they cut off his head. Taking it with them, they traveled all night by way of the Arabah. [8]They brought the head of Ish-Bosheth to David at Hebron and said to the king, "Here is the head of Ish-Bosheth son of Saul, your enemy, who tried to kill you. This day the LORD has avenged my lord the king against Saul and his offspring."

[9]David answered Rekab and his brother Baanah, the sons of Rimmon the Beerothite, "As surely as the LORD lives, who has delivered me out of every trouble, [10]when someone told me, 'Saul is dead,' and thought he was bringing good news, I seized him and put him to death in Ziklag. That was the reward I gave him for his news! [11]How much more — when wicked men have killed an innocent man in his own house and on his own bed — should I not now demand his blood from your hand and rid the earth of you!"

[12]So David gave an order to his men, and they killed them. They cut off their hands and feet and hung the bodies by the pool in Hebron. But they took the head of Ish-Bosheth and buried it in Abner's tomb at Hebron.

David Becomes King Over Israel

5 All the tribes of Israel came to David at Hebron and said, "We are your own flesh and blood. [2]In the past, while Saul was king over us, you were the one who led Israel on their military campaigns. And the LORD said to you, 'You will shepherd my people Israel, and you will become their ruler.' "

[3]When all the elders of Israel had come to King David at Hebron, the king made a covenant with them at Hebron before the LORD, and they anointed David king over Israel.

[4]David was thirty years old when he became king, and he reigned forty years. [5]In Hebron he reigned over Judah seven years and six months, and in Jerusalem he reigned over all Israel and Judah thirty-three years.

David Conquers Jerusalem

[6]The king and his men marched to Jerusalem to attack the Jebusites, who lived there. The Jebusites said to David, "You will not get in here; even the blind and the lame can ward

you off." They thought, "David cannot get in here." [7]Nevertheless, David captured the fortress of Zion — which is the City of David.

[8]On that day David had said, "Anyone who conquers the Jebusites will have to use the water shaft to reach those 'lame and blind' who are David's enemies.[a]" That is why they say, "The 'blind and lame' will not enter the palace."

[9]David then took up residence in the fortress and called it the City of David. He built up the area around it, from the terraces[b] inward. [10]And he became more and more powerful, because the LORD God Almighty was with him.

[11]Now Hiram king of Tyre sent envoys to David, along with cedar logs and carpenters and stonemasons, and they built a palace for David. [12]Then David knew that the LORD had established him as king over Israel and had exalted his kingdom for the sake of his people Israel.

[13]After he left Hebron, David took more concubines and wives in Jerusalem, and more sons and daughters were born to him. [14]These are the names of the children born to him there: Shammua, Shobab, Nathan, Solomon, [15]Ibhar, Elishua, Nepheg, Japhia, [16]Elishama, Eliada and Eliphelet.

David Defeats the Philistines

[17]When the Philistines heard that David had been anointed king over Israel, they went up in full force to search for him, but David heard about it and went down to the stronghold. [18]Now the Philistines had come and spread out in the Valley of Rephaim; [19]so David inquired of the LORD, "Shall I go and attack the Philistines? Will you deliver them into my hands?"

The LORD answered him, "Go, for I will surely deliver the Philistines into your hands."

[20]So David went to Baal Perazim, and there he defeated them. He said, "As waters break out, the LORD has broken out against my enemies before me." So that place was called Baal Perazim.[c] [21]The Philistines abandoned their idols there, and David and his men carried them off.

[22]Once more the Philistines came up and spread out in the Valley of Rephaim; [23]so

---

[a] 8 Or *are hated by David*   [b] 9 Or *the Millo*   [c] 20 *Baal Perazim* means *the lord who breaks out*.

David inquired of the LORD, and he answered, "Do not go straight up, but circle around behind them and attack them in front of the poplar trees. [24]As soon as you hear the sound of marching in the tops of the poplar trees, move quickly, because that will mean the LORD has gone out in front of you to strike the Philistine army." [25]So David did as the LORD commanded him, and he struck down the Philistines all the way from Gibeon[a] to Gezer.

The Ark Brought to Jerusalem

6 David again brought together all the able young men of Israel—thirty thousand. [2]He and all his men went to Baalah[b] in Judah to bring up from there the ark of God, which is called by the Name,[c] the name of the LORD Almighty, who is enthroned between the cherubim on the ark. [3]They set the ark of God on a new cart and brought it from the house of Abinadab, which was on the hill. Uzzah and Ahio, sons of Abinadab, were guiding the new cart [4]with the ark of God on it,[d] and Ahio was walking in front of it. [5]David and all Israel were celebrating with all their might before the LORD, with castanets,[e] harps, lyres, timbrels, sistrums and cymbals.

[6]When they came to the threshing floor of Nakon, Uzzah reached out and took hold of the ark of God, because the oxen stumbled. [7]The LORD's anger burned against Uzzah because of his irreverent act; therefore God struck him down, and he died there beside the ark of God.

[8]Then David was angry because the LORD's wrath had broken out against Uzzah, and to this day that place is called Perez Uzzah.[f]

[9]David was afraid of the LORD that day and said, "How can the ark of the LORD ever come to me?" [10]He was not willing to take the ark of the LORD to be with him in the City of David. Instead, he took it to the house of Obed-Edom the Gittite. [11]The ark of the LORD remained in the house of Obed-Edom the Gittite for three months, and the LORD blessed him and his entire household.

[12]Now King David was told, "The LORD has blessed the household of Obed-Edom and everything he has, because of the ark of God." So David went to bring up the ark of God from the house of Obed-Edom to the City of David with rejoicing. [13]When those who were carrying the ark of the LORD had taken six steps, he sacrificed a bull and a fattened calf. [14]Wearing a linen ephod, David was dancing before the LORD with all his might, [15]while he and all Israel were bringing up the ark of the LORD with shouts and the sound of trumpets.

[16]As the ark of the LORD was entering the City of David, Michal daughter of Saul watched from a window. And when she saw King David leaping and dancing before the LORD, she despised him in her heart.

[17]They brought the ark of the LORD and set it in its place inside the tent that David had pitched for it, and David sacrificed burnt offerings and fellowship offerings before the LORD. [18]After he had finished sacrificing the burnt offerings and fellowship offerings, he blessed the people in the name of the LORD Almighty. [19]Then he gave a loaf of bread, a cake of dates and a cake of raisins to each person in the whole crowd of Israelites, both men and women. And all the people went to their homes.

[20]When David returned home to bless his household, Michal daughter of Saul came out to meet him and said, "How the king of Israel has distinguished himself today, going around half-naked in full view of the slave girls of his servants as any vulgar fellow would!"

[21]David said to Michal, "It was before the LORD, who chose me rather than your father or anyone from his house when he appointed me ruler over the LORD's people Israel—I will celebrate before the LORD. [22]I will become even more undignified than this, and I will be humiliated in my own eyes. But by these slave girls you spoke of, I will be held in honor."

[23]And Michal daughter of Saul had no children to the day of her death.

God's Promise to David

7 After the king was settled in his palace and the LORD had given him rest from

---

a 25 Septuagint (see also 1 Chron. 14:16); Hebrew *Geba*   *b 2* That is, Kiriath Jearim (see 1 Chron. 13:6)   *c 2* Hebrew; Septuagint and Vulgate do not have *the Name.*   *d 3,4* Dead Sea Scrolls and some Septuagint manuscripts; Masoretic Text *cart* *4and they brought it with the ark of God from the house of Abinadab, which was on the hill*   *e 5* Masoretic Text; Dead Sea Scrolls and Septuagint (see also 1 Chron. 13:8) *songs*   *f 8* *Perez Uzzah* means *outbreak against Uzzah.*

all his enemies around him, [2]he said to Nathan the prophet, "Here I am, living in a house of cedar, while the ark of God remains in a tent."

[3]Nathan replied to the king, "Whatever you have in mind, go ahead and do it, for the LORD is with you."

[4]But that night the word of the LORD came to Nathan, saying:

[5]"Go and tell my servant David, 'This is what the LORD says: Are you the one to build me a house to dwell in? [6]I have not dwelt in a house from the day I brought the Israelites up out of Egypt to this day. I have been moving from place to place with a tent as my dwelling. [7]Wherever I have moved with all the Israelites, did I ever say to any of their rulers whom I commanded to shepherd my people Israel, "Why have you not built me a house of cedar?" '

[8]"Now then, tell my servant David, 'This is what the LORD Almighty says: I took you from the pasture, from tending the flock, and appointed you ruler over my people Israel. [9]I have been with you wherever you have gone, and I have cut off all your enemies from before you. Now I will make your name great, like the names of the greatest men on earth. [10]And I will provide a place for my people Israel and will plant them so that they can have a home of their own and no longer be disturbed. Wicked people will not oppress them anymore, as they did at the beginning [11]and have done ever since the time I appointed leaders[a] over my people Israel. I will also give you rest from all your enemies.

"'The LORD declares to you that the LORD himself will establish a house for you: [12]When your days are over and you rest with your ancestors, I will raise up your offspring to succeed you, your own flesh and blood, and I will establish his kingdom. [13]He is the one who will build a house for my Name, and I will establish the throne of his kingdom forever. [14]I will be his father, and he will be my son. When he does wrong, I will punish him with a rod wielded by men, with floggings inflicted by human hands. [15]But my love will never be taken away from him, as I took it away from Saul, whom I removed from before you. [16]Your house and your kingdom will endure forever before me[b]; your throne will be established forever.' "

[17]Nathan reported to David all the words of this entire revelation.

David's Prayer

[18]Then King David went in and sat before the LORD, and he said:

"Who am I, Sovereign LORD, and what is my family, that you have brought me this far? [19]And as if this were not enough in your sight, Sovereign LORD, you have also spoken about the future of the house of your servant — and this decree, Sovereign LORD, is for a mere human![c]

[20]"What more can David say to you? For you know your servant, Sovereign LORD. [21]For the sake of your word and according to your will, you have done this great thing and made it known to your servant.

[22]"How great you are, Sovereign LORD! There is no one like you, and there is no God but you, as we have heard with our own ears. [23]And who is like your people Israel — the one nation on earth that God went out to redeem as a people for himself, and to make a name for himself, and to perform great and awesome wonders by driving out nations and their gods from before your people, whom you redeemed from Egypt?[d] [24]You have established your people Israel as your very own forever, and you, LORD, have become their God.

[25]"And now, LORD God, keep forever the promise you have made concerning your servant and his house. Do as you promised, [26]so that your name will be great forever. Then people will say, 'The LORD Almighty is God over Israel!' And

---

[a] 11 Traditionally *judges*   [b] 16 Some Hebrew manuscripts and Septuagint; most Hebrew manuscripts *you*   [c] 19 Or *for the human race*   [d] 23 See Septuagint and 1 Chron. 17:21; Hebrew *wonders for your land and before your people, whom you redeemed from Egypt, from the nations and their gods.*

NATHAN

But that night the word of the LORD came to Nathan, saying: "Go and tell my servant David, 'This is what the LORD says...'" 2 SAMUEL 7:4-5

HIS NAME MEANS: "giver" or "gift"
READ HIS STORY: *2 Samuel 7:1-17, 12:1-20; 1 Kings 1*

M E N

OF THE BIBLE

ust as King Saul had been advised by the prophet Samuel, Nathan served as prophet to King David throughout his reign and at the beginning of the reign of David's son, King Solomon.

Nathan took his position seriously and worked hard to help both kings know God better and honor his ways. When King David told Nathan he planned to build a temple to honor God, Nathan heard a special message from God that said David's son would be the one to build the temple instead. This message also declared that David's throne would be established forever, which we know was fulfilled through Jesus, the "son of David" (Matthew 1:1). Nathan was faithful to report the entire message to the king.

Nathan reported encouraging messages from God, but he was not afraid to give a message of discipline when it was needed. Later in David's reign, God sent Nathan to confront David for his sins related to Bathsheba and her husband (2 Samuel 12:1-14). In those days, someone who accused a king of evil-doing could have been killed, but Nathan stayed true to God's messages.

Sometime later, when David and Bathsheba had their son Solomon, God sent Nathan to tell them this child was loved by the Lord (2 Samuel 12:25). Through Nathan and his faithful ministry as prophet, we can see God more clearly and better understand who God is. Nathan was a reminder that God is with us through good times and bad, to counsel and guide us, to comfort us and give us hope.

the house of your servant David will be established in your sight.

[27] "LORD Almighty, God of Israel, you have revealed this to your servant, saying, 'I will build a house for you.' So your servant has found courage to pray this prayer to you. [28] Sovereign LORD, you are God! Your covenant is trustworthy, and you have promised these good things to your servant. [29] Now be pleased to bless the house of your servant, that it may continue forever in your sight; for you, Sovereign LORD, have spoken, and with your blessing the house of your servant will be blessed forever."

David's Victories

8 In the course of time, David defeated the Philistines and subdued them, and he took Metheg Ammah from the control of the Philistines.

[2] David also defeated the Moabites. He made them lie down on the ground and measured them off with a length of cord. Every two lengths of them were put to death, and the third length was allowed to live. So the Moabites became subject to David and brought him tribute.

[3] Moreover, David defeated Hadadezer son of Rehob, king of Zobah, when he went to restore his monument at[a] the Euphrates River. [4] David captured a thousand of his chariots, seven thousand charioteers[b] and twenty thousand foot soldiers. He hamstrung all but a hundred of the chariot horses.

[5] When the Arameans of Damascus came to help Hadadezer king of Zobah, David struck down twenty-two thousand of them. [6] He put garrisons in the Aramean kingdom of Damascus, and the Arameans became subject to him and brought tribute. The LORD gave David victory wherever he went.

[7] David took the gold shields that belonged to the officers of Hadadezer and brought them to Jerusalem. [8] From Tebah[c] and Berothai, towns that belonged to Had-

adezer, King David took a great quantity of bronze.

[9] When Tou[d] king of Hamath heard that David had defeated the entire army of Hadadezer, [10] he sent his son Joram[e] to King David to greet him and congratulate him on his victory in battle over Hadadezer, who had been at war with Tou. Joram brought with him articles of silver, of gold and of bronze.

[11] King David dedicated these articles to the LORD, as he had done with the silver and gold from all the nations he had subdued: [12] Edom[f] and Moab, the Ammonites and the Philistines, and Amalek. He also dedicated the plunder taken from Hadadezer son of Rehob, king of Zobah.

[13] And David became famous after he returned from striking down eighteen thousand Edomites[g] in the Valley of Salt.

[14] He put garrisons throughout Edom, and all the Edomites became subject to David. The LORD gave David victory wherever he went.

David's Officials

[15] David reigned over all Israel, doing what was just and right for all his people. [16] Joab son of Zeruiah was over the army; Jehoshaphat son of Ahilud was recorder; [17] Zadok son of Ahitub and Ahimelek son of Abiathar were priests; Seraiah was secretary; [18] Benaiah son of Jehoiada was over the Kerethites and Pelethites; and David's sons were priests.[h]

David and Mephibosheth

9 David asked, "Is there anyone still left of the house of Saul to whom I can show kindness for Jonathan's sake?"

[2] Now there was a servant of Saul's household named Ziba. They summoned him to appear before David, and the king said to him, "Are you Ziba?"

"At your service," he replied.

[3] The king asked, "Is there no one still alive from the house of Saul to whom I can show God's kindness?"

---

[a] 3 Or *his control along*   [b] 4 Septuagint (see also Dead Sea Scrolls and 1 Chron. 18:4); Masoretic Text *captured seventeen hundred of his charioteers*   [c] 8 See some Septuagint manuscripts (see also 1 Chron. 18:8); Hebrew *Betah*.   [d] 9 Hebrew *Toi*, a variant of *Tou*; also in verse 10   [e] 10 A variant of *Hadoram*   [f] 12 Some Hebrew manuscripts, Septuagint and Syriac (see also 1 Chron. 18:11); most Hebrew manuscripts *Aram*   [g] 13 A few Hebrew manuscripts, Septuagint and Syriac (see also 1 Chron. 18:12); most Hebrew manuscripts *Aram* (that is, Arameans)   [h] 18 Or *were chief officials* (see Septuagint and Targum; see also 1 Chron. 18:17)

WHAT'S THE PROPORTION?

READ: 2 SAMUEL 7:25-29

The more you pray, the bigger your imagination becomes because the Holy Spirit supersizes it with God-sized dreams. A good test of spiritual maturity is whether your dreams are getting bigger or smaller. The older you get, the more faith you should have, because you've experienced more of God's faithfulness. And it's God's faithfulness that should increase our faith and expand our vision.

If you keep praying, you'll keep dreaming, and better yet, if you keep dreaming, you'll keep praying. Dreaming really is a form of praying, and praying is a form of dreaming.

The day we stop dreaming is the day we start dying. When vision is sacrificed on the altar of logic, God is robbed of the glory that rightfully belongs to him. In fact, the death of a dream is often a subtle form of idolatry. We lose faith in the God who gave us the big dream and settle for a small dream that we can accomplish without his help.

BUILDING

FAITH

WISDOM

STRENGTH

We go after dreams that don't require divine intervention. Lame.

Nothing honors God more than a big dream that is way beyond our ability to accomplish. Why? Because there's no way we can take credit for it. And nothing is better for our spiritual development than a big dream because it keeps us on our knees in raw dependence on God.

Taken from *The Circle Maker Student Edition* by Mark Batterson with Parker Batterson, copyright © 2012 by Mark Batterson, published by Zondervan.

Ziba answered the king, "There is still a son of Jonathan; he is lame in both feet."

⁴ "Where is he?" the king asked.

Ziba answered, "He is at the house of Makir son of Ammiel in Lo Debar."

⁵ So King David had him brought from Lo Debar, from the house of Makir son of Ammiel.

⁶ When Mephibosheth son of Jonathan, the son of Saul, came to David, he bowed down to pay him honor.

David said, "Mephibosheth!"

"At your service," he replied.

⁷ "Don't be afraid," David said to him, "for I will surely show you kindness for the sake of your father Jonathan. I will restore to you all the land that belonged to your grandfather Saul, and you will always eat at my table."

⁸ Mephibosheth bowed down and said, "What is your servant, that you should notice a dead dog like me?"

⁹ Then the king summoned Ziba, Saul's steward, and said to him, "I have given your master's grandson everything that belonged to Saul and his family. ¹⁰ You and your sons and your servants are to farm the land for him and bring in the crops, so that your master's grandson may be provided for. And Mephibosheth, grandson of your master, will always eat at my table." (Now Ziba had fifteen sons and twenty servants.)

¹¹ Then Ziba said to the king, "Your servant will do whatever my lord the king commands his servant to do." So Mephibosheth ate at David's*ᵃ* table like one of the king's sons.

¹² Mephibosheth had a young son named Mika, and all the members of Ziba's household were servants of Mephibosheth. ¹³ And Mephibosheth lived in Jerusalem, because he always ate at the king's table; he was lame in both feet.

David Defeats the Ammonites

10 In the course of time, the king of the Ammonites died, and his son Hanun succeeded him as king. ² David thought, "I will show kindness to Hanun son of Nahash, just as his father showed kindness to me." So David sent a delegation to express his sympathy to Hanun concerning his father.

When David's men came to the land of the Ammonites, ³ the Ammonite commanders said to Hanun their lord, "Do you think David is honoring your father by sending envoys to you to express sympathy? Hasn't David sent them to you only to explore the city and spy it out and overthrow it?" ⁴ So Hanun seized David's envoys, shaved off half of each man's beard, cut off their garments at the buttocks, and sent them away.

⁵ When David was told about this, he sent messengers to meet the men, for they were greatly humiliated. The king said, "Stay at Jericho till your beards have grown, and then come back."

⁶ When the Ammonites realized that they had become obnoxious to David, they hired twenty thousand Aramean foot soldiers from Beth Rehob and Zobah, as well as the king of Maakah with a thousand men, and also twelve thousand men from Tob.

⁷ On hearing this, David sent Joab out with the entire army of fighting men. ⁸ The Ammonites came out and drew up in battle formation at the entrance of their city gate, while the Arameans of Zobah and Rehob and the men of Tob and Maakah were by themselves in the open country.

⁹ Joab saw that there were battle lines in front of him and behind him; so he selected some of the best troops in Israel and deployed them against the Arameans. ¹⁰ He put the rest of the men under the command of Abishai his brother and deployed them against the Ammonites. ¹¹ Joab said, "If the Arameans are too strong for me, then you are to come to my rescue; but if the Ammonites are too strong for you, then I will come to rescue you. ¹² Be strong, and let us fight bravely for our people and the cities of our God. The LORD will do what is good in his sight."

¹³ Then Joab and the troops with him advanced to fight the Arameans, and they fled before him. ¹⁴ When the Ammonites realized that the Arameans were fleeing, they fled before Abishai and went inside the city. So Joab returned from fighting the Ammonites and came to Jerusalem.

¹⁵ After the Arameans saw that they had been routed by Israel, they regrouped. ¹⁶ Hadadezer had Arameans brought from beyond the Euphrates River; they went to

---

ᵃ 11 Septuagint; Hebrew *my*

Helam, with Shobak the commander of Hadadezer's army leading them.

[17] When David was told of this, he gathered all Israel, crossed the Jordan and went to Helam. The Arameans formed their battle lines to meet David and fought against him. [18] But they fled before Israel, and David killed seven hundred of their charioteers and forty thousand of their foot soldiers.[a] He also struck down Shobak the commander of their army, and he died there. [19] When all the kings who were vassals of Hadadezer saw that they had been routed by Israel, they made peace with the Israelites and became subject to them.

So the Arameans were afraid to help the Ammonites anymore.

David and Bathsheba

11 In the spring, at the time when kings go off to war, David sent Joab out with the king's men and the whole Israelite army. They destroyed the Ammonites and besieged Rabbah. But David remained in Jerusalem.

[2] One evening David got up from his bed and walked around on the roof of the palace. From the roof he saw a woman bathing. The woman was very beautiful, [3] and David sent someone to find out about her. The man said, "She is Bathsheba, the daughter of Eliam and the wife of Uriah the Hittite." [4] Then David sent messengers to get her. She came to him, and he slept with her. (Now she was purifying herself from her monthly uncleanness.) Then she went back home. [5] The woman conceived and sent word to David, saying, "I am pregnant."

[6] So David sent this word to Joab: "Send me Uriah the Hittite." And Joab sent him to David. [7] When Uriah came to him, David asked him how Joab was, how the soldiers were and how the war was going. [8] Then David said to Uriah, "Go down to your house and wash your feet." So Uriah left the palace, and a gift from the king was sent after him. [9] But Uriah slept at the entrance to the palace with all his master's servants and did not go down to his house.

[10] David was told, "Uriah did not go home." So he asked Uriah, "Haven't you just come from a military campaign? Why didn't you go home?"

[11] Uriah said to David, "The ark and Israel and Judah are staying in tents,[b] and my commander Joab and my lord's men are camped in the open country. How could I go to my house to eat and drink and make love to my wife? As surely as you live, I will not do such a thing!"

[12] Then David said to him, "Stay here one more day, and tomorrow I will send you back." So Uriah remained in Jerusalem that day and the next. [13] At David's invitation, he ate and drank with him, and David made him drunk. But in the evening Uriah went out to sleep on his mat among his master's servants; he did not go home.

[14] In the morning David wrote a letter to Joab and sent it with Uriah. [15] In it he wrote, "Put Uriah out in front where the fighting is fiercest. Then withdraw from him so he will be struck down and die."

[16] So while Joab had the city under siege, he put Uriah at a place where he knew the strongest defenders were. [17] When the men of the city came out and fought against Joab, some of the men in David's army fell; moreover, Uriah the Hittite died.

[18] Joab sent David a full account of the battle. [19] He instructed the messenger: "When you have finished giving the king this account of the battle, [20] the king's anger may flare up, and he may ask you, 'Why did you get so close to the city to fight? Didn't you know they would shoot arrows from the wall? [21] Who killed Abimelek son of Jerub-Besheth[c]? Didn't a woman drop an upper millstone on him from the wall, so that he died in Thebez? Why did you get so close to the wall?' If he asks you this, then say to him, 'Moreover, your servant Uriah the Hittite is dead.'"

[22] The messenger set out, and when he arrived he told David everything Joab had sent him to say. [23] The messenger said to David, "The men overpowered us and came out against us in the open, but we drove them back to the entrance of the city gate. [24] Then the archers shot arrows at your servants from the wall, and some of the king's men died. Moreover, your servant Uriah the Hittite is dead."

---

[a] 18 Some Septuagint manuscripts (see also 1 Chron. 19:18); Hebrew *horsemen*   [b] 11 Or *staying at Sukkoth*   [c] 21 Also known as *Jerub-Baal* (that is, Gideon)

ROADBLOCKS NEEDED

READ: 2 SAMUEL 11:1-5, 14-17

I know I can be the first guy to cave in to temptation. I do go there. I do jump into this. I do click on that. I do flip to that channel. How did I get there? Because that's what hearts do. They're made of flesh.

Even though I try to guard my heart so it will stay bent toward God, I still need to set up some roadblocks that will help when my heart gets fickle and tries to pull away from the Lord.

You don't have to struggle with viewing inappropriate websites to know the Internet is a hazard. It's out there, and Satan steers it straight to you. Maybe porn isn't your issue. You may need to erect roadblocks in the gym to make sure you don't turn fitness into the pursuit of a body that becomes your idol. The Enemy knows your buttons. So put up roadblocks that prevent you from even going there in your thoughts.

BUILDING
FAITH
WISDOM
STRENGTH

Let's be willing to set up barriers. We all want to be able to say we did the right thing because our heart is right with God. But the truth is that sometimes we need to be safe—even when we do have an intimate walk with the Lord.

The best roadblock is to have a friend to whom you give the right to get into your business. The arrangement, however, needs to be authentic. If you want it, mean it.

²⁵David told the messenger, "Say this to Joab: 'Don't let this upset you; the sword devours one as well as another. Press the attack against the city and destroy it.' Say this to encourage Joab."

²⁶When Uriah's wife heard that her husband was dead, she mourned for him. ²⁷After the time of mourning was over, David had her brought to his house, and she became his wife and bore him a son. But the thing David had done displeased the LORD.

Nathan Rebukes David

12 The LORD sent Nathan to David. When he came to him, he said, "There were two men in a certain town, one rich and the other poor. ²The rich man had a very large number of sheep and cattle, ³but the poor man had nothing except one little ewe lamb he had bought. He raised it, and it grew up with him and his children. It shared his food, drank from his cup and even slept in his arms. It was like a daughter to him.

⁴"Now a traveler came to the rich man, but the rich man refrained from taking one of his own sheep or cattle to prepare a meal for the traveler who had come to him. Instead, he took the ewe lamb that belonged to the poor man and prepared it for the one who had come to him."

⁵David burned with anger against the man and said to Nathan, "As surely as the LORD lives, the man who did this must die! ⁶He must pay for that lamb four times over, because he did such a thing and had no pity."

⁷Then Nathan said to David, "You are the man! This is what the LORD, the God of Israel, says: 'I anointed you king over Israel, and I delivered you from the hand of Saul. ⁸I gave your master's house to you, and your master's wives into your arms. I gave you all Israel and Judah. And if all this had been too little, I would have given you even more. ⁹Why did you despise the word of the LORD by doing what is evil in his eyes? You struck down Uriah the Hittite with the sword and took his wife to be your own. You killed him with the sword of the Ammonites. ¹⁰Now, therefore, the sword will never depart from your house, because you despised me and took the wife of Uriah the Hittite to be your own.'

¹¹"This is what the LORD says: 'Out of your own household I am going to bring calamity on you. Before your very eyes I will take your wives and give them to one who is close to you, and he will sleep with your wives in broad daylight. ¹²You did it in secret, but I will do this thing in broad daylight before all Israel.'"

¹³Then David said to Nathan, "I have sinned against the LORD."

Nathan replied, "The LORD has taken away your sin. You are not going to die. ¹⁴But because by doing this you have shown utter contempt for[a] the LORD, the son born to you will die."

¹⁵After Nathan had gone home, the LORD struck the child that Uriah's wife had borne to David, and he became ill. ¹⁶David pleaded with God for the child. He fasted and spent the nights lying in sackcloth[b] on the ground. ¹⁷The elders of his household stood beside him to get him up from the ground, but he refused, and he would not eat any food with them.

¹⁸On the seventh day the child died. David's attendants were afraid to tell him that the child was dead, for they thought, "While the child was still living, he wouldn't listen to us when we spoke to him. How can we now tell him the child is dead? He may do something desperate."

¹⁹David noticed that his attendants were whispering among themselves, and he realized the child was dead. "Is the child dead?" he asked.

"Yes," they replied, "he is dead."

²⁰Then David got up from the ground. After he had washed, put on lotions and changed his clothes, he went into the house of the LORD and worshiped. Then he went to his own house, and at his request they served him food, and he ate.

²¹His attendants asked him, "Why are you acting this way? While the child was alive, you fasted and wept, but now that the child is dead, you get up and eat!"

²²He answered, "While the child was still alive, I fasted and wept. I thought, 'Who knows? The LORD may be gracious to me and let the child live.' ²³But now that he is dead, why should I go on fasting? Can I bring him back again? I will go to him, but he will not return to me."

---

a 14 An ancient Hebrew scribal tradition; Masoretic Text *for the enemies of*   *b* 16 Dead Sea Scrolls and Septuagint; Masoretic Text does not have *in sackcloth*.

²⁴Then David comforted his wife Bathsheba, and he went to her and made love to her. She gave birth to a son, and they named him Solomon. The LORD loved him; ²⁵and because the LORD loved him, he sent word through Nathan the prophet to name him Jedidiah.ᵃ

²⁶Meanwhile Joab fought against Rabbah of the Ammonites and captured the royal citadel. ²⁷Joab then sent messengers to David, saying, "I have fought against Rabbah and taken its water supply. ²⁸Now muster the rest of the troops and besiege the city and capture it. Otherwise I will take the city, and it will be named after me."

²⁹So David mustered the entire army and went to Rabbah, and attacked and captured it. ³⁰David took the crown from their king'sᵇ head, and it was placed on his own head. It weighed a talentᶜ of gold, and it was set with precious stones. David took a great quantity of plunder from the city ³¹and brought out the people who were there, consigning them to labor with saws and with iron picks and axes, and he made them work at brickmaking.ᵈ David did this to all the Ammonite towns. Then he and his entire army returned to Jerusalem.

Amnon and Tamar

13 In the course of time, Amnon son of David fell in love with Tamar, the beautiful sister of Absalom son of David.

²Amnon became so obsessed with his sister Tamar that he made himself ill. She was a virgin, and it seemed impossible for him to do anything to her.

³Now Amnon had an adviser named Jonadab son of Shimeah, David's brother. Jonadab was a very shrewd man. ⁴He asked Amnon, "Why do you, the king's son, look so haggard morning after morning? Won't you tell me?"

Amnon said to him, "I'm in love with Tamar, my brother Absalom's sister."

⁵"Go to bed and pretend to be ill," Jonadab said. "When your father comes to see you, say to him, 'I would like my sister Tamar to come and give me something to eat. Let her prepare the food in my sight so I may watch her and then eat it from her hand.'"

⁶So Amnon lay down and pretended to be ill. When the king came to see him, Amnon said to him, "I would like my sister Tamar to come and make some special bread in my sight, so I may eat from her hand."

⁷David sent word to Tamar at the palace: "Go to the house of your brother Amnon and prepare some food for him." ⁸So Tamar went to the house of her brother Amnon, who was lying down. She took some dough, kneaded it, made the bread in his sight and baked it. ⁹Then she took the pan and served him the bread, but he refused to eat.

"Send everyone out of here," Amnon said. So everyone left him. ¹⁰Then Amnon said to Tamar, "Bring the food here into my bedroom so I may eat from your hand." And Tamar took the bread she had prepared and brought it to her brother Amnon in his bedroom. ¹¹But when she took it to him to eat, he grabbed her and said, "Come to bed with me, my sister."

¹²"No, my brother!" she said to him. "Don't force me! Such a thing should not be done in Israel! Don't do this wicked thing. ¹³What about me? Where could I get rid of my disgrace? And what about you? You would be like one of the wicked fools in Israel. Please speak to the king; he will not keep me from being married to you." ¹⁴But he refused to listen to her, and since he was stronger than she, he raped her.

¹⁵Then Amnon hated her with intense hatred. In fact, he hated her more than he had loved her. Amnon said to her, "Get up and get out!"

¹⁶"No!" she said to him. "Sending me away would be a greater wrong than what you have already done to me."

But he refused to listen to her. ¹⁷He called his personal servant and said, "Get this woman out of my sight and bolt the door after her." ¹⁸So his servant put her out and bolted the door after her. She was wearing an ornateᵉ robe, for this was the kind of garment the virgin daughters of the king wore. ¹⁹Tamar put ashes on her head and tore the ornate robe she was wearing. She put her hands on her head and went away, weeping aloud as she went.

²⁰Her brother Absalom said to her, "Has

ᵃ 25 *Jedidiah* means *loved by the* LORD.   ᵇ 30 Or *from Milkom's* (that is, Molek's)   ᶜ 30 That is, about 75 pounds or about 34 kilograms   ᵈ 31 The meaning of the Hebrew for this clause is uncertain.
ᵉ 18 The meaning of the Hebrew for this word is uncertain; also in verse 19.

BLIND LUST

READ: 2 SAMUEL 13

Amnon's sexual sin brought incredible devastation, not just upon his family but on the entire nation. The disruption to a royal family means disruption to a country. Everything spiraled wildly out of control. And where did it all begin? Amnon spent countless hours lusting after Tamar until it became his obsession.

So let me ask you, have the thoughts, or even pursuit, of sexual pleasure become an obsession? Is it the last thing you think about at night and the first thing that comes to mind in the morning? Do you daydream about it at school, risk your reputation, friendships, and relationships for it? Do you feel the presence of God fading into a cloud of deepening shame?

Amnon would tell you to buckle up and slow down, because he discovered there wasn't any real or lasting pleasure in the god of sex. Just a quick release and then a whole lot of shame, pain, and emptiness. He had to have known his actions had consequences.

Tamar told her full brother, Absalom, what had happened. Absalom burned with rage, but he waited for his moment. Notice that Absalom had an impulse to act on too; his happened to be a lust for revenge rather than sexual release. But his choice was just as destructive.

What if Amnon could've looked into the future and seen the results? On one side would be a fleeting moment of sensual pleasure. On the other, his death, a civil war, and many lost lives. Why hadn't the whisper of lust included all of that?

BUILDING FAITH WISDOM STRENGTH

Taken from *Gods at War Student Edition* by Kyle Idleman, copyright © 2014 by City on a Hill Studio, LLC, published by Zondervan.

that Amnon, your brother, been with you? Be quiet for now, my sister; he is your brother. Don't take this thing to heart." And Tamar lived in her brother Absalom's house, a desolate woman.

²¹When King David heard all this, he was furious. ²²And Absalom never said a word to Amnon, either good or bad; he hated Amnon because he had disgraced his sister Tamar.

Absalom Kills Amnon

²³Two years later, when Absalom's sheepshearers were at Baal Hazor near the border of Ephraim, he invited all the king's sons to come there. ²⁴Absalom went to the king and said, "Your servant has had shearers come. Will the king and his attendants please join me?"

²⁵"No, my son," the king replied. "All of us should not go; we would only be a burden to you." Although Absalom urged him, he still refused to go but gave him his blessing.

²⁶Then Absalom said, "If not, please let my brother Amnon come with us."

The king asked him, "Why should he go with you?" ²⁷But Absalom urged him, so he sent with him Amnon and the rest of the king's sons.

²⁸Absalom ordered his men, "Listen! When Amnon is in high spirits from drinking wine and I say to you, 'Strike Amnon down,' then kill him. Don't be afraid. Haven't I given you this order? Be strong and brave." ²⁹So Absalom's men did to Amnon what Absalom had ordered. Then all the king's sons got up, mounted their mules and fled.

³⁰While they were on their way, the report came to David: "Absalom has struck down all the king's sons; not one of them is left." ³¹The king stood up, tore his clothes and lay down on the ground; and all his attendants stood by with their clothes torn.

³²But Jonadab son of Shimeah, David's brother, said, "My lord should not think that they killed all the princes; only Amnon is dead. This has been Absalom's express intention ever since the day Amnon raped his sister Tamar. ³³My lord the king should not be concerned about the report that all the king's sons are dead. Only Amnon is dead."

³⁴Meanwhile, Absalom had fled.

Now the man standing watch looked up and saw many people on the road west of him, coming down the side of the hill. The watchman went and told the king, "I see men in the direction of Horonaim, on the side of the hill."^a

³⁵Jonadab said to the king, "See, the king's sons have come; it has happened just as your servant said."

³⁶As he finished speaking, the king's sons came in, wailing loudly. The king, too, and all his attendants wept very bitterly.

³⁷Absalom fled and went to Talmai son of Ammihud, the king of Geshur. But King David mourned many days for his son.

³⁸After Absalom fled and went to Geshur, he stayed there three years. ³⁹And King David longed to go to Absalom, for he was consoled concerning Amnon's death.

Absalom Returns to Jerusalem

14 Joab son of Zeruiah knew that the king's heart longed for Absalom. ²So Joab sent someone to Tekoa and had a wise woman brought from there. He said to her, "Pretend you are in mourning. Dress in mourning clothes, and don't use any cosmetic lotions. Act like a woman who has spent many days grieving for the dead. ³Then go to the king and speak these words to him." And Joab put the words in her mouth.

⁴When the woman from Tekoa went^b to the king, she fell with her face to the ground to pay him honor, and she said, "Help me, Your Majesty!"

⁵The king asked her, "What is troubling you?"

She said, "I am a widow; my husband is dead. ⁶I your servant had two sons. They got into a fight with each other in the field, and no one was there to separate them. One struck the other and killed him. ⁷Now the whole clan has risen up against your servant; they say, 'Hand over the one who struck his brother down, so that we may put him to death for the life of his brother whom he killed; then we will get rid of the heir as well.' They would put out the only burning coal I have left, leaving my husband neither name nor descendant on the face of the earth."

⁸The king said to the woman, "Go home, and I will issue an order in your behalf."

---

^a 34 Septuagint; Hebrew does not have this sentence. Vulgate and Syriac; most Hebrew manuscripts *spoke*

^b 4 Many Hebrew manuscripts, Septuagint,

[9]But the woman from Tekoa said to him, "Let my lord the king pardon me and my family, and let the king and his throne be without guilt."

[10]The king replied, "If anyone says anything to you, bring them to me, and they will not bother you again."

[11]She said, "Then let the king invoke the LORD his God to prevent the avenger of blood from adding to the destruction, so that my son will not be destroyed."

"As surely as the LORD lives," he said, "not one hair of your son's head will fall to the ground."

[12]Then the woman said, "Let your servant speak a word to my lord the king."

"Speak," he replied.

[13]The woman said, "Why then have you devised a thing like this against the people of God? When the king says this, does he not convict himself, for the king has not brought back his banished son? [14]Like water spilled on the ground, which cannot be recovered, so we must die. But that is not what God desires; rather, he devises ways so that a banished person does not remain banished from him.

[15]"And now I have come to say this to my lord the king because the people have made me afraid. Your servant thought, 'I will speak to the king; perhaps he will grant his servant's request. [16]Perhaps the king will agree to deliver his servant from the hand of the man who is trying to cut off both me and my son from God's inheritance.'

[17]"And now your servant says, 'May the word of my lord the king secure my inheritance, for my lord the king is like an angel of God in discerning good and evil. May the LORD your God be with you.'"

[18]Then the king said to the woman, "Don't keep from me the answer to what I am going to ask you."

"Let my lord the king speak," the woman said.

[19]The king asked, "Isn't the hand of Joab with you in all this?"

The woman answered, "As surely as you live, my lord the king, no one can turn to the right or to the left from anything my lord the king says. Yes, it was your servant Joab who instructed me to do this and who put all these words into the mouth of your servant.

[20]Your servant Joab did this to change the present situation. My lord has wisdom like that of an angel of God—he knows everything that happens in the land."

[21]The king said to Joab, "Very well, I will do it. Go, bring back the young man Absalom."

[22]Joab fell with his face to the ground to pay him honor, and he blessed the king. Joab said, "Today your servant knows that he has found favor in your eyes, my lord the king, because the king has granted his servant's request."

[23]Then Joab went to Geshur and brought Absalom back to Jerusalem. [24]But the king said, "He must go to his own house; he must not see my face." So Absalom went to his own house and did not see the face of the king.

[25]In all Israel there was not a man so highly praised for his handsome appearance as Absalom. From the top of his head to the sole of his foot there was no blemish in him. [26]Whenever he cut the hair of his head—he used to cut his hair once a year because it became too heavy for him—he would weigh it, and its weight was two hundred shekels[a] by the royal standard.

[27]Three sons and a daughter were born to Absalom. His daughter's name was Tamar, and she became a beautiful woman.

[28]Absalom lived two years in Jerusalem without seeing the king's face. [29]Then Absalom sent for Joab in order to send him to the king, but Joab refused to come to him. So he sent a second time, but he refused to come. [30]Then he said to his servants, "Look, Joab's field is next to mine, and he has barley there. Go and set it on fire." So Absalom's servants set the field on fire.

[31]Then Joab did go to Absalom's house, and he said to him, "Why have your servants set my field on fire?"

[32]Absalom said to Joab, "Look, I sent word to you and said, 'Come here so I can send you to the king to ask, "Why have I come from Geshur? It would be better for me if I were still there!"' Now then, I want to see the king's face, and if I am guilty of anything, let him put me to death."

[33]So Joab went to the king and told him this. Then the king summoned Absalom, and he came in and bowed down with his face to the ground before the king. And the king kissed Absalom.

---

[a] 26 That is, about 5 pounds or about 2.3 kilograms

Absalom's Conspiracy

15 In the course of time, Absalom provided himself with a chariot and horses and with fifty men to run ahead of him. [2] He would get up early and stand by the side of the road leading to the city gate. Whenever anyone came with a complaint to be placed before the king for a decision, Absalom would call out to him, "What town are you from?" He would answer, "Your servant is from one of the tribes of Israel." [3] Then Absalom would say to him, "Look, your claims are valid and proper, but there is no representative of the king to hear you." [4] And Absalom would add, "If only I were appointed judge in the land! Then everyone who has a complaint or case could come to me and I would see that they receive justice." [5] Also, whenever anyone approached him to bow down before him, Absalom would reach out his hand, take hold of him and kiss him. [6] Absalom behaved in this way toward all the Israelites who came to the king asking for justice, and so he stole the hearts of the people of Israel.

[7] At the end of four[a] years, Absalom said to the king, "Let me go to Hebron and fulfill a vow I made to the LORD. [8] While your servant was living at Geshur in Aram, I made this vow: 'If the LORD takes me back to Jerusalem, I will worship the LORD in Hebron.[b] '"

[9] The king said to him, "Go in peace." So he went to Hebron.

[10] Then Absalom sent secret messengers throughout the tribes of Israel to say, "As soon as you hear the sound of the trumpets, then say, 'Absalom is king in Hebron.' " [11] Two hundred men from Jerusalem had accompanied Absalom. They had been invited as guests and went quite innocently, knowing nothing about the matter. [12] While Absalom was offering sacrifices, he also sent for Ahithophel the Gilonite, David's counselor, to come from Giloh, his hometown. And so the conspiracy gained strength, and Absalom's following kept on increasing.

David Flees

[13] A messenger came and told David, "The hearts of the people of Israel are with Absalom."

[14] Then David said to all his officials who were with him in Jerusalem, "Come! We must flee, or none of us will escape from Absalom. We must leave immediately, or he will move quickly to overtake us and bring ruin on us and put the city to the sword."

[15] The king's officials answered him, "Your servants are ready to do whatever our lord the king chooses."

[16] The king set out, with his entire household following him; but he left ten concubines to take care of the palace. [17] So the king set out, with all the people following him, and they halted at the edge of the city. [18] All his men marched past him, along with all the Kerethites and Pelethites; and all the six hundred Gittites who had accompanied him from Gath marched before the king.

[19] The king said to Ittai the Gittite, "Why should you come along with us? Go back and stay with King Absalom. You are a foreigner, an exile from your homeland. [20] You came only yesterday. And today shall I make you wander about with us, when I do not know where I am going? Go back, and take your people with you. May the LORD show you kindness and faithfulness."[c]

[21] But Ittai replied to the king, "As surely as the LORD lives, and as my lord the king lives, wherever my lord the king may be, whether it means life or death, there will your servant be."

[22] David said to Ittai, "Go ahead, march on." So Ittai the Gittite marched on with all his men and the families that were with him.

[23] The whole countryside wept aloud as all the people passed by. The king also crossed the Kidron Valley, and all the people moved on toward the wilderness.

[24] Zadok was there, too, and all the Levites who were with him were carrying the ark of the covenant of God. They set down the ark of God, and Abiathar offered sacrifices until all the people had finished leaving the city.

[25] Then the king said to Zadok, "Take the ark of God back into the city. If I find favor in the LORD's eyes, he will bring me back and let me see it and his dwelling place again. [26] But if he says, 'I am not pleased with you,' then I am ready; let him do to me whatever seems good to him."

---

[a] 7 Some Septuagint manuscripts, Syriac and Josephus; Hebrew *forty*   [b] 8 Some Septuagint manuscripts; Hebrew does not have *in Hebron*.   [c] 20 Septuagint; Hebrew *May kindness and faithfulness be with you*

²⁷The king also said to Zadok the priest, "Do you understand? Go back to the city with my blessing. Take your son Ahimaaz with you, and also Abiathar's son Jonathan. You and Abiathar return with your two sons. ²⁸I will wait at the fords in the wilderness until word comes from you to inform me." ²⁹So Zadok and Abiathar took the ark of God back to Jerusalem and stayed there.

³⁰But David continued up the Mount of Olives, weeping as he went; his head was covered and he was barefoot. All the people with him covered their heads too and were weeping as they went up. ³¹Now David had been told, "Ahithophel is among the conspirators with Absalom." So David prayed, "Lord, turn Ahithophel's counsel into foolishness."

³²When David arrived at the summit, where people used to worship God, Hushai the Arkite was there to meet him, his robe torn and dust on his head. ³³David said to him, "If you go with me, you will be a burden to me. ³⁴But if you return to the city and say to Absalom, 'Your Majesty, I will be your servant; I was your father's servant in the past, but now I will be your servant,' then you can help me by frustrating Ahithophel's advice. ³⁵Won't the priests Zadok and Abiathar be there with you? Tell them anything you hear in the king's palace. ³⁶Their two sons, Ahimaaz son of Zadok and Jonathan son of Abiathar, are there with them. Send them to me with anything you hear."

³⁷So Hushai, David's confidant, arrived at Jerusalem as Absalom was entering the city.

David and Ziba

16 When David had gone a short distance beyond the summit, there was Ziba, the steward of Mephibosheth, waiting to meet him. He had a string of donkeys saddled and loaded with two hundred loaves of bread, a hundred cakes of raisins, a hundred cakes of figs and a skin of wine.

²The king asked Ziba, "Why have you brought these?"

Ziba answered, "The donkeys are for the king's household to ride on, the bread and fruit are for the men to eat, and the wine is to refresh those who become exhausted in the wilderness."

³The king then asked, "Where is your master's grandson?"

Ziba said to him, "He is staying in Jerusalem, because he thinks, 'Today the Israelites will restore to me my grandfather's kingdom.'"

⁴Then the king said to Ziba, "All that belonged to Mephibosheth is now yours."

"I humbly bow," Ziba said. "May I find favor in your eyes, my lord the king."

Shimei Curses David

⁵As King David approached Bahurim, a man from the same clan as Saul's family came out from there. His name was Shimei son of Gera, and he cursed as he came out. ⁶He pelted David and all the king's officials with stones, though all the troops and the special guard were on David's right and left. ⁷As he cursed, Shimei said, "Get out, get out, you murderer, you scoundrel! ⁸The Lord has repaid you for all the blood you shed in the household of Saul, in whose place you have reigned. The Lord has given the kingdom into the hands of your son Absalom. You have come to ruin because you are a murderer!"

⁹Then Abishai son of Zeruiah said to the king, "Why should this dead dog curse my lord the king? Let me go over and cut off his head."

¹⁰But the king said, "What does this have to do with you, you sons of Zeruiah? If he is cursing because the Lord said to him, 'Curse David,' who can ask, 'Why do you do this?'"

¹¹David then said to Abishai and all his officials, "My son, my own flesh and blood, is trying to kill me. How much more, then, this Benjamite! Leave him alone; let him curse, for the Lord has told him to. ¹²It may be that the Lord will look upon my misery and restore to me his covenant blessing instead of his curse today."

¹³So David and his men continued along the road while Shimei was going along the hillside opposite him, cursing as he went and throwing stones at him and showering him with dirt. ¹⁴The king and all the people with him arrived at their destination exhausted. And there he refreshed himself.

The Advice of Ahithophel and Hushai

¹⁵Meanwhile, Absalom and all the men of Israel came to Jerusalem, and Ahithophel was with him. ¹⁶Then Hushai the Arkite, David's

confidant, went to Absalom and said to him, "Long live the king! Long live the king!"

[17] Absalom said to Hushai, "So this is the love you show your friend? If he's your friend, why didn't you go with him?"

[18] Hushai said to Absalom, "No, the one chosen by the LORD, by these people, and by all the men of Israel — his I will be, and I will remain with him. [19] Furthermore, whom should I serve? Should I not serve the son? Just as I served your father, so I will serve you."

[20] Absalom said to Ahithophel, "Give us your advice. What should we do?"

[21] Ahithophel answered, "Sleep with your father's concubines whom he left to take care of the palace. Then all Israel will hear that you have made yourself obnoxious to your father, and the hands of everyone with you will be more resolute." [22] So they pitched a tent for Absalom on the roof, and he slept with his father's concubines in the sight of all Israel.

[23] Now in those days the advice Ahithophel gave was like that of one who inquires of God. That was how both David and Absalom regarded all of Ahithophel's advice.

17 Ahithophel said to Absalom, "I would[a] choose twelve thousand men and set out tonight in pursuit of David. [2] I would attack him while he is weary and weak. I would strike him with terror, and then all the people with him will flee. I would strike down only the king [3] and bring all the people back to you. The death of the man you seek will mean the return of all; all the people will be unharmed." [4] This plan seemed good to Absalom and to all the elders of Israel.

[5] But Absalom said, "Summon also Hushai the Arkite, so we can hear what he has to say as well." [6] When Hushai came to him, Absalom said, "Ahithophel has given this advice. Should we do what he says? If not, give us your opinion."

[7] Hushai replied to Absalom, "The advice Ahithophel has given is not good this time. [8] You know your father and his men; they are fighters, and as fierce as a wild bear robbed of her cubs. Besides, your father is an experienced fighter; he will not spend the night with the troops. [9] Even now, he is hidden in a cave or some other place. If he should attack your troops first,[b] whoever hears about it will say, 'There has been a slaughter among the troops who follow Absalom.' [10] Then even the bravest soldier, whose heart is like the heart of a lion, will melt with fear, for all Israel knows that your father is a fighter and that those with him are brave.

[11] "So I advise you: Let all Israel, from Dan to Beersheba — as numerous as the sand on the seashore — be gathered to you, with you yourself leading them into battle. [12] Then we will attack him wherever he may be found, and we will fall on him as dew settles on the ground. Neither he nor any of his men will be left alive. [13] If he withdraws into a city, then all Israel will bring ropes to that city, and we will drag it down to the valley until not so much as a pebble is left."

[14] Absalom and all the men of Israel said, "The advice of Hushai the Arkite is better than that of Ahithophel." For the LORD had determined to frustrate the good advice of Ahithophel in order to bring disaster on Absalom.

[15] Hushai told Zadok and Abiathar, the priests, "Ahithophel has advised Absalom and the elders of Israel to do such and such, but I have advised them to do so and so. [16] Now send a message at once and tell David, 'Do not spend the night at the fords in the wilderness; cross over without fail, or the king and all the people with him will be swallowed up.'"

[17] Jonathan and Ahimaaz were staying at En Rogel. A female servant was to go and inform them, and they were to go and tell King David, for they could not risk being seen entering the city. [18] But a young man saw them and told Absalom. So the two of them left at once and went to the house of a man in Bahurim. He had a well in his courtyard, and they climbed down into it. [19] His wife took a covering and spread it out over the opening of the well and scattered grain over it. No one knew anything about it.

[20] When Absalom's men came to the woman at the house, they asked, "Where are Ahimaaz and Jonathan?"

The woman answered them, "They crossed over the brook."[c] The men searched but found no one, so they returned to Jerusalem.

[21] After they had gone, the two climbed out of the well and went to inform King David. They said to him, "Set out and cross the

---

[a] 1 Or Let me   [b] 9 Or When some of the men fall at the first attack   [c] 20 Or "They passed by the sheep pen toward the water."

river at once; Ahithophel has advised such and such against you." ²²So David and all the people with him set out and crossed the Jordan. By daybreak, no one was left who had not crossed the Jordan.

²³When Ahithophel saw that his advice had not been followed, he saddled his donkey and set out for his house in his hometown. He put his house in order and then hanged himself. So he died and was buried in his father's tomb.

Absalom's Death

²⁴David went to Mahanaim, and Absalom crossed the Jordan with all the men of Israel. ²⁵Absalom had appointed Amasa over the army in place of Joab. Amasa was the son of Jether,ᵃ an Ishmaeliteᵇ who had married Abigail,ᶜ the daughter of Nahash and sister of Zeruiah the mother of Joab. ²⁶The Israelites and Absalom camped in the land of Gilead.

²⁷When David came to Mahanaim, Shobi son of Nahash from Rabbah of the Ammonites, and Makir son of Ammiel from Lo Debar, and Barzillai the Gileadite from Rogelim ²⁸brought bedding and bowls and articles of pottery. They also brought wheat and barley, flour and roasted grain, beans and lentils,ᵈ ²⁹honey and curds, sheep, and cheese from cows' milk for David and his people to eat. For they said, "The people have become exhausted and hungry and thirsty in the wilderness."

18 David mustered the men who were with him and appointed over them commanders of thousands and commanders of hundreds. ²David sent out his troops, a third under the command of Joab, a third under Joab's brother Abishai son of Zeruiah, and a third under Ittai the Gittite. The king told the troops, "I myself will surely march out with you."

³But the men said, "You must not go out; if we are forced to flee, they won't care about us. Even if half of us die, they won't care; but you are worth ten thousand of us.ᵉ It would be better now for you to give us support from the city."

⁴The king answered, "I will do whatever seems best to you."

So the king stood beside the gate while all his men marched out in units of hundreds and of thousands. ⁵The king commanded Joab, Abishai and Ittai, "Be gentle with the young man Absalom for my sake." And all the troops heard the king giving orders concerning Absalom to each of the commanders.

⁶David's army marched out of the city to fight Israel, and the battle took place in the forest of Ephraim. ⁷There Israel's troops were routed by David's men, and the casualties that day were great—twenty thousand men. ⁸The battle spread out over the whole countryside, and the forest swallowed up more men that day than the sword.

⁹Now Absalom happened to meet David's men. He was riding his mule, and as the mule went under the thick branches of a large oak, Absalom's hair got caught in the tree. He was left hanging in midair, while the mule he was riding kept on going.

¹⁰When one of the men saw what had happened, he told Joab, "I just saw Absalom hanging in an oak tree."

¹¹Joab said to the man who had told him this, "What! You saw him? Why didn't you strike him to the ground right there? Then I would have had to give you ten shekelsᶠ of silver and a warrior's belt."

¹²But the man replied, "Even if a thousand shekelsᵍ were weighed out into my hands, I would not lay a hand on the king's son. In our hearing the king commanded you and Abishai and Ittai, 'Protect the young man Absalom for my sake.'ʰ ¹³And if I had put my life in jeopardyⁱ—and nothing is hidden from the king—you would have kept your distance from me."

¹⁴Joab said, "I'm not going to wait like this for you." So he took three javelins in his hand and plunged them into Absalom's heart while Absalom was still alive in the oak tree. ¹⁵And ten of Joab's armor-bearers surrounded Absalom, struck him and killed him.

ᵃ 25 Hebrew *Ithra,* a variant of *Jether*   ᵇ 25 Some Septuagint manuscripts (see also 1 Chron. 2:17); Hebrew and other Septuagint manuscripts *Israelite*   ᶜ 25 Hebrew *Abigal,* a variant of *Abigail*   ᵈ 28 Most Septuagint manuscripts and Syriac; Hebrew *lentils, and roasted grain*   ᵉ 3 Two Hebrew manuscripts, some Septuagint manuscripts and Vulgate; most Hebrew manuscripts *care; for now there are ten thousand like us*   ᶠ 11 That is, about 4 ounces or about 115 grams   ᵍ 12 That is, about 25 pounds or about 12 kilograms   ʰ 12 A few Hebrew manuscripts, Septuagint, Vulgate and Syriac; most Hebrew manuscripts may be translated *Absalom, whoever you may be.*   ⁱ 13 Or *Otherwise, if I had acted treacherously toward him*

¹⁶Then Joab sounded the trumpet, and the troops stopped pursuing Israel, for Joab halted them. ¹⁷They took Absalom, threw him into a big pit in the forest and piled up a large heap of rocks over him. Meanwhile, all the Israelites fled to their homes.

¹⁸During his lifetime Absalom had taken a pillar and erected it in the King's Valley as a monument to himself, for he thought, "I have no son to carry on the memory of my name." He named the pillar after himself, and it is called Absalom's Monument to this day.

David Mourns

¹⁹Now Ahimaaz son of Zadok said, "Let me run and take the news to the king that the LORD has vindicated him by delivering him from the hand of his enemies."

²⁰"You are not the one to take the news today," Joab told him. "You may take the news another time, but you must not do so today, because the king's son is dead."

²¹Then Joab said to a Cushite, "Go, tell the king what you have seen." The Cushite bowed down before Joab and ran off.

²²Ahimaaz son of Zadok again said to Joab, "Come what may, please let me run behind the Cushite."

But Joab replied, "My son, why do you want to go? You don't have any news that will bring you a reward."

²³He said, "Come what may, I want to run."

So Joab said, "Run!" Then Ahimaaz ran by way of the plain*ᵃ* and outran the Cushite.

²⁴While David was sitting between the inner and outer gates, the watchman went up to the roof of the gateway by the wall. As he looked out, he saw a man running alone. ²⁵The watchman called out to the king and reported it.

The king said, "If he is alone, he must have good news." And the runner came closer and closer.

²⁶Then the watchman saw another runner, and he called down to the gatekeeper, "Look, another man running alone!"

The king said, "He must be bringing good news, too."

²⁷The watchman said, "It seems to me that the first one runs like Ahimaaz son of Zadok."

"He's a good man," the king said. "He comes with good news."

²⁸Then Ahimaaz called out to the king, "All is well!" He bowed down before the king with his face to the ground and said, "Praise be to the LORD your God! He has delivered up those who lifted their hands against my lord the king."

²⁹The king asked, "Is the young man Absalom safe?"

Ahimaaz answered, "I saw great confusion just as Joab was about to send the king's servant and me, your servant, but I don't know what it was."

³⁰The king said, "Stand aside and wait here." So he stepped aside and stood there.

³¹Then the Cushite arrived and said, "My lord the king, hear the good news! The LORD has vindicated you today by delivering you from the hand of all who rose up against you."

³²The king asked the Cushite, "Is the young man Absalom safe?"

The Cushite replied, "May the enemies of my lord the king and all who rise up to harm you be like that young man."

³³The king was shaken. He went up to the room over the gateway and wept. As he went, he said: "O my son Absalom! My son, my son Absalom! If only I had died instead of you— O Absalom, my son, my son!"*ᵇ*

19ᶜ Joab was told, "The king is weeping and mourning for Absalom." ²And for the whole army the victory that day was turned into mourning, because on that day the troops heard it said, "The king is grieving for his son." ³The men stole into the city that day as men steal in who are ashamed when they flee from battle. ⁴The king covered his face and cried aloud, "O my son Absalom! O Absalom, my son, my son!"

⁵Then Joab went into the house to the king and said, "Today you have humiliated all your men, who have just saved your life and the lives of your sons and daughters and the lives of your wives and concubines. ⁶You love those who hate you and hate those who love you. You have made it clear today that the commanders and their men mean nothing to you. I see that you would be pleased if Absalom were alive today and all of us were dead. ⁷Now go out and encourage your men. I swear by the LORD that if you don't go out,

---

ᵃ 23 That is, the plain of the Jordan   *ᵇ 33* In Hebrew texts this verse (18:33) is numbered 19:1.
ᶜ In Hebrew texts 19:1-43 is numbered 19:2-44.

STOP SMALL SINS

READ: 2 SAMUEL 18:33

Even the best believers sometimes make bad choices that bring disastrous consequences. The sad scenes playing out in 2 Samuel go all the way back to David's sin against Bathsheba and Uriah.

The Lord had picked David to take Saul's place as king because he was a guy with God's heart (1 Samuel 13:14). But that extreme passion for God didn't make David a perfect man. After David's own sexual offense with Bathsheba, his son Amnon raped Tamar, who was David's daughter and Amnon's half sister. Although that act of violence enraged David, he did nothing to bring his son to justice (2 Samuel 13:21).

BUILDING FAITH WISDOM STRENGTH

Two years later, another of David's sons, Absalom, killed Amnon to avenge the rape. Absalom fled, and for three years David wouldn't speak to his son. During that time, Absalom gained a crowd of followers. He eventually staged a coup and drove his father from the throne, then slept with his father's concubines as the prophet Nathan had predicted (12:11). The rebellion ended with Absalom dead and David brokenhearted. "My son, my son Absalom!" he wailed. "If only I had died instead of you" (18:33).

David's ongoing bad choices only made these problems worse. And the scenes you observe in 2 Samuel show what happens when you let evil get out of hand. Don't miss the point that sin is best stopped when it's small. Problems are best fixed before they get completely twisted.

not a man will be left with you by nightfall. This will be worse for you than all the calamities that have come on you from your youth till now."

⁸So the king got up and took his seat in the gateway. When the men were told, "The king is sitting in the gateway," they all came before him.

Meanwhile, the Israelites had fled to their homes.

David Returns to Jerusalem

⁹Throughout the tribes of Israel, all the people were arguing among themselves, saying, "The king delivered us from the hand of our enemies; he is the one who rescued us from the hand of the Philistines. But now he has fled the country to escape from Absalom; ¹⁰and Absalom, whom we anointed to rule over us, has died in battle. So why do you say nothing about bringing the king back?"

¹¹King David sent this message to Zadok and Abiathar, the priests: "Ask the elders of Judah, 'Why should you be the last to bring the king back to his palace, since what is being said throughout Israel has reached the king at his quarters? ¹²You are my relatives, my own flesh and blood. So why should you be the last to bring back the king?' ¹³And say to Amasa, 'Are you not my own flesh and blood? May God deal with me, be it ever so severely, if you are not the commander of my army for life in place of Joab.'"

¹⁴He won over the hearts of the men of Judah so that they were all of one mind. They sent word to the king, "Return, you and all your men." ¹⁵Then the king returned and went as far as the Jordan.

Now the men of Judah had come to Gilgal to go out and meet the king and bring him across the Jordan. ¹⁶Shimei son of Gera, the Benjamite from Bahurim, hurried down with the men of Judah to meet King David. ¹⁷With him were a thousand Benjamites, along with Ziba, the steward of Saul's household, and his fifteen sons and twenty servants. They rushed to the Jordan, where the king was. ¹⁸They crossed at the ford to take the king's household over and to do whatever he wished.

When Shimei son of Gera crossed the Jordan, he fell prostrate before the king ¹⁹and said to him, "May my lord not hold me guilty. Do not remember how your servant did wrong on the day my lord the king left Jerusalem. May the king put it out of his mind. ²⁰For I your servant know that I have sinned, but today I have come here as the first from the tribes of Joseph to come down and meet my lord the king."

²¹Then Abishai son of Zeruiah said, "Shouldn't Shimei be put to death for this? He cursed the LORD's anointed."

²²David replied, "What does this have to do with you, you sons of Zeruiah? What right do you have to interfere? Should anyone be put to death in Israel today? Don't I know that today I am king over Israel?" ²³So the king said to Shimei, "You shall not die." And the king promised him on oath.

²⁴Mephibosheth, Saul's grandson, also went down to meet the king. He had not taken care of his feet or trimmed his mustache or washed his clothes from the day the king left until the day he returned safely. ²⁵When he came from Jerusalem to meet the king, the king asked him, "Why didn't you go with me, Mephibosheth?"

²⁶He said, "My lord the king, since I your servant am lame, I said, 'I will have my donkey saddled and will ride on it, so I can go with the king.' But Ziba my servant betrayed me. ²⁷And he has slandered your servant to my lord the king. My lord the king is like an angel of God; so do whatever you wish. ²⁸All my grandfather's descendants deserved nothing but death from my lord the king, but you gave your servant a place among those who eat at your table. So what right do I have to make any more appeals to the king?"

²⁹The king said to him, "Why say more? I order you and Ziba to divide the land."

³⁰Mephibosheth said to the king, "Let him take everything, now that my lord the king has returned home safely."

³¹Barzillai the Gileadite also came down from Rogelim to cross the Jordan with the king and to send him on his way from there. ³²Now Barzillai was very old, eighty years of age. He had provided for the king during his stay in Mahanaim, for he was a very wealthy man. ³³The king said to Barzillai, "Cross over with me and stay with me in Jerusalem, and I will provide for you."

³⁴But Barzillai answered the king, "How many more years will I live, that I should go up to Jerusalem with the king? ³⁵I am now

eighty years old. Can I tell the difference between what is enjoyable and what is not? Can your servant taste what he eats and drinks? Can I still hear the voices of male and female singers? Why should your servant be an added burden to my lord the king? ³⁶Your servant will cross over the Jordan with the king for a short distance, but why should the king reward me in this way? ³⁷Let your servant return, that I may die in my own town near the tomb of my father and mother. But here is your servant Kimham. Let him cross over with my lord the king. Do for him whatever you wish."

³⁸The king said, "Kimham shall cross over with me, and I will do for him whatever you wish. And anything you desire from me I will do for you."

³⁹So all the people crossed the Jordan, and then the king crossed over. The king kissed Barzillai and bid him farewell, and Barzillai returned to his home.

⁴⁰When the king crossed over to Gilgal, Kimham crossed with him. All the troops of Judah and half the troops of Israel had taken the king over.

⁴¹Soon all the men of Israel were coming to the king and saying to him, "Why did our brothers, the men of Judah, steal the king away and bring him and his household across the Jordan, together with all his men?"

⁴²All the men of Judah answered the men of Israel, "We did this because the king is closely related to us. Why are you angry about it? Have we eaten any of the king's provisions? Have we taken anything for ourselves?"

⁴³Then the men of Israel answered the men of Judah, "We have ten shares in the king; so we have a greater claim on David than you have. Why then do you treat us with contempt? Weren't we the first to speak of bringing back our king?"

But the men of Judah pressed their claims even more forcefully than the men of Israel.

Sheba Rebels Against David

20 Now a troublemaker named Sheba son of Bikri, a Benjamite, happened to be there. He sounded the trumpet and shouted,

"We have no share in David,
   no part in Jesse's son!
Every man to his tent, Israel!"

²So all the men of Israel deserted David to follow Sheba son of Bikri. But the men of Judah stayed by their king all the way from the Jordan to Jerusalem.

³When David returned to his palace in Jerusalem, he took the ten concubines he had left to take care of the palace and put them in a house under guard. He provided for them but had no sexual relations with them. They were kept in confinement till the day of their death, living as widows.

⁴Then the king said to Amasa, "Summon the men of Judah to come to me within three days, and be here yourself." ⁵But when Amasa went to summon Judah, he took longer than the time the king had set for him.

⁶David said to Abishai, "Now Sheba son of Bikri will do us more harm than Absalom did. Take your master's men and pursue him, or he will find fortified cities and escape from us."ᵃ ⁷So Joab's men and the Kerethites and Pelethites and all the mighty warriors went out under the command of Abishai. They marched out from Jerusalem to pursue Sheba son of Bikri.

⁸While they were at the great rock in Gibeon, Amasa came to meet them. Joab was wearing his military tunic, and strapped over it at his waist was a belt with a dagger in its sheath. As he stepped forward, it dropped out of its sheath.

⁹Joab said to Amasa, "How are you, my brother?" Then Joab took Amasa by the beard with his right hand to kiss him. ¹⁰Amasa was not on his guard against the dagger in Joab's hand, and Joab plunged it into his belly, and his intestines spilled out on the ground. Without being stabbed again, Amasa died. Then Joab and his brother Abishai pursued Sheba son of Bikri.

¹¹One of Joab's men stood beside Amasa and said, "Whoever favors Joab, and whoever is for David, let him follow Joab!" ¹²Amasa lay wallowing in his blood in the middle of the road, and the man saw that all the troops came to a halt there. When he realized that everyone who came up to Amasa stopped, he dragged him from the road into a field and threw a garment over him. ¹³After Amasa

---

ᵃ 6 Or *and do us serious injury*

had been removed from the road, everyone went on with Joab to pursue Sheba son of Bikri.

[14] Sheba passed through all the tribes of Israel to Abel Beth Maakah and through the entire region of the Bikrites,[a] who gathered together and followed him. [15] All the troops with Joab came and besieged Sheba in Abel Beth Maakah. They built a siege ramp up to the city, and it stood against the outer fortifications. While they were battering the wall to bring it down, [16] a wise woman called from the city, "Listen! Listen! Tell Joab to come here so I can speak to him." [17] He went toward her, and she asked, "Are you Joab?"

"I am," he answered.

She said, "Listen to what your servant has to say."

"I'm listening," he said.

[18] She continued, "Long ago they used to say, 'Get your answer at Abel,' and that settled it. [19] We are the peaceful and faithful in Israel. You are trying to destroy a city that is a mother in Israel. Why do you want to swallow up the LORD's inheritance?"

[20] "Far be it from me!" Joab replied, "Far be it from me to swallow up or destroy! [21] That is not the case. A man named Sheba son of Bikri, from the hill country of Ephraim, has lifted up his hand against the king, against David. Hand over this one man, and I'll withdraw from the city."

The woman said to Joab, "His head will be thrown to you from the wall."

[22] Then the woman went to all the people with her wise advice, and they cut off the head of Sheba son of Bikri and threw it to Joab. So he sounded the trumpet, and his men dispersed from the city, each returning to his home. And Joab went back to the king in Jerusalem.

David's Officials

[23] Joab was over Israel's entire army; Benaiah son of Jehoiada was over the Kerethites and Pelethites; [24] Adoniram[b] was in charge of forced labor; Jehoshaphat son of Ahilud was recorder; [25] Sheva was secretary; Zadok and Abiathar were priests; [26] and Ira the Jairite[c] was David's priest.

The Gibeonites Avenged

21 During the reign of David, there was a famine for three successive years; so David sought the face of the LORD. The LORD said, "It is on account of Saul and his blood-stained house; it is because he put the Gibeonites to death."

[2] The king summoned the Gibeonites and spoke to them. (Now the Gibeonites were not a part of Israel but were survivors of the Amorites; the Israelites had sworn to spare them, but Saul in his zeal for Israel and Judah had tried to annihilate them.) [3] David asked the Gibeonites, "What shall I do for you? How shall I make atonement so that you will bless the LORD's inheritance?"

[4] The Gibeonites answered him, "We have no right to demand silver or gold from Saul or his family, nor do we have the right to put anyone in Israel to death."

"What do you want me to do for you?" David asked.

[5] They answered the king, "As for the man who destroyed us and plotted against us so that we have been decimated and have no place anywhere in Israel, [6] let seven of his male descendants be given to us to be killed and their bodies exposed before the LORD at Gibeah of Saul — the LORD's chosen one."

So the king said, "I will give them to you."

[7] The king spared Mephibosheth son of Jonathan, the son of Saul, because of the oath before the LORD between David and Jonathan son of Saul. [8] But the king took Armoni and Mephibosheth, the two sons of Aiah's daughter Rizpah, whom she had borne to Saul, together with the five sons of Saul's daughter Merab,[d] whom she had borne to Adriel son of Barzillai the Meholathite. [9] He handed them over to the Gibeonites, who killed them and exposed their bodies on a hill before the LORD. All seven of them fell together; they were put to death during the first days of the harvest, just as the barley harvest was beginning.

[10] Rizpah daughter of Aiah took sackcloth and spread it out for herself on a rock. From the beginning of the harvest till the rain poured down from the heavens on the bodies, she did not let the birds touch them by

---

[a] 14 See Septuagint and Vulgate; Hebrew *Berites*.   [b] 24 Some Septuagint manuscripts (see also 1 Kings 4:6 and 5:14); Hebrew *Adoram*   [c] 26 Hebrew; some Septuagint manuscripts and Syriac (see also 23:38) *Ithrite*   [d] 8 Two Hebrew manuscripts, some Septuagint manuscripts and Syriac (see also 1 Samuel 18:19); most Hebrew and Septuagint manuscripts *Michal*

day or the wild animals by night. ¹¹When David was told what Aiah's daughter Rizpah, Saul's concubine, had done, ¹²he went and took the bones of Saul and his son Jonathan from the citizens of Jabesh Gilead. (They had stolen their bodies from the public square at Beth Shan, where the Philistines had hung them after they struck Saul down on Gilboa.) ¹³David brought the bones of Saul and his son Jonathan from there, and the bones of those who had been killed and exposed were gathered up.

¹⁴They buried the bones of Saul and his son Jonathan in the tomb of Saul's father Kish, at Zela in Benjamin, and did everything the king commanded. After that, God answered prayer in behalf of the land.

Wars Against the Philistines

¹⁵Once again there was a battle between the Philistines and Israel. David went down with his men to fight against the Philistines, and he became exhausted. ¹⁶And Ishbi-Benob, one of the descendants of Rapha, whose bronze spearhead weighed three hundred shekels[a] and who was armed with a new sword, said he would kill David. ¹⁷But Abishai son of Zeruiah came to David's rescue; he struck the Philistine down and killed him. Then David's men swore to him, saying, "Never again will you go out with us to battle, so that the lamp of Israel will not be extinguished."

¹⁸In the course of time, there was another battle with the Philistines, at Gob. At that time Sibbekai the Hushathite killed Saph, one of the descendants of Rapha.

¹⁹In another battle with the Philistines at Gob, Elhanan son of Jair[b] the Bethlehemite killed the brother of[c] Goliath the Gittite, who had a spear with a shaft like a weaver's rod.

²⁰In still another battle, which took place at Gath, there was a huge man with six fingers on each hand and six toes on each foot—twenty-four in all. He also was descended from Rapha. ²¹When he taunted Israel, Jonathan son of Shimeah, David's brother, killed him.

²²These four were descendants of Rapha

in Gath, and they fell at the hands of David and his men.

David's Song of Praise

22 David sang to the LORD the words of this song when the LORD delivered him from the hand of all his enemies and from the hand of Saul. ²He said:

"The LORD is my rock, my fortress and my deliverer;
³ my God is my rock, in whom I take refuge,
my shield[d] and the horn[e] of my salvation.
He is my stronghold, my refuge and my savior—
from violent people you save me.

⁴"I called to the LORD, who is worthy of praise,
and have been saved from my enemies.
⁵The waves of death swirled about me;
the torrents of destruction overwhelmed me.
⁶The cords of the grave coiled around me;
the snares of death confronted me.

⁷"In my distress I called to the LORD;
I called out to my God.
From his temple he heard my voice;
my cry came to his ears.
⁸The earth trembled and quaked,
the foundations of the heavens[f] shook;
they trembled because he was angry.
⁹Smoke rose from his nostrils;
consuming fire came from his mouth,
burning coals blazed out of it.
¹⁰He parted the heavens and came down;
dark clouds were under his feet.
¹¹He mounted the cherubim and flew;
he soared[g] on the wings of the wind.
¹²He made darkness his canopy around him—
the dark[h] rain clouds of the sky.
¹³Out of the brightness of his presence
bolts of lightning blazed forth.
¹⁴The LORD thundered from heaven;
the voice of the Most High resounded.

---

[a] 16 That is, about 7 1/2 pounds or about 3.5 kilograms   [b] 19 See 1 Chron. 20:5; Hebrew *Jaare-Oregim.*
[c] 19 See 1 Chron. 20:5; Hebrew does not have *the brother of.*   [d] 3 Or *sovereign*   [e] 3 *Horn* here symbolizes strength.   [f] 8 Hebrew; Vulgate and Syriac (see also Psalm 18:7) *mountains*   [g] 11 Many Hebrew manuscripts (see also Psalm 18:10); most Hebrew manuscripts *appeared*   [h] 12 Septuagint (see also Psalm 18:11); Hebrew *massed*

¹⁵ He shot his arrows and scattered the
    enemy,
    with great bolts of lightning he routed
    them.
¹⁶ The valleys of the sea were exposed
    and the foundations of the earth laid
    bare
    at the rebuke of the LORD,
    at the blast of breath from his nostrils.

¹⁷ "He reached down from on high and took
    hold of me;
    he drew me out of deep waters.
¹⁸ He rescued me from my powerful enemy,
    from my foes, who were too strong for
    me.
¹⁹ They confronted me in the day of my
    disaster,
    but the LORD was my support.
²⁰ He brought me out into a spacious place;
    he rescued me because he delighted
    in me.

²¹ "The LORD has dealt with me according
    to my righteousness;
    according to the cleanness of my
    hands he has rewarded me.
²² For I have kept the ways of the LORD;
    I am not guilty of turning from my God.
²³ All his laws are before me;
    I have not turned away from his
    decrees.
²⁴ I have been blameless before him
    and have kept myself from sin.
²⁵ The LORD has rewarded me according to
    my righteousness,
    according to my cleanness^a in his
    sight.

²⁶ "To the faithful you show yourself
    faithful,
    to the blameless you show yourself
    blameless,
²⁷ to the pure you show yourself pure,
    but to the devious you show yourself
    shrewd.
²⁸ You save the humble,
    but your eyes are on the haughty to
    bring them low.
²⁹ You, LORD, are my lamp;
    the LORD turns my darkness into light.

³⁰ With your help I can advance against a
    troop^b;
    with my God I can scale a wall.

³¹ "As for God, his way is perfect:
    The LORD's word is flawless;
    he shields all who take refuge in him.
³² For who is God besides the LORD?
    And who is the Rock except our God?
³³ It is God who arms me with strength^c
    and keeps my way secure.
³⁴ He makes my feet like the feet of a deer;
    he causes me to stand on the heights.
³⁵ He trains my hands for battle;
    my arms can bend a bow of bronze.
³⁶ You make your saving help my shield;
    your help has made^d me great.
³⁷ You provide a broad path for my feet,
    so that my ankles do not give way.

³⁸ "I pursued my enemies and crushed them;
    I did not turn back till they were
    destroyed.
³⁹ I crushed them completely, and they
    could not rise;
    they fell beneath my feet.
⁴⁰ You armed me with strength for battle;
    you humbled my adversaries before me.
⁴¹ You made my enemies turn their backs
    in flight,
    and I destroyed my foes.
⁴² They cried for help, but there was no one
    to save them—
    to the LORD, but he did not answer.
⁴³ I beat them as fine as the dust of the
    earth;
    I pounded and trampled them like
    mud in the streets.

⁴⁴ "You have delivered me from the attacks
    of the peoples;
    you have preserved me as the head of
    nations.
    People I did not know now serve me,
⁴⁵   foreigners cower before me;
    as soon as they hear of me, they
    obey me.
⁴⁶ They all lose heart;
    they come trembling^e from their
    strongholds.

---

^{a} 25 Hebrew; Septuagint and Vulgate (see also Psalm 18:24) *to the cleanness of my hands* ^{b} 30 Or *can run through a barricade* ^{c} 33 Dead Sea Scrolls, some Septuagint manuscripts, Vulgate and Syriac (see also Psalm 18:32); Masoretic Text *who is my strong refuge* ^{d} 36 Dead Sea Scrolls; Masoretic Text *shield; / you stoop down to make* ^{e} 46 Some Septuagint manuscripts and Vulgate (see also Psalm 18:45); Masoretic Text *they arm themselves*

PUT YOUR FOOT DOWN

READ: 2 SAMUEL 22:34,37

The first followers of Christ left a footprint with every step. Their lives made a mark. Their actions touched the souls of those they encountered. Their footprints are left in the sand for us to see and to marvel at the determined path walked by each one.

When I watch people graduate from high school or college, I wonder, *What footprints will they leave? What path will they ultimately take?* I wonder if they see the potential they have within them to do mighty, footprint-leaving, world-denting things. Most often, I see students with a bucket full of stuff (textbooks, a major, some fun ideas, debt) but with no real direction—just a hope that they'll find something to occupy themselves until they die, or until they ultimately discover a purpose. I see people easily distracted.

BUILDING FAITH WISDOM STRENGTH

You were designed to leave a unique footprint. Not five years from now, but right now. Not after twenty years of seeking and hunting. Right now. Immediately.

Take a look at your feet. Those two flat pieces of flesh are God's metaphors for our lives. The more we put our feet to the earth and walk the planet for God, the more lives are changed. We talk so much about being on a journey, but let's not just talk—let's actually journey.

Discover who you are now so you can use who you are for God's glory. Toss certainty and concrete living aside. Leave rules, steps, and guidelines behind you, and step off into the journey. Waiting is not an option.

Taken from *Leave a Footprint—Change the World* by Tim Baker, copyright © 2009 by Tim Baker, published by Zondervan.

47 "The LORD lives! Praise be to my Rock!
    Exalted be my God, the Rock, my
        Savior!
48 He is the God who avenges me,
    who puts the nations under me,
49   who sets me free from my enemies.
    You exalted me above my foes;
        from a violent man you rescued me.
50 Therefore I will praise you, LORD, among
        the nations;
    I will sing the praises of your name.

51 "He gives his king great victories;
    he shows unfailing kindness to his
        anointed,
        to David and his descendants
            forever."

David's Last Words

23 These are the last words of David:

"The inspired utterance of David son
        of Jesse,
    the utterance of the man exalted by the
        Most High,
the man anointed by the God of Jacob,
    the hero of Israel's songs:

2 "The Spirit of the LORD spoke through me;
    his word was on my tongue.
3 The God of Israel spoke,
    the Rock of Israel said to me:
    'When one rules over people in
        righteousness,
        when he rules in the fear of God,
4 he is like the light of morning at sunrise
    on a cloudless morning,
    like the brightness after rain
        that brings grass from the earth.'

5 "If my house were not right with God,
    surely he would not have made with
        me an everlasting covenant,
    arranged and secured in every part;
surely he would not bring to fruition my
        salvation
    and grant me my every desire.
6 But evil men are all to be cast aside like
        thorns,
    which are not gathered with the hand.
7 Whoever touches thorns

uses a tool of iron or the shaft of
        a spear;
    they are burned up where they lie."

David's Mighty Warriors

8 These are the names of David's mighty
warriors:

Josheb-Basshebeth,[a] a Tahkemonite,[b] was
chief of the Three; he raised his spear against
eight hundred men, whom he killed[c] in one
encounter.

9 Next to him was Eleazar son of Dodai
the Ahohite. As one of the three mighty warriors, he was with David when they taunted
the Philistines gathered at Pas Dammim[d] for
battle. Then the Israelites retreated, 10 but
Eleazar stood his ground and struck down
the Philistines till his hand grew tired and
froze to the sword. The LORD brought about
a great victory that day. The troops returned
to Eleazar, but only to strip the dead.

11 Next to him was Shammah son of Agee
the Hararite. When the Philistines banded
together at a place where there was a field
full of lentils, Israel's troops fled from them.
12 But Shammah took his stand in the middle of the field. He defended it and struck
the Philistines down, and the LORD brought
about a great victory.

13 During harvest time, three of the thirty chief warriors came down to David at the
cave of Adullam, while a band of Philistines
was encamped in the Valley of Rephaim.
14 At that time David was in the stronghold,
and the Philistine garrison was at Bethlehem. 15 David longed for water and said,
"Oh, that someone would get me a drink of
water from the well near the gate of Bethlehem!" 16 So the three mighty warriors broke
through the Philistine lines, drew water
from the well near the gate of Bethlehem
and carried it back to David. But he refused
to drink it; instead, he poured it out before
the LORD. 17 "Far be it from me, LORD, to do
this!" he said. "Is it not the blood of men who
went at the risk of their lives?" And David
would not drink it.

Such were the exploits of the three mighty
warriors.

---

a 8 Hebrew; some Septuagint manuscripts suggest *Ish-Bosheth,* that is, *Esh-Baal* (see also 1 Chron. 11:11
Jashobeam).   *b 8* Probably a variant of *Hakmonite* (see 1 Chron. 11:11)   *c 8* Some Septuagint
manuscripts (see also 1 Chron. 11:11); Hebrew and other Septuagint manuscripts *Three; it was Adino the
Eznite who killed eight hundred men*   *d 9* See 1 Chron. 11:13; Hebrew *gathered there.*

[18] Abishai the brother of Joab son of Zeruiah was chief of the Three.[a] He raised his spear against three hundred men, whom he killed, and so he became as famous as the Three. [19] Was he not held in greater honor than the Three? He became their commander, even though he was not included among them.

[20] Benaiah son of Jehoiada, a valiant fighter from Kabzeel, performed great exploits. He struck down Moab's two mightiest warriors. He also went down into a pit on a snowy day and killed a lion. [21] And he struck down a huge Egyptian. Although the Egyptian had a spear in his hand, Benaiah went against him with a club. He snatched the spear from the Egyptian's hand and killed him with his own spear. [22] Such were the exploits of Benaiah son of Jehoiada; he too was as famous as the three mighty warriors. [23] He was held in greater honor than any of the Thirty, but he was not included among the Three. And David put him in charge of his bodyguard.

[24] Among the Thirty were:
Asahel the brother of Joab,
Elhanan son of Dodo from Bethlehem,
[25] Shammah the Harodite,
Elika the Harodite,
[26] Helez the Paltite,
Ira son of Ikkesh from Tekoa,
[27] Abiezer from Anathoth,
Sibbekai[b] the Hushathite,
[28] Zalmon the Ahohite,
Maharai the Netophathite,
[29] Heled[c] son of Baanah the Netophathite,
Ithai son of Ribai from Gibeah in Benjamin,
[30] Benaiah the Pirathonite,
Hiddai[d] from the ravines of Gaash,
[31] Abi-Albon the Arbathite,
Azmaveth the Barhumite,
[32] Eliahba the Shaalbonite,
the sons of Jashen,

Jonathan [33] son of[e] Shammah the Hararite,
Ahiam son of Sharar[f] the Hararite,
[34] Eliphelet son of Ahasbai the Maakathite,
Eliam son of Ahithophel the Gilonite,
[35] Hezro the Carmelite,
Paarai the Arbite,
[36] Igal son of Nathan from Zobah,
the son of Hagri,[g]
[37] Zelek the Ammonite,
Naharai the Beerothite, the armorbearer of Joab son of Zeruiah,
[38] Ira the Ithrite,
Gareb the Ithrite
[39] and Uriah the Hittite.
There were thirty-seven in all.

David Enrolls the Fighting Men

24 Again the anger of the LORD burned against Israel, and he incited David against them, saying, "Go and take a census of Israel and Judah."

[2] So the king said to Joab and the army commanders[h] with him, "Go throughout the tribes of Israel from Dan to Beersheba and enroll the fighting men, so that I may know how many there are."

[3] But Joab replied to the king, "May the LORD your God multiply the troops a hundred times over, and may the eyes of my lord the king see it. But why does my lord the king want to do such a thing?"

[4] The king's word, however, overruled Joab and the army commanders; so they left the presence of the king to enroll the fighting men of Israel.

[5] After crossing the Jordan, they camped near Aroer, south of the town in the gorge, and then went through Gad and on to Jazer. [6] They went to Gilead and the region of Tahtim Hodshi, and on to Dan Jaan and around toward Sidon. [7] Then they went toward the fortress of Tyre and all the towns of the Hivites and Canaanites. Finally, they went on to Beersheba in the Negev of Judah.

---

[a] 18 Most Hebrew manuscripts (see also 1 Chron. 11:20); two Hebrew manuscripts and Syriac *Thirty* [b] 27 Some Septuagint manuscripts (see also 21:18; 1 Chron. 11:29); Hebrew *Mebunnai* [c] 29 Some Hebrew manuscripts and Vulgate (see also 1 Chron. 11:30); most Hebrew manuscripts *Heleb* [d] 30 Hebrew; some Septuagint manuscripts (see also 1 Chron. 11:32) *Hurai* [e] 33 Some Septuagint manuscripts (see also 1 Chron. 11:34); Hebrew does not have *son of*. [f] 33 Hebrew; some Septuagint manuscripts (see also 1 Chron. 11:35) *Sakar* [g] 36 Some Septuagint manuscripts (see also 1 Chron. 11:38); Hebrew *Haggadi* [h] 2 Septuagint (see also verse 4 and 1 Chron. 21:2); Hebrew *Joab the army commander*

COUNTING ON THE WRONG THING

C ounting soldiers sounds smart. If you're a king about to go to war, it seems wise to know how many people stand on your side of the battle line. But God had a different view of the census David undertook.

Fighters gathered around David as soon as he fled Saul, soon numbering in the hundreds (1 Samuel 22:1-2). Starting as a band of misfits, these men became known for daring exploits. During his reign as king, David had his three mighty warriors and the thirty mighty men, along with a trio of additional well-known warriors.

Yet something goes awry when David counts the troops under his command. The plan is opposed by his commanders, but the king's word wins out. When David discovers he has more than a million soldiers at hand, he knows he has sinned.

David needed an army to defend the nation. But his census was evidence he had unwisely turned to human might instead of to the Lord. As David himself once wrote, "Some trust in chariots and some in horses, but we trust in the name of the LORD our God. They are brought to their knees and fall, but we rise up and stand firm" (Psalm 20:7-8). God gives you abilities, resources, and everything else you need to thrive. But as soon as you count on those gifts more than God, you're acting like David. And that doesn't end well.

BUILDING FAITH WISDOM STRENGTH

[8]After they had gone through the entire land, they came back to Jerusalem at the end of nine months and twenty days.

[9]Joab reported the number of the fighting men to the king: In Israel there were eight hundred thousand able-bodied men who could handle a sword, and in Judah five hundred thousand.

[10]David was conscience-stricken after he had counted the fighting men, and he said to the LORD, "I have sinned greatly in what I have done. Now, LORD, I beg you, take away the guilt of your servant. I have done a very foolish thing."

[11]Before David got up the next morning, the word of the LORD had come to Gad the prophet, David's seer: [12]"Go and tell David, 'This is what the LORD says: I am giving you three options. Choose one of them for me to carry out against you.'"

[13]So Gad went to David and said to him, "Shall there come on you three[a] years of famine in your land? Or three months of fleeing from your enemies while they pursue you? Or three days of plague in your land? Now then, think it over and decide how I should answer the one who sent me."

[14]David said to Gad, "I am in deep distress. Let us fall into the hands of the LORD, for his mercy is great; but do not let me fall into human hands."

[15]So the LORD sent a plague on Israel from that morning until the end of the time designated, and seventy thousand of the people from Dan to Beersheba died. [16]When the angel stretched out his hand to destroy Jerusalem, the LORD relented concerning the disaster and said to the angel who was afflicting the people, "Enough! Withdraw your hand." The angel of the LORD was then at the threshing floor of Araunah the Jebusite.

[17]When David saw the angel who was striking down the people, he said to the LORD, "I have sinned; I, the shepherd,[b] have done wrong. These are but sheep. What have they done? Let your hand fall on me and my family."

David Builds an Altar

[18]On that day Gad went to David and said to him, "Go up and build an altar to the LORD on the threshing floor of Araunah the Jebusite." [19]So David went up, as the LORD had commanded through Gad. [20]When Araunah looked and saw the king and his officials coming toward him, he went out and bowed down before the king with his face to the ground.

[21]Araunah said, "Why has my lord the king come to his servant?"

"To buy your threshing floor," David answered, "so I can build an altar to the LORD, that the plague on the people may be stopped."

[22]Araunah said to David, "Let my lord the king take whatever he wishes and offer it up. Here are oxen for the burnt offering, and here are threshing sledges and ox yokes for the wood. [23]Your Majesty, Araunah[c] gives all this to the king." Araunah also said to him, "May the LORD your God accept you."

[24]But the king replied to Araunah, "No, I insist on paying you for it. I will not sacrifice to the LORD my God burnt offerings that cost me nothing."

So David bought the threshing floor and the oxen and paid fifty shekels[d] of silver for them. [25]David built an altar to the LORD there and sacrificed burnt offerings and fellowship offerings. Then the LORD answered his prayer in behalf of the land, and the plague on Israel was stopped.

---

[a] 13 Septuagint (see also 1 Chron. 21:12); Hebrew *seven*   [b] 17 Dead Sea Scrolls and Septuagint; Masoretic Text does not have *the shepherd*.   [c] 23 Some Hebrew manuscripts and Septuagint; most Hebrew manuscripts *King Araunah*   [d] 24 That is, about 1 1/4 pounds or about 575 grams

1 KINGS

⮕ ## WHEN DID THIS HAPPEN?

About 970–840 B.C. in the land of Israel—divided into the northern kingdom of Israel and the southern kingdom of Judah

⮕ ## WHO IS IN THIS BOOK?

Solomon

Elijah

Micaiah

Jeroboam

Ahab

Jezebel

the prophets of Baal

⮕ ## VERSES YOU MIGHT RECOGNIZE

1 KINGS 2:3B

"Walk in obedience to him, and keep his decrees and commands, his laws and regulations, as written in the Law of Moses. Do this so that you may prosper in all you do and wherever you go."

1 KINGS 18:21

"Elijah went before the people and said, 'How long will you waver between two opinions? If the LORD is God, follow him; but if Baal is God, follow him.'"

WHAT'S IT ABOUT?

Abijah, Asa, Baasha and Elah. These might sound like the names of foreign cities, but they are actually the names of kings who ruled Israel. This book opens during King David's final days. After David died, his son, Solomon, took the throne. Solomon started out strong by asking God for wisdom (which God gives him) and building the temple, but eventually Solomon became distracted by his wealth and his many wives, and he quit putting God first.

After Solomon, very few of the kings followed God, so God used prophets, like Elijah, to remind the people of his commands. In this book, you'll read the exciting story of Elijah's confrontation with the prophets of Baal. The longer that wicked kings ruled Israel, the more the people forgot about God's plan for them. They disobeyed the laws God had given them through Moses, set up idols, and worshiped false gods. The kings who reigned under God's authority experienced his favor and blessing, but those who did evil in his sight brought trouble on the entire nation.

1 KINGS

Adonijah Sets Himself Up as King

1 When King David was very old, he could not keep warm even when they put covers over him. ²So his attendants said to him, "Let us look for a young virgin to serve the king and take care of him. She can lie beside him so that our lord the king may keep warm."

³Then they searched throughout Israel for a beautiful young woman and found Abishag, a Shunammite, and brought her to the king. ⁴The woman was very beautiful; she took care of the king and waited on him, but the king had no sexual relations with her.

⁵Now Adonijah, whose mother was Haggith, put himself forward and said, "I will be king." So he got chariots and horses*a* ready, with fifty men to run ahead of him. ⁶(His father had never rebuked him by asking, "Why do you behave as you do?" He was also very handsome and was born next after Absalom.)

⁷Adonijah conferred with Joab son of Zeruiah and with Abiathar the priest, and they gave him their support. ⁸But Zadok the priest, Benaiah son of Jehoiada, Nathan the prophet, Shimei and Rei and David's special guard did not join Adonijah.

⁹Adonijah then sacrificed sheep, cattle and fattened calves at the Stone of Zoheleth near En Rogel. He invited all his brothers, the king's sons, and all the royal officials of Judah, ¹⁰but he did not invite Nathan the prophet or Benaiah or the special guard or his brother Solomon.

¹¹Then Nathan asked Bathsheba, Solomon's mother, "Have you not heard that Adonijah, the son of Haggith, has become king, and our lord David knows nothing about it? ¹²Now then, let me advise you how you can save your own life and the life of your son Solomon. ¹³Go in to King David and say to him, 'My lord the king, did you not swear to me your servant: "Surely Solomon your son shall be king after me, and he will sit on my throne"? Why then has Adonijah become king?' ¹⁴While you are still there talking to the king, I will come in and add my word to what you have said."

¹⁵So Bathsheba went to see the aged king in his room, where Abishag the Shunammite was attending him. ¹⁶Bathsheba bowed down, prostrating herself before the king.

"What is it you want?" the king asked.

¹⁷She said to him, "My lord, you yourself swore to me your servant by the LORD your God: 'Solomon your son shall be king after me, and he will sit on my throne.' ¹⁸But now Adonijah has become king, and you, my lord the king, do not know about it. ¹⁹He has sacrificed great numbers of cattle, fattened calves, and sheep, and has invited all the king's sons, Abiathar the priest and Joab the commander of the army, but he has not invited Solomon your servant. ²⁰My lord the king, the eyes of all Israel are on you, to learn from you who will sit on the throne of my lord the king after him. ²¹Otherwise, as soon as my lord the king is laid to rest with his ancestors, I and my son Solomon will be treated as criminals."

²²While she was still speaking with the king, Nathan the prophet arrived. ²³And the king was told, "Nathan the prophet is here." So he went before the king and bowed with his face to the ground.

²⁴Nathan said, "Have you, my lord the king, declared that Adonijah shall be king after you, and that he will sit on your throne? ²⁵Today he has gone down and sacrificed great numbers of cattle, fattened calves, and sheep. He has invited all the king's sons, the commanders of the army and Abiathar the priest. Right now they are eating and drinking with him and saying, 'Long live King Adonijah!' ²⁶But me your servant, and Zadok the priest, and Benaiah son of Jehoiada, and your servant Solomon he did not invite. ²⁷Is this something my lord the king has done without letting his servants know who should sit on the throne of my lord the king after him?"

a 5 Or charioteers

David Makes Solomon King

28 Then King David said, "Call in Bathsheba." So she came into the king's presence and stood before him.

29 The king then took an oath: "As surely as the LORD lives, who has delivered me out of every trouble, 30 I will surely carry out this very day what I swore to you by the LORD, the God of Israel: Solomon your son shall be king after me, and he will sit on my throne in my place."

31 Then Bathsheba bowed down with her face to the ground, prostrating herself before the king, and said, "May my lord King David live forever!"

32 King David said, "Call in Zadok the priest, Nathan the prophet and Benaiah son of Jehoiada." When they came before the king, 33 he said to them: "Take your lord's servants with you and have Solomon my son mount my own mule and take him down to Gihon. 34 There have Zadok the priest and Nathan the prophet anoint him king over Israel. Blow the trumpet and shout, 'Long live King Solomon!' 35 Then you are to go up with him, and he is to come and sit on my throne and reign in my place. I have appointed him ruler over Israel and Judah."

36 Benaiah son of Jehoiada answered the king, "Amen! May the LORD, the God of my lord the king, so declare it. 37 As the LORD was with my lord the king, so may he be with Solomon to make his throne even greater than the throne of my lord King David!"

38 So Zadok the priest, Nathan the prophet, Benaiah son of Jehoiada, the Kerethites and the Pelethites went down and had Solomon mount King David's mule, and they escorted him to Gihon. 39 Zadok the priest took the horn of oil from the sacred tent and anointed Solomon. Then they sounded the trumpet and all the people shouted, "Long live King Solomon!" 40 And all the people went up after him, playing pipes and rejoicing greatly, so that the ground shook with the sound.

41 Adonijah and all the guests who were with him heard it as they were finishing their feast. On hearing the sound of the trumpet, Joab asked, "What's the meaning of all the noise in the city?"

42 Even as he was speaking, Jonathan son of Abiathar the priest arrived. Adonijah said, "Come in. A worthy man like you must be bringing good news."

43 "Not at all!" Jonathan answered. "Our lord King David has made Solomon king. 44 The king has sent with him Zadok the priest, Nathan the prophet, Benaiah son of Jehoiada, the Kerethites and the Pelethites, and they have put him on the king's mule, 45 and Zadok the priest and Nathan the prophet have anointed him king at Gihon. From there they have gone up cheering, and the city resounds with it. That's the noise you hear. 46 Moreover, Solomon has taken his seat on the royal throne. 47 Also, the royal officials have come to congratulate our lord King David, saying, 'May your God make Solomon's name more famous than yours and his throne greater than yours!' And the king bowed in worship on his bed 48 and said, 'Praise be to the LORD, the God of Israel, who has allowed my eyes to see a successor on my throne today.'"

49 At this, all Adonijah's guests rose in alarm and dispersed. 50 But Adonijah, in fear of Solomon, went and took hold of the horns of the altar. 51 Then Solomon was told, "Adonijah is afraid of King Solomon and is clinging to the horns of the altar. He says, 'Let King Solomon swear to me today that he will not put his servant to death with the sword.'"

52 Solomon replied, "If he shows himself to be worthy, not a hair of his head will fall to the ground; but if evil is found in him, he will die." 53 Then King Solomon sent men, and they brought him down from the altar. And Adonijah came and bowed down to King Solomon, and Solomon said, "Go to your home."

David's Charge to Solomon

2 When the time drew near for David to die, he gave a charge to Solomon his son.

2 "I am about to go the way of all the earth," he said. "So be strong, act like a man, 3 and observe what the LORD your God requires: Walk in obedience to him, and keep his decrees and commands, his laws and regulations, as written in the Law of Moses. Do this so that you may prosper in all you do and wherever you go 4 and that the LORD may keep his promise to me: 'If your descendants watch how they live, and if they walk faithfully before me with all their heart and soul, you will never fail to have a successor on the throne of Israel.'

5 "Now you yourself know what Joab son of

Zeruiah did to me — what he did to the two commanders of Israel's armies, Abner son of Ner and Amasa son of Jether. He killed them, shedding their blood in peacetime as if in battle, and with that blood he stained the belt around his waist and the sandals on his feet. [6] Deal with him according to your wisdom, but do not let his gray head go down to the grave in peace.

[7] "But show kindness to the sons of Barzillai of Gilead and let them be among those who eat at your table. They stood by me when I fled from your brother Absalom.

[8] "And remember, you have with you Shimei son of Gera, the Benjamite from Bahurim, who called down bitter curses on me the day I went to Mahanaim. When he came down to meet me at the Jordan, I swore to him by the LORD: 'I will not put you to death by the sword.' [9] But now, do not consider him innocent. You are a man of wisdom; you will know what to do to him. Bring his gray head down to the grave in blood."

[10] Then David rested with his ancestors and was buried in the City of David. [11] He had reigned forty years over Israel — seven years in Hebron and thirty-three in Jerusalem. [12] So Solomon sat on the throne of his father David, and his rule was firmly established.

Solomon's Throne Established

[13] Now Adonijah, the son of Haggith, went to Bathsheba, Solomon's mother. Bathsheba asked him, "Do you come peacefully?"

He answered, "Yes, peacefully." [14] Then he added, "I have something to say to you."

"You may say it," she replied.

[15] "As you know," he said, "the kingdom was mine. All Israel looked to me as their king. But things changed, and the kingdom has gone to my brother; for it has come to him from the LORD. [16] Now I have one request to make of you. Do not refuse me."

"You may make it," she said.

[17] So he continued, "Please ask King Solomon — he will not refuse you — to give me Abishag the Shunammite as my wife."

[18] "Very well," Bathsheba replied, "I will speak to the king for you."

[19] When Bathsheba went to King Solomon to speak to him for Adonijah, the king stood up to meet her, bowed down to her and sat down on his throne. He had a throne brought for the king's mother, and she sat down at his right hand.

[20] "I have one small request to make of you," she said. "Do not refuse me."

The king replied, "Make it, my mother; I will not refuse you."

[21] So she said, "Let Abishag the Shunammite be given in marriage to your brother Adonijah."

[22] King Solomon answered his mother, "Why do you request Abishag the Shunammite for Adonijah? You might as well request the kingdom for him — after all, he is my older brother — yes, for him and for Abiathar the priest and Joab son of Zeruiah!"

[23] Then King Solomon swore by the LORD: "May God deal with me, be it ever so severely, if Adonijah does not pay with his life for this request! [24] And now, as surely as the LORD lives — he who has established me securely on the throne of my father David and has founded a dynasty for me as he promised — Adonijah shall be put to death today!" [25] So King Solomon gave orders to Benaiah son of Jehoiada, and he struck down Adonijah and he died.

[26] To Abiathar the priest the king said, "Go back to your fields in Anathoth. You deserve to die, but I will not put you to death now, because you carried the ark of the Sovereign LORD before my father David and shared all my father's hardships." [27] So Solomon removed Abiathar from the priesthood of the LORD, fulfilling the word the LORD had spoken at Shiloh about the house of Eli.

[28] When the news reached Joab, who had conspired with Adonijah though not with Absalom, he fled to the tent of the LORD and took hold of the horns of the altar. [29] King Solomon was told that Joab had fled to the tent of the LORD and was beside the altar. Then Solomon ordered Benaiah son of Jehoiada, "Go, strike him down!"

[30] So Benaiah entered the tent of the LORD and said to Joab, "The king says, 'Come out!'"

But he answered, "No, I will die here."

Benaiah reported to the king, "This is how Joab answered me."

[31] Then the king commanded Benaiah, "Do as he says. Strike him down and bury him, and so clear me and my whole family of the guilt of the innocent blood that Joab shed. [32] The LORD will repay him for the blood he shed, because without my father David

knowing it he attacked two men and killed them with the sword. Both of them—Abner son of Ner, commander of Israel's army, and Amasa son of Jether, commander of Judah's army—were better men and more upright than he. ³³May the guilt of their blood rest on the head of Joab and his descendants forever. But on David and his descendants, his house and his throne, may there be the LORD's peace forever."

³⁴So Benaiah son of Jehoiada went up and struck down Joab and killed him, and he was buried at his home out in the country. ³⁵The king put Benaiah son of Jehoiada over the army in Joab's position and replaced Abiathar with Zadok the priest.

³⁶Then the king sent for Shimei and said to him, "Build yourself a house in Jerusalem and live there, but do not go anywhere else. ³⁷The day you leave and cross the Kidron Valley, you can be sure you will die; your blood will be on your own head."

³⁸Shimei answered the king, "What you say is good. Your servant will do as my lord the king has said." And Shimei stayed in Jerusalem for a long time.

³⁹But three years later, two of Shimei's slaves ran off to Achish son of Maakah, king of Gath, and Shimei was told, "Your slaves are in Gath." ⁴⁰At this, he saddled his donkey and went to Achish at Gath in search of his slaves. So Shimei went away and brought the slaves back from Gath.

⁴¹When Solomon was told that Shimei had gone from Jerusalem to Gath and had returned, ⁴²the king summoned Shimei and said to him, "Did I not make you swear by the LORD and warn you, 'On the day you leave to go anywhere else, you can be sure you will die'? At that time you said to me, 'What you say is good. I will obey.' ⁴³Why then did you not keep your oath to the LORD and obey the command I gave you?"

⁴⁴The king also said to Shimei, "You know in your heart all the wrong you did to my father David. Now the LORD will repay you for your wrongdoing. ⁴⁵But King Solomon will be blessed, and David's throne will remain secure before the LORD forever."

⁴⁶Then the king gave the order to Benaiah son of Jehoiada, and he went out and struck Shimei down and he died.

The kingdom was now established in Solomon's hands.

Solomon Asks for Wisdom

3 Solomon made an alliance with Pharaoh king of Egypt and married his daughter. He brought her to the City of David until he finished building his palace and the temple of the LORD, and the wall around Jerusalem. ²The people, however, were still sacrificing at the high places, because a temple had not yet been built for the Name of the LORD. ³Solomon showed his love for the LORD by walking according to the instructions given him by his father David, except that he offered sacrifices and burned incense on the high places.

⁴The king went to Gibeon to offer sacrifices, for that was the most important high place, and Solomon offered a thousand burnt offerings on that altar. ⁵At Gibeon the LORD appeared to Solomon during the night in a dream, and God said, "Ask for whatever you want me to give you."

⁶Solomon answered, "You have shown great kindness to your servant, my father David, because he was faithful to you and righteous and upright in heart. You have continued this great kindness to him and have given him a son to sit on his throne this very day.

⁷"Now, LORD my God, you have made your servant king in place of my father David. But I am only a little child and do not know how to carry out my duties. ⁸Your servant is here among the people you have chosen, a great people, too numerous to count or number. ⁹So give your servant a discerning heart to govern your people and to distinguish between right and wrong. For who is able to govern this great people of yours?"

¹⁰The Lord was pleased that Solomon had asked for this. ¹¹So God said to him, "Since you have asked for this and not for long life or wealth for yourself, nor have asked for the death of your enemies but for discernment in administering justice, ¹²I will do what you have asked. I will give you a wise and discerning heart, so that there will never have been anyone like you, nor will there ever be. ¹³Moreover, I will give you what you have not asked for—both wealth and honor—so that in your lifetime you will have no equal among kings. ¹⁴And if you walk in obedience to me and keep my decrees and commands as David your father did, I will give you a long life." ¹⁵Then Solomon awoke—and he realized it had been a dream.

He returned to Jerusalem, stood before the ark of the Lord's covenant and sacrificed burnt offerings and fellowship offerings. Then he gave a feast for all his court.

A Wise Ruling

[16]Now two prostitutes came to the king and stood before him. [17]One of them said, "Pardon me, my lord. This woman and I live in the same house, and I had a baby while she was there with me. [18]The third day after my child was born, this woman also had a baby. We were alone; there was no one in the house but the two of us.

[19]"During the night this woman's son died because she lay on him. [20]So she got up in the middle of the night and took my son from my side while I your servant was asleep. She put him by her breast and put her dead son by my breast. [21]The next morning, I got up to nurse my son—and he was dead! But when I looked at him closely in the morning light, I saw that it wasn't the son I had borne."

[22]The other woman said, "No! The living one is my son; the dead one is yours."

But the first one insisted, "No! The dead one is yours; the living one is mine." And so they argued before the king.

[23]The king said, "This one says, 'My son is alive and your son is dead,' while that one says, 'No! Your son is dead and mine is alive.'"

[24]Then the king said, "Bring me a sword." So they brought a sword for the king. [25]He then gave an order: "Cut the living child in two and give half to one and half to the other."

[26]The woman whose son was alive was deeply moved out of love for her son and said to the king, "Please, my lord, give her the living baby! Don't kill him!"

But the other said, "Neither I nor you shall have him. Cut him in two!"

[27]Then the king gave his ruling: "Give the living baby to the first woman. Do not kill him; she is his mother."

[28]When all Israel heard the verdict the king had given, they held the king in awe, because they saw that he had wisdom from God to administer justice.

Solomon's Officials and Governors

4 So King Solomon ruled over all Israel. [2]And these were his chief officials:

Azariah son of Zadok—the priest;

[3]Elihoreph and Ahijah, sons of Shisha—secretaries;

Jehoshaphat son of Ahilud—recorder;

[4]Benaiah son of Jehoiada—commander in chief;

Zadok and Abiathar—priests;

[5]Azariah son of Nathan—in charge of the district governors;

Zabud son of Nathan—a priest and adviser to the king;

[6]Ahishar—palace administrator;

Adoniram son of Abda—in charge of forced labor.

[7]Solomon had twelve district governors over all Israel, who supplied provisions for the king and the royal household. Each one had to provide supplies for one month in the year. [8]These are their names:

Ben-Hur—in the hill country of Ephraim;

[9]Ben-Deker—in Makaz, Shaalbim, Beth Shemesh and Elon Bethhanan;

[10]Ben-Hesed—in Arubboth (Sokoh and all the land of Hepher were his);

[11]Ben-Abinadab—in Naphoth Dor (he was married to Taphath daughter of Solomon);

[12]Baana son of Ahilud—in Taanach and Megiddo, and in all of Beth Shan next to Zarethan below Jezreel, from Beth Shan to Abel Meholah across to Jokmeam;

[13]Ben-Geber—in Ramoth Gilead (the settlements of Jair son of Manasseh in Gilead were his, as well as the region of Argob in Bashan and its sixty large walled cities with bronze gate bars);

[14]Ahinadab son of Iddo—in Mahanaim;

[15]Ahimaaz—in Naphtali (he had married Basemath daughter of Solomon);

[16]Baana son of Hushai—in Asher and in Aloth;

[17]Jehoshaphat son of Paruah—in Issachar;

[18]Shimei son of Ela—in Benjamin;

[19]Geber son of Uri—in Gilead (the country of Sihon king of the Amorites and the country of Og king of Bashan). He was the only governor over the district.

Solomon's Daily Provisions

²⁰The people of Judah and Israel were as numerous as the sand on the seashore; they ate, they drank and they were happy. ²¹And Solomon ruled over all the kingdoms from the Euphrates River to the land of the Philistines, as far as the border of Egypt. These countries brought tribute and were Solomon's subjects all his life.

²²Solomon's daily provisions were thirty cors*ᵃ* of the finest flour and sixty cors*ᵇ* of meal, ²³ten head of stall-fed cattle, twenty of pasture-fed cattle and a hundred sheep and goats, as well as deer, gazelles, roebucks and choice fowl. ²⁴For he ruled over all the kingdoms west of the Euphrates River, from Tiphsah to Gaza, and had peace on all sides. ²⁵During Solomon's lifetime Judah and Israel, from Dan to Beersheba, lived in safety, everyone under their own vine and under their own fig tree.

²⁶Solomon had four*ᶜ* thousand stalls for chariot horses, and twelve thousand horses.*ᵈ* ²⁷The district governors, each in his month, supplied provisions for King Solomon and all who came to the king's table. They saw to it that nothing was lacking. ²⁸They also brought to the proper place their quotas of barley and straw for the chariot horses and the other horses.

Solomon's Wisdom

²⁹God gave Solomon wisdom and very great insight, and a breadth of understanding as measureless as the sand on the seashore. ³⁰Solomon's wisdom was greater than the wisdom of all the people of the East, and greater than all the wisdom of Egypt. ³¹He was wiser than anyone else, including Ethan the Ezrahite — wiser than Heman, Kalkol and Darda, the sons of Mahol. And his fame spread to all the surrounding nations. ³²He spoke three thousand proverbs and his songs numbered a thousand and five. ³³He spoke about plant life, from the cedar of Lebanon to the hyssop that grows out of walls. He also spoke about animals and birds, reptiles and fish. ³⁴From all nations people came to listen to Solomon's wisdom, sent by all the kings of the world, who had heard of his wisdom.*ᵉ*

Preparations for Building the Temple

5*ᶠ* When Hiram king of Tyre heard that Solomon had been anointed king to succeed his father David, he sent his envoys to Solomon, because he had always been on friendly terms with David. ²Solomon sent back this message to Hiram:

³"You know that because of the wars waged against my father David from all sides, he could not build a temple for the Name of the LORD his God until the LORD put his enemies under his feet. ⁴But now the LORD my God has given me rest on every side, and there is no adversary or disaster. ⁵I intend, therefore, to build a temple for the Name of the LORD my God, as the LORD told my father David, when he said, 'Your son whom I will put on the throne in your place will build the temple for my Name.'

⁶"So give orders that cedars of Lebanon be cut for me. My men will work with yours, and I will pay you for your men whatever wages you set. You know that we have no one so skilled in felling timber as the Sidonians."

⁷When Hiram heard Solomon's message, he was greatly pleased and said, "Praise be to the LORD today, for he has given David a wise son to rule over this great nation."

⁸So Hiram sent word to Solomon:

"I have received the message you sent me and will do all you want in providing the cedar and juniper logs. ⁹My men will haul them down from Lebanon to the Mediterranean Sea, and I will float them as rafts by sea to the place you specify. There I will separate them and you can take them away. And you are to grant my wish by providing food for my royal household."

¹⁰In this way Hiram kept Solomon supplied with all the cedar and juniper logs he wanted, ¹¹and Solomon gave Hiram twenty

---

ᵃ 22 That is, probably about 5 1/2 tons or about 5 metric tons　*ᵇ 22* That is, probably about 11 tons or about 10 metric tons　*ᶜ 26* Some Septuagint manuscripts (see also 2 Chron. 9:25); Hebrew *forty*　*ᵈ 26* Or *charioteers*　*ᵉ 34* In Hebrew texts 4:21-34 is numbered 5:1-14.　*ᶠ* In Hebrew texts 5:1-18 is numbered 5:15-32.

thousand cors[a] of wheat as food for his household, in addition to twenty thousand baths[b,c] of pressed olive oil. Solomon continued to do this for Hiram year after year. [12]The LORD gave Solomon wisdom, just as he had promised him. There were peaceful relations between Hiram and Solomon, and the two of them made a treaty.

[13]King Solomon conscripted laborers from all Israel—thirty thousand men. [14]He sent them off to Lebanon in shifts of ten thousand a month, so that they spent one month in Lebanon and two months at home. Adoniram was in charge of the forced labor. [15]Solomon had seventy thousand carriers and eighty thousand stonecutters in the hills, [16]as well as thirty-three hundred[d] foremen who supervised the project and directed the workers. [17]At the king's command they removed from the quarry large blocks of high-grade stone to provide a foundation of dressed stone for the temple. [18]The craftsmen of Solomon and Hiram and workers from Byblos cut and prepared the timber and stone for the building of the temple.

Solomon Builds the Temple

6 In the four hundred and eightieth[e] year after the Israelites came out of Egypt, in the fourth year of Solomon's reign over Israel, in the month of Ziv, the second month, he began to build the temple of the LORD.

[2]The temple that King Solomon built for the LORD was sixty cubits long, twenty wide and thirty high.[f] [3]The portico at the front of the main hall of the temple extended the width of the temple, that is twenty cubits,[g] and projected ten cubits[h] from the front of the temple. [4]He made narrow windows high up in the temple walls. [5]Against the walls of the main hall and inner sanctuary he built a structure around the building, in which there were side rooms. [6]The lowest floor was five cubits[i] wide, the middle floor six cubits[j] and the third floor seven.[k] He made offset ledges around the outside of the temple so

that nothing would be inserted into the temple walls.

[7]In building the temple, only blocks dressed at the quarry were used, and no hammer, chisel or any other iron tool was heard at the temple site while it was being built.

[8]The entrance to the lowest[l] floor was on the south side of the temple; a stairway led up to the middle level and from there to the third. [9]So he built the temple and completed it, roofing it with beams and cedar planks. [10]And he built the side rooms all along the temple. The height of each was five cubits, and they were attached to the temple by beams of cedar.

[11]The word of the LORD came to Solomon: [12]"As for this temple you are building, if you follow my decrees, observe my laws and keep all my commands and obey them, I will fulfill through you the promise I gave to David your father. [13]And I will live among the Israelites and will not abandon my people Israel."

[14]So Solomon built the temple and completed it. [15]He lined its interior walls with cedar boards, paneling them from the floor of the temple to the ceiling, and covered the floor of the temple with planks of juniper. [16]He partitioned off twenty cubits at the rear of the temple with cedar boards from floor to ceiling to form within the temple an inner sanctuary, the Most Holy Place. [17]The main hall in front of this room was forty cubits[m] long. [18]The inside of the temple was cedar, carved with gourds and open flowers. Everything was cedar; no stone was to be seen.

[19]He prepared the inner sanctuary within the temple to set the ark of the covenant of the LORD there. [20]The inner sanctuary was twenty cubits long, twenty wide and twenty high. He overlaid the inside with pure gold, and he also overlaid the altar of cedar. [21]Solomon covered the inside of the temple with pure gold, and he extended gold chains across the front of the inner sanctuary, which

---

[a] 11 That is, probably about 3,600 tons or about 3,250 metric tons   [b] 11 Septuagint (see also 2 Chron. 2:10); Hebrew *twenty cors*   [c] 11 That is, about 120,000 gallons or about 440,000 liters   [d] 16 Hebrew; some Septuagint manuscripts (see also 2 Chron. 2:2,18) *thirty-six hundred*   [e] 1 Hebrew; Septuagint *four hundred and fortieth*   [f] 2 That is, about 90 feet long, 30 feet wide and 45 feet high or about 27 meters long, 9 meters wide and 14 meters high   [g] 3 That is, about 30 feet or about 9 meters; also in verses 16 and 20   [h] 3 That is, about 15 feet or about 4.5 meters; also in verses 23-26   [i] 6 That is, about 7 1/2 feet or about 2.3 meters; also in verses 10 and 24   [j] 6 That is, about 9 feet or about 2.7 meters   [k] 6 That is, about 11 feet or about 3.2 meters   [l] 8 Septuagint; Hebrew *middle*   [m] 17 That is, about 60 feet or about 18 meters

was overlaid with gold. ²²So he overlaid the whole interior with gold. He also overlaid with gold the altar that belonged to the inner sanctuary.

²³For the inner sanctuary he made a pair of cherubim out of olive wood, each ten cubits high. ²⁴One wing of the first cherub was five cubits long, and the other wing five cubits — ten cubits from wing tip to wing tip. ²⁵The second cherub also measured ten cubits, for the two cherubim were identical in size and shape. ²⁶The height of each cherub was ten cubits. ²⁷He placed the cherubim inside the innermost room of the temple, with their wings spread out. The wing of one cherub touched one wall, while the wing of the other touched the other wall, and their wings touched each other in the middle of the room. ²⁸He overlaid the cherubim with gold.

²⁹On the walls all around the temple, in both the inner and outer rooms, he carved cherubim, palm trees and open flowers. ³⁰He also covered the floors of both the inner and outer rooms of the temple with gold.

³¹For the entrance to the inner sanctuary he made doors out of olive wood that were one fifth of the width of the sanctuary. ³²And on the two olive-wood doors he carved cherubim, palm trees and open flowers, and overlaid the cherubim and palm trees with hammered gold. ³³In the same way, for the entrance to the main hall he made doorframes out of olive wood that were one fourth of the width of the hall. ³⁴He also made two doors out of juniper wood, each having two leaves that turned in sockets. ³⁵He carved cherubim, palm trees and open flowers on them and overlaid them with gold hammered evenly over the carvings.

³⁶And he built the inner courtyard of three courses of dressed stone and one course of trimmed cedar beams.

³⁷The foundation of the temple of the LORD was laid in the fourth year, in the month of Ziv. ³⁸In the eleventh year in the month of Bul, the eighth month, the temple was finished in all its details according to its specifications. He had spent seven years building it.

Solomon Builds His Palace

7 It took Solomon thirteen years, however, to complete the construction of his palace. ²He built the Palace of the Forest of Lebanon a hundred cubits long, fifty wide and thirty high,ᵃ with four rows of cedar columns supporting trimmed cedar beams. ³It was roofed with cedar above the beams that rested on the columns — forty-five beams, fifteen to a row. ⁴Its windows were placed high in sets of three, facing each other. ⁵All the doorways had rectangular frames; they were in the front part in sets of three, facing each other.ᵇ

⁶He made a colonnade fifty cubits long and thirty wide.ᶜ In front of it was a portico, and in front of that were pillars and an overhanging roof.

⁷He built the throne hall, the Hall of Justice, where he was to judge, and he covered it with cedar from floor to ceiling.ᵈ ⁸And the palace in which he was to live, set farther back, was similar in design. Solomon also made a palace like this hall for Pharaoh's daughter, whom he had married.

⁹All these structures, from the outside to the great courtyard and from foundation to eaves, were made of blocks of high-grade stone cut to size and smoothed on their inner and outer faces. ¹⁰The foundations were laid with large stones of good quality, some measuring ten cubitsᵉ and some eight.ᶠ ¹¹Above were high-grade stones, cut to size, and cedar beams. ¹²The great courtyard was surrounded by a wall of three courses of dressed stone and one course of trimmed cedar beams, as was the inner courtyard of the temple of the LORD with its portico.

The Temple's Furnishings

¹³King Solomon sent to Tyre and brought Huram,ᵍ ¹⁴whose mother was a widow from the tribe of Naphtali and whose father was from Tyre and a skilled craftsman in bronze. Huram was filled with wisdom, with understanding and with knowledge to do all kinds of bronze work. He came to King Solomon and did all the work assigned to him.

ᵃ 2 That is, about 150 feet long, 75 feet wide and 45 feet high or about 45 meters long, 23 meters wide and 14 meters high   ᵇ 5 The meaning of the Hebrew for this verse is uncertain.   ᶜ 6 That is, about 75 feet long and 45 feet wide or about 23 meters long and 14 meters wide   ᵈ 7 Vulgate and Syriac; Hebrew *floor*   ᵉ 10 That is, about 15 feet or about 4.5 meters; also in verse 23   ᶠ 10 That is, about 12 feet or about 3.6 meters   ᵍ 13 Hebrew *Hiram,* a variant of *Huram;* also in verses 40 and 45

WORSHIP EVERYWHERE

READ: 1 KINGS 6:38

Seven years is roughly the span you will spend in middle school and high school. It's not forever, but it's hardly the blink of an eye. That's how long Solomon dedicated to building a temple to worship God.

For an Old Testament believer, there was only one correct place to worship. At first, that was the tabernacle, a tent-like worship structure (Exodus 25:1-8). As David settled into his reign as king, he felt embarrassed luxuriating in a palace while the Lord dwelled in a tent. God, however, didn't think it was right for David, a man of war, to build his new home. That job would fall to his son, Solomon (2 Samuel 7:1-17).

BUILDING

FAITH

WISDOM

STRENGTH

Solomon constructed an exquisite building to honor God, filling it with silver and gold and all the furnishings necessary for worship. The temple became the only place on earth where Old Testament believers could legally offer the all-important sacrifices the Lord prescribed. Sacrificing anywhere else was as sinful as worshiping a foreign god.

When Jesus died and rose, he did away not only with having to follow the Old Testament rituals for salvation, but needing to worship in the temple where those rituals took place (Hebrews 10:10-18). Nowadays you might prefer to praise God on a mountain peak, in a stained-glass cathedral or modern auditorium, at school or out in the street. Where you worship isn't important. What matters is that you give God all the honor he deserves.

¹⁵He cast two bronze pillars, each eighteen cubits high and twelve cubits in circumference.ᵃ ¹⁶He also made two capitals of cast bronze to set on the tops of the pillars; each capital was five cubitsᵇ high. ¹⁷A network of interwoven chains adorned the capitals on top of the pillars, seven for each capital. ¹⁸He made pomegranates in two rowsᶜ encircling each network to decorate the capitals on top of the pillars.ᵈ He did the same for each capital. ¹⁹The capitals on top of the pillars in the portico were in the shape of lilies, four cubitsᵉ high. ²⁰On the capitals of both pillars, above the bowl-shaped part next to the network, were the two hundred pomegranates in rows all around. ²¹He erected the pillars at the portico of the temple. The pillar to the south he named Jakinᶠ and the one to the north Boaz.ᵍ ²²The capitals on top were in the shape of lilies. And so the work on the pillars was completed.

²³He made the Sea of cast metal, circular in shape, measuring ten cubits from rim to rim and five cubits high. It took a line of thirty cubitsʰ to measure around it. ²⁴Below the rim, gourds encircled it — ten to a cubit. The gourds were cast in two rows in one piece with the Sea.

²⁵The Sea stood on twelve bulls, three facing north, three facing west, three facing south and three facing east. The Sea rested on top of them, and their hindquarters were toward the center. ²⁶It was a handbreadthⁱ in thickness, and its rim was like the rim of a cup, like a lily blossom. It held two thousand baths.ʲ

²⁷He also made ten movable stands of bronze; each was four cubits long, four wide and three high.ᵏ ²⁸This is how the stands were made: They had side panels attached to uprights. ²⁹On the panels between the uprights were lions, bulls and cherubim — and on the uprights as well. Above and below the lions and bulls were wreaths of hammered work. ³⁰Each stand had four bronze wheels with bronze axles, and each had a basin resting on four supports, cast with wreaths on each side. ³¹On the inside of the stand there was an opening that had a circular frame one cubitˡ deep. This opening was round, and with its basework it measured a cubit and a half.ᵐ Around its opening there was engraving. The panels of the stands were square, not round. ³²The four wheels were under the panels, and the axles of the wheels were attached to the stand. The diameter of each wheel was a cubit and a half. ³³The wheels were made like chariot wheels; the axles, rims, spokes and hubs were all of cast metal.

³⁴Each stand had four handles, one on each corner, projecting from the stand. ³⁵At the top of the stand there was a circular band half a cubitⁿ deep. The supports and panels were attached to the top of the stand. ³⁶He engraved cherubim, lions and palm trees on the surfaces of the supports and on the panels, in every available space, with wreaths all around. ³⁷This is the way he made the ten stands. They were all cast in the same molds and were identical in size and shape.

³⁸He then made ten bronze basins, each holding forty bathsᵒ and measuring four cubits across, one basin to go on each of the ten stands. ³⁹He placed five of the stands on the south side of the temple and five on the north. He placed the Sea on the south side, at the southeast corner of the temple. ⁴⁰He also made the potsᵖ and shovels and sprinkling bowls.

So Huram finished all the work he had undertaken for King Solomon in the temple of the Lord:

ᵃ 15 That is, about 27 feet high and 18 feet in circumference or about 8.1 meters high and 5.4 meters in circumference   ᵇ 16 That is, about 7 1/2 feet or about 2.3 meters; also in verse 23   ᶜ 18 Two Hebrew manuscripts and Septuagint; most Hebrew manuscripts *made the pillars, and there were two rows*   ᵈ 18 Many Hebrew manuscripts and Syriac; most Hebrew manuscripts *pomegranates*   ᵉ 19 That is, about 6 feet or about 1.8 meters; also in verse 38   ᶠ 21 *Jakin* probably means *he establishes.*   ᵍ 21 *Boaz* probably means *in him is strength.*   ʰ 23 That is, about 45 feet or about 14 meters   ⁱ 26 That is, about 3 inches or about 7.5 centimeters   ʲ 26 That is, about 12,000 gallons or about 44,000 liters; the Septuagint does not have this sentence.   ᵏ 27 That is, about 6 feet long and wide and about 4 1/2 feet high or about 1.8 meters long and wide and 1.4 meters high   ˡ 31 That is, about 18 inches or about 45 centimeters   ᵐ 31 That is, about 2 1/4 feet or about 68 centimeters; also in verse 32   ⁿ 35 That is, about 9 inches or about 23 centimeters   ᵒ 38 That is, about 240 gallons or about 880 liters   ᵖ 40 Many Hebrew manuscripts, Septuagint, Syriac and Vulgate (see also verse 45 and 2 Chron. 4:11); many other Hebrew manuscripts *basins*

⁴¹ the two pillars;

the two bowl-shaped capitals on top of
the pillars;

the two sets of network decorating the
two bowl-shaped capitals on top of
the pillars;

⁴² the four hundred pomegranates for
the two sets of network (two rows of
pomegranates for each network decorating the bowl-shaped capitals on
top of the pillars);

⁴³ the ten stands with their ten basins;

⁴⁴ the Sea and the twelve bulls under it;

⁴⁵ the pots, shovels and sprinkling bowls.

All these objects that Huram made for
King Solomon for the temple of the LORD
were of burnished bronze. ⁴⁶The king had
them cast in clay molds in the plain of the
Jordan between Sukkoth and Zarethan.
⁴⁷ Solomon left all these things unweighed,
because there were so many; the weight of
the bronze was not determined.

⁴⁸ Solomon also made all the furnishings
that were in the LORD's temple:

the golden altar;

the golden table on which was the
bread of the Presence;

⁴⁹ the lampstands of pure gold (five on the
right and five on the left, in front of
the inner sanctuary);

the gold floral work and lamps and
tongs;

⁵⁰ the pure gold basins, wick trimmers,
sprinkling bowls, dishes and censers;

and the gold sockets for the doors of
the innermost room, the Most Holy
Place, and also for the doors of the
main hall of the temple.

⁵¹ When all the work King Solomon had
done for the temple of the LORD was finished, he brought in the things his father David had dedicated — the silver and gold and
the furnishings — and he placed them in the
treasuries of the LORD's temple.

The Ark Brought to the Temple

8 Then King Solomon summoned into his
presence at Jerusalem the elders of Israel, all the heads of the tribes and the chiefs
of the Israelite families, to bring up the ark
of the LORD's covenant from Zion, the City
of David. ²All the Israelites came together
to King Solomon at the time of the festival in
the month of Ethanim, the seventh month.

³ When all the elders of Israel had arrived, the priests took up the ark, ⁴and they
brought up the ark of the LORD and the tent
of meeting and all the sacred furnishings in
it. The priests and Levites carried them up,
⁵ and King Solomon and the entire assembly
of Israel that had gathered about him were
before the ark, sacrificing so many sheep
and cattle that they could not be recorded or
counted.

⁶ The priests then brought the ark of the
LORD's covenant to its place in the inner
sanctuary of the temple, the Most Holy Place,
and put it beneath the wings of the cherubim. ⁷The cherubim spread their wings over
the place of the ark and overshadowed the
ark and its carrying poles. ⁸These poles were
so long that their ends could be seen from
the Holy Place in front of the inner sanctuary, but not from outside the Holy Place; and
they are still there today. ⁹There was nothing
in the ark except the two stone tablets that
Moses had placed in it at Horeb, where the
LORD made a covenant with the Israelites after they came out of Egypt.

¹⁰ When the priests withdrew from the
Holy Place, the cloud filled the temple of the
LORD. ¹¹And the priests could not perform
their service because of the cloud, for the
glory of the LORD filled his temple.

¹² Then Solomon said, "The LORD has said
that he would dwell in a dark cloud; ¹³I have
indeed built a magnificent temple for you, a
place for you to dwell forever."

¹⁴ While the whole assembly of Israel was
standing there, the king turned around and
blessed them. ¹⁵Then he said:

"Praise be to the LORD, the God of
Israel, who with his own hand has fulfilled what he promised with his own
mouth to my father David. For he said,
¹⁶ 'Since the day I brought my people
Israel out of Egypt, I have not chosen a
city in any tribe of Israel to have a temple built so that my Name might be
there, but I have chosen David to rule
my people Israel.'

¹⁷ "My father David had it in his heart
to build a temple for the Name of the
LORD, the God of Israel. ¹⁸But the LORD

said to my father David, 'You did well to have it in your heart to build a temple for my Name. ¹⁹Nevertheless, you are not the one to build the temple, but your son, your own flesh and blood—he is the one who will build the temple for my Name.'

²⁰"The LORD has kept the promise he made: I have succeeded David my father and now I sit on the throne of Israel, just as the LORD promised, and I have built the temple for the Name of the LORD, the God of Israel. ²¹I have provided a place there for the ark, in which is the covenant of the LORD that he made with our ancestors when he brought them out of Egypt."

Solomon's Prayer of Dedication

²²Then Solomon stood before the altar of the LORD in front of the whole assembly of Israel, spread out his hands toward heaven ²³and said:

"LORD, the God of Israel, there is no God like you in heaven above or on earth below—you who keep your covenant of love with your servants who continue wholeheartedly in your way. ²⁴You have kept your promise to your servant David my father; with your mouth you have promised and with your hand you have fulfilled it—as it is today.

²⁵"Now LORD, the God of Israel, keep for your servant David my father the promises you made to him when you said, 'You shall never fail to have a successor to sit before me on the throne of Israel, if only your descendants are careful in all they do to walk before me faithfully as you have done.' ²⁶And now, God of Israel, let your word that you promised your servant David my father come true.

²⁷"But will God really dwell on earth? The heavens, even the highest heaven, cannot contain you. How much less this temple I have built! ²⁸Yet give attention to your servant's prayer and his plea for mercy, LORD my God. Hear the cry and the prayer that your servant is praying in your presence this day. ²⁹May your eyes be open toward this temple night and day, this place of which you said, 'My Name shall be there,' so that you will hear the prayer your servant prays toward this place. ³⁰Hear the supplication of your servant and of your people Israel when they pray toward this place. Hear from heaven, your dwelling place, and when you hear, forgive.

³¹"When anyone wrongs their neighbor and is required to take an oath and they come and swear the oath before your altar in this temple, ³²then hear from heaven and act. Judge between your servants, condemning the guilty by bringing down on their heads what they have done, and vindicating the innocent by treating them in accordance with their innocence.

³³"When your people Israel have been defeated by an enemy because they have sinned against you, and when they turn back to you and give praise to your name, praying and making supplication to you in this temple, ³⁴then hear from heaven and forgive the sin of your people Israel and bring them back to the land you gave to their ancestors.

³⁵"When the heavens are shut up and there is no rain because your people have sinned against you, and when they pray toward this place and give praise to your name and turn from their sin because you have afflicted them, ³⁶then hear from heaven and forgive the sin of your servants, your people Israel. Teach them the right way to live, and send rain on the land you gave your people for an inheritance.

³⁷"When famine or plague comes to the land, or blight or mildew, locusts or grasshoppers, or when an enemy besieges them in any of their cities, whatever disaster or disease may come, ³⁸and when a prayer or plea is made by anyone among your people Israel—being aware of the afflictions of their own hearts, and spreading out their hands toward this temple— ³⁹then hear from heaven, your dwelling place. Forgive and act; deal with everyone according to all they do, since you know their hearts (for you alone know every human

heart), ⁴⁰ so that they will fear you all the time they live in the land you gave our ancestors.

⁴¹ "As for the foreigner who does not belong to your people Israel but has come from a distant land because of your name— ⁴² for they will hear of your great name and your mighty hand and your outstretched arm—when they come and pray toward this temple, ⁴³ then hear from heaven, your dwelling place. Do whatever the foreigner asks of you, so that all the peoples of the earth may know your name and fear you, as do your own people Israel, and may know that this house I have built bears your Name.

⁴⁴ "When your people go to war against their enemies, wherever you send them, and when they pray to the LORD toward the city you have chosen and the temple I have built for your Name, ⁴⁵ then hear from heaven their prayer and their plea, and uphold their cause.

⁴⁶ "When they sin against you—for there is no one who does not sin— and you become angry with them and give them over to their enemies, who take them captive to their own lands, far away or near; ⁴⁷ and if they have a change of heart in the land where they are held captive, and repent and plead with you in the land of their captors and say, 'We have sinned, we have done wrong, we have acted wickedly'; ⁴⁸ and if they turn back to you with all their heart and soul in the land of their enemies who took them captive, and pray to you toward the land you gave their ancestors, toward the city you have chosen and the temple I have built for your Name; ⁴⁹ then from heaven, your dwelling place, hear their prayer and their plea, and uphold their cause. ⁵⁰ And forgive your people, who have sinned against you; forgive all the offenses they have committed against you, and cause their captors to show them mercy; ⁵¹ for they are your people and your inheritance, whom you brought out of Egypt, out of that iron-smelting furnace.

⁵² "May your eyes be open to your ser-

vant's plea and to the plea of your people Israel, and may you listen to them whenever they cry out to you. ⁵³ For you singled them out from all the nations of the world to be your own inheritance, just as you declared through your servant Moses when you, Sovereign LORD, brought our ancestors out of Egypt."

⁵⁴ When Solomon had finished all these prayers and supplications to the LORD, he rose from before the altar of the LORD, where he had been kneeling with his hands spread out toward heaven. ⁵⁵ He stood and blessed the whole assembly of Israel in a loud voice, saying:

⁵⁶ "Praise be to the LORD, who has given rest to his people Israel just as he promised. Not one word has failed of all the good promises he gave through his servant Moses. ⁵⁷ May the LORD our God be with us as he was with our ancestors; may he never leave us nor forsake us. ⁵⁸ May he turn our hearts to him, to walk in obedience to him and keep the commands, decrees and laws he gave our ancestors. ⁵⁹ And may these words of mine, which I have prayed before the LORD, be near to the LORD our God day and night, that he may uphold the cause of his servant and the cause of his people Israel according to each day's need, ⁶⁰ so that all the peoples of the earth may know that the LORD is God and that there is no other. ⁶¹ And may your hearts be fully committed to the LORD our God, to live by his decrees and obey his commands, as at this time."

The Dedication of the Temple

⁶² Then the king and all Israel with him offered sacrifices before the LORD. ⁶³ Solomon offered a sacrifice of fellowship offerings to the LORD: twenty-two thousand cattle and a hundred and twenty thousand sheep and goats. So the king and all the Israelites dedicated the temple of the LORD.

⁶⁴ On that same day the king consecrated the middle part of the courtyard in front of the temple of the LORD, and there he offered burnt offerings, grain offerings and the fat of the fellowship offerings, because the bronze altar that stood before the LORD was too

CAN YOU COMMIT?

READ: 1 KINGS 8:58-61

Committed isn't a word that's often used to describe people nowadays. Though perhaps you have grandparents, or perhaps great-grandparents, who were part of what's called the "Greatest Generation"—the one that fought the Second World War. This group of people was known for commitment. They worked one job, lived in one home, and attended one church for the duration of their adulthood. People were committed to companies, communities, congregations, and their families.

In our times, families commonly live a nomadic existence, moving from city to city and from church to church. Our eyes are always on the horizon, looking for the better cell phone, the cuter girlfriend, the happier life. We're always watching for a better deal. We live in a world where "no strings attached" is a popular choice when it comes to relationships. We seem to be a generation with one commitment: keeping our options open.

BUILDING
FAITH
WISDOM
STRENGTH

While keeping our options open is not necessarily all bad, we should recognize that this quality makes it much more difficult to appreciate the seriousness of idolatry. The only relationship God is interested in is one that is exclusive and completely committed. He is not interested in an "open relationship" with you. He won't consider sharing space on the loveseat of your heart. His throne has only one seat.

Who's on it?

small to hold the burnt offerings, the grain offerings and the fat of the fellowship offerings.

[65] So Solomon observed the festival at that time, and all Israel with him—a vast assembly, people from Lebo Hamath to the Wadi of Egypt. They celebrated it before the LORD our God for seven days and seven days more, fourteen days in all. [66] On the following day he sent the people away. They blessed the king and then went home, joyful and glad in heart for all the good things the LORD had done for his servant David and his people Israel.

The LORD Appears to Solomon

9 When Solomon had finished building the temple of the LORD and the royal palace, and had achieved all he had desired to do, [2] the LORD appeared to him a second time, as he had appeared to him at Gibeon. [3] The LORD said to him:

"I have heard the prayer and plea you have made before me; I have consecrated this temple, which you have built, by putting my Name there forever. My eyes and my heart will always be there.

[4] "As for you, if you walk before me faithfully with integrity of heart and uprightness, as David your father did, and do all I command and observe my decrees and laws, [5] I will establish your royal throne over Israel forever, as I promised David your father when I said, 'You shall never fail to have a successor on the throne of Israel.'

[6] "But if you[a] or your descendants turn away from me and do not observe the commands and decrees I have given you[a] and go off to serve other gods and worship them, [7] then I will cut off Israel from the land I have given them and will reject this temple I have consecrated for my Name. Israel will then become a byword and an object of ridicule among all peoples. [8] This temple will become a heap of rubble. All[b] who pass by will be appalled and will scoff and say, 'Why has the LORD done such

a thing to this land and to this temple?' [9] People will answer, 'Because they have forsaken the LORD their God, who brought their ancestors out of Egypt, and have embraced other gods, worshiping and serving them—that is why the LORD brought all this disaster on them.'"

Solomon's Other Activities

[10] At the end of twenty years, during which Solomon built these two buildings—the temple of the LORD and the royal palace—[11] King Solomon gave twenty towns in Galilee to Hiram king of Tyre, because Hiram had supplied him with all the cedar and juniper and gold he wanted. [12] But when Hiram went from Tyre to see the towns that Solomon had given him, he was not pleased with them. [13] "What kind of towns are these you have given me, my brother?" he asked. And he called them the Land of Kabul,[c] a name they have to this day. [14] Now Hiram had sent to the king 120 talents[d] of gold.

[15] Here is the account of the forced labor King Solomon conscripted to build the LORD's temple, his own palace, the terraces,[e] the wall of Jerusalem, and Hazor, Megiddo and Gezer. [16] (Pharaoh king of Egypt had attacked and captured Gezer. He had set it on fire. He killed its Canaanite inhabitants and then gave it as a wedding gift to his daughter, Solomon's wife. [17] And Solomon rebuilt Gezer.) He built up Lower Beth Horon, [18] Baalath, and Tadmor[f] in the desert, within his land, [19] as well as all his store cities and the towns for his chariots and for his horses[g]—whatever he desired to build in Jerusalem, in Lebanon and throughout all the territory he ruled.

[20] There were still people left from the Amorites, Hittites, Perizzites, Hivites and Jebusites (these peoples were not Israelites). [21] Solomon conscripted the descendants of all these peoples remaining in the land—whom the Israelites could not exterminate[h]—to serve as slave labor, as it is to this day. [22] But Solomon did not make slaves of any of the Israelites; they were his fighting

---

[a] 6 The Hebrew is plural.   [b] 8 See some Septuagint manuscripts, Old Latin, Syriac, Arabic and Targum; Hebrew *And though this temple is now imposing, all*   [c] 13 *Kabul* sounds like the Hebrew for *good-for-nothing.*   [d] 14 That is, about 4 1/2 tons or about 4 metric tons   [e] 15 Or *the Millo*; also in verse 24   [f] 18 The Hebrew may also be read *Tamar.*   [g] 19 Or *charioteers*   [h] 21 The Hebrew term refers to the irrevocable giving over of things or persons to the LORD, often by totally destroying them.

men, his government officials, his officers, his captains, and the commanders of his chariots and charioteers. ²³They were also the chief officials in charge of Solomon's projects — 550 officials supervising those who did the work.

²⁴After Pharaoh's daughter had come up from the City of David to the palace Solomon had built for her, he constructed the terraces.

²⁵Three times a year Solomon sacrificed burnt offerings and fellowship offerings on the altar he had built for the LORD, burning incense before the LORD along with them, and so fulfilled the temple obligations.

²⁶King Solomon also built ships at Ezion Geber, which is near Elath in Edom, on the shore of the Red Sea.ᵃ ²⁷And Hiram sent his men — sailors who knew the sea — to serve in the fleet with Solomon's men. ²⁸They sailed to Ophir and brought back 420 talentsᵇ of gold, which they delivered to King Solomon.

The Queen of Sheba Visits Solomon

10 When the queen of Sheba heard about the fame of Solomon and his relationship to the LORD, she came to test Solomon with hard questions. ²Arriving at Jerusalem with a very great caravan — with camels carrying spices, large quantities of gold, and precious stones — she came to Solomon and talked with him about all that she had on her mind. ³Solomon answered all her questions; nothing was too hard for the king to explain to her. ⁴When the queen of Sheba saw all the wisdom of Solomon and the palace he had built, ⁵the food on his table, the seating of his officials, the attending servants in their robes, his cupbearers, and the burnt offerings he made atᶜ the temple of the LORD, she was overwhelmed.

⁶She said to the king, "The report I heard in my own country about your achievements and your wisdom is true. ⁷But I did not believe these things until I came and saw with my own eyes. Indeed, not even half was told me; in wisdom and wealth you have

far exceeded the report I heard. ⁸How happy your people must be! How happy your officials, who continually stand before you and hear your wisdom! ⁹Praise be to the LORD your God, who has delighted in you and placed you on the throne of Israel. Because of the LORD's eternal love for Israel, he has made you king to maintain justice and righteousness."

¹⁰And she gave the king 120 talentsᵈ of gold, large quantities of spices, and precious stones. Never again were so many spices brought in as those the queen of Sheba gave to King Solomon.

¹¹(Hiram's ships brought gold from Ophir; and from there they brought great cargoes of almugwoodᵉ and precious stones. ¹²The king used the almugwood to make supportsᶠ for the temple of the LORD and for the royal palace, and to make harps and lyres for the musicians. So much almugwood has never been imported or seen since that day.)

¹³King Solomon gave the queen of Sheba all she desired and asked for, besides what he had given her out of his royal bounty. Then she left and returned with her retinue to her own country.

Solomon's Splendor

¹⁴The weight of the gold that Solomon received yearly was 666 talents,ᵍ ¹⁵not including the revenues from merchants and traders and from all the Arabian kings and the governors of the territories.

¹⁶King Solomon made two hundred large shields of hammered gold; six hundred shekelsʰ of gold went into each shield. ¹⁷He also made three hundred small shields of hammered gold, with three minasⁱ of gold in each shield. The king put them in the Palace of the Forest of Lebanon.

¹⁸Then the king made a great throne covered with ivory and overlaid with fine gold. ¹⁹The throne had six steps, and its back had a rounded top. On both sides of the seat were armrests, with a lion standing beside each of them. ²⁰Twelve lions stood on the six steps, one at either end of each step. Nothing like it

---

ᵃ 26 Or the Sea of Reeds   ᵇ 28 That is, about 16 tons or about 14 metric tons   ᶜ 5 Or the ascent by which he went up to   ᵈ 10 That is, about 4 1/2 tons or about 4 metric tons   ᵉ 11 Probably a variant of algumwood; also in verse 12   ᶠ 12 The meaning of the Hebrew for this word is uncertain.   ᵍ 14 That is, about 25 tons or about 23 metric tons   ʰ 16 That is, about 15 pounds or about 6.9 kilograms; also in verse 29   ⁱ 17 That is, about 3 3/4 pounds or about 1.7 kilograms; or perhaps reference is to double minas, that is, about 7 1/2 pounds or about 3.5 kilograms.

had ever been made for any other kingdom. [21] All King Solomon's goblets were gold, and all the household articles in the Palace of the Forest of Lebanon were pure gold. Nothing was made of silver, because silver was considered of little value in Solomon's days. [22] The king had a fleet of trading ships[a] at sea along with the ships of Hiram. Once every three years it returned, carrying gold, silver and ivory, and apes and baboons.

[23] King Solomon was greater in riches and wisdom than all the other kings of the earth. [24] The whole world sought audience with Solomon to hear the wisdom God had put in his heart. [25] Year after year, everyone who came brought a gift — articles of silver and gold, robes, weapons and spices, and horses and mules.

[26] Solomon accumulated chariots and horses; he had fourteen hundred chariots and twelve thousand horses,[b] which he kept in the chariot cities and also with him in Jerusalem. [27] The king made silver as common in Jerusalem as stones, and cedar as plentiful as sycamore-fig trees in the foothills. [28] Solomon's horses were imported from Egypt and from Kue[c] — the royal merchants purchased them from Kue at the current price. [29] They imported a chariot from Egypt for six hundred shekels of silver, and a horse for a hundred and fifty.[d] They also exported them to all the kings of the Hittites and of the Arameans.

Solomon's Wives

11 King Solomon, however, loved many foreign women besides Pharaoh's daughter — Moabites, Ammonites, Edomites, Sidonians and Hittites. [2] They were from nations about which the LORD had told the Israelites, "You must not intermarry with them, because they will surely turn your hearts after their gods." Nevertheless, Solomon held fast to them in love. [3] He had seven hundred wives of royal birth and three hundred concubines, and his wives led him astray. [4] As Solomon grew old, his wives turned his heart after other gods, and his heart was not fully devoted to the LORD his God, as the heart of David his father had been. [5] He followed Ashtoreth the goddess of the Sidonians, and Molek the detestable god of the Ammonites. [6] So

Solomon did evil in the eyes of the LORD; he did not follow the LORD completely, as David his father had done.

[7] On a hill east of Jerusalem, Solomon built a high place for Chemosh the detestable god of Moab, and for Molek the detestable god of the Ammonites. [8] He did the same for all his foreign wives, who burned incense and offered sacrifices to their gods.

[9] The LORD became angry with Solomon because his heart had turned away from the LORD, the God of Israel, who had appeared to him twice. [10] Although he had forbidden Solomon to follow other gods, Solomon did not keep the LORD's command. [11] So the LORD said to Solomon, "Since this is your attitude and you have not kept my covenant and my decrees, which I commanded you, I will most certainly tear the kingdom away from you and give it to one of your subordinates. [12] Nevertheless, for the sake of David your father, I will not do it during your lifetime. I will tear it out of the hand of your son. [13] Yet I will not tear the whole kingdom from him, but will give him one tribe for the sake of David my servant and for the sake of Jerusalem, which I have chosen."

Solomon's Adversaries

[14] Then the LORD raised up against Solomon an adversary, Hadad the Edomite, from the royal line of Edom. [15] Earlier when David was fighting with Edom, Joab the commander of the army, who had gone up to bury the dead, had struck down all the men in Edom. [16] Joab and all the Israelites stayed there for six months, until they had destroyed all the men in Edom. [17] But Hadad, still only a boy, fled to Egypt with some Edomite officials who had served his father. [18] They set out from Midian and went to Paran. Then taking people from Paran with them, they went to Egypt, to Pharaoh king of Egypt, who gave Hadad a house and land and provided him with food.

[19] Pharaoh was so pleased with Hadad that he gave him a sister of his own wife, Queen Tahpenes, in marriage. [20] The sister of Tahpenes bore him a son named Genubath, whom Tahpenes brought up in the royal palace. There Genubath lived with Pharaoh's own children.

---

[a] 22 Hebrew *of ships of Tarshish*   [b] 26 Or *charioteers*   [c] 28 Probably *Cilicia*   [d] 29 That is, about 3 3/4 pounds or about 1.7 kilograms

GOOD CONNECTIONS

READ: 1 KINGS 11:4

One glance at the Ten Commandments tells you instantly what matters most to God.

Rule number one: "You shall have no other gods before me" (Exodus 20:3). If you aim to put God first, then you guard against anything that can knock him out of that top spot, like falling for girls not totally devoted to him.

In the Old Testament the Lord laid down clear rules against marrying worshipers of other gods. He said, "Do not intermarry with them. Do not give your daughters to their sons or take their daughters for your sons, for they will turn your children away from following me to serve other gods" (Deuteronomy 7:3–4). And the Lord didn't drop that rule in the New Testament. The apostle Paul writes, "Do not be yoked together with unbelievers. For what do righteousness and wickedness have in common? Or what fellowship can light have with darkness?" (2 Corinthians 6:14).

Solomon brought catastrophe on himself by disobeying that core command. Having hundreds of wives wasn't against the law in his day. But when his foreign wives pulled him into sin, the Lord ripped away most of his kingdom.

You're not likely looking for a spouse right now, but the principle still applies. If you bind yourself to nonbelievers—like you do in dating, marriage, and some other partnerships and friendships—you risk everything that matters most.

BUILDING
FAITH
WISDOM
STRENGTH

²¹While he was in Egypt, Hadad heard that David rested with his ancestors and that Joab the commander of the army was also dead. Then Hadad said to Pharaoh, "Let me go, that I may return to my own country."

²²"What have you lacked here that you want to go back to your own country?" Pharaoh asked.

"Nothing," Hadad replied, "but do let me go!"

²³And God raised up against Solomon another adversary, Rezon son of Eliada, who had fled from his master, Hadadezer king of Zobah. ²⁴When David destroyed Zobah's army, Rezon gathered a band of men around him and became their leader; they went to Damascus, where they settled and took control. ²⁵Rezon was Israel's adversary as long as Solomon lived, adding to the trouble caused by Hadad. So Rezon ruled in Aram and was hostile toward Israel.

Jeroboam Rebels Against Solomon

²⁶Also, Jeroboam son of Nebat rebelled against the king. He was one of Solomon's officials, an Ephraimite from Zeredah, and his mother was a widow named Zeruah.

²⁷Here is the account of how he rebelled against the king: Solomon had built the terraces*ᵃ* and had filled in the gap in the wall of the city of David his father. ²⁸Now Jeroboam was a man of standing, and when Solomon saw how well the young man did his work, he put him in charge of the whole labor force of the tribes of Joseph.

²⁹About that time Jeroboam was going out of Jerusalem, and Ahijah the prophet of Shiloh met him on the way, wearing a new cloak. The two of them were alone out in the country, ³⁰and Ahijah took hold of the new cloak he was wearing and tore it into twelve pieces. ³¹Then he said to Jeroboam, "Take ten pieces for yourself, for this is what the LORD, the God of Israel, says: 'See, I am going to tear the kingdom out of Solomon's hand and give you ten tribes. ³²But for the sake of my servant David and the city of Jerusalem, which I have chosen out of all the tribes of Israel, he will have one tribe. ³³I will do this because they have*ᵇ* forsaken me and worshiped Ashtoreth the goddess of the Sidonians, Chemosh the god of the Moabites, and

Molek the god of the Ammonites, and have not walked in obedience to me, nor done what is right in my eyes, nor kept my decrees and laws as David, Solomon's father, did.

³⁴"'But I will not take the whole kingdom out of Solomon's hand; I have made him ruler all the days of his life for the sake of David my servant, whom I chose and who obeyed my commands and decrees. ³⁵I will take the kingdom from his son's hands and give you ten tribes. ³⁶I will give one tribe to his son so that David my servant may always have a lamp before me in Jerusalem, the city where I chose to put my Name. ³⁷However, as for you, I will take you, and you will rule over all that your heart desires; you will be king over Israel. ³⁸If you do whatever I command you and walk in obedience to me and do what is right in my eyes by obeying my decrees and commands, as David my servant did, I will be with you. I will build you a dynasty as enduring as the one I built for David and will give Israel to you. ³⁹I will humble David's descendants because of this, but not forever.'"

⁴⁰Solomon tried to kill Jeroboam, but Jeroboam fled to Egypt, to Shishak the king, and stayed there until Solomon's death.

Solomon's Death

⁴¹As for the other events of Solomon's reign—all he did and the wisdom he displayed—are they not written in the book of the annals of Solomon? ⁴²Solomon reigned in Jerusalem over all Israel forty years. ⁴³Then he rested with his ancestors and was buried in the city of David his father. And Rehoboam his son succeeded him as king.

Israel Rebels Against Rehoboam

12 Rehoboam went to Shechem, for all Israel had gone there to make him king. ²When Jeroboam son of Nebat heard this (he was still in Egypt, where he had fled from King Solomon), he returned from*ᶜ* Egypt. ³So they sent for Jeroboam, and he and the whole assembly of Israel went to Rehoboam and said to him: ⁴"Your father put a heavy yoke on us, but now lighten the harsh labor and the heavy yoke he put on us, and we will serve you."

⁵Rehoboam answered, "Go away for three

days and then come back to me." So the people went away.

⁶Then King Rehoboam consulted the elders who had served his father Solomon during his lifetime. "How would you advise me to answer these people?" he asked.

⁷They replied, "If today you will be a servant to these people and serve them and give them a favorable answer, they will always be your servants."

⁸But Rehoboam rejected the advice the elders gave him and consulted the young men who had grown up with him and were serving him. ⁹He asked them, "What is your advice? How should we answer these people who say to me, 'Lighten the yoke your father put on us'?"

¹⁰The young men who had grown up with him replied, "These people have said to you, 'Your father put a heavy yoke on us, but make our yoke lighter.' Now tell them, 'My little finger is thicker than my father's waist. ¹¹My father laid on you a heavy yoke; I will make it even heavier. My father scourged you with whips; I will scourge you with scorpions.'"

¹²Three days later Jeroboam and all the people returned to Rehoboam, as the king had said, "Come back to me in three days." ¹³The king answered the people harshly. Rejecting the advice given him by the elders, ¹⁴he followed the advice of the young men and said, "My father made your yoke heavy; I will make it even heavier. My father scourged you with whips; I will scourge you with scorpions." ¹⁵So the king did not listen to the people, for this turn of events was from the LORD, to fulfill the word the LORD had spoken to Jeroboam son of Nebat through Ahijah the Shilonite.

¹⁶When all Israel saw that the king refused to listen to them, they answered the king:

"What share do we have in David,
    what part in Jesse's son?
To your tents, Israel!
    Look after your own house, David!"

So the Israelites went home. ¹⁷But as for the Israelites who were living in the towns of Judah, Rehoboam still ruled over them.

¹⁸King Rehoboam sent out Adoniram,ᵃ who was in charge of forced labor, but all Israel stoned him to death. King Rehoboam, however, managed to get into his chariot and escape to Jerusalem. ¹⁹So Israel has been in rebellion against the house of David to this day.

²⁰When all the Israelites heard that Jeroboam had returned, they sent and called him to the assembly and made him king over all Israel. Only the tribe of Judah remained loyal to the house of David.

²¹When Rehoboam arrived in Jerusalem, he mustered all Judah and the tribe of Benjamin—a hundred and eighty thousand able young men—to go to war against Israel and to regain the kingdom for Rehoboam son of Solomon.

²²But this word of God came to Shemaiah the man of God: ²³"Say to Rehoboam son of Solomon king of Judah, to all Judah and Benjamin, and to the rest of the people, ²⁴'This is what the LORD says: Do not go up to fight against your brothers, the Israelites. Go home, every one of you, for this is my doing.'" So they obeyed the word of the LORD and went home again, as the LORD had ordered.

Golden Calves at Bethel and Dan

²⁵Then Jeroboam fortified Shechem in the hill country of Ephraim and lived there. From there he went out and built up Peniel.ᵇ

²⁶Jeroboam thought to himself, "The kingdom will now likely revert to the house of David. ²⁷If these people go up to offer sacrifices at the temple of the LORD in Jerusalem, they will again give their allegiance to their lord, Rehoboam king of Judah. They will kill me and return to King Rehoboam."

²⁸After seeking advice, the king made two golden calves. He said to the people, "It is too much for you to go up to Jerusalem. Here are your gods, Israel, who brought you up out of Egypt." ²⁹One he set up in Bethel, and the other in Dan. ³⁰And this thing became a sin; the people came to worship the one at Bethel and went as far as Dan to worship the other.ᶜ

³¹Jeroboam built shrines on high places and appointed priests from all sorts of people, even though they were not Levites. ³²He instituted a festival on the fifteenth day of the eighth month, like the festival held in Judah,

---

ᵃ 18 Some Septuagint manuscripts and Syriac (see also 4:6 and 5:14); Hebrew *Adoram*   ᵇ 25 Hebrew *Penuel*, a variant of *Peniel*   ᶜ 30 Probable reading of the original Hebrew text; Masoretic Text *people went to the one as far as Dan* and offered sacrifices on the altar. This he did in Bethel, sacrificing to the calves he had made. And at Bethel he also installed priests at the high places he had made. ³³On the fifteenth day of the eighth month, a month of his own choosing, he offered sacrifices on the altar he had built at Bethel. So he instituted the festival for the Israelites and went up to the altar to make offerings.

The Man of God From Judah

13 By the word of the LORD a man of God came from Judah to Bethel, as Jeroboam was standing by the altar to make an offering. ²By the word of the LORD he cried out against the altar: "Altar, altar! This is what the LORD says: 'A son named Josiah will be born to the house of David. On you he will sacrifice the priests of the high places who make offerings here, and human bones will be burned on you.'" ³That same day the man of God gave a sign: "This is the sign the LORD has declared: The altar will be split apart and the ashes on it will be poured out."

⁴When King Jeroboam heard what the man of God cried out against the altar at Bethel, he stretched out his hand from the altar and said, "Seize him!" But the hand he stretched out toward the man shriveled up, so that he could not pull it back. ⁵Also, the altar was split apart and its ashes poured out according to the sign given by the man of God by the word of the LORD.

⁶Then the king said to the man of God, "Intercede with the LORD your God and pray for me that my hand may be restored." So the man of God interceded with the LORD, and the king's hand was restored and became as it was before.

⁷The king said to the man of God, "Come home with me for a meal, and I will give you a gift."

⁸But the man of God answered the king, "Even if you were to give me half your possessions, I would not go with you, nor would I eat bread or drink water here. ⁹For I was commanded by the word of the LORD: 'You must not eat bread or drink water or return by the way you came.'" ¹⁰So he took another road and did not return by the way he had come to Bethel.

¹¹Now there was a certain old prophet living in Bethel, whose sons came and told him all that the man of God had done there

that day. They also told their father what he had said to the king. ¹²Their father asked them, "Which way did he go?" And his sons showed him which road the man of God from Judah had taken. ¹³So he said to his sons, "Saddle the donkey for me." And when they had saddled the donkey for him, he mounted it ¹⁴and rode after the man of God. He found him sitting under an oak tree and asked, "Are you the man of God who came from Judah?"

"I am," he replied.

¹⁵So the prophet said to him, "Come home with me and eat."

¹⁶The man of God said, "I cannot turn back and go with you, nor can I eat bread or drink water with you in this place. ¹⁷I have been told by the word of the LORD: 'You must not eat bread or drink water there or return by the way you came.'"

¹⁸The old prophet answered, "I too am a prophet, as you are. And an angel said to me by the word of the LORD: 'Bring him back with you to your house so that he may eat bread and drink water.'" (But he was lying to him.) ¹⁹So the man of God returned with him and ate and drank in his house.

²⁰While they were sitting at the table, the word of the LORD came to the old prophet who had brought him back. ²¹He cried out to the man of God who had come from Judah, "This is what the LORD says: 'You have defied the word of the LORD and have not kept the command the LORD your God gave you. ²²You came back and ate bread and drank water in the place where he told you not to eat or drink. Therefore your body will not be buried in the tomb of your ancestors.'"

²³When the man of God had finished eating and drinking, the prophet who had brought him back saddled his donkey for him. ²⁴As he went on his way, a lion met him on the road and killed him, and his body was left lying on the road, with both the donkey and the lion standing beside it. ²⁵Some people who passed by saw the body lying there, with the lion standing beside the body, and they went and reported it in the city where the old prophet lived.

²⁶When the prophet who had brought him back from his journey heard of it, he said, "It is the man of God who defied the word of the LORD. The LORD has given him over to the lion, which has mauled him and killed him, as the word of the LORD had warned him."

PRAYER ORIGINS

READ: 1 KINGS 13:6, 18:36

Every miracle has a genealogy. If you trace those miracles all the way back to their origin, you'll find prayer. Miracles are the by-product of prayers that were prayed by you or for you. And that should be all the motivation you need to pray. God has determined that certain expressions of his power will only be exercised in response to prayer. Simply put, God won't do it unless you pray for it. We have not because we ask not. The greatest tragedy in life is the prayers that go unanswered because they go unasked.

Now here's the good news: If you do pray, all bets are off. You aren't called to live in the shadow of doubt. Instead, you can live with a holy anticipation because you never know how or when or where God is going to answer your prayers. But I promise you this: He will answer.

He may not answer when or how you want. But it will be the right answer at the right time. And his answers are not limited by your requests. We pray out of our ignorance, but God answers out of his omniscience. We pray out of our limited human understanding, but God answers out of his unlimited knowledge. God has the ability to answer the prayers we should have prayed but lacked the knowledge or ability to even ask.

BUILDING FAITH WISDOM STRENGTH

²⁷The prophet said to his sons, "Saddle the donkey for me," and they did so. ²⁸Then he went out and found the body lying on the road, with the donkey and the lion standing beside it. The lion had neither eaten the body nor mauled the donkey. ²⁹So the prophet picked up the body of the man of God, laid it on the donkey, and brought it back to his own city to mourn for him and bury him. ³⁰Then he laid the body in his own tomb, and they mourned over him and said, "Alas, my brother!"

³¹After burying him, he said to his sons, "When I die, bury me in the grave where the man of God is buried; lay my bones beside his bones. ³²For the message he declared by the word of the LORD against the altar in Bethel and against all the shrines on the high places in the towns of Samaria will certainly come true."

³³Even after this, Jeroboam did not change his evil ways, but once more appointed priests for the high places from all sorts of people. Anyone who wanted to become a priest he consecrated for the high places. ³⁴This was the sin of the house of Jeroboam that led to its downfall and to its destruction from the face of the earth.

Ahijah's Prophecy Against Jeroboam

14 At that time Abijah son of Jeroboam became ill, ²and Jeroboam said to his wife, "Go, disguise yourself, so you won't be recognized as the wife of Jeroboam. Then go to Shiloh. Ahijah the prophet is there — the one who told me I would be king over this people. ³Take ten loaves of bread with you, some cakes and a jar of honey, and go to him. He will tell you what will happen to the boy." ⁴So Jeroboam's wife did what he said and went to Ahijah's house in Shiloh.

Now Ahijah could not see; his sight was gone because of his age. ⁵But the LORD had told Ahijah, "Jeroboam's wife is coming to ask you about her son, for he is ill, and you are to give her such and such an answer. When she arrives, she will pretend to be someone else."

⁶So when Ahijah heard the sound of her footsteps at the door, he said, "Come in, wife of Jeroboam. Why this pretense? I have been sent to you with bad news. ⁷Go, tell Jeroboam that this is what the LORD, the God of Israel, says: 'I raised you up from among the people and appointed you ruler over my people Israel. ⁸I tore the kingdom away from the house of David and gave it to you, but you have not been like my servant David, who kept my commands and followed me with all his heart, doing only what was right in my eyes. ⁹You have done more evil than all who lived before you. You have made for yourself other gods, idols made of metal; you have aroused my anger and turned your back on me.

¹⁰ "'Because of this, I am going to bring disaster on the house of Jeroboam. I will cut off from Jeroboam every last male in Israel — slave or free.ᵃ I will burn up the house of Jeroboam as one burns dung, until it is all gone. ¹¹Dogs will eat those belonging to Jeroboam who die in the city, and the birds will feed on those who die in the country. The LORD has spoken!'

¹²"As for you, go back home. When you set foot in your city, the boy will die. ¹³All Israel will mourn for him and bury him. He is the only one belonging to Jeroboam who will be buried, because he is the only one in the house of Jeroboam in whom the LORD, the God of Israel, has found anything good.

¹⁴"The LORD will raise up for himself a king over Israel who will cut off the family of Jeroboam. Even now this is beginning to happen.ᵇ ¹⁵And the LORD will strike Israel, so that it will be like a reed swaying in the water. He will uproot Israel from this good land that he gave to their ancestors and scatter them beyond the Euphrates River, because they aroused the LORD's anger by making Asherah poles.ᶜ ¹⁶And he will give Israel up because of the sins Jeroboam has committed and has caused Israel to commit."

¹⁷Then Jeroboam's wife got up and left and went to Tirzah. As soon as she stepped over the threshold of the house, the boy died. ¹⁸They buried him, and all Israel mourned for him, as the LORD had said through his servant the prophet Ahijah.

¹⁹The other events of Jeroboam's reign, his wars and how he ruled, are written in the book of the annals of the kings of Israel. ²⁰He reigned for twenty-two years and then rested with his ancestors. And Nadab his son succeeded him as king.

ᵃ10 Or Israel — every ruler or leader   ᵇ 14 The meaning of the Hebrew for this sentence is uncertain.
ᶜ 15 That is, wooden symbols of the goddess Asherah; here and elsewhere in 1 Kings

Rehoboam King of Judah

²¹Rehoboam son of Solomon was king in Judah. He was forty-one years old when he became king, and he reigned seventeen years in Jerusalem, the city the LORD had chosen out of all the tribes of Israel in which to put his Name. His mother's name was Naamah; she was an Ammonite.

²²Judah did evil in the eyes of the LORD. By the sins they committed they stirred up his jealous anger more than those who were before them had done. ²³They also set up for themselves high places, sacred stones and Asherah poles on every high hill and under every spreading tree. ²⁴There were even male shrine prostitutes in the land; the people engaged in all the detestable practices of the nations the LORD had driven out before the Israelites.

²⁵In the fifth year of King Rehoboam, Shishak king of Egypt attacked Jerusalem. ²⁶He carried off the treasures of the temple of the LORD and the treasures of the royal palace. He took everything, including all the gold shields Solomon had made. ²⁷So King Rehoboam made bronze shields to replace them and assigned these to the commanders of the guard on duty at the entrance to the royal palace. ²⁸Whenever the king went to the LORD's temple, the guards bore the shields, and afterward they returned them to the guardroom.

²⁹As for the other events of Rehoboam's reign, and all he did, are they not written in the book of the annals of the kings of Judah? ³⁰There was continual warfare between Rehoboam and Jeroboam. ³¹And Rehoboam rested with his ancestors and was buried with them in the City of David. His mother's name was Naamah; she was an Ammonite. And Abijah[a] his son succeeded him as king.

Abijah King of Judah

15 In the eighteenth year of the reign of Jeroboam son of Nebat, Abijah[b] became king of Judah, ²and he reigned in Jerusalem three years. His mother's name was Maakah daughter of Abishalom.[c]

³He committed all the sins his father had done before him; his heart was not fully devoted to the LORD his God, as the heart of David his forefather had been. ⁴Nevertheless, for David's sake the LORD his God gave him a lamp in Jerusalem by raising up a son to succeed him and by making Jerusalem strong. ⁵For David had done what was right in the eyes of the LORD and had not failed to keep any of the LORD's commands all the days of his life — except in the case of Uriah the Hittite.

⁶There was war between Abijah[d] and Jeroboam throughout Abijah's lifetime. ⁷As for the other events of Abijah's reign, and all he did, are they not written in the book of the annals of the kings of Judah? There was war between Abijah and Jeroboam. ⁸And Abijah rested with his ancestors and was buried in the City of David. And Asa his son succeeded him as king.

Asa King of Judah

⁹In the twentieth year of Jeroboam king of Israel, Asa became king of Judah, ¹⁰and he reigned in Jerusalem forty-one years. His grandmother's name was Maakah daughter of Abishalom.

¹¹Asa did what was right in the eyes of the LORD, as his father David had done. ¹²He expelled the male shrine prostitutes from the land and got rid of all the idols his ancestors had made. ¹³He even deposed his grandmother Maakah from her position as queen mother, because she had made a repulsive image for the worship of Asherah. Asa cut it down and burned it in the Kidron Valley. ¹⁴Although he did not remove the high places, Asa's heart was fully committed to the LORD all his life. ¹⁵He brought into the temple of the LORD the silver and gold and the articles that he and his father had dedicated.

¹⁶There was war between Asa and Baasha king of Israel throughout their reigns. ¹⁷Baasha king of Israel went up against Judah and fortified Ramah to prevent anyone from leaving or entering the territory of Asa king of Judah.

¹⁸Asa then took all the silver and gold that was left in the treasuries of the LORD's temple and of his own palace. He entrusted it to his officials and sent them to Ben-Hadad son

---

a 31 Some Hebrew manuscripts and Septuagint (see also 2 Chron. 12:16); most Hebrew manuscripts *Abijam*   *b 1* Some Hebrew manuscripts and Septuagint (see also 2 Chron. 12:16); most Hebrew manuscripts *Abijam*; also in verses 7 and 8   *c 2* A variant of *Absalom*; also in verse 10   *d 6* Some Hebrew manuscripts and Syriac *Abijam* (that is, Abijah); most Hebrew manuscripts *Rehoboam* of Tabrimmon, the son of Hezion, the king of Aram, who was ruling in Damascus. ¹⁹"Let there be a treaty between me and you," he said, "as there was between my father and your father. See, I am sending you a gift of silver and gold. Now break your treaty with Baasha king of Israel so he will withdraw from me."

²⁰Ben-Hadad agreed with King Asa and sent the commanders of his forces against the towns of Israel. He conquered Ijon, Dan, Abel Beth Maakah and all Kinnereth in addition to Naphtali. ²¹When Baasha heard this, he stopped building Ramah and withdrew to Tirzah. ²²Then King Asa issued an order to all Judah — no one was exempt — and they carried away from Ramah the stones and timber Baasha had been using there. With them King Asa built up Geba in Benjamin, and also Mizpah.

²³As for all the other events of Asa's reign, all his achievements, all he did and the cities he built, are they not written in the book of the annals of the kings of Judah? In his old age, however, his feet became diseased. ²⁴Then Asa rested with his ancestors and was buried with them in the city of his father David. And Jehoshaphat his son succeeded him as king.

Nadab King of Israel

²⁵Nadab son of Jeroboam became king of Israel in the second year of Asa king of Judah, and he reigned over Israel two years. ²⁶He did evil in the eyes of the LORD, following the ways of his father and committing the same sin his father had caused Israel to commit.

²⁷Baasha son of Ahijah from the tribe of Issachar plotted against him, and he struck him down at Gibbethon, a Philistine town, while Nadab and all Israel were besieging it. ²⁸Baasha killed Nadab in the third year of Asa king of Judah and succeeded him as king.

²⁹As soon as he began to reign, he killed Jeroboam's whole family. He did not leave Jeroboam anyone that breathed, but destroyed them all, according to the word of the LORD given through his servant Ahijah the Shilonite. ³⁰This happened because of the sins Jeroboam had committed and had caused Israel to commit, and because he aroused the anger of the LORD, the God of Israel.

³¹As for the other events of Nadab's reign, and all he did, are they not written in the book of the annals of the kings of Israel? ³²There was war between Asa and Baasha king of Israel throughout their reigns.

Baasha King of Israel

³³In the third year of Asa king of Judah, Baasha son of Ahijah became king of all Israel in Tirzah, and he reigned twenty-four years. ³⁴He did evil in the eyes of the LORD, following the ways of Jeroboam and committing the same sin Jeroboam had caused Israel to commit.

16 Then the word of the LORD came to Jehu son of Hanani concerning Baasha: ²"I lifted you up from the dust and appointed you ruler over my people Israel, but you followed the ways of Jeroboam and caused my people Israel to sin and to arouse my anger by their sins. ³So I am about to wipe out Baasha and his house, and I will make your house like that of Jeroboam son of Nebat. ⁴Dogs will eat those belonging to Baasha who die in the city, and birds will feed on those who die in the country."

⁵As for the other events of Baasha's reign, what he did and his achievements, are they not written in the book of the annals of the kings of Israel? ⁶Baasha rested with his ancestors and was buried in Tirzah. And Elah his son succeeded him as king.

⁷Moreover, the word of the LORD came through the prophet Jehu son of Hanani to Baasha and his house, because of all the evil he had done in the eyes of the LORD, arousing his anger by the things he did, becoming like the house of Jeroboam — and also because he destroyed it.

Elah King of Israel

⁸In the twenty-sixth year of Asa king of Judah, Elah son of Baasha became king of Israel, and he reigned in Tirzah two years.

⁹Zimri, one of his officials, who had command of half his chariots, plotted against him. Elah was in Tirzah at the time, getting drunk in the home of Arza, the palace administrator at Tirzah. ¹⁰Zimri came in, struck him down and killed him in the twenty-seventh year of Asa king of Judah. Then he succeeded him as king.

¹¹As soon as he began to reign and was seated on the throne, he killed off Baasha's

whole family. He did not spare a single male, whether relative or friend. ¹²So Zimri destroyed the whole family of Baasha, in accordance with the word of the LORD spoken against Baasha through the prophet Jehu— ¹³because of all the sins Baasha and his son Elah had committed and had caused Israel to commit, so that they aroused the anger of the LORD, the God of Israel, by their worthless idols.

¹⁴As for the other events of Elah's reign, and all he did, are they not written in the book of the annals of the kings of Israel?

Zimri King of Israel

¹⁵In the twenty-seventh year of Asa king of Judah, Zimri reigned in Tirzah seven days. The army was encamped near Gibbethon, a Philistine town. ¹⁶When the Israelites in the camp heard that Zimri had plotted against the king and murdered him, they proclaimed Omri, the commander of the army, king over Israel that very day there in the camp. ¹⁷Then Omri and all the Israelites with him withdrew from Gibbethon and laid siege to Tirzah. ¹⁸When Zimri saw that the city was taken, he went into the citadel of the royal palace and set the palace on fire around him. So he died, ¹⁹because of the sins he had committed, doing evil in the eyes of the LORD and following the ways of Jeroboam and committing the same sin Jeroboam had caused Israel to commit.

²⁰As for the other events of Zimri's reign, and the rebellion he carried out, are they not written in the book of the annals of the kings of Israel?

Omri King of Israel

²¹Then the people of Israel were split into two factions; half supported Tibni son of Ginath for king, and the other half supported Omri. ²²But Omri's followers proved stronger than those of Tibni son of Ginath. So Tibni died and Omri became king.

²³In the thirty-first year of Asa king of Judah, Omri became king of Israel, and he reigned twelve years, six of them in Tirzah. ²⁴He bought the hill of Samaria from Shemer for two talents[a] of silver and built a city on the hill, calling it Samaria, after Shemer, the name of the former owner of the hill.

²⁵But Omri did evil in the eyes of the LORD and sinned more than all those before him. ²⁶He followed completely the ways of Jeroboam son of Nebat, committing the same sin Jeroboam had caused Israel to commit, so that they aroused the anger of the LORD, the God of Israel, by their worthless idols.

²⁷As for the other events of Omri's reign, what he did and the things he achieved, are they not written in the book of the annals of the kings of Israel? ²⁸Omri rested with his ancestors and was buried in Samaria. And Ahab his son succeeded him as king.

Ahab Becomes King of Israel

²⁹In the thirty-eighth year of Asa king of Judah, Ahab son of Omri became king of Israel, and he reigned in Samaria over Israel twenty-two years. ³⁰Ahab son of Omri did more evil in the eyes of the LORD than any of those before him. ³¹He not only considered it trivial to commit the sins of Jeroboam son of Nebat, but he also married Jezebel daughter of Ethbaal king of the Sidonians, and began to serve Baal and worship him. ³²He set up an altar for Baal in the temple of Baal that he built in Samaria. ³³Ahab also made an Asherah pole and did more to arouse the anger of the LORD, the God of Israel, than did all the kings of Israel before him.

³⁴In Ahab's time, Hiel of Bethel rebuilt Jericho. He laid its foundations at the cost of his firstborn son Abiram, and he set up its gates at the cost of his youngest son Segub, in accordance with the word of the LORD spoken by Joshua son of Nun.

Elijah Announces a Great Drought

17 Now Elijah the Tishbite, from Tishbe[b] in Gilead, said to Ahab, "As the LORD, the God of Israel, lives, whom I serve, there will be neither dew nor rain in the next few years except at my word."

Elijah Fed by Ravens

²Then the word of the LORD came to Elijah: ³"Leave here, turn eastward and hide in the Kerith Ravine, east of the Jordan. ⁴You will drink from the brook, and I have directed the ravens to supply you with food there." ⁵So he did what the LORD had told him. He went to the Kerith Ravine, east of the Jordan,

---

ᵃ 24 That is, about 150 pounds or about 68 kilograms   ᵇ 1 Or *Tishbite, of the settlers* and stayed there. [6]The ravens brought him bread and meat in the morning and bread and meat in the evening, and he drank from the brook.

Elijah and the Widow at Zarephath

[7]Some time later the brook dried up because there had been no rain in the land. [8]Then the word of the LORD came to him: [9]"Go at once to Zarephath in the region of Sidon and stay there. I have directed a widow there to supply you with food." [10]So he went to Zarephath. When he came to the town gate, a widow was there gathering sticks. He called to her and asked, "Would you bring me a little water in a jar so I may have a drink?" [11]As she was going to get it, he called, "And bring me, please, a piece of bread."

[12]"As surely as the LORD your God lives," she replied, "I don't have any bread—only a handful of flour in a jar and a little olive oil in a jug. I am gathering a few sticks to take home and make a meal for myself and my son, that we may eat it—and die."

[13]Elijah said to her, "Don't be afraid. Go home and do as you have said. But first make a small loaf of bread for me from what you have and bring it to me, and then make something for yourself and your son. [14]For this is what the LORD, the God of Israel, says: 'The jar of flour will not be used up and the jug of oil will not run dry until the day the LORD sends rain on the land.'"

[15]She went away and did as Elijah had told her. So there was food every day for Elijah and for the woman and her family. [16]For the jar of flour was not used up and the jug of oil did not run dry, in keeping with the word of the LORD spoken by Elijah.

[17]Some time later the son of the woman who owned the house became ill. He grew worse and worse, and finally stopped breathing. [18]She said to Elijah, "What do you have against me, man of God? Did you come to remind me of my sin and kill my son?"

[19]"Give me your son," Elijah replied. He took him from her arms, carried him to the upper room where he was staying, and laid him on his bed. [20]Then he cried out to the LORD, "LORD my God, have you brought tragedy even on this widow I am staying with, by causing her son to die?" [21]Then he stretched himself out on the boy three times and cried out to the LORD, "LORD my God, let this boy's life return to him!"

[22]The LORD heard Elijah's cry, and the boy's life returned to him, and he lived. [23]Elijah picked up the child and carried him down from the room into the house. He gave him to his mother and said, "Look, your son is alive!"

[24]Then the woman said to Elijah, "Now I know that you are a man of God and that the word of the LORD from your mouth is the truth."

Elijah and Obadiah

18 After a long time, in the third year, the word of the LORD came to Elijah: "Go and present yourself to Ahab, and I will send rain on the land." [2]So Elijah went to present himself to Ahab.

Now the famine was severe in Samaria, [3]and Ahab had summoned Obadiah, his palace administrator. (Obadiah was a devout believer in the LORD. [4]While Jezebel was killing off the LORD's prophets, Obadiah had taken a hundred prophets and hidden them in two caves, fifty in each, and had supplied them with food and water.) [5]Ahab had said to Obadiah, "Go through the land to all the springs and valleys. Maybe we can find some grass to keep the horses and mules alive so we will not have to kill any of our animals." [6]So they divided the land they were to cover, Ahab going in one direction and Obadiah in another.

[7]As Obadiah was walking along, Elijah met him. Obadiah recognized him, bowed down to the ground, and said, "Is it really you, my lord Elijah?"

[8]"Yes," he replied. "Go tell your master, 'Elijah is here.'"

[9]"What have I done wrong," asked Obadiah, "that you are handing your servant over to Ahab to be put to death? [10]As surely as the LORD your God lives, there is not a nation or kingdom where my master has not sent someone to look for you. And whenever a nation or kingdom claimed you were not there, he made them swear they could not find you. [11]But now you tell me to go to my master and say, 'Elijah is here.' [12]I don't know where the Spirit of the LORD may carry you when I leave you. If I go and tell Ahab and he doesn't find you, he will kill me. Yet I your servant have worshiped the LORD since my

ELIJAH

Elijah said to them, "I am the only one of the LORD's prophets left, but Baal has four hundred and fifty prophets." 1 KINGS 18:22

HIS NAME MEANS: "the LORD is my God"
READ HIS STORY: *1 Kings 17–19; 21; 2 Kings 2*

Have you ever felt alone in your faith? The prophet Elijah felt that way. He lived when King Ahab "did more to arouse the anger of the LORD, the God of Israel, than did all the kings of Israel before him" (1 Kings 16:33). And it's not like the other kings were stand-up guys. But Ahab was evil. He and Queen Jezebel killed God's prophets, built altars to false gods and led the people away from the Lord.

God called Elijah to go before Ahab and tell him it wouldn't rain in Israel for years. This didn't make Elijah very popular. But the Lord hid Elijah in a ravine so he was safe from danger. Ravens brought him bread and meat. Elijah drank from a brook to quench his thirst. About three years passed without rain before the Lord led Elijah back to Ahab. Elijah told Ahab to gather the people to witness a holy smackdown on Mount Carmel (1 Kings 18:16–40). On one side, Elijah. On the other, 450 prophets of Baal and 400 prophets of Asherah, a goddess affiliated with Baal. The challenge: sacrifice a bull and see which god answers with fire.

It was a slaughter. Literally. The Lord answered Elijah's prayer with an all-consuming blaze. The people saw the truth and killed the false prophets.

Elijah is possibly the most famous prophet who ever lived, but we don't know much about where he came from. We do know where he went. After faithfully serving the Lord and mentoring Elisha, Elijah was swept by a fiery chariot into heaven (2 Kings 2:11).

youth. ¹³Haven't you heard, my lord, what I did while Jezebel was killing the prophets of the LORD? I hid a hundred of the LORD's prophets in two caves, fifty in each, and supplied them with food and water. ¹⁴And now you tell me to go to my master and say, 'Elijah is here.' He will kill me!"

¹⁵Elijah said, "As the LORD Almighty lives, whom I serve, I will surely present myself to Ahab today."

Elijah on Mount Carmel

¹⁶So Obadiah went to meet Ahab and told him, and Ahab went to meet Elijah. ¹⁷When he saw Elijah, he said to him, "Is that you, you troubler of Israel?"

¹⁸"I have not made trouble for Israel," Elijah replied. "But you and your father's family have. You have abandoned the LORD's commands and have followed the Baals. ¹⁹Now summon the people from all over Israel to meet me on Mount Carmel. And bring the four hundred and fifty prophets of Baal and the four hundred prophets of Asherah, who eat at Jezebel's table."

²⁰So Ahab sent word throughout all Israel and assembled the prophets on Mount Carmel. ²¹Elijah went before the people and said, "How long will you waver between two opinions? If the LORD is God, follow him; but if Baal is God, follow him."

But the people said nothing.

²²Then Elijah said to them, "I am the only one of the LORD's prophets left, but Baal has four hundred and fifty prophets. ²³Get two bulls for us. Let Baal's prophets choose one for themselves, and let them cut it into pieces and put it on the wood but not set fire to it. I will prepare the other bull and put it on the wood but not set fire to it. ²⁴Then you call on the name of your god, and I will call on the name of the LORD. The god who answers by fire—he is God."

Then all the people said, "What you say is good."

²⁵Elijah said to the prophets of Baal, "Choose one of the bulls and prepare it first, since there are so many of you. Call on the name of your god, but do not light the fire." ²⁶So they took the bull given them and prepared it.

Then they called on the name of Baal from morning till noon. "Baal, answer us!" they shouted. But there was no response; no one answered. And they danced around the altar they had made.

²⁷At noon Elijah began to taunt them. "Shout louder!" he said. "Surely he is a god! Perhaps he is deep in thought, or busy, or traveling. Maybe he is sleeping and must be awakened." ²⁸So they shouted louder and slashed themselves with swords and spears, as was their custom, until their blood flowed. ²⁹Midday passed, and they continued their frantic prophesying until the time for the evening sacrifice. But there was no response, no one answered, no one paid attention.

³⁰Then Elijah said to all the people, "Come here to me." They came to him, and he repaired the altar of the LORD, which had been torn down. ³¹Elijah took twelve stones, one for each of the tribes descended from Jacob, to whom the word of the LORD had come, saying, "Your name shall be Israel." ³²With the stones he built an altar in the name of the LORD, and he dug a trench around it large enough to hold two seahs*a* of seed. ³³He arranged the wood, cut the bull into pieces and laid it on the wood. Then he said to them, "Fill four large jars with water and pour it on the offering and on the wood."

³⁴"Do it again," he said, and they did it again.

"Do it a third time," he ordered, and they did it the third time. ³⁵The water ran down around the altar and even filled the trench.

³⁶At the time of sacrifice, the prophet Elijah stepped forward and prayed: "LORD, the God of Abraham, Isaac and Israel, let it be known today that you are God in Israel and that I am your servant and have done all these things at your command. ³⁷Answer me, LORD, answer me, so these people will know that you, LORD, are God, and that you are turning their hearts back again."

³⁸Then the fire of the LORD fell and burned up the sacrifice, the wood, the stones and the soil, and also licked up the water in the trench.

³⁹When all the people saw this, they fell prostrate and cried, "The LORD—he is God! The LORD—he is God!"

⁴⁰Then Elijah commanded them, "Seize the prophets of Baal. Don't let anyone get

---

a 32 That is, probably about 24 pounds or about 11 kilograms

DOUBLE, TRIPLE, QUADRUPLE CHECK

READ: 1 KINGS 18:41-45

For three long years, there was no puddle jumping in Israel. Then the Lord promised Elijah that he would send rain, but like every good promise, Elijah still had to circle it with persistent prayer. Most of us would give up right around two or three times, right? We can't see any real difference with our natural eyes, so we stop praying. But when we do that, we allow our circumstances to get between God and us instead of putting God between us and our circumstances.

Elijah held his holy ground. He stood on the promise God had given him. I think Elijah would have prayed ten thousand times if that's what it took, but between the sixth and seventh prayer, there was a subtle shift in atmospheric pressure. Elijah's nearsighted servant strained his eyes and saw a small cloud the size of a man's hand rising from the sea.

What if Elijah had quit praying after the sixth time? The miracle would have been forfeited, of course.

It's easy to give up on dreams, miracles, and promises. We lose heart, lose patience, lose faith. Worst part is, it's like a slow leak; it happens without us even knowing, until our prayer life is completely flat. The reason many of us give up too soon is that we feel like we've failed somehow if God doesn't answer our prayer. That isn't failure. The only way you can fail is if you stop praying. I love that approach to prayer. I love that approach to life too!

BUILDING FAITH WISDOM STRENGTH

Taken from *The Circle Maker Student Edition* by Mark Batterson with Parker Batterson, copyright © 2012 by Mark Batterson, published by Zondervan.

away!" They seized them, and Elijah had them brought down to the Kishon Valley and slaughtered there.

⁴¹And Elijah said to Ahab, "Go, eat and drink, for there is the sound of a heavy rain." ⁴²So Ahab went off to eat and drink, but Elijah climbed to the top of Carmel, bent down to the ground and put his face between his knees.

⁴³"Go and look toward the sea," he told his servant. And he went up and looked.

"There is nothing there," he said.

Seven times Elijah said, "Go back."

⁴⁴The seventh time the servant reported, "A cloud as small as a man's hand is rising from the sea."

So Elijah said, "Go and tell Ahab, 'Hitch up your chariot and go down before the rain stops you.'"

⁴⁵Meanwhile, the sky grew black with clouds, the wind rose, a heavy rain started falling and Ahab rode off to Jezreel. ⁴⁶The power of the LORD came on Elijah and, tucking his cloak into his belt, he ran ahead of Ahab all the way to Jezreel.

Elijah Flees to Horeb

19 Now Ahab told Jezebel everything Elijah had done and how he had killed all the prophets with the sword. ²So Jezebel sent a messenger to Elijah to say, "May the gods deal with me, be it ever so severely, if by this time tomorrow I do not make your life like that of one of them."

³Elijah was afraid*ᵃ* and ran for his life. When he came to Beersheba in Judah, he left his servant there, ⁴while he himself went a day's journey into the wilderness. He came to a broom bush, sat down under it and prayed that he might die. "I have had enough, LORD," he said. "Take my life; I am no better than my ancestors." ⁵Then he lay down under the bush and fell asleep.

All at once an angel touched him and said, "Get up and eat." ⁶He looked around, and there by his head was some bread baked over hot coals, and a jar of water. He ate and drank and then lay down again.

⁷The angel of the LORD came back a second time and touched him and said, "Get up and eat, for the journey is too much for you." ⁸So he got up and ate and drank. Strength-

ened by that food, he traveled forty days and forty nights until he reached Horeb, the mountain of God. ⁹There he went into a cave and spent the night.

The LORD Appears to Elijah

And the word of the LORD came to him: "What are you doing here, Elijah?"

¹⁰He replied, "I have been very zealous for the LORD God Almighty. The Israelites have rejected your covenant, torn down your altars, and put your prophets to death with the sword. I am the only one left, and now they are trying to kill me too."

¹¹The LORD said, "Go out and stand on the mountain in the presence of the LORD, for the LORD is about to pass by."

Then a great and powerful wind tore the mountains apart and shattered the rocks before the LORD, but the LORD was not in the wind. After the wind there was an earthquake, but the LORD was not in the earthquake. ¹²After the earthquake came a fire, but the LORD was not in the fire. And after the fire came a gentle whisper. ¹³When Elijah heard it, he pulled his cloak over his face and went out and stood at the mouth of the cave.

Then a voice said to him, "What are you doing here, Elijah?"

¹⁴He replied, "I have been very zealous for the LORD God Almighty. The Israelites have rejected your covenant, torn down your altars, and put your prophets to death with the sword. I am the only one left, and now they are trying to kill me too."

¹⁵The LORD said to him, "Go back the way you came, and go to the Desert of Damascus. When you get there, anoint Hazael king over Aram. ¹⁶Also, anoint Jehu son of Nimshi king over Israel, and anoint Elisha son of Shaphat from Abel Meholah to succeed you as prophet. ¹⁷Jehu will put to death any who escape the sword of Hazael, and Elisha will put to death any who escape the sword of Jehu. ¹⁸Yet I reserve seven thousand in Israel—all whose knees have not bowed down to Baal and whose mouths have not kissed him."

The Call of Elisha

¹⁹So Elijah went from there and found Elisha son of Shaphat. He was plowing with

---

ᵃ 3 Or *Elijah saw*

THE LET DOWN

READ: 1 KINGS 19:10

Nothing makes you want to give up on following God like feeling as if you're all alone. That's how the prophet Elijah felt after his spectacular clash with the prophets of the false god Baal.

Elijah appeared on the scene in 1 Kings 17 to confront the evil king Ahab, who gave Baal equal status with the Lord. Because of this terrible sin, Elijah vowed that no rain would fall in Israel until he called for it (v. 1).

Three years later, the land was parched and the nation starving. Then Elijah threw down a challenge to hundreds of prophets of Baal and Asherah. He assembled a large sacrifice and invited his opponents to do the same. When their gods didn't answer loud prayers to set their offering ablaze, the Lord sent fire that consumed not only Elijah's sacrifice but a water-drenched wood and rock altar.

BUILDING FAITH WISDOM STRENGTH

After that confrontation, Elijah fled for his life. He soon found himself alone and despairing, convinced he was the only one who followed God. But the Lord didn't leave Elijah to suffer alone. He gave the prophet food and rest. He made a stunning appearance and promised to give Elijah an assistant and thousands of others to support him.

When you commit your life to God, you're never as alone as you might fear. God himself is with you, and he will surround you with others who follow him too.

twelve yoke of oxen, and he himself was driving the twelfth pair. Elijah went up to him and threw his cloak around him. ²⁰Elisha then left his oxen and ran after Elijah. "Let me kiss my father and mother goodbye," he said, "and then I will come with you."

"Go back," Elijah replied. "What have I done to you?"

²¹So Elisha left him and went back. He took his yoke of oxen and slaughtered them. He burned the plowing equipment to cook the meat and gave it to the people, and they ate. Then he set out to follow Elijah and became his servant.

Ben-Hadad Attacks Samaria

20 Now Ben-Hadad king of Aram mustered his entire army. Accompanied by thirty-two kings with their horses and chariots, he went up and besieged Samaria and attacked it. ²He sent messengers into the city to Ahab king of Israel, saying, "This is what Ben-Hadad says: ³'Your silver and gold are mine, and the best of your wives and children are mine.'"

⁴The king of Israel answered, "Just as you say, my lord the king. I and all I have are yours."

⁵The messengers came again and said, "This is what Ben-Hadad says: 'I sent to demand your silver and gold, your wives and your children. ⁶But about this time tomorrow I am going to send my officials to search your palace and the houses of your officials. They will seize everything you value and carry it away.'"

⁷The king of Israel summoned all the elders of the land and said to them, "See how this man is looking for trouble! When he sent for my wives and my children, my silver and my gold, I did not refuse him."

⁸The elders and the people all answered, "Don't listen to him or agree to his demands."

⁹So he replied to Ben-Hadad's messengers, "Tell my lord the king, 'Your servant will do all you demanded the first time, but this demand I cannot meet.'" They left and took the answer back to Ben-Hadad.

¹⁰Then Ben-Hadad sent another message to Ahab: "May the gods deal with me, be it ever so severely, if enough dust remains in Samaria to give each of my men a handful."

¹¹The king of Israel answered, "Tell him: 'One who puts on his armor should not boast like one who takes it off.'"

¹²Ben-Hadad heard this message while he and the kings were drinking in their tents,^a and he ordered his men: "Prepare to attack." So they prepared to attack the city.

Ahab Defeats Ben-Hadad

¹³Meanwhile a prophet came to Ahab king of Israel and announced, "This is what the LORD says: 'Do you see this vast army? I will give it into your hand today, and then you will know that I am the LORD.'"

¹⁴"But who will do this?" asked Ahab.

The prophet replied, "This is what the LORD says: 'The junior officers under the provincial commanders will do it.'"

"And who will start the battle?" he asked.

The prophet answered, "You will."

¹⁵So Ahab summoned the 232 junior officers under the provincial commanders. Then he assembled the rest of the Israelites, 7,000 in all. ¹⁶They set out at noon while Ben-Hadad and the 32 kings allied with him were in their tents getting drunk. ¹⁷The junior officers under the provincial commanders went out first.

Now Ben-Hadad had dispatched scouts, who reported, "Men are advancing from Samaria."

¹⁸He said, "If they have come out for peace, take them alive; if they have come out for war, take them alive."

¹⁹The junior officers under the provincial commanders marched out of the city with the army behind them ²⁰and each one struck down his opponent. At that, the Arameans fled, with the Israelites in pursuit. But Ben-Hadad king of Aram escaped on horseback with some of his horsemen. ²¹The king of Israel advanced and overpowered the horses and chariots and inflicted heavy losses on the Arameans.

²²Afterward, the prophet came to the king of Israel and said, "Strengthen your position and see what must be done, because next spring the king of Aram will attack you again."

²³Meanwhile, the officials of the king of Aram advised him, "Their gods are gods of the hills. That is why they were too strong for

---

^a 12 Or *in Sukkoth*; also in verse 16

BURN IT ALL

READ: 1 KINGS 19:21

There are moments when we need to burn the ships of our past—eliminating the possibility of sailing back to the old world we left behind. You burn the ships named Past Failure and Past Success. You burn the ship named Bad Habit. You burn the ship named Regret. You burn the ship named Guilt.

That is precisely what Elisha did when he turned his plowing equipment into kindling and barbequed his oxen. He said bye-bye to his old life by throwing a party for his friends. They shared a meal and stories into the wee hours. But the bonfire made it the most meaningful night of his life.

Burning the plowing equipment was Elisha's way of burning the ships. He couldn't go back because he destroyed the stuff he needed to go back. Elisha the farmer was finished. This was the beginning of Elisha the prophet.

It doesn't matter whether you're trying to lose weight, get into a school, or write a book. The first step is always the longest and the hardest. You wonder why you keep hooking up with your ex? Because you text her all day! Delete the number from your phone.

Stop and think about the symbolism of what Elisha did. He literally cooked his old way of life and ate it for dinner. And forgive me if this is taking it too far, but after digesting it, he definitely got his "old ways" out of his system.

You've got to eliminate the possibility of moving backward into the past. Burn 'em, baby.

BUILDING FAITH WISDOM STRENGTH

us. But if we fight them on the plains, surely we will be stronger than they. ²⁴Do this: Remove all the kings from their commands and replace them with other officers. ²⁵You must also raise an army like the one you lost—horse for horse and chariot for chariot—so we can fight Israel on the plains. Then surely we will be stronger than they." He agreed with them and acted accordingly.

²⁶The next spring Ben-Hadad mustered the Arameans and went up to Aphek to fight against Israel. ²⁷When the Israelites were also mustered and given provisions, they marched out to meet them. The Israelites camped opposite them like two small flocks of goats, while the Arameans covered the countryside.

²⁸The man of God came up and told the king of Israel, "This is what the Lord says: 'Because the Arameans think the Lord is a god of the hills and not a god of the valleys, I will deliver this vast army into your hands, and you will know that I am the Lord.'"

²⁹For seven days they camped opposite each other, and on the seventh day the battle was joined. The Israelites inflicted a hundred thousand casualties on the Aramean foot soldiers in one day. ³⁰The rest of them escaped to the city of Aphek, where the wall collapsed on twenty-seven thousand of them. And Ben-Hadad fled to the city and hid in an inner room.

³¹His officials said to him, "Look, we have heard that the kings of Israel are merciful. Let us go to the king of Israel with sackcloth around our waists and ropes around our heads. Perhaps he will spare your life."

³²Wearing sackcloth around their waists and ropes around their heads, they went to the king of Israel and said, "Your servant Ben-Hadad says: 'Please let me live.'"

The king answered, "Is he still alive? He is my brother."

³³The men took this as a good sign and were quick to pick up his word. "Yes, your brother Ben-Hadad!" they said.

"Go and get him," the king said. When Ben-Hadad came out, Ahab had him come up into his chariot.

³⁴"I will return the cities my father took from your father," Ben-Hadad offered. "You may set up your own market areas in Damascus, as my father did in Samaria."

Ahab said, "On the basis of a treaty I will set you free." So he made a treaty with him, and let him go.

A Prophet Condemns Ahab

³⁵By the word of the Lord one of the company of the prophets said to his companion, "Strike me with your weapon," but he refused.

³⁶So the prophet said, "Because you have not obeyed the Lord, as soon as you leave me a lion will kill you." And after the man went away, a lion found him and killed him.

³⁷The prophet found another man and said, "Strike me, please." So the man struck him and wounded him. ³⁸Then the prophet went and stood by the road waiting for the king. He disguised himself with his headband down over his eyes. ³⁹As the king passed by, the prophet called out to him, "Your servant went into the thick of the battle, and someone came to me with a captive and said, 'Guard this man. If he is missing, it will be your life for his life, or you must pay a talent^a of silver.' ⁴⁰While your servant was busy here and there, the man disappeared."

"That is your sentence," the king of Israel said. "You have pronounced it yourself."

⁴¹Then the prophet quickly removed the headband from his eyes, and the king of Israel recognized him as one of the prophets. ⁴²He said to the king, "This is what the Lord says: 'You have set free a man I had determined should die.^b Therefore it is your life for his life, your people for his people.'" ⁴³Sullen and angry, the king of Israel went to his palace in Samaria.

Naboth's Vineyard

21 Some time later there was an incident involving a vineyard belonging to Naboth the Jezreelite. The vineyard was in Jezreel, close to the palace of Ahab king of Samaria. ²Ahab said to Naboth, "Let me have your vineyard to use for a vegetable garden, since it is close to my palace. In exchange I will give you a better vineyard or, if you prefer, I will pay you whatever it is worth."

³But Naboth replied, "The Lord forbid that I should give you the inheritance of my ancestors."

---

^a 39 That is, about 75 pounds or about 34 kilograms   ^b 42 The Hebrew term refers to the irrevocable giving over of things or persons to the Lord, often by totally destroying them.

⁴So Ahab went home, sullen and angry because Naboth the Jezreelite had said, "I will not give you the inheritance of my ancestors." He lay on his bed sulking and refused to eat.

⁵His wife Jezebel came in and asked him, "Why are you so sullen? Why won't you eat?"

⁶He answered her, "Because I said to Naboth the Jezreelite, 'Sell me your vineyard; or if you prefer, I will give you another vineyard in its place.' But he said, 'I will not give you my vineyard.'"

⁷Jezebel his wife said, "Is this how you act as king over Israel? Get up and eat! Cheer up. I'll get you the vineyard of Naboth the Jezreelite."

⁸So she wrote letters in Ahab's name, placed his seal on them, and sent them to the elders and nobles who lived in Naboth's city with him. ⁹In those letters she wrote:

> "Proclaim a day of fasting and seat Naboth in a prominent place among the people. ¹⁰But seat two scoundrels opposite him and have them bring charges that he has cursed both God and the king. Then take him out and stone him to death."

¹¹So the elders and nobles who lived in Naboth's city did as Jezebel directed in the letters she had written to them. ¹²They proclaimed a fast and seated Naboth in a prominent place among the people. ¹³Then two scoundrels came and sat opposite him and brought charges against Naboth before the people, saying, "Naboth has cursed both God and the king." So they took him outside the city and stoned him to death. ¹⁴Then they sent word to Jezebel: "Naboth has been stoned to death."

¹⁵As soon as Jezebel heard that Naboth had been stoned to death, she said to Ahab, "Get up and take possession of the vineyard of Naboth the Jezreelite that he refused to sell you. He is no longer alive, but dead." ¹⁶When Ahab heard that Naboth was dead, he got up and went down to take possession of Naboth's vineyard.

¹⁷Then the word of the LORD came to Elijah the Tishbite: ¹⁸"Go down to meet Ahab king of Israel, who rules in Samaria. He is now in Naboth's vineyard, where he has gone to take possession of it. ¹⁹Say to him, 'This is what the LORD says: Have you not murdered a man and seized his property?' Then say to him, 'This is what the LORD says: In the place where dogs licked up Naboth's blood, dogs will lick up your blood—yes, yours!'"

²⁰Ahab said to Elijah, "So you have found me, my enemy!"

"I have found you," he answered, "because you have sold yourself to do evil in the eyes of the LORD. ²¹He says, 'I am going to bring disaster on you. I will wipe out your descendants and cut off from Ahab every last male in Israel—slave or free.ᵃ ²²I will make your house like that of Jeroboam son of Nebat and that of Baasha son of Ahijah, because you have aroused my anger and have caused Israel to sin.'

²³"And also concerning Jezebel the LORD says: 'Dogs will devour Jezebel by the wall ofᵇ Jezreel.'

²⁴"Dogs will eat those belonging to Ahab who die in the city, and the birds will feed on those who die in the country."

²⁵(There was never anyone like Ahab, who sold himself to do evil in the eyes of the LORD, urged on by Jezebel his wife. ²⁶He behaved in the vilest manner by going after idols, like the Amorites the LORD drove out before Israel.)

²⁷When Ahab heard these words, he tore his clothes, put on sackcloth and fasted. He lay in sackcloth and went around meekly.

²⁸Then the word of the LORD came to Elijah the Tishbite: ²⁹"Have you noticed how Ahab has humbled himself before me? Because he has humbled himself, I will not bring this disaster in his day, but I will bring it on his house in the days of his son."

Micaiah Prophesies Against Ahab

22 For three years there was no war between Aram and Israel. ²But in the third year Jehoshaphat king of Judah went down to see the king of Israel. ³The king of Israel had said to his officials, "Don't you know that Ramoth Gilead belongs to us and yet we are doing nothing to retake it from the king of Aram?"

⁴So he asked Jehoshaphat, "Will you go with me to fight against Ramoth Gilead?"

ᵃ 21 Or *Israel—every ruler or leader*   ᵇ 23 Most Hebrew manuscripts; a few Hebrew manuscripts, Vulgate and Syriac (see also 2 Kings 9:26) *the plot of ground at*

Jehoshaphat replied to the king of Israel, "I am as you are, my people as your people, my horses as your horses." ⁵But Jehoshaphat also said to the king of Israel, "First seek the counsel of the LORD."

⁶So the king of Israel brought together the prophets — about four hundred men — and asked them, "Shall I go to war against Ramoth Gilead, or shall I refrain?"

"Go," they answered, "for the Lord will give it into the king's hand."

⁷But Jehoshaphat asked, "Is there no longer a prophet of the LORD here whom we can inquire of?"

⁸The king of Israel answered Jehoshaphat, "There is still one prophet through whom we can inquire of the LORD, but I hate him because he never prophesies anything good about me, but always bad. He is Micaiah son of Imlah."

"The king should not say such a thing," Jehoshaphat replied.

⁹So the king of Israel called one of his officials and said, "Bring Micaiah son of Imlah at once."

¹⁰Dressed in their royal robes, the king of Israel and Jehoshaphat king of Judah were sitting on their thrones at the threshing floor by the entrance of the gate of Samaria, with all the prophets prophesying before them. ¹¹Now Zedekiah son of Kenaanah had made iron horns and he declared, "This is what the LORD says: 'With these you will gore the Arameans until they are destroyed.'"

¹²All the other prophets were prophesying the same thing. "Attack Ramoth Gilead and be victorious," they said, "for the LORD will give it into the king's hand."

¹³The messenger who had gone to summon Micaiah said to him, "Look, the other prophets without exception are predicting success for the king. Let your word agree with theirs, and speak favorably."

¹⁴But Micaiah said, "As surely as the LORD lives, I can tell him only what the LORD tells me."

¹⁵When he arrived, the king asked him, "Micaiah, shall we go to war against Ramoth Gilead, or not?"

"Attack and be victorious," he answered, "for the LORD will give it into the king's hand."

¹⁶The king said to him, "How many times must I make you swear to tell me nothing but the truth in the name of the LORD?"

¹⁷Then Micaiah answered, "I saw all Israel scattered on the hills like sheep without a shepherd, and the LORD said, 'These people have no master. Let each one go home in peace.'"

¹⁸The king of Israel said to Jehoshaphat, "Didn't I tell you that he never prophesies anything good about me, but only bad?"

¹⁹Micaiah continued, "Therefore hear the word of the LORD: I saw the LORD sitting on his throne with all the multitudes of heaven standing around him on his right and on his left. ²⁰And the LORD said, 'Who will entice Ahab into attacking Ramoth Gilead and going to his death there?'

"One suggested this, and another that. ²¹Finally, a spirit came forward, stood before the LORD and said, 'I will entice him.'

²²"'By what means?' the LORD asked.

"'I will go out and be a deceiving spirit in the mouths of all his prophets,' he said.

"'You will succeed in enticing him,' said the LORD. 'Go and do it.'

²³"So now the LORD has put a deceiving spirit in the mouths of all these prophets of yours. The LORD has decreed disaster for you."

²⁴Then Zedekiah son of Kenaanah went up and slapped Micaiah in the face. "Which way did the spirit from*ᵃ* the LORD go when he went from me to speak to you?" he asked.

²⁵Micaiah replied, "You will find out on the day you go to hide in an inner room."

²⁶The king of Israel then ordered, "Take Micaiah and send him back to Amon the ruler of the city and to Joash the king's son ²⁷and say, 'This is what the king says: Put this fellow in prison and give him nothing but bread and water until I return safely.'"

²⁸Micaiah declared, "If you ever return safely, the LORD has not spoken through me." Then he added, "Mark my words, all you people!"

Ahab Killed at Ramoth Gilead

²⁹So the king of Israel and Jehoshaphat king of Judah went up to Ramoth Gilead. ³⁰The king of Israel said to Jehoshaphat, "I will enter the battle in disguise, but you wear

---

ᵃ 24 Or *Spirit of*

your royal robes." So the king of Israel disguised himself and went into battle.

³¹Now the king of Aram had ordered his thirty-two chariot commanders, "Do not fight with anyone, small or great, except the king of Israel." ³²When the chariot commanders saw Jehoshaphat, they thought, "Surely this is the king of Israel." So they turned to attack him, but when Jehoshaphat cried out, ³³the chariot commanders saw that he was not the king of Israel and stopped pursuing him.

³⁴But someone drew his bow at random and hit the king of Israel between the sections of his armor. The king told his chariot driver, "Wheel around and get me out of the fighting. I've been wounded." ³⁵All day long the battle raged, and the king was propped up in his chariot facing the Arameans. The blood from his wound ran onto the floor of the chariot, and that evening he died. ³⁶As the sun was setting, a cry spread through the army: "Every man to his town. Every man to his land!"

³⁷So the king died and was brought to Samaria, and they buried him there. ³⁸They washed the chariot at a pool in Samaria (where the prostitutes bathed),ᵃ and the dogs licked up his blood, as the word of the LORD had declared.

³⁹As for the other events of Ahab's reign, including all he did, the palace he built and adorned with ivory, and the cities he fortified, are they not written in the book of the annals of the kings of Israel? ⁴⁰Ahab rested with his ancestors. And Ahaziah his son succeeded him as king.

Jehoshaphat King of Judah

⁴¹Jehoshaphat son of Asa became king of Judah in the fourth year of Ahab king of Israel. ⁴²Jehoshaphat was thirty-five years old when he became king, and he reigned in Jerusalem twenty-five years. His mother's name was Azubah daughter of Shilhi. ⁴³In everything he followed the ways of his father Asa and did not stray from them; he did what was right in the eyes of the LORD. The high places, however, were not removed, and the people continued to offer sacrifices and burn incense there.ᵇ ⁴⁴Jehoshaphat was also at peace with the king of Israel.

⁴⁵As for the other events of Jehoshaphat's reign, the things he achieved and his military exploits, are they not written in the book of the annals of the kings of Judah? ⁴⁶He rid the land of the rest of the male shrine prostitutes who remained there even after the reign of his father Asa. ⁴⁷There was then no king in Edom; a provincial governor ruled.

⁴⁸Now Jehoshaphat built a fleet of trading shipsᶜ to go to Ophir for gold, but they never set sail—they were wrecked at Ezion Geber. ⁴⁹At that time Ahaziah son of Ahab said to Jehoshaphat, "Let my men sail with yours," but Jehoshaphat refused.

⁵⁰Then Jehoshaphat rested with his ancestors and was buried with them in the city of David his father. And Jehoram his son succeeded him as king.

Ahaziah King of Israel

⁵¹Ahaziah son of Ahab became king of Israel in Samaria in the seventeenth year of Jehoshaphat king of Judah, and he reigned over Israel two years. ⁵²He did evil in the eyes of the LORD, because he followed the ways of his father and mother and of Jeroboam son of Nebat, who caused Israel to sin. ⁵³He served and worshiped Baal and aroused the anger of the LORD, the God of Israel, just as his father had done.

ᵃ 38 Or *Samaria and cleaned the weapons*   ᵇ 43 In Hebrew texts this sentence (22:43b) is numbered 22:44, and 22:44-53 is numbered 22:45-54.   ᶜ 48 Hebrew *of ships of Tarshish*

2 KINGS

WHEN DID THIS HAPPEN?

WHEN DID THIS HAPPEN?

About 840–560 B.C. in the land of Israel—divided into the northern kingdom of Israel and the southern kingdom of Judah

WHO IS IN THIS BOOK?

Elisha
Naaman
Joash
Isaiah
Hezekiah
Josiah

VERSES YOU MIGHT RECOGNIZE

2 KINGS 17:38

"Do not forget the covenant I have made with you, and do not worship other gods."

2 KINGS 23:25

"Neither before nor after Josiah was there a king like him who turned to the LORD as he did—with all his heart and with all his soul and with all his strength."

WHAT'S IT ABOUT?

A sequel to 1 Kings, this book continues telling the history of Israel. Appointing human kings did not work out well for God's people. One wicked king after another took the throne, and the nation drifted farther and farther away from God. The prophets Elijah and Elisha warned the people to turn back to God before it was too late. Later, yet other prophets warned that as punishment, the people would be captured by other nations. After King Solomon's death, the nation of Israel had been divided into two parts—the southern kingdom, known as Judah, and the northern kingdom, called Israel. Judah was the first to be captured by Babylon. Later, Assyria captured Israel.

As the heartbroken Israelites watched their promised land slip away, they must have wondered what God was doing. Though they were being punished for turning to other gods, God had no intention of leaving them or breaking his promises. He would still do amazing things for those who obeyed him.

2 KINGS

The LORD's Judgment on Ahaziah

1 After Ahab's death, Moab rebelled against Israel. ²Now Ahaziah had fallen through the lattice of his upper room in Samaria and injured himself. So he sent messengers, saying to them, "Go and consult Baal-Zebub, the god of Ekron, to see if I will recover from this injury."

³But the angel of the LORD said to Elijah the Tishbite, "Go up and meet the messengers of the king of Samaria and ask them, 'Is it because there is no God in Israel that you are going off to consult Baal-Zebub, the god of Ekron?' ⁴Therefore this is what the LORD says: 'You will not leave the bed you are lying on. You will certainly die!'" So Elijah went.

⁵When the messengers returned to the king, he asked them, "Why have you come back?"

⁶"A man came to meet us," they replied. "And he said to us, 'Go back to the king who sent you and tell him, "This is what the LORD says: Is it because there is no God in Israel that you are sending messengers to consult Baal-Zebub, the god of Ekron? Therefore you will not leave the bed you are lying on. You will certainly die!"'"

⁷The king asked them, "What kind of man was it who came to meet you and told you this?"

⁸They replied, "He had a garment of hair[a] and had a leather belt around his waist."

The king said, "That was Elijah the Tishbite."

⁹Then he sent to Elijah a captain with his company of fifty men. The captain went up to Elijah, who was sitting on the top of a hill, and said to him, "Man of God, the king says, 'Come down!'"

¹⁰Elijah answered the captain, "If I am a man of God, may fire come down from heaven and consume you and your fifty men!" Then fire fell from heaven and consumed the captain and his men.

¹¹At this the king sent to Elijah another captain with his fifty men. The captain said to him, "Man of God, this is what the king says, 'Come down at once!'"

¹²"If I am a man of God," Elijah replied, "may fire come down from heaven and consume you and your fifty men!" Then the fire of God fell from heaven and consumed him and his fifty men.

¹³So the king sent a third captain with his fifty men. This third captain went up and fell on his knees before Elijah. "Man of God," he begged, "please have respect for my life and the lives of these fifty men, your servants! ¹⁴See, fire has fallen from heaven and consumed the first two captains and all their men. But now have respect for my life!"

¹⁵The angel of the LORD said to Elijah, "Go down with him; do not be afraid of him." So Elijah got up and went down with him to the king.

¹⁶He told the king, "This is what the LORD says: Is it because there is no God in Israel for you to consult that you have sent messengers to consult Baal-Zebub, the god of Ekron? Because you have done this, you will never leave the bed you are lying on. You will certainly die!" ¹⁷So he died, according to the word of the LORD that Elijah had spoken.

Because Ahaziah had no son, Joram[b] succeeded him as king in the second year of Jehoram son of Jehoshaphat king of Judah. ¹⁸As for all the other events of Ahaziah's reign, and what he did, are they not written in the book of the annals of the kings of Israel?

Elijah Taken Up to Heaven

2 When the LORD was about to take Elijah up to heaven in a whirlwind, Elijah and Elisha were on their way from Gilgal. ²Elijah said to Elisha, "Stay here; the LORD has sent me to Bethel."

But Elisha said, "As surely as the LORD lives and as you live, I will not leave you." So they went down to Bethel.

---

[a] 8 Or *He was a hairy man*   [b] 17 Hebrew *Jehoram*, a variant of *Joram*

³The company of the prophets at Bethel came out to Elisha and asked, "Do you know that the LORD is going to take your master from you today?"

"Yes, I know," Elisha replied, "so be quiet."

⁴Then Elijah said to him, "Stay here, Elisha; the LORD has sent me to Jericho."

And he replied, "As surely as the LORD lives and as you live, I will not leave you." So they went to Jericho.

⁵The company of the prophets at Jericho went up to Elisha and asked him, "Do you know that the LORD is going to take your master from you today?"

"Yes, I know," he replied, "so be quiet."

⁶Then Elijah said to him, "Stay here; the LORD has sent me to the Jordan."

And he replied, "As surely as the LORD lives and as you live, I will not leave you." So the two of them walked on.

⁷Fifty men from the company of the prophets went and stood at a distance, facing the place where Elijah and Elisha had stopped at the Jordan. ⁸Elijah took his cloak, rolled it up and struck the water with it. The water divided to the right and to the left, and the two of them crossed over on dry ground.

⁹When they had crossed, Elijah said to Elisha, "Tell me, what can I do for you before I am taken from you?"

"Let me inherit a double portion of your spirit," Elisha replied.

¹⁰"You have asked a difficult thing," Elijah said, "yet if you see me when I am taken from you, it will be yours — otherwise, it will not."

¹¹As they were walking along and talking together, suddenly a chariot of fire and horses of fire appeared and separated the two of them, and Elijah went up to heaven in a whirlwind. ¹²Elisha saw this and cried out, "My father! My father! The chariots and horsemen of Israel!" And Elisha saw him no more. Then he took hold of his garment and tore it in two.

¹³Elisha then picked up Elijah's cloak that had fallen from him and went back and stood on the bank of the Jordan. ¹⁴He took the cloak that had fallen from Elijah and struck the water with it. "Where now is the LORD, the God of Elijah?" he asked. When he struck the water, it divided to the right and to the left, and he crossed over.

¹⁵The company of the prophets from Jericho, who were watching, said, "The spirit of Elijah is resting on Elisha." And they went to meet him and bowed to the ground before him. ¹⁶"Look," they said, "we your servants have fifty able men. Let them go and look for your master. Perhaps the Spirit of the LORD has picked him up and set him down on some mountain or in some valley."

"No," Elisha replied, "do not send them."

¹⁷But they persisted until he was too embarrassed to refuse. So he said, "Send them." And they sent fifty men, who searched for three days but did not find him. ¹⁸When they returned to Elisha, who was staying in Jericho, he said to them, "Didn't I tell you not to go?"

Healing of the Water

¹⁹The people of the city said to Elisha, "Look, our lord, this town is well situated, as you can see, but the water is bad and the land is unproductive."

²⁰"Bring me a new bowl," he said, "and put salt in it." So they brought it to him.

²¹Then he went out to the spring and threw the salt into it, saying, "This is what the LORD says: 'I have healed this water. Never again will it cause death or make the land unproductive.'" ²²And the water has remained pure to this day, according to the word Elisha had spoken.

Elisha Is Jeered

²³From there Elisha went up to Bethel. As he was walking along the road, some boys came out of the town and jeered at him. "Get out of here, baldy!" they said. "Get out of here, baldy!" ²⁴He turned around, looked at them and called down a curse on them in the name of the LORD. Then two bears came out of the woods and mauled forty-two of the boys. ²⁵And he went on to Mount Carmel and from there returned to Samaria.

Moab Revolts

3 Joram*a* son of Ahab became king of Israel in Samaria in the eighteenth year of Jehoshaphat king of Judah, and he reigned twelve years. ²He did evil in the eyes of the LORD, but not as his father and mother had done. He got rid of the sacred stone of Baal

---

a 1 Hebrew *Jehoram*, a variant of *Joram*; also in verse 6

BACK TO THE BEGINNING

READ: 2 KINGS 2:9

It's tough to rank the prophets, but if there were an ancient fantasy league in Israel, Elisha would be a first-round pick. Elisha gets some big points for parting the Jordan River, raising a boy from the dead, and making an iron axhead float. That's some serious fantasy points!

So why did God give Elisha a double portion? For starters, Elisha asked for it. Then he backed it up by his willingness to go back to the beginning and start all over again. Elisha didn't hold out on God so God didn't hold out on Elisha.

Elisha gave up his life for an unpaid internship with a crazy prophet whose name was almost the same. In one day he went from the top of the totem pole to the bottom. He got the jobs no one else wanted to do as an intern. But you have to be willing to start at the bottom.

BUILDING FAITH WISDOM STRENGTH

Every black belt starts as a white belt.

Every musician starts with scales.

Every PhD starts in kindergarten.

If you aren't willing to begin at the beginning, God just can't use you. You're too thick. You've got to be willing to leave the seat of honor and take the lowest place at the table. You've got to be willing to go from first to last. Isn't that the example Jesus set? The all-powerful Creator became a servant. If you follow suit, there is nothing God can't do in you and through you.

that his father had made. ³Nevertheless he clung to the sins of Jeroboam son of Nebat, which he had caused Israel to commit; he did not turn away from them.

⁴Now Mesha king of Moab raised sheep, and he had to pay the king of Israel a tribute of a hundred thousand lambs and the wool of a hundred thousand rams. ⁵But after Ahab died, the king of Moab rebelled against the king of Israel. ⁶So at that time King Joram set out from Samaria and mobilized all Israel. ⁷He also sent this message to Jehoshaphat king of Judah: "The king of Moab has rebelled against me. Will you go with me to fight against Moab?"

"I will go with you," he replied. "I am as you are, my people as your people, my horses as your horses."

⁸"By what route shall we attack?" he asked.

"Through the Desert of Edom," he answered.

⁹So the king of Israel set out with the king of Judah and the king of Edom. After a roundabout march of seven days, the army had no more water for themselves or for the animals with them.

¹⁰"What!" exclaimed the king of Israel. "Has the LORD called us three kings together only to deliver us into the hands of Moab?"

¹¹But Jehoshaphat asked, "Is there no prophet of the LORD here, through whom we may inquire of the LORD?"

An officer of the king of Israel answered, "Elisha son of Shaphat is here. He used to pour water on the hands of Elijah.ᵃ"

¹²Jehoshaphat said, "The word of the LORD is with him." So the king of Israel and Jehoshaphat and the king of Edom went down to him.

¹³Elisha said to the king of Israel, "Why do you want to involve me? Go to the prophets of your father and the prophets of your mother."

"No," the king of Israel answered, "because it was the LORD who called us three kings together to deliver us into the hands of Moab."

¹⁴Elisha said, "As surely as the LORD Almighty lives, whom I serve, if I did not have respect for the presence of Jehoshaphat king of Judah, I would not pay any attention to you. ¹⁵But now bring me a harpist."

While the harpist was playing, the hand of the LORD came on Elisha ¹⁶and he said, "This is what the LORD says: I will fill this valley with pools of water. ¹⁷For this is what the LORD says: You will see neither wind nor rain, yet this valley will be filled with water, and you, your cattle and your other animals will drink. ¹⁸This is an easy thing in the eyes of the LORD; he will also deliver Moab into your hands. ¹⁹You will overthrow every fortified city and every major town. You will cut down every good tree, stop up all the springs, and ruin every good field with stones."

²⁰The next morning, about the time for offering the sacrifice, there it was — water flowing from the direction of Edom! And the land was filled with water.

²¹Now all the Moabites had heard that the kings had come to fight against them; so every man, young and old, who could bear arms was called up and stationed on the border. ²²When they got up early in the morning, the sun was shining on the water. To the Moabites across the way, the water looked red — like blood. ²³"That's blood!" they said. "Those kings must have fought and slaughtered each other. Now to the plunder, Moab!"

²⁴But when the Moabites came to the camp of Israel, the Israelites rose up and fought them until they fled. And the Israelites invaded the land and slaughtered the Moabites. ²⁵They destroyed the towns, and each man threw a stone on every good field until it was covered. They stopped up all the springs and cut down every good tree. Only Kir Hareseth was left with its stones in place, but men armed with slings surrounded it and attacked it.

²⁶When the king of Moab saw that the battle had gone against him, he took with him seven hundred swordsmen to break through to the king of Edom, but they failed. ²⁷Then he took his firstborn son, who was to succeed him as king, and offered him as a sacrifice on the city wall. The fury against Israel was great; they withdrew and returned to their own land.

The Widow's Olive Oil

4 The wife of a man from the company of the prophets cried out to Elisha, "Your servant my husband is dead, and you know

---

ᵃ *11* That is, he was Elijah's personal servant.

that he revered the LORD. But now his creditor is coming to take my two boys as his slaves."

²Elisha replied to her, "How can I help you? Tell me, what do you have in your house?"

"Your servant has nothing there at all," she said, "except a small jar of olive oil."

³Elisha said, "Go around and ask all your neighbors for empty jars. Don't ask for just a few. ⁴Then go inside and shut the door behind you and your sons. Pour oil into all the jars, and as each is filled, put it to one side."

⁵She left him and shut the door behind her and her sons. They brought the jars to her and she kept pouring. ⁶When all the jars were full, she said to her son, "Bring me another one."

But he replied, "There is not a jar left." Then the oil stopped flowing.

⁷She went and told the man of God, and he said, "Go, sell the oil and pay your debts. You and your sons can live on what is left."

The Shunammite's Son Restored to Life

⁸One day Elisha went to Shunem. And a well-to-do woman was there, who urged him to stay for a meal. So whenever he came by, he stopped there to eat. ⁹She said to her husband, "I know that this man who often comes our way is a holy man of God. ¹⁰Let's make a small room on the roof and put in it a bed and a table, a chair and a lamp for him. Then he can stay there whenever he comes to us."

¹¹One day when Elisha came, he went up to his room and lay down there. ¹²He said to his servant Gehazi, "Call the Shunammite." So he called her, and she stood before him. ¹³Elisha said to him, "Tell her, 'You have gone to all this trouble for us. Now what can be done for you? Can we speak on your behalf to the king or the commander of the army?'"

She replied, "I have a home among my own people."

¹⁴"What can be done for her?" Elisha asked.

Gehazi said, "She has no son, and her husband is old."

¹⁵Then Elisha said, "Call her." So he called her, and she stood in the doorway. ¹⁶"About this time next year," Elisha said, "you will hold a son in your arms."

"No, my lord!" she objected. "Please, man of God, don't mislead your servant!"

¹⁷But the woman became pregnant, and the next year about that same time she gave birth to a son, just as Elisha had told her.

¹⁸The child grew, and one day he went out to his father, who was with the reapers. ¹⁹He said to his father, "My head! My head!"

His father told a servant, "Carry him to his mother." ²⁰After the servant had lifted him up and carried him to his mother, the boy sat on her lap until noon, and then he died. ²¹She went up and laid him on the bed of the man of God, then shut the door and went out.

²²She called her husband and said, "Please send me one of the servants and a donkey so I can go to the man of God quickly and return."

²³"Why go to him today?" he asked. "It's not the New Moon or the Sabbath."

"That's all right," she said.

²⁴She saddled the donkey and said to her servant, "Lead on; don't slow down for me unless I tell you." ²⁵So she set out and came to the man of God at Mount Carmel.

When he saw her in the distance, the man of God said to his servant Gehazi, "Look! There's the Shunammite! ²⁶Run to meet her and ask her, 'Are you all right? Is your husband all right? Is your child all right?'"

"Everything is all right," she said.

²⁷When she reached the man of God at the mountain, she took hold of his feet. Gehazi came over to push her away, but the man of God said, "Leave her alone! She is in bitter distress, but the LORD has hidden it from me and has not told me why."

²⁸"Did I ask you for a son, my lord?" she said. "Didn't I tell you, 'Don't raise my hopes'?"

²⁹Elisha said to Gehazi, "Tuck your cloak into your belt, take my staff in your hand and run. Don't greet anyone you meet, and if anyone greets you, do not answer. Lay my staff on the boy's face."

³⁰But the child's mother said, "As surely as the LORD lives and as you live, I will not leave you." So he got up and followed her.

³¹Gehazi went on ahead and laid the staff on the boy's face, but there was no sound or response. So Gehazi went back to meet Elisha and told him, "The boy has not awakened."

³²When Elisha reached the house, there was the boy lying dead on his couch. ³³He went in, shut the door on the two of them and prayed to the LORD. ³⁴Then he got on

GAME OF CHICKEN

READ: 2 KINGS 4:1-7

Remember the game Chicken? From first grade? God must love the game of Chicken because he plays it with us all the time. He has this habit of waiting until the very last moment to answer our prayer to see if we'll chicken out or pray through. If we chicken out, we miss out on the miracle; if we pray through, God will come through, but it may well be at the last moment possible. And, of course, if you chicken out of the game of Chicken, God will always give you another chance to get back in the game and play another round.

The classic last-second provision is repeated throughout Scripture, and I think it reveals God's playful personality. Sometimes we're so focused on the character of God that we forget that God has a personality too. He loves hiding around corners and jumping out and scaring the mess out of us with blessings. You can't convince me that Jesus didn't have fun sneaking up on the disciples in the middle of the night in the middle of the lake by walking on water. I can just imagine them waking up everyone around the lake with girly cries of "Help! It's a ghost!" There's no way God didn't enjoy the befuddled look on Moses' face when he heard the talking bush. Probably why he chose a bush!

BUILDING

FAITH

WISDOM

STRENGTH

As I read Scripture, I can come to no other conclusion than this: God loves showing up in unexpected ways at unexpected times. I love this part of God's personality.

the bed and lay on the boy, mouth to mouth, eyes to eyes, hands to hands. As he stretched himself out on him, the boy's body grew warm. ³⁵Elisha turned away and walked back and forth in the room and then got on the bed and stretched out on him once more. The boy sneezed seven times and opened his eyes.

³⁶Elisha summoned Gehazi and said, "Call the Shunammite." And he did. When she came, he said, "Take your son." ³⁷She came in, fell at his feet and bowed to the ground. Then she took her son and went out.

Death in the Pot

³⁸Elisha returned to Gilgal and there was a famine in that region. While the company of the prophets was meeting with him, he said to his servant, "Put on the large pot and cook some stew for these prophets."

³⁹One of them went out into the fields to gather herbs and found a wild vine and picked as many of its gourds as his garment could hold. When he returned, he cut them up into the pot of stew, though no one knew what they were. ⁴⁰The stew was poured out for the men, but as they began to eat it, they cried out, "Man of God, there is death in the pot!" And they could not eat it.

⁴¹Elisha said, "Get some flour." He put it into the pot and said, "Serve it to the people to eat." And there was nothing harmful in the pot.

Feeding of a Hundred

⁴²A man came from Baal Shalishah, bringing the man of God twenty loaves of barley bread baked from the first ripe grain, along with some heads of new grain. "Give it to the people to eat," Elisha said.

⁴³"How can I set this before a hundred men?" his servant asked.

But Elisha answered, "Give it to the people to eat. For this is what the Lord says: 'They will eat and have some left over.'" ⁴⁴Then he set it before them, and they ate and had some left over, according to the word of the Lord.

Naaman Healed of Leprosy

5 Now Naaman was commander of the army of the king of Aram. He was a great man in the sight of his master and highly regarded, because through him the Lord had given victory to Aram. He was a valiant soldier, but he had leprosy.ᵃ

²Now bands of raiders from Aram had gone out and had taken captive a young girl from Israel, and she served Naaman's wife. ³She said to her mistress, "If only my master would see the prophet who is in Samaria! He would cure him of his leprosy."

⁴Naaman went to his master and told him what the girl from Israel had said. ⁵"By all means, go," the king of Aram replied. "I will send a letter to the king of Israel." So Naaman left, taking with him ten talentsᵇ of silver, six thousand shekelsᶜ of gold and ten sets of clothing. ⁶The letter that he took to the king of Israel read: "With this letter I am sending my servant Naaman to you so that you may cure him of his leprosy."

⁷As soon as the king of Israel read the letter, he tore his robes and said, "Am I God? Can I kill and bring back to life? Why does this fellow send someone to me to be cured of his leprosy? See how he is trying to pick a quarrel with me!"

⁸When Elisha the man of God heard that the king of Israel had torn his robes, he sent him this message: "Why have you torn your robes? Have the man come to me and he will know that there is a prophet in Israel." ⁹So Naaman went with his horses and chariots and stopped at the door of Elisha's house. ¹⁰Elisha sent a messenger to say to him, "Go, wash yourself seven times in the Jordan, and your flesh will be restored and you will be cleansed."

¹¹But Naaman went away angry and said, "I thought that he would surely come out to me and stand and call on the name of the Lord his God, wave his hand over the spot and cure me of my leprosy. ¹²Are not Abana and Pharpar, the rivers of Damascus, better than all the waters of Israel? Couldn't I wash in them and be cleansed?" So he turned and went off in a rage.

¹³Naaman's servants went to him and said, "My father, if the prophet had told you to do some great thing, would you not have done it? How much more, then, when he tells you, 'Wash and be cleansed'!" ¹⁴So he went down and dipped himself in the Jordan sev-

---

ᵃ 1 The Hebrew for *leprosy* was used for various diseases affecting the skin; also in verses 3, 6, 7, 11 and 27.
ᵇ 5 That is, about 750 pounds or about 340 kilograms   ᶜ 5 That is, about 150 pounds or about 69 kilograms

NO STRINGS ATTACHED

READ: 2 KINGS 5:10

Suppose you have a huge prayer you want God to answer. You try to entice him to say yes by making him an equally huge promise. Whatever you dream up as a bribe to the Lord can't compare to what Naaman offered for his healing—an outrageous haul including 750 pounds of silver and 150 pounds of gold.

Naaman was the general of the army of Aram, an area roughly equivalent to modern Syria. He was afflicted with leprosy, the same dreaded skin disease seen in Luke 17:11–19. Naaman's master, the king of Aram, sent him to Israel with a rich gift for God's prophet, hoping for a cure. But Elisha wanted none of the wealth. He sent the general to do a ridiculously simple task, dipping seven times in an ordinary nearby river.

Naaman almost left without getting the healing God had in store for him, but by the time he went home he gained a couple of crucial lessons. First, God doesn't need a bribe to do us good. His gifts come free, no strings attached. Second, the Lord is the one and only God. Naaman vowed to never worship any other god, and took home a film of river dirt as a reminder.

When you need something from God, don't show up with a bribe. Just always put God first. Tell the Lord what you need, and watch for his answer.

BUILDING

FAITH

WISDOM

STRENGTH

en times, as the man of God had told him, and his flesh was restored and became clean like that of a young boy.

¹⁵Then Naaman and all his attendants went back to the man of God. He stood before him and said, "Now I know that there is no God in all the world except in Israel. So please accept a gift from your servant."

¹⁶The prophet answered, "As surely as the LORD lives, whom I serve, I will not accept a thing." And even though Naaman urged him, he refused.

¹⁷"If you will not," said Naaman, "please let me, your servant, be given as much earth as a pair of mules can carry, for your servant will never again make burnt offerings and sacrifices to any other god but the LORD. ¹⁸But may the LORD forgive your servant for this one thing: When my master enters the temple of Rimmon to bow down and he is leaning on my arm and I have to bow there also — when I bow down in the temple of Rimmon, may the LORD forgive your servant for this."

¹⁹"Go in peace," Elisha said.

After Naaman had traveled some distance, ²⁰Gehazi, the servant of Elisha the man of God, said to himself, "My master was too easy on Naaman, this Aramean, by not accepting from him what he brought. As surely as the LORD lives, I will run after him and get something from him."

²¹So Gehazi hurried after Naaman. When Naaman saw him running toward him, he got down from the chariot to meet him. "Is everything all right?" he asked.

²²"Everything is all right," Gehazi answered. "My master sent me to say, 'Two young men from the company of the prophets have just come to me from the hill country of Ephraim. Please give them a talent*a* of silver and two sets of clothing.'"

²³"By all means, take two talents," said Naaman. He urged Gehazi to accept them, and then tied up the two talents of silver in two bags, with two sets of clothing. He gave them to two of his servants, and they carried them ahead of Gehazi. ²⁴When Gehazi came to the hill, he took the things from the servants and put them away in the house. He sent the men away and they left.

²⁵When he went in and stood before his master, Elisha asked him, "Where have you been, Gehazi?"

"Your servant didn't go anywhere," Gehazi answered.

²⁶But Elisha said to him, "Was not my spirit with you when the man got down from his chariot to meet you? Is this the time to take money or to accept clothes — or olive groves and vineyards, or flocks and herds, or male and female slaves? ²⁷Naaman's leprosy will cling to you and to your descendants forever." Then Gehazi went from Elisha's presence and his skin was leprous — it had become as white as snow.

An Axhead Floats

6 The company of the prophets said to Elisha, "Look, the place where we meet with you is too small for us. ²Let us go to the Jordan, where each of us can get a pole; and let us build a place there for us to meet."

And he said, "Go."

³Then one of them said, "Won't you please come with your servants?"

"I will," Elisha replied. ⁴And he went with them.

They went to the Jordan and began to cut down trees. ⁵As one of them was cutting down a tree, the iron axhead fell into the water. "Oh no, my lord!" he cried out. "It was borrowed!"

⁶The man of God asked, "Where did it fall?" When he showed him the place, Elisha cut a stick and threw it there, and made the iron float. ⁷"Lift it out," he said. Then the man reached out his hand and took it.

Elisha Traps Blinded Arameans

⁸Now the king of Aram was at war with Israel. After conferring with his officers, he said, "I will set up my camp in such and such a place."

⁹The man of God sent word to the king of Israel: "Beware of passing that place, because the Arameans are going down there." ¹⁰So the king of Israel checked on the place indicated by the man of God. Time and again Elisha warned the king, so that he was on his guard in such places.

¹¹This enraged the king of Aram. He summoned his officers and demanded of them, "Tell me! Which of us is on the side of the king of Israel?"

a 22 That is, about 75 pounds or about 34 kilograms

ELISHA

The prophet answered, "As surely as the LORD lives, whom I serve, I will not accept a thing." 2 KINGS 5:16

HIS NAME MEANS: "God is salvation"
READ HIS STORY: *1 Kings 19:19–21; 2 Kings 2–7; 8:1–14*

We can learn several lessons by looking at Elisha. Lesson One: When we're confident of God's call on our life, we must act. When the prophet Elijah approached Elisha as he plowed a field behind a pair of oxen, the younger man immediately understood his calling. There was no turning back. Elisha was likely in his twenties, if not his teens, so he was committed to following Elijah—and God—for the long haul.

Lesson Two: Never make fun of God's servants. Once when Elisha was walking along a road, some teenage boys mocked him, yelling, "Get out of here, baldy!" Elisha turned and called down a curse. Two bears ran out of the forest and mauled forty-two of the boys because they mocked one of the Lord's representatives (2 Kings 2:24).

Lesson Three: God's power flows through his people. Elisha performed miracle after miracle in God's name. He made rancid water pure, raised a boy from the dead, healed Naaman from leprosy, made an axhead float, temporarily blinded enemy soldiers, fed a hundred men with some small loaves of bread and saw water mysteriously fill a valley to save Israel's army. Not bad for a former farmer.

Elisha was no lone ranger. He often traveled with a servant and called other prophets to help him do God's work. There's another lesson: We're stronger when we serve God together.

¹²"None of us, my lord the king," said one of his officers, "but Elisha, the prophet who is in Israel, tells the king of Israel the very words you speak in your bedroom."

¹³"Go, find out where he is," the king ordered, "so I can send men and capture him." The report came back: "He is in Dothan." ¹⁴Then he sent horses and chariots and a strong force there. They went by night and surrounded the city.

¹⁵When the servant of the man of God got up and went out early the next morning, an army with horses and chariots had surrounded the city. "Oh no, my lord! What shall we do?" the servant asked.

¹⁶"Don't be afraid," the prophet answered. "Those who are with us are more than those who are with them."

¹⁷And Elisha prayed, "Open his eyes, Lord, so that he may see." Then the Lord opened the servant's eyes, and he looked and saw the hills full of horses and chariots of fire all around Elisha.

¹⁸As the enemy came down toward him, Elisha prayed to the Lord, "Strike this army with blindness." So he struck them with blindness, as Elisha had asked.

¹⁹Elisha told them, "This is not the road and this is not the city. Follow me, and I will lead you to the man you are looking for." And he led them to Samaria.

²⁰After they entered the city, Elisha said, "Lord, open the eyes of these men so they can see." Then the Lord opened their eyes and they looked, and there they were, inside Samaria.

²¹When the king of Israel saw them, he asked Elisha, "Shall I kill them, my father? Shall I kill them?"

²²"Do not kill them," he answered. "Would you kill those you have captured with your own sword or bow? Set food and water before them so that they may eat and drink and then go back to their master." ²³So he prepared a great feast for them, and after they had finished eating and drinking, he sent them away, and they returned to their master. So the bands from Aram stopped raiding Israel's territory.

Famine in Besieged Samaria

²⁴Some time later, Ben-Hadad king of Aram mobilized his entire army and marched up and laid siege to Samaria. ²⁵There was a great famine in the city; the siege lasted so long that a donkey's head sold for eighty shekels[a] of silver, and a quarter of a cab[b] of seed pods[c] for five shekels.[d]

²⁶As the king of Israel was passing by on the wall, a woman cried to him, "Help me, my lord the king!"

²⁷The king replied, "If the Lord does not help you, where can I get help for you? From the threshing floor? From the winepress?" ²⁸Then he asked her, "What's the matter?"

She answered, "This woman said to me, 'Give up your son so we may eat him today, and tomorrow we'll eat my son.' ²⁹So we cooked my son and ate him. The next day I said to her, 'Give up your son so we may eat him,' but she had hidden him."

³⁰When the king heard the woman's words, he tore his robes. As he went along the wall, the people looked, and they saw that, under his robes, he had sackcloth on his body. ³¹He said, "May God deal with me, be it ever so severely, if the head of Elisha son of Shaphat remains on his shoulders today!"

³²Now Elisha was sitting in his house, and the elders were sitting with him. The king sent a messenger ahead, but before he arrived, Elisha said to the elders, "Don't you see how this murderer is sending someone to cut off my head? Look, when the messenger comes, shut the door and hold it shut against him. Is not the sound of his master's footsteps behind him?" ³³While he was still talking to them, the messenger came down to him.

The king said, "This disaster is from the Lord. Why should I wait for the Lord any longer?"

7 Elisha replied, "Hear the word of the Lord. This is what the Lord says: About this time tomorrow, a seah[e] of the finest flour will sell for a shekel[f] and two seahs[g] of barley for a shekel at the gate of Samaria."

²The officer on whose arm the king was leaning said to the man of God, "Look, even

---

[a] 25 That is, about 2 pounds or about 920 grams   [b] 25 That is, probably about 1/4 pound or about 100 grams   [c] 25 Or *of doves' dung*   [d] 25 That is, about 2 ounces or about 58 grams   [e] 1 That is, probably about 12 pounds or about 5.5 kilograms of flour; also in verses 16 and 18   [f] 1 That is, about 2/5 ounce or about 12 grams; also in verses 16 and 18   [g] 1 That is, probably about 20 pounds or about 9 kilograms of barley; also in verses 16 and 18

if the LORD should open the floodgates of the heavens, could this happen?"

"You will see it with your own eyes," answered Elisha, "but you will not eat any of it!"

The Siege Lifted

³Now there were four men with leprosy[a] at the entrance of the city gate. They said to each other, "Why stay here until we die? ⁴If we say, 'We'll go into the city'—the famine is there, and we will die. And if we stay here, we will die. So let's go over to the camp of the Arameans and surrender. If they spare us, we live; if they kill us, then we die."

⁵At dusk they got up and went to the camp of the Arameans. When they reached the edge of the camp, no one was there, ⁶for the Lord had caused the Arameans to hear the sound of chariots and horses and a great army, so that they said to one another, "Look, the king of Israel has hired the Hittite and Egyptian kings to attack us!" ⁷So they got up and fled in the dusk and abandoned their tents and their horses and donkeys. They left the camp as it was and ran for their lives.

⁸The men who had leprosy reached the edge of the camp, entered one of the tents and ate and drank. Then they took silver, gold and clothes, and went off and hid them. They returned and entered another tent and took some things from it and hid them also.

⁹Then they said to each other, "What we're doing is not right. This is a day of good news and we are keeping it to ourselves. If we wait until daylight, punishment will overtake us. Let's go at once and report this to the royal palace."

¹⁰So they went and called out to the city gatekeepers and told them, "We went into the Aramean camp and no one was there—not a sound of anyone—only tethered horses and donkeys, and the tents left just as they were." ¹¹The gatekeepers shouted the news, and it was reported within the palace.

¹²The king got up in the night and said to his officers, "I will tell you what the Arameans have done to us. They know we are starving; so they have left the camp to hide in the countryside, thinking, 'They will surely come out, and then we will take them alive and get into the city.'"

¹³One of his officers answered, "Have some men take five of the horses that are left in the city. Their plight will be like that of all the Israelites left here—yes, they will only be like all these Israelites who are doomed. So let us send them to find out what happened."

¹⁴So they selected two chariots with their horses, and the king sent them after the Aramean army. He commanded the drivers, "Go and find out what has happened." ¹⁵They followed them as far as the Jordan, and they found the whole road strewn with the clothing and equipment the Arameans had thrown away in their headlong flight. So the messengers returned and reported to the king. ¹⁶Then the people went out and plundered the camp of the Arameans. So a seah of the finest flour sold for a shekel, and two seahs of barley sold for a shekel, as the LORD had said.

¹⁷Now the king had put the officer on whose arm he leaned in charge of the gate, and the people trampled him in the gateway, and he died, just as the man of God had foretold when the king came down to his house. ¹⁸It happened as the man of God had said to the king: "About this time tomorrow, a seah of the finest flour will sell for a shekel and two seahs of barley for a shekel at the gate of Samaria."

¹⁹The officer had said to the man of God, "Look, even if the LORD should open the floodgates of the heavens, could this happen?" The man of God had replied, "You will see it with your own eyes, but you will not eat any of it!" ²⁰And that is exactly what happened to him, for the people trampled him in the gateway, and he died.

The Shunammite's Land Restored

8 Now Elisha had said to the woman whose son he had restored to life, "Go away with your family and stay for a while wherever you can, because the LORD has decreed a famine in the land that will last seven years." ²The woman proceeded to do as the man of God said. She and her family went away and stayed in the land of the Philistines seven years.

³At the end of the seven years she came back from the land of the Philistines and

---

ᵃ 3 The Hebrew for *leprosy* was used for various diseases affecting the skin; also in verse 8.

went to appeal to the king for her house and land. ⁴The king was talking to Gehazi, the servant of the man of God, and had said, "Tell me about all the great things Elisha has done." ⁵Just as Gehazi was telling the king how Elisha had restored the dead to life, the woman whose son Elisha had brought back to life came to appeal to the king for her house and land.

Gehazi said, "This is the woman, my lord the king, and this is her son whom Elisha restored to life." ⁶The king asked the woman about it, and she told him.

Then he assigned an official to her case and said to him, "Give back everything that belonged to her, including all the income from her land from the day she left the country until now."

Hazael Murders Ben-Hadad

⁷Elisha went to Damascus, and Ben-Hadad king of Aram was ill. When the king was told, "The man of God has come all the way up here," ⁸he said to Hazael, "Take a gift with you and go to meet the man of God. Consult the Lord through him; ask him, 'Will I recover from this illness?'"

⁹Hazael went to meet Elisha, taking with him as a gift forty camel-loads of all the finest wares of Damascus. He went in and stood before him, and said, "Your son Ben-Hadad king of Aram has sent me to ask, 'Will I recover from this illness?'"

¹⁰Elisha answered, "Go and say to him, 'You will certainly recover.' Nevertheless,ᵃ the Lord has revealed to me that he will in fact die." ¹¹He stared at him with a fixed gaze until Hazael was embarrassed. Then the man of God began to weep.

¹²"Why is my lord weeping?" asked Hazael.

"Because I know the harm you will do to the Israelites," he answered. "You will set fire to their fortified places, kill their young men with the sword, dash their little children to the ground, and rip open their pregnant women."

¹³Hazael said, "How could your servant, a mere dog, accomplish such a feat?"

"The Lord has shown me that you will become king of Aram," answered Elisha.

¹⁴Then Hazael left Elisha and returned to his master. When Ben-Hadad asked, "What did Elisha say to you?" Hazael replied, "He told me that you would certainly recover." ¹⁵But the next day he took a thick cloth, soaked it in water and spread it over the king's face, so that he died. Then Hazael succeeded him as king.

Jehoram King of Judah

¹⁶In the fifth year of Joram son of Ahab king of Israel, when Jehoshaphat was king of Judah, Jehoram son of Jehoshaphat began his reign as king of Judah. ¹⁷He was thirty-two years old when he became king, and he reigned in Jerusalem eight years. ¹⁸He followed the ways of the kings of Israel, as the house of Ahab had done, for he married a daughter of Ahab. He did evil in the eyes of the Lord. ¹⁹Nevertheless, for the sake of his servant David, the Lord was not willing to destroy Judah. He had promised to maintain a lamp for David and his descendants forever.

²⁰In the time of Jehoram, Edom rebelled against Judah and set up its own king. ²¹So Jehoramᵇ went to Zair with all his chariots. The Edomites surrounded him and his chariot commanders, but he rose up and broke through by night; his army, however, fled back home. ²²To this day Edom has been in rebellion against Judah. Libnah revolted at the same time.

²³As for the other events of Jehoram's reign, and all he did, are they not written in the book of the annals of the kings of Judah? ²⁴Jehoram rested with his ancestors and was buried with them in the City of David. And Ahaziah his son succeeded him as king.

Ahaziah King of Judah

²⁵In the twelfth year of Joram son of Ahab king of Israel, Ahaziah son of Jehoram king of Judah began to reign. ²⁶Ahaziah was twenty-two years old when he became king, and he reigned in Jerusalem one year. His mother's name was Athaliah, a granddaughter of Omri king of Israel. ²⁷He followed the ways of the house of Ahab and did evil in the eyes of the Lord, as the house of Ahab had done, for he was related by marriage to Ahab's family.

²⁸Ahaziah went with Joram son of Ahab to war against Hazael king of Aram at Ramoth

---

ᵃ 10 The Hebrew may also be read *Go and say, 'You will certainly not recover,' for.*   ᵇ 21 Hebrew *Joram,* a variant of *Jehoram*; also in verses 23 and 24

Gilead. The Arameans wounded Joram; ²⁹so King Joram returned to Jezreel to recover from the wounds the Arameans had inflicted on him at Ramoth*ᵃ* in his battle with Hazael king of Aram.

Then Ahaziah son of Jehoram king of Judah went down to Jezreel to see Joram son of Ahab, because he had been wounded.

Jehu Anointed King of Israel

9 The prophet Elisha summoned a man from the company of the prophets and said to him, "Tuck your cloak into your belt, take this flask of olive oil with you and go to Ramoth Gilead. ²When you get there, look for Jehu son of Jehoshaphat, the son of Nimshi. Go to him, get him away from his companions and take him into an inner room. ³Then take the flask and pour the oil on his head and declare, 'This is what the LORD says: I anoint you king over Israel.' Then open the door and run; don't delay!"

⁴So the young prophet went to Ramoth Gilead. ⁵When he arrived, he found the army officers sitting together. "I have a message for you, commander," he said.

"For which of us?" asked Jehu.

"For you, commander," he replied.

⁶Jehu got up and went into the house. Then the prophet poured the oil on Jehu's head and declared, "This is what the LORD, the God of Israel, says: 'I anoint you king over the LORD's people Israel. ⁷You are to destroy the house of Ahab your master, and I will avenge the blood of my servants the prophets and the blood of all the LORD's servants shed by Jezebel. ⁸The whole house of Ahab will perish. I will cut off from Ahab every last male in Israel—slave or free.*ᵇ* ⁹I will make the house of Ahab like the house of Jeroboam son of Nebat and like the house of Baasha son of Ahijah. ¹⁰As for Jezebel, dogs will devour her on the plot of ground at Jezreel, and no one will bury her.'" Then he opened the door and ran.

¹¹When Jehu went out to his fellow officers, one of them asked him, "Is everything all right? Why did this maniac come to you?"

"You know the man and the sort of things he says," Jehu replied.

¹²"That's not true!" they said. "Tell us."

Jehu said, "Here is what he told me: 'This is what the LORD says: I anoint you king over Israel.'"

¹³They quickly took their cloaks and spread them under him on the bare steps. Then they blew the trumpet and shouted, "Jehu is king!"

Jehu Kills Joram and Ahaziah

¹⁴So Jehu son of Jehoshaphat, the son of Nimshi, conspired against Joram. (Now Joram and all Israel had been defending Ramoth Gilead against Hazael king of Aram, ¹⁵but King Joram*ᶜ* had returned to Jezreel to recover from the wounds the Arameans had inflicted on him in the battle with Hazael king of Aram.) Jehu said, "If you desire to make me king, don't let anyone slip out of the city to go and tell the news in Jezreel." ¹⁶Then he got into his chariot and rode to Jezreel, because Joram was resting there and Ahaziah king of Judah had gone down to see him.

¹⁷When the lookout standing on the tower in Jezreel saw Jehu's troops approaching, he called out, "I see some troops coming."

"Get a horseman," Joram ordered. "Send him to meet them and ask, 'Do you come in peace?'"

¹⁸The horseman rode off to meet Jehu and said, "This is what the king says: 'Do you come in peace?'"

"What do you have to do with peace?" Jehu replied. "Fall in behind me."

The lookout reported, "The messenger has reached them, but he isn't coming back."

¹⁹So the king sent out a second horseman. When he came to them he said, "This is what the king says: 'Do you come in peace?'"

Jehu replied, "What do you have to do with peace? Fall in behind me."

²⁰The lookout reported, "He has reached them, but he isn't coming back either. The driving is like that of Jehu son of Nimshi—he drives like a maniac."

²¹"Hitch up my chariot," Joram ordered. And when it was hitched up, Joram king of Israel and Ahaziah king of Judah rode out, each in his own chariot, to meet Jehu. They met him at the plot of ground that had belonged to Naboth the Jezreelite. ²²When Joram saw Jehu he asked, "Have you come in peace, Jehu?"

ᵃ 29 Hebrew *Ramah,* a variant of *Ramoth*   *ᵇ 8* Or *Israel—every ruler or leader*   *ᶜ 15* Hebrew *Jehoram,* a variant of *Joram;* also in verses 17 and 21-24

"How can there be peace," Jehu replied, "as long as all the idolatry and witchcraft of your mother Jezebel abound?"

²³Joram turned about and fled, calling out to Ahaziah, "Treachery, Ahaziah!"

²⁴Then Jehu drew his bow and shot Joram between the shoulders. The arrow pierced his heart and he slumped down in his chariot. ²⁵Jehu said to Bidkar, his chariot officer, "Pick him up and throw him on the field that belonged to Naboth the Jezreelite. Remember how you and I were riding together in chariots behind Ahab his father when the LORD spoke this prophecy against him: ²⁶'Yesterday I saw the blood of Naboth and the blood of his sons, declares the LORD, and I will surely make you pay for it on this plot of ground, declares the LORD.'ᵃ Now then, pick him up and throw him on that plot, in accordance with the word of the LORD."

²⁷When Ahaziah king of Judah saw what had happened, he fled up the road to Beth Haggan.ᵇ Jehu chased him, shouting, "Kill him too!" They wounded him in his chariot on the way up to Gur near Ibleam, but he escaped to Megiddo and died there. ²⁸His servants took him by chariot to Jerusalem and buried him with his ancestors in his tomb in the City of David. ²⁹(In the eleventh year of Joram son of Ahab, Ahaziah had become king of Judah.)

Jezebel Killed

³⁰Then Jehu went to Jezreel. When Jezebel heard about it, she put on eye makeup, arranged her hair and looked out of a window. ³¹As Jehu entered the gate, she asked, "Have you come in peace, you Zimri, you murderer of your master?"ᶜ

³²He looked up at the window and called out, "Who is on my side? Who?" Two or three eunuchs looked down at him. ³³"Throw her down!" Jehu said. So they threw her down, and some of her blood spattered the wall and the horses as they trampled her underfoot.

³⁴Jehu went in and ate and drank. "Take care of that cursed woman," he said, "and bury her, for she was a king's daughter." ³⁵But when they went out to bury her, they found nothing except her skull, her feet and her hands. ³⁶They went back and told Jehu, who said, "This is the word of the LORD that he spoke through his servant Elijah the Tishbite: On the plot of ground at Jezreel dogs will devour Jezebel's flesh.ᵈ ³⁷Jezebel's body will be like dung on the ground in the plot at Jezreel, so that no one will be able to say, 'This is Jezebel.'"

Ahab's Family Killed

10 Now there were in Samaria seventy sons of the house of Ahab. So Jehu wrote letters and sent them to Samaria: to the officials of Jezreel,ᵉ to the elders and to the guardians of Ahab's children. He said, ²"You have your master's sons with you and you have chariots and horses, a fortified city and weapons. Now as soon as this letter reaches you, ³choose the best and most worthy of your master's sons and set him on his father's throne. Then fight for your master's house."

⁴But they were terrified and said, "If two kings could not resist him, how can we?"

⁵So the palace administrator, the city governor, the elders and the guardians sent this message to Jehu: "We are your servants and we will do anything you say. We will not appoint anyone as king; you do whatever you think best."

⁶Then Jehu wrote them a second letter, saying, "If you are on my side and will obey me, take the heads of your master's sons and come to me in Jezreel by this time tomorrow."

Now the royal princes, seventy of them, were with the leading men of the city, who were rearing them. ⁷When the letter arrived, these men took the princes and slaughtered all seventy of them. They put their heads in baskets and sent them to Jehu in Jezreel. ⁸When the messenger arrived, he told Jehu, "They have brought the heads of the princes."

Then Jehu ordered, "Put them in two piles at the entrance of the city gate until morning."

⁹The next morning Jehu went out. He stood before all the people and said, "You are innocent. It was I who conspired against my master and killed him, but who killed all these? ¹⁰Know, then, that not a word the LORD has spoken against the house of Ahab will fail. The LORD has done what he

---

ᵃ 26 See 1 Kings 21:19.   ᵇ 27 Or fled by way of the garden house   ᶜ 31 Or "Was there peace for Zimri, who murdered his master?"   ᵈ 36 See 1 Kings 21:23.   ᵉ 1 Hebrew; some Septuagint manuscripts and Vulgate of the city

FINALLY, JUSTICE

READ: 2 KINGS 9:30

Jezebel's story reads more like a reality TV script than the usual Bible account. But here you see an evil queen meet an ugly death.

Jezebel first appears as the wife of Israel's King Ahab (1 Kings 16:31). Her systematic attempt to kill off God's prophets forced Elijah to flee for his life after his victory against the prophets of the false god Baal (19:1-9).

Ahab and Jezebel made a frightening pair. Like the Bible says, "There was never anyone like Ahab, who sold himself to do evil in the eyes of the LORD, urged on by Jezebel his wife" (21:25). Even after Ahab was killed in battle, Jezebel continued to exert terrible control through her sons Joram and Ahaziah.

When a man named Jehu was anointed the next king of Israel, the Lord commanded him to destroy Ahab's household. Jehu drove his chariot "like a maniac" (2 Kings 9:20) to hunt down Joram and Ahaziah. When Jezebel heard Jehu closing in on the palace, she did herself up like a queen. She put on makeup, fixed her hair, and posed in a window. A push from her servants sent her to a bloody death on the street below, where dogs devoured her body.

BUILDING

FAITH

WISDOM

STRENGTH

There's nothing happy in Jezebel's story, but it signals that God is just. He doesn't let evil people live forever. He puts a stop to blatant sin.

announced through his servant Elijah." [11] So Jehu killed everyone in Jezreel who remained of the house of Ahab, as well as all his chief men, his close friends and his priests, leaving him no survivor.

[12] Jehu then set out and went toward Samaria. At Beth Eked of the Shepherds, [13] he met some relatives of Ahaziah king of Judah and asked, "Who are you?"

They said, "We are relatives of Ahaziah, and we have come down to greet the families of the king and of the queen mother."

[14] "Take them alive!" he ordered. So they took them alive and slaughtered them by the well of Beth Eked—forty-two of them. He left no survivor.

[15] After he left there, he came upon Jehonadab son of Rekab, who was on his way to meet him. Jehu greeted him and said, "Are you in accord with me, as I am with you?"

"I am," Jehonadab answered.

"If so," said Jehu, "give me your hand." So he did, and Jehu helped him up into the chariot. [16] Jehu said, "Come with me and see my zeal for the LORD." Then he had him ride along in his chariot.

[17] When Jehu came to Samaria, he killed all who were left there of Ahab's family; he destroyed them, according to the word of the LORD spoken to Elijah.

Servants of Baal Killed

[18] Then Jehu brought all the people together and said to them, "Ahab served Baal a little; Jehu will serve him much. [19] Now summon all the prophets of Baal, all his servants and all his priests. See that no one is missing, because I am going to hold a great sacrifice for Baal. Anyone who fails to come will no longer live." But Jehu was acting deceptively in order to destroy the servants of Baal.

[20] Jehu said, "Call an assembly in honor of Baal." So they proclaimed it. [21] Then he sent word throughout Israel, and all the servants of Baal came; not one stayed away. They crowded into the temple of Baal until it was full from one end to the other. [22] And Jehu said to the keeper of the wardrobe, "Bring robes for all the servants of Baal." So he brought out robes for them.

[23] Then Jehu and Jehonadab son of Rekab went into the temple of Baal. Jehu said to the servants of Baal, "Look around and see that no one who serves the LORD is here with you—only servants of Baal." [24] So they went in to make sacrifices and burnt offerings. Now Jehu had posted eighty men outside with this warning: "If one of you lets any of the men I am placing in your hands escape, it will be your life for his life."

[25] As soon as Jehu had finished making the burnt offering, he ordered the guards and officers: "Go in and kill them; let no one escape." So they cut them down with the sword. The guards and officers threw the bodies out and then entered the inner shrine of the temple of Baal. [26] They brought the sacred stone out of the temple of Baal and burned it. [27] They demolished the sacred stone of Baal and tore down the temple of Baal, and people have used it for a latrine to this day.

[28] So Jehu destroyed Baal worship in Israel. [29] However, he did not turn away from the sins of Jeroboam son of Nebat, which he had caused Israel to commit—the worship of the golden calves at Bethel and Dan.

[30] The LORD said to Jehu, "Because you have done well in accomplishing what is right in my eyes and have done to the house of Ahab all I had in mind to do, your descendants will sit on the throne of Israel to the fourth generation." [31] Yet Jehu was not careful to keep the law of the LORD, the God of Israel, with all his heart. He did not turn away from the sins of Jeroboam, which he had caused Israel to commit.

[32] In those days the LORD began to reduce the size of Israel. Hazael overpowered the Israelites throughout their territory [33] east of the Jordan in all the land of Gilead (the region of Gad, Reuben and Manasseh), from Aroer by the Arnon Gorge through Gilead to Bashan.

[34] As for the other events of Jehu's reign, all he did, and all his achievements, are they not written in the book of the annals of the kings of Israel?

[35] Jehu rested with his ancestors and was buried in Samaria. And Jehoahaz his son succeeded him as king. [36] The time that Jehu reigned over Israel in Samaria was twenty-eight years.

Athaliah and Joash

11 When Athaliah the mother of Ahaziah saw that her son was dead, she proceeded to destroy the whole royal family.

²But Jehosheba, the daughter of King Jehoram[a] and sister of Ahaziah, took Joash son of Ahaziah and stole him away from among the royal princes, who were about to be murdered. She put him and his nurse in a bedroom to hide him from Athaliah; so he was not killed. ³He remained hidden with his nurse at the temple of the LORD for six years while Athaliah ruled the land.

⁴In the seventh year Jehoiada sent for the commanders of units of a hundred, the Carites and the guards and had them brought to him at the temple of the LORD. He made a covenant with them and put them under oath at the temple of the LORD. Then he showed them the king's son. ⁵He commanded them, saying, "This is what you are to do: You who are in the three companies that are going on duty on the Sabbath — a third of you guarding the royal palace, ⁶a third at the Sur Gate, and a third at the gate behind the guard, who take turns guarding the temple — ⁷and you who are in the other two companies that normally go off Sabbath duty are all to guard the temple for the king. ⁸Station yourselves around the king, each of you with weapon in hand. Anyone who approaches your ranks[b] is to be put to death. Stay close to the king wherever he goes."

⁹The commanders of units of a hundred did just as Jehoiada the priest ordered. Each one took his men — those who were going on duty on the Sabbath and those who were going off duty — and came to Jehoiada the priest. ¹⁰Then he gave the commanders the spears and shields that had belonged to King David and that were in the temple of the LORD. ¹¹The guards, each with weapon in hand, stationed themselves around the king — near the altar and the temple, from the south side to the north side of the temple.

¹²Jehoiada brought out the king's son and put the crown on him; he presented him with a copy of the covenant and proclaimed him king. They anointed him, and the people clapped their hands and shouted, "Long live the king!"

¹³When Athaliah heard the noise made by the guards and the people, she went to the people at the temple of the LORD. ¹⁴She looked and there was the king, standing by the pillar, as the custom was. The officers and the trumpeters were beside the king, and all the people of the land were rejoicing and blowing trumpets. Then Athaliah tore her robes and called out, "Treason! Treason!"

¹⁵Jehoiada the priest ordered the commanders of units of a hundred, who were in charge of the troops: "Bring her out between the ranks[c] and put to the sword anyone who follows her." For the priest had said, "She must not be put to death in the temple of the LORD." ¹⁶So they seized her as she reached the place where the horses enter the palace grounds, and there she was put to death.

¹⁷Jehoiada then made a covenant between the LORD and the king and people that they would be the LORD's people. He also made a covenant between the king and the people. ¹⁸All the people of the land went to the temple of Baal and tore it down. They smashed the altars and idols to pieces and killed Mattan the priest of Baal in front of the altars.

Then Jehoiada the priest posted guards at the temple of the LORD. ¹⁹He took with him the commanders of hundreds, the Carites, the guards and all the people of the land, and together they brought the king down from the temple of the LORD and went into the palace, entering by way of the gate of the guards. The king then took his place on the royal throne. ²⁰All the people of the land rejoiced, and the city was calm, because Athaliah had been slain with the sword at the palace.

²¹Joash[d] was seven years old when he began to reign.[e]

Joash Repairs the Temple

12[f] In the seventh year of Jehu, Joash[g] became king, and he reigned in Jerusalem forty years. His mother's name was Zibiah; she was from Beersheba. ²Joash did what was right in the eyes of the LORD all the years Jehoiada the priest instructed him. ³The high places, however, were not removed; the people continued to offer sacrifices and burn incense there.

⁴Joash said to the priests, "Collect all the

---

[a] 2 Hebrew *Joram*, a variant of *Jehoram*   [b] 8 Or *approaches the precincts*   [c] 15 Or *out from the precincts*
[d] 21 Hebrew *Jehoash*, a variant of *Joash*   [e] 21 In Hebrew texts this verse (11:21) is numbered 12:1.   [f] In
Hebrew texts 12:1-21 is numbered 12:2-22.   [g] 1 Hebrew *Jehoash*, a variant of *Joash*; also in verses 2, 4, 6,
7 and 18

money that is brought as sacred offerings to the temple of the LORD — the money collected in the census, the money received from personal vows and the money brought voluntarily to the temple. ⁵Let every priest receive the money from one of the treasurers, then use it to repair whatever damage is found in the temple."

⁶But by the twenty-third year of King Joash the priests still had not repaired the temple. ⁷Therefore King Joash summoned Jehoiada the priest and the other priests and asked them, "Why aren't you repairing the damage done to the temple? Take no more money from your treasurers, but hand it over for repairing the temple." ⁸The priests agreed that they would not collect any more money from the people and that they would not repair the temple themselves.

⁹Jehoiada the priest took a chest and bored a hole in its lid. He placed it beside the altar, on the right side as one enters the temple of the LORD. The priests who guarded the entrance put into the chest all the money that was brought to the temple of the LORD. ¹⁰Whenever they saw that there was a large amount of money in the chest, the royal secretary and the high priest came, counted the money that had been brought into the temple of the LORD and put it into bags. ¹¹When the amount had been determined, they gave the money to the men appointed to supervise the work on the temple. With it they paid those who worked on the temple of the LORD — the carpenters and builders, ¹²the masons and stonecutters. They purchased timber and blocks of dressed stone for the repair of the temple of the LORD, and met all the other expenses of restoring the temple.

¹³The money brought into the temple was not spent for making silver basins, wick trimmers, sprinkling bowls, trumpets or any other articles of gold or silver for the temple of the LORD; ¹⁴it was paid to the workers, who used it to repair the temple. ¹⁵They did not require an accounting from those to whom they gave the money to pay the workers, because they acted with complete honesty. ¹⁶The money from the guilt offerings and sin offerings[a] was not brought into the temple of the LORD; it belonged to the priests.

¹⁷About this time Hazael king of Aram went up and attacked Gath and captured it. Then he turned to attack Jerusalem. ¹⁸But Joash king of Judah took all the sacred objects dedicated by his predecessors — Jehoshaphat, Jehoram and Ahaziah, the kings of Judah — and the gifts he himself had dedicated and all the gold found in the treasuries of the temple of the LORD and of the royal palace, and he sent them to Hazael king of Aram, who then withdrew from Jerusalem.

¹⁹As for the other events of the reign of Joash, and all he did, are they not written in the book of the annals of the kings of Judah? ²⁰His officials conspired against him and assassinated him at Beth Millo, on the road down to Silla. ²¹The officials who murdered him were Jozabad son of Shimeath and Jehozabad son of Shomer. He died and was buried with his ancestors in the City of David. And Amaziah his son succeeded him as king.

Jehoahaz King of Israel

13 In the twenty-third year of Joash son of Ahaziah king of Judah, Jehoahaz son of Jehu became king of Israel in Samaria, and he reigned seventeen years. ²He did evil in the eyes of the LORD by following the sins of Jeroboam son of Nebat, which he had caused Israel to commit, and he did not turn away from them. ³So the LORD's anger burned against Israel, and for a long time he kept them under the power of Hazael king of Aram and Ben-Hadad his son.

⁴Then Jehoahaz sought the LORD's favor, and the LORD listened to him, for he saw how severely the king of Aram was oppressing Israel. ⁵The LORD provided a deliverer for Israel, and they escaped from the power of Aram. So the Israelites lived in their own homes as they had before. ⁶But they did not turn away from the sins of the house of Jeroboam, which he had caused Israel to commit; they continued in them. Also, the Asherah pole[b] remained standing in Samaria.

⁷Nothing had been left of the army of Jehoahaz except fifty horsemen, ten chariots and ten thousand foot soldiers, for the king of Aram had destroyed the rest and made them like the dust at threshing time.

⁸As for the other events of the reign of Jehoahaz, all he did and his achievements, are

---

a 16 Or *purification offerings*   *b 6* That is, a wooden symbol of the goddess Asherah; here and elsewhere in 2 Kings they not written in the book of the annals of the kings of Israel? [9] Jehoahaz rested with his ancestors and was buried in Samaria. And Jehoash[a] his son succeeded him as king.

Jehoash King of Israel

[10] In the thirty-seventh year of Joash king of Judah, Jehoash son of Jehoahaz became king of Israel in Samaria, and he reigned sixteen years. [11] He did evil in the eyes of the LORD and did not turn away from any of the sins of Jeroboam son of Nebat, which he had caused Israel to commit; he continued in them.

[12] As for the other events of the reign of Jehoash, all he did and his achievements, including his war against Amaziah king of Judah, are they not written in the book of the annals of the kings of Israel? [13] Jehoash rested with his ancestors, and Jeroboam succeeded him on the throne. Jehoash was buried in Samaria with the kings of Israel.

[14] Now Elisha had been suffering from the illness from which he died. Jehoash king of Israel went down to see him and wept over him. "My father! My father!" he cried. "The chariots and horsemen of Israel!"

[15] Elisha said, "Get a bow and some arrows," and he did so. [16] "Take the bow in your hands," he said to the king of Israel. When he had taken it, Elisha put his hands on the king's hands.

[17] "Open the east window," he said, and he opened it. "Shoot!" Elisha said, and he shot. "The LORD's arrow of victory, the arrow of victory over Aram!" Elisha declared. "You will completely destroy the Arameans at Aphek."

[18] Then he said, "Take the arrows," and the king took them. Elisha told him, "Strike the ground." He struck it three times and stopped. [19] The man of God was angry with him and said, "You should have struck the ground five or six times; then you would have defeated Aram and completely destroyed it. But now you will defeat it only three times."

[20] Elisha died and was buried.

Now Moabite raiders used to enter the country every spring. [21] Once while some Israelites were burying a man, suddenly they saw a band of raiders; so they threw the man's body into Elisha's tomb. When the body touched Elisha's bones, the man came to life and stood up on his feet.

[22] Hazael king of Aram oppressed Israel throughout the reign of Jehoahaz. [23] But the LORD was gracious to them and had compassion and showed concern for them because of his covenant with Abraham, Isaac and Jacob. To this day he has been unwilling to destroy them or banish them from his presence.

[24] Hazael king of Aram died, and Ben-Hadad his son succeeded him as king. [25] Then Jehoash son of Jehoahaz recaptured from Ben-Hadad son of Hazael the towns he had taken in battle from his father Jehoahaz. Three times Jehoash defeated him, and so he recovered the Israelite towns.

Amaziah King of Judah

14 In the second year of Jehoash[b] son of Jehoahaz king of Israel, Amaziah son of Joash king of Judah began to reign. [2] He was twenty-five years old when he became king, and he reigned in Jerusalem twenty-nine years. His mother's name was Jehoaddan; she was from Jerusalem. [3] He did what was right in the eyes of the LORD, but not as his father David had done. In everything he followed the example of his father Joash. [4] The high places, however, were not removed; the people continued to offer sacrifices and burn incense there.

[5] After the kingdom was firmly in his grasp, he executed the officials who had murdered his father the king. [6] Yet he did not put the children of the assassins to death, in accordance with what is written in the Book of the Law of Moses where the LORD commanded: "Parents are not to be put to death for their children, nor children put to death for their parents; each will die for their own sin."[c]

[7] He was the one who defeated ten thousand Edomites in the Valley of Salt and captured Sela in battle, calling it Joktheel, the name it has to this day.

[8] Then Amaziah sent messengers to Jehoash son of Jehoahaz, the son of Jehu, king of Israel, with the challenge: "Come, let us face each other in battle."

[9] But Jehoash king of Israel replied to Amaziah king of Judah: "A thistle in Lebanon sent

---

a 9 Hebrew *Joash,* a variant of *Jehoash*; also in verses 12-14 and 25 *b* 1 Hebrew *Joash,* a variant of *Jehoash*; also in verses 13, 23 and 27 *c* 6 Deut. 24:16

a message to a cedar in Lebanon, 'Give your daughter to my son in marriage.' Then a wild beast in Lebanon came along and trampled the thistle underfoot. [10]You have indeed defeated Edom and now you are arrogant. Glory in your victory, but stay at home! Why ask for trouble and cause your own downfall and that of Judah also?"

[11]Amaziah, however, would not listen, so Jehoash king of Israel attacked. He and Amaziah king of Judah faced each other at Beth Shemesh in Judah. [12]Judah was routed by Israel, and every man fled to his home. [13]Jehoash king of Israel captured Amaziah king of Judah, the son of Joash, the son of Ahaziah, at Beth Shemesh. Then Jehoash went to Jerusalem and broke down the wall of Jerusalem from the Ephraim Gate to the Corner Gate — a section about four hundred cubits long.[a] [14]He took all the gold and silver and all the articles found in the temple of the LORD and in the treasuries of the royal palace. He also took hostages and returned to Samaria.

[15]As for the other events of the reign of Jehoash, what he did and his achievements, including his war against Amaziah king of Judah, are they not written in the book of the annals of the kings of Israel? [16]Jehoash rested with his ancestors and was buried in Samaria with the kings of Israel. And Jeroboam his son succeeded him as king.

[17]Amaziah son of Joash king of Judah lived for fifteen years after the death of Jehoash son of Jehoahaz king of Israel. [18]As for the other events of Amaziah's reign, are they not written in the book of the annals of the kings of Judah?

[19]They conspired against him in Jerusalem, and he fled to Lachish, but they sent men after him to Lachish and killed him there. [20]He was brought back by horse and was buried in Jerusalem with his ancestors, in the City of David.

[21]Then all the people of Judah took Azariah,[b] who was sixteen years old, and made him king in place of his father Amaziah. [22]He was the one who rebuilt Elath and restored it to Judah after Amaziah rested with his ancestors.

Jeroboam II King of Israel

[23]In the fifteenth year of Amaziah son of Joash king of Judah, Jeroboam son of Jehoash king of Israel became king in Samaria, and he reigned forty-one years. [24]He did evil in the eyes of the LORD and did not turn away from any of the sins of Jeroboam son of Nebat, which he had caused Israel to commit. [25]He was the one who restored the boundaries of Israel from Lebo Hamath to the Dead Sea,[c] in accordance with the word of the LORD, the God of Israel, spoken through his servant Jonah son of Amittai, the prophet from Gath Hepher.

[26]The LORD had seen how bitterly everyone in Israel, whether slave or free, was suffering;[d] there was no one to help them. [27]And since the LORD had not said he would blot out the name of Israel from under heaven, he saved them by the hand of Jeroboam son of Jehoash.

[28]As for the other events of Jeroboam's reign, all he did, and his military achievements, including how he recovered for Israel both Damascus and Hamath, which had belonged to Judah, are they not written in the book of the annals of the kings of Israel? [29]Jeroboam rested with his ancestors, the kings of Israel. And Zechariah his son succeeded him as king.

Azariah King of Judah

15 In the twenty-seventh year of Jeroboam king of Israel, Azariah[e] son of Amaziah king of Judah began to reign. [2]He was sixteen years old when he became king, and he reigned in Jerusalem fifty-two years. His mother's name was Jekoliah; she was from Jerusalem. [3]He did what was right in the eyes of the LORD, just as his father Amaziah had done. [4]The high places, however, were not removed; the people continued to offer sacrifices and burn incense there.

[5]The LORD afflicted the king with leprosy[f] until the day he died, and he lived in a separate house.[g] Jotham the king's son had charge of the palace and governed the people of the land.

[6]As for the other events of Azariah's reign, and all he did, are they not written in the

---

[a] 13 That is, about 600 feet or about 180 meters   [b] 21 Also called *Uzziah*   [c] 25 Hebrew *the Sea of the Arabah*   [d] 26 Or *Israel was suffering. They were without a ruler or leader, and*   [e] 1 Also called *Uzziah*; also in verses 6, 7, 8, 17, 23 and 27   [f] 5 The Hebrew for *leprosy* was used for various diseases affecting the skin.   [g] 5 Or *in a house where he was relieved of responsibilities*

CHOOSE GOD NOW

READ: 2 KINGS 14:23-24

You're not alone if all the Bible kings confuse you. Nearly four dozen ruled in the hundreds of years after King Saul came to Israel's throne (1 Samuel 10:1-27). The list of kings is extra long because after King Solomon, the nation split into a northern kingdom (Israel) and a southern kingdom (Judah), creating two royal lines.

The staggered sequence of these rulers show up in the introduction of each king. For example, Jeroboam became king of Israel fifteen years into the rule of King Amaziah of Judah (2 Kings 14:23). Far more important than the chronology, however, is the description of each king. A few do right, yet many completely reject God.

You probably know families where everyone takes the wrong path in life until someone finally chooses a better way. While all of Israel's kings consistently did evil, some of Judah's kings broke loose from past sinful patterns to live for God. A few even built on the godly habits of the previous king, like Azariah, also known as Uzziah (15:1-7), and Jotham, his son (vv. 33-38).

You might be surrounded by people who don't follow God. Your own family might not be fully committed to him. But these old royal stories prove it's possible for you to do something completely new. You can choose God now.

BUILDING

FAITH

WISDOM

STRENGTH

book of the annals of the kings of Judah? [7]Azariah rested with his ancestors and was buried near them in the City of David. And Jotham his son succeeded him as king.

Zechariah King of Israel

[8]In the thirty-eighth year of Azariah king of Judah, Zechariah son of Jeroboam became king of Israel in Samaria, and he reigned six months. [9]He did evil in the eyes of the LORD, as his predecessors had done. He did not turn away from the sins of Jeroboam son of Nebat, which he had caused Israel to commit.

[10]Shallum son of Jabesh conspired against Zechariah. He attacked him in front of the people,[a] assassinated him and succeeded him as king. [11]The other events of Zechariah's reign are written in the book of the annals of the kings of Israel. [12]So the word of the LORD spoken to Jehu was fulfilled: "Your descendants will sit on the throne of Israel to the fourth generation."[b]

Shallum King of Israel

[13]Shallum son of Jabesh became king in the thirty-ninth year of Uzziah king of Judah, and he reigned in Samaria one month. [14]Then Menahem son of Gadi went from Tirzah up to Samaria. He attacked Shallum son of Jabesh in Samaria, assassinated him and succeeded him as king.

[15]The other events of Shallum's reign, and the conspiracy he led, are written in the book of the annals of the kings of Israel.

[16]At that time Menahem, starting out from Tirzah, attacked Tiphsah and everyone in the city and its vicinity, because they refused to open their gates. He sacked Tiphsah and ripped open all the pregnant women.

Menahem King of Israel

[17]In the thirty-ninth year of Azariah king of Judah, Menahem son of Gadi became king of Israel, and he reigned in Samaria ten years. [18]He did evil in the eyes of the LORD. During his entire reign he did not turn away from the sins of Jeroboam son of Nebat, which he had caused Israel to commit.

[19]Then Pul[c] king of Assyria invaded the land, and Menahem gave him a thousand talents[d] of silver to gain his support and strengthen his own hold on the kingdom. [20]Menahem exacted this money from Israel. Every wealthy person had to contribute fifty shekels[e] of silver to be given to the king of Assyria. So the king of Assyria withdrew and stayed in the land no longer.

[21]As for the other events of Menahem's reign, and all he did, are they not written in the book of the annals of the kings of Israel? [22]Menahem rested with his ancestors. And Pekahiah his son succeeded him as king.

Pekahiah King of Israel

[23]In the fiftieth year of Azariah king of Judah, Pekahiah son of Menahem became king of Israel in Samaria, and he reigned two years. [24]Pekahiah did evil in the eyes of the LORD. He did not turn away from the sins of Jeroboam son of Nebat, which he had caused Israel to commit. [25]One of his chief officers, Pekah son of Remaliah, conspired against him. Taking fifty men of Gilead with him, he assassinated Pekahiah, along with Argob and Arieh, in the citadel of the royal palace at Samaria. So Pekah killed Pekahiah and succeeded him as king.

[26]The other events of Pekahiah's reign, and all he did, are written in the book of the annals of the kings of Israel.

Pekah King of Israel

[27]In the fifty-second year of Azariah king of Judah, Pekah son of Remaliah became king of Israel in Samaria, and he reigned twenty years. [28]He did evil in the eyes of the LORD. He did not turn away from the sins of Jeroboam son of Nebat, which he had caused Israel to commit.

[29]In the time of Pekah king of Israel, Tiglath-Pileser king of Assyria came and took Ijon, Abel Beth Maakah, Janoah, Kedesh and Hazor. He took Gilead and Galilee, including all the land of Naphtali, and deported the people to Assyria. [30]Then Hoshea son of Elah conspired against Pekah son of Remaliah. He attacked and assassinated him, and then succeeded him as king in the twentieth year of Jotham son of Uzziah.

[31]As for the other events of Pekah's reign,

---

[a] 10 Hebrew; some Septuagint manuscripts *in Ibleam*   [b] 12 2 Kings 10:30   [c] 19 Also called *Tiglath-Pileser*   [d] 19 That is, about 38 tons or about 34 metric tons   [e] 20 That is, about 1 1/4 pounds or about 575 grams

and all he did, are they not written in the book of the annals of the kings of Israel?

Jotham King of Judah

³²In the second year of Pekah son of Remaliah king of Israel, Jotham son of Uzziah king of Judah began to reign. ³³He was twenty-five years old when he became king, and he reigned in Jerusalem sixteen years. His mother's name was Jerusha daughter of Zadok. ³⁴He did what was right in the eyes of the LORD, just as his father Uzziah had done. ³⁵The high places, however, were not removed; the people continued to offer sacrifices and burn incense there. Jotham rebuilt the Upper Gate of the temple of the LORD.

³⁶As for the other events of Jotham's reign, and what he did, are they not written in the book of the annals of the kings of Judah? ³⁷(In those days the LORD began to send Rezin king of Aram and Pekah son of Remaliah against Judah.) ³⁸Jotham rested with his ancestors and was buried with them in the City of David, the city of his father. And Ahaz his son succeeded him as king.

Ahaz King of Judah

16 In the seventeenth year of Pekah son of Remaliah, Ahaz son of Jotham king of Judah began to reign. ²Ahaz was twenty years old when he became king, and he reigned in Jerusalem sixteen years. Unlike David his father, he did not do what was right in the eyes of the LORD his God. ³He followed the ways of the kings of Israel and even sacrificed his son in the fire, engaging in the detestable practices of the nations the LORD had driven out before the Israelites. ⁴He offered sacrifices and burned incense at the high places, on the hilltops and under every spreading tree.

⁵Then Rezin king of Aram and Pekah son of Remaliah king of Israel marched up to fight against Jerusalem and besieged Ahaz, but they could not overpower him. ⁶At that time, Rezin king of Aram recovered Elath for Aram by driving out the people of Judah. Edomites then moved into Elath and have lived there to this day.

⁷Ahaz sent messengers to say to Tiglath-Pileser king of Assyria, "I am your servant and vassal. Come up and save me out of the hand of the king of Aram and of the king of Israel, who are attacking me." ⁸And Ahaz took the silver and gold found in the temple of the LORD and in the treasuries of the royal palace and sent it as a gift to the king of Assyria. ⁹The king of Assyria complied by attacking Damascus and capturing it. He deported its inhabitants to Kir and put Rezin to death.

¹⁰Then King Ahaz went to Damascus to meet Tiglath-Pileser king of Assyria. He saw an altar in Damascus and sent to Uriah the priest a sketch of the altar, with detailed plans for its construction. ¹¹So Uriah the priest built an altar in accordance with all the plans that King Ahaz had sent from Damascus and finished it before King Ahaz returned. ¹²When the king came back from Damascus and saw the altar, he approached it and presented offerings*a* on it. ¹³He offered up his burnt offering and grain offering, poured out his drink offering, and splashed the blood of his fellowship offerings against the altar. ¹⁴As for the bronze altar that stood before the LORD, he brought it from the front of the temple—from between the new altar and the temple of the LORD—and put it on the north side of the new altar.

¹⁵King Ahaz then gave these orders to Uriah the priest: "On the large new altar, offer the morning burnt offering and the evening grain offering, the king's burnt offering and his grain offering, and the burnt offering of all the people of the land, and their grain offering and their drink offering. Splash against this altar the blood of all the burnt offerings and sacrifices. But I will use the bronze altar for seeking guidance." ¹⁶And Uriah the priest did just as King Ahaz had ordered.

¹⁷King Ahaz cut off the side panels and removed the basins from the movable stands. He removed the Sea from the bronze bulls that supported it and set it on a stone base. ¹⁸He took away the Sabbath canopy*b* that had been built at the temple and removed the royal entryway outside the temple of the LORD, in deference to the king of Assyria.

¹⁹As for the other events of the reign of Ahaz, and what he did, are they not written in the book of the annals of the kings of Judah? ²⁰Ahaz rested with his ancestors and was buried with them in the City of David.

---

a 12 Or *and went up*   *b* 18 Or *the dais of his throne* (see Septuagint)

And Hezekiah his son succeeded him as king.

Hoshea Last King of Israel

17 In the twelfth year of Ahaz king of Judah, Hoshea son of Elah became king of Israel in Samaria, and he reigned nine years. [2]He did evil in the eyes of the LORD, but not like the kings of Israel who preceded him.

[3]Shalmaneser king of Assyria came up to attack Hoshea, who had been Shalmaneser's vassal and had paid him tribute. [4]But the king of Assyria discovered that Hoshea was a traitor, for he had sent envoys to So[a] king of Egypt, and he no longer paid tribute to the king of Assyria, as he had done year by year. Therefore Shalmaneser seized him and put him in prison. [5]The king of Assyria invaded the entire land, marched against Samaria and laid siege to it for three years. [6]In the ninth year of Hoshea, the king of Assyria captured Samaria and deported the Israelites to Assyria. He settled them in Halah, in Gozan on the Habor River and in the towns of the Medes.

Israel Exiled Because of Sin

[7]All this took place because the Israelites had sinned against the LORD their God, who had brought them up out of Egypt from under the power of Pharaoh king of Egypt. They worshiped other gods [8]and followed the practices of the nations the LORD had driven out before them, as well as the practices that the kings of Israel had introduced. [9]The Israelites secretly did things against the LORD their God that were not right. From watchtower to fortified city they built themselves high places in all their towns. [10]They set up sacred stones and Asherah poles on every high hill and under every spreading tree. [11]At every high place they burned incense, as the nations whom the LORD had driven out before them had done. They did wicked things that aroused the LORD's anger. [12]They worshiped idols, though the LORD had said, "You shall not do this."[b] [13]The LORD warned Israel and Judah through all his prophets and seers: "Turn from your evil ways. Observe my commands and decrees, in accordance with the entire Law that I commanded

your ancestors to obey and that I delivered to you through my servants the prophets."

[14]But they would not listen and were as stiff-necked as their ancestors, who did not trust in the LORD their God. [15]They rejected his decrees and the covenant he had made with their ancestors and the statutes he had warned them to keep. They followed worthless idols and themselves became worthless. They imitated the nations around them although the LORD had ordered them, "Do not do as they do."

[16]They forsook all the commands of the LORD their God and made for themselves two idols cast in the shape of calves, and an Asherah pole. They bowed down to all the starry hosts, and they worshiped Baal. [17]They sacrificed their sons and daughters in the fire. They practiced divination and sought omens and sold themselves to do evil in the eyes of the LORD, arousing his anger.

[18]So the LORD was very angry with Israel and removed them from his presence. Only the tribe of Judah was left, [19]and even Judah did not keep the commands of the LORD their God. They followed the practices Israel had introduced. [20]Therefore the LORD rejected all the people of Israel; he afflicted them and gave them into the hands of plunderers, until he thrust them from his presence.

[21]When he tore Israel away from the house of David, they made Jeroboam son of Nebat their king. Jeroboam enticed Israel away from following the LORD and caused them to commit a great sin. [22]The Israelites persisted in all the sins of Jeroboam and did not turn away from them [23]until the LORD removed them from his presence, as he had warned through all his servants the prophets. So the people of Israel were taken from their homeland into exile in Assyria, and they are still there.

Samaria Resettled

[24]The king of Assyria brought people from Babylon, Kuthah, Avva, Hamath and Sepharvaim and settled them in the towns of Samaria to replace the Israelites. They took over Samaria and lived in its towns. [25]When they first lived there, they did not worship the LORD; so he sent lions among them and they killed some of the people. [26]It was reported

---

[a] 4 So is probably an abbreviation for Osorkon.   [b] 12 Exodus 20:4,5

to the king of Assyria: "The people you deported and resettled in the towns of Samaria do not know what the god of that country requires. He has sent lions among them, which are killing them off, because the people do not know what he requires."

27 Then the king of Assyria gave this order: "Have one of the priests you took captive from Samaria go back to live there and teach the people what the god of the land requires." 28 So one of the priests who had been exiled from Samaria came to live in Bethel and taught them how to worship the LORD.

29 Nevertheless, each national group made its own gods in the several towns where they settled, and set them up in the shrines the people of Samaria had made at the high places. 30 The people from Babylon made Sukkoth Benoth, those from Kuthah made Nergal, and those from Hamath made Ashima; 31 the Avvites made Nibhaz and Tartak, and the Sepharvites burned their children in the fire as sacrifices to Adrammelek and Anammelek, the gods of Sepharvaim. 32 They worshiped the LORD, but they also appointed all sorts of their own people to officiate for them as priests in the shrines at the high places. 33 They worshiped the LORD, but they also served their own gods in accordance with the customs of the nations from which they had been brought.

34 To this day they persist in their former practices. They neither worship the LORD nor adhere to the decrees and regulations, the laws and commands that the LORD gave the descendants of Jacob, whom he named Israel. 35 When the LORD made a covenant with the Israelites, he commanded them: "Do not worship any other gods or bow down to them, serve them or sacrifice to them. 36 But the LORD, who brought you up out of Egypt with mighty power and outstretched arm, is the one you must worship. To him you shall bow down and to him offer sacrifices. 37 You must always be careful to keep the decrees and regulations, the laws and commands he wrote for you. Do not worship other gods. 38 Do not forget the covenant I have made with you, and do not worship other gods. 39 Rather, worship the LORD your God; it is he who will deliver you from the hand of all your enemies."

40 They would not listen, however, but persisted in their former practices. 41 Even while these people were worshiping the LORD, they were serving their idols. To this day their children and grandchildren continue to do as their ancestors did.

Hezekiah King of Judah

18 In the third year of Hoshea son of Elah king of Israel, Hezekiah son of Ahaz king of Judah began to reign. 2 He was twenty-five years old when he became king, and he reigned in Jerusalem twenty-nine years. His mother's name was Abijah*a* daughter of Zechariah. 3 He did what was right in the eyes of the LORD, just as his father David had done. 4 He removed the high places, smashed the sacred stones and cut down the Asherah poles. He broke into pieces the bronze snake Moses had made, for up to that time the Israelites had been burning incense to it. (It was called Nehushtan.*b*)

5 Hezekiah trusted in the LORD, the God of Israel. There was no one like him among all the kings of Judah, either before him or after him. 6 He held fast to the LORD and did not stop following him; he kept the commands the LORD had given Moses. 7 And the LORD was with him; he was successful in whatever he undertook. He rebelled against the king of Assyria and did not serve him. 8 From watchtower to fortified city, he defeated the Philistines, as far as Gaza and its territory.

9 In King Hezekiah's fourth year, which was the seventh year of Hoshea son of Elah king of Israel, Shalmaneser king of Assyria marched against Samaria and laid siege to it. 10 At the end of three years the Assyrians took it. So Samaria was captured in Hezekiah's sixth year, which was the ninth year of Hoshea king of Israel. 11 The king of Assyria deported Israel to Assyria and settled them in Halah, in Gozan on the Habor River and in towns of the Medes. 12 This happened because they had not obeyed the LORD their God, but had violated his covenant—all that Moses the servant of the LORD commanded. They neither listened to the commands nor carried them out.

13 In the fourteenth year of King Hezekiah's reign, Sennacherib king of Assyria attacked all the fortified cities of Judah and

---

a 2 Hebrew *Abi*, a variant of *Abijah*   *b* 4 *Nehushtan* sounds like the Hebrew for both *bronze* and *snake*.

captured them. [14]So Hezekiah king of Judah sent this message to the king of Assyria at Lachish: "I have done wrong. Withdraw from me, and I will pay whatever you demand of me." The king of Assyria exacted from Hezekiah king of Judah three hundred talents[a] of silver and thirty talents[b] of gold. [15]So Hezekiah gave him all the silver that was found in the temple of the LORD and in the treasuries of the royal palace.

[16]At this time Hezekiah king of Judah stripped off the gold with which he had covered the doors and doorposts of the temple of the LORD, and gave it to the king of Assyria.

Sennacherib Threatens Jerusalem

[17]The king of Assyria sent his supreme commander, his chief officer and his field commander with a large army, from Lachish to King Hezekiah at Jerusalem. They came up to Jerusalem and stopped at the aqueduct of the Upper Pool, on the road to the Washerman's Field. [18]They called for the king; and Eliakim son of Hilkiah the palace administrator, Shebna the secretary, and Joah son of Asaph the recorder went out to them.

[19]The field commander said to them, "Tell Hezekiah:

"'This is what the great king, the king of Assyria, says: On what are you basing this confidence of yours? [20]You say you have the counsel and the might for war—but you speak only empty words. On whom are you depending, that you rebel against me? [21]Look, I know you are depending on Egypt, that splintered reed of a staff, which pierces the hand of anyone who leans on it! Such is Pharaoh king of Egypt to all who depend on him. [22]But if you say to me, "We are depending on the LORD our God"—isn't he the one whose high places and altars Hezekiah removed, saying to Judah and Jerusalem, "You must worship before this altar in Jerusalem"?

[23]"'Come now, make a bargain with my master, the king of Assyria: I will give you two thousand horses—if you can put riders on them! [24]How can you repulse one officer of the least of my master's officials, even though you are depending on Egypt for chariots and horsemen[c]? [25]Furthermore, have I come to attack and destroy this place without word from the LORD? The LORD himself told me to march against this country and destroy it.'"

[26]Then Eliakim son of Hilkiah, and Shebna and Joah said to the field commander, "Please speak to your servants in Aramaic, since we understand it. Don't speak to us in Hebrew in the hearing of the people on the wall."

[27]But the commander replied, "Was it only to your master and you that my master sent me to say these things, and not to the people sitting on the wall—who, like you, will have to eat their own excrement and drink their own urine?"

[28]Then the commander stood and called out in Hebrew, "Hear the word of the great king, the king of Assyria! [29]This is what the king says: Do not let Hezekiah deceive you. He cannot deliver you from my hand. [30]Do not let Hezekiah persuade you to trust in the LORD when he says, 'The LORD will surely deliver us; this city will not be given into the hand of the king of Assyria.'

[31]"Do not listen to Hezekiah. This is what the king of Assyria says: Make peace with me and come out to me. Then each of you will eat fruit from your own vine and fig tree and drink water from your own cistern, [32]until I come and take you to a land like your own— a land of grain and new wine, a land of bread and vineyards, a land of olive trees and honey. Choose life and not death!

"Do not listen to Hezekiah, for he is misleading you when he says, 'The LORD will deliver us.' [33]Has the god of any nation ever delivered his land from the hand of the king of Assyria? [34]Where are the gods of Hamath and Arpad? Where are the gods of Sepharvaim, Hena and Ivvah? Have they rescued Samaria from my hand? [35]Who of all the gods of these countries has been able to save his land from me? How then can the LORD deliver Jerusalem from my hand?"

[36]But the people remained silent and said nothing in reply, because the king had commanded, "Do not answer him."

---

[a] 14 That is, about 11 tons or about 10 metric tons   [b] 14 That is, about 1 ton or about 1 metric ton
[c] 24 Or charioteers

[37] Then Eliakim son of Hilkiah the palace administrator, Shebna the secretary, and Joah son of Asaph the recorder went to Hezekiah, with their clothes torn, and told him what the field commander had said.

Jerusalem's Deliverance Foretold

19 When King Hezekiah heard this, he tore his clothes and put on sackcloth and went into the temple of the LORD. [2] He sent Eliakim the palace administrator, Shebna the secretary and the leading priests, all wearing sackcloth, to the prophet Isaiah son of Amoz. [3] They told him, "This is what Hezekiah says: This day is a day of distress and rebuke and disgrace, as when children come to the moment of birth and there is no strength to deliver them. [4] It may be that the LORD your God will hear all the words of the field commander, whom his master, the king of Assyria, has sent to ridicule the living God, and that he will rebuke him for the words the LORD your God has heard. Therefore pray for the remnant that still survives."

[5] When King Hezekiah's officials came to Isaiah, [6] Isaiah said to them, "Tell your master, 'This is what the LORD says: Do not be afraid of what you have heard — those words with which the underlings of the king of Assyria have blasphemed me. [7] Listen! When he hears a certain report, I will make him want to return to his own country, and there I will have him cut down with the sword.' "

[8] When the field commander heard that the king of Assyria had left Lachish, he withdrew and found the king fighting against Libnah.

[9] Now Sennacherib received a report that Tirhakah, the king of Cush,[a] was marching out to fight against him. So he again sent messengers to Hezekiah with this word: [10] "Say to Hezekiah king of Judah: Do not let the god you depend on deceive you when he says, 'Jerusalem will not be given into the hands of the king of Assyria.' [11] Surely you have heard what the kings of Assyria have done to all the countries, destroying them completely. And will you be delivered? [12] Did the gods of the nations that were destroyed by my predecessors deliver them — the gods of Gozan, Harran, Rezeph and the people of Eden who were in Tel Assar? [13] Where is the king of Hamath or the king of Arpad? Where are the kings of Lair, Sepharvaim, Hena and Ivvah?"

Hezekiah's Prayer

[14] Hezekiah received the letter from the messengers and read it. Then he went up to the temple of the LORD and spread it out before the LORD. [15] And Hezekiah prayed to the LORD: "LORD, the God of Israel, enthroned between the cherubim, you alone are God over all the kingdoms of the earth. You have made heaven and earth. [16] Give ear, LORD, and hear; open your eyes, LORD, and see; listen to the words Sennacherib has sent to ridicule the living God.

[17] "It is true, LORD, that the Assyrian kings have laid waste these nations and their lands. [18] They have thrown their gods into the fire and destroyed them, for they were not gods but only wood and stone, fashioned by human hands. [19] Now, LORD our God, deliver us from his hand, so that all the kingdoms of the earth may know that you alone, LORD, are God."

Isaiah Prophesies Sennacherib's Fall

[20] Then Isaiah son of Amoz sent a message to Hezekiah: "This is what the LORD, the God of Israel, says: I have heard your prayer concerning Sennacherib king of Assyria. [21] This is the word that the LORD has spoken against him:

> " 'Virgin Daughter Zion
>   despises you and mocks you.
> Daughter Jerusalem
>   tosses her head as you flee.
> [22] Who is it you have ridiculed and
>   blasphemed?
>   Against whom have you raised your
>   voice
> and lifted your eyes in pride?
>   Against the Holy One of Israel!
> [23] By your messengers
>   you have ridiculed the Lord.
> And you have said,
>   "With my many chariots
> I have ascended the heights of the
>   mountains,
>   the utmost heights of Lebanon.
> I have cut down its tallest cedars,
>   the choicest of its junipers.

---

[a] 9 That is, the upper Nile region

TROUBLE WILL COME

READ: 2 KINGS 19:14-15

Hezekiah was unlike any king of Judah before or after him. Check how the Bible sums him up: "He held fast to the LORD and did not stop following him; he kept the commands the LORD had given Moses. And the LORD was with him; he was successful in whatever he undertook" (2 Kings 18:6-7).

Living close to God didn't mean Hezekiah escaped difficult times. Six years into his reign, forces of the Assyrian empire obliterated the northern kingdom of Israel forever (v. 10). Eight years later, all of the walled cities of his own southern kingdom of Judah had fallen (v. 13).

Hezekiah had reason to be terrified, because his royal city of Jerusalem was the last thing left for the Assyrians to attack. Their commander mocked God and hurled insults at the king, even threatening that common people would grow so hungry they would eat their own waste (vv. 17-37). When the king received a final threatening letter predicting his defeat, he knew exactly what to do. He went to the temple and laid the letter before the Lord. Then he prayed. He praised the Lord's greatness and pleaded for help.

Hezekiah didn't escape deadly trouble, and neither will you. But you too can run to God and lay all your problems before him. Don't hesitate for a moment to tell him what you need.

BUILDING
FAITH
WISDOM
STRENGTH

I have reached its remotest parts,
  the finest of its forests.
²⁴ I have dug wells in foreign lands
  and drunk the water there.
With the soles of my feet
  I have dried up all the streams of
    Egypt."

²⁵ " 'Have you not heard?
  Long ago I ordained it.
In days of old I planned it;
  now I have brought it to pass,
that you have turned fortified cities
  into piles of stone.
²⁶ Their people, drained of power,
  are dismayed and put to shame.
They are like plants in the field,
  like tender green shoots,
like grass sprouting on the roof,
  scorched before it grows up.

²⁷ " 'But I know where you are
  and when you come and go
  and how you rage against me.
²⁸ Because you rage against me
  and because your insolence has
    reached my ears,
I will put my hook in your nose
  and my bit in your mouth,
and I will make you return
  by the way you came.'

²⁹ "This will be the sign for you, Hezekiah:

"This year you will eat what grows by
    itself,
  and the second year what springs from
    that.
But in the third year sow and reap,
  plant vineyards and eat their fruit.
³⁰ Once more a remnant of the kingdom of
    Judah
  will take root below and bear fruit
    above.
³¹ For out of Jerusalem will come a
    remnant,
  and out of Mount Zion a band of
    survivors.

"The zeal of the LORD Almighty will accomplish this.

³² "Therefore this is what the LORD says
concerning the king of Assyria:

" 'He will not enter this city
  or shoot an arrow here.

He will not come before it with shield
  or build a siege ramp against it.
³³ By the way that he came he will return;
  he will not enter this city,
            declares the LORD.
³⁴ I will defend this city and save it,
  for my sake and for the sake of David
    my servant.' "

³⁵ That night the angel of the LORD went out
and put to death a hundred and eighty-five
thousand in the Assyrian camp. When the
people got up the next morning — there were
all the dead bodies! ³⁶ So Sennacherib king
of Assyria broke camp and withdrew. He returned to Nineveh and stayed there.

³⁷ One day, while he was worshiping in the
temple of his god Nisrok, his sons Adrammelek and Sharezer killed him with the sword,
and they escaped to the land of Ararat. And
Esarhaddon his son succeeded him as king.

Hezekiah's Illness

20 In those days Hezekiah became ill
and was at the point of death. The
prophet Isaiah son of Amoz went to him and
said, "This is what the LORD says: Put your
house in order, because you are going to die;
you will not recover."

² Hezekiah turned his face to the wall and
prayed to the LORD, ³ "Remember, LORD,
how I have walked before you faithfully and
with wholehearted devotion and have done
what is good in your eyes." And Hezekiah
wept bitterly.

⁴ Before Isaiah had left the middle court,
the word of the LORD came to him: ⁵ "Go
back and tell Hezekiah, the ruler of my people, 'This is what the LORD, the God of your
father David, says: I have heard your prayer
and seen your tears; I will heal you. On the
third day from now you will go up to the temple of the LORD. ⁶ I will add fifteen years to
your life. And I will deliver you and this city
from the hand of the king of Assyria. I will
defend this city for my sake and for the sake
of my servant David.' "

⁷ Then Isaiah said, "Prepare a poultice of
figs." They did so and applied it to the boil,
and he recovered.

⁸ Hezekiah had asked Isaiah, "What will
be the sign that the LORD will heal me and
that I will go up to the temple of the LORD on
the third day from now?"

⁹Isaiah answered, "This is the LORD's sign to you that the LORD will do what he has promised: Shall the shadow go forward ten steps, or shall it go back ten steps?"

¹⁰"It is a simple matter for the shadow to go forward ten steps," said Hezekiah. "Rather, have it go back ten steps."

¹¹Then the prophet Isaiah called on the LORD, and the LORD made the shadow go back the ten steps it had gone down on the stairway of Ahaz.

Envoys From Babylon

¹²At that time Marduk-Baladan son of Baladan king of Babylon sent Hezekiah letters and a gift, because he had heard of Hezekiah's illness. ¹³Hezekiah received the envoys and showed them all that was in his storehouses—the silver, the gold, the spices and the fine olive oil—his armory and everything found among his treasures. There was nothing in his palace or in all his kingdom that Hezekiah did not show them.

¹⁴Then Isaiah the prophet went to King Hezekiah and asked, "What did those men say, and where did they come from?"

"From a distant land," Hezekiah replied. "They came from Babylon."

¹⁵The prophet asked, "What did they see in your palace?"

"They saw everything in my palace," Hezekiah said. "There is nothing among my treasures that I did not show them."

¹⁶Then Isaiah said to Hezekiah, "Hear the word of the LORD: ¹⁷The time will surely come when everything in your palace, and all that your predecessors have stored up until this day, will be carried off to Babylon. Nothing will be left, says the LORD. ¹⁸And some of your descendants, your own flesh and blood who will be born to you, will be taken away, and they will become eunuchs in the palace of the king of Babylon."

¹⁹"The word of the LORD you have spoken is good," Hezekiah replied. For he thought, "Will there not be peace and security in my lifetime?"

²⁰As for the other events of Hezekiah's reign, all his achievements and how he made the pool and the tunnel by which he brought water into the city, are they not written in the book of the annals of the kings of Judah? ²¹Hezekiah rested with his ancestors. And Manasseh his son succeeded him as king.

Manasseh King of Judah

21 Manasseh was twelve years old when he became king, and he reigned in Jerusalem fifty-five years. His mother's name was Hephzibah. ²He did evil in the eyes of the LORD, following the detestable practices of the nations the LORD had driven out before the Israelites. ³He rebuilt the high places his father Hezekiah had destroyed; he also erected altars to Baal and made an Asherah pole, as Ahab king of Israel had done. He bowed down to all the starry hosts and worshiped them. ⁴He built altars in the temple of the LORD, of which the LORD had said, "In Jerusalem I will put my Name." ⁵In the two courts of the temple of the LORD, he built altars to all the starry hosts. ⁶He sacrificed his own son in the fire, practiced divination, sought omens, and consulted mediums and spiritists. He did much evil in the eyes of the LORD, arousing his anger.

⁷He took the carved Asherah pole he had made and put it in the temple, of which the LORD had said to David and to his son Solomon, "In this temple and in Jerusalem, which I have chosen out of all the tribes of Israel, I will put my Name forever. ⁸I will not again make the feet of the Israelites wander from the land I gave their ancestors, if only they will be careful to do everything I commanded them and will keep the whole Law that my servant Moses gave them." ⁹But the people did not listen. Manasseh led them astray, so that they did more evil than the nations the LORD had destroyed before the Israelites.

¹⁰The LORD said through his servants the prophets: ¹¹"Manasseh king of Judah has committed these detestable sins. He has done more evil than the Amorites who preceded him and has led Judah into sin with his idols. ¹²Therefore this is what the LORD, the God of Israel, says: I am going to bring such disaster on Jerusalem and Judah that the ears of everyone who hears of it will tingle. ¹³I will stretch out over Jerusalem the measuring line used against Samaria and the plumb line used against the house of Ahab. I will wipe out Jerusalem as one wipes a dish, wiping it and turning it upside down. ¹⁴I will forsake the remnant of my inheritance and give them into the hands of enemies. They will be looted and plundered by all their enemies; ¹⁵they have done evil in

my eyes and have aroused my anger from the day their ancestors came out of Egypt until this day."

[16] Moreover, Manasseh also shed so much innocent blood that he filled Jerusalem from end to end — besides the sin that he had caused Judah to commit, so that they did evil in the eyes of the LORD.

[17] As for the other events of Manasseh's reign, and all he did, including the sin he committed, are they not written in the book of the annals of the kings of Judah? [18] Manasseh rested with his ancestors and was buried in his palace garden, the garden of Uzza. And Amon his son succeeded him as king.

Amon King of Judah

[19] Amon was twenty-two years old when he became king, and he reigned in Jerusalem two years. His mother's name was Meshullemeth daughter of Haruz; she was from Jotbah. [20] He did evil in the eyes of the LORD, as his father Manasseh had done. [21] He followed completely the ways of his father, worshiping the idols his father had worshiped, and bowing down to them. [22] He forsook the LORD, the God of his ancestors, and did not walk in obedience to him.

[23] Amon's officials conspired against him and assassinated the king in his palace. [24] Then the people of the land killed all who had plotted against King Amon, and they made Josiah his son king in his place.

[25] As for the other events of Amon's reign, and what he did, are they not written in the book of the annals of the kings of Judah? [26] He was buried in his tomb in the garden of Uzza. And Josiah his son succeeded him as king.

The Book of the Law Found

22 Josiah was eight years old when he became king, and he reigned in Jerusalem thirty-one years. His mother's name was Jedidah daughter of Adaiah; she was from Bozkath. [2] He did what was right in the eyes of the LORD and followed completely the ways of his father David, not turning aside to the right or to the left.

[3] In the eighteenth year of his reign, King Josiah sent the secretary, Shaphan son of Azaliah, the son of Meshullam, to the temple of the LORD. He said: [4] "Go up to Hilkiah the high priest and have him get ready the money that has been brought into the temple of the LORD, which the doorkeepers have collected from the people. [5] Have them entrust it to the men appointed to supervise the work on the temple. And have these men pay the workers who repair the temple of the LORD — [6] the carpenters, the builders and the masons. Also have them purchase timber and dressed stone to repair the temple. [7] But they need not account for the money entrusted to them, because they are honest in their dealings."

[8] Hilkiah the high priest said to Shaphan the secretary, "I have found the Book of the Law in the temple of the LORD." He gave it to Shaphan, who read it. [9] Then Shaphan the secretary went to the king and reported to him: "Your officials have paid out the money that was in the temple of the LORD and have entrusted it to the workers and supervisors at the temple." [10] Then Shaphan the secretary informed the king, "Hilkiah the priest has given me a book." And Shaphan read from it in the presence of the king.

[11] When the king heard the words of the Book of the Law, he tore his robes. [12] He gave these orders to Hilkiah the priest, Ahikam son of Shaphan, Akbor son of Micaiah, Shaphan the secretary and Asaiah the king's attendant: [13] "Go and inquire of the LORD for me and for the people and for all Judah about what is written in this book that has been found. Great is the LORD's anger that burns against us because those who have gone before us have not obeyed the words of this book; they have not acted in accordance with all that is written there concerning us."

[14] Hilkiah the priest, Ahikam, Akbor, Shaphan and Asaiah went to speak to the prophet Huldah, who was the wife of Shallum son of Tikvah, the son of Harhas, keeper of the wardrobe. She lived in Jerusalem, in the New Quarter.

[15] She said to them, "This is what the LORD, the God of Israel, says: Tell the man who sent you to me, [16] 'This is what the LORD says: I am going to bring disaster on this place and its people, according to everything written in the book the king of Judah has read. [17] Because they have forsaken me and burned incense to other gods and aroused my anger by all the idols their hands have made,[a] my anger will burn against this place and will not

_____
[a] 17 Or _by everything they have done_

JOSIAH

Neither before nor after Josiah was there a king like him who turned to the LORD as he did—with all his heart and with all his soul and with all this strength, in accordance with all the Law of Moses. 2 KINGS 23:25

HIS NAME MEANS: "the LORD supports"
READ HIS STORY: *2 Kings 21:23—23:30; 2 Chronicles 34-35*

MEN OF THE BIBLE

Josiah was just eight years old when he was crowned the king of Judah. Yet he didn't follow in the footsteps of the evil kings before him. "In the eighth year of his reign, while he was still young, he began to seek the God of his father David" (2 Chronicles 34:3).

What does it mean to seek God? First of all, Josiah spent time with God. He prayed and talked with God, even weeping because of sin (2 Chronicles 34:27). When the priests found the Book of the Law in the temple, Josiah had the priests read it to him. King Josiah went up to the temple and read God's Word to the people himself, leading them in renewing their covenant with God. Josiah also led the people to worship God during the celebration of the Passover as no other king in Israel had ever done before.

Josiah was still young when he began to seek after God. His age didn't deter him. If he were around today, we'd probably label him a radical. He purged the entire country of its idols, reformed their ways and repaired the temple. He was passionate for God and for his people. And God's wisdom made him one of Judah's best kings.

So what's holding you back from being a great follower of God? Talk with God every day. Seek him with all your heart and all your soul and all your strength—just as King Josiah did.

be quenched.' [18]Tell the king of Judah, who sent you to inquire of the LORD, 'This is what the LORD, the God of Israel, says concerning the words you heard: [19]Because your heart was responsive and you humbled yourself before the LORD when you heard what I have spoken against this place and its people — that they would become a curse[a] and be laid waste — and because you tore your robes and wept in my presence, I also have heard you, declares the LORD. [20]Therefore I will gather you to your ancestors, and you will be buried in peace. Your eyes will not see all the disaster I am going to bring on this place.' "

So they took her answer back to the king.

Josiah Renews the Covenant

23 Then the king called together all the elders of Judah and Jerusalem. [2]He went up to the temple of the LORD with the people of Judah, the inhabitants of Jerusalem, the priests and the prophets — all the people from the least to the greatest. He read in their hearing all the words of the Book of the Covenant, which had been found in the temple of the LORD. [3]The king stood by the pillar and renewed the covenant in the presence of the LORD — to follow the LORD and keep his commands, statutes and decrees with all his heart and all his soul, thus confirming the words of the covenant written in this book. Then all the people pledged themselves to the covenant.

[4]The king ordered Hilkiah the high priest, the priests next in rank and the doorkeepers to remove from the temple of the LORD all the articles made for Baal and Asherah and all the starry hosts. He burned them outside Jerusalem in the fields of the Kidron Valley and took the ashes to Bethel. [5]He did away with the idolatrous priests appointed by the kings of Judah to burn incense on the high places of the towns of Judah and on those around Jerusalem — those who burned incense to Baal, to the sun and moon, to the constellations and to all the starry hosts. [6]He took the Asherah pole from the temple of the LORD to the Kidron Valley outside Jerusalem and burned it there. He ground it to powder and scattered the dust over the graves of the common people. [7]He also tore down the quarters of the male shrine prostitutes that were in the temple of the LORD, the quarters where women did weaving for Asherah.

[8]Josiah brought all the priests from the towns of Judah and desecrated the high places, from Geba to Beersheba, where the priests had burned incense. He broke down the gateway at the entrance of the Gate of Joshua, the city governor, which was on the left of the city gate. [9]Although the priests of the high places did not serve at the altar of the LORD in Jerusalem, they ate unleavened bread with their fellow priests.

[10]He desecrated Topheth, which was in the Valley of Ben Hinnom, so no one could use it to sacrifice their son or daughter in the fire to Molek. [11]He removed from the entrance to the temple of the LORD the horses that the kings of Judah had dedicated to the sun. They were in the court[b] near the room of an official named Nathan-Melek. Josiah then burned the chariots dedicated to the sun.

[12]He pulled down the altars the kings of Judah had erected on the roof near the upper room of Ahaz, and the altars Manasseh had built in the two courts of the temple of the LORD. He removed them from there, smashed them to pieces and threw the rubble into the Kidron Valley. [13]The king also desecrated the high places that were east of Jerusalem on the south of the Hill of Corruption — the ones Solomon king of Israel had built for Ashtoreth the vile goddess of the Sidonians, for Chemosh the vile god of Moab, and for Molek the detestable god of the people of Ammon. [14]Josiah smashed the sacred stones and cut down the Asherah poles and covered the sites with human bones.

[15]Even the altar at Bethel, the high place made by Jeroboam son of Nebat, who had caused Israel to sin — even that altar and high place he demolished. He burned the high place and ground it to powder, and burned the Asherah pole also. [16]Then Josiah looked around, and when he saw the tombs that were there on the hillside, he had the bones removed from them and burned on the altar to defile it, in accordance with the word of the LORD proclaimed by the man of God who foretold these things.

[17]The king asked, "What is that tombstone I see?"

---

[a] 19 That is, their names would be used in cursing (see Jer. 29:22); or, others would see that they are cursed.   [b] 11 The meaning of the Hebrew for this word is uncertain.

The people of the city said, "It marks the tomb of the man of God who came from Judah and pronounced against the altar of Bethel the very things you have done to it."

[18]"Leave it alone," he said. "Don't let anyone disturb his bones." So they spared his bones and those of the prophet who had come from Samaria.

[19]Just as he had done at Bethel, Josiah removed all the shrines at the high places that the kings of Israel had built in the towns of Samaria and that had aroused the LORD's anger. [20]Josiah slaughtered all the priests of those high places on the altars and burned human bones on them. Then he went back to Jerusalem.

[21]The king gave this order to all the people: "Celebrate the Passover to the LORD your God, as it is written in this Book of the Covenant." [22]Neither in the days of the judges who led Israel nor in the days of the kings of Israel and the kings of Judah had any such Passover been observed. [23]But in the eighteenth year of King Josiah, this Passover was celebrated to the LORD in Jerusalem.

[24]Furthermore, Josiah got rid of the mediums and spiritists, the household gods, the idols and all the other detestable things seen in Judah and Jerusalem. This he did to fulfill the requirements of the law written in the book that Hilkiah the priest had discovered in the temple of the LORD. [25]Neither before nor after Josiah was there a king like him who turned to the LORD as he did—with all his heart and with all his soul and with all his strength, in accordance with all the Law of Moses.

[26]Nevertheless, the LORD did not turn away from the heat of his fierce anger, which burned against Judah because of all that Manasseh had done to arouse his anger. [27]So the LORD said, "I will remove Judah also from my presence as I removed Israel, and I will reject Jerusalem, the city I chose, and this temple, about which I said, 'My Name shall be there.'[a]"

[28]As for the other events of Josiah's reign, and all he did, are they not written in the book of the annals of the kings of Judah?

[29]While Josiah was king, Pharaoh Necho king of Egypt went up to the Euphrates River to help the king of Assyria. King Josiah marched out to meet him in battle, but Necho faced him and killed him at Megiddo. [30]Josiah's servants brought his body in a chariot from Megiddo to Jerusalem and buried him in his own tomb. And the people of the land took Jehoahaz son of Josiah and anointed him and made him king in place of his father.

Jehoahaz King of Judah

[31]Jehoahaz was twenty-three years old when he became king, and he reigned in Jerusalem three months. His mother's name was Hamutal daughter of Jeremiah; she was from Libnah. [32]He did evil in the eyes of the LORD, just as his predecessors had done. [33]Pharaoh Necho put him in chains at Riblah in the land of Hamath so that he might not reign in Jerusalem, and he imposed on Judah a levy of a hundred talents[b] of silver and a talent[c] of gold. [34]Pharaoh Necho made Eliakim son of Josiah king in place of his father Josiah and changed Eliakim's name to Jehoiakim. But he took Jehoahaz and carried him off to Egypt, and there he died. [35]Jehoiakim paid Pharaoh Necho the silver and gold he demanded. In order to do so, he taxed the land and exacted the silver and gold from the people of the land according to their assessments.

Jehoiakim King of Judah

[36]Jehoiakim was twenty-five years old when he became king, and he reigned in Jerusalem eleven years. His mother's name was Zebidah daughter of Pedaiah; she was from Rumah. [37]And he did evil in the eyes of the LORD, just as his predecessors had done.

24 During Jehoiakim's reign, Nebuchadnezzar king of Babylon invaded the land, and Jehoiakim became his vassal for three years. But then he turned against Nebuchadnezzar and rebelled. [2]The LORD sent Babylonian,[d] Aramean, Moabite and Ammonite raiders against him to destroy Judah, in accordance with the word of the LORD proclaimed by his servants the prophets. [3]Surely these things happened to Judah according to the LORD's command, in order to remove them from his presence because of the sins of Manasseh and all he had done, [4]including the shedding of innocent blood. For he had

---

[a] 27 1 Kings 8:29   [b] 33 That is, about 3 3/4 tons or about 3.4 metric tons   [c] 33 That is, about 75 pounds or about 34 kilograms   [d] 2 Or *Chaldean*

filled Jerusalem with innocent blood, and the LORD was not willing to forgive.

[5] As for the other events of Jehoiakim's reign, and all he did, are they not written in the book of the annals of the kings of Judah? [6] Jehoiakim rested with his ancestors. And Jehoiachin his son succeeded him as king.

[7] The king of Egypt did not march out from his own country again, because the king of Babylon had taken all his territory, from the Wadi of Egypt to the Euphrates River.

Jehoiachin King of Judah

[8] Jehoiachin was eighteen years old when he became king, and he reigned in Jerusalem three months. His mother's name was Nehushta daughter of Elnathan; she was from Jerusalem. [9] He did evil in the eyes of the LORD, just as his father had done.

[10] At that time the officers of Nebuchadnezzar king of Babylon advanced on Jerusalem and laid siege to it, [11] and Nebuchadnezzar himself came up to the city while his officers were besieging it. [12] Jehoiachin king of Judah, his mother, his attendants, his nobles and his officials all surrendered to him.

In the eighth year of the reign of the king of Babylon, he took Jehoiachin prisoner. [13] As the LORD had declared, Nebuchadnezzar removed the treasures from the temple of the LORD and from the royal palace, and cut up the gold articles that Solomon king of Israel had made for the temple of the LORD. [14] He carried all Jerusalem into exile: all the officers and fighting men, and all the skilled workers and artisans — a total of ten thousand. Only the poorest people of the land were left.

[15] Nebuchadnezzar took Jehoiachin captive to Babylon. He also took from Jerusalem to Babylon the king's mother, his wives, his officials and the prominent people of the land. [16] The king of Babylon also deported to Babylon the entire force of seven thousand fighting men, strong and fit for war, and a thousand skilled workers and artisans. [17] He made Mattaniah, Jehoiachin's uncle, king in his place and changed his name to Zedekiah.

Zedekiah King of Judah

[18] Zedekiah was twenty-one years old when he became king, and he reigned in Jerusalem eleven years. His mother's name was Hamutal daughter of Jeremiah; she was from Libnah. [19] He did evil in the eyes of the LORD, just as Jehoiakim had done. [20] It was because of the LORD's anger that all this happened to Jerusalem and Judah, and in the end he thrust them from his presence.

The Fall of Jerusalem

Now Zedekiah rebelled against the king of Babylon.

25 So in the ninth year of Zedekiah's reign, on the tenth day of the tenth month, Nebuchadnezzar king of Babylon marched against Jerusalem with his whole army. He encamped outside the city and built siege works all around it. [2] The city was kept under siege until the eleventh year of King Zedekiah.

[3] By the ninth day of the fourth[a] month the famine in the city had become so severe that there was no food for the people to eat. [4] Then the city wall was broken through, and the whole army fled at night through the gate between the two walls near the king's garden, though the Babylonians[b] were surrounding the city. They fled toward the Arabah,[c] [5] but the Babylonian[d] army pursued the king and overtook him in the plains of Jericho. All his soldiers were separated from him and scattered, [6] and he was captured.

He was taken to the king of Babylon at Riblah, where sentence was pronounced on him. [7] They killed the sons of Zedekiah before his eyes. Then they put out his eyes, bound him with bronze shackles and took him to Babylon.

[8] On the seventh day of the fifth month, in the nineteenth year of Nebuchadnezzar king of Babylon, Nebuzaradan commander of the imperial guard, an official of the king of Babylon, came to Jerusalem. [9] He set fire to the temple of the LORD, the royal palace and all the houses of Jerusalem. Every important building he burned down. [10] The whole Babylonian army under the commander of the imperial guard broke down the walls around Jerusalem. [11] Nebuzaradan the commander of the guard carried into exile the people who remained in the city, along with the rest of the populace and those who had deserted

---

[a] 3 Probable reading of the original Hebrew text (see Jer. 52:6); Masoretic Text does not have *fourth*.
[b] 4 Or *Chaldeans*; also in verses 13, 25 and 26   [c] 4 Or *the Jordan Valley*   [d] 5 Or *Chaldean*; also in verses 10 and 24

TAKE GOD'S DISCIPLINE

READ: 2 KINGS 25:11

You know about God's discipline. The Bible asserts that his correction is a sign of his love (Proverbs 3:12). Keep that fact in mind as you watch the final events of 2 Kings unfold.

Decades before the drama of 2 Kings 24-25, Josiah had led the nation of Judah back to God by teaching the people all the laws the Lord had spoken to Moses. The king's passion for God ushered in some of the best years in the nation's history (22:1–23:30). But the Lord was still fed up with the sins committed by rulers before Josiah, and rulers after him quickly returned to doing evil (2:31-37).

Remember that many hundreds of years earlier, the Lord had threatened to drive his people from the land he had promised them if they disobeyed his commands. "I will scatter you among the nations," he said. "Your land will be laid waste, and your cities will lie in ruins" (Leviticus 26:33). As a consequence of sin, God had allowed Israel to be conquered by the Assyrians (2 Kings 18:10). 2 Kings records how Judah fell to the Babylonians, and its people were led as slaves to a distant land.

Exile was the Lord's ultimate discipline. As strange as it might seem, this toughness was an act of love. Whenever the Lord disciplines you, his aim is to bring you back to himself and teach you to follow him.

BUILDING

FAITH

WISDOM

STRENGTH

to the king of Babylon. [12] But the commander left behind some of the poorest people of the land to work the vineyards and fields.

[13] The Babylonians broke up the bronze pillars, the movable stands and the bronze Sea that were at the temple of the LORD and they carried the bronze to Babylon. [14] They also took away the pots, shovels, wick trimmers, dishes and all the bronze articles used in the temple service. [15] The commander of the imperial guard took away the censers and sprinkling bowls — all that were made of pure gold or silver.

[16] The bronze from the two pillars, the Sea and the movable stands, which Solomon had made for the temple of the LORD, was more than could be weighed. [17] Each pillar was eighteen cubits[a] high. The bronze capital on top of one pillar was three cubits[b] high and was decorated with a network and pomegranates of bronze all around. The other pillar, with its network, was similar.

[18] The commander of the guard took as prisoners Seraiah the chief priest, Zephaniah the priest next in rank and the three doorkeepers. [19] Of those still in the city, he took the officer in charge of the fighting men, and five royal advisers. He also took the secretary who was chief officer in charge of conscripting the people of the land and sixty of the conscripts who were found in the city. [20] Nebuzaradan the commander took them all and brought them to the king of Babylon at Riblah. [21] There at Riblah, in the land of Hamath, the king had them executed.

So Judah went into captivity, away from her land.

[22] Nebuchadnezzar king of Babylon appointed Gedaliah son of Ahikam, the son of Shaphan, to be over the people he had left behind in Judah. [23] When all the army officers and their men heard that the king of Babylon had appointed Gedaliah as governor, they came to Gedaliah at Mizpah — Ishmael son of Nethaniah, Johanan son of Kareah, Seraiah son of Tanhumeth the Netophathite, Jaazaniah the son of the Maakathite, and their men. [24] Gedaliah took an oath to reassure them and their men. "Do not be afraid of the Babylonian officials," he said. "Settle down in the land and serve the king of Babylon, and it will go well with you."

[25] In the seventh month, however, Ishmael son of Nethaniah, the son of Elishama, who was of royal blood, came with ten men and assassinated Gedaliah and also the men of Judah and the Babylonians who were with him at Mizpah. [26] At this, all the people from the least to the greatest, together with the army officers, fled to Egypt for fear of the Babylonians.

Jehoiachin Released

[27] In the thirty-seventh year of the exile of Jehoiachin king of Judah, in the year Awel-Marduk became king of Babylon, he released Jehoiachin king of Judah from prison. He did this on the twenty-seventh day of the twelfth month. [28] He spoke kindly to him and gave him a seat of honor higher than those of the other kings who were with him in Babylon. [29] So Jehoiachin put aside his prison clothes and for the rest of his life ate regularly at the king's table. [30] Day by day the king gave Jehoiachin a regular allowance as long as he lived.

---

[a] 17 That is, about 27 feet or about 8.1 meters   [b] 17 That is, about 4 1/2 feet or about 1.4 meters

1 CHRONICLES

WHAT'S IT ABOUT?

I f this book sounds familiar, that's because it covers the same time period as 2 Samuel and 1 Kings. Written by an unnamed chronicler (possibly Ezra), this book is a historical record of King David's reign. It was written much later than the books of Samuel and Kings for the people returning to Judah from the Babylonian exile. To remind the people that God blesses obedience, this book shows how God worked through King David, a ruler devoted to him, to give Israel victory when they followed him.

Why do we need 1 Chronicles when we have the other books? Chronicles presents Israel's history with a specific purpose. Samuel and Kings emphasize the sins of the people that led to exile. But Chronicles focuses on God's law, his blessing of David's obedience, and the special purpose and plan for the temple. Returning from the exile, Israel needed to be reminded that God would keep the promises he made to David and that he was working out a plan to reconcile all people to himself.

1 CHRONICLES

Historical Records From Adam to Abraham

To Noah's Sons

1 Adam, Seth, Enosh, ²Kenan, Mahalalel, Jared, ³Enoch, Methuselah, Lamech, Noah.

⁴The sons of Noah:[a]
Shem, Ham and Japheth.

The Japhethites

⁵The sons[b] of Japheth:
Gomer, Magog, Madai, Javan, Tubal, Meshek and Tiras.
⁶The sons of Gomer:
Ashkenaz, Riphath[c] and Togarmah.
⁷The sons of Javan:
Elishah, Tarshish, the Kittites and the Rodanites.

The Hamites

⁸The sons of Ham:
Cush, Egypt, Put and Canaan.
⁹The sons of Cush:
Seba, Havilah, Sabta, Raamah and Sabteka.
The sons of Raamah:
Sheba and Dedan.
¹⁰Cush was the father[d] of
Nimrod, who became a mighty warrior on earth.
¹¹Egypt was the father of
the Ludites, Anamites, Lehabites, Naphtuhites, ¹²Pathrusites, Kasluhites (from whom the Philistines came) and Caphtorites.
¹³Canaan was the father of
Sidon his firstborn,[e] and of the Hittites, ¹⁴Jebusites, Amorites, Girgashites, ¹⁵Hivites, Arkites, Sinites, ¹⁶Arvadites, Zemarites and Hamathites.

The Semites

¹⁷The sons of Shem:
Elam, Ashur, Arphaxad, Lud and Aram.
The sons of Aram:[f]
Uz, Hul, Gether and Meshek.
¹⁸Arphaxad was the father of Shelah, and Shelah the father of Eber.
¹⁹Two sons were born to Eber:
One was named Peleg,[g] because in his time the earth was divided; his brother was named Joktan.
²⁰Joktan was the father of
Almodad, Sheleph, Hazarmaveth, Jerah, ²¹Hadoram, Uzal, Diklah, ²²Obal,[h] Abimael, Sheba, ²³Ophir, Havilah and Jobab. All these were sons of Joktan.

²⁴Shem, Arphaxad,[i] Shelah,
²⁵Eber, Peleg, Reu,
²⁶Serug, Nahor, Terah
²⁷and Abram (that is, Abraham).

The Family of Abraham

²⁸The sons of Abraham:
Isaac and Ishmael.

Descendants of Hagar

²⁹These were their descendants:
Nebaioth the firstborn of Ishmael, Kedar, Adbeel, Mibsam, ³⁰Mishma, Dumah, Massa, Hadad, Tema, ³¹Jetur, Naphish and Kedemah. These were the sons of Ishmael.

---

[a] 4 Septuagint; Hebrew does not have this line.   [b] 5 *Sons* may mean *descendants* or *successors* or *nations*; also in verses 6-9, 17 and 23.   [c] 6 Many Hebrew manuscripts and Vulgate (see also Septuagint and Gen. 10:3); most Hebrew manuscripts *Diphath*   [d] 10 *Father* may mean *ancestor* or *predecessor* or *founder*; also in verses 11, 13, 18 and 20.   [e] 13 Or *of the Sidonians, the foremost*   [f] 17 One Hebrew manuscript and some Septuagint manuscripts (see also Gen. 10:23); most Hebrew manuscripts do not have this line.   [g] 19 *Peleg* means *division*.   [h] 22 Some Hebrew manuscripts and Syriac (see also Gen. 10:28); most Hebrew manuscripts *Ebal*   [i] 24 Hebrew; some Septuagint manuscripts *Arphaxad, Cainan* (see also note at Gen. 11:10)

Descendants of Keturah

32 The sons born to Keturah, Abraham's concubine:

Zimran, Jokshan, Medan, Midian, Ishbak and Shuah.

The sons of Jokshan:

Sheba and Dedan.

33 The sons of Midian:

Ephah, Epher, Hanok, Abida and El-daah.

All these were descendants of Keturah.

Descendants of Sarah

34 Abraham was the father of Isaac.

The sons of Isaac:

Esau and Israel.

Esau's Sons

35 The sons of Esau:

Eliphaz, Reuel, Jeush, Jalam and Korah.

36 The sons of Eliphaz:

Teman, Omar, Zepho,*a* Gatam and Kenaz;

by Timna: Amalek.*b*

37 The sons of Reuel:

Nahath, Zerah, Shammah and Mizzah.

The People of Seir in Edom

38 The sons of Seir:

Lotan, Shobal, Zibeon, Anah, Dishon, Ezer and Dishan.

39 The sons of Lotan:

Hori and Homam. Timna was Lotan's sister.

40 The sons of Shobal:

Alvan,*c* Manahath, Ebal, Shepho and Onam.

The sons of Zibeon:

Aiah and Anah.

41 The son of Anah:

Dishon.

The sons of Dishon:

Hemdan,*d* Eshban, Ithran and Keran.

42 The sons of Ezer:

Bilhan, Zaavan and Akan.*e*

The sons of Dishan*f*:

Uz and Aran.

The Rulers of Edom

43 These were the kings who reigned in Edom before any Israelite king reigned:

Bela son of Beor, whose city was named Dinhabah.

44 When Bela died, Jobab son of Zerah from Bozrah succeeded him as king.

45 When Jobab died, Husham from the land of the Temanites succeeded him as king.

46 When Husham died, Hadad son of Bedad, who defeated Midian in the country of Moab, succeeded him as king. His city was named Avith.

47 When Hadad died, Samlah from Masrekah succeeded him as king.

48 When Samlah died, Shaul from Rehoboth on the river*g* succeeded him as king.

49 When Shaul died, Baal-Hanan son of Akbor succeeded him as king.

50 When Baal-Hanan died, Hadad succeeded him as king. His city was named Pau,*h* and his wife's name was Mehetabel daughter of Matred, the daughter of Me-Zahab. 51 Hadad also died.

The chiefs of Edom were:

Timna, Alvah, Jetheth, 52 Oholibamah, Elah, Pinon, 53 Kenaz, Teman, Mibzar, 54 Magdiel and Iram. These were the chiefs of Edom.

Israel's Sons

2 These were the sons of Israel:

Reuben, Simeon, Levi, Judah, Issachar, Zebulun, 2 Dan, Joseph, Benjamin, Naphtali, Gad and Asher.

Judah

To Hezron's Sons

3 The sons of Judah:

Er, Onan and Shelah. These three

---

a 36 Many Hebrew manuscripts, some Septuagint manuscripts and Syriac (see also Gen. 36:11); most Hebrew manuscripts *Zephi*   *b 36* Some Septuagint manuscripts (see also Gen. 36:12); Hebrew *Gatam, Kenaz, Timna and Amalek*   *c 40* Many Hebrew manuscripts and some Septuagint manuscripts (see also Gen. 36:23); most Hebrew manuscripts *Alian*   *d 41* Many Hebrew manuscripts and some Septuagint manuscripts (see also Gen. 36:26); most Hebrew manuscripts *Hamran*   *e 42* Many Hebrew and Septuagint manuscripts (see also Gen. 36:27); most Hebrew manuscripts *Zaavan, Jaakan*   *f 42* See Gen. 36:28; Hebrew *Dishon*, a variant of *Dishan*   *g 48* Possibly the Euphrates   *h 50* Many Hebrew manuscripts, some Septuagint manuscripts, Vulgate and Syriac (see also Gen. 36:39); most Hebrew manuscripts *Pai* were born to him by a Canaanite woman, the daughter of Shua. Er, Judah's firstborn, was wicked in the LORD's sight; so the LORD put him to death. ⁴Judah's daughter-in-law Tamar bore Perez and Zerah to Judah. He had five sons in all.

⁵The sons of Perez:
Hezron and Hamul.

⁶The sons of Zerah:
Zimri, Ethan, Heman, Kalkol and Darda*ᵃ*—five in all.

⁷The son of Karmi:
Achar,*ᵇ* who brought trouble on Israel by violating the ban on taking devoted things.*ᶜ*

⁸The son of Ethan:
Azariah.

⁹The sons born to Hezron were:
Jerahmeel, Ram and Caleb.*ᵈ*

From Ram Son of Hezron

¹⁰Ram was the father of
Amminadab, and Amminadab the father of Nahshon, the leader of the people of Judah. ¹¹Nahshon was the father of Salmon,*ᵉ* Salmon the father of Boaz, ¹²Boaz the father of Obed and Obed the father of Jesse.

¹³Jesse was the father of
Eliab his firstborn; the second son was Abinadab, the third Shimea, ¹⁴the fourth Nethanel, the fifth Raddai, ¹⁵the sixth Ozem and the seventh David. ¹⁶Their sisters were Zeruiah and Abigail. Zeruiah's three sons were Abishai, Joab and Asahel. ¹⁷Abigail was the mother of Amasa, whose father was Jether the Ishmaelite.

Caleb Son of Hezron

¹⁸Caleb son of Hezron had children by his wife Azubah (and by Jerioth). These were her sons: Jesher, Shobab and Ardon. ¹⁹When Azubah died, Caleb married Ephrath, who bore

him Hur. ²⁰Hur was the father of Uri, and Uri the father of Bezalel.

²¹Later, Hezron, when he was sixty years old, married the daughter of Makir the father of Gilead. He made love to her, and she bore him Segub. ²²Segub was the father of Jair, who controlled twenty-three towns in Gilead. ²³(But Geshur and Aram captured Havvoth Jair,*ᶠ* as well as Kenath with its surrounding settlements—sixty towns.) All these were descendants of Makir the father of Gilead.

²⁴After Hezron died in Caleb Ephrathah, Abijah the wife of Hezron bore him Ashhur the father*ᵍ* of Tekoa.

Jerahmeel Son of Hezron

²⁵The sons of Jerahmeel the firstborn of Hezron:
Ram his firstborn, Bunah, Oren, Ozem and*ʰ* Ahijah. ²⁶Jerahmeel had another wife, whose name was Atarah; she was the mother of Onam.

²⁷The sons of Ram the firstborn of Jerahmeel:
Maaz, Jamin and Eker.

²⁸The sons of Onam:
Shammai and Jada.
The sons of Shammai:
Nadab and Abishur.

²⁹Abishur's wife was named Abihail, who bore him Ahban and Molid.

³⁰The sons of Nadab:
Seled and Appaim. Seled died without children.

³¹The son of Appaim:
Ishi, who was the father of Sheshan. Sheshan was the father of Ahlai.

³²The sons of Jada, Shammai's brother:
Jether and Jonathan. Jether died without children.

³³The sons of Jonathan:
Peleth and Zaza.
These were the descendants of Jerahmeel.

ᵃ 6 Many Hebrew manuscripts, some Septuagint manuscripts and Syriac (see also 1 Kings 4:31); most Hebrew manuscripts *Dara*   *ᵇ 7 Achar* means *trouble; Achar* is called *Achan* in Joshua.
ᶜ 7 The Hebrew term refers to the irrevocable giving over of things or persons to the LORD, often by totally destroying them.   *ᵈ 9* Hebrew *Kelubai,* a variant of *Caleb*   *ᵉ 11* Septuagint (see also Ruth 4:21); Hebrew *Salma*   *ᶠ 23* Or *captured the settlements of Jair*   *ᵍ 24 Father* may mean *civic leader* or *military leader;* also in verses 42, 45, 49-52 and possibly elsewhere.   *ʰ 25* Or *Oren and Ozem, by*

34 Sheshan had no sons — only daughters. He had an Egyptian servant named Jarha. 35 Sheshan gave his daughter in marriage to his servant Jarha, and she bore him Attai. 36 Attai was the father of Nathan,

Nathan the father of Zabad,
37 Zabad the father of Ephlal,
Ephlal the father of Obed,
38 Obed the father of Jehu,
Jehu the father of Azariah,
39 Azariah the father of Helez,
Helez the father of Eleasah,
40 Eleasah the father of Sismai,
Sismai the father of Shallum,
41 Shallum the father of Jekamiah,
and Jekamiah the father of Elishama.

The Clans of Caleb

42 The sons of Caleb the brother of Jerahmeel:

Mesha his firstborn, who was the father of Ziph, and his son Mareshah,*a* who was the father of Hebron.
43 The sons of Hebron:

Korah, Tappuah, Rekem and Shema. 44 Shema was the father of Raham, and Raham the father of Jorkeam. Rekem was the father of Shammai. 45 The son of Shammai was Maon, and Maon was the father of Beth Zur.
46 Caleb's concubine Ephah was the mother of Haran, Moza and Gazez. Haran was the father of Gazez.
47 The sons of Jahdai:

Regem, Jotham, Geshan, Pelet, Ephah and Shaaph.
48 Caleb's concubine Maakah was the mother of Sheber and Tirhanah. 49 She also gave birth to Shaaph the father of Madmannah and to Sheva the father of Makbenah and Gibea. Caleb's daughter was Aksah. 50 These were the descendants of Caleb.

The sons of Hur the firstborn of Ephrathah:

Shobal the father of Kiriath Jearim, 51 Salma the father of Bethlehem, and Hareph the father of Beth Gader.

52 The descendants of Shobal the father of Kiriath Jearim were:

Haroeh, half the Manahathites, 53 and the clans of Kiriath Jearim: the Ithrites, Puthites, Shumathites and Mishraites. From these descended the Zorathites and Eshtaolites.
54 The descendants of Salma:

Bethlehem, the Netophathites, Atroth Beth Joab, half the Manahathites, the Zorites, 55 and the clans of scribes*b* who lived at Jabez: the Tirathites, Shimeathites and Sucathites. These are the Kenites who came from Hammath, the father of the Rekabites.*c*

The Sons of David

3 These were the sons of David born to him in Hebron:

The firstborn was Amnon the son of Ahinoam of Jezreel;
the second, Daniel the son of Abigail of Carmel;
2 the third, Absalom the son of Maakah daughter of Talmai king of Geshur;
the fourth, Adonijah the son of Haggith;
3 the fifth, Shephatiah the son of Abital;
and the sixth, Ithream, by his wife Eglah.
4 These six were born to David in Hebron, where he reigned seven years and six months.

David reigned in Jerusalem thirty-three years, 5 and these were the children born to him there:

Shammua,*d* Shobab, Nathan and Solomon. These four were by Bathsheba*e* daughter of Ammiel. 6 There were also Ibhar, Elishua,*f* Eliphelet, 7 Nogah, Nepheg, Japhia, 8 Elishama, Eliada and Eliphelet — nine in all. 9 All these were the sons of David, besides his sons by his concubines. And Tamar was their sister.

The Kings of Judah

10 Solomon's son was Rehoboam,
Abijah his son,

---

a 42 The meaning of the Hebrew for this phrase is uncertain.   *b 55* Or *of the Sopherites*   *c 55* Or *father of Beth Rekab*   *d 5* Hebrew *Shimea,* a variant of *Shammua*   *e 5* One Hebrew manuscript and Vulgate (see also Septuagint and 2 Samuel 11:3); most Hebrew manuscripts *Bathshua*   *f 6* Two Hebrew manuscripts (see also 2 Samuel 5:15 and 1 Chron. 14:5); most Hebrew manuscripts *Elishama*

Asa his son,
Jehoshaphat his son,
[11] Jehoram[a] his son,
Ahaziah his son,
Joash his son,
[12] Amaziah his son,
Azariah his son,
Jotham his son,
[13] Ahaz his son,
Hezekiah his son,
Manasseh his son,
[14] Amon his son,
Josiah his son.
[15] The sons of Josiah:
Johanan the firstborn,
Jehoiakim the second son,
Zedekiah the third,
Shallum the fourth.
[16] The successors of Jehoiakim:
Jehoiachin[b] his son,
and Zedekiah.

The Royal Line After the Exile

[17] The descendants of Jehoiachin the captive:
Shealtiel his son, [18] Malkiram, Pedaiah, Shenazzar, Jekamiah, Hoshama and Nedabiah.
[19] The sons of Pedaiah:
Zerubbabel and Shimei.
The sons of Zerubbabel:
Meshullam and Hananiah.
Shelomith was their sister.
[20] There were also five others:
Hashubah, Ohel, Berekiah, Hasadiah and Jushab-Hesed.
[21] The descendants of Hananiah:
Pelatiah and Jeshaiah, and the sons of Rephaiah, of Arnan, of Obadiah and of Shekaniah.
[22] The descendants of Shekaniah:
Shemaiah and his sons:
Hattush, Igal, Bariah, Neariah and Shaphat—six in all.
[23] The sons of Neariah:
Elioenai, Hizkiah and Azrikam—three in all.
[24] The sons of Elioenai:
Hodaviah, Eliashib, Pelaiah, Akkub,

Johanan, Delaiah and Anani—seven in all.

Other Clans of Judah

4 The descendants of Judah:
Perez, Hezron, Karmi, Hur and Shobal.
[2] Reaiah son of Shobal was the father of Jahath, and Jahath the father of Ahumai and Lahad. These were the clans of the Zorathites.
[3] These were the sons[c] of Etam:
Jezreel, Ishma and Idbash. Their sister was named Hazzelelponi. [4] Penuel was the father of Gedor, and Ezer the father of Hushah.
These were the descendants of Hur, the firstborn of Ephrathah and father[d] of Bethlehem.
[5] Ashhur the father of Tekoa had two wives, Helah and Naarah.
[6] Naarah bore him Ahuzzam, Hepher, Temeni and Haahashtari. These were the descendants of Naarah.
[7] The sons of Helah:
Zereth, Zohar, Ethnan, [8] and Koz, who was the father of Anub and Hazzobebah and of the clans of Aharhel son of Harum.

[9] Jabez was more honorable than his brothers. His mother had named him Jabez,[e] saying, "I gave birth to him in pain." [10] Jabez cried out to the God of Israel, "Oh, that you would bless me and enlarge my territory! Let your hand be with me, and keep me from harm so that I will be free from pain." And God granted his request.

[11] Kelub, Shuhah's brother, was the father of Mehir, who was the father of Eshton. [12] Eshton was the father of Beth Rapha, Paseah and Tehinnah the father of Ir Nahash.[f] These were the men of Rekah.

[13] The sons of Kenaz:
Othniel and Seraiah.
The sons of Othniel:
Hathath and Meonothai.[g] [14] Meonothai was the father of Ophrah.

---

[a] 11 Hebrew *Joram*, a variant of *Jehoram*   [b] 16 Hebrew *Jeconiah*, a variant of *Jehoiachin*; also in verse 17   [c] 3 Some Septuagint manuscripts (see also Vulgate); Hebrew *father*   [d] 4 *Father* may mean *civic leader* or *military leader*; also in verses 12, 14, 17, 18 and possibly elsewhere.   [e] 9 *Jabez* sounds like the Hebrew for *pain*.   [f] 12 Or *of the city of Nahash*   [g] 13 Some Septuagint manuscripts and Vulgate; Hebrew does not have *and Meonothai*.

PLAY OFFENSE

READ: 1 CHRONICLES 4:10

There's an old saying: opportunity knocks. It's a lie. Usually, you are the one who needs to do the knocking. And sometimes you even have to knock the door down. Don't wait for it to come to you. You need to go get it. Don't just sit around, waiting for something to happen. Make it happen.

It doesn't matter how many times you've been knocked down, only how many you've gotten up.

It doesn't matter how tough it has been before, but only that you continue the fight.

Is there a dream you've given up on? Go back and try again. Don't give up!

Failure isn't the opposite of success. It's the nearest ally! I could have given up after a failed church plant, but I got back up and tried again. I could have given up after thirteen years of attempting to write a book, but I didn't wave the white flag.

BUILDING

FAITH

WISDOM

STRENGTH

Everyone has had a moment in his life when his dreams seemed so far off that he couldn't think of anything else to do but give up. You might even be heavily tempted right now to give up on your plans for college or your dream job. Hang in there. Even if there's no back-up and no ammunition, you need to charge the problem, charge the dream, charge the goal.

Taken from *All In Student Edition* by Mark Batterson and Parker Batterson, copyright © 2014 by Mark Batterson, published by Zondervan.

Seraiah was the father of Joab,
the father of Ge Harashim.[a] It was
called this because its people were
skilled workers.

[15]The sons of Caleb son of Jephunneh:
Iru, Elah and Naam.

The son of Elah:
Kenaz.

[16]The sons of Jehallelel:
Ziph, Ziphah, Tiria and Asarel.

[17]The sons of Ezrah:
Jether, Mered, Epher and Jalon. One
of Mered's wives gave birth to Miriam, Shammai and Ishbah the father
of Eshtemoa. [18](His wife from the
tribe of Judah gave birth to Jered the
father of Gedor, Heber the father of
Soko, and Jekuthiel the father of Zanoah.) These were the children of
Pharaoh's daughter Bithiah, whom
Mered had married.

[19]The sons of Hodiah's wife, the sister of
Naham:
the father of Keilah the Garmite, and
Eshtemoa the Maakathite.

[20]The sons of Shimon:
Amnon, Rinnah, Ben-Hanan and Tilon.

The descendants of Ishi:
Zoheth and Ben-Zoheth.

[21]The sons of Shelah son of Judah:
Er the father of Lekah, Laadah the father of Mareshah and the clans of the
linen workers at Beth Ashbea, [22]Jokim, the men of Kozeba, and Joash
and Saraph, who ruled in Moab and
Jashubi Lehem. (These records are
from ancient times.) [23]They were the
potters who lived at Netaim and Gederah; they stayed there and worked
for the king.

Simeon

[24]The descendants of Simeon:
Nemuel, Jamin, Jarib, Zerah and
Shaul;

[25]Shallum was Shaul's son, Mibsam
his son and Mishma his son.

[26]The descendants of Mishma:
Hammuel his son, Zakkur his son
and Shimei his son.

[27]Shimei had sixteen sons and six daughters, but his brothers did not have many children; so their entire clan did not become as numerous as the people of Judah. [28]They lived in Beersheba, Moladah, Hazar Shual, [29]Bilhah, Ezem, Tolad, [30]Bethuel, Hormah, Ziklag, [31]Beth Markaboth, Hazar Susim, Beth Biri and Shaaraim. These were their towns until the reign of David. [32]Their surrounding villages were Etam, Ain, Rimmon, Token and Ashan — five towns — [33]and all the villages around these towns as far as Baalath.[b] These were their settlements. And they kept a genealogical record.

[34]Meshobab, Jamlech, Joshah son of Amaziah, [35]Joel, Jehu son of Joshibiah, the son of Seraiah, the son of Asiel, [36]also Elioenai, Jaakobah, Jeshohaiah, Asaiah, Adiel, Jesimiel, Benaiah, [37]and Ziza son of Shiphi, the son of Allon, the son of Jedaiah, the son of Shimri, the son of Shemaiah.

[38]The men listed above by name were leaders of their clans. Their families increased greatly, [39]and they went to the outskirts of Gedor to the east of the valley in search of pasture for their flocks. [40]They found rich, good pasture, and the land was spacious, peaceful and quiet. Some Hamites had lived there formerly.

[41]The men whose names were listed came in the days of Hezekiah king of Judah. They attacked the Hamites in their dwellings and also the Meunites who were there and completely destroyed[c] them, as is evident to this day. Then they settled in their place, because there was pasture for their flocks. [42]And five hundred of these Simeonites, led by Pelatiah, Neariah, Rephaiah and Uzziel, the sons of Ishi, invaded the hill country of Seir. [43]They killed the remaining Amalekites who had escaped, and they have lived there to this day.

Reuben

5 The sons of Reuben the firstborn of Israel (he was the firstborn, but when he defiled his father's marriage bed, his rights as firstborn were given to the sons of Joseph

---

[a] 14 *Ge Harashim* means *valley of skilled workers.* 19:8); Hebrew *Baal*   [c] 41 The Hebrew term refers to the irrevocable giving over of things or persons to the LORD, often by totally destroying them.   [b] 33 Some Septuagint manuscripts (see also Joshua

JABEZ

His mother had named him Jabez, saying, "I gave birth to him in pain." Jabez cried out to the God of Israel, "Oh, that you would bless me and enlarge my territory! Let your hand be with me, and keep me from harm so that I will be free from pain." And God granted his request. 1 CHRONICLES 4:9-10

HIS NAME MEANS: "he causes pain"
READ HIS STORY: *1 Chronicles 4:9-10*

Hidden within a list of genealogies and names, the story of Jabez is like finding a pearl in an oyster. What makes this story so special? It's the voice of an underdog who cries out for help. But Jabez didn't just ask for help in a small way. His prayer is a great big request because he knew he was calling out to a great big God.

Everything seemed to be against Jabez from the day he was born. Even his mother seemed against him, giving him a name that meant "He causes pain." Yet Jabez asked God to bless him in spite of it all.

Not only did Jabez ask for blessings, he also asked for *bigger* and *better*. He also asked for God's hand of protection to be with him wherever he went so that he wouldn't live up to his name and bring pain to others. Those are some big requests—and God said yes to each one.

God helped Jabez in his day of trouble and granted his request. God wants to help you too. You are precious in God's sight. He loves you and wants to help you, just as he helped Jabez. God wants to turn your biggest sorrows into blessings so large you won't be able to contain your joy.

son of Israel; so he could not be listed in the genealogical record in accordance with his birthright, ²and though Judah was the strongest of his brothers and a ruler came from him, the rights of the firstborn belonged to Joseph)— ³the sons of Reuben the firstborn of Israel:

Hanok, Pallu, Hezron and Karmi.

⁴The descendants of Joel:

Shemaiah his son, Gog his son, Shimei his son, ⁵Micah his son, Reaiah his son, Baal his son,

⁶and Beerah his son, whom Tiglath-Pileser*ᵃ* king of Assyria took into exile. Beerah was a leader of the Reubenites.

⁷Their relatives by clans, listed according to their genealogical records:

Jeiel the chief, Zechariah, ⁸and Bela son of Azaz, the son of Shema, the son of Joel. They settled in the area from Aroer to Nebo and Baal Meon. ⁹To the east they occupied the land up to the edge of the desert that extends to the Euphrates River, because their livestock had increased in Gilead.

¹⁰During Saul's reign they waged war against the Hagrites, who were defeated at their hands; they occupied the dwellings of the Hagrites throughout the entire region east of Gilead.

Gad

¹¹The Gadites lived next to them in Bashan, as far as Salekah:

¹²Joel was the chief, Shapham the second, then Janai and Shaphat, in Bashan.

¹³Their relatives, by families, were:

Michael, Meshullam, Sheba, Jorai, Jakan, Zia and Eber—seven in all. ¹⁴These were the sons of Abihail son of Huri, the son of Jaroah, the son of Gilead, the son of Michael, the son of Jeshishai, the son of Jahdo, the son of Buz.

¹⁵Ahi son of Abdiel, the son of Guni, was head of their family.

¹⁶The Gadites lived in Gilead, in Bashan and its outlying villages, and on all the pasturelands of Sharon as far as they extended.

¹⁷All these were entered in the genealogical records during the reigns of Jotham king of Judah and Jeroboam king of Israel.

¹⁸The Reubenites, the Gadites and the half-tribe of Manasseh had 44,760 men ready for military service—able-bodied men who could handle shield and sword, who could use a bow, and who were trained for battle. ¹⁹They waged war against the Hagrites, Jetur, Naphish and Nodab. ²⁰They were helped in fighting them, and God delivered the Hagrites and all their allies into their hands, because they cried out to him during the battle. He answered their prayers, because they trusted in him. ²¹They seized the livestock of the Hagrites—fifty thousand camels, two hundred fifty thousand sheep and two thousand donkeys. They also took one hundred thousand people captive, ²²and many others fell slain, because the battle was God's. And they occupied the land until the exile.

The Half-Tribe of Manasseh

²³The people of the half-tribe of Manasseh were numerous; they settled in the land from Bashan to Baal Hermon, that is, to Senir (Mount Hermon).

²⁴These were the heads of their families: Epher, Ishi, Eliel, Azriel, Jeremiah, Hodaviah and Jahdiel. They were brave warriors, famous men, and heads of their families. ²⁵But they were unfaithful to the God of their ancestors and prostituted themselves to the gods of the peoples of the land, whom God had destroyed before them. ²⁶So the God of Israel stirred up the spirit of Pul king of Assyria (that is, Tiglath-Pileser king of Assyria), who took the Reubenites, the Gadites and the half-tribe of Manasseh into exile. He took them to Halah, Habor, Hara and the river of Gozan, where they are to this day.

Levi

6ᵇ The sons of Levi:

Gershon, Kohath and Merari.

²The sons of Kohath:

Amram, Izhar, Hebron and Uzziel.

³The children of Amram:

Aaron, Moses and Miriam.

ᵃ 6 Hebrew *Tilgath-Pilneser*, a variant of *Tiglath-Pileser*; also in verse 26   *ᵇ* In Hebrew texts 6:1-15 is numbered 5:27-41, and 6:16-81 is numbered 6:1-66.

The sons of Aaron:
Nadab, Abihu, Eleazar and Ithamar.
⁴ Eleazar was the father of Phinehas,
Phinehas the father of Abishua,
⁵ Abishua the father of Bukki,
Bukki the father of Uzzi,
⁶ Uzzi the father of Zerahiah,
Zerahiah the father of Meraioth,
⁷ Meraioth the father of Amariah,
Amariah the father of Ahitub,
⁸ Ahitub the father of Zadok,
Zadok the father of Ahimaaz,
⁹ Ahimaaz the father of Azariah,
Azariah the father of Johanan,
¹⁰ Johanan the father of Azariah (it was
he who served as priest in the temple
Solomon built in Jerusalem),
¹¹ Azariah the father of Amariah,
Amariah the father of Ahitub,
¹² Ahitub the father of Zadok,
Zadok the father of Shallum,
¹³ Shallum the father of Hilkiah,
Hilkiah the father of Azariah,
¹⁴ Azariah the father of Seraiah,
and Seraiah the father of Jozadak.ᵃ
¹⁵ Jozadak was deported when the Lᴏʀᴅ
sent Judah and Jerusalem into exile by
the hand of Nebuchadnezzar.

¹⁶ The sons of Levi:
Gershon,ᵇ Kohath and Merari.
¹⁷ These are the names of the sons of Ger-
shon:
Libni and Shimei.
¹⁸ The sons of Kohath:
Amram, Izhar, Hebron and Uzziel.
¹⁹ The sons of Merari:
Mahli and Mushi.
These are the clans of the Levites listed
according to their fathers:
²⁰ Of Gershon:
Libni his son, Jahath his son,
Zimmah his son, ²¹ Joah his son,
Iddo his son, Zerah his son
and Jeatherai his son.
²² The descendants of Kohath:
Amminadab his son, Korah his son,
Assir his son, ²³ Elkanah his son,
Ebiasaph his son, Assir his son,

²⁴ Tahath his son, Uriel his son,
Uzziah his son and Shaul his son.
²⁵ The descendants of Elkanah:
Amasai, Ahimoth,
²⁶ Elkanah his son,ᶜ Zophai his son,
Nahath his son, ²⁷ Eliab his son,
Jeroham his son, Elkanah his son
and Samuel his son.ᵈ
²⁸ The sons of Samuel:
Joelᵉ the firstborn
and Abijah the second son.
²⁹ The descendants of Merari:
Mahli, Libni his son,
Shimei his son, Uzzah his son,
³⁰ Shimea his son, Haggiah his son
and Asaiah his son.

The Temple Musicians

³¹ These are the men David put in charge
of the music in the house of the Lᴏʀᴅ after
the ark came to rest there. ³² They ministered
with music before the tabernacle, the tent
of meeting, until Solomon built the temple
of the Lᴏʀᴅ in Jerusalem. They performed
their duties according to the regulations laid
down for them.

³³ Here are the men who served, together
with their sons:
From the Kohathites:
Heman, the musician,
the son of Joel, the son of Samuel,
³⁴ the son of Elkanah, the son of Jeroham,
the son of Eliel, the son of Toah,
³⁵ the son of Zuph, the son of Elkanah,
the son of Mahath, the son of Amasai,
³⁶ the son of Elkanah, the son of Joel,
the son of Azariah, the son of Zephaniah,
³⁷ the son of Tahath, the son of Assir,
the son of Ebiasaph, the son of Korah,
³⁸ the son of Izhar, the son of Kohath,
the son of Levi, the son of Israel;
³⁹ and Heman's associate Asaph, who
served at his right hand:
Asaph son of Berekiah, the son of
Shimea,
⁴⁰ the son of Michael, the son of Baase-
iah,ᶠ

ᵃ 14 Hebrew *Jehozadak*, a variant of *Jozadak*; also in verse 15   ᵇ 16 Hebrew *Gershom*, a variant of *Gershon*;
also in verses 17, 20, 43, 62 and 71   ᶜ 26 Some Hebrew manuscripts, Septuagint and Syriac; most Hebrew
manuscripts *Ahimoth* ²⁶*and Elkanah. The sons of Elkanah:*   ᵈ 27 Some Septuagint manuscripts (see also
1 Samuel 1:19,20 and 1 Chron. 6:33,34); Hebrew does not have *and Samuel his son.*   ᵉ 28 Some Septuagint
manuscripts and Syriac (see also 1 Samuel 8:2 and 1 Chron. 6:33); Hebrew does not have *Joel.*   ᶠ 40 Most
Hebrew manuscripts; some Hebrew manuscripts, one Septuagint manuscript and Syriac *Maaseiah*

THE REASON FOR THE LISTS

READ: 1 CHRONICLES 6:31

Don't let your eyes glaze over when you read the lists of temple workers in 1 Chronicles. Each of those people had a place in the Lord's plans. So do you.

The musicians, priests, and temple assistants remembered here are long gone. Yet they were actual people. They were born and they died, and for all the days they had breath they served God. Aaron and his sons (1 Chronicles 6:3) served as priests. Asaph and his boys (1 Chronicles 6:39) come in a long succession of musicians. Thousands of years later, his family is still famous for writing at least twelve Old Testament psalms (Psalms 50, 73–83).

This passage describes the parcels of land given to these servants of God. As they took responsibility for the spiritual leadership of Israel, the Lord made sure their practical needs were met. These lists aren't all that different from names and faces that appear on a modern church website: people paid to work as pastors, youth directors, or other staff members.

There are also real-life principles here. You can be part of supporting your spiritual leaders, because the Lord cares about their needs (1 Timothy 5:17–18). And whenever and however you serve God, you can be certain he watches out for you.

BUILDING

FAITH

WISDOM

STRENGTH

the son of Malkijah, [41]the son of Ethni, the son of Zerah, the son of Adaiah, [42]the son of Ethan, the son of Zimmah, the son of Shimei, [43]the son of Jahath, the son of Gershon, the son of Levi;

[44]and from their associates, the Merarites, at his left hand:

Ethan son of Kishi, the son of Abdi, the son of Malluk, [45]the son of Hashabiah,

the son of Amaziah, the son of Hilkiah,

[46]the son of Amzi, the son of Bani, the son of Shemer, [47]the son of Mahli, the son of Mushi, the son of Merari, the son of Levi.

[48]Their fellow Levites were assigned to all the other duties of the tabernacle, the house of God. [49]But Aaron and his descendants were the ones who presented offerings on the altar of burnt offering and on the altar of incense in connection with all that was done in the Most Holy Place, making atonement for Israel, in accordance with all that Moses the servant of God had commanded.

[50]These were the descendants of Aaron:

Eleazar his son, Phinehas his son, Abishua his son, [51]Bukki his son, Uzzi his son, Zerahiah his son, [52]Meraioth his son, Amariah his son, Ahitub his son, [53]Zadok his son and Ahimaaz his son.

[54]These were the locations of their settlements allotted as their territory (they were assigned to the descendants of Aaron who were from the Kohathite clan, because the first lot was for them):

[55]They were given Hebron in Judah with its surrounding pasturelands. [56]But the fields and villages around the city were given to Caleb son of Jephunneh. [57]So the descendants of Aaron were given Hebron (a city of refuge), and Libnah,[a] Jattir, Eshtemoa, [58]Hilen, Debir, [59]Ashan, Juttah[b] and Beth Shemesh, together with their pasturelands. [60]And from the tribe of Benjamin they were given Gibeon,[c] Geba, Alemeth

and Anathoth, together with their pasturelands.

The total number of towns distributed among the Kohathite clans came to thirteen.

[61]The rest of Kohath's descendants were allotted ten towns from the clans of half the tribe of Manasseh.

[62]The descendants of Gershon, clan by clan, were allotted thirteen towns from the tribes of Issachar, Asher and Naphtali, and from the part of the tribe of Manasseh that is in Bashan.

[63]The descendants of Merari, clan by clan, were allotted twelve towns from the tribes of Reuben, Gad and Zebulun.

[64]So the Israelites gave the Levites these towns and their pasturelands. [65]From the tribes of Judah, Simeon and Benjamin they allotted the previously named towns.

[66]Some of the Kohathite clans were given as their territory towns from the tribe of Ephraim.

[67]In the hill country of Ephraim they were given Shechem (a city of refuge), and Gezer,[d] [68]Jokmeam, Beth Horon, [69]Aijalon and Gath Rimmon, together with their pasturelands.

[70]And from half the tribe of Manasseh the Israelites gave Aner and Bileam, together with their pasturelands, to the rest of the Kohathite clans.

[71]The Gershonites received the following:

From the clan of the half-tribe of Manasseh

they received Golan in Bashan and also Ashtaroth, together with their pasturelands;

[72]from the tribe of Issachar

they received Kedesh, Daberath, [73]Ramoth and Anem, together with their pasturelands;

[74]from the tribe of Asher

they received Mashal, Abdon, [75]Hukok and Rehob, together with their pasturelands;

[76]and from the tribe of Naphtali

they received Kedesh in Galilee, Hammon and Kiriathaim, together with their pasturelands.

---

[a] 57 See Joshua 21:13; Hebrew *given the cities of refuge: Hebron, Libnah.*   [b] 59 Syriac (see also Septuagint and Joshua 21:16); Hebrew does not have *Juttah.*   [c] 60 See Joshua 21:17; Hebrew does not have *Gibeon.*   [d] 67 See Joshua 21:21; Hebrew *given the cities of refuge: Shechem, Gezer.*

⁷⁷The Merarites (the rest of the Levites) received the following:

> From the tribe of Zebulun
> they received Jokneam, Kartah,^a
> Rimmono and Tabor, together with
> their pasturelands;

⁷⁸from the tribe of Reuben across the Jordan east of Jericho

> they received Bezer in the wilderness, Jahzah, ⁷⁹Kedemoth and Mephaath, together with their pasturelands;

⁸⁰and from the tribe of Gad

> they received Ramoth in Gilead, Mahanaim, ⁸¹Heshbon and Jazer, together with their pasturelands.

Issachar

7 The sons of Issachar:

> Tola, Puah, Jashub and Shimron—four in all.

²The sons of Tola:

> Uzzi, Rephaiah, Jeriel, Jahmai, Ibsam and Samuel—heads of their families. During the reign of David, the descendants of Tola listed as fighting men in their genealogy numbered 22,600.

³The son of Uzzi:

> Izrahiah.

The sons of Izrahiah:

> Michael, Obadiah, Joel and Ishiah. All five of them were chiefs. ⁴According to their family genealogy, they had 36,000 men ready for battle, for they had many wives and children.

⁵The relatives who were fighting men belonging to all the clans of Issachar, as listed in their genealogy, were 87,000 in all.

Benjamin

⁶Three sons of Benjamin:

> Bela, Beker and Jediael.

⁷The sons of Bela:

> Ezbon, Uzzi, Uzziel, Jerimoth and Iri, heads of families—five in all. Their genealogical record listed 22,034 fighting men.

⁸The sons of Beker:

> Zemirah, Joash, Eliezer, Elioenai, Omri, Jeremoth, Abijah, Anathoth and Alemeth. All these were the sons of Beker. ⁹Their genealogical record listed the heads of families and 20,200 fighting men.

¹⁰The son of Jediael:

> Bilhan.

The sons of Bilhan:

> Jeush, Benjamin, Ehud, Kenaanah, Zethan, Tarshish and Ahishahar. ¹¹All these sons of Jediael were heads of families. There were 17,200 fighting men ready to go out to war.

¹²The Shuppites and Huppites were the descendants of Ir, and the Hushites^b the descendants of Aher.

Naphtali

¹³The sons of Naphtali:

> Jahziel, Guni, Jezer and Shillem^c—the descendants of Bilhah.

Manasseh

¹⁴The descendants of Manasseh:

> Asriel was his descendant through his Aramean concubine. She gave birth to Makir the father of Gilead. ¹⁵Makir took a wife from among the Huppites and Shuppites. His sister's name was Maakah.

> Another descendant was named Zelophehad, who had only daughters.

¹⁶Makir's wife Maakah gave birth to a son and named him Peresh. His brother was named Sheresh, and his sons were Ulam and Rakem.

¹⁷The son of Ulam:

> Bedan.

These were the sons of Gilead son of Makir, the son of Manasseh. ¹⁸His sister Hammoleketh gave birth to Ishhod, Abiezer and Mahlah.

¹⁹The sons of Shemida were:

> Ahian, Shechem, Likhi and Aniam.

Ephraim

²⁰The descendants of Ephraim:

> Shuthelah, Bered his son,
> Tahath his son, Eleadah his son,

---

^a 77 See Septuagint and Joshua 21:34; Hebrew does not have *Jokneam, Kartah.*   ^b 12 Or *Ir. The sons of Dan: Hushim,* (see Gen. 46:23); Hebrew does not have *The sons of Dan.*   ^c 13 Some Hebrew and Septuagint manuscripts (see also Gen. 46:24 and Num. 26:49); most Hebrew manuscripts *Shallum*

Tahath his son, [21]Zabad his son and Shuthelah his son.

Ezer and Elead were killed by the native-born men of Gath, when they went down to seize their livestock. [22]Their father Ephraim mourned for them many days, and his relatives came to comfort him. [23]Then he made love to his wife again, and she became pregnant and gave birth to a son. He named him Beriah,[a] because there had been misfortune in his family. [24]His daughter was Sheerah, who built Lower and Upper Beth Horon as well as Uzzen Sheerah.

[25]Rephah was his son, Resheph his son,[b] Telah his son, Tahan his son, [26]Ladan his son, Ammihud his son, Elishama his son, [27]Nun his son and Joshua his son.

[28]Their lands and settlements included Bethel and its surrounding villages, Naaran to the east, Gezer and its villages to the west, and Shechem and its villages all the way to Ayyah and its villages. [29]Along the borders of Manasseh were Beth Shan, Taanach, Megiddo and Dor, together with their villages. The descendants of Joseph son of Israel lived in these towns.

Asher

[30]The sons of Asher:

Imnah, Ishvah, Ishvi and Beriah. Their sister was Serah.

[31]The sons of Beriah:

Heber and Malkiel, who was the father of Birzaith.

[32]Heber was the father of Japhlet, Shomer and Hotham and of their sister Shua.

[33]The sons of Japhlet:

Pasak, Bimhal and Ashvath. These were Japhlet's sons.

[34]The sons of Shomer:

Ahi, Rohgah,[c] Hubbah and Aram.

[35]The sons of his brother Helem:

Zophah, Imna, Shelesh and Amal.

[36]The sons of Zophah:

Suah, Harnepher, Shual, Beri, Imrah, [37]Bezer, Hod, Shamma, Shilshah, Ithran[d] and Beera.

[38]The sons of Jether:

Jephunneh, Pispah and Ara.

[39]The sons of Ulla:

Arah, Hanniel and Rizia.

[40]All these were descendants of Asher — heads of families, choice men, brave warriors and outstanding leaders. The number of men ready for battle, as listed in their genealogy, was 26,000.

The Genealogy of Saul the Benjamite

8 Benjamin was the father of Bela his firstborn,

Ashbel the second son, Aharah the third,

[2]Nohah the fourth and Rapha the fifth.

[3]The sons of Bela were:

Addar, Gera, Abihud,[e] [4]Abishua, Naaman, Ahoah, [5]Gera, Shephuphan and Huram.

[6]These were the descendants of Ehud, who were heads of families of those living in Geba and were deported to Manahath:

[7]Naaman, Ahijah, and Gera, who deported them and who was the father of Uzza and Ahihud.

[8]Sons were born to Shaharaim in Moab after he had divorced his wives Hushim and Baara. [9]By his wife Hodesh he had Jobab, Zibia, Mesha, Malkam, [10]Jeuz, Sakia and Mirmah. These were his sons, heads of families. [11]By Hushim he had Abitub and Elpaal.

[12]The sons of Elpaal:

Eber, Misham, Shemed (who built Ono and Lod with its surrounding villages), [13]and Beriah and Shema, who were heads of families of those living in Aijalon and who drove out the inhabitants of Gath.

[14]Ahio, Shashak, Jeremoth, [15]Zebadiah, Arad, Eder, [16]Michael, Ishpah and Joha were the sons of Beriah.

[17]Zebadiah, Meshullam, Hizki, Heber, [18]Ishmerai, Izliah and Jobab were the sons of Elpaal.

[19]Jakim, Zikri, Zabdi, [20]Elienai, Zillethai, Eliel, [21]Adaiah, Beraiah and Shimrath were the sons of Shimei.

[22]Ishpan, Eber, Eliel, [23]Abdon, Zikri, Hanan, [24]Hananiah, Elam, Anthothijah,

---

[a] 23 Beriah sounds like the Hebrew for misfortune.   [b] 25 Some Septuagint manuscripts; Hebrew does not have his son.   [c] 34 Or of his brother Shomer: Rohgah   [d] 37 Possibly a variant of Jether   [e] 3 Or Gera the father of Ehud

²⁵Iphdeiah and Penuel were the sons of Shashak.

²⁶Shamsherai, Shehariah, Athaliah, ²⁷Jaareshiah, Elijah and Zikri were the sons of Jeroham.

²⁸All these were heads of families, chiefs as listed in their genealogy, and they lived in Jerusalem.

²⁹Jeiel[a] the father[b] of Gibeon lived in Gibeon.

His wife's name was Maakah, ³⁰and his firstborn son was Abdon, followed by Zur, Kish, Baal, Ner,[c] Nadab, ³¹Gedor, Ahio, Zeker ³²and Mikloth, who was the father of Shimeah. They too lived near their relatives in Jerusalem.

³³Ner was the father of Kish, Kish the father of Saul, and Saul the father of Jonathan, Malki-Shua, Abinadab and Esh-Baal.[d]

³⁴The son of Jonathan:

Merib-Baal,[e] who was the father of Micah.

³⁵The sons of Micah:

Pithon, Melek, Tarea and Ahaz.

³⁶Ahaz was the father of Jehoaddah, Jehoaddah was the father of Alemeth, Azmaveth and Zimri, and Zimri was the father of Moza. ³⁷Moza was the father of Binea; Raphah was his son, Eleasah his son and Azel his son.

³⁸Azel had six sons, and these were their names:

Azrikam, Bokeru, Ishmael, Sheariah, Obadiah and Hanan. All these were the sons of Azel.

³⁹The sons of his brother Eshek:

Ulam his firstborn, Jeush the second son and Eliphelet the third. ⁴⁰The sons of Ulam were brave warriors who could handle the bow. They had many sons and grandsons—150 in all.

All these were the descendants of Benjamin.

9 All Israel was listed in the genealogies recorded in the book of the kings of Israel and Judah. They were taken captive to Babylon because of their unfaithfulness.

The People in Jerusalem

²Now the first to resettle on their own property in their own towns were some Israelites, priests, Levites and temple servants.

³Those from Judah, from Benjamin, and from Ephraim and Manasseh who lived in Jerusalem were:

⁴Uthai son of Ammihud, the son of Omri, the son of Imri, the son of Bani, a descendant of Perez son of Judah.

⁵Of the Shelanites[f]:

Asaiah the firstborn and his sons.

⁶Of the Zerahites:

Jeuel.

The people from Judah numbered 690.

⁷Of the Benjamites:

Sallu son of Meshullam, the son of Hodaviah, the son of Hassenuah;

⁸Ibneiah son of Jeroham; Elah son of Uzzi, the son of Mikri; and Meshullam son of Shephatiah, the son of Reuel, the son of Ibnijah.

⁹The people from Benjamin, as listed in their genealogy, numbered 956. All these men were heads of their families.

¹⁰Of the priests:

Jedaiah; Jehoiarib; Jakin;

¹¹Azariah son of Hilkiah, the son of Meshullam, the son of Zadok, the son of Meraioth, the son of Ahitub, the official in charge of the house of God;

¹²Adaiah son of Jeroham, the son of Pashhur, the son of Malkijah; and Maasai son of Adiel, the son of Jahzerah, the son of Meshullam, the son of Meshillemith, the son of Immer.

¹³The priests, who were heads of families, numbered 1,760. They were able men, responsible for ministering in the house of God.

¹⁴Of the Levites:

Shemaiah son of Hasshub, the son of Azrikam, the son of Hashabiah, a Merarite; ¹⁵Bakbakkar, Heresh, Galal and Mattaniah son of Mika, the son of Zikri, the son of Asaph; ¹⁶Obadiah son of Shemaiah, the son

---

ᵃ 29 Some Septuagint manuscripts (see also 9:35); Hebrew does not have *Jeiel.*   ᵇ 29 *Father* may mean *civic leader* or *military leader.*   ᶜ 30 Some Septuagint manuscripts (see also 9:36); Hebrew does not have *Ner.*   ᵈ 33 Also known as *Ish-Bosheth*   ᵉ 34 Also known as *Mephibosheth*   ᶠ 5 See Num. 26:20; Hebrew *Shilonites.*

of Galal, the son of Jeduthun; and Berekiah son of Asa, the son of Elkanah, who lived in the villages of the Netophathites.

¹⁷ The gatekeepers:

Shallum, Akkub, Talmon, Ahiman and their fellow Levites, Shallum their chief ¹⁸ being stationed at the King's Gate on the east, up to the present time. These were the gatekeepers belonging to the camp of the Levites. ¹⁹ Shallum son of Kore, the son of Ebiasaph, the son of Korah, and his fellow gatekeepers from his family (the Korahites) were responsible for guarding the thresholds of the tent just as their ancestors had been responsible for guarding the entrance to the dwelling of the LORD. ²⁰ In earlier times Phinehas son of Eleazar was the official in charge of the gatekeepers, and the LORD was with him. ²¹ Zechariah son of Meshelemiah was the gatekeeper at the entrance to the tent of meeting.

²² Altogether, those chosen to be gatekeepers at the thresholds numbered 212. They were registered by genealogy in their villages. The gatekeepers had been assigned to their positions of trust by David and Samuel the seer. ²³ They and their descendants were in charge of guarding the gates of the house of the LORD — the house called the tent of meeting. ²⁴ The gatekeepers were on the four sides: east, west, north and south. ²⁵ Their fellow Levites in their villages had to come from time to time and share their duties for seven-day periods. ²⁶ But the four principal gatekeepers, who were Levites, were entrusted with the responsibility for the rooms and treasuries in the house of God. ²⁷ They would spend the night stationed around the house of God, because they had to guard it; and they had charge of the key for opening it each morning.

²⁸ Some of them were in charge of the articles used in the temple service; they counted them when they were brought in and when they were taken out. ²⁹ Others were assigned to take care of the furnishings and all the other articles of the sanctuary, as well as the special flour and wine, and the olive oil, incense and spices. ³⁰ But some of the priests took care of mixing the spices. ³¹ A Levite named Mattithiah, the firstborn son of Shallum the Korahite, was entrusted with the responsibility for baking the offering bread. ³² Some of the Kohathites, their fellow Levites, were in charge of preparing for every Sabbath the bread set out on the table.

³³ Those who were musicians, heads of Levite families, stayed in the rooms of the temple and were exempt from other duties because they were responsible for the work day and night.

³⁴ All these were heads of Levite families, chiefs as listed in their genealogy, and they lived in Jerusalem.

The Genealogy of Saul

³⁵ Jeiel the father[a] of Gibeon lived in Gibeon.

His wife's name was Maakah, ³⁶ and his firstborn son was Abdon, followed by Zur, Kish, Baal, Ner, Nadab, ³⁷ Gedor, Ahio, Zechariah and Mikloth. ³⁸ Mikloth was the father of Shimeam. They too lived near their relatives in Jerusalem.

³⁹ Ner was the father of Kish, Kish the father of Saul, and Saul the father of Jonathan, Malki-Shua, Abinadab and Esh-Baal.[b]

⁴⁰ The son of Jonathan:

Merib-Baal,[c] who was the father of Micah.

⁴¹ The sons of Micah:

Pithon, Melek, Tahrea and Ahaz.[d]

⁴² Ahaz was the father of Jadah, Jadah[e] was the father of Alemeth, Azmaveth and Zimri, and Zimri was the father of Moza. ⁴³ Moza was the father of Binea; Rephaiah was his son, Eleasah his son and Azel his son.

⁴⁴ Azel had six sons, and these were their names:

Azrikam, Bokeru, Ishmael, Sheariah, Obadiah and Hanan. These were the sons of Azel.

---

a 35 *Father* may mean *civic leader* or *military leader.* *b 39* Also known as *Ish-Bosheth* *c 40* Also known as *Mephibosheth* *d 41* Vulgate and Syriac (see also Septuagint and 8:35); Hebrew does not have *and Ahaz.* *e 42* Some Hebrew manuscripts and Septuagint (see also 8:36); most Hebrew manuscripts *Jarah, Jarah*

Saul Takes His Life

10 Now the Philistines fought against Israel; the Israelites fled before them, and many fell dead on Mount Gilboa. ²The Philistines were in hot pursuit of Saul and his sons, and they killed his sons Jonathan, Abinadab and Malki-Shua. ³The fighting grew fierce around Saul, and when the archers overtook him, they wounded him.

⁴Saul said to his armor-bearer, "Draw your sword and run me through, or these uncircumcised fellows will come and abuse me."

But his armor-bearer was terrified and would not do it; so Saul took his own sword and fell on it. ⁵When the armor-bearer saw that Saul was dead, he too fell on his sword and died. ⁶So Saul and his three sons died, and all his house died together.

⁷When all the Israelites in the valley saw that the army had fled and that Saul and his sons had died, they abandoned their towns and fled. And the Philistines came and occupied them.

⁸The next day, when the Philistines came to strip the dead, they found Saul and his sons fallen on Mount Gilboa. ⁹They stripped him and took his head and his armor, and sent messengers throughout the land of the Philistines to proclaim the news among their idols and their people. ¹⁰They put his armor in the temple of their gods and hung up his head in the temple of Dagon.

¹¹When all the inhabitants of Jabesh Gilead heard what the Philistines had done to Saul, ¹²all their valiant men went and took the bodies of Saul and his sons and brought them to Jabesh. Then they buried their bones under the great tree in Jabesh, and they fasted seven days.

¹³Saul died because he was unfaithful to the Lord; he did not keep the word of the Lord and even consulted a medium for guidance, ¹⁴and did not inquire of the Lord. So the Lord put him to death and turned the kingdom over to David son of Jesse.

David Becomes King Over Israel

11 All Israel came together to David at Hebron and said, "We are your own flesh and blood. ²In the past, even while Saul was king, you were the one who led Israel on their military campaigns. And the Lord your God said to you, 'You will shepherd my people Israel, and you will become their ruler.'"

³When all the elders of Israel had come to King David at Hebron, he made a covenant with them at Hebron before the Lord, and they anointed David king over Israel, as the Lord had promised through Samuel.

David Conquers Jerusalem

⁴David and all the Israelites marched to Jerusalem (that is, Jebus). The Jebusites who lived there ⁵said to David, "You will not get in here." Nevertheless, David captured the fortress of Zion—which is the City of David.

⁶David had said, "Whoever leads the attack on the Jebusites will become commander-in-chief." Joab son of Zeruiah went up first, and so he received the command.

⁷David then took up residence in the fortress, and so it was called the City of David. ⁸He built up the city around it, from the terraces*a* to the surrounding wall, while Joab restored the rest of the city. ⁹And David became more and more powerful, because the Lord Almighty was with him.

David's Mighty Warriors

¹⁰These were the chiefs of David's mighty warriors—they, together with all Israel, gave his kingship strong support to extend it over the whole land, as the Lord had promised— ¹¹this is the list of David's mighty warriors:

Jashobeam,*b* a Hakmonite, was chief of the officers*c*; he raised his spear against three hundred men, whom he killed in one encounter.

¹²Next to him was Eleazar son of Dodai the Ahohite, one of the three mighty warriors. ¹³He was with David at Pas Dammim when the Philistines gathered there for battle. At a place where there was a field full of barley, the troops fled from the Philistines. ¹⁴But they took their stand in the middle of the field. They defended it and struck the Philistines down, and the Lord brought about a great victory.

¹⁵Three of the thirty chiefs came down to David to the rock at the cave of Adullam, while a band of Philistines was encamped

---

a 8 Or *the Millo*   *b 11* Possibly a variant of *Jashob-Baal*   *c 11* Or *Thirty*; some Septuagint manuscripts *Three* (see also 2 Samuel 23:8)

SUPPORT SYSTEM

READ: 1 CHRONICLES 11:10

I mmense accomplishments sound all the more amazing when they're done solo—like shattering a home run record, scaling Mount Everest, or circling the globe in a sailboat. Yet no great feat happens without help.

The Lord had a plan for David that started with his appointment as king over Israel, an act of blessing initiated through Samuel (1 Samuel 16:13). God later made an astonishing promise that one of David's descendants would always rule on the throne (2 Samuel 7:16), a vow fulfilled when Jesus the eternal King was born to David's line (Matthew 1:1-17).

David's forty-year reign was marked by significant deeds. He attacked the supposedly unbeatable city and made it his capital, Jerusalem. He brought the ark of God to the city, giving worship its rightful place at the heart of the nation. He calmed tensions between northern and southern tribes, and he extended peace in every direction. But it took the strong support of his mighty warriors for David to make his kingship strong throughout the land.

BUILDING FAITH WISDOM STRENGTH

There's nothing truly great you can accomplish on your own. You need parents, pastors, teachers, coaches, friends, and countless others behind you no matter what you want to accomplish. And if there's something you think you can do well on your own, remind yourself that you will do even better if you partner with others.

in the Valley of Rephaim. ¹⁶At that time David was in the stronghold, and the Philistine garrison was at Bethlehem. ¹⁷David longed for water and said, "Oh, that someone would get me a drink of water from the well near the gate of Bethlehem!" ¹⁸So the Three broke through the Philistine lines, drew water from the well near the gate of Bethlehem and carried it back to David. But he refused to drink it; instead, he poured it out to the LORD. ¹⁹"God forbid that I should do this!" he said. "Should I drink the blood of these men who went at the risk of their lives?" Because they risked their lives to bring it back, David would not drink it.

Such were the exploits of the three mighty warriors.

²⁰Abishai the brother of Joab was chief of the Three. He raised his spear against three hundred men, whom he killed, and so he became as famous as the Three. ²¹He was doubly honored above the Three and became their commander, even though he was not included among them.

²²Benaiah son of Jehoiada, a valiant fighter from Kabzeel, performed great exploits. He struck down Moab's two mightiest warriors. He also went down into a pit on a snowy day and killed a lion. ²³And he struck down an Egyptian who was five cubits*a* tall. Although the Egyptian had a spear like a weaver's rod in his hand, Benaiah went against him with a club. He snatched the spear from the Egyptian's hand and killed him with his own spear. ²⁴Such were the exploits of Benaiah son of Jehoiada; he too was as famous as the three mighty warriors. ²⁵He was held in greater honor than any of the Thirty, but he was not included among the Three. And David put him in charge of his bodyguard.

²⁶The mighty warriors were:

Asahel the brother of Joab,
Elhanan son of Dodo from Bethlehem,
²⁷Shammoth the Harorite,
Helez the Pelonite,
²⁸Ira son of Ikkesh from Tekoa,
Abiezer from Anathoth,
²⁹Sibbekai the Hushathite,
Ilai the Ahohite,
³⁰Maharai the Netophathite,

Heled son of Baanah the Netophathite,
³¹Ithai son of Ribai from Gibeah in Benjamin,
Benaiah the Pirathonite,
³²Hurai from the ravines of Gaash,
Abiel the Arbathite,
³³Azmaveth the Baharumite,
Eliahba the Shaalbonite,
³⁴the sons of Hashem the Gizonite,
Jonathan son of Shagee the Hararite,
³⁵Ahiam son of Sakar the Hararite,
Eliphal son of Ur,
³⁶Hepher the Mekerathite,
Ahijah the Pelonite,
³⁷Hezro the Carmelite,
Naarai son of Ezbai,
³⁸Joel the brother of Nathan,
Mibhar son of Hagri,
³⁹Zelek the Ammonite,
Naharai the Berothite, the armorbearer of Joab son of Zeruiah,
⁴⁰Ira the Ithrite,
Gareb the Ithrite,
⁴¹Uriah the Hittite,
Zabad son of Ahlai,
⁴²Adina son of Shiza the Reubenite, who was chief of the Reubenites, and the thirty with him,
⁴³Hanan son of Maakah,
Joshaphat the Mithnite,
⁴⁴Uzzia the Ashterathite,
Shama and Jeiel the sons of Hotham the Aroerite,
⁴⁵Jediael son of Shimri,
his brother Joha the Tizite,
⁴⁶Eliel the Mahavite,
Jeribai and Joshaviah the sons of Elnaam,
Ithmah the Moabite,
⁴⁷Eliel, Obed and Jaasiel the Mezobaite.

Warriors Join David

12 These were the men who came to David at Ziklag, while he was banished from the presence of Saul son of Kish (they were among the warriors who helped him in battle; ²they were armed with bows and were able to shoot arrows or to sling stones right-handed or left-handed; they were relatives of Saul from the tribe of Benjamin):

³Ahiezer their chief and Joash the sons of Shemaah the Gibeathite; Jeziel and

---

a 23 That is, about 7 feet 6 inches or about 2.3 meters

Pelet the sons of Azmaveth; Berakah, Jehu the Anathothite, ⁴and Ishmaiah the Gibeonite, a mighty warrior among the Thirty, who was a leader of the Thirty; Jeremiah, Jahaziel, Johanan, Jozabad the Gederathite,ᵃ ⁵Eluzai, Jerimoth, Bealiah, Shemariah and Shephatiah the Haruphite; ⁶Elkanah, Ishiah, Azarel, Joezer and Jashobeam the Korahites; ⁷and Joelah and Zebadiah the sons of Jeroham from Gedor.

⁸Some Gadites defected to David at his stronghold in the wilderness. They were brave warriors, ready for battle and able to handle the shield and spear. Their faces were the faces of lions, and they were as swift as gazelles in the mountains.

⁹Ezer was the chief,
Obadiah the second in command, Eliab the third,
¹⁰Mishmannah the fourth, Jeremiah the fifth,
¹¹Attai the sixth, Eliel the seventh,
¹²Johanan the eighth, Elzabad the ninth,
¹³Jeremiah the tenth and Makbannai the eleventh.

¹⁴These Gadites were army commanders; the least was a match for a hundred, and the greatest for a thousand. ¹⁵It was they who crossed the Jordan in the first month when it was overflowing all its banks, and they put to flight everyone living in the valleys, to the east and to the west.

¹⁶Other Benjamites and some men from Judah also came to David in his stronghold. ¹⁷David went out to meet them and said to them, "If you have come to me in peace to help me, I am ready for you to join me. But if you have come to betray me to my enemies when my hands are free from violence, may the God of our ancestors see it and judge you." ¹⁸Then the Spirit came on Amasai, chief of the Thirty, and he said:

"We are yours, David!
We are with you, son of Jesse!
Success, success to you,
and success to those who help you,
for your God will help you."

So David received them and made them leaders of his raiding bands.

¹⁹Some of the tribe of Manasseh defected to David when he went with the Philistines to fight against Saul. (He and his men did not help the Philistines because, after consultation, their rulers sent him away. They said, "It will cost us our heads if he deserts to his master Saul.") ²⁰When David went to Ziklag, these were the men of Manasseh who defected to him: Adnah, Jozabad, Jediael, Michael, Jozabad, Elihu and Zillethai, leaders of units of a thousand in Manasseh. ²¹They helped David against raiding bands, for all of them were brave warriors, and they were commanders in his army. ²²Day after day men came to help David, until he had a great army, like the army of God.ᵇ

Others Join David at Hebron

²³These are the numbers of the men armed for battle who came to David at Hebron to turn Saul's kingdom over to him, as the LORD had said:

²⁴from Judah, carrying shield and spear—6,800 armed for battle;
²⁵from Simeon, warriors ready for battle—7,100;
²⁶from Levi—4,600, ²⁷including Jehoiada, leader of the family of Aaron, with 3,700 men, ²⁸and Zadok, a brave young warrior, with 22 officers from his family;
²⁹from Benjamin, Saul's tribe—3,000, most of whom had remained loyal to Saul's house until then;
³⁰from Ephraim, brave warriors, famous in their own clans—20,800;
³¹from half the tribe of Manasseh, designated by name to come and make David king—18,000;
³²from Issachar, men who understood the times and knew what Israel should do—200 chiefs, with all their relatives under their command;
³³from Zebulun, experienced soldiers prepared for battle with every type of weapon, to help David with undivided loyalty—50,000;
³⁴from Naphtali—1,000 officers, together with 37,000 men carrying shields and spears;
³⁵from Dan, ready for battle—28,600;

ᵃ 4 In Hebrew texts the second half of this verse (*Jeremiah . . . Gederathite*) is numbered 12:5, and 12:5-40 is numbered 12:6-41.   ᵇ 22 Or *a great and mighty army*

³⁶ from Asher, experienced soldiers prepared for battle — 40,000; ³⁷ and from east of the Jordan, from Reuben, Gad and the half-tribe of Manasseh, armed with every type of weapon — 120,000.

³⁸ All these were fighting men who volunteered to serve in the ranks. They came to Hebron fully determined to make David king over all Israel. All the rest of the Israelites were also of one mind to make David king. ³⁹ The men spent three days there with David, eating and drinking, for their families had supplied provisions for them. ⁴⁰ Also, their neighbors from as far away as Issachar, Zebulun and Naphtali came bringing food on donkeys, camels, mules and oxen. There were plentiful supplies of flour, fig cakes, raisin cakes, wine, olive oil, cattle and sheep, for there was joy in Israel.

Bringing Back the Ark

13 David conferred with each of his officers, the commanders of thousands and commanders of hundreds. ² He then said to the whole assembly of Israel, "If it seems good to you and if it is the will of the LORD our God, let us send word far and wide to the rest of our people throughout the territories of Israel, and also to the priests and Levites who are with them in their towns and pasturelands, to come and join us. ³ Let us bring the ark of our God back to us, for we did not inquire of ᵃ it ᵇ during the reign of Saul." ⁴ The whole assembly agreed to do this, because it seemed right to all the people.

⁵ So David assembled all Israel, from the Shihor River in Egypt to Lebo Hamath, to bring the ark of God from Kiriath Jearim. ⁶ David and all Israel went to Baalah of Judah (Kiriath Jearim) to bring up from there the ark of God the LORD, who is enthroned between the cherubim — the ark that is called by the Name.

⁷ They moved the ark of God from Abinadab's house on a new cart, with Uzzah and Ahio guiding it. ⁸ David and all the Israelites were celebrating with all their might before God, with songs and with harps, lyres, timbrels, cymbals and trumpets. ⁹ When they came to the threshing floor of Kidon, Uzzah reached out his hand to steady the ark, because the oxen stumbled. ¹⁰ The LORD's anger burned against Uzzah, and he struck him down because he had put his hand on the ark. So he died there before God.

¹¹ Then David was angry because the LORD's wrath had broken out against Uzzah, and to this day that place is called Perez Uzzah.ᶜ

¹² David was afraid of God that day and asked, "How can I ever bring the ark of God to me?" ¹³ He did not take the ark to be with him in the City of David. Instead, he took it to the house of Obed-Edom the Gittite. ¹⁴ The ark of God remained with the family of Obed-Edom in his house for three months, and the LORD blessed his household and everything he had.

David's House and Family

14 Now Hiram king of Tyre sent messengers to David, along with cedar logs, stonemasons and carpenters to build a palace for him. ² And David knew that the LORD had established him as king over Israel and that his kingdom had been highly exalted for the sake of his people Israel.

³ In Jerusalem David took more wives and became the father of more sons and daughters. ⁴ These are the names of the children born to him there: Shammua, Shobab, Nathan, Solomon, ⁵ Ibhar, Elishua, Elpelet, ⁶ Nogah, Nepheg, Japhia, ⁷ Elishama, Beeliadaᵈ and Eliphelet.

David Defeats the Philistines

⁸ When the Philistines heard that David had been anointed king over all Israel, they went up in full force to search for him, but David heard about it and went out to meet them. ⁹ Now the Philistines had come and raided the Valley of Rephaim; ¹⁰ so David inquired of God: "Shall I go and attack the Philistines? Will you deliver them into my hands?"

The LORD answered him, "Go, I will deliver them into your hands."

¹¹ So David and his men went up to Baal Perazim, and there he defeated them. He said, "As waters break out, God has broken out against my enemies by my hand." So that place was called Baal Perazim.ᵉ ¹² The

---

ᵃ 3 Or *we neglected*   ᵇ 3 Or *him*   ᶜ 11 *Perez Uzzah* means *outbreak against Uzzah.*   ᵈ 7 A variant of *Eliada*   ᵉ 11 *Baal Perazim* means *the lord who breaks out.*

Philistines had abandoned their gods there, and David gave orders to burn them in the fire.

¹³Once more the Philistines raided the valley; ¹⁴so David inquired of God again, and God answered him, "Do not go directly after them, but circle around them and attack them in front of the poplar trees. ¹⁵As soon as you hear the sound of marching in the tops of the poplar trees, move out to battle, because that will mean God has gone out in front of you to strike the Philistine army." ¹⁶So David did as God commanded him, and they struck down the Philistine army, all the way from Gibeon to Gezer.

¹⁷So David's fame spread throughout every land, and the LORD made all the nations fear him.

The Ark Brought to Jerusalem

15 After David had constructed buildings for himself in the City of David, he prepared a place for the ark of God and pitched a tent for it. ²Then David said, "No one but the Levites may carry the ark of God, because the LORD chose them to carry the ark of the LORD and to minister before him forever."

³David assembled all Israel in Jerusalem to bring up the ark of the LORD to the place he had prepared for it. ⁴He called together the descendants of Aaron and the Levites:

⁵From the descendants of Kohath,
  Uriel the leader and 120 relatives;
⁶from the descendants of Merari,
  Asaiah the leader and 220 relatives;
⁷from the descendants of Gershon,ᵃ
  Joel the leader and 130 relatives;
⁸from the descendants of Elizaphan,
  Shemaiah the leader and 200 relatives;
⁹from the descendants of Hebron,
  Eliel the leader and 80 relatives;
¹⁰from the descendants of Uzziel,
  Amminadab the leader and 112 relatives.

¹¹Then David summoned Zadok and Abiathar the priests, and Uriel, Asaiah, Joel, Shemaiah, Eliel and Amminadab the Levites. ¹²He said to them, "You are the heads of the Levitical families; you and your fellow Levites are to consecrate yourselves and bring up the ark of the LORD, the God of Israel, to the place I have prepared for it. ¹³It was because you, the Levites, did not bring it up the first time that the LORD our God broke out in anger against us. We did not inquire of him about how to do it in the prescribed way." ¹⁴So the priests and Levites consecrated themselves in order to bring up the ark of the LORD, the God of Israel. ¹⁵And the Levites carried the ark of God with the poles on their shoulders, as Moses had commanded in accordance with the word of the LORD.

¹⁶David told the leaders of the Levites to appoint their fellow Levites as musicians to make a joyful sound with musical instruments: lyres, harps and cymbals.

¹⁷So the Levites appointed Heman son of Joel; from his relatives, Asaph son of Berekiah; and from their relatives the Merarites, Ethan son of Kushaiah; ¹⁸and with them their relatives next in rank: Zechariah,ᵇ Jaaziel, Shemiramoth, Jehiel, Unni, Eliab, Benaiah, Maaseiah, Mattithiah, Eliphelehu, Mikneiah, Obed-Edom and Jeiel,ᶜ the gatekeepers.

¹⁹The musicians Heman, Asaph and Ethan were to sound the bronze cymbals; ²⁰Zechariah, Jaaziel,ᵈ Shemiramoth, Jehiel, Unni, Eliab, Maaseiah and Benaiah were to play the lyres according to *alamoth*,ᵉ ²¹and Mattithiah, Eliphelehu, Mikneiah, Obed-Edom, Jeiel and Azaziah were to play the harps, directing according to *sheminith*.ᵉ ²²Kenaniah the head Levite was in charge of the singing; that was his responsibility because he was skillful at it.

²³Berekiah and Elkanah were to be doorkeepers for the ark. ²⁴Shebaniah, Joshaphat, Nethanel, Amasai, Zechariah, Benaiah and Eliezer the priests were to blow trumpets before the ark of God. Obed-Edom and Jehiah were also to be doorkeepers for the ark.

²⁵So David and the elders of Israel and the commanders of units of a thousand went to bring up the ark of the covenant of the LORD from the house of Obed-Edom, with rejoicing. ²⁶Because God had helped the Levites who were carrying the ark of the covenant of

---

ᵃ 7 Hebrew *Gershom*, a variant of *Gershon*   ᵇ 18 Three Hebrew manuscripts and most Septuagint manuscripts (see also verse 20 and 16:5); most Hebrew manuscripts *Zechariah son and* or *Zechariah, Ben and*   ᶜ 18 Hebrew; Septuagint (see also verse 21) *Jeiel and Azaziah*   ᵈ 20 See verse 18; Hebrew *Aziel*, a variant of *Jaaziel*.   ᵉ 20,21 Probably a musical term the LORD, seven bulls and seven rams were sacrificed. ²⁷Now David was clothed in a robe of fine linen, as were all the Levites who were carrying the ark, and as were the musicians, and Kenaniah, who was in charge of the singing of the choirs. David also wore a linen ephod. ²⁸So all Israel brought up the ark of the covenant of the LORD with shouts, with the sounding of rams' horns and trumpets, and of cymbals, and the playing of lyres and harps.

²⁹As the ark of the covenant of the LORD was entering the City of David, Michal daughter of Saul watched from a window. And when she saw King David dancing and celebrating, she despised him in her heart.

Ministering Before the Ark

16 They brought the ark of God and set it inside the tent that David had pitched for it, and they presented burnt offerings and fellowship offerings before God. ²After David had finished sacrificing the burnt offerings and fellowship offerings, he blessed the people in the name of the LORD. ³Then he gave a loaf of bread, a cake of dates and a cake of raisins to each Israelite man and woman.

⁴He appointed some of the Levites to minister before the ark of the LORD, to extol,ª thank, and praise the LORD, the God of Israel: ⁵Asaph was the chief, and next to him in rank were Zechariah, then Jaaziel,ᵇ Shemiramoth, Jehiel, Mattithiah, Eliab, Benaiah, Obed-Edom and Jeiel. They were to play the lyres and harps, Asaph was to sound the cymbals, ⁶and Benaiah and Jahaziel the priests were to blow the trumpets regularly before the ark of the covenant of God.

⁷That day David first appointed Asaph and his associates to give praise to the LORD in this manner:

⁸Give praise to the LORD, proclaim his name;
    make known among the nations what he has done.
⁹Sing to him, sing praise to him;
    tell of all his wonderful acts.
¹⁰Glory in his holy name;

let the hearts of those who seek the LORD rejoice.
¹¹Look to the LORD and his strength;
    seek his face always.

¹²Remember the wonders he has done,
    his miracles, and the judgments he pronounced,
¹³you his servants, the descendants of Israel,
    his chosen ones, the children of Jacob.
¹⁴He is the LORD our God;
    his judgments are in all the earth.

¹⁵He remembersᶜ his covenant forever,
    the promise he made, for a thousand generations,
¹⁶the covenant he made with Abraham,
    the oath he swore to Isaac.
¹⁷He confirmed it to Jacob as a decree,
    to Israel as an everlasting covenant:
¹⁸"To you I will give the land of Canaan
    as the portion you will inherit."

¹⁹When they were but few in number,
    few indeed, and strangers in it,
²⁰theyᵈ wandered from nation to nation,
    from one kingdom to another.
²¹He allowed no one to oppress them;
    for their sake he rebuked kings:
²²"Do not touch my anointed ones;
    do my prophets no harm."

²³Sing to the LORD, all the earth;
    proclaim his salvation day after day.
²⁴Declare his glory among the nations,
    his marvelous deeds among all peoples.

²⁵For great is the LORD and most worthy of praise;
    he is to be feared above all gods.
²⁶For all the gods of the nations are idols,
    but the LORD made the heavens.
²⁷Splendor and majesty are before him;
    strength and joy are in his dwelling place.

²⁸Ascribe to the LORD, all you families of nations,
    ascribe to the LORD glory and strength.
²⁹Ascribe to the LORD the glory due his name;

ª 4 Or *petition*; or *invoke*   ᵇ 5 See 15:18,20; Hebrew *Jeiel*, possibly another name for *Jaaziel*.
ᶜ 15 Some Septuagint manuscripts (see also Psalm 105:8); Hebrew *Remember*   ᵈ 18-20 One Hebrew manuscript, Septuagint and Vulgate (see also Psalm 105:12); most Hebrew manuscripts *inherit*, / ¹⁹*though you are but few in number, / few indeed, and strangers in it.*" / ²⁰*They*

EXTREME JOY

READ: **1 CHRONICLES 15:29**

It might not fit your style to dance with enthusiasm for the Lord. But David couldn't help celebrating when he brought the ark of God into Jerusalem. He wasn't about to let anyone halt his extreme joy.

The ark had been a physical sign of the Lord's spiritual presence with Israel since the days of wandering in the desert (Deuteronomy 31:9). After God's people entered the promised land, they parked the ark for centuries at Shiloh (Joshua 18:1). David moved it to Jerusalem, where later it would find its home in the new temple Solomon built (1 Kings 8:6).

BUILDING FAITH WISDOM STRENGTH

Ushering the ark into the holy city was an epic event, and David is so overflowing with happiness that he strips to a loincloth and dances wildly before God. His wife Michal accuses the king of prancing half naked in front of the slave girls, but David says he would rather become even more undignified and humiliated than refrain from celebrating God (2 Samuel 6:20-22). David doesn't care what anyone thinks about his deep love for God. He would rather look like an idiot than fail to give the Lord the honor he deserves.

The world is jam-packed with people who look down at your faith. They especially don't understand your enthusiasm for following Jesus. But don't be afraid to let them know what you think and feel. Your God is real. So is your passion for him.

bring an offering and come before
him.
Worship the LORD in the splendor of his[a]
holiness.

[30] Tremble before him, all the earth!
The world is firmly established; it
cannot be moved.

[31] Let the heavens rejoice, let the earth be
glad;
let them say among the nations, "The
LORD reigns!"
[32] Let the sea resound, and all that is in it;
let the fields be jubilant, and
everything in them!
[33] Let the trees of the forest sing,
let them sing for joy before the LORD,
for he comes to judge the earth.

[34] Give thanks to the LORD, for he is good;
his love endures forever.
[35] Cry out, "Save us, God our Savior;
gather us and deliver us from the
nations,
that we may give thanks to your holy
name,
and glory in your praise."
[36] Praise be to the LORD, the God of Israel,
from everlasting to everlasting.

Then all the people said "Amen" and "Praise
the LORD."

[37] David left Asaph and his associates before the ark of the covenant of the LORD to
minister there regularly, according to each
day's requirements. [38] He also left Obed-
Edom and his sixty-eight associates to minister with them. Obed-Edom son of Jeduthun, and also Hosah, were gatekeepers.

[39] David left Zadok the priest and his fellow priests before the tabernacle of the LORD
at the high place in Gibeon [40] to present
burnt offerings to the LORD on the altar of
burnt offering regularly, morning and evening, in accordance with everything written
in the Law of the LORD, which he had given
Israel. [41] With them were Heman and Jeduthun and the rest of those chosen and designated by name to give thanks to the LORD,
"for his love endures forever." [42] Heman and
Jeduthun were responsible for the sounding of the trumpets and cymbals and for the
playing of the other instruments for sacred

song. The sons of Jeduthun were stationed at
the gate.
[43] Then all the people left, each for their
own home, and David returned home to
bless his family.

God's Promise to David

17 After David was settled in his palace,
he said to Nathan the prophet, "Here
I am, living in a house of cedar, while the ark
of the covenant of the LORD is under a tent."

[2] Nathan replied to David, "Whatever you
have in mind, do it, for God is with you."

[3] But that night the word of God came to
Nathan, saying:

[4] "Go and tell my servant David, 'This
is what the LORD says: You are not the
one to build me a house to dwell in. [5] I
have not dwelt in a house from the day
I brought Israel up out of Egypt to this
day. I have moved from one tent site
to another, from one dwelling place to
another. [6] Wherever I have moved with
all the Israelites, did I ever say to any of
their leaders[b] whom I commanded to
shepherd my people, "Why have you
not built me a house of cedar?"'

[7] "Now then, tell my servant David,
'This is what the LORD Almighty says:
I took you from the pasture, from tending the flock, and appointed you ruler over my people Israel. [8] I have been
with you wherever you have gone, and
I have cut off all your enemies from before you. Now I will make your name
like the names of the greatest men on
earth. [9] And I will provide a place for
my people Israel and will plant them so
that they can have a home of their own
and no longer be disturbed. Wicked
people will not oppress them anymore,
as they did at the beginning [10] and have
done ever since the time I appointed
leaders over my people Israel. I will also
subdue all your enemies.

"'I declare to you that the LORD will
build a house for you: [11] When your days
are over and you go to be with your ancestors, I will raise up your offspring to
succeed you, one of your own sons, and
I will establish his kingdom. [12] He is the
one who will build a house for me, and I

---

[a] 29 Or LORD *with the splendor of*   [b] 6 Traditionally *judges*; also in verse 10

will establish his throne forever. [13] I will be his father, and he will be my son. I will never take my love away from him, as I took it away from your predecessor. [14] I will set him over my house and my kingdom forever; his throne will be established forever.' "

[15] Nathan reported to David all the words of this entire revelation.

David's Prayer

[16] Then King David went in and sat before the LORD, and he said:

"Who am I, LORD God, and what is my family, that you have brought me this far? [17] And as if this were not enough in your sight, my God, you have spoken about the future of the house of your servant. You, LORD God, have looked on me as though I were the most exalted of men.

[18] "What more can David say to you for honoring your servant? For you know your servant, [19] LORD. For the sake of your servant and according to your will, you have done this great thing and made known all these great promises.

[20] "There is no one like you, LORD, and there is no God but you, as we have heard with our own ears. [21] And who is like your people Israel — the one nation on earth whose God went out to redeem a people for himself, and to make a name for yourself, and to perform great and awesome wonders by driving out nations from before your people, whom you redeemed from Egypt? [22] You made your people Israel your very own forever, and you, LORD, have become their God.

[23] "And now, LORD, let the promise you have made concerning your servant and his house be established forever. Do as you promised, [24] so that it will be established and that your name will be great forever. Then people will say, 'The LORD Almighty, the God over Israel, is Israel's God!' And the house of your servant David will be established before you.

[25] "You, my God, have revealed to your servant that you will build a house for him. So your servant has found courage to pray to you. [26] You, LORD, are God! You have promised these good things to your servant. [27] Now you have been pleased to bless the house of your servant, that it may continue forever in your sight; for you, LORD, have blessed it, and it will be blessed forever."

David's Victories

18 In the course of time, David defeated the Philistines and subdued them, and he took Gath and its surrounding villages from the control of the Philistines.

[2] David also defeated the Moabites, and they became subject to him and brought him tribute.

[3] Moreover, David defeated Hadadezer king of Zobah, in the vicinity of Hamath, when he went to set up his monument at[a] the Euphrates River. [4] David captured a thousand of his chariots, seven thousand charioteers and twenty thousand foot soldiers. He hamstrung all but a hundred of the chariot horses.

[5] When the Arameans of Damascus came to help Hadadezer king of Zobah, David struck down twenty-two thousand of them. [6] He put garrisons in the Aramean kingdom of Damascus, and the Arameans became subject to him and brought him tribute. The LORD gave David victory wherever he went.

[7] David took the gold shields carried by the officers of Hadadezer and brought them to Jerusalem. [8] From Tebah[b] and Kun, towns that belonged to Hadadezer, David took a great quantity of bronze, which Solomon used to make the bronze Sea, the pillars and various bronze articles.

[9] When Tou king of Hamath heard that David had defeated the entire army of Hadadezer king of Zobah, [10] he sent his son Hadoram to King David to greet him and congratulate him on his victory in battle over Hadadezer, who had been at war with Tou. Hadoram brought all kinds of articles of gold, of silver and of bronze.

[11] King David dedicated these articles to the LORD, as he had done with the silver and gold he had taken from all these nations:

---

[a] 3 Or *to restore his control over*   [b] 8 Hebrew *Tibhath*, a variant of *Tebah*

Edom and Moab, the Ammonites and the Philistines, and Amalek. [12]Abishai son of Zeruiah struck down eighteen thousand Edomites in the Valley of Salt. [13]He put garrisons in Edom, and all the Edomites became subject to David. The LORD gave David victory wherever he went.

David's Officials

[14]David reigned over all Israel, doing what was just and right for all his people. [15]Joab son of Zeruiah was over the army; Jehoshaphat son of Ahilud was recorder; [16]Zadok son of Ahitub and Ahimelek[a] son of Abiathar were priests; Shavsha was secretary; [17]Benaiah son of Jehoiada was over the Kerethites and Pelethites; and David's sons were chief officials at the king's side.

David Defeats the Ammonites

19 In the course of time, Nahash king of the Ammonites died, and his son succeeded him as king. [2]David thought, "I will show kindness to Hanun son of Nahash, because his father showed kindness to me." So David sent a delegation to express his sympathy to Hanun concerning his father.

When David's envoys came to Hanun in the land of the Ammonites to express sympathy to him, [3]the Ammonite commanders said to Hanun, "Do you think David is honoring your father by sending envoys to you to express sympathy? Haven't his envoys come to you only to explore and spy out the country and overthrow it?" [4]So Hanun seized David's envoys, shaved them, cut off their garments at the buttocks, and sent them away.

[5]When someone came and told David about the men, he sent messengers to meet them, for they were greatly humiliated. The king said, "Stay at Jericho till your beards have grown, and then come back."

[6]When the Ammonites realized that they had become obnoxious to David, Hanun and the Ammonites sent a thousand talents[b] of silver to hire chariots and charioteers from Aram Naharaim,[c] Aram Maakah and Zobah. [7]They hired thirty-two thousand chariots and charioteers, as well as the king of Maakah with his troops, who came and camped near Medeba, while the Ammonites were mustered from their towns and moved out for battle.

[8]On hearing this, David sent Joab out with the entire army of fighting men. [9]The Ammonites came out and drew up in battle formation at the entrance to their city, while the kings who had come were by themselves in the open country.

[10]Joab saw that there were battle lines in front of him and behind him; so he selected some of the best troops in Israel and deployed them against the Arameans. [11]He put the rest of the men under the command of Abishai his brother, and they were deployed against the Ammonites. [12]Joab said, "If the Arameans are too strong for me, then you are to rescue me; but if the Ammonites are too strong for you, then I will rescue you. [13]Be strong, and let us fight bravely for our people and the cities of our God. The LORD will do what is good in his sight."

[14]Then Joab and the troops with him advanced to fight the Arameans, and they fled before him. [15]When the Ammonites realized that the Arameans were fleeing, they too fled before his brother Abishai and went inside the city. So Joab went back to Jerusalem.

[16]After the Arameans saw that they had been routed by Israel, they sent messengers and had Arameans brought from beyond the Euphrates River, with Shophak the commander of Hadadezer's army leading them.

[17]When David was told of this, he gathered all Israel and crossed the Jordan; he advanced against them and formed his battle lines opposite them. David formed his lines to meet the Arameans in battle, and they fought against him. [18]But they fled before Israel, and David killed seven thousand of their charioteers and forty thousand of their foot soldiers. He also killed Shophak the commander of their army.

[19]When the vassals of Hadadezer saw that they had been routed by Israel, they made peace with David and became subject to him.

So the Arameans were not willing to help the Ammonites anymore.

The Capture of Rabbah

20 In the spring, at the time when kings go off to war, Joab led out the armed forces. He laid waste the land of the Ammonites and went to Rabbah and besieged

---

[a] 16 Some Hebrew manuscripts, Vulgate and Syriac (see also 2 Samuel 8:17); most Hebrew manuscripts *Abimelek* [b] 6 That is, about 38 tons or about 34 metric tons [c] 6 That is, Northwest Mesopotamia

it, but David remained in Jerusalem. Joab attacked Rabbah and left it in ruins. ²David took the crown from the head of their king*ᵃ* — its weight was found to be a talent*ᵇ* of gold, and it was set with precious stones — and it was placed on David's head. He took a great quantity of plunder from the city ³and brought out the people who were there, consigning them to labor with saws and with iron picks and axes. David did this to all the Ammonite towns. Then David and his entire army returned to Jerusalem.

War With the Philistines

⁴In the course of time, war broke out with the Philistines, at Gezer. At that time Sibbekai the Hushathite killed Sippai, one of the descendants of the Rephaites, and the Philistines were subjugated.

⁵In another battle with the Philistines, Elhanan son of Jair killed Lahmi the brother of Goliath the Gittite, who had a spear with a shaft like a weaver's rod.

⁶In still another battle, which took place at Gath, there was a huge man with six fingers on each hand and six toes on each foot — twenty-four in all. He also was descended from Rapha. ⁷When he taunted Israel, Jonathan son of Shimea, David's brother, killed him.

⁸These were descendants of Rapha in Gath, and they fell at the hands of David and his men.

David Counts the Fighting Men

21 Satan rose up against Israel and incited David to take a census of Israel. ²So David said to Joab and the commanders of the troops, "Go and count the Israelites from Beersheba to Dan. Then report back to me so that I may know how many there are."

³But Joab replied, "May the LORD multiply his troops a hundred times over. My lord the king, are they not all my lord's subjects? Why does my lord want to do this? Why should he bring guilt on Israel?"

⁴The king's word, however, overruled Joab; so Joab left and went throughout Israel and then came back to Jerusalem. ⁵Joab reported the number of the fighting men

to David: In all Israel there were one million one hundred thousand men who could handle a sword, including four hundred and seventy thousand in Judah.

⁶But Joab did not include Levi and Benjamin in the numbering, because the king's command was repulsive to him. ⁷This command was also evil in the sight of God; so he punished Israel.

⁸Then David said to God, "I have sinned greatly by doing this. Now, I beg you, take away the guilt of your servant. I have done a very foolish thing."

⁹The LORD said to Gad, David's seer, ¹⁰"Go and tell David, 'This is what the LORD says: I am giving you three options. Choose one of them for me to carry out against you.'"

¹¹So Gad went to David and said to him, "This is what the LORD says: 'Take your choice: ¹²three years of famine, three months of being swept away*ᶜ* before your enemies, with their swords overtaking you, or three days of the sword of the LORD — days of plague in the land, with the angel of the LORD ravaging every part of Israel.' Now then, decide how I should answer the one who sent me."

¹³David said to Gad, "I am in deep distress. Let me fall into the hands of the LORD, for his mercy is very great; but do not let me fall into human hands."

¹⁴So the LORD sent a plague on Israel, and seventy thousand men of Israel fell dead. ¹⁵And God sent an angel to destroy Jerusalem. But as the angel was doing so, the LORD saw it and relented concerning the disaster and said to the angel who was destroying the people, "Enough! Withdraw your hand." The angel of the LORD was then standing at the threshing floor of Araunah*ᵈ* the Jebusite.

¹⁶David looked up and saw the angel of the LORD standing between heaven and earth, with a drawn sword in his hand extended over Jerusalem. Then David and the elders, clothed in sackcloth, fell facedown.

¹⁷David said to God, "Was it not I who ordered the fighting men to be counted? I, the shepherd,*ᵉ* have sinned and done wrong. These are but sheep. What have they done? LORD my God, let your hand fall on me and

---

ᵃ 2 Or *of Milkom,* that is, Molek   *ᵇ 2* That is, about 75 pounds or about 34 kilograms   *ᶜ 12* Hebrew; Septuagint and Vulgate (see also 2 Samuel 24:13) *of fleeing*   *ᵈ 15* Hebrew *Ornan,* a variant of *Araunah;* also in verses 18-28   *ᵉ 17* Probable reading of the original Hebrew text (see 2 Samuel 24:17 and note); Masoretic Text does not have *the shepherd.*

my family, but do not let this plague remain on your people."

David Builds an Altar

[18]Then the angel of the LORD ordered Gad to tell David to go up and build an altar to the LORD on the threshing floor of Araunah the Jebusite. [19]So David went up in obedience to the word that Gad had spoken in the name of the LORD.

[20]While Araunah was threshing wheat, he turned and saw the angel; his four sons who were with him hid themselves. [21]Then David approached, and when Araunah looked and saw him, he left the threshing floor and bowed down before David with his face to the ground.

[22]David said to him, "Let me have the site of your threshing floor so I can build an altar to the LORD, that the plague on the people may be stopped. Sell it to me at the full price."

[23]Araunah said to David, "Take it! Let my lord the king do whatever pleases him. Look, I will give the oxen for the burnt offerings, the threshing sledges for the wood, and the wheat for the grain offering. I will give all this."

[24]But King David replied to Araunah, "No, I insist on paying the full price. I will not take for the LORD what is yours, or sacrifice a burnt offering that costs me nothing."

[25]So David paid Araunah six hundred shekels[a] of gold for the site. [26]David built an altar to the LORD there and sacrificed burnt offerings and fellowship offerings. He called on the LORD, and the LORD answered him with fire from heaven on the altar of burnt offering.

[27]Then the LORD spoke to the angel, and he put his sword back into its sheath. [28]At that time, when David saw that the LORD had answered him on the threshing floor of Araunah the Jebusite, he offered sacrifices there. [29]The tabernacle of the LORD, which Moses had made in the wilderness, and the altar of burnt offering were at that time on the high place at Gibeon. [30]But David could not go before it to inquire of God, because he was afraid of the sword of the angel of the LORD.

22 Then David said, "The house of the LORD God is to be here, and also the altar of burnt offering for Israel."

Preparations for the Temple

[2]So David gave orders to assemble the foreigners residing in Israel, and from among them he appointed stonecutters to prepare dressed stone for building the house of God. [3]He provided a large amount of iron to make nails for the doors of the gateways and for the fittings, and more bronze than could be weighed. [4]He also provided more cedar logs than could be counted, for the Sidonians and Tyrians had brought large numbers of them to David.

[5]David said, "My son Solomon is young and inexperienced, and the house to be built for the LORD should be of great magnificence and fame and splendor in the sight of all the nations. Therefore I will make preparations for it." So David made extensive preparations before his death.

[6]Then he called for his son Solomon and charged him to build a house for the LORD, the God of Israel. [7]David said to Solomon: "My son, I had it in my heart to build a house for the Name of the LORD my God. [8]But this word of the LORD came to me: 'You have shed much blood and have fought many wars. You are not to build a house for my Name, because you have shed much blood on the earth in my sight. [9]But you will have a son who will be a man of peace and rest, and I will give him rest from all his enemies on every side. His name will be Solomon,[b] and I will grant Israel peace and quiet during his reign. [10]He is the one who will build a house for my Name. He will be my son, and I will be his father. And I will establish the throne of his kingdom over Israel forever.'

[11]"Now, my son, the LORD be with you, and may you have success and build the house of the LORD your God, as he said you would. [12]May the LORD give you discretion and understanding when he puts you in command over Israel, so that you may keep the law of the LORD your God. [13]Then you will have success if you are careful to observe the decrees and laws that the LORD gave Moses for

---

[a] 25 That is, about 15 pounds or about 6.9 kilograms the Hebrew for *peace*.

[b] 9 *Solomon* sounds like and may be derived from

UNKNOWN REASONS

READ: 1 CHRONICLES 22:1-10

When I graduated from high school, I went to the University of Chicago on a full-ride scholarship and earned a starting position on the basketball team by the end of my freshman year. Then I transferred to Central Bible College, where I earned first-team all-American honors my senior season.

I was having my best season ever, and I wasn't just playing well; I was playing for God. I wanted to win a national championship because I thought it would be a great way to glorify God, but that dream died with one cut to the basket when my right knee buckled. Two weeks before the national tournament, my basketball career came to a painful end.

To be honest, the spiritual pain was worse than the physical pain. At first, I was angry. *God, I was playing for you. How could you let this happen?* Eventually, my anger turned to mourning. I remember begging God to heal my knee. I knew he could do it, but he chose not to. In the grand scheme of things, I realize that a game is a game, but it was a bitter disappointment. And I still don't know why.

Some of the hardest moments in life are when you actually do pray hard but the answer is no and you don't know why. And you may never know why, but it's part of the trust test. Do you trust that God is for you even when he doesn't give you what you asked for? Do you trust that his plan is better than yours?

BUILDING FAITH WISDOM STRENGTH

Israel. Be strong and courageous. Do not be afraid or discouraged.

¹⁴ "I have taken great pains to provide for the temple of the LORD a hundred thousand talents*a* of gold, a million talents*b* of silver, quantities of bronze and iron too great to be weighed, and wood and stone. And you may add to them. ¹⁵ You have many workers: stonecutters, masons and carpenters, as well as those skilled in every kind of work ¹⁶ in gold and silver, bronze and iron — craftsmen beyond number. Now begin the work, and the LORD be with you."

¹⁷ Then David ordered all the leaders of Israel to help his son Solomon. ¹⁸ He said to them, "Is not the LORD your God with you? And has he not granted you rest on every side? For he has given the inhabitants of the land into my hands, and the land is subject to the LORD and to his people. ¹⁹ Now devote your heart and soul to seeking the LORD your God. Begin to build the sanctuary of the LORD God, so that you may bring the ark of the covenant of the LORD and the sacred articles belonging to God into the temple that will be built for the Name of the LORD."

The Levites

23 When David was old and full of years, he made his son Solomon king over Israel.

² He also gathered together all the leaders of Israel, as well as the priests and Levites. ³ The Levites thirty years old or more were counted, and the total number of men was thirty-eight thousand. ⁴ David said, "Of these, twenty-four thousand are to be in charge of the work of the temple of the LORD and six thousand are to be officials and judges. ⁵ Four thousand are to be gatekeepers and four thousand are to praise the LORD with the musical instruments I have provided for that purpose."

⁶ David separated the Levites into divisions corresponding to the sons of Levi: Gershon, Kohath and Merari.

Gershonites

⁷ Belonging to the Gershonites:
Ladan and Shimei.
⁸ The sons of Ladan:

Jehiel the first, Zetham and Joel —
three in all.
⁹ The sons of Shimei:
Shelomoth, Haziel and Haran —
three in all.
These were the heads of the families of Ladan.
¹⁰ And the sons of Shimei:
Jahath, Ziza,*c* Jeush and Beriah.
These were the sons of Shimei — four in all.
¹¹ Jahath was the first and Ziza the second, but Jeush and Beriah did not have many sons; so they were counted as one family with one assignment.

Kohathites

¹² The sons of Kohath:
Amram, Izhar, Hebron and Uzziel —
four in all.
¹³ The sons of Amram:
Aaron and Moses.
Aaron was set apart, he and his descendants forever, to consecrate the most holy things, to offer sacrifices before the LORD, to minister before him and to pronounce blessings in his name forever. ¹⁴ The sons of Moses the man of God were counted as part of the tribe of Levi.
¹⁵ The sons of Moses:
Gershom and Eliezer.
¹⁶ The descendants of Gershom:
Shubael was the first.
¹⁷ The descendants of Eliezer:
Rehabiah was the first.
Eliezer had no other sons, but the sons of Rehabiah were very numerous.
¹⁸ The sons of Izhar:
Shelomith was the first.
¹⁹ The sons of Hebron:
Jeriah the first, Amariah the second, Jahaziel the third and Jekameam the fourth.
²⁰ The sons of Uzziel:
Micah the first and Ishiah the second.

Merarites

²¹ The sons of Merari:
Mahli and Mushi.

---

a 14 That is, about 3,750 tons or about 3,400 metric tons   *b* 14 That is, about 37,500 tons or about 34,000 metric tons   *c* 10 One Hebrew manuscript, Septuagint and Vulgate (see also verse 11); most Hebrew manuscripts *Zina*

The sons of Mahli:
Eleazar and Kish.
²²Eleazar died without having sons: he had only daughters. Their cousins, the sons of Kish, married them.
²³The sons of Mushi:
Mahli, Eder and Jerimoth — three in all.

²⁴These were the descendants of Levi by their families — the heads of families as they were registered under their names and counted individually, that is, the workers twenty years old or more who served in the temple of the Lord. ²⁵For David had said, "Since the Lord, the God of Israel, has granted rest to his people and has come to dwell in Jerusalem forever, ²⁶the Levites no longer need to carry the tabernacle or any of the articles used in its service." ²⁷According to the last instructions of David, the Levites were counted from those twenty years old or more.

²⁸The duty of the Levites was to help Aaron's descendants in the service of the temple of the Lord: to be in charge of the courtyards, the side rooms, the purification of all sacred things and the performance of other duties at the house of God. ²⁹They were in charge of the bread set out on the table, the special flour for the grain offerings, the thin loaves made without yeast, the baking and the mixing, and all measurements of quantity and size. ³⁰They were also to stand every morning to thank and praise the Lord. They were to do the same in the evening ³¹and whenever burnt offerings were presented to the Lord on the Sabbaths, at the New Moon feasts and at the appointed festivals. They were to serve before the Lord regularly in the proper number and in the way prescribed for them.

³²And so the Levites carried out their responsibilities for the tent of meeting, for the Holy Place and, under their relatives the descendants of Aaron, for the service of the temple of the Lord.

The Divisions of Priests

24 These were the divisions of the descendants of Aaron:

The sons of Aaron were Nadab, Abihu, Eleazar and Ithamar. ²But Nadab and Abihu died before their father did, and they had no sons; so Eleazar and Ithamar served as the priests. ³With the help of Zadok a descendant of Eleazar and Ahimelek a descendant of Ithamar, David separated them into divisions for their appointed order of ministering. ⁴A larger number of leaders were found among Eleazar's descendants than among Ithamar's, and they were divided accordingly: sixteen heads of families from Eleazar's descendants and eight heads of families from Ithamar's descendants. ⁵They divided them impartially by casting lots, for there were officials of the sanctuary and officials of God among the descendants of both Eleazar and Ithamar.

⁶The scribe Shemaiah son of Nethanel, a Levite, recorded their names in the presence of the king and of the officials: Zadok the priest, Ahimelek son of Abiathar and the heads of families of the priests and of the Levites — one family being taken from Eleazar and then one from Ithamar.

⁷The first lot fell to Jehoiarib,
the second to Jedaiah,
⁸the third to Harim,
the fourth to Seorim,
⁹the fifth to Malkijah,
the sixth to Mijamin,
¹⁰the seventh to Hakkoz,
the eighth to Abijah,
¹¹the ninth to Jeshua,
the tenth to Shekaniah,
¹²the eleventh to Eliashib,
the twelfth to Jakim,
¹³the thirteenth to Huppah,
the fourteenth to Jeshebeab,
¹⁴the fifteenth to Bilgah,
the sixteenth to Immer,
¹⁵the seventeenth to Hezir,
the eighteenth to Happizzez,
¹⁶the nineteenth to Pethahiah,
the twentieth to Jehezkel,
¹⁷the twenty-first to Jakin,
the twenty-second to Gamul,
¹⁸the twenty-third to Delaiah
and the twenty-fourth to Maaziah.

¹⁹This was their appointed order of ministering when they entered the temple of the Lord, according to the regulations prescribed for them by their ancestor Aaron, as the Lord, the God of Israel, had commanded him.

The Rest of the Levites

²⁰As for the rest of the descendants of Levi:
from the sons of Amram: Shubael;
from the sons of Shubael: Jehdeiah.

²¹ As for Rehabiah, from his sons:
Ishiah was the first.
²² From the Izharites: Shelomoth;
from the sons of Shelomoth: Jahath.
²³ The sons of Hebron: Jeriah the first,ᵃ
Amariah the second, Jahaziel the
third and Jekameam the fourth.
²⁴ The son of Uzziel: Micah;
from the sons of Micah: Shamir.
²⁵ The brother of Micah: Ishiah;
from the sons of Ishiah: Zechariah.
²⁶ The sons of Merari: Mahli and Mushi.
The son of Jaaziah: Beno.
²⁷ The sons of Merari:
from Jaaziah: Beno, Shoham, Zakkur
and Ibri.
²⁸ From Mahli: Eleazar, who had no sons.
²⁹ From Kish: the son of Kish:
Jerahmeel.
³⁰ And the sons of Mushi: Mahli, Eder and
Jerimoth.

These were the Levites, according to their families. ³¹ They also cast lots, just as their relatives the descendants of Aaron did, in the presence of King David and of Zadok, Ahimelek, and the heads of families of the priests and of the Levites. The families of the oldest brother were treated the same as those of the youngest.

The Musicians

25 David, together with the commanders of the army, set apart some of the sons of Asaph, Heman and Jeduthun for the ministry of prophesying, accompanied by harps, lyres and cymbals. Here is the list of the men who performed this service:

² From the sons of Asaph:
Zakkur, Joseph, Nethaniah and Asarelah. The sons of Asaph were under the supervision of Asaph, who prophesied under the king's supervision.
³ As for Jeduthun, from his sons:
Gedaliah, Zeri, Jeshaiah, Shimei,ᵇ Hashabiah and Mattithiah, six in all, under the supervision of their father Jeduthun, who prophesied, using the harp in thanking and praising the LORD.

⁴ As for Heman, from his sons:
Bukkiah, Mattaniah, Uzziel, Shubael and Jerimoth; Hananiah, Hanani, Eliathah, Giddalti and Romamti-Ezer; Joshbekashah, Mallothi, Hothir and Mahazioth. ⁵ (All these were sons of Heman the king's seer. They were given him through the promises of God to exalt him. God gave Heman fourteen sons and three daughters.)

⁶ All these men were under the supervision of their father for the music of the temple of the LORD, with cymbals, lyres and harps, for the ministry at the house of God. Asaph, Jeduthun and Heman were under the supervision of the king. ⁷ Along with their relatives—all of them trained and skilled in music for the LORD—they numbered 288. ⁸ Young and old alike, teacher as well as student, cast lots for their duties.

⁹ The first lot, which was for Asaph,
fell to Joseph,
his sons and relativesᶜ   12ᵈ
the second to Gedaliah,
him and his relatives and sons   12
¹⁰ the third to Zakkur,
his sons and relatives   12
¹¹ the fourth to Izri,ᵉ
his sons and relatives   12
¹² the fifth to Nethaniah,
his sons and relatives   12
¹³ the sixth to Bukkiah,
his sons and relatives   12
¹⁴ the seventh to Jesarelah,ᶠ
his sons and relatives   12
¹⁵ the eighth to Jeshaiah,
his sons and relatives   12
¹⁶ the ninth to Mattaniah,
his sons and relatives   12
¹⁷ the tenth to Shimei,
his sons and relatives   12
¹⁸ the eleventh to Azarel,ᵍ
his sons and relatives   12
¹⁹ the twelfth to Hashabiah,
his sons and relatives   12
²⁰ the thirteenth to Shubael,
his sons and relatives   12
²¹ the fourteenth to Mattithiah,
his sons and relatives   12

ᵃ 23 Two Hebrew manuscripts and some Septuagint manuscripts (see also 23:19); most Hebrew manuscripts *The sons of Jeriah:*   ᵇ 3 One Hebrew manuscript and some Septuagint manuscripts (see also verse 17); most Hebrew manuscripts do not have *Shimei.*   ᶜ 9 See Septuagint; Hebrew does not have *his sons and relatives.*   ᵈ 9 See the total in verse 7; Hebrew does not have *twelve.*   ᵉ 11 A variant of *Zeri*   ᶠ 14 A variant of *Asarelah*   ᵍ 18 A variant of *Uzziel*

²²the fifteenth to Jerimoth,
   his sons and relatives   12
²³the sixteenth to Hananiah,
   his sons and relatives   12
²⁴the seventeenth to Joshbekashah,
   his sons and relatives   12
²⁵the eighteenth to Hanani,
   his sons and relatives   12
²⁶the nineteenth to Mallothi,
   his sons and relatives   12
²⁷the twentieth to Eliathah,
   his sons and relatives   12
²⁸the twenty-first to Hothir,
   his sons and relatives   12
²⁹the twenty-second to Giddalti,
   his sons and relatives   12
³⁰the twenty-third to Mahazioth,
   his sons and relatives   12
³¹the twenty-fourth to Romamti-Ezer,
   his sons and relatives   12.

The Gatekeepers

26 The divisions of the gatekeepers:

From the Korahites: Meshelemiah son of Kore, one of the sons of Asaph.

²Meshelemiah had sons:
   Zechariah the firstborn,
   Jediael the second,
   Zebadiah the third,
   Jathniel the fourth,
³Elam the fifth,
   Jehohanan the sixth
   and Eliehoenai the seventh.
⁴Obed-Edom also had sons:
   Shemaiah the firstborn,
   Jehozabad the second,
   Joah the third,
   Sakar the fourth,
   Nethanel the fifth,
⁵Ammiel the sixth,
   Issachar the seventh
   and Peullethai the eighth.
   (For God had blessed Obed-Edom.)

⁶Obed-Edom's son Shemaiah also had sons, who were leaders in their father's family because they were very capable men. ⁷The sons of Shemaiah: Othni, Rephael, Obed and Elzabad; his relatives Elihu and Sema-

kiah were also able men. ⁸All these were descendants of Obed-Edom; they and their sons and their relatives were capable men with the strength to do the work—descendants of Obed-Edom, 62 in all.
⁹Meshelemiah had sons and relatives, who were able men—18 in all.

¹⁰Hosah the Merarite had sons: Shimri the first (although he was not the firstborn, his father had appointed him the first), ¹¹Hilkiah the second, Tabaliah the third and Zechariah the fourth. The sons and relatives of Hosah were 13 in all.
¹²These divisions of the gatekeepers, through their leaders, had duties for ministering in the temple of the Lord, just as their relatives had. ¹³Lots were cast for each gate, according to their families, young and old alike.
¹⁴The lot for the East Gate fell to Shelemiah.ᵃ Then lots were cast for his son Zechariah, a wise counselor, and the lot for the North Gate fell to him. ¹⁵The lot for the South Gate fell to Obed-Edom, and the lot for the storehouse fell to his sons. ¹⁶The lots for the West Gate and the Shalleketh Gate on the upper road fell to Shuppim and Hosah.

Guard was alongside of guard: ¹⁷There were six Levites a day on the east, four a day on the north, four a day on the south and two at a time at the storehouse. ¹⁸As for the courtᵇ to the west, there were four at the road and two at the courtᵇ itself.
¹⁹These were the divisions of the gatekeepers who were descendants of Korah and Merari.

The Treasurers and Other Officials

²⁰Their fellow Levites wereᶜ in charge of the treasuries of the house of God and the treasuries for the dedicated things.
²¹The descendants of Ladan, who were Gershonites through Ladan and who were heads of families belonging to Ladan the Gershonite, were Jehieli, ²²the sons of Jehieli, Zetham and his brother Joel. They were in charge of the treasuries of the temple of the Lord.
²³From the Amramites, the Izharites, the Hebronites and the Uzzielites:

ᵃ *14* A variant of *Meshelemiah*   ᵇ *18* The meaning of the Hebrew for this word is uncertain.
ᶜ *20* Septuagint; Hebrew *As for the Levites, Ahijah was*

²⁴Shubael, a descendant of Gershom son of Moses, was the official in charge of the treasuries. ²⁵His relatives through Eliezer: Rehabiah his son, Jeshaiah his son, Joram his son, Zikri his son and Shelomith his son. ²⁶Shelomith and his relatives were in charge of all the treasuries for the things dedicated by King David, by the heads of families who were the commanders of thousands and commanders of hundreds, and by the other army commanders. ²⁷Some of the plunder taken in battle they dedicated for the repair of the temple of the LORD. ²⁸And everything dedicated by Samuel the seer and by Saul son of Kish, Abner son of Ner and Joab son of Zeruiah, and all the other dedicated things were in the care of Shelomith and his relatives.

²⁹From the Izharites: Kenaniah and his sons were assigned duties away from the temple, as officials and judges over Israel.

³⁰From the Hebronites: Hashabiah and his relatives — seventeen hundred able men — were responsible in Israel west of the Jordan for all the work of the LORD and for the king's service. ³¹As for the Hebronites, Jeriah was their chief according to the genealogical records of their families. In the fortieth year of David's reign a search was made in the records, and capable men among the Hebronites were found at Jazer in Gilead. ³²Jeriah had twenty-seven hundred relatives, who were able men and heads of families, and King David put them in charge of the Reubenites, the Gadites and the half-tribe of Manasseh for every matter pertaining to God and for the affairs of the king.

Army Divisions

27 This is the list of the Israelites — heads of families, commanders of thousands and commanders of hundreds, and their officers, who served the king in all that concerned the army divisions that were on duty month by month throughout the year. Each division consisted of 24,000 men.

²In charge of the first division, for the first month, was Jashobeam son of Zabdiel. There were 24,000 men in his division. ³He was a descendant of Perez and chief of all the army officers for the first month.

⁴In charge of the division for the second month was Dodai the Ahohite; Mikloth was the leader of his division. There were 24,000 men in his division.

⁵The third army commander, for the third month, was Benaiah son of Jehoiada the priest. He was chief and there were 24,000 men in his division. ⁶This was the Benaiah who was a mighty warrior among the Thirty and was over the Thirty. His son Ammizabad was in charge of his division.

⁷The fourth, for the fourth month, was Asahel the brother of Joab; his son Zebadiah was his successor. There were 24,000 men in his division.

⁸The fifth, for the fifth month, was the commander Shamhuth the Izrahite. There were 24,000 men in his division.

⁹The sixth, for the sixth month, was Ira the son of Ikkesh the Tekoite. There were 24,000 men in his division.

¹⁰The seventh, for the seventh month, was Helez the Pelonite, an Ephraimite. There were 24,000 men in his division.

¹¹The eighth, for the eighth month, was Sibbekai the Hushathite, a Zerahite. There were 24,000 men in his division.

¹²The ninth, for the ninth month, was Abiezer the Anathothite, a Benjamite. There were 24,000 men in his division.

¹³The tenth, for the tenth month, was Maharai the Netophathite, a Zerahite. There were 24,000 men in his division.

¹⁴The eleventh, for the eleventh month, was Benaiah the Pirathonite, an Ephraimite. There were 24,000 men in his division.

¹⁵The twelfth, for the twelfth month, was Heldai the Netophathite, from the family of Othniel. There were 24,000 men in his division.

Leaders of the Tribes

¹⁶The leaders of the tribes of Israel:

over the Reubenites: Eliezer son of Zikri;
over the Simeonites: Shephatiah son of Maakah;

¹⁷ over Levi: Hashabiah son of Kemuel;
over Aaron: Zadok;
¹⁸ over Judah: Elihu, a brother of David;
over Issachar: Omri son of Michael;
¹⁹ over Zebulun: Ishmaiah son of Obadiah;
over Naphtali: Jerimoth son of Azriel;
²⁰ over the Ephraimites: Hoshea son of
Azaziah;
over half the tribe of Manasseh: Joel
son of Pedaiah;
²¹ over the half-tribe of Manasseh in Gilead: Iddo son of Zechariah;
over Benjamin: Jaasiel son of Abner;
²² over Dan: Azarel son of Jeroham.

These were the leaders of the tribes of Israel.

²³ David did not take the number of the
men twenty years old or less, because the
LORD had promised to make Israel as numerous as the stars in the sky. ²⁴ Joab son of
Zeruiah began to count the men but did not
finish. God's wrath came on Israel on account of this numbering, and the number
was not entered in the book*ᵃ* of the annals of
King David.

The King's Overseers

²⁵ Azmaveth son of Adiel was in charge of
the royal storehouses.

Jonathan son of Uzziah was in charge of
the storehouses in the outlying districts, in
the towns, the villages and the watchtowers.

²⁶ Ezri son of Kelub was in charge of the
workers who farmed the land.

²⁷ Shimei the Ramathite was in charge of
the vineyards.

Zabdi the Shiphmite was in charge of the
produce of the vineyards for the wine vats.

²⁸ Baal-Hanan the Gederite was in charge
of the olive and sycamore-fig trees in the
western foothills.

Joash was in charge of the supplies of olive oil.

²⁹ Shitrai the Sharonite was in charge of
the herds grazing in Sharon.

Shaphat son of Adlai was in charge of the
herds in the valleys.

³⁰ Obil the Ishmaelite was in charge of the
camels.

Jehdeiah the Meronothite was in charge
of the donkeys.

³¹ Jaziz the Hagrite was in charge of the
flocks.

All these were the officials in charge of
King David's property.

³² Jonathan, David's uncle, was a counsel-
or, a man of insight and a scribe. Jehiel son of
Hakmoni took care of the king's sons.

³³ Ahithophel was the king's counselor.
Hushai the Arkite was the king's confidant. ³⁴ Ahithophel was succeeded by Jehoiada son of Benaiah and by Abiathar.

Joab was the commander of the royal
army.

David's Plans for the Temple

28 David summoned all the officials of
Israel to assemble at Jerusalem: the
officers over the tribes, the commanders of
the divisions in the service of the king, the
commanders of thousands and commanders of hundreds, and the officials in charge
of all the property and livestock belonging to
the king and his sons, together with the palace officials, the warriors and all the brave
fighting men.

²King David rose to his feet and said:
"Listen to me, my fellow Israelites, my people. I had it in my heart to build a house as
a place of rest for the ark of the covenant of
the LORD, for the footstool of our God, and I
made plans to build it. ³But God said to me,
'You are not to build a house for my Name,
because you are a warrior and have shed
blood.'

⁴"Yet the LORD, the God of Israel, chose
me from my whole family to be king over Israel forever. He chose Judah as leader, and
from the tribe of Judah he chose my family,
and from my father's sons he was pleased
to make me king over all Israel. ⁵Of all my
sons — and the LORD has given me many —
he has chosen my son Solomon to sit on the
throne of the kingdom of the LORD over Israel. ⁶He said to me: 'Solomon your son is the
one who will build my house and my courts,
for I have chosen him to be my son, and I will
be his father. ⁷I will establish his kingdom
forever if he is unswerving in carrying out
my commands and laws, as is being done at
this time.'

⁸"So now I charge you in the sight of all
Israel and of the assembly of the LORD, and
in the hearing of our God: Be careful to follow all the commands of the LORD your God,

ᵃ 24 Septuagint; Hebrew *number*

that you may possess this good land and pass it on as an inheritance to your descendants forever.

⁹ "And you, my son Solomon, acknowledge the God of your father, and serve him with wholehearted devotion and with a willing mind, for the LORD searches every heart and understands every desire and every thought. If you seek him, he will be found by you; but if you forsake him, he will reject you forever. ¹⁰ Consider now, for the LORD has chosen you to build a house as the sanctuary. Be strong and do the work."

¹¹ Then David gave his son Solomon the plans for the portico of the temple, its buildings, its storerooms, its upper parts, its inner rooms and the place of atonement. ¹² He gave him the plans of all that the Spirit had put in his mind for the courts of the temple of the LORD and all the surrounding rooms, for the treasuries of the temple of God and for the treasuries for the dedicated things. ¹³ He gave him instructions for the divisions of the priests and Levites, and for all the work of serving in the temple of the LORD, as well as for all the articles to be used in its service. ¹⁴ He designated the weight of gold for all the gold articles to be used in various kinds of service, and the weight of silver for all the silver articles to be used in various kinds of service: ¹⁵ the weight of gold for the gold lampstands and their lamps, with the weight for each lampstand and its lamps; and the weight of silver for each silver lampstand and its lamps, according to the use of each lampstand; ¹⁶ the weight of gold for each table for consecrated bread; the weight of silver for the silver tables; ¹⁷ the weight of pure gold for the forks, sprinkling bowls and pitchers; the weight of gold for each gold dish; the weight of silver for each silver dish; ¹⁸ and the weight of the refined gold for the altar of incense. He also gave him the plan for the chariot, that is, the cherubim of gold that spread their wings and overshadow the ark of the covenant of the LORD.

¹⁹ "All this," David said, "I have in writing as a result of the LORD's hand on me, and he enabled me to understand all the details of the plan."

²⁰ David also said to Solomon his son, "Be strong and courageous, and do the work. Do not be afraid or discouraged, for the LORD God, my God, is with you. He will not fail you or forsake you until all the work for the service of the temple of the LORD is finished. ²¹ The divisions of the priests and Levites are ready for all the work on the temple of God, and every willing person skilled in any craft will help you in all the work. The officials and all the people will obey your every command."

Gifts for Building the Temple

29 Then King David said to the whole assembly: "My son Solomon, the one whom God has chosen, is young and inexperienced. The task is great, because this palatial structure is not for man but for the LORD God. ² With all my resources I have provided for the temple of my God — gold for the gold work, silver for the silver, bronze for the bronze, iron for the iron and wood for the wood, as well as onyx for the settings, turquoise,ᵃ stones of various colors, and all kinds of fine stone and marble — all of these in large quantities. ³ Besides, in my devotion to the temple of my God I now give my personal treasures of gold and silver for the temple of my God, over and above everything I have provided for this holy temple: ⁴ three thousand talentsᵇ of gold (gold of Ophir) and seven thousand talentsᶜ of refined silver, for the overlaying of the walls of the buildings, ⁵ for the gold work and the silver work, and for all the work to be done by the craftsmen. Now, who is willing to consecrate themselves to the LORD today?"

⁶ Then the leaders of families, the officers of the tribes of Israel, the commanders of thousands and commanders of hundreds, and the officials in charge of the king's work gave willingly. ⁷ They gave toward the work on the temple of God five thousand talentsᵈ and ten thousand daricsᵉ of gold, ten thousand talentsᶠ of silver, eighteen thousand talentsᵍ of bronze and a hundred thousand talentsʰ of iron. ⁸ Anyone who had precious stones gave them to the treasury of the temple of the

---

ᵃ 2 The meaning of the Hebrew for this word is uncertain.   ᵇ 4 That is, about 110 tons or about 100 metric tons   ᶜ 4 That is, about 260 tons or about 235 metric tons   ᵈ 7 That is, about 190 tons or about 170 metric tons   ᵉ 7 That is, about 185 pounds or about 84 kilograms   ᶠ 7 That is, about 380 tons or about 340 metric tons   ᵍ 7 That is, about 675 tons or about 610 metric tons   ʰ 7 That is, about 3,800 tons or about 3,400 metric tons

ABLE-BODIED

READ: 1 CHRONICLES 28:12

God gives us our abilities, combining them with passions, desires, dreams, and personality quirks that temper and refine them. To be honest, I don't understand why we aren't all famous for the abilities he's given us.

I don't understand why God would give two people the ability to play the guitar, yet they'd become known for it in entirely different ways. The way God uses that ability in us is also at his disposal; some of us use it for his glory on the stage, and others use it for his glory in front of our grandmothers. Either way, it's for his glory.

Maybe you're like me, and you struggle to really believe you're good at anything. I don't feel comfortable with my abilities—and talking about the areas of my life where I feel like a total wimp makes me even more uncomfortable. But we all have strengths. None of us is an empty blob with no skills at all.

Time usually tells the truth about our abilities—and that's true whether we're talking about natural talents, skills we've perfected with practice, or abilities we've acquired from necessity. Think about what kinds of things you've been consistently good at, what people have complimented you about. Those are the abilities God has given you. Sometimes it takes a little time and effort to discover what you're really good at.

BUILDING

FAITH

WISDOM

STRENGTH

Lord in the custody of Jehiel the Gershonite.
[9]The people rejoiced at the willing response of their leaders, for they had given freely and wholeheartedly to the Lord. David the king also rejoiced greatly.

David's Prayer

[10]David praised the Lord in the presence of the whole assembly, saying,

"Praise be to you, Lord,
  the God of our father Israel,
  from everlasting to everlasting.
[11]Yours, Lord, is the greatness and the
    power
  and the glory and the majesty and the
    splendor,
  for everything in heaven and earth is
    yours.
Yours, Lord, is the kingdom;
  you are exalted as head over all.
[12]Wealth and honor come from you;
  you are the ruler of all things.
In your hands are strength and power
  to exalt and give strength to all.
[13]Now, our God, we give you thanks,
  and praise your glorious name.

[14]"But who am I, and who are my people, that we should be able to give as generously as this? Everything comes from you, and we have given you only what comes from your hand. [15]We are foreigners and strangers in your sight, as were all our ancestors. Our days on earth are like a shadow, without hope. [16]Lord our God, all this abundance that we have provided for building you a temple for your Holy Name comes from your hand, and all of it belongs to you. [17]I know, my God, that you test the heart and are pleased with integrity. All these things I have given willingly and with honest intent. And now I have seen with joy how willingly your people who are here have given to you. [18]Lord, the God of our fathers Abraham, Isaac and Israel, keep these desires and thoughts in the hearts of your people forever, and keep their hearts loyal to you. [19]And give my son Solomon the wholehearted devotion to keep your commands, statutes and decrees and to do everything to build the palatial structure for which I have provided."

[20]Then David said to the whole assembly, "Praise the Lord your God." So they all praised the Lord, the God of their fathers; they bowed down, prostrating themselves before the Lord and the king.

Solomon Acknowledged as King

[21]The next day they made sacrifices to the Lord and presented burnt offerings to him: a thousand bulls, a thousand rams and a thousand male lambs, together with their drink offerings, and other sacrifices in abundance for all Israel. [22]They ate and drank with great joy in the presence of the Lord that day.

Then they acknowledged Solomon son of David as king a second time, anointing him before the Lord to be ruler and Zadok to be priest. [23]So Solomon sat on the throne of the Lord as king in place of his father David. He prospered and all Israel obeyed him. [24]All the officers and warriors, as well as all of King David's sons, pledged their submission to King Solomon.

[25]The Lord highly exalted Solomon in the sight of all Israel and bestowed on him royal splendor such as no king over Israel ever had before.

The Death of David

[26]David son of Jesse was king over all Israel. [27]He ruled over Israel forty years—seven in Hebron and thirty-three in Jerusalem. [28]He died at a good old age, having enjoyed long life, wealth and honor. His son Solomon succeeded him as king.

[29]As for the events of King David's reign, from beginning to end, they are written in the records of Samuel the seer, the records of Nathan the prophet and the records of Gad the seer, [30]together with the details of his reign and power, and the circumstances that surrounded him and Israel and the kingdoms of all the other lands.

2 CHRONICLES

➡ **WHEN DID THIS HAPPEN?**

About 970–560 B.C. in the land of Israel—divided into the northern kingdom of Israel and the southern kingdom of Judah

➡ **WHO IS IN THIS BOOK?**

Solomon
Asa
Jehoshaphat
Joash
Hezekiah
Josiah

➡ **VERSES YOU MIGHT RECOGNIZE**

2 CHRONICLES 7:14
"If my people, who are called by my name, will humble themselves and pray and seek my face and turn from their wicked ways, then I will hear from heaven, and I will forgive their sin and will heal their land."

2 CHRONICLES 32:8
"'With him is only the arm of flesh, but with us is the LORD our God to help us and to fight our battles.' And the people gained confidence from what Hezekiah the king of Judah said."

WHAT'S IT ABOUT?

Like 1 Chronicles, this book is a retelling of the time period covered in 1 and 2 Kings. Written for the Israelites returning from captivity, it records the history of the southern kingdom of Judah from King Solomon's reign to the end of the Babylonian exile.

Once again, the chronicler (possibly Ezra) emphasized Israel's successes rather than its failures. The stars of this book are the kings who follow God and seek to turn Israel back to him. Not much is said about the bad kings or the failures of the godly kings. The point is to show how God worked through obedient rulers, such as Solomon, Jehoshaphat, Joash, Josiah and Hezekiah. Israel needed to remember that God could still do amazing things through them if they would obey. The references to kings in this book look ahead to the true King of kings—Jesus Christ. One day, Jesus would sit on the throne as David's heir and rule in perfect righteousness, something none of Israel's kings could achieve.

2 CHRONICLES

Solomon Asks for Wisdom

1 Solomon son of David established himself firmly over his kingdom, for the LORD his God was with him and made him exceedingly great.

2 Then Solomon spoke to all Israel — to the commanders of thousands and commanders of hundreds, to the judges and to all the leaders in Israel, the heads of families — 3 and Solomon and the whole assembly went to the high place at Gibeon, for God's tent of meeting was there, which Moses the LORD's servant had made in the wilderness. 4 Now David had brought up the ark of God from Kiriath Jearim to the place he had prepared for it, because he had pitched a tent for it in Jerusalem. 5 But the bronze altar that Bezalel son of Uri, the son of Hur, had made was in Gibeon in front of the tabernacle of the LORD; so Solomon and the assembly inquired of him there. 6 Solomon went up to the bronze altar before the LORD in the tent of meeting and offered a thousand burnt offerings on it.

7 That night God appeared to Solomon and said to him, "Ask for whatever you want me to give you."

8 Solomon answered God, "You have shown great kindness to David my father and have made me king in his place. 9 Now, LORD God, let your promise to my father David be confirmed, for you have made me king over a people who are as numerous as the dust of the earth. 10 Give me wisdom and knowledge, that I may lead this people, for who is able to govern this great people of yours?"

11 God said to Solomon, "Since this is your heart's desire and you have not asked for wealth, possessions or honor, nor for the death of your enemies, and since you have not asked for a long life but for wisdom and knowledge to govern my people over whom I have made you king, 12 therefore wisdom and knowledge will be given you. And I will also give you wealth, possessions and honor, such as no king who was before you ever had and none after you will have."

13 Then Solomon went to Jerusalem from the high place at Gibeon, from before the tent of meeting. And he reigned over Israel.

14 Solomon accumulated chariots and horses; he had fourteen hundred chariots and twelve thousand horses,[a] which he kept in the chariot cities and also with him in Jerusalem. 15 The king made silver and gold as common in Jerusalem as stones, and cedar as plentiful as sycamore-fig trees in the foothills. 16 Solomon's horses were imported from Egypt and from Kue[b] — the royal merchants purchased them from Kue at the current price. 17 They imported a chariot from Egypt for six hundred shekels[c] of silver, and a horse for a hundred and fifty.[d] They also exported them to all the kings of the Hittites and of the Arameans.

Preparations for Building the Temple

2[e] Solomon gave orders to build a temple for the Name of the LORD and a royal palace for himself. 2 He conscripted 70,000 men as carriers and 80,000 as stonecutters in the hills and 3,600 as foremen over them.

3 Solomon sent this message to Hiram[f] king of Tyre:

"Send me cedar logs as you did for my father David when you sent him cedar to build a palace to live in. 4 Now I am about to build a temple for the Name of the LORD my God and to dedicate it to him for burning fragrant incense before him, for setting out the consecrated bread regularly, and for making burnt offerings every morning and evening and on the Sabbaths, at the New Moons and at the appointed

---

a 14 Or *charioteers*   *b 16* Probably Cilicia   *c 17* That is, about 15 pounds or about 6.9 kilograms   *d 17* That is, about 3 3/4 pounds or about 1.7 kilograms   *e* In Hebrew texts 2:1 is numbered 1:18, and 2:2-18 is numbered 2:1-17.   *f 3* Hebrew *Huram*, a variant of *Hiram*; also in verses 11 and 12 festivals of the LORD our God. This is a lasting ordinance for Israel.

⁵ "The temple I am going to build will be great, because our God is greater than all other gods. ⁶ But who is able to build a temple for him, since the heavens, even the highest heavens, cannot contain him? Who then am I to build a temple for him, except as a place to burn sacrifices before him?

⁷ "Send me, therefore, a man skilled to work in gold and silver, bronze and iron, and in purple, crimson and blue yarn, and experienced in the art of engraving, to work in Judah and Jerusalem with my skilled workers, whom my father David provided.

⁸ "Send me also cedar, juniper and algum*ᵃ* logs from Lebanon, for I know that your servants are skilled in cutting timber there. My servants will work with yours ⁹ to provide me with plenty of lumber, because the temple I build must be large and magnificent. ¹⁰ I will give your servants, the woodsmen who cut the timber, twenty thousand cors*ᵇ* of ground wheat, twenty thousand cors*ᶜ* of barley, twenty thousand baths*ᵈ* of wine and twenty thousand baths of olive oil."

¹¹ Hiram king of Tyre replied by letter to Solomon:

"Because the LORD loves his people, he has made you their king."

¹² And Hiram added:

"Praise be to the LORD, the God of Israel, who made heaven and earth! He has given King David a wise son, endowed with intelligence and discernment, who will build a temple for the LORD and a palace for himself.

¹³ "I am sending you Huram-Abi, a man of great skill, ¹⁴ whose mother was from Dan and whose father was from Tyre. He is trained to work in gold and silver, bronze and iron, stone and wood, and with purple and blue and crimson yarn and fine linen. He is experienced in all kinds of engraving and can execute any design given to him. He will work with your skilled workers and with those of my lord, David your father.

¹⁵ "Now let my lord send his servants the wheat and barley and the olive oil and wine he promised, ¹⁶ and we will cut all the logs from Lebanon that you need and will float them as rafts by sea down to Joppa. You can then take them up to Jerusalem."

¹⁷ Solomon took a census of all the foreigners residing in Israel, after the census his father David had taken; and they were found to be 153,600. ¹⁸ He assigned 70,000 of them to be carriers and 80,000 to be stonecutters in the hills, with 3,600 foremen over them to keep the people working.

Solomon Builds the Temple

3 Then Solomon began to build the temple of the LORD in Jerusalem on Mount Moriah, where the LORD had appeared to his father David. It was on the threshing floor of Araunah*ᵉ* the Jebusite, the place provided by David. ² He began building on the second day of the second month in the fourth year of his reign.

³ The foundation Solomon laid for building the temple of God was sixty cubits long and twenty cubits wide*ᶠ* (using the cubit of the old standard). ⁴ The portico at the front of the temple was twenty cubits*ᵍ* long across the width of the building and twenty*ʰ* cubits high.

He overlaid the inside with pure gold. ⁵ He paneled the main hall with juniper and covered it with fine gold and decorated it with palm tree and chain designs. ⁶ He adorned the temple with precious stones. And the gold he used was gold of Parvaim. ⁷ He overlaid the ceiling beams, doorframes, walls and doors of the temple with gold, and he carved cherubim on the walls.

ᵃ 8 Probably a variant of *almug*   *ᵇ 10* That is, probably about 3,600 tons or about 3,200 metric tons of wheat   *ᶜ 10* That is, probably about 3,000 tons or about 2,700 metric tons of barley   *ᵈ 10* That is, about 120,000 gallons or about 440,000 liters   *ᵉ 1* Hebrew *Ornan*, a variant of *Araunah*   *ᶠ 3* That is, about 90 feet long and 30 feet wide or about 27 meters long and 9 meters wide   *ᵍ 4* That is, about 30 feet or about 9 meters; also in verses 8, 11 and 13   *ʰ 4* Some Septuagint and Syriac manuscripts; Hebrew *and a hundred and twenty*

UNBELIEVING FRIENDS

READ: 2 CHRONICLES 2:11

Back in the times of David and Solomon, the area surrounding the city of Tyre was famed for its thick cedar forests, much like northern California is known for giant redwoods. A stand of surviving trees is protected in a preserve in modern Lebanon called the "Cedars of God."

It's no surprise that King Solomon turned to Hiram, king of Tyre, for beautiful wood and skilled help to build the temple. Hiram had long been friends with Solomon's father, David, and he provided timber and labor for David's royal palace (1 Chronicles 14:1). So Solomon asked for cedar logs and an artisan skilled in working precious metals and rich yarns.

When Hiram replied, he declared that God must love his people to have given them a king like Solomon. He recognized that the Lord had given David's son intelligence and solid judgment. He promised to send the materials and the worker Solomon needed. And Hiram praised the Lord, whom he called "the God of Israel, who made heaven and earth!" (2 Chronicles 2:12).

BUILDING FAITH WISDOM STRENGTH

Hiram knew Solomon. He even knew something about Solomon's God. The king of Tyre no doubt worshiped the gods of his own land, so it is strange that he would say Solomon's God is the ultimate ruler of the universe. Perhaps he accepted God as one among many. These two men likely disagreed about God, yet they made the most of their friendship. They let you glimpse how you can get along with people who don't follow Jesus.

[8]He built the Most Holy Place, its length corresponding to the width of the temple—twenty cubits long and twenty cubits wide. He overlaid the inside with six hundred talents[a] of fine gold. [9]The gold nails weighed fifty shekels.[b] He also overlaid the upper parts with gold.

[10]For the Most Holy Place he made a pair of sculptured cherubim and overlaid them with gold. [11]The total wingspan of the cherubim was twenty cubits. One wing of the first cherub was five cubits[c] long and touched the temple wall, while its other wing, also five cubits long, touched the wing of the other cherub. [12]Similarly one wing of the second cherub was five cubits long and touched the other temple wall, and its other wing, also five cubits long, touched the wing of the first cherub. [13]The wings of these cherubim extended twenty cubits. They stood on their feet, facing the main hall.[d]

[14]He made the curtain of blue, purple and crimson yarn and fine linen, with cherubim worked into it.

[15]For the front of the temple he made two pillars, which together were thirty-five cubits[e] long, each with a capital five cubits high. [16]He made interwoven chains[f] and put them on top of the pillars. He also made a hundred pomegranates and attached them to the chains. [17]He erected the pillars in the front of the temple, one to the south and one to the north. The one to the south he named Jakin[g] and the one to the north Boaz.[h]

The Temple's Furnishings

4 He made a bronze altar twenty cubits long, twenty cubits wide and ten cubits high.[i] [2]He made the Sea of cast metal, circular in shape, measuring ten cubits from rim to rim and five cubits[j] high. It took a line of thirty cubits[k] to measure around it. [3]Below the rim, figures of bulls encircled it—ten to a cubit.[l] The bulls were cast in two rows in one piece with the Sea.

[4]The Sea stood on twelve bulls, three facing north, three facing west, three facing south and three facing east. The Sea rested on top of them, and their hindquarters were toward the center. [5]It was a handbreadth[m] in thickness, and its rim was like the rim of a cup, like a lily blossom. It held three thousand baths.[n]

[6]He then made ten basins for washing and placed five on the south side and five on the north. In them the things to be used for the burnt offerings were rinsed, but the Sea was to be used by the priests for washing.

[7]He made ten gold lampstands according to the specifications for them and placed them in the temple, five on the south side and five on the north.

[8]He made ten tables and placed them in the temple, five on the south side and five on the north. He also made a hundred gold sprinkling bowls.

[9]He made the courtyard of the priests, and the large court and the doors for the court, and overlaid the doors with bronze. [10]He placed the Sea on the south side, at the southeast corner.

[11]And Huram also made the pots and shovels and sprinkling bowls.

So Huram finished the work he had undertaken for King Solomon in the temple of God:

[12]the two pillars;
the two bowl-shaped capitals on top of the pillars;
the two sets of network decorating the two bowl-shaped capitals on top of the pillars;
[13]the four hundred pomegranates for the two sets of network (two rows of pomegranates for each network, decorating the bowl-shaped capitals on top of the pillars);
[14]the stands with their basins;
[15]the Sea and the twelve bulls under it;
[16]the pots, shovels, meat forks and all related articles.

---

[a] 8 That is, about 23 tons or about 21 metric tons   [b] 9 That is, about 1 1/4 pounds or about 575 grams   [c] 11 That is, about 7 1/2 feet or about 2.3 meters; also in verse 15   [d] 13 Or facing inward   [e] 15 That is, about 53 feet or about 16 meters   [f] 16 Or possibly made chains in the inner sanctuary; the meaning of the Hebrew for this phrase is uncertain.   [g] 17 Jakin probably means he establishes.   [h] 17 Boaz probably means in him is strength.   [i] 1 That is, about 30 feet long and wide and 15 feet high or about 9 meters long and wide and 4.5 meters high   [j] 2 That is, about 7 1/2 feet or about 2.3 meters   [k] 2 That is, about 45 feet or about 14 meters   [l] 3 That is, about 18 inches or about 45 centimeters   [m] 5 That is, about 3 inches or about 7.5 centimeters   [n] 5 That is, about 18,000 gallons or about 66,000 liters

All the objects that Huram-Abi made for King Solomon for the temple of the LORD were of polished bronze. ¹⁷The king had them cast in clay molds in the plain of the Jordan between Sukkoth and Zarethan.ᵃ ¹⁸All these things that Solomon made amounted to so much that the weight of the bronze could not be calculated.

¹⁹Solomon also made all the furnishings that were in God's temple:

the golden altar;
the tables on which was the bread of the Presence;
²⁰the lampstands of pure gold with their lamps, to burn in front of the inner sanctuary as prescribed;
²¹the gold floral work and lamps and tongs (they were solid gold);
²²the pure gold wick trimmers, sprinkling bowls, dishes and censers; and the gold doors of the temple: the inner doors to the Most Holy Place and the doors of the main hall.

5 When all the work Solomon had done for the temple of the LORD was finished, he brought in the things his father David had dedicated—the silver and gold and all the furnishings—and he placed them in the treasuries of God's temple.

The Ark Brought to the Temple

²Then Solomon summoned to Jerusalem the elders of Israel, all the heads of the tribes and the chiefs of the Israelite families, to bring up the ark of the LORD's covenant from Zion, the City of David. ³And all the Israelites came together to the king at the time of the festival in the seventh month.

⁴When all the elders of Israel had arrived, the Levites took up the ark, ⁵and they brought up the ark and the tent of meeting and all the sacred furnishings in it. The Levitical priests carried them up; ⁶and King Solomon and the entire assembly of Israel that had gathered about him were before the ark, sacrificing so many sheep and cattle that they could not be recorded or counted.

⁷The priests then brought the ark of the LORD's covenant to its place in the inner sanctuary of the temple, the Most Holy Place, and put it beneath the wings of the cherubim. ⁸The cherubim spread their wings over the place of the ark and covered the ark and its carrying poles. ⁹These poles were so long that their ends, extending from the ark, could be seen from in front of the inner sanctuary, but not from outside the Holy Place; and they are still there today. ¹⁰There was nothing in the ark except the two tablets that Moses had placed in it at Horeb, where the LORD made a covenant with the Israelites after they came out of Egypt.

¹¹The priests then withdrew from the Holy Place. All the priests who were there had consecrated themselves, regardless of their divisions. ¹²All the Levites who were musicians—Asaph, Heman, Jeduthun and their sons and relatives—stood on the east side of the altar, dressed in fine linen and playing cymbals, harps and lyres. They were accompanied by 120 priests sounding trumpets. ¹³The trumpeters and musicians joined in unison to give praise and thanks to the LORD. Accompanied by trumpets, cymbals and other instruments, the singers raised their voices in praise to the LORD and sang:

"He is good;
his love endures forever."

Then the temple of the LORD was filled with the cloud, ¹⁴and the priests could not perform their service because of the cloud, for the glory of the LORD filled the temple of God.

6 Then Solomon said, "The LORD has said that he would dwell in a dark cloud; ²I have built a magnificent temple for you, a place for you to dwell forever."

³While the whole assembly of Israel was standing there, the king turned around and blessed them. ⁴Then he said:

"Praise be to the LORD, the God of Israel, who with his hands has fulfilled what he promised with his mouth to my father David. For he said, ⁵'Since the day I brought my people out of Egypt, I have not chosen a city in any tribe of Israel to have a temple built so that my Name might be there, nor have I chosen anyone to be ruler over my people Israel. ⁶But now I have chosen Jerusalem for my Name to be there, and I have chosen David to rule my people Israel.'

ᵃ 17 Hebrew *Zeredatha*, a variant of *Zarethan*

[7] "My father David had it in his heart to build a temple for the Name of the LORD, the God of Israel. [8] But the LORD said to my father David, 'You did well to have it in your heart to build a temple for my Name. [9] Nevertheless, you are not the one to build the temple, but your son, your own flesh and blood—he is the one who will build the temple for my Name.'

[10] "The LORD has kept the promise he made. I have succeeded David my father and now I sit on the throne of Israel, just as the LORD promised, and I have built the temple for the Name of the LORD, the God of Israel. [11] There I have placed the ark, in which is the covenant of the LORD that he made with the people of Israel."

Solomon's Prayer of Dedication

[12] Then Solomon stood before the altar of the LORD in front of the whole assembly of Israel and spread out his hands. [13] Now he had made a bronze platform, five cubits long, five cubits wide and three cubits high,[a] and had placed it in the center of the outer court. He stood on the platform and then knelt down before the whole assembly of Israel and spread out his hands toward heaven. [14] He said:

"LORD, the God of Israel, there is no God like you in heaven or on earth—you who keep your covenant of love with your servants who continue wholeheartedly in your way. [15] You have kept your promise to your servant David my father; with your mouth you have promised and with your hand you have fulfilled it—as it is today.

[16] "Now, LORD, the God of Israel, keep for your servant David my father the promises you made to him when you said, 'You shall never fail to have a successor to sit before me on the throne of Israel, if only your descendants are careful in all they do to walk before me according to my law, as you have done.' [17] And now, LORD, the God of Israel, let your word that you promised your servant David come true.

[18] "But will God really dwell on earth with humans? The heavens, even the highest heavens, cannot contain you. How much less this temple I have built! [19] Yet, LORD my God, give attention to your servant's prayer and his plea for mercy. Hear the cry and the prayer that your servant is praying in your presence. [20] May your eyes be open toward this temple day and night, this place of which you said you would put your Name there. May you hear the prayer your servant prays toward this place. [21] Hear the supplications of your servant and of your people Israel when they pray toward this place. Hear from heaven, your dwelling place; and when you hear, forgive.

[22] "When anyone wrongs their neighbor and is required to take an oath and they come and swear the oath before your altar in this temple, [23] then hear from heaven and act. Judge between your servants, condemning the guilty and bringing down on their heads what they have done, and vindicating the innocent by treating them in accordance with their innocence.

[24] "When your people Israel have been defeated by an enemy because they have sinned against you and when they turn back and give praise to your name, praying and making supplication before you in this temple, [25] then hear from heaven and forgive the sin of your people Israel and bring them back to the land you gave to them and their ancestors.

[26] "When the heavens are shut up and there is no rain because your people have sinned against you, and when they pray toward this place and give praise to your name and turn from their sin because you have afflicted them, [27] then hear from heaven and forgive the sin of your servants, your people Israel. Teach them the right way to live, and send rain on the land you gave your people for an inheritance.

[28] "When famine or plague comes to the land, or blight or mildew, locusts or grasshoppers, or when enemies besiege

---

[a] 13 That is, about 7 1/2 feet long and wide and 4 1/2 feet high or about 2.3 meters long and wide and 1.4 meters high

them in any of their cities, whatever disaster or disease may come, ²⁹ and when a prayer or plea is made by anyone among your people Israel — being aware of their afflictions and pains, and spreading out their hands toward this temple — ³⁰ then hear from heaven, your dwelling place. Forgive, and deal with everyone according to all they do, since you know their hearts (for you alone know the human heart), ³¹ so that they will fear you and walk in obedience to you all the time they live in the land you gave our ancestors.

³² "As for the foreigner who does not belong to your people Israel but has come from a distant land because of your great name and your mighty hand and your outstretched arm — when they come and pray toward this temple, ³³ then hear from heaven, your dwelling place. Do whatever the foreigner asks of you, so that all the peoples of the earth may know your name and fear you, as do your own people Israel, and may know that this house I have built bears your Name.

³⁴ "When your people go to war against their enemies, wherever you send them, and when they pray to you toward this city you have chosen and the temple I have built for your Name, ³⁵ then hear from heaven their prayer and their plea, and uphold their cause.

³⁶ "When they sin against you — for there is no one who does not sin — and you become angry with them and give them over to the enemy, who takes them captive to a land far away or near; ³⁷ and if they have a change of heart in the land where they are held captive, and repent and plead with you in the land of their captivity and say, 'We have sinned, we have done wrong and acted wickedly'; ³⁸ and if they turn back to you with all their heart and soul in the land of their captivity where they were taken, and pray toward the land you gave their ancestors, toward the city you have chosen and toward the temple I have built for your Name; ³⁹ then from heaven, your dwelling place, hear their prayer and their pleas, and uphold their cause. And forgive your people, who have sinned against you.

⁴⁰ "Now, my God, may your eyes be open and your ears attentive to the prayers offered in this place.

⁴¹ "Now arise, Lord God, and come
  to your resting place,
  you and the ark of your might.
May your priests, Lord God, be
  clothed with salvation,
  may your faithful people
  rejoice in your goodness.
⁴² Lord God, do not reject your
  anointed one.
  Remember the great love
  promised to David your
  servant."

The Dedication of the Temple

7 When Solomon finished praying, fire came down from heaven and consumed the burnt offering and the sacrifices, and the glory of the Lord filled the temple. ² The priests could not enter the temple of the Lord because the glory of the Lord filled it. ³ When all the Israelites saw the fire coming down and the glory of the Lord above the temple, they knelt on the pavement with their faces to the ground, and they worshiped and gave thanks to the Lord, saying,

"He is good;
  his love endures forever."

⁴ Then the king and all the people offered sacrifices before the Lord. ⁵ And King Solomon offered a sacrifice of twenty-two thousand head of cattle and a hundred and twenty thousand sheep and goats. So the king and all the people dedicated the temple of God. ⁶ The priests took their positions, as did the Levites with the Lord's musical instruments, which King David had made for praising the Lord and which were used when he gave thanks, saying, "His love endures forever." Opposite the Levites, the priests blew their trumpets, and all the Israelites were standing.

⁷ Solomon consecrated the middle part of the courtyard in front of the temple of the Lord, and there he offered burnt offerings and the fat of the fellowship offerings, because the bronze altar he had made could not hold the burnt offerings, the grain offerings and the fat portions.

⁸ So Solomon observed the festival at that time for seven days, and all Israel with

him—a vast assembly, people from Lebo Hamath to the Wadi of Egypt. [9]On the eighth day they held an assembly, for they had celebrated the dedication of the altar for seven days and the festival for seven days more. [10]On the twenty-third day of the seventh month he sent the people to their homes, joyful and glad in heart for the good things the LORD had done for David and Solomon and for his people Israel.

The LORD Appears to Solomon

[11]When Solomon had finished the temple of the LORD and the royal palace, and had succeeded in carrying out all he had in mind to do in the temple of the LORD and in his own palace, [12]the LORD appeared to him at night and said:

"I have heard your prayer and have chosen this place for myself as a temple for sacrifices.

[13]"When I shut up the heavens so that there is no rain, or command locusts to devour the land or send a plague among my people, [14]if my people, who are called by my name, will humble themselves and pray and seek my face and turn from their wicked ways, then I will hear from heaven, and I will forgive their sin and will heal their land. [15]Now my eyes will be open and my ears attentive to the prayers offered in this place. [16]I have chosen and consecrated this temple so that my Name may be there forever. My eyes and my heart will always be there.

[17]"As for you, if you walk before me faithfully as David your father did, and do all I command, and observe my decrees and laws, [18]I will establish your royal throne, as I covenanted with David your father when I said, 'You shall never fail to have a successor to rule over Israel.'

[19]"But if you[a] turn away and forsake the decrees and commands I have given you[a] and go off to serve other gods and worship them, [20]then I will uproot Israel from my land, which I have given them, and will reject this temple I have

consecrated for my Name. I will make it a byword and an object of ridicule among all peoples. [21]This temple will become a heap of rubble. All[b] who pass by will be appalled and say, 'Why has the LORD done such a thing to this land and to this temple?' [22]People will answer, 'Because they have forsaken the LORD, the God of their ancestors, who brought them out of Egypt, and have embraced other gods, worshiping and serving them—that is why he brought all this disaster on them.'"

Solomon's Other Activities

8 At the end of twenty years, during which Solomon built the temple of the LORD and his own palace, [2]Solomon rebuilt the villages that Hiram[c] had given him, and settled Israelites in them. [3]Solomon then went to Hamath Zobah and captured it. [4]He also built up Tadmor in the desert and all the store cities he had built in Hamath. [5]He rebuilt Upper Beth Horon and Lower Beth Horon as fortified cities, with walls and with gates and bars, [6]as well as Baalath and all his store cities, and all the cities for his chariots and for his horses[d]—whatever he desired to build in Jerusalem, in Lebanon and throughout all the territory he ruled.

[7]There were still people left from the Hittites, Amorites, Perizzites, Hivites and Jebusites (these people were not Israelites). [8]Solomon conscripted the descendants of all these people remaining in the land—whom the Israelites had not destroyed—to serve as slave labor, as it is to this day. [9]But Solomon did not make slaves of the Israelites for his work; they were his fighting men, commanders of his captains, and commanders of his chariots and charioteers. [10]They were also King Solomon's chief officials—two hundred and fifty officials supervising the men.

[11]Solomon brought Pharaoh's daughter up from the City of David to the palace he had built for her, for he said, "My wife must not live in the palace of David king of Israel, because the places the ark of the LORD has entered are holy."

[12]On the altar of the LORD that he had built

---

[a] 19 The Hebrew is plural.   [b] 21 See some Septuagint manuscripts, Old Latin, Syriac, Arabic and Targum; Hebrew *And though this temple is now so imposing, all*   [c] 2 Hebrew *Huram,* a variant of *Hiram;* also in verse 18   [d] 6 Or *charioteers*

in front of the portico, Solomon sacrificed burnt offerings to the LORD, ¹³according to the daily requirement for offerings commanded by Moses for the Sabbaths, the New Moons and the three annual festivals—the Festival of Unleavened Bread, the Festival of Weeks and the Festival of Tabernacles. ¹⁴In keeping with the ordinance of his father David, he appointed the divisions of the priests for their duties, and the Levites to lead the praise and to assist the priests according to each day's requirement. He also appointed the gatekeepers by divisions for the various gates, because this was what David the man of God had ordered. ¹⁵They did not deviate from the king's commands to the priests or to the Levites in any matter, including that of the treasuries.

¹⁶All Solomon's work was carried out, from the day the foundation of the temple of the LORD was laid until its completion. So the temple of the LORD was finished.

¹⁷Then Solomon went to Ezion Geber and Elath on the coast of Edom. ¹⁸And Hiram sent him ships commanded by his own men, sailors who knew the sea. These, with Solomon's men, sailed to Ophir and brought back four hundred and fifty talents*ᵃ* of gold, which they delivered to King Solomon.

The Queen of Sheba Visits Solomon

9 When the queen of Sheba heard of Solomon's fame, she came to Jerusalem to test him with hard questions. Arriving with a very great caravan—with camels carrying spices, large quantities of gold, and precious stones—she came to Solomon and talked with him about all she had on her mind. ²Solomon answered all her questions; nothing was too hard for him to explain to her. ³When the queen of Sheba saw the wisdom of Solomon, as well as the palace he had built, ⁴the food on his table, the seating of his officials, the attending servants in their robes, the cupbearers in their robes and the burnt offerings he made at*ᵇ* the temple of the LORD, she was overwhelmed.

⁵She said to the king, "The report I heard in my own country about your achievements and your wisdom is true. ⁶But I did not believe what they said until I came and saw with my own eyes. Indeed, not even half the greatness of your wisdom was told me; you have far exceeded the report I heard. ⁷How happy your people must be! How happy your officials, who continually stand before you and hear your wisdom! ⁸Praise be to the LORD your God, who has delighted in you and placed you on his throne as king to rule for the LORD your God. Because of the love of your God for Israel and his desire to uphold them forever, he has made you king over them, to maintain justice and righteousness."

⁹Then she gave the king 120 talents*ᶜ* of gold, large quantities of spices, and precious stones. There had never been such spices as those the queen of Sheba gave to King Solomon.

¹⁰(The servants of Hiram and the servants of Solomon brought gold from Ophir; they also brought algumwood*ᵈ* and precious stones. ¹¹The king used the algumwood to make steps for the temple of the LORD and for the royal palace, and to make harps and lyres for the musicians. Nothing like them had ever been seen in Judah.)

¹²King Solomon gave the queen of Sheba all she desired and asked for; he gave her more than she had brought to him. Then she left and returned with her retinue to her own country.

Solomon's Splendor

¹³The weight of the gold that Solomon received yearly was 666 talents,*ᵉ* ¹⁴not including the revenues brought in by merchants and traders. Also all the kings of Arabia and the governors of the territories brought gold and silver to Solomon.

¹⁵King Solomon made two hundred large shields of hammered gold; six hundred shekels*ᶠ* of hammered gold went into each shield. ¹⁶He also made three hundred small shields of hammered gold, with three hundred shekels*ᵍ* of gold in each shield. The king put them in the Palace of the Forest of Lebanon.

¹⁷Then the king made a great throne covered with ivory and overlaid with pure

---

ᵃ 18 That is, about 17 tons or about 15 metric tons   *ᵇ 4* Or *and the ascent by which he went up to*
ᶜ 9 That is, about 4 1/2 tons or about 4 metric tons   *ᵈ 10* Probably a variant of *almugwood*   *ᵉ 13* That
is, about 25 tons or about 23 metric tons   *ᶠ 15* That is, about 15 pounds or about 6.9 kilograms
ᵍ 16 That is, about 7 1/2 pounds or about 3.5 kilograms

SOLOMON

All the kings of the earth sought audience with Solomon to hear the wisdom God had put in his heart. 2 CHRONICLES 9:23

HIS NAME MEANS: "peace," "peaceable"

READ HIS STORY: *1 Kings 1–3; 6·10; Ecclesiastes 1:12–18; 2 Chronicles 1, 9*

OF THE BIBLE

I f God appeared in a dream and offered anything you wanted, what would you ask for? Money? Talent? A long life? Solomon didn't ask for these things. As the son of King David and Bathsheba, Solomon had just become Israel's ruler. As a result, he asked the Lord for a discerning heart, so he could govern well and know right from wrong (1 Kings 3:9). God was so pleased by Solomon's answer that he gave the king wisdom but also promised riches and honor.

Solomon's wisdom became legendary. He settled disputes. Foreign leaders sought advice and brought gifts—gold, silver, weapons, horses . . . even their daughters. Back then countries often sealed agreements with a wedding. As Solomon's power grew, so did his number of wives. Solomon had 700 wives of royal birth and 300 concubines (1 Kings 11:3). His wealth was even more staggering. Experts estimate that Solomon brought in about a billion in gold every year through taxes and gifts. That doesn't account for his other treasures.

Solomon was a man who had it all and experienced it all. We can learn from his wisdom by reading the book of Proverbs. But we can learn from his mistakes by reading the book of Ecclesiastes. Solomon discovered that pleasure, wealth and wisdom were meaningless. God gave him wisdom, but Solomon got sidetracked by women and money. In the end, he concluded, the best thing we can do is "fear God and keep his commandments . . . For God will bring every deed into judgment, including every hidden thing, whether it is good or evil" (Ecclesiastes 12:13–14).

gold. ¹⁸The throne had six steps, and a foot-stool of gold was attached to it. On both sides of the seat were armrests, with a lion standing beside each of them. ¹⁹Twelve lions stood on the six steps, one at either end of each step. Nothing like it had ever been made for any other kingdom. ²⁰All King Solomon's goblets were gold, and all the household articles in the Palace of the Forest of Lebanon were pure gold. Nothing was made of silver, because silver was considered of little value in Solomon's day. ²¹The king had a fleet of trading ships*ᵃ* manned by Hiram's*ᵇ* servants. Once every three years it returned, carrying gold, silver and ivory, and apes and baboons.

²²King Solomon was greater in riches and wisdom than all the other kings of the earth. ²³All the kings of the earth sought audience with Solomon to hear the wisdom God had put in his heart. ²⁴Year after year, everyone who came brought a gift—articles of silver and gold, and robes, weapons and spices, and horses and mules.

²⁵Solomon had four thousand stalls for horses and chariots, and twelve thousand horses,*ᶜ* which he kept in the chariot cities and also with him in Jerusalem. ²⁶He ruled over all the kings from the Euphrates River to the land of the Philistines, as far as the border of Egypt. ²⁷The king made silver as common in Jerusalem as stones, and cedar as plentiful as sycamore-fig trees in the foothills. ²⁸Solomon's horses were imported from Egypt and from all other countries.

Solomon's Death

²⁹As for the other events of Solomon's reign, from beginning to end, are they not written in the records of Nathan the prophet, in the prophecy of Ahijah the Shilonite and in the visions of Iddo the seer concerning Jeroboam son of Nebat? ³⁰Solomon reigned in Jerusalem over all Israel forty years. ³¹Then he rested with his ancestors and was buried in the city of David his father. And Rehoboam his son succeeded him as king.

Israel Rebels Against Rehoboam

10 Rehoboam went to Shechem, for all Israel had gone there to make him king. ²When Jeroboam son of Nebat heard this (he was in Egypt, where he had fled from King Solomon), he returned from Egypt. ³So they sent for Jeroboam, and he and all Israel went to Rehoboam and said to him: ⁴"Your father put a heavy yoke on us, but now lighten the harsh labor and the heavy yoke he put on us, and we will serve you."

⁵Rehoboam answered, "Come back to me in three days." So the people went away.

⁶Then King Rehoboam consulted the elders who had served his father Solomon during his lifetime. "How would you advise me to answer these people?" he asked.

⁷They replied, "If you will be kind to these people and please them and give them a favorable answer, they will always be your servants."

⁸But Rehoboam rejected the advice the elders gave him and consulted the young men who had grown up with him and were serving him. ⁹He asked them, "What is your advice? How should we answer these people who say to me, 'Lighten the yoke your father put on us'?"

¹⁰The young men who had grown up with him replied, "The people have said to you, 'Your father put a heavy yoke on us, but make our yoke lighter.' Now tell them, 'My little finger is thicker than my father's waist. ¹¹My father laid on you a heavy yoke; I will make it even heavier. My father scourged you with whips; I will scourge you with scorpions.'"

¹²Three days later Jeroboam and all the people returned to Rehoboam, as the king had said, "Come back to me in three days." ¹³The king answered them harshly. Rejecting the advice of the elders, ¹⁴he followed the advice of the young men and said, "My father made your yoke heavy; I will make it even heavier. My father scourged you with whips; I will scourge you with scorpions." ¹⁵So the king did not listen to the people, for this turn of events was from God, to fulfill the word the LORD had spoken to Jeroboam son of Nebat through Ahijah the Shilonite.

¹⁶When all Israel saw that the king refused to listen to them, they answered the king:

"What share do we have in David,
 what part in Jesse's son?
To your tents, Israel!
 Look after your own house, David!"

ᵃ 21 Hebrew *of ships that could go to Tarshish*   *ᵇ 21* Hebrew *Huram,* a variant of *Hiram*
ᶜ 25 Or *charioteers*

PICKY ADVICE

READ: 2 CHRONICLES 10:8

The Israelites should have spotted this ugly scene coming. Years earlier, God grew angry at King Solomon for worshiping the pagan gods of his many foreign wives. The Lord vowed to rip away much of Solomon's kingdom as a consequence of sin, though not until after the king's death (1 Kings 11:9-13).

After Solomon dies, his son Rehoboam ascended to the throne. An old enemy named Jeroboam (vv. 26-40) returned from Egypt to plead with Rehoboam for relief from the heavy burdens of taxation and forced labor Solomon had put on the people to undertake his lavish building projects (v. 28). Jeroboam spoke not just for himself but for the entire nation.

BUILDING FAITH WISDOM STRENGTH

Older advisors told Rehoboam that showing kindness to his new subjects would earn their undying affection. Yet younger counselors urged Rehoboam to pile even more severe loads on the people and to beat them not merely with whips embedded with razor-sharp metal but with poisonous scorpions. When Rehoboam thundered his verdict, the kingdom split just as God had predicted.

Proverbs 19:20 says, "Listen to advice and accept discipline, and at the end you will be counted among the wise." But foolish advice doesn't do you any good. When you turn to others for wisdom, not just any voice will do. Choose carefully whom you listen to. Bad advice is worse than no advice at all.

So all the Israelites went home. [17]But as for the Israelites who were living in the towns of Judah, Rehoboam still ruled over them.

[18]King Rehoboam sent out Adoniram,[a] who was in charge of forced labor, but the Israelites stoned him to death. King Rehoboam, however, managed to get into his chariot and escape to Jerusalem. [19]So Israel has been in rebellion against the house of David to this day.

11 When Rehoboam arrived in Jerusalem, he mustered Judah and Benjamin — a hundred and eighty thousand able young men — to go to war against Israel and to regain the kingdom for Rehoboam.

[2]But this word of the LORD came to Shemaiah the man of God: [3]"Say to Rehoboam son of Solomon king of Judah and to all Israel in Judah and Benjamin, [4]'This is what the LORD says: Do not go up to fight against your fellow Israelites. Go home, every one of you, for this is my doing.'" So they obeyed the words of the LORD and turned back from marching against Jeroboam.

Rehoboam Fortifies Judah

[5]Rehoboam lived in Jerusalem and built up towns for defense in Judah: [6]Bethlehem, Etam, Tekoa, [7]Beth Zur, Soko, Adullam, [8]Gath, Mareshah, Ziph, [9]Adoraim, Lachish, Azekah, [10]Zorah, Aijalon and Hebron. These were fortified cities in Judah and Benjamin. [11]He strengthened their defenses and put commanders in them, with supplies of food, olive oil and wine. [12]He put shields and spears in all the cities, and made them very strong. So Judah and Benjamin were his.

[13]The priests and Levites from all their districts throughout Israel sided with him. [14]The Levites even abandoned their pasturelands and property and came to Judah and Jerusalem, because Jeroboam and his sons had rejected them as priests of the LORD [15]when he appointed his own priests for the high places and for the goat and calf idols he had made. [16]Those from every tribe of Israel who set their hearts on seeking the LORD, the God of Israel, followed the Levites to Jerusalem to offer sacrifices to the LORD, the God of their ancestors. [17]They strengthened the kingdom of Judah and supported

Rehoboam son of Solomon three years, following the ways of David and Solomon during this time.

Rehoboam's Family

[18]Rehoboam married Mahalath, who was the daughter of David's son Jerimoth and of Abihail, the daughter of Jesse's son Eliab. [19]She bore him sons: Jeush, Shemariah and Zaham. [20]Then he married Maakah daughter of Absalom, who bore him Abijah, Attai, Ziza and Shelomith. [21]Rehoboam loved Maakah daughter of Absalom more than any of his other wives and concubines. In all, he had eighteen wives and sixty concubines, twenty-eight sons and sixty daughters.

[22]Rehoboam appointed Abijah son of Maakah as crown prince among his brothers, in order to make him king. [23]He acted wisely, dispersing some of his sons throughout the districts of Judah and Benjamin, and to all the fortified cities. He gave them abundant provisions and took many wives for them.

Shishak Attacks Jerusalem

12 After Rehoboam's position as king was established and he had become strong, he and all Israel[b] with him abandoned the law of the LORD. [2]Because they had been unfaithful to the LORD, Shishak king of Egypt attacked Jerusalem in the fifth year of King Rehoboam. [3]With twelve hundred chariots and sixty thousand horsemen and the innumerable troops of Libyans, Sukkites and Cushites[c] that came with him from Egypt, [4]he captured the fortified cities of Judah and came as far as Jerusalem.

[5]Then the prophet Shemaiah came to Rehoboam and to the leaders of Judah who had assembled in Jerusalem for fear of Shishak, and he said to them, "This is what the LORD says, 'You have abandoned me; therefore, I now abandon you to Shishak.'"

[6]The leaders of Israel and the king humbled themselves and said, "The LORD is just."

[7]When the LORD saw that they humbled themselves, this word of the LORD came to Shemaiah: "Since they have humbled themselves, I will not destroy them but will soon give them deliverance. My wrath will not be poured out on Jerusalem through Shishak.

---

[a] 18 Hebrew *Hadoram*, a variant of *Adoniram*   [b] 1 That is, Judah, as frequently in 2 Chronicles
[c] 3 That is, people from the upper Nile region

[8]They will, however, become subject to him, so that they may learn the difference between serving me and serving the kings of other lands."

[9]When Shishak king of Egypt attacked Jerusalem, he carried off the treasures of the temple of the LORD and the treasures of the royal palace. He took everything, including the gold shields Solomon had made. [10]So King Rehoboam made bronze shields to replace them and assigned these to the commanders of the guard on duty at the entrance to the royal palace. [11]Whenever the king went to the LORD's temple, the guards went with him, bearing the shields, and afterward they returned them to the guardroom.

[12]Because Rehoboam humbled himself, the LORD's anger turned from him, and he was not totally destroyed. Indeed, there was some good in Judah.

[13]King Rehoboam established himself firmly in Jerusalem and continued as king. He was forty-one years old when he became king, and he reigned seventeen years in Jerusalem, the city the LORD had chosen out of all the tribes of Israel in which to put his Name. His mother's name was Naamah; she was an Ammonite. [14]He did evil because he had not set his heart on seeking the LORD.

[15]As for the events of Rehoboam's reign, from beginning to end, are they not written in the records of Shemaiah the prophet and of Iddo the seer that deal with genealogies? There was continual warfare between Rehoboam and Jeroboam. [16]Rehoboam rested with his ancestors and was buried in the City of David. And Abijah his son succeeded him as king.

Abijah King of Judah

13 In the eighteenth year of the reign of Jeroboam, Abijah became king of Judah, [2]and he reigned in Jerusalem three years. His mother's name was Maakah,[a] a daughter[b] of Uriel of Gibeah.

There was war between Abijah and Jeroboam. [3]Abijah went into battle with an army of four hundred thousand able fighting men, and Jeroboam drew up a battle line against him with eight hundred thousand able troops.

[4]Abijah stood on Mount Zemaraim, in the hill country of Ephraim, and said, "Jeroboam and all Israel, listen to me! [5]Don't you know that the LORD, the God of Israel, has given the kingship of Israel to David and his descendants forever by a covenant of salt? [6]Yet Jeroboam son of Nebat, an official of Solomon son of David, rebelled against his master. [7]Some worthless scoundrels gathered around him and opposed Rehoboam son of Solomon when he was young and indecisive and not strong enough to resist them.

[8]"And now you plan to resist the kingdom of the LORD, which is in the hands of David's descendants. You are indeed a vast army and have with you the golden calves that Jeroboam made to be your gods. [9]But didn't you drive out the priests of the LORD, the sons of Aaron, and the Levites, and make priests of your own as the peoples of other lands do? Whoever comes to consecrate himself with a young bull and seven rams may become a priest of what are not gods.

[10]"As for us, the LORD is our God, and we have not forsaken him. The priests who serve the LORD are sons of Aaron, and the Levites assist them. [11]Every morning and evening they present burnt offerings and fragrant incense to the LORD. They set out the bread on the ceremonially clean table and light the lamps on the gold lampstand every evening. We are observing the requirements of the LORD our God. But you have forsaken him. [12]God is with us; he is our leader. His priests with their trumpets will sound the battle cry against you. People of Israel, do not fight against the LORD, the God of your ancestors, for you will not succeed."

[13]Now Jeroboam had sent troops around to the rear, so that while he was in front of Judah the ambush was behind them. [14]Judah turned and saw that they were being attacked at both front and rear. Then they cried out to the LORD. The priests blew their trumpets [15]and the men of Judah raised the battle cry. At the sound of their battle cry, God routed Jeroboam and all Israel before Abijah and Judah. [16]The Israelites fled before Judah, and God delivered them into their hands. [17]Abijah and his troops inflicted heavy losses on them, so that there were five

---

[a] 2 Most Septuagint manuscripts and Syriac (see also 11:20 and 1 Kings 15:2); Hebrew *Micaiah*
[b] 2 Or *granddaughter*

hundred thousand casualties among Israel's able men. [18] The Israelites were subdued on that occasion, and the people of Judah were victorious because they relied on the LORD, the God of their ancestors.

[19] Abijah pursued Jeroboam and took from him the towns of Bethel, Jeshanah and Ephron, with their surrounding villages. [20] Jeroboam did not regain power during the time of Abijah. And the LORD struck him down and he died.

[21] But Abijah grew in strength. He married fourteen wives and had twenty-two sons and sixteen daughters.

[22] The other events of Abijah's reign, what he did and what he said, are written in the annotations of the prophet Iddo.

14[a] And Abijah rested with his ancestors and was buried in the City of David. Asa his son succeeded him as king, and in his days the country was at peace for ten years.

Asa King of Judah

[2] Asa did what was good and right in the eyes of the LORD his God. [3] He removed the foreign altars and the high places, smashed the sacred stones and cut down the Asherah poles.[b] [4] He commanded Judah to seek the LORD, the God of their ancestors, and to obey his laws and commands. [5] He removed the high places and incense altars in every town in Judah, and the kingdom was at peace under him. [6] He built up the fortified cities of Judah, since the land was at peace. No one was at war with him during those years, for the LORD gave him rest.

[7] "Let us build up these towns," he said to Judah, "and put walls around them, with towers, gates and bars. The land is still ours, because we have sought the LORD our God; we sought him and he has given us rest on every side." So they built and prospered.

[8] Asa had an army of three hundred thousand men from Judah, equipped with large shields and with spears, and two hundred and eighty thousand from Benjamin, armed with small shields and with bows. All these were brave fighting men.

[9] Zerah the Cushite marched out against them with an army of thousands upon thousands and three hundred chariots, and came as far as Mareshah. [10] Asa went out to meet him, and they took up battle positions in the Valley of Zephathah near Mareshah.

[11] Then Asa called to the LORD his God and said, "LORD, there is no one like you to help the powerless against the mighty. Help us, LORD our God, for we rely on you, and in your name we have come against this vast army. LORD, you are our God; do not let mere mortals prevail against you."

[12] The LORD struck down the Cushites before Asa and Judah. The Cushites fled, [13] and Asa and his army pursued them as far as Gerar. Such a great number of Cushites fell that they could not recover; they were crushed before the LORD and his forces. The men of Judah carried off a large amount of plunder. [14] They destroyed all the villages around Gerar, for the terror of the LORD had fallen on them. They looted all these villages, since there was much plunder there. [15] They also attacked the camps of the herders and carried off droves of sheep and goats and camels. Then they returned to Jerusalem.

Asa's Reform

15 The Spirit of God came on Azariah son of Oded. [2] He went out to meet Asa and said to him, "Listen to me, Asa and all Judah and Benjamin. The LORD is with you when you are with him. If you seek him, he will be found by you, but if you forsake him, he will forsake you. [3] For a long time Israel was without the true God, without a priest to teach and without the law. [4] But in their distress they turned to the LORD, the God of Israel, and sought him, and he was found by them. [5] In those days it was not safe to travel about, for all the inhabitants of the lands were in great turmoil. [6] One nation was being crushed by another and one city by another, because God was troubling them with every kind of distress. [7] But as for you, be strong and do not give up, for your work will be rewarded."

[8] When Asa heard these words and the prophecy of Azariah son of[c] Oded the prophet, he took courage. He removed the detestable idols from the whole land of Judah and Benjamin and from the towns he had captured

---

[a] In Hebrew texts 14:1 is numbered 13:23, and 14:2-15 is numbered 14:1-14.   [b] 3 That is, wooden symbols of the goddess Asherah; here and elsewhere in 2 Chronicles   [c] 8 Vulgate and Syriac (see also Septuagint and verse 1); Hebrew does not have *Azariah son of*.

START HERE

READ: 2 CHRONICLES 15:2-4

The most common reason people give for not following Jesus is they want to get their lives together first. It sounds noble, like you are taking the invitation of Jesus so seriously you want to wait to start following him until you get your life turned around and going in the right direction. But when Jesus invites you to follow him, his invitation comes to you right where you are. He wants you to say yes today and he will lead you out of where you are now.

I tend to think I know where I'm going, even when I don't. For the most part, every time I use the GPS, I've tried finding something myself but have managed to get lost. When I do type in my destination, the first question that comes on the screen is this: "Directions from current location?" In other words, "Do you want to start where you are?" And then it begins calculating my route, not from where I started, or the direction I should be headed, but from where I am currently located.

BUILDING

FAITH

WISDOM

STRENGTH

When Jesus invites you to follow he wants you to start right now from your current location. You don't have to go back to where you started. You don't need to get a little closer on your own. He reaches out to you with grace and love and invites you to follow him.

Taken from *Not a Fan Student Edition* by Kyle Idleman, copyright © 2012 by City on the Hill Studio, Inc., published by Zondervan.

in the hills of Ephraim. He repaired the altar of the LORD that was in front of the portico of the LORD's temple.

⁹Then he assembled all Judah and Benjamin and the people from Ephraim, Manasseh and Simeon who had settled among them, for large numbers had come over to him from Israel when they saw that the LORD his God was with him.

¹⁰They assembled at Jerusalem in the third month of the fifteenth year of Asa's reign. ¹¹At that time they sacrificed to the LORD seven hundred head of cattle and seven thousand sheep and goats from the plunder they had brought back. ¹²They entered into a covenant to seek the LORD, the God of their ancestors, with all their heart and soul. ¹³All who would not seek the LORD, the God of Israel, were to be put to death, whether small or great, man or woman. ¹⁴They took an oath to the LORD with loud acclamation, with shouting and with trumpets and horns. ¹⁵All Judah rejoiced about the oath because they had sworn it wholeheartedly. They sought God eagerly, and he was found by them. So the LORD gave them rest on every side.

¹⁶King Asa also deposed his grandmother Maakah from her position as queen mother, because she had made a repulsive image for the worship of Asherah. Asa cut it down, broke it up and burned it in the Kidron Valley. ¹⁷Although he did not remove the high places from Israel, Asa's heart was fully committed to the LORD all his life. ¹⁸He brought into the temple of God the silver and gold and the articles that he and his father had dedicated.

¹⁹There was no more war until the thirty-fifth year of Asa's reign.

Asa's Last Years

16 In the thirty-sixth year of Asa's reign Baasha king of Israel went up against Judah and fortified Ramah to prevent anyone from leaving or entering the territory of Asa king of Judah.

²Asa then took the silver and gold out of the treasuries of the LORD's temple and of his own palace and sent it to Ben-Hadad king of Aram, who was ruling in Damascus. ³"Let there be a treaty between me and you," he said, "as there was between my father and your father. See, I am sending you silver and gold. Now break your treaty with Baasha king of Israel so he will withdraw from me."

⁴Ben-Hadad agreed with King Asa and sent the commanders of his forces against the towns of Israel. They conquered Ijon, Dan, Abel Maim*a* and all the store cities of Naphtali. ⁵When Baasha heard this, he stopped building Ramah and abandoned his work. ⁶Then King Asa brought all the men of Judah, and they carried away from Ramah the stones and timber Baasha had been using. With them he built up Geba and Mizpah.

⁷At that time Hanani the seer came to Asa king of Judah and said to him: "Because you relied on the king of Aram and not on the LORD your God, the army of the king of Aram has escaped from your hand. ⁸Were not the Cushites*b* and Libyans a mighty army with great numbers of chariots and horsemen*c*? Yet when you relied on the LORD, he delivered them into your hand. ⁹For the eyes of the LORD range throughout the earth to strengthen those whose hearts are fully committed to him. You have done a foolish thing, and from now on you will be at war."

¹⁰Asa was angry with the seer because of this; he was so enraged that he put him in prison. At the same time Asa brutally oppressed some of the people.

¹¹The events of Asa's reign, from beginning to end, are written in the book of the kings of Judah and Israel. ¹²In the thirty-ninth year of his reign Asa was afflicted with a disease in his feet. Though his disease was severe, even in his illness he did not seek help from the LORD, but only from the physicians. ¹³Then in the forty-first year of his reign Asa died and rested with his ancestors. ¹⁴They buried him in the tomb that he had cut out for himself in the City of David. They laid him on a bier covered with spices and various blended perfumes, and they made a huge fire in his honor.

Jehoshaphat King of Judah

17 Jehoshaphat his son succeeded him as king and strengthened himself against Israel. ²He stationed troops in all the fortified cities of Judah and put garrisons in

a 4 Also known as *Abel Beth Maakah*   *b 8* That is, people from the upper Nile region
c 8 Or *charioteers*

Judah and in the towns of Ephraim that his father Asa had captured.

[3] The LORD was with Jehoshaphat because he followed the ways of his father David before him. He did not consult the Baals [4] but sought the God of his father and followed his commands rather than the practices of Israel. [5] The LORD established the kingdom under his control; and all Judah brought gifts to Jehoshaphat, so that he had great wealth and honor. [6] His heart was devoted to the ways of the LORD; furthermore, he removed the high places and the Asherah poles from Judah.

[7] In the third year of his reign he sent his officials Ben-Hail, Obadiah, Zechariah, Nethanel and Micaiah to teach in the towns of Judah. [8] With them were certain Levites — Shemaiah, Nethaniah, Zebadiah, Asahel, Shemiramoth, Jehonathan, Adonijah, Tobijah and Tob-Adonijah — and the priests Elishama and Jehoram. [9] They taught throughout Judah, taking with them the Book of the Law of the LORD; they went around to all the towns of Judah and taught the people.

[10] The fear of the LORD fell on all the kingdoms of the lands surrounding Judah, so that they did not go to war against Jehoshaphat. [11] Some Philistines brought Jehoshaphat gifts and silver as tribute, and the Arabs brought him flocks: seven thousand seven hundred rams and seven thousand seven hundred goats.

[12] Jehoshaphat became more and more powerful; he built forts and store cities in Judah [13] and had large supplies in the towns of Judah. He also kept experienced fighting men in Jerusalem. [14] Their enrollment by families was as follows:

From Judah, commanders of units of 1,000:

Adnah the commander, with 300,000 fighting men;

[15] next, Jehohanan the commander, with 280,000;

[16] next, Amasiah son of Zikri, who volunteered himself for the service of the LORD, with 200,000.

[17] From Benjamin:

Eliada, a valiant soldier, with 200,000 men armed with bows and shields;

[18] next, Jehozabad, with 180,000 men armed for battle.

[19] These were the men who served the king, besides those he stationed in the fortified cities throughout Judah.

Micaiah Prophesies Against Ahab

18 Now Jehoshaphat had great wealth and honor, and he allied himself with Ahab by marriage. [2] Some years later he went down to see Ahab in Samaria. Ahab slaughtered many sheep and cattle for him and the people with him and urged him to attack Ramoth Gilead. [3] Ahab king of Israel asked Jehoshaphat king of Judah, "Will you go with me against Ramoth Gilead?"

Jehoshaphat replied, "I am as you are, and my people as your people; we will join you in the war." [4] But Jehoshaphat also said to the king of Israel, "First seek the counsel of the LORD."

[5] So the king of Israel brought together the prophets — four hundred men — and asked them, "Shall we go to war against Ramoth Gilead, or shall I not?"

"Go," they answered, "for God will give it into the king's hand."

[6] But Jehoshaphat asked, "Is there no longer a prophet of the LORD here whom we can inquire of?"

[7] The king of Israel answered Jehoshaphat, "There is still one prophet through whom we can inquire of the LORD, but I hate him because he never prophesies anything good about me, but always bad. He is Micaiah son of Imlah."

"The king should not say such a thing," Jehoshaphat replied.

[8] So the king of Israel called one of his officials and said, "Bring Micaiah son of Imlah at once."

[9] Dressed in their royal robes, the king of Israel and Jehoshaphat king of Judah were sitting on their thrones at the threshing floor by the entrance of the gate of Samaria, with all the prophets prophesying before them. [10] Now Zedekiah son of Kenaanah had made iron horns, and he declared, "This is what the LORD says: 'With these you will gore the Arameans until they are destroyed.'"

[11] All the other prophets were prophesying the same thing. "Attack Ramoth Gilead and be victorious," they said, "for the LORD will give it into the king's hand."

[12] The messenger who had gone to summon Micaiah said to him, "Look, the other

UNWISE DUDES

READ: 2 CHRONICLES 18:9-27

The Bible is full of more subtle examples of the bad influences of others. Think about the first family: Adam fell with a little help from Eve (Genesis 3:6). Jesus' disciples constantly needled each other about who would be greatest among them (Luke 9:46–48; 22:24–27). James and John dragged their mother into the fray (Matthew 20:20–22). Jesus healed ten men with leprosy, yet only one returned to thank him; the other nine did the peer pressure thing (Luke 17:11–19).

Our friends mold our thoughts, tastes, and even our patterns of speech. What we put into our heads and hearts today will influence our choices tomorrow.

We don't prearrange life-changing moments. We don't punch a date in our cell phones to schedule our next fork in the road—they just happen. And when they do, who do we turn to? It's usually the people right beside us. We have to surround ourselves with people who stretch and challenge us, people we respect and admire and want to emulate. We hang with them and ask questions. We watch and listen more than we talk. We take wise counsel.

Our counsel consists of the people, things, and ideas that pour into us, shaping our thoughts and sparking our actions. To delight in the law of the Lord is to absorb infinitely wise counsel. The believer has no greater need.

BUILDING
FAITH
WISDOM
STRENGTH

prophets without exception are predicting success for the king. Let your word agree with theirs, and speak favorably."

¹³ But Micaiah said, "As surely as the LORD lives, I can tell him only what my God says."

¹⁴ When he arrived, the king asked him, "Micaiah, shall we go to war against Ramoth Gilead, or shall I not?"

"Attack and be victorious," he answered, "for they will be given into your hand."

¹⁵ The king said to him, "How many times must I make you swear to tell me nothing but the truth in the name of the LORD?"

¹⁶ Then Micaiah answered, "I saw all Israel scattered on the hills like sheep without a shepherd, and the LORD said, 'These people have no master. Let each one go home in peace.'"

¹⁷ The king of Israel said to Jehoshaphat, "Didn't I tell you that he never prophesies anything good about me, but only bad?"

¹⁸ Micaiah continued, "Therefore hear the word of the LORD: I saw the LORD sitting on his throne with all the multitudes of heaven standing on his right and on his left. ¹⁹ And the LORD said, 'Who will entice Ahab king of Israel into attacking Ramoth Gilead and going to his death there?'

"One suggested this, and another that. ²⁰ Finally, a spirit came forward, stood before the LORD and said, 'I will entice him.'

"'By what means?' the LORD asked.

²¹ "'I will go and be a deceiving spirit in the mouths of all his prophets,' he said.

"'You will succeed in enticing him,' said the LORD. 'Go and do it.'

²² "So now the LORD has put a deceiving spirit in the mouths of these prophets of yours. The LORD has decreed disaster for you."

²³ Then Zedekiah son of Kenaanah went up and slapped Micaiah in the face. "Which way did the spirit from*a* the LORD go when he went from me to speak to you?" he asked.

²⁴ Micaiah replied, "You will find out on the day you go to hide in an inner room."

²⁵ The king of Israel then ordered, "Take Micaiah and send him back to Amon the ruler of the city and to Joash the king's son, ²⁶ and say, 'This is what the king says: Put this fellow in prison and give him nothing but bread and water until I return safely.'"

²⁷ Micaiah declared, "If you ever return safely, the LORD has not spoken through me." Then he added, "Mark my words, all you people!"

Ahab Killed at Ramoth Gilead

²⁸ So the king of Israel and Jehoshaphat king of Judah went up to Ramoth Gilead. ²⁹ The king of Israel said to Jehoshaphat, "I will enter the battle in disguise, but you wear your royal robes." So the king of Israel disguised himself and went into battle.

³⁰ Now the king of Aram had ordered his chariot commanders, "Do not fight with anyone, small or great, except the king of Israel." ³¹ When the chariot commanders saw Jehoshaphat, they thought, "This is the king of Israel." So they turned to attack him, but Jehoshaphat cried out, and the LORD helped him. God drew them away from him, ³² for when the chariot commanders saw that he was not the king of Israel, they stopped pursuing him.

³³ But someone drew his bow at random and hit the king of Israel between the breastplate and the scale armor. The king told the chariot driver, "Wheel around and get me out of the fighting. I've been wounded." ³⁴ All day long the battle raged, and the king of Israel propped himself up in his chariot facing the Arameans until evening. Then at sunset he died.

19 When Jehoshaphat king of Judah returned safely to his palace in Jerusalem, ² Jehu the seer, the son of Hanani, went out to meet him and said to the king, "Should you help the wicked and love*b* those who hate the LORD? Because of this, the wrath of the LORD is on you. ³ There is, however, some good in you, for you have rid the land of the Asherah poles and have set your heart on seeking God."

Jehoshaphat Appoints Judges

⁴ Jehoshaphat lived in Jerusalem, and he went out again among the people from Beersheba to the hill country of Ephraim and turned them back to the LORD, the God of their ancestors. ⁵ He appointed judges in the land, in each of the fortified cities of Judah. ⁶ He told them, "Consider carefully what you do, because you are not judging for mere

---

a 23 Or *Spirit of*   *b* 2 Or *and make alliances with*

STRONG BELIEVER

READ: 2 CHRONICLES 19:2

When Jehu the prophet challenges King Jehoshaphat about helping the wicked and loving people who hate God, it might sound like he's going against Jesus' command to "love your enemies and pray for those who persecute you" (Matthew 5:44). But Jehu was out to make a different point.

Jehoshaphat ruled the southern kingdom of Judah at the same time Ahab reigned in the northern kingdom of Israel. Ahab and his wife Jezebel had a reputation as the most evil leaders in the history of God's people. When Jehoshaphat allied himself with Ahab by letting his son marry Ahab's daughter (2 Chronicles 18:1), God wasn't happy with the cozy relationship between the royal families.

When Jehoshaphat goes into battle with Ahab against a common enemy, the king of Aram, the Lord grows even more upset. That's when Jehu the prophet speaks up. Jehoshaphat sinned by teaming up with a king bent on evil. The king wasn't merely befriending notorious Ahab; he had become a partner in crime.

All day long you meet people who don't know God. They need your love and help, and the Bible is jammed with ideas for reaching out to them. But you have to be honest with yourself and not cross an important line. If you let nonbelievers lead you into sin, you're not exactly demonstrating God's kindness.

BUILDING FAITH WISDOM STRENGTH

mortals but for the LORD, who is with you whenever you give a verdict. ⁷Now let the fear of the LORD be on you. Judge carefully, for with the LORD our God there is no injustice or partiality or bribery."

⁸In Jerusalem also, Jehoshaphat appointed some of the Levites, priests and heads of Israelite families to administer the law of the LORD and to settle disputes. And they lived in Jerusalem. ⁹He gave them these orders: "You must serve faithfully and wholeheartedly in the fear of the LORD. ¹⁰In every case that comes before you from your people who live in the cities — whether bloodshed or other concerns of the law, commands, decrees or regulations — you are to warn them not to sin against the LORD; otherwise his wrath will come on you and your people. Do this, and you will not sin.

¹¹"Amariah the chief priest will be over you in any matter concerning the LORD, and Zebadiah son of Ishmael, the leader of the tribe of Judah, will be over you in any matter concerning the king, and the Levites will serve as officials before you. Act with courage, and may the LORD be with those who do well."

Jehoshaphat Defeats Moab and Ammon

20 After this, the Moabites and Ammonites with some of the Meunites*ᵃ* came to wage war against Jehoshaphat.

²Some people came and told Jehoshaphat, "A vast army is coming against you from Edom,*ᵇ* from the other side of the Dead Sea. It is already in Hazezon Tamar" (that is, En Gedi). ³Alarmed, Jehoshaphat resolved to inquire of the LORD, and he proclaimed a fast for all Judah. ⁴The people of Judah came together to seek help from the LORD; indeed, they came from every town in Judah to seek him.

⁵Then Jehoshaphat stood up in the assembly of Judah and Jerusalem at the temple of the LORD in the front of the new courtyard ⁶and said:

"LORD, the God of our ancestors, are you not the God who is in heaven? You rule over all the kingdoms of the nations. Power and might are in your hand, and no one can withstand you.

⁷Our God, did you not drive out the inhabitants of this land before your people Israel and give it forever to the descendants of Abraham your friend? ⁸They have lived in it and have built in it a sanctuary for your Name, saying, ⁹'If calamity comes upon us, whether the sword of judgment, or plague or famine, we will stand in your presence before this temple that bears your Name and will cry out to you in our distress, and you will hear us and save us.'

¹⁰"But now here are men from Ammon, Moab and Mount Seir, whose territory you would not allow Israel to invade when they came from Egypt; so they turned away from them and did not destroy them. ¹¹See how they are repaying us by coming to drive us out of the possession you gave us as an inheritance. ¹²Our God, will you not judge them? For we have no power to face this vast army that is attacking us. We do not know what to do, but our eyes are on you."

¹³All the men of Judah, with their wives and children and little ones, stood there before the LORD.

¹⁴Then the Spirit of the LORD came on Jahaziel son of Zechariah, the son of Benaiah, the son of Jeiel, the son of Mattaniah, a Levite and descendant of Asaph, as he stood in the assembly.

¹⁵He said: "Listen, King Jehoshaphat and all who live in Judah and Jerusalem! This is what the LORD says to you: 'Do not be afraid or discouraged because of this vast army. For the battle is not yours, but God's. ¹⁶Tomorrow march down against them. They will be climbing up by the Pass of Ziz, and you will find them at the end of the gorge in the Desert of Jeruel. ¹⁷You will not have to fight this battle. Take up your positions; stand firm and see the deliverance the LORD will give you, Judah and Jerusalem. Do not be afraid; do not be discouraged. Go out to face them tomorrow, and the LORD will be with you.'"

¹⁸Jehoshaphat bowed down with his face to the ground, and all the people of Judah and Jerusalem fell down in worship before the LORD. ¹⁹Then some Levites from the

---

ᵃ 1 Some Septuagint manuscripts; Hebrew *Ammonites*   *ᵇ 2* One Hebrew manuscript; most Hebrew manuscripts, Septuagint and Vulgate *Aram*

Kohathites and Korahites stood up and praised the LORD, the God of Israel, with a very loud voice.

²⁰Early in the morning they left for the Desert of Tekoa. As they set out, Jehoshaphat stood and said, "Listen to me, Judah and people of Jerusalem! Have faith in the LORD your God and you will be upheld; have faith in his prophets and you will be successful." ²¹After consulting the people, Jehoshaphat appointed men to sing to the LORD and to praise him for the splendor of his*ᵃ* holiness as they went out at the head of the army, saying:

"Give thanks to the LORD,
for his love endures forever."

²²As they began to sing and praise, the LORD set ambushes against the men of Ammon and Moab and Mount Seir who were invading Judah, and they were defeated. ²³The Ammonites and Moabites rose up against the men from Mount Seir to destroy and annihilate them. After they finished slaughtering the men from Seir, they helped to destroy one another.

²⁴When the men of Judah came to the place that overlooks the desert and looked toward the vast army, they saw only dead bodies lying on the ground; no one had escaped. ²⁵So Jehoshaphat and his men went to carry off their plunder, and they found among them a great amount of equipment and clothing*ᵇ* and also articles of value—more than they could take away. There was so much plunder that it took three days to collect it. ²⁶On the fourth day they assembled in the Valley of Berakah, where they praised the LORD. This is why it is called the Valley of Berakah*ᶜ* to this day.

²⁷Then, led by Jehoshaphat, all the men of Judah and Jerusalem returned joyfully to Jerusalem, for the LORD had given them cause to rejoice over their enemies. ²⁸They entered Jerusalem and went to the temple of the LORD with harps and lyres and trumpets.

²⁹The fear of God came on all the surrounding kingdoms when they heard how the LORD had fought against the enemies of Israel. ³⁰And the kingdom of Jehoshaphat was at peace, for his God had given him rest on every side.

The End of Jehoshaphat's Reign

³¹So Jehoshaphat reigned over Judah. He was thirty-five years old when he became king of Judah, and he reigned in Jerusalem twenty-five years. His mother's name was Azubah daughter of Shilhi. ³²He followed the ways of his father Asa and did not stray from them; he did what was right in the eyes of the LORD. ³³The high places, however, were not removed, and the people still had not set their hearts on the God of their ancestors.

³⁴The other events of Jehoshaphat's reign, from beginning to end, are written in the annals of Jehu son of Hanani, which are recorded in the book of the kings of Israel.

³⁵Later, Jehoshaphat king of Judah made an alliance with Ahaziah king of Israel, whose ways were wicked. ³⁶He agreed with him to construct a fleet of trading ships.*ᵈ* After these were built at Ezion Geber, ³⁷Eliezer son of Dodavahu of Mareshah prophesied against Jehoshaphat, saying, "Because you have made an alliance with Ahaziah, the LORD will destroy what you have made." The ships were wrecked and were not able to set sail to trade.*ᵉ*

21 Then Jehoshaphat rested with his ancestors and was buried with them in the City of David. And Jehoram his son succeeded him as king. ²Jehoram's brothers, the sons of Jehoshaphat, were Azariah, Jehiel, Zechariah, Azariahu, Michael and Shephatiah. All these were sons of Jehoshaphat king of Israel.*ᶠ* ³Their father had given them many gifts of silver and gold and articles of value, as well as fortified cities in Judah, but he had given the kingdom to Jehoram because he was his firstborn son.

Jehoram King of Judah

⁴When Jehoram established himself firmly over his father's kingdom, he put all his brothers to the sword along with some of the officials of Israel. ⁵Jehoram was thirty-two years old when he became king, and he reigned in Jerusalem eight years. ⁶He followed the ways of the kings of Israel, as the house of Ahab had done, for he married a daughter of Ahab. He did evil in the eyes of

---

ᵃ 21 Or *him with the splendor of*   *ᵇ 25* Some Hebrew manuscripts and Vulgate; most Hebrew manuscripts *corpses*   *ᶜ 26 Berakah* means *praise.*   *ᵈ 36* Hebrew *of ships that could go to Tarshish*   *ᵉ 37* Hebrew *sail for Tarshish*   *ᶠ 2* That is, Judah, as frequently in 2 Chronicles

JEHOSHAPHAT

Jehoshaphat stood and said, "Listen to me, Judah and people of Jerusalem! Have faith in the LORD your God and you will be upheld." 2 CHRONICLES 20:20

HIS NAME MEANS: "the LORD is judge"
READ HIS STORY: *1 Kings 22:41–50; 2 Kings 3; 2 Chronicles 17:1–21:1*

OF THE BIBLE

Jehoshaphat followed after the Lord and even sent teachers and priests throughout the land to teach the people God's Word. Jehoshaphat was king over Judah when news came that a huge army was on its way to attack and destroy him. This news was so terrible that 2 Chronicles 20:3-4 says, "Alarmed, Jehoshaphat resolved to inquire of the LORD, and he proclaimed a fast for all Judah. The people of Judah came together to seek help from the LORD; indeed, they came from every town in Judah to seek him."

When he was afraid, Jehoshaphat called on the Lord for help. He knew that ultimately God was the one in control. God had the answers. It was then that a message came from the Lord. In 2 Chronicles 20:15, Jahaziel said, "Listen, King Jehoshaphat and all who live in Judah and Jerusalem! This is what the LORD says to you: 'Do not be afraid or discouraged because of this vast army. For the battle is not yours, but God's.'"

Jehoshaphat was strong but humble. He listened to God's messengers and took time to seek the Lord, setting an example of faithfulness for his family and nation even when faced with battle and hard choices.

Is there something that overwhelms you today? Is your heart filled with fear, worry, or dread? Call out to God. Ask him to help you. Then cling to the same promise God gave to Jehoshaphat. The battle belongs to the Lord.

the Lord. **7** Nevertheless, because of the covenant the Lord had made with David, the Lord was not willing to destroy the house of David. He had promised to maintain a lamp for him and his descendants forever.

8 In the time of Jehoram, Edom rebelled against Judah and set up its own king. **9** So Jehoram went there with his officers and all his chariots. The Edomites surrounded him and his chariot commanders, but he rose up and broke through by night. **10** To this day Edom has been in rebellion against Judah.

Libnah revolted at the same time, because Jehoram had forsaken the Lord, the God of his ancestors. **11** He had also built high places on the hills of Judah and had caused the people of Jerusalem to prostitute themselves and had led Judah astray.

12 Jehoram received a letter from Elijah the prophet, which said:

"This is what the Lord, the God of your father David, says: 'You have not followed the ways of your father Jehoshaphat or of Asa king of Judah. **13** But you have followed the ways of the kings of Israel, and you have led Judah and the people of Jerusalem to prostitute themselves, just as the house of Ahab did. You have also murdered your own brothers, members of your own family, men who were better than you. **14** So now the Lord is about to strike your people, your sons, your wives and everything that is yours, with a heavy blow. **15** You yourself will be very ill with a lingering disease of the bowels, until the disease causes your bowels to come out.' "

16 The Lord aroused against Jehoram the hostility of the Philistines and of the Arabs who lived near the Cushites. **17** They attacked Judah, invaded it and carried off all the goods found in the king's palace, together with his sons and wives. Not a son was left to him except Ahaziah,[a] the youngest.

18 After all this, the Lord afflicted Jehoram with an incurable disease of the bowels. **19** In the course of time, at the end of the second year, his bowels came out because of the disease, and he died in great pain. His people made no funeral fire in his honor, as they had for his predecessors.

20 Jehoram was thirty-two years old when he became king, and he reigned in Jerusalem eight years. He passed away, to no one's regret, and was buried in the City of David, but not in the tombs of the kings.

Ahaziah King of Judah

22 The people of Jerusalem made Ahaziah, Jehoram's youngest son, king in his place, since the raiders, who came with the Arabs into the camp, had killed all the older sons. So Ahaziah son of Jehoram king of Judah began to reign.

2 Ahaziah was twenty-two[b] years old when he became king, and he reigned in Jerusalem one year. His mother's name was Athaliah, a granddaughter of Omri.

3 He too followed the ways of the house of Ahab, for his mother encouraged him to act wickedly. **4** He did evil in the eyes of the Lord, as the house of Ahab had done, for after his father's death they became his advisers, to his undoing. **5** He also followed their counsel when he went with Joram[c] son of Ahab king of Israel to wage war against Hazael king of Aram at Ramoth Gilead. The Arameans wounded Joram; **6** so he returned to Jezreel to recover from the wounds they had inflicted on him at Ramoth[d] in his battle with Hazael king of Aram.

Then Ahaziah[e] son of Jehoram king of Judah went down to Jezreel to see Joram son of Ahab because he had been wounded.

7 Through Ahaziah's visit to Joram, God brought about Ahaziah's downfall. When Ahaziah arrived, he went out with Joram to meet Jehu son of Nimshi, whom the Lord had anointed to destroy the house of Ahab. **8** While Jehu was executing judgment on the house of Ahab, he found the officials of Judah and the sons of Ahaziah's relatives, who had been attending Ahaziah, and he killed them. **9** He then went in search of Ahaziah, and his men captured him while he was hiding in Samaria. He was brought to Jehu and put to death. They buried him, for they said, "He was a son of Jehoshaphat, who sought

---

a 17 Hebrew *Jehoahaz,* a variant of *Ahaziah*   *b 2* Some Septuagint manuscripts and Syriac (see also 2 Kings 8:26); Hebrew *forty-two*   *c 5* Hebrew *Jehoram,* a variant of *Joram;* also in verses 6 and 7
d 6 Hebrew *Ramah,* a variant of *Ramoth*   *e 6* Some Hebrew manuscripts, Septuagint, Vulgate and Syriac (see also 2 Kings 8:29); most Hebrew manuscripts *Azariah*

the Lord with all his heart." So there was no one in the house of Ahaziah powerful enough to retain the kingdom.

Athaliah and Joash

¹⁰When Athaliah the mother of Ahaziah saw that her son was dead, she proceeded to destroy the whole royal family of the house of Judah. ¹¹But Jehosheba,ᵃ the daughter of King Jehoram, took Joash son of Ahaziah and stole him away from among the royal princes who were about to be murdered and put him and his nurse in a bedroom. Because Jehosheba,ᵃ the daughter of King Jehoram and wife of the priest Jehoiada, was Ahaziah's sister, she hid the child from Athaliah so she could not kill him. ¹²He remained hidden with them at the temple of God for six years while Athaliah ruled the land.

23 In the seventh year Jehoiada showed his strength. He made a covenant with the commanders of units of a hundred: Azariah son of Jeroham, Ishmael son of Jehohanan, Azariah son of Obed, Maaseiah son of Adaiah, and Elishaphat son of Zikri. ²They went throughout Judah and gathered the Levites and the heads of Israelite families from all the towns. When they came to Jerusalem, ³the whole assembly made a covenant with the king at the temple of God.

Jehoiada said to them, "The king's son shall reign, as the Lord promised concerning the descendants of David. ⁴Now this is what you are to do: A third of you priests and Levites who are going on duty on the Sabbath are to keep watch at the doors, ⁵a third of you at the royal palace and a third at the Foundation Gate, and all the others are to be in the courtyards of the temple of the Lord. ⁶No one is to enter the temple of the Lord except the priests and Levites on duty; they may enter because they are consecrated, but all the others are to observe the Lord's command not to enter.ᵇ ⁷The Levites are to station themselves around the king, each with weapon in hand. Anyone who enters the temple is to be put to death. Stay close to the king wherever he goes."

⁸The Levites and all the men of Judah did just as Jehoiada the priest ordered. Each one took his men—those who were going on duty on the Sabbath and those who were going off duty—for Jehoiada the priest had not released any of the divisions. ⁹Then he gave the commanders of units of a hundred the spears and the large and small shields that had belonged to King David and that were in the temple of God. ¹⁰He stationed all the men, each with his weapon in his hand, around the king—near the altar and the temple, from the south side to the north side of the temple.

¹¹Jehoiada and his sons brought out the king's son and put the crown on him; they presented him with a copy of the covenant and proclaimed him king. They anointed him and shouted, "Long live the king!"

¹²When Athaliah heard the noise of the people running and cheering the king, she went to them at the temple of the Lord. ¹³She looked, and there was the king, standing by his pillar at the entrance. The officers and the trumpeters were beside the king, and all the people of the land were rejoicing and blowing trumpets, and musicians with their instruments were leading the praises. Then Athaliah tore her robes and shouted, "Treason! Treason!"

¹⁴Jehoiada the priest sent out the commanders of units of a hundred, who were in charge of the troops, and said to them: "Bring her out between the ranksᶜ and put to the sword anyone who follows her." For the priest had said, "Do not put her to death at the temple of the Lord." ¹⁵So they seized her as she reached the entrance of the Horse Gate on the palace grounds, and there they put her to death.

¹⁶Jehoiada then made a covenant that he, the people and the kingᵈ would be the Lord's people. ¹⁷All the people went to the temple of Baal and tore it down. They smashed the altars and idols and killed Mattan the priest of Baal in front of the altars.

¹⁸Then Jehoiada placed the oversight of the temple of the Lord in the hands of the Levitical priests, to whom David had made assignments in the temple, to present the burnt offerings of the Lord as written in the Law of Moses, with rejoicing and singing, as David had ordered. ¹⁹He also stationed gatekeepers at the gates of the Lord's temple

ᵃ 11 Hebrew *Jehoshabeath,* a variant of *Jehosheba*   ᵇ 6 Or *are to stand guard where the Lord has assigned them*   ᶜ 14 Or *out from the precincts*   ᵈ 16 Or *covenant between the Lord and the people and the king that they* (see 2 Kings 11:17) so that no one who was in any way unclean might enter. [20]He took with him the commanders of hundreds, the nobles, the rulers of the people and all the people of the land and brought the king down from the temple of the LORD. They went into the palace through the Upper Gate and seated the king on the royal throne. [21]All the people of the land rejoiced, and the city was calm, because Athaliah had been slain with the sword.

Joash Repairs the Temple

24 Joash was seven years old when he became king, and he reigned in Jerusalem forty years. His mother's name was Zibiah; she was from Beersheba. [2]Joash did what was right in the eyes of the LORD all the years of Jehoiada the priest. [3]Jehoiada chose two wives for him, and he had sons and daughters.

[4]Some time later Joash decided to restore the temple of the LORD. [5]He called together the priests and Levites and said to them, "Go to the towns of Judah and collect the money due annually from all Israel, to repair the temple of your God. Do it now." But the Levites did not act at once.

[6]Therefore the king summoned Jehoiada the chief priest and said to him, "Why haven't you required the Levites to bring in from Judah and Jerusalem the tax imposed by Moses the servant of the LORD and by the assembly of Israel for the tent of the covenant law?"

[7]Now the sons of that wicked woman Athaliah had broken into the temple of God and had used even its sacred objects for the Baals.

[8]At the king's command, a chest was made and placed outside, at the gate of the temple of the LORD. [9]A proclamation was then issued in Judah and Jerusalem that they should bring to the LORD the tax that Moses the servant of God had required of Israel in the wilderness. [10]All the officials and all the people brought their contributions gladly, dropping them into the chest until it was full. [11]Whenever the chest was brought in by the Levites to the king's officials and they saw that there was a large amount of money, the royal secretary and the officer of the chief priest would come and empty the chest and carry it back to its place. They did this regularly and collected a great amount of money. [12]The king and Jehoiada gave it to those who carried out the work required for the temple of the LORD. They hired masons and carpenters to restore the LORD's temple, and also workers in iron and bronze to repair the temple.

[13]The men in charge of the work were diligent, and the repairs progressed under them. They rebuilt the temple of God according to its original design and reinforced it. [14]When they had finished, they brought the rest of the money to the king and Jehoiada, and with it were made articles for the LORD's temple: articles for the service and for the burnt offerings, and also dishes and other objects of gold and silver. As long as Jehoiada lived, burnt offerings were presented continually in the temple of the LORD.

[15]Now Jehoiada was old and full of years, and he died at the age of a hundred and thirty. [16]He was buried with the kings in the City of David, because of the good he had done in Israel for God and his temple.

The Wickedness of Joash

[17]After the death of Jehoiada, the officials of Judah came and paid homage to the king, and he listened to them. [18]They abandoned the temple of the LORD, the God of their ancestors, and worshiped Asherah poles and idols. Because of their guilt, God's anger came on Judah and Jerusalem. [19]Although the LORD sent prophets to the people to bring them back to him, and though they testified against them, they would not listen.

[20]Then the Spirit of God came on Zechariah son of Jehoiada the priest. He stood before the people and said, "This is what God says: 'Why do you disobey the LORD's commands? You will not prosper. Because you have forsaken the LORD, he has forsaken you.' "

[21]But they plotted against him, and by order of the king they stoned him to death in the courtyard of the LORD's temple. [22]King Joash did not remember the kindness Zechariah's father Jehoiada had shown him but killed his son, who said as he lay dying, "May the LORD see this and call you to account."

[23]At the turn of the year,[a] the army of

---

[a] 23 Probably in the spring

JOASH

Joash was seven years old when he became king, and he reigned in Jerusalem forty years ... Joash did what was right in the eyes of the LORD all the years of Jehoiada the priest. 2 CHRONICLES 24:1–2

HIS NAME MEANS: "the LORD has given"
READ HIS STORY: *2 Kings 11–12; 2 Chronicles 22:10–24:27*

The target of an assassination attempt as a baby, Joash started life on the run. He spent his first six years in hiding with a nurse. No outside contact, no playmates, and no parents.

A few godly people—his nurse, and his aunt Jehosheba, and his uncle Jehoiada (who was a priest)—saved Joash's life so he would rightfully inherit the throne. At seven years old, Joash came out of hiding and became king. Needless to say, he was a little young and sheltered for such a big job. He had to trust the few people who had protected him. And he did. He relied on Jehoiada as his counselor and guide. Joash followed everything Jehoiada told him to do, following God's ways to a T.

As Joash grew up, however, he never *grew up*. He relied so much on those around him—which is usually a good thing—that he never developed the maturity and wisdom to make his own decisions and lead his people confidently. This wasn't a problem while Jehoiada was alive and well. But once his uncle died (at 130 years old), Joash had to find someone else to lean on. He didn't choose God. The officials who ran to his side had no any interest in keeping Jehoiada's legacy (2 Chronicles 24:17-19). Unfortunately, Joash followed their lead, forgot everything Jehoiada had ever taught him and fell away from God.

Aram marched against Joash; it invaded Judah and Jerusalem and killed all the leaders of the people. They sent all the plunder to their king in Damascus. ²⁴Although the Aramean army had come with only a few men, the LORD delivered into their hands a much larger army. Because Judah had forsaken the LORD, the God of their ancestors, judgment was executed on Joash. ²⁵When the Arameans withdrew, they left Joash severely wounded. His officials conspired against him for murdering the son of Jehoiada the priest, and they killed him in his bed. So he died and was buried in the City of David, but not in the tombs of the kings.

²⁶Those who conspired against him were Zabad,ᵃ son of Shimeath an Ammonite woman, and Jehozabad, son of Shimrithᵇ a Moabite woman. ²⁷The account of his sons, the many prophecies about him, and the record of the restoration of the temple of God are written in the annotations on the book of the kings. And Amaziah his son succeeded him as king.

Amaziah King of Judah

25 Amaziah was twenty-five years old when he became king, and he reigned in Jerusalem twenty-nine years. His mother's name was Jehoaddan; she was from Jerusalem. ²He did what was right in the eyes of the LORD, but not wholeheartedly. ³After the kingdom was firmly in his control, he executed the officials who had murdered his father the king. ⁴Yet he did not put their children to death, but acted in accordance with what is written in the Law, in the Book of Moses, where the LORD commanded: "Parents shall not be put to death for their children, nor children be put to death for their parents; each will die for their own sin."ᶜ

⁵Amaziah called the people of Judah together and assigned them according to their families to commanders of thousands and commanders of hundreds for all Judah and Benjamin. He then mustered those twenty years old or more and found that there were three hundred thousand men fit for military service, able to handle the spear and shield. ⁶He also hired a hundred thousand fighting men from Israel for a hundred talentsᵈ of silver.

⁷But a man of God came to him and said, "Your Majesty, these troops from Israel must not march with you, for the LORD is not with Israel—not with any of the people of Ephraim. ⁸Even if you go and fight courageously in battle, God will overthrow you before the enemy, for God has the power to help or to overthrow."

⁹Amaziah asked the man of God, "But what about the hundred talents I paid for these Israelite troops?"

The man of God replied, "The LORD can give you much more than that."

¹⁰So Amaziah dismissed the troops who had come to him from Ephraim and sent them home. They were furious with Judah and left for home in a great rage.

¹¹Amaziah then marshaled his strength and led his army to the Valley of Salt, where he killed ten thousand men of Seir. ¹²The army of Judah also captured ten thousand men alive, took them to the top of a cliff and threw them down so that all were dashed to pieces.

¹³Meanwhile the troops that Amaziah had sent back and had not allowed to take part in the war raided towns belonging to Judah from Samaria to Beth Horon. They killed three thousand people and carried off great quantities of plunder.

¹⁴When Amaziah returned from slaughtering the Edomites, he brought back the gods of the people of Seir. He set them up as his own gods, bowed down to them and burned sacrifices to them. ¹⁵The anger of the LORD burned against Amaziah, and he sent a prophet to him, who said, "Why do you consult this people's gods, which could not save their own people from your hand?"

¹⁶While he was still speaking, the king said to him, "Have we appointed you an adviser to the king? Stop! Why be struck down?"

So the prophet stopped but said, "I know that God has determined to destroy you, because you have done this and have not listened to my counsel."

¹⁷After Amaziah king of Judah consulted his advisers, he sent this challenge to Jehoashᵉ son of Jehoahaz, the son of Jehu, king of Israel: "Come, let us face each other in battle."

ᵃ 26 A variant of *Jozabad*   ᵇ 26 A variant of *Shomer*   ᶜ 4 Deut. 24:16   ᵈ 6 That is, about 3 3/4 tons or about 3.4 metric tons; also in verse 9   ᵉ 17 Hebrew *Joash*, a variant of *Jehoash*; also in verses 18, 21, 23 and 25

[18] But Jehoash king of Israel replied to Amaziah king of Judah: "A thistle in Lebanon sent a message to a cedar in Lebanon, 'Give your daughter to my son in marriage.' Then a wild beast in Lebanon came along and trampled the thistle underfoot. [19] You say to yourself that you have defeated Edom, and now you are arrogant and proud. But stay at home! Why ask for trouble and cause your own downfall and that of Judah also?"

[20] Amaziah, however, would not listen, for God so worked that he might deliver them into the hands of Jehoash, because they sought the gods of Edom. [21] So Jehoash king of Israel attacked. He and Amaziah king of Judah faced each other at Beth Shemesh in Judah. [22] Judah was routed by Israel, and every man fled to his home. [23] Jehoash king of Israel captured Amaziah king of Judah, the son of Joash, the son of Ahaziah,[a] at Beth Shemesh. Then Jehoash brought him to Jerusalem and broke down the wall of Jerusalem from the Ephraim Gate to the Corner Gate — a section about four hundred cubits[b] long. [24] He took all the gold and silver and all the articles found in the temple of God that had been in the care of Obed-Edom, together with the palace treasures and the hostages, and returned to Samaria.

[25] Amaziah son of Joash king of Judah lived for fifteen years after the death of Jehoash son of Jehoahaz king of Israel. [26] As for the other events of Amaziah's reign, from beginning to end, are they not written in the book of the kings of Judah and Israel? [27] From the time that Amaziah turned away from following the LORD, they conspired against him in Jerusalem and he fled to Lachish, but they sent men after him to Lachish and killed him there. [28] He was brought back by horse and was buried with his ancestors in the City of Judah.[c]

Uzziah King of Judah

26 Then all the people of Judah took Uzziah,[d] who was sixteen years old, and made him king in place of his father Amaziah. [2] He was the one who rebuilt Elath and restored it to Judah after Amaziah rested with his ancestors.

[3] Uzziah was sixteen years old when he became king, and he reigned in Jerusalem fifty-two years. His mother's name was Jekoliah; she was from Jerusalem. [4] He did what was right in the eyes of the LORD, just as his father Amaziah had done. [5] He sought God during the days of Zechariah, who instructed him in the fear[e] of God. As long as he sought the LORD, God gave him success.

[6] He went to war against the Philistines and broke down the walls of Gath, Jabneh and Ashdod. He then rebuilt towns near Ashdod and elsewhere among the Philistines. [7] God helped him against the Philistines and against the Arabs who lived in Gur Baal and against the Meunites. [8] The Ammonites brought tribute to Uzziah, and his fame spread as far as the border of Egypt, because he had become very powerful.

[9] Uzziah built towers in Jerusalem at the Corner Gate, at the Valley Gate and at the angle of the wall, and he fortified them. [10] He also built towers in the wilderness and dug many cisterns, because he had much livestock in the foothills and in the plain. He had people working his fields and vineyards in the hills and in the fertile lands, for he loved the soil.

[11] Uzziah had a well-trained army, ready to go out by divisions according to their numbers as mustered by Jeiel the secretary and Maaseiah the officer under the direction of Hananiah, one of the royal officials. [12] The total number of family leaders over the fighting men was 2,600. [13] Under their command was an army of 307,500 men trained for war, a powerful force to support the king against his enemies. [14] Uzziah provided shields, spears, helmets, coats of armor, bows and slingstones for the entire army. [15] In Jerusalem he made devices invented for use on the towers and on the corner defenses so that soldiers could shoot arrows and hurl large stones from the walls. His fame spread far and wide, for he was greatly helped until he became powerful.

[16] But after Uzziah became powerful, his pride led to his downfall. He was unfaithful to the LORD his God, and entered the temple of the LORD to burn incense on the altar

---

[a] 23 Hebrew *Jehoahaz*, a variant of *Ahaziah*   [b] 23 That is, about 600 feet or about 180 meters
[c] 28 Most Hebrew manuscripts; some Hebrew manuscripts, Septuagint, Vulgate and Syriac (see also 2 Kings 14:20) *David*   [d] 1 Also called *Azariah*   [e] 5 Many Hebrew manuscripts, Septuagint and Syriac; other Hebrew manuscripts *vision*

of incense. [17]Azariah the priest with eighty other courageous priests of the LORD followed him in. [18]They confronted King Uzziah and said, "It is not right for you, Uzziah, to burn incense to the LORD. That is for the priests, the descendants of Aaron, who have been consecrated to burn incense. Leave the sanctuary, for you have been unfaithful; and you will not be honored by the LORD God."

[19]Uzziah, who had a censer in his hand ready to burn incense, became angry. While he was raging at the priests in their presence before the incense altar in the LORD's temple, leprosy[a] broke out on his forehead. [20]When Azariah the chief priest and all the other priests looked at him, they saw that he had leprosy on his forehead, so they hurried him out. Indeed, he himself was eager to leave, because the LORD had afflicted him. [21]King Uzziah had leprosy until the day he died. He lived in a separate house[b] — leprous, and banned from the temple of the LORD. Jotham his son had charge of the palace and governed the people of the land.

[22]The other events of Uzziah's reign, from beginning to end, are recorded by the prophet Isaiah son of Amoz. [23]Uzziah rested with his ancestors and was buried near them in a cemetery that belonged to the kings, for people said, "He had leprosy." And Jotham his son succeeded him as king.

Jotham King of Judah

27 Jotham was twenty-five years old when he became king, and he reigned in Jerusalem sixteen years. His mother's name was Jerusha daughter of Zadok. [2]He did what was right in the eyes of the LORD, just as his father Uzziah had done, but unlike him he did not enter the temple of the LORD. The people, however, continued their corrupt practices. [3]Jotham rebuilt the Upper Gate of the temple of the LORD and did extensive work on the wall at the hill of Ophel. [4]He built towns in the hill country of Judah and forts and towers in the wooded areas.

[5]Jotham waged war against the king of the Ammonites and conquered them. That year the Ammonites paid him a hundred talents[c] of silver, ten thousand cors[d] of wheat and ten

thousand cors[e] of barley. The Ammonites brought him the same amount also in the second and third years.

[6]Jotham grew powerful because he walked steadfastly before the LORD his God.

[7]The other events in Jotham's reign, including all his wars and the other things he did, are written in the book of the kings of Israel and Judah. [8]He was twenty-five years old when he became king, and he reigned in Jerusalem sixteen years. [9]Jotham rested with his ancestors and was buried in the City of David. And Ahaz his son succeeded him as king.

Ahaz King of Judah

28 Ahaz was twenty years old when he became king, and he reigned in Jerusalem sixteen years. Unlike David his father, he did not do what was right in the eyes of the LORD. [2]He followed the ways of the kings of Israel and also made idols for worshiping the Baals. [3]He burned sacrifices in the Valley of Ben Hinnom and sacrificed his children in the fire, engaging in the detestable practices of the nations the LORD had driven out before the Israelites. [4]He offered sacrifices and burned incense at the high places, on the hilltops and under every spreading tree.

[5]Therefore the LORD his God delivered him into the hands of the king of Aram. The Arameans defeated him and took many of his people as prisoners and brought them to Damascus.

He was also given into the hands of the king of Israel, who inflicted heavy casualties on him. [6]In one day Pekah son of Remaliah killed a hundred and twenty thousand soldiers in Judah — because Judah had forsaken the LORD, the God of their ancestors. [7]Zikri, an Ephraimite warrior, killed Maaseiah the king's son, Azrikam the officer in charge of the palace, and Elkanah, second to the king. [8]The men of Israel took captive from their fellow Israelites who were from Judah two hundred thousand wives, sons and daughters. They also took a great deal of plunder, which they carried back to Samaria.

[9]But a prophet of the LORD named Oded was there, and he went out to meet the army

---

[a] 19 The Hebrew for *leprosy* was used for various diseases affecting the skin; also in verses 20, 21 and 23.
[b] 21 Or *in a house where he was relieved of responsibilities*   [c] 5 That is, about 3 3/4 tons or about 3.4 metric tons   [d] 5 That is, probably about 1,800 tons or about 1,600 metric tons of wheat   [e] 5 That is, probably about 1,500 tons or about 1,350 metric tons of barley

when it returned to Samaria. He said to them, "Because the LORD, the God of your ancestors, was angry with Judah, he gave them into your hand. But you have slaughtered them in a rage that reaches to heaven. [10]And now you intend to make the men and women of Judah and Jerusalem your slaves. But aren't you also guilty of sins against the LORD your God? [11]Now listen to me! Send back your fellow Israelites you have taken as prisoners, for the LORD's fierce anger rests on you."

[12]Then some of the leaders in Ephraim—Azariah son of Jehohanan, Berekiah son of Meshillemoth, Jehizkiah son of Shallum, and Amasa son of Hadlai—confronted those who were arriving from the war. [13]"You must not bring those prisoners here," they said, "or we will be guilty before the LORD. Do you intend to add to our sin and guilt? For our guilt is already great, and his fierce anger rests on Israel."

[14]So the soldiers gave up the prisoners and plunder in the presence of the officials and all the assembly. [15]The men designated by name took the prisoners, and from the plunder they clothed all who were naked. They provided them with clothes and sandals, food and drink, and healing balm. All those who were weak they put on donkeys. So they took them back to their fellow Israelites at Jericho, the City of Palms, and returned to Samaria.

[16]At that time King Ahaz sent to the kings[a] of Assyria for help. [17]The Edomites had again come and attacked Judah and carried away prisoners, [18]while the Philistines had raided towns in the foothills and in the Negev of Judah. They captured and occupied Beth Shemesh, Aijalon and Gederoth, as well as Soko, Timnah and Gimzo, with their surrounding villages. [19]The LORD had humbled Judah because of Ahaz king of Israel,[b] for he had promoted wickedness in Judah and had been most unfaithful to the LORD. [20]Tiglath-Pileser[c] king of Assyria came to him, but he gave him trouble instead of help. [21]Ahaz took some of the things from the temple of the LORD and from the royal palace and from the officials and presented them to the king of Assyria, but that did not help him.

[22]In his time of trouble King Ahaz became even more unfaithful to the LORD. [23]He offered sacrifices to the gods of Damascus, who had defeated him; for he thought, "Since the gods of the kings of Aram have helped them, I will sacrifice to them so they will help me." But they were his downfall and the downfall of all Israel.

[24]Ahaz gathered together the furnishings from the temple of God and cut them in pieces. He shut the doors of the LORD's temple and set up altars at every street corner in Jerusalem. [25]In every town in Judah he built high places to burn sacrifices to other gods and aroused the anger of the LORD, the God of his ancestors.

[26]The other events of his reign and all his ways, from beginning to end, are written in the book of the kings of Judah and Israel. [27]Ahaz rested with his ancestors and was buried in the city of Jerusalem, but he was not placed in the tombs of the kings of Israel. And Hezekiah his son succeeded him as king.

Hezekiah Purifies the Temple

29 Hezekiah was twenty-five years old when he became king, and he reigned in Jerusalem twenty-nine years. His mother's name was Abijah daughter of Zechariah. [2]He did what was right in the eyes of the LORD, just as his father David had done.

[3]In the first month of the first year of his reign, he opened the doors of the temple of the LORD and repaired them. [4]He brought in the priests and the Levites, assembled them in the square on the east side [5]and said: "Listen to me, Levites! Consecrate yourselves now and consecrate the temple of the LORD, the God of your ancestors. Remove all defilement from the sanctuary. [6]Our parents were unfaithful; they did evil in the eyes of the LORD our God and forsook him. They turned their faces away from the LORD's dwelling place and turned their backs on him. [7]They also shut the doors of the portico and put out the lamps. They did not burn incense or present any burnt offerings at the sanctuary to the God of Israel. [8]Therefore, the anger of the LORD has fallen on Judah and Jerusalem; he has made them an object of dread and

---

[a] 16 Most Hebrew manuscripts; one Hebrew manuscript, Septuagint and Vulgate (see also 2 Kings 16:7) king   [b] 19 That is, Judah, as frequently in 2 Chronicles   [c] 20 Hebrew Tilgath-Pilneser, a variant of Tiglath-Pileser

horror and scorn, as you can see with your own eyes. ⁹This is why our fathers have fallen by the sword and why our sons and daughters and our wives are in captivity. ¹⁰Now I intend to make a covenant with the LORD, the God of Israel, so that his fierce anger will turn away from us. ¹¹My sons, do not be negligent now, for the LORD has chosen you to stand before him and serve him, to minister before him and to burn incense."

¹²Then these Levites set to work:

from the Kohathites,

Mahath son of Amasai and Joel son of Azariah;

from the Merarites,

Kish son of Abdi and Azariah son of Jehallelel;

from the Gershonites,

Joah son of Zimmah and Eden son of Joah;

¹³from the descendants of Elizaphan,

Shimri and Jeiel;

from the descendants of Asaph,

Zechariah and Mattaniah;

¹⁴from the descendants of Heman,

Jehiel and Shimei;

from the descendants of Jeduthun,

Shemaiah and Uzziel.

¹⁵When they had assembled their fellow Levites and consecrated themselves, they went in to purify the temple of the LORD, as the king had ordered, following the word of the LORD. ¹⁶The priests went into the sanctuary of the LORD to purify it. They brought out to the courtyard of the LORD's temple everything unclean that they found in the temple of the LORD. The Levites took it and carried it out to the Kidron Valley. ¹⁷They began the consecration on the first day of the first month, and by the eighth day of the month they reached the portico of the LORD. For eight more days they consecrated the temple of the LORD itself, finishing on the sixteenth day of the first month.

¹⁸Then they went in to King Hezekiah and reported: "We have purified the entire temple of the LORD, the altar of burnt offering with all its utensils, and the table for setting out the consecrated bread, with all its articles. ¹⁹We have prepared and consecrated all the articles that King Ahaz removed in his unfaithfulness while he was king. They are now in front of the LORD's altar."

²⁰Early the next morning King Hezekiah gathered the city officials together and went up to the temple of the LORD. ²¹They brought seven bulls, seven rams, seven male lambs and seven male goats as a sin offering*a* for the kingdom, for the sanctuary and for Judah. The king commanded the priests, the descendants of Aaron, to offer these on the altar of the LORD. ²²So they slaughtered the bulls, and the priests took the blood and splashed it against the altar; next they slaughtered the rams and splashed their blood against the altar; then they slaughtered the lambs and splashed their blood against the altar. ²³The goats for the sin offering were brought before the king and the assembly, and they laid their hands on them. ²⁴The priests then slaughtered the goats and presented their blood on the altar for a sin offering to atone for all Israel, because the king had ordered the burnt offering and the sin offering for all Israel.

²⁵He stationed the Levites in the temple of the LORD with cymbals, harps and lyres in the way prescribed by David and Gad the king's seer and Nathan the prophet; this was commanded by the LORD through his prophets. ²⁶So the Levites stood ready with David's instruments, and the priests with their trumpets.

²⁷Hezekiah gave the order to sacrifice the burnt offering on the altar. As the offering began, singing to the LORD began also, accompanied by trumpets and the instruments of David king of Israel. ²⁸The whole assembly bowed in worship, while the musicians played and the trumpets sounded. All this continued until the sacrifice of the burnt offering was completed.

²⁹When the offerings were finished, the king and everyone present with him knelt down and worshiped. ³⁰King Hezekiah and his officials ordered the Levites to praise the LORD with the words of David and of Asaph the seer. So they sang praises with gladness and bowed down and worshiped.

³¹Then Hezekiah said, "You have now dedicated yourselves to the LORD. Come and bring sacrifices and thank offerings to the temple of the LORD." So the assembly brought sacrifices and thank offerings, and all whose hearts were willing brought burnt offerings.

---

a 21 Or *purification offering*; also in verses 23 and 24

[32] The number of burnt offerings the assembly brought was seventy bulls, a hundred rams and two hundred male lambs — all of them for burnt offerings to the LORD. [33] The animals consecrated as sacrifices amounted to six hundred bulls and three thousand sheep and goats. [34] The priests, however, were too few to skin all the burnt offerings; so their relatives the Levites helped them until the task was finished and until other priests had been consecrated, for the Levites had been more conscientious in consecrating themselves than the priests had been. [35] There were burnt offerings in abundance, together with the fat of the fellowship offerings and the drink offerings that accompanied the burnt offerings.

So the service of the temple of the LORD was reestablished. [36] Hezekiah and all the people rejoiced at what God had brought about for his people, because it was done so quickly.

Hezekiah Celebrates the Passover

30 Hezekiah sent word to all Israel and Judah and also wrote letters to Ephraim and Manasseh, inviting them to come to the temple of the LORD in Jerusalem and celebrate the Passover to the LORD, the God of Israel. [2] The king and his officials and the whole assembly in Jerusalem decided to celebrate the Passover in the second month. [3] They had not been able to celebrate it at the regular time because not enough priests had consecrated themselves and the people had not assembled in Jerusalem. [4] The plan seemed right both to the king and to the whole assembly. [5] They decided to send a proclamation throughout Israel, from Beersheba to Dan, calling the people to come to Jerusalem and celebrate the Passover to the LORD, the God of Israel. It had not been celebrated in large numbers according to what was written.

[6] At the king's command, couriers went throughout Israel and Judah with letters from the king and from his officials, which read:

"People of Israel, return to the LORD,
the God of Abraham, Isaac and Israel,
that he may return to you who are left,
who have escaped from the hand of the
kings of Assyria. [7] Do not be like your parents and your fellow Israelites, who were unfaithful to the LORD, the God of their ancestors, so that he made them an object of horror, as you see. [8] Do not be stiff-necked, as your ancestors were; submit to the LORD. Come to his sanctuary, which he has consecrated forever. Serve the LORD your God, so that his fierce anger will turn away from you. [9] If you return to the LORD, then your fellow Israelites and your children will be shown compassion by their captors and will return to this land, for the LORD your God is gracious and compassionate. He will not turn his face from you if you return to him."

[10] The couriers went from town to town in Ephraim and Manasseh, as far as Zebulun, but people scorned and ridiculed them. [11] Nevertheless, some from Asher, Manasseh and Zebulun humbled themselves and went to Jerusalem. [12] Also in Judah the hand of God was on the people to give them unity of mind to carry out what the king and his officials had ordered, following the word of the LORD.

[13] A very large crowd of people assembled in Jerusalem to celebrate the Festival of Unleavened Bread in the second month. [14] They removed the altars in Jerusalem and cleared away the incense altars and threw them into the Kidron Valley.

[15] They slaughtered the Passover lamb on the fourteenth day of the second month. The priests and the Levites were ashamed and consecrated themselves and brought burnt offerings to the temple of the LORD. [16] Then they took up their regular positions as prescribed in the Law of Moses the man of God. The priests splashed against the altar the blood handed to them by the Levites. [17] Since many in the crowd had not consecrated themselves, the Levites had to kill the Passover lambs for all those who were not ceremonially clean and could not consecrate their lambs[a] to the LORD. [18] Although most of the many people who came from Ephraim, Manasseh, Issachar and Zebulun had not purified themselves, yet they ate the Passover, contrary to what was written. But Hezekiah prayed for them, saying, "May the

---

[a] 17 Or consecrate themselves

LORD, who is good, pardon everyone [19]who sets their heart on seeking God—the LORD, the God of their ancestors—even if they are not clean according to the rules of the sanctuary." [20]And the LORD heard Hezekiah and healed the people.

[21]The Israelites who were present in Jerusalem celebrated the Festival of Unleavened Bread for seven days with great rejoicing, while the Levites and priests praised the LORD every day with resounding instruments dedicated to the LORD.[a]

[22]Hezekiah spoke encouragingly to all the Levites, who showed good understanding of the service of the LORD. For the seven days they ate their assigned portion and offered fellowship offerings and praised[b] the LORD, the God of their ancestors.

[23]The whole assembly then agreed to celebrate the festival seven more days; so for another seven days they celebrated joyfully. [24]Hezekiah king of Judah provided a thousand bulls and seven thousand sheep and goats for the assembly, and the officials provided them with a thousand bulls and ten thousand sheep and goats. A great number of priests consecrated themselves. [25]The entire assembly of Judah rejoiced, along with the priests and Levites and all who had assembled from Israel, including the foreigners who had come from Israel and also those who resided in Judah. [26]There was great joy in Jerusalem, for since the days of Solomon son of David king of Israel there had been nothing like this in Jerusalem. [27]The priests and the Levites stood to bless the people, and God heard them, for their prayer reached heaven, his holy dwelling place.

31 When all this had ended, the Israelites who were there went out to the towns of Judah, smashed the sacred stones and cut down the Asherah poles. They destroyed the high places and the altars throughout Judah and Benjamin and in Ephraim and Manasseh. After they had destroyed all of them, the Israelites returned to their own towns and to their own property.

Contributions for Worship

[2]Hezekiah assigned the priests and Levites to divisions—each of them according to their duties as priests or Levites—to offer burnt offerings and fellowship offerings, to minister, to give thanks and to sing praises at the gates of the LORD's dwelling. [3]The king contributed from his own possessions for the morning and evening burnt offerings and for the burnt offerings on the Sabbaths, at the New Moons and at the appointed festivals as written in the Law of the LORD. [4]He ordered the people living in Jerusalem to give the portion due the priests and Levites so they could devote themselves to the Law of the LORD. [5]As soon as the order went out, the Israelites generously gave the firstfruits of their grain, new wine, olive oil and honey and all that the fields produced. They brought a great amount, a tithe of everything. [6]The people of Israel and Judah who lived in the towns of Judah also brought a tithe of their herds and flocks and a tithe of the holy things dedicated to the LORD their God, and they piled them in heaps. [7]They began doing this in the third month and finished in the seventh month. [8]When Hezekiah and his officials came and saw the heaps, they praised the LORD and blessed his people Israel.

[9]Hezekiah asked the priests and Levites about the heaps; [10]and Azariah the chief priest, from the family of Zadok, answered, "Since the people began to bring their contributions to the temple of the LORD, we have had enough to eat and plenty to spare, because the LORD has blessed his people, and this great amount is left over."

[11]Hezekiah gave orders to prepare storerooms in the temple of the LORD, and this was done. [12]Then they faithfully brought in the contributions, tithes and dedicated gifts. Konaniah, a Levite, was the overseer in charge of these things, and his brother Shimei was next in rank. [13]Jehiel, Azaziah, Nahath, Asahel, Jerimoth, Jozabad, Eliel, Ismakiah, Mahath and Benaiah were assistants of Konaniah and Shimei his brother. All these served by appointment of King Hezekiah and Azariah the official in charge of the temple of God.

[14]Kore son of Imnah the Levite, keeper of the East Gate, was in charge of the freewill offerings given to God, distributing the contributions made to the LORD and also the consecrated gifts. [15]Eden, Miniamin,

---

[a] 21 Or *priests sang to the LORD every day, accompanied by the LORD's instruments of praise*   [b] 22 Or *and confessed their sins to*

Jeshua, Shemaiah, Amariah and Shekaniah assisted him faithfully in the towns of the priests, distributing to their fellow priests according to their divisions, old and young alike.

[16] In addition, they distributed to the males three years old or more whose names were in the genealogical records — all who would enter the temple of the LORD to perform the daily duties of their various tasks, according to their responsibilities and their divisions. [17] And they distributed to the priests enrolled by their families in the genealogical records and likewise to the Levites twenty years old or more, according to their responsibilities and their divisions. [18] They included all the little ones, the wives, and the sons and daughters of the whole community listed in these genealogical records. For they were faithful in consecrating themselves.

[19] As for the priests, the descendants of Aaron, who lived on the farmlands around their towns or in any other towns, men were designated by name to distribute portions to every male among them and to all who were recorded in the genealogies of the Levites.

[20] This is what Hezekiah did throughout Judah, doing what was good and right and faithful before the LORD his God. [21] In everything that he undertook in the service of God's temple and in obedience to the law and the commands, he sought his God and worked wholeheartedly. And so he prospered.

Sennacherib Threatens Jerusalem

32 After all that Hezekiah had so faithfully done, Sennacherib king of Assyria came and invaded Judah. He laid siege to the fortified cities, thinking to conquer them for himself. [2] When Hezekiah saw that Sennacherib had come and that he intended to wage war against Jerusalem, [3] he consulted with his officials and military staff about blocking off the water from the springs outside the city, and they helped him. [4] They gathered a large group of people who blocked all the springs and the stream that flowed through the land. "Why should the kings[a] of Assyria come and find plenty of water?" they said. [5] Then he worked hard

repairing all the broken sections of the wall and building towers on it. He built another wall outside that one and reinforced the terraces[b] of the City of David. He also made large numbers of weapons and shields.

[6] He appointed military officers over the people and assembled them before him in the square at the city gate and encouraged them with these words: [7] "Be strong and courageous. Do not be afraid or discouraged because of the king of Assyria and the vast army with him, for there is a greater power with us than with him. [8] With him is only the arm of flesh, but with us is the LORD our God to help us and to fight our battles." And the people gained confidence from what Hezekiah the king of Judah said.

[9] Later, when Sennacherib king of Assyria and all his forces were laying siege to Lachish, he sent his officers to Jerusalem with this message for Hezekiah king of Judah and for all the people of Judah who were there:

[10] "This is what Sennacherib king of Assyria says: On what are you basing your confidence, that you remain in Jerusalem under siege? [11] When Hezekiah says, 'The LORD our God will save us from the hand of the king of Assyria,' he is misleading you, to let you die of hunger and thirst. [12] Did not Hezekiah himself remove this god's high places and altars, saying to Judah and Jerusalem, 'You must worship before one altar and burn sacrifices on it'?

[13] "Do you not know what I and my predecessors have done to all the peoples of the other lands? Were the gods of those nations ever able to deliver their land from my hand? [14] Who of all the gods of these nations that my predecessors destroyed has been able to save his people from me? How then can your god deliver you from my hand? [15] Now do not let Hezekiah deceive you and mislead you like this. Do not believe him, for no god of any nation or kingdom has been able to deliver his people from my hand or the hand of my predecessors. How much less will your god deliver you from my hand!"

[16] Sennacherib's officers spoke further against the LORD God and against his servant

---

[a] 4 Hebrew; Septuagint and Syriac *king*   [b] 5 Or *the Millo*

Hezekiah. ¹⁷The king also wrote letters ridiculing the LORD, the God of Israel, and saying this against him: "Just as the gods of the peoples of the other lands did not rescue their people from my hand, so the god of Hezekiah will not rescue his people from my hand." ¹⁸Then they called out in Hebrew to the people of Jerusalem who were on the wall, to terrify them and make them afraid in order to capture the city. ¹⁹They spoke about the God of Jerusalem as they did about the gods of the other peoples of the world—the work of human hands.

²⁰King Hezekiah and the prophet Isaiah son of Amoz cried out in prayer to heaven about this. ²¹And the LORD sent an angel, who annihilated all the fighting men and the commanders and officers in the camp of the Assyrian king. So he withdrew to his own land in disgrace. And when he went into the temple of his god, some of his sons, his own flesh and blood, cut him down with the sword.

²²So the LORD saved Hezekiah and the people of Jerusalem from the hand of Sennacherib king of Assyria and from the hand of all others. He took care of them*a* on every side. ²³Many brought offerings to Jerusalem for the LORD and valuable gifts for Hezekiah king of Judah. From then on he was highly regarded by all the nations.

Hezekiah's Pride, Success and Death

²⁴In those days Hezekiah became ill and was at the point of death. He prayed to the LORD, who answered him and gave him a miraculous sign. ²⁵But Hezekiah's heart was proud and he did not respond to the kindness shown him; therefore the LORD's wrath was on him and on Judah and Jerusalem. ²⁶Then Hezekiah repented of the pride of his heart, as did the people of Jerusalem; therefore the LORD's wrath did not come on them during the days of Hezekiah.

²⁷Hezekiah had very great wealth and honor, and he made treasuries for his silver and gold and for his precious stones, spices, shields and all kinds of valuables. ²⁸He also made buildings to store the harvest of grain, new wine and olive oil; and he made stalls for various kinds of cattle, and pens for the flocks. ²⁹He built villages and acquired great numbers of flocks and herds, for God had given him very great riches.

³⁰It was Hezekiah who blocked the upper outlet of the Gihon spring and channeled the water down to the west side of the City of David. He succeeded in everything he undertook. ³¹But when envoys were sent by the rulers of Babylon to ask him about the miraculous sign that had occurred in the land, God left him to test him and to know everything that was in his heart.

³²The other events of Hezekiah's reign and his acts of devotion are written in the vision of the prophet Isaiah son of Amoz in the book of the kings of Judah and Israel. ³³Hezekiah rested with his ancestors and was buried on the hill where the tombs of David's descendants are. All Judah and the people of Jerusalem honored him when he died. And Manasseh his son succeeded him as king.

Manasseh King of Judah

33 Manasseh was twelve years old when he became king, and he reigned in Jerusalem fifty-five years. ²He did evil in the eyes of the LORD, following the detestable practices of the nations the LORD had driven out before the Israelites. ³He rebuilt the high places his father Hezekiah had demolished; he also erected altars to the Baals and made Asherah poles. He bowed down to all the starry hosts and worshiped them. ⁴He built altars in the temple of the LORD, of which the LORD had said, "My Name will remain in Jerusalem forever." ⁵In both courts of the temple of the LORD, he built altars to all the starry hosts. ⁶He sacrificed his children in the fire in the Valley of Ben Hinnom, practiced divination and witchcraft, sought omens, and consulted mediums and spiritists. He did much evil in the eyes of the LORD, arousing his anger.

⁷He took the image he had made and put it in God's temple, of which God had said to David and to his son Solomon, "In this temple and in Jerusalem, which I have chosen out of all the tribes of Israel, I will put my Name forever. ⁸I will not again make the feet of the Israelites leave the land I assigned to your ancestors, if only they will be careful to do everything I commanded them concerning all the laws, decrees and regulations

---

a 22 Hebrew; Septuagint and Vulgate *He gave them rest*

ALWAYS WELCOME

READ: 2 CHRONICLES 33:1

Hezekiah ruled as one of the godliest and most accomplished kings in the royal line of Judah. Toward the end of his life he grew proud and ignored God's kindness, but he turned back to God before he died.

Manasseh came to the throne at age twelve and committed unspeakable evil, undoing much of the good his father Hezekiah had done. He reestablished the high places, illegal worship sites built atop hills and mountains. He built altars to pagan gods and worshiped the sun and stars. He even put altars to false gods within the Lord's temple. He practiced witchcraft and turned to mediums to contact the dead on his behalf. And he burnt his children alive as sacrifices to idols (2 Chronicles 33:1-6).

When the Lord spoke up to stop these evils, Manasseh ignored him. Not until an invading army led the king away in chains with a hook in his nose did he humble himself and turn back to the Lord. He then did everything in his power to lead the nation back to worship the one true God.

No matter who you are or what you have done, the Lord always invites you to repent—to quit sinning and turn to him. Whenever you feel like you have wandered far from God, he's always eager to welcome you home.

BUILDING

FAITH

WISDOM

STRENGTH

given through Moses." ⁹But Manasseh led Judah and the people of Jerusalem astray, so that they did more evil than the nations the LORD had destroyed before the Israelites.

¹⁰The LORD spoke to Manasseh and his people, but they paid no attention. ¹¹So the LORD brought against them the army commanders of the king of Assyria, who took Manasseh prisoner, put a hook in his nose, bound him with bronze shackles and took him to Babylon. ¹²In his distress he sought the favor of the LORD his God and humbled himself greatly before the God of his ancestors. ¹³And when he prayed to him, the LORD was moved by his entreaty and listened to his plea; so he brought him back to Jerusalem and to his kingdom. Then Manasseh knew that the LORD is God.

¹⁴Afterward he rebuilt the outer wall of the City of David, west of the Gihon spring in the valley, as far as the entrance of the Fish Gate and encircling the hill of Ophel; he also made it much higher. He stationed military commanders in all the fortified cities in Judah.

¹⁵He got rid of the foreign gods and removed the image from the temple of the LORD, as well as all the altars he had built on the temple hill and in Jerusalem; and he threw them out of the city. ¹⁶Then he restored the altar of the LORD and sacrificed fellowship offerings and thank offerings on it, and told Judah to serve the LORD, the God of Israel. ¹⁷The people, however, continued to sacrifice at the high places, but only to the LORD their God.

¹⁸The other events of Manasseh's reign, including his prayer to his God and the words the seers spoke to him in the name of the LORD, the God of Israel, are written in the annals of the kings of Israel.[a] ¹⁹His prayer and how God was moved by his entreaty, as well as all his sins and unfaithfulness, and the sites where he built high places and set up Asherah poles and idols before he humbled himself — all these are written in the records of the seers.[b] ²⁰Manasseh rested with his ancestors and was buried in his palace. And Amon his son succeeded him as king.

Amon King of Judah

²¹Amon was twenty-two years old when he became king, and he reigned in Jerusa-

lem two years. ²²He did evil in the eyes of the LORD, as his father Manasseh had done. Amon worshiped and offered sacrifices to all the idols Manasseh had made. ²³But unlike his father Manasseh, he did not humble himself before the LORD; Amon increased his guilt.

²⁴Amon's officials conspired against him and assassinated him in his palace. ²⁵Then the people of the land killed all who had plotted against King Amon, and they made Josiah his son king in his place.

Josiah's Reforms

34 Josiah was eight years old when he became king, and he reigned in Jerusalem thirty-one years. ²He did what was right in the eyes of the LORD and followed the ways of his father David, not turning aside to the right or to the left.

³In the eighth year of his reign, while he was still young, he began to seek the God of his father David. In his twelfth year he began to purge Judah and Jerusalem of high places, Asherah poles and idols. ⁴Under his direction the altars of the Baals were torn down; he cut to pieces the incense altars that were above them, and smashed the Asherah poles and the idols. These he broke to pieces and scattered over the graves of those who had sacrificed to them. ⁵He burned the bones of the priests on their altars, and so he purged Judah and Jerusalem. ⁶In the towns of Manasseh, Ephraim and Simeon, as far as Naphtali, and in the ruins around them, ⁷he tore down the altars and the Asherah poles and crushed the idols to powder and cut to pieces all the incense altars throughout Israel. Then he went back to Jerusalem.

⁸In the eighteenth year of Josiah's reign, to purify the land and the temple, he sent Shaphan son of Azaliah and Maaseiah the ruler of the city, with Joah son of Joahaz, the recorder, to repair the temple of the LORD his God.

⁹They went to Hilkiah the high priest and gave him the money that had been brought into the temple of God, which the Levites who were the gatekeepers had collected from the people of Manasseh, Ephraim and the entire remnant of Israel and from all the people of Judah and Benjamin and the

---

[a] 18   That is, Judah, as frequently in 2 Chronicles   [b] 19   One Hebrew manuscript and Septuagint; most Hebrew manuscripts *of Hozai*

inhabitants of Jerusalem. [10]Then they entrusted it to the men appointed to supervise the work on the LORD's temple. These men paid the workers who repaired and restored the temple. [11]They also gave money to the carpenters and builders to purchase dressed stone, and timber for joists and beams for the buildings that the kings of Judah had allowed to fall into ruin.

[12]The workers labored faithfully. Over them to direct them were Jahath and Obadiah, Levites descended from Merari, and Zechariah and Meshullam, descended from Kohath. The Levites — all who were skilled in playing musical instruments — [13]had charge of the laborers and supervised all the workers from job to job. Some of the Levites were secretaries, scribes and gatekeepers.

The Book of the Law Found

[14]While they were bringing out the money that had been taken into the temple of the LORD, Hilkiah the priest found the Book of the Law of the LORD that had been given through Moses. [15]Hilkiah said to Shaphan the secretary, "I have found the Book of the Law in the temple of the LORD." He gave it to Shaphan.

[16]Then Shaphan took the book to the king and reported to him: "Your officials are doing everything that has been committed to them. [17]They have paid out the money that was in the temple of the LORD and have entrusted it to the supervisors and workers." [18]Then Shaphan the secretary informed the king, "Hilkiah the priest has given me a book." And Shaphan read from it in the presence of the king.

[19]When the king heard the words of the Law, he tore his robes. [20]He gave these orders to Hilkiah, Ahikam son of Shaphan, Abdon son of Micah,[a] Shaphan the secretary and Asaiah the king's attendant: [21]"Go and inquire of the LORD for me and for the remnant in Israel and Judah about what is written in this book that has been found. Great is the LORD's anger that is poured out on us because those who have gone before us have not kept the word of the LORD; they have not acted in accordance with all that is written in this book."

[22]Hilkiah and those the king had sent with him[b] went to speak to the prophet Huldah, who was the wife of Shallum son of Tokhath,[c] the son of Hasrah,[d] keeper of the wardrobe. She lived in Jerusalem, in the New Quarter.

[23]She said to them, "This is what the LORD, the God of Israel, says: Tell the man who sent you to me, [24]'This is what the LORD says: I am going to bring disaster on this place and its people — all the curses written in the book that has been read in the presence of the king of Judah. [25]Because they have forsaken me and burned incense to other gods and aroused my anger by all that their hands have made,[e] my anger will be poured out on this place and will not be quenched.' [26]Tell the king of Judah, who sent you to inquire of the LORD, 'This is what the LORD, the God of Israel, says concerning the words you heard: [27]Because your heart was responsive and you humbled yourself before God when you heard what he spoke against this place and its people, and because you humbled yourself before me and tore your robes and wept in my presence, I have heard you, declares the LORD. [28]Now I will gather you to your ancestors, and you will be buried in peace. Your eyes will not see all the disaster I am going to bring on this place and on those who live here.'"

So they took her answer back to the king.

[29]Then the king called together all the elders of Judah and Jerusalem. [30]He went up to the temple of the LORD with the people of Judah, the inhabitants of Jerusalem, the priests and the Levites — all the people from the least to the greatest. He read in their hearing all the words of the Book of the Covenant, which had been found in the temple of the LORD. [31]The king stood by his pillar and renewed the covenant in the presence of the LORD — to follow the LORD and keep his commands, statutes and decrees with all his heart and all his soul, and to obey the words of the covenant written in this book.

[32]Then he had everyone in Jerusalem and Benjamin pledge themselves to it; the people of Jerusalem did this in accordance with the covenant of God, the God of their ancestors.

[33]Josiah removed all the detestable idols

---

[a] 20 Also called *Akbor son of Micaiah*   [b] 22 One Hebrew manuscript, Vulgate and Syriac; most Hebrew manuscripts do not have *had sent with him*.   [c] 22 Also called *Tikvah*   [d] 22 Also called *Harhas*
[e] 25 Or *by everything they have done*

from all the territory belonging to the Israelites, and he had all who were present in Israel serve the LORD their God. As long as he lived, they did not fail to follow the LORD, the God of their ancestors.

Josiah Celebrates the Passover

35 Josiah celebrated the Passover to the LORD in Jerusalem, and the Passover lamb was slaughtered on the fourteenth day of the first month. ²He appointed the priests to their duties and encouraged them in the service of the LORD's temple. ³He said to the Levites, who instructed all Israel and who had been consecrated to the LORD: "Put the sacred ark in the temple that Solomon son of David king of Israel built. It is not to be carried about on your shoulders. Now serve the LORD your God and his people Israel. ⁴Prepare yourselves by families in your divisions, according to the instructions written by David king of Israel and by his son Solomon.

⁵"Stand in the holy place with a group of Levites for each subdivision of the families of your fellow Israelites, the lay people. ⁶Slaughter the Passover lambs, consecrate yourselves and prepare the lambs for your fellow Israelites, doing what the LORD commanded through Moses."

⁷Josiah provided for all the lay people who were there a total of thirty thousand lambs and goats for the Passover offerings, and also three thousand cattle — all from the king's own possessions.

⁸His officials also contributed voluntarily to the people and the priests and Levites. Hilkiah, Zechariah and Jehiel, the officials in charge of God's temple, gave the priests twenty-six hundred Passover offerings and three hundred cattle. ⁹Also Konaniah along with Shemaiah and Nethanel, his brothers, and Hashabiah, Jeiel and Jozabad, the leaders of the Levites, provided five thousand Passover offerings and five hundred head of cattle for the Levites.

¹⁰The service was arranged and the priests stood in their places with the Levites in their divisions as the king had ordered. ¹¹The Passover lambs were slaughtered, and the priests splashed against the altar the blood handed to them, while the Levites skinned the animals. ¹²They set aside the burnt offerings to give them to the subdivisions of the families of the people to offer to the LORD, as it is written in the Book of Moses. They did the same with the cattle. ¹³They roasted the Passover animals over the fire as prescribed, and boiled the holy offerings in pots, caldrons and pans and served them quickly to all the people. ¹⁴After this, they made preparations for themselves and for the priests, because the priests, the descendants of Aaron, were sacrificing the burnt offerings and the fat portions until nightfall. So the Levites made preparations for themselves and for the Aaronic priests.

¹⁵The musicians, the descendants of Asaph, were in the places prescribed by David, Asaph, Heman and Jeduthun the king's seer. The gatekeepers at each gate did not need to leave their posts, because their fellow Levites made the preparations for them.

¹⁶So at that time the entire service of the LORD was carried out for the celebration of the Passover and the offering of burnt offerings on the altar of the LORD, as King Josiah had ordered. ¹⁷The Israelites who were present celebrated the Passover at that time and observed the Festival of Unleavened Bread for seven days. ¹⁸The Passover had not been observed like this in Israel since the days of the prophet Samuel; and none of the kings of Israel had ever celebrated such a Passover as did Josiah, with the priests, the Levites and all Judah and Israel who were there with the people of Jerusalem. ¹⁹This Passover was celebrated in the eighteenth year of Josiah's reign.

The Death of Josiah

²⁰After all this, when Josiah had set the temple in order, Necho king of Egypt went up to fight at Carchemish on the Euphrates, and Josiah marched out to meet him in battle. ²¹But Necho sent messengers to him, saying, "What quarrel is there, king of Judah, between you and me? It is not you I am attacking at this time, but the house with which I am at war. God has told me to hurry; so stop opposing God, who is with me, or he will destroy you."

²²Josiah, however, would not turn away from him, but disguised himself to engage him in battle. He would not listen to what Necho had said at God's command but went to fight him on the plain of Megiddo.

²³Archers shot King Josiah, and he told his

ALL OUT

READ: 2 CHRONICLES 35:18

Josiah not only led his people in destroying all other gods in their lives, but he also showed them how to worship. Since God first led his people out of Egypt, the Israelites had celebrated Passover. But in the eighteenth year of Josiah's reign, the king put on a Passover to end all other Passovers. Talk about a party! He provided 30,000 sheep and goats and 3,000 cattle as Passover offerings. Musicians played and the people ate, danced, and celebrated for seven days. The king gave away much of his material wealth to celebrate God.

In our modern thinking, many people associate worship with religion. If someone doesn't have a drawer in the dresser of their life labeled "organized religion," then they assume that the question of what god they worship doesn't apply to them.

The problem, of course, is they misunderstand what worship is.

When you subtract the religious language, worship is the built-in human reflex to put your hope in something or someone and then chase after it. The end result, of course, is that our lives begin to take the shape of what we care about most. The object of your worship will determine your future and define your life. It's the one choice that all other choices are motivated by. Josiah chose to worship God with his possessions, his words, his actions, and his heart. And God blessed him for his decision.

BUILDING FAITH WISDOM STRENGTH

Taken from *Gods at War Student Edition* by Kyle Idleman, copyright © 2014 by City on a Hill Studio, LLC, published by Zondervan.

officers, "Take me away; I am badly wounded." [24] So they took him out of his chariot, put him in his other chariot and brought him to Jerusalem, where he died. He was buried in the tombs of his ancestors, and all Judah and Jerusalem mourned for him.

[25] Jeremiah composed laments for Josiah, and to this day all the male and female singers commemorate Josiah in the laments. These became a tradition in Israel and are written in the Laments.

[26] The other events of Josiah's reign and his acts of devotion in accordance with what is written in the Law of the LORD — [27] all the events, from beginning to end, are written in the book of the kings of Israel and Judah. [36][1] And the people of the land took Jehoahaz son of Josiah and made him king in Jerusalem in place of his father.

Jehoahaz King of Judah

[2] Jehoahaz[a] was twenty-three years old when he became king, and he reigned in Jerusalem three months. [3] The king of Egypt dethroned him in Jerusalem and imposed on Judah a levy of a hundred talents[b] of silver and a talent[c] of gold. [4] The king of Egypt made Eliakim, a brother of Jehoahaz, king over Judah and Jerusalem and changed Eliakim's name to Jehoiakim. But Necho took Eliakim's brother Jehoahaz and carried him off to Egypt.

Jehoiakim King of Judah

[5] Jehoiakim was twenty-five years old when he became king, and he reigned in Jerusalem eleven years. He did evil in the eyes of the LORD his God. [6] Nebuchadnezzar king of Babylon attacked him and bound him with bronze shackles to take him to Babylon. [7] Nebuchadnezzar also took to Babylon articles from the temple of the LORD and put them in his temple[d] there.

[8] The other events of Jehoiakim's reign, the detestable things he did and all that was found against him, are written in the book of the kings of Israel and Judah. And Jehoiachin his son succeeded him as king.

Jehoiachin King of Judah

[9] Jehoiachin was eighteen[e] years old when he became king, and he reigned in Jerusalem three months and ten days. He did evil in the eyes of the LORD. [10] In the spring, King Nebuchadnezzar sent for him and brought him to Babylon, together with articles of value from the temple of the LORD, and he made Jehoiachin's uncle,[f] Zedekiah, king over Judah and Jerusalem.

Zedekiah King of Judah

[11] Zedekiah was twenty-one years old when he became king, and he reigned in Jerusalem eleven years. [12] He did evil in the eyes of the LORD his God and did not humble himself before Jeremiah the prophet, who spoke the word of the LORD. [13] He also rebelled against King Nebuchadnezzar, who had made him take an oath in God's name. He became stiff-necked and hardened his heart and would not turn to the LORD, the God of Israel. [14] Furthermore, all the leaders of the priests and the people became more and more unfaithful, following all the detestable practices of the nations and defiling the temple of the LORD, which he had consecrated in Jerusalem.

The Fall of Jerusalem

[15] The LORD, the God of their ancestors, sent word to them through his messengers again and again, because he had pity on his people and on his dwelling place. [16] But they mocked God's messengers, despised his words and scoffed at his prophets until the wrath of the LORD was aroused against his people and there was no remedy. [17] He brought up against them the king of the Babylonians,[g] who killed their young men with the sword in the sanctuary, and did not spare young men or young women, the elderly or the infirm. God gave them all into the hands of Nebuchadnezzar. [18] He carried to Babylon all the articles from the temple of God, both large and small, and the treasures of the LORD's temple and the treasures of the king and his officials. [19] They set fire to God's temple and broke down the wall of Jerusalem; they burned all the palaces and destroyed everything of value there.

[20] He carried into exile to Babylon the remnant, who escaped from the sword, and

---

[a] 2 Hebrew *Joahaz*, a variant of *Jehoahaz*; also in verse 4   [b] 3 That is, about 3 3/4 tons or about 3.4 metric tons   [c] 3 That is, about 75 pounds or about 34 kilograms   [d] 7 Or *palace*   [e] 9 One Hebrew manuscript, some Septuagint manuscripts and Syriac (see also 2 Kings 24:8); most Hebrew manuscripts *eight*   [f] 10 Hebrew *brother,* that is, relative (see 2 Kings 24:17)   [g] 17 Or *Chaldeans*

they became servants to him and his successors until the kingdom of Persia came to power. [21] The land enjoyed its sabbath rests; all the time of its desolation it rested, until the seventy years were completed in fulfillment of the word of the LORD spoken by Jeremiah.

[22] In the first year of Cyrus king of Persia, in order to fulfill the word of the LORD spoken by Jeremiah, the LORD moved the heart of Cyrus king of Persia to make a proclamation throughout his realm and also to put it in writing:

[23] "This is what Cyrus king of Persia says:

" 'The LORD, the God of heaven, has given me all the kingdoms of the earth and he has appointed me to build a temple for him at Jerusalem in Judah. Any of his people among you may go up, and may the LORD their God be with them.' "

EZRA

WHEN DID THIS HAPPEN?

Around 521–460 B.C. in the land of Israel—specifically, in what was the southern kingdom of Judah

WHO IS IN THIS BOOK?

King Cyrus
Ezra
Zerubbabel

VERSES YOU MIGHT RECOGNIZE

EZRA 3:11

"And all the people gave a great shout of praise to the LORD, because the foundation of the house of the LORD was laid."

EZRA 7:10

"For Ezra had devoted himself to the study and observance of the Law of the LORD, and to teaching its decrees and laws in Israel."

WHAT'S IT ABOUT?

After being captives in Babylon for 60 years, the Israelites—now known as Jews—were allowed to return to Judah, where they rebuilt the temple. Sixty years after that, a scribe named Ezra led a group of Jews back to Jerusalem.

This book records two separate time periods right after the 70-year exile in Babylon. Ezra 1–6 records the first return of the exiles under a governor named Zerubbabel. Ezra 7–10 jumps ahead more than 60 years to tell about Ezra leading the second group of exiles back to Israel.

The exile had been a painful reminder to the Jews that God's help and blessing can only come through obedience to his commands. Though they had failed, they were ready to try again. Ezra reminded them that God had kept his promise to bring them back to Israel, and he led them in confessing their sins and recommitting themselves to God. By the end of the book, Israel had renewed its covenant with God and started acting in obedience. God had not forgotten his promises to Abraham and David. In a little more than 400 years, God would keep his greatest promise of all—to send a Messiah.

Cyrus Helps the Exiles to Return

1 In the first year of Cyrus king of Persia, in order to fulfill the word of the LORD spoken by Jeremiah, the LORD moved the heart of Cyrus king of Persia to make a proclamation throughout his realm and also to put it in writing:

2 "This is what Cyrus king of Persia says:

"'The LORD, the God of heaven, has given me all the kingdoms of the earth and he has appointed me to build a temple for him at Jerusalem in Judah. 3 Any of his people among you may go up to Jerusalem in Judah and build the temple of the LORD, the God of Israel, the God who is in Jerusalem, and may their God be with them. 4 And in any locality where survivors may now be living, the people are to provide them with silver and gold, with goods and livestock, and with freewill offerings for the temple of God in Jerusalem.'"

5 Then the family heads of Judah and Benjamin, and the priests and Levites — everyone whose heart God had moved — prepared to go up and build the house of the LORD in Jerusalem. 6 All their neighbors assisted them with articles of silver and gold, with goods and livestock, and with valuable gifts, in addition to all the freewill offerings.

7 Moreover, King Cyrus brought out the articles belonging to the temple of the LORD, which Nebuchadnezzar had carried away from Jerusalem and had placed in the temple of his god.[a] 8 Cyrus king of Persia had them brought by Mithredath the treasurer, who counted them out to Sheshbazzar the prince of Judah.

9 This was the inventory:

gold dishes	30
silver dishes	1,000
silver pans[b]	29
10 gold bowls	30
matching silver bowls	410
other articles	1,000

11 In all, there were 5,400 articles of gold and of silver. Sheshbazzar brought all these along with the exiles when they came up from Babylon to Jerusalem.

The List of the Exiles Who Returned

2 Now these are the people of the province who came up from the captivity of the exiles, whom Nebuchadnezzar king of Babylon had taken captive to Babylon (they returned to Jerusalem and Judah, each to their own town, 2 in company with Zerubbabel, Joshua, Nehemiah, Seraiah, Reelaiah, Mordecai, Bilshan, Mispar, Bigvai, Rehum and Baanah):

The list of the men of the people of Israel:

3 the descendants of Parosh	2,172
4 of Shephatiah	372
5 of Arah	775
6 of Pahath-Moab (through the line of Jeshua and Joab)	2,812
7 of Elam	1,254
8 of Zattu	945
9 of Zakkai	760
10 of Bani	642
11 of Bebai	623
12 of Azgad	1,222
13 of Adonikam	666
14 of Bigvai	2,056
15 of Adin	454
16 of Ater (through Hezekiah)	98
17 of Bezai	323
18 of Jorah	112
19 of Hashum	223
20 of Gibbar	95
21 the men of Bethlehem	123
22 of Netophah	56
23 of Anathoth	128
24 of Azmaveth	42

---

a 7 Or gods   b 9 The meaning of the Hebrew for this word is uncertain.

²⁵ of Kiriath Jearim,ᵃ Kephirah
and Beeroth 743
²⁶ of Ramah and Geba 621
²⁷ of Mikmash 122
²⁸ of Bethel and Ai 223
²⁹ of Nebo 52
³⁰ of Magbish 156
³¹ of the other Elam 1,254
³² of Harim 320
³³ of Lod, Hadid and Ono 725
³⁴ of Jericho 345
³⁵ of Senaah 3,630

³⁶ The priests:

the descendants of Jedaiah
(through the family of
Jeshua) 973
³⁷ of Immer 1,052
³⁸ of Pashhur 1,247
³⁹ of Harim 1,017

⁴⁰ The Levites:

the descendants of Jeshua
and Kadmiel (of the line
of Hodaviah) 74

⁴¹ The musicians:

the descendants of Asaph 128

⁴² The gatekeepers of the temple:

the descendants of
Shallum, Ater, Talmon,
Akkub, Hatita and Shobai 139

⁴³ The temple servants:

the descendants of
Ziha, Hasupha, Tabbaoth,
⁴⁴ Keros, Siaha, Padon,
⁴⁵ Lebanah, Hagabah, Akkub,
⁴⁶ Hagab, Shalmai, Hanan,
⁴⁷ Giddel, Gahar, Reaiah,
⁴⁸ Rezin, Nekoda, Gazzam,
⁴⁹ Uzza, Paseah, Besai,
⁵⁰ Asnah, Meunim, Nephusim,
⁵¹ Bakbuk, Hakupha, Harhur,
⁵² Bazluth, Mehida, Harsha,
⁵³ Barkos, Sisera, Temah,
⁵⁴ Neziah and Hatipha

⁵⁵ The descendants of the servants of
Solomon:

the descendants of
Sotai, Hassophereth, Peruda,

⁵⁶ Jaala, Darkon, Giddel,
⁵⁷ Shephatiah, Hattil,
Pokereth-Hazzebaim and Ami

⁵⁸ The temple servants and the
descendants of the servants
of Solomon 392

⁵⁹ The following came up from the
towns of Tel Melah, Tel Harsha, Kerub,
Addon and Immer, but they could not
show that their families were descended from Israel:

⁶⁰ The descendants of
Delaiah, Tobiah and Nekoda 652

⁶¹ And from among the priests:

The descendants of
Hobaiah, Hakkoz and Barzillai (a
man who had married a daughter
of Barzillai the Gileadite and was
called by that name).

⁶² These searched for their family records, but they could not find them and
so were excluded from the priesthood
as unclean. ⁶³ The governor ordered
them not to eat any of the most sacred
food until there was a priest ministering with the Urim and Thummim.

⁶⁴ The whole company numbered
42,360, ⁶⁵ besides their 7,337 male and
female slaves; and they also had 200
male and female singers. ⁶⁶ They had
736 horses, 245 mules, ⁶⁷ 435 camels
and 6,720 donkeys.

⁶⁸ When they arrived at the house of
the LORD in Jerusalem, some of the heads of the
families gave freewill offerings toward the rebuilding of the house of God on its site. ⁶⁹ According to their ability they gave to the treasury for this work 61,000 daricsᵇ of gold, 5,000
minasᶜ of silver and 100 priestly garments.

⁷⁰ The priests, the Levites, the musicians,
the gatekeepers and the temple servants settled in their own towns, along with some of
the other people, and the rest of the Israelites
settled in their towns.

Rebuilding the Altar

3 When the seventh month came and the
Israelites had settled in their towns, the

ᵃ 25 See Septuagint (see also Neh. 7:29); Hebrew *Kiriath Arim.*   ᵇ 69 That is, about 1,100 pounds or
about 500 kilograms   ᶜ 69 That is, about 3 tons or about 2.8 metric tons

people assembled together as one in Jerusalem. ²Then Joshua son of Jozadak and his fellow priests and Zerubbabel son of Shealtiel and his associates began to build the altar of the God of Israel to sacrifice burnt offerings on it, in accordance with what is written in the Law of Moses the man of God. ³Despite their fear of the peoples around them, they built the altar on its foundation and sacrificed burnt offerings on it to the LORD, both the morning and evening sacrifices. ⁴Then in accordance with what is written, they celebrated the Festival of Tabernacles with the required number of burnt offerings prescribed for each day. ⁵After that, they presented the regular burnt offerings, the New Moon sacrifices and the sacrifices for all the appointed sacred festivals of the LORD, as well as those brought as freewill offerings to the LORD. ⁶On the first day of the seventh month they began to offer burnt offerings to the LORD, though the foundation of the LORD's temple had not yet been laid.

Rebuilding the Temple

⁷Then they gave money to the masons and carpenters, and gave food and drink and olive oil to the people of Sidon and Tyre, so that they would bring cedar logs by sea from Lebanon to Joppa, as authorized by Cyrus king of Persia.

⁸In the second month of the second year after their arrival at the house of God in Jerusalem, Zerubbabel son of Shealtiel, Joshua son of Jozadak and the rest of the people (the priests and the Levites and all who had returned from the captivity to Jerusalem) began the work. They appointed Levites twenty years old and older to supervise the building of the house of the LORD. ⁹Joshua and his sons and brothers and Kadmiel and his sons (descendants of Hodaviah*ᵃ*) and the sons of Henadad and their sons and brothers — all Levites — joined together in supervising those working on the house of God.

¹⁰When the builders laid the foundation of the temple of the LORD, the priests in their vestments and with trumpets, and the Levites (the sons of Asaph) with cymbals, took their places to praise the LORD, as prescribed by David king of Israel. ¹¹With praise and thanksgiving they sang to the LORD:

"He is good;
    his love toward Israel endures forever."

And all the people gave a great shout of praise to the LORD, because the foundation of the house of the LORD was laid. ¹²But many of the older priests and Levites and family heads, who had seen the former temple, wept aloud when they saw the foundation of this temple being laid, while many others shouted for joy. ¹³No one could distinguish the sound of the shouts of joy from the sound of weeping, because the people made so much noise. And the sound was heard far away.

Opposition to the Rebuilding

4 When the enemies of Judah and Benjamin heard that the exiles were building a temple for the LORD, the God of Israel, ²they came to Zerubbabel and to the heads of the families and said, "Let us help you build because, like you, we seek your God and have been sacrificing to him since the time of Esarhaddon king of Assyria, who brought us here."

³But Zerubbabel, Joshua and the rest of the heads of the families of Israel answered, "You have no part with us in building a temple to our God. We alone will build it for the LORD, the God of Israel, as King Cyrus, the king of Persia, commanded us."

⁴Then the peoples around them set out to discourage the people of Judah and make them afraid to go on building.*ᵇ* ⁵They bribed officials to work against them and frustrate their plans during the entire reign of Cyrus king of Persia and down to the reign of Darius king of Persia.

Later Opposition Under Xerxes and Artaxerxes

⁶At the beginning of the reign of Xerxes,*ᶜ* they lodged an accusation against the people of Judah and Jerusalem.

⁷And in the days of Artaxerxes king of Persia, Bishlam, Mithredath, Tabeel and the rest of his associates wrote a letter to Artaxerxes. The letter was written in Aramaic script and in the Aramaic language.*ᵈ,ᵉ*

⁸Rehum the commanding officer and Shimshai the secretary wrote a letter against Jerusalem to Artaxerxes the king as follows:

ᵃ 9 Hebrew *Yehudah,* a variant of *Hodaviah*   *ᵇ* 4 Or *and troubled them as they built*   *ᶜ* 6 Hebrew *Ahasuerus*   *ᵈ* 7 Or *written in Aramaic and translated*   *ᵉ* 7 The text of 4:8 – 6:18 is in Aramaic.

DON'T GET DISTRACTED

READ: EZRA 3:11

The book of Ezra begins by announcing extraordinary news: Cyrus, king of Persia, decided to set God's people free from captivity in Babylon to return to their homeland in Judah. Cyrus acknowledged that the Lord had set him on the throne of a vast empire, and he directed the returning captives to build a temple to God in Jerusalem (Ezra 1:1-3).

The most astonishing part of this news is that more than a hundred years before Cyrus issued his decree, Isaiah prophesied that the king would give exactly that order (Isaiah 44:28). As the people traveled hundreds of miles back to their homeland, they could be sure they had God's blessing on their task.

A man named Zerubbabel led the group homeward. He and Joshua the high priest immediately set up an altar for burnt offerings and began rebuilding the temple. The people celebrated and applauded God when the foundation was complete. But enemies soon brought the work to a halt for nearly two decades (Ezra 4:5). In the meantime, everyone became preoccupied with building themselves lavish houses instead of completing the house of worship (Haggai 1:2-4).

God sets you free to live for him. But if you let opposition and distractions pull you away from his plans for you, you miss out on his best blessings. Stay on task and you'll have real reason to celebrate.

BUILDING FAITH WISDOM STRENGTH

[9] Rehum the commanding officer and Shimshai the secretary, together with the rest of their associates — the judges, officials and administrators over the people from Persia, Uruk and Babylon, the Elamites of Susa, [10] and the other people whom the great and honorable Ashurbanipal deported and settled in the city of Samaria and elsewhere in Trans-Euphrates.

[11] (This is a copy of the letter they sent him.)

To King Artaxerxes,

From your servants in Trans-Euphrates:

[12] The king should know that the people who came up to us from you have gone to Jerusalem and are rebuilding that rebellious and wicked city. They are restoring the walls and repairing the foundations.

[13] Furthermore, the king should know that if this city is built and its walls are restored, no more taxes, tribute or duty will be paid, and eventually the royal revenues will suffer.[a] [14] Now since we are under obligation to the palace and it is not proper for us to see the king dishonored, we are sending this message to inform the king, [15] so that a search may be made in the archives of your predecessors. In these records you will find that this city is a rebellious city, troublesome to kings and provinces, a place with a long history of sedition. That is why this city was destroyed. [16] We inform the king that if this city is built and its walls are restored, you will be left with nothing in Trans-Euphrates.

[17] The king sent this reply:

To Rehum the commanding officer, Shimshai the secretary and the rest of their associates living in Samaria and elsewhere in Trans-Euphrates:

Greetings.

[18] The letter you sent us has been read and translated in my presence. [19] I issued an order and a search was made, and it was found that this city has a long history of revolt against kings and has been a place of rebellion and sedition. [20] Jerusalem has had powerful kings ruling over the whole of Trans-Euphrates, and taxes, tribute and duty were paid to them. [21] Now issue an order to these men to stop work, so that this city will not be rebuilt until I so order. [22] Be careful not to neglect this matter. Why let this threat grow, to the detriment of the royal interests?

[23] As soon as the copy of the letter of King Artaxerxes was read to Rehum and Shimshai the secretary and their associates, they went immediately to the Jews in Jerusalem and compelled them by force to stop.

[24] Thus the work on the house of God in Jerusalem came to a standstill until the second year of the reign of Darius king of Persia.

Tattenai's Letter to Darius

5 Now Haggai the prophet and Zechariah the prophet, a descendant of Iddo, prophesied to the Jews in Judah and Jerusalem in the name of the God of Israel, who was over them. [2] Then Zerubbabel son of Shealtiel and Joshua son of Jozadak set to work to rebuild the house of God in Jerusalem. And the prophets of God were with them, supporting them.

[3] At that time Tattenai, governor of Trans-Euphrates, and Shethar-Bozenai and their associates went to them and asked, "Who authorized you to rebuild this temple and to finish it?" [4] They[b] also asked, "What are the names of those who are constructing this building?" [5] But the eye of their God was watching over the elders of the Jews, and they were not stopped until a report could go to Darius and his written reply be received.

[6] This is a copy of the letter that Tattenai, governor of Trans-Euphrates, and Shethar-Bozenai and their associates, the officials of Trans-Euphrates, sent to King Darius. [7] The report they sent him read as follows:

To King Darius:

Cordial greetings.

[8] The king should know that we went to the district of Judah, to the temple of

---

[a] 13 The meaning of the Aramaic for this clause is uncertain.   [b] 4 See Septuagint; Aramaic *We*.

the great God. The people are building it with large stones and placing the timbers in the walls. The work is being carried on with diligence and is making rapid progress under their direction.

[9] We questioned the elders and asked them, "Who authorized you to rebuild this temple and to finish it?" [10] We also asked them their names, so that we could write down the names of their leaders for your information.

[11] This is the answer they gave us:

"We are the servants of the God of heaven and earth, and we are rebuilding the temple that was built many years ago, one that a great king of Israel built and finished. [12] But because our ancestors angered the God of heaven, he gave them into the hands of Nebuchadnezzar the Chaldean, king of Babylon, who destroyed this temple and deported the people to Babylon.

[13] "However, in the first year of Cyrus king of Babylon, King Cyrus issued a decree to rebuild this house of God. [14] He even removed from the temple[a] of Babylon the gold and silver articles of the house of God, which Nebuchadnezzar had taken from the temple in Jerusalem and brought to the temple[a] in Babylon. Then King Cyrus gave them to a man named Sheshbazzar, whom he had appointed governor, [15] and he told him, 'Take these articles and go and deposit them in the temple in Jerusalem. And rebuild the house of God on its site.'

[16] "So this Sheshbazzar came and laid the foundations of the house of God in Jerusalem. From that day to the present it has been under construction but is not yet finished."

[17] Now if it pleases the king, let a search be made in the royal archives of Babylon to see if King Cyrus did in fact issue a decree to rebuild this house of God in Jerusalem. Then let the king send us his decision in this matter.

The Decree of Darius

6 King Darius then issued an order, and they searched in the archives stored in the treasury at Babylon. [2] A scroll was found in the citadel of Ecbatana in the province of Media, and this was written on it:

Memorandum:

[3] In the first year of King Cyrus, the king issued a decree concerning the temple of God in Jerusalem:

Let the temple be rebuilt as a place to present sacrifices, and let its foundations be laid. It is to be sixty cubits[b] high and sixty cubits wide, [4] with three courses of large stones and one of timbers. The costs are to be paid by the royal treasury. [5] Also, the gold and silver articles of the house of God, which Nebuchadnezzar took from the temple in Jerusalem and brought to Babylon, are to be returned to their places in the temple in Jerusalem; they are to be deposited in the house of God.

[6] Now then, Tattenai, governor of Trans-Euphrates, and Shethar-Bozenai and you other officials of that province, stay away from there. [7] Do not interfere with the work on this temple of God. Let the governor of the Jews and the Jewish elders rebuild this house of God on its site.

[8] Moreover, I hereby decree what you are to do for these elders of the Jews in the construction of this house of God:

Their expenses are to be fully paid out of the royal treasury, from the revenues of Trans-Euphrates, so that the work will not stop. [9] Whatever is needed — young bulls, rams, male lambs for burnt offerings to the God of heaven, and wheat, salt, wine and olive oil, as requested by the priests in Jerusalem — must be given them daily without fail, [10] so that they may offer sacrifices pleasing to the God of heaven and pray for the well-being of the king and his sons.

[11] Furthermore, I decree that if anyone defies this edict, a beam is to be pulled from their house and they are to be impaled on it. And for this crime their house is to be made a pile of rubble. [12] May God, who has caused his Name to dwell there, overthrow any

---

[a] 14 Or *palace*   [b] 3 That is, about 90 feet or about 27 meters

king or people who lifts a hand to change this decree or to destroy this temple in Jerusalem.

I Darius have decreed it. Let it be carried out with diligence.

Completion and Dedication of the Temple

[13]Then, because of the decree King Darius had sent, Tattenai, governor of Trans-Euphrates, and Shethar-Bozenai and their associates carried it out with diligence. [14]So the elders of the Jews continued to build and prosper under the preaching of Haggai the prophet and Zechariah, a descendant of Iddo. They finished building the temple according to the command of the God of Israel and the decrees of Cyrus, Darius and Artaxerxes, kings of Persia. [15]The temple was completed on the third day of the month Adar, in the sixth year of the reign of King Darius.

[16]Then the people of Israel—the priests, the Levites and the rest of the exiles—celebrated the dedication of the house of God with joy. [17]For the dedication of this house of God they offered a hundred bulls, two hundred rams, four hundred male lambs and, as a sin offering[a] for all Israel, twelve male goats, one for each of the tribes of Israel. [18]And they installed the priests in their divisions and the Levites in their groups for the service of God at Jerusalem, according to what is written in the Book of Moses.

The Passover

[19]On the fourteenth day of the first month, the exiles celebrated the Passover. [20]The priests and Levites had purified themselves and were all ceremonially clean. The Levites slaughtered the Passover lamb for all the exiles, for their relatives the priests and for themselves. [21]So the Israelites who had returned from the exile ate it, together with all who had separated themselves from the unclean practices of their Gentile neighbors in order to seek the LORD, the God of Israel. [22]For seven days they celebrated with joy the Festival of Unleavened Bread, because the LORD had filled them with joy by changing the attitude of the king of Assyria so that he assisted them in the work on the house of God, the God of Israel.

Ezra Comes to Jerusalem

7 After these things, during the reign of Artaxerxes king of Persia, Ezra son of Seraiah, the son of Azariah, the son of Hilkiah, [2]the son of Shallum, the son of Zadok, the son of Ahitub, [3]the son of Amariah, the son of Azariah, the son of Meraioth, [4]the son of Zerahiah, the son of Uzzi, the son of Bukki, [5]the son of Abishua, the son of Phinehas, the son of Eleazar, the son of Aaron the chief priest— [6]this Ezra came up from Babylon. He was a teacher well versed in the Law of Moses, which the LORD, the God of Israel, had given. The king had granted him everything he asked, for the hand of the LORD his God was on him. [7]Some of the Israelites, including priests, Levites, musicians, gatekeepers and temple servants, also came up to Jerusalem in the seventh year of King Artaxerxes.

[8]Ezra arrived in Jerusalem in the fifth month of the seventh year of the king. [9]He had begun his journey from Babylon on the first day of the first month, and he arrived in Jerusalem on the first day of the fifth month, for the gracious hand of his God was on him. [10]For Ezra had devoted himself to the study and observance of the Law of the LORD, and to teaching its decrees and laws in Israel.

King Artaxerxes' Letter to Ezra

[11]This is a copy of the letter King Artaxerxes had given to Ezra the priest, a teacher of the Law, a man learned in matters concerning the commands and decrees of the LORD for Israel:

[12]Artaxerxes, king of kings,

To Ezra the priest, teacher of the Law of the God of heaven:

Greetings.

[13]Now I decree that any of the Israelites in my kingdom, including priests and Levites, who volunteer to go to Jerusalem with you, may go. [14]You are sent by the king and his seven advisers to inquire about Judah and Jerusalem with regard to the Law of your God, which is in your hand. [15]Moreover, you are to take with you the silver and gold that the king and his advisers have

A JOB WELL DONE

READ: EZRA 6:16

God's people finally had a real reason to celebrate. Their work on the temple got off to a nice start, then stalled. Two decades later they had pushed through every kind of opposition. Now their job was done.

Opposition to building the temple began when Judah's neighbors heard about the project. Their offer of assistance sounded good at first, but these sly enemies weren't part of God's people. They had been forcibly resettled in the land just as the people of Judah had been taken captive to Babylon. To them the Lord was merely one of many gods. They didn't even know his proper name, Yahweh (Ezra 4:1-5).

Their opposition made the people afraid to build, and their complaints to a new king, Artaxerxes, forced the work to stop altogether. Only when the prophets Haggai and Zechariah came on the scene did work begin again (5:1-3). They stood up for their right to rebuild the temple, convincing yet another king, Darius, to let them proceed. Darius even stepped up and paid for the project from his royal treasury, supplying everything needed for the task.

When you set your mind on serving God, he will ensure you accomplish his plans. Yet his help doesn't mean you won't face ferocious opposition. If you give up at the first sign of trouble, you might never know what he can accomplish through you.

BUILDING FAITH WISDOM STRENGTH

freely given to the God of Israel, whose dwelling is in Jerusalem, ¹⁶together with all the silver and gold you may obtain from the province of Babylon, as well as the freewill offerings of the people and priests for the temple of their God in Jerusalem. ¹⁷With this money be sure to buy bulls, rams and male lambs, together with their grain offerings and drink offerings, and sacrifice them on the altar of the temple of your God in Jerusalem.

¹⁸You and your fellow Israelites may then do whatever seems best with the rest of the silver and gold, in accordance with the will of your God. ¹⁹Deliver to the God of Jerusalem all the articles entrusted to you for worship in the temple of your God. ²⁰And anything else needed for the temple of your God that you are responsible to supply, you may provide from the royal treasury.

²¹Now I, King Artaxerxes, decree that all the treasurers of Trans-Euphrates are to provide with diligence whatever Ezra the priest, the teacher of the Law of the God of heaven, may ask of you — ²²up to a hundred talents[a] of silver, a hundred cors[b] of wheat, a hundred baths[c] of wine, a hundred baths[c] of olive oil, and salt without limit. ²³Whatever the God of heaven has prescribed, let it be done with diligence for the temple of the God of heaven. Why should his wrath fall on the realm of the king and of his sons? ²⁴You are also to know that you have no authority to impose taxes, tribute or duty on any of the priests, Levites, musicians, gatekeepers, temple servants or other workers at this house of God.

²⁵And you, Ezra, in accordance with the wisdom of your God, which you possess, appoint magistrates and judges to administer justice to all the people of Trans-Euphrates — all who know the laws of your God. And you are to teach any who do not know them. ²⁶Whoever does not obey the law of your God and the law of the king must surely be punished by death, banishment, confiscation of property, or imprisonment.[d]

²⁷Praise be to the Lᴏʀᴅ, the God of our ancestors, who has put it into the king's heart to bring honor to the house of the Lᴏʀᴅ in Jerusalem in this way ²⁸and who has extended his good favor to me before the king and his advisers and all the king's powerful officials. Because the hand of the Lᴏʀᴅ my God was on me, I took courage and gathered leaders from Israel to go up with me.

List of the Family Heads Returning With Ezra

8 These are the family heads and those registered with them who came up with me from Babylon during the reign of King Artaxerxes:

²of the descendants of Phinehas, Gershom;

of the descendants of Ithamar, Daniel;

of the descendants of David, Hattush ³of the descendants of Shekaniah;

of the descendants of Parosh, Zechariah, and with him were registered 150 men;

⁴of the descendants of Pahath-Moab, Eliehoenai son of Zerahiah, and with him 200 men;

⁵of the descendants of Zattu,[e] Shekaniah son of Jahaziel, and with him 300 men;

⁶of the descendants of Adin, Ebed son of Jonathan, and with him 50 men;

⁷of the descendants of Elam, Jeshaiah son of Athaliah, and with him 70 men;

⁸of the descendants of Shephatiah, Zebadiah son of Michael, and with him 80 men;

⁹of the descendants of Joab, Obadiah son of Jehiel, and with him 218 men;

¹⁰of the descendants of Bani,[f] Shelomith son of Josiphiah, and with him 160 men;

¹¹of the descendants of Bebai, Zechariah son of Bebai, and with him 28 men;

---

a 22 That is, about 3 3/4 tons or about 3.4 metric tons   *b 22* That is, probably about 18 tons or about 16 metric tons   *c 22* That is, about 600 gallons or about 2,200 liters   *d 26* The text of 7:12-26 is in Aramaic.   *e 5* Some Septuagint manuscripts (also 1 Esdras 8:32); Hebrew does not have *Zattu*.   *f 10* Some Septuagint manuscripts (also 1 Esdras 8:36); Hebrew does not have *Bani*.

¹² of the descendants of Azgad, Johanan son of Hakkatan, and with him 110 men;

¹³ of the descendants of Adonikam, the last ones, whose names were Eliphelet, Jeuel and Shemaiah, and with them 60 men;

¹⁴ of the descendants of Bigvai, Uthai and Zakkur, and with them 70 men.

The Return to Jerusalem

¹⁵ I assembled them at the canal that flows toward Ahava, and we camped there three days. When I checked among the people and the priests, I found no Levites there. ¹⁶ So I summoned Eliezer, Ariel, Shemaiah, Elnathan, Jarib, Elnathan, Nathan, Zechariah and Meshullam, who were leaders, and Joiarib and Elnathan, who were men of learning, ¹⁷ and I ordered them to go to Iddo, the leader in Kasiphia. I told them what to say to Iddo and his fellow Levites, the temple servants in Kasiphia, so that they might bring attendants to us for the house of our God. ¹⁸ Because the gracious hand of our God was on us, they brought us Sherebiah, a capable man, from the descendants of Mahli son of Levi, the son of Israel, and Sherebiah's sons and brothers, 18 in all; ¹⁹ and Hashabiah, together with Jeshaiah from the descendants of Merari, and his brothers and nephews, 20 in all. ²⁰ They also brought 220 of the temple servants — a body that David and the officials had established to assist the Levites. All were registered by name.

²¹ There, by the Ahava Canal, I proclaimed a fast, so that we might humble ourselves before our God and ask him for a safe journey for us and our children, with all our possessions. ²² I was ashamed to ask the king for soldiers and horsemen to protect us from enemies on the road, because we had told the king, "The gracious hand of our God is on everyone who looks to him, but his great anger is against all who forsake him." ²³ So we fasted and petitioned our God about this, and he answered our prayer.

²⁴ Then I set apart twelve of the leading priests, namely, Sherebiah, Hashabiah and ten of their brothers, ²⁵ and I weighed out to them the offering of silver and gold and the articles that the king, his advisers, his officials and all Israel present there had donated for the house of our God. ²⁶ I weighed out to them 650 talents[a] of silver, silver articles weighing 100 talents,[b] 100 talents[b] of gold, ²⁷ 20 bowls of gold valued at 1,000 darics,[c] and two fine articles of polished bronze, as precious as gold.

²⁸ I said to them, "You as well as these articles are consecrated to the LORD. The silver and gold are a freewill offering to the LORD, the God of your ancestors. ²⁹ Guard them carefully until you weigh them out in the chambers of the house of the LORD in Jerusalem before the leading priests and the Levites and the family heads of Israel." ³⁰ Then the priests and Levites received the silver and gold and sacred articles that had been weighed out to be taken to the house of our God in Jerusalem.

³¹ On the twelfth day of the first month we set out from the Ahava Canal to go to Jerusalem. The hand of our God was on us, and he protected us from enemies and bandits along the way. ³² So we arrived in Jerusalem, where we rested three days.

³³ On the fourth day, in the house of our God, we weighed out the silver and gold and the sacred articles into the hands of Meremoth son of Uriah, the priest. Eleazar son of Phinehas was with him, and so were the Levites Jozabad son of Jeshua and Noadiah son of Binnui. ³⁴ Everything was accounted for by number and weight, and the entire weight was recorded at that time.

³⁵ Then the exiles who had returned from captivity sacrificed burnt offerings to the God of Israel: twelve bulls for all Israel, ninety-six rams, seventy-seven male lambs and, as a sin offering,[d] twelve male goats. All this was a burnt offering to the LORD. ³⁶ They also delivered the king's orders to the royal satraps and to the governors of Trans-Euphrates, who then gave assistance to the people and to the house of God.

Ezra's Prayer About Intermarriage

9 After these things had been done, the leaders came to me and said, "The people of Israel, including the priests and the Levites, have not kept themselves separate from the neighboring peoples with their detestable practices, like those of the Canaanites,

---

[a] 26 That is, about 24 tons or about 22 metric tons
[b] 26 That is, about 3 3/4 tons or about 3.4 metric tons
[c] 27 That is, about 19 pounds or about 8.4 kilograms
[d] 35 Or purification offering

EZRA

Ezra came up from Babylon. He was a teacher well versed in the Law of Moses, which the LORD, the God of Israel, had given. The king had granted him everything he asked, for the hand of the LORD his God was on him. EZRA 7:6

HIS NAME MEANS: "help"
READ HIS STORY: *Ezra 7–10; Nehemiah 8*

MEN OF THE BIBLE

As a priest, Ezra could trace his ancestry straight back to Aaron, the brother of Moses. While living in Babylon more than a century after the exile, Ezra got permission from King Artaxerxes to lead a caravan of Israelites to return to Jerusalem. His powerful leadership brought reform and change as he encouraged fellow Jews to confess their sins and live a holy life dedicated to following God's Word.

As a teacher of the Law, he had to diligently study, interpret and preserve God's words. Ezra knew the power of God's Word. In it he found laws and truth that changed his life and the direction of his nation.

Ezra knew the delight of God's Word. This means he loved to read it through and through, over and over. He was so filled with joy from the discoveries he made when he read the Scriptures that he couldn't hold it inside—he just had to share and teach others all about it. He inspired his fellow Israelites to love God's Word too; they listened to him read Scripture from early morning until noon one day (Nehemiah 8:2–3).

Have you discovered the treasure of reading God's Word as Ezra did? Read the Bible every day. You'll find strength to face whatever challenge may come your way. You'll find the answers to questions that overwhelm you. You'll discover that its wisdom will nourish your soul, sustain your spirit and help you grow.

Hittites, Perizzites, Jebusites, Ammonites, Moabites, Egyptians and Amorites. [2]They have taken some of their daughters as wives for themselves and their sons, and have mingled the holy race with the peoples around them. And the leaders and officials have led the way in this unfaithfulness."

[3]When I heard this, I tore my tunic and cloak, pulled hair from my head and beard and sat down appalled. [4]Then everyone who trembled at the words of the God of Israel gathered around me because of this unfaithfulness of the exiles. And I sat there appalled until the evening sacrifice.

[5]Then, at the evening sacrifice, I rose from my self-abasement, with my tunic and cloak torn, and fell on my knees with my hands spread out to the LORD my God [6]and prayed:

"I am too ashamed and disgraced, my God, to lift up my face to you, because our sins are higher than our heads and our guilt has reached to the heavens. [7]From the days of our ancestors until now, our guilt has been great. Because of our sins, we and our kings and our priests have been subjected to the sword and captivity, to pillage and humiliation at the hand of foreign kings, as it is today.

[8]"But now, for a brief moment, the LORD our God has been gracious in leaving us a remnant and giving us a firm place[a] in his sanctuary, and so our God gives light to our eyes and a little relief in our bondage. [9]Though we are slaves, our God has not forsaken us in our bondage. He has shown us kindness in the sight of the kings of Persia: He has granted us new life to rebuild the house of our God and repair its ruins, and he has given us a wall of protection in Judah and Jerusalem.

[10]"But now, our God, what can we say after this? For we have forsaken the commands [11]you gave through your servants the prophets when you said: 'The land you are entering to possess is a land polluted by the corruption of its peoples. By their detestable practices they have filled it with their impurity from one end to the other. [12]Therefore, do not give your daughters in marriage to their sons or take their daughters for your sons. Do not seek a treaty of friendship with them at any time, that you may be strong and eat the good things of the land and leave it to your children as an everlasting inheritance.'

[13]"What has happened to us is a result of our evil deeds and our great guilt, and yet, our God, you have punished us less than our sins deserved and have given us a remnant like this. [14]Shall we then break your commands again and intermarry with the peoples who commit such detestable practices? Would you not be angry enough with us to destroy us, leaving us no remnant or survivor? [15]LORD, the God of Israel, you are righteous! We are left this day as a remnant. Here we are before you in our guilt, though because of it not one of us can stand in your presence."

The People's Confession of Sin

10 While Ezra was praying and confessing, weeping and throwing himself down before the house of God, a large crowd of Israelites — men, women and children — gathered around him. They too wept bitterly. [2]Then Shekaniah son of Jehiel, one of the descendants of Elam, said to Ezra, "We have been unfaithful to our God by marrying foreign women from the peoples around us. But in spite of this, there is still hope for Israel. [3]Now let us make a covenant before our God to send away all these women and their children, in accordance with the counsel of my lord and of those who fear the commands of our God. Let it be done according to the Law. [4]Rise up; this matter is in your hands. We will support you, so take courage and do it."

[5]So Ezra rose up and put the leading priests and Levites and all Israel under oath to do what had been suggested. And they took the oath. [6]Then Ezra withdrew from before the house of God and went to the room of Jehohanan son of Eliashib. While he was there, he ate no food and drank no water, because he continued to mourn over the unfaithfulness of the exiles.

[7]A proclamation was then issued throughout Judah and Jerusalem for all the exiles to assemble in Jerusalem. [8]Anyone who failed

---

[a] 8 Or *a foothold*

to appear within three days would forfeit all his property, in accordance with the decision of the officials and elders, and would himself be expelled from the assembly of the exiles.

⁹Within the three days, all the men of Judah and Benjamin had gathered in Jerusalem. And on the twentieth day of the ninth month, all the people were sitting in the square before the house of God, greatly distressed by the occasion and because of the rain. ¹⁰Then Ezra the priest stood up and said to them, "You have been unfaithful; you have married foreign women, adding to Israel's guilt. ¹¹Now honor[a] the LORD, the God of your ancestors, and do his will. Separate yourselves from the peoples around you and from your foreign wives."

¹²The whole assembly responded with a loud voice: "You are right! We must do as you say. ¹³But there are many people here and it is the rainy season; so we cannot stand outside. Besides, this matter cannot be taken care of in a day or two, because we have sinned greatly in this thing. ¹⁴Let our officials act for the whole assembly. Then let everyone in our towns who has married a foreign woman come at a set time, along with the elders and judges of each town, until the fierce anger of our God in this matter is turned away from us." ¹⁵Only Jonathan son of Asahel and Jahzeiah son of Tikvah, supported by Meshullam and Shabbethai the Levite, opposed this.

¹⁶So the exiles did as was proposed. Ezra the priest selected men who were family heads, one from each family division, and all of them designated by name. On the first day of the tenth month they sat down to investigate the cases, ¹⁷and by the first day of the first month they finished dealing with all the men who had married foreign women.

Those Guilty of Intermarriage

¹⁸Among the descendants of the priests, the following had married foreign women:

From the descendants of Joshua son of Jozadak, and his brothers: Maaseiah, Eliezer, Jarib and Gedaliah. ¹⁹(They all gave their hands in pledge to put away their wives, and for their guilt they each presented a ram from the flock as a guilt offering.)

²⁰From the descendants of Immer:
Hanani and Zebadiah.

²¹From the descendants of Harim:
Maaseiah, Elijah, Shemaiah, Jehiel and Uzziah.

²²From the descendants of Pashhur:
Elioenai, Maaseiah, Ishmael, Nethanel, Jozabad and Elasah.

²³Among the Levites:

Jozabad, Shimei, Kelaiah (that is, Kelita), Pethahiah, Judah and Eliezer.

²⁴From the musicians:
Eliashib.
From the gatekeepers:
Shallum, Telem and Uri.

²⁵And among the other Israelites:

From the descendants of Parosh:
Ramiah, Izziah, Malkijah, Mijamin, Eleazar, Malkijah and Benaiah.

²⁶From the descendants of Elam:
Mattaniah, Zechariah, Jehiel, Abdi, Jeremoth and Elijah.

²⁷From the descendants of Zattu:
Elioenai, Eliashib, Mattaniah, Jeremoth, Zabad and Aziza.

²⁸From the descendants of Bebai:
Jehohanan, Hananiah, Zabbai and Athlai.

²⁹From the descendants of Bani:
Meshullam, Malluk, Adaiah, Jashub, Sheal and Jeremoth.

³⁰From the descendants of Pahath-Moab:
Adna, Kelal, Benaiah, Maaseiah, Mattaniah, Bezalel, Binnui and Manasseh.

³¹From the descendants of Harim:
Eliezer, Ishijah, Malkijah, Shemaiah, Shimeon, ³²Benjamin, Malluk and Shemariah.

³³From the descendants of Hashum:
Mattenai, Mattattah, Zabad, Eliphelet, Jeremai, Manasseh and Shimei.

³⁴From the descendants of Bani:
Maadai, Amram, Uel, ³⁵Benaiah, Bedeiah, Keluhi, ³⁶Vaniah, Meremoth, Eliashib, ³⁷Mattaniah, Mattenai and Jaasu.

ᵃ 11 Or *Now make confession to*

38 From the descendants of Binnui:[a]
   Shimei, 39 Shelemiah, Nathan, Adaiah, 40 Maknadebai, Shashai, Sharai,
   41 Azarel, Shelemiah, Shemariah,
   42 Shallum, Amariah and Joseph.
43 From the descendants of Nebo:

Jeiel, Mattithiah, Zabad, Zebina, Jad-
dai, Joel and Benaiah.

44 All these had married foreign women,
and some of them had children by these
wives.[b]

NEHEMIAH

WHEN DID THIS HAPPEN?

Around 445 B.C. in Jerusalem, in the land of Israel

WHO IS IN THIS BOOK?

Nehemiah
King Artaxerxes
Ezra
Sanballat
Tobiah

VERSES YOU MIGHT RECOGNIZE

NEHEMIAH 1:10

"They are your servants and your people, whom you redeemed by your great strength and your mighty hand."

NEHEMIAH 8:10

"This day is holy to our Lord. Do not grieve, for the joy of the LORD is your strength."

WHAT'S IT ABOUT?

Nehemiah is a little like a sequel to Ezra. In fact, many scholars believe the two books were once one. Thirteen years after Ezra's return to Jerusalem, Nehemiah, a Jewish cupbearer to the Persian king, Artaxerxes, heard that the temple in Jerusalem was being rebuilt. He became anxious, knowing that the city had no wall to protect it from foreign invaders. The king gave Nehemiah his blessing—and the supplies—to go to Jerusalem and rebuild the walls around the city.

Even with some major challenges—attacks from the Samaritans and arguments among his own people—Nehemiah led the Jews in rebuilding the wall in fifty-two days! Twelve years later, the walls still stood, but the Jews couldn't seem to consistently obey God. So Nehemiah gave them a refresher course on God's law.

NEHEMIAH

Nehemiah's Prayer

1 The words of Nehemiah son of Hakaliah:

In the month of Kislev in the twentieth year, while I was in the citadel of Susa, ²Hanani, one of my brothers, came from Judah with some other men, and I questioned them about the Jewish remnant that had survived the exile, and also about Jerusalem.

³They said to me, "Those who survived the exile and are back in the province are in great trouble and disgrace. The wall of Jerusalem is broken down, and its gates have been burned with fire."

⁴When I heard these things, I sat down and wept. For some days I mourned and fasted and prayed before the God of heaven. ⁵Then I said:

"LORD, the God of heaven, the great and awesome God, who keeps his covenant of love with those who love him and keep his commandments, ⁶let your ear be attentive and your eyes open to hear the prayer your servant is praying before you day and night for your servants, the people of Israel. I confess the sins we Israelites, including myself and my father's family, have committed against you. ⁷We have acted very wickedly toward you. We have not obeyed the commands, decrees and laws you gave your servant Moses.

⁸"Remember the instruction you gave your servant Moses, saying, 'If you are unfaithful, I will scatter you among the nations, ⁹but if you return to me and obey my commands, then even if your exiled people are at the farthest horizon, I will gather them from there and bring them to the place I have chosen as a dwelling for my Name.'

¹⁰"They are your servants and your people, whom you redeemed by your great strength and your mighty hand. ¹¹Lord, let your ear be attentive to the prayer of this your servant and to the prayer of your servants who delight in revering your name. Give your servant success today by granting him favor in the presence of this man."

I was cupbearer to the king.

Artaxerxes Sends Nehemiah to Jerusalem

2 In the month of Nisan in the twentieth year of King Artaxerxes, when wine was brought for him, I took the wine and gave it to the king. I had not been sad in his presence before, ²so the king asked me, "Why does your face look so sad when you are not ill? This can be nothing but sadness of heart."

I was very much afraid, ³but I said to the king, "May the king live forever! Why should my face not look sad when the city where my ancestors are buried lies in ruins, and its gates have been destroyed by fire?"

⁴The king said to me, "What is it you want?"

Then I prayed to the God of heaven, ⁵and I answered the king, "If it pleases the king and if your servant has found favor in his sight, let him send me to the city in Judah where my ancestors are buried so that I can rebuild it."

⁶Then the king, with the queen sitting beside him, asked me, "How long will your journey take, and when will you get back?" It pleased the king to send me; so I set a time.

⁷I also said to him, "If it pleases the king, may I have letters to the governors of Trans-Euphrates, so that they will provide me safe-conduct until I arrive in Judah? ⁸And may I have a letter to Asaph, keeper of the royal park, so he will give me timber to make beams for the gates of the citadel by the temple and for the city wall and for the residence I will occupy?" And because the gracious hand of my God was on me, the king granted my requests. ⁹So I went to the governors of Trans-Euphrates and gave them the king's letters. The king had also sent army officers and cavalry with me.

MAKE A DIFFERENCE

READ: NEHEMIAH 1:3

Almost a century after captives returned from Babylon to rebuild God's temple in Jerusalem, Nehemiah receives an urgent message from home. He discovers the returnees are still struggling to survive, with the holy city's protective walls flattened and its thick gates burned.

Nehemiah weeps at this news. For days, he grieves and goes without food. Then he prays. He reminds his awesome God of his loving care. He begs God to pay attention to his words. He confesses wrongs done by him and the entire nation. Then he pleads with the Lord to keep his promises to protect his people.

Nehemiah serves as the king of Persia's trusted cupbearer, the guy who samples royal food and drink to ensure it isn't poisoned. He lives hundreds of miles from Jerusalem, yet he refuses to forget about far-off troubles. He seeks help from his powerful boss, then travels in secret to Jerusalem. He surveys the damage and gathers his fellow citizens to reconstruct the wall.

BUILDING FAITH WISDOM STRENGTH

This smart and compassionate man demonstrates steps you can take to make a difference in your hurting world. Start with prayer, make a plan, and then do your part. You can press the Lord to solve the problem, then do everything in your power to work hard and rally others to the cause. You won't accomplish anything if you pray and then stop. Dig in and get things done.

[10] When Sanballat the Horonite and Tobiah the Ammonite official heard about this, they were very much disturbed that someone had come to promote the welfare of the Israelites.

Nehemiah Inspects Jerusalem's Walls

[11] I went to Jerusalem, and after staying there three days [12] I set out during the night with a few others. I had not told anyone what my God had put in my heart to do for Jerusalem. There were no mounts with me except the one I was riding on. [13] By night I went out through the Valley Gate toward the Jackal[a] Well and the Dung Gate, examining the walls of Jerusalem, which had been broken down, and its gates, which had been destroyed by fire. [14] Then I moved on toward the Fountain Gate and the King's Pool, but there was not enough room for my mount to get through; [15] so I went up the valley by night, examining the wall. Finally, I turned back and reentered through the Valley Gate. [16] The officials did not know where I had gone or what I was doing, because as yet I had said nothing to the Jews or the priests or nobles or officials or any others who would be doing the work.

[17] Then I said to them, "You see the trouble we are in: Jerusalem lies in ruins, and its gates have been burned with fire. Come, let us rebuild the wall of Jerusalem, and we will no longer be in disgrace." [18] I also told them about the gracious hand of my God on me and what the king had said to me.

They replied, "Let us start rebuilding." So they began this good work.

[19] But when Sanballat the Horonite, Tobiah the Ammonite official and Geshem the Arab heard about it, they mocked and ridiculed us. "What is this you are doing?" they asked. "Are you rebelling against the king?"

[20] I answered them by saying, "The God of heaven will give us success. We his servants will start rebuilding, but as for you, you have no share in Jerusalem or any claim or historic right to it."

Builders of the Wall

3 Eliashib the high priest and his fellow priests went to work and rebuilt the Sheep Gate. They dedicated it and set its doors in place, building as far as the Tower of the Hundred, which they dedicated, and as far as the Tower of Hananel. [2] The men of Jericho built the adjoining section, and Zakkur son of Imri built next to them.

[3] The Fish Gate was rebuilt by the sons of Hassenaah. They laid its beams and put its doors and bolts and bars in place. [4] Meremoth son of Uriah, the son of Hakkoz, repaired the next section. Next to him Meshullam son of Berekiah, the son of Meshezabel, made repairs, and next to him Zadok son of Baana also made repairs. [5] The next section was repaired by the men of Tekoa, but their nobles would not put their shoulders to the work under their supervisors.[b]

[6] The Jeshanah[c] Gate was repaired by Joiada son of Paseah and Meshullam son of Besodeiah. They laid its beams and put its doors with their bolts and bars in place. [7] Next to them, repairs were made by men from Gibeon and Mizpah—Melatiah of Gibeon and Jadon of Meronoth—places under the authority of the governor of Trans-Euphrates. [8] Uzziel son of Harhaiah, one of the goldsmiths, repaired the next section; and Hananiah, one of the perfume-makers, made repairs next to that. They restored Jerusalem as far as the Broad Wall. [9] Rephaiah son of Hur, ruler of a half-district of Jerusalem, repaired the next section. [10] Adjoining this, Jedaiah son of Harumaph made repairs opposite his house, and Hattush son of Hashabneiah made repairs next to him. [11] Malkijah son of Harim and Hasshub son of Pahath-Moab repaired another section and the Tower of the Ovens. [12] Shallum son of Hallohesh, ruler of a half-district of Jerusalem, repaired the next section with the help of his daughters.

[13] The Valley Gate was repaired by Hanun and the residents of Zanoah. They rebuilt it and put its doors with their bolts and bars in place. They also repaired a thousand cubits[d] of the wall as far as the Dung Gate.

[14] The Dung Gate was repaired by Malkijah son of Rekab, ruler of the district of Beth Hakkerem. He rebuilt it and put its doors with their bolts and bars in place.

[15] The Fountain Gate was repaired by Shallun son of Kol-Hozeh, ruler of the district of

---

[a] 13 Or *Serpent* or *Fig*   [b] 5 Or *their Lord* or *the governor*   [c] 6 Or *Old*   [d] 13 That is, about 1,500 feet or about 450 meters

NEHEMIAH

Remember me with favor, my God, for all I have done for these people. NEHEMIAH 5:19

HIS NAME MEANS: "the LORD comforts"
READ HIS STORY: *Nehemiah 1–13*

Nehemiah started out as a cupbearer for the Persian king Artaxerxes, an honored role. Then through a miraculous set of circumstances Nehemiah was appointed governor of Judah. After making the long journey to Jerusalem, he led the Israelites in rebuilding the wall around the city, and then he joined with Ezra to bring spiritual revival.

Most of all, Nehemiah was a godly leader. A man of prayer, he constantly prayed to God, confessing his sins and the sins of his nation, asking for help, and affirming his trust in the Lord. Unlike some previous officials, he was truthful, honest and worked hard to ease the financial burden of his people.

Up against terrible threats from non-Jewish political leaders, Nehemiah acted with wisdom, a steady head and careful planning. He was not afraid to lead God's people in the midst of extremely dangerous times and threats of attack, but encouraged everyone who was rebuilding the wall around Jerusalem. In Nehemiah 4:14, he said, "Don't be afraid of them. Remember the Lord, who is great and awesome, and fight for your families, your sons and your daughters, your wives and your homes." As a leader, Nehemiah always stood for what was right and constantly encouraged those in his care.

Do you plan to run for student leadership or have a political career? Ask God to give you the same heart and same anointing as Nehemiah. Study his life. Make his prayers your prayers. Follow in the footsteps of this godly leader and let God use you to rebuild what is broken and bring revival.

Mizpah. He rebuilt it, roofing it over and putting its doors and bolts and bars in place. He also repaired the wall of the Pool of Siloam,[a] by the King's Garden, as far as the steps going down from the City of David. [16]Beyond him, Nehemiah son of Azbuk, ruler of a half-district of Beth Zur, made repairs up to a point opposite the tombs[b] of David, as far as the artificial pool and the House of the Heroes.

[17]Next to him, the repairs were made by the Levites under Rehum son of Bani. Beside him, Hashabiah, ruler of half the district of Keilah, carried out repairs for his district. [18]Next to him, the repairs were made by their fellow Levites under Binnui[c] son of Henadad, ruler of the other half-district of Keilah. [19]Next to him, Ezer son of Jeshua, ruler of Mizpah, repaired another section, from a point facing the ascent to the armory as far as the angle of the wall. [20]Next to him, Baruch son of Zabbai zealously repaired another section, from the angle to the entrance of the house of Eliashib the high priest. [21]Next to him, Meremoth son of Uriah, the son of Hakkoz, repaired another section, from the entrance of Eliashib's house to the end of it.

[22]The repairs next to him were made by the priests from the surrounding region. [23]Beyond them, Benjamin and Hasshub made repairs in front of their house; and next to them, Azariah son of Maaseiah, the son of Ananiah, made repairs beside his house. [24]Next to him, Binnui son of Henadad repaired another section, from Azariah's house to the angle and the corner, [25]and Palal son of Uzai worked opposite the angle and the tower projecting from the upper palace near the court of the guard. Next to him, Pedaiah son of Parosh [26]and the temple servants living on the hill of Ophel made repairs up to a point opposite the Water Gate toward the east and the projecting tower. [27]Next to them, the men of Tekoa repaired another section, from the great projecting tower to the wall of Ophel.

[28]Above the Horse Gate, the priests made repairs, each in front of his own house. [29]Next to them, Zadok son of Immer made repairs opposite his house. Next to him, Shemaiah son of Shekaniah, the guard at the East Gate, made repairs. [30]Next to him, Hananiah son of Shelemiah, and Hanun, the sixth son of Zalaph, repaired another section. Next to them, Meshullam son of Berekiah made repairs opposite his living quarters. [31]Next to him, Malkijah, one of the goldsmiths, made repairs as far as the house of the temple servants and the merchants, opposite the Inspection Gate, and as far as the room above the corner; [32]and between the room above the corner and the Sheep Gate the goldsmiths and merchants made repairs.

Opposition to the Rebuilding

4[d] When Sanballat heard that we were rebuilding the wall, he became angry and was greatly incensed. He ridiculed the Jews, [2]and in the presence of his associates and the army of Samaria, he said, "What are those feeble Jews doing? Will they restore their wall? Will they offer sacrifices? Will they finish in a day? Can they bring the stones back to life from those heaps of rubble—burned as they are?"

[3]Tobiah the Ammonite, who was at his side, said, "What they are building—even a fox climbing up on it would break down their wall of stones!"

[4]Hear us, our God, for we are despised. Turn their insults back on their own heads. Give them over as plunder in a land of captivity. [5]Do not cover up their guilt or blot out their sins from your sight, for they have thrown insults in the face of[e] the builders.

[6]So we rebuilt the wall till all of it reached half its height, for the people worked with all their heart.

[7]But when Sanballat, Tobiah, the Arabs, the Ammonites and the people of Ashdod heard that the repairs to Jerusalem's walls had gone ahead and that the gaps were being closed, they were very angry. [8]They all plotted together to come and fight against Jerusalem and stir up trouble against it. [9]But we prayed to our God and posted a guard day and night to meet this threat.

[10]Meanwhile, the people in Judah said, "The strength of the laborers is giving out,

---

[a] 15 Hebrew *Shelah,* a variant of *Shiloah,* that is, Siloam   [b] 16 Hebrew; Septuagint, some Vulgate manuscripts and Syriac *tomb*   [c] 18 Two Hebrew manuscripts and Syriac (see also Septuagint and verse 24); most Hebrew manuscripts *Bavvai*   [d] In Hebrew texts 4:1-6 is numbered 3:33-38, and 4:7-23 is numbered 4:1-17.   [e] 5 Or *have aroused your anger before*

and there is so much rubble that we cannot rebuild the wall."

¹¹Also our enemies said, "Before they know it or see us, we will be right there among them and will kill them and put an end to the work."

¹²Then the Jews who lived near them came and told us ten times over, "Wherever you turn, they will attack us."

¹³Therefore I stationed some of the people behind the lowest points of the wall at the exposed places, posting them by families, with their swords, spears and bows. ¹⁴After I looked things over, I stood up and said to the nobles, the officials and the rest of the people, "Don't be afraid of them. Remember the Lord, who is great and awesome, and fight for your families, your sons and your daughters, your wives and your homes."

¹⁵When our enemies heard that we were aware of their plot and that God had frustrated it, we all returned to the wall, each to our own work.

¹⁶From that day on, half of my men did the work, while the other half were equipped with spears, shields, bows and armor. The officers posted themselves behind all the people of Judah ¹⁷who were building the wall. Those who carried materials did their work with one hand and held a weapon in the other, ¹⁸and each of the builders wore his sword at his side as he worked. But the man who sounded the trumpet stayed with me.

¹⁹Then I said to the nobles, the officials and the rest of the people, "The work is extensive and spread out, and we are widely separated from each other along the wall. ²⁰Wherever you hear the sound of the trumpet, join us there. Our God will fight for us!"

²¹So we continued the work with half the men holding spears, from the first light of dawn till the stars came out. ²²At that time I also said to the people, "Have every man and his helper stay inside Jerusalem at night, so they can serve us as guards by night and as workers by day." ²³Neither I nor my brothers nor my men nor the guards with me took off our clothes; each had his weapon, even when he went for water.ᵃ

Nehemiah Helps the Poor

5 Now the men and their wives raised a great outcry against their fellow Jews.

²Some were saying, "We and our sons and daughters are numerous; in order for us to eat and stay alive, we must get grain."

³Others were saying, "We are mortgaging our fields, our vineyards and our homes to get grain during the famine."

⁴Still others were saying, "We have had to borrow money to pay the king's tax on our fields and vineyards. ⁵Although we are of the same flesh and blood as our fellow Jews and though our children are as good as theirs, yet we have to subject our sons and daughters to slavery. Some of our daughters have already been enslaved, but we are powerless, because our fields and our vineyards belong to others."

⁶When I heard their outcry and these charges, I was very angry. ⁷I pondered them in my mind and then accused the nobles and officials. I told them, "You are charging your own people interest!" So I called together a large meeting to deal with them ⁸and said: "As far as possible, we have bought back our fellow Jews who were sold to the Gentiles. Now you are selling your own people, only for them to be sold back to us!" They kept quiet, because they could find nothing to say.

⁹So I continued, "What you are doing is not right. Shouldn't you walk in the fear of our God to avoid the reproach of our Gentile enemies? ¹⁰I and my brothers and my men are also lending the people money and grain. But let us stop charging interest! ¹¹Give back to them immediately their fields, vineyards, olive groves and houses, and also the interest you are charging them — one percent of the money, grain, new wine and olive oil."

¹²"We will give it back," they said. "And we will not demand anything more from them. We will do as you say."

Then I summoned the priests and made the nobles and officials take an oath to do what they had promised. ¹³I also shook out the folds of my robe and said, "In this way may God shake out of their house and possessions anyone who does not keep this promise. So may such a person be shaken out and emptied!"

At this the whole assembly said, "Amen," and praised the Lord. And the people did as they had promised.

¹⁴Moreover, from the twentieth year of

ᵃ 23 The meaning of the Hebrew for this clause is uncertain.

King Artaxerxes, when I was appointed to be their governor in the land of Judah, until his thirty-second year — twelve years — neither I nor my brothers ate the food allotted to the governor. [15]But the earlier governors — those preceding me — placed a heavy burden on the people and took forty shekels[a] of silver from them in addition to food and wine. Their assistants also lorded it over the people. But out of reverence for God I did not act like that. [16]Instead, I devoted myself to the work on this wall. All my men were assembled there for the work; we[b] did not acquire any land.

[17]Furthermore, a hundred and fifty Jews and officials ate at my table, as well as those who came to us from the surrounding nations. [18]Each day one ox, six choice sheep and some poultry were prepared for me, and every ten days an abundant supply of wine of all kinds. In spite of all this, I never demanded the food allotted to the governor, because the demands were heavy on these people.

[19]Remember me with favor, my God, for all I have done for these people.

Further Opposition to the Rebuilding

6 When word came to Sanballat, Tobiah, Geshem the Arab and the rest of our enemies that I had rebuilt the wall and not a gap was left in it — though up to that time I had not set the doors in the gates — [2]Sanballat and Geshem sent me this message: "Come, let us meet together in one of the villages[c] on the plain of Ono."

But they were scheming to harm me; [3]so I sent messengers to them with this reply: "I am carrying on a great project and cannot go down. Why should the work stop while I leave it and go down to you?" [4]Four times they sent me the same message, and each time I gave them the same answer.

[5]Then, the fifth time, Sanballat sent his aide to me with the same message, and in his hand was an unsealed letter [6]in which was written:

"It is reported among the nations — and Geshem[d] says it is true — that you and the Jews are plotting to revolt, and therefore you are building the wall. Moreover, according to these reports you are about to become their king

[7]and have even appointed prophets to make this proclamation about you in Jerusalem: 'There is a king in Judah!' Now this report will get back to the king; so come, let us meet together."

[8]I sent him this reply: "Nothing like what you are saying is happening; you are just making it up out of your head."

[9]They were all trying to frighten us, thinking, "Their hands will get too weak for the work, and it will not be completed."

But I prayed, "Now strengthen my hands."

[10]One day I went to the house of Shemaiah son of Delaiah, the son of Mehetabel, who was shut in at his home. He said, "Let us meet in the house of God, inside the temple, and let us close the temple doors, because men are coming to kill you — by night they are coming to kill you."

[11]But I said, "Should a man like me run away? Or should someone like me go into the temple to save his life? I will not go!" [12]I realized that God had not sent him, but that he had prophesied against me because Tobiah and Sanballat had hired him. [13]He had been hired to intimidate me so that I would commit a sin by doing this, and then they would give me a bad name to discredit me.

[14]Remember Tobiah and Sanballat, my God, because of what they have done; remember also the prophet Noadiah and how she and the rest of the prophets have been trying to intimidate me. [15]So the wall was completed on the twenty-fifth of Elul, in fifty-two days.

Opposition to the Completed Wall

[16]When all our enemies heard about this, all the surrounding nations were afraid and lost their self-confidence, because they realized that this work had been done with the help of our God.

[17]Also, in those days the nobles of Judah were sending many letters to Tobiah, and replies from Tobiah kept coming to them. [18]For many in Judah were under oath to him, since he was son-in-law to Shekaniah son of Arah, and his son Jehohanan had married the daughter of Meshullam son of Berekiah. [19]Moreover, they kept reporting to me his

---

[a] 15 That is, about 1 pound or about 460 grams   [b] 16 Most Hebrew manuscripts; some Hebrew manuscripts, Septuagint, Vulgate and Syriac I of Geshem   [c] 2 Or in Kephirim   [d] 6 Hebrew Gashmu, a variant

GOD-SIZED SOLUTION

READ: NEHEMIAH 6:16

Jerusalem's residents got to work as soon as Nehemiah persuaded them it was possible to rebuild the protective wall that ringed the city. Even when they endured fierce opposition, they didn't stop until they were done.

Don't skip over key details of this divine construction project. Right from the start the builders face ridicule and lies (Nehemiah 2:19). People take responsibility for specific portions of the job (3:1–32). A few popular people refuse to lift a finger to help (v. 5). When enemies mock, workers pray (4:1–5). Because almost everyone decides to work hard, the wall quickly reaches half its height (v. 6).

Those problems and solutions fit any job you will ever do. And there's more. When enemies threaten to attack, the people think smart, both praying to God and posting a guard night and day (v. 9). The builders depend on the Lord for protection and strength (v. 14). When the wall is finished, everyone near and far knows only God could have powered their work.

BUILDING

FAITH

WISDOM

STRENGTH

The book of Nehemiah is all about seeing a problem, getting a God-sized solution, and working hard to finish the task. Don't think you can accomplish that kind of job on your own. No matter what tasks you need to get done today, God wants you to lean on him for power and encouragement.

good deeds and then telling him what I said. And Tobiah sent letters to intimidate me.

7 After the wall had been rebuilt and I had set the doors in place, the gatekeepers, the musicians and the Levites were appointed. ²I put in charge of Jerusalem my brother Hanani, along with Hananiah the commander of the citadel, because he was a man of integrity and feared God more than most people do. ³I said to them, "The gates of Jerusalem are not to be opened until the sun is hot. While the gatekeepers are still on duty, have them shut the doors and bar them. Also appoint residents of Jerusalem as guards, some at their posts and some near their own houses."

The List of the Exiles Who Returned

⁴Now the city was large and spacious, but there were few people in it, and the houses had not yet been rebuilt. ⁵So my God put it into my heart to assemble the nobles, the officials and the common people for registration by families. I found the genealogical record of those who had been the first to return. This is what I found written there:

⁶These are the people of the province who came up from the captivity of the exiles whom Nebuchadnezzar king of Babylon had taken captive (they returned to Jerusalem and Judah, each to his own town, ⁷in company with Zerubbabel, Joshua, Nehemiah, Azariah, Raamiah, Nahamani, Mordecai, Bilshan, Mispereth, Bigvai, Nehum and Baanah):

The list of the men of Israel:

⁸	the descendants of Parosh	2,172
⁹	of Shephatiah	372
¹⁰	of Arah	652
¹¹	of Pahath-Moab (through the line of Jeshua and Joab)	2,818
¹²	of Elam	1,254
¹³	of Zattu	845
¹⁴	of Zakkai	760
¹⁵	of Binnui	648
¹⁶	of Bebai	628
¹⁷	of Azgad	2,322
¹⁸	of Adonikam	667
¹⁹	of Bigvai	2,067
²⁰	of Adin	655
²¹	of Ater (through Hezekiah)	98
²²	of Hashum	328
²³	of Bezai	324
²⁴	of Hariph	112
²⁵	of Gibeon	95
²⁶	the men of Bethlehem and Netophah	188
²⁷	of Anathoth	128
²⁸	of Beth Azmaveth	42
²⁹	of Kiriath Jearim, Kephirah and Beeroth	743
³⁰	of Ramah and Geba	621
³¹	of Mikmash	122
³²	of Bethel and Ai	123
³³	of the other Nebo	52
³⁴	of the other Elam	1,254
³⁵	of Harim	320
³⁶	of Jericho	345
³⁷	of Lod, Hadid and Ono	721
³⁸	of Senaah	3,930

³⁹The priests:

the descendants of Jedaiah (through the family of Jeshua)	973
⁴⁰ of Immer	1,052
⁴¹ of Pashhur	1,247
⁴² of Harim	1,017

⁴³The Levites:

the descendants of Jeshua (through Kadmiel through the line of Hodaviah)	74

⁴⁴The musicians:

the descendants of Asaph	148

⁴⁵The gatekeepers:

the descendants of Shallum, Ater, Talmon, Akkub, Hatita and Shobai	138

⁴⁶The temple servants:

the descendants of
Ziha, Hasupha, Tabbaoth,
⁴⁷Keros, Sia, Padon,
⁴⁸Lebana, Hagaba, Shalmai,
⁴⁹Hanan, Giddel, Gahar,
⁵⁰Reaiah, Rezin, Nekoda,
⁵¹Gazzam, Uzza, Paseah,
⁵²Besai, Meunim, Nephusim,
⁵³Bakbuk, Hakupha, Harhur,
⁵⁴Bazluth, Mehida, Harsha,
⁵⁵Barkos, Sisera, Temah,
⁵⁶Neziah and Hatipha

⁵⁷The descendants of the servants of Solomon:

the descendants of
Sotai, Sophereth, Perida,
58 Jaala, Darkon, Giddel,
59 Shephatiah, Hattil,
Pokereth-Hazzebaim and Amon

60 The temple servants and the
descendants of the servants of
Solomon   392

61 The following came up from the towns of Tel Melah, Tel Harsha, Kerub, Addon and Immer, but they could not show that their families were descended from Israel:

62 the descendants of
Delaiah, Tobiah and Nekoda 642

63 And from among the priests:

the descendants of
Hobaiah, Hakkoz and Barzillai (a man who had married a daughter of Barzillai the Gileadite and was called by that name).

64 These searched for their family records, but they could not find them and so were excluded from the priesthood as unclean. 65 The governor, therefore, ordered them not to eat any of the most sacred food until there should be a priest ministering with the Urim and Thummim.

66 The whole company numbered 42,360, 67 besides their 7,337 male and female slaves; and they also had 245 male and female singers. 68 There were 736 horses, 245 mules,*a* 69 435 camels and 6,720 donkeys.

70 Some of the heads of the families contributed to the work. The governor gave to the treasury 1,000 darics*b* of gold, 50 bowls and 530 garments for priests. 71 Some of the heads of the families gave to the treasury for the work 20,000 darics*c* of gold and 2,200 minas*d* of silver. 72 The total given by the rest of the people was 20,000 darics of gold, 2,000 minas*e* of silver and 67 garments for priests.

73 The priests, the Levites, the gatekeepers, the musicians and the temple servants, along with certain of the people and the rest of the Israelites, settled in their own towns.

Ezra Reads the Law

When the seventh month came and the Israelites had settled in their towns, 1 all the people came together as one in the square before the Water Gate. They told Ezra the teacher of the Law to bring out the Book of the Law of Moses, which the LORD had commanded for Israel.

2 So on the first day of the seventh month Ezra the priest brought the Law before the assembly, which was made up of men and women and all who were able to understand. 3 He read it aloud from daybreak till noon as he faced the square before the Water Gate in the presence of the men, women and others who could understand. And all the people listened attentively to the Book of the Law.

4 Ezra the teacher of the Law stood on a high wooden platform built for the occasion. Beside him on his right stood Mattithiah, Shema, Anaiah, Uriah, Hilkiah and Maaseiah; and on his left were Pedaiah, Mishael, Malkijah, Hashum, Hashbaddanah, Zechariah and Meshullam.

5 Ezra opened the book. All the people could see him because he was standing above them; and as he opened it, the people all stood up. 6 Ezra praised the LORD, the great God; and all the people lifted their hands and responded, "Amen! Amen!" Then they bowed down and worshiped the LORD with their faces to the ground.

7 The Levites—Jeshua, Bani, Sherebiah, Jamin, Akkub, Shabbethai, Hodiah, Maaseiah, Kelita, Azariah, Jozabad, Hanan and Pelaiah—instructed the people in the Law while the people were standing there. 8 They read from the Book of the Law of God, making it clear*f* and giving the meaning so that the people understood what was being read.

9 Then Nehemiah the governor, Ezra the priest and teacher of the Law, and the Levites who were instructing the people said to them all, "This day is holy to the LORD your

---

a 68 Some Hebrew manuscripts (see also Ezra 2:66); most Hebrew manuscripts do not have this verse.
b 70 That is, about 19 pounds or about 8.4 kilograms   *c* 71 That is, about 375 pounds or about 170 kilograms; also in verse 72   *d* 71 That is, about 1 1/3 tons or about 1.2 metric tons   *e* 72 That is, about 1 1/4 tons or about 1.1 metric tons   *f* 8 Or God, translating it

GOOD RETURNS

READ: NEHEMIAH 8:6

My biggest worship time comes when I'm alone in the car. Most of my songwriting time comes after worshiping God right there behind the wheel.

Worship is taking God's best and giving it back to him. This can happen in serving, in giving, in singing, in admiring his majesty in creation. A butterfly can lead to tears of adoration for a holy God.

An attitude of worship is the vanguard of our hearts. The idea that citizens of Jerusalem placed palm branches on the ground and sang hosannas for five days before they screamed, "Crucify him!" shows how quickly we can focus on ourselves (see John 12:12-14; 19:6-15). Worship is not praising the God you want. It's praising the God who is. Worship is what we're created for, and we're never more at peace than when we're doing what we're created to do. Worship is God's gift to us, and through worship we enjoy fellowship with him (community!). But he didn't give us worship because we have to remind God of how good he is. He's God. He gave us worship as a gift so we can do what we're created to do.

A sign of spiritual maturity is when we show that we know the gift is to be given back. God is so awesome that even in a moment that is all about him, he pours everything out on us and fills us with a sense of his presence. May our hearts spill out such gratitude that we're never hesitant, never bashful, to lift our voices to praise him.

BUILDING FAITH WISDOM STRENGTH

God. Do not mourn or weep." For all the people had been weeping as they listened to the words of the Law.

[10] Nehemiah said, "Go and enjoy choice food and sweet drinks, and send some to those who have nothing prepared. This day is holy to our Lord. Do not grieve, for the joy of the LORD is your strength."

[11] The Levites calmed all the people, saying, "Be still, for this is a holy day. Do not grieve."

[12] Then all the people went away to eat and drink, to send portions of food and to celebrate with great joy, because they now understood the words that had been made known to them.

[13] On the second day of the month, the heads of all the families, along with the priests and the Levites, gathered around Ezra the teacher to give attention to the words of the Law. [14] They found written in the Law, which the LORD had commanded through Moses, that the Israelites were to live in temporary shelters during the festival of the seventh month [15] and that they should proclaim this word and spread it throughout their towns and in Jerusalem: "Go out into the hill country and bring back branches from olive and wild olive trees, and from myrtles, palms and shade trees, to make temporary shelters" — as it is written.[a]

[16] So the people went out and brought back branches and built themselves temporary shelters on their own roofs, in their courtyards, in the courts of the house of God and in the square by the Water Gate and the one by the Gate of Ephraim. [17] The whole company that had returned from exile built temporary shelters and lived in them. From the days of Joshua son of Nun until that day, the Israelites had not celebrated it like this. And their joy was very great.

[18] Day after day, from the first day to the last, Ezra read from the Book of the Law of God. They celebrated the festival for seven days, and on the eighth day, in accordance with the regulation, there was an assembly.

The Israelites Confess Their Sins

9 On the twenty-fourth day of the same month, the Israelites gathered together, fasting and wearing sackcloth and putting dust on their heads. [2] Those of Israelite descent had separated themselves from all foreigners. They stood in their places and confessed their sins and the sins of their ancestors. [3] They stood where they were and read from the Book of the Law of the LORD their God for a quarter of the day, and spent another quarter in confession and in worshiping the LORD their God. [4] Standing on the stairs of the Levites were Jeshua, Bani, Kadmiel, Shebaniah, Bunni, Sherebiah, Bani and Kenani. They cried out with loud voices to the LORD their God. [5] And the Levites — Jeshua, Kadmiel, Bani, Hashabneiah, Sherebiah, Hodiah, Shebaniah and Pethahiah — said: "Stand up and praise the LORD your God, who is from everlasting to everlasting.[b]"

"Blessed be your glorious name, and may it be exalted above all blessing and praise. [6] You alone are the LORD. You made the heavens, even the highest heavens, and all their starry host, the earth and all that is on it, the seas and all that is in them. You give life to everything, and the multitudes of heaven worship you.

[7] "You are the LORD God, who chose Abram and brought him out of Ur of the Chaldeans and named him Abraham. [8] You found his heart faithful to you, and you made a covenant with him to give to his descendants the land of the Canaanites, Hittites, Amorites, Perizzites, Jebusites and Girgashites. You have kept your promise because you are righteous.

[9] "You saw the suffering of our ancestors in Egypt; you heard their cry at the Red Sea.[c] [10] You sent signs and wonders against Pharaoh, against all his officials and all the people of his land, for you knew how arrogantly the Egyptians treated them. You made a name for yourself, which remains to this day. [11] You divided the sea before them, so that they passed through it on dry ground, but you hurled their pursuers into the depths, like a stone into mighty waters. [12] By day you led them with a pillar of cloud, and by night with a pillar of fire to give them light on the way they were to take.

---

[a] 15 See Lev. 23:37-40.   [b] 5 Or *God for ever and ever*   [c] 9 Or *the Sea of Reeds*

COMPARISON CHECK

READ: NEHEMIAH 9:5

Who is it that you love so much that you'd lay down your life for them? Take a moment to compare the sacrifices you are willing to make for that person with the sacrifices you have made to follow Jesus. Can you tell a story of how you personally sacrificed out of your commitment and devotion to Christ?

To what extent does this person, or persons, determine your state of mind?

To what extent have you organized your life around this relationship?

It's worth comparing the emotions you experience in worship. Though worship can be a quieter and more introspective experience, can you say that you experience feelings that approach the depth of what you experience with your friends or family? Yeah, I know, it's a tough question.

BUILDING

FAITH

WISDOM

STRENGTH

The sources of our greatest and deepest emotional expression provide a strong clue to who or what controls us.

Imagine your life as a fully devoted worshiper of God and follower of Jesus Christ. Envision yourself laying your relationships at the altar, along with every other part of you. You tell God, "I can't do this right. I worship you and you alone, and I trust you to make me the son/daughter/friend I need to be. I love these people deeply, but they will no longer be the meaning of my life. Only you will be. Help me be the person I need to be, so that you can bless these relationships. May these beautiful gifts from you make my heart more completely yours."

13 "You came down on Mount Sinai; you spoke to them from heaven. You gave them regulations and laws that are just and right, and decrees and commands that are good. 14 You made known to them your holy Sabbath and gave them commands, decrees and laws through your servant Moses. 15 In their hunger you gave them bread from heaven and in their thirst you brought them water from the rock; you told them to go in and take possession of the land you had sworn with uplifted hand to give them.

16 "But they, our ancestors, became arrogant and stiff-necked, and they did not obey your commands. 17 They refused to listen and failed to remember the miracles you performed among them. They became stiff-necked and in their rebellion appointed a leader in order to return to their slavery. But you are a forgiving God, gracious and compassionate, slow to anger and abounding in love. Therefore you did not desert them, 18 even when they cast for themselves an image of a calf and said, 'This is your god, who brought you up out of Egypt,' or when they committed awful blasphemies.

19 "Because of your great compassion you did not abandon them in the wilderness. By day the pillar of cloud did not fail to guide them on their path, nor the pillar of fire by night to shine on the way they were to take. 20 You gave your good Spirit to instruct them. You did not withhold your manna from their mouths, and you gave them water for their thirst. 21 For forty years you sustained them in the wilderness; they lacked nothing, their clothes did not wear out nor did their feet become swollen.

22 "You gave them kingdoms and nations, allotting to them even the remotest frontiers. They took over the country of Sihon[a] king of Heshbon and the country of Og king of Bashan. 23 You made their children as numerous as the stars in the sky, and you brought them into the land that you told their parents to enter and possess. 24 Their children went in and took possession of the land. You subdued before them the Canaanites, who lived in the land; you gave the Canaanites into their hands, along with their kings and the peoples of the land, to deal with them as they pleased. 25 They captured fortified cities and fertile land; they took possession of houses filled with all kinds of good things, wells already dug, vineyards, olive groves and fruit trees in abundance. They ate to the full and were well-nourished; they reveled in your great goodness.

26 "But they were disobedient and rebelled against you; they turned their backs on your law. They killed your prophets, who had warned them in order to turn them back to you; they committed awful blasphemies. 27 So you delivered them into the hands of their enemies, who oppressed them. But when they were oppressed they cried out to you. From heaven you heard them, and in your great compassion you gave them deliverers, who rescued them from the hand of their enemies.

28 "But as soon as they were at rest, they again did what was evil in your sight. Then you abandoned them to the hand of their enemies so that they ruled over them. And when they cried out to you again, you heard from heaven, and in your compassion you delivered them time after time.

29 "You warned them in order to turn them back to your law, but they became arrogant and disobeyed your commands. They sinned against your ordinances, of which you said, 'The person who obeys them will live by them.' Stubbornly they turned their backs on you, became stiff-necked and refused to listen. 30 For many years you were patient with them. By your Spirit you warned them through your prophets. Yet they paid no attention, so you gave them into the hands of the neighboring peoples. 31 But in your great mercy you did not put an end to them or abandon them, for you are a gracious and merciful God.

32 "Now therefore, our God, the great

___

a 22 One Hebrew manuscript and Septuagint; most Hebrew manuscripts *Sihon, that is, the country of the*

God, mighty and awesome, who keeps his covenant of love, do not let all this hardship seem trifling in your eyes — the hardship that has come on us, on our kings and leaders, on our priests and prophets, on our ancestors and all your people, from the days of the kings of Assyria until today. ³³ In all that has happened to us, you have remained righteous; you have acted faithfully, while we acted wickedly. ³⁴ Our kings, our leaders, our priests and our ancestors did not follow your law; they did not pay attention to your commands or the statutes you warned them to keep. ³⁵ Even while they were in their kingdom, enjoying your great goodness to them in the spacious and fertile land you gave them, they did not serve you or turn from their evil ways.

³⁶ "But see, we are slaves today, slaves in the land you gave our ancestors so they could eat its fruit and the other good things it produces. ³⁷ Because of our sins, its abundant harvest goes to the kings you have placed over us. They rule over our bodies and our cattle as they please. We are in great distress.

The Agreement of the People

³⁸ "In view of all this, we are making a binding agreement, putting it in writing, and our leaders, our Levites and our priests are affixing their seals to it." ^a

10 ^b Those who sealed it were:

Nehemiah the governor, the son of Hakaliah.

Zedekiah, ² Seraiah, Azariah, Jeremiah, ³ Pashhur, Amariah, Malkijah, ⁴ Hattush, Shebaniah, Malluk, ⁵ Harim, Meremoth, Obadiah, ⁶ Daniel, Ginnethon, Baruch, ⁷ Meshullam, Abijah, Mijamin, ⁸ Maaziah, Bilgai and Shemaiah.
These were the priests.

⁹ The Levites:

Jeshua son of Azaniah, Binnui of the sons of Henadad, Kadmiel,

¹⁰ and their associates: Shebaniah, Hodiah, Kelita, Pelaiah, Hanan, ¹¹ Mika, Rehob, Hashabiah, ¹² Zakkur, Sherebiah, Shebaniah, ¹³ Hodiah, Bani and Beninu.

¹⁴ The leaders of the people:

Parosh, Pahath-Moab, Elam, Zattu, Bani, ¹⁵ Bunni, Azgad, Bebai, ¹⁶ Adonijah, Bigvai, Adin, ¹⁷ Ater, Hezekiah, Azzur, ¹⁸ Hodiah, Hashum, Bezai, ¹⁹ Hariph, Anathoth, Nebai, ²⁰ Magpiash, Meshullam, Hezir, ²¹ Meshezabel, Zadok, Jaddua, ²² Pelatiah, Hanan, Anaiah, ²³ Hoshea, Hananiah, Hasshub, ²⁴ Hallohesh, Pilha, Shobek, ²⁵ Rehum, Hashabnah, Maaseiah, ²⁶ Ahiah, Hanan, Anan, ²⁷ Malluk, Harim and Baanah.

²⁸ "The rest of the people — priests, Levites, gatekeepers, musicians, temple servants and all who separated themselves from the neighboring peoples for the sake of the Law of God, together with their wives and all their sons and daughters who are able to understand — ²⁹ all these now join their fellow Israelites the nobles, and bind themselves with a curse and an oath to follow the Law of God given through Moses the servant of God and to obey carefully all the commands, regulations and decrees of the LORD our Lord.

³⁰ "We promise not to give our daughters in marriage to the peoples around us or take their daughters for our sons.

³¹ "When the neighboring peoples bring merchandise or grain to sell on the Sabbath, we will not buy from them on the Sabbath or on any holy day. Every seventh year we will forgo working the land and will cancel all debts.

³² "We assume the responsibility for carrying out the commands to give a third of a shekel ^c each year for the service of the house of our God: ³³ for the bread set out on the table; for the regular

---

^a 38 In Hebrew texts this verse (9:38) is numbered 10:1.
^c 32 That is, about 1/8 ounce or about 4 grams

^b In Hebrew texts 10:1-39 is numbered 10:2-40.

grain offerings and burnt offerings; for the offerings on the Sabbaths, at the New Moon feasts and at the appointed festivals; for the holy offerings; for sin offerings[a] to make atonement for Israel; and for all the duties of the house of our God.

³⁴ "We — the priests, the Levites and the people — have cast lots to determine when each of our families is to bring to the house of our God at set times each year a contribution of wood to burn on the altar of the LORD our God, as it is written in the Law.

³⁵ "We also assume responsibility for bringing to the house of the LORD each year the firstfruits of our crops and of every fruit tree.

³⁶ "As it is also written in the Law, we will bring the firstborn of our sons and of our cattle, of our herds and of our flocks to the house of our God, to the priests ministering there.

³⁷ "Moreover, we will bring to the storerooms of the house of our God, to the priests, the first of our ground meal, of our grain offerings, of the fruit of all our trees and of our new wine and olive oil. And we will bring a tithe of our crops to the Levites, for it is the Levites who collect the tithes in all the towns where we work. ³⁸ A priest descended from Aaron is to accompany the Levites when they receive the tithes, and the Levites are to bring a tenth of the tithes up to the house of our God, to the storerooms of the treasury. ³⁹ The people of Israel, including the Levites, are to bring their contributions of grain, new wine and olive oil to the storerooms, where the articles for the sanctuary and for the ministering priests, the gatekeepers and the musicians are also kept.

"We will not neglect the house of our God."

The New Residents of Jerusalem

11 Now the leaders of the people settled in Jerusalem. The rest of the people cast lots to bring one out of every ten of them to live in Jerusalem, the holy city, while the remaining nine were to stay in their own towns. ² The people commended all who volunteered to live in Jerusalem.

³ These are the provincial leaders who settled in Jerusalem (now some Israelites, priests, Levites, temple servants and descendants of Solomon's servants lived in the towns of Judah, each on their own property in the various towns, ⁴ while other people from both Judah and Benjamin lived in Jerusalem):

From the descendants of Judah:

Athaiah son of Uzziah, the son of Zechariah, the son of Amariah, the son of Shephatiah, the son of Mahalalel, a descendant of Perez; ⁵ and Maaseiah son of Baruch, the son of Kol-Hozeh, the son of Hazaiah, the son of Adaiah, the son of Joiarib, the son of Zechariah, a descendant of Shelah. ⁶ The descendants of Perez who lived in Jerusalem totaled 468 men of standing.

⁷ From the descendants of Benjamin:

Sallu son of Meshullam, the son of Joed, the son of Pedaiah, the son of Kolaiah, the son of Maaseiah, the son of Ithiel, the son of Jeshaiah, ⁸ and his followers, Gabbai and Sallai — 928 men. ⁹ Joel son of Zikri was their chief officer, and Judah son of Hassenuah was over the New Quarter of the city.

¹⁰ From the priests:

Jedaiah; the son of Joiarib; Jakin; ¹¹ Seraiah son of Hilkiah, the son of Meshullam, the son of Zadok, the son of Meraioth, the son of Ahitub, the official in charge of the house of God, ¹² and their associates, who carried on work for the temple — 822 men; Adaiah son of Jeroham, the son of Pelaliah, the son of Amzi, the son of Zechariah, the son of Pashhur, the son of Malkijah, ¹³ and his associates, who were heads of families — 242 men; Amashsai son of Azarel, the son of Ahzai, the son of Meshillemoth, the son of Immer, ¹⁴ and his[b] associates, who were men of standing — 128. Their chief officer was Zabdiel son of Haggedolim.

¹⁵ From the Levites:

Shemaiah son of Hasshub, the son of Azrikam, the son of Hashabiah, the son

---

of Bunni; [16]Shabbethai and Jozabad, two of the heads of the Levites, who had charge of the outside work of the house of God; [17]Mattaniah son of Mika, the son of Zabdi, the son of Asaph, the director who led in thanksgiving and prayer; Bakbukiah, second among his associates; and Abda son of Shammua, the son of Galal, the son of Jeduthun. [18]The Levites in the holy city totaled 284.

[19]The gatekeepers:

Akkub, Talmon and their associates, who kept watch at the gates — 172 men.

[20]The rest of the Israelites, with the priests and Levites, were in all the towns of Judah, each on their ancestral property.

[21]The temple servants lived on the hill of Ophel, and Ziha and Gishpa were in charge of them.

[22]The chief officer of the Levites in Jerusalem was Uzzi son of Bani, the son of Hashabiah, the son of Mattaniah, the son of Mika. Uzzi was one of Asaph's descendants, who were the musicians responsible for the service of the house of God. [23]The musicians were under the king's orders, which regulated their daily activity.

[24]Pethahiah son of Meshezabel, one of the descendants of Zerah son of Judah, was the king's agent in all affairs relating to the people.

[25]As for the villages with their fields, some of the people of Judah lived in Kiriath Arba and its surrounding settlements, in Dibon and its settlements, in Jekabzeel and its villages, [26]in Jeshua, in Moladah, in Beth Pelet, [27]in Hazar Shual, in Beersheba and its settlements, [28]in Ziklag, in Mekonah and its settlements, [29]in En Rimmon, in Zorah, in Jarmuth, [30]Zanoah, Adullam and their villages, in Lachish and its fields, and in Azekah and its settlements. So they were living all the way from Beersheba to the Valley of Hinnom.

[31]The descendants of the Benjamites from Geba lived in Mikmash, Aija, Bethel and its settlements, [32]in Anathoth, Nob and Ananiah, [33]in Hazor, Ramah and Gittaim, [34]in Hadid, Zeboim and Neballat, [35]in Lod and Ono, and in Ge Harashim.

[36]Some of the divisions of the Levites of Judah settled in Benjamin.

Priests and Levites

12 These were the priests and Levites who returned with Zerubbabel son of Shealtiel and with Joshua:

Seraiah, Jeremiah, Ezra,
[2]Amariah, Malluk, Hattush,
[3]Shekaniah, Rehum, Meremoth,
[4]Iddo, Ginnethon,[a] Abijah,
[5]Mijamin,[b] Moadiah, Bilgah,
[6]Shemaiah, Joiarib, Jedaiah,
[7]Sallu, Amok, Hilkiah and Jedaiah.

These were the leaders of the priests and their associates in the days of Joshua.

[8]The Levites were Jeshua, Binnui, Kadmiel, Sherebiah, Judah, and also Mattaniah, who, together with his associates, was in charge of the songs of thanksgiving. [9]Bakbukiah and Unni, their associates, stood opposite them in the services.

[10]Joshua was the father of Joiakim, Joiakim the father of Eliashib, Eliashib the father of Joiada, [11]Joiada the father of Jonathan, and Jonathan the father of Jaddua.

[12]In the days of Joiakim, these were the heads of the priestly families:

of Seraiah's family, Meraiah;
of Jeremiah's, Hananiah;
[13]of Ezra's, Meshullam;
of Amariah's, Jehohanan;
[14]of Malluk's, Jonathan;
of Shekaniah's,[c] Joseph;
[15]of Harim's, Adna;
of Meremoth's,[d] Helkai;
[16]of Iddo's, Zechariah;
of Ginnethon's, Meshullam;
[17]of Abijah's, Zikri;
of Miniamin's and of Moadiah's, Piltai;
[18]of Bilgah's, Shammua;
of Shemaiah's, Jehonathan;
[19]of Joiarib's, Mattenai;
of Jedaiah's, Uzzi;
[20]of Sallu's, Kallai;
of Amok's, Eber;
[21]of Hilkiah's, Hashabiah;
of Jedaiah's, Nethanel.

[a] 4 Many Hebrew manuscripts and Vulgate (see also verse 16); most Hebrew manuscripts *Ginnethoi*
[b] 5 A variant of *Miniamin*   [c] 14 Very many Hebrew manuscripts, some Septuagint manuscripts and Syriac (see also verse 3); most Hebrew manuscripts *Shebaniah's*   [d] 15 Some Septuagint manuscripts (see also verse 3); Hebrew *Meraioth's*

²²The family heads of the Levites in the days of Eliashib, Joiada, Johanan and Jaddua, as well as those of the priests, were recorded in the reign of Darius the Persian. ²³The family heads among the descendants of Levi up to the time of Johanan son of Eliashib were recorded in the book of the annals. ²⁴And the leaders of the Levites were Hashabiah, Sherebiah, Jeshua son of Kadmiel, and their associates, who stood opposite them to give praise and thanksgiving, one section responding to the other, as prescribed by David the man of God.

²⁵Mattaniah, Bakbukiah, Obadiah, Meshullam, Talmon and Akkub were gatekeepers who guarded the storerooms at the gates. ²⁶They served in the days of Joiakim son of Joshua, the son of Jozadak, and in the days of Nehemiah the governor and of Ezra the priest, the teacher of the Law.

Dedication of the Wall of Jerusalem

²⁷At the dedication of the wall of Jerusalem, the Levites were sought out from where they lived and were brought to Jerusalem to celebrate joyfully the dedication with songs of thanksgiving and with the music of cymbals, harps and lyres. ²⁸The musicians also were brought together from the region around Jerusalem—from the villages of the Netophathites, ²⁹from Beth Gilgal, and from the area of Geba and Azmaveth, for the musicians had built villages for themselves around Jerusalem. ³⁰When the priests and Levites had purified themselves ceremonially, they purified the people, the gates and the wall.

³¹I had the leaders of Judah go up on top of^a the wall. I also assigned two large choirs to give thanks. One was to proceed on top of^b the wall to the right, toward the Dung Gate. ³²Hoshaiah and half the leaders of Judah followed them, ³³along with Azariah, Ezra, Meshullam, ³⁴Judah, Benjamin, Shemaiah, Jeremiah, ³⁵as well as some priests with trumpets, and also Zechariah son of Jonathan, the son of Shemaiah, the son of Mattaniah, the son of Micaiah, the son of Zakkur, the son of Asaph, ³⁶and his associates—Shemaiah, Azarel, Milalai, Gilalai, Maai, Nethanel, Judah and Hanani—with musical instruments prescribed by David the man of God. Ezra the teacher of the Law led the procession. ³⁷At the Fountain Gate they continued directly up the steps of the City of David on the ascent to the wall and passed above the site of David's palace to the Water Gate on the east.

³⁸The second choir proceeded in the opposite direction. I followed them on top of^c the wall, together with half the people—past the Tower of the Ovens to the Broad Wall, ³⁹over the Gate of Ephraim, the Jeshanah^d Gate, the Fish Gate, the Tower of Hananel and the Tower of the Hundred, as far as the Sheep Gate. At the Gate of the Guard they stopped.

⁴⁰The two choirs that gave thanks then took their places in the house of God; so did I, together with half the officials, ⁴¹as well as the priests—Eliakim, Maaseiah, Miniamin, Micaiah, Elioenai, Zechariah and Hananiah with their trumpets— ⁴²and also Maaseiah, Shemaiah, Eleazar, Uzzi, Jehohanan, Malkijah, Elam and Ezer. The choirs sang under the direction of Jezrahiah. ⁴³And on that day they offered great sacrifices, rejoicing because God had given them great joy. The women and children also rejoiced. The sound of rejoicing in Jerusalem could be heard far away.

⁴⁴At that time men were appointed to be in charge of the storerooms for the contributions, firstfruits and tithes. From the fields around the towns they were to bring into the storerooms the portions required by the Law for the priests and the Levites, for Judah was pleased with the ministering priests and Levites. ⁴⁵They performed the service of their God and the service of purification, as did also the musicians and gatekeepers, according to the commands of David and his son Solomon. ⁴⁶For long ago, in the days of David and Asaph, there had been directors for the musicians and for the songs of praise and thanksgiving to God. ⁴⁷So in the days of Zerubbabel and of Nehemiah, all Israel contributed the daily portions for the musicians and the gatekeepers. They also set aside the portion for the other Levites, and the Levites set aside the portion for the descendants of Aaron.

Nehemiah's Final Reforms

13 On that day the Book of Moses was read aloud in the hearing of the people and there it was found written that no Ammonite or Moabite should ever be admitted into the assembly of God, ²because

---

^{a} 31 Or go alongside ^{b} 31 Or proceed alongside ^{c} 38 Or them alongside ^{d} 39 Or Old they had not met the Israelites with food and water but had hired Balaam to call a curse down on them. (Our God, however, turned the curse into a blessing.) [3]When the people heard this law, they excluded from Israel all who were of foreign descent.

[4]Before this, Eliashib the priest had been put in charge of the storerooms of the house of our God. He was closely associated with Tobiah, [5]and he had provided him with a large room formerly used to store the grain offerings and incense and temple articles, and also the tithes of grain, new wine and olive oil prescribed for the Levites, musicians and gatekeepers, as well as the contributions for the priests.

[6]But while all this was going on, I was not in Jerusalem, for in the thirty-second year of Artaxerxes king of Babylon I had returned to the king. Some time later I asked his permission [7]and came back to Jerusalem. Here I learned about the evil thing Eliashib had done in providing Tobiah a room in the courts of the house of God. [8]I was greatly displeased and threw all Tobiah's household goods out of the room. [9]I gave orders to purify the rooms, and then I put back into them the equipment of the house of God, with the grain offerings and the incense.

[10]I also learned that the portions assigned to the Levites had not been given to them, and that all the Levites and musicians responsible for the service had gone back to their own fields. [11]So I rebuked the officials and asked them, "Why is the house of God neglected?" Then I called them together and stationed them at their posts.

[12]All Judah brought the tithes of grain, new wine and olive oil into the storerooms. [13]I put Shelemiah the priest, Zadok the scribe, and a Levite named Pedaiah in charge of the storerooms and made Hanan son of Zakkur, the son of Mattaniah, their assistant, because they were considered trustworthy. They were made responsible for distributing the supplies to their fellow Levites.

[14]Remember me for this, my God, and do not blot out what I have so faithfully done for the house of my God and its services.

[15]In those days I saw people in Judah treading winepresses on the Sabbath and bringing in grain and loading it on donkeys, together with wine, grapes, figs and all oth-

er kinds of loads. And they were bringing all this into Jerusalem on the Sabbath. Therefore I warned them against selling food on that day. [16]People from Tyre who lived in Jerusalem were bringing in fish and all kinds of merchandise and selling them in Jerusalem on the Sabbath to the people of Judah. [17]I rebuked the nobles of Judah and said to them, "What is this wicked thing you are doing—desecrating the Sabbath day? [18]Didn't your ancestors do the same things, so that our God brought all this calamity on us and on this city? Now you are stirring up more wrath against Israel by desecrating the Sabbath."

[19]When evening shadows fell on the gates of Jerusalem before the Sabbath, I ordered the doors to be shut and not opened until the Sabbath was over. I stationed some of my own men at the gates so that no load could be brought in on the Sabbath day. [20]Once or twice the merchants and sellers of all kinds of goods spent the night outside Jerusalem. [21]But I warned them and said, "Why do you spend the night by the wall? If you do this again, I will arrest you." From that time on they no longer came on the Sabbath. [22]Then I commanded the Levites to purify themselves and go and guard the gates in order to keep the Sabbath day holy.

Remember me for this also, my God, and show mercy to me according to your great love.

[23]Moreover, in those days I saw men of Judah who had married women from Ashdod, Ammon and Moab. [24]Half of their children spoke the language of Ashdod or the language of one of the other peoples, and did not know how to speak the language of Judah. [25]I rebuked them and called curses down on them. I beat some of the men and pulled out their hair. I made them take an oath in God's name and said: "You are not to give your daughters in marriage to their sons, nor are you to take their daughters in marriage for your sons or for yourselves. [26]Was it not because of marriages like these that Solomon king of Israel sinned? Among the many nations there was no king like him. He was loved by his God, and God made him king over all Israel, but even he was led into sin by foreign women. [27]Must we hear now that you too are doing all this terrible wickedness and are being unfaithful to our God by marrying foreign women?"

²⁸One of the sons of Joiada son of Eliashib the high priest was son-in-law to Sanballat the Horonite. And I drove him away from me.

²⁹Remember them, my God, because they defiled the priestly office and the covenant of the priesthood and of the Levites.

³⁰So I purified the priests and the Levites of everything foreign, and assigned them duties, each to his own task. ³¹I also made provision for contributions of wood at designated times, and for the firstfruits.

Remember me with favor, my God.

ESTHER

WHEN DID THIS HAPPEN?

Around 485–465 B.C. in Susa, the capital of the Persian empire

WHO IS IN THIS BOOK?

Xerxes
Vashti
Esther
Mordecai
Haman

VERSES YOU MIGHT RECOGNIZE

ESTHER 4:14

"Who knows but that you have come to your royal position for such a time as this?"

ESTHER 5:2

"When he saw Queen Esther standing in the court, he was pleased with her and held out to her the gold scepter that was in his hand. So Esther approached and touched the tip of the scepter."

WHAT'S IT ABOUT?

This book is about God's people, the Jews, living in a foreign land just after the Babylonian exile. The story takes place sometime between the Jews' first return to Judah and Ezra and Nehemiah's return. Some of the Jews were back in Israel, but others remained in Persia, the nation that had conquered Babylon.

God is never mentioned in this book, but his sovereignty and plan are evident. When Queen Vashti offended King Xerxes, she was banished from his presence, and a beauty contest was held to find her replacement. Esther, a beautiful Jewish woman, gained favor with everyone she met and became queen.

Like an exciting movie, this book contains clear "good guys" and "bad guys" and lots of drama. Esther's cousin, Mordecai, was the good guy who uncovered a murder plot against the king. Haman was the bad guy who plotted to kill all of the Jews. But before that could happen, Esther bravely stepped forward and revealed her true identity as a Jew, risking her life and saving her people. Even in a foreign land, God delivers the Jews.

ESTHER

Queen Vashti Deposed

1 This is what happened during the time of Xerxes,[a] the Xerxes who ruled over 127 provinces stretching from India to Cush[b]: [2]At that time King Xerxes reigned from his royal throne in the citadel of Susa, [3]and in the third year of his reign he gave a banquet for all his nobles and officials. The military leaders of Persia and Media, the princes, and the nobles of the provinces were present.

[4]For a full 180 days he displayed the vast wealth of his kingdom and the splendor and glory of his majesty. [5]When these days were over, the king gave a banquet, lasting seven days, in the enclosed garden of the king's palace, for all the people from the least to the greatest who were in the citadel of Susa. [6]The garden had hangings of white and blue linen, fastened with cords of white linen and purple material to silver rings on marble pillars. There were couches of gold and silver on a mosaic pavement of porphyry, marble, mother-of-pearl and other costly stones. [7]Wine was served in goblets of gold, each one different from the other, and the royal wine was abundant, in keeping with the king's liberality. [8]By the king's command each guest was allowed to drink with no restrictions, for the king instructed all the wine stewards to serve each man what he wished.

[9]Queen Vashti also gave a banquet for the women in the royal palace of King Xerxes.

[10]On the seventh day, when King Xerxes was in high spirits from wine, he commanded the seven eunuchs who served him — Mehuman, Biztha, Harbona, Bigtha, Abagtha, Zethar and Karkas — [11]to bring before him Queen Vashti, wearing her royal crown, in order to display her beauty to the people and nobles, for she was lovely to look at. [12]But when the attendants delivered the king's command, Queen Vashti refused to come. Then the king became furious and burned with anger.

[13]Since it was customary for the king to consult experts in matters of law and justice, he spoke with the wise men who understood the times [14]and were closest to the king — Karshena, Shethar, Admatha, Tarshish, Meres, Marsena and Memukan, the seven nobles of Persia and Media who had special access to the king and were highest in the kingdom.

[15]"According to law, what must be done to Queen Vashti?" he asked. "She has not obeyed the command of King Xerxes that the eunuchs have taken to her."

[16]Then Memukan replied in the presence of the king and the nobles, "Queen Vashti has done wrong, not only against the king but also against all the nobles and the peoples of all the provinces of King Xerxes. [17]For the queen's conduct will become known to all the women, and so they will despise their husbands and say, 'King Xerxes commanded Queen Vashti to be brought before him, but she would not come.' [18]This very day the Persian and Median women of the nobility who have heard about the queen's conduct will respond to all the king's nobles in the same way. There will be no end of disrespect and discord.

[19]"Therefore, if it pleases the king, let him issue a royal decree and let it be written in the laws of Persia and Media, which cannot be repealed, that Vashti is never again to enter the presence of King Xerxes. Also let the king give her royal position to someone else who is better than she. [20]Then when the king's edict is proclaimed throughout all his vast realm, all the women will respect their husbands, from the least to the greatest."

[21]The king and his nobles were pleased with this advice, so the king did as Memukan proposed. [22]He sent dispatches to all parts of the kingdom, to each province in its own script and to each people in their own language, proclaiming that every man should be ruler over his own household, using his native tongue.

---

[a] 1 Hebrew *Ahasuerus*; here and throughout Esther   [b] 1 That is, the upper Nile region

Esther Made Queen

2 Later when King Xerxes' fury had subsided, he remembered Vashti and what she had done and what he had decreed about her. [2] Then the king's personal attendants proposed, "Let a search be made for beautiful young virgins for the king. [3] Let the king appoint commissioners in every province of his realm to bring all these beautiful young women into the harem at the citadel of Susa. Let them be placed under the care of Hegai, the king's eunuch, who is in charge of the women; and let beauty treatments be given to them. [4] Then let the young woman who pleases the king be queen instead of Vashti." This advice appealed to the king, and he followed it.

[5] Now there was in the citadel of Susa a Jew of the tribe of Benjamin, named Mordecai son of Jair, the son of Shimei, the son of Kish, [6] who had been carried into exile from Jerusalem by Nebuchadnezzar king of Babylon, among those taken captive with Jehoiachin[a] king of Judah. [7] Mordecai had a cousin named Hadassah, whom he had brought up because she had neither father nor mother. This young woman, who was also known as Esther, had a lovely figure and was beautiful. Mordecai had taken her as his own daughter when her father and mother died.

[8] When the king's order and edict had been proclaimed, many young women were brought to the citadel of Susa and put under the care of Hegai. Esther also was taken to the king's palace and entrusted to Hegai, who had charge of the harem. [9] She pleased him and won his favor. Immediately he provided her with her beauty treatments and special food. He assigned to her seven female attendants selected from the king's palace and moved her and her attendants into the best place in the harem.

[10] Esther had not revealed her nationality and family background, because Mordecai had forbidden her to do so. [11] Every day he walked back and forth near the courtyard of the harem to find out how Esther was and what was happening to her.

[12] Before a young woman's turn came to go in to King Xerxes, she had to complete twelve months of beauty treatments prescribed for the women, six months with oil of myrrh and six with perfumes and cosmetics. [13] And this is how she would go to the king: Anything she wanted was given her to take with her from the harem to the king's palace. [14] In the evening she would go there and in the morning return to another part of the harem to the care of Shaashgaz, the king's eunuch who was in charge of the concubines. She would not return to the king unless he was pleased with her and summoned her by name.

[15] When the turn came for Esther (the young woman Mordecai had adopted, the daughter of his uncle Abihail) to go to the king, she asked for nothing other than what Hegai, the king's eunuch who was in charge of the harem, suggested. And Esther won the favor of everyone who saw her. [16] She was taken to King Xerxes in the royal residence in the tenth month, the month of Tebeth, in the seventh year of his reign.

[17] Now the king was attracted to Esther more than to any of the other women, and she won his favor and approval more than any of the other virgins. So he set a royal crown on her head and made her queen instead of Vashti. [18] And the king gave a great banquet, Esther's banquet, for all his nobles and officials. He proclaimed a holiday throughout the provinces and distributed gifts with royal liberality.

Mordecai Uncovers a Conspiracy

[19] When the virgins were assembled a second time, Mordecai was sitting at the king's gate. [20] But Esther had kept secret her family background and nationality just as Mordecai had told her to do, for she continued to follow Mordecai's instructions as she had done when he was bringing her up.

[21] During the time Mordecai was sitting at the king's gate, Bigthana[b] and Teresh, two of the king's officers who guarded the doorway, became angry and conspired to assassinate King Xerxes. [22] But Mordecai found out about the plot and told Queen Esther, who in turn reported it to the king, giving credit to Mordecai. [23] And when the report was investigated and found to be true, the two officials were impaled on poles. All this was recorded in the book of the annals in the presence of the king.

---

[a] 6 Hebrew *Jeconiah*, a variant of *Jehoiachin* [b] 21 Hebrew *Bigthan*, a variant of *Bigthana*

BROKEN FAMILIES

READ: ESTHER 2:5-7

J ust in case you've always thought God works only in perfect families, I've got news for you: God is at work in every family. Your family doesn't have to be perfect, beautiful, or even "normal." I grew up in a divorced family, and I resented my broken one for the longest time. I don't blame my parents or myself or anyone else for the damage that surrounded me then, or even now. Sometimes families just fall apart. But as I look back I can definitely see God's hand in my uncomfortable family.

We may want to think we just happened into our particular families, or that God just set us there randomly. But that's not true. Each of us was masterfully placed by God's hand in the exact family where he wanted us, to be raised in a certain way and to have certain experiences that shape us into the people he's designed us to be.

Think of your family and their influence on you like a masterfully designed jigsaw puzzle. God brought everything together to make you who you are. Your parents, your siblings, your other relatives, your home environment—they are all pieces of the puzzle that tells the bigger story of who you are. The more you try to understand that puzzle, the more you understand who you are and what you're made to do.

BUILDING

FAITH

WISDOM

STRENGTH

Haman's Plot to Destroy the Jews

3 After these events, King Xerxes honored Haman son of Hammedatha, the Agagite, elevating him and giving him a seat of honor higher than that of all the other nobles. [2] All the royal officials at the king's gate knelt down and paid honor to Haman, for the king had commanded this concerning him. But Mordecai would not kneel down or pay him honor.

[3] Then the royal officials at the king's gate asked Mordecai, "Why do you disobey the king's command?" [4] Day after day they spoke to him but he refused to comply. Therefore they told Haman about it to see whether Mordecai's behavior would be tolerated, for he had told them he was a Jew.

[5] When Haman saw that Mordecai would not kneel down or pay him honor, he was enraged. [6] Yet having learned who Mordecai's people were, he scorned the idea of killing only Mordecai. Instead Haman looked for a way to destroy all Mordecai's people, the Jews, throughout the whole kingdom of Xerxes.

[7] In the twelfth year of King Xerxes, in the first month, the month of Nisan, the *pur* (that is, the lot) was cast in the presence of Haman to select a day and month. And the lot fell on[a] the twelfth month, the month of Adar.

[8] Then Haman said to King Xerxes, "There is a certain people dispersed among the peoples in all the provinces of your kingdom who keep themselves separate. Their customs are different from those of all other people, and they do not obey the king's laws; it is not in the king's best interest to tolerate them. [9] If it pleases the king, let a decree be issued to destroy them, and I will give ten thousand talents[b] of silver to the king's administrators for the royal treasury."

[10] So the king took his signet ring from his finger and gave it to Haman son of Hammedatha, the Agagite, the enemy of the Jews. [11] "Keep the money," the king said to Haman, "and do with the people as you please."

[12] Then on the thirteenth day of the first month the royal secretaries were summoned. They wrote out in the script of each province and in the language of each people all Haman's orders to the king's satraps, the governors of the various provinces and the nobles of the various peoples. These were written in the name of King Xerxes himself and sealed with his own ring. [13] Dispatches were sent by couriers to all the king's provinces with the order to destroy, kill and annihilate all the Jews—young and old, women and children—on a single day, the thirteenth day of the twelfth month, the month of Adar, and to plunder their goods. [14] A copy of the text of the edict was to be issued as law in every province and made known to the people of every nationality so they would be ready for that day.

[15] The couriers went out, spurred on by the king's command, and the edict was issued in the citadel of Susa. The king and Haman sat down to drink, but the city of Susa was bewildered.

Mordecai Persuades Esther to Help

4 When Mordecai learned of all that had been done, he tore his clothes, put on sackcloth and ashes, and went out into the city, wailing loudly and bitterly. [2] But he went only as far as the king's gate, because no one clothed in sackcloth was allowed to enter it. [3] In every province to which the edict and order of the king came, there was great mourning among the Jews, with fasting, weeping and wailing. Many lay in sackcloth and ashes.

[4] When Esther's eunuchs and female attendants came and told her about Mordecai, she was in great distress. She sent clothes for him to put on instead of his sackcloth, but he would not accept them. [5] Then Esther summoned Hathak, one of the king's eunuchs assigned to attend her, and ordered him to find out what was troubling Mordecai and why.

[6] So Hathak went out to Mordecai in the open square of the city in front of the king's gate. [7] Mordecai told him everything that had happened to him, including the exact amount of money Haman had promised to pay into the royal treasury for the destruction of the Jews. [8] He also gave him a copy of the text of the edict for their annihilation, which had been published in Susa, to show to Esther and explain it to her, and he told him to instruct her to go into the king's

---

[a] 7 Septuagint; Hebrew does not have *And the lot fell on.*   [b] 9 That is, about 375 tons or about 340 metric tons

presence to beg for mercy and plead with him for her people.

⁹Hathak went back and reported to Esther what Mordecai had said. ¹⁰Then she instructed him to say to Mordecai, ¹¹"All the king's officials and the people of the royal provinces know that for any man or woman who approaches the king in the inner court without being summoned the king has but one law: that they be put to death unless the king extends the gold scepter to them and spares their lives. But thirty days have passed since I was called to go to the king."

¹²When Esther's words were reported to Mordecai, ¹³he sent back this answer: "Do not think that because you are in the king's house you alone of all the Jews will escape. ¹⁴For if you remain silent at this time, relief and deliverance for the Jews will arise from another place, but you and your father's family will perish. And who knows but that you have come to your royal position for such a time as this?"

¹⁵Then Esther sent this reply to Mordecai: ¹⁶"Go, gather together all the Jews who are in Susa, and fast for me. Do not eat or drink for three days, night or day. I and my attendants will fast as you do. When this is done, I will go to the king, even though it is against the law. And if I perish, I perish."

¹⁷So Mordecai went away and carried out all of Esther's instructions.

Esther's Request to the King

5 On the third day Esther put on her royal robes and stood in the inner court of the palace, in front of the king's hall. The king was sitting on his royal throne in the hall, facing the entrance. ²When he saw Queen Esther standing in the court, he was pleased with her and held out to her the gold scepter that was in his hand. So Esther approached and touched the tip of the scepter.

³Then the king asked, "What is it, Queen Esther? What is your request? Even up to half the kingdom, it will be given you."

⁴"If it pleases the king," replied Esther, "let the king, together with Haman, come today to a banquet I have prepared for him."

⁵"Bring Haman at once," the king said, "so that we may do what Esther asks."

So the king and Haman went to the banquet Esther had prepared. ⁶As they were drinking wine, the king again asked Esther, "Now what is your petition? It will be given you. And what is your request? Even up to half the kingdom, it will be granted."

⁷Esther replied, "My petition and my request is this: ⁸If the king regards me with favor and if it pleases the king to grant my petition and fulfill my request, let the king and Haman come tomorrow to the banquet I will prepare for them. Then I will answer the king's question."

Haman's Rage Against Mordecai

⁹Haman went out that day happy and in high spirits. But when he saw Mordecai at the king's gate and observed that he neither rose nor showed fear in his presence, he was filled with rage against Mordecai. ¹⁰Nevertheless, Haman restrained himself and went home.

Calling together his friends and Zeresh, his wife, ¹¹Haman boasted to them about his vast wealth, his many sons, and all the ways the king had honored him and how he had elevated him above the other nobles and officials. ¹²"And that's not all," Haman added. "I'm the only person Queen Esther invited to accompany the king to the banquet she gave. And she has invited me along with the king tomorrow. ¹³But all this gives me no satisfaction as long as I see that Jew Mordecai sitting at the king's gate."

¹⁴His wife Zeresh and all his friends said to him, "Have a pole set up, reaching to a height of fifty cubits,ᵃ and ask the king in the morning to have Mordecai impaled on it. Then go with the king to the banquet and enjoy yourself." This suggestion delighted Haman, and he had the pole set up.

Mordecai Honored

6 That night the king could not sleep; so he ordered the book of the chronicles, the record of his reign, to be brought in and read to him. ²It was found recorded there that Mordecai had exposed Bigthana and Teresh, two of the king's officers who guarded the doorway, who had conspired to assassinate King Xerxes.

³"What honor and recognition has Mordecai received for this?" the king asked.

"Nothing has been done for him," his attendants answered.

ᵃ 14 That is, about 75 feet or about 23 meters

DON'T GO IT ALONE

READ: ESTHER 4:15-17

Ask any builder—the taller the building, the deeper the workers have to go to dig the foundation. A believer's foundation is his root system, and God has made a way for us to deepen our roots through spiritual disciplines. The Bible stresses the necessity of worship, prayer, and study of Scripture. Those are the Big Three essentials in growing as a believer.

A fourth discipline is often overlooked. While it may not immediately come to mind as a discipline, an argument can be made that Jesus elevated it to be among his top priorities. Community.

When I say community, I mean sharing life with other followers of Christ. Of all the Bible's descriptions of the church, perhaps none is more appropriate than "the body of Christ." If we're the body of Christ, then by nature we are a collection of individual parts grouped into a purposed whole.

Community is more than connecting with your friends and attending a worship service; it's part of digging in your roots. If you're only a roots person, full of knowledge without any reach, you're useless. At the same time, if you dig in alone, not only are you useless as a reach person; you also don't have a good picture of God. God is community. Even in his essence, he is three Persons in one—Father, Son, and Holy Spirit—and they're always together.

BUILDING

FAITH

WISDOM

STRENGTH

Taken from *Thrive Student Edition* by Mark Hall with Tim Luke, copyright © 2014 by Mark Hall, published by Zondervan.

[4]The king said, "Who is in the court?" Now Haman had just entered the outer court of the palace to speak to the king about impaling Mordecai on the pole he had set up for him.

[5]His attendants answered, "Haman is standing in the court."

"Bring him in," the king ordered.

[6]When Haman entered, the king asked him, "What should be done for the man the king delights to honor?"

Now Haman thought to himself, "Who is there that the king would rather honor than me?" [7]So he answered the king, "For the man the king delights to honor, [8]have them bring a royal robe the king has worn and a horse the king has ridden, one with a royal crest placed on its head. [9]Then let the robe and horse be entrusted to one of the king's most noble princes. Let them robe the man the king delights to honor, and lead him on the horse through the city streets, proclaiming before him, 'This is what is done for the man the king delights to honor!' "

[10]"Go at once," the king commanded Haman. "Get the robe and the horse and do just as you have suggested for Mordecai the Jew, who sits at the king's gate. Do not neglect anything you have recommended."

[11]So Haman got the robe and the horse. He robed Mordecai, and led him on horseback through the city streets, proclaiming before him, "This is what is done for the man the king delights to honor!"

[12]Afterward Mordecai returned to the king's gate. But Haman rushed home, with his head covered in grief, [13]and told Zeresh his wife and all his friends everything that had happened to him.

His advisers and his wife Zeresh said to him, "Since Mordecai, before whom your downfall has started, is of Jewish origin, you cannot stand against him—you will surely come to ruin!" [14]While they were still talking with him, the king's eunuchs arrived and hurried Haman away to the banquet Esther had prepared.

Haman Impaled

7 So the king and Haman went to Queen Esther's banquet, [2]and as they were drinking wine on the second day, the king again asked, "Queen Esther, what is your petition? It will be given you. What is your request? Even up to half the kingdom, it will be granted."

[3]Then Queen Esther answered, "If I have found favor with you, Your Majesty, and if it pleases you, grant me my life—this is my petition. And spare my people—this is my request. [4]For I and my people have been sold to be destroyed, killed and annihilated. If we had merely been sold as male and female slaves, I would have kept quiet, because no such distress would justify disturbing the king.[a]"

[5]King Xerxes asked Queen Esther, "Who is he? Where is he—the man who has dared to do such a thing?"

[6]Esther said, "An adversary and enemy! This vile Haman!"

Then Haman was terrified before the king and queen. [7]The king got up in a rage, left his wine and went out into the palace garden. But Haman, realizing that the king had already decided his fate, stayed behind to beg Queen Esther for his life.

[8]Just as the king returned from the palace garden to the banquet hall, Haman was falling on the couch where Esther was reclining.

The king exclaimed, "Will he even molest the queen while she is with me in the house?"

As soon as the word left the king's mouth, they covered Haman's face. [9]Then Harbona, one of the eunuchs attending the king, said, "A pole reaching to a height of fifty cubits[b] stands by Haman's house. He had it set up for Mordecai, who spoke up to help the king."

The king said, "Impale him on it!" [10]So they impaled Haman on the pole he had set up for Mordecai. Then the king's fury subsided.

The King's Edict in Behalf of the Jews

8 That same day King Xerxes gave Queen Esther the estate of Haman, the enemy of the Jews. And Mordecai came into the presence of the king, for Esther had told how he was related to her. [2]The king took off his signet ring, which he had reclaimed from Haman, and presented it to Mordecai. And Esther appointed him over Haman's estate.

[3]Esther again pleaded with the king, falling at his feet and weeping. She begged him to

---

[a] 4 Or *quiet, but the compensation our adversary offers cannot be compared with the loss the king would suffer*   [b] 9 That is, about 75 feet or about 23 meters

put an end to the evil plan of Haman the Agagite, which he had devised against the Jews. [4] Then the king extended the gold scepter to Esther and she arose and stood before him.

[5] "If it pleases the king," she said, "and if he regards me with favor and thinks it the right thing to do, and if he is pleased with me, let an order be written overruling the dispatches that Haman son of Hammedatha, the Agagite, devised and wrote to destroy the Jews in all the king's provinces. [6] For how can I bear to see disaster fall on my people? How can I bear to see the destruction of my family?"

[7] King Xerxes replied to Queen Esther and to Mordecai the Jew, "Because Haman attacked the Jews, I have given his estate to Esther, and they have impaled him on the pole he set up. [8] Now write another decree in the king's name in behalf of the Jews as seems best to you, and seal it with the king's signet ring—for no document written in the king's name and sealed with his ring can be revoked."

[9] At once the royal secretaries were summoned—on the twenty-third day of the third month, the month of Sivan. They wrote out all Mordecai's orders to the Jews, and to the satraps, governors and nobles of the 127 provinces stretching from India to Cush.[a] These orders were written in the script of each province and the language of each people and also to the Jews in their own script and language. [10] Mordecai wrote in the name of King Xerxes, sealed the dispatches with the king's signet ring, and sent them by mounted couriers, who rode fast horses especially bred for the king.

[11] The king's edict granted the Jews in every city the right to assemble and protect themselves; to destroy, kill and annihilate the armed men of any nationality or province who might attack them and their women and children,[b] and to plunder the property of their enemies. [12] The day appointed for the Jews to do this in all the provinces of King Xerxes was the thirteenth day of the twelfth month, the month of Adar. [13] A copy of the text of the edict was to be issued as law in every province and made known to the people of every nationality so that the Jews would be ready on that day to avenge themselves on their enemies.

[14] The couriers, riding the royal horses, went out, spurred on by the king's command, and the edict was issued in the citadel of Susa.

The Triumph of the Jews

[15] When Mordecai left the king's presence, he was wearing royal garments of blue and white, a large crown of gold and a purple robe of fine linen. And the city of Susa held a joyous celebration. [16] For the Jews it was a time of happiness and joy, gladness and honor. [17] In every province and in every city to which the edict of the king came, there was joy and gladness among the Jews, with feasting and celebrating. And many people of other nationalities became Jews because fear of the Jews had seized them.

9 On the thirteenth day of the twelfth month, the month of Adar, the edict commanded by the king was to be carried out. On this day the enemies of the Jews had hoped to overpower them, but now the tables were turned and the Jews got the upper hand over those who hated them. [2] The Jews assembled in their cities in all the provinces of King Xerxes to attack those determined to destroy them. No one could stand against them, because the people of all the other nationalities were afraid of them. [3] And all the nobles of the provinces, the satraps, the governors and the king's administrators helped the Jews, because fear of Mordecai had seized them. [4] Mordecai was prominent in the palace; his reputation spread throughout the provinces, and he became more and more powerful.

[5] The Jews struck down all their enemies with the sword, killing and destroying them, and they did what they pleased to those who hated them. [6] In the citadel of Susa, the Jews killed and destroyed five hundred men. [7] They also killed Parshandatha, Dalphon, Aspatha, [8] Poratha, Adalia, Aridatha, [9] Parmashta, Arisai, Aridai and Vaizatha, [10] the ten sons of Haman son of Hammedatha, the enemy of the Jews. But they did not lay their hands on the plunder.

[11] The number of those killed in the citadel of Susa was reported to the king that same day. [12] The king said to Queen Esther, "The Jews have killed and destroyed five hundred men and the ten sons of Haman in

---

[a] 9 That is, the upper Nile region   [b] 11 Or *province, together with their women and children, who might attack them;*

WORTH LIVING FOR

READ: ESTHER 8:6

Plenty of action has swept by since Esther won the role of queen in a royal beauty pageant.

Not long after Esther rose to the throne, her elder cousin Mordecai courts trouble for refusing to bow to an arrogant government official named Haman. In a fit of revenge, Haman plots to kill not just the disrespectful Mordecai but all his people (Esther 3:5-6). Mordecai and the Jews weep and wail at their impending death, and Mordecai pleads with Esther to bring the matter to the attention of the king. Xerxes doesn't yet realize his young queen was born to the people his own edict allows to be killed. Yet Esther protests that she can't approach the king without being called into his presence, as entering without permission is an offense that carries a sentence of death. (4:1-11).

BUILDING

FAITH

WISDOM

STRENGTH

Esther faces a choice to brave the king's wrath and put her life on the line for the sake of her people. Mordecai warns that Esther won't escape the slaughter even if she hides her true identity, and he suggests God has made her queen "for such a time as this" (4:14).

You might never face a situation where you have to risk your life or physical safety for the sake of your family or people. But if you know what you're willing to die for, you know what's worth living for.

the citadel of Susa. What have they done in the rest of the king's provinces? Now what is your petition? It will be given you. What is your request? It will also be granted."

¹³"If it pleases the king," Esther answered, "give the Jews in Susa permission to carry out this day's edict tomorrow also, and let Haman's ten sons be impaled on poles."

¹⁴So the king commanded that this be done. An edict was issued in Susa, and they impaled the ten sons of Haman. ¹⁵The Jews in Susa came together on the fourteenth day of the month of Adar, and they put to death in Susa three hundred men, but they did not lay their hands on the plunder.

¹⁶Meanwhile, the remainder of the Jews who were in the king's provinces also assembled to protect themselves and get relief from their enemies. They killed seventy-five thousand of them but did not lay their hands on the plunder. ¹⁷This happened on the thirteenth day of the month of Adar, and on the fourteenth they rested and made it a day of feasting and joy.

¹⁸The Jews in Susa, however, had assembled on the thirteenth and fourteenth, and then on the fifteenth they rested and made it a day of feasting and joy.

¹⁹That is why rural Jews — those living in villages — observe the fourteenth of the month of Adar as a day of joy and feasting, a day for giving presents to each other.

Purim Established

²⁰Mordecai recorded these events, and he sent letters to all the Jews throughout the provinces of King Xerxes, near and far, ²¹to have them celebrate annually the fourteenth and fifteenth days of the month of Adar ²²as the time when the Jews got relief from their enemies, and as the month when their sorrow was turned into joy and their mourning into a day of celebration. He wrote them to observe the days as days of feasting and joy and giving presents of food to one another and gifts to the poor.

²³So the Jews agreed to continue the celebration they had begun, doing what Mordecai had written to them. ²⁴For Haman son of Hammedatha, the Agagite, the enemy of all the Jews, had plotted against the Jews to destroy them and had cast the *pur* (that is, the lot) for their ruin and destruction. ²⁵But when the plot came to the king's attention,ᵃ he issued written orders that the evil scheme Haman had devised against the Jews should come back onto his own head, and that he and his sons should be impaled on poles. ²⁶(Therefore these days were called Purim, from the word *pur*.) Because of everything written in this letter and because of what they had seen and what had happened to them, ²⁷the Jews took it on themselves to establish the custom that they and their descendants and all who join them should without fail observe these two days every year, in the way prescribed and at the time appointed. ²⁸These days should be remembered and observed in every generation by every family, and in every province and in every city. And these days of Purim should never fail to be celebrated by the Jews — nor should the memory of these days die out among their descendants.

²⁹So Queen Esther, daughter of Abihail, along with Mordecai the Jew, wrote with full authority to confirm this second letter concerning Purim. ³⁰And Mordecai sent letters to all the Jews in the 127 provinces of Xerxes' kingdom — words of goodwill and assurance — ³¹to establish these days of Purim at their designated times, as Mordecai the Jew and Queen Esther had decreed for them, and as they had established for themselves and their descendants in regard to their times of fasting and lamentation. ³²Esther's decree confirmed these regulations about Purim, and it was written down in the records.

The Greatness of Mordecai

10 King Xerxes imposed tribute throughout the empire, to its distant shores. ²And all his acts of power and might, together with a full account of the greatness of Mordecai, whom the king had promoted, are they not written in the book of the annals of the kings of Media and Persia? ³Mordecai the Jew was second in rank to King Xerxes, preeminent among the Jews, and held in high esteem by his many fellow Jews, because he worked for the good of his people and spoke up for the welfare of all the Jews.

ᵃ 25 Or *when Esther came before the king*

JOB

➤ ## WHEN DID THIS HAPPEN?

Unknown, but likely around or just after the time Abraham lived

➤ ## WHO IS IN THIS BOOK?

Job
Job's wife
Eliphaz
Bildad
Zophar
Elihu

➤ ## VERSES YOU MIGHT RECOGNIZE

JOB 13:15

"Though he slay me, yet will I hope in him; I will surely defend my ways to his face."

JOB 19:25

"I know that my redeemer lives, and that in the end he will stand on the earth."

WHAT'S IT ABOUT?

Job is the first of the wisdom books, which also include Psalms, Proverbs and Ecclesiastes. The story of Job takes place way back during the time of Abraham. Even though Job was not an Israelite, we learn that he was "blameless and upright" and feared God. What happens to Job is painful to read about. Satan staged a deliberate attack on Job and Job lost everything—his animals, his riches, his children and even his health.

Covered head to toe in painful, disgusting sores, Job withstood the criticism of his wife and the questioning of his friends, who believed he must have done *something* to bring about his hardship. Job asked God some tough questions, but he held on to his faith in his redeemer and was rewarded in the end. This book shows us how to respond when bad things happen and we don't understand why. God is always trustworthy, even when we can't see his loving plan.

JOB

Prologue

1 In the land of Uz there lived a man whose name was Job. This man was blameless and upright; he feared God and shunned evil. ²He had seven sons and three daughters, ³and he owned seven thousand sheep, three thousand camels, five hundred yoke of oxen and five hundred donkeys, and had a large number of servants. He was the greatest man among all the people of the East.

⁴His sons used to hold feasts in their homes on their birthdays, and they would invite their three sisters to eat and drink with them. ⁵When a period of feasting had run its course, Job would make arrangements for them to be purified. Early in the morning he would sacrifice a burnt offering for each of them, thinking, "Perhaps my children have sinned and cursed God in their hearts." This was Job's regular custom.

⁶One day the angels[a] came to present themselves before the LORD, and Satan[b] also came with them. ⁷The LORD said to Satan, "Where have you come from?"

Satan answered the LORD, "From roaming throughout the earth, going back and forth on it."

⁸Then the LORD said to Satan, "Have you considered my servant Job? There is no one on earth like him; he is blameless and upright, a man who fears God and shuns evil."

⁹"Does Job fear God for nothing?" Satan replied. ¹⁰"Have you not put a hedge around him and his household and everything he has? You have blessed the work of his hands, so that his flocks and herds are spread throughout the land. ¹¹But now stretch out your hand and strike everything he has, and he will surely curse you to your face."

¹²The LORD said to Satan, "Very well, then, everything he has is in your power, but on the man himself do not lay a finger."

Then Satan went out from the presence of the LORD.

¹³One day when Job's sons and daughters were feasting and drinking wine at the oldest brother's house, ¹⁴a messenger came to Job and said, "The oxen were plowing and the donkeys were grazing nearby, ¹⁵and the Sabeans attacked and made off with them. They put the servants to the sword, and I am the only one who has escaped to tell you!"

¹⁶While he was still speaking, another messenger came and said, "The fire of God fell from the heavens and burned up the sheep and the servants, and I am the only one who has escaped to tell you!"

¹⁷While he was still speaking, another messenger came and said, "The Chaldeans formed three raiding parties and swept down on your camels and made off with them. They put the servants to the sword, and I am the only one who has escaped to tell you!"

¹⁸While he was still speaking, yet another messenger came and said, "Your sons and daughters were feasting and drinking wine at the oldest brother's house, ¹⁹when suddenly a mighty wind swept in from the desert and struck the four corners of the house. It collapsed on them and they are dead, and I am the only one who has escaped to tell you!"

²⁰At this, Job got up and tore his robe and shaved his head. Then he fell to the ground in worship ²¹and said:

"Naked I came from my mother's womb,
    and naked I will depart.[c]
The LORD gave and the LORD has taken
        away;
    may the name of the LORD be praised."

²²In all this, Job did not sin by charging God with wrongdoing.

2 On another day the angels[a] came to present themselves before the LORD, and Satan also came with them to present himself before him. ²And the LORD said to Satan, "Where have you come from?"

Satan answered the LORD, "From roaming

ᵃ 6,1 Hebrew *the sons of God*   ᵇ 6 Hebrew *satan* means *adversary*.   ᶜ 21 Or *will return there*

WHAT TO SAY, WHAT NOT TO SAY

READ: JOB 1:21

The man Job (rhymes with "robe") ranks near the top of any list of the Bible's most prominent people. His story was probably written in King Solomon's era, and his reputation as "the greatest man among all the peoples of the East" (Job 1:3) likely locates him in the ancient land of Edom. But the Bible's account of Job's suffering intrigues people in every time and place.

Satan was conversing with the Lord when he suggested that Job lived uprightly only because the Lord filled his life with so many blessings. God agreed to let Satan prove his point by testing Job. Soon fire and marauders destroyed Job's wealth. Wind killed his children. Oozing sores afflicted his body from head to toe.

Whether blessings come or go, Job still trusted God, even though his wife told him to curse the Lord and die. When three friends showed up, they barely recognized him. They sat with him and wept night and day for a week, unable to say anything because of Job's horrible pain. When they finally spoke, their words weren't exactly comforting.

BUILDING

FAITH

WISDOM

STRENGTH

The book of Job helps you think through tough issues like why good people suffer. It teaches you what to say—or not say—to hurting friends. In the end you find that questions about good and evil aren't always easy to answer. But you can be sure that no matter what you suffer, the Lord is worth trusting.

throughout the earth, going back and forth on it."

³ Then the LORD said to Satan, "Have you considered my servant Job? There is no one on earth like him; he is blameless and upright, a man who fears God and shuns evil. And he still maintains his integrity, though you incited me against him to ruin him without any reason."

⁴ "Skin for skin!" Satan replied. "A man will give all he has for his own life. ⁵ But now stretch out your hand and strike his flesh and bones, and he will surely curse you to your face."

⁶ The LORD said to Satan, "Very well, then, he is in your hands; but you must spare his life."

⁷ So Satan went out from the presence of the LORD and afflicted Job with painful sores from the soles of his feet to the crown of his head. ⁸ Then Job took a piece of broken pottery and scraped himself with it as he sat among the ashes.

⁹ His wife said to him, "Are you still maintaining your integrity? Curse God and die!"

¹⁰ He replied, "You are talking like a foolish*ᵃ* woman. Shall we accept good from God, and not trouble?"

In all this, Job did not sin in what he said.

¹¹ When Job's three friends, Eliphaz the Temanite, Bildad the Shuhite and Zophar the Naamathite, heard about all the troubles that had come upon him, they set out from their homes and met together by agreement to go and sympathize with him and comfort him. ¹² When they saw him from a distance, they could hardly recognize him; they began to weep aloud, and they tore their robes and sprinkled dust on their heads. ¹³ Then they sat on the ground with him for seven days and seven nights. No one said a word to him, because they saw how great his suffering was.

Job Speaks

3 After this, Job opened his mouth and cursed the day of his birth. ² He said:

³ "May the day of my birth perish,
    and the night that said, 'A boy is
        conceived!'
⁴ That day — may it turn to darkness;

may God above not care about it;
    may no light shine on it.
⁵ May gloom and utter darkness claim it
        once more;
    may a cloud settle over it;
    may blackness overwhelm it.
⁶ That night — may thick darkness seize it;
    may it not be included among the days
        of the year
    nor be entered in any of the months.
⁷ May that night be barren;
    may no shout of joy be heard in it.
⁸ May those who curse days*ᵇ* curse that
        day,
    those who are ready to rouse
        Leviathan.
⁹ May its morning stars become dark;
    may it wait for daylight in vain
    and not see the first rays of dawn,
¹⁰ for it did not shut the doors of the womb
        on me
    to hide trouble from my eyes.

¹¹ "Why did I not perish at birth,
    and die as I came from the womb?
¹² Why were there knees to receive me
    and breasts that I might be nursed?
¹³ For now I would be lying down in peace;
    I would be asleep and at rest
¹⁴ with kings and rulers of the earth,
    who built for themselves places now
        lying in ruins,
¹⁵ with princes who had gold,
    who filled their houses with silver.
¹⁶ Or why was I not hidden away in the
        ground like a stillborn child,
    like an infant who never saw the light
        of day?
¹⁷ There the wicked cease from turmoil,
    and there the weary are at rest.
¹⁸ Captives also enjoy their ease;
    they no longer hear the slave driver's
        shout.
¹⁹ The small and the great are there,
    and the slaves are freed from their
        owners.

²⁰ "Why is light given to those in misery,
    and life to the bitter of soul,
²¹ to those who long for death that does not
        come,
    who search for it more than for hidden
        treasure,

ᵃ 10 The Hebrew word rendered *foolish* denotes moral deficiency.   ᵇ 8 Or *curse the sea*

CLASSIC MOVE

READ: JOB 2:4-10

When I was a kid, my dad would make us watch Westerns with him. I'd be in the middle of *Bugs Bunny*, and during a commercial he would turn the channel to a Western and say, "This is a classic, son. It's a classic!" I'd have to sit there and watch it, which I hated at the time.

Usually, it was a movie about cowboys and Indians. Dad would say the same thing every time. "All they gotta do is kill that Indian chief. If they can cut down that chief, it's all over because nobody will know what to do."

One truth believers often have to learn the hard way is that the first thing the Enemy goes after is our time with God. It's basic military strategy— cut off communication, and all the soldiers run around and don't know what to do.

BUILDING

FAITH

WISDOM

STRENGTH

Satan wants to go after our communication with God to make us useless. We scurry into all manner of trouble when we don't hear God's voice. I've seen it in my own life. I see how I thrive when I draw from Jesus on a regular basis, and I see how I dive when I don't.

At these times I have to remind myself of the difference between false guilt and God's conviction. Satan throws guilt at us to tell us we're the worst Christian and biggest hypocrite ever. The Lord gently convicts us of a particular sin, maybe using a particular Scripture, and in his kindness he leads us to repentance.

Taken from *Thrive Student Edition* by Mark Hall with Tim Luke, copyright © 2014 by Mark Hall, published by Zondervan.

22 who are filled with gladness
    and rejoice when they reach the grave?
23 Why is life given to a man
    whose way is hidden,
    whom God has hedged in?
24 For sighing has become my daily food;
    my groans pour out like water.
25 What I feared has come upon me;
    what I dreaded has happened to me.
26 I have no peace, no quietness;
    I have no rest, but only turmoil."

Eliphaz

4 Then Eliphaz the Temanite replied:

2 "If someone ventures a word with you,
    will you be impatient?
    But who can keep from speaking?
3 Think how you have instructed many,
    how you have strengthened feeble
    hands.
4 Your words have supported those who
    stumbled;
    you have strengthened faltering knees.
5 But now trouble comes to you, and you
    are discouraged;
    it strikes you, and you are dismayed.
6 Should not your piety be your confidence
    and your blameless ways your hope?

7 "Consider now: Who, being innocent, has
    ever perished?
    Where were the upright ever
    destroyed?
8 As I have observed, those who plow evil
    and those who sow trouble reap it.
9 At the breath of God they perish;
    at the blast of his anger they are no
    more.
10 The lions may roar and growl,
    yet the teeth of the great lions are
    broken.
11 The lion perishes for lack of prey,
    and the cubs of the lioness are
    scattered.

12 "A word was secretly brought to me,
    my ears caught a whisper of it.
13 Amid disquieting dreams in the night,
    when deep sleep falls on people,
14 fear and trembling seized me
    and made all my bones shake.
15 A spirit glided past my face,
    and the hair on my body stood on end.
16 It stopped,

but I could not tell what it was.
A form stood before my eyes,
    and I heard a hushed voice:
17 'Can a mortal be more righteous than
    God?
    Can even a strong man be more pure
    than his Maker?
18 If God places no trust in his servants,
    if he charges his angels with error,
19 how much more those who live in houses
    of clay,
    whose foundations are in the dust,
    who are crushed more readily than a
    moth!
20 Between dawn and dusk they are broken
    to pieces;
    unnoticed, they perish forever.
21 Are not the cords of their tent pulled up,
    so that they die without wisdom?'

5 "Call if you will, but who will answer
    you?
    To which of the holy ones will you
    turn?
2 Resentment kills a fool,
    and envy slays the simple.
3 I myself have seen a fool taking root,
    but suddenly his house was cursed.
4 His children are far from safety,
    crushed in court without a defender.
5 The hungry consume his harvest,
    taking it even from among thorns,
    and the thirsty pant after his wealth.
6 For hardship does not spring from the
    soil,
    nor does trouble sprout from the
    ground.
7 Yet man is born to trouble
    as surely as sparks fly upward.

8 "But if I were you, I would appeal to God;
    I would lay my cause before him.
9 He performs wonders that cannot be
    fathomed,
    miracles that cannot be counted.
10 He provides rain for the earth;
    he sends water on the countryside.
11 The lowly he sets on high,
    and those who mourn are lifted to
    safety.
12 He thwarts the plans of the crafty,
    so that their hands achieve no success.
13 He catches the wise in their craftiness,
    and the schemes of the wily are swept
    away.

STRAIGHT-TALKING FRIENDS

READ: JOB 3:1, 4:1-6

I 'm grateful for people who are serious about thinking and rethinking what they believe to be true about God and who aren't too concerned about stepping on toes. I've got friends like that; do you? They include both Christians and non-Christians, people I love who don't mind kicking around the theological dirt with me, considering the what ifs and how dids about God.

Despite both my education and calling, at first I was terrified of having such conversations. What would people think if I asked questions about my own core beliefs? Was I willing to admit that some of them knew more about theology than I did? Would they be confused if I continued to love them even if we disagreed? Is it really possible for us to maintain our love for God and the body of Christ while still questioning some of what we've understood to be true for so long? Could we really hold one another in check without feeling guilty for asking questions?

BUILDING FAITH WISDOM STRENGTH

Oddly enough, I think having these concerns and sharing them with one another helps us from getting too far off base. Maybe it's the Holy Spirit who reminds us that caution is both necessary and healthy as we seek to discover more about God. But caution should never be an excuse to stop asking questions or considering new ideas.

Taken from *Jesus Is for Liars: A Hypocrite's Guide to Authenticity* by Tim Baker, copyright © 2009 by Tim Baker, published by Zondervan.

¹⁴ Darkness comes upon them in the
daytime;
at noon they grope as in the night.
¹⁵ He saves the needy from the sword in
their mouth;
he saves them from the clutches of the
powerful.
¹⁶ So the poor have hope,
and injustice shuts its mouth.

¹⁷ "Blessed is the one whom God corrects;
so do not despise the discipline of the
Almighty.ᵃ
¹⁸ For he wounds, but he also binds up;
he injures, but his hands also heal.
¹⁹ From six calamities he will rescue you;
in seven no harm will touch you.
²⁰ In famine he will deliver you from death,
and in battle from the stroke of the
sword.
²¹ You will be protected from the lash of the
tongue,
and need not fear when destruction
comes.
²² You will laugh at destruction and famine,
and need not fear the wild animals.
²³ For you will have a covenant with the
stones of the field,
and the wild animals will be at peace
with you.
²⁴ You will know that your tent is secure;
you will take stock of your property
and find nothing missing.
²⁵ You will know that your children will be
many,
and your descendants like the grass of
the earth.
²⁶ You will come to the grave in full vigor,
like sheaves gathered in season.

²⁷ "We have examined this, and it is true.
So hear it and apply it to yourself."

Job

6 Then Job replied:

² "If only my anguish could be weighed
and all my misery be placed on the
scales!
³ It would surely outweigh the sand of the
seas—
no wonder my words have been
impetuous.

⁴ The arrows of the Almighty are in me,
my spirit drinks in their poison;
God's terrors are marshaled against
me.
⁵ Does a wild donkey bray when it has
grass,
or an ox bellow when it has fodder?
⁶ Is tasteless food eaten without salt,
or is there flavor in the sap of the
mallowᵇ?
⁷ I refuse to touch it;
such food makes me ill.

⁸ "Oh, that I might have my request,
that God would grant what I hope for,
⁹ that God would be willing to crush me,
to let loose his hand and cut off my life!
¹⁰ Then I would still have this
consolation—
my joy in unrelenting pain—
that I had not denied the words of the
Holy One.

¹¹ "What strength do I have, that I should
still hope?
What prospects, that I should be
patient?
¹² Do I have the strength of stone?
Is my flesh bronze?
¹³ Do I have any power to help myself,
now that success has been driven from
me?

¹⁴ "Anyone who withholds kindness from a
friend
forsakes the fear of the Almighty.
¹⁵ But my brothers are as undependable as
intermittent streams,
as the streams that overflow
¹⁶ when darkened by thawing ice
and swollen with melting snow,
¹⁷ but that stop flowing in the dry season,
and in the heat vanish from their
channels.
¹⁸ Caravans turn aside from their routes;
they go off into the wasteland and
perish.
¹⁹ The caravans of Tema look for water,
the traveling merchants of Sheba look
in hope.
²⁰ They are distressed, because they had
been confident;
they arrive there, only to be
disappointed.

ᵃ 17 Hebrew *Shaddai*; here and throughout Job ᵇ 6 The meaning of the Hebrew for this phrase is
uncertain.

²¹ Now you too have proved to be of no help;
　　 you see something dreadful and are
　　 afraid.
²² Have I ever said, 'Give something on my
　　 behalf,
　　 pay a ransom for me from your wealth,
²³ deliver me from the hand of the enemy,
　　 rescue me from the clutches of the
　　 ruthless'?

²⁴ "Teach me, and I will be quiet;
　　 show me where I have been wrong.
²⁵ How painful are honest words!
　　 But what do your arguments prove?
²⁶ Do you mean to correct what I say,
　　 and treat my desperate words as wind?
²⁷ You would even cast lots for the fatherless
　　 and barter away your friend.

²⁸ "But now be so kind as to look at me.
　　 Would I lie to your face?
²⁹ Relent, do not be unjust;
　　 reconsider, for my integrity is at stake.[a]
³⁰ Is there any wickedness on my lips?
　　 Can my mouth not discern malice?

7 "Do not mortals have hard service on
　　 earth?
　　 Are not their days like those of hired
　　 laborers?
² Like a slave longing for the evening
　　 shadows,
　　 or a hired laborer waiting to be paid,
³ so I have been allotted months of futility,
　　 and nights of misery have been
　　 assigned to me.
⁴ When I lie down I think, 'How long before
　　 I get up?'
　　 The night drags on, and I toss and turn
　　 until dawn.
⁵ My body is clothed with worms and scabs,
　　 my skin is broken and festering.

⁶ "My days are swifter than a weaver's
　　 shuttle,
　　 and they come to an end without hope.
⁷ Remember, O God, that my life is but a
　　 breath;
　　 my eyes will never see happiness
　　 again.
⁸ The eye that now sees me will see me no
　　 longer;
　　 you will look for me, but I will be no
　　 more.

⁹ As a cloud vanishes and is gone,
　　 so one who goes down to the grave
　　 does not return.
¹⁰ He will never come to his house again;
　　 his place will know him no more.

¹¹ "Therefore I will not keep silent;
　　 I will speak out in the anguish of my
　　 spirit,
　　 I will complain in the bitterness of my
　　 soul.
¹² Am I the sea, or the monster of the deep,
　　 that you put me under guard?
¹³ When I think my bed will comfort me
　　 and my couch will ease my complaint,
¹⁴ even then you frighten me with dreams
　　 and terrify me with visions,
¹⁵ so that I prefer strangling and death,
　　 rather than this body of mine.
¹⁶ I despise my life; I would not live forever.
　　 Let me alone; my days have no
　　 meaning.

¹⁷ "What is mankind that you make so
　　 much of them,
　　 that you give them so much attention,
¹⁸ that you examine them every morning
　　 and test them every moment?
¹⁹ Will you never look away from me,
　　 or let me alone even for an instant?
²⁰ If I have sinned, what have I done to you,
　　 you who see everything we do?
　　 Why have you made me your target?
　　 Have I become a burden to you?[b]
²¹ Why do you not pardon my offenses
　　 and forgive my sins?
　　 For I will soon lie down in the dust;
　　 you will search for me, but I will be no
　　 more."

Bildad

8 Then Bildad the Shuhite replied:

² "How long will you say such things?
　　 Your words are a blustering wind.
³ Does God pervert justice?
　　 Does the Almighty pervert what is
　　 right?
⁴ When your children sinned against him,
　　 he gave them over to the penalty of
　　 their sin.
⁵ But if you will seek God earnestly
　　 and plead with the Almighty,

---

[a] 29 Or *my righteousness still stands*　　[b] 20 A few manuscripts of the Masoretic Text, an ancient Hebrew scribal tradition and Septuagint; most manuscripts of the Masoretic Text *I have become a burden to myself.*

BEING PRESENT

READ: JOB 8:3-4

At the start of Job's story, his friends couldn't have been more helpful. They rush to his side. They weep at his pain. They stay close with a man whose only relief is scraping open sores with a slice of broken pottery. And they don't try to give quick and easy answers to a situation too bad for words. Counselors call this "being present" for people.

Then the three friends open their mouths. Their arguments sound impressive, but they give their hurting friend messed-up advice. Eliphaz speaks first, arguing that Job must have purposely sinned to deserve such pain. Bildad commands Job to stop questioning God. And Zophar orders Job to repent—to quit sinning and turn to God. These three men each speak several times during the book. Job counters their arguments each time.

BUILDING

FAITH

WISDOM

STRENGTH

Eliphaz, Bildad, and Zophar all mistakenly argue that bad things always happen as a result of someone's sin. Because Job faces terrible pain, they think he must have committed terrible sins. The more Job protests his innocence, the more they continue to heap guilt on him.

You know the inside scoop on Job: God knows Job is a good man. Even Satan realizes Job's righteousness. Job is undergoing a spiritual test, but none of the humans in the story can see that. People can try with all their might to figure out pain and suffering, but only the Lord knows the whole truth.

⁶ if you are pure and upright,
  even now he will rouse himself on
    your behalf
  and restore you to your prosperous
    state.
⁷ Your beginnings will seem humble,
  so prosperous will your future be.

⁸ "Ask the former generation
  and find out what their ancestors
    learned,
⁹ for we were born only yesterday and
    know nothing,
  and our days on earth are but a
    shadow.
¹⁰ Will they not instruct you and tell you?
  Will they not bring forth words from
    their understanding?
¹¹ Can papyrus grow tall where there is
    no marsh?
  Can reeds thrive without water?
¹² While still growing and uncut,
  they wither more quickly than
    grass.
¹³ Such is the destiny of all who forget
    God;
  so perishes the hope of the godless.
¹⁴ What they trust in is fragile*ᵃ*;
  what they rely on is a spider's web.
¹⁵ They lean on the web, but it gives way;
  they cling to it, but it does not hold.
¹⁶ They are like a well-watered plant in the
    sunshine,
  spreading its shoots over the garden;
¹⁷ it entwines its roots around a pile of
    rocks
  and looks for a place among the
    stones.
¹⁸ But when it is torn from its spot,
  that place disowns it and says, 'I never
    saw you.'
¹⁹ Surely its life withers away,
  and*ᵇ* from the soil other plants grow.

²⁰ "Surely God does not reject one who is
    blameless
  or strengthen the hands of evildoers.
²¹ He will yet fill your mouth with
    laughter
  and your lips with shouts of joy.
²² Your enemies will be clothed in shame,
  and the tents of the wicked will be
    no more."

Job

9 Then Job replied:

² "Indeed, I know that this is true.
  But how can mere mortals prove their
    innocence before God?
³ Though they wished to dispute with him,
  they could not answer him one time
    out of a thousand.
⁴ His wisdom is profound, his power is
    vast.
  Who has resisted him and come out
    unscathed?
⁵ He moves mountains without their
    knowing it
  and overturns them in his anger.
⁶ He shakes the earth from its place
  and makes its pillars tremble.
⁷ He speaks to the sun and it does not
    shine;
  he seals off the light of the stars.
⁸ He alone stretches out the heavens
  and treads on the waves of the sea.
⁹ He is the Maker of the Bear*ᶜ* and Orion,
  the Pleiades and the constellations of
    the south.
¹⁰ He performs wonders that cannot be
    fathomed,
  miracles that cannot be counted.
¹¹ When he passes me, I cannot see him;
  when he goes by, I cannot perceive
    him.
¹² If he snatches away, who can stop him?
  Who can say to him, 'What are you
    doing?'
¹³ God does not restrain his anger;
  even the cohorts of Rahab cowered at
    his feet.

¹⁴ "How then can I dispute with him?
  How can I find words to argue with
    him?
¹⁵ Though I were innocent, I could not
    answer him;
  I could only plead with my Judge for
    mercy.
¹⁶ Even if I summoned him and he
    responded,
  I do not believe he would give me a
    hearing.
¹⁷ He would crush me with a storm
  and multiply my wounds for no reason.

ᵃ 14 The meaning of the Hebrew for this word is uncertain.   ᵇ 19 Or *Surely all the joy it has / is that*
ᶜ 9 Or *of Leo*

¹⁸ He would not let me catch my breath
    but would overwhelm me with misery.
¹⁹ If it is a matter of strength, he is mighty!
    And if it is a matter of justice, who can
        challenge him*a*?
²⁰ Even if I were innocent, my mouth would
        condemn me;
    if I were blameless, it would pronounce
        me guilty.

²¹ "Although I am blameless,
    I have no concern for myself;
    I despise my own life.
²² It is all the same; that is why I say,
    'He destroys both the blameless and
        the wicked.'
²³ When a scourge brings sudden death,
    he mocks the despair of the innocent.
²⁴ When a land falls into the hands of the
        wicked,
    he blindfolds its judges.
    If it is not he, then who is it?

²⁵ "My days are swifter than a runner;
    they fly away without a glimpse of joy.
²⁶ They skim past like boats of papyrus,
    like eagles swooping down on their
        prey.
²⁷ If I say, 'I will forget my complaint,
    I will change my expression, and
        smile,'
²⁸ I still dread all my sufferings,
    for I know you will not hold me
        innocent.
²⁹ Since I am already found guilty,
    why should I struggle in vain?
³⁰ Even if I washed myself with soap
    and my hands with cleansing powder,
³¹ you would plunge me into a slime pit
    so that even my clothes would detest
        me.

³² "He is not a mere mortal like me that I
        might answer him,
    that we might confront each other in
        court.
³³ If only there were someone to mediate
        between us,
    someone to bring us together,
³⁴ someone to remove God's rod from me,
    so that his terror would frighten me no
        more.
³⁵ Then I would speak up without fear of
        him,

but as it now stands with me,
    I cannot.

10 "I loathe my very life;
    therefore I will give free rein to my
        complaint
    and speak out in the bitterness of
        my soul.
² I say to God: Do not declare me guilty,
    but tell me what charges you have
        against me.
³ Does it please you to oppress me,
    to spurn the work of your hands,
    while you smile on the plans of the
        wicked?
⁴ Do you have eyes of flesh?
    Do you see as a mortal sees?
⁵ Are your days like those of a mortal
    or your years like those of a strong
        man,
⁶ that you must search out my faults
    and probe after my sin—
⁷ though you know that I am not guilty
    and that no one can rescue me from
        your hand?

⁸ "Your hands shaped me and made me.
    Will you now turn and destroy me?
⁹ Remember that you molded me like clay.
    Will you now turn me to dust again?
¹⁰ Did you not pour me out like milk
    and curdle me like cheese,
¹¹ clothe me with skin and flesh
    and knit me together with bones and
        sinews?
¹² You gave me life and showed me
        kindness,
    and in your providence watched over
        my spirit.

¹³ "But this is what you concealed in your
        heart,
    and I know that this was in your
        mind:
¹⁴ If I sinned, you would be watching me
    and would not let my offense go
        unpunished.
¹⁵ If I am guilty—woe to me!
    Even if I am innocent, I cannot lift my
        head,
    for I am full of shame
    and drowned in*b* my affliction.
¹⁶ If I hold my head high, you stalk me like
        a lion

---

a 19 See Septuagint; Hebrew *me*.   *b* 15 Or *and aware of*

and again display your awesome
power against me.
¹⁷ You bring new witnesses against me
and increase your anger toward me;
your forces come against me wave
upon wave.

¹⁸ "Why then did you bring me out of the
womb?
I wish I had died before any eye saw me.
¹⁹ If only I had never come into being,
or had been carried straight from the
womb to the grave!
²⁰ Are not my few days almost over?
Turn away from me so I can have a
moment's joy
²¹ before I go to the place of no return,
to the land of gloom and utter
darkness,
²² to the land of deepest night,
of utter darkness and disorder,
where even the light is like darkness."

Zophar

11 Then Zophar the Naamathite replied:

² "Are all these words to go unanswered?
Is this talker to be vindicated?
³ Will your idle talk reduce others to
silence?
Will no one rebuke you when you
mock?
⁴ You say to God, 'My beliefs are flawless
and I am pure in your sight.'
⁵ Oh, how I wish that God would speak,
that he would open his lips against you
⁶ and disclose to you the secrets of
wisdom,
for true wisdom has two sides.
Know this: God has even forgotten
some of your sin.

⁷ "Can you fathom the mysteries of God?
Can you probe the limits of the
Almighty?
⁸ They are higher than the heavens
above—what can you do?
They are deeper than the depths
below—what can you know?
⁹ Their measure is longer than the earth
and wider than the sea.

¹⁰ "If he comes along and confines you in
prison

and convenes a court, who can oppose
him?
¹¹ Surely he recognizes deceivers;
and when he sees evil, does he not take
note?
¹² But the witless can no more become wise
than a wild donkey's colt can be born
human.^a

¹³ "Yet if you devote your heart to him
and stretch out your hands to him,
¹⁴ if you put away the sin that is in your
hand
and allow no evil to dwell in your tent,
¹⁵ then, free of fault, you will lift up your
face;
you will stand firm and without fear.
¹⁶ You will surely forget your trouble,
recalling it only as waters gone by.
¹⁷ Life will be brighter than noonday,
and darkness will become like
morning.
¹⁸ You will be secure, because there
is hope;
you will look about you and take your
rest in safety.
¹⁹ You will lie down, with no one to make
you afraid,
and many will court your favor.
²⁰ But the eyes of the wicked will fail,
and escape will elude them;
their hope will become a dying gasp."

Job

12 Then Job replied:

² "Doubtless you are the only people who
matter,
and wisdom will die with you!
³ But I have a mind as well as you;
I am not inferior to you.
Who does not know all these things?

⁴ "I have become a laughingstock to my
friends,
though I called on God and he
answered—
a mere laughingstock, though
righteous and blameless!
⁵ Those who are at ease have contempt for
misfortune
as the fate of those whose feet are
slipping.

^a 12 Or *wild donkey can be born tame*

⁶The tents of marauders are undisturbed,
  and those who provoke God are
    secure —
  those God has in his hand.ᵃ

⁷"But ask the animals, and they will teach
    you,
  or the birds in the sky, and they will
    tell you;
⁸or speak to the earth, and it will teach you,
  or let the fish in the sea inform you.
⁹Which of all these does not know
  that the hand of the LORD has done
    this?
¹⁰In his hand is the life of every creature
  and the breath of all mankind.
¹¹Does not the ear test words
  as the tongue tastes food?
¹²Is not wisdom found among the aged?
  Does not long life bring
    understanding?

¹³"To God belong wisdom and power;
  counsel and understanding are his.
¹⁴What he tears down cannot be rebuilt;
  those he imprisons cannot be released.
¹⁵If he holds back the waters, there is
    drought;
  if he lets them loose, they devastate the
    land.
¹⁶To him belong strength and insight;
  both deceived and deceiver are his.
¹⁷He leads rulers away stripped
  and makes fools of judges.
¹⁸He takes off the shackles put on by kings
  and ties a loinclothᵇ around their
    waist.
¹⁹He leads priests away stripped
  and overthrows officials long
    established.
²⁰He silences the lips of trusted advisers
  and takes away the discernment of
    elders.
²¹He pours contempt on nobles
  and disarms the mighty.
²²He reveals the deep things of darkness
  and brings utter darkness into the
    light.
²³He makes nations great, and destroys
    them;
  he enlarges nations, and disperses
    them.

²⁴He deprives the leaders of the earth of
    their reason;
  he makes them wander in a trackless
    waste.
²⁵They grope in darkness with no light;
  he makes them stagger like drunkards.

13 "My eyes have seen all this,
  my ears have heard and
    understood it.
²What you know, I also know;
  I am not inferior to you.
³But I desire to speak to the Almighty
  and to argue my case with God.
⁴You, however, smear me with lies;
  you are worthless physicians, all
    of you!
⁵If only you would be altogether silent!
  For you, that would be wisdom.
⁶Hear now my argument;
  listen to the pleas of my lips.
⁷Will you speak wickedly on God's behalf?
  Will you speak deceitfully for him?
⁸Will you show him partiality?
  Will you argue the case for God?
⁹Would it turn out well if he examined
    you?
  Could you deceive him as you might
    deceive a mortal?
¹⁰He would surely call you to account
  if you secretly showed partiality.
¹¹Would not his splendor terrify you?
  Would not the dread of him fall on
    you?
¹²Your maxims are proverbs of ashes;
  your defenses are defenses of clay.

¹³"Keep silent and let me speak;
  then let come to me what may.
¹⁴Why do I put myself in jeopardy
  and take my life in my hands?
¹⁵Though he slay me, yet will I hope in him;
  I will surelyᶜ defend my ways to his
    face.
¹⁶Indeed, this will turn out for my
    deliverance,
  for no godless person would dare come
    before him!
¹⁷Listen carefully to what I say;
  let my words ring in your ears.
¹⁸Now that I have prepared my case,
  I know I will be vindicated.

ᵃ 6 Or *those whose god is in their own hand*   ᵇ 18 Or *shackles of kings / and ties a belt*   ᶜ 15 Or *He will*
surely slay me; I have no hope — / yet I will

¹⁹ Can anyone bring charges against me?
    If so, I will be silent and die.

²⁰ "Only grant me these two things, God,
    and then I will not hide from you:
²¹ Withdraw your hand far from me,
    and stop frightening me with your
        terrors.
²² Then summon me and I will answer,
    or let me speak, and you reply to me.
²³ How many wrongs and sins have I
        committed?
    Show me my offense and my sin.
²⁴ Why do you hide your face
    and consider me your enemy?
²⁵ Will you torment a windblown leaf?
    Will you chase after dry chaff?
²⁶ For you write down bitter things
        against me
    and make me reap the sins of my
        youth.
²⁷ You fasten my feet in shackles;
    you keep close watch on all my paths
    by putting marks on the soles of my
        feet.

²⁸ "So man wastes away like something
        rotten,
    like a garment eaten by moths.

14 "Mortals, born of woman,
    are of few days and full of trouble.
² They spring up like flowers and wither
        away;
    like fleeting shadows, they do not
        endure.
³ Do you fix your eye on them?
    Will you bring them^a before you for
        judgment?
⁴ Who can bring what is pure from the
        impure?
    No one!
⁵ A person's days are determined;
    you have decreed the number of his
        months
    and have set limits he cannot exceed.
⁶ So look away from him and let him alone,
    till he has put in his time like a hired
        laborer.

⁷ "At least there is hope for a tree:
    If it is cut down, it will sprout again,
    and its new shoots will not fail.
⁸ Its roots may grow old in the ground
    and its stump die in the soil,

⁹ yet at the scent of water it will bud
    and put forth shoots like a plant.
¹⁰ But a man dies and is laid low;
    he breathes his last and is no more.
¹¹ As the water of a lake dries up
    or a riverbed becomes parched
        and dry,
¹² so he lies down and does not rise;
    till the heavens are no more, people
        will not awake
    or be roused from their sleep.

¹³ "If only you would hide me in the grave
    and conceal me till your anger has
        passed!
    If only you would set me a time
    and then remember me!
¹⁴ If someone dies, will they live again?
    All the days of my hard service
    I will wait for my renewal^b to come.
¹⁵ You will call and I will answer you;
    you will long for the creature your
        hands have made.
¹⁶ Surely then you will count my steps
    but not keep track of my sin.
¹⁷ My offenses will be sealed up in a bag;
    you will cover over my sin.

¹⁸ "But as a mountain erodes and crumbles
    and as a rock is moved from its place,
¹⁹ as water wears away stones
    and torrents wash away the soil,
    so you destroy a person's hope.
²⁰ You overpower them once for all, and
        they are gone;
    you change their countenance and
        send them away.
²¹ If their children are honored, they do not
        know it;
    if their offspring are brought low, they
        do not see it.
²² They feel but the pain of their own bodies
    and mourn only for themselves."

Eliphaz

15 Then Eliphaz the Temanite replied:

² "Would a wise person answer with empty
        notions
    or fill their belly with the hot east
        wind?
³ Would they argue with useless words,
    with speeches that have no value?

---

^a 3 Septuagint, Vulgate and Syriac; Hebrew *me*   ^b 14 Or *release*

⁴But you even undermine piety
and hinder devotion to God.
⁵Your sin prompts your mouth;
you adopt the tongue of the crafty.
⁶Your own mouth condemns you, not
mine;
your own lips testify against you.

⁷"Are you the first man ever born?
Were you brought forth before the
hills?
⁸Do you listen in on God's council?
Do you have a monopoly on wisdom?
⁹What do you know that we do not know?
What insights do you have that we do
not have?
¹⁰The gray-haired and the aged are on our
side,
men even older than your father.
¹¹Are God's consolations not enough
for you,
words spoken gently to you?
¹²Why has your heart carried you away,
and why do your eyes flash,
¹³so that you vent your rage against God
and pour out such words from your
mouth?

¹⁴"What are mortals, that they could be
pure,
or those born of woman, that they
could be righteous?
¹⁵If God places no trust in his holy ones,
if even the heavens are not pure in
his eyes,
¹⁶how much less mortals, who are vile and
corrupt,
who drink up evil like water!

¹⁷"Listen to me and I will explain to you;
let me tell you what I have seen,
¹⁸what the wise have declared,
hiding nothing received from their
ancestors
¹⁹(to whom alone the land was given
when no foreigners moved among
them):
²⁰All his days the wicked man suffers
torment,
the ruthless man through all the years
stored up for him.
²¹Terrifying sounds fill his ears;
when all seems well, marauders attack
him.
²²He despairs of escaping the realm of
darkness;

he is marked for the sword.
²³He wanders about for food like a vulture;
he knows the day of darkness is at
hand.
²⁴Distress and anguish fill him with terror;
troubles overwhelm him, like a king
poised to attack,
²⁵because he shakes his fist at God
and vaunts himself against the
Almighty,
²⁶defiantly charging against him
with a thick, strong shield.

²⁷"Though his face is covered with fat
and his waist bulges with flesh,
²⁸he will inhabit ruined towns
and houses where no one lives,
houses crumbling to rubble.
²⁹He will no longer be rich and his wealth
will not endure,
nor will his possessions spread over
the land.
³⁰He will not escape the darkness;
a flame will wither his shoots,
and the breath of God's mouth will
carry him away.
³¹Let him not deceive himself by trusting
what is worthless,
for he will get nothing in return.
³²Before his time he will wither,
and his branches will not flourish.
³³He will be like a vine stripped of its
unripe grapes,
like an olive tree shedding its
blossoms.
³⁴For the company of the godless will be
barren,
and fire will consume the tents of
those who love bribes.
³⁵They conceive trouble and give birth
to evil;
their womb fashions deceit."

Job

16 Then Job replied:

²"I have heard many things like these;
you are miserable comforters, all
of you!
³Will your long-winded speeches never
end?
What ails you that you keep on
arguing?
⁴I also could speak like you,
if you were in my place;

I could make fine speeches against you
    and shake my head at you.
⁵ But my mouth would encourage you;
    comfort from my lips would bring you
        relief.

⁶ "Yet if I speak, my pain is not relieved;
    and if I refrain, it does not go away.
⁷ Surely, God, you have worn me out;
    you have devastated my entire
        household.
⁸ You have shriveled me up — and it has
        become a witness;
    my gauntness rises up and testifies
        against me.
⁹ God assails me and tears me in his anger
        and gnashes his teeth at me;
    my opponent fastens on me his
        piercing eyes.
¹⁰ People open their mouths to jeer at me;
    they strike my cheek in scorn
        and unite together against me.
¹¹ God has turned me over to the ungodly
    and thrown me into the clutches of the
        wicked.
¹² All was well with me, but he shattered
        me;
    he seized me by the neck and crushed
        me.
    He has made me his target;
¹³   his archers surround me.
    Without pity, he pierces my kidneys
        and spills my gall on the ground.
¹⁴ Again and again he bursts upon me;
    he rushes at me like a warrior.

¹⁵ "I have sewed sackcloth over my skin
    and buried my brow in the dust.
¹⁶ My face is red with weeping,
    dark shadows ring my eyes;
¹⁷ yet my hands have been free of violence
    and my prayer is pure.

¹⁸ "Earth, do not cover my blood;
    may my cry never be laid to rest!
¹⁹ Even now my witness is in heaven;
    my advocate is on high.
²⁰ My intercessor is my friend*ᵃ*
    as my eyes pour out tears to God;
²¹ on behalf of a man he pleads with God
    as one pleads for a friend.

²² "Only a few years will pass
    before I take the path of no return.

17 ¹ My spirit is broken,
    my days are cut short,
    the grave awaits me.
² Surely mockers surround me;
    my eyes must dwell on their hostility.

³ "Give me, O God, the pledge you demand.
    Who else will put up security for me?
⁴ You have closed their minds to
        understanding;
    therefore you will not let them
        triumph.
⁵ If anyone denounces their friends for
        reward,
    the eyes of their children will fail.

⁶ "God has made me a byword to everyone,
    a man in whose face people spit.
⁷ My eyes have grown dim with grief;
    my whole frame is but a shadow.
⁸ The upright are appalled at this;
    the innocent are aroused against the
        ungodly.
⁹ Nevertheless, the righteous will hold to
        their ways,
    and those with clean hands will grow
        stronger.

¹⁰ "But come on, all of you, try again!
    I will not find a wise man among you.
¹¹ My days have passed, my plans are
        shattered.
    Yet the desires of my heart
¹² turn night into day;
    in the face of the darkness light is near.
¹³ If the only home I hope for is the grave,
    if I spread out my bed in the realm of
        darkness,
¹⁴ if I say to corruption, 'You are my father,'
    and to the worm, 'My mother' or 'My
        sister,'
¹⁵ where then is my hope —
    who can see any hope for me?
¹⁶ Will it go down to the gates of death?
    Will we descend together into the
        dust?"

Bildad

18 Then Bildad the Shuhite replied:

² "When will you end these speeches?
    Be sensible, and then we can talk.
³ Why are we regarded as cattle
    and considered stupid in your sight?

ᵃ 20 Or *My friends treat me with scorn*

⁴You who tear yourself to pieces in your anger,
is the earth to be abandoned for your sake?
Or must the rocks be moved from their place?

⁵ "The lamp of a wicked man is snuffed out;
the flame of his fire stops burning.
⁶The light in his tent becomes dark;
the lamp beside him goes out.
⁷The vigor of his step is weakened;
his own schemes throw him down.
⁸His feet thrust him into a net;
he wanders into its mesh.
⁹A trap seizes him by the heel;
a snare holds him fast.
¹⁰A noose is hidden for him on the ground;
a trap lies in his path.
¹¹Terrors startle him on every side
and dog his every step.
¹²Calamity is hungry for him;
disaster is ready for him when he falls.
¹³It eats away parts of his skin;
death's firstborn devours his limbs.
¹⁴He is torn from the security of his tent
and marched off to the king of terrors.
¹⁵Fire resides*a* in his tent;
burning sulfur is scattered over his dwelling.
¹⁶His roots dry up below
and his branches wither above.
¹⁷The memory of him perishes from the earth;
he has no name in the land.
¹⁸He is driven from light into the realm of darkness
and is banished from the world.
¹⁹He has no offspring or descendants among his people,
no survivor where once he lived.
²⁰People of the west are appalled at his fate;
those of the east are seized with horror.
²¹Surely such is the dwelling of an evil man;
such is the place of one who does not know God."

Job

19

Then Job replied:

² "How long will you torment me
and crush me with words?

³Ten times now you have reproached me;
shamelessly you attack me.
⁴If it is true that I have gone astray,
my error remains my concern alone.
⁵If indeed you would exalt yourselves above me
and use my humiliation against me,
⁶then know that God has wronged me
and drawn his net around me.

⁷ "Though I cry, 'Violence!' I get no response;
though I call for help, there is no justice.
⁸He has blocked my way so I cannot pass;
he has shrouded my paths in darkness.
⁹He has stripped me of my honor
and removed the crown from my head.
¹⁰He tears me down on every side till I am gone;
he uproots my hope like a tree.
¹¹His anger burns against me;
he counts me among his enemies.
¹²His troops advance in force;
they build a siege ramp against me
and encamp around my tent.

¹³ "He has alienated my family from me;
my acquaintances are completely estranged from me.
¹⁴My relatives have gone away;
my closest friends have forgotten me.
¹⁵My guests and my female servants count me a foreigner;
they look on me as on a stranger.
¹⁶I summon my servant, but he does not answer,
though I beg him with my own mouth.
¹⁷My breath is offensive to my wife;
I am loathsome to my own family.
¹⁸Even the little boys scorn me;
when I appear, they ridicule me.
¹⁹All my intimate friends detest me;
those I love have turned against me.
²⁰I am nothing but skin and bones;
I have escaped only by the skin of my teeth.*b*

²¹ "Have pity on me, my friends, have pity,
for the hand of God has struck me.
²²Why do you pursue me as God does?
Will you never get enough of my flesh?

²³ "Oh, that my words were recorded,
that they were written on a scroll,

---

a 15 Or *Nothing he had remains*   *b* 20 Or *only by my gums*

²⁴ that they were inscribed with an iron tool
on*a* lead,
  or engraved in rock forever!
²⁵ I know that my redeemer*b* lives,
  and that in the end he will stand on the
earth.*c*
²⁶ And after my skin has been destroyed,
yet*d* in*e* my flesh I will see God;
²⁷ I myself will see him
  with my own eyes — I, and not another.
  How my heart yearns within me!

²⁸ "If you say, 'How we will hound him,
  since the root of the trouble lies in
him,*f*'
²⁹ you should fear the sword yourselves;
  for wrath will bring punishment by the
sword,
  and then you will know that there is
judgment.*g*"

Zophar

20 Then Zophar the Naamathite replied:

² "My troubled thoughts prompt me to
answer
  because I am greatly disturbed.
³ I hear a rebuke that dishonors me,
  and my understanding inspires me
to reply.

⁴ "Surely you know how it has been from
of old,
  ever since mankind*h* was placed on
the earth,
⁵ that the mirth of the wicked is brief,
  the joy of the godless lasts but a
moment.
⁶ Though the pride of the godless person
reaches to the heavens
  and his head touches the clouds,
⁷ he will perish forever, like his own
dung;
  those who have seen him will say,
  'Where is he?'
⁸ Like a dream he flies away, no more to
be found,
  banished like a vision of the night.
⁹ The eye that saw him will not see him
again;
  his place will look on him no more.

¹⁰ His children must make amends to the
poor;
  his own hands must give back his
wealth.
¹¹ The youthful vigor that fills his bones
  will lie with him in the dust.

¹² "Though evil is sweet in his mouth
  and he hides it under his tongue,
¹³ though he cannot bear to let it go
  and lets it linger in his mouth,
¹⁴ yet his food will turn sour in his
stomach;
  it will become the venom of serpents
within him.
¹⁵ He will spit out the riches he swallowed;
  God will make his stomach vomit
them up.
¹⁶ He will suck the poison of serpents;
  the fangs of an adder will kill him.
¹⁷ He will not enjoy the streams,
  the rivers flowing with honey and
cream.
¹⁸ What he toiled for he must give back
uneaten;
  he will not enjoy the profit from his
trading.
¹⁹ For he has oppressed the poor and left
them destitute;
  he has seized houses he did not build.

²⁰ "Surely he will have no respite from his
craving;
  he cannot save himself by his treasure.
²¹ Nothing is left for him to devour;
  his prosperity will not endure.
²² In the midst of his plenty, distress will
overtake him;
  the full force of misery will come upon
him.
²³ When he has filled his belly,
  God will vent his burning anger
against him
  and rain down his blows on him.
²⁴ Though he flees from an iron weapon,
  a bronze-tipped arrow pierces him.
²⁵ He pulls it out of his back,
  the gleaming point out of his liver.
  Terrors will come over him;
²⁶   total darkness lies in wait for his
treasures.

---

a 24 Or *and*   *b* 25 Or *vindicator*   *c* 25 Or *on my grave
has been destroyed, / then*   *e* 26 Or *destroyed, / apart from*   *d* 26 Or *And after I awake, / though this body*   *f* 28 Many Hebrew manuscripts,
Septuagint and Vulgate; most Hebrew manuscripts *me*   *g* 29 Or *sword, / that you may come to know the
Almighty*   *h* 4 Or *Adam*

ZOPHAR

When Job's three friends, Eliphaz the Temanite, Bildad the Shuhite and Zophar the Naamathite, heard about all the troubles that had come upon him, they set out from their homes . . . to go and sympathize with him and comfort him. JOB 2:11

HIS NAME MEANS: "hairy"
READ HIS STORY: *Job 2:11–13, 11, 20, 42:7–9*

OF THE BIBLE

With friends like Job's, it was good he didn't have enemies. At first his "friends" sat and comforted him. Always a good idea. After all, Job had just lost ten children, a large number of servants and 11,000 animals. Painful sores had broken out all over his body. His family, fortune and health had been obliterated . But his friends' words of encouragement soon turned into accusations. Certainly Job had committed some horrible sin to deserve the terrible things that happened to him, they thought. Zophar was the most tactless and harsh of the three speakers.

Zophar acted like he knew the mind of God. Job's problems were caused by hidden sin. Zophar tells Job, "You say to God, 'My beliefs are flawless and I am pure in your sight.' Oh, how I wish that God would speak, that he would open his lips against you" (Job 11:4–5). But no person on earth knew that God had already spoken about Job and called him blameless (Job 1:8).

Zophar believed if we live right, we cruise through life. If we suffer, it's because of sin. But we don't control God with our behavior. We can't earn God's favor. He gives us grace. At the same time, we live in a world where bad things happen to good people. Sometimes God uses difficulties in our lives to draw us to him. Other times suffering is a consequence of being a member of the fallen human race.

If we're going to speak for God, we better be right. Zophar misspoke, and God was angry with him and his friends. In the end, Job prayed on Zophar's behalf and God forgave his arrogance (Job 42:7–9).

A fire unfanned will consume him
and devour what is left in his tent.
²⁷ The heavens will expose his guilt;
the earth will rise up against him.
²⁸ A flood will carry off his house,
rushing waters^a on the day of God's
wrath.
²⁹ Such is the fate God allots the wicked,
the heritage appointed for them
by God."

Job

21

Then Job replied:

² "Listen carefully to my words;
let this be the consolation you give me.
³ Bear with me while I speak,
and after I have spoken, mock on.

⁴ "Is my complaint directed to a human
being?
Why should I not be impatient?
⁵ Look at me and be appalled;
clap your hand over your mouth.
⁶ When I think about this, I am terrified;
trembling seizes my body.
⁷ Why do the wicked live on,
growing old and increasing in power?
⁸ They see their children established
around them,
their offspring before their eyes.
⁹ Their homes are safe and free from fear;
the rod of God is not on them.
¹⁰ Their bulls never fail to breed;
their cows calve and do not miscarry.
¹¹ They send forth their children as a flock;
their little ones dance about.
¹² They sing to the music of timbrel and
lyre;
they make merry to the sound of the
pipe.
¹³ They spend their years in prosperity
and go down to the grave in peace.^b
¹⁴ Yet they say to God, 'Leave us alone!
We have no desire to know your ways.
¹⁵ Who is the Almighty, that we should
serve him?
What would we gain by praying to
him?'
¹⁶ But their prosperity is not in their own
hands,

so I stand aloof from the plans of the
wicked.

¹⁷ "Yet how often is the lamp of the wicked
snuffed out?
How often does calamity come upon
them,
the fate God allots in his anger?
¹⁸ How often are they like straw before the
wind,
like chaff swept away by a gale?
¹⁹ It is said, 'God stores up the punishment
of the wicked for their children.'
Let him repay the wicked, so that they
themselves will experience it!
²⁰ Let their own eyes see their destruction;
let them drink the cup of the wrath of
the Almighty.
²¹ For what do they care about the families
they leave behind
when their allotted months come to an
end?

²² "Can anyone teach knowledge to God,
since he judges even the highest?
²³ One person dies in full vigor,
completely secure and at ease,
²⁴ well nourished in body,^c
bones rich with marrow.
²⁵ Another dies in bitterness of soul,
never having enjoyed anything good.
²⁶ Side by side they lie in the dust,
and worms cover them both.

²⁷ "I know full well what you are thinking,
the schemes by which you would
wrong me.
²⁸ You say, 'Where now is the house of the
great,
the tents where the wicked lived?'
²⁹ Have you never questioned those who
travel?
Have you paid no regard to their
accounts—
³⁰ that the wicked are spared from the day
of calamity,
that they are delivered from^d the day
of wrath?
³¹ Who denounces their conduct to their
face?
Who repays them for what they have
done?

---

^a 28 Or *The possessions in his house will be carried off, / washed away*   ^b 13 Or *in an instant*
^c 24 The meaning of the Hebrew for this word is uncertain.   ^d 30 Or *wicked are reserved for the day of calamity, / that they are brought forth to*

³² They are carried to the grave,
and watch is kept over their tombs.
³³ The soil in the valley is sweet to them;
everyone follows after them,
and a countless throng goes^a before
them.

³⁴ "So how can you console me with your
nonsense?
Nothing is left of your answers but
falsehood!"

Eliphaz

22 Then Eliphaz the Temanite replied:

² "Can a man be of benefit to God?
Can even a wise person benefit him?
³ What pleasure would it give the Almighty
if you were righteous?
What would he gain if your ways were
blameless?

⁴ "Is it for your piety that he rebukes you
and brings charges against you?
⁵ Is not your wickedness great?
Are not your sins endless?
⁶ You demanded security from your
relatives for no reason;
you stripped people of their clothing,
leaving them naked.
⁷ You gave no water to the weary
and you withheld food from the
hungry,
⁸ though you were a powerful man,
owning land—
an honored man, living on it.
⁹ And you sent widows away empty-
handed
and broke the strength of the
fatherless.
¹⁰ That is why snares are all around you,
why sudden peril terrifies you,
¹¹ why it is so dark you cannot see,
and why a flood of water covers you.

¹² "Is not God in the heights of heaven?
And see how lofty are the highest stars!
¹³ Yet you say, 'What does God know?
Does he judge through such darkness?
¹⁴ Thick clouds veil him, so he does not
see us
as he goes about in the vaulted
heavens.'

¹⁵ Will you keep to the old path
that the wicked have trod?
¹⁶ They were carried off before their time,
their foundations washed away by a
flood.
¹⁷ They said to God, 'Leave us alone!
What can the Almighty do to us?'
¹⁸ Yet it was he who filled their houses with
good things,
so I stand aloof from the plans of the
wicked.
¹⁹ The righteous see their ruin and rejoice;
the innocent mock them, saying,
²⁰ 'Surely our foes are destroyed,
and fire devours their wealth.'

²¹ "Submit to God and be at peace with him;
in this way prosperity will come
to you.
²² Accept instruction from his mouth
and lay up his words in your heart.
²³ If you return to the Almighty, you will
be restored:
If you remove wickedness far from
your tent
²⁴ and assign your nuggets to the dust,
your gold of Ophir to the rocks in the
ravines,
²⁵ then the Almighty will be your gold,
the choicest silver for you.
²⁶ Surely then you will find delight in the
Almighty
and will lift up your face to God.
²⁷ You will pray to him, and he will hear
you,
and you will fulfill your vows.
²⁸ What you decide on will be done,
and light will shine on your ways.
²⁹ When people are brought low and you
say, 'Lift them up!'
then he will save the downcast.
³⁰ He will deliver even one who is not
innocent,
who will be delivered through the
cleanness of your hands."

Job

23 Then Job replied:

² "Even today my complaint is bitter;
his hand^b is heavy in spite of^c my
groaning.

---

^a 33 Or *them, / as a countless throng went*   ^b 2 Septuagint and Syriac; Hebrew / *the hand on me*
^c 2 Or *heavy on me in*

EASY TARGET

READ: JOB 22:4-5

As if it isn't bad enough that Job had to put up with the loss of everything that mattered to him—his family, riches, and health—he now had to listen to his so-called friends pelt him with lies.

Eliphaz, Bildad, and Zophar all started with a wrong assumption that life's painful experiences are the Lord's payback for wrongdoing. They thought God automatically and instantly sent consequences for sin. In their eyes someone's suffering was therefore undeniable proof of their evil behavior.

Jesus himself debunks that way of thinking. He points out that all people do wrong and will one day die if they don't repent—if they don't quit sinning and turn to God. But experiencing a disaster doesn't make someone more guilty than anyone else (Luke 13:1-5).

Since the start of this book, Job has protested his innocence. When Eliphaz can't spot anything Job has done wrong, he makes up false accusations. He says Job has cheated the poor, refused to feed the hungry, and mistreated orphans (Job 24:7-10).

BUILDING FAITH WISDOM STRENGTH

When people decide to make you a target, you often can't shut them up. If they can't find a fault to pick at, they invent one. Your only real choice in that situation is to do what Job did. You keep trusting God (Psalm 25:1-2). Keep believing in yourself (17:3). And keep doing right (1 Peter 3:8-17).

³ If only I knew where to find him;
    if only I could go to his dwelling!
⁴ I would state my case before him
    and fill my mouth with arguments.
⁵ I would find out what he would answer me,
    and consider what he would say to me.
⁶ Would he vigorously oppose me?
    No, he would not press charges
        against me.
⁷ There the upright can establish their
        innocence before him,
    and there I would be delivered forever
        from my judge.

⁸ "But if I go to the east, he is not there;
    if I go to the west, I do not find him.
⁹ When he is at work in the north, I do not
        see him;
    when he turns to the south, I catch no
        glimpse of him.
¹⁰ But he knows the way that I take;
    when he has tested me, I will come
        forth as gold.
¹¹ My feet have closely followed his steps;
    I have kept to his way without turning
        aside.
¹² I have not departed from the commands
        of his lips;
    I have treasured the words of his
        mouth more than my daily bread.

¹³ "But he stands alone, and who can
        oppose him?
    He does whatever he pleases.
¹⁴ He carries out his decree against me,
    and many such plans he still has in
        store.
¹⁵ That is why I am terrified before him;
    when I think of all this, I fear him.
¹⁶ God has made my heart faint;
    the Almighty has terrified me.
¹⁷ Yet I am not silenced by the darkness,
    by the thick darkness that covers
        my face.

24 "Why does the Almighty not set
        times for judgment?
    Why must those who know him look in
        vain for such days?
² There are those who move boundary
        stones;
    they pasture flocks they have stolen.
³ They drive away the orphan's donkey
    and take the widow's ox in pledge.

⁴ They thrust the needy from the path
    and force all the poor of the land into
        hiding.
⁵ Like wild donkeys in the desert,
    the poor go about their labor of
        foraging food;
    the wasteland provides food for their
        children.
⁶ They gather fodder in the fields
    and glean in the vineyards of the
        wicked.
⁷ Lacking clothes, they spend the night
        naked;
    they have nothing to cover themselves
        in the cold.
⁸ They are drenched by mountain rains
    and hug the rocks for lack of shelter.
⁹ The fatherless child is snatched from the
        breast;
    the infant of the poor is seized for a
        debt.
¹⁰ Lacking clothes, they go about naked;
    they carry the sheaves, but still go
        hungry.
¹¹ They crush olives among the terraces[a];
    they tread the winepresses, yet suffer
        thirst.
¹² The groans of the dying rise from the city,
    and the souls of the wounded cry out
        for help.
    But God charges no one with
        wrongdoing.

¹³ "There are those who rebel against
        the light,
    who do not know its ways
    or stay in its paths.
¹⁴ When daylight is gone, the murderer
        rises up,
    kills the poor and needy,
    and in the night steals forth like a thief.
¹⁵ The eye of the adulterer watches for dusk;
    he thinks, 'No eye will see me,'
    and he keeps his face concealed.
¹⁶ In the dark, thieves break into houses,
    but by day they shut themselves in;
    they want nothing to do with the light.
¹⁷ For all of them, midnight is their
        morning;
    they make friends with the terrors
        of darkness.

¹⁸ "Yet they are foam on the surface of
        the water;

---

[a] 11 The meaning of the Hebrew for this word is uncertain.

their portion of the land is cursed,
so that no one goes to the vineyards.

¹⁹ As heat and drought snatch away the
melted snow,
so the grave snatches away those who
have sinned.

²⁰ The womb forgets them,
the worm feasts on them;
the wicked are no longer remembered
but are broken like a tree.

²¹ They prey on the barren and childless
woman,
and to the widow they show no
kindness.

²² But God drags away the mighty by his
power;
though they become established, they
have no assurance of life.

²³ He may let them rest in a feeling of
security,
but his eyes are on their ways.

²⁴ For a little while they are exalted, and
then they are gone;
they are brought low and gathered up
like all others;
they are cut off like heads of grain.

²⁵ "If this is not so, who can prove me false
and reduce my words to nothing?"

Bildad

25 Then Bildad the Shuhite replied:

² "Dominion and awe belong to God;
he establishes order in the heights of
heaven.

³ Can his forces be numbered?
On whom does his light not rise?

⁴ How then can a mortal be righteous
before God?
How can one born of woman be pure?

⁵ If even the moon is not bright
and the stars are not pure in his eyes,

⁶ how much less a mortal, who is but a
maggot —
a human being, who is only a worm!"

Job

26 Then Job replied:

² "How you have helped the powerless!
How you have saved the arm that is
feeble!

³ What advice you have offered to one
without wisdom!
And what great insight you have
displayed!

⁴ Who has helped you utter these words?
And whose spirit spoke from your
mouth?

⁵ "The dead are in deep anguish,
those beneath the waters and all that
live in them.

⁶ The realm of the dead is naked before
God;
Destruction*a* lies uncovered.

⁷ He spreads out the northern skies over
empty space;
he suspends the earth over nothing.

⁸ He wraps up the waters in his clouds,
yet the clouds do not burst under their
weight.

⁹ He covers the face of the full moon,
spreading his clouds over it.

¹⁰ He marks out the horizon on the face of
the waters
for a boundary between light and
darkness.

¹¹ The pillars of the heavens quake,
aghast at his rebuke.

¹² By his power he churned up the sea;
by his wisdom he cut Rahab to pieces.

¹³ By his breath the skies became fair;
his hand pierced the gliding serpent.

¹⁴ And these are but the outer fringe of his
works;
how faint the whisper we hear of him!
Who then can understand the thunder
of his power?"

Job's Final Word to His Friends

27 And Job continued his discourse:

² "As surely as God lives, who has denied
me justice,
the Almighty, who has made my life
bitter,

³ as long as I have life within me,
the breath of God in my nostrils,

⁴ my lips will not say anything wicked,
and my tongue will not utter lies.

⁵ I will never admit you are in the right;
till I die, I will not deny my integrity.

⁶ I will maintain my innocence and never
let go of it;

---

a 6 Hebrew *Abaddon*

my conscience will not reproach me as long as I live.

7 "May my enemy be like the wicked,
my adversary like the unjust!
8 For what hope have the godless when they are cut off,
when God takes away their life?
9 Does God listen to their cry
when distress comes upon them?
10 Will they find delight in the Almighty?
Will they call on God at all times?

11 "I will teach you about the power of God;
the ways of the Almighty I will not conceal.
12 You have all seen this yourselves.
Why then this meaningless talk?

13 "Here is the fate God allots to the wicked,
the heritage a ruthless man receives from the Almighty:
14 However many his children, their fate is the sword;
his offspring will never have enough to eat.
15 The plague will bury those who survive him,
and their widows will not weep for them.
16 Though he heaps up silver like dust
and clothes like piles of clay,
17 what he lays up the righteous will wear,
and the innocent will divide his silver.
18 The house he builds is like a moth's cocoon,
like a hut made by a watchman.
19 He lies down wealthy, but will do so no more;
when he opens his eyes, all is gone.
20 Terrors overtake him like a flood;
a tempest snatches him away in the night.
21 The east wind carries him off, and he is gone;
it sweeps him out of his place.
22 It hurls itself against him without mercy
as he flees headlong from its power.
23 It claps its hands in derision
and hisses him out of his place."

Interlude: Where Wisdom Is Found

28 There is a mine for silver
and a place where gold is refined.
2 Iron is taken from the earth,
and copper is smelted from ore.
3 Mortals put an end to the darkness;
they search out the farthest recesses
for ore in the blackest darkness.
4 Far from human dwellings they cut a shaft,
in places untouched by human feet;
far from other people they dangle and sway.
5 The earth, from which food comes,
is transformed below as by fire;
6 lapis lazuli comes from its rocks,
and its dust contains nuggets of gold.
7 No bird of prey knows that hidden path,
no falcon's eye has seen it.
8 Proud beasts do not set foot on it,
and no lion prowls there.
9 People assault the flinty rock with their hands
and lay bare the roots of the mountains.
10 They tunnel through the rock;
their eyes see all its treasures.
11 They search[a] the sources of the rivers
and bring hidden things to light.

12 But where can wisdom be found?
Where does understanding dwell?
13 No mortal comprehends its worth;
it cannot be found in the land of the living.
14 The deep says, "It is not in me";
the sea says, "It is not with me."
15 It cannot be bought with the finest gold,
nor can its price be weighed out in silver.
16 It cannot be bought with the gold of Ophir,
with precious onyx or lapis lazuli.
17 Neither gold nor crystal can compare with it,
nor can it be had for jewels of gold.
18 Coral and jasper are not worthy of mention;
the price of wisdom is beyond rubies.
19 The topaz of Cush cannot compare with it;
it cannot be bought with pure gold.

20 Where then does wisdom come from?
Where does understanding dwell?
21 It is hidden from the eyes of every living thing,

---

a 11 Septuagint, Aquila and Vulgate; Hebrew *They dam up*

concealed even from the birds in
the sky.
²² Destruction^a and Death say,
"Only a rumor of it has reached our
ears."
²³ God understands the way to it
and he alone knows where it dwells,
²⁴ for he views the ends of the earth
and sees everything under the
heavens.
²⁵ When he established the force of
the wind
and measured out the waters,
²⁶ when he made a decree for the rain
and a path for the thunderstorm,
²⁷ then he looked at wisdom and
appraised it;
he confirmed it and tested it.
²⁸ And he said to the human race,
"The fear of the Lord — that is wisdom,
and to shun evil is understanding."

Job's Final Defense

29 Job continued his discourse:

² "How I long for the months gone by,
for the days when God watched
over me,
³ when his lamp shone on my head
and by his light I walked through
darkness!
⁴ Oh, for the days when I was in my prime,
when God's intimate friendship
blessed my house,
⁵ when the Almighty was still with me
and my children were around me,
⁶ when my path was drenched with cream
and the rock poured out for me
streams of olive oil.

⁷ "When I went to the gate of the city
and took my seat in the public square,
⁸ the young men saw me and stepped
aside
and the old men rose to their feet;
⁹ the chief men refrained from speaking
and covered their mouths with their
hands;
¹⁰ the voices of the nobles were hushed,
and their tongues stuck to the roof of
their mouths.
¹¹ Whoever heard me spoke well of me,
and those who saw me commended me,

¹² because I rescued the poor who cried
for help,
and the fatherless who had none to
assist them.
¹³ The one who was dying blessed me;
I made the widow's heart sing.
¹⁴ I put on righteousness as my clothing;
justice was my robe and my turban.
¹⁵ I was eyes to the blind
and feet to the lame.
¹⁶ I was a father to the needy;
I took up the case of the stranger.
¹⁷ I broke the fangs of the wicked
and snatched the victims from their
teeth.

¹⁸ "I thought, 'I will die in my own house,
my days as numerous as the grains
of sand.
¹⁹ My roots will reach to the water,
and the dew will lie all night on my
branches.
²⁰ My glory will not fade;
the bow will be ever new in my hand.'

²¹ "People listened to me expectantly,
waiting in silence for my counsel.
²² After I had spoken, they spoke no more;
my words fell gently on their ears.
²³ They waited for me as for showers
and drank in my words as the spring
rain.
²⁴ When I smiled at them, they scarcely
believed it;
the light of my face was precious
to them.^b
²⁵ I chose the way for them and sat as their
chief;
I dwelt as a king among his troops;
I was like one who comforts
mourners.

30 "But now they mock me,
men younger than I,
whose fathers I would have disdained
to put with my sheep dogs.
² Of what use was the strength of their
hands to me,
since their vigor had gone from
them?
³ Haggard from want and hunger,
they roamed^c the parched land
in desolate wastelands at night.
⁴ In the brush they gathered salt herbs,

---

^a 22 Hebrew *Abaddon*   ^b 24 The meaning of the Hebrew for this clause is uncertain.   ^c 3 Or *gnawed*

INSIDE JUSTICE

READ: JOB 29:14-16

Where did we get this idea of justice and injustice? Is it just a feeling? Or is it something real in the world? This concept didn't come from society, for people have often sought justice against society and even changed society. Today, every headline in the newspaper talks about corruption in economics, world politics, international sanctions, and pollution.

People desire justice with an intensity that comes from a standard inside of them. With that standard they want to make things right for themselves and for others. The law of right and wrong is deeper and larger than science, society, instincts, or family.

The best explanation I have found is that the spiritual, smart, strong being is also the Justice-Giver. We call this being God—and God has built a moral law within us. That would explain why everyone else— in every culture—has this sense of justice too. No culture believes it's okay, for instance, for a neighbor to bully, terrorize, and kill all of their friends. And we call cultures that believe otherwise twisted and wrong (sometimes we even use words such as *primitive* or *savage*). And we praise international organizations that rescue kids abused in sex trafficking and stolen for war.

God, through justice, gives us a strong sense of how things ought to be. In the entire human race, this awareness of justice is present. Some may disagree about the details, but it's difficult to deny that the law of right and wrong exists to help people figure out those details.

BUILDING

FAITH

WISDOM

STRENGTH

and their food*a* was the root of the
broom bush.
⁵ They were banished from human society,
shouted at as if they were thieves.
⁶ They were forced to live in the dry stream
beds,
among the rocks and in holes in the
ground.
⁷ They brayed among the bushes
and huddled in the undergrowth.
⁸ A base and nameless brood,
they were driven out of the land.

⁹ "And now those young men mock me
in song;
I have become a byword among them.
¹⁰ They detest me and keep their distance;
they do not hesitate to spit in my face.
¹¹ Now that God has unstrung my bow and
afflicted me,
they throw off restraint in my
presence.
¹² On my right the tribe*b* attacks;
they lay snares for my feet,
they build their siege ramps
against me.
¹³ They break up my road;
they succeed in destroying me.
'No one can help him,' they say.
¹⁴ They advance as through a gaping
breach;
amid the ruins they come rolling in.
¹⁵ Terrors overwhelm me;
my dignity is driven away as by the
wind,
my safety vanishes like a cloud.

¹⁶ "And now my life ebbs away;
days of suffering grip me.
¹⁷ Night pierces my bones;
my gnawing pains never rest.
¹⁸ In his great power God becomes like
clothing to me*c*;
he binds me like the neck of my
garment.
¹⁹ He throws me into the mud,
and I am reduced to dust and ashes.

²⁰ "I cry out to you, God, but you do not
answer;
I stand up, but you merely look at me.
²¹ You turn on me ruthlessly;
with the might of your hand you
attack me.

²² You snatch me up and drive me before
the wind;
you toss me about in the storm.
²³ I know you will bring me down to death,
to the place appointed for all the
living.

²⁴ "Surely no one lays a hand on a broken
man
when he cries for help in his distress.
²⁵ Have I not wept for those in trouble?
Has not my soul grieved for the poor?
²⁶ Yet when I hoped for good, evil came;
when I looked for light, then came
darkness.
²⁷ The churning inside me never stops;
days of suffering confront me.
²⁸ I go about blackened, but not by the sun;
I stand up in the assembly and cry
for help.
²⁹ I have become a brother of jackals,
a companion of owls.
³⁰ My skin grows black and peels;
my body burns with fever.
³¹ My lyre is tuned to mourning,
and my pipe to the sound of wailing.

31 "I made a covenant with my eyes
not to look lustfully at a young
woman.
² For what is our lot from God above,
our heritage from the Almighty on
high?
³ Is it not ruin for the wicked,
disaster for those who do wrong?
⁴ Does he not see my ways
and count my every step?

⁵ "If I have walked with falsehood
or my foot has hurried after deceit—
⁶ let God weigh me in honest scales
and he will know that I am
blameless—
⁷ if my steps have turned from the path,
if my heart has been led by my eyes,
or if my hands have been defiled,
⁸ then may others eat what I have sown,
and may my crops be uprooted.

⁹ "If my heart has been enticed by a
woman,
or if I have lurked at my neighbor's
door,

---

a 4 Or *fuel*   *b 12* The meaning of the Hebrew for this word is uncertain.   *c 18* Hebrew; Septuagint *power he grasps my clothing*

¹⁰ then may my wife grind another man's
grain,
and may other men sleep with her.
¹¹ For that would have been wicked,
a sin to be judged.
¹² It is a fire that burns to Destruction^a;
it would have uprooted my harvest.

¹³ "If I have denied justice to any of my
servants,
whether male or female,
when they had a grievance against me,
¹⁴ what will I do when God confronts me?
What will I answer when called to
account?
¹⁵ Did not he who made me in the womb
make them?
Did not the same one form us both
within our mothers?

¹⁶ "If I have denied the desires of the poor
or let the eyes of the widow grow
weary,
¹⁷ if I have kept my bread to myself,
not sharing it with the fatherless —
¹⁸ but from my youth I reared them as a
father would,
and from my birth I guided the
widow —
¹⁹ if I have seen anyone perishing for lack of
clothing,
or the needy without garments,
²⁰ and their hearts did not bless me
for warming them with the fleece from
my sheep,
²¹ if I have raised my hand against the
fatherless,
knowing that I had influence in court,
²² then let my arm fall from the shoulder,
let it be broken off at the joint.
²³ For I dreaded destruction from God,
and for fear of his splendor I could not
do such things.

²⁴ "If I have put my trust in gold
or said to pure gold, 'You are my
security,'
²⁵ if I have rejoiced over my great wealth,
the fortune my hands had gained,
²⁶ if I have regarded the sun in its radiance
or the moon moving in splendor,
²⁷ so that my heart was secretly enticed
and my hand offered them a kiss of
homage,

²⁸ then these also would be sins to be
judged,
for I would have been unfaithful to
God on high.

²⁹ "If I have rejoiced at my enemy's
misfortune
or gloated over the trouble that came
to him —
³⁰ I have not allowed my mouth to sin
by invoking a curse against their life —
³¹ if those of my household have never said,
'Who has not been filled with Job's
meat?' —
³² but no stranger had to spend the night in
the street,
for my door was always open to the
traveler —
³³ if I have concealed my sin as people do,^b
by hiding my guilt in my heart
³⁴ because I so feared the crowd
and so dreaded the contempt of the
clans
that I kept silent and would not go
outside —

³⁵ ("Oh, that I had someone to hear me!
I sign now my defense — let the
Almighty answer me;
let my accuser put his indictment in
writing.
³⁶ Surely I would wear it on my shoulder,
I would put it on like a crown.
³⁷ I would give him an account of my every
step;
I would present it to him as to a
ruler.) —

³⁸ "if my land cries out against me
and all its furrows are wet with tears,
³⁹ if I have devoured its yield without
payment
or broken the spirit of its tenants,
⁴⁰ then let briers come up instead of wheat
and stinkweed instead of barley."

The words of Job are ended.

Elihu

32 So these three men stopped answer-
ing Job, because he was righteous in
his own eyes. ² But Elihu son of Barakel the
Buzite, of the family of Ram, became very
angry with Job for justifying himself rather

---

^a 12 Hebrew *Abaddon*   ^b 33 Or *as Adam did*

than God. ³He was also angry with the three friends, because they had found no way to refute Job, and yet had condemned him.ᵃ ⁴Now Elihu had waited before speaking to Job because they were older than he. ⁵But when he saw that the three men had nothing more to say, his anger was aroused.

⁶So Elihu son of Barakel the Buzite said:

"I am young in years,
    and you are old;
that is why I was fearful,
    not daring to tell you what I know.
⁷I thought, 'Age should speak;
    advanced years should teach wisdom.'
⁸But it is the spiritᵇ in a person,
    the breath of the Almighty, that gives
        them understanding.
⁹It is not only the oldᶜ who are wise,
    not only the aged who understand
        what is right.

¹⁰"Therefore I say: Listen to me;
    I too will tell you what I know.
¹¹I waited while you spoke,
    I listened to your reasoning;
while you were searching for words,
¹²   I gave you my full attention.
    But not one of you has proved Job wrong;
        none of you has answered his
            arguments.
¹³Do not say, 'We have found wisdom;
    let God, not a man, refute him.'
¹⁴But Job has not marshaled his words
        against me,
    and I will not answer him with your
        arguments.

¹⁵"They are dismayed and have no more
        to say;
    words have failed them.
¹⁶Must I wait, now that they are silent,
    now that they stand there with no
        reply?
¹⁷I too will have my say;
    I too will tell what I know.
¹⁸For I am full of words,
    and the spirit within me compels me;
¹⁹inside I am like bottled-up wine,
    like new wineskins ready to burst.
²⁰I must speak and find relief;
    I must open my lips and reply.

²¹I will show no partiality,
    nor will I flatter anyone;
²²for if I were skilled in flattery,
    my Maker would soon take me away.

33 "But now, Job, listen to my words;
    pay attention to everything I say.
²I am about to open my mouth;
    my words are on the tip of my tongue.
³My words come from an upright heart;
    my lips sincerely speak what I know.
⁴The Spirit of God has made me;
    the breath of the Almighty gives
        me life.
⁵Answer me then, if you can;
    stand up and argue your case
        before me.
⁶I am the same as you in God's sight;
    I too am a piece of clay.
⁷No fear of me should alarm you,
    nor should my hand be heavy on you.

⁸"But you have said in my hearing—
    I heard the very words—
⁹'I am pure, I have done no wrong;
    I am clean and free from sin.
¹⁰Yet God has found fault with me;
    he considers me his enemy.
¹¹He fastens my feet in shackles;
    he keeps close watch on all my paths.'

¹²"But I tell you, in this you are not right,
    for God is greater than any mortal.
¹³Why do you complain to him
    that he responds to no one's wordsᵈ?
¹⁴For God does speak—now one way, now
        another—
    though no one perceives it.
¹⁵In a dream, in a vision of the night,
    when deep sleep falls on people
        as they slumber in their beds,
¹⁶he may speak in their ears
    and terrify them with warnings,
¹⁷to turn them from wrongdoing
    and keep them from pride,
¹⁸to preserve them from the pit,
    their lives from perishing by the
        sword.ᵉ

¹⁹"Or someone may be chastened on a bed
        of pain
    with constant distress in their bones,

ᵃ 3 Masoretic Text; an ancient Hebrew scribal tradition *Job, and so had condemned God*   ᵇ 8 Or *Spirit*; also in verse 18   ᶜ 9 Or *many*; or *great*   ᵈ 13 Or *that he does not answer for any of his actions* ᵉ 18 Or *from crossing the river*

²⁰ so that their body finds food repulsive
and their soul loathes the choicest
meal.
²¹ Their flesh wastes away to nothing,
and their bones, once hidden, now
stick out.
²² They draw near to the pit,
and their life to the messengers of
death.ᵃ
²³ Yet if there is an angel at their side,
a messenger, one out of a thousand,
sent to tell them how to be upright,
²⁴ and he is gracious to that person and says
to God,
'Spare them from going down to
the pit;
I have found a ransom for them—
²⁵ let their flesh be renewed like a child's;
let them be restored as in the days of
their youth'—
²⁶ then that person can pray to God and
find favor with him,
they will see God's face and shout
for joy;
he will restore them to full well-being.
²⁷ And they will go to others and say,
'I have sinned, I have perverted what
is right,
but I did not get what I deserved.
²⁸ God has delivered me from going down
to the pit,
and I shall live to enjoy the light of life.'

²⁹ "God does all these things to a person—
twice, even three times—
³⁰ to turn them back from the pit,
that the light of life may shine on them.

³¹ "Pay attention, Job, and listen to me;
be silent, and I will speak.
³² If you have anything to say, answer me;
speak up, for I want to vindicate you.
³³ But if not, then listen to me;
be silent, and I will teach you wisdom."

34

Then Elihu said:

² "Hear my words, you wise men;
listen to me, you men of learning.
³ For the ear tests words
as the tongue tastes food.
⁴ Let us discern for ourselves what is right;
let us learn together what is good.

⁵ "Job says, 'I am innocent,
but God denies me justice.
⁶ Although I am right,
I am considered a liar;
although I am guiltless,
his arrow inflicts an incurable wound.'
⁷ Is there anyone like Job,
who drinks scorn like water?
⁸ He keeps company with evildoers;
he associates with the wicked.
⁹ For he says, 'There is no profit
in trying to please God.'

¹⁰ "So listen to me, you men of
understanding.
Far be it from God to do evil,
from the Almighty to do wrong.
¹¹ He repays everyone for what they have
done;
he brings on them what their conduct
deserves.
¹² It is unthinkable that God would do
wrong,
that the Almighty would pervert
justice.
¹³ Who appointed him over the earth?
Who put him in charge of the whole
world?
¹⁴ If it were his intention
and he withdrew his spiritᵇ and breath,
¹⁵ all humanity would perish together
and mankind would return to the dust.

¹⁶ "If you have understanding, hear this;
listen to what I say.
¹⁷ Can someone who hates justice govern?
Will you condemn the just and mighty
One?
¹⁸ Is he not the One who says to kings, 'You
are worthless,'
and to nobles, 'You are wicked,'
¹⁹ who shows no partiality to princes
and does not favor the rich over the
poor,
for they are all the work of his hands?
²⁰ They die in an instant, in the middle of
the night;
the people are shaken and they pass
away;
the mighty are removed without
human hand.

²¹ "His eyes are on the ways of mortals;
he sees their every step.

ᵃ 22 Or *to the place of the dead*   ᵇ 14 Or *Spirit*

²² There is no deep shadow, no utter
    darkness,
    where evildoers can hide.
²³ God has no need to examine people
    further,
    that they should come before him for
    judgment.
²⁴ Without inquiry he shatters the mighty
    and sets up others in their place.
²⁵ Because he takes note of their deeds,
    he overthrows them in the night and
    they are crushed.
²⁶ He punishes them for their wickedness
    where everyone can see them,
²⁷ because they turned from following him
    and had no regard for any of his ways.
²⁸ They caused the cry of the poor to come
    before him,
    so that he heard the cry of the needy.
²⁹ But if he remains silent, who can
    condemn him?
    If he hides his face, who can see him?
    Yet he is over individual and nation alike,
³⁰   to keep the godless from ruling,
    from laying snares for the people.

³¹ "Suppose someone says to God,
    'I am guilty but will offend no more.
³² Teach me what I cannot see;
    if I have done wrong, I will not do so
    again.'
³³ Should God then reward you on your
    terms,
    when you refuse to repent?
    You must decide, not I;
    so tell me what you know.

³⁴ "Men of understanding declare,
    wise men who hear me say to me,
³⁵ 'Job speaks without knowledge;
    his words lack insight.'
³⁶ Oh, that Job might be tested to the
    utmost
    for answering like a wicked man!
³⁷ To his sin he adds rebellion;
    scornfully he claps his hands
        among us
    and multiplies his words against God."

35 Then Elihu said:

² "Do you think this is just?
    You say, 'I am in the right, not God.'

³ Yet you ask him, 'What profit is it to me,[a]
    and what do I gain by not sinning?'

⁴ "I would like to reply to you
    and to your friends with you.
⁵ Look up at the heavens and see;
    gaze at the clouds so high above you.
⁶ If you sin, how does that affect him?
    If your sins are many, what does that
        do to him?
⁷ If you are righteous, what do you give
        to him,
    or what does he receive from your
        hand?
⁸ Your wickedness only affects humans
        like yourself,
    and your righteousness only other
        people.

⁹ "People cry out under a load of
        oppression;
    they plead for relief from the arm of the
        powerful.
¹⁰ But no one says, 'Where is God my Maker,
    who gives songs in the night,
¹¹ who teaches us more than he teaches[b]
        the beasts of the earth
    and makes us wiser than[c] the birds in
        the sky?'
¹² He does not answer when people cry out
    because of the arrogance of the
        wicked.
¹³ Indeed, God does not listen to their
        empty plea;
    the Almighty pays no attention to it.
¹⁴ How much less, then, will he listen
    when you say that you do not see him,
    that your case is before him
    and you must wait for him,
¹⁵ and further, that his anger never
        punishes
    and he does not take the least notice of
        wickedness.[d]
¹⁶ So Job opens his mouth with empty talk;
    without knowledge he multiplies
        words."

36 Elihu continued:

² "Bear with me a little longer and I will
        show you
    that there is more to be said in God's
        behalf.

---

^a 3 Or *you*   ^b 10,11 Or *night,* / ¹¹*who teaches us by*   ^c 11 Or *us wise by*   ^d 15 Symmachus, Theodotion
and Vulgate; the meaning of the Hebrew for this word is uncertain.

³ I get my knowledge from afar;
  I will ascribe justice to my Maker.
⁴ Be assured that my words are not false;
  one who has perfect knowledge is
    with you.

⁵ "God is mighty, but despises no one;
  he is mighty, and firm in his purpose.
⁶ He does not keep the wicked alive
  but gives the afflicted their rights.
⁷ He does not take his eyes off the
    righteous;
  he enthrones them with kings
  and exalts them forever.
⁸ But if people are bound in chains,
  held fast by cords of affliction,
⁹ he tells them what they have done —
  that they have sinned arrogantly.
¹⁰ He makes them listen to correction
  and commands them to repent of
    their evil.
¹¹ If they obey and serve him,
  they will spend the rest of their days
    in prosperity
  and their years in contentment.
¹² But if they do not listen,
  they will perish by the sword*a*
  and die without knowledge.

¹³ "The godless in heart harbor resentment;
  even when he fetters them, they do not
    cry for help.
¹⁴ They die in their youth,
  among male prostitutes of the shrines.
¹⁵ But those who suffer he delivers in their
    suffering;
  he speaks to them in their affliction.

¹⁶ "He is wooing you from the jaws of
    distress
  to a spacious place free from
    restriction,
  to the comfort of your table laden with
    choice food.
¹⁷ But now you are laden with the judgment
    due the wicked;
  judgment and justice have taken hold
    of you.
¹⁸ Be careful that no one entices you by
    riches;
  do not let a large bribe turn you
    aside.

¹⁹ Would your wealth or even all your
    mighty efforts
  sustain you so you would not be in
    distress?
²⁰ Do not long for the night,
  to drag people away from their
    homes.*b*
²¹ Beware of turning to evil,
  which you seem to prefer to affliction.

²² "God is exalted in his power.
  Who is a teacher like him?
²³ Who has prescribed his ways for him,
  or said to him, 'You have done wrong'?
²⁴ Remember to extol his work,
  which people have praised in song.
²⁵ All humanity has seen it;
  mortals gaze on it from afar.
²⁶ How great is God — beyond our
    understanding!
  The number of his years is past
    finding out.

²⁷ "He draws up the drops of water,
  which distill as rain to the streams*c*;
²⁸ the clouds pour down their moisture
  and abundant showers fall on
    mankind.
²⁹ Who can understand how he spreads out
    the clouds,
  how he thunders from his pavilion?
³⁰ See how he scatters his lightning about
    him,
  bathing the depths of the sea.
³¹ This is the way he governs*d* the nations
  and provides food in abundance.
³² He fills his hands with lightning
  and commands it to strike its mark.
³³ His thunder announces the coming
    storm;
  even the cattle make known its
    approach.*e*

37

  "At this my heart pounds
  and leaps from its place.
² Listen! Listen to the roar of his voice,
  to the rumbling that comes from his
    mouth.
³ He unleashes his lightning beneath the
    whole heaven
  and sends it to the ends of the earth.
⁴ After that comes the sound of his roar;

---

a 12 Or *will cross the river*   *b 20* The meaning of the Hebrew for verses 18-20 is uncertain.
c 27 Or *distill from the mist as rain*   *d 31* Or *nourishes*   *e 33* Or *announces his coming — / the One zealous against evil*

he thunders with his majestic
voice.
When his voice resounds,
he holds nothing back.
[5] God's voice thunders in marvelous ways;
he does great things beyond our
understanding.
[6] He says to the snow, 'Fall on the earth,'
and to the rain shower, 'Be a mighty
downpour.'
[7] So that everyone he has made may know
his work,
he stops all people from their labor.[a]
[8] The animals take cover;
they remain in their dens.
[9] The tempest comes out from its chamber,
the cold from the driving winds.
[10] The breath of God produces ice,
and the broad waters become frozen.
[11] He loads the clouds with moisture;
he scatters his lightning through them.
[12] At his direction they swirl around
over the face of the whole earth
to do whatever he commands them.
[13] He brings the clouds to punish people,
or to water his earth and show his love.

[14] "Listen to this, Job;
stop and consider God's wonders.
[15] Do you know how God controls the
clouds
and makes his lightning flash?
[16] Do you know how the clouds hang
poised,
those wonders of him who has perfect
knowledge?
[17] You who swelter in your clothes
when the land lies hushed under the
south wind,
[18] can you join him in spreading out the
skies,
hard as a mirror of cast bronze?

[19] "Tell us what we should say to him;
we cannot draw up our case because of
our darkness.
[20] Should he be told that I want to speak?
Would anyone ask to be swallowed up?
[21] Now no one can look at the sun,
bright as it is in the skies
after the wind has swept them clean.
[22] Out of the north he comes in golden
splendor;

God comes in awesome majesty.
[23] The Almighty is beyond our reach and
exalted in power;
in his justice and great righteousness,
he does not oppress.
[24] Therefore, people revere him,
for does he not have regard for all the
wise in heart?[b]"

The LORD Speaks

38 Then the LORD spoke to Job out of the
storm. He said:

[2] "Who is this that obscures my plans
with words without knowledge?
[3] Brace yourself like a man;
I will question you,
and you shall answer me.

[4] "Where were you when I laid the earth's
foundation?
Tell me, if you understand.
[5] Who marked off its dimensions? Surely
you know!
Who stretched a measuring line
across it?
[6] On what were its footings set,
or who laid its cornerstone—
[7] while the morning stars sang together
and all the angels[c] shouted for joy?

[8] "Who shut up the sea behind doors
when it burst forth from the womb,
[9] when I made the clouds its garment
and wrapped it in thick darkness,
[10] when I fixed limits for it
and set its doors and bars in place,
[11] when I said, 'This far you may come and
no farther;
here is where your proud waves halt'?

[12] "Have you ever given orders to the
morning,
or shown the dawn its place,
[13] that it might take the earth by the edges
and shake the wicked out of it?
[14] The earth takes shape like clay under
a seal;
its features stand out like those of a
garment.
[15] The wicked are denied their light,
and their upraised arm is broken.

[16] "Have you journeyed to the springs of
the sea

---

[a] 7 Or *work, / he fills all people with fear by his power
think they are wise.*   [c] 7 Hebrew *the sons of God*

[b] 24 Or *for he does not have regard for any who*

TALK TO GOD

READ: JOB 38:1-2

At first Eliphaz, Bildad, and Zophar won't stop talking. After their longwinded speeches fail to persuade Job to drop his defenses and quit complaining about God, young Elihu chimes in, angry that his elders can't silence one pitiful man (Job 32:3). As these four men take turns speaking throughout the book, Job answers them point by point.

Suddenly it's the Lord's turn to speak, and you catch right away he isn't happy with all the words these guys have spoken. After Job has uttered countless questions for God, now it's God's turn to probe Job.

Job shrinks as the Lord hits him with impossible questions. This troubled man wasn't around when God laid the earth's foundations (38:4). He doesn't tell the stars when to move (v. 31). The creatures of the earth don't serve him (39:27). When the Lord invites Job to answer, Job realizes he has nothing left to say (40:1-5). He concludes that God knows everything and can do anything (42:1-6). When Job repents, the Lord restores everything Job had lost (vv. 7-17).

God welcomes your big questions. He listens to your complaints. He hears your agonizing cries. But he won't settle for anything less than your total respect. Even when you can't understand everything life throws at you, God is in control. He always cares.

BUILDING

FAITH

WISDOM

STRENGTH

or walked in the recesses of the
deep?
17 Have the gates of death been shown
to you?
Have you seen the gates of the deepest
darkness?
18 Have you comprehended the vast
expanses of the earth?
Tell me, if you know all this.

19 "What is the way to the abode of light?
And where does darkness reside?
20 Can you take them to their places?
Do you know the paths to their
dwellings?
21 Surely you know, for you were already
born!
You have lived so many years!

22 "Have you entered the storehouses of
the snow
or seen the storehouses of the hail,
23 which I reserve for times of trouble,
for days of war and battle?
24 What is the way to the place where the
lightning is dispersed,
or the place where the east winds are
scattered over the earth?
25 Who cuts a channel for the torrents
of rain,
and a path for the thunderstorm,
26 to water a land where no one lives,
an uninhabited desert,
27 to satisfy a desolate wasteland
and make it sprout with grass?
28 Does the rain have a father?
Who fathers the drops of dew?
29 From whose womb comes the ice?
Who gives birth to the frost from the
heavens
30 when the waters become hard as stone,
when the surface of the deep is frozen?

31 "Can you bind the chains*a* of the
Pleiades?
Can you loosen Orion's belt?
32 Can you bring forth the constellations in
their seasons*b*
or lead out the Bear*c* with its cubs?
33 Do you know the laws of the heavens?
Can you set up God's*d* dominion over
the earth?

34 "Can you raise your voice to the clouds
and cover yourself with a flood of
water?
35 Do you send the lightning bolts on
their way?
Do they report to you, 'Here we are'?
36 Who gives the ibis wisdom*e*
or gives the rooster understanding?*f*
37 Who has the wisdom to count the clouds?
Who can tip over the water jars of the
heavens
38 when the dust becomes hard
and the clods of earth stick together?

39 "Do you hunt the prey for the lioness
and satisfy the hunger of the lions
40 when they crouch in their dens
or lie in wait in a thicket?
41 Who provides food for the raven
when its young cry out to God
and wander about for lack of food?

39 "Do you know when the mountain
goats give birth?
Do you watch when the doe bears her
fawn?
2 Do you count the months till they bear?
Do you know the time they give birth?
3 They crouch down and bring forth their
young;
their labor pains are ended.
4 Their young thrive and grow strong in
the wilds;
they leave and do not return.

5 "Who let the wild donkey go free?
Who untied its ropes?
6 I gave it the wasteland as its home,
the salt flats as its habitat.
7 It laughs at the commotion in the town;
it does not hear a driver's shout.
8 It ranges the hills for its pasture
and searches for any green thing.

9 "Will the wild ox consent to serve you?
Will it stay by your manger at night?
10 Can you hold it to the furrow with a
harness?
Will it till the valleys behind you?
11 Will you rely on it for its great strength?
Will you leave your heavy work to it?
12 Can you trust it to haul in your grain
and bring it to your threshing floor?

---

a 31 Septuagint; Hebrew *beauty*   *b* 32 Or *the morning star in its season*   *c* 32 Or *out Leo*
d 33 Or *their*   *e* 36 That is, wisdom about the flooding of the Nile   *f* 36 That is, understanding of when
to crow; the meaning of the Hebrew for this verse is uncertain.

¹³ "The wings of the ostrich flap joyfully,
    though they cannot compare
      with the wings and feathers of the
        stork.
¹⁴ She lays her eggs on the ground
    and lets them warm in the sand,
¹⁵ unmindful that a foot may crush them,
    that some wild animal may trample
      them.
¹⁶ She treats her young harshly, as if they
      were not hers;
    she cares not that her labor was in
      vain,
¹⁷ for God did not endow her with wisdom
    or give her a share of good sense.
¹⁸ Yet when she spreads her feathers to run,
    she laughs at horse and rider.

¹⁹ "Do you give the horse its strength
    or clothe its neck with a flowing mane?
²⁰ Do you make it leap like a locust,
    striking terror with its proud snorting?
²¹ It paws fiercely, rejoicing in its strength,
    and charges into the fray.
²² It laughs at fear, afraid of nothing;
    it does not shy away from the sword.
²³ The quiver rattles against its side,
    along with the flashing spear and
      lance.
²⁴ In frenzied excitement it eats up the
      ground;
    it cannot stand still when the trumpet
      sounds.
²⁵ At the blast of the trumpet it snorts, 'Aha!'
    It catches the scent of battle from afar,
    the shout of commanders and the
      battle cry.

²⁶ "Does the hawk take flight by your
      wisdom
    and spread its wings toward the south?
²⁷ Does the eagle soar at your command
    and build its nest on high?
²⁸ It dwells on a cliff and stays there at
      night;
    a rocky crag is its stronghold.
²⁹ From there it looks for food;
    its eyes detect it from afar.
³⁰ Its young ones feast on blood,
    and where the slain are, there it is."

40 The LORD said to Job:

² "Will the one who contends with the
    Almighty correct him?

Let him who accuses God answer him!"

³ Then Job answered the LORD:

⁴ "I am unworthy — how can I reply to you?
    I put my hand over my mouth.
⁵ I spoke once, but I have no answer —
    twice, but I will say no more."

⁶ Then the LORD spoke to Job out of the
storm:

⁷ "Brace yourself like a man;
    I will question you,
    and you shall answer me.

⁸ "Would you discredit my justice?
    Would you condemn me to justify
      yourself?
⁹ Do you have an arm like God's,
    and can your voice thunder like his?
¹⁰ Then adorn yourself with glory and
      splendor,
    and clothe yourself in honor and
      majesty.
¹¹ Unleash the fury of your wrath,
    look at all who are proud and bring
      them low,
¹² look at all who are proud and humble
      them,
    crush the wicked where they stand.
¹³ Bury them all in the dust together;
    shroud their faces in the grave.
¹⁴ Then I myself will admit to you
    that your own right hand can save you.

¹⁵ "Look at Behemoth,
    which I made along with you
    and which feeds on grass like an ox.
¹⁶ What strength it has in its loins,
    what power in the muscles of its belly!
¹⁷ Its tail sways like a cedar;
    the sinews of its thighs are close-knit.
¹⁸ Its bones are tubes of bronze,
    its limbs like rods of iron.
¹⁹ It ranks first among the works of God,
    yet its Maker can approach it with his
      sword.
²⁰ The hills bring it their produce,
    and all the wild animals play nearby.
²¹ Under the lotus plants it lies,
    hidden among the reeds in the marsh.
²² The lotuses conceal it in their shadow;
    the poplars by the stream surround it.
²³ A raging river does not alarm it;
    it is secure, though the Jordan should
      surge against its mouth.

SEEMS PALTRY

READ: JOB 40:6-9

God is omnipotent, which means by definition, there's nothing God can't do. Yet many of us pray as if our problems are bigger than God. So let me remind you of this high-octane truth that should fuel your faith: God is infinitely bigger than your biggest problem or biggest dream. And while we're on the topic, his grace is infinitely bigger than your biggest sin.

It's our low view of God that is the cause of all lesser problems, and it's a high view of God that is the solution. Your biggest problem isn't a broken relationship, your parents' divorce, or a bad grade. Please understand, I'm not making light of your dating, family, or academic issues. I certainly don't want to minimize the overwhelming challenges you may be facing. But in order to obtain a godly perspective on your problems, you have to answer this question: Are your problems bigger than God, or is God bigger than your problems? Our biggest problem is our low view of God.

BUILDING FAITH WISDOM STRENGTH

How big is your God? Is he big enough to help you find the right person for your future or heal your broken family? Is he bigger than a bad grade or a bad game? Is he bigger than your secret sin or secret dream?

Once you embrace the unlimited power of God, you'll draw bigger and bigger prayer circles around your God-given, God-sized dreams.

Taken from *The Circle Maker Student Edition* by Mark Batterson with Parker Batterson, copyright © 2012 by Mark Batterson, published by Zondervan.

²⁴ Can anyone capture it by the eyes,
   or trap it and pierce its nose?

41 ᵃ "Can you pull in Leviathan with a
      fishhook
   or tie down its tongue with a rope?
² Can you put a cord through its nose
   or pierce its jaw with a hook?
³ Will it keep begging you for mercy?
   Will it speak to you with gentle
      words?
⁴ Will it make an agreement with you
   for you to take it as your slave for life?
⁵ Can you make a pet of it like a bird
   or put it on a leash for the young
      women in your house?
⁶ Will traders barter for it?
   Will they divide it up among the
      merchants?
⁷ Can you fill its hide with harpoons
   or its head with fishing spears?
⁸ If you lay a hand on it,
   you will remember the struggle and
      never do it again!
⁹ Any hope of subduing it is false;
   the mere sight of it is overpowering.
¹⁰ No one is fierce enough to rouse it.
   Who then is able to stand against me?
¹¹ Who has a claim against me that I must
      pay?
   Everything under heaven belongs
      to me.

¹² "I will not fail to speak of Leviathan's
      limbs,
   its strength and its graceful form.
¹³ Who can strip off its outer coat?
   Who can penetrate its double coat of
      armor ᵇ?
¹⁴ Who dares open the doors of its mouth,
   ringed about with fearsome teeth?
¹⁵ Its back has ᶜ rows of shields
   tightly sealed together;
¹⁶ each is so close to the next
   that no air can pass between.
¹⁷ They are joined fast to one another;
   they cling together and cannot be
      parted.
¹⁸ Its snorting throws out flashes of light;
   its eyes are like the rays of dawn.
¹⁹ Flames stream from its mouth;
   sparks of fire shoot out.

²⁰ Smoke pours from its nostrils
   as from a boiling pot over burning
      reeds.
²¹ Its breath sets coals ablaze,
   and flames dart from its mouth.
²² Strength resides in its neck;
   dismay goes before it.
²³ The folds of its flesh are tightly joined;
   they are firm and immovable.
²⁴ Its chest is hard as rock,
   hard as a lower millstone.
²⁵ When it rises up, the mighty are terrified;
   they retreat before its thrashing.
²⁶ The sword that reaches it has no effect,
   nor does the spear or the dart or the
      javelin.
²⁷ Iron it treats like straw
   and bronze like rotten wood.
²⁸ Arrows do not make it flee;
   slingstones are like chaff to it.
²⁹ A club seems to it but a piece of straw;
   it laughs at the rattling of the lance.
³⁰ Its undersides are jagged potsherds,
   leaving a trail in the mud like a
      threshing sledge.
³¹ It makes the depths churn like a boiling
      caldron
   and stirs up the sea like a pot of
      ointment.
³² It leaves a glistening wake behind it;
   one would think the deep had white
      hair.
³³ Nothing on earth is its equal —
   a creature without fear.
³⁴ It looks down on all that are haughty;
   it is king over all that are proud."

Job

42 Then Job replied to the LORD:

² "I know that you can do all things;
   no purpose of yours can be thwarted.
³ You asked, 'Who is this that obscures my
      plans without knowledge?'
   Surely I spoke of things I did not
      understand,
   things too wonderful for me to know.

⁴ "You said, 'Listen now, and I will
      speak;
   I will question you,
   and you shall answer me.'

ᵃ In Hebrew texts 41:1-8 is numbered 40:25-32, and 41:9-34 is numbered 41:1-26.   ᵇ 13 Septuagint;
Hebrew *double bridle*   ᶜ 15 Or *Its pride is its*

⁵My ears had heard of you
  but now my eyes have seen you.
⁶Therefore I despise myself
  and repent in dust and ashes."

Epilogue

⁷After the Lord had said these things to Job, he said to Eliphaz the Temanite, "I am angry with you and your two friends, because you have not spoken the truth about me, as my servant Job has. ⁸So now take seven bulls and seven rams and go to my servant Job and sacrifice a burnt offering for yourselves. My servant Job will pray for you, and I will accept his prayer and not deal with you according to your folly. You have not spoken the truth about me, as my servant Job has." ⁹So Eliphaz the Temanite, Bildad the Shuhite and Zophar the Naamathite did what the Lord told them; and the Lord accepted Job's prayer.

¹⁰After Job had prayed for his friends, the Lord restored his fortunes and gave him twice as much as he had before. ¹¹All his brothers and sisters and everyone who had known him before came and ate with him in his house. They comforted and consoled him over all the trouble the Lord had brought on him, and each one gave him a piece of silver*ᵃ* and a gold ring.

¹²The Lord blessed the latter part of Job's life more than the former part. He had fourteen thousand sheep, six thousand camels, a thousand yoke of oxen and a thousand donkeys. ¹³And he also had seven sons and three daughters. ¹⁴The first daughter he named Jemimah, the second Keziah and the third Keren-Happuch. ¹⁵Nowhere in all the land were there found women as beautiful as Job's daughters, and their father granted them an inheritance along with their brothers.

¹⁶After this, Job lived a hundred and forty years; he saw his children and their children to the fourth generation. ¹⁷And so Job died, an old man and full of years.

ᵃ 11 Hebrew *him a kesitah*; a kesitah was a unit of money of unknown weight and value.

PSALMS

WHEN DID THIS HAPPEN?

Composed between 1400 and 400 B.C.

WHO IS IN THIS BOOK?

the Psalmists: David, Asaph, the Sons of Korah, Solomon, Heman, Ethan and Moses

the wicked

enemies

foes

VERSES YOU MIGHT RECOGNIZE

PSALM 28:7

"The LORD is my strength and my shield; my heart trusts in him, and he helps me."

PSALM 51:10

"Create in me a pure heart, O God, and renew a steadfast spirit within me."

PSALM 104:24

"How many are your works, LORD! In wisdom you made them all; the earth is full of your creatures."

WHAT'S IT ABOUT?

This book is a collection of worship songs and poems written by a variety of authors over the course of 1,000 years. You'll recognize the names of some of the writers. King David wrote almost half of the 150 psalms. In these poems, he often asked God for help and forgiveness. Sometimes he cried out in anger or frustration about his circumstances. But he always ended up praising and thanking God for who God is.

Not all psalms are the same. Here are a few different kinds you'll discover in this book:

- *Hallel psalms* (one example is Psalm 113) praise God for his character.
- *Wisdom psalms* (one example is Psalm 37) talk about how to follow God and make wise choices.
- *Lament psalms* (one example is Psalm 4) cry out to God for help or rescue.

There are also *imprecatory psalms* (calls to punish the wicked), *penitential psalms* (confession of sin), *Messianic psalms* (foreshadowing Jesus), *thanksgiving psalms* (praise) and *songs of ascent* (songs for religious holidays). The emotional highs and lows of the psalms remind us that we are not alone in our feelings. More importantly, they encourage us to trust in a loving God who is bigger than our problems.

BOOK I

Psalms 1–41

Psalm 1

¹ Blessed is the one
    who does not walk in step with the
      wicked
  or stand in the way that sinners take
  or sit in the company of mockers,
² but whose delight is in the law of the Lord,
    and who meditates on his law day and
      night.
³ That person is like a tree planted by
    streams of water,
  which yields its fruit in season
  and whose leaf does not wither —
    whatever they do prospers.

⁴ Not so the wicked!
    They are like chaff
  that the wind blows away.
⁵ Therefore the wicked will not stand in the
    judgment,
  nor sinners in the assembly of the
    righteous.

⁶ For the Lord watches over the way of the
    righteous,
  but the way of the wicked leads to
    destruction.

Psalm 2

¹ Why do the nations conspire*a*
    and the peoples plot in vain?
² The kings of the earth rise up
    and the rulers band together
  against the Lord and against his
    anointed, saying,
³ "Let us break their chains
    and throw off their shackles."

⁴ The One enthroned in heaven laughs;
    the Lord scoffs at them.

⁵ He rebukes them in his anger
    and terrifies them in his wrath, saying,
⁶ "I have installed my king
    on Zion, my holy mountain."

⁷ I will proclaim the Lord's decree:

He said to me, "You are my son;
    today I have become your father.
⁸ Ask me,
    and I will make the nations your
      inheritance,
  the ends of the earth your possession.
⁹ You will break them with a rod of iron*b*;
    you will dash them to pieces like
      pottery."

¹⁰ Therefore, you kings, be wise;
    be warned, you rulers of the earth.
¹¹ Serve the Lord with fear
    and celebrate his rule with trembling.
¹² Kiss his son, or he will be angry
    and your way will lead to your
      destruction,
  for his wrath can flare up in a moment.
    Blessed are all who take refuge in him.

Psalm 3*c*

A psalm of David.
When he fled from his son Absalom.

¹ Lord, how many are my foes!
    How many rise up against me!
² Many are saying of me,
    "God will not deliver him."*d*

³ But you, Lord, are a shield around me,
    my glory, the One who lifts my head
      high.
⁴ I call out to the Lord,
    and he answers me from his holy
      mountain.

⁵ I lie down and sleep;
    I wake again, because the Lord
      sustains me.

---

a 1 Hebrew; Septuagint *rage*   *b 9* Or *will rule them with an iron scepter* (see Septuagint and Syriac)
c In Hebrew texts 3:1-8 is numbered 3:2-9.   *d 2* The Hebrew has *Selah* (a word of uncertain meaning)
here and at the end of verses 4 and 8.

REBEL

READ: PSALM 2:2

Everyone knows what it's like to make another person angry. But only God knows what it's like to have the whole human race up in arms against him.

Human rebellion started back with Adam and Eve in the garden of Eden (Genesis 3:1–24). But sin quickly spread to every person and place on earth. Psalm 2 shows the entire world rising up against the Lord. Nations scheme. Groups hatch useless plots. The earth's rulers want to break loose from God's control.

God studies this crowd of puny rebels and laughs because their might is nothing compared to his. And the Lord has a secret power: he has installed his Son as ruler over the earth. That's an astonishing Old Testament picture. Hundreds of years before Jesus showed up as a baby in Bethlehem, this Scripture reveals him reigning as king of everything. Even when human beings join together to fight God, they can't beat his "anointed," or chosen one. The whole world belongs to Jesus, and wise people everywhere submit to his authority. No one can stop the Lord's plan to save people, and he blesses everyone who runs to him for help.

Glance around and you'll see plenty of people living against God. But you can serve God with utter respect. You can celebrate his reign. You can bow to him with every part of who you are.

BUILDING FAITH WISDOM STRENGTH

⁶ I will not fear though tens of thousands
    assail me on every side.

⁷ Arise, LORD!
    Deliver me, my God!
  Strike all my enemies on the jaw;
    break the teeth of the wicked.

⁸ From the LORD comes deliverance.
    May your blessing be on your people.

Psalm 4ᵃ

For the director of music.
With stringed instruments. A psalm of David.

¹ Answer me when I call to you,
    my righteous God.
  Give me relief from my distress;
    have mercy on me and hear my prayer.

² How long will you people turn my glory
    into shame?
  How long will you love delusions and
    seek false godsᵇ?ᶜ
³ Know that the LORD has set apart his
    faithful servant for himself;
  the LORD hears when I call to him.

⁴ Tremble andᵈ do not sin;
    when you are on your beds,
    search your hearts and be silent.
⁵ Offer the sacrifices of the righteous
    and trust in the LORD.

⁶ Many, LORD, are asking, "Who will bring
    us prosperity?"
  Let the light of your face shine on us.
⁷ Fill my heart with joy
    when their grain and new wine abound.

⁸ In peace I will lie down and sleep,
    for you alone, LORD,
    make me dwell in safety.

Psalm 5ᵉ

For the director of music. For pipes.
A psalm of David.

¹ Listen to my words, LORD,
    consider my lament.
² Hear my cry for help,
    my King and my God,
    for to you I pray.

³ In the morning, LORD, you hear my
    voice;
  in the morning I lay my requests
    before you
    and wait expectantly.
⁴ For you are not a God who is pleased with
    wickedness;
  with you, evil people are not welcome.
⁵ The arrogant cannot stand
    in your presence.
  You hate all who do wrong;
⁶   you destroy those who tell lies.
  The bloodthirsty and deceitful
    you, LORD, detest.
⁷ But I, by your great love,
    can come into your house;
  in reverence I bow down
    toward your holy temple.

⁸ Lead me, LORD, in your righteousness
    because of my enemies—
    make your way straight before me.
⁹ Not a word from their mouth can be
    trusted;
    their heart is filled with malice.
  Their throat is an open grave;
    with their tongues they tell lies.
¹⁰ Declare them guilty, O God!
    Let their intrigues be their downfall.
  Banish them for their many sins,
    for they have rebelled against you.
¹¹ But let all who take refuge in you be glad;
    let them ever sing for joy.
  Spread your protection over them,
    that those who love your name may
    rejoice in you.

¹² Surely, LORD, you bless the righteous;
    you surround them with your favor as
    with a shield.

Psalm 6ᶠ

For the director of music. With stringed
instruments. According to sheminith.ᵍ
A psalm of David.

¹ LORD, do not rebuke me in your anger
    or discipline me in your wrath.
² Have mercy on me, LORD, for I am faint;
    heal me, LORD, for my bones are in
    agony.
³ My soul is in deep anguish.
    How long, LORD, how long?

ᵃ In Hebrew texts 4:1-8 is numbered 4:2-9.   ᵇ 2 Or *seek lies*   ᶜ 2 The Hebrew has *Selah* (a word of uncertain meaning) here and at the end of verse 4.   ᵈ 4 Or *In your anger* (see Septuagint)   ᵉ In Hebrew texts 5:1-12 is numbered 5:2-13.   ᶠ In Hebrew texts 6:1-10 is numbered 6:2-11.   ᵍ Title: Probably a musical term

THE BEST LISTENER

READ: PSALM 4:1

Picture collapsing on your bed after your most unpleasant day ever. It's not hard to recall what pushed you into the misery zone. But you might wonder if God was around when you were hurting. He was. And he is.

Psalm 4 doesn't say why King David wrote these words, but the shape of his problem isn't hard to detect. He'd prayed but hadn't received an answer. He'd waited for compassionate relief from distress, after being humiliated by people who don't worship God. He trembled on his bed, trying to figure out where he went wrong. He was so tired of people doubting God's goodness that he just wanted to fall asleep and forget the day.

David's head was spinning with frustration. His heart was thick with sadness. But he fought back with true facts. He reminded himself that God watches over his followers and hears their cries. His own shaking wasn't an excuse to sin in what he thought, said, or did. His pain was a chance to trust, look for God's shining brilliance, and enjoy the Lord's simple gifts. He could sleep peacefully because the Lord kept him safe.

When you feel overwhelmed, you can be sure you're not praying to empty sky. God was listening when you felt deep pain. He's listening now.

BUILDING

FAITH

WISDOM

STRENGTH

⁴Turn, LORD, and deliver me;
  save me because of your unfailing love.
⁵Among the dead no one proclaims
      your name.
  Who praises you from the grave?

⁶I am worn out from my groaning.

  All night long I flood my bed with weeping
    and drench my couch with tears.
⁷My eyes grow weak with sorrow;
    they fail because of all my foes.

⁸Away from me, all you who do evil,
    for the LORD has heard my weeping.
⁹The LORD has heard my cry for mercy;
    the LORD accepts my prayer.
¹⁰All my enemies will be overwhelmed
      with shame and anguish;
    they will turn back and suddenly be
      put to shame.

Psalm 7ᵃ

*A shiggaionᵇ of David,
which he sang to the LORD concerning
Cush, a Benjamite.*

¹LORD my God, I take refuge in you;
    save and deliver me from all who
      pursue me,
²or they will tear me apart like a lion
    and rip me to pieces with no one to
      rescue me.

³LORD my God, if I have done this
    and there is guilt on my hands—
⁴if I have repaid my ally with evil
    or without cause have robbed my foe—
⁵then let my enemy pursue and
      overtake me;
    let him trample my life to the ground
    and make me sleep in the dust.ᶜ

⁶Arise, LORD, in your anger;
    rise up against the rage of my enemies.
  Awake, my God; decree justice.
⁷Let the assembled peoples gather
      around you,
    while you sit enthroned over them
      on high.
⁸ Let the LORD judge the peoples.
  Vindicate me, LORD, according to my
      righteousness,

according to my integrity, O Most High.
⁹Bring to an end the violence of the wicked
    and make the righteous secure—
  you, the righteous God
    who probes minds and hearts.

¹⁰My shieldᵈ is God Most High,
    who saves the upright in heart.
¹¹God is a righteous judge,
    a God who displays his wrath every day.
¹²If he does not relent,
    heᵉ will sharpen his sword;
    he will bend and string his bow.
¹³He has prepared his deadly weapons;
    he makes ready his flaming arrows.

¹⁴Whoever is pregnant with evil
    conceives trouble and gives birth to
      disillusionment.
¹⁵Whoever digs a hole and scoops it out
    falls into the pit they have made.
¹⁶The trouble they cause recoils on them;
    their violence comes down on their
      own heads.

¹⁷I will give thanks to the LORD because of
      his righteousness;
    I will sing the praises of the name of
      the LORD Most High.

Psalm 8ᶠ

For the director of music. According to gittith.ᵍ
A psalm of David.

¹LORD, our Lord,
    how majestic is your name in all the
      earth!

  You have set your glory
    in the heavens.
²Through the praise of children and
      infants
    you have established a stronghold
      against your enemies,
    to silence the foe and the avenger.
³When I consider your heavens,
    the work of your fingers,
  the moon and the stars,
    which you have set in place,
⁴what is mankind that you are mindful of
      them,
    human beings that you care for them?ʰ

ᵃ In Hebrew texts 7:1-17 is numbered 7:2-18.   ᵇ Title: Probably a literary or musical term   ᶜ 5 The
Hebrew has *Selah* (a word of uncertain meaning) here.   ᵈ 10 Or *sovereign*   ᵉ 12 Or *If anyone does
not repent, / God*   ᶠ In Hebrew texts 8:1-9 is numbered 8:2-10.   ᵍ Title: Probably a musical term
ʰ 4 Or *what is a human being that you are mindful of him, / a son of man that you care for him?*

⁵You have made them*ᵃ* a little lower than
the angels*ᵇ*
and crowned them*ᵃ* with glory and
honor.
⁶You made them rulers over the works of
your hands;
you put everything under their*ᶜ* feet:
⁷all flocks and herds,
and the animals of the wild,
⁸the birds in the sky,
and the fish in the sea,
all that swim the paths of the seas.

⁹Lord, our Lord,
how majestic is your name in all
the earth!

Psalm 9*ᵈ,ᵉ*

For the director of music.
To the tune of "The Death of the Son."
A psalm of David.

¹I will give thanks to you, Lord, with all
my heart;
I will tell of all your wonderful deeds.
²I will be glad and rejoice in you;
I will sing the praises of your name,
O Most High.

³My enemies turn back;
they stumble and perish before you.
⁴For you have upheld my right and my
cause,
sitting enthroned as the righteous
judge.
⁵You have rebuked the nations and
destroyed the wicked;
you have blotted out their name for
ever and ever.
⁶Endless ruin has overtaken my enemies,
you have uprooted their cities;
even the memory of them has
perished.

⁷The Lord reigns forever;
he has established his throne for
judgment.
⁸He rules the world in righteousness
and judges the peoples with equity.
⁹The Lord is a refuge for the oppressed,
a stronghold in times of trouble.

¹⁰Those who know your name trust in you,
for you, Lord, have never forsaken
those who seek you.

¹¹Sing the praises of the Lord, enthroned
in Zion;
proclaim among the nations what he
has done.
¹²For he who avenges blood remembers;
he does not ignore the cries of the
afflicted.

¹³Lord, see how my enemies persecute me!
Have mercy and lift me up from the
gates of death,
¹⁴that I may declare your praises
in the gates of Daughter Zion,
and there rejoice in your salvation.

¹⁵The nations have fallen into the pit they
have dug;
their feet are caught in the net they
have hidden.
¹⁶The Lord is known by his acts of justice;
the wicked are ensnared by the work of
their hands.*ᶠ*

¹⁷The wicked go down to the realm of
the dead,
all the nations that forget God.
¹⁸But God will never forget the needy;
the hope of the afflicted will never
perish.

¹⁹Arise, Lord, do not let mortals triumph;
let the nations be judged in your
presence.
²⁰Strike them with terror, Lord;
let the nations know they are only
mortal.

Psalm 10*ᵈ*

¹Why, Lord, do you stand far off?
Why do you hide yourself in times of
trouble?

²In his arrogance the wicked man hunts
down the weak,
who are caught in the schemes he
devises.
³He boasts about the cravings of his
heart;

ᵃ 5 Or *him*   *ᵇ* 5 Or *than God*   *ᶜ* 6 Or *made him ruler ...; / ... his*   *ᵈ* Psalms 9 and 10 may originally
have been a single acrostic poem in which alternating lines began with the successive letters of the
Hebrew alphabet. In the Septuagint they constitute one psalm.   *ᵉ* In Hebrew texts 9:1-20 is numbered
9:2-21.   *ᶠ* 16 The Hebrew has *Higgaion* and *Selah* (words of uncertain meaning) here; *Selah* occurs also
at the end of verse 20.

UP TO YOU

READ: PSALM 9:10

Maybe your parents decided to have you baptized as a baby, but you've never personally come after him. Or it has been your family's tradition to come to church and call themselves Christians, but you don't ever remember going to church because you wanted to. Mom made you. Dad said you had to.

The truth is you call yourself a Christian mostly because you always have. Besides, what would people say if you didn't? You're not pursuing a relationship with Jesus; you're just putting up with him to keep up other relationships.

Pursuing Jesus is your choice, and Jesus will settle for nothing less than to be the great love and pursuit of your life. That's what he wants. At church, we sometimes talk about how "God wants your time" or "God wants your money" or "God wants your worship."

BUILDING FAITH WISDOM STRENGTH

But do you understand why we talk about those things? It's not because God needs your time. It's not because he needs your money. If God needed your money he could take it. It's not that God needs your worship. The reason we talk about those things is not because God needs or wants those things; it's because he wants you.

He wants your love. He longs for you to passionately pursue him, and all those things are come after indicators. They are outer signs that point to an inner reality that you love Jesus more than anything else.

Taken from *Not a Fan Student Edition* by Kyle Idleman, copyright © 2012 by City on the Hill Studio, Inc., published by Zondervan.

he blesses the greedy and reviles the
LORD.
⁴ In his pride the wicked man does not
seek him;
in all his thoughts there is no room
for God.
⁵ His ways are always prosperous;
your laws are rejected by*a* him;
he sneers at all his enemies.
⁶ He says to himself, "Nothing will ever
shake me."
He swears, "No one will ever do me
harm."

⁷ His mouth is full of lies and threats;
trouble and evil are under his tongue.
⁸ He lies in wait near the villages;
from ambush he murders the
innocent.
His eyes watch in secret for his victims;
⁹   like a lion in cover he lies in wait.
He lies in wait to catch the helpless;
he catches the helpless and drags them
off in his net.
¹⁰ His victims are crushed, they collapse;
they fall under his strength.
¹¹ He says to himself, "God will never notice;
he covers his face and never sees."

¹² Arise, LORD! Lift up your hand, O God.
Do not forget the helpless.
¹³ Why does the wicked man revile God?
Why does he say to himself,
"He won't call me to account"?
¹⁴ But you, God, see the trouble of the
afflicted;
you consider their grief and take it
in hand.
The victims commit themselves to you;
you are the helper of the fatherless.
¹⁵ Break the arm of the wicked man;
call the evildoer to account for his
wickedness
that would not otherwise be found out.

¹⁶ The LORD is King for ever and ever;
the nations will perish from his land.
¹⁷ You, LORD, hear the desire of the
afflicted;
you encourage them, and you listen to
their cry,
¹⁸ defending the fatherless and the
oppressed,

so that mere earthly mortals
will never again strike terror.

Psalm 11

For the director of music. Of David.

¹ In the LORD I take refuge.
How then can you say to me:
"Flee like a bird to your mountain.
² For look, the wicked bend their bows;
they set their arrows against the
strings
to shoot from the shadows
at the upright in heart.
³ When the foundations are being
destroyed,
what can the righteous do?"

⁴ The LORD is in his holy temple;
the LORD is on his heavenly throne.
He observes everyone on earth;
his eyes examine them.
⁵ The LORD examines the righteous,
but the wicked, those who love
violence,
he hates with a passion.
⁶ On the wicked he will rain
fiery coals and burning sulfur;
a scorching wind will be their lot.

⁷ For the LORD is righteous,
he loves justice;
the upright will see his face.

Psalm 12*b*

For the director of music.
According to sheminith.*c* *A psalm of David.*

¹ Help, LORD, for no one is faithful anymore;
those who are loyal have vanished
from the human race.
² Everyone lies to their neighbor;
they flatter with their lips
but harbor deception in their hearts.

³ May the LORD silence all flattering lips
and every boastful tongue —
⁴ those who say,
"By our tongues we will prevail;
our own lips will defend us — who is
lord over us?"

⁵ "Because the poor are plundered and the
needy groan,

---

a 5 See Septuagint; Hebrew / *they are haughty, and your laws are far from*   *b* In Hebrew texts 12:1-8 is
numbered 12:2-9.   *c* Title: Probably a musical term

I will now arise," says the LORD.
"I will protect them from those who
malign them."
[6] And the words of the LORD are flawless,
like silver purified in a crucible,
like gold[a] refined seven times.

[7] You, LORD, will keep the needy safe
and will protect us forever from the
wicked,
[8] who freely strut about
when what is vile is honored by the
human race.

Psalm 13[b]

For the director of music. A psalm of David.

[1] How long, LORD? Will you forget me
forever?
How long will you hide your face
from me?
[2] How long must I wrestle with my
thoughts
and day after day have sorrow in
my heart?
How long will my enemy triumph
over me?

[3] Look on me and answer, LORD my God.
Give light to my eyes, or I will sleep in
death,
[4] and my enemy will say, "I have overcome
him,"
and my foes will rejoice when I fall.

[5] But I trust in your unfailing love;
my heart rejoices in your salvation.
[6] I will sing the LORD's praise,
for he has been good to me.

Psalm 14

For the director of music. Of David.

[1] The fool[c] says in his heart,
"There is no God."
They are corrupt, their deeds are vile;
there is no one who does good.

[2] The LORD looks down from heaven
on all mankind
to see if there are any who understand,
any who seek God.

[3] All have turned away, all have become
corrupt;
there is no one who does good,
not even one.

[4] Do all these evildoers know nothing?

They devour my people as though eating
bread;
they never call on the LORD.
[5] But there they are, overwhelmed with
dread,
for God is present in the company of
the righteous.
[6] You evildoers frustrate the plans of
the poor,
but the LORD is their refuge.

[7] Oh, that salvation for Israel would come
out of Zion!
When the LORD restores his people,
let Jacob rejoice and Israel be glad!

Psalm 15

A psalm of David.

[1] LORD, who may dwell in your sacred tent?
Who may live on your holy mountain?

[2] The one whose walk is blameless,
who does what is righteous,
who speaks the truth from their heart;
[3] whose tongue utters no slander,
who does no wrong to a neighbor,
and casts no slur on others;
[4] who despises a vile person
but honors those who fear the LORD;
who keeps an oath even when it hurts,
and does not change their mind;
[5] who lends money to the poor without
interest;
who does not accept a bribe against
the innocent.

Whoever does these things
will never be shaken.

Psalm 16

A miktam[d] of David.

[1] Keep me safe, my God,
for in you I take refuge.

[2] I say to the LORD, "You are my Lord;
apart from you I have no good thing."

---

[a] 6 Probable reading of the original Hebrew text; Masoretic Text *earth*   [b] In Hebrew texts 13:1-6 is
numbered 13:2-6.   [c] 1 The Hebrew words rendered *fool* in Psalms denote one who is morally deficient.
[d] Title: Probably a literary or musical term

COME NEAR TO GOD

READ: **PSALM 15:1**

David sounds like a sly teacher as he pens Psalm 15, asking a trick question even the smartest students might miss: "Who is good enough to get near God?"

David wonders aloud who can approach the "sacred tent" on the Lord's "holy mountain." Both phrases refer to the place set aside to worship the Lord—the tent-like tabernacle used in David's day and the beautiful temple his son Solomon built in its place.

David then lists all the qualifications of people good enough to get close to the Lord. They must live without fault. They must never lie or speak ill of a neighbor. They must honor God's friends, do right even when it hurts, and watch out for the poor.

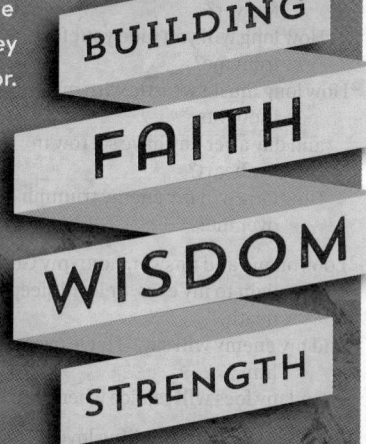

The tricky part is that the question has two correct answers. One is that none of us meets those rigorous demands. Our sins make us spiritually unclean, unfit to enter the presence of a holy God (Psalm 14:1-3).

But there's another, even better, answer. When Jesus died on the cross for your sins, he made you righteous, as pure as if you never did wrong. If you trust in his death on your behalf, you can be sure God will welcome you near (Hebrews 10:19-23). He invites you to live close to him now, and one day he will usher you home to heaven.

3 I say of the holy people who are in the
land,
"They are the noble ones in whom is all
my delight."
4 Those who run after other gods will
suffer more and more.
I will not pour out libations of blood to
such gods
or take up their names on my lips.

5 LORD, you alone are my portion and
my cup;
you make my lot secure.
6 The boundary lines have fallen for me in
pleasant places;
surely I have a delightful inheritance.
7 I will praise the LORD, who counsels me;
even at night my heart instructs me.
8 I keep my eyes always on the LORD.
With him at my right hand, I will not
be shaken.

9 Therefore my heart is glad and my tongue
rejoices;
my body also will rest secure,
10 because you will not abandon me to the
realm of the dead,
nor will you let your faithful*a* one see
decay.
11 You make known to me the path of life;
you will fill me with joy in your
presence,
with eternal pleasures at your right
hand.

Psalm 17

A prayer of David.

1 Hear me, LORD, my plea is just;
listen to my cry.
Hear my prayer—
it does not rise from deceitful lips.
2 Let my vindication come from you;
may your eyes see what is right.

3 Though you probe my heart,
though you examine me at night and
test me,
you will find that I have planned no evil;
my mouth has not transgressed.
4 Though people tried to bribe me,
I have kept myself from the ways of
the violent
through what your lips have
commanded.

5 My steps have held to your paths;
my feet have not stumbled.
6 I call on you, my God, for you will
answer me;
turn your ear to me and hear my
prayer.
7 Show me the wonders of your great love,
you who save by your right hand
those who take refuge in you from
their foes.
8 Keep me as the apple of your eye;
hide me in the shadow of your wings
9 from the wicked who are out to destroy me,
from my mortal enemies who
surround me.

10 They close up their callous hearts,
and their mouths speak with
arrogance.
11 They have tracked me down, they now
surround me,
with eyes alert, to throw me to the
ground.
12 They are like a lion hungry for prey,
like a fierce lion crouching in cover.

13 Rise up, LORD, confront them, bring
them down;
with your sword rescue me from the
wicked.
14 By your hand save me from such people,
LORD,
from those of this world whose reward
is in this life.
May what you have stored up for the
wicked fill their bellies;
may their children gorge themselves
on it,
and may there be leftovers for their
little ones.

15 As for me, I will be vindicated and will
see your face;
when I awake, I will be satisfied with
seeing your likeness.

Psalm 18*b*

*For the director of music. Of David the servant of
the LORD. He sang to the LORD the words of this song
when the LORD delivered him from the hand of all
his enemies and from the hand of Saul. He said:*

1 I love you, LORD, my strength.

2 The LORD is my rock, my fortress and my
deliverer;

---

a 10 Or *holy*   *b* In Hebrew texts 18:1-50 is numbered 18:2-51.

my God is my rock, in whom I take
refuge,
my shield[a] and the horn[b] of my
salvation, my stronghold.

³ I called to the LORD, who is worthy of
praise,
and I have been saved from my
enemies.
⁴ The cords of death entangled me;
the torrents of destruction
overwhelmed me.
⁵ The cords of the grave coiled around me;
the snares of death confronted me.

⁶ In my distress I called to the LORD;
I cried to my God for help.
From his temple he heard my voice;
my cry came before him, into his ears.
⁷ The earth trembled and quaked,
and the foundations of the mountains
shook;
they trembled because he was angry.
⁸ Smoke rose from his nostrils;
consuming fire came from his mouth,
burning coals blazed out of it.
⁹ He parted the heavens and came down;
dark clouds were under his feet.
¹⁰ He mounted the cherubim and flew;
he soared on the wings of the wind.
¹¹ He made darkness his covering, his
canopy around him —
the dark rain clouds of the sky.
¹² Out of the brightness of his presence
clouds advanced,
with hailstones and bolts of lightning.
¹³ The LORD thundered from heaven;
the voice of the Most High resounded.[c]
¹⁴ He shot his arrows and scattered the
enemy,
with great bolts of lightning he routed
them.
¹⁵ The valleys of the sea were exposed
and the foundations of the earth laid
bare
at your rebuke, LORD,
at the blast of breath from your
nostrils.
¹⁶ He reached down from on high and took
hold of me;
he drew me out of deep waters.

¹⁷ He rescued me from my powerful enemy,
from my foes, who were too strong
for me.
¹⁸ They confronted me in the day of my
disaster,
but the LORD was my support.
¹⁹ He brought me out into a spacious place;
he rescued me because he delighted
in me.

²⁰ The LORD has dealt with me according to
my righteousness;
according to the cleanness of my
hands he has rewarded me.
²¹ For I have kept the ways of the LORD;
I am not guilty of turning from my God.
²² All his laws are before me;
I have not turned away from his
decrees.
²³ I have been blameless before him
and have kept myself from sin.
²⁴ The LORD has rewarded me according to
my righteousness,
according to the cleanness of my
hands in his sight.

²⁵ To the faithful you show yourself faithful,
to the blameless you show yourself
blameless,
²⁶ to the pure you show yourself pure,
but to the devious you show yourself
shrewd.
²⁷ You save the humble
but bring low those whose eyes are
haughty.
²⁸ You, LORD, keep my lamp burning;
my God turns my darkness into light.
²⁹ With your help I can advance against
a troop[d];
with my God I can scale a wall.

³⁰ As for God, his way is perfect:
The LORD's word is flawless;
he shields all who take refuge in him.
³¹ For who is God besides the LORD?
And who is the Rock except our God?
³² It is God who arms me with strength
and keeps my way secure.
³³ He makes my feet like the feet of a deer;
he causes me to stand on the heights.
³⁴ He trains my hands for battle;
my arms can bend a bow of bronze.

---

a 2 Or *sovereign*   *b 2* *Horn* here symbolizes strength.   *c 13* Some Hebrew manuscripts and
Septuagint (see also 2 Samuel 22:14); most Hebrew manuscripts *resounded, / amid hailstones and bolts of
lightning*   *d 29* Or *can run through a barricade*

35 You make your saving help my shield,
  and your right hand sustains me;
  your help has made me great.
36 You provide a broad path for my feet,
  so that my ankles do not give way.

37 I pursued my enemies and overtook
    them;
  I did not turn back till they were
    destroyed.
38 I crushed them so that they could
    not rise;
  they fell beneath my feet.
39 You armed me with strength for battle;
  you humbled my adversaries
    before me.
40 You made my enemies turn their backs
    in flight,
  and I destroyed my foes.
41 They cried for help, but there was no one
    to save them —
  to the LORD, but he did not answer.
42 I beat them as fine as windblown dust;
  I trampled them*a* like mud in the
    streets.

43 You have delivered me from the attacks of
    the people;
  you have made me the head of nations.
  People I did not know now serve me,
44   foreigners cower before me;
  as soon as they hear of me, they
    obey me.
45 They all lose heart;
  they come trembling from their
    strongholds.

46 The LORD lives! Praise be to my Rock!
  Exalted be God my Savior!
47 He is the God who avenges me,
  who subdues nations under me,
48   who saves me from my enemies.
  You exalted me above my foes;
  from a violent man you rescued me.
49 Therefore I will praise you, LORD, among
    the nations;
  I will sing the praises of your name.

50 He gives his king great victories;
  he shows unfailing love to his
    anointed,
  to David and to his descendants
    forever.

Psalm 19*b*

For the director of music. A psalm of David.

1 The heavens declare the glory of God;
  the skies proclaim the work of his
    hands.
2 Day after day they pour forth speech;
  night after night they reveal
    knowledge.
3 They have no speech, they use no words;
  no sound is heard from them.
4 Yet their voice*c* goes out into all the earth,
  their words to the ends of the world.
  In the heavens God has pitched a tent for
    the sun.
5   It is like a bridegroom coming out of
    his chamber,
  like a champion rejoicing to run his
    course.
6 It rises at one end of the heavens
  and makes its circuit to the other;
  nothing is deprived of its warmth.

7 The law of the LORD is perfect,
  refreshing the soul.
  The statutes of the LORD are trustworthy,
    making wise the simple.
8 The precepts of the LORD are right,
  giving joy to the heart.
  The commands of the LORD are radiant,
    giving light to the eyes.
9 The fear of the LORD is pure,
  enduring forever.
  The decrees of the LORD are firm,
    and all of them are righteous.

10 They are more precious than gold,
  than much pure gold;
  they are sweeter than honey,
    than honey from the honeycomb.
11 By them your servant is warned;
  in keeping them there is great reward.
12 But who can discern their own errors?
  Forgive my hidden faults.
13 Keep your servant also from willful sins;
  may they not rule over me.
  Then I will be blameless,
    innocent of great transgression.

14 May these words of my mouth and this
    meditation of my heart
  be pleasing in your sight,
  LORD, my Rock and my Redeemer.

a 42 Many Hebrew manuscripts, Septuagint, Syriac and Targum (see also 2 Samuel 22:43); Masoretic Text
I poured them out   *b* In Hebrew texts 19:1-14 is numbered 19:2-15.   *c 4* Septuagint, Jerome and Syriac;
Hebrew *measuring line*

WHO'S AFRAID OF THE . . .?

READ: PSALM 19:14

D o you like to go swimming in the ocean at night? Anybody who has seen *Jaws* doesn't want to do that, even four decades after the movie debuted. Old, dilapidated houses are automatically "haunted" because of horror flicks. Going into the basement in the dark is taboo because of the most scary movies you've ever seen. In unsettling moments, we are convinced that things lurk under our beds and in our closets—all because movies have redefined how we see them.

The images we put into our brains matter. The music we pump into our heads matters. It's all going somewhere and eventually will come out, but it's never going away. I can go into a restaurant and hear a song from my high school years and tell you where I was when I heard it back in the day. I can tell you how the room smelled. It's seared into my brain.

BUILDING
FAITH
WISDOM
STRENGTH

It's amazing how scary movies can redefine reality and make us uneasy about things that never bothered us before. Toilets are not scary; little kids' toys are not scary; birds are not scary—but they all were redefined and became scary to me because of the effects of one movie.

This is why it is essential that believers saturate themselves in God's Word. When the world launches its multimedia guns at us, we can overcome the trash with the purity and tranquility of God's truth.

Psalm 20[a]

For the director of music. A psalm of David.

[1] May the Lord answer you when you are
in distress;
may the name of the God of Jacob
protect you.
[2] May he send you help from the sanctuary
and grant you support from Zion.
[3] May he remember all your sacrifices
and accept your burnt offerings.[b]
[4] May he give you the desire of your heart
and make all your plans succeed.
[5] May we shout for joy over your victory
and lift up our banners in the name of
our God.

May the Lord grant all your requests.

[6] Now this I know:
The Lord gives victory to his anointed.
He answers him from his heavenly
sanctuary
with the victorious power of his right
hand.
[7] Some trust in chariots and some in
horses,
but we trust in the name of the Lord
our God.
[8] They are brought to their knees and fall,
but we rise up and stand firm.
[9] Lord, give victory to the king!
Answer us when we call!

Psalm 21[c]

For the director of music. A psalm of David.

[1] The king rejoices in your strength, Lord.
How great is his joy in the victories
you give!

[2] You have granted him his heart's desire
and have not withheld the request of
his lips.[b]
[3] You came to greet him with rich blessings
and placed a crown of pure gold on his
head.
[4] He asked you for life, and you gave it
to him—
length of days, for ever and ever.
[5] Through the victories you gave, his glory
is great;

you have bestowed on him splendor
and majesty.
[6] Surely you have granted him unending
blessings
and made him glad with the joy of your
presence.
[7] For the king trusts in the Lord;
through the unfailing love of the Most
High
he will not be shaken.

[8] Your hand will lay hold on all your
enemies;
your right hand will seize your foes.
[9] When you appear for battle,
you will burn them up as in a blazing
furnace.
The Lord will swallow them up in his
wrath,
and his fire will consume them.
[10] You will destroy their descendants from
the earth,
their posterity from mankind.
[11] Though they plot evil against you
and devise wicked schemes, they
cannot succeed.
[12] You will make them turn their backs
when you aim at them with drawn
bow.

[13] Be exalted in your strength, Lord;
we will sing and praise your might.

Psalm 22[d]

*For the director of music. To the tune of
"The Doe of the Morning." A psalm of David.*

[1] My God, my God, why have you
forsaken me?
Why are you so far from saving me,
so far from my cries of anguish?
[2] My God, I cry out by day, but you do not
answer,
by night, but I find no rest.[e]

[3] Yet you are enthroned as the Holy One;
you are the one Israel praises.[f]
[4] In you our ancestors put their trust;
they trusted and you delivered them.
[5] To you they cried out and were saved;
in you they trusted and were not put
to shame.

---

[a] In Hebrew texts 20:1-9 is numbered 20:2-10. [b] 3,2 The Hebrew has *Selah* (a word of uncertain
meaning) here. [c] In Hebrew texts 21:1-13 is numbered 21:2-14. [d] In Hebrew texts 22:1-31 is numbered
22:2-32. [e] 2 Or *night, and am not silent* [f] 3 Or *Yet you are holy, / enthroned on the praises of Israel*

⁶ But I am a worm and not a man,
     scorned by everyone, despised by the
         people.
⁷ All who see me mock me;
     they hurl insults, shaking their heads.
⁸ "He trusts in the LORD," they say,
     "let the LORD rescue him.
   Let him deliver him,
     since he delights in him."

⁹ Yet you brought me out of the womb;
     you made me trust in you, even at my
         mother's breast.
¹⁰ From birth I was cast on you;
     from my mother's womb you have
         been my God.

¹¹ Do not be far from me,
     for trouble is near
     and there is no one to help.

¹² Many bulls surround me;
     strong bulls of Bashan encircle me.
¹³ Roaring lions that tear their prey
     open their mouths wide against me.
¹⁴ I am poured out like water,
     and all my bones are out of joint.
   My heart has turned to wax;
     it has melted within me.
¹⁵ My mouth*ᵃ* is dried up like a potsherd,
     and my tongue sticks to the roof of my
         mouth;
   you lay me in the dust of death.

¹⁶ Dogs surround me,
     a pack of villains encircles me;
   they pierce*ᵇ* my hands and my feet.
¹⁷ All my bones are on display;
     people stare and gloat over me.
¹⁸ They divide my clothes among them
     and cast lots for my garment.

¹⁹ But you, LORD, do not be far from me.
     You are my strength; come quickly to
         help me.
²⁰ Deliver me from the sword,
     my precious life from the power of
         the dogs.
²¹ Rescue me from the mouth of the
         lions;
     save me from the horns of the wild
         oxen.

²² I will declare your name to my people;
     in the assembly I will praise you.
²³ You who fear the LORD, praise him!
     All you descendants of Jacob, honor
         him!
     Revere him, all you descendants of
         Israel!
²⁴ For he has not despised or scorned
     the suffering of the afflicted one;
   he has not hidden his face from him
     but has listened to his cry for help.

²⁵ From you comes the theme of my praise
     in the great assembly;
   before those who fear you*ᶜ* I will fulfill
         my vows.
²⁶ The poor will eat and be satisfied;
     those who seek the LORD will praise
         him—
     may your hearts live forever!

²⁷ All the ends of the earth
     will remember and turn to the LORD,
   and all the families of the nations
     will bow down before him,
²⁸ for dominion belongs to the LORD
     and he rules over the nations.

²⁹ All the rich of the earth will feast and
         worship;
     all who go down to the dust will kneel
         before him—
     those who cannot keep themselves
         alive.
³⁰ Posterity will serve him;
     future generations will be told about
         the Lord.
³¹ They will proclaim his righteousness,
     declaring to a people yet unborn:
     He has done it!

Psalm 23

A psalm of David.

¹ The LORD is my shepherd, I lack nothing.
²   He makes me lie down in green
         pastures,
   he leads me beside quiet waters,
³   he refreshes my soul.
   He guides me along the right paths
     for his name's sake.

ᵃ 15 Probable reading of the original Hebrew text; Masoretic Text *strength*   *ᵇ 16* Dead Sea Scrolls and some manuscripts of the Masoretic Text, Septuagint and Syriac; most manuscripts of the Masoretic Text *me, / like a lion*   *ᶜ 25* Hebrew *him*

FIERCE SAFETY

READ: **PSALM 23:1-3**

There's a good chance someone will read the cherished words of Psalm 23 at your funeral, beginning with "The Lord is my shepherd, I shall not want . . ." But God doesn't reserve those words for a moment you're no longer around to hear them. They're encouragement to live by right now.

Long before David became king of Israel he watched his father's flocks (1 Samuel 16:11), even killing a lion and bear to protect the family's sheep (17:36). So David knew shepherding up close. He pictured the Lord as the best shepherd ever.

You don't have to know much about sheep to catch this imagery. With the Lord as your shepherd, there's nothing you need. He shows you safe places to rest and leads you to drink at waters that won't spook your timid soul. He stakes his honor on leading you to good places and protecting you from death. Evil doesn't scare you when you're under God's care. His protection is fierce. He blesses you in front of your enemies, giving you luxurious provisions and honoring you with perfumed oils. He lavishes you with gifts you don't deserve.

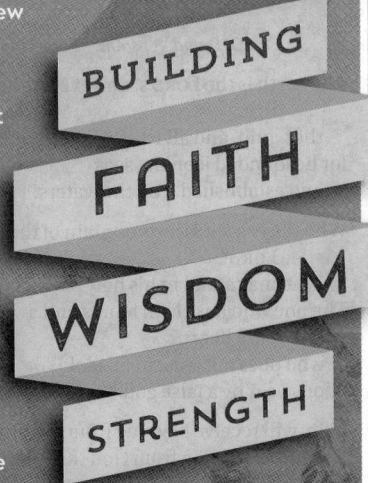

When the Lord is your shepherd, you will experience his loyal love every day of your life. And one day he will bring you home to heaven to live even closer to him.

⁴Even though I walk
    through the darkest valley,ᵃ
I will fear no evil,
    for you are with me;
your rod and your staff,
    they comfort me.

⁵You prepare a table before me
    in the presence of my enemies.
You anoint my head with oil;
    my cup overflows.
⁶Surely your goodness and love will
        follow me
    all the days of my life,
and I will dwell in the house of the LORD
    forever.

Psalm 24

Of David. A psalm.

¹The earth is the LORD's, and everything
        in it,
    the world, and all who live in it;
²for he founded it on the seas
    and established it on the waters.

³Who may ascend the mountain of the
        LORD?
    Who may stand in his holy place?
⁴The one who has clean hands and a
        pure heart,
    who does not trust in an idol
    or swear by a false god.ᵇ

⁵They will receive blessing from the LORD
    and vindication from God their Savior.
⁶Such is the generation of those who
        seek him,
    who seek your face, God of Jacob.ᶜ,ᵈ

⁷Lift up your heads, you gates;
    be lifted up, you ancient doors,
    that the King of glory may come in.
⁸Who is this King of glory?
    The LORD strong and mighty,
    the LORD mighty in battle.
⁹Lift up your heads, you gates;
    lift them up, you ancient doors,
    that the King of glory may come in.
¹⁰Who is he, this King of glory?
    The LORD Almighty—
    he is the King of glory.

Psalm 25ᵉ

Of David.

¹In you, LORD my God,
    I put my trust.

²I trust in you;
    do not let me be put to shame,
    nor let my enemies triumph over me.
³No one who hopes in you
    will ever be put to shame,
but shame will come on those
    who are treacherous without cause.

⁴Show me your ways, LORD,
    teach me your paths.
⁵Guide me in your truth and teach me,
    for you are God my Savior,
    and my hope is in you all day long.
⁶Remember, LORD, your great mercy
        and love,
    for they are from of old.
⁷Do not remember the sins of my youth
    and my rebellious ways;
according to your love remember me,
    for you, LORD, are good.

⁸Good and upright is the LORD;
    therefore he instructs sinners in
        his ways.
⁹He guides the humble in what is right
    and teaches them his way.
¹⁰All the ways of the LORD are loving and
        faithful
    toward those who keep the demands of
        his covenant.
¹¹For the sake of your name, LORD,
    forgive my iniquity, though it is great.

¹²Who, then, are those who fear the LORD?
    He will instruct them in the ways they
        should choose.ᶠ
¹³They will spend their days in prosperity,
    and their descendants will inherit
        the land.
¹⁴The LORD confides in those who fear him;
    he makes his covenant known
        to them.
¹⁵My eyes are ever on the LORD,
    for only he will release my feet from
        the snare.

ᵃ 4 Or *the valley of the shadow of death*   ᵇ 4 Or *swear falsely*   ᶜ 6 Two Hebrew manuscripts and Syriac
(see also Septuagint); most Hebrew manuscripts *face, Jacob*   ᵈ 6 The Hebrew has *Selah* (a word of
uncertain meaning) here and at the end of verse 10.   ᵉ This psalm is an acrostic poem, the verses of
which begin with the successive letters of the Hebrew alphabet.   ᶠ 12 Or *ways he chooses*

ADD A BEAT

READ: PSALM 25:14

Prayer is conversation. That's why I like to start prayer with worship, because worship is going to God without asking for anything. It's just praising God for who he is and what he's done.

I heard a preacher say one time, "If you want to know how selfish you are, just start praying and see how long you can go without asking for anything." I frowned. A little pompous and determined to prove him wrong, I set out to pray with no petitions. I lasted maybe three, four sentences. I instinctively asked for something. I didn't know how not to ask.

When I first learned about the psalms, I understood them to be songs. That's what the word *psalms* means. It took me a while to realize that they were really prayers put to music.

David and other writers of the psalms showed how worship and prayer correlate. And what does David do in the psalms? He opens his heart and dumps out everything to the Lord. He is unreserved. He is unashamed. He is transparent. He even asks God to destroy those who want to destroy him. David is real. I learned how to pray by studying the book of Psalms.

It dawned on me that God wants us to converse with him because, as Psalm 25:14 makes clear, he is our friend.

Our worship, our clapping real hard, and even our believing in God doesn't make him more or less of who he is. Our worship does, however, reveal who we are and what we believe about God.

BUILDING
FAITH
WISDOM
STRENGTH

Taken from *Thrive Student Edition* by Mark Hall with Tim Luke, copyright © 2014 by Mark Hall, published by Zondervan.

¹⁶Turn to me and be gracious to me,
  for I am lonely and afflicted.
¹⁷Relieve the troubles of my heart
  and free me from my anguish.
¹⁸Look on my affliction and my distress
  and take away all my sins.
¹⁹See how numerous are my enemies
  and how fiercely they hate me!

²⁰Guard my life and rescue me;
  do not let me be put to shame,
  for I take refuge in you.
²¹May integrity and uprightness
    protect me,
  because my hope, LORD,^a is in you.

²²Deliver Israel, O God,
  from all their troubles!

Psalm 26

Of David.

¹Vindicate me, LORD,
  for I have led a blameless life;
 I have trusted in the LORD
  and have not faltered.
²Test me, LORD, and try me,
  examine my heart and my mind;
³for I have always been mindful of your
    unfailing love
  and have lived in reliance on your
    faithfulness.

⁴I do not sit with the deceitful,
  nor do I associate with hypocrites.
⁵I abhor the assembly of evildoers
  and refuse to sit with the wicked.
⁶I wash my hands in innocence,
  and go about your altar, LORD,
⁷proclaiming aloud your praise
  and telling of all your wonderful deeds.

⁸LORD, I love the house where you live,
  the place where your glory dwells.
⁹Do not take away my soul along with
    sinners,
  my life with those who are
    bloodthirsty,
¹⁰in whose hands are wicked schemes,
  whose right hands are full of bribes.
¹¹I lead a blameless life;
  deliver me and be merciful to me.

¹²My feet stand on level ground;

 in the great congregation I will praise
  the LORD.

Psalm 27

Of David.

¹The LORD is my light and my salvation —
  whom shall I fear?
 The LORD is the stronghold of my life —
  of whom shall I be afraid?

²When the wicked advance against me
    to devour^b me,
 it is my enemies and my foes
  who will stumble and fall.
³Though an army besiege me,
  my heart will not fear;
 though war break out against me,
  even then I will be confident.

⁴One thing I ask from the LORD,
  this only do I seek:
 that I may dwell in the house of the LORD
  all the days of my life,
 to gaze on the beauty of the LORD
  and to seek him in his temple.
⁵For in the day of trouble
  he will keep me safe in his dwelling;
 he will hide me in the shelter of his
    sacred tent
  and set me high upon a rock.

⁶Then my head will be exalted
  above the enemies who surround me;
 at his sacred tent I will sacrifice with
    shouts of joy;
  I will sing and make music to the
    LORD.

⁷Hear my voice when I call, LORD;
  be merciful to me and answer me.
⁸My heart says of you, "Seek his face!"
  Your face, LORD, I will seek.
⁹Do not hide your face from me,
  do not turn your servant away in anger;
  you have been my helper.
 Do not reject me or forsake me,
  God my Savior.
¹⁰Though my father and mother
    forsake me,
  the LORD will receive me.
¹¹Teach me your way, LORD;
  lead me in a straight path
  because of my oppressors.

WILLING?

READ: PSALM 27:10

A few years ago I was pretty deep into some tribal areas of Africa. One night I finished preaching to a few dozen people. I presented the gospel and the invitation of Jesus to follow him. There were two young men, probably in their twenties, who accepted Christ and committed to follow him. The following afternoon these two men showed up at the house where we were staying. They each carried a good-sized bag over their shoulder. I asked the local missionary why they were here. He explained that these two men would no longer be welcomed by their families or in their village. When I heard that, I was afraid that maybe this was going to be more than they would be willing to go along with. About that time the missionary said to me, "They knew this would happen when they made the decision."

They were choosing Jesus over their families. They were choosing Jesus over their own comfort and convenience.

BUILDING

FAITH

WISDOM

STRENGTH

True followers are willing to deny themselves and say, "I choose Jesus over money. I choose Jesus over my guidance counselor's career advice. I am his completely. I choose Jesus over my game system. I choose Jesus over shopping. I choose Jesus over the person I'm dating. I choose Jesus over looking at porn. I choose Jesus over my freedom. I choose Jesus over what other people may think of me." A follower makes a decision every day to deny himself and choose Jesus ... even if it costs everything.

¹²Do not turn me over to the desire of
my foes,
for false witnesses rise up against me,
spouting malicious accusations.

¹³I remain confident of this:
I will see the goodness of the LORD
in the land of the living.
¹⁴Wait for the LORD;
be strong and take heart
and wait for the LORD.

Psalm 28

Of David.

¹To you, LORD, I call;
you are my Rock,
do not turn a deaf ear to me.
For if you remain silent,
I will be like those who go down to
the pit.
²Hear my cry for mercy
as I call to you for help,
as I lift up my hands
toward your Most Holy Place.

³Do not drag me away with the wicked,
with those who do evil,
who speak cordially with their neighbors
but harbor malice in their hearts.
⁴Repay them for their deeds
and for their evil work;
repay them for what their hands have
done
and bring back on them what they
deserve.

⁵Because they have no regard for the
deeds of the LORD
and what his hands have done,
he will tear them down
and never build them up again.

⁶Praise be to the LORD,
for he has heard my cry for mercy.
⁷The LORD is my strength and my shield;
my heart trusts in him, and he
helps me.
My heart leaps for joy,
and with my song I praise him.

⁸The LORD is the strength of his people,
a fortress of salvation for his anointed
one.

⁹Save your people and bless your
inheritance;
be their shepherd and carry them
forever.

Psalm 29

A psalm of David.

¹Ascribe to the LORD, you heavenly
beings,
ascribe to the LORD glory and strength.
²Ascribe to the LORD the glory due his
name;
worship the LORD in the splendor of
his*ᵃ* holiness.

³The voice of the LORD is over the waters;
the God of glory thunders,
the LORD thunders over the mighty
waters.
⁴The voice of the LORD is powerful;
the voice of the LORD is majestic.
⁵The voice of the LORD breaks the cedars;
the LORD breaks in pieces the cedars
of Lebanon.
⁶He makes Lebanon leap like a calf,
Sirion*ᵇ* like a young wild ox.
⁷The voice of the LORD strikes
with flashes of lightning.
⁸The voice of the LORD shakes the desert;
the LORD shakes the Desert of Kadesh.
⁹The voice of the LORD twists the oaks*ᶜ*
and strips the forests bare.
And in his temple all cry, "Glory!"

¹⁰The LORD sits enthroned over the flood;
the LORD is enthroned as King forever.
¹¹The LORD gives strength to his people;
the LORD blesses his people with
peace.

Psalm 30*ᵈ*

A psalm. A song.
*For the dedication of the temple.*ᵉ *Of David.*

¹I will exalt you, LORD,
for you lifted me out of the depths
and did not let my enemies gloat
over me.
²LORD my God, I called to you for help,
and you healed me.
³You, LORD, brought me up from the realm
of the dead;

ᵃ 2 Or LORD *with the splendor of*   *ᵇ* 6 That is, Mount Hermon   *ᶜ* 9 Or LORD *makes the deer give birth*
ᵈ In Hebrew texts 30:1-12 is numbered 30:2-13.   *ᵉ* Title: Or *palace*

HIS UNMATCHED WORTH

READ: **PSALM 29:1**

I t's not every day you get to order angels around. Yet that's what David dares to do in Psalm 29. He begins his song by telling heavenly beings to give the Lord all the worship he deserves. Yet that command doesn't just apply to angels. David wraps up his song by instructing everyone in the Lord's temple to cry, "Glory!"

Worship isn't worship if it has to be dragged from your mouth. Authentic praise is a natural response to understanding God's unsurpassed worth. It doesn't invent warm feelings about the Lord. It simply reflects on who he is. So David spells out why the Lord deserves your worship.

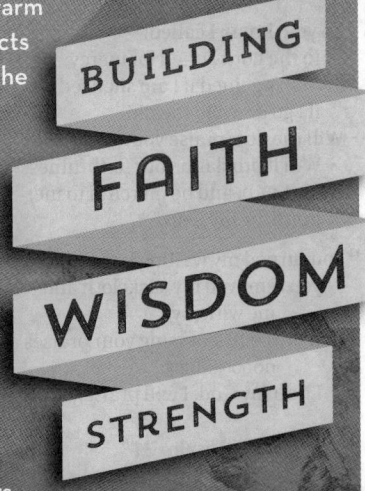
BUILDING FAITH WISDOM STRENGTH

Start where David ends. God rules as King forever. He isn't Lord of a little corner of earth but of the entire universe. He isn't a temporary ruler to be replaced in the next election, but the only being who will reign for all eternity.

This eternal king is full of brilliant glory and matchless strength. He is holy, absolutely pure. And the Lord is incredibly powerful. His voice thunders louder than the roar of an ocean. It strips bark from tall cedars and twists strong oaks. No wonder everyone should cry, "Glory!"

This mighty Lord is enthroned forever. But he doesn't reside in a distant castle—he's enthroned in our hearts as well. Count on him today to give you strength. He will give you his peace.

you spared me from going down to
the pit.

⁴ Sing the praises of the LORD, you his
faithful people;
praise his holy name.
⁵ For his anger lasts only a moment,
but his favor lasts a lifetime;
weeping may stay for the night,
but rejoicing comes in the morning.

⁶ When I felt secure, I said,
"I will never be shaken."
⁷ LORD, when you favored me,
you made my royal mountain*ᵃ* stand
firm;
but when you hid your face,
I was dismayed.

⁸ To you, LORD, I called;
to the Lord I cried for mercy:
⁹ "What is gained if I am silenced,
if I go down to the pit?
Will the dust praise you?
Will it proclaim your faithfulness?
¹⁰ Hear, LORD, and be merciful to me;
LORD, be my help."

¹¹ You turned my wailing into dancing;
you removed my sackcloth and clothed
me with joy,
¹² that my heart may sing your praises and
not be silent.
LORD my God, I will praise you forever.

Psalm 31*ᵇ*

*For the director of music.
A psalm of David.*

¹ In you, LORD, I have taken refuge;
let me never be put to shame;
deliver me in your righteousness.
² Turn your ear to me,
come quickly to my rescue;
be my rock of refuge,
a strong fortress to save me.
³ Since you are my rock and my fortress,
for the sake of your name lead and
guide me.
⁴ Keep me free from the trap that is set
for me,
for you are my refuge.
⁵ Into your hands I commit my spirit;
deliver me, LORD, my faithful God.

⁶ I hate those who cling to worthless idols;
as for me, I trust in the LORD.
⁷ I will be glad and rejoice in your love,
for you saw my affliction
and knew the anguish of my soul.
⁸ You have not given me into the hands of
the enemy
but have set my feet in a spacious
place.

⁹ Be merciful to me, LORD, for I am in
distress;
my eyes grow weak with sorrow,
my soul and body with grief.
¹⁰ My life is consumed by anguish
and my years by groaning;
my strength fails because of my
affliction,*ᶜ*
and my bones grow weak.
¹¹ Because of all my enemies,
I am the utter contempt of my
neighbors
and an object of dread to my closest
friends —
those who see me on the street flee
from me.
¹² I am forgotten as though I were dead;
I have become like broken pottery.
¹³ For I hear many whispering,
"Terror on every side!"
They conspire against me
and plot to take my life.

¹⁴ But I trust in you, LORD;
I say, "You are my God."
¹⁵ My times are in your hands;
deliver me from the hands of my
enemies,
from those who pursue me.
¹⁶ Let your face shine on your servant;
save me in your unfailing love.
¹⁷ Let me not be put to shame, LORD,
for I have cried out to you;
but let the wicked be put to shame
and be silent in the realm of the dead.
¹⁸ Let their lying lips be silenced,
for with pride and contempt
they speak arrogantly against the
righteous.

¹⁹ How abundant are the good things
that you have stored up for those who
fear you,
that you bestow in the sight of all,
on those who take refuge in you.

ᵃ 7 That is, Mount Zion   *ᵇ* In Hebrew texts 31:1-24 is numbered 31:2-25.   *ᶜ* 10 Or *guilt*

20 In the shelter of your presence you
        hide them
    from all human intrigues;
  you keep them safe in your dwelling
      from accusing tongues.

21 Praise be to the LORD,
    for he showed me the wonders of
        his love
    when I was in a city under siege.
22 In my alarm I said,
    "I am cut off from your sight!"
  Yet you heard my cry for mercy
    when I called to you for help.

23 Love the LORD, all his faithful people!
    The LORD preserves those who are true
        to him,
  but the proud he pays back in full.
24 Be strong and take heart,
    all you who hope in the LORD.

Psalm 32

Of David. A maskil.[a]

1 Blessed is the one
    whose transgressions are forgiven,
    whose sins are covered.
2 Blessed is the one
    whose sin the LORD does not count
        against them
    and in whose spirit is no deceit.

3 When I kept silent,
    my bones wasted away
    through my groaning all day long.
4 For day and night
    your hand was heavy on me;
  my strength was sapped
    as in the heat of summer.[b]

5 Then I acknowledged my sin to you
    and did not cover up my iniquity.
  I said, "I will confess
    my transgressions to the LORD."
  And you forgave
    the guilt of my sin.

6 Therefore let all the faithful pray to you
    while you may be found;
  surely the rising of the mighty waters
    will not reach them.
7 You are my hiding place;
    you will protect me from trouble

and surround me with songs of
        deliverance.

8 I will instruct you and teach you in the
        way you should go;
    I will counsel you with my loving eye
        on you.
9 Do not be like the horse or the mule,
    which have no understanding
  but must be controlled by bit and bridle
    or they will not come to you.
10 Many are the woes of the wicked,
    but the LORD's unfailing love
    surrounds the one who trusts in him.

11 Rejoice in the LORD and be glad, you
        righteous;
    sing, all you who are upright in heart!

Psalm 33

1 Sing joyfully to the LORD, you righteous;
    it is fitting for the upright to praise
        him.
2 Praise the LORD with the harp;
    make music to him on the ten-stringed
        lyre.
3 Sing to him a new song;
    play skillfully, and shout for joy.

4 For the word of the LORD is right and true;
    he is faithful in all he does.
5 The LORD loves righteousness and
        justice;
    the earth is full of his unfailing love.

6 By the word of the LORD the heavens were
        made,
    their starry host by the breath of his
        mouth.
7 He gathers the waters of the sea into jars[c];
    he puts the deep into storehouses.
8 Let all the earth fear the LORD;
    let all the people of the world revere
        him.
9 For he spoke, and it came to be;
    he commanded, and it stood firm.

10 The LORD foils the plans of the nations;
    he thwarts the purposes of the
        peoples.
11 But the plans of the LORD stand firm
        forever,
    the purposes of his heart through all
        generations.

---

a Title: Probably a literary or musical term   *b 4* The Hebrew has *Selah* (a word of uncertain meaning)
here and at the end of verses 5 and 7.   *c 7* Or *sea as into a heap*

¹²Blessed is the nation whose God is the
LORD,
   the people he chose for his
      inheritance.
¹³From heaven the LORD looks down
   and sees all mankind;
¹⁴from his dwelling place he watches
   all who live on earth—
¹⁵he who forms the hearts of all,
   who considers everything they do.

¹⁶No king is saved by the size of his army;
   no warrior escapes by his great
      strength.
¹⁷A horse is a vain hope for deliverance;
   despite all its great strength it cannot
      save.
¹⁸But the eyes of the LORD are on those who
      fear him,
   on those whose hope is in his unfailing
      love,
¹⁹to deliver them from death
   and keep them alive in famine.

²⁰We wait in hope for the LORD;
   he is our help and our shield.
²¹In him our hearts rejoice,
   for we trust in his holy name.
²²May your unfailing love be with us, LORD,
   even as we put our hope in you.

Psalm 34[a,b]

*Of David. When he pretended to be insane
before Abimelek, who drove him away, and he left.*

¹I will extol the LORD at all times;
   his praise will always be on my lips.
²I will glory in the LORD;
   let the afflicted hear and rejoice.
³Glorify the LORD with me;
   let us exalt his name together.

⁴I sought the LORD, and he answered me;
   he delivered me from all my fears.
⁵Those who look to him are radiant;
   their faces are never covered with
      shame.
⁶This poor man called, and the LORD
      heard him;
   he saved him out of all his troubles.
⁷The angel of the LORD encamps around
      those who fear him,
   and he delivers them.

⁸Taste and see that the LORD is good;
   blessed is the one who takes refuge
      in him.
⁹Fear the LORD, you his holy people,
   for those who fear him lack nothing.
¹⁰The lions may grow weak and hungry,
   but those who seek the LORD lack no
      good thing.
¹¹Come, my children, listen to me;
   I will teach you the fear of the LORD.
¹²Whoever of you loves life
   and desires to see many good days,
¹³keep your tongue from evil
   and your lips from telling lies.
¹⁴Turn from evil and do good;
   seek peace and pursue it.

¹⁵The eyes of the LORD are on the
      righteous,
   and his ears are attentive to their cry;
¹⁶but the face of the LORD is against those
      who do evil,
   to blot out their name from the earth.

¹⁷The righteous cry out, and the LORD
      hears them;
   he delivers them from all their
      troubles.
¹⁸The LORD is close to the brokenhearted
   and saves those who are crushed in
      spirit.

¹⁹The righteous person may have many
      troubles,
   but the LORD delivers him from
      them all;
²⁰he protects all his bones,
   not one of them will be broken.

²¹Evil will slay the wicked;
   the foes of the righteous will be
      condemned.
²²The LORD will rescue his servants;
   no one who takes refuge in him will be
      condemned.

Psalm 35

Of David.

¹Contend, LORD, with those who contend
      with me;
   fight against those who fight against me.
²Take up shield and armor;
   arise and come to my aid.

---

^a This psalm is an acrostic poem, the verses of which begin with the successive letters of the Hebrew
alphabet.   ^b In Hebrew texts 34:1-22 is numbered 34:2-23.

SORTA PLANNING

READ: **PSALM 33:11–15**

I believe in planning. Failing to plan is planning to fail. But I also believe this: One bold prayer can accomplish more than a thousand well-laid plans. So go ahead and plan, but make sure you circle your plans in prayer. If your plans aren't soaked with prayer, they won't succeed. This much I know from personal experience. When I was twenty-two and planting a church in Chicago, I had a twenty-five-year plan. That "well-laid" plan was a project for one of my seminary classes, and I actually got an A on it. In reality, I should have gotten an F because it failed. I still have that twenty-five-year plan in my files.

Few things sting more than a failed plan, but I've always drawn a little bit of humor and humility from the old saying, "If you want to make God laugh, tell him your plans." It's not a vindictive chuckle, as if God enjoys our failure. I just think God is sometimes amazed at how small our plans are. He allows our small plans to fail so that his big dream for us can prevail. The glass is half full, my friends! So keep planning like it depends on you, but make sure you pray like it depends on God. Prayer is the alpha and omega, the beginning and the end, of planning. Don't just brainstorm; praystorm.

BUILDING

FAITH

WISDOM

STRENGTH

Taken from *The Circle Maker Student Edition* by Mark Batterson with Parker Batterson, copyright © 2012 by Mark Batterson, published by Zondervan.

³Brandish spear and javelin[a]
    against those who pursue me.
Say to me,
    "I am your salvation."

⁴May those who seek my life
    be disgraced and put to shame;
may those who plot my ruin
    be turned back in dismay.
⁵May they be like chaff before the wind,
    with the angel of the LORD driving
        them away;
⁶may their path be dark and slippery,
    with the angel of the LORD pursuing
        them.

⁷Since they hid their net for me without
        cause
    and without cause dug a pit for me,
⁸may ruin overtake them by surprise —
    may the net they hid entangle them,
    may they fall into the pit, to their ruin.
⁹Then my soul will rejoice in the LORD
    and delight in his salvation.
¹⁰My whole being will exclaim,
    "Who is like you, LORD?
You rescue the poor from those too
        strong for them,
    the poor and needy from those who
        rob them."

¹¹Ruthless witnesses come forward;
    they question me on things I know
        nothing about.
¹²They repay me evil for good
    and leave me like one bereaved.
¹³Yet when they were ill, I put on sackcloth
    and humbled myself with fasting.
When my prayers returned to me
        unanswered,
¹⁴ I went about mourning
    as though for my friend or brother.
I bowed my head in grief
    as though weeping for my mother.
¹⁵But when I stumbled, they gathered
        in glee;
    assailants gathered against me
        without my knowledge.
    They slandered me without ceasing.
¹⁶Like the ungodly they maliciously
        mocked;[b]
    they gnashed their teeth at me.

¹⁷How long, Lord, will you look on?
    Rescue me from their ravages,
    my precious life from these lions.
¹⁸I will give you thanks in the great
        assembly;
    among the throngs I will praise you.
¹⁹Do not let those gloat over me
    who are my enemies without cause;
do not let those who hate me without
        reason
    maliciously wink the eye.
²⁰They do not speak peaceably,
    but devise false accusations
    against those who live quietly in
        the land.
²¹They sneer at me and say, "Aha! Aha!
    With our own eyes we have seen it."

²²LORD, you have seen this; do not be silent.
    Do not be far from me, Lord.
²³Awake, and rise to my defense!
    Contend for me, my God and Lord.
²⁴Vindicate me in your righteousness,
    LORD my God;
    do not let them gloat over me.
²⁵Do not let them think, "Aha, just what
        we wanted!"
    or say, "We have swallowed him up."

²⁶May all who gloat over my distress
    be put to shame and confusion;
may all who exalt themselves over me
    be clothed with shame and disgrace.
²⁷May those who delight in my vindication
    shout for joy and gladness;
may they always say, "The LORD be
        exalted,
    who delights in the well-being of his
        servant."

²⁸My tongue will proclaim your
        righteousness,
    your praises all day long.

Psalm 36[c]

For the director of music.
Of David the servant of the LORD.

¹I have a message from God in my heart
    concerning the sinfulness of the
        wicked:[d]
There is no fear of God
    before their eyes.

---

[a] 3 Or *and block the way*   [b] 16 Septuagint; Hebrew may mean *Like an ungodly circle of mockers,*   [c] In Hebrew texts 36:1-12 is numbered 36:2-13.   [d] 1 Or *A message from God: The transgression of the wicked / resides in their hearts.*

² In their own eyes they flatter themselves
 too much to detect or hate their sin.
³ The words of their mouths are wicked
 and deceitful;
 they fail to act wisely or do good.
⁴ Even on their beds they plot evil;
 they commit themselves to a sinful
  course
 and do not reject what is wrong.

⁵ Your love, LORD, reaches to the heavens,
 your faithfulness to the skies.
⁶ Your righteousness is like the highest
 mountains,
 your justice like the great deep.
 You, LORD, preserve both people and
  animals.
⁷ How priceless is your unfailing love,
 O God!
 People take refuge in the shadow of
  your wings.
⁸ They feast on the abundance of your
 house;
 you give them drink from your river
  of delights.
⁹ For with you is the fountain of life;
 in your light we see light.

¹⁰ Continue your love to those who
 know you,
 your righteousness to the upright in
  heart.
¹¹ May the foot of the proud not come
 against me,
 nor the hand of the wicked drive
  me away.
¹² See how the evildoers lie fallen —
 thrown down, not able to rise!

Psalm 37 ᵃ

Of David.

¹ Do not fret because of those who are evil
 or be envious of those who do wrong;
² for like the grass they will soon wither,
 like green plants they will soon die
  away.

³ Trust in the LORD and do good;
 dwell in the land and enjoy safe
  pasture.
⁴ Take delight in the LORD,
 and he will give you the desires of your
  heart.

⁵ Commit your way to the LORD;
 trust in him and he will do this:
⁶ He will make your righteous reward
 shine like the dawn,
 your vindication like the noonday sun.

⁷ Be still before the LORD
 and wait patiently for him;
do not fret when people succeed in
 their ways,
 when they carry out their wicked
  schemes.

⁸ Refrain from anger and turn from wrath;
 do not fret — it leads only to evil.
⁹ For those who are evil will be destroyed,
 but those who hope in the LORD will
  inherit the land.

¹⁰ A little while, and the wicked will be no
 more;
 though you look for them, they will not
  be found.
¹¹ But the meek will inherit the land
 and enjoy peace and prosperity.

¹² The wicked plot against the righteous
 and gnash their teeth at them;
¹³ but the Lord laughs at the wicked,
 for he knows their day is coming.

¹⁴ The wicked draw the sword
 and bend the bow
to bring down the poor and needy,
 to slay those whose ways are upright.
¹⁵ But their swords will pierce their own
 hearts,
 and their bows will be broken.

¹⁶ Better the little that the righteous have
 than the wealth of many wicked;
¹⁷ for the power of the wicked will be
 broken,
 but the LORD upholds the righteous.

¹⁸ The blameless spend their days under the
 LORD's care,
 and their inheritance will endure
  forever.
¹⁹ In times of disaster they will not wither;
 in days of famine they will enjoy
  plenty.

²⁰ But the wicked will perish:
 Though the LORD's enemies are like
  the flowers of the field,

ᵃ This psalm is an acrostic poem, the stanzas of which begin with the successive letters of the Hebrew
alphabet.

they will be consumed, they will go up
in smoke.

²¹ The wicked borrow and do not repay,
but the righteous give generously;
²² those the LORD blesses will inherit the
land,
but those he curses will be destroyed.

²³ The LORD makes firm the steps
of the one who delights in him;
²⁴ though he may stumble, he will not fall,
for the LORD upholds him with his
hand.

²⁵ I was young and now I am old,
yet I have never seen the righteous
forsaken
or their children begging bread.
²⁶ They are always generous and lend
freely;
their children will be a blessing.^a

²⁷ Turn from evil and do good;
then you will dwell in the land forever.
²⁸ For the LORD loves the just
and will not forsake his faithful ones.

Wrongdoers will be completely
destroyed^b;
the offspring of the wicked will perish.
²⁹ The righteous will inherit the land
and dwell in it forever.

³⁰ The mouths of the righteous utter
wisdom,
and their tongues speak what is just.
³¹ The law of their God is in their hearts;
their feet do not slip.

³² The wicked lie in wait for the righteous,
intent on putting them to death;
³³ but the LORD will not leave them in the
power of the wicked
or let them be condemned when
brought to trial.

³⁴ Hope in the LORD
and keep his way.
He will exalt you to inherit the land;
when the wicked are destroyed, you
will see it.

³⁵ I have seen a wicked and ruthless man
flourishing like a luxuriant native tree,

³⁶ but he soon passed away and was no more;
though I looked for him, he could not
be found.

³⁷ Consider the blameless, observe the
upright;
a future awaits those who seek peace.^c
³⁸ But all sinners will be destroyed;
there will be no future^d for the wicked.

³⁹ The salvation of the righteous comes
from the LORD;
he is their stronghold in time of
trouble.
⁴⁰ The LORD helps them and delivers them;
he delivers them from the wicked and
saves them,
because they take refuge in him.

Psalm 38^e

A psalm of David. A petition.

¹ LORD, do not rebuke me in your anger
or discipline me in your wrath.
² Your arrows have pierced me,
and your hand has come down on me.
³ Because of your wrath there is no health
in my body;
there is no soundness in my bones
because of my sin.
⁴ My guilt has overwhelmed me
like a burden too heavy to bear.

⁵ My wounds fester and are loathsome
because of my sinful folly.
⁶ I am bowed down and brought very low;
all day long I go about mourning.
⁷ My back is filled with searing pain;
there is no health in my body.
⁸ I am feeble and utterly crushed;
I groan in anguish of heart.

⁹ All my longings lie open before you,
Lord;
my sighing is not hidden from you.
¹⁰ My heart pounds, my strength fails me;
even the light has gone from my eyes.
¹¹ My friends and companions avoid me
because of my wounds;
my neighbors stay far away.
¹² Those who want to kill me set their
traps,

---

^a 26 Or *freely; / the names of their children will be used in blessings* (see Gen. 48:20); or *freely; / others will
see that their children are blessed*   ^b 28 See Septuagint; Hebrew *They will be protected forever*
^c 37 Or *upright; / those who seek peace will have posterity*   ^d 38 Or *posterity*   ^e In Hebrew texts 38:1-22
is numbered 38:2-23.

WATCH YOUR STEP

READ: PSALM 37:37

A hundred times a day you stand at a fork in the road, faced with a decision to go God's way or down some other path. You might hear that either choice is as good as the other. But one leads to a future. The other doesn't.

In this psalm David describes an evil and ruthless person who flourishes like a native green tree. Even if you're underwhelmed by a nearby stand of oaks or pines, a tree thriving in Israel's arid climate makes an impressive sight. But this prosperous man soon dies. Not only that, he disappears. He's nowhere in sight. No matter how hard everyone looks, a guy who looked successful and safe is gone.

That destiny awaits everyone who lives against God. In God's time and way, they vanish. But a real future lies ahead for people who "hope in the LORD and keep his way" (Psalm 37:34). These are the people who try hard to do right and consistently seek peace. The Lord won't let them be overpowered by evil, and in the end, they will inherit everything good.

You probably don't plan to go chasing down a path of all-out evil. But whenever you compromise any of the Lord's commands, you take a step away from him. Small steps can add up to big leaps until you find yourself distant from God. And there's no future in that.

BUILDING

FAITH

WISDOM

STRENGTH

those who would harm me talk of
my ruin;
all day long they scheme and lie.
[13] I am like the deaf, who cannot hear,
like the mute, who cannot speak;
[14] I have become like one who does
not hear,
whose mouth can offer no reply.
[15] LORD, I wait for you;
you will answer, Lord my God.
[16] For I said, "Do not let them gloat
or exalt themselves over me when my
feet slip."

[17] For I am about to fall,
and my pain is ever with me.
[18] I confess my iniquity;
I am troubled by my sin.
[19] Many have become my enemies without
cause[a];
those who hate me without reason are
numerous.
[20] Those who repay my good with evil
lodge accusations against me,
though I seek only to do what is good.

[21] LORD, do not forsake me;
do not be far from me, my God.
[22] Come quickly to help me,
my Lord and my Savior.

Psalm 39[b]

For the director of music.
For Jeduthun. A psalm of David.

[1] I said, "I will watch my ways
and keep my tongue from sin;
I will put a muzzle on my mouth
while in the presence of the wicked."
[2] So I remained utterly silent,
not even saying anything good.
But my anguish increased;
[3]   my heart grew hot within me.
While I meditated, the fire burned;
then I spoke with my tongue:

[4] "Show me, LORD, my life's end
and the number of my days;
let me know how fleeting my life is.
[5] You have made my days a mere
handbreadth;
the span of my years is as nothing
before you.

Everyone is but a breath,
even those who seem secure.[c]
[6] "Surely everyone goes around like a mere
phantom;
in vain they rush about, heaping up
wealth
without knowing whose it will
finally be.

[7] "But now, Lord, what do I look for?
My hope is in you.
[8] Save me from all my transgressions;
do not make me the scorn of fools.
[9] I was silent; I would not open my mouth,
for you are the one who has done this.
[10] Remove your scourge from me;
I am overcome by the blow of your
hand.
[11] When you rebuke and discipline anyone
for their sin,
you consume their wealth like a
moth —
surely everyone is but a breath.

[12] "Hear my prayer, LORD,
listen to my cry for help;
do not be deaf to my weeping.
I dwell with you as a foreigner,
a stranger, as all my ancestors were.
[13] Look away from me, that I may enjoy life
again
before I depart and am no more."

Psalm 40[d]

For the director of music.
Of David. A psalm.

[1] I waited patiently for the LORD;
he turned to me and heard my cry.
[2] He lifted me out of the slimy pit,
out of the mud and mire;
he set my feet on a rock
and gave me a firm place to stand.
[3] He put a new song in my mouth,
a hymn of praise to our God.
Many will see and fear the LORD
and put their trust in him.

[4] Blessed is the one
who trusts in the LORD,
who does not look to the proud,
to those who turn aside to false gods.[e]

---

[a] *19* One Dead Sea Scrolls manuscript; Masoretic Text *my vigorous enemies*   [b] In Hebrew texts 39:1-13 is
numbered 39:2-14.   [c] *5* The Hebrew has *Selah* (a word of uncertain meaning) here and at the end of
verse 11.   [d] In Hebrew texts 40:1-17 is numbered 40:2-18.   [e] *4* Or *to lies*

⁵Many, Lᴏʀᴅ my God,
  are the wonders you have done,
  the things you planned for us.
None can compare with you;
  were I to speak and tell of your deeds,
  they would be too many to declare.

⁶Sacrifice and offering you did not
    desire—
  but my ears you have opened^a—
  burnt offerings and sin offerings^b you
    did not require.
⁷Then I said, "Here I am, I have come—
  it is written about me in the scroll.^c
⁸I desire to do your will, my God;
  your law is within my heart."

⁹I proclaim your saving acts in the great
    assembly;
  I do not seal my lips, Lᴏʀᴅ,
  as you know.
¹⁰I do not hide your righteousness in my
    heart;
  I speak of your faithfulness and your
    saving help.
I do not conceal your love and your
    faithfulness
  from the great assembly.

¹¹Do not withhold your mercy from me,
    Lᴏʀᴅ;
  may your love and faithfulness always
    protect me.
¹²For troubles without number surround
    me;
  my sins have overtaken me, and I
    cannot see.
They are more than the hairs of my head,
  and my heart fails within me.
¹³Be pleased to save me, Lᴏʀᴅ;
  come quickly, Lᴏʀᴅ, to help me.

¹⁴May all who want to take my life
  be put to shame and confusion;
  may all who desire my ruin
  be turned back in disgrace.
¹⁵May those who say to me, "Aha! Aha!"
  be appalled at their own shame.
¹⁶But may all who seek you
  rejoice and be glad in you;
  may those who long for your saving help
    always say,
  "The Lᴏʀᴅ is great!"

¹⁷But as for me, I am poor and needy;
  may the Lord think of me.
You are my help and my deliverer;
  you are my God, do not delay.

Psalm 41^d

For the director of music. A psalm of David.

¹Blessed are those who have regard for
    the weak;
  the Lᴏʀᴅ delivers them in times of
    trouble.
²The Lᴏʀᴅ protects and preserves them—
  they are counted among the blessed in
    the land—
  he does not give them over to the
    desire of their foes.
³The Lᴏʀᴅ sustains them on their sickbed
  and restores them from their bed of
    illness.

⁴I said, "Have mercy on me, Lᴏʀᴅ;
  heal me, for I have sinned against you."
⁵My enemies say of me in malice,
  "When will he die and his name
    perish?"
⁶When one of them comes to see me,
  he speaks falsely, while his heart
    gathers slander;
  then he goes out and spreads it around.

⁷All my enemies whisper together
    against me;
  they imagine the worst for me, saying,
⁸"A vile disease has afflicted him;
  he will never get up from the place
    where he lies."
⁹Even my close friend,
    someone I trusted,
  one who shared my bread,
  has turned^e against me.

¹⁰But may you have mercy on me, Lᴏʀᴅ;
  raise me up, that I may repay them.
¹¹I know that you are pleased with me,
  for my enemy does not triumph
    over me.
¹²Because of my integrity you uphold me
  and set me in your presence forever.

¹³Praise be to the Lᴏʀᴅ, the God of Israel,
  from everlasting to everlasting.
    Amen and Amen.

---

^a 6 Hebrew; some Septuagint manuscripts *but a body you have prepared for me*   ^b 6 Or *purification offerings*   ^c 7 Or *come / with the scroll written for me*   ^d In Hebrew texts 41:1-13 is numbered 41:2-14.   ^e 9 Hebrew *has lifted up his heel*

BOOK II

Psalms 42–72

Psalm 42[a,b]

For the director of music.
A maskil[c] of the Sons of Korah.

[1] As the deer pants for streams of water,
   so my soul pants for you, my God.
[2] My soul thirsts for God, for the living God.
   When can I go and meet with God?
[3] My tears have been my food
      day and night,
   while people say to me all day long,
      "Where is your God?"
[4] These things I remember
      as I pour out my soul:
   how I used to go to the house of God
      under the protection of the
         Mighty One[d]
   with shouts of joy and praise
      among the festive throng.

[5] Why, my soul, are you downcast?
      Why so disturbed within me?
   Put your hope in God,
      for I will yet praise him,
      my Savior and my God.

[6] My soul is downcast within me;
      therefore I will remember you
   from the land of the Jordan,
      the heights of Hermon — from Mount
         Mizar.
[7] Deep calls to deep
      in the roar of your waterfalls;
   all your waves and breakers
      have swept over me.

[8] By day the LORD directs his love,
      at night his song is with me —
   a prayer to the God of my life.

[9] I say to God my Rock,
      "Why have you forgotten me?
   Why must I go about mourning,
      oppressed by the enemy?"
[10] My bones suffer mortal agony
      as my foes taunt me,
   saying to me all day long,
      "Where is your God?"

[11] Why, my soul, are you downcast?
      Why so disturbed within me?
   Put your hope in God,
      for I will yet praise him,
      my Savior and my God.

Psalm 43[a]

[1] Vindicate me, my God,
      and plead my cause
      against an unfaithful nation.
   Rescue me from those who are
      deceitful and wicked.
[2] You are God my stronghold.
      Why have you rejected me?
   Why must I go about mourning,
      oppressed by the enemy?
[3] Send me your light and your faithful care,
      let them lead me;
   let them bring me to your holy
         mountain,
      to the place where you dwell.
[4] Then I will go to the altar of God,
      to God, my joy and my delight.
   I will praise you with the lyre,
      O God, my God.

[5] Why, my soul, are you downcast?
      Why so disturbed within me?
   Put your hope in God,
      for I will yet praise him,
      my Savior and my God.

Psalm 44[e]

For the director of music.
Of the Sons of Korah. A maskil.[c]

[1] We have heard it with our ears, O God;
      our ancestors have told us
   what you did in their days,
      in days long ago.
[2] With your hand you drove out the nations
      and planted our ancestors;
   you crushed the peoples
      and made our ancestors flourish.
[3] It was not by their sword that they won
         the land,
      nor did their arm bring them victory;
   it was your right hand, your arm,
      and the light of your face, for you
         loved them.

---

[a] In many Hebrew manuscripts Psalms 42 and 43 constitute one psalm.   [b] In Hebrew texts 42:1-11 is numbered 42:2-12.   [c] Title: Probably a literary or musical term   [d] 4 See Septuagint and Syriac; the meaning of the Hebrew for this line is uncertain.   [e] In Hebrew texts 44:1-26 is numbered 44:2-27.

THIRST QUENCHER

READ: PSALM 42:1

No one had to teach you to feel thirsty. That craving for fluids results from a complex bodily system that measures water volume along with the presence of minerals like salt. When your fluid levels drop out of balance, your brain forces you to quench your thirst.

So picture yourself as the deer in Psalm 42. You bounce through the forest, expecting to happen upon a stream. When you don't find the refreshment you're looking for, you sniff the air for moisture. Then your pace slows to a deliberate hunt. Soon every instinct tells you the only thing that matters is finding water. That's what real longing for God feels like.

When you truly thirst for God, the deepest part of you wonders where and how you can connect with him. Like in Psalm 42, maybe you feel beat up by an awful sadness, as if you have consumed nothing for days except tears. Or maybe everyone around sees your pain and mockingly wonders why God hasn't helped you.

BUILDING FAITH WISDOM STRENGTH

This song hints at a couple of ways to quench your thirst. You can keep hoping in God, trusting that soon you won't feel so far from him. And you can purposely go on the hunt for God's people, finding ways to both hang out with people and worship God. Whatever you do, don't give up on finding God. You must obey your thirst.

⁴You are my King and my God,
  who decrees*a* victories for Jacob.
⁵Through you we push back our enemies;
  through your name we trample
    our foes.
⁶I put no trust in my bow,
  my sword does not bring me victory;
⁷but you give us victory over our enemies,
  you put our adversaries to shame.
⁸In God we make our boast all day long,
  and we will praise your name forever.*b*

⁹But now you have rejected and
    humbled us;
  you no longer go out with our armies.
¹⁰You made us retreat before the enemy,
  and our adversaries have plundered us.
¹¹You gave us up to be devoured like sheep
  and have scattered us among the
    nations.
¹²You sold your people for a pittance,
  gaining nothing from their sale.

¹³You have made us a reproach to our
    neighbors,
  the scorn and derision of those
    around us.
¹⁴You have made us a byword among the
    nations;
  the peoples shake their heads at us.
¹⁵I live in disgrace all day long,
  and my face is covered with shame
¹⁶at the taunts of those who reproach and
    revile me,
  because of the enemy, who is bent on
    revenge.

¹⁷All this came upon us,
  though we had not forgotten you;
  we had not been false to your
    covenant.
¹⁸Our hearts had not turned back;
  our feet had not strayed from your
    path.
¹⁹But you crushed us and made us a haunt
    for jackals;
  you covered us over with deep
    darkness.

²⁰If we had forgotten the name of our God
  or spread out our hands to a foreign
    god,

²¹would not God have discovered it,
  since he knows the secrets of the
    heart?
²²Yet for your sake we face death all day long;
  we are considered as sheep to be
    slaughtered.

²³Awake, Lord! Why do you sleep?
  Rouse yourself! Do not reject us forever.
²⁴Why do you hide your face
  and forget our misery and oppression?

²⁵We are brought down to the dust;
  our bodies cling to the ground.
²⁶Rise up and help us;
  rescue us because of your unfailing
    love.

Psalm 45*c*

For the director of music. To the tune of "Lilies."
Of the Sons of Korah. A maskil.d A wedding song.

¹My heart is stirred by a noble theme
  as I recite my verses for the king;
  my tongue is the pen of a skillful writer.

²You are the most excellent of men
  and your lips have been anointed with
    grace,
  since God has blessed you forever.

³Gird your sword on your side, you
    mighty one;
  clothe yourself with splendor and
    majesty.
⁴In your majesty ride forth victoriously
  in the cause of truth, humility and
    justice;
  let your right hand achieve awesome
    deeds.
⁵Let your sharp arrows pierce the hearts of
    the king's enemies;
  let the nations fall beneath your feet.
⁶Your throne, O God,*e* will last for ever
    and ever;
  a scepter of justice will be the scepter
    of your kingdom.
⁷You love righteousness and hate
    wickedness;
  therefore God, your God, has set you
    above your companions
  by anointing you with the oil of joy.

---

a 4 Septuagint, Aquila and Syriac; Hebrew *King, O God; / command*   *b* 8 The Hebrew has *Selah* (a word of uncertain meaning) here.   *c* In Hebrew texts 45:1-17 is numbered 45:2-18.   *d* Title: Probably a literary or musical term   *e* 6 Here the king is addressed as God's representative.

GOD'S GOT TIME FOR YOU

READ: PSALM 44:23-24

It can be frustrating when you can't get someone's attention. Now imagine if that someone is your god, to whom you've dedicated your life. When priests of the false god Baal couldn't persuade their master to answer their prayers, the prophet Elijah unleashed a great taunt. He told them, "Shout louder! . . . Perhaps he is deep in thought, or busy, or traveling. Maybe he is sleeping and must be awakened" (1 Kings 18:27).

"Busy" is actually a polite way to say, "Perhaps your God is visiting the bathroom." Yet worshipers of ancient gods had even bigger worries. Their deities often dozed off, and they had to be awakened by loud cultic rituals. So the worshipers of Baal not only screamed but slashed themselves "until their blood flowed" (v. 28).

A god can't do you much good if he can't keep his eyes open or if you have to torture yourself to get his attention. But Scripture tells us that the God who watches over us "will neither slumber nor sleep" (Psalm 121:4). That's a vivid way to remember that the Lord's care never ends.

BUILDING FAITH WISDOM STRENGTH

Knowing that the Lord doesn't sleep might not quiet the worries expressed in Psalm 44—that God needs to be prodded, or that he's rejected you. Yet the last lines of this song answer that concern. God will rise up. He will help you. He will rescue you. Why? Not because of anything special you do. You can count on his care because of his unfailing love.

⁸All your robes are fragrant with myrrh
and aloes and cassia;
from palaces adorned with ivory
the music of the strings makes you
glad.
⁹Daughters of kings are among your
honored women;
at your right hand is the royal bride in
gold of Ophir.

¹⁰Listen, daughter, and pay careful
attention:
Forget your people and your father's
house.
¹¹Let the king be enthralled by your
beauty;
honor him, for he is your lord.
¹²The city of Tyre will come with a gift,ᵃ
people of wealth will seek your favor.
¹³All glorious is the princess within her
chamber;
her gown is interwoven with gold.
¹⁴In embroidered garments she is led to
the king;
her virgin companions follow her —
those brought to be with her.
¹⁵Led in with joy and gladness,
they enter the palace of the king.

¹⁶Your sons will take the place of your
fathers;
you will make them princes
throughout the land.

¹⁷I will perpetuate your memory through
all generations;
therefore the nations will praise you
for ever and ever.

Psalm 46ᵇ

*For the director of music. Of the Sons of Korah.
According to* alamoth.ᶜ *A song.*

¹God is our refuge and strength,
an ever-present help in trouble.
²Therefore we will not fear, though the
earth give way
and the mountains fall into the heart
of the sea,
³though its waters roar and foam
and the mountains quake with their
surging.ᵈ

⁴There is a river whose streams make glad
the city of God,
the holy place where the Most High
dwells.
⁵God is within her, she will not fall;
God will help her at break of day.
⁶Nations are in uproar, kingdoms fall;
he lifts his voice, the earth melts.

⁷The Lord Almighty is with us;
the God of Jacob is our fortress.

⁸Come and see what the Lord has done,
the desolations he has brought on
the earth.
⁹He makes wars cease
to the ends of the earth.
He breaks the bow and shatters the
spear;
he burns the shieldsᵉ with fire.
¹⁰He says, "Be still, and know that I
am God;
I will be exalted among the nations,
I will be exalted in the earth."

¹¹The Lord Almighty is with us;
the God of Jacob is our fortress.

Psalm 47ᶠ

*For the director of music.
Of the Sons of Korah. A psalm.*

¹Clap your hands, all you nations;
shout to God with cries of joy.

²For the Lord Most High is awesome,
the great King over all the earth.
³He subdued nations under us,
peoples under our feet.
⁴He chose our inheritance for us,
the pride of Jacob, whom he loved.ᵍ

⁵God has ascended amid shouts of joy,
the Lord amid the sounding of
trumpets.
⁶Sing praises to God, sing praises;
sing praises to our King, sing praises.
⁷For God is the King of all the earth;
sing to him a psalm of praise.

⁸God reigns over the nations;
God is seated on his holy throne.
⁹The nobles of the nations assemble
as the people of the God of Abraham,

ᵃ 12 Or *A Tyrian robe is among the gifts*   ᵇ In Hebrew texts 46:1-11 is numbered 46:2-12.   ᶜ Title:
Probably a musical term   ᵈ 3 The Hebrew has *Selah* (a word of uncertain meaning) here and at the end
of verses 7 and 11.   ᵉ 9 Or *chariots*   ᶠ In Hebrew texts 47:1-9 is numbered 47:2-10.   ᵍ 4 The Hebrew
has *Selah* (a word of uncertain meaning) here.

for the kings*ᵃ* of the earth belong to God;
he is greatly exalted.

Psalm 48*ᵇ*

A song. A psalm of the Sons of Korah.

¹ Great is the Lᴏʀᴅ, and most worthy of
praise,
in the city of our God, his holy
mountain.

² Beautiful in its loftiness,
the joy of the whole earth,
like the heights of Zaphon*ᶜ* is Mount Zion,
the city of the Great King.
³ God is in her citadels;
he has shown himself to be her fortress.

⁴ When the kings joined forces,
when they advanced together,
⁵ they saw her and were astounded;
they fled in terror.
⁶ Trembling seized them there,
pain like that of a woman in labor.
⁷ You destroyed them like ships of Tarshish
shattered by an east wind.

⁸ As we have heard,
so we have seen
in the city of the Lᴏʀᴅ Almighty,
in the city of our God:
God makes her secure
forever.*ᵈ*

⁹ Within your temple, O God,
we meditate on your unfailing love.
¹⁰ Like your name, O God,
your praise reaches to the ends of the
earth;
your right hand is filled with
righteousness.
¹¹ Mount Zion rejoices,
the villages of Judah are glad
because of your judgments.

¹² Walk about Zion, go around her,
count her towers,
¹³ consider well her ramparts,
view her citadels,
that you may tell of them
to the next generation.

¹⁴ For this God is our God for ever and ever;
he will be our guide even to the end.

Psalm 49*ᵉ*

For the director of music.
Of the Sons of Korah. A psalm.

¹ Hear this, all you peoples;
listen, all who live in this world,
² both low and high,
rich and poor alike:
³ My mouth will speak words of wisdom;
the meditation of my heart will give
you understanding.
⁴ I will turn my ear to a proverb;
with the harp I will expound my
riddle:

⁵ Why should I fear when evil days come,
when wicked deceivers surround me—
⁶ those who trust in their wealth
and boast of their great riches?
⁷ No one can redeem the life of another
or give to God a ransom for them—
⁸ the ransom for a life is costly,
no payment is ever enough—
⁹ so that they should live on forever
and not see decay.
¹⁰ For all can see that the wise die,
that the foolish and the senseless also
perish,
leaving their wealth to others.
¹¹ Their tombs will remain their houses*ᶠ*
forever,
their dwellings for endless
generations,
though they had*ᵍ* named lands after
themselves.

¹² People, despite their wealth, do not
endure;
they are like the beasts that perish.

¹³ This is the fate of those who trust in
themselves,
and of their followers, who approve
their sayings.*ʰ*
¹⁴ They are like sheep and are destined
to die;
death will be their shepherd

ᵃ 9 Or *shields*   *ᵇ* In Hebrew texts 48:1-14 is numbered 48:2-15.   *ᶜ 2 Zaphon* was the most sacred
mountain of the Canaanites.   *ᵈ 8* The Hebrew has *Selah* (a word of uncertain meaning) here.   *ᵉ* In
Hebrew texts 49:1-20 is numbered 49:2-21.   *ᶠ 11* Septuagint and Syriac; Hebrew *In their thoughts their
houses will remain*   *ᵍ 11* Or *generations, / for they have*   *ʰ 13* The Hebrew has *Selah* (a word of
uncertain meaning) here and at the end of verse 15.

(but the upright will prevail over them
in the morning).
Their forms will decay in the grave,
far from their princely mansions.
¹⁵ But God will redeem me from the realm
of the dead;
he will surely take me to himself.
¹⁶ Do not be overawed when others grow
rich,
when the splendor of their houses
increases;
¹⁷ for they will take nothing with them
when they die,
their splendor will not descend
with them.
¹⁸ Though while they live they count
themselves blessed —
and people praise you when you
prosper —
¹⁹ they will join those who have gone
before them,
who will never again see the light
of life.
²⁰ People who have wealth but lack
understanding
are like the beasts that perish.

Psalm 50

A psalm of Asaph.

¹ The Mighty One, God, the Lord,
speaks and summons the earth
from the rising of the sun to where
it sets.
² From Zion, perfect in beauty,
God shines forth.
³ Our God comes
and will not be silent;
a fire devours before him,
and around him a tempest rages.
⁴ He summons the heavens above,
and the earth, that he may judge
his people:
⁵ "Gather to me this consecrated
people,
who made a covenant with me by
sacrifice."
⁶ And the heavens proclaim his
righteousness,
for he is a God of justice.*ᵃ,ᵇ*

⁷ "Listen, my people, and I will speak;
I will testify against you, Israel:
I am God, your God.
⁸ I bring no charges against you
concerning your sacrifices
or concerning your burnt offerings,
which are ever before me.
⁹ I have no need of a bull from your stall
or of goats from your pens,
¹⁰ for every animal of the forest is mine,
and the cattle on a thousand hills.
¹¹ I know every bird in the mountains,
and the insects in the fields are
mine.
¹² If I were hungry I would not tell you,
for the world is mine, and all that is
in it.
¹³ Do I eat the flesh of bulls
or drink the blood of goats?
¹⁴ "Sacrifice thank offerings to God,
fulfill your vows to the Most High,
¹⁵ and call on me in the day of trouble;
I will deliver you, and you will
honor me."

¹⁶ But to the wicked person, God says:

"What right have you to recite my laws
or take my covenant on your lips?
¹⁷ You hate my instruction
and cast my words behind you.
¹⁸ When you see a thief, you join
with him;
you throw in your lot with
adulterers.
¹⁹ You use your mouth for evil
and harness your tongue to deceit.
²⁰ You sit and testify against your brother
and slander your own mother's son.
²¹ When you did these things and I kept
silent,
you thought I was exactly*ᶜ* like you.
But I now arraign you
and set my accusations before you.
²² "Consider this, you who forget God,
or I will tear you to pieces, with no one
to rescue you:
²³ Those who sacrifice thank offerings
honor me,
and to the blameless*ᵈ* I will show my
salvation."

ᵃ 6 With a different word division of the Hebrew; Masoretic Text *for God himself is judge*   *ᵇ 6* The
Hebrew has *Selah* (a word of uncertain meaning) here.   *ᶜ 21* Or *thought the 'I am' was*   *ᵈ 23* Probable
reading of the original Hebrew text; the meaning of the Masoretic Text for this phrase is uncertain.

Psalm 51[a]

For the director of music. A psalm of David.
When the prophet Nathan came to him after
David had committed adultery with Bathsheba.

[1] Have mercy on me, O God,
    according to your unfailing love;
according to your great compassion
    blot out my transgressions.
[2] Wash away all my iniquity
    and cleanse me from my sin.

[3] For I know my transgressions,
    and my sin is always before me.
[4] Against you, you only, have I sinned
    and done what is evil in your sight;
so you are right in your verdict
    and justified when you judge.
[5] Surely I was sinful at birth,
    sinful from the time my mother
        conceived me.
[6] Yet you desired faithfulness even in
        the womb;
    you taught me wisdom in that secret
        place.

[7] Cleanse me with hyssop, and I will be
        clean;
    wash me, and I will be whiter than
        snow.
[8] Let me hear joy and gladness;
    let the bones you have crushed rejoice.
[9] Hide your face from my sins
    and blot out all my iniquity.

[10] Create in me a pure heart, O God,
    and renew a steadfast spirit within me.
[11] Do not cast me from your presence
    or take your Holy Spirit from me.
[12] Restore to me the joy of your salvation
    and grant me a willing spirit, to
        sustain me.

[13] Then I will teach transgressors your ways,
    so that sinners will turn back to you.
[14] Deliver me from the guilt of bloodshed,
        O God,
    you who are God my Savior,
    and my tongue will sing of your
        righteousness.
[15] Open my lips, Lord,
    and my mouth will declare your
        praise.

[16] You do not delight in sacrifice, or I would
        bring it;
    you do not take pleasure in burnt
        offerings.
[17] My sacrifice, O God, is[b] a broken spirit;
    a broken and contrite heart
    you, God, will not despise.

[18] May it please you to prosper Zion,
    to build up the walls of Jerusalem.
[19] Then you will delight in the sacrifices of
        the righteous,
    in burnt offerings offered whole;
    then bulls will be offered on your altar.

Psalm 52[c]

For the director of music. A maskil[d] *of David.*
When Doeg the Edomite had gone to Saul and told
him: "David has gone to the house of Ahimelek."

[1] Why do you boast of evil, you mighty
        hero?
    Why do you boast all day long,
    you who are a disgrace in the eyes
        of God?
[2] You who practice deceit,
    your tongue plots destruction;
    it is like a sharpened razor.
[3] You love evil rather than good,
    falsehood rather than speaking the
        truth.[e]
[4] You love every harmful word,
    you deceitful tongue!

[5] Surely God will bring you down to
        everlasting ruin:
    He will snatch you up and pluck you
        from your tent;
    he will uproot you from the land of
        the living.
[6] The righteous will see and fear;
    they will laugh at you, saying,
[7] "Here now is the man
    who did not make God his stronghold
    but trusted in his great wealth
    and grew strong by destroying others!"

[8] But I am like an olive tree
    flourishing in the house of God;
I trust in God's unfailing love
    for ever and ever.
[9] For what you have done I will always
        praise you

---

[a] In Hebrew texts 51:1-19 is numbered 51:3-21.   [b] *17* Or *The sacrifices of God are*   [c] In Hebrew texts
52:1-9 is numbered 52:3-11.   [d] Title: Probably a literary or musical term   [e] *3* The Hebrew has *Selah*
(a word of uncertain meaning) here and at the end of verse 5.

SAY YOU'RE SORRY

READ: PSALM 51:1

From the time you were little your parents taught you to say, "I'm sorry." After a while they prodded you to "Say it like you mean it." If you're truly fortunate, they told you, "Tell God you're sorry too."

There's a specific story behind Psalm 51, the Bible's famed song of confession. The heading says King David penned these words after the prophet Nathan called out his sin with Bathsheba.

David should have been leading his troops in battle, but he was lounging around the palace when he spied a beautiful woman bathing. David sent for her, slept with her, and got her pregnant. If that weren't enough, he conspired to kill her husband, sending a loyal soldier into the heat of battle (2 Samuel 11:1–27). When God sent Nathan to confront David, the prophet compared the king to a wealthy rancher who stole a poor man's only lamb (12:1–14). That's when David poured out his heart to God. He admitted all the evil he had done against the Lord.

BUILDING FAITH WISDOM STRENGTH

Everyone sins, but the big choice is always what you do about your failures. Admitting you're wrong to God and others might be the toughest thing you ever do, but you get a head start when you make David's words your own. Pray them and invite God to wash you clean.

in the presence of your faithful
    people.
And I will hope in your name,
    for your name is good.

Psalm 53[a]

For the director of music.
According to mahalath.[b] *A* maskil[c] *of David.*

[1] The fool says in his heart,
    "There is no God."
They are corrupt, and their ways are vile;
    there is no one who does good.

[2] God looks down from heaven
    on all mankind
to see if there are any who understand,
    any who seek God.
[3] Everyone has turned away, all have
    become corrupt;
    there is no one who does good,
    not even one.

[4] Do all these evildoers know nothing?

They devour my people as though eating
    bread;
    they never call on God.
[5] But there they are, overwhelmed with
    dread,
    where there was nothing to dread.
God scattered the bones of those who
    attacked you;
    you put them to shame, for God
    despised them.

[6] Oh, that salvation for Israel would come
    out of Zion!
    When God restores his people,
    let Jacob rejoice and Israel be glad!

Psalm 54[d]

For the director of music.
With stringed instruments. A maskil[c] *of David.*
When the Ziphites had gone to Saul and said,
    "Is not David hiding among us?"

[1] Save me, O God, by your name;
    vindicate me by your might.
[2] Hear my prayer, O God;
    listen to the words of my mouth.

[3] Arrogant foes are attacking me;
    ruthless people are trying to kill me—
    people without regard for God.[e]

[4] Surely God is my help;
    the Lord is the one who sustains me.

[5] Let evil recoil on those who slander me;
    in your faithfulness destroy them.

[6] I will sacrifice a freewill offering to you;
    I will praise your name, LORD, for it
    is good.
[7] You have delivered me from all my
    troubles,
    and my eyes have looked in triumph
    on my foes.

Psalm 55[f]

For the director of music. With stringed
instruments. A maskil[c] *of David.*

[1] Listen to my prayer, O God,
    do not ignore my plea;
[2]   hear me and answer me.
My thoughts trouble me and I am
    distraught
[3]   because of what my enemy is saying,
    because of the threats of the wicked;
for they bring down suffering on me
    and assail me in their anger.

[4] My heart is in anguish within me;
    the terrors of death have fallen on me.
[5] Fear and trembling have beset me;
    horror has overwhelmed me.
[6] I said, "Oh, that I had the wings of
    a dove!
    I would fly away and be at rest.
[7] I would flee far away
    and stay in the desert;[g]
[8] I would hurry to my place of shelter,
    far from the tempest and storm."

[9] Lord, confuse the wicked, confound
    their words,
    for I see violence and strife in the city.
[10] Day and night they prowl about on its
    walls;
    malice and abuse are within it.
[11] Destructive forces are at work in the city;
    threats and lies never leave its streets.

---

[a] In Hebrew texts 53:1-6 is numbered 53:2-7.   [b] Title: Probably a musical term   [c] Title: Probably a
literary or musical term   [d] In Hebrew texts 54:1-7 is numbered 54:3-9.   [e] 3 The Hebrew has *Selah* (a
word of uncertain meaning) here.   [f] In Hebrew texts 55:1-23 is numbered 55:2-24.   [g] 7 The Hebrew
has *Selah* (a word of uncertain meaning) here and in the middle of verse 19.

TASTE TEST

READ: **PSALM 53:2**

What kind of people would we become if our lives were marked by a constant, unending desire to know all that we can know of God? The road that leads out of a dead-end spirituality is a road we often must create ourselves.

You know the phrase, "Don't put God in a box"? I think we end up doing that much more than we realize. At first, we use theological words, philosophical ideas, and denominational beliefs in a genuine effort to understand more about the God we love. But too often we let those words define God's limits more than they describe his limitlessness. We start to imagine that we've got God all figured out, that we know exactly how God works—and how God would never work.

BUILDING FAITH WISDOM STRENGTH

The Living God cries from eternity to be released from the boxes we've built around him. God wants to be discovered, to be learned about.

Are there places we dare not go, ones that might lead us into dangerous territory? Certainly. But God wants us to know him better. As the psalmist says, "Taste and see that the Lord is good" (Psalm 34:8). God invites you to discover him, to try him over and over. His goodness is not experienced in just one bite, it's discovered over a lifetime of continued tasting.

¹²If an enemy were insulting me,
    I could endure it;
if a foe were rising against me,
    I could hide.
¹³But it is you, a man like myself,
    my companion, my close friend,
¹⁴with whom I once enjoyed sweet
        fellowship
    at the house of God,
as we walked about
    among the worshipers.

¹⁵Let death take my enemies by surprise;
    let them go down alive to the realm of
        the dead,
    for evil finds lodging among them.

¹⁶As for me, I call to God,
    and the LORD saves me.
¹⁷Evening, morning and noon
    I cry out in distress,
    and he hears my voice.
¹⁸He rescues me unharmed
    from the battle waged against me,
    even though many oppose me.
¹⁹God, who is enthroned from of old,
    who does not change —
    he will hear them and humble them,
    because they have no fear of God.

²⁰My companion attacks his friends;
    he violates his covenant.
²¹His talk is smooth as butter,
    yet war is in his heart;
his words are more soothing than oil,
    yet they are drawn swords.

²²Cast your cares on the LORD
    and he will sustain you;
he will never let
    the righteous be shaken.
²³But you, God, will bring down the wicked
    into the pit of decay;
    the bloodthirsty and deceitful
        will not live out half their days.

But as for me, I trust in you.

Psalm 56ᵃ

For the director of music. To the tune of
"A Dove on Distant Oaks." Of David. A miktam.ᵇ
When the Philistines had seized him in Gath.

¹Be merciful to me, my God,
    for my enemies are in hot pursuit;

all day long they press their
        attack.
²My adversaries pursue me all day long;
    in their pride many are attacking me.

³When I am afraid, I put my trust in you.
⁴   In God, whose word I praise —
    in God I trust and am not afraid.
    What can mere mortals do to me?

⁵All day long they twist my words;
    all their schemes are for my ruin.
⁶They conspire, they lurk,
    they watch my steps,
    hoping to take my life.
⁷Because of their wickedness do notᶜ let
        them escape;
    in your anger, God, bring the nations
        down.

⁸Record my misery;
    list my tears on your scrollᵈ —
    are they not in your record?
⁹Then my enemies will turn back
    when I call for help.
    By this I will know that God is for me.

¹⁰In God, whose word I praise,
    in the LORD, whose word I praise —
¹¹in God I trust and am not afraid.
    What can man do to me?

¹²I am under vows to you, my God;
    I will present my thank offerings
        to you.
¹³For you have delivered me from death
    and my feet from stumbling,
that I may walk before God
    in the light of life.

Psalm 57ᵉ

For the director of music. To the tune of
"Do Not Destroy." Of David. A miktam.ᵇ
When he had fled from Saul into the cave.

¹Have mercy on me, my God, have mercy
        on me,
    for in you I take refuge.
I will take refuge in the shadow of your
        wings
    until the disaster has passed.

²I cry out to God Most High,
    to God, who vindicates me.

ᵃ In Hebrew texts 56:1-13 is numbered 56:2-14.   ᵇ Title: Probably a literary or musical term
ᶜ 7 Probable reading of the original Hebrew text; Masoretic Text does not have *do not*.   ᵈ 8 Or *misery; /*
put my tears in your wineskin   ᵉ In Hebrew texts 57:1-11 is numbered 57:2-12.

[3] He sends from heaven and saves me,
rebuking those who hotly pursue
me — [a]
God sends forth his love and his
faithfulness.

[4] I am in the midst of lions;
I am forced to dwell among ravenous
beasts —
men whose teeth are spears and arrows,
whose tongues are sharp swords.

[5] Be exalted, O God, above the heavens;
let your glory be over all the earth.

[6] They spread a net for my feet —
I was bowed down in distress.
They dug a pit in my path —
but they have fallen into it themselves.

[7] My heart, O God, is steadfast,
my heart is steadfast;
I will sing and make music.
[8] Awake, my soul!
Awake, harp and lyre!
I will awaken the dawn.

[9] I will praise you, Lord, among the
nations;
I will sing of you among the peoples.
[10] For great is your love, reaching to the
heavens;
your faithfulness reaches to the skies.

[11] Be exalted, O God, above the heavens;
let your glory be over all the earth.

Psalm 58[b]

*For the director of music. To the tune of
"Do Not Destroy." Of David. A* miktam.[c]

[1] Do you rulers indeed speak justly?
Do you judge people with equity?
[2] No, in your heart you devise injustice,
and your hands mete out violence on
the earth.

[3] Even from birth the wicked go astray;
from the womb they are wayward,
spreading lies.
[4] Their venom is like the venom of a snake,
like that of a cobra that has stopped
its ears,

[5] that will not heed the tune of the
charmer,
however skillful the enchanter
may be.

[6] Break the teeth in their mouths, O God;
LORD, tear out the fangs of those
lions!
[7] Let them vanish like water that flows
away;
when they draw the bow, let their
arrows fall short.
[8] May they be like a slug that melts away as
it moves along,
like a stillborn child that never sees
the sun.

[9] Before your pots can feel the heat of the
thorns —
whether they be green or dry — the
wicked will be swept away.[d]
[10] The righteous will be glad when they are
avenged,
when they dip their feet in the blood of
the wicked.
[11] Then people will say,
"Surely the righteous still are
rewarded;
surely there is a God who judges the
earth."

Psalm 59[e]

*For the director of music. To the tune of
"Do Not Destroy." Of David. A* miktam.[c]
*When Saul had sent men to watch David's
house in order to kill him.*

[1] Deliver me from my enemies, O God;
be my fortress against those who are
attacking me.
[2] Deliver me from evildoers
and save me from those who are after
my blood.

[3] See how they lie in wait for me!
Fierce men conspire against me
for no offense or sin of mine, LORD.
[4] I have done no wrong, yet they are ready
to attack me.
Arise to help me; look on my plight!
[5] You, LORD God Almighty,
you who are the God of Israel,

---

[a] 3 The Hebrew has *Selah* (a word of uncertain meaning) here and at the end of verse 6.   [b] In Hebrew
texts 58:1-11 is numbered 58:2-12.   [c] Title: Probably a literary or musical term   [d] 9 The meaning of the
Hebrew for this verse is uncertain.   [e] In Hebrew texts 59:1-17 is numbered 59:2-18.

rouse yourself to punish all the
    nations;
    show no mercy to wicked traitors. *a*

6 They return at evening,
    snarling like dogs,
    and prowl about the city.
7 See what they spew from their
    mouths —
    the words from their lips are sharp
    as swords,
    and they think, "Who can hear us?"
8 But you laugh at them, LORD;
    you scoff at all those nations.

9 You are my strength, I watch for you;
    you, God, are my fortress,
10   my God on whom I can rely.

God will go before me
    and will let me gloat over those who
    slander me.
11 But do not kill them, Lord our shield, *b*
    or my people will forget.
In your might uproot them
    and bring them down.
12 For the sins of their mouths,
    for the words of their lips,
    let them be caught in their pride.
For the curses and lies they utter,
13   consume them in your wrath,
    consume them till they are no
    more.
Then it will be known to the ends of
    the earth
    that God rules over Jacob.

14 They return at evening,
    snarling like dogs,
    and prowl about the city.
15 They wander about for food
    and howl if not satisfied.
16 But I will sing of your strength,
    in the morning I will sing of your
    love;
for you are my fortress,
    my refuge in times of trouble.

17 You are my strength, I sing praise
    to you;
    you, God, are my fortress,
    my God on whom I can rely.

Psalm 60 *c*

For the director of music. To the tune of "The Lily of
the Covenant." A miktam *d* *of David. For teaching.*
When he fought Aram Naharaim *e* *and Aram*
Zobah, *f* *and when Joab returned and struck down*
twelve thousand Edomites in the Valley of Salt.

1 You have rejected us, God, and burst
    upon us;
    you have been angry — now restore us!
2 You have shaken the land and torn it
    open;
    mend its fractures, for it is quaking.
3 You have shown your people desperate
    times;
    you have given us wine that makes us
    stagger.
4 But for those who fear you, you have
    raised a banner
    to be unfurled against the bow. *g*

5 Save us and help us with your right hand,
    that those you love may be delivered.
6 God has spoken from his sanctuary:
    "In triumph I will parcel out Shechem
    and measure off the Valley of Sukkoth.
7 Gilead is mine, and Manasseh is mine;
    Ephraim is my helmet,
    Judah is my scepter.
8 Moab is my washbasin,
    on Edom I toss my sandal;
    over Philistia I shout in triumph."

9 Who will bring me to the fortified city?
    Who will lead me to Edom?
10 Is it not you, God, you who have now
    rejected us
    and no longer go out with our armies?
11 Give us aid against the enemy,
    for human help is worthless.
12 With God we will gain the victory,
    and he will trample down our enemies.

Psalm 61 *h*

For the director of music.
With stringed instruments. Of David.

1 Hear my cry, O God;
    listen to my prayer.

2 From the ends of the earth I call to you,
    I call as my heart grows faint;

---

a 5 The Hebrew has *Selah* (a word of uncertain meaning) here and at the end of verse 13.   *b 11* Or *sovereign*
c In Hebrew texts 60:1-12 is numbered 60:3-14.   *d* Title: Probably a literary or musical term   *e* Title: That
is, Arameans of Northwest Mesopotamia   *f* Title: That is, Arameans of central Syria   *g 4* The Hebrew
has *Selah* (a word of uncertain meaning) here.   *h* In Hebrew texts 61:1-8 is numbered 61:2-9.

SONGWRITER

READ: PSALM 61:2

Many psalms sound pretty, but they're far more than lush words. David and others wrote their songs to express their thoughts and emotions. They divulged real-life struggles and celebrated hard-fought triumphs. By creating these songs for ancient public worship, they let you in on their experience of God.

Instead of rushing through these words, look for what they say line by line. David says "hear my cry" (Psalm 61:1) because he wants the Lord to pay attention to everything that follows. "From the ends of the earth" (v. 2) says he feels as far away from God as he can get. "As my heart grows faint" (v. 2) means his emotions, thoughts, and will are about to collapse. "The rock that is higher than I" (v. 2) isn't just a picturesque safe place, but a name for God himself. "Refuge" and "strong tower" are fortresses that give protection from a "foe" (v. 3) in war. David wants nothing more than to "dwell in your tent forever" (v. 4), to live close to God in the tabernacle. He longs to take refuge under the Lord's "wings" (v. 4), the only place young birds find complete safety.

BUILDING
FAITH
WISDOM
STRENGTH

You can pray these powerful words as your own. Or you can write your own songs to God. What thoughts and emotions do you need to tell him? What struggles or triumphs do you want him to know about? Or what images describe how you picture the Lord?

lead me to the rock that is higher
than I.
³ For you have been my refuge,
a strong tower against the foe.

⁴ I long to dwell in your tent forever
and take refuge in the shelter of your
wings.ᵃ
⁵ For you, God, have heard my vows;
you have given me the heritage of
those who fear your name.

⁶ Increase the days of the king's life,
his years for many generations.
⁷ May he be enthroned in God's presence
forever;
appoint your love and faithfulness to
protect him.

⁸ Then I will ever sing in praise of your
name
and fulfill my vows day after day.

Psalm 62ᵇ

For the director of music.
For Jeduthun. A psalm of David.

¹ Truly my soul finds rest in God;
my salvation comes from him.
² Truly he is my rock and my salvation;
he is my fortress, I will never be
shaken.

³ How long will you assault me?
Would all of you throw me down —
this leaning wall, this tottering fence?
⁴ Surely they intend to topple me
from my lofty place;
they take delight in lies.
With their mouths they bless,
but in their hearts they curse.ᶜ

⁵ Yes, my soul, find rest in God;
my hope comes from him.
⁶ Truly he is my rock and my salvation;
he is my fortress, I will not be shaken.
⁷ My salvation and my honor depend
on God ᵈ;
he is my mighty rock, my refuge.
⁸ Trust in him at all times, you people;
pour out your hearts to him,
for God is our refuge.

⁹ Surely the lowborn are but a breath,
the highborn are but a lie.

If weighed on a balance, they are
nothing;
together they are only a breath.
¹⁰ Do not trust in extortion
or put vain hope in stolen goods;
though your riches increase,
do not set your heart on them.

¹¹ One thing God has spoken,
two things I have heard:
"Power belongs to you, God,
¹²   and with you, Lord, is unfailing love";
and, "You reward everyone
according to what they have done."

Psalm 63ᵉ

A psalm of David.
When he was in the Desert of Judah.

¹ You, God, are my God,
earnestly I seek you;
I thirst for you,
my whole being longs for you,
in a dry and parched land
where there is no water.

² I have seen you in the sanctuary
and beheld your power and your
glory.
³ Because your love is better than life,
my lips will glorify you.
⁴ I will praise you as long as I live,
and in your name I will lift up my
hands.
⁵ I will be fully satisfied as with the richest
of foods;
with singing lips my mouth will
praise you.

⁶ On my bed I remember you;
I think of you through the watches of
the night.
⁷ Because you are my help,
I sing in the shadow of your wings.
⁸ I cling to you;
your right hand upholds me.

⁹ Those who want to kill me will be
destroyed;
they will go down to the depths of
the earth.
¹⁰ They will be given over to the sword
and become food for jackals.

ᵃ 4 The Hebrew has *Selah* (a word of uncertain meaning) here.   ᵇ In Hebrew texts 62:1-12 is numbered 62:2-13.   ᶜ 4 The Hebrew has *Selah* (a word of uncertain meaning) here and at the end of verse 8.   ᵈ 7 Or / *God Most High is my salvation and my honor*   ᵉ In Hebrew texts 63:1-11 is numbered 63:2-12.

[11] But the king will rejoice in God;
  all who swear by God will glory in him,
  while the mouths of liars will be
    silenced.

Psalm 64[a]

For the director of music.
A psalm of David.

[1] Hear me, my God, as I voice my
    complaint;
  protect my life from the threat of the
    enemy.

[2] Hide me from the conspiracy of the
    wicked,
  from the plots of evildoers.

[3] They sharpen their tongues like swords
  and aim cruel words like deadly
    arrows.

[4] They shoot from ambush at the innocent;
  they shoot suddenly, without fear.

[5] They encourage each other in evil plans,
  they talk about hiding their snares;
  they say, "Who will see it[b]?"

[6] They plot injustice and say,
  "We have devised a perfect plan!"
  Surely the human mind and heart are
    cunning.

[7] But God will shoot them with his arrows;
  they will suddenly be struck down.

[8] He will turn their own tongues against
    them
  and bring them to ruin;
  all who see them will shake their
    heads in scorn.

[9] All people will fear;
  they will proclaim the works of God
  and ponder what he has done.

[10] The righteous will rejoice in the LORD
  and take refuge in him;
  all the upright in heart will glory
    in him!

Psalm 65[c]

For the director of music.
A psalm of David. A song.

[1] Praise awaits[d] you, our God, in Zion;
  to you our vows will be fulfilled.

[2] You who answer prayer,
  to you all people will come.

[3] When we were overwhelmed by sins,
  you forgave[e] our transgressions.

[4] Blessed are those you choose
  and bring near to live in your courts!
  We are filled with the good things of your
    house,
  of your holy temple.

[5] You answer us with awesome and
    righteous deeds,
  God our Savior,
  the hope of all the ends of the earth
  and of the farthest seas,

[6] who formed the mountains by your
    power,
  having armed yourself with strength,

[7] who stilled the roaring of the seas,
  the roaring of their waves,
  and the turmoil of the nations.

[8] The whole earth is filled with awe at your
    wonders;
  where morning dawns, where evening
    fades,
  you call forth songs of joy.

[9] You care for the land and water it;
  you enrich it abundantly.
  The streams of God are filled with water
  to provide the people with grain,
  for so you have ordained it.[f]

[10] You drench its furrows and level its
    ridges;
  you soften it with showers and bless
    its crops.

[11] You crown the year with your bounty,
  and your carts overflow with
    abundance.

[12] The grasslands of the wilderness
    overflow;
  the hills are clothed with gladness.

[13] The meadows are covered with flocks
  and the valleys are mantled with
    grain;
  they shout for joy and sing.

Psalm 66

For the director of music. A song. A psalm.

[1] Shout for joy to God, all the earth!
[2]   Sing the glory of his name;
  make his praise glorious.

---

[a] In Hebrew texts 64:1-10 is numbered 64:2-11.   [b] 5 Or *us*   [c] In Hebrew texts 65:1-13 is numbered 65:2-
14.   [d] 1 Or *befits*; the meaning of the Hebrew for this word is uncertain.   [e] 3 Or *made atonement for*
[f] 9 Or *for that is how you prepare the land*

GOING HAITIAN

READ: **PSALM 65:4**

I 'll never forget the first time I went to a church service in Haiti. I had heard from other friends who'd made similar mission trips about worship services lasting four to six hours. Most preachers in the States would tell you that they start losing people if the church service goes much longer than an hour.

So when I got to Haiti, I spoke to the local Haitian pastor about the time differences in our services. I said, "What is it about the Haitian people that keeps them worshiping at church for so many hours?" I was hoping for a profound answer that would redefine my sermons and church services. He laughed and said, "In Haiti, we have nothing else to do." I laughed, but then I was immediately struck by the weight of his answer. They didn't have televisions, radios, phones, computers, theaters. The Lord God didn't have much competition. And then I realized the implications of that.

BUILDING

FAITH

WISDOM

STRENGTH

What if you "went Haitian" for a week or two? What if you had a media fast, other than the requirements of your schoolwork? Can I challenge you to eliminate God's competition, just for a test, and see what happens?

Turn off the TV.
Turn down the music.
Unplug the game console.
Shut down the laptop.
Turn your eyes to the Lord.

Taken from *Gods at War Student Edition* by Kyle Idleman, copyright © 2014 by City on a Hill Studio, LLC, published by Zondervan.

³ Say to God, "How awesome are your
deeds!
So great is your power
that your enemies cringe before you.
⁴ All the earth bows down to you;
they sing praise to you,
they sing the praises of your name."ᵃ

⁵ Come and see what God has done,
his awesome deeds for mankind!
⁶ He turned the sea into dry land,
they passed through the waters on
foot —
come, let us rejoice in him.
⁷ He rules forever by his power,
his eyes watch the nations —
let not the rebellious rise up
against him.

⁸ Praise our God, all peoples,
let the sound of his praise be heard;
⁹ he has preserved our lives
and kept our feet from slipping.
¹⁰ For you, God, tested us;
you refined us like silver.
¹¹ You brought us into prison
and laid burdens on our backs.
¹² You let people ride over our heads;
we went through fire and water,
but you brought us to a place of
abundance.

¹³ I will come to your temple with burnt
offerings
and fulfill my vows to you —
¹⁴ vows my lips promised and my mouth
spoke
when I was in trouble.
¹⁵ I will sacrifice fat animals to you
and an offering of rams;
I will offer bulls and goats.

¹⁶ Come and hear, all you who fear God;
let me tell you what he has done for me.
¹⁷ I cried out to him with my mouth;
his praise was on my tongue.
¹⁸ If I had cherished sin in my heart,
the Lord would not have listened;
¹⁹ but God has surely listened
and has heard my prayer.
²⁰ Praise be to God,
who has not rejected my prayer
or withheld his love from me!

Psalm 67ᵇ

*For the director of music. With stringed
instruments. A psalm. A song.*

¹ May God be gracious to us and bless us
and make his face shine on us — ᶜ
² so that your ways may be known on
earth,
your salvation among all nations.

³ May the peoples praise you, God;
may all the peoples praise you.
⁴ May the nations be glad and sing for joy,
for you rule the peoples with equity
and guide the nations of the earth.
⁵ May the peoples praise you, God;
may all the peoples praise you.

⁶ The land yields its harvest;
God, our God, blesses us.
⁷ May God bless us still,
so that all the ends of the earth will
fear him.

Psalm 68ᵈ

*For the director of music. Of David.
A psalm. A song.*

¹ May God arise, may his enemies be
scattered;
may his foes flee before him.
² May you blow them away like smoke —
as wax melts before the fire,
may the wicked perish before God.
³ But may the righteous be glad
and rejoice before God;
may they be happy and joyful.

⁴ Sing to God, sing in praise of his name,
extol him who rides on the cloudsᵉ;
rejoice before him — his name is
the LORD.
⁵ A father to the fatherless, a defender of
widows,
is God in his holy dwelling.
⁶ God sets the lonely in families,ᶠ
he leads out the prisoners with
singing;
but the rebellious live in a sun-
scorched land.

⁷ When you, God, went out before your
people,

ᵃ 4 The Hebrew has *Selah* (a word of uncertain meaning) here and at the end of verses 7 and 15.   ᵇ In
Hebrew texts 67:1-7 is numbered 67:2-8.   ᶜ 1 The Hebrew has *Selah* (a word of uncertain meaning) here
and at the end of verse 4.   ᵈ In Hebrew texts 68:1-35 is numbered 68:2-36.   ᵉ 4 Or *name, / prepare the
way for him who rides through the deserts*   ᶠ 6 Or *the desolate in a homeland*

IN THE GREAT EXPANSE

READ: PSALM 66:4

While I was in college, I found a dock that hung out over a bay. I spent many evening hours there, away from everything—just sitting, thinking, and wrestling with my thoughts about dating relationships, project deadlines, friends, and the ways of college. I wanted to find some peace and know that Someone may be watching, speaking, and comforting me. I often sat and listened.

A fish jumped.

The waves moved softly over the still water and onto the shore.

The bay mirrored the tiny specks of light in the black, velvety sky.

Unheard music flowed from the celestial bodies above, moving in their patterns and throwing their beams to earth like an extended, friendly hand. The ancients called this unheard music, "the harmony of the spheres."

Dangling my feet over the dock, I was comforted by the sea air, the star song, and the calm bay. I was not alone, but I was part of something bigger than my own questions. I was just a creature on a planet teeming with countless other creatures, where everything had its place and worked in harmony. The earth is filled with peace and fury, lights and fire, delicate sea foam and surging waves.

BUILDING
FAITH
WISDOM
STRENGTH

Creation blanketed me and provided enrichment for my body and soul. Yet creation is also created. Nature and I have this in common: we are both mortal. Nature is my friend and the habitat of my home—built by a God who loves.

Taken from *Living with Questions* by Dale Fincher, copyright © 2007 by Charles Dale Fincher, published by Zondervan.

when you marched through the
wilderness,[a]
8 the earth shook, the heavens poured
down rain,
before God, the One of Sinai,
before God, the God of Israel.
9 You gave abundant showers, O God;
you refreshed your weary inheritance.
10 Your people settled in it,
and from your bounty, God, you
provided for the poor.

11 The Lord announces the word,
and the women who proclaim it are a
mighty throng:
12 "Kings and armies flee in haste;
the women at home divide the
plunder.
13 Even while you sleep among the sheep
pens,[b]
the wings of my dove are sheathed
with silver,
its feathers with shining gold."
14 When the Almighty[c] scattered the kings
in the land,
it was like snow fallen on Mount
Zalmon.

15 Mount Bashan, majestic mountain,
Mount Bashan, rugged mountain,
16 why gaze in envy, you rugged mountain,
at the mountain where God chooses to
reign,
where the LORD himself will dwell
forever?
17 The chariots of God are tens of thousands
and thousands of thousands;
the Lord has come from Sinai into his
sanctuary.[d]
18 When you ascended on high,
you took many captives;
you received gifts from people,
even from[e] the rebellious —
that you,[f] LORD God, might dwell there.

19 Praise be to the Lord, to God our Savior,
who daily bears our burdens.
20 Our God is a God who saves;
from the Sovereign LORD comes
escape from death.

21 Surely God will crush the heads of his
enemies,
the hairy crowns of those who go on in
their sins.
22 The Lord says, "I will bring them from
Bashan;
I will bring them from the depths of
the sea,
23 that your feet may wade in the blood
of your foes,
while the tongues of your dogs have
their share."

24 Your procession, God, has come into
view,
the procession of my God and King
into the sanctuary.
25 In front are the singers, after them the
musicians;
with them are the young women
playing the timbrels.
26 Praise God in the great congregation;
praise the LORD in the assembly of
Israel.
27 There is the little tribe of Benjamin,
leading them,
there the great throng of Judah's
princes,
and there the princes of Zebulun and
of Naphtali.

28 Summon your power, God[g];
show us your strength, our God, as you
have done before.
29 Because of your temple at Jerusalem
kings will bring you gifts.
30 Rebuke the beast among the reeds,
the herd of bulls among the calves of
the nations.
Humbled, may the beast bring bars of
silver.
Scatter the nations who delight in war.
31 Envoys will come from Egypt;
Cush[h] will submit herself to God.

32 Sing to God, you kingdoms of the earth,
sing praise to the Lord,
33 to him who rides across the highest
heavens, the ancient heavens,
who thunders with mighty voice.

---

[a] 7 The Hebrew has *Selah* (a word of uncertain meaning) here and at the end of verses 19 and 32.
[b] 13 Or *the campfires;* or *the saddlebags*   [c] 14 Hebrew *Shaddai*   [d] 17 Probable reading of the original
Hebrew text; Masoretic Text *Lord is among them at Sinai in holiness*   [e] 18 Or *gifts for people, / even*
[f] 18 Or *they*   [g] 28 Many Hebrew manuscripts, Septuagint and Syriac; most Hebrew manuscripts *Your
God has summoned power for you*   [h] 31 That is, the upper Nile region

³⁴ Proclaim the power of God,
  whose majesty is over Israel,
  whose power is in the heavens.
³⁵ You, God, are awesome in your
    sanctuary;
  the God of Israel gives power and
    strength to his people.

Praise be to God!

Psalm 69^a

For the director of music.
To the tune of "Lilies." Of David.

¹ Save me, O God,
  for the waters have come up to
    my neck.
² I sink in the miry depths,
  where there is no foothold.
I have come into the deep waters;
  the floods engulf me.
³ I am worn out calling for help;
  my throat is parched.
My eyes fail,
  looking for my God.
⁴ Those who hate me without reason
  outnumber the hairs of my head;
many are my enemies without cause,
  those who seek to destroy me.
I am forced to restore
  what I did not steal.

⁵ You, God, know my folly;
  my guilt is not hidden from you.

⁶ Lord, the LORD Almighty,
  may those who hope in you
  not be disgraced because of me;
God of Israel,
  may those who seek you
  not be put to shame because of me.
⁷ For I endure scorn for your sake,
  and shame covers my face.
⁸ I am a foreigner to my own family,
  a stranger to my own mother's
    children;
⁹ for zeal for your house consumes me,
  and the insults of those who insult you
    fall on me.
¹⁰ When I weep and fast,
  I must endure scorn;
¹¹ when I put on sackcloth,
  people make sport of me.

¹² Those who sit at the gate mock me,
  and I am the song of the drunkards.

¹³ But I pray to you, LORD,
  in the time of your favor;
in your great love, O God,
  answer me with your sure salvation.
¹⁴ Rescue me from the mire,
  do not let me sink;
deliver me from those who hate me,
  from the deep waters.
¹⁵ Do not let the floodwaters engulf me
  or the depths swallow me up
  or the pit close its mouth over me.

¹⁶ Answer me, LORD, out of the goodness of
    your love;
  in your great mercy turn to me.
¹⁷ Do not hide your face from your servant;
  answer me quickly, for I am in trouble.
¹⁸ Come near and rescue me;
  deliver me because of my foes.

¹⁹ You know how I am scorned, disgraced
    and shamed;
  all my enemies are before you.
²⁰ Scorn has broken my heart
  and has left me helpless;
I looked for sympathy, but there was
    none,
  for comforters, but I found none.
²¹ They put gall in my food
  and gave me vinegar for my thirst.

²² May the table set before them become
    a snare;
  may it become retribution and^b a trap.
²³ May their eyes be darkened so they
    cannot see,
  and their backs be bent forever.
²⁴ Pour out your wrath on them;
  let your fierce anger overtake them.
²⁵ May their place be deserted;
  let there be no one to dwell in their
    tents.
²⁶ For they persecute those you wound
  and talk about the pain of those
    you hurt.
²⁷ Charge them with crime upon crime;
  do not let them share in your salvation.
²⁸ May they be blotted out of the book of life
  and not be listed with the righteous.

²⁹ But as for me, afflicted and in pain —
  may your salvation, God, protect me.

---

^a In Hebrew texts 69:1-36 is numbered 69:2-37.   ^b 22 Or *snare / and their fellowship become*

30 I will praise God's name in song
  and glorify him with thanksgiving.
31 This will please the LORD more than
      an ox,
  more than a bull with its horns and
      hooves.
32 The poor will see and be glad —
  you who seek God, may your hearts
      live!
33 The LORD hears the needy
  and does not despise his captive
      people.

34 Let heaven and earth praise him,
  the seas and all that move in them,
35 for God will save Zion
  and rebuild the cities of Judah.
  Then people will settle there and
      possess it;
36 the children of his servants will
      inherit it,
  and those who love his name will
      dwell there.

Psalm 70[a]

For the director of music. Of David. A petition.

1 Hasten, O God, to save me;
  come quickly, LORD, to help me.

2 May those who want to take my life
  be put to shame and confusion;
  may all who desire my ruin
  be turned back in disgrace.
3 May those who say to me, "Aha! Aha!"
  turn back because of their shame.
4 But may all who seek you
  rejoice and be glad in you;
  may those who long for your saving help
      always say,
  "The LORD is great!"

5 But as for me, I am poor and needy;
  come quickly to me, O God.
  You are my help and my deliverer;
  LORD, do not delay.

Psalm 71

1 In you, LORD, I have taken refuge;
  let me never be put to shame.
2 In your righteousness, rescue me and
      deliver me;
  turn your ear to me and save me.

3 Be my rock of refuge,
  to which I can always go;
  give the command to save me,
  for you are my rock and my fortress.
4 Deliver me, my God, from the hand of the
      wicked,
  from the grasp of those who are evil
      and cruel.

5 For you have been my hope, Sovereign
      LORD,
  my confidence since my youth.
6 From birth I have relied on you;
  you brought me forth from my
      mother's womb.
  I will ever praise you.
7 I have become a sign to many;
  you are my strong refuge.
8 My mouth is filled with your praise,
  declaring your splendor all day long.

9 Do not cast me away when I am old;
  do not forsake me when my strength
      is gone.
10 For my enemies speak against me;
  those who wait to kill me conspire
      together.
11 They say, "God has forsaken him;
  pursue him and seize him,
  for no one will rescue him."
12 Do not be far from me, my God;
  come quickly, God, to help me.
13 May my accusers perish in shame;
  may those who want to harm me
  be covered with scorn and disgrace.

14 As for me, I will always have hope;
  I will praise you more and more.
15 My mouth will tell of your righteous
      deeds,
  of your saving acts all day long —
  though I know not how to relate
      them all.
16 I will come and proclaim your mighty
      acts, Sovereign LORD;
  I will proclaim your righteous deeds,
  yours alone.
17 Since my youth, God, you have taught me,
  and to this day I declare your
      marvelous deeds.
18 Even when I am old and gray,
  do not forsake me, my God,
  till I declare your power to the next
      generation,

---

a In Hebrew texts 70:1-5 is numbered 70:2-6.

HELPING HANDS

READ: PSALM 69:33

It's easy to look the other way when you walk by someone begging money. Or to forget about the hundreds of homeless people in any sizeable city. Or to shut out images and sounds of a billion hungry people around the globe. But God never closes his eyes or plugs his ears to the needy.

At first glance Psalm 69 isn't all about the poor. David starts by asking the Lord to save him from waters that have risen to his neck. He can't find a foothold. Waters keep washing over him. He's almost out of energy to call for help (vv. 1–3).

Then David goes on to tell God that people hate him for no reason. He feels like an alien among his own family. His heart breaks with weeping. When he hungers, his enemies feed him "gall," a bitter, poisonous herb. When he thirsts, they give him "vinegar," a drink made from sour wine (vv. 4–21).

Those details all add up to a solid description of the experience of people who struggle with poverty, and at the end of this song David offers hope to the poor. They will be glad when they praise the Lord. Their hearts will live when they seek God. Why? Because "The Lord hears the needy" (v. 33).

When you connect with God's heart, you can't help but care about people who don't have much in this world.

your mighty acts to all who are to
 come.

¹⁹ Your righteousness, God, reaches to the
 heavens,
 you who have done great things.
 Who is like you, God?
²⁰ Though you have made me see
 troubles,
 many and bitter,
 you will restore my life again;
 from the depths of the earth
 you will again bring me up.
²¹ You will increase my honor
 and comfort me once more.

²² I will praise you with the harp
 for your faithfulness, my God;
 I will sing praise to you with the lyre,
 Holy One of Israel.
²³ My lips will shout for joy
 when I sing praise to you—
 I whom you have delivered.
²⁴ My tongue will tell of your righteous acts
 all day long,
 for those who wanted to harm me
 have been put to shame and
 confusion.

Psalm 72

Of Solomon.

¹ Endow the king with your justice,
 O God,
 the royal son with your righteousness.
² May he judge your people in
 righteousness,
 your afflicted ones with justice.

³ May the mountains bring prosperity to
 the people,
 the hills the fruit of righteousness.
⁴ May he defend the afflicted among the
 people
 and save the children of the needy;
 may he crush the oppressor.
⁵ May he endure*ᵃ* as long as the sun,
 as long as the moon, through all
 generations.
⁶ May he be like rain falling on a mown
 field,
 like showers watering the earth.

⁷ In his days may the righteous flourish
 and prosperity abound till the moon
 is no more.
⁸ May he rule from sea to sea
 and from the River*ᵇ* to the ends of
 the earth.
⁹ May the desert tribes bow before him
 and his enemies lick the dust.
¹⁰ May the kings of Tarshish and of distant
 shores
 bring tribute to him.
 May the kings of Sheba and Seba
 present him gifts.
¹¹ May all kings bow down to him
 and all nations serve him.

¹² For he will deliver the needy who cry out,
 the afflicted who have no one to help.
¹³ He will take pity on the weak and the
 needy
 and save the needy from death.
¹⁴ He will rescue them from oppression and
 violence,
 for precious is their blood in his sight.

¹⁵ Long may he live!
 May gold from Sheba be given him.
 May people ever pray for him
 and bless him all day long.
¹⁶ May grain abound throughout the
 land;
 on the tops of the hills may it sway.
 May the crops flourish like Lebanon
 and thrive*ᶜ* like the grass of the field.
¹⁷ May his name endure forever;
 may it continue as long as the sun.

 Then all nations will be blessed through
 him,*ᵈ*
 and they will call him blessed.

¹⁸ Praise be to the LORD God, the God
 of Israel,
 who alone does marvelous deeds.
¹⁹ Praise be to his glorious name forever;
 may the whole earth be filled with
 his glory.
 Amen and Amen.

²⁰ This concludes the prayers of David
 son of Jesse.

ᵃ 5 Septuagint; Hebrew *You will be feared*   *ᵇ 8* That is, the Euphrates   *ᶜ 16* Probable reading of the
original Hebrew text; Masoretic Text *Lebanon, / from the city*   *ᵈ 17* Or *will use his name in blessings* (see
Gen. 48:20)

BOOK III

Psalms 73–89

Psalm 73

A psalm of Asaph.

¹ Surely God is good to Israel,
   to those who are pure in heart.

² But as for me, my feet had almost slipped;
   I had nearly lost my foothold.
³ For I envied the arrogant
   when I saw the prosperity of the
      wicked.

⁴ They have no struggles;
   their bodies are healthy and strong.*ᵃ*
⁵ They are free from common human
      burdens;
   they are not plagued by human ills.
⁶ Therefore pride is their necklace;
   they clothe themselves with violence.
⁷ From their callous hearts comes
      iniquity*ᵇ*;
   their evil imaginations have no limits.
⁸ They scoff, and speak with malice;
   with arrogance they threaten
      oppression.
⁹ Their mouths lay claim to heaven,
   and their tongues take possession of
      the earth.
¹⁰ Therefore their people turn to them
   and drink up waters in abundance.*ᶜ*
¹¹ They say, "How would God know?
   Does the Most High know anything?"

¹² This is what the wicked are like —
   always free of care, they go on
      amassing wealth.

¹³ Surely in vain I have kept my heart pure
   and have washed my hands in
      innocence.
¹⁴ All day long I have been afflicted,
   and every morning brings new
      punishments.

¹⁵ If I had spoken out like that,
   I would have betrayed your children.
¹⁶ When I tried to understand all this,
   it troubled me deeply
¹⁷ till I entered the sanctuary of God;
   then I understood their final destiny.

¹⁸ Surely you place them on slippery
      ground;
   you cast them down to ruin.
¹⁹ How suddenly are they destroyed,
   completely swept away by terrors!
²⁰ They are like a dream when one awakes;
   when you arise, Lord,
   you will despise them as fantasies.

²¹ When my heart was grieved
   and my spirit embittered,
²² I was senseless and ignorant;
   I was a brute beast before you.

²³ Yet I am always with you;
   you hold me by my right hand.
²⁴ You guide me with your counsel,
   and afterward you will take me into
      glory.
²⁵ Whom have I in heaven but you?
   And earth has nothing I desire
      besides you.
²⁶ My flesh and my heart may fail,
   but God is the strength of my heart
   and my portion forever.

²⁷ Those who are far from you will perish;
   you destroy all who are unfaithful
      to you.
²⁸ But as for me, it is good to be near God.
   I have made the Sovereign LORD my
      refuge;
   I will tell of all your deeds.

Psalm 74

*A maskil*ᵈ *of Asaph.*

¹ O God, why have you rejected us forever?
   Why does your anger smolder against
      the sheep of your pasture?
² Remember the nation you purchased
      long ago,
   the people of your inheritance, whom
      you redeemed —
   Mount Zion, where you dwelt.
³ Turn your steps toward these everlasting
      ruins,
   all this destruction the enemy has
      brought on the sanctuary.

⁴ Your foes roared in the place where you
      met with us;
   they set up their standards as signs.

ᵃ 4 With a different word division of the Hebrew; Masoretic Text *struggles at their death; / their bodies are healthy*   *ᵇ 7* Syriac (see also Septuagint); Hebrew *Their eyes bulge with fat*   *ᶜ 10* The meaning of the Hebrew for this verse is uncertain.   *ᵈ Title:* Probably a literary or musical term

PLAY IT OVER AND OVER

READ: PSALM 73:2-3

You might want to make Psalm 73 your new favorite song. If it rocked with a solid tune, it would echo through your heart and mind more than anything you have loaded on a playlist.

This song is credited to Asaph, a guy who clanged cymbals when the ark of God moved to Jerusalem (1 Chronicles 15:16-19). Asaph might be the actual lyricist, or the song might have been written by someone in his family (25:1-9).

Asaph was surrounded by evil people enjoying wild success. He was so envious of their prosperity that he almost quit trusting God. He observed that evil people didn't struggle. Their bodies didn't break. Because they didn't have problems like normal people, they wore pride as a necklace and violence like the latest fashion. They had plenty of time to dream up ways to sin, and they thought God wouldn't notice. In Psalm 73, Asaph wonders if it's been a waste to stay pure.

BUILDING
FAITH
WISDOM
STRENGTH

Keep reading the rest of this song to find out what happens to these evildoers. It isn't pretty. In the end, Asaph discovers the Lord has grabbed him by the hand and will never let go.

Whenever you feel like Asaph, remind yourself that you serve a just God. If your life falls apart, recall that you still have everything you need. You have God. And if you're near him, that's enough.

5 They behaved like men wielding axes
    to cut through a thicket of trees.
6 They smashed all the carved paneling
    with their axes and hatchets.
7 They burned your sanctuary to the
      ground;
    they defiled the dwelling place of your
      Name.
8 They said in their hearts, "We will crush
      them completely!"
    They burned every place where God
      was worshiped in the land.

9 We are given no signs from God;
    no prophets are left,
    and none of us knows how long this
      will be.
10 How long will the enemy mock you, God?
    Will the foe revile your name forever?
11 Why do you hold back your hand, your
      right hand?
    Take it from the folds of your garment
      and destroy them!

12 But God is my King from long ago;
    he brings salvation on the earth.

13 It was you who split open the sea by your
      power;
    you broke the heads of the monster in
      the waters.
14 It was you who crushed the heads of
      Leviathan
    and gave it as food to the creatures
      of the desert.
15 It was you who opened up springs and
      streams;
    you dried up the ever-flowing rivers.
16 The day is yours, and yours also the
      night;
    you established the sun and moon.
17 It was you who set all the boundaries of
      the earth;
    you made both summer and winter.

18 Remember how the enemy has mocked
      you, Lord,
    how foolish people have reviled your
      name.
19 Do not hand over the life of your dove to
      wild beasts;
    do not forget the lives of your afflicted
      people forever.

20 Have regard for your covenant,
    because haunts of violence fill the dark
      places of the land.
21 Do not let the oppressed retreat in
      disgrace;
    may the poor and needy praise your
      name.
22 Rise up, O God, and defend your cause;
    remember how fools mock you all
      day long.
23 Do not ignore the clamor of your
      adversaries,
    the uproar of your enemies, which
      rises continually.

Psalm 75 [a]

*For the director of music.
To the tune of "Do Not Destroy."
A psalm of Asaph. A song.*

1 We praise you, God,
    we praise you, for your Name is near;
    people tell of your wonderful deeds.

2 You say, "I choose the appointed time;
    it is I who judge with equity.
3 When the earth and all its people quake,
    it is I who hold its pillars firm. [b]
4 To the arrogant I say, 'Boast no more,'
    and to the wicked, 'Do not lift up your
      horns. [c]
5 Do not lift your horns against heaven;
    do not speak so defiantly.' "

6 No one from the east or the west
    or from the desert can exalt
      themselves.
7 It is God who judges:
    He brings one down, he exalts another.
8 In the hand of the Lord is a cup
    full of foaming wine mixed with
      spices;
  he pours it out, and all the wicked of
      the earth
    drink it down to its very dregs.

9 As for me, I will declare this forever;
    I will sing praise to the God of Jacob,
10 who says, "I will cut off the horns of all
      the wicked,
    but the horns of the righteous will be
      lifted up."

a In Hebrew texts 75:1-10 is numbered 75:2-11.   *b 3* The Hebrew has *Selah* (a word of uncertain meaning)
here.   *c 4 Horns* here symbolize strength; also in verses 5 and 10.

PLENTY OF EVIDENCE

READ: **PSALM 74:12**

S ome people give God no respect. They expect the Lord to prove himself by sending an instant answer to prayer or doing an on-demand miraculous act. When God ignores their tests, they "mock," attacking the Lord and defying his commands. They "revile," abusing him with harsh words (Psalm 74:10).

When the Lord seems to let these insults go on forever, Psalm 74 asks him to powerfully halt them. But then the song offers a longer and bigger view of God. It lists the Lord's powerful actions in making and governing the world, wrapping his accomplishments in poetic language. His power split the sea from land, a picture drawn from creation (Genesis 1:6-8). He took on "Leviathan," a sea monster in pagan literature, crushing that serpent's head and proving his dominance over evil. He opened springs in the desert to quench his people's thirst (Numbers 20:8-13), and he dried up waters to let them march onward (Exodus 14:21-31). He rules the day, night, and seasons.

BUILDING FAITH WISDOM STRENGTH

When people challenge your faith, you don't need on-the-spot proof of God's power. You can look back to everything he's already done, all the ways he has shown he's your King "from long ago" (Psalm 74:12). And you can point people to Jesus, the one who "brings salvation on the earth" (v. 12). He's the best sign of God's existence, power, and love.

Psalm 76[a]

For the director of music. With stringed instruments. A psalm of Asaph. A song.

[1] God is renowned in Judah;
in Israel his name is great.
[2] His tent is in Salem,
his dwelling place in Zion.
[3] There he broke the flashing arrows,
the shields and the swords, the
weapons of war.[b]

[4] You are radiant with light,
more majestic than mountains rich
with game.
[5] The valiant lie plundered,
they sleep their last sleep;
not one of the warriors
can lift his hands.
[6] At your rebuke, God of Jacob,
both horse and chariot lie still.

[7] It is you alone who are to be feared.
Who can stand before you when you
are angry?
[8] From heaven you pronounced judgment,
and the land feared and was quiet—
[9] when you, God, rose up to judge,
to save all the afflicted of the land.
[10] Surely your wrath against mankind
brings you praise,
and the survivors of your wrath are
restrained.[c]

[11] Make vows to the LORD your God and
fulfill them;
let all the neighboring lands
bring gifts to the One to be feared.
[12] He breaks the spirit of rulers;
he is feared by the kings of the earth.

Psalm 77[d]

*For the director of music.
For Jeduthun. Of Asaph. A psalm.*

[1] I cried out to God for help;
I cried out to God to hear me.
[2] When I was in distress, I sought the
Lord;
at night I stretched out untiring hands,
and I would not be comforted.

[3] I remembered you, God, and I groaned;
I meditated, and my spirit grew faint.[e]
[4] You kept my eyes from closing;
I was too troubled to speak.
[5] I thought about the former days,
the years of long ago;
[6] I remembered my songs in the night.
My heart meditated and my spirit
asked:

[7] "Will the Lord reject forever?
Will he never show his favor again?
[8] Has his unfailing love vanished forever?
Has his promise failed for all time?
[9] Has God forgotten to be merciful?
Has he in anger withheld his
compassion?"

[10] Then I thought, "To this I will appeal:
the years when the Most High
stretched out his right hand.
[11] I will remember the deeds of the LORD;
yes, I will remember your miracles of
long ago.
[12] I will consider all your works
and meditate on all your mighty deeds."

[13] Your ways, God, are holy.
What god is as great as our God?
[14] You are the God who performs miracles;
you display your power among the
peoples.
[15] With your mighty arm you redeemed
your people,
the descendants of Jacob and Joseph.

[16] The waters saw you, God,
the waters saw you and writhed;
the very depths were convulsed.
[17] The clouds poured down water,
the heavens resounded with thunder;
your arrows flashed back and forth.
[18] Your thunder was heard in the
whirlwind,
your lightning lit up the world;
the earth trembled and quaked.
[19] Your path led through the sea,
your way through the mighty waters,
though your footprints were not seen.
[20] You led your people like a flock
by the hand of Moses and Aaron.

---

[a] In Hebrew texts 76:1-12 is numbered 76:2-13.   [b] 3 The Hebrew has *Selah* (a word of uncertain meaning) here and at the end of verse 9.   [c] 10 Or *Surely the wrath of mankind brings you praise, / and with the remainder of wrath you arm yourself*   [d] In Hebrew texts 77:1-20 is numbered 77:2-21.   [e] 3 The Hebrew has *Selah* (a word of uncertain meaning) here and at the end of verses 9 and 15.

REMEMBER AND TRUST

READ: **PSALM 77:13**

You're in trouble, so you cry to God for help, hoping he hears all your moaning. The more you think about your situation, the more you ache. You can't sleep, and you don't have words big enough to describe your pain. You wonder if God will always feel so distant. Maybe he's forgotten to be sympathetic and forgiving, or he's so angry he's out of compassion for you.

That's the gist of Psalm 77:1–9. The first part of this song from Asaph acts like a giant question, asking what many believers feel when they hit life's tough spots. What's going on? Where is God? Why bother to trust him?

The rest of Psalm 77 serves up the answer. Asaph decides to purposely remember all the good things God has already done. He remembers the years when the Lord's power in his life was obvious. He recalls God's amazing miracles. He won't stop rolling these thoughts around in his mind.

Asaph thinks back to creation and the Lord's choice of Israel, but you can make your own list of reasons you look to God, trusting his love and power. Whether you keep your list in your head or write it down, it gives you facts to think about whenever you get discouraged. And you can put verse 13 at the top of your list. Your God is always perfectly pure and right. There's no one who compares to him.

BUILDING

FAITH

WISDOM

STRENGTH

Psalm 78

A maskil[a] of Asaph.

¹ My people, hear my teaching;
  listen to the words of my mouth.
² I will open my mouth with a parable;
  I will utter hidden things, things from
    of old —
³ things we have heard and known,
  things our ancestors have told us.
⁴ We will not hide them from their
    descendants;
  we will tell the next generation
  the praiseworthy deeds of the LORD,
    his power, and the wonders he has
      done.
⁵ He decreed statutes for Jacob
  and established the law in Israel,
  which he commanded our ancestors
    to teach their children,
⁶ so the next generation would know them,
  even the children yet to be born,
  and they in turn would tell their
    children.
⁷ Then they would put their trust in God
  and would not forget his deeds
  but would keep his commands.
⁸ They would not be like their ancestors —
  a stubborn and rebellious generation,
  whose hearts were not loyal to God,
  whose spirits were not faithful to him.

⁹ The men of Ephraim, though armed with
    bows,
  turned back on the day of battle;
¹⁰ they did not keep God's covenant
  and refused to live by his law.
¹¹ They forgot what he had done,
  the wonders he had shown them.
¹² He did miracles in the sight of their
    ancestors
  in the land of Egypt, in the region of
    Zoan.
¹³ He divided the sea and led them through;
  he made the water stand up like
    a wall.
¹⁴ He guided them with the cloud by day
  and with light from the fire all night.
¹⁵ He split the rocks in the wilderness
  and gave them water as abundant as
    the seas;
¹⁶ he brought streams out of a rocky crag
  and made water flow down like rivers.

¹⁷ But they continued to sin against him,
  rebelling in the wilderness against the
    Most High.
¹⁸ They willfully put God to the test
  by demanding the food they craved.
¹⁹ They spoke against God;
  they said, "Can God really
  spread a table in the wilderness?
²⁰ True, he struck the rock,
  and water gushed out,
  streams flowed abundantly,
  but can he also give us bread?
  Can he supply meat for his people?"
²¹ When the LORD heard them, he was
    furious;
  his fire broke out against Jacob,
  and his wrath rose against Israel,
²² for they did not believe in God
  or trust in his deliverance.
²³ Yet he gave a command to the skies above
  and opened the doors of the heavens;
²⁴ he rained down manna for the people
    to eat,
  he gave them the grain of heaven.
²⁵ Human beings ate the bread of angels;
  he sent them all the food they could eat.
²⁶ He let loose the east wind from the
    heavens
  and by his power made the south
    wind blow.
²⁷ He rained meat down on them like dust,
  birds like sand on the seashore.
²⁸ He made them come down inside their
    camp,
  all around their tents.
²⁹ They ate till they were gorged —
  he had given them what they craved.
³⁰ But before they turned from what they
    craved,
  even while the food was still in their
    mouths,
³¹ God's anger rose against them;
  he put to death the sturdiest among
    them,
  cutting down the young men of Israel.

³² In spite of all this, they kept on sinning;
  in spite of his wonders, they did not
    believe.
³³ So he ended their days in futility
  and their years in terror.
³⁴ Whenever God slew them, they would
    seek him;
  they eagerly turned to him again.

a Title: Probably a literary or musical term

35 They remembered that God was their
    Rock,
        that God Most High was their
        Redeemer.
36 But then they would flatter him with
    their mouths,
        lying to him with their tongues;
37 their hearts were not loyal to him,
        they were not faithful to his covenant.
38 Yet he was merciful;
        he forgave their iniquities
        and did not destroy them.
    Time after time he restrained his anger
        and did not stir up his full wrath.
39 He remembered that they were but flesh,
        a passing breeze that does not return.

40 How often they rebelled against him in
    the wilderness
        and grieved him in the wasteland!
41 Again and again they put God to the test;
        they vexed the Holy One of Israel.
42 They did not remember his power —
        the day he redeemed them from the
        oppressor,
43 the day he displayed his signs in Egypt,
        his wonders in the region of Zoan.
44 He turned their river into blood;
        they could not drink from their
        streams.
45 He sent swarms of flies that devoured
    them,
        and frogs that devastated them.
46 He gave their crops to the grasshopper,
        their produce to the locust.
47 He destroyed their vines with hail
        and their sycamore-figs with sleet.
48 He gave over their cattle to the hail,
        their livestock to bolts of lightning.
49 He unleashed against them his hot anger,
        his wrath, indignation and hostility —
        a band of destroying angels.
50 He prepared a path for his anger;
        he did not spare them from death
        but gave them over to the plague.
51 He struck down all the firstborn of Egypt,
        the firstfruits of manhood in the tents
        of Ham.
52 But he brought his people out like a flock;
        he led them like sheep through the
        wilderness.
53 He guided them safely, so they were
    unafraid;
        but the sea engulfed their enemies.

54 And so he brought them to the border of
    his holy land,
        to the hill country his right hand had
        taken.
55 He drove out nations before them
        and allotted their lands to them as an
        inheritance;
        he settled the tribes of Israel in their
        homes.

56 But they put God to the test
        and rebelled against the Most High;
        they did not keep his statutes.
57 Like their ancestors they were disloyal
    and faithless,
        as unreliable as a faulty bow.
58 They angered him with their high places;
        they aroused his jealousy with their
        idols.
59 When God heard them, he was furious;
        he rejected Israel completely.
60 He abandoned the tabernacle of Shiloh,
        the tent he had set up among humans.
61 He sent the ark of his might into captivity,
        his splendor into the hands of the
        enemy.
62 He gave his people over to the sword;
        he was furious with his inheritance.
63 Fire consumed their young men,
        and their young women had no
        wedding songs;
64 their priests were put to the sword,
        and their widows could not weep.

65 Then the Lord awoke as from sleep,
        as a warrior wakes from the stupor
        of wine.
66 He beat back his enemies;
        he put them to everlasting shame.
67 Then he rejected the tents of Joseph,
        he did not choose the tribe of
        Ephraim;
68 but he chose the tribe of Judah,
        Mount Zion, which he loved.
69 He built his sanctuary like the heights,
        like the earth that he established
        forever.
70 He chose David his servant
        and took him from the sheep pens;
71 from tending the sheep he brought him
        to be the shepherd of his people Jacob,
        of Israel his inheritance.
72 And David shepherded them with
        integrity of heart;
        with skillful hands he led them.

Psalm 79

A psalm of Asaph.

[1] O God, the nations have invaded your
  inheritance;
  they have defiled your holy temple,
  they have reduced Jerusalem to
  rubble.
[2] They have left the dead bodies of your
  servants
  as food for the birds of the sky,
  the flesh of your own people for the
  animals of the wild.
[3] They have poured out blood like water
  all around Jerusalem,
  and there is no one to bury the dead.
[4] We are objects of contempt to our
  neighbors,
  of scorn and derision to those
  around us.

[5] How long, LORD? Will you be angry
  forever?
  How long will your jealousy burn
  like fire?
[6] Pour out your wrath on the nations
  that do not acknowledge you,
  on the kingdoms
  that do not call on your name;
[7] for they have devoured Jacob
  and devastated his homeland.

[8] Do not hold against us the sins of past
  generations;
  may your mercy come quickly to
  meet us,
  for we are in desperate need.
[9] Help us, God our Savior,
  for the glory of your name;
  deliver us and forgive our sins
  for your name's sake.
[10] Why should the nations say,
  "Where is their God?"

  Before our eyes, make known among the
  nations
  that you avenge the outpoured blood
  of your servants.
[11] May the groans of the prisoners come
  before you;
  with your strong arm preserve those
  condemned to die.
[12] Pay back into the laps of our neighbors
  seven times

the contempt they have hurled at
  you, Lord.
[13] Then we your people, the sheep of your
  pasture,
  will praise you forever;
  from generation to generation
  we will proclaim your praise.

Psalm 80[a]

For the director of music. To the tune of
"The Lilies of the Covenant." Of Asaph. A psalm.

[1] Hear us, Shepherd of Israel,
  you who lead Joseph like a flock.
  You who sit enthroned between the
  cherubim,
  shine forth [2] before Ephraim,
  Benjamin and Manasseh.
  Awaken your might;
  come and save us.

[3] Restore us, O God;
  make your face shine on us,
  that we may be saved.

[4] How long, LORD God Almighty,
  will your anger smolder
  against the prayers of your people?
[5] You have fed them with the bread of
  tears;
  you have made them drink tears by
  the bowlful.
[6] You have made us an object of derision[b]
  to our neighbors,
  and our enemies mock us.

[7] Restore us, God Almighty;
  make your face shine on us,
  that we may be saved.

[8] You transplanted a vine from Egypt;
  you drove out the nations and
  planted it.
[9] You cleared the ground for it,
  and it took root and filled the land.
[10] The mountains were covered with its
  shade,
  the mighty cedars with its branches.
[11] Its branches reached as far as the Sea,[c]
  its shoots as far as the River.[d]
[12] Why have you broken down its walls
  so that all who pass by pick its grapes?
[13] Boars from the forest ravage it,
  and insects from the fields feed on it.

---

[a] In Hebrew texts 80:1-19 is numbered 80:2-20.   [b] 6 Probable reading of the original Hebrew text;
Masoretic Text *contention*   [c] 11 Probably the Mediterranean   [d] 11 That is, the Euphrates

¹⁴ Return to us, God Almighty!
  Look down from heaven and see!
Watch over this vine,
¹⁵   the root your right hand has planted,
    the son*a* you have raised up for
      yourself.

¹⁶ Your vine is cut down, it is burned with
    fire;
  at your rebuke your people perish.
¹⁷ Let your hand rest on the man at your
    right hand,
  the son of man you have raised up for
    yourself.
¹⁸ Then we will not turn away from you;
  revive us, and we will call on your
    name.

¹⁹ Restore us, LORD God Almighty;
  make your face shine on us,
  that we may be saved.

Psalm 81*b*

For the director of music. According to gittith.*c*
  Of Asaph.

¹ Sing for joy to God our strength;
  shout aloud to the God of Jacob!
² Begin the music, strike the timbrel,
  play the melodious harp and lyre.

³ Sound the ram's horn at the New Moon,
  and when the moon is full, on the day
    of our festival;
⁴ this is a decree for Israel,
  an ordinance of the God of Jacob.
⁵ When God went out against Egypt,
  he established it as a statute for
    Joseph.

I heard an unknown voice say:

⁶ "I removed the burden from their
    shoulders;
  their hands were set free from the
    basket.
⁷ In your distress you called and I rescued
    you,
  I answered you out of a thundercloud;
  I tested you at the waters of Meribah.*d*
⁸ Hear me, my people, and I will warn
    you —
  if you would only listen to me, Israel!
⁹ You shall have no foreign god among you;

you shall not worship any god other
    than me.
¹⁰ I am the LORD your God,
  who brought you up out of Egypt.
  Open wide your mouth and I will fill it.

¹¹ "But my people would not listen to me;
  Israel would not submit to me.
¹² So I gave them over to their stubborn
    hearts
  to follow their own devices.

¹³ "If my people would only listen to me,
  if Israel would only follow my ways,
¹⁴ how quickly I would subdue their
    enemies
  and turn my hand against their foes!
¹⁵ Those who hate the LORD would cringe
    before him,
  and their punishment would last
    forever.
¹⁶ But you would be fed with the finest of
    wheat;
  with honey from the rock I would
    satisfy you."

Psalm 82

A psalm of Asaph.

¹ God presides in the great assembly;
  he renders judgment among the "gods":

² "How long will you*e* defend the unjust
  and show partiality to the wicked?*d*
³ Defend the weak and the fatherless;
  uphold the cause of the poor and the
    oppressed.
⁴ Rescue the weak and the needy;
  deliver them from the hand of the
    wicked.

⁵ "The 'gods' know nothing, they
    understand nothing.
  They walk about in darkness;
  all the foundations of the earth are
    shaken.

⁶ "I said, 'You are "gods";
  you are all sons of the Most High.'
⁷ But you will die like mere mortals;
  you will fall like every other ruler."

⁸ Rise up, O God, judge the earth,
  for all the nations are your
    inheritance.

---

a 15 Or *branch*   *b* In Hebrew texts 81:1-16 is numbered 81:2-17.   *c* Title: Probably a musical term
d 7,2 The Hebrew has *Selah* (a word of uncertain meaning) here.   *e* 2 The Hebrew is plural.

FILL UP

READ: **PSALM 81:10**

My car ran out of gas a while back. I knew it was running low, yet I kept driving around, thinking prices would drop a penny or two if I held out. Eventually, the car wheezed to a stop. I climbed out seething with anger. But I wasn't mad at myself, I was angry at my car.

I slammed its door to let it know how I felt. I kicked its tire to express my disappointment. How could the car do this to me? I know that's ridiculous, but we all have our irrational moments. It's irrational to expect a car to do what it was never designed to do. It's just as irrational to become upset at someone else for failing to give us happiness and satisfaction that it's not in their power to give.

BUILDING

FAITH

WISDOM

STRENGTH

If I am constantly critical of others for the emptiness I feel or if I am always giving the ones I love a hard time for not meeting my needs, it's most likely because I'm asking them to do something they weren't made to do. They can give me love and happiness, but there's a deeper satisfaction and contentment that must come from God alone. Criticism often marks our families and relationships because we want someone to do for us what only God can do and they are always falling short.

We can't expect things or people to fill a God-shaped void.

Taken from *Gods at War Student Edition* by Kyle Idleman, copyright © 2014 by City on a Hill Studio, LLC, published by Zondervan.

Psalm 83[a]

A song. A psalm of Asaph.

[1] O God, do not remain silent;
  do not turn a deaf ear,
  do not stand aloof, O God.
[2] See how your enemies growl,
  how your foes rear their heads.
[3] With cunning they conspire against your
    people;
  they plot against those you cherish.
[4] "Come," they say, "let us destroy them as
    a nation,
  so that Israel's name is remembered
    no more."

[5] With one mind they plot together;
  they form an alliance against you —
[6] the tents of Edom and the Ishmaelites,
  of Moab and the Hagrites,
[7] Byblos, Ammon and Amalek,
  Philistia, with the people of Tyre.
[8] Even Assyria has joined them
  to reinforce Lot's descendants.[b]

[9] Do to them as you did to Midian,
  as you did to Sisera and Jabin at the
    river Kishon,
[10] who perished at Endor
  and became like dung on the ground.
[11] Make their nobles like Oreb and Zeeb,
  all their princes like Zebah and
    Zalmunna,
[12] who said, "Let us take possession
  of the pasturelands of God."

[13] Make them like tumbleweed, my God,
  like chaff before the wind.
[14] As fire consumes the forest
  or a flame sets the mountains
    ablaze,
[15] so pursue them with your tempest
  and terrify them with your storm.
[16] Cover their faces with shame, LORD,
  so that they will seek your name.

[17] May they ever be ashamed and
    dismayed;
  may they perish in disgrace.
[18] Let them know that you, whose name is
    the LORD —

that you alone are the Most High over
  all the earth.

Psalm 84[c]

For the director of music.
According to gittith.[d] *Of the Sons of Korah.*
A psalm.

[1] How lovely is your dwelling place,
  LORD Almighty!
[2] My soul yearns, even faints,
  for the courts of the LORD;
  my heart and my flesh cry out
  for the living God.
[3] Even the sparrow has found a home,
  and the swallow a nest for herself,
  where she may have her young —
  a place near your altar,
  LORD Almighty, my King and my God.
[4] Blessed are those who dwell in your
    house;
  they are ever praising you.[e]

[5] Blessed are those whose strength is
    in you,
  whose hearts are set on pilgrimage.
[6] As they pass through the Valley of Baka,
  they make it a place of springs;
  the autumn rains also cover it with
    pools.[f]
[7] They go from strength to strength,
  till each appears before God in Zion.

[8] Hear my prayer, LORD God Almighty;
  listen to me, God of Jacob.
[9] Look on our shield,[g] O God;
  look with favor on your anointed
    one.

[10] Better is one day in your courts
  than a thousand elsewhere;
  I would rather be a doorkeeper in the
    house of my God
  than dwell in the tents of the wicked.
[11] For the LORD God is a sun and shield;
  the LORD bestows favor and honor;
  no good thing does he withhold
  from those whose walk is blameless.

[12] LORD Almighty,
  blessed is the one who trusts in you.

---

[a] In Hebrew texts 83:1-18 is numbered 83:2-19.   [b] 8 The Hebrew has *Selah* (a word of uncertain
meaning) here.   [c] In Hebrew texts 84:1-12 is numbered 84:2-13.   [d] Title: Probably a musical term
[e] 4 The Hebrew has *Selah* (a word of uncertain meaning) here and at the end of verse 8.   [f] 6 Or *blessings*
[g] 9 Or *sovereign*

BIGGER AND BETTER THINGS

READ: PSALM 83:1

There's no worse sensation than feeling like God is standing in some far-off corner of the universe with his back turned to you and his hands plugging his ears, ignoring your desperate prayers.

In Psalm 83 Asaph writes of growling enemies who form cunning conspiracies to destroy God's people. He names all the surrounding nations as allies in a plot against the Lord. He pleads for God to blow them away like tumbleweed, and he wants everyone to know the Most High rules the entire earth. And as Asaph waits for an answer, he worries that God isn't listening.

You can be sure that the Lord hears your prayers. Psalm 116:1 shouts, "I love the LORD, for he heard my voice." Not only does he hear your prayers, but his answers are superior to anything you can ask. They're more immense than your biggest dreams. Ephesians 3:20 praises God as the one "who is able to do immeasurably more than all we ask or imagine."

That same verse adds an intriguing twist. The Lord does bigger and better things "according to his power that is at work within us." You might be waiting for God to alter your situation. Yet he might be working to change something about you. As you glance around for the Lord's answers to your prayers, don't just look outside. Check what he's doing inside too.

BUILDING
FAITH
WISDOM
STRENGTH

Psalm 85[a]

For the director of music.
Of the Sons of Korah. A psalm.

[1] You, LORD, showed favor to your land;
    you restored the fortunes of Jacob.
[2] You forgave the iniquity of your people
    and covered all their sins.[b]
[3] You set aside all your wrath
    and turned from your fierce anger.

[4] Restore us again, God our Savior,
    and put away your displeasure toward
        us.
[5] Will you be angry with us forever?
    Will you prolong your anger through
        all generations?
[6] Will you not revive us again,
    that your people may rejoice in you?
[7] Show us your unfailing love, LORD,
    and grant us your salvation.

[8] I will listen to what God the LORD says;
    he promises peace to his people, his
        faithful servants—
    but let them not turn to folly.
[9] Surely his salvation is near those who
        fear him,
    that his glory may dwell in our land.

[10] Love and faithfulness meet together;
    righteousness and peace kiss each
        other.
[11] Faithfulness springs forth from the earth,
    and righteousness looks down from
        heaven.
[12] The LORD will indeed give what is good,
    and our land will yield its harvest.
[13] Righteousness goes before him
    and prepares the way for his steps.

Psalm 86

A prayer of David.

[1] Hear me, LORD, and answer me,
    for I am poor and needy.
[2] Guard my life, for I am faithful to you;
    save your servant who trusts in you.
    You are my God; [3] have mercy on me,
        Lord,
    for I call to you all day long.
[4] Bring joy to your servant, Lord,
    for I put my trust in you.

[5] You, Lord, are forgiving and good,
    abounding in love to all who call
        to you.
[6] Hear my prayer, LORD;
    listen to my cry for mercy.
[7] When I am in distress, I call to you,
    because you answer me.

[8] Among the gods there is none like
        you, Lord;
    no deeds can compare with yours.
[9] All the nations you have made
    will come and worship before you, Lord;
    they will bring glory to your name.
[10] For you are great and do marvelous
        deeds;
    you alone are God.

[11] Teach me your way, LORD,
    that I may rely on your faithfulness;
    give me an undivided heart,
    that I may fear your name.
[12] I will praise you, Lord my God, with all
        my heart;
    I will glorify your name forever.
[13] For great is your love toward me;
    you have delivered me from the
        depths,
    from the realm of the dead.

[14] Arrogant foes are attacking me, O God;
    ruthless people are trying to kill me—
    they have no regard for you.
[15] But you, Lord, are a compassionate and
        gracious God,
    slow to anger, abounding in love and
        faithfulness.
[16] Turn to me and have mercy on me;
    show your strength in behalf of your
        servant;
    save me, because I serve you
    just as my mother did.
[17] Give me a sign of your goodness,
    that my enemies may see it and be put
        to shame,
    for you, LORD, have helped me and
        comforted me.

Psalm 87

Of the Sons of Korah. A psalm. A song.

[1] He has founded his city on the holy
        mountain.

---

[a] In Hebrew texts 85:1-13 is numbered 85:2-14.   [b] 2   The Hebrew has *Selah* (a word of uncertain
meaning) here.

² The Lord loves the gates of Zion
    more than all the other dwellings of
        Jacob.

³ Glorious things are said of you,
    city of God:[a]
⁴ "I will record Rahab[b] and Babylon
    among those who acknowledge me—
Philistia too, and Tyre, along with
        Cush[c]—
    and will say, 'This one was born in
        Zion.'"[d]
⁵ Indeed, of Zion it will be said,
    "This one and that one were born in
        her,
    and the Most High himself will
        establish her."
⁶ The Lord will write in the register of the
        peoples:
    "This one was born in Zion."

⁷ As they make music they will sing,
    "All my fountains are in you."

Psalm 88[e]

*A song. A psalm of the Sons of Korah. For the
director of music. According to* mahalath
leannoth.[f] *A* maskil[g] *of Heman the Ezrahite.*

¹ Lord, you are the God who saves me;
    day and night I cry out to you.
² May my prayer come before you;
    turn your ear to my cry.

³ I am overwhelmed with troubles
    and my life draws near to death.
⁴ I am counted among those who go down
        to the pit;
    I am like one without strength.
⁵ I am set apart with the dead,
    like the slain who lie in the grave,
whom you remember no more,
    who are cut off from your care.

⁶ You have put me in the lowest pit,
    in the darkest depths.
⁷ Your wrath lies heavily on me;
    you have overwhelmed me with all
        your waves.[h]

⁸ You have taken from me my closest
        friends
    and have made me repulsive to them.
    I am confined and cannot escape;
⁹   my eyes are dim with grief.

    I call to you, Lord, every day;
    I spread out my hands to you.
¹⁰ Do you show your wonders to the dead?
    Do their spirits rise up and praise you?
¹¹ Is your love declared in the grave,
    your faithfulness in Destruction[i]?
¹² Are your wonders known in the place of
        darkness,
    or your righteous deeds in the land of
        oblivion?

¹³ But I cry to you for help, Lord;
    in the morning my prayer comes
        before you.
¹⁴ Why, Lord, do you reject me
    and hide your face from me?

¹⁵ From my youth I have suffered and been
        close to death;
    I have borne your terrors and am in
        despair.
¹⁶ Your wrath has swept over me;
    your terrors have destroyed me.
¹⁷ All day long they surround me like a
        flood;
    they have completely engulfed me.
¹⁸ You have taken from me friend and
        neighbor—
    darkness is my closest friend.

Psalm 89[j]

A maskil[g] *of Ethan the Ezrahite.*

¹ I will sing of the Lord's great love forever;
    with my mouth I will make your
        faithfulness known
    through all generations.
² I will declare that your love stands firm
        forever,
    that you have established your
        faithfulness in heaven itself.
³ You said, "I have made a covenant with
        my chosen one,

---

[a] 3 The Hebrew has *Selah* (a word of uncertain meaning) here and at the end of verse 6.   [b] 4 A poetic
name for Egypt   [c] 4 That is, the upper Nile region   [d] 4 Or *"I will record concerning those who
acknowledge me: / 'This one was born in Zion.' / Hear this, Rahab and Babylon, / and you too, Philistia, Tyre
and Cush."*   [e] In Hebrew texts 88:1-18 is numbered 88:2-19.   [f] Title: Possibly a tune, "The Suffering of
Affliction"   [g] Title: Probably a literary or musical term   [h] 7 The Hebrew has *Selah* (a word of
uncertain meaning) here and at the end of verse 10.   [i] 11 Hebrew *Abaddon*   [j] In Hebrew texts 89:1-52
is numbered 89:2-53.

I have sworn to David my servant,
⁴'I will establish your line forever
and make your throne firm through all
generations.'"ᵃ

⁵The heavens praise your wonders, LORD,
your faithfulness too, in the assembly
of the holy ones.
⁶For who in the skies above can compare
with the LORD?
Who is like the LORD among the
heavenly beings?
⁷In the council of the holy ones God is
greatly feared;
he is more awesome than all who
surround him.
⁸Who is like you, LORD God Almighty?
You, LORD, are mighty, and your
faithfulness surrounds you.

⁹You rule over the surging sea;
when its waves mount up, you still
them.
¹⁰You crushed Rahab like one of the slain;
with your strong arm you scattered
your enemies.
¹¹The heavens are yours, and yours also
the earth;
you founded the world and all that
is in it.
¹²You created the north and the south;
Tabor and Hermon sing for joy at your
name.
¹³Your arm is endowed with power;
your hand is strong, your right hand
exalted.

¹⁴Righteousness and justice are the
foundation of your throne;
love and faithfulness go before you.
¹⁵Blessed are those who have learned to
acclaim you,
who walk in the light of your presence,
LORD.
¹⁶They rejoice in your name all day long;
they celebrate your righteousness.
¹⁷For you are their glory and strength,
and by your favor you exalt our horn.ᵇ
¹⁸Indeed, our shieldᶜ belongs to the LORD,
our king to the Holy One of Israel.

¹⁹Once you spoke in a vision,
to your faithful people you said:

"I have bestowed strength on a warrior;
I have raised up a young man from
among the people.
²⁰I have found David my servant;
with my sacred oil I have anointed him.
²¹My hand will sustain him;
surely my arm will strengthen him.
²²The enemy will not get the better of him;
the wicked will not oppress him.
²³I will crush his foes before him
and strike down his adversaries.
²⁴My faithful love will be with him,
and through my name his hornᵈ will
be exalted.
²⁵I will set his hand over the sea,
his right hand over the rivers.
²⁶He will call out to me, 'You are my Father,
my God, the Rock my Savior.'
²⁷And I will appoint him to be my firstborn,
the most exalted of the kings of the
earth.
²⁸I will maintain my love to him forever,
and my covenant with him will
never fail.
²⁹I will establish his line forever,
his throne as long as the heavens
endure.

³⁰"If his sons forsake my law
and do not follow my statutes,
³¹if they violate my decrees
and fail to keep my commands,
³²I will punish their sin with the rod,
their iniquity with flogging;
³³but I will not take my love from him,
nor will I ever betray my faithfulness.
³⁴I will not violate my covenant
or alter what my lips have uttered.
³⁵Once for all, I have sworn by my
holiness—
and I will not lie to David—
³⁶that his line will continue forever
and his throne endure before me like
the sun;
³⁷it will be established forever like the
moon,
the faithful witness in the sky."

³⁸But you have rejected, you have
spurned,
you have been very angry with your
anointed one.

ᵃ 4 The Hebrew has *Selah* (a word of uncertain meaning) here and at the end of verses 37, 45 and 48.
ᵇ 17 *Horn* here symbolizes strong one.   ᶜ 18 Or *sovereign*   ᵈ 24 *Horn* here symbolizes strength.

DIG IN

READ: PSALM 89:9

The Bible sometimes makes you feel like you're on the outside of an inside joke. Or you're part of a whispered conversation you're sure was intended to exclude you. You can scratch your head about what the Lord intended to say through Scripture, or you can try to solve the book's puzzles.

This passage starts with words able to boost your worst day. What's not to like about a God who rules the surging sea? He flattens waves that threaten to drown you. But what's the point about Rahab? Maybe you remember Rahab as a prostitute who bravely helped two Israelite spies escape their enemies in Joshua 2:1–24. But that's not the Rahab mentioned here, because the spelling is different in the Hebrew language used to write the Old Testament. This Rahab happens to be a symbolic name for Egypt (Psalm 87:4). So this song celebrates God crushing a nation that forced his people into slavery.

BUILDING

FAITH

WISDOM

STRENGTH

Then there's "Tabor" and "Hermon." Those names sound like long-lost great uncles, but they're actually mountains significant in Israel's history, with Hermon the likely site of Jesus' transfiguration (Matthew 17:1). These peaks show off God's enormous power.

It's easy to skip parts of the Bible you don't understand. But you can ask a pastor where to find a solid Bible dictionary. Or look for resources online. Easy digging often lets you track with the action.

³⁹ You have renounced the covenant with
your servant
and have defiled his crown in the
dust.
⁴⁰ You have broken through all his walls
and reduced his strongholds to ruins.
⁴¹ All who pass by have plundered him;
he has become the scorn of his
neighbors.
⁴² You have exalted the right hand of his foes;
you have made all his enemies rejoice.
⁴³ Indeed, you have turned back the edge of
his sword
and have not supported him in battle.
⁴⁴ You have put an end to his splendor
and cast his throne to the ground.
⁴⁵ You have cut short the days of his youth;
you have covered him with a mantle
of shame.

⁴⁶ How long, Lord? Will you hide yourself
forever?
How long will your wrath burn like fire?
⁴⁷ Remember how fleeting is my life.
For what futility you have created all
humanity!
⁴⁸ Who can live and not see death,
or who can escape the power of the
grave?
⁴⁹ Lord, where is your former great love,
which in your faithfulness you swore
to David?
⁵⁰ Remember, Lord, how your servant has^a
been mocked,
how I bear in my heart the taunts of all
the nations,
⁵¹ the taunts with which your enemies,
Lord, have mocked,
with which they have mocked every
step of your anointed one.

⁵² Praise be to the Lord forever!
Amen and Amen.

BOOK IV

Psalms 90–106

Psalm 90

A prayer of Moses the man of God.

¹ Lord, you have been our dwelling place
throughout all generations.

² Before the mountains were born
or you brought forth the whole world,
from everlasting to everlasting you
are God.

³ You turn people back to dust,
saying, "Return to dust, you mortals."
⁴ A thousand years in your sight
are like a day that has just gone by,
or like a watch in the night.
⁵ Yet you sweep people away in the sleep of
death—
they are like the new grass of the
morning:
⁶ In the morning it springs up new,
but by evening it is dry and withered.

⁷ We are consumed by your anger
and terrified by your indignation.
⁸ You have set our iniquities before you,
our secret sins in the light of your
presence.
⁹ All our days pass away under your wrath;
we finish our years with a moan.
¹⁰ Our days may come to seventy years,
or eighty, if our strength endures;
yet the best of them are but trouble and
sorrow,
for they quickly pass, and we fly away.
¹¹ If only we knew the power of your anger!
Your wrath is as great as the fear that is
your due.
¹² Teach us to number our days,
that we may gain a heart of wisdom.

¹³ Relent, Lord! How long will it be?
Have compassion on your servants.
¹⁴ Satisfy us in the morning with your
unfailing love,
that we may sing for joy and be glad all
our days.
¹⁵ Make us glad for as many days as you
have afflicted us,
for as many years as we have seen
trouble.
¹⁶ May your deeds be shown to your
servants,
your splendor to their children.

¹⁷ May the favor^b of the Lord our God rest
on us;
establish the work of our hands
for us—
yes, establish the work of our hands.

---

^a 50 Or *your servants have*   ^b 17 Or *beauty*

Psalm 91

¹ Whoever dwells in the shelter of the
  Most High
    will rest in the shadow of the
    Almighty.ᵃ
² I will say of the LORD, "He is my refuge
  and my fortress,
    my God, in whom I trust."

³ Surely he will save you
  from the fowler's snare
  and from the deadly pestilence.
⁴ He will cover you with his feathers,
  and under his wings you will find
    refuge;
    his faithfulness will be your shield and
    rampart.
⁵ You will not fear the terror of night,
  nor the arrow that flies by day,
⁶ nor the pestilence that stalks in the
    darkness,
  nor the plague that destroys at midday.
⁷ A thousand may fall at your side,
  ten thousand at your right hand,
  but it will not come near you.
⁸ You will only observe with your eyes
  and see the punishment of the wicked.

⁹ If you say, "The LORD is my refuge,"
  and you make the Most High your
    dwelling,
¹⁰ no harm will overtake you,
  no disaster will come near your tent.
¹¹ For he will command his angels
    concerning you
  to guard you in all your ways;
¹² they will lift you up in their hands,
  so that you will not strike your foot
    against a stone.
¹³ You will tread on the lion and the cobra;
  you will trample the great lion and the
    serpent.

¹⁴ "Because heᵇ loves me," says the LORD, "I
    will rescue him;
  I will protect him, for he acknowledges
    my name.
¹⁵ He will call on me, and I will answer him;
  I will be with him in trouble,
  I will deliver him and honor him.
¹⁶ With long life I will satisfy him
  and show him my salvation."

Psalm 92ᶜ

A psalm. A song. For the Sabbath day.

¹ It is good to praise the LORD
  and make music to your name,
    O Most High,
² proclaiming your love in the morning
  and your faithfulness at night,
³ to the music of the ten-stringed lyre
  and the melody of the harp.

⁴ For you make me glad by your deeds,
    LORD;
  I sing for joy at what your hands have
    done.
⁵ How great are your works, LORD,
  how profound your thoughts!
⁶ Senseless people do not know,
  fools do not understand,
⁷ that though the wicked spring up like
    grass
  and all evildoers flourish,
  they will be destroyed forever.

⁸ But you, LORD, are forever exalted.

⁹ For surely your enemies, LORD,
  surely your enemies will perish;
  all evildoers will be scattered.
¹⁰ You have exalted my hornᵈ like that of
    a wild ox;
  fine oils have been poured on me.
¹¹ My eyes have seen the defeat of my
    adversaries;
  my ears have heard the rout of my
    wicked foes.

¹² The righteous will flourish like a palm
    tree,
  they will grow like a cedar of Lebanon;
¹³ planted in the house of the LORD,
  they will flourish in the courts of
    our God.
¹⁴ They will still bear fruit in old age,
  they will stay fresh and green,
¹⁵ proclaiming, "The LORD is upright;
  he is my Rock, and there is no
    wickedness in him."

Psalm 93

¹ The LORD reigns, he is robed in majesty;
  the LORD is robed in majesty and
    armed with strength;

ᵃ 1 Hebrew *Shaddai*   ᵇ 14 That is, probably the king   ᶜ In Hebrew texts 92:1-15 is numbered 92:2-16.
ᵈ 10 *Horn* here symbolizes strength.

POETIC EXPRESSION

READ: PSALM 91:4

Scriptural poetry gives us the words Jewish people prayed and sang. While this verse is about a literal God who provides real safety, God does not literally have wings. Three common-sense rules of poetry interpretation will guide you to read poetry better.

1. Tools of poetic interpretation teach us to expect imagery, metaphor, simile, and so on. Feathers and wings describe God with a word picture. David's metaphor paints a living picture of how he feels protected and sheltered by God's care.

2. Much biblical poetry is emotional. We must read it again and again, getting into the shoes of the writer, if we want to understand the feelings of the poet. Biblical poetry demonstrates that human joy, fear, delight, depression, sexual passion, and even rage are appropriate topics about which to speak to God. Some of Jesus' last words before death echoed Psalm 22, revealing that our Savior relied on poetry to express his own pain.

3. Poetry is honest. Look for surprising, shocking bits of real people crafting their feelings into beautiful stanzas. While almost every biblical book includes poetic songs, noted by indentations or stanzas such as Miriam's song in Exodus 15, the Beatitudes in Matthew 5, and the poetic creed in Philippians 2:5–11, you can find concentrated sections of poetry in the Psalms, parts of Job, Song of Songs, and Lamentations.

BUILDING

FAITH

WISDOM

STRENGTH

Taken from *Coffee Shop Conversations* by Dale Fincher and Jonalyn Fincher, copyright © 2010 by Charles Dale Fincher and Jonalyn Grace Fincher, published by Zondervan.

indeed, the world is established, firm
and secure.
2 Your throne was established long ago;
you are from all eternity.

3 The seas have lifted up, LORD,
the seas have lifted up their voice;
the seas have lifted up their pounding
waves.
4 Mightier than the thunder of the great
waters,
mightier than the breakers of the
sea—
the LORD on high is mighty.

5 Your statutes, LORD, stand firm;
holiness adorns your house
for endless days.

Psalm 94

1 The LORD is a God who avenges.
O God who avenges, shine forth.
2 Rise up, Judge of the earth;
pay back to the proud what they
deserve.
3 How long, LORD, will the wicked,
how long will the wicked be jubilant?

4 They pour out arrogant words;
all the evildoers are full of boasting.
5 They crush your people, LORD;
they oppress your inheritance.
6 They slay the widow and the foreigner;
they murder the fatherless.
7 They say, "The LORD does not see;
the God of Jacob takes no notice."

8 Take notice, you senseless ones among
the people;
you fools, when will you become wise?
9 Does he who fashioned the ear not hear?
Does he who formed the eye not see?
10 Does he who disciplines nations not
punish?
Does he who teaches mankind lack
knowledge?
11 The LORD knows all human plans;
he knows that they are futile.

12 Blessed is the one you discipline, LORD,
the one you teach from your law;
13 you grant them relief from days of
trouble,
till a pit is dug for the wicked.
14 For the LORD will not reject his people;
he will never forsake his inheritance.

15 Judgment will again be founded on
righteousness,
and all the upright in heart will
follow it.

16 Who will rise up for me against the
wicked?
Who will take a stand for me against
evildoers?
17 Unless the LORD had given me help,
I would soon have dwelt in the silence
of death.
18 When I said, "My foot is slipping,"
your unfailing love, LORD,
supported me.
19 When anxiety was great within me,
your consolation brought me joy.

20 Can a corrupt throne be allied with
you—
a throne that brings on misery by its
decrees?
21 The wicked band together against the
righteous
and condemn the innocent to death.
22 But the LORD has become my fortress,
and my God the rock in whom I take
refuge.
23 He will repay them for their sins
and destroy them for their
wickedness;
the LORD our God will destroy them.

Psalm 95

1 Come, let us sing for joy to the LORD;
let us shout aloud to the Rock of our
salvation.
2 Let us come before him with
thanksgiving
and extol him with music and song.

3 For the LORD is the great God,
the great King above all gods.
4 In his hand are the depths of the earth,
and the mountain peaks belong to
him.
5 The sea is his, for he made it,
and his hands formed the dry land.

6 Come, let us bow down in worship,
let us kneel before the LORD our
Maker;
7 for he is our God
and we are the people of his pasture,
the flock under his care.

Today, if only you would hear his voice,
⁸ "Do not harden your hearts as you did at
Meribah,ᵃ
as you did that day at Massahᵇ in the
wilderness,
⁹ where your ancestors tested me;
they tried me, though they had seen
what I did.
¹⁰ For forty years I was angry with that
generation;
I said, 'They are a people whose hearts
go astray,
and they have not known my ways.'
¹¹ So I declared on oath in my anger,
'They shall never enter my rest.'"

Psalm 96

¹ Sing to the Lᴏʀᴅ a new song;
sing to the Lᴏʀᴅ, all the earth.
² Sing to the Lᴏʀᴅ, praise his name;
proclaim his salvation day after day.
³ Declare his glory among the nations,
his marvelous deeds among all peoples.

⁴ For great is the Lᴏʀᴅ and most worthy of
praise;
he is to be feared above all gods.
⁵ For all the gods of the nations are idols,
but the Lᴏʀᴅ made the heavens.
⁶ Splendor and majesty are before him;
strength and glory are in his
sanctuary.

⁷ Ascribe to the Lᴏʀᴅ, all you families of
nations,
ascribe to the Lᴏʀᴅ glory and strength.
⁸ Ascribe to the Lᴏʀᴅ the glory due his
name;
bring an offering and come into his
courts.
⁹ Worship the Lᴏʀᴅ in the splendor of hisᶜ
holiness;
tremble before him, all the earth.
¹⁰ Say among the nations, "The Lᴏʀᴅ
reigns."
The world is firmly established, it
cannot be moved;
he will judge the peoples with equity.

¹¹ Let the heavens rejoice, let the earth
be glad;
let the sea resound, and all that is in it.

¹² Let the fields be jubilant, and everything
in them;
let all the trees of the forest sing for joy.
¹³ Let all creation rejoice before the Lᴏʀᴅ,
for he comes,
he comes to judge the earth.
He will judge the world in righteousness
and the peoples in his faithfulness.

Psalm 97

¹ The Lᴏʀᴅ reigns, let the earth be glad;
let the distant shores rejoice.
² Clouds and thick darkness surround
him;
righteousness and justice are the
foundation of his throne.
³ Fire goes before him
and consumes his foes on every side.
⁴ His lightning lights up the world;
the earth sees and trembles.
⁵ The mountains melt like wax before the
Lᴏʀᴅ,
before the Lord of all the earth.
⁶ The heavens proclaim his righteousness,
and all peoples see his glory.

⁷ All who worship images are put to shame,
those who boast in idols—
worship him, all you gods!

⁸ Zion hears and rejoices
and the villages of Judah are glad
because of your judgments, Lᴏʀᴅ.
⁹ For you, Lᴏʀᴅ, are the Most High over all
the earth;
you are exalted far above all gods.
¹⁰ Let those who love the Lᴏʀᴅ hate evil,
for he guards the lives of his faithful
ones
and delivers them from the hand of the
wicked.
¹¹ Light shinesᵈ on the righteous
and joy on the upright in heart.
¹² Rejoice in the Lᴏʀᴅ, you who are
righteous,
and praise his holy name.

Psalm 98

A psalm.

¹ Sing to the Lᴏʀᴅ a new song,
for he has done marvelous things;

ᵃ *8* Meribah means *quarreling.*   ᵇ *8* Massah means *testing.*   ᶜ *9* Or Lᴏʀᴅ *with the splendor of*   ᵈ *11* One
Hebrew manuscript and ancient versions (see also 112:4); most Hebrew manuscripts *Light is sown*

WHAT ARE YOU WORSHIPING?

READ: PSALM 96:4-5

All of us are worshipers. Worship is hardwired into who we are. It's true of every culture and every civilization—everyone worships. When I was in college, I spent a month in Africa with a medical missions team. We went off-road and visited several tribes that had no contact with the outside world. As we entered their communities, the question was not, "Are they worshipers?" The question was, "Who or what do they worship?"

Wherever you go, you see that people have chosen. You will too. You can go to places where they have old-school idols, rituals, and sacrifices. Or you can go to the most technologically advanced cities, where folks think they're way past that "religious mumbo jumbo." But upon closer inspection you will find that they are sacrificing a great deal on the altars of power or pleasure or finance. It's really all the same. People are choosing their gods and bringing their offerings. At the end of the day, the real offering is themselves.

BUILDING

FAITH

WISDOM

STRENGTH

Here's where we get confused; in our modern thinking, we associate worship with religion. But since we all worship, everybody follows a religion. It may be the religion of pleasure or money or relationships. There are lots of options, with one exception: the option to opt out. Again, there is no box for "none of the above." So choose for yourself; otherwise, you will float through life, until you find yourself inside a temple bowing to a god you never consciously chose.

his right hand and his holy arm
   have worked salvation for him.
² The LORD has made his salvation known
   and revealed his righteousness to the
      nations.
³ He has remembered his love
   and his faithfulness to Israel;
all the ends of the earth have seen
   the salvation of our God.

⁴ Shout for joy to the LORD, all the earth,
   burst into jubilant song with music;
⁵ make music to the LORD with the harp,
   with the harp and the sound of
      singing,
⁶ with trumpets and the blast of the ram's
      horn—
   shout for joy before the LORD, the King.

⁷ Let the sea resound, and everything in it,
   the world, and all who live in it.
⁸ Let the rivers clap their hands,
   let the mountains sing together for joy;
⁹ let them sing before the LORD,
   for he comes to judge the earth.
He will judge the world in righteousness
   and the peoples with equity.

Psalm 99

¹ The LORD reigns,
   let the nations tremble;
he sits enthroned between the cherubim,
   let the earth shake.
² Great is the LORD in Zion;
   he is exalted over all the nations.
³ Let them praise your great and awesome
      name—
   he is holy.

⁴ The King is mighty, he loves justice—
   you have established equity;
in Jacob you have done
   what is just and right.
⁵ Exalt the LORD our God
   and worship at his footstool;
   he is holy.

⁶ Moses and Aaron were among his
      priests,
   Samuel was among those who called
      on his name;
they called on the LORD
   and he answered them.
⁷ He spoke to them from the pillar of cloud;

they kept his statutes and the decrees
   he gave them.
⁸ LORD our God,
   you answered them;
you were to Israel a forgiving God,
   though you punished their misdeeds.ᵃ
⁹ Exalt the LORD our God
   and worship at his holy mountain,
   for the LORD our God is holy.

Psalm 100

A psalm. For giving grateful praise.

¹ Shout for joy to the LORD, all the earth.
²   Worship the LORD with gladness;
   come before him with joyful songs.
³ Know that the LORD is God.
   It is he who made us, and we are his;ᵇ
   we are his people, the sheep of his
      pasture.

⁴ Enter his gates with thanksgiving
   and his courts with praise;
   give thanks to him and praise his
      name.
⁵ For the LORD is good and his love endures
      forever;
   his faithfulness continues through all
      generations.

Psalm 101

Of David. A psalm.

¹ I will sing of your love and justice;
   to you, LORD, I will sing praise.
² I will be careful to lead a blameless life—
   when will you come to me?

I will conduct the affairs of my house
   with a blameless heart.
³ I will not look with approval
   on anything that is vile.

I hate what faithless people do;
   I will have no part in it.
⁴ The perverse of heart shall be far from me;
   I will have nothing to do with what
      is evil.

⁵ Whoever slanders their neighbor in
      secret,
   I will put to silence;
whoever has haughty eyes and a proud
      heart,
   I will not tolerate.

ᵃ 8 Or *God, / an avenger of the wrongs done to them*   ᵇ 3 Or *and not we ourselves*

⁶My eyes will be on the faithful in the
land,
that they may dwell with me;
the one whose walk is blameless
will minister to me.

⁷No one who practices deceit
will dwell in my house;
no one who speaks falsely
will stand in my presence.

⁸Every morning I will put to silence
all the wicked in the land;
I will cut off every evildoer
from the city of the LORD.

Psalm 102ᵃ

*A prayer of an afflicted person who has grown
weak and pours out a lament before the LORD.*

¹Hear my prayer, LORD;
let my cry for help come to you.
²Do not hide your face from me
when I am in distress.
Turn your ear to me;
when I call, answer me quickly.

³For my days vanish like smoke;
my bones burn like glowing embers.
⁴My heart is blighted and withered like
grass;
I forget to eat my food.
⁵In my distress I groan aloud
and am reduced to skin and bones.
⁶I am like a desert owl,
like an owl among the ruins.
⁷I lie awake; I have become
like a bird alone on a roof.
⁸All day long my enemies taunt me;
those who rail against me use my
name as a curse.
⁹For I eat ashes as my food
and mingle my drink with tears
¹⁰because of your great wrath,
for you have taken me up and thrown
me aside.
¹¹My days are like the evening shadow;
I wither away like grass.

¹²But you, LORD, sit enthroned forever;
your renown endures through all
generations.
¹³You will arise and have compassion
on Zion,

for it is time to show favor to her;
the appointed time has come.
¹⁴For her stones are dear to your
servants;
her very dust moves them to pity.
¹⁵The nations will fear the name of the
LORD,
all the kings of the earth will revere
your glory.
¹⁶For the LORD will rebuild Zion
and appear in his glory.
¹⁷He will respond to the prayer of the
destitute;
he will not despise their plea.

¹⁸Let this be written for a future
generation,
that a people not yet created may
praise the LORD:
¹⁹"The LORD looked down from his
sanctuary on high,
from heaven he viewed the earth,
²⁰to hear the groans of the prisoners
and release those condemned to
death."
²¹So the name of the LORD will be declared
in Zion
and his praise in Jerusalem
²²when the peoples and the kingdoms
assemble to worship the LORD.

²³In the course of my lifeᵇ he broke my
strength;
he cut short my days.
²⁴So I said:
"Do not take me away, my God, in the
midst of my days;
your years go on through all
generations.
²⁵In the beginning you laid the foundations
of the earth,
and the heavens are the work of your
hands.
²⁶They will perish, but you remain;
they will all wear out like a garment.
Like clothing you will change them
and they will be discarded.
²⁷But you remain the same,
and your years will never end.
²⁸The children of your servants will live in
your presence;
their descendants will be established
before you."

ᵃ In Hebrew texts 102:1-28 is numbered 102:2-29.   ᵇ 23 Or *By his power*

Psalm 103

Of David.

¹ Praise the LORD, my soul;
    all my inmost being, praise his holy
        name.
² Praise the LORD, my soul,
    and forget not all his benefits —
³ who forgives all your sins
    and heals all your diseases,
⁴ who redeems your life from the pit
    and crowns you with love and
        compassion,
⁵ who satisfies your desires with good
        things
    so that your youth is renewed like the
        eagle's.

⁶ The LORD works righteousness
    and justice for all the oppressed.

⁷ He made known his ways to Moses,
    his deeds to the people of Israel:
⁸ The LORD is compassionate and gracious,
    slow to anger, abounding in love.
⁹ He will not always accuse,
    nor will he harbor his anger forever;
¹⁰ he does not treat us as our sins deserve
    or repay us according to our iniquities.
¹¹ For as high as the heavens are above
        the earth,
    so great is his love for those who fear
        him;
¹² as far as the east is from the west,
    so far has he removed our
        transgressions from us.

¹³ As a father has compassion on his
        children,
    so the LORD has compassion on those
        who fear him;
¹⁴ for he knows how we are formed,
    he remembers that we are dust.
¹⁵ The life of mortals is like grass,
    they flourish like a flower of the field;
¹⁶ the wind blows over it and it is gone,
    and its place remembers it no more.
¹⁷ But from everlasting to everlasting
    the LORD's love is with those who fear
        him,
    and his righteousness with their
        children's children —
¹⁸ with those who keep his covenant
    and remember to obey his precepts.

¹⁹ The LORD has established his throne
        in heaven,
    and his kingdom rules over all.

²⁰ Praise the LORD, you his angels,
    you mighty ones who do his bidding,
    who obey his word.
²¹ Praise the LORD, all his heavenly hosts,
    you his servants who do his will.
²² Praise the LORD, all his works
    everywhere in his dominion.

    Praise the LORD, my soul.

Psalm 104

¹ Praise the LORD, my soul.

    LORD my God, you are very great;
        you are clothed with splendor and
            majesty.

² The LORD wraps himself in light as with a
        garment;
    he stretches out the heavens like a tent
³   and lays the beams of his upper
        chambers on their waters.
    He makes the clouds his chariot
        and rides on the wings of the wind.
⁴ He makes winds his messengers,ᵃ
    flames of fire his servants.

⁵ He set the earth on its foundations;
    it can never be moved.
⁶ You covered it with the watery depths as
        with a garment;
    the waters stood above the mountains.
⁷ But at your rebuke the waters fled,
    at the sound of your thunder they took
        to flight;
⁸ they flowed over the mountains,
    they went down into the valleys,
    to the place you assigned for them.
⁹ You set a boundary they cannot cross;
    never again will they cover the earth.

¹⁰ He makes springs pour water into the
        ravines;
    it flows between the mountains.
¹¹ They give water to all the beasts of the
        field;
    the wild donkeys quench their thirst.
¹² The birds of the sky nest by the waters;
    they sing among the branches.
¹³ He waters the mountains from his upper
        chambers;

ᵃ 4 Or *angels*

I GOT THIS

READ: PSALM 103:12

When you make God's story yours, he covers you in Christ. You wear him like a vest. Old labels no longer apply—only labels that would be appropriately worn by Jesus Christ.

How far is the east from the west? Farther and farther by the moment. Travel west and you can make laps around the globe and never go east. Journey east and, if you desire, maintain an easterly course indefinitely.

East and west have no turning points. Neither does God. When he sends your sins to the east and you to the west, you can be sure of this: he doesn't see you in your sins. His forgiveness is irreversible.

Headline this truth: when God sees you, he sees his Son, not your sin. No probation. No exception. No reversals. He did his due diligence. He saw your secret deeds and heard your unsaid thoughts. The lies, the lusts, the longings—he knows them all. God assessed your life from first day to last, from worst moment to best, and made his decision.

BUILDING

FAITH

WISDOM

STRENGTH

"I want that child in my kingdom." You cannot convince him otherwise. Your name is written in the Book of the Lamb. Not in pencil marks that can be erased, but with blood that will not be removed. No need to keep God happy; he is satisfied. No need to pay the price; Jesus paid it. All.

Taken from *God's Story, Your Story: Youth Edition* by Max Lucado, copyright © 2011 by Max Lucado, published by Zondervan.

the land is satisfied by the fruit of
his work.
¹⁴He makes grass grow for the cattle,
and plants for people to cultivate—
bringing forth food from the earth:
¹⁵wine that gladdens human hearts,
oil to make their faces shine,
and bread that sustains their hearts.
¹⁶The trees of the Lord are well watered,
the cedars of Lebanon that he planted.
¹⁷There the birds make their nests;
the stork has its home in the junipers.
¹⁸The high mountains belong to the wild
goats;
the crags are a refuge for the hyrax.

¹⁹He made the moon to mark the seasons,
and the sun knows when to go down.
²⁰You bring darkness, it becomes night,
and all the beasts of the forest prowl.
²¹The lions roar for their prey
and seek their food from God.
²²The sun rises, and they steal away;
they return and lie down in their dens.
²³Then people go out to their work,
to their labor until evening.

²⁴How many are your works, Lord!
In wisdom you made them all;
the earth is full of your creatures.
²⁵There is the sea, vast and spacious,
teeming with creatures beyond
number—
living things both large and small.
²⁶There the ships go to and fro,
and Leviathan, which you formed to
frolic there.

²⁷All creatures look to you
to give them their food at the proper
time.
²⁸When you give it to them,
they gather it up;
when you open your hand,
they are satisfied with good things.
²⁹When you hide your face,
they are terrified;
when you take away their breath,
they die and return to the dust.
³⁰When you send your Spirit,
they are created,
and you renew the face of the ground.

³¹May the glory of the Lord endure forever;
may the Lord rejoice in his works—

³²he who looks at the earth, and it trembles,
who touches the mountains, and they
smoke.

³³I will sing to the Lord all my life;
I will sing praise to my God as long as
I live.
³⁴May my meditation be pleasing to him,
as I rejoice in the Lord.
³⁵But may sinners vanish from the earth
and the wicked be no more.

Praise the Lord, my soul.

Praise the Lord.^a

Psalm 105

¹Give praise to the Lord, proclaim his
name;
make known among the nations what
he has done.
²Sing to him, sing praise to him;
tell of all his wonderful acts.
³Glory in his holy name;
let the hearts of those who seek the
Lord rejoice.
⁴Look to the Lord and his strength;
seek his face always.

⁵Remember the wonders he has done,
his miracles, and the judgments he
pronounced,
⁶you his servants, the descendants of
Abraham,
his chosen ones, the children of Jacob.
⁷He is the Lord our God;
his judgments are in all the earth.

⁸He remembers his covenant forever,
the promise he made, for a thousand
generations,
⁹the covenant he made with Abraham,
the oath he swore to Isaac.
¹⁰He confirmed it to Jacob as a decree,
to Israel as an everlasting covenant:
¹¹"To you I will give the land of Canaan
as the portion you will inherit."

¹²When they were but few in number,
few indeed, and strangers in it,
¹³they wandered from nation to nation,
from one kingdom to another.
¹⁴He allowed no one to oppress them;
for their sake he rebuked kings:
¹⁵"Do not touch my anointed ones;
do my prophets no harm."

---

^a 35 Hebrew *Hallelu Yah*; in the Septuagint this line stands at the beginning of Psalm 105.

¹⁶ He called down famine on the land
and destroyed all their supplies
of food;
¹⁷ and he sent a man before them —
Joseph, sold as a slave.
¹⁸ They bruised his feet with shackles,
his neck was put in irons,
¹⁹ till what he foretold came to pass,
till the word of the LORD proved
him true.
²⁰ The king sent and released him,
the ruler of peoples set him free.
²¹ He made him master of his household,
ruler over all he possessed,
²² to instruct his princes as he pleased
and teach his elders wisdom.

²³ Then Israel entered Egypt;
Jacob resided as a foreigner in the land
of Ham.
²⁴ The LORD made his people very fruitful;
he made them too numerous for their
foes,
²⁵ whose hearts he turned to hate his
people,
to conspire against his servants.
²⁶ He sent Moses his servant,
and Aaron, whom he had chosen.
²⁷ They performed his signs among them,
his wonders in the land of Ham.
²⁸ He sent darkness and made the land
dark —
for had they not rebelled against his
words?
²⁹ He turned their waters into blood,
causing their fish to die.
³⁰ Their land teemed with frogs,
which went up into the bedrooms of
their rulers.
³¹ He spoke, and there came swarms of flies,
and gnats throughout their country.
³² He turned their rain into hail,
with lightning throughout their land;
³³ he struck down their vines and fig trees
and shattered the trees of their
country.
³⁴ He spoke, and the locusts came,
grasshoppers without number;
³⁵ they ate up every green thing in their land,
ate up the produce of their soil.
³⁶ Then he struck down all the firstborn in
their land,
the firstfruits of all their manhood.

³⁷ He brought out Israel, laden with silver
and gold,
and from among their tribes no one
faltered.
³⁸ Egypt was glad when they left,
because dread of Israel had fallen
on them.

³⁹ He spread out a cloud as a covering,
and a fire to give light at night.
⁴⁰ They asked, and he brought them quail;
he fed them well with the bread of
heaven.
⁴¹ He opened the rock, and water gushed
out;
it flowed like a river in the desert.

⁴² For he remembered his holy promise
given to his servant Abraham.
⁴³ He brought out his people with rejoicing,
his chosen ones with shouts of joy;
⁴⁴ he gave them the lands of the nations,
and they fell heir to what others had
toiled for —
⁴⁵ that they might keep his precepts
and observe his laws.

Praise the LORD.ᵃ

Psalm 106

¹ Praise the LORD.ᵇ

Give thanks to the LORD, for he is good;
his love endures forever.

² Who can proclaim the mighty acts of
the LORD
or fully declare his praise?
³ Blessed are those who act justly,
who always do what is right.

⁴ Remember me, LORD, when you show
favor to your people,
come to my aid when you save them,
⁵ that I may enjoy the prosperity of your
chosen ones,
that I may share in the joy of your
nation
and join your inheritance in giving
praise.

⁶ We have sinned, even as our ancestors
did;
we have done wrong and acted
wickedly.
⁷ When our ancestors were in Egypt,

ᵃ 45 Hebrew *Hallelu Yah*   ᵇ 1 Hebrew *Hallelu Yah*; also in verse 48

they gave no thought to your
    miracles;
they did not remember your many
    kindnesses,
    and they rebelled by the sea, the
        Red Sea.[a]
[8] Yet he saved them for his name's sake,
    to make his mighty power known.
[9] He rebuked the Red Sea, and it dried up;
    he led them through the depths as
        through a desert.
[10] He saved them from the hand of the foe;
    from the hand of the enemy he
        redeemed them.
[11] The waters covered their adversaries;
    not one of them survived.
[12] Then they believed his promises
    and sang his praise.

[13] But they soon forgot what he had done
    and did not wait for his plan to unfold.
[14] In the desert they gave in to their craving;
    in the wilderness they put God to
        the test.
[15] So he gave them what they asked for,
    but sent a wasting disease among them.

[16] In the camp they grew envious of Moses
    and of Aaron, who was consecrated to
        the LORD.
[17] The earth opened up and swallowed
        Dathan;
    it buried the company of Abiram.
[18] Fire blazed among their followers;
    a flame consumed the wicked.
[19] At Horeb they made a calf
    and worshiped an idol cast from metal.
[20] They exchanged their glorious God
    for an image of a bull, which eats grass.
[21] They forgot the God who saved them,
    who had done great things in Egypt,
[22] miracles in the land of Ham
    and awesome deeds by the Red Sea.
[23] So he said he would destroy them —
    had not Moses, his chosen one,
    stood in the breach before him
    to keep his wrath from destroying
        them.

[24] Then they despised the pleasant land;
    they did not believe his promise.
[25] They grumbled in their tents
    and did not obey the LORD.
[26] So he swore to them with uplifted hand

that he would make them fall in the
    wilderness,
[27] make their descendants fall among the
        nations
    and scatter them throughout the lands.

[28] They yoked themselves to the Baal of Peor
    and ate sacrifices offered to lifeless
        gods;
[29] they aroused the LORD's anger by their
        wicked deeds,
    and a plague broke out among them.
[30] But Phinehas stood up and intervened,
    and the plague was checked.
[31] This was credited to him as
        righteousness
    for endless generations to come.
[32] By the waters of Meribah they angered
        the LORD,
    and trouble came to Moses because
        of them;
[33] for they rebelled against the Spirit of God,
    and rash words came from Moses' lips.[b]

[34] They did not destroy the peoples
    as the LORD had commanded them,
[35] but they mingled with the nations
    and adopted their customs.
[36] They worshiped their idols,
    which became a snare to them.
[37] They sacrificed their sons
    and their daughters to false gods.
[38] They shed innocent blood,
    the blood of their sons and daughters,
    whom they sacrificed to the idols of
        Canaan,
    and the land was desecrated by their
        blood.
[39] They defiled themselves by what
        they did;
    by their deeds they prostituted
        themselves.

[40] Therefore the LORD was angry with his
        people
    and abhorred his inheritance.
[41] He gave them into the hands of the
        nations,
    and their foes ruled over them.
[42] Their enemies oppressed them
    and subjected them to their power.
[43] Many times he delivered them,
    but they were bent on rebellion
    and they wasted away in their sin.

---

a 7 Or *the Sea of Reeds*; also in verses 9 and 22   *b* 33 Or *against his spirit, / and rash words came from his lips*

44 Yet he took note of their distress
    when he heard their cry;
45 for their sake he remembered his
    covenant
    and out of his great love he relented.
46 He caused all who held them captive
    to show them mercy.

47 Save us, Lord our God,
    and gather us from the nations,
    that we may give thanks to your holy name
    and glory in your praise.

48 Praise be to the Lord, the God of Israel,
    from everlasting to everlasting.

Let all the people say, "Amen!"

Praise the Lord.

BOOK V

Psalms 107 – 150

Psalm 107

1 Give thanks to the Lord, for he is good;
    his love endures forever.

2 Let the redeemed of the Lord tell their
    story—
    those he redeemed from the hand of
    the foe,
3 those he gathered from the lands,
    from east and west, from north and
    south.^a

4 Some wandered in desert wastelands,
    finding no way to a city where they
    could settle.
5 They were hungry and thirsty,
    and their lives ebbed away.
6 Then they cried out to the Lord in their
    trouble,
    and he delivered them from their
    distress.
7 He led them by a straight way
    to a city where they could settle.
8 Let them give thanks to the Lord for his
    unfailing love
    and his wonderful deeds for mankind,
9 for he satisfies the thirsty
    and fills the hungry with good things.

10 Some sat in darkness, in utter darkness,
    prisoners suffering in iron chains,
11 because they rebelled against God's
    commands
    and despised the plans of the Most
    High.
12 So he subjected them to bitter labor;
    they stumbled, and there was no one
    to help.
13 Then they cried to the Lord in their
    trouble,
    and he saved them from their distress.
14 He brought them out of darkness, the
    utter darkness,
    and broke away their chains.
15 Let them give thanks to the Lord for his
    unfailing love
    and his wonderful deeds for mankind,
16 for he breaks down gates of bronze
    and cuts through bars of iron.

17 Some became fools through their
    rebellious ways
    and suffered affliction because of their
    iniquities.
18 They loathed all food
    and drew near the gates of death.
19 Then they cried to the Lord in their
    trouble,
    and he saved them from their distress.
20 He sent out his word and healed them;
    he rescued them from the grave.
21 Let them give thanks to the Lord for his
    unfailing love
    and his wonderful deeds for mankind.
22 Let them sacrifice thank offerings
    and tell of his works with songs of joy.

23 Some went out on the sea in ships;
    they were merchants on the mighty
    waters.
24 They saw the works of the Lord,
    his wonderful deeds in the deep.
25 For he spoke and stirred up a tempest
    that lifted high the waves.
26 They mounted up to the heavens and
    went down to the depths;
    in their peril their courage melted
    away.
27 They reeled and staggered like
    drunkards;
    they were at their wits' end.
28 Then they cried out to the Lord in their
    trouble,
    and he brought them out of their
    distress.

---

^a 3 Hebrew *north and the sea*

²⁹ He stilled the storm to a whisper;
   the waves of the sea^a were hushed.
³⁰ They were glad when it grew calm,
   and he guided them to their desired
      haven.
³¹ Let them give thanks to the LORD for his
      unfailing love
   and his wonderful deeds for mankind.
³² Let them exalt him in the assembly of the
      people
   and praise him in the council of the
      elders.

³³ He turned rivers into a desert,
   flowing springs into thirsty ground,
³⁴ and fruitful land into a salt waste,
   because of the wickedness of those
      who lived there.
³⁵ He turned the desert into pools of water
   and the parched ground into flowing
      springs;
³⁶ there he brought the hungry to live,
   and they founded a city where they
      could settle.
³⁷ They sowed fields and planted vineyards
   that yielded a fruitful harvest;
³⁸ he blessed them, and their numbers
      greatly increased,
   and he did not let their herds diminish.

³⁹ Then their numbers decreased, and they
      were humbled
   by oppression, calamity and sorrow;
⁴⁰ he who pours contempt on nobles
   made them wander in a trackless
      waste.
⁴¹ But he lifted the needy out of their
      affliction
   and increased their families like
      flocks.
⁴² The upright see and rejoice,
   but all the wicked shut their mouths.

⁴³ Let the one who is wise heed these things
   and ponder the loving deeds of the
      LORD.

Psalm 108^b

A song. A psalm of David.

¹ My heart, O God, is steadfast;
   I will sing and make music with all my
      soul.
² Awake, harp and lyre!

   I will awaken the dawn.
³ I will praise you, LORD, among the
      nations;
   I will sing of you among the peoples.
⁴ For great is your love, higher than the
      heavens;
   your faithfulness reaches to the skies.
⁵ Be exalted, O God, above the heavens;
   let your glory be over all the earth.

⁶ Save us and help us with your right hand,
   that those you love may be delivered.
⁷ God has spoken from his sanctuary:
   "In triumph I will parcel out Shechem
   and measure off the Valley of Sukkoth.
⁸ Gilead is mine, Manasseh is mine;
   Ephraim is my helmet,
   Judah is my scepter.
⁹ Moab is my washbasin,
   on Edom I toss my sandal;
   over Philistia I shout in triumph."

¹⁰ Who will bring me to the fortified city?
   Who will lead me to Edom?
¹¹ Is it not you, God, you who have
      rejected us
   and no longer go out with our armies?
¹² Give us aid against the enemy,
   for human help is worthless.
¹³ With God we will gain the victory,
   and he will trample down our
      enemies.

Psalm 109

For the director of music.
Of David. A psalm.

¹ My God, whom I praise,
   do not remain silent,
² for people who are wicked and deceitful
   have opened their mouths against me;
   they have spoken against me with
      lying tongues.
³ With words of hatred they surround me;
   they attack me without cause.
⁴ In return for my friendship they
      accuse me,
   but I am a man of prayer.
⁵ They repay me evil for good,
   and hatred for my friendship.

⁶ Appoint someone evil to oppose my
      enemy;
   let an accuser stand at his right hand.

---

^a 29 Dead Sea Scrolls; Masoretic Text / *their waves*   ^b In Hebrew texts 108:1-13 is numbered 108:2-14.

PERFECT TIMING

READ: **PSALM 107:35-36**

God knows what you need exactly when you need it. He works his wonders at precisely the right time. He constantly gives you specific reasons to give thanks for his unfailing love. That's the point of Psalm 107.

Psalm 107 looks like the previous two psalms in a same-but-not-the-same sort of way. Each song recites a story. Psalm 105 recaps the Israelites' miraculous escape from slavery in Egypt. Psalm 106 helps you learn the lessons of their most rebellious moments. And Psalm 107 thanks the Lord for redeeming his people, releasing them from all kinds of everyday hardships.

Psalm 107 shows how God thunders to the rescue of people with real-life needs. He satisfies hungry and thirsty desert wanderers (v. 4). He breaks the chains of captives held in darkness (v. 14). His wise words heal the foolish (v. 20). He stills storms to a whisper (v. 29) and pumps the desert full of life-giving pools (v. 35). He multiplies a decimated nation (v. 39).

BUILDING
FAITH
WISDOM
STRENGTH

You might not notice that God does good things for you all the time, but you can be sure that everything sweet comes from him. When you spot him acting on your behalf, make sure you stop and "give thanks to the Lord for his unfailing love and his wonderful deeds for mankind" (v. 31).

⁷ When he is tried, let him be found guilty,
  and may his prayers condemn him.
⁸ May his days be few;
  may another take his place of
    leadership.
⁹ May his children be fatherless
  and his wife a widow.
¹⁰ May his children be wandering beggars;
  may they be driven*a* from their ruined
    homes.
¹¹ May a creditor seize all he has;
  may strangers plunder the fruits of
    his labor.
¹² May no one extend kindness to him
  or take pity on his fatherless children.
¹³ May his descendants be cut off,
  their names blotted out from the next
    generation.
¹⁴ May the iniquity of his fathers be
    remembered before the LORD;
  may the sin of his mother never be
    blotted out.
¹⁵ May their sins always remain before the
    LORD,
  that he may blot out their name from
    the earth.

¹⁶ For he never thought of doing a kindness,
  but hounded to death the poor
  and the needy and the brokenhearted.
¹⁷ He loved to pronounce a curse —
  may it come back on him.
  He found no pleasure in blessing —
  may it be far from him.
¹⁸ He wore cursing as his garment;
  it entered into his body like water,
  into his bones like oil.
¹⁹ May it be like a cloak wrapped about him,
  like a belt tied forever around him.
²⁰ May this be the LORD's payment to my
    accusers,
  to those who speak evil of me.

²¹ But you, Sovereign LORD,
  help me for your name's sake;
  out of the goodness of your love,
    deliver me.
²² For I am poor and needy,
  and my heart is wounded within me.
²³ I fade away like an evening shadow;
  I am shaken off like a locust.
²⁴ My knees give way from fasting;
  my body is thin and gaunt.

²⁵ I am an object of scorn to my accusers;
  when they see me, they shake their
    heads.
²⁶ Help me, LORD my God;
  save me according to your unfailing
    love.
²⁷ Let them know that it is your hand,
  that you, LORD, have done it.
²⁸ While they curse, may you bless;
  may those who attack me be put to
    shame,
  but may your servant rejoice.
²⁹ May my accusers be clothed with
    disgrace
  and wrapped in shame as in a cloak.

³⁰ With my mouth I will greatly extol the
    LORD;
  in the great throng of worshipers I will
    praise him.
³¹ For he stands at the right hand of the
    needy,
  to save their lives from those who
    would condemn them.

Psalm 110

Of David. A psalm.

¹ The LORD says to my lord:*b*

"Sit at my right hand
  until I make your enemies
  a footstool for your feet."

² The LORD will extend your mighty
    scepter from Zion, saying,
  "Rule in the midst of your enemies!"
³ Your troops will be willing
  on your day of battle.
  Arrayed in holy splendor,
  your young men will come to you
  like dew from the morning's womb.*c*

⁴ The LORD has sworn
  and will not change his mind:
  "You are a priest forever,
  in the order of Melchizedek."

⁵ The Lord is at your right hand*d*;
  he will crush kings on the day of his
    wrath.
⁶ He will judge the nations, heaping up
    the dead
  and crushing the rulers of the whole
    earth.

---

a 10 Septuagint; Hebrew *sought*   *b 1* Or *Lord*   *c 3* The meaning of the Hebrew for this sentence is
uncertain.   *d 5* Or *My lord is at your right hand,* LORD

⁷ He will drink from a brook along the way,ᵃ
  and so he will lift his head high.

Psalm 111ᵇ

¹ Praise the LORD.ᶜ

I will extol the LORD with all my heart
  in the council of the upright and in the
    assembly.

² Great are the works of the LORD;
  they are pondered by all who delight
    in them.

³ Glorious and majestic are his deeds,
  and his righteousness endures forever.

⁴ He has caused his wonders to be
    remembered;
  the LORD is gracious and
    compassionate.

⁵ He provides food for those who fear him;
  he remembers his covenant forever.

⁶ He has shown his people the power of
    his works,
  giving them the lands of other nations.

⁷ The works of his hands are faithful and
    just;
  all his precepts are trustworthy.

⁸ They are established for ever and ever,
  enacted in faithfulness and
    uprightness.

⁹ He provided redemption for his people;
  he ordained his covenant forever —
    holy and awesome is his name.

¹⁰ The fear of the LORD is the beginning of
    wisdom;
  all who follow his precepts have good
    understanding.
  To him belongs eternal praise.

Psalm 112ᵇ

¹ Praise the LORD.ᶜ

Blessed are those who fear the LORD,
  who find great delight in his
    commands.

² Their children will be mighty in the
    land;
  the generation of the upright will be
    blessed.

³ Wealth and riches are in their houses,

and their righteousness endures
    forever.

⁴ Even in darkness light dawns for the
    upright,
  for those who are gracious and
    compassionate and righteous.

⁵ Good will come to those who are
    generous and lend freely,
  who conduct their affairs with justice.

⁶ Surely the righteous will never be
    shaken;
  they will be remembered forever.

⁷ They will have no fear of bad news;
  their hearts are steadfast, trusting in
    the LORD.

⁸ Their hearts are secure, they will have
    no fear;
  in the end they will look in triumph on
    their foes.

⁹ They have freely scattered their gifts to
    the poor,
  their righteousness endures forever;
  their hornᵈ will be lifted high in honor.

¹⁰ The wicked will see and be vexed,
  they will gnash their teeth and waste
    away;
  the longings of the wicked will come
    to nothing.

Psalm 113

¹ Praise the LORD.ᵉ

Praise the LORD, you his servants;
  praise the name of the LORD.

² Let the name of the LORD be praised,
  both now and forevermore.

³ From the rising of the sun to the place
    where it sets,
  the name of the LORD is to be praised.

⁴ The LORD is exalted over all the nations,
  his glory above the heavens.

⁵ Who is like the LORD our God,
  the One who sits enthroned on high,

⁶ who stoops down to look
  on the heavens and the earth?

⁷ He raises the poor from the dust
  and lifts the needy from the ash heap;

⁸ he seats them with princes,
  with the princes of his people.

ᵃ 7 The meaning of the Hebrew for this clause is uncertain.
ᵇ This psalm is an acrostic poem, the lines of
which begin with the successive letters of the Hebrew alphabet.   ᶜ 1 Hebrew *Hallelu Yah*   ᵈ 9 *Horn* here
symbolizes dignity.   ᵉ 1 Hebrew *Hallelu Yah*; also in verse 9

9 He settles the childless woman in her
home
    as a happy mother of children.

Praise the LORD.

Psalm 114

1 When Israel came out of Egypt,
    Jacob from a people of foreign tongue,
2 Judah became God's sanctuary,
    Israel his dominion.

3 The sea looked and fled,
    the Jordan turned back;
4 the mountains leaped like rams,
    the hills like lambs.

5 Why was it, sea, that you fled?
    Why, Jordan, did you turn back?
6 Why, mountains, did you leap like rams,
    you hills, like lambs?

7 Tremble, earth, at the presence of the
Lord,
    at the presence of the God of Jacob,
8 who turned the rock into a pool,
    the hard rock into springs of water.

Psalm 115

1 Not to us, LORD, not to us
    but to your name be the glory,
    because of your love and faithfulness.

2 Why do the nations say,
    "Where is their God?"
3 Our God is in heaven;
    he does whatever pleases him.
4 But their idols are silver and gold,
    made by human hands.
5 They have mouths, but cannot speak,
    eyes, but cannot see.
6 They have ears, but cannot hear,
    noses, but cannot smell.
7 They have hands, but cannot feel,
    feet, but cannot walk,
    nor can they utter a sound with their
    throats.
8 Those who make them will be like them,
    and so will all who trust in them.

9 All you Israelites, trust in the LORD —
    he is their help and shield.
10 House of Aaron, trust in the LORD —
    he is their help and shield.

11 You who fear him, trust in the LORD —
    he is their help and shield.

12 The LORD remembers us and will
    bless us:
    He will bless his people Israel,
    he will bless the house of Aaron,
13 he will bless those who fear the LORD —
    small and great alike.

14 May the LORD cause you to flourish,
    both you and your children.
15 May you be blessed by the LORD,
    the Maker of heaven and earth.

16 The highest heavens belong to the LORD,
    but the earth he has given to mankind.
17 It is not the dead who praise the LORD,
    those who go down to the place of
    silence;
18 it is we who extol the LORD,
    both now and forevermore.

Praise the LORD.ᵃ

Psalm 116

1 I love the LORD, for he heard my voice;
    he heard my cry for mercy.
2 Because he turned his ear to me,
    I will call on him as long as I live.

3 The cords of death entangled me,
    the anguish of the grave came over me;
    I was overcome by distress and sorrow.
4 Then I called on the name of the LORD:
    "LORD, save me!"

5 The LORD is gracious and righteous;
    our God is full of compassion.
6 The LORD protects the unwary;
    when I was brought low, he saved me.

7 Return to your rest, my soul,
    for the LORD has been good to you.

8 For you, LORD, have delivered me from
    death,
    my eyes from tears,
    my feet from stumbling,
9 that I may walk before the LORD
    in the land of the living.

10 I trusted in the LORD when I said,
    "I am greatly afflicted";
11 in my alarm I said,
    "Everyone is a liar."

ᵃ 18 Hebrew *Hallelu Yah*

¹² What shall I return to the Lord
　　for all his goodness to me?

¹³ I will lift up the cup of salvation
　　and call on the name of the Lord.
¹⁴ I will fulfill my vows to the Lord
　　in the presence of all his people.

¹⁵ Precious in the sight of the Lord
　　is the death of his faithful servants.
¹⁶ Truly I am your servant, Lord;
　　I serve you just as my mother did;
　　you have freed me from my chains.

¹⁷ I will sacrifice a thank offering to you
　　and call on the name of the Lord.
¹⁸ I will fulfill my vows to the Lord
　　in the presence of all his people,
¹⁹ in the courts of the house of the Lord —
　　in your midst, Jerusalem.

　　Praise the Lord.*a*

Psalm 117

¹ Praise the Lord, all you nations;
　　extol him, all you peoples.
² For great is his love toward us,
　　and the faithfulness of the Lord
　　endures forever.

　　Praise the Lord.*a*

Psalm 118

¹ Give thanks to the Lord, for he is good;
　　his love endures forever.

² Let Israel say:
　　"His love endures forever."
³ Let the house of Aaron say:
　　"His love endures forever."
⁴ Let those who fear the Lord say:
　　"His love endures forever."

⁵ When hard pressed, I cried to the Lord;
　　he brought me into a spacious place.
⁶ The Lord is with me; I will not be afraid.
　　What can mere mortals do to me?
⁷ The Lord is with me; he is my helper.
　　I look in triumph on my enemies.

⁸ It is better to take refuge in the Lord
　　than to trust in humans.
⁹ It is better to take refuge in the Lord
　　than to trust in princes.
¹⁰ All the nations surrounded me,

but in the name of the Lord I cut
　　them down.
¹¹ They surrounded me on every side,
　　but in the name of the Lord I cut them
　　down.
¹² They swarmed around me like bees,
　　but they were consumed as quickly as
　　burning thorns;
　　in the name of the Lord I cut them
　　down.
¹³ I was pushed back and about to fall,
　　but the Lord helped me.
¹⁴ The Lord is my strength and my
　　defense*b*;
　　he has become my salvation.

¹⁵ Shouts of joy and victory
　　resound in the tents of the righteous:
　　"The Lord's right hand has done mighty
　　things!
¹⁶　　The Lord's right hand is lifted high;
　　the Lord's right hand has done mighty
　　things!"

¹⁷ I will not die but live,
　　and will proclaim what the Lord has
　　done.
¹⁸ The Lord has chastened me severely,
　　but he has not given me over to death.
¹⁹ Open for me the gates of the righteous;
　　I will enter and give thanks to the
　　Lord.
²⁰ This is the gate of the Lord
　　through which the righteous may
　　enter.
²¹ I will give you thanks, for you answered
　　me;
　　you have become my salvation.

²² The stone the builders rejected
　　has become the cornerstone;
²³ the Lord has done this,
　　and it is marvelous in our eyes.
²⁴ The Lord has done it this very day;
　　let us rejoice today and be glad.

²⁵ Lord, save us!
　　Lord, grant us success!

²⁶ Blessed is he who comes in the name of
　　the Lord.
　　From the house of the Lord we bless
　　you.*c*
²⁷ The Lord is God,
　　and he has made his light shine on us.

---

a 19,2 Hebrew *Hallelu Yah*　　*b 14* Or *song*　　*c 26* The Hebrew is plural.

With boughs in hand, join in the festal
procession
up^a to the horns of the altar.

²⁸ You are my God, and I will praise you;
you are my God, and I will exalt you.

²⁹ Give thanks to the LORD, for he is good;
his love endures forever.

Psalm 119^b

א Aleph

¹ Blessed are those whose ways are
blameless,
who walk according to the law of the
LORD.
² Blessed are those who keep his statutes
and seek him with all their heart —
³ they do no wrong
but follow his ways.
⁴ You have laid down precepts
that are to be fully obeyed.
⁵ Oh, that my ways were steadfast
in obeying your decrees!
⁶ Then I would not be put to shame
when I consider all your commands.
⁷ I will praise you with an upright heart
as I learn your righteous laws.
⁸ I will obey your decrees;
do not utterly forsake me.

ב Beth

⁹ How can a young person stay on the path
of purity?
By living according to your word.
¹⁰ I seek you with all my heart;
do not let me stray from your
commands.
¹¹ I have hidden your word in my heart
that I might not sin against you.
¹² Praise be to you, LORD;
teach me your decrees.
¹³ With my lips I recount
all the laws that come from your mouth.
¹⁴ I rejoice in following your statutes
as one rejoices in great riches.
¹⁵ I meditate on your precepts
and consider your ways.
¹⁶ I delight in your decrees;
I will not neglect your word.

ג Gimel

¹⁷ Be good to your servant while I live,
that I may obey your word.
¹⁸ Open my eyes that I may see
wonderful things in your law.
¹⁹ I am a stranger on earth;
do not hide your commands from me.
²⁰ My soul is consumed with longing
for your laws at all times.
²¹ You rebuke the arrogant, who are
accursed,
those who stray from your commands.
²² Remove from me their scorn and
contempt,
for I keep your statutes.
²³ Though rulers sit together and slander me,
your servant will meditate on your
decrees.
²⁴ Your statutes are my delight;
they are my counselors.

ד Daleth

²⁵ I am laid low in the dust;
preserve my life according to your word.
²⁶ I gave an account of my ways and you
answered me;
teach me your decrees.
²⁷ Cause me to understand the way of your
precepts,
that I may meditate on your wonderful
deeds.
²⁸ My soul is weary with sorrow;
strengthen me according to your word.
²⁹ Keep me from deceitful ways;
be gracious to me and teach me your
law.
³⁰ I have chosen the way of faithfulness;
I have set my heart on your laws.
³¹ I hold fast to your statutes, LORD;
do not let me be put to shame.
³² I run in the path of your commands,
for you have broadened my
understanding.

ה He

³³ Teach me, LORD, the way of your decrees,
that I may follow it to the end.^c
³⁴ Give me understanding, so that I may
keep your law
and obey it with all my heart.

^a 27 Or *Bind the festal sacrifice with ropes / and take it*   ^b This psalm is an acrostic poem, the stanzas of
which begin with successive letters of the Hebrew alphabet; moreover, the verses of each stanza begin with
the same letter of the Hebrew alphabet.   ^c 33 Or *follow it for its reward*

THE LINK

READ: PSALM 119:28, 43

I'm going to share something that I think could change the way you pray and read the Bible. We often view prayer and Scripture reading as two separate spiritual practices without much in common, but what if they were meant to be linked? What if reading became a form of praying and praying became a form of reading?

One of the biggest reasons we don't pray through is because we run out of things to say! Our lack of persistence is just a lack of conversation pieces. "Well. This is awkward . . . Talk to you later, God!" And when that happens, our prayer turns into clichés and vague requests and small talk.

BUILDING

FAITH

WISDOM

STRENGTH

The solution? Pray through the Bible. Prayer was never meant to be a one-sided conversation; it was meant to be a dialogue! Think of Scripture as God's part of the script; prayer's our part. Scripture is God's way of initiating a conversation, and prayer is just our response. The shift happens when you realize that the Bible wasn't just meant to be read through; the Bible was meant to be prayed through. And if you pray through it, you'll never run out of things to talk about.

You think you've read it all? Not if you haven't prayed it. As you pray, the Holy Spirit will highlight certain promises to your spirit. It's very difficult to predict what and when and where and how, but over time, the promises of God will become your promises.

Taken from *The Circle Maker Student Edition* by Mark Batterson with Parker Batterson, copyright © 2012 by Mark Batterson, published by Zondervan.

³⁵ Direct me in the path of your commands,
for there I find delight.
³⁶ Turn my heart toward your statutes
and not toward selfish gain.
³⁷ Turn my eyes away from worthless
things;
preserve my life according to your
word.ᵃ
³⁸ Fulfill your promise to your servant,
so that you may be feared.
³⁹ Take away the disgrace I dread,
for your laws are good.
⁴⁰ How I long for your precepts!
In your righteousness preserve my life.

וWaw

⁴¹ May your unfailing love come to me,
LORD,
your salvation, according to your
promise;
⁴² then I can answer anyone who taunts me,
for I trust in your word.
⁴³ Never take your word of truth from my
mouth,
for I have put my hope in your laws.
⁴⁴ I will always obey your law,
for ever and ever.
⁴⁵ I will walk about in freedom,
for I have sought out your precepts.
⁴⁶ I will speak of your statutes before kings
and will not be put to shame,
⁴⁷ for I delight in your commands
because I love them.
⁴⁸ I reach out for your commands, which I
love,
that I may meditate on your decrees.

זZayin

⁴⁹ Remember your word to your servant,
for you have given me hope.
⁵⁰ My comfort in my suffering is this:
Your promise preserves my life.
⁵¹ The arrogant mock me unmercifully,
but I do not turn from your law.
⁵² I remember, LORD, your ancient laws,
and I find comfort in them.
⁵³ Indignation grips me because of the
wicked,
who have forsaken your law.
⁵⁴ Your decrees are the theme of my song
wherever I lodge.

⁵⁵ In the night, LORD, I remember your
name,
that I may keep your law.
⁵⁶ This has been my practice:
I obey your precepts.

חHeth

⁵⁷ You are my portion, LORD;
I have promised to obey your words.
⁵⁸ I have sought your face with all my heart;
be gracious to me according to your
promise.
⁵⁹ I have considered my ways
and have turned my steps to your
statutes.
⁶⁰ I will hasten and not delay
to obey your commands.
⁶¹ Though the wicked bind me with ropes,
I will not forget your law.
⁶² At midnight I rise to give you thanks
for your righteous laws.
⁶³ I am a friend to all who fear you,
to all who follow your precepts.
⁶⁴ The earth is filled with your love, LORD;
teach me your decrees.

טTeth

⁶⁵ Do good to your servant
according to your word, LORD.
⁶⁶ Teach me knowledge and good judgment,
for I trust your commands.
⁶⁷ Before I was afflicted I went astray,
but now I obey your word.
⁶⁸ You are good, and what you do is good;
teach me your decrees.
⁶⁹ Though the arrogant have smeared me
with lies,
I keep your precepts with all my heart.
⁷⁰ Their hearts are callous and unfeeling,
but I delight in your law.
⁷¹ It was good for me to be afflicted
so that I might learn your decrees.
⁷² The law from your mouth is more
precious to me
than thousands of pieces of silver and
gold.

יYodh

⁷³ Your hands made me and formed me;
give me understanding to learn your
commands.

ᵃ 37 Two manuscripts of the Masoretic Text and Dead Sea Scrolls; most manuscripts of the Masoretic Text *life
in your way*

INVERTED

READ: **PSALM 119:36**

An astronomer named Nicolaus Copernicus challenged the belief that the earth was the center of the universe. Copernicus suggested that the sun didn't revolve around the earth, but that the earth revolved around the sun. The Copernican Revolution turned the scientific world upside down.

We all need to experience a little Copernican Revolution in our own lives. That change happens once we come to terms with the fact that the world doesn't revolve around us. That's what babies do: let the world feed them and change their diapers. Anyone and everyone in our presence is there to serve us. It's as if we're alive solely to have people wait on us. And that's an okay mindset if you're an infant. If you're seventeen, it's a problem!

Heads up: You're not the center of the universe!

All that to say, sinfulness is selfishness. It's placing yourself above all others—your desires, your "needs," your plans—above everyone else. You might still seek God, but you definitely don't seek him first. And that's the truth. You seek him second or third or seventh. Even if you sing, "Jesus at the center of it all," what you really want is for others to bow down to you because you bow down to Christ. That right there is a sneaky form of selfishness disguised as holiness, but is not truly Jesus centered. It's all about you. It's less about us serving his purposes and more about him serving our purposes. I like to call it the inverted gospel.

BUILDING FAITH WISDOM STRENGTH

Taken from *All In Student Edition* by Mark Batterson and Parker Batterson, copyright © 2014 by Mark Batterson, published by Zondervan.

⁷⁴ May those who fear you rejoice when
they see me,
for I have put my hope in your word.
⁷⁵ I know, Lᴏʀᴅ, that your laws are
righteous,
and that in faithfulness you have
afflicted me.
⁷⁶ May your unfailing love be my comfort,
according to your promise to your
servant.
⁷⁷ Let your compassion come to me that I
may live,
for your law is my delight.
⁷⁸ May the arrogant be put to shame for
wronging me without cause;
but I will meditate on your precepts.
⁷⁹ May those who fear you turn to me,
those who understand your statutes.
⁸⁰ May I wholeheartedly follow your decrees,
that I may not be put to shame.

 כ Kaph

⁸¹ My soul faints with longing for your
salvation,
but I have put my hope in your word.
⁸² My eyes fail, looking for your promise;
I say, "When will you comfort me?"
⁸³ Though I am like a wineskin in the smoke,
I do not forget your decrees.
⁸⁴ How long must your servant wait?
When will you punish my persecutors?
⁸⁵ The arrogant dig pits to trap me,
contrary to your law.
⁸⁶ All your commands are trustworthy;
help me, for I am being persecuted
without cause.
⁸⁷ They almost wiped me from the earth,
but I have not forsaken your precepts.
⁸⁸ In your unfailing love preserve my life,
that I may obey the statutes of your
mouth.

ל Lamedh

⁸⁹ Your word, Lᴏʀᴅ, is eternal;
it stands firm in the heavens.
⁹⁰ Your faithfulness continues through all
generations;
you established the earth, and it
endures.
⁹¹ Your laws endure to this day,
for all things serve you.
⁹² If your law had not been my delight,

I would have perished in my
affliction.
⁹³ I will never forget your precepts,
for by them you have preserved my life.
⁹⁴ Save me, for I am yours;
I have sought out your precepts.
⁹⁵ The wicked are waiting to destroy me,
but I will ponder your statutes.
⁹⁶ To all perfection I see a limit,
but your commands are boundless.

מ Mem

⁹⁷ Oh, how I love your law!
I meditate on it all day long.
⁹⁸ Your commands are always with me
and make me wiser than my enemies.
⁹⁹ I have more insight than all my teachers,
for I meditate on your statutes.
¹⁰⁰ I have more understanding than the
elders,
for I obey your precepts.
¹⁰¹ I have kept my feet from every evil path
so that I might obey your word.
¹⁰² I have not departed from your laws,
for you yourself have taught me.
¹⁰³ How sweet are your words to my taste,
sweeter than honey to my mouth!
¹⁰⁴ I gain understanding from your
precepts;
therefore I hate every wrong path.

נ Nun

¹⁰⁵ Your word is a lamp for my feet,
a light on my path.
¹⁰⁶ I have taken an oath and confirmed it,
that I will follow your righteous laws.
¹⁰⁷ I have suffered much;
preserve my life, Lᴏʀᴅ, according to
your word.
¹⁰⁸ Accept, Lᴏʀᴅ, the willing praise of my
mouth,
and teach me your laws.
¹⁰⁹ Though I constantly take my life in my
hands,
I will not forget your law.
¹¹⁰ The wicked have set a snare for me,
but I have not strayed from your
precepts.
¹¹¹ Your statutes are my heritage forever;
they are the joy of my heart.
¹¹² My heart is set on keeping your decrees
to the very end.^a

---

^a 112 Or *decrees* / *for their enduring reward*

ס Samekh

¹¹³ I hate double-minded people,
   but I love your law.
¹¹⁴ You are my refuge and my shield;
   I have put my hope in your word.
¹¹⁵ Away from me, you evildoers,
   that I may keep the commands of
      my God!
¹¹⁶ Sustain me, my God, according to your
      promise, and I will live;
   do not let my hopes be dashed.
¹¹⁷ Uphold me, and I will be delivered;
   I will always have regard for your
      decrees.
¹¹⁸ You reject all who stray from your
      decrees,
   for their delusions come to nothing.
¹¹⁹ All the wicked of the earth you discard
      like dross;
   therefore I love your statutes.
¹²⁰ My flesh trembles in fear of you;
   I stand in awe of your laws.

ע Ayin

¹²¹ I have done what is righteous and just;
   do not leave me to my oppressors.
¹²² Ensure your servant's well-being;
   do not let the arrogant oppress me.
¹²³ My eyes fail, looking for your salvation,
   looking for your righteous promise.
¹²⁴ Deal with your servant according to
      your love
   and teach me your decrees.
¹²⁵ I am your servant; give me discernment
   that I may understand your statutes.
¹²⁶ It is time for you to act, LORD;
   your law is being broken.
¹²⁷ Because I love your commands
   more than gold, more than pure gold,
¹²⁸ and because I consider all your precepts
      right,
   I hate every wrong path.

פ Pe

¹²⁹ Your statutes are wonderful;
   therefore I obey them.
¹³⁰ The unfolding of your words gives light;
   it gives understanding to the simple.
¹³¹ I open my mouth and pant,
   longing for your commands.
¹³² Turn to me and have mercy on me,
   as you always do to those who love
      your name.

¹³³ Direct my footsteps according to your
      word;
   let no sin rule over me.
¹³⁴ Redeem me from human oppression,
   that I may obey your precepts.
¹³⁵ Make your face shine on your servant
   and teach me your decrees.
¹³⁶ Streams of tears flow from my eyes,
   for your law is not obeyed.

צ Tsadhe

¹³⁷ You are righteous, LORD,
   and your laws are right.
¹³⁸ The statutes you have laid down are
      righteous;
   they are fully trustworthy.
¹³⁹ My zeal wears me out,
   for my enemies ignore your words.
¹⁴⁰ Your promises have been thoroughly
      tested,
   and your servant loves them.
¹⁴¹ Though I am lowly and despised,
   I do not forget your precepts.
¹⁴² Your righteousness is everlasting
   and your law is true.
¹⁴³ Trouble and distress have come
      upon me,
   but your commands give me delight.
¹⁴⁴ Your statutes are always righteous;
   give me understanding that I may live.

ק Qoph

¹⁴⁵ I call with all my heart; answer me,
      LORD,
   and I will obey your decrees.
¹⁴⁶ I call out to you; save me
   and I will keep your statutes.
¹⁴⁷ I rise before dawn and cry for help;
   I have put my hope in your word.
¹⁴⁸ My eyes stay open through the watches
      of the night,
   that I may meditate on your promises.
¹⁴⁹ Hear my voice in accordance with your
      love;
   preserve my life, LORD, according to
      your laws.
¹⁵⁰ Those who devise wicked schemes are
      near,
   but they are far from your law.
¹⁵¹ Yet you are near, LORD,
   and all your commands are true.
¹⁵² Long ago I learned from your statutes
   that you established them to last
      forever.

CHECK OUT HIS PROMISES

READ: **PSALM 119:140**

Occasionally chairs snap, brakes fail, and roller coasters take flight. But you throw your weight on a chair because it's caught you a thousand times. You push on a brake pedal because it's never failed to halt your car. You dare to ride a roller coaster because it's always stayed on the tracks.

The Lord's words do even better. For thousands of years, millions of people have thoroughly tested them and found them flawless. Time after time his promises have proven trustworthy. They never break. That's good reason to fall in love with your Lord's words.

Jesus once invited his followers to test his words. He said, "If you hold to my teaching, you are really my disciples. Then you will know the truth, and the truth will set you free" (John 8:31–32). Every time you apply the Lord's words to a part of your life, you demonstrate that you're his follower. You get a chance to see if they're true. And you discover that you can count on every promise that comes from the Lord's lips. No one has to force you to trust him. You're free.

Even if countless throngs of people have tested God's promises, you still need to check them out for yourself. That isn't a mind game, an exercise you can do in your head. You need to dare to act on the Lord's promises. Then you can figure out for yourself that they're true.

BUILDING

FAITH

WISDOM

STRENGTH

ר Resh

¹⁵³ Look on my suffering and deliver me,
for I have not forgotten your law.
¹⁵⁴ Defend my cause and redeem me;
preserve my life according to your
promise.
¹⁵⁵ Salvation is far from the wicked,
for they do not seek out your decrees.
¹⁵⁶ Your compassion, LORD, is great;
preserve my life according to your
laws.
¹⁵⁷ Many are the foes who persecute me,
but I have not turned from your
statutes.
¹⁵⁸ I look on the faithless with loathing,
for they do not obey your word.
¹⁵⁹ See how I love your precepts;
preserve my life, LORD, in accordance
with your love.
¹⁶⁰ All your words are true;
all your righteous laws are eternal.

ש Sin and Shin

¹⁶¹ Rulers persecute me without cause,
but my heart trembles at your word.
¹⁶² I rejoice in your promise
like one who finds great spoil.
¹⁶³ I hate and detest falsehood
but I love your law.
¹⁶⁴ Seven times a day I praise you
for your righteous laws.
¹⁶⁵ Great peace have those who love your
law,
and nothing can make them stumble.
¹⁶⁶ I wait for your salvation, LORD,
and I follow your commands.
¹⁶⁷ I obey your statutes,
for I love them greatly.
¹⁶⁸ I obey your precepts and your statutes,
for all my ways are known to you.

ת Taw

¹⁶⁹ May my cry come before you, LORD;
give me understanding according to
your word.
¹⁷⁰ May my supplication come before you;
deliver me according to your promise.
¹⁷¹ May my lips overflow with praise,
for you teach me your decrees.
¹⁷² May my tongue sing of your word,
for all your commands are righteous.
¹⁷³ May your hand be ready to help me,
for I have chosen your precepts.

¹⁷⁴ I long for your salvation, LORD,
and your law gives me delight.
¹⁷⁵ Let me live that I may praise you,
and may your laws sustain me.
¹⁷⁶ I have strayed like a lost sheep.
Seek your servant,
for I have not forgotten your commands.

Psalm 120

A song of ascents.

¹ I call on the LORD in my distress,
and he answers me.
² Save me, LORD,
from lying lips
and from deceitful tongues.

³ What will he do to you,
and what more besides,
you deceitful tongue?
⁴ He will punish you with a warrior's sharp
arrows,
with burning coals of the broom bush.

⁵ Woe to me that I dwell in Meshek,
that I live among the tents of Kedar!
⁶ Too long have I lived
among those who hate peace.
⁷ I am for peace;
but when I speak, they are for war.

Psalm 121

A song of ascents.

¹ I lift up my eyes to the mountains —
where does my help come from?
² My help comes from the LORD,
the Maker of heaven and earth.

³ He will not let your foot slip —
he who watches over you will not
slumber;
⁴ indeed, he who watches over Israel
will neither slumber nor sleep.

⁵ The LORD watches over you —
the LORD is your shade at your right
hand;
⁶ the sun will not harm you by day,
nor the moon by night.

⁷ The LORD will keep you from all harm —
he will watch over your life;
⁸ the LORD will watch over your coming
and going
both now and forevermore.

Psalm 122

A song of ascents. Of David.

1 I rejoiced with those who said to me,
  "Let us go to the house of the LORD."
2 Our feet are standing
  in your gates, Jerusalem.

3 Jerusalem is built like a city
  that is closely compacted together.
4 That is where the tribes go up —
  the tribes of the LORD —
to praise the name of the LORD
  according to the statute given to Israel.
5 There stand the thrones for judgment,
  the thrones of the house of David.

6 Pray for the peace of Jerusalem:
  "May those who love you be secure.
7 May there be peace within your walls
  and security within your citadels."
8 For the sake of my family and friends,
  I will say, "Peace be within you."
9 For the sake of the house of the LORD
  our God,
  I will seek your prosperity.

Psalm 123

A song of ascents.

1 I lift up my eyes to you,
  to you who sit enthroned in heaven.
2 As the eyes of slaves look to the hand of
  their master,
  as the eyes of a female slave look to the
  hand of her mistress,
so our eyes look to the LORD our God,
  till he shows us his mercy.

3 Have mercy on us, LORD, have mercy
  on us,
  for we have endured no end of
  contempt.
4 We have endured no end
  of ridicule from the arrogant,
  of contempt from the proud.

Psalm 124

A song of ascents. Of David.

1 If the LORD had not been on our side —
  let Israel say —
2 if the LORD had not been on our side
  when people attacked us,

3 they would have swallowed us alive
  when their anger flared against us;
4 the flood would have engulfed us,
  the torrent would have swept over us,
5 the raging waters
  would have swept us away.

6 Praise be to the LORD,
  who has not let us be torn by their teeth.
7 We have escaped like a bird
  from the fowler's snare;
the snare has been broken,
  and we have escaped.
8 Our help is in the name of the LORD,
  the Maker of heaven and earth.

Psalm 125

A song of ascents.

1 Those who trust in the LORD are like
    Mount Zion,
  which cannot be shaken but endures
    forever.
2 As the mountains surround Jerusalem,
  so the LORD surrounds his people
  both now and forevermore.

3 The scepter of the wicked will not remain
  over the land allotted to the righteous,
for then the righteous might use
  their hands to do evil.

4 LORD, do good to those who are good,
  to those who are upright in heart.
5 But those who turn to crooked ways
  the LORD will banish with the evildoers.

  Peace be on Israel.

Psalm 126

A song of ascents.

1 When the LORD restored the fortunes
    of*a* Zion,
  we were like those who dreamed.*b*
2 Our mouths were filled with laughter,
  our tongues with songs of joy.
Then it was said among the nations,
  "The LORD has done great things for
    them."
3 The LORD has done great things for us,
  and we are filled with joy.

4 Restore our fortunes,*c* LORD,
  like streams in the Negev.

---

a 1 Or LORD *brought back the captives to*   *b* 1 Or *those restored to health*   *c* 4 Or *Bring back our captives*

LET'S GO

READ: PSALM 122:1

"A song of ascents" appears fifteen times in the titles of songs in the book of Psalms (Psalms 120–134). "Ascents" literally means "goings up." Believers sang these tunes while "going up" to Jerusalem to worship. Several times a year thousands of pilgrims traveled to the holy city from every direction to offer sacrifices and participate in religious festivals.

The book of Isaiah fills out that scene. It says, "And you will sing as on the night you celebrate a holy festival; your hearts will rejoice as when people playing pipes go up to the mountain of the LORD" (30:29).

The psalmist says he's gleefully happy when others invite him on a trip to the temple. He likes the crowded feel of the compact city. He recognizes Jerusalem not only as a place to praise the Lord but also as the home of government, "the thrones of the house of David" (Psalm 122:5). He unites with other worshipers who pray for God's peace to reign in the city and overflow with blessings to their family and friends.

BUILDING

FAITH

WISDOM

STRENGTH

You don't have to trek to Jerusalem to get that same rush of excitement. Every time you and your friends get together to worship, you're "going up" to God's holy home. Give each other an encouraging nudge to get moving. Then praise God together and experience his blessings.

ALL YOU NEED IS . . .

The Lord is better than any late night comic at filling you with laughter and belly-rocking joy. Yet that happiness comes from an unusual source. It's all because he does astonishing things for you.

Don't miss the fact that this song of ascent comes from the era after Israel's captivity in Babylon. It's a radical change from what you read in a passage like Psalm 137, which expresses the deep grief the exiles felt. They sat by the rivers in that distant place and wept as they remembered their homeland. They hung up their harps and refused to sing for their tormenters. But now the Lord has brought them home.

That news is so good that these believers wonder if they're dreaming. Their mouths once were full of the mournful funeral songs you read in the book of Lamentations, but now they spill over with laughter. They all recognize the great acts the Lord has done on their behalf. They're like starving people who go to the fields to plant seed and return home carrying bundles of grain.

BUILDING FAITH WISDOM STRENGTH

God didn't stop doing stunning things back in the Bible. He sends you streams when you feel stuck in dry places. He feeds you when you feel like you're about to starve. He brings you home when you feel far away. Ask him to meet your needs in surprising ways. He will fill you with joy when he does great things.

⁵ Those who sow with tears
   will reap with songs of joy.
⁶ Those who go out weeping,
   carrying seed to sow,
 will return with songs of joy,
   carrying sheaves with them.

Psalm 127

A song of ascents. Of Solomon.

¹ Unless the LORD builds the house,
   the builders labor in vain.
 Unless the LORD watches over the city,
   the guards stand watch in vain.
² In vain you rise early
   and stay up late,
 toiling for food to eat —
   for he grants sleep to*ᵃ* those he
     loves.

³ Children are a heritage from the
     LORD,
   offspring a reward from him.
⁴ Like arrows in the hands of a warrior
   are children born in one's youth.
⁵ Blessed is the man
   whose quiver is full of them.
 They will not be put to shame
   when they contend with their
     opponents in court.

Psalm 128

A song of ascents.

¹ Blessed are all who fear the LORD,
   who walk in obedience to him.
² You will eat the fruit of your labor;
   blessings and prosperity will
     be yours.
³ Your wife will be like a fruitful vine
   within your house;
 your children will be like olive shoots
   around your table.
⁴ Yes, this will be the blessing
   for the man who fears the LORD.

⁵ May the LORD bless you from Zion;
   may you see the prosperity of
     Jerusalem
 all the days of your life.
⁶ May you live to see your children's
     children —
   peace be on Israel.

Psalm 129

A song of ascents.

¹ "They have greatly oppressed me from
     my youth,"
   let Israel say;
² "they have greatly oppressed me from
     my youth,
   but they have not gained the victory
     over me.
³ Plowmen have plowed my back
   and made their furrows long.
⁴ But the LORD is righteous;
   he has cut me free from the cords of
     the wicked."

⁵ May all who hate Zion
   be turned back in shame.
⁶ May they be like grass on the roof,
   which withers before it can grow;
⁷ a reaper cannot fill his hands with it,
   nor one who gathers fill his arms.
⁸ May those who pass by not say to them,
   "The blessing of the LORD be on you;
   we bless you in the name of the LORD."

Psalm 130

A song of ascents.

¹ Out of the depths I cry to you, LORD;
²   Lord, hear my voice.
 Let your ears be attentive
   to my cry for mercy.

³ If you, LORD, kept a record of sins,
   Lord, who could stand?
⁴ But with you there is forgiveness,
   so that we can, with reverence,
     serve you.

⁵ I wait for the LORD, my whole being
     waits,
   and in his word I put my hope.
⁶ I wait for the Lord
   more than watchmen wait for the
     morning,
   more than watchmen wait for the
     morning.

⁷ Israel, put your hope in the LORD,
   for with the LORD is unfailing love
   and with him is full redemption.
⁸ He himself will redeem Israel
   from all their sins.

ᵃ 2 Or eat — / for while they sleep he provides for

CLEAN RECORD

READ: **PSALM 130:3-4**

I magine being confronted with a list of everything you have ever done wrong. The list spells out every big sin and every small mistake. It details deeds you did on purpose and wrongs you're not even aware of. It covers every mishap, whether thoughts, words, or actions.

How many trees would the Lord have to kill to put all your faults on paper? Maybe not a whole forest, but far more than a little twig. The sweet reality is that you can banish that imaginary list from your mind, because the Bible promises that the Lord doesn't keep a record of your sins.

You can run to God and get forgiveness whenever you need it. But the Lord doesn't forgive your wrongdoing so you can go and sin some more. If sin is bad enough for Jesus to die for, it's bad enough to get rid of from your life. This song informs you that the Lord throws away every record of your sin so you can serve him with reverence, living for him with utter respect.

BUILDING

FAITH

WISDOM

STRENGTH

Forgiveness seems like a prime excuse to purposely go on sinning over and over. But that would be an act of total contempt for your God, showing disrespect for "the riches of his kindness, forbearance and patience" (Romans 2:4). The Lord has wiped your record clean. Don't abuse his kindness.

Psalm 131

A song of ascents. Of David.

¹ My heart is not proud, LORD,
  my eyes are not haughty;
I do not concern myself with great matters
  or things too wonderful for me.
² But I have calmed and quieted myself,
  I am like a weaned child with its
    mother;
  like a weaned child I am content.

³ Israel, put your hope in the LORD
  both now and forevermore.

Psalm 132

A song of ascents.

¹ LORD, remember David
  and all his self-denial.

² He swore an oath to the LORD,
  he made a vow to the Mighty One
    of Jacob:
³ "I will not enter my house
  or go to my bed,
⁴ I will allow no sleep to my eyes
  or slumber to my eyelids,
⁵ till I find a place for the LORD,
  a dwelling for the Mighty One of Jacob."

⁶ We heard it in Ephrathah,
  we came upon it in the fields of Jaar:[a]
⁷ "Let us go to his dwelling place,
  let us worship at his footstool, saying,
⁸ 'Arise, LORD, and come to your resting
    place,
  you and the ark of your might.
⁹ May your priests be clothed with your
    righteousness;
  may your faithful people sing for joy.' "

¹⁰ For the sake of your servant David,
  do not reject your anointed one.

¹¹ The LORD swore an oath to David,
  a sure oath he will not revoke:
  "One of your own descendants
    I will place on your throne.
¹² If your sons keep my covenant
  and the statutes I teach them,
then their sons will sit
  on your throne for ever and ever."

¹³ For the LORD has chosen Zion,
  he has desired it for his dwelling,
    saying,
¹⁴ "This is my resting place for ever and ever;
  here I will sit enthroned, for I have
    desired it.
¹⁵ I will bless her with abundant provisions;
  her poor I will satisfy with food.
¹⁶ I will clothe her priests with salvation,
  and her faithful people will ever sing
    for joy.

¹⁷ "Here I will make a horn[b] grow for David
  and set up a lamp for my anointed one.
¹⁸ I will clothe his enemies with shame,
  but his head will be adorned with a
    radiant crown."

Psalm 133

A song of ascents. Of David.

¹ How good and pleasant it is
  when God's people live together in
    unity!

² It is like precious oil poured on the head,
  running down on the beard,
running down on Aaron's beard,
  down on the collar of his robe.
³ It is as if the dew of Hermon
  were falling on Mount Zion.
For there the LORD bestows his blessing,
  even life forevermore.

Psalm 134

A song of ascents.

¹ Praise the LORD, all you servants of the
    LORD
  who minister by night in the house of
    the LORD.
² Lift up your hands in the sanctuary
  and praise the LORD.

³ May the LORD bless you from Zion,
  he who is the Maker of heaven and
    earth.

Psalm 135

¹ Praise the LORD.[c]

Praise the name of the LORD;
  praise him, you servants of the LORD,

---

[a] 6 Or *heard of it in Ephrathah, / we found it in the fields of Jearim.* (See 1 Chron. 13:5,6) (And no quotation marks around verses 7-9)   [b] 17 *Horn* here symbolizes strong one, that is, king.   [c] 1 Hebrew *Hallelu Yah*; also in verses 3 and 21

² you who minister in the house of the
   LORD,
   in the courts of the house of our God.

³ Praise the LORD, for the LORD is good;
   sing praise to his name, for that is
      pleasant.
⁴ For the LORD has chosen Jacob to be
      his own,
   Israel to be his treasured possession.

⁵ I know that the LORD is great,
   that our Lord is greater than all gods.
⁶ The LORD does whatever pleases him,
   in the heavens and on the earth,
   in the seas and all their depths.
⁷ He makes clouds rise from the ends of
      the earth;
   he sends lightning with the rain
   and brings out the wind from his
      storehouses.

⁸ He struck down the firstborn of Egypt,
   the firstborn of people and animals.
⁹ He sent his signs and wonders into your
      midst, Egypt,
   against Pharaoh and all his servants.
¹⁰ He struck down many nations
   and killed mighty kings —
¹¹ Sihon king of the Amorites,
   Og king of Bashan,
   and all the kings of Canaan —
¹² and he gave their land as an inheritance,
   an inheritance to his people Israel.

¹³ Your name, LORD, endures forever,
   your renown, LORD, through all
      generations.
¹⁴ For the LORD will vindicate his people
   and have compassion on his servants.

¹⁵ The idols of the nations are silver and gold,
   made by human hands.
¹⁶ They have mouths, but cannot speak,
   eyes, but cannot see.
¹⁷ They have ears, but cannot hear,
   nor is there breath in their mouths.
¹⁸ Those who make them will be like them,
   and so will all who trust in them.

¹⁹ All you Israelites, praise the LORD;
   house of Aaron, praise the LORD;
²⁰ house of Levi, praise the LORD;
   you who fear him, praise the LORD.
²¹ Praise be to the LORD from Zion,
   to him who dwells in Jerusalem.

   Praise the LORD.

---

a 13 Or *the Sea of Reeds*; also in verse 15

Psalm 136

¹ Give thanks to the LORD, for he is good.
   His love endures forever.
² Give thanks to the God of gods.
   His love endures forever.
³ Give thanks to the Lord of lords:
   His love endures forever.

⁴ to him who alone does great wonders,
   His love endures forever.
⁵ who by his understanding made the
      heavens,
   His love endures forever.
⁶ who spread out the earth upon the waters,
   His love endures forever.
⁷ who made the great lights —
   His love endures forever.
⁸ the sun to govern the day,
   His love endures forever.
⁹ the moon and stars to govern the night;
   His love endures forever.

¹⁰ to him who struck down the firstborn
      of Egypt
   His love endures forever.
¹¹ and brought Israel out from among them
   His love endures forever.
¹² with a mighty hand and outstretched
      arm;
   His love endures forever.
¹³ to him who divided the Red Sea*a* asunder
   His love endures forever.
¹⁴ and brought Israel through the midst of it,
   His love endures forever.
¹⁵ but swept Pharaoh and his army into the
      Red Sea;
   His love endures forever.

¹⁶ to him who led his people through the
      wilderness;
   His love endures forever.

¹⁷ to him who struck down great kings,
   His love endures forever.
¹⁸ and killed mighty kings —
   His love endures forever.
¹⁹ Sihon king of the Amorites
   His love endures forever.
²⁰ and Og king of Bashan —
   His love endures forever.
²¹ and gave their land as an inheritance,
   His love endures forever.
²² an inheritance to his servant Israel.
   His love endures forever.

²³ He remembered us in our low estate
>> *His love endures forever.*
²⁴ and freed us from our enemies.
>> *His love endures forever.*
²⁵ He gives food to every creature.
>> *His love endures forever.*

²⁶ Give thanks to the God of heaven.
>> *His love endures forever.*

Psalm 137

¹ By the rivers of Babylon we sat and wept
>> when we remembered Zion.
² There on the poplars
>> we hung our harps,
³ for there our captors asked us for songs,
>> our tormentors demanded songs
>> of joy;
>> they said, "Sing us one of the songs
>> of Zion!"

⁴ How can we sing the songs of the Lord
>> while in a foreign land?
⁵ If I forget you, Jerusalem,
>> may my right hand forget its skill.
⁶ May my tongue cling to the roof of my
>> mouth
>> if I do not remember you,
>> if I do not consider Jerusalem
>> my highest joy.

⁷ Remember, Lord, what the Edomites did
>> on the day Jerusalem fell.
>> "Tear it down," they cried,
>> "tear it down to its foundations!"
⁸ Daughter Babylon, doomed to
>> destruction,
>> happy is the one who repays you
>> according to what you have done to us.
⁹ Happy is the one who seizes your infants
>> and dashes them against the rocks.

Psalm 138

Of David.

¹ I will praise you, Lord, with all my heart;
>> before the "gods" I will sing your
>> praise.
² I will bow down toward your holy temple
>> and will praise your name
>> for your unfailing love and your
>> faithfulness,
>> for you have so exalted your solemn
>> decree
>> that it surpasses your fame.

³ When I called, you answered me;
>> you greatly emboldened me.

⁴ May all the kings of the earth praise you,
>> Lord,
>> when they hear what you have
>> decreed.
⁵ May they sing of the ways of the Lord,
>> for the glory of the Lord is great.

⁶ Though the Lord is exalted, he looks
>> kindly on the lowly;
>> though lofty, he sees them from afar.
⁷ Though I walk in the midst of trouble,
>> you preserve my life.
>> You stretch out your hand against the
>> anger of my foes;
>> with your right hand you save me.
⁸ The Lord will vindicate me;
>> your love, Lord, endures forever —
>> do not abandon the works of your
>> hands.

Psalm 139

For the director of music.
Of David. A psalm.

¹ You have searched me, Lord,
>> and you know me.
² You know when I sit and when I rise;
>> you perceive my thoughts from afar.
³ You discern my going out and my lying
>> down;
>> you are familiar with all my ways.
⁴ Before a word is on my tongue
>> you, Lord, know it completely.
⁵ You hem me in behind and before,
>> and you lay your hand upon me.
⁶ Such knowledge is too wonderful for me,
>> too lofty for me to attain.

⁷ Where can I go from your Spirit?
>> Where can I flee from your presence?
⁸ If I go up to the heavens, you are there;
>> if I make my bed in the depths, you are
>> there.
⁹ If I rise on the wings of the dawn,
>> if I settle on the far side of the sea,
¹⁰ even there your hand will guide me,
>> your right hand will hold me fast.
¹¹ If I say, "Surely the darkness will hide me
>> and the light become night around me,"
¹² even the darkness will not be dark to you;
>> the night will shine like the day,
>> for darkness is as light to you.

ON REPEAT

READ: PSALM 136:26

People know what to expect when you open your mouth. You have signature words or comic lines everyone knows. You might have jokes you constantly repeat or lyrics you sing in your sleep. If you move your lips, you have phrases you say over and over.

Psalm 136 contains an obvious repeated refrain: His love endures forever. This song starts by telling you to "Give thanks to the LORD, for he is good" (v. 1) and ends the same way (v. 26). The lines between start and finish recite good things the Lord has done, concrete things the psalmist is grateful for. Some describe God's stunning acts of creation. Others come from ancient Israelite history. Still others sound straight out of your life. But every line illustrates that obvious theme: His love endures forever.

That "love" is the Lord's "mercy" or "loyal love," and it's the Psalms' most significant description of God. It's the kind of love that leads the Lord to help people in misery. It's a love that lasts forever. It's part of his unchanging eternal character.

BUILDING FAITH WISDOM STRENGTH

If you want to add a new line to your vocabulary of most-used words, this is a good one. No matter what God gives you, his love endures forever. Whenever he leads you through a rough patch, his love endures forever. Don't let a day slip by without inserting that line into your life.

¹³ For you created my inmost being;
    you knit me together in my mother's
        womb.
¹⁴ I praise you because I am fearfully and
        wonderfully made;
    your works are wonderful,
    I know that full well.
¹⁵ My frame was not hidden from you
    when I was made in the secret place,
    when I was woven together in the
        depths of the earth.
¹⁶ Your eyes saw my unformed body;
    all the days ordained for me were
        written in your book
    before one of them came to be.
¹⁷ How precious to me are your thoughts,ᵃ
        God!
    How vast is the sum of them!
¹⁸ Were I to count them,
    they would outnumber the grains of
        sand —
    when I awake, I am still with you.

¹⁹ If only you, God, would slay the wicked!
    Away from me, you who are
        bloodthirsty!
²⁰ They speak of you with evil intent;
    your adversaries misuse your name.
²¹ Do I not hate those who hate you, LORD,
    and abhor those who are in rebellion
        against you?
²² I have nothing but hatred for them;
    I count them my enemies.
²³ Search me, God, and know my heart;
    test me and know my anxious
        thoughts.
²⁴ See if there is any offensive way in me,
    and lead me in the way everlasting.

Psalm 140ᵇ

For the director of music.
A psalm of David.

¹ Rescue me, LORD, from evildoers;
    protect me from the violent,
² who devise evil plans in their hearts
    and stir up war every day.
³ They make their tongues as sharp as a
        serpent's;
    the poison of vipers is on their lips.ᶜ

⁴ Keep me safe, LORD, from the hands of
        the wicked;
    protect me from the violent,
    who devise ways to trip my feet.
⁵ The arrogant have hidden a snare for me;
    they have spread out the cords of
        their net
    and have set traps for me along my
        path.

⁶ I say to the LORD, "You are my God."
    Hear, LORD, my cry for mercy.
⁷ Sovereign LORD, my strong deliverer,
    you shield my head in the day of battle.
⁸ Do not grant the wicked their desires,
        LORD;
    do not let their plans succeed.

⁹ Those who surround me proudly rear
        their heads;
    may the mischief of their lips engulf
        them.
¹⁰ May burning coals fall on them;
    may they be thrown into the fire,
    into miry pits, never to rise.
¹¹ May slanderers not be established in the
        land;
    may disaster hunt down the violent.

¹² I know that the LORD secures justice for
        the poor
    and upholds the cause of the needy.
¹³ Surely the righteous will praise your name,
    and the upright will live in your
        presence.

Psalm 141

A psalm of David.

¹ I call to you, LORD, come quickly to me;
    hear me when I call to you.
² May my prayer be set before you like
        incense;
    may the lifting up of my hands be like
        the evening sacrifice.

³ Set a guard over my mouth, LORD;
    keep watch over the door of my lips.
⁴ Do not let my heart be drawn to what is
        evil
    so that I take part in wicked deeds
    along with those who are evildoers;
    do not let me eat their delicacies.

⁵ Let a righteous man strike me — that is a
        kindness;

ᵃ 17 Or *How amazing are your thoughts concerning me*   ᵇ In Hebrew texts 140:1-13 is numbered 140:2-14.
ᶜ 3 The Hebrew has *Selah* (a word of uncertain meaning) here and at the end of verses 5 and 8.

MADE JUST RIGHT

READ: PSALM 139:13-14

There are two groups of people spreading their opinions on what God thinks about humanity. One group seems intent on reminding us about how trashy and sinful we are. They are constantly reminding us about how unworthy we are in the presence of God's greatness. Oh yeah, God loves us, but his love endures through our rottenness. We are God's much-loved, fantastic disappointment.

I'm in the other camp. I believe God loves us so much that he made us perfectly unique. In love, God made every single one of us different from every other and, in love, each of us is perfect to him. If your nose is big, if your hair is a freaky color, if you have chronically bad breath—God wanted you that way. He made you unique.

BUILDING

FAITH

WISDOM

STRENGTH

There are really important words there: *knit*, *fearfully* and *wonderfully*, *frame*, *woven*, *unformed*. Can you tell the author of the psalm was trying to describe the indescribable?

That uniqueness includes your personality, your looks, your smell, your tastes in clothes and food, your abilities—anything that makes you unlike anyone else. Your uniqueness is God's stamp of creativity. If you embrace God's wonderful creativity, you'll see yourself as an interesting world just waiting to be discovered. Living in God's love encourages us to discover more about who he made us to be.

Taken from *Leave a Footprint—Change the World* by Tim Baker, copyright © 2009 by Tim Baker, published by Zondervan.

let him rebuke me — that is oil on
    my head.
My head will not refuse it,
    for my prayer will still be against the
        deeds of evildoers.

6 Their rulers will be thrown down from
        the cliffs,
    and the wicked will learn that my
        words were well spoken.
7 They will say, "As one plows and breaks
        up the earth,
    so our bones have been scattered at
        the mouth of the grave."

8 But my eyes are fixed on you, Sovereign
        LORD;
    in you I take refuge — do not give me
        over to death.
9 Keep me safe from the traps set by
        evildoers,
    from the snares they have laid for me.
10 Let the wicked fall into their own nets,
    while I pass by in safety.

Psalm 142[a]

*A maskil[b] of David. When he was in the cave.
A prayer.*

1 I cry aloud to the LORD;
    I lift up my voice to the LORD for mercy.
2 I pour out before him my complaint;
    before him I tell my trouble.

3 When my spirit grows faint within me,
    it is you who watch over my way.
In the path where I walk
    people have hidden a snare for me.
4 Look and see, there is no one at my right
        hand;
    no one is concerned for me.
I have no refuge;
    no one cares for my life.

5 I cry to you, LORD;
    I say, "You are my refuge,
    my portion in the land of the living."

6 Listen to my cry,
    for I am in desperate need;
rescue me from those who pursue me,
    for they are too strong for me.
7 Set me free from my prison,
    that I may praise your name.

Then the righteous will gather about me
    because of your goodness to me.

Psalm 143

A psalm of David.

1 LORD, hear my prayer,
    listen to my cry for mercy;
in your faithfulness and righteousness
    come to my relief.
2 Do not bring your servant into
        judgment,
    for no one living is righteous before
        you.
3 The enemy pursues me,
    he crushes me to the ground;
he makes me dwell in the darkness
    like those long dead.
4 So my spirit grows faint within me;
    my heart within me is dismayed.
5 I remember the days of long ago;
    I meditate on all your works
    and consider what your hands have
        done.
6 I spread out my hands to you;
    I thirst for you like a parched land.[c]

7 Answer me quickly, LORD;
    my spirit fails.
Do not hide your face from me
    or I will be like those who go down to
        the pit.
8 Let the morning bring me word of your
        unfailing love,
    for I have put my trust in you.
Show me the way I should go,
    for to you I entrust my life.
9 Rescue me from my enemies, LORD,
    for I hide myself in you.
10 Teach me to do your will,
    for you are my God;
may your good Spirit
    lead me on level ground.

11 For your name's sake, LORD, preserve
        my life;
    in your righteousness, bring me out
        of trouble.
12 In your unfailing love, silence my
        enemies;
    destroy all my foes,
    for I am your servant.

---

[a] In Hebrew texts 142:1-7 is numbered 142:2-8.   [b] Title: Probably a literary or musical term   [c] 6 The
Hebrew has *Selah* (a word of uncertain meaning) here.

Psalm 144

Of David.

[1] Praise be to the LORD my Rock,
  who trains my hands for war,
  my fingers for battle.
[2] He is my loving God and my fortress,
  my stronghold and my deliverer,
  my shield, in whom I take refuge,
  who subdues peoples[a] under me.

[3] LORD, what are human beings that you
    care for them,
  mere mortals that you think of them?
[4] They are like a breath;
  their days are like a fleeting shadow.

[5] Part your heavens, LORD, and come
    down;
  touch the mountains, so that they
    smoke.
[6] Send forth lightning and scatter the
    enemy;
  shoot your arrows and rout them.
[7] Reach down your hand from on high;
  deliver me and rescue me
from the mighty waters,
  from the hands of foreigners
[8] whose mouths are full of lies,
  whose right hands are deceitful.

[9] I will sing a new song to you, my God;
  on the ten-stringed lyre I will make
    music to you,
[10] to the One who gives victory to kings,
  who delivers his servant David.

From the deadly sword [11] deliver me;
  rescue me from the hands of foreigners
whose mouths are full of lies,
  whose right hands are deceitful.

[12] Then our sons in their youth
  will be like well-nurtured plants,
and our daughters will be like pillars
  carved to adorn a palace.
[13] Our barns will be filled
  with every kind of provision.
Our sheep will increase by thousands,
  by tens of thousands in our fields;
[14]   our oxen will draw heavy loads.[b]

There will be no breaching of walls,
  no going into captivity,
  no cry of distress in our streets.
[15] Blessed is the people of whom this is true;
  blessed is the people whose God is the
    LORD.

Psalm 145[c]

A psalm of praise. Of David.

[1] I will exalt you, my God the King;
  I will praise your name for ever and
    ever.
[2] Every day I will praise you
  and extol your name for ever and ever.

[3] Great is the LORD and most worthy of
    praise;
  his greatness no one can fathom.
[4] One generation commends your works to
    another;
  they tell of your mighty acts.
[5] They speak of the glorious splendor of
    your majesty—
  and I will meditate on your wonderful
    works.[d]
[6] They tell of the power of your awesome
    works—
  and I will proclaim your great deeds.
[7] They celebrate your abundant goodness
  and joyfully sing of your
    righteousness.

[8] The LORD is gracious and compassionate,
  slow to anger and rich in love.

[9] The LORD is good to all;
  he has compassion on all he has
    made.
[10] All your works praise you, LORD;
  your faithful people extol you.
[11] They tell of the glory of your kingdom
  and speak of your might,
[12] so that all people may know of your
    mighty acts
  and the glorious splendor of your
    kingdom.
[13] Your kingdom is an everlasting kingdom,
  and your dominion endures through
    all generations.

---

[a] 2 Many manuscripts of the Masoretic Text, Dead Sea Scrolls, Aquila, Jerome and Syriac; most manuscripts of the Masoretic Text *subdues my people*   [b] 14 Or *our chieftains will be firmly established*   [c] This psalm is an acrostic poem, the verses of which (including verse 13b) begin with the successive letters of the Hebrew alphabet.   [d] 5 Dead Sea Scrolls and Syriac (see also Septuagint); Masoretic Text *On the glorious splendor of your majesty / and on your wonderful works I will meditate*

BIG ASK

READ: PSALM 144:5-6

D avid doesn't want small favors from God. He begs the Lord to rip open heaven. He urges God to stretch out his hand and make mountains smoke. He wants bolts of lightning to send his enemies running. And those are just a few of the items on his list of prayer requests.

David needs an unusual brand of divine assistance to help him rule Israel. His enemies pursue him with deadly swords (Psalm 144:10). He fends off foreigners spewing lies (v. 8). He worries about enemies breaking through city walls, and he hopes he never hears cries of distress rise from the streets (v. 14). So he asks the Lord for military victory. He praises God for training him to win at war. He counts on God to make entire peoples submit to him (vv. 1-2).

As David watches over the nation, he looks for God's blessings not just for him but for every person under his care. He wants young women and men to grow up like well-fed plants (v. 12). He prays for barns full of crops and fields covered with flocks (v. 13).

BUILDING FAITH WISDOM STRENGTH

David's requests for military triumph might not resemble what you need from God. But you can make your own bold requests of the Lord, asking him to meet your real needs. He knows you're a mere mortal. Your life is but a breath. But because he is your God, you can count on his care.

FULL YET?

READ: PSALM 145:16

If God is as good as all indications say he is, then God knows our needs.

Imagine wanting the best for someone or something. What if you had a new puppy? Would you let the dog nibble on a dead rat in the backyard while you had some juicy, meaty dog food for him inside the house? It would only make sense to give the best to the puppy. That's what good owners do.

What if the puppy felt threatened when you said to him, "Eating that dead rat will make you sick!" What if he stuck up his head and replied, "You're not a good owner. You should leave me to my own business."

We are not God's pets. But some of this analogy really fits our situation. If God is the maker and owner of this world, which includes us, God knows when we're doing something that hurts us. God knows if we can live better lives. God knows the best way to be human, the best way to enjoy reality.

BUILDING FAITH WISDOM STRENGTH

What is the best we could have in God's wide world? Many times we nibble on lesser foods for our souls—diversions such as feeding on a friend's approval, moping in a puddle of self-consciousness, running after desires for things we know aren't good for us, licking our own proverbial dead rats—when God is offering us real food.

Our souls' food is God himself. We were made to run on the life of God.

The Lord is trustworthy in all he
   promises
   and faithful in all he does.[a]
[14] The Lord upholds all who fall
   and lifts up all who are bowed down.
[15] The eyes of all look to you,
   and you give them their food at the
   proper time.
[16] You open your hand
   and satisfy the desires of every living
   thing.

[17] The Lord is righteous in all his ways
   and faithful in all he does.
[18] The Lord is near to all who call on him,
   to all who call on him in truth.
[19] He fulfills the desires of those who fear
   him;
   he hears their cry and saves them.
[20] The Lord watches over all who love him,
   but all the wicked he will destroy.

[21] My mouth will speak in praise of the Lord.
   Let every creature praise his holy name
   for ever and ever.

Psalm 146

[1] Praise the Lord.[b]

Praise the Lord, my soul.

[2] I will praise the Lord all my life;
   I will sing praise to my God as long as
   I live.
[3] Do not put your trust in princes,
   in human beings, who cannot save.
[4] When their spirit departs, they return to
   the ground;
   on that very day their plans come to
   nothing.
[5] Blessed are those whose help is the God
   of Jacob,
   whose hope is in the Lord their God.

[6] He is the Maker of heaven and earth,
   the sea, and everything in them—
   he remains faithful forever.
[7] He upholds the cause of the oppressed
   and gives food to the hungry.
   The Lord sets prisoners free,
[8]   the Lord gives sight to the blind,
   the Lord lifts up those who are bowed
   down,

the Lord loves the righteous.
[9] The Lord watches over the foreigner
   and sustains the fatherless and the
   widow,
   but he frustrates the ways of the
   wicked.

[10] The Lord reigns forever,
   your God, O Zion, for all generations.

Praise the Lord.

Psalm 147

[1] Praise the Lord.[c]

How good it is to sing praises to our God,
   how pleasant and fitting to praise him!

[2] The Lord builds up Jerusalem;
   he gathers the exiles of Israel.
[3] He heals the brokenhearted
   and binds up their wounds.
[4] He determines the number of the stars
   and calls them each by name.
[5] Great is our Lord and mighty in power;
   his understanding has no limit.
[6] The Lord sustains the humble
   but casts the wicked to the ground.

[7] Sing to the Lord with grateful praise;
   make music to our God on the harp.

[8] He covers the sky with clouds;
   he supplies the earth with rain
   and makes grass grow on the hills.
[9] He provides food for the cattle
   and for the young ravens when they
   call.

[10] His pleasure is not in the strength of the
   horse,
   nor his delight in the legs of the
   warrior;
[11] the Lord delights in those who fear him,
   who put their hope in his unfailing
   love.

[12] Extol the Lord, Jerusalem;
   praise your God, Zion.
[13] He strengthens the bars of your gates
   and blesses your people within you.
[14] He grants peace to your borders
   and satisfies you with the finest of
   wheat.

---

[a] 13 One manuscript of the Masoretic Text, Dead Sea Scrolls and Syriac (see also Septuagint); most manuscripts of the Masoretic Text do not have the last two lines of verse 13.   [b] 1 Hebrew *Hallelu Yah*; also in verse 10   [c] 1 Hebrew *Hallelu Yah*; also in verse 20

THIS IS GOD

READ: PSALM 147:5,11

God is imagined in countless ways on this planet. Maybe he lives on Mount Olympus, as the Greeks thought, and comes to earth only when he's bored. Maybe "he" is actually an entire pantheon of gods, as the Hindus have it. Maybe God is just another word for nature, as the pantheists believe, meaning that the tree outside my window is God; this chair is God; hey, you and I are God! Maybe there is no God as a separate being, as the Buddhists have it; the answers are supposedly within us.

Christianity offers a view of God that is strikingly different from any other. In Christianity, there is one God. He is all-powerful. His most striking feature is not anger or power or transcendence or even creativity, but instead is his relentless, all-consuming love. No one would have made up such a God. The idea is too outrageous.

This is a God who comes from heaven, from all of his perfection and purity and might, to us, in all of our weakness and impurity. He puts on skin, taking the form of a helpless baby all in pursuit of your heart. This is God who, when turned down, ignored, rejected—even violently, even blasphemously—finds a new way to express his love and issue the invitation. This is a God who has never given up on winning your heart. Never.

BUILDING FAITH WISDOM STRENGTH

¹⁵ He sends his command to the earth;
　　his word runs swiftly.
¹⁶ He spreads the snow like wool
　　and scatters the frost like ashes.
¹⁷ He hurls down his hail like pebbles.
　　Who can withstand his icy blast?
¹⁸ He sends his word and melts them;
　　he stirs up his breezes, and the
　　　waters flow.

¹⁹ He has revealed his word to Jacob,
　　his laws and decrees to Israel.
²⁰ He has done this for no other nation;
　　they do not know his laws.ᵃ

　　Praise the LORD.

Psalm 148

¹ Praise the LORD.ᵇ

Praise the LORD from the heavens;
　　praise him in the heights above.
² Praise him, all his angels;
　　praise him, all his heavenly hosts.
³ Praise him, sun and moon;
　　praise him, all you shining stars.
⁴ Praise him, you highest heavens
　　and you waters above the skies.

⁵ Let them praise the name of the LORD,
　　for at his command they were
　　　created,
⁶ and he established them for ever and
　　　ever —
　　he issued a decree that will never pass
　　　away.

⁷ Praise the LORD from the earth,
　　you great sea creatures and all ocean
　　　depths,
⁸ lightning and hail, snow and clouds,
　　stormy winds that do his bidding,
⁹ you mountains and all hills,
　　fruit trees and all cedars,
¹⁰ wild animals and all cattle,
　　small creatures and flying birds,
¹¹ kings of the earth and all nations,
　　you princes and all rulers on earth,
¹² young men and women,
　　old men and children.

¹³ Let them praise the name of the LORD,
　　for his name alone is exalted;

his splendor is above the earth and the
　　heavens.
¹⁴ And he has raised up for his people a
　　horn,ᶜ
　　the praise of all his faithful servants,
　　of Israel, the people close to his heart.

Praise the LORD.

Psalm 149

¹ Praise the LORD.ᵈ

Sing to the LORD a new song,
　　his praise in the assembly of his
　　　faithful people.

² Let Israel rejoice in their Maker;
　　let the people of Zion be glad in their
　　　King.
³ Let them praise his name with dancing
　　and make music to him with timbrel
　　　and harp.
⁴ For the LORD takes delight in his
　　people;
　　he crowns the humble with victory.
⁵ Let his faithful people rejoice in this
　　honor
　　and sing for joy on their beds.

⁶ May the praise of God be in their
　　mouths
　　and a double-edged sword in their
　　　hands,
⁷ to inflict vengeance on the nations
　　and punishment on the peoples,
⁸ to bind their kings with fetters,
　　their nobles with shackles of iron,
⁹ to carry out the sentence written against
　　them —
　　this is the glory of all his faithful
　　　people.

Praise the LORD.

Psalm 150

¹ Praise the LORD.ᵉ

Praise God in his sanctuary;
　　praise him in his mighty heavens.
² Praise him for his acts of power;
　　praise him for his surpassing
　　　greatness.

ᵃ *20* Masoretic Text; Dead Sea Scrolls and Septuagint *nation; / he has not made his laws known to them*
ᵇ *1* Hebrew *Hallelu Yah*; also in verse 14   ᶜ *14* *Horn* here symbolizes strength.   ᵈ *1* Hebrew *Hallelu Yah*;
also in verse 9   ᵉ *1* Hebrew *Hallelu Yah*; also in verse 6

JOIN THE WORLD

READ: PSALM 148:3

When you worship the Lord, you join a cosmic choir that includes more than human beings. Psalm 19:1 says, "The heavens declare the glory of God; the skies proclaim the work of his hands." And the sky isn't the only thing in the universe that opens its mouth wide to praise God.

Psalm 148 shows every part of the Lord's creation bowing in worship. Praise starts in the heavens, "the heights above" (Psalm 148:1). It rings out among the angels, the Lord's heavenly army. It echoes from the sun, moon, and stars to the farthest reaches of space. All of these examples of the Lord's handiwork praise him because his command created them. He spoke and they sprang into existence (Genesis 1:3–14).

The Lord's earthbound creation joins the song. Sea creatures and fish swimming the ocean depths sing. The weather waves its praise. Mountains large and small are joined by all kinds of trees. Wild and domestic beasts on land and in the air can't help but worship. Rulers from every part of the world worship the Lord along with men and women of every age (Psalm 148:7–12)

Only God deserves this kind of intense worship. His splendor rises above the entire universe (v. 13). When you praise God, you might think you're the only one singing. But the whole world joins with you. Praise the Lord!

BUILDING
FAITH
WISDOM
STRENGTH

³ Praise him with the sounding of the
    trumpet,
  praise him with the harp and lyre,
⁴ praise him with timbrel and dancing,
  praise him with the strings and
    pipe,

⁵ praise him with the clash of cymbals,
  praise him with resounding cymbals.

⁶ Let everything that has breath praise
  the LORD.

  Praise the LORD.

PROVERBS

WHEN DID THIS HAPPEN?

This book was written around 970 B.C. in the land of Israel

WHO IS IN THIS BOOK?

wisdom
mockers
sinners
fools

VERSES YOU MIGHT RECOGNIZE

PROVERBS 1:7

"The fear of the LORD is the beginning of knowledge, but fools despise wisdom and instruction."

PROVERBS 31:30

"Charm is deceptive, and beauty is fleeting; but a woman who fears the LORD is to be praised."

WHAT'S IT ABOUT?

Where does wisdom come from? Written by the wisest man who ever lived, King Solomon, this book focuses on the benefits that come from fearing the Lord. Does that mean you have to be afraid of God? No. Fearing the Lord means giving God the respect he deserves, following his instructions and honoring him with your actions. This book tells us that fearing the Lord is the way to wisdom.

Covering topics such as money, friendship, work, sexual purity and family, Proverbs is a series of common-sense instructions for living life in a wise way. These "proverbs" can be applied to many different people and circumstances. But here's the bottom line: Wise choices lead to a happy life, while foolish decisions lead to destruction.

Purpose and Theme

1 The proverbs of Solomon son of David,
king of Israel:

² for gaining wisdom and instruction;
for understanding words of insight;
³ for receiving instruction in prudent
behavior,
doing what is right and just and fair;
⁴ for giving prudence to those who are
simple,ᵃ
knowledge and discretion to the
young—
⁵ let the wise listen and add to their
learning,
and let the discerning get guidance—
⁶ for understanding proverbs and parables,
the sayings and riddles of the wise.ᵇ

⁷ The fear of the Lᴏʀᴅ is the beginning of
knowledge,
but foolsᶜ despise wisdom and
instruction.

Prologue:
Exhortations to Embrace Wisdom

Warning Against the Invitation
of Sinful Men

⁸ Listen, my son, to your father's
instruction
and do not forsake your mother's
teaching.
⁹ They are a garland to grace your head
and a chain to adorn your neck.

¹⁰ My son, if sinful men entice you,
do not give in to them.
¹¹ If they say, "Come along with us;
let's lie in wait for innocent blood,
let's ambush some harmless soul;
¹² let's swallow them alive, like the grave,
and whole, like those who go down to
the pit;

¹³ we will get all sorts of valuable things
and fill our houses with plunder;
¹⁴ cast lots with us;
we will all share the loot"—
¹⁵ my son, do not go along with them,
do not set foot on their paths;
¹⁶ for their feet rush into evil,
they are swift to shed blood.
¹⁷ How useless to spread a net
where every bird can see it!
¹⁸ These men lie in wait for their own blood;
they ambush only themselves!
¹⁹ Such are the paths of all who go after ill-
gotten gain;
it takes away the life of those who get it.

Wisdom's Rebuke

²⁰ Out in the open wisdom calls aloud,
she raises her voice in the public
square;
²¹ on top of the wallᵈ she cries out,
at the city gate she makes her speech:

²² "How long will you who are simple love
your simple ways?
How long will mockers delight in
mockery
and fools hate knowledge?
²³ Repent at my rebuke!
Then I will pour out my thoughts to you,
I will make known to you my
teachings.
²⁴ But since you refuse to listen when I call
and no one pays attention when I
stretch out my hand,
²⁵ since you disregard all my advice
and do not accept my rebuke,
²⁶ I in turn will laugh when disaster
strikes you;
I will mock when calamity overtakes
you—
²⁷ when calamity overtakes you like a
storm,

ᵃ 4 The Hebrew word rendered *simple* in Proverbs denotes a person who is gullible, without moral
direction and inclined to evil.   ᵇ 6 Or *understanding a proverb, namely, a parable, / and the sayings of
the wise, their riddles*   ᶜ 7 The Hebrew words rendered *fool* in Proverbs, and often elsewhere in the Old
Testament, denote a person who is morally deficient.   ᵈ 21 Septuagint; Hebrew / *at noisy street corners*

DON'T BE A FOOL

Fearing God might not sound fun. But again and again Scripture says it's your first step to getting the wisdom you need to survive real life.

The meaning of the word for "fear" ranges from feeling terror in the midst of a deadly storm (Jonah 1:10) to overflowing with awe in a king's presence (1 Kings 3:28). When you experience "the fear of the Lord" you simultaneously wonder about backing away in dread but can't help but draw close in amazement. This healthy reverence doesn't leave you quaking. It does remind you to honor God and not treat him casually, like some kind of heavenly buddy.

Proverbs says good things result when you choose to live for God with utter respect. You get insight, a grasp of what's sensible, right, and fair. Everyone will notice you're wise beyond your years, and your understanding will stay fresh until your final breath. You will gain an intelligence that guards you from acting recklessly or caving into evil peer pressure.

Proverbs is the Bible's most densely packed collection of wisdom. If you respect God, you will think hard about the instructions you find in these pages. And you won't hesitate to put your discoveries into action. After all, rejecting the Lord's choice wisdom will send you tripping down a fool's path. And nothing about that sounds enjoyable.

BUILDING
FAITH
WISDOM
STRENGTH

when disaster sweeps over you like a
whirlwind,
when distress and trouble overwhelm
you.
28 "Then they will call to me but I will not
answer;
they will look for me but will not
find me,
29 since they hated knowledge
and did not choose to fear the LORD.
30 Since they would not accept my advice
and spurned my rebuke,
31 they will eat the fruit of their ways
and be filled with the fruit of their
schemes.
32 For the waywardness of the simple will
kill them,
and the complacency of fools will
destroy them;
33 but whoever listens to me will live in
safety
and be at ease, without fear of harm."

Moral Benefits of Wisdom

2 My son, if you accept my words
and store up my commands within you,
2 turning your ear to wisdom
and applying your heart to
understanding—
3 indeed, if you call out for insight
and cry aloud for understanding,
4 and if you look for it as for silver
and search for it as for hidden treasure,
5 then you will understand the fear of the
LORD
and find the knowledge of God.
6 For the LORD gives wisdom;
from his mouth come knowledge and
understanding.
7 He holds success in store for the upright,
he is a shield to those whose walk is
blameless,
8 for he guards the course of the just
and protects the way of his faithful ones.
9 Then you will understand what is right
and just
and fair — every good path.
10 For wisdom will enter your heart,
and knowledge will be pleasant to
your soul.
11 Discretion will protect you,
and understanding will guard you.

12 Wisdom will save you from the ways of
wicked men,
from men whose words are perverse,
13 who have left the straight paths
to walk in dark ways,
14 who delight in doing wrong
and rejoice in the perverseness of evil,
15 whose paths are crooked
and who are devious in their ways.

16 Wisdom will save you also from the
adulterous woman,
from the wayward woman with her
seductive words,
17 who has left the partner of her youth
and ignored the covenant she made
before God.[a]
18 Surely her house leads down to death
and her paths to the spirits of the dead.
19 None who go to her return
or attain the paths of life.

20 Thus you will walk in the ways of the
good
and keep to the paths of the righteous.
21 For the upright will live in the land,
and the blameless will remain in it;
22 but the wicked will be cut off from the
land,
and the unfaithful will be torn from it.

Wisdom Bestows Well-Being

3 My son, do not forget my teaching,
but keep my commands in your heart,
2 for they will prolong your life many years
and bring you peace and prosperity.

3 Let love and faithfulness never leave you;
bind them around your neck,
write them on the tablet of your heart.
4 Then you will win favor and a good name
in the sight of God and man.

5 Trust in the LORD with all your heart
and lean not on your own
understanding;
6 in all your ways submit to him,
and he will make your paths straight.[b]

7 Do not be wise in your own eyes;
fear the LORD and shun evil.
8 This will bring health to your body
and nourishment to your bones.

9 Honor the LORD with your wealth,
with the firstfruits of all your crops;

---

[a] 17 Or *covenant of her God*   [b] 6 Or *will direct your paths*

¹⁰ then your barns will be filled to
  overflowing,
  and your vats will brim over with
  new wine.

¹¹ My son, do not despise the LORD's
  discipline,
  and do not resent his rebuke,
¹² because the LORD disciplines those
  he loves,
  as a father the son he delights in.ᵃ

¹³ Blessed are those who find wisdom,
  those who gain understanding,
¹⁴ for she is more profitable than silver
  and yields better returns than gold.
¹⁵ She is more precious than rubies;
  nothing you desire can compare
  with her.
¹⁶ Long life is in her right hand;
  in her left hand are riches and honor.
¹⁷ Her ways are pleasant ways,
  and all her paths are peace.
¹⁸ She is a tree of life to those who take hold
  of her;
  those who hold her fast will be
  blessed.

¹⁹ By wisdom the LORD laid the earth's
  foundations,
  by understanding he set the heavens
  in place;
²⁰ by his knowledge the watery depths were
  divided,
  and the clouds let drop the dew.

²¹ My son, do not let wisdom and
  understanding out of your sight,
  preserve sound judgment and
  discretion;
²² they will be life for you,
  an ornament to grace your neck.
²³ Then you will go on your way in safety,
  and your foot will not stumble.
²⁴ When you lie down, you will not be
  afraid;
  when you lie down, your sleep will be
  sweet.
²⁵ Have no fear of sudden disaster
  or of the ruin that overtakes the
  wicked,
²⁶ for the LORD will be at your side
  and will keep your foot from being
  snared.

²⁷ Do not withhold good from those to
  whom it is due,
  when it is in your power to act.
²⁸ Do not say to your neighbor,
  "Come back tomorrow and I'll give it
  to you" —
  when you already have it with you.
²⁹ Do not plot harm against your neighbor,
  who lives trustfully near you.
³⁰ Do not accuse anyone for no reason —
  when they have done you no harm.
³¹ Do not envy the violent
  or choose any of their ways.
³² For the LORD detests the perverse
  but takes the upright into his
  confidence.
³³ The LORD's curse is on the house of the
  wicked,
  but he blesses the home of the
  righteous.
³⁴ He mocks proud mockers
  but shows favor to the humble and
  oppressed.
³⁵ The wise inherit honor,
  but fools get only shame.

Get Wisdom at Any Cost

4 Listen, my sons, to a father's
  instruction;
  pay attention and gain understanding.
² I give you sound learning,
  so do not forsake my teaching.
³ For I too was a son to my father,
  still tender, and cherished by my
  mother.
⁴ Then he taught me, and he said to me,
  "Take hold of my words with all your
  heart;
  keep my commands, and you will live.
⁵ Get wisdom, get understanding;
  do not forget my words or turn away
  from them.
⁶ Do not forsake wisdom, and she will
  protect you;
  love her, and she will watch over you.
⁷ The beginning of wisdom is this: Getᵇ
  wisdom.
  Though it cost all you have,ᶜ get
  understanding.
⁸ Cherish her, and she will exalt you;
  embrace her, and she will honor you.

ᵃ 12 Hebrew; Septuagint *loves, / and he chastens everyone he accepts as his child*   ᵇ 7 Or *Wisdom is supreme; therefore get*   ᶜ 7 Or *wisdom. / Whatever else you get*

GOD-SIZED GOALS

READ: PROVERBS 4:25-26

Y ou'll never achieve the goals you don't set. The brain is a goal-seeking organism. Setting a goal creates structural tension in your brain, which will seek to close the gap between where you are and where you want to be, who you are and who you want to be.

Goal setting is good stewardship of your right-brain imagination. It's also great for your prayer life! What does goal setting have to do with praying hard and thinking long? Goals are the cause and effect of praying hard. The more you pray, the more God-sized goals you'll be inspired to go after. Goals give you a prayer target. And prayer gives your goals wheels.

Goals are a great way of thinking long. I have checked off nearly a quarter of my life goal list. Some goals, like speaking for an NFL chapel or coaching a sports team for each of my kids, I've checked off numerous times. But a few of my life goals will take a lifetime to achieve. It might take until I'm seventy-five to write twenty-five books. And I have no idea when I'll be part of baptizing three thousand people in the same place at the same time, like the day of Pentecost, but it's on my life goal list.

BUILDING

FAITH

WISDOM

STRENGTH

If you set goals in the context of prayer, there is a much higher likelihood that your goals will glorify God, and if they don't glorify God, then they aren't worth setting in the first place. Prayer is breakthrough number one; goal setting is breakthrough number two!

⁹ She will give you a garland to grace
your head
and present you with a glorious crown."

¹⁰ Listen, my son, accept what I say,
and the years of your life will be many.
¹¹ I instruct you in the way of wisdom
and lead you along straight paths.
¹² When you walk, your steps will not be
hampered;
when you run, you will not stumble.
¹³ Hold on to instruction, do not let it go;
guard it well, for it is your life.
¹⁴ Do not set foot on the path of the wicked
or walk in the way of evildoers.
¹⁵ Avoid it, do not travel on it;
turn from it and go on your way.
¹⁶ For they cannot rest until they do evil;
they are robbed of sleep till they make
someone stumble.
¹⁷ They eat the bread of wickedness
and drink the wine of violence.

¹⁸ The path of the righteous is like the
morning sun,
shining ever brighter till the full light
of day.
¹⁹ But the way of the wicked is like deep
darkness;
they do not know what makes them
stumble.

²⁰ My son, pay attention to what I say;
turn your ear to my words.
²¹ Do not let them out of your sight,
keep them within your heart;
²² for they are life to those who find them
and health to one's whole body.
²³ Above all else, guard your heart,
for everything you do flows from it.
²⁴ Keep your mouth free of perversity;
keep corrupt talk far from your lips.
²⁵ Let your eyes look straight ahead;
fix your gaze directly before you.
²⁶ Give careful thought to the*ᵃ* paths for
your feet
and be steadfast in all your ways.
²⁷ Do not turn to the right or the left;
keep your foot from evil.

Warning Against Adultery

5 My son, pay attention to my wisdom,
turn your ear to my words of insight,
² that you may maintain discretion
and your lips may preserve knowledge.

³ For the lips of the adulterous woman drip
honey,
and her speech is smoother than oil;
⁴ but in the end she is bitter as gall,
sharp as a double-edged sword.
⁵ Her feet go down to death;
her steps lead straight to the grave.
⁶ She gives no thought to the way of life;
her paths wander aimlessly, but she
does not know it.

⁷ Now then, my sons, listen to me;
do not turn aside from what I say.
⁸ Keep to a path far from her,
do not go near the door of her house,
⁹ lest you lose your honor to others
and your dignityᵇ to one who is cruel,
¹⁰ lest strangers feast on your wealth
and your toil enrich the house of
another.
¹¹ At the end of your life you will groan,
when your flesh and body are spent.
¹² You will say, "How I hated discipline!
How my heart spurned correction!
¹³ I would not obey my teachers
or turn my ear to my instructors.
¹⁴ And I was soon in serious trouble
in the assembly of God's people."

¹⁵ Drink water from your own cistern,
running water from your own well.
¹⁶ Should your springs overflow in the
streets,
your streams of water in the public
squares?
¹⁷ Let them be yours alone,
never to be shared with strangers.
¹⁸ May your fountain be blessed,
and may you rejoice in the wife of your
youth.
¹⁹ A loving doe, a graceful deer —
may her breasts satisfy you always,
may you ever be intoxicated with
her love.
²⁰ Why, my son, be intoxicated with another
man's wife?
Why embrace the bosom of a wayward
woman?

²¹ For your ways are in full view of the LORD,
and he examines all your paths.
²² The evil deeds of the wicked ensnare
them;
the cords of their sins hold them fast.

ᵃ 26 Or *Make level*   ᵇ 9 Or *years*

SACRED SEX

READ: **PROVERBS 5:16–17**

Anyone who thinks God dislikes sex obviously hasn't read Proverbs 5. While the chapter starts with stern warnings about misusing one of the Lord's maximum gifts, that portion merely sets up a song of love.

This voice in this passage assumes the person benefiting from this wisdom is a young man, but every point here matters just as much to a young woman. You might be startled to read these words in your Bible, but there they are. God lays it all out. His design for sex is satisfying. His plan is intoxicating.

God's main point in this honest passage is that sexual intimacy is so outstanding that it shouldn't be wasted. It's anything but casual. It's a treasure a husband and wife can enjoy for life, and it's for them alone.

Sex with anyone other than your mate for life is like spilling your most valuable possession in the streets. It's like letting strangers splash in your priceless fountain. So sex is "never to be shared with strangers." It isn't a recreational activity with someone who wanders into your life and tries to lead you astray. It isn't a gulp of water you grab wherever you can.

God examines everywhere you go and sees everything you do. He's pointing you down the path to real life, challenging you to wait for his very best.

BUILDING
FAITH
WISDOM
STRENGTH

²³ For lack of discipline they will die,
   led astray by their own great folly.

Warnings Against Folly

6 My son, if you have put up security for
   your neighbor,
   if you have shaken hands in pledge for
   a stranger,
² you have been trapped by what you said,
   ensnared by the words of your mouth.
³ So do this, my son, to free yourself,
   since you have fallen into your
   neighbor's hands:
   Go — to the point of exhaustion — ᵃ
   and give your neighbor no rest!
⁴ Allow no sleep to your eyes,
   no slumber to your eyelids.
⁵ Free yourself, like a gazelle from the
   hand of the hunter,
   like a bird from the snare of the fowler.

⁶ Go to the ant, you sluggard;
   consider its ways and be wise!
⁷ It has no commander,
   no overseer or ruler,
⁸ yet it stores its provisions in summer
   and gathers its food at harvest.

⁹ How long will you lie there, you sluggard?
   When will you get up from your sleep?
¹⁰ A little sleep, a little slumber,
   a little folding of the hands to rest —
¹¹ and poverty will come on you like a thief
   and scarcity like an armed man.

¹² A troublemaker and a villain,
   who goes about with a corrupt mouth,
¹³   who winks maliciously with his eye,
   signals with his feet
   and motions with his fingers,
¹⁴   who plots evil with deceit in his
   heart —
   he always stirs up conflict.
¹⁵ Therefore disaster will overtake him in
   an instant;
   he will suddenly be destroyed —
   without remedy.

¹⁶ There are six things the LORD hates,
   seven that are detestable to him:
¹⁷   haughty eyes,
   a lying tongue,
   hands that shed innocent blood,
¹⁸   a heart that devises wicked schemes,
   feet that are quick to rush into evil,

¹⁹   a false witness who pours out lies
   and a person who stirs up conflict in
   the community.

Warning Against Adultery

²⁰ My son, keep your father's command
   and do not forsake your mother's
   teaching.
²¹ Bind them always on your heart;
   fasten them around your neck.
²² When you walk, they will guide you;
   when you sleep, they will watch over
   you;
   when you awake, they will speak to you.
²³ For this command is a lamp,
   this teaching is a light,
   and correction and instruction
   are the way to life,
²⁴ keeping you from your neighbor's wife,
   from the smooth talk of a wayward
   woman.

²⁵ Do not lust in your heart after her beauty
   or let her captivate you with her eyes.

²⁶ For a prostitute can be had for a loaf of
   bread,
   but another man's wife preys on your
   very life.
²⁷ Can a man scoop fire into his lap
   without his clothes being burned?
²⁸ Can a man walk on hot coals
   without his feet being scorched?
²⁹ So is he who sleeps with another man's
   wife;
   no one who touches her will go
   unpunished.

³⁰ People do not despise a thief if he steals
   to satisfy his hunger when he is
   starving.
³¹ Yet if he is caught, he must pay sevenfold,
   though it costs him all the wealth of
   his house.
³² But a man who commits adultery has
   no sense;
   whoever does so destroys himself.
³³ Blows and disgrace are his lot,
   and his shame will never be wiped
   away.

³⁴ For jealousy arouses a husband's fury,
   and he will show no mercy when he
   takes revenge.

ᵃ 3 Or *Go and humble yourself,*

BACK TO OLD HABITS

READ: PROVERBS 6:16

I was researching "the seven deadly sins." I was curious about how that list developed. It turns out that years ago the literacy rate was low and people weren't reading the Bible for themselves. Some early church leaders got together and made a list of the worst sins so at least people would know what *not* to do.

As I was reading about the seven deadly sins, I discovered something about the one sin on that list that seemed out of place: sloth. I understand that laziness isn't good, but it hardly seems deadly. But I discovered that the word *sloth* is translated from the word *acedia*. A better way to convey what the early church leaders were getting at would be "spiritual apathy." You reach a point where you simply say, "I don't care." God loves you and sent his Son to die on the cross to forgive your sins, and you shrug your shoulders.

So what do you do if you find yourself in a place of acedia? Notice what Jesus tells the church in Ephesus. He says to repent and do the things you did at first.

Confess the sin of acedia and then get on your knees and talk to God. Turn on some worship music and sing along. Start reading and meditating on God's Word. Gather with followers who are passionately pursuing Jesus. You'll find their passion to be contagious. Even if you don't initially feel like doing some of those things, it will begin to stir the fire that has grown dim.

BUILDING
FAITH
WISDOM
STRENGTH

35 He will not accept any compensation;
    he will refuse a bribe, however great
        it is.

Warning Against the Adulterous Woman

7 My son, keep my words
    and store up my commands within you.
2 Keep my commands and you will live;
    guard my teachings as the apple of
      your eye.
3 Bind them on your fingers;
    write them on the tablet of your heart.
4 Say to wisdom, "You are my sister,"
    and to insight, "You are my relative."
5 They will keep you from the adulterous
      woman,
    from the wayward woman with her
      seductive words.

6 At the window of my house
    I looked down through the lattice.
7 I saw among the simple,
    I noticed among the young men,
    a youth who had no sense.
8 He was going down the street near her
      corner,
    walking along in the direction of her
      house
9 at twilight, as the day was fading,
    as the dark of night set in.

10 Then out came a woman to meet him,
    dressed like a prostitute and with
      crafty intent.
11 (She is unruly and defiant,
    her feet never stay at home;
12 now in the street, now in the squares,
    at every corner she lurks.)
13 She took hold of him and kissed him
    and with a brazen face she said:

14 "Today I fulfilled my vows,
    and I have food from my fellowship
      offering at home.
15 So I came out to meet you;
    I looked for you and have found you!
16 I have covered my bed
    with colored linens from Egypt.
17 I have perfumed my bed
    with myrrh, aloes and cinnamon.
18 Come, let's drink deeply of love till
      morning;
    let's enjoy ourselves with love!

19 My husband is not at home;
    he has gone on a long journey.
20 He took his purse filled with money
    and will not be home till full moon."

21 With persuasive words she led him
      astray;
    she seduced him with her smooth talk.
22 All at once he followed her
    like an ox going to the slaughter,
  like a deer[a] stepping into a noose[b]
23   till an arrow pierces his liver,
    like a bird darting into a snare,
      little knowing it will cost him his life.

24 Now then, my sons, listen to me;
    pay attention to what I say.
25 Do not let your heart turn to her ways
    or stray into her paths.
26 Many are the victims she has brought
      down;
    her slain are a mighty throng.
27 Her house is a highway to the grave,
    leading down to the chambers of
      death.

Wisdom's Call

8 Does not wisdom call out?
    Does not understanding raise her
      voice?
2 At the highest point along the way,
    where the paths meet, she takes her
      stand;
3 beside the gate leading into the city,
    at the entrance, she cries aloud:
4 "To you, O people, I call out;
    I raise my voice to all mankind.
5 You who are simple, gain prudence;
    you who are foolish, set your hearts
      on it.[c]
6 Listen, for I have trustworthy things
      to say;
    I open my lips to speak what is right.
7 My mouth speaks what is true,
    for my lips detest wickedness.
8 All the words of my mouth are just;
    none of them is crooked or perverse.
9 To the discerning all of them are right;
    they are upright to those who have
      found knowledge.
10 Choose my instruction instead of silver,
    knowledge rather than choice gold,

---

a 22 Syriac (see also Septuagint); Hebrew *fool*   *b* 22 The meaning of the Hebrew for this line is
uncertain.   *c* 5 Septuagint; Hebrew *foolish, instruct your minds*

[11] for wisdom is more precious than rubies,
   and nothing you desire can compare
      with her.

[12] "I, wisdom, dwell together with
      prudence;
   I possess knowledge and discretion.
[13] To fear the LORD is to hate evil;
   I hate pride and arrogance,
      evil behavior and perverse speech.
[14] Counsel and sound judgment are mine;
   I have insight, I have power.
[15] By me kings reign
   and rulers issue decrees that are just;
[16] by me princes govern,
   and nobles — all who rule on earth.[a]
[17] I love those who love me,
   and those who seek me find me.
[18] With me are riches and honor,
   enduring wealth and prosperity.
[19] My fruit is better than fine gold;
   what I yield surpasses choice silver.
[20] I walk in the way of righteousness,
   along the paths of justice,
[21] bestowing a rich inheritance on those
      who love me
   and making their treasuries full.

[22] "The LORD brought me forth as the first of
      his works,[b,c]
   before his deeds of old;
[23] I was formed long ages ago,
   at the very beginning, when the world
      came to be.
[24] When there were no watery depths, I was
      given birth,
   when there were no springs
      overflowing with water;
[25] before the mountains were settled in
      place,
   before the hills, I was given birth,
[26] before he made the world or its fields
   or any of the dust of the earth.
[27] I was there when he set the heavens in
      place,
   when he marked out the horizon on
      the face of the deep,
[28] when he established the clouds above
   and fixed securely the fountains of
      the deep,

[29] when he gave the sea its boundary
   so the waters would not overstep his
      command,
   and when he marked out the foundations
      of the earth.
[30]   Then I was constantly[d] at his side.
   I was filled with delight day after day,
   rejoicing always in his presence,
[31] rejoicing in his whole world
   and delighting in mankind.

[32] "Now then, my children, listen to me;
   blessed are those who keep my ways.
[33] Listen to my instruction and be wise;
   do not disregard it.
[34] Blessed are those who listen to me,
   watching daily at my doors,
   waiting at my doorway.
[35] For those who find me find life
   and receive favor from the LORD.
[36] But those who fail to find me harm
      themselves;
   all who hate me love death."

Invitations of Wisdom and Folly

9 Wisdom has built her house;
   she has set up[e] its seven pillars.
[2] She has prepared her meat and mixed
      her wine;
   she has also set her table.
[3] She has sent out her servants, and she
      calls
   from the highest point of the city,
[4]   "Let all who are simple come to my
      house!"
   To those who have no sense she says,
[5]   "Come, eat my food
   and drink the wine I have mixed.
[6] Leave your simple ways and you will live;
   walk in the way of insight."

[7] Whoever corrects a mocker invites
      insults;
   whoever rebukes the wicked incurs
      abuse.
[8] Do not rebuke mockers or they will
      hate you;
   rebuke the wise and they will love you.
[9] Instruct the wise and they will be wiser
      still;

---

[a] 16 Some Hebrew manuscripts and Septuagint; other Hebrew manuscripts *all righteous rulers*
[b] 22 Or *way*; or *dominion*   [c] 22 Or *The LORD possessed me at the beginning of his work*; or *The LORD brought me forth at the beginning of his work*   [d] 30 Or *was the artisan*; or *was a little child*
[e] 1 Septuagint, Syriac and Targum; Hebrew *has hewn out*

teach the righteous and they will add
  to their learning.

¹⁰ The fear of the LORD is the beginning of
    wisdom,
  and knowledge of the Holy One is
    understanding.
¹¹ For through wisdom*ᵃ* your days will
    be many,
  and years will be added to your life.
¹² If you are wise, your wisdom will reward
    you;
  if you are a mocker, you alone will
    suffer.

¹³ Folly is an unruly woman;
  she is simple and knows nothing.
¹⁴ She sits at the door of her house,
  on a seat at the highest point of the
    city,
¹⁵ calling out to those who pass by,
  who go straight on their way,
¹⁶ "Let all who are simple come to my
    house!"
  To those who have no sense she says,
¹⁷ "Stolen water is sweet;
    food eaten in secret is delicious!"
¹⁸ But little do they know that the dead are
    there,
  that her guests are deep in the realm of
    the dead.

Proverbs of Solomon

10 The proverbs of Solomon:

A wise son brings joy to his father,
  but a foolish son brings grief to his
    mother.

² Ill-gotten treasures have no lasting value,
  but righteousness delivers from death.

³ The LORD does not let the righteous go
    hungry,
  but he thwarts the craving of the
    wicked.

⁴ Lazy hands make for poverty,
  but diligent hands bring wealth.

⁵ He who gathers crops in summer is a
    prudent son,
  but he who sleeps during harvest is a
    disgraceful son.

⁶ Blessings crown the head of the
    righteous,
  but violence overwhelms the mouth of
    the wicked.*ᵇ*

⁷ The name of the righteous is used in
    blessings,*ᶜ*
  but the name of the wicked will rot.

⁸ The wise in heart accept commands,
  but a chattering fool comes to ruin.

⁹ Whoever walks in integrity walks
    securely,
  but whoever takes crooked paths will
    be found out.

¹⁰ Whoever winks maliciously causes grief,
  and a chattering fool comes to ruin.

¹¹ The mouth of the righteous is a fountain
    of life,
  but the mouth of the wicked conceals
    violence.

¹² Hatred stirs up conflict,
  but love covers over all wrongs.

¹³ Wisdom is found on the lips of the
    discerning,
  but a rod is for the back of one who has
    no sense.

¹⁴ The wise store up knowledge,
  but the mouth of a fool invites ruin.

¹⁵ The wealth of the rich is their fortified
    city,
  but poverty is the ruin of the poor.

¹⁶ The wages of the righteous is life,
  but the earnings of the wicked are sin
    and death.

¹⁷ Whoever heeds discipline shows the way
    to life,
  but whoever ignores correction leads
    others astray.

¹⁸ Whoever conceals hatred with lying lips
  and spreads slander is a fool.

¹⁹ Sin is not ended by multiplying words,
  but the prudent hold their tongues.

²⁰ The tongue of the righteous is choice
    silver,
  but the heart of the wicked is of little
    value.

ᵃ 11 Septuagint, Syriac and Targum; Hebrew *me*
conceals violence *ᶜ 7* See Gen. 48:20. *ᵇ 6* Or *righteous, / but the mouth of the wicked*

WISDOM AND FOLLY

READ: PROVERBS 9:13

You already met the wise woman of Proverbs 8. She's the personification of the Lord's practical intelligence, the knowledge you need to thrive in real life. Call that lady "Wisdom." Now you get to meet a rowdy woman. She's named "Folly," and she embodies everything unwise.

These two women couldn't be more different, but their profiles in Proverbs 9:1–6 and 9:13–18 fit together almost line-by-line. Make sure to read them both, comparing where they match or differ.

Folly is unruly, meaning she's loud and undisciplined. She's also simple, unsure about her path in life. She knows absolutely nothing, so she can't tell the difference between right and wrong. Like Wisdom, she calls out from her house high atop the city. Also like Wisdom, she beckons naive people to come close, inviting everyone who lacks sense. But unlike Wisdom, she serves stolen water (5:15–16) and secret food (30:20). Little do visitors know that her house is jammed with dead bodies. By entering her home, her guests have already expired.

If you live against God, you're hanging out in Folly's house. You're also missing out on the grand banquet Wisdom serves. She has fine food and fresh drinks. Everyone who enters her home learns how to escape their simple ways, and she points them down a sophisticated path. And none of Wisdom's guests ever drop dead.

BUILDING

FAITH

WISDOM

STRENGTH

²¹ The lips of the righteous nourish many,
    but fools die for lack of sense.

²² The blessing of the LORD brings wealth,
    without painful toil for it.

²³ A fool finds pleasure in wicked schemes,
    but a person of understanding delights
    in wisdom.

²⁴ What the wicked dread will overtake
    them;
    what the righteous desire will be
    granted.

²⁵ When the storm has swept by, the wicked
    are gone,
    but the righteous stand firm forever.

²⁶ As vinegar to the teeth and smoke to the
    eyes,
    so are sluggards to those who send
    them.

²⁷ The fear of the LORD adds length to life,
    but the years of the wicked are cut
    short.

²⁸ The prospect of the righteous is joy,
    but the hopes of the wicked come to
    nothing.

²⁹ The way of the LORD is a refuge for the
    blameless,
    but it is the ruin of those who do evil.

³⁰ The righteous will never be uprooted,
    but the wicked will not remain in
    the land.

³¹ From the mouth of the righteous comes
    the fruit of wisdom,
    but a perverse tongue will be silenced.

³² The lips of the righteous know what finds
    favor,
    but the mouth of the wicked only what
    is perverse.

11 The LORD detests dishonest scales,
    but accurate weights find favor with
    him.

² When pride comes, then comes disgrace,
    but with humility comes wisdom.

³ The integrity of the upright guides them,
    but the unfaithful are destroyed by
    their duplicity.

⁴ Wealth is worthless in the day of wrath,
    but righteousness delivers from death.

⁵ The righteousness of the blameless
    makes their paths straight,
    but the wicked are brought down by
    their own wickedness.

⁶ The righteousness of the upright delivers
    them,
    but the unfaithful are trapped by evil
    desires.

⁷ Hopes placed in mortals die with them;
    all the promise of*ᵃ* their power comes
    to nothing.

⁸ The righteous person is rescued from
    trouble,
    and it falls on the wicked instead.

⁹ With their mouths the godless destroy
    their neighbors,
    but through knowledge the righteous
    escape.

¹⁰ When the righteous prosper, the city
    rejoices;
    when the wicked perish, there are
    shouts of joy.

¹¹ Through the blessing of the upright a city
    is exalted,
    but by the mouth of the wicked it is
    destroyed.

¹² Whoever derides their neighbor has no
    sense,
    but the one who has understanding
    holds their tongue.

¹³ A gossip betrays a confidence,
    but a trustworthy person keeps a
    secret.

¹⁴ For lack of guidance a nation falls,
    but victory is won through many
    advisers.

¹⁵ Whoever puts up security for a stranger
    will surely suffer,
    but whoever refuses to shake hands in
    pledge is safe.

¹⁶ A kindhearted woman gains honor,
    but ruthless men gain only wealth.

¹⁷ Those who are kind benefit themselves,
    but the cruel bring ruin on themselves.

ᵃ 7 Two Hebrew manuscripts; most Hebrew manuscripts, Vulgate, Syriac and Targum *When the wicked die, their hope perishes; / all they expected from*

GIVING BLESSING

READ: PROVERBS 11:25

You can watch a professional golfer to learn how to swing, or you can study a hack to learn what not to do. Proverbs 11 gives you that same option. You can see how righteous people act and the good results that follow, or you can witness the disasters that befall people who live against God.

Proverbs goes out of its way to give you good and bad examples of handling money. Like this one: "One person gives freely, yet gains even more; another withholds unduly, but comes to poverty" (Proverbs 11:24). Logic says making a habit of giving will leave you impoverished. But that's not how the Lord works. When you give away your time, money, or energy, he gives you more. When you hang on to what you have, you finish with even less.

When you refresh others, God makes sure you receive what you need. When you give, you often get even more. Jesus once said, "Give, and it will be given to you. A good measure, pressed down, shaken together and running over, will be poured into your lap. For with the measure you use, it will be measured to you" (Luke 6:38).

There's one catch. If you give just to get more, the Lord sniffs that out. You spoil the joy of real generosity, and that's not the kind of giving the Lord rewards.

BUILDING FAITH WISDOM STRENGTH

¹⁸ A wicked person earns deceptive wages,
 but the one who sows righteousness
  reaps a sure reward.

¹⁹ Truly the righteous attain life,
 but whoever pursues evil finds death.

²⁰ The Lord detests those whose hearts are
  perverse,
 but he delights in those whose ways
  are blameless.

²¹ Be sure of this: The wicked will not go
  unpunished,
 but those who are righteous will go free.

²² Like a gold ring in a pig's snout
 is a beautiful woman who shows no
  discretion.

²³ The desire of the righteous ends only in
  good,
 but the hope of the wicked only in
  wrath.

²⁴ One person gives freely, yet gains even
  more;
 another withholds unduly, but comes
  to poverty.

²⁵ A generous person will prosper;
 whoever refreshes others will be
  refreshed.

²⁶ People curse the one who hoards grain,
 but they pray God's blessing on the one
  who is willing to sell.

²⁷ Whoever seeks good finds favor,
 but evil comes to one who searches
  for it.

²⁸ Those who trust in their riches will fall,
 but the righteous will thrive like a
  green leaf.

²⁹ Whoever brings ruin on their family will
  inherit only wind,
 and the fool will be servant to the wise.

³⁰ The fruit of the righteous is a tree of life,
 and the one who is wise saves lives.

³¹ If the righteous receive their due on
  earth,
 how much more the ungodly and the
  sinner!

12 Whoever loves discipline loves
   knowledge,
 but whoever hates correction is stupid.

² Good people obtain favor from the Lord,
 but he condemns those who devise
  wicked schemes.

³ No one can be established through
  wickedness,
 but the righteous cannot be uprooted.

⁴ A wife of noble character is her husband's
  crown,
 but a disgraceful wife is like decay in
  his bones.

⁵ The plans of the righteous are just,
 but the advice of the wicked is
  deceitful.

⁶ The words of the wicked lie in wait for
  blood,
 but the speech of the upright rescues
  them.

⁷ The wicked are overthrown and are no
  more,
 but the house of the righteous stands
  firm.

⁸ A person is praised according to their
  prudence,
 and one with a warped mind is
  despised.

⁹ Better to be a nobody and yet have a
  servant
 than pretend to be somebody and have
  no food.

¹⁰ The righteous care for the needs of their
  animals,
 but the kindest acts of the wicked are
  cruel.

¹¹ Those who work their land will have
  abundant food,
 but those who chase fantasies have no
  sense.

¹² The wicked desire the stronghold of
  evildoers,
 but the root of the righteous endures.

¹³ Evildoers are trapped by their sinful talk,
 and so the innocent escape trouble.

¹⁴ From the fruit of their lips people are
  filled with good things,
 and the work of their hands brings
  them reward.

¹⁵ The way of fools seems right to them,
 but the wise listen to advice.

BEYOND SURVIVAL

READ: PROVERBS 11:28

When I was in high school, it felt like the best I could do was to survive. As I struggled with attention deficit disorder and dyslexia, school days felt like a mix of labor camp, summer camp, and the next embarrassment that lurked right around the corner. At times, I feel like I'm still trying to survive.

If we are honest, we can look back on the last year and say we only survived it. We survived school. We survived with most of our relationships intact.

Some of us have not survived very well. Maybe our circle of friends has changed. Maybe our families are different than they were this time last year, and we have survived some major storms. In fact, a lot of us are in survival mode right now.

I remember looking at the clock in high school and thinking, *Only eleven more minutes. I don't think they're ever going to pass. I'm never going to get out of this place. I'm going to grow old and die in this room. If I can survive just eleven more minutes, I'm done with this.*

BUILDING

FAITH

WISDOM

STRENGTH

If you're not careful, you will live your life with that same survival attitude.

You were not made to survive life. Or to survive school. Or your family. You were not made to exist until you can get over the next hump or get to the next break. You were created for one purpose: to know God and to make him known. You were meant to thrive.

Taken from *Thrive Student Edition* by Mark Hall with Tim Luke, copyright © 2014 by Mark Hall, published by Zondervan.

¹⁶Fools show their annoyance at once,
but the prudent overlook an insult.

¹⁷An honest witness tells the truth,
but a false witness tells lies.

¹⁸The words of the reckless pierce like
swords,
but the tongue of the wise brings
healing.

¹⁹Truthful lips endure forever,
but a lying tongue lasts only a moment.

²⁰Deceit is in the hearts of those who plot
evil,
but those who promote peace have joy.

²¹No harm overtakes the righteous,
but the wicked have their fill of
trouble.

²²The LORD detests lying lips,
but he delights in people who are
trustworthy.

²³The prudent keep their knowledge to
themselves,
but a fool's heart blurts out folly.

²⁴Diligent hands will rule,
but laziness ends in forced labor.

²⁵Anxiety weighs down the heart,
but a kind word cheers it up.

²⁶The righteous choose their friends
carefully,
but the way of the wicked leads them
astray.

²⁷The lazy do not roast^a any game,
but the diligent feed on the riches of
the hunt.

²⁸In the way of righteousness there is life;
along that path is immortality.

13 A wise son heeds his father's
instruction,
but a mocker does not respond to
rebukes.

²From the fruit of their lips people enjoy
good things,
but the unfaithful have an appetite for
violence.

³Those who guard their lips preserve their
lives,

but those who speak rashly will come
to ruin.

⁴A sluggard's appetite is never filled,
but the desires of the diligent are fully
satisfied.

⁵The righteous hate what is false,
but the wicked make themselves
a stench
and bring shame on themselves.

⁶Righteousness guards the person of
integrity,
but wickedness overthrows the
sinner.

⁷One person pretends to be rich, yet has
nothing;
another pretends to be poor, yet has
great wealth.

⁸A person's riches may ransom their life,
but the poor cannot respond to
threatening rebukes.

⁹The light of the righteous shines
brightly,
but the lamp of the wicked is snuffed
out.

¹⁰Where there is strife, there is pride,
but wisdom is found in those who take
advice.

¹¹Dishonest money dwindles away,
but whoever gathers money little by
little makes it grow.

¹²Hope deferred makes the heart sick,
but a longing fulfilled is a tree of life.

¹³Whoever scorns instruction will pay
for it,
but whoever respects a command is
rewarded.

¹⁴The teaching of the wise is a fountain
of life,
turning a person from the snares of
death.

¹⁵Good judgment wins favor,
but the way of the unfaithful leads to
their destruction.^b

¹⁶All who are prudent act with^c knowledge,
but fools expose their folly.

^a 27 The meaning of the Hebrew for this word is uncertain.   ^b 15 Septuagint and Syriac; the meaning of
the Hebrew for this phrase is uncertain.   ^c 16 Or *prudent protect themselves through*

THE TWO SIDES OF PRIDE

READ: PROVERBS 13:10

There's a reason people don't get along. Battles happen when we don't back down from what we want. Maybe you have never thought of that as "pride," but that's what it is. Proverbs points out that whenever you encounter strife, there's an evil pride behind it.

There's a good kind of pride that gives you healthy self-respect. It helps you stand up for yourself when others try to slam you down, and it doesn't hesitate to celebrate accomplishments (Galatians 6:4). But there's also a dark pride that's one of the sins God hates most (Proverbs 6:16–17). It caused Satan to rebel against the Lord and get ejected from heaven (Ezekiel 28:15–17). It makes human beings think they deserve more honor than God (Isaiah 2:11). And it causes conflict between you and the people around you.

The pride Proverbs is talking about makes people push themselves ahead of others and demand their own way. The apostle James details the outcome. He writes, "For where you have envy and selfish ambition, there you find disorder and every evil practice" (James 3:16). Self-centeredness causes turmoil and all kinds of bickering.

When you find yourself at odds with someone, you're rarely the whole cause of the problem. But you can study yourself to see how your pride might have started or intensified the conflict. Realizing your own faults is the first step to ending whatever battle you face.

BUILDING
FAITH
WISDOM
STRENGTH

¹⁷ A wicked messenger falls into trouble,
  but a trustworthy envoy brings
    healing.

¹⁸ Whoever disregards discipline comes to
    poverty and shame,
  but whoever heeds correction is
    honored.

¹⁹ A longing fulfilled is sweet to the soul,
  but fools detest turning from evil.

²⁰ Walk with the wise and become wise,
  for a companion of fools suffers harm.

²¹ Trouble pursues the sinner,
  but the righteous are rewarded with
    good things.

²² A good person leaves an inheritance for
    their children's children,
  but a sinner's wealth is stored up for
    the righteous.

²³ An unplowed field produces food for the
    poor,
  but injustice sweeps it away.

²⁴ Whoever spares the rod hates their
    children,
  but the one who loves their children is
    careful to discipline them.

²⁵ The righteous eat to their hearts' content,
  but the stomach of the wicked goes
    hungry.

14

The wise woman builds her house,
  but with her own hands the foolish
    one tears hers down.

² Whoever fears the LORD walks uprightly,
  but those who despise him are devious
    in their ways.

³ A fool's mouth lashes out with pride,
  but the lips of the wise protect them.

⁴ Where there are no oxen, the manger is
    empty,
  but from the strength of an ox come
    abundant harvests.

⁵ An honest witness does not deceive,
  but a false witness pours out lies.

⁶ The mocker seeks wisdom and finds
    none,
  but knowledge comes easily to the
    discerning.

⁷ Stay away from a fool,
  for you will not find knowledge on
    their lips.

⁸ The wisdom of the prudent is to give
    thought to their ways,
  but the folly of fools is deception.

⁹ Fools mock at making amends for sin,
  but goodwill is found among the
    upright.

¹⁰ Each heart knows its own bitterness,
  and no one else can share its joy.

¹¹ The house of the wicked will be
    destroyed,
  but the tent of the upright will
    flourish.

¹² There is a way that appears to be right,
  but in the end it leads to death.

¹³ Even in laughter the heart may ache,
  and rejoicing may end in grief.

¹⁴ The faithless will be fully repaid for their
    ways,
  and the good rewarded for theirs.

¹⁵ The simple believe anything,
  but the prudent give thought to their
    steps.

¹⁶ The wise fear the LORD and shun evil,
  but a fool is hotheaded and yet feels
    secure.

¹⁷ A quick-tempered person does foolish
    things,
  and the one who devises evil schemes
    is hated.

¹⁸ The simple inherit folly,
  but the prudent are crowned with
    knowledge.

¹⁹ Evildoers will bow down in the presence
    of the good,
  and the wicked at the gates of the
    righteous.

²⁰ The poor are shunned even by their
    neighbors,
  but the rich have many friends.

²¹ It is a sin to despise one's neighbor,
  but blessed is the one who is kind to
    the needy.

²² Do not those who plot evil go astray?

But those who plan what is good find[a]
love and faithfulness.

23 All hard work brings a profit,
but mere talk leads only to poverty.

24 The wealth of the wise is their crown,
but the folly of fools yields folly.

25 A truthful witness saves lives,
but a false witness is deceitful.

26 Whoever fears the LORD has a secure
fortress,
and for their children it will be a refuge.

27 The fear of the LORD is a fountain of life,
turning a person from the snares of
death.

28 A large population is a king's glory,
but without subjects a prince is ruined.

29 Whoever is patient has great
understanding,
but one who is quick-tempered
displays folly.

30 A heart at peace gives life to the body,
but envy rots the bones.

31 Whoever oppresses the poor shows
contempt for their Maker,
but whoever is kind to the needy
honors God.

32 When calamity comes, the wicked are
brought down,
but even in death the righteous seek
refuge in God.

33 Wisdom reposes in the heart of the
discerning
and even among fools she lets herself
be known.[b]

34 Righteousness exalts a nation,
but sin condemns any people.

35 A king delights in a wise servant,
but a shameful servant arouses
his fury.

15 A gentle answer turns away wrath,
but a harsh word stirs up anger.

2 The tongue of the wise adorns
knowledge,
but the mouth of the fool gushes folly.

3 The eyes of the LORD are everywhere,
keeping watch on the wicked and the
good.

4 The soothing tongue is a tree of life,
but a perverse tongue crushes the spirit.

5 A fool spurns a parent's discipline,
but whoever heeds correction shows
prudence.

6 The house of the righteous contains great
treasure,
but the income of the wicked brings
ruin.

7 The lips of the wise spread knowledge,
but the hearts of fools are not upright.

8 The LORD detests the sacrifice of the
wicked,
but the prayer of the upright pleases
him.

9 The LORD detests the way of the wicked,
but he loves those who pursue
righteousness.

10 Stern discipline awaits anyone who
leaves the path;
the one who hates correction will die.

11 Death and Destruction[c] lie open before
the LORD —
how much more do human hearts!

12 Mockers resent correction,
so they avoid the wise.

13 A happy heart makes the face cheerful,
but heartache crushes the spirit.

14 The discerning heart seeks knowledge,
but the mouth of a fool feeds on folly.

15 All the days of the oppressed are
wretched,
but the cheerful heart has a continual
feast.

16 Better a little with the fear of the LORD
than great wealth with turmoil.

17 Better a small serving of vegetables with
love
than a fattened calf with hatred.

18 A hot-tempered person stirs up conflict,
but the one who is patient calms a
quarrel.

a 22 Or *show*   b 33 Hebrew; Septuagint and Syriac *discerning / but in the heart of fools she is not known*
c 11 Hebrew *Abaddon*

TAKE A DRINK

READ: PROVERBS 14:27

You can easily flip a faucet to access an endless stream of water for drinking, cooking, and getting clean, but the Israelites never took water for granted.

After escaping slavery in Egypt, God's people spent forty years wandering in a desert. When they couldn't locate an adequate supply of water, they experienced desperate and deadly thirst (Exodus 17:1-7). When the people arrived in the promised land, they found more than milk and honey: the land's springs gave them reliable fresh water for people, animals, and crops. Yet in that dry and scorching hot region, water was always a precious commodity (2 Chronicles 32:2-4).

When the Bible declares that "the fear of the LORD is a fountain of life" (Proverbs 14:27), it's saying that living for God with awe-filled respect is as good as stumbling across water in the desert. Relating to him with reverence is the difference between living and dying. And awe for the Lord is like a "fountain," a free-flowing supply of fresh water. That's a source far better than rain collected in cisterns that quickly turns warm and stagnant.

The book of Jeremiah calls it a sin to turn away from the Lord, "the spring of living water," to rely on a cistern you dig for yourself (Jeremiah 2:13). But when you choose to respect God, you experience his thirst-quenching, life-saving waters.

BUILDING
FAITH
WISDOM
STRENGTH

¹⁹ The way of the sluggard is blocked with
  thorns,
  but the path of the upright is a
  highway.

²⁰ A wise son brings joy to his father,
  but a foolish man despises his mother.

²¹ Folly brings joy to one who has no sense,
  but whoever has understanding keeps
  a straight course.

²² Plans fail for lack of counsel,
  but with many advisers they succeed.

²³ A person finds joy in giving an apt reply—
  and how good is a timely word!

²⁴ The path of life leads upward for the
  prudent
  to keep them from going down to the
  realm of the dead.

²⁵ The LORD tears down the house of the
  proud,
  but he sets the widow's boundary
  stones in place.

²⁶ The LORD detests the thoughts of the
  wicked,
  but gracious words are pure in his
  sight.

²⁷ The greedy bring ruin to their
  households,
  but the one who hates bribes will live.

²⁸ The heart of the righteous weighs its
  answers,
  but the mouth of the wicked gushes
  evil.

²⁹ The LORD is far from the wicked,
  but he hears the prayer of the
  righteous.

³⁰ Light in a messenger's eyes brings joy to
  the heart,
  and good news gives health to the
  bones.

³¹ Whoever heeds life-giving correction
  will be at home among the wise.

³² Those who disregard discipline despise
  themselves,
  but the one who heeds correction
  gains understanding.

³³ Wisdom's instruction is to fear the LORD,
  and humility comes before honor.

16 To humans belong the plans of the
  heart,
  but from the LORD comes the proper
  answer of the tongue.

² All a person's ways seem pure to them,
  but motives are weighed by the LORD.

³ Commit to the LORD whatever you do,
  and he will establish your plans.

⁴ The LORD works out everything to its
  proper end—
  even the wicked for a day of disaster.

⁵ The LORD detests all the proud of heart.
  Be sure of this: They will not go
  unpunished.

⁶ Through love and faithfulness sin is
  atoned for;
  through the fear of the LORD evil is
  avoided.

⁷ When the LORD takes pleasure in
  anyone's way,
  he causes their enemies to make peace
  with them.

⁸ Better a little with righteousness
  than much gain with injustice.

⁹ In their hearts humans plan their
  course,
  but the LORD establishes their steps.

¹⁰ The lips of a king speak as an oracle,
  and his mouth does not betray justice.

¹¹ Honest scales and balances belong to the
  LORD;
  all the weights in the bag are of his
  making.

¹² Kings detest wrongdoing,
  for a throne is established through
  righteousness.

¹³ Kings take pleasure in honest lips;
  they value the one who speaks what
  is right.

¹⁴ A king's wrath is a messenger of death,
  but the wise will appease it.

¹⁵ When a king's face brightens, it means
  life;
  his favor is like a rain cloud in spring.

¹⁶ How much better to get wisdom
  than gold,
  to get insight rather than silver!

THANKS FOR THE CORRECTION

READ: **PROVERBS 15:32**

You know how it goes. You act up and do something wrong, and your parents come back at you with some variety of discipline. Back when you were little, you might have gotten a time out. Now you're more likely to lose a privilege or end up doing extra chores. But do you learn from that experience?

The Bible tries hard to convince you that discipline—no matter where it comes from—is one of the best gifts you can ever receive. Correction gives life (Proverbs 15:31). Learning from discipline gives you wise friends (v. 31). Paying attention to tough lessons makes you smart (v. 32). Discipline assures you of God's love (3:12). Hating correction means you're stupid (12:1).

You're wise if you accept those statements as facts so true you can't wait to put them into action. And here's another intriguing piece of information you don't want to ignore: "Those who disregard discipline despise themselves" (15:32).

To "despise" yourself means you consider yourself worthless or even hate the core of who you are. When you refuse to learn from correction—whether it's doled out by parents, teachers, coaches, pastors, or God himself—you're doomed to go on doing wrong. You continue to injure others. You no doubt offend God again and again. And along with all that, you tell everyone how much you disrespect yourself.

BUILDING

FAITH

WISDOM

STRENGTH

¹⁷ The highway of the upright avoids evil;
   those who guard their ways preserve
      their lives.

¹⁸ Pride goes before destruction,
   a haughty spirit before a fall.

¹⁹ Better to be lowly in spirit along with the
      oppressed
   than to share plunder with the proud.

²⁰ Whoever gives heed to instruction
      prospers,ᵃ
   and blessed is the one who trusts in
      the LORD.

²¹ The wise in heart are called discerning,
   and gracious words promote
      instruction.ᵇ

²² Prudence is a fountain of life to the
      prudent,
   but folly brings punishment to fools.

²³ The hearts of the wise make their mouths
      prudent,
   and their lips promote instruction.ᶜ

²⁴ Gracious words are a honeycomb,
   sweet to the soul and healing to the
      bones.

²⁵ There is a way that appears to be right,
   but in the end it leads to death.

²⁶ The appetite of laborers works for them;
   their hunger drives them on.

²⁷ A scoundrel plots evil,
   and on their lips it is like a scorching
      fire.

²⁸ A perverse person stirs up conflict,
   and a gossip separates close friends.

²⁹ A violent person entices their neighbor
   and leads them down a path that is not
      good.

³⁰ Whoever winks with their eye is plotting
      perversity;
   whoever purses their lips is bent on
      evil.

³¹ Gray hair is a crown of splendor;
   it is attained in the way of
      righteousness.

³² Better a patient person than a warrior,
   one with self-control than one who
      takes a city.

³³ The lot is cast into the lap,
   but its every decision is from
      the LORD.

17 Better a dry crust with peace and
      quiet
   than a house full of feasting, with
      strife.

² A prudent servant will rule over a
      disgraceful son
   and will share the inheritance as one
      of the family.

³ The crucible for silver and the furnace
      for gold,
   but the LORD tests the heart.

⁴ A wicked person listens to deceitful lips;
   a liar pays attention to a destructive
      tongue.

⁵ Whoever mocks the poor shows
      contempt for their Maker;
   whoever gloats over disaster will not
      go unpunished.

⁶ Children's children are a crown to the
      aged,
   and parents are the pride of their
      children.

⁷ Eloquent lips are unsuited to a godless
      fool —
   how much worse lying lips to a ruler!

⁸ A bribe is seen as a charm by the one who
      gives it;
   they think success will come at every
      turn.

⁹ Whoever would foster love covers over an
      offense,
   but whoever repeats the matter
      separates close friends.

¹⁰ A rebuke impresses a discerning person
   more than a hundred lashes a fool.

¹¹ Evildoers foster rebellion against God;
   the messenger of death will be sent
      against them.

¹² Better to meet a bear robbed of her cubs
   than a fool bent on folly.

¹³ Evil will never leave the house
   of one who pays back evil for good.

ᵃ 20 Or *whoever speaks prudently finds what is good*   ᵇ 21 Or *words make a person persuasive*
ᶜ 23 Or *prudent / and make their lips persuasive*

FIGHT OR FLIGHT

READ: PROVERBS 17:14

People usually deal with conflict in one of two ways. You either avoid the situation—or dig in and fight. Put another way, you either pretend everything's okay—or you lash out until others crumble.

Jesus said, "Blessed are the peacemakers" (Matthew 5:9), but don't take that to mean Christians are pushovers. God doesn't want you to "fake peace," pretending that everything's okay when it's not. He also doesn't want you to "break peace," winning a battle at any cost. The Lord filled the Bible with wise ways of handling conflict, no matter who you butt heads with or why you fight.

The apostle Paul wrote, for example, "If it is possible, as far as it depends on you, live at peace with everyone" (Romans 12:18). Those words recognize that peace should be your goal, but solving a problem isn't completely in your control. Paul also said, "Do not let the sun go down while you are still angry" (Ephesians 4:26). That's not a command to solve every problem before bedtime, but not to let an issue linger. Jesus himself provided a series of courageous practical steps to take when someone wrongs you (Matthew 18:15-17).

Most fights aren't worth the air it takes to argue. So the next time you see a conflict coming, check if you can put Proverbs 17:14 into action. Try to stop the fight before it starts.

BUILDING
FAITH
WISDOM
STRENGTH

¹⁴ Starting a quarrel is like breaching
      a dam;
   so drop the matter before a dispute
      breaks out.

¹⁵ Acquitting the guilty and condemning
      the innocent—
   the LORD detests them both.

¹⁶ Why should fools have money in hand to
      buy wisdom,
   when they are not able to understand it?

¹⁷ A friend loves at all times,
   and a brother is born for a time of
      adversity.

¹⁸ One who has no sense shakes hands in
      pledge
   and puts up security for a neighbor.

¹⁹ Whoever loves a quarrel loves sin;
   whoever builds a high gate invites
      destruction.

²⁰ One whose heart is corrupt does not
      prosper;
   one whose tongue is perverse falls into
      trouble.

²¹ To have a fool for a child brings grief;
   there is no joy for the parent of a
      godless fool.

²² A cheerful heart is good medicine,
   but a crushed spirit dries up the bones.

²³ The wicked accept bribes in secret
   to pervert the course of justice.

²⁴ A discerning person keeps wisdom in
      view,
   but a fool's eyes wander to the ends of
      the earth.

²⁵ A foolish son brings grief to his father
   and bitterness to the mother who bore
      him.

²⁶ If imposing a fine on the innocent is not
      good,
   surely to flog honest officials is not
      right.

²⁷ The one who has knowledge uses words
      with restraint,
   and whoever has understanding is
      even-tempered.

²⁸ Even fools are thought wise if they keep
      silent,

and discerning if they hold their
   tongues.

18 An unfriendly person pursues
      selfish ends
   and against all sound judgment starts
      quarrels.

² Fools find no pleasure in understanding
   but delight in airing their own
      opinions.

³ When wickedness comes, so does
      contempt,
   and with shame comes reproach.

⁴ The words of the mouth are deep waters,
   but the fountain of wisdom is a rushing
      stream.

⁵ It is not good to be partial to the wicked
   and so deprive the innocent of justice.

⁶ The lips of fools bring them strife,
   and their mouths invite a beating.

⁷ The mouths of fools are their undoing,
   and their lips are a snare to their very
      lives.

⁸ The words of a gossip are like choice
      morsels;
   they go down to the inmost parts.

⁹ One who is slack in his work
   is brother to one who destroys.

¹⁰ The name of the LORD is a fortified tower;
   the righteous run to it and are safe.

¹¹ The wealth of the rich is their fortified
      city;
   they imagine it a wall too high to scale.

¹² Before a downfall the heart is haughty,
   but humility comes before honor.

¹³ To answer before listening—
   that is folly and shame.

¹⁴ The human spirit can endure in sickness,
   but a crushed spirit who can bear?

¹⁵ The heart of the discerning acquires
      knowledge,
   for the ears of the wise seek it out.

¹⁶ A gift opens the way
   and ushers the giver into the presence
      of the great.

¹⁷ In a lawsuit the first to speak seems right,
   until someone comes forward and
      cross-examines.

¹⁸ Casting the lot settles disputes
    and keeps strong opponents apart.

¹⁹ A brother wronged is more unyielding
        than a fortified city;
    disputes are like the barred gates of
        a citadel.

²⁰ From the fruit of their mouth a person's
        stomach is filled;
    with the harvest of their lips they are
        satisfied.

²¹ The tongue has the power of life and
        death,
    and those who love it will eat
        its fruit.

²² He who finds a wife finds what is good
    and receives favor from the LORD.

²³ The poor plead for mercy,
    but the rich answer harshly.

²⁴ One who has unreliable friends soon
        comes to ruin,
    but there is a friend who sticks closer
        than a brother.

19 Better the poor whose walk is
        blameless
    than a fool whose lips are perverse.

² Desire without knowledge is not good—
    how much more will hasty feet miss
        the way!

³ A person's own folly leads to their ruin,
    yet their heart rages against the LORD.

⁴ Wealth attracts many friends,
    but even the closest friend of the poor
        person deserts them.

⁵ A false witness will not go unpunished,
    and whoever pours out lies will not
        go free.

⁶ Many curry favor with a ruler,
    and everyone is the friend of one who
        gives gifts.

⁷ The poor are shunned by all their
        relatives—
    how much more do their friends avoid
        them!
    Though the poor pursue them with
        pleading,
    they are nowhere to be found.ᵃ

⁸ The one who gets wisdom loves life;
    the one who cherishes understanding
        will soon prosper.

⁹ A false witness will not go unpunished,
    and whoever pours out lies will perish.

¹⁰ It is not fitting for a fool to live in luxury—
    how much worse for a slave to rule over
        princes!

¹¹ A person's wisdom yields patience;
    it is to one's glory to overlook an offense.

¹² A king's rage is like the roar of a lion,
    but his favor is like dew on the grass.

¹³ A foolish child is a father's ruin,
    and a quarrelsome wife is like
    the constant dripping of a leaky roof.

¹⁴ Houses and wealth are inherited from
        parents,
    but a prudent wife is from the LORD.

¹⁵ Laziness brings on deep sleep,
    and the shiftless go hungry.

¹⁶ Whoever keeps commandments keeps
        their life,
    but whoever shows contempt for their
        ways will die.

¹⁷ Whoever is kind to the poor lends to the
        LORD,
    and he will reward them for what they
        have done.

¹⁸ Discipline your children, for in that there
        is hope;
    do not be a willing party to their death.

¹⁹ A hot-tempered person must pay the
        penalty;
    rescue them, and you will have to do
        it again.

²⁰ Listen to advice and accept discipline,
    and at the end you will be counted
        among the wise.

²¹ Many are the plans in a person's heart,
    but it is the LORD's purpose that
        prevails.

²² What a person desires is unfailing loveᵇ;
    better to be poor than a liar.

²³ The fear of the LORD leads to life;
    then one rests content, untouched by
        trouble.

ᵃ 7 The meaning of the Hebrew for this sentence is uncertain.   ᵇ 22 Or *Greed is a person's shame*

FOR OR AGAINST . . . YOUR PARENT?

READ: **PROVERBS 19:18**

Parents aren't all that tough to understand. Just try to look at yourself through their eyes. What do they see—and hope to see? Then try taking a few mental steps in their shoes. What are they responsible for—at home, at work, and in raising you?

God gives parents a staggering opportunity. He commands them to nurture children to know him well and thrive in every part of life. The Bible tells parents to "start children off on the way they should go," so that "even when they are old they will not turn from it" (Proverbs 22:6). They should train you to follow God's commands, talking about them "when you sit at home and when you walk along the road, when you lie down and when you get up" (Deuteronomy 6:7). God expects them to bring you up "in the training and instruction of the Lord" (Ephesians 6:4).

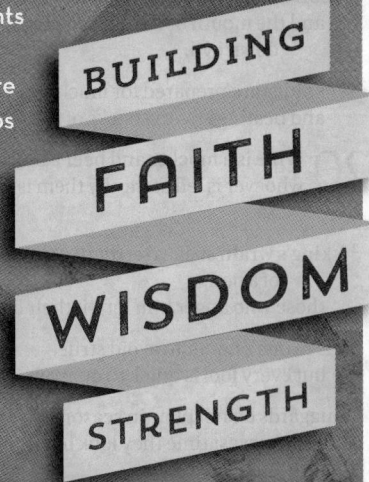

BUILDING FAITH WISDOM STRENGTH

The Lord knows that parents aren't perfect. They discipline you the best they know how (Hebrews 12:10). After all, guiding and correcting you is their only good option. If they don't discipline you, they risk watching you walk off a cliff, hurting yourself spiritually, emotionally, physically, morally. You have a choice today to work with your parents or against them. When you let them do their job, you avoid doing yourself harm that will do you in.

²⁴ A sluggard buries his hand in the dish;
  he will not even bring it back to his
    mouth!

²⁵ Flog a mocker, and the simple will learn
    prudence;
  rebuke the discerning, and they will
    gain knowledge.

²⁶ Whoever robs their father and drives out
    their mother
  is a child who brings shame and
    disgrace.

²⁷ Stop listening to instruction, my son,
  and you will stray from the words of
    knowledge.

²⁸ A corrupt witness mocks at justice,
  and the mouth of the wicked gulps
    down evil.

²⁹ Penalties are prepared for mockers,
  and beatings for the backs of fools.

20 Wine is a mocker and beer a brawler;
  whoever is led astray by them is not
    wise.

² A king's wrath strikes terror like the roar
    of a lion;
  those who anger him forfeit their lives.

³ It is to one's honor to avoid strife,
  but every fool is quick to quarrel.

⁴ Sluggards do not plow in season;
  so at harvest time they look but find
    nothing.

⁵ The purposes of a person's heart are deep
    waters,
  but one who has insight draws
    them out.

⁶ Many claim to have unfailing love,
  but a faithful person who can find?

⁷ The righteous lead blameless lives;
  blessed are their children after them.

⁸ When a king sits on his throne to judge,
  he winnows out all evil with his eyes.

⁹ Who can say, "I have kept my heart
    pure;
  I am clean and without sin"?

¹⁰ Differing weights and differing
    measures—
  the Lord detests them both.

¹¹ Even small children are known by their
    actions,
  so is their conduct really pure and
    upright?

¹² Ears that hear and eyes that see—
  the Lord has made them both.

¹³ Do not love sleep or you will grow poor;
  stay awake and you will have food
    to spare.

¹⁴ "It's no good, it's no good!" says the
    buyer—
  then goes off and boasts about the
    purchase.

¹⁵ Gold there is, and rubies in abundance,
  but lips that speak knowledge are a
    rare jewel.

¹⁶ Take the garment of one who puts up
    security for a stranger;
  hold it in pledge if it is done for an
    outsider.

¹⁷ Food gained by fraud tastes sweet,
  but one ends up with a mouth full
    of gravel.

¹⁸ Plans are established by seeking advice;
  so if you wage war, obtain guidance.

¹⁹ A gossip betrays a confidence;
  so avoid anyone who talks too much.

²⁰ If someone curses their father or mother,
  their lamp will be snuffed out in pitch
    darkness.

²¹ An inheritance claimed too soon
  will not be blessed at the end.

²² Do not say, "I'll pay you back for this
    wrong!"
  Wait for the Lord, and he will avenge
    you.

²³ The Lord detests differing weights,
  and dishonest scales do not please him.

²⁴ A person's steps are directed by the Lord.
  How then can anyone understand
    their own way?

²⁵ It is a trap to dedicate something
    rashly
  and only later to consider one's vows.

²⁶ A wise king winnows out the wicked;
  he drives the threshing wheel over
    them.

²⁷ The human spirit is^a the lamp of the LORD
that sheds light on one's inmost being.

²⁸ Love and faithfulness keep a king safe;
through love his throne is made
secure.

²⁹ The glory of young men is their strength,
gray hair the splendor of the old.

³⁰ Blows and wounds scrub away evil,
and beatings purge the inmost being.

21 In the LORD's hand the king's heart
is a stream of water
that he channels toward all who
please him.

² A person may think their own ways are
right,
but the LORD weighs the heart.

³ To do what is right and just
is more acceptable to the LORD than
sacrifice.

⁴ Haughty eyes and a proud heart —
the unplowed field of the wicked —
produce sin.

⁵ The plans of the diligent lead to profit
as surely as haste leads to poverty.

⁶ A fortune made by a lying tongue
is a fleeting vapor and a deadly snare.^b

⁷ The violence of the wicked will drag them
away,
for they refuse to do what is right.

⁸ The way of the guilty is devious,
but the conduct of the innocent is
upright.

⁹ Better to live on a corner of the roof
than share a house with a quarrelsome
wife.

¹⁰ The wicked crave evil;
their neighbors get no mercy from them.

¹¹ When a mocker is punished, the simple
gain wisdom;
by paying attention to the wise they get
knowledge.

¹² The Righteous One^c takes note of the
house of the wicked
and brings the wicked to ruin.

¹³ Whoever shuts their ears to the cry of the
poor
will also cry out and not be answered.

¹⁴ A gift given in secret soothes anger,
and a bribe concealed in the cloak
pacifies great wrath.

¹⁵ When justice is done, it brings joy to the
righteous
but terror to evildoers.

¹⁶ Whoever strays from the path of
prudence
comes to rest in the company of the
dead.

¹⁷ Whoever loves pleasure will become
poor;
whoever loves wine and olive oil will
never be rich.

¹⁸ The wicked become a ransom for the
righteous,
and the unfaithful for the upright.

¹⁹ Better to live in a desert
than with a quarrelsome and nagging
wife.

²⁰ The wise store up choice food and
olive oil,
but fools gulp theirs down.

²¹ Whoever pursues righteousness and love
finds life, prosperity^d and honor.

²² One who is wise can go up against the
city of the mighty
and pull down the stronghold in which
they trust.

²³ Those who guard their mouths and their
tongues
keep themselves from calamity.

²⁴ The proud and arrogant person —
"Mocker" is his name —
behaves with insolent fury.

²⁵ The craving of a sluggard will be the
death of him,
because his hands refuse to work.

²⁶ All day long he craves for more,
but the righteous give without sparing.

²⁷ The sacrifice of the wicked is
detestable —

---

^a 27 Or *A person's words are*   ^b 6 Some Hebrew manuscripts, Septuagint and Vulgate; most Hebrew
manuscripts *vapor for those who seek death*   ^c 12 Or *The righteous person*   ^d 21 Or *righteousness*

how much more so when brought with
evil intent!

²⁸ A false witness will perish,
but a careful listener will testify
successfully.

²⁹ The wicked put up a bold front,
but the upright give thought to their
ways.

³⁰ There is no wisdom, no insight, no plan
that can succeed against the LORD.

³¹ The horse is made ready for the day of
battle,
but victory rests with the LORD.

22 A good name is more desirable than
great riches;
to be esteemed is better than silver
or gold.

² Rich and poor have this in common:
The LORD is the Maker of them all.

³ The prudent see danger and take refuge,
but the simple keep going and pay the
penalty.

⁴ Humility is the fear of the LORD;
its wages are riches and honor and life.

⁵ In the paths of the wicked are snares and
pitfalls,
but those who would preserve their life
stay far from them.

⁶ Start children off on the way they
should go,
and even when they are old they will
not turn from it.

⁷ The rich rule over the poor,
and the borrower is slave to the lender.

⁸ Whoever sows injustice reaps calamity,
and the rod they wield in fury will be
broken.

⁹ The generous will themselves be blessed,
for they share their food with the poor.

¹⁰ Drive out the mocker, and out goes strife;
quarrels and insults are ended.

¹¹ One who loves a pure heart and who
speaks with grace
will have the king for a friend.

¹² The eyes of the LORD keep watch over
knowledge,

but he frustrates the words of the
unfaithful.

¹³ The sluggard says, "There's a lion outside!
I'll be killed in the public square!"

¹⁴ The mouth of an adulterous woman is a
deep pit;
a man who is under the LORD's wrath
falls into it.

¹⁵ Folly is bound up in the heart of a child,
but the rod of discipline will drive it
far away.

¹⁶ One who oppresses the poor to increase
his wealth
and one who gives gifts to the rich—
both come to poverty.

Thirty Sayings of the Wise

Saying 1
¹⁷ Pay attention and turn your ear to the
sayings of the wise;
apply your heart to what I teach,
¹⁸ for it is pleasing when you keep them in
your heart
and have all of them ready on your
lips.
¹⁹ So that your trust may be in the LORD,
I teach you today, even you.
²⁰ Have I not written thirty sayings for you,
sayings of counsel and knowledge,
²¹ teaching you to be honest and to speak
the truth,
so that you bring back truthful reports
to those you serve?

Saying 2
²² Do not exploit the poor because they
are poor
and do not crush the needy in court,
²³ for the LORD will take up their case
and will exact life for life.

Saying 3
²⁴ Do not make friends with a hot-tempered
person,
do not associate with one easily
angered,
²⁵ or you may learn their ways
and get yourself ensnared.

Saying 4
²⁶ Do not be one who shakes hands in
pledge
or puts up security for debts;

ANGER MANAGEMENT

READ: PROVERBS 22:24-25

That "hot-tempered person" in Proverbs 22:24 might sound like someone you know. Maybe even you. Hanging out with a friend with a short fuse puts you in danger of deadly blow-ups.

The Bible doesn't say all anger is wrong. Ephesians 4:26 says, "In your anger do not sin," showing that anger and sin are two different things. Yet it hints that anger often leads to sin. So the Bible says to not let anger burn but to sort out issues quickly (v. 26). If you don't, you give Satan entry to your life (v. 27). The Bible also points out that human anger doesn't produce the good lives God wants (James 1:20). It says there are times when it's wise to overlook wrongs done to you rather than get angry (Proverbs 19:11).

People with anger management issues aren't any better or worse than everyone else in the sins they struggle to overcome. But they do require careful handling. Getting too close can get you burned. Anger acts like fire, with bad tempers leaping from person to person like flames spread across dry grass.

BUILDING FAITH WISDOM STRENGTH

Anger isn't just a personality issue. God wants you to get rid of it, along with bitterness and rage (Ephesians 4:31). He aims for you to deal kindly and patiently with others, just like he puts up with you (v. 2).

²⁷ if you lack the means to pay,
  your very bed will be snatched from
    under you.

Saying 5

²⁸ Do not move an ancient boundary stone
  set up by your ancestors.

Saying 6

²⁹ Do you see someone skilled in their
    work?
  They will serve before kings;
  they will not serve before officials of
    low rank.

Saying 7

23 When you sit to dine with a ruler,
  note well what^a is before you,
² and put a knife to your throat
  if you are given to gluttony.
³ Do not crave his delicacies,
  for that food is deceptive.

Saying 8

⁴ Do not wear yourself out to get rich;
  do not trust your own cleverness.
⁵ Cast but a glance at riches, and they
    are gone,
  for they will surely sprout wings
  and fly off to the sky like an eagle.

Saying 9

⁶ Do not eat the food of a begrudging host,
  do not crave his delicacies;
⁷ for he is the kind of person
  who is always thinking about the cost.^b
  "Eat and drink," he says to you,
  but his heart is not with you.
⁸ You will vomit up the little you have
    eaten
  and will have wasted your
    compliments.

Saying 10

⁹ Do not speak to fools,
  for they will scorn your prudent words.

Saying 11

¹⁰ Do not move an ancient boundary stone
  or encroach on the fields of the
    fatherless,
¹¹ for their Defender is strong;
  he will take up their case against you.

Saying 12

¹² Apply your heart to instruction
  and your ears to words of knowledge.

Saying 13

¹³ Do not withhold discipline from a child;
  if you punish them with the rod, they
    will not die.
¹⁴ Punish them with the rod
  and save them from death.

Saying 14

¹⁵ My son, if your heart is wise,
  then my heart will be glad indeed;
¹⁶ my inmost being will rejoice
  when your lips speak what is right.

Saying 15

¹⁷ Do not let your heart envy sinners,
  but always be zealous for the fear of
    the LORD.
¹⁸ There is surely a future hope for you,
  and your hope will not be cut off.

Saying 16

¹⁹ Listen, my son, and be wise,
  and set your heart on the right path:
²⁰ Do not join those who drink too much
    wine
  or gorge themselves on meat,
²¹ for drunkards and gluttons become poor,
  and drowsiness clothes them in rags.

Saying 17

²² Listen to your father, who gave you life,
  and do not despise your mother when
    she is old.
²³ Buy the truth and do not sell it —
  wisdom, instruction and insight as
    well.
²⁴ The father of a righteous child has great
    joy;
  a man who fathers a wise son rejoices
    in him.
²⁵ May your father and mother rejoice;
  may she who gave you birth be joyful!

Saying 18

²⁶ My son, give me your heart
  and let your eyes delight in my ways,
²⁷ for an adulterous woman is a deep pit,
  and a wayward wife is a narrow well.

---

^a 1 Or *who*   ^b 7 Or *for as he thinks within himself, / so he is*; or *for as he puts on a feast, / so he is*

²⁸ Like a bandit she lies in wait
     and multiplies the unfaithful
          among men.

Saying 19

²⁹ Who has woe? Who has sorrow?
     Who has strife? Who has complaints?
     Who has needless bruises? Who has
          bloodshot eyes?
³⁰ Those who linger over wine,
     who go to sample bowls of mixed wine.
³¹ Do not gaze at wine when it is red,
     when it sparkles in the cup,
     when it goes down smoothly!
³² In the end it bites like a snake
     and poisons like a viper.
³³ Your eyes will see strange sights,
     and your mind will imagine confusing
          things.
³⁴ You will be like one sleeping on the high
          seas,
     lying on top of the rigging.
³⁵ "They hit me," you will say, "but I'm not
          hurt!
     They beat me, but I don't feel it!
     When will I wake up
          so I can find another drink?"

Saying 20

24 Do not envy the wicked,
     do not desire their company;
² for their hearts plot violence,
     and their lips talk about making
          trouble.

Saying 21

³ By wisdom a house is built,
     and through understanding it is
          established;
⁴ through knowledge its rooms are filled
     with rare and beautiful treasures.

Saying 22

⁵ The wise prevail through great power,
     and those who have knowledge muster
          their strength.
⁶ Surely you need guidance to wage war,
     and victory is won through many
          advisers.

Saying 23

⁷ Wisdom is too high for fools;
     in the assembly at the gate they must
          not open their mouths.

Saying 24

⁸ Whoever plots evil
     will be known as a schemer.
⁹ The schemes of folly are sin,
     and people detest a mocker.

Saying 25

¹⁰ If you falter in a time of trouble,
     how small is your strength!
¹¹ Rescue those being led away to death;
     hold back those staggering toward
          slaughter.
¹² If you say, "But we knew nothing about
          this,"
     does not he who weighs the heart
          perceive it?
     Does not he who guards your life
          know it?
     Will he not repay everyone according
          to what they have done?

Saying 26

¹³ Eat honey, my son, for it is good;
     honey from the comb is sweet to your
          taste.
¹⁴ Know also that wisdom is like honey for
          you:
     If you find it, there is a future hope
          for you,
     and your hope will not be cut off.

Saying 27

¹⁵ Do not lurk like a thief near the house of
          the righteous,
     do not plunder their dwelling place;
¹⁶ for though the righteous fall seven times,
          they rise again,
     but the wicked stumble when calamity
          strikes.

Saying 28

¹⁷ Do not gloat when your enemy falls;
     when they stumble, do not let your
          heart rejoice,
¹⁸ or the Lord will see and disapprove
     and turn his wrath away from
          them.

Saying 29

¹⁹ Do not fret because of evildoers
     or be envious of the wicked,
²⁰ for the evildoer has no future hope,
     and the lamp of the wicked will be
          snuffed out.

BEYOND THE SMOOTH TASTE

READ: **PROVERBS 23:31-32**

E ither you control alcohol, or it controls you. There's not much middle ground.

Proverbs declares that all kinds of terrible effects track back to excessive drinking. Proverbs 23:29-30 says it brings "woe," a deep grief or affliction. It causes "sorrow," extreme sadness and the total opposite of joy. When people get drunk, they spout "complaints," they sport "needless bruises," and they greet the world with "bloodshot eyes."

That's just the start. People who drink too much "see strange sights" and their brains "imagine confusing things" (v. 33). Even when they lie down to rest, their bodies heave "like one sleeping on the high seas," strung up high in a sailing ship's rigging (v. 34). They get thrashed but feel no pain, so they keep going back for more. All they can think about is finding another drink (v. 35).

BUILDING

FAITH

WISDOM

STRENGTH

The Bible doesn't ban all alcohol consumption, but this passage makes it clear that drunkenness stings like the bite of a poisonous snake. The problem starts when people don't see any further than alcohol's sparkle and smooth taste.

Your parents and other mentors can teach you the best ways to deal with alcohol when you're of age. But for now it's out of bounds, usually illegal and surely against what God wants for you. Don't miss the main point of this passage: alcohol isn't the giant party everyone says it is.

Saying 30

21 Fear the LORD and the king, my son,
  and do not join with rebellious
    officials,
22 for those two will send sudden
    destruction on them,
  and who knows what calamities they
    can bring?

Further Sayings of the Wise

23 These also are sayings of the wise:

To show partiality in judging is not good:
24 Whoever says to the guilty, "You are
    innocent,"
  will be cursed by peoples and
    denounced by nations.
25 But it will go well with those who convict
    the guilty,
  and rich blessing will come on them.

26 An honest answer
  is like a kiss on the lips.

27 Put your outdoor work in order
    and get your fields ready;
  after that, build your house.

28 Do not testify against your neighbor
    without cause —
  would you use your lips to mislead?
29 Do not say, "I'll do to them as they have
    done to me;
  I'll pay them back for what they did."

30 I went past the field of a sluggard,
  past the vineyard of someone who has
    no sense;
31 thorns had come up everywhere,
  the ground was covered with weeds,
    and the stone wall was in ruins.
32 I applied my heart to what I observed
  and learned a lesson from what I saw:
33 A little sleep, a little slumber,
  a little folding of the hands to rest—
34 and poverty will come on you like a thief
  and scarcity like an armed man.

More Proverbs of Solomon

25 These are more proverbs of Solomon,
  compiled by the men of Hezekiah
king of Judah:

2 It is the glory of God to conceal a matter;
  to search out a matter is the glory of
    kings.
3 As the heavens are high and the earth is
    deep,
  so the hearts of kings are
    unsearchable.

4 Remove the dross from the silver,
  and a silversmith can produce a vessel;
5 remove wicked officials from the king's
    presence,
  and his throne will be established
    through righteousness.

6 Do not exalt yourself in the king's
    presence,
  and do not claim a place among his
    great men;
7 it is better for him to say to you, "Come up
    here,"
  than for him to humiliate you before
    his nobles.

What you have seen with your eyes
8   do not bring*a* hastily to court,
  for what will you do in the end
    if your neighbor puts you to shame?

9 If you take your neighbor to court,
  do not betray another's confidence,
10 or the one who hears it may shame you
  and the charge against you will stand.

11 Like apples*b* of gold in settings of silver
  is a ruling rightly given.
12 Like an earring of gold or an ornament of
    fine gold
  is the rebuke of a wise judge to a
    listening ear.

13 Like a snow-cooled drink at harvest time
  is a trustworthy messenger to the one
    who sends him;
  he refreshes the spirit of his master.
14 Like clouds and wind without rain
  is one who boasts of gifts never given.

15 Through patience a ruler can be
    persuaded,
  and a gentle tongue can break a bone.

16 If you find honey, eat just enough—
  too much of it, and you will vomit.
17 Seldom set foot in your neighbor's
    house—
  too much of you, and they will hate you.

---

a 7,8 Or *nobles / on whom you had set your eyes. / *8*Do not go*   *b* 11 Or possibly *apricots*

SKIMMING OFF IMPURITIES

READ: **PROVERBS 25:4**

Dross" is the name for solids that rise to the surface of metal that has been blasted with heat to the point of melting. Skimming these floating impurities off the top results in pure metal ready to pour into a mold to make something useful or beautiful. Liquefying silver sounds amusing if you're experimenting in science or art class. It's not so happy if you're the stuff feeling the heat.

Impurities in a metal weaken a vessel and prevent it from performing up to its potential. They spoil the vessel's beauty. Impurities inside you keep you from accomplishing all the Lord has planned for you. Those flaws spoil your outward appearance as a believer or your inward devotion to God.

God puts every follower of Jesus through a process of purification. He aims to rid you of every little piece of crud that doesn't belong in your life. First he goes after obvious outward sins. But he doesn't miss hurtful secret habits or bad attitudes. And sometimes he turns up the heat to get rid of flaws you don't even know are there. God says in Isaiah 1:25, "I will thoroughly purge away your dross and remove all your impurities."

You never know what process the Lord will use to make you pure. But when he lets you feel the heat, you can be sure he's forging you into a stunning work of art.

BUILDING
FAITH
WISDOM
STRENGTH

¹⁸ Like a club or a sword or a sharp arrow
   is one who gives false testimony
      against a neighbor.
¹⁹ Like a broken tooth or a lame foot
   is reliance on the unfaithful in a time
      of trouble.
²⁰ Like one who takes away a garment on a
      cold day,
   or like vinegar poured on a wound,
   is one who sings songs to a heavy
      heart.

²¹ If your enemy is hungry, give him food
      to eat;
   if he is thirsty, give him water to drink.
²² In doing this, you will heap burning coals
      on his head,
   and the LORD will reward you.

²³ Like a north wind that brings unexpected
      rain
   is a sly tongue — which provokes a
      horrified look.

²⁴ Better to live on a corner of the roof
   than share a house with a quarrelsome
      wife.

²⁵ Like cold water to a weary soul
   is good news from a distant land.
²⁶ Like a muddied spring or a polluted well
   are the righteous who give way to the
      wicked.

²⁷ It is not good to eat too much honey,
   nor is it honorable to search out
      matters that are too deep.

²⁸ Like a city whose walls are broken
      through
   is a person who lacks self-control.

26 Like snow in summer or rain in
      harvest,
   honor is not fitting for a fool.
² Like a fluttering sparrow or a darting
      swallow,
   an undeserved curse does not come
      to rest.
³ A whip for the horse, a bridle for the
      donkey,
   and a rod for the backs of fools!
⁴ Do not answer a fool according to his folly,
   or you yourself will be just like him.
⁵ Answer a fool according to his folly,
   or he will be wise in his own eyes.

⁶ Sending a message by the hands of a fool
   is like cutting off one's feet or drinking
      poison.
⁷ Like the useless legs of one who is lame
   is a proverb in the mouth of a fool.
⁸ Like tying a stone in a sling
   is the giving of honor to a fool.
⁹ Like a thornbush in a drunkard's hand
   is a proverb in the mouth of a fool.
¹⁰ Like an archer who wounds at random
   is one who hires a fool or any passer-by.
¹¹ As a dog returns to its vomit,
   so fools repeat their folly.
¹² Do you see a person wise in their own
      eyes?
   There is more hope for a fool than
      for them.

¹³ A sluggard says, "There's a lion in the
      road,
   a fierce lion roaming the streets!"
¹⁴ As a door turns on its hinges,
   so a sluggard turns on his bed.
¹⁵ A sluggard buries his hand in the dish;
   he is too lazy to bring it back to his
      mouth.
¹⁶ A sluggard is wiser in his own eyes
   than seven people who answer
      discreetly.

¹⁷ Like one who grabs a stray dog by
      the ears
   is someone who rushes into a quarrel
      not their own.

¹⁸ Like a maniac shooting
   flaming arrows of death
¹⁹ is one who deceives their neighbor
   and says, "I was only joking!"

²⁰ Without wood a fire goes out;
   without a gossip a quarrel dies down.
²¹ As charcoal to embers and as wood
      to fire,
   so is a quarrelsome person for kindling
      strife.
²² The words of a gossip are like choice
      morsels;
   they go down to the inmost parts.

²³ Like a coating of silver dross on
      earthenware
   are fervent*ᵃ* lips with an evil heart.
²⁴ Enemies disguise themselves with their
      lips,
   but in their hearts they harbor deceit.

ᵃ 23 Hebrew; Septuagint *smooth*

²⁵Though their speech is charming, do not
believe them,
for seven abominations fill their hearts.
²⁶Their malice may be concealed by
deception,
but their wickedness will be exposed
in the assembly.
²⁷Whoever digs a pit will fall into it;
if someone rolls a stone, it will roll back
on them.
²⁸A lying tongue hates those it hurts,
and a flattering mouth works ruin.

27 Do not boast about tomorrow,
for you do not know what a day may
bring.

²Let someone else praise you, and not
your own mouth;
an outsider, and not your own lips.

³Stone is heavy and sand a burden,
but a fool's provocation is heavier
than both.

⁴Anger is cruel and fury overwhelming,
but who can stand before jealousy?

⁵Better is open rebuke
than hidden love.

⁶Wounds from a friend can be trusted,
but an enemy multiplies kisses.

⁷One who is full loathes honey from the
comb,
but to the hungry even what is bitter
tastes sweet.

⁸Like a bird that flees its nest
is anyone who flees from home.

⁹Perfume and incense bring joy to the
heart,
and the pleasantness of a friend
springs from their heartfelt advice.

¹⁰Do not forsake your friend or a friend of
your family,
and do not go to your relative's house
when disaster strikes you —
better a neighbor nearby than a
relative far away.

¹¹Be wise, my son, and bring joy to my
heart;
then I can answer anyone who treats
me with contempt.

¹²The prudent see danger and take refuge,
but the simple keep going and pay
the penalty.

¹³Take the garment of one who puts up
security for a stranger;
hold it in pledge if it is done for an
outsider.

¹⁴If anyone loudly blesses their neighbor
early in the morning,
it will be taken as a curse.

¹⁵A quarrelsome wife is like the dripping
of a leaky roof in a rainstorm;
¹⁶restraining her is like restraining
the wind
or grasping oil with the hand.

¹⁷As iron sharpens iron,
so one person sharpens another.

¹⁸The one who guards a fig tree will eat
its fruit,
and whoever protects their master will
be honored.

¹⁹As water reflects the face,
so one's life reflects the heart.^a

²⁰Death and Destruction^b are never
satisfied,
and neither are human eyes.

²¹The crucible for silver and the furnace
for gold,
but people are tested by their praise.

²²Though you grind a fool in a mortar,
grinding them like grain with a pestle,
you will not remove their folly
from them.

²³Be sure you know the condition of your
flocks,
give careful attention to your herds;
²⁴for riches do not endure forever,
and a crown is not secure for all
generations.
²⁵When the hay is removed and new
growth appears
and the grass from the hills is
gathered in,
²⁶the lambs will provide you with clothing,
and the goats with the price of a field.
²⁷You will have plenty of goats' milk to feed
your family
and to nourish your female servants.

^a 19 Or *so others reflect your heart back to you*   ^b 20 Hebrew *Abaddon*

STEERING CLEAR

READ: PROVERBS 27:12

When you get behind the wheel of a car, nothing keeps you safer than gluing your eyes to the road. You can't often stop another driver from slamming you from behind. But as long as you stay alert, you can look ahead and steer around all kinds of accidents.

"Prudence" is a common Bible word for the skill, common sense, and good judgment you need to navigate life safely. It's not at all the same thing as running through life scared. Paranoid people see danger where it doesn't exist. They flee imaginary threats, and their insides churn with fear. But the prudent spot real danger even when others can't see it. They recognize genuine threats. They know when fear is appropriate, and prudence lets them walk through life with calm confidence.

The Lord aims to train you to be prudent. He wants to teach you the skill of looking down a road to avoid danger. Less attentive people plow right ahead, and they pay the price. The Bible calls them "simple." They lack sense and intelligence but abound in ignorance.

Prudence means choosing to be alert about what lies ahead and the harm it can cause you. So think through your day. What threatens to injure you spiritually, emotionally, or physically? Who wants to help you get closer to the Lord—and who wants to drag you away? What might destroy you if you don't pay attention?

BUILDING

FAITH

WISDOM

STRENGTH

THE CORE

READ: **PROVERBS 27:19**

Your heart defines who you are, how you think, and what you do. Because everything flows from it. What do we mean when we speak of "the heart"? In science, we know that it's the blood-pumping organ that makes the body run. It doesn't think; it doesn't feel. But in Hebrew culture, the heart was seen differently. It was a metaphor for the center, or core, of a personality. It was the spiritual hub. The ancients knew that you could lightly touch the wrist and feel a soft beating—what we call a pulse. That same pulse could be felt in the neck and elsewhere.

But place the hand over the heart, which is the center of a person, and that beating was more powerful. So it stood to reason that everything flowed from the heart—not only blood, but also personality, motives, emotions, and will. The Hebrews understood that all along. In Hebrew, the word heart means "the kernel of the nut."

BUILDING **FAITH** WISDOM STRENGTH

Your "heart" reflects your true identity.

Overlooking the heart and focusing just on what's downstream could be described as "behavior modification." Behavior modification, popular in mid-twentieth century psychology, is the idea of trying to bring about change by targeting things we can observe and measure. It's symptom-based care, quick-fix methodology.

This is not a condemnation of setting limits or working harder. It's simply that the heart of the issue is an issue of the heart.

28

The wicked flee though no one pursues,
but the righteous are as bold as a lion.

² When a country is rebellious, it has many rulers,
but a ruler with discernment and knowledge maintains order.

³ A ruler[a] who oppresses the poor
is like a driving rain that leaves no crops.

⁴ Those who forsake instruction praise the wicked,
but those who heed it resist them.

⁵ Evildoers do not understand what is right,
but those who seek the LORD understand it fully.

⁶ Better the poor whose walk is blameless
than the rich whose ways are perverse.

⁷ A discerning son heeds instruction,
but a companion of gluttons disgraces his father.

⁸ Whoever increases wealth by taking interest or profit from the poor
amasses it for another, who will be kind to the poor.

⁹ If anyone turns a deaf ear to my instruction,
even their prayers are detestable.

¹⁰ Whoever leads the upright along an evil path
will fall into their own trap,
but the blameless will receive a good inheritance.

¹¹ The rich are wise in their own eyes;
one who is poor and discerning sees how deluded they are.

¹² When the righteous triumph, there is great elation;
but when the wicked rise to power, people go into hiding.

¹³ Whoever conceals their sins does not prosper,
but the one who confesses and renounces them finds mercy.

¹⁴ Blessed is the one who always trembles before God,
but whoever hardens their heart falls into trouble.

¹⁵ Like a roaring lion or a charging bear
is a wicked ruler over a helpless people.

¹⁶ A tyrannical ruler practices extortion,
but one who hates ill-gotten gain will enjoy a long reign.

¹⁷ Anyone tormented by the guilt of murder
will seek refuge in the grave;
let no one hold them back.

¹⁸ The one whose walk is blameless is kept safe,
but the one whose ways are perverse will fall into the pit.[b]

¹⁹ Those who work their land will have abundant food,
but those who chase fantasies will have their fill of poverty.

²⁰ A faithful person will be richly blessed,
but one eager to get rich will not go unpunished.

²¹ To show partiality is not good—
yet a person will do wrong for a piece of bread.

²² The stingy are eager to get rich
and are unaware that poverty awaits them.

²³ Whoever rebukes a person will in the end gain favor
rather than one who has a flattering tongue.

²⁴ Whoever robs their father or mother
and says, "It's not wrong,"
is partner to one who destroys.

²⁵ The greedy stir up conflict,
but those who trust in the LORD will prosper.

²⁶ Those who trust in themselves are fools,
but those who walk in wisdom are kept safe.

²⁷ Those who give to the poor will lack nothing,
but those who close their eyes to them receive many curses.

---

a 3 Or *A poor person*   *b* 18 Syriac (see Septuagint); Hebrew *into one*

28 When the wicked rise to power, people go
　　into hiding;
　　but when the wicked perish, the
　　righteous thrive.

29 Whoever remains stiff-necked after
　　many rebukes
　　will suddenly be destroyed—without
　　remedy.

2 When the righteous thrive, the people
　　rejoice;
　　when the wicked rule, the people groan.

3 A man who loves wisdom brings joy to
　　his father,
　　but a companion of prostitutes
　　squanders his wealth.

4 By justice a king gives a country stability,
　　but those who are greedy for[a] bribes
　　tear it down.

5 Those who flatter their neighbors
　　are spreading nets for their feet.

6 Evildoers are snared by their own sin,
　　but the righteous shout for joy and
　　are glad.

7 The righteous care about justice for the
　　poor,
　　but the wicked have no such concern.

8 Mockers stir up a city,
　　but the wise turn away anger.

9 If a wise person goes to court with a fool,
　　the fool rages and scoffs, and there is
　　no peace.

10 The bloodthirsty hate a person of
　　integrity
　　and seek to kill the upright.

11 Fools give full vent to their rage,
　　but the wise bring calm in the end.

12 If a ruler listens to lies,
　　all his officials become wicked.

13 The poor and the oppressor have this in
　　common:
　　The LORD gives sight to the eyes of both.

14 If a king judges the poor with fairness,
　　his throne will be established forever.

15 A rod and a reprimand impart wisdom,
　　but a child left undisciplined disgraces
　　its mother.

16 When the wicked thrive, so does sin,
　　but the righteous will see their
　　downfall.

17 Discipline your children, and they will
　　give you peace;
　　they will bring you the delights you
　　desire.

18 Where there is no revelation, people cast
　　off restraint;
　　but blessed is the one who heeds
　　wisdom's instruction.

19 Servants cannot be corrected by mere
　　words;
　　though they understand, they will not
　　respond.

20 Do you see someone who speaks in haste?
　　There is more hope for a fool than for
　　them.

21 A servant pampered from youth
　　will turn out to be insolent.

22 An angry person stirs up conflict,
　　and a hot-tempered person commits
　　many sins.

23 Pride brings a person low,
　　but the lowly in spirit gain honor.

24 The accomplices of thieves are their own
　　enemies;
　　they are put under oath and dare not
　　testify.

25 Fear of man will prove to be a snare,
　　but whoever trusts in the LORD is
　　kept safe.

26 Many seek an audience with a ruler,
　　but it is from the LORD that one gets
　　justice.

27 The righteous detest the dishonest;
　　the wicked detest the upright.

Sayings of Agur

30 The sayings of Agur son of Jakeh—
　　an inspired utterance.

This man's utterance to Ithiel:

"I am weary, God,
　　but I can prevail.[b]
2 Surely I am only a brute, not a man;
　　I do not have human understanding.

---

[a] 4 Or who give　　[b] 1 With a different word division of the Hebrew; Masoretic Text utterance to Ithiel, / to Ithiel and Ukal:

WHISPERING SIN

READ: **PROVERBS 29:1**

There's something that happens in the back of your head before you choose to do wrong. It's not as obvious as a cartoon devil popping up on your shoulder, but a little voice whispers that "it's okay . . . it doesn't hurt anyone . . . nothing will happen . . . you won't get caught." But the truth is it's not okay . . . it does hurt someone . . . something will happen . . . and you will get caught. You just never know when the consequences of sin will kick in.

That's the point of Proverbs 29:1. A "rebuke" is a sharp correction. The person described here is literally "a man of rebukes," someone corrected so often it's as if "rebuke" is now part of his name. To be "stiff-necked" means the opposite of physically bending your neck, a sign of submission. This stubborn person doesn't see destruction coming, and when it does arrive, there will be no way to put him back together again.

You're smart enough not to do wildly stupid things like driving drunk, knowing that sooner or later you will maim or kill yourself or someone else. When you can foresee the consequences of all sins, it's a sign you're starting to think clearly. Sure, you might think you'll get away with sin sometimes. But there are usually consequences.

Maybe your sin will become a habit that will hook you forever. Or it will cause destruction you can't avoid forever. So get smart. When the Lord corrects you, don't ignore him.

BUILDING

FAITH

WISDOM

STRENGTH

³ I have not learned wisdom,
  nor have I attained to the knowledge of
    the Holy One.
⁴ Who has gone up to heaven and come
      down?
  Whose hands have gathered up the
    wind?
  Who has wrapped up the waters in a
    cloak?
  Who has established all the ends of the
    earth?
  What is his name, and what is the name
    of his son?
  Surely you know!

⁵ "Every word of God is flawless;
  he is a shield to those who take refuge
    in him.
⁶ Do not add to his words,
  or he will rebuke you and prove you
    a liar.

⁷ "Two things I ask of you, Lord;
  do not refuse me before I die:
⁸ Keep falsehood and lies far from me;
  give me neither poverty nor riches,
  but give me only my daily bread.
⁹ Otherwise, I may have too much and
    disown you
  and say, 'Who is the Lord?'
  Or I may become poor and steal,
  and so dishonor the name of my God.

¹⁰ "Do not slander a servant to their master,
  or they will curse you, and you will
    pay for it.

¹¹ "There are those who curse their fathers
  and do not bless their mothers;
¹² those who are pure in their own eyes
  and yet are not cleansed of their filth;
¹³ those whose eyes are ever so haughty,
  whose glances are so disdainful;
¹⁴ those whose teeth are swords
  and whose jaws are set with knives
  to devour the poor from the earth
  and the needy from among mankind.

¹⁵ "The leech has two daughters.
  'Give! Give!' they cry.

  "There are three things that are never
    satisfied,
  four that never say, 'Enough!':
¹⁶ the grave, the barren womb,

land, which is never satisfied with
    water,
  and fire, which never says, 'Enough!'

¹⁷ "The eye that mocks a father,
  that scorns an aged mother,
  will be pecked out by the ravens of the
    valley,
  will be eaten by the vultures.

¹⁸ "There are three things that are too
      amazing for me,
  four that I do not understand:
¹⁹ the way of an eagle in the sky,
  the way of a snake on a rock,
  the way of a ship on the high seas,
  and the way of a man with a young
    woman.

²⁰ "This is the way of an adulterous
      woman:
  She eats and wipes her mouth
  and says, 'I've done nothing wrong.'

²¹ "Under three things the earth trembles,
  under four it cannot bear up:
²² a servant who becomes king,
  a godless fool who gets plenty to eat,
²³ a contemptible woman who gets married,
  and a servant who displaces her
    mistress.

²⁴ "Four things on earth are small,
  yet they are extremely wise:
²⁵ Ants are creatures of little strength,
  yet they store up their food in the
    summer;
²⁶ hyraxes are creatures of little power,
  yet they make their home in
    the crags;
²⁷ locusts have no king,
  yet they advance together in ranks;
²⁸ a lizard can be caught with the hand,
  yet it is found in kings' palaces.

²⁹ "There are three things that are stately in
      their stride,
  four that move with stately bearing:
³⁰ a lion, mighty among beasts,
  who retreats before nothing;
³¹ a strutting rooster, a he-goat,
  and a king secure against revolt.[a]

³² "If you play the fool and exalt yourself,
  or if you plan evil,
  clap your hand over your mouth!

[a] 31 The meaning of the Hebrew for this phrase is uncertain.

³³ For as churning cream produces butter,
　and as twisting the nose produces
　　blood,
　so stirring up anger produces strife."

Sayings of King Lemuel

31 The sayings of King Lemuel — an inspired utterance his mother taught
him.

² Listen, my son! Listen, son of my womb!
　Listen, my son, the answer to my
　　prayers!
³ Do not spend your strength[a] on women,
　your vigor on those who ruin kings.

⁴ It is not for kings, Lemuel —
　it is not for kings to drink wine,
　not for rulers to crave beer,
⁵ lest they drink and forget what has been
　　decreed,
　and deprive all the oppressed of their
　　rights.
⁶ Let beer be for those who are perishing,
　wine for those who are in anguish!
⁷ Let them drink and forget their poverty
　and remember their misery no more.

⁸ Speak up for those who cannot speak for
　　themselves,
　for the rights of all who are destitute.
⁹ Speak up and judge fairly;
　defend the rights of the poor and
　　needy.

Epilogue: The Wife of Noble Character

¹⁰ [b] A wife of noble character who can find?
　She is worth far more than rubies.
¹¹ Her husband has full confidence in her
　and lacks nothing of value.
¹² She brings him good, not harm,
　all the days of her life.
¹³ She selects wool and flax
　and works with eager hands.
¹⁴ She is like the merchant ships,
　bringing her food from afar.

¹⁵ She gets up while it is still night;
　she provides food for her family
　and portions for her female servants.
¹⁶ She considers a field and buys it;
　out of her earnings she plants a
　　vineyard.
¹⁷ She sets about her work vigorously;
　her arms are strong for her tasks.
¹⁸ She sees that her trading is profitable,
　and her lamp does not go out at night.
¹⁹ In her hand she holds the distaff
　and grasps the spindle with her
　　fingers.
²⁰ She opens her arms to the poor
　and extends her hands to the needy.
²¹ When it snows, she has no fear for her
　　household;
　for all of them are clothed in scarlet.
²² She makes coverings for her bed;
　she is clothed in fine linen and purple.
²³ Her husband is respected at the city gate,
　where he takes his seat among the
　　elders of the land.
²⁴ She makes linen garments and sells them,
　and supplies the merchants with
　　sashes.
²⁵ She is clothed with strength and dignity;
　she can laugh at the days to come.
²⁶ She speaks with wisdom,
　and faithful instruction is on her
　　tongue.
²⁷ She watches over the affairs of her
　　household
　and does not eat the bread of idleness.
²⁸ Her children arise and call her blessed;
　her husband also, and he praises her:
²⁹ "Many women do noble things,
　but you surpass them all."
³⁰ Charm is deceptive, and beauty is
　　fleeting;
　but a woman who fears the LORD is to
　　be praised.
³¹ Honor her for all that her hands have
　　done,
　and let her works bring her praise at
　　the city gate.

---

[a] 3 Or *wealth*　　[b] 10 Verses 10-31 are an acrostic poem, the verses of which begin with the successive
letters of the Hebrew alphabet.

ECCLESIASTES

➡️ **WHEN DID THIS HAPPEN?**

Written around 930 B.C. in the land of Israel

➡️ **WHO IS IN THIS BOOK?**

the Teacher

➡️ **VERSES YOU MIGHT RECOGNIZE**

ECCLESIASTES 4:9

"Two are better than one, because they have a good return for their labor."

ECCLESIASTES 7:20

"There is no one on earth who is righteous, no one who does what is right and never sins."

WHAT'S IT ABOUT?

What is the meaning of life? The writer of Ecclesiastes set out to answer this question. The writer, who called himself "the Teacher," also identified himself as "the son of David, King of Jerusalem" and one who had "increased in wisdom more than anyone who has ruled over Jerusalem before me." Sound familiar? Most scholars agree that King Solomon probably wrote this book.

The Teacher examined the many things people chase after—work, money, success, relationships—and came to discover that life is meaningless apart from God. Worldly pursuits, such as pleasure and lots of money, are not satisfying. Solomon knew this from experience. Even with unprecedented wisdom, unimaginable wealth and many beautiful wives, Solomon was not happy. As the wisest man who ever lived, he realized the only way to be truly satisfied in this life is to walk closely with God and enjoy the blessings he gives us.

ECCLESIASTES

Everything Is Meaningless

1 The words of the Teacher,[a] son of David, king in Jerusalem:

2 "Meaningless! Meaningless!"
   says the Teacher.
"Utterly meaningless!
   Everything is meaningless."

3 What do people gain from all their labors
   at which they toil under the sun?
4 Generations come and generations go,
   but the earth remains forever.
5 The sun rises and the sun sets,
   and hurries back to where it rises.
6 The wind blows to the south
   and turns to the north;
round and round it goes,
   ever returning on its course.
7 All streams flow into the sea,
   yet the sea is never full.
To the place the streams come from,
   there they return again.
8 All things are wearisome,
   more than one can say.
The eye never has enough of seeing,
   nor the ear its fill of hearing.
9 What has been will be again,
   what has been done will be done again;
   there is nothing new under the sun.
10 Is there anything of which one can say,
   "Look! This is something new"?
It was here already, long ago;
   it was here before our time.
11 No one remembers the former
      generations,
   and even those yet to come
will not be remembered
   by those who follow them.

Wisdom Is Meaningless

12 I, the Teacher, was king over Israel in Jerusalem. 13 I applied my mind to study and to explore by wisdom all that is done under the heavens. What a heavy burden God has laid on mankind! 14 I have seen all the things that are done under the sun; all of them are meaningless, a chasing after the wind.

15 What is crooked cannot be straightened;
   what is lacking cannot be counted.

16 I said to myself, "Look, I have increased in wisdom more than anyone who has ruled over Jerusalem before me; I have experienced much of wisdom and knowledge." 17 Then I applied myself to the understanding of wisdom, and also of madness and folly, but I learned that this, too, is a chasing after the wind.

18 For with much wisdom comes much
      sorrow;
   the more knowledge, the more grief.

Pleasures Are Meaningless

2 I said to myself, "Come now, I will test you with pleasure to find out what is good." But that also proved to be meaningless. 2 "Laughter," I said, "is madness. And what does pleasure accomplish?" 3 I tried cheering myself with wine, and embracing folly — my mind still guiding me with wisdom. I wanted to see what was good for people to do under the heavens during the few days of their lives.

4 I undertook great projects: I built houses for myself and planted vineyards. 5 I made gardens and parks and planted all kinds of fruit trees in them. 6 I made reservoirs to water groves of flourishing trees. 7 I bought male and female slaves and had other slaves who were born in my house. I also owned more herds and flocks than anyone in Jerusalem before me. 8 I amassed silver and gold for myself, and the treasure of kings and provinces. I acquired male and female singers, and a harem[b] as well — the delights of a man's heart. 9 I became greater by far than anyone in Jerusalem before me. In all this my wisdom stayed with me.

---

[a] 1 Or *the leader of the assembly*; also in verses 2 and 12 is uncertain.   [b] 8 The meaning of the Hebrew for this phrase

ULTIMATE SPREE

READ: ECCLESIASTES 1:14-2:3

Solomon, one of the greatest figures of the Old Testament, pursued entertainment relentlessly, looking for pleasure. Ecclesiastes is basically the journal he kept while he pursued pleasure. Solomon has incredible wealth and power, and he spares no expense in trying to entertain himself. He begins with laughter. He tunes into the comedy channel and hires the comedian of his day as a court jester. But he soon concludes that it's meaningless. There's no lasting joy in it.

He tries the life of partying, but sees the emptiness of it quickly. He entertains himself by taking on great projects. He builds houses, plants vineyards, and creates parks. He is a man of many interests, trying to find which, if any, will fill the void in his soul. He has all the luxuries that vast wealth can afford. He has servants, butlers, maids, chauffeurs, massage therapists, personal shoppers, and even ongoing live entertainment. Ecclesiastes 2:8 tells us that he brought in a choir of men and women—and of course, a harem.

BUILDING FAITH WISDOM STRENGTH

Most people have heard about the harem. The Bible says he had 700 wives and 300 concubines. There are women from every nation, food from every culture, books of wisdom from every civilization.

Solomon covers all the bases. He's going to find pleasure if it kills him!

And how does it end? With this exclamation: "Meaningless! Meaningless! Utterly meaningless!" (Ecclesiastes 1:2).

[10] I denied myself nothing my eyes desired;
   I refused my heart no pleasure.
My heart took delight in all my labor,
   and this was the reward for all my toil.
[11] Yet when I surveyed all that my hands
      had done
   and what I had toiled to achieve,
everything was meaningless, a chasing
      after the wind;
   nothing was gained under the sun.

Wisdom and Folly Are Meaningless

[12] Then I turned my thoughts to consider
      wisdom,
   and also madness and folly.
What more can the king's successor do
   than what has already been done?
[13] I saw that wisdom is better than folly,
   just as light is better than darkness.
[14] The wise have eyes in their heads,
   while the fool walks in the darkness;
but I came to realize
   that the same fate overtakes them
      both.

[15] Then I said to myself,

"The fate of the fool will overtake me
      also.
   What then do I gain by being wise?"
I said to myself,
   "This too is meaningless."
[16] For the wise, like the fool, will not be long
      remembered;
   the days have already come when both
      have been forgotten.
Like the fool, the wise too must die!

Toil Is Meaningless

[17] So I hated life, because the work that is done under the sun was grievous to me. All of it is meaningless, a chasing after the wind. [18] I hated all the things I had toiled for under the sun, because I must leave them to the one who comes after me. [19] And who knows whether that person will be wise or foolish? Yet they will have control over all the fruit of my toil into which I have poured my effort and skill under the sun. This too is meaningless. [20] So my heart began to despair over all my toilsome labor under the sun. [21] For a person may labor with wisdom, knowledge and skill, and then they must leave all they

own to another who has not toiled for it. This too is meaningless and a great misfortune. [22] What do people get for all the toil and anxious striving with which they labor under the sun? [23] All their days their work is grief and pain; even at night their minds do not rest. This too is meaningless.

[24] A person can do nothing better than to eat and drink and find satisfaction in their own toil. This too, I see, is from the hand of God, [25] for without him, who can eat or find enjoyment? [26] To the person who pleases him, God gives wisdom, knowledge and happiness, but to the sinner he gives the task of gathering and storing up wealth to hand it over to the one who pleases God. This too is meaningless, a chasing after the wind.

A Time for Everything

3 There is a time for everything,
   and a season for every activity under
      the heavens:

[2]   a time to be born and a time to die,
   a time to plant and a time to uproot,
[3]   a time to kill and a time to heal,
   a time to tear down and a time to
      build,
[4]   a time to weep and a time to laugh,
   a time to mourn and a time to dance,
[5]   a time to scatter stones and a time to
      gather them,
   a time to embrace and a time to refrain
      from embracing,
[6]   a time to search and a time to give up,
   a time to keep and a time to throw
      away,
[7]   a time to tear and a time to mend,
   a time to be silent and a time to speak,
[8]   a time to love and a time to hate,
   a time for war and a time for peace.

[9] What do workers gain from their toil? [10] I have seen the burden God has laid on the human race. [11] He has made everything beautiful in its time. He has also set eternity in the human heart; yet[a] no one can fathom what God has done from beginning to end. [12] I know that there is nothing better for people than to be happy and to do good while they live. [13] That each of them may eat and drink, and find satisfaction in all their toil — this is the gift of God. [14] I know that everything God does will endure forever; nothing

---

[a] 11 Or *also placed ignorance in the human heart, so that*

MORE CHAPTERS TO COME

READ: ECCLESIASTES 3:11

While on an airplane, I looked around at fellow passengers, and I saw content people. Thanks to books, pillows, and crossword puzzles, they passed the time quite nicely. But suppose this announcement were heard: "Ladies and Gentlemen, this flight is your final destination. We will never land. Your home is this plane, so enjoy the journey."

Passengers would become mutineers. We'd take over the cockpit and seek out a landing strip. We wouldn't settle for such an idea. The journey is not the destination. The vessel is not the goal. Those who are content with nothing more than joy in the journey are settling for too little satisfaction. Our hearts tell us there is more to this life than this life.

In God's story, life on earth is but the beginning: the first letter of the first sentence in the first chapter of the great story God is writing with your life. You will do your best work in heaven.

BUILDING FAITH WISDOM STRENGTH

Do you regret something you've done that you can't seem to escape? So do I. We have an eternity to make up for lost time. God is polishing you for your place in his kingdom. Your biggest moments lie ahead, on the other side of the grave.

Thank God that this life is not your real life, that you have a home beyond this world where every broken thing will be perfect.

can be added to it and nothing taken from it. God does it so that people will fear him.

¹⁵ Whatever is has already been,
and what will be has been before;
and God will call the past to account.^a

¹⁶ And I saw something else under the sun:

In the place of judgment — wickedness
was there,
in the place of justice — wickedness
was there.

¹⁷ I said to myself,

"God will bring into judgment
both the righteous and the wicked,
for there will be a time for every activity,
a time to judge every deed."

¹⁸ I also said to myself, "As for humans, God tests them so that they may see that they are like the animals. ¹⁹ Surely the fate of human beings is like that of the animals; the same fate awaits them both: As one dies, so dies the other. All have the same breath^b; humans have no advantage over animals. Everything is meaningless. ²⁰ All go to the same place; all come from dust, and to dust all return. ²¹ Who knows if the human spirit rises upward and if the spirit of the animal goes down into the earth?"

²² So I saw that there is nothing better for a person than to enjoy their work, because that is their lot. For who can bring them to see what will happen after them?

Oppression, Toil, Friendlessness

4 Again I looked and saw all the oppression that was taking place under the sun:

I saw the tears of the oppressed —
and they have no comforter;
power was on the side of their
oppressors —
and they have no comforter.
² And I declared that the dead,
who had already died,
are happier than the living,
who are still alive.
³ But better than both
is the one who has never been born,
who has not seen the evil
that is done under the sun.

⁴ And I saw that all toil and all achievement spring from one person's envy of another. This too is meaningless, a chasing after the wind.

⁵ Fools fold their hands
and ruin themselves.
⁶ Better one handful with tranquillity
than two handfuls with toil
and chasing after the wind.

⁷ Again I saw something meaningless under the sun:

⁸ There was a man all alone;
he had neither son nor brother.
There was no end to his toil,
yet his eyes were not content with
his wealth.
"For whom am I toiling," he asked,
"and why am I depriving myself of
enjoyment?"
This too is meaningless —
a miserable business!

⁹ Two are better than one,
because they have a good return for
their labor:
¹⁰ If either of them falls down,
one can help the other up.
But pity anyone who falls
and has no one to help them up.
¹¹ Also, if two lie down together, they will
keep warm.
But how can one keep warm
alone?
¹² Though one may be overpowered,
two can defend themselves.
A cord of three strands is not quickly
broken.

Advancement Is Meaningless

¹³ Better a poor but wise youth than an old but foolish king who no longer knows how to heed a warning. ¹⁴ The youth may have come from prison to the kingship, or he may have been born in poverty within his kingdom. ¹⁵ I saw that all who lived and walked under the sun followed the youth, the king's successor. ¹⁶ There was no end to all the people who were before them. But those who came later were not pleased with the successor. This too is meaningless, a chasing after the wind.

^a 15 Or *God calls back the past*   ^b 19 Or *spirit*

Fulfill Your Vow to God

5 [a] Guard your steps when you go to the house of God. Go near to listen rather than to offer the sacrifice of fools, who do not know that they do wrong.

2 Do not be quick with your mouth,
    do not be hasty in your heart
    to utter anything before God.
  God is in heaven
    and you are on earth,
    so let your words be few.
3 A dream comes when there are many
    cares,
    and many words mark the speech of
    a fool.

4 When you make a vow to God, do not delay to fulfill it. He has no pleasure in fools; fulfill your vow. 5 It is better not to make a vow than to make one and not fulfill it. 6 Do not let your mouth lead you into sin. And do not protest to the temple messenger, "My vow was a mistake." Why should God be angry at what you say and destroy the work of your hands? 7 Much dreaming and many words are meaningless. Therefore fear God.

Riches Are Meaningless

8 If you see the poor oppressed in a district, and justice and rights denied, do not be surprised at such things; for one official is eyed by a higher one, and over them both are others higher still. 9 The increase from the land is taken by all; the king himself profits from the fields.

10 Whoever loves money never has enough;
    whoever loves wealth is never satisfied
    with their income.
  This too is meaningless.

11 As goods increase,
    so do those who consume them.
  And what benefit are they to the owners
    except to feast their eyes on them?

12 The sleep of a laborer is sweet,
    whether they eat little or much,
  but as for the rich, their abundance
    permits them no sleep.

13 I have seen a grievous evil under the sun:

  wealth hoarded to the harm of its
    owners,

14   or wealth lost through some
        misfortune,
  so that when they have children
    there is nothing left for them to inherit.
15 Everyone comes naked from their
        mother's womb,
    and as everyone comes, so they depart.
  They take nothing from their toil
    that they can carry in their hands.

16 This too is a grievous evil:

  As everyone comes, so they depart,
    and what do they gain,
    since they toil for the wind?
17 All their days they eat in darkness,
    with great frustration, affliction and
        anger.

18 This is what I have observed to be good: that it is appropriate for a person to eat, to drink and to find satisfaction in their toilsome labor under the sun during the few days of life God has given them—for this is their lot. 19 Moreover, when God gives someone wealth and possessions, and the ability to enjoy them, to accept their lot and be happy in their toil—this is a gift of God. 20 They seldom reflect on the days of their life, because God keeps them occupied with gladness of heart.

6 I have seen another evil under the sun, and it weighs heavily on mankind: 2 God gives some people wealth, possessions and honor, so that they lack nothing their hearts desire, but God does not grant them the ability to enjoy them, and strangers enjoy them instead. This is meaningless, a grievous evil.

3 A man may have a hundred children and live many years; yet no matter how long he lives, if he cannot enjoy his prosperity and does not receive proper burial, I say that a stillborn child is better off than he. 4 It comes without meaning, it departs in darkness, and in darkness its name is shrouded. 5 Though it never saw the sun or knew anything, it has more rest than does that man— 6 even if he lives a thousand years twice over but fails to enjoy his prosperity. Do not all go to the same place?

7 Everyone's toil is for their mouth,
    yet their appetite is never satisfied.

---

[a] In Hebrew texts 5:1 is numbered 4:17, and 5:2-20 is numbered 5:1-19.

IT'S NOT ABOUT FUN

READ: ECCLESIASTES 5:10-12, 18-19

Have you ever thought about the place of pleasure in modern life? I'm talking about the plain old pursuit of fun in all its forms. There have always been games, stories, jokes, and songs, but today pleasure is something close to the theme of daily living. We even expect school and our daily responsibilities to be pleasurable. That's not how our ancestors looked at things. In a society based on agriculture, nobody said, "Know what? Plowing and tending cattle aren't enough fun for me." But these days if it isn't fun, we don't want to do it.

In a postindustrial society, our survival needs are met. We sold the farm, after all, and we've gathered in cities where we have food, shelter, plenty of water, and a surplus of time.

I know what you're thinking: *No one has a surplus of time. I'm busier than ever.* Fair enough, but what are we busy doing? Quite often, the answer is chasing pleasure.

BUILDING FAITH WISDOM STRENGTH

Just to be clear, I want to say that food, sex, and entertainment are not sinful or evil in and of themselves. In fact these things all have the potential to be good gifts from God that draw our hearts to him all the more. But inside the temple of pleasure, when forced to choose between the Lord God and the god of pleasure, we say nothing. Why? Because we want both.

God cannot and will not give us a sense of lasting pleasure apart from him, because it violates his purpose and our design.

Taken from *Gods at War Student Edition* by Kyle Idleman, copyright © 2014 by City on a Hill Studio, LLC, published by Zondervan.

⁸ What advantage have the wise over fools?
What do the poor gain
　　by knowing how to conduct themselves
　　　before others?
⁹ Better what the eye sees
　　than the roving of the appetite.
This too is meaningless,
　　a chasing after the wind.

¹⁰ Whatever exists has already been named,
　　and what humanity is has been
　　　known;
no one can contend
　　with someone who is stronger.
¹¹ The more the words,
　　the less the meaning,
　　and how does that profit anyone?

¹² For who knows what is good for a person
in life, during the few and meaningless days
they pass through like a shadow? Who can
tell them what will happen under the sun after they are gone?

Wisdom

7 A good name is better than fine
　　perfume,
　　and the day of death better than the
　　　day of birth.
² It is better to go to a house of mourning
　　than to go to a house of feasting,
for death is the destiny of everyone;
　　the living should take this to heart.
³ Frustration is better than laughter,
　　because a sad face is good for the
　　　heart.
⁴ The heart of the wise is in the house of
　　mourning,
　　but the heart of fools is in the house of
　　　pleasure.
⁵ It is better to heed the rebuke of a wise
　　person
　　than to listen to the song of fools.
⁶ Like the crackling of thorns under the
　　pot,
　　so is the laughter of fools.
　　This too is meaningless.

⁷ Extortion turns a wise person into a fool,
　　and a bribe corrupts the heart.

⁸ The end of a matter is better than its
　　beginning,
　　and patience is better than pride.

⁹ Do not be quickly provoked in your spirit,
　　for anger resides in the lap of fools.

¹⁰ Do not say, "Why were the old days better
　　than these?"
　　For it is not wise to ask such questions.

¹¹ Wisdom, like an inheritance, is a good
　　thing
　　and benefits those who see the sun.
¹² Wisdom is a shelter
　　as money is a shelter,
but the advantage of knowledge is this:
　　Wisdom preserves those who have it.

¹³ Consider what God has done:

Who can straighten
　　what he has made crooked?
¹⁴ When times are good, be happy;
　　but when times are bad, consider this:
God has made the one
　　as well as the other.
Therefore, no one can discover
　　anything about their future.

¹⁵ In this meaningless life of mine I have
seen both of these:

the righteous perishing in their
　　righteousness,
　　and the wicked living long in their
　　　wickedness.
¹⁶ Do not be overrighteous,
　　neither be overwise—
　　why destroy yourself?
¹⁷ Do not be overwicked,
　　and do not be a fool—
　　why die before your time?
¹⁸ It is good to grasp the one
　　and not let go of the other.
　　Whoever fears God will avoid all
　　　extremes.ᵃ

¹⁹ Wisdom makes one wise person more
　　powerful
　　than ten rulers in a city.

²⁰ Indeed, there is no one on earth who is
　　righteous,
　　no one who does what is right and
　　　never sins.

²¹ Do not pay attention to every word
　　people say,
　　or you may hear your servant cursing
　　　you—

ᵃ 18 Or *will follow them both*

²²for you know in your heart
    that many times you yourself have
        cursed others.

²³All this I tested by wisdom and I said,

"I am determined to be wise" —
    but this was beyond me.
²⁴Whatever exists is far off and most
        profound —
    who can discover it?
²⁵So I turned my mind to understand,
    to investigate and to search out
        wisdom and the scheme of things
and to understand the stupidity of
    wickedness
    and the madness of folly.

²⁶I find more bitter than death
    the woman who is a snare,
whose heart is a trap
    and whose hands are chains.
The man who pleases God will escape
    her,
    but the sinner she will ensnare.

²⁷"Look," says the Teacher,[a] "this is what I
have discovered:

"Adding one thing to another to discover
        the scheme of things —
²⁸   while I was still searching
        but not finding —
    I found one upright man among a
        thousand,
        but not one upright woman among
            them all.
²⁹This only have I found:
    God created mankind upright,
    but they have gone in search of many
        schemes."

8 Who is like the wise?
    Who knows the explanation of things?
A person's wisdom brightens their face
    and changes its hard appearance.

Obey the King

²Obey the king's command, I say, because
you took an oath before God. ³Do not be in
a hurry to leave the king's presence. Do not
stand up for a bad cause, for he will do whatever he pleases. ⁴Since a king's word is supreme,
who can say to him, "What are you doing?"

⁵Whoever obeys his command will come
        to no harm,
    and the wise heart will know the
        proper time and procedure.
⁶For there is a proper time and procedure
        for every matter,
    though a person may be weighed down
        by misery.

⁷Since no one knows the future,
    who can tell someone else what is to
        come?
⁸As no one has power over the wind to
        contain it,
    so[b] no one has power over the time of
        their death.
As no one is discharged in time of war,
    so wickedness will not release those
        who practice it.

⁹All this I saw, as I applied my mind to
everything done under the sun. There is a
time when a man lords it over others to his
own[c] hurt. ¹⁰Then too, I saw the wicked buried — those who used to come and go from
the holy place and receive praise[d] in the city
where they did this. This too is meaningless.
¹¹When the sentence for a crime is not
quickly carried out, people's hearts are
filled with schemes to do wrong. ¹²Although
a wicked person who commits a hundred
crimes may live a long time, I know that it
will go better with those who fear God, who
are reverent before him. ¹³Yet because the
wicked do not fear God, it will not go well
with them, and their days will not lengthen
like a shadow.

¹⁴There is something else meaningless
that occurs on earth: the righteous who get
what the wicked deserve, and the wicked
who get what the righteous deserve. This
too, I say, is meaningless. ¹⁵So I commend
the enjoyment of life, because there is nothing better for a person under the sun than to
eat and drink and be glad. Then joy will accompany them in their toil all the days of the
life God has given them under the sun.

¹⁶When I applied my mind to know wisdom and to observe the labor that is done
on earth — people getting no sleep day or
night — ¹⁷then I saw all that God has done.
No one can comprehend what goes on under

---

[a] 27 Or *the leader of the assembly*   [b] 8 Or *over the human spirit to retain it, / and so*   [c] 9 Or *to their*
[d] 10 Some Hebrew manuscripts and Septuagint (Aquila); most Hebrew manuscripts *and are forgotten*

the sun. Despite all their efforts to search it out, no one can discover its meaning. Even if the wise claim they know, they cannot really comprehend it.

A Common Destiny for All

9 So I reflected on all this and concluded that the righteous and the wise and what they do are in God's hands, but no one knows whether love or hate awaits them. ²All share a common destiny—the righteous and the wicked, the good and the bad,ᵃ the clean and the unclean, those who offer sacrifices and those who do not.

As it is with the good,
　so with the sinful;
as it is with those who take oaths,
　so with those who are afraid to take them.

³This is the evil in everything that happens under the sun: The same destiny overtakes all. The hearts of people, moreover, are full of evil and there is madness in their hearts while they live, and afterward they join the dead. ⁴Anyone who is among the living has hopeᵇ—even a live dog is better off than a dead lion!

⁵For the living know that they will die,
　but the dead know nothing;
they have no further reward,
　and even their name is forgotten.
⁶Their love, their hate
　and their jealousy have long since vanished;
never again will they have a part
　in anything that happens under the sun.

⁷Go, eat your food with gladness, and drink your wine with a joyful heart, for God has already approved what you do. ⁸Always be clothed in white, and always anoint your head with oil. ⁹Enjoy life with your wife, whom you love, all the days of this meaningless life that God has given you under the sun—all your meaningless days. For this is your lot in life and in your toilsome labor under the sun. ¹⁰Whatever your hand finds to do, do it with all your might, for in the realm of the dead, where you are going, there is nei-

ther working nor planning nor knowledge nor wisdom.

¹¹I have seen something else under the sun:

The race is not to the swift
　or the battle to the strong,
nor does food come to the wise
　or wealth to the brilliant
　or favor to the learned;
but time and chance happen to them all.

¹²Moreover, no one knows when their hour will come:

As fish are caught in a cruel net,
　or birds are taken in a snare,
so people are trapped by evil times
　that fall unexpectedly upon them.

Wisdom Better Than Folly

¹³I also saw under the sun this example of wisdom that greatly impressed me: ¹⁴There was once a small city with only a few people in it. And a powerful king came against it, surrounded it and built huge siege works against it. ¹⁵Now there lived in that city a man poor but wise, and he saved the city by his wisdom. But nobody remembered that poor man. ¹⁶So I said, "Wisdom is better than strength." But the poor man's wisdom is despised, and his words are no longer heeded.

¹⁷The quiet words of the wise are more to be heeded
　than the shouts of a ruler of fools.
¹⁸Wisdom is better than weapons of war,
　but one sinner destroys much good.

10 As dead flies give perfume a bad smell,
　so a little folly outweighs wisdom and honor.
²The heart of the wise inclines to the right,
　but the heart of the fool to the left.
³Even as fools walk along the road,
　they lack sense
　and show everyone how stupid they are.
⁴If a ruler's anger rises against you,
　do not leave your post;
　calmness can lay great offenses to rest.

⁵There is an evil I have seen under the sun,
　the sort of error that arises from a ruler:

ᵃ 2 Septuagint (Aquila), Vulgate and Syriac; Hebrew does not have *and the bad.*　　ᵇ 4 Or *What then is to be chosen? With all who live, there is hope*

⁶Fools are put in many high positions,
while the rich occupy the low ones.
⁷I have seen slaves on horseback,
while princes go on foot like slaves.

⁸Whoever digs a pit may fall into it;
whoever breaks through a wall may be
bitten by a snake.
⁹Whoever quarries stones may be injured
by them;
whoever splits logs may be endangered
by them.

¹⁰If the ax is dull
and its edge unsharpened,
more strength is needed,
but skill will bring success.

¹¹If a snake bites before it is charmed,
the charmer receives no fee.

¹²Words from the mouth of the wise are
gracious,
but fools are consumed by their
own lips.
¹³At the beginning their words are folly;
at the end they are wicked madness—
¹⁴   and fools multiply words.

No one knows what is coming—
who can tell someone else what will
happen after them?

¹⁵The toil of fools wearies them;
they do not know the way to town.

¹⁶Woe to the land whose king was a
servant*a*
and whose princes feast in the
morning.
¹⁷Blessed is the land whose king is of noble
birth
and whose princes eat at a proper
time—
for strength and not for drunkenness.

¹⁸Through laziness, the rafters sag;
because of idle hands, the house leaks.

¹⁹A feast is made for laughter,
wine makes life merry,
and money is the answer for
everything.

²⁰Do not revile the king even in your
thoughts,
or curse the rich in your bedroom,

because a bird in the sky may carry your
words,
and a bird on the wing may report
what you say.

Invest in Many Ventures

11 Ship your grain across the sea;
after many days you may receive a
return.
²Invest in seven ventures, yes, in eight;
you do not know what disaster may
come upon the land.

³If clouds are full of water,
they pour rain on the earth.
Whether a tree falls to the south or to the
north,
in the place where it falls, there it
will lie.
⁴Whoever watches the wind will not plant;
whoever looks at the clouds will not
reap.

⁵As you do not know the path of the wind,
or how the body is formed*b* in a
mother's womb,
so you cannot understand the work
of God,
the Maker of all things.

⁶Sow your seed in the morning,
and at evening let your hands not
be idle,
for you do not know which will succeed,
whether this or that,
or whether both will do equally well.

Remember Your Creator While Young

⁷Light is sweet,
and it pleases the eyes to see the sun.
⁸However many years anyone may live,
let them enjoy them all.
But let them remember the days of
darkness,
for there will be many.
Everything to come is meaningless.

⁹You who are young, be happy while you
are young,
and let your heart give you joy in the
days of your youth.
Follow the ways of your heart
and whatever your eyes see,
but know that for all these things
God will bring you into judgment.

a 16 Or *king is a child*   *b* 5 Or *know how life* (or *the spirit*) / *enters the body being formed*

THINKING ABOUT GOD

READ: ECCLESIASTES 12:1

The Teacher tried everything and said it was all meaningless. "I have seen all the things that are done under the sun," he says. "All of them are meaningless, a chasing after the wind" (Ecclesiastes 1:14).

But not everything in life feels utterly absurd.

The Teacher finds pleasure in simple things. He says, "A person can do nothing better than to eat and drink and find satisfaction in their own toil. This too, I see, is from the hand of God, for without him, who can eat or find enjoyment?" (2:24–25). The Teacher also recognizes God blesses his followers. He declares, "To the person who pleases him, God gives wisdom, knowledge and happiness" (v. 2:26). And the Teacher realizes love brings meaning to life. He says, "Enjoy life with your wife, whom you love" (9:9).

BUILDING
FAITH
WISDOM
STRENGTH

The last pages of this book reveal the Teacher's ultimate answers to his quest for meaning. He instructs you first of all to remember God when you're still young. That's not telling you just to think about the Lord once in a while but to act every day on what you already know. And then the Teacher announces your core duty. You're to give God the respect he deserves and keep all his commands, because he's the one thing you can count on to give your life meaning (12:13).

[10] So then, banish anxiety from your heart
and cast off the troubles of your body,
for youth and vigor are meaningless.

12 Remember your Creator
in the days of your youth,
before the days of trouble come
and the years approach when you
will say,
"I find no pleasure in them" —
[2] before the sun and the light
and the moon and the stars grow dark,
and the clouds return after the rain;
[3] when the keepers of the house tremble,
and the strong men stoop,
when the grinders cease because they
are few,
and those looking through the
windows grow dim;
[4] when the doors to the street are closed
and the sound of grinding fades;
when people rise up at the sound of birds,
but all their songs grow faint;
[5] when people are afraid of heights
and of dangers in the streets;
when the almond tree blossoms
and the grasshopper drags itself along
and desire no longer is stirred.
Then people go to their eternal home
and mourners go about the streets.

[6] Remember him — before the silver cord is
severed,
and the golden bowl is broken;

before the pitcher is shattered at the
spring,
and the wheel broken at the well,
[7] and the dust returns to the ground it
came from,
and the spirit returns to God who
gave it.

[8] "Meaningless! Meaningless!" says the
Teacher.[a]
"Everything is meaningless!"

The Conclusion of the Matter

[9] Not only was the Teacher wise, but he also imparted knowledge to the people. He pondered and searched out and set in order many proverbs. [10] The Teacher searched to find just the right words, and what he wrote was upright and true.

[11] The words of the wise are like goads, their collected sayings like firmly embedded nails — given by one shepherd.[b] [12] Be warned, my son, of anything in addition to them.

Of making many books there is no end, and much study wearies the body.

[13] Now all has been heard;
here is the conclusion of the matter:
Fear God and keep his commandments,
for this is the duty of all mankind.
[14] For God will bring every deed into
judgment,
including every hidden thing,
whether it is good or evil.

---

[a] 8 Or *the leader of the assembly*; also in verses 9 and 10   [b] 11 Or *Shepherd*

SONG OF SONGS

➡️ **WHEN DID THIS HAPPEN?**

Around 965 B.C.

➡️ **WHO IS IN THIS BOOK?**

friends

she

he

➡️ **VERSES YOU MIGHT RECOGNIZE**

SONG OF SONGS 2:1

"I am a rose of Sharon, a lily of the valleys."

SONG OF SONGS 3:5B

"Do not arouse or awaken love until it so desires."

WHAT'S IT ABOUT?

This book, written as a poetic song, looks at God's wonderful design for love and sex. Much like a fairy tale, the man and woman in the song—a peasant girl and a king—meet, fall in love and get married. While their relationship isn't perfect, they delight in each other and love one another passionately. More than just a love story about a bride and groom, Song of Songs is also a picture of how God loves his people—faithfully, passionately, joyfully.

While it may feel strange to be reading about sex in the Bible, this book provides a picture of God's wonderful plan for intimacy. Waiting until you're married to have sex isn't a popular idea in the world, but like all of God's ideas, it brings the greatest satisfaction and joy. Song of Songs shows how going about love in the right way allows true romance to blossom in God's timing.

SONG OF SONGS

1 Solomon's Song of Songs.

She[a]

2 Let him kiss me with the kisses of his
     mouth—
   for your love is more delightful than
     wine.
3 Pleasing is the fragrance of your
     perfumes;
   your name is like perfume poured out.
   No wonder the young women love you!
4 Take me away with you—let us hurry!
   Let the king bring me into his
     chambers.

Friends

   We rejoice and delight in you[b];
   we will praise your love more than
     wine.

She

   How right they are to adore you!

5 Dark am I, yet lovely,
     daughters of Jerusalem,
   dark like the tents of Kedar,
     like the tent curtains of Solomon.[c]
6 Do not stare at me because I am dark,
     because I am darkened by the sun.
   My mother's sons were angry with me
     and made me take care of the
       vineyards;
   my own vineyard I had to neglect.
7 Tell me, you whom I love,
     where you graze your flock
   and where you rest your sheep at
       midday.
   Why should I be like a veiled woman
     beside the flocks of your friends?

Friends

8 If you do not know, most beautiful of
     women,
   follow the tracks of the sheep

and graze your young goats
   by the tents of the shepherds.

He

9 I liken you, my darling, to a mare
     among Pharaoh's chariot horses.
10 Your cheeks are beautiful with
       earrings,
   your neck with strings of jewels.
11 We will make you earrings of gold,
     studded with silver.

She

12 While the king was at his table,
     my perfume spread its fragrance.
13 My beloved is to me a sachet of myrrh
     resting between my breasts.
14 My beloved is to me a cluster of henna
       blossoms
   from the vineyards of En Gedi.

He

15 How beautiful you are, my darling!
     Oh, how beautiful!
   Your eyes are doves.

She

16 How handsome you are, my beloved!
     Oh, how charming!
   And our bed is verdant.

He

17 The beams of our house are cedars;
     our rafters are firs.

She[d]

2 I am a rose[e] of Sharon,
   a lily of the valleys.

He

2 Like a lily among thorns
     is my darling among the young
       women.

---

[a] The main male and female speakers (identified primarily on the basis of the gender of the relevant Hebrew forms) are indicated by the captions *He* and *She* respectively. The words of others are marked *Friends*. In some instances the divisions and their captions are debatable.   [b] 4 The Hebrew is masculine singular.   [c] 5 Or *Salma*   [d] Or *He*   [e] 1 Probably a member of the crocus family

She

3 Like an apple*a* tree among the trees of
    the forest
  is my beloved among the young men.
  I delight to sit in his shade,
    and his fruit is sweet to my taste.
4 Let him lead me to the banquet hall,
    and let his banner over me be love.
5 Strengthen me with raisins,
    refresh me with apples,
    for I am faint with love.
6 His left arm is under my head,
    and his right arm embraces me.
7 Daughters of Jerusalem, I charge you
    by the gazelles and by the does of
      the field:
  Do not arouse or awaken love
    until it so desires.

8 Listen! My beloved!
    Look! Here he comes,
  leaping across the mountains,
  bounding over the hills.
9 My beloved is like a gazelle or a young
    stag.
  Look! There he stands behind our wall,
  gazing through the windows,
  peering through the lattice.
10 My beloved spoke and said to me,
    "Arise, my darling,
    my beautiful one, come with me.
11 See! The winter is past;
    the rains are over and gone.
12 Flowers appear on the earth;
    the season of singing has come,
  the cooing of doves
  is heard in our land.
13 The fig tree forms its early fruit;
    the blossoming vines spread their
      fragrance.
  Arise, come, my darling;
    my beautiful one, come with me."

He

14 My dove in the clefts of the rock,
    in the hiding places on the
      mountainside,
  show me your face,
    let me hear your voice;
  for your voice is sweet,
    and your face is lovely.
15 Catch for us the foxes,
    the little foxes

that ruin the vineyards,
    our vineyards that are in bloom.

She

16 My beloved is mine and I am his;
    he browses among the lilies.
17 Until the day breaks
    and the shadows flee,
  turn, my beloved,
    and be like a gazelle
  or like a young stag
    on the rugged hills.*b*

3 All night long on my bed
    I looked for the one my heart loves;
    I looked for him but did not find him.
2 I will get up now and go about the city,
    through its streets and squares;
  I will search for the one my heart loves.
    So I looked for him but did not find him.
3 The watchmen found me
    as they made their rounds in the city.
    "Have you seen the one my heart
      loves?"
4 Scarcely had I passed them
    when I found the one my heart loves.
  I held him and would not let him go
    till I had brought him to my mother's
      house,
    to the room of the one who
      conceived me.
5 Daughters of Jerusalem, I charge you
    by the gazelles and by the does of
      the field:
  Do not arouse or awaken love
    until it so desires.

6 Who is this coming up from the
      wilderness
    like a column of smoke,
  perfumed with myrrh and incense
    made from all the spices of the
      merchant?
7 Look! It is Solomon's carriage,
    escorted by sixty warriors,
    the noblest of Israel,
8 all of them wearing the sword,
    all experienced in battle,
  each with his sword at his side,
    prepared for the terrors of the night.
9 King Solomon made for himself the
      carriage;
  he made it of wood from Lebanon.

---

a 3 Or possibly *apricot*; here and elsewhere in Song of Songs   *b 17* Or *the hills of Bether*

OH, ROMEO

READ: SONG OF SONGS 3:1-5

Our culture holds up romantic love as the noblest of pursuits. We are led to believe that the need for romantic affection is built into every single one of us, so that we instinctively yearn for that tingly, bubbly feeling that we call "falling in love."

The message to those who aren't dating someone is that you won't be content or complete unless you're in a relationship. It starts early.

For many, romantic love becomes the focus of their lives. Pop music tells us that love makes the world go round and that all you need is love. Pick your cliché, but what seems clear is that romantic love is the be-all and end-all. Nearly all of our music is about this kind of love, and it's been that way for a long time.

But romantic love as the great quest, an obsession, something we must have or be miserable, is a more recent cultural invention. God has wired most of us for intimate fellowship, for a special mate, someone to complement us. But in modern times we've inflated that idea to crazy proportions. We look to romantic love as the secret to our satisfaction and the missing piece to make life feel complete.

When we put our hope in romantic love and sacrifice for it, we have to ask if this beautiful gift from God has actually replaced him. When that happens, the ending is rarely "happily ever after."

BUILDING FAITH WISDOM STRENGTH

¹⁰ Its posts he made of silver,
  its base of gold.
 Its seat was upholstered with purple,
  its interior inlaid with love.
 Daughters of Jerusalem, ¹¹ come out,
  and look, you daughters of Zion.
 Look[a] on King Solomon wearing a crown,
  the crown with which his mother
   crowned him
 on the day of his wedding,
  the day his heart rejoiced.

He

4 How beautiful you are, my darling!
  Oh, how beautiful!
  Your eyes behind your veil are doves.
 Your hair is like a flock of goats
  descending from the hills of Gilead.
² Your teeth are like a flock of sheep just
   shorn,
  coming up from the washing.
 Each has its twin;
  not one of them is alone.
³ Your lips are like a scarlet ribbon;
  your mouth is lovely.
 Your temples behind your veil
  are like the halves of a pomegranate.
⁴ Your neck is like the tower of David,
  built with courses of stone[b];
 on it hang a thousand shields,
  all of them shields of warriors.
⁵ Your breasts are like two fawns,
  like twin fawns of a gazelle
  that browse among the lilies.
⁶ Until the day breaks
  and the shadows flee,
 I will go to the mountain of myrrh
  and to the hill of incense.
⁷ You are altogether beautiful, my darling;
  there is no flaw in you.

⁸ Come with me from Lebanon, my bride,
  come with me from Lebanon.
 Descend from the crest of Amana,
  from the top of Senir, the summit of
   Hermon,
 from the lions' dens
  and the mountain haunts of leopards.
⁹ You have stolen my heart, my sister, my
   bride;
  you have stolen my heart
 with one glance of your eyes,
  with one jewel of your necklace.

¹⁰ How delightful is your love, my sister, my
   bride!
 How much more pleasing is your love
   than wine,
  and the fragrance of your perfume
   more than any spice!
¹¹ Your lips drop sweetness as the
   honeycomb, my bride;
  milk and honey are under your tongue.
 The fragrance of your garments
  is like the fragrance of Lebanon.
¹² You are a garden locked up, my sister,
   my bride;
  you are a spring enclosed, a sealed
   fountain.
¹³ Your plants are an orchard of
   pomegranates
  with choice fruits,
  with henna and nard,
¹⁴ nard and saffron,
  calamus and cinnamon,
  with every kind of incense tree,
  with myrrh and aloes
  and all the finest spices.
¹⁵ You are[c] a garden fountain,
  a well of flowing water
  streaming down from Lebanon.

She

¹⁶ Awake, north wind,
  and come, south wind!
 Blow on my garden,
  that its fragrance may spread
   everywhere.
 Let my beloved come into his garden
  and taste its choice fruits.

He

5 I have come into my garden, my sister,
  my bride;
 I have gathered my myrrh with my
   spice.
 I have eaten my honeycomb and my
   honey;
 I have drunk my wine and my milk.

Friends

 Eat, friends, and drink;
  drink your fill of love.

She

² I slept but my heart was awake.
 Listen! My beloved is knocking:

---

[a] *10,11* Or *interior lovingly inlaid / by the daughters of Jerusalem. / ¹¹Come out, you daughters of Zion, / and
look*   [b] *4* The meaning of the Hebrew for this phrase is uncertain.   [c] *15* Or *I am* (spoken by *She*)

LOVE SONGS

READ: SONG OF SONGS 4:1-2

S ome day you might want to take a stab at writing love poetry, but it's not likely to come out sounding like the Song of Songs. This tale of love celebrates human affection with imagery and honesty that might catch you by surprise.

Some readers see this book as a picture of God's love for his people. They say it honors the love between God and his Old Testament people, the Israelites, or the love shared by Jesus and his New Testament people, the church. But the most obvious way to interpret these words is simple and straightforward. They picture a man and woman who are crazy about each other.

This book doesn't hide the passion that flows between the author and a young country girl. You quickly learn that the Bible isn't bashful about physical love. After all, God created man and woman to bond in heart, mind, and body. Adam saw Eve and thought she was perfect, and the Lord planned right from the start that husband and wife would become "one flesh" (Genesis 2:24). That first couple felt no shame in being naked (v. 25).

The Song of Songs makes an unmistakable push for purity, waiting for sexual intimacy until marriage. Solomon's bride kept herself pure as she grew up (Song of Songs 8:8-10). And the book challenges you to "not arouse or awaken love" until God's right time (2:7).

BUILDING
FAITH
WISDOM
STRENGTH

"Open to me, my sister, my darling,
my dove, my flawless one.
My head is drenched with dew,
my hair with the dampness of the
night."
³ I have taken off my robe —
must I put it on again?
I have washed my feet —
must I soil them again?
⁴ My beloved thrust his hand through the
latch-opening;
my heart began to pound for him.
⁵ I arose to open for my beloved,
and my hands dripped with myrrh,
my fingers with flowing myrrh,
on the handles of the bolt.
⁶ I opened for my beloved,
but my beloved had left; he was gone.
My heart sank at his departure.ᵃ
I looked for him but did not find him.
I called him but he did not answer.
⁷ The watchmen found me
as they made their rounds in the city.
They beat me, they bruised me;
they took away my cloak,
those watchmen of the walls!
⁸ Daughters of Jerusalem, I charge you —
if you find my beloved,
what will you tell him?
Tell him I am faint with love.

Friends

⁹ How is your beloved better than others,
most beautiful of women?
How is your beloved better than others,
that you so charge us?

She

¹⁰ My beloved is radiant and ruddy,
outstanding among ten thousand.
¹¹ His head is purest gold;
his hair is wavy
and black as a raven.
¹² His eyes are like doves
by the water streams,
washed in milk,
mounted like jewels.
¹³ His cheeks are like beds of spice
yielding perfume.
His lips are like lilies
dripping with myrrh.
¹⁴ His arms are rods of gold
set with topaz.

His body is like polished ivory
decorated with lapis lazuli.
¹⁵ His legs are pillars of marble
set on bases of pure gold.
His appearance is like Lebanon,
choice as its cedars.
¹⁶ His mouth is sweetness itself;
he is altogether lovely.
This is my beloved, this is my friend,
daughters of Jerusalem.

Friends

6 Where has your beloved gone,
most beautiful of women?
Which way did your beloved turn,
that we may look for him with you?

She

² My beloved has gone down to his garden,
to the beds of spices,
to browse in the gardens
and to gather lilies.
³ I am my beloved's and my beloved is mine;
he browses among the lilies.

He

⁴ You are as beautiful as Tirzah, my darling,
as lovely as Jerusalem,
as majestic as troops with banners.
⁵ Turn your eyes from me;
they overwhelm me.
Your hair is like a flock of goats
descending from Gilead.
⁶ Your teeth are like a flock of sheep
coming up from the washing.
Each has its twin,
not one of them is missing.
⁷ Your temples behind your veil
are like the halves of a pomegranate.
⁸ Sixty queens there may be,
and eighty concubines,
and virgins beyond number;
⁹ but my dove, my perfect one, is unique,
the only daughter of her mother,
the favorite of the one who bore her.
The young women saw her and called
her blessed;
the queens and concubines praised her.

Friends

¹⁰ Who is this that appears like the dawn,
fair as the moon, bright as the sun,
majestic as the stars in procession?

ᵃ 6 Or *heart had gone out to him when he spoke*

He

¹¹ I went down to the grove of nut trees
    to look at the new growth in the valley,
  to see if the vines had budded
    or the pomegranates were in bloom.
¹² Before I realized it,
    my desire set me among the royal
      chariots of my people.[a]

Friends

¹³ Come back, come back, O Shulammite;
    come back, come back, that we may
      gaze on you!

He

Why would you gaze on the Shulammite
  as on the dance of Mahanaim?[b]

7[c] How beautiful your sandaled feet,
    O prince's daughter!
Your graceful legs are like jewels,
    the work of an artist's hands.
² Your navel is a rounded goblet
    that never lacks blended wine.
Your waist is a mound of wheat
    encircled by lilies.
³ Your breasts are like two fawns,
    like twin fawns of a gazelle.
⁴ Your neck is like an ivory tower.
Your eyes are the pools of Heshbon
    by the gate of Bath Rabbim.
Your nose is like the tower of Lebanon
    looking toward Damascus.
⁵ Your head crowns you like Mount Carmel.
    Your hair is like royal tapestry;
    the king is held captive by its tresses.
⁶ How beautiful you are and how pleasing,
    my love, with your delights!
⁷ Your stature is like that of the palm,
    and your breasts like clusters of fruit.
⁸ I said, "I will climb the palm tree;
    I will take hold of its fruit."
May your breasts be like clusters of
      grapes on the vine,
    the fragrance of your breath like apples,
⁹   and your mouth like the best wine.

She

May the wine go straight to my beloved,
    flowing gently over lips and teeth.[d]

¹⁰ I belong to my beloved,
    and his desire is for me.
¹¹ Come, my beloved, let us go to the
      countryside,
    let us spend the night in the villages.[e]
¹² Let us go early to the vineyards
    to see if the vines have budded,
  if their blossoms have opened,
    and if the pomegranates are in
      bloom—
    there I will give you my love.
¹³ The mandrakes send out their fragrance,
    and at our door is every delicacy,
  both new and old,
    that I have stored up for you, my
      beloved.

8 If only you were to me like a brother,
    who was nursed at my mother's
      breasts!
Then, if I found you outside,
    I would kiss you,
    and no one would despise me.
² I would lead you
    and bring you to my mother's house—
    she who has taught me.
I would give you spiced wine to drink,
    the nectar of my pomegranates.
³ His left arm is under my head
    and his right arm embraces me.
⁴ Daughters of Jerusalem, I charge you:
    Do not arouse or awaken love
    until it so desires.

Friends

⁵ Who is this coming up from the
      wilderness
    leaning on her beloved?

She

Under the apple tree I roused you;
    there your mother conceived you,
    there she who was in labor gave you
      birth.
⁶ Place me like a seal over your heart,
    like a seal on your arm;
for love is as strong as death,
    its jealousy[f] unyielding as the grave.
It burns like blazing fire,
    like a mighty flame.[g]

---

[a] 12 Or *among the chariots of Amminadab*; or *among the chariots of the people of the prince*   [b] 13 In Hebrew texts this verse (6:13) is numbered 7:1.   [c] In Hebrew texts 7:1-13 is numbered 7:2-14.   [d] 9 Septuagint, Aquila, Vulgate and Syriac; Hebrew *lips of sleepers*   [e] 11 Or *the henna bushes*   [f] 6 Or *ardor*   [g] 6 Or *fire, / like the very flame of the* Lord

[7] Many waters cannot quench love;
  rivers cannot sweep it away.
If one were to give
  all the wealth of one's house for love,
  it[a] would be utterly scorned.

Friends

[8] We have a little sister,
  and her breasts are not yet grown.
What shall we do for our sister
  on the day she is spoken for?
[9] If she is a wall,
  we will build towers of silver on her.
If she is a door,
  we will enclose her with panels of cedar.

She

[10] I am a wall,
  and my breasts are like towers.
Thus I have become in his eyes
  like one bringing contentment.

[11] Solomon had a vineyard in Baal
    Hamon;
  he let out his vineyard to tenants.
Each was to bring for its fruit
  a thousand shekels[b] of silver.
[12] But my own vineyard is mine to give;
  the thousand shekels are for you,
    Solomon,
  and two hundred[c] are for those who
    tend its fruit.

He

[13] You who dwell in the gardens
  with friends in attendance,
  let me hear your voice!

She

[14] Come away, my beloved,
  and be like a gazelle
  or like a young stag
  on the spice-laden mountains.

---

[a] 7 Or *he*   [b] 11 That is, about 25 pounds or about 12 kilograms; also in verse 12   [c] 12 That is, about 5 pounds or about 2.3 kilograms

ISAIAH

➡ **WHEN DID THIS HAPPEN?**

Around 740 B.C. in the southern kingdom of Judah

➡ **WHO IS IN THIS BOOK?**

Isaiah
Hezekiah
Sennacherib

➡ **VERSES YOU MIGHT RECOGNIZE**

ISAIAH 9:6

"For to us a child is born, to us a son is given, and the government will be on his shoulders. And he will be called Wonderful Counselor, Mighty God, Everlasting Father, Prince of Peace."

ISAIAH 43:10

"'You are my witnesses,' declares the LORD, 'and my servant whom I have chosen.'"

WHAT'S IT ABOUT?

Written before the Babylonian exile, during the period described in 2 Kings, this book proclaims judgment on Judah for its many sins. The Israelites had turned away from God, and they needed a prophet to wake them up. The book is divided into two halves. In chapters 1-39, Isaiah listed Israel's sins and warned them of an Assyrian invasion. In chapters 40-66, he comforted Israel during their exile to Babylon. God must punish sin, but he is also compassionate and will provide a way of salvation.

This book also paints the clearest picture of the coming Messiah—Jesus. It foreshadows his virgin birth, his message of good news and even his sacrificial death. The list of Israel's failures reveals their great need for a Savior, but God still wants a relationship with them. He will be faithful to his promises and provide the salvation they need. The only question is if they will accept his offer.

ISAIAH

1 The vision concerning Judah and Jerusalem that Isaiah son of Amoz saw during the reigns of Uzziah, Jotham, Ahaz and Hezekiah, kings of Judah.

A Rebellious Nation

² Hear me, you heavens! Listen, earth!
    For the LORD has spoken:
"I reared children and brought them up,
    but they have rebelled against me.
³ The ox knows its master,
    the donkey its owner's manger,
but Israel does not know,
    my people do not understand."

⁴ Woe to the sinful nation,
    a people whose guilt is great,
a brood of evildoers,
    children given to corruption!
They have forsaken the LORD;
    they have spurned the Holy One of
        Israel
    and turned their backs on him.

⁵ Why should you be beaten anymore?
    Why do you persist in rebellion?
Your whole head is injured,
    your whole heart afflicted.
⁶ From the sole of your foot to the top of
        your head
    there is no soundness—
only wounds and welts
    and open sores,
not cleansed or bandaged
    or soothed with olive oil.

⁷ Your country is desolate,
    your cities burned with fire;
your fields are being stripped by
        foreigners
    right before you,
    laid waste as when overthrown by
        strangers.
⁸ Daughter Zion is left
    like a shelter in a vineyard,
like a hut in a cucumber field,
    like a city under siege.

⁹ Unless the LORD Almighty
    had left us some survivors,
we would have become like Sodom,
    we would have been like Gomorrah.

¹⁰ Hear the word of the LORD,
    you rulers of Sodom;
listen to the instruction of our God,
    you people of Gomorrah!
¹¹ "The multitude of your sacrifices—
    what are they to me?" says the LORD.
"I have more than enough of burnt
        offerings,
    of rams and the fat of fattened animals;
I have no pleasure
    in the blood of bulls and lambs and
        goats.
¹² When you come to appear before me,
    who has asked this of you,
    this trampling of my courts?
¹³ Stop bringing meaningless offerings!
    Your incense is detestable to me.
New Moons, Sabbaths and
        convocations—
    I cannot bear your worthless
        assemblies.
¹⁴ Your New Moon feasts and your
        appointed festivals
    I hate with all my being.
They have become a burden to me;
    I am weary of bearing them.
¹⁵ When you spread out your hands in
        prayer,
    I hide my eyes from you;
even when you offer many prayers,
    I am not listening.

Your hands are full of blood!

¹⁶ Wash and make yourselves clean.
    Take your evil deeds out of my sight;
    stop doing wrong.
¹⁷ Learn to do right; seek justice.
    Defend the oppressed.[a]
Take up the cause of the fatherless;
    plead the case of the widow.

ᵃ 17 Or *justice. / Correct the oppressor*

18 "Come now, let us settle the matter,"
    says the LORD.
  "Though your sins are like scarlet,
    they shall be as white as snow;
  though they are red as crimson,
    they shall be like wool.
19 If you are willing and obedient,
    you will eat the good things of the
        land;
20 but if you resist and rebel,
    you will be devoured by the sword."
          For the mouth of the LORD
                has spoken.

21 See how the faithful city
    has become a prostitute!
  She once was full of justice;
    righteousness used to dwell in her —
    but now murderers!
22 Your silver has become dross,
    your choice wine is diluted with water.
23 Your rulers are rebels,
    partners with thieves;
  they all love bribes
    and chase after gifts.
  They do not defend the cause of the
        fatherless;
    the widow's case does not come before
        them.

24 Therefore the Lord, the LORD Almighty,
    the Mighty One of Israel, declares:
  "Ah! I will vent my wrath on my foes
    and avenge myself on my enemies.
25 I will turn my hand against you;[a]
    I will thoroughly purge away your
        dross
    and remove all your impurities.
26 I will restore your leaders as in days
        of old,
    your rulers as at the beginning.
  Afterward you will be called
    the City of Righteousness,
    the Faithful City."

27 Zion will be delivered with justice,
    her penitent ones with righteousness.
28 But rebels and sinners will both be
        broken,
    and those who forsake the LORD will
        perish.

29 "You will be ashamed because of the
        sacred oaks
    in which you have delighted;

you will be disgraced because of the
        gardens
    that you have chosen.
30 You will be like an oak with fading leaves,
    like a garden without water.
31 The mighty man will become tinder
    and his work a spark;
  both will burn together,
    with no one to quench the fire."

The Mountain of the Lord

2 This is what Isaiah son of Amoz saw
  concerning Judah and Jerusalem:

2 In the last days

the mountain of the LORD's temple will
        be established
    as the highest of the mountains;
  it will be exalted above the hills,
    and all nations will stream to it.

3 Many peoples will come and say,

  "Come, let us go up to the mountain of
        the LORD,
    to the temple of the God of Jacob.
  He will teach us his ways,
    so that we may walk in his paths."
  The law will go out from Zion,
    the word of the LORD from Jerusalem.
4 He will judge between the nations
    and will settle disputes for many
        peoples.
  They will beat their swords into
        plowshares
    and their spears into pruning hooks.
  Nation will not take up sword against
        nation,
    nor will they train for war anymore.

5 Come, descendants of Jacob,
    let us walk in the light of the LORD.

The Day of the Lord

6 You, LORD, have abandoned your people,
    the descendants of Jacob.
  They are full of superstitions from the East;
    they practice divination like the
        Philistines
    and embrace pagan customs.
7 Their land is full of silver and gold;
    there is no end to their treasures.
  Their land is full of horses;
    there is no end to their chariots.

a 25 That is, against Jerusalem

⁸Their land is full of idols;
    they bow down to the work of their
       hands,
    to what their fingers have made.
⁹So people will be brought low
    and everyone humbled —
    do not forgive them.ᵃ

¹⁰Go into the rocks, hide in the ground
    from the fearful presence of the Lᴏʀᴅ
    and the splendor of his majesty!
¹¹The eyes of the arrogant will be humbled
    and human pride brought low;
    the Lᴏʀᴅ alone will be exalted in
       that day.

¹²The Lᴏʀᴅ Almighty has a day in store
    for all the proud and lofty,
    for all that is exalted
       (and they will be humbled),
¹³for all the cedars of Lebanon, tall and
       lofty,
    and all the oaks of Bashan,
¹⁴for all the towering mountains
    and all the high hills,
¹⁵for every lofty tower
    and every fortified wall,
¹⁶for every trading shipᵇ
    and every stately vessel.
¹⁷The arrogance of man will be
       brought low
    and human pride humbled;
    the Lᴏʀᴅ alone will be exalted in
       that day,
¹⁸   and the idols will totally disappear.

¹⁹People will flee to caves in the rocks
    and to holes in the ground
    from the fearful presence of the Lᴏʀᴅ
    and the splendor of his majesty,
    when he rises to shake the earth.
²⁰In that day people will throw away
    to the moles and bats
    their idols of silver and idols of gold,
    which they made to worship.
²¹They will flee to caverns in the rocks
    and to the overhanging crags
    from the fearful presence of the Lᴏʀᴅ
    and the splendor of his majesty,
    when he rises to shake the earth.

²²Stop trusting in mere humans,
    who have but a breath in their nostrils.
    Why hold them in esteem?

Judgment on Jerusalem and Judah

3 See now, the Lord,
    the Lᴏʀᴅ Almighty,
  is about to take from Jerusalem and
       Judah
    both supply and support:
  all supplies of food and all supplies of
       water,
²   the hero and the warrior,
  the judge and the prophet,
    the diviner and the elder,
³the captain of fifty and the man of rank,
    the counselor, skilled craftsman and
       clever enchanter.

⁴"I will make mere youths their officials;
    children will rule over them."

⁵People will oppress each other —
    man against man, neighbor against
       neighbor.
  The young will rise up against the old,
    the nobody against the honored.

⁶A man will seize one of his brothers
    in his father's house, and say,
  "You have a cloak, you be our leader;
    take charge of this heap of ruins!"
⁷But in that day he will cry out,
    "I have no remedy.
  I have no food or clothing in my house;
    do not make me the leader of the
       people."

⁸Jerusalem staggers,
    Judah is falling;
  their words and deeds are against the
       Lᴏʀᴅ,
    defying his glorious presence.
⁹The look on their faces testifies against
       them;
    they parade their sin like Sodom;
    they do not hide it.
  Woe to them!
    They have brought disaster upon
       themselves.

¹⁰Tell the righteous it will be well with
       them,
    for they will enjoy the fruit of their
       deeds.
¹¹Woe to the wicked!
    Disaster is upon them!
  They will be paid back
    for what their hands have done.

ᵃ 9 Or *not raise them up*   ᵇ 16 Hebrew *every ship of Tarshish*

¹² Youths oppress my people,
  women rule over them.
My people, your guides lead you astray;
  they turn you from the path.

¹³ The LORD takes his place in court;
  he rises to judge the people.
¹⁴ The LORD enters into judgment
  against the elders and leaders of his
    people:
"It is you who have ruined my vineyard;
  the plunder from the poor is in your
    houses.
¹⁵ What do you mean by crushing my
    people
  and grinding the faces of the poor?"
      declares the Lord,
        the LORD Almighty.

¹⁶ The LORD says,
"The women of Zion are haughty,
  walking along with outstretched necks,
  flirting with their eyes,
strutting along with swaying hips,
  with ornaments jingling on their
    ankles.
¹⁷ Therefore the Lord will bring sores on the
    heads of the women of Zion;
  the LORD will make their scalps bald."

¹⁸ In that day the Lord will snatch away
their finery: the bangles and headbands
and crescent necklaces, ¹⁹ the earrings and
bracelets and veils, ²⁰ the headdresses and
anklets and sashes, the perfume bottles and
charms, ²¹ the signet rings and nose rings,
²² the fine robes and the capes and cloaks,
the purses ²³ and mirrors, and the linen garments and tiaras and shawls.

²⁴ Instead of fragrance there will be a stench;
  instead of a sash, a rope;
instead of well-dressed hair, baldness;
  instead of fine clothing, sackcloth;
  instead of beauty, branding.
²⁵ Your men will fall by the sword,
  your warriors in battle.
²⁶ The gates of Zion will lament and mourn;
  destitute, she will sit on the ground.

4 ¹ In that day seven women
  will take hold of one man
and say, "We will eat our own food
  and provide our own clothes;
only let us be called by your name.
  Take away our disgrace!"

The Branch of the Lord

² In that day the Branch of the LORD will
be beautiful and glorious, and the fruit of the
land will be the pride and glory of the survivors in Israel. ³ Those who are left in Zion,
who remain in Jerusalem, will be called
holy, all who are recorded among the living
in Jerusalem. ⁴ The Lord will wash away the
filth of the women of Zion; he will cleanse
the bloodstains from Jerusalem by a spirit[a] of judgment and a spirit[a] of fire. ⁵ Then
the LORD will create over all of Mount Zion
and over those who assemble there a cloud
of smoke by day and a glow of flaming fire
by night; over everything the glory[b] will be a
canopy. ⁶ It will be a shelter and shade from
the heat of the day, and a refuge and hiding
place from the storm and rain.

The Song of the Vineyard

5 I will sing for the one I love
  a song about his vineyard:
My loved one had a vineyard
  on a fertile hillside.
² He dug it up and cleared it of stones
  and planted it with the choicest vines.
He built a watchtower in it
  and cut out a winepress as well.
Then he looked for a crop of good grapes,
  but it yielded only bad fruit.

³ "Now you dwellers in Jerusalem and
    people of Judah,
  judge between me and my vineyard.
⁴ What more could have been done for my
    vineyard
  than I have done for it?
When I looked for good grapes,
  why did it yield only bad?
⁵ Now I will tell you
  what I am going to do to my vineyard:
I will take away its hedge,
  and it will be destroyed;
I will break down its wall,
  and it will be trampled.
⁶ I will make it a wasteland,
  neither pruned nor cultivated,
  and briers and thorns will grow there.
I will command the clouds
  not to rain on it."

⁷ The vineyard of the LORD Almighty
  is the nation of Israel,

ᵃ 4 Or *the Spirit*   ᵇ 5 Or *over all the glory there*

and the people of Judah
are the vines he delighted in.
And he looked for justice, but saw
bloodshed;
for righteousness, but heard cries of
distress.

Woes and Judgments

⁸ Woe to you who add house to house
and join field to field
till no space is left
and you live alone in the land.

⁹ The LORD Almighty has declared in my
hearing:

"Surely the great houses will become
desolate,
the fine mansions left without
occupants.
¹⁰ A ten-acre vineyard will produce only a
bath*ᵃ* of wine;
a homer*ᵇ* of seed will yield only an
ephah*ᶜ* of grain."

¹¹ Woe to those who rise early in the
morning
to run after their drinks,
who stay up late at night
till they are inflamed with wine.
¹² They have harps and lyres at their
banquets,
pipes and timbrels and wine,
but they have no regard for the deeds of
the LORD,
no respect for the work of his hands.
¹³ Therefore my people will go into exile
for lack of understanding;
those of high rank will die of hunger
and the common people will be
parched with thirst.
¹⁴ Therefore Death expands its jaws,
opening wide its mouth;
into it will descend their nobles and
masses
with all their brawlers and revelers.
¹⁵ So people will be brought low
and everyone humbled,
the eyes of the arrogant humbled.
¹⁶ But the LORD Almighty will be exalted by
his justice,
and the holy God will be proved holy
by his righteous acts.

¹⁷ Then sheep will graze as in their own
pasture;
lambs will feed*ᵈ* among the ruins of
the rich.

¹⁸ Woe to those who draw sin along with
cords of deceit,
and wickedness as with cart ropes,
¹⁹ to those who say, "Let God hurry;
let him hasten his work
so we may see it.
The plan of the Holy One of Israel —
let it approach, let it come into view,
so we may know it."

²⁰ Woe to those who call evil good
and good evil,
who put darkness for light
and light for darkness,
who put bitter for sweet
and sweet for bitter.

²¹ Woe to those who are wise in their
own eyes
and clever in their own sight.

²² Woe to those who are heroes at drinking
wine
and champions at mixing drinks,
²³ who acquit the guilty for a bribe,
but deny justice to the innocent.
²⁴ Therefore, as tongues of fire lick up straw
and as dry grass sinks down in the
flames,
so their roots will decay
and their flowers blow away like dust;
for they have rejected the law of the LORD
Almighty
and spurned the word of the Holy One
of Israel.
²⁵ Therefore the LORD's anger burns against
his people;
his hand is raised and he strikes them
down.
The mountains shake,
and the dead bodies are like refuse in
the streets.

Yet for all this, his anger is not turned
away,
his hand is still upraised.

²⁶ He lifts up a banner for the distant
nations,

ᵃ 10 That is, about 6 gallons or about 22 liters   *ᵇ 10* That is, probably about 360 pounds or about 160
kilograms   *ᶜ 10* That is, probably about 36 pounds or about 16 kilograms   *ᵈ 17* Septuagint; Hebrew
/ strangers will eat

he whistles for those at the ends of the
earth.
Here they come,
swiftly and speedily!
²⁷ Not one of them grows tired or stumbles,
not one slumbers or sleeps;
not a belt is loosened at the waist,
not a sandal strap is broken.
²⁸ Their arrows are sharp,
all their bows are strung;
their horses' hooves seem like flint,
their chariot wheels like a whirlwind.
²⁹ Their roar is like that of the lion,
they roar like young lions;
they growl as they seize their prey
and carry it off with no one to rescue.
³⁰ In that day they will roar over it
like the roaring of the sea.
And if one looks at the land,
there is only darkness and distress;
even the sun will be darkened by
clouds.

Isaiah's Commission

6 In the year that King Uzziah died, I saw
the Lord, high and exalted, seated on a
throne; and the train of his robe filled the
temple. ²Above him were seraphim, each
with six wings: With two wings they covered
their faces, with two they covered their feet,
and with two they were flying. ³And they
were calling to one another:

"Holy, holy, holy is the LORD Almighty;
the whole earth is full of his glory."

⁴At the sound of their voices the doorposts
and thresholds shook and the temple was
filled with smoke.

⁵"Woe to me!" I cried. "I am ruined! For I
am a man of unclean lips, and I live among
a people of unclean lips, and my eyes have
seen the King, the LORD Almighty."

⁶Then one of the seraphim flew to me
with a live coal in his hand, which he had
taken with tongs from the altar. ⁷With it he
touched my mouth and said, "See, this has
touched your lips; your guilt is taken away
and your sin atoned for."

⁸Then I heard the voice of the Lord saying, "Whom shall I send? And who will go
for us?"

And I said, "Here am I. Send me!"
⁹He said, "Go and tell this people:

"'Be ever hearing, but never
understanding;
be ever seeing, but never perceiving.'
¹⁰ Make the heart of this people calloused;
make their ears dull
and close their eyes.ᵃ
Otherwise they might see with their eyes,
hear with their ears,
understand with their hearts,
and turn and be healed."

¹¹ Then I said, "For how long, Lord?"
And he answered:

"Until the cities lie ruined
and without inhabitant,
until the houses are left deserted
and the fields ruined and ravaged,
¹² until the LORD has sent everyone far
away
and the land is utterly forsaken.
¹³ And though a tenth remains in the land,
it will again be laid waste.
But as the terebinth and oak
leave stumps when they are cut down,
so the holy seed will be the stump in
the land."

The Sign of Immanuel

7 When Ahaz son of Jotham, the son of
Uzziah, was king of Judah, King Rezin of
Aram and Pekah son of Remaliah king of Israel marched up to fight against Jerusalem,
but they could not overpower it.

²Now the house of David was told, "Aram
has allied itself withᵇ Ephraim"; so the hearts
of Ahaz and his people were shaken, as the
trees of the forest are shaken by the wind.

³Then the LORD said to Isaiah, "Go out,
you and your son Shear-Jashub,ᶜ to meet
Ahaz at the end of the aqueduct of the Upper
Pool, on the road to the Launderer's Field.
⁴Say to him, 'Be careful, keep calm and don't
be afraid. Do not lose heart because of these
two smoldering stubs of firewood—because
of the fierce anger of Rezin and Aram and of
the son of Remaliah. ⁵Aram, Ephraim and
Remaliah's son have plotted your ruin, saying, ⁶"Let us invade Judah; let us tear it apart
and divide it among ourselves, and make the

ᵃ 9,10 Hebrew; Septuagint *'You will be ever hearing, but never understanding; / you will be ever seeing, but
never perceiving.' / ¹⁰This people's heart has become calloused; / they hardly hear with their ears, / and they
have closed their eyes*   ᵇ 2 Or *has set up camp in*   ᶜ 3 *Shear-Jashub* means *a remnant will return.*

RISKY ANSWER

READ: ISAIAH 6:8

Abraham. Jacob. Joseph. Moses. Samuel. David. Isaiah. They all have one thing in common. Every one of them said, "Here am I."

All we have to do is simply say, "Here am I" and God will take it from there. Don't stress about money or your age or parents. It'll happen in time! It's God's job to get us where he wants us to go, not ours. Our job is to be available anytime, anyplace. Sometimes it's a calling to move halfway around the world or sometimes it's moving over one lunch table. But it always starts with the little three-word prayer: Here am I.

That's what Samuel said when he heard the still small voice of the Holy Spirit.

That's what Moses said at the burning bush.

That's what Caleb said when he finally stepped foot into the promised land.

That's what Isaiah said when King Uzziah died.

You need to be willing to do something a little crazy!

It would've been so easy for any of them to talk their way out of it: "I don't have the right weapon. I can't do this by myself." These aren't even my people. If we look for an excuse, we'll always find one. When it comes to making excuses, we are infinitely creative. What if we channeled that creativity into finding solutions?

BUILDING FAITH WISDOM STRENGTH

son of Tabeel king over it." ⁷Yet this is what the Sovereign LORD says:

" 'It will not take place,
    it will not happen,
⁸for the head of Aram is Damascus,
    and the head of Damascus is only
        Rezin.
Within sixty-five years
    Ephraim will be too shattered to be a
        people.
⁹The head of Ephraim is Samaria,
    and the head of Samaria is only
        Remaliah's son.
If you do not stand firm in your faith,
    you will not stand at all.' "

¹⁰Again the LORD spoke to Ahaz, ¹¹"Ask the LORD your God for a sign, whether in the deepest depths or in the highest heights."

¹²But Ahaz said, "I will not ask; I will not put the LORD to the test."

¹³Then Isaiah said, "Hear now, you house of David! Is it not enough to try the patience of humans? Will you try the patience of my God also? ¹⁴Therefore the Lord himself will give you*ᵃ* a sign: The virgin*ᵇ* will conceive and give birth to a son, and*ᶜ* will call him Immanuel.*ᵈ* ¹⁵He will be eating curds and honey when he knows enough to reject the wrong and choose the right, ¹⁶for before the boy knows enough to reject the wrong and choose the right, the land of the two kings you dread will be laid waste. ¹⁷The LORD will bring on you and on your people and on the house of your father a time unlike any since Ephraim broke away from Judah — he will bring the king of Assyria."

Assyria, the Lord's Instrument

¹⁸In that day the LORD will whistle for flies from the Nile delta in Egypt and for bees from the land of Assyria. ¹⁹They will all come and settle in the steep ravines and in the crevices in the rocks, on all the thornbushes and at all the water holes. ²⁰In that day the Lord will use a razor hired from beyond the Euphrates River — the king of Assyria — to shave your head and private parts, and to cut off your beard also. ²¹In that day, a person will keep alive a young cow and two goats. ²²And because of the abundance of the milk they give, there will be curds to eat. All who remain in the land will eat curds and honey. ²³In that day, in every place where there were a thousand vines worth a thousand silver shekels,*ᵉ* there will be only briers and thorns. ²⁴Hunters will go there with bow and arrow, for the land will be covered with briers and thorns. ²⁵As for all the hills once cultivated by the hoe, you will no longer go there for fear of the briers and thorns; they will become places where cattle are turned loose and where sheep run.

Isaiah and His Children as Signs

8 The LORD said to me, "Take a large scroll and write on it with an ordinary pen: Maher-Shalal-Hash-Baz."*ᶠ* ²So I called in Uriah the priest and Zechariah son of Jeberekiah as reliable witnesses for me. ³Then I made love to the prophetess, and she conceived and gave birth to a son. And the LORD said to me, "Name him Maher-Shalal-Hash-Baz. ⁴For before the boy knows how to say 'My father' or 'My mother,' the wealth of Damascus and the plunder of Samaria will be carried off by the king of Assyria."

⁵The LORD spoke to me again:

⁶"Because this people has rejected
    the gently flowing waters of Shiloah
and rejoices over Rezin
    and the son of Remaliah,
⁷therefore the Lord is about to bring
        against them
    the mighty floodwaters of the
        Euphrates —
    the king of Assyria with all his pomp.
It will overflow all its channels,
    run over all its banks
⁸and sweep on into Judah, swirling over it,
    passing through it and reaching up to
        the neck.
Its outspread wings will cover the
        breadth of your land,
    Immanuel*ᵈ*!"

⁹Raise the war cry,*ᵍ* you nations, and be
        shattered!
    Listen, all you distant lands.

ᵃ 14 The Hebrew is plural.   ᵇ 14 Or *young woman* or *son, and they*   ᵈ 14,8 *Immanuel* means *God with us.*   ᶜ 14 Masoretic Text; Dead Sea Scrolls *son, and he*   ᵉ 23 That is, about 25 pounds or about 12 kilograms   ᶠ 1 *Maher-Shalal-Hash-Baz* means *quick to the plunder, swift to the spoil*; also in verse 3.   ᵍ 9 Or *Do your worst*

Prepare for battle, and be shattered!
Prepare for battle, and be shattered!
[10] Devise your strategy, but it will be
thwarted;
propose your plan, but it will not stand,
for God is with us.[a]

[11] This is what the LORD says to me with
his strong hand upon me, warning me not to
follow the way of this people:

[12] "Do not call conspiracy
everything this people calls a
conspiracy;
do not fear what they fear,
and do not dread it.
[13] The LORD Almighty is the one you are to
regard as holy,
he is the one you are to fear,
he is the one you are to dread.
[14] He will be a holy place;
for both Israel and Judah he will be
a stone that causes people to stumble
and a rock that makes them fall.
And for the people of Jerusalem he will be
a trap and a snare.
[15] Many of them will stumble;
they will fall and be broken,
they will be snared and captured."

[16] Bind up this testimony of warning
and seal up God's instruction among
my disciples.
[17] I will wait for the LORD,
who is hiding his face from the
descendants of Jacob.
I will put my trust in him.

[18] Here am I, and the children the LORD
has given me. We are signs and symbols in
Israel from the LORD Almighty, who dwells
on Mount Zion.

The Darkness Turns to Light

[19] When someone tells you to consult mediums and spiritists, who whisper and mutter, should not a people inquire of their God?
Why consult the dead on behalf of the living?
[20] Consult God's instruction and the testimony of warning. If anyone does not speak
according to this word, they have no light
of dawn. [21] Distressed and hungry, they will
roam through the land; when they are famished, they will become enraged and, looking upward, will curse their king and their
God. [22] Then they will look toward the earth
and see only distress and darkness and fearful gloom, and they will be thrust into utter
darkness.

9^b Nevertheless, there will be no more
gloom for those who were in distress. In
the past he humbled the land of Zebulun and
the land of Naphtali, but in the future he will
honor Galilee of the nations, by the Way of
the Sea, beyond the Jordan —

[2] The people walking in darkness
have seen a great light;
on those living in the land of deep
darkness
a light has dawned.
[3] You have enlarged the nation
and increased their joy;
they rejoice before you
as people rejoice at the harvest,
as warriors rejoice
when dividing the plunder.
[4] For as in the day of Midian's defeat,
you have shattered
the yoke that burdens them,
the bar across their shoulders,
the rod of their oppressor.
[5] Every warrior's boot used in battle
and every garment rolled in blood
will be destined for burning,
will be fuel for the fire.
[6] For to us a child is born,
to us a son is given,
and the government will be on his
shoulders.
And he will be called
Wonderful Counselor, Mighty God,
Everlasting Father, Prince of Peace.
[7] Of the greatness of his government and
peace
there will be no end.
He will reign on David's throne
and over his kingdom,
establishing and upholding it
with justice and righteousness
from that time on and forever.
The zeal of the LORD Almighty
will accomplish this.

The Lord's Anger Against Israel

[8] The Lord has sent a message against
Jacob;
it will fall on Israel.

---

[a] 10 Hebrew *Immanuel*   [b] In Hebrew texts 9:1 is numbered 8:23, and 9:2-21 is numbered 9:1-20.

9 All the people will know it—
  Ephraim and the inhabitants of
    Samaria—
who say with pride
  and arrogance of heart,
10 "The bricks have fallen down,
  but we will rebuild with dressed stone;
the fig trees have been felled,
  but we will replace them with cedars."
11 But the LORD has strengthened Rezin's
    foes against them
  and has spurred their enemies on.
12 Arameans from the east and Philistines
    from the west
  have devoured Israel with open
    mouth.

Yet for all this, his anger is not turned
    away,
  his hand is still upraised.

13 But the people have not returned to him
    who struck them,
  nor have they sought the LORD
    Almighty.
14 So the LORD will cut off from Israel both
    head and tail,
  both palm branch and reed in a single
    day;
15 the elders and dignitaries are the head,
  the prophets who teach lies are the
    tail.
16 Those who guide this people mislead
    them,
  and those who are guided are led
    astray.
17 Therefore the Lord will take no pleasure
    in the young men,
  nor will he pity the fatherless and
    widows,
for everyone is ungodly and wicked,
  every mouth speaks folly.

Yet for all this, his anger is not turned
    away,
  his hand is still upraised.

18 Surely wickedness burns like a fire;
  it consumes briers and thorns,
it sets the forest thickets ablaze,
  so that it rolls upward in a column of
    smoke.
19 By the wrath of the LORD Almighty
  the land will be scorched

and the people will be fuel for the fire;
  they will not spare one another.
20 On the right they will devour,
  but still be hungry;
on the left they will eat,
  but not be satisfied.
Each will feed on the flesh of their own
    offspring[a]:
21   Manasseh will feed on Ephraim, and
    Ephraim on Manasseh;
  together they will turn against Judah.

Yet for all this, his anger is not turned
    away,
  his hand is still upraised.

10 Woe to those who make unjust laws,
  to those who issue oppressive
    decrees,
2 to deprive the poor of their rights
  and withhold justice from the
    oppressed of my people,
making widows their prey
  and robbing the fatherless.
3 What will you do on the day of reckoning,
  when disaster comes from afar?
To whom will you run for help?
  Where will you leave your riches?
4 Nothing will remain but to cringe among
    the captives
  or fall among the slain.

Yet for all this, his anger is not turned
    away,
  his hand is still upraised.

God's Judgment on Assyria

5 "Woe to the Assyrian, the rod of my
    anger,
  in whose hand is the club of my wrath!
6 I send him against a godless nation,
  I dispatch him against a people who
    anger me,
to seize loot and snatch plunder,
  and to trample them down like mud in
    the streets.
7 But this is not what he intends,
  this is not what he has in mind;
his purpose is to destroy,
  to put an end to many nations.
8 'Are not my commanders all kings?' he
    says.
9   'Has not Kalno fared like Carchemish?

a 20 Or arm

Is not Hamath like Arpad,
and Samaria like Damascus?
¹⁰ As my hand seized the kingdoms of the
idols,
kingdoms whose images excelled
those of Jerusalem and
Samaria—
¹¹ shall I not deal with Jerusalem and her
images
as I dealt with Samaria and her idols?' "

¹² When the Lord has finished all his work
against Mount Zion and Jerusalem, he will
say, "I will punish the king of Assyria for the
willful pride of his heart and the haughty
look in his eyes. ¹³ For he says:

" 'By the strength of my hand I have done
this,
and by my wisdom, because I have
understanding.
I removed the boundaries of nations,
I plundered their treasures;
like a mighty one I subdued*ᵃ their kings.
¹⁴ As one reaches into a nest,
so my hand reached for the wealth of
the nations;
as people gather abandoned eggs,
so I gathered all the countries;
not one flapped a wing,
or opened its mouth to chirp.' "

¹⁵ Does the ax raise itself above the person
who swings it,
or the saw boast against the one who
uses it?
As if a rod were to wield the person who
lifts it up,
or a club brandish the one who is not
wood!
¹⁶ Therefore, the Lord, the LORD Almighty,
will send a wasting disease upon his
sturdy warriors;
under his pomp a fire will be kindled
like a blazing flame.
¹⁷ The Light of Israel will become a fire,
their Holy One a flame;
in a single day it will burn and consume
his thorns and his briers.
¹⁸ The splendor of his forests and fertile
fields
it will completely destroy,
as when a sick person wastes away.

¹⁹ And the remaining trees of his forests
will be so few
that a child could write them down.

The Remnant of Israel

²⁰ In that day the remnant of Israel,
the survivors of Jacob,
will no longer rely on him
who struck them down
but will truly rely on the LORD,
the Holy One of Israel.
²¹ A remnant will return,ᵇ a remnant of
Jacob
will return to the Mighty God.
²² Though your people be like the sand by
the sea, Israel,
only a remnant will return.
Destruction has been decreed,
overwhelming and righteous.
²³ The Lord, the LORD Almighty, will
carry out
the destruction decreed upon the
whole land.

²⁴ Therefore this is what the Lord, the
LORD Almighty, says:

"My people who live in Zion,
do not be afraid of the Assyrians,
who beat you with a rod
and lift up a club against you, as
Egypt did.
²⁵ Very soon my anger against you will end
and my wrath will be directed to their
destruction."

²⁶ The LORD Almighty will lash them with
a whip,
as when he struck down Midian at the
rock of Oreb;
and he will raise his staff over the waters,
as he did in Egypt.
²⁷ In that day their burden will be lifted
from your shoulders,
their yoke from your neck;
the yoke will be broken
because you have grown so fat.ᶜ

²⁸ They enter Aiath;
they pass through Migron;
they store supplies at Mikmash.
²⁹ They go over the pass, and say,
"We will camp overnight at Geba."

ᵃ 13 Or treasures; / I subdued the mighty,   ᵇ 21 Hebrew shear-jashub (see 7:3 and note); also in verse 22
ᶜ 27 Hebrew; Septuagint broken / from your shoulders

Ramah trembles;
  Gibeah of Saul flees.
³⁰Cry out, Daughter Gallim!
  Listen, Laishah!
  Poor Anathoth!
³¹Madmenah is in flight;
  the people of Gebim take cover.
³²This day they will halt at Nob;
  they will shake their fist
  at the mount of Daughter Zion,
  at the hill of Jerusalem.

³³See, the Lord, the LORD Almighty,
  will lop off the boughs with great
    power.
  The lofty trees will be felled,
  the tall ones will be brought low.
³⁴He will cut down the forest thickets with
    an ax;
  Lebanon will fall before the Mighty
    One.

The Branch From Jesse

11 A shoot will come up from the stump
    of Jesse;
  from his roots a Branch will bear fruit.
²The Spirit of the LORD will rest on him —
  the Spirit of wisdom and of
    understanding,
  the Spirit of counsel and of might,
  the Spirit of the knowledge and fear of
    the LORD —
³and he will delight in the fear of the
  LORD.

He will not judge by what he sees with
    his eyes,
  or decide by what he hears with his
    ears;
⁴but with righteousness he will judge the
    needy,
  with justice he will give decisions for
    the poor of the earth.
He will strike the earth with the rod of his
    mouth;
  with the breath of his lips he will slay
    the wicked.
⁵Righteousness will be his belt
  and faithfulness the sash around his
    waist.

⁶The wolf will live with the lamb,
  the leopard will lie down with the goat,
the calf and the lion and the yearling^a
    together;
  and a little child will lead them.
⁷The cow will feed with the bear,
  their young will lie down together,
  and the lion will eat straw like the ox.
⁸The infant will play near the cobra's den,
  and the young child will put its hand
    into the viper's nest.
⁹They will neither harm nor destroy
  on all my holy mountain,
for the earth will be filled with the
    knowledge of the LORD
  as the waters cover the sea.

¹⁰In that day the Root of Jesse will stand as a banner for the peoples; the nations will rally to him, and his resting place will be glorious. ¹¹In that day the Lord will reach out his hand a second time to reclaim the surviving remnant of his people from Assyria, from Lower Egypt, from Upper Egypt, from Cush,^b from Elam, from Babylonia,^c from Hamath and from the islands of the Mediterranean.

¹²He will raise a banner for the nations
  and gather the exiles of Israel;
he will assemble the scattered people of
    Judah
  from the four quarters of the earth.
¹³Ephraim's jealousy will vanish,
  and Judah's enemies^d will be
    destroyed;
  Ephraim will not be jealous of Judah,
  nor Judah hostile toward Ephraim.
¹⁴They will swoop down on the slopes of
    Philistia to the west;
  together they will plunder the people
    to the east.
They will subdue Edom and Moab,
  and the Ammonites will be subject to
    them.
¹⁵The LORD will dry up
  the gulf of the Egyptian sea;
with a scorching wind he will sweep his
    hand
  over the Euphrates River.
He will break it up into seven streams
  so that anyone can cross over in
    sandals.
¹⁶There will be a highway for the remnant
    of his people
  that is left from Assyria,

---

^a 6 Hebrew; Septuagint *lion will feed*   ^b 11 That is, the upper Nile region   ^c 11 Hebrew *Shinar*
^d 13 Or *hostility*

as there was for Israel
when they came up from Egypt.

Songs of Praise

12 In that day you will say:

"I will praise you, LORD.
    Although you were angry with me,
your anger has turned away
    and you have comforted me.
² Surely God is my salvation;
    I will trust and not be afraid.
The LORD, the LORD himself, is my
        strength and my defense*a*;
    he has become my salvation."
³ With joy you will draw water
    from the wells of salvation.

⁴ In that day you will say:

"Give praise to the LORD, proclaim his
        name;
    make known among the nations what
        he has done,
    and proclaim that his name is exalted.
⁵ Sing to the LORD, for he has done glorious
        things;
    let this be known to all the world.
⁶ Shout aloud and sing for joy, people of
        Zion,
    for great is the Holy One of Israel
        among you."

A Prophecy Against Babylon

13 A prophecy against Babylon that Isaiah son of Amoz saw:

² Raise a banner on a bare hilltop,
    shout to them;
beckon to them
    to enter the gates of the nobles.
³ I have commanded those I prepared for
        battle;
    I have summoned my warriors to carry
        out my wrath —
    those who rejoice in my triumph.

⁴ Listen, a noise on the mountains,
    like that of a great multitude!
Listen, an uproar among the kingdoms,
    like nations massing together!
The LORD Almighty is mustering
    an army for war.
⁵ They come from faraway lands,
    from the ends of the heavens —

the LORD and the weapons of his wrath —
    to destroy the whole country.

⁶ Wail, for the day of the LORD is near;
    it will come like destruction from the
        Almighty.*b*
⁷ Because of this, all hands will go limp,
    every heart will melt with fear.
⁸ Terror will seize them,
    pain and anguish will grip them;
    they will writhe like a woman in labor.
They will look aghast at each other,
    their faces aflame.

⁹ See, the day of the LORD is coming
    — a cruel day, with wrath and fierce
        anger —
to make the land desolate
    and destroy the sinners within it.
¹⁰ The stars of heaven and their
        constellations
    will not show their light.
The rising sun will be darkened
    and the moon will not give its light.
¹¹ I will punish the world for its evil,
    the wicked for their sins.
I will put an end to the arrogance of the
        haughty
    and will humble the pride of the
        ruthless.
¹² I will make people scarcer than pure
        gold,
    more rare than the gold of Ophir.
¹³ Therefore I will make the heavens
        tremble;
    and the earth will shake from its place
at the wrath of the LORD Almighty,
    in the day of his burning anger.

¹⁴ Like a hunted gazelle,
    like sheep without a shepherd,
they will all return to their own people,
    they will flee to their native land.
¹⁵ Whoever is captured will be thrust
        through;
    all who are caught will fall by the
        sword.
¹⁶ Their infants will be dashed to pieces
        before their eyes;
    their houses will be looted and their
        wives violated.

¹⁷ See, I will stir up against them the Medes,
    who do not care for silver
    and have no delight in gold.

---

a 2 Or *song*   *b* 6 Hebrew *Shaddai*

¹⁸ Their bows will strike down the young
men;
they will have no mercy on infants,
nor will they look with compassion on
children.
¹⁹ Babylon, the jewel of kingdoms,
the pride and glory of the
Babylonians,^a
will be overthrown by God
like Sodom and Gomorrah.
²⁰ She will never be inhabited
or lived in through all generations;
there no nomads will pitch their tents,
there no shepherds will rest their
flocks.
²¹ But desert creatures will lie there,
jackals will fill her houses;
there the owls will dwell,
and there the wild goats will leap
about.
²² Hyenas will inhabit her strongholds,
jackals her luxurious palaces.
Her time is at hand,
and her days will not be prolonged.

14 The LORD will have compassion on
Jacob;
once again he will choose Israel
and will settle them in their own land.
Foreigners will join them
and unite with the descendants of
Jacob.
² Nations will take them
and bring them to their own place.
And Israel will take possession of the
nations
and make them male and female
servants in the LORD's land.
They will make captives of their captors
and rule over their oppressors.

³ On the day the LORD gives you relief from
your suffering and turmoil and from the
harsh labor forced on you, ⁴ you will take up
this taunt against the king of Babylon:

How the oppressor has come to an end!
How his fury^b has ended!
⁵ The LORD has broken the rod of the
wicked,
the scepter of the rulers,

⁶ which in anger struck down peoples
with unceasing blows,
and in fury subdued nations
with relentless aggression.
⁷ All the lands are at rest and at peace;
they break into singing.
⁸ Even the junipers and the cedars of
Lebanon
gloat over you and say,
"Now that you have been laid low,
no one comes to cut us down."

⁹ The realm of the dead below is all astir
to meet you at your coming;
it rouses the spirits of the departed to
greet you —
all those who were leaders in the world;
it makes them rise from their thrones —
all those who were kings over the
nations.
¹⁰ They will all respond,
they will say to you,
"You also have become weak, as we are;
you have become like us."
¹¹ All your pomp has been brought down to
the grave,
along with the noise of your harps;
maggots are spread out beneath you
and worms cover you.

¹² How you have fallen from heaven,
morning star, son of the dawn!
You have been cast down to the earth,
you who once laid low the nations!
¹³ You said in your heart,
"I will ascend to the heavens;
I will raise my throne
above the stars of God;
I will sit enthroned on the mount of
assembly,
on the utmost heights of Mount
Zaphon.^c
¹⁴ I will ascend above the tops of the clouds;
I will make myself like the Most High."
¹⁵ But you are brought down to the realm of
the dead,
to the depths of the pit.

¹⁶ Those who see you stare at you,
they ponder your fate:
"Is this the man who shook the earth
and made kingdoms tremble,

---

^a 19 Or *Chaldeans*   ^b 4 Dead Sea Scrolls, Septuagint and Syriac; the meaning of the word in the
Masoretic Text is uncertain.   ^c 13 Or *of the north*; Zaphon was the most sacred mountain of the
Canaanites.

USURPER

READ: ISAIAH 14:13-14

Satan wants worship. He wants you and me to tell him how great he is. He wants to write his own story in which he is the hero and God is an afterthought. He admitted as much. Satan wants to take God's place, but God isn't moving. Satan covets the throne of heaven, but God isn't leaving.

Satan wants to win you to his side, but God will never let you go. You have his word. Even more, you have God's help. We shout, and God runs at the right moment. God places himself prior to our need, and just before we encounter that need, he gives us what we need.

You don't have to face Satan alone. You know his schemes. He will attack your weak spots first. He will tell you to meet your own needs. When you question your identity as a child of God, that is Satan speaking.

Pray. We cannot do battle with Satan on our own. He is a roaring lion, a fallen angel, an experienced fighter, and a trained soldier. He is angry—angry because he knows that his time is short (Revelation 12:12) and that God's victory is secure.

But there is wonderful news for the Christian: Christ reigns as our protector and provider. Arm yourself with God's Word. Load your pistol with Scriptures and keep a finger on the trigger.

BUILDING FAITH WISDOM STRENGTH

Taken from *God's Story, Your Story: Youth Edition* by Max Lucado, copyright © 2011 by Max Lucado, published by Zondervan.

¹⁷the man who made the world a
     wilderness,
  who overthrew its cities
  and would not let his captives go
     home?"

¹⁸All the kings of the nations lie in state,
  each in his own tomb.
¹⁹But you are cast out of your tomb
  like a rejected branch;
you are covered with the slain,
  with those pierced by the sword,
  those who descend to the stones of
     the pit.
Like a corpse trampled underfoot,
²⁰ you will not join them in burial,
for you have destroyed your land
  and killed your people.

Let the offspring of the wicked
  never be mentioned again.
²¹Prepare a place to slaughter his children
  for the sins of their ancestors;
they are not to rise to inherit the land
  and cover the earth with their cities.

²²"I will rise up against them,"
  declares the LORD Almighty.
"I will wipe out Babylon's name and
     survivors,
  her offspring and descendants,"
                    declares the LORD.
²³"I will turn her into a place for owls
  and into swampland;
I will sweep her with the broom of
     destruction,"
  declares the LORD Almighty.

²⁴The LORD Almighty has sworn,

"Surely, as I have planned, so it will be,
  and as I have purposed, so it will
     happen.
²⁵I will crush the Assyrian in my land;
  on my mountains I will trample him
     down.
His yoke will be taken from my people,
  and his burden removed from their
     shoulders."

²⁶This is the plan determined for the whole
     world;
  this is the hand stretched out over all
     nations.
²⁷For the LORD Almighty has purposed,
  and who can thwart him?

His hand is stretched out, and who can
  turn it back?

A Prophecy Against the Philistines

²⁸This prophecy came in the year King
Ahaz died:

²⁹Do not rejoice, all you Philistines,
  that the rod that struck you is broken;
from the root of that snake will spring up
     a viper,
  its fruit will be a darting, venomous
     serpent.
³⁰The poorest of the poor will find pasture,
  and the needy will lie down in safety.
But your root I will destroy by famine;
  it will slay your survivors.

³¹Wail, you gate! Howl, you city!
  Melt away, all you Philistines!
A cloud of smoke comes from the north,
  and there is not a straggler in its ranks.
³²What answer shall be given
  to the envoys of that nation?
"The LORD has established Zion,
  and in her his afflicted people will find
     refuge."

A Prophecy Against Moab

15 A prophecy against Moab:

Ar in Moab is ruined,
  destroyed in a night!
Kir in Moab is ruined,
  destroyed in a night!
²Dibon goes up to its temple,
  to its high places to weep;
  Moab wails over Nebo and Medeba.
Every head is shaved
  and every beard cut off.
³In the streets they wear sackcloth;
  on the roofs and in the public squares
they all wail,
  prostrate with weeping.
⁴Heshbon and Elealeh cry out,
  their voices are heard all the way to
     Jahaz.
Therefore the armed men of Moab
     cry out,
  and their hearts are faint.

⁵My heart cries out over Moab;
  her fugitives flee as far as Zoar,
  as far as Eglath Shelishiyah.
They go up the hill to Luhith,
  weeping as they go;

on the road to Horonaim
they lament their destruction.
6 The waters of Nimrim are dried up
and the grass is withered;
the vegetation is gone
and nothing green is left.
7 So the wealth they have acquired and
stored up
they carry away over the Ravine of the
Poplars.
8 Their outcry echoes along the border
of Moab;
their wailing reaches as far as Eglaim,
their lamentation as far as Beer Elim.
9 The waters of Dimon[a] are full of blood,
but I will bring still more upon
Dimon[a]—
a lion upon the fugitives of Moab
and upon those who remain in the
land.

16 Send lambs as tribute
to the ruler of the land,
from Sela, across the desert,
to the mount of Daughter Zion.
2 Like fluttering birds
pushed from the nest,
so are the women of Moab
at the fords of the Arnon.

3 "Make up your mind," Moab says.
"Render a decision.
Make your shadow like night—
at high noon.
Hide the fugitives,
do not betray the refugees.
4 Let the Moabite fugitives stay with you;
be their shelter from the destroyer."

The oppressor will come to an end,
and destruction will cease;
the aggressor will vanish from the land.
5 In love a throne will be established;
in faithfulness a man will sit on it—
one from the house[b] of David—
one who in judging seeks justice
and speeds the cause of righteousness.

6 We have heard of Moab's pride—
how great is her arrogance!—
of her conceit, her pride and her
insolence;
but her boasts are empty.

7 Therefore the Moabites wail,
they wail together for Moab.
Lament and grieve
for the raisin cakes of Kir Hareseth.
8 The fields of Heshbon wither,
the vines of Sibmah also.
The rulers of the nations
have trampled down the choicest
vines,
which once reached Jazer
and spread toward the desert.
Their shoots spread out
and went as far as the sea.[c]
9 So I weep, as Jazer weeps,
for the vines of Sibmah.
Heshbon and Elealeh,
I drench you with tears!
The shouts of joy over your ripened fruit
and over your harvests have been
stilled.
10 Joy and gladness are taken away from the
orchards;
no one sings or shouts in the
vineyards;
no one treads out wine at the presses,
for I have put an end to the shouting.
11 My heart laments for Moab like a harp,
my inmost being for Kir Hareseth.
12 When Moab appears at her high place,
she only wears herself out;
when she goes to her shrine to pray,
it is to no avail.

13 This is the word the LORD has already
spoken concerning Moab. 14 But now the
LORD says: "Within three years, as a servant
bound by contract would count them, Moab's splendor and all her many people will
be despised, and her survivors will be very
few and feeble."

A Prophecy Against Damascus

17 A prophecy against Damascus:

"See, Damascus will no longer be a city
but will become a heap of ruins.
2 The cities of Aroer will be deserted
and left to flocks, which will lie down,
with no one to make them afraid.
3 The fortified city will disappear from
Ephraim,
and royal power from Damascus;

---

[a] 9 *Dimon*, a wordplay on *Dibon* (see verse 2), sounds like the Hebrew for *blood*.   [b] 5 Hebrew *tent*
[c] 8 Probably the Dead Sea

the remnant of Aram will be
  like the glory of the Israelites,"
        declares the LORD Almighty.

4 "In that day the glory of Jacob will fade;
  the fat of his body will waste away.
5 It will be as when reapers harvest the
    standing grain,
  gathering the grain in their arms —
as when someone gleans heads of grain
  in the Valley of Rephaim.
6 Yet some gleanings will remain,
  as when an olive tree is beaten,
leaving two or three olives on the
    topmost branches,
  four or five on the fruitful boughs,"
        declares the LORD, the God
            of Israel.

7 In that day people will look to their
    Maker
  and turn their eyes to the Holy One of
    Israel.
8 They will not look to the altars,
  the work of their hands,
and they will have no regard for the
    Asherah poles[a]
  and the incense altars their fingers
    have made.

9 In that day their strong cities, which they
left because of the Israelites, will be like
places abandoned to thickets and undergrowth. And all will be desolation.

10 You have forgotten God your Savior;
  you have not remembered the Rock,
    your fortress.
Therefore, though you set out the finest
    plants
  and plant imported vines,
11 though on the day you set them out, you
    make them grow,
  and on the morning when you plant
    them, you bring them to bud,
yet the harvest will be as nothing
  in the day of disease and incurable
    pain.

12 Woe to the many nations that rage —
  they rage like the raging sea!
Woe to the peoples who roar —
  they roar like the roaring of great
    waters!

13 Although the peoples roar like the roar of
    surging waters,
  when he rebukes them they flee far
    away,
driven before the wind like chaff on the
    hills,
  like tumbleweed before a gale.
14 In the evening, sudden terror!
  Before the morning, they are gone!
This is the portion of those who loot us,
  the lot of those who plunder us.

A Prophecy Against Cush

18 Woe to the land of whirring wings[b]
    along the rivers of Cush,[c]
2 which sends envoys by sea
  in papyrus boats over the water.

Go, swift messengers,
  to a people tall and smooth-skinned,
to a people feared far and wide,
an aggressive nation of strange speech,
  whose land is divided by rivers.

3 All you people of the world,
  you who live on the earth,
when a banner is raised on the
    mountains,
  you will see it,
and when a trumpet sounds,
  you will hear it.
4 This is what the LORD says to me:
  "I will remain quiet and will look on
    from my dwelling place,
like shimmering heat in the sunshine,
  like a cloud of dew in the heat of
    harvest."
5 For, before the harvest, when the blossom
    is gone
  and the flower becomes a ripening
    grape,
he will cut off the shoots with pruning
    knives,
  and cut down and take away the
    spreading branches.
6 They will all be left to the mountain birds
    of prey
  and to the wild animals;
the birds will feed on them all summer,
  the wild animals all winter.

7 At that time gifts will be brought to the
LORD Almighty

---

[a] 8 That is, wooden symbols of the goddess Asherah   [b] 1 Or of locusts   [c] 1 That is, the upper
Nile region

from a people tall and smooth-skinned,
  from a people feared far and wide,
an aggressive nation of strange speech,
  whose land is divided by rivers —

the gifts will be brought to Mount Zion, the place of the Name of the LORD Almighty.

A Prophecy Against Egypt

19 A prophecy against Egypt:

See, the LORD rides on a swift cloud
  and is coming to Egypt.
The idols of Egypt tremble before him,
  and the hearts of the Egyptians melt
    with fear.

2 "I will stir up Egyptian against
    Egyptian —
  brother will fight against brother,
  neighbor against neighbor,
  city against city,
  kingdom against kingdom.
3 The Egyptians will lose heart,
  and I will bring their plans to nothing;
they will consult the idols and the spirits
    of the dead,
  the mediums and the spiritists.
4 I will hand the Egyptians over
  to the power of a cruel master,
and a fierce king will rule over them,"
  declares the Lord, the LORD Almighty.

5 The waters of the river will dry up,
  and the riverbed will be parched
    and dry.
6 The canals will stink;
  the streams of Egypt will dwindle and
    dry up.
The reeds and rushes will wither,
7   also the plants along the Nile,
  at the mouth of the river.
Every sown field along the Nile
  will become parched, will blow away
    and be no more.
8 The fishermen will groan and lament,
  all who cast hooks into the Nile;
those who throw nets on the water
  will pine away.
9 Those who work with combed flax will
    despair,
  the weavers of fine linen will lose
    hope.

10 The workers in cloth will be dejected,
  and all the wage earners will be sick
    at heart.

11 The officials of Zoan are nothing but
    fools;
  the wise counselors of Pharaoh give
    senseless advice.
How can you say to Pharaoh,
  "I am one of the wise men,
  a disciple of the ancient kings"?

12 Where are your wise men now?
  Let them show you and make known
what the LORD Almighty
  has planned against Egypt.
13 The officials of Zoan have become fools,
  the leaders of Memphis are deceived;
the cornerstones of her peoples
  have led Egypt astray.
14 The LORD has poured into them
  a spirit of dizziness;
they make Egypt stagger in all that she
    does,
  as a drunkard staggers around in his
    vomit.
15 There is nothing Egypt can do —
  head or tail, palm branch or reed.

16 In that day the Egyptians will become weaklings. They will shudder with fear at the uplifted hand that the LORD Almighty raises against them. 17 And the land of Judah will bring terror to the Egyptians; everyone to whom Judah is mentioned will be terrified, because of what the LORD Almighty is planning against them.

18 In that day five cities in Egypt will speak the language of Canaan and swear allegiance to the LORD Almighty. One of them will be called the City of the Sun.[a]

19 In that day there will be an altar to the LORD in the heart of Egypt, and a monument to the LORD at its border. 20 It will be a sign and witness to the LORD Almighty in the land of Egypt. When they cry out to the LORD because of their oppressors, he will send them a savior and defender, and he will rescue them. 21 So the LORD will make himself known to the Egyptians, and in that day they will acknowledge the LORD. They will worship with sacrifices and grain offerings; they will make vows to the LORD and keep them.

---

[a] 18 Some manuscripts of the Masoretic Text, Dead Sea Scrolls, Symmachus and Vulgate; most manuscripts of the Masoretic Text *City of Destruction*

²²The LORD will strike Egypt with a plague; he will strike them and heal them. They will turn to the LORD, and he will respond to their pleas and heal them.

²³In that day there will be a highway from Egypt to Assyria. The Assyrians will go to Egypt and the Egyptians to Assyria. The Egyptians and Assyrians will worship together. ²⁴In that day Israel will be the third, along with Egypt and Assyria, a blessing*ᵃ* on the earth. ²⁵The LORD Almighty will bless them, saying, "Blessed be Egypt my people, Assyria my handiwork, and Israel my inheritance."

A Prophecy Against Egypt and Cush

20 In the year that the supreme commander, sent by Sargon king of Assyria, came to Ashdod and attacked and captured it— ²at that time the LORD spoke through Isaiah son of Amoz. He said to him, "Take off the sackcloth from your body and the sandals from your feet." And he did so, going around stripped and barefoot.

³Then the LORD said, "Just as my servant Isaiah has gone stripped and barefoot for three years, as a sign and portent against Egypt and Cush,*ᵇ* ⁴so the king of Assyria will lead away stripped and barefoot the Egyptian captives and Cushite exiles, young and old, with buttocks bared—to Egypt's shame. ⁵Those who trusted in Cush and boasted in Egypt will be dismayed and put to shame. ⁶In that day the people who live on this coast will say, 'See what has happened to those we relied on, those we fled to for help and deliverance from the king of Assyria! How then can we escape?'"

A Prophecy Against Babylon

21 A prophecy against the Desert by the Sea:

Like whirlwinds sweeping through the southland,
an invader comes from the desert,
from a land of terror.

²A dire vision has been shown to me:
The traitor betrays, the looter takes loot.
Elam, attack! Media, lay siege!

I will bring to an end all the groaning
she caused.

³At this my body is racked with pain,
pangs seize me, like those of a woman
in labor;
I am staggered by what I hear,
I am bewildered by what I see.
⁴My heart falters,
fear makes me tremble;
the twilight I longed for
has become a horror to me.

⁵They set the tables,
they spread the rugs,
they eat, they drink!
Get up, you officers,
oil the shields!

⁶This is what the Lord says to me:

"Go, post a lookout
and have him report what he sees.
⁷When he sees chariots
with teams of horses,
riders on donkeys
or riders on camels,
let him be alert,
fully alert."

⁸And the lookout*ᶜ* shouted,

"Day after day, my lord, I stand on the
watchtower;
every night I stay at my post.
⁹Look, here comes a man in a chariot
with a team of horses.
And he gives back the answer:
'Babylon has fallen, has fallen!
All the images of its gods
lie shattered on the ground!'"

¹⁰My people who are crushed on the
threshing floor,
I tell you what I have heard
from the LORD Almighty,
from the God of Israel.

A Prophecy Against Edom

¹¹A prophecy against Dumah*ᵈ*:

Someone calls to me from Seir,
"Watchman, what is left of the night?
Watchman, what is left of the night?"

ᵃ 24 Or *Assyria, whose names will be used in blessings* (see Gen. 48:20); or *Assyria, who will be seen by others as blessed*   *ᵇ 3* That is, the upper Nile region; also in verse 5   *ᶜ 8* Dead Sea Scrolls and Syriac; Masoretic Text *A lion*   *ᵈ 11 Dumah*, a wordplay on *Edom*, means *silence* or *stillness*.

ISAIAH

At that time the LORD spoke through Isaiah son of Amoz. He said to him, "Take off the sackcloth from your body and the sandals from your feet." And he did so, going around stripped and barefoot. ISAIAH 20:2

HIS NAME MEANS: "the LORD is salvation"
READ HIS STORY: Isaiah 1:1; 6; 36–39

Isaiah had one of the toughest prophet jobs around. He was constantly a walking illustration of God's judgment. He even gave his sons names that were prophetically and politically symbolic (Isaiah 7:3, 8:1–4). This guy's radical obedience to God required equally radical boldness. Granted, his call to ministry was unforgettable—a vision of the Lord with smoke and flying seraphim!

After seeing God's glory, Isaiah knew without a doubt what he was called to do. No one else's opinion mattered. He went all out for God. No task questioned. No job too big or too embarrassing or too tough.

His prophecies and messages to Israel's people and kings were poetic, vivid and challenging. Naked preaching to warn what could happen to Judah if they didn't trust the Lord? He was in. Whatever God asked. No matter how crazy.

It might seem like his behavior should have landed him in prison. Yet he counseled royalty, and remained an active prophet for at least forty, if not sixty, years. Perhaps it was his delivery; though his book sounds a clear and strong warning of God's judgment, he was the eternal optimist, reminding God's people of his love and salvation. He had personally experienced both—and those truths were the grand motivation behind everything Isaiah did or said.

OF THE BIBLE

¹²The watchman replies,
  "Morning is coming, but also the
    night.
  If you would ask, then ask;
    and come back yet again."

A Prophecy Against Arabia

¹³A prophecy against Arabia:

You caravans of Dedanites,
  who camp in the thickets of Arabia,
¹⁴ bring water for the thirsty;
you who live in Tema,
  bring food for the fugitives.
¹⁵They flee from the sword,
  from the drawn sword,
from the bent bow
  and from the heat of battle.

¹⁶This is what the Lord says to me: "Within one year, as a servant bound by contract would count it, all the splendor of Kedar will come to an end. ¹⁷The survivors of the archers, the warriors of Kedar, will be few." The LORD, the God of Israel, has spoken.

A Prophecy About Jerusalem

22 A prophecy against the Valley of Vision:

What troubles you now,
  that you have all gone up on the roofs,
²you town so full of commotion,
  you city of tumult and revelry?
Your slain were not killed by the sword,
  nor did they die in battle.
³All your leaders have fled together;
  they have been captured without using
    the bow.
All you who were caught were taken
    prisoner together,
  having fled while the enemy was still
    far away.
⁴Therefore I said, "Turn away from me;
  let me weep bitterly.
Do not try to console me
  over the destruction of my people."

⁵The Lord, the LORD Almighty, has a day
  of tumult and trampling and terror
    in the Valley of Vision,
a day of battering down walls
  and of crying out to the mountains.
⁶Elam takes up the quiver,
  with her charioteers and horses;
Kir uncovers the shield.

⁷Your choicest valleys are full of chariots,
  and horsemen are posted at the city
    gates.
⁸The Lord stripped away the defenses of
    Judah,
  and you looked in that day
  to the weapons in the Palace of the
    Forest.
⁹You saw that the walls of the City of David
  were broken through in many places;
you stored up water
  in the Lower Pool.
¹⁰You counted the buildings in Jerusalem
  and tore down houses to strengthen
    the wall.
¹¹You built a reservoir between the two
    walls
  for the water of the Old Pool,
but you did not look to the One who
    made it,
  or have regard for the One who
    planned it long ago.

¹²The Lord, the LORD Almighty,
  called you on that day
to weep and to wail,
  to tear out your hair and put on
    sackcloth.
¹³But see, there is joy and revelry,
  slaughtering of cattle and killing of
    sheep,
  eating of meat and drinking of wine!
"Let us eat and drink," you say,
  "for tomorrow we die!"

¹⁴The LORD Almighty has revealed this in my hearing: "Till your dying day this sin will not be atoned for," says the Lord, the LORD Almighty.

¹⁵This is what the Lord, the LORD Almighty, says:

"Go, say to this steward,
  to Shebna the palace administrator:
¹⁶What are you doing here and who gave
    you permission
  to cut out a grave for yourself here,
hewing your grave on the height
  and chiseling your resting place in
    the rock?

¹⁷"Beware, the LORD is about to take firm
    hold of you
  and hurl you away, you mighty man.

[18] He will roll you up tightly like a ball
  and throw you into a large country.
There you will die
  and there the chariots you were so
    proud of
  will become a disgrace to your
    master's house.
[19] I will depose you from your office,
  and you will be ousted from your
    position.

[20] "In that day I will summon my servant,
Eliakim son of Hilkiah. [21] I will clothe him
with your robe and fasten your sash around
him and hand your authority over to him.
He will be a father to those who live in Jerusalem and to the people of Judah. [22] I will
place on his shoulder the key to the house of
David; what he opens no one can shut, and
what he shuts no one can open. [23] I will drive
him like a peg into a firm place; he will become a seat[a] of honor for the house of his
father. [24] All the glory of his family will hang
on him: its offspring and offshoots — all its
lesser vessels, from the bowls to all the jars.

[25] "In that day," declares the LORD Almighty, "the peg driven into the firm place
will give way; it will be sheared off and will
fall, and the load hanging on it will be cut
down." The LORD has spoken.

A Prophecy Against Tyre

23 A prophecy against Tyre:

  Wail, you ships of Tarshish!
    For Tyre is destroyed
    and left without house or harbor.
  From the land of Cyprus
    word has come to them.

[2] Be silent, you people of the island
  and you merchants of Sidon,
  whom the seafarers have enriched.
[3] On the great waters
    came the grain of the Shihor;
  the harvest of the Nile[b] was the revenue
    of Tyre,
  and she became the marketplace of
    the nations.

[4] Be ashamed, Sidon, and you fortress of
    the sea,

for the sea has spoken:
"I have neither been in labor nor given
    birth;
  I have neither reared sons nor brought
    up daughters."
[5] When word comes to Egypt,
  they will be in anguish at the report
    from Tyre.

[6] Cross over to Tarshish;
  wail, you people of the island.
[7] Is this your city of revelry,
  the old, old city,
whose feet have taken her
  to settle in far-off lands?
[8] Who planned this against Tyre,
  the bestower of crowns,
whose merchants are princes,
  whose traders are renowned in the
    earth?
[9] The LORD Almighty planned it,
  to bring down her pride in all her
    splendor
  and to humble all who are renowned
    on the earth.

[10] Till[c] your land as they do along the Nile,
    Daughter Tarshish,
  for you no longer have a harbor.
[11] The LORD has stretched out his hand over
    the sea
  and made its kingdoms tremble.
He has given an order concerning
    Phoenicia
  that her fortresses be destroyed.
[12] He said, "No more of your reveling,
  Virgin Daughter Sidon, now crushed!

  "Up, cross over to Cyprus;
    even there you will find no rest."
[13] Look at the land of the Babylonians,[d]
  this people that is now of no account!
The Assyrians have made it
  a place for desert creatures;
they raised up their siege towers,
  they stripped its fortresses bare
  and turned it into a ruin.

[14] Wail, you ships of Tarshish;
  your fortress is destroyed!

[15] At that time Tyre will be forgotten for
seventy years, the span of a king's life. But at

---

[a] 23 Or *throne*   [b] 2,3 Masoretic Text; Dead Sea Scrolls *Sidon, / who cross over the sea; / your envoys* [3] *are
on the great waters. / The grain of the Shihor, / the harvest of the Nile,*   [c] 10 Dead Sea Scrolls and some
Septuagint manuscripts; Masoretic Text *Go through*   [d] 13 Or *Chaldeans*

the end of these seventy years, it will happen to Tyre as in the song of the prostitute:

¹⁶ "Take up a harp, walk through the city,
  you forgotten prostitute;
play the harp well, sing many a song,
  so that you will be remembered."

¹⁷ At the end of seventy years, the LORD will deal with Tyre. She will return to her lucrative prostitution and will ply her trade with all the kingdoms on the face of the earth. ¹⁸ Yet her profit and her earnings will be set apart for the LORD; they will not be stored up or hoarded. Her profits will go to those who live before the LORD, for abundant food and fine clothes.

The Lord's Devastation of the Earth

24 See, the LORD is going to lay waste
    the earth
  and devastate it;
he will ruin its face
  and scatter its inhabitants—
² it will be the same
  for priest as for people,
  for the master as for his servant,
  for the mistress as for her servant,
  for seller as for buyer,
  for borrower as for lender,
  for debtor as for creditor.
³ The earth will be completely laid waste
  and totally plundered.
    The LORD has spoken this word.

⁴ The earth dries up and withers,
  the world languishes and withers,
  the heavens languish with the earth.
⁵ The earth is defiled by its people;
  they have disobeyed the laws,
  violated the statutes
  and broken the everlasting covenant.
⁶ Therefore a curse consumes the earth;
  its people must bear their guilt.
  Therefore earth's inhabitants are
    burned up,
  and very few are left.
⁷ The new wine dries up and the vine
    withers;
  all the merrymakers groan.
⁸ The joyful timbrels are stilled,
  the noise of the revelers has stopped,
  the joyful harp is silent.
⁹ No longer do they drink wine with a song;
  the beer is bitter to its drinkers.

¹⁰ The ruined city lies desolate;
  the entrance to every house is barred.
¹¹ In the streets they cry out for wine;
  all joy turns to gloom,
  all joyful sounds are banished from
    the earth.
¹² The city is left in ruins,
  its gate is battered to pieces.
¹³ So will it be on the earth
  and among the nations,
  as when an olive tree is beaten,
  or as when gleanings are left after the
    grape harvest.

¹⁴ They raise their voices, they shout for joy;
  from the west they acclaim the LORD's
    majesty.
¹⁵ Therefore in the east give glory to the
    LORD;
  exalt the name of the LORD, the God
    of Israel,
  in the islands of the sea.
¹⁶ From the ends of the earth we hear
    singing:
  "Glory to the Righteous One."

But I said, "I waste away, I waste away!
    Woe to me!
The treacherous betray!
  With treachery the treacherous
    betray!"
¹⁷ Terror and pit and snare await you,
  people of the earth.
¹⁸ Whoever flees at the sound of terror
  will fall into a pit;
whoever climbs out of the pit
  will be caught in a snare.

The floodgates of the heavens are
    opened,
  the foundations of the earth shake.
¹⁹ The earth is broken up,
  the earth is split asunder,
  the earth is violently shaken.
²⁰ The earth reels like a drunkard,
  it sways like a hut in the wind;
so heavy upon it is the guilt of its
    rebellion
  that it falls—never to rise again.

²¹ In that day the LORD will punish
  the powers in the heavens above
  and the kings on the earth below.
²² They will be herded together
  like prisoners bound in a
    dungeon;

they will be shut up in prison
and be punished[a] after many days.
²³ The moon will be dismayed,
the sun ashamed;
for the LORD Almighty will reign
on Mount Zion and in Jerusalem,
and before its elders — with great glory.

Praise to the Lord

25 LORD, you are my God;
I will exalt you and praise your
name,
for in perfect faithfulness
you have done wonderful things,
things planned long ago.
² You have made the city a heap of rubble,
the fortified town a ruin,
the foreigners' stronghold a city no more;
it will never be rebuilt.
³ Therefore strong peoples will honor you;
cities of ruthless nations will revere you.
⁴ You have been a refuge for the poor,
a refuge for the needy in their distress,
a shelter from the storm
and a shade from the heat.
For the breath of the ruthless
is like a storm driving against a wall
⁵ and like the heat of the desert.
You silence the uproar of foreigners;
as heat is reduced by the shadow of a
cloud,
so the song of the ruthless is stilled.

⁶ On this mountain the LORD Almighty
will prepare
a feast of rich food for all peoples,
a banquet of aged wine —
the best of meats and the finest of
wines.
⁷ On this mountain he will destroy
the shroud that enfolds all peoples,
the sheet that covers all nations;
⁸ he will swallow up death forever.
The Sovereign LORD will wipe away
the tears
from all faces;
he will remove his people's disgrace
from all the earth.
The LORD has spoken.

⁹ In that day they will say,

"Surely this is our God;
we trusted in him, and he saved us.

This is the LORD, we trusted in him;
let us rejoice and be glad in his
salvation."

¹⁰ The hand of the LORD will rest on this
mountain;
but Moab will be trampled in their
land
as straw is trampled down in the
manure.
¹¹ They will stretch out their hands in it,
as swimmers stretch out their hands
to swim.
God will bring down their pride
despite the cleverness[b] of their hands.
¹² He will bring down your high fortified
walls
and lay them low;
he will bring them down to the ground,
to the very dust.

A Song of Praise

26 In that day this song will be sung in
the land of Judah:

We have a strong city;
God makes salvation
its walls and ramparts.
² Open the gates
that the righteous nation may enter,
the nation that keeps faith.
³ You will keep in perfect peace
those whose minds are steadfast,
because they trust in you.
⁴ Trust in the LORD forever,
for the LORD, the LORD himself, is the
Rock eternal.
⁵ He humbles those who dwell on high,
he lays the lofty city low;
he levels it to the ground
and casts it down to the dust.
⁶ Feet trample it down —
the feet of the oppressed,
the footsteps of the poor.

⁷ The path of the righteous is level;
you, the Upright One, make the way of
the righteous smooth.
⁸ Yes, LORD, walking in the way of your
laws,[c]
we wait for you;
your name and renown
are the desire of our hearts.

---

[a] 22 Or *released*   [b] 11 The meaning of the Hebrew for this word is uncertain.   [c] 8 Or *judgments*

⁹My soul yearns for you in the night;
  in the morning my spirit longs for you.
When your judgments come upon the
    earth,
  the people of the world learn
    righteousness.
¹⁰But when grace is shown to the wicked,
  they do not learn righteousness;
even in a land of uprightness they go on
    doing evil
  and do not regard the majesty of the
    LORD.
¹¹LORD, your hand is lifted high,
  but they do not see it.
Let them see your zeal for your people
    and be put to shame;
  let the fire reserved for your enemies
    consume them.

¹²LORD, you establish peace for us;
  all that we have accomplished you
    have done for us.
¹³LORD our God, other lords besides you
    have ruled over us,
  but your name alone do we honor.
¹⁴They are now dead, they live no more;
    their spirits do not rise.
You punished them and brought them to
    ruin;
  you wiped out all memory of them.
¹⁵You have enlarged the nation, LORD;
  you have enlarged the nation.
You have gained glory for yourself;
  you have extended all the borders of
    the land.

¹⁶LORD, they came to you in their distress;
  when you disciplined them,
  they could barely whisper a prayer.ᵃ
¹⁷As a pregnant woman about to give birth
  writhes and cries out in her pain,
  so were we in your presence, LORD.
¹⁸We were with child, we writhed in labor,
  but we gave birth to wind.
We have not brought salvation to the
    earth,
  and the people of the world have not
    come to life.

¹⁹But your dead will live, LORD;
  their bodies will rise —
let those who dwell in the dust
  wake up and shout for joy —

your dew is like the dew of the morning;
  the earth will give birth to her dead.

²⁰Go, my people, enter your rooms
  and shut the doors behind you;
hide yourselves for a little while
  until his wrath has passed by.
²¹See, the LORD is coming out of his
    dwelling
  to punish the people of the earth for
    their sins.
The earth will disclose the blood shed
    on it;
  the earth will conceal its slain no
    longer.

Deliverance of Israel

27 In that day,

the LORD will punish with his sword —
  his fierce, great and powerful sword —
Leviathan the gliding serpent,
  Leviathan the coiling serpent;
he will slay the monster of the sea.

²In that day —

"Sing about a fruitful vineyard:
³   I, the LORD, watch over it;
  I water it continually.
I guard it day and night
  so that no one may harm it.
⁴   I am not angry.
If only there were briers and thorns
    confronting me!
  I would march against them in battle;
  I would set them all on fire.
⁵Or else let them come to me for refuge;
  let them make peace with me,
  yes, let them make peace with me."

⁶In days to come Jacob will take root,
  Israel will bud and blossom
  and fill all the world with fruit.

⁷Has the LORD struck her
  as he struck down those who struck
    her?
Has she been killed
  as those were killed who killed her?
⁸By warfareᵇ and exile you contend with
    her —
  with his fierce blast he drives her out,
  as on a day the east wind blows.

ᵃ 16 The meaning of the Hebrew for this clause is uncertain.   ᵇ 8 See Septuagint; the meaning of the
Hebrew for this word is uncertain.

⁹By this, then, will Jacob's guilt be
　　atoned for,
　　and this will be the full fruit of the
　　　removal of his sin:
When he makes all the altar stones
　　to be like limestone crushed to pieces,
　　no Asherah poles*ᵃ* or incense altars
　　will be left standing.
¹⁰The fortified city stands desolate,
　　an abandoned settlement, forsaken
　　　like the wilderness;
there the calves graze,
　　there they lie down;
　　they strip its branches bare.
¹¹When its twigs are dry, they are
　　　broken off
　　and women come and make fires with
　　　them.
For this is a people without
　　　understanding;
　　so their Maker has no compassion on
　　　them,
　　and their Creator shows them no favor.

¹²In that day the Lᴏʀᴅ will thresh from
the flowing Euphrates to the Wadi of Egypt,
and you, Israel, will be gathered up one by
one. ¹³And in that day a great trumpet will
sound. Those who were perishing in Assyria and those who were exiled in Egypt will
come and worship the Lᴏʀᴅ on the holy
mountain in Jerusalem.

Woe to the Leaders of Ephraim and Judah

28 Woe to that wreath, the pride of
　　　Ephraim's drunkards,
　　to the fading flower, his glorious
　　　beauty,
　　set on the head of a fertile valley—
　　to that city, the pride of those laid low
　　　by wine!
²See, the Lord has one who is powerful
　　　and strong.
　　Like a hailstorm and a destructive
　　　wind,
　　like a driving rain and a flooding
　　　downpour,
　　he will throw it forcefully to the
　　　ground.
³That wreath, the pride of Ephraim's
　　　drunkards,

　　will be trampled underfoot.
⁴That fading flower, his glorious beauty,
　　set on the head of a fertile valley,
　　will be like figs ripe before harvest—
　　as soon as people see them and take
　　　them in hand,
　　they swallow them.

⁵In that day the Lᴏʀᴅ Almighty
　　will be a glorious crown,
　　a beautiful wreath
　　for the remnant of his people.
⁶He will be a spirit of justice
　　to the one who sits in judgment,
　　a source of strength
　　to those who turn back the battle at
　　　the gate.

⁷And these also stagger from wine
　　and reel from beer:
Priests and prophets stagger from beer
　　and are befuddled with wine;
they reel from beer,
　　they stagger when seeing visions,
　　they stumble when rendering
　　　decisions.
⁸All the tables are covered with vomit
　　and there is not a spot without filth.

⁹"Who is it he is trying to teach?
　　To whom is he explaining his message?
To children weaned from their milk,
　　to those just taken from the breast?
¹⁰For it is:
　　Do this, do that,
　　a rule for this, a rule for that*ᵇ*;
　　a little here, a little there."

¹¹Very well then, with foreign lips and
　　　strange tongues
　　God will speak to this people,
¹²to whom he said,
　　"This is the resting place, let the
　　　weary rest";
and, "This is the place of repose"—
　　but they would not listen.
¹³So then, the word of the Lᴏʀᴅ to them
　　　will become:
　　Do this, do that,
　　a rule for this, a rule for that;
　　a little here, a little there—
so that as they go they will fall
　　　backward;

ᵃ 9 That is, wooden symbols of the goddess Asherah　　*ᵇ 10* Hebrew / *sav lasav sav lasav / kav lakav kav
lakav* (probably meaningless sounds mimicking the prophet's words); also in verse 13

they will be injured and snared and
captured.

¹⁴ Therefore hear the word of the LORD, you
scoffers
who rule this people in Jerusalem.
¹⁵ You boast, "We have entered into a
covenant with death,
with the realm of the dead we have
made an agreement.
When an overwhelming scourge
sweeps by,
it cannot touch us,
for we have made a lie our refuge
and falsehood^a our hiding place."

¹⁶ So this is what the Sovereign LORD says:

"See, I lay a stone in Zion, a tested stone,
a precious cornerstone for a sure
foundation;
the one who relies on it
will never be stricken with panic.
¹⁷ I will make justice the measuring line
and righteousness the plumb line;
hail will sweep away your refuge, the lie,
and water will overflow your hiding
place.
¹⁸ Your covenant with death will be
annulled;
your agreement with the realm of the
dead will not stand.
When the overwhelming scourge
sweeps by,
you will be beaten down by it.
¹⁹ As often as it comes it will carry you away;
morning after morning, by day and
by night,
it will sweep through."

The understanding of this message
will bring sheer terror.
²⁰ The bed is too short to stretch out on,
the blanket too narrow to wrap
around you.
²¹ The LORD will rise up as he did at Mount
Perazim,
he will rouse himself as in the Valley of
Gibeon —
to do his work, his strange work,
and perform his task, his alien task.
²² Now stop your mocking,
or your chains will become heavier;
the Lord, the LORD Almighty, has told me

of the destruction decreed against the
whole land.

²³ Listen and hear my voice;
pay attention and hear what I say.
²⁴ When a farmer plows for planting, does
he plow continually?
Does he keep on breaking up and
working the soil?
²⁵ When he has leveled the surface,
does he not sow caraway and scatter
cumin?
Does he not plant wheat in its place,^b
barley in its plot,^b
and spelt in its field?
²⁶ His God instructs him
and teaches him the right way.

²⁷ Caraway is not threshed with a sledge,
nor is the wheel of a cart rolled over
cumin;
caraway is beaten out with a rod,
and cumin with a stick.
²⁸ Grain must be ground to make bread;
so one does not go on threshing it
forever.
The wheels of a threshing cart may be
rolled over it,
but one does not use horses to grind
grain.
²⁹ All this also comes from the LORD
Almighty,
whose plan is wonderful,
whose wisdom is magnificent.

Woe to David's City

29 Woe to you, Ariel, Ariel,
the city where David settled!
Add year to year
and let your cycle of festivals go on.
² Yet I will besiege Ariel;
she will mourn and lament,
she will be to me like an altar hearth.^c
³ I will encamp against you on all sides;
I will encircle you with towers
and set up my siege works against you.
⁴ Brought low, you will speak from the
ground;
your speech will mumble out of the
dust.
Your voice will come ghostlike from the
earth;

---

^a 15 Or *false gods*   ^b 25 The meaning of the Hebrew for this word is uncertain.   ^c 2 The Hebrew for
altar hearth sounds like the Hebrew for *Ariel.*

out of the dust your speech will
 whisper.

⁵ But your many enemies will become like
 fine dust,
 the ruthless hordes like blown chaff.
 Suddenly, in an instant,
⁶   the LORD Almighty will come
with thunder and earthquake and great
 noise,
 with windstorm and tempest and
 flames of a devouring fire.
⁷ Then the hordes of all the nations that
 fight against Ariel,
 that attack her and her fortress and
 besiege her,
will be as it is with a dream,
 with a vision in the night —
⁸ as when a hungry person dreams of
 eating,
 but awakens hungry still;
as when a thirsty person dreams of
 drinking,
 but awakens faint and thirsty still.
So will it be with the hordes of all the
 nations
 that fight against Mount Zion.

⁹ Be stunned and amazed,
 blind yourselves and be sightless;
be drunk, but not from wine,
 stagger, but not from beer.
¹⁰ The LORD has brought over you a deep
 sleep:
 He has sealed your eyes (the prophets);
 he has covered your heads (the seers).

¹¹ For you this whole vision is nothing
but words sealed in a scroll. And if you give
the scroll to someone who can read, and
say, "Read this, please," they will answer, "I
can't; it is sealed." ¹² Or if you give the scroll
to someone who cannot read, and say, "Read
this, please," they will answer, "I don't know
how to read."

¹³ The Lord says:

"These people come near to me with
 their mouth
 and honor me with their lips,
 but their hearts are far from me.
Their worship of me
 is based on merely human rules they
 have been taught.ᵃ

¹⁴ Therefore once more I will astound these
 people
 with wonder upon wonder;
the wisdom of the wise will perish,
 the intelligence of the intelligent will
 vanish."
¹⁵ Woe to those who go to great depths
 to hide their plans from the LORD,
who do their work in darkness and think,
 "Who sees us? Who will know?"
¹⁶ You turn things upside down,
 as if the potter were thought to be like
 the clay!
Shall what is formed say to the one who
 formed it,
 "You did not make me"?
Can the pot say to the potter,
 "You know nothing"?

¹⁷ In a very short time, will not Lebanon be
 turned into a fertile field
 and the fertile field seem like a forest?
¹⁸ In that day the deaf will hear the words of
 the scroll,
 and out of gloom and darkness
 the eyes of the blind will see.
¹⁹ Once more the humble will rejoice in the
 LORD;
 the needy will rejoice in the Holy One
 of Israel.
²⁰ The ruthless will vanish,
 the mockers will disappear,
 and all who have an eye for evil will be
 cut down —
²¹ those who with a word make someone
 out to be guilty,
 who ensnare the defender in court
 and with false testimony deprive the
 innocent of justice.

²² Therefore this is what the LORD, who redeemed Abraham, says to the descendants
of Jacob:

"No longer will Jacob be ashamed;
 no longer will their faces grow pale.
²³ When they see among them their
 children,
 the work of my hands,
they will keep my name holy;
 they will acknowledge the holiness of
 the Holy One of Jacob,
 and will stand in awe of the God of
 Israel.

ᵃ 13 Hebrew; Septuagint *They worship me in vain; / their teachings are merely human rules*

ANYTHING BUT BORING

READ: ISAIAH 29:13

My greatest concern as a pastor is that people can go to church every week of their lives and never go all in with Jesus Christ. They'll follow the rules but never follow Christ. We've cheapened the gospel by allowing people to buy in without selling out (even though Jesus says to sell everything). We've made it way too convenient, and too comfortable. We've given people just enough Jesus to be bored but not enough to feel the surge of holy adrenaline that courses through your veins when you decide to follow him no matter what, no matter where, no matter when.

A guy from Denmark named Søren Kierkegaard believed that boredom was the root of all evil. In other words, boredom isn't just boring. It's wrong. You cannot be in the presence of God and be bored at the same time. You just can't be in the will of God and be bored at the same time. If you follow in the footsteps of Jesus, it will be anything but boring.

BUILDING FAITH WISDOM STRENGTH

When you look back on your life, the greatest moments will be the ones where you went all in. It's as true today as it was the day Abraham placed Isaac on the altar, the day Jonathan climbed a cliff to fight the Philistines, and the day Peter got out of the boat and walked on water.

Taken from *All In Student Edition* by Mark Batterson and Parker Batterson, copyright © 2014 by Mark Batterson, published by Zondervan.

²⁴ Those who are wayward in spirit will
gain understanding;
those who complain will accept
instruction."

Woe to the Obstinate Nation

30 "Woe to the obstinate children,"
declares the LORD,
"to those who carry out plans that are not
mine,
forming an alliance, but not by my
Spirit,
heaping sin upon sin;
² who go down to Egypt
without consulting me;
who look for help to Pharaoh's protection,
to Egypt's shade for refuge.
³ But Pharaoh's protection will be to your
shame,
Egypt's shade will bring you disgrace.
⁴ Though they have officials in Zoan
and their envoys have arrived in
Hanes,
⁵ everyone will be put to shame
because of a people useless to them,
who bring neither help nor advantage,
but only shame and disgrace."

⁶ A prophecy concerning the animals of
the Negev:

Through a land of hardship and distress,
of lions and lionesses,
of adders and darting snakes,
the envoys carry their riches on donkeys'
backs,
their treasures on the humps of
camels,
to that unprofitable nation,
⁷ to Egypt, whose help is utterly useless.
Therefore I call her
Rahab the Do-Nothing.

⁸ Go now, write it on a tablet for them,
inscribe it on a scroll,
that for the days to come
it may be an everlasting witness.
⁹ For these are rebellious people, deceitful
children,
children unwilling to listen to the
LORD's instruction.
¹⁰ They say to the seers,
"See no more visions!"
and to the prophets,
"Give us no more visions of what
is right!

Tell us pleasant things,
prophesy illusions.
¹¹ Leave this way,
get off this path,
and stop confronting us
with the Holy One of Israel!"

¹² Therefore this is what the Holy One of
Israel says:

"Because you have rejected this message,
relied on oppression
and depended on deceit,
¹³ this sin will become for you
like a high wall, cracked and bulging,
that collapses suddenly, in an instant.
¹⁴ It will break in pieces like pottery,
shattered so mercilessly
that among its pieces not a fragment will
be found
for taking coals from a hearth
or scooping water out of a cistern."

¹⁵ This is what the Sovereign LORD, the
Holy One of Israel, says:

"In repentance and rest is your salvation,
in quietness and trust is your strength,
but you would have none of it.
¹⁶ You said, 'No, we will flee on horses.'
Therefore you will flee!
You said, 'We will ride off on swift
horses.'
Therefore your pursuers will be swift!
¹⁷ A thousand will flee
at the threat of one;
at the threat of five
you will all flee away,
till you are left
like a flagstaff on a mountaintop,
like a banner on a hill."

¹⁸ Yet the LORD longs to be gracious to you;
therefore he will rise up to show you
compassion.
For the LORD is a God of justice.
Blessed are all who wait for him!

¹⁹ People of Zion, who live in Jerusalem,
you will weep no more. How gracious he
will be when you cry for help! As soon as he
hears, he will answer you. ²⁰ Although the
Lord gives you the bread of adversity and
the water of affliction, your teachers will be
hidden no more; with your own eyes you will
see them. ²¹ Whether you turn to the right or
to the left, your ears will hear a voice behind

you, saying, "This is the way; walk in it." [22] Then you will desecrate your idols overlaid with silver and your images covered with gold; you will throw them away like a menstrual cloth and say to them, "Away with you!"

[23] He will also send you rain for the seed you sow in the ground, and the food that comes from the land will be rich and plentiful. In that day your cattle will graze in broad meadows. [24] The oxen and donkeys that work the soil will eat fodder and mash, spread out with fork and shovel. [25] In the day of great slaughter, when the towers fall, streams of water will flow on every high mountain and every lofty hill. [26] The moon will shine like the sun, and the sunlight will be seven times brighter, like the light of seven full days, when the LORD binds up the bruises of his people and heals the wounds he inflicted.

[27] See, the Name of the LORD comes from afar,
  with burning anger and dense clouds of smoke;
his lips are full of wrath,
  and his tongue is a consuming fire.
[28] His breath is like a rushing torrent,
  rising up to the neck.
He shakes the nations in the sieve of destruction;
  he places in the jaws of the peoples
  a bit that leads them astray.
[29] And you will sing
  as on the night you celebrate a holy festival;
your hearts will rejoice
  as when people playing pipes go up
to the mountain of the LORD,
  to the Rock of Israel.
[30] The LORD will cause people to hear his majestic voice
  and will make them see his arm coming down
with raging anger and consuming fire,
  with cloudburst, thunderstorm and hail.
[31] The voice of the LORD will shatter Assyria;
  with his rod he will strike them down.
[32] Every stroke the LORD lays on them
  with his punishing club
will be to the music of timbrels and harps,

as he fights them in battle with the blows of his arm.
[33] Topheth has long been prepared;
  it has been made ready for the king.
Its fire pit has been made deep and wide,
  with an abundance of fire and wood;
the breath of the LORD,
  like a stream of burning sulfur,
  sets it ablaze.

Woe to Those Who Rely on Egypt

31 Woe to those who go down to Egypt for help,
  who rely on horses,
who trust in the multitude of their chariots
  and in the great strength of their horsemen,
but do not look to the Holy One of Israel,
  or seek help from the LORD.
[2] Yet he too is wise and can bring disaster;
  he does not take back his words.
He will rise up against that wicked nation,
  against those who help evildoers.
[3] But the Egyptians are mere mortals and not God;
  their horses are flesh and not spirit.
When the LORD stretches out his hand,
  those who help will stumble,
  those who are helped will fall;
  all will perish together.

[4] This is what the LORD says to me:

"As a lion growls,
  a great lion over its prey—
and though a whole band of shepherds
  is called together against it,
it is not frightened by their shouts
  or disturbed by their clamor—
so the LORD Almighty will come down
  to do battle on Mount Zion and on its heights.
[5] Like birds hovering overhead,
  the LORD Almighty will shield Jerusalem;
he will shield it and deliver it,
  he will 'pass over' it and will rescue it."

[6] Return, you Israelites, to the One you have so greatly revolted against. [7] For in that day every one of you will reject the idols of silver and gold your sinful hands have made.

8 "Assyria will fall by no human sword;
　　a sword, not of mortals, will devour
　　　them.
They will flee before the sword
　and their young men will be put to
　　　forced labor.
9 Their stronghold will fall because of terror;
　at the sight of the battle standard their
　　　commanders will panic,"
declares the Lord,
　whose fire is in Zion,
　whose furnace is in Jerusalem.

The Kingdom of Righteousness

32 See, a king will reign in righteousness
　and rulers will rule with justice.
2 Each one will be like a shelter from
　　　the wind
　and a refuge from the storm,
like streams of water in the desert
　and the shadow of a great rock in a
　　　thirsty land.

3 Then the eyes of those who see will no
　　　longer be closed,
　and the ears of those who hear will
　　　listen.
4 The fearful heart will know and
　　　understand,
　and the stammering tongue will be
　　　fluent and clear.
5 No longer will the fool be called noble
　nor the scoundrel be highly respected.
6 For fools speak folly,
　　their hearts are bent on evil:
They practice ungodliness
　and spread error concerning the Lord;
the hungry they leave empty
　and from the thirsty they withhold
　　　water.
7 Scoundrels use wicked methods,
　they make up evil schemes
to destroy the poor with lies,
　even when the plea of the needy is just.
8 But the noble make noble plans,
　and by noble deeds they stand.

The Women of Jerusalem

9 You women who are so complacent,
　rise up and listen to me;
you daughters who feel secure,
　hear what I have to say!
10 In little more than a year
　you who feel secure will tremble;

the grape harvest will fail,
　and the harvest of fruit will not come.
11 Tremble, you complacent women;
　shudder, you daughters who feel
　　　secure!
Strip off your fine clothes
　and wrap yourselves in rags.
12 Beat your breasts for the pleasant fields,
　for the fruitful vines
13 and for the land of my people,
　a land overgrown with thorns and
　　　briers —
yes, mourn for all houses of merriment
　and for this city of revelry.
14 The fortress will be abandoned,
　the noisy city deserted;
citadel and watchtower will become a
　　　wasteland forever,
　the delight of donkeys, a pasture for
　　　flocks,
15 till the Spirit is poured on us from
　　　on high,
　and the desert becomes a fertile field,
　and the fertile field seems like a forest.
16 The Lord's justice will dwell in the
　　　desert,
　his righteousness live in the fertile field.
17 The fruit of that righteousness will be
　　　peace;
　its effect will be quietness and
　　　confidence forever.
18 My people will live in peaceful dwelling
　　　places,
　in secure homes,
　in undisturbed places of rest.
19 Though hail flattens the forest
　and the city is leveled completely,
20 how blessed you will be,
　sowing your seed by every stream,
　and letting your cattle and donkeys
　　　range free.

Distress and Help

33 Woe to you, destroyer,
　you who have not been destroyed!
Woe to you, betrayer,
　you who have not been betrayed!
When you stop destroying,
　you will be destroyed;
when you stop betraying,
　you will be betrayed.

2 Lord, be gracious to us;
　we long for you.

Be our strength every morning,
    our salvation in time of distress.
³ At the uproar of your army, the peoples
    flee;
    when you rise up, the nations scatter.
⁴ Your plunder, O nations, is harvested as
    by young locusts;
    like a swarm of locusts people pounce
    on it.

⁵ The LORD is exalted, for he dwells
    on high;
    he will fill Zion with his justice and
    righteousness.
⁶ He will be the sure foundation for your
    times,
    a rich store of salvation and wisdom
    and knowledge;
    the fear of the LORD is the key to this
    treasure.ᵃ

⁷ Look, their brave men cry aloud in
    the streets;
    the envoys of peace weep bitterly.
⁸ The highways are deserted,
    no travelers are on the roads.
The treaty is broken,
    its witnessesᵇ are despised,
    no one is respected.
⁹ The land dries up and wastes away,
    Lebanon is ashamed and withers;
Sharon is like the Arabah,
    and Bashan and Carmel drop their
    leaves.

¹⁰ "Now will I arise," says the LORD.
    "Now will I be exalted;
    now will I be lifted up.
¹¹ You conceive chaff,
    you give birth to straw;
    your breath is a fire that consumes
    you.
¹² The peoples will be burned to ashes;
    like cut thornbushes they will be set
    ablaze."

¹³ You who are far away, hear what I have
    done;
    you who are near, acknowledge my
    power!
¹⁴ The sinners in Zion are terrified;
    trembling grips the godless:
"Who of us can dwell with the consuming
    fire?

Who of us can dwell with everlasting
    burning?"
¹⁵ Those who walk righteously
    and speak what is right,
who reject gain from extortion
    and keep their hands from accepting
    bribes,
who stop their ears against plots of
    murder
    and shut their eyes against
    contemplating evil—
¹⁶ they are the ones who will dwell on the
    heights,
    whose refuge will be the mountain
    fortress.
Their bread will be supplied,
    and water will not fail them.

¹⁷ Your eyes will see the king in his beauty
    and view a land that stretches afar.
¹⁸ In your thoughts you will ponder the
    former terror:
    "Where is that chief officer?
Where is the one who took the revenue?
    Where is the officer in charge of the
    towers?"
¹⁹ You will see those arrogant people no
    more,
    people whose speech is obscure,
    whose language is strange and
    incomprehensible.

²⁰ Look on Zion, the city of our festivals;
    your eyes will see Jerusalem,
    a peaceful abode, a tent that will not be
    moved;
    its stakes will never be pulled up,
    nor any of its ropes broken.
²¹ There the LORD will be our Mighty One.
    It will be like a place of broad rivers
    and streams.
No galley with oars will ride them,
    no mighty ship will sail them.
²² For the LORD is our judge,
    the LORD is our lawgiver,
the LORD is our king;
    it is he who will save us.

²³ Your rigging hangs loose:
    The mast is not held secure,
    the sail is not spread.
Then an abundance of spoils will be
    divided
    and even the lame will carry off
    plunder.

²⁴ No one living in Zion will say, "I am ill";
and the sins of those who dwell there
will be forgiven.

Judgment Against the Nations

34 Come near, you nations, and listen;
pay attention, you peoples!
Let the earth hear, and all that is in it,
the world, and all that comes out of it!
² The LORD is angry with all nations;
his wrath is on all their armies.
He will totally destroy[a] them,
he will give them over to slaughter.
³ Their slain will be thrown out,
their dead bodies will stink;
the mountains will be soaked with
their blood.
⁴ All the stars in the sky will be dissolved
and the heavens rolled up like a scroll;
all the starry host will fall
like withered leaves from the vine,
like shriveled figs from the fig tree.

⁵ My sword has drunk its fill in the
heavens;
see, it descends in judgment on Edom,
the people I have totally destroyed.
⁶ The sword of the LORD is bathed in blood,
it is covered with fat—
the blood of lambs and goats,
fat from the kidneys of rams.
For the LORD has a sacrifice in Bozrah
and a great slaughter in the land of
Edom.
⁷ And the wild oxen will fall with them,
the bull calves and the great bulls.
Their land will be drenched with blood,
and the dust will be soaked with fat.

⁸ For the LORD has a day of vengeance,
a year of retribution, to uphold Zion's
cause.
⁹ Edom's streams will be turned into pitch,
her dust into burning sulfur;
her land will become blazing pitch!
¹⁰ It will not be quenched night or day;
its smoke will rise forever.
From generation to generation it will lie
desolate;
no one will ever pass through it again.
¹¹ The desert owl[b] and screech owl[b] will
possess it;

the great owl[b] and the raven will nest
there.
God will stretch out over Edom
the measuring line of chaos
and the plumb line of desolation.
¹² Her nobles will have nothing there to be
called a kingdom,
all her princes will vanish away.
¹³ Thorns will overrun her citadels,
nettles and brambles her strongholds.
She will become a haunt for jackals,
a home for owls.
¹⁴ Desert creatures will meet with hyenas,
and wild goats will bleat to each other;
there the night creatures will also lie
down
and find for themselves places of rest.
¹⁵ The owl will nest there and lay eggs,
she will hatch them, and care for her
young
under the shadow of her wings;
there also the falcons will gather,
each with its mate.

¹⁶ Look in the scroll of the LORD and read:

None of these will be missing,
not one will lack her mate.
For it is his mouth that has given the
order,
and his Spirit will gather them
together.
¹⁷ He allots their portions;
his hand distributes them by measure.
They will possess it forever
and dwell there from generation to
generation.

Joy of the Redeemed

35 The desert and the parched land
will be glad;
the wilderness will rejoice and
blossom.
Like the crocus, ² it will burst into bloom;
it will rejoice greatly and shout for joy.
The glory of Lebanon will be given to it,
the splendor of Carmel and Sharon;
they will see the glory of the LORD,
the splendor of our God.

³ Strengthen the feeble hands,
steady the knees that give way;
⁴ say to those with fearful hearts,

---

a 2 The Hebrew term refers to the irrevocable giving over of things or persons to the LORD, often by totally
destroying them; also in verse 5.   *b 11* The precise identification of these birds is uncertain.

"Be strong, do not fear;
　your God will come,
　　he will come with vengeance;
　　with divine retribution
　　　he will come to save you."

⁵ Then will the eyes of the blind be opened
　and the ears of the deaf unstopped.
⁶ Then will the lame leap like a deer,
　and the mute tongue shout for joy.
Water will gush forth in the wilderness
　and streams in the desert.
⁷ The burning sand will become a pool,
　the thirsty ground bubbling springs.
In the haunts where jackals once lay,
　grass and reeds and papyrus will grow.

⁸ And a highway will be there;
　it will be called the Way of Holiness;
　it will be for those who walk on
　　that Way.
The unclean will not journey on it;
　wicked fools will not go about on it.
⁹ No lion will be there,
　nor any ravenous beast;
　they will not be found there.
But only the redeemed will walk there,
¹⁰ 　and those the LORD has rescued will
　　　return.
They will enter Zion with singing;
　everlasting joy will crown their heads.
Gladness and joy will overtake them,
　and sorrow and sighing will flee away.

Sennacherib Threatens Jerusalem

36 In the fourteenth year of King Hezekiah's reign, Sennacherib king of Assyria attacked all the fortified cities of Judah and captured them. ²Then the king of Assyria sent his field commander with a large army from Lachish to King Hezekiah at Jerusalem. When the commander stopped at the aqueduct of the Upper Pool, on the road to the Launderer's Field, ³Eliakim son of Hilkiah the palace administrator, Shebna the secretary, and Joah son of Asaph the recorder went out to him.

⁴The field commander said to them, "Tell Hezekiah:

"'This is what the great king, the king of Assyria, says: On what are you basing this confidence of yours? ⁵You say you have counsel and might for war—but you speak only empty words. On whom are you depending, that you rebel against me? ⁶Look, I know you are depending on Egypt, that splintered reed of a staff, which pierces the hand of anyone who leans on it! Such is Pharaoh king of Egypt to all who depend on him. ⁷But if you say to me, "We are depending on the LORD our God"— isn't he the one whose high places and altars Hezekiah removed, saying to Judah and Jerusalem, "You must worship before this altar"?

⁸"'Come now, make a bargain with my master, the king of Assyria: I will give you two thousand horses—if you can put riders on them! ⁹How then can you repulse one officer of the least of my master's officials, even though you are depending on Egypt for chariots and horsemen[a]? ¹⁰Furthermore, have I come to attack and destroy this land without the LORD? The LORD himself told me to march against this country and destroy it.'"

¹¹Then Eliakim, Shebna and Joah said to the field commander, "Please speak to your servants in Aramaic, since we understand it. Don't speak to us in Hebrew in the hearing of the people on the wall."

¹²But the commander replied, "Was it only to your master and you that my master sent me to say these things, and not to the people sitting on the wall—who, like you, will have to eat their own excrement and drink their own urine?"

¹³Then the commander stood and called out in Hebrew, "Hear the words of the great king, the king of Assyria! ¹⁴This is what the king says: Do not let Hezekiah deceive you. He cannot deliver you! ¹⁵Do not let Hezekiah persuade you to trust in the LORD when he says, 'The LORD will surely deliver us; this city will not be given into the hand of the king of Assyria.'

¹⁶"Do not listen to Hezekiah. This is what the king of Assyria says: Make peace with me and come out to me. Then each of you will eat fruit from your own vine and fig tree and drink water from your own cistern, ¹⁷until I come and take you to a land like your own— a land of grain and new wine, a land of bread and vineyards.

_____
ᵃ 9 Or *charioteers*

WALK THAT WAY

READ: ISAIAH 35:8

Holiness" is God's awesome trait that combines "separation" and "brightness" to describe his unique glory. His holiness means he's completely pure and without fault. This passage from the prophet Isaiah says the Lord has plans for you to trek along his holy highway.

Ancient peoples built vast transportation systems, including a quarter million miles of roadways crossing the Roman empire, but no one ever put down pavement across the shifting sands of vast deserts. God decides to change that. He promises to make the wilderness burst into bloom, with glory that causes it to shout for joy (Isaiah 35:1–2). He will transform burning sand into pools and let springs bubble up from thirsty ground (vv. 6–7).

Across this new landscape God lays down a "Way of Holiness." The path refers in part to the physical highways worshipers followed on their way to religious feasts at the temple in Jerusalem. God also had a broader idea in mind. For you to "walk on that Way" means you go around "doing holiness" and following God's path of right behavior.

Some people won't step foot on that path. But for you and God's people, "the redeemed," it's smooth pavement. When you walk today in the purity God intends for you, "sorrow and sighing will flee away," and "everlasting joy" will take you by surprise (v. 10). Others will chase down other paths, but this is the route you want to hike.

BUILDING

FAITH

WISDOM

STRENGTH

[18] "Do not let Hezekiah mislead you when he says, 'The LORD will deliver us.' Have the gods of any nations ever delivered their lands from the hand of the king of Assyria? [19] Where are the gods of Hamath and Arpad? Where are the gods of Sepharvaim? Have they rescued Samaria from my hand? [20] Who of all the gods of these countries have been able to save their lands from me? How then can the LORD deliver Jerusalem from my hand?"

[21] But the people remained silent and said nothing in reply, because the king had commanded, "Do not answer him."

[22] Then Eliakim son of Hilkiah the palace administrator, Shebna the secretary and Joah son of Asaph the recorder went to Hezekiah, with their clothes torn, and told him what the field commander had said.

Jerusalem's Deliverance Foretold

37 When King Hezekiah heard this, he tore his clothes and put on sackcloth and went into the temple of the LORD. [2] He sent Eliakim the palace administrator, Shebna the secretary, and the leading priests, all wearing sackcloth, to the prophet Isaiah son of Amoz. [3] They told him, "This is what Hezekiah says: This day is a day of distress and rebuke and disgrace, as when children come to the moment of birth and there is no strength to deliver them. [4] It may be that the LORD your God will hear the words of the field commander, whom his master, the king of Assyria, has sent to ridicule the living God, and that he will rebuke him for the words the LORD your God has heard. Therefore pray for the remnant that still survives."

[5] When King Hezekiah's officials came to Isaiah, [6] Isaiah said to them, "Tell your master, 'This is what the LORD says: Do not be afraid of what you have heard — those words with which the underlings of the king of Assyria have blasphemed me. [7] Listen! When he hears a certain report, I will make him want to return to his own country, and there I will have him cut down with the sword.' "

[8] When the field commander heard that the king of Assyria had left Lachish, he withdrew and found the king fighting against Libnah.

[9] Now Sennacherib received a report that Tirhakah, the king of Cush,[a] was marching out to fight against him. When he heard it, he sent messengers to Hezekiah with this word: [10] "Say to Hezekiah king of Judah: Do not let the god you depend on deceive you when he says, 'Jerusalem will not be given into the hands of the king of Assyria.' [11] Surely you have heard what the kings of Assyria have done to all the countries, destroying them completely. And will you be delivered? [12] Did the gods of the nations that were destroyed by my predecessors deliver them — the gods of Gozan, Harran, Rezeph and the people of Eden who were in Tel Assar? [13] Where is the king of Hamath or the king of Arpad? Where are the kings of Lair, Sepharvaim, Hena and Ivvah?"

Hezekiah's Prayer

[14] Hezekiah received the letter from the messengers and read it. Then he went up to the temple of the LORD and spread it out before the LORD. [15] And Hezekiah prayed to the LORD: [16] "LORD Almighty, the God of Israel, enthroned between the cherubim, you alone are God over all the kingdoms of the earth. You have made heaven and earth. [17] Give ear, LORD, and hear; open your eyes, LORD, and see; listen to all the words Sennacherib has sent to ridicule the living God.

[18] "It is true, LORD, that the Assyrian kings have laid waste all these peoples and their lands. [19] They have thrown their gods into the fire and destroyed them, for they were not gods but only wood and stone, fashioned by human hands. [20] Now, LORD our God, deliver us from his hand, so that all the kingdoms of the earth may know that you, LORD, are the only God.[b]"

Sennacherib's Fall

[21] Then Isaiah son of Amoz sent a message to Hezekiah: "This is what the LORD, the God of Israel, says: Because you have prayed to me concerning Sennacherib king of Assyria, [22] this is the word the LORD has spoken against him:

"Virgin Daughter Zion
    despises and mocks you.
Daughter Jerusalem
    tosses her head as you flee.

---

[a] 9 That is, the upper Nile region   [b] 20 Dead Sea Scrolls (see also 2 Kings 19:19); Masoretic Text *you alone are the LORD*

²³ Who is it you have ridiculed and
　　blasphemed?
　Against whom have you raised your
　　voice
　and lifted your eyes in pride?
　Against the Holy One of Israel!
²⁴ By your messengers
　you have ridiculed the Lord.
And you have said,
　'With my many chariots
　I have ascended the heights of the
　　mountains,
　the utmost heights of Lebanon.
I have cut down its tallest cedars,
　the choicest of its junipers.
I have reached its remotest heights,
　the finest of its forests.
²⁵ I have dug wells in foreign lands*ᵃ*
　and drunk the water there.
With the soles of my feet
　I have dried up all the streams of
　　Egypt.'
²⁶ "Have you not heard?
　Long ago I ordained it.
In days of old I planned it;
　now I have brought it to pass,
　that you have turned fortified cities
　　into piles of stone.
²⁷ Their people, drained of power,
　are dismayed and put to shame.
They are like plants in the field,
　like tender green shoots,
like grass sprouting on the roof,
　scorched*ᵇ* before it grows up.
²⁸ "But I know where you are
　and when you come and go
　and how you rage against me.
²⁹ Because you rage against me
　and because your insolence has
　　reached my ears,
I will put my hook in your nose
　and my bit in your mouth,
and I will make you return
　by the way you came.
³⁰ "This will be the sign for you, Hezekiah:

　"This year you will eat what grows by
　　itself,
　and the second year what springs
　　from that.

But in the third year sow and reap,
　plant vineyards and eat their fruit.
³¹ Once more a remnant of the kingdom of
　Judah
　will take root below and bear fruit
　　above.
³² For out of Jerusalem will come a
　remnant,
　and out of Mount Zion a band of
　　survivors.
The zeal of the LORD Almighty
　will accomplish this.

³³ "Therefore this is what the LORD says
concerning the king of Assyria:

　"He will not enter this city
　　or shoot an arrow here.
　He will not come before it with shield
　　or build a siege ramp against it.
³⁴ By the way that he came he will return;
　he will not enter this city,"
　　　　　　　　　　　　declares the LORD.
³⁵ "I will defend this city and save it,
　for my sake and for the sake of David
　　my servant!"

³⁶ Then the angel of the LORD went out and
put to death a hundred and eighty-five thousand in the Assyrian camp. When the people got up the next morning—there were all
the dead bodies! ³⁷ So Sennacherib king of
Assyria broke camp and withdrew. He returned to Nineveh and stayed there.

³⁸ One day, while he was worshiping in the
temple of his god Nisrok, his sons Adrammelek and Sharezer killed him with the sword,
and they escaped to the land of Ararat. And
Esarhaddon his son succeeded him as king.

Hezekiah's Illness

38 In those days Hezekiah became ill
and was at the point of death. The
prophet Isaiah son of Amoz went to him and
said, "This is what the LORD says: Put your
house in order, because you are going to die;
you will not recover." ² Hezekiah turned his face to the wall and
prayed to the LORD, ³ "Remember, LORD,
how I have walked before you faithfully and
with wholehearted devotion and have done
what is good in your eyes." And Hezekiah
wept bitterly.

ᵃ 25 Dead Sea Scrolls (see also 2 Kings 19:24); Masoretic Text does not have *in foreign lands.* *ᵇ 27* Some
manuscripts of the Masoretic Text, Dead Sea Scrolls and some Septuagint manuscripts (see also 2 Kings
19:26); most manuscripts of the Masoretic Text *roof / and terraced fields*

[4] Then the word of the LORD came to Isaiah: [5] "Go and tell Hezekiah, 'This is what the LORD, the God of your father David, says: I have heard your prayer and seen your tears; I will add fifteen years to your life. [6] And I will deliver you and this city from the hand of the king of Assyria. I will defend this city.

[7] "'This is the LORD's sign to you that the LORD will do what he has promised: [8] I will make the shadow cast by the sun go back the ten steps it has gone down on the stairway of Ahaz.' " So the sunlight went back the ten steps it had gone down.

[9] A writing of Hezekiah king of Judah after his illness and recovery:

[10] I said, "In the prime of my life
    must I go through the gates of death
    and be robbed of the rest of my years?"
[11] I said, "I will not again see the LORD
    himself
    in the land of the living;
no longer will I look on my fellow man,
    or be with those who now dwell in this
        world.
[12] Like a shepherd's tent my house
    has been pulled down and taken
        from me.
Like a weaver I have rolled up my life,
    and he has cut me off from the loom;
    day and night you made an end of me.
[13] I waited patiently till dawn,
    but like a lion he broke all my bones;
    day and night you made an end of me.
[14] I cried like a swift or thrush,
    I moaned like a mourning dove.
My eyes grew weak as I looked to the
        heavens.
    I am being threatened; Lord, come to
        my aid!"

[15] But what can I say?
    He has spoken to me, and he himself
        has done this.
I will walk humbly all my years
    because of this anguish of my soul.
[16] Lord, by such things people live;
    and my spirit finds life in them too.
You restored me to health
    and let me live.
[17] Surely it was for my benefit
    that I suffered such anguish.
In your love you kept me
    from the pit of destruction;

you have put all my sins
    behind your back.
[18] For the grave cannot praise you,
    death cannot sing your praise;
those who go down to the pit
    cannot hope for your faithfulness.
[19] The living, the living — they praise you,
    as I am doing today;
parents tell their children
    about your faithfulness.

[20] The LORD will save me,
    and we will sing with stringed
        instruments
all the days of our lives
    in the temple of the LORD.

[21] Isaiah had said, "Prepare a poultice of figs and apply it to the boil, and he will recover."

[22] Hezekiah had asked, "What will be the sign that I will go up to the temple of the LORD?"

Envoys From Babylon

39 At that time Marduk-Baladan son of Baladan king of Babylon sent Hezekiah letters and a gift, because he had heard of his illness and recovery. [2] Hezekiah received the envoys gladly and showed them what was in his storehouses — the silver, the gold, the spices, the fine olive oil — his entire armory and everything found among his treasures. There was nothing in his palace or in all his kingdom that Hezekiah did not show them.

[3] Then Isaiah the prophet went to King Hezekiah and asked, "What did those men say, and where did they come from?"

"From a distant land," Hezekiah replied. "They came to me from Babylon."

[4] The prophet asked, "What did they see in your palace?"

"They saw everything in my palace," Hezekiah said. "There is nothing among my treasures that I did not show them."

[5] Then Isaiah said to Hezekiah, "Hear the word of the LORD Almighty: [6] The time will surely come when everything in your palace, and all that your predecessors have stored up until this day, will be carried off to Babylon. Nothing will be left, says the LORD. [7] And some of your descendants, your own flesh and blood who will be born to you, will

be taken away, and they will become eunuchs in the palace of the king of Babylon."

⁸ "The word of the LORD you have spoken is good," Hezekiah replied. For he thought, "There will be peace and security in my lifetime."

Comfort for God's People

40 Comfort, comfort my people,
    says your God.
² Speak tenderly to Jerusalem,
    and proclaim to her
that her hard service has been
    completed,
    that her sin has been paid for,
that she has received from the LORD's
    hand
    double for all her sins.

³ A voice of one calling:
"In the wilderness prepare
    the way for the LORD*a*;
make straight in the desert
    a highway for our God.*b*
⁴ Every valley shall be raised up,
    every mountain and hill made low;
the rough ground shall become level,
    the rugged places a plain.
⁵ And the glory of the LORD will be
    revealed,
    and all people will see it together.
                For the mouth of the LORD
                        has spoken."

⁶ A voice says, "Cry out."
    And I said, "What shall I cry?"

"All people are like grass,
    and all their faithfulness is like the
        flowers of the field.
⁷ The grass withers and the flowers fall,
    because the breath of the LORD blows
        on them.
    Surely the people are grass.
⁸ The grass withers and the flowers fall,
    but the word of our God endures
        forever."

⁹ You who bring good news to Zion,
    go up on a high mountain.
You who bring good news to Jerusalem,*c*
    lift up your voice with a shout,
    lift it up, do not be afraid;

say to the towns of Judah,
    "Here is your God!"
¹⁰ See, the Sovereign LORD comes with
        power,
    and he rules with a mighty arm.
See, his reward is with him,
    and his recompense accompanies
        him.
¹¹ He tends his flock like a shepherd:
    He gathers the lambs in his arms
and carries them close to his heart;
    he gently leads those that have young.

¹² Who has measured the waters in the
        hollow of his hand,
    or with the breadth of his hand marked
        off the heavens?
Who has held the dust of the earth in a
        basket,
    or weighed the mountains on the
        scales
    and the hills in a balance?
¹³ Who can fathom the Spirit*d* of the LORD,
    or instruct the LORD as his counselor?
¹⁴ Whom did the LORD consult to enlighten
        him,
    and who taught him the right way?
Who was it that taught him knowledge,
    or showed him the path of
        understanding?

¹⁵ Surely the nations are like a drop in a
        bucket;
    they are regarded as dust on the scales;
    he weighs the islands as though they
        were fine dust.
¹⁶ Lebanon is not sufficient for altar fires,
    nor its animals enough for burnt
        offerings.
¹⁷ Before him all the nations are as nothing;
    they are regarded by him as worthless
        and less than nothing.

¹⁸ With whom, then, will you compare God?
    To what image will you liken him?
¹⁹ As for an idol, a metalworker casts it,
    and a goldsmith overlays it with gold
        and fashions silver chains for it.
²⁰ A person too poor to present such an
        offering
    selects wood that will not rot;
they look for a skilled worker
    to set up an idol that will not topple.

---

a 3 Or *A voice of one calling in the wilderness: / "Prepare the way for the LORD*   *b 3* Hebrew; Septuagint
make straight the paths of our God   *c 9* Or *Zion, bringer of good news, / go up on a high mountain. /*
Jerusalem, bringer of good news   *d 13* Or *mind*

²¹ Do you not know?
  Have you not heard?
Has it not been told you from the
    beginning?
  Have you not understood since the
    earth was founded?
²² He sits enthroned above the circle of the
    earth,
  and its people are like grasshoppers.
He stretches out the heavens like a
    canopy,
  and spreads them out like a tent to
    live in.
²³ He brings princes to naught
  and reduces the rulers of this world to
    nothing.
²⁴ No sooner are they planted,
  no sooner are they sown,
  no sooner do they take root in the
    ground,
than he blows on them and they wither,
  and a whirlwind sweeps them away
    like chaff.

²⁵ "To whom will you compare me?
  Or who is my equal?" says the Holy One.
²⁶ Lift up your eyes and look to the heavens:
  Who created all these?
He who brings out the starry host one
    by one
  and calls forth each of them by
    name.
Because of his great power and mighty
    strength,
  not one of them is missing.

²⁷ Why do you complain, Jacob?
  Why do you say, Israel,
"My way is hidden from the LORD;
  my cause is disregarded by my God"?
²⁸ Do you not know?
  Have you not heard?
The LORD is the everlasting God,
  the Creator of the ends of the earth.
He will not grow tired or weary,
  and his understanding no one can
    fathom.
²⁹ He gives strength to the weary
  and increases the power of the weak.
³⁰ Even youths grow tired and weary,
  and young men stumble and fall;
³¹ but those who hope in the LORD
  will renew their strength.

They will soar on wings like eagles;
  they will run and not grow weary,
  they will walk and not be faint.

The Helper of Israel

41 "Be silent before me, you islands!
  Let the nations renew their strength!
Let them come forward and speak;
  let us meet together at the place of
    judgment.

² "Who has stirred up one from the east,
  calling him in righteousness to his
    service*ᵃ*?
He hands nations over to him
  and subdues kings before him.
He turns them to dust with his sword,
  to windblown chaff with his bow.
³ He pursues them and moves on
    unscathed,
  by a path his feet have not traveled
    before.
⁴ Who has done this and carried it
    through,
  calling forth the generations from the
    beginning?
I, the LORD — with the first of them
  and with the last — I am he."

⁵ The islands have seen it and fear;
  the ends of the earth tremble.
They approach and come forward;
⁶   they help each other
  and say to their companions, "Be
    strong!"
⁷ The metalworker encourages the
    goldsmith,
  and the one who smooths with the
    hammer
  spurs on the one who strikes the anvil.
One says of the welding, "It is good."
  The other nails down the idol so it will
    not topple.

⁸ "But you, Israel, my servant,
  Jacob, whom I have chosen,
  you descendants of Abraham my
    friend,
⁹ I took you from the ends of the earth,
  from its farthest corners I called you.
I said, 'You are my servant';
  I have chosen you and have not
    rejected you.

ᵃ 2 Or east, / whom victory meets at every step

¹⁰ So do not fear, for I am with you;
    do not be dismayed, for I am your God.
I will strengthen you and help you;
    I will uphold you with my righteous
      right hand.

¹¹ "All who rage against you
    will surely be ashamed and disgraced;
those who oppose you
    will be as nothing and perish.
¹² Though you search for your enemies,
    you will not find them.
Those who wage war against you
    will be as nothing at all.
¹³ For I am the LORD your God
    who takes hold of your right hand
and says to you, Do not fear;
    I will help you.
¹⁴ Do not be afraid, you worm Jacob,
    little Israel, do not fear,
for I myself will help you," declares the
    LORD,
    your Redeemer, the Holy One of Israel.
¹⁵ "See, I will make you into a threshing
    sledge,
    new and sharp, with many teeth.
You will thresh the mountains and crush
    them,
    and reduce the hills to chaff.
¹⁶ You will winnow them, the wind will pick
    them up,
    and a gale will blow them away.
But you will rejoice in the LORD
    and glory in the Holy One of Israel.

¹⁷ "The poor and needy search for water,
    but there is none;
    their tongues are parched with thirst.
But I the LORD will answer them;
    I, the God of Israel, will not forsake
     them.
¹⁸ I will make rivers flow on barren heights,
    and springs within the valleys.
I will turn the desert into pools of water,
    and the parched ground into springs.
¹⁹ I will put in the desert
    the cedar and the acacia, the myrtle
     and the olive.
I will set junipers in the wasteland,
    the fir and the cypress together,
²⁰ so that people may see and know,
    may consider and understand,
that the hand of the LORD has done this,
    that the Holy One of Israel has
     created it.

²¹ "Present your case," says the LORD.
    "Set forth your arguments," says
     Jacob's King.
²² "Tell us, you idols,
    what is going to happen.
Tell us what the former things were,
    so that we may consider them
    and know their final outcome.
Or declare to us the things to come,
²³   tell us what the future holds,
    so we may know that you are gods.
Do something, whether good or bad,
    so that we will be dismayed and filled
     with fear.
²⁴ But you are less than nothing
    and your works are utterly worthless;
    whoever chooses you is detestable.

²⁵ "I have stirred up one from the north, and
    he comes —
    one from the rising sun who calls on
     my name.
He treads on rulers as if they were
    mortar,
    as if he were a potter treading the clay.
²⁶ Who told of this from the beginning, so
    we could know,
    or beforehand, so we could say, 'He
     was right'?
No one told of this,
    no one foretold it,
    no one heard any words from you.
²⁷ I was the first to tell Zion, 'Look, here
    they are!'
    I gave to Jerusalem a messenger of
     good news.
²⁸ I look but there is no one —
    no one among the gods to give counsel,
    no one to give answer when I ask them.
²⁹ See, they are all false!
    Their deeds amount to nothing;
    their images are but wind and
     confusion.

The Servant of the Lord

42   "Here is my servant, whom I uphold,
    my chosen one in whom I delight;
I will put my Spirit on him,
    and he will bring justice to the nations.
² He will not shout or cry out,
    or raise his voice in the streets.
³ A bruised reed he will not break,
    and a smoldering wick he will not
     snuff out.

PREDICTIONS ABOUT JESUS

READ: ISAIAH 42:1

I f the Bible could do a dramatic drum roll, it would start in Isaiah 42. It's the beginning of several impressive revelations of a unique servant of God. These intriguing passages point to Jesus hundreds of years before he arrives on earth. Four "servant songs" describe this servant in Isaiah 42:1-9, 49:1-7, 50:4-9, and 52:13-53:12. The first introduces the Lord's chosen servant. Some of the descriptions you read there could apply to any representative of God, including the prophet Isaiah.

Other points appear to describe God's plan to show off his glory through the nation of Israel. But as you read these words it's hard not to see a picture of Jesus. God promises to put his Spirit on this servant, a pledge that comes true in Matthew 3:16-17 when the Spirit floats down like a dove and lands on Jesus. God says his servant will be his new "covenant" or "agreement" (Isaiah 42:6) with everyone on earth, a claim Jesus made about himself in Luke 22:20 and fulfilled when he died on the cross for the sins of every human being.

As you read these servant songs throughout the next dozen chapters of Isaiah, you'll get to know a deep side of Jesus. He's someone you can't help but like. He's a hero who inspires your total admiration. He's a Savior absolutely worth following.

BUILDING

FAITH

WISDOM

STRENGTH

In faithfulness he will bring forth justice;
4   he will not falter or be discouraged
till he establishes justice on earth.
    In his teaching the islands will put
        their hope."

5 This is what God the LORD says—
the Creator of the heavens, who stretches
        them out,
    who spreads out the earth with all that
        springs from it,
    who gives breath to its people,
    and life to those who walk on it:
6 "I, the LORD, have called you in
        righteousness;
    I will take hold of your hand.
I will keep you and will make you
    to be a covenant for the people
    and a light for the Gentiles,
7 to open eyes that are blind,
    to free captives from prison
    and to release from the dungeon those
        who sit in darkness.

8 "I am the LORD; that is my name!
    I will not yield my glory to another
    or my praise to idols.
9 See, the former things have taken place,
    and new things I declare;
before they spring into being
    I announce them to you."

Song of Praise to the Lord

10 Sing to the LORD a new song,
    his praise from the ends of the earth,
you who go down to the sea, and all that
        is in it,
    you islands, and all who live in them.
11 Let the wilderness and its towns raise
        their voices;
    let the settlements where Kedar lives
        rejoice.
Let the people of Sela sing for joy;
    let them shout from the mountaintops.
12 Let them give glory to the LORD
    and proclaim his praise in the islands.
13 The LORD will march out like a
        champion,
    like a warrior he will stir up his zeal;
with a shout he will raise the battle cry
    and will triumph over his enemies.

14 "For a long time I have kept silent,
    I have been quiet and held myself back.
But now, like a woman in childbirth,
    I cry out, I gasp and pant.

15 I will lay waste the mountains and hills
    and dry up all their vegetation;
I will turn rivers into islands
    and dry up the pools.
16 I will lead the blind by ways they have not
        known,
    along unfamiliar paths I will guide
        them;
I will turn the darkness into light before
        them
    and make the rough places smooth.
These are the things I will do;
    I will not forsake them.
17 But those who trust in idols,
    who say to images, 'You are our gods,'
    will be turned back in utter shame.

Israel Blind and Deaf

18 "Hear, you deaf;
    look, you blind, and see!
19 Who is blind but my servant,
    and deaf like the messenger I send?
Who is blind like the one in covenant
        with me,
    blind like the servant of the LORD?
20 You have seen many things, but you pay
        no attention;
    your ears are open, but you do not
        listen."
21 It pleased the LORD
    for the sake of his righteousness
    to make his law great and glorious.
22 But this is a people plundered and looted,
    all of them trapped in pits
    or hidden away in prisons.
They have become plunder,
    with no one to rescue them;
they have been made loot,
    with no one to say, "Send them back."

23 Which of you will listen to this
    or pay close attention in time to come?
24 Who handed Jacob over to become loot,
    and Israel to the plunderers?
Was it not the LORD,
    against whom we have sinned?
For they would not follow his ways;
    they did not obey his law.
25 So he poured out on them his burning
        anger,
    the violence of war.
It enveloped them in flames, yet they did
        not understand;
    it consumed them, but they did not
        take it to heart.

Israel's Only Savior

43 But now, this is what the LORD
says—
he who created you, Jacob,
he who formed you, Israel:
"Do not fear, for I have redeemed you;
I have summoned you by name; you
are mine.
² When you pass through the waters,
I will be with you;
and when you pass through the rivers,
they will not sweep over you.
When you walk through the fire,
you will not be burned;
the flames will not set you ablaze.
³ For I am the LORD your God,
the Holy One of Israel, your Savior;
I give Egypt for your ransom,
Cush[a] and Seba in your stead.
⁴ Since you are precious and honored in
my sight,
and because I love you,
I will give people in exchange for you,
nations in exchange for your life.
⁵ Do not be afraid, for I am with you;
I will bring your children from the east
and gather you from the west.
⁶ I will say to the north, 'Give them up!'
and to the south, 'Do not hold them
back.'
Bring my sons from afar
and my daughters from the ends of the
earth—
⁷ everyone who is called by my name,
whom I created for my glory,
whom I formed and made."

⁸ Lead out those who have eyes but are
blind,
who have ears but are deaf.
⁹ All the nations gather together
and the peoples assemble.
Which of their gods foretold this
and proclaimed to us the former
things?
Let them bring in their witnesses to prove
they were right,
so that others may hear and say, "It is
true."
¹⁰ "You are my witnesses," declares the LORD,
"and my servant whom I have chosen,
so that you may know and believe me
and understand that I am he.

Before me no god was formed,
nor will there be one after me.
¹¹ I, even I, am the LORD,
and apart from me there is no savior.
¹² I have revealed and saved and
proclaimed—
I, and not some foreign god among you.
You are my witnesses," declares the
LORD, "that I am God.
¹³   Yes, and from ancient days I am he.
No one can deliver out of my hand.
When I act, who can reverse it?"

God's Mercy and Israel's Unfaithfulness

¹⁴ This is what the LORD says—
your Redeemer, the Holy One of Israel:
"For your sake I will send to Babylon
and bring down as fugitives all the
Babylonians,[b]
in the ships in which they took pride.
¹⁵ I am the LORD, your Holy One,
Israel's Creator, your King."

¹⁶ This is what the LORD says—
he who made a way through the sea,
a path through the mighty waters,
¹⁷ who drew out the chariots and horses,
the army and reinforcements together,
and they lay there, never to rise again,
extinguished, snuffed out like a wick:
¹⁸ "Forget the former things;
do not dwell on the past.
¹⁹ See, I am doing a new thing!
Now it springs up; do you not
perceive it?
I am making a way in the wilderness
and streams in the wasteland.
²⁰ The wild animals honor me,
the jackals and the owls,
because I provide water in the wilderness
and streams in the wasteland,
to give drink to my people, my chosen,
²¹   the people I formed for myself
that they may proclaim my praise.

²² "Yet you have not called on me, Jacob,
you have not wearied yourselves for[c]
me, Israel.
²³ You have not brought me sheep for burnt
offerings,
nor honored me with your sacrifices.
I have not burdened you with grain
offerings

---

[a] 3 That is, the upper Nile region   [b] 14 Or *Chaldeans*   [c] 22 Or *Jacob; / surely you have grown weary of*

nor wearied you with demands for
incense.
24 You have not bought any fragrant
calamus for me,
or lavished on me the fat of your
sacrifices.
But you have burdened me with your sins
and wearied me with your offenses.

25 "I, even I, am he who blots out
your transgressions, for my own
sake,
and remembers your sins no more.
26 Review the past for me,
let us argue the matter together;
state the case for your innocence.
27 Your first father sinned;
those I sent to teach you rebelled
against me.
28 So I disgraced the dignitaries of your
temple;
I consigned Jacob to destruction*a*
and Israel to scorn.

Israel the Chosen

44 "But now listen, Jacob, my servant,
Israel, whom I have chosen.
2 This is what the LORD says —
he who made you, who formed you in
the womb,
and who will help you:
Do not be afraid, Jacob, my servant,
Jeshurun,*b* whom I have chosen.
3 For I will pour water on the thirsty land,
and streams on the dry ground;
I will pour out my Spirit on your
offspring,
and my blessing on your descendants.
4 They will spring up like grass in a
meadow,
like poplar trees by flowing streams.
5 Some will say, 'I belong to the LORD';
others will call themselves by the
name of Jacob;
still others will write on their hand, 'The
LORD's,'
and will take the name Israel.

The Lord, Not Idols

6 "This is what the LORD says —
Israel's King and Redeemer, the LORD
Almighty:

I am the first and I am the last;
apart from me there is no God.
7 Who then is like me? Let him proclaim it.
Let him declare and lay out before me
what has happened since I established
my ancient people,
and what is yet to come —
yes, let them foretell what will come.
8 Do not tremble, do not be afraid.
Did I not proclaim this and foretell it
long ago?
You are my witnesses. Is there any God
besides me?
No, there is no other Rock; I know
not one."

9 All who make idols are nothing,
and the things they treasure are
worthless.
Those who would speak up for them are
blind;
they are ignorant, to their own shame.
10 Who shapes a god and casts an idol,
which can profit nothing?
11 People who do that will be put to shame;
such craftsmen are only human
beings.
Let them all come together and take their
stand;
they will be brought down to terror
and shame.

12 The blacksmith takes a tool
and works with it in the coals;
he shapes an idol with hammers,
he forges it with the might of his arm.
He gets hungry and loses his strength;
he drinks no water and grows faint.
13 The carpenter measures with a line
and makes an outline with a
marker;
he roughs it out with chisels
and marks it with compasses.
He shapes it in human form,
human form in all its glory,
that it may dwell in a shrine.
14 He cut down cedars,
or perhaps took a cypress or oak.
He let it grow among the trees of the
forest,
or planted a pine, and the rain made
it grow.

---

a 28 The Hebrew term refers to the irrevocable giving over of things or persons to the LORD, often by
totally destroying them.   *b* 2 *Jeshurun* means *the upright one,* that is, Israel.

OUT TO SEA

READ: ISAIAH 43:25

God says he drops our sins into his sea of forgetfulness. No one else forgets our sin. A sea of forgetfulness doesn't make sense when everyone else is ready to throw us into a mud puddle of remembrance. The world continually reminds us of our failure and rubs our noses in it. Sometimes we believers struggle on that sea, riding its swells and billows to the point of sickness as we base our worth and identity on worldly pursuits and opinions.

The most liberating truth in all of Scripture is that we are liberated. God is not a God bound by human logic. God is not like our teacher, friend, or significant other. When God says he forgives us, he is speaking the truth because he is truth (1 Thessalonians 2:13; Titus 1:2). When God says he forgives, he isn't talking about a sappy, sentimental moment in which we talked him into being good to us. He is referring to a decision he makes to extend grace to an undeserving person.

BUILDING FAITH WISDOM STRENGTH

He did this by killing his Son. This is a blunt statement, but it's true. John 3:16 states that God gave his Son. At the same time, Jesus, who is God, laid down his life (John 10:17–18). Why? So he could offer us the truth of 2 Corinthians 5:21: "God made him who had no sin to be sin for us, so that in him we might become the righteousness of God." Jesus became sin for us. Gnaw on that one. That's how serious God is about forgiveness.

¹⁵ It is used as fuel for burning;
  some of it he takes and warms himself,
  he kindles a fire and bakes bread.
But he also fashions a god and
    worships it;
  he makes an idol and bows down to it.
¹⁶ Half of the wood he burns in the fire;
  over it he prepares his meal,
  he roasts his meat and eats his fill.
He also warms himself and says,
  "Ah! I am warm; I see the fire."
¹⁷ From the rest he makes a god, his idol;
  he bows down to it and worships.
He prays to it and says,
  "Save me! You are my god!"
¹⁸ They know nothing, they understand
    nothing;
  their eyes are plastered over so they
    cannot see,
  and their minds closed so they cannot
    understand.
¹⁹ No one stops to think,
  no one has the knowledge or
    understanding to say,
"Half of it I used for fuel;
  I even baked bread over its coals,
  I roasted meat and I ate.
Shall I make a detestable thing from what
    is left?
  Shall I bow down to a block of wood?"
²⁰ Such a person feeds on ashes; a deluded
    heart misleads him;
  he cannot save himself, or say,
  "Is not this thing in my right hand a
    lie?"

²¹ "Remember these things, Jacob,
  for you, Israel, are my servant.
I have made you, you are my servant;
  Israel, I will not forget you.
²² I have swept away your offenses like a
    cloud,
  your sins like the morning mist.
Return to me,
  for I have redeemed you."

²³ Sing for joy, you heavens, for the LORD
    has done this;
  shout aloud, you earth beneath.
Burst into song, you mountains,
  you forests and all your trees,
for the LORD has redeemed Jacob,
  he displays his glory in Israel.

Jerusalem to Be Inhabited

²⁴ "This is what the LORD says —
  your Redeemer, who formed you in the
    womb:

I am the LORD,
  the Maker of all things,
  who stretches out the heavens,
  who spreads out the earth by myself,
²⁵ who foils the signs of false prophets
  and makes fools of diviners,
who overthrows the learning of the wise
  and turns it into nonsense,
²⁶ who carries out the words of his servants
  and fulfills the predictions of his
    messengers,

who says of Jerusalem, 'It shall be
    inhabited,'
  of the towns of Judah, 'They shall be
    rebuilt,'
  and of their ruins, 'I will restore them,'
²⁷ who says to the watery deep, 'Be dry,
  and I will dry up your streams,'
²⁸ who says of Cyrus, 'He is my shepherd
  and will accomplish all that I please;
he will say of Jerusalem, "Let it be
    rebuilt,"
  and of the temple, "Let its foundations
    be laid." '

45 "This is what the LORD says to his
      anointed,
  to Cyrus, whose right hand I take
    hold of
to subdue nations before him
  and to strip kings of their armor,
to open doors before him
  so that gates will not be shut:
² I will go before you
  and will level the mountains*;
I will break down gates of bronze
  and cut through bars of iron.
³ I will give you hidden treasures,
  riches stored in secret places,
so that you may know that I am the LORD,
  the God of Israel, who summons you
    by name.
⁴ For the sake of Jacob my servant,
  of Israel my chosen,
I summon you by name
  and bestow on you a title of honor,
  though you do not acknowledge me.

---

a 2 Dead Sea Scrolls and Septuagint; the meaning of the word in the Masoretic Text is uncertain.

ACT LIKE IT

READ: ISAIAH 44:21-23

I have to use the eyes of Jesus when I look at my past. I have to accept that his Word says my past is paid for and my slate is wiped clean. Jesus took my sin and spread it as far as the east is from the west. It's gone.

But . . .

But I can't act like it didn't happen. Instead of my past—even as recent as yesterday—haunting me and dragging me back into it, I can use it. If I see my past through the eyes of Jesus, then I see it as fodder for another soul.

Your scars are your road map to God's grace in your life. If we act like we have it all together, not only is it untrue, but everyone sees through the façade as well. Phony never led anyone to Jesus. If we would see some of the bad choices we've made as a way to point other people to Jesus, we would allow Jesus to go Romans 8:28 on our past and turn it into good. Some people believe their past is so bad that not even God can redeem it, but God said he makes all things new (Revelation 21:5).

When you seek see your past in a different light, it doesn't scare you anymore. You don't worry about people discovering your skeletons. You don't freak out about your weaknesses anymore because you see that the Bible is full of fools, outlaws, and ordinary people. God used them, and his Word will convince you that he'll use you too.

BUILDING
FAITH
WISDOM
STRENGTH

⁵ I am the LORD, and there is no other;
  apart from me there is no God.
I will strengthen you,
  though you have not acknowledged me,
⁶ so that from the rising of the sun
  to the place of its setting
people may know there is none
      besides me.
  I am the LORD, and there is no other.
⁷ I form the light and create darkness,
  I bring prosperity and create disaster;
  I, the LORD, do all these things.

⁸ "You heavens above, rain down my
      righteousness;
  let the clouds shower it down.
Let the earth open wide,
  let salvation spring up,
let righteousness flourish with it;
  I, the LORD, have created it.

⁹ "Woe to those who quarrel with their
      Maker,
  those who are nothing but potsherds
  among the potsherds on the ground.
Does the clay say to the potter,
  'What are you making?'
Does your work say,
  'The potter has no hands'?
¹⁰ Woe to the one who says to a father,
  'What have you begotten?'
or to a mother,
  'What have you brought to birth?'

¹¹ "This is what the LORD says —
  the Holy One of Israel, and its Maker:
Concerning things to come,
  do you question me about my children,
  or give me orders about the work of
      my hands?
¹² It is I who made the earth
  and created mankind on it.
My own hands stretched out the heavens;
  I marshaled their starry hosts.
¹³ I will raise up Cyrus[a] in my
      righteousness:
  I will make all his ways straight.
He will rebuild my city
  and set my exiles free,
but not for a price or reward,
  says the LORD Almighty."

¹⁴ This is what the LORD says:

"The products of Egypt and the
      merchandise of Cush,[b]

and those tall Sabeans —
they will come over to you
  and will be yours;
they will trudge behind you,
  coming over to you in chains.
They will bow down before you
  and plead with you, saying,
'Surely God is with you, and there is no
      other;
  there is no other god.' "

¹⁵ Truly you are a God who has been hiding
      himself,
  the God and Savior of Israel.
¹⁶ All the makers of idols will be put to
      shame and disgraced;
  they will go off into disgrace together.
¹⁷ But Israel will be saved by the LORD
  with an everlasting salvation;
you will never be put to shame or
      disgraced,
  to ages everlasting.

¹⁸ For this is what the LORD says —
he who created the heavens,
  he is God;
he who fashioned and made the earth,
  he founded it;
he did not create it to be empty,
  but formed it to be inhabited —
he says:
"I am the LORD,
  and there is no other.
¹⁹ I have not spoken in secret,
  from somewhere in a land of darkness;
I have not said to Jacob's descendants,
  'Seek me in vain.'
I, the LORD, speak the truth;
  I declare what is right.

²⁰ "Gather together and come;
  assemble, you fugitives from the
      nations.
Ignorant are those who carry about idols
      of wood,
  who pray to gods that cannot save.
²¹ Declare what is to be, present it —
  let them take counsel together.
Who foretold this long ago,
  who declared it from the distant past?
Was it not I, the LORD?
  And there is no God apart from me,
a righteous God and a Savior;
  there is none but me.

---

a 13 Hebrew *him*   *b 14* That is, the upper Nile region

²² "Turn to me and be saved,
  all you ends of the earth;
  for I am God, and there is no other.
²³ By myself I have sworn,
  my mouth has uttered in all integrity
  a word that will not be revoked:
Before me every knee will bow;
  by me every tongue will swear.
²⁴ They will say of me, 'In the LORD alone
  are deliverance and strength.' "
All who have raged against him
  will come to him and be put to shame.
²⁵ But all the descendants of Israel
  will find deliverance in the LORD
  and will make their boast in him.

Gods of Babylon

46 Bel bows down, Nebo stoops low;
  their idols are borne by beasts of
  burden.ᵃ
The images that are carried about are
  burdensome,
  a burden for the weary.
² They stoop and bow down together;
  unable to rescue the burden,
  they themselves go off into captivity.

³ "Listen to me, you descendants of Jacob,
  all the remnant of the people of Israel,
you whom I have upheld since your birth,
  and have carried since you were born.
⁴ Even to your old age and gray hairs
  I am he, I am he who will sustain you.
I have made you and I will carry you;
  I will sustain you and I will rescue you.

⁵ "With whom will you compare me or
  count me equal?
To whom will you liken me that we
  may be compared?
⁶ Some pour out gold from their bags
  and weigh out silver on the scales;
they hire a goldsmith to make it into
  a god,
  and they bow down and worship it.
⁷ They lift it to their shoulders and carry it;
  they set it up in its place, and there it
  stands.
From that spot it cannot move.
Even though someone cries out to it, it
  cannot answer;
  it cannot save them from their
  troubles.

⁸ "Remember this, keep it in mind,
  take it to heart, you rebels.
⁹ Remember the former things, those of
  long ago;
I am God, and there is no other;
  I am God, and there is none like me.
¹⁰ I make known the end from the
  beginning,
  from ancient times, what is still to come.
I say, 'My purpose will stand,
  and I will do all that I please.'
¹¹ From the east I summon a bird of prey;
  from a far-off land, a man to fulfill my
  purpose.
What I have said, that I will bring about;
  what I have planned, that I will do.
¹² Listen to me, you stubborn-hearted,
  you who are now far from my
  righteousness.
¹³ I am bringing my righteousness near,
  it is not far away;
  and my salvation will not be delayed.
I will grant salvation to Zion,
  my splendor to Israel.

The Fall of Babylon

47 "Go down, sit in the dust,
  Virgin Daughter Babylon;
sit on the ground without a throne,
  queen city of the Babylonians.ᵇ
No more will you be called
  tender or delicate.
² Take millstones and grind flour;
  take off your veil.
Lift up your skirts, bare your legs,
  and wade through the streams.
³ Your nakedness will be exposed
  and your shame uncovered.
I will take vengeance;
  I will spare no one."

⁴ Our Redeemer — the LORD Almighty is
  his name —
  is the Holy One of Israel.

⁵ "Sit in silence, go into darkness,
  queen city of the Babylonians;
no more will you be called
  queen of kingdoms.
⁶ I was angry with my people
  and desecrated my inheritance;
I gave them into your hand,
  and you showed them no mercy.

ᵃ 1 Or *are but beasts and cattle*   ᵇ 1 Or *Chaldeans*; also in verse 5

Even on the aged
  you laid a very heavy yoke.
[7] You said, 'I am forever—
    the eternal queen!'
But you did not consider these things
  or reflect on what might happen.

[8] "Now then, listen, you lover of pleasure,
    lounging in your security
and saying to yourself,
    'I am, and there is none besides me.
I will never be a widow
    or suffer the loss of children.'
[9] Both of these will overtake you
    in a moment, on a single day:
    loss of children and widowhood.
They will come upon you in full measure,
    in spite of your many sorceries
    and all your potent spells.

[10] You have trusted in your wickedness
    and have said, 'No one sees me.'
Your wisdom and knowledge mislead you
    when you say to yourself,
    'I am, and there is none besides me.'
[11] Disaster will come upon you,
    and you will not know how to conjure
      it away.
A calamity will fall upon you
    that you cannot ward off with a
      ransom;
a catastrophe you cannot foresee
    will suddenly come upon you.

[12] "Keep on, then, with your magic spells
    and with your many sorceries,
    which you have labored at since
      childhood.
Perhaps you will succeed,
    perhaps you will cause terror.
[13] All the counsel you have received has
      only worn you out!
Let your astrologers come forward,
    those stargazers who make predictions
      month by month,
    let them save you from what is coming
      upon you.
[14] Surely they are like stubble;
    the fire will burn them up.
They cannot even save themselves
    from the power of the flame.
These are not coals for warmth;
    this is not a fire to sit by.
[15] That is all they are to you—
    these you have dealt with
    and labored with since childhood.

All of them go on in their error;
  there is not one that can save you.

Stubborn Israel

48 "Listen to this, you descendants
      of Jacob,
    you who are called by the name of
      Israel
and come from the line of Judah,
    you who take oaths in the name of the
      LORD
and invoke the God of Israel—
    but not in truth or righteousness—
[2] you who call yourselves citizens of the
      holy city
    and claim to rely on the God of Israel—
    the LORD Almighty is his name:
[3] I foretold the former things long ago,
    my mouth announced them and I
      made them known;
    then suddenly I acted, and they came
      to pass.
[4] For I knew how stubborn you were;
    your neck muscles were iron,
    your forehead was bronze.
[5] Therefore I told you these things long ago;
    before they happened I announced
      them to you
so that you could not say,
    'My images brought them about;
    my wooden image and metal god
      ordained them.'
[6] You have heard these things; look at
      them all.
    Will you not admit them?

"From now on I will tell you of new
      things,
    of hidden things unknown to you.
[7] They are created now, and not long ago;
    you have not heard of them before
      today.
So you cannot say,
    'Yes, I knew of them.'
[8] You have neither heard nor understood;
    from of old your ears have not been
      open.
Well do I know how treacherous you are;
    you were called a rebel from birth.
[9] For my own name's sake I delay my
      wrath;
    for the sake of my praise I hold it back
      from you,
    so as not to destroy you completely.

STUBBORNNESS WORKS HOW?

READ: ISAIAH 48:4

Y ou might hit the gym to get muscles as solid as iron. Think of the boards you could break with a forehead as hard as bronze. But that kind of toughness is out of line when it comes to you getting along with God. The book of Isaiah communicates blunt warnings from the Lord mixed with assurances of his nonstop care for his people. In Isaiah 48 the Lord blasts their stubborn resistance to him.

God notes that his people happily use his name to pray and make solemn pledges. They're glad to call themselves citizens of Jerusalem, and they claim they rely on him. But when the people see their world shake, they interpret it as proof of their false gods' power, giving credit to their wooden and metal idols. That's why the Lord calls them stubborn. He vows to announce his mighty acts ahead of time so that no one doubts they come from him.

BUILDING FAITH WISDOM STRENGTH

The Lord doesn't stop with those warnings. He goes on to remind Israel of his tenderness, and in Isaiah 49:1–7 a "servant song" divulges more about his plan to send a messenger to show off his splendor and make the whole world bow.

There's always a better choice than stubbornness. If you pay attention to him and keep his commands, his peace will refresh you like a river rushing through a desert (48:18).

¹⁰ See, I have refined you, though not as
silver;
I have tested you in the furnace of
affliction.
¹¹ For my own sake, for my own sake, I do
this.
How can I let myself be defamed?
I will not yield my glory to another.

Israel Freed

¹² "Listen to me, Jacob,
Israel, whom I have called:
I am he;
I am the first and I am the last.
¹³ My own hand laid the foundations of the
earth,
and my right hand spread out the
heavens;
when I summon them,
they all stand up together.

¹⁴ "Come together, all of you, and listen:
Which of the idols has foretold these
things?
The LORD's chosen ally
will carry out his purpose against
Babylon;
his arm will be against the
Babylonians.ᵃ
¹⁵ I, even I, have spoken;
yes, I have called him.
I will bring him,
and he will succeed in his mission.

¹⁶ "Come near me and listen to this:

"From the first announcement I have not
spoken in secret;
at the time it happens, I am there."

And now the Sovereign LORD has sent me,
endowed with his Spirit.

¹⁷ This is what the LORD says—
your Redeemer, the Holy One of Israel:
"I am the LORD your God,
who teaches you what is best for you,
who directs you in the way you
should go.
¹⁸ If only you had paid attention to my
commands,
your peace would have been like a
river,
your well-being like the waves of
the sea.

¹⁹ Your descendants would have been like
the sand,
your children like its numberless
grains;
their name would never be blotted out
nor destroyed from before me."

²⁰ Leave Babylon,
flee from the Babylonians!
Announce this with shouts of joy
and proclaim it.
Send it out to the ends of the earth;
say, "The LORD has redeemed his
servant Jacob."
²¹ They did not thirst when he led them
through the deserts;
he made water flow for them from the
rock;
he split the rock
and water gushed out.

²² "There is no peace," says the LORD, "for
the wicked."

The Servant of the Lord

49 Listen to me, you islands;
hear this, you distant nations:
Before I was born the LORD called me;
from my mother's womb he has spoken
my name.
² He made my mouth like a sharpened
sword,
in the shadow of his hand he hid me;
he made me into a polished arrow
and concealed me in his quiver.
³ He said to me, "You are my servant,
Israel, in whom I will display my
splendor."
⁴ But I said, "I have labored in vain;
I have spent my strength for nothing
at all.
Yet what is due me is in the LORD's hand,
and my reward is with my God."

⁵ And now the LORD says—
he who formed me in the womb to be
his servant
to bring Jacob back to him
and gather Israel to himself,
for I amᵇ honored in the eyes of the LORD
and my God has been my strength—
⁶ he says:
"It is too small a thing for you to be my
servant

ᵃ 14 Or *Chaldeans*; also in verse 20   ᵇ 5 Or *him, / but Israel would not be gathered; / yet I will be*

to restore the tribes of Jacob
and bring back those of Israel I have
kept.
I will also make you a light for the
Gentiles,
that my salvation may reach to the
ends of the earth."

⁷ This is what the LORD says—
the Redeemer and Holy One of Israel—
to him who was despised and abhorred
by the nation,
to the servant of rulers:
"Kings will see you and stand up,
princes will see and bow down,
because of the LORD, who is faithful,
the Holy One of Israel, who has
chosen you."

Restoration of Israel

⁸ This is what the LORD says:

"In the time of my favor I will answer you,
and in the day of salvation I will help
you;
I will keep you and will make you
to be a covenant for the people,
to restore the land
and to reassign its desolate
inheritances,
⁹ to say to the captives, 'Come out,'
and to those in darkness, 'Be free!'

"They will feed beside the roads
and find pasture on every barren hill.
¹⁰ They will neither hunger nor thirst,
nor will the desert heat or the sun beat
down on them.
He who has compassion on them will
guide them
and lead them beside springs of water.
¹¹ I will turn all my mountains into roads,
and my highways will be raised up.
¹² See, they will come from afar—
some from the north, some from
the west,
some from the region of Aswan.ᵃ"

¹³ Shout for joy, you heavens;
rejoice, you earth;
burst into song, you mountains!
For the LORD comforts his people
and will have compassion on his
afflicted ones.

¹⁴ But Zion said, "The LORD has
forsaken me,
the Lord has forgotten me."

¹⁵ "Can a mother forget the baby at her
breast
and have no compassion on the child
she has borne?
Though she may forget,
I will not forget you!
¹⁶ See, I have engraved you on the palms of
my hands;
your walls are ever before me.
¹⁷ Your children hasten back,
and those who laid you waste depart
from you.
¹⁸ Lift up your eyes and look around;
all your children gather and come
to you.
As surely as I live," declares the LORD,
"you will wear them all as ornaments;
you will put them on, like a bride.

¹⁹ "Though you were ruined and made
desolate
and your land laid waste,
now you will be too small for your people,
and those who devoured you will be
far away.
²⁰ The children born during your
bereavement
will yet say in your hearing,
'This place is too small for us;
give us more space to live in.'
²¹ Then you will say in your heart,
'Who bore me these?
I was bereaved and barren;
I was exiled and rejected.
Who brought these up?
I was left all alone,
but these—where have they come
from?'"

²² This is what the Sovereign LORD says:

"See, I will beckon to the nations,
I will lift up my banner to the peoples;
they will bring your sons in their arms
and carry your daughters on their hips.
²³ Kings will be your foster fathers,
and their queens your nursing
mothers.
They will bow down before you with their
faces to the ground;
they will lick the dust at your feet.

ᵃ 12 Dead Sea Scrolls; Masoretic Text *Sinim*

Then you will know that I am the LORD;
those who hope in me will not be
disappointed."

24 Can plunder be taken from warriors,
or captives be rescued from the
fierce*a*?

25 But this is what the LORD says:

"Yes, captives will be taken from
warriors,
and plunder retrieved from the fierce;
I will contend with those who contend
with you,
and your children I will save.
26 I will make your oppressors eat their
own flesh;
they will be drunk on their own blood,
as with wine.
Then all mankind will know
that I, the LORD, am your Savior,
your Redeemer, the Mighty One of
Jacob."

Israel's Sin and the Servant's Obedience

50 This is what the LORD says:

"Where is your mother's certificate of
divorce
with which I sent her away?
Or to which of my creditors
did I sell you?
Because of your sins you were sold;
because of your transgressions your
mother was sent away.
2 When I came, why was there no one?
When I called, why was there no one to
answer?
Was my arm too short to deliver you?
Do I lack the strength to rescue you?
By a mere rebuke I dry up the sea,
I turn rivers into a desert;
their fish rot for lack of water
and die of thirst.
3 I clothe the heavens with darkness
and make sackcloth its covering."

4 The Sovereign LORD has given me a well-
instructed tongue,
to know the word that sustains the
weary.
He wakens me morning by morning,

wakens my ear to listen like one being
instructed.
5 The Sovereign LORD has opened my ears;
I have not been rebellious,
I have not turned away.
6 I offered my back to those who beat me,
my cheeks to those who pulled out my
beard;
I did not hide my face
from mocking and spitting.
7 Because the Sovereign LORD helps me,
I will not be disgraced.
Therefore have I set my face like flint,
and I know I will not be put to shame.
8 He who vindicates me is near.
Who then will bring charges
against me?
Let us face each other!
Who is my accuser?
Let him confront me!
9 It is the Sovereign LORD who helps me.
Who will condemn me?
They will all wear out like a garment;
the moths will eat them up.

10 Who among you fears the LORD
and obeys the word of his servant?
Let the one who walks in the dark,
who has no light,
trust in the name of the LORD
and rely on their God.
11 But now, all you who light fires
and provide yourselves with flaming
torches,
go, walk in the light of your fires
and of the torches you have set ablaze.
This is what you shall receive from my
hand:
You will lie down in torment.

Everlasting Salvation for Zion

51 "Listen to me, you who pursue
righteousness
and who seek the LORD:
Look to the rock from which you were cut
and to the quarry from which you were
hewn;
2 look to Abraham, your father,
and to Sarah, who gave you birth.
When I called him he was only one man,
and I blessed him and made him
many.
3 The LORD will surely comfort Zion

---

a 24 Dead Sea Scrolls, Vulgate and Syriac (see also Septuagint and verse 25); Masoretic Text *righteous*

and will look with compassion on all
her ruins;
he will make her deserts like Eden,
her wastelands like the garden of the
LORD.
Joy and gladness will be found in her,
thanksgiving and the sound of singing.

⁴ "Listen to me, my people;
hear me, my nation:
Instruction will go out from me;
my justice will become a light to
the nations.
⁵ My righteousness draws near speedily,
my salvation is on the way,
and my arm will bring justice to the
nations.
The islands will look to me
and wait in hope for my arm.
⁶ Lift up your eyes to the heavens,
look at the earth beneath;
the heavens will vanish like smoke,
the earth will wear out like a garment
and its inhabitants die like flies.
But my salvation will last forever,
my righteousness will never fail.

⁷ "Hear me, you who know what is right,
you people who have taken my
instruction to heart:
Do not fear the reproach of mere mortals
or be terrified by their insults.
⁸ For the moth will eat them up like a
garment;
the worm will devour them like wool.
But my righteousness will last forever,
my salvation through all generations."

⁹ Awake, awake, arm of the LORD,
clothe yourself with strength!
Awake, as in days gone by,
as in generations of old.
Was it not you who cut Rahab to pieces,
who pierced that monster through?
¹⁰ Was it not you who dried up the sea,
the waters of the great deep,
who made a road in the depths of the sea
so that the redeemed might cross
over?
¹¹ Those the LORD has rescued will return.
They will enter Zion with singing;
everlasting joy will crown their heads.
Gladness and joy will overtake them,
and sorrow and sighing will flee away.

¹² "I, even I, am he who comforts you.
Who are you that you fear mere
mortals,
human beings who are but grass,
¹³ that you forget the LORD your Maker,
who stretches out the heavens
and who lays the foundations of the
earth,
that you live in constant terror every day
because of the wrath of the oppressor,
who is bent on destruction?
For where is the wrath of the oppressor?
¹⁴   The cowering prisoners will soon be
set free;
they will not die in their dungeon,
nor will they lack bread.
¹⁵ For I am the LORD your God,
who stirs up the sea so that its waves
roar —
the LORD Almighty is his name.
¹⁶ I have put my words in your mouth
and covered you with the shadow of
my hand —
I who set the heavens in place,
who laid the foundations of the earth,
and who say to Zion, 'You are my
people.' "

The Cup of the Lord's Wrath

¹⁷ Awake, awake!
Rise up, Jerusalem,
you who have drunk from the hand of the
LORD
the cup of his wrath,
you who have drained to its dregs
the goblet that makes people stagger.
¹⁸ Among all the children she bore
there was none to guide her;
among all the children she reared
there was none to take her by the hand.
¹⁹ These double calamities have come
upon you —
who can comfort you? —
ruin and destruction, famine and
sword —
who can*ᵃ* console you?
²⁰ Your children have fainted;
they lie at every street corner,
like antelope caught in a net.
They are filled with the wrath of the
LORD,
with the rebuke of your God.

ᵃ 19 Dead Sea Scrolls, Septuagint, Vulgate and Syriac; Masoretic Text / *how can I*

²¹ Therefore hear this, you afflicted one,
  made drunk, but not with wine.
²² This is what your Sovereign LORD says,
  your God, who defends his people:
  "See, I have taken out of your hand
    the cup that made you stagger;
  from that cup, the goblet of my wrath,
    you will never drink again.
²³ I will put it into the hands of your
    tormentors,
  who said to you,
    'Fall prostrate that we may walk on you.'
  And you made your back like the ground,
    like a street to be walked on."

52 Awake, awake, Zion,
    clothe yourself with strength!
  Put on your garments of splendor,
    Jerusalem, the holy city.
  The uncircumcised and defiled
    will not enter you again.
² Shake off your dust;
  rise up, sit enthroned, Jerusalem.
  Free yourself from the chains on your
    neck,
  Daughter Zion, now a captive.

³ For this is what the LORD says:

  "You were sold for nothing,
    and without money you will be
    redeemed."

⁴ For this is what the Sovereign LORD says:

  "At first my people went down to Egypt
    to live;
    lately, Assyria has oppressed them.

⁵ "And now what do I have here?" declares
the LORD.

  "For my people have been taken away for
    nothing,
    and those who rule them mock,ᵃ"
                          declares the LORD.
  "And all day long
    my name is constantly blasphemed.
⁶ Therefore my people will know my name;
    therefore in that day they will know
    that it is I who foretold it.
    Yes, it is I."

⁷ How beautiful on the mountains
  are the feet of those who bring good
    news,

who proclaim peace,
  who bring good tidings,
  who proclaim salvation,
who say to Zion,
  "Your God reigns!"
⁸ Listen! Your watchmen lift up their voices;
  together they shout for joy.
When the LORD returns to Zion,
  they will see it with their own eyes.
⁹ Burst into songs of joy together,
  you ruins of Jerusalem,
for the LORD has comforted his people,
  he has redeemed Jerusalem.
¹⁰ The LORD will lay bare his holy arm
  in the sight of all the nations,
and all the ends of the earth will see
  the salvation of our God.

¹¹ Depart, depart, go out from there!
  Touch no unclean thing!
Come out from it and be pure,
  you who carry the articles of the
    LORD's house.
¹² But you will not leave in haste
  or go in flight;
for the LORD will go before you,
  the God of Israel will be your rear
    guard.

The Suffering and Glory of the Servant

¹³ See, my servant will act wiselyᵇ;
  he will be raised and lifted up and
    highly exalted.
¹⁴ Just as there were many who were
    appalled at himᶜ—
  his appearance was so disfigured
    beyond that of any human being
  and his form marred beyond human
    likeness—
¹⁵ so he will sprinkle many nations,ᵈ
  and kings will shut their mouths
    because of him.
For what they were not told, they will see,
  and what they have not heard, they
    will understand.

53 Who has believed our message
    and to whom has the arm of the
    LORD been revealed?
² He grew up before him like a tender
    shoot,
  and like a root out of dry ground.

ᵃ 5 Dead Sea Scrolls and Vulgate; Masoretic Text *wail*   ᵇ 13 Or *will prosper*   ᶜ 14 Hebrew *you*
ᵈ 15 Or *so will many nations be amazed at him* (see also Septuagint)

SEEING INTO THE FUTURE

READ: ISAIAH 53:5

I f you snip Isaiah 52:13–53:12 from your Bible, place it in front of an assortment of people, and ask them whom the passage is about, many will say "Jesus." Yet these Old Testament words were spoken hundreds of years before he came on the scene. Amazing!

This passage is the last of four "servant songs" in Isaiah, although other sections in the book also point to Christ. Isaiah 7:14 predicts that a virgin will give birth to a son called "God with us" (Matthew 1:23). Isaiah 61:1–2 records the striking words quoted by Jesus in his hometown near the start of his ministry (Luke 4:14-21). This passage gives deep insights into Jesus' death on the cross.

Isaiah foretells some of the details of that death, like the fact that the Lord's servant will be beaten to the point of being disfigured (Isaiah 52:14, Matthew 27:30) and that he will suffer without complaint (Isaiah 53:7, Mark 14:61). Even more important, it explains what the servant will accomplish on the cross. His body is pierced for our sins. God lets him suffer for our rebellion. His punishment brings us peace.

BUILDING
FAITH
WISDOM
STRENGTH

Jesus's death wasn't just another bloody execution inflicted by a potent ancient empire. When he went to the cross, he carried out God's own plan, paying the penalty for the world's sins. Do you believe he died for you?

He had no beauty or majesty to attract us
to him,
nothing in his appearance that we
should desire him.
[3] He was despised and rejected by
mankind,
a man of suffering, and familiar with
pain.
Like one from whom people hide their
faces
he was despised, and we held him in
low esteem.

[4] Surely he took up our pain
and bore our suffering,
yet we considered him punished by God,
stricken by him, and afflicted.
[5] But he was pierced for our transgressions,
he was crushed for our iniquities;
the punishment that brought us peace
was on him,
and by his wounds we are healed.
[6] We all, like sheep, have gone astray,
each of us has turned to our own way;
and the LORD has laid on him
the iniquity of us all.

[7] He was oppressed and afflicted,
yet he did not open his mouth;
he was led like a lamb to the slaughter,
and as a sheep before its shearers is
silent,
so he did not open his mouth.
[8] By oppression[a] and judgment he was
taken away.
Yet who of his generation protested?
For he was cut off from the land of the
living;
for the transgression of my people he
was punished.[b]
[9] He was assigned a grave with the wicked,
and with the rich in his death,
though he had done no violence,
nor was any deceit in his mouth.

[10] Yet it was the LORD's will to crush him
and cause him to suffer,
and though the LORD makes[c] his life
an offering for sin,
he will see his offspring and prolong his
days,

and the will of the LORD will prosper in
his hand.
[11] After he has suffered,
he will see the light of life[d] and be
satisfied[e];
by his knowledge[f] my righteous servant
will justify many,
and he will bear their iniquities.
[12] Therefore I will give him a portion among
the great,[g]
and he will divide the spoils with the
strong,[h]
because he poured out his life unto
death,
and was numbered with the
transgressors.
For he bore the sin of many,
and made intercession for the
transgressors.

The Future Glory of Zion

54 "Sing, barren woman,
you who never bore a child;
burst into song, shout for joy,
you who were never in labor;
because more are the children of the
desolate woman
than of her who has a husband,"
says the LORD.
[2] "Enlarge the place of your tent,
stretch your tent curtains wide,
do not hold back;
lengthen your cords,
strengthen your stakes.
[3] For you will spread out to the right and to
the left;
your descendants will dispossess
nations
and settle in their desolate cities.

[4] "Do not be afraid; you will not be put to
shame.
Do not fear disgrace; you will not be
humiliated.
You will forget the shame of your youth
and remember no more the reproach
of your widowhood.
[5] For your Maker is your husband—
the LORD Almighty is his name—

---

[a] 8 Or *From arrest*   [b] 8 Or *generation considered / that he was cut off from the land of the living, / that he
was punished for the transgression of my people?*   [c] 10 Hebrew *though you make*   [d] 11 Dead Sea
Scrolls (see also Septuagint); Masoretic Text does not have *the light of life.*   [e] 11 Or (with Masoretic Text)
[11]*He will see the fruit of his suffering / and will be satisfied*   [f] 11 Or *by knowledge of him*   [g] 12 Or *many*
[h] 12 Or *numerous*

the Holy One of Israel is your Redeemer;
he is called the God of all the
earth.
⁶ The LORD will call you back
as if you were a wife deserted and
distressed in spirit —
a wife who married young,
only to be rejected," says your God.
⁷ "For a brief moment I abandoned you,
but with deep compassion I will bring
you back.
⁸ In a surge of anger
I hid my face from you for a moment,
but with everlasting kindness
I will have compassion on you,"
says the LORD your Redeemer.

⁹ "To me this is like the days of Noah,
when I swore that the waters of Noah
would never again cover the
earth.
So now I have sworn not to be angry
with you,
never to rebuke you again.
¹⁰ Though the mountains be shaken
and the hills be removed,
yet my unfailing love for you will not be
shaken
nor my covenant of peace be
removed,"
says the LORD, who has compassion
on you.

¹¹ "Afflicted city, lashed by storms and not
comforted,
I will rebuild you with stones of
turquoise,ᵃ
your foundations with lapis lazuli.
¹² I will make your battlements of rubies,
your gates of sparkling jewels,
and all your walls of precious stones.
¹³ All your children will be taught by the
LORD,
and great will be their peace.
¹⁴ In righteousness you will be established:
Tyranny will be far from you;
you will have nothing to fear.
Terror will be far removed;
it will not come near you.
¹⁵ If anyone does attack you, it will not be
my doing;
whoever attacks you will surrender
to you.

¹⁶ "See, it is I who created the blacksmith
who fans the coals into flame
and forges a weapon fit for its work.
And it is I who have created the destroyer
to wreak havoc;
¹⁷   no weapon forged against you will
prevail,
and you will refute every tongue that
accuses you.
This is the heritage of the servants of the
LORD,
and this is their vindication from me,"
declares the LORD.

Invitation to the Thirsty

55 "Come, all you who are thirsty,
come to the waters;
and you who have no money,
come, buy and eat!
Come, buy wine and milk
without money and without cost.
² Why spend money on what is not bread,
and your labor on what does not
satisfy?
Listen, listen to me, and eat what is good,
and you will delight in the richest
of fare.
³ Give ear and come to me;
listen, that you may live.
I will make an everlasting covenant
with you,
my faithful love promised to David.
⁴ See, I have made him a witness to the
peoples,
a ruler and commander of the peoples.
⁵ Surely you will summon nations you
know not,
and nations you do not know will come
running to you,
because of the LORD your God,
the Holy One of Israel,
for he has endowed you with
splendor."

⁶ Seek the LORD while he may be found;
call on him while he is near.
⁷ Let the wicked forsake their ways
and the unrighteous their thoughts.
Let them turn to the LORD, and he will
have mercy on them,
and to our God, for he will freely
pardon.

ᵃ 11 The meaning of the Hebrew for this word is uncertain.

8 "For my thoughts are not your thoughts,
    neither are your ways my ways,"
                    declares the LORD.
9 "As the heavens are higher than
        the earth,
    so are my ways higher than your ways
    and my thoughts than your thoughts.
10 As the rain and the snow
        come down from heaven,
    and do not return to it
        without watering the earth
    and making it bud and flourish,
        so that it yields seed for the sower and
            bread for the eater,
11 so is my word that goes out from my
        mouth:
    It will not return to me empty,
    but will accomplish what I desire
        and achieve the purpose for which
            I sent it.
12 You will go out in joy
        and be led forth in peace;
    the mountains and hills
        will burst into song before you,
    and all the trees of the field
        will clap their hands.
13 Instead of the thornbush will grow the
        juniper,
    and instead of briers the myrtle will
        grow.
    This will be for the LORD's renown,
        for an everlasting sign,
        that will endure forever."

Salvation for Others

56 This is what the LORD says:

"Maintain justice
    and do what is right,
    for my salvation is close at hand
        and my righteousness will soon be
            revealed.
2 Blessed is the one who does this—
        the person who holds it fast,
    who keeps the Sabbath without
        desecrating it,
    and keeps their hands from doing any
        evil."

3 Let no foreigner who is bound to the
        LORD say,
    "The LORD will surely exclude me from
        his people."
    And let no eunuch complain,
        "I am only a dry tree."

4 For this is what the LORD says:

"To the eunuchs who keep my
        Sabbaths,
    who choose what pleases me
    and hold fast to my covenant—
5 to them I will give within my temple
        and its walls
    a memorial and a name
    better than sons and daughters;
    I will give them an everlasting name
        that will endure forever.
6 And foreigners who bind themselves
        to the LORD
    to minister to him,
    to love the name of the LORD,
        and to be his servants,
    all who keep the Sabbath without
        desecrating it
    and who hold fast to my covenant—
7 these I will bring to my holy mountain
        and give them joy in my house of
            prayer.
    Their burnt offerings and sacrifices
        will be accepted on my altar;
    for my house will be called
        a house of prayer for all nations."
8 The Sovereign LORD declares—
        he who gathers the exiles of Israel:
    "I will gather still others to them
        besides those already gathered."

God's Accusation Against
the Wicked

9 Come, all you beasts of the field,
        come and devour, all you beasts of
            the forest!
10 Israel's watchmen are blind,
        they all lack knowledge;
    they are all mute dogs,
        they cannot bark;
    they lie around and dream,
        they love to sleep.
11 They are dogs with mighty appetites;
        they never have enough.
    They are shepherds who lack
        understanding;
    they all turn to their own way,
        they seek their own gain.
12 "Come," each one cries, "let me get
        wine!
    Let us drink our fill of beer!
    And tomorrow will be like today,
        or even far better."

LIGHT YEARS' DIFFERENCE

READ: ISAIAH 55:8-11

While God's power is technically measureless, the prophet Isaiah gives us a glimpse of God's omnipotence by comparing it to the size of the universe. The distance between his wisdom and ours, his power and ours, is likened to the distance from one side of the universe to the other.

The universe is larger than we can imagine, but let me try to put it into perspective. The basic unit of measurement is a light-year. Light travels at 186,000 miles per second, which is so fast that in the time it takes to snap your fingers, light circles the globe half a dozen times. (You just snapped your fingers, didn't you?) The sun is 94.4 million miles away from the earth at its farthest distance from us. If you could drive to the sun traveling 65 miles per hour, 24 hours a day, 365 days a year, it would take you more than 163 years to get there. The light that warms your face on a sunny day, on the other hand, left the surface of the sun only 8 minutes ago. So while 94.4 million miles may seem like a long distance by earthly standards, it's our next-door neighbor by astronomical measurements.

BUILDING FAITH WISDOM STRENGTH

The outer edge of the universe, according to astrophysicists, is 15.5 billion light-years away! It's virtually unimaginable. Yet God says that this is the distance between his thoughts and our thoughts. So here's my thought: Your best thought on your best day falls 15.5 billion light-years short of how great and how good God really is.

57

The righteous perish,
  and no one takes it to heart;
the devout are taken away,
  and no one understands
that the righteous are taken away
  to be spared from evil.
² Those who walk uprightly
  enter into peace;
  they find rest as they lie in death.

³ "But you — come here, you children of a
    sorceress,
  you offspring of adulterers and
    prostitutes!
⁴ Who are you mocking?
  At whom do you sneer
    and stick out your tongue?
Are you not a brood of rebels,
  the offspring of liars?
⁵ You burn with lust among the oaks
  and under every spreading tree;
you sacrifice your children in the
    ravines
  and under the overhanging crags.
⁶ The idols among the smooth stones of the
    ravines are your portion;
  indeed, they are your lot.
Yes, to them you have poured out drink
    offerings
  and offered grain offerings.
  In view of all this, should I relent?
⁷ You have made your bed on a high and
    lofty hill;
  there you went up to offer your
    sacrifices.
⁸ Behind your doors and your doorposts
  you have put your pagan symbols.
Forsaking me, you uncovered your bed,
  you climbed into it and opened it wide;
you made a pact with those whose beds
    you love,
  and you looked with lust on their
    naked bodies.
⁹ You went to Molek*ᵃ* with olive oil
  and increased your perfumes.
You sent your ambassadors*ᵇ* far away;
  you descended to the very realm of
    the dead!
¹⁰ You wearied yourself by such going
    about,
  but you would not say, 'It is hopeless.'
You found renewal of your strength,
  and so you did not faint.

¹¹ "Whom have you so dreaded and feared
  that you have not been true to me,
and have neither remembered me
  nor taken this to heart?
Is it not because I have long been silent
  that you do not fear me?
¹² I will expose your righteousness and
    your works,
  and they will not benefit you.
¹³ When you cry out for help,
  let your collection of idols save you!
The wind will carry all of them off,
  a mere breath will blow them away.
But whoever takes refuge in me
  will inherit the land
  and possess my holy mountain."

Comfort for the Contrite

¹⁴ And it will be said:

"Build up, build up, prepare the road!
  Remove the obstacles out of the way of
    my people."
¹⁵ For this is what the high and exalted
    One says —
  he who lives forever, whose name is
    holy:
"I live in a high and holy place,
  but also with the one who is contrite
    and lowly in spirit,
to revive the spirit of the lowly
  and to revive the heart of the contrite.
¹⁶ I will not accuse them forever,
  nor will I always be angry,
for then they would faint away because
    of me —
  the very people I have created.
¹⁷ I was enraged by their sinful greed;
  I punished them, and hid my face in
    anger,
  yet they kept on in their willful ways.
¹⁸ I have seen their ways, but I will heal
    them;
  I will guide them and restore comfort
    to Israel's mourners,
¹⁹   creating praise on their lips.
Peace, peace, to those far and near,"
  says the LORD. "And I will heal them."
²⁰ But the wicked are like the tossing sea,
  which cannot rest,
  whose waves cast up mire and mud.
²¹ "There is no peace," says my God, "for the
    wicked."

ᵃ 9 Or *to the king*   *ᵇ* 9 Or *idols*

True Fasting

58 "Shout it aloud, do not hold back.
Raise your voice like a trumpet.
Declare to my people their rebellion
and to the descendants of Jacob their
sins.
² For day after day they seek me out;
they seem eager to know my ways,
as if they were a nation that does what
is right
and has not forsaken the commands of
its God.
They ask me for just decisions
and seem eager for God to come near
them.
³ 'Why have we fasted,' they say,
'and you have not seen it?
Why have we humbled ourselves,
and you have not noticed?'

"Yet on the day of your fasting, you do as
you please
and exploit all your workers.
⁴ Your fasting ends in quarreling and strife,
and in striking each other with wicked
fists.
You cannot fast as you do today
and expect your voice to be heard
on high.
⁵ Is this the kind of fast I have chosen,
only a day for people to humble
themselves?
Is it only for bowing one's head like a reed
and for lying in sackcloth and ashes?
Is that what you call a fast,
a day acceptable to the LORD?

⁶ "Is not this the kind of fasting I have
chosen:
to loose the chains of injustice
and untie the cords of the yoke,
to set the oppressed free
and break every yoke?
⁷ Is it not to share your food with the
hungry
and to provide the poor wanderer with
shelter—
when you see the naked, to clothe them,
and not to turn away from your own
flesh and blood?
⁸ Then your light will break forth like
the dawn,
and your healing will quickly appear;

then your righteousness*a* will go
before you,
and the glory of the LORD will be your
rear guard.
⁹ Then you will call, and the LORD will
answer;
you will cry for help, and he will say:
Here am I.

"If you do away with the yoke of
oppression,
with the pointing finger and malicious
talk,
¹⁰ and if you spend yourselves in behalf of
the hungry
and satisfy the needs of the oppressed,
then your light will rise in the darkness,
and your night will become like the
noonday.
¹¹ The LORD will guide you always;
he will satisfy your needs in a sun-
scorched land
and will strengthen your frame.
You will be like a well-watered garden,
like a spring whose waters never fail.
¹² Your people will rebuild the ancient ruins
and will raise up the age-old
foundations;
you will be called Repairer of Broken
Walls,
Restorer of Streets with Dwellings.

¹³ "If you keep your feet from breaking the
Sabbath
and from doing as you please on my
holy day,
if you call the Sabbath a delight
and the LORD's holy day honorable,
and if you honor it by not going your
own way
and not doing as you please or
speaking idle words,
¹⁴ then you will find your joy in the LORD,
and I will cause you to ride in triumph
on the heights of the land
and to feast on the inheritance of your
father Jacob."
For the mouth of the LORD
has spoken.

Sin, Confession and Redemption

59 Surely the arm of the LORD is not too
short to save,
nor his ear too dull to hear.

---

a 8 Or *your righteous One*

2 But your iniquities have separated
you from your God;
your sins have hidden his face from you,
so that he will not hear.
3 For your hands are stained with blood,
your fingers with guilt.
Your lips have spoken falsely,
and your tongue mutters wicked things.
4 No one calls for justice;
no one pleads a case with integrity.
They rely on empty arguments, they
utter lies;
they conceive trouble and give birth
to evil.
5 They hatch the eggs of vipers
and spin a spider's web.
Whoever eats their eggs will die,
and when one is broken, an adder is
hatched.
6 Their cobwebs are useless for clothing;
they cannot cover themselves with
what they make.
Their deeds are evil deeds,
and acts of violence are in their hands.
7 Their feet rush into sin;
they are swift to shed innocent blood.
They pursue evil schemes;
acts of violence mark their ways.
8 The way of peace they do not know;
there is no justice in their paths.
They have turned them into crooked
roads;
no one who walks along them will
know peace.

9 So justice is far from us,
and righteousness does not reach us.
We look for light, but all is darkness;
for brightness, but we walk in deep
shadows.
10 Like the blind we grope along the wall,
feeling our way like people without
eyes.
At midday we stumble as if it were
twilight;
among the strong, we are like the dead.
11 We all growl like bears;
we moan mournfully like doves.
We look for justice, but find none;
for deliverance, but it is far away.
12 For our offenses are many in your sight,
and our sins testify against us.

Our offenses are ever with us,
and we acknowledge our iniquities:
13 rebellion and treachery against the LORD,
turning our backs on our God,
inciting revolt and oppression,
uttering lies our hearts have
conceived.
14 So justice is driven back,
and righteousness stands at a distance;
truth has stumbled in the streets,
honesty cannot enter.
15 Truth is nowhere to be found,
and whoever shuns evil becomes
a prey.

The LORD looked and was displeased
that there was no justice.
16 He saw that there was no one,
he was appalled that there was no one
to intervene;
so his own arm achieved salvation
for him,
and his own righteousness sustained
him.
17 He put on righteousness as his
breastplate,
and the helmet of salvation on his
head;
he put on the garments of vengeance
and wrapped himself in zeal as in
a cloak.
18 According to what they have done,
so will he repay
wrath to his enemies
and retribution to his foes;
he will repay the islands their due.
19 From the west, people will fear the name
of the LORD,
and from the rising of the sun, they
will revere his glory.
For he will come like a pent-up flood
that the breath of the LORD drives
along.[a]
20 "The Redeemer will come to Zion,
to those in Jacob who repent of
their sins,"
declares the LORD.

21 "As for me, this is my covenant with
them," says the LORD. "My Spirit, who is on
you, will not depart from you, and my words
that I have put in your mouth will always be
on your lips, on the lips of your children and

---

[a] 19 Or *When enemies come in like a flood, / the Spirit of the LORD will put them to flight*

on the lips of their descendants—from this time on and forever," says the LORD.

The Glory of Zion

60 "Arise, shine, for your light has come,
and the glory of the LORD rises upon you.
2 See, darkness covers the earth
and thick darkness is over the peoples,
but the LORD rises upon you
and his glory appears over you.
3 Nations will come to your light,
and kings to the brightness of your dawn.

4 "Lift up your eyes and look about you:
All assemble and come to you;
your sons come from afar,
and your daughters are carried on the hip.
5 Then you will look and be radiant,
your heart will throb and swell with joy;
the wealth on the seas will be brought to you,
to you the riches of the nations will come.
6 Herds of camels will cover your land,
young camels of Midian and Ephah.
And all from Sheba will come,
bearing gold and incense
and proclaiming the praise of the LORD.
7 All Kedar's flocks will be gathered to you,
the rams of Nebaioth will serve you;
they will be accepted as offerings on my altar,
and I will adorn my glorious temple.

8 "Who are these that fly along like clouds,
like doves to their nests?
9 Surely the islands look to me;
in the lead are the ships of Tarshish,[a]
bringing your children from afar,
with their silver and gold,
to the honor of the LORD your God,
the Holy One of Israel,
for he has endowed you with splendor.

10 "Foreigners will rebuild your walls,
and their kings will serve you.
Though in anger I struck you,
in favor I will show you compassion.
11 Your gates will always stand open,
they will never be shut, day or night,
so that people may bring you the wealth of the nations—
their kings led in triumphal procession.
12 For the nation or kingdom that will not serve you will perish;
it will be utterly ruined.

13 "The glory of Lebanon will come to you,
the juniper, the fir and the cypress together,
to adorn my sanctuary;
and I will glorify the place for my feet.
14 The children of your oppressors will come bowing before you;
all who despise you will bow down at your feet
and will call you the City of the LORD,
Zion of the Holy One of Israel.

15 "Although you have been forsaken and hated,
with no one traveling through,
I will make you the everlasting pride
and the joy of all generations.
16 You will drink the milk of nations
and be nursed at royal breasts.
Then you will know that I, the LORD, am your Savior,
your Redeemer, the Mighty One of Jacob.
17 Instead of bronze I will bring you gold,
and silver in place of iron.
Instead of wood I will bring you bronze,
and iron in place of stones.
I will make peace your governor
and well-being your ruler.
18 No longer will violence be heard in your land,
nor ruin or destruction within your borders,
but you will call your walls Salvation
and your gates Praise.
19 The sun will no more be your light by day,
nor will the brightness of the moon shine on you,
for the LORD will be your everlasting light,
and your God will be your glory.
20 Your sun will never set again,
and your moon will wane no more;

---

a 9 Or the trading ships

the LORD will be your everlasting light,
and your days of sorrow will end.
²¹ Then all your people will be righteous
and they will possess the land forever.
They are the shoot I have planted,
the work of my hands,
for the display of my splendor.
²² The least of you will become a thousand,
the smallest a mighty nation.
I am the LORD;
in its time I will do this swiftly."

The Year of the Lord's Favor

61 The Spirit of the Sovereign LORD is
on me,
because the LORD has anointed me
to proclaim good news to the poor.
He has sent me to bind up the
brokenhearted,
to proclaim freedom for the captives
and release from darkness for the
prisoners,ᵃ
² to proclaim the year of the LORD's favor
and the day of vengeance of our God,
to comfort all who mourn,
³ and provide for those who grieve
in Zion—
to bestow on them a crown of beauty
instead of ashes,
the oil of joy
instead of mourning,
and a garment of praise
instead of a spirit of despair.
They will be called oaks of righteousness,
a planting of the LORD
for the display of his splendor.

⁴ They will rebuild the ancient ruins
and restore the places long devastated;
they will renew the ruined cities
that have been devastated for
generations.
⁵ Strangers will shepherd your flocks;
foreigners will work your fields and
vineyards.
⁶ And you will be called priests of the LORD,
you will be named ministers of
our God.
You will feed on the wealth of nations,
and in their riches you will boast.
⁷ Instead of your shame
you will receive a double portion,

and instead of disgrace
you will rejoice in your inheritance.
And so you will inherit a double portion
in your land,
and everlasting joy will be yours.

⁸ "For I, the LORD, love justice;
I hate robbery and wrongdoing.
In my faithfulness I will reward my
people
and make an everlasting covenant
with them.
⁹ Their descendants will be known among
the nations
and their offspring among the peoples.
All who see them will acknowledge
that they are a people the LORD has
blessed."

¹⁰ I delight greatly in the LORD;
my soul rejoices in my God.
For he has clothed me with garments of
salvation
and arrayed me in a robe of his
righteousness,
as a bridegroom adorns his head like a
priest,
and as a bride adorns herself with her
jewels.
¹¹ For as the soil makes the sprout come up
and a garden causes seeds to grow,
so the Sovereign LORD will make
righteousness
and praise spring up before all nations.

Zion's New Name

62 For Zion's sake I will not keep silent,
for Jerusalem's sake I will not
remain quiet,
till her vindication shines out like the
dawn,
her salvation like a blazing torch.
² The nations will see your vindication,
and all kings your glory;
you will be called by a new name
that the mouth of the LORD will
bestow.
³ You will be a crown of splendor in the
LORD's hand,
a royal diadem in the hand of
your God.
⁴ No longer will they call you Deserted,
or name your land Desolate.

ᵃ 1 Hebrew; Septuagint the blind

But you will be called Hephzibah,[a]
  and your land Beulah[b];
for the Lord will take delight in you,
  and your land will be married.
[5] As a young man marries a young woman,
  so will your Builder marry you;
as a bridegroom rejoices over his bride,
  so will your God rejoice over you.

[6] I have posted watchmen on your walls,
  Jerusalem;
  they will never be silent day or night.
You who call on the Lord,
  give yourselves no rest,
[7] and give him no rest till he establishes
  Jerusalem
  and makes her the praise of the earth.

[8] The Lord has sworn by his right hand
  and by his mighty arm:
"Never again will I give your grain
  as food for your enemies,
and never again will foreigners drink the
  new wine
  for which you have toiled;
[9] but those who harvest it will eat it
  and praise the Lord,
and those who gather the grapes will
  drink it
  in the courts of my sanctuary."

[10] Pass through, pass through the gates!
  Prepare the way for the people.
Build up, build up the highway!
  Remove the stones.
Raise a banner for the nations.

[11] The Lord has made proclamation
  to the ends of the earth:
"Say to Daughter Zion,
  'See, your Savior comes!
See, his reward is with him,
  and his recompense accompanies
  him.'"
[12] They will be called the Holy People,
  the Redeemed of the Lord;
and you will be called Sought After,
  the City No Longer Deserted.

God's Day of Vengeance and Redemption

63 Who is this coming from Edom,
  from Bozrah, with his garments
  stained crimson?

Who is this, robed in splendor,
  striding forward in the greatness of his
  strength?

"It is I, proclaiming victory,
  mighty to save."

[2] Why are your garments red,
  like those of one treading the
  winepress?

[3] "I have trodden the winepress alone;
  from the nations no one was with me.
I trampled them in my anger
  and trod them down in my wrath;
their blood spattered my garments,
  and I stained all my clothing.
[4] It was for me the day of vengeance;
  the year for me to redeem had come.
[5] I looked, but there was no one to help,
  I was appalled that no one gave
  support;
so my own arm achieved salvation
  for me,
  and my own wrath sustained me.
[6] I trampled the nations in my anger;
  in my wrath I made them drunk
  and poured their blood on the
  ground."

Praise and Prayer

[7] I will tell of the kindnesses of the Lord,
  the deeds for which he is to be praised,
  according to all the Lord has done
  for us—
yes, the many good things
  he has done for Israel,
  according to his compassion and
  many kindnesses.
[8] He said, "Surely they are my people,
  children who will be true to me";
  and so he became their Savior.
[9] In all their distress he too was distressed,
  and the angel of his presence saved
  them.[c]
In his love and mercy he redeemed
  them;
  he lifted them up and carried them
  all the days of old.
[10] Yet they rebelled
  and grieved his Holy Spirit.
So he turned and became their enemy
  and he himself fought against them.

---

[a] 4 Hephzibah means my delight is in her.   [b] 4 Beulah means married.   [c] 9 Or Savior [9] in their distress.
/ It was no envoy or angel / but his own presence that saved them

ARE YOU IN STEP?

READ: ISAIAH 63:10

Some time ago I purchased a new cartridge for my computer printer. But when I used it, no letters appeared on the page. It was half an hour before I noticed the thin strip of tape covering the outlet of the cartridge. There was plenty of ink, but until the tape was removed, no impression could be made.

Is there anything in your life that needs to be removed? Any impediment to the impression of God's Spirit? We can grieve the Spirit with our angry words (Ephesians 4:29-30; Isaiah 63:10) and resist the Spirit in our disobedience (Acts 7:51). We can test or conspire against the Spirit in our plottings (Acts 5:9). We can even quench the Spirit by having no regard for God's teachings.

BUILDING FAITH WISDOM STRENGTH

Here is something that helps me stay in step with the Spirit. We know that the fruit of the Spirit is love, joy, peace, patience, kindness, goodness, faithfulness, gentleness, self-control (Galatians 5:22–23). God's Spirit creates and distributes these characteristics. They are indicators on my spiritual dashboard. So whenever I sense them, I know I am walking in the Spirit. Whenever I lack them, I know I am out of step with the Spirit.

When God's Spirit directs us, we actually "keep in step with the Spirit" (Galatians 5:25). He is the drum major; we are the marching band. He is the sergeant; we are the platoon. He directs and leads; we obey and follow.

Taken from *God's Story, Your Story: Youth Edition* by Max Lucado, copyright © 2011 by Max Lucado, published by Zondervan.

¹¹ Then his people recalled^a the days of old,
the days of Moses and his people —
where is he who brought them through
the sea,
with the shepherd of his flock?
Where is he who set
his Holy Spirit among them,
¹² who sent his glorious arm of power
to be at Moses' right hand,
who divided the waters before them,
to gain for himself everlasting renown,
¹³ who led them through the depths?
Like a horse in open country,
they did not stumble;
¹⁴ like cattle that go down to the plain,
they were given rest by the Spirit of the
Lord.
This is how you guided your people
to make for yourself a glorious name.

¹⁵ Look down from heaven and see,
from your lofty throne, holy and
glorious.
Where are your zeal and your might?
Your tenderness and compassion are
withheld from us.
¹⁶ But you are our Father,
though Abraham does not know us
or Israel acknowledge us;
you, Lord, are our Father,
our Redeemer from of old is your
name.
¹⁷ Why, Lord, do you make us wander from
your ways
and harden our hearts so we do not
revere you?
Return for the sake of your servants,
the tribes that are your inheritance.
¹⁸ For a little while your people possessed
your holy place,
but now our enemies have trampled
down your sanctuary.
¹⁹ We are yours from of old;
but you have not ruled over them,
they have not been called^b by your
name.

64^c Oh, that you would rend the
heavens and come down,
that the mountains would tremble
before you!

² As when fire sets twigs ablaze
and causes water to boil,
come down to make your name known to
your enemies
and cause the nations to quake before
you!
³ For when you did awesome things that
we did not expect,
you came down, and the mountains
trembled before you.
⁴ Since ancient times no one has heard,
no ear has perceived,
no eye has seen any God besides you,
who acts on behalf of those who wait
for him.
⁵ You come to the help of those who gladly
do right,
who remember your ways.
But when we continued to sin against
them,
you were angry.
How then can we be saved?
⁶ All of us have become like one who is
unclean,
and all our righteous acts are like
filthy rags;
we all shrivel up like a leaf,
and like the wind our sins sweep us
away.
⁷ No one calls on your name
or strives to lay hold of you;
for you have hidden your face from us
and have given us over to^d our sins.

⁸ Yet you, Lord, are our Father.
We are the clay, you are the potter;
we are all the work of your hand.
⁹ Do not be angry beyond measure, Lord;
do not remember our sins forever.
Oh, look on us, we pray,
for we are all your people.
¹⁰ Your sacred cities have become a
wasteland;
even Zion is a wasteland, Jerusalem a
desolation.
¹¹ Our holy and glorious temple, where our
ancestors praised you,
has been burned with fire,
and all that we treasured lies in ruins.
¹² After all this, Lord, will you hold
yourself back?

^a 11 Or *But may he recall*   ^b 19 Or *We are like those you have never ruled, / like those never called*   ^c In
Hebrew texts 64:1 is numbered 63:19b, and 64:2-12 are numbered 64:1-11.   ^d 7 Septuagint, Syriac and
Targum; Hebrew *have made us melt because of*

THE STRONG ARM

READ: ISAIAH 64:1

When the prophet Isaiah begs the Lord to rip open the heavens and come to earth, he's hoping for more than a dose of excitement to break up his day. He wants to see the earth tremble. Just as a match can set twigs ablaze to make a pot boil, the Lord's arrival will make the world quake.

Isaiah remembers awesome and unexpected things the Lord did in the past, instances where he shook mountains. He no doubt recalls the Lord's thundering appearance at Mount Sinai, where he gave Moses the Ten Commandments (Exodus 19:16-18).

There's a catch if you invite the Lord to show up and smash evil. It's tough to ask him to step in and halt sin if you're part of the problem. Even though you want God to act at once, you aren't so happy if he's quick to correct your own wrongdoing. Isaiah admits that the Lord's people have broken his commands. No one struggles to know God, and even their best actions are just filthy rags (Isaiah 64:6).

BUILDING
FAITH
WISDOM
STRENGTH

The good news is that we don't have to be in fear of God's instant wrath for our sin. The apostle Paul said it like this: "God demonstrates his own love for us in this: While we were still sinners, Christ died for us" (Romans 5:8). That's not an excuse to sin; it's an opportunity for you to turn to him.

Will you keep silent and punish us
beyond measure?

Judgment and Salvation

65 "I revealed myself to those who did
not ask for me;
I was found by those who did not
seek me.
To a nation that did not call on my name,
I said, 'Here am I, here am I.'
[2] All day long I have held out my hands
to an obstinate people,
who walk in ways not good,
pursuing their own imaginations—
[3] a people who continually provoke me
to my very face,
offering sacrifices in gardens
and burning incense on altars of brick;
[4] who sit among the graves
and spend their nights keeping secret
vigil;
who eat the flesh of pigs,
and whose pots hold broth of impure
meat;
[5] who say, 'Keep away; don't come near me,
for I am too sacred for you!'
Such people are smoke in my nostrils,
a fire that keeps burning all day.

[6] "See, it stands written before me:
I will not keep silent but will pay back
in full;
I will pay it back into their laps—
[7] both your sins and the sins of your
ancestors,"
says the LORD.
"Because they burned sacrifices on the
mountains
and defied me on the hills,
I will measure into their laps
the full payment for their former
deeds."

[8] This is what the LORD says:

"As when juice is still found in a cluster
of grapes
and people say, 'Don't destroy it,
there is still a blessing in it,'
so will I do in behalf of my servants;
I will not destroy them all.
[9] I will bring forth descendants from
Jacob,
and from Judah those who will possess
my mountains;

my chosen people will inherit them,
and there will my servants live.
[10] Sharon will become a pasture for flocks,
and the Valley of Achor a resting place
for herds,
for my people who seek me.

[11] "But as for you who forsake the LORD
and forget my holy mountain,
who spread a table for Fortune
and fill bowls of mixed wine for
Destiny,
[12] I will destine you for the sword,
and all of you will fall in the slaughter;
for I called but you did not answer,
I spoke but you did not listen.
You did evil in my sight
and chose what displeases me."

[13] Therefore this is what the Sovereign
LORD says:

"My servants will eat,
but you will go hungry;
my servants will drink,
but you will go thirsty;
my servants will rejoice,
but you will be put to shame.
[14] My servants will sing
out of the joy of their hearts,
but you will cry out
from anguish of heart
and wail in brokenness of spirit.
[15] You will leave your name
for my chosen ones to use in their
curses;
the Sovereign LORD will put you to death,
but to his servants he will give another
name.
[16] Whoever invokes a blessing in the land
will do so by the one true God;
whoever takes an oath in the land
will swear by the one true God.
For the past troubles will be forgotten
and hidden from my eyes.

New Heavens and a New Earth

[17] "See, I will create
new heavens and a new earth.
The former things will not be
remembered,
nor will they come to mind.
[18] But be glad and rejoice forever
in what I will create,
for I will create Jerusalem to be a delight
and its people a joy.

¹⁹ I will rejoice over Jerusalem
    and take delight in my people;
the sound of weeping and of crying
    will be heard in it no more.

²⁰ "Never again will there be in it
    an infant who lives but a few days,
    or an old man who does not live out
        his years;
the one who dies at a hundred
    will be thought a mere child;
the one who fails to reach*a* a hundred
    will be considered accursed.
²¹ They will build houses and dwell in
        them;
    they will plant vineyards and eat
        their fruit.
²² No longer will they build houses and
        others live in them,
    or plant and others eat.
For as the days of a tree,
    so will be the days of my people;
my chosen ones will long enjoy
    the work of their hands.
²³ They will not labor in vain,
    nor will they bear children doomed to
        misfortune;
for they will be a people blessed by
    the LORD,
    they and their descendants with them.
²⁴ Before they call I will answer;
    while they are still speaking I will hear.
²⁵ The wolf and the lamb will feed together,
    and the lion will eat straw like the ox,
    and dust will be the serpent's food.
They will neither harm nor destroy
    on all my holy mountain,"
                            says the LORD.

Judgment and Hope

66 This is what the LORD says:

"Heaven is my throne,
    and the earth is my footstool.
Where is the house you will build for me?
    Where will my resting place be?
² Has not my hand made all these things,
    and so they came into being?"
                            declares the LORD.

"These are the ones I look on with favor:
    those who are humble and contrite in
        spirit,

and who tremble at my word.
³ But whoever sacrifices a bull
    is like one who kills a person,
and whoever offers a lamb
    is like one who breaks a dog's neck;
whoever makes a grain offering
    is like one who presents pig's blood,
and whoever burns memorial incense
    is like one who worships an idol.
They have chosen their own ways,
    and they delight in their
        abominations;
⁴ so I also will choose harsh treatment
        for them
    and will bring on them what they
        dread.
For when I called, no one answered,
    when I spoke, no one listened.
They did evil in my sight
    and chose what displeases me."

⁵ Hear the word of the LORD,
    you who tremble at his word:
"Your own people who hate you,
    and exclude you because of my name,
        have said,
'Let the LORD be glorified,
    that we may see your joy!'
    Yet they will be put to shame.
⁶ Hear that uproar from the city,
    hear that noise from the temple!
It is the sound of the LORD
    repaying his enemies all they deserve.

⁷ "Before she goes into labor,
    she gives birth;
before the pains come upon her,
    she delivers a son.
⁸ Who has ever heard of such things?
    Who has ever seen things like this?
Can a country be born in a day
    or a nation be brought forth in a
        moment?
Yet no sooner is Zion in labor
    than she gives birth to her children.
⁹ Do I bring to the moment of birth
    and not give delivery?" says the LORD.
"Do I close up the womb
    when I bring to delivery?" says
        your God.
¹⁰ "Rejoice with Jerusalem and be glad
        for her,
    all you who love her;

---

a 20 Or *the sinner who reaches*

rejoice greatly with her,
all you who mourn over her.
¹¹ For you will nurse and be satisfied
at her comforting breasts;
you will drink deeply
and delight in her overflowing
abundance."

¹² For this is what the LORD says:

"I will extend peace to her like a river,
and the wealth of nations like a
flooding stream;
you will nurse and be carried on her arm
and dandled on her knees.
¹³ As a mother comforts her child,
so will I comfort you;
and you will be comforted over
Jerusalem."

¹⁴ When you see this, your heart will rejoice
and you will flourish like grass;
the hand of the LORD will be made
known to his servants,
but his fury will be shown to his foes.
¹⁵ See, the LORD is coming with fire,
and his chariots are like a whirlwind;
he will bring down his anger with fury,
and his rebuke with flames of fire.
¹⁶ For with fire and with his sword
the LORD will execute judgment on all
people,
and many will be those slain by the
LORD.

¹⁷ "Those who consecrate and purify
themselves to go into the gardens, following
one who is among those who eat the flesh of
pigs, rats and other unclean things — they
will meet their end together with the one
they follow," declares the LORD.

¹⁸ "And I, because of what they have
planned and done, am about to come[a] and
gather the people of all nations and languages, and they will come and see my glory.

¹⁹ "I will set a sign among them, and I
will send some of those who survive to the
nations — to Tarshish, to the Libyans[b] and
Lydians (famous as archers), to Tubal and
Greece, and to the distant islands that have
not heard of my fame or seen my glory. They
will proclaim my glory among the nations.
²⁰ And they will bring all your people, from
all the nations, to my holy mountain in Jerusalem as an offering to the LORD — on horses, in chariots and wagons, and on mules
and camels," says the LORD. "They will bring
them, as the Israelites bring their grain offerings, to the temple of the LORD in ceremonially clean vessels. ²¹ And I will select some
of them also to be priests and Levites," says
the LORD.

²² "As the new heavens and the new earth
that I make will endure before me," declares
the LORD, "so will your name and descendants endure. ²³ From one New Moon to another and from one Sabbath to another, all
mankind will come and bow down before
me," says the LORD. ²⁴ "And they will go out
and look on the dead bodies of those who rebelled against me; the worms that eat them
will not die, the fire that burns them will not
be quenched, and they will be loathsome to
all mankind."

ᵃ 18 The meaning of the Hebrew for this clause is uncertain.   ᵇ 19 Some Septuagint manuscripts Put
(Libyans); Hebrew Pul

JEREMIAH

WHEN DID THIS HAPPEN?

Around 626 B.C. in the southern kingdom of Judah

WHO IS IN THIS BOOK?

Jeremiah
Baruch
Shallum
Jehoiachin
Hananiah

VERSES YOU MIGHT RECOGNIZE

JEREMIAH 29:11

"'For I know the plans I have for you,' declares the LORD, 'plans to prosper you and not to harm you, plans to give you hope and a future.'"

JEREMIAH 31:3

"The LORD appeared to us in the past, saying: 'I have loved you with an everlasting love; I have drawn you with unfailing kindness.'"

WHAT'S IT ABOUT?

Jeremiah prophesied during the reign of Israel's last five kings; the same time period depicted in 2 Kings. Even after hearing the prophet Isaiah's warnings, the people of Israel continued to worship false gods and ignore God's commands. Jeremiah is sometimes called "the weeping prophet" because he was so distraught over the message he had to deliver. He told the people living in Judah that they were about to face judgment for their sins and they would be taken captive by Babylon.

But there was still hope: as always, God would keep his promises and restore his people. This book gives the first clear picture of the new covenant God was going to establish with Israel. The law would be written on their minds and in their hearts instead of on tablets of stone (Jeremiah 31:33). Through Jeremiah, God promised that his people would know him directly. That would happen through his Son, Jesus Christ.

1 The words of Jeremiah son of Hilkiah, one of the priests at Anathoth in the territory of Benjamin. ²The word of the LORD came to him in the thirteenth year of the reign of Josiah son of Amon king of Judah, ³and through the reign of Jehoiakim son of Josiah king of Judah, down to the fifth month of the eleventh year of Zedekiah son of Josiah king of Judah, when the people of Jerusalem went into exile.

The Call of Jeremiah

⁴The word of the LORD came to me, saying,

⁵ "Before I formed you in the womb
    I knew*ᵃ* you,
  before you were born I set you apart;
  I appointed you as a prophet to the
    nations."

⁶ "Alas, Sovereign LORD," I said, "I do not know how to speak; I am too young."

⁷But the LORD said to me, "Do not say, 'I am too young.' You must go to everyone I send you to and say whatever I command you. ⁸Do not be afraid of them, for I am with you and will rescue you," declares the LORD.

⁹Then the LORD reached out his hand and touched my mouth and said to me, "I have put my words in your mouth. ¹⁰See, today I appoint you over nations and kingdoms to uproot and tear down, to destroy and overthrow, to build and to plant."

¹¹The word of the LORD came to me: "What do you see, Jeremiah?"

"I see the branch of an almond tree," I replied.

¹²The LORD said to me, "You have seen correctly, for I am watching*ᵇ* to see that my word is fulfilled."

¹³The word of the LORD came to me again: "What do you see?"

"I see a pot that is boiling," I answered. "It is tilting toward us from the north."

¹⁴The LORD said to me, "From the north disaster will be poured out on all who live in the land. ¹⁵I am about to summon all the peoples of the northern kingdoms," declares the LORD.

"Their kings will come and set up their
    thrones
  in the entrance of the gates of
    Jerusalem;
they will come against all her
    surrounding walls
  and against all the towns of Judah.
¹⁶ I will pronounce my judgments on my
    people
  because of their wickedness in
    forsaking me,
in burning incense to other gods
  and in worshiping what their hands
    have made.

¹⁷ "Get yourself ready! Stand up and say to them whatever I command you. Do not be terrified by them, or I will terrify you before them. ¹⁸Today I have made you a fortified city, an iron pillar and a bronze wall to stand against the whole land — against the kings of Judah, its officials, its priests and the people of the land. ¹⁹They will fight against you but will not overcome you, for I am with you and will rescue you," declares the LORD.

Israel Forsakes God

2 The word of the LORD came to me: ² "Go and proclaim in the hearing of Jerusalem:

"This is what the LORD says:

" 'I remember the devotion of your youth,
  how as a bride you loved me
and followed me through the wilderness,
  through a land not sown.
³ Israel was holy to the LORD,
  the firstfruits of his harvest;
all who devoured her were held guilty,
  and disaster overtook them,' "
                            declares the LORD.

⁴ Hear the word of the LORD, you
    descendants of Jacob,
  all you clans of Israel.

ᵃ 5 Or *chose*   *ᵇ* 12 The Hebrew for *watching* sounds like the Hebrew for *almond tree.*

NO TIME LIKE NOW

READ: JEREMIAH 1:5

God doesn't make you wait until you're old to serve him. He's thought hard about how he can move you into action. The apostle Paul wrote, "For we are God's handiwork, created in Christ Jesus to do good works, which God prepared in advance for us to do" (Ephesians 2:10).

The Lord had his eye on Jeremiah even before he was conceived. The fact that God "knew" Jeremiah wasn't merely a fuzzy awareness that he would someday be born. It means the Lord already had a relationship with Jeremiah and approved of him. No one knows exactly how old Jeremiah was when God commanded him to preach, but his ministry lasted forty years. He prophesied until the final days of the southern kingdom of Judah.

BUILDING

FAITH

WISDOM

STRENGTH

Jeremiah feels overwhelmed at the thought of taking the Lord's message to the world. First he argues he can't speak. Then he protests he's too young. God swats down both excuses. He promises to go with Jeremiah, to protect him, and to fully equip him for the task.

God has a plan to use you to do his work in the world. He says, "Get yourself ready!" (Jeremiah 1:17). He knows the unique opportunities he prepared for you long ago, and he commands you to be fearless as you accomplish whatever he has in store for you. When God sends you, he takes away your terror.

⁵This is what the LORD says:

"What fault did your ancestors find
      in me,
   that they strayed so far from me?
They followed worthless idols
   and became worthless themselves.
⁶They did not ask, 'Where is the LORD,
   who brought us up out of Egypt
and led us through the barren
      wilderness,
   through a land of deserts and
      ravines,
a land of drought and utter darkness,
   a land where no one travels and no
      one lives?'
⁷I brought you into a fertile land
   to eat its fruit and rich produce.
But you came and defiled my land
   and made my inheritance detestable.
⁸The priests did not ask,
   'Where is the LORD?'
Those who deal with the law did not
      know me;
   the leaders rebelled against me.
The prophets prophesied by Baal,
   following worthless idols.

⁹"Therefore I bring charges against you
      again,"
                  declares the LORD.
   "And I will bring charges against your
      children's children.
¹⁰Cross over to the coasts of Cyprus and
      look,
   send to Kedar* and observe closely;
   see if there has ever been anything
      like this:
¹¹Has a nation ever changed its gods?
   (Yet they are not gods at all.)
But my people have exchanged their
      glorious God
   for worthless idols.
¹²Be appalled at this, you heavens,
   and shudder with great horror,"
                  declares the LORD.
¹³"My people have committed two sins:
They have forsaken me,
   the spring of living water,
and have dug their own cisterns,
   broken cisterns that cannot hold water.
¹⁴Is Israel a servant, a slave by birth?
   Why then has he become plunder?

¹⁵Lions have roared;
   they have growled at him.
They have laid waste his land;
   his towns are burned and deserted.
¹⁶Also, the men of Memphis and
      Tahpanhes
   have cracked your skull.
¹⁷Have you not brought this on yourselves
   by forsaking the LORD your God
   when he led you in the way?
¹⁸Now why go to Egypt
   to drink water from the Nile*?
And why go to Assyria
   to drink water from the Euphrates?
¹⁹Your wickedness will punish you;
   your backsliding will rebuke you.
Consider then and realize
   how evil and bitter it is for you
when you forsake the LORD your God
   and have no awe of me,"
                  declares the Lord,
                  the LORD Almighty.

²⁰"Long ago you broke off your yoke
   and tore off your bonds;
   you said, 'I will not serve you!'
Indeed, on every high hill
   and under every spreading tree
   you lay down as a prostitute.
²¹I had planted you like a choice vine
   of sound and reliable stock.
How then did you turn against me
   into a corrupt, wild vine?
²²Although you wash yourself with soap
   and use an abundance of cleansing
      powder,
   the stain of your guilt is still before
      me,"
                  declares the Sovereign LORD.
²³"How can you say, 'I am not defiled;
   I have not run after the Baals'?
See how you behaved in the valley;
   consider what you have done.
You are a swift she-camel
   running here and there,
²⁴a wild donkey accustomed to the desert,
   sniffing the wind in her craving—
   in her heat who can restrain her?
Any males that pursue her need not tire
      themselves;
   at mating time they will find her.
²⁵Do not run until your feet are bare
   and your throat is dry.

---

a 10 In the Syro-Arabian desert   *b 18* Hebrew *Shihor*; that is, a branch of the Nile

DRINK UP

READ: JEREMIAH 2:9-13

I n Israel, rain was scarce about half the year, so the people in those days would dig cisterns and line them with bricks and plaster to hold the water. But cisterns were always breaking and losing water. Even when they didn't break, the water would often become stagnant or the supply would be inadequate.

The people would have thought of Jeremiah's metaphor was ridiculous. No one would ever choose a cistern as his water source when a spring of crystal clear water was available. But that captures the ridiculousness of looking to something or someone to do for us what God was meant to do for us.

Instead of looking to God as our source of significance, we turn to our accomplishments.

Instead of looking to God as our source of joy, we look to our family, friends, or girlfriend.

Instead of looking to God as our source of truth, we look to popular opinion, entertainment, and what teachers and those in authority tell us.

BUILDING
FAITH
WISDOM
STRENGTH

The things we look to for help aren't necessarily bad in and of themselves. In fact, God may use them to accomplish his purpose, but the questions are: Have they become broken cisterns that we turn to instead of the living water? Am I putting my hope in something that doesn't hold water?

As God tells Jeremiah, the heavens look on with great horror at the sight of God's children drinking from the nasty cisterns and rejecting the fresh living water. It's one of the most heartbreaking things for God the Father to watch.

But you said, 'It's no use!
    I love foreign gods,
    and I must go after them.'

26 "As a thief is disgraced when he is
       caught,
    so the people of Israel are disgraced —
  they, their kings and their officials,
    their priests and their prophets.
27 They say to wood, 'You are my father,'
    and to stone, 'You gave me birth.'
They have turned their backs to me
    and not their faces;
yet when they are in trouble, they say,
    'Come and save us!'
28 Where then are the gods you made for
      yourselves?
    Let them come if they can save you
    when you are in trouble!
For you, Judah, have as many gods
    as you have towns.

29 "Why do you bring charges against me?
    You have all rebelled against me,"
                    declares the LORD.
30 "In vain I punished your people;
    they did not respond to correction.
Your sword has devoured your prophets
    like a ravenous lion.

31 "You of this generation, consider the
word of the LORD:

"Have I been a desert to Israel
    or a land of great darkness?
Why do my people say, 'We are free to
      roam;
    we will come to you no more'?
32 Does a young woman forget her jewelry,
    a bride her wedding ornaments?
Yet my people have forgotten me,
    days without number.
33 How skilled you are at pursuing love!
    Even the worst of women can learn
      from your ways.
34 On your clothes is found
    the lifeblood of the innocent poor,
    though you did not catch them
      breaking in.
Yet in spite of all this
35   you say, 'I am innocent;
    he is not angry with me.'
But I will pass judgment on you
    because you say, 'I have not sinned.'
36 Why do you go about so much,
    changing your ways?

You will be disappointed by Egypt
    as you were by Assyria.
37 You will also leave that place
    with your hands on your head,
for the LORD has rejected those you trust;
    you will not be helped by them.

3 "If a man divorces his wife
    and she leaves him and marries
      another man,
should he return to her again?
    Would not the land be completely
      defiled?
But you have lived as a prostitute with
      many lovers —
    would you now return to me?"
                    declares the LORD.

2 "Look up to the barren heights and see.
    Is there any place where you have not
      been ravished?
By the roadside you sat waiting for lovers,
    sat like a nomad in the desert.
You have defiled the land
    with your prostitution and
      wickedness.
3 Therefore the showers have been
      withheld,
    and no spring rains have fallen.
Yet you have the brazen look of a
      prostitute;
    you refuse to blush with shame.
4 Have you not just called to me:
    'My Father, my friend from my youth,
5 will you always be angry?
    Will your wrath continue forever?'
This is how you talk,
    but you do all the evil you can."

Unfaithful Israel

6 During the reign of King Josiah, the LORD said to me, "Have you seen what faithless Israel has done? She has gone up on every high hill and under every spreading tree and has committed adultery there. 7 I thought that after she had done all this she would return to me but she did not, and her unfaithful sister Judah saw it. 8 I gave faithless Israel her certificate of divorce and sent her away because of all her adulteries. Yet I saw that her unfaithful sister Judah had no fear; she also went out and committed adultery. 9 Because Israel's immorality mattered so little to her, she defiled the land and committed adultery with stone and wood. 10 In spite of all this,

JEREMIAH

The word of the LORD came to me, saying, "Before I formed you in the womb I knew you, before you were born I set you apart; I appointed you as a prophet to the nations." JEREMIAH 1:4-5

HIS NAME MEANS: Exact meaning unknown; suggestions include "the LORD exalts" or "the LORD establishes"

READ HIS STORY: *Jeremiah 1, 36-43*

MEN OF THE BIBLE

eremiah grew up around the same time as King Josiah. He lived during the tragic final days of the nation of Judah, when the city of Jerusalem was destroyed, the temple burnt and the people either killed or carried off to Babylon. As a result, Jeremiah has become known as the "weeping prophet."

During the lifetime of Jeremiah, the Israelites turned their backs on God and worshiped detestable idols instead. Jeremiah's ministry was focused on calling his people to repentance in hopes they would turn back to God. For the most part, his message fell on deaf ears. Even worse, his ministry created a lot of enemies. Even the other priests and prophets wanted to kill him (Jeremiah 26:7-8). They threw him into a dungeon, put him in stocks and tossed him into a muddy well (Jeremiah 20:2; 37:16; 38:6)—all in hopes he would die. Persecuted. Scorned. Rejected.

Yet Jeremiah knew the heart of God. The Israelites were breaking the Lord's heart and bringing disaster upon themselves. So Jeremiah was faithful to call them out of their sin. But he wrestled with God through his trials, especially when he was mocked and hurt over and over. Even in his deepest struggles, Jeremiah stayed close to God and relied on his hope. During such a time of great evil, his journey was one of solitude and sorrow. Yet his faith and mission of forty years was constant.

her unfaithful sister Judah did not return to me with all her heart, but only in pretense," declares the LORD.

¹¹ The LORD said to me, "Faithless Israel is more righteous than unfaithful Judah. ¹²Go, proclaim this message toward the north:

"'Return, faithless Israel,' declares
     the LORD,
  'I will frown on you no longer,
for I am faithful,' declares the LORD,
  'I will not be angry forever.
¹³ Only acknowledge your guilt—
     you have rebelled against the LORD
        your God,
  you have scattered your favors to foreign
        gods
     under every spreading tree,
     and have not obeyed me,'"
                    declares the LORD.

¹⁴ "Return, faithless people," declares the LORD, "for I am your husband. I will choose you—one from a town and two from a clan—and bring you to Zion. ¹⁵Then I will give you shepherds after my own heart, who will lead you with knowledge and understanding. ¹⁶In those days, when your numbers have increased greatly in the land," declares the LORD, "people will no longer say, 'The ark of the covenant of the LORD.' It will never enter their minds or be remembered; it will not be missed, nor will another one be made. ¹⁷At that time they will call Jerusalem The Throne of the LORD, and all nations will gather in Jerusalem to honor the name of the LORD. No longer will they follow the stubbornness of their evil hearts. ¹⁸In those days the people of Judah will join the people of Israel, and together they will come from a northern land to the land I gave your ancestors as an inheritance.

¹⁹ "I myself said,

"'How gladly would I treat you like my
        children
     and give you a pleasant land,
     the most beautiful inheritance of any
        nation.'
  I thought you would call me 'Father'
     and not turn away from following me.
²⁰ But like a woman unfaithful to her
        husband,
     so you, Israel, have been unfaithful
        to me,"
                    declares the LORD.

²¹ A cry is heard on the barren heights,
     the weeping and pleading of the
        people of Israel,
  because they have perverted their ways
     and have forgotten the LORD
        their God.

²² "Return, faithless people;
     I will cure you of backsliding."

  "Yes, we will come to you,
     for you are the LORD our God.
²³ Surely the idolatrous commotion on
        the hills
     and mountains is a deception;
  surely in the LORD our God
     is the salvation of Israel.
²⁴ From our youth shameful gods have
        consumed
     the fruits of our ancestors' labor—
  their flocks and herds,
     their sons and daughters.
²⁵ Let us lie down in our shame,
     and let our disgrace cover us.
  We have sinned against the LORD
        our God,
     both we and our ancestors;
  from our youth till this day
     we have not obeyed the LORD
        our God."

4 "If you, Israel, will return,
     then return to me,"
                    declares the LORD.
  "If you put your detestable idols out of
        my sight
     and no longer go astray,
² and if in a truthful, just and righteous
        way
     you swear, 'As surely as the LORD lives,'
  then the nations will invoke blessings
        by him
     and in him they will boast."

³ This is what the LORD says to the people of Judah and to Jerusalem:

  "Break up your unplowed ground
     and do not sow among thorns.
⁴ Circumcise yourselves to the LORD,
     circumcise your hearts,
  you people of Judah and inhabitants of
        Jerusalem,
  or my wrath will flare up and burn like
        fire
     because of the evil you have done—
  burn with no one to quench it.

Disaster From the North

5 "Announce in Judah and proclaim in
   Jerusalem and say:
   'Sound the trumpet throughout the
      land!'
   Cry aloud and say:
   'Gather together!
   Let us flee to the fortified cities!'
6 Raise the signal to go to Zion!
   Flee for safety without delay!
   For I am bringing disaster from the north,
      even terrible destruction."

7 A lion has come out of his lair;
   a destroyer of nations has set out.
   He has left his place
      to lay waste your land.
   Your towns will lie in ruins
      without inhabitant.
8 So put on sackcloth,
      lament and wail,
   for the fierce anger of the LORD
      has not turned away from us.

9 "In that day," declares the LORD,
   "the king and the officials will lose
      heart,
   the priests will be horrified,
      and the prophets will be appalled."

10 Then I said, "Alas, Sovereign LORD! How
completely you have deceived this people and Jerusalem by saying, 'You will have
peace,' when the sword is at our throats!"

11 At that time this people and Jerusalem
will be told, "A scorching wind from the barren heights in the desert blows toward my
people, but not to winnow or cleanse; 12 a
wind too strong for that comes from me. Now
I pronounce my judgments against them."

13 Look! He advances like the clouds,
   his chariots come like a whirlwind,
   his horses are swifter than eagles.
      Woe to us! We are ruined!
14 Jerusalem, wash the evil from your heart
      and be saved.
   How long will you harbor wicked
      thoughts?
15 A voice is announcing from Dan,
   proclaiming disaster from the hills of
      Ephraim.
16 "Tell this to the nations,
   proclaim concerning Jerusalem:
   'A besieging army is coming from a
      distant land,

   raising a war cry against the cities of
      Judah.
17 They surround her like men guarding
      a field,
   because she has rebelled against me,'"
                        declares the LORD.
18 "Your own conduct and actions
      have brought this on you.
   This is your punishment.
      How bitter it is!
      How it pierces to the heart!"

19 Oh, my anguish, my anguish!
   I writhe in pain.
   Oh, the agony of my heart!
      My heart pounds within me,
      I cannot keep silent.
   For I have heard the sound of the
      trumpet;
      I have heard the battle cry.
20 Disaster follows disaster;
   the whole land lies in ruins.
   In an instant my tents are destroyed,
      my shelter in a moment.
21 How long must I see the battle standard
   and hear the sound of the trumpet?

22 "My people are fools;
   they do not know me.
   They are senseless children;
      they have no understanding.
   They are skilled in doing evil;
      they know not how to do good."

23 I looked at the earth,
      and it was formless and empty;
   and at the heavens,
      and their light was gone.
24 I looked at the mountains,
      and they were quaking;
   all the hills were swaying.
25 I looked, and there were no people;
   every bird in the sky had flown away.
26 I looked, and the fruitful land was a
      desert;
   all its towns lay in ruins
   before the LORD, before his fierce anger.

27 This is what the LORD says:

"The whole land will be ruined,
   though I will not destroy it completely.
28 Therefore the earth will mourn
      and the heavens above grow dark,
   because I have spoken and will not
      relent,
   I have decided and will not turn back."

LET YOUR HEART BREAK

READ: JEREMIAH 4:19

Your chest thumps with compassion when you hear about hungry children. You get angry at the facts about human trafficking. You churn with frustration if your friends refuse to follow Jesus. Those are all signs you care about God and his goals for the world.

People call Jeremiah "the weeping prophet" because his heart breaks for the broken state of the Lord's people. The people of Judah had abandoned God and thrown themselves into sin (Jeremiah 1:16). They were once like a young bride devoted to the Lord (2:2) but now they act like a prostitute chasing other lovers (3:1). They seek military power from other nations instead of relying on God (2:18), and they worship the false god Baal (v. 23).

Jeremiah speaks the Lord's message, urging the people to come back to God and admit their guilt (4:1). But their refusal invites an attack from a distant army, and Jeremiah twists in pain as he announces sin's painful consequences for the nation. He feels their pain and won't quit caring.

Sometimes you might wish you could shut off your passion for God and not care about the world's troubles. But you can choose to be like Jeremiah. You can keep obeying God. You can continue doing the job he gives you. The Lord doesn't give up on the world, and neither should you.

BUILDING
FAITH
WISDOM
STRENGTH

²⁹ At the sound of horsemen and archers
   every town takes to flight.
Some go into the thickets;
   some climb up among the rocks.
All the towns are deserted;
   no one lives in them.

³⁰ What are you doing, you devastated one?
   Why dress yourself in scarlet
   and put on jewels of gold?
Why highlight your eyes with makeup?
   You adorn yourself in vain.
Your lovers despise you;
   they want to kill you.

³¹ I hear a cry as of a woman in labor,
   a groan as of one bearing her first
      child —
the cry of Daughter Zion gasping for
      breath,
   stretching out her hands and saying,
"Alas! I am fainting;
   my life is given over to murderers."

Not One Is Upright

5 "Go up and down the streets of
      Jerusalem,
   look around and consider,
   search through her squares.
If you can find but one person
   who deals honestly and seeks the truth,
   I will forgive this city.
² Although they say, 'As surely as the
      LORD lives,'
   still they are swearing falsely."

³ LORD, do not your eyes look for truth?
   You struck them, but they felt no pain;
   you crushed them, but they refused
      correction.
They made their faces harder than stone
   and refused to repent.
⁴ I thought, "These are only the poor;
   they are foolish,
for they do not know the way of the LORD,
   the requirements of their God.
⁵ So I will go to the leaders
   and speak to them;
surely they know the way of the LORD,
   the requirements of their God."
But with one accord they too had broken
      off the yoke
   and torn off the bonds.
⁶ Therefore a lion from the forest will
      attack them,

a wolf from the desert will ravage
      them,
a leopard will lie in wait near their towns
   to tear to pieces any who venture out,
for their rebellion is great
   and their backslidings many.

⁷ "Why should I forgive you?
   Your children have forsaken me
   and sworn by gods that are not gods.
I supplied all their needs,
   yet they committed adultery
   and thronged to the houses of
      prostitutes.
⁸ They are well-fed, lusty stallions,
   each neighing for another man's wife.
⁹ Should I not punish them for this?"
   declares the LORD.
"Should I not avenge myself
   on such a nation as this?

¹⁰ "Go through her vineyards and ravage
      them,
   but do not destroy them completely.
Strip off her branches,
   for these people do not belong to the
      LORD.
¹¹ The people of Israel and the people of
      Judah
   have been utterly unfaithful to me,"
      declares the LORD.

¹² They have lied about the LORD;
   they said, "He will do nothing!
No harm will come to us;
   we will never see sword or famine.
¹³ The prophets are but wind
   and the word is not in them;
   so let what they say be done to them."

¹⁴ Therefore this is what the LORD God Almighty says:

"Because the people have spoken these
      words,
I will make my words in your mouth
      a fire
and these people the wood it
      consumes.
¹⁵ People of Israel," declares the LORD,
   "I am bringing a distant nation against
      you —
an ancient and enduring nation,
   a people whose language you do not
      know,
   whose speech you do not understand.

¹⁶ Their quivers are like an open grave;
   all of them are mighty warriors.
¹⁷ They will devour your harvests and food,
   devour your sons and daughters;
 they will devour your flocks and herds,
   devour your vines and fig trees.
 With the sword they will destroy
   the fortified cities in which you trust.

¹⁸ "Yet even in those days," declares the
Lord, "I will not destroy you completely.
¹⁹ And when the people ask, 'Why has the
Lord our God done all this to us?' you will
tell them, 'As you have forsaken me and
served foreign gods in your own land, so
now you will serve foreigners in a land not
your own.'

²⁰ "Announce this to the descendants
      of Jacob
   and proclaim it in Judah:
²¹ Hear this, you foolish and senseless
      people,
   who have eyes but do not see,
   who have ears but do not hear:
²² Should you not fear me?" declares
      the Lord.
   "Should you not tremble in my
      presence?
 I made the sand a boundary for the sea,
   an everlasting barrier it cannot cross.
 The waves may roll, but they cannot
      prevail;
   they may roar, but they cannot cross it.
²³ But these people have stubborn and
      rebellious hearts;
   they have turned aside and gone away.
²⁴ They do not say to themselves,
   'Let us fear the Lord our God,
 who gives autumn and spring rains in
      season,
   who assures us of the regular weeks
      of harvest.'
²⁵ Your wrongdoings have kept these away;
   your sins have deprived you of good.

²⁶ "Among my people are the wicked
   who lie in wait like men who snare
      birds
   and like those who set traps to catch
      people.
²⁷ Like cages full of birds,
   their houses are full of deceit;
 they have become rich and powerful
²⁸   and have grown fat and sleek.

 Their evil deeds have no limit;
   they do not seek justice.
 They do not promote the case of the
      fatherless;
   they do not defend the just cause of
      the poor.
²⁹ Should I not punish them for this?"
   declares the Lord.
 "Should I not avenge myself
   on such a nation as this?

³⁰ "A horrible and shocking thing
   has happened in the land:
³¹ The prophets prophesy lies,
   the priests rule by their own authority,
 and my people love it this way.
   But what will you do in the end?

Jerusalem Under Siege

6 "Flee for safety, people of Benjamin!
   Flee from Jerusalem!
 Sound the trumpet in Tekoa!
   Raise the signal over Beth Hakkerem!
 For disaster looms out of the north,
   even terrible destruction.
² I will destroy Daughter Zion,
   so beautiful and delicate.
³ Shepherds with their flocks will come
      against her;
   they will pitch their tents around her,
   each tending his own portion."

⁴ "Prepare for battle against her!
   Arise, let us attack at noon!
 But, alas, the daylight is fading,
   and the shadows of evening grow long.
⁵ So arise, let us attack at night
   and destroy her fortresses!"

⁶ This is what the Lord Almighty says:

 "Cut down the trees
   and build siege ramps against
      Jerusalem.
 This city must be punished;
   it is filled with oppression.
⁷ As a well pours out its water,
   so she pours out her wickedness.
 Violence and destruction resound
      in her;
   her sickness and wounds are ever
      before me.
⁸ Take warning, Jerusalem,
   or I will turn away from you
 and make your land desolate
   so no one can live in it."

⁹This is what the LORD Almighty says:

"Let them glean the remnant of Israel
    as thoroughly as a vine;
pass your hand over the branches again,
    like one gathering grapes."

¹⁰To whom can I speak and give warning?
    Who will listen to me?
Their ears are closed*ᵃ*
    so they cannot hear.
The word of the LORD is offensive
    to them;
    they find no pleasure in it.
¹¹But I am full of the wrath of the LORD,
    and I cannot hold it in.

"Pour it out on the children in the street
    and on the young men gathered
        together;
both husband and wife will be caught
    in it,
    and the old, those weighed down with
        years.
¹²Their houses will be turned over to
        others,
    together with their fields and their
        wives,
when I stretch out my hand
    against those who live in the land,"
                    declares the LORD.
¹³"From the least to the greatest,
    all are greedy for gain;
prophets and priests alike,
    all practice deceit.
¹⁴They dress the wound of my people
    as though it were not serious.
'Peace, peace,' they say,
    when there is no peace.
¹⁵Are they ashamed of their detestable
        conduct?
    No, they have no shame at all;
    they do not even know how to blush.
So they will fall among the fallen;
    they will be brought down when I
        punish them,"
                    says the LORD.

¹⁶This is what the LORD says:

"Stand at the crossroads and look;
    ask for the ancient paths,
ask where the good way is, and walk in it,
    and you will find rest for your souls.
    But you said, 'We will not walk in it.'

¹⁷I appointed watchmen over you and said,
    'Listen to the sound of the trumpet!'
    But you said, 'We will not listen.'
¹⁸Therefore hear, you nations;
    you who are witnesses,
    observe what will happen to them.
¹⁹Hear, you earth:
    I am bringing disaster on this people,
        the fruit of their schemes,
because they have not listened to my
        words
    and have rejected my law.
²⁰What do I care about incense from Sheba
    or sweet calamus from a distant land?
Your burnt offerings are not acceptable;
    your sacrifices do not please me."

²¹Therefore this is what the LORD says:

"I will put obstacles before this people.
    Parents and children alike will
        stumble over them;
    neighbors and friends will perish."

²²This is what the LORD says:

"Look, an army is coming
    from the land of the north;
a great nation is being stirred up
    from the ends of the earth.
²³They are armed with bow and spear;
    they are cruel and show no mercy.
They sound like the roaring sea
    as they ride on their horses;
they come like men in battle formation
    to attack you, Daughter Zion."

²⁴We have heard reports about them,
    and our hands hang limp.
Anguish has gripped us,
    pain like that of a woman in labor.
²⁵Do not go out to the fields
    or walk on the roads,
for the enemy has a sword,
    and there is terror on every side.
²⁶Put on sackcloth, my people,
    and roll in ashes;
mourn with bitter wailing
    as for an only son,
for suddenly the destroyer
    will come upon us.

²⁷"I have made you a tester of metals
    and my people the ore,
that you may observe
    and test their ways.

ᵃ 10 Hebrew *uncircumcised*

²⁸ They are all hardened rebels,
      going about to slander.
  They are bronze and iron;
      they all act corruptly.
²⁹ The bellows blow fiercely
      to burn away the lead with fire,
  but the refining goes on in vain;
      the wicked are not purged out.
³⁰ They are called rejected silver,
      because the LORD has rejected them."

False Religion Worthless

7 This is the word that came to Jeremiah from the LORD: ² "Stand at the gate of the LORD's house and there proclaim this message:

" 'Hear the word of the LORD, all you people of Judah who come through these gates to worship the LORD. ³ This is what the LORD Almighty, the God of Israel, says: Reform your ways and your actions, and I will let you live in this place. ⁴ Do not trust in deceptive words and say, "This is the temple of the LORD, the temple of the LORD, the temple of the LORD!" ⁵ If you really change your ways and your actions and deal with each other justly, ⁶ if you do not oppress the foreigner, the fatherless or the widow and do not shed innocent blood in this place, and if you do not follow other gods to your own harm, ⁷ then I will let you live in this place, in the land I gave your ancestors for ever and ever. ⁸ But look, you are trusting in deceptive words that are worthless.

⁹ " 'Will you steal and murder, commit adultery and perjury,*ᵃ* burn incense to Baal and follow other gods you have not known, ¹⁰ and then come and stand before me in this house, which bears my Name, and say, "We are safe" — safe to do all these detestable things? ¹¹ Has this house, which bears my Name, become a den of robbers to you? But I have been watching! declares the LORD.

¹² " 'Go now to the place in Shiloh where I first made a dwelling for my Name, and see what I did to it because of the wickedness of my people Israel. ¹³ While you were doing all these things, declares the LORD, I spoke to you again and again, but you did not listen; I called you, but you did not answer. ¹⁴ Therefore, what I did to Shiloh I will now do to the house that bears my Name, the temple you

trust in, the place I gave to you and your ancestors. ¹⁵ I will thrust you from my presence, just as I did all your fellow Israelites, the people of Ephraim.'

¹⁶ "So do not pray for this people nor offer any plea or petition for them; do not plead with me, for I will not listen to you. ¹⁷ Do you not see what they are doing in the towns of Judah and in the streets of Jerusalem? ¹⁸ The children gather wood, the fathers light the fire, and the women knead the dough and make cakes to offer to the Queen of Heaven. They pour out drink offerings to other gods to arouse my anger. ¹⁹ But am I the one they are provoking? declares the LORD. Are they not rather harming themselves, to their own shame?

²⁰ " 'Therefore this is what the Sovereign LORD says: My anger and my wrath will be poured out on this place — on man and beast, on the trees of the field and on the crops of your land — and it will burn and not be quenched.

²¹ " 'This is what the LORD Almighty, the God of Israel, says: Go ahead, add your burnt offerings to your other sacrifices and eat the meat yourselves! ²² For when I brought your ancestors out of Egypt and spoke to them, I did not just give them commands about burnt offerings and sacrifices, ²³ but I gave them this command: Obey me, and I will be your God and you will be my people. Walk in obedience to all I command you, that it may go well with you. ²⁴ But they did not listen or pay attention; instead, they followed the stubborn inclinations of their evil hearts. They went backward and not forward. ²⁵ From the time your ancestors left Egypt until now, day after day, again and again I sent you my servants the prophets. ²⁶ But they did not listen to me or pay attention. They were stiff-necked and did more evil than their ancestors.'

²⁷ "When you tell them all this, they will not listen to you; when you call to them, they will not answer. ²⁸ Therefore say to them, 'This is the nation that has not obeyed the LORD its God or responded to correction. Truth has perished; it has vanished from their lips.

²⁹ " 'Cut off your hair and throw it away; take up a lament on the barren heights, for

---

ᵃ 9 Or *and swear by false gods*

UM, YEAH, ABOUT THAT . . .

READ: JEREMIAH 7:22–24

At the church where I am a pastor, someone sent an email asking to be removed from the church membership. The stated reason for leaving read as follows: "I don't like Kyle's sermons."

That's all it said. That begs for some kind of explanation, so I decided to call the person. I checked the name of the person and got the phone number. When he answered I simply said, "Hey, this is Kyle Idleman. I understand you're leaving the church because you don't like my sermons."

There was a brief silence. It was awkward for a moment, and then he started trying to express what he meant. What he said was not meant to be encouraging, but his words caused me to breathe such a sigh of relief that tears came to my eyes.

BUILDING

FAITH

WISDOM

STRENGTH

"Well . . . whenever I listen to one of the messages I feel like you are trying to interfere with my life."

Yeah, umm, that's kind of like my job description. But do you hear what he was saying? He's saying—I believe in Jesus, I'm a big fan, but don't ask me to follow. I don't mind coming to church on the weekends. I'll pray before meals. I'll do a bit of recycling. I'll even slap a Jesus fish on my bumper. But I don't want Jesus to interfere with my life.

When Jesus defines the relationship he wants with us he makes it clear that being a fan who believes without making any real commitment to follow isn't an option.

Taken from *Not a Fan Student Edition* by Kyle Idleman, copyright © 2012 by City on the Hill Studio, Inc., published by Zondervan.

the LORD has rejected and abandoned this generation that is under his wrath.

The Valley of Slaughter

[30] " 'The people of Judah have done evil in my eyes, declares the LORD. They have set up their detestable idols in the house that bears my Name and have defiled it. [31] They have built the high places of Topheth in the Valley of Ben Hinnom to burn their sons and daughters in the fire — something I did not command, nor did it enter my mind. [32] So beware, the days are coming, declares the LORD, when people will no longer call it Topheth or the Valley of Ben Hinnom, but the Valley of Slaughter, for they will bury the dead in Topheth until there is no more room. [33] Then the carcasses of this people will become food for the birds and the wild animals, and there will be no one to frighten them away. [34] I will bring an end to the sounds of joy and gladness and to the voices of bride and bridegroom in the towns of Judah and the streets of Jerusalem, for the land will become desolate.

8 " 'At that time, declares the LORD, the bones of the kings and officials of Judah, the bones of the priests and prophets, and the bones of the people of Jerusalem will be removed from their graves. [2] They will be exposed to the sun and the moon and all the stars of the heavens, which they have loved and served and which they have followed and consulted and worshiped. They will not be gathered up or buried, but will be like dung lying on the ground. [3] Wherever I banish them, all the survivors of this evil nation will prefer death to life, declares the LORD Almighty.'

Sin and Punishment

[4] "Say to them, 'This is what the LORD says:

" 'When people fall down, do they not
  get up?
 When someone turns away, do they
  not return?
[5] Why then have these people turned
  away?
 Why does Jerusalem always turn away?
 They cling to deceit;
  they refuse to return.
[6] I have listened attentively,

but they do not say what is right.
None of them repent of their wickedness,
  saying, "What have I done?"
Each pursues their own course
  like a horse charging into battle.
[7] Even the stork in the sky
  knows her appointed seasons,
and the dove, the swift and the thrush
  observe the time of their migration.
But my people do not know
  the requirements of the LORD.

[8] " 'How can you say, "We are wise,
  for we have the law of the LORD,"
when actually the lying pen of the
  scribes
  has handled it falsely?
[9] The wise will be put to shame;
  they will be dismayed and trapped.
Since they have rejected the word of
  the LORD,
  what kind of wisdom do they have?
[10] Therefore I will give their wives to
  other men
  and their fields to new owners.
From the least to the greatest,
  all are greedy for gain;
prophets and priests alike,
  all practice deceit.
[11] They dress the wound of my people
  as though it were not serious.
"Peace, peace," they say,
  when there is no peace.
[12] Are they ashamed of their detestable
  conduct?
 No, they have no shame at all;
  they do not even know how to blush.
So they will fall among the fallen;
  they will be brought down when they
  are punished,
                              says the LORD.

[13] " 'I will take away their harvest,
                  declares the LORD.
 There will be no grapes on the vine.
There will be no figs on the tree,
  and their leaves will wither.
What I have given them
  will be taken from them.[a] ' "

[14] Why are we sitting here?
  Gather together!
Let us flee to the fortified cities
  and perish there!

---

[a] 13 The meaning of the Hebrew for this sentence is uncertain.

For the LORD our God has doomed us
to perish
and given us poisoned water to drink,
because we have sinned against him.
¹⁵ We hoped for peace
but no good has come,
for a time of healing
but there is only terror.
¹⁶ The snorting of the enemy's horses
is heard from Dan;
at the neighing of their stallions
the whole land trembles.
They have come to devour
the land and everything in it,
the city and all who live there.

¹⁷ "See, I will send venomous snakes
among you,
vipers that cannot be charmed,
and they will bite you,"
declares the LORD.

¹⁸ You who are my Comforter[a] in sorrow,
my heart is faint within me.
¹⁹ Listen to the cry of my people
from a land far away:
"Is the LORD not in Zion?
Is her King no longer there?"

"Why have they aroused my anger with
their images,
with their worthless foreign idols?"

²⁰ "The harvest is past,
the summer has ended,
and we are not saved."

²¹ Since my people are crushed, I am
crushed;
I mourn, and horror grips me.
²² Is there no balm in Gilead?
Is there no physician there?
Why then is there no healing
for the wound of my people?

9[b] ¹ Oh, that my head were a spring of
water
and my eyes a fountain of tears!
I would weep day and night
for the slain of my people.
² Oh, that I had in the desert
a lodging place for travelers,
so that I might leave my people
and go away from them;

for they are all adulterers,
a crowd of unfaithful people.

³ "They make ready their tongue
like a bow, to shoot lies;
it is not by truth
that they triumph[c] in the land.
They go from one sin to another;
they do not acknowledge me,"
declares the LORD.
⁴ "Beware of your friends;
do not trust anyone in your clan.
For every one of them is a deceiver,[d]
and every friend a slanderer.
⁵ Friend deceives friend,
and no one speaks the truth.
They have taught their tongues to lie;
they weary themselves with sinning.
⁶ You[e] live in the midst of deception;
in their deceit they refuse to
acknowledge me,"
declares the LORD.

⁷ Therefore this is what the LORD Almighty
says:

"See, I will refine and test them,
for what else can I do
because of the sin of my people?
⁸ Their tongue is a deadly arrow;
it speaks deceitfully.
With their mouths they all speak
cordially to their neighbors,
but in their hearts they set traps for
them.
⁹ Should I not punish them for this?"
declares the LORD.
"Should I not avenge myself
on such a nation as this?"

¹⁰ I will weep and wail for the mountains
and take up a lament concerning the
wilderness grasslands.
They are desolate and untraveled,
and the lowing of cattle is not
heard.
The birds have all fled
and the animals are gone.

¹¹ "I will make Jerusalem a heap of ruins,
a haunt of jackals;
and I will lay waste the towns of Judah
so no one can live there."

---

a 18 The meaning of the Hebrew for this word is uncertain.   *b* In Hebrew texts 9:1 is numbered 8:23,
and 9:2-26 is numbered 9:1-25.   *c 3* Or *lies; / they are not valiant for truth*   *d 4* Or *a deceiving Jacob*
e 6 That is, Jeremiah (the Hebrew is singular)

¹²Who is wise enough to understand this? Who has been instructed by the LORD and can explain it? Why has the land been ruined and laid waste like a desert that no one can cross?

¹³The LORD said, "It is because they have forsaken my law, which I set before them; they have not obeyed me or followed my law. ¹⁴Instead, they have followed the stubbornness of their hearts; they have followed the Baals, as their ancestors taught them." ¹⁵Therefore this is what the LORD Almighty, the God of Israel, says: "See, I will make this people eat bitter food and drink poisoned water. ¹⁶I will scatter them among nations that neither they nor their ancestors have known, and I will pursue them with the sword until I have made an end of them."

¹⁷This is what the LORD Almighty says:

"Consider now! Call for the wailing
       women to come;
   send for the most skillful of them.
¹⁸Let them come quickly
   and wail over us
till our eyes overflow with tears
   and water streams from our eyelids.
¹⁹The sound of wailing is heard from
       Zion:
   'How ruined we are!
   How great is our shame!
We must leave our land
   because our houses are in ruins.' "

²⁰Now, you women, hear the word of
       the LORD;
   open your ears to the words of his
       mouth.
Teach your daughters how to wail;
   teach one another a lament.
²¹Death has climbed in through our
       windows
   and has entered our fortresses;
it has removed the children from the
       streets
   and the young men from the public
       squares.

²²Say, "This is what the LORD declares:

" 'Dead bodies will lie
   like dung on the open field,
like cut grain behind the reaper,
   with no one to gather them.' "

²³This is what the LORD says:

"Let not the wise boast of their wisdom
   or the strong boast of their strength
   or the rich boast of their riches,
²⁴but let the one who boasts boast about
       this:
   that they have the understanding to
       know me,
   that I am the LORD, who exercises
       kindness,
   justice and righteousness on earth,
   for in these I delight,"
                   declares the LORD.

²⁵"The days are coming," declares the LORD, "when I will punish all who are circumcised only in the flesh— ²⁶Egypt, Judah, Edom, Ammon, Moab and all who live in the wilderness in distant places.ᵃ For all these nations are really uncircumcised, and even the whole house of Israel is uncircumcised in heart."

God and Idols

10 Hear what the LORD says to you, people of Israel. ²This is what the LORD says:

"Do not learn the ways of the nations
   or be terrified by signs in the heavens,
   though the nations are terrified by
       them.
³For the practices of the peoples are
       worthless;
   they cut a tree out of the forest,
   and a craftsman shapes it with his
       chisel.
⁴They adorn it with silver and gold;
   they fasten it with hammer and nails
   so it will not totter.
⁵Like a scarecrow in a cucumber field,
   their idols cannot speak;
they must be carried
   because they cannot walk.
Do not fear them;
   they can do no harm
   nor can they do any good."

⁶No one is like you, LORD;
   you are great,
   and your name is mighty in power.
⁷Who should not fear you,
   King of the nations?
   This is your due.

ᵃ 26 Or *wilderness and who clip the hair by their foreheads*

ONLY ONE THING

READ: JEREMIAH 9:24

Darkness was creeping across the land of Judah. As Jerusalem falls to the attacking Babylonian army, women who make a job out of loud public wailing take their place in the city's dramatic downfall (Jeremiah 9:17). The entire nation joins their cries for the ruined land. Death has climbed in the windows of homes and forts. Children and young people die in the streets (v. 21).

The nation flails, hoping for anything to save it. Some people think they're smart enough to escape the violence. Others say their strength will let them outrun their enemies. Still others trust their wealth to buy them peace. Then God sends a piercing message through the prophet Jeremiah. In his people's grim time of need, the Lord says, "Let not the wise boast of their wisdom or the strong boast of their strength or the rich boast of their riches" (v. 23). None of those things can rescue God's people. Only the Lord himself deserves their trust.

BUILDING FAITH WISDOM STRENGTH

You might be bright, but that's not enough to save you from truly sticky situations. You might be buff, but the Lord possesses infinitely more power. You might be wealthy, but money can vanish in an instant. In your worst and best moments, there's only one thing worth bragging about—that you know and understand God. He's the one you can count on to always treat you with kindness, justice, and righteousness.

Among all the wise leaders of the nations
and in all their kingdoms,
there is no one like you.

8 They are all senseless and foolish;
they are taught by worthless wooden
idols.
9 Hammered silver is brought from Tarshish
and gold from Uphaz.
What the craftsman and goldsmith
have made
is then dressed in blue and purple —
all made by skilled workers.
10 But the LORD is the true God;
he is the living God, the eternal King.
When he is angry, the earth trembles;
the nations cannot endure his wrath.

11 "Tell them this: 'These gods, who did
not make the heavens and the earth, will
perish from the earth and from under the
heavens.' " *a*

12 But God made the earth by his power;
he founded the world by his wisdom
and stretched out the heavens by his
understanding.
13 When he thunders, the waters in the
heavens roar;
he makes clouds rise from the ends of
the earth.
He sends lightning with the rain
and brings out the wind from his
storehouses.

14 Everyone is senseless and without
knowledge;
every goldsmith is shamed by his idols.
The images he makes are a fraud;
they have no breath in them.
15 They are worthless, the objects of
mockery;
when their judgment comes, they will
perish.
16 He who is the Portion of Jacob is not
like these,
for he is the Maker of all things,
including Israel, the people of his
inheritance —
the LORD Almighty is his name.

Coming Destruction

17 Gather up your belongings to leave
the land,
you who live under siege.

18 For this is what the LORD says:
"At this time I will hurl out
those who live in this land;
I will bring distress on them
so that they may be captured."

19 Woe to me because of my injury!
My wound is incurable!
Yet I said to myself,
"This is my sickness, and I must
endure it."
20 My tent is destroyed;
all its ropes are snapped.
My children are gone from me and are
no more;
no one is left now to pitch my tent
or to set up my shelter.
21 The shepherds are senseless
and do not inquire of the LORD;
so they do not prosper
and all their flock is scattered.
22 Listen! The report is coming —
a great commotion from the land of
the north!
It will make the towns of Judah desolate,
a haunt of jackals.

Jeremiah's Prayer

23 LORD, I know that people's lives are not
their own;
it is not for them to direct their steps.
24 Discipline me, LORD, but only in due
measure —
not in your anger,
or you will reduce me to nothing.
25 Pour out your wrath on the nations
that do not acknowledge you,
on the peoples who do not call on your
name.
For they have devoured Jacob;
they have devoured him completely
and destroyed his homeland.

The Covenant Is Broken

11 This is the word that came to Jeremiah from the LORD: 2 "Listen to the terms of this covenant and tell them to the people of Judah and to those who live in Jerusalem. 3 Tell them that this is what the LORD, the God of Israel, says: 'Cursed is the one who does not obey the terms of this covenant — 4 the terms I commanded your ancestors when I brought them out of Egypt,

a 11 The text of this verse is in Aramaic.

out of the iron-smelting furnace.' I said, 'Obey me and do everything I command you, and you will be my people, and I will be your God. ⁵Then I will fulfill the oath I swore to your ancestors, to give them a land flowing with milk and honey'—the land you possess today."

I answered, "Amen, LORD."

⁶The LORD said to me, "Proclaim all these words in the towns of Judah and in the streets of Jerusalem: 'Listen to the terms of this covenant and follow them. ⁷From the time I brought your ancestors up from Egypt until today, I warned them again and again, saying, "Obey me." ⁸But they did not listen or pay attention; instead, they followed the stubbornness of their evil hearts. So I brought on them all the curses of the covenant I had commanded them to follow but that they did not keep.'"

⁹Then the LORD said to me, "There is a conspiracy among the people of Judah and those who live in Jerusalem. ¹⁰They have returned to the sins of their ancestors, who refused to listen to my words. They have followed other gods to serve them. Both Israel and Judah have broken the covenant I made with their ancestors. ¹¹Therefore this is what the LORD says: 'I will bring on them a disaster they cannot escape. Although they cry out to me, I will not listen to them. ¹²The towns of Judah and the people of Jerusalem will go and cry out to the gods to whom they burn incense, but they will not help them at all when disaster strikes. ¹³You, Judah, have as many gods as you have towns; and the altars you have set up to burn incense to that shameful god Baal are as many as the streets of Jerusalem.'

¹⁴"Do not pray for this people or offer any plea or petition for them, because I will not listen when they call to me in the time of their distress.

¹⁵"What is my beloved doing in my temple
    as she, with many others, works out
      her evil schemes?
  Can consecrated meat avert your
    punishment?
When you engage in your wickedness,
  then you rejoice.ᵃ"

¹⁶The LORD called you a thriving olive tree
  with fruit beautiful in form.

But with the roar of a mighty storm
  he will set it on fire,
    and its branches will be broken.

¹⁷The LORD Almighty, who planted you, has decreed disaster for you, because the people of both Israel and Judah have done evil and aroused my anger by burning incense to Baal.

Plot Against Jeremiah

¹⁸Because the LORD revealed their plot to me, I knew it, for at that time he showed me what they were doing. ¹⁹I had been like a gentle lamb led to the slaughter; I did not realize that they had plotted against me, saying,

"Let us destroy the tree and its fruit;
  let us cut him off from the land of the
    living,
  that his name be remembered no
    more."
²⁰But you, LORD Almighty, who judge
    righteously
  and test the heart and mind,
let me see your vengeance on them,
  for to you I have committed my cause.

²¹Therefore this is what the LORD says about the people of Anathoth who are threatening to kill you, saying, "Do not prophesy in the name of the LORD or you will die by our hands"— ²²therefore this is what the LORD Almighty says: "I will punish them. Their young men will die by the sword, their sons and daughters by famine. ²³Not even a remnant will be left to them, because I will bring disaster on the people of Anathoth in the year of their punishment."

Jeremiah's Complaint

12 You are always righteous, LORD,
  when I bring a case before you.
Yet I would speak with you about your
    justice:
  Why does the way of the wicked
    prosper?
  Why do all the faithless live at ease?
²You have planted them, and they have
    taken root;
  they grow and bear fruit.
You are always on their lips
  but far from their hearts.

ᵃ 15 Or *Could consecrated meat avert your punishment? / Then you would rejoice*

³Yet you know me, LORD;
  you see me and test my thoughts
    about you.
Drag them off like sheep to be butchered!
  Set them apart for the day of slaughter!
⁴How long will the land lie parched
  and the grass in every field be
    withered?
Because those who live in it are wicked,
  the animals and birds have perished.
Moreover, the people are saying,
  "He will not see what happens to us."

God's Answer

⁵"If you have raced with men on foot
  and they have worn you out,
    how can you compete with horses?
If you stumble*ᵃ* in safe country,
  how will you manage in the thickets
    by*ᵇ* the Jordan?
⁶Your relatives, members of your own
    family—
  even they have betrayed you;
    they have raised a loud cry against
      you.
Do not trust them,
  though they speak well of you.

⁷"I will forsake my house,
  abandon my inheritance;
I will give the one I love
  into the hands of her enemies.
⁸My inheritance has become to me
  like a lion in the forest.
She roars at me;
  therefore I hate her.
⁹Has not my inheritance become to me
  like a speckled bird of prey
    that other birds of prey surround and
      attack?
Go and gather all the wild beasts;
  bring them to devour.
¹⁰Many shepherds will ruin my vineyard
  and trample down my field;
they will turn my pleasant field
  into a desolate wasteland.
¹¹It will be made a wasteland,
  parched and desolate before me;
the whole land will be laid waste
  because there is no one who cares.
¹²Over all the barren heights in the desert
  destroyers will swarm,
for the sword of the LORD will devour

from one end of the land to the other;
  no one will be safe.
¹³They will sow wheat but reap thorns;
  they will wear themselves out but gain
    nothing.
They will bear the shame of their harvest
  because of the LORD's fierce anger."

¹⁴This is what the LORD says: "As for all my wicked neighbors who seize the inheritance I gave my people Israel, I will uproot them from their lands and I will uproot the people of Judah from among them. ¹⁵But after I uproot them, I will again have compassion and will bring each of them back to their own inheritance and their own country. ¹⁶And if they learn well the ways of my people and swear by my name, saying, 'As surely as the LORD lives'—even as they once taught my people to swear by Baal—then they will be established among my people. ¹⁷But if any nation does not listen, I will completely uproot and destroy it," declares the LORD.

A Linen Belt

13 This is what the LORD said to me: "Go and buy a linen belt and put it around your waist, but do not let it touch water." ²So I bought a belt, as the LORD directed, and put it around my waist.

³Then the word of the LORD came to me a second time: ⁴"Take the belt you bought and are wearing around your waist, and go now to Perath*ᶜ* and hide it there in a crevice in the rocks." ⁵So I went and hid it at Perath, as the LORD told me.

⁶Many days later the LORD said to me, "Go now to Perath and get the belt I told you to hide there." ⁷So I went to Perath and dug up the belt and took it from the place where I had hidden it, but now it was ruined and completely useless.

⁸Then the word of the LORD came to me: ⁹"This is what the LORD says: 'In the same way I will ruin the pride of Judah and the great pride of Jerusalem. ¹⁰These wicked people, who refuse to listen to my words, who follow the stubbornness of their hearts and go after other gods to serve and worship them, will be like this belt—completely useless! ¹¹For as a belt is bound around the waist, so I bound all the people of Israel and all the people of Judah to me,' declares the

---

ᵃ 5 Or *you feel secure only*   *ᵇ 5* Or *the flooding of*   *ᶜ 4* Or possibly *to the Euphrates*; similarly in verses 5-7

WHAT DO YOU REALLY KNOW?

READ: JEREMIAH 12:3

For as long as I can remember, I've had the books of the Bible memorized in order. Not only that, I can actually say the books of the Bible in one breath. (Don't try to act like you're not impressed.)

The truth is that Jesus doesn't care that I can do that. He's not impressed with my knowledge. Admittedly, I kind of wish he was. I was born into a Christian home and rarely missed a weekend of church. From before I can remember I could quote the Lord's Prayer, John 3:16, and the 23rd Psalm. By thirteen, I felt pressure to have the "Baptist blow-dry" hairstyle that my father was somewhat of a legend for perfecting. When I was in junior high, I even had a picture of Jesus hanging on my wall right next to the poster of Michael Jordan. That is a visual example of how I would define my relationship with Jesus at the time. I was a fan of Jesus, like I was a fan of Mike.

If you would have confronted me on being just a fan of Jesus and not a completely committed follower, I would have pointed to my impressive record whenever I competed in a "quote off." A "quote off" is similar to a "dance off" except you quote Bible verses.

Instead of describing a relationship where I truly knew Jesus, I would have told you what I knew *about* Jesus. But when there is knowledge without intimacy, you're really no more than a fan.

BUILDING

FAITH

WISDOM

STRENGTH

Taken from *Not a Fan Student Edition* by Kyle Idleman, copyright © 2012 by City on the Hill Studio, Inc., published by Zondervan.

LORD, 'to be my people for my renown and praise and honor. But they have not listened.'

Wineskins

¹² "Say to them: 'This is what the LORD, the God of Israel, says: Every wineskin should be filled with wine.' And if they say to you, 'Don't we know that every wineskin should be filled with wine?' ¹³ then tell them, 'This is what the LORD says: I am going to fill with drunkenness all who live in this land, including the kings who sit on David's throne, the priests, the prophets and all those living in Jerusalem. ¹⁴ I will smash them one against the other, parents and children alike, declares the LORD. I will allow no pity or mercy or compassion to keep me from destroying them.'"

Threat of Captivity

¹⁵ Hear and pay attention,
do not be arrogant,
for the LORD has spoken.
¹⁶ Give glory to the LORD your God
before he brings the darkness,
before your feet stumble
on the darkening hills.
You hope for light,
but he will turn it to utter darkness
and change it to deep gloom.
¹⁷ If you do not listen,
I will weep in secret
because of your pride;
my eyes will weep bitterly,
overflowing with tears,
because the LORD's flock will be taken
captive.
¹⁸ Say to the king and to the queen mother,
"Come down from your thrones,
for your glorious crowns
will fall from your heads."
¹⁹ The cities in the Negev will be shut up,
and there will be no one to open them.
All Judah will be carried into exile,
carried completely away.
²⁰ Look up and see
those who are coming from the north.
Where is the flock that was entrusted
to you,
the sheep of which you boasted?
²¹ What will you say when the LORD sets
over you

those you cultivated as your special
allies?
Will not pain grip you
like that of a woman in labor?
²² And if you ask yourself,
"Why has this happened to me?" —
it is because of your many sins
that your skirts have been torn off
and your body mistreated.
²³ Can an Ethiopian*a* change his skin
or a leopard its spots?
Neither can you do good
who are accustomed to doing evil.
²⁴ "I will scatter you like chaff
driven by the desert wind.
²⁵ This is your lot,
the portion I have decreed for you,"
declares the LORD,
"because you have forgotten me
and trusted in false gods.
²⁶ I will pull up your skirts over your face
that your shame may be seen —
²⁷ your adulteries and lustful neighings,
your shameless prostitution!
I have seen your detestable acts
on the hills and in the fields.
Woe to you, Jerusalem!
How long will you be unclean?"

Drought, Famine, Sword

14 This is the word of the LORD that came to Jeremiah concerning the drought:

² "Judah mourns,
her cities languish;
they wail for the land,
and a cry goes up from Jerusalem.
³ The nobles send their servants for water;
they go to the cisterns
but find no water.
They return with their jars unfilled;
dismayed and despairing,
they cover their heads.
⁴ The ground is cracked
because there is no rain in the land;
the farmers are dismayed
and cover their heads.
⁵ Even the doe in the field
deserts her newborn fawn
because there is no grass.
⁶ Wild donkeys stand on the barren
heights

---

a 23 Hebrew *Cushite* (probably a person from the upper Nile region)

and pant like jackals;
their eyes fail
for lack of food."

7 Although our sins testify against us,
do something, LORD, for the sake of
your name.
For we have often rebelled;
we have sinned against you.
8 You who are the hope of Israel,
its Savior in times of distress,
why are you like a stranger in the land,
like a traveler who stays only a night?
9 Why are you like a man taken by surprise,
like a warrior powerless to save?
You are among us, LORD,
and we bear your name;
do not forsake us!

10 This is what the LORD says about this
people:

"They greatly love to wander;
they do not restrain their feet.
So the LORD does not accept them;
he will now remember their
wickedness
and punish them for their sins."

11 Then the LORD said to me, "Do not pray
for the well-being of this people. 12 Although
they fast, I will not listen to their cry; though
they offer burnt offerings and grain offerings, I will not accept them. Instead, I will
destroy them with the sword, famine and
plague."

13 But I said, "Alas, Sovereign LORD! The
prophets keep telling them, 'You will not
see the sword or suffer famine. Indeed, I will
give you lasting peace in this place.'"

14 Then the LORD said to me, "The prophets are prophesying lies in my name. I have
not sent them or appointed them or spoken
to them. They are prophesying to you false
visions, divinations, idolatries[a] and the delusions of their own minds. 15 Therefore this
is what the LORD says about the prophets
who are prophesying in my name: I did not
send them, yet they are saying, 'No sword
or famine will touch this land.' Those same
prophets will perish by sword and famine.
16 And the people they are prophesying to
will be thrown out into the streets of Jerusalem because of the famine and sword. There

will be no one to bury them, their wives,
their sons and their daughters. I will pour
out on them the calamity they deserve.

17 "Speak this word to them:

"'Let my eyes overflow with tears
night and day without ceasing;
for the Virgin Daughter, my people,
has suffered a grievous wound,
a crushing blow.
18 If I go into the country,
I see those slain by the sword;
if I go into the city,
I see the ravages of famine.
Both prophet and priest
have gone to a land they know not.'"

19 Have you rejected Judah completely?
Do you despise Zion?
Why have you afflicted us
so that we cannot be healed?
We hoped for peace
but no good has come,
for a time of healing
but there is only terror.
20 We acknowledge our wickedness, LORD,
and the guilt of our ancestors;
we have indeed sinned against you.
21 For the sake of your name do not
despise us;
do not dishonor your glorious throne.
Remember your covenant with us
and do not break it.
22 Do any of the worthless idols of the
nations bring rain?
Do the skies themselves send down
showers?
No, it is you, LORD our God.
Therefore our hope is in you,
for you are the one who does all this.

15 Then the LORD said to me: "Even if
Moses and Samuel were to stand before me, my heart would not go out to this
people. Send them away from my presence!
Let them go! 2 And if they ask you, 'Where
shall we go?' tell them, 'This is what the
LORD says:

"'Those destined for death, to death;
those for the sword, to the sword;
those for starvation, to starvation;
those for captivity, to captivity.'

---

a 14 Or *visions, worthless divinations*

³ "I will send four kinds of destroyers against them," declares the LORD, "the sword to kill and the dogs to drag away and the birds and the wild animals to devour and destroy. ⁴ I will make them abhorrent to all the kingdoms of the earth because of what Manasseh son of Hezekiah king of Judah did in Jerusalem.

⁵ "Who will have pity on you, Jerusalem?
    Who will mourn for you?
    Who will stop to ask how you are?
⁶ You have rejected me," declares the LORD.
    "You keep on backsliding.
So I will reach out and destroy you;
    I am tired of holding back.
⁷ I will winnow them with a winnowing
        fork
    at the city gates of the land.
I will bring bereavement and destruction
        on my people,
    for they have not changed their ways.
⁸ I will make their widows more numerous
        than the sand of the sea.
At midday I will bring a destroyer
    against the mothers of their young men;
suddenly I will bring down on them
    anguish and terror.
⁹ The mother of seven will grow faint
    and breathe her last.
Her sun will set while it is still day;
    she will be disgraced and humiliated.
I will put the survivors to the sword
    before their enemies,"
                        declares the LORD.

¹⁰ Alas, my mother, that you gave me
        birth,
    a man with whom the whole land
        strives and contends!
I have neither lent nor borrowed,
    yet everyone curses me.

¹¹ The LORD said,

"Surely I will deliver you for a good
        purpose;
    surely I will make your enemies plead
        with you
    in times of disaster and times of
        distress.

¹² "Can a man break iron —
    iron from the north — or bronze?

¹³ "Your wealth and your treasures
    I will give as plunder, without charge,
because of all your sins
    throughout your country.
¹⁴ I will enslave you to your enemies
    in*ᵃ* a land you do not know,
for my anger will kindle a fire
    that will burn against you."

¹⁵ LORD, you understand;
    remember me and care for me.
    Avenge me on my persecutors.
You are long-suffering — do not take me
        away;
    think of how I suffer reproach for
        your sake.
¹⁶ When your words came, I ate them;
    they were my joy and my heart's
        delight,
for I bear your name,
    LORD God Almighty.
¹⁷ I never sat in the company of revelers,
    never made merry with them;
I sat alone because your hand was
        on me
    and you had filled me with
        indignation.
¹⁸ Why is my pain unending
    and my wound grievous and
        incurable?
You are to me like a deceptive brook,
    like a spring that fails.

¹⁹ Therefore this is what the LORD says:

"If you repent, I will restore you
    that you may serve me;
if you utter worthy, not worthless,
        words,
    you will be my spokesman.
Let this people turn to you,
    but you must not turn to them.
²⁰ I will make you a wall to this people,
    a fortified wall of bronze;
they will fight against you
    but will not overcome you,
for I am with you
    to rescue and save you,"
                        declares the LORD.
²¹ "I will save you from the hands of the
        wicked
    and deliver you from the grasp of
        the cruel."

ᵃ 14 Some Hebrew manuscripts, Septuagint and Syriac (see also 17:4); most Hebrew manuscripts *I will cause your enemies to bring you / into*

Day of Disaster

16 Then the word of the LORD came to me: [2] "You must not marry and have sons or daughters in this place." [3] For this is what the LORD says about the sons and daughters born in this land and about the women who are their mothers and the men who are their fathers: [4] "They will die of deadly diseases. They will not be mourned or buried but will be like dung lying on the ground. They will perish by sword and famine, and their dead bodies will become food for the birds and the wild animals."

[5] For this is what the LORD says: "Do not enter a house where there is a funeral meal; do not go to mourn or show sympathy, because I have withdrawn my blessing, my love and my pity from this people," declares the LORD. [6] "Both high and low will die in this land. They will not be buried or mourned, and no one will cut themselves or shave their head for the dead. [7] No one will offer food to comfort those who mourn for the dead — not even for a father or a mother — nor will anyone give them a drink to console them.

[8] "And do not enter a house where there is feasting and sit down to eat and drink. [9] For this is what the LORD Almighty, the God of Israel, says: Before your eyes and in your days I will bring an end to the sounds of joy and gladness and to the voices of bride and bridegroom in this place.

[10] "When you tell these people all this and they ask you, 'Why has the LORD decreed such a great disaster against us? What wrong have we done? What sin have we committed against the LORD our God?' [11] then say to them, 'It is because your ancestors forsook me,' declares the LORD, 'and followed other gods and served and worshiped them. They forsook me and did not keep my law. [12] But you have behaved more wickedly than your ancestors. See how all of you are following the stubbornness of your evil hearts instead of obeying me. [13] So I will throw you out of this land into a land neither you nor your ancestors have known, and there you will serve other gods day and night, for I will show you no favor.'

[14] "However, the days are coming," declares the LORD, "when it will no longer be said, 'As surely as the LORD lives, who brought the Israelites up out of Egypt,' [15] but it will be said, 'As surely as the LORD lives, who brought the Israelites up out of the land of the north and out of all the countries where he had banished them.' For I will restore them to the land I gave their ancestors.

[16] "But now I will send for many fishermen," declares the LORD, "and they will catch them. After that I will send for many hunters, and they will hunt them down on every mountain and hill and from the crevices of the rocks. [17] My eyes are on all their ways; they are not hidden from me, nor is their sin concealed from my eyes. [18] I will repay them double for their wickedness and their sin, because they have defiled my land with the lifeless forms of their vile images and have filled my inheritance with their detestable idols."

[19] LORD, my strength and my fortress,
my refuge in time of distress,
to you the nations will come
from the ends of the earth and say,
"Our ancestors possessed nothing but
false gods,
worthless idols that did them no good.
[20] Do people make their own gods?
Yes, but they are not gods!"

[21] "Therefore I will teach them —
this time I will teach them
my power and might.
Then they will know
that my name is the LORD.

17 "Judah's sin is engraved with an iron tool,
inscribed with a flint point,
on the tablets of their hearts
and on the horns of their altars.
[2] Even their children remember
their altars and Asherah poles[a]
beside the spreading trees
and on the high hills.
[3] My mountain in the land
and your[b] wealth and all your
treasures
I will give away as plunder,
together with your high places,
because of sin throughout your
country.
[4] Through your own fault you will lose
the inheritance I gave you.

---

[a] 2 That is, wooden symbols of the goddess Asherah   [b] 2,3 Or hills / [3] and the mountains of the land. / Your

I will enslave you to your enemies
  in a land you do not know,
for you have kindled my anger,
  and it will burn forever."

⁵This is what the LORD says:

"Cursed is the one who trusts in man,
  who draws strength from mere flesh
  and whose heart turns away from the
    LORD.
⁶That person will be like a bush in the
    wastelands;
  they will not see prosperity when it
    comes.
They will dwell in the parched places of
    the desert,
  in a salt land where no one lives.

⁷"But blessed is the one who trusts in
    the LORD,
  whose confidence is in him.
⁸They will be like a tree planted by the
    water
  that sends out its roots by the stream.
It does not fear when heat comes;
  its leaves are always green.
It has no worries in a year of drought
  and never fails to bear fruit."

⁹The heart is deceitful above all things
  and beyond cure.
  Who can understand it?

¹⁰"I the LORD search the heart
  and examine the mind,
to reward each person according to their
    conduct,
  according to what their deeds
    deserve."

¹¹Like a partridge that hatches eggs it did
    not lay
  are those who gain riches by unjust
    means.
When their lives are half gone, their
    riches will desert them,
  and in the end they will prove to be
    fools.

¹²A glorious throne, exalted from the
    beginning,
  is the place of our sanctuary.
¹³LORD, you are the hope of Israel;
  all who forsake you will be put to
    shame.

Those who turn away from you will be
    written in the dust
  because they have forsaken the LORD,
    the spring of living water.

¹⁴Heal me, LORD, and I will be healed;
  save me and I will be saved,
  for you are the one I praise.
¹⁵They keep saying to me,
  "Where is the word of the LORD?
  Let it now be fulfilled!"
¹⁶I have not run away from being your
    shepherd;
  you know I have not desired the day of
    despair.
  What passes my lips is open before
    you.
¹⁷Do not be a terror to me;
  you are my refuge in the day of
    disaster.
¹⁸Let my persecutors be put to shame,
  but keep me from shame;
let them be terrified,
  but keep me from terror.
Bring on them the day of disaster;
  destroy them with double destruction.

Keeping the Sabbath Day Holy

¹⁹This is what the LORD said to me: "Go
and stand at the Gate of the People,ᵃ through
which the kings of Judah go in and out; stand
also at all the other gates of Jerusalem. ²⁰Say
to them, 'Hear the word of the LORD, you
kings of Judah and all people of Judah and
everyone living in Jerusalem who come
through these gates. ²¹This is what the LORD
says: Be careful not to carry a load on the
Sabbath day or bring it through the gates of
Jerusalem. ²²Do not bring a load out of your
houses or do any work on the Sabbath, but
keep the Sabbath day holy, as I commanded your ancestors. ²³Yet they did not listen
or pay attention; they were stiff-necked and
would not listen or respond to discipline.
²⁴But if you are careful to obey me, declares
the LORD, and bring no load through the
gates of this city on the Sabbath, but keep
the Sabbath day holy by not doing any work
on it, ²⁵then kings who sit on David's throne
will come through the gates of this city with
their officials. They and their officials will
come riding in chariots and on horses, accompanied by the men of Judah and those

---

ᵃ 19 Or *Army*

TIME TO REDEFINE

READ: JEREMIAH 17:14

How we face the future and how we make decisions are based on what we believe about God and what we believe about ourselves. We can say God is in control, but our lives often suggest that we don't totally buy it. We can say that God forgives sin and wipes it away forever, but we still live under guilt.

God wants to renew our minds and redefine our ideas of who he is and who we are in him. We believe about him only what we've seen. We have fuzzy notions of him and partially believe what we've read, heard, and sung about him. But we'd be amazed to realize how much of our faith is still not ours.

I discovered this in how we pray for people. When somebody else is dangerously sick, we pray for "God's will," not for healing, because we're afraid the person won't pull through and we don't want to stick out our necks in public. But if it's my brother or dad, I'm not praying for "God's will." That's my family, and I'm begging God to heal him! Our just-in-case prayers tell us something about our view of God.

BUILDING

FAITH

WISDOM

STRENGTH

I have to dig deep into my roots so God can show me who he is and who I am in him. He has to redefine what saved me and keeps me saved. He has to redefine real fruit. I let him redefine wrong ideas about him and about me. I let him search me and know my heart. I let him have his way.

living in Jerusalem, and this city will be inhabited forever. ²⁶People will come from the towns of Judah and the villages around Jerusalem, from the territory of Benjamin and the western foothills, from the hill country and the Negev, bringing burnt offerings and sacrifices, grain offerings and incense, and bringing thank offerings to the house of the LORD. ²⁷But if you do not obey me to keep the Sabbath day holy by not carrying any load as you come through the gates of Jerusalem on the Sabbath day, then I will kindle an unquenchable fire in the gates of Jerusalem that will consume her fortresses.' "

At the Potter's House

18 This is the word that came to Jeremiah from the LORD: ²"Go down to the potter's house, and there I will give you my message." ³So I went down to the potter's house, and I saw him working at the wheel. ⁴But the pot he was shaping from the clay was marred in his hands; so the potter formed it into another pot, shaping it as seemed best to him.

⁵Then the word of the LORD came to me. ⁶He said, "Can I not do with you, Israel, as this potter does?" declares the LORD. "Like clay in the hand of the potter, so are you in my hand, Israel. ⁷If at any time I announce that a nation or kingdom is to be uprooted, torn down and destroyed, ⁸and if that nation I warned repents of its evil, then I will relent and not inflict on it the disaster I had planned. ⁹And if at another time I announce that a nation or kingdom is to be built up and planted, ¹⁰and if it does evil in my sight and does not obey me, then I will reconsider the good I had intended to do for it.

¹¹"Now therefore say to the people of Judah and those living in Jerusalem, 'This is what the LORD says: Look! I am preparing a disaster for you and devising a plan against you. So turn from your evil ways, each one of you, and reform your ways and your actions.' ¹²But they will reply, 'It's no use. We will continue with our own plans; we will all follow the stubbornness of our evil hearts.' "

¹³Therefore this is what the LORD says:

"Inquire among the nations:
  Who has ever heard anything like this?
A most horrible thing has been done
  by Virgin Israel.
¹⁴Does the snow of Lebanon
  ever vanish from its rocky slopes?
Do its cool waters from distant sources
  ever stop flowing?^a
¹⁵Yet my people have forgotten me;
  they burn incense to worthless idols,
which made them stumble in their ways,
  in the ancient paths.
They made them walk in byways,
  on roads not built up.
¹⁶Their land will be an object of horror
  and of lasting scorn;
all who pass by will be appalled
  and will shake their heads.
¹⁷Like a wind from the east,
  I will scatter them before their
    enemies;
I will show them my back and not my face
  in the day of their disaster."

¹⁸They said, "Come, let's make plans against Jeremiah; for the teaching of the law by the priest will not cease, nor will counsel from the wise, nor the word from the prophets. So come, let's attack him with our tongues and pay no attention to anything he says."

¹⁹Listen to me, LORD;
  hear what my accusers are saying!
²⁰Should good be repaid with evil?
  Yet they have dug a pit for me.
Remember that I stood before you
  and spoke in their behalf
to turn your wrath away from them.
²¹So give their children over to famine;
  hand them over to the power of the
    sword.
Let their wives be made childless and
    widows;
  let their men be put to death,
  their young men slain by the sword in
    battle.
²²Let a cry be heard from their houses
  when you suddenly bring invaders
    against them,
for they have dug a pit to capture me
  and have hidden snares for my feet.
²³But you, LORD, know
  all their plots to kill me.
Do not forgive their crimes
  or blot out their sins from your sight.

^a 14 The meaning of the Hebrew for this sentence is uncertain.

Let them be overthrown before you;
   deal with them in the time of your
      anger.

19 This is what the LORD says: "Go and
buy a clay jar from a potter. Take
along some of the elders of the people and
of the priests ²and go out to the Valley of
Ben Hinnom, near the entrance of the Potsherd Gate. There proclaim the words I tell
you, ³and say, 'Hear the word of the LORD,
you kings of Judah and people of Jerusalem.
This is what the LORD Almighty, the God of
Israel, says: Listen! I am going to bring a disaster on this place that will make the ears
of everyone who hears of it tingle. ⁴For they
have forsaken me and made this a place of
foreign gods; they have burned incense in it
to gods that neither they nor their ancestors
nor the kings of Judah ever knew, and they
have filled this place with the blood of the
innocent. ⁵They have built the high places
of Baal to burn their children in the fire as
offerings to Baal — something I did not command or mention, nor did it enter my mind.
⁶So beware, the days are coming, declares
the LORD, when people will no longer call
this place Topheth or the Valley of Ben Hinnom, but the Valley of Slaughter.

⁷ "'In this place I will ruin*ᵃ* the plans of Judah and Jerusalem. I will make them fall by
the sword before their enemies, at the hands
of those who want to kill them, and I will
give their carcasses as food to the birds and
the wild animals. ⁸I will devastate this city
and make it an object of horror and scorn; all
who pass by will be appalled and will scoff
because of all its wounds. ⁹I will make them
eat the flesh of their sons and daughters, and
they will eat one another's flesh because
their enemies will press the siege so hard
against them to destroy them.'

¹⁰ "Then break the jar while those who go
with you are watching, ¹¹and say to them,
'This is what the LORD Almighty says: I will
smash this nation and this city just as this
potter's jar is smashed and cannot be repaired. They will bury the dead in Topheth
until there is no more room. ¹²This is what
I will do to this place and to those who live
here, declares the LORD. I will make this city
like Topheth. ¹³The houses in Jerusalem

and those of the kings of Judah will be defiled like this place, Topheth — all the houses where they burned incense on the roofs
to all the starry hosts and poured out drink
offerings to other gods.'"

¹⁴Jeremiah then returned from Topheth,
where the LORD had sent him to prophesy,
and stood in the court of the LORD's temple
and said to all the people, ¹⁵"This is what
the LORD Almighty, the God of Israel, says:
'Listen! I am going to bring on this city and
all the villages around it every disaster I
pronounced against them, because they
were stiff-necked and would not listen to my
words.'"

Jeremiah and Pashhur

20 When the priest Pashhur son of Immer, the official in charge of the temple of the LORD, heard Jeremiah prophesying
these things, ²he had Jeremiah the prophet
beaten and put in the stocks at the Upper Gate of Benjamin at the LORD's temple.
³The next day, when Pashhur released him
from the stocks, Jeremiah said to him, "The
LORD's name for you is not Pashhur, but Terror on Every Side. ⁴For this is what the LORD
says: 'I will make you a terror to yourself and
to all your friends; with your own eyes you
will see them fall by the sword of their enemies. I will give all Judah into the hands
of the king of Babylon, who will carry them
away to Babylon or put them to the sword.
⁵I will deliver all the wealth of this city into
the hands of their enemies — all its products, all its valuables and all the treasures
of the kings of Judah. They will take it away
as plunder and carry it off to Babylon. ⁶And
you, Pashhur, and all who live in your house
will go into exile to Babylon. There you will
die and be buried, you and all your friends to
whom you have prophesied lies.'"

Jeremiah's Complaint

⁷You deceived*ᵇ* me, LORD, and I was
    deceived*ᵇ*;
  you overpowered me and prevailed.
  I am ridiculed all day long;
    everyone mocks me.
⁸Whenever I speak, I cry out
    proclaiming violence and
      destruction.

ᵃ 7 The Hebrew for *ruin* sounds like the Hebrew for *jar* (see verses 1 and 10).   *ᵇ* 7 Or *persuaded*

So the word of the Lord has brought me
 insult and reproach all day long.
⁹ But if I say, "I will not mention his word
 or speak anymore in his name,"
his word is in my heart like a fire,
 a fire shut up in my bones.
I am weary of holding it in;
 indeed, I cannot.
¹⁰ I hear many whispering,
 "Terror on every side!
 Denounce him! Let's denounce
 him!"
All my friends
 are waiting for me to slip, saying,
 "Perhaps he will be deceived;
 then we will prevail over him
 and take our revenge on him."

¹¹ But the Lord is with me like a mighty
 warrior;
 so my persecutors will stumble and
 not prevail.
They will fail and be thoroughly
 disgraced;
 their dishonor will never be forgotten.
¹² Lord Almighty, you who examine the
 righteous
 and probe the heart and mind,
let me see your vengeance on them,
 for to you I have committed my cause.

¹³ Sing to the Lord!
 Give praise to the Lord!
He rescues the life of the needy
 from the hands of the wicked.

¹⁴ Cursed be the day I was born!
 May the day my mother bore me not be
 blessed!
¹⁵ Cursed be the man who brought my
 father the news,
 who made him very glad, saying,
 "A child is born to you — a son!"
¹⁶ May that man be like the towns
 the Lord overthrew without pity.
May he hear wailing in the morning,
 a battle cry at noon.
¹⁷ For he did not kill me in the womb,
 with my mother as my grave,
 her womb enlarged forever.
¹⁸ Why did I ever come out of the womb
 to see trouble and sorrow
 and to end my days in shame?

God Rejects Zedekiah's Request

21 The word came to Jeremiah from the Lord when King Zedekiah sent to him Pashhur son of Malkijah and the priest Zephaniah son of Maaseiah. They said: ² "Inquire now of the Lord for us because Nebuchadnezzar[a] king of Babylon is attacking us. Perhaps the Lord will perform wonders for us as in times past so that he will withdraw from us."

³ But Jeremiah answered them, "Tell Zedekiah, ⁴ 'This is what the Lord, the God of Israel, says: I am about to turn against you the weapons of war that are in your hands, which you are using to fight the king of Babylon and the Babylonians[b] who are outside the wall besieging you. And I will gather them inside this city. ⁵ I myself will fight against you with an outstretched hand and a mighty arm in furious anger and in great wrath. ⁶ I will strike down those who live in this city — both man and beast — and they will die of a terrible plague. ⁷ After that, declares the Lord, I will give Zedekiah king of Judah, his officials and the people in this city who survive the plague, sword and famine, into the hands of Nebuchadnezzar king of Babylon and to their enemies who want to kill them. He will put them to the sword; he will show them no mercy or pity or compassion.'

⁸ "Furthermore, tell the people, 'This is what the Lord says: See, I am setting before you the way of life and the way of death. ⁹ Whoever stays in this city will die by the sword, famine or plague. But whoever goes out and surrenders to the Babylonians who are besieging you will live; they will escape with their lives. ¹⁰ I have determined to do this city harm and not good, declares the Lord. It will be given into the hands of the king of Babylon, and he will destroy it with fire.'

¹¹ "Moreover, say to the royal house of Judah, 'Hear the word of the Lord. ¹² This is what the Lord says to you, house of David:

" 'Administer justice every morning;
 rescue from the hand of the oppressor
 the one who has been robbed,
or my wrath will break out and burn
 like fire

---

[a] 2 Hebrew *Nebuchadrezzar*, of which *Nebuchadnezzar* is a variant; here and often in Jeremiah and Ezekiel   [b] 4 Or *Chaldeans*; also in verse 9

because of the evil you have done —
   burn with no one to quench it.
¹³ I am against you, Jerusalem,
   you who live above this valley
   on the rocky plateau, declares the
      LORD —
you who say, "Who can come against us?
   Who can enter our refuge?"
¹⁴ I will punish you as your deeds deserve,
   declares the LORD.
I will kindle a fire in your forests
   that will consume everything
      around you.'"

Judgment Against Wicked Kings

22 This is what the LORD says: "Go down to the palace of the king of Judah and proclaim this message there: ²'Hear the word of the LORD to you, king of Judah, you who sit on David's throne — you, your officials and your people who come through these gates. ³This is what the LORD says: Do what is just and right. Rescue from the hand of the oppressor the one who has been robbed. Do no wrong or violence to the foreigner, the fatherless or the widow, and do not shed innocent blood in this place. ⁴For if you are careful to carry out these commands, then kings who sit on David's throne will come through the gates of this palace, riding in chariots and on horses, accompanied by their officials and their people. ⁵But if you do not obey these commands, declares the LORD, I swear by myself that this palace will become a ruin.'"

⁶For this is what the LORD says about the palace of the king of Judah:

"Though you are like Gilead to me,
   like the summit of Lebanon,
I will surely make you like a wasteland,
   like towns not inhabited.
⁷I will send destroyers against you,
   each man with his weapons,
and they will cut up your fine cedar
      beams
   and throw them into the fire.

⁸"People from many nations will pass by this city and will ask one another, 'Why has the LORD done such a thing to this great city?' ⁹And the answer will be: 'Because they have forsaken the covenant of the LORD

their God and have worshiped and served other gods.'"

¹⁰ Do not weep for the dead king or mourn
      his loss;
   rather, weep bitterly for him who is
      exiled,
because he will never return
   nor see his native land again.

¹¹For this is what the LORD says about Shallum[a] son of Josiah, who succeeded his father as king of Judah but has gone from this place: "He will never return. ¹²He will die in the place where they have led him captive; he will not see this land again."

¹³ "Woe to him who builds his palace by
      unrighteousness,
   his upper rooms by injustice,
making his own people work for nothing,
   not paying them for their labor.
¹⁴ He says, 'I will build myself a great palace
   with spacious upper rooms.'
So he makes large windows in it,
   panels it with cedar
   and decorates it in red.

¹⁵ "Does it make you a king
   to have more and more cedar?
Did not your father have food and drink?
   He did what was right and just,
      so all went well with him.
¹⁶ He defended the cause of the poor
      and needy,
   and so all went well.
Is that not what it means to know me?"
   declares the LORD.
¹⁷ "But your eyes and your heart
   are set only on dishonest gain,
on shedding innocent blood
   and on oppression and extortion."

¹⁸Therefore this is what the LORD says about Jehoiakim son of Josiah king of Judah:

"They will not mourn for him:
   'Alas, my brother! Alas, my sister!'
They will not mourn for him:
   'Alas, my master! Alas, his splendor!'
¹⁹ He will have the burial of a donkey —
   dragged away and thrown
   outside the gates of Jerusalem."

²⁰ "Go up to Lebanon and cry out,
   let your voice be heard in Bashan,

---

a 11 Also called *Jehoahaz*

cry out from Abarim,
for all your allies are crushed.
²¹ I warned you when you felt secure,
but you said, 'I will not listen!'
This has been your way from your youth;
you have not obeyed me.
²² The wind will drive all your shepherds
away,
and your allies will go into exile.
Then you will be ashamed and disgraced
because of all your wickedness.
²³ You who live in 'Lebanon,'ᵃ
who are nestled in cedar buildings,
how you will groan when pangs come
upon you,
pain like that of a woman in labor!

²⁴ "As surely as I live," declares the LORD, "even if you, Jehoiachinᵇ son of Jehoiakim king of Judah, were a signet ring on my right hand, I would still pull you off. ²⁵ I will deliver you into the hands of those who want to kill you, those you fear—Nebuchadnezzar king of Babylon and the Babylonians.ᶜ ²⁶ I will hurl you and the mother who gave you birth into another country, where neither of you was born, and there you both will die. ²⁷ You will never come back to the land you long to return to."

²⁸ Is this man Jehoiachin a despised,
broken pot,
an object no one wants?
Why will he and his children be
hurled out,
cast into a land they do not know?
²⁹ O land, land, land,
hear the word of the LORD!
³⁰ This is what the LORD says:
"Record this man as if childless,
a man who will not prosper in his
lifetime,
for none of his offspring will prosper,
none will sit on the throne of David
or rule anymore in Judah."

The Righteous Branch

23 "Woe to the shepherds who are destroying and scattering the sheep of my pasture!" declares the LORD. ² Therefore this is what the LORD, the God of Israel, says to the shepherds who tend my people:

"Because you have scattered my flock and driven them away and have not bestowed care on them, I will bestow punishment on you for the evil you have done," declares the LORD. ³ "I myself will gather the remnant of my flock out of all the countries where I have driven them and will bring them back to their pasture, where they will be fruitful and increase in number. ⁴ I will place shepherds over them who will tend them, and they will no longer be afraid or terrified, nor will any be missing," declares the LORD.

⁵ "The days are coming," declares the
LORD,
"when I will raise up for Davidᵈ a
righteous Branch,
a King who will reign wisely
and do what is just and right in
the land.
⁶ In his days Judah will be saved
and Israel will live in safety.
This is the name by which he will
be called:
The LORD Our Righteous Savior.

⁷ "So then, the days are coming," declares the LORD, "when people will no longer say, 'As surely as the LORD lives, who brought the Israelites up out of Egypt,' ⁸ but they will say, 'As surely as the LORD lives, who brought the descendants of Israel up out of the land of the north and out of all the countries where he had banished them.' Then they will live in their own land."

Lying Prophets

⁹ Concerning the prophets:

My heart is broken within me;
all my bones tremble.
I am like a drunken man,
like a strong man overcome by wine,
because of the LORD
and his holy words.
¹⁰ The land is full of adulterers;
because of the curseᵉ the land lies
parched
and the pastures in the wilderness are
withered.
The prophets follow an evil course
and use their power unjustly.

ᵃ 23 That is, the palace in Jerusalem (see 1 Kings 7:2) in verse 28   ᶜ 25 Or *Chaldeans*   ᵈ 5 Or *up from David's line*   ᵇ 24 Hebrew *Koniah*, a variant of *Jehoiachin*; also   ᵉ 10 Or *because of these things*

¹¹ "Both prophet and priest are godless;
    even in my temple I find their
        wickedness,"
                    declares the LORD.
¹² "Therefore their path will become
        slippery;
    they will be banished to darkness
    and there they will fall.
I will bring disaster on them
    in the year they are punished,"
                    declares the LORD.

¹³ "Among the prophets of Samaria
        I saw this repulsive thing:
They prophesied by Baal
    and led my people Israel astray.
¹⁴ And among the prophets of Jerusalem
        I have seen something horrible:
    They commit adultery and live a lie.
They strengthen the hands of evildoers,
    so that not one of them turns from
        their wickedness.
They are all like Sodom to me;
    the people of Jerusalem are like
        Gomorrah."

¹⁵ Therefore this is what the LORD Almighty says concerning the prophets:

"I will make them eat bitter food
    and drink poisoned water,
because from the prophets of Jerusalem
    ungodliness has spread throughout
        the land.'"

¹⁶ This is what the LORD Almighty says:

"Do not listen to what the prophets are
        prophesying to you;
    they fill you with false hopes.
They speak visions from their own
        minds,
    not from the mouth of the LORD.
¹⁷ They keep saying to those who
        despise me,
    'The LORD says: You will have peace.'
And to all who follow the stubbornness of
        their hearts
    they say, 'No harm will come to you.'
¹⁸ But which of them has stood in the
        council of the LORD
    to see or to hear his word?
    Who has listened and heard his word?
¹⁹ See, the storm of the LORD
    will burst out in wrath,
a whirlwind swirling down
    on the heads of the wicked.

²⁰ The anger of the LORD will not turn back
    until he fully accomplishes
        the purposes of his heart.
In days to come
    you will understand it clearly.
²¹ I did not send these prophets,
    yet they have run with their message;
I did not speak to them,
    yet they have prophesied.
²² But if they had stood in my council,
    they would have proclaimed my words
        to my people
and would have turned them from their
        evil ways
    and from their evil deeds.

²³ "Am I only a God nearby,"
                    declares the LORD,
    "and not a God far away?
²⁴ Who can hide in secret places
    so that I cannot see them?"
                    declares the LORD.
    "Do not I fill heaven and earth?"
                    declares the LORD.

²⁵ "I have heard what the prophets say who prophesy lies in my name. They say, 'I had a dream! I had a dream!' ²⁶ How long will this continue in the hearts of these lying prophets, who prophesy the delusions of their own minds? ²⁷ They think the dreams they tell one another will make my people forget my name, just as their ancestors forgot my name through Baal worship. ²⁸ Let the prophet who has a dream recount the dream, but let the one who has my word speak it faithfully. For what has straw to do with grain?" declares the LORD. ²⁹ "Is not my word like fire," declares the LORD, "and like a hammer that breaks a rock in pieces?

³⁰ "Therefore," declares the LORD, "I am against the prophets who steal from one another words supposedly from me. ³¹ Yes," declares the LORD, "I am against the prophets who wag their own tongues and yet declare, 'The LORD declares.' ³² Indeed, I am against those who prophesy false dreams," declares the LORD. "They tell them and lead my people astray with their reckless lies, yet I did not send or appoint them. They do not benefit these people in the least," declares the LORD.

False Prophecy

³³ "When these people, or a prophet or a priest, ask you, 'What is the message from

FAKERS

READ: JEREMIAH 23:16

Ancient Judah was awash in people who claimed to speak for God. After all the tough messages Jeremiah brought from the Lord, it's no surprise that an assortment of preachers popped up who spoke happier words. As Jeremiah prophesied destruction, these false prophets uttered things like "You will have peace" and "No harm will come to you" (Jeremiah 23:17).

Jeremiah calls out these fake prophets. He points out that none of them has listened to God and heard his word (v. 18). The Lord hadn't sent them (v. 21). A genuine prophet turns people from their evil ways (v. 22). And the Lord himself wonders how long people will believe these delusions (v. 26).

Back in Deuteronomy 13:1–18 the Lord told his Old Testament people to get rid of false prophets who tempted them away from worshiping the one true God. As a New Testament believer it's not your job to stone people who disagree with the Lord. But often it's still wise to tune out a conversation, change a channel, or surf to another site. Unless you're teaming up with other believers to understand and defend your true faith, feeding on false ideas will pull you away from the Lord.

Like the days of Jeremiah, your world is awash with misguided people who speak lies about God. Look for real spokespeople whose words and actions point to the Lord, and listen closely to them.

BUILDING FAITH WISDOM STRENGTH

the Lord?' say to them, 'What message? I will forsake you, declares the Lord.' ³⁴If a prophet or a priest or anyone else claims, 'This is a message from the Lord,' I will punish them and their household. ³⁵This is what each of you keeps saying to your friends and other Israelites: 'What is the Lord's answer?' or 'What has the Lord spoken?' ³⁶But you must not mention 'a message from the Lord' again, because each one's word becomes their own message. So you distort the words of the living God, the Lord Almighty, our God. ³⁷This is what you keep saying to a prophet: 'What is the Lord's answer to you?' or 'What has the Lord spoken?' ³⁸Although you claim, 'This is a message from the Lord,' this is what the Lord says: You used the words, 'This is a message from the Lord,' even though I told you that you must not claim, 'This is a message from the Lord.' ³⁹Therefore, I will surely forget you and cast you out of my presence along with the city I gave to you and your ancestors. ⁴⁰I will bring on you everlasting disgrace — everlasting shame that will not be forgotten."

Two Baskets of Figs

24 After Jehoiachin[a] son of Jehoiakim king of Judah and the officials, the skilled workers and the artisans of Judah were carried into exile from Jerusalem to Babylon by Nebuchadnezzar king of Babylon, the Lord showed me two baskets of figs placed in front of the temple of the Lord. ²One basket had very good figs, like those that ripen early; the other basket had very bad figs, so bad they could not be eaten.

³Then the Lord asked me, "What do you see, Jeremiah?"

"Figs," I answered. "The good ones are very good, but the bad ones are so bad they cannot be eaten."

⁴Then the word of the Lord came to me: ⁵"This is what the Lord, the God of Israel, says: 'Like these good figs, I regard as good the exiles from Judah, whom I sent away from this place to the land of the Babylonians.[b] ⁶My eyes will watch over them for their good, and I will bring them back to this land. I will build them up and not tear them down; I will plant them and not uproot them. ⁷I will

give them a heart to know me, that I am the Lord. They will be my people, and I will be their God, for they will return to me with all their heart.

⁸"But like the bad figs, which are so bad they cannot be eaten,' says the Lord, 'so will I deal with Zedekiah king of Judah, his officials and the survivors from Jerusalem, whether they remain in this land or live in Egypt. ⁹I will make them abhorrent and an offense to all the kingdoms of the earth, a reproach and a byword, a curse[c] and an object of ridicule, wherever I banish them. ¹⁰I will send the sword, famine and plague against them until they are destroyed from the land I gave to them and their ancestors.' "

Seventy Years of Captivity

25 The word came to Jeremiah concerning all the people of Judah in the fourth year of Jehoiakim son of Josiah king of Judah, which was the first year of Nebuchadnezzar king of Babylon. ²So Jeremiah the prophet said to all the people of Judah and to all those living in Jerusalem: ³For twenty-three years — from the thirteenth year of Josiah son of Amon king of Judah until this very day — the word of the Lord has come to me and I have spoken to you again and again, but you have not listened.

⁴And though the Lord has sent all his servants the prophets to you again and again, you have not listened or paid any attention. ⁵They said, "Turn now, each of you, from your evil ways and your evil practices, and you can stay in the land the Lord gave to you and your ancestors for ever and ever. ⁶Do not follow other gods to serve and worship them; do not arouse my anger with what your hands have made. Then I will not harm you."

⁷"But you did not listen to me," declares the Lord, "and you have aroused my anger with what your hands have made, and you have brought harm to yourselves."

⁸Therefore the Lord Almighty says this: "Because you have not listened to my words, ⁹I will summon all the peoples of the north and my servant Nebuchadnezzar king of Babylon," declares the Lord, "and I will bring them against this land and its inhabitants and against all the surrounding nations.

---

[a] 1 Hebrew *Jeconiah,* a variant of *Jehoiachin*   [b] 5 Or *Chaldeans*   [c] 9 That is, their names will be used in cursing (see 29:22); or, others will see that they are cursed.

I will completely destroy[a] them and make them an object of horror and scorn, and an everlasting ruin. [10]I will banish from them the sounds of joy and gladness, the voices of bride and bridegroom, the sound of millstones and the light of the lamp. [11]This whole country will become a desolate wasteland, and these nations will serve the king of Babylon seventy years.

[12]"But when the seventy years are fulfilled, I will punish the king of Babylon and his nation, the land of the Babylonians,[b] for their guilt," declares the LORD, "and will make it desolate forever. [13]I will bring on that land all the things I have spoken against it, all that are written in this book and prophesied by Jeremiah against all the nations. [14]They themselves will be enslaved by many nations and great kings; I will repay them according to their deeds and the work of their hands."

The Cup of God's Wrath

[15]This is what the LORD, the God of Israel, said to me: "Take from my hand this cup filled with the wine of my wrath and make all the nations to whom I send you drink it. [16]When they drink it, they will stagger and go mad because of the sword I will send among them."

[17]So I took the cup from the LORD's hand and made all the nations to whom he sent me drink it: [18]Jerusalem and the towns of Judah, its kings and officials, to make them a ruin and an object of horror and scorn, a curse[c] — as they are today; [19]Pharaoh king of Egypt, his attendants, his officials and all his people, [20]and all the foreign people there; all the kings of Uz; all the kings of the Philistines (those of Ashkelon, Gaza, Ekron, and the people left at Ashdod); [21]Edom, Moab and Ammon; [22]all the kings of Tyre and Sidon; the kings of the coastlands across the sea; [23]Dedan, Tema, Buz and all who are in distant places[d]; [24]all the kings of Arabia and all the kings of the foreign people who live in the wilderness; [25]all the kings of Zimri, Elam and Media; [26]and all the kings of the north, near and far, one after the other — all the kingdoms on the face of the earth. And after all of them, the king of Sheshak[e] will drink it too.

[27]"Then tell them, 'This is what the LORD Almighty, the God of Israel, says: Drink, get drunk and vomit, and fall to rise no more because of the sword I will send among you.' [28]But if they refuse to take the cup from your hand and drink, tell them, 'This is what the LORD Almighty says: You must drink it! [29]See, I am beginning to bring disaster on the city that bears my Name, and will you indeed go unpunished? You will not go unpunished, for I am calling down a sword on all who live on the earth, declares the LORD Almighty.'

[30]"Now prophesy all these words against them and say to them:

" 'The LORD will roar from on high;
    he will thunder from his holy dwelling
      and roar mightily against his land.
He will shout like those who tread the grapes,
    shout against all who live on the earth.
[31]The tumult will resound to the ends of the earth,
    for the LORD will bring charges against the nations;
he will bring judgment on all mankind
    and put the wicked to the sword,' "
                declares the LORD.

[32]This is what the LORD Almighty says:

"Look! Disaster is spreading
    from nation to nation;
a mighty storm is rising
    from the ends of the earth."

[33]At that time those slain by the LORD will be everywhere — from one end of the earth to the other. They will not be mourned or gathered up or buried, but will be like dung lying on the ground.

[34]Weep and wail, you shepherds;
    roll in the dust, you leaders of the flock.
For your time to be slaughtered has come;
    you will fall like the best of the rams.[f]
[35]The shepherds will have nowhere to flee,
    the leaders of the flock no place to escape.

---

[a] 9 The Hebrew term refers to the irrevocable giving over of things or persons to the LORD, often by totally destroying them.   [b] 12 Or *Chaldeans*   [c] 18 That is, their names to be used in cursing (see 29:22); or, to be seen by others as cursed   [d] 23 Or *who clip the hair by their foreheads*   [e] 26 *Sheshak* is a cryptogram for Babylon.   [f] 34 Septuagint; Hebrew *fall and be shattered like fine pottery*

³⁶Hear the cry of the shepherds,
　　the wailing of the leaders of the flock,
　　for the LORD is destroying their
　　　pasture.
³⁷The peaceful meadows will be laid waste
　　because of the fierce anger of the
　　　LORD.
³⁸Like a lion he will leave his lair,
　　and their land will become desolate
　　because of the sword*a* of the oppressor
　　and because of the LORD's fierce anger.

Jeremiah Threatened With Death

26 Early in the reign of Jehoiakim son of Josiah king of Judah, this word came from the LORD: ²"This is what the LORD says: Stand in the courtyard of the LORD's house and speak to all the people of the towns of Judah who come to worship in the house of the LORD. Tell them everything I command you; do not omit a word. ³Perhaps they will listen and each will turn from their evil ways. Then I will relent and not inflict on them the disaster I was planning because of the evil they have done. ⁴Say to them, 'This is what the LORD says: If you do not listen to me and follow my law, which I have set before you, ⁵and if you do not listen to the words of my servants the prophets, whom I have sent to you again and again (though you have not listened), ⁶then I will make this house like Shiloh and this city a curse*b* among all the nations of the earth.'"

⁷The priests, the prophets and all the people heard Jeremiah speak these words in the house of the LORD. ⁸But as soon as Jeremiah finished telling all the people everything the LORD had commanded him to say, the priests, the prophets and all the people seized him and said, "You must die! ⁹Why do you prophesy in the LORD's name that this house will be like Shiloh and this city will be desolate and deserted?" And all the people crowded around Jeremiah in the house of the LORD.

¹⁰When the officials of Judah heard about these things, they went up from the royal palace to the house of the LORD and took their places at the entrance of the New Gate of the LORD's house. ¹¹Then the priests and the prophets said to the officials and all the

people, "This man should be sentenced to death because he has prophesied against this city. You have heard it with your own ears!"

¹²Then Jeremiah said to all the officials and all the people: "The LORD sent me to prophesy against this house and this city all the things you have heard. ¹³Now reform your ways and your actions and obey the LORD your God. Then the LORD will relent and not bring the disaster he has pronounced against you. ¹⁴As for me, I am in your hands; do with me whatever you think is good and right. ¹⁵Be assured, however, that if you put me to death, you will bring the guilt of innocent blood on yourselves and on this city and on those who live in it, for in truth the LORD has sent me to you to speak all these words in your hearing."

¹⁶Then the officials and all the people said to the priests and the prophets, "This man should not be sentenced to death! He has spoken to us in the name of the LORD our God."

¹⁷Some of the elders of the land stepped forward and said to the entire assembly of people, ¹⁸"Micah of Moresheth prophesied in the days of Hezekiah king of Judah. He told all the people of Judah, 'This is what the LORD Almighty says:

　"'Zion will be plowed like a field,
　　Jerusalem will become a heap of
　　　rubble,
　　the temple hill a mound overgrown
　　　with thickets.'*c*

¹⁹"Did Hezekiah king of Judah or anyone else in Judah put him to death? Did not Hezekiah fear the LORD and seek his favor? And did not the LORD relent, so that he did not bring the disaster he pronounced against them? We are about to bring a terrible disaster on ourselves!"

²⁰(Now Uriah son of Shemaiah from Kiriath Jearim was another man who prophesied in the name of the LORD; he prophesied the same things against this city and this land as Jeremiah did. ²¹When King Jehoiakim and all his officers and officials heard his words, the king was determined to put him to death. But Uriah heard of it and fled

---

a 38 Some Hebrew manuscripts and Septuagint (see also 46:16 and 50:16); most Hebrew manuscripts
anger　　*b 6* That is, its name will be used in cursing (see 29:22); or, others will see that it is cursed.
c 18 Micah 3:12

THE STRAIGHT TRUTH ON SIN

READ: JEREMIAH 26:1-6

et's not talk about sin," said one friend. "It's so negative; let's talk about positive things." Many dislike sin because it sounds judgmental, negative, hopeless. Careless religious leaders use sin as a bully stick, beating people into repentance or forcing them to try harder. To most people, sin only pops up in a conversation to warn them that someone is getting religious. However, God talks about sin to help us diagnose what's wrong in our lives.

Despite its popularity in religious circles, sin isn't a religious idea as much as a human idea. Sin is universal. From our childhood, we begin wondering why we have a hard time making good decisions. We ignore unpopular people. We tell partial truths. We defend ourselves when we're wrong. We fail to love the unlovely. We abuse our power over others. We admit we waste time and need discipline.

BUILDING FAITH WISDOM STRENGTH

Sin takes a good thing, like a chocolate cake, and uses it wrongly, lacing it with arsenic. Sin takes the goodness of sexual passion and uses it for the wrong person, at the wrong time. Sin always preys on the good.

Don't we all twist and warp the good? G. K. Chesterton found sin such an obvious issue he said it was as "practical as potatoes." If we sin any time we twist something good, we can begin to realize how God's laws are more than arbitrary rules; they actually safeguard us. We can see how something like the Ten Commandments protects us from twisting our souls and our relationships.

in fear to Egypt. [22]King Jehoiakim, however, sent Elnathan son of Akbor to Egypt, along with some other men. [23]They brought Uriah out of Egypt and took him to King Jehoiakim, who had him struck down with a sword and his body thrown into the burial place of the common people.)

[24]Furthermore, Ahikam son of Shaphan supported Jeremiah, and so he was not handed over to the people to be put to death.

Judah to Serve Nebuchadnezzar

27 Early in the reign of Zedekiah[a] son of Josiah king of Judah, this word came to Jeremiah from the LORD: [2]This is what the LORD said to me: "Make a yoke out of straps and crossbars and put it on your neck. [3]Then send word to the kings of Edom, Moab, Ammon, Tyre and Sidon through the envoys who have come to Jerusalem to Zedekiah king of Judah. [4]Give them a message for their masters and say, 'This is what the LORD Almighty, the God of Israel, says: "Tell this to your masters: [5]With my great power and outstretched arm I made the earth and its people and the animals that are on it, and I give it to anyone I please. [6]Now I will give all your countries into the hands of my servant Nebuchadnezzar king of Babylon; I will make even the wild animals subject to him. [7]All nations will serve him and his son and his grandson until the time for his land comes; then many nations and great kings will subjugate him.

[8]"'"If, however, any nation or kingdom will not serve Nebuchadnezzar king of Babylon or bow its neck under his yoke, I will punish that nation with the sword, famine and plague, declares the LORD, until I destroy it by his hand. [9]So do not listen to your prophets, your diviners, your interpreters of dreams, your mediums or your sorcerers who tell you, 'You will not serve the king of Babylon.' [10]They prophesy lies to you that will only serve to remove you far from your lands; I will banish you and you will perish. [11]But if any nation will bow its neck under the yoke of the king of Babylon and serve him, I will let that nation remain in its own land to till it and to live there, declares the LORD.'"'"

[12]I gave the same message to Zedekiah king of Judah. I said, "Bow your neck under the yoke of the king of Babylon; serve him and his people, and you will live. [13]Why will you and your people die by the sword, famine and plague with which the LORD has threatened any nation that will not serve the king of Babylon? [14]Do not listen to the words of the prophets who say to you, 'You will not serve the king of Babylon,' for they are prophesying lies to you. [15]'I have not sent them,' declares the LORD. 'They are prophesying lies in my name. Therefore, I will banish you and you will perish, both you and the prophets who prophesy to you.'"

[16]Then I said to the priests and all these people, "This is what the LORD says: Do not listen to the prophets who say, 'Very soon now the articles from the LORD's house will be brought back from Babylon.' They are prophesying lies to you. [17]Do not listen to them. Serve the king of Babylon, and you will live. Why should this city become a ruin? [18]If they are prophets and have the word of the LORD, let them plead with the LORD Almighty that the articles remaining in the house of the LORD and in the palace of the king of Judah and in Jerusalem not be taken to Babylon. [19]For this is what the LORD Almighty says about the pillars, the bronze Sea, the movable stands and the other articles that are left in this city, [20]which Nebuchadnezzar king of Babylon did not take away when he carried Jehoiachin[b] son of Jehoiakim king of Judah into exile from Jerusalem to Babylon, along with all the nobles of Judah and Jerusalem— [21]yes, this is what the LORD Almighty, the God of Israel, says about the things that are left in the house of the LORD and in the palace of the king of Judah and in Jerusalem: [22]'They will be taken to Babylon and there they will remain until the day I come for them,' declares the LORD. 'Then I will bring them back and restore them to this place.'"

The False Prophet Hananiah

28 In the fifth month of that same year, the fourth year, early in the reign of Zedekiah king of Judah, the prophet Hananiah son of Azzur, who was from Gibeon, said

---

[a] *1* A few Hebrew manuscripts and Syriac (see also 27:3,12 and 28:1); most Hebrew manuscripts *Jehoiakim* (Most Septuagint manuscripts do not have this verse.)   [b] *20* Hebrew *Jeconiah*, a variant of *Jehoiachin*

to me in the house of the LORD in the presence of the priests and all the people: ² "This is what the LORD Almighty, the God of Israel, says: 'I will break the yoke of the king of Babylon. ³ Within two years I will bring back to this place all the articles of the LORD's house that Nebuchadnezzar king of Babylon removed from here and took to Babylon. ⁴ I will also bring back to this place Jehoiachin[a] son of Jehoiakim king of Judah and all the other exiles from Judah who went to Babylon,' declares the LORD, 'for I will break the yoke of the king of Babylon.' "

⁵ Then the prophet Jeremiah replied to the prophet Hananiah before the priests and all the people who were standing in the house of the LORD. ⁶ He said, "Amen! May the LORD do so! May the LORD fulfill the words you have prophesied by bringing the articles of the LORD's house and all the exiles back to this place from Babylon. ⁷ Nevertheless, listen to what I have to say in your hearing and in the hearing of all the people: ⁸ From early times the prophets who preceded you and me have prophesied war, disaster and plague against many countries and great kingdoms. ⁹ But the prophet who prophesies peace will be recognized as one truly sent by the LORD only if his prediction comes true."

¹⁰ Then the prophet Hananiah took the yoke off the neck of the prophet Jeremiah and broke it, ¹¹ and he said before all the people, "This is what the LORD says: 'In the same way I will break the yoke of Nebuchadnezzar king of Babylon off the neck of all the nations within two years.' " At this, the prophet Jeremiah went on his way.

¹² After the prophet Hananiah had broken the yoke off the neck of the prophet Jeremiah, the word of the LORD came to Jeremiah: ¹³ "Go and tell Hananiah, 'This is what the LORD says: You have broken a wooden yoke, but in its place you will get a yoke of iron. ¹⁴ This is what the LORD Almighty, the God of Israel, says: I will put an iron yoke on the necks of all these nations to make them serve Nebuchadnezzar king of Babylon, and they will serve him. I will even give him control over the wild animals.' "

¹⁵ Then the prophet Jeremiah said to Hananiah the prophet, "Listen, Hananiah! The LORD has not sent you, yet you have persuaded this nation to trust in lies. ¹⁶ Therefore this is what the LORD says: 'I am about to remove you from the face of the earth. This very year you are going to die, because you have preached rebellion against the LORD.' "

¹⁷ In the seventh month of that same year, Hananiah the prophet died.

A Letter to the Exiles

29 This is the text of the letter that the prophet Jeremiah sent from Jerusalem to the surviving elders among the exiles and to the priests, the prophets and all the other people Nebuchadnezzar had carried into exile from Jerusalem to Babylon. ² (This was after King Jehoiachin[a] and the queen mother, the court officials and the leaders of Judah and Jerusalem, the skilled workers and the artisans had gone into exile from Jerusalem.) ³ He entrusted the letter to Elasah son of Shaphan and to Gemariah son of Hilkiah, whom Zedekiah king of Judah sent to King Nebuchadnezzar in Babylon. It said:

⁴ This is what the LORD Almighty, the God of Israel, says to all those I carried into exile from Jerusalem to Babylon: ⁵ "Build houses and settle down; plant gardens and eat what they produce. ⁶ Marry and have sons and daughters; find wives for your sons and give your daughters in marriage, so that they too may have sons and daughters. Increase in number there; do not decrease. ⁷ Also, seek the peace and prosperity of the city to which I have carried you into exile. Pray to the LORD for it, because if it prospers, you too will prosper." ⁸ Yes, this is what the LORD Almighty, the God of Israel, says: "Do not let the prophets and diviners among you deceive you. Do not listen to the dreams you encourage them to have. ⁹ They are prophesying lies to you in my name. I have not sent them," declares the LORD.

¹⁰ This is what the LORD says: "When seventy years are completed for Babylon, I will come to you and fulfill my good promise to bring you back to this place. ¹¹ For I know the plans I have for you," declares the LORD, "plans to prosper you and not to harm you, plans to give you hope and a future. ¹² Then you

---

[a] 4,2 Hebrew *Jeconiah*, a variant of *Jehoiachin*

will call on me and come and pray to me, and I will listen to you. ¹³You will seek me and find me when you seek me with all your heart. ¹⁴I will be found by you," declares the Lord, "and will bring you back from captivity.ᵃ I will gather you from all the nations and places where I have banished you," declares the Lord, "and will bring you back to the place from which I carried you into exile."

¹⁵You may say, "The Lord has raised up prophets for us in Babylon," ¹⁶but this is what the Lord says about the king who sits on David's throne and all the people who remain in this city, your fellow citizens who did not go with you into exile — ¹⁷yes, this is what the Lord Almighty says: "I will send the sword, famine and plague against them and I will make them like figs that are so bad they cannot be eaten. ¹⁸I will pursue them with the sword, famine and plague and will make them abhorrent to all the kingdoms of the earth, a curseᵇ and an object of horror, of scorn and reproach, among all the nations where I drive them. ¹⁹For they have not listened to my words," declares the Lord, "words that I sent to them again and again by my servants the prophets. And you exiles have not listened either," declares the Lord.

²⁰Therefore, hear the word of the Lord, all you exiles whom I have sent away from Jerusalem to Babylon. ²¹This is what the Lord Almighty, the God of Israel, says about Ahab son of Kolaiah and Zedekiah son of Maaseiah, who are prophesying lies to you in my name: "I will deliver them into the hands of Nebuchadnezzar king of Babylon, and he will put them to death before your very eyes. ²²Because of them, all the exiles from Judah who are in Babylon will use this curse: 'May the Lord treat you like Zedekiah and Ahab, whom the king of Babylon burned in the fire.' ²³For they have done outrageous things in Israel; they have committed adultery with their neighbors' wives, and in my name they have uttered lies — which I did not

authorize. I know it and am a witness to it," declares the Lord.

Message to Shemaiah

²⁴Tell Shemaiah the Nehelamite, ²⁵"This is what the Lord Almighty, the God of Israel, says: You sent letters in your own name to all the people in Jerusalem, to the priest Zephaniah son of Maaseiah, and to all the other priests. You said to Zephaniah, ²⁶'The Lord has appointed you priest in place of Jehoiada to be in charge of the house of the Lord; you should put any maniac who acts like a prophet into the stocks and neck-irons. ²⁷So why have you not reprimanded Jeremiah from Anathoth, who poses as a prophet among you? ²⁸He has sent this message to us in Babylon: It will be a long time. Therefore build houses and settle down; plant gardens and eat what they produce.'"

²⁹Zephaniah the priest, however, read the letter to Jeremiah the prophet. ³⁰Then the word of the Lord came to Jeremiah: ³¹"Send this message to all the exiles: 'This is what the Lord says about Shemaiah the Nehelamite: Because Shemaiah has prophesied to you, even though I did not send him, and has persuaded you to trust in lies, ³²this is what the Lord says: I will surely punish Shemaiah the Nehelamite and his descendants. He will have no one left among this people, nor will he see the good things I will do for my people, declares the Lord, because he has preached rebellion against me.'"

Restoration of Israel

30 This is the word that came to Jeremiah from the Lord: ²"This is what the Lord, the God of Israel, says: 'Write in a book all the words I have spoken to you. ³The days are coming,' declares the Lord, 'when I will bring my people Israel and Judah back from captivityᶜ and restore them to the land I gave their ancestors to possess,' says the Lord."

⁴These are the words the Lord spoke concerning Israel and Judah: ⁵"This is what the Lord says:

"'Cries of fear are heard —
    terror, not peace.
⁶Ask and see:
    Can a man bear children?

ᵃ 14 Or *will restore your fortunes*   ᵇ 18 That is, their names will be used in cursing (see verse 22); or, others will see that they are cursed.   ᶜ 3 Or *will restore the fortunes of my people Israel and Judah*

Then why do I see every strong man
    with his hands on his stomach like a
        woman in labor,
    every face turned deathly pale?
⁷ How awful that day will be!
    No other will be like it.
It will be a time of trouble for Jacob,
    but he will be saved out of it.

⁸ " 'In that day,' declares the LORD
        Almighty,
    'I will break the yoke off their necks
and will tear off their bonds;
    no longer will foreigners enslave them.
⁹ Instead, they will serve the LORD
        their God
    and David their king,
    whom I will raise up for them.

¹⁰ " 'So do not be afraid, Jacob my servant;
    do not be dismayed, Israel,'
                declares the LORD.
    'I will surely save you out of a distant
        place,
    your descendants from the land of
        their exile.
Jacob will again have peace and security,
    and no one will make him afraid.
¹¹ I am with you and will save you,'
        declares the LORD.
    'Though I completely destroy all the
        nations
    among which I scatter you,
    I will not completely destroy you.
I will discipline you but only in due
        measure;
    I will not let you go entirely
        unpunished.'

¹² "This is what the LORD says:

" 'Your wound is incurable,
    your injury beyond healing.
¹³ There is no one to plead your cause,
    no remedy for your sore,
    no healing for you.
¹⁴ All your allies have forgotten you;
    they care nothing for you.
I have struck you as an enemy would
    and punished you as would the cruel,
because your guilt is so great
    and your sins so many.
¹⁵ Why do you cry out over your wound,
    your pain that has no cure?
Because of your great guilt and many sins
    I have done these things to you.

¹⁶ " 'But all who devour you will be
        devoured;
    all your enemies will go into exile.
Those who plunder you will be
        plundered;
    all who make spoil of you I will despoil.
¹⁷ But I will restore you to health
    and heal your wounds,'
                declares the LORD,
'because you are called an outcast,
    Zion for whom no one cares.'

¹⁸ "This is what the LORD says:

" 'I will restore the fortunes of Jacob's
        tents
    and have compassion on his dwellings;
the city will be rebuilt on her ruins,
    and the palace will stand in its proper
        place.
¹⁹ From them will come songs of
        thanksgiving
    and the sound of rejoicing.
I will add to their numbers,
    and they will not be decreased;
I will bring them honor,
    and they will not be disdained.
²⁰ Their children will be as in days of old,
    and their community will be
        established before me;
    I will punish all who oppress them.
²¹ Their leader will be one of their own;
    their ruler will arise from among them.
I will bring him near and he will come
        close to me—
    for who is he who will devote himself
        to be close to me?'
                declares the LORD.
²² " 'So you will be my people,
    and I will be your God.' "

²³ See, the storm of the LORD
    will burst out in wrath,
a driving wind swirling down
    on the heads of the wicked.
²⁴ The fierce anger of the LORD will not turn
        back
    until he fully accomplishes
    the purposes of his heart.
In days to come
    you will understand this.

31 "At that time," declares the LORD, "I
will be the God of all the families of
Israel, and they will be my people."

[2] This is what the LORD says:

"The people who survive the sword
     will find favor in the wilderness;
I will come to give rest to Israel."

[3] The LORD appeared to us in the past,[a]
saying:

"I have loved you with an everlasting
          love;
I have drawn you with unfailing
          kindness.
[4] I will build you up again,
     and you, Virgin Israel, will be rebuilt.
Again you will take up your timbrels
     and go out to dance with the joyful.
[5] Again you will plant vineyards
     on the hills of Samaria;
the farmers will plant them
     and enjoy their fruit.
[6] There will be a day when watchmen
          cry out
     on the hills of Ephraim,
'Come, let us go up to Zion,
     to the LORD our God.' "

[7] This is what the LORD says:

"Sing with joy for Jacob;
     shout for the foremost of the nations.
Make your praises heard, and say,
     'LORD, save your people,
     the remnant of Israel.'
[8] See, I will bring them from the land of
          the north
     and gather them from the ends of the
          earth.
Among them will be the blind and the
          lame,
     expectant mothers and women in
          labor;
     a great throng will return.
[9] They will come with weeping;
     they will pray as I bring them back.
I will lead them beside streams of water
     on a level path where they will not
          stumble,
because I am Israel's father,
     and Ephraim is my firstborn son.

[10] "Hear the word of the LORD, you
          nations;
     proclaim it in distant coastlands:
'He who scattered Israel will gather them

and will watch over his flock like a
          shepherd.'
[11] For the LORD will deliver Jacob
     and redeem them from the hand of
          those stronger than they.
[12] They will come and shout for joy on the
          heights of Zion;
     they will rejoice in the bounty of the
          LORD —
the grain, the new wine and the olive oil,
     the young of the flocks and herds.
They will be like a well-watered garden,
     and they will sorrow no more.
[13] Then young women will dance and
          be glad,
     young men and old as well.
I will turn their mourning into gladness;
     I will give them comfort and joy
          instead of sorrow.
[14] I will satisfy the priests with abundance,
     and my people will be filled with my
          bounty,"
                         declares the LORD.

[15] This is what the LORD says:

"A voice is heard in Ramah,
     mourning and great weeping,
Rachel weeping for her children
     and refusing to be comforted,
     because they are no more."

[16] This is what the LORD says:

"Restrain your voice from weeping
     and your eyes from tears,
for your work will be rewarded,"
                         declares the LORD.
"They will return from the land of the
          enemy.
[17] So there is hope for your descendants,"
                         declares the LORD.
"Your children will return to their own
          land.

[18] "I have surely heard Ephraim's moaning:
'You disciplined me like an unruly
          calf,
     and I have been disciplined.
Restore me, and I will return,
     because you are the LORD my God.
[19] After I strayed,
     I repented;
after I came to understand,
     I beat my breast.

I was ashamed and humiliated
   because I bore the disgrace of my
      youth.'
20 Is not Ephraim my dear son,
   the child in whom I delight?
Though I often speak against him,
   I still remember him.
Therefore my heart yearns for him;
   I have great compassion for him,"
               declares the LORD.

21 "Set up road signs;
   put up guideposts.
Take note of the highway,
   the road that you take.
Return, Virgin Israel,
   return to your towns.
22 How long will you wander,
   unfaithful Daughter Israel?
The LORD will create a new thing on
      earth—
   the woman will return to*a* the man."

23 This is what the LORD Almighty, the God of Israel, says: "When I bring them back from captivity,*b* the people in the land of Judah and in its towns will once again use these words: 'The LORD bless you, you prosperous city, you sacred mountain.' 24 People will live together in Judah and all its towns—farmers and those who move about with their flocks. 25 I will refresh the weary and satisfy the faint."

26 At this I awoke and looked around. My sleep had been pleasant to me.

27 "The days are coming," declares the LORD, "when I will plant the kingdoms of Israel and Judah with the offspring of people and of animals. 28 Just as I watched over them to uproot and tear down, and to overthrow, destroy and bring disaster, so I will watch over them to build and to plant," declares the LORD. 29 "In those days people will no longer say,

  'The parents have eaten sour grapes,
    and the children's teeth are set
      on edge.'

30 Instead, everyone will die for their own sin; whoever eats sour grapes—their own teeth will be set on edge.

31 "The days are coming," declares the
   LORD,

"when I will make a new covenant
with the people of Israel
   and with the people of Judah.
32 It will not be like the covenant
   I made with their ancestors
when I took them by the hand
   to lead them out of Egypt,
because they broke my covenant,
   though I was a husband to*c* them,*d*"
               declares the LORD.
33 "This is the covenant I will make with the
     people of Israel
   after that time," declares the LORD.
"I will put my law in their minds
   and write it on their hearts.
I will be their God,
   and they will be my people.
34 No longer will they teach their neighbor,
   or say to one another, 'Know the LORD,'
because they will all know me,
   from the least of them to the greatest,"
               declares the LORD.
"For I will forgive their wickedness
   and will remember their sins no more."

35 This is what the LORD says,

he who appoints the sun
   to shine by day,
who decrees the moon and stars
   to shine by night,
who stirs up the sea
   so that its waves roar—
   the LORD Almighty is his name:
36 "Only if these decrees vanish from my
     sight,"
   declares the LORD,
"will Israel ever cease
   being a nation before me."

37 This is what the LORD says:

"Only if the heavens above can be
     measured
   and the foundations of the earth below
     be searched out
will I reject all the descendants of Israel
   because of all they have done,"
               declares the LORD.

38 "The days are coming," declares the LORD, "when this city will be rebuilt for me from the Tower of Hananel to the Corner Gate. 39 The measuring line will stretch from

---

a 22 Or *will protect*   *b 23* Or *I restore their fortunes away from*   *d 32* Or *was their master*   *c 32* Hebrew; Septuagint and Syriac */ and I turned*

BOLD PLAN

READ: JEREMIAH 31:31-32

The old "covenant" or "agreement" between God and people wasn't working. Nothing was wrong with the plan the Lord had laid out. He had grabbed his people by the hand and loosed them from slavery in Egypt. But as soon as the people had their freedom, they bowed to other gods.

God needed a bold new plan. The old covenant was a list of rules on tablets of stone, inscribed by God's finger and passed down through Moses (Exodus 31:18). Those laws came at people from the outside, telling people to obey but giving them no power to do good. But now the Lord promises to make a new and better agreement with his people. He says, "I will put my law in their minds and write it on their hearts" (Jeremiah 31:33). He will be their God, and they will be his people. Everyone will know him well, and he will totally forgive their evil ways.

BUILDING

FAITH

WISDOM

STRENGTH

The New Testament shows you that better agreement between God and people. It's a fresh plan for how they get along. It calls Jesus "the mediator of a new covenant" (Hebrews 12:24) begun at the cross. As a Christian, you're part of that new covenant. Through Jesus, he provides a way for you to be forgiven. Through the Holy Spirit, he gives you all the power you need to obey. God wants you to get with his bold new plan.

there straight to the hill of Gareb and then turn to Goah. [40] The whole valley where dead bodies and ashes are thrown, and all the terraces out to the Kidron Valley on the east as far as the corner of the Horse Gate, will be holy to the LORD. The city will never again be uprooted or demolished."

Jeremiah Buys a Field

32 This is the word that came to Jeremiah from the LORD in the tenth year of Zedekiah king of Judah, which was the eighteenth year of Nebuchadnezzar. [2] The army of the king of Babylon was then besieging Jerusalem, and Jeremiah the prophet was confined in the courtyard of the guard in the royal palace of Judah.

[3] Now Zedekiah king of Judah had imprisoned him there, saying, "Why do you prophesy as you do? You say, 'This is what the LORD says: I am about to give this city into the hands of the king of Babylon, and he will capture it. [4] Zedekiah king of Judah will not escape the Babylonians[a] but will certainly be given into the hands of the king of Babylon, and will speak with him face to face and see him with his own eyes. [5] He will take Zedekiah to Babylon, where he will remain until I deal with him, declares the LORD. If you fight against the Babylonians, you will not succeed.'"

[6] Jeremiah said, "The word of the LORD came to me: [7] Hanamel son of Shallum your uncle is going to come to you and say, 'Buy my field at Anathoth, because as nearest relative it is your right and duty to buy it.'

[8] "Then, just as the LORD had said, my cousin Hanamel came to me in the courtyard of the guard and said, 'Buy my field at Anathoth in the territory of Benjamin. Since it is your right to redeem it and possess it, buy it for yourself.'

"I knew that this was the word of the LORD; [9] so I bought the field at Anathoth from my cousin Hanamel and weighed out for him seventeen shekels[b] of silver. [10] I signed and sealed the deed, had it witnessed, and weighed out the silver on the scales. [11] I took the deed of purchase — the sealed copy containing the terms and conditions, as well as the unsealed copy — [12] and I gave this deed to Baruch son of Neriah, the son of Mahse-

iah, in the presence of my cousin Hanamel and of the witnesses who had signed the deed and of all the Jews sitting in the courtyard of the guard.

[13] "In their presence I gave Baruch these instructions: [14] 'This is what the LORD Almighty, the God of Israel, says: Take these documents, both the sealed and unsealed copies of the deed of purchase, and put them in a clay jar so they will last a long time. [15] For this is what the LORD Almighty, the God of Israel, says: Houses, fields and vineyards will again be bought in this land.'

[16] "After I had given the deed of purchase to Baruch son of Neriah, I prayed to the LORD:

[17] "Ah, Sovereign LORD, you have made the heavens and the earth by your great power and outstretched arm. Nothing is too hard for you. [18] You show love to thousands but bring the punishment for the parents' sins into the laps of their children after them. Great and mighty God, whose name is the LORD Almighty, [19] great are your purposes and mighty are your deeds. Your eyes are open to the ways of all mankind; you reward each person according to their conduct and as their deeds deserve. [20] You performed signs and wonders in Egypt and have continued them to this day, in Israel and among all mankind, and have gained the renown that is still yours. [21] You brought your people Israel out of Egypt with signs and wonders, by a mighty hand and an outstretched arm and with great terror. [22] You gave them this land you had sworn to give their ancestors, a land flowing with milk and honey. [23] They came in and took possession of it, but they did not obey you or follow your law; they did not do what you commanded them to do. So you brought all this disaster on them.

[24] "See how the siege ramps are built up to take the city. Because of the sword, famine and plague, the city will be given into the hands of the Babylonians who are attacking it. What you said has happened, as you now see. [25] And though the city will be given into the

---

[a] 4 Or *Chaldeans*; also in verses 5, 24, 25, 28, 29 and 43   [b] 9 That is, about 7 ounces or about 200 grams

hands of the Babylonians, you, Sovereign Lᴏʀᴅ, say to me, 'Buy the field with silver and have the transaction witnessed.'"

²⁶Then the word of the Lᴏʀᴅ came to Jeremiah: ²⁷"I am the Lᴏʀᴅ, the God of all mankind. Is anything too hard for me? ²⁸Therefore this is what the Lᴏʀᴅ says: I am about to give this city into the hands of the Babylonians and to Nebuchadnezzar king of Babylon, who will capture it. ²⁹The Babylonians who are attacking this city will come in and set it on fire; they will burn it down, along with the houses where the people aroused my anger by burning incense on the roofs to Baal and by pouring out drink offerings to other gods.

³⁰"The people of Israel and Judah have done nothing but evil in my sight from their youth; indeed, the people of Israel have done nothing but arouse my anger with what their hands have made, declares the Lᴏʀᴅ. ³¹From the day it was built until now, this city has so aroused my anger and wrath that I must remove it from my sight. ³²The people of Israel and Judah have provoked me by all the evil they have done—they, their kings and officials, their priests and prophets, the people of Judah and those living in Jerusalem. ³³They turned their backs to me and not their faces; though I taught them again and again, they would not listen or respond to discipline. ³⁴They set up their vile images in the house that bears my Name and defiled it. ³⁵They built high places for Baal in the Valley of Ben Hinnom to sacrifice their sons and daughters to Molek, though I never commanded—nor did it enter my mind—that they should do such a detestable thing and so make Judah sin.

³⁶"You are saying about this city, 'By the sword, famine and plague it will be given into the hands of the king of Babylon'; but this is what the Lᴏʀᴅ, the God of Israel, says: ³⁷I will surely gather them from all the lands where I banish them in my furious anger and great wrath; I will bring them back to this place and let them live in safety. ³⁸They will be my people, and I will be their God. ³⁹I will give them singleness of heart and action, so that they will always fear me and that all will then go well for them and for their children after them. ⁴⁰I will make an everlasting covenant with them: I will never stop doing good to them, and I will inspire them to fear me, so that they will never turn away from me. ⁴¹I will rejoice in doing them good and will assuredly plant them in this land with all my heart and soul.

⁴²"This is what the Lᴏʀᴅ says: As I have brought all this great calamity on this people, so I will give them all the prosperity I have promised them. ⁴³Once more fields will be bought in this land of which you say, 'It is a desolate waste, without people or animals, for it has been given into the hands of the Babylonians.' ⁴⁴Fields will be bought for silver, and deeds will be signed, sealed and witnessed in the territory of Benjamin, in the villages around Jerusalem, in the towns of Judah and in the towns of the hill country, of the western foothills and of the Negev, because I will restore their fortunes,ᵃ declares the Lᴏʀᴅ."

Promise of Restoration

33 While Jeremiah was still confined in the courtyard of the guard, the word of the Lᴏʀᴅ came to him a second time: ²"This is what the Lᴏʀᴅ says, he who made the earth, the Lᴏʀᴅ who formed it and established it—the Lᴏʀᴅ is his name: ³'Call to me and I will answer you and tell you great and unsearchable things you do not know.' ⁴For this is what the Lᴏʀᴅ, the God of Israel, says about the houses in this city and the royal palaces of Judah that have been torn down to be used against the siege ramps and the sword ⁵in the fight with the Babylonians*ᵇ*: 'They will be filled with the dead bodies of the people I will slay in my anger and wrath. I will hide my face from this city because of all its wickedness.

⁶"'Nevertheless, I will bring health and healing to it; I will heal my people and will let them enjoy abundant peace and security. ⁷I will bring Judah and Israel back from captivityᶜ and will rebuild them as they were before. ⁸I will cleanse them from all the sin they have committed against me and will forgive all their sins of rebellion against me. ⁹Then this city will bring me renown, joy, praise and honor before all nations on earth

---

ᵃ 44 Or *will bring them back from captivity and Israel*   ᵇ 5 Or *Chaldeans*   ᶜ 7 Or *will restore the fortunes of Judah*

WATCHING AND WAITING

READ: JEREMIAH 33:6-9

No normal kid gets to open presents before a birthday or Christmas. Operative word: normal. That's not my family. My mom used to beg me to open my gifts because she could hardly wait to give them! "Are you sure? Not even one? Here, just this small one! C'mon!" And now I do with our kids what she did with me.

I think that's how the Heavenly Father feels about the art of gift giving. He can hardly wait to keep his promises. He can hardly wait to act on his Word. He can hardly wait to answer our prayers. And when we take him at his Word, he can hardly contain his joy. True story.

BUILDING

FAITH

WISDOM

STRENGTH

We sometimes pray like God doesn't want to keep his promises, and we have to beg him to. You have no idea how badly God wants to keep his promises! That's why he made them in the first place. We sometimes pray as if our bold prayers that circle the promises of God might offend the God who made them. Are you kidding me? God is offended by anything less! There's nothing God loves more than showing off his power. We only doubt God because we doubt ourselves.

God isn't holding out or holding back. It's not in his nature to withhold any good thing from us. He won't bless disobedience, straight up, but he'll definitely bless obedience. And his capacity to give is far greater than your capacity to receive.

Taken from *The Circle Maker Student Edition* by Mark Batterson with Parker Batterson, copyright © 2012 by Mark Batterson, published by Zondervan.

that hear of all the good things I do for it; and they will be in awe and will tremble at the abundant prosperity and peace I provide for it.'

¹⁰"This is what the LORD says: 'You say about this place, "It is a desolate waste, without people or animals." Yet in the towns of Judah and the streets of Jerusalem that are deserted, inhabited by neither people nor animals, there will be heard once more ¹¹ the sounds of joy and gladness, the voices of bride and bridegroom, and the voices of those who bring thank offerings to the house of the LORD, saying,

> "Give thanks to the LORD Almighty,
>   for the LORD is good;
>   his love endures forever."

For I will restore the fortunes of the land as they were before,' says the LORD.

¹²"This is what the LORD Almighty says: 'In this place, desolate and without people or animals—in all its towns there will again be pastures for shepherds to rest their flocks. ¹³ In the towns of the hill country, of the western foothills and of the Negev, in the territory of Benjamin, in the villages around Jerusalem and in the towns of Judah, flocks will again pass under the hand of the one who counts them,' says the LORD.

¹⁴"'The days are coming,' declares the LORD, 'when I will fulfill the good promise I made to the people of Israel and Judah.

¹⁵"'In those days and at that time
>   I will make a righteous Branch sprout
>   from David's line;
>   he will do what is just and right in the
>   land.
¹⁶ In those days Judah will be saved
>   and Jerusalem will live in safety.
>   This is the name by which it^a will be
>   called:
>   The LORD Our Righteous Savior.'

¹⁷For this is what the LORD says: 'David will never fail to have a man to sit on the throne of Israel, ¹⁸ nor will the Levitical priests ever fail to have a man to stand before me continually to offer burnt offerings, to burn grain offerings and to present sacrifices.'"

¹⁹The word of the LORD came to Jeremiah: ²⁰"This is what the LORD says: 'If you can break my covenant with the day and my covenant with the night, so that day and night no longer come at their appointed time, ²¹ then my covenant with David my servant—and my covenant with the Levites who are priests ministering before me—can be broken and David will no longer have a descendant to reign on his throne. ²² I will make the descendants of David my servant and the Levites who minister before me as countless as the stars in the sky and as measureless as the sand on the seashore.'"

²³The word of the LORD came to Jeremiah: ²⁴"Have you not noticed that these people are saying, 'The LORD has rejected the two kingdoms^b he chose'? So they despise my people and no longer regard them as a nation. ²⁵ This is what the LORD says: 'If I have not made my covenant with day and night and established the laws of heaven and earth, ²⁶ then I will reject the descendants of Jacob and David my servant and will not choose one of his sons to rule over the descendants of Abraham, Isaac and Jacob. For I will restore their fortunes^c and have compassion on them.'"

Warning to Zedekiah

34 While Nebuchadnezzar king of Babylon and all his army and all the kingdoms and peoples in the empire he ruled were fighting against Jerusalem and all its surrounding towns, this word came to Jeremiah from the LORD: ²"This is what the LORD, the God of Israel, says: Go to Zedekiah king of Judah and tell him, 'This is what the LORD says: I am about to give this city into the hands of the king of Babylon, and he will burn it down. ³You will not escape from his grasp but will surely be captured and given into his hands. You will see the king of Babylon with your own eyes, and he will speak with you face to face. And you will go to Babylon.

⁴"'Yet hear the LORD's promise to you, Zedekiah king of Judah. This is what the LORD says concerning you: You will not die by the sword; ⁵you will die peacefully. As people made a funeral fire in honor of your predecessors, the kings who ruled before you, so they will make a fire in your honor and lament, "Alas, master!" I myself make this promise, declares the LORD.'"

---

^a 16 Or he   ^b 24 Or families   ^c 26 Or will bring them back from captivity

⁶Then Jeremiah the prophet told all this to Zedekiah king of Judah, in Jerusalem, ⁷while the army of the king of Babylon was fighting against Jerusalem and the other cities of Judah that were still holding out—Lachish and Azekah. These were the only fortified cities left in Judah.

Freedom for Slaves

⁸The word came to Jeremiah from the LORD after King Zedekiah had made a covenant with all the people in Jerusalem to proclaim freedom for the slaves. ⁹Everyone was to free their Hebrew slaves, both male and female; no one was to hold a fellow Hebrew in bondage. ¹⁰So all the officials and people who entered into this covenant agreed that they would free their male and female slaves and no longer hold them in bondage. They agreed, and set them free. ¹¹But afterward they changed their minds and took back the slaves they had freed and enslaved them again.

¹²Then the word of the LORD came to Jeremiah: ¹³"This is what the LORD, the God of Israel, says: I made a covenant with your ancestors when I brought them out of Egypt, out of the land of slavery. I said, ¹⁴'Every seventh year each of you must free any fellow Hebrews who have sold themselves to you. After they have served you six years, you must let them go free.'ᵃ Your ancestors, however, did not listen to me or pay attention to me. ¹⁵Recently you repented and did what is right in my sight: Each of you proclaimed freedom to your own people. You even made a covenant before me in the house that bears my Name. ¹⁶But now you have turned around and profaned my name; each of you has taken back the male and female slaves you had set free to go where they wished. You have forced them to become your slaves again.

¹⁷"Therefore this is what the LORD says: You have not obeyed me; you have not proclaimed freedom to your own people. So I now proclaim 'freedom' for you, declares the LORD—'freedom' to fall by the sword, plague and famine. I will make you abhorrent to all the kingdoms of the earth. ¹⁸Those who have violated my covenant and have not fulfilled the terms of the covenant they made before me, I will treat like the calf they cut in two and then walked between its pieces. ¹⁹The leaders of Judah and Jerusalem, the court officials, the priests and all the people of the land who walked between the pieces of the calf, ²⁰I will deliver into the hands of their enemies who want to kill them. Their dead bodies will become food for the birds and the wild animals.

²¹"I will deliver Zedekiah king of Judah and his officials into the hands of their enemies who want to kill them, to the army of the king of Babylon, which has withdrawn from you. ²²I am going to give the order, declares the LORD, and I will bring them back to this city. They will fight against it, take it and burn it down. And I will lay waste the towns of Judah so no one can live there."

The Rekabites

35 This is the word that came to Jeremiah from the LORD during the reign of Jehoiakim son of Josiah king of Judah: ²"Go to the Rekabite family and invite them to come to one of the side rooms of the house of the LORD and give them wine to drink."

³So I went to get Jaazaniah son of Jeremiah, the son of Habazziniah, and his brothers and all his sons—the whole family of the Rekabites. ⁴I brought them into the house of the LORD, into the room of the sons of Hanan son of Igdaliah the man of God. It was next to the room of the officials, which was over that of Maaseiah son of Shallum the doorkeeper. ⁵Then I set bowls full of wine and some cups before the Rekabites and said to them, "Drink some wine."

⁶But they replied, "We do not drink wine, because our forefather Jehonadabᵇ son of Rekab gave us this command: 'Neither you nor your descendants must ever drink wine. ⁷Also you must never build houses, sow seed or plant vineyards; you must never have any of these things, but must always live in tents. Then you will live a long time in the land where you are nomads.' ⁸We have obeyed everything our forefather Jehonadab son of Rekab commanded us. Neither we nor our wives nor our sons and daughters have ever drunk wine ⁹or built houses to live in or had vineyards, fields or crops. ¹⁰We have lived in tents and have fully obeyed everything our

---

ᵃ 14 Deut. 15:12   ᵇ 6 Hebrew *Jonadab*, a variant of *Jehonadab*; here and often in this chapter forefather Jehonadab commanded us. [11] But when Nebuchadnezzar king of Babylon invaded this land, we said, 'Come, we must go to Jerusalem to escape the Babylonian[a] and Aramean armies.' So we have remained in Jerusalem."

[12] Then the word of the LORD came to Jeremiah, saying: [13] "This is what the LORD Almighty, the God of Israel, says: Go and tell the people of Judah and those living in Jerusalem, 'Will you not learn a lesson and obey my words?' declares the LORD. [14] 'Jehonadab son of Rekab ordered his descendants not to drink wine and this command has been kept. To this day they do not drink wine, because they obey their forefather's command. But I have spoken to you again and again, yet you have not obeyed me. [15] Again and again I sent all my servants the prophets to you. They said, "Each of you must turn from your wicked ways and reform your actions; do not follow other gods to serve them. Then you will live in the land I have given to you and your ancestors." But you have not paid attention or listened to me. [16] The descendants of Jehonadab son of Rekab have carried out the command their forefather gave them, but these people have not obeyed me.'

[17] "Therefore this is what the LORD God Almighty, the God of Israel, says: 'Listen! I am going to bring on Judah and on everyone living in Jerusalem every disaster I pronounced against them. I spoke to them, but they did not listen; I called to them, but they did not answer.'"

[18] Then Jeremiah said to the family of the Rekabites, "This is what the LORD Almighty, the God of Israel, says: 'You have obeyed the command of your forefather Jehonadab and have followed all his instructions and have done everything he ordered.' [19] Therefore this is what the LORD Almighty, the God of Israel, says: 'Jehonadab son of Rekab will never fail to have a descendant to serve me.'"

Jehoiakim Burns Jeremiah's Scroll

36 In the fourth year of Jehoiakim son of Josiah king of Judah, this word came to Jeremiah from the LORD: [2] "Take a scroll and write on it all the words I have spoken to you concerning Israel, Judah and all the other nations from the time I began speaking to you in the reign of Josiah till now. [3] Perhaps when the people of Judah hear about every disaster I plan to inflict on them, they will each turn from their wicked ways; then I will forgive their wickedness and their sin."

[4] So Jeremiah called Baruch son of Neriah, and while Jeremiah dictated all the words the LORD had spoken to him, Baruch wrote them on the scroll. [5] Then Jeremiah told Baruch, "I am restricted; I am not allowed to go to the LORD's temple. [6] So you go to the house of the LORD on a day of fasting and read to the people from the scroll the words of the LORD that you wrote as I dictated. Read them to all the people of Judah who come in from their towns. [7] Perhaps they will bring their petition before the LORD and will each turn from their wicked ways, for the anger and wrath pronounced against this people by the LORD are great."

[8] Baruch son of Neriah did everything Jeremiah the prophet told him to do; at the LORD's temple he read the words of the LORD from the scroll. [9] In the ninth month of the fifth year of Jehoiakim son of Josiah king of Judah, a time of fasting before the LORD was proclaimed for all the people in Jerusalem and those who had come from the towns of Judah. [10] From the room of Gemariah son of Shaphan the secretary, which was in the upper courtyard at the entrance of the New Gate of the temple, Baruch read to all the people at the LORD's temple the words of Jeremiah from the scroll.

[11] When Micaiah son of Gemariah, the son of Shaphan, heard all the words of the LORD from the scroll, [12] he went down to the secretary's room in the royal palace, where all the officials were sitting: Elishama the secretary, Delaiah son of Shemaiah, Elnathan son of Akbor, Gemariah son of Shaphan, Zedekiah son of Hananiah, and all the other officials. [13] After Micaiah told them everything he had heard Baruch read to the people from the scroll, [14] all the officials sent Jehudi son of Nethaniah, the son of Shelemiah, the son of Cushi, to say to Baruch, "Bring the scroll from which you have read to the people and come." So Baruch son of Neriah went to them with the scroll in his hand. [15] They said to him, "Sit down, please, and read it to us."

So Baruch read it to them. [16] When they

---

[a] 11 Or *Chaldean*

heard all these words, they looked at each other in fear and said to Baruch, "We must report all these words to the king." ¹⁷Then they asked Baruch, "Tell us, how did you come to write all this? Did Jeremiah dictate it?"

¹⁸"Yes," Baruch replied, "he dictated all these words to me, and I wrote them in ink on the scroll."

¹⁹Then the officials said to Baruch, "You and Jeremiah, go and hide. Don't let anyone know where you are."

²⁰After they put the scroll in the room of Elishama the secretary, they went to the king in the courtyard and reported everything to him. ²¹The king sent Jehudi to get the scroll, and Jehudi brought it from the room of Elishama the secretary and read it to the king and all the officials standing beside him. ²²It was the ninth month and the king was sitting in the winter apartment, with a fire burning in the firepot in front of him. ²³Whenever Jehudi had read three or four columns of the scroll, the king cut them off with a scribe's knife and threw them into the firepot, until the entire scroll was burned in the fire. ²⁴The king and all his attendants who heard all these words showed no fear, nor did they tear their clothes. ²⁵Even though Elnathan, Delaiah and Gemariah urged the king not to burn the scroll, he would not listen to them. ²⁶Instead, the king commanded Jerahmeel, a son of the king, Seraiah son of Azriel and Shelemiah son of Abdeel to arrest Baruch the scribe and Jeremiah the prophet. But the LORD had hidden them.

²⁷After the king burned the scroll containing the words that Baruch had written at Jeremiah's dictation, the word of the LORD came to Jeremiah: ²⁸"Take another scroll and write on it all the words that were on the first scroll, which Jehoiakim king of Judah burned up. ²⁹Also tell Jehoiakim king of Judah, 'This is what the LORD says: You burned that scroll and said, "Why did you write on it that the king of Babylon would certainly come and destroy this land and wipe from it both man and beast?" ³⁰Therefore this is what the LORD says about Jehoiakim king of Judah: He will have no one to sit on the throne of David; his body will be thrown out and exposed to the heat by day and the frost

by night. ³¹I will punish him and his children and his attendants for their wickedness; I will bring on them and those living in Jerusalem and the people of Judah every disaster I pronounced against them, because they have not listened.'"

³²So Jeremiah took another scroll and gave it to the scribe Baruch son of Neriah, and as Jeremiah dictated, Baruch wrote on it all the words of the scroll that Jehoiakim king of Judah had burned in the fire. And many similar words were added to them.

Jeremiah in Prison

37 Zedekiah son of Josiah was made king of Judah by Nebuchadnezzar king of Babylon; he reigned in place of Jehoiachin[a] son of Jehoiakim. ²Neither he nor his attendants nor the people of the land paid any attention to the words the LORD had spoken through Jeremiah the prophet.

³King Zedekiah, however, sent Jehukal son of Shelemiah with the priest Zephaniah son of Maaseiah to Jeremiah the prophet with this message: "Please pray to the LORD our God for us."

⁴Now Jeremiah was free to come and go among the people, for he had not yet been put in prison. ⁵Pharaoh's army had marched out of Egypt, and when the Babylonians[b] who were besieging Jerusalem heard the report about them, they withdrew from Jerusalem.

⁶Then the word of the LORD came to Jeremiah the prophet: ⁷"This is what the LORD, the God of Israel, says: Tell the king of Judah, who sent you to inquire of me, 'Pharaoh's army, which has marched out to support you, will go back to its own land, to Egypt. ⁸Then the Babylonians will return and attack this city; they will capture it and burn it down.'

⁹"This is what the LORD says: Do not deceive yourselves, thinking, 'The Babylonians will surely leave us.' They will not! ¹⁰Even if you were to defeat the entire Babylonian[c] army that is attacking you and only wounded men were left in their tents, they would come out and burn this city down."

¹¹After the Babylonian army had withdrawn from Jerusalem because of Pharaoh's

---

a 1 Hebrew *Koniah,* a variant of *Jehoiachin*   *b 5* Or *Chaldeans;* also in verses 8, 9, 13 and 14
c 10 Or *Chaldean;* also in verse 11

SHARE YOUR FAITH

READ: JEREMIAH 36:23

Friends might ignore you when you try to tell them about Jesus. Or they might unmistakably signal you to shut up. But you haven't likely experienced the outrageous hostility the prophet Jeremiah faces from King Jehoiakim.

Jeremiah 36 shows the prophet listening carefully to every word the Lord speaks about the fate of Israel, Judah, and the surrounding nations. The Lord threatens disaster, hoping his people will turn from evil and seek forgiveness. Jeremiah dictates God's message to his scribe, Baruch, who reads the Lord's words in the temple. When royal officials hear these words, fear pierces their hearts. They insist the king hear the message.

As Jehudi, Jeremiah's secretary/assistant, reads the Lord's words, King Jehoiakim slices the scroll, tossing it column by column into the fire. The king and his attendants show no trepidation. They don't rip their clothing, an ancient sign of alarm and grief. Rather than turning from evil and seeking forgiveness, the king tries to silence Jeremiah and Baruch. He orders their arrest, and the Lord responds with a promise to carry out all his threats for Judah's destruction.

Your friends might not be eager to listen to God. But that shouldn't stop you from paying attention to the Lord's words and putting them into action—and respectfully sharing what he says.

BUILDING FAITH WISDOM STRENGTH

army, [12]Jeremiah started to leave the city to go to the territory of Benjamin to get his share of the property among the people there. [13]But when he reached the Benjamin Gate, the captain of the guard, whose name was Irijah son of Shelemiah, the son of Hananiah, arrested him and said, "You are deserting to the Babylonians!"

[14]"That's not true!" Jeremiah said. "I am not deserting to the Babylonians." But Irijah would not listen to him; instead, he arrested Jeremiah and brought him to the officials. [15]They were angry with Jeremiah and had him beaten and imprisoned in the house of Jonathan the secretary, which they had made into a prison.

[16]Jeremiah was put into a vaulted cell in a dungeon, where he remained a long time. [17]Then King Zedekiah sent for him and had him brought to the palace, where he asked him privately, "Is there any word from the LORD?"

"Yes," Jeremiah replied, "you will be delivered into the hands of the king of Babylon."

[18]Then Jeremiah said to King Zedekiah, "What crime have I committed against you or your attendants or this people, that you have put me in prison? [19]Where are your prophets who prophesied to you, 'The king of Babylon will not attack you or this land'? [20]But now, my lord the king, please listen. Let me bring my petition before you: Do not send me back to the house of Jonathan the secretary, or I will die there."

[21]King Zedekiah then gave orders for Jeremiah to be placed in the courtyard of the guard and given a loaf of bread from the street of the bakers each day until all the bread in the city was gone. So Jeremiah remained in the courtyard of the guard.

Jeremiah Thrown Into a Cistern

38 Shephatiah son of Mattan, Gedaliah son of Pashhur, Jehukal[a] son of Shelemiah, and Pashhur son of Malkijah heard what Jeremiah was telling all the people when he said, [2]"This is what the LORD says: 'Whoever stays in this city will die by the sword, famine or plague, but whoever goes over to the Babylonians[b] will live. They will escape with their lives; they will live.'

[3]And this is what the LORD says: 'This city will certainly be given into the hands of the army of the king of Babylon, who will capture it.' "

[4]Then the officials said to the king, "This man should be put to death. He is discouraging the soldiers who are left in this city, as well as all the people, by the things he is saying to them. This man is not seeking the good of these people but their ruin."

[5]"He is in your hands," King Zedekiah answered. "The king can do nothing to oppose you."

[6]So they took Jeremiah and put him into the cistern of Malkijah, the king's son, which was in the courtyard of the guard. They lowered Jeremiah by ropes into the cistern; it had no water in it, only mud, and Jeremiah sank down into the mud.

[7]But Ebed-Melek, a Cushite,[c] an official[d] in the royal palace, heard that they had put Jeremiah into the cistern. While the king was sitting in the Benjamin Gate, [8]Ebed-Melek went out of the palace and said to him, [9]"My lord the king, these men have acted wickedly in all they have done to Jeremiah the prophet. They have thrown him into a cistern, where he will starve to death when there is no longer any bread in the city."

[10]Then the king commanded Ebed-Melek the Cushite, "Take thirty men from here with you and lift Jeremiah the prophet out of the cistern before he dies."

[11]So Ebed-Melek took the men with him and went to a room under the treasury in the palace. He took some old rags and worn-out clothes from there and let them down with ropes to Jeremiah in the cistern. [12]Ebed-Melek the Cushite said to Jeremiah, "Put these old rags and worn-out clothes under your arms to pad the ropes." Jeremiah did so, [13]and they pulled him up with the ropes and lifted him out of the cistern. And Jeremiah remained in the courtyard of the guard.

Zedekiah Questions Jeremiah Again

[14]Then King Zedekiah sent for Jeremiah the prophet and had him brought to the third entrance to the temple of the LORD. "I am going to ask you something," the king said to Jeremiah. "Do not hide anything from me."

---

[a] 1 Hebrew *Jukal*, a variant of *Jehukal*   [b] 2 Or *Chaldeans*; also in verses 18, 19 and 23   [c] 7 Probably from the upper Nile region   [d] 7 Or *a eunuch*

[15] Jeremiah said to Zedekiah, "If I give you an answer, will you not kill me? Even if I did give you counsel, you would not listen to me."

[16] But King Zedekiah swore this oath secretly to Jeremiah: "As surely as the LORD lives, who has given us breath, I will neither kill you nor hand you over to those who want to kill you."

[17] Then Jeremiah said to Zedekiah, "This is what the LORD God Almighty, the God of Israel, says: 'If you surrender to the officers of the king of Babylon, your life will be spared and this city will not be burned down; you and your family will live. [18] But if you will not surrender to the officers of the king of Babylon, this city will be given into the hands of the Babylonians and they will burn it down; you yourself will not escape from them.'"

[19] King Zedekiah said to Jeremiah, "I am afraid of the Jews who have gone over to the Babylonians, for the Babylonians may hand me over to them and they will mistreat me."

[20] "They will not hand you over," Jeremiah replied. "Obey the LORD by doing what I tell you. Then it will go well with you, and your life will be spared. [21] But if you refuse to surrender, this is what the LORD has revealed to me: [22] All the women left in the palace of the king of Judah will be brought out to the officials of the king of Babylon. Those women will say to you:

"'They misled you and overcame you—
    those trusted friends of yours.
Your feet are sunk in the mud;
    your friends have deserted you.'

[23] "All your wives and children will be brought out to the Babylonians. You yourself will not escape from their hands but will be captured by the king of Babylon; and this city will[a] be burned down."

[24] Then Zedekiah said to Jeremiah, "Do not let anyone know about this conversation, or you may die. [25] If the officials hear that I talked with you, and they come to you and say, 'Tell us what you said to the king and what the king said to you; do not hide it from us or we will kill you,' [26] then tell them, 'I was pleading with the king not to send me back to Jonathan's house to die there.'"

[27] All the officials did come to Jeremiah and question him, and he told them everything the king had ordered him to say. So they said no more to him, for no one had heard his conversation with the king.

[28] And Jeremiah remained in the courtyard of the guard until the day Jerusalem was captured.

The Fall of Jerusalem

39 This is how Jerusalem was taken: [1] In the ninth year of Zedekiah king of Judah, in the tenth month, Nebuchadnezzar king of Babylon marched against Jerusalem with his whole army and laid siege to it. [2] And on the ninth day of the fourth month of Zedekiah's eleventh year, the city wall was broken through. [3] Then all the officials of the king of Babylon came and took seats in the Middle Gate: Nergal-Sharezer of Samgar, Nebo-Sarsekim a chief officer, Nergal-Sharezer a high official and all the other officials of the king of Babylon. [4] When Zedekiah king of Judah and all the soldiers saw them, they fled; they left the city at night by way of the king's garden, through the gate between the two walls, and headed toward the Arabah.[b]

[5] But the Babylonian[c] army pursued them and overtook Zedekiah in the plains of Jericho. They captured him and took him to Nebuchadnezzar king of Babylon at Riblah in the land of Hamath, where he pronounced sentence on him. [6] There at Riblah the king of Babylon slaughtered the sons of Zedekiah before his eyes and also killed all the nobles of Judah. [7] Then he put out Zedekiah's eyes and bound him with bronze shackles to take him to Babylon.

[8] The Babylonians[d] set fire to the royal palace and the houses of the people and broke down the walls of Jerusalem. [9] Nebuzaradan commander of the imperial guard carried into exile to Babylon the people who remained in the city, along with those who had gone over to him, and the rest of the people. [10] But Nebuzaradan the commander of the guard left behind in the land of Judah some of the poor people, who owned nothing; and at that time he gave them vineyards and fields.

[11] Now Nebuchadnezzar king of Babylon had given these orders about Jeremiah through Nebuzaradan commander of the

---

[a] 23 Or *and you will cause this city to*   [b] 4 Or *the Jordan Valley*   [c] 5 Or *Chaldean*   [d] 8 Or *Chaldeans*

imperial guard: ¹²"Take him and look after him; don't harm him but do for him whatever he asks." ¹³So Nebuzaradan the commander of the guard, Nebushazban a chief officer, Nergal-Sharezer a high official and all the other officers of the king of Babylon ¹⁴sent and had Jeremiah taken out of the courtyard of the guard. They turned him over to Gedaliah son of Ahikam, the son of Shaphan, to take him back to his home. So he remained among his own people.

¹⁵While Jeremiah had been confined in the courtyard of the guard, the word of the LORD came to him: ¹⁶"Go and tell Ebed-Melek the Cushite, 'This is what the LORD Almighty, the God of Israel, says: I am about to fulfill my words against this city—words concerning disaster, not prosperity. At that time they will be fulfilled before your eyes. ¹⁷But I will rescue you on that day, declares the LORD; you will not be given into the hands of those you fear. ¹⁸I will save you; you will not fall by the sword but will escape with your life, because you trust in me, declares the LORD.'"

Jeremiah Freed

40 The word came to Jeremiah from the LORD after Nebuzaradan commander of the imperial guard had released him at Ramah. He had found Jeremiah bound in chains among all the captives from Jerusalem and Judah who were being carried into exile to Babylon. ²When the commander of the guard found Jeremiah, he said to him, "The LORD your God decreed this disaster for this place. ³And now the LORD has brought it about; he has done just as he said he would. All this happened because you people sinned against the LORD and did not obey him. ⁴But today I am freeing you from the chains on your wrists. Come with me to Babylon, if you like, and I will look after you; but if you do not want to, then don't come. Look, the whole country lies before you; go wherever you please." ⁵However, before Jeremiah turned to go,ᵃ Nebuzaradan added, "Go back to Gedaliah son of Ahikam, the son of Shaphan, whom the king of Babylon has appointed over the towns of Judah, and live with him among the people, or go anywhere else you please."

Then the commander gave him provisions and a present and let him go. ⁶So Jeremiah went to Gedaliah son of Ahikam at Mizpah and stayed with him among the people who were left behind in the land.

Gedaliah Assassinated

⁷When all the army officers and their men who were still in the open country heard that the king of Babylon had appointed Gedaliah son of Ahikam as governor over the land and had put him in charge of the men, women and children who were the poorest in the land and who had not been carried into exile to Babylon, ⁸they came to Gedaliah at Mizpah—Ishmael son of Nethaniah, Johanan and Jonathan the sons of Kareah, Seraiah son of Tanhumeth, the sons of Ephai the Netophathite, and Jaazaniahᵇ the son of the Maakathite, and their men. ⁹Gedaliah son of Ahikam, the son of Shaphan, took an oath to reassure them and their men. "Do not be afraid to serve the Babylonians,ᶜ" he said. "Settle down in the land and serve the king of Babylon, and it will go well with you. ¹⁰I myself will stay at Mizpah to represent you before the Babylonians who come to us, but you are to harvest the wine, summer fruit and olive oil, and put them in your storage jars, and live in the towns you have taken over."

¹¹When all the Jews in Moab, Ammon, Edom and all the other countries heard that the king of Babylon had left a remnant in Judah and had appointed Gedaliah son of Ahikam, the son of Shaphan, as governor over them, ¹²they all came back to the land of Judah, to Gedaliah at Mizpah, from all the countries where they had been scattered. And they harvested an abundance of wine and summer fruit.

¹³Johanan son of Kareah and all the army officers still in the open country came to Gedaliah at Mizpah ¹⁴and said to him, "Don't you know that Baalis king of the Ammonites has sent Ishmael son of Nethaniah to take your life?" But Gedaliah son of Ahikam did not believe them.

¹⁵Then Johanan son of Kareah said privately to Gedaliah in Mizpah, "Let me go and kill Ishmael son of Nethaniah, and no

---

ᵃ 5 Or *Jeremiah answered*   ᵇ 8 Hebrew *Jezaniah*, a variant of *Jaazaniah*   ᶜ 9 Or *Chaldeans*; also in verse 10 one will know it. Why should he take your life and cause all the Jews who are gathered around you to be scattered and the remnant of Judah to perish?"

[16]But Gedaliah son of Ahikam said to Johanan son of Kareah, "Don't do such a thing! What you are saying about Ishmael is not true."

41 In the seventh month Ishmael son of Nethaniah, the son of Elishama, who was of royal blood and had been one of the king's officers, came with ten men to Gedaliah son of Ahikam at Mizpah. While they were eating together there, [2]Ishmael son of Nethaniah and the ten men who were with him got up and struck down Gedaliah son of Ahikam, the son of Shaphan, with the sword, killing the one whom the king of Babylon had appointed as governor over the land. [3]Ishmael also killed all the men of Judah who were with Gedaliah at Mizpah, as well as the Babylonian[a] soldiers who were there.

[4]The day after Gedaliah's assassination, before anyone knew about it, [5]eighty men who had shaved off their beards, torn their clothes and cut themselves came from Shechem, Shiloh and Samaria, bringing grain offerings and incense with them to the house of the LORD. [6]Ishmael son of Nethaniah went out from Mizpah to meet them, weeping as he went. When he met them, he said, "Come to Gedaliah son of Ahikam." [7]When they went into the city, Ishmael son of Nethaniah and the men who were with him slaughtered them and threw them into a cistern. [8]But ten of them said to Ishmael, "Don't kill us! We have wheat and barley, olive oil and honey, hidden in a field." So he let them alone and did not kill them with the others. [9]Now the cistern where he threw all the bodies of the men he had killed along with Gedaliah was the one King Asa had made as part of his defense against Baasha king of Israel. Ishmael son of Nethaniah filled it with the dead.

[10]Ishmael made captives of all the rest of the people who were in Mizpah—the king's daughters along with all the others who were left there, over whom Nebuzaradan commander of the imperial guard had appointed Gedaliah son of Ahikam. Ishmael son of Nethaniah took them captive and set out to cross over to the Ammonites.

[11]When Johanan son of Kareah and all the army officers who were with him heard about all the crimes Ishmael son of Nethaniah had committed, [12]they took all their men and went to fight Ishmael son of Nethaniah. They caught up with him near the great pool in Gibeon. [13]When all the people Ishmael had with him saw Johanan son of Kareah and the army officers who were with him, they were glad. [14]All the people Ishmael had taken captive at Mizpah turned and went over to Johanan son of Kareah. [15]But Ishmael son of Nethaniah and eight of his men escaped from Johanan and fled to the Ammonites.

Flight to Egypt

[16]Then Johanan son of Kareah and all the army officers who were with him led away all the people of Mizpah who had survived, whom Johanan had recovered from Ishmael son of Nethaniah after Ishmael had assassinated Gedaliah son of Ahikam—the soldiers, women, children and court officials he had recovered from Gibeon. [17]And they went on, stopping at Geruth Kimham near Bethlehem on their way to Egypt [18]to escape the Babylonians.[b] They were afraid of them because Ishmael son of Nethaniah had killed Gedaliah son of Ahikam, whom the king of Babylon had appointed as governor over the land.

42 Then all the army officers, including Johanan son of Kareah and Jezaniah[c] son of Hoshaiah, and all the people from the least to the greatest approached [2]Jeremiah the prophet and said to him, "Please hear our petition and pray to the LORD your God for this entire remnant. For as you now see, though we were once many, now only a few are left. [3]Pray that the LORD your God will tell us where we should go and what we should do."

[4]"I have heard you," replied Jeremiah the prophet. "I will certainly pray to the LORD your God as you have requested; I will tell you everything the LORD says and will keep nothing back from you."

[5]Then they said to Jeremiah, "May the LORD be a true and faithful witness against us if we do not act in accordance with everything the LORD your God sends you to tell us.

---

[a] 3 Or *Chaldean*   [b] 18 Or *Chaldeans*   [c] 1 Hebrew; Septuagint (see also 43:2) *Azariah*

TOUGH OBEDIENCE

READ: JEREMIAH 42:3

In 586 B.C. the Lord's most dire threats against his people come true. King Nebuchadnezzar and the Babylonian army lay siege to Jerusalem. When they break through the city wall, King Zedekiah of Judah flees. Enemy soldiers catch the king and slaughter his sons and put out his eyes. The Babylonians burn the city and drag all but the poorest people back to Babylon (Jeremiah 39:1–10).

The Ammonites are another of Israel's enemies, and soon an Ammonite named Ishmael assassinates the land's new governor, Gedaliah. He takes scores of other Israelites captive, but they're freed by Johanan and other army officers (41:1–15).

That victory puts Johanan and his allies in a tough spot. They worry Nebuchadnezzar will wrongly strike back at them for Gedaliah's death. So they beg Jeremiah to ask the Lord what they should do. They pledge to obey God's instruction "whether it is favorable or unfavorable" (42:6). Days later the Lord replies that they shouldn't fear Nebuchadnezzar. He commands them to stay in Judah and warns that running away to Egypt will lead to their deaths. Johanan angrily rejects this message. He leads a mass escape of God's people south to Egypt, kidnapping Jeremiah and taking him along (43:1–7).

The lesson? Don't tell God you want to know what he thinks if you aren't ready to do what he says. He deserves your utter obedience, even in those tough times when you question his commands.

BUILDING FAITH WISDOM STRENGTH

⁶Whether it is favorable or unfavorable, we will obey the LORD our God, to whom we are sending you, so that it will go well with us, for we will obey the LORD our God."

⁷Ten days later the word of the LORD came to Jeremiah. ⁸So he called together Johanan son of Kareah and all the army officers who were with him and all the people from the least to the greatest. ⁹He said to them, "This is what the LORD, the God of Israel, to whom you sent me to present your petition, says: ¹⁰'If you stay in this land, I will build you up and not tear you down; I will plant you and not uproot you, for I have relented concerning the disaster I have inflicted on you. ¹¹Do not be afraid of the king of Babylon, whom you now fear. Do not be afraid of him, declares the LORD, for I am with you and will save you and deliver you from his hands. ¹²I will show you compassion so that he will have compassion on you and restore you to your land.'

¹³"However, if you say, 'We will not stay in this land,' and so disobey the LORD your God, ¹⁴and if you say, 'No, we will go and live in Egypt, where we will not see war or hear the trumpet or be hungry for bread,' ¹⁵then hear the word of the LORD, you remnant of Judah. This is what the LORD Almighty, the God of Israel, says: 'If you are determined to go to Egypt and you do go to settle there, ¹⁶then the sword you fear will overtake you there, and the famine you dread will follow you into Egypt, and there you will die. ¹⁷Indeed, all who are determined to go to Egypt to settle there will die by the sword, famine and plague; not one of them will survive or escape the disaster I will bring on them.' ¹⁸This is what the LORD Almighty, the God of Israel, says: 'As my anger and wrath have been poured out on those who lived in Jerusalem, so will my wrath be poured out on you when you go to Egypt. You will be a curse[a] and an object of horror, a curse[a] and an object of reproach; you will never see this place again.'

¹⁹"Remnant of Judah, the LORD has told you, 'Do not go to Egypt.' Be sure of this: I warn you today ²⁰that you made a fatal mistake when you sent me to the LORD your God and said, 'Pray to the LORD our God for us; tell us everything he says and we will do it.' ²¹I have told you today, but you still have not obeyed the LORD your God in all he sent me to tell you. ²²So now, be sure of this: You will die by the sword, famine and plague in the place where you want to go to settle."

43 When Jeremiah had finished telling the people all the words of the LORD their God—everything the LORD had sent him to tell them— ²Azariah son of Hoshaiah and Johanan son of Kareah and all the arrogant men said to Jeremiah, "You are lying! The LORD our God has not sent you to say, 'You must not go to Egypt to settle there.' ³But Baruch son of Neriah is inciting you against us to hand us over to the Babylonians,[b] so they may kill us or carry us into exile to Babylon."

⁴So Johanan son of Kareah and all the army officers and all the people disobeyed the LORD's command to stay in the land of Judah. ⁵Instead, Johanan son of Kareah and all the army officers led away all the remnant of Judah who had come back to live in the land of Judah from all the nations where they had been scattered. ⁶They also led away all those whom Nebuzaradan commander of the imperial guard had left with Gedaliah son of Ahikam, the son of Shaphan—the men, the women, the children and the king's daughters. And they took Jeremiah the prophet and Baruch son of Neriah along with them. ⁷So they entered Egypt in disobedience to the LORD and went as far as Tahpanhes.

⁸In Tahpanhes the word of the LORD came to Jeremiah: ⁹"While the Jews are watching, take some large stones with you and bury them in clay in the brick pavement at the entrance to Pharaoh's palace in Tahpanhes. ¹⁰Then say to them, 'This is what the LORD Almighty, the God of Israel, says: I will send for my servant Nebuchadnezzar king of Babylon, and I will set his throne over these stones I have buried here; he will spread his royal canopy above them. ¹¹He will come and attack Egypt, bringing death to those destined for death, captivity to those destined for captivity, and the sword to those destined for the sword. ¹²He will set fire to the temples of the gods of Egypt; he will burn their temples and take their gods captive. As a shepherd picks his garment clean of lice, so he will pick Egypt clean and depart. ¹³There in the temple of the sun[c] in Egypt he will

---

ᵃ 18 That is, your name will be used in cursing (see 29:22); or, others will see that you are cursed.
ᵇ 3 Or *Chaldeans*   ᶜ 13 Or *in Heliopolis*

demolish the sacred pillars and will burn down the temples of the gods of Egypt.'"

Disaster Because of Idolatry

44 This word came to Jeremiah concerning all the Jews living in Lower Egypt—in Migdol, Tahpanhes and Memphis—and in Upper Egypt: ²"This is what the LORD Almighty, the God of Israel, says: You saw the great disaster I brought on Jerusalem and on all the towns of Judah. Today they lie deserted and in ruins ³because of the evil they have done. They aroused my anger by burning incense to and worshiping other gods that neither they nor you nor your ancestors ever knew. ⁴Again and again I sent my servants the prophets, who said, 'Do not do this detestable thing that I hate!' ⁵But they did not listen or pay attention; they did not turn from their wickedness or stop burning incense to other gods. ⁶Therefore, my fierce anger was poured out; it raged against the towns of Judah and the streets of Jerusalem and made them the desolate ruins they are today.

⁷"Now this is what the LORD God Almighty, the God of Israel, says: Why bring such great disaster on yourselves by cutting off from Judah the men and women, the children and infants, and so leave yourselves without a remnant? ⁸Why arouse my anger with what your hands have made, burning incense to other gods in Egypt, where you have come to live? You will destroy yourselves and make yourselves a curse^a and an object of reproach among all the nations on earth. ⁹Have you forgotten the wickedness committed by your ancestors and by the kings and queens of Judah and the wickedness committed by you and your wives in the land of Judah and the streets of Jerusalem? ¹⁰To this day they have not humbled themselves or shown reverence, nor have they followed my law and the decrees I set before you and your ancestors.

¹¹"Therefore this is what the LORD Almighty, the God of Israel, says: I am determined to bring disaster on you and to destroy all Judah. ¹²I will take away the remnant of Judah who were determined to go to Egypt to settle there. They will all perish in Egypt; they will fall by the sword or die from famine. From the least to the greatest, they will die by sword or famine. They will become a curse and an object of horror, a curse and an object of reproach. ¹³I will punish those who live in Egypt with the sword, famine and plague, as I punished Jerusalem. ¹⁴None of the remnant of Judah who have gone to live in Egypt will escape or survive to return to the land of Judah, to which they long to return and live; none will return except a few fugitives."

¹⁵Then all the men who knew that their wives were burning incense to other gods, along with all the women who were present—a large assembly—and all the people living in Lower and Upper Egypt, said to Jeremiah, ¹⁶"We will not listen to the message you have spoken to us in the name of the LORD! ¹⁷We will certainly do everything we said we would: We will burn incense to the Queen of Heaven and will pour out drink offerings to her just as we and our ancestors, our kings and our officials did in the towns of Judah and in the streets of Jerusalem. At that time we had plenty of food and were well off and suffered no harm. ¹⁸But ever since we stopped burning incense to the Queen of Heaven and pouring out drink offerings to her, we have had nothing and have been perishing by sword and famine."

¹⁹The women added, "When we burned incense to the Queen of Heaven and poured out drink offerings to her, did not our husbands know that we were making cakes impressed with her image and pouring out drink offerings to her?"

²⁰Then Jeremiah said to all the people, both men and women, who were answering him, ²¹"Did not the LORD remember and call to mind the incense burned in the towns of Judah and the streets of Jerusalem by you and your ancestors, your kings and your officials and the people of the land? ²²When the LORD could no longer endure your wicked actions and the detestable things you did, your land became a curse and a desolate waste without inhabitants, as it is today. ²³Because you have burned incense and have sinned against the LORD and have not obeyed him or followed his law or his decrees or his stipulations, this disaster has come upon you, as you now see."

---

^a 8 That is, your name will be used in cursing (see 29:22); or, others will see that you are cursed; also in verse 12; similarly in verse 22.

²⁴Then Jeremiah said to all the people, including the women, "Hear the word of the Lord, all you people of Judah in Egypt. ²⁵This is what the Lord Almighty, the God of Israel, says: You and your wives have done what you said you would do when you promised, 'We will certainly carry out the vows we made to burn incense and pour out drink offerings to the Queen of Heaven.'

"Go ahead then, do what you promised! Keep your vows! ²⁶But hear the word of the Lord, all you Jews living in Egypt: 'I swear by my great name,' says the Lord, 'that no one from Judah living anywhere in Egypt will ever again invoke my name or swear, "As surely as the Sovereign Lord lives." ²⁷For I am watching over them for harm, not for good; the Jews in Egypt will perish by sword and famine until they are all destroyed. ²⁸Those who escape the sword and return to the land of Judah from Egypt will be very few. Then the whole remnant of Judah who came to live in Egypt will know whose word will stand—mine or theirs.

²⁹"'This will be the sign to you that I will punish you in this place,' declares the Lord, 'so that you will know that my threats of harm against you will surely stand.' ³⁰This is what the Lord says: 'I am going to deliver Pharaoh Hophra king of Egypt into the hands of his enemies who want to kill him, just as I gave Zedekiah king of Judah into the hands of Nebuchadnezzar king of Babylon, the enemy who wanted to kill him.'"

A Message to Baruch

45 When Baruch son of Neriah wrote on a scroll the words Jeremiah the prophet dictated in the fourth year of Jehoiakim son of Josiah king of Judah, Jeremiah said this to Baruch: ²"This is what the Lord, the God of Israel, says to you, Baruch: ³You said, 'Woe to me! The Lord has added sorrow to my pain; I am worn out with groaning and find no rest.' ⁴But the Lord has told me to say to you, 'This is what the Lord says: I will overthrow what I have built and uproot what I have planted, throughout the earth. ⁵Should you then seek great things for yourself? Do not seek them. For I will bring disaster on all people, declares the Lord, but wherever you go I will let you escape with your life.'"

A Message About Egypt

46 This is the word of the Lord that came to Jeremiah the prophet concerning the nations:

²Concerning Egypt:

This is the message against the army of Pharaoh Necho king of Egypt, which was defeated at Carchemish on the Euphrates River by Nebuchadnezzar king of Babylon in the fourth year of Jehoiakim son of Josiah king of Judah:

³"Prepare your shields, both large and small,
    and march out for battle!
⁴Harness the horses,
    mount the steeds!
Take your positions
    with helmets on!
Polish your spears,
    put on your armor!
⁵What do I see?
    They are terrified,
they are retreating,
    their warriors are defeated.
They flee in haste
    without looking back,
    and there is terror on every side,"
            declares the Lord.
⁶"The swift cannot flee
    nor the strong escape.
In the north by the River Euphrates
    they stumble and fall.

⁷"Who is this that rises like the Nile,
    like rivers of surging waters?
⁸Egypt rises like the Nile,
    like rivers of surging waters.
She says, 'I will rise and cover the earth;
    I will destroy cities and their people.'
⁹Charge, you horses!
    Drive furiously, you charioteers!
March on, you warriors—men of Cush^a
    and Put who carry shields,
    men of Lydia who draw the bow.
¹⁰But that day belongs to the Lord, the
    Lord Almighty—
    a day of vengeance, for vengeance on
    his foes.
The sword will devour till it is satisfied,
    till it has quenched its thirst with
    blood.

---

^a 9 That is, the upper Nile region

For the Lord, the LORD Almighty, will
  offer sacrifice
  in the land of the north by the River
    Euphrates.

¹¹ "Go up to Gilead and get balm,
  Virgin Daughter Egypt.
But you try many medicines in vain;
  there is no healing for you.
¹²The nations will hear of your shame;
  your cries will fill the earth.
One warrior will stumble over another;
  both will fall down together."

¹³This is the message the LORD spoke to
Jeremiah the prophet about the coming of
Nebuchadnezzar king of Babylon to attack
Egypt:

¹⁴ "Announce this in Egypt, and proclaim it
    in Migdol;
  proclaim it also in Memphis and
    Tahpanhes:
'Take your positions and get ready,
  for the sword devours those around
    you.'
¹⁵Why will your warriors be laid low?
  They cannot stand, for the LORD
    will push them down.
¹⁶They will stumble repeatedly;
  they will fall over each other.
They will say, 'Get up, let us go back
  to our own people and our native
    lands,
  away from the sword of the oppressor.'
¹⁷There they will exclaim,
  'Pharaoh king of Egypt is only a loud
    noise;
  he has missed his opportunity.'

¹⁸ "As surely as I live," declares the King,
  whose name is the LORD Almighty,
"one will come who is like Tabor among
    the mountains,
  like Carmel by the sea.
¹⁹Pack your belongings for exile,
  you who live in Egypt,
for Memphis will be laid waste
  and lie in ruins without inhabitant.

²⁰ "Egypt is a beautiful heifer,
  but a gadfly is coming
  against her from the north.
²¹The mercenaries in her ranks
  are like fattened calves.
They too will turn and flee together,
  they will not stand their ground,

for the day of disaster is coming upon
    them,
  the time for them to be punished.
²²Egypt will hiss like a fleeing serpent
  as the enemy advances in force;
they will come against her with axes,
  like men who cut down trees.
²³They will chop down her forest,"
                declares the LORD,
  "dense though it be.
They are more numerous than locusts,
  they cannot be counted.
²⁴Daughter Egypt will be put to shame,
  given into the hands of the people of
    the north."

²⁵The LORD Almighty, the God of Israel,
says: "I am about to bring punishment on
Amon god of Thebes, on Pharaoh, on Egypt
and her gods and her kings, and on those
who rely on Pharaoh. ²⁶I will give them into
the hands of those who want to kill them—
Nebuchadnezzar king of Babylon and his officers. Later, however, Egypt will be inhabited as in times past," declares the LORD.

²⁷ "Do not be afraid, Jacob my servant;
  do not be dismayed, Israel.
I will surely save you out of a distant
    place,
  your descendants from the land of
    their exile.
Jacob will again have peace and security,
  and no one will make him afraid.
²⁸Do not be afraid, Jacob my servant,
  for I am with you," declares the LORD.
"Though I completely destroy all the
    nations
  among which I scatter you,
I will not completely destroy you.
I will discipline you but only in due
    measure;
  I will not let you go entirely
    unpunished."

A Message About the Philistines

47 This is the word of the LORD that
  came to Jeremiah the prophet concerning the Philistines before Pharaoh attacked Gaza:

²This is what the LORD says:

"See how the waters are rising in the
    north;

they will become an overflowing
torrent.
They will overflow the land and
everything in it,
the towns and those who live in them.
The people will cry out;
all who dwell in the land will wail
³ at the sound of the hooves of galloping
steeds,
at the noise of enemy chariots
and the rumble of their wheels.
Parents will not turn to help their
children;
their hands will hang limp.
⁴ For the day has come
to destroy all the Philistines
and to remove all survivors
who could help Tyre and Sidon.
The LORD is about to destroy the
Philistines,
the remnant from the coasts of
Caphtor.ᵃ
⁵ Gaza will shave her head in mourning;
Ashkelon will be silenced.
You remnant on the plain,
how long will you cut yourselves?

⁶ " 'Alas, sword of the LORD,
how long till you rest?
Return to your sheath;
cease and be still.'
⁷ But how can it rest
when the LORD has commanded it,
when he has ordered it
to attack Ashkelon and the coast?"

A Message About Moab

48
Concerning Moab:

This is what the LORD Almighty, the God
of Israel, says:

"Woe to Nebo, for it will be ruined.
Kiriathaim will be disgraced and
captured;
the strongholdᵇ will be disgraced and
shattered.
² Moab will be praised no more;
in Heshbonᶜ people will plot her
downfall:
'Come, let us put an end to that nation.'
You, the people of Madmen,ᵈ will also be
silenced;

the sword will pursue you.
³ Cries of anguish arise from Horonaim,
cries of great havoc and destruction.
⁴ Moab will be broken;
her little ones will cry out.ᵉ
⁵ They go up the hill to Luhith,
weeping bitterly as they go;
on the road down to Horonaim
anguished cries over the destruction
are heard.
⁶ Flee! Run for your lives;
become like a bushᶠ in the desert.
⁷ Since you trust in your deeds and riches,
you too will be taken captive,
and Chemosh will go into exile,
together with his priests and officials.
⁸ The destroyer will come against every
town,
and not a town will escape.
The valley will be ruined
and the plateau destroyed,
because the LORD has spoken.
⁹ Put salt on Moab,
for she will be laid wasteᵍ;
her towns will become desolate,
with no one to live in them.

¹⁰ "A curse on anyone who is lax in doing
the LORD's work!
A curse on anyone who keeps their
sword from bloodshed!

¹¹ "Moab has been at rest from youth,
like wine left on its dregs,
not poured from one jar to another—
she has not gone into exile.
So she tastes as she did,
and her aroma is unchanged.
¹² But days are coming,"
declares the LORD,
"when I will send men who pour from
pitchers,
and they will pour her out;
they will empty her pitchers
and smash her jars.
¹³ Then Moab will be ashamed of
Chemosh,
as Israel was ashamed
when they trusted in Bethel.

¹⁴ "How can you say, 'We are warriors,
men valiant in battle'?

ᵃ 4 That is, Crete   ᵇ 1 Or captured; / Misgab   ᶜ 2 The Hebrew for Heshbon sounds like the Hebrew for
plot.   ᵈ 2 The name of the Moabite town Madmen sounds like the Hebrew for be silenced.   ᵉ 4 Hebrew;
Septuagint / proclaim it to Zoar   ᶠ 6 Or like Aroer   ᵍ 9 Or Give wings to Moab, / for she will fly away

¹⁵ Moab will be destroyed and her towns
        invaded;
    her finest young men will go down in
        the slaughter,"
    declares the King, whose name is the
        LORD Almighty.
¹⁶ "The fall of Moab is at hand;
    her calamity will come quickly.
¹⁷ Mourn for her, all who live around her,
    all who know her fame;
    say, 'How broken is the mighty scepter,
    how broken the glorious staff!'

¹⁸ "Come down from your glory
        and sit on the parched ground,
        you inhabitants of Daughter Dibon,
    for the one who destroys Moab
        will come up against you
        and ruin your fortified cities.
¹⁹ Stand by the road and watch,
    you who live in Aroer.
    Ask the man fleeing and the woman
        escaping,
        ask them, 'What has happened?'
²⁰ Moab is disgraced, for she is shattered.
        Wail and cry out!
    Announce by the Arnon
        that Moab is destroyed.
²¹ Judgment has come to the plateau —
        to Holon, Jahzah and Mephaath,
²²   to Dibon, Nebo and Beth Diblathaim,
²³   to Kiriathaim, Beth Gamul and Beth
        Meon,
²⁴   to Kerioth and Bozrah —
    to all the towns of Moab, far and near.
²⁵ Moab's horn*ᵃ* is cut off;
    her arm is broken,"
                declares the LORD.

²⁶ "Make her drunk,
    for she has defied the LORD.
    Let Moab wallow in her vomit;
        let her be an object of ridicule.
²⁷ Was not Israel the object of your
        ridicule?
    Was she caught among thieves,
    that you shake your head in scorn
        whenever you speak of her?
²⁸ Abandon your towns and dwell among
        the rocks,
        you who live in Moab.
    Be like a dove that makes its nest
        at the mouth of a cave.

²⁹ "We have heard of Moab's pride —
        how great is her arrogance! —
    of her insolence, her pride, her conceit
        and the haughtiness of her heart.
³⁰ I know her insolence but it is futile,"
                declares the LORD,
    "and her boasts accomplish nothing.
³¹ Therefore I wail over Moab,
        for all Moab I cry out,
    I moan for the people of Kir Hareseth.
³² I weep for you, as Jazer weeps,
        you vines of Sibmah.
    Your branches spread as far as the sea*ᵇ*;
        they reached as far as*ᶜ* Jazer.
    The destroyer has fallen
        on your ripened fruit and grapes.
³³ Joy and gladness are gone
        from the orchards and fields of
        Moab.
    I have stopped the flow of wine from the
        presses;
        no one treads them with shouts of joy.
    Although there are shouts,
        they are not shouts of joy.

³⁴ "The sound of their cry rises
        from Heshbon to Elealeh and Jahaz,
    from Zoar as far as Horonaim and Eglath
        Shelishiyah,
    for even the waters of Nimrim are
        dried up.
³⁵ In Moab I will put an end
        to those who make offerings on the
        high places
    and burn incense to their gods,"
                declares the LORD.
³⁶ "So my heart laments for Moab like the
        music of a pipe;
    it laments like a pipe for the people of
        Kir Hareseth.
    The wealth they acquired is gone.
³⁷ Every head is shaved
        and every beard cut off;
    every hand is slashed
        and every waist is covered with
        sackcloth.
³⁸ On all the roofs in Moab
        and in the public squares
    there is nothing but mourning,
        for I have broken Moab
        like a jar that no one wants,"
                declares the LORD.

ᵃ 25 Horn here symbolizes strength.   *ᵇ 32* Probably the Dead Sea   *ᶜ 32* Two Hebrew manuscripts and
Septuagint; most Hebrew manuscripts *as far as the Sea of*

³⁹ "How shattered she is! How they wail!
How Moab turns her back in shame!
Moab has become an object of ridicule,
an object of horror to all those
around her."

⁴⁰ This is what the LORD says:

"Look! An eagle is swooping down,
spreading its wings over Moab.
⁴¹ Kerioth*a* will be captured
and the strongholds taken.
In that day the hearts of Moab's warriors
will be like the heart of a woman in
labor.
⁴² Moab will be destroyed as a nation
because she defied the LORD.
⁴³ Terror and pit and snare await you,
you people of Moab,"
declares the LORD.
⁴⁴ "Whoever flees from the terror
will fall into a pit,
whoever climbs out of the pit
will be caught in a snare;
for I will bring on Moab
the year of her punishment,"
declares the LORD.
⁴⁵ "In the shadow of Heshbon
the fugitives stand helpless,
for a fire has gone out from Heshbon,
a blaze from the midst of Sihon;
it burns the foreheads of Moab,
the skulls of the noisy boasters.
⁴⁶ Woe to you, Moab!
The people of Chemosh are destroyed;
your sons are taken into exile
and your daughters into captivity.

⁴⁷ "Yet I will restore the fortunes of Moab
in days to come,"
declares the LORD.

Here ends the judgment on Moab.

A Message About Ammon

49 Concerning the Ammonites:

This is what the LORD says:

"Has Israel no sons?
Has Israel no heir?
Why then has Molek*b* taken possession
of Gad?
Why do his people live in its towns?

² But the days are coming,"
declares the LORD,
"when I will sound the battle cry
against Rabbah of the Ammonites;
it will become a mound of ruins,
and its surrounding villages will be set
on fire.
Then Israel will drive out
those who drove her out,"
says the LORD.
³ "Wail, Heshbon, for Ai is destroyed!
Cry out, you inhabitants of Rabbah!
Put on sackcloth and mourn;
rush here and there inside the walls,
for Molek will go into exile,
together with his priests and officials.
⁴ Why do you boast of your valleys,
boast of your valleys so fruitful?
Unfaithful Daughter Ammon,
you trust in your riches and say,
'Who will attack me?'
⁵ I will bring terror on you
from all those around you,"
declares the Lord,
the LORD Almighty.
"Every one of you will be driven away,
and no one will gather the fugitives.

⁶ "Yet afterward, I will restore the fortunes
of the Ammonites,"
declares the LORD.

A Message About Edom

⁷ Concerning Edom:

This is what the LORD Almighty says:

"Is there no longer wisdom in Teman?
Has counsel perished from the
prudent?
Has their wisdom decayed?
⁸ Turn and flee, hide in deep caves,
you who live in Dedan,
for I will bring disaster on Esau
at the time when I punish him.
⁹ If grape pickers came to you,
would they not leave a few grapes?
If thieves came during the night,
would they not steal only as much as
they wanted?
¹⁰ But I will strip Esau bare;
I will uncover his hiding places,
so that he cannot conceal himself.
His armed men are destroyed,

---

a 41 Or *The cities*   *b* 1 Or *their king*; also in verse 3

also his allies and neighbors,
so there is no one to say,

¹¹ 'Leave your fatherless children; I will
keep them alive.
Your widows too can depend on me.' "

¹² This is what the LORD says: "If those who do not deserve to drink the cup must drink it, why should you go unpunished? You will not go unpunished, but must drink it. ¹³ I swear by myself," declares the LORD, "that Bozrah will become a ruin and a curse,^a an object of horror and reproach; and all its towns will be in ruins forever."

¹⁴ I have heard a message from the LORD;
an envoy was sent to the nations to say,
"Assemble yourselves to attack it!
Rise up for battle!"

¹⁵ "Now I will make you small among the
nations,
despised by mankind.
¹⁶ The terror you inspire
and the pride of your heart have
deceived you,
you who live in the clefts of the rocks,
who occupy the heights of the hill.
Though you build your nest as high as the
eagle's,
from there I will bring you down,"
declares the LORD.
¹⁷ "Edom will become an object of horror;
all who pass by will be appalled and
will scoff
because of all its wounds.
¹⁸ As Sodom and Gomorrah were
overthrown,
along with their neighboring towns,"
says the LORD,
"so no one will live there;
no people will dwell in it.

¹⁹ "Like a lion coming up from Jordan's
thickets
to a rich pastureland,
I will chase Edom from its land in an
instant.
Who is the chosen one I will appoint
for this?
Who is like me and who can challenge me?
And what shepherd can stand
against me?"

²⁰ Therefore, hear what the LORD has
planned against Edom,
what he has purposed against those
who live in Teman:
The young of the flock will be dragged
away;
their pasture will be appalled at
their fate.
²¹ At the sound of their fall the earth will
tremble;
their cry will resound to the Red Sea.^b
²² Look! An eagle will soar and swoop down,
spreading its wings over Bozrah.
In that day the hearts of Edom's warriors
will be like the heart of a woman in
labor.

A Message About Damascus

²³ Concerning Damascus:

"Hamath and Arpad are dismayed,
for they have heard bad news.
They are disheartened,
troubled like^c the restless sea.
²⁴ Damascus has become feeble,
she has turned to flee
and panic has gripped her;
anguish and pain have seized her,
pain like that of a woman in labor.
²⁵ Why has the city of renown not been
abandoned,
the town in which I delight?
²⁶ Surely, her young men will fall in the
streets;
all her soldiers will be silenced in that
day,"
declares the LORD Almighty.
²⁷ "I will set fire to the walls of Damascus;
it will consume the fortresses of Ben-
Hadad."

A Message About Kedar and Hazor

²⁸ Concerning Kedar and the kingdoms of Hazor, which Nebuchadnezzar king of Babylon attacked:

This is what the LORD says:

"Arise, and attack Kedar
and destroy the people of the East.
²⁹ Their tents and their flocks will be taken;
their shelters will be carried off
with all their goods and camels.

---

^a 13 That is, its name will be used in cursing (see 29:22); or, others will see that it is cursed.   ^b 21 Or the Sea of Reeds   ^c 23 Hebrew on or by

People will shout to them,
  'Terror on every side!'

30 "Flee quickly away!
  Stay in deep caves, you who live in
    Hazor,"
          declares the LORD.
"Nebuchadnezzar king of Babylon has
  plotted against you;
he has devised a plan against you.

31 "Arise and attack a nation at ease,
  which lives in confidence,"
          declares the LORD,
"a nation that has neither gates nor bars;
  its people live far from danger.
32 Their camels will become plunder,
  and their large herds will be spoils
    of war.
I will scatter to the winds those who are
  in distant places[a]
  and will bring disaster on them from
    every side,"
          declares the LORD.
33 "Hazor will become a haunt of jackals,
  a desolate place forever.
No one will live there;
  no people will dwell in it."

A Message About Elam

34 This is the word of the LORD that came
to Jeremiah the prophet concerning Elam,
early in the reign of Zedekiah king of Judah:

35 This is what the LORD Almighty says:

"See, I will break the bow of Elam,
  the mainstay of their might.
36 I will bring against Elam the four
    winds
  from the four quarters of heaven;
I will scatter them to the four winds,
  and there will not be a nation
  where Elam's exiles do not go.
37 I will shatter Elam before their foes,
  before those who want to kill them;
I will bring disaster on them,
  even my fierce anger,"
          declares the LORD.
"I will pursue them with the sword
  until I have made an end of them.
38 I will set my throne in Elam
  and destroy her king and officials,"
          declares the LORD.

39 "Yet I will restore the fortunes of Elam
  in days to come,"
          declares the LORD.

A Message About Babylon

50 This is the word the LORD spoke
through Jeremiah the prophet concerning Babylon and the land of the Babylonians[b]:

2 "Announce and proclaim among the
    nations,
  lift up a banner and proclaim it;
  keep nothing back, but say,
'Babylon will be captured;
  Bel will be put to shame,
  Marduk filled with terror.
Her images will be put to shame
  and her idols filled with terror.'
3 A nation from the north will attack her
  and lay waste her land.
No one will live in it;
  both people and animals will flee
    away.

4 "In those days, at that time,"
    declares the LORD,
"the people of Israel and the people of
    Judah together
  will go in tears to seek the LORD
    their God.
5 They will ask the way to Zion
  and turn their faces toward it.
They will come and bind themselves to
    the LORD
  in an everlasting covenant
  that will not be forgotten.

6 "My people have been lost sheep;
  their shepherds have led them astray
  and caused them to roam on the
    mountains.
They wandered over mountain and hill
  and forgot their own resting place.
7 Whoever found them devoured them;
  their enemies said, 'We are not guilty,
for they sinned against the LORD, their
    verdant pasture,
  the LORD, the hope of their ancestors.'

8 "Flee out of Babylon;
  leave the land of the Babylonians,
  and be like the goats that lead
    the flock.

---

[a] 32 Or *who clip the hair by their foreheads*   [b] 1 Or *Chaldeans*; also in verses 8, 25, 35 and 45

⁹For I will stir up and bring against
  Babylon
    an alliance of great nations from the
      land of the north.
  They will take up their positions
    against her,
    and from the north she will be
      captured.
  Their arrows will be like skilled warriors
    who do not return empty-handed.
¹⁰So Babylonia*ᵃ* will be plundered;
    all who plunder her will have their fill,"
                            declares the LORD.

¹¹"Because you rejoice and are glad,
    you who pillage my inheritance,
  because you frolic like a heifer threshing
      grain
    and neigh like stallions,
¹²your mother will be greatly ashamed;
    she who gave you birth will be
      disgraced.
  She will be the least of the nations —
    a wilderness, a dry land, a desert.
¹³Because of the LORD's anger she will not
      be inhabited
    but will be completely desolate.
  All who pass Babylon will be appalled;
    they will scoff because of all her
      wounds.
¹⁴"Take up your positions around Babylon,
    all you who draw the bow.
  Shoot at her! Spare no arrows,
    for she has sinned against the LORD.
¹⁵Shout against her on every side!
    She surrenders, her towers fall,
      her walls are torn down.
  Since this is the vengeance of the LORD,
    take vengeance on her;
    do to her as she has done to others.
¹⁶Cut off from Babylon the sower,
    and the reaper with his sickle at
      harvest.
  Because of the sword of the oppressor
    let everyone return to their own
      people,
    let everyone flee to their own land.

¹⁷"Israel is a scattered flock
    that lions have chased away.
  The first to devour them
    was the king of Assyria;

the last to crush their bones
    was Nebuchadnezzar king of
      Babylon."

¹⁸Therefore this is what the LORD Almighty, the God of Israel, says:

"I will punish the king of Babylon and
      his land
    as I punished the king of Assyria.
¹⁹But I will bring Israel back to their own
      pasture,
    and they will graze on Carmel and
      Bashan;
  their appetite will be satisfied
    on the hills of Ephraim and Gilead.
²⁰In those days, at that time,"
                      declares the LORD,
  "search will be made for Israel's guilt,
    but there will be none,
  and for the sins of Judah,
    but none will be found,
    for I will forgive the remnant I spare.

²¹"Attack the land of Merathaim
    and those who live in Pekod.
  Pursue, kill and completely destroy*ᵇ*
      them,"
                            declares the LORD.
  "Do everything I have commanded
      you.
²²The noise of battle is in the land,
    the noise of great destruction!
²³How broken and shattered
    is the hammer of the whole earth!
  How desolate is Babylon
    among the nations!
²⁴I set a trap for you, Babylon,
    and you were caught before you
      knew it;
  you were found and captured
    because you opposed the LORD.
²⁵The LORD has opened his arsenal
    and brought out the weapons of his
      wrath,
  for the Sovereign LORD Almighty has
      work to do
    in the land of the Babylonians.
²⁶Come against her from afar.
    Break open her granaries;
    pile her up like heaps of grain.
  Completely destroy her
    and leave her no remnant.

ᵃ 10 Or *Chaldea*   *ᵇ 21* The Hebrew term refers to the irrevocable giving over of things or persons to the
LORD, often by totally destroying them; also in verse 26.

²⁷ Kill all her young bulls;
let them go down to the slaughter!
Woe to them! For their day has come,
the time for them to be punished.
²⁸ Listen to the fugitives and refugees from
Babylon
declaring in Zion
how the LORD our God has taken
vengeance,
vengeance for his temple.

²⁹ "Summon archers against Babylon,
all those who draw the bow.
Encamp all around her;
let no one escape.
Repay her for her deeds;
do to her as she has done.
For she has defied the LORD,
the Holy One of Israel.
³⁰ Therefore, her young men will fall in the
streets;
all her soldiers will be silenced in
that day,"
declares the LORD.
³¹ "See, I am against you, you arrogant one,"
declares the Lord, the LORD Almighty,
"for your day has come,
the time for you to be punished.
³² The arrogant one will stumble and fall
and no one will help her up;
I will kindle a fire in her towns
that will consume all who are
around her."

³³ This is what the LORD Almighty says:

"The people of Israel are oppressed,
and the people of Judah as well.
All their captors hold them fast,
refusing to let them go.
³⁴ Yet their Redeemer is strong;
the LORD Almighty is his name.
He will vigorously defend their cause
so that he may bring rest to their land,
but unrest to those who live in
Babylon.

³⁵ "A sword against the Babylonians!"
declares the LORD —
"against those who live in Babylon
and against her officials and wise men!
³⁶ A sword against her false prophets!
They will become fools.
A sword against her warriors!

They will be filled with terror.
³⁷ A sword against her horses and chariots
and all the foreigners in her ranks!
They will become weaklings.
A sword against her treasures!
They will be plundered.
³⁸ A drought on^a her waters!
They will dry up.
For it is a land of idols,
idols that will go mad with terror.

³⁹ "So desert creatures and hyenas will
live there,
and there the owl will dwell.
It will never again be inhabited
or lived in from generation to
generation.
⁴⁰ As I overthrew Sodom and Gomorrah
along with their neighboring towns,"
declares the LORD,
"so no one will live there;
no people will dwell in it.

⁴¹ "Look! An army is coming from the
north;
a great nation and many kings
are being stirred up from the ends of
the earth.
⁴² They are armed with bows and spears;
they are cruel and without mercy.
They sound like the roaring sea
as they ride on their horses;
they come like men in battle formation
to attack you, Daughter Babylon.
⁴³ The king of Babylon has heard reports
about them,
and his hands hang limp.
Anguish has gripped him,
pain like that of a woman in labor.
⁴⁴ Like a lion coming up from Jordan's
thickets
to a rich pastureland,
I will chase Babylon from its land in an
instant.
Who is the chosen one I will appoint
for this?
Who is like me and who can challenge me?
And what shepherd can stand
against me?"

⁴⁵ Therefore, hear what the LORD has
planned against Babylon,
what he has purposed against the land
of the Babylonians:

^a 38 Or *A sword against*

The young of the flock will be dragged
away;
    their pasture will be appalled at
    their fate.
⁴⁶ At the sound of Babylon's capture the
    earth will tremble;
    its cry will resound among the nations.

51 This is what the LORD says:

"See, I will stir up the spirit of a destroyer
    against Babylon and the people of Leb
    Kamai.ᵃ
² I will send foreigners to Babylon
    to winnow her and to devastate
    her land;
they will oppose her on every side
    in the day of her disaster.
³ Let not the archer string his bow,
    nor let him put on his armor.
Do not spare her young men;
    completely destroyᵇ her army.
⁴ They will fall down slain in Babylon,ᶜ
    fatally wounded in her streets.
⁵ For Israel and Judah have not been
    forsaken
    by their God, the LORD Almighty,
though their landᵈ is full of guilt
    before the Holy One of Israel.

⁶ "Flee from Babylon!
    Run for your lives!
    Do not be destroyed because of
    her sins.
It is time for the LORD's vengeance;
    he will repay her what she deserves.
⁷ Babylon was a gold cup in the LORD's
    hand;
    she made the whole earth drunk.
The nations drank her wine;
    therefore they have now gone mad.
⁸ Babylon will suddenly fall and be broken.
    Wail over her!
Get balm for her pain;
    perhaps she can be healed.

⁹ " 'We would have healed Babylon,
    but she cannot be healed;
let us leave her and each go to our own
    land,
    for her judgment reaches to the skies,
    it rises as high as the heavens.'

¹⁰ " 'The LORD has vindicated us;
    come, let us tell in Zion
    what the LORD our God has done.'

¹¹ "Sharpen the arrows,
    take up the shields!
The LORD has stirred up the kings of
    the Medes,
    because his purpose is to destroy
    Babylon.
The LORD will take vengeance,
    vengeance for his temple.
¹² Lift up a banner against the walls of
    Babylon!
    Reinforce the guard,
station the watchmen,
    prepare an ambush!
The LORD will carry out his purpose,
    his decree against the people of
    Babylon.

¹³ You who live by many waters
    and are rich in treasures,
your end has come,
    the time for you to be destroyed.
¹⁴ The LORD Almighty has sworn by
    himself:
    I will surely fill you with troops, as
    with a swarm of locusts,
    and they will shout in triumph
    over you.

¹⁵ "He made the earth by his power;
    he founded the world by his wisdom
    and stretched out the heavens by his
    understanding.
¹⁶ When he thunders, the waters in the
    heavens roar;
    he makes clouds rise from the ends of
    the earth.
He sends lightning with the rain
    and brings out the wind from his
    storehouses.

¹⁷ "Everyone is senseless and without
    knowledge;
    every goldsmith is shamed by his idols.
The images he makes are a fraud;
    they have no breath in them.
¹⁸ They are worthless, the objects of
    mockery;
    when their judgment comes, they will
    perish.

ᵃ 1 Leb Kamai is a cryptogram for Chaldea, that is, Babylonia.   ᵇ 3 The Hebrew term refers to the
irrevocable giving over of things or persons to the LORD, often by totally destroying them.
ᶜ 4 Or Chaldea   ᵈ 5 Or Almighty, / and the land of the Babylonians

¹⁹ He who is the Portion of Jacob is not like
these,
for he is the Maker of all things,
including the people of his inheritance —
the LORD Almighty is his name.

²⁰ "You are my war club,
my weapon for battle —
with you I shatter nations,
with you I destroy kingdoms,
²¹ with you I shatter horse and rider,
with you I shatter chariot and driver,
²² with you I shatter man and woman,
with you I shatter old man and youth,
with you I shatter young man and
young woman,
²³ with you I shatter shepherd and flock,
with you I shatter farmer and oxen,
with you I shatter governors and
officials.

²⁴ "Before your eyes I will repay Babylon
and all who live in Babylonia^a for all the
wrong they have done in Zion," declares the
LORD.

²⁵ "I am against you, you destroying
mountain,
you who destroy the whole earth,"
declares the LORD.
"I will stretch out my hand against you,
roll you off the cliffs,
and make you a burned-out mountain.
²⁶ No rock will be taken from you for a
cornerstone,
nor any stone for a foundation,
for you will be desolate forever,"
declares the LORD.

²⁷ "Lift up a banner in the land!
Blow the trumpet among the nations!
Prepare the nations for battle against her;
summon against her these kingdoms:
Ararat, Minni and Ashkenaz.
Appoint a commander against her;
send up horses like a swarm of locusts.
²⁸ Prepare the nations for battle against
her —
the kings of the Medes,
their governors and all their officials,
and all the countries they rule.
²⁹ The land trembles and writhes,
for the LORD's purposes against
Babylon stand —

to lay waste the land of Babylon
so that no one will live there.
³⁰ Babylon's warriors have stopped fighting;
they remain in their strongholds.
Their strength is exhausted;
they have become weaklings.
Her dwellings are set on fire;
the bars of her gates are broken.
³¹ One courier follows another
and messenger follows messenger
to announce to the king of Babylon
that his entire city is captured,
³² the river crossings seized,
the marshes set on fire,
and the soldiers terrified."

³³ This is what the LORD Almighty, the
God of Israel, says:

"Daughter Babylon is like a threshing
floor
at the time it is trampled;
the time to harvest her will soon
come."

³⁴ "Nebuchadnezzar king of Babylon has
devoured us,
he has thrown us into confusion,
he has made us an empty jar.
Like a serpent he has swallowed us
and filled his stomach with our
delicacies,
and then has spewed us out.
³⁵ May the violence done to our flesh^b be on
Babylon,"
say the inhabitants of Zion.
"May our blood be on those who live in
Babylonia,"
says Jerusalem.

³⁶ Therefore this is what the LORD says:

"See, I will defend your cause
and avenge you;
I will dry up her sea
and make her springs dry.
³⁷ Babylon will be a heap of ruins,
a haunt of jackals,
an object of horror and scorn,
a place where no one lives.
³⁸ Her people all roar like young lions,
they growl like lion cubs.
³⁹ But while they are aroused,
I will set out a feast for them
and make them drunk,

---

^a 24 Or *Chaldea*; also in verse 35   ^b 35 Or *done to us and to our children*

so that they shout with laughter —
  then sleep forever and not awake,"
            declares the LORD.
40 "I will bring them down
  like lambs to the slaughter,
  like rams and goats.

41 "How Sheshak[a] will be captured,
  the boast of the whole earth seized!
 How desolate Babylon will be
  among the nations!
42 The sea will rise over Babylon;
  its roaring waves will cover her.
43 Her towns will be desolate,
  a dry and desert land,
  a land where no one lives,
  through which no one travels.
44 I will punish Bel in Babylon
  and make him spew out what he has
    swallowed.
 The nations will no longer stream
    to him.
 And the wall of Babylon will fall.

45 "Come out of her, my people!
  Run for your lives!
  Run from the fierce anger of the LORD.
46 Do not lose heart or be afraid
  when rumors are heard in the land;
 one rumor comes this year, another
    the next,
  rumors of violence in the land
  and of ruler against ruler.
47 For the time will surely come
  when I will punish the idols of
    Babylon;
 her whole land will be disgraced
  and her slain will all lie fallen
    within her.
48 Then heaven and earth and all that is in
    them
  will shout for joy over Babylon,
 for out of the north
  destroyers will attack her,"
            declares the LORD.

49 "Babylon must fall because of Israel's
    slain,
  just as the slain in all the earth
  have fallen because of Babylon.
50 You who have escaped the sword,
  leave and do not linger!
 Remember the LORD in a distant land,
  and call to mind Jerusalem."

51 "We are disgraced,
  for we have been insulted
 and shame covers our faces,
  because foreigners have entered
  the holy places of the LORD's house."

52 "But days are coming," declares the LORD,
  "when I will punish her idols,
 and throughout her land
  the wounded will groan.
53 Even if Babylon ascends to the heavens
  and fortifies her lofty stronghold,
 I will send destroyers against her,"
            declares the LORD.

54 "The sound of a cry comes from Babylon,
  the sound of great destruction
  from the land of the Babylonians.[b]
55 The LORD will destroy Babylon;
  he will silence her noisy din.
 Waves of enemies will rage like great
    waters;
  the roar of their voices will resound.
56 A destroyer will come against Babylon;
  her warriors will be captured,
  and their bows will be broken.
 For the LORD is a God of retribution;
  he will repay in full.
57 I will make her officials and wise men
    drunk,
  her governors, officers and warriors
    as well;
 they will sleep forever and not awake,"
  declares the King, whose name is the
    LORD Almighty.

58 This is what the LORD Almighty says:

"Babylon's thick wall will be leveled
  and her high gates set on fire;
 the peoples exhaust themselves for
    nothing,
  the nations' labor is only fuel for the
    flames."

59 This is the message Jeremiah the prophet gave to the staff officer Seraiah son of Neriah, the son of Mahseiah, when he went to Babylon with Zedekiah king of Judah in the fourth year of his reign. 60 Jeremiah had written on a scroll about all the disasters that would come upon Babylon — all that had been recorded concerning Babylon. 61 He said to Seraiah, "When you get to Babylon, see that you read all these words aloud.

---

a 41 Sheshak is a cryptogram for Babylon.   b 54 Or Chaldeans

⁶²Then say, 'LORD, you have said you will destroy this place, so that neither people nor animals will live in it; it will be desolate forever.' ⁶³When you finish reading this scroll, tie a stone to it and throw it into the Euphrates. ⁶⁴Then say, 'So will Babylon sink to rise no more because of the disaster I will bring on her. And her people will fall.'"

The words of Jeremiah end here.

The Fall of Jerusalem

52 Zedekiah was twenty-one years old when he became king, and he reigned in Jerusalem eleven years. His mother's name was Hamutal daughter of Jeremiah; she was from Libnah. ²He did evil in the eyes of the LORD, just as Jehoiakim had done. ³It was because of the LORD's anger that all this happened to Jerusalem and Judah, and in the end he thrust them from his presence.

Now Zedekiah rebelled against the king of Babylon.

⁴So in the ninth year of Zedekiah's reign, on the tenth day of the tenth month, Nebuchadnezzar king of Babylon marched against Jerusalem with his whole army. They encamped outside the city and built siege works all around it. ⁵The city was kept under siege until the eleventh year of King Zedekiah.

⁶By the ninth day of the fourth month the famine in the city had become so severe that there was no food for the people to eat. ⁷Then the city wall was broken through, and the whole army fled. They left the city at night through the gate between the two walls near the king's garden, though the Babylonians*a* were surrounding the city. They fled toward the Arabah,*b* ⁸but the Babylonian*c* army pursued King Zedekiah and overtook him in the plains of Jericho. All his soldiers were separated from him and scattered, ⁹and he was captured.

He was taken to the king of Babylon at Riblah in the land of Hamath, where he pronounced sentence on him. ¹⁰There at Riblah the king of Babylon killed the sons of Zedekiah before his eyes; he also killed all the officials of Judah. ¹¹Then he put out Zedekiah's eyes, bound him with bronze shackles

and took him to Babylon, where he put him in prison till the day of his death.

¹²On the tenth day of the fifth month, in the nineteenth year of Nebuchadnezzar king of Babylon, Nebuzaradan commander of the imperial guard, who served the king of Babylon, came to Jerusalem. ¹³He set fire to the temple of the LORD, the royal palace and all the houses of Jerusalem. Every important building he burned down. ¹⁴The whole Babylonian army, under the commander of the imperial guard, broke down all the walls around Jerusalem. ¹⁵Nebuzaradan the commander of the guard carried into exile some of the poorest people and those who remained in the city, along with the rest of the craftsmen*d* and those who had deserted to the king of Babylon. ¹⁶But Nebuzaradan left behind the rest of the poorest people of the land to work the vineyards and fields.

¹⁷The Babylonians broke up the bronze pillars, the movable stands and the bronze Sea that were at the temple of the LORD and they carried all the bronze to Babylon. ¹⁸They also took away the pots, shovels, wick trimmers, sprinkling bowls, dishes and all the bronze articles used in the temple service. ¹⁹The commander of the imperial guard took away the basins, censers, sprinkling bowls, pots, lampstands, dishes and bowls used for drink offerings — all that were made of pure gold or silver.

²⁰The bronze from the two pillars, the Sea and the twelve bronze bulls under it, and the movable stands, which King Solomon had made for the temple of the LORD, was more than could be weighed. ²¹Each pillar was eighteen cubits high and twelve cubits in circumference*e*; each was four fingers thick, and hollow. ²²The bronze capital on top of one pillar was five cubits*f* high and was decorated with a network and pomegranates of bronze all around. The other pillar, with its pomegranates, was similar. ²³There were ninety-six pomegranates on the sides; the total number of pomegranates above the surrounding network was a hundred.

²⁴The commander of the guard took as

---

a 7 Or *Chaldeans*; also in verse 17   *b 7* Or *the Jordan Valley*   *c 8* Or *Chaldean*; also in verse 14
d 15 Or *the populace*   *e 21* That is, about 27 feet high and 18 feet in circumference or about 8.1 meters high and 5.4 meters in circumference   *f 22* That is, about 7 1/2 feet or about 2.3 meters

prisoners Seraiah the chief priest, Zephaniah the priest next in rank and the three doorkeepers. ²⁵Of those still in the city, he took the officer in charge of the fighting men, and seven royal advisers. He also took the secretary who was chief officer in charge of conscripting the people of the land, sixty of whom were found in the city. ²⁶Nebuzaradan the commander took them all and brought them to the king of Babylon at Riblah. ²⁷There at Riblah, in the land of Hamath, the king had them executed.

So Judah went into captivity, away from her land. ²⁸This is the number of the people Nebuchadnezzar carried into exile:

in the seventh year, 3,023 Jews;
²⁹in Nebuchadnezzar's eighteenth year,
832 people from Jerusalem;
³⁰in his twenty-third year,

745 Jews taken into exile by Nebuzaradan the commander of the imperial guard.

There were 4,600 people in all.

Jehoiachin Released

³¹In the thirty-seventh year of the exile of Jehoiachin king of Judah, in the year Awel-Marduk became king of Babylon, on the twenty-fifth day of the twelfth month, he released Jehoiachin king of Judah and freed him from prison. ³²He spoke kindly to him and gave him a seat of honor higher than those of the other kings who were with him in Babylon. ³³So Jehoiachin put aside his prison clothes and for the rest of his life ate regularly at the king's table. ³⁴Day by day the king of Babylon gave Jehoiachin a regular allowance as long as he lived, till the day of his death.

LAMENTATIONS

WHEN DID THIS HAPPEN?

Around 586 B.C. in Jerusalem, in the southern kingdom of Judah

WHO IS IN THIS BOOK?

the writer

VERSE YOU MIGHT RECOGNIZE

LAMENTATIONS 3:22–23

"Because of the LORD's great love we are not consumed, for his compassions never fail. They are new every morning; great is your faithfulness."

WHAT'S IT ABOUT?

How deserted lies the city, once so full of people!" These sad words begin the book of Lamentations, a group of poems written after Jerusalem was destroyed and the Jews were taken captive by Babylon. Like final respects spoken at a funeral, this book mourns what has happened to Jerusalem as the writer (who may have been Jeremiah) witnesses the invasion of Jerusalem and the destruction of the once great city. The people of Israel finally understand that they are being punished for their sins and begin to mourn.

Although these poems talk about the specific consequences of Israel's sin, which at times are gruesome, the book is also hopeful. This hope is found in God's promise to never leave them and to restore them regardless of what they have done. The author wrote, "Because of the LORD's great love we are not consumed, for his compassions never fail" (3:22). Even in the worst of circumstances, which the people of Israel brought upon themselves, they could take hope in God's love for them and his plan for their ultimate salvation.

LAMENTATIONS

1 ^a How deserted lies the city,
　once so full of people!
How like a widow is she,
　who once was great among the
　　nations!
She who was queen among the provinces
　has now become a slave.

² Bitterly she weeps at night,
　tears are on her cheeks.
Among all her lovers
　there is no one to comfort her.
All her friends have betrayed her;
　they have become her enemies.

³ After affliction and harsh labor,
　Judah has gone into exile.
She dwells among the nations;
　she finds no resting place.
All who pursue her have overtaken her
　in the midst of her distress.

⁴ The roads to Zion mourn,
　for no one comes to her appointed
　　festivals.
All her gateways are desolate,
　her priests groan,
her young women grieve,
　and she is in bitter anguish.

⁵ Her foes have become her masters;
　her enemies are at ease.
The LORD has brought her grief
　because of her many sins.
Her children have gone into exile,
　captive before the foe.

⁶ All the splendor has departed
　from Daughter Zion.
Her princes are like deer
　that find no pasture;
in weakness they have fled
　before the pursuer.

⁷ In the days of her affliction and
　　wandering
　Jerusalem remembers all the treasures
that were hers in days of old.
When her people fell into enemy hands,
　there was no one to help her.
Her enemies looked at her
　and laughed at her destruction.

⁸ Jerusalem has sinned greatly
　and so has become unclean.
All who honored her despise her,
　for they have all seen her naked;
she herself groans
　and turns away.

⁹ Her filthiness clung to her skirts;
　she did not consider her future.
Her fall was astounding;
　there was none to comfort her.
"Look, LORD, on my affliction,
　for the enemy has triumphed."

¹⁰ The enemy laid hands
　on all her treasures;
she saw pagan nations
　enter her sanctuary—
those you had forbidden
　to enter your assembly.

¹¹ All her people groan
　as they search for bread;
they barter their treasures for food
　to keep themselves alive.
"Look, LORD, and consider,
　for I am despised."

¹² "Is it nothing to you, all you who pass by?
　Look around and see.
Is any suffering like my suffering
　that was inflicted on me,
that the LORD brought on me
　in the day of his fierce anger?

¹³ "From on high he sent fire,
　sent it down into my bones.
He spread a net for my feet
　and turned me back.
He made me desolate,
　faint all the day long.

^a This chapter is an acrostic poem, the verses of which begin with the successive letters of the Hebrew alphabet.

¹⁴ "My sins have been bound into a yoke^a;
 by his hands they were woven
  together.
They have been hung on my neck,
 and the Lord has sapped my strength.
He has given me into the hands
 of those I cannot withstand.

¹⁵ "The Lord has rejected
 all the warriors in my midst;
he has summoned an army against me
 to^b crush my young men.
In his winepress the Lord has trampled
 Virgin Daughter Judah.

¹⁶ "This is why I weep
 and my eyes overflow with tears.
No one is near to comfort me,
 no one to restore my spirit.
My children are destitute
 because the enemy has prevailed."

¹⁷ Zion stretches out her hands,
 but there is no one to comfort her.
The LORD has decreed for Jacob
 that his neighbors become his foes;
Jerusalem has become
 an unclean thing among them.

¹⁸ "The LORD is righteous,
 yet I rebelled against his command.
Listen, all you peoples;
 look on my suffering.
My young men and young women
 have gone into exile.

¹⁹ "I called to my allies
 but they betrayed me.
My priests and my elders
 perished in the city
while they searched for food
 to keep themselves alive.

²⁰ "See, LORD, how distressed I am!
 I am in torment within,
and in my heart I am disturbed,
 for I have been most rebellious.
Outside, the sword bereaves;
 inside, there is only death.

²¹ "People have heard my groaning,
 but there is no one to comfort me.
All my enemies have heard of my
  distress;

they rejoice at what you have
  done.
May you bring the day you have
  announced
so they may become like me.

²² "Let all their wickedness come
  before you;
 deal with them
as you have dealt with me
 because of all my sins.
My groans are many
 and my heart is faint."

2^c How the Lord has covered Daughter
   Zion
 with the cloud of his anger^d!
He has hurled down the splendor of
  Israel
 from heaven to earth;
he has not remembered his footstool
 in the day of his anger.

² Without pity the Lord has swallowed up
 all the dwellings of Jacob;
in his wrath he has torn down
 the strongholds of Daughter Judah.
He has brought her kingdom and its
  princes
 down to the ground in dishonor.

³ In fierce anger he has cut off
 every horn^{e,f} of Israel.
He has withdrawn his right hand
 at the approach of the enemy.
He has burned in Jacob like a flaming fire
 that consumes everything around it.

⁴ Like an enemy he has strung his bow;
 his right hand is ready.
Like a foe he has slain
 all who were pleasing to the eye;
he has poured out his wrath like fire
 on the tent of Daughter Zion.

⁵ The Lord is like an enemy;
 he has swallowed up Israel.
He has swallowed up all her palaces
 and destroyed her strongholds.
He has multiplied mourning and
  lamentation
 for Daughter Judah.

---

^a 14 Most Hebrew manuscripts; many Hebrew manuscripts and Septuagint *He kept watch over my sins*
^b 15 Or *has set a time for me / when he will*   ^c This chapter is an acrostic poem, the verses of which begin
with the successive letters of the Hebrew alphabet.   ^d 1 Or *How the Lord in his anger / has treated Daughter
Zion with contempt*   ^e 3 Or *off / all the strength*; or *every king*   ^f 3 *Horn* here symbolizes strength.

⁶ He has laid waste his dwelling like a
    garden;
  he has destroyed his place of meeting.
The LORD has made Zion forget
    her appointed festivals and her
    Sabbaths;
  in his fierce anger he has spurned
    both king and priest.

⁷ The Lord has rejected his altar
    and abandoned his sanctuary.
He has given the walls of her palaces
    into the hands of the enemy;
  they have raised a shout in the house of
    the LORD
    as on the day of an appointed
    festival.

⁸ The LORD determined to tear down
    the wall around Daughter Zion.
He stretched out a measuring line
    and did not withhold his hand from
    destroying.
He made ramparts and walls lament;
    together they wasted away.

⁹ Her gates have sunk into the ground;
    their bars he has broken and
    destroyed.
Her king and her princes are exiled
    among the nations,
    the law is no more,
  and her prophets no longer find
    visions from the LORD.

¹⁰ The elders of Daughter Zion
    sit on the ground in silence;
  they have sprinkled dust on their heads
    and put on sackcloth.
The young women of Jerusalem
    have bowed their heads to the ground.

¹¹ My eyes fail from weeping,
    I am in torment within;
  my heart is poured out on the ground
    because my people are destroyed,
  because children and infants faint
    in the streets of the city.

¹² They say to their mothers,
    "Where is bread and wine?"
  as they faint like the wounded
    in the streets of the city,
  as their lives ebb away
    in their mothers' arms.

¹³ What can I say for you?
    With what can I compare you,
    Daughter Jerusalem?
To what can I liken you,
    that I may comfort you,
    Virgin Daughter Zion?
Your wound is as deep as the sea.
    Who can heal you?

¹⁴ The visions of your prophets
    were false and worthless;
  they did not expose your sin
    to ward off your captivity.
The prophecies they gave you
    were false and misleading.

¹⁵ All who pass your way
    clap their hands at you;
  they scoff and shake their heads
    at Daughter Jerusalem:
  "Is this the city that was called
    the perfection of beauty,
    the joy of the whole earth?"

¹⁶ All your enemies open their mouths
    wide against you;
  they scoff and gnash their teeth
    and say, "We have swallowed her up.
  This is the day we have waited for;
    we have lived to see it."

¹⁷ The LORD has done what he planned;
    he has fulfilled his word,
    which he decreed long ago.
He has overthrown you without pity,
    he has let the enemy gloat over you,
    he has exalted the horn[a] of your foes.

¹⁸ The hearts of the people
    cry out to the Lord.
You walls of Daughter Zion,
    let your tears flow like a river
    day and night;
  give yourself no relief,
    your eyes no rest.

¹⁹ Arise, cry out in the night,
    as the watches of the night begin;
  pour out your heart like water
    in the presence of the Lord.
Lift up your hands to him
    for the lives of your children,
  who faint from hunger
    at every street corner.

²⁰ "Look, LORD, and consider:

ᵃ 17 *Horn* here symbolizes strength.

Whom have you ever treated like this?
Should women eat their offspring,
    the children they have cared for?
Should priest and prophet be killed
    in the sanctuary of the Lord?

21 "Young and old lie together
    in the dust of the streets;
my young men and young women
    have fallen by the sword.
You have slain them in the day of your
    anger;
    you have slaughtered them
    without pity.

22 "As you summon to a feast day,
    so you summoned against me terrors
    on every side.
In the day of the LORD's anger
    no one escaped or survived;
those I cared for and reared
    my enemy has destroyed."

3ᵃ I am the man who has seen affliction
    by the rod of the LORD's wrath.
2 He has driven me away and made me walk
    in darkness rather than light;
3 indeed, he has turned his hand
        against me
    again and again, all day long.

4 He has made my skin and my flesh
        grow old
    and has broken my bones.
5 He has besieged me and surrounded me
    with bitterness and hardship.
6 He has made me dwell in darkness
    like those long dead.

7 He has walled me in so I cannot escape;
    he has weighed me down with chains.
8 Even when I call out or cry for help,
    he shuts out my prayer.
9 He has barred my way with blocks
        of stone;
    he has made my paths crooked.

10 Like a bear lying in wait,
    like a lion in hiding,
11 he dragged me from the path and
        mangled me
    and left me without help.
12 He drew his bow
    and made me the target for his arrows.

13 He pierced my heart
    with arrows from his quiver.
14 I became the laughingstock of all my
        people;
    they mock me in song all day long.
15 He has filled me with bitter herbs
    and given me gall to drink.

16 He has broken my teeth with gravel;
    he has trampled me in the dust.
17 I have been deprived of peace;
    I have forgotten what prosperity is.
18 So I say, "My splendor is gone
    and all that I had hoped from the LORD."

19 I remember my affliction and my
        wandering,
    the bitterness and the gall.
20 I well remember them,
    and my soul is downcast within me.
21 Yet this I call to mind
    and therefore I have hope:

22 Because of the LORD's great love we are
        not consumed,
    for his compassions never fail.
23 They are new every morning;
    great is your faithfulness.
24 I say to myself, "The LORD is my portion;
    therefore I will wait for him."

25 The LORD is good to those whose hope is
        in him,
    to the one who seeks him;
26 it is good to wait quietly
    for the salvation of the LORD.
27 It is good for a man to bear the yoke
    while he is young.

28 Let him sit alone in silence,
    for the LORD has laid it on him.
29 Let him bury his face in the dust —
    there may yet be hope.
30 Let him offer his cheek to one who would
        strike him,
    and let him be filled with disgrace.

31 For no one is cast off
    by the Lord forever.
32 Though he brings grief, he will show
        compassion,
    so great is his unfailing love.
33 For he does not willingly bring affliction
    or grief to anyone.

ᵃ This chapter is an acrostic poem; the verses of each stanza begin with the successive letters of the
Hebrew alphabet, and the verses within each stanza begin with the same letter.

PLENTY TO CRY ABOUT

READ: **LAMENTATIONS 3:22-23**

Ancient Hebrews didn't grieve privately or quietly. When an individual died, relatives wailed. Neighbors ran to join the crying. Families even hired professional mourners to add to the volume of shrieks and sobs.

Don't expect to stumble upon much happiness in the book of Lamentations. Many scholars credit this book to the prophet Jeremiah, the "weeping prophet," but it expresses a whole nation's grief for the loss of its land, capital, and spiritual center. Each of the book's five chapters records a sad poem for the holy city of Jerusalem after the Babylonians burned it to the ground. These "laments" are dirges, songs meant to be sung at a funeral.

BUILDING FAITH WISDOM STRENGTH

This book gives plenty of reasons to cry. It explains why God let his people be taken as prisoners to a distant nation. It describes the desolation of their home city. It announces the people's shame and anguish. It cries out in anguish for God to rush to rescue his people. Yet the book also shouts hope; the Lord's people remain alive because of his steady love. His compassion keeps showing up morning after morning. His faithfulness never stops. So his people can wait patiently for him.

Don't ever give up when you face a bad situation, even when sadness overwhelms you. The Lord can carry you through your worst circumstances and set you free from your darkest feelings. His care for you never fades or fails.

³⁴ To crush underfoot
all prisoners in the land,
³⁵ to deny people their rights
before the Most High,
³⁶ to deprive them of justice —
would not the Lord see such things?

³⁷ Who can speak and have it happen
if the Lord has not decreed it?
³⁸ Is it not from the mouth of the Most High
that both calamities and good things
come?
³⁹ Why should the living complain
when punished for their sins?

⁴⁰ Let us examine our ways and test them,
and let us return to the Lord.
⁴¹ Let us lift up our hearts and our hands
to God in heaven, and say:
⁴² "We have sinned and rebelled
and you have not forgiven.

⁴³ "You have covered yourself with anger
and pursued us;
you have slain without pity.
⁴⁴ You have covered yourself with a cloud
so that no prayer can get through.
⁴⁵ You have made us scum and refuse
among the nations.

⁴⁶ "All our enemies have opened their
mouths
wide against us.
⁴⁷ We have suffered terror and pitfalls,
ruin and destruction."
⁴⁸ Streams of tears flow from my eyes
because my people are destroyed.

⁴⁹ My eyes will flow unceasingly,
without relief,
⁵⁰ until the Lord looks down
from heaven and sees.
⁵¹ What I see brings grief to my soul
because of all the women of my city.

⁵² Those who were my enemies without
cause
hunted me like a bird.
⁵³ They tried to end my life in a pit
and threw stones at me;
⁵⁴ the waters closed over my head,
and I thought I was about to perish.

⁵⁵ I called on your name, Lord,
from the depths of the pit.

⁵⁶ You heard my plea: "Do not close
your ears
to my cry for relief."
⁵⁷ You came near when I called you,
and you said, "Do not fear."

⁵⁸ You, Lord, took up my case;
you redeemed my life.
⁵⁹ Lord, you have seen the wrong done
to me.
Uphold my cause!
⁶⁰ You have seen the depth of their
vengeance,
all their plots against me.

⁶¹ Lord, you have heard their insults,
all their plots against me —
⁶² what my enemies whisper and mutter
against me all day long.
⁶³ Look at them! Sitting or standing,
they mock me in their songs.

⁶⁴ Pay them back what they deserve,
Lord,
for what their hands have done.
⁶⁵ Put a veil over their hearts,
and may your curse be on them!
⁶⁶ Pursue them in anger and destroy them
from under the heavens of the Lord.

4 ᵃ How the gold has lost its luster,
the fine gold become dull!
The sacred gems are scattered
at every street corner.

² How the precious children of Zion,
once worth their weight in gold,
are now considered as pots of clay,
the work of a potter's hands!

³ Even jackals offer their breasts
to nurse their young,
but my people have become
heartless
like ostriches in the desert.

⁴ Because of thirst the infant's tongue
sticks to the roof of its mouth;
the children beg for bread,
but no one gives it to them.

⁵ Those who once ate delicacies
are destitute in the streets.
Those brought up in royal purple
now lie on ash heaps.

ᵃ This chapter is an acrostic poem, the verses of which begin with the successive letters of the Hebrew alphabet.

⁶ The punishment of my people
is greater than that of Sodom,
which was overthrown in a moment
without a hand turned to help her.

⁷ Their princes were brighter than snow
and whiter than milk,
their bodies more ruddy than rubies,
their appearance like lapis lazuli.

⁸ But now they are blacker than soot;
they are not recognized in the streets.
Their skin has shriveled on their bones;
it has become as dry as a stick.

⁹ Those killed by the sword are better off
than those who die of famine;
racked with hunger, they waste away
for lack of food from the field.

¹⁰ With their own hands compassionate
women
have cooked their own children,
who became their food
when my people were destroyed.

¹¹ The LORD has given full vent to his wrath;
he has poured out his fierce anger.
He kindled a fire in Zion
that consumed her foundations.

¹² The kings of the earth did not believe,
nor did any of the peoples of the world,
that enemies and foes could enter
the gates of Jerusalem.

¹³ But it happened because of the sins of her
prophets
and the iniquities of her priests,
who shed within her
the blood of the righteous.

¹⁴ Now they grope through the streets
as if they were blind.
They are so defiled with blood
that no one dares to touch their
garments.

¹⁵ "Go away! You are unclean!" people cry
to them.
"Away! Away! Don't touch us!"
When they flee and wander about,
people among the nations say,
"They can stay here no longer."

¹⁶ The LORD himself has scattered them;
he no longer watches over them.
The priests are shown no honor,
the elders no favor.

¹⁷ Moreover, our eyes failed,
looking in vain for help;
from our towers we watched
for a nation that could not save us.

¹⁸ People stalked us at every step,
so we could not walk in our streets.
Our end was near, our days were
numbered,
for our end had come.

¹⁹ Our pursuers were swifter
than eagles in the sky;
they chased us over the mountains
and lay in wait for us in the desert.

²⁰ The LORD's anointed, our very life breath,
was caught in their traps.
We thought that under his shadow
we would live among the nations.

²¹ Rejoice and be glad, Daughter Edom,
you who live in the land of Uz.
But to you also the cup will be passed;
you will be drunk and stripped naked.

²² Your punishment will end, Daughter
Zion;
he will not prolong your exile.
But he will punish your sin, Daughter
Edom,
and expose your wickedness.

5 Remember, LORD, what has happened
to us;
look, and see our disgrace.
² Our inheritance has been turned over to
strangers,
our homes to foreigners.
³ We have become fatherless,
our mothers are widows.
⁴ We must buy the water we drink;
our wood can be had only at a price.
⁵ Those who pursue us are at our heels;
we are weary and find no rest.
⁶ We submitted to Egypt and Assyria
to get enough bread.
⁷ Our ancestors sinned and are no more,
and we bear their punishment.
⁸ Slaves rule over us,
and there is no one to free us from
their hands.
⁹ We get our bread at the risk of our lives
because of the sword in the desert.
¹⁰ Our skin is hot as an oven,
feverish from hunger.

¹¹ Women have been violated in Zion,
and virgins in the towns of Judah.
¹² Princes have been hung up by their
hands;
elders are shown no respect.
¹³ Young men toil at the millstones;
boys stagger under loads of wood.
¹⁴ The elders are gone from the city gate;
the young men have stopped their
music.
¹⁵ Joy is gone from our hearts;
our dancing has turned to mourning.
¹⁶ The crown has fallen from our head.
Woe to us, for we have sinned!
¹⁷ Because of this our hearts are faint,

because of these things our eyes
grow dim
¹⁸ for Mount Zion, which lies desolate,
with jackals prowling over it.

¹⁹ You, LORD, reign forever;
your throne endures from generation
to generation.
²⁰ Why do you always forget us?
Why do you forsake us so long?
²¹ Restore us to yourself, LORD, that we may
return;
renew our days as of old
²² unless you have utterly rejected us
and are angry with us beyond
measure.

EZEKIEL

➤ **WHEN DID THIS HAPPEN?**

Between 593 and 571 B.C. in Babylon

➤ **WHO IS IN THIS BOOK?**

Ezekiel

➤ **VERSES YOU MIGHT RECOGNIZE**

EZEKIEL 33:11A

"Say to them, 'As surely as I live,' declares the Sovereign LORD, I take no pleasure in the death of the wicked, but rather that they turn from their ways and live.'"

EZEKIEL 36:26

"I will give you a new heart and put a new spirit in you; I will remove from you your heart of stone and give you a heart of flesh."

WHAT'S IT ABOUT?

Dry bones standing up and walking around. This is the picture God gave to the prophet Ezekiel of how God would restore Israel. Ezekiel was a priest exiled into Babylon with the Jews. He pronounced judgment on Israel and the surrounding nations for their sin and rebellion, but he also reminded them that God was the same I AM who delivered them from Egypt. He had delivered them once, and he would do it again. Despite their sinful ways, God would eventually bring his people back to Jerusalem.

Ezekiel also offered a picture of the new temple in Jerusalem, including the return of God's glory. He even looked forward to Israel's worship after Christ's return in the end times, when he would rule all people from his throne in Jerusalem for a thousand years. The Jews needed to be reminded of God's strength and their own weakness and failure, but God did not leave them without hope. He would give them new hearts and put a "new spirit" within them.

EZEKIEL

Ezekiel's Inaugural Vision

1 In my thirtieth year, in the fourth month on the fifth day, while I was among the exiles by the Kebar River, the heavens were opened and I saw visions of God.

[2] On the fifth of the month — it was the fifth year of the exile of King Jehoiachin — [3] the word of the LORD came to Ezekiel the priest, the son of Buzi, by the Kebar River in the land of the Babylonians.[a] There the hand of the LORD was on him.

[4] I looked, and I saw a windstorm coming out of the north — an immense cloud with flashing lightning and surrounded by brilliant light. The center of the fire looked like glowing metal, [5] and in the fire was what looked like four living creatures. In appearance their form was human, [6] but each of them had four faces and four wings. [7] Their legs were straight; their feet were like those of a calf and gleamed like burnished bronze. [8] Under their wings on their four sides they had human hands. All four of them had faces and wings, [9] and the wings of one touched the wings of another. Each one went straight ahead; they did not turn as they moved.

[10] Their faces looked like this: Each of the four had the face of a human being, and on the right side each had the face of a lion, and on the left the face of an ox; each also had the face of an eagle. [11] Such were their faces. They each had two wings spreading out upward, each wing touching that of the creature on either side; and each had two other wings covering its body. [12] Each one went straight ahead. Wherever the spirit would go, they would go, without turning as they went. [13] The appearance of the living creatures was like burning coals of fire or like torches. Fire moved back and forth among the creatures; it was bright, and lightning flashed out of it. [14] The creatures sped back and forth like flashes of lightning.

[15] As I looked at the living creatures, I saw a wheel on the ground beside each creature with its four faces. [16] This was the appearance and structure of the wheels: They sparkled like topaz, and all four looked alike. Each appeared to be made like a wheel intersecting a wheel. [17] As they moved, they would go in any one of the four directions the creatures faced; the wheels did not change direction as the creatures went. [18] Their rims were high and awesome, and all four rims were full of eyes all around.

[19] When the living creatures moved, the wheels beside them moved; and when the living creatures rose from the ground, the wheels also rose. [20] Wherever the spirit would go, they would go, and the wheels would rise along with them, because the spirit of the living creatures was in the wheels. [21] When the creatures moved, they also moved; when the creatures stood still, they also stood still; and when the creatures rose from the ground, the wheels rose along with them, because the spirit of the living creatures was in the wheels.

[22] Spread out above the heads of the living creatures was what looked something like a vault, sparkling like crystal, and awesome. [23] Under the vault their wings were stretched out one toward the other, and each had two wings covering its body. [24] When the creatures moved, I heard the sound of their wings, like the roar of rushing waters, like the voice of the Almighty,[b] like the tumult of an army. When they stood still, they lowered their wings.

[25] Then there came a voice from above the vault over their heads as they stood with lowered wings. [26] Above the vault over their heads was what looked like a throne of lapis lazuli, and high above on the throne was a figure like that of a man. [27] I saw that from what appeared to be his waist up he looked like glowing metal, as if full of fire, and that from there down he looked like fire; and brilliant light surrounded him. [28] Like the

---

[a] 3 Or *Chaldeans*   [b] 24 Hebrew *Shaddai*

EPIC DRAMA

READ: EZEKIEL 1:1

The book of Ezekiel doesn't make much sense if you don't understand its setting right from the start. The prophet Ezekiel is thirty years old (Ezekiel 1:1). Five years have passed since he and some of his fellow Israelites were dragged into captivity by the Babylonians (v. 2). He's hundreds of miles from home living with other exiles along Babylon's Kebar River.

That's when heaven splits open and Ezekiel experiences a wild vision of God. He sees strange angelic creatures high overhead. Wheels spin within wheels. God outshines everything else. It feels like Ezekiel doesn't have words to describe what he sees, so don't be surprised if his descriptions puzzle you too.

Ezekiel sees the Lord and falls on his face. Then God speaks, sending him to speak to the Lord's stubborn people. The rest of this book records the prophet's visions, words, and sometimes bizarre actions meant to help the captives come back to God.

You might not always track with the action of this dramatic book. But don't miss its main point: God never turns his back on his people. Even when you rebel against him, he never stops loving you. He never quits trying to win you back.

BUILDING FAITH WISDOM STRENGTH

appearance of a rainbow in the clouds on a rainy day, so was the radiance around him.

This was the appearance of the likeness of the glory of the LORD. When I saw it, I fell facedown, and I heard the voice of one speaking.

Ezekiel's Call to Be a Prophet

2 He said to me, "Son of man,[a] stand up on your feet and I will speak to you." ²As he spoke, the Spirit came into me and raised me to my feet, and I heard him speaking to me.

³He said: "Son of man, I am sending you to the Israelites, to a rebellious nation that has rebelled against me; they and their ancestors have been in revolt against me to this very day. ⁴The people to whom I am sending you are obstinate and stubborn. Say to them, 'This is what the Sovereign LORD says.' ⁵And whether they listen or fail to listen—for they are a rebellious people—they will know that a prophet has been among them. ⁶And you, son of man, do not be afraid of them or their words. Do not be afraid, though briers and thorns are all around you and you live among scorpions. Do not be afraid of what they say or be terrified by them, though they are a rebellious people. ⁷You must speak my words to them, whether they listen or fail to listen, for they are rebellious. ⁸But you, son of man, listen to what I say to you. Do not rebel like that rebellious people; open your mouth and eat what I give you."

⁹Then I looked, and I saw a hand stretched out to me. In it was a scroll, ¹⁰which he unrolled before me. On both sides of it were written words of lament and mourning and woe.

3 And he said to me, "Son of man, eat what is before you, eat this scroll; then go and speak to the people of Israel." ²So I opened my mouth, and he gave me the scroll to eat.

³Then he said to me, "Son of man, eat this scroll I am giving you and fill your stomach with it." So I ate it, and it tasted as sweet as honey in my mouth.

⁴He then said to me: "Son of man, go now to the people of Israel and speak my words to them. ⁵You are not being sent to a people of obscure speech and strange language, but to

the people of Israel— ⁶not to many peoples of obscure speech and strange language, whose words you cannot understand. Surely if I had sent you to them, they would have listened to you. ⁷But the people of Israel are not willing to listen to you because they are not willing to listen to me, for all the Israelites are hardened and obstinate. ⁸But I will make you as unyielding and hardened as they are. ⁹I will make your forehead like the hardest stone, harder than flint. Do not be afraid of them or terrified by them, though they are a rebellious people."

¹⁰And he said to me, "Son of man, listen carefully and take to heart all the words I speak to you. ¹¹Go now to your people in exile and speak to them. Say to them, 'This is what the Sovereign LORD says,' whether they listen or fail to listen."

¹²Then the Spirit lifted me up, and I heard behind me a loud rumbling sound as the glory of the LORD rose from the place where it was standing.[b] ¹³It was the sound of the wings of the living creatures brushing against each other and the sound of the wheels beside them, a loud rumbling sound. ¹⁴The Spirit then lifted me up and took me away, and I went in bitterness and in the anger of my spirit, with the strong hand of the LORD on me. ¹⁵I came to the exiles who lived at Tel Aviv near the Kebar River. And there, where they were living, I sat among them for seven days—deeply distressed.

Ezekiel's Task as Watchman

¹⁶At the end of seven days the word of the LORD came to me: ¹⁷"Son of man, I have made you a watchman for the people of Israel; so hear the word I speak and give them warning from me. ¹⁸When I say to a wicked person, 'You will surely die,' and you do not warn them or speak out to dissuade them from their evil ways in order to save their life, that wicked person will die for[c] their sin, and I will hold you accountable for their blood. ¹⁹But if you do warn the wicked person and they do not turn from their wickedness or from their evil ways, they will die for their sin; but you will have saved yourself.

²⁰"Again, when a righteous person turns

a 1 The Hebrew phrase *ben adam* means *human being.* The phrase *son of man* is retained as a form of address here and throughout Ezekiel because of its possible association with "Son of Man" in the New Testament. *b 12* Probable reading of the original Hebrew text; Masoretic Text *sound—may the glory of the LORD be praised from his place* *c 18* Or *in*; also in verses 19 and 20 from their righteousness and does evil, and I put a stumbling block before them, they will die. Since you did not warn them, they will die for their sin. The righteous things that person did will not be remembered, and I will hold you accountable for their blood. ²¹But if you do warn the righteous person not to sin and they do not sin, they will surely live because they took warning, and you will have saved yourself."

²²The hand of the LORD was on me there, and he said to me, "Get up and go out to the plain, and there I will speak to you." ²³So I got up and went out to the plain. And the glory of the LORD was standing there, like the glory I had seen by the Kebar River, and I fell facedown.

²⁴Then the Spirit came into me and raised me to my feet. He spoke to me and said: "Go, shut yourself inside your house. ²⁵And you, son of man, they will tie with ropes; you will be bound so that you cannot go out among the people. ²⁶I will make your tongue stick to the roof of your mouth so that you will be silent and unable to rebuke them, for they are a rebellious people. ²⁷But when I speak to you, I will open your mouth and you shall say to them, 'This is what the Sovereign LORD says.' Whoever will listen let them listen, and whoever will refuse let them refuse; for they are a rebellious people.

Siege of Jerusalem Symbolized

4 "Now, son of man, take a block of clay, put it in front of you and draw the city of Jerusalem on it. ²Then lay siege to it: Erect siege works against it, build a ramp up to it, set up camps against it and put battering rams around it. ³Then take an iron pan, place it as an iron wall between you and the city and turn your face toward it. It will be under siege, and you shall besiege it. This will be a sign to the people of Israel.

⁴"Then lie on your left side and put the sin of the people of Israel upon yourself.ᵃ You are to bear their sin for the number of days you lie on your side. ⁵I have assigned you the same number of days as the years of their sin. So for 390 days you will bear the sin of the people of Israel.

⁶"After you have finished this, lie down again, this time on your right side, and bear the sin of the people of Judah. I have assigned you 40 days, a day for each year. ⁷Turn your face toward the siege of Jerusalem and with bared arm prophesy against her. ⁸I will tie you up with ropes so that you cannot turn from one side to the other until you have finished the days of your siege.

⁹"Take wheat and barley, beans and lentils, millet and spelt; put them in a storage jar and use them to make bread for yourself. You are to eat it during the 390 days you lie on your side. ¹⁰Weigh out twenty shekelsᵇ of food to eat each day and eat it at set times. ¹¹Also measure out a sixth of a hinᶜ of water and drink it at set times. ¹²Eat the food as you would a loaf of barley bread; bake it in the sight of the people, using human excrement for fuel." ¹³The LORD said, "In this way the people of Israel will eat defiled food among the nations where I will drive them."

¹⁴Then I said, "Not so, Sovereign LORD! I have never defiled myself. From my youth until now I have never eaten anything found dead or torn by wild animals. No impure meat has ever entered my mouth."

¹⁵"Very well," he said, "I will let you bake your bread over cow dung instead of human excrement."

¹⁶He then said to me: "Son of man, I am about to cut off the food supply in Jerusalem. The people will eat rationed food in anxiety and drink rationed water in despair, ¹⁷for food and water will be scarce. They will be appalled at the sight of each other and will waste away because ofᵈ their sin.

God's Razor of Judgment

5 "Now, son of man, take a sharp sword and use it as a barber's razor to shave your head and your beard. Then take a set of scales and divide up the hair. ²When the days of your siege come to an end, burn a third of the hair inside the city. Take a third and strike it with the sword all around the city. And scatter a third to the wind. For I will pursue them with drawn sword. ³But take a few hairs and tuck them away in the folds of your garment. ⁴Again, take a few of these and throw them into the fire and burn them up. A fire will spread from there to all Israel.

ᵃ 4 Or *upon your side*   ᵇ 10 That is, about 8 ounces or about 230 grams   ᶜ 11 That is, about 2/3 quart or about 0.6 liter   ᵈ 17 Or *away in*

⁵"This is what the Sovereign LORD says: This is Jerusalem, which I have set in the center of the nations, with countries all around her. ⁶Yet in her wickedness she has rebelled against my laws and decrees more than the nations and countries around her. She has rejected my laws and has not followed my decrees.

⁷"Therefore this is what the Sovereign LORD says: You have been more unruly than the nations around you and have not followed my decrees or kept my laws. You have not even*ᵃ* conformed to the standards of the nations around you.

⁸"Therefore this is what the Sovereign LORD says: I myself am against you, Jerusalem, and I will inflict punishment on you in the sight of the nations. ⁹Because of all your detestable idols, I will do to you what I have never done before and will never do again. ¹⁰Therefore in your midst parents will eat their children, and children will eat their parents. I will inflict punishment on you and will scatter all your survivors to the winds. ¹¹Therefore as surely as I live, declares the Sovereign LORD, because you have defiled my sanctuary with all your vile images and detestable practices, I myself will shave you; I will not look on you with pity or spare you. ¹²A third of your people will die of the plague or perish by famine inside you; a third will fall by the sword outside your walls; and a third I will scatter to the winds and pursue with drawn sword.

¹³"Then my anger will cease and my wrath against them will subside, and I will be avenged. And when I have spent my wrath on them, they will know that I the LORD have spoken in my zeal.

¹⁴"I will make you a ruin and a reproach among the nations around you, in the sight of all who pass by. ¹⁵You will be a reproach and a taunt, a warning and an object of horror to the nations around you when I inflict punishment on you in anger and in wrath and with stinging rebuke. I the LORD have spoken. ¹⁶When I shoot at you with my deadly and destructive arrows of famine, I will shoot to destroy you. I will bring more and more famine upon you and cut off your supply of food. ¹⁷I will send famine and wild beasts against you, and they will leave you

childless. Plague and bloodshed will sweep through you, and I will bring the sword against you. I the LORD have spoken."

Doom for the Mountains of Israel

6 The word of the LORD came to me: ²"Son of man, set your face against the mountains of Israel; prophesy against them ³and say: 'You mountains of Israel, hear the word of the Sovereign LORD. This is what the Sovereign LORD says to the mountains and hills, to the ravines and valleys: I am about to bring a sword against you, and I will destroy your high places. ⁴Your altars will be demolished and your incense altars will be smashed; and I will slay your people in front of your idols. ⁵I will lay the dead bodies of the Israelites in front of their idols, and I will scatter your bones around your altars. ⁶Wherever you live, the towns will be laid waste and the high places demolished, so that your altars will be laid waste and devastated, your idols smashed and ruined, your incense altars broken down, and what you have made wiped out. ⁷Your people will fall slain among you, and you will know that I am the LORD.

⁸"'But I will spare some, for some of you will escape the sword when you are scattered among the lands and nations. ⁹Then in the nations where they have been carried captive, those who escape will remember me—how I have been grieved by their adulterous hearts, which have turned away from me, and by their eyes, which have lusted after their idols. They will loathe themselves for the evil they have done and for all their detestable practices. ¹⁰And they will know that I am the LORD; I did not threaten in vain to bring this calamity on them.

¹¹"'This is what the Sovereign LORD says: Strike your hands together and stamp your feet and cry out "Alas!" because of all the wicked and detestable practices of the people of Israel, for they will fall by the sword, famine and plague. ¹²One who is far away will die of the plague, and one who is near will fall by the sword, and anyone who survives and is spared will die of famine. So will I pour out my wrath on them. ¹³And they will know that I am the LORD, when their people lie slain among their idols around their altars, on

---

ᵃ 7 Most Hebrew manuscripts; some Hebrew manuscripts and Syriac *You have*

IDOL MAKEOVER

READ: EZEKIEL 6:6-9

One of our problems in identifying today's gods is that their identities not only lack the usual trappings of religion, they are also things that often aren't even wrong. Is God against pleasure? Sex? Money? Popularity?

These things are not immoral. They are morally neutral—and sometimes even commendable—until they become something else. It could be friendships or the pursuit of getting into your dream college. It could be a worthy cause. You could even be feeding the hungry and healing the sick. All of those are good things.

BUILDING FAITH WISDOM STRENGTH

The problem is that the instant something takes the place of God, the moment it becomes an end in itself rather than something to lay at God's throne, it becomes an idol. When someone or something replaces the Lord God in the position of glory in our lives, then that person or thing by definition has become our god.

So to identify some gods, look at what you are chasing. Another way to identify the gods in your life is to look at what you create.

Just because we call them by different names doesn't change what they are. We may not have the god of knowledge, the god of agriculture, the god of sex, or the god of the hunt. But we do have GPAs, cars, pornography, and sports. If it walks like an idol, and quacks like an idol, it's probably . . . (Hint: The answer isn't "a duck.")

Taken from *Gods at War Student Edition* by Kyle Idleman, copyright © 2014 by City on a Hill Studio, LLC, published by Zondervan.

every high hill and on all the mountaintops, under every spreading tree and every leafy oak—places where they offered fragrant incense to all their idols. [14] And I will stretch out my hand against them and make the land a desolate waste from the desert to Diblah[a]— wherever they live. Then they will know that I am the LORD.' "

The End Has Come

7 The word of the LORD came to me: [2] "Son of man, this is what the Sovereign LORD says to the land of Israel:

" 'The end! The end has come
  upon the four corners of the land!
[3] The end is now upon you,
  and I will unleash my anger against
    you.
I will judge you according to your
    conduct
  and repay you for all your detestable
    practices.
[4] I will not look on you with pity;
  I will not spare you.
I will surely repay you for your conduct
  and for the detestable practices
    among you.

" 'Then you will know that I am the LORD.'

[5] "This is what the Sovereign LORD says:

" 'Disaster! Unheard-of[b] disaster!
  See, it comes!
[6] The end has come!
  The end has come!
It has roused itself against you.
  See, it comes!
[7] Doom has come upon you,
  upon you who dwell in the land.
The time has come! The day is near!
  There is panic, not joy, on the
    mountains.
[8] I am about to pour out my wrath on you
  and spend my anger against you.
I will judge you according to your
    conduct
  and repay you for all your detestable
    practices.
[9] I will not look on you with pity;
  I will not spare you.
I will repay you for your conduct

and for the detestable practices
  among you.

" 'Then you will know that it is I the LORD
who strikes you.

[10] " 'See, the day!
  See, it comes!
Doom has burst forth,
  the rod has budded,
  arrogance has blossomed!
[11] Violence has arisen,[c]
  a rod to punish the wicked.
None of the people will be left,
  none of that crowd—
none of their wealth,
  nothing of value.
[12] The time has come!
  The day has arrived!
Let not the buyer rejoice
  nor the seller grieve,
  for my wrath is on the whole crowd.
[13] The seller will not recover
  the property that was sold—
  as long as both buyer and seller live.
For the vision concerning the whole
    crowd
  will not be reversed.
Because of their sins, not one of them
  will preserve their life.

[14] " 'They have blown the trumpet,
  they have made all things ready,
but no one will go into battle,
  for my wrath is on the whole crowd.
[15] Outside is the sword;
  inside are plague and famine.
Those in the country
  will die by the sword;
those in the city
  will be devoured by famine and
    plague.
[16] The fugitives who escape
  will flee to the mountains.
Like doves of the valleys,
  they will all moan,
  each for their own sins.
[17] Every hand will go limp;
  every leg will be wet with urine.
[18] They will put on sackcloth
  and be clothed with terror.
Every face will be covered with shame,
  and every head will be shaved.

---

[a] 14 Most Hebrew manuscripts; a few Hebrew manuscripts *Riblah*   [b] 5 Most Hebrew manuscripts;
some Hebrew manuscripts and Syriac *Disaster after*   [c] 11 Or *The violent one has become*

19 " 'They will throw their silver into the
    streets,
  and their gold will be treated as a thing
    unclean.
  Their silver and gold
    will not be able to deliver them
    in the day of the LORD's wrath.
  It will not satisfy their hunger
    or fill their stomachs,
  for it has caused them to stumble
    into sin.
20 They took pride in their beautiful jewelry
    and used it to make their detestable
    idols.
  They made it into vile images;
    therefore I will make it a thing unclean
    for them.
21 I will give their wealth as plunder to
    foreigners
  and as loot to the wicked of the earth,
    who will defile it.
22 I will turn my face away from the people,
    and robbers will desecrate the place
    I treasure.
  They will enter it
    and will defile it.

23 " 'Prepare chains!
  For the land is full of bloodshed,
    and the city is full of violence.
24 I will bring the most wicked of nations
    to take possession of their houses.
  I will put an end to the pride of the
    mighty,
    and their sanctuaries will be
    desecrated.
25 When terror comes,
    they will seek peace in vain.
26 Calamity upon calamity will come,
    and rumor upon rumor.
  They will go searching for a vision from
    the prophet,
  priestly instruction in the law will
    cease,
  the counsel of the elders will come to
    an end.
27 The king will mourn,
    the prince will be clothed with
    despair,
  and the hands of the people of the land
    will tremble.
  I will deal with them according to their
    conduct,

  and by their own standards I will
    judge them.

" 'Then they will know that I am the LORD.' "

Idolatry in the Temple

8 In the sixth year, in the sixth month on the fifth day, while I was sitting in my house and the elders of Judah were sitting before me, the hand of the Sovereign LORD came on me there. ²I looked, and I saw a figure like that of a man.ᵃ From what appeared to be his waist down he was like fire, and from there up his appearance was as bright as glowing metal. ³He stretched out what looked like a hand and took me by the hair of my head. The Spirit lifted me up between earth and heaven and in visions of God he took me to Jerusalem, to the entrance of the north gate of the inner court, where the idol that provokes to jealousy stood. ⁴And there before me was the glory of the God of Israel, as in the vision I had seen in the plain.

⁵Then he said to me, "Son of man, look toward the north." So I looked, and in the entrance north of the gate of the altar I saw this idol of jealousy.

⁶And he said to me, "Son of man, do you see what they are doing — the utterly detestable things the Israelites are doing here, things that will drive me far from my sanctuary? But you will see things that are even more detestable."

⁷Then he brought me to the entrance to the court. I looked, and I saw a hole in the wall. ⁸He said to me, "Son of man, now dig into the wall." So I dug into the wall and saw a doorway there.

⁹And he said to me, "Go in and see the wicked and detestable things they are doing here." ¹⁰So I went in and looked, and I saw portrayed all over the walls all kinds of crawling things and unclean animals and all the idols of Israel. ¹¹In front of them stood seventy elders of Israel, and Jaazaniah son of Shaphan was standing among them. Each had a censer in his hand, and a fragrant cloud of incense was rising.

¹²He said to me, "Son of man, have you seen what the elders of Israel are doing in the darkness, each at the shrine of his own idol? They say, 'The LORD does not see us; the LORD has forsaken the land.' " ¹³Again,

---

ᵃ 2 Or *saw a fiery figure*

HIDDEN ROOMS

READ: EZEKIEL 8:3

The prophet Ezekiel has a vision of an idol that is dubbed "the idol that provokes to jealousy." Scholars believe the idol referenced is the Canaanite goddess of fertility. So basically their sex god.

We look down on those ancient pagans carving their own idols and then bowing down to some wood statue. Usually an audible scoff follows. But are we any different? We're just sophisticated sinners now.

The fact that pornography is a $100 billion dollar industry is proof that the god of lust is also worshiped secretly and addictively everywhere else. What I'm getting at is this: we're still bowing down to the Canaanite goddess of fertility. And like every other idol, it has to be dethroned.

The Canaanite goddess of sex was the most visible idol in the temple, but it was just the tip of the iceberg. When Ezekiel peered through a peephole into a hidden room within the temple, he saw crawling things and unclean animals portrayed on the walls in ancient hieroglyphics.

BUILDING

FAITH

WISDOM

STRENGTH

What's etched on the walls of your mind and concealed in the hidden rooms of your heart?

It's not enough to invite Jesus into the outer court. You have to let him into the inner court. He wants to renovate every corner and crevice of your heart, but you have to open the door to your hidden room.

he said, "You will see them doing things that are even more detestable."

[14] Then he brought me to the entrance of the north gate of the house of the LORD, and I saw women sitting there, mourning the god Tammuz. [15] He said to me, "Do you see this, son of man? You will see things that are even more detestable than this."

[16] He then brought me into the inner court of the house of the LORD, and there at the entrance to the temple, between the portico and the altar, were about twenty-five men. With their backs toward the temple of the LORD and their faces toward the east, they were bowing down to the sun in the east.

[17] He said to me, "Have you seen this, son of man? Is it a trivial matter for the people of Judah to do the detestable things they are doing here? Must they also fill the land with violence and continually arouse my anger? Look at them putting the branch to their nose! [18] Therefore I will deal with them in anger; I will not look on them with pity or spare them. Although they shout in my ears, I will not listen to them."

Judgment on the Idolaters

9 Then I heard him call out in a loud voice, "Bring near those who are appointed to execute judgment on the city, each with a weapon in his hand." [2] And I saw six men coming from the direction of the upper gate, which faces north, each with a deadly weapon in his hand. With them was a man clothed in linen who had a writing kit at his side. They came in and stood beside the bronze altar.

[3] Now the glory of the God of Israel went up from above the cherubim, where it had been, and moved to the threshold of the temple. Then the LORD called to the man clothed in linen who had the writing kit at his side [4] and said to him, "Go throughout the city of Jerusalem and put a mark on the foreheads of those who grieve and lament over all the detestable things that are done in it."

[5] As I listened, he said to the others, "Follow him through the city and kill, without showing pity or compassion. [6] Slaughter the old men, the young men and women, the mothers and children, but do not touch anyone who has the mark. Begin at my sanctuary." So they began with the old men who were in front of the temple.

[7] Then he said to them, "Defile the temple and fill the courts with the slain. Go!" So they went out and began killing throughout the city. [8] While they were killing and I was left alone, I fell facedown, crying out, "Alas, Sovereign LORD! Are you going to destroy the entire remnant of Israel in this outpouring of your wrath on Jerusalem?"

[9] He answered me, "The sin of the people of Israel and Judah is exceedingly great; the land is full of bloodshed and the city is full of injustice. They say, 'The LORD has forsaken the land; the LORD does not see.' [10] So I will not look on them with pity or spare them, but I will bring down on their own heads what they have done."

[11] Then the man in linen with the writing kit at his side brought back word, saying, "I have done as you commanded."

God's Glory Departs From the Temple

10 I looked, and I saw the likeness of a throne of lapis lazuli above the vault that was over the heads of the cherubim. [2] The LORD said to the man clothed in linen, "Go in among the wheels beneath the cherubim. Fill your hands with burning coals from among the cherubim and scatter them over the city." And as I watched, he went in.

[3] Now the cherubim were standing on the south side of the temple when the man went in, and a cloud filled the inner court. [4] Then the glory of the LORD rose from above the cherubim and moved to the threshold of the temple. The cloud filled the temple, and the court was full of the radiance of the glory of the LORD. [5] The sound of the wings of the cherubim could be heard as far away as the outer court, like the voice of God Almighty[a] when he speaks.

[6] When the LORD commanded the man in linen, "Take fire from among the wheels, from among the cherubim," the man went in and stood beside a wheel. [7] Then one of the cherubim reached out his hand to the fire that was among them. He took up some of it and put it into the hands of the man in linen, who took it and went out. [8] (Under the wings of the cherubim could be seen what looked like human hands.)

[a] 5 Hebrew *El-Shaddai*

⁹I looked, and I saw beside the cherubim four wheels, one beside each of the cherubim; the wheels sparkled like topaz. ¹⁰As for their appearance, the four of them looked alike; each was like a wheel intersecting a wheel. ¹¹As they moved, they would go in any one of the four directions the cherubim faced; the wheels did not turn about[a] as the cherubim went. The cherubim went in whatever direction the head faced, without turning as they went. ¹²Their entire bodies, including their backs, their hands and their wings, were completely full of eyes, as were their four wheels. ¹³I heard the wheels being called "the whirling wheels." ¹⁴Each of the cherubim had four faces: One face was that of a cherub, the second the face of a human being, the third the face of a lion, and the fourth the face of an eagle.

¹⁵Then the cherubim rose upward. These were the living creatures I had seen by the Kebar River. ¹⁶When the cherubim moved, the wheels beside them moved; and when the cherubim spread their wings to rise from the ground, the wheels did not leave their side. ¹⁷When the cherubim stood still, they also stood still; and when the cherubim rose, they rose with them, because the spirit of the living creatures was in them.

¹⁸Then the glory of the LORD departed from over the threshold of the temple and stopped above the cherubim. ¹⁹While I watched, the cherubim spread their wings and rose from the ground, and as they went, the wheels went with them. They stopped at the entrance of the east gate of the LORD's house, and the glory of the God of Israel was above them.

²⁰These were the living creatures I had seen beneath the God of Israel by the Kebar River, and I realized that they were cherubim. ²¹Each had four faces and four wings, and under their wings was what looked like human hands. ²²Their faces had the same appearance as those I had seen by the Kebar River. Each one went straight ahead.

God's Sure Judgment on Jerusalem

11 Then the Spirit lifted me up and brought me to the gate of the house of the LORD that faces east. There at the entrance of the gate were twenty-five men, and I saw among them Jaazaniah son of Azzur and Pelatiah son of Benaiah, leaders of the people. ²The LORD said to me, "Son of man, these are the men who are plotting evil and giving wicked advice in this city. ³They say, 'Haven't our houses been recently rebuilt? This city is a pot, and we are the meat in it.' ⁴Therefore prophesy against them; prophesy, son of man."

⁵Then the Spirit of the LORD came on me, and he told me to say: "This is what the LORD says: That is what you are saying, you leaders in Israel, but I know what is going through your mind. ⁶You have killed many people in this city and filled its streets with the dead.

⁷"Therefore this is what the Sovereign LORD says: The bodies you have thrown there are the meat and this city is the pot, but I will drive you out of it. ⁸You fear the sword, and the sword is what I will bring against you, declares the Sovereign LORD. ⁹I will drive you out of the city and deliver you into the hands of foreigners and inflict punishment on you. ¹⁰You will fall by the sword, and I will execute judgment on you at the borders of Israel. Then you will know that I am the LORD. ¹¹This city will not be a pot for you, nor will you be the meat in it; I will execute judgment on you at the borders of Israel. ¹²And you will know that I am the LORD, for you have not followed my decrees or kept my laws but have conformed to the standards of the nations around you."

¹³Now as I was prophesying, Pelatiah son of Benaiah died. Then I fell facedown and cried out in a loud voice, "Alas, Sovereign LORD! Will you completely destroy the remnant of Israel?"

The Promise of Israel's Return

¹⁴The word of the LORD came to me: ¹⁵"Son of man, the people of Jerusalem have said of your fellow exiles and all the other Israelites, 'They are far away from the LORD; this land was given to us as our possession.'

¹⁶"Therefore say: 'This is what the Sovereign LORD says: Although I sent them far away among the nations and scattered them among the countries, yet for a little while I have been a sanctuary for them in the countries where they have gone.'

---

[a] 11 Or *aside*

ADMIT IT

READ: EZEKIEL 10:18

Solomon was smart enough to know God didn't literally live in the temple, as if he had a physical body and needed a kitchen and bed in a back room. The king said to his friend Hiram about the Lord, "But who is able to build a temple for him, since the heavens, even the highest heavens, cannot contain him? Who then am I to build a temple for him, except as a place to burn sacrifices before him?" (2 Chronicles 2:6).

Nevertheless, the Lord had promised to make the temple the one and only place of his intense presence. Just as God dwelled in the old tabernacle (Exodus 40:34–36), he made the temple his new home. When Solomon finished praying to dedicate the temple, "fire came down from heaven and consumed the burnt offering and the sacrifices, and the glory of the LORD filled the temple" (2 Chronicles 7:1).

BUILDING

FAITH

WISDOM

STRENGTH

Those facts help you understand why it's such a colossal tragedy when the Lord's glory leaves the temple. Because of Israel's habitual idolatry and other sins, the Lord's presence up and exits. It's one of the most heart-wrenching scenes of the Old Testament.

Today you are the Lord's temple—through the Holy Spirit a part of God resides in you (1 Corinthians 6:19–20). Even though he promises to never leave you (Hebrews 13:5), sin makes him feel far away. So admit when you do wrong. Let him know you want his presence in every bit of your life.

[17] "Therefore say: 'This is what the Sovereign LORD says: I will gather you from the nations and bring you back from the countries where you have been scattered, and I will give you back the land of Israel again.'

[18] "They will return to it and remove all its vile images and detestable idols. [19] I will give them an undivided heart and put a new spirit in them; I will remove from them their heart of stone and give them a heart of flesh. [20] Then they will follow my decrees and be careful to keep my laws. They will be my people, and I will be their God. [21] But as for those whose hearts are devoted to their vile images and detestable idols, I will bring down on their own heads what they have done, declares the Sovereign LORD."

[22] Then the cherubim, with the wheels beside them, spread their wings, and the glory of the God of Israel was above them. [23] The glory of the LORD went up from within the city and stopped above the mountain east of it. [24] The Spirit lifted me up and brought me to the exiles in Babylonia[a] in the vision given by the Spirit of God.

Then the vision I had seen went up from me, [25] and I told the exiles everything the LORD had shown me.

The Exile Symbolized

12 The word of the LORD came to me: [2] "Son of man, you are living among a rebellious people. They have eyes to see but do not see and ears to hear but do not hear, for they are a rebellious people.

[3] "Therefore, son of man, pack your belongings for exile and in the daytime, as they watch, set out and go from where you are to another place. Perhaps they will understand, though they are a rebellious people. [4] During the daytime, while they watch, bring out your belongings packed for exile. Then in the evening, while they are watching, go out like those who go into exile. [5] While they watch, dig through the wall and take your belongings out through it. [6] Put them on your shoulder as they are watching and carry them out at dusk. Cover your face so that you cannot see the land, for I have made you a sign to the Israelites."

[7] So I did as I was commanded. During the day I brought out my things packed for exile. Then in the evening I dug through the wall with my hands. I took my belongings out at dusk, carrying them on my shoulders while they watched.

[8] In the morning the word of the LORD came to me: [9] "Son of man, did not the Israelites, that rebellious people, ask you, 'What are you doing?'

[10] "Say to them, 'This is what the Sovereign LORD says: This prophecy concerns the prince in Jerusalem and all the Israelites who are there.' [11] Say to them, 'I am a sign to you.'

"As I have done, so it will be done to them. They will go into exile as captives.

[12] "The prince among them will put his things on his shoulder at dusk and leave, and a hole will be dug in the wall for him to go through. He will cover his face so that he cannot see the land. [13] I will spread my net for him, and he will be caught in my snare; I will bring him to Babylonia, the land of the Chaldeans, but he will not see it, and there he will die. [14] I will scatter to the winds all those around him — his staff and all his troops — and I will pursue them with drawn sword.

[15] "They will know that I am the LORD, when I disperse them among the nations and scatter them through the countries. [16] But I will spare a few of them from the sword, famine and plague, so that in the nations where they go they may acknowledge all their detestable practices. Then they will know that I am the LORD."

[17] The word of the LORD came to me: [18] "Son of man, tremble as you eat your food, and shudder in fear as you drink your water. [19] Say to the people of the land: 'This is what the Sovereign LORD says about those living in Jerusalem and in the land of Israel: They will eat their food in anxiety and drink their water in despair, for their land will be stripped of everything in it because of the violence of all who live there. [20] The inhabited towns will be laid waste and the land will be desolate. Then you will know that I am the LORD.' "

There Will Be No Delay

[21] The word of the LORD came to me: [22] "Son of man, what is this proverb you have in the land of Israel: 'The days go by and every

_____
[a] 24 Or *Chaldea*

vision comes to nothing'? ²³Say to them, 'This is what the Sovereign LORD says: I am going to put an end to this proverb, and they will no longer quote it in Israel.' Say to them, 'The days are near when every vision will be fulfilled. ²⁴For there will be no more false visions or flattering divinations among the people of Israel. ²⁵But I the LORD will speak what I will, and it shall be fulfilled without delay. For in your days, you rebellious people, I will fulfill whatever I say, declares the Sovereign LORD.'"

²⁶The word of the LORD came to me: ²⁷"Son of man, the Israelites are saying, 'The vision he sees is for many years from now, and he prophesies about the distant future.' ²⁸"Therefore say to them, 'This is what the Sovereign LORD says: None of my words will be delayed any longer; whatever I say will be fulfilled, declares the Sovereign LORD.'"

False Prophets Condemned

13 The word of the LORD came to me: ²"Son of man, prophesy against the prophets of Israel who are now prophesying. Say to those who prophesy out of their own imagination: 'Hear the word of the LORD! ³This is what the Sovereign LORD says: Woe to the foolish^a prophets who follow their own spirit and have seen nothing! ⁴Your prophets, Israel, are like jackals among ruins. ⁵You have not gone up to the breaches in the wall to repair it for the people of Israel so that it will stand firm in the battle on the day of the LORD. ⁶Their visions are false and their divinations a lie. Even though the LORD has not sent them, they say, "The LORD declares," and expect him to fulfill their words. ⁷Have you not seen false visions and uttered lying divinations when you say, "The LORD declares," though I have not spoken?

⁸"'Therefore this is what the Sovereign LORD says: Because of your false words and lying visions, I am against you, declares the Sovereign LORD. ⁹My hand will be against the prophets who see false visions and utter lying divinations. They will not belong to the council of my people or be listed in the records of Israel, nor will they enter the land of Israel. Then you will know that I am the Sovereign LORD.

¹⁰"'Because they lead my people astray, saying, "Peace," when there is no peace, and because, when a flimsy wall is built, they cover it with whitewash, ¹¹therefore tell those who cover it with whitewash that it is going to fall. Rain will come in torrents, and I will send hailstones hurtling down, and violent winds will burst forth. ¹²When the wall collapses, will people not ask you, "Where is the whitewash you covered it with?"

¹³"'Therefore this is what the Sovereign LORD says: In my wrath I will unleash a violent wind, and in my anger hailstones and torrents of rain will fall with destructive fury. ¹⁴I will tear down the wall you have covered with whitewash and will level it to the ground so that its foundation will be laid bare. When it^b falls, you will be destroyed in it; and you will know that I am the LORD. ¹⁵So I will pour out my wrath against the wall and against those who covered it with whitewash. I will say to you, "The wall is gone and so are those who whitewashed it, ¹⁶those prophets of Israel who prophesied to Jerusalem and saw visions of peace for her when there was no peace, declares the Sovereign LORD."'

¹⁷"Now, son of man, set your face against the daughters of your people who prophesy out of their own imagination. Prophesy against them ¹⁸and say, 'This is what the Sovereign LORD says: Woe to the women who sew magic charms on all their wrists and make veils of various lengths for their heads in order to ensnare people. Will you ensnare the lives of my people but preserve your own? ¹⁹You have profaned me among my people for a few handfuls of barley and scraps of bread. By lying to my people, who listen to lies, you have killed those who should not have died and have spared those who should not live.

²⁰"'Therefore this is what the Sovereign LORD says: I am against your magic charms with which you ensnare people like birds and I will tear them from your arms; I will set free the people that you ensnare like birds. ²¹I will tear off your veils and save my people from your hands, and they will no longer fall prey to your power. Then you will know that I am the LORD. ²²Because you disheartened the righteous with your lies, when I had brought them no grief, and

^a 3 Or *wicked*   ^b 14 Or *the city*

ON GUARD

READ: EZEKIEL 13:18

God didn't drop the Bible into the world with a handy timeline to inform you when the action takes place. Even so, scholars use Scripture's hints to do the math and calculate the timing of significant events.

Obvious dates in the records of Ezekiel and Jeremiah make clear the two prophets preach at roughly the same time. Ezekiel is swept up and transported to Babylon with a group of exiles a decade before the fall of Jerusalem in 586 B.C. Jeremiah remains in Judah until after the city's destruction, and he keeps preaching even after being abducted to Egypt (Jeremiah 43-44). The messages of these guys separated by hundreds of miles frequently overlap.

Jeremiah goes nose-to-nose with false prophets in Judah who claim to speak for God (Jeremiah 23:9-32). Ezekiel battles women who likewise speak false prophecies, inventing speeches in their own imaginations. Ezekiel confronts these false prophetesses for using sorcery to cast death spells. Their charms and veils are dark magic accessories that symbolize tying up victims to hunt them down. Apparently many people died as a result of the deception spread by these women.

You might wonder why God's people listened to these liars. Yet once people reject the truth of the Lord's real words, even the most obvious and destructive lies become believable. If you're not on guard, you can fall for anything.

BUILDING

FAITH

WISDOM

STRENGTH

because you encouraged the wicked not to turn from their evil ways and so save their lives, ²³therefore you will no longer see false visions or practice divination. I will save my people from your hands. And then you will know that I am the LORD.' "

Idolaters Condemned

14 Some of the elders of Israel came to me and sat down in front of me. ²Then the word of the LORD came to me: ³"Son of man, these men have set up idols in their hearts and put wicked stumbling blocks before their faces. Should I let them inquire of me at all? ⁴Therefore speak to them and tell them, 'This is what the Sovereign LORD says: When any of the Israelites set up idols in their hearts and put a wicked stumbling block before their faces and then go to a prophet, I the LORD will answer them myself in keeping with their great idolatry. ⁵I will do this to recapture the hearts of the people of Israel, who have all deserted me for their idols.'

⁶"Therefore say to the people of Israel, 'This is what the Sovereign LORD says: Repent! Turn from your idols and renounce all your detestable practices!

⁷" 'When any of the Israelites or any foreigner residing in Israel separate themselves from me and set up idols in their hearts and put a wicked stumbling block before their faces and then go to a prophet to inquire of me, I the LORD will answer them myself. ⁸I will set my face against them and make them an example and a byword. I will remove them from my people. Then you will know that I am the LORD.

⁹" 'And if the prophet is enticed to utter a prophecy, I the LORD have enticed that prophet, and I will stretch out my hand against him and destroy him from among my people Israel. ¹⁰They will bear their guilt—the prophet will be as guilty as the one who consults him. ¹¹Then the people of Israel will no longer stray from me, nor will they defile themselves anymore with all their sins. They will be my people, and I will be their God, declares the Sovereign LORD.' "

Jerusalem's Judgment Inescapable

¹²The word of the LORD came to me: ¹³"Son of man, if a country sins against me by being unfaithful and I stretch out my hand against it to cut off its food supply and send famine upon it and kill its people and their animals, ¹⁴even if these three men—Noah, Daniel[a] and Job—were in it, they could save only themselves by their righteousness, declares the Sovereign LORD.

¹⁵"Or if I send wild beasts through that country and they leave it childless and it becomes desolate so that no one can pass through it because of the beasts, ¹⁶as surely as I live, declares the Sovereign LORD, even if these three men were in it, they could not save their own sons or daughters. They alone would be saved, but the land would be desolate.

¹⁷"Or if I bring a sword against that country and say, 'Let the sword pass throughout the land,' and I kill its people and their animals, ¹⁸as surely as I live, declares the Sovereign LORD, even if these three men were in it, they could not save their own sons or daughters. They alone would be saved.

¹⁹"Or if I send a plague into that land and pour out my wrath on it through bloodshed, killing its people and their animals, ²⁰as surely as I live, declares the Sovereign LORD, even if Noah, Daniel and Job were in it, they could save neither son nor daughter. They would save only themselves by their righteousness.

²¹"For this is what the Sovereign LORD says: How much worse will it be when I send against Jerusalem my four dreadful judgments—sword and famine and wild beasts and plague—to kill its men and their animals! ²²Yet there will be some survivors—sons and daughters who will be brought out of it. They will come to you, and when you see their conduct and their actions, you will be consoled regarding the disaster I have brought on Jerusalem—every disaster I have brought on it. ²³You will be consoled when you see their conduct and their actions, for you will know that I have done nothing in it without cause, declares the Sovereign LORD."

Jerusalem as a Useless Vine

15 The word of the LORD came to me: ²"Son of man, how is the wood of a vine different from that of a branch from any

^a 14 Or *Danel*, a man of renown in ancient literature; also in verse 20

of the trees in the forest? ³Is wood ever taken from it to make anything useful? Do they make pegs from it to hang things on? ⁴And after it is thrown on the fire as fuel and the fire burns both ends and chars the middle, is it then useful for anything? ⁵If it was not useful for anything when it was whole, how much less can it be made into something useful when the fire has burned it and it is charred?

⁶"Therefore this is what the Sovereign LORD says: As I have given the wood of the vine among the trees of the forest as fuel for the fire, so will I treat the people living in Jerusalem. ⁷I will set my face against them. Although they have come out of the fire, the fire will yet consume them. And when I set my face against them, you will know that I am the LORD. ⁸I will make the land desolate because they have been unfaithful, declares the Sovereign LORD."

Jerusalem as an Adulterous Wife

16 The word of the LORD came to me: ²"Son of man, confront Jerusalem with her detestable practices ³and say, 'This is what the Sovereign LORD says to Jerusalem: Your ancestry and birth were in the land of the Canaanites; your father was an Amorite and your mother a Hittite. ⁴On the day you were born your cord was not cut, nor were you washed with water to make you clean, nor were you rubbed with salt or wrapped in cloths. ⁵No one looked on you with pity or had compassion enough to do any of these things for you. Rather, you were thrown out into the open field, for on the day you were born you were despised.

⁶"'Then I passed by and saw you kicking about in your blood, and as you lay there in your blood I said to you, "Live!"ᵃ ⁷I made you grow like a plant of the field. You grew and developed and entered puberty. Your breasts had formed and your hair had grown, yet you were stark naked.

⁸"'Later I passed by, and when I looked at you and saw that you were old enough for love, I spread the corner of my garment over you and covered your naked body. I gave you my solemn oath and entered into a covenant with you, declares the Sovereign LORD, and you became mine.

⁹"'I bathed you with water and washed the blood from you and put ointments on you. ¹⁰I clothed you with an embroidered dress and put sandals of fine leather on you. I dressed you in fine linen and covered you with costly garments. ¹¹I adorned you with jewelry: I put bracelets on your arms and a necklace around your neck, ¹²and I put a ring on your nose, earrings on your ears and a beautiful crown on your head. ¹³So you were adorned with gold and silver; your clothes were of fine linen and costly fabric and embroidered cloth. Your food was honey, olive oil and the finest flour. You became very beautiful and rose to be a queen. ¹⁴And your fame spread among the nations on account of your beauty, because the splendor I had given you made your beauty perfect, declares the Sovereign LORD.

¹⁵"'But you trusted in your beauty and used your fame to become a prostitute. You lavished your favors on anyone who passed by and your beauty became his. ¹⁶You took some of your garments to make gaudy high places, where you carried on your prostitution. You went to him, and he possessed your beauty.ᵇ ¹⁷You also took the fine jewelry I gave you, the jewelry made of my gold and silver, and you made for yourself male idols and engaged in prostitution with them. ¹⁸And you took your embroidered clothes to put on them, and you offered my oil and incense before them. ¹⁹Also the food I provided for you—the flour, olive oil and honey I gave you to eat—you offered as fragrant incense before them. That is what happened, declares the Sovereign LORD.

²⁰"'And you took your sons and daughters whom you bore to me and sacrificed them as food to the idols. Was your prostitution not enough? ²¹You slaughtered my children and sacrificed them to the idols. ²²In all your detestable practices and your prostitution you did not remember the days of your youth, when you were naked and bare, kicking about in your blood.

²³"'Woe! Woe to you, declares the Sovereign LORD. In addition to all your other wickedness, ²⁴you built a mound for yourself and made a lofty shrine in every public square. ²⁵At every street corner you built your lofty

---

ᵃ 6 A few Hebrew manuscripts, Septuagint and Syriac; most Hebrew manuscripts repeat *and as you lay there in your blood I said to you, "Live!"*   ᵇ 16 The meaning of the Hebrew for this sentence is uncertain.

shrines and degraded your beauty, spreading your legs with increasing promiscuity to anyone who passed by. ²⁶You engaged in prostitution with the Egyptians, your neighbors with large genitals, and aroused my anger with your increasing promiscuity. ²⁷So I stretched out my hand against you and reduced your territory; I gave you over to the greed of your enemies, the daughters of the Philistines, who were shocked by your lewd conduct. ²⁸You engaged in prostitution with the Assyrians too, because you were insatiable; and even after that, you still were not satisfied. ²⁹Then you increased your promiscuity to include Babylonia,^a a land of merchants, but even with this you were not satisfied.

³⁰" 'I am filled with fury against you,^b declares the Sovereign LORD, when you do all these things, acting like a brazen prostitute! ³¹When you built your mounds at every street corner and made your lofty shrines in every public square, you were unlike a prostitute, because you scorned payment.

³²" 'You adulterous wife! You prefer strangers to your own husband! ³³All prostitutes receive gifts, but you give gifts to all your lovers, bribing them to come to you from everywhere for your illicit favors. ³⁴So in your prostitution you are the opposite of others; no one runs after you for your favors. You are the very opposite, for you give payment and none is given to you.

³⁵" 'Therefore, you prostitute, hear the word of the LORD! ³⁶This is what the Sovereign LORD says: Because you poured out your lust and exposed your naked body in your promiscuity with your lovers, and because of all your detestable idols, and because you gave them your children's blood, ³⁷therefore I am going to gather all your lovers, with whom you found pleasure, those you loved as well as those you hated. I will gather them against you from all around and will strip you in front of them, and they will see you stark naked. ³⁸I will sentence you to the punishment of women who commit adultery and who shed blood; I will bring on you the blood vengeance of my wrath and jealous anger. ³⁹Then I will deliver you into the hands of your lovers, and they will tear down your mounds and destroy your lofty shrines. They will strip you of your clothes and take your fine jewelry and leave you stark naked. ⁴⁰They will bring a mob against you, who will stone you and hack you to pieces with their swords. ⁴¹They will burn down your houses and inflict punishment on you in the sight of many women. I will put a stop to your prostitution, and you will no longer pay your lovers. ⁴²Then my wrath against you will subside and my jealous anger will turn away from you; I will be calm and no longer angry.

⁴³" 'Because you did not remember the days of your youth but enraged me with all these things, I will surely bring down on your head what you have done, declares the Sovereign LORD. Did you not add lewdness to all your other detestable practices?

⁴⁴" 'Everyone who quotes proverbs will quote this proverb about you: "Like mother, like daughter." ⁴⁵You are a true daughter of your mother, who despised her husband and her children; and you are a true sister of your sisters, who despised their husbands and their children. Your mother was a Hittite and your father an Amorite. ⁴⁶Your older sister was Samaria, who lived to the north of you with her daughters; and your younger sister, who lived to the south of you with her daughters, was Sodom. ⁴⁷You not only followed their ways and copied their detestable practices, but in all your ways you soon became more depraved than they. ⁴⁸As surely as I live, declares the Sovereign LORD, your sister Sodom and her daughters never did what you and your daughters have done.

⁴⁹" 'Now this was the sin of your sister Sodom: She and her daughters were arrogant, overfed and unconcerned; they did not help the poor and needy. ⁵⁰They were haughty and did detestable things before me. Therefore I did away with them as you have seen. ⁵¹Samaria did not commit half the sins you did. You have done more detestable things than they, and have made your sisters seem righteous by all these things you have done. ⁵²Bear your disgrace, for you have furnished some justification for your sisters. Because your sins were more vile than theirs, they appear more righteous than you. So then, be ashamed and bear your disgrace, for you have made your sisters appear righteous.

⁵³" 'However, I will restore the fortunes of Sodom and her daughters and of Samaria

---

^a 29 Or *Chaldea*   ^b 30 Or *How feverish is your heart,*

and her daughters, and your fortunes along with them, ⁵⁴so that you may bear your disgrace and be ashamed of all you have done in giving them comfort. ⁵⁵And your sisters, Sodom with her daughters and Samaria with her daughters, will return to what they were before; and you and your daughters will return to what you were before. ⁵⁶You would not even mention your sister Sodom in the day of your pride, ⁵⁷before your wickedness was uncovered. Even so, you are now scorned by the daughters of Edom*ᵃ* and all her neighbors and the daughters of the Philistines — all those around you who despise you. ⁵⁸You will bear the consequences of your lewdness and your detestable practices, declares the LORD.

⁵⁹ "This is what the Sovereign LORD says: I will deal with you as you deserve, because you have despised my oath by breaking the covenant. ⁶⁰Yet I will remember the covenant I made with you in the days of your youth, and I will establish an everlasting covenant with you. ⁶¹Then you will remember your ways and be ashamed when you receive your sisters, both those who are older than you and those who are younger. I will give them to you as daughters, but not on the basis of my covenant with you. ⁶²So I will establish my covenant with you, and you will know that I am the LORD. ⁶³Then, when I make atonement for you for all you have done, you will remember and be ashamed and never again open your mouth because of your humiliation, declares the Sovereign LORD.' "

Two Eagles and a Vine

17 The word of the LORD came to me: ²"Son of man, set forth an allegory and tell it to the Israelites as a parable. ³Say to them, 'This is what the Sovereign LORD says: A great eagle with powerful wings, long feathers and full plumage of varied colors came to Lebanon. Taking hold of the top of a cedar, ⁴he broke off its topmost shoot and carried it away to a land of merchants, where he planted it in a city of traders.

⁵ "He took one of the seedlings of the land and put it in fertile soil. He planted it like a willow by abundant water, ⁶and it sprouted and became a low, spreading vine. Its branches turned toward him, but its roots remained under it. So it became a vine and produced branches and put out leafy boughs.

⁷ "'But there was another great eagle with powerful wings and full plumage. The vine now sent out its roots toward him from the plot where it was planted and stretched out its branches to him for water. ⁸It had been planted in good soil by abundant water so that it would produce branches, bear fruit and become a splendid vine.'

⁹"Say to them, 'This is what the Sovereign LORD says: Will it thrive? Will it not be uprooted and stripped of its fruit so that it withers? All its new growth will wither. It will not take a strong arm or many people to pull it up by the roots. ¹⁰It has been planted, but will it thrive? Will it not wither completely when the east wind strikes it — wither away in the plot where it grew?' "

¹¹Then the word of the LORD came to me: ¹²"Say to this rebellious people, 'Do you not know what these things mean?' Say to them: 'The king of Babylon went to Jerusalem and carried off her king and her nobles, bringing them back with him to Babylon. ¹³Then he took a member of the royal family and made a treaty with him, putting him under oath. He also carried away the leading men of the land, ¹⁴so that the kingdom would be brought low, unable to rise again, surviving only by keeping his treaty. ¹⁵But the king rebelled against him by sending his envoys to Egypt to get horses and a large army. Will he succeed? Will he who does such things escape? Will he break the treaty and yet escape?

¹⁶ "'As surely as I live, declares the Sovereign LORD, he shall die in Babylon, in the land of the king who put him on the throne, whose oath he despised and whose treaty he broke. ¹⁷Pharaoh with his mighty army and great horde will be of no help to him in war, when ramps are built and siege works erected to destroy many lives. ¹⁸He despised the oath by breaking the covenant. Because he had given his hand in pledge and yet did all these things, he shall not escape.

¹⁹ "'Therefore this is what the Sovereign LORD says: As surely as I live, I will repay him for despising my oath and breaking my covenant. ²⁰I will spread my net for him, and

---

ᵃ 57 Many Hebrew manuscripts and Syriac; most Hebrew manuscripts, Septuagint and Vulgate *Aram* he will be caught in my snare. I will bring him to Babylon and execute judgment on him there because he was unfaithful to me. ²¹ All his choice troops will fall by the sword, and the survivors will be scattered to the winds. Then you will know that I the LORD have spoken.

²² "'This is what the Sovereign LORD says: I myself will take a shoot from the very top of a cedar and plant it; I will break off a tender sprig from its topmost shoots and plant it on a high and lofty mountain. ²³ On the mountain heights of Israel I will plant it; it will produce branches and bear fruit and become a splendid cedar. Birds of every kind will nest in it; they will find shelter in the shade of its branches. ²⁴ All the trees of the forest will know that I the LORD bring down the tall tree and make the low tree grow tall. I dry up the green tree and make the dry tree flourish.

"'I the LORD have spoken, and I will do it.'"

The One Who Sins Will Die

18 The word of the LORD came to me: ² "What do you people mean by quoting this proverb about the land of Israel:

"'The parents eat sour grapes,
and the children's teeth are set on
edge'?

³ "As surely as I live, declares the Sovereign LORD, you will no longer quote this proverb in Israel. ⁴ For everyone belongs to me, the parent as well as the child — both alike belong to me. The one who sins is the one who will die.

⁵ "Suppose there is a righteous man
who does what is just and right.
⁶ He does not eat at the mountain shrines
or look to the idols of Israel.
He does not defile his neighbor's wife
or have sexual relations with a woman
during her period.
⁷ He does not oppress anyone,
but returns what he took in pledge
for a loan.
He does not commit robbery
but gives his food to the hungry
and provides clothing for the naked.
⁸ He does not lend to them at interest
or take a profit from them.

He withholds his hand from doing wrong
and judges fairly between two parties.
⁹ He follows my decrees
and faithfully keeps my laws.
That man is righteous;
he will surely live,
declares the Sovereign LORD.

¹⁰ "Suppose he has a violent son, who sheds blood or does any of these other things*ᵃ* ¹¹ (though the father has done none of them):

"He eats at the mountain shrines.
He defiles his neighbor's wife.
¹² He oppresses the poor and needy.
He commits robbery.
He does not return what he took in
pledge.
He looks to the idols.
He does detestable things.
¹³ He lends at interest and takes a profit.

Will such a man live? He will not! Because he has done all these detestable things, he is to be put to death; his blood will be on his own head.

¹⁴ "But suppose this son has a son who sees all the sins his father commits, and though he sees them, he does not do such things:

¹⁵ "He does not eat at the mountain shrines
or look to the idols of Israel.
He does not defile his neighbor's wife.
¹⁶ He does not oppress anyone
or require a pledge for a loan.
He does not commit robbery
but gives his food to the hungry
and provides clothing for the naked.
¹⁷ He withholds his hand from mistreating
the poor
and takes no interest or profit
from them.
He keeps my laws and follows my
decrees.

He will not die for his father's sin; he will surely live. ¹⁸ But his father will die for his own sin, because he practiced extortion, robbed his brother and did what was wrong among his people.

¹⁹ "Yet you ask, 'Why does the son not share the guilt of his father?' Since the son has done what is just and right and has been careful to keep all my decrees, he will surely

---

ᵃ 10 Or *things to a brother*

live. ²⁰The one who sins is the one who will die. The child will not share the guilt of the parent, nor will the parent share the guilt of the child. The righteousness of the righteous will be credited to them, and the wickedness of the wicked will be charged against them.

²¹ "But if a wicked person turns away from all the sins they have committed and keeps all my decrees and does what is just and right, that person will surely live; they will not die. ²²None of the offenses they have committed will be remembered against them. Because of the righteous things they have done, they will live. ²³Do I take any pleasure in the death of the wicked? declares the Sovereign LORD. Rather, am I not pleased when they turn from their ways and live?

²⁴ "But if a righteous person turns from their righteousness and commits sin and does the same detestable things the wicked person does, will they live? None of the righteous things that person has done will be remembered. Because of the unfaithfulness they are guilty of and because of the sins they have committed, they will die.

²⁵ "Yet you say, 'The way of the Lord is not just.' Hear, you Israelites: Is my way unjust? Is it not your ways that are unjust? ²⁶If a righteous person turns from their righteousness and commits sin, they will die for it; because of the sin they have committed they will die. ²⁷But if a wicked person turns away from the wickedness they have committed and does what is just and right, they will save their life. ²⁸Because they consider all the offenses they have committed and turn away from them, that person will surely live; they will not die. ²⁹Yet the Israelites say, 'The way of the Lord is not just.' Are my ways unjust, people of Israel? Is it not your ways that are unjust?

³⁰ "Therefore, you Israelites, I will judge each of you according to your own ways, declares the Sovereign LORD. Repent! Turn away from all your offenses; then sin will not be your downfall. ³¹Rid yourselves of all the offenses you have committed, and get a new heart and a new spirit. Why will you die, people of Israel? ³²For I take no pleasure in the death of anyone, declares the Sovereign LORD. Repent and live!

A Lament Over Israel's Princes

19 "Take up a lament concerning the princes of Israel ²and say:

" 'What a lioness was your mother
    among the lions!
She lay down among them
    and reared her cubs.
³ She brought up one of her cubs,
    and he became a strong lion.
He learned to tear the prey
    and he became a man-eater.
⁴ The nations heard about him,
    and he was trapped in their pit.
They led him with hooks
    to the land of Egypt.

⁵ " 'When she saw her hope unfulfilled,
    her expectation gone,
she took another of her cubs
    and made him a strong lion.
⁶ He prowled among the lions,
    for he was now a strong lion.
He learned to tear the prey
    and he became a man-eater.
⁷ He broke down^a their strongholds
    and devastated their towns.
The land and all who were in it
    were terrified by his roaring.
⁸ Then the nations came against him,
    those from regions round about.
They spread their net for him,
    and he was trapped in their pit.
⁹ With hooks they pulled him into a cage
    and brought him to the king of
        Babylon.
They put him in prison,
    so his roar was heard no longer
        on the mountains of Israel.

¹⁰ " 'Your mother was like a vine in your
        vineyard^b
    planted by the water;
it was fruitful and full of branches
    because of abundant water.
¹¹ Its branches were strong,
    fit for a ruler's scepter.
It towered high
    above the thick foliage,
conspicuous for its height
    and for its many branches.
¹² But it was uprooted in fury
    and thrown to the ground.

---

^a 7 Targum (see Septuagint); Hebrew *He knew*   ^b 10 Two Hebrew manuscripts; most Hebrew manuscripts *your blood*

The east wind made it shrivel,
    it was stripped of its fruit;
its strong branches withered
    and fire consumed them.
¹³ Now it is planted in the desert,
    in a dry and thirsty land.
¹⁴ Fire spread from one of its main[a]
        branches
    and consumed its fruit.
No strong branch is left on it
    fit for a ruler's scepter.'

"This is a lament and is to be used as a lament."

Rebellious Israel Purged

20 In the seventh year, in the fifth month on the tenth day, some of the elders of Israel came to inquire of the LORD, and they sat down in front of me.

² Then the word of the LORD came to me: ³ "Son of man, speak to the elders of Israel and say to them, 'This is what the Sovereign LORD says: Have you come to inquire of me? As surely as I live, I will not let you inquire of me, declares the Sovereign LORD.'

⁴ "Will you judge them? Will you judge them, son of man? Then confront them with the detestable practices of their ancestors ⁵ and say to them: 'This is what the Sovereign LORD says: On the day I chose Israel, I swore with uplifted hand to the descendants of Jacob and revealed myself to them in Egypt. With uplifted hand I said to them, "I am the LORD your God." ⁶ On that day I swore to them that I would bring them out of Egypt into a land I had searched out for them, a land flowing with milk and honey, the most beautiful of all lands. ⁷ And I said to them, "Each of you, get rid of the vile images you have set your eyes on, and do not defile yourselves with the idols of Egypt. I am the LORD your God."

⁸ "'But they rebelled against me and would not listen to me; they did not get rid of the vile images they had set their eyes on, nor did they forsake the idols of Egypt. So I said I would pour out my wrath on them and spend my anger against them in Egypt. ⁹ But for the sake of my name, I brought them out of Egypt. I did it to keep my name from being profaned in the eyes of the nations among whom they lived and in whose sight I had revealed myself to the Israelites. ¹⁰ Therefore I led them out of Egypt and brought them into the wilderness. ¹¹ I gave them my decrees and made known to them my laws, by which the person who obeys them will live. ¹² Also I gave them my Sabbaths as a sign between us, so they would know that I the LORD made them holy.

¹³ "'Yet the people of Israel rebelled against me in the wilderness. They did not follow my decrees but rejected my laws — by which the person who obeys them will live — and they utterly desecrated my Sabbaths. So I said I would pour out my wrath on them and destroy them in the wilderness. ¹⁴ But for the sake of my name I did what would keep it from being profaned in the eyes of the nations in whose sight I had brought them out. ¹⁵ Also with uplifted hand I swore to them in the wilderness that I would not bring them into the land I had given them — a land flowing with milk and honey, the most beautiful of all lands — ¹⁶ because they rejected my laws and did not follow my decrees and desecrated my Sabbaths. For their hearts were devoted to their idols. ¹⁷ Yet I looked on them with pity and did not destroy them or put an end to them in the wilderness. ¹⁸ I said to their children in the wilderness, "Do not follow the statutes of your parents or keep their laws or defile yourselves with their idols. ¹⁹ I am the LORD your God; follow my decrees and be careful to keep my laws. ²⁰ Keep my Sabbaths holy, that they may be a sign between us. Then you will know that I am the LORD your God."

²¹ "'But the children rebelled against me: They did not follow my decrees, they were not careful to keep my laws, of which I said, "The person who obeys them will live by them," and they desecrated my Sabbaths. So I said I would pour out my wrath on them and spend my anger against them in the wilderness. ²² But I withheld my hand, and for the sake of my name I did what would keep it from being profaned in the eyes of the nations in whose sight I had brought them out. ²³ Also with uplifted hand I swore to them in the wilderness that I would disperse them among the nations and scatter them through the countries, ²⁴ because they had not obeyed my laws but had rejected my decrees and desecrated my Sabbaths, and their

---

[a] 14 Or *from under its*

EZEKIEL

In the seventh year, in the fifth month on the tenth day, some of the elders of Israel came to inquire of the LORD, and they sat down in front of me. Then the word of the LORD came to me: "Son of man, speak to the elders of Israel and say to them, 'This is what the Sovereign LORD says: Have you come to inquire of me? As surely as I live, I will not let you inquire of me, declares the Sovereign LORD.'" EZEKIEL 20:1-3

HIS NAME MEANS: "God is strong"
READ HIS STORY: *Ezekiel 1-3, 8, 24:15-27, 33*

When the armies of Nebuchadnezzar marched into Judah, Ezekiel was one of 10,000 men taken captive to Babylon in the second of three deportations (2 Kings 24:10-14). There, Ezekiel—who was a priest—was called to be a prophet. He saw many visions about the wonders in heaven, angelic beings, future world events, the blueprint of an amazing temple and God's final restoration of his people.

One of the unique things about Ezekiel was the way he served in ministry. God often had Ezekiel show the people vivid illustrations of what God's messages meant. For example, one time Ezekiel built a model of the city of Jerusalem to demonstrate what it would look like when it was under siege. Then he lay down on his left side for 390 days and then turned over on his right side for 40 more days to demonstrate the number of years Israel and Judah had sinned against God (Ezekiel 4:1-8).

The hearts of God's children had become unfaithful, stubborn and filled with sin. Ezekiel, however, taught them about the faithfulness of God. In Ezekiel 36:26-27, the prophet shared God's promise of transformation: "I will give you a new heart and put a new spirit in you; I will remove from you your heart of stone and give you a heart of flesh. And I will put my Spirit in you and move you to follow my decrees and be careful to keep my laws."

eyes lusted after their parents' idols. ²⁵So I gave them other statutes that were not good and laws through which they could not live; ²⁶I defiled them through their gifts — the sacrifice of every firstborn — that I might fill them with horror so they would know that I am the LORD.'

²⁷"Therefore, son of man, speak to the people of Israel and say to them, 'This is what the Sovereign LORD says: In this also your ancestors blasphemed me by being unfaithful to me: ²⁸When I brought them into the land I had sworn to give them and they saw any high hill or any leafy tree, there they offered their sacrifices, made offerings that aroused my anger, presented their fragrant incense and poured out their drink offerings. ²⁹Then I said to them: What is this high place you go to?' " (It is called Bamahᵃ to this day.)

Rebellious Israel Renewed

³⁰"Therefore say to the Israelites: 'This is what the Sovereign LORD says: Will you defile yourselves the way your ancestors did and lust after their vile images? ³¹When you offer your gifts — the sacrifice of your children in the fire — you continue to defile yourselves with all your idols to this day. Am I to let you inquire of me, you Israelites? As surely as I live, declares the Sovereign LORD, I will not let you inquire of me.

³²"'You say, "We want to be like the nations, like the peoples of the world, who serve wood and stone." But what you have in mind will never happen. ³³As surely as I live, declares the Sovereign LORD, I will reign over you with a mighty hand and an outstretched arm and with outpoured wrath. ³⁴I will bring you from the nations and gather you from the countries where you have been scattered — with a mighty hand and an outstretched arm and with outpoured wrath. ³⁵I will bring you into the wilderness of the nations and there, face to face, I will execute judgment upon you. ³⁶As I judged your ancestors in the wilderness of the land of Egypt, so I will judge you, declares the Sovereign LORD. ³⁷I will take note of you as you pass under my rod, and I will bring you into the bond of the covenant. ³⁸I will purge you of those who revolt and rebel against me. Although I will bring them out of the land

where they are living, yet they will not enter the land of Israel. Then you will know that I am the LORD.

³⁹"'As for you, people of Israel, this is what the Sovereign LORD says: Go and serve your idols, every one of you! But afterward you will surely listen to me and no longer profane my holy name with your gifts and idols. ⁴⁰For on my holy mountain, the high mountain of Israel, declares the Sovereign LORD, there in the land all the people of Israel will serve me, and there I will accept them. There I will require your offerings and your choice gifts,ᵇ along with all your holy sacrifices. ⁴¹I will accept you as fragrant incense when I bring you out from the nations and gather you from the countries where you have been scattered, and I will be proved holy through you in the sight of the nations. ⁴²Then you will know that I am the LORD, when I bring you into the land of Israel, the land I had sworn with uplifted hand to give to your ancestors. ⁴³There you will remember your conduct and all the actions by which you have defiled yourselves, and you will loathe yourselves for all the evil you have done. ⁴⁴You will know that I am the LORD, when I deal with you for my name's sake and not according to your evil ways and your corrupt practices, you people of Israel, declares the Sovereign LORD.'"

Prophecy Against the South

⁴⁵The word of the LORD came to me: ⁴⁶"Son of man, set your face toward the south; preach against the south and prophesy against the forest of the southland. ⁴⁷Say to the southern forest: 'Hear the word of the LORD. This is what the Sovereign LORD says: I am about to set fire to you, and it will consume all your trees, both green and dry. The blazing flame will not be quenched, and every face from south to north will be scorched by it. ⁴⁸Everyone will see that I the LORD have kindled it; it will not be quenched.'"

⁴⁹Then I said, "Sovereign LORD, they are saying of me, 'Isn't he just telling parables?'"ᶜ

Babylon as God's Sword of Judgment

21ᵈ The word of the LORD came to me: ²"Son of man, set your face against Jerusalem and preach against the sanctuary.

ᵃ 29 *Bamah* means *high place.*   ᵇ 40 Or *and the gifts of your firstfruits*   ᶜ 49 In Hebrew texts 20:45-49 is numbered 21:1-5.   ᵈ In Hebrew texts 21:1-32 is numbered 21:6-37.

Prophesy against the land of Israel ³and say to her: 'This is what the LORD says: I am against you. I will draw my sword from its sheath and cut off from you both the righteous and the wicked. ⁴Because I am going to cut off the righteous and the wicked, my sword will be unsheathed against everyone from south to north. ⁵Then all people will know that I the LORD have drawn my sword from its sheath; it will not return again.'

⁶"Therefore groan, son of man! Groan before them with broken heart and bitter grief. ⁷And when they ask you, 'Why are you groaning?' you shall say, 'Because of the news that is coming. Every heart will melt with fear and every hand go limp; every spirit will become faint and every leg will be wet with urine.' It is coming! It will surely take place, declares the Sovereign LORD."

⁸The word of the LORD came to me: ⁹"Son of man, prophesy and say, 'This is what the Lord says:

"'A sword, a sword,
    sharpened and polished—
¹⁰sharpened for the slaughter,
    polished to flash like lightning!

"'Shall we rejoice in the scepter of my royal son? The sword despises every such stick.

¹¹"'The sword is appointed to be polished,
    to be grasped with the hand;
it is sharpened and polished,
    made ready for the hand of the slayer.
¹²Cry out and wail, son of man,
    for it is against my people;
    it is against all the princes of Israel.
They are thrown to the sword
    along with my people.
Therefore beat your breast.

¹³"'Testing will surely come. And what if even the scepter, which the sword despises, does not continue? declares the Sovereign LORD.'

¹⁴"So then, son of man, prophesy
    and strike your hands together.
Let the sword strike twice,
    even three times.
It is a sword for slaughter—
    a sword for great slaughter,
    closing in on them from every side.

¹⁵So that hearts may melt with fear
    and the fallen be many,
I have stationed the sword for slaughter[a]
    at all their gates.
Look! It is forged to strike like lightning,
    it is grasped for slaughter.
¹⁶Slash to the right, you sword,
    then to the left,
    wherever your blade is turned.
¹⁷I too will strike my hands together,
    and my wrath will subside.
I the LORD have spoken."

¹⁸The word of the LORD came to me: ¹⁹"Son of man, mark out two roads for the sword of the king of Babylon to take, both starting from the same country. Make a signpost where the road branches off to the city. ²⁰Mark out one road for the sword to come against Rabbah of the Ammonites and another against Judah and fortified Jerusalem. ²¹For the king of Babylon will stop at the fork in the road, at the junction of the two roads, to seek an omen: He will cast lots with arrows, he will consult his idols, he will examine the liver. ²²Into his right hand will come the lot for Jerusalem, where he is to set up battering rams, to give the command to slaughter, to sound the battle cry, to set battering rams against the gates, to build a ramp and to erect siege works. ²³It will seem like a false omen to those who have sworn allegiance to him, but he will remind them of their guilt and take them captive.

²⁴"Therefore this is what the Sovereign LORD says: 'Because you people have brought to mind your guilt by your open rebellion, revealing your sins in all that you do—because you have done this, you will be taken captive.

²⁵"'You profane and wicked prince of Israel, whose day has come, whose time of punishment has reached its climax, ²⁶this is what the Sovereign LORD says: Take off the turban, remove the crown. It will not be as it was: The lowly will be exalted and the exalted will be brought low. ²⁷A ruin! A ruin! I will make it a ruin! The crown will not be restored until he to whom it rightfully belongs shall come; to him I will give it.'

²⁸"And you, son of man, prophesy and say, 'This is what the Sovereign LORD says about the Ammonites and their insults:

---

a 15 Septuagint; the meaning of the Hebrew for this word is uncertain.

" 'A sword, a sword,
    drawn for the slaughter,
    polished to consume
    and to flash like lightning!
²⁹ Despite false visions concerning you
    and lying divinations about you,
    it will be laid on the necks
    of the wicked who are to be slain,
    whose day has come,
    whose time of punishment has
    reached its climax.

³⁰ " 'Let the sword return to its sheath.
    In the place where you were created,
    in the land of your ancestry,
    I will judge you.
³¹ I will pour out my wrath on you
    and breathe out my fiery anger
    against you;
    I will deliver you into the hands of
    brutal men,
    men skilled in destruction.
³² You will be fuel for the fire,
    your blood will be shed in your land,
    you will be remembered no more;
    for I the LORD have spoken.' "

Judgment on Jerusalem's Sins

22 The word of the LORD came to me: ² "Son of man, will you judge her? Will you judge this city of bloodshed? Then confront her with all her detestable practices ³ and say: 'This is what the Sovereign LORD says: You city that brings on herself doom by shedding blood in her midst and defiles herself by making idols, ⁴ you have become guilty because of the blood you have shed and have become defiled by the idols you have made. You have brought your days to a close, and the end of your years has come. Therefore I will make you an object of scorn to the nations and a laughingstock to all the countries. ⁵ Those who are near and those who are far away will mock you, you infamous city, full of turmoil.

⁶ " 'See how each of the princes of Israel who are in you uses his power to shed blood. ⁷ In you they have treated father and mother with contempt; in you they have oppressed the foreigner and mistreated the fatherless and the widow. ⁸ You have despised my holy things and desecrated my Sabbaths. ⁹ In you are slanderers who are bent on shedding blood; in you are those who eat at the mountain shrines and commit lewd acts. ¹⁰ In you are those who dishonor their father's bed; in you are those who violate women during their period, when they are ceremonially unclean. ¹¹ In you one man commits a detestable offense with his neighbor's wife, another shamefully defiles his daughter-in-law, and another violates his sister, his own father's daughter. ¹² In you are people who accept bribes to shed blood; you take interest and make a profit from the poor. You extort unjust gain from your neighbors. And you have forgotten me, declares the Sovereign LORD.

¹³ " 'I will surely strike my hands together at the unjust gain you have made and at the blood you have shed in your midst. ¹⁴ Will your courage endure or your hands be strong in the day I deal with you? I the LORD have spoken, and I will do it. ¹⁵ I will disperse you among the nations and scatter you through the countries; and I will put an end to your uncleanness. ¹⁶ When you have been defiled[a] in the eyes of the nations, you will know that I am the LORD.' "

¹⁷ Then the word of the LORD came to me: ¹⁸ "Son of man, the people of Israel have become dross to me; all of them are the copper, tin, iron and lead left inside a furnace. They are but the dross of silver. ¹⁹ Therefore this is what the Sovereign LORD says: 'Because you have all become dross, I will gather you into Jerusalem. ²⁰ As silver, copper, iron, lead and tin are gathered into a furnace to be melted with a fiery blast, so will I gather you in my anger and my wrath and put you inside the city and melt you. ²¹ I will gather you and I will blow on you with my fiery wrath, and you will be melted inside her. ²² As silver is melted in a furnace, so you will be melted inside her, and you will know that I the LORD have poured out my wrath on you.' "

²³ Again the word of the LORD came to me: ²⁴ "Son of man, say to the land, 'You are a land that has not been cleansed or rained on in the day of wrath.' ²⁵ There is a conspiracy of her princes[b] within her like a roaring lion tearing its prey; they devour people, take treasures and precious things and make many widows within her. ²⁶ Her

---

ᵃ 16 Or *When I have allotted you your inheritance*   ᵇ 25 Septuagint; Hebrew *prophets* priests do violence to my law and profane my holy things; they do not distinguish between the holy and the common; they teach that there is no difference between the unclean and the clean; and they shut their eyes to the keeping of my Sabbaths, so that I am profaned among them. ²⁷Her officials within her are like wolves tearing their prey; they shed blood and kill people to make unjust gain. ²⁸Her prophets whitewash these deeds for them by false visions and lying divinations. They say, 'This is what the Sovereign Lord says' — when the Lord has not spoken. ²⁹The people of the land practice extortion and commit robbery; they oppress the poor and needy and mistreat the foreigner, denying them justice.

³⁰"I looked for someone among them who would build up the wall and stand before me in the gap on behalf of the land so I would not have to destroy it, but I found no one. ³¹So I will pour out my wrath on them and consume them with my fiery anger, bringing down on their own heads all they have done, declares the Sovereign Lord."

Two Adulterous Sisters

23 The word of the Lord came to me: ²"Son of man, there were two women, daughters of the same mother. ³They became prostitutes in Egypt, engaging in prostitution from their youth. In that land their breasts were fondled and their virgin bosoms caressed. ⁴The older was named Oholah, and her sister was Oholibah. They were mine and gave birth to sons and daughters. Oholah is Samaria, and Oholibah is Jerusalem.

⁵"Oholah engaged in prostitution while she was still mine; and she lusted after her lovers, the Assyrians — warriors ⁶clothed in blue, governors and commanders, all of them handsome young men, and mounted horsemen. ⁷She gave herself as a prostitute to all the elite of the Assyrians and defiled herself with all the idols of everyone she lusted after. ⁸She did not give up the prostitution she began in Egypt, when during her youth men slept with her, caressed her virgin bosom and poured out their lust on her.

⁹"Therefore I delivered her into the hands of her lovers, the Assyrians, for whom she lusted. ¹⁰They stripped her naked, took away her sons and daughters and killed her with the sword. She became a byword among women, and punishment was inflicted on her.

¹¹"Her sister Oholibah saw this, yet in her lust and prostitution she was more depraved than her sister. ¹²She too lusted after the Assyrians — governors and commanders, warriors in full dress, mounted horsemen, all handsome young men. ¹³I saw that she too defiled herself; both of them went the same way.

¹⁴"But she carried her prostitution still further. She saw men portrayed on a wall, figures of Chaldeans*ᵃ* portrayed in red, ¹⁵with belts around their waists and flowing turbans on their heads; all of them looked like Babylonian chariot officers, natives of Chaldea.*ᵇ* ¹⁶As soon as she saw them, she lusted after them and sent messengers to them in Chaldea. ¹⁷Then the Babylonians came to her, to the bed of love, and in their lust they defiled her. After she had been defiled by them, she turned away from them in disgust. ¹⁸When she carried on her prostitution openly and exposed her naked body, I turned away from her in disgust, just as I had turned away from her sister. ¹⁹Yet she became more and more promiscuous as she recalled the days of her youth, when she was a prostitute in Egypt. ²⁰There she lusted after her lovers, whose genitals were like those of donkeys and whose emission was like that of horses. ²¹So you longed for the lewdness of your youth, when in Egypt your bosom was caressed and your young breasts fondled.*ᶜ*

²²"Therefore, Oholibah, this is what the Sovereign Lord says: I will stir up your lovers against you, those you turned away from in disgust, and I will bring them against you from every side — ²³the Babylonians and all the Chaldeans, the men of Pekod and Shoa and Koa, and all the Assyrians with them, handsome young men, all of them governors and commanders, chariot officers and men of high rank, all mounted on horses. ²⁴They will come against you with weapons,*ᵈ* chariots and wagons and with a throng of people; they will take up positions against you on every side with large and small shields and

---

ᵃ 14 Or *Babylonians*   *ᵇ 15* Or *Babylonia*; also in verse 16   *ᶜ 21* Syriac (see also verse 3); Hebrew *caressed because of your young breasts*   *ᵈ 24* The meaning of the Hebrew for this word is uncertain.

with helmets. I will turn you over to them for punishment, and they will punish you according to their standards. ²⁵ I will direct my jealous anger against you, and they will deal with you in fury. They will cut off your noses and your ears, and those of you who are left will fall by the sword. They will take away your sons and daughters, and those of you who are left will be consumed by fire. ²⁶ They will also strip you of your clothes and take your fine jewelry. ²⁷ So I will put a stop to the lewdness and prostitution you began in Egypt. You will not look on these things with longing or remember Egypt anymore.

²⁸ "For this is what the Sovereign LORD says: I am about to deliver you into the hands of those you hate, to those you turned away from in disgust. ²⁹ They will deal with you in hatred and take away everything you have worked for. They will leave you stark naked, and the shame of your prostitution will be exposed. Your lewdness and promiscuity ³⁰ have brought this on you, because you lusted after the nations and defiled yourself with their idols. ³¹ You have gone the way of your sister; so I will put her cup into your hand.

³² "This is what the Sovereign LORD says:

"You will drink your sister's cup,
  a cup large and deep;
it will bring scorn and derision,
  for it holds so much.
³³ You will be filled with drunkenness and
    sorrow,
  the cup of ruin and desolation,
  the cup of your sister Samaria.
³⁴ You will drink it and drain it dry
  and chew on its pieces —
  and you will tear your breasts.

I have spoken, declares the Sovereign LORD.

³⁵ "Therefore this is what the Sovereign LORD says: Since you have forgotten me and turned your back on me, you must bear the consequences of your lewdness and prostitution."

³⁶ The LORD said to me: "Son of man, will you judge Oholah and Oholibah? Then confront them with their detestable practices, ³⁷ for they have committed adultery and blood is on their hands. They committed adultery with their idols; they even sacrificed their children, whom they bore to me,

as food for them. ³⁸ They have also done this to me: At that same time they defiled my sanctuary and desecrated my Sabbaths. ³⁹ On the very day they sacrificed their children to their idols, they entered my sanctuary and desecrated it. That is what they did in my house.

⁴⁰ "They even sent messengers for men who came from far away, and when they arrived you bathed yourself for them, applied eye makeup and put on your jewelry. ⁴¹ You sat on an elegant couch, with a table spread before it on which you had placed the incense and olive oil that belonged to me.

⁴² "The noise of a carefree crowd was around her; drunkards were brought from the desert along with men from the rabble, and they put bracelets on the wrists of the woman and her sister and beautiful crowns on their heads. ⁴³ Then I said about the one worn out by adultery, 'Now let them use her as a prostitute, for that is all she is.' ⁴⁴ And they slept with her. As men sleep with a prostitute, so they slept with those lewd women, Oholah and Oholibah. ⁴⁵ But righteous judges will sentence them to the punishment of women who commit adultery and shed blood, because they are adulterous and blood is on their hands.

⁴⁶ "This is what the Sovereign LORD says: Bring a mob against them and give them over to terror and plunder. ⁴⁷ The mob will stone them and cut them down with their swords; they will kill their sons and daughters and burn down their houses.

⁴⁸ "So I will put an end to lewdness in the land, that all women may take warning and not imitate you. ⁴⁹ You will suffer the penalty for your lewdness and bear the consequences of your sins of idolatry. Then you will know that I am the Sovereign LORD."

Jerusalem as a Cooking Pot

24 In the ninth year, in the tenth month on the tenth day, the word of the LORD came to me: ² "Son of man, record this date, this very date, because the king of Babylon has laid siege to Jerusalem this very day. ³ Tell this rebellious people a parable and say to them: 'This is what the Sovereign LORD says:

"'Put on the cooking pot; put it on
  and pour water into it.

⁴Put into it the pieces of meat,
all the choice pieces—the leg and the
shoulder.
Fill it with the best of these bones;
⁵ take the pick of the flock.
Pile wood beneath it for the bones;
bring it to a boil
and cook the bones in it.

⁶"'For this is what the Sovereign LORD says:

"'Woe to the city of bloodshed,
to the pot now encrusted,
whose deposit will not go away!
Take the meat out piece by piece
in whatever order it comes.

⁷"'For the blood she shed is in her midst:
She poured it on the bare rock;
she did not pour it on the ground,
where the dust would cover it.
⁸To stir up wrath and take revenge
I put her blood on the bare rock,
so that it would not be covered.

⁹"'Therefore this is what the Sovereign LORD says:

"'Woe to the city of bloodshed!
I, too, will pile the wood high.
¹⁰So heap on the wood
and kindle the fire.
Cook the meat well,
mixing in the spices;
and let the bones be charred.
¹¹Then set the empty pot on the coals
till it becomes hot and its copper
glows,
so that its impurities may be melted
and its deposit burned away.
¹²It has frustrated all efforts;
its heavy deposit has not been
removed,
not even by fire.

¹³"'Now your impurity is lewdness. Because I tried to cleanse you but you would not be cleansed from your impurity, you will not be clean again until my wrath against you has subsided.

¹⁴"'I the LORD have spoken. The time has come for me to act. I will not hold back; I will not have pity, nor will I relent. You will be judged according to your conduct and your actions, declares the Sovereign LORD.'"

Ezekiel's Wife Dies

¹⁵The word of the LORD came to me: ¹⁶"Son of man, with one blow I am about to take away from you the delight of your eyes. Yet do not lament or weep or shed any tears. ¹⁷Groan quietly; do not mourn for the dead. Keep your turban fastened and your sandals on your feet; do not cover your mustache and beard or eat the customary food of mourners."

¹⁸So I spoke to the people in the morning, and in the evening my wife died. The next morning I did as I had been commanded.

¹⁹Then the people asked me, "Won't you tell us what these things have to do with us? Why are you acting like this?"

²⁰So I said to them, "The word of the LORD came to me: ²¹Say to the people of Israel, 'This is what the Sovereign LORD says: I am about to desecrate my sanctuary—the stronghold in which you take pride, the delight of your eyes, the object of your affection. The sons and daughters you left behind will fall by the sword. ²²And you will do as I have done. You will not cover your mustache and beard or eat the customary food of mourners. ²³You will keep your turbans on your heads and your sandals on your feet. You will not mourn or weep but will waste away because of[a] your sins and groan among yourselves. ²⁴Ezekiel will be a sign to you; you will do just as he has done. When this happens, you will know that I am the Sovereign LORD.'

²⁵"And you, son of man, on the day I take away their stronghold, their joy and glory, the delight of their eyes, their heart's desire, and their sons and daughters as well— ²⁶on that day a fugitive will come to tell you the news. ²⁷At that time your mouth will be opened; you will speak with him and will no longer be silent. So you will be a sign to them, and they will know that I am the LORD."

A Prophecy Against Ammon

25 The word of the LORD came to me: ²"Son of man, set your face against the Ammonites and prophesy against them. ³Say to them, 'Hear the word of the Sovereign LORD. This is what the Sovereign LORD says: Because you said "Aha!" over my sanctuary when it was desecrated and over the

---

a 23 Or *away in*

land of Israel when it was laid waste and over the people of Judah when they went into exile, [4]therefore I am going to give you to the people of the East as a possession. They will set up their camps and pitch their tents among you; they will eat your fruit and drink your milk. [5]I will turn Rabbah into a pasture for camels and Ammon into a resting place for sheep. Then you will know that I am the LORD. [6]For this is what the Sovereign LORD says: Because you have clapped your hands and stamped your feet, rejoicing with all the malice of your heart against the land of Israel, [7]therefore I will stretch out my hand against you and give you as plunder to the nations. I will wipe you out from among the nations and exterminate you from the countries. I will destroy you, and you will know that I am the LORD.'"

A Prophecy Against Moab

[8]"This is what the Sovereign LORD says: 'Because Moab and Seir said, "Look, Judah has become like all the other nations," [9]therefore I will expose the flank of Moab, beginning at its frontier towns — Beth Jeshimoth, Baal Meon and Kiriathaim — the glory of that land. [10]I will give Moab along with the Ammonites to the people of the East as a possession, so that the Ammonites will not be remembered among the nations; [11]and I will inflict punishment on Moab. Then they will know that I am the LORD.'"

A Prophecy Against Edom

[12]"This is what the Sovereign LORD says: 'Because Edom took revenge on Judah and became very guilty by doing so, [13]therefore this is what the Sovereign LORD says: I will stretch out my hand against Edom and kill both man and beast. I will lay it waste, and from Teman to Dedan they will fall by the sword. [14]I will take vengeance on Edom by the hand of my people Israel, and they will deal with Edom in accordance with my anger and my wrath; they will know my vengeance, declares the Sovereign LORD.'"

A Prophecy Against Philistia

[15]"This is what the Sovereign LORD says: 'Because the Philistines acted in vengeance and took revenge with malice in their hearts, and with ancient hostility sought to destroy Judah, [16]therefore this is what the Sovereign LORD says: I am about to stretch out my hand against the Philistines, and I will wipe out the Kerethites and destroy those remaining along the coast. [17]I will carry out great vengeance on them and punish them in my wrath. Then they will know that I am the LORD, when I take vengeance on them.'"

A Prophecy Against Tyre

26 In the eleventh month of the twelfth[a] year, on the first day of the month, the word of the LORD came to me: [2]"Son of man, because Tyre has said of Jerusalem, 'Aha! The gate to the nations is broken, and its doors have swung open to me; now that she lies in ruins I will prosper,' [3]therefore this is what the Sovereign LORD says: I am against you, Tyre, and I will bring many nations against you, like the sea casting up its waves. [4]They will destroy the walls of Tyre and pull down her towers; I will scrape away her rubble and make her a bare rock. [5]Out in the sea she will become a place to spread fishnets, for I have spoken, declares the Sovereign LORD. She will become plunder for the nations, [6]and her settlements on the mainland will be ravaged by the sword. Then they will know that I am the LORD.

[7]"For this is what the Sovereign LORD says: From the north I am going to bring against Tyre Nebuchadnezzar[b] king of Babylon, king of kings, with horses and chariots, with horsemen and a great army. [8]He will ravage your settlements on the mainland with the sword; he will set up siege works against you, build a ramp up to your walls and raise his shields against you. [9]He will direct the blows of his battering rams against your walls and demolish your towers with his weapons. [10]His horses will be so many that they will cover you with dust. Your walls will tremble at the noise of the warhorses, wagons and chariots when he enters your gates as men enter a city whose walls have been broken through. [11]The hooves of his horses will trample all your streets; he will kill your people with the sword, and your strong pillars will fall to the ground. [12]They will plunder your wealth and loot your merchandise;

---

[a] 1 Probable reading of the original Hebrew text; Masoretic Text does not have *month of the twelfth*.
[b] 7 Hebrew *Nebuchadrezzar*, of which *Nebuchadnezzar* is a variant; here and often in Ezekiel and Jeremiah

they will break down your walls and demolish your fine houses and throw your stones, timber and rubble into the sea. [13]I will put an end to your noisy songs, and the music of your harps will be heard no more. [14]I will make you a bare rock, and you will become a place to spread fishnets. You will never be rebuilt, for I the LORD have spoken, declares the Sovereign LORD.

[15]"This is what the Sovereign LORD says to Tyre: Will not the coastlands tremble at the sound of your fall, when the wounded groan and the slaughter takes place in you? [16]Then all the princes of the coast will step down from their thrones and lay aside their robes and take off their embroidered garments. Clothed with terror, they will sit on the ground, trembling every moment, appalled at you. [17]Then they will take up a lament concerning you and say to you:

"'How you are destroyed, city of renown,
    peopled by men of the sea!
You were a power on the seas,
    you and your citizens;
you put your terror
    on all who lived there.
[18]Now the coastlands tremble
    on the day of your fall;
the islands in the sea
    are terrified at your collapse.'

[19]"This is what the Sovereign LORD says: When I make you a desolate city, like cities no longer inhabited, and when I bring the ocean depths over you and its vast waters cover you, [20]then I will bring you down with those who go down to the pit, to the people of long ago. I will make you dwell in the earth below, as in ancient ruins, with those who go down to the pit, and you will not return or take your place[a] in the land of the living. [21]I will bring you to a horrible end and you will be no more. You will be sought, but you will never again be found, declares the Sovereign LORD."

A Lament Over Tyre

27 The word of the LORD came to me: [2]"Son of man, take up a lament concerning Tyre. [3]Say to Tyre, situated at the gateway to the sea, merchant of peoples on many coasts, 'This is what the Sovereign LORD says:

"'You say, Tyre,
    "I am perfect in beauty."
[4]Your domain was on the high seas;
    your builders brought your beauty to
        perfection.
[5]They made all your timbers
    of juniper from Senir[b];
they took a cedar from Lebanon
    to make a mast for you.
[6]Of oaks from Bashan
    they made your oars;
of cypress wood[c] from the coasts
    of Cyprus
    they made your deck, adorned with
        ivory.
[7]Fine embroidered linen from Egypt was
        your sail
    and served as your banner;
your awnings were of blue and purple
    from the coasts of Elishah.
[8]Men of Sidon and Arvad were your
        oarsmen;
    your skilled men, Tyre, were aboard as
        your sailors.
[9]Veteran craftsmen of Byblos were on
        board
    as shipwrights to caulk your seams.
All the ships of the sea and their sailors
    came alongside to trade for your
        wares.

[10]"'Men of Persia, Lydia and Put
    served as soldiers in your army.
They hung their shields and helmets on
        your walls,
    bringing you splendor.
[11]Men of Arvad and Helek
    guarded your walls on every side;
men of Gammad
    were in your towers.
They hung their shields around your
        walls;
    they brought your beauty to
        perfection.

[12]"'Tarshish did business with you because of your great wealth of goods; they exchanged silver, iron, tin and lead for your merchandise.

[13]"'Greece, Tubal and Meshek did business

---

[a] 20 Septuagint; Hebrew *return, and I will give glory*   [b] 5 That is, Mount Hermon   [c] 6 Targum; the Masoretic Text has a different division of the consonants.

with you; they traded human beings and articles of bronze for your wares.

14 " 'Men of Beth Togarmah exchanged chariot horses, cavalry horses and mules for your merchandise.

15 " 'The men of Rhodes[a] traded with you, and many coastlands were your customers; they paid you with ivory tusks and ebony.

16 " 'Aram[b] did business with you because of your many products; they exchanged turquoise, purple fabric, embroidered work, fine linen, coral and rubies for your merchandise.

17 " 'Judah and Israel traded with you; they exchanged wheat from Minnith and confections,[c] honey, olive oil and balm for your wares.

18 " 'Damascus did business with you because of your many products and great wealth of goods. They offered wine from Helbon, wool from Zahar 19 and casks of wine from Izal in exchange for your wares: wrought iron, cassia and calamus.

20 " 'Dedan traded in saddle blankets with you.

21 " 'Arabia and all the princes of Kedar were your customers; they did business with you in lambs, rams and goats.

22 " 'The merchants of Sheba and Raamah traded with you; for your merchandise they exchanged the finest of all kinds of spices and precious stones, and gold.

23 " 'Harran, Kanneh and Eden and merchants of Sheba, Ashur and Kilmad traded with you. 24 In your marketplace they traded with you beautiful garments, blue fabric, embroidered work and multicolored rugs with cords twisted and tightly knotted.

25 " 'The ships of Tarshish serve
as carriers for your wares.
You are filled with heavy cargo
as you sail the sea.
26 Your oarsmen take you
out to the high seas.
But the east wind will break you to pieces
far out at sea.
27 Your wealth, merchandise and wares,
your mariners, sailors and
shipwrights,
your merchants and all your soldiers,
and everyone else on board

will sink into the heart of the sea
on the day of your shipwreck.
28 The shorelands will quake
when your sailors cry out.
29 All who handle the oars
will abandon their ships;
the mariners and all the sailors
will stand on the shore.
30 They will raise their voice
and cry bitterly over you;
they will sprinkle dust on their heads
and roll in ashes.
31 They will shave their heads because
of you
and will put on sackcloth.
They will weep over you with anguish
of soul
and with bitter mourning.
32 As they wail and mourn over you,
they will take up a lament concerning
you:
"Who was ever silenced like Tyre,
surrounded by the sea?"
33 When your merchandise went out on the
seas,
you satisfied many nations;
with your great wealth and your wares
you enriched the kings of the earth.
34 Now you are shattered by the sea
in the depths of the waters;
your wares and all your company
have gone down with you.
35 All who live in the coastlands
are appalled at you;
their kings shudder with horror
and their faces are distorted with fear.
36 The merchants among the nations scoff
at you;
you have come to a horrible end
and will be no more.' "

A Prophecy Against the King of Tyre

28 The word of the LORD came to me:
2 "Son of man, say to the ruler of Tyre,
'This is what the Sovereign LORD says:

" 'In the pride of your heart
you say, "I am a god;
I sit on the throne of a god
in the heart of the seas."
But you are a mere mortal and
not a god,

---

[a] 15 Septuagint; Hebrew *Dedan*   [b] 16 Most Hebrew manuscripts; some Hebrew manuscripts and Syriac *Edom*   [c] 17 The meaning of the Hebrew for this word is uncertain.

HIM OR ME?

READ: EZEKIEL 28:2

I n my brokenness, I feel the pull to worship me. I hear the whispered lie that Adam and Eve first heard: "Your eyes will be opened, and you will be like God" (Genesis 3:5). Why serve? You rule! You have everything you need to be your own god. Every day is a trip to that orchard where the snake is waiting. I must face this same choice: Will I worship God, and find my true place in this universe, the perfect place he has arranged for me? Or will I worship myself and decide I can somehow come up with a better life than the Creator of all could design?

You'll confront many of the gods in our lineup at some point in your life. But the god of me is one you'll grapple with every single day—multiple times per day.

There are some symptoms that start to show up when the god of me edges himself onto the throne of my heart. One symptom is arrogance. *I'm always right. My way is the best way.* The god of me won't listen to the wisdom of others.

BUILDING
FAITH
WISDOM
STRENGTH

Another symptom that surfaces when I start to worship the god of me is insecurity. The god of me is consumed with what others think and terrified of trying something and failing. You can't help but be self-conscious, because when you're god, it's all about you.

But the god of me, in all its forms, always leaves you disappointed and disillusioned.

Taken from *Gods at War Student Edition* by Kyle Idleman, copyright © 2014 by City on a Hill Studio, LLC, published by Zondervan.

though you think you are as wise as
a god.
³ Are you wiser than Daniel*ᵃ*?
Is no secret hidden from you?
⁴ By your wisdom and understanding
you have gained wealth for yourself
and amassed gold and silver
in your treasuries.
⁵ By your great skill in trading
you have increased your wealth,
and because of your wealth
your heart has grown proud.

⁶ " 'Therefore this is what the Sovereign
LORD says:

" 'Because you think you are wise,
as wise as a god,
⁷ I am going to bring foreigners against
you,
the most ruthless of nations;
they will draw their swords against your
beauty and wisdom
and pierce your shining splendor.
⁸ They will bring you down to the pit,
and you will die a violent death
in the heart of the seas.
⁹ Will you then say, "I am a god,"
in the presence of those who kill you?
You will be but a mortal, not a god,
in the hands of those who slay you.
¹⁰ You will die the death of the
uncircumcised
at the hands of foreigners.

I have spoken, declares the Sovereign
LORD.' "

¹¹ The word of the LORD came to me:
¹² "Son of man, take up a lament concerning
the king of Tyre and say to him: 'This is what
the Sovereign LORD says:

" 'You were the seal of perfection,
full of wisdom and perfect in beauty.
¹³ You were in Eden,
the garden of God;
every precious stone adorned you:
carnelian, chrysolite and emerald,
topaz, onyx and jasper,
lapis lazuli, turquoise and beryl.*ᵇ*
Your settings and mountings*ᶜ* were made
of gold;

on the day you were created they were
prepared.
¹⁴ You were anointed as a guardian cherub,
for so I ordained you.
You were on the holy mount of God;
you walked among the fiery stones.
¹⁵ You were blameless in your ways
from the day you were created
till wickedness was found in you.
¹⁶ Through your widespread trade
you were filled with violence,
and you sinned.
So I drove you in disgrace from the
mount of God,
and I expelled you, guardian cherub,
from among the fiery stones.
¹⁷ Your heart became proud
on account of your beauty,
and you corrupted your wisdom
because of your splendor.
So I threw you to the earth;
I made a spectacle of you before
kings.
¹⁸ By your many sins and dishonest trade
you have desecrated your sanctuaries.
So I made a fire come out from you,
and it consumed you,
and I reduced you to ashes on the ground
in the sight of all who were watching.
¹⁹ All the nations who knew you
are appalled at you;
you have come to a horrible end
and will be no more.' "

A Prophecy Against Sidon

²⁰ The word of the LORD came to me:
²¹ "Son of man, set your face against Sidon;
prophesy against her ²² and say: 'This is what
the Sovereign LORD says:

" 'I am against you, Sidon,
and among you I will display my glory.
You will know that I am the LORD,
when I inflict punishment on you
and within you am proved to be holy.
²³ I will send a plague upon you
and make blood flow in your streets.
The slain will fall within you,
with the sword against you on
every side.
Then you will know that I am the LORD.

ᵃ 3 Or *Danel*, a man of renown in ancient literature   *ᵇ 13* The precise identification of some of these
precious stones is uncertain.   *ᶜ 13* The meaning of the Hebrew for this phrase is uncertain.

²⁴ "'No longer will the people of Israel have malicious neighbors who are painful briers and sharp thorns. Then they will know that I am the Sovereign Lord.

²⁵ "'This is what the Sovereign Lord says: When I gather the people of Israel from the nations where they have been scattered, I will be proved holy through them in the sight of the nations. Then they will live in their own land, which I gave to my servant Jacob. ²⁶ They will live there in safety and will build houses and plant vineyards; they will live in safety when I inflict punishment on all their neighbors who maligned them. Then they will know that I am the Lord their God.'"

A Prophecy Against Egypt
Judgment on Pharaoh

29 In the tenth year, in the tenth month on the twelfth day, the word of the Lord came to me: ²"Son of man, set your face against Pharaoh king of Egypt and prophesy against him and against all Egypt. ³Speak to him and say: 'This is what the Sovereign Lord says:

"'I am against you, Pharaoh king of Egypt,
    you great monster lying among your
        streams.
You say, "The Nile belongs to me;
    I made it for myself."
⁴ But I will put hooks in your jaws
    and make the fish of your streams stick
        to your scales.
I will pull you out from among your
        streams,
    with all the fish sticking to your scales.
⁵ I will leave you in the desert,
    you and all the fish of your streams.
You will fall on the open field
    and not be gathered or picked up.
I will give you as food
    to the beasts of the earth and the birds
        of the sky.

⁶ Then all who live in Egypt will know that I am the Lord.

"'You have been a staff of reed for the people of Israel. ⁷When they grasped you with their hands, you splintered and you tore open their shoulders; when they leaned on you, you broke and their backs were wrenched.ᵃ

⁸ "'Therefore this is what the Sovereign Lord says: I will bring a sword against you and kill both man and beast. ⁹Egypt will become a desolate wasteland. Then they will know that I am the Lord.

"'Because you said, "The Nile is mine; I made it," ¹⁰therefore I am against you and against your streams, and I will make the land of Egypt a ruin and a desolate waste from Migdol to Aswan, as far as the border of Cush.ᵇ ¹¹The foot of neither man nor beast will pass through it; no one will live there for forty years. ¹²I will make the land of Egypt desolate among devastated lands, and her cities will lie desolate forty years among ruined cities. And I will disperse the Egyptians among the nations and scatter them through the countries.

¹³ "'Yet this is what the Sovereign Lord says: At the end of forty years I will gather the Egyptians from the nations where they were scattered. ¹⁴I will bring them back from captivity and return them to Upper Egypt, the land of their ancestry. There they will be a lowly kingdom. ¹⁵It will be the lowliest of kingdoms and will never again exalt itself above the other nations. I will make it so weak that it will never again rule over the nations. ¹⁶Egypt will no longer be a source of confidence for the people of Israel but will be a reminder of their sin in turning to her for help. Then they will know that I am the Sovereign Lord.'"

Nebuchadnezzar's Reward

¹⁷In the twenty-seventh year, in the first month on the first day, the word of the Lord came to me: ¹⁸"Son of man, Nebuchadnezzar king of Babylon drove his army in a hard campaign against Tyre; every head was rubbed bare and every shoulder made raw. Yet he and his army got no reward from the campaign he led against Tyre. ¹⁹Therefore this is what the Sovereign Lord says: I am going to give Egypt to Nebuchadnezzar king of Babylon, and he will carry off its wealth. He will loot and plunder the land as pay for his army. ²⁰I have given him Egypt as a reward for his efforts because he and his army did it for me, declares the Sovereign Lord. ²¹"On that day I will make a hornᶜ grow for the Israelites, and I will open your mouth

---

ᵃ 7 Syriac (see also Septuagint and Vulgate); Hebrew *and you caused their backs to stand*   ᵇ 10 That is, the upper Nile region   ᶜ 21 *Horn* here symbolizes strength.

among them. Then they will know that I am the Lord."

A Lament Over Egypt

30 The word of the Lord came to me: ² "Son of man, prophesy and say: 'This is what the Sovereign Lord says:

" 'Wail and say,
"Alas for that day!"
³ For the day is near,
the day of the Lord is near —
a day of clouds,
a time of doom for the nations.
⁴ A sword will come against Egypt,
and anguish will come upon Cush.ᵃ
When the slain fall in Egypt,
her wealth will be carried away
and her foundations torn down.

⁵ Cush and Libya, Lydia and all Arabia, Kub and the people of the covenant land will fall by the sword along with Egypt.

⁶ " 'This is what the Lord says:

" 'The allies of Egypt will fall
and her proud strength will fail.
From Migdol to Aswan
they will fall by the sword within her,
declares the Sovereign Lord.
⁷ " 'They will be desolate
among desolate lands,
and their cities will lie
among ruined cities.
⁸ Then they will know that I am the Lord,
when I set fire to Egypt
and all her helpers are crushed.

⁹ " 'On that day messengers will go out from me in ships to frighten Cush out of her complacency. Anguish will take hold of them on the day of Egypt's doom, for it is sure to come.

¹⁰ " 'This is what the Sovereign Lord says:

" 'I will put an end to the hordes of Egypt
by the hand of Nebuchadnezzar king
of Babylon.
¹¹ He and his army — the most ruthless of
nations —
will be brought in to destroy the land.
They will draw their swords against
Egypt
and fill the land with the slain.

¹² I will dry up the waters of the Nile
and sell the land to an evil nation;
by the hand of foreigners
I will lay waste the land and
everything in it.

I the Lord have spoken.

¹³ " 'This is what the Sovereign Lord says:

" 'I will destroy the idols
and put an end to the images in
Memphis.
No longer will there be a prince in Egypt,
and I will spread fear throughout
the land.
¹⁴ I will lay waste Upper Egypt,
set fire to Zoan
and inflict punishment on Thebes.
¹⁵ I will pour out my wrath on Pelusium,
the stronghold of Egypt,
and wipe out the hordes of Thebes.
¹⁶ I will set fire to Egypt;
Pelusium will writhe in agony.
Thebes will be taken by storm;
Memphis will be in constant distress.
¹⁷ The young men of Heliopolis and
Bubastis
will fall by the sword,
and the cities themselves will go into
captivity.
¹⁸ Dark will be the day at Tahpanhes
when I break the yoke of Egypt;
there her proud strength will come to
an end.
She will be covered with clouds,
and her villages will go into captivity.
¹⁹ So I will inflict punishment on Egypt,
and they will know that I am the
Lord.' "

Pharaoh's Arms Are Broken

²⁰ In the eleventh year, in the first month on the seventh day, the word of the Lord came to me: ²¹ "Son of man, I have broken the arm of Pharaoh king of Egypt. It has not been bound up to be healed or put in a splint so that it may become strong enough to hold a sword. ²² Therefore this is what the Sovereign Lord says: I am against Pharaoh king of Egypt. I will break both his arms, the good arm as well as the broken one, and make the sword fall from his hand. ²³ I will disperse the Egyptians among the nations

ᵃ 4 That is, the upper Nile region; also in verses 5 and 9

and scatter them through the countries. ²⁴I will strengthen the arms of the king of Babylon and put my sword in his hand, but I will break the arms of Pharaoh, and he will groan before him like a mortally wounded man. ²⁵I will strengthen the arms of the king of Babylon, but the arms of Pharaoh will fall limp. Then they will know that I am the LORD, when I put my sword into the hand of the king of Babylon and he brandishes it against Egypt. ²⁶I will disperse the Egyptians among the nations and scatter them through the countries. Then they will know that I am the LORD."

Pharaoh as a Felled Cedar of Lebanon

31 In the eleventh year, in the third month on the first day, the word of the LORD came to me: ²"Son of man, say to Pharaoh king of Egypt and to his hordes:

"'Who can be compared with you in
    majesty?
³ Consider Assyria, once a cedar in
    Lebanon,
  with beautiful branches
    overshadowing the forest;
  it towered on high,
    its top above the thick foliage.
⁴ The waters nourished it,
    deep springs made it grow tall;
  their streams flowed
    all around its base
  and sent their channels
    to all the trees of the field.
⁵ So it towered higher
    than all the trees of the field;
  its boughs increased
    and its branches grew long,
  spreading because of abundant
    waters.
⁶ All the birds of the sky
    nested in its boughs,
  all the animals of the wild
    gave birth under its branches;
  all the great nations
    lived in its shade.
⁷ It was majestic in beauty,
    with its spreading boughs,
  for its roots went down
    to abundant waters.
⁸ The cedars in the garden of God
    could not rival it,
  nor could the junipers
    equal its boughs,

nor could the plane trees
    compare with its branches—
  no tree in the garden of God
    could match its beauty.
⁹ I made it beautiful
    with abundant branches,
  the envy of all the trees of Eden
    in the garden of God.

¹⁰ "'Therefore this is what the Sovereign LORD says: Because the great cedar towered over the thick foliage, and because it was proud of its height, ¹¹I gave it into the hands of the ruler of the nations, for him to deal with according to its wickedness. I cast it aside, ¹²and the most ruthless of foreign nations cut it down and left it. Its boughs fell on the mountains and in all the valleys; its branches lay broken in all the ravines of the land. All the nations of the earth came out from under its shade and left it. ¹³All the birds settled on the fallen tree, and all the wild animals lived among its branches. ¹⁴Therefore no other trees by the waters are ever to tower proudly on high, lifting their tops above the thick foliage. No other trees so well-watered are ever to reach such a height; they are all destined for death, for the earth below, among mortals who go down to the realm of the dead.

¹⁵ "'This is what the Sovereign LORD says: On the day it was brought down to the realm of the dead I covered the deep springs with mourning for it; I held back its streams, and its abundant waters were restrained. Because of it I clothed Lebanon with gloom, and all the trees of the field withered away. ¹⁶I made the nations tremble at the sound of its fall when I brought it down to the realm of the dead to be with those who go down to the pit. Then all the trees of Eden, the choicest and best of Lebanon, the well-watered trees, were consoled in the earth below. ¹⁷They too, like the great cedar, had gone down to the realm of the dead, to those killed by the sword, along with the armed men who lived in its shade among the nations.

¹⁸ "'Which of the trees of Eden can be compared with you in splendor and majesty? Yet you, too, will be brought down with the trees of Eden to the earth below; you will lie among the uncircumcised, with those killed by the sword.

"'This is Pharaoh and all his hordes, declares the Sovereign LORD.'"

A Lament Over Pharaoh

32 In the twelfth year, in the twelfth month on the first day, the word of the LORD came to me: [2] "Son of man, take up a lament concerning Pharaoh king of Egypt and say to him:

"'You are like a lion among the nations;
  you are like a monster in the seas
thrashing about in your streams,
  churning the water with your feet
  and muddying the streams.

[3] "'This is what the Sovereign LORD says:

"'With a great throng of people
  I will cast my net over you,
  and they will haul you up in my net.
[4] I will throw you on the land
  and hurl you on the open field.
I will let all the birds of the sky settle
  on you
  and all the animals of the wild gorge
  themselves on you.
[5] I will spread your flesh on the mountains
  and fill the valleys with your remains.
[6] I will drench the land with your flowing
  blood
  all the way to the mountains,
  and the ravines will be filled with your
  flesh.
[7] When I snuff you out, I will cover the
  heavens
  and darken their stars;
I will cover the sun with a cloud,
  and the moon will not give its light.
[8] All the shining lights in the heavens
  I will darken over you;
  I will bring darkness over your land,
    declares the Sovereign LORD.
[9] I will trouble the hearts of many peoples
  when I bring about your destruction
    among the nations,
  among[a] lands you have not known.
[10] I will cause many peoples to be appalled
    at you,
  and their kings will shudder with
    horror because of you
  when I brandish my sword before them.
On the day of your downfall
  each of them will tremble
  every moment for his life.

[11] "'For this is what the Sovereign LORD says:

"'The sword of the king of Babylon
  will come against you.
[12] I will cause your hordes to fall
  by the swords of mighty men —
  the most ruthless of all nations.
They will shatter the pride of Egypt,
  and all her hordes will be overthrown.
[13] I will destroy all her cattle
  from beside abundant waters
no longer to be stirred by the foot of man
  or muddied by the hooves of cattle.
[14] Then I will let her waters settle
  and make her streams flow like oil,
    declares the Sovereign LORD.
[15] When I make Egypt desolate
  and strip the land of everything in it,
  when I strike down all who live there,
  then they will know that I am the LORD.'

[16] "This is the lament they will chant for her. The daughters of the nations will chant it; for Egypt and all her hordes they will chant it, declares the Sovereign LORD."

Egypt's Descent Into the Realm of the Dead

[17] In the twelfth year, on the fifteenth day of the month, the word of the LORD came to me: [18] "Son of man, wail for the hordes of Egypt and consign to the earth below both her and the daughters of mighty nations, along with those who go down to the pit. [19] Say to them, 'Are you more favored than others? Go down and be laid among the uncircumcised.' [20] They will fall among those killed by the sword. The sword is drawn; let her be dragged off with all her hordes. [21] From within the realm of the dead the mighty leaders will say of Egypt and her allies, 'They have come down and they lie with the uncircumcised, with those killed by the sword.'

[22] "Assyria is there with her whole army; she is surrounded by the graves of all her slain, all who have fallen by the sword. [23] Their graves are in the depths of the pit and her army lies around her grave. All who had spread terror in the land of the living are slain, fallen by the sword.

[24] "Elam is there, with all her hordes around her grave. All of them are slain, fallen by the sword. All who had spread terror in the land of the living went down uncircumcised to the earth below. They bear their

---

a 9 Hebrew; Septuagint *bring you into captivity among the nations, / to* shame with those who go down to the pit. ²⁵A bed is made for her among the slain, with all her hordes around her grave. All of them are uncircumcised, killed by the sword. Because their terror had spread in the land of the living, they bear their shame with those who go down to the pit; they are laid among the slain.

²⁶ "Meshek and Tubal are there, with all their hordes around their graves. All of them are uncircumcised, killed by the sword because they spread their terror in the land of the living. ²⁷But they do not lie with the fallen warriors of old,ᵃ who went down to the realm of the dead with their weapons of war — their swords placed under their heads and their shieldsᵇ resting on their bones — though these warriors also had terrorized the land of the living.

²⁸ "You too, Pharaoh, will be broken and will lie among the uncircumcised, with those killed by the sword.

²⁹ "Edom is there, her kings and all her princes; despite their power, they are laid with those killed by the sword. They lie with the uncircumcised, with those who go down to the pit.

³⁰ "All the princes of the north and all the Sidonians are there; they went down with the slain in disgrace despite the terror caused by their power. They lie uncircumcised with those killed by the sword and bear their shame with those who go down to the pit.

³¹ "Pharaoh — he and all his army — will see them and he will be consoled for all his hordes that were killed by the sword, declares the Sovereign LORD. ³²Although I had him spread terror in the land of the living, Pharaoh and all his hordes will be laid among the uncircumcised, with those killed by the sword, declares the Sovereign LORD."

Renewal of Ezekiel's Call as Watchman

33 The word of the LORD came to me: ² "Son of man, speak to your people and say to them: 'When I bring the sword against a land, and the people of the land choose one of their men and make him their watchman, ³and he sees the sword coming against the land and blows the trumpet to warn the people, ⁴then if anyone hears the trumpet but does not heed the warning and the sword comes and takes their life, their blood will be on their own head. ⁵Since they heard the sound of the trumpet but did not heed the warning, their blood will be on their own head. If they had heeded the warning, they would have saved themselves. ⁶But if the watchman sees the sword coming and does not blow the trumpet to warn the people and the sword comes and takes someone's life, that person's life will be taken because of their sin, but I will hold the watchman accountable for their blood.'

⁷ "Son of man, I have made you a watchman for the people of Israel; so hear the word I speak and give them warning from me. ⁸When I say to the wicked, 'You wicked person, you will surely die,' and you do not speak out to dissuade them from their ways, that wicked person will die forᶜ their sin, and I will hold you accountable for their blood. ⁹But if you do warn the wicked person to turn from their ways and they do not do so, they will die for their sin, though you yourself will be saved.

¹⁰ "Son of man, say to the Israelites, 'This is what you are saying: "Our offenses and sins weigh us down, and we are wasting away because ofᵈ them. How then can we live?" ' ¹¹Say to them, 'As surely as I live, declares the Sovereign LORD, I take no pleasure in the death of the wicked, but rather that they turn from their ways and live. Turn! Turn from your evil ways! Why will you die, people of Israel?'

¹² "Therefore, son of man, say to your people, 'If someone who is righteous disobeys, that person's former righteousness will count for nothing. And if someone who is wicked repents, that person's former wickedness will not bring condemnation. The righteous person who sins will not be allowed to live even though they were formerly righteous.' ¹³If I tell a righteous person that they will surely live, but then they trust in their righteousness and do evil, none of the righteous things that person has done will be remembered; they will die for the evil they have done. ¹⁴And if I say to a wicked person, 'You will surely die,' but they then turn away from their sin and do what is just and right — ¹⁵if they give back what

---

ᵃ 27 Septuagint; Hebrew *warriors who were uncircumcised*   ᵇ 27 Probable reading of the original Hebrew text; Masoretic Text *punishment*   ᶜ 8 Or *in*; also in verse 9   ᵈ 10 Or *away in*

THE WATCHMEN

READ: EZEKIEL 33:7

The Bible's first murder was no mystery. Cain and Abel each present an offering to the Lord. Older brother Cain fumes when God looks down on his sacrifice, then he kills his brother. When the Lord asks where Abel is, Cain gives a notorious response. "I don't know," he says. "Am I my brother's keeper?" (Genesis 4:9)

The Lord made the prophet Ezekiel his brothers' keeper and more. He serves as a "watchman" for the entire nation of Israel, standing guard like an army lookout, blowing a trumpet to warn the Lord's people of danger. If a watchman sounds the alarm and no one heeds the warning, the people have no one but themselves to blame for their own deaths. But if a watchman sees danger and fails to warn the people, the Lord holds the watchman accountable for their blood.

Ezekiel faces the daunting job as a spiritual watchman of trying to turn God's people from their evil habits. The Lord doesn't want the wicked to die. He wants them to turn from their sin and live. If Ezekiel fails to pass along this message, the Lord will hold him accountable. You might not know it, but you're indeed your brothers' and sisters' keeper. You're appointed to stand guard over others within your reach. Show them the Lord's compassion. Sound the alarm when danger heads their way.

BUILDING

FAITH

WISDOM

STRENGTH

they took in pledge for a loan, return what they have stolen, follow the decrees that give life, and do no evil—that person will surely live; they will not die. [16]None of the sins that person has committed will be remembered against them. They have done what is just and right; they will surely live.

[17]"Yet your people say, 'The way of the Lord is not just.' But it is their way that is not just. [18]If a righteous person turns from their righteousness and does evil, they will die for it. [19]And if a wicked person turns away from their wickedness and does what is just and right, they will live by doing so. [20]Yet you Israelites say, 'The way of the Lord is not just.' But I will judge each of you according to your own ways."

Jerusalem's Fall Explained

[21]In the twelfth year of our exile, in the tenth month on the fifth day, a man who had escaped from Jerusalem came to me and said, "The city has fallen!" [22]Now the evening before the man arrived, the hand of the LORD was on me, and he opened my mouth before the man came to me in the morning. So my mouth was opened and I was no longer silent.

[23]Then the word of the LORD came to me: [24]"Son of man, the people living in those ruins in the land of Israel are saying, 'Abraham was only one man, yet he possessed the land. But we are many; surely the land has been given to us as our possession.' [25]Therefore say to them, 'This is what the Sovereign LORD says: Since you eat meat with the blood still in it and look to your idols and shed blood, should you then possess the land? [26]You rely on your sword, you do detestable things, and each of you defiles his neighbor's wife. Should you then possess the land?'

[27]"Say this to them: 'This is what the Sovereign LORD says: As surely as I live, those who are left in the ruins will fall by the sword, those out in the country I will give to the wild animals to be devoured, and those in strongholds and caves will die of a plague. [28]I will make the land a desolate waste, and her proud strength will come to an end, and the mountains of Israel will become desolate so that no one will cross them. [29]Then they will know that I am the LORD, when I have made the land a desolate waste because of all the detestable things they have done.'

[30]"As for you, son of man, your people are talking together about you by the walls and at the doors of the houses, saying to each other, 'Come and hear the message that has come from the LORD.' [31]My people come to you, as they usually do, and sit before you to hear your words, but they do not put them into practice. Their mouths speak of love, but their hearts are greedy for unjust gain. [32]Indeed, to them you are nothing more than one who sings love songs with a beautiful voice and plays an instrument well, for they hear your words but do not put them into practice.

[33]"When all this comes true—and it surely will—then they will know that a prophet has been among them."

The Lord Will Be Israel's Shepherd

34 The word of the LORD came to me: [2]"Son of man, prophesy against the shepherds of Israel; prophesy and say to them: 'This is what the Sovereign LORD says: Woe to you shepherds of Israel who only take care of yourselves! Should not shepherds take care of the flock? [3]You eat the curds, clothe yourselves with the wool and slaughter the choice animals, but you do not take care of the flock. [4]You have not strengthened the weak or healed the sick or bound up the injured. You have not brought back the strays or searched for the lost. You have ruled them harshly and brutally. [5]So they were scattered because there was no shepherd, and when they were scattered they became food for all the wild animals. [6]My sheep wandered over all the mountains and on every high hill. They were scattered over the whole earth, and no one searched or looked for them.

[7]"'Therefore, you shepherds, hear the word of the LORD: [8]As surely as I live, declares the Sovereign LORD, because my flock lacks a shepherd and so has been plundered and has become food for all the wild animals, and because my shepherds did not search for my flock but cared for themselves rather than for my flock, [9]therefore, you shepherds, hear the word of the LORD: [10]This is what the Sovereign LORD says: I am against the shepherds and will hold them accountable for my flock. I will remove them from tending the flock so that the shepherds can no longer feed themselves. I will rescue

my flock from their mouths, and it will no longer be food for them.

[11] "'For this is what the Sovereign LORD says: I myself will search for my sheep and look after them. [12] As a shepherd looks after his scattered flock when he is with them, so will I look after my sheep. I will rescue them from all the places where they were scattered on a day of clouds and darkness. [13] I will bring them out from the nations and gather them from the countries, and I will bring them into their own land. I will pasture them on the mountains of Israel, in the ravines and in all the settlements in the land. [14] I will tend them in a good pasture, and the mountain heights of Israel will be their grazing land. There they will lie down in good grazing land, and there they will feed in a rich pasture on the mountains of Israel. [15] I myself will tend my sheep and have them lie down, declares the Sovereign LORD. [16] I will search for the lost and bring back the strays. I will bind up the injured and strengthen the weak, but the sleek and the strong I will destroy. I will shepherd the flock with justice.

[17] "'As for you, my flock, this is what the Sovereign LORD says: I will judge between one sheep and another, and between rams and goats. [18] Is it not enough for you to feed on the good pasture? Must you also trample the rest of your pasture with your feet? Is it not enough for you to drink clear water? Must you also muddy the rest with your feet? [19] Must my flock feed on what you have trampled and drink what you have muddied with your feet?

[20] "'Therefore this is what the Sovereign LORD says to them: See, I myself will judge between the fat sheep and the lean sheep. [21] Because you shove with flank and shoulder, butting all the weak sheep with your horns until you have driven them away, [22] I will save my flock, and they will no longer be plundered. I will judge between one sheep and another. [23] I will place over them one shepherd, my servant David, and he will tend them; he will tend them and be their shepherd. [24] I the LORD will be their God, and my servant David will be prince among them. I the LORD have spoken.

[25] "'I will make a covenant of peace with them and rid the land of savage beasts so that they may live in the wilderness and sleep in the forests in safety. [26] I will make them and the places surrounding my hill a blessing.[a] I will send down showers in season; there will be showers of blessing. [27] The trees will yield their fruit and the ground will yield its crops; the people will be secure in their land. They will know that I am the LORD, when I break the bars of their yoke and rescue them from the hands of those who enslaved them. [28] They will no longer be plundered by the nations, nor will wild animals devour them. They will live in safety, and no one will make them afraid. [29] I will provide for them a land renowned for its crops, and they will no longer be victims of famine in the land or bear the scorn of the nations. [30] Then they will know that I, the LORD their God, am with them and that they, the Israelites, are my people, declares the Sovereign LORD. [31] You are my sheep, the sheep of my pasture, and I am your God, declares the Sovereign LORD.'"

A Prophecy Against Edom

35 The word of the LORD came to me: [2] "Son of man, set your face against Mount Seir; prophesy against it [3] and say: 'This is what the Sovereign LORD says: I am against you, Mount Seir, and I will stretch out my hand against you and make you a desolate waste. [4] I will turn your towns into ruins and you will be desolate. Then you will know that I am the LORD.

[5] "'Because you harbored an ancient hostility and delivered the Israelites over to the sword at the time of their calamity, the time their punishment reached its climax, [6] therefore as surely as I live, declares the Sovereign LORD, I will give you over to bloodshed and it will pursue you. Since you did not hate bloodshed, bloodshed will pursue you. [7] I will make Mount Seir a desolate waste and cut off from it all who come and go. [8] I will fill your mountains with the slain; those killed by the sword will fall on your hills and in your valleys and in all your ravines. [9] I will make you desolate forever; your towns will not be inhabited. Then you will know that I am the LORD.

[10] "'Because you have said, "These two nations and countries will be ours and we

---

[a] 26 Or *I will cause them and the places surrounding my hill to be named in blessings* (see Gen. 48:20); or *I will cause them and the places surrounding my hill to be seen as blessed*

will take possession of them," even though I the LORD was there, ¹¹therefore as surely as I live, declares the Sovereign LORD, I will treat you in accordance with the anger and jealousy you showed in your hatred of them and I will make myself known among them when I judge you. ¹²Then you will know that I the LORD have heard all the contemptible things you have said against the mountains of Israel. You said, "They have been laid waste and have been given over to us to devour." ¹³You boasted against me and spoke against me without restraint, and I heard it. ¹⁴This is what the Sovereign LORD says: While the whole earth rejoices, I will make you desolate. ¹⁵Because you rejoiced when the inheritance of Israel became desolate, that is how I will treat you. You will be desolate, Mount Seir, you and all of Edom. Then they will know that I am the LORD.' "

Hope for the Mountains of Israel

36 "Son of man, prophesy to the mountains of Israel and say, 'Mountains of Israel, hear the word of the LORD. ²This is what the Sovereign LORD says: The enemy said of you, "Aha! The ancient heights have become our possession." ' ³Therefore prophesy and say, 'This is what the Sovereign LORD says: Because they ravaged and crushed you from every side so that you became the possession of the rest of the nations and the object of people's malicious talk and slander, ⁴therefore, mountains of Israel, hear the word of the Sovereign LORD: This is what the Sovereign LORD says to the mountains and hills, to the ravines and valleys, to the desolate ruins and the deserted towns that have been plundered and ridiculed by the rest of the nations around you— ⁵this is what the Sovereign LORD says: In my burning zeal I have spoken against the rest of the nations, and against all Edom, for with glee and with malice in their hearts they made my land their own possession so that they might plunder its pastureland.' ⁶Therefore prophesy concerning the land of Israel and say to the mountains and hills, to the ravines and valleys: 'This is what the Sovereign LORD says: I speak in my jealous wrath because you have suffered the scorn of the nations. ⁷Therefore this is what the Sovereign LORD says: I swear with uplifted hand that the nations around you will also suffer scorn.

⁸" 'But you, mountains of Israel, will produce branches and fruit for my people Israel, for they will soon come home. ⁹I am concerned for you and will look on you with favor; you will be plowed and sown, ¹⁰and I will cause many people to live on you—yes, all of Israel. The towns will be inhabited and the ruins rebuilt. ¹¹I will increase the number of people and animals living on you, and they will be fruitful and become numerous. I will settle people on you as in the past and will make you prosper more than before. Then you will know that I am the LORD. ¹²I will cause people, my people Israel, to live on you. They will possess you, and you will be their inheritance; you will never again deprive them of their children.

¹³" 'This is what the Sovereign LORD says: Because some say to you, "You devour people and deprive your nation of its children," ¹⁴therefore you will no longer devour people or make your nation childless, declares the Sovereign LORD. ¹⁵No longer will I make you hear the taunts of the nations, and no longer will you suffer the scorn of the peoples or cause your nation to fall, declares the Sovereign LORD.' "

Israel's Restoration Assured

¹⁶Again the word of the LORD came to me: ¹⁷"Son of man, when the people of Israel were living in their own land, they defiled it by their conduct and their actions. Their conduct was like a woman's monthly uncleanness in my sight. ¹⁸So I poured out my wrath on them because they had shed blood in the land and because they had defiled it with their idols. ¹⁹I dispersed them among the nations, and they were scattered through the countries; I judged them according to their conduct and their actions. ²⁰And wherever they went among the nations they profaned my holy name, for it was said of them, 'These are the LORD's people, and yet they had to leave his land.' ²¹I had concern for my holy name, which the people of Israel profaned among the nations where they had gone.

²²"Therefore say to the Israelites, 'This is what the Sovereign LORD says: It is not for your sake, people of Israel, that I am going to do these things, but for the sake of my holy name, which you have profaned among the nations where you have gone. ²³I will

show the holiness of my great name, which has been profaned among the nations, the name you have profaned among them. Then the nations will know that I am the LORD, declares the Sovereign LORD, when I am proved holy through you before their eyes.

²⁴ " 'For I will take you out of the nations; I will gather you from all the countries and bring you back into your own land. ²⁵I will sprinkle clean water on you, and you will be clean; I will cleanse you from all your impurities and from all your idols. ²⁶I will give you a new heart and put a new spirit in you; I will remove from you your heart of stone and give you a heart of flesh. ²⁷And I will put my Spirit in you and move you to follow my decrees and be careful to keep my laws. ²⁸Then you will live in the land I gave your ancestors; you will be my people, and I will be your God. ²⁹I will save you from all your uncleanness. I will call for the grain and make it plentiful and will not bring famine upon you. ³⁰I will increase the fruit of the trees and the crops of the field, so that you will no longer suffer disgrace among the nations because of famine. ³¹Then you will remember your evil ways and wicked deeds, and you will loathe yourselves for your sins and detestable practices. ³²I want you to know that I am not doing this for your sake, declares the Sovereign LORD. Be ashamed and disgraced for your conduct, people of Israel!

³³ " 'This is what the Sovereign LORD says: On the day I cleanse you from all your sins, I will resettle your towns, and the ruins will be rebuilt. ³⁴The desolate land will be cultivated instead of lying desolate in the sight of all who pass through it. ³⁵They will say, "This land that was laid waste has become like the garden of Eden; the cities that were lying in ruins, desolate and destroyed, are now fortified and inhabited." ³⁶Then the nations around you that remain will know that I the LORD have rebuilt what was destroyed and have replanted what was desolate. I the LORD have spoken, and I will do it.'

³⁷ "This is what the Sovereign LORD says: Once again I will yield to Israel's plea and do this for them: I will make their people as numerous as sheep, ³⁸as numerous as the flocks for offerings at Jerusalem during her appointed festivals. So will the ruined cities be filled with flocks of people. Then they will know that I am the LORD."

The Valley of Dry Bones

37 The hand of the LORD was on me, and he brought me out by the Spirit of the LORD and set me in the middle of a valley; it was full of bones. ²He led me back and forth among them, and I saw a great many bones on the floor of the valley, bones that were very dry. ³He asked me, "Son of man, can these bones live?"

I said, "Sovereign LORD, you alone know."

⁴Then he said to me, "Prophesy to these bones and say to them, 'Dry bones, hear the word of the LORD! ⁵This is what the Sovereign LORD says to these bones: I will make breath*ᵃ* enter you, and you will come to life. ⁶I will attach tendons to you and make flesh come upon you and cover you with skin; I will put breath in you, and you will come to life. Then you will know that I am the LORD.' "

⁷So I prophesied as I was commanded. And as I was prophesying, there was a noise, a rattling sound, and the bones came together, bone to bone. ⁸I looked, and tendons and flesh appeared on them and skin covered them, but there was no breath in them.

⁹Then he said to me, "Prophesy to the breath; prophesy, son of man, and say to it, 'This is what the Sovereign LORD says: Come, breath, from the four winds and breathe into these slain, that they may live.' " ¹⁰So I prophesied as he commanded me, and breath entered them; they came to life and stood up on their feet—a vast army.

¹¹Then he said to me: "Son of man, these bones are the people of Israel. They say, 'Our bones are dried up and our hope is gone; we are cut off.' ¹²Therefore prophesy and say to them: 'This is what the Sovereign LORD says: My people, I am going to open your graves and bring you up from them; I will bring you back to the land of Israel. ¹³Then you, my people, will know that I am the LORD, when I open your graves and bring you up from them. ¹⁴I will put my Spirit in you and you will live, and I will settle you in your own land. Then you will know that I the LORD have spoken, and I have done it, declares the LORD.' "

ᵃ 5 The Hebrew for this word can also mean *wind* or *spirit* (see verses 6-14).

One Nation Under One King

¹⁵The word of the LORD came to me: ¹⁶"Son of man, take a stick of wood and write on it, 'Belonging to Judah and the Israelites associated with him.' Then take another stick of wood, and write on it, 'Belonging to Joseph (that is, to Ephraim) and all the Israelites associated with him.' ¹⁷Join them together into one stick so that they will become one in your hand.

¹⁸"When your people ask you, 'Won't you tell us what you mean by this?' ¹⁹say to them, 'This is what the Sovereign LORD says: I am going to take the stick of Joseph—which is in Ephraim's hand—and of the Israelite tribes associated with him, and join it to Judah's stick. I will make them into a single stick of wood, and they will become one in my hand.' ²⁰Hold before their eyes the sticks you have written on ²¹and say to them, 'This is what the Sovereign LORD says: I will take the Israelites out of the nations where they have gone. I will gather them from all around and bring them back into their own land. ²²I will make them one nation in the land, on the mountains of Israel. There will be one king over all of them and they will never again be two nations or be divided into two kingdoms. ²³They will no longer defile themselves with their idols and vile images or with any of their offenses, for I will save them from all their sinful backsliding,^a and I will cleanse them. They will be my people, and I will be their God.

²⁴"'My servant David will be king over them, and they will all have one shepherd. They will follow my laws and be careful to keep my decrees. ²⁵They will live in the land I gave to my servant Jacob, the land where your ancestors lived. They and their children and their children's children will live there forever, and David my servant will be their prince forever. ²⁶I will make a covenant of peace with them; it will be an everlasting covenant. I will establish them and increase their numbers, and I will put my sanctuary among them forever. ²⁷My dwelling place will be with them; I will be their God, and they will be my people. ²⁸Then the nations will know that I the LORD make Israel holy, when my sanctuary is among them forever.'"

The Lord's Great Victory Over the Nations

38 The word of the LORD came to me: ²"Son of man, set your face against Gog, of the land of Magog, the chief prince of^b Meshek and Tubal; prophesy against him ³and say: 'This is what the Sovereign LORD says: I am against you, Gog, chief prince of^c Meshek and Tubal. ⁴I will turn you around, put hooks in your jaws and bring you out with your whole army—your horses, your horsemen fully armed, and a great horde with large and small shields, all of them brandishing their swords. ⁵Persia, Cush^d and Put will be with them, all with shields and helmets, ⁶also Gomer with all its troops, and Beth Togarmah from the far north with all its troops—the many nations with you.

⁷"'Get ready; be prepared, you and all the hordes gathered about you, and take command of them. ⁸After many days you will be called to arms. In future years you will invade a land that has recovered from war, whose people were gathered from many nations to the mountains of Israel, which had long been desolate. They had been brought out from the nations, and now all of them live in safety. ⁹You and all your troops and the many nations with you will go up, advancing like a storm; you will be like a cloud covering the land.

¹⁰"'This is what the Sovereign LORD says: On that day thoughts will come into your mind and you will devise an evil scheme. ¹¹You will say, "I will invade a land of unwalled villages; I will attack a peaceful and unsuspecting people—all of them living without walls and without gates and bars. ¹²I will plunder and loot and turn my hand against the resettled ruins and the people gathered from the nations, rich in livestock and goods, living at the center of the land.^e" ¹³Sheba and Dedan and the merchants of Tarshish and all her villages^f will say to you, "Have you come to plunder? Have you gathered your hordes to loot, to carry off silver and gold, to take away livestock and goods and to seize much plunder?"'

¹⁴"Therefore, son of man, prophesy and say to Gog: 'This is what the Sovereign LORD

---

^a 23 Many Hebrew manuscripts (see also Septuagint); most Hebrew manuscripts *all their dwelling places where they sinned*   ^b 2 Or *the prince of Rosh,*   ^c 3 Or *Gog, prince of Rosh,*   ^d 5 That is, the upper Nile region   ^e 12 The Hebrew for this phrase means *the navel of the earth.*   ^f 13 Or *her strong lions*

IN THE END

READ: EZEKIEL 38:3-4

First the prophet Ezekiel sees a vision of the Lord making a valley of dry bones rattle back to life (Ezekiel 37:1-14). Then God promises to raise up an eternal king from the line of David (15-28), a clear prediction of Jesus' arrival on earth. And now God offers a glimpse into a mighty battle at the end of time (38:1–39:29).

This prophecy says many nations will join a ruler named Gog to invade Israel. These troops will "be like a cloud covering the land" (38:9), coming from the north to plunder the nation. But the Lord will arise with fiery wrath, shaking the land and overturning mountains. He will pour hailstones and burning sulfur on the invaders. All this will happen so the world will see that God is in control. He proclaims that everyone will see his greatness and holiness, and know he is Lord (v. 23).

BUILDING FAITH WISDOM STRENGTH

This is an extraordinary battle. "After many days" and "in future years" (v. 8) are unusual terms that point to the final days of earth. At the end of the Bible, Gog shows up to march against God's people (Revelation 20:7-8). Though all the details aren't clear, this passage assures you of firm facts: At the end of time, God wins. Evil loses. So choose the right side.

says: In that day, when my people Israel are living in safety, will you not take notice of it? ¹⁵You will come from your place in the far north, you and many nations with you, all of them riding on horses, a great horde, a mighty army. ¹⁶You will advance against my people Israel like a cloud that covers the land. In days to come, Gog, I will bring you against my land, so that the nations may know me when I am proved holy through you before their eyes.

¹⁷"'This is what the Sovereign LORD says: You are the one I spoke of in former days by my servants the prophets of Israel. At that time they prophesied for years that I would bring you against them. ¹⁸This is what will happen in that day: When Gog attacks the land of Israel, my hot anger will be aroused, declares the Sovereign LORD. ¹⁹In my zeal and fiery wrath I declare that at that time there shall be a great earthquake in the land of Israel. ²⁰The fish in the sea, the birds in the sky, the beasts of the field, every creature that moves along the ground, and all the people on the face of the earth will tremble at my presence. The mountains will be overturned, the cliffs will crumble and every wall will fall to the ground. ²¹I will summon a sword against Gog on all my mountains, declares the Sovereign LORD. Every man's sword will be against his brother. ²²I will execute judgment on him with plague and bloodshed; I will pour down torrents of rain, hailstones and burning sulfur on him and on his troops and on the many nations with him. ²³And so I will show my greatness and my holiness, and I will make myself known in the sight of many nations. Then they will know that I am the LORD.'

39 "Son of man, prophesy against Gog and say: 'This is what the Sovereign LORD says: I am against you, Gog, chief prince of[a] Meshek and Tubal. ²I will turn you around and drag you along. I will bring you from the far north and send you against the mountains of Israel. ³Then I will strike your bow from your left hand and make your arrows drop from your right hand. ⁴On the mountains of Israel you will fall, you and all your troops and the nations with you. I will give you as food to all kinds of carrion birds and to the wild animals. ⁵You will

fall in the open field, for I have spoken, declares the Sovereign LORD. ⁶I will send fire on Magog and on those who live in safety in the coastlands, and they will know that I am the LORD.

⁷"'I will make known my holy name among my people Israel. I will no longer let my holy name be profaned, and the nations will know that I the LORD am the Holy One in Israel. ⁸It is coming! It will surely take place, declares the Sovereign LORD. This is the day I have spoken of.

⁹"'Then those who live in the towns of Israel will go out and use the weapons for fuel and burn them up — the small and large shields, the bows and arrows, the war clubs and spears. For seven years they will use them for fuel. ¹⁰They will not need to gather wood from the fields or cut it from the forests, because they will use the weapons for fuel. And they will plunder those who plundered them and loot those who looted them, declares the Sovereign LORD.

¹¹"'On that day I will give Gog a burial place in Israel, in the valley of those who travel east of the Sea. It will block the way of travelers, because Gog and all his hordes will be buried there. So it will be called the Valley of Hamon Gog.[b]

¹²"'For seven months the Israelites will be burying them in order to cleanse the land. ¹³All the people of the land will bury them, and the day I display my glory will be a memorable day for them, declares the Sovereign LORD. ¹⁴People will be continually employed in cleansing the land. They will spread out across the land and, along with others, they will bury any bodies that are lying on the ground.

"'After the seven months they will carry out a more detailed search. ¹⁵As they go through the land, anyone who sees a human bone will leave a marker beside it until the gravediggers bury it in the Valley of Hamon Gog, ¹⁶near a town called Hamonah.[c] And so they will cleanse the land.'

¹⁷"Son of man, this is what the Sovereign LORD says: Call out to every kind of bird and all the wild animals: 'Assemble and come together from all around to the sacrifice I am preparing for you, the great sacrifice on the mountains of Israel. There you will eat flesh

---

[a] 1 Or Gog, prince of Rosh,   [b] 11 Hamon Gog means hordes of Gog.   [c] 16 Hamonah means horde.

and drink blood. [18]You will eat the flesh of mighty men and drink the blood of the princes of the earth as if they were rams and lambs, goats and bulls — all of them fattened animals from Bashan. [19]At the sacrifice I am preparing for you, you will eat fat till you are glutted and drink blood till you are drunk. [20]At my table you will eat your fill of horses and riders, mighty men and soldiers of every kind,' declares the Sovereign LORD.

[21]"I will display my glory among the nations, and all the nations will see the punishment I inflict and the hand I lay on them. [22]From that day forward the people of Israel will know that I am the LORD their God. [23]And the nations will know that the people of Israel went into exile for their sin, because they were unfaithful to me. So I hid my face from them and handed them over to their enemies, and they all fell by the sword. [24]I dealt with them according to their uncleanness and their offenses, and I hid my face from them.

[25]"Therefore this is what the Sovereign LORD says: I will now restore the fortunes of Jacob[a] and will have compassion on all the people of Israel, and I will be zealous for my holy name. [26]They will forget their shame and all the unfaithfulness they showed toward me when they lived in safety in their land with no one to make them afraid. [27]When I have brought them back from the nations and have gathered them from the countries of their enemies, I will be proved holy through them in the sight of many nations. [28]Then they will know that I am the LORD their God, for though I sent them into exile among the nations, I will gather them to their own land, not leaving any behind. [29]I will no longer hide my face from them, for I will pour out my Spirit on the people of Israel, declares the Sovereign LORD."

The Temple Area Restored

40 In the twenty-fifth year of our exile, at the beginning of the year, on the tenth of the month, in the fourteenth year after the fall of the city — on that very day the hand of the LORD was on me and he took me there. [2]In visions of God he took me to the land of Israel and set me on a very high mountain, on whose south side were some buildings that looked like a city. [3]He took me there, and I saw a man whose appearance was like bronze; he was standing in the gateway with a linen cord and a measuring rod in his hand. [4]The man said to me, "Son of man, look carefully and listen closely and pay attention to everything I am going to show you, for that is why you have been brought here. Tell the people of Israel everything you see."

The East Gate to the Outer Court

[5]I saw a wall completely surrounding the temple area. The length of the measuring rod in the man's hand was six long cubits,[b] each of which was a cubit and a handbreadth. He measured the wall; it was one measuring rod thick and one rod high.

[6]Then he went to the east gate. He climbed its steps and measured the threshold of the gate; it was one rod deep. [7]The alcoves for the guards were one rod long and one rod wide, and the projecting walls between the alcoves were five cubits[c] thick. And the threshold of the gate next to the portico facing the temple was one rod deep.

[8]Then he measured the portico of the gateway; [9]it[d] was eight cubits[e] deep and its jambs were two cubits[f] thick. The portico of the gateway faced the temple.

[10]Inside the east gate were three alcoves on each side; the three had the same measurements, and the faces of the projecting walls on each side had the same measurements. [11]Then he measured the width of the entrance of the gateway; it was ten cubits and its length was thirteen cubits.[g] [12]In front of each alcove was a wall one cubit high, and the alcoves were six cubits square. [13]Then he measured the gateway from the top of the rear wall of one alcove to the top of the opposite one; the distance was twenty-five

---

[a] 25 Or *now bring Jacob back from captivity*   [b] 5 That is, about 11 feet or about 3.2 meters; also in verse 12. The long cubit of about 21 inches or about 53 centimeters is the basic unit of measurement of length throughout chapters 40 – 48.   [c] 7 That is, about 8 3/4 feet or about 2.7 meters; also in verse 48   [d] 8,9 Many Hebrew manuscripts, Septuagint, Vulgate and Syriac; most Hebrew manuscripts *gateway facing the temple; it was one rod deep.* [9]*Then he measured the portico of the gateway; it*   [e] 9 That is, about 14 feet or about 4.2 meters   [f] 9 That is, about 3 1/2 feet or about 1 meter   [g] 11 That is, about 18 feet wide and 23 feet long or about 5.3 meters wide and 6.9 meters long

cubits*a* from one parapet opening to the opposite one. ¹⁴He measured along the faces of the projecting walls all around the inside of the gateway — sixty cubits.*b* The measurement was up to the portico*c* facing the courtyard.*d* ¹⁵The distance from the entrance of the gateway to the far end of its portico was fifty cubits.*e* ¹⁶The alcoves and the projecting walls inside the gateway were surmounted by narrow parapet openings all around, as was the portico; the openings all around faced inward. The faces of the projecting walls were decorated with palm trees.

The Outer Court

¹⁷Then he brought me into the outer court. There I saw some rooms and a pavement that had been constructed all around the court; there were thirty rooms along the pavement. ¹⁸It abutted the sides of the gateways and was as wide as they were long; this was the lower pavement. ¹⁹Then he measured the distance from the inside of the lower gateway to the outside of the inner court; it was a hundred cubits*f* on the east side as well as on the north.

The North Gate

²⁰Then he measured the length and width of the north gate, leading into the outer court. ²¹Its alcoves — three on each side — its projecting walls and its portico had the same measurements as those of the first gateway. It was fifty cubits long and twenty-five cubits wide. ²²Its openings, its portico and its palm tree decorations had the same measurements as those of the gate facing east. Seven steps led up to it, with its portico opposite them. ²³There was a gate to the inner court facing the north gate, just as there was on the east. He measured from one gate to the opposite one; it was a hundred cubits.

The South Gate

²⁴Then he led me to the south side and I saw the south gate. He measured its jambs and its portico, and they had the same measurements as the others. ²⁵The gateway and its portico had narrow openings all around, like the openings of the others. It was fifty cubits long and twenty-five cubits wide. ²⁶Seven steps led up to it, with its portico opposite them; it had palm tree decorations on the faces of the projecting walls on each side. ²⁷The inner court also had a gate facing south, and he measured from this gate to the outer gate on the south side; it was a hundred cubits.

The Gates to the Inner Court

²⁸Then he brought me into the inner court through the south gate, and he measured the south gate; it had the same measurements as the others. ²⁹Its alcoves, its projecting walls and its portico had the same measurements as the others. The gateway and its portico had openings all around. It was fifty cubits long and twenty-five cubits wide. ³⁰(The porticoes of the gateways around the inner court were twenty-five cubits wide and five cubits deep.) ³¹Its portico faced the outer court; palm trees decorated its jambs, and eight steps led up to it.

³²Then he brought me to the inner court on the east side, and he measured the gateway; it had the same measurements as the others. ³³Its alcoves, its projecting walls and its portico had the same measurements as the others. The gateway and its portico had openings all around. It was fifty cubits long and twenty-five cubits wide. ³⁴Its portico faced the outer court; palm trees decorated the jambs on either side, and eight steps led up to it.

³⁵Then he brought me to the north gate and measured it. It had the same measurements as the others, ³⁶as did its alcoves, its projecting walls and its portico, and it had openings all around. It was fifty cubits long and twenty-five cubits wide. ³⁷Its portico*g* faced the outer court; palm trees decorated the jambs on either side, and eight steps led up to it.

The Rooms for Preparing Sacrifices

³⁸A room with a doorway was by the portico in each of the inner gateways, where the burnt offerings were washed. ³⁹In the

---

a *13* That is, about 44 feet or about 13 meters; also in verses 21, 25, 29, 30, 33 and 36   *b* *14* That is, about 105 feet or about 32 meters   *c* *14* Septuagint; Hebrew *projecting wall*   *d* *14* The meaning of the Hebrew for this verse is uncertain.   *e* *15* That is, about 88 feet or about 27 meters; also in verses 21, 25, 29, 33 and 36   *f* *19* That is, about 175 feet or about 53 meters; also in verses 23, 27 and 47   *g* *37* Septuagint (see also verses 31 and 34); Hebrew *jambs* portico of the gateway were two tables on each side, on which the burnt offerings, sin offerings[a] and guilt offerings were slaughtered. [40]By the outside wall of the portico of the gateway, near the steps at the entrance of the north gateway were two tables, and on the other side of the steps were two tables. [41]So there were four tables on one side of the gateway and four on the other—eight tables in all—on which the sacrifices were slaughtered. [42]There were also four tables of dressed stone for the burnt offerings, each a cubit and a half long, a cubit and a half wide and a cubit high.[b] On them were placed the utensils for slaughtering the burnt offerings and the other sacrifices. [43]And double-pronged hooks, each a handbreadth[c] long, were attached to the wall all around. The tables were for the flesh of the offerings.

The Rooms for the Priests

[44]Outside the inner gate, within the inner court, were two rooms, one[d] at the side of the north gate and facing south, and another at the side of the south[e] gate and facing north. [45]He said to me, "The room facing south is for the priests who guard the temple, [46]and the room facing north is for the priests who guard the altar. These are the sons of Zadok, who are the only Levites who may draw near to the LORD to minister before him."

[47]Then he measured the court: It was square—a hundred cubits long and a hundred cubits wide. And the altar was in front of the temple.

The New Temple

[48]He brought me to the portico of the temple and measured the jambs of the portico; they were five cubits wide on either side. The width of the entrance was fourteen cubits[f] and its projecting walls were[g] three cubits[h] wide on either side. [49]The portico was twenty cubits[i] wide, and twelve[j] cubits[k] from front to back. It was reached by a flight of stairs,[l] and there were pillars on each side of the jambs.

41 Then the man brought me to the main hall and measured the jambs; the width of the jambs was six cubits[m] on each side.[n] [2]The entrance was ten cubits[o] wide, and the projecting walls on each side of it were five cubits[p] wide. He also measured the main hall; it was forty cubits long and twenty cubits wide.[q]

[3]Then he went into the inner sanctuary and measured the jambs of the entrance; each was two cubits[r] wide. The entrance was six cubits wide, and the projecting walls on each side of it were seven cubits[s] wide. [4]And he measured the length of the inner sanctuary; it was twenty cubits, and its width was twenty cubits across the end of the main hall. He said to me, "This is the Most Holy Place."

[5]Then he measured the wall of the temple; it was six cubits thick, and each side room around the temple was four cubits[t] wide. [6]The side rooms were on three levels, one above another, thirty on each level. There were ledges all around the wall of the temple to serve as supports for the side rooms, so that the supports were not inserted into the wall of the temple. [7]The side rooms all around the temple were wider at each successive level. The structure surrounding the temple was built in ascending stages, so that the rooms widened as one went upward. A stairway went up from the lowest floor to the top floor through the middle floor.

[8]I saw that the temple had a raised base all around it, forming the foundation of the side rooms. It was the length of the rod, six long cubits. [9]The outer wall of the side rooms was five cubits thick. The open area between the side rooms of the temple [10]and

---

[a] 39 Or *purification offerings*   [b] 42 That is, about 2 2/3 feet long and wide and 21 inches high or about 80 centimeters long and wide and 53 centimeters high   [c] 43 That is, about 3 1/2 inches or about 9 centimeters   [d] 44 Septuagint; Hebrew *were rooms for singers, which were*   [e] 44 Septuagint; Hebrew *east*   [f] 48 That is, about 25 feet or about 7.4 meters   [g] 48 Septuagint; Hebrew *entrance was*   [h] 48 That is, about 5 1/4 feet or about 1.6 meters   [i] 49 That is, about 35 feet or about 11 meters   [j] 49 Septuagint; Hebrew *eleven*   [k] 49 That is, about 21 feet or about 6.4 meters   [l] 49 Hebrew; Septuagint *Ten steps led up to it*   [m] 1 That is, about 11 feet or about 3.2 meters; also in verses 3, 5 and 8   [n] 1 One Hebrew manuscript and Septuagint; most Hebrew manuscripts *side, the width of the tent*   [o] 2 That is, about 18 feet or about 5.3 meters   [p] 2 That is, about 8 3/4 feet or about 2.7 meters; also in verses 9, 11 and 12   [q] 2 That is, about 70 feet long and 35 feet wide or about 21 meters long and 11 meters wide   [r] 3 That is, about 3 1/2 feet or about 1.1 meters; also in verse 22   [s] 3 That is, about 12 feet or about 3.7 meters   [t] 5 That is, about 7 feet or about 2.1 meters

the priests' rooms was twenty cubits wide all around the temple. [11]There were entrances to the side rooms from the open area, one on the north and another on the south; and the base adjoining the open area was five cubits wide all around.

[12]The building facing the temple courtyard on the west side was seventy cubits[a] wide. The wall of the building was five cubits thick all around, and its length was ninety cubits.[b]

[13]Then he measured the temple; it was a hundred cubits[c] long, and the temple courtyard and the building with its walls were also a hundred cubits long. [14]The width of the temple courtyard on the east, including the front of the temple, was a hundred cubits.

[15]Then he measured the length of the building facing the courtyard at the rear of the temple, including its galleries on each side; it was a hundred cubits.

The main hall, the inner sanctuary and the portico facing the court, [16]as well as the thresholds and the narrow windows and galleries around the three of them — everything beyond and including the threshold was covered with wood. The floor, the wall up to the windows, and the windows were covered. [17]In the space above the outside of the entrance to the inner sanctuary and on the walls at regular intervals all around the inner and outer sanctuary [18]were carved cherubim and palm trees. Palm trees alternated with cherubim. Each cherub had two faces: [19]the face of a human being toward the palm tree on one side and the face of a lion toward the palm tree on the other. They were carved all around the whole temple. [20]From the floor to the area above the entrance, cherubim and palm trees were carved on the wall of the main hall.

[21]The main hall had a rectangular doorframe, and the one at the front of the Most Holy Place was similar. [22]There was a wooden altar three cubits[d] high and two cubits square[e]; its corners, its base[f] and its sides were of wood. The man said to me, "This is

the table that is before the LORD." [23]Both the main hall and the Most Holy Place had double doors. [24]Each door had two leaves — two hinged leaves for each door. [25]And on the doors of the main hall were carved cherubim and palm trees like those carved on the walls, and there was a wooden overhang on the front of the portico. [26]On the sidewalls of the portico were narrow windows with palm trees carved on each side. The side rooms of the temple also had overhangs.

The Rooms for the Priests

42 Then the man led me northward into the outer court and brought me to the rooms opposite the temple courtyard and opposite the outer wall on the north side. [2]The building whose door faced north was a hundred cubits long and fifty cubits wide.[g] [3]Both in the section twenty cubits[h] from the inner court and in the section opposite the pavement of the outer court, gallery faced gallery at the three levels. [4]In front of the rooms was an inner passageway ten cubits wide and a hundred cubits[i] long.[j] Their doors were on the north. [5]Now the upper rooms were narrower, for the galleries took more space from them than from the rooms on the lower and middle floors of the building. [6]The rooms on the top floor had no pillars, as the courts had; so they were smaller in floor space than those on the lower and middle floors. [7]There was an outer wall parallel to the rooms and the outer court; it extended in front of the rooms for fifty cubits. [8]While the row of rooms on the side next to the outer court was fifty cubits long, the row on the side nearest the sanctuary was a hundred cubits long. [9]The lower rooms had an entrance on the east side as one enters them from the outer court.

[10]On the south side[k] along the length of the wall of the outer court, adjoining the temple courtyard and opposite the outer wall, were rooms [11]with a passageway in front of them. These were like the rooms on the north; they had the same length and width, with similar exits and dimensions.

---

[a] 12 That is, about 123 feet or about 37 meters   [b] 12 That is, about 158 feet or about 48 meters
[c] 13 That is, about 175 feet or about 53 meters; also in verses 14 and 15   [d] 22 That is, about 5 1/4 feet or about 1.5 meters   [e] 22 Septuagint; Hebrew long   [f] 22 Septuagint; Hebrew length   [g] 2 That is, about 175 feet long and 88 feet wide or about 53 meters long and 27 meters wide   [h] 3 That is, about 35 feet or about 11 meters   [i] 4 Septuagint and Syriac; Hebrew and one cubit   [j] 4 That is, about 18 feet wide and 175 feet long or about 5.3 meters wide and 53 meters long   [k] 10 Septuagint; Hebrew Eastward

Similar to the doorways on the north [12]were the doorways of the rooms on the south. There was a doorway at the beginning of the passageway that was parallel to the corresponding wall extending eastward, by which one enters the rooms.

[13]Then he said to me, "The north and south rooms facing the temple courtyard are the priests' rooms, where the priests who approach the LORD will eat the most holy offerings. There they will put the most holy offerings — the grain offerings, the sin offerings[a] and the guilt offerings — for the place is holy. [14]Once the priests enter the holy precincts, they are not to go into the outer court until they leave behind the garments in which they minister, for these are holy. They are to put on other clothes before they go near the places that are for the people."

[15]When he had finished measuring what was inside the temple area, he led me out by the east gate and measured the area all around: [16]He measured the east side with the measuring rod; it was five hundred cubits.[b,c] [17]He measured the north side; it was five hundred cubits[d] by the measuring rod. [18]He measured the south side; it was five hundred cubits by the measuring rod. [19]Then he turned to the west side and measured; it was five hundred cubits by the measuring rod. [20]So he measured the area on all four sides. It had a wall around it, five hundred cubits long and five hundred cubits wide, to separate the holy from the common.

God's Glory Returns to the Temple

43 Then the man brought me to the gate facing east, [2]and I saw the glory of the God of Israel coming from the east. His voice was like the roar of rushing waters, and the land was radiant with his glory. [3]The vision I saw was like the vision I had seen when he[e] came to destroy the city and like the visions I had seen by the Kebar River, and I fell facedown. [4]The glory of the LORD entered the temple through the gate facing east. [5]Then

the Spirit lifted me up and brought me into the inner court, and the glory of the LORD filled the temple.

[6]While the man was standing beside me, I heard someone speaking to me from inside the temple. [7]He said: "Son of man, this is the place of my throne and the place for the soles of my feet. This is where I will live among the Israelites forever. The people of Israel will never again defile my holy name — neither they nor their kings — by their prostitution and the funeral offerings[f] for their kings at their death.[g] [8]When they placed their threshold next to my threshold and their doorposts beside my doorposts, with only a wall between me and them, they defiled my holy name by their detestable practices. So I destroyed them in my anger. [9]Now let them put away from me their prostitution and the funeral offerings for their kings, and I will live among them forever.

[10]"Son of man, describe the temple to the people of Israel, that they may be ashamed of their sins. Let them consider its perfection, [11]and if they are ashamed of all they have done, make known to them the design of the temple — its arrangement, its exits and entrances — its whole design and all its regulations[h] and laws. Write these down before them so that they may be faithful to its design and follow all its regulations.

[12]"This is the law of the temple: All the surrounding area on top of the mountain will be most holy. Such is the law of the temple.

The Great Altar Restored

[13]"These are the measurements of the altar in long cubits,[i] that cubit being a cubit and a handbreadth: Its gutter is a cubit deep and a cubit wide, with a rim of one span[j] around the edge. And this is the height of the altar: [14]From the gutter on the ground up to the lower ledge that goes around the altar it is two cubits high, and the ledge is a cubit wide.[k] From this lower ledge to the upper ledge that goes around the altar it is four

---

[a] 13 Or *purification offerings*   [b] 16 See Septuagint of verse 17; Hebrew *rods*; also in verses 18 and 19.
[c] 16 Five hundred cubits equal about 875 feet or about 265 meters; also in verses 17, 18 and 19.
[d] 17 Septuagint; Hebrew *rods*   [e] 3 Some Hebrew manuscripts and Vulgate; most Hebrew manuscripts *I*
[f] 7 Or *the memorial monuments*; also in verse 9   [g] 7 Or *their high places*   [h] 11 Some Hebrew
manuscripts and Septuagint; most Hebrew manuscripts *regulations and its whole design*   [i] 13 That is,
about 21 inches or about 53 centimeters; also in verses 14 and 17. The long cubit is the basic unit for linear
measurement throughout Ezekiel 40-48.   [j] 13 That is, about 11 inches or about 27 centimeters
[k] 14 That is, about 3 1/2 feet high and 1 3/4 feet wide or about 105 centimeters high and 53 centimeters wide

cubits high, and that ledge is also a cubit wide.*ᵃ* ¹⁵Above that, the altar hearth is four cubits high, and four horns project upward from the hearth. ¹⁶The altar hearth is square, twelve cubits*ᵇ* long and twelve cubits wide. ¹⁷The upper ledge also is square, fourteen cubits*ᶜ* long and fourteen cubits wide. All around the altar is a gutter of one cubit with a rim of half a cubit.*ᵈ* The steps of the altar face east."

¹⁸Then he said to me, "Son of man, this is what the Sovereign LORD says: These will be the regulations for sacrificing burnt offerings and splashing blood against the altar when it is built: ¹⁹You are to give a young bull as a sin offering*ᵉ* to the Levitical priests of the family of Zadok, who come near to minister before me, declares the Sovereign LORD. ²⁰You are to take some of its blood and put it on the four horns of the altar and on the four corners of the upper ledge and all around the rim, and so purify the altar and make atonement for it. ²¹You are to take the bull for the sin offering and burn it in the designated part of the temple area outside the sanctuary.

²²"On the second day you are to offer a male goat without defect for a sin offering, and the altar is to be purified as it was purified with the bull. ²³When you have finished purifying it, you are to offer a young bull and a ram from the flock, both without defect. ²⁴You are to offer them before the LORD, and the priests are to sprinkle salt on them and sacrifice them as a burnt offering to the LORD.

²⁵"For seven days you are to provide a male goat daily for a sin offering; you are also to provide a young bull and a ram from the flock, both without defect. ²⁶For seven days they are to make atonement for the altar and cleanse it; thus they will dedicate it. ²⁷At the end of these days, from the eighth day on, the priests are to present your burnt offerings and fellowship offerings on the altar. Then I will accept you, declares the Sovereign LORD."

The Priesthood Restored

44 Then the man brought me back to the outer gate of the sanctuary, the one facing east, and it was shut. ²The LORD said to me, "This gate is to remain shut. It must not be opened; no one may enter through it. It is to remain shut because the LORD, the God of Israel, has entered through it. ³The prince himself is the only one who may sit inside the gateway to eat in the presence of the LORD. He is to enter by way of the portico of the gateway and go out the same way."

⁴Then the man brought me by way of the north gate to the front of the temple. I looked and saw the glory of the LORD filling the temple of the LORD, and I fell facedown.

⁵The LORD said to me, "Son of man, look carefully, listen closely and give attention to everything I tell you concerning all the regulations and instructions regarding the temple of the LORD. Give attention to the entrance to the temple and all the exits of the sanctuary. ⁶Say to rebellious Israel, 'This is what the Sovereign LORD says: Enough of your detestable practices, people of Israel! ⁷In addition to all your other detestable practices, you brought foreigners uncircumcised in heart and flesh into my sanctuary, desecrating my temple while you offered me food, fat and blood, and you broke my covenant. ⁸Instead of carrying out your duty in regard to my holy things, you put others in charge of my sanctuary. ⁹This is what the Sovereign LORD says: No foreigner uncircumcised in heart and flesh is to enter my sanctuary, not even the foreigners who live among the Israelites.

¹⁰"'The Levites who went far from me when Israel went astray and who wandered from me after their idols must bear the consequences of their sin. ¹¹They may serve in my sanctuary, having charge of the gates of the temple and serving in it; they may slaughter the burnt offerings and sacrifices for the people and stand before the people and serve them. ¹²But because they served them in the presence of their idols and made the people of Israel fall into sin, therefore I have sworn with uplifted hand that they must bear the consequences of their sin, declares the Sovereign LORD. ¹³They are not to come near to serve me as priests or come near any of my holy things or my most holy offerings; they must bear the shame of their

---

ᵃ 14 That is, about 7 feet high and 1 3/4 feet wide or about 2.1 meters high and 53 centimeters wide   *ᵇ 16* That is, about 21 feet or about 6.4 meters   *ᶜ 17* That is, about 25 feet or about 7.4 meters   *ᵈ 17* That is, about 11 inches or about 27 centimeters   *ᵉ 19* Or *purification offering; also in verses 21, 22 and 25* detestable practices. [14]And I will appoint them to guard the temple for all the work that is to be done in it.

[15] " 'But the Levitical priests, who are descendants of Zadok and who guarded my sanctuary when the Israelites went astray from me, are to come near to minister before me; they are to stand before me to offer sacrifices of fat and blood, declares the Sovereign LORD. [16]They alone are to enter my sanctuary; they alone are to come near my table to minister before me and serve me as guards.

[17] " 'When they enter the gates of the inner court, they are to wear linen clothes; they must not wear any woolen garment while ministering at the gates of the inner court or inside the temple. [18]They are to wear linen turbans on their heads and linen undergarments around their waists. They must not wear anything that makes them perspire. [19]When they go out into the outer court where the people are, they are to take off the clothes they have been ministering in and are to leave them in the sacred rooms, and put on other clothes, so that the people are not consecrated through contact with their garments.

[20] " 'They must not shave their heads or let their hair grow long, but they are to keep the hair of their heads trimmed. [21]No priest is to drink wine when he enters the inner court. [22]They must not marry widows or divorced women; they may marry only virgins of Israelite descent or widows of priests. [23]They are to teach my people the difference between the holy and the common and show them how to distinguish between the unclean and the clean.

[24] " 'In any dispute, the priests are to serve as judges and decide it according to my ordinances. They are to keep my laws and my decrees for all my appointed festivals, and they are to keep my Sabbaths holy.

[25] " 'A priest must not defile himself by going near a dead person; however, if the dead person was his father or mother, son or daughter, brother or unmarried sister, then he may defile himself. [26]After he is cleansed, he must wait seven days. [27]On the day he goes into the inner court of the sanctuary to minister in the sanctuary, he is to offer a sin offering[a] for himself, declares the Sovereign LORD.

[28] " 'I am to be the only inheritance the priests have. You are to give them no possession in Israel; I will be their possession. [29]They will eat the grain offerings, the sin offerings and the guilt offerings; and everything in Israel devoted[b] to the LORD will belong to them. [30]The best of all the firstfruits and of all your special gifts will belong to the priests. You are to give them the first portion of your ground meal so that a blessing may rest on your household. [31]The priests must not eat anything, whether bird or animal, found dead or torn by wild animals.

Israel Fully Restored

45 " 'When you allot the land as an inheritance, you are to present to the LORD a portion of the land as a sacred district, 25,000 cubits[c] long and 20,000[d] cubits[e] wide; the entire area will be holy. [2]Of this, a section 500 cubits[f] square is to be for the sanctuary, with 50 cubits[g] around it for open land. [3]In the sacred district, measure off a section 25,000 cubits long and 10,000 cubits[h] wide. In it will be the sanctuary, the Most Holy Place. [4]It will be the sacred portion of the land for the priests, who minister in the sanctuary and who draw near to minister before the LORD. It will be a place for their houses as well as a holy place for the sanctuary. [5]An area 25,000 cubits long and 10,000 cubits wide will belong to the Levites, who serve in the temple, as their possession for towns to live in.[i]

[6] " 'You are to give the city as its property an area 5,000 cubits[j] wide and 25,000 cubits long, adjoining the sacred portion; it will belong to all Israel.

[7] " 'The prince will have the land bordering each side of the area formed by the sacred district and the property of the city. It will extend westward from the west side and

---

[a] 27 Or *purification offering*; also in verse 29   [b] 29 The Hebrew term refers to the irrevocable giving over of things or persons to the LORD.   [c] 1 That is, about 8 miles or about 13 kilometers; also in verses 3, 5 and 6   [d] 1 Septuagint (see also verses 3 and 5 and 48:9); Hebrew *10,000*   [e] 1 That is, about 6 1/2 miles or about 11 kilometers   [f] 2 That is, about 875 feet or about 265 meters   [g] 2 That is, about 88 feet or about 27 meters   [h] 3 That is, about 3 1/3 miles or about 5.3 kilometers; also in verse 5   [i] 5 Septuagint; Hebrew *temple; they will have as their possession 20 rooms*   [j] 6 That is, about 1 2/3 miles or about 2.7 kilometers

eastward from the east side, running lengthwise from the western to the eastern border parallel to one of the tribal portions. ⁸This land will be his possession in Israel. And my princes will no longer oppress my people but will allow the people of Israel to possess the land according to their tribes.

⁹ " 'This is what the Sovereign LORD says: You have gone far enough, princes of Israel! Give up your violence and oppression and do what is just and right. Stop dispossessing my people, declares the Sovereign LORD. ¹⁰You are to use accurate scales, an accurate ephah[a] and an accurate bath.[b] ¹¹The ephah and the bath are to be the same size, the bath containing a tenth of a homer and the ephah a tenth of a homer; the homer is to be the standard measure for both. ¹²The shekel[c] is to consist of twenty gerahs. Twenty shekels plus twenty-five shekels plus fifteen shekels equal one mina.[d]

¹³ " 'This is the special gift you are to offer: a sixth of an ephah[e] from each homer of wheat and a sixth of an ephah[f] from each homer of barley. ¹⁴The prescribed portion of olive oil, measured by the bath, is a tenth of a bath[g] from each cor (which consists of ten baths or one homer, for ten baths are equivalent to a homer). ¹⁵Also one sheep is to be taken from every flock of two hundred from the well-watered pastures of Israel. These will be used for the grain offerings, burnt offerings and fellowship offerings to make atonement for the people, declares the Sovereign LORD. ¹⁶All the people of the land will be required to give this special offering to the prince in Israel. ¹⁷It will be the duty of the prince to provide the burnt offerings, grain offerings and drink offerings at the festivals, the New Moons and the Sabbaths — at all the appointed festivals of Israel. He will provide the sin offerings,[h] grain offerings, burnt offerings and fellowship offerings to make atonement for the Israelites.

¹⁸ " 'This is what the Sovereign LORD says: In the first month on the first day you are to take a young bull without defect and purify the sanctuary. ¹⁹The priest is to take some of the blood of the sin offering and put it on the doorposts of the temple, on the four corners of the upper ledge of the altar and on the gateposts of the inner court. ²⁰You are to do the same on the seventh day of the month for anyone who sins unintentionally or through ignorance; so you are to make atonement for the temple.

²¹ " 'In the first month on the fourteenth day you are to observe the Passover, a festival lasting seven days, during which you shall eat bread made without yeast. ²²On that day the prince is to provide a bull as a sin offering for himself and for all the people of the land. ²³Every day during the seven days of the festival he is to provide seven bulls and seven rams without defect as a burnt offering to the LORD, and a male goat for a sin offering. ²⁴He is to provide as a grain offering an ephah for each bull and an ephah for each ram, along with a hin[i] of olive oil for each ephah.

²⁵ " 'During the seven days of the festival, which begins in the seventh month on the fifteenth day, he is to make the same provision for sin offerings, burnt offerings, grain offerings and oil.

46 " 'This is what the Sovereign LORD says: The gate of the inner court facing east is to be shut on the six working days, but on the Sabbath day and on the day of the New Moon it is to be opened. ²The prince is to enter from the outside through the portico of the gateway and stand by the gatepost. The priests are to sacrifice his burnt offering and his fellowship offerings. He is to bow down in worship at the threshold of the gateway and then go out, but the gate will not be shut until evening. ³On the Sabbaths and New Moons the people of the land are to worship in the presence of the LORD at the entrance of that gateway. ⁴The burnt offering the prince brings to the LORD on the Sabbath day is to be six male lambs and a ram, all without defect. ⁵The grain offering given with the ram is to be an

---

a 10 An ephah was a dry measure having the capacity of about 3/5 bushel or about 22 liters.   *b 10* A bath was a liquid measure equaling about 6 gallons or about 22 liters.   *c 12* A shekel weighed about 2/5 ounce or about 12 grams.   *d 12* That is, 60 shekels; the common mina was 50 shekels. Sixty shekels were about 1 1/2 pounds or about 690 grams.   *e 13* That is, probably about 6 pounds or about 2.7 kilograms *f 13* That is, probably about 5 pounds or about 2.3 kilograms   *g 14* That is, about 2 1/2 quarts or about 2.2 liters   *h 17* Or *purification offerings*; also in verses 19, 22, 23 and 25   *i 24* That is, about 1 gallon or about 3.8 liters ephah,[a] and the grain offering with the lambs is to be as much as he pleases, along with a hin[b] of olive oil for each ephah. [6]On the day of the New Moon he is to offer a young bull, six lambs and a ram, all without defect. [7]He is to provide as a grain offering one ephah with the bull, one ephah with the ram, and with the lambs as much as he wants to give, along with a hin of oil for each ephah. [8]When the prince enters, he is to go in through the portico of the gateway, and he is to come out the same way.

[9]"'When the people of the land come before the LORD at the appointed festivals, whoever enters by the north gate to worship is to go out the south gate; and whoever enters by the south gate is to go out the north gate. No one is to return through the gate by which they entered, but each is to go out the opposite gate. [10]The prince is to be among them, going in when they go in and going out when they go out. [11]At the feasts and the appointed festivals, the grain offering is to be an ephah with a bull, an ephah with a ram, and with the lambs as much as he pleases, along with a hin of oil for each ephah.

[12]"'When the prince provides a freewill offering to the LORD—whether a burnt offering or fellowship offerings—the gate facing east is to be opened for him. He shall offer his burnt offering or his fellowship offerings as he does on the Sabbath day. Then he shall go out, and after he has gone out, the gate will be shut.

[13]"'Every day you are to provide a year-old lamb without defect for a burnt offering to the LORD; morning by morning you shall provide it. [14]You are also to provide with it morning by morning a grain offering, consisting of a sixth of an ephah[c] with a third of a hin[d] of oil to moisten the flour. The presenting of this grain offering to the LORD is a lasting ordinance. [15]So the lamb and the grain offering and the oil shall be provided morning by morning for a regular burnt offering.

[16]"'This is what the Sovereign LORD says: If the prince makes a gift from his inheritance to one of his sons, it will also belong to his descendants; it is to be their property by inheritance. [17]If, however, he makes a gift from his inheritance to one of his servants, the servant may keep it until the year of freedom; then it will revert to the prince. His inheritance belongs to his sons only; it is theirs. [18]The prince must not take any of the inheritance of the people, driving them off their property. He is to give his sons their inheritance out of his own property, so that not one of my people will be separated from their property.'"

[19]Then the man brought me through the entrance at the side of the gate to the sacred rooms facing north, which belonged to the priests, and showed me a place at the western end. [20]He said to me, "This is the place where the priests are to cook the guilt offering and the sin offering[e] and bake the grain offering, to avoid bringing them into the outer court and consecrating the people."

[21]He then brought me to the outer court and led me around to its four corners, and I saw in each corner another court. [22]In the four corners of the outer court were enclosed[f] courts, forty cubits long and thirty cubits wide;[g] each of the courts in the four corners was the same size. [23]Around the inside of each of the four courts was a ledge of stone, with places for fire built all around under the ledge. [24]He said to me, "These are the kitchens where those who minister at the temple are to cook the sacrifices of the people."

The River From the Temple

47 The man brought me back to the entrance to the temple, and I saw water coming out from under the threshold of the temple toward the east (for the temple faced east). The water was coming down from under the south side of the temple, south of the altar. [2]He then brought me out through the north gate and led me around the outside to the outer gate facing east, and the water was trickling from the south side.

[3]As the man went eastward with a measuring line in his hand, he measured off a

---

[a] 5 That is, probably about 35 pounds or about 16 kilograms; also in verses 7 and 11   [b] 5 That is, about 1 gallon or about 3.8 liters; also in verses 7 and 11   [c] 14 That is, probably about 6 pounds or about 2.7 kilograms   [d] 14 That is, about 1 1/2 quarts or about 1.3 liters   [e] 20 Or *purification offering*   [f] 22 The meaning of the Hebrew for this word is uncertain.   [g] 22 That is, about 70 feet long and 53 feet wide or about 21 meters long and 16 meters wide

thousand cubits[a] and then led me through water that was ankle-deep. [4]He measured off another thousand cubits and led me through water that was knee-deep. He measured off another thousand and led me through water that was up to the waist. [5]He measured off another thousand, but now it was a river that I could not cross, because the water had risen and was deep enough to swim in — a river that no one could cross. [6]He asked me, "Son of man, do you see this?"

Then he led me back to the bank of the river. [7]When I arrived there, I saw a great number of trees on each side of the river. [8]He said to me, "This water flows toward the eastern region and goes down into the Arabah,[b] where it enters the Dead Sea. When it empties into the sea, the salty water there becomes fresh. [9]Swarms of living creatures will live wherever the river flows. There will be large numbers of fish, because this water flows there and makes the salt water fresh; so where the river flows everything will live. [10]Fishermen will stand along the shore; from En Gedi to En Eglaim there will be places for spreading nets. The fish will be of many kinds — like the fish of the Mediterranean Sea. [11]But the swamps and marshes will not become fresh; they will be left for salt. [12]Fruit trees of all kinds will grow on both banks of the river. Their leaves will not wither, nor will their fruit fail. Every month they will bear fruit, because the water from the sanctuary flows to them. Their fruit will serve for food and their leaves for healing."

The Boundaries of the Land

[13]This is what the Sovereign LORD says: "These are the boundaries of the land that you will divide among the twelve tribes of Israel as their inheritance, with two portions for Joseph. [14]You are to divide it equally among them. Because I swore with uplifted hand to give it to your ancestors, this land will become your inheritance.

[15]"This is to be the boundary of the land:

"On the north side it will run from the Mediterranean Sea by the Hethlon road past Lebo Hamath to Zedad, [16]Berothah[c]

and Sibraim (which lies on the border between Damascus and Hamath), as far as Hazer Hattikon, which is on the border of Hauran. [17]The boundary will extend from the sea to Hazar Enan,[d] along the northern border of Damascus, with the border of Hamath to the north. This will be the northern boundary.

[18]"On the east side the boundary will run between Hauran and Damascus, along the Jordan between Gilead and the land of Israel, to the Dead Sea and as far as Tamar.[e] This will be the eastern boundary.

[19]"On the south side it will run from Tamar as far as the waters of Meribah Kadesh, then along the Wadi of Egypt to the Mediterranean Sea. This will be the southern boundary.

[20]"On the west side, the Mediterranean Sea will be the boundary to a point opposite Lebo Hamath. This will be the western boundary.

[21]"You are to distribute this land among yourselves according to the tribes of Israel. [22]You are to allot it as an inheritance for yourselves and for the foreigners residing among you and who have children. You are to consider them as native-born Israelites; along with you they are to be allotted an inheritance among the tribes of Israel. [23]In whatever tribe a foreigner resides, there you are to give them their inheritance," declares the Sovereign LORD.

The Division of the Land

48 "These are the tribes, listed by name: At the northern frontier, Dan will have one portion; it will follow the Hethlon road to Lebo Hamath; Hazar Enan and the northern border of Damascus next to Hamath will be part of its border from the east side to the west side.

[2]"Asher will have one portion; it will border the territory of Dan from east to west.

[3]"Naphtali will have one portion; it will border the territory of Asher from east to west.

[4]"Manasseh will have one portion; it will border the territory of Naphtali from east to west.

---

[a] 3 That is, about 1,700 feet or about 530 meters   [b] 8 Or *the Jordan Valley*   [c] 15,16 See Septuagint and 48:1; Hebrew *road to go into Zedad,* [16]*Hamath, Berothah.*   [d] 17 Hebrew *Enon,* a variant of *Enan*
[e] 18 See Syriac; Hebrew *Israel. You will measure to the Dead Sea.*

⁵ "Ephraim will have one portion; it will border the territory of Manasseh from east to west.

⁶ "Reuben will have one portion; it will border the territory of Ephraim from east to west.

⁷ "Judah will have one portion; it will border the territory of Reuben from east to west.

⁸ "Bordering the territory of Judah from east to west will be the portion you are to present as a special gift. It will be 25,000 cubits*ᵃ* wide, and its length from east to west will equal one of the tribal portions; the sanctuary will be in the center of it.

⁹ "The special portion you are to offer to the LORD will be 25,000 cubits long and 10,000 cubits*ᵇ* wide. ¹⁰ This will be the sacred portion for the priests. It will be 25,000 cubits long on the north side, 10,000 cubits wide on the west side, 10,000 cubits wide on the east side and 25,000 cubits long on the south side. In the center of it will be the sanctuary of the LORD. ¹¹ This will be for the consecrated priests, the Zadokites, who were faithful in serving me and did not go astray as the Levites did when the Israelites went astray. ¹² It will be a special gift to them from the sacred portion of the land, a most holy portion, bordering the territory of the Levites.

¹³ "Alongside the territory of the priests, the Levites will have an allotment 25,000 cubits long and 10,000 cubits wide. Its total length will be 25,000 cubits and its width 10,000 cubits. ¹⁴ They must not sell or exchange any of it. This is the best of the land and must not pass into other hands, because it is holy to the LORD.

¹⁵ "The remaining area, 5,000 cubits*ᶜ* wide and 25,000 cubits long, will be for the common use of the city, for houses and for pastureland. The city will be in the center of it ¹⁶ and will have these measurements: the north side 4,500 cubits,*ᵈ* the south side 4,500 cubits, the east side 4,500 cubits, and the west side 4,500 cubits. ¹⁷ The pastureland for the city will be 250 cubits*ᵉ* on the north, 250 cubits on the south, 250 cubits on the east, and 250 cubits on the west. ¹⁸ What remains of the area, bordering on the sacred portion and running the length of it, will be 10,000

cubits on the east side and 10,000 cubits on the west side. Its produce will supply food for the workers of the city. ¹⁹ The workers from the city who farm it will come from all the tribes of Israel. ²⁰ The entire portion will be a square, 25,000 cubits on each side. As a special gift you will set aside the sacred portion, along with the property of the city.

²¹ "What remains on both sides of the area formed by the sacred portion and the property of the city will belong to the prince. It will extend eastward from the 25,000 cubits of the sacred portion to the eastern border, and westward from the 25,000 cubits to the western border. Both these areas running the length of the tribal portions will belong to the prince, and the sacred portion with the temple sanctuary will be in the center of them. ²² So the property of the Levites and the property of the city will lie in the center of the area that belongs to the prince. The area belonging to the prince will lie between the border of Judah and the border of Benjamin.

²³ "As for the rest of the tribes: Benjamin will have one portion; it will extend from the east side to the west side.

²⁴ "Simeon will have one portion; it will border the territory of Benjamin from east to west.

²⁵ "Issachar will have one portion; it will border the territory of Simeon from east to west.

²⁶ "Zebulun will have one portion; it will border the territory of Issachar from east to west.

²⁷ "Gad will have one portion; it will border the territory of Zebulun from east to west.

²⁸ "The southern boundary of Gad will run south from Tamar to the waters of Meribah Kadesh, then along the Wadi of Egypt to the Mediterranean Sea.

²⁹ "This is the land you are to allot as an inheritance to the tribes of Israel, and these will be their portions," declares the Sovereign LORD.

The Gates of the New City

³⁰ "These will be the exits of the city: Beginning on the north side, which is 4,500 cubits long, ³¹ the gates of the city will be named

---

ᵃ 8 That is, about 8 miles or about 13 kilometers; also in verses 9, 10, 13, 15, 20 and 21   *ᵇ 9* That is, about 3 1/3 miles or about 5.3 kilometers; also in verses 10, 13 and 18   *ᶜ 15* That is, about 1 2/3 miles or about 2.7 kilometers   *ᵈ 16* That is, about 1 1/2 miles or about 2.4 kilometers; also in verses 30, 32, 33 and 34   *ᵉ 17* That is, about 440 feet or about 135 meters after the tribes of Israel. The three gates on the north side will be the gate of Reuben, the gate of Judah and the gate of Levi.

³²"On the east side, which is 4,500 cubits long, will be three gates: the gate of Joseph, the gate of Benjamin and the gate of Dan.

³³"On the south side, which measures 4,500 cubits, will be three gates: the gate of Simeon, the gate of Issachar and the gate of Zebulun.

³⁴"On the west side, which is 4,500 cubits long, will be three gates: the gate of Gad, the gate of Asher and the gate of Naphtali.

³⁵"The distance all around will be 18,000 cubits.^a

"And the name of the city from that time on will be:

THE LORD IS THERE."

---

^a 35 That is, about 6 miles or about 9.5 kilometers

DANIEL

⟹ **WHEN DID THIS HAPPEN?**

Between 605 and 536 B.C. in Babylon and Persia

⟹ **WHO IS IN THIS BOOK?**

Daniel
Shadrach
Meshach
Abednego
Nebuchadnezzar
Darius

⟹ **VERSES YOU MIGHT RECOGNIZE**

DANIEL 2:20–21

"Praise be to the name of God for ever and ever; wisdom and power are his ... He gives wisdom to the wise and knowledge to the discerning."

DANIEL 6:22A

"My God sent his angel, and he shut the mouths of the lions. They have not hurt me, because I was found innocent in his sight."

WHAT'S IT ABOUT?

Daniel's story began about eighteen years before the major exile the prophet Ezekiel experienced. Daniel and his friends were taken captive early by Babylon to be used in service to the king.

The story of Daniel gives an example of how God's people should live during exile. Surrounded by foreign gods and sinful practices and forced to study the occult, would Daniel and his friends stay loyal to God and worship him alone? Yes, and even during captivity, God could protect and sustain those who obeyed him. In fact, Daniel eventually rose to become one of the top four rulers in the land.

The book of Daniel is packed with exciting stories you may recognize, such as Shadrach, Meshach and Abednego in the fiery furnace and Daniel in the lion's den. God's protection of those who honor him is epic. But Daniel also gave information about the end times. Daniel's visions recorded in this book predicted what would happen to the Jews in the future—leading up to the coming of Christ. His point: God is the supreme ruler of heaven and earth, and in dark times there is always hope.

DANIEL

Daniel's Training in Babylon

1 In the third year of the reign of Jehoiakim king of Judah, Nebuchadnezzar king of Babylon came to Jerusalem and besieged it. ²And the Lord delivered Jehoiakim king of Judah into his hand, along with some of the articles from the temple of God. These he carried off to the temple of his god in Babylonia*a* and put in the treasure house of his god.

³Then the king ordered Ashpenaz, chief of his court officials, to bring into the king's service some of the Israelites from the royal family and the nobility— ⁴young men without any physical defect, handsome, showing aptitude for every kind of learning, well informed, quick to understand, and qualified to serve in the king's palace. He was to teach them the language and literature of the Babylonians.*b* ⁵The king assigned them a daily amount of food and wine from the king's table. They were to be trained for three years, and after that they were to enter the king's service.

⁶Among those who were chosen were some from Judah: Daniel, Hananiah, Mishael and Azariah. ⁷The chief official gave them new names: to Daniel, the name Belteshazzar; to Hananiah, Shadrach; to Mishael, Meshach; and to Azariah, Abednego.

⁸But Daniel resolved not to defile himself with the royal food and wine, and he asked the chief official for permission not to defile himself this way. ⁹Now God had caused the official to show favor and compassion to Daniel, ¹⁰but the official told Daniel, "I am afraid of my lord the king, who has assigned your*c* food and drink. Why should he see you looking worse than the other young men your age? The king would then have my head because of you."

¹¹Daniel then said to the guard whom the chief official had appointed over Daniel, Hananiah, Mishael and Azariah, ¹²"Please test your servants for ten days: Give us nothing but vegetables to eat and water to drink. ¹³Then compare our appearance with that of the young men who eat the royal food, and treat your servants in accordance with what you see." ¹⁴So he agreed to this and tested them for ten days.

¹⁵At the end of the ten days they looked healthier and better nourished than any of the young men who ate the royal food. ¹⁶So the guard took away their choice food and the wine they were to drink and gave them vegetables instead.

¹⁷To these four young men God gave knowledge and understanding of all kinds of literature and learning. And Daniel could understand visions and dreams of all kinds.

¹⁸At the end of the time set by the king to bring them into his service, the chief official presented them to Nebuchadnezzar. ¹⁹The king talked with them, and he found none equal to Daniel, Hananiah, Mishael and Azariah; so they entered the king's service. ²⁰In every matter of wisdom and understanding about which the king questioned them, he found them ten times better than all the magicians and enchanters in his whole kingdom.

²¹And Daniel remained there until the first year of King Cyrus.

Nebuchadnezzar's Dream

2 In the second year of his reign, Nebuchadnezzar had dreams; his mind was troubled and he could not sleep. ²So the king summoned the magicians, enchanters, sorcerers and astrologers*d* to tell him what he had dreamed. When they came in and stood before the king, ³he said to them, "I have had a dream that troubles me and I want to know what it means.*e*"

⁴Then the astrologers answered the king,*f*

---

a 2 Hebrew *Shinar*   *b 4* Or *Chaldeans*   *c 10* The Hebrew for *your* and *you* in this verse is plural.
d 2 Or *Chaldeans*; also in verses 4, 5 and 10   *e 3* Or *was*   *f 4* At this point the Hebrew text has *in Aramaic*, indicating that the text from here through the end of chapter 7 is in Aramaic.

TO THEIR KNEES

READ: DANIEL 1:19-21, 2:24-28

Daniel ranks as one of the most brilliant minds the ancient world has ever known. He was a Renaissance man 2,000 years before the Renaissance. He was a genius philosopher and scientist. He could explain riddles and solve problems unlike anyone in his generation, and no one could dream or interpret dreams like Daniel. But the thing that set him apart wasn't his IQ. Daniel prayed circles around the greatest superpower on earth, and because he got on his knees, he brought kings and kingdoms to their knees.

Physical posture is an important part of prayer. It's like a prayer within a prayer. Posture is related to prayer like tone is related to communication. You've probably heard plenty about tone from your parents! If words are what you say, then posture is how you say it. There's a reason that Scripture recommends a wide variety of postures such as kneeling (Psalm 95:6), falling on one's face (1 Chronicles 29:20), the laying on of hands (Luke 4:40), and anointing someone's head with oil (James 5:14). Physical postures help posture our hearts and minds.

BUILDING
FAITH
WISDOM
STRENGTH

When I extend out my hands in worship, it symbolizes my surrender to God. Sometimes I'll raise a clenched fist to celebrate what Christ has accomplished for me on the cross and declare the victory he's won. We do it after a great play, so why not during a great song?

All I know is this: Humility honors God, and God honors humility. Why not kneel? It certainly can't hurt.

Taken from *The Circle Maker Student Edition* by Mark Batterson with Parker Batterson, copyright © 2012 by Mark Batterson, published by Zondervan.

"May the king live forever! Tell your servants the dream, and we will interpret it."

⁵The king replied to the astrologers, "This is what I have firmly decided: If you do not tell me what my dream was and interpret it, I will have you cut into pieces and your houses turned into piles of rubble. ⁶But if you tell me the dream and explain it, you will receive from me gifts and rewards and great honor. So tell me the dream and interpret it for me."

⁷Once more they replied, "Let the king tell his servants the dream, and we will interpret it."

⁸Then the king answered, "I am certain that you are trying to gain time, because you realize that this is what I have firmly decided: ⁹If you do not tell me the dream, there is only one penalty for you. You have conspired to tell me misleading and wicked things, hoping the situation will change. So then, tell me the dream, and I will know that you can interpret it for me."

¹⁰The astrologers answered the king, "There is no one on earth who can do what the king asks! No king, however great and mighty, has ever asked such a thing of any magician or enchanter or astrologer. ¹¹What the king asks is too difficult. No one can reveal it to the king except the gods, and they do not live among humans."

¹²This made the king so angry and furious that he ordered the execution of all the wise men of Babylon. ¹³So the decree was issued to put the wise men to death, and men were sent to look for Daniel and his friends to put them to death.

¹⁴When Arioch, the commander of the king's guard, had gone out to put to death the wise men of Babylon, Daniel spoke to him with wisdom and tact. ¹⁵He asked the king's officer, "Why did the king issue such a harsh decree?" Arioch then explained the matter to Daniel. ¹⁶At this, Daniel went in to the king and asked for time, so that he might interpret the dream for him.

¹⁷Then Daniel returned to his house and explained the matter to his friends Hananiah, Mishael and Azariah. ¹⁸He urged them to plead for mercy from the God of heaven concerning this mystery, so that he and his friends might not be executed with the rest of the wise men of Babylon. ¹⁹During the night the mystery was revealed to Daniel in a vision. Then Daniel praised the God of heaven ²⁰and said:

"Praise be to the name of God for ever
    and ever;
    wisdom and power are his.
²¹He changes times and seasons;
    he deposes kings and raises up others.
He gives wisdom to the wise
    and knowledge to the discerning.
²²He reveals deep and hidden things;
    he knows what lies in darkness,
    and light dwells with him.
²³I thank and praise you, God of my
        ancestors:
    You have given me wisdom and power,
    you have made known to me what we
        asked of you,
    you have made known to us the dream
        of the king."

Daniel Interprets the Dream

²⁴Then Daniel went to Arioch, whom the king had appointed to execute the wise men of Babylon, and said to him, "Do not execute the wise men of Babylon. Take me to the king, and I will interpret his dream for him."

²⁵Arioch took Daniel to the king at once and said, "I have found a man among the exiles from Judah who can tell the king what his dream means."

²⁶The king asked Daniel (also called Belteshazzar), "Are you able to tell me what I saw in my dream and interpret it?"

²⁷Daniel replied, "No wise man, enchanter, magician or diviner can explain to the king the mystery he has asked about, ²⁸but there is a God in heaven who reveals mysteries. He has shown King Nebuchadnezzar what will happen in days to come. Your dream and the visions that passed through your mind as you were lying in bed are these:

²⁹"As Your Majesty was lying there, your mind turned to things to come, and the revealer of mysteries showed you what is going to happen. ³⁰As for me, this mystery has been revealed to me, not because I have greater wisdom than anyone else alive, but so that Your Majesty may know the interpretation and that you may understand what went through your mind.

³¹"Your Majesty looked, and there before you stood a large statue—an enormous, dazzling statue, awesome in appearance. ³²The head of the statue was made of pure gold, its chest and arms of silver, its belly and thighs of bronze, ³³its legs of iron, its feet partly of

iron and partly of baked clay. [34]While you were watching, a rock was cut out, but not by human hands. It struck the statue on its feet of iron and clay and smashed them. [35]Then the iron, the clay, the bronze, the silver and the gold were all broken to pieces and became like chaff on a threshing floor in the summer. The wind swept them away without leaving a trace. But the rock that struck the statue became a huge mountain and filled the whole earth.

[36]"This was the dream, and now we will interpret it to the king. [37]Your Majesty, you are the king of kings. The God of heaven has given you dominion and power and might and glory; [38]in your hands he has placed all mankind and the beasts of the field and the birds in the sky. Wherever they live, he has made you ruler over them all. You are that head of gold.

[39]"After you, another kingdom will arise, inferior to yours. Next, a third kingdom, one of bronze, will rule over the whole earth. [40]Finally, there will be a fourth kingdom, strong as iron—for iron breaks and smashes everything—and as iron breaks things to pieces, so it will crush and break all the others. [41]Just as you saw that the feet and toes were partly of baked clay and partly of iron, so this will be a divided kingdom; yet it will have some of the strength of iron in it, even as you saw iron mixed with clay. [42]As the toes were partly iron and partly clay, so this kingdom will be partly strong and partly brittle. [43]And just as you saw the iron mixed with baked clay, so the people will be a mixture and will not remain united, any more than iron mixes with clay.

[44]"In the time of those kings, the God of heaven will set up a kingdom that will never be destroyed, nor will it be left to another people. It will crush all those kingdoms and bring them to an end, but it will itself endure forever. [45]This is the meaning of the vision of the rock cut out of a mountain, but not by human hands—a rock that broke the iron, the bronze, the clay, the silver and the gold to pieces.

"The great God has shown the king what will take place in the future. The dream is true and its interpretation is trustworthy."

[46]Then King Nebuchadnezzar fell prostrate before Daniel and paid him honor and ordered that an offering and incense be presented to him. [47]The king said to Daniel, "Surely your God is the God of gods and the Lord of kings and a revealer of mysteries, for you were able to reveal this mystery."

[48]Then the king placed Daniel in a high position and lavished many gifts on him. He made him ruler over the entire province of Babylon and placed him in charge of all its wise men. [49]Moreover, at Daniel's request the king appointed Shadrach, Meshach and Abednego administrators over the province of Babylon, while Daniel himself remained at the royal court.

The Image of Gold and the Blazing Furnace

3 King Nebuchadnezzar made an image of gold, sixty cubits high and six cubits wide,[a] and set it up on the plain of Dura in the province of Babylon. [2]He then summoned the satraps, prefects, governors, advisers, treasurers, judges, magistrates and all the other provincial officials to come to the dedication of the image he had set up. [3]So the satraps, prefects, governors, advisers, treasurers, judges, magistrates and all the other provincial officials assembled for the dedication of the image that King Nebuchadnezzar had set up, and they stood before it.

[4]Then the herald loudly proclaimed, "Nations and peoples of every language, this is what you are commanded to do: [5]As soon as you hear the sound of the horn, flute, zither, lyre, harp, pipe and all kinds of music, you must fall down and worship the image of gold that King Nebuchadnezzar has set up. [6]Whoever does not fall down and worship will immediately be thrown into a blazing furnace."

[7]Therefore, as soon as they heard the sound of the horn, flute, zither, lyre, harp and all kinds of music, all the nations and peoples of every language fell down and worshiped the image of gold that King Nebuchadnezzar had set up.

[8]At this time some astrologers[b] came forward and denounced the Jews. [9]They said to

---

[a] 1 That is, about 90 feet high and 9 feet wide or about 27 meters high and 2.7 meters wide
[b] 8 Or Chaldeans

King Nebuchadnezzar, "May the king live forever! [10]Your Majesty has issued a decree that everyone who hears the sound of the horn, flute, zither, lyre, harp, pipe and all kinds of music must fall down and worship the image of gold, [11]and that whoever does not fall down and worship will be thrown into a blazing furnace. [12]But there are some Jews whom you have set over the affairs of the province of Babylon—Shadrach, Meshach and Abednego—who pay no attention to you, Your Majesty. They neither serve your gods nor worship the image of gold you have set up."

[13]Furious with rage, Nebuchadnezzar summoned Shadrach, Meshach and Abednego. So these men were brought before the king, [14]and Nebuchadnezzar said to them, "Is it true, Shadrach, Meshach and Abednego, that you do not serve my gods or worship the image of gold I have set up? [15]Now when you hear the sound of the horn, flute, zither, lyre, harp, pipe and all kinds of music, if you are ready to fall down and worship the image I made, very good. But if you do not worship it, you will be thrown immediately into a blazing furnace. Then what god will be able to rescue you from my hand?"

[16]Shadrach, Meshach and Abednego replied to him, "King Nebuchadnezzar, we do not need to defend ourselves before you in this matter. [17]If we are thrown into the blazing furnace, the God we serve is able to deliver us from it, and he will deliver us[a] from Your Majesty's hand. [18]But even if he does not, we want you to know, Your Majesty, that we will not serve your gods or worship the image of gold you have set up."

[19]Then Nebuchadnezzar was furious with Shadrach, Meshach and Abednego, and his attitude toward them changed. He ordered the furnace heated seven times hotter than usual [20]and commanded some of the strongest soldiers in his army to tie up Shadrach, Meshach and Abednego and throw them into the blazing furnace. [21]So these men, wearing their robes, trousers, turbans and other clothes, were bound and thrown into the blazing furnace. [22]The king's command was so urgent and the furnace so hot that the flames of the fire killed the soldiers who took up Shadrach, Meshach and Abednego, [23]and these three men, firmly tied, fell into the blazing furnace.

[24]Then King Nebuchadnezzar leaped to his feet in amazement and asked his advisers, "Weren't there three men that we tied up and threw into the fire?"

They replied, "Certainly, Your Majesty."

[25]He said, "Look! I see four men walking around in the fire, unbound and unharmed, and the fourth looks like a son of the gods."

[26]Nebuchadnezzar then approached the opening of the blazing furnace and shouted, "Shadrach, Meshach and Abednego, servants of the Most High God, come out! Come here!"

So Shadrach, Meshach and Abednego came out of the fire, [27]and the satraps, prefects, governors and royal advisers crowded around them. They saw that the fire had not harmed their bodies, nor was a hair of their heads singed; their robes were not scorched, and there was no smell of fire on them.

[28]Then Nebuchadnezzar said, "Praise be to the God of Shadrach, Meshach and Abednego, who has sent his angel and rescued his servants! They trusted in him and defied the king's command and were willing to give up their lives rather than serve or worship any god except their own God. [29]Therefore I decree that the people of any nation or language who say anything against the God of Shadrach, Meshach and Abednego be cut into pieces and their houses be turned into piles of rubble, for no other god can save in this way."

[30]Then the king promoted Shadrach, Meshach and Abednego in the province of Babylon.

Nebuchadnezzar's Dream of a Tree

4[b] King Nebuchadnezzar,

To the nations and peoples of every language, who live in all the earth:

May you prosper greatly!

[2]It is my pleasure to tell you about the miraculous signs and wonders that the Most High God has performed for me.

[3]How great are his signs,
how mighty his wonders!

---

[a] 17 Or *If the God we serve is able to deliver us, then he will deliver us from the blazing furnace and*
[b] In Aramaic texts 4:1-3 is numbered 3:31-33, and 4:4-37 is numbered 4:1-34.

WELCOME DEATH SENTENCE

READ: DANIEL 3

I don't know of a near-death experience that's more intense than Shadrach, Meshach, and Abednego being chucked into a furnace. It was a death sentence.

But they obviously feared God more than they feared death. They would've rather died in that furnace (supposedly the most painful possible death) than dishonor God. So they made a defining decision to stand up for what was right rather than bow down to ninety feet of wrongness. All or nothing, now or never, life or death.

To be honest, I could've come up with a million reasons to bow down to that sucker. *I'm bowing on the outside, but I'm not bowing on the inside. I'll ask for forgiveness right after I get back up. My fingers are crossed. I'm only breaking one of the Ten Commandments. What good am I to God if I'm dead?* When it comes to sinful rationalizations, we get very creative. But it's our lame rationalizations that block his revelations.

BUILDING FAITH WISDOM STRENGTH

When we lose our integrity, we don't leave room for divine intervention. When we take matters into our own hands, we take God out of the picture. When we try to manipulate a situation, we miss out on the miracle.

Stop and think about this. If Shadrach, Meshach, and Abednego had just bowed down to the statue, they would have been delivered from the fiery furnace. But it would have been by Nebuchadnezzar, not by God. They would have lost the epic testimony by failing the test.

His kingdom is an eternal
kingdom;
his dominion endures from
generation to generation.

⁴I, Nebuchadnezzar, was at home in my palace, contented and prosperous. ⁵I had a dream that made me afraid. As I was lying in bed, the images and visions that passed through my mind terrified me. ⁶So I commanded that all the wise men of Babylon be brought before me to interpret the dream for me. ⁷When the magicians, enchanters, astrologers[a] and diviners came, I told them the dream, but they could not interpret it for me. ⁸Finally, Daniel came into my presence and I told him the dream. (He is called Belteshazzar, after the name of my god, and the spirit of the holy gods is in him.)

⁹I said, "Belteshazzar, chief of the magicians, I know that the spirit of the holy gods is in you, and no mystery is too difficult for you. Here is my dream; interpret it for me. ¹⁰These are the visions I saw while lying in bed: I looked, and there before me stood a tree in the middle of the land. Its height was enormous. ¹¹The tree grew large and strong and its top touched the sky; it was visible to the ends of the earth. ¹²Its leaves were beautiful, its fruit abundant, and on it was food for all. Under it the wild animals found shelter, and the birds lived in its branches; from it every creature was fed.

¹³"In the visions I saw while lying in bed, I looked, and there before me was a holy one, a messenger,[b] coming down from heaven. ¹⁴He called in a loud voice: 'Cut down the tree and trim off its branches; strip off its leaves and scatter its fruit. Let the animals flee from under it and the birds from its branches. ¹⁵But let the stump and its roots, bound with iron and bronze, remain in the ground, in the grass of the field.

" 'Let him be drenched with the dew of heaven, and let him live with the animals among the plants of the earth. ¹⁶Let his mind be changed from that of a man and let him be given the mind

of an animal, till seven times[c] pass by for him.

¹⁷" 'The decision is announced by messengers, the holy ones declare the verdict, so that the living may know that the Most High is sovereign over all kingdoms on earth and gives them to anyone he wishes and sets over them the lowliest of people.'

¹⁸"This is the dream that I, King Nebuchadnezzar, had. Now, Belteshazzar, tell me what it means, for none of the wise men in my kingdom can interpret it for me. But you can, because the spirit of the holy gods is in you."

Daniel Interprets the Dream

¹⁹Then Daniel (also called Belteshazzar) was greatly perplexed for a time, and his thoughts terrified him. So the king said, "Belteshazzar, do not let the dream or its meaning alarm you."

Belteshazzar answered, "My lord, if only the dream applied to your enemies and its meaning to your adversaries! ²⁰The tree you saw, which grew large and strong, with its top touching the sky, visible to the whole earth, ²¹with beautiful leaves and abundant fruit, providing food for all, giving shelter to the wild animals, and having nesting places in its branches for the birds— ²²Your Majesty, you are that tree! You have become great and strong; your greatness has grown until it reaches the sky, and your dominion extends to distant parts of the earth.

²³"Your Majesty saw a holy one, a messenger, coming down from heaven and saying, 'Cut down the tree and destroy it, but leave the stump, bound with iron and bronze, in the grass of the field, while its roots remain in the ground. Let him be drenched with the dew of heaven; let him live with the wild animals, until seven times pass by for him.'

²⁴"This is the interpretation, Your Majesty, and this is the decree the Most High has issued against my lord the king: ²⁵You will be driven away from people and will live with the wild

---

ᵃ 7 Or *Chaldeans*   ᵇ 13 Or *watchman*; also in verses 17 and 23   ᶜ 16 Or *years*; also in verses 23, 25 and 32 animals; you will eat grass like the ox and be drenched with the dew of heaven. Seven times will pass by for you until you acknowledge that the Most High is sovereign over all kingdoms on earth and gives them to anyone he wishes. ²⁶The command to leave the stump of the tree with its roots means that your kingdom will be restored to you when you acknowledge that Heaven rules. ²⁷Therefore, Your Majesty, be pleased to accept my advice: Renounce your sins by doing what is right, and your wickedness by being kind to the oppressed. It may be that then your prosperity will continue."

The Dream Is Fulfilled

²⁸All this happened to King Nebuchadnezzar. ²⁹Twelve months later, as the king was walking on the roof of the royal palace of Babylon, ³⁰he said, "Is not this the great Babylon I have built as the royal residence, by my mighty power and for the glory of my majesty?"

³¹Even as the words were on his lips, a voice came from heaven, "This is what is decreed for you, King Nebuchadnezzar: Your royal authority has been taken from you. ³²You will be driven away from people and will live with the wild animals; you will eat grass like the ox. Seven times will pass by for you until you acknowledge that the Most High is sovereign over all kingdoms on earth and gives them to anyone he wishes."

³³Immediately what had been said about Nebuchadnezzar was fulfilled. He was driven away from people and ate grass like the ox. His body was drenched with the dew of heaven until his hair grew like the feathers of an eagle and his nails like the claws of a bird.

³⁴At the end of that time, I, Nebuchadnezzar, raised my eyes toward heaven, and my sanity was restored. Then I praised the Most High; I honored and glorified him who lives forever.

His dominion is an eternal dominion;
his kingdom endures from generation
to generation.

³⁵All the peoples of the earth
are regarded as nothing.
He does as he pleases
with the powers of heaven
and the peoples of the earth.
No one can hold back his hand
or say to him: "What have you done?"

³⁶At the same time that my sanity was restored, my honor and splendor were returned to me for the glory of my kingdom. My advisers and nobles sought me out, and I was restored to my throne and became even greater than before. ³⁷Now I, Nebuchadnezzar, praise and exalt and glorify the King of heaven, because everything he does is right and all his ways are just. And those who walk in pride he is able to humble.

The Writing on the Wall

5 King Belshazzar gave a great banquet for a thousand of his nobles and drank wine with them. ²While Belshazzar was drinking his wine, he gave orders to bring in the gold and silver goblets that Nebuchadnezzar his father^a had taken from the temple in Jerusalem, so that the king and his nobles, his wives and his concubines might drink from them. ³So they brought in the gold goblets that had been taken from the temple of God in Jerusalem, and the king and his nobles, his wives and his concubines drank from them. ⁴As they drank the wine, they praised the gods of gold and silver, of bronze, iron, wood and stone.

⁵Suddenly the fingers of a human hand appeared and wrote on the plaster of the wall, near the lampstand in the royal palace. The king watched the hand as it wrote. ⁶His face turned pale and he was so frightened that his legs became weak and his knees were knocking.

⁷The king summoned the enchanters, astrologers^b and diviners. Then he said to these wise men of Babylon, "Whoever reads this writing and tells me what it means will be clothed in purple and have a gold chain placed around his neck, and he will be made the third highest ruler in the kingdom."

⁸Then all the king's wise men came in, but they could not read the writing or tell the

---

^a 2 Or *ancestor*; or *predecessor*; also in verses 11, 13 and 18   ^b 7 Or *Chaldeans*; also in verse 11

king what it meant. [9] So King Belshazzar became even more terrified and his face grew more pale. His nobles were baffled.

[10] The queen,[a] hearing the voices of the king and his nobles, came into the banquet hall. "May the king live forever!" she said. "Don't be alarmed! Don't look so pale! [11] There is a man in your kingdom who has the spirit of the holy gods in him. In the time of your father he was found to have insight and intelligence and wisdom like that of the gods. Your father, King Nebuchadnezzar, appointed him chief of the magicians, enchanters, astrologers and diviners. [12] He did this because Daniel, whom the king called Belteshazzar, was found to have a keen mind and knowledge and understanding, and also the ability to interpret dreams, explain riddles and solve difficult problems. Call for Daniel, and he will tell you what the writing means."

[13] So Daniel was brought before the king, and the king said to him, "Are you Daniel, one of the exiles my father the king brought from Judah? [14] I have heard that the spirit of the gods is in you and that you have insight, intelligence and outstanding wisdom. [15] The wise men and enchanters were brought before me to read this writing and tell me what it means, but they could not explain it. [16] Now I have heard that you are able to give interpretations and to solve difficult problems. If you can read this writing and tell me what it means, you will be clothed in purple and have a gold chain placed around your neck, and you will be made the third highest ruler in the kingdom."

[17] Then Daniel answered the king, "You may keep your gifts for yourself and give your rewards to someone else. Nevertheless, I will read the writing for the king and tell him what it means.

[18] "Your Majesty, the Most High God gave your father Nebuchadnezzar sovereignty and greatness and glory and splendor. [19] Because of the high position he gave him, all the nations and peoples of every language dreaded and feared him. Those the king wanted to put to death, he put to death; those he wanted to spare, he spared; those

he wanted to promote, he promoted; and those he wanted to humble, he humbled. [20] But when his heart became arrogant and hardened with pride, he was deposed from his royal throne and stripped of his glory. [21] He was driven away from people and given the mind of an animal; he lived with the wild donkeys and ate grass like the ox; and his body was drenched with the dew of heaven, until he acknowledged that the Most High God is sovereign over all kingdoms on earth and sets over them anyone he wishes.

[22] "But you, Belshazzar, his son,[b] have not humbled yourself, though you knew all this. [23] Instead, you have set yourself up against the Lord of heaven. You had the goblets from his temple brought to you, and you and your nobles, your wives and your concubines drank wine from them. You praised the gods of silver and gold, of bronze, iron, wood and stone, which cannot see or hear or understand. But you did not honor the God who holds in his hand your life and all your ways. [24] Therefore he sent the hand that wrote the inscription.

[25] "This is the inscription that was written:

MENE, MENE, TEKEL, PARSIN

[26] "Here is what these words mean:

Mene[c]: God has numbered the days of your reign and brought it to an end.

[27] Tekel[d]: You have been weighed on the scales and found wanting.

[28] Peres[e]: Your kingdom is divided and given to the Medes and Persians."

[29] Then at Belshazzar's command, Daniel was clothed in purple, a gold chain was placed around his neck, and he was proclaimed the third highest ruler in the kingdom.

[30] That very night Belshazzar, king of the Babylonians,[f] was slain, [31] and Darius the Mede took over the kingdom, at the age of sixty-two.[g]

---

[a] 10 Or queen mother   [b] 22 Or descendant; or successor   [c] 26 Mene can mean numbered or mina (a unit of money).   [d] 27 Tekel can mean weighed or shekel.   [e] 28 Peres (the singular of Parsin) can mean divided or Persia or a half mina or a half shekel.   [f] 30 Or Chaldeans   [g] 31 In Aramaic texts this verse (5:31) is numbered 6:1.

DANIEL

Daniel so distinguished himself among the administrators and the satraps by his exceptional qualities that the king planned to set him over the whole kingdom. DANIEL 6:3

HIS NAME MEANS: "God is my judge"
READ HIS STORY: *Daniel 1-2, 4-6*

D aniel lived with integrity, even when he was forced to serve in a foreign land 900 miles from his home. His consistent living made it impossible for anyone—except his enemies—to say anything bad about him.

Daniel was born around 600 years before Jesus. Early in his life, the Babylonians stormed into Jerusalem for the first of three times. Nebuchadnezzar, king of Babylon, ordered his officials to take the best and brightest young men of royalty or nobility to his palace. Daniel was one of those teens, along with Hananiah, Mishael and Azariah (whose names were changed to Shadrach, Meshach and Abednego). Immediately, these young men stood out. They didn't compromise in what they ate or how they acted. God gave Daniel the ability to understand dreams and make amazing prophecies—even predictions about the end times. He became one of King Nebuchadnezzar's greatest advisors and also worked in the court of Belshazzar, the last king of the Babylonian empire, and in the courts of Darius and Cyrus of the Persian empire.

Daniel lived most of his long life away from his homeland, but he never stopped serving God. The Babylonians and Persians had numerous gods and idols, even kings who wanted to be worshiped as gods (Daniel 6:7). Daniel prayed to God three times a day. He didn't hide his devotion. People in the palace knew Daniel went to his upstairs room, got on his knees and prayed facing Jerusalem. Daniel's consistent prayers got him thrown into the lions' den when his enemies tricked King Darius. God answered Daniel's prayers, saved him and ultimately raised him to a place of honor—on earth and in history.

MEN

OF THE BIBLE

Daniel in the Den of Lions

6 [a] It pleased Darius to appoint 120 satraps to rule throughout the kingdom, [2] with three administrators over them, one of whom was Daniel. The satraps were made accountable to them so that the king might not suffer loss. [3] Now Daniel so distinguished himself among the administrators and the satraps by his exceptional qualities that the king planned to set him over the whole kingdom. [4] At this, the administrators and the satraps tried to find grounds for charges against Daniel in his conduct of government affairs, but they were unable to do so. They could find no corruption in him, because he was trustworthy and neither corrupt nor negligent. [5] Finally these men said, "We will never find any basis for charges against this man Daniel unless it has something to do with the law of his God."

[6] So these administrators and satraps went as a group to the king and said: "May King Darius live forever! [7] The royal administrators, prefects, satraps, advisers and governors have all agreed that the king should issue an edict and enforce the decree that anyone who prays to any god or human being during the next thirty days, except to you, Your Majesty, shall be thrown into the lions' den. [8] Now, Your Majesty, issue the decree and put it in writing so that it cannot be altered—in accordance with the law of the Medes and Persians, which cannot be repealed." [9] So King Darius put the decree in writing.

[10] Now when Daniel learned that the decree had been published, he went home to his upstairs room where the windows opened toward Jerusalem. Three times a day he got down on his knees and prayed, giving thanks to his God, just as he had done before. [11] Then these men went as a group and found Daniel praying and asking God for help. [12] So they went to the king and spoke to him about his royal decree: "Did you not publish a decree that during the next thirty days anyone who prays to any god or human being except to you, Your Majesty, would be thrown into the lions' den?"

The king answered, "The decree stands—in accordance with the law of the Medes and Persians, which cannot be repealed."

[13] Then they said to the king, "Daniel, who is one of the exiles from Judah, pays no attention to you, Your Majesty, or to the decree you put in writing. He still prays three times a day." [14] When the king heard this, he was greatly distressed; he was determined to rescue Daniel and made every effort until sundown to save him.

[15] Then the men went as a group to King Darius and said to him, "Remember, Your Majesty, that according to the law of the Medes and Persians no decree or edict that the king issues can be changed."

[16] So the king gave the order, and they brought Daniel and threw him into the lions' den. The king said to Daniel, "May your God, whom you serve continually, rescue you!"

[17] A stone was brought and placed over the mouth of the den, and the king sealed it with his own signet ring and with the rings of his nobles, so that Daniel's situation might not be changed. [18] Then the king returned to his palace and spent the night without eating and without any entertainment being brought to him. And he could not sleep.

[19] At the first light of dawn, the king got up and hurried to the lions' den. [20] When he came near the den, he called to Daniel in an anguished voice, "Daniel, servant of the living God, has your God, whom you serve continually, been able to rescue you from the lions?"

[21] Daniel answered, "May the king live forever! [22] My God sent his angel, and he shut the mouths of the lions. They have not hurt me, because I was found innocent in his sight. Nor have I ever done any wrong before you, Your Majesty."

[23] The king was overjoyed and gave orders to lift Daniel out of the den. And when Daniel was lifted from the den, no wound was found on him, because he had trusted in his God.

[24] At the king's command, the men who had falsely accused Daniel were brought in and thrown into the lions' den, along with their wives and children. And before they reached the floor of the den, the lions overpowered them and crushed all their bones.

[25] Then King Darius wrote to all the nations and peoples of every language in all the earth:

---

[a] In Aramaic texts 6:1-28 is numbered 6:2-29.

WE DON'T GET THE CREDIT

READ: DANIEL 6:10-11

We all want to spend eternity with God. We just don't want to spend time with him. We sit and stare from a distance—satisfied with superficiality. We Facebook more than we seek his face. And our eyes aren't fixed on Jesus—they're plastered to our iPhones and iPads—emphasis on "i." Then, we wonder why God feels so distant. We wonder why we're bored with our faith. It's because we're holding out! We want joy without sacrifice. We want character without suffering. We want success without failure. We want gain without pain. We want a testimony without the test. Are you starting to see what's wrong with that?

You don't get to know God by looking at him from a distance. You have to hike into the depths of his power and the heights of his holiness. And if you take a single Spirit-led step of faith in God's direction, spiritual adrenaline will surge through your veins once again.

BUILDING FAITH WISDOM STRENGTH

Sitting in a church service for sixty minutes does squat. Don't get me wrong, going to church is a good thing, a biblical thing, the right thing. But you don't do anybody any favors by just sitting there. Churches are filled with spiritual sightseers who feel like they've done their religious duty by sitting and listening. We don't get credit for an audit. That's not quite how it works. Stop letting someone else worship for you, study for you, fast for you, journal for you, and pray for you.

"May you prosper greatly!

²⁶"I issue a decree that in every part of my kingdom people must fear and reverence the God of Daniel.

"For he is the living God
  and he endures forever;
his kingdom will not be destroyed,
  his dominion will never end.
²⁷He rescues and he saves;
  he performs signs and wonders
  in the heavens and on the earth.
He has rescued Daniel
  from the power of the lions."

²⁸So Daniel prospered during the reign of Darius and the reign of Cyrus*ᵃ* the Persian.

Daniel's Dream of Four Beasts

7 In the first year of Belshazzar king of Babylon, Daniel had a dream, and visions passed through his mind as he was lying in bed. He wrote down the substance of his dream.

²Daniel said: "In my vision at night I looked, and there before me were the four winds of heaven churning up the great sea. ³Four great beasts, each different from the others, came up out of the sea.

⁴"The first was like a lion, and it had the wings of an eagle. I watched until its wings were torn off and it was lifted from the ground so that it stood on two feet like a human being, and the mind of a human was given to it.

⁵"And there before me was a second beast, which looked like a bear. It was raised up on one of its sides, and it had three ribs in its mouth between its teeth. It was told, 'Get up and eat your fill of flesh!'

⁶"After that, I looked, and there before me was another beast, one that looked like a leopard. And on its back it had four wings like those of a bird. This beast had four heads, and it was given authority to rule.

⁷"After that, in my vision at night I looked, and there before me was a fourth beast—terrifying and frightening and very powerful. It had large iron teeth; it crushed and devoured its victims and trampled underfoot whatever was left. It was different from all the former beasts, and it had ten horns.

⁸"While I was thinking about the horns, there before me was another horn, a little one, which came up among them; and three of the first horns were uprooted before it. This horn had eyes like the eyes of a human being and a mouth that spoke boastfully.
⁹"As I looked,

"thrones were set in place,
  and the Ancient of Days took his seat.
His clothing was as white as snow;
  the hair of his head was white like
    wool.
His throne was flaming with fire,
  and its wheels were all ablaze.
¹⁰A river of fire was flowing,
  coming out from before him.
Thousands upon thousands attended
    him;
  ten thousand times ten thousand
    stood before him.
The court was seated,
  and the books were opened.

¹¹"Then I continued to watch because of the boastful words the horn was speaking. I kept looking until the beast was slain and its body destroyed and thrown into the blazing fire. ¹²(The other beasts had been stripped of their authority, but were allowed to live for a period of time.)

¹³"In my vision at night I looked, and there before me was one like a son of man,*ᵇ* coming with the clouds of heaven. He approached the Ancient of Days and was led into his presence. ¹⁴He was given authority, glory and sovereign power; all nations and peoples of every language worshiped him. His dominion is an everlasting dominion that will not pass away, and his kingdom is one that will never be destroyed.

The Interpretation of the Dream

¹⁵"I, Daniel, was troubled in spirit, and the visions that passed through my mind disturbed me. ¹⁶I approached one of those standing there and asked him the meaning of all this.

"So he told me and gave me the interpretation of these things: ¹⁷'The four great beasts are four kings that will rise from the earth. ¹⁸But the holy people of the Most High

---

ᵃ 28 Or *Darius, that is, the reign of Cyrus*   *ᵇ 13* The Aramaic phrase *bar enash* means *human being.* The phrase *son of man* is retained here because of its use in the New Testament as a title of Jesus, probably based largely on this verse.

will receive the kingdom and will possess it forever—yes, for ever and ever.'

¹⁹ "Then I wanted to know the meaning of the fourth beast, which was different from all the others and most terrifying, with its iron teeth and bronze claws—the beast that crushed and devoured its victims and trampled underfoot whatever was left. ²⁰I also wanted to know about the ten horns on its head and about the other horn that came up, before which three of them fell—the horn that looked more imposing than the others and that had eyes and a mouth that spoke boastfully. ²¹As I watched, this horn was waging war against the holy people and defeating them, ²²until the Ancient of Days came and pronounced judgment in favor of the holy people of the Most High, and the time came when they possessed the kingdom.

²³ "He gave me this explanation: 'The fourth beast is a fourth kingdom that will appear on earth. It will be different from all the other kingdoms and will devour the whole earth, trampling it down and crushing it. ²⁴The ten horns are ten kings who will come from this kingdom. After them another king will arise, different from the earlier ones; he will subdue three kings. ²⁵He will speak against the Most High and oppress his holy people and try to change the set times and the laws. The holy people will be delivered into his hands for a time, times and half a time.ᵃ

²⁶ " 'But the court will sit, and his power will be taken away and completely destroyed forever. ²⁷Then the sovereignty, power and greatness of all the kingdoms under heaven will be handed over to the holy people of the Most High. His kingdom will be an everlasting kingdom, and all rulers will worship and obey him.'

²⁸ "This is the end of the matter. I, Daniel, was deeply troubled by my thoughts, and my face turned pale, but I kept the matter to myself."

Daniel's Vision of a Ram and a Goat

8 In the third year of King Belshazzar's reign, I, Daniel, had a vision, after the one that had already appeared to me. ²In my vision I saw myself in the citadel of Susa in the province of Elam; in the vision I was beside the Ulai Canal. ³I looked up, and there before me was a ram with two horns, standing beside the canal, and the horns were long. One of the horns was longer than the other but grew up later. ⁴I watched the ram as it charged toward the west and the north and the south. No animal could stand against it, and none could rescue from its power. It did as it pleased and became great.

⁵As I was thinking about this, suddenly a goat with a prominent horn between its eyes came from the west, crossing the whole earth without touching the ground. ⁶It came toward the two-horned ram I had seen standing beside the canal and charged at it in great rage. ⁷I saw it attack the ram furiously, striking the ram and shattering its two horns. The ram was powerless to stand against it; the goat knocked it to the ground and trampled on it, and none could rescue the ram from its power. ⁸The goat became very great, but at the height of its power the large horn was broken off, and in its place four prominent horns grew up toward the four winds of heaven.

⁹Out of one of them came another horn, which started small but grew in power to the south and to the east and toward the Beautiful Land. ¹⁰It grew until it reached the host of the heavens, and it threw some of the starry host down to the earth and trampled on them. ¹¹It set itself up to be as great as the commander of the army of the LORD; it took away the daily sacrifice from the LORD, and his sanctuary was thrown down. ¹²Because of rebellion, the LORD's peopleᵇ and the daily sacrifice were given over to it. It prospered in everything it did, and truth was thrown to the ground.

¹³Then I heard a holy one speaking, and another holy one said to him, "How long will it take for the vision to be fulfilled—the vision concerning the daily sacrifice, the rebellion that causes desolation, the surrender of the sanctuary and the trampling underfoot of the LORD's people?"

¹⁴He said to me, "It will take 2,300 evenings and mornings; then the sanctuary will be reconsecrated."

The Interpretation of the Vision

¹⁵While I, Daniel, was watching the vision and trying to understand it, there before me

---

ᵃ 25 Or *for a year, two years and half a year*   ᵇ 12 Or *rebellion, the armies* stood one who looked like a man. ¹⁶And I heard a man's voice from the Ulai calling, "Gabriel, tell this man the meaning of the vision."

¹⁷As he came near the place where I was standing, I was terrified and fell prostrate. "Son of man,"*ᵃ* he said to me, "understand that the vision concerns the time of the end."

¹⁸While he was speaking to me, I was in a deep sleep, with my face to the ground. Then he touched me and raised me to my feet.

¹⁹He said: "I am going to tell you what will happen later in the time of wrath, because the vision concerns the appointed time of the end.*ᵇ* ²⁰The two-horned ram that you saw represents the kings of Media and Persia. ²¹The shaggy goat is the king of Greece, and the large horn between its eyes is the first king. ²²The four horns that replaced the one that was broken off represent four kingdoms that will emerge from his nation but will not have the same power.

²³"In the latter part of their reign, when rebels have become completely wicked, a fierce-looking king, a master of intrigue, will arise. ²⁴He will become very strong, but not by his own power. He will cause astounding devastation and will succeed in whatever he does. He will destroy those who are mighty, the holy people. ²⁵He will cause deceit to prosper, and he will consider himself superior. When they feel secure, he will destroy many and take his stand against the Prince of princes. Yet he will be destroyed, but not by human power.

²⁶"The vision of the evenings and mornings that has been given you is true, but seal up the vision, for it concerns the distant future."

²⁷I, Daniel, was worn out. I lay exhausted for several days. Then I got up and went about the king's business. I was appalled by the vision; it was beyond understanding.

Daniel's Prayer

9 In the first year of Darius son of Xerxes*ᶜ* (a Mede by descent), who was made ruler over the Babylonian*ᵈ* kingdom — ²in the first year of his reign, I, Daniel, understood from the Scriptures, according to the word of the LORD given to Jeremiah the prophet, that the desolation of Jerusalem would last seventy years. ³So I turned to the Lord God and pleaded with him in prayer and petition, in fasting, and in sackcloth and ashes.

⁴I prayed to the LORD my God and confessed:

"Lord, the great and awesome God, who keeps his covenant of love with those who love him and keep his commandments, ⁵we have sinned and done wrong. We have been wicked and have rebelled; we have turned away from your commands and laws. ⁶We have not listened to your servants the prophets, who spoke in your name to our kings, our princes and our ancestors, and to all the people of the land.

⁷"Lord, you are righteous, but this day we are covered with shame — the people of Judah and the inhabitants of Jerusalem and all Israel, both near and far, in all the countries where you have scattered us because of our unfaithfulness to you. ⁸We and our kings, our princes and our ancestors are covered with shame, LORD, because we have sinned against you. ⁹The Lord our God is merciful and forgiving, even though we have rebelled against him; ¹⁰we have not obeyed the LORD our God or kept the laws he gave us through his servants the prophets. ¹¹All Israel has transgressed your law and turned away, refusing to obey you.

"Therefore the curses and sworn judgments written in the Law of Moses, the servant of God, have been poured out on us, because we have sinned against you. ¹²You have fulfilled the words spoken against us and against our rulers by bringing on us great disaster. Under the whole heaven nothing has ever been done like what has been done to Jerusalem. ¹³Just as it is written in the Law of Moses, all this disaster has come on us, yet we have not sought the favor of the LORD our God by turning from our sins and giving attention to your truth. ¹⁴The LORD did not

---

ᵃ 17 The Hebrew phrase *ben adam* means *human being*. The phrase *son of man* is retained as a form of address here because of its possible association with "Son of Man" in the New Testament.
ᵇ 19 Or *because the end will be at the appointed time*   ᶜ 1 Hebrew *Ahasuerus*   ᵈ 1 Or *Chaldean*

hesitate to bring the disaster on us, for the LORD our God is righteous in everything he does; yet we have not obeyed him.

15 "Now, Lord our God, who brought your people out of Egypt with a mighty hand and who made for yourself a name that endures to this day, we have sinned, we have done wrong. 16 Lord, in keeping with all your righteous acts, turn away your anger and your wrath from Jerusalem, your city, your holy hill. Our sins and the iniquities of our ancestors have made Jerusalem and your people an object of scorn to all those around us.

17 "Now, our God, hear the prayers and petitions of your servant. For your sake, Lord, look with favor on your desolate sanctuary. 18 Give ear, our God, and hear; open your eyes and see the desolation of the city that bears your Name. We do not make requests of you because we are righteous, but because of your great mercy. 19 Lord, listen! Lord, forgive! Lord, hear and act! For your sake, my God, do not delay, because your city and your people bear your Name."

The Seventy "Sevens"

20 While I was speaking and praying, confessing my sin and the sin of my people Israel and making my request to the LORD my God for his holy hill— 21 while I was still in prayer, Gabriel, the man I had seen in the earlier vision, came to me in swift flight about the time of the evening sacrifice. 22 He instructed me and said to me, "Daniel, I have now come to give you insight and understanding. 23 As soon as you began to pray, a word went out, which I have come to tell you, for you are highly esteemed. Therefore, consider the word and understand the vision:

24 "Seventy 'sevens'*a* are decreed for your people and your holy city to finish*b* transgression, to put an end to sin, to atone for wickedness, to bring in everlasting righteousness, to seal up vision and prophecy and to anoint the Most Holy Place.*c*

25 "Know and understand this: From the time the word goes out to restore and rebuild Jerusalem until the Anointed One,*d* the ruler, comes, there will be seven 'sevens,' and sixty-two 'sevens.' It will be rebuilt with streets and a trench, but in times of trouble. 26 After the sixty-two 'sevens,' the Anointed One will be put to death and will have nothing.*e* The people of the ruler who will come will destroy the city and the sanctuary. The end will come like a flood: War will continue until the end, and desolations have been decreed. 27 He will confirm a covenant with many for one 'seven.'*f* In the middle of the 'seven'*f* he will put an end to sacrifice and offering. And at the temple*g* he will set up an abomination that causes desolation, until the end that is decreed is poured out on him.*h" i*

Daniel's Vision of a Man

10 In the third year of Cyrus king of Persia, a revelation was given to Daniel (who was called Belteshazzar). Its message was true and it concerned a great war.*j* The understanding of the message came to him in a vision.

2 At that time I, Daniel, mourned for three weeks. 3 I ate no choice food; no meat or wine touched my lips; and I used no lotions at all until the three weeks were over.

4 On the twenty-fourth day of the first month, as I was standing on the bank of the great river, the Tigris, 5 I looked up and there before me was a man dressed in linen, with a belt of fine gold from Uphaz around his waist. 6 His body was like topaz, his face like lightning, his eyes like flaming torches, his arms and legs like the gleam of burnished bronze, and his voice like the sound of a multitude.

7 I, Daniel, was the only one who saw the vision; those who were with me did not see it, but such terror overwhelmed them that they fled and hid themselves. 8 So I was left alone, gazing at this great vision; I had no strength left, my face turned deathly pale and I was helpless. 9 Then I heard him speaking, and as I listened to him, I fell into a deep sleep, my face to the ground.

---

a 24 Or 'weeks'; also in verses 25 and 26   *b* 24 Or restrain   *c* 24 Or the most holy One   *d* 25 Or an anointed one; also in verse 26   *e* 26 Or death and will have no one; or death, but not for himself   *f* 27 Or 'week'   *g* 27 Septuagint and Theodotion; Hebrew wing   *h* 27 Or it   *i* 27 Or And one who causes desolation will come upon the wing of the abominable temple, until the end that is decreed is poured out on the desolated city   *j* 1 Or true and burdensome

POWER FAST

READ: DANIEL 10:1-3

A t critical intervals in my life I've done a Daniel fast. It's called a Daniel fast because it's inspired by the intense fasts that Daniel did at critical intervals in his life. It's different from an absolute fast because the diet generally consists of fruits, vegetables, and water. And it's typically done with a specific goal and defined timeline in mind. It was a ten-day fast that kick-started Daniel's sudden and dramatic climb to political power; it was a twenty-one-day fast that ended with an angelic encounter.

Fasting and praying is awesome as a package deal. It's almost like those moving sidewalks that get you to your destination in like half the time. They call it fasting for a reason—it has a way of fast-tracking our prayers! Because fasting is physically harder than praying, fasting is a form of praying hard. In my experience, it's the shortest distance to a breakthrough.

BUILDING FAITH WISDOM STRENGTH

Let's get counterfactual: What if Daniel had quit praying through on day twenty, hour 23, minute 59? The answer is simple: Daniel would have forfeited the miracle the day before the day. Those are important questions to ask because you don't want to miss miracles. I don't know where you are on the timeline between praying through and breaking through. Maybe you're at day one; maybe you're at day twenty. Either way, you can pray with a holy confidence, knowing that with each prayer you are one prayer closer. Don't give up. Just like Daniel, the answer is on the way.

¹⁰A hand touched me and set me trembling on my hands and knees. ¹¹He said, "Daniel, you who are highly esteemed, consider carefully the words I am about to speak to you, and stand up, for I have now been sent to you." And when he said this to me, I stood up trembling.

¹²Then he continued, "Do not be afraid, Daniel. Since the first day that you set your mind to gain understanding and to humble yourself before your God, your words were heard, and I have come in response to them. ¹³But the prince of the Persian kingdom resisted me twenty-one days. Then Michael, one of the chief princes, came to help me, because I was detained there with the king of Persia. ¹⁴Now I have come to explain to you what will happen to your people in the future, for the vision concerns a time yet to come."

¹⁵While he was saying this to me, I bowed with my face toward the ground and was speechless. ¹⁶Then one who looked like a man[a] touched my lips, and I opened my mouth and began to speak. I said to the one standing before me, "I am overcome with anguish because of the vision, my lord, and I feel very weak. ¹⁷How can I, your servant, talk with you, my lord? My strength is gone and I can hardly breathe."

¹⁸Again the one who looked like a man touched me and gave me strength. ¹⁹"Do not be afraid, you who are highly esteemed," he said. "Peace! Be strong now; be strong."

When he spoke to me, I was strengthened and said, "Speak, my lord, since you have given me strength."

²⁰So he said, "Do you know why I have come to you? Soon I will return to fight against the prince of Persia, and when I go, the prince of Greece will come; ²¹but first I will tell you what is written in the Book of Truth. (No one supports me against them except Michael, your prince. ¹And in the first year of Darius the Mede, I took my stand to support and protect him.)

The Kings of the South and the North

²"Now then, I tell you the truth: Three more kings will arise in Persia, and then a fourth, who will be far richer than all the others. When he has gained power by his wealth, he will stir up everyone against the kingdom of Greece. ³Then a mighty king will arise, who will rule with great power and do as he pleases. ⁴After he has arisen, his empire will be broken up and parceled out toward the four winds of heaven. It will not go to his descendants, nor will it have the power he exercised, because his empire will be uprooted and given to others.

⁵"The king of the South will become strong, but one of his commanders will become even stronger than he and will rule his own kingdom with great power. ⁶After some years, they will become allies. The daughter of the king of the South will go to the king of the North to make an alliance, but she will not retain her power, and he and his power[b] will not last. In those days she will be betrayed, together with her royal escort and her father[c] and the one who supported her.

⁷"One from her family line will arise to take her place. He will attack the forces of the king of the North and enter his fortress; he will fight against them and be victorious. ⁸He will also seize their gods, their metal images and their valuable articles of silver and gold and carry them off to Egypt. For some years he will leave the king of the North alone. ⁹Then the king of the North will invade the realm of the king of the South but will retreat to his own country. ¹⁰His sons will prepare for war and assemble a great army, which will sweep on like an irresistible flood and carry the battle as far as his fortress.

¹¹"Then the king of the South will march out in a rage and fight against the king of the North, who will raise a large army, but it will be defeated. ¹²When the army is carried off, the king of the South will be filled with pride and will slaughter many thousands, yet he will not remain triumphant. ¹³For the king of the North will muster another army, larger than the first; and after several years, he will advance with a huge army fully equipped.

¹⁴"In those times many will rise against the king of the South. Those who are violent among your own people will rebel in fulfillment of the vision, but without success.

---

a 16 Most manuscripts of the Masoretic Text; one manuscript of the Masoretic Text, Dead Sea Scrolls and Septuagint *Then something that looked like a human hand*   *b 6* Or *offspring*   *c 6* Or *child* (see Vulgate and Syriac)

¹⁵Then the king of the North will come and build up siege ramps and will capture a fortified city. The forces of the South will be powerless to resist; even their best troops will not have the strength to stand. ¹⁶The invader will do as he pleases; no one will be able to stand against him. He will establish himself in the Beautiful Land and will have the power to destroy it. ¹⁷He will determine to come with the might of his entire kingdom and will make an alliance with the king of the South. And he will give him a daughter in marriage in order to overthrow the kingdom, but his plans*a* will not succeed or help him. ¹⁸Then he will turn his attention to the coastlands and will take many of them, but a commander will put an end to his insolence and will turn his insolence back on him. ¹⁹After this, he will turn back toward the fortresses of his own country but will stumble and fall, to be seen no more.

²⁰"His successor will send out a tax collector to maintain the royal splendor. In a few years, however, he will be destroyed, yet not in anger or in battle.

²¹"He will be succeeded by a contemptible person who has not been given the honor of royalty. He will invade the kingdom when its people feel secure, and he will seize it through intrigue. ²²Then an overwhelming army will be swept away before him; both it and a prince of the covenant will be destroyed. ²³After coming to an agreement with him, he will act deceitfully, and with only a few people he will rise to power. ²⁴When the richest provinces feel secure, he will invade them and will achieve what neither his fathers nor his forefathers did. He will distribute plunder, loot and wealth among his followers. He will plot the overthrow of fortresses—but only for a time.

²⁵"With a large army he will stir up his strength and courage against the king of the South. The king of the South will wage war with a large and very powerful army, but he will not be able to stand because of the plots devised against him. ²⁶Those who eat from the king's provisions will try to destroy him; his army will be swept away, and many will fall in battle. ²⁷The two kings, with their hearts bent on evil, will sit at the same table and lie to each other, but to no avail, because

an end will still come at the appointed time. ²⁸The king of the North will return to his own country with great wealth, but his heart will be set against the holy covenant. He will take action against it and then return to his own country.

²⁹"At the appointed time he will invade the South again, but this time the outcome will be different from what it was before. ³⁰Ships of the western coastlands will oppose him, and he will lose heart. Then he will turn back and vent his fury against the holy covenant. He will return and show favor to those who forsake the holy covenant.

³¹"His armed forces will rise up to desecrate the temple fortress and will abolish the daily sacrifice. Then they will set up the abomination that causes desolation. ³²With flattery he will corrupt those who have violated the covenant, but the people who know their God will firmly resist him.

³³"Those who are wise will instruct many, though for a time they will fall by the sword or be burned or captured or plundered. ³⁴When they fall, they will receive a little help, and many who are not sincere will join them. ³⁵Some of the wise will stumble, so that they may be refined, purified and made spotless until the time of the end, for it will still come at the appointed time.

The King Who Exalts Himself

³⁶"The king will do as he pleases. He will exalt and magnify himself above every god and will say unheard-of things against the God of gods. He will be successful until the time of wrath is completed, for what has been determined must take place. ³⁷He will show no regard for the gods of his ancestors or for the one desired by women, nor will he regard any god, but will exalt himself above them all. ³⁸Instead of them, he will honor a god of fortresses; a god unknown to his ancestors he will honor with gold and silver, with precious stones and costly gifts. ³⁹He will attack the mightiest fortresses with the help of a foreign god and will greatly honor those who acknowledge him. He will make them rulers over many people and will distribute the land at a price.*b*

⁴⁰"At the time of the end the king of the South will engage him in battle, and the

---

a 17 Or *but she*   *b 39* Or *land for a reward*

king of the North will storm out against him with chariots and cavalry and a great fleet of ships. He will invade many countries and sweep through them like a flood. ⁴¹ He will also invade the Beautiful Land. Many countries will fall, but Edom, Moab and the leaders of Ammon will be delivered from his hand. ⁴² He will extend his power over many countries; Egypt will not escape. ⁴³ He will gain control of the treasures of gold and silver and all the riches of Egypt, with the Libyans and Cushites*ᵃ* in submission. ⁴⁴ But reports from the east and the north will alarm him, and he will set out in a great rage to destroy and annihilate many. ⁴⁵ He will pitch his royal tents between the seas at*ᵇ* the beautiful holy mountain. Yet he will come to his end, and no one will help him.

The End Times

12 "At that time Michael, the great prince who protects your people, will arise. There will be a time of distress such as has not happened from the beginning of nations until then. But at that time your people — everyone whose name is found written in the book — will be delivered. ² Multitudes who sleep in the dust of the earth will awake: some to everlasting life, others to shame and everlasting contempt. ³ Those who are wise*ᶜ* will shine like the brightness of the heavens, and those who lead many to righteousness, like the stars for ever and ever. ⁴ But you, Daniel, roll up and seal the words of the scroll until the time of the end. Many will go here and there to increase knowledge."

⁵ Then I, Daniel, looked, and there before me stood two others, one on this bank of the river and one on the opposite bank. ⁶ One of them said to the man clothed in linen, who was above the waters of the river, "How long will it be before these astonishing things are fulfilled?"

⁷ The man clothed in linen, who was above the waters of the river, lifted his right hand and his left hand toward heaven, and I heard him swear by him who lives forever, saying, "It will be for a time, times and half a time.*ᵈ* When the power of the holy people has been finally broken, all these things will be completed."

⁸ I heard, but I did not understand. So I asked, "My lord, what will the outcome of all this be?"

⁹ He replied, "Go your way, Daniel, because the words are rolled up and sealed until the time of the end. ¹⁰ Many will be purified, made spotless and refined, but the wicked will continue to be wicked. None of the wicked will understand, but those who are wise will understand.

¹¹ "From the time that the daily sacrifice is abolished and the abomination that causes desolation is set up, there will be 1,290 days. ¹² Blessed is the one who waits for and reaches the end of the 1,335 days.

¹³ "As for you, go your way till the end. You will rest, and then at the end of the days you will rise to receive your allotted inheritance."

ᵃ 43 That is, people from the upper Nile region *ᵇ 45* Or *the sea and* *ᶜ 3* Or *who impart wisdom*
ᵈ 7 Or *a year, two years and half a year*

HOSEA

 WHEN DID THIS HAPPEN?

Between 753 and 715 B.C. in the northern kingdom of Israel

 WHO IS IN THIS BOOK?

Hosea
Gomer

 VERSES YOU MIGHT RECOGNIZE

HOSEA 12:6
"But you must return to your God; maintain love and justice, and wait for your God always."

HOSEA 14:4
"I will heal their waywardness and love them freely, for my anger has turned away from them."

WHAT'S IT ABOUT?

This book, written around the same time as Isaiah's ministry—before the Assyrian invasion of the northern kingdom—is about God's love for his people. Using a real-life illustration, God told his prophet Hosea to marry a promiscuous woman named Gomer. Gomer's unfaithfulness was an example of how Israel was unfaithful to God by turning to idols and practicing injustice.

The book begins with warnings for Jeroboam II, one of Israel's wicked kings, followed by five cycles of judgment and restoration. All the while, Hosea personally lived this cycle with his unfaithful wife. The amazing part is that despite all of Gomer's failings, Hosea still loved her—just as God still loved Israel. Hosea called the people to turn from their sins, but he also reminded them of God's unwavering faithfulness and his promise to Abraham to make them as numerous as the sand on the seashore (see 1:10).

HOSEA

1 The word of the LORD that came to Hosea son of Beeri during the reigns of Uzziah, Jotham, Ahaz and Hezekiah, kings of
Judah, and during the reign of Jeroboam son
of Jehoash[a] king of Israel:

Hosea's Wife and Children

²When the LORD began to speak through
Hosea, the LORD said to him, "Go, marry a
promiscuous woman and have children
with her, for like an adulterous wife this land
is guilty of unfaithfulness to the LORD." ³So
he married Gomer daughter of Diblaim, and
she conceived and bore him a son.

⁴Then the LORD said to Hosea, "Call him
Jezreel, because I will soon punish the house
of Jehu for the massacre at Jezreel, and I will
put an end to the kingdom of Israel. ⁵In that
day I will break Israel's bow in the Valley of
Jezreel."

⁶Gomer conceived again and gave birth to a
daughter. Then the LORD said to Hosea, "Call
her Lo-Ruhamah (which means "not loved"),
for I will no longer show love to Israel, that I
should at all forgive them. ⁷Yet I will show love
to Judah; and I will save them—not by bow,
sword or battle, or by horses and horsemen,
but I, the LORD their God, will save them."

⁸After she had weaned Lo-Ruhamah, Gomer had another son. ⁹Then the LORD said,
"Call him Lo-Ammi (which means "not my
people"), for you are not my people, and I am
not your God.[b]

¹⁰"Yet the Israelites will be like the sand
on the seashore, which cannot be measured
or counted. In the place where it was said
to them, 'You are not my people,' they will
be called 'children of the living God.' ¹¹The
people of Judah and the people of Israel will
come together; they will appoint one leader
and will come up out of the land, for great
will be the day of Jezreel.[c]

2[d] "Say of your brothers, 'My people,' and
of your sisters, 'My loved one.'

Israel Punished and Restored

²"Rebuke your mother, rebuke her,
    for she is not my wife,
    and I am not her husband.
Let her remove the adulterous look from
        her face
    and the unfaithfulness from between
        her breasts.
³Otherwise I will strip her naked
    and make her as bare as on the day she
        was born;
I will make her like a desert,
    turn her into a parched land,
    and slay her with thirst.
⁴I will not show my love to her children,
    because they are the children of
        adultery.
⁵Their mother has been unfaithful
    and has conceived them in disgrace.
She said, 'I will go after my lovers,
    who give me my food and my water,
    my wool and my linen, my olive oil and
        my drink.'
⁶Therefore I will block her path with
        thornbushes;
    I will wall her in so that she cannot
        find her way.
⁷She will chase after her lovers but not
        catch them;
    she will look for them but not find
        them.
Then she will say,
    'I will go back to my husband as at first,
    for then I was better off than now.'
⁸She has not acknowledged that I was
        the one
    who gave her the grain, the new wine
        and oil,
who lavished on her the silver and gold—
    which they used for Baal.

⁹"Therefore I will take away my grain
        when it ripens,
    and my new wine when it is ready.

---

[a] 1 Hebrew *Joash*, a variant of *Jehoash*   [b] 9 Or *your I AM*   [c] 11 In Hebrew texts 1:10,11 is numbered
2:1,2.   [d] In Hebrew texts 2:1-23 is numbered 2:3-25.

I will take back my wool and my linen,
   intended to cover her naked body.
¹⁰ So now I will expose her lewdness
   before the eyes of her lovers;
   no one will take her out of my hands.
¹¹ I will stop all her celebrations:
   her yearly festivals, her New Moons,
   her Sabbath days — all her appointed
      festivals.
¹² I will ruin her vines and her fig trees,
   which she said were her pay from her
      lovers;
I will make them a thicket,
   and wild animals will devour them.
¹³ I will punish her for the days
   she burned incense to the Baals;
she decked herself with rings and
      jewelry,
   and went after her lovers,
   but me she forgot,"
                    declares the LORD.

¹⁴ "Therefore I am now going to allure her;
   I will lead her into the wilderness
   and speak tenderly to her.
¹⁵ There I will give her back her vineyards,
   and will make the Valley of Achor[a] a
      door of hope.
There she will respond[b] as in the days of
      her youth,
   as in the day she came up out of Egypt.

¹⁶ "In that day," declares the LORD,
   "you will call me 'my husband';
   you will no longer call me 'my master.'[c]
¹⁷ I will remove the names of the Baals from
      her lips;
   no longer will their names be invoked.
¹⁸ In that day I will make a covenant for
      them
   with the beasts of the field, the birds in
      the sky
   and the creatures that move along the
      ground.
Bow and sword and battle
   I will abolish from the land,
   so that all may lie down in safety.
¹⁹ I will betroth you to me forever;
   I will betroth you in[d] righteousness
      and justice,
   in[d] love and compassion.

²⁰ I will betroth you in[d] faithfulness,
   and you will acknowledge the LORD.

²¹ "In that day I will respond,"
   declares the LORD —
"I will respond to the skies,
   and they will respond to the earth;
²² and the earth will respond to the grain,
   the new wine and the olive oil,
   and they will respond to Jezreel.[e]
²³ I will plant her for myself in the land;
   I will show my love to the one I called
      'Not my loved one.'[f]
I will say to those called 'Not my people,'[g]
      'You are my people';
   and they will say, 'You are my God.' "

Hosea's Reconciliation With His Wife

3 The LORD said to me, "Go, show your
love to your wife again, though she is
loved by another man and is an adulteress.
Love her as the LORD loves the Israelites,
though they turn to other gods and love the
sacred raisin cakes."

² So I bought her for fifteen shekels[h] of silver and about a homer and a lethek[i] of barley. ³ Then I told her, "You are to live with me
many days; you must not be a prostitute or
be intimate with any man, and I will behave
the same way toward you."

⁴ For the Israelites will live many days
without king or prince, without sacrifice or
sacred stones, without ephod or household
gods. ⁵ Afterward the Israelites will return
and seek the LORD their God and David their
king. They will come trembling to the LORD
and to his blessings in the last days.

The Charge Against Israel

4 Hear the word of the LORD, you
Israelites,
   because the LORD has a charge
      to bring
   against you who live in the land:
"There is no faithfulness, no love,
   no acknowledgment of God in
      the land.
² There is only cursing,[j] lying and murder,
   stealing and adultery;

---

[a] 15 Achor means trouble.   [b] 15 Or sing   [c] 16 Hebrew baal   [d] 19,20 Or with   [e] 22 Jezreel means
God plants.   [f] 23 Hebrew Lo-Ruhamah (see 1:6)   [g] 23 Hebrew Lo-Ammi (see 1:9)   [h] 2 That is, about
6 ounces or about 170 grams   [i] 2 A homer and a lethek possibly weighed about 430 pounds or about 195
kilograms.   [j] 2 That is, to pronounce a curse on

DON'T TRY THIS AT HOME

READ: HOSEA 2:19

The book of Hosea should come with a warning label: "Don't try this at home." The Lord commands Hosea to do an outrageous deed, instructing him to marry a prostitute and have children with her. It's a true-life illustration showing how Israel acts toward God like an unfaithful spouse.

This book doesn't say whether Hosea and his wife, Gomer, ever laughed and enjoyed happy days together. The couple soon gives birth to three children, assigning them painful names like "Not-Loved" and "Not-My-People" (Hosea 1:6, 9). A couple chapters later you learn that Gomer is living with another man, having become not only his lover but also his property. Hosea can't simply persuade his wife to come home. He has to buy her back with fifteen shekels of silver as well as over four hundred pounds of barley, the price of a female slave (3:1–2). This time he insists she stay faithful to him (v. 3). Hosea loves his wife despite her adulterous behavior. Obeying God's command had to be as tough for the prophet as it would be for any other rejected husband. Yet his love for Gomer illustrates the Lord's intense passion for his people.

BUILDING

FAITH

WISDOM

STRENGTH

This story's explicit language helps you sense the Lord's pain. He feels betrayed by his people as they chase other gods. This book isn't easy to read. But it shows how God feels when his people choose to leave him.

HOSEA

For I desire mercy, not sacrifice, and acknowledgment of God rather than burnt offerings. HOSEA 6:6

HIS NAME MEANS: "salvation"
READ HIS STORY: *Hosea 1–3*

Hosea loved his wife. No big deal, right? Well, she was an adulteress *and* a prostitute. In other words, his wife slept around—a lot. It had to be hard to love her.

Want to hear something that sounds crazy? God wanted Hosea to marry an unfaithful woman so the prophet could feel what it's like to love—and forgive—someone who's unfaithful. Throughout the Old Testament, God's people turned from the Lord, ignored his rules and worshiped other gods. God loves his people just like a husband loves his wife. When his people worshiped other gods, to him it felt like a wife who was cheating on her husband.

So what did Hosea do? He continued to love his wife. He forgave her. He told her to stop sleeping around and invited her back home.

What an amazing story! But it's not just Hosea's story; it's our story. Some have called Hosea the first prophet of grace. Through his life and in his prophecies, we see a picture of God's grace. God is always ready to forgive. No sin is too great. No rebelliousness unforgiveable. Hosea said that God would "heal [the Israelites'] waywardness and love them freely" (Hosea 14:4).

Hosea may be known as a *minor* prophet, but his story is majorly important. By experiencing the heartbreak of betrayal, Hosea helps God's people see their sinful actions, understand God's anger toward them and realize that God's love is unconditional and everlasting ... no matter what they've done.

they break all bounds,
and bloodshed follows bloodshed.
³Because of this the land dries up,
and all who live in it waste away;
the beasts of the field, the birds in
the sky
and the fish in the sea are swept away.

⁴"But let no one bring a charge,
let no one accuse another,
for your people are like those
who bring charges against a priest.
⁵You stumble day and night,
and the prophets stumble with you.
So I will destroy your mother—
⁶   my people are destroyed from lack of
knowledge.

"Because you have rejected knowledge,
I also reject you as my priests;
because you have ignored the law of
your God,
I also will ignore your children.
⁷The more priests there were,
the more they sinned against me;
they exchanged their glorious God*ᵃ* for
something disgraceful.
⁸They feed on the sins of my people
and relish their wickedness.
⁹And it will be: Like people, like priests.
I will punish both of them for their
ways
and repay them for their deeds.

¹⁰"They will eat but not have enough;
they will engage in prostitution but not
flourish,
because they have deserted the LORD
to give themselves ¹¹to prostitution;
old wine and new wine
take away their understanding.
¹²My people consult a wooden idol,
and a diviner's rod speaks to them.
A spirit of prostitution leads them
astray;
they are unfaithful to their God.
¹³They sacrifice on the mountaintops
and burn offerings on the hills,
under oak, poplar and terebinth,
where the shade is pleasant.
Therefore your daughters turn to
prostitution
and your daughters-in-law to adultery.

¹⁴"I will not punish your daughters
when they turn to prostitution,
nor your daughters-in-law
when they commit adultery,
because the men themselves consort
with harlots
and sacrifice with shrine prostitutes—
a people without understanding will
come to ruin!

¹⁵"Though you, Israel, commit adultery,
do not let Judah become guilty.

"Do not go to Gilgal;
do not go up to Beth Aven.*ᵇ*
And do not swear, 'As surely as the
LORD lives!'
¹⁶The Israelites are stubborn,
like a stubborn heifer.
How then can the LORD pasture them
like lambs in a meadow?
¹⁷Ephraim is joined to idols;
leave him alone!
¹⁸Even when their drinks are gone,
they continue their prostitution;
their rulers dearly love shameful ways.
¹⁹A whirlwind will sweep them away,
and their sacrifices will bring them
shame.

Judgment Against Israel

5 "Hear this, you priests!
Pay attention, you Israelites!
Listen, royal house!
This judgment is against you:
You have been a snare at Mizpah,
a net spread out on Tabor.
²The rebels are knee-deep in slaughter.
I will discipline all of them.
³I know all about Ephraim;
Israel is not hidden from me.
Ephraim, you have now turned to
prostitution;
Israel is corrupt.

⁴"Their deeds do not permit them
to return to their God.
A spirit of prostitution is in their heart;
they do not acknowledge the LORD.
⁵Israel's arrogance testifies against them;
the Israelites, even Ephraim, stumble
in their sin;
Judah also stumbles with them.

ᵃ 7 Syriac (see also an ancient Hebrew scribal tradition); Masoretic Text *me; / I will exchange their glory*
ᵇ 15 Beth Aven means *house of wickedness* (a derogatory name for Bethel, which means *house of God*).

⁶When they go with their flocks and herds
  to seek the LORD,
they will not find him;
  he has withdrawn himself from them.
⁷They are unfaithful to the LORD;
  they give birth to illegitimate children.
When they celebrate their New Moon
    feasts,
  he will devour*a* their fields.

⁸"Sound the trumpet in Gibeah,
  the horn in Ramah.
Raise the battle cry in Beth Aven*b*;
  lead on, Benjamin.
⁹Ephraim will be laid waste
  on the day of reckoning.
Among the tribes of Israel
  I proclaim what is certain.
¹⁰Judah's leaders are like those
  who move boundary stones.
I will pour out my wrath on them
  like a flood of water.
¹¹Ephraim is oppressed,
  trampled in judgment,
  intent on pursuing idols.*c*
¹²I am like a moth to Ephraim,
  like rot to the people of Judah.

¹³"When Ephraim saw his sickness,
  and Judah his sores,
then Ephraim turned to Assyria,
  and sent to the great king for help.
But he is not able to cure you,
  not able to heal your sores.
¹⁴For I will be like a lion to Ephraim,
  like a great lion to Judah.
I will tear them to pieces and go away;
  I will carry them off, with no one to
    rescue them.
¹⁵Then I will return to my lair
  until they have borne their guilt
  and seek my face —
in their misery
  they will earnestly seek me."

Israel Unrepentant

6 "Come, let us return to the LORD.
  He has torn us to pieces
  but he will heal us;
he has injured us
  but he will bind up our wounds.

²After two days he will revive us;
  on the third day he will restore us,
  that we may live in his presence.
³Let us acknowledge the LORD;
  let us press on to acknowledge him.
As surely as the sun rises,
  he will appear;
he will come to us like the winter rains,
  like the spring rains that water the
    earth."

⁴"What can I do with you, Ephraim?
  What can I do with you, Judah?
Your love is like the morning mist,
  like the early dew that disappears.
⁵Therefore I cut you in pieces with my
    prophets,
  I killed you with the words of my
    mouth —
  then my judgments go forth like
    the sun.*d*
⁶For I desire mercy, not sacrifice,
  and acknowledgment of God rather
    than burnt offerings.
⁷As at Adam,*e* they have broken the
    covenant;
  they were unfaithful to me there.
⁸Gilead is a city of evildoers,
  stained with footprints of blood.
⁹As marauders lie in ambush for a victim,
  so do bands of priests;
they murder on the road to Shechem,
  carrying out their wicked schemes.
¹⁰I have seen a horrible thing in Israel:
  There Ephraim is given to prostitution,
  Israel is defiled.

¹¹"Also for you, Judah,
  a harvest is appointed.

"Whenever I would restore the fortunes
  of my people,

7 ¹whenever I would heal Israel,
  the sins of Ephraim are exposed
  and the crimes of Samaria revealed.
They practice deceit,
  thieves break into houses,
  bandits rob in the streets;
²but they do not realize
  that I remember all their evil deeds.
Their sins engulf them;
  they are always before me.

---

a 7 Or *Now their New Moon feasts / will devour them and*
derogatory name for Bethel, which means *house of God*).
is uncertain.   *d* 5 The meaning of the Hebrew for this line is uncertain.   *e* 7 Or *Like Adam*; or *Like human beings*
b 8 *Beth Aven* means *house of wickedness* (a
c 11 The meaning of the Hebrew for this word

3 "They delight the king with their
wickedness,
   the princes with their lies.
4 They are all adulterers,
   burning like an oven
whose fire the baker need not stir
   from the kneading of the dough till
   it rises.
5 On the day of the festival of our king
   the princes become inflamed with
   wine,
   and he joins hands with the mockers.
6 Their hearts are like an oven;
   they approach him with intrigue.
Their passion smolders all night;
   in the morning it blazes like a
   flaming fire.
7 All of them are hot as an oven;
   they devour their rulers.
All their kings fall,
   and none of them calls on me.

8 "Ephraim mixes with the nations;
   Ephraim is a flat loaf not turned over.
9 Foreigners sap his strength,
   but he does not realize it.
His hair is sprinkled with gray,
   but he does not notice.
10 Israel's arrogance testifies against him,
   but despite all this
he does not return to the LORD his God
   or search for him.

11 "Ephraim is like a dove,
   easily deceived and senseless —
now calling to Egypt,
   now turning to Assyria.
12 When they go, I will throw my net over
   them;
   I will pull them down like the birds in
   the sky.
When I hear them flocking together,
   I will catch them.
13 Woe to them,
   because they have strayed from me!
Destruction to them,
   because they have rebelled
   against me!
I long to redeem them
   but they speak about me falsely.
14 They do not cry out to me from their
   hearts
   but wail on their beds.

They slash themselves,[a] appealing to
their gods
   for grain and new wine,
   but they turn away from me.
15 I trained them and strengthened
their arms,
   but they plot evil against me.
16 They do not turn to the Most High;
   they are like a faulty bow.
Their leaders will fall by the sword
   because of their insolent words.
For this they will be ridiculed
   in the land of Egypt.

Israel to Reap the Whirlwind

8 "Put the trumpet to your lips!
   An eagle is over the house of the LORD
because the people have broken my
   covenant
   and rebelled against my law.
2 Israel cries out to me,
   'Our God, we acknowledge you!'
3 But Israel has rejected what is good;
   an enemy will pursue him.
4 They set up kings without my consent;
   they choose princes without my
   approval.
With their silver and gold
   they make idols for themselves
   to their own destruction.
5 Samaria, throw out your calf-idol!
   My anger burns against them.
How long will they be incapable of
   purity?
6   They are from Israel!
This calf — a metalworker has made it;
   it is not God.
It will be broken in pieces,
   that calf of Samaria.

7 "They sow the wind
   and reap the whirlwind.
The stalk has no head;
   it will produce no flour.
Were it to yield grain,
   foreigners would swallow it up.
8 Israel is swallowed up;
   now she is among the nations
   like something no one wants.
9 For they have gone up to Assyria
   like a wild donkey wandering alone.
   Ephraim has sold herself to lovers.

---

a 14 Some Hebrew manuscripts and Septuagint; most Hebrew manuscripts *They gather together*

[10] Although they have sold themselves
  among the nations,
 I will now gather them together.
 They will begin to waste away
  under the oppression of the mighty
  king.

[11] "Though Ephraim built many altars for
  sin offerings,
 these have become altars for sinning.
[12] I wrote for them the many things of
  my law,
 but they regarded them as something
  foreign.
[13] Though they offer sacrifices as gifts
  to me,
 and though they eat the meat,
  the LORD is not pleased with them.
 Now he will remember their wickedness
  and punish their sins:
 They will return to Egypt.
[14] Israel has forgotten their Maker
  and built palaces;
 Judah has fortified many towns.
 But I will send fire on their cities
  that will consume their fortresses."

Punishment for Israel

9 Do not rejoice, Israel;
  do not be jubilant like the other
  nations.
 For you have been unfaithful to your God;
  you love the wages of a prostitute
  at every threshing floor.
[2] Threshing floors and winepresses will
  not feed the people;
  the new wine will fail them.
[3] They will not remain in the LORD's land;
  Ephraim will return to Egypt
  and eat unclean food in Assyria.
[4] They will not pour out wine offerings to
  the LORD,
 nor will their sacrifices please him.
 Such sacrifices will be to them like the
  bread of mourners;
 all who eat them will be unclean.
 This food will be for themselves;
  it will not come into the temple of
  the LORD.
[5] What will you do on the day of your
  appointed festivals,
  on the feast days of the LORD?

[6] Even if they escape from destruction,
  Egypt will gather them,
  and Memphis will bury them.
 Their treasures of silver will be taken
  over by briers,
  and thorns will overrun their tents.
[7] The days of punishment are coming,
  the days of reckoning are at hand.
  Let Israel know this.
 Because your sins are so many
  and your hostility so great,
 the prophet is considered a fool,
  the inspired person a maniac.
[8] The prophet, along with my God,
  is the watchman over Ephraim,[a]
 yet snares await him on all his paths,
  and hostility in the house of his God.
[9] They have sunk deep into corruption,
  as in the days of Gibeah.
 God will remember their wickedness
  and punish them for their sins.

[10] "When I found Israel,
  it was like finding grapes in the desert;
 when I saw your ancestors,
  it was like seeing the early fruit on the
  fig tree.
 But when they came to Baal Peor,
  they consecrated themselves to that
  shameful idol
  and became as vile as the thing they
  loved.
[11] Ephraim's glory will fly away like a bird —
  no birth, no pregnancy, no conception.
[12] Even if they rear children,
  I will bereave them of every one.
 Woe to them
  when I turn away from them!
[13] I have seen Ephraim, like Tyre,
  planted in a pleasant place.
 But Ephraim will bring out
  their children to the slayer."

[14] Give them, LORD —
  what will you give them?
 Give them wombs that miscarry
  and breasts that are dry.

[15] "Because of all their wickedness in Gilgal,
  I hated them there.
 Because of their sinful deeds,
  I will drive them out of my house.
 I will no longer love them;
  all their leaders are rebellious.

---

a 8 Or *The prophet is the watchman over Ephraim, / the people of my God*

16 Ephraim is blighted,
    their root is withered,
    they yield no fruit.
Even if they bear children,
    I will slay their cherished offspring."

17 My God will reject them
    because they have not obeyed him;
    they will be wanderers among the
        nations.

10 Israel was a spreading vine;
    he brought forth fruit for himself.
As his fruit increased,
    he built more altars;
as his land prospered,
    he adorned his sacred stones.
2 Their heart is deceitful,
    and now they must bear their guilt.
The LORD will demolish their altars
    and destroy their sacred stones.

3 Then they will say, "We have no king
    because we did not revere the LORD.
But even if we had a king,
    what could he do for us?"
4 They make many promises,
    take false oaths
    and make agreements;
therefore lawsuits spring up
    like poisonous weeds in a plowed field.
5 The people who live in Samaria fear
    for the calf-idol of Beth Aven.ᵃ
Its people will mourn over it,
    and so will its idolatrous priests,
those who had rejoiced over its
        splendor,
    because it is taken from them into
        exile.
6 It will be carried to Assyria
    as tribute for the great king.
Ephraim will be disgraced;
    Israel will be ashamed of its foreign
        alliances.
7 Samaria's king will be destroyed,
    swept away like a twig on the surface
        of the waters.
8 The high places of wickednessᵇ will be
        destroyed —
    it is the sin of Israel.
Thorns and thistles will grow up
    and cover their altars.

Then they will say to the mountains,
    "Cover us!"
and to the hills, "Fall on us!"

9 "Since the days of Gibeah, you have
        sinned, Israel,
    and there you have remained.ᶜ
Will not war again overtake
    the evildoers in Gibeah?
10 When I please, I will punish them;
    nations will be gathered against them
to put them in bonds for their
        double sin.
11 Ephraim is a trained heifer
    that loves to thresh;
so I will put a yoke
    on her fair neck.
I will drive Ephraim,
    Judah must plow,
    and Jacob must break up the ground.
12 Sow righteousness for yourselves,
    reap the fruit of unfailing love,
and break up your unplowed ground;
    for it is time to seek the LORD,
until he comes
    and showers his righteousness on you.
13 But you have planted wickedness,
    you have reaped evil,
    you have eaten the fruit of deception.
Because you have depended on your own
        strength
    and on your many warriors,
14 the roar of battle will rise against your
        people,
    so that all your fortresses will be
        devastated —
as Shalman devastated Beth Arbel on the
        day of battle,
    when mothers were dashed to the
        ground with their children.
15 So will it happen to you, Bethel,
    because your wickedness is great.
When that day dawns,
    the king of Israel will be completely
        destroyed.

God's Love for Israel

11 "When Israel was a child, I loved
        him,
    and out of Egypt I called my son.
2 But the more they were called,

ᵃ 5 *Beth Aven* means *house of wickedness* (a derogatory name for Bethel, which means *house of God*).
ᵇ 8 Hebrew *aven,* a reference to Beth Aven (a derogatory name for Bethel); see verse 5.   ᶜ 9 Or *there a stand was taken*

the more they went away
    from me.*a*
They sacrificed to the Baals
    and they burned incense to images.
³ It was I who taught Ephraim to walk,
    taking them by the arms;
but they did not realize
    it was I who healed them.
⁴ I led them with cords of human kindness,
    with ties of love.
To them I was like one who lifts
    a little child to the cheek,
    and I bent down to feed them.

⁵ "Will they not return to Egypt
    and will not Assyria rule over them
    because they refuse to repent?
⁶ A sword will flash in their cities;
    it will devour their false prophets
    and put an end to their plans.
⁷ My people are determined to turn
    from me.
    Even though they call me God Most
    High,
I will by no means exalt them.

⁸ "How can I give you up, Ephraim?
    How can I hand you over, Israel?
How can I treat you like Admah?
    How can I make you like Zeboyim?
My heart is changed within me;
    all my compassion is aroused.
⁹ I will not carry out my fierce anger,
    nor will I devastate Ephraim again.
For I am God, and not a man—
    the Holy One among you.
I will not come against their cities.
¹⁰ They will follow the LORD;
    he will roar like a lion.
When he roars,
    his children will come trembling from
    the west.
¹¹ They will come from Egypt,
    trembling like sparrows,
    from Assyria, fluttering like doves.
I will settle them in their homes,"
    declares the LORD.

Israel's Sin

¹² Ephraim has surrounded me with lies,
    Israel with deceit.
And Judah is unruly against God,

even against the faithful
    Holy One.*b*

12 *c* ¹ Ephraim feeds on the wind;
    he pursues the east wind all day
    and multiplies lies and violence.
He makes a treaty with Assyria
    and sends olive oil to Egypt.
² The LORD has a charge to bring against
    Judah;
he will punish Jacob*d* according to
    his ways
    and repay him according to his deeds.
³ In the womb he grasped his brother's
    heel;
    as a man he struggled with God.
⁴ He struggled with the angel and
    overcame him;
    he wept and begged for his favor.
He found him at Bethel
    and talked with him there—
⁵ the LORD God Almighty,
    the LORD is his name!
⁶ But you must return to your God;
    maintain love and justice,
    and wait for your God always.

⁷ The merchant uses dishonest scales
    and loves to defraud.
⁸ Ephraim boasts,
    "I am very rich; I have become wealthy.
With all my wealth they will not find
    in me
    any iniquity or sin."

⁹ "I have been the LORD your God
    ever since you came out of Egypt;
I will make you live in tents again,
    as in the days of your appointed
    festivals.
¹⁰ I spoke to the prophets,
    gave them many visions
    and told parables through them."

¹¹ Is Gilead wicked?
    Its people are worthless!
Do they sacrifice bulls in Gilgal?
    Their altars will be like piles of
    stones
    on a plowed field.
¹² Jacob fled to the country of Aram*e*;
    Israel served to get a wife,
    and to pay for her he tended sheep.

---

a 2 Septuagint; Hebrew *them*   *b* 12 In Hebrew texts this verse (11:12) is numbered 12:1.   *c* In Hebrew
texts 12:1-14 is numbered 12:2-15.   *d* 2 *Jacob* means *he grasps the heel*, a Hebrew idiom for *he takes
advantage of* or *he deceives.*   *e* 12 That is, Northwest Mesopotamia

¹³ The Lᴏʀᴅ used a prophet to bring Israel
     up from Egypt,
    by a prophet he cared for him.
¹⁴ But Ephraim has aroused his bitter
     anger;
    his Lord will leave on him the guilt of
     his bloodshed
    and will repay him for his contempt.

The Lord's Anger Against Israel

13 When Ephraim spoke, people
     trembled;
    he was exalted in Israel.
    But he became guilty of Baal worship
     and died.
² Now they sin more and more;
    they make idols for themselves from
     their silver,
    cleverly fashioned images,
     all of them the work of craftsmen.
    It is said of these people,
     "They offer human sacrifices!
     They kiss^a calf-idols!"
³ Therefore they will be like the morning
     mist,
    like the early dew that disappears,
    like chaff swirling from a threshing
     floor,
    like smoke escaping through a
     window.

⁴ "But I have been the Lᴏʀᴅ your God
     ever since you came out of Egypt.
    You shall acknowledge no God but me,
     no Savior except me.
⁵ I cared for you in the wilderness,
    in the land of burning heat.
⁶ When I fed them, they were satisfied;
    when they were satisfied, they became
     proud;
    then they forgot me.
⁷ So I will be like a lion to them,
    like a leopard I will lurk by the path.
⁸ Like a bear robbed of her cubs,
    I will attack them and rip them open;
    like a lion I will devour them —
     a wild animal will tear them apart.

⁹ "You are destroyed, Israel,
    because you are against me, against
     your helper.
¹⁰ Where is your king, that he may save you?

Where are your rulers in all your
     towns,
of whom you said,
    'Give me a king and princes'?
¹¹ So in my anger I gave you a king,
    and in my wrath I took him away.
¹² The guilt of Ephraim is stored up,
    his sins are kept on record.
¹³ Pains as of a woman in childbirth come
     to him,
    but he is a child without wisdom;
when the time arrives,
    he doesn't have the sense to come out
     of the womb.

¹⁴ "I will deliver this people from the power
     of the grave;
    I will redeem them from death.
    Where, O death, are your plagues?
    Where, O grave, is your destruction?

    "I will have no compassion,
¹⁵   even though he thrives among his
     brothers.
An east wind from the Lᴏʀᴅ will come,
    blowing in from the desert;
his spring will fail
    and his well dry up.
His storehouse will be plundered
    of all its treasures.
¹⁶ The people of Samaria must bear their
     guilt,
    because they have rebelled against
     their God.
They will fall by the sword;
    their little ones will be dashed to the
     ground,
    their pregnant women ripped open."^b

Repentance to Bring Blessing

14 ^c Return, Israel, to the Lᴏʀᴅ your
     God.
    Your sins have been your downfall!
² Take words with you
    and return to the Lᴏʀᴅ.
Say to him:
    "Forgive all our sins
and receive us graciously,
    that we may offer the fruit of our lips.^d
³ Assyria cannot save us;
    we will not mount warhorses.
We will never again say 'Our gods'

---

^a 2 Or *"Men who sacrifice / kiss*
texts 14:1-9 is numbered 14:2-10.
^b 16 In Hebrew texts this verse (13:16) is numbered 14:1.
^c In Hebrew
^d 2 Or *offer our lips as sacrifices of bulls*

to what our own hands have made,
 for in you the fatherless find
  compassion."

4 "I will heal their waywardness
 and love them freely,
  for my anger has turned away
   from them.
5 I will be like the dew to Israel;
 he will blossom like a lily.
 Like a cedar of Lebanon
 he will send down his roots;
6 his young shoots will grow.
 His splendor will be like an olive tree,
  his fragrance like a cedar of Lebanon.
7 People will dwell again in his shade;
 they will flourish like the grain,

they will blossom like the vine —
 Israel's fame will be like the wine
  of Lebanon.
8 Ephraim, what more have I*a* to do
  with idols?
 I will answer him and care
  for him.
 I am like a flourishing juniper;
  your fruitfulness comes from me."

9 Who is wise? Let them realize these
  things.
 Who is discerning? Let them
  understand.
 The ways of the LORD are right;
  the righteous walk in them,
  but the rebellious stumble in them.

---

a 8 Or Hebrew; Septuagint What more has Ephraim

JOEL

WHEN DID THIS HAPPEN?

About 835 B.C. in the southern kingdom of Judah

WHO IS IN THIS BOOK?

Joel

VERSES YOU MIGHT RECOGNIZE

JOEL 2:13

"Return to the LORD your God, for he is gracious and compassionate, slow to anger and abounding in love."

JOEL 2:32

"And everyone who calls on the name of the LORD will be saved."

WHAT'S IT ABOUT?

Days covered in darkness. A mighty army consuming everything in its path. The moon turning to blood. The description of "the day of the LORD" in the book of Joel paints a frightening picture. In the prophet's own words, "The day of the LORD is great; it is dreadful. Who can endure it?" (2:11).

We don't know exactly when Joel lived, but clues in this book point to early in the life of King Joash (see 2 Kings 11–12), at the same time as the prophet Elisha. During a severe locust plague in Judah, Joel delivered God's message of judgment to Judah and the surrounding nations, but he also offered the people hope if they repented of their sins. The "day of the LORD" Joel talked about refers to more than just a locust plague. He also wrote of a final judgment day when God would judge all people and bring the righteous into his kingdom. This future event is also written about in 2 Thessalonians 2 and Revelation 16.

JOEL

1

The word of the LORD that came to Joel son of Pethuel.

An Invasion of Locusts

² Hear this, you elders;
  listen, all who live in the land.
Has anything like this ever happened in
    your days
  or in the days of your ancestors?
³ Tell it to your children,
  and let your children tell it to their
    children,
  and their children to the next
    generation.
⁴ What the locust swarm has left
  the great locusts have eaten;
what the great locusts have left
  the young locusts have eaten;
what the young locusts have left
  other locusts[a] have eaten.

⁵ Wake up, you drunkards, and weep!
  Wail, all you drinkers of wine;
wail because of the new wine,
  for it has been snatched from your lips.
⁶ A nation has invaded my land,
  a mighty army without number;
it has the teeth of a lion,
  the fangs of a lioness.
⁷ It has laid waste my vines
  and ruined my fig trees.
It has stripped off their bark
  and thrown it away,
  leaving their branches white.

⁸ Mourn like a virgin in sackcloth
  grieving for the betrothed of her youth.
⁹ Grain offerings and drink offerings
  are cut off from the house of the LORD.
The priests are in mourning,
  those who minister before the LORD.
¹⁰ The fields are ruined,
  the ground is dried up;
the grain is destroyed,
  the new wine is dried up,
  the olive oil fails.

¹¹ Despair, you farmers,
  wail, you vine growers;
grieve for the wheat and the barley,
  because the harvest of the field is
    destroyed.
¹² The vine is dried up
  and the fig tree is withered;
the pomegranate, the palm and the
    apple[b] tree —
  all the trees of the field — are dried up.
Surely the people's joy
  is withered away.

A Call to Lamentation

¹³ Put on sackcloth, you priests, and mourn;
  wail, you who minister before the
    altar.
Come, spend the night in sackcloth,
  you who minister before my God;
for the grain offerings and drink offerings
  are withheld from the house of your
    God.
¹⁴ Declare a holy fast;
  call a sacred assembly.
Summon the elders
  and all who live in the land
to the house of the LORD your God,
  and cry out to the LORD.

¹⁵ Alas for that day!
  For the day of the LORD is near;
  it will come like destruction from the
    Almighty.[c]

¹⁶ Has not the food been cut off
  before our very eyes —
joy and gladness
  from the house of our God?
¹⁷ The seeds are shriveled
  beneath the clods.[d]
The storehouses are in ruins,
  the granaries have been broken down,
  for the grain has dried up.
¹⁸ How the cattle moan!
  The herds mill about

---

a 4 The precise meaning of the four Hebrew words used here for locusts is uncertain.   b 12 Or possibly
apricot   c 15 Hebrew *Shaddai*   d 17 The meaning of the Hebrew for this word is uncertain.

IN SUFFERING

READ: JOEL 1:19-20

The pain and suffering in this world sometimes challenges everything we say we believe about God. Life doesn't always make sense—and it can shake our faith. It can leave us questioning what we think we know about God. Are those definitions lies? Mistakes? Half-truths? How does our understanding of God connect with the world in which we live?

I live through moments where, after hearing stories about starving people in war-torn countries, about people who are dying for lack of clean drinking water, about the hopelessness and despair some people experience with their employment, and on and on, I stop believing God is love, and I start wondering if maybe God isn't just plain disinterested in what's happening in our lives.

BUILDING FAITH WISDOM STRENGTH

Every struggle we face might be a great learning or testing opportunity, but it's not always from God. The dark clouds that storm into our lives don't always have silver linings. The simple truth is that we don't always know what God is up to. We don't always know why he allows what he does.

If all we do is tell God how much we don't like his decision, if all we do is shout, we've just created a one-sided anger diatribe. But if we say what we have to say and then stop and listen to what God might be saying back to us, that feels healthier. We need to be open to yelling our hearts out at God, but we need to be open to hearing back from God in response.

Taken from *Jesus Is for Liars: A Hypocrite's Guide to Authenticity* by Tim Baker, copyright © 2009 by Tim Baker, published by Zondervan.

because they have no pasture;
even the flocks of sheep are suffering.

¹⁹ To you, LORD, I call,
for fire has devoured the pastures in
the wilderness
and flames have burned up all the
trees of the field.
²⁰ Even the wild animals pant for you;
the streams of water have dried up
and fire has devoured the pastures in
the wilderness.

An Army of Locusts

2 Blow the trumpet in Zion;
sound the alarm on my holy hill.

Let all who live in the land tremble,
for the day of the LORD is coming.
It is close at hand—
² a day of darkness and gloom,
a day of clouds and blackness.
Like dawn spreading across the
mountains
a large and mighty army comes,
such as never was in ancient times
nor ever will be in ages to come.

³ Before them fire devours,
behind them a flame blazes.
Before them the land is like the garden
of Eden,
behind them, a desert waste—
nothing escapes them.
⁴ They have the appearance of horses;
they gallop along like cavalry.
⁵ With a noise like that of chariots
they leap over the mountaintops,
like a crackling fire consuming stubble,
like a mighty army drawn up for battle.

⁶ At the sight of them, nations are in
anguish;
every face turns pale.
⁷ They charge like warriors;
they scale walls like soldiers.
They all march in line,
not swerving from their course.
⁸ They do not jostle each other;
each marches straight ahead.
They plunge through defenses
without breaking ranks.
⁹ They rush upon the city;
they run along the wall.
They climb into the houses;

like thieves they enter through the
windows.

¹⁰ Before them the earth shakes,
the heavens tremble,
the sun and moon are darkened,
and the stars no longer shine.
¹¹ The LORD thunders
at the head of his army;
his forces are beyond number,
and mighty is the army that obeys
his command.
The day of the LORD is great;
it is dreadful.
Who can endure it?

Rend Your Heart

¹² "Even now," declares the LORD,
"return to me with all your heart,
with fasting and weeping and
mourning."

¹³ Rend your heart
and not your garments.
Return to the LORD your God,
for he is gracious and compassionate,
slow to anger and abounding in love,
and he relents from sending
calamity.
¹⁴ Who knows? He may turn and relent
and leave behind a blessing—
grain offerings and drink offerings
for the LORD your God.

¹⁵ Blow the trumpet in Zion,
declare a holy fast,
call a sacred assembly.
¹⁶ Gather the people,
consecrate the assembly;
bring together the elders,
gather the children,
those nursing at the breast.
Let the bridegroom leave his room
and the bride her chamber.
¹⁷ Let the priests, who minister before
the LORD,
weep between the portico and
the altar.
Let them say, "Spare your people, LORD.
Do not make your inheritance an
object of scorn,
a byword among the nations.
Why should they say among the
peoples,
'Where is their God?' "

JOEL

Return to the LORD your God, for he is gracious and compassionate, slow to anger and abounding in love. JOEL 2:13

HIS NAME MEANS: "the LORD is God"
READ HIS STORY: *Joel 1–2*

OF THE BIBLE

God raised up prophets to speak for him. They often warned of coming judgment and encouraged God's people to follow his teachings. Prophets had special access to God, through his Spirit, to know his mind and foresee future events.

Of all the prophets, we may know the least about Joel. Other prophets mentioned specific kings or events in their writings, so we can ascertain when they lived. Joel does not. He doesn't talk about himself, except to say he was the son of Pethuel. We do know he wrote to God's people in Judah.

While we don't know exactly when Joel was writing, we do know locusts had just swarmed Judah. The insects ravaged crops, creating a famine that killed people and livestock. Joel warned that there would be a judgement against Judah, unless the people fasted, prayed and turned to God.

Joel most likely lived near Jerusalem, because he referenced the capital city. The apostle Peter quoted from Joel in light of the Holy Spirit descending on the followers of Jesus at Pentecost (Acts 2:17–21).

THE GOOD KIND OF JEALOUS

READ: JOEL 2:18

God is not jealous of anything. He can't be. But the Creator is jealous for everything because it all belongs to him. Including you and me.

"There is not a square inch in the whole domain of our human existence over which Christ, who is Sovereign over all, does not cry, 'Mine!'" Abraham Kuyper said that. That's good stuff right there.

Everything was created by him . . . for him.

There never has been and never will be anyone like you, but that's thanks to the God who created you. And that means no one can worship God like you or for you. You're downright irreplaceable in God's grand scheme. And God is jealous for you. He's the one who causes your synapses to fire. He's the one who conceives desires within your heart of hearts. That's pretty cool to be so intensely sought after by someone so excellent.

Jealousy isn't a character trait that we sing about or write about often. We ignore it because we don't understand it. Jealousy has a negative connotation because for us it's usually the by-product of pride. But God's jealousy is a beautiful expression of his love. It's a jealous love that wants all of you—all to himself. And if you've ever been in love, you know what I'm talking about.

BUILDING FAITH WISDOM STRENGTH

The Lord's Answer

¹⁸ Then the LORD was jealous for his land
    and took pity on his people.

¹⁹ The LORD replied*ᵃ* to them:

"I am sending you grain, new wine and
    olive oil,
    enough to satisfy you fully;
never again will I make you
    an object of scorn to the nations.

²⁰ "I will drive the northern horde far
    from you,
    pushing it into a parched and barren
    land;
its eastern ranks will drown in the
    Dead Sea
    and its western ranks in the
    Mediterranean Sea.
And its stench will go up;
    its smell will rise."

Surely he has done great things!
²¹   Do not be afraid, land of Judah;
    be glad and rejoice.
Surely the LORD has done great things!
²²   Do not be afraid, you wild animals,
    for the pastures in the wilderness are
    becoming green.
The trees are bearing their fruit;
    the fig tree and the vine yield their
    riches.
²³ Be glad, people of Zion,
    rejoice in the LORD your God,
for he has given you the autumn rains
    because he is faithful.
He sends you abundant showers,
    both autumn and spring rains, as
    before.
²⁴ The threshing floors will be filled with
    grain;
    the vats will overflow with new wine
    and oil.

²⁵ "I will repay you for the years the locusts
    have eaten —
    the great locust and the young
    locust,
    the other locusts and the locust
    swarm*ᵇ* —
my great army that I sent among you.

²⁶ You will have plenty to eat, until you
    are full,
    and you will praise the name of the
    LORD your God,
    who has worked wonders for you;
never again will my people be shamed.
²⁷ Then you will know that I am in Israel,
    that I am the LORD your God,
    and that there is no other;
never again will my people be shamed.

The Day of the Lord

²⁸ "And afterward,
    I will pour out my Spirit on all people.
Your sons and daughters will prophesy,
    your old men will dream dreams,
    your young men will see visions.
²⁹ Even on my servants, both men and
    women,
    I will pour out my Spirit in those days.
³⁰ I will show wonders in the heavens
    and on the earth,
    blood and fire and billows of smoke.
³¹ The sun will be turned to darkness
    and the moon to blood
    before the coming of the great and
    dreadful day of the LORD.
³² And everyone who calls
    on the name of the LORD will be
    saved;
for on Mount Zion and in Jerusalem
    there will be deliverance,
    as the LORD has said,
even among the survivors
    whom the LORD calls.*ᶜ*

The Nations Judged

3^d "In those days and at that time,
    when I restore the fortunes of Judah
    and Jerusalem,
² I will gather all nations
    and bring them down to the Valley of
    Jehoshaphat.*ᵉ*
There I will put them on trial
    for what they did to my inheritance,
    my people Israel,
because they scattered my people among
    the nations
    and divided up my land.

ᵃ 18,19 Or *LORD will be jealous . . . / and take pity . . . / ¹⁹The LORD will reply*   *ᵇ 25* The precise meaning of the four Hebrew words used here for locusts is uncertain.   *ᶜ 32* In Hebrew texts 2:28-32 is numbered 3:1-5.   *ᵈ* In Hebrew texts 3:1-21 is numbered 4:1-21.   *ᵉ 2 Jehoshaphat* means *the LORD judges*; also in verse 12.

³ They cast lots for my people
    and traded boys for prostitutes;
    they sold girls for wine to drink.

⁴ "Now what have you against me, Tyre and Sidon and all you regions of Philistia? Are you repaying me for something I have done? If you are paying me back, I will swiftly and speedily return on your own heads what you have done. ⁵ For you took my silver and my gold and carried off my finest treasures to your temples.ᵃ ⁶ You sold the people of Judah and Jerusalem to the Greeks, that you might send them far from their homeland.

⁷ "See, I am going to rouse them out of the places to which you sold them, and I will return on your own heads what you have done. ⁸ I will sell your sons and daughters to the people of Judah, and they will sell them to the Sabeans, a nation far away." The LORD has spoken.

⁹ Proclaim this among the nations:
    Prepare for war!
    Rouse the warriors!
    Let all the fighting men draw near and
        attack.
¹⁰ Beat your plowshares into swords
    and your pruning hooks into spears.
    Let the weakling say,
        "I am strong!"
¹¹ Come quickly, all you nations from every
        side,
    and assemble there.

    Bring down your warriors, LORD!

¹² "Let the nations be roused;
    let them advance into the Valley of
        Jehoshaphat,
    for there I will sit
    to judge all the nations on every side.
¹³ Swing the sickle,
    for the harvest is ripe.
    Come, trample the grapes,
    for the winepress is full

and the vats overflow—
    so great is their wickedness!"

¹⁴ Multitudes, multitudes
    in the valley of decision!
For the day of the LORD is near
    in the valley of decision.
¹⁵ The sun and moon will be darkened,
    and the stars no longer shine.
¹⁶ The LORD will roar from Zion
    and thunder from Jerusalem;
    the earth and the heavens will
        tremble.
But the LORD will be a refuge for his
        people,
    a stronghold for the people of Israel.

Blessings for God's People

¹⁷ "Then you will know that I, the LORD
        your God,
    dwell in Zion, my holy hill.
Jerusalem will be holy;
    never again will foreigners invade her.

¹⁸ "In that day the mountains will drip
        new wine,
    and the hills will flow with milk;
    all the ravines of Judah will run with
        water.
A fountain will flow out of the LORD's
        house
    and will water the valley of acacias.ᵇ
¹⁹ But Egypt will be desolate,
    Edom a desert waste,
because of violence done to the people
        of Judah,
    in whose land they shed innocent
        blood.
²⁰ Judah will be inhabited forever
    and Jerusalem through all
        generations.
²¹ Shall I leave their innocent blood
        unavenged?
    No, I will not."

    The LORD dwells in Zion!

ᵃ 5 Or *palaces*   ᵇ 18 Or *Valley of Shittim*

AMOS

➤ **WHEN DID THIS HAPPEN?**
About 760 B.C. in the northern kingdom of Israel

➤ **WHO IS IN THIS BOOK?**
Amos

➤ **VERSES YOU MIGHT RECOGNIZE**

AMOS 4:13
"He who forms the mountains, who creates the wind, and who reveals his thoughts to mankind, who turns dawn to darkness, and treads on the heights of the earth—the LORD God Almighty is his name."

AMOS 5:24
"But let justice roll on like a river, righteousness like a never-failing stream!"

WHAT'S IT ABOUT?

Amos, a shepherd from Judah, delivered God's message to the northern kingdom of Israel. After speaking judgment against the surrounding nations of Damascus, Gaza, Tyre, Edom, Ammon and Moab, Amos pointed out Israel's many sins. At the top of the list was injustice toward the weak and the poor. The people were rich and successful because of their own greed and violence, but they would be punished for the wicked and unjust ways they treated others.

Written 160 years before the Babylonian exile begins, Amos predicted that Israel would one day be judged for breaking God's law. Unlike some of the other prophetic books, this one doesn't mix in a message of God's love and restoration until the very end. Even that promise—that God will "restore David's fallen shelter" by providing a Messiah from David's bloodline—was directed to Judah, not the more rebellious northern kingdom of Israel.

AMOS

1 The words of Amos, one of the shepherds of Tekoa — the vision he saw concerning Israel two years before the earthquake, when Uzziah was king of Judah and Jeroboam son of Jehoash[a] was king of Israel. ²He said:

"The LORD roars from Zion
   and thunders from Jerusalem;
the pastures of the shepherds dry up,
   and the top of Carmel withers."

Judgment on Israel's Neighbors

³This is what the LORD says:

"For three sins of Damascus,
   even for four, I will not relent.
Because she threshed Gilead
   with sledges having iron teeth,
⁴I will send fire on the house of Hazael
   that will consume the fortresses of
      Ben-Hadad.
⁵I will break down the gate of Damascus;
   I will destroy the king who is in[b] the
      Valley of Aven[c]
and the one who holds the scepter in
      Beth Eden.
   The people of Aram will go into exile
      to Kir,"
                              says the LORD.

⁶This is what the LORD says:

"For three sins of Gaza,
   even for four, I will not relent.
Because she took captive whole
      communities
   and sold them to Edom,
⁷I will send fire on the walls of Gaza
   that will consume her fortresses.
⁸I will destroy the king[d] of Ashdod
   and the one who holds the scepter in
      Ashkelon.
I will turn my hand against Ekron,
   till the last of the Philistines are dead,"
                  says the Sovereign LORD.

⁹This is what the LORD says:

"For three sins of Tyre,
   even for four, I will not relent.
Because she sold whole communities of
      captives to Edom,
   disregarding a treaty of brotherhood,
¹⁰I will send fire on the walls of Tyre
   that will consume her fortresses."

¹¹This is what the LORD says:

"For three sins of Edom,
   even for four, I will not relent.
Because he pursued his brother with
      a sword
   and slaughtered the women of
      the land,
because his anger raged continually
   and his fury flamed unchecked,
¹²I will send fire on Teman
   that will consume the fortresses
      of Bozrah."

¹³This is what the LORD says:

"For three sins of Ammon,
   even for four, I will not relent.
Because he ripped open the pregnant
      women of Gilead
   in order to extend his borders,
¹⁴I will set fire to the walls of Rabbah
   that will consume her fortresses
amid war cries on the day of battle,
   amid violent winds on a
      stormy day.
¹⁵Her king[e] will go into exile,
   he and his officials together,"
                              says the LORD.

2 This is what the LORD says:

"For three sins of Moab,
   even for four, I will not relent.
Because he burned to ashes
   the bones of Edom's king,
²I will send fire on Moab

---

[a] 1 Hebrew *Joash*, a variant of *Jehoash*   [b] 5 Or *the inhabitants of*   [c] 5 *Aven* means *wickedness*.
[d] 8 Or *inhabitants*   [e] 15 Or / Molek

that will consume the fortresses of
   Kerioth.*a*
Moab will go down in great tumult
   amid war cries and the blast of the
   trumpet.
³ I will destroy her ruler
   and kill all her officials with him,"
                                    says the LORD.

⁴ This is what the LORD says:

"For three sins of Judah,
   even for four, I will not relent.
Because they have rejected the law of
   the LORD
   and have not kept his decrees,
because they have been led astray by
   false gods,*b*
   the gods*c* their ancestors followed,
⁵ I will send fire on Judah
   that will consume the fortresses of
   Jerusalem."

Judgment on Israel

⁶ This is what the LORD says:

"For three sins of Israel,
   even for four, I will not relent.
They sell the innocent for silver,
   and the needy for a pair of sandals.
⁷ They trample on the heads of the poor
   as on the dust of the ground
   and deny justice to the oppressed.
Father and son use the same girl
   and so profane my holy name.
⁸ They lie down beside every altar
   on garments taken in pledge.
In the house of their god
   they drink wine taken as fines.

⁹ "Yet I destroyed the Amorites before
   them,
   though they were tall as the cedars
   and strong as the oaks.
I destroyed their fruit above
   and their roots below.
¹⁰ I brought you up out of Egypt
   and led you forty years in the
   wilderness
   to give you the land of the Amorites.

¹¹ "I also raised up prophets from among
   your children
   and Nazirites from among your
   youths.

Is this not true, people of Israel?"
                                 declares the LORD.
¹² "But you made the Nazirites drink wine
   and commanded the prophets not
   to prophesy.

¹³ "Now then, I will crush you
   as a cart crushes when loaded with
   grain.
¹⁴ The swift will not escape,
   the strong will not muster their
   strength,
   and the warrior will not save his life.
¹⁵ The archer will not stand his ground,
   the fleet-footed soldier will not get
   away,
   and the horseman will not save his
   life.
¹⁶ Even the bravest warriors
   will flee naked on that day,"
                                 declares the LORD.

Witnesses Summoned Against Israel

3 Hear this word, people of Israel, the
   word the LORD has spoken against
you—against the whole family I brought up
out of Egypt:

² "You only have I chosen
   of all the families of the earth;
therefore I will punish you
   for all your sins."

³ Do two walk together
   unless they have agreed to do so?
⁴ Does a lion roar in the thicket
   when it has no prey?
Does it growl in its den
   when it has caught nothing?
⁵ Does a bird swoop down to a trap on
   the ground
   when no bait is there?
Does a trap spring up from the ground
   if it has not caught anything?
⁶ When a trumpet sounds in a city,
   do not the people tremble?
When disaster comes to a city,
   has not the LORD caused it?

⁷ Surely the Sovereign LORD does nothing
   without revealing his plan
   to his servants the prophets.

⁸ The lion has roared—
   who will not fear?

---

a 2 Or *of her cities*   *b 4* Or *by lies*   *c 4* Or *lies*

I'LL GO

READ: AMOS 2:6

God is fed up with his people's constant wrongdoing. You can hear him burst with anger as he speaks through the prophet Amos. Amos thunders against Israel (the northern kingdom) even though he comes from Judah (the southern kingdom). The Bible mentions his hometown, Tekoa (Amos 1:1), a village a few miles south of Jerusalem. Amos comes on the scene "two years before the earthquake" (v. 1), an event historians can't precisely date.

This real-life guy never planned on becoming the Lord's spokesperson. He wasn't born to a line of prophets, priests, or other religious workers. When pressed for his credentials, he explains, "I was neither a prophet nor the son of a prophet, but I was a shepherd, and I also took care of sycamore-fig trees" (7:14). Yet the Lord compels him to speak up. As Amos puts it, "The LORD took me from tending the flock and said to me, 'Go, prophesy to my people Israel'" (v. 15).

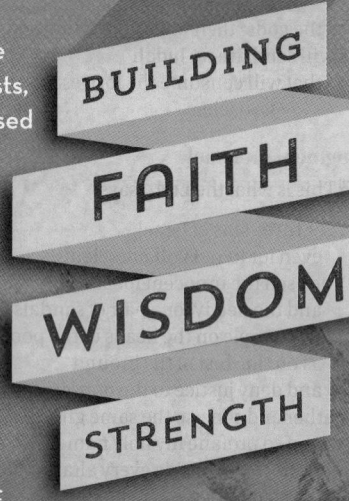

This prophet speaks against Israel's neighbors before turning to the sins of God's people. He rebukes them for abandoning God's laws and following false gods. He repeatedly denounces Israel's treatment of the poor, a key theme of his preaching.

Amos illustrates that God can pluck you out of your everyday life and send you to places you never expected, doing things you could never foresee. Tell him you're willing to serve him wherever and however he wants.

The Sovereign LORD has spoken —
who can but prophesy?

⁹ Proclaim to the fortresses of Ashdod
and to the fortresses of Egypt:
"Assemble yourselves on the mountains
of Samaria;
see the great unrest within her
and the oppression among her people."

¹⁰ "They do not know how to do right,"
declares the LORD,
"who store up in their fortresses
what they have plundered and looted."

¹¹ Therefore this is what the Sovereign
LORD says:

"An enemy will overrun your land,
pull down your strongholds
and plunder your fortresses."

¹² This is what the LORD says:

"As a shepherd rescues from the lion's
mouth
only two leg bones or a piece of an ear,
so will the Israelites living in Samaria be
rescued,
with only the head of a bed
and a piece of fabric*a* from a couch.*b*"

¹³ "Hear this and testify against the descendants of Jacob," declares the Lord, the
LORD God Almighty.

¹⁴ "On the day I punish Israel for her sins,
I will destroy the altars of Bethel;
the horns of the altar will be cut off
and fall to the ground.
¹⁵ I will tear down the winter house
along with the summer house;
the houses adorned with ivory will be
destroyed
and the mansions will be demolished,"
declares the LORD.

Israel Has Not Returned to God

4 Hear this word, you cows of Bashan on
Mount Samaria,
you women who oppress the poor and
crush the needy
and say to your husbands, "Bring us
some drinks!"

² The Sovereign LORD has sworn by his
holiness:
"The time will surely come
when you will be taken away with hooks,
the last of you with fishhooks.*c*
³ You will each go straight out
through breaches in the wall,
and you will be cast out toward
Harmon,*d*"
declares the LORD.

⁴ "Go to Bethel and sin;
go to Gilgal and sin yet more.
Bring your sacrifices every morning,
your tithes every three years.*e*
⁵ Burn leavened bread as a thank offering
and brag about your freewill
offerings —
boast about them, you Israelites,
for this is what you love to do,"
declares the Sovereign LORD.

⁶ "I gave you empty stomachs in every city
and lack of bread in every town,
yet you have not returned to me,"
declares the LORD.

⁷ "I also withheld rain from you
when the harvest was still three
months away.
I sent rain on one town,
but withheld it from another.
One field had rain;
another had none and dried up.
⁸ People staggered from town to town for
water
but did not get enough to drink,
yet you have not returned to me,"
declares the LORD.

⁹ "Many times I struck your gardens and
vineyards,
destroying them with blight and
mildew.
Locusts devoured your fig and olive
trees,
yet you have not returned to me,"
declares the LORD.

¹⁰ "I sent plagues among you
as I did to Egypt.
I killed your young men with the sword,
along with your captured horses.

---

a 12 The meaning of the Hebrew for this phrase is uncertain.   *b* 12 Or *Israelites be rescued, / those who
sit in Samaria / on the edge of their beds / and in Damascus on their couches.*   *c* 2 Or *away in baskets, /
the last of you in fish baskets*   *d* 3 Masoretic Text; with a different word division of the Hebrew (see
Septuagint) *out, you mountain of oppression*   *e* 4 Or *days*

I filled your nostrils with the stench of
your camps,
yet you have not returned to me,"
declares the LORD.

¹¹ "I overthrew some of you
as I overthrew Sodom and
Gomorrah.
You were like a burning stick snatched
from the fire,
yet you have not returned to me,"
declares the LORD.

¹² "Therefore this is what I will do to you,
Israel,
and because I will do this to you,
Israel,
prepare to meet your God."

¹³ He who forms the mountains,
who creates the wind,
and who reveals his thoughts to
mankind,
who turns dawn to darkness,
and treads on the heights of the
earth —
the LORD God Almighty is his name.

A Lament and Call to Repentance

5 Hear this word, Israel, this lament I take
up concerning you:

² "Fallen is Virgin Israel,
never to rise again,
deserted in her own land,
with no one to lift her up."

³ This is what the Sovereign LORD says to
Israel:

"Your city that marches out a thousand
strong
will have only a hundred left;
your town that marches out a hundred
strong
will have only ten left."

⁴ This is what the LORD says to Israel:

"Seek me and live;
⁵ do not seek Bethel,
do not go to Gilgal,
do not journey to Beersheba.
For Gilgal will surely go into exile,
and Bethel will be reduced to
nothing.^a"

⁶ Seek the LORD and live,
or he will sweep through the tribes of
Joseph like a fire;
it will devour them,
and Bethel will have no one to
quench it.

⁷ There are those who turn justice into
bitterness
and cast righteousness to the ground.

⁸ He who made the Pleiades and Orion,
who turns midnight into dawn
and darkens day into night,
who calls for the waters of the sea
and pours them out over the face of
the land —
the LORD is his name.
⁹ With a blinding flash he destroys the
stronghold
and brings the fortified city to ruin.

¹⁰ There are those who hate the one who
upholds justice in court
and detest the one who tells the truth.

¹¹ You levy a straw tax on the poor
and impose a tax on their grain.
Therefore, though you have built stone
mansions,
you will not live in them;
though you have planted lush vineyards,
you will not drink their wine.
¹² For I know how many are your offenses
and how great your sins.

There are those who oppress the
innocent and take bribes
and deprive the poor of justice in the
courts.
¹³ Therefore the prudent keep quiet in
such times,
for the times are evil.

¹⁴ Seek good, not evil,
that you may live.
Then the LORD God Almighty will be
with you,
just as you say he is.
¹⁵ Hate evil, love good;
maintain justice in the courts.
Perhaps the LORD God Almighty will
have mercy
on the remnant of Joseph.

¹⁶ Therefore this is what the Lord, the LORD
God Almighty, says:

---

^a 5 Hebrew *aven*, a reference to Beth Aven (a derogatory name for Bethel); see Hosea 4:15.

"There will be wailing in all the streets
   and cries of anguish in every public
      square.
The farmers will be summoned to weep
   and the mourners to wail.
¹⁷ There will be wailing in all the vineyards,
   for I will pass through your midst,"
                              says the LORD.

The Day of the Lord

¹⁸ Woe to you who long
   for the day of the LORD!
Why do you long for the day of the LORD?
   That day will be darkness, not light.
¹⁹ It will be as though a man fled from a lion
   only to meet a bear,
as though he entered his house
   and rested his hand on the wall
   only to have a snake bite him.
²⁰ Will not the day of the LORD be darkness,
   not light—
   pitch-dark, without a ray of
      brightness?

²¹ "I hate, I despise your religious festivals;
   your assemblies are a stench to me.
²² Even though you bring me burnt
      offerings and grain offerings,
   I will not accept them.
Though you bring choice fellowship
      offerings,
   I will have no regard for them.
²³ Away with the noise of your songs!
   I will not listen to the music of your
      harps.
²⁴ But let justice roll on like a river,
   righteousness like a never-failing
      stream!

²⁵ "Did you bring me sacrifices and
      offerings
   forty years in the wilderness, people
      of Israel?
²⁶ You have lifted up the shrine of
      your king,
   the pedestal of your idols,
   the star of your god[a]—
   which you made for yourselves.
²⁷ Therefore I will send you into exile
      beyond Damascus,"
   says the LORD, whose name is God
      Almighty.

Woe to the Complacent

6 Woe to you who are complacent
      in Zion,
   and to you who feel secure on Mount
      Samaria,
you notable men of the foremost
      nation,
   to whom the people of Israel come!
² Go to Kalneh and look at it;
   go from there to great Hamath,
   and then go down to Gath in Philistia.
Are they better off than your two
      kingdoms?
   Is their land larger than yours?
³ You put off the day of disaster
   and bring near a reign of terror.
⁴ You lie on beds adorned with ivory
   and lounge on your couches.
You dine on choice lambs
   and fattened calves.
⁵ You strum away on your harps like David
   and improvise on musical
      instruments.
⁶ You drink wine by the bowlful
   and use the finest lotions,
   but you do not grieve over the ruin of
      Joseph.
⁷ Therefore you will be among the first to
      go into exile;
   your feasting and lounging will end.

The Lord Abhors the Pride of Israel

⁸ The Sovereign LORD has sworn by himself—the LORD God Almighty declares:

   "I abhor the pride of Jacob
      and detest his fortresses;
   I will deliver up the city
      and everything in it."

⁹ If ten people are left in one house, they
too will die. ¹⁰ And if the relative who comes
to carry the bodies out of the house to burn
them[b] asks anyone who might be hiding
there, "Is anyone else with you?" and he
says, "No," then he will go on to say, "Hush!
We must not mention the name of the LORD."

¹¹ For the LORD has given the command,
      and he will smash the great house into
      pieces
      and the small house into bits.

_a 26_ Or _lifted up Sakkuth your king / and Kaiwan your idols, / your star-gods_; Septuagint _lifted up the shrine
of Molek / and the star of your god Rephan, / their idols_   _b 10_ Or _to make a funeral fire in honor of the dead_

LET IT ROLL

READ: AMOS 5:24

You never have to wonder what the prophet Amos is thinking. As soon as he opens his mouth you discover he has a message burning inside. He aims to rescue the poor and oppressed.

Amos points out the obvious idolatry and immorality of God's people. But right from the start the prophet attacks people who mistreat the weakest members of society. He says the Israelites "sell the innocent for silver, and the needy for a pair of sandals" (Amos 2:6), forcing neighbors into slavery and selling them for the price of cheap flip-flops.

When the Israelites go to court, "they trample on the heads of the poor as on the dust of the ground and deny justice to the oppressed" (v. 7).

The prophet compares rich women to well-fed cows who force their husbands to crush the needy (4:1). Even though the wealthy have money to build stone mansions, the poor are taxed to the point of starvation (5:11). Merchants cheat the poor with dishonest scales (8:5).

There's no evidence that Israel ever listened to Amos, and a few decades later the kingdom fell to invading Assyrians. But even now the words of Amos push you to work to overcome injustice. For example, around the world, thousands of people are working in sweatshops to create the clothes we buy, and you can affect change by being aware of where your clothing and other products are made. People are living with day-to-day starvation, and you can find an organization that helps meet their needs. Like the prophet said, "Let justice roll on like a river, righteousness like a never failing stream!" (5:24).

BUILDING

FAITH

WISDOM

STRENGTH

12 Do horses run on the rocky crags?
  Does one plow the sea*a* with oxen?
But you have turned justice into poison
  and the fruit of righteousness into
    bitterness—
13 you who rejoice in the conquest of Lo
    Debar*b*
  and say, "Did we not take Karnaim*c*
    by our own strength?"

14 For the LORD God Almighty declares,
  "I will stir up a nation against you,
    Israel,
that will oppress you all the way
  from Lebo Hamath to the valley of the
    Arabah."

Locusts, Fire and a Plumb Line

7 This is what the Sovereign LORD showed
  me: He was preparing swarms of locusts
after the king's share had been harvested
and just as the late crops were coming up.
2 When they had stripped the land clean, I
cried out, "Sovereign LORD, forgive! How can
Jacob survive? He is so small!"

3 So the LORD relented.

"This will not happen," the LORD said.

4 This is what the Sovereign LORD showed
me: The Sovereign LORD was calling for
judgment by fire; it dried up the great deep
and devoured the land. 5 Then I cried out,
"Sovereign LORD, I beg you, stop! How can
Jacob survive? He is so small!"

6 So the LORD relented.

"This will not happen either," the Sovereign LORD said.

7 This is what he showed me: The Lord was
standing by a wall that had been built true
to plumb,*d* with a plumb line*e* in his hand.
8 And the LORD asked me, "What do you see,
Amos?"

"A plumb line," I replied.

Then the Lord said, "Look, I am setting a
plumb line among my people Israel; I will
spare them no longer.

9 "The high places of Isaac will be
    destroyed
  and the sanctuaries of Israel will be
    ruined;

with my sword I will rise against the
  house of Jeroboam."

Amos and Amaziah

10 Then Amaziah the priest of Bethel sent a
message to Jeroboam king of Israel: "Amos is
raising a conspiracy against you in the very
heart of Israel. The land cannot bear all his
words. 11 For this is what Amos is saying:

" 'Jeroboam will die by the sword,
  and Israel will surely go into exile,
    away from their native land.' "

12 Then Amaziah said to Amos, "Get out,
you seer! Go back to the land of Judah. Earn
your bread there and do your prophesying
there. 13 Don't prophesy anymore at Bethel,
because this is the king's sanctuary and the
temple of the kingdom."

14 Amos answered Amaziah, "I was neither a prophet nor the son of a prophet, but I
was a shepherd, and I also took care of sycamore-fig trees. 15 But the LORD took me from
tending the flock and said to me, 'Go, prophesy to my people Israel.' 16 Now then, hear
the word of the LORD. You say,

" 'Do not prophesy against Israel,
  and stop preaching against the
    descendants of Isaac.'

17 "Therefore this is what the LORD says:

" 'Your wife will become a prostitute in
    the city,
  and your sons and daughters will fall
    by the sword.
Your land will be measured and
    divided up,
  and you yourself will die in a pagan*f*
    country.
And Israel will surely go into exile,
  away from their native land.' "

A Basket of Ripe Fruit

8 This is what the Sovereign LORD showed
  me: a basket of ripe fruit. 2 "What do you
see, Amos?" he asked.

"A basket of ripe fruit," I answered.

Then the LORD said to me, "The time is
ripe for my people Israel; I will spare them
no longer.

---

a 12 With a different word division of the Hebrew; Masoretic Text *plow there*   *b 13 Lo Debar* means
nothing.   *c 13 Karnaim* means *horns; horn* here symbolizes strength.   *d 7* The meaning of the
Hebrew for this phrase is uncertain.   *e 7* The meaning of the Hebrew for this phrase is uncertain; also
in verse 8.   *f 17* Hebrew *an unclean*

TAKE A STAND

READ: AMOS 7:12-14

On October 31, 1517, a monk named Martin Luther picked a great fight. He attacked the selling of indulgences. Indulgences were sold by the Catholic Church, and could "erase" a sin or reduce your time in "purgatory." Luther posted ninety-five reasons why they were dead wrong on the doors of All Saints' Church in Wittenberg, Germany, and ignited the Protestant Reformation.

What I love about the story is how a little-known monk in a tiny town in the middle of nowhere could impact history the way he did. I don't think Martin Luther knew he was making history as he made history, but our small acts of courage can have a domino effect. All we need to do is stand up, step in, or step out.

Holy Roman emperor Charles V put the poor guy on trial in 1521, but Martin refused to back down: "My conscience is taken captive by God's Word, I cannot and will not recant anything."

BUILDING FAITH WISDOM STRENGTH

Let me bring it a little closer to home. Who do you need to stand up for? The homeless? The fatherless? The voiceless? Stop reading for a minute and actually think about that. Maybe it's a friend or issue you care about deeply.

It may feel like an overwhelming problem or challenge or dream, but don't let what you can't do keep you from doing what you can. Take the first step. Step up and make a difference.

³ "In that day," declares the Sovereign LORD, "the songs in the temple will turn to wailing.^a Many, many bodies — flung everywhere! Silence!"

⁴ Hear this, you who trample the needy
  and do away with the poor of the land,

⁵ saying,

"When will the New Moon be over
  that we may sell grain,
and the Sabbath be ended
  that we may market wheat?" —
skimping on the measure,
  boosting the price
and cheating with dishonest scales,
⁶ buying the poor with silver
  and the needy for a pair of sandals,
  selling even the sweepings with the
    wheat.

⁷ The LORD has sworn by himself, the Pride of Jacob: "I will never forget anything they have done.

⁸ "Will not the land tremble for this,
  and all who live in it mourn?
The whole land will rise like the Nile;
  it will be stirred up and then sink
  like the river of Egypt.

⁹ "In that day," declares the Sovereign LORD,

"I will make the sun go down at noon
  and darken the earth in broad
    daylight.
¹⁰ I will turn your religious festivals into
    mourning
  and all your singing into weeping.
I will make all of you wear sackcloth
  and shave your heads.
I will make that time like mourning for
    an only son
  and the end of it like a bitter day.

¹¹ "The days are coming," declares the
    Sovereign LORD,
  "when I will send a famine through the
    land —
not a famine of food or a thirst for water,
  but a famine of hearing the words of
    the LORD.
¹² People will stagger from sea to sea
  and wander from north to east,

searching for the word of the LORD,
  but they will not find it.

¹³ "In that day

"the lovely young women and strong
    young men
  will faint because of thirst.
¹⁴ Those who swear by the sin of Samaria —
  who say, 'As surely as your god lives,
    Dan,'
or, 'As surely as the god^b of Beersheba
    lives' —
  they will fall, never to rise again."

Israel to Be Destroyed

9 I saw the Lord standing by the altar, and he said:

"Strike the tops of the pillars
  so that the thresholds shake.
Bring them down on the heads of all the
    people;
  those who are left I will kill with the
    sword.
Not one will get away,
  none will escape.
² Though they dig down to the depths
    below,
  from there my hand will take them.
Though they climb up to the heavens
    above,
  from there I will bring them down.
³ Though they hide themselves on the top
    of Carmel,
  there I will hunt them down and seize
    them.
Though they hide from my eyes at the
    bottom of the sea,
  there I will command the serpent to
    bite them.
⁴ Though they are driven into exile by their
    enemies,
  there I will command the sword to
    slay them.

"I will keep my eye on them
  for harm and not for good."

⁵ The Lord, the LORD Almighty —
  he touches the earth and it melts,
    and all who live in it mourn;
the whole land rises like the Nile,
    then sinks like the river of Egypt;

---

^a 3 Or "the temple singers will wail   ^b 14 Hebrew the way

AMOS

MEN

OF THE BIBLE

"I was neither a prophet nor the son of a prophet, but I was a shepherd, and I also took care of sycamore-fig trees. But the LORD took me from tending the flock and said to me, 'Go, prophesy to my people Israel.'"AMOS 7:14-15

HIS NAME MEANS: "burden-bearer"
READ HIS STORY: *Amos 1:1–2; 7, 9*

A
mos was an ordinary man. He was a shepherd and a farmer. Yet he had an extraordinary boldness for God.

Amos lived in the southern kingdom of Judah in the village of Tekoa, located south of Bethlehem. One day Amos left the comfort of his village and his quiet days on his farm to travel to the northern kingdom of Israel with an important message for the people there. He never considered himself a prophet or someone meant to do full-time ministry, but when God called him, he went.

His mission was to address the people of both Israel and Judah (who were refusing to follow God) and the neighboring nations (who were fighting violently against each other). Even when the world was going crazy around him, Amos boldly declared God's message. He stood strong in his faith even when important leaders told him to shut his mouth and go away.

Are you surrounded by ungodly people? Other teens who don't care what's right or wrong? Teachers or other adults who push their agenda of wrong-doing or scoff at your faith? Family members who tell you to keep quiet and get lost?

Stand firm in your beliefs based on the truth of God's Word. You follow the Mighty God, the Creator of the universe. Nothing compares with that. That's why Amos was confident—he knew who he was following. He declared in Amos 4:13, "He who forms the mountains, who creates the wind, and who reveals his thoughts to mankind, who turns dawn to darkness, and treads on the heights of the earth— the LORD God Almighty is his name."

[6] he builds his lofty palace[a] in the
  heavens
  and sets its foundation[b] on the earth;
he calls for the waters of the sea
  and pours them out over the face of
  the land —
  the LORD is his name.

[7] "Are not you Israelites
  the same to me as the Cushites[c]?"
  declares the LORD.
"Did I not bring Israel up from Egypt,
  the Philistines from Caphtor[d]
  and the Arameans from Kir?

[8] "Surely the eyes of the Sovereign LORD
  are on the sinful kingdom.
I will destroy it
  from the face of the earth.
Yet I will not totally destroy
  the descendants of Jacob,"
  declares the LORD.

[9] "For I will give the command,
  and I will shake the people
  of Israel
  among all the nations
as grain is shaken in a sieve,
  and not a pebble will reach the
  ground.

[10] All the sinners among my people
  will die by the sword,
all those who say,
  'Disaster will not overtake or
  meet us.'

Israel's Restoration

[11] "In that day

"I will restore David's fallen shelter —
  I will repair its broken walls
  and restore its ruins —
  and will rebuild it as it used to be,
[12] so that they may possess the remnant
  of Edom
  and all the nations that bear my name,[e]"
  declares the LORD, who will
  do these things.

[13] "The days are coming," declares the
LORD,

"when the reaper will be overtaken by
  the plowman
  and the planter by the one treading
  grapes.
New wine will drip from the mountains
  and flow from all the hills,
[14] and I will bring my people Israel back
  from exile.[f]

"They will rebuild the ruined cities and
  live in them.
They will plant vineyards and drink
  their wine;
they will make gardens and eat their
  fruit.
[15] I will plant Israel in their own land,
  never again to be uprooted
  from the land I have given them,"

says the LORD your God.

---

[a] 6 The meaning of the Hebrew for this phrase is uncertain.   [b] 6 The meaning of the Hebrew for this word is uncertain.   [c] 7 That is, people from the upper Nile region   [d] 7 That is, Crete   [e] 12 Hebrew; Septuagint *so that the remnant of people / and all the nations that bear my name may seek me*   [f] 14 Or *will restore the fortunes of my people Israel*

OBADIAH

WHEN DID THIS HAPPEN?

Unknown, but possibly around 605 B.C.

WHO IS IN THIS BOOK?

Obadiah

Jacob

Esau

VERSE YOU MIGHT RECOGNIZE

OBADIAH 1:17

"But on Mount Zion will be deliverance; it will be holy, and Jacob will possess his inheritance."

WHAT'S IT ABOUT?

At just twenty-one verses, Obadiah is the shortest book in the Old Testament. Obadiah delivered a prophecy against Edom, a nation that had been hurting Israel. When Babylon took the Jews captive, Edom rejoiced in their destruction, mocked them, and even took the opportunity to loot Jerusalem. Through Obadiah, God told Edom that he would destroy their nation forever and redeem Israel.

The Edomites and the Israelites were actually related. The two nations were descendants of twin brothers—Jacob (who was renamed Israel) and Esau. Throughout history, the two nations fought. Many years before this book was written, God had made a promise to Abraham and Israel; "Whoever curses you I will curse" (Genesis 12:3). That was true of Edom, a nation that does not exist today. Obadiah's point was clear: Even though Israel was far from perfect, God would defend his chosen people against anyone who hurt them.

OBADIAH

Obadiah's Vision

¹ The vision of Obadiah.

This is what the Sovereign Lord says about Edom—

We have heard a message from the Lord:
    An envoy was sent to the nations to say,
"Rise, let us go against her for battle"—

² "See, I will make you small among the nations;
    you will be utterly despised.
³ The pride of your heart has deceived you,
    you who live in the clefts of the rocks*a*
and make your home on the heights,
you who say to yourself,
    'Who can bring me down to the ground?'
⁴ Though you soar like the eagle
    and make your nest among the stars,
from there I will bring you down,"
               declares the Lord.
⁵ "If thieves came to you,
    if robbers in the night—
oh, what a disaster awaits you!—
    would they not steal only as much as they wanted?
If grape pickers came to you,
    would they not leave a few grapes?
⁶ But how Esau will be ransacked,
    his hidden treasures pillaged!
⁷ All your allies will force you to the border;
    your friends will deceive and overpower you;
those who eat your bread will set a trap for you,*b*
    but you will not detect it.

⁸ "In that day," declares the Lord,
    "will I not destroy the wise men of Edom,
those of understanding in the mountains of Esau?
⁹ Your warriors, Teman, will be terrified,
and everyone in Esau's mountains
    will be cut down in the slaughter.
¹⁰ Because of the violence against your brother Jacob,
    you will be covered with shame;
    you will be destroyed forever.
¹¹ On the day you stood aloof
    while strangers carried off his wealth
and foreigners entered his gates
    and cast lots for Jerusalem,
    you were like one of them.
¹² You should not gloat over your brother
    in the day of his misfortune,
nor rejoice over the people of Judah
    in the day of their destruction,
nor boast so much
    in the day of their trouble.
¹³ You should not march through the gates of my people
    in the day of their disaster,
nor gloat over them in their calamity
    in the day of their disaster,
nor seize their wealth
    in the day of their disaster.
¹⁴ You should not wait at the crossroads
    to cut down their fugitives,
nor hand over their survivors
    in the day of their trouble.

¹⁵ "The day of the Lord is near
    for all nations.
As you have done, it will be done to you;
    your deeds will return upon your own head.
¹⁶ Just as you drank on my holy hill,
    so all the nations will drink continually;
they will drink and drink
    and be as if they had never been.
¹⁷ But on Mount Zion will be deliverance;
    it will be holy,
    and Jacob will possess his inheritance.
¹⁸ Jacob will be a fire
    and Joseph a flame;

---

a 3 Or *of Sela*   *b 7* The meaning of the Hebrew for this clause is uncertain.

OBADIAH

On the day you stood aloof while strangers carried off his wealth and foreigners entered his gates and cast lots for Jerusalem, you were like one of them. OBADIAH 11

HIS NAME MEANS: "servant" or "worshiper of the Lord"
READ HIS STORY: *Obadiah*

OF THE BIBLE

Obadiah was a prophet who spoke a powerful message from God to the Edomites, neighbors of Judah. His message was clear: God would bring judgment upon the people of Edom because they turned their back on the people of Judah and took advantage of their desperate plight.

Nothing much is known about the prophet who wrote the book except for his name. He delivered the message, however, with such a lively and passionate voice that it reveals the heartfelt passion of the man who wrote it.

Obadiah pronounced judgment against the Edomites because they didn't care about what happened to the people of Judah in their day of distress. They didn't try to help. In fact, the Edomites went so far as to treat the Jewish fugitives poorly (verse 14).

Obadiah's message reminds us how precious God's people are to the Lord. And that God will watch over his people, even when they sin, protecting them those who wish to harm.

Esau will be stubble,
    and they will set him on fire and
        destroy him.
There will be no survivors
    from Esau."

                    The LORD has spoken.

[19] People from the Negev will occupy
    the mountains of Esau,
and people from the foothills will possess
    the land of the Philistines.
They will occupy the fields of Ephraim
    and Samaria,
and Benjamin will possess
    Gilead.
[20] This company of Israelite exiles who
    are in Canaan
will possess the land as far as
    Zarephath;
the exiles from Jerusalem who are in
    Sepharad
will possess the towns of the Negev.
[21] Deliverers will go up on[a] Mount Zion
    to govern the mountains of Esau.
And the kingdom will be the LORD's.

JONAH

**WHEN DID THIS
HAPPEN?**

Around 760 B.C. in Assyria

**WHO IS IN THIS
BOOK?**

Jonah

the Ninevites

**VERSES YOU MIGHT
RECOGNIZE**

JONAH 2:2

*"In my distress I called to the
LORD, and he answered me.
From deep in the realm of the
dead I called for help, and
you listened to my cry."*

JONAH 4:2B

*"I knew that you are a
gracious and compassionate
God, slow to anger and
abounding in love, a God
who relents from sending
calamity."*

WHAT'S IT ABOUT?

Jonah lived at the same time as the prophets Hosea and Amos, a time when Israel had grown rich because of its greed and injustice. But instead of having Jonah deliver a message of judgment to his own people, God sent Jonah to Nineveh, the capital city of Assyria. Jonah didn't believe these cruel enemies of Israel deserved God's mercy, so he boarded a ship headed in the opposite direction.

When a violent storm arose, Jonah convinced the other passengers to throw him overboard. Instead of drowning, Jonah was swallowed by a big fish. God showed Jonah the very mercy he wanted to extend to Nineveh. Jonah eventually preached a message of judgment in Nineveh, and the people repented.

Jonah is one of only four writer prophets mentioned by Jesus, who talked about the "sign of Jonah." Just as Jonah spent three days inside the big fish, Jesus would spend three days in the grave (see Matthew 12:39–40). The book of Jonah foreshadows Jesus' death and resurrection centuries before these events happened.

Jonah Flees From the Lord

1 The word of the LORD came to Jonah son of Amittai: ² "Go to the great city of Nineveh and preach against it, because its wickedness has come up before me."

³ But Jonah ran away from the LORD and headed for Tarshish. He went down to Joppa, where he found a ship bound for that port. After paying the fare, he went aboard and sailed for Tarshish to flee from the LORD.

⁴ Then the LORD sent a great wind on the sea, and such a violent storm arose that the ship threatened to break up. ⁵ All the sailors were afraid and each cried out to his own god. And they threw the cargo into the sea to lighten the ship.

But Jonah had gone below deck, where he lay down and fell into a deep sleep. ⁶ The captain went to him and said, "How can you sleep? Get up and call on your god! Maybe he will take notice of us so that we will not perish."

⁷ Then the sailors said to each other, "Come, let us cast lots to find out who is responsible for this calamity." They cast lots and the lot fell on Jonah. ⁸ So they asked him, "Tell us, who is responsible for making all this trouble for us? What kind of work do you do? Where do you come from? What is your country? From what people are you?"

⁹ He answered, "I am a Hebrew and I worship the LORD, the God of heaven, who made the sea and the dry land."

¹⁰ This terrified them and they asked, "What have you done?" (They knew he was running away from the LORD, because he had already told them so.)

¹¹ The sea was getting rougher and rougher. So they asked him, "What should we do to you to make the sea calm down for us?"

¹² "Pick me up and throw me into the sea," he replied, "and it will become calm. I know that it is my fault that this great storm has come upon you."

¹³ Instead, the men did their best to row back to land. But they could not, for the sea grew even wilder than before. ¹⁴ Then they cried out to the LORD, "Please, LORD, do not let us die for taking this man's life. Do not hold us accountable for killing an innocent man, for you, LORD, have done as you pleased." ¹⁵ Then they took Jonah and threw him overboard, and the raging sea grew calm. ¹⁶ At this the men greatly feared the LORD, and they offered a sacrifice to the LORD and made vows to him.

Jonah's Prayer

¹⁷ Now the LORD provided a huge fish to swallow Jonah, and Jonah was in the belly of

2ᵃ the fish three days and three nights. ¹ From inside the fish Jonah prayed to the LORD his God. ² He said:

"In my distress I called to the LORD,
 and he answered me.
From deep in the realm of the dead I
  called for help,
 and you listened to my cry.
³ You hurled me into the depths,
  into the very heart of the seas,
  and the currents swirled about me;
 all your waves and breakers
  swept over me.
⁴ I said, 'I have been banished
  from your sight;
 yet I will look again
  toward your holy temple.'
⁵ The engulfing waters threatened me,ᵇ
  the deep surrounded me;
  seaweed was wrapped around
   my head.
⁶ To the roots of the mountains I sank
   down;
  the earth beneath barred me in
   forever.
But you, LORD my God,
 brought my life up from the pit.

⁷ "When my life was ebbing away,
  I remembered you, LORD,

ᵃ In Hebrew texts 2:1 is numbered 1:17, and 2:1-10 is numbered 2:2-11.   ᵇ 5 Or *waters were at my throat*

MERCY WAITING

READ: JONAH 1:17

Bible critics say the book of Jonah is nothing more than a big fish story. But Jesus seemed to accept this account as literal history, using Jonah's three days in a fish belly to make a point about his own death and resurrection (Matthew 12:40). Despite this debate, the book's lesson is obvious: Your God longs to show mercy. The Lord tells Jonah to preach to the hated enemy city of Nineveh, capital of the Assyrian empire, a kingdom famous for rampant sin and brutal military tactics.

The Assyrians had overrun Israel and conquered it, so you can imagine they weren't Jonah's favorite people. Jonah runs from the Lord, boarding a ship and heading as far and fast as he can in the opposite direction. God whips up a storm, and Jonah's shipmates toss him overboard to save their own lives.

When the Lord sends a huge fish to swallow Jonah, it might seem like he's lashing out. But that fish actually rescues the prophet from drowning. As soon as Jonah admits his foolishness, the fish vomits him onto land (Jonah 2:10).

BUILDING FAITH WISDOM STRENGTH

The Ninevites surprise Jonah by believing God's message. Even the king gets rid of his royal clothes and mourns. Because they turn from their evil ways, God doesn't destroy them.

You might not like that God wants to show kindness to your enemies. It's especially aggravating that he uses you to demonstrate his love. But the Lord always longs to give mercy. He gave it to you, so pass it along.

JONAH

The word of the LORD came to Jonah a second time: "Go to the great city of Nineveh and proclaim to it the message I give you." JONAH 3:1-2

HIS NAME MEANS: "dove"
READ HIS STORY: *2 Kings 14:25; Jonah 1-4*

When someone realizes their sinfulness and turns to God for forgiveness, it's a reason to celebrate. Jesus said that the angels rejoice when one sinner repents (Luke 15:10). But when tens of thousands of people turned from their wicked ways in the great city of Nineveh in Assyria, the prophet Jonah wasn't throwing a party. Actually, he did throw a party—a pity party.

He was angry with God. Jonah looked to the heavens and said, "I knew that you are a gracious and compassionate God, slow to anger and abounding in love, a God who relents from sending calamity. Now, LORD, take away my life, for it is better for me to die than to live" (Jonah 4:2-3).

Why the strange reaction when people actually listened to him and turned from evil? Simply put: Jonah hated the Ninevites. Assyria and Israel were enemies. He wanted to see them wiped from the planet as God promised would happen if they didn't repent. Had Nineveh been destroyed, it would've been a victory for Israel.

That's one reason why, when the Lord told Jonah to go to Nineveh and preach against it, he ran from God. More precisely, he boarded a boat at Joppa that was headed to Tarshish, which was perhaps in modern-day Spain. Nineveh was located near what now is known as Mosul, Iraq—the opposite way. God used a great fish to turn Jonah around. The good news was, being swallowed whole gave Jonah some time to think and decide to obey God by traveling to Ninevah. The bad news was that reluctant Jonah was still reluctant. Though he preached God's message of repentance to the Ninevites, he did it hoping he would fail.

and my prayer rose to you,
to your holy temple.

[8] "Those who cling to worthless idols
turn away from God's love for them.
[9] But I, with shouts of grateful praise,
will sacrifice to you.
What I have vowed I will make good.
I will say, 'Salvation comes from
the Lord.' "

[10] And the Lord commanded the fish, and it vomited Jonah onto dry land.

Jonah Goes to Nineveh

3 Then the word of the Lord came to Jonah a second time: [2] "Go to the great city of Nineveh and proclaim to it the message I give you."

[3] Jonah obeyed the word of the Lord and went to Nineveh. Now Nineveh was a very large city; it took three days to go through it. [4] Jonah began by going a day's journey into the city, proclaiming, "Forty more days and Nineveh will be overthrown." [5] The Ninevites believed God. A fast was proclaimed, and all of them, from the greatest to the least, put on sackcloth.

[6] When Jonah's warning reached the king of Nineveh, he rose from his throne, took off his royal robes, covered himself with sackcloth and sat down in the dust. [7] This is the proclamation he issued in Nineveh:

"By the decree of the king and his nobles:

Do not let people or animals, herds or flocks, taste anything; do not let them eat or drink. [8] But let people and animals be covered with sackcloth. Let everyone call urgently on God. Let them give up their evil ways and their violence. [9] Who knows? God may yet relent and with compassion turn from his fierce anger so that we will not perish."

[10] When God saw what they did and how they turned from their evil ways, he relented and did not bring on them the destruction he had threatened.

Jonah's Anger at the Lord's Compassion

4 But to Jonah this seemed very wrong, and he became angry. [2] He prayed to the Lord, "Isn't this what I said, Lord, when I was still at home? That is what I tried to forestall by fleeing to Tarshish. I knew that you are a gracious and compassionate God, slow to anger and abounding in love, a God who relents from sending calamity. [3] Now, Lord, take away my life, for it is better for me to die than to live."

[4] But the Lord replied, "Is it right for you to be angry?"

[5] Jonah had gone out and sat down at a place east of the city. There he made himself a shelter, sat in its shade and waited to see what would happen to the city. [6] Then the Lord God provided a leafy plant[a] and made it grow up over Jonah to give shade for his head to ease his discomfort, and Jonah was very happy about the plant. [7] But at dawn the next day God provided a worm, which chewed the plant so that it withered. [8] When the sun rose, God provided a scorching east wind, and the sun blazed on Jonah's head so that he grew faint. He wanted to die, and said, "It would be better for me to die than to live."

[9] But God said to Jonah, "Is it right for you to be angry about the plant?"

"It is," he said. "And I'm so angry I wish I were dead."

[10] But the Lord said, "You have been concerned about this plant, though you did not tend it or make it grow. It sprang up overnight and died overnight. [11] And should I not have concern for the great city of Nineveh, in which there are more than a hundred and twenty thousand people who cannot tell their right hand from their left—and also many animals?"

---

[a] 6 The precise identification of this plant is uncertain; also in verses 7, 9 and 10.

MICAH

WHEN DID THIS HAPPEN?

Between 742 and 687 B.C. in the southern kingdom of Judah

WHO IS IN THIS BOOK?

Micah

VERSES YOU MIGHT RECOGNIZE

MICAH 6:8

"And what does the LORD require of you? To act justly and to love mercy and to walk humbly with your God."

MICAH 7:18

"You do not stay angry forever but delight to show mercy."

WHAT'S IT ABOUT?

Micah prophesied during the years surrounding Israel's fall to the Assyrians. He delivered a stern message of judgment to Judah and Israel for their unjust ways. People were taking land that didn't belong to them, cheating the poor and mistreating women and children. As Israel slipped deeper and deeper into sin, Micah told the people God's will for them: "To act justly and to love mercy and to walk humbly with your God."

Micah lived at the same time as the prophets Isaiah and Hosea. Like those prophets, Micah also proclaimed judgment on Israel for their many sins. Micah's prophecy ended with a dramatic courtroom scene where Israel stood trial before God for rejecting him and mistreating others. But Micah also offered hope as he described a future Savior and shepherd for Israel. He even predicted that the Messiah would be born in Bethlehem (see Micah 5:2).

MICAH

The word of the LORD that came to Micah of Moresheth during the reigns of Jotham, Ahaz and Hezekiah, kings of Judah—the vision he saw concerning Samaria and Jerusalem.

² Hear, you peoples, all of you,
    listen, earth and all who live in it,
that the Sovereign LORD may bear
        witness against you,
    the Lord from his holy temple.

Judgment Against Samaria and Jerusalem

³ Look! The LORD is coming from his
        dwelling place;
    he comes down and treads on the
        heights of the earth.
⁴ The mountains melt beneath him
    and the valleys split apart,
like wax before the fire,
    like water rushing down a slope.
⁵ All this is because of Jacob's
        transgression,
    because of the sins of the people
        of Israel.
What is Jacob's transgression?
    Is it not Samaria?
What is Judah's high place?
    Is it not Jerusalem?

⁶ "Therefore I will make Samaria a heap
        of rubble,
    a place for planting vineyards.
I will pour her stones into the valley
    and lay bare her foundations.
⁷ All her idols will be broken to pieces;
    all her temple gifts will be burned
        with fire;
    I will destroy all her images.
Since she gathered her gifts from the
        wages of prostitutes,
    as the wages of prostitutes they will
        again be used."

Weeping and Mourning

⁸ Because of this I will weep and wail;
    I will go about barefoot and naked.
I will howl like a jackal
    and moan like an owl.
⁹ For Samaria's plague is incurable;
    it has spread to Judah.
It has reached the very gate of my people,
    even to Jerusalem itself.
¹⁰ Tell it not in Gath*a*;
    weep not at all.
In Beth Ophrah*b*
    roll in the dust.
¹¹ Pass by naked and in shame,
    you who live in Shaphir.*c*
Those who live in Zaanan*d*
    will not come out.
Beth Ezel is in mourning;
    it no longer protects you.
¹² Those who live in Maroth*e* writhe
        in pain,
    waiting for relief,
because disaster has come from
        the LORD,
    even to the gate of Jerusalem.
¹³ You who live in Lachish,
    harness fast horses to the chariot.
You are where the sin of Daughter Zion
        began,
    for the transgressions of Israel were
        found in you.
¹⁴ Therefore you will give parting gifts
    to Moresheth Gath.
The town of Akzib*f* will prove deceptive
    to the kings of Israel.
¹⁵ I will bring a conqueror against you
    who live in Mareshah.*g*
The nobles of Israel
    will flee to Adullam.
¹⁶ Shave your head in mourning
    for the children in whom you delight;
make yourself as bald as the vulture,
    for they will go from you into exile.

---

a 10 Gath sounds like the Hebrew for *tell*.   *b 10 Beth Ophrah* means *house of dust*.   *c 11 Shaphir* means *pleasant*.   *d 11 Zaanan* sounds like the Hebrew for *come out*.   *e 12 Maroth* sounds like the Hebrew for *bitter*.   *f 14 Akzib* means *deception*.   *g 15 Mareshah* sounds like the Hebrew for *conqueror*.

Human Plans and God's Plans

2 Woe to those who plan iniquity,
  to those who plot evil on their beds!
At morning's light they carry it out
  because it is in their power to do it.
[2] They covet fields and seize them,
  and houses, and take them.
They defraud people of their homes,
  they rob them of their inheritance.

[3] Therefore, the LORD says:

"I am planning disaster against this
    people,
  from which you cannot save
    yourselves.
You will no longer walk proudly,
  for it will be a time of calamity.
[4] In that day people will ridicule you;
  they will taunt you with this mournful
    song:
'We are utterly ruined;
  my people's possession is divided up.
He takes it from me!
  He assigns our fields to traitors.' "

[5] Therefore you will have no one in the
    assembly of the LORD
  to divide the land by lot.

False Prophets

[6] "Do not prophesy," their prophets say.
  "Do not prophesy about these things;
  disgrace will not overtake us."
[7] You descendants of Jacob, should it
    be said,
  "Does the LORD become[a] impatient?
  Does he do such things?"

"Do not my words do good
  to the one whose ways are upright?
[8] Lately my people have risen up
  like an enemy.
You strip off the rich robe
  from those who pass by without a care,
  like men returning from battle.
[9] You drive the women of my people
  from their pleasant homes.
You take away my blessing
  from their children forever.
[10] Get up, go away!
  For this is not your resting place,
because it is defiled,
  it is ruined, beyond all remedy.

[11] If a liar and deceiver comes and says,
  'I will prophesy for you plenty of wine
    and beer,'
  that would be just the prophet for this
    people!

Deliverance Promised

[12] "I will surely gather all of you, Jacob;
  I will surely bring together the
    remnant of Israel.
I will bring them together like sheep
    in a pen,
  like a flock in its pasture;
  the place will throng with people.
[13] The One who breaks open the way will
    go up before them;
  they will break through the gate and
    go out.
Their King will pass through before
    them,
  the LORD at their head."

Leaders and Prophets Rebuked

3 Then I said,

"Listen, you leaders of Jacob,
  you rulers of Israel.
Should you not embrace justice,
[2]   you who hate good and love evil;
who tear the skin from my people
  and the flesh from their bones;
[3] who eat my people's flesh,
  strip off their skin
  and break their bones in pieces;
who chop them up like meat for the pan,
  like flesh for the pot?"

[4] Then they will cry out to the LORD,
  but he will not answer them.
At that time he will hide his face from
    them
  because of the evil they have done.

[5] This is what the LORD says:

"As for the prophets
  who lead my people astray,
they proclaim 'peace'
  if they have something to eat,
but prepare to wage war against anyone
  who refuses to feed them.
[6] Therefore night will come over you,
    without visions,
  and darkness, without divination.

[a] 7 Or *Is the Spirit of the LORD*

MICAH

What does the LORD require of you? To act justly and to love mercy and to walk humbly with your God. MICAH 6:8

HIS NAME MEANS: "who is like the LORD?"
READ HIS STORY: *Micah 1:1-2; Jeremiah 26:17-19; Matthew 2:1-6*

Ever wondered what God wants us to do? The prophet Micah summed it up in a sentence: To act justly and to love mercy and to walk humbly with your God. The life of faith isn't rocket science, and it doesn't take a rocket scientist to understand it, live it out and encourage others to do the same. Micah is a testament to that fact.

Micah came from Moresheth, a tiny town more than twenty miles southwest of Jerusalem. He spoke against corruption, such as rulers and judges taking bribes and priests and prophets operating merely for the money they received. Because of such corruption and disrespect for God's ways, Micah foretold that "Zion will be plowed like a field, Jerusalem will become a heap of rubble" (Micah 3:12). That prophecy came true, and so did the one Micah made more than 700 years before Jesus was born: "But you, Bethlehem Ephrathah, though you are small among the clans of Judah, out of you will come for me one who will be ruler over Israel, whose origins are from of old, from ancient times" (Micah 5:2). Micah ministered about the same time as the prophets Isaiah, Amos and Hosea. Growing up in a rural village a fair distance from Jerusalem, Micah didn't speak before kings like Isaiah did. But like his contemporaries, Micah preached courageously and with conviction. He pointed out sin, called for repentance, assured God's people of forgiveness and foretold the coming Messiah.

The sun will set for the prophets,
and the day will go dark for them.
⁷The seers will be ashamed
and the diviners disgraced.
They will all cover their faces
because there is no answer
from God."
⁸But as for me, I am filled with power,
with the Spirit of the LORD,
and with justice and might,
to declare to Jacob his transgression,
to Israel his sin.

⁹Hear this, you leaders of Jacob,
you rulers of Israel,
who despise justice
and distort all that is right;
¹⁰who build Zion with bloodshed,
and Jerusalem with wickedness.
¹¹Her leaders judge for a bribe,
her priests teach for a price,
and her prophets tell fortunes for
money.
Yet they look for the LORD's support
and say,
"Is not the LORD among us?
No disaster will come upon us."
¹²Therefore because of you,
Zion will be plowed like a field,
Jerusalem will become a heap of rubble,
the temple hill a mound overgrown
with thickets.

The Mountain of the Lord

4 In the last days

the mountain of the LORD's temple will
be established
as the highest of the mountains;
it will be exalted above the hills,
and peoples will stream to it.

²Many nations will come and say,

"Come, let us go up to the mountain of
the LORD,
to the temple of the God of Jacob.
He will teach us his ways,
so that we may walk in his paths."
The law will go out from Zion,
the word of the LORD from Jerusalem.
³He will judge between many peoples
and will settle disputes for strong
nations far and wide.

They will beat their swords into
plowshares
and their spears into pruning hooks.
Nation will not take up sword against
nation,
nor will they train for war anymore.
⁴Everyone will sit under their own vine
and under their own fig tree,
and no one will make them afraid,
for the LORD Almighty has spoken.
⁵All the nations may walk
in the name of their gods,
but we will walk in the name of the LORD
our God for ever and ever.

The Lord's Plan

⁶"In that day," declares the LORD,

"I will gather the lame;
I will assemble the exiles
and those I have brought to grief.
⁷I will make the lame my remnant,
those driven away a strong nation.
The LORD will rule over them in Mount
Zion
from that day and forever.
⁸As for you, watchtower of the flock,
stronghold*ᵃ* of Daughter Zion,
the former dominion will be restored to
you;
kingship will come to Daughter
Jerusalem."

⁹Why do you now cry aloud —
have you no king*ᵇ*?
Has your ruler*ᶜ* perished,
that pain seizes you like that of a
woman in labor?
¹⁰Writhe in agony, Daughter Zion,
like a woman in labor,
for now you must leave the city
to camp in the open field.
You will go to Babylon;
there you will be rescued.
There the LORD will redeem you
out of the hand of your enemies.
¹¹But now many nations
are gathered against you.
They say, "Let her be defiled,
let our eyes gloat over Zion!"
¹²But they do not know
the thoughts of the LORD;
they do not understand his plan,

ᵃ 8 Or *hill*   *ᵇ 9* Or *King*   *ᶜ 9* Or *Ruler*

that he has gathered them like sheaves
 to the threshing floor.
13 "Rise and thresh, Daughter Zion,
 for I will give you horns of iron;
I will give you hooves of bronze,
 and you will break to pieces many
  nations."
You will devote their ill-gotten gains to
  the LORD,
 their wealth to the Lord of all the earth.

A Promised Ruler From Bethlehem

5 *a* Marshal your troops now, city of
  troops,
 for a siege is laid against us.
They will strike Israel's ruler
 on the cheek with a rod.

2 "But you, Bethlehem Ephrathah,
 though you are small among the clans*b*
  of Judah,
out of you will come for me
 one who will be ruler over Israel,
whose origins are from of old,
 from ancient times."

3 Therefore Israel will be abandoned
 until the time when she who is in labor
  bears a son,
and the rest of his brothers return
 to join the Israelites.

4 He will stand and shepherd his flock
 in the strength of the LORD,
 in the majesty of the name of the LORD
  his God.
And they will live securely, for then his
  greatness
 will reach to the ends of the earth.

5 And he will be our peace
 when the Assyrians invade our land
 and march through our fortresses.
We will raise against them seven
  shepherds,
 even eight commanders,
6 who will rule*c* the land of Assyria with
  the sword,
 the land of Nimrod with drawn
  sword.*d*
He will deliver us from the Assyrians
 when they invade our land
 and march across our borders.

7 The remnant of Jacob will be
 in the midst of many peoples
like dew from the LORD,
 like showers on the grass,
which do not wait for anyone
 or depend on man.
8 The remnant of Jacob will be among
  the nations,
 in the midst of many peoples,
like a lion among the beasts of the forest,
 like a young lion among flocks of
  sheep,
which mauls and mangles as it goes,
 and no one can rescue.
9 Your hand will be lifted up in triumph
  over your enemies,
 and all your foes will be destroyed.

10 "In that day," declares the LORD,

"I will destroy your horses from
  among you
 and demolish your chariots.
11 I will destroy the cities of your land
 and tear down all your strongholds.
12 I will destroy your witchcraft
 and you will no longer cast spells.
13 I will destroy your idols
 and your sacred stones from
  among you;
you will no longer bow down
 to the work of your hands.
14 I will uproot from among you your
  Asherah poles*e*
 when I demolish your cities.
15 I will take vengeance in anger and wrath
 on the nations that have not
  obeyed me."

The Lord's Case Against Israel

6 Listen to what the LORD says:

"Stand up, plead my case before the
  mountains;
 let the hills hear what you have to say.

2 "Hear, you mountains, the LORD's
  accusation;
 listen, you everlasting foundations of
  the earth.
For the LORD has a case against his
  people;
 he is lodging a charge against Israel.

---

a In Hebrew texts 5:1 is numbered 4:14, and 5:2-15 is numbered 5:1-14. *b* 2 Or *rulers* *c* 6 Or *crush*
d 6 Or *Nimrod in its gates* *e* 14 That is, wooden symbols of the goddess Asherah

STANDING IN LINE

READ: MICAH 7:7

A lot of times, when we tell stories about our spiritual lives, we focus on some big roller-coaster moment. But where do you really get to know Jesus? You get to know him when you're in line. Every day as you pray, dig into his Word, go to school, sit at lunch, and do homework, you grow in Christ as you take time in your heart and mind to stand in line with the Lord.

As much as we think the high points shape us, they only reveal how we've attended to our spiritual lives to that point. It's the same with our quiet times. We go into our quiet times wanting the earth to move. We want Billy Graham thunder to fall. But it's not about the roller-coaster ride anymore. It's just you and God, and you're not in it for the buzz of an emotional experience.

BUILDING

FAITH

WISDOM

STRENGTH

Think about your best friend. You're not looking for an adventure every time you hang out with him or her. You just hang out and talk about nothing, and you're fine. Let's aspire to be so intimate with God.

Another factor that can detract from our time with God is that we often go into it wanting a win. We want to take the problem of the day to the Lord and have it fixed now. The impatience of the American culture maims our walk with Jesus. We need to soak in God's Word, not so that something good will happen but so that we get to know him.

³ "My people, what have I done to you?
 How have I burdened you? Answer me.
⁴ I brought you up out of Egypt
 and redeemed you from the land of
 slavery.
 I sent Moses to lead you,
 also Aaron and Miriam.
⁵ My people, remember
 what Balak king of Moab plotted
 and what Balaam son of Beor
 answered.
 Remember your journey from Shittim to
 Gilgal,
 that you may know the righteous acts
 of the LORD."

⁶ With what shall I come before the LORD
 and bow down before the exalted God?
 Shall I come before him with burnt
 offerings,
 with calves a year old?
⁷ Will the LORD be pleased with thousands
 of rams,
 with ten thousand rivers of olive oil?
 Shall I offer my firstborn for my
 transgression,
 the fruit of my body for the sin of
 my soul?
⁸ He has shown you, O mortal, what is
 good.
 And what does the LORD require
 of you?
 To act justly and to love mercy
 and to walk humbly*a* with your God.

Israel's Guilt and Punishment

⁹ Listen! The LORD is calling to the city —
 and to fear your name is wisdom —
 "Heed the rod and the One who
 appointed it.*b*
¹⁰ Am I still to forget your ill-gotten
 treasures, you wicked house,
 and the short ephah,*c* which is
 accursed?
¹¹ Shall I acquit someone with dishonest
 scales,
 with a bag of false weights?
¹² Your rich people are violent;
 your inhabitants are liars
 and their tongues speak deceitfully.

¹³ Therefore, I have begun to destroy you,
 to ruin*d* you because of your sins.
¹⁴ You will eat but not be satisfied;
 your stomach will still be empty.*e*
 You will store up but save nothing,
 because what you save*f* I will give to
 the sword.
¹⁵ You will plant but not harvest;
 you will press olives but not use the oil,
 you will crush grapes but not drink the
 wine.
¹⁶ You have observed the statutes of Omri
 and all the practices of Ahab's house;
 you have followed their traditions.
 Therefore I will give you over to ruin
 and your people to derision;
 you will bear the scorn of the
 nations.*g*"

Israel's Misery

7 What misery is mine!
 I am like one who gathers summer fruit
 at the gleaning of the vineyard;
 there is no cluster of grapes to eat,
 none of the early figs that I crave.
² The faithful have been swept from the
 land;
 not one upright person remains.
 Everyone lies in wait to shed blood;
 they hunt each other with nets.
³ Both hands are skilled in doing evil;
 the ruler demands gifts,
 the judge accepts bribes,
 the powerful dictate what they
 desire —
 they all conspire together.
⁴ The best of them is like a brier,
 the most upright worse than a thorn
 hedge.
 The day God visits you has come,
 the day your watchmen sound the
 alarm.
 Now is the time of your confusion.
⁵ Do not trust a neighbor;
 put no confidence in a friend.
 Even with the woman who lies in your
 embrace
 guard the words of your lips.
⁶ For a son dishonors his father,
 a daughter rises up against her mother,

---

a 8 Or *prudently*   *b* 9 The meaning of the Hebrew for this line is uncertain.   *c* 10 An ephah was a dry
measure.   *d* 13 Or *Therefore, I will make you ill and destroy you; / I will ruin*   *e* 14 The meaning of the
Hebrew for this word is uncertain.   *f* 14 Or *You will press toward birth but not give birth, / and what you
bring to birth*   *g* 16 Septuagint; Hebrew *scorn due my people*

FLAWED LOGIC

READ: MICAH 7:19

When I forgive someone, what that person did to me seems always to hover in the back of my mind. I can't help but make decisions based on my memory of what happened. How can God, whose memory is perfect, be any different? We assume there's no way God can forgive without condition and without end.

God-sized forgiveness doesn't compute. It just makes sense that God will give up on us sooner or later. We hold forgiveness up to the light, inspect it from every conceivable angle, shake it, thump it, and bring it to our ear to see if it's ever going to say something back to us. Then we decide it's too good to be true.

But that's human logic.

We live as if we believe that God follows human logic. Three strikes, and you're out. You get so many detentions, and you're suspended. You get too many speeding tickets, and you lose your license. You commit this sin too many times, and God is going to leave you too. It just makes sense.

BUILDING
FAITH
WISDOM
STRENGTH

This logic originates with our false belief that we did something to make God love us in the first place. We think we're so lovable that God can't help but love us. But really the opposite is true. While we were still sinners, Christ died for us.

When we understand that our relationship with God is something he starts, maintains, and completes (Philippians 1:6), we can begin to accept the truth that God's forgiveness is forever.

a daughter-in-law against her mother-
in-law —
a man's enemies are the members of
his own household.

⁷ But as for me, I watch in hope for the LORD,
I wait for God my Savior;
my God will hear me.

Israel Will Rise

⁸ Do not gloat over me, my enemy!
Though I have fallen, I will rise.
Though I sit in darkness,
the LORD will be my light.
⁹ Because I have sinned against him,
I will bear the LORD's wrath,
until he pleads my case
and upholds my cause.
He will bring me out into the light;
I will see his righteousness.
¹⁰ Then my enemy will see it
and will be covered with shame,
she who said to me,
"Where is the LORD your God?"
My eyes will see her downfall;
even now she will be trampled
underfoot
like mire in the streets.

¹¹ The day for building your walls will come,
the day for extending your boundaries.
¹² In that day people will come to you
from Assyria and the cities of Egypt,
even from Egypt to the Euphrates
and from sea to sea
and from mountain to mountain.
¹³ The earth will become desolate because
of its inhabitants,
as the result of their deeds.

Prayer and Praise

¹⁴ Shepherd your people with your staff,
the flock of your inheritance,
which lives by itself in a forest,
in fertile pasturelands.ᵃ
Let them feed in Bashan and Gilead
as in days long ago.

¹⁵ "As in the days when you came out
of Egypt,
I will show them my wonders."

¹⁶ Nations will see and be ashamed,
deprived of all their power.
They will put their hands over their
mouths
and their ears will become deaf.
¹⁷ They will lick dust like a snake,
like creatures that crawl on the
ground.
They will come trembling out of their
dens;
they will turn in fear to the LORD
our God
and will be afraid of you.
¹⁸ Who is a God like you,
who pardons sin and forgives the
transgression
of the remnant of his inheritance?
You do not stay angry forever
but delight to show mercy.
¹⁹ You will again have compassion on us;
you will tread our sins underfoot
and hurl all our iniquities into the
depths of the sea.
²⁰ You will be faithful to Jacob,
and show love to Abraham,
as you pledged on oath to our ancestors
in days long ago.

ᵃ 14 Or *in the middle of Carmel*

NAHUM

➤ **WHEN DID THIS HAPPEN?**

Between 645 and 620 B.C. in the southern kingdom of Judah

➤ **WHO IS IN THIS BOOK?**

Nahum

➤ **VERSES YOU MIGHT RECOGNIZE**

NAHUM 1:7

"The LORD is good, a refuge in times of trouble. He cares for those who trust in him."

NAHUM 1:15A

"Look, there on the mountains, the feet of one who brings good news, who proclaims peace!"

WHAT'S IT ABOUT?

This book was written 150 years after Jonah preached to Nineveh. Fifty years after Jonah's message, Assyria totally destroyed the northern kingdom of Israel and took its people captive. Since that time, Assyria had attacked the kingdom of Judah repeatedly, and the people lived in fear of this great empire. They needed encouragement that God was bigger and stronger than this powerful enemy.

Nahum announced that Nineveh, the capital city of Assyria, would be destroyed—an event that happened in 612 B.C. Filled with hope and encouragement for Israel, Nahum's prophecy reminded them of God's love for them. He would punish the enemies of his people.

You may think Nahum's comforting prophecy came at a time when the people were following God. But that's not the case. Nahum preached during one of Judah's darkest periods, when evil King Manasseh ruled and the people worshiped idols. God's grace for them was so big and so unstoppable that he sent them a message of mercy at the very time they least deserved it.

NAHUM

1 A prophecy concerning Nineveh. The book of the vision of Nahum the Elkoshite.

The Lord's Anger Against Nineveh

[2] The LORD is a jealous and avenging God;
  the LORD takes vengeance and is filled
    with wrath.
The LORD takes vengeance on his foes
  and vents his wrath against his
    enemies.
[3] The LORD is slow to anger but great in
    power;
  the LORD will not leave the guilty
    unpunished.
His way is in the whirlwind and the
    storm,
  and clouds are the dust of his feet.
[4] He rebukes the sea and dries it up;
  he makes all the rivers run dry.
Bashan and Carmel wither
  and the blossoms of Lebanon fade.
[5] The mountains quake before him
  and the hills melt away.
The earth trembles at his presence,
  the world and all who live in it.
[6] Who can withstand his indignation?
  Who can endure his fierce anger?
His wrath is poured out like fire;
  the rocks are shattered before him.

[7] The LORD is good,
  a refuge in times of trouble.
He cares for those who trust in him,
[8] but with an overwhelming flood
he will make an end of Nineveh;
  he will pursue his foes into the realm
    of darkness.

[9] Whatever they plot against the LORD
  he will bring[a] to an end;
  trouble will not come a second time.
[10] They will be entangled among thorns
  and drunk from their wine;

they will be consumed like dry
    stubble.[b]
[11] From you, Nineveh, has one come forth
  who plots evil against the LORD
  and devises wicked plans.

[12] This is what the LORD says:

"Although they have allies and are
    numerous,
  they will be destroyed and pass away.
Although I have afflicted you, Judah,
  I will afflict you no more.
[13] Now I will break their yoke from
    your neck
  and tear your shackles away."

[14] The LORD has given a command
    concerning you, Nineveh:
  "You will have no descendants to bear
    your name.
I will destroy the images and idols
  that are in the temple of your gods.
I will prepare your grave,
  for you are vile."

[15] Look, there on the mountains,
  the feet of one who brings good news,
  who proclaims peace!
Celebrate your festivals, Judah,
  and fulfill your vows.
No more will the wicked invade you;
  they will be completely destroyed.[c]

Nineveh to Fall

2[d] An attacker advances against you,
    Nineveh.
  Guard the fortress,
  watch the road,
  brace yourselves,
  marshal all your strength!

[2] The LORD will restore the splendor
    of Jacob
  like the splendor of Israel,

---

[a] 9 Or *What do you foes plot against the LORD? / He will bring it*   [b] 10 The meaning of the Hebrew for this verse is uncertain.   [c] 15 In Hebrew texts this verse (1:15) is numbered 2:1.   [d] In Hebrew texts 2:1-13 is numbered 2:2-14.

though destroyers have laid them waste
and have ruined their vines.

³ The shields of the soldiers are red;
the warriors are clad in scarlet.
The metal on the chariots flashes
on the day they are made ready;
the spears of juniper are brandished.ᵃ
⁴ The chariots storm through the streets,
rushing back and forth through the
squares.
They look like flaming torches;
they dart about like lightning.

⁵ Nineveh summons her picked troops,
yet they stumble on their way.
They dash to the city wall;
the protective shield is put in place.
⁶ The river gates are thrown open
and the palace collapses.
⁷ It is decreedᵇ that Nineveh
be exiled and carried away.
Her female slaves moan like doves
and beat on their breasts.
⁸ Nineveh is like a pool
whose water is draining away.
"Stop! Stop!" they cry,
but no one turns back.
⁹ Plunder the silver!
Plunder the gold!
The supply is endless,
the wealth from all its treasures!
¹⁰ She is pillaged, plundered, stripped!
Hearts melt, knees give way,
bodies tremble, every face grows pale.

¹¹ Where now is the lions' den,
the place where they fed their young,
where the lion and lioness went,
and the cubs, with nothing to fear?
¹² The lion killed enough for his cubs
and strangled the prey for his mate,
filling his lairs with the kill
and his dens with the prey.

¹³ "I am against you,"
declares the LORD Almighty.
"I will burn up your chariots in smoke,
and the sword will devour your
young lions.
I will leave you no prey on the earth.
The voices of your messengers
will no longer be heard."

Woe to Nineveh

3 Woe to the city of blood,
full of lies,
full of plunder,
never without victims!
² The crack of whips,
the clatter of wheels,
galloping horses
and jolting chariots!
³ Charging cavalry,
flashing swords
and glittering spears!
Many casualties,
piles of dead,
bodies without number,
people stumbling over the corpses —
⁴ all because of the wanton lust of a
prostitute,
alluring, the mistress of sorceries,
who enslaved nations by her prostitution
and peoples by her witchcraft.

⁵ "I am against you," declares the LORD
Almighty.
"I will lift your skirts over your face.
I will show the nations your nakedness
and the kingdoms your shame.
⁶ I will pelt you with filth,
I will treat you with contempt
and make you a spectacle.
⁷ All who see you will flee from you and
say,
'Nineveh is in ruins — who will mourn
for her?'
Where can I find anyone to comfort
you?"

⁸ Are you better than Thebes,
situated on the Nile,
with water around her?
The river was her defense,
the waters her wall.
⁹ Cushᶜ and Egypt were her boundless
strength;
Put and Libya were among her allies.
¹⁰ Yet she was taken captive
and went into exile.
Her infants were dashed to pieces
at every street corner.
Lots were cast for her nobles,
and all her great men were put in
chains.

ᵃ 3 Hebrew; Septuagint and Syriac *ready; / the horsemen rush to and fro.*   ᵇ 7 The meaning of the
Hebrew for this word is uncertain.   ᶜ 9 That is, the upper Nile region

[11] You too will become drunk;
   you will go into hiding
   and seek refuge from the enemy.

[12] All your fortresses are like fig trees
   with their first ripe fruit;
when they are shaken,
   the figs fall into the mouth of the
      eater.
[13] Look at your troops —
   they are all weaklings.
The gates of your land
   are wide open to your enemies;
   fire has consumed the bars of
      your gates.

[14] Draw water for the siege,
   strengthen your defenses!
Work the clay,
   tread the mortar,
   repair the brickwork!
[15] There the fire will consume you;
   the sword will cut you down —
   they will devour you like a swarm
      of locusts.

Multiply like grasshoppers,
   multiply like locusts!
[16] You have increased the number of your
      merchants
   till they are more numerous than the
      stars in the sky,
but like locusts they strip the land
   and then fly away.
[17] Your guards are like locusts,
   your officials like swarms of locusts
   that settle in the walls on a cold day —
but when the sun appears they fly away,
   and no one knows where.

[18] King of Assyria, your shepherds[a] slumber;
   your nobles lie down to rest.
Your people are scattered on the
      mountains
   with no one to gather them.
[19] Nothing can heal you;
   your wound is fatal.
All who hear the news about you
   clap their hands at your fall,
for who has not felt
   your endless cruelty?

---

[a] 18 That is, rulers

HABAKKUK

WHEN DID THIS HAPPEN?

Between 605 and 588 B.C. in the southern kingdom of Judah

WHO IS IN THIS BOOK?

Habakkuk

VERSES YOU MIGHT RECOGNIZE

HABAKKUK 3:2

"LORD, I have heard of your fame; I stand in awe of your deeds, LORD. Repeat them in our day, in our time make them known; in wrath remember mercy."

HABAKKUK 3:19

"The Sovereign LORD is my strength; he makes my feet like the feet of a deer, he enables me to tread on the heights."

WHAT'S IT ABOUT?

How long, LORD?" This was the cry of the prophet Habakkuk. While most of the prophets delivered a message *from* God to the people, Habakkuk directed his message *to* God. Habakkuk, who was probably over 70 years old, complained that God was not judging the southern kingdom for its evil ways. He asked how long God would allow their sin to continue. God told him that punishment was coming—Babylon would soon conquer Judah.

This answer didn't make Habakkuk happy, because Babylon was even more sinful than Judah! God assured the prophet that Babylon would also be punished. Evil would not prevail and God's justice would be satisfied. The book ends with Habakkuk's prayer, which praises God for who he is and asks for mercy for his people. The people of Judah would soon experience a difficult time, but Habakkuk trusted that God would be with them. He ends by affirming that the Lord is his strength (see Habakkuk 3:19).

HABAKKUK

1

The prophecy that Habakkuk the prophet received.

Habakkuk's Complaint

² How long, LORD, must I call for help,
  but you do not listen?
Or cry out to you, "Violence!"
  but you do not save?
³ Why do you make me look at injustice?
  Why do you tolerate wrongdoing?
Destruction and violence are before me;
  there is strife, and conflict abounds.
⁴ Therefore the law is paralyzed,
  and justice never prevails.
The wicked hem in the righteous,
  so that justice is perverted.

The Lord's Answer

⁵ "Look at the nations and watch—
  and be utterly amazed.
For I am going to do something in
    your days
  that you would not believe,
  even if you were told.
⁶ I am raising up the Babylonians,ᵃ
  that ruthless and impetuous people,
who sweep across the whole earth
  to seize dwellings not their own.
⁷ They are a feared and dreaded people;
  they are a law to themselves
  and promote their own honor.
⁸ Their horses are swifter than leopards,
  fiercer than wolves at dusk.
Their cavalry gallops headlong;
  their horsemen come from afar.
They fly like an eagle swooping to
    devour;
⁹   they all come intent on violence.
Their hordesᵇ advance like a desert
    wind
  and gather prisoners like sand.
¹⁰ They mock kings
  and scoff at rulers.
They laugh at all fortified cities;

by building earthen ramps they
    capture them.
¹¹ Then they sweep past like the wind and
    go on—
  guilty people, whose own strength is
    their god."

Habakkuk's Second Complaint

¹² LORD, are you not from everlasting?
  My God, my Holy One, youᶜ will
    never die.
You, LORD, have appointed them to
    execute judgment;
  you, my Rock, have ordained them to
    punish.
¹³ Your eyes are too pure to look on evil;
  you cannot tolerate wrongdoing.
Why then do you tolerate the
    treacherous?
Why are you silent while the wicked
  swallow up those more righteous than
    themselves?
¹⁴ You have made people like the fish in
    the sea,
  like the sea creatures that have no
    ruler.
¹⁵ The wicked foe pulls all of them up
    with hooks,
he catches them in his net,
  he gathers them up in his dragnet;
  and so he rejoices and is glad.
¹⁶ Therefore he sacrifices to his net
  and burns incense to his dragnet,
for by his net he lives in luxury
  and enjoys the choicest food.
¹⁷ Is he to keep on emptying his net,
  destroying nations without
    mercy?

2

I will stand at my watch
  and station myself on the ramparts;
I will look to see what he will say to me,
  and what answer I am to give to this
    complaint.ᵈ

ᵃ 6 Or *Chaldeans*   ᵇ 9 The meaning of the Hebrew for this word is uncertain.   ᶜ 12 An ancient
Hebrew scribal tradition; Masoretic Text *we*   ᵈ 1 Or *and what to answer when I am rebuked*

HABAKKUK

How long, LORD, must I call for help, but you do not listen? Or cry out to you, "Violence!" but you do not save? HABAKKUK 1:2

HIS NAME MEANS: The name is probably Babylonian, and refers to a kind of garden plant

READ HIS STORY: *Habakkuk 1–3*

MEN OF THE BIBLE

Do you ever wonder why bad guys prosper while good guys experience trouble? The prophet Habakkuk struggled with the very same question, and the book he wrote records his discussion with God.

Habakkuk detested sin. Yet all around him God's chosen people were living sinful lives. Habakkuk wanted justice. He called out for God's judgment against the sinners, because for many years their sins had gone unpunished. But Habakkuk wasn't expecting God's answer to his complaint. Habakkuk lived when the evil nation of Babylon was rising to power; and the Lord told his prophet that he was going to use the Babylonians, known to be cruel conquerors, to punish his people. How could God do such a thing? The Babylonians were worse than the people of Judah!

In the end, Habakkuk learned to put his trust in God. Yes, many of his questions were still unanswered. Yes, the ways of God were not easy for him to understand. But he chose to trust God.

Habakkuk's final message is this: Don't look at the circumstances around you, but keep your eyes on God. The prophet himself says in Habakkuk 3:17-19, "Though the fig tree does not bud and there are no grapes on the vines, though the olive crop fails and the fields produce no food, though there are no sheep in the pen and no cattle in the stalls, yet I will rejoice in the LORD, I will be joyful in God my Savior. The Sovereign LORD is my strength; he makes my feet like the feet of a deer, he enables me to tread on the heights."

The Lord's Answer

² Then the LORD replied:

"Write down the revelation
and make it plain on tablets
so that a herald[a] may run with it.
³ For the revelation awaits an appointed
time;
it speaks of the end
and will not prove false.
Though it linger, wait for it;
it[b] will certainly come
and will not delay.

⁴ "See, the enemy is puffed up;
his desires are not upright —
but the righteous person will live by
his faithfulness[c] —
⁵ indeed, wine betrays him;
he is arrogant and never at rest.
Because he is as greedy as the grave
and like death is never satisfied,
he gathers to himself all the nations
and takes captive all the peoples.

⁶ "Will not all of them taunt him with ridicule and scorn, saying,

" 'Woe to him who piles up stolen goods
and makes himself wealthy by
extortion!
How long must this go on?'
⁷ Will not your creditors suddenly arise?
Will they not wake up and make you
tremble?
Then you will become their prey.
⁸ Because you have plundered many
nations,
the peoples who are left will plunder
you.
For you have shed human blood;
you have destroyed lands and cities
and everyone in them.

⁹ "Woe to him who builds his house by
unjust gain,
setting his nest on high
to escape the clutches of ruin!
¹⁰ You have plotted the ruin of many
peoples,
shaming your own house and
forfeiting your life.
¹¹ The stones of the wall will cry out,

and the beams of the woodwork will
echo it.

¹² "Woe to him who builds a city with
bloodshed
and establishes a town by injustice!
¹³ Has not the LORD Almighty determined
that the people's labor is only fuel
for the fire,
that the nations exhaust themselves
for nothing?
¹⁴ For the earth will be filled with the
knowledge of the glory of
the LORD
as the waters cover the sea.

¹⁵ "Woe to him who gives drink to his
neighbors,
pouring it from the wineskin till they
are drunk,
so that he can gaze on their naked
bodies!
¹⁶ You will be filled with shame instead
of glory.
Now it is your turn! Drink and let your
nakedness be exposed[d]!
The cup from the LORD's right hand is
coming around to you,
and disgrace will cover your glory.
¹⁷ The violence you have done to Lebanon
will overwhelm you,
and your destruction of animals will
terrify you.
For you have shed human blood;
you have destroyed lands and cities
and everyone in them.

¹⁸ "Of what value is an idol carved by a
craftsman?
Or an image that teaches lies?
For the one who makes it trusts in his
own creation;
he makes idols that cannot speak.
¹⁹ Woe to him who says to wood, 'Come
to life!'
Or to lifeless stone, 'Wake up!'
Can it give guidance?
It is covered with gold and silver;
there is no breath in it."

²⁰ The LORD is in his holy temple;
let all the earth be silent
before him.

---

a 2 Or *so that whoever reads it*   *b 3* Or *Though he linger, wait for him; / he*   *c 4* Or *faith*
d 16 Masoretic Text; Dead Sea Scrolls, Aquila, Vulgate and Syriac (see also Septuagint) *and stagger*

THE IDOL WAR

READ: HABAKKUK 2:18

The whole subject of idolatry seems obsolete. As for those thousand or so references to idolatry in the Bible, haven't they expired? We don't know anyone who kneels before golden statues or bows down before carved images. Hasn't idolatry gone the way of parachute pants, beehive hairstyles, and three layers of grungy flannel shirts? Idolatry seems so primitive. So irrelevant.

And yet idolatry is the number one issue in the Bible. That should catch our attention. Idolatry shows up in every book. More than fifty of the laws in the Bible's first five books are aimed at this issue. In all of Judaism, it was one of only four sins that came with the death penalty attached.

Seeing my faith and life through the lens of idolatry has rebuilt my relationship with God from the ground up. As I've talked with my friends and people at church about it, they've agreed this issue is a game changer.

BUILDING FAITH WISDOM STRENGTH

What if it's not about statues? What if the gods of here and now take identities that are so ordinary that we don't recognize them as "gods" at all? What if we do our "kneeling" and our "bowing" with our imaginations, our cash, our search engines, our calendars?

The gods are at war, and their strength is not to be underestimated. These gods clash for the throne of your heart, and a lot is at stake. Everything about me, everything I do, every relationship I have, everything I hope or dream or wish to become, depends upon what god wins that war.

Habakkuk's Prayer

3 A prayer of Habakkuk the prophet. On *shigionoth.*[a]

² LORD, I have heard of your fame;
  I stand in awe of your deeds, LORD.
Repeat them in our day,
  in our time make them known;
  in wrath remember mercy.

³ God came from Teman,
  the Holy One from Mount Paran.[b]
His glory covered the heavens
  and his praise filled the earth.
⁴ His splendor was like the sunrise;
  rays flashed from his hand,
  where his power was hidden.
⁵ Plague went before him;
  pestilence followed his steps.
⁶ He stood, and shook the earth;
  he looked, and made the nations
    tremble.
The ancient mountains crumbled
  and the age-old hills collapsed —
  but he marches on forever.
⁷ I saw the tents of Cushan in distress,
  the dwellings of Midian in anguish.

⁸ Were you angry with the rivers, LORD?
  Was your wrath against the streams?
Did you rage against the sea
  when you rode your horses
  and your chariots to victory?
⁹ You uncovered your bow,
  you called for many arrows.
You split the earth with rivers;
¹⁰   the mountains saw you and writhed.
Torrents of water swept by;
  the deep roared
  and lifted its waves on high.

¹¹ Sun and moon stood still in the heavens
  at the glint of your flying arrows,
  at the lightning of your flashing spear.
¹² In wrath you strode through the earth
  and in anger you threshed the nations.
¹³ You came out to deliver your people,
  to save your anointed one.
You crushed the leader of the land of
    wickedness,
  you stripped him from head to foot.
¹⁴ With his own spear you pierced his head
  when his warriors stormed out to
    scatter us,
gloating as though about to devour
  the wretched who were in hiding.
¹⁵ You trampled the sea with your horses,
  churning the great waters.

¹⁶ I heard and my heart pounded,
  my lips quivered at the sound;
decay crept into my bones,
  and my legs trembled.
Yet I will wait patiently for the day of
    calamity
  to come on the nation invading us.
¹⁷ Though the fig tree does not bud
  and there are no grapes on the vines,
though the olive crop fails
  and the fields produce no food,
though there are no sheep in the pen
  and no cattle in the stalls,
¹⁸ yet I will rejoice in the LORD,
  I will be joyful in God my Savior.

¹⁹ The Sovereign LORD is my strength;
  he makes my feet like the feet of a deer,
  he enables me to tread on the heights.

For the director of music. On my stringed
  instruments.

---

[a] *1* Probably a literary or musical term   [b] *3* The Hebrew has *Selah* (a word of uncertain meaning) here and at the middle of verse 9 and at the end of verse 13.

ZEPHANIAH

WHEN DID THIS HAPPEN?

Between 640 and 627 B.C. in the southern kingdom of Judah

WHO IS IN THIS BOOK?

Zephaniah

VERSE YOU MIGHT RECOGNIZE

ZEPHANIAH 3:17

"He will take great delight in you; in his love he will no longer rebuke you, but will rejoice over you with singing."

WHAT'S IT ABOUT?

Zephaniah was a descendent of Hezekiah—one of Judah's few good kings—and he prophesied during the reign of King Josiah. Like Joel, Zephaniah predicted the day of the Lord, a judgment day when God's wrath would be poured out on his people as punishment for their sins. For Judah, the day of the Lord would come when they were conquered by Babylon and taken captive. But Zephaniah was also talking about the future day of the Lord at the end of history.

King Josiah's grandfather, Manasseh, and father, Amon, had led the people in many evil practices, including child sacrifice and idol worship. During King Josiah's reign, the young ruler discovered the scrolls of the law and had God's Word read to the people. Zephaniah's prophecy may have helped turn people to God during King Josiah's reign.

Unfortunately, the changes wouldn't last, and the first Jews would be taken into captivity a few short years later. Zephaniah offered encouragement that after this time of God's wrath and judgment, restoration would come. God would be with his people and rejoice over them.

ZEPHANIAH

1 The word of the LORD that came to Zephaniah son of Cushi, the son of Gedaliah, the son of Amariah, the son of Hezekiah, during the reign of Josiah son of Amon king of Judah:

Judgment on the Whole Earth in the Day of the Lord

² "I will sweep away everything
  from the face of the earth,"
      declares the LORD.
³ "I will sweep away both man and beast;
  I will sweep away the birds in the sky
  and the fish in the sea—
  and the idols that cause the wicked to
    stumble."*a*

"When I destroy all mankind
  on the face of the earth,"
      declares the LORD,
⁴ "I will stretch out my hand against
    Judah
  and against all who live in Jerusalem.
I will destroy every remnant of Baal
    worship in this place,
  the very names of the idolatrous
    priests—
⁵ those who bow down on the roofs
  to worship the starry host,
those who bow down and swear by the
    LORD
  and who also swear by Molek,*b*
⁶ those who turn back from following
    the LORD
  and neither seek the LORD nor inquire
    of him."

⁷ Be silent before the Sovereign LORD,
  for the day of the LORD is near.
The LORD has prepared a sacrifice;
  he has consecrated those he has
    invited.

⁸ "On the day of the LORD's sacrifice
  I will punish the officials
  and the king's sons

and all those clad
  in foreign clothes.
⁹ On that day I will punish
  all who avoid stepping on the
    threshold,*c*
who fill the temple of their gods
  with violence and deceit.

¹⁰ "On that day,"
  declares the LORD,
"a cry will go up from the Fish Gate,
  wailing from the New Quarter,
  and a loud crash from the hills.
¹¹ Wail, you who live in the market district*d*;
  all your merchants will be wiped out,
  all who trade with*e* silver will be
    destroyed.
¹² At that time I will search Jerusalem
    with lamps
  and punish those who are
    complacent,
  who are like wine left on its dregs,
who think, 'The LORD will do nothing,
  either good or bad.'
¹³ Their wealth will be plundered,
  their houses demolished.
Though they build houses,
  they will not live in them;
though they plant vineyards,
  they will not drink the wine."

¹⁴ The great day of the LORD is near—
  near and coming quickly.
The cry on the day of the LORD is
    bitter;
  the Mighty Warrior shouts his
    battle cry.
¹⁵ That day will be a day of wrath—
  a day of distress and anguish,
    a day of trouble and ruin,
  a day of darkness and gloom,
    a day of clouds and blackness—
¹⁶ a day of trumpet and battle cry
against the fortified cities
  and against the corner towers.

---

a 3 The meaning of the Hebrew for this line is uncertain.   *b 5* Hebrew *Malkam*   *c 9* See 1 Samuel 5:5.
d 11 Or *the Mortar*   *e 11* Or *in*

ZEPHANIAH

Seek the LORD, all you humble of the land, you who do what he commands. Seek righteousness, seek humility; perhaps you will be sheltered on the day of the LORD's anger. ZEPHANIAH 2:3

HIS NAME MEANS: "the LORD hides" or "the LORD protects"
READ HIS STORY: *Zephaniah 1–3*

Zephaniah's great-great grandfather was King Hezekiah. Of the twenty kings of Judah, the Bible says only eight were good. (All twenty of Israel's kings were wicked.) Hezekiah was a good king. Due to his royal lineage, experts believe Zephaniah held a prominent social position. He prophesied during the time of King Josiah—another good king—making him a contemporary of the prophets Jeremiah and Nahum.

Even with the influence of these good kings, many people who claimed to follow God also pursued wickedness. They worshiped the stars from their rooftops and bowed down to the fire-god Molek (Zephaniah 1:5). The priests defiled the temple and neglected the law (Zephaniah 3:4). Zephaniah's knowledge of events in the temple could indicate that Zephaniah was connected to the religious *and* political culture of Jerusalem. Amid this filth, Zephaniah tried to raise people up to follow the one true God.

Over and over, he warned the day of the Lord was near. God wasn't coming in celebration; he was coming to judge. Zephaniah paints a terrible picture of wrath, distress, anguish, trouble, ruin, darkness and gloom where the sinful would have their blood poured out like dust (Zephaniah 1:17).

Zephaniah didn't see much likelihood of most people turning back to God. He knew the day of the Lord was coming. But he did see hope for the righteous to find shelter in God. True followers would be saved and would grow again into a great nation.

17 "I will bring such distress on all people
   that they will grope about like those
      who are blind,
   because they have sinned against
      the LORD.
Their blood will be poured out like dust
   and their entrails like dung.
18 Neither their silver nor their gold
   will be able to save them
   on the day of the LORD's wrath."

In the fire of his jealousy
   the whole earth will be consumed,
   for he will make a sudden end
   of all who live on the earth.

Judah and Jerusalem Judged Along With the Nations

Judah Summoned to Repent

2 Gather together, gather yourselves
   together,
   you shameful nation,
2 before the decree takes effect
   and that day passes like windblown
      chaff,
   before the LORD's fierce anger
      comes upon you,
   before the day of the LORD's wrath
      comes upon you.
3 Seek the LORD, all you humble of
      the land,
   you who do what he commands.
Seek righteousness, seek humility;
   perhaps you will be sheltered
   on the day of the LORD's anger.

Philistia

4 Gaza will be abandoned
   and Ashkelon left in ruins.
At midday Ashdod will be emptied
   and Ekron uprooted.
5 Woe to you who live by the sea,
   you Kerethite people;
the word of the LORD is against you,
   Canaan, land of the Philistines.
He says, "I will destroy you,
   and none will be left."
6 The land by the sea will become pastures
   having wells for shepherds
   and pens for flocks.
7 That land will belong
   to the remnant of the people of Judah;
   there they will find pasture.

In the evening they will lie down
   in the houses of Ashkelon.
The LORD their God will care for them;
   he will restore their fortunes.[a]

Moab and Ammon

8 "I have heard the insults of Moab
   and the taunts of the Ammonites,
who insulted my people
   and made threats against their land.
9 Therefore, as surely as I live,"
   declares the LORD Almighty,
   the God of Israel,
"surely Moab will become like Sodom,
   the Ammonites like Gomorrah—
a place of weeds and salt pits,
   a wasteland forever.
The remnant of my people will plunder
      them;
   the survivors of my nation will inherit
      their land."

10 This is what they will get in return for
      their pride,
   for insulting and mocking
   the people of the LORD Almighty.
11 The LORD will be awesome to them
   when he destroys all the gods of the
      earth.
Distant nations will bow down to him,
   all of them in their own lands.

Cush

12 "You Cushites,[b] too,
   will be slain by my sword."

Assyria

13 He will stretch out his hand against
      the north
   and destroy Assyria,
leaving Nineveh utterly desolate
   and dry as the desert.
14 Flocks and herds will lie down there,
   creatures of every kind.
The desert owl and the screech owl
   will roost on her columns.
Their hooting will echo through the
      windows,
   rubble will fill the doorways,
   the beams of cedar will be
      exposed.
15 This is the city of revelry
   that lived in safety.

---

a 7 Or *will bring back their captives*   *b 12* That is, people from the upper Nile region

She said to herself,
"I am the one! And there is none
besides me."
What a ruin she has become,
a lair for wild beasts!
All who pass by her scoff
and shake their fists.

Jerusalem

3 Woe to the city of oppressors,
rebellious and defiled!
² She obeys no one,
she accepts no correction.
She does not trust in the LORD,
she does not draw near to her God.
³ Her officials within her
are roaring lions;
her rulers are evening wolves,
who leave nothing for the morning.
⁴ Her prophets are unprincipled;
they are treacherous people.
Her priests profane the sanctuary
and do violence to the law.
⁵ The LORD within her is righteous;
he does no wrong.
Morning by morning he dispenses his
justice,
and every new day he does not fail,
yet the unrighteous know no
shame.

Jerusalem Remains Unrepentant

⁶ "I have destroyed nations;
their strongholds are demolished.
I have left their streets deserted,
with no one passing through.
Their cities are laid waste;
they are deserted and empty.
⁷ Of Jerusalem I thought,
'Surely you will fear me
and accept correction!'
Then her place of refuge*a* would not be
destroyed,
nor all my punishments come
upon*b* her.
But they were still eager
to act corruptly in all they did.
⁸ Therefore wait for me,"
declares the LORD,
"for the day I will stand up to testify.*c*
I have decided to assemble the nations,
to gather the kingdoms

and to pour out my wrath on them —
all my fierce anger.
The whole world will be consumed
by the fire of my jealous anger.

Restoration of Israel's Remnant

⁹ "Then I will purify the lips of the
peoples,
that all of them may call on the name
of the LORD
and serve him shoulder to shoulder.
¹⁰ From beyond the rivers of Cush*d*
my worshipers, my scattered people,
will bring me offerings.
¹¹ On that day you, Jerusalem, will not be
put to shame
for all the wrongs you have done to me,
because I will remove from you
your arrogant boasters.
Never again will you be haughty
on my holy hill.
¹² But I will leave within you
the meek and humble.
The remnant of Israel
will trust in the name of the LORD.
¹³ They will do no wrong;
they will tell no lies.
A deceitful tongue
will not be found in their mouths.
They will eat and lie down
and no one will make them afraid."

¹⁴ Sing, Daughter Zion;
shout aloud, Israel!
Be glad and rejoice with all your heart,
Daughter Jerusalem!
¹⁵ The LORD has taken away your
punishment,
he has turned back your enemy.
The LORD, the King of Israel, is with you;
never again will you fear any harm.
¹⁶ On that day
they will say to Jerusalem,
"Do not fear, Zion;
do not let your hands hang limp.
¹⁷ The LORD your God is with you,
the Mighty Warrior who saves.
He will take great delight in you;
in his love he will no longer rebuke
you,
but will rejoice over you with singing."

¹⁸ "I will remove from you

---

a 7 Or *her sanctuary*   *b 7* Or *all those I appointed over*
to plunder   *d 10* That is, the upper Nile region
c 8 Septuagint and Syriac; Hebrew *will rise up*

100 PERCENT

READ: ZEPHANIAH 3:14

The phrase *with all your heart* means "with more energy than you have." It means giving it everything you've got. And then some. The issue isn't what you're doing. The real issue is why you do it, how you do it, and who you do it for. That's key.

Ultimately, I hope when you get a full-time job you'll love what you do and do what you love. I hope you work at a job that you would want to do even if you didn't get paid to do it. But sometimes you need to have a job you don't like, and you need to still glorify God by doing a good job at a bad job.

One of my summer jobs during college was working as a ditch digger. Yes, a ditch digger. We called ourselves earth relocation engineers, but it was backbreaking work that was impossible for anyone to enjoy. But I made the most of it. Anybody can do a good job at a good job, but there is something God-glorifying about doing a good job at a bad job. Anybody can be nice to a nice boss or teacher, but there is something God-glorifying when you love like Jesus in a godless work or school environment.

BUILDING

FAITH

WISDOM

STRENGTH

It's not about success and failure. It's not about good days and bad days. It's not about wealth or poverty. It's not about health or sickness. It's not even really about life or death. It's about glorifying God in whatever circumstance you find yourself in.

Whenever. Wherever. Whatever.

all who mourn over the loss of your
appointed festivals,
which is a burden and reproach
for you.
¹⁹ At that time I will deal
with all who oppressed you.
I will rescue the lame;
I will gather the exiles.
I will give them praise and honor

in every land where they have suffered
shame.
²⁰ At that time I will gather you;
at that time I will bring you home.
I will give you honor and praise
among all the peoples of the earth
when I restore your fortunes[a]
before your very eyes,"

says the LORD.

HAGGAI

WHEN DID THIS HAPPEN?

520–480 B.C. in Judah, the southern kingdom of Israel

WHO IS IN THIS BOOK?

Haggai
Zerubbabel
Joshua the high priest

VERSE YOU MIGHT RECOGNIZE

HAGGAI 1:5

"Now this is what the LORD Almighty says: 'Give careful thought to your ways.'"

WHAT'S IT ABOUT?

Haggai was one of three prophets (along with Zechariah and Malachi) who delivered prophecies to the first Jews returning from exile. Sixteen years after the first group of Jews returned to Judah, the people still hadn't rebuilt God's temple. They had returned to their land hopeful, but when enemies stopped them from building the temple, they had given up (see Ezra 4:24). The people went on with their lives and adjusted to the new normal.

Haggai delivered four short messages, telling the people that they had put their own comfort before the Lord and that their hardships—such as not having food and clothing—were a result of not putting God first by rebuilding the temple.

For once, the people of Judah listened! Haggai's prophecies inspired them to finish rebuilding the temple and to have hope for the future of their nation. Haggai also reaffirmed God's promises to David through a prophecy about Zerubbabel, a descendent of David (see Haggai 2:23).

HAGGAI

A Call to Build the House of the Lord

1 In the second year of King Darius, on the first day of the sixth month, the word of the LORD came through the prophet Haggai to Zerubbabel son of Shealtiel, governor of Judah, and to Joshua son of Jozadak, the high priest:

²This is what the LORD Almighty says: "These people say, 'The time has not yet come to rebuild the LORD's house.'"

³Then the word of the LORD came through the prophet Haggai: ⁴"Is it a time for you yourselves to be living in your paneled houses, while this house remains a ruin?"

⁵Now this is what the LORD Almighty says: "Give careful thought to your ways. ⁶You have planted much, but harvested little. You eat, but never have enough. You drink, but never have your fill. You put on clothes, but are not warm. You earn wages, only to put them in a purse with holes in it."

⁷This is what the LORD Almighty says: "Give careful thought to your ways. ⁸Go up into the mountains and bring down timber and build my house, so that I may take pleasure in it and be honored," says the LORD. ⁹"You expected much, but see, it turned out to be little. What you brought home, I blew away. Why?" declares the LORD Almighty. "Because of my house, which remains a ruin, while each of you is busy with your own house. ¹⁰Therefore, because of you the heavens have withheld their dew and the earth its crops. ¹¹I called for a drought on the fields and the mountains, on the grain, the new wine, the olive oil and everything else the ground produces, on people and livestock, and on all the labor of your hands."

¹²Then Zerubbabel son of Shealtiel, Joshua son of Jozadak, the high priest, and the whole remnant of the people obeyed the voice of the LORD their God and the message of the prophet Haggai, because the LORD their God had sent him. And the people feared the LORD.

¹³Then Haggai, the LORD's messenger, gave this message of the LORD to the people: "I am with you," declares the LORD. ¹⁴So the LORD stirred up the spirit of Zerubbabel son of Shealtiel, governor of Judah, and the spirit of Joshua son of Jozadak, the high priest, and the spirit of the whole remnant of the people. They came and began to work on the house of the LORD Almighty, their God, ¹⁵on the twenty-fourth day of the sixth month.

The Promised Glory of the New House

2 In the second year of King Darius, ¹on the twenty-first day of the seventh month, the word of the LORD came through the prophet Haggai: ²"Speak to Zerubbabel son of Shealtiel, governor of Judah, to Joshua son of Jozadak,ᵃ the high priest, and to the remnant of the people. Ask them, ³'Who of you is left who saw this house in its former glory? How does it look to you now? Does it not seem to you like nothing? ⁴But now be strong, Zerubbabel,' declares the LORD. 'Be strong, Joshua son of Jozadak, the high priest. Be strong, all you people of the land,' declares the LORD, 'and work. For I am with you,' declares the LORD Almighty. ⁵'This is what I covenanted with you when you came out of Egypt. And my Spirit remains among you. Do not fear.'

⁶"This is what the LORD Almighty says: 'In a little while I will once more shake the heavens and the earth, the sea and the dry land. ⁷I will shake all nations, and what is desired by all nations will come, and I will fill this house with glory,' says the LORD Almighty. ⁸'The silver is mine and the gold is mine,' declares the LORD Almighty. ⁹'The glory of this present house will be greater than the glory of the former house,' says the LORD Almighty. 'And in this place I will grant peace,' declares the LORD Almighty."

ᵃ 2 Hebrew *Jehozadak*, a variant of *Jozadak*; also in verse 4

TOP PRIORITY

READ: HAGGAI 1:3-4

The Jews arrived home from exile in Babylon nearly two decades before the start of this book. Immediately after their return, they erect an altar for burnt offerings and begin to rebuild the temple. When the foundation is complete, they celebrate and praise God. But opposition and their own concerns soon distract them, and the work halts (Ezra 4:24).

The prophet Haggai comes on the scene and confronts God's people. The Lord has noticed they live in houses with fine wood paneling while his own home remains a heap of rocks. The Lord commands his people to head to the mountains and bring back enough timber to finally finish the temple.

People who remembered the first temple aren't impressed by this new house of worship. But the Lord tells his people to be strong. He promises to help Zerubbabel the governor and Joshua the high priest. He will make this house even more glorious than the first.

BUILDING FAITH WISDOM STRENGTH

This ancient scene shows how easy it is to pay attention to your own interests and forget about the Lord and his concerns. But God repeats a caution that can help you keep your priorities straight. He says, "Give careful thought to your ways" (Haggai 1:5, 7; 2:15, 18). If you think hard about how you live, you will know what it means to put God first.

HAGGAI

Then the word of the LORD came through the prophet Haggai: "Is it a time for you yourselves to be living in your paneled houses, while this house remains a ruin?"
HAGGAI 1:3–4

HIS NAME MEANS: "festal," perhaps because he was born during a festival

READ HIS STORY: *Haggai 1–2; Ezra 5–6*

MEN OF THE BIBLE

Not much is known about Haggai's personal life, but we do know he lived during a difficult time in the history of Israel. Sixty-six years before Haggai declared the Lord's messages, King Nebuchadnezzar conquered Judah and took the people into exile in Babylon. During Haggai's lifetime, some Jews returned to Jerusalem with plans to rebuild the temple the Babylonians had destroyed. Haggai and Zechariah were like tag-team prophets, bringing God's word to the Israelites during these years of reconstruction.

Haggai's messages were to his fellow Jews, who had become distracted from their goal. Enemies threatened them, crops failed and times were hard financially. Eventually the construction of the temple stopped completely. People focused instead on building their own houses and pursuing their own interests. Haggai wouldn't stand for that.

He told the people and their leaders to get their priorities right and put God first. It had been sixteen years since the new ruler, King Cyrus of Persia, had permitted the Israelites to return to rebuild the temple. And lately they'd been languishing. So Haggai urged them to finish the work they had started.

Unlike many other prophets, whom the people scorned, Haggai got their attention. However, he didn't just rebuke them; he encouraged them and foretold of God's blessings for their obedience. His words were so powerful that the people got back to work and soon the temple was completed.

What message would Haggai speak to us if he were living today? Once again, he would challenge each one of us to put God first.

Blessings for a Defiled People

¹⁰On the twenty-fourth day of the ninth month, in the second year of Darius, the word of the LORD came to the prophet Haggai: ¹¹"This is what the LORD Almighty says: 'Ask the priests what the law says: ¹²If someone carries consecrated meat in the fold of their garment, and that fold touches some bread or stew, some wine, olive oil or other food, does it become consecrated?'"

The priests answered, "No."

¹³Then Haggai said, "If a person defiled by contact with a dead body touches one of these things, does it become defiled?"

"Yes," the priests replied, "it becomes defiled."

¹⁴Then Haggai said, "'So it is with this people and this nation in my sight,' declares the LORD. 'Whatever they do and whatever they offer there is defiled.

¹⁵"'Now give careful thought to this from this day on[a]—consider how things were before one stone was laid on another in the LORD's temple. ¹⁶When anyone came to a heap of twenty measures, there were only ten. When anyone went to a wine vat to draw fifty measures, there were only twenty. ¹⁷I

struck all the work of your hands with blight, mildew and hail, yet you did not return to me,' declares the LORD. ¹⁸'From this day on, from this twenty-fourth day of the ninth month, give careful thought to the day when the foundation of the LORD's temple was laid. Give careful thought: ¹⁹Is there yet any seed left in the barn? Until now, the vine and the fig tree, the pomegranate and the olive tree have not borne fruit.

"'From this day on I will bless you.'"

Zerubbabel the Lord's Signet Ring

²⁰The word of the LORD came to Haggai a second time on the twenty-fourth day of the month: ²¹"Tell Zerubbabel governor of Judah that I am going to shake the heavens and the earth. ²²I will overturn royal thrones and shatter the power of the foreign kingdoms. I will overthrow chariots and their drivers; horses and their riders will fall, each by the sword of his brother.

²³"'On that day,' declares the LORD Almighty, 'I will take you, my servant Zerubbabel son of Shealtiel,' declares the LORD, 'and I will make you like my signet ring, for I have chosen you,' declares the LORD Almighty."

ᵃ 15 Or *to the days past*

ZECHARIAH

➤ **WHEN DID THIS HAPPEN?**

Between 520 and 480 B.C. in Judah, the southern kingdom of Israel

➤ **WHO IS IN THIS BOOK?**

Zechariah

➤ **VERSES YOU MIGHT RECOGNIZE**

ZECHARIAH 1:3

"'Return to me,' declares the LORD Almighty, 'and I will return to you.'"

ZECHARIAH 9:9

"Rejoice greatly, Daughter Zion! Shout, Daughter Jerusalem! See, your king comes to you, righteous and victorious, lowly and riding on a donkey."

WHAT'S IT ABOUT?

Zechariah's message was similar to Haggai's: return to the Lord and he will return to you (see Zechariah 1:3). The people had returned from exile, but they still didn't have their priorities straight. The Jews had returned to the land, but they no longer owned it and were now subject to the authorities already there. Following God was the only way they could experience peace and joy.

Through a series of prophetic visions, God revealed to Zechariah some of the incredible things he had in store for Israel: the completion of the temple, judgment on the nation's enemies and the witness of the Jews to the nations through the coming Messiah.

This book also contains the most messianic prophecies (prophecies about Jesus) of any other of the minor prophets (short prophetic books). One of the most recognizable is Zechariah 9:9: "See, your king comes to you, righteous and victorious, lowly and riding on a donkey." One day Jesus will come, not only as a judge and a high priest, but also as a king to rule on his throne in Jerusalem.

ZECHARIAH

A Call to Return to the Lord

1 In the eighth month of the second year of Darius, the word of the LORD came to the prophet Zechariah son of Berekiah, the son of Iddo:

2 "The LORD was very angry with your ancestors. 3 Therefore tell the people: This is what the LORD Almighty says: 'Return to me,' declares the LORD Almighty, 'and I will return to you,' says the LORD Almighty. 4 Do not be like your ancestors, to whom the earlier prophets proclaimed: This is what the LORD Almighty says: 'Turn from your evil ways and your evil practices.' But they would not listen or pay attention to me, declares the LORD. 5 Where are your ancestors now? And the prophets, do they live forever? 6 But did not my words and my decrees, which I commanded my servants the prophets, overtake your ancestors?

"Then they repented and said, 'The LORD Almighty has done to us what our ways and practices deserve, just as he determined to do.'"

The Man Among the Myrtle Trees

7 On the twenty-fourth day of the eleventh month, the month of Shebat, in the second year of Darius, the word of the LORD came to the prophet Zechariah son of Berekiah, the son of Iddo.

8 During the night I had a vision, and there before me was a man mounted on a red horse. He was standing among the myrtle trees in a ravine. Behind him were red, brown and white horses.

9 I asked, "What are these, my lord?"

The angel who was talking with me answered, "I will show you what they are."

10 Then the man standing among the myrtle trees explained, "They are the ones the LORD has sent to go throughout the earth."

11 And they reported to the angel of the LORD who was standing among the myrtle trees, "We have gone throughout the earth and found the whole world at rest and in peace."

12 Then the angel of the LORD said, "LORD Almighty, how long will you withhold mercy from Jerusalem and from the towns of Judah, which you have been angry with these seventy years?" 13 So the LORD spoke kind and comforting words to the angel who talked with me.

14 Then the angel who was speaking to me said, "Proclaim this word: This is what the LORD Almighty says: 'I am very jealous for Jerusalem and Zion, 15 and I am very angry with the nations that feel secure. I was only a little angry, but they went too far with the punishment.'

16 "Therefore this is what the LORD says: 'I will return to Jerusalem with mercy, and there my house will be rebuilt. And the measuring line will be stretched out over Jerusalem,' declares the LORD Almighty.

17 "Proclaim further: This is what the LORD Almighty says: 'My towns will again overflow with prosperity, and the LORD will again comfort Zion and choose Jerusalem.'"

Four Horns and Four Craftsmen

18 Then I looked up, and there before me were four horns. 19 I asked the angel who was speaking to me, "What are these?"

He answered me, "These are the horns that scattered Judah, Israel and Jerusalem."

20 Then the LORD showed me four craftsmen. 21 I asked, "What are these coming to do?"

He answered, "These are the horns that scattered Judah so that no one could raise their head, but the craftsmen have come to terrify them and throw down these horns of the nations who lifted up their horns against the land of Judah to scatter its people."[a]

A Man With a Measuring Line

2[b] Then I looked up, and there before me was a man with a measuring line in his hand. 2 I asked, "Where are you going?"

---

[a] 21 In Hebrew texts 1:18-21 is numbered 2:1-4.   [b] In Hebrew texts 2:1-13 is numbered 2:5-17.

ZECHARIAH

Zechariah the prophet, a descendant of Iddo, prophesied to the Jews in Judah and Jerusalem in the name of the God of Israel, who was over them. EZRA 5:1

HIS NAME MEANS: "the LORD remembers"
READ HIS STORY: *Zechariah 1:1, 9–12; Ezra 5–6*

OF THE BIBLE

Hope gives us the determination to keep going, even in difficult times. Before Babylon destroyed Jerusalem and dispersed God's people, the prophet Jeremiah promised them "hope and a future" (Jeremiah 29:11). The visions Zechariah received speak to the continued hope of those who trust in the Lord.

Zechariah was the son of a priest. Historians believe he was born in Babylon during the exile but returned with his family to Jerusalem around 537 B.C. By this time, Persia had defeated Babylon. Darius the Great (not the King Darius mentioned by Daniel) ruled the Persian empire. By dating his visions according to Darius's reign, we know Zechariah wrote his book about 520 B.C.

He begins by telling the people how angry the Lord was with their ancestors. They'd strayed from the Lord and followed false gods. Then through eight visions, Zechariah shows how repentance can lead to restoration. Zechariah encouraged God's people to rebuild the temple. But Zechariah didn't want to just give hope for the present; he preached about the coming Messiah. Bible scholars note that only Isaiah wrote more frequent prophecies about Jesus than Zechariah.

Zechariah 9:9 tells us the coming king of Israel will ride in on "a colt, a foal of a donkey." Jesus did exactly that (Luke 19:29-36). In Zechariah 11:13, he talks about thirty pieces of silver—the amount Judas was paid for betraying Jesus (Matthew 26:14-16). Zechariah 12:10 indicates that the Messiah would suffer and be pierced, and this prophecy is quoted in John 19:37. All these truths we see in Jesus, the source of true hope.

He answered me, "To measure Jerusalem, to find out how wide and how long it is."

[3] While the angel who was speaking to me was leaving, another angel came to meet him [4] and said to him: "Run, tell that young man, 'Jerusalem will be a city without walls because of the great number of people and animals in it. [5] And I myself will be a wall of fire around it,' declares the LORD, 'and I will be its glory within.'

[6] "Come! Come! Flee from the land of the north," declares the LORD, "for I have scattered you to the four winds of heaven," declares the LORD.

[7] "Come, Zion! Escape, you who live in Daughter Babylon!" [8] For this is what the LORD Almighty says: "After the Glorious One has sent me against the nations that have plundered you — for whoever touches you touches the apple of his eye — [9] I will surely raise my hand against them so that their slaves will plunder them.[a] Then you will know that the LORD Almighty has sent me.

[10] "Shout and be glad, Daughter Zion. For I am coming, and I will live among you," declares the LORD. [11] "Many nations will be joined with the LORD in that day and will become my people. I will live among you and you will know that the LORD Almighty has sent me to you. [12] The LORD will inherit Judah as his portion in the holy land and will again choose Jerusalem. [13] Be still before the LORD, all mankind, because he has roused himself from his holy dwelling."

Clean Garments for the High Priest

3 Then he showed me Joshua the high priest standing before the angel of the LORD, and Satan[b] standing at his right side to accuse him. [2] The LORD said to Satan, "The LORD rebuke you, Satan! The LORD, who has chosen Jerusalem, rebuke you! Is not this man a burning stick snatched from the fire?"

[3] Now Joshua was dressed in filthy clothes as he stood before the angel. [4] The angel said to those who were standing before him, "Take off his filthy clothes."

Then he said to Joshua, "See, I have taken away your sin, and I will put fine garments on you."

[5] Then I said, "Put a clean turban on his head." So they put a clean turban on his head and clothed him, while the angel of the LORD stood by.

[6] The angel of the LORD gave this charge to Joshua: [7] "This is what the LORD Almighty says: 'If you will walk in obedience to me and keep my requirements, then you will govern my house and have charge of my courts, and I will give you a place among these standing here.

[8] "'Listen, High Priest Joshua, you and your associates seated before you, who are men symbolic of things to come: I am going to bring my servant, the Branch. [9] See, the stone I have set in front of Joshua! There are seven eyes[c] on that one stone, and I will engrave an inscription on it,' says the LORD Almighty, 'and I will remove the sin of this land in a single day.

[10] "'In that day each of you will invite your neighbor to sit under your vine and fig tree,' declares the LORD Almighty."

The Gold Lampstand and the Two Olive Trees

4 Then the angel who talked with me returned and woke me up, like someone awakened from sleep. [2] He asked me, "What do you see?"

I answered, "I see a solid gold lampstand with a bowl at the top and seven lamps on it, with seven channels to the lamps. [3] Also there are two olive trees by it, one on the right of the bowl and the other on its left."

[4] I asked the angel who talked with me, "What are these, my lord?"

[5] He answered, "Do you not know what these are?"

"No, my lord," I replied.

[6] So he said to me, "This is the word of the LORD to Zerubbabel: 'Not by might nor by power, but by my Spirit,' says the LORD Almighty.

[7] "What are you, mighty mountain? Before Zerubbabel you will become level ground. Then he will bring out the capstone to shouts of 'God bless it! God bless it!' "

[8] Then the word of the LORD came to me: [9] "The hands of Zerubbabel have laid the foundation of this temple; his hands will also complete it. Then you will know that the LORD Almighty has sent me to you.

---

[a] 8,9 Or *says after . . . eye:* [9] *"I . . . plunder them."*   [b] 1 Hebrew *satan* means *adversary.*   [c] 9 Or *facets*

¹⁰"Who dares despise the day of small things, since the seven eyes of the LORD that range throughout the earth will rejoice when they see the chosen capstone*ᵃ* in the hand of Zerubbabel?"

¹¹Then I asked the angel, "What are these two olive trees on the right and the left of the lampstand?"

¹²Again I asked him, "What are these two olive branches beside the two gold pipes that pour out golden oil?"

¹³He replied, "Do you not know what these are?"

"No, my lord," I said.

¹⁴So he said, "These are the two who are anointed to*ᵇ* serve the Lord of all the earth."

The Flying Scroll

5 I looked again, and there before me was a flying scroll.

²He asked me, "What do you see?"

I answered, "I see a flying scroll, twenty cubits long and ten cubits wide.*ᶜ*"

³And he said to me, "This is the curse that is going out over the whole land; for according to what it says on one side, every thief will be banished, and according to what it says on the other, everyone who swears falsely will be banished. ⁴The LORD Almighty declares, 'I will send it out, and it will enter the house of the thief and the house of anyone who swears falsely by my name. It will remain in that house and destroy it completely, both its timbers and its stones.' "

The Woman in a Basket

⁵Then the angel who was speaking to me came forward and said to me, "Look up and see what is appearing."

⁶I asked, "What is it?"

He replied, "It is a basket." And he added, "This is the iniquity*ᵈ* of the people throughout the land."

⁷Then the cover of lead was raised, and there in the basket sat a woman! ⁸He said, "This is wickedness," and he pushed her back into the basket and pushed its lead cover down on it.

⁹Then I looked up — and there before me were two women, with the wind in their wings! They had wings like those of a stork,

and they lifted up the basket between heaven and earth.

¹⁰"Where are they taking the basket?" I asked the angel who was speaking to me.

¹¹He replied, "To the country of Babylonia*ᵉ* to build a house for it. When the house is ready, the basket will be set there in its place."

Four Chariots

6 I looked up again, and there before me were four chariots coming out from between two mountains — mountains of bronze. ²The first chariot had red horses, the second black, ³the third white, and the fourth dappled — all of them powerful. ⁴I asked the angel who was speaking to me, "What are these, my lord?"

⁵The angel answered me, "These are the four spirits*ᶠ* of heaven, going out from standing in the presence of the Lord of the whole world. ⁶The one with the black horses is going toward the north country, the one with the white horses toward the west,*ᵍ* and the one with the dappled horses toward the south."

⁷When the powerful horses went out, they were straining to go throughout the earth. And he said, "Go throughout the earth!" So they went throughout the earth.

⁸Then he called to me, "Look, those going toward the north country have given my Spirit*ʰ* rest in the land of the north."

A Crown for Joshua

⁹The word of the LORD came to me: ¹⁰"Take silver and gold from the exiles Heldai, Tobijah and Jedaiah, who have arrived from Babylon. Go the same day to the house of Josiah son of Zephaniah. ¹¹Take the silver and gold and make a crown, and set it on the head of the high priest, Joshua son of Jozadak.*ⁱ* ¹²Tell him this is what the LORD Almighty says: 'Here is the man whose name is the Branch, and he will branch out from his place and build the temple of the LORD. ¹³It is he who will build the temple of the LORD, and he will be clothed with majesty and will sit and rule on his throne. And he*ʲ* will be a priest on his throne. And there will be harmony between the two.'

ᵃ 10 Or *the plumb line*   *ᵇ* 14 Or *two who bring oil and* or about 9 meters long and 4.5 meters wide   *ᵈ* 6 Or *appearance*   *ᵉ* 11 Hebrew *Shinar*   *ᶠ* 5 Or *winds* *ᵍ* 6 Or *horses after them*   *ʰ* 8 Or *spirit*   *ⁱ* 11 Hebrew *Jehozadak,* a variant of *Jozadak*   *ʲ* 13 Or *there*   *ᶜ* 2 That is, about 30 feet long and 15 feet wide

[14]The crown will be given to Heldai,[a] Tobijah, Jedaiah and Hen[b] son of Zephaniah as a memorial in the temple of the LORD. [15]Those who are far away will come and help to build the temple of the LORD, and you will know that the LORD Almighty has sent me to you. This will happen if you diligently obey the LORD your God."

Justice and Mercy, Not Fasting

7 In the fourth year of King Darius, the word of the LORD came to Zechariah on the fourth day of the ninth month, the month of Kislev. [2]The people of Bethel had sent Sharezer and Regem-Melek, together with their men, to entreat the LORD [3]by asking the priests of the house of the LORD Almighty and the prophets, "Should I mourn and fast in the fifth month, as I have done for so many years?"

[4]Then the word of the LORD Almighty came to me: [5]"Ask all the people of the land and the priests, 'When you fasted and mourned in the fifth and seventh months for the past seventy years, was it really for me that you fasted? [6]And when you were eating and drinking, were you not just feasting for yourselves? [7]Are these not the words the LORD proclaimed through the earlier prophets when Jerusalem and its surrounding towns were at rest and prosperous, and the Negev and the western foothills were settled?' "

[8]And the word of the LORD came again to Zechariah: [9]"This is what the LORD Almighty said: 'Administer true justice; show mercy and compassion to one another. [10]Do not oppress the widow or the fatherless, the foreigner or the poor. Do not plot evil against each other.'

[11]"But they refused to pay attention; stubbornly they turned their backs and covered their ears. [12]They made their hearts as hard as flint and would not listen to the law or to the words that the LORD Almighty had sent by his Spirit through the earlier prophets. So the LORD Almighty was very angry.

[13]" 'When I called, they did not listen; so when they called, I would not listen,' says the LORD Almighty. [14]'I scattered them with a whirlwind among all the nations, where they were strangers. The land they left behind them was so desolate that no one traveled through it. This is how they made the pleasant land desolate.' "

The Lord Promises to Bless Jerusalem

8 The word of the LORD Almighty came to me. [2]This is what the LORD Almighty says: "I am very jealous for Zion; I am burning with jealousy for her."

[3]This is what the LORD says: "I will return to Zion and dwell in Jerusalem. Then Jerusalem will be called the Faithful City, and the mountain of the LORD Almighty will be called the Holy Mountain."

[4]This is what the LORD Almighty says: "Once again men and women of ripe old age will sit in the streets of Jerusalem, each of them with cane in hand because of their age. [5]The city streets will be filled with boys and girls playing there."

[6]This is what the LORD Almighty says: "It may seem marvelous to the remnant of this people at that time, but will it seem marvelous to me?" declares the LORD Almighty.

[7]This is what the LORD Almighty says: "I will save my people from the countries of the east and the west. [8]I will bring them back to live in Jerusalem; they will be my people, and I will be faithful and righteous to them as their God."

[9]This is what the LORD Almighty says: "Now hear these words, 'Let your hands be strong so that the temple may be built.' This is also what the prophets said who were present when the foundation was laid for the house of the LORD Almighty. [10]Before that time there were no wages for people or hire for animals. No one could go about their business safely because of their enemies, since I had turned everyone against their neighbor. [11]But now I will not deal with the remnant of this people as I did in the past," declares the LORD Almighty.

[12]"The seed will grow well, the vine will yield its fruit, the ground will produce its crops, and the heavens will drop their dew. I will give all these things as an inheritance to the remnant of this people. [13]Just as you, Judah and Israel, have been a curse[c] among

---

[a] 14 Syriac; Hebrew *Helem*   [b] 14 Or *and the gracious one, the*   [c] 13 That is, your name has been used in cursing (see Jer. 29:22); or, you have been regarded as under a curse.

the nations, so I will save you, and you will be a blessing.[a] Do not be afraid, but let your hands be strong."

¹⁴ This is what the LORD Almighty says: "Just as I had determined to bring disaster on you and showed no pity when your ancestors angered me," says the LORD Almighty, ¹⁵ "so now I have determined to do good again to Jerusalem and Judah. Do not be afraid. ¹⁶ These are the things you are to do: Speak the truth to each other, and render true and sound judgment in your courts; ¹⁷ do not plot evil against each other, and do not love to swear falsely. I hate all this," declares the LORD.

¹⁸ The word of the LORD Almighty came to me.

¹⁹ This is what the LORD Almighty says: "The fasts of the fourth, fifth, seventh and tenth months will become joyful and glad occasions and happy festivals for Judah. Therefore love truth and peace."

²⁰ This is what the LORD Almighty says: "Many peoples and the inhabitants of many cities will yet come, ²¹ and the inhabitants of one city will go to another and say, 'Let us go at once to entreat the LORD and seek the LORD Almighty. I myself am going.' ²² And many peoples and powerful nations will come to Jerusalem to seek the LORD Almighty and to entreat him."

²³ This is what the LORD Almighty says: "In those days ten people from all languages and nations will take firm hold of one Jew by the hem of his robe and say, 'Let us go with you, because we have heard that God is with you.'"

Judgment on Israel's Enemies

9 A prophecy:

The word of the LORD is against the land of Hadrak
　　and will come to rest on Damascus —
for the eyes of all people and all the tribes of Israel
　　are on the LORD —[b]
² and on Hamath too, which borders on it,
　　and on Tyre and Sidon, though they
　　are very skillful.
³ Tyre has built herself a stronghold;

she has heaped up silver like dust,
　　and gold like the dirt of the streets.
⁴ But the Lord will take away her
　　possessions
　　and destroy her power on the sea,
　　and she will be consumed by fire.
⁵ Ashkelon will see it and fear;
　　Gaza will writhe in agony,
　　and Ekron too, for her hope will wither.
Gaza will lose her king
　　and Ashkelon will be deserted.
⁶ A mongrel people will occupy Ashdod,
　　and I will put an end to the pride of the
　　Philistines.
⁷ I will take the blood from their mouths,
　　the forbidden food from between their
　　teeth.
Those who are left will belong to our God
　　and become a clan in Judah,
　　and Ekron will be like the Jebusites.
⁸ But I will encamp at my temple
　　to guard it against marauding forces.
Never again will an oppressor overrun
　　my people,
　　for now I am keeping watch.

The Coming of Zion's King

⁹ Rejoice greatly, Daughter Zion!
　　Shout, Daughter Jerusalem!
See, your king comes to you,
　　righteous and victorious,
lowly and riding on a donkey,
　　on a colt, the foal of a donkey.
¹⁰ I will take away the chariots from
　　Ephraim
　　and the warhorses from Jerusalem,
　　and the battle bow will be broken.
He will proclaim peace to the nations.
　　His rule will extend from sea to sea
　　and from the River[c] to the ends of
　　the earth.
¹¹ As for you, because of the blood of my
　　covenant with you,
　　I will free your prisoners from the
　　waterless pit.
¹² Return to your fortress, you prisoners
　　of hope;
　　even now I announce that I will restore
　　twice as much to you.
¹³ I will bend Judah as I bend my bow
　　and fill it with Ephraim.

---

[a] 13 Or and your name will be used in blessings (see Gen. 48:20); or and you will be seen as blessed
[b] 1 Or Damascus. / For the eye of the LORD is on all people, / as well as on the tribes of Israel,
[c] 10 That is, the Euphrates

I will rouse your sons, Zion,
  against your sons, Greece,
  and make you like a warrior's
    sword.

The Lord Will Appear

¹⁴ Then the LORD will appear over them;
  his arrow will flash like lightning.
The Sovereign LORD will sound the
    trumpet;
  he will march in the storms of the
    south,
¹⁵   and the LORD Almighty will shield
    them.
They will destroy
  and overcome with slingstones.
They will drink and roar as with wine;
  they will be full like a bowl
  used for sprinkling*ᵃ* the corners of
    the altar.
¹⁶ The LORD their God will save his people
    on that day
  as a shepherd saves his flock.
They will sparkle in his land
  like jewels in a crown.
¹⁷ How attractive and beautiful they will be!
  Grain will make the young men thrive,
  and new wine the young women.

The Lord Will Care for Judah

10 Ask the LORD for rain in the
    springtime;
  it is the LORD who sends the
    thunderstorms.
He gives showers of rain to all people,
  and plants of the field to everyone.
² The idols speak deceitfully,
  diviners see visions that lie;
they tell dreams that are false,
  they give comfort in vain.
Therefore the people wander like sheep
  oppressed for lack of a shepherd.

³ "My anger burns against the shepherds,
  and I will punish the leaders;
for the LORD Almighty will care
  for his flock, the people of Judah,
  and make them like a proud horse in
    battle.
⁴ From Judah will come the cornerstone,
  from him the tent peg,
from him the battle bow,
  from him every ruler.

⁵ Together they*ᵇ* will be like warriors
    in battle
  trampling their enemy into the mud
    of the streets.
They will fight because the LORD is with
    them,
  and they will put the enemy horsemen
    to shame.
⁶ "I will strengthen Judah
  and save the tribes of Joseph.
I will restore them
  because I have compassion on them.
They will be as though
  I had not rejected them,
for I am the LORD their God
  and I will answer them.
⁷ The Ephraimites will become like
    warriors,
  and their hearts will be glad as with
    wine.
Their children will see it and be joyful;
  their hearts will rejoice in the LORD.
⁸ I will signal for them
  and gather them in.
Surely I will redeem them;
  they will be as numerous as before.
⁹ Though I scatter them among the
    peoples,
  yet in distant lands they will
    remember me.
They and their children will survive,
  and they will return.
¹⁰ I will bring them back from Egypt
  and gather them from Assyria.
I will bring them to Gilead and Lebanon,
  and there will not be room enough
    for them.
¹¹ They will pass through the sea of trouble;
  the surging sea will be subdued
  and all the depths of the Nile will
    dry up.
Assyria's pride will be brought down
  and Egypt's scepter will pass away.
¹² I will strengthen them in the LORD
  and in his name they will live
    securely,"
              declares the LORD.

11 Open your doors, Lebanon,
  so that fire may devour your cedars!
² Wail, you juniper, for the cedar has fallen;
  the stately trees are ruined!

ᵃ 15 Or *bowl, / like*   *ᵇ* 4,5 Or *ruler, all of them together. /* ⁵*They*

Wail, oaks of Bashan;
   the dense forest has been cut down!
³Listen to the wail of the shepherds;
   their rich pastures are destroyed!
Listen to the roar of the lions;
   the lush thicket of the Jordan is ruined!

Two Shepherds

⁴This is what the Lord my God says: "Shepherd the flock marked for slaughter. ⁵Their buyers slaughter them and go unpunished. Those who sell them say, 'Praise the Lord, I am rich!' Their own shepherds do not spare them. ⁶For I will no longer have pity on the people of the land," declares the Lord. "I will give everyone into the hands of their neighbors and their king. They will devastate the land, and I will not rescue anyone from their hands."

⁷So I shepherded the flock marked for slaughter, particularly the oppressed of the flock. Then I took two staffs and called one Favor and the other Union, and I shepherded the flock. ⁸In one month I got rid of the three shepherds.

The flock detested me, and I grew weary of them ⁹and said, "I will not be your shepherd. Let the dying die, and the perishing perish. Let those who are left eat one another's flesh."

¹⁰Then I took my staff called Favor and broke it, revoking the covenant I had made with all the nations. ¹¹It was revoked on that day, and so the oppressed of the flock who were watching me knew it was the word of the Lord.

¹²I told them, "If you think it best, give me my pay; but if not, keep it." So they paid me thirty pieces of silver.

¹³And the Lord said to me, "Throw it to the potter"—the handsome price at which they valued me! So I took the thirty pieces of silver and threw them to the potter at the house of the Lord.

¹⁴Then I broke my second staff called Union, breaking the family bond between Judah and Israel.

¹⁵Then the Lord said to me, "Take again the equipment of a foolish shepherd. ¹⁶For I am going to raise up a shepherd over the land who will not care for the lost, or seek the young, or heal the injured, or feed the healthy, but will eat the meat of the choice sheep, tearing off their hooves.

¹⁷ "Woe to the worthless shepherd,
   who deserts the flock!
May the sword strike his arm and his
      right eye!
May his arm be completely withered,
   his right eye totally blinded!"

Jerusalem's Enemies to Be Destroyed

12 A prophecy: The word of the Lord concerning Israel.

The Lord, who stretches out the heavens, who lays the foundation of the earth, and who forms the human spirit within a person, declares: ² "I am going to make Jerusalem a cup that sends all the surrounding peoples reeling. Judah will be besieged as well as Jerusalem. ³On that day, when all the nations of the earth are gathered against her, I will make Jerusalem an immovable rock for all the nations. All who try to move it will injure themselves. ⁴On that day I will strike every horse with panic and its rider with madness," declares the Lord. "I will keep a watchful eye over Judah, but I will blind all the horses of the nations. ⁵Then the clans of Judah will say in their hearts, 'The people of Jerusalem are strong, because the Lord Almighty is their God.'

⁶ "On that day I will make the clans of Judah like a firepot in a woodpile, like a flaming torch among sheaves. They will consume all the surrounding peoples right and left, but Jerusalem will remain intact in her place.

⁷ "The Lord will save the dwellings of Judah first, so that the honor of the house of David and of Jerusalem's inhabitants may not be greater than that of Judah. ⁸On that day the Lord will shield those who live in Jerusalem, so that the feeblest among them will be like David, and the house of David will be like God, like the angel of the Lord going before them. ⁹On that day I will set out to destroy all the nations that attack Jerusalem.

Mourning for the One They Pierced

¹⁰ "And I will pour out on the house of David and the inhabitants of Jerusalem a spirit^a of grace and supplication. They will look on^b me, the one they have pierced, and they

^a 10 Or *the Spirit*   ^b 10 Or *to*

SIGNS OF A SAVIOR

READ: **ZECHARIAH 12:10**

You can find Jesus all over the pages of the book of Zechariah. The man behind this book started prophesying as a young guy (Zechariah 2:4), a couple of months after Haggai wrapped up his preaching, and both men call the nation back from its selfishness to finish rebuilding the temple. But Zechariah preaches about more than God's house. He highlights the greatness of the Messiah promised by the Lord.

Zechariah describes this coming Savior as "the Branch" (Zechariah 3:8) who would serve as both king and priest (6:12–13). That's an exact description of Jesus' role on earth (Hebrews 1:1–4).

Details of the story of Palm Sunday show up here (Zechariah 9:9) hundreds of years before Jesus rides a donkey into Jerusalem (Matthew 21:1–9). His arrival on such a humble animal shows he's a king who comes in peace.

You catch facts about Judas' betrayal of Jesus both here (Zechariah 11:12–13) and in the New Testament (Matthew 26:15). And the prediction that Jerusalem's people will grieve for one they pierce (Zechariah 12:10) comes to pass as Jesus hangs on the cross (John 19:34, 37).

God had a plan from the very beginning to save you through Jesus. He laid out the details long in advance so you could recognize the Savior when he showed up on earth. It's all a sign of his one-of-a-kind care for you.

BUILDING

FAITH

WISDOM

STRENGTH

will mourn for him as one mourns for an only child, and grieve bitterly for him as one grieves for a firstborn son. ¹¹On that day the weeping in Jerusalem will be as great as the weeping of Hadad Rimmon in the plain of Megiddo. ¹²The land will mourn, each clan by itself, with their wives by themselves: the clan of the house of David and their wives, the clan of the house of Nathan and their wives, ¹³the clan of the house of Levi and their wives, the clan of Shimei and their wives, ¹⁴and all the rest of the clans and their wives.

Cleansing From Sin

13 "On that day a fountain will be opened to the house of David and the inhabitants of Jerusalem, to cleanse them from sin and impurity.

²"On that day, I will banish the names of the idols from the land, and they will be remembered no more," declares the Lord Almighty. "I will remove both the prophets and the spirit of impurity from the land. ³And if anyone still prophesies, their father and mother, to whom they were born, will say to them, 'You must die, because you have told lies in the Lord's name.' Then their own parents will stab the one who prophesies.

⁴"On that day every prophet will be ashamed of their prophetic vision. They will not put on a prophet's garment of hair in order to deceive. ⁵Each will say, 'I am not a prophet. I am a farmer; the land has been my livelihood since my youth.'ᵃ ⁶If someone asks, 'What are these wounds on your bodyᵇ?' they will answer, 'The wounds I was given at the house of my friends.'

The Shepherd Struck, the Sheep Scattered

⁷"Awake, sword, against my shepherd,
    against the man who is close to me!"
    declares the Lord Almighty.
"Strike the shepherd,
    and the sheep will be scattered,
    and I will turn my hand against the
      little ones.
⁸In the whole land," declares the Lord,
    "two-thirds will be struck down and
      perish;
    yet one-third will be left in it.

⁹This third I will put into the fire;
    I will refine them like silver
    and test them like gold.
They will call on my name
    and I will answer them;
I will say, 'They are my people,'
    and they will say, 'The Lord is
      our God.'"

The Lord Comes and Reigns

14 A day of the Lord is coming, Jerusalem, when your possessions will be plundered and divided up within your very walls.

²I will gather all the nations to Jerusalem to fight against it; the city will be captured, the houses ransacked, and the women raped. Half of the city will go into exile, but the rest of the people will not be taken from the city. ³Then the Lord will go out and fight against those nations, as he fights on a day of battle. ⁴On that day his feet will stand on the Mount of Olives, east of Jerusalem, and the Mount of Olives will be split in two from east to west, forming a great valley, with half of the mountain moving north and half moving south. ⁵You will flee by my mountain valley, for it will extend to Azel. You will flee as you fled from the earthquakeᶜ in the days of Uzziah king of Judah. Then the Lord my God will come, and all the holy ones with him.

⁶On that day there will be neither sunlight nor cold, frosty darkness. ⁷It will be a unique day — a day known only to the Lord — with no distinction between day and night. When evening comes, there will be light.

⁸On that day living water will flow out from Jerusalem, half of it east to the Dead Sea and half of it west to the Mediterranean Sea, in summer and in winter.

⁹The Lord will be king over the whole earth. On that day there will be one Lord, and his name the only name.

¹⁰The whole land, from Geba to Rimmon, south of Jerusalem, will become like the Arabah. But Jerusalem will be raised up high from the Benjamin Gate to the site of the First Gate, to the Corner Gate, and from the Tower of Hananel to the royal winepresses, and will remain in its place. ¹¹It will be inhabited;

ᵃ 5 Or *farmer; a man sold me in my youth*   ᵇ 6 Or *wounds between your hands*   ᶜ 5 Or *⁵My mountain valley will be blocked and will extend to Azel. It will be blocked as it was blocked because of the earthquake*

THE GIVER

READ: ZECHARIAH 13:9

God will never tempt you. He can't. On the contrary, he promises to provide an escape route for every tempting situation. And I can promise you this: God will test your faith. And those tests won't get easier. They'll probably get harder. Sorry! And those tests always involve what's most important to you.

What do you find your identity in?

God will test you to make sure your identity is in Jesus Christ and nothing else. You don't have to live in fear that God is going to take away what's most important to you. If the gift ever becomes more important than the Gift Giver, then there's a problem.

God-given gifts are great things and dangerous things. One of my constant prayers is this: "Lord, don't let my gifts take me farther than my character can sustain me." As we grow in the gifts God has given us, it's easy to start relying on those gifts instead of relying on God. That's when our greatest strength becomes our greatest weakness.

BUILDING

FAITH

WISDOM

STRENGTH

It was God who gave Lucifer a beautiful voice. Those musical gifts were originally used to glorify God. Then Lucifer started looking in the mirror (which is always dangerous). He glorified the gift he had been given instead of glorifying God. Don't be a Lucifer. And remember this: whatever you don't turn into praise turns into pride.

never again will it be destroyed. Jerusalem will be secure.

¹²This is the plague with which the Lord will strike all the nations that fought against Jerusalem: Their flesh will rot while they are still standing on their feet, their eyes will rot in their sockets, and their tongues will rot in their mouths. ¹³On that day people will be stricken by the Lord with great panic. They will seize each other by the hand and attack one another. ¹⁴Judah too will fight at Jerusalem. The wealth of all the surrounding nations will be collected — great quantities of gold and silver and clothing. ¹⁵A similar plague will strike the horses and mules, the camels and donkeys, and all the animals in those camps.

¹⁶Then the survivors from all the nations that have attacked Jerusalem will go up year after year to worship the King, the Lord Almighty, and to celebrate the Festival of Tabernacles. ¹⁷If any of the peoples of the earth do not go up to Jerusalem to worship the King, the Lord Almighty, they will have no rain. ¹⁸If the Egyptian people do not go up and take part, they will have no rain. The Lord[a] will bring on them the plague he inflicts on the nations that do not go up to celebrate the Festival of Tabernacles. ¹⁹This will be the punishment of Egypt and the punishment of all the nations that do not go up to celebrate the Festival of Tabernacles.

²⁰On that day HOLY TO THE LORD will be inscribed on the bells of the horses, and the cooking pots in the Lord's house will be like the sacred bowls in front of the altar. ²¹Every pot in Jerusalem and Judah will be holy to the Lord Almighty, and all who come to sacrifice will take some of the pots and cook in them. And on that day there will no longer be a Canaanite[b] in the house of the Lord Almighty.

MALACHI

WHEN DID THIS HAPPEN?

About 430 B.C. in the southern kingdom of Judah

WHO IS IN THIS BOOK?

Malachi

VERSES YOU MIGHT RECOGNIZE

MALACHI 1:11

"My name will be great among the nations, from where the sun rises to where it sets."

MALACHI 3:7

"'Return to me, and I will return to you,' says the LORD Almighty."

WHAT'S IT ABOUT?

When Malachi delivered his message, the Jews had been back in Judah for more than 100 years. The people had rebuilt the temple and Jerusalem's walls, but they had become apathetic about following God's ways, and they doubted God's love for them.

Malachi pointed out the ways they had not lived up to their side of the deal in their covenant with God. They had not offered the correct sacrifices, they had withheld money that should have been given to the Lord, and they had married those who served foreign gods. The people's unfaithfulness served to highlight God's perfect faithfulness throughout Israel's history.

Malachi wrapped up his writing by reminding them of what God had done for them during the time of Moses and predicting that the great prophet Elijah would come again to help them in future days. God would keep his promise to send a Messiah. But the people had to wait 400 more years.

1 A prophecy: The word of the LORD to Israel through Malachi.[a]

Israel Doubts God's Love

2 "I have loved you," says the LORD.

"But you ask, 'How have you loved us?'

"Was not Esau Jacob's brother?" declares the LORD. "Yet I have loved Jacob, 3 but Esau I have hated, and I have turned his hill country into a wasteland and left his inheritance to the desert jackals."

4 Edom may say, "Though we have been crushed, we will rebuild the ruins."

But this is what the LORD Almighty says: "They may build, but I will demolish. They will be called the Wicked Land, a people always under the wrath of the LORD. 5 You will see it with your own eyes and say, 'Great is the LORD—even beyond the borders of Israel!'

Breaking Covenant Through Blemished Sacrifices

6 "A son honors his father, and a slave his master. If I am a father, where is the honor due me? If I am a master, where is the respect due me?" says the LORD Almighty.

"It is you priests who show contempt for my name.

"But you ask, 'How have we shown contempt for your name?'

7 "By offering defiled food on my altar.

"But you ask, 'How have we defiled you?'

"By saying that the LORD's table is contemptible. 8 When you offer blind animals for sacrifice, is that not wrong? When you sacrifice lame or diseased animals, is that not wrong? Try offering them to your governor! Would he be pleased with you? Would he accept you?" says the LORD Almighty.

9 "Now plead with God to be gracious to us. With such offerings from your hands, will he accept you?"—says the LORD Almighty.

10 "Oh, that one of you would shut the temple doors, so that you would not light useless fires on my altar! I am not pleased with you," says the LORD Almighty, "and I will accept no offering from your hands. 11 My name will be great among the nations, from where the sun rises to where it sets. In every place incense and pure offerings will be brought to me, because my name will be great among the nations," says the LORD Almighty.

12 "But you profane it by saying, 'The Lord's table is defiled,' and, 'Its food is contemptible.' 13 And you say, 'What a burden!' and you sniff at it contemptuously," says the LORD Almighty.

"When you bring injured, lame or diseased animals and offer them as sacrifices, should I accept them from your hands?" says the LORD. 14 "Cursed is the cheat who has an acceptable male in his flock and vows to give it, but then sacrifices a blemished animal to the Lord. For I am a great king," says the LORD Almighty, "and my name is to be feared among the nations.

Additional Warning to the Priests

2 "And now, you priests, this warning is for you. 2 If you do not listen, and if you do not resolve to honor my name," says the LORD Almighty, "I will send a curse on you, and I will curse your blessings. Yes, I have already cursed them, because you have not resolved to honor me.

3 "Because of you I will rebuke your descendants[b]; I will smear on your faces the dung from your festival sacrifices, and you will be carried off with it. 4 And you will know that I have sent you this warning so that my covenant with Levi may continue," says the LORD Almighty. 5 "My covenant was with him, a covenant of life and peace, and I gave them to him; this called for reverence and he revered me and stood in awe of my name. 6 True instruction was in his mouth and nothing false was found on his lips. He walked with me in peace and uprightness, and turned many from sin.

ARE YOU TIGHT?

READ: MALACHI 1:2

The Israelites felt so far from God that they started to doubt God's love. When he said, "I love you," they said, "Really? Why should we believe that?"

God always adored his chosen people. He didn't pick Israel because they were the best among the nations. He simply made a choice to love them (Deuteronomy 7:7). He saw their plight as slaves and plucked them from death. He would never quit loving them. That didn't mean God wouldn't set consequences for sin, any more than good parents quit setting boundaries for their children. And it didn't mean Israel would never feel distant from him. But when they felt far away, it wasn't his fault. It was their doing.

The Lord reminds the people that they aren't giving him their all. They bring imperfect animals for sacrifices, like handing a best friend a broken gift (Malachi 1:6-14). Priests fail to teach truth (2:1-9). Husbands and wives break God's commands against divorce (vv. 10-16). Everyone acts unjustly (2:17–3:5) and they don't bring the offerings due him (3:6-12).

When you don't give the Lord your best, it's no surprise he seems distant. You can't live far from God and expect to feel like he's your tight friend. Pull close to him, and he pulls close to you (James 4:8).

BUILDING

FAITH

WISDOM

STRENGTH

MALACHI

Then those who feared the LORD talked with each other, and the LORD listened and heard. A scroll of remembrance was written in his presence concerning those who feared the LORD and honored his name.
MALACHI 3:16

HIS NAME MEANS: "my messenger"
READ HIS STORY: *Malachi 1–4*

Since the world "Malachi" means "my messenger," a common term for prophets and priests, some people believe it's possible Malachi was written by an anonymous person. Chances are, though, that Malachi is the author's actual name. Scholars agree that the author of this book lived during the same time as Ezra, Nehemiah and Zerubbabel, about one hundred years after the first Jews returned from exile in Babylon to Jerusalem.

Malachi was the last of the biblical prophets before several centuries of silence in Israel's history. God didn't speak again through a prophet until John the Baptist, who was born just before Jesus.

Even though we don't know much about the man who wrote this book, we do know the message he gave. Malachi's message declared how unfaithful the nation of Israel had been to God. In the midst of the nation's unfaithfulness, however, there were those who stayed true to God. Malachi encouraged these faithful few. He told them how each time they mentioned God and talked about him with each other, it was written down in a special memory book called a "scroll of remembrance" (Malachi 3:16).

Do you love to talk with your friends and people at church about the good things God does? Each time you do, he hears what you say and remembers.

⁷"For the lips of a priest ought to preserve knowledge, because he is the messenger of the Lord Almighty and people seek instruction from his mouth. ⁸But you have turned from the way and by your teaching have caused many to stumble; you have violated the covenant with Levi," says the Lord Almighty. ⁹"So I have caused you to be despised and humiliated before all the people, because you have not followed my ways but have shown partiality in matters of the law."

Breaking Covenant Through Divorce

¹⁰Do we not all have one Father[a]? Did not one God create us? Why do we profane the covenant of our ancestors by being unfaithful to one another?

¹¹Judah has been unfaithful. A detestable thing has been committed in Israel and in Jerusalem: Judah has desecrated the sanctuary the Lord loves by marrying women who worship a foreign god. ¹²As for the man who does this, whoever he may be, may the Lord remove him from the tents of Jacob[b] — even though he brings an offering to the Lord Almighty.

¹³Another thing you do: You flood the Lord's altar with tears. You weep and wail because he no longer looks with favor on your offerings or accepts them with pleasure from your hands. ¹⁴You ask, "Why?" It is because the Lord is the witness between you and the wife of your youth. You have been unfaithful to her, though she is your partner, the wife of your marriage covenant.

¹⁵Has not the one God made you? You belong to him in body and spirit. And what does the one God seek? Godly offspring.[c] So be on your guard, and do not be unfaithful to the wife of your youth.

¹⁶"The man who hates and divorces his wife," says the Lord, the God of Israel, "does violence to the one he should protect,"[d] says the Lord Almighty.

So be on your guard, and do not be unfaithful.

Breaking Covenant Through Injustice

¹⁷You have wearied the Lord with your words.

"How have we wearied him?" you ask.

By saying, "All who do evil are good in the eyes of the Lord, and he is pleased with them" or "Where is the God of justice?"

3 "I will send my messenger, who will prepare the way before me. Then suddenly the Lord you are seeking will come to his temple; the messenger of the covenant, whom you desire, will come," says the Lord Almighty.

²But who can endure the day of his coming? Who can stand when he appears? For he will be like a refiner's fire or a launderer's soap. ³He will sit as a refiner and purifier of silver; he will purify the Levites and refine them like gold and silver. Then the Lord will have men who will bring offerings in righteousness, ⁴and the offerings of Judah and Jerusalem will be acceptable to the Lord, as in days gone by, as in former years.

⁵"So I will come to put you on trial. I will be quick to testify against sorcerers, adulterers and perjurers, against those who defraud laborers of their wages, who oppress the widows and the fatherless, and deprive the foreigners among you of justice, but do not fear me," says the Lord Almighty.

Breaking Covenant by Withholding Tithes

⁶"I the Lord do not change. So you, the descendants of Jacob, are not destroyed. ⁷Ever since the time of your ancestors you have turned away from my decrees and have not kept them. Return to me, and I will return to you," says the Lord Almighty.

"But you ask, 'How are we to return?'

⁸"Will a mere mortal rob God? Yet you rob me.

"But you ask, 'How are we robbing you?'

"In tithes and offerings. ⁹You are under a curse — your whole nation — because you are robbing me. ¹⁰Bring the whole tithe into the storehouse, that there may be food in my house. Test me in this," says the Lord Almighty, "and see if I will not throw open the floodgates of heaven and pour out so much blessing that there will not be room enough to store it. ¹¹I will prevent pests from devouring your crops, and the vines in your fields

---

a 10 Or *father*   *b 12* Or *¹²May the Lord remove from the tents of Jacob anyone who gives testimony in behalf of the man who does this*   *c 15* The meaning of the Hebrew for the first part of this verse is uncertain.   *d 16* Or *"I hate divorce," says the Lord, the God of Israel, "because the man who divorces his wife covers his garment with violence,"*

PROPHECY 101

READ: MALACHI 3:6-12

P rophecy can seem both exciting and cryptic when we try to apply it to our lives. But this genre often gets abused as a guide for what will happen in our near future, quoted with the daily news. Our credibility as Christians has eroded because of the mishandling of this single genre of Scripture. More than 90 percent of biblical prophecy outlines Israel's immediate future—events that have already occurred. Prophecy is generally less about our future—ancient Hebrews were not writing specifically about twenty-first-century Americans—than it is about seeing how God fulfills his promises to his people in history. Since most of prophecy is about Israel's immediate future, we can keep these four characteristics in mind as we try to better understand God's Word.

BUILDING FAITH WISDOM STRENGTH

1. God used prophets to warn his people about their unfaithfulness. Prophets were ambassadors from a heavenly court, speaking not on their own initiative, but as God instructed them. They endured hard lives.
2. Prophecy will not make sense if you do not understand the covenant that the prophets reference. A little Bible background reading teaches us that Israel willingly entered into a covenant that required specific actions from both Israel and God.
3. Outside reading is enormously helpful. Bible dictionaries or encyclopedias provide the historical setting of each book.
4. Prophets often spoke as poets to ensure their messages would ring convincingly and memorably in their oral culture.

WHO'S FOLLOWING?

READ: MALACHI 3:17-18

If you walk into most churches, most people think they're following Jesus when actually they've invited Jesus to follow them. Believe me, I used to be one of them. I wanted to go down my own path and have Jesus tag along. I wanted Jesus to provide me with what I wanted, and to follow through with my will.

Honestly, I didn't play God very well. Not to mention how tiring it became. I quit trying to "find myself" and decided to seek the Lord first. And I couldn't get enough of his Word! I got up early to pray. I actually fasted for the first time in my life. I had never truly put God first, but this time I did.

So I took the first step toward God's plan for me. I walked into the admissions office at the University of Chicago to transfer to a Bible college to pursue ministry full time. It's safe to say that the guidance counselor thought I was out of my mind. Most of my friends and family thought I was making a mistake too. I was giving up a full-ride scholarship to a top-ranked university. Sometimes it didn't even make sense to me. But I knew what God was telling me to do, and this was my now-or-never moment.

BUILDING FAITH WISDOM STRENGTH

That day I finally stopped asking Jesus to follow me, and I started following him.

Let me ask the question: Who's following who?

Are you following Jesus?

Or have you made it your game and asked Jesus to follow you?

will not drop their fruit before it is ripe," says the LORD Almighty. ¹²"Then all the nations will call you blessed, for yours will be a delightful land," says the LORD Almighty.

Israel Speaks Arrogantly Against God

¹³"You have spoken arrogantly against me," says the LORD.

"Yet you ask, 'What have we said against you?'

¹⁴"You have said, 'It is futile to serve God. What do we gain by carrying out his requirements and going about like mourners before the LORD Almighty? ¹⁵But now we call the arrogant blessed. Certainly evildoers prosper, and even when they put God to the test, they get away with it.'"

The Faithful Remnant

¹⁶Then those who feared the LORD talked with each other, and the LORD listened and heard. A scroll of remembrance was written in his presence concerning those who feared the LORD and honored his name.

¹⁷"On the day when I act," says the LORD Almighty, "they will be my treasured possession. I will spare them, just as a father has compassion and spares his son who serves him. ¹⁸And you will again see the distinction between the righteous and the wicked, between those who serve God and those who do not.

Judgment and Covenant Renewal

4 *ᵃ* "Surely the day is coming; it will burn like a furnace. All the arrogant and every evildoer will be stubble, and the day that is coming will set them on fire," says the LORD Almighty. "Not a root or a branch will be left to them. ²But for you who revere my name, the sun of righteousness will rise with healing in its rays. And you will go out and frolic like well-fed calves. ³Then you will trample on the wicked; they will be ashes under the soles of your feet on the day when I act," says the LORD Almighty.

⁴"Remember the law of my servant Moses, the decrees and laws I gave him at Horeb for all Israel.

⁵"See, I will send the prophet Elijah to you before that great and dreadful day of the LORD comes. ⁶He will turn the hearts of the parents to their children, and the hearts of the children to their parents; or else I will come and strike the land with total destruction."

ᵃ In Hebrew texts 4:1-6 is numbered 3:19-24.

THE NEW TESTAMENT

MATTHEW

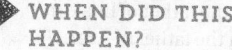

WHEN DID THIS HAPPEN?

A.D. 1 to 36 in Palestine

WHO IS IN THIS BOOK?

Mary
Joseph
John the Baptist
Judas
Jesus
Herod
Magi
the disciples
Matthew
Caiaphas
Barabbas

VERSES YOU MIGHT RECOGNIZE

MATTHEW 5:6

"Blessed are those who hunger and thirst for righteousness, for they will be filled."

MATTHEW 21:22

"If you believe, you will receive whatever you ask for in prayer."

WHAT'S IT ABOUT?

The book of Matthew picks up where Malachi left off ... kind of. This book is the first of three "synoptic gospels." Synoptic means "seen together," and gospel means "good news." The gospels of Matthew, Mark and Luke tell the good news about Jesus and are similar in the events they include and even some of the words they use. Still, each writer had a specific purpose.

Matthew was writing to the Jews, and his main goal was to reveal that Jesus was the long-awaited Messiah that the prophets had foretold. That's why the first thing we read in Matthew is a genealogy. It may seem like a boring way to introduce the Savior, but it was important to the Jews to see that Jesus was in the bloodline of their ancestors David and Abraham. Matthew also quoted prophecies from Isaiah, Jeremiah and Hosea, and he said that Jesus fulfilled them.

Matthew told the story of Jesus, beginning with his birth to a virgin named Mary and her husband, Joseph. We also meet John the Baptist, a new prophet who prepares people for Christ. Jesus chose disciples and began a three-year-long ministry of teaching and healing. The book of Matthew contains the Sermon on the Mount, the beatitudes ("blessed are") and many parables. Ultimately, Jesus died, was buried and rose again, fulfilling his destiny as the Messiah who saves people from their sins.

MATTHEW

The Genealogy of Jesus the Messiah

1 This is the genealogy[a] of Jesus the Messiah[b] the son of David, the son of Abraham:

2 Abraham was the father of Isaac,
Isaac the father of Jacob,
Jacob the father of Judah and his brothers,
3 Judah the father of Perez and Zerah, whose mother was Tamar,
Perez the father of Hezron,
Hezron the father of Ram,
4 Ram the father of Amminadab,
Amminadab the father of Nahshon,
Nahshon the father of Salmon,
5 Salmon the father of Boaz, whose mother was Rahab,
Boaz the father of Obed, whose mother was Ruth,
Obed the father of Jesse,
6 and Jesse the father of King David.

David was the father of Solomon, whose mother had been Uriah's wife,
7 Solomon the father of Rehoboam,
Rehoboam the father of Abijah,
Abijah the father of Asa,
8 Asa the father of Jehoshaphat,
Jehoshaphat the father of Jehoram,
Jehoram the father of Uzziah,
9 Uzziah the father of Jotham,
Jotham the father of Ahaz,
Ahaz the father of Hezekiah,
10 Hezekiah the father of Manasseh,
Manasseh the father of Amon,
Amon the father of Josiah,
11 and Josiah the father of Jeconiah[c] and his brothers at the time of the exile to Babylon.

12 After the exile to Babylon:
Jeconiah was the father of Shealtiel,
Shealtiel the father of Zerubbabel,
13 Zerubbabel the father of Abihud,
Abihud the father of Eliakim,
Eliakim the father of Azor,
14 Azor the father of Zadok,
Zadok the father of Akim,
Akim the father of Elihud,
15 Elihud the father of Eleazar,
Eleazar the father of Matthan,
Matthan the father of Jacob,
16 and Jacob the father of Joseph, the husband of Mary, and Mary was the mother of Jesus who is called the Messiah.

17 Thus there were fourteen generations in all from Abraham to David, fourteen from David to the exile to Babylon, and fourteen from the exile to the Messiah.

Joseph Accepts Jesus as His Son

18 This is how the birth of Jesus the Messiah came about[d]: His mother Mary was pledged to be married to Joseph, but before they came together, she was found to be pregnant through the Holy Spirit. 19 Because Joseph her husband was faithful to the law, and yet[e] did not want to expose her to public disgrace, he had in mind to divorce her quietly.

20 But after he had considered this, an angel of the Lord appeared to him in a dream and said, "Joseph son of David, do not be afraid to take Mary home as your wife, because what is conceived in her is from the Holy Spirit. 21 She will give birth to a son, and you are to give him the name Jesus,[f] because he will save his people from their sins."

22 All this took place to fulfill what the Lord had said through the prophet: 23 "The virgin will conceive and give birth to a son, and they will call him Immanuel"[g] (which means "God with us").

24 When Joseph woke up, he did what the

HEROD THE GREAT

He gave orders to kill all the boys in Bethlehem and its vicinity who were two years old and under. MATTHEW 2:16

HIS NAME MEANS: "son of the hero"
READ HIS STORY: *Matthew 2*

Herod the Great was a major player during this time in history. In 63 B.C., Julius Caesar expanded his empire into Palestine. Sixteen years later, Caesar appointed Antipater over the Roman government of this area. Antipater made his oldest son governor of Jerusalem and his second son, Herod, governor of Galilee.

Once Herod tasted power, he didn't want to lose it. In 40 B.C., the Parthians invaded Palestine. Herod retreated to Rome, where his friend Mark Antony resided. He used his political connections to be appointed king of Judea by the Roman senate. He was given an army, returned to Palestine, and reclaimed the land for Rome. Herod was just thirty-six years old when he began his rule.

Herod earned his title of "the Great" through an aggressive building campaign. He constructed a glorious port city, rebuilt the temple and fortified the land.

As great as his buildings may have been, his insecurities were even greater. If he felt a bid for his power, Herod killed the challengers—including his wife, three of his sons and other family members. So guess Herod's thoughts when the wise men showed up and asked, "Where is the one who has been born king of the Jews?" (Matthew 2:2)? That was a title Herod had fought and killed for. Nobody was going to take his power. He killed every baby boy in and around Bethlehem in an attempt to stop the coming king. But God's plan can't be thwarted. Jesus escaped with his parents to Egypt and returned to Palestine in 4 B.C., when Herod the Great died.

angel of the Lord had commanded him and took Mary home as his wife. [25]But he did not consummate their marriage until she gave birth to a son. And he gave him the name Jesus.

The Magi Visit the Messiah

2 After Jesus was born in Bethlehem in Judea, during the time of King Herod, Magi[a] from the east came to Jerusalem [2]and asked, "Where is the one who has been born king of the Jews? We saw his star when it rose and have come to worship him."

[3]When King Herod heard this he was disturbed, and all Jerusalem with him. [4]When he had called together all the people's chief priests and teachers of the law, he asked them where the Messiah was to be born. [5]"In Bethlehem in Judea," they replied, "for this is what the prophet has written:

[6] " 'But you, Bethlehem, in the land of
      Judah,
   are by no means least among the rulers
      of Judah;
for out of you will come a ruler
   who will shepherd my people Israel.'[b]"

[7]Then Herod called the Magi secretly and found out from them the exact time the star had appeared. [8]He sent them to Bethlehem and said, "Go and search carefully for the child. As soon as you find him, report to me, so that I too may go and worship him." [9]After they had heard the king, they went on their way, and the star they had seen when it rose went ahead of them until it stopped over the place where the child was. [10]When they saw the star, they were overjoyed. [11]On coming to the house, they saw the child with his mother Mary, and they bowed down and worshiped him. Then they opened their treasures and presented him with gifts of gold, frankincense and myrrh. [12]And having been warned in a dream not to go back to Herod, they returned to their country by another route.

The Escape to Egypt

[13]When they had gone, an angel of the Lord appeared to Joseph in a dream. "Get up," he said, "take the child and his mother and escape to Egypt. Stay there until I tell you, for Herod is going to search for the child to kill him."

[14]So he got up, took the child and his mother during the night and left for Egypt, [15]where he stayed until the death of Herod. And so was fulfilled what the Lord had said through the prophet: "Out of Egypt I called my son."[c]

[16]When Herod realized that he had been outwitted by the Magi, he was furious, and he gave orders to kill all the boys in Bethlehem and its vicinity who were two years old and under, in accordance with the time he had learned from the Magi. [17]Then what was said through the prophet Jeremiah was fulfilled:

[18]"A voice is heard in Ramah,
      weeping and great mourning,
   Rachel weeping for her children
      and refusing to be comforted,
      because they are no more."[d]

The Return to Nazareth

[19]After Herod died, an angel of the Lord appeared in a dream to Joseph in Egypt [20]and said, "Get up, take the child and his mother and go to the land of Israel, for those who were trying to take the child's life are dead."

[21]So he got up, took the child and his mother and went to the land of Israel. [22]But when he heard that Archelaus was reigning in Judea in place of his father Herod, he was afraid to go there. Having been warned in a dream, he withdrew to the district of Galilee, [23]and he went and lived in a town called Nazareth. So was fulfilled what was said through the prophets, that he would be called a Nazarene.

John the Baptist Prepares the Way

3 In those days John the Baptist came, preaching in the wilderness of Judea [2]and saying, "Repent, for the kingdom of heaven has come near." [3]This is he who was spoken of through the prophet Isaiah:

"A voice of one calling in the wilderness,
   'Prepare the way for the Lord,
      make straight paths for him.' "[e]

[4]John's clothes were made of camel's hair, and he had a leather belt around his waist.

---

[a] 1 Traditionally *wise men*   [b] 6 Micah 5:2,4   [c] 15 Hosea 11:1   [d] 18 Jer. 31:15   [e] 3 Isaiah 40:3

BE PREPARED

READ: MATTHEW 3:1-2

Even before Jesus began to teach and do miracles, people knew someone amazing was on the way. That's because John the Baptist had come on the scene and prepared people to meet the Lord. John's arrival was no surprise. Isaiah, the Old Testament prophet, once predicted a voice in the wilderness would clear a path for God (Isaiah 40:3). And an angel announced that Elizabeth, a relative of Mary the mother of Jesus, would give birth to the Lord's messenger.

John wore rough clothes and ate a plain diet. His grueling life in the desert reminded everyone of God's ancient messengers. When he commanded everyone to repent—to stop sinning and turn back to God—his challenging words drew crowds from every direction. John confronted not only the masses but Pharisees and Sadducees, religious rule-keepers who considered themselves too good to need cleansing from sin. He baptized everyone who accepted his message, dipping them in the Jordan River as a way of demonstrating remorse for doing wrong. His every word and action pointed to one fact: someone much greater was coming.

BUILDING
FAITH
WISDOM
STRENGTH

You would be startled if John the Baptist showed up shouting in your street. But his message hits home no matter where you live. You want to be prepared for Jesus. You need to recognize the awfulness of sin and be ready to meet your Savior.

His food was locusts and wild honey. [5]People went out to him from Jerusalem and all Judea and the whole region of the Jordan. [6]Confessing their sins, they were baptized by him in the Jordan River.

[7]But when he saw many of the Pharisees and Sadducees coming to where he was baptizing, he said to them: "You brood of vipers! Who warned you to flee from the coming wrath? [8]Produce fruit in keeping with repentance. [9]And do not think you can say to yourselves, 'We have Abraham as our father.' I tell you that out of these stones God can raise up children for Abraham. [10]The ax is already at the root of the trees, and every tree that does not produce good fruit will be cut down and thrown into the fire.

[11]"I baptize you with[a] water for repentance. But after me comes one who is more powerful than I, whose sandals I am not worthy to carry. He will baptize you with[a] the Holy Spirit and fire. [12]His winnowing fork is in his hand, and he will clear his threshing floor, gathering his wheat into the barn and burning up the chaff with unquenchable fire."

The Baptism of Jesus

[13]Then Jesus came from Galilee to the Jordan to be baptized by John. [14]But John tried to deter him, saying, "I need to be baptized by you, and do you come to me?"

[15]Jesus replied, "Let it be so now; it is proper for us to do this to fulfill all righteousness." Then John consented.

[16]As soon as Jesus was baptized, he went up out of the water. At that moment heaven was opened, and he saw the Spirit of God descending like a dove and alighting on him. [17]And a voice from heaven said, "This is my Son, whom I love; with him I am well pleased."

Jesus Is Tested in the Wilderness

4 Then Jesus was led by the Spirit into the wilderness to be tempted[b] by the devil. [2]After fasting forty days and forty nights, he was hungry. [3]The tempter came to him and said, "If you are the Son of God, tell these stones to become bread."

[4]Jesus answered, "It is written: 'Man shall not live on bread alone, but on every word that comes from the mouth of God.'[c]"

[5]Then the devil took him to the holy city and had him stand on the highest point of the temple. [6]"If you are the Son of God," he said, "throw yourself down. For it is written:

" 'He will command his angels
    concerning you,
  and they will lift you up in their hands,
    so that you will not strike your foot
      against a stone.'[d]"

[7]Jesus answered him, "It is also written: 'Do not put the Lord your God to the test.'[e]"

[8]Again, the devil took him to a very high mountain and showed him all the kingdoms of the world and their splendor. [9]"All this I will give you," he said, "if you will bow down and worship me."

[10]Jesus said to him, "Away from me, Satan! For it is written: 'Worship the Lord your God, and serve him only.'[f]"

[11]Then the devil left him, and angels came and attended him.

Jesus Begins to Preach

[12]When Jesus heard that John had been put in prison, he withdrew to Galilee. [13]Leaving Nazareth, he went and lived in Capernaum, which was by the lake in the area of Zebulun and Naphtali — [14]to fulfill what was said through the prophet Isaiah:

[15]"Land of Zebulun and land of Naphtali,
    the Way of the Sea, beyond the Jordan,
    Galilee of the Gentiles —
[16]the people living in darkness
    have seen a great light;
  on those living in the land of the shadow
      of death
    a light has dawned."[g]

[17]From that time on Jesus began to preach, "Repent, for the kingdom of heaven has come near."

Jesus Calls His First Disciples

[18]As Jesus was walking beside the Sea of Galilee, he saw two brothers, Simon called Peter and his brother Andrew. They were casting a net into the lake, for they were fishermen. [19]"Come, follow me," Jesus said, "and

---

[a] 11 Or in   [b] 1 The Greek for tempted can also mean tested.   [c] 4 Deut. 8:3   [d] 6 Psalm 91:11,12
[e] 7 Deut. 6:16   [f] 10 Deut. 6:13   [g] 16 Isaiah 9:1,2

WHAT ABOUT NOW?

READ: MATTHEW 4:18-20

There is a tendency to treat our relationship with Jesus like the diet we keep meaning to start. I'm going to start eating right, as soon as I finish off this chicken chimichanga. Tomorrow for sure.

On the invitation Jesus gives to follow him there is an RSVP date and it reads: TODAY. The word *tomorrow* is not in the Holy Spirit's vocabulary. When Jesus calls us to follow, he means right now.

The question is, how long have you been saying tomorrow? Technically, if you said it yesterday, then today is tomorrow and that means the time is now.

Jesus hasn't just been whispering "Follow me" to some of you. He's been shouting, hoping to get your attention before you lose any more in the Land of Tomorrow.

The most dangerous part of following Jesus tomorrow isn't what you will lose between now and then. That's not the worst thing that can happen. The worst thing that can happen is that tomorrow might never come. The truth is the longer you put him off, the more likely it is that following him will never happen.

Don't tell yourself, *Tomorrow I'm going to surrender my secret sin.* Don't tell yourself, *Tomorrow I'm going to start being generous to those in need.* Don't tell yourself, *Tomorrow I'm going to check into a mission trip or sign up for a Bible study or volunteer at . . .*

The time is now. The day is today.

BUILDING

FAITH

WISDOM

STRENGTH

I will send you out to fish for people." ²⁰At once they left their nets and followed him.
²¹Going on from there, he saw two other brothers, James son of Zebedee and his brother John. They were in a boat with their father Zebedee, preparing their nets. Jesus called them, ²²and immediately they left the boat and their father and followed him.

Jesus Heals the Sick

²³Jesus went throughout Galilee, teaching in their synagogues, proclaiming the good news of the kingdom, and healing every disease and sickness among the people. ²⁴News about him spread all over Syria, and people brought to him all who were ill with various diseases, those suffering severe pain, the demon-possessed, those having seizures, and the paralyzed; and he healed them. ²⁵Large crowds from Galilee, the Decapolis,^a Jerusalem, Judea and the region across the Jordan followed him.

Introduction to the Sermon on the Mount

5 Now when Jesus saw the crowds, he went up on a mountainside and sat down. His disciples came to him, ²and he began to teach them.

The Beatitudes

He said:

³ "Blessed are the poor in spirit,
　　for theirs is the kingdom of heaven.
⁴ Blessed are those who mourn,
　　for they will be comforted.
⁵ Blessed are the meek,
　　for they will inherit the earth.
⁶ Blessed are those who hunger and thirst
　　　for righteousness,
　　for they will be filled.
⁷ Blessed are the merciful,
　　for they will be shown mercy.
⁸ Blessed are the pure in heart,
　　for they will see God.
⁹ Blessed are the peacemakers,
　　for they will be called children of God.
¹⁰ Blessed are those who are persecuted
　　　because of righteousness,
　　for theirs is the kingdom of heaven.

¹¹ "Blessed are you when people insult you, persecute you and falsely say all kinds of evil against you because of me. ¹²Rejoice and be glad, because great is your reward in heaven, for in the same way they persecuted the prophets who were before you.

Salt and Light

¹³ "You are the salt of the earth. But if the salt loses its saltiness, how can it be made salty again? It is no longer good for anything, except to be thrown out and trampled underfoot.

¹⁴ "You are the light of the world. A town built on a hill cannot be hidden. ¹⁵Neither do people light a lamp and put it under a bowl. Instead they put it on its stand, and it gives light to everyone in the house. ¹⁶In the same way, let your light shine before others, that they may see your good deeds and glorify your Father in heaven.

The Fulfillment of the Law

¹⁷ "Do not think that I have come to abolish the Law or the Prophets; I have not come to abolish them but to fulfill them. ¹⁸For truly I tell you, until heaven and earth disappear, not the smallest letter, not the least stroke of a pen, will by any means disappear from the Law until everything is accomplished. ¹⁹Therefore anyone who sets aside one of the least of these commands and teaches others accordingly will be called least in the kingdom of heaven, but whoever practices and teaches these commands will be called great in the kingdom of heaven. ²⁰For I tell you that unless your righteousness surpasses that of the Pharisees and the teachers of the law, you will certainly not enter the kingdom of heaven.

Murder

²¹ "You have heard that it was said to the people long ago, 'You shall not murder,^b and anyone who murders will be subject to judgment.' ²²But I tell you that anyone who is angry with a brother or sister^{c,d} will be subject to judgment. Again, anyone who says to a brother or sister, 'Raca,'^e is answerable to the court. And anyone who says, 'You fool!' will be in danger of the fire of hell.

---

^a 25 That is, the Ten Cities　　^b 21 Exodus 20:13　　^c 22 The Greek word for *brother or sister* (*adelphos*) refers here to a fellow disciple, whether man or woman; also in verse 23.　　^d 22 Some manuscripts *brother or sister without cause*　　^e 22 An Aramaic term of contempt

WHAT'S MOTIVATING YOU?

READ: MATTHEW 5:3-12

I was in Mexico, on a mission trip with students. We were there for a lot of reasons—to try to help the people in that poverty-stricken community, to lead small children into a better understanding of who God is, to pray with and for people, and to learn what it's like to live in another culture. Throughout that week, I felt God leading me to read the Sermon on the Mount.

As I read that great sermon, I began to feel like Jesus' words about the hypocrisy of the religious leaders of his day were directed right to me. I'd not been the kind of man I'd always thought I was. My actions were often just a carefully constructed veneer that was modeled on what I thought a Christian was supposed to think and do. It was a lot of well-intentioned pretending.

Each day in Mexico, when I got up early and read my Bible (something I hadn't done regularly in years, despite all my talk about how much I love the Bible), I felt an inescapable call from Christ, a challenge to live differently. Jesus' words rang out clearly in my heart, a reminder that what I'd been doing with my hands and my feet, the physical me, didn't matter as much as the attitude that motivated the movement of my hands and feet. His words in those passages are focused on our hearts, our intent, and our honesty.

BUILDING FAITH WISDOM STRENGTH

[23] "Therefore, if you are offering your gift at the altar and there remember that your brother or sister has something against you, [24] leave your gift there in front of the altar. First go and be reconciled to them; then come and offer your gift.

[25] "Settle matters quickly with your adversary who is taking you to court. Do it while you are still together on the way, or your adversary may hand you over to the judge, and the judge may hand you over to the officer, and you may be thrown into prison. [26] Truly I tell you, you will not get out until you have paid the last penny.

Adultery

[27] "You have heard that it was said, 'You shall not commit adultery.'[a] [28] But I tell you that anyone who looks at a woman lustfully has already committed adultery with her in his heart. [29] If your right eye causes you to stumble, gouge it out and throw it away. It is better for you to lose one part of your body than for your whole body to be thrown into hell. [30] And if your right hand causes you to stumble, cut it off and throw it away. It is better for you to lose one part of your body than for your whole body to go into hell.

Divorce

[31] "It has been said, 'Anyone who divorces his wife must give her a certificate of divorce.'[b] [32] But I tell you that anyone who divorces his wife, except for sexual immorality, makes her the victim of adultery, and anyone who marries a divorced woman commits adultery.

Oaths

[33] "Again, you have heard that it was said to the people long ago, 'Do not break your oath, but fulfill to the Lord the vows you have made.' [34] But I tell you, do not swear an oath at all: either by heaven, for it is God's throne; [35] or by the earth, for it is his footstool; or by Jerusalem, for it is the city of the Great King. [36] And do not swear by your head, for you cannot make even one hair white or black. [37] All you need to say is simply 'Yes' or 'No'; anything beyond this comes from the evil one.[c]

Eye for Eye

[38] "You have heard that it was said, 'Eye for eye, and tooth for tooth.'[d] [39] But I tell you, do not resist an evil person. If anyone slaps you on the right cheek, turn to them the other cheek also. [40] And if anyone wants to sue you and take your shirt, hand over your coat as well. [41] If anyone forces you to go one mile, go with them two miles. [42] Give to the one who asks you, and do not turn away from the one who wants to borrow from you.

Love for Enemies

[43] "You have heard that it was said, 'Love your neighbor[e] and hate your enemy.' [44] But I tell you, love your enemies and pray for those who persecute you, [45] that you may be children of your Father in heaven. He causes his sun to rise on the evil and the good, and sends rain on the righteous and the unrighteous. [46] If you love those who love you, what reward will you get? Are not even the tax collectors doing that? [47] And if you greet only your own people, what are you doing more than others? Do not even pagans do that? [48] Be perfect, therefore, as your heavenly Father is perfect.

Giving to the Needy

6 "Be careful not to practice your righteousness in front of others to be seen by them. If you do, you will have no reward from your Father in heaven.

[2] "So when you give to the needy, do not announce it with trumpets, as the hypocrites do in the synagogues and on the streets, to be honored by others. Truly I tell you, they have received their reward in full. [3] But when you give to the needy, do not let your left hand know what your right hand is doing, [4] so that your giving may be in secret. Then your Father, who sees what is done in secret, will reward you.

Prayer

[5] "And when you pray, do not be like the hypocrites, for they love to pray standing in the synagogues and on the street corners to be seen by others. Truly I tell you, they have received their reward in full. [6] But when you pray, go into your room, close the door and

---

[a] 27 Exodus 20:14   [b] 31 Deut. 24:1   [c] 37 Or *from evil*   [d] 38 Exodus 21:24; Lev. 24:20; Deut. 19:21
[e] 43 Lev. 19:18

pray to your Father, who is unseen. Then your Father, who sees what is done in secret, will reward you. [7] And when you pray, do not keep on babbling like pagans, for they think they will be heard because of their many words. [8] Do not be like them, for your Father knows what you need before you ask him.

[9] "This, then, is how you should pray:

> "'Our Father in heaven,
> hallowed be your name,
> [10] your kingdom come,
> your will be done,
> on earth as it is in heaven.
> [11] Give us today our daily bread.
> [12] And forgive us our debts,
> as we also have forgiven our debtors.
> [13] And lead us not into temptation,[a]
> but deliver us from the evil one.[b]'

[14] For if you forgive other people when they sin against you, your heavenly Father will also forgive you. [15] But if you do not forgive others their sins, your Father will not forgive your sins.

Fasting

[16] "When you fast, do not look somber as the hypocrites do, for they disfigure their faces to show others they are fasting. Truly I tell you, they have received their reward in full. [17] But when you fast, put oil on your head and wash your face, [18] so that it will not be obvious to others that you are fasting, but only to your Father, who is unseen; and your Father, who sees what is done in secret, will reward you.

Treasures in Heaven

[19] "Do not store up for yourselves treasures on earth, where moths and vermin destroy, and where thieves break in and steal. [20] But store up for yourselves treasures in heaven, where moths and vermin do not destroy, and where thieves do not break in and steal. [21] For where your treasure is, there your heart will be also.

[22] "The eye is the lamp of the body. If your eyes are healthy,[c] your whole body will be full of light. [23] But if your eyes are unhealthy,[d] your whole body will be full of darkness. If then the light within you is darkness, how great is that darkness!

[24] "No one can serve two masters. Either you will hate the one and love the other, or you will be devoted to the one and despise the other. You cannot serve both God and money.

Do Not Worry

[25] "Therefore I tell you, do not worry about your life, what you will eat or drink; or about your body, what you will wear. Is not life more than food, and the body more than clothes? [26] Look at the birds of the air; they do not sow or reap or store away in barns, and yet your heavenly Father feeds them. Are you not much more valuable than they? [27] Can any one of you by worrying add a single hour to your life[e]? [28] "And why do you worry about clothes? See how the flowers of the field grow. They do not labor or spin. [29] Yet I tell you that not even Solomon in all his splendor was dressed like one of these. [30] If that is how God clothes the grass of the field, which is here today and tomorrow is thrown into the fire, will he not much more clothe you — you of little faith? [31] So do not worry, saying, 'What shall we eat?' or 'What shall we drink?' or 'What shall we wear?' [32] For the pagans run after all these things, and your heavenly Father knows that you need them. [33] But seek first his kingdom and his righteousness, and all these things will be given to you as well. [34] Therefore do not worry about tomorrow, for tomorrow will worry about itself. Each day has enough trouble of its own.

Judging Others

7 "Do not judge, or you too will be judged. [2] For in the same way you judge others, you will be judged, and with the measure you use, it will be measured to you.

[3] "Why do you look at the speck of sawdust in your brother's eye and pay no attention to the plank in your own eye? [4] How can you say to your brother, 'Let me take the speck out of your eye,' when all the time there is a plank in your own eye? [5] You hypocrite, first take the plank out of your own eye, and then

---

[a] 13 The Greek for *temptation* can also mean *testing*.   [b] 13 Or *from evil*; some late manuscripts one, / for
yours is the kingdom and the power and the glory forever. Amen.   [c] 22 The Greek for *healthy* here implies
generous.   [d] 23 The Greek for *unhealthy* here implies *stingy*.   [e] 27 Or *single cubit to your height*

THE FIRST STEP TOWARD FORGIVENESS

READ: MATTHEW 6:12-14

Most people are not familiar with the biblical idea of forgiveness. Some think forgiveness means to forget or to give someone another chance. Others confuse forgiveness with pretending someone's offense doesn't hurt us anymore. But biblical forgiveness begins with acknowledging someone hurt us, deeply.

Forgiveness begins when we journey with Jesus back into the memory of the pain. As we name the pain, we often feel worse, even weaker, at first. We admit our pain to ourselves, and to God, but not necessarily to the offender. That's how David handled his pain. "They close up their callous hearts, and their mouths speak with arrogance. They have tracked me down, they now surround me with eyes alert, to throw me to the ground" (Psalm 17:10-11). This is not the speech of a man in denial. He spared no details of how he felt and what he wanted God to do on his behalf. He wasn't ready to forgive; but David begins the process by inviting God to see his pain.

Jesus showed us that forgiveness doesn't include forgetting or approving the evil. When Jesus hung on the cross, he didn't approve of the embarrassment or the pain he felt. Jesus did not forget who accused him, who tortured him, who nailed him to the cross. Jesus didn't die pretending the evil wasn't so bad.

Forgiveness means we refuse to believe the lie that we can remain embittered against someone without harming ourselves. Forgiveness means we invite Jesus' power to absorb evil, releasing the person from our punishment.

BUILDING

FAITH

WISDOM

STRENGTH

HE'S GOT IT COVERED

READ: MATTHEW 6:24-34

I often talk to young people who are scared to death that they won't make it into college or they'll flunk out once they get there. I have one answer for them: "Do you realize you're mortified over college, and yet God is watching you walk across the stage to accept your degree right now? Because he is. He's already there."

We're all guilty of living in anticipation of a fork in the road. There is no fork in your road. God didn't ask you to make any huge decisions. All he said was, "Lean on me, see like I see, and realize your past is gone and your future is mine. All I ask is that you get to know me and make me known."

God hasn't called us to something in a year. We're called for the here and now. We were not made to survive today for some potential future endeavor, something that maybe he'll do through us one day.

BUILDING

FAITH

WISDOM

STRENGTH

We're looking so forward to tomorrow that we're tripping over today. Then when we get to tomorrow, we start worrying about the next tomorrow. Everything counts, especially today.

God has placed you where you are totally on purpose. Don't spoil it by anticipating or dreading your future. God didn't call you to figure out what happens next. He's already there. He's at the end of your life looking back on it right now. He wants you to rest in that truth.

Taken from *Thrive Student Edition* by Mark Hall with Tim Luke, copyright © 2014 by Mark Hall, published by Zondervan.

you will see clearly to remove the speck from your brother's eye.

⁶"Do not give dogs what is sacred; do not throw your pearls to pigs. If you do, they may trample them under their feet, and turn and tear you to pieces.

Ask, Seek, Knock

⁷"Ask and it will be given to you; seek and you will find; knock and the door will be opened to you. ⁸For everyone who asks receives; the one who seeks finds; and to the one who knocks, the door will be opened.

⁹"Which of you, if your son asks for bread, will give him a stone? ¹⁰Or if he asks for a fish, will give him a snake? ¹¹If you, then, though you are evil, know how to give good gifts to your children, how much more will your Father in heaven give good gifts to those who ask him! ¹²So in everything, do to others what you would have them do to you, for this sums up the Law and the Prophets.

The Narrow and Wide Gates

¹³"Enter through the narrow gate. For wide is the gate and broad is the road that leads to destruction, and many enter through it. ¹⁴But small is the gate and narrow the road that leads to life, and only a few find it.

True and False Prophets

¹⁵"Watch out for false prophets. They come to you in sheep's clothing, but inwardly they are ferocious wolves. ¹⁶By their fruit you will recognize them. Do people pick grapes from thornbushes, or figs from thistles? ¹⁷Likewise, every good tree bears good fruit, but a bad tree bears bad fruit. ¹⁸A good tree cannot bear bad fruit, and a bad tree cannot bear good fruit. ¹⁹Every tree that does not bear good fruit is cut down and thrown into the fire. ²⁰Thus, by their fruit you will recognize them.

True and False Disciples

²¹"Not everyone who says to me, 'Lord, Lord,' will enter the kingdom of heaven, but only the one who does the will of my Father who is in heaven. ²²Many will say to me on that day, 'Lord, Lord, did we not prophesy in your name and in your name drive out de-

mons and in your name perform many miracles?' ²³Then I will tell them plainly, 'I never knew you. Away from me, you evildoers!'

The Wise and Foolish Builders

²⁴"Therefore everyone who hears these words of mine and puts them into practice is like a wise man who built his house on the rock. ²⁵The rain came down, the streams rose, and the winds blew and beat against that house; yet it did not fall, because it had its foundation on the rock. ²⁶But everyone who hears these words of mine and does not put them into practice is like a foolish man who built his house on sand. ²⁷The rain came down, the streams rose, and the winds blew and beat against that house, and it fell with a great crash."

²⁸When Jesus had finished saying these things, the crowds were amazed at his teaching, ²⁹because he taught as one who had authority, and not as their teachers of the law.

Jesus Heals a Man With Leprosy

8 When Jesus came down from the mountainside, large crowds followed him. ²A man with leprosy[a] came and knelt before him and said, "Lord, if you are willing, you can make me clean."

³Jesus reached out his hand and touched the man. "I am willing," he said. "Be clean!" Immediately he was cleansed of his leprosy. ⁴Then Jesus said to him, "See that you don't tell anyone. But go, show yourself to the priest and offer the gift Moses commanded, as a testimony to them."

The Faith of the Centurion

⁵When Jesus had entered Capernaum, a centurion came to him, asking for help. ⁶"Lord," he said, "my servant lies at home paralyzed, suffering terribly."

⁷Jesus said to him, "Shall I come and heal him?"

⁸The centurion replied, "Lord, I do not deserve to have you come under my roof. But just say the word, and my servant will be healed. ⁹For I myself am a man under authority, with soldiers under me. I tell this one, 'Go,' and he goes; and that one, 'Come,' and he comes. I say to my servant, 'Do this,' and he does it."

---

[a] 2 The Greek word traditionally translated *leprosy* was used for various diseases affecting the skin.

CHECK YOUR DIRECTIONS

READ: MATTHEW 7:13-14

Not long ago I was returning to Louisville from a quick trip to Cincinnati. The highway between Cincinnati and Louisville called I-71 is a straight shot and takes about an hour. I was heading home in plenty of time to have dinner with my family. The radio was turned up, it was a beautiful day, and I was enjoying the journey. After about an hour, I knew I was getting close to Louisville, but then I saw a sign that said, "Welcome to Lexington." What?

There is a place right outside Cincinnati where, if you're not real careful, you can easily miss where I-71 toward Louisville splits off from I-75 toward Lexington. It never occurred to me that I might be going the wrong way.

Many people take the wrong road; few find the narrow path. If that is true, then wouldn't it make sense for us to hit the brakes, pull over, and make sure that we are on the road that leads to life?

BUILDING

FAITH

WISDOM

STRENGTH

This teaching of Jesus is the conclusion of "The Sermon on the Mount." It's a sermon that has been all about raising the bar of the commitment for those who would follow him. It's a narrow road, but it's a road that leads to life.

I'm just wondering, is it possible that you have set cruise control, turned up the Christian radio, and are traveling down the road of destruction? Before you continue driving, slow down the car, look at some of the signs, and ask yourself what road you are on.

[10] When Jesus heard this, he was amazed and said to those following him, "Truly I tell you, I have not found anyone in Israel with such great faith. [11] I say to you that many will come from the east and the west, and will take their places at the feast with Abraham, Isaac and Jacob in the kingdom of heaven. [12] But the subjects of the kingdom will be thrown outside, into the darkness, where there will be weeping and gnashing of teeth."

[13] Then Jesus said to the centurion, "Go! Let it be done just as you believed it would." And his servant was healed at that moment.

Jesus Heals Many

[14] When Jesus came into Peter's house, he saw Peter's mother-in-law lying in bed with a fever. [15] He touched her hand and the fever left her, and she got up and began to wait on him.

[16] When evening came, many who were demon-possessed were brought to him, and he drove out the spirits with a word and healed all the sick. [17] This was to fulfill what was spoken through the prophet Isaiah:

> "He took up our infirmities
>   and bore our diseases."[a]

The Cost of Following Jesus

[18] When Jesus saw the crowd around him, he gave orders to cross to the other side of the lake. [19] Then a teacher of the law came to him and said, "Teacher, I will follow you wherever you go."

[20] Jesus replied, "Foxes have dens and birds have nests, but the Son of Man has no place to lay his head."

[21] Another disciple said to him, "Lord, first let me go and bury my father."

[22] But Jesus told him, "Follow me, and let the dead bury their own dead."

Jesus Calms the Storm

[23] Then he got into the boat and his disciples followed him. [24] Suddenly a furious storm came up on the lake, so that the waves swept over the boat. But Jesus was sleeping. [25] The disciples went and woke him, saying, "Lord, save us! We're going to drown!"

[26] He replied, "You of little faith, why are you so afraid?" Then he got up and rebuked the winds and the waves, and it was completely calm.

[27] The men were amazed and asked, "What kind of man is this? Even the winds and the waves obey him!"

Jesus Restores Two Demon-Possessed Men

[28] When he arrived at the other side in the region of the Gadarenes,[b] two demon-possessed men coming from the tombs met him. They were so violent that no one could pass that way. [29] "What do you want with us, Son of God?" they shouted. "Have you come here to torture us before the appointed time?"

[30] Some distance from them a large herd of pigs was feeding. [31] The demons begged Jesus, "If you drive us out, send us into the herd of pigs."

[32] He said to them, "Go!" So they came out and went into the pigs, and the whole herd rushed down the steep bank into the lake and died in the water. [33] Those tending the pigs ran off, went into the town and reported all this, including what had happened to the demon-possessed men. [34] Then the whole town went out to meet Jesus. And when they saw him, they pleaded with him to leave their region.

Jesus Forgives and Heals a Paralyzed Man

9 Jesus stepped into a boat, crossed over and came to his own town. [2] Some men brought to him a paralyzed man, lying on a mat. When Jesus saw their faith, he said to the man, "Take heart, son; your sins are forgiven."

[3] At this, some of the teachers of the law said to themselves, "This fellow is blaspheming!"

[4] Knowing their thoughts, Jesus said, "Why do you entertain evil thoughts in your hearts? [5] Which is easier: to say, 'Your sins are forgiven,' or to say, 'Get up and walk'? [6] But I want you to know that the Son of Man has authority on earth to forgive sins." So he said to the paralyzed man, "Get up, take your mat and go home." [7] Then the man got up and went home. [8] When the crowd saw this, they were filled with awe; and they praised God, who had given such authority to man.

---

[a] 17 Isaiah 53:4 (see Septuagint)   [b] 28 Some manuscripts *Gergesenes*; other manuscripts *Gerasenes*

YEP, HE'S INVITED TOO

READ: MATTHEW 9:9

Jesus has invited *anyone* to follow him, but when they come to church they find that there is an asterisk. The not-so-subtle message is we have to let you in here because Jesus told us to, but we are going be keeping an eye on you. I can't help but wonder if that's how the other disciples must have felt when Jesus invited Matthew. What about his qualifications? What about his past history? Jesus, surely you don't really mean *anyone*? But when Jesus says *anyone*, it turns out what he really means is *anyone*.

So here Matthew sits at his tax collector's booth, mulling over this rabbi's offer. There is no doubt that Matthew knew what this invitation involved. He understood that it meant giving up everything. He received an invitation, but there was no way he could respond to it and stay the same. Saying yes to following Jesus would mean saying no to his lucrative business.

BUILDING

FAITH

WISDOM

STRENGTH

It's important to understand that the grace of God doesn't simply invite us to follow ... it teaches us to follow. Just because Matthew left his past behind and started following didn't mean he was perfect. Far from it. Even after we decide to follow Jesus, we continue to need his grace for the journey. Each morning I receive the same grace-filled invitation that Jesus spoke to Matthew: "Follow me."

The Calling of Matthew

9As Jesus went on from there, he saw a man named Matthew sitting at the tax collector's booth. "Follow me," he told him, and Matthew got up and followed him.

10While Jesus was having dinner at Matthew's house, many tax collectors and sinners came and ate with him and his disciples. **11**When the Pharisees saw this, they asked his disciples, "Why does your teacher eat with tax collectors and sinners?"

12On hearing this, Jesus said, "It is not the healthy who need a doctor, but the sick. **13**But go and learn what this means: 'I desire mercy, not sacrifice.'*a* For I have not come to call the righteous, but sinners."

Jesus Questioned About Fasting

14Then John's disciples came and asked him, "How is it that we and the Pharisees fast often, but your disciples do not fast?"

15Jesus answered, "How can the guests of the bridegroom mourn while he is with them? The time will come when the bridegroom will be taken from them; then they will fast.

16"No one sews a patch of unshrunk cloth on an old garment, for the patch will pull away from the garment, making the tear worse. **17**Neither do people pour new wine into old wineskins. If they do, the skins will burst; the wine will run out and the wineskins will be ruined. No, they pour new wine into new wineskins, and both are preserved."

Jesus Raises a Dead Girl and Heals a Sick Woman

18While he was saying this, a synagogue leader came and knelt before him and said, "My daughter has just died. But come and put your hand on her, and she will live." **19**Jesus got up and went with him, and so did his disciples.

20Just then a woman who had been subject to bleeding for twelve years came up behind him and touched the edge of his cloak. **21**She said to herself, "If I only touch his cloak, I will be healed."

22Jesus turned and saw her. "Take heart, daughter," he said, "your faith has healed you." And the woman was healed at that moment.

23When Jesus entered the synagogue leader's house and saw the noisy crowd and people playing pipes, **24**he said, "Go away. The girl is not dead but asleep." But they laughed at him. **25**After the crowd had been put outside, he went in and took the girl by the hand, and she got up. **26**News of this spread through all that region.

Jesus Heals the Blind and the Mute

27As Jesus went on from there, two blind men followed him, calling out, "Have mercy on us, Son of David!"

28When he had gone indoors, the blind men came to him, and he asked them, "Do you believe that I am able to do this?"

"Yes, Lord," they replied.

29Then he touched their eyes and said, "According to your faith let it be done to you"; **30**and their sight was restored. Jesus warned them sternly, "See that no one knows about this." **31**But they went out and spread the news about him all over that region.

32While they were going out, a man who was demon-possessed and could not talk was brought to Jesus. **33**And when the demon was driven out, the man who had been mute spoke. The crowd was amazed and said, "Nothing like this has ever been seen in Israel."

34But the Pharisees said, "It is by the prince of demons that he drives out demons."

The Workers Are Few

35Jesus went through all the towns and villages, teaching in their synagogues, proclaiming the good news of the kingdom and healing every disease and sickness. **36**When he saw the crowds, he had compassion on them, because they were harassed and helpless, like sheep without a shepherd. **37**Then he said to his disciples, "The harvest is plentiful but the workers are few. **38**Ask the Lord of the harvest, therefore, to send out workers into his harvest field."

Jesus Sends Out the Twelve

10 Jesus called his twelve disciples to him and gave them authority to drive out impure spirits and to heal every disease and sickness.

2These are the names of the twelve apostles: first, Simon (who is called Peter) and

a 13 Hosea 6:6

MATTHEW

[Jesus] saw a man named Matthew sitting at the tax collector's booth. "Follow me," he told him, and Matthew got up and followed him. MATTHEW 9:9

HIS NAME MEANS: "gift of the LORD"
READ HIS STORY: *Matthew 9:9-13, 10:1-8; Luke 5:27-32; Acts 1:12-14*

Leeches—that's what tax collectors were considered in Jesus' day. These Jewish men worked for Rome, sitting in booths and collecting money. The tax collectors had to pay the Roman government what it demanded, but they could charge the people whatever they wanted and keep the rest. Many were corrupt . . . and rich.

Matthew's booth was likely located by a main road in Capernaum. Here he collected duties on goods brought in by farmers, merchants and caravans. Jesus lived in Capernaum and would've passed Matthew's booth many times. While others looked at Matthew (also called Levi) with hatred and as a traitor of his people, Jesus looked at him with compassion. The Lord called him to stop following money and instead follow a heavenly king.

Matthew took Jesus to his house and threw a large banquet. He invited his friends to celebrate his new career path. Matthew didn't have his life together before choosing to follow Jesus. But he knew serving Christ was worth leaving everything behind. When the Pharisees saw the party guests, they were shocked Jesus would socialize with tax collectors and sinners. Jesus heard their complaints and said, "It is not the healthy who need a doctor, but the sick" (Matthew 9:12).

The great physician had come. Matthew knew it and followed Jesus to the end. And Matthew's accurate record keeping—something he developed as a tax collector—shows in the writing of his gospel.

SO ANNOYING!

READ: MATTHEW 9:35-38

Ministry is great until people show up. We can be fired up about doing really cool spiritual things, and then when people get in front of us, life gets hard. They don't listen. They have their own ideas. It's easy to shy away and decide, *I just prefer to be a very deep believer.* If all we do is suck in knowledge, we'll find that it puffs up. On the other hand, love builds up.

Matthew 9:35-38 describes a typical scene in Jesus' earthly ministry. One particular word stands out in the middle of this story. It's only three letters long: s-a-w. "When he saw the crowds, he had compassion on them." Sure, the images of these people registered on the retinas of the disciples. But they did not see these people. Jesus did.

There is something about the way Jesus sees people that causes me to want to know him more. The more I walk with God—not practicing religion or doing ministry but getting to know the person of Jesus—the more I see people the way he sees them. When I start seeing people like he sees them, I start hurting like he does. When you walk into your school, do you see people as road cones on your way to bigger and better things? Or do you see them as God's providential appointments to reach for him?

BUILDING
FAITH
WISDOM
STRENGTH

his brother Andrew; James son of Zebedee, and his brother John; [3] Philip and Bartholomew; Thomas and Matthew the tax collector; James son of Alphaeus, and Thaddaeus; [4] Simon the Zealot and Judas Iscariot, who betrayed him.

[5] These twelve Jesus sent out with the following instructions: "Do not go among the Gentiles or enter any town of the Samaritans. [6] Go rather to the lost sheep of Israel. [7] As you go, proclaim this message: 'The kingdom of heaven has come near.' [8] Heal the sick, raise the dead, cleanse those who have leprosy,[a] drive out demons. Freely you have received; freely give.

[9] "Do not get any gold or silver or copper to take with you in your belts— [10] no bag for the journey or extra shirt or sandals or a staff, for the worker is worth his keep. [11] Whatever town or village you enter, search there for some worthy person and stay at their house until you leave. [12] As you enter the home, give it your greeting. [13] If the home is deserving, let your peace rest on it; if it is not, let your peace return to you. [14] If anyone will not welcome you or listen to your words, leave that home or town and shake the dust off your feet. [15] Truly I tell you, it will be more bearable for Sodom and Gomorrah on the day of judgment than for that town.

[16] "I am sending you out like sheep among wolves. Therefore be as shrewd as snakes and as innocent as doves. [17] Be on your guard; you will be handed over to the local councils and be flogged in the synagogues. [18] On my account you will be brought before governors and kings as witnesses to them and to the Gentiles. [19] But when they arrest you, do not worry about what to say or how to say it. At that time you will be given what to say, [20] for it will not be you speaking, but the Spirit of your Father speaking through you.

[21] "Brother will betray brother to death, and a father his child; children will rebel against their parents and have them put to death. [22] You will be hated by everyone because of me, but the one who stands firm to the end will be saved. [23] When you are persecuted in one place, flee to another. Truly I tell you, you will not finish going through the towns of Israel before the Son of Man comes.

[24] "The student is not above the teacher, nor a servant above his master. [25] It is enough for students to be like their teachers, and servants like their masters. If the head of the house has been called Beelzebul, how much more the members of his household!

[26] "So do not be afraid of them, for there is nothing concealed that will not be disclosed, or hidden that will not be made known. [27] What I tell you in the dark, speak in the daylight; what is whispered in your ear, proclaim from the roofs. [28] Do not be afraid of those who kill the body but cannot kill the soul. Rather, be afraid of the One who can destroy both soul and body in hell. [29] Are not two sparrows sold for a penny? Yet not one of them will fall to the ground outside your Father's care.[b] [30] And even the very hairs of your head are all numbered. [31] So don't be afraid; you are worth more than many sparrows.

[32] "Whoever acknowledges me before others, I will also acknowledge before my Father in heaven. [33] But whoever disowns me before others, I will disown before my Father in heaven.

[34] "Do not suppose that I have come to bring peace to the earth. I did not come to bring peace, but a sword. [35] For I have come to turn

" 'a man against his father,
    a daughter against her mother,
  a daughter-in-law against her mother-
      in-law—
[36]   a man's enemies will be the members
     of his own household.'[c]

[37] "Anyone who loves their father or mother more than me is not worthy of me; anyone who loves their son or daughter more than me is not worthy of me. [38] Whoever does not take up their cross and follow me is not worthy of me. [39] Whoever finds their life will lose it, and whoever loses their life for my sake will find it.

[40] "Anyone who welcomes you welcomes me, and anyone who welcomes me welcomes the one who sent me. [41] Whoever welcomes a prophet as a prophet will receive a prophet's reward, and whoever welcomes a righteous person as a righteous person will receive a righteous person's reward. [42] And if

---

[a] 8 The Greek word traditionally translated *leprosy* was used for various diseases affecting the skin.
[b] 29 Or *will*; or *knowledge* [c] 36 Micah 7:6

anyone gives even a cup of cold water to one of these little ones who is my disciple, truly I tell you, that person will certainly not lose their reward."

Jesus and John the Baptist

11 After Jesus had finished instructing his twelve disciples, he went on from there to teach and preach in the towns of Galilee.[a]

2 When John, who was in prison, heard about the deeds of the Messiah, he sent his disciples 3 to ask him, "Are you the one who is to come, or should we expect someone else?"

4 Jesus replied, "Go back and report to John what you hear and see: 5 The blind receive sight, the lame walk, those who have leprosy[b] are cleansed, the deaf hear, the dead are raised, and the good news is proclaimed to the poor. 6 Blessed is anyone who does not stumble on account of me."

7 As John's disciples were leaving, Jesus began to speak to the crowd about John: "What did you go out into the wilderness to see? A reed swayed by the wind? 8 If not, what did you go out to see? A man dressed in fine clothes? No, those who wear fine clothes are in kings' palaces. 9 Then what did you go out to see? A prophet? Yes, I tell you, and more than a prophet. 10 This is the one about whom it is written:

" 'I will send my messenger ahead
   of you,
   who will prepare your way
      before you.'[c]

11 Truly I tell you, among those born of women there has not risen anyone greater than John the Baptist; yet whoever is least in the kingdom of heaven is greater than he. 12 From the days of John the Baptist until now, the kingdom of heaven has been subjected to violence,[d] and violent people have been raiding it. 13 For all the Prophets and the Law prophesied until John. 14 And if you are willing to accept it, he is the Elijah who was to come. 15 Whoever has ears, let them hear.

16 "To what can I compare this generation? They are like children sitting in the marketplaces and calling out to others:

17 " 'We played the pipe for you,
      and you did not dance;

we sang a dirge,
   and you did not mourn.'

18 For John came neither eating nor drinking, and they say, 'He has a demon.' 19 The Son of Man came eating and drinking, and they say, 'Here is a glutton and a drunkard, a friend of tax collectors and sinners.' But wisdom is proved right by her deeds."

Woe on Unrepentant Towns

20 Then Jesus began to denounce the towns in which most of his miracles had been performed, because they did not repent. 21 "Woe to you, Chorazin! Woe to you, Bethsaida! For if the miracles that were performed in you had been performed in Tyre and Sidon, they would have repented long ago in sackcloth and ashes. 22 But I tell you, it will be more bearable for Tyre and Sidon on the day of judgment than for you. 23 And you, Capernaum, will you be lifted to the heavens? No, you will go down to Hades.[e] For if the miracles that were performed in you had been performed in Sodom, it would have remained to this day. 24 But I tell you that it will be more bearable for Sodom on the day of judgment than for you."

The Father Revealed in the Son

25 At that time Jesus said, "I praise you, Father, Lord of heaven and earth, because you have hidden these things from the wise and learned, and revealed them to little children. 26 Yes, Father, for this is what you were pleased to do.

27 "All things have been committed to me by my Father. No one knows the Son except the Father, and no one knows the Father except the Son and those to whom the Son chooses to reveal him.

28 "Come to me, all you who are weary and burdened, and I will give you rest. 29 Take my yoke upon you and learn from me, for I am gentle and humble in heart, and you will find rest for your souls. 30 For my yoke is easy and my burden is light."

Jesus Is Lord of the Sabbath

12 At that time Jesus went through the grainfields on the Sabbath. His disciples were hungry and began to pick some heads of grain and eat them. 2 When the

---

[a] 1 Greek in their towns   [b] 5 The Greek word traditionally translated leprosy was used for various diseases affecting the skin.   [c] 10 Mal. 3:1   [d] 12 Or been forcefully advancing   [e] 23 That is, the realm of the dead

Pharisees saw this, they said to him, "Look! Your disciples are doing what is unlawful on the Sabbath."

³He answered, "Haven't you read what David did when he and his companions were hungry? ⁴He entered the house of God, and he and his companions ate the consecrated bread — which was not lawful for them to do, but only for the priests. ⁵Or haven't you read in the Law that the priests on Sabbath duty in the temple desecrate the Sabbath and yet are innocent? ⁶I tell you that something greater than the temple is here. ⁷If you had known what these words mean, 'I desire mercy, not sacrifice,'ᵃ you would not have condemned the innocent. ⁸For the Son of Man is Lord of the Sabbath."

⁹Going on from that place, he went into their synagogue, ¹⁰and a man with a shriveled hand was there. Looking for a reason to bring charges against Jesus, they asked him, "Is it lawful to heal on the Sabbath?"

¹¹He said to them, "If any of you has a sheep and it falls into a pit on the Sabbath, will you not take hold of it and lift it out? ¹²How much more valuable is a person than a sheep! Therefore it is lawful to do good on the Sabbath."

¹³Then he said to the man, "Stretch out your hand." So he stretched it out and it was completely restored, just as sound as the other. ¹⁴But the Pharisees went out and plotted how they might kill Jesus.

God's Chosen Servant

¹⁵Aware of this, Jesus withdrew from that place. A large crowd followed him, and he healed all who were ill. ¹⁶He warned them not to tell others about him. ¹⁷This was to fulfill what was spoken through the prophet Isaiah:

¹⁸ "Here is my servant whom I have chosen,
    the one I love, in whom I delight;
I will put my Spirit on him,
    and he will proclaim justice to the
      nations.
¹⁹ He will not quarrel or cry out;
    no one will hear his voice in the
      streets.
²⁰ A bruised reed he will not break,
    and a smoldering wick he will not
      snuff out,
till he has brought justice through to
    victory.
²¹ In his name the nations will put
    their hope."ᵇ

Jesus and Beelzebul

²²Then they brought him a demon-possessed man who was blind and mute, and Jesus healed him, so that he could both talk and see. ²³All the people were astonished and said, "Could this be the Son of David?"

²⁴But when the Pharisees heard this, they said, "It is only by Beelzebul, the prince of demons, that this fellow drives out demons."

²⁵Jesus knew their thoughts and said to them, "Every kingdom divided against itself will be ruined, and every city or household divided against itself will not stand. ²⁶If Satan drives out Satan, he is divided against himself. How then can his kingdom stand? ²⁷And if I drive out demons by Beelzebul, by whom do your people drive them out? So then, they will be your judges. ²⁸But if it is by the Spirit of God that I drive out demons, then the kingdom of God has come upon you.

²⁹ "Or again, how can anyone enter a strong man's house and carry off his possessions unless he first ties up the strong man? Then he can plunder his house.

³⁰ "Whoever is not with me is against me, and whoever does not gather with me scatters. ³¹And so I tell you, every kind of sin and slander can be forgiven, but blasphemy against the Spirit will not be forgiven. ³²Anyone who speaks a word against the Son of Man will be forgiven, but anyone who speaks against the Holy Spirit will not be forgiven, either in this age or in the age to come.

³³ "Make a tree good and its fruit will be good, or make a tree bad and its fruit will be bad, for a tree is recognized by its fruit. ³⁴You brood of vipers, how can you who are evil say anything good? For the mouth speaks what the heart is full of. ³⁵A good man brings good things out of the good stored up in him, and an evil man brings evil things out of the evil stored up in him. ³⁶But I tell you that everyone will have to give account on the day of judgment for every empty word they have spoken. ³⁷For by your words you will

ᵃ 7 Hosea 6:6   ᵇ 21 Isaiah 42:1-4

be acquitted, and by your words you will be condemned."

The Sign of Jonah

38 Then some of the Pharisees and teachers of the law said to him, "Teacher, we want to see a sign from you."

39 He answered, "A wicked and adulterous generation asks for a sign! But none will be given it except the sign of the prophet Jonah. 40 For as Jonah was three days and three nights in the belly of a huge fish, so the Son of Man will be three days and three nights in the heart of the earth. 41 The men of Nineveh will stand up at the judgment with this generation and condemn it; for they repented at the preaching of Jonah, and now something greater than Jonah is here. 42 The Queen of the South will rise at the judgment with this generation and condemn it; for she came from the ends of the earth to listen to Solomon's wisdom, and now something greater than Solomon is here.

43 "When an impure spirit comes out of a person, it goes through arid places seeking rest and does not find it. 44 Then it says, 'I will return to the house I left.' When it arrives, it finds the house unoccupied, swept clean and put in order. 45 Then it goes and takes with it seven other spirits more wicked than itself, and they go in and live there. And the final condition of that person is worse than the first. That is how it will be with this wicked generation."

Jesus' Mother and Brothers

46 While Jesus was still talking to the crowd, his mother and brothers stood outside, wanting to speak to him. 47 Someone told him, "Your mother and brothers are standing outside, wanting to speak to you."

48 He replied to him, "Who is my mother, and who are my brothers?" 49 Pointing to his disciples, he said, "Here are my mother and my brothers. 50 For whoever does the will of my Father in heaven is my brother and sister and mother."

The Parable of the Sower

13 That same day Jesus went out of the house and sat by the lake. 2 Such large crowds gathered around him that he got into a boat and sat in it, while all the people stood on the shore. 3 Then he told them many things in parables, saying: "A farmer went out to sow his seed. 4 As he was scattering the seed, some fell along the path, and the birds came and ate it up. 5 Some fell on rocky places, where it did not have much soil. It sprang up quickly, because the soil was shallow. 6 But when the sun came up, the plants were scorched, and they withered because they had no root. 7 Other seed fell among thorns, which grew up and choked the plants. 8 Still other seed fell on good soil, where it produced a crop — a hundred, sixty or thirty times what was sown. 9 Whoever has ears, let them hear."

10 The disciples came to him and asked, "Why do you speak to the people in parables?"

11 He replied, "Because the knowledge of the secrets of the kingdom of heaven has been given to you, but not to them. 12 Whoever has will be given more, and they will have an abundance. Whoever does not have, even what they have will be taken from them. 13 This is why I speak to them in parables:

"Though seeing, they do not see;
    though hearing, they do not hear or
        understand.

14 In them is fulfilled the prophecy of Isaiah:

" 'You will be ever hearing but never
        understanding;
    you will be ever seeing but never
        perceiving.
15 For this people's heart has become
        calloused;
    they hardly hear with their ears,
    and they have closed their eyes.
Otherwise they might see with their eyes,
    hear with their ears,
    understand with their hearts
and turn, and I would heal them.'*a*

16 But blessed are your eyes because they see, and your ears because they hear. 17 For truly I tell you, many prophets and righteous people longed to see what you see but did not see it, and to hear what you hear but did not hear it.

---

a 15 Isaiah 6:9,10 (see Septuagint)

18 "Listen then to what the parable of the sower means: 19 When anyone hears the message about the kingdom and does not understand it, the evil one comes and snatches away what was sown in their heart. This is the seed sown along the path. 20 The seed falling on rocky ground refers to someone who hears the word and at once receives it with joy. 21 But since they have no root, they last only a short time. When trouble or persecution comes because of the word, they quickly fall away. 22 The seed falling among the thorns refers to someone who hears the word, but the worries of this life and the deceitfulness of wealth choke the word, making it unfruitful. 23 But the seed falling on good soil refers to someone who hears the word and understands it. This is the one who produces a crop, yielding a hundred, sixty or thirty times what was sown."

The Parable of the Weeds

24 Jesus told them another parable: "The kingdom of heaven is like a man who sowed good seed in his field. 25 But while everyone was sleeping, his enemy came and sowed weeds among the wheat, and went away. 26 When the wheat sprouted and formed heads, then the weeds also appeared.

27 "The owner's servants came to him and said, 'Sir, didn't you sow good seed in your field? Where then did the weeds come from?'

28 " 'An enemy did this,' he replied.

"The servants asked him, 'Do you want us to go and pull them up?'

29 " 'No,' he answered, 'because while you are pulling the weeds, you may uproot the wheat with them. 30 Let both grow together until the harvest. At that time I will tell the harvesters: First collect the weeds and tie them in bundles to be burned; then gather the wheat and bring it into my barn.' "

The Parables of the Mustard Seed and the Yeast

31 He told them another parable: "The kingdom of heaven is like a mustard seed, which a man took and planted in his field. 32 Though it is the smallest of all seeds, yet when it grows, it is the largest of garden plants and becomes a tree, so that the birds come and perch in its branches."

33 He told them still another parable: "The kingdom of heaven is like yeast that a woman took and mixed into about sixty pounds[a] of flour until it worked all through the dough."

34 Jesus spoke all these things to the crowd in parables; he did not say anything to them without using a parable. 35 So was fulfilled what was spoken through the prophet:

"I will open my mouth in parables,
    I will utter things hidden since the
        creation of the world."[b]

The Parable of the Weeds Explained

36 Then he left the crowd and went into the house. His disciples came to him and said, "Explain to us the parable of the weeds in the field."

37 He answered, "The one who sowed the good seed is the Son of Man. 38 The field is the world, and the good seed stands for the people of the kingdom. The weeds are the people of the evil one, 39 and the enemy who sows them is the devil. The harvest is the end of the age, and the harvesters are angels.

40 "As the weeds are pulled up and burned in the fire, so it will be at the end of the age. 41 The Son of Man will send out his angels, and they will weed out of his kingdom everything that causes sin and all who do evil. 42 They will throw them into the blazing furnace, where there will be weeping and gnashing of teeth. 43 Then the righteous will shine like the sun in the kingdom of their Father. Whoever has ears, let them hear.

The Parables of the Hidden Treasure and the Pearl

44 "The kingdom of heaven is like treasure hidden in a field. When a man found it, he hid it again, and then in his joy went and sold all he had and bought that field.

45 "Again, the kingdom of heaven is like a merchant looking for fine pearls. 46 When he found one of great value, he went away and sold everything he had and bought it.

The Parable of the Net

47 "Once again, the kingdom of heaven is like a net that was let down into the lake and caught all kinds of fish. 48 When it was full, the fishermen pulled it up on the shore. Then they sat down and collected the good

---

a 33 Or about 27 kilograms   *b 35* Psalm 78:2

HIDDEN GOLD

READ: MATTHEW 13:44-46

I n Bible times people would often bury their savings in the ground. It was considered safe, especially during times of war or government upheaval. It would not have been uncommon for someone to bury their treasure in the ground and then be killed while away at war.

Jesus describes a scenario where years later a hired hand discovers a buried treasure chest while plowing. He can't believe his eyes! There are thousands of dollars' worth of precious gems glistening in the sun. His heart pounds with excitement. He quickly reburies the treasure and continues working, but the whole time he is carefully plotting his course of action. He is desperate to buy that field so the treasure will be his. That evening he liquidates his assets. He sells everything—his house, his oxen, his cart. Friends and family begin to talk. They think he's lost his mind. It just doesn't make sense. But the truth is, this is the best investment that he could possibly make.

BUILDING FAITH WISDOM STRENGTH

When we discover the life that we can have in Jesus, we are to come after him like this man pursued this pearl of great price. Following Jesus is a pursuit that may cost us everything, but it is the best investment we could ever make.

In the parable of "The Pearl of Great Price" the man sold everything he had to get the treasure, but once he had the treasure, did you notice his response? Sacrificing everything he had for the treasure brought him great joy because he knew it was worth it.

Taken from *Not a Fan Student Edition* by Kyle Idleman, copyright © 2012 by City on the Hill Studio, Inc., published by Zondervan.

fish in baskets, but threw the bad away. [49]This is how it will be at the end of the age. The angels will come and separate the wicked from the righteous [50]and throw them into the blazing furnace, where there will be weeping and gnashing of teeth.

[51]"Have you understood all these things?" Jesus asked.

"Yes," they replied.

[52]He said to them, "Therefore every teacher of the law who has become a disciple in the kingdom of heaven is like the owner of a house who brings out of his storeroom new treasures as well as old."

A Prophet Without Honor

[53]When Jesus had finished these parables, he moved on from there. [54]Coming to his hometown, he began teaching the people in their synagogue, and they were amazed. "Where did this man get this wisdom and these miraculous powers?" they asked. [55]"Isn't this the carpenter's son? Isn't his mother's name Mary, and aren't his brothers James, Joseph, Simon and Judas? [56]Aren't all his sisters with us? Where then did this man get all these things?" [57]And they took offense at him.

But Jesus said to them, "A prophet is not without honor except in his own town and in his own home."

[58]And he did not do many miracles there because of their lack of faith.

John the Baptist Beheaded

14 At that time Herod the tetrarch heard the reports about Jesus, [2]and he said to his attendants, "This is John the Baptist; he has risen from the dead! That is why miraculous powers are at work in him."

[3]Now Herod had arrested John and bound him and put him in prison because of Herodias, his brother Philip's wife, [4]for John had been saying to him: "It is not lawful for you to have her." [5]Herod wanted to kill John, but he was afraid of the people, because they considered John a prophet.

[6]On Herod's birthday the daughter of Herodias danced for the guests and pleased Herod so much [7]that he promised with an oath to give her whatever she asked. [8]Prompted by her mother, she said, "Give me here on a platter the head of John the Baptist." [9]The king was distressed, but because of his oaths and his dinner guests, he ordered that her request be granted [10]and had John beheaded in the prison. [11]His head was brought in on a platter and given to the girl, who carried it to her mother. [12]John's disciples came and took his body and buried it. Then they went and told Jesus.

Jesus Feeds the Five Thousand

[13]When Jesus heard what had happened, he withdrew by boat privately to a solitary place. Hearing of this, the crowds followed him on foot from the towns. [14]When Jesus landed and saw a large crowd, he had compassion on them and healed their sick.

[15]As evening approached, the disciples came to him and said, "This is a remote place, and it's already getting late. Send the crowds away, so they can go to the villages and buy themselves some food."

[16]Jesus replied, "They do not need to go away. You give them something to eat."

[17]"We have here only five loaves of bread and two fish," they answered.

[18]"Bring them here to me," he said. [19]And he directed the people to sit down on the grass. Taking the five loaves and the two fish and looking up to heaven, he gave thanks and broke the loaves. Then he gave them to the disciples, and the disciples gave them to the people. [20]They all ate and were satisfied, and the disciples picked up twelve basketfuls of broken pieces that were left over. [21]The number of those who ate was about five thousand men, besides women and children.

Jesus Walks on the Water

[22]Immediately Jesus made the disciples get into the boat and go on ahead of him to the other side, while he dismissed the crowd. [23]After he had dismissed them, he went up on a mountainside by himself to pray. Later that night, he was there alone, [24]and the boat was already a considerable distance from land, buffeted by the waves because the wind was against it.

[25]Shortly before dawn Jesus went out to them, walking on the lake. [26]When the disciples saw him walking on the lake, they were terrified. "It's a ghost," they said, and cried out in fear.

[27]But Jesus immediately said to them: "Take courage! It is I. Don't be afraid."

EXAMINING FAITH

READ: MATTHEW 14:22-32

Faith has less to do with figuring out if something is true and more to do with trust as we enter relationships.

Let's look at a chair. First, it makes good sense to say the chair exists. My eyesight (perception) shows me that it exists. My touching it (perception) shows me that it exists. It doesn't take any faith to know the chair exists.

Now I must examine the character of the chair. How is it constructed? Is it sturdy enough to hold a person? Has it held people in the past (memory)? We have knowledge of the character of the chair. None of this deduction requires an ignorant form of faith to study the existence and character of the chair. So where does faith come in? Faith happens the moment I rely on the evidence and actually trust the chair to hold my weight.

Notice carefully that faith is not the opposite of evidence or reason or truth. In fact, faith is what happens when I choose to follow the evidence to its proper conclusion.

BUILDING

FAITH

WISDOM

STRENGTH

The same statements I made about the chair can also be made about God. Evidence about God's character is found in the Bible (testimony), in the world around me (perception, memory), and even in history (testimony). Throughout the Old Testament, we see how well God keeps his promises.

Faith happens when I enter into relationship with God, when I rely on the evidence and actually trust that God will keep his promise to me.

Taken from *Living with Questions* by Dale Fincher, copyright © 2007 by Charles Dale Fincher, published by Zondervan.

28"Lord, if it's you," Peter replied, "tell me to come to you on the water."

29"Come," he said.

Then Peter got down out of the boat, walked on the water and came toward Jesus. 30But when he saw the wind, he was afraid and, beginning to sink, cried out, "Lord, save me!"

31Immediately Jesus reached out his hand and caught him. "You of little faith," he said, "why did you doubt?"

32And when they climbed into the boat, the wind died down. 33Then those who were in the boat worshiped him, saying, "Truly you are the Son of God."

34When they had crossed over, they landed at Gennesaret. 35And when the men of that place recognized Jesus, they sent word to all the surrounding country. People brought all their sick to him 36and begged him to let the sick just touch the edge of his cloak, and all who touched it were healed.

That Which Defiles

15 Then some Pharisees and teachers of the law came to Jesus from Jerusalem and asked, 2"Why do your disciples break the tradition of the elders? They don't wash their hands before they eat!"

3Jesus replied, "And why do you break the command of God for the sake of your tradition? 4For God said, 'Honor your father and mother'*a* and 'Anyone who curses their father or mother is to be put to death.'*b* 5But you say that if anyone declares that what might have been used to help their father or mother is 'devoted to God,' 6they are not to 'honor their father or mother' with it. Thus you nullify the word of God for the sake of your tradition. 7You hypocrites! Isaiah was right when he prophesied about you:

8 "'These people honor me with their lips,
    but their hearts are far from me.
9They worship me in vain;
    their teachings are merely human rules.'*c*"

10Jesus called the crowd to him and said, "Listen and understand. 11What goes into someone's mouth does not defile them, but what comes out of their mouth, that is what defiles them."

12Then the disciples came to him and asked, "Do you know that the Pharisees were offended when they heard this?"

13He replied, "Every plant that my heavenly Father has not planted will be pulled up by the roots. 14Leave them; they are blind guides.*d* If the blind lead the blind, both will fall into a pit."

15Peter said, "Explain the parable to us."

16"Are you still so dull?" Jesus asked them. 17"Don't you see that whatever enters the mouth goes into the stomach and then out of the body? 18But the things that come out of a person's mouth come from the heart, and these defile them. 19For out of the heart come evil thoughts — murder, adultery, sexual immorality, theft, false testimony, slander. 20These are what defile a person; but eating with unwashed hands does not defile them."

The Faith of a Canaanite Woman

21Leaving that place, Jesus withdrew to the region of Tyre and Sidon. 22A Canaanite woman from that vicinity came to him, crying out, "Lord, Son of David, have mercy on me! My daughter is demon-possessed and suffering terribly."

23Jesus did not answer a word. So his disciples came to him and urged him, "Send her away, for she keeps crying out after us."

24He answered, "I was sent only to the lost sheep of Israel."

25The woman came and knelt before him. "Lord, help me!" she said.

26He replied, "It is not right to take the children's bread and toss it to the dogs."

27"Yes it is, Lord," she said. "Even the dogs eat the crumbs that fall from their master's table."

28Then Jesus said to her, "Woman, you have great faith! Your request is granted." And her daughter was healed at that moment.

Jesus Feeds the Four Thousand

29Jesus left there and went along the Sea of Galilee. Then he went up on a mountainside and sat down. 30Great crowds came to

---

a 4 Exodus 20:12; Deut. 5:16   *b 4* Exodus 21:17; Lev. 20:9   *c 9* Isaiah 29:13   *d 14* Some manuscripts *blind guides of the blind* him, bringing the lame, the blind, the crippled, the mute and many others, and laid them at his feet; and he healed them. [31]The people were amazed when they saw the mute speaking, the crippled made well, the lame walking and the blind seeing. And they praised the God of Israel.

[32]Jesus called his disciples to him and said, "I have compassion for these people; they have already been with me three days and have nothing to eat. I do not want to send them away hungry, or they may collapse on the way."

[33]His disciples answered, "Where could we get enough bread in this remote place to feed such a crowd?"

[34]"How many loaves do you have?" Jesus asked.

"Seven," they replied, "and a few small fish."

[35]He told the crowd to sit down on the ground. [36]Then he took the seven loaves and the fish, and when he had given thanks, he broke them and gave them to the disciples, and they in turn to the people. [37]They all ate and were satisfied. Afterward the disciples picked up seven basketfuls of broken pieces that were left over. [38]The number of those who ate was four thousand men, besides women and children. [39]After Jesus had sent the crowd away, he got into the boat and went to the vicinity of Magadan.

The Demand for a Sign

16 The Pharisees and Sadducees came to Jesus and tested him by asking him to show them a sign from heaven.

[2]He replied, "When evening comes, you say, 'It will be fair weather, for the sky is red,' [3]and in the morning, 'Today it will be stormy, for the sky is red and overcast.' You know how to interpret the appearance of the sky, but you cannot interpret the signs of the times.[a] [4]A wicked and adulterous generation looks for a sign, but none will be given it except the sign of Jonah." Jesus then left them and went away.

The Yeast of the Pharisees and Sadducees

[5]When they went across the lake, the disciples forgot to take bread. [6]"Be careful," Jesus said to them. "Be on your guard against the yeast of the Pharisees and Sadducees."

[7]They discussed this among themselves and said, "It is because we didn't bring any bread."

[8]Aware of their discussion, Jesus asked, "You of little faith, why are you talking among yourselves about having no bread? [9]Do you still not understand? Don't you remember the five loaves for the five thousand, and how many basketfuls you gathered? [10]Or the seven loaves for the four thousand, and how many basketfuls you gathered? [11]How is it you don't understand that I was not talking to you about bread? But be on your guard against the yeast of the Pharisees and Sadducees." [12]Then they understood that he was not telling them to guard against the yeast used in bread, but against the teaching of the Pharisees and Sadducees.

Peter Declares That Jesus Is the Messiah

[13]When Jesus came to the region of Caesarea Philippi, he asked his disciples, "Who do people say the Son of Man is?"

[14]They replied, "Some say John the Baptist; others say Elijah; and still others, Jeremiah or one of the prophets."

[15]"But what about you?" he asked. "Who do you say I am?"

[16]Simon Peter answered, "You are the Messiah, the Son of the living God."

[17]Jesus replied, "Blessed are you, Simon son of Jonah, for this was not revealed to you by flesh and blood, but by my Father in heaven. [18]And I tell you that you are Peter,[b] and on this rock I will build my church, and the gates of Hades[c] will not overcome it. [19]I will give you the keys of the kingdom of heaven; whatever you bind on earth will be[d] bound in heaven, and whatever you loose on earth will be[d] loosed in heaven." [20]Then he ordered his disciples not to tell anyone that he was the Messiah.

Jesus Predicts His Death

[21]From that time on Jesus began to explain to his disciples that he must go to Jerusalem and suffer many things at the hands of the elders, the chief priests and the teachers

---

[a] 2,3 Some early manuscripts do not have When evening comes . . . of the times.   [b] 18 The Greek word for Peter means rock.   [c] 18 That is, the realm of the dead   [d] 19 Or will have been

THE REAL D.T.R.

READ: MATTHEW 16:24-28

D o you want to guess what D.T.R. stands for? For a young man involved in a romantic relationship, these letters are often enough to strike fear into his heart. Define the Relationship. You want to see where things stand and find out if what you have is real.

So in your mind, picture yourself walking into a local coffee shop. You grab a snack and get a drink and then walk towards the back where it isn't crowded and you find a seat at a small table. Now, imagine that Jesus comes in and sits down next to you. You know it's him because of the blue sash.

Jesus skips past the small talk and gets right to the point. He looks you in the eye and says, "It's time we define this relationship." He wants to know how you feel about him. How would your relationship with him be defined? What exactly is your level of commitment?

Whether you've called yourself a Christian since childhood, or all of this is new to you, Jesus would clearly define what kind of relationship he wants to have with you. He wouldn't sugarcoat it or dress it up. He would tell you exactly what it means to follow him. As you're sitting in that coffee shop listening to Jesus give you the unedited version of what kind of relationship he wants with you, I can't help but wonder if that question, "Are you a follower of Jesus?" would be a little more challenging to answer.

BUILDING

FAITH

WISDOM

STRENGTH

Taken from *Not a Fan Student Edition* by Kyle Idleman, copyright © 2012 by City on the Hill Studio, Inc., published by Zondervan.

of the law, and that he must be killed and on the third day be raised to life.

²²Peter took him aside and began to rebuke him. "Never, Lord!" he said. "This shall never happen to you!"

²³Jesus turned and said to Peter, "Get behind me, Satan! You are a stumbling block to me; you do not have in mind the concerns of God, but merely human concerns."

²⁴Then Jesus said to his disciples, "Whoever wants to be my disciple must deny themselves and take up their cross and follow me. ²⁵For whoever wants to save their life*a* will lose it, but whoever loses their life for me will find it. ²⁶What good will it be for someone to gain the whole world, yet forfeit their soul? Or what can anyone give in exchange for their soul? ²⁷For the Son of Man is going to come in his Father's glory with his angels, and then he will reward each person according to what they have done.

²⁸"Truly I tell you, some who are standing here will not taste death before they see the Son of Man coming in his kingdom."

The Transfiguration

17 After six days Jesus took with him Peter, James and John the brother of James, and led them up a high mountain by themselves. ²There he was transfigured before them. His face shone like the sun, and his clothes became as white as the light. ³Just then there appeared before them Moses and Elijah, talking with Jesus.

⁴Peter said to Jesus, "Lord, it is good for us to be here. If you wish, I will put up three shelters — one for you, one for Moses and one for Elijah."

⁵While he was still speaking, a bright cloud covered them, and a voice from the cloud said, "This is my Son, whom I love; with him I am well pleased. Listen to him!"

⁶When the disciples heard this, they fell facedown to the ground, terrified. ⁷But Jesus came and touched them. "Get up," he said. "Don't be afraid." ⁸When they looked up, they saw no one except Jesus.

⁹As they were coming down the mountain, Jesus instructed them, "Don't tell anyone what you have seen, until the Son of Man has been raised from the dead."

¹⁰The disciples asked him, "Why then do the teachers of the law say that Elijah must come first?"

¹¹Jesus replied, "To be sure, Elijah comes and will restore all things. ¹²But I tell you, Elijah has already come, and they did not recognize him, but have done to him everything they wished. In the same way the Son of Man is going to suffer at their hands." ¹³Then the disciples understood that he was talking to them about John the Baptist.

Jesus Heals a Demon-Possessed Boy

¹⁴When they came to the crowd, a man approached Jesus and knelt before him. ¹⁵"Lord, have mercy on my son," he said. "He has seizures and is suffering greatly. He often falls into the fire or into the water. ¹⁶I brought him to your disciples, but they could not heal him."

¹⁷"You unbelieving and perverse generation," Jesus replied, "how long shall I stay with you? How long shall I put up with you? Bring the boy here to me." ¹⁸Jesus rebuked the demon, and it came out of the boy, and he was healed at that moment.

¹⁹Then the disciples came to Jesus in private and asked, "Why couldn't we drive it out?"

²⁰He replied, "Because you have so little faith. Truly I tell you, if you have faith as small as a mustard seed, you can say to this mountain, 'Move from here to there,' and it will move. Nothing will be impossible for you." [21]*b*

Jesus Predicts His Death a Second Time

²²When they came together in Galilee, he said to them, "The Son of Man is going to be delivered into the hands of men. ²³They will kill him, and on the third day he will be raised to life." And the disciples were filled with grief.

The Temple Tax

²⁴After Jesus and his disciples arrived in Capernaum, the collectors of the two-drachma temple tax came to Peter and asked, "Doesn't your teacher pay the temple tax?"

²⁵"Yes, he does," he replied.

---

a 25 The Greek word means either *life* or *soul*; also in verse 26.   *b 21* Some manuscripts include here words similar to Mark 9:29.

GO FISH

READ: MATTHEW 17:24-27

Part of me wonders if Peter thought Jesus was joking. He was probably a little off-balance, because I'm sure Jesus had pulled more than one prank on Peter.

Jesus could have provided the four-drachma coin in the normal way by giving it to him, but he tells Peter to go fish for it. I think there are a few reasons he did it this way. First, God loves doing different miracles in different ways because it reveals different dimensions of his power and personality.

But I wonder if the biggest reason is that Jesus wanted to see if Peter would trust him in the realm where Peter had the greatest professional expertise. As a professional fisherman, fishing was the one area where Peter would have been most tempted to think he didn't need Jesus. If you've caught hundreds of thousands of fish, none of which has ever had a coin in its mouth, how do you have the faith to believe that the next one will have a four-drachma coin? It seems kind of impossible, doesn't it? But there's only one way to find out if God will keep his promise: Obey the crazy nudges.

Let me spell it out: If you want to see crazy miracles, obey the crazy promptings of the Holy Spirit. Grab your pole, head to the lake, row the boat, cast the line, set the hook, and reel it in. You never know what you'll catch, but you can expect miracles.

BUILDING FAITH WISDOM STRENGTH

Taken from *The Circle Maker Student Edition* by Mark Batterson with Parker Batterson, copyright © 2012 by Mark Batterson, published by Zondervan.

When Peter came into the house, Jesus was the first to speak. "What do you think, Simon?" he asked. "From whom do the kings of the earth collect duty and taxes—from their own children or from others?"

26 "From others," Peter answered.

"Then the children are exempt," Jesus said to him. 27 "But so that we may not cause offense, go to the lake and throw out your line. Take the first fish you catch; open its mouth and you will find a four-drachma coin. Take it and give it to them for my tax and yours."

The Greatest in the Kingdom of Heaven

18 At that time the disciples came to Jesus and asked, "Who, then, is the greatest in the kingdom of heaven?"

2 He called a little child to him, and placed the child among them. 3 And he said: "Truly I tell you, unless you change and become like little children, you will never enter the kingdom of heaven. 4 Therefore, whoever takes the lowly position of this child is the greatest in the kingdom of heaven. 5 And whoever welcomes one such child in my name welcomes me.

Causing to Stumble

6 "If anyone causes one of these little ones—those who believe in me—to stumble, it would be better for them to have a large millstone hung around their neck and to be drowned in the depths of the sea. 7 Woe to the world because of the things that cause people to stumble! Such things must come, but woe to the person through whom they come! 8 If your hand or your foot causes you to stumble, cut it off and throw it away. It is better for you to enter life maimed or crippled than to have two hands or two feet and be thrown into eternal fire. 9 And if your eye causes you to stumble, gouge it out and throw it away. It is better for you to enter life with one eye than to have two eyes and be thrown into the fire of hell.

The Parable of the Wandering Sheep

10 "See that you do not despise one of these little ones. For I tell you that their angels in heaven always see the face of my Father in heaven. [11]a

12 "What do you think? If a man owns a hundred sheep, and one of them wanders away, will he not leave the ninety-nine on the hills and go to look for the one that wandered off? 13 And if he finds it, truly I tell you, he is happier about that one sheep than about the ninety-nine that did not wander off. 14 In the same way your Father in heaven is not willing that any of these little ones should perish.

Dealing With Sin in the Church

15 "If your brother or sister b sins, c go and point out their fault, just between the two of you. If they listen to you, you have won them over. 16 But if they will not listen, take one or two others along, so that 'every matter may be established by the testimony of two or three witnesses.'d 17 If they still refuse to listen, tell it to the church; and if they refuse to listen even to the church, treat them as you would a pagan or a tax collector.

18 "Truly I tell you, whatever you bind on earth will be e bound in heaven, and whatever you loose on earth will be e loosed in heaven.

19 "Again, truly I tell you that if two of you on earth agree about anything they ask for, it will be done for them by my Father in heaven. 20 For where two or three gather in my name, there am I with them."

The Parable of the Unmerciful Servant

21 Then Peter came to Jesus and asked, "Lord, how many times shall I forgive my brother or sister who sins against me? Up to seven times?"

22 Jesus answered, "I tell you, not seven times, but seventy-seven times.f

23 "Therefore, the kingdom of heaven is like a king who wanted to settle accounts with his servants. 24 As he began the settlement, a man who owed him ten thousand bags of goldg was brought to him. 25 Since he was not able to pay, the master ordered that he and his wife and his children and all that he had be sold to repay the debt.

---

a 11 Some manuscripts include here the words of Luke 19:10.   b 15 The Greek word for *brother or sister* (*adelphos*) refers here to a fellow disciple, whether man or woman; also in verses 21 and 35.   c 15 Some manuscripts *sins against you*   d 16 Deut. 19:15   e 18 Or *will have been*   f 22 Or *seventy times seven* g 24 Greek *ten thousand talents*; a talent was worth about 20 years of a day laborer's wages.

26 "At this the servant fell on his knees before him. 'Be patient with me,' he begged, 'and I will pay back everything.' 27 The servant's master took pity on him, canceled the debt and let him go.

28 "But when that servant went out, he found one of his fellow servants who owed him a hundred silver coins.[a] He grabbed him and began to choke him. 'Pay back what you owe me!' he demanded.

29 "His fellow servant fell to his knees and begged him, 'Be patient with me, and I will pay it back.'

30 "But he refused. Instead, he went off and had the man thrown into prison until he could pay the debt. 31 When the other servants saw what had happened, they were outraged and went and told their master everything that had happened.

32 "Then the master called the servant in. 'You wicked servant,' he said, 'I canceled all that debt of yours because you begged me to. 33 Shouldn't you have had mercy on your fellow servant just as I had on you?' 34 In anger his master handed him over to the jailers to be tortured, until he should pay back all he owed.

35 "This is how my heavenly Father will treat each of you unless you forgive your brother or sister from your heart."

Divorce

19 When Jesus had finished saying these things, he left Galilee and went into the region of Judea to the other side of the Jordan. 2 Large crowds followed him, and he healed them there.

3 Some Pharisees came to him to test him. They asked, "Is it lawful for a man to divorce his wife for any and every reason?"

4 "Haven't you read," he replied, "that at the beginning the Creator 'made them male and female,'[b] 5 and said, 'For this reason a man will leave his father and mother and be united to his wife, and the two will become one flesh'[c]? 6 So they are no longer two, but one flesh. Therefore what God has joined together, let no one separate."

7 "Why then," they asked, "did Moses command that a man give his wife a certificate of divorce and send her away?"

8 Jesus replied, "Moses permitted you to divorce your wives because your hearts were hard. But it was not this way from the beginning. 9 I tell you that anyone who divorces his wife, except for sexual immorality, and marries another woman commits adultery."

10 The disciples said to him, "If this is the situation between a husband and wife, it is better not to marry."

11 Jesus replied, "Not everyone can accept this word, but only those to whom it has been given. 12 For there are eunuchs who were born that way, and there are eunuchs who have been made eunuchs by others—and there are those who choose to live like eunuchs for the sake of the kingdom of heaven. The one who can accept this should accept it."

The Little Children and Jesus

13 Then people brought little children to Jesus for him to place his hands on them and pray for them. But the disciples rebuked them.

14 Jesus said, "Let the little children come to me, and do not hinder them, for the kingdom of heaven belongs to such as these." 15 When he had placed his hands on them, he went on from there.

The Rich and the Kingdom of God

16 Just then a man came up to Jesus and asked, "Teacher, what good thing must I do to get eternal life?"

17 "Why do you ask me about what is good?" Jesus replied. "There is only One who is good. If you want to enter life, keep the commandments."

18 "Which ones?" he inquired.

Jesus replied, "'You shall not murder, you shall not commit adultery, you shall not steal, you shall not give false testimony, 19 honor your father and mother,'[d] and 'love your neighbor as yourself.'[e]"

20 "All these I have kept," the young man said. "What do I still lack?"

21 Jesus answered, "If you want to be perfect, go, sell your possessions and give to the poor, and you will have treasure in heaven. Then come, follow me."

22 When the young man heard this, he went away sad, because he had great wealth.

---

a 28 Greek a hundred denarii; a denarius was the usual daily wage of a day laborer (see 20:2).
b 4 Gen. 1:27   c 5 Gen. 2:24   d 19 Exodus 20:12-16; Deut. 5:16-20   e 19 Lev. 19:18

[23] Then Jesus said to his disciples, "Truly I tell you, it is hard for someone who is rich to enter the kingdom of heaven. [24] Again I tell you, it is easier for a camel to go through the eye of a needle than for someone who is rich to enter the kingdom of God."

[25] When the disciples heard this, they were greatly astonished and asked, "Who then can be saved?"

[26] Jesus looked at them and said, "With man this is impossible, but with God all things are possible."

[27] Peter answered him, "We have left everything to follow you! What then will there be for us?"

[28] Jesus said to them, "Truly I tell you, at the renewal of all things, when the Son of Man sits on his glorious throne, you who have followed me will also sit on twelve thrones, judging the twelve tribes of Israel. [29] And everyone who has left houses or brothers or sisters or father or mother or wife[a] or children or fields for my sake will receive a hundred times as much and will inherit eternal life. [30] But many who are first will be last, and many who are last will be first.

The Parable of the Workers in the Vineyard

20 "For the kingdom of heaven is like a landowner who went out early in the morning to hire workers for his vineyard. [2] He agreed to pay them a denarius[b] for the day and sent them into his vineyard.

[3] "About nine in the morning he went out and saw others standing in the marketplace doing nothing. [4] He told them, 'You also go and work in my vineyard, and I will pay you whatever is right.' [5] So they went.

"He went out again about noon and about three in the afternoon and did the same thing. [6] About five in the afternoon he went out and found still others standing around. He asked them, 'Why have you been standing here all day long doing nothing?'

[7] "'Because no one has hired us,' they answered.

"He said to them, 'You also go and work in my vineyard.'

[8] "When evening came, the owner of the vineyard said to his foreman, 'Call the workers and pay them their wages, beginning with the last ones hired and going on to the first.'

[9] "The workers who were hired about five in the afternoon came and each received a denarius. [10] So when those came who were hired first, they expected to receive more. But each one of them also received a denarius. [11] When they received it, they began to grumble against the landowner. [12] 'These who were hired last worked only one hour,' they said, 'and you have made them equal to us who have borne the burden of the work and the heat of the day.'

[13] "But he answered one of them, 'I am not being unfair to you, friend. Didn't you agree to work for a denarius? [14] Take your pay and go. I want to give the one who was hired last the same as I gave you. [15] Don't I have the right to do what I want with my own money? Or are you envious because I am generous?'

[16] "So the last will be first, and the first will be last."

Jesus Predicts His Death a Third Time

[17] Now Jesus was going up to Jerusalem. On the way, he took the Twelve aside and said to them, [18] "We are going up to Jerusalem, and the Son of Man will be delivered over to the chief priests and the teachers of the law. They will condemn him to death [19] and will hand him over to the Gentiles to be mocked and flogged and crucified. On the third day he will be raised to life!"

A Mother's Request

[20] Then the mother of Zebedee's sons came to Jesus with her sons and, kneeling down, asked a favor of him.

[21] "What is it you want?" he asked.

She said, "Grant that one of these two sons of mine may sit at your right and the other at your left in your kingdom."

[22] "You don't know what you are asking," Jesus said to them. "Can you drink the cup I am going to drink?"

"We can," they answered.

[23] Jesus said to them, "You will indeed drink from my cup, but to sit at my right or left is not for me to grant. These places belong to those for whom they have been prepared by my Father."

---

[a] 29 Some manuscripts do not have *or wife*.   [b] 2 A denarius was the usual daily wage of a day laborer.

²⁴When the ten heard about this, they were indignant with the two brothers. ²⁵Jesus called them together and said, "You know that the rulers of the Gentiles lord it over them, and their high officials exercise authority over them. ²⁶Not so with you. Instead, whoever wants to become great among you must be your servant, ²⁷and whoever wants to be first must be your slave — ²⁸just as the Son of Man did not come to be served, but to serve, and to give his life as a ransom for many."

Two Blind Men Receive Sight

²⁹As Jesus and his disciples were leaving Jericho, a large crowd followed him. ³⁰Two blind men were sitting by the roadside, and when they heard that Jesus was going by, they shouted, "Lord, Son of David, have mercy on us!"

³¹The crowd rebuked them and told them to be quiet, but they shouted all the louder, "Lord, Son of David, have mercy on us!"

³²Jesus stopped and called them. "What do you want me to do for you?" he asked.

³³"Lord," they answered, "we want our sight."

³⁴Jesus had compassion on them and touched their eyes. Immediately they received their sight and followed him.

Jesus Comes to Jerusalem as King

21 As they approached Jerusalem and came to Bethphage on the Mount of Olives, Jesus sent two disciples, ²saying to them, "Go to the village ahead of you, and at once you will find a donkey tied there, with her colt by her. Untie them and bring them to me. ³If anyone says anything to you, say that the Lord needs them, and he will send them right away."

⁴This took place to fulfill what was spoken through the prophet:

⁵ "Say to Daughter Zion,
    'See, your king comes to you,
 gentle and riding on a donkey,
    and on a colt, the foal of
       a donkey.' "ᵃ

⁶The disciples went and did as Jesus had instructed them. ⁷They brought the donkey and the colt and placed their cloaks on them for Jesus to sit on. ⁸A very large crowd spread their cloaks on the road, while others cut branches from the trees and spread them on the road. ⁹The crowds that went ahead of him and those that followed shouted,

"Hosannaᵇ to the Son of David!"

"Blessed is he who comes in the name of
    the Lord!"ᶜ

"Hosannaᵇ in the highest heaven!"

¹⁰When Jesus entered Jerusalem, the whole city was stirred and asked, "Who is this?"

¹¹The crowds answered, "This is Jesus, the prophet from Nazareth in Galilee."

Jesus at the Temple

¹²Jesus entered the temple courts and drove out all who were buying and selling there. He overturned the tables of the money changers and the benches of those selling doves. ¹³"It is written," he said to them, " 'My house will be called a house of prayer,'ᵈ but you are making it 'a den of robbers.'ᵉ"

¹⁴The blind and the lame came to him at the temple, and he healed them. ¹⁵But when the chief priests and the teachers of the law saw the wonderful things he did and the children shouting in the temple courts, "Hosanna to the Son of David," they were indignant.

¹⁶"Do you hear what these children are saying?" they asked him.

"Yes," replied Jesus, "have you never read,

" 'From the lips of children and infants
    you, Lord, have called forth your
       praise'ᶠ?"

¹⁷And he left them and went out of the city to Bethany, where he spent the night.

Jesus Curses a Fig Tree

¹⁸Early in the morning, as Jesus was on his way back to the city, he was hungry. ¹⁹Seeing a fig tree by the road, he went up to it but found nothing on it except leaves. Then he said to it, "May you never bear fruit again!" Immediately the tree withered.

²⁰When the disciples saw this, they were amazed. "How did the fig tree wither so quickly?" they asked.

ᵃ 5 Zech. 9:9   ᵇ 9 A Hebrew expression meaning "Save!" which became an exclamation of praise; also in verse 15   ᶜ 9 Psalm 118:25,26   ᵈ 13 Isaiah 56:7   ᵉ 13 Jer. 7:11   ᶠ 16 Psalm 8:2 (see Septuagint)

YOUR ANSWER PLEASE

READ: MATTHEW 20:29-34

Jesus sees this as a divine appointment. So he stops and responds with a pointed question: "What do you want me to do for you?"

Seriously? Is that question even necessary? Isn't it obvious what they want? They're blind. Yet Jesus forced them to define exactly what they wanted. He made them spell it out, but it wasn't because Jesus didn't know what they wanted (believe me, he knew); he wanted to make sure they knew what they wanted.

What if Jesus were to ask you this very same question: What do you want me to do for you? Would you be able to spell out the promises, miracles, and dreams God has put in your heart? I'm afraid many of us would be dumbfounded. Sure there are things we could ask him for, but really, what's worth asking Jesus for? If we can't answer this question, then we're as blind spiritually as these blind men were physically.

BUILDING

FAITH

WISDOM

STRENGTH

So while God is for us, most of us have no idea what we want God to do for us. And that's why our prayers aren't just boring to us; they are uninspiring to God. When there's no real thought behind your prayers, it's as lame for him to listen as it is for you to pray it. If faith is being sure of what we hope for, then being unsure of what we hope for is the exact opposite of faith, isn't it? Well-developed faith results in well-defined prayers, and well-defined prayers result in a well-lived life.

Taken from *The Circle Maker Student Edition* by Mark Batterson with Parker Batterson, copyright © 2012 by Mark Batterson, published by Zondervan.

[21] Jesus replied, "Truly I tell you, if you have faith and do not doubt, not only can you do what was done to the fig tree, but also you can say to this mountain, 'Go, throw yourself into the sea,' and it will be done. [22] If you believe, you will receive whatever you ask for in prayer."

The Authority of Jesus Questioned

[23] Jesus entered the temple courts, and, while he was teaching, the chief priests and the elders of the people came to him. "By what authority are you doing these things?" they asked. "And who gave you this authority?"

[24] Jesus replied, "I will also ask you one question. If you answer me, I will tell you by what authority I am doing these things. [25] John's baptism—where did it come from? Was it from heaven, or of human origin?"

They discussed it among themselves and said, "If we say, 'From heaven,' he will ask, 'Then why didn't you believe him?' [26] But if we say, 'Of human origin'—we are afraid of the people, for they all hold that John was a prophet."

[27] So they answered Jesus, "We don't know."

Then he said, "Neither will I tell you by what authority I am doing these things.

The Parable of the Two Sons

[28] "What do you think? There was a man who had two sons. He went to the first and said, 'Son, go and work today in the vineyard.'

[29] "'I will not,' he answered, but later he changed his mind and went.

[30] "Then the father went to the other son and said the same thing. He answered, 'I will, sir,' but he did not go.

[31] "Which of the two did what his father wanted?"

"The first," they answered.

Jesus said to them, "Truly I tell you, the tax collectors and the prostitutes are entering the kingdom of God ahead of you. [32] For John came to you to show you the way of righteousness, and you did not believe him, but the tax collectors and the prostitutes did. And even after you saw this, you did not repent and believe him.

The Parable of the Tenants

[33] "Listen to another parable: There was a landowner who planted a vineyard. He put a wall around it, dug a winepress in it and built a watchtower. Then he rented the vineyard to some farmers and moved to another place. [34] When the harvest time approached, he sent his servants to the tenants to collect his fruit.

[35] "The tenants seized his servants; they beat one, killed another, and stoned a third. [36] Then he sent other servants to them, more than the first time, and the tenants treated them the same way. [37] Last of all, he sent his son to them. 'They will respect my son,' he said.

[38] "But when the tenants saw the son, they said to each other, 'This is the heir. Come, let's kill him and take his inheritance.' [39] So they took him and threw him out of the vineyard and killed him.

[40] "Therefore, when the owner of the vineyard comes, what will he do to those tenants?"

[41] "He will bring those wretches to a wretched end," they replied, "and he will rent the vineyard to other tenants, who will give him his share of the crop at harvest time."

[42] Jesus said to them, "Have you never read in the Scriptures:

> "'The stone the builders rejected
> has become the cornerstone;
> the Lord has done this,
> and it is marvelous in our eyes'[a]?

[43] "Therefore I tell you that the kingdom of God will be taken away from you and given to a people who will produce its fruit. [44] Anyone who falls on this stone will be broken to pieces; anyone on whom it falls will be crushed."[b]

[45] When the chief priests and the Pharisees heard Jesus' parables, they knew he was talking about them. [46] They looked for a way to arrest him, but they were afraid of the crowd because the people held that he was a prophet.

The Parable of the Wedding Banquet

22 Jesus spoke to them again in parables, saying: [2] "The kingdom of heaven is like a king who prepared a wedding banquet for his son. [3] He sent his servants to those who had been invited to the banquet to tell them to come, but they refused to come.

---

[a] 42 Psalm 118:22,23   [b] 44 Some manuscripts do not have verse 44.

IT'S PERSONAL

READ: MATTHEW 21:9-11

When we're caught in the cycle of compromise, we can become guilt-ridden and try and try to do our best. We feel we have to do something, anything, to pacify an angry God, so we sometimes substitute ritual for relationship. We're trying religiously to earn God's favor, never realizing that Jesus is already standing beside us.

If we feel secure in the Christian life only when we're at church, then we've signed up for Big Group Jesus. Big Group Jesus is what I call the weird phenomenon when a bunch of believers get together, and the music and preaching are just right. It gets louder, the emotion intensifies, and the people sing and respond with more passion. Half of them don't even know why they're doing it, but they're only mimicking the authentic worship of others. For many, it's just that—an experience going on around them—and they're seeing and feeling the effects of it. But it's not in their hearts.

BUILDING

FAITH

WISDOM

STRENGTH

This is what happens when we don't have our own Jesus. There is a huge difference between Big Group Jesus and real fellowship with God.

What about you? Your own Jesus—and no one else's—should go home with you when the night is over. Your own Jesus should have gone with you in the first place.

4 "Then he sent some more servants and said, 'Tell those who have been invited that I have prepared my dinner: My oxen and fattened cattle have been butchered, and everything is ready. Come to the wedding banquet.'

5 "But they paid no attention and went off — one to his field, another to his business. 6 The rest seized his servants, mistreated them and killed them. 7 The king was enraged. He sent his army and destroyed those murderers and burned their city.

8 "Then he said to his servants, 'The wedding banquet is ready, but those I invited did not deserve to come. 9 So go to the street corners and invite to the banquet anyone you find.' 10 So the servants went out into the streets and gathered all the people they could find, the bad as well as the good, and the wedding hall was filled with guests.

11 "But when the king came in to see the guests, he noticed a man there who was not wearing wedding clothes. 12 He asked, 'How did you get in here without wedding clothes, friend?' The man was speechless.

13 "Then the king told the attendants, 'Tie him hand and foot, and throw him outside, into the darkness, where there will be weeping and gnashing of teeth.'

14 "For many are invited, but few are chosen."

Paying the Imperial Tax to Caesar

15 Then the Pharisees went out and laid plans to trap him in his words. 16 They sent their disciples to him along with the Herodians. "Teacher," they said, "we know that you are a man of integrity and that you teach the way of God in accordance with the truth. You aren't swayed by others, because you pay no attention to who they are. 17 Tell us then, what is your opinion? Is it right to pay the imperial tax[a] to Caesar or not?"

18 But Jesus, knowing their evil intent, said, "You hypocrites, why are you trying to trap me? 19 Show me the coin used for paying the tax." They brought him a denarius, 20 and he asked them, "Whose image is this? And whose inscription?"

21 "Caesar's," they replied.

Then he said to them, "So give back to Caesar what is Caesar's, and to God what is God's."

22 When they heard this, they were amazed. So they left him and went away.

Marriage at the Resurrection

23 That same day the Sadducees, who say there is no resurrection, came to him with a question. 24 "Teacher," they said, "Moses told us that if a man dies without having children, his brother must marry the widow and raise up offspring for him. 25 Now there were seven brothers among us. The first one married and died, and since he had no children, he left his wife to his brother. 26 The same thing happened to the second and third brother, right on down to the seventh. 27 Finally, the woman died. 28 Now then, at the resurrection, whose wife will she be of the seven, since all of them were married to her?"

29 Jesus replied, "You are in error because you do not know the Scriptures or the power of God. 30 At the resurrection people will neither marry nor be given in marriage; they will be like the angels in heaven. 31 But about the resurrection of the dead — have you not read what God said to you, 32 'I am the God of Abraham, the God of Isaac, and the God of Jacob'[b]? He is not the God of the dead but of the living."

33 When the crowds heard this, they were astonished at his teaching.

The Greatest Commandment

34 Hearing that Jesus had silenced the Sadducees, the Pharisees got together. 35 One of them, an expert in the law, tested him with this question: 36 "Teacher, which is the greatest commandment in the Law?"

37 Jesus replied: "'Love the Lord your God with all your heart and with all your soul and with all your mind.'[c] 38 This is the first and greatest commandment. 39 And the second is like it: 'Love your neighbor as yourself.'[d] 40 All the Law and the Prophets hang on these two commandments."

Whose Son Is the Messiah?

41 While the Pharisees were gathered together, Jesus asked them, 42 "What do you think about the Messiah? Whose son is he?"

"The son of David," they replied.

43 He said to them, "How is it then that

---

[a] 17 A special tax levied on subject peoples, not on Roman citizens   [b] 32 Exodus 3:6   [c] 37 Deut. 6:5
[d] 39 Lev. 19:18

David, speaking by the Spirit, calls him 'Lord'? For he says,

⁴⁴ " 'The Lord said to my Lord:
  "Sit at my right hand
  until I put your enemies
    under your feet." ' ᵃ

⁴⁵If then David calls him 'Lord,' how can he be his son?" ⁴⁶No one could say a word in reply, and from that day on no one dared to ask him any more questions.

A Warning Against Hypocrisy

23 Then Jesus said to the crowds and to his disciples: ²"The teachers of the law and the Pharisees sit in Moses' seat. ³So you must be careful to do everything they tell you. But do not do what they do, for they do not practice what they preach. ⁴They tie up heavy, cumbersome loads and put them on other people's shoulders, but they themselves are not willing to lift a finger to move them.

⁵"Everything they do is done for people to see: They make their phylacteriesᵇ wide and the tassels on their garments long; ⁶they love the place of honor at banquets and the most important seats in the synagogues; ⁷they love to be greeted with respect in the marketplaces and to be called 'Rabbi' by others.

⁸"But you are not to be called 'Rabbi,' for you have one Teacher, and you are all brothers. ⁹And do not call anyone on earth 'father,' for you have one Father, and he is in heaven. ¹⁰Nor are you to be called instructors, for you have one Instructor, the Messiah. ¹¹The greatest among you will be your servant. ¹²For those who exalt themselves will be humbled, and those who humble themselves will be exalted.

Seven Woes on the Teachers of the Law and the Pharisees

¹³"Woe to you, teachers of the law and Pharisees, you hypocrites! You shut the door of the kingdom of heaven in people's faces. You yourselves do not enter, nor will you let those enter who are trying to. [14]ᶜ

¹⁵"Woe to you, teachers of the law and Pharisees, you hypocrites! You travel over land and sea to win a single convert, and when you have succeeded, you make them twice as much a child of hell as you are.

¹⁶"Woe to you, blind guides! You say, 'If anyone swears by the temple, it means nothing; but anyone who swears by the gold of the temple is bound by that oath.' ¹⁷You blind fools! Which is greater: the gold, or the temple that makes the gold sacred? ¹⁸You also say, 'If anyone swears by the altar, it means nothing; but anyone who swears by the gift on the altar is bound by that oath.' ¹⁹You blind men! Which is greater: the gift, or the altar that makes the gift sacred? ²⁰Therefore, anyone who swears by the altar swears by it and by everything on it. ²¹And anyone who swears by the temple swears by it and by the one who dwells in it. ²²And anyone who swears by heaven swears by God's throne and by the one who sits on it.

²³"Woe to you, teachers of the law and Pharisees, you hypocrites! You give a tenth of your spices—mint, dill and cumin. But you have neglected the more important matters of the law—justice, mercy and faithfulness. You should have practiced the latter, without neglecting the former. ²⁴You blind guides! You strain out a gnat but swallow a camel.

²⁵"Woe to you, teachers of the law and Pharisees, you hypocrites! You clean the outside of the cup and dish, but inside they are full of greed and self-indulgence. ²⁶Blind Pharisee! First clean the inside of the cup and dish, and then the outside also will be clean.

²⁷"Woe to you, teachers of the law and Pharisees, you hypocrites! You are like whitewashed tombs, which look beautiful on the outside but on the inside are full of the bones of the dead and everything unclean. ²⁸In the same way, on the outside you appear to people as righteous but on the inside you are full of hypocrisy and wickedness.

²⁹"Woe to you, teachers of the law and Pharisees, you hypocrites! You build tombs for the prophets and decorate the graves of the righteous. ³⁰And you say, 'If we had lived in the days of our ancestors, we would not have taken part with them in shedding the blood of the prophets.' ³¹So you testify

---

ᵃ 44 Psalm 110:1   ᵇ 5 That is, boxes containing Scripture verses, worn on forehead and arm
ᶜ 14 Some manuscripts include here words similar to Mark 12:40 and Luke 20:47.

CLEAN INSIDES

READ: MATTHEW 23:25-26

You can learn a lot from hypocrites—if you carefully study what they do and pursue the opposite.

Scripture shows Jesus speaking harsh words to the Pharisees almost every time they meet. These religious rule-keepers focused so intently on the smallest of God's laws that they forgot about the Lord himself. They constantly called out the failings of ordinary "sinners," anyone who didn't fit in their exclusive group.

Jesus faults the Pharisees for loving applause and grabbing the most visible seats in their synagogues, local places of worship. He picks apart how they pile rules upon rules, as if their misguided devotion would get them closer to God. They carefully measure out offerings from their spice jars, but they forget to show mercy.

Yet there's one habit of the Pharisees you truly want to watch— and do differently. Jesus condemns the Pharisees for putting all their effort into looking spotless on the outside. Jesus knows that inside they're still full of sin and death.

BUILDING

FAITH

WISDOM

STRENGTH

True followers of God get clean from the inside out. It's like scrubbing the grime from the inside of a dirty glass. By the time you get to the outside, the whole cup sparkles.

You can wash your insides by letting the Lord wash you with forgiveness. Then let him scrub your thoughts and attitudes. By the time he's done, your actions will be pure as well.

against yourselves that you are the descendants of those who murdered the prophets. ³²Go ahead, then, and complete what your ancestors started!

³³"You snakes! You brood of vipers! How will you escape being condemned to hell? ³⁴Therefore I am sending you prophets and sages and teachers. Some of them you will kill and crucify; others you will flog in your synagogues and pursue from town to town. ³⁵And so upon you will come all the righteous blood that has been shed on earth, from the blood of righteous Abel to the blood of Zechariah son of Berekiah, whom you murdered between the temple and the altar. ³⁶Truly I tell you, all this will come on this generation.

³⁷"Jerusalem, Jerusalem, you who kill the prophets and stone those sent to you, how often I have longed to gather your children together, as a hen gathers her chicks under her wings, and you were not willing. ³⁸Look, your house is left to you desolate. ³⁹For I tell you, you will not see me again until you say, 'Blessed is he who comes in the name of the Lord.'[a]"

The Destruction of the Temple and Signs of the End Times

24 Jesus left the temple and was walking away when his disciples came up to him to call his attention to its buildings. ²"Do you see all these things?" he asked. "Truly I tell you, not one stone here will be left on another; every one will be thrown down."

³As Jesus was sitting on the Mount of Olives, the disciples came to him privately. "Tell us," they said, "when will this happen, and what will be the sign of your coming and of the end of the age?"

⁴Jesus answered: "Watch out that no one deceives you. ⁵For many will come in my name, claiming, 'I am the Messiah,' and will deceive many. ⁶You will hear of wars and rumors of wars, but see to it that you are not alarmed. Such things must happen, but the end is still to come. ⁷Nation will rise against nation, and kingdom against kingdom. There will be famines and earthquakes in various places. ⁸All these are the beginning of birth pains.

⁹"Then you will be handed over to be persecuted and put to death, and you will be hated by all nations because of me. ¹⁰At that time many will turn away from the faith and will betray and hate each other, ¹¹and many false prophets will appear and deceive many people. ¹²Because of the increase of wickedness, the love of most will grow cold, ¹³but the one who stands firm to the end will be saved. ¹⁴And this gospel of the kingdom will be preached in the whole world as a testimony to all nations, and then the end will come.

¹⁵"So when you see standing in the holy place 'the abomination that causes desolation,'[b] spoken of through the prophet Daniel—let the reader understand— ¹⁶then let those who are in Judea flee to the mountains. ¹⁷Let no one on the housetop go down to take anything out of the house. ¹⁸Let no one in the field go back to get their cloak. ¹⁹How dreadful it will be in those days for pregnant women and nursing mothers! ²⁰Pray that your flight will not take place in winter or on the Sabbath. ²¹For then there will be great distress, unequaled from the beginning of the world until now—and never to be equaled again.

²²"If those days had not been cut short, no one would survive, but for the sake of the elect those days will be shortened. ²³At that time if anyone says to you, 'Look, here is the Messiah!' or, 'There he is!' do not believe it. ²⁴For false messiahs and false prophets will appear and perform great signs and wonders to deceive, if possible, even the elect. ²⁵See, I have told you ahead of time.

²⁶"So if anyone tells you, 'There he is, out in the wilderness,' do not go out; or, 'Here he is, in the inner rooms,' do not believe it. ²⁷For as lightning that comes from the east is visible even in the west, so will be the coming of the Son of Man. ²⁸Wherever there is a carcass, there the vultures will gather.

²⁹"Immediately after the distress of those days

"'the sun will be darkened,
    and the moon will not give
        its light;
the stars will fall from the sky,
    and the heavenly bodies will be
        shaken.'[c]

a 39 Psalm 118:26   *b* 15 Daniel 9:27; 11:31; 12:11   *c* 29 Isaiah 13:10; 34:4

³⁰"Then will appear the sign of the Son of Man in heaven. And then all the peoples of the earth*ᵃ* will mourn when they see the Son of Man coming on the clouds of heaven, with power and great glory.*ᵇ* ³¹And he will send his angels with a loud trumpet call, and they will gather his elect from the four winds, from one end of the heavens to the other.

³²"Now learn this lesson from the fig tree: As soon as its twigs get tender and its leaves come out, you know that summer is near. ³³Even so, when you see all these things, you know that it*ᶜ* is near, right at the door. ³⁴Truly I tell you, this generation will certainly not pass away until all these things have happened. ³⁵Heaven and earth will pass away, but my words will never pass away.

The Day and Hour Unknown

³⁶"But about that day or hour no one knows, not even the angels in heaven, nor the Son,*ᵈ* but only the Father. ³⁷As it was in the days of Noah, so it will be at the coming of the Son of Man. ³⁸For in the days before the flood, people were eating and drinking, marrying and giving in marriage, up to the day Noah entered the ark; ³⁹and they knew nothing about what would happen until the flood came and took them all away. That is how it will be at the coming of the Son of Man. ⁴⁰Two men will be in the field; one will be taken and the other left. ⁴¹Two women will be grinding with a hand mill; one will be taken and the other left.

⁴²"Therefore keep watch, because you do not know on what day your Lord will come. ⁴³But understand this: If the owner of the house had known at what time of night the thief was coming, he would have kept watch and would not have let his house be broken into. ⁴⁴So you also must be ready, because the Son of Man will come at an hour when you do not expect him.

⁴⁵"Who then is the faithful and wise servant, whom the master has put in charge of the servants in his household to give them their food at the proper time? ⁴⁶It will be good for that servant whose master finds him doing so when he returns. ⁴⁷Truly I tell you, he will put him in charge of all his possessions. ⁴⁸But suppose that servant is wick-

ed and says to himself, 'My master is staying away a long time,' ⁴⁹and he then begins to beat his fellow servants and to eat and drink with drunkards. ⁵⁰The master of that servant will come on a day when he does not expect him and at an hour he is not aware of. ⁵¹He will cut him to pieces and assign him a place with the hypocrites, where there will be weeping and gnashing of teeth.

The Parable of the Ten Virgins

25 "At that time the kingdom of heaven will be like ten virgins who took their lamps and went out to meet the bridegroom. ²Five of them were foolish and five were wise. ³The foolish ones took their lamps but did not take any oil with them. ⁴The wise ones, however, took oil in jars along with their lamps. ⁵The bridegroom was a long time in coming, and they all became drowsy and fell asleep.

⁶"At midnight the cry rang out: 'Here's the bridegroom! Come out to meet him!'

⁷"Then all the virgins woke up and trimmed their lamps. ⁸The foolish ones said to the wise, 'Give us some of your oil; our lamps are going out.'

⁹"'No,' they replied, 'there may not be enough for both us and you. Instead, go to those who sell oil and buy some for yourselves.'

¹⁰"But while they were on their way to buy the oil, the bridegroom arrived. The virgins who were ready went in with him to the wedding banquet. And the door was shut.

¹¹"Later the others also came. 'Lord, Lord,' they said, 'open the door for us!'

¹²"But he replied, 'Truly I tell you, I don't know you.'

¹³"Therefore keep watch, because you do not know the day or the hour.

The Parable of the Bags of Gold

¹⁴"Again, it will be like a man going on a journey, who called his servants and entrusted his wealth to them. ¹⁵To one he gave five bags of gold, to another two bags, and to another one bag,*ᵉ* each according to his ability. Then he went on his journey. ¹⁶The man who had received five bags of gold went at once and put his money to work and gained five

---

ᵃ 30 Or *the tribes of the land*   *ᵇ 30* See Daniel 7:13-14.   *ᶜ 33* Or *he*   *ᵈ 36* Some manuscripts do not have *nor the Son.*   *ᵉ 15* Greek *five talents . . . two talents . . . one talent*; also throughout this parable; a talent was worth about 20 years of a day laborer's wage.

bags more. [17] So also, the one with two bags of gold gained two more. [18] But the man who had received one bag went off, dug a hole in the ground and hid his master's money.

[19] "After a long time the master of those servants returned and settled accounts with them. [20] The man who had received five bags of gold brought the other five. 'Master,' he said, 'you entrusted me with five bags of gold. See, I have gained five more.'

[21] "His master replied, 'Well done, good and faithful servant! You have been faithful with a few things; I will put you in charge of many things. Come and share your master's happiness!'

[22] "The man with two bags of gold also came. 'Master,' he said, 'you entrusted me with two bags of gold; see, I have gained two more.'

[23] "His master replied, 'Well done, good and faithful servant! You have been faithful with a few things; I will put you in charge of many things. Come and share your master's happiness!'

[24] "Then the man who had received one bag of gold came. 'Master,' he said, 'I knew that you are a hard man, harvesting where you have not sown and gathering where you have not scattered seed. [25] So I was afraid and went out and hid your gold in the ground. See, here is what belongs to you.'

[26] "His master replied, 'You wicked, lazy servant! So you knew that I harvest where I have not sown and gather where I have not scattered seed? [27] Well then, you should have put my money on deposit with the bankers, so that when I returned I would have received it back with interest.

[28] "'So take the bag of gold from him and give it to the one who has ten bags. [29] For whoever has will be given more, and they will have an abundance. Whoever does not have, even what they have will be taken from them. [30] And throw that worthless servant outside, into the darkness, where there will be weeping and gnashing of teeth.'

The Sheep and the Goats

[31] "When the Son of Man comes in his glory, and all the angels with him, he will sit on his glorious throne. [32] All the nations will be gathered before him, and he will separate the people one from another as a shepherd separates the sheep from the goats. [33] He will put the sheep on his right and the goats on his left.

[34] "Then the King will say to those on his right, 'Come, you who are blessed by my Father; take your inheritance, the kingdom prepared for you since the creation of the world. [35] For I was hungry and you gave me something to eat, I was thirsty and you gave me something to drink, I was a stranger and you invited me in, [36] I needed clothes and you clothed me, I was sick and you looked after me, I was in prison and you came to visit me.'

[37] "Then the righteous will answer him, 'Lord, when did we see you hungry and feed you, or thirsty and give you something to drink? [38] When did we see you a stranger and invite you in, or needing clothes and clothe you? [39] When did we see you sick or in prison and go to visit you?'

[40] "The King will reply, 'Truly I tell you, whatever you did for one of the least of these brothers and sisters of mine, you did for me.'

[41] "Then he will say to those on his left, 'Depart from me, you who are cursed, into the eternal fire prepared for the devil and his angels. [42] For I was hungry and you gave me nothing to eat, I was thirsty and you gave me nothing to drink, [43] I was a stranger and you did not invite me in, I needed clothes and you did not clothe me, I was sick and in prison and you did not look after me.'

[44] "They also will answer, 'Lord, when did we see you hungry or thirsty or a stranger or needing clothes or sick or in prison, and did not help you?'

[45] "He will reply, 'Truly I tell you, whatever you did not do for one of the least of these, you did not do for me.'

[46] "Then they will go away to eternal punishment, but the righteous to eternal life."

The Plot Against Jesus

26 When Jesus had finished saying all these things, he said to his disciples, [2] "As you know, the Passover is two days away — and the Son of Man will be handed over to be crucified."

[3] Then the chief priests and the elders of the people assembled in the palace of the high priest, whose name was Caiaphas, [4] and they schemed to arrest Jesus secretly and kill him. [5] "But not during the festival," they said, "or there may be a riot among the people."

GIVE YOUR ALL

READ: MATTHEW 25:21

S uppose someone asked you to invest a sack of gold that was worth something just short of a million dollars. Or maybe two bags. Or five. What wise thing would you do with the money?

That's an important question, because that's roughly the value of the significant sums Jesus describes in Matthew 25. He tells a story of three men. Two wisely invest their master's cash and make more. One buries his master's money in the ground, the equivalent of stashing it in a super-safe vault. When the master returns, the third man earns nothing but condemnation.

While Jesus spins an intriguing story about big money, he isn't giving a lecture on Wall Street investing. His topic is investing your life, as part of a longer teaching about being ready for his return.

Jesus had said that your key task from now until his return is to get busy doing what the Father wants (Matthew 24:46). The lesson of the Parable of the Bags of Gold is that God has entrusted you with something of enormous value—everything that adds up to you. Each person gets a different mix of resources—talent, money, energy—but each should put it all to work for the Lord. When you do that, you can count on the Lord being happy with your work. He will give you even more ways to do well for him.

BUILDING

FAITH

WISDOM

STRENGTH

Jesus Anointed at Bethany

[6] While Jesus was in Bethany in the home of Simon the Leper, [7] a woman came to him with an alabaster jar of very expensive perfume, which she poured on his head as he was reclining at the table.

[8] When the disciples saw this, they were indignant. "Why this waste?" they asked. [9] "This perfume could have been sold at a high price and the money given to the poor."

[10] Aware of this, Jesus said to them, "Why are you bothering this woman? She has done a beautiful thing to me. [11] The poor you will always have with you,[a] but you will not always have me. [12] When she poured this perfume on my body, she did it to prepare me for burial. [13] Truly I tell you, wherever this gospel is preached throughout the world, what she has done will also be told, in memory of her."

Judas Agrees to Betray Jesus

[14] Then one of the Twelve — the one called Judas Iscariot — went to the chief priests [15] and asked, "What are you willing to give me if I deliver him over to you?" So they counted out for him thirty pieces of silver. [16] From then on Judas watched for an opportunity to hand him over.

The Last Supper

[17] On the first day of the Festival of Unleavened Bread, the disciples came to Jesus and asked, "Where do you want us to make preparations for you to eat the Passover?"

[18] He replied, "Go into the city to a certain man and tell him, 'The Teacher says: My appointed time is near. I am going to celebrate the Passover with my disciples at your house.'" [19] So the disciples did as Jesus had directed them and prepared the Passover.

[20] When evening came, Jesus was reclining at the table with the Twelve. [21] And while they were eating, he said, "Truly I tell you, one of you will betray me."

[22] They were very sad and began to say to him one after the other, "Surely you don't mean me, Lord?"

[23] Jesus replied, "The one who has dipped his hand into the bowl with me will betray me. [24] The Son of Man will go just as it is written about him. But woe to that man who betrays the Son of Man! It would be better for him if he had not been born."

[25] Then Judas, the one who would betray him, said, "Surely you don't mean me, Rabbi?"

Jesus answered, "You have said so."

[26] While they were eating, Jesus took bread, and when he had given thanks, he broke it and gave it to his disciples, saying, "Take and eat; this is my body."

[27] Then he took a cup, and when he had given thanks, he gave it to them, saying, "Drink from it, all of you. [28] This is my blood of the[b] covenant, which is poured out for many for the forgiveness of sins. [29] I tell you, I will not drink from this fruit of the vine from now on until that day when I drink it new with you in my Father's kingdom."

[30] When they had sung a hymn, they went out to the Mount of Olives.

Jesus Predicts Peter's Denial

[31] Then Jesus told them, "This very night you will all fall away on account of me, for it is written:

> "'I will strike the shepherd,
>   and the sheep of the flock will be
>   scattered.'[c]

[32] But after I have risen, I will go ahead of you into Galilee."

[33] Peter replied, "Even if all fall away on account of you, I never will."

[34] "Truly I tell you," Jesus answered, "this very night, before the rooster crows, you will disown me three times."

[35] But Peter declared, "Even if I have to die with you, I will never disown you." And all the other disciples said the same.

Gethsemane

[36] Then Jesus went with his disciples to a place called Gethsemane, and he said to them, "Sit here while I go over there and pray." [37] He took Peter and the two sons of Zebedee along with him, and he began to be sorrowful and troubled. [38] Then he said to them, "My soul is overwhelmed with sorrow to the point of death. Stay here and keep watch with me."

[39] Going a little farther, he fell with his face to the ground and prayed, "My Father, if it is

---

[a] 11 See Deut. 15:11.   [b] 28 Some manuscripts *the new*   [c] 31 Zech. 13:7

THIRTY PIECES

READ: **MATTHEW 26:14-15**

J udas Iscariot would have been a "one marshmallow now" kind of guy. He couldn't keep his hand out of the cookie jar.

He betrayed Jesus (the Son of God . . .) for thirty pieces of silver.

His lack of integrity from the get-go says a lot.

Judas' famous betrayal wasn't a spur-of-the-moment mistake. He betrayed Jesus each and every time he took a little something—something for himself from the money pot. And while most of us can't imagine pickpocketing Jesus, we do it all the time in a thousand different ways. We rob God of the glory he demands and deserves by not living up to our full, God-given potential.

BUILDING FAITH WISDOM STRENGTH

No matter how we slice it, sin leaves us with the short end of the stick. Sin always over-promises and under-delivers. Righteousness pays for eternity. Yet we sell out for something now instead of holding out for something better later.

Esau sold his birthright for a bowl of stew.

Samson sold his secret for a one-night stand.

Judas sold his soul for thirty pieces of silver.

What were they thinking? You're right, they weren't. Nothing is more illogical than sin. It's just poor judgment. And we have no alibi, except the cross of Jesus, who is Christ.

It's not worth it, and we know it.

Yet we do it anyway. We sell out for something dead lame, instead of going all in for something so excellent.

Taken from *All In Student Edition* by Mark Batterson and Parker Batterson, copyright © 2014 by Mark Batterson, published by Zondervan.

possible, may this cup be taken from me. Yet not as I will, but as you will."

[40] Then he returned to his disciples and found them sleeping. "Couldn't you men keep watch with me for one hour?" he asked Peter. [41] "Watch and pray so that you will not fall into temptation. The spirit is willing, but the flesh is weak."

[42] He went away a second time and prayed, "My Father, if it is not possible for this cup to be taken away unless I drink it, may your will be done."

[43] When he came back, he again found them sleeping, because their eyes were heavy. [44] So he left them and went away once more and prayed the third time, saying the same thing.

[45] Then he returned to the disciples and said to them, "Are you still sleeping and resting? Look, the hour has come, and the Son of Man is delivered into the hands of sinners. [46] Rise! Let us go! Here comes my betrayer!"

Jesus Arrested

[47] While he was still speaking, Judas, one of the Twelve, arrived. With him was a large crowd armed with swords and clubs, sent from the chief priests and the elders of the people. [48] Now the betrayer had arranged a signal with them: "The one I kiss is the man; arrest him." [49] Going at once to Jesus, Judas said, "Greetings, Rabbi!" and kissed him.

[50] Jesus replied, "Do what you came for, friend."[a]

Then the men stepped forward, seized Jesus and arrested him. [51] With that, one of Jesus' companions reached for his sword, drew it out and struck the servant of the high priest, cutting off his ear.

[52] "Put your sword back in its place," Jesus said to him, "for all who draw the sword will die by the sword. [53] Do you think I cannot call on my Father, and he will at once put at my disposal more than twelve legions of angels? [54] But how then would the Scriptures be fulfilled that say it must happen in this way?"

[55] In that hour Jesus said to the crowd, "Am I leading a rebellion, that you have come out with swords and clubs to capture me? Every day I sat in the temple courts teaching, and you did not arrest me. [56] But this has all taken place that the writings of the prophets might be fulfilled." Then all the disciples deserted him and fled.

Jesus Before the Sanhedrin

[57] Those who had arrested Jesus took him to Caiaphas the high priest, where the teachers of the law and the elders had assembled. [58] But Peter followed him at a distance, right up to the courtyard of the high priest. He entered and sat down with the guards to see the outcome.

[59] The chief priests and the whole Sanhedrin were looking for false evidence against Jesus so that they could put him to death. [60] But they did not find any, though many false witnesses came forward.

Finally two came forward [61] and declared, "This fellow said, 'I am able to destroy the temple of God and rebuild it in three days.'"

[62] Then the high priest stood up and said to Jesus, "Are you not going to answer? What is this testimony that these men are bringing against you?" [63] But Jesus remained silent.

The high priest said to him, "I charge you under oath by the living God: Tell us if you are the Messiah, the Son of God."

[64] "You have said so," Jesus replied. "But I say to all of you: From now on you will see the Son of Man sitting at the right hand of the Mighty One and coming on the clouds of heaven."[b]

[65] Then the high priest tore his clothes and said, "He has spoken blasphemy! Why do we need any more witnesses? Look, now you have heard the blasphemy. [66] What do you think?"

"He is worthy of death," they answered.

[67] Then they spit in his face and struck him with their fists. Others slapped him [68] and said, "Prophesy to us, Messiah. Who hit you?"

Peter Disowns Jesus

[69] Now Peter was sitting out in the courtyard, and a servant girl came to him. "You also were with Jesus of Galilee," she said.

[70] But he denied it before them all. "I don't know what you're talking about," he said.

[71] Then he went out to the gateway, where another servant girl saw him and said to the people there, "This fellow was with Jesus of Nazareth."

---

[a] 50 Or *"Why have you come, friend?"*   [b] 64 See Psalm 110:1; Daniel 7:13.

[72] He denied it again, with an oath: "I don't know the man!"

[73] After a little while, those standing there went up to Peter and said, "Surely you are one of them; your accent gives you away."

[74] Then he began to call down curses, and he swore to them, "I don't know the man!"

Immediately a rooster crowed. [75] Then Peter remembered the word Jesus had spoken: "Before the rooster crows, you will disown me three times." And he went outside and wept bitterly.

Judas Hangs Himself

27 Early in the morning, all the chief priests and the elders of the people made their plans how to have Jesus executed. [2] So they bound him, led him away and handed him over to Pilate the governor.

[3] When Judas, who had betrayed him, saw that Jesus was condemned, he was seized with remorse and returned the thirty pieces of silver to the chief priests and the elders. [4] "I have sinned," he said, "for I have betrayed innocent blood."

"What is that to us?" they replied. "That's your responsibility."

[5] So Judas threw the money into the temple and left. Then he went away and hanged himself.

[6] The chief priests picked up the coins and said, "It is against the law to put this into the treasury, since it is blood money." [7] So they decided to use the money to buy the potter's field as a burial place for foreigners. [8] That is why it has been called the Field of Blood to this day. [9] Then what was spoken by Jeremiah the prophet was fulfilled: "They took the thirty pieces of silver, the price set on him by the people of Israel, [10] and they used them to buy the potter's field, as the Lord commanded me."[a]

Jesus Before Pilate

[11] Meanwhile Jesus stood before the governor, and the governor asked him, "Are you the king of the Jews?"

"You have said so," Jesus replied.

[12] When he was accused by the chief priests and the elders, he gave no answer. [13] Then Pilate asked him, "Don't you hear the testimony they are bringing against you?"

[14] But Jesus made no reply, not even to a single charge — to the great amazement of the governor.

[15] Now it was the governor's custom at the festival to release a prisoner chosen by the crowd. [16] At that time they had a well-known prisoner whose name was Jesus[b] Barabbas. [17] So when the crowd had gathered, Pilate asked them, "Which one do you want me to release to you: Jesus Barabbas, or Jesus who is called the Messiah?" [18] For he knew it was out of self-interest that they had handed Jesus over to him.

[19] While Pilate was sitting on the judge's seat, his wife sent him this message: "Don't have anything to do with that innocent man, for I have suffered a great deal today in a dream because of him."

[20] But the chief priests and the elders persuaded the crowd to ask for Barabbas and to have Jesus executed.

[21] "Which of the two do you want me to release to you?" asked the governor.

"Barabbas," they answered.

[22] "What shall I do, then, with Jesus who is called the Messiah?" Pilate asked.

They all answered, "Crucify him!"

[23] "Why? What crime has he committed?" asked Pilate.

But they shouted all the louder, "Crucify him!"

[24] When Pilate saw that he was getting nowhere, but that instead an uproar was starting, he took water and washed his hands in front of the crowd. "I am innocent of this man's blood," he said. "It is your responsibility!"

[25] All the people answered, "His blood is on us and on our children!"

[26] Then he released Barabbas to them. But he had Jesus flogged, and handed him over to be crucified.

The Soldiers Mock Jesus

[27] Then the governor's soldiers took Jesus into the Praetorium and gathered the whole company of soldiers around him. [28] They stripped him and put a scarlet robe on him, [29] and then twisted together a crown of thorns and set it on his head. They put a staff in his right hand. Then they knelt in front of him and mocked him. "Hail, king of the Jews!" they said. [30] They spit on him, and

---

a 10 See Zech. 11:12,13; Jer. 19:1-13; 32:6-9.   *b* 16 Many manuscripts do not have *Jesus*; also in verse 17.

took the staff and struck him on the head again and again. [31]After they had mocked him, they took off the robe and put his own clothes on him. Then they led him away to crucify him.

The Crucifixion of Jesus

[32]As they were going out, they met a man from Cyrene, named Simon, and they forced him to carry the cross. [33]They came to a place called Golgotha (which means "the place of the skull"). [34]There they offered Jesus wine to drink, mixed with gall; but after tasting it, he refused to drink it. [35]When they had crucified him, they divided up his clothes by casting lots. [36]And sitting down, they kept watch over him there. [37]Above his head they placed the written charge against him: THIS IS JESUS, THE KING OF THE JEWS.

[38]Two rebels were crucified with him, one on his right and one on his left. [39]Those who passed by hurled insults at him, shaking their heads [40]and saying, "You who are going to destroy the temple and build it in three days, save yourself! Come down from the cross, if you are the Son of God!" [41]In the same way the chief priests, the teachers of the law and the elders mocked him. [42]"He saved others," they said, "but he can't save himself! He's the king of Israel! Let him come down now from the cross, and we will believe in him. [43]He trusts in God. Let God rescue him now if he wants him, for he said, 'I am the Son of God.'" [44]In the same way the rebels who were crucified with him also heaped insults on him.

The Death of Jesus

[45]From noon until three in the afternoon darkness came over all the land. [46]About three in the afternoon Jesus cried out in a loud voice, *"Eli, Eli,[a] lema sabachthani?"* (which means "My God, my God, why have you forsaken me?").[b]

[47]When some of those standing there heard this, they said, "He's calling Elijah."

[48]Immediately one of them ran and got a sponge. He filled it with wine vinegar, put it on a staff, and offered it to Jesus to drink. [49]The rest said, "Now leave him alone. Let's see if Elijah comes to save him."

[50]And when Jesus had cried out again in a loud voice, he gave up his spirit.

[51]At that moment the curtain of the temple was torn in two from top to bottom. The earth shook, the rocks split [52]and the tombs broke open. The bodies of many holy people who had died were raised to life. [53]They came out of the tombs after Jesus' resurrection and[c] went into the holy city and appeared to many people.

[54]When the centurion and those with him who were guarding Jesus saw the earthquake and all that had happened, they were terrified, and exclaimed, "Surely he was the Son of God!"

[55]Many women were there, watching from a distance. They had followed Jesus from Galilee to care for his needs. [56]Among them were Mary Magdalene, Mary the mother of James and Joseph,[d] and the mother of Zebedee's sons.

The Burial of Jesus

[57]As evening approached, there came a rich man from Arimathea, named Joseph, who had himself become a disciple of Jesus. [58]Going to Pilate, he asked for Jesus' body, and Pilate ordered that it be given to him. [59]Joseph took the body, wrapped it in a clean linen cloth, [60]and placed it in his own new tomb that he had cut out of the rock. He rolled a big stone in front of the entrance to the tomb and went away. [61]Mary Magdalene and the other Mary were sitting there opposite the tomb.

The Guard at the Tomb

[62]The next day, the one after Preparation Day, the chief priests and the Pharisees went to Pilate. [63]"Sir," they said, "we remember that while he was still alive that deceiver said, 'After three days I will rise again.' [64]So give the order for the tomb to be made secure until the third day. Otherwise, his disciples may come and steal the body and tell the people that he has been raised from the dead. This last deception will be worse than the first."

[65]"Take a guard," Pilate answered. "Go, make the tomb as secure as you know how." [66]So they went and made the tomb secure by

---

[a] 46 Some manuscripts *Eloi, Eloi*   [b] 46 Psalm 22:1   [c] 53 Or *tombs, and after Jesus' resurrection they*
[d] 56 Greek *Joses*, a variant of *Joseph*

PONTIUS PILATE

When Pilate saw that he was getting nowhere, but that instead an uproar was starting, he took water and washed his hands in front of the crowd. "I am innocent of this man's blood," he said. "It is your responsibility!"
MATTHEW 27:24

HIS NAME MEANS: "one armed with a dart (or javelin)"
READ HIS STORY: *Matthew 27:11–26; Mark 15:1–15, 42–46; Luke 23:1–25; John 18:28—19:22*

Pontius Pilate was the Roman governor appointed over Judea from A.D. 26-36. We don't read much about him, except for a passing reference in Luke 3:1, until Jesus' crucifixion. As governor, Pilate was the supreme judge. Normally only he could sentence a criminal to die. According to Roman law, calling yourself king was an act of treason and could be punished by death. So when Jesus went before Pilate, one of the first things Pilate asked was, "Are you the king of the Jews?"

"You have said so," Jesus replied (Matthew 27:11).

Even after hearing the accusations of the chief priests against Jesus, Pilate could tell he was innocent. Plus, Pilate's wife had a dream and sent word to her husband not to "have anything to do with that innocent man" (Matthew 27:19).

Instead of doing the right thing, Pilate allowed the crowd to sway him. The people shouted for Jesus to be crucified. Pilate asked the crowd, "What crime has he committed?" (Matthew 27:23). They didn't listen to reason. They were set on blood and wanted Jesus crucified.

As a final act, Pilate "washed his hands" of Jesus' death. He could've stood firm in his convictions about Jesus, but he went along with the crowd and told the people it was their responsibility (Matthew 27:24).

Pilate will forever be remembered for handing Jesus over to be crucified. But we should also remember him as a leader who failed to step up when pressured by popular opinion.

putting a seal on the stone and posting the guard.

Jesus Has Risen

28 After the Sabbath, at dawn on the first day of the week, Mary Magdalene and the other Mary went to look at the tomb.

²There was a violent earthquake, for an angel of the Lord came down from heaven and, going to the tomb, rolled back the stone and sat on it. ³His appearance was like lightning, and his clothes were white as snow. ⁴The guards were so afraid of him that they shook and became like dead men.

⁵The angel said to the women, "Do not be afraid, for I know that you are looking for Jesus, who was crucified. ⁶He is not here; he has risen, just as he said. Come and see the place where he lay. ⁷Then go quickly and tell his disciples: 'He has risen from the dead and is going ahead of you into Galilee. There you will see him.' Now I have told you."

⁸So the women hurried away from the tomb, afraid yet filled with joy, and ran to tell his disciples. ⁹Suddenly Jesus met them. "Greetings," he said. They came to him, clasped his feet and worshiped him. ¹⁰Then Jesus said to them, "Do not be afraid. Go and tell my brothers to go to Galilee; there they will see me."

The Guards' Report

¹¹While the women were on their way, some of the guards went into the city and reported to the chief priests everything that had happened. ¹²When the chief priests had met with the elders and devised a plan, they gave the soldiers a large sum of money, ¹³telling them, "You are to say, 'His disciples came during the night and stole him away while we were asleep.' ¹⁴If this report gets to the governor, we will satisfy him and keep you out of trouble." ¹⁵So the soldiers took the money and did as they were instructed. And this story has been widely circulated among the Jews to this very day.

The Great Commission

¹⁶Then the eleven disciples went to Galilee, to the mountain where Jesus had told them to go. ¹⁷When they saw him, they worshiped him; but some doubted. ¹⁸Then Jesus came to them and said, "All authority in heaven and on earth has been given to me. ¹⁹Therefore go and make disciples of all nations, baptizing them in the name of the Father and of the Son and of the Holy Spirit, ²⁰and teaching them to obey everything I have commanded you. And surely I am with you always, to the very end of the age."

MARK

WHEN DID THIS HAPPEN?

A.D. 1 to 36 in Palestine

WHO IS IN THIS BOOK?

Jesus

the disciples

Bartimaeus

Pilate

Simon of Cyrene

Joseph of Arimathea

VERSES YOU MIGHT RECOGNIZE

MARK 1:17

"'Come, follow me,' Jesus said, 'and I will send you out to fish for people.'"

MARK 16:15

"Go into all the world and preach the good news to all creation."

WHAT'S IT ABOUT?

The second of the synoptic gospels, the book of Mark jumps right into the action, skipping the story of Jesus' birth and going straight to the start of his ministry. Like an action movie, Mark is fast-paced, covering Jesus' miracles and the most important events of his life, death and resurrection.

Mark wrote for a non-Jewish audience, so he didn't include the prophecies that Matthew did. Even someone who hadn't read the Old Testament could easily see that Jesus was God from the miracles he performed. Mark, who is mentioned in the book of Acts, got his information from the disciple Peter.

Where Matthew's gospel portrays Jesus as Messiah and King, Mark's gospel portrays him as the ultimate servant. It shows him serving the poor, the sick, and even children. He would serve humanity by paying the ultimate price, giving "his life as a ransom for many" (Mark 10:45). His death and resurrection would change everything, freeing those who believe from the bondage of their sin.

MARK

John the Baptist Prepares the Way

1 The beginning of the good news about Jesus the Messiah,[a] the Son of God,[b] [2] as it is written in Isaiah the prophet:

"I will send my messenger ahead of you,
who will prepare your way"[c] —
[3] "a voice of one calling in the wilderness,
'Prepare the way for the Lord,
make straight paths for him.'"[d]

[4] And so John the Baptist appeared in the wilderness, preaching a baptism of repentance for the forgiveness of sins. [5] The whole Judean countryside and all the people of Jerusalem went out to him. Confessing their sins, they were baptized by him in the Jordan River. [6] John wore clothing made of camel's hair, with a leather belt around his waist, and he ate locusts and wild honey. [7] And this was his message: "After me comes the one more powerful than I, the straps of whose sandals I am not worthy to stoop down and untie. [8] I baptize you with[e] water, but he will baptize you with[e] the Holy Spirit."

The Baptism and Testing of Jesus

[9] At that time Jesus came from Nazareth in Galilee and was baptized by John in the Jordan. [10] Just as Jesus was coming up out of the water, he saw heaven being torn open and the Spirit descending on him like a dove. [11] And a voice came from heaven: "You are my Son, whom I love; with you I am well pleased."

[12] At once the Spirit sent him out into the wilderness, [13] and he was in the wilderness forty days, being tempted[f] by Satan. He was with the wild animals, and angels attended him.

Jesus Announces the Good News

[14] After John was put in prison, Jesus went into Galilee, proclaiming the good news of God. [15] "The time has come," he said. "The kingdom of God has come near. Repent and believe the good news!"

Jesus Calls His First Disciples

[16] As Jesus walked beside the Sea of Galilee, he saw Simon and his brother Andrew casting a net into the lake, for they were fishermen. [17] "Come, follow me," Jesus said, "and I will send you out to fish for people." [18] At once they left their nets and followed him.

[19] When he had gone a little farther, he saw James son of Zebedee and his brother John in a boat, preparing their nets. [20] Without delay he called them, and they left their father Zebedee in the boat with the hired men and followed him.

Jesus Drives Out an Impure Spirit

[21] They went to Capernaum, and when the Sabbath came, Jesus went into the synagogue and began to teach. [22] The people were amazed at his teaching, because he taught them as one who had authority, not as the teachers of the law. [23] Just then a man in their synagogue who was possessed by an impure spirit cried out, [24] "What do you want with us, Jesus of Nazareth? Have you come to destroy us? I know who you are — the Holy One of God!"

[25] "Be quiet!" said Jesus sternly. "Come out of him!" [26] The impure spirit shook the man violently and came out of him with a shriek.

[27] The people were all so amazed that they asked each other, "What is this? A new teaching — and with authority! He even gives orders to impure spirits and they obey him." [28] News about him spread quickly over the whole region of Galilee.

Jesus Heals Many

[29] As soon as they left the synagogue, they went with James and John to the home of

---

[a] 1 Or *Jesus Christ. Messiah* (Hebrew) and *Christ* (Greek) both mean *Anointed One.*   [b] 1 Some manuscripts do not have *the Son of God.*   [c] 2 Mal. 3:1   [d] 3 Isaiah 40:3   [e] 8 Or *in*   [f] 13 The Greek for *tempted* can also mean *tested.*

TIME TO FOLLOW

READ: MARK 1:16-20

Many have made a decision to believe in Jesus without making a commitment to follow Jesus. The gospel allows for no such distinction. Biblical belief is more than just accepting something as fact in your mind or saying the right things.

We tend to define belief as the acceptance of something as real or true. But biblical belief is more than just an intellectual acceptance or a heartfelt acknowledgment; it is a commitment to follow. *Following* by definition requires more than a decision you make in your head while sitting in a pew; *following* calls for movement. Our churches sometimes have separated the message of "believe" from the message of "follow." After separating the two messages, they get out of balance.

BUILDING

FAITH

WISDOM

STRENGTH

If you read through the four Gospels that tell of Christ's life, you'll find that Jesus says "Believe in me" about five times. But care to guess how many times Jesus said "Follow me"? About twenty times. Now I'm not saying that following is more important than believing. What I am saying is that the two are firmly connected. They are the heart and lungs of faith. One can't live without the other. If you try and separate the message of *follow* from the message of *believe*, belief dies in the process. Our churches will continue to be full of fans rather than followers, until we bring together these words that should never have been separated to begin with. Following is part of believing. To truly believe is to follow.

Simon and Andrew. ³⁰Simon's mother-in-law was in bed with a fever, and they immediately told Jesus about her. ³¹So he went to her, took her hand and helped her up. The fever left her and she began to wait on them.

³²That evening after sunset the people brought to Jesus all the sick and demon-possessed. ³³The whole town gathered at the door, ³⁴and Jesus healed many who had various diseases. He also drove out many demons, but he would not let the demons speak because they knew who he was.

Jesus Prays in a Solitary Place

³⁵Very early in the morning, while it was still dark, Jesus got up, left the house and went off to a solitary place, where he prayed. ³⁶Simon and his companions went to look for him, ³⁷and when they found him, they exclaimed: "Everyone is looking for you!"

³⁸Jesus replied, "Let us go somewhere else — to the nearby villages — so I can preach there also. That is why I have come." ³⁹So he traveled throughout Galilee, preaching in their synagogues and driving out demons.

Jesus Heals a Man With Leprosy

⁴⁰A man with leprosy*ᵃ* came to him and begged him on his knees, "If you are willing, you can make me clean."

⁴¹Jesus was indignant.*ᵇ* He reached out his hand and touched the man. "I am willing," he said. "Be clean!" ⁴²Immediately the leprosy left him and he was cleansed.

⁴³Jesus sent him away at once with a strong warning: ⁴⁴"See that you don't tell this to anyone. But go, show yourself to the priest and offer the sacrifices that Moses commanded for your cleansing, as a testimony to them." ⁴⁵Instead he went out and began to talk freely, spreading the news. As a result, Jesus could no longer enter a town openly but stayed outside in lonely places. Yet the people still came to him from everywhere.

Jesus Forgives and Heals a Paralyzed Man

2 A few days later, when Jesus again entered Capernaum, the people heard that he had come home. ²They gathered in such large numbers that there was no room left, not even outside the door, and he preached the word to them. ³Some men came, bringing to him a paralyzed man, carried by four of them. ⁴Since they could not get him to Jesus because of the crowd, they made an opening in the roof above Jesus by digging through it and then lowered the mat the man was lying on. ⁵When Jesus saw their faith, he said to the paralyzed man, "Son, your sins are forgiven."

⁶Now some teachers of the law were sitting there, thinking to themselves, ⁷"Why does this fellow talk like that? He's blaspheming! Who can forgive sins but God alone?"

⁸Immediately Jesus knew in his spirit that this was what they were thinking in their hearts, and he said to them, "Why are you thinking these things? ⁹Which is easier: to say to this paralyzed man, 'Your sins are forgiven,' or to say, 'Get up, take your mat and walk'? ¹⁰But I want you to know that the Son of Man has authority on earth to forgive sins." So he said to the man, ¹¹"I tell you, get up, take your mat and go home." ¹²He got up, took his mat and walked out in full view of them all. This amazed everyone and they praised God, saying, "We have never seen anything like this!"

Jesus Calls Levi and Eats With Sinners

¹³Once again Jesus went out beside the lake. A large crowd came to him, and he began to teach them. ¹⁴As he walked along, he saw Levi son of Alphaeus sitting at the tax collector's booth. "Follow me," Jesus told him, and Levi got up and followed him.

¹⁵While Jesus was having dinner at Levi's house, many tax collectors and sinners were eating with him and his disciples, for there were many who followed him. ¹⁶When the teachers of the law who were Pharisees saw him eating with the sinners and tax collectors, they asked his disciples: "Why does he eat with tax collectors and sinners?"

¹⁷On hearing this, Jesus said to them, "It is not the healthy who need a doctor, but the sick. I have not come to call the righteous, but sinners."

ᵃ 40 The Greek word traditionally translated *leprosy* was used for various diseases affecting the skin.
ᵇ 41 Many manuscripts *Jesus was filled with compassion*

ACCEPTING GOD'S HELP

READ: **MARK 2:17**

Suppose you were a doctor dropped into the rubble of a natural catastrophe. As you survey countless injured and dying, you stumble on a group that eyes you suspiciously. They're as badly wounded as everyone else, but they claim they don't need your care. When they reject your treatment, you wouldn't hesitate to move on to others begging for help.

That's the scene in Mark 2. Jesus had just called a follower named Levi, better known as Matthew. He was a despised tax collector, hated not only for cheating fellow citizens but also for collaborating with the Romans who occupied Israel. Everyone regarded Levi as one of the worst sinners of his day, yet Jesus didn't shy away from dining with him. It flashed a powerful sign of acceptance and fellowship.

BUILDING

FAITH

WISDOM

STRENGTH

The Pharisees couldn't understand why Jesus ate with sinners. They didn't want to join up with Jesus as friends. And they certainly weren't eager to obey his teachings. Jesus didn't get hung up on their criticisms. Those religious rule keepers were like dying people living in denial of their condition. They could pretend to be well, but they were as needy as everyone else.

The Lord comes to people who recognize they have problems. If you're honest, you realize that's all of us. But you have to want his help.

Jesus Questioned About Fasting

[18] Now John's disciples and the Pharisees were fasting. Some people came and asked Jesus, "How is it that John's disciples and the disciples of the Pharisees are fasting, but yours are not?"

[19] Jesus answered, "How can the guests of the bridegroom fast while he is with them? They cannot, so long as they have him with them. [20] But the time will come when the bridegroom will be taken from them, and on that day they will fast.

[21] "No one sews a patch of unshrunk cloth on an old garment. Otherwise, the new piece will pull away from the old, making the tear worse. [22] And no one pours new wine into old wineskins. Otherwise, the wine will burst the skins, and both the wine and the wineskins will be ruined. No, they pour new wine into new wineskins."

Jesus Is Lord of the Sabbath

[23] One Sabbath Jesus was going through the grainfields, and as his disciples walked along, they began to pick some heads of grain. [24] The Pharisees said to him, "Look, why are they doing what is unlawful on the Sabbath?"

[25] He answered, "Have you never read what David did when he and his companions were hungry and in need? [26] In the days of Abiathar the high priest, he entered the house of God and ate the consecrated bread, which is lawful only for priests to eat. And he also gave some to his companions."

[27] Then he said to them, "The Sabbath was made for man, not man for the Sabbath. [28] So the Son of Man is Lord even of the Sabbath."

Jesus Heals on the Sabbath

3 Another time Jesus went into the synagogue, and a man with a shriveled hand was there. [2] Some of them were looking for a reason to accuse Jesus, so they watched him closely to see if he would heal him on the Sabbath. [3] Jesus said to the man with the shriveled hand, "Stand up in front of everyone."

[4] Then Jesus asked them, "Which is lawful on the Sabbath: to do good or to do evil, to save life or to kill?" But they remained silent.

[5] He looked around at them in anger and,

deeply distressed at their stubborn hearts, said to the man, "Stretch out your hand." He stretched it out, and his hand was completely restored. [6] Then the Pharisees went out and began to plot with the Herodians how they might kill Jesus.

Crowds Follow Jesus

[7] Jesus withdrew with his disciples to the lake, and a large crowd from Galilee followed. [8] When they heard about all he was doing, many people came to him from Judea, Jerusalem, Idumea, and the regions across the Jordan and around Tyre and Sidon. [9] Because of the crowd he told his disciples to have a small boat ready for him, to keep the people from crowding him. [10] For he had healed many, so that those with diseases were pushing forward to touch him. [11] Whenever the impure spirits saw him, they fell down before him and cried out, "You are the Son of God." [12] But he gave them strict orders not to tell others about him.

Jesus Appoints the Twelve

[13] Jesus went up on a mountainside and called to him those he wanted, and they came to him. [14] He appointed twelve[a] that they might be with him and that he might send them out to preach [15] and to have authority to drive out demons. [16] These are the twelve he appointed: Simon (to whom he gave the name Peter), [17] James son of Zebedee and his brother John (to them he gave the name Boanerges, which means "sons of thunder"), [18] Andrew, Philip, Bartholomew, Matthew, Thomas, James son of Alphaeus, Thaddaeus, Simon the Zealot [19] and Judas Iscariot, who betrayed him.

Jesus Accused by His Family and by Teachers of the Law

[20] Then Jesus entered a house, and again a crowd gathered, so that he and his disciples were not even able to eat. [21] When his family[b] heard about this, they went to take charge of him, for they said, "He is out of his mind."

[22] And the teachers of the law who came down from Jerusalem said, "He is possessed by Beelzebul! By the prince of demons he is driving out demons."

[23] So Jesus called them over to him and

---

[a] 14 Some manuscripts *twelve—designating them apostles—*   [b] 21 Or *his associates*

began to speak to them in parables: "How can Satan drive out Satan? ²⁴If a kingdom is divided against itself, that kingdom cannot stand. ²⁵If a house is divided against itself, that house cannot stand. ²⁶And if Satan opposes himself and is divided, he cannot stand; his end has come. ²⁷In fact, no one can enter a strong man's house without first tying him up. Then he can plunder the strong man's house. ²⁸Truly I tell you, people can be forgiven all their sins and every slander they utter, ²⁹but whoever blasphemes against the Holy Spirit will never be forgiven; they are guilty of an eternal sin."

³⁰He said this because they were saying, "He has an impure spirit."

³¹Then Jesus' mother and brothers arrived. Standing outside, they sent someone in to call him. ³²A crowd was sitting around him, and they told him, "Your mother and brothers are outside looking for you."

³³"Who are my mother and my brothers?" he asked.

³⁴Then he looked at those seated in a circle around him and said, "Here are my mother and my brothers! ³⁵Whoever does God's will is my brother and sister and mother."

The Parable of the Sower

4 Again Jesus began to teach by the lake. The crowd that gathered around him was so large that he got into a boat and sat in it out on the lake, while all the people were along the shore at the water's edge. ²He taught them many things by parables, and in his teaching said: ³"Listen! A farmer went out to sow his seed. ⁴As he was scattering the seed, some fell along the path, and the birds came and ate it up. ⁵Some fell on rocky places, where it did not have much soil. It sprang up quickly, because the soil was shallow. ⁶But when the sun came up, the plants were scorched, and they withered because they had no root. ⁷Other seed fell among thorns, which grew up and choked the plants, so that they did not bear grain. ⁸Still other seed fell on good soil. It came up, grew and produced a crop, some multiplying thirty, some sixty, some a hundred times."

⁹Then Jesus said, "Whoever has ears to hear, let them hear."

¹⁰When he was alone, the Twelve and the others around him asked him about the parables. ¹¹He told them, "The secret of the kingdom of God has been given to you. But to those on the outside everything is said in parables ¹²so that,

"'they may be ever seeing but never
        perceiving,
    and ever hearing but never
        understanding;
otherwise they might turn and be
        forgiven!'ᵃ

¹³Then Jesus said to them, "Don't you understand this parable? How then will you understand any parable? ¹⁴The farmer sows the word. ¹⁵Some people are like seed along the path, where the word is sown. As soon as they hear it, Satan comes and takes away the word that was sown in them. ¹⁶Others, like seed sown on rocky places, hear the word and at once receive it with joy. ¹⁷But since they have no root, they last only a short time. When trouble or persecution comes because of the word, they quickly fall away. ¹⁸Still others, like seed sown among thorns, hear the word; ¹⁹but the worries of this life, the deceitfulness of wealth and the desires for other things come in and choke the word, making it unfruitful. ²⁰Others, like seed sown on good soil, hear the word, accept it, and produce a crop — some thirty, some sixty, some a hundred times what was sown."

A Lamp on a Stand

²¹He said to them, "Do you bring in a lamp to put it under a bowl or a bed? Instead, don't you put it on its stand? ²²For whatever is hidden is meant to be disclosed, and whatever is concealed is meant to be brought out into the open. ²³If anyone has ears to hear, let them hear."

²⁴"Consider carefully what you hear," he continued. "With the measure you use, it will be measured to you — and even more. ²⁵Whoever has will be given more; whoever does not have, even what they have will be taken from them."

The Parable of the Growing Seed

²⁶He also said, "This is what the kingdom of God is like. A man scatters seed on the ground. ²⁷Night and day, whether he sleeps

---

ᵃ 12 Isaiah 6:9,10

or gets up, the seed sprouts and grows, though he does not know how. [28]All by itself the soil produces grain—first the stalk, then the head, then the full kernel in the head. [29]As soon as the grain is ripe, he puts the sickle to it, because the harvest has come."

The Parable of the Mustard Seed

[30]Again he said, "What shall we say the kingdom of God is like, or what parable shall we use to describe it? [31]It is like a mustard seed, which is the smallest of all seeds on earth. [32]Yet when planted, it grows and becomes the largest of all garden plants, with such big branches that the birds can perch in its shade."

[33]With many similar parables Jesus spoke the word to them, as much as they could understand. [34]He did not say anything to them without using a parable. But when he was alone with his own disciples, he explained everything.

Jesus Calms the Storm

[35]That day when evening came, he said to his disciples, "Let us go over to the other side." [36]Leaving the crowd behind, they took him along, just as he was, in the boat. There were also other boats with him. [37]A furious squall came up, and the waves broke over the boat, so that it was nearly swamped. [38]Jesus was in the stern, sleeping on a cushion. The disciples woke him and said to him, "Teacher, don't you care if we drown?"

[39]He got up, rebuked the wind and said to the waves, "Quiet! Be still!" Then the wind died down and it was completely calm.

[40]He said to his disciples, "Why are you so afraid? Do you still have no faith?"

[41]They were terrified and asked each other, "Who is this? Even the wind and the waves obey him!"

Jesus Restores a Demon-Possessed Man

5 They went across the lake to the region of the Gerasenes.[a] [2]When Jesus got out of the boat, a man with an impure spirit came from the tombs to meet him. [3]This man lived in the tombs, and no one could bind him anymore, not even with a chain. [4]For he had often been chained hand and foot, but he tore the chains apart and broke the irons on his feet. No one was strong enough to subdue him. [5]Night and day among the tombs and in the hills he would cry out and cut himself with stones.

[6]When he saw Jesus from a distance, he ran and fell on his knees in front of him. [7]He shouted at the top of his voice, "What do you want with me, Jesus, Son of the Most High God? In God's name don't torture me!" [8]For Jesus had said to him, "Come out of this man, you impure spirit!"

[9]Then Jesus asked him, "What is your name?"

"My name is Legion," he replied, "for we are many." [10]And he begged Jesus again and again not to send them out of the area.

[11]A large herd of pigs was feeding on the nearby hillside. [12]The demons begged Jesus, "Send us among the pigs; allow us to go into them." [13]He gave them permission, and the impure spirits came out and went into the pigs. The herd, about two thousand in number, rushed down the steep bank into the lake and were drowned.

[14]Those tending the pigs ran off and reported this in the town and countryside, and the people went out to see what had happened. [15]When they came to Jesus, they saw the man who had been possessed by the legion of demons, sitting there, dressed and in his right mind; and they were afraid. [16]Those who had seen it told the people what had happened to the demon-possessed man—and told about the pigs as well. [17]Then the people began to plead with Jesus to leave their region.

[18]As Jesus was getting into the boat, the man who had been demon-possessed begged to go with him. [19]Jesus did not let him, but said, "Go home to your own people and tell them how much the Lord has done for you, and how he has had mercy on you." [20]So the man went away and began to tell in the Decapolis[b] how much Jesus had done for him. And all the people were amazed.

Jesus Raises a Dead Girl and Heals a Sick Woman

[21]When Jesus had again crossed over by boat to the other side of the lake, a large crowd gathered around him while he was by

---

[a] 1 Some manuscripts *Gadarenes*; other manuscripts *Gergesenes*   [b] 20 That is, the Ten Cities

the lake. [22] Then one of the synagogue leaders, named Jairus, came, and when he saw Jesus, he fell at his feet. [23] He pleaded earnestly with him, "My little daughter is dying. Please come and put your hands on her so that she will be healed and live." [24] So Jesus went with him.

A large crowd followed and pressed around him. [25] And a woman was there who had been subject to bleeding for twelve years. [26] She had suffered a great deal under the care of many doctors and had spent all she had, yet instead of getting better she grew worse. [27] When she heard about Jesus, she came up behind him in the crowd and touched his cloak, [28] because she thought, "If I just touch his clothes, I will be healed." [29] Immediately her bleeding stopped and she felt in her body that she was freed from her suffering.

[30] At once Jesus realized that power had gone out from him. He turned around in the crowd and asked, "Who touched my clothes?"

[31] "You see the people crowding against you," his disciples answered, "and yet you can ask, 'Who touched me?'"

[32] But Jesus kept looking around to see who had done it. [33] Then the woman, knowing what had happened to her, came and fell at his feet and, trembling with fear, told him the whole truth. [34] He said to her, "Daughter, your faith has healed you. Go in peace and be freed from your suffering."

[35] While Jesus was still speaking, some people came from the house of Jairus, the synagogue leader. "Your daughter is dead," they said. "Why bother the teacher anymore?"

[36] Overhearing[a] what they said, Jesus told him, "Don't be afraid; just believe."

[37] He did not let anyone follow him except Peter, James and John the brother of James. [38] When they came to the home of the synagogue leader, Jesus saw a commotion, with people crying and wailing loudly. [39] He went in and said to them, "Why all this commotion and wailing? The child is not dead but asleep." [40] But they laughed at him.

After he put them all out, he took the child's father and mother and the disciples who were with him, and went in where the child was. [41] He took her by the hand and said to her, *"Talitha koum!"* (which means "Little girl, I say to you, get up!"). [42] Immediately the girl stood up and began to walk around (she was twelve years old). At this they were completely astonished. [43] He gave strict orders not to let anyone know about this, and told them to give her something to eat.

A Prophet Without Honor

6 Jesus left there and went to his hometown, accompanied by his disciples. [2] When the Sabbath came, he began to teach in the synagogue, and many who heard him were amazed.

"Where did this man get these things?" they asked. "What's this wisdom that has been given him? What are these remarkable miracles he is performing? [3] Isn't this the carpenter? Isn't this Mary's son and the brother of James, Joseph,[b] Judas and Simon? Aren't his sisters here with us?" And they took offense at him.

[4] Jesus said to them, "A prophet is not without honor except in his own town, among his relatives and in his own home." [5] He could not do any miracles there, except lay his hands on a few sick people and heal them. [6] He was amazed at their lack of faith.

Jesus Sends Out the Twelve

Then Jesus went around teaching from village to village. [7] Calling the Twelve to him, he began to send them out two by two and gave them authority over impure spirits.

[8] These were his instructions: "Take nothing for the journey except a staff—no bread, no bag, no money in your belts. [9] Wear sandals but not an extra shirt. [10] Whenever you enter a house, stay there until you leave that town. [11] And if any place will not welcome you or listen to you, leave that place and shake the dust off your feet as a testimony against them."

[12] They went out and preached that people should repent. [13] They drove out many demons and anointed many sick people with oil and healed them.

John the Baptist Beheaded

[14] King Herod heard about this, for Jesus' name had become well known. Some were saying,[c] "John the Baptist has been raised

---

[a] 36 Or *Ignoring*   [b] 3 Greek *Joses,* a variant of *Joseph*   [c] 14 Some early manuscripts *He was saying*

from the dead, and that is why miraculous powers are at work in him."

¹⁵ Others said, "He is Elijah."

And still others claimed, "He is a prophet, like one of the prophets of long ago."

¹⁶ But when Herod heard this, he said, "John, whom I beheaded, has been raised from the dead!"

¹⁷ For Herod himself had given orders to have John arrested, and he had him bound and put in prison. He did this because of Herodias, his brother Philip's wife, whom he had married. ¹⁸ For John had been saying to Herod, "It is not lawful for you to have your brother's wife." ¹⁹ So Herodias nursed a grudge against John and wanted to kill him. But she was not able to, ²⁰ because Herod feared John and protected him, knowing him to be a righteous and holy man. When Herod heard John, he was greatly puzzled[a]; yet he liked to listen to him.

²¹ Finally the opportune time came. On his birthday Herod gave a banquet for his high officials and military commanders and the leading men of Galilee. ²² When the daughter of[b] Herodias came in and danced, she pleased Herod and his dinner guests.

The king said to the girl, "Ask me for anything you want, and I'll give it to you." ²³ And he promised her with an oath, "Whatever you ask I will give you, up to half my kingdom."

²⁴ She went out and said to her mother, "What shall I ask for?"

"The head of John the Baptist," she answered.

²⁵ At once the girl hurried in to the king with the request: "I want you to give me right now the head of John the Baptist on a platter."

²⁶ The king was greatly distressed, but because of his oaths and his dinner guests, he did not want to refuse her. ²⁷ So he immediately sent an executioner with orders to bring John's head. The man went, beheaded John in the prison, ²⁸ and brought back his head on a platter. He presented it to the girl, and she gave it to her mother. ²⁹ On hearing of this, John's disciples came and took his body and laid it in a tomb.

Jesus Feeds the Five Thousand

³⁰ The apostles gathered around Jesus and reported to him all they had done and taught. ³¹ Then, because so many people were coming and going that they did not even have a chance to eat, he said to them, "Come with me by yourselves to a quiet place and get some rest."

³² So they went away by themselves in a boat to a solitary place. ³³ But many who saw them leaving recognized them and ran on foot from all the towns and got there ahead of them. ³⁴ When Jesus landed and saw a large crowd, he had compassion on them, because they were like sheep without a shepherd. So he began teaching them many things.

³⁵ By this time it was late in the day, so his disciples came to him. "This is a remote place," they said, "and it's already very late. ³⁶ Send the people away so that they can go to the surrounding countryside and villages and buy themselves something to eat." ³⁷ But he answered, "You give them something to eat."

They said to him, "That would take more than half a year's wages[c]! Are we to go and spend that much on bread and give it to them to eat?"

³⁸ "How many loaves do you have?" he asked. "Go and see."

When they found out, they said, "Five—and two fish."

³⁹ Then Jesus directed them to have all the people sit down in groups on the green grass. ⁴⁰ So they sat down in groups of hundreds and fifties. ⁴¹ Taking the five loaves and the two fish and looking up to heaven, he gave thanks and broke the loaves. Then he gave them to his disciples to distribute to the people. He also divided the two fish among them all. ⁴² They all ate and were satisfied, ⁴³ and the disciples picked up twelve basketfuls of broken pieces of bread and fish. ⁴⁴ The number of the men who had eaten was five thousand.

Jesus Walks on the Water

⁴⁵ Immediately Jesus made his disciples get into the boat and go on ahead of him to Bethsaida, while he dismissed the crowd. ⁴⁶ After leaving them, he went up on a mountainside to pray.

⁴⁷ Later that night, the boat was in the middle of the lake, and he was alone on land. ⁴⁸ He saw the disciples straining at the oars,

---

[a] 20 Some early manuscripts *he did many things* [b] 22 Some early manuscripts *When his daughter*
[c] 37 Greek *take two hundred denarii*

because the wind was against them. Shortly before dawn he went out to them, walking on the lake. He was about to pass by them, [49]but when they saw him walking on the lake, they thought he was a ghost. They cried out, [50]because they all saw him and were terrified.

Immediately he spoke to them and said, "Take courage! It is I. Don't be afraid." [51]Then he climbed into the boat with them, and the wind died down. They were completely amazed, [52]for they had not understood about the loaves; their hearts were hardened.

[53]When they had crossed over, they landed at Gennesaret and anchored there. [54]As soon as they got out of the boat, people recognized Jesus. [55]They ran throughout that whole region and carried the sick on mats to wherever they heard he was. [56]And wherever he went — into villages, towns or countryside — they placed the sick in the marketplaces. They begged him to let them touch even the edge of his cloak, and all who touched it were healed.

That Which Defiles

7 The Pharisees and some of the teachers of the law who had come from Jerusalem gathered around Jesus [2]and saw some of his disciples eating food with hands that were defiled, that is, unwashed. [3](The Pharisees and all the Jews do not eat unless they give their hands a ceremonial washing, holding to the tradition of the elders. [4]When they come from the marketplace they do not eat unless they wash. And they observe many other traditions, such as the washing of cups, pitchers and kettles.[a])

[5]So the Pharisees and teachers of the law asked Jesus, "Why don't your disciples live according to the tradition of the elders instead of eating their food with defiled hands?"

[6]He replied, "Isaiah was right when he prophesied about you hypocrites; as it is written:

"'These people honor me with their lips,
  but their hearts are far from me.
[7]They worship me in vain;
  their teachings are merely human
    rules.'[b]

[8]You have let go of the commands of God and are holding on to human traditions."

[9]And he continued, "You have a fine way of setting aside the commands of God in order to observe[c] your own traditions! [10]For Moses said, 'Honor your father and mother,'[d] and, 'Anyone who curses their father or mother is to be put to death.'[e] [11]But you say that if anyone declares that what might have been used to help their father or mother is Corban (that is, devoted to God) — [12]then you no longer let them do anything for their father or mother. [13]Thus you nullify the word of God by your tradition that you have handed down. And you do many things like that."

[14]Again Jesus called the crowd to him and said, "Listen to me, everyone, and understand this. [15]Nothing outside a person can defile them by going into them. Rather, it is what comes out of a person that defiles them." [16][f]

[17]After he had left the crowd and entered the house, his disciples asked him about this parable. [18]"Are you so dull?" he asked. "Don't you see that nothing that enters a person from the outside can defile them? [19]For it doesn't go into their heart but into their stomach, and then out of the body." (In saying this, Jesus declared all foods clean.)

[20]He went on: "What comes out of a person is what defiles them. [21]For it is from within, out of a person's heart, that evil thoughts come — sexual immorality, theft, murder, [22]adultery, greed, malice, deceit, lewdness, envy, slander, arrogance and folly. [23]All these evils come from inside and defile a person."

Jesus Honors a Syrophoenician Woman's Faith

[24]Jesus left that place and went to the vicinity of Tyre.[g] He entered a house and did not want anyone to know it; yet he could not keep his presence secret. [25]In fact, as soon as she heard about him, a woman whose little daughter was possessed by an impure spirit came and fell at his feet. [26]The woman was a Greek, born in Syrian Phoenicia. She begged Jesus to drive the demon out of her daughter.

[27]"First let the children eat all they want,"

---

[a] 4 Some early manuscripts *pitchers, kettles and dining couches*   [b] 6,7 Isaiah 29:13   [c] 9 Some manuscripts *set up*   [d] 10 Exodus 20:12; Deut. 5:16   [e] 10 Exodus 21:17; Lev. 20:9   [f] 16 Some manuscripts include here the words of 4:23.   [g] 24 Many early manuscripts *Tyre and Sidon*

he told her, "for it is not right to take the children's bread and toss it to the dogs."

²⁸"Lord," she replied, "even the dogs under the table eat the children's crumbs."

²⁹Then he told her, "For such a reply, you may go; the demon has left your daughter."

³⁰She went home and found her child lying on the bed, and the demon gone.

Jesus Heals a Deaf and Mute Man

³¹Then Jesus left the vicinity of Tyre and went through Sidon, down to the Sea of Galilee and into the region of the Decapolis.ᵃ ³²There some people brought to him a man who was deaf and could hardly talk, and they begged Jesus to place his hand on him.

³³After he took him aside, away from the crowd, Jesus put his fingers into the man's ears. Then he spit and touched the man's tongue. ³⁴He looked up to heaven and with a deep sigh said to him, *"Ephphatha!"* (which means "Be opened!"). ³⁵At this, the man's ears were opened, his tongue was loosened and he began to speak plainly.

³⁶Jesus commanded them not to tell anyone. But the more he did so, the more they kept talking about it. ³⁷People were overwhelmed with amazement. "He has done everything well," they said. "He even makes the deaf hear and the mute speak."

Jesus Feeds the Four Thousand

8 During those days another large crowd gathered. Since they had nothing to eat, Jesus called his disciples to him and said, ²"I have compassion for these people; they have already been with me three days and have nothing to eat. ³If I send them home hungry, they will collapse on the way, because some of them have come a long distance."

⁴His disciples answered, "But where in this remote place can anyone get enough bread to feed them?"

⁵"How many loaves do you have?" Jesus asked.

"Seven," they replied.

⁶He told the crowd to sit down on the ground. When he had taken the seven loaves and given thanks, he broke them and gave them to his disciples to distribute to the people, and they did so. ⁷They had a few small fish as well; he gave thanks for them also and

told the disciples to distribute them. ⁸The people ate and were satisfied. Afterward the disciples picked up seven basketfuls of broken pieces that were left over. ⁹About four thousand were present. After he had sent them away, ¹⁰he got into the boat with his disciples and went to the region of Dalmanutha.

¹¹The Pharisees came and began to question Jesus. To test him, they asked him for a sign from heaven. ¹²He sighed deeply and said, "Why does this generation ask for a sign? Truly I tell you, no sign will be given to it." ¹³Then he left them, got back into the boat and crossed to the other side.

The Yeast of the Pharisees and Herod

¹⁴The disciples had forgotten to bring bread, except for one loaf they had with them in the boat. ¹⁵"Be careful," Jesus warned them. "Watch out for the yeast of the Pharisees and that of Herod."

¹⁶They discussed this with one another and said, "It is because we have no bread."

¹⁷Aware of their discussion, Jesus asked them: "Why are you talking about having no bread? Do you still not see or understand? Are your hearts hardened? ¹⁸Do you have eyes but fail to see, and ears but fail to hear? And don't you remember? ¹⁹When I broke the five loaves for the five thousand, how many basketfuls of pieces did you pick up?"

"Twelve," they replied.

²⁰"And when I broke the seven loaves for the four thousand, how many basketfuls of pieces did you pick up?"

They answered, "Seven."

²¹He said to them, "Do you still not understand?"

Jesus Heals a Blind Man at Bethsaida

²²They came to Bethsaida, and some people brought a blind man and begged Jesus to touch him. ²³He took the blind man by the hand and led him outside the village. When he had spit on the man's eyes and put his hands on him, Jesus asked, "Do you see anything?"

²⁴He looked up and said, "I see people; they look like trees walking around."

²⁵Once more Jesus put his hands on the man's eyes. Then his eyes were opened, his

---

ᵃ 31 That is, the Ten Cities

BRAND SPANKIN' NEW

READ: MARK 7:33-35

Everything about this healing stands out. The way Jesus separates the man from the crowd. The tongue and ear touching. But it's the sigh that we notice. This is a sigh of sadness, a deep breath, and a heavenly glance that resolves, "It won't be this way for long."

Jesus will heal all who seek healing in him. There are no exceptions to this promise—no nuances, fine-print conditions, or caveats. To say some will be healed beyond the grave by no means diminishes the promise. We shall graduate from this version of life into his likeness. You'll have a spiritual body.

In your current state, your flesh battles your spirit. Your eyes look where they shouldn't. Your taste buds desire the wrong drinks. Your heart knows you shouldn't be anxious, but your mind still worries.

Your "parts" will no longer rebel in heaven. Your new body will be a spiritual body, with all members cooperating toward one end.

BUILDING FAITH WISDOM STRENGTH

Sin will no longer be at war with our flesh. Eyes won't lust, thoughts won't wander, hands won't steal, our minds won't judge, appetites won't rage, and our tongues won't lie. We will be brand new.

Some of you live in such road-weary bodies. Others exited the womb on an uphill ride. While I have no easy answers for your struggle, I implore you to see your challenge in the scope of God's story. View these days on earth as but the opening lines of his sweeping saga.

Taken from *God's Story, Your Story: Youth Edition* by Max Lucado, copyright © 2011 by Max Lucado, published by Zondervan.

sight was restored, and he saw everything clearly. [26] Jesus sent him home, saying, "Don't even go into[a] the village."

Peter Declares That Jesus Is the Messiah

[27] Jesus and his disciples went on to the villages around Caesarea Philippi. On the way he asked them, "Who do people say I am?"

[28] They replied, "Some say John the Baptist; others say Elijah; and still others, one of the prophets."

[29] "But what about you?" he asked. "Who do you say I am?"

Peter answered, "You are the Messiah."

[30] Jesus warned them not to tell anyone about him.

Jesus Predicts His Death

[31] He then began to teach them that the Son of Man must suffer many things and be rejected by the elders, the chief priests and the teachers of the law, and that he must be killed and after three days rise again. [32] He spoke plainly about this, and Peter took him aside and began to rebuke him.

[33] But when Jesus turned and looked at his disciples, he rebuked Peter. "Get behind me, Satan!" he said. "You do not have in mind the concerns of God, but merely human concerns."

The Way of the Cross

[34] Then he called the crowd to him along with his disciples and said: "Whoever wants to be my disciple must deny themselves and take up their cross and follow me. [35] For whoever wants to save their life[b] will lose it, but whoever loses their life for me and for the gospel will save it. [36] What good is it for someone to gain the whole world, yet forfeit their soul? [37] Or what can anyone give in exchange for their soul? [38] If anyone is ashamed of me and my words in this adulterous and sinful generation, the Son of Man will be ashamed of them when he comes in his Father's glory with the holy angels."

9 And he said to them, "Truly I tell you, some who are standing here will not taste death before they see that the kingdom of God has come with power."

The Transfiguration

[2] After six days Jesus took Peter, James and John with him and led them up a high mountain, where they were all alone. There he was transfigured before them. [3] His clothes became dazzling white, whiter than anyone in the world could bleach them. [4] And there appeared before them Elijah and Moses, who were talking with Jesus.

[5] Peter said to Jesus, "Rabbi, it is good for us to be here. Let us put up three shelters—one for you, one for Moses and one for Elijah." [6] (He did not know what to say, they were so frightened.)

[7] Then a cloud appeared and covered them, and a voice came from the cloud: "This is my Son, whom I love. Listen to him!"

[8] Suddenly, when they looked around, they no longer saw anyone with them except Jesus.

[9] As they were coming down the mountain, Jesus gave them orders not to tell anyone what they had seen until the Son of Man had risen from the dead. [10] They kept the matter to themselves, discussing what "rising from the dead" meant.

[11] And they asked him, "Why do the teachers of the law say that Elijah must come first?"

[12] Jesus replied, "To be sure, Elijah does come first, and restores all things. Why then is it written that the Son of Man must suffer much and be rejected? [13] But I tell you, Elijah has come, and they have done to him everything they wished, just as it is written about him."

Jesus Heals a Boy Possessed by an Impure Spirit

[14] When they came to the other disciples, they saw a large crowd around them and the teachers of the law arguing with them. [15] As soon as all the people saw Jesus, they were overwhelmed with wonder and ran to greet him.

[16] "What are you arguing with them about?" he asked.

[17] A man in the crowd answered, "Teacher, I brought you my son, who is possessed by a spirit that has robbed him of speech. [18] Whenever it seizes him, it throws him to the ground.

---

[a] 26 Some manuscripts *go and tell anyone in* verses 36 and 37.   [b] 35 The Greek word means either *life* or *soul*; also in

EVERY SINGLE THING

READ: MARK 8:34-35

My dad would often do the old school revivals at different churches and bring me along with him. Every night when he would finish preaching he would use the same invitation hymn, "I Surrender All." I knew the song backward and forward: "All to Jesus I surrender; humbly at his feet I bow. Worldly pleasures all forsaken; take me Jesus, take me now. I surrender all." But one night when I was about ten years old, I decided to surrender all. I stood next to him down front and sang along with the church to the final words of the song.

But as I got older, I didn't. It was one thing to sing those words as a general commitment, but when surrendering became more specific, the song I was singing wasn't "I Surrender All," it was "I Surrender Some." I didn't surrender my pride, and I was often motivated more out of a desire to impress people. I didn't surrender my plans; God was welcome to come along, but I did what I wanted to do. I didn't surrender my selfish desires. I didn't surrender my lustful thoughts. I didn't surrender my entertainment choices. I didn't surrender my money; God got the leftovers.

BUILDING

FAITH

WISDOM

STRENGTH

Where is the one place you find it most difficult to follow Jesus? What about in your own home? What about at school? What about on the court or on the field? What about in the neighborhood? What about when you're hanging out with old friends?

He foams at the mouth, gnashes his teeth and becomes rigid. I asked your disciples to drive out the spirit, but they could not."

¹⁹ "You unbelieving generation," Jesus replied, "how long shall I stay with you? How long shall I put up with you? Bring the boy to me."

²⁰ So they brought him. When the spirit saw Jesus, it immediately threw the boy into a convulsion. He fell to the ground and rolled around, foaming at the mouth.

²¹ Jesus asked the boy's father, "How long has he been like this?"

"From childhood," he answered. ²² "It has often thrown him into fire or water to kill him. But if you can do anything, take pity on us and help us."

²³ " 'If you can'?" said Jesus. "Everything is possible for one who believes."

²⁴ Immediately the boy's father exclaimed, "I do believe; help me overcome my unbelief!"

²⁵ When Jesus saw that a crowd was running to the scene, he rebuked the impure spirit. "You deaf and mute spirit," he said, "I command you, come out of him and never enter him again."

²⁶ The spirit shrieked, convulsed him violently and came out. The boy looked so much like a corpse that many said, "He's dead." ²⁷ But Jesus took him by the hand and lifted him to his feet, and he stood up.

²⁸ After Jesus had gone indoors, his disciples asked him privately, "Why couldn't we drive it out?"

²⁹ He replied, "This kind can come out only by prayer.ᵃ"

Jesus Predicts His Death a Second Time

³⁰ They left that place and passed through Galilee. Jesus did not want anyone to know where they were, ³¹ because he was teaching his disciples. He said to them, "The Son of Man is going to be delivered into the hands of men. They will kill him, and after three days he will rise." ³² But they did not understand what he meant and were afraid to ask him about it.

³³ They came to Capernaum. When he was in the house, he asked them, "What were you arguing about on the road?" ³⁴ But they kept quiet because on the way they had argued about who was the greatest.

³⁵ Sitting down, Jesus called the Twelve and said, "Anyone who wants to be first must be the very last, and the servant of all."

³⁶ He took a little child whom he placed among them. Taking the child in his arms, he said to them, ³⁷ "Whoever welcomes one of these little children in my name welcomes me; and whoever welcomes me does not welcome me but the one who sent me."

Whoever Is Not Against Us Is for Us

³⁸ "Teacher," said John, "we saw someone driving out demons in your name and we told him to stop, because he was not one of us."

³⁹ "Do not stop him," Jesus said. "For no one who does a miracle in my name can in the next moment say anything bad about me, ⁴⁰ for whoever is not against us is for us. ⁴¹ Truly I tell you, anyone who gives you a cup of water in my name because you belong to the Messiah will certainly not lose their reward.

Causing to Stumble

⁴² "If anyone causes one of these little ones — those who believe in me — to stumble, it would be better for them if a large millstone were hung around their neck and they were thrown into the sea. ⁴³ If your hand causes you to stumble, cut it off. It is better for you to enter life maimed than with two hands to go into hell, where the fire never goes out. [⁴⁴]ᵇ ⁴⁵ And if your foot causes you to stumble, cut it off. It is better for you to enter life crippled than to have two feet and be thrown into hell. [⁴⁶]ᵇ ⁴⁷ And if your eye causes you to stumble, pluck it out. It is better for you to enter the kingdom of God with one eye than to have two eyes and be thrown into hell, ⁴⁸ where

" 'the worms that eat them do not die,
    and the fire is not quenched.'ᶜ

⁴⁹ Everyone will be salted with fire.

⁵⁰ "Salt is good, but if it loses its saltiness, how can you make it salty again? Have salt among yourselves, and be at peace with each other."

Divorce

10 Jesus then left that place and went into the region of Judea and across

---

ᵃ 29 Some manuscripts *prayer and fasting* of verse 48.   ᶜ 48 Isaiah 66:24   ᵇ 44,46 Some manuscripts include here the words of verse 48.

OVERCOMING UNBELIEF

READ: MARK 9:25

You probably haven't spotted demons hanging around in your world. Maybe you were also astounded to read about your Lord shining with heavenly glory. Supernatural spiritual happenings might not seem real life, but Jesus' coming to earth as God in the flesh provoked intense activity by dark forces.

Mark gives an account of a boy who brought his parents sadness and terror from birth onward. They watched him violently tossed around, sometimes nearly killed in fire or water. The boy foamed at the mouth and gnashed his teeth. These parents were desperate for help, but this wasn't an ordinary physical or psychological problem. It had a spiritual source.

This episode is one of many in the Gospels—the first four books of the New Testament—that show Jesus exerting power over demons. In the story, his disciple attempted to drive out the spirit possessing the boy, but couldn't. Jesus speaks sharply to the impure spirit, commanding it to come out. The spirit shrieks and leaves the boy.

BUILDING

FAITH

WISDOM

STRENGTH

The Lord challenged his disciples—and the boy's father—to believe in his power. And that dad offered a prayer to Jesus that's worth repeating every time you encounter a challenge you can't understand or defeat: "I do believe; help me overcome my unbelief!" (Mark 9:24). God wants you to trust in him. He also wants to help grow your faith.

the Jordan. Again crowds of people came to him, and as was his custom, he taught them.

² Some Pharisees came and tested him by asking, "Is it lawful for a man to divorce his wife?"

³ "What did Moses command you?" he replied.

⁴ They said, "Moses permitted a man to write a certificate of divorce and send her away."

⁵ "It was because your hearts were hard that Moses wrote you this law," Jesus replied. ⁶ "But at the beginning of creation God 'made them male and female.'*a* ⁷ 'For this reason a man will leave his father and mother and be united to his wife,*b* ⁸ and the two will become one flesh.'*c* So they are no longer two, but one flesh. ⁹ Therefore what God has joined together, let no one separate."

¹⁰ When they were in the house again, the disciples asked Jesus about this. ¹¹ He answered, "Anyone who divorces his wife and marries another woman commits adultery against her. ¹² And if she divorces her husband and marries another man, she commits adultery."

The Little Children and Jesus

¹³ People were bringing little children to Jesus for him to place his hands on them, but the disciples rebuked them. ¹⁴ When Jesus saw this, he was indignant. He said to them, "Let the little children come to me, and do not hinder them, for the kingdom of God belongs to such as these. ¹⁵ Truly I tell you, anyone who will not receive the kingdom of God like a little child will never enter it." ¹⁶ And he took the children in his arms, placed his hands on them and blessed them.

The Rich and the Kingdom of God

¹⁷ As Jesus started on his way, a man ran up to him and fell on his knees before him. "Good teacher," he asked, "what must I do to inherit eternal life?"

¹⁸ "Why do you call me good?" Jesus answered. "No one is good—except God alone. ¹⁹ You know the commandments: 'You shall not murder, you shall not commit adultery, you shall not steal, you shall not give false

testimony, you shall not defraud, honor your father and mother.'*d*"

²⁰ "Teacher," he declared, "all these I have kept since I was a boy."

²¹ Jesus looked at him and loved him. "One thing you lack," he said. "Go, sell everything you have and give to the poor, and you will have treasure in heaven. Then come, follow me."

²² At this the man's face fell. He went away sad, because he had great wealth.

²³ Jesus looked around and said to his disciples, "How hard it is for the rich to enter the kingdom of God!"

²⁴ The disciples were amazed at his words. But Jesus said again, "Children, how hard it is*e* to enter the kingdom of God! ²⁵ It is easier for a camel to go through the eye of a needle than for someone who is rich to enter the kingdom of God."

²⁶ The disciples were even more amazed, and said to each other, "Who then can be saved?"

²⁷ Jesus looked at them and said, "With man this is impossible, but not with God; all things are possible with God."

²⁸ Then Peter spoke up, "We have left everything to follow you!"

²⁹ "Truly I tell you," Jesus replied, "no one who has left home or brothers or sisters or mother or father or children or fields for me and the gospel ³⁰ will fail to receive a hundred times as much in this present age: homes, brothers, sisters, mothers, children and fields—along with persecutions—and in the age to come eternal life. ³¹ But many who are first will be last, and the last first."

Jesus Predicts His Death a Third Time

³² They were on their way up to Jerusalem, with Jesus leading the way, and the disciples were astonished, while those who followed were afraid. Again he took the Twelve aside and told them what was going to happen to him. ³³ "We are going up to Jerusalem," he said, "and the Son of Man will be delivered over to the chief priests and the teachers of the law. They will condemn him to death and will hand him over to the Gentiles, ³⁴ who will mock him and spit on him, flog him and kill him. Three days later he will rise."

---

a 6 Gen. 1:27   *b* 7 Some early manuscripts do not have *and be united to his wife.*   *c* 8 Gen. 2:24
d 19 Exodus 20:12-16; Deut. 5:16-20   *e* 24 Some manuscripts *is for those who trust in riches*

The Request of James and John

[35] Then James and John, the sons of Zebedee, came to him. "Teacher," they said, "we want you to do for us whatever we ask."

[36] "What do you want me to do for you?" he asked.

[37] They replied, "Let one of us sit at your right and the other at your left in your glory."

[38] "You don't know what you are asking," Jesus said. "Can you drink the cup I drink or be baptized with the baptism I am baptized with?"

[39] "We can," they answered.

Jesus said to them, "You will drink the cup I drink and be baptized with the baptism I am baptized with, [40] but to sit at my right or left is not for me to grant. These places belong to those for whom they have been prepared."

[41] When the ten heard about this, they became indignant with James and John. [42] Jesus called them together and said, "You know that those who are regarded as rulers of the Gentiles lord it over them, and their high officials exercise authority over them. [43] Not so with you. Instead, whoever wants to become great among you must be your servant, [44] and whoever wants to be first must be slave of all. [45] For even the Son of Man did not come to be served, but to serve, and to give his life as a ransom for many."

Blind Bartimaeus Receives His Sight

[46] Then they came to Jericho. As Jesus and his disciples, together with a large crowd, were leaving the city, a blind man, Bartimaeus (which means "son of Timaeus"), was sitting by the roadside begging. [47] When he heard that it was Jesus of Nazareth, he began to shout, "Jesus, Son of David, have mercy on me!"

[48] Many rebuked him and told him to be quiet, but he shouted all the more, "Son of David, have mercy on me!"

[49] Jesus stopped and said, "Call him."

So they called to the blind man, "Cheer up! On your feet! He's calling you." [50] Throwing his cloak aside, he jumped to his feet and came to Jesus.

[51] "What do you want me to do for you?" Jesus asked him.

The blind man said, "Rabbi, I want to see."

[52] "Go," said Jesus, "your faith has healed you." Immediately he received his sight and followed Jesus along the road.

Jesus Comes to Jerusalem as King

11 As they approached Jerusalem and came to Bethphage and Bethany at the Mount of Olives, Jesus sent two of his disciples, [2] saying to them, "Go to the village ahead of you, and just as you enter it, you will find a colt tied there, which no one has ever ridden. Untie it and bring it here. [3] If anyone asks you, 'Why are you doing this?' say, 'The Lord needs it and will send it back here shortly.'"

[4] They went and found a colt outside in the street, tied at a doorway. As they untied it, [5] some people standing there asked, "What are you doing, untying that colt?" [6] They answered as Jesus had told them to, and the people let them go. [7] When they brought the colt to Jesus and threw their cloaks over it, he sat on it. [8] Many people spread their cloaks on the road, while others spread branches they had cut in the fields. [9] Those who went ahead and those who followed shouted,

"Hosanna!*ᵃ*"

"Blessed is he who comes in the name of
the Lord!"*ᵇ*

[10] "Blessed is the coming kingdom of our
father David!"

"Hosanna in the highest heaven!"

[11] Jesus entered Jerusalem and went into the temple courts. He looked around at everything, but since it was already late, he went out to Bethany with the Twelve.

Jesus Curses a Fig Tree and Clears the Temple Courts

[12] The next day as they were leaving Bethany, Jesus was hungry. [13] Seeing in the distance a fig tree in leaf, he went to find out if it had any fruit. When he reached it, he found nothing but leaves, because it was not the season for figs. [14] Then he said to the tree, "May no one ever eat fruit from you again." And his disciples heard him say it.

[15] On reaching Jerusalem, Jesus entered the temple courts and began driving out

---

ᵃ 9 A Hebrew expression meaning "Save!" which became an exclamation of praise; also in verse 10
ᵇ 9 Psalm 118:25,26

those who were buying and selling there. He overturned the tables of the money changers and the benches of those selling doves, ¹⁶and would not allow anyone to carry merchandise through the temple courts. ¹⁷And as he taught them, he said, "Is it not written:

'My house will be called a house of prayer for all nations'ᵃ? But you have made it 'a den of robbers.'ᵇ"

¹⁸The chief priests and the teachers of the law heard this and began looking for a way to kill him, for they feared him, because the whole crowd was amazed at his teaching.

¹⁹When evening came, Jesus and his disciplesᶜ went out of the city.

²⁰In the morning, as they went along, they saw the fig tree withered from the roots. ²¹Peter remembered and said to Jesus, "Rabbi, look! The fig tree you cursed has withered!"

²²"Have faith in God," Jesus answered. ²³"Trulyᵈ I tell you, if anyone says to this mountain, 'Go, throw yourself into the sea,' and does not doubt in their heart but believes that what they say will happen, it will be done for them. ²⁴Therefore I tell you, whatever you ask for in prayer, believe that you have received it, and it will be yours. ²⁵And when you stand praying, if you hold anything against anyone, forgive them, so that your Father in heaven may forgive you your sins." [26]ᵉ

The Authority of Jesus Questioned

²⁷They arrived again in Jerusalem, and while Jesus was walking in the temple courts, the chief priests, the teachers of the law and the elders came to him. ²⁸"By what authority are you doing these things?" they asked. "And who gave you authority to do this?"

²⁹Jesus replied, "I will ask you one question. Answer me, and I will tell you by what authority I am doing these things. ³⁰John's baptism — was it from heaven, or of human origin? Tell me!"

³¹They discussed it among themselves and said, "If we say, 'From heaven,' he will ask, 'Then why didn't you believe him?' ³²But if we say, 'Of human origin' . . ." (They feared the people, for everyone held that John really was a prophet.)

³³So they answered Jesus, "We don't know."

Jesus said, "Neither will I tell you by what authority I am doing these things."

The Parable of the Tenants

12 Jesus then began to speak to them in parables: "A man planted a vineyard. He put a wall around it, dug a pit for the winepress and built a watchtower. Then he rented the vineyard to some farmers and moved to another place. ²At harvest time he sent a servant to the tenants to collect from them some of the fruit of the vineyard. ³But they seized him, beat him and sent him away empty-handed. ⁴Then he sent another servant to them; they struck this man on the head and treated him shamefully. ⁵He sent still another, and that one they killed. He sent many others; some of them they beat, others they killed.

⁶"He had one left to send, a son, whom he loved. He sent him last of all, saying, 'They will respect my son.'

⁷"But the tenants said to one another, 'This is the heir. Come, let's kill him, and the inheritance will be ours.' ⁸So they took him and killed him, and threw him out of the vineyard.

⁹"What then will the owner of the vineyard do? He will come and kill those tenants and give the vineyard to others. ¹⁰Haven't you read this passage of Scripture:

"'The stone the builders rejected
    has become the cornerstone;
¹¹the Lord has done this,
    and it is marvelous in our eyes'ᶠ?"

¹²Then the chief priests, the teachers of the law and the elders looked for a way to arrest him because they knew he had spoken the parable against them. But they were afraid of the crowd; so they left him and went away.

Paying the Imperial Tax to Caesar

¹³Later they sent some of the Pharisees and Herodians to Jesus to catch him in his words. ¹⁴They came to him and said, "Teacher, we know that you are a man of integrity. You aren't swayed by others, because you pay

---

ᵃ 17 Isaiah 56:7   ᵇ 17 Jer. 7:11   ᶜ 19 Some early manuscripts came, Jesus   ᵈ 22,23 Some early manuscripts "If you have faith in God," Jesus answered, ²³"truly   ᵉ 26 Some manuscripts include here words similar to Matt. 6:15.   ᶠ 11 Psalm 118:22,23

JUMP!

READ: MARK 11:22-23

I don't know about you, but I always wish God would reveal the second step before I take the first step (the one that requires faith). But I've discovered that if I don't take the first step, God's not going to just let me have the second one. This is why we get stuck spiritually. We want more revelation before we obey more, but God wants more obedience before he reveals more. Or we want God to lay out some optional plans and then let us pick our favorite. But that's not quite how it works!

Most of us will only follow Christ to a place where we've been before. But no farther. And as a result, we give up all the new gifts, new anointings, and new dreams that God has waiting for us.

If you want God to do something new, you can't keep doing what you've always done. Push past the fear of the unknown. You've obviously got to do something different.

We need to step into the conflict without knowing if we can resolve it. We need to share our faith without knowing how our friends will react to it. We need to pray for a miracle without knowing how God will answer. We need to put ourselves in a situation that activates a spiritual gift we've never exercised before. And we need to go after a dream that'll fail without divine intervention.

And when we do, we develop a spiritual hunger for the miraculous and lose our appetite for the habitual.

BUILDING

FAITH

WISDOM

STRENGTH

Taken from *All In Student Edition* by Mark Batterson and Parker Batterson, copyright © 2014 by Mark Batterson, published by Zondervan.

no attention to who they are; but you teach the way of God in accordance with the truth. Is it right to pay the imperial tax[a] to Caesar or not? [15]Should we pay or shouldn't we?"

But Jesus knew their hypocrisy. "Why are you trying to trap me?" he asked. "Bring me a denarius and let me look at it." [16]They brought the coin, and he asked them, "Whose image is this? And whose inscription?"

"Caesar's," they replied.

[17]Then Jesus said to them, "Give back to Caesar what is Caesar's and to God what is God's."

And they were amazed at him.

Marriage at the Resurrection

[18]Then the Sadducees, who say there is no resurrection, came to him with a question. [19]"Teacher," they said, "Moses wrote for us that if a man's brother dies and leaves a wife but no children, the man must marry the widow and raise up offspring for his brother. [20]Now there were seven brothers. The first one married and died without leaving any children. [21]The second one married the widow, but he also died, leaving no child. It was the same with the third. [22]In fact, none of the seven left any children. Last of all, the woman died too. [23]At the resurrection[b] whose wife will she be, since the seven were married to her?"

[24]Jesus replied, "Are you not in error because you do not know the Scriptures or the power of God? [25]When the dead rise, they will neither marry nor be given in marriage; they will be like the angels in heaven. [26]Now about the dead rising—have you not read in the Book of Moses, in the account of the burning bush, how God said to him, 'I am the God of Abraham, the God of Isaac, and the God of Jacob'[c]? [27]He is not the God of the dead, but of the living. You are badly mistaken!"

The Greatest Commandment

[28]One of the teachers of the law came and heard them debating. Noticing that Jesus had given them a good answer, he asked him, "Of all the commandments, which is the most important?"

[29]"The most important one," answered Jesus, "is this: 'Hear, O Israel: The Lord our God, the Lord is one.[d] [30]Love the Lord your God with all your heart and with all your soul and with all your mind and with all your strength.'[e] [31]The second is this: 'Love your neighbor as yourself.'[f] There is no commandment greater than these."

[32]"Well said, teacher," the man replied. "You are right in saying that God is one and there is no other but him. [33]To love him with all your heart, with all your understanding and with all your strength, and to love your neighbor as yourself is more important than all burnt offerings and sacrifices."

[34]When Jesus saw that he had answered wisely, he said to him, "You are not far from the kingdom of God." And from then on no one dared ask him any more questions.

Whose Son Is the Messiah?

[35]While Jesus was teaching in the temple courts, he asked, "Why do the teachers of the law say that the Messiah is the son of David? [36]David himself, speaking by the Holy Spirit, declared:

" 'The Lord said to my Lord:
"Sit at my right hand
until I put your enemies
under your feet." '[g]

[37]David himself calls him 'Lord.' How then can he be his son?"

The large crowd listened to him with delight.

Warning Against the Teachers of the Law

[38]As he taught, Jesus said, "Watch out for the teachers of the law. They like to walk around in flowing robes and be greeted with respect in the marketplaces, [39]and have the most important seats in the synagogues and the places of honor at banquets. [40]They devour widows' houses and for a show make lengthy prayers. These men will be punished most severely."

The Widow's Offering

[41]Jesus sat down opposite the place where the offerings were put and watched the crowd putting their money into the temple treasury. Many rich people threw in large

---

a 14 A special tax levied on subject peoples, not on Roman citizens   *b 23* Some manuscripts *resurrection, when people rise from the dead,*   *c 26* Exodus 3:6   *d 29* Or *The Lord our God is one Lord*   *e 30* Deut. 6:4,5   *f 31* Lev. 19:18   *g 36* Psalm 110:1

amounts. [42]But a poor widow came and put in two very small copper coins, worth only a few cents.

[43]Calling his disciples to him, Jesus said, "Truly I tell you, this poor widow has put more into the treasury than all the others. [44]They all gave out of their wealth; but she, out of her poverty, put in everything—all she had to live on."

The Destruction of the Temple and Signs of the End Times

13 As Jesus was leaving the temple, one of his disciples said to him, "Look, Teacher! What massive stones! What magnificent buildings!"

[2]"Do you see all these great buildings?" replied Jesus. "Not one stone here will be left on another; every one will be thrown down."

[3]As Jesus was sitting on the Mount of Olives opposite the temple, Peter, James, John and Andrew asked him privately, [4]"Tell us, when will these things happen? And what will be the sign that they are all about to be fulfilled?"

[5]Jesus said to them: "Watch out that no one deceives you. [6]Many will come in my name, claiming, 'I am he,' and will deceive many. [7]When you hear of wars and rumors of wars, do not be alarmed. Such things must happen, but the end is still to come. [8]Nation will rise against nation, and kingdom against kingdom. There will be earthquakes in various places, and famines. These are the beginning of birth pains.

[9]"You must be on your guard. You will be handed over to the local councils and flogged in the synagogues. On account of me you will stand before governors and kings as witnesses to them. [10]And the gospel must first be preached to all nations. [11]Whenever you are arrested and brought to trial, do not worry beforehand about what to say. Just say whatever is given you at the time, for it is not you speaking, but the Holy Spirit.

[12]"Brother will betray brother to death, and a father his child. Children will rebel against their parents and have them put to death. [13]Everyone will hate you because of me, but the one who stands firm to the end will be saved.

[14]"When you see 'the abomination that causes desolation'[a] standing where it[b] does not belong—let the reader understand—then let those who are in Judea flee to the mountains. [15]Let no one on the housetop go down or enter the house to take anything out. [16]Let no one in the field go back to get their cloak. [17]How dreadful it will be in those days for pregnant women and nursing mothers! [18]Pray that this will not take place in winter, [19]because those will be days of distress unequaled from the beginning, when God created the world, until now—and never to be equaled again.

[20]"If the Lord had not cut short those days, no one would survive. But for the sake of the elect, whom he has chosen, he has shortened them. [21]At that time if anyone says to you, 'Look, here is the Messiah!' or, 'Look, there he is!' do not believe it. [22]For false messiahs and false prophets will appear and perform signs and wonders to deceive, if possible, even the elect. [23]So be on your guard; I have told you everything ahead of time.

[24]"But in those days, following that distress,

"'the sun will be darkened,
    and the moon will not give its light;
[25]the stars will fall from the sky,
    and the heavenly bodies will be
        shaken.'[c]

[26]"At that time people will see the Son of Man coming in clouds with great power and glory. [27]And he will send his angels and gather his elect from the four winds, from the ends of the earth to the ends of the heavens.

[28]"Now learn this lesson from the fig tree: As soon as its twigs get tender and its leaves come out, you know that summer is near. [29]Even so, when you see these things happening, you know that it[b] is near, right at the door. [30]Truly I tell you, this generation will certainly not pass away until all these things have happened. [31]Heaven and earth will pass away, but my words will never pass away.

The Day and Hour Unknown

[32]"But about that day or hour no one knows, not even the angels in heaven, nor the Son, but only the Father. [33]Be on guard!

---

[a] 14 Daniel 9:27; 11:31; 12:11   [b] 14,29 Or *he*   [c] 25 Isaiah 13:10; 34:4

Be alert[a]! You do not know when that time will come. [34]It's like a man going away: He leaves his house and puts his servants in charge, each with their assigned task, and tells the one at the door to keep watch.

[35]"Therefore keep watch because you do not know when the owner of the house will come back — whether in the evening, or at midnight, or when the rooster crows, or at dawn. [36]If he comes suddenly, do not let him find you sleeping. [37]What I say to you, I say to everyone: 'Watch!'"

Jesus Anointed at Bethany

14 Now the Passover and the Festival of Unleavened Bread were only two days away, and the chief priests and the teachers of the law were scheming to arrest Jesus secretly and kill him. [2]"But not during the festival," they said, "or the people may riot."

[3]While he was in Bethany, reclining at the table in the home of Simon the Leper, a woman came with an alabaster jar of very expensive perfume, made of pure nard. She broke the jar and poured the perfume on his head.

[4]Some of those present were saying indignantly to one another, "Why this waste of perfume? [5]It could have been sold for more than a year's wages[b] and the money given to the poor." And they rebuked her harshly.

[6]"Leave her alone," said Jesus. "Why are you bothering her? She has done a beautiful thing to me. [7]The poor you will always have with you,[c] and you can help them any time you want. But you will not always have me. [8]She did what she could. She poured perfume on my body beforehand to prepare for my burial. [9]Truly I tell you, wherever the gospel is preached throughout the world, what she has done will also be told, in memory of her."

[10]Then Judas Iscariot, one of the Twelve, went to the chief priests to betray Jesus to them. [11]They were delighted to hear this and promised to give him money. So he watched for an opportunity to hand him over.

The Last Supper

[12]On the first day of the Festival of Unleavened Bread, when it was customary to sacrifice the Passover lamb, Jesus' disciples asked him, "Where do you want us to go and make preparations for you to eat the Passover?"

[13]So he sent two of his disciples, telling them, "Go into the city, and a man carrying a jar of water will meet you. Follow him. [14]Say to the owner of the house he enters, 'The Teacher asks: Where is my guest room, where I may eat the Passover with my disciples?' [15]He will show you a large room upstairs, furnished and ready. Make preparations for us there."

[16]The disciples left, went into the city and found things just as Jesus had told them. So they prepared the Passover.

[17]When evening came, Jesus arrived with the Twelve. [18]While they were reclining at the table eating, he said, "Truly I tell you, one of you will betray me — one who is eating with me."

[19]They were saddened, and one by one they said to him, "Surely you don't mean me?"

[20]"It is one of the Twelve," he replied, "one who dips bread into the bowl with me. [21]The Son of Man will go just as it is written about him. But woe to that man who betrays the Son of Man! It would be better for him if he had not been born."

[22]While they were eating, Jesus took bread, and when he had given thanks, he broke it and gave it to his disciples, saying, "Take it; this is my body."

[23]Then he took a cup, and when he had given thanks, he gave it to them, and they all drank from it.

[24]"This is my blood of the[d] covenant, which is poured out for many," he said to them. [25]"Truly I tell you, I will not drink again from the fruit of the vine until that day when I drink it new in the kingdom of God."

[26]When they had sung a hymn, they went out to the Mount of Olives.

Jesus Predicts Peter's Denial

[27]"You will all fall away," Jesus told them, "for it is written:

"'I will strike the shepherd,
    and the sheep will be scattered.'[e]

[28]But after I have risen, I will go ahead of you into Galilee."

---

[a] 33 Some manuscripts *alert and pray*   [b] 5 Greek *than three hundred denarii*   [c] 7 See Deut. 15:11.
[d] 24 Some manuscripts *the new*   [e] 27 Zech. 13:7

²⁹Peter declared, "Even if all fall away, I will not."

³⁰"Truly I tell you," Jesus answered, "today — yes, tonight — before the rooster crows twice*a* you yourself will disown me three times."

³¹But Peter insisted emphatically, "Even if I have to die with you, I will never disown you." And all the others said the same.

Gethsemane

³²They went to a place called Gethsemane, and Jesus said to his disciples, "Sit here while I pray." ³³He took Peter, James and John along with him, and he began to be deeply distressed and troubled. ³⁴"My soul is overwhelmed with sorrow to the point of death," he said to them. "Stay here and keep watch."

³⁵Going a little farther, he fell to the ground and prayed that if possible the hour might pass from him. ³⁶"*Abba,*b* Father," he said, "everything is possible for you. Take this cup from me. Yet not what I will, but what you will."

³⁷Then he returned to his disciples and found them sleeping. "Simon," he said to Peter, "are you asleep? Couldn't you keep watch for one hour? ³⁸Watch and pray so that you will not fall into temptation. The spirit is willing, but the flesh is weak."

³⁹Once more he went away and prayed the same thing. ⁴⁰When he came back, he again found them sleeping, because their eyes were heavy. They did not know what to say to him.

⁴¹Returning the third time, he said to them, "Are you still sleeping and resting? Enough! The hour has come. Look, the Son of Man is delivered into the hands of sinners. ⁴²Rise! Let us go! Here comes my betrayer!"

Jesus Arrested

⁴³Just as he was speaking, Judas, one of the Twelve, appeared. With him was a crowd armed with swords and clubs, sent from the chief priests, the teachers of the law, and the elders. ⁴⁴Now the betrayer had arranged a signal with them: "The one I kiss is the man; arrest him and lead him away under guard." ⁴⁵Going at once to Jesus, Judas said, "Rabbi!" and kissed him. ⁴⁶The men seized Jesus and arrested him. ⁴⁷Then one of those standing near drew his sword and struck the servant of the high priest, cutting off his ear.

⁴⁸"Am I leading a rebellion," said Jesus, "that you have come out with swords and clubs to capture me? ⁴⁹Every day I was with you, teaching in the temple courts, and you did not arrest me. But the Scriptures must be fulfilled." ⁵⁰Then everyone deserted him and fled.

⁵¹A young man, wearing nothing but a linen garment, was following Jesus. When they seized him, ⁵²he fled naked, leaving his garment behind.

Jesus Before the Sanhedrin

⁵³They took Jesus to the high priest, and all the chief priests, the elders and the teachers of the law came together. ⁵⁴Peter followed him at a distance, right into the courtyard of the high priest. There he sat with the guards and warmed himself at the fire.

⁵⁵The chief priests and the whole Sanhedrin were looking for evidence against Jesus so that they could put him to death, but they did not find any. ⁵⁶Many testified falsely against him, but their statements did not agree.

⁵⁷Then some stood up and gave this false testimony against him: ⁵⁸"We heard him say, 'I will destroy this temple made with human hands and in three days will build another, not made with hands.'" ⁵⁹Yet even then their testimony did not agree.

⁶⁰Then the high priest stood up before them and asked Jesus, "Are you not going to answer? What is this testimony that these men are bringing against you?" ⁶¹But Jesus remained silent and gave no answer.

Again the high priest asked him, "Are you the Messiah, the Son of the Blessed One?"

⁶²"I am," said Jesus. "And you will see the Son of Man sitting at the right hand of the Mighty One and coming on the clouds of heaven."

⁶³The high priest tore his clothes. "Why do we need any more witnesses?" he asked. ⁶⁴"You have heard the blasphemy. What do you think?"

They all condemned him as worthy of death. ⁶⁵Then some began to spit at him;

---

a 30 Some early manuscripts do not have *twice.*   *b 36* Aramaic for *father* they blindfolded him, struck him with their fists, and said, "Prophesy!" And the guards took him and beat him.

Peter Disowns Jesus

[66]While Peter was below in the courtyard, one of the servant girls of the high priest came by. [67]When she saw Peter warming himself, she looked closely at him.

"You also were with that Nazarene, Jesus," she said.

[68]But he denied it. "I don't know or understand what you're talking about," he said, and went out into the entryway.[a]

[69]When the servant girl saw him there, she said again to those standing around, "This fellow is one of them." [70]Again he denied it.

After a little while, those standing near said to Peter, "Surely you are one of them, for you are a Galilean."

[71]He began to call down curses, and he swore to them, "I don't know this man you're talking about."

[72]Immediately the rooster crowed the second time.[b] Then Peter remembered the word Jesus had spoken to him: "Before the rooster crows twice[c] you will disown me three times." And he broke down and wept.

Jesus Before Pilate

15 Very early in the morning, the chief priests, with the elders, the teachers of the law and the whole Sanhedrin, made their plans. So they bound Jesus, led him away and handed him over to Pilate.

[2]"Are you the king of the Jews?" asked Pilate.

"You have said so," Jesus replied.

[3]The chief priests accused him of many things. [4]So again Pilate asked him, "Aren't you going to answer? See how many things they are accusing you of."

[5]But Jesus still made no reply, and Pilate was amazed.

[6]Now it was the custom at the festival to release a prisoner whom the people requested. [7]A man called Barabbas was in prison with the insurrectionists who had committed murder in the uprising. [8]The crowd came up and asked Pilate to do for them what he usually did.

[9]"Do you want me to release to you the king of the Jews?" asked Pilate, [10]knowing it was out of self-interest that the chief priests had handed Jesus over to him. [11]But the chief priests stirred up the crowd to have Pilate release Barabbas instead.

[12]"What shall I do, then, with the one you call the king of the Jews?" Pilate asked them.

[13]"Crucify him!" they shouted.

[14]"Why? What crime has he committed?" asked Pilate.

But they shouted all the louder, "Crucify him!"

[15]Wanting to satisfy the crowd, Pilate released Barabbas to them. He had Jesus flogged, and handed him over to be crucified.

The Soldiers Mock Jesus

[16]The soldiers led Jesus away into the palace (that is, the Praetorium) and called together the whole company of soldiers. [17]They put a purple robe on him, then twisted together a crown of thorns and set it on him. [18]And they began to call out to him, "Hail, king of the Jews!" [19]Again and again they struck him on the head with a staff and spit on him. Falling on their knees, they paid homage to him. [20]And when they had mocked him, they took off the purple robe and put his own clothes on him. Then they led him out to crucify him.

The Crucifixion of Jesus

[21]A certain man from Cyrene, Simon, the father of Alexander and Rufus, was passing by on his way in from the country, and they forced him to carry the cross. [22]They brought Jesus to the place called Golgotha (which means "the place of the skull"). [23]Then they offered him wine mixed with myrrh, but he did not take it. [24]And they crucified him. Dividing up his clothes, they cast lots to see what each would get.

[25]It was nine in the morning when they crucified him. [26]The written notice of the charge against him read: THE KING OF THE JEWS.

[27]They crucified two rebels with him, one on his right and one on his left. [28][d] [29]Those who passed by hurled insults at him, shaking

---

[a] 68 Some early manuscripts *entryway and the rooster crowed*   [b] 72 Some early manuscripts do not have *the second time.*   [c] 72 Some early manuscripts do not have *twice.*   [d] 28 Some manuscripts include here words similar to Luke 22:37.

HOW COULD HE DO THAT?

READ: MARK 15:27-34

Jesus: bloodied, beaten. More crimson than clean. Every sinew afire with pain.

And God: He ebonized the sky and shook the earth. He cleaved the rocks and ripped the temple curtain. He untombed the entombed and unveiled the Holy of Holies in the temple.

But first he heard the cry of his Son.

Forsaken. Visceral, painful. The word reminds us of abandonment, of desertion, of being left helpless, alone, cast out, of being completely forgotten. Jesus forsaken? Does Scripture not declare, "I have never seen the righteous forsaken," and assure that "the Lord . . . will not forsake his faithful ones" (Psalm 37:25, 28)?

Indeed it does. But in that hour Jesus was anything but righteous. This was the moment in which our sins were put on Christ. He wrapped himself around us and felt the full force of the fall. He took the unrelaxed punishment of the guilty. He died, not like a sinner, but as a sinner—in our place. His sacrifice is a sufficient one. Our accomplishments don't enhance it. Our stumbles don't diminish it. The sacrifice of Christ is a total and unceasing and accomplished work. "It is finished," Jesus announced (John 19:30). His prayer of abandonment is followed by a cry of accomplishment. Not "It is begun" or "It is initiated" or "It is a work in progress." No, "It is finished."

BUILDING FAITH WISDOM STRENGTH

Taken from *God's Story, Your Story: Youth Edition* by Max Lucado, copyright © 2011 by Max Lucado, published by Zondervan.

their heads and saying, "So! You who are going to destroy the temple and build it in three days, **30** come down from the cross and save yourself!" **31** In the same way the chief priests and the teachers of the law mocked him among themselves. "He saved others," they said, "but he can't save himself! **32** Let this Messiah, this king of Israel, come down now from the cross, that we may see and believe." Those crucified with him also heaped insults on him.

The Death of Jesus

33 At noon, darkness came over the whole land until three in the afternoon. **34** And at three in the afternoon Jesus cried out in a loud voice, *"Eloi, Eloi, lema sabachthani?"* (which means "My God, my God, why have you forsaken me?").*ᵃ*

35 When some of those standing near heard this, they said, "Listen, he's calling Elijah."

36 Someone ran, filled a sponge with wine vinegar, put it on a staff, and offered it to Jesus to drink. "Now leave him alone. Let's see if Elijah comes to take him down," he said.

37 With a loud cry, Jesus breathed his last.

38 The curtain of the temple was torn in two from top to bottom. **39** And when the centurion, who stood there in front of Jesus, saw how he died,*ᵇ* he said, "Surely this man was the Son of God!"

40 Some women were watching from a distance. Among them were Mary Magdalene, Mary the mother of James the younger and of Joseph,*ᶜ* and Salome. **41** In Galilee these women had followed him and cared for his needs. Many other women who had come up with him to Jerusalem were also there.

The Burial of Jesus

42 It was Preparation Day (that is, the day before the Sabbath). So as evening approached, **43** Joseph of Arimathea, a prominent member of the Council, who was himself waiting for the kingdom of God, went boldly to Pilate and asked for Jesus' body. **44** Pilate was surprised to hear that he was

already dead. Summoning the centurion, he asked him if Jesus had already died. **45** When he learned from the centurion that it was so, he gave the body to Joseph. **46** So Joseph bought some linen cloth, took down the body, wrapped it in the linen, and placed it in a tomb cut out of rock. Then he rolled a stone against the entrance of the tomb. **47** Mary Magdalene and Mary the mother of Joseph saw where he was laid.

Jesus Has Risen

16 When the Sabbath was over, Mary Magdalene, Mary the mother of James, and Salome bought spices so that they might go to anoint Jesus' body. **2** Very early on the first day of the week, just after sunrise, they were on their way to the tomb **3** and they asked each other, "Who will roll the stone away from the entrance of the tomb?"

4 But when they looked up, they saw that the stone, which was very large, had been rolled away. **5** As they entered the tomb, they saw a young man dressed in a white robe sitting on the right side, and they were alarmed.

6 "Don't be alarmed," he said. "You are looking for Jesus the Nazarene, who was crucified. He has risen! He is not here. See the place where they laid him. **7** But go, tell his disciples and Peter, 'He is going ahead of you into Galilee. There you will see him, just as he told you.'"

8 Trembling and bewildered, the women went out and fled from the tomb. They said nothing to anyone, because they were afraid.*ᵈ*

[The earliest manuscripts and some other ancient witnesses do not have verses 9–20.]

9 When Jesus rose early on the first day of the week, he appeared first to Mary Magdalene, out of whom he had driven seven demons. 10 She went and told those who had been with him and who were mourning and weeping. 11 When they heard that Jesus was alive and that she had seen him, they did not believe it.

ᵃ 34 Psalm 22:1   *ᵇ 39* Some manuscripts *saw that he died with such a cry*   *ᶜ 40* Greek *Joses,* a variant of *Joseph;* also in verse 47   *ᵈ 8* Some manuscripts have the following ending between verses 8 and 9, and one manuscript has it after verse 8 (omitting verses 9-20): *Then they quickly reported all these instructions to those around Peter. After this, Jesus himself also sent out through them from east to west the sacred and imperishable proclamation of eternal salvation. Amen.*

KINDA UNEXPECTED

READ: **MARK 16:1-7**

No one dreamed of a Sunday morning miracle. Peter didn't ask John, "What will you say when you see Jesus?" Mary didn't ponder, *How will he appear?* They didn't encourage each other with quotes of his promised return. They could have. At least four times Jesus had said words like these: "The Messiah will suffer and rise from the dead on the third day" (Matthew 12:40, 27:63; Luke 18:33, 24:46). You'd think someone would mention this prophecy and do the math. "Hmm, he died yesterday. Today is the second day. He promised to rise on the third day. Tomorrow is the third day ... Friends, I think we'd better wake up early tomorrow."

Easter parade? Victory march? Hardly. More like a funeral procession.

It was left to the angel to lead them into Sunday. God shook up the cemetery. Trees swayed, and the ground trembled. The women struggled to maintain their balance. They looked in the direction of the tomb only to see the guards—scared stiff, paralyzed, and sprawled on the ground. Hard to miss the irony: the guards of the dead appear dead, while the dead one appears to be living. And then the announcement. "He has risen."

The bodily resurrection means everything. If Jesus lives on only in spirit and deeds, he is but one of a thousand dead heroes. But if he lives on in flesh and bone, he is the King who pressed his heel against the head of death.

BUILDING

FAITH

WISDOM

STRENGTH

Taken from *God's Story, Your Story: Youth Edition* by Max Lucado, copyright © 2011 by Max Lucado, published by Zondervan.

[12] Afterward Jesus appeared in a different form to two of them while they were walking in the country. [13] These returned and reported it to the rest; but they did not believe them either.

[14] Later Jesus appeared to the Eleven as they were eating; he rebuked them for their lack of faith and their stubborn refusal to believe those who had seen him after he had risen.

[15] He said to them, "Go into all the world and preach the gospel to all creation. [16] Whoever believes and is baptized will be saved, but whoever does not believe will be condemned. [17] And these signs will accompany those who believe: In my name they will drive out demons; they will speak in new tongues; [18] they will pick up snakes with their hands; and when they drink deadly poison, it will not hurt them at all; they will place their hands on sick people, and they will get well."

[19] After the Lord Jesus had spoken to them, he was taken up into heaven and he sat at the right hand of God. [20] Then the disciples went out and preached everywhere, and the Lord worked with them and confirmed his word by the signs that accompanied it.

LUKE

➥ **WHEN DID THIS HAPPEN?**

A.D. 1 to 36 in Palestine

➥ **WHO IS IN THIS BOOK?**

Zechariah
Elizabeth
Mary
Joseph
John the Baptist
Jesus
the shepherds
Anna
Simeon
Zacchaeus

➥ **VERSES YOU MIGHT RECOGNIZE**

LUKE 9:23

"Whoever wants to be my disciple must deny themselves and take up their cross daily and follow me."

LUKE 19:10

"For the Son of Man came to seek and to save the lost."

WHAT'S IT ABOUT?

Taking the approach of a newspaper reporter, Luke wrote a well-researched report on Jesus' life for someone named Theophilus. Luke, a Gentile doctor who also wrote the book of Acts, gathered his information from eyewitness accounts. Luke showed Jesus' special compassion for outcasts and disrespected people, such as women, children and the poor. He also showed Jesus' love for sinners, including immoral women, tax collectors and the thieves who hung next to him on the cross.

Where Matthew focused on Jesus the Messiah and Mark examined Jesus the servant, Luke captured Jesus' human side, frequently using "Son of Man," a name Jesus used for himself. This synoptic gospel shows Jesus reaching out to individuals. One of the most memorable people is Zacchaeus, a vertically challenged tax collector who climbed a tree to get a view of Jesus. The Rabbi invited himself over to Zacchaeus' house for dinner and radically changed the man's life. In the book of Luke, Jesus is the perfect man, able to save the lost.

LUKE

Introduction

1 Many have undertaken to draw up an account of the things that have been fulfilled[a] among us, [2] just as they were handed down to us by those who from the first were eyewitnesses and servants of the word. [3] With this in mind, since I myself have carefully investigated everything from the beginning, I too decided to write an orderly account for you, most excellent Theophilus, [4] so that you may know the certainty of the things you have been taught.

The Birth of John the Baptist Foretold

[5] In the time of Herod king of Judea there was a priest named Zechariah, who belonged to the priestly division of Abijah; his wife Elizabeth was also a descendant of Aaron. [6] Both of them were righteous in the sight of God, observing all the Lord's commands and decrees blamelessly. [7] But they were childless because Elizabeth was not able to conceive, and they were both very old.

[8] Once when Zechariah's division was on duty and he was serving as priest before God, [9] he was chosen by lot, according to the custom of the priesthood, to go into the temple of the Lord and burn incense. [10] And when the time for the burning of incense came, all the assembled worshipers were praying outside.

[11] Then an angel of the Lord appeared to him, standing at the right side of the altar of incense. [12] When Zechariah saw him, he was startled and was gripped with fear. [13] But the angel said to him: "Do not be afraid, Zechariah; your prayer has been heard. Your wife Elizabeth will bear you a son, and you are to call him John. [14] He will be a joy and delight to you, and many will rejoice because of his birth, [15] for he will be great in the sight of the Lord. He is never to take wine or other fermented drink, and he will be filled with the Holy Spirit even before he is born. [16] He will bring back many of the people of Israel to the Lord their God. [17] And he will go on before the Lord, in the spirit and power of Elijah, to turn the hearts of the parents to their children and the disobedient to the wisdom of the righteous — to make ready a people prepared for the Lord."

[18] Zechariah asked the angel, "How can I be sure of this? I am an old man and my wife is well along in years."

[19] The angel said to him, "I am Gabriel. I stand in the presence of God, and I have been sent to speak to you and to tell you this good news. [20] And now you will be silent and not able to speak until the day this happens, because you did not believe my words, which will come true at their appointed time."

[21] Meanwhile, the people were waiting for Zechariah and wondering why he stayed so long in the temple. [22] When he came out, he could not speak to them. They realized he had seen a vision in the temple, for he kept making signs to them but remained unable to speak.

[23] When his time of service was completed, he returned home. [24] After this his wife Elizabeth became pregnant and for five months remained in seclusion. [25] "The Lord has done this for me," she said. "In these days he has shown his favor and taken away my disgrace among the people."

The Birth of Jesus Foretold

[26] In the sixth month of Elizabeth's pregnancy, God sent the angel Gabriel to Nazareth, a town in Galilee, [27] to a virgin pledged to be married to a man named Joseph, a descendant of David. The virgin's name was Mary. [28] The angel went to her and said, "Greetings, you who are highly favored! The Lord is with you."

[29] Mary was greatly troubled at his words and wondered what kind of greeting this might be. [30] But the angel said to her, "Do not be afraid, Mary; you have found favor with God. [31] You will conceive and give birth

---

[a] 1 Or been surely believed

TRUE STORY

READ: LUKE 1:3-4

Bible critics suggest the Bible is a collection of made-up stories. But that isn't the picture that emerges from the pages of Scripture. Luke, for example, purposely set out to write trustworthy history.

Luke begins his book about Jesus by acknowledging that others had already written about events everyone had seen and heard. These writers didn't invent stories about the Lord but relied on the reports of eyewitnesses. As someone who has "carefully investigated everything from the beginning" (Luke 1:3), Luke decides to write an orderly history for someone he calls Theophilus, or "lover of wisdom." This person might have been a new believer or someone especially interested in testing the claims of Christianity. Luke presents facts to help his reader be convinced of the truth about the Lord.

When you read about Jesus in Scripture, you can be sure you aren't reading a tale slapped together by a writer careless with facts. Luke penned both this gospel and the book of Acts, works that contain details that can be checked against archaeology and ancient documents. Luke's accuracy astounds historians, not only intelligent believers but also scholars hostile to the idea of God.

When Luke tells you about Jesus, he begins with key details surrounding his birth. What Luke writes is valuable history. But he has a bigger point. He wants to assure you that your Savior is on his way.

BUILDING FAITH WISDOM STRENGTH

JOHN THE BAPTIST

In those days John the Baptist came, preaching in the wilderness of Judea and saying, "Repent, for the kingdom of heaven has come near." MATTHEW 3:1-2

HIS NAME MEANS: "the LORD is gracious"
READ HIS STORY: *Matthew 3, 11, 14; Luke 1*

John the Baptist wouldn't have won "Best Dressed" in the school yearbook. And he definitely wouldn't have been voted "Most Likely to Succeed." Yet John succeeded in accomplishing everything God called him to do.

John was Jesus' cousin. Even before the two of them were born, John recognized God's Son by leaping in his mom's womb when Mary, who was pregnant with Jesus, came to visit (Luke 1:41). The next time we see John in the Bible, he's living in the desert, wearing clothes made from camel's hair and eating bugs. But instead of avoiding this crazy-looking man, people flock to him. They confess their sins, and John baptizes them in the Jordan River.

People wondered if John might be the Messiah. But he knew his role in God's kingdom. "After me comes one who is more powerful than I, whose sandals I am not worthy to carry," John said in Matthew 3:11. "He will baptize you with the Holy Spirit and fire."

Jesus walked from Nazareth to the Jordan to be baptized by John. When John saw the Lord, he said Jesus should baptize him instead. But Jesus insisted. John dunked Jesus in the river. When he came out of the water, God spoke from heaven.

John died (Herod Antipas, son of Herod the Great, beheaded him) proclaiming that the King of kings had come. In his short ministry, he made a powerful impact as a truth-telling, desert-dwelling, smelling-like-a-camel prophet of God who paved the way for Jesus.

to a son, and you are to call him Jesus. ³²He will be great and will be called the Son of the Most High. The Lord God will give him the throne of his father David, ³³and he will reign over Jacob's descendants forever; his kingdom will never end."

³⁴"How will this be," Mary asked the angel, "since I am a virgin?"

³⁵The angel answered, "The Holy Spirit will come on you, and the power of the Most High will overshadow you. So the holy one to be born will be called^a the Son of God. ³⁶Even Elizabeth your relative is going to have a child in her old age, and she who was said to be unable to conceive is in her sixth month. ³⁷For no word from God will ever fail."

³⁸"I am the Lord's servant," Mary answered. "May your word to me be fulfilled." Then the angel left her.

Mary Visits Elizabeth

³⁹At that time Mary got ready and hurried to a town in the hill country of Judea, ⁴⁰where she entered Zechariah's home and greeted Elizabeth. ⁴¹When Elizabeth heard Mary's greeting, the baby leaped in her womb, and Elizabeth was filled with the Holy Spirit. ⁴²In a loud voice she exclaimed: "Blessed are you among women, and blessed is the child you will bear! ⁴³But why am I so favored, that the mother of my Lord should come to me? ⁴⁴As soon as the sound of your greeting reached my ears, the baby in my womb leaped for joy. ⁴⁵Blessed is she who has believed that the Lord would fulfill his promises to her!"

Mary's Song

⁴⁶And Mary said:

"My soul glorifies the Lord
⁴⁷   and my spirit rejoices in God my
          Savior,
⁴⁸for he has been mindful
          of the humble state of his servant.
     From now on all generations will call
          me blessed,
⁴⁹   for the Mighty One has done great
          things for me —
          holy is his name.
⁵⁰His mercy extends to those who
          fear him,
          from generation to generation.

⁵¹He has performed mighty deeds with
          his arm;
     he has scattered those who are proud
          in their inmost thoughts.
⁵²He has brought down rulers from their
          thrones
     but has lifted up the humble.
⁵³He has filled the hungry with good things
     but has sent the rich away empty.
⁵⁴He has helped his servant Israel,
          remembering to be merciful
⁵⁵to Abraham and his descendants forever,
     just as he promised our ancestors."

⁵⁶Mary stayed with Elizabeth for about three months and then returned home.

The Birth of John the Baptist

⁵⁷When it was time for Elizabeth to have her baby, she gave birth to a son. ⁵⁸Her neighbors and relatives heard that the Lord had shown her great mercy, and they shared her joy.

⁵⁹On the eighth day they came to circumcise the child, and they were going to name him after his father Zechariah, ⁶⁰but his mother spoke up and said, "No! He is to be called John."

⁶¹They said to her, "There is no one among your relatives who has that name."

⁶²Then they made signs to his father, to find out what he would like to name the child. ⁶³He asked for a writing tablet, and to everyone's astonishment he wrote, "His name is John." ⁶⁴Immediately his mouth was opened and his tongue set free, and he began to speak, praising God. ⁶⁵All the neighbors were filled with awe, and throughout the hill country of Judea people were talking about all these things. ⁶⁶Everyone who heard this wondered about it, asking, "What then is this child going to be?" For the Lord's hand was with him.

Zechariah's Song

⁶⁷His father Zechariah was filled with the Holy Spirit and prophesied:

⁶⁸"Praise be to the Lord, the God of Israel,
          because he has come to his people and
          redeemed them.
⁶⁹He has raised up a horn^b of salvation
          for us
     in the house of his servant David

---

^a 35 Or *So the child to be born will be called holy,*   ^b 69 *Horn* here symbolizes a strong king.

[70] (as he said through his holy prophets
of long ago),
[71] salvation from our enemies
and from the hand of all who
hate us —
[72] to show mercy to our ancestors
and to remember his holy covenant,
[73] the oath he swore to our father
Abraham:
[74] to rescue us from the hand of our
enemies,
and to enable us to serve him without
fear
[75] in holiness and righteousness before
him all our days.

[76] And you, my child, will be called a
prophet of the Most High;
for you will go on before the Lord to
prepare the way for him,
[77] to give his people the knowledge of
salvation
through the forgiveness of their sins,
[78] because of the tender mercy of our God,
by which the rising sun will come to
us from heaven
[79] to shine on those living in darkness
and in the shadow of death,
to guide our feet into the path
of peace."

[80] And the child grew and became strong
in spirit[a]; and he lived in the wilderness until he appeared publicly to Israel.

The Birth of Jesus

2 In those days Caesar Augustus issued a
decree that a census should be taken of
the entire Roman world. [2](This was the first
census that took place while[b] Quirinius was
governor of Syria.) [3] And everyone went to
their own town to register.

[4] So Joseph also went up from the town of
Nazareth in Galilee to Judea, to Bethlehem
the town of David, because he belonged to
the house and line of David. [5] He went there
to register with Mary, who was pledged to be
married to him and was expecting a child.
[6] While they were there, the time came for
the baby to be born, [7] and she gave birth to
her firstborn, a son. She wrapped him in
cloths and placed him in a manger, because
there was no guest room available for them.

[8] And there were shepherds living out in
the fields nearby, keeping watch over their
flocks at night. [9] An angel of the Lord appeared to them, and the glory of the Lord
shone around them, and they were terrified. [10] But the angel said to them, "Do not be
afraid. I bring you good news that will cause
great joy for all the people. [11] Today in the
town of David a Savior has been born to you;
he is the Messiah, the Lord. [12] This will be a
sign to you: You will find a baby wrapped in
cloths and lying in a manger."

[13] Suddenly a great company of the heavenly host appeared with the angel, praising
God and saying,

[14] "Glory to God in the highest heaven,
and on earth peace to those on whom
his favor rests."

[15] When the angels had left them and gone
into heaven, the shepherds said to one another, "Let's go to Bethlehem and see this
thing that has happened, which the Lord has
told us about."

[16] So they hurried off and found Mary
and Joseph, and the baby, who was lying
in the manger. [17] When they had seen him,
they spread the word concerning what had
been told them about this child, [18] and all
who heard it were amazed at what the shepherds said to them. [19] But Mary treasured up
all these things and pondered them in her
heart. [20] The shepherds returned, glorifying
and praising God for all the things they had
heard and seen, which were just as they had
been told.

[21] On the eighth day, when it was time to
circumcise the child, he was named Jesus,
the name the angel had given him before he
was conceived.

Jesus Presented in the Temple

[22] When the time came for the purification rites required by the Law of Moses, Joseph and Mary took him to Jerusalem to present him to the Lord [23](as it is written in the
Law of the Lord, "Every firstborn male is to
be consecrated to the Lord"[c]), [24] and to offer a sacrifice in keeping with what is said in
the Law of the Lord: "a pair of doves or two
young pigeons."[d]

[25] Now there was a man in Jerusalem called

---

[a] 80 Or *in the Spirit*   [b] 2 Or *This census took place before*   [c] 23 Exodus 13:2,12   [d] 24 Lev. 12:8

MEN

OF THE BIBLE

JESUS

Today in the town of David a Savior has been born to you; he is the Messiah, the Lord. LUKE 2:11

HIS NAME MEANS: "the LORD saves"

READ HIS STORY: *The Gospels of Matthew, Mark, Luke and John*

Different people and different religions have different definitions of who Jesus is. But who is Jesus *really*? He actually told us when he lived on earth.

In Mark 2:5, Jesus said to a paralyzed man, "Son, your sins are forgiven." Since only God can forgive sins, Jesus had just announced that he is God.

Another time Jesus told the people that he existed prior to Abraham, even though Abraham lived 2,000 years earlier. In John 8:58, Jesus said, "Before Abraham was born, I am!" Since God's name is "I am" (Exodus 3:14), once again Jesus had announced he is God.

Don't stop with the words Jesus said, however. Look at what Jesus did to show us who he is. He gave sight to the blind and made the deaf hear. He brought dead people back to life. The miracles Jesus did prove that he is God.

When Jesus died on the cross and rose again, he revealed that he is the Messiah, the Savior of the world—the only one who could pay the punishment for all our sins. Over a period of forty days after his resurrection, he met with his followers (Acts 1:3). He showed them the wounds where his hands were nailed to the cross and where the soldiers pierced his side with a spear (John 19:34; 20:20-27). He showed them he is alive forever and mighty to save.

Who is Jesus?

Jesus is God's Son. He is our Savior. He died so you may live forever with God if you choose to trust in him to save you.

Simeon, who was righteous and devout. He was waiting for the consolation of Israel, and the Holy Spirit was on him. ²⁶It had been revealed to him by the Holy Spirit that he would not die before he had seen the Lord's Messiah. ²⁷Moved by the Spirit, he went into the temple courts. When the parents brought in the child Jesus to do for him what the custom of the Law required, ²⁸Simeon took him in his arms and praised God, saying:

²⁹"Sovereign Lord, as you have promised,
    you may now dismiss*ᵃ* your servant
        in peace.
³⁰For my eyes have seen your salvation,
³¹   which you have prepared in the
        sight of all nations:
³²a light for revelation to the Gentiles,
    and the glory of your people
        Israel."

³³The child's father and mother marveled at what was said about him. ³⁴Then Simeon blessed them and said to Mary, his mother: "This child is destined to cause the falling and rising of many in Israel, and to be a sign that will be spoken against, ³⁵so that the thoughts of many hearts will be revealed. And a sword will pierce your own soul too."

³⁶There was also a prophet, Anna, the daughter of Penuel, of the tribe of Asher. She was very old; she had lived with her husband seven years after her marriage, ³⁷and then was a widow until she was eighty-four.ᵇ She never left the temple but worshiped night and day, fasting and praying. ³⁸Coming up to them at that very moment, she gave thanks to God and spoke about the child to all who were looking forward to the redemption of Jerusalem.

³⁹When Joseph and Mary had done everything required by the Law of the Lord, they returned to Galilee to their own town of Nazareth. ⁴⁰And the child grew and became strong; he was filled with wisdom, and the grace of God was on him.

The Boy Jesus at the Temple

⁴¹Every year Jesus' parents went to Jerusalem for the Festival of the Passover. ⁴²When he was twelve years old, they went up to the festival, according to the custom. ⁴³After the festival was over, while his par-

ents were returning home, the boy Jesus stayed behind in Jerusalem, but they were unaware of it. ⁴⁴Thinking he was in their company, they traveled on for a day. Then they began looking for him among their relatives and friends. ⁴⁵When they did not find him, they went back to Jerusalem to look for him. ⁴⁶After three days they found him in the temple courts, sitting among the teachers, listening to them and asking them questions. ⁴⁷Everyone who heard him was amazed at his understanding and his answers. ⁴⁸When his parents saw him, they were astonished. His mother said to him, "Son, why have you treated us like this? Your father and I have been anxiously searching for you."

⁴⁹"Why were you searching for me?" he asked. "Didn't you know I had to be in my Father's house?"ᶜ ⁵⁰But they did not understand what he was saying to them.

⁵¹Then he went down to Nazareth with them and was obedient to them. But his mother treasured all these things in her heart. ⁵²And Jesus grew in wisdom and stature, and in favor with God and man.

John the Baptist Prepares the Way

3 In the fifteenth year of the reign of Tiberius Caesar—when Pontius Pilate was governor of Judea, Herod tetrarch of Galilee, his brother Philip tetrarch of Iturea and Traconitis, and Lysanias tetrarch of Abilene— ²during the high-priesthood of Annas and Caiaphas, the word of God came to John son of Zechariah in the wilderness. ³He went into all the country around the Jordan, preaching a baptism of repentance for the forgiveness of sins. ⁴As it is written in the book of the words of Isaiah the prophet:

"A voice of one calling in the
    wilderness,
'Prepare the way for the Lord,
    make straight paths for him.
⁵Every valley shall be filled in,
    every mountain and hill made low.
The crooked roads shall become
    straight,
    the rough ways smooth.
⁶And all people will see God's
    salvation.'"ᵈ

ᵃ 29 Or *promised, / now dismiss*   ᵇ 37 Or *then had been a widow for eighty-four years.*   ᶜ 49 Or *be about my Father's business*   ᵈ 6 Isaiah 40:3-5

[7]John said to the crowds coming out to be baptized by him, "You brood of vipers! Who warned you to flee from the coming wrath? [8]Produce fruit in keeping with repentance. And do not begin to say to yourselves, 'We have Abraham as our father.' For I tell you that out of these stones God can raise up children for Abraham. [9]The ax is already at the root of the trees, and every tree that does not produce good fruit will be cut down and thrown into the fire."

[10]"What should we do then?" the crowd asked.

[11]John answered, "Anyone who has two shirts should share with the one who has none, and anyone who has food should do the same."

[12]Even tax collectors came to be baptized. "Teacher," they asked, "what should we do?"

[13]"Don't collect any more than you are required to," he told them.

[14]Then some soldiers asked him, "And what should we do?"

He replied, "Don't extort money and don't accuse people falsely — be content with your pay."

[15]The people were waiting expectantly and were all wondering in their hearts if John might possibly be the Messiah. [16]John answered them all, "I baptize you with[a] water. But one who is more powerful than I will come, the straps of whose sandals I am not worthy to untie. He will baptize you with[a] the Holy Spirit and fire. [17]His winnowing fork is in his hand to clear his threshing floor and to gather the wheat into his barn, but he will burn up the chaff with unquenchable fire." [18]And with many other words John exhorted the people and proclaimed the good news to them.

[19]But when John rebuked Herod the tetrarch because of his marriage to Herodias, his brother's wife, and all the other evil things he had done, [20]Herod added this to them all: He locked John up in prison.

The Baptism and Genealogy of Jesus

[21]When all the people were being baptized, Jesus was baptized too. And as he was praying, heaven was opened [22]and the Holy Spirit descended on him in bodily form like a dove. And a voice came from heaven: "You are my Son, whom I love; with you I am well pleased."

[23]Now Jesus himself was about thirty years old when he began his ministry. He was the son, so it was thought, of Joseph,

the son of Heli, [24]the son of Matthat,
the son of Levi, the son of Melki,
the son of Jannai, the son of Joseph,
[25]the son of Mattathias, the son of Amos,
the son of Nahum, the son of Esli,
the son of Naggai, [26]the son of Maath,
the son of Mattathias, the son of Semein,
the son of Josek, the son of Joda,
[27]the son of Joanan, the son of Rhesa,
the son of Zerubbabel, the son of Shealtiel,
the son of Neri, [28]the son of Melki,
the son of Addi, the son of Cosam,
the son of Elmadam, the son of Er,
[29]the son of Joshua, the son of Eliezer,
the son of Jorim, the son of Matthat,
the son of Levi, [30]the son of Simeon,
the son of Judah, the son of Joseph,
the son of Jonam, the son of Eliakim,
[31]the son of Melea, the son of Menna,
the son of Mattatha, the son of Nathan,
the son of David, [32]the son of Jesse,
the son of Obed, the son of Boaz,
the son of Salmon,[b] the son of Nahshon,
[33]the son of Amminadab, the son of Ram,[c]
the son of Hezron, the son of Perez,
the son of Judah, [34]the son of Jacob,
the son of Isaac, the son of Abraham,
the son of Terah, the son of Nahor,
[35]the son of Serug, the son of Reu,
the son of Peleg, the son of Eber,
the son of Shelah, [36]the son of Cainan,
the son of Arphaxad, the son of Shem,
the son of Noah, the son of Lamech,
[37]the son of Methuselah, the son of Enoch,
the son of Jared, the son of Mahalalel,
the son of Kenan, [38]the son of Enosh,
the son of Seth, the son of Adam,
the son of God.

Jesus Is Tested in the Wilderness

4 Jesus, full of the Holy Spirit, left the Jordan and was led by the Spirit into the wilderness, [2]where for forty days he was tempted[d] by the devil. He ate nothing during

---

[a] 16 Or in [b] 32 Some early manuscripts *Sala the son of Arni;* other manuscripts vary widely. [c] 33 Some manuscripts *Amminadab, the son of Admin,* [d] 2 The Greek for *tempted* can also mean *tested.*

those days, and at the end of them he was hungry.

³The devil said to him, "If you are the Son of God, tell this stone to become bread."

⁴Jesus answered, "It is written: 'Man shall not live on bread alone.'ᵃ"

⁵The devil led him up to a high place and showed him in an instant all the kingdoms of the world. ⁶And he said to him, "I will give you all their authority and splendor; it has been given to me, and I can give it to anyone I want to. ⁷If you worship me, it will all be yours."

⁸Jesus answered, "It is written: 'Worship the Lord your God and serve him only.'ᵇ"

⁹The devil led him to Jerusalem and had him stand on the highest point of the temple. "If you are the Son of God," he said, "throw yourself down from here. ¹⁰For it is written:

"'He will command his angels
  concerning you
  to guard you carefully;
¹¹they will lift you up in their hands,
  so that you will not strike your foot
  against a stone.'ᶜ"

¹²Jesus answered, "It is said: 'Do not put the Lord your God to the test.'ᵈ"

¹³When the devil had finished all this tempting, he left him until an opportune time.

Jesus Rejected at Nazareth

¹⁴Jesus returned to Galilee in the power of the Spirit, and news about him spread through the whole countryside. ¹⁵He was teaching in their synagogues, and everyone praised him.

¹⁶He went to Nazareth, where he had been brought up, and on the Sabbath day he went into the synagogue, as was his custom. He stood up to read, ¹⁷and the scroll of the prophet Isaiah was handed to him. Unrolling it, he found the place where it is written:

¹⁸ "The Spirit of the Lord is on me,
  because he has anointed me
  to proclaim good news to the poor.
He has sent me to proclaim freedom for
  the prisoners

and recovery of sight for the blind,
  to set the oppressed free,
¹⁹ to proclaim the year of the Lord's
    favor."ᵉ

²⁰Then he rolled up the scroll, gave it back to the attendant and sat down. The eyes of everyone in the synagogue were fastened on him. ²¹He began by saying to them, "Today this scripture is fulfilled in your hearing."

²²All spoke well of him and were amazed at the gracious words that came from his lips. "Isn't this Joseph's son?" they asked.

²³Jesus said to them, "Surely you will quote this proverb to me: 'Physician, heal yourself!' And you will tell me, 'Do here in your hometown what we have heard that you did in Capernaum.'"

²⁴"Truly I tell you," he continued, "no prophet is accepted in his hometown. ²⁵I assure you that there were many widows in Israel in Elijah's time, when the sky was shut for three and a half years and there was a severe famine throughout the land. ²⁶Yet Elijah was not sent to any of them, but to a widow in Zarephath in the region of Sidon. ²⁷And there were many in Israel with leprosyᶠ in the time of Elisha the prophet, yet not one of them was cleansed—only Naaman the Syrian."

²⁸All the people in the synagogue were furious when they heard this. ²⁹They got up, drove him out of the town, and took him to the brow of the hill on which the town was built, in order to throw him off the cliff. ³⁰But he walked right through the crowd and went on his way.

Jesus Drives Out an Impure Spirit

³¹Then he went down to Capernaum, a town in Galilee, and on the Sabbath he taught the people. ³²They were amazed at his teaching, because his words had authority.

³³In the synagogue there was a man possessed by a demon, an impure spirit. He cried out at the top of his voice, ³⁴"Go away! What do you want with us, Jesus of Nazareth? Have you come to destroy us? I know who you are—the Holy One of God!"

³⁵"Be quiet!" Jesus said sternly. "Come

ᵃ 4 Deut. 8:3   ᵇ 8 Deut. 6:13   ᶜ 11 Psalm 91:11,12   ᵈ 12 Deut. 6:16   ᵉ 19 Isaiah 61:1,2 (see Septuagint); Isaiah 58:6   ᶠ 27 The Greek word traditionally translated *leprosy* was used for various diseases affecting the skin.

THE WEAK SPOT

READ: LUKE 4:1-13

Jesus didn't doubt the reality of the devil. The Savior strode into the badlands with one goal, to unmask Satan, and made him the first stop on his itinerary.

Does God do the same with us? Might the Spirit of God lead us into the wilderness? If I were the devil, I'd tell you no. I would want you to think that I, on occasion, snooker heaven. That I catch God napping. That I sneak in when he isn't looking and snatch his children out of his hand. I'd leave you sleeping with one eye open. But Scripture reveals otherwise.

BUILDING FAITH WISDOM STRENGTH

The next time you hear the phrase "all hell broke loose," correct the speaker. Hell does not break loose. God uses Satan's temptation to strengthen us. (If I were the devil, that would aggravate me to no end.) Times of testing are actually times of training, purification, and strength building.

We know Satan will attack weak spots first. Forty days of fasting left Jesus famished, so Satan began with the topic of bread. Jesus' stomach was empty, so to the stomach Satan turned.

Where are you empty? Are you hungry for attention, craving success, longing for intimacy? Be aware of your weaknesses. Bring them to God before Satan brings them to you. Satan will tell you to turn stones into bread. In other words, meet your own needs, take matters into your own hands, leave God out of the picture.

out of him!" Then the demon threw the man down before them all and came out without injuring him.

³⁶All the people were amazed and said to each other, "What words these are! With authority and power he gives orders to impure spirits and they come out!" ³⁷And the news about him spread throughout the surrounding area.

Jesus Heals Many

³⁸Jesus left the synagogue and went to the home of Simon. Now Simon's mother-in-law was suffering from a high fever, and they asked Jesus to help her. ³⁹So he bent over her and rebuked the fever, and it left her. She got up at once and began to wait on them.

⁴⁰At sunset, the people brought to Jesus all who had various kinds of sickness, and laying his hands on each one, he healed them. ⁴¹Moreover, demons came out of many people, shouting, "You are the Son of God!" But he rebuked them and would not allow them to speak, because they knew he was the Messiah.

⁴²At daybreak, Jesus went out to a solitary place. The people were looking for him and when they came to where he was, they tried to keep him from leaving them. ⁴³But he said, "I must proclaim the good news of the kingdom of God to the other towns also, because that is why I was sent." ⁴⁴And he kept on preaching in the synagogues of Judea.

Jesus Calls His First Disciples

5 One day as Jesus was standing by the Lake of Gennesaret,ᵃ the people were crowding around him and listening to the word of God. ²He saw at the water's edge two boats, left there by the fishermen, who were washing their nets. ³He got into one of the boats, the one belonging to Simon, and asked him to put out a little from shore. Then he sat down and taught the people from the boat.

⁴When he had finished speaking, he said to Simon, "Put out into deep water, and let down the nets for a catch."

⁵Simon answered, "Master, we've worked hard all night and haven't caught anything. But because you say so, I will let down the nets."

⁶When they had done so, they caught such a large number of fish that their nets began to break. ⁷So they signaled their partners in the other boat to come and help them, and they came and filled both boats so full that they began to sink.

⁸When Simon Peter saw this, he fell at Jesus' knees and said, "Go away from me, Lord; I am a sinful man!" ⁹For he and all his companions were astonished at the catch of fish they had taken, ¹⁰and so were James and John, the sons of Zebedee, Simon's partners.

Then Jesus said to Simon, "Don't be afraid; from now on you will fish for people." ¹¹So they pulled their boats up on shore, left everything and followed him.

Jesus Heals a Man With Leprosy

¹²While Jesus was in one of the towns, a man came along who was covered with leprosy.ᵇ When he saw Jesus, he fell with his face to the ground and begged him, "Lord, if you are willing, you can make me clean."

¹³Jesus reached out his hand and touched the man. "I am willing," he said. "Be clean!" And immediately the leprosy left him.

¹⁴Then Jesus ordered him, "Don't tell anyone, but go, show yourself to the priest and offer the sacrifices that Moses commanded for your cleansing, as a testimony to them."

¹⁵Yet the news about him spread all the more, so that crowds of people came to hear him and to be healed of their sicknesses. ¹⁶But Jesus often withdrew to lonely places and prayed.

Jesus Forgives and Heals a Paralyzed Man

¹⁷One day Jesus was teaching, and Pharisees and teachers of the law were sitting there. They had come from every village of Galilee and from Judea and Jerusalem. And the power of the Lord was with Jesus to heal the sick. ¹⁸Some men came carrying a paralyzed man on a mat and tried to take him into the house to lay him before Jesus. ¹⁹When they could not find a way to do this because of the crowd, they went up on the roof and lowered him on his mat through the tiles into the middle of the crowd, right in front of Jesus.

ᵃ 1 That is, the Sea of Galilee   ᵇ 12 The Greek word traditionally translated *leprosy* was used for various diseases affecting the skin.

²⁰When Jesus saw their faith, he said, "Friend, your sins are forgiven."

²¹The Pharisees and the teachers of the law began thinking to themselves, "Who is this fellow who speaks blasphemy? Who can forgive sins but God alone?"

²²Jesus knew what they were thinking and asked, "Why are you thinking these things in your hearts? ²³Which is easier: to say, 'Your sins are forgiven,' or to say, 'Get up and walk'? ²⁴But I want you to know that the Son of Man has authority on earth to forgive sins." So he said to the paralyzed man, "I tell you, get up, take your mat and go home." ²⁵Immediately he stood up in front of them, took what he had been lying on and went home praising God. ²⁶Everyone was amazed and gave praise to God. They were filled with awe and said, "We have seen remarkable things today."

Jesus Calls Levi and Eats With Sinners

²⁷After this, Jesus went out and saw a tax collector by the name of Levi sitting at his tax booth. "Follow me," Jesus said to him, ²⁸and Levi got up, left everything and followed him.

²⁹Then Levi held a great banquet for Jesus at his house, and a large crowd of tax collectors and others were eating with them. ³⁰But the Pharisees and the teachers of the law who belonged to their sect complained to his disciples, "Why do you eat and drink with tax collectors and sinners?"

³¹Jesus answered them, "It is not the healthy who need a doctor, but the sick. ³²I have not come to call the righteous, but sinners to repentance."

Jesus Questioned About Fasting

³³They said to him, "John's disciples often fast and pray, and so do the disciples of the Pharisees, but yours go on eating and drinking."

³⁴Jesus answered, "Can you make the friends of the bridegroom fast while he is with them? ³⁵But the time will come when the bridegroom will be taken from them; in those days they will fast."

³⁶He told them this parable: "No one tears a piece out of a new garment to patch an old one. Otherwise, they will have torn the new garment, and the patch from the new will not match the old. ³⁷And no one pours new wine into old wineskins. Otherwise, the new wine will burst the skins; the wine will run out and the wineskins will be ruined. ³⁸No, new wine must be poured into new wineskins. ³⁹And no one after drinking old wine wants the new, for they say, 'The old is better.' "

Jesus Is Lord of the Sabbath

6 One Sabbath Jesus was going through the grainfields, and his disciples began to pick some heads of grain, rub them in their hands and eat the kernels. ²Some of the Pharisees asked, "Why are you doing what is unlawful on the Sabbath?"

³Jesus answered them, "Have you never read what David did when he and his companions were hungry? ⁴He entered the house of God, and taking the consecrated bread, he ate what is lawful only for priests to eat. And he also gave some to his companions." ⁵Then Jesus said to them, "The Son of Man is Lord of the Sabbath."

⁶On another Sabbath he went into the synagogue and was teaching, and a man was there whose right hand was shriveled. ⁷The Pharisees and the teachers of the law were looking for a reason to accuse Jesus, so they watched him closely to see if he would heal on the Sabbath. ⁸But Jesus knew what they were thinking and said to the man with the shriveled hand, "Get up and stand in front of everyone." So he got up and stood there.

⁹Then Jesus said to them, "I ask you, which is lawful on the Sabbath: to do good or to do evil, to save life or to destroy it?"

¹⁰He looked around at them all, and then said to the man, "Stretch out your hand." He did so, and his hand was completely restored. ¹¹But the Pharisees and the teachers of the law were furious and began to discuss with one another what they might do to Jesus.

The Twelve Apostles

¹²One of those days Jesus went out to a mountainside to pray, and spent the night praying to God. ¹³When morning came, he called his disciples to him and chose twelve of them, whom he also designated apostles: ¹⁴Simon (whom he named Peter), his brother Andrew, James, John, Philip, Bartholomew, ¹⁵Matthew, Thomas, James son of Alphaeus, Simon who was called the Zealot, ¹⁶Judas

son of James, and Judas Iscariot, who became a traitor.

Blessings and Woes

¹⁷He went down with them and stood on a level place. A large crowd of his disciples was there and a great number of people from all over Judea, from Jerusalem, and from the coastal region around Tyre and Sidon, ¹⁸who had come to hear him and to be healed of their diseases. Those troubled by impure spirits were cured, ¹⁹and the people all tried to touch him, because power was coming from him and healing them all.

²⁰Looking at his disciples, he said:

"Blessed are you who are poor,
for yours is the kingdom of God.
²¹Blessed are you who hunger now,
for you will be satisfied.
Blessed are you who weep now,
for you will laugh.
²²Blessed are you when people hate you,
when they exclude you and insult you
and reject your name as evil,
because of the Son of Man.

²³"Rejoice in that day and leap for joy, because great is your reward in heaven. For that is how their ancestors treated the prophets.

²⁴"But woe to you who are rich,
for you have already received your
comfort.
²⁵Woe to you who are well fed now,
for you will go hungry.
Woe to you who laugh now,
for you will mourn and weep.
²⁶Woe to you when everyone speaks well
of you,
for that is how their ancestors treated
the false prophets.

Love for Enemies

²⁷"But to you who are listening I say: Love your enemies, do good to those who hate you, ²⁸bless those who curse you, pray for those who mistreat you. ²⁹If someone slaps you on one cheek, turn to them the other also. If someone takes your coat, do not withhold your shirt from them. ³⁰Give to everyone who asks you, and if anyone takes what belongs to you, do not demand it back. ³¹Do to others as you would have them do to you.

³²"If you love those who love you, what credit is that to you? Even sinners love those who love them. ³³And if you do good to those who are good to you, what credit is that to you? Even sinners do that. ³⁴And if you lend to those from whom you expect repayment, what credit is that to you? Even sinners lend to sinners, expecting to be repaid in full. ³⁵But love your enemies, do good to them, and lend to them without expecting to get anything back. Then your reward will be great, and you will be children of the Most High, because he is kind to the ungrateful and wicked. ³⁶Be merciful, just as your Father is merciful.

Judging Others

³⁷"Do not judge, and you will not be judged. Do not condemn, and you will not be condemned. Forgive, and you will be forgiven. ³⁸Give, and it will be given to you. A good measure, pressed down, shaken together and running over, will be poured into your lap. For with the measure you use, it will be measured to you."

³⁹He also told them this parable: "Can the blind lead the blind? Will they not both fall into a pit? ⁴⁰The student is not above the teacher, but everyone who is fully trained will be like their teacher.

⁴¹"Why do you look at the speck of sawdust in your brother's eye and pay no attention to the plank in your own eye? ⁴²How can you say to your brother, 'Brother, let me take the speck out of your eye,' when you yourself fail to see the plank in your own eye? You hypocrite, first take the plank out of your eye, and then you will see clearly to remove the speck from your brother's eye.

A Tree and Its Fruit

⁴³"No good tree bears bad fruit, nor does a bad tree bear good fruit. ⁴⁴Each tree is recognized by its own fruit. People do not pick figs from thornbushes, or grapes from briers. ⁴⁵A good man brings good things out of the good stored up in his heart, and an evil man brings evil things out of the evil stored up in his heart. For the mouth speaks what the heart is full of.

The Wise and Foolish Builders

⁴⁶"Why do you call me, 'Lord, Lord,' and do not do what I say? ⁴⁷As for everyone who

INSIDE JOB

READ: LUKE 6:42

The main problem Jesus had with these religious leaders is they were hypocrites. I'm not guessing at that, that's what he calls them. To their faces. Eight times. The problem that Jesus had with these teachers is that what they were teaching wasn't a reflection of who they really were. Jesus has harsh words for those who were trying to impress others through their religious credentials. It's interesting to note that as severe as Jesus was with these religious leaders he is just as tender and encouraging to those who have genuinely given him their hearts, even if they don't have it all together on the outside. Please don't miss this: Jesus doesn't expect followers to be perfect, but he does call them to be authentic.

BUILDING FAITH WISDOM STRENGTH

Every week I get a chance to sit down with the people who are new to our church. On any given week there are anywhere from two to twenty people sitting around a table. There are those who are new to Christ and the church. They haven't learned the rules. And when they tell their stories, they'll tell about eating disorders, gambling problems, suicide attempts, and drug addictions. They just don't know any better. And I hope nobody tells them that they're supposed to act like they've got it all together. You don't often get to see people without a mask. And it's such a beautiful thing.

That's what Christ wants in a follower—someone who isn't pretending on the outside to have it all together.

Taken from *Not a Fan Student Edition* by Kyle Idleman, copyright © 2012 by City on the Hill Studio, Inc., published by Zondervan.

comes to me and hears my words and puts them into practice, I will show you what they are like. ⁴⁸They are like a man building a house, who dug down deep and laid the foundation on rock. When a flood came, the torrent struck that house but could not shake it, because it was well built. ⁴⁹But the one who hears my words and does not put them into practice is like a man who built a house on the ground without a foundation. The moment the torrent struck that house, it collapsed and its destruction was complete."

The Faith of the Centurion

7 When Jesus had finished saying all this to the people who were listening, he entered Capernaum. ²There a centurion's servant, whom his master valued highly, was sick and about to die. ³The centurion heard of Jesus and sent some elders of the Jews to him, asking him to come and heal his servant. ⁴When they came to Jesus, they pleaded earnestly with him, "This man deserves to have you do this, ⁵because he loves our nation and has built our synagogue." ⁶So Jesus went with them.

He was not far from the house when the centurion sent friends to say to him: "Lord, don't trouble yourself, for I do not deserve to have you come under my roof. ⁷That is why I did not even consider myself worthy to come to you. But say the word, and my servant will be healed. ⁸For I myself am a man under authority, with soldiers under me. I tell this one, 'Go,' and he goes; and that one, 'Come,' and he comes. I say to my servant, 'Do this,' and he does it."

⁹When Jesus heard this, he was amazed at him, and turning to the crowd following him, he said, "I tell you, I have not found such great faith even in Israel." ¹⁰Then the men who had been sent returned to the house and found the servant well.

Jesus Raises a Widow's Son

¹¹Soon afterward, Jesus went to a town called Nain, and his disciples and a large crowd went along with him. ¹²As he approached the town gate, a dead person was being carried out — the only son of his mother, and she was a widow. And a large crowd from the town was with her. ¹³When the Lord saw her, his heart went out to her and he said, "Don't cry."

¹⁴Then he went up and touched the bier they were carrying him on, and the bearers stood still. He said, "Young man, I say to you, get up!" ¹⁵The dead man sat up and began to talk, and Jesus gave him back to his mother.

¹⁶They were all filled with awe and praised God. "A great prophet has appeared among us," they said. "God has come to help his people." ¹⁷This news about Jesus spread throughout Judea and the surrounding country.

Jesus and John the Baptist

¹⁸John's disciples told him about all these things. Calling two of them, ¹⁹he sent them to the Lord to ask, "Are you the one who is to come, or should we expect someone else?"

²⁰When the men came to Jesus, they said, "John the Baptist sent us to you to ask, 'Are you the one who is to come, or should we expect someone else?'"

²¹At that very time Jesus cured many who had diseases, sicknesses and evil spirits, and gave sight to many who were blind. ²²So he replied to the messengers, "Go back and report to John what you have seen and heard: The blind receive sight, the lame walk, those who have leprosy*ᵃ* are cleansed, the deaf hear, the dead are raised, and the good news is proclaimed to the poor. ²³Blessed is anyone who does not stumble on account of me."

²⁴After John's messengers left, Jesus began to speak to the crowd about John: "What did you go out into the wilderness to see? A reed swayed by the wind? ²⁵If not, what did you go out to see? A man dressed in fine clothes? No, those who wear expensive clothes and indulge in luxury are in palaces. ²⁶But what did you go out to see? A prophet? Yes, I tell you, and more than a prophet. ²⁷This is the one about whom it is written:

"'I will send my messenger ahead of you,
  who will prepare your way before you.'*ᵇ*

²⁸I tell you, among those born of women there is no one greater than John; yet the one who is least in the kingdom of God is greater than he."

ᵃ 22 The Greek word traditionally translated *leprosy* was used for various diseases affecting the skin.
ᵇ 27 Mal. 3:1

²⁹(All the people, even the tax collectors, when they heard Jesus' words, acknowledged that God's way was right, because they had been baptized by John. ³⁰But the Pharisees and the experts in the law rejected God's purpose for themselves, because they had not been baptized by John.)

³¹Jesus went on to say, "To what, then, can I compare the people of this generation? What are they like? ³²They are like children sitting in the marketplace and calling out to each other:

" 'We played the pipe for you,
    and you did not dance;
  we sang a dirge,
    and you did not cry.'

³³For John the Baptist came neither eating bread nor drinking wine, and you say, 'He has a demon.' ³⁴The Son of Man came eating and drinking, and you say, 'Here is a glutton and a drunkard, a friend of tax collectors and sinners.' ³⁵But wisdom is proved right by all her children."

Jesus Anointed by a Sinful Woman

³⁶When one of the Pharisees invited Jesus to have dinner with him, he went to the Pharisee's house and reclined at the table. ³⁷A woman in that town who lived a sinful life learned that Jesus was eating at the Pharisee's house, so she came there with an alabaster jar of perfume. ³⁸As she stood behind him at his feet weeping, she began to wet his feet with her tears. Then she wiped them with her hair, kissed them and poured perfume on them.

³⁹When the Pharisee who had invited him saw this, he said to himself, "If this man were a prophet, he would know who is touching him and what kind of woman she is — that she is a sinner."

⁴⁰Jesus answered him, "Simon, I have something to tell you."

"Tell me, teacher," he said.

⁴¹"Two people owed money to a certain moneylender. One owed him five hundred denarii,ᵃ and the other fifty. ⁴²Neither of them had the money to pay him back, so he forgave the debts of both. Now which of them will love him more?"

⁴³Simon replied, "I suppose the one who had the bigger debt forgiven."

"You have judged correctly," Jesus said.

⁴⁴Then he turned toward the woman and said to Simon, "Do you see this woman? I came into your house. You did not give me any water for my feet, but she wet my feet with her tears and wiped them with her hair. ⁴⁵You did not give me a kiss, but this woman, from the time I entered, has not stopped kissing my feet. ⁴⁶You did not put oil on my head, but she has poured perfume on my feet. ⁴⁷Therefore, I tell you, her many sins have been forgiven — as her great love has shown. But whoever has been forgiven little loves little."

⁴⁸Then Jesus said to her, "Your sins are forgiven."

⁴⁹The other guests began to say among themselves, "Who is this who even forgives sins?"

⁵⁰Jesus said to the woman, "Your faith has saved you; go in peace."

The Parable of the Sower

8 After this, Jesus traveled about from one town and village to another, proclaiming the good news of the kingdom of God. The Twelve were with him, ²and also some women who had been cured of evil spirits and diseases: Mary (called Magdalene) from whom seven demons had come out; ³Joanna the wife of Chuza, the manager of Herod's household; Susanna; and many others. These women were helping to support them out of their own means.

⁴While a large crowd was gathering and people were coming to Jesus from town after town, he told this parable: ⁵"A farmer went out to sow his seed. As he was scattering the seed, some fell along the path; it was trampled on, and the birds ate it up. ⁶Some fell on rocky ground, and when it came up, the plants withered because they had no moisture. ⁷Other seed fell among thorns, which grew up with it and choked the plants. ⁸Still other seed fell on good soil. It came up and yielded a crop, a hundred times more than was sown."

When he said this, he called out, "Whoever has ears to hear, let them hear."

⁹His disciples asked him what this parable meant. ¹⁰He said, "The knowledge of the secrets of the kingdom of God has been given

---

ᵃ 41 A denarius was the usual daily wage of a day laborer (see Matt. 20:2).

BOLD AND AWKWARD

READ: LUKE 7:36-38

This is a classic. A party hosted by a Pharisee? Come on, that's classy humor—how fun could it have been? No deejay. No punch. And definitely no pigs in blankets because that wouldn't be kosher! The party favors were probably phylacteries. This is the definition of "lame party."

Then in walks this woman.

Jesus had a twinkle in his eye, guaranteed. He knew it was about to get offensive: the best kind of fun. If you follow in his footsteps, you'll eventually offend some Pharisees too. Can you imagine the look on the Pharisees' faces when this woman makes her surprise appearance? They start coughing uncontrollably when she busts out her jar of perfume.

BUILDING FAITH WISDOM STRENGTH

And then she starts wiping Jesus' feet with her hair.

Can you say awkward?

But she definitely made a statement, didn't she? This is one of the most intense, beautiful acts of worship and faith in all of Scripture. She risked her reputation (what little she had left of it) to honor Jesus. She knew the Pharisees stoned women like her, but that didn't keep her from going for it.

She used her most precious possession, an alabaster jar of perfume. And this is some beautiful irony: the perfume she used as a prostitute would become her profession of faith. She poured out every last drop at the feet of Jesus.

We all need to come clean sooner or later. This is that moment for this woman. Quit acting like sin disqualifies you from the grace of God. That's the only thing that qualifies us.

to you, but to others I speak in parables, so that,

> " 'though seeing, they may not see;
> though hearing, they may not
> understand.'[a]

[11] "This is the meaning of the parable: The seed is the word of God. [12] Those along the path are the ones who hear, and then the devil comes and takes away the word from their hearts, so that they may not believe and be saved. [13] Those on the rocky ground are the ones who receive the word with joy when they hear it, but they have no root. They believe for a while, but in the time of testing they fall away. [14] The seed that fell among thorns stands for those who hear, but as they go on their way they are choked by life's worries, riches and pleasures, and they do not mature. [15] But the seed on good soil stands for those with a noble and good heart, who hear the word, retain it, and by persevering produce a crop.

A Lamp on a Stand

[16] "No one lights a lamp and hides it in a clay jar or puts it under a bed. Instead, they put it on a stand, so that those who come in can see the light. [17] For there is nothing hidden that will not be disclosed, and nothing concealed that will not be known or brought out into the open. [18] Therefore consider carefully how you listen. Whoever has will be given more; whoever does not have, even what they think they have will be taken from them."

Jesus' Mother and Brothers

[19] Now Jesus' mother and brothers came to see him, but they were not able to get near him because of the crowd. [20] Someone told him, "Your mother and brothers are standing outside, wanting to see you."

[21] He replied, "My mother and brothers are those who hear God's word and put it into practice."

Jesus Calms the Storm

[22] One day Jesus said to his disciples, "Let us go over to the other side of the lake." So they got into a boat and set out. [23] As they sailed, he fell asleep. A squall came down on the lake, so that the boat was being swamped, and they were in great danger.

[24] The disciples went and woke him, saying, "Master, Master, we're going to drown!"

He got up and rebuked the wind and the raging waters; the storm subsided, and all was calm. [25] "Where is your faith?" he asked his disciples.

In fear and amazement they asked one another, "Who is this? He commands even the winds and the water, and they obey him."

Jesus Restores a Demon-Possessed Man

[26] They sailed to the region of the Gerasenes,[b] which is across the lake from Galilee. [27] When Jesus stepped ashore, he was met by a demon-possessed man from the town. For a long time this man had not worn clothes or lived in a house, but had lived in the tombs. [28] When he saw Jesus, he cried out and fell at his feet, shouting at the top of his voice, "What do you want with me, Jesus, Son of the Most High God? I beg you, don't torture me!" [29] For Jesus had commanded the impure spirit to come out of the man. Many times it had seized him, and though he was chained hand and foot and kept under guard, he had broken his chains and had been driven by the demon into solitary places.

[30] Jesus asked him, "What is your name?"

"Legion," he replied, because many demons had gone into him. [31] And they begged Jesus repeatedly not to order them to go into the Abyss.

[32] A large herd of pigs was feeding there on the hillside. The demons begged Jesus to let them go into the pigs, and he gave them permission. [33] When the demons came out of the man, they went into the pigs, and the herd rushed down the steep bank into the lake and was drowned.

[34] When those tending the pigs saw what had happened, they ran off and reported this in the town and countryside, [35] and the people went out to see what had happened. When they came to Jesus, they found the man from whom the demons had gone out, sitting at Jesus' feet, dressed and in his right mind; and they were afraid. [36] Those who had seen it told the people how the demon-possessed

---

a 10 Isaiah 6:9   *b* 26 Some manuscripts *Gadarenes*; other manuscripts *Gergesenes*; also in verse 37

JAIRUS

Then a man named Jairus, a synagogue leader, came and fell at Jesus' feet, pleading with him to come to his house because his only daughter, a girl of about twelve, was dying. LUKE 8:41-42

HIS NAME MEANS: "he will enlighten"

READ HIS STORY: *Matthew 9:18–26; Mark 5:21–43; Luke 8:40–56*

airus was an important man. He was a leader in a synagogue, so he was well-known and respected as a religious authority. Yet when Jairus had a problem, who did he turn to? Pharisees, scribes or other synagogue leaders? No. He turned to Jesus.

Jairus' twelve-year-old daughter was dying. He didn't stay home with the rest of his friends and family, overcome with grief. In his distress and sadness, Jairus left the others behind and went to find Jesus. When he did locate Jesus, Jairus fell at his feet. He didn't care who saw him or what people would think. He was desperate and knew that Jesus was the only one with the power to help him. Mark 5:23 says, "He pleaded earnestly with him, 'My little daughter is dying. Please come and put your hands on her so that she will be healed and live.'"

After that, however, the situation got worse, not better. Someone arrived to say his daughter had already died. But Jairus didn't give up when he heard the news. It was then that Jesus comforted Jairus and told him not to fear. They continued on to Jairus' house. And Jesus gave his healing touch—he brought the little girl back to life.

Do you have an overwhelming, insurmountable problem? Seek after Jesus. Fall at his feet as Jairus did. Speak earnestly with him and place the situation, whatever it may be, into his capable and loving hands.

man had been cured. [37] Then all the people of the region of the Gerasenes asked Jesus to leave them, because they were overcome with fear. So he got into the boat and left.

[38] The man from whom the demons had gone out begged to go with him, but Jesus sent him away, saying, [39] "Return home and tell how much God has done for you." So the man went away and told all over town how much Jesus had done for him.

Jesus Raises a Dead Girl and Heals a Sick Woman

[40] Now when Jesus returned, a crowd welcomed him, for they were all expecting him. [41] Then a man named Jairus, a synagogue leader, came and fell at Jesus' feet, pleading with him to come to his house [42] because his only daughter, a girl of about twelve, was dying.

As Jesus was on his way, the crowds almost crushed him. [43] And a woman was there who had been subject to bleeding for twelve years,[a] but no one could heal her. [44] She came up behind him and touched the edge of his cloak, and immediately her bleeding stopped.

[45] "Who touched me?" Jesus asked.

When they all denied it, Peter said, "Master, the people are crowding and pressing against you."

[46] But Jesus said, "Someone touched me; I know that power has gone out from me."

[47] Then the woman, seeing that she could not go unnoticed, came trembling and fell at his feet. In the presence of all the people, she told why she had touched him and how she had been instantly healed. [48] Then he said to her, "Daughter, your faith has healed you. Go in peace."

[49] While Jesus was still speaking, someone came from the house of Jairus, the synagogue leader. "Your daughter is dead," he said. "Don't bother the teacher anymore."

[50] Hearing this, Jesus said to Jairus, "Don't be afraid; just believe, and she will be healed."

[51] When he arrived at the house of Jairus, he did not let anyone go in with him except Peter, John and James, and the child's father and mother. [52] Meanwhile, all the people were wailing and mourning for her. "Stop wailing," Jesus said. "She is not dead but asleep."

[53] They laughed at him, knowing that she was dead. [54] But he took her by the hand and said, "My child, get up!" [55] Her spirit returned, and at once she stood up. Then Jesus told them to give her something to eat. [56] Her parents were astonished, but he ordered them not to tell anyone what had happened.

Jesus Sends Out the Twelve

9 When Jesus had called the Twelve together, he gave them power and authority to drive out all demons and to cure diseases, [2] and he sent them out to proclaim the kingdom of God and to heal the sick. [3] He told them: "Take nothing for the journey — no staff, no bag, no bread, no money, no extra shirt. [4] Whatever house you enter, stay there until you leave that town. [5] If people do not welcome you, leave their town and shake the dust off your feet as a testimony against them." [6] So they set out and went from village to village, proclaiming the good news and healing people everywhere.

[7] Now Herod the tetrarch heard about all that was going on. And he was perplexed because some were saying that John had been raised from the dead, [8] others that Elijah had appeared, and still others that one of the prophets of long ago had come back to life. [9] But Herod said, "I beheaded John. Who, then, is this I hear such things about?" And he tried to see him.

Jesus Feeds the Five Thousand

[10] When the apostles returned, they reported to Jesus what they had done. Then he took them with him and they withdrew by themselves to a town called Bethsaida, [11] but the crowds learned about it and followed him. He welcomed them and spoke to them about the kingdom of God, and healed those who needed healing.

[12] Late in the afternoon the Twelve came to him and said, "Send the crowd away so they can go to the surrounding villages and countryside and find food and lodging, because we are in a remote place here."

[13] He replied, "You give them something to eat."

They answered, "We have only five loaves

---

a 43 Many manuscripts *years, and she had spent all she had on doctors* of bread and two fish — unless we go and buy food for all this crowd." [14](About five thousand men were there.)

But he said to his disciples, "Have them sit down in groups of about fifty each." [15]The disciples did so, and everyone sat down. [16]Taking the five loaves and the two fish and looking up to heaven, he gave thanks and broke them. Then he gave them to the disciples to distribute to the people. [17]They all ate and were satisfied, and the disciples picked up twelve basketfuls of broken pieces that were left over.

Peter Declares That Jesus Is the Messiah

[18]Once when Jesus was praying in private and his disciples were with him, he asked them, "Who do the crowds say I am?"

[19]They replied, "Some say John the Baptist; others say Elijah; and still others, that one of the prophets of long ago has come back to life."

[20]"But what about you?" he asked. "Who do you say I am?"

Peter answered, "God's Messiah."

Jesus Predicts His Death

[21]Jesus strictly warned them not to tell this to anyone. [22]And he said, "The Son of Man must suffer many things and be rejected by the elders, the chief priests and the teachers of the law, and he must be killed and on the third day be raised to life."

[23]Then he said to them all: "Whoever wants to be my disciple must deny themselves and take up their cross daily and follow me. [24]For whoever wants to save their life will lose it, but whoever loses their life for me will save it. [25]What good is it for someone to gain the whole world, and yet lose or forfeit their very self? [26]Whoever is ashamed of me and my words, the Son of Man will be ashamed of them when he comes in his glory and in the glory of the Father and of the holy angels.

[27]"Truly I tell you, some who are standing here will not taste death before they see the kingdom of God."

The Transfiguration

[28]About eight days after Jesus said this, he took Peter, John and James with him and went up onto a mountain to pray. [29]As he was praying, the appearance of his face changed, and his clothes became as bright as a flash of lightning. [30]Two men, Moses and Elijah, appeared in glorious splendor, talking with Jesus. [31]They spoke about his departure,[a] which he was about to bring to fulfillment at Jerusalem. [32]Peter and his companions were very sleepy, but when they became fully awake, they saw his glory and the two men standing with him. [33]As the men were leaving Jesus, Peter said to him, "Master, it is good for us to be here. Let us put up three shelters — one for you, one for Moses and one for Elijah." (He did not know what he was saying.)

[34]While he was speaking, a cloud appeared and covered them, and they were afraid as they entered the cloud. [35]A voice came from the cloud, saying, "This is my Son, whom I have chosen; listen to him." [36]When the voice had spoken, they found that Jesus was alone. The disciples kept this to themselves and did not tell anyone at that time what they had seen.

Jesus Heals a Demon-Possessed Boy

[37]The next day, when they came down from the mountain, a large crowd met him. [38]A man in the crowd called out, "Teacher, I beg you to look at my son, for he is my only child. [39]A spirit seizes him and he suddenly screams; it throws him into convulsions so that he foams at the mouth. It scarcely ever leaves him and is destroying him. [40]I begged your disciples to drive it out, but they could not."

[41]"You unbelieving and perverse generation," Jesus replied, "how long shall I stay with you and put up with you? Bring your son here."

[42]Even while the boy was coming, the demon threw him to the ground in a convulsion. But Jesus rebuked the impure spirit, healed the boy and gave him back to his father. [43]And they were all amazed at the greatness of God.

Jesus Predicts His Death a Second Time

While everyone was marveling at all that Jesus did, he said to his disciples, [44]"Listen carefully to what I am about to tell you: The Son of Man is going to be delivered into the

---

[a] 31 Greek *exodos*

DENIED FOR SACRIFICE

READ: LUKE 9:23

The selfish part of us has a little freak-out allergic reaction to the word *deny*. It's tough to do when we live in the lap of luxury. Listen: the biggest problem with indulgence (the luxury we experience is America) is that enough is never enough. The more we indulge ourselves in food or sex or any of the toys we have, the less we'll enjoy them. It's not until we go all in with God that we discover that true joy is only found on the sacrificial side of life.

The more you give away, the more you will enjoy what you have. True story. If you give God the tithe, you'll enjoy the 90 percent you keep 10 percent more. Which also means you'll enjoy the 80 percent you keep 20 percent more! And eventually you'll enjoy the 70 percent you keep 30 percent more! And so on. One of the life goals of my family is to reverse tithe and live off 10 percent and give away 90 percent. When we get there, I'm confident we'll enjoy the 10 percent we keep 90 percent more.

BUILDING

FAITH

WISDOM

STRENGTH

You probably heard this classy playground rule when you were a kid: finders keepers, losers weepers. It's the exact opposite in God's kingdom: finders weepers, losers keepers. The first will be last and the last will be first.

hands of men." ⁴⁵But they did not understand what this meant. It was hidden from them, so that they did not grasp it, and they were afraid to ask him about it.

⁴⁶An argument started among the disciples as to which of them would be the greatest. ⁴⁷Jesus, knowing their thoughts, took a little child and had him stand beside him. ⁴⁸Then he said to them, "Whoever welcomes this little child in my name welcomes me; and whoever welcomes me welcomes the one who sent me. For it is the one who is least among you all who is the greatest."

⁴⁹"Master," said John, "we saw someone driving out demons in your name and we tried to stop him, because he is not one of us."

⁵⁰"Do not stop him," Jesus said, "for whoever is not against you is for you."

Samaritan Opposition

⁵¹As the time approached for him to be taken up to heaven, Jesus resolutely set out for Jerusalem. ⁵²And he sent messengers on ahead, who went into a Samaritan village to get things ready for him; ⁵³but the people there did not welcome him, because he was heading for Jerusalem. ⁵⁴When the disciples James and John saw this, they asked, "Lord, do you want us to call fire down from heaven to destroy them*a*?" ⁵⁵But Jesus turned and rebuked them. ⁵⁶Then he and his disciples went to another village.

The Cost of Following Jesus

⁵⁷As they were walking along the road, a man said to him, "I will follow you wherever you go."

⁵⁸Jesus replied, "Foxes have dens and birds have nests, but the Son of Man has no place to lay his head."

⁵⁹He said to another man, "Follow me."

But he replied, "Lord, first let me go and bury my father."

⁶⁰Jesus said to him, "Let the dead bury their own dead, but you go and proclaim the kingdom of God."

⁶¹Still another said, "I will follow you, Lord; but first let me go back and say goodbye to my family."

⁶²Jesus replied, "No one who puts a hand to the plow and looks back is fit for service in the kingdom of God."

Jesus Sends Out the Seventy-Two

10 After this the Lord appointed seventy-two*b* others and sent them two by two ahead of him to every town and place where he was about to go. ²He told them, "The harvest is plentiful, but the workers are few. Ask the Lord of the harvest, therefore, to send out workers into his harvest field. ³Go! I am sending you out like lambs among wolves. ⁴Do not take a purse or bag or sandals; and do not greet anyone on the road.

⁵"When you enter a house, first say, 'Peace to this house.' ⁶If someone who promotes peace is there, your peace will rest on them; if not, it will return to you. ⁷Stay there, eating and drinking whatever they give you, for the worker deserves his wages. Do not move around from house to house.

⁸"When you enter a town and are welcomed, eat what is offered to you. ⁹Heal the sick who are there and tell them, 'The kingdom of God has come near to you.' ¹⁰But when you enter a town and are not welcomed, go into its streets and say, ¹¹'Even the dust of your town we wipe from our feet as a warning to you. Yet be sure of this: The kingdom of God has come near.' ¹²I tell you, it will be more bearable on that day for Sodom than for that town.

¹³"Woe to you, Chorazin! Woe to you, Bethsaida! For if the miracles that were performed in you had been performed in Tyre and Sidon, they would have repented long ago, sitting in sackcloth and ashes. ¹⁴But it will be more bearable for Tyre and Sidon at the judgment than for you. ¹⁵And you, Capernaum, will you be lifted to the heavens? No, you will go down to Hades.*c*

¹⁶"Whoever listens to you listens to me; whoever rejects you rejects me; but whoever rejects me rejects him who sent me."

¹⁷The seventy-two returned with joy and said, "Lord, even the demons submit to us in your name."

¹⁸He replied, "I saw Satan fall like lightning from heaven. ¹⁹I have given you authority to trample on snakes and scorpions and to overcome all the power of the enemy; nothing will harm you. ²⁰However, do not

---

a 54 Some manuscripts *them, just as Elijah did*   *b 1* Some manuscripts *seventy*; also in verse 17
c 15 That is, the realm of the dead

rejoice that the spirits submit to you, but rejoice that your names are written in heaven."

²¹At that time Jesus, full of joy through the Holy Spirit, said, "I praise you, Father, Lord of heaven and earth, because you have hidden these things from the wise and learned, and revealed them to little children. Yes, Father, for this is what you were pleased to do.

²²"All things have been committed to me by my Father. No one knows who the Son is except the Father, and no one knows who the Father is except the Son and those to whom the Son chooses to reveal him."

²³Then he turned to his disciples and said privately, "Blessed are the eyes that see what you see. ²⁴For I tell you that many prophets and kings wanted to see what you see but did not see it, and to hear what you hear but did not hear it."

The Parable of the Good Samaritan

²⁵On one occasion an expert in the law stood up to test Jesus. "Teacher," he asked, "what must I do to inherit eternal life?"

²⁶"What is written in the Law?" he replied. "How do you read it?"

²⁷He answered, "'Love the Lord your God with all your heart and with all your soul and with all your strength and with all your mind'*a*; and, 'Love your neighbor as yourself.'*b*"

²⁸"You have answered correctly," Jesus replied. "Do this and you will live."

²⁹But he wanted to justify himself, so he asked Jesus, "And who is my neighbor?"

³⁰In reply Jesus said: "A man was going down from Jerusalem to Jericho, when he was attacked by robbers. They stripped him of his clothes, beat him and went away, leaving him half dead. ³¹A priest happened to be going down the same road, and when he saw the man, he passed by on the other side. ³²So too, a Levite, when he came to the place and saw him, passed by on the other side. ³³But a Samaritan, as he traveled, came where the man was; and when he saw him, he took pity on him. ³⁴He went to him and bandaged his wounds, pouring on oil and wine. Then he put the man on his own donkey, brought him to an inn and took care of him. ³⁵The next

day he took out two denarii*c* and gave them to the innkeeper. 'Look after him,' he said, 'and when I return, I will reimburse you for any extra expense you may have.'

³⁶"Which of these three do you think was a neighbor to the man who fell into the hands of robbers?"

³⁷The expert in the law replied, "The one who had mercy on him."

Jesus told him, "Go and do likewise."

At the Home of Martha and Mary

³⁸As Jesus and his disciples were on their way, he came to a village where a woman named Martha opened her home to him. ³⁹She had a sister called Mary, who sat at the Lord's feet listening to what he said. ⁴⁰But Martha was distracted by all the preparations that had to be made. She came to him and asked, "Lord, don't you care that my sister has left me to do the work by myself? Tell her to help me!"

⁴¹"Martha, Martha," the Lord answered, "you are worried and upset about many things, ⁴²but few things are needed — or indeed only one.*d* Mary has chosen what is better, and it will not be taken away from her."

Jesus' Teaching on Prayer

11 One day Jesus was praying in a certain place. When he finished, one of his disciples said to him, "Lord, teach us to pray, just as John taught his disciples."

²He said to them, "When you pray, say:

"'Father,*e*
hallowed be your name,
your kingdom come.*f*
³Give us each day our daily bread.
⁴Forgive us our sins,
    for we also forgive everyone who sins
        against us.*g*
And lead us not into temptation.*h*'"

⁵Then Jesus said to them, "Suppose you have a friend, and you go to him at midnight and say, 'Friend, lend me three loaves of bread; ⁶a friend of mine on a journey has come to me, and I have no food to offer him.'

---

a 27 Deut. 6:5   *b* 27 Lev. 19:18   *c* 35 A denarius was the usual daily wage of a day laborer (see Matt. 20:2).   *d* 42 Some manuscripts *but only one thing is needed*   *e* 2 Some manuscripts *Our Father in heaven*   *f* 2 Some manuscripts *come. May your will be done on earth as it is in heaven.*   *g* 4 Greek *everyone who is indebted to us*   *h* 4 Some manuscripts *temptation, but deliver us from the evil one*

CHILL FOR A SEC

READ: LUKE 10:38-42

Most of us resonate with Martha because we are an achievement-based culture. This is the ADHD generation. We're always on the move, always trying to get something done. Our phones are constantly dinging to let us know there is a text we need to return, a post we need to make, or something important we're going to be late for.

How many times have we been so distracted that we've missed a divine moment? How many things does God long to say to us, but he keeps getting our voicemail because we're too busy to pick up? Busyness appears to be based on virtue and traditional values—and all those "apply yourself" talks your parents might be fond of giving. Work hard. Don't be like that loafer, Mary! Who's going to get this stuff done?

I wonder how important that stuff was to Martha after her friend had been crucified, resurrected, and taken up into heaven. I wonder what she would have given for just a few moments to sit at his feet. "Mary has chosen what is better."

BUILDING FAITH WISDOM STRENGTH

That's a choice we can make every single day when we choose to make our relationship with God more important than anything else on our to-do list. I want to be clear: Working hard and achieving goals are an important part of leading a God-glorifying life. But they are not life. They are not even a measuring stick for the worth of life.

⁷And suppose the one inside answers, 'Don't bother me. The door is already locked, and my children and I are in bed. I can't get up and give you anything.' ⁸I tell you, even though he will not get up and give you the bread because of friendship, yet because of your shameless audacity*ᵃ* he will surely get up and give you as much as you need.

⁹"So I say to you: Ask and it will be given to you; seek and you will find; knock and the door will be opened to you. ¹⁰For everyone who asks receives; the one who seeks finds; and to the one who knocks, the door will be opened.

¹¹"Which of you fathers, if your son asks for*ᵇ* a fish, will give him a snake instead? ¹²Or if he asks for an egg, will give him a scorpion? ¹³If you then, though you are evil, know how to give good gifts to your children, how much more will your Father in heaven give the Holy Spirit to those who ask him!"

Jesus and Beelzebul

¹⁴Jesus was driving out a demon that was mute. When the demon left, the man who had been mute spoke, and the crowd was amazed. ¹⁵But some of them said, "By Beelzebul, the prince of demons, he is driving out demons." ¹⁶Others tested him by asking for a sign from heaven.

¹⁷Jesus knew their thoughts and said to them: "Any kingdom divided against itself will be ruined, and a house divided against itself will fall. ¹⁸If Satan is divided against himself, how can his kingdom stand? I say this because you claim that I drive out demons by Beelzebul. ¹⁹Now if I drive out demons by Beelzebul, by whom do your followers drive them out? So then, they will be your judges. ²⁰But if I drive out demons by the finger of God, then the kingdom of God has come upon you.

²¹"When a strong man, fully armed, guards his own house, his possessions are safe. ²²But when someone stronger attacks and overpowers him, he takes away the armor in which the man trusted and divides up his plunder.

²³"Whoever is not with me is against me, and whoever does not gather with me scatters.

²⁴"When an impure spirit comes out of a person, it goes through arid places seeking rest and does not find it. Then it says, 'I will return to the house I left.' ²⁵When it arrives, it finds the house swept clean and put in order. ²⁶Then it goes and takes seven other spirits more wicked than itself, and they go in and live there. And the final condition of that person is worse than the first."

²⁷As Jesus was saying these things, a woman in the crowd called out, "Blessed is the mother who gave you birth and nursed you."

²⁸He replied, "Blessed rather are those who hear the word of God and obey it."

The Sign of Jonah

²⁹As the crowds increased, Jesus said, "This is a wicked generation. It asks for a sign, but none will be given it except the sign of Jonah. ³⁰For as Jonah was a sign to the Ninevites, so also will the Son of Man be to this generation. ³¹The Queen of the South will rise at the judgment with the people of this generation and condemn them, for she came from the ends of the earth to listen to Solomon's wisdom; and now something greater than Solomon is here. ³²The men of Nineveh will stand up at the judgment with this generation and condemn it, for they repented at the preaching of Jonah; and now something greater than Jonah is here.

The Lamp of the Body

³³"No one lights a lamp and puts it in a place where it will be hidden, or under a bowl. Instead they put it on its stand, so that those who come in may see the light. ³⁴Your eye is the lamp of your body. When your eyes are healthy,*ᶜ* your whole body also is full of light. But when they are unhealthy,*ᵈ* your body also is full of darkness. ³⁵See to it, then, that the light within you is not darkness. ³⁶Therefore, if your whole body is full of light, and no part of it dark, it will be just as full of light as when a lamp shines its light on you."

Woes on the Pharisees and the Experts in the Law

³⁷When Jesus had finished speaking, a Pharisee invited him to eat with him; so he went in and reclined at the table. ³⁸But the Pharisee was surprised when he noticed that Jesus did not first wash before the meal.

ᵃ 8 Or *yet to preserve his good name*   *ᵇ 11* Some manuscripts *for bread, will give him a stone? Or if he asks for*   *ᶜ 34* The Greek for *healthy* here implies *generous.*   *ᵈ 34* The Greek for *unhealthy* here implies *stingy.*

[39] Then the Lord said to him, "Now then, you Pharisees clean the outside of the cup and dish, but inside you are full of greed and wickedness. [40] You foolish people! Did not the one who made the outside make the inside also? [41] But now as for what is inside you — be generous to the poor, and everything will be clean for you.

[42] "Woe to you Pharisees, because you give God a tenth of your mint, rue and all other kinds of garden herbs, but you neglect justice and the love of God. You should have practiced the latter without leaving the former undone.

[43] "Woe to you Pharisees, because you love the most important seats in the synagogues and respectful greetings in the marketplaces.

[44] "Woe to you, because you are like unmarked graves, which people walk over without knowing it."

[45] One of the experts in the law answered him, "Teacher, when you say these things, you insult us also."

[46] Jesus replied, "And you experts in the law, woe to you, because you load people down with burdens they can hardly carry, and you yourselves will not lift one finger to help them.

[47] "Woe to you, because you build tombs for the prophets, and it was your ancestors who killed them. [48] So you testify that you approve of what your ancestors did; they killed the prophets, and you build their tombs. [49] Because of this, God in his wisdom said, 'I will send them prophets and apostles, some of whom they will kill and others they will persecute.' [50] Therefore this generation will be held responsible for the blood of all the prophets that has been shed since the beginning of the world, [51] from the blood of Abel to the blood of Zechariah, who was killed between the altar and the sanctuary. Yes, I tell you, this generation will be held responsible for it all.

[52] "Woe to you experts in the law, because you have taken away the key to knowledge. You yourselves have not entered, and you have hindered those who were entering."

[53] When Jesus went outside, the Pharisees and the teachers of the law began to oppose him fiercely and to besiege him with questions, [54] waiting to catch him in something he might say.

Warnings and Encouragements

12 Meanwhile, when a crowd of many thousands had gathered, so that they were trampling on one another, Jesus began to speak first to his disciples, saying: "Be[a] on your guard against the yeast of the Pharisees, which is hypocrisy. [2] There is nothing concealed that will not be disclosed, or hidden that will not be made known. [3] What you have said in the dark will be heard in the daylight, and what you have whispered in the ear in the inner rooms will be proclaimed from the roofs.

[4] "I tell you, my friends, do not be afraid of those who kill the body and after that can do no more. [5] But I will show you whom you should fear: Fear him who, after your body has been killed, has authority to throw you into hell. Yes, I tell you, fear him. [6] Are not five sparrows sold for two pennies? Yet not one of them is forgotten by God. [7] Indeed, the very hairs of your head are all numbered. Don't be afraid; you are worth more than many sparrows.

[8] "I tell you, whoever publicly acknowledges me before others, the Son of Man will also acknowledge before the angels of God. [9] But whoever disowns me before others will be disowned before the angels of God. [10] And everyone who speaks a word against the Son of Man will be forgiven, but anyone who blasphemes against the Holy Spirit will not be forgiven.

[11] "When you are brought before synagogues, rulers and authorities, do not worry about how you will defend yourselves or what you will say, [12] for the Holy Spirit will teach you at that time what you should say."

The Parable of the Rich Fool

[13] Someone in the crowd said to him, "Teacher, tell my brother to divide the inheritance with me."

[14] Jesus replied, "Man, who appointed me a judge or an arbiter between you?" [15] Then he said to them, "Watch out! Be on your guard against all kinds of greed; life does not consist in an abundance of possessions."

[16] And he told them this parable: "The ground of a certain rich man yielded an abundant harvest. [17] He thought to himself, 'What shall I do? I have no place to store my crops.'

---

[a] 1 Or *speak to his disciples, saying:* "First of all, be

SO NOT MINE

READ: LUKE 12:16-19

I f you look closely, you'll notice that the man refers to himself nine times in two verses. He speaks of my crops, my barns, my grain. But who gave him the good crops? Who gave him the ability to get rich? It doesn't seem to occur to him that he has what he has because God has given it to him.

The key to keeping materialism in its right place is to remember that everything belongs to God. Whatever we have is on loan from our heavenly Father. Solomon reminds us in Ecclesiastes 5:15, "Everyone comes naked from their mother's womb, and as everyone comes, so they depart. They take nothing from their toil that they can carry in their hands." Psalm 24:1 simply puts it this way: "The earth is the LORD's, and everything in it." When we keep that perspective, we understand our dependence on God and we worship him as the provider.

BUILDING FAITH WISDOM STRENGTH

God has given us the use of his resources here on earth. If we stop and think about it, we have much to be grateful for. Go through your day sometime recognizing that everything is God's. Get out of God's bed, walk into God's bathroom, and turn on God's shower. Then put on God's jeans and zip up God's hoodie. Eat God's cereal. Drink God's orange juice. Get in God's car and head to school.

When we start to see every possession as God's, it helps us develop an attitude of gratitude that leads to a heart of worship.

¹⁸"Then he said, 'This is what I'll do. I will tear down my barns and build bigger ones, and there I will store my surplus grain. ¹⁹And I'll say to myself, "You have plenty of grain laid up for many years. Take life easy; eat, drink and be merry."'

²⁰"But God said to him, 'You fool! This very night your life will be demanded from you. Then who will get what you have prepared for yourself?'

²¹"This is how it will be with whoever stores up things for themselves but is not rich toward God."

Do Not Worry

²²Then Jesus said to his disciples: "Therefore I tell you, do not worry about your life, what you will eat; or about your body, what you will wear. ²³For life is more than food, and the body more than clothes. ²⁴Consider the ravens: They do not sow or reap, they have no storeroom or barn; yet God feeds them. And how much more valuable you are than birds! ²⁵Who of you by worrying can add a single hour to your life*a*? ²⁶Since you cannot do this very little thing, why do you worry about the rest?

²⁷"Consider how the wild flowers grow. They do not labor or spin. Yet I tell you, not even Solomon in all his splendor was dressed like one of these. ²⁸If that is how God clothes the grass of the field, which is here today, and tomorrow is thrown into the fire, how much more will he clothe you—you of little faith! ²⁹And do not set your heart on what you will eat or drink; do not worry about it. ³⁰For the pagan world runs after all such things, and your Father knows that you need them. ³¹But seek his kingdom, and these things will be given to you as well.

³²"Do not be afraid, little flock, for your Father has been pleased to give you the kingdom. ³³Sell your possessions and give to the poor. Provide purses for yourselves that will not wear out, a treasure in heaven that will never fail, where no thief comes near and no moth destroys. ³⁴For where your treasure is, there your heart will be also.

Watchfulness

³⁵"Be dressed ready for service and keep your lamps burning, ³⁶like servants waiting for their master to return from a wedding banquet, so that when he comes and knocks they can immediately open the door for him. ³⁷It will be good for those servants whose master finds them watching when he comes. Truly I tell you, he will dress himself to serve, will have them recline at the table and will come and wait on them. ³⁸It will be good for those servants whose master finds them ready, even if he comes in the middle of the night or toward daybreak. ³⁹But understand this: If the owner of the house had known at what hour the thief was coming, he would not have let his house be broken into. ⁴⁰You also must be ready, because the Son of Man will come at an hour when you do not expect him."

⁴¹Peter asked, "Lord, are you telling this parable to us, or to everyone?"

⁴²The Lord answered, "Who then is the faithful and wise manager, whom the master puts in charge of his servants to give them their food allowance at the proper time? ⁴³It will be good for that servant whom the master finds doing so when he returns. ⁴⁴Truly I tell you, he will put him in charge of all his possessions. ⁴⁵But suppose the servant says to himself, 'My master is taking a long time in coming,' and he then begins to beat the other servants, both men and women, and to eat and drink and get drunk. ⁴⁶The master of that servant will come on a day when he does not expect him and at an hour he is not aware of. He will cut him to pieces and assign him a place with the unbelievers.

⁴⁷"The servant who knows the master's will and does not get ready or does not do what the master wants will be beaten with many blows. ⁴⁸But the one who does not know and does things deserving punishment will be beaten with few blows. From everyone who has been given much, much will be demanded; and from the one who has been entrusted with much, much more will be asked.

Not Peace but Division

⁴⁹"I have come to bring fire on the earth, and how I wish it were already kindled! ⁵⁰But I have a baptism to undergo, and what constraint I am under until it is completed! ⁵¹Do you think I came to bring peace on

---

a 25 Or *single cubit to your height*

earth? No, I tell you, but division. ⁵²From now on there will be five in one family divided against each other, three against two and two against three. ⁵³They will be divided, father against son and son against father, mother against daughter and daughter against mother, mother-in-law against daughter-in-law and daughter-in-law against mother-in-law."

Interpreting the Times

⁵⁴He said to the crowd: "When you see a cloud rising in the west, immediately you say, 'It's going to rain,' and it does. ⁵⁵And when the south wind blows, you say, 'It's going to be hot,' and it is. ⁵⁶Hypocrites! You know how to interpret the appearance of the earth and the sky. How is it that you don't know how to interpret this present time?

⁵⁷"Why don't you judge for yourselves what is right? ⁵⁸As you are going with your adversary to the magistrate, try hard to be reconciled on the way, or your adversary may drag you off to the judge, and the judge turn you over to the officer, and the officer throw you into prison. ⁵⁹I tell you, you will not get out until you have paid the last penny."

Repent or Perish

13 Now there were some present at that time who told Jesus about the Galileans whose blood Pilate had mixed with their sacrifices. ²Jesus answered, "Do you think that these Galileans were worse sinners than all the other Galileans because they suffered this way? ³I tell you, no! But unless you repent, you too will all perish. ⁴Or those eighteen who died when the tower in Siloam fell on them—do you think they were more guilty than all the others living in Jerusalem? ⁵I tell you, no! But unless you repent, you too will all perish."

⁶Then he told this parable: "A man had a fig tree growing in his vineyard, and he went to look for fruit on it but did not find any. ⁷So he said to the man who took care of the vineyard, 'For three years now I've been coming to look for fruit on this fig tree and haven't found any. Cut it down! Why should it use up the soil?'

⁸"'Sir,' the man replied, 'leave it alone for one more year, and I'll dig around it and fer-

tilize it. ⁹If it bears fruit next year, fine! If not, then cut it down.'"

Jesus Heals a Crippled Woman on the Sabbath

¹⁰On a Sabbath Jesus was teaching in one of the synagogues, ¹¹and a woman was there who had been crippled by a spirit for eighteen years. She was bent over and could not straighten up at all. ¹²When Jesus saw her, he called her forward and said to her, "Woman, you are set free from your infirmity." ¹³Then he put his hands on her, and immediately she straightened up and praised God.

¹⁴Indignant because Jesus had healed on the Sabbath, the synagogue leader said to the people, "There are six days for work. So come and be healed on those days, not on the Sabbath."

¹⁵The Lord answered him, "You hypocrites! Doesn't each of you on the Sabbath untie your ox or donkey from the stall and lead it out to give it water? ¹⁶Then should not this woman, a daughter of Abraham, whom Satan has kept bound for eighteen long years, be set free on the Sabbath day from what bound her?"

¹⁷When he said this, all his opponents were humiliated, but the people were delighted with all the wonderful things he was doing.

The Parables of the Mustard Seed and the Yeast

¹⁸Then Jesus asked, "What is the kingdom of God like? What shall I compare it to? ¹⁹It is like a mustard seed, which a man took and planted in his garden. It grew and became a tree, and the birds perched in its branches."

²⁰Again he asked, "What shall I compare the kingdom of God to? ²¹It is like yeast that a woman took and mixed into about sixty pounds[a] of flour until it worked all through the dough."

The Narrow Door

²²Then Jesus went through the towns and villages, teaching as he made his way to Jerusalem. ²³Someone asked him, "Lord, are only a few people going to be saved?"

He said to them, ²⁴"Make every effort to enter through the narrow door, because

---

[a] 21 Or about 27 kilograms

TRAGIC ENDINGS

READ: LUKE 13:2-3

A mom gets cancer and dies. A terrorist guns down a camp full of teenagers. An airplane crashes and hundreds lose their lives. Some say such episodes of evil have a quick and easy explanation: Bad things happen to bad people.

That's the assumption between the lines at the start of this scene. Unidentified sources tell Jesus about victims "whose blood Pilate had mixed with their sacrifices" (Luke 13:1). Though the Bible doesn't offer more details, it sounds like people from northern Israel had died at the hand of the Roman governor while offering their usual animal sacrifices at the Jerusalem temple.

The person who brought this news must have worn a face that said, "They got what they deserved," because Jesus immediately declares that tragedy doesn't work that way. The Galileans were no worse sinners than those who escaped dying that day. Nor were people crushed by a falling tower any more evil than their neighbors.

Jesus doesn't want us pointing fingers when bad things happen. For that matter, you don't need to be buried with guilt when tragedy hits you. Bad things happen to everyone, and in God's sight, all human beings are sinners (Romans 3:23). We all have the same need, whether life seems smooth or sad. The Lord wants all of us to repent—to quit sinning and turn to him.

BUILDING

FAITH

WISDOM

STRENGTH

many, I tell you, will try to enter and will not be able to. ²⁵Once the owner of the house gets up and closes the door, you will stand outside knocking and pleading, 'Sir, open the door for us.'

"But he will answer, 'I don't know you or where you come from.'

²⁶"Then you will say, 'We ate and drank with you, and you taught in our streets.'

²⁷"But he will reply, 'I don't know you or where you come from. Away from me, all you evildoers!'

²⁸"There will be weeping there, and gnashing of teeth, when you see Abraham, Isaac and Jacob and all the prophets in the kingdom of God, but you yourselves thrown out. ²⁹People will come from east and west and north and south, and will take their places at the feast in the kingdom of God. ³⁰Indeed there are those who are last who will be first, and first who will be last."

Jesus' Sorrow for Jerusalem

³¹At that time some Pharisees came to Jesus and said to him, "Leave this place and go somewhere else. Herod wants to kill you."

³²He replied, "Go tell that fox, 'I will keep on driving out demons and healing people today and tomorrow, and on the third day I will reach my goal.' ³³In any case, I must press on today and tomorrow and the next day—for surely no prophet can die outside Jerusalem!

³⁴"Jerusalem, Jerusalem, you who kill the prophets and stone those sent to you, how often I have longed to gather your children together, as a hen gathers her chicks under her wings, and you were not willing. ³⁵Look, your house is left to you desolate. I tell you, you will not see me again until you say, 'Blessed is he who comes in the name of the Lord.'ᵃ"

Jesus at a Pharisee's House

14 One Sabbath, when Jesus went to eat in the house of a prominent Pharisee, he was being carefully watched. ²There in front of him was a man suffering from abnormal swelling of his body. ³Jesus asked the Pharisees and experts in the law, "Is it lawful to heal on the Sabbath or not?" ⁴But they remained silent. So taking hold of the man, he healed him and sent him on his way.

⁵Then he asked them, "If one of you has a childᵇ or an ox that falls into a well on the Sabbath day, will you not immediately pull it out?" ⁶And they had nothing to say.

⁷When he noticed how the guests picked the places of honor at the table, he told them this parable: ⁸"When someone invites you to a wedding feast, do not take the place of honor, for a person more distinguished than you may have been invited. ⁹If so, the host who invited both of you will come and say to you, 'Give this person your seat.' Then, humiliated, you will have to take the least important place. ¹⁰But when you are invited, take the lowest place, so that when your host comes, he will say to you, 'Friend, move up to a better place.' Then you will be honored in the presence of all the other guests. ¹¹For all those who exalt themselves will be humbled, and those who humble themselves will be exalted."

¹²Then Jesus said to his host, "When you give a luncheon or dinner, do not invite your friends, your brothers or sisters, your relatives, or your rich neighbors; if you do, they may invite you back and so you will be repaid. ¹³But when you give a banquet, invite the poor, the crippled, the lame, the blind, ¹⁴and you will be blessed. Although they cannot repay you, you will be repaid at the resurrection of the righteous."

The Parable of the Great Banquet

¹⁵When one of those at the table with him heard this, he said to Jesus, "Blessed is the one who will eat at the feast in the kingdom of God."

¹⁶Jesus replied: "A certain man was preparing a great banquet and invited many guests. ¹⁷At the time of the banquet he sent his servant to tell those who had been invited, 'Come, for everything is now ready.'

¹⁸"But they all alike began to make excuses. The first said, 'I have just bought a field, and I must go and see it. Please excuse me.'

¹⁹"Another said, 'I have just bought five yoke of oxen, and I'm on my way to try them out. Please excuse me.'

²⁰"Still another said, 'I just got married, so I can't come.'

²¹"The servant came back and reported this to his master. Then the owner of the

---

ᵃ 35 Psalm 118:26   ᵇ 5 Some manuscripts *donkey*

house became angry and ordered his servant, 'Go out quickly into the streets and alleys of the town and bring in the poor, the crippled, the blind and the lame.'

²²"'Sir,' the servant said, 'what you ordered has been done, but there is still room.'

²³"Then the master told his servant, 'Go out to the roads and country lanes and compel them to come in, so that my house will be full. ²⁴I tell you, not one of those who were invited will get a taste of my banquet.'"

The Cost of Being a Disciple

²⁵Large crowds were traveling with Jesus, and turning to them he said: ²⁶"If anyone comes to me and does not hate father and mother, wife and children, brothers and sisters — yes, even their own life — such a person cannot be my disciple. ²⁷And whoever does not carry their cross and follow me cannot be my disciple.

²⁸"Suppose one of you wants to build a tower. Won't you first sit down and estimate the cost to see if you have enough money to complete it? ²⁹For if you lay the foundation and are not able to finish it, everyone who sees it will ridicule you, ³⁰saying, 'This person began to build and wasn't able to finish.'

³¹"Or suppose a king is about to go to war against another king. Won't he first sit down and consider whether he is able with ten thousand men to oppose the one coming against him with twenty thousand? ³²If he is not able, he will send a delegation while the other is still a long way off and will ask for terms of peace. ³³In the same way, those of you who do not give up everything you have cannot be my disciples.

³⁴"Salt is good, but if it loses its saltiness, how can it be made salty again? ³⁵It is fit neither for the soil nor for the manure pile; it is thrown out.

"Whoever has ears to hear, let them hear."

The Parable of the Lost Sheep

15 Now the tax collectors and sinners were all gathering around to hear Jesus. ²But the Pharisees and the teachers of the law muttered, "This man welcomes sinners and eats with them."

³Then Jesus told them this parable: ⁴"Suppose one of you has a hundred sheep and loses one of them. Doesn't he leave the ninety-nine in the open country and go after the lost sheep until he finds it? ⁵And when he finds it, he joyfully puts it on his shoulders ⁶and goes home. Then he calls his friends and neighbors together and says, 'Rejoice with me; I have found my lost sheep.' ⁷I tell you that in the same way there will be more rejoicing in heaven over one sinner who repents than over ninety-nine righteous persons who do not need to repent.

The Parable of the Lost Coin

⁸"Or suppose a woman has ten silver coins[a] and loses one. Doesn't she light a lamp, sweep the house and search carefully until she finds it? ⁹And when she finds it, she calls her friends and neighbors together and says, 'Rejoice with me; I have found my lost coin.' ¹⁰In the same way, I tell you, there is rejoicing in the presence of the angels of God over one sinner who repents."

The Parable of the Lost Son

¹¹Jesus continued: "There was a man who had two sons. ¹²The younger one said to his father, 'Father, give me my share of the estate.' So he divided his property between them.

¹³"Not long after that, the younger son got together all he had, set off for a distant country and there squandered his wealth in wild living. ¹⁴After he had spent everything, there was a severe famine in that whole country, and he began to be in need. ¹⁵So he went and hired himself out to a citizen of that country, who sent him to his fields to feed pigs. ¹⁶He longed to fill his stomach with the pods that the pigs were eating, but no one gave him anything.

¹⁷"When he came to his senses, he said, 'How many of my father's hired servants have food to spare, and here I am starving to death! ¹⁸I will set out and go back to my father and say to him: Father, I have sinned against heaven and against you. ¹⁹I am no longer worthy to be called your son; make me like one of your hired servants.' ²⁰So he got up and went to his father.

"But while he was still a long way off, his father saw him and was filled with compassion for him; he ran to his son, threw his arms around him and kissed him.

---

[a] 8 Greek *ten drachmas*, each worth about a day's wages

²¹"The son said to him, 'Father, I have sinned against heaven and against you. I am no longer worthy to be called your son.'

²²"But the father said to his servants, 'Quick! Bring the best robe and put it on him. Put a ring on his finger and sandals on his feet. ²³Bring the fattened calf and kill it. Let's have a feast and celebrate. ²⁴For this son of mine was dead and is alive again; he was lost and is found.' So they began to celebrate.

²⁵"Meanwhile, the older son was in the field. When he came near the house, he heard music and dancing. ²⁶So he called one of the servants and asked him what was going on. ²⁷'Your brother has come,' he replied, 'and your father has killed the fattened calf because he has him back safe and sound.'

²⁸"The older brother became angry and refused to go in. So his father went out and pleaded with him. ²⁹But he answered his father, 'Look! All these years I've been slaving for you and never disobeyed your orders. Yet you never gave me even a young goat so I could celebrate with my friends. ³⁰But when this son of yours who has squandered your property with prostitutes comes home, you kill the fattened calf for him!'

³¹"'My son,' the father said, 'you are always with me, and everything I have is yours. ³²But we had to celebrate and be glad, because this brother of yours was dead and is alive again; he was lost and is found.' "

The Parable of the Shrewd Manager

16 Jesus told his disciples: "There was a rich man whose manager was accused of wasting his possessions. ²So he called him in and asked him, 'What is this I hear about you? Give an account of your management, because you cannot be manager any longer.'

³"The manager said to himself, 'What shall I do now? My master is taking away my job. I'm not strong enough to dig, and I'm ashamed to beg— ⁴I know what I'll do so that, when I lose my job here, people will welcome me into their houses.'

⁵"So he called in each one of his master's debtors. He asked the first, 'How much do you owe my master?'

⁶"'Nine hundred gallons*ᵃ* of olive oil,' he replied.

"The manager told him, 'Take your bill, sit down quickly, and make it four hundred and fifty.'

⁷"Then he asked the second, 'And how much do you owe?'

"'A thousand bushels*ᵇ* of wheat,' he replied.

"He told him, 'Take your bill and make it eight hundred.'

⁸"The master commended the dishonest manager because he had acted shrewdly. For the people of this world are more shrewd in dealing with their own kind than are the people of the light. ⁹I tell you, use worldly wealth to gain friends for yourselves, so that when it is gone, you will be welcomed into eternal dwellings.

¹⁰"Whoever can be trusted with very little can also be trusted with much, and whoever is dishonest with very little will also be dishonest with much. ¹¹So if you have not been trustworthy in handling worldly wealth, who will trust you with true riches? ¹²And if you have not been trustworthy with someone else's property, who will give you property of your own?

¹³"No one can serve two masters. Either you will hate the one and love the other, or you will be devoted to the one and despise the other. You cannot serve both God and money."

¹⁴The Pharisees, who loved money, heard all this and were sneering at Jesus. ¹⁵He said to them, "You are the ones who justify yourselves in the eyes of others, but God knows your hearts. What people value highly is detestable in God's sight.

Additional Teachings

¹⁶"The Law and the Prophets were proclaimed until John. Since that time, the good news of the kingdom of God is being preached, and everyone is forcing their way into it. ¹⁷It is easier for heaven and earth to disappear than for the least stroke of a pen to drop out of the Law.

¹⁸"Anyone who divorces his wife and marries another woman commits adultery, and the man who marries a divorced woman commits adultery.

The Rich Man and Lazarus

¹⁹"There was a rich man who was dressed in purple and fine linen and lived in luxury

---

ᵃ 6 Or about 3,000 liters   *ᵇ* 7 Or about 30 tons

every day. ²⁰At his gate was laid a beggar named Lazarus, covered with sores ²¹and longing to eat what fell from the rich man's table. Even the dogs came and licked his sores.

²²"The time came when the beggar died and the angels carried him to Abraham's side. The rich man also died and was buried. ²³In Hades, where he was in torment, he looked up and saw Abraham far away, with Lazarus by his side. ²⁴So he called to him, 'Father Abraham, have pity on me and send Lazarus to dip the tip of his finger in water and cool my tongue, because I am in agony in this fire.'

²⁵"But Abraham replied, 'Son, remember that in your lifetime you received your good things, while Lazarus received bad things, but now he is comforted here and you are in agony. ²⁶And besides all this, between us and you a great chasm has been set in place, so that those who want to go from here to you cannot, nor can anyone cross over from there to us.'

²⁷"He answered, 'Then I beg you, father, send Lazarus to my family, ²⁸for I have five brothers. Let him warn them, so that they will not also come to this place of torment.'

²⁹"Abraham replied, 'They have Moses and the Prophets; let them listen to them.'

³⁰"'No, father Abraham,' he said, 'but if someone from the dead goes to them, they will repent.'

³¹"He said to him, 'If they do not listen to Moses and the Prophets, they will not be convinced even if someone rises from the dead.'"

Sin, Faith, Duty

17 Jesus said to his disciples: "Things that cause people to stumble are bound to come, but woe to anyone through whom they come. ²It would be better for them to be thrown into the sea with a millstone tied around their neck than to cause one of these little ones to stumble. ³So watch yourselves.

"If your brother or sister*a* sins against you, rebuke them; and if they repent, forgive them. ⁴Even if they sin against you seven times in a day and seven times come back to you saying 'I repent,' you must forgive them."

⁵The apostles said to the Lord, "Increase our faith!"

⁶He replied, "If you have faith as small as a mustard seed, you can say to this mulberry tree, 'Be uprooted and planted in the sea,' and it will obey you.

⁷"Suppose one of you has a servant plowing or looking after the sheep. Will he say to the servant when he comes in from the field, 'Come along now and sit down to eat'? ⁸Won't he rather say, 'Prepare my supper, get yourself ready and wait on me while I eat and drink; after that you may eat and drink'? ⁹Will he thank the servant because he did what he was told to do? ¹⁰So you also, when you have done everything you were told to do, should say, 'We are unworthy servants; we have only done our duty.'"

Jesus Heals Ten Men With Leprosy

¹¹Now on his way to Jerusalem, Jesus traveled along the border between Samaria and Galilee. ¹²As he was going into a village, ten men who had leprosy*b* met him. They stood at a distance ¹³and called out in a loud voice, "Jesus, Master, have pity on us!"

¹⁴When he saw them, he said, "Go, show yourselves to the priests." And as they went, they were cleansed.

¹⁵One of them, when he saw he was healed, came back, praising God in a loud voice. ¹⁶He threw himself at Jesus' feet and thanked him—and he was a Samaritan.

¹⁷Jesus asked, "Were not all ten cleansed? Where are the other nine? ¹⁸Has no one returned to give praise to God except this foreigner?" ¹⁹Then he said to him, "Rise and go; your faith has made you well."

The Coming of the Kingdom of God

²⁰Once, on being asked by the Pharisees when the kingdom of God would come, Jesus replied, "The coming of the kingdom of God is not something that can be observed, ²¹nor will people say, 'Here it is,' or 'There it is,' because the kingdom of God is in your midst."*c*

²²Then he said to his disciples, "The time is coming when you will long to see one of the days of the Son of Man, but you will not see it. ²³People will tell you, 'There he is!'

---

a 3 The Greek word for *brother or sister* (*adelphos*) refers here to a fellow disciple, whether man or woman.
b 12 The Greek word traditionally translated *leprosy* was used for various diseases affecting the skin.
c 21 Or *is within you*

or 'Here he is!' Do not go running off after them. [24]For the Son of Man in his day[a] will be like the lightning, which flashes and lights up the sky from one end to the other. [25]But first he must suffer many things and be rejected by this generation.

[26]"Just as it was in the days of Noah, so also will it be in the days of the Son of Man. [27]People were eating, drinking, marrying and being given in marriage up to the day Noah entered the ark. Then the flood came and destroyed them all.

[28]"It was the same in the days of Lot. People were eating and drinking, buying and selling, planting and building. [29]But the day Lot left Sodom, fire and sulfur rained down from heaven and destroyed them all.

[30]"It will be just like this on the day the Son of Man is revealed. [31]On that day no one who is on the housetop, with possessions inside, should go down to get them. Likewise, no one in the field should go back for anything. [32]Remember Lot's wife! [33]Whoever tries to keep their life will lose it, and whoever loses their life will preserve it. [34]I tell you, on that night two people will be in one bed; one will be taken and the other left. [35]Two women will be grinding grain together; one will be taken and the other left." [36][b]

[37]"Where, Lord?" they asked.

He replied, "Where there is a dead body, there the vultures will gather."

The Parable of the Persistent Widow

18 Then Jesus told his disciples a parable to show them that they should always pray and not give up. [2]He said: "In a certain town there was a judge who neither feared God nor cared what people thought. [3]And there was a widow in that town who kept coming to him with the plea, 'Grant me justice against my adversary.'

[4]"For some time he refused. But finally he said to himself, 'Even though I don't fear God or care what people think, [5]yet because this widow keeps bothering me, I will see that she gets justice, so that she won't eventually come and attack me!'"

[6]And the Lord said, "Listen to what the unjust judge says. [7]And will not God bring about justice for his chosen ones, who cry out to him day and night? Will he keep putting them off? [8]I tell you, he will see that they get justice, and quickly. However, when the Son of Man comes, will he find faith on the earth?"

The Parable of the Pharisee and the Tax Collector

[9]To some who were confident of their own righteousness and looked down on everyone else, Jesus told this parable: [10]"Two men went up to the temple to pray, one a Pharisee and the other a tax collector. [11]The Pharisee stood by himself and prayed: 'God, I thank you that I am not like other people — robbers, evildoers, adulterers — or even like this tax collector. [12]I fast twice a week and give a tenth of all I get.'

[13]"But the tax collector stood at a distance. He would not even look up to heaven, but beat his breast and said, 'God, have mercy on me, a sinner.'

[14]"I tell you that this man, rather than the other, went home justified before God. For all those who exalt themselves will be humbled, and those who humble themselves will be exalted."

The Little Children and Jesus

[15]People were also bringing babies to Jesus for him to place his hands on them. When the disciples saw this, they rebuked them. [16]But Jesus called the children to him and said, "Let the little children come to me, and do not hinder them, for the kingdom of God belongs to such as these. [17]Truly I tell you, anyone who will not receive the kingdom of God like a little child will never enter it."

The Rich and the Kingdom of God

[18]A certain ruler asked him, "Good teacher, what must I do to inherit eternal life?"

[19]"Why do you call me good?" Jesus answered. "No one is good — except God alone. [20]You know the commandments: 'You shall not commit adultery, you shall not murder, you shall not steal, you shall not give false testimony, honor your father and mother.'[c]"

[21]"All these I have kept since I was a boy," he said.

---

[a] 24 Some manuscripts do not have *in his day*. [b] 36 Some manuscripts include here words similar to Matt. 24:40. [c] 20 Exodus 20:12-16; Deut. 5:16-20

HOW MANY ROUNDS WILL YOU GO?

READ: **LUKE 18:1-6**

This parable of the persistent widow shows us what praying hard looks like: knocking until your knuckles are raw, crying out until your voice is lost, and pleading until you're out of tears. If you pray through, God will come through. But remember that it will be on God's timeline and in God's way.

There's a phrase used to describe the widow's persistence: "She is wearing me out." That's boxing terminology, and it's appropriate because praying hard sometimes feels like going twelve rounds with God. A heavyweight prayer bout with God Almighty can be excruciating and exhausting, but that is how the greatest prayer victories are won. Praying hard is more than words; it's blood, sweat, and tears.

BUILDING

FAITH

WISDOM

STRENGTH

Praying hard is two-dimensional: praying like it depends on God and working like it depends on you. It's praying until God answers, no matter how long it takes. It's doing whatever it takes to show God you're serious.

There will come a day when you need to break the rules of decorum, drop to your knees, and pray for the impossible. And there will be a moment when you need to muster every ounce of faith you have and call down rain from heaven. For the persistent widow, this was that moment.

How desperate are you for the miracle? Desperate enough to pray through the night? How many times are you willing to circle the promise? Until the day you die? How long and loud will you knock on the door of opportunity? Until you knock the door down?

Taken from *The Circle Maker Student Edition* by Mark Batterson with Parker Batterson, copyright © 2012 by Mark Batterson, published by Zondervan.

[22] When Jesus heard this, he said to him, "You still lack one thing. Sell everything you have and give to the poor, and you will have treasure in heaven. Then come, follow me."

[23] When he heard this, he became very sad, because he was very wealthy. [24] Jesus looked at him and said, "How hard it is for the rich to enter the kingdom of God! [25] Indeed, it is easier for a camel to go through the eye of a needle than for someone who is rich to enter the kingdom of God."

[26] Those who heard this asked, "Who then can be saved?"

[27] Jesus replied, "What is impossible with man is possible with God."

[28] Peter said to him, "We have left all we had to follow you!"

[29] "Truly I tell you," Jesus said to them, "no one who has left home or wife or brothers or sisters or parents or children for the sake of the kingdom of God [30] will fail to receive many times as much in this age, and in the age to come eternal life."

Jesus Predicts His Death a Third Time

[31] Jesus took the Twelve aside and told them, "We are going up to Jerusalem, and everything that is written by the prophets about the Son of Man will be fulfilled. [32] He will be delivered over to the Gentiles. They will mock him, insult him and spit on him; [33] they will flog him and kill him. On the third day he will rise again."

[34] The disciples did not understand any of this. Its meaning was hidden from them, and they did not know what he was talking about.

A Blind Beggar Receives His Sight

[35] As Jesus approached Jericho, a blind man was sitting by the roadside begging. [36] When he heard the crowd going by, he asked what was happening. [37] They told him, "Jesus of Nazareth is passing by."

[38] He called out, "Jesus, Son of David, have mercy on me!"

[39] Those who led the way rebuked him and told him to be quiet, but he shouted all the more, "Son of David, have mercy on me!"

[40] Jesus stopped and ordered the man to be brought to him. When he came near, Jesus asked him, [41] "What do you want me to do for you?"

"Lord, I want to see," he replied.

[42] Jesus said to him, "Receive your sight; your faith has healed you." [43] Immediately he received his sight and followed Jesus, praising God. When all the people saw it, they also praised God.

Zacchaeus the Tax Collector

19 Jesus entered Jericho and was passing through. [2] A man was there by the name of Zacchaeus; he was a chief tax collector and was wealthy. [3] He wanted to see who Jesus was, but because he was short he could not see over the crowd. [4] So he ran ahead and climbed a sycamore-fig tree to see him, since Jesus was coming that way.

[5] When Jesus reached the spot, he looked up and said to him, "Zacchaeus, come down immediately. I must stay at your house today." [6] So he came down at once and welcomed him gladly.

[7] All the people saw this and began to mutter, "He has gone to be the guest of a sinner."

[8] But Zacchaeus stood up and said to the Lord, "Look, Lord! Here and now I give half of my possessions to the poor, and if I have cheated anybody out of anything, I will pay back four times the amount."

[9] Jesus said to him, "Today salvation has come to this house, because this man, too, is a son of Abraham. [10] For the Son of Man came to seek and to save the lost."

The Parable of the Ten Minas

[11] While they were listening to this, he went on to tell them a parable, because he was near Jerusalem and the people thought that the kingdom of God was going to appear at once. [12] He said: "A man of noble birth went to a distant country to have himself appointed king and then to return. [13] So he called ten of his servants and gave them ten minas.[a] 'Put this money to work,' he said, 'until I come back.'

[14] "But his subjects hated him and sent a delegation after him to say, 'We don't want this man to be our king.'

[15] "He was made king, however, and returned home. Then he sent for the servants to whom he had given the money, in order to find out what they had gained with it.

[16] "The first one came and said, 'Sir, your mina has earned ten more.'

---

[a] 13 A mina was about three months' wages.

THANKS, BUT I'LL PASS

READ: LUKE 18:18-30

Be honest: Do you ever feel bad for the rich young ruler? Part of me feels like Jesus was asking for too much. Are you sure you want to ask for everything? Why don't you start with the tithe? But Jesus goes right in with the sucker punch. He asks the poor guy to cough it all up! Why? Because he loved the rich young ruler too much to ask for anything less.

We focus on what Jesus asked him to give up but fail to consider what he offered in exchange. Jesus invited the rich young ruler to follow him. That's the offer of a lifetime, right there!

I live in the internship capital of the world. Trillions of twenty-somethings flock to D.C. every summer because the right internship with the right person can open the right door. It's all about building your résumé. I don't think anyone in the history of humankind has ever been offered a better internship opportunity than the rich young ruler. An internship with the Creator of the Universe? Come on, that'll look good on a job application. What a reference! But the rich young ruler says no. What!?

BUILDING

FAITH

WISDOM

STRENGTH

So if you feel bad for the rich young ruler, it shouldn't be because of what Jesus asked him to give up. It should be because of the opportunity he passed up.

Taken from *All In Student Edition* by Mark Batterson and Parker Batterson, copyright © 2014 by Mark Batterson, published by Zondervan.

¹⁷ " 'Well done, my good servant!' his master replied. 'Because you have been trustworthy in a very small matter, take charge of ten cities.'

¹⁸ "The second came and said, 'Sir, your mina has earned five more.'

¹⁹ "His master answered, 'You take charge of five cities.'

²⁰ "Then another servant came and said, 'Sir, here is your mina; I have kept it laid away in a piece of cloth. ²¹ I was afraid of you, because you are a hard man. You take out what you did not put in and reap what you did not sow.'

²² "His master replied, 'I will judge you by your own words, you wicked servant! You knew, did you, that I am a hard man, taking out what I did not put in, and reaping what I did not sow? ²³ Why then didn't you put my money on deposit, so that when I came back, I could have collected it with interest?'

²⁴ "Then he said to those standing by, 'Take his mina away from him and give it to the one who has ten minas.'

²⁵ " 'Sir,' they said, 'he already has ten!'

²⁶ "He replied, 'I tell you that to everyone who has, more will be given, but as for the one who has nothing, even what they have will be taken away. ²⁷ But those enemies of mine who did not want me to be king over them — bring them here and kill them in front of me.' "

Jesus Comes to Jerusalem as King

²⁸ After Jesus had said this, he went on ahead, going up to Jerusalem. ²⁹ As he approached Bethphage and Bethany at the hill called the Mount of Olives, he sent two of his disciples, saying to them, ³⁰ "Go to the village ahead of you, and as you enter it, you will find a colt tied there, which no one has ever ridden. Untie it and bring it here. ³¹ If anyone asks you, 'Why are you untying it?' say, 'The Lord needs it.' "

³² Those who were sent ahead went and found it just as he had told them. ³³ As they were untying the colt, its owners asked them, "Why are you untying the colt?"

³⁴ They replied, "The Lord needs it."

³⁵ They brought it to Jesus, threw their cloaks on the colt and put Jesus on it. ³⁶ As he went along, people spread their cloaks on the road.

³⁷ When he came near the place where the road goes down the Mount of Olives, the whole crowd of disciples began joyfully to praise God in loud voices for all the miracles they had seen:

³⁸ "Blessed is the king who comes in the
　　name of the Lord!"ᵃ
"Peace in heaven and glory in the highest!"

³⁹ Some of the Pharisees in the crowd said to Jesus, "Teacher, rebuke your disciples!"

⁴⁰ "I tell you," he replied, "if they keep quiet, the stones will cry out."

⁴¹ As he approached Jerusalem and saw the city, he wept over it ⁴² and said, "If you, even you, had only known on this day what would bring you peace — but now it is hidden from your eyes. ⁴³ The days will come upon you when your enemies will build an embankment against you and encircle you and hem you in on every side. ⁴⁴ They will dash you to the ground, you and the children within your walls. They will not leave one stone on another, because you did not recognize the time of God's coming to you."

Jesus at the Temple

⁴⁵ When Jesus entered the temple courts, he began to drive out those who were selling. ⁴⁶ "It is written," he said to them, " 'My house will be a house of prayer'ᵇ; but you have made it 'a den of robbers.'ᶜ"

⁴⁷ Every day he was teaching at the temple. But the chief priests, the teachers of the law and the leaders among the people were trying to kill him. ⁴⁸ Yet they could not find any way to do it, because all the people hung on his words.

The Authority of Jesus Questioned

20 One day as Jesus was teaching the people in the temple courts and proclaiming the good news, the chief priests and the teachers of the law, together with the elders, came up to him. ² "Tell us by what authority you are doing these things," they said. "Who gave you this authority?"

³ He replied, "I will also ask you a question. Tell me: ⁴ John's baptism — was it from heaven, or of human origin?"

⁵ They discussed it among themselves and said, "If we say, 'From heaven,' he will ask,

---

ᵃ *38* Psalm 118:26　　ᵇ*46* Isaiah 56:7　　ᶜ *46* Jer. 7:11

'Why didn't you believe him?' ⁶But if we say, 'Of human origin,' all the people will stone us, because they are persuaded that John was a prophet."

⁷So they answered, "We don't know where it was from."

⁸Jesus said, "Neither will I tell you by what authority I am doing these things."

The Parable of the Tenants

⁹He went on to tell the people this parable: "A man planted a vineyard, rented it to some farmers and went away for a long time. ¹⁰At harvest time he sent a servant to the tenants so they would give him some of the fruit of the vineyard. But the tenants beat him and sent him away empty-handed. ¹¹He sent another servant, but that one also they beat and treated shamefully and sent away empty-handed. ¹²He sent still a third, and they wounded him and threw him out.

¹³"Then the owner of the vineyard said, 'What shall I do? I will send my son, whom I love; perhaps they will respect him.'

¹⁴"But when the tenants saw him, they talked the matter over. 'This is the heir,' they said. 'Let's kill him, and the inheritance will be ours.' ¹⁵So they threw him out of the vineyard and killed him.

"What then will the owner of the vineyard do to them? ¹⁶He will come and kill those tenants and give the vineyard to others."

When the people heard this, they said, "God forbid!"

¹⁷Jesus looked directly at them and asked, "Then what is the meaning of that which is written:

" 'The stone the builders rejected
has become the cornerstone'ᵃ?

¹⁸Everyone who falls on that stone will be broken to pieces; anyone on whom it falls will be crushed."

¹⁹The teachers of the law and the chief priests looked for a way to arrest him immediately, because they knew he had spoken this parable against them. But they were afraid of the people.

Paying Taxes to Caesar

²⁰Keeping a close watch on him, they sent spies, who pretended to be sincere. They hoped to catch Jesus in something he said, so that they might hand him over to the power and authority of the governor. ²¹So the spies questioned him: "Teacher, we know that you speak and teach what is right, and that you do not show partiality but teach the way of God in accordance with the truth. ²²Is it right for us to pay taxes to Caesar or not?"

²³He saw through their duplicity and said to them, ²⁴"Show me a denarius. Whose image and inscription are on it?"

"Caesar's," they replied.

²⁵He said to them, "Then give back to Caesar what is Caesar's, and to God what is God's."

²⁶They were unable to trap him in what he had said there in public. And astonished by his answer, they became silent.

The Resurrection and Marriage

²⁷Some of the Sadducees, who say there is no resurrection, came to Jesus with a question. ²⁸"Teacher," they said, "Moses wrote for us that if a man's brother dies and leaves a wife but no children, the man must marry the widow and raise up offspring for his brother. ²⁹Now there were seven brothers. The first one married a woman and died childless. ³⁰The second ³¹and then the third married her, and in the same way the seven died, leaving no children. ³²Finally, the woman died too. ³³Now then, at the resurrection whose wife will she be, since the seven were married to her?"

³⁴Jesus replied, "The people of this age marry and are given in marriage. ³⁵But those who are considered worthy of taking part in the age to come and in the resurrection from the dead will neither marry nor be given in marriage, ³⁶and they can no longer die; for they are like the angels. They are God's children, since they are children of the resurrection. ³⁷But in the account of the burning bush, even Moses showed that the dead rise, for he calls the Lord 'the God of Abraham, and the God of Isaac, and the God of Jacob.'ᵇ ³⁸He is not the God of the dead, but of the living, for to him all are alive."

³⁹Some of the teachers of the law responded, "Well said, teacher!" ⁴⁰And no one dared to ask him any more questions.

ᵃ 17 Psalm 118:22   ᵇ 37 Exodus 3:6

Whose Son Is the Messiah?

[41] Then Jesus said to them, "Why is it said that the Messiah is the son of David? [42] David himself declares in the Book of Psalms:

" 'The Lord said to my Lord:
  "Sit at my right hand
[43] until I make your enemies
  a footstool for your feet." ' [a]

[44] David calls him 'Lord.' How then can he be his son?"

Warning Against the Teachers of the Law

[45] While all the people were listening, Jesus said to his disciples, [46] "Beware of the teachers of the law. They like to walk around in flowing robes and love to be greeted with respect in the marketplaces and have the most important seats in the synagogues and the places of honor at banquets. [47] They devour widows' houses and for a show make lengthy prayers. These men will be punished most severely."

The Widow's Offering

21 As Jesus looked up, he saw the rich putting their gifts into the temple treasury. [2] He also saw a poor widow put in two very small copper coins. [3] "Truly I tell you," he said, "this poor widow has put in more than all the others. [4] All these people gave their gifts out of their wealth; but she out of her poverty put in all she had to live on."

The Destruction of the Temple and Signs of the End Times

[5] Some of his disciples were remarking about how the temple was adorned with beautiful stones and with gifts dedicated to God. But Jesus said, [6] "As for what you see here, the time will come when not one stone will be left on another; every one of them will be thrown down."

[7] "Teacher," they asked, "when will these things happen? And what will be the sign that they are about to take place?"

[8] He replied: "Watch out that you are not deceived. For many will come in my name, claiming, 'I am he,' and, 'The time is near.'

Do not follow them. [9] When you hear of wars and uprisings, do not be frightened. These things must happen first, but the end will not come right away."

[10] Then he said to them: "Nation will rise against nation, and kingdom against kingdom. [11] There will be great earthquakes, famines and pestilences in various places, and fearful events and great signs from heaven.

[12] "But before all this, they will seize you and persecute you. They will hand you over to synagogues and put you in prison, and you will be brought before kings and governors, and all on account of my name. [13] And so you will bear testimony to me. [14] But make up your mind not to worry beforehand how you will defend yourselves. [15] For I will give you words and wisdom that none of your adversaries will be able to resist or contradict. [16] You will be betrayed even by parents, brothers and sisters, relatives and friends, and they will put some of you to death. [17] Everyone will hate you because of me. [18] But not a hair of your head will perish. [19] Stand firm, and you will win life.

[20] "When you see Jerusalem being surrounded by armies, you will know that its desolation is near. [21] Then let those who are in Judea flee to the mountains, let those in the city get out, and let those in the country not enter the city. [22] For this is the time of punishment in fulfillment of all that has been written. [23] How dreadful it will be in those days for pregnant women and nursing mothers! There will be great distress in the land and wrath against this people. [24] They will fall by the sword and will be taken as prisoners to all the nations. Jerusalem will be trampled on by the Gentiles until the times of the Gentiles are fulfilled.

[25] "There will be signs in the sun, moon and stars. On the earth, nations will be in anguish and perplexity at the roaring and tossing of the sea. [26] People will faint from terror, apprehensive of what is coming on the world, for the heavenly bodies will be shaken. [27] At that time they will see the Son of Man coming in a cloud with power and great glory. [28] When these things begin to take place, stand up and lift up your heads, because your redemption is drawing near."

[a] 43 Psalm 110:1

[29] He told them this parable: "Look at the fig tree and all the trees. [30] When they sprout leaves, you can see for yourselves and know that summer is near. [31] Even so, when you see these things happening, you know that the kingdom of God is near.

[32] "Truly I tell you, this generation will certainly not pass away until all these things have happened. [33] Heaven and earth will pass away, but my words will never pass away.

[34] "Be careful, or your hearts will be weighed down with carousing, drunkenness and the anxieties of life, and that day will close on you suddenly like a trap. [35] For it will come on all those who live on the face of the whole earth. [36] Be always on the watch, and pray that you may be able to escape all that is about to happen, and that you may be able to stand before the Son of Man."

[37] Each day Jesus was teaching at the temple, and each evening he went out to spend the night on the hill called the Mount of Olives, [38] and all the people came early in the morning to hear him at the temple.

Judas Agrees to Betray Jesus

22 Now the Festival of Unleavened Bread, called the Passover, was approaching, [2] and the chief priests and the teachers of the law were looking for some way to get rid of Jesus, for they were afraid of the people. [3] Then Satan entered Judas, called Iscariot, one of the Twelve. [4] And Judas went to the chief priests and the officers of the temple guard and discussed with them how he might betray Jesus. [5] They were delighted and agreed to give him money. [6] He consented, and watched for an opportunity to hand Jesus over to them when no crowd was present.

The Last Supper

[7] Then came the day of Unleavened Bread on which the Passover lamb had to be sacrificed. [8] Jesus sent Peter and John, saying, "Go and make preparations for us to eat the Passover."

[9] "Where do you want us to prepare for it?" they asked.

[10] He replied, "As you enter the city, a man carrying a jar of water will meet you. Follow him to the house that he enters, [11] and say to the owner of the house, 'The Teacher asks: Where is the guest room, where I may eat the Passover with my disciples?' [12] He will show you a large room upstairs, all furnished. Make preparations there."

[13] They left and found things just as Jesus had told them. So they prepared the Passover.

[14] When the hour came, Jesus and his apostles reclined at the table. [15] And he said to them, "I have eagerly desired to eat this Passover with you before I suffer. [16] For I tell you, I will not eat it again until it finds fulfillment in the kingdom of God."

[17] After taking the cup, he gave thanks and said, "Take this and divide it among you. [18] For I tell you I will not drink again from the fruit of the vine until the kingdom of God comes."

[19] And he took bread, gave thanks and broke it, and gave it to them, saying, "This is my body given for you; do this in remembrance of me."

[20] In the same way, after the supper he took the cup, saying, "This cup is the new covenant in my blood, which is poured out for you.[a] [21] But the hand of him who is going to betray me is with mine on the table. [22] The Son of Man will go as it has been decreed. But woe to that man who betrays him!" [23] They began to question among themselves which of them it might be who would do this.

[24] A dispute also arose among them as to which of them was considered to be greatest. [25] Jesus said to them, "The kings of the Gentiles lord it over them; and those who exercise authority over them call themselves Benefactors. [26] But you are not to be like that. Instead, the greatest among you should be like the youngest, and the one who rules like the one who serves. [27] For who is greater, the one who is at the table or the one who serves? Is it not the one who is at the table? But I am among you as one who serves. [28] You are those who have stood by me in my trials. [29] And I confer on you a kingdom, just as my Father conferred one on me, [30] so that you may eat and drink at my table in my kingdom and sit on thrones, judging the twelve tribes of Israel.

---

[a] 19,20 Some manuscripts do not have *given for you . . . poured out for you.*

³¹"Simon, Simon, Satan has asked to sift all of you as wheat. ³²But I have prayed for you, Simon, that your faith may not fail. And when you have turned back, strengthen your brothers."

³³But he replied, "Lord, I am ready to go with you to prison and to death."

³⁴Jesus answered, "I tell you, Peter, before the rooster crows today, you will deny three times that you know me."

³⁵Then Jesus asked them, "When I sent you without purse, bag or sandals, did you lack anything?"

"Nothing," they answered.

³⁶He said to them, "But now if you have a purse, take it, and also a bag; and if you don't have a sword, sell your cloak and buy one. ³⁷It is written: 'And he was numbered with the transgressors'ᵃ; and I tell you that this must be fulfilled in me. Yes, what is written about me is reaching its fulfillment."

³⁸The disciples said, "See, Lord, here are two swords."

"That's enough!" he replied.

Jesus Prays on the Mount of Olives

³⁹Jesus went out as usual to the Mount of Olives, and his disciples followed him. ⁴⁰On reaching the place, he said to them, "Pray that you will not fall into temptation." ⁴¹He withdrew about a stone's throw beyond them, knelt down and prayed, ⁴²"Father, if you are willing, take this cup from me; yet not my will, but yours be done." ⁴³An angel from heaven appeared to him and strengthened him. ⁴⁴And being in anguish, he prayed more earnestly, and his sweat was like drops of blood falling to the ground.ᵇ

⁴⁵When he rose from prayer and went back to the disciples, he found them asleep, exhausted from sorrow. ⁴⁶"Why are you sleeping?" he asked them. "Get up and pray so that you will not fall into temptation."

Jesus Arrested

⁴⁷While he was still speaking a crowd came up, and the man who was called Judas, one of the Twelve, was leading them. He approached Jesus to kiss him, ⁴⁸but Jesus asked him, "Judas, are you betraying the Son of Man with a kiss?"

⁴⁹When Jesus' followers saw what was going to happen, they said, "Lord, should we strike with our swords?" ⁵⁰And one of them struck the servant of the high priest, cutting off his right ear.

⁵¹But Jesus answered, "No more of this!" And he touched the man's ear and healed him.

⁵²Then Jesus said to the chief priests, the officers of the temple guard, and the elders, who had come for him, "Am I leading a rebellion, that you have come with swords and clubs? ⁵³Every day I was with you in the temple courts, and you did not lay a hand on me. But this is your hour—when darkness reigns."

Peter Disowns Jesus

⁵⁴Then seizing him, they led him away and took him into the house of the high priest. Peter followed at a distance. ⁵⁵And when some there had kindled a fire in the middle of the courtyard and had sat down together, Peter sat down with them. ⁵⁶A servant girl saw him seated there in the firelight. She looked closely at him and said, "This man was with him."

⁵⁷But he denied it. "Woman, I don't know him," he said.

⁵⁸A little later someone else saw him and said, "You also are one of them."

"Man, I am not!" Peter replied.

⁵⁹About an hour later another asserted, "Certainly this fellow was with him, for he is a Galilean."

⁶⁰Peter replied, "Man, I don't know what you're talking about!" Just as he was speaking, the rooster crowed. ⁶¹The Lord turned and looked straight at Peter. Then Peter remembered the word the Lord had spoken to him: "Before the rooster crows today, you will disown me three times." ⁶²And he went outside and wept bitterly.

The Guards Mock Jesus

⁶³The men who were guarding Jesus began mocking and beating him. ⁶⁴They blindfolded him and demanded, "Prophesy! Who hit you?" ⁶⁵And they said many other insulting things to him.

Jesus Before Pilate and Herod

⁶⁶At daybreak the council of the elders of the people, both the chief priests and the

---

ᵃ 37 Isaiah 53:12   ᵇ 43,44 Many early manuscripts do not have verses 43 and 44.

TOTALLY BLEW IT

READ: **LUKE 22:54-61**

Peter got scared, because that's what people do. We're weak. As long as we have this skin on, we'll do some of the dumbest things imaginable.

In that one moment, when all eyes were on him, Peter choked. Three times. The last of the three times he even called down curses on himself. I can't even imagine how Peter felt about this.

Or can I?

When I fail, the Enemy lies to me. He wants me to remain a failure. "Are you sure you're even saved? Look at what you're doing." He wants me out of the Word and into the mirror. If Satan can get me out of the Word to focus on my circumstances and on myself, he can mire me in numbing guilt and neutralize me. I recognize that, despite trying to live for Jesus, I've failed badly. Before long, I decide, *Oh, well. I guess that was my shot.*

Just when we're starting to thrive, the Enemy will try to derail us. He'll throw our past at us. He'll bring obstacles right now. He'll make us doubt our future. He'll even make us doubt whether all of this is real and whether we really belong to God. Sometimes, we'll want to quit. But God is always faithful. Jesus always comes looking for us. He's always waiting on the shore, calling out to me.

BUILDING

FAITH

WISDOM

STRENGTH

Taken from *Thrive Student Edition* by Mark Hall with Tim Luke, copyright © 2014 by Mark Hall, published by Zondervan.

teachers of the law, met together, and Jesus was led before them. [67] "If you are the Messiah," they said, "tell us."

Jesus answered, "If I tell you, you will not believe me, [68] and if I asked you, you would not answer. [69] But from now on, the Son of Man will be seated at the right hand of the mighty God."

[70] They all asked, "Are you then the Son of God?"

He replied, "You say that I am."

[71] Then they said, "Why do we need any more testimony? We have heard it from his own lips."

23 Then the whole assembly rose and led him off to Pilate. [2] And they began to accuse him, saying, "We have found this man subverting our nation. He opposes payment of taxes to Caesar and claims to be Messiah, a king."

[3] So Pilate asked Jesus, "Are you the king of the Jews?"

"You have said so," Jesus replied.

[4] Then Pilate announced to the chief priests and the crowd, "I find no basis for a charge against this man."

[5] But they insisted, "He stirs up the people all over Judea by his teaching. He started in Galilee and has come all the way here."

[6] On hearing this, Pilate asked if the man was a Galilean. [7] When he learned that Jesus was under Herod's jurisdiction, he sent him to Herod, who was also in Jerusalem at that time.

[8] When Herod saw Jesus, he was greatly pleased, because for a long time he had been wanting to see him. From what he had heard about him, he hoped to see him perform a sign of some sort. [9] He plied him with many questions, but Jesus gave him no answer. [10] The chief priests and the teachers of the law were standing there, vehemently accusing him. [11] Then Herod and his soldiers ridiculed and mocked him. Dressing him in an elegant robe, they sent him back to Pilate. [12] That day Herod and Pilate became friends—before this they had been enemies.

[13] Pilate called together the chief priests, the rulers and the people, [14] and said to them, "You brought me this man as one who was inciting the people to rebellion. I have

examined him in your presence and have found no basis for your charges against him. [15] Neither has Herod, for he sent him back to us; as you can see, he has done nothing to deserve death. [16] Therefore, I will punish him and then release him." [17] [a]

[18] But the whole crowd shouted, "Away with this man! Release Barabbas to us!" [19] (Barabbas had been thrown into prison for an insurrection in the city, and for murder.)

[20] Wanting to release Jesus, Pilate appealed to them again. [21] But they kept shouting, "Crucify him! Crucify him!"

[22] For the third time he spoke to them: "Why? What crime has this man committed? I have found in him no grounds for the death penalty. Therefore I will have him punished and then release him."

[23] But with loud shouts they insistently demanded that he be crucified, and their shouts prevailed. [24] So Pilate decided to grant their demand. [25] He released the man who had been thrown into prison for insurrection and murder, the one they asked for, and surrendered Jesus to their will.

The Crucifixion of Jesus

[26] As the soldiers led him away, they seized Simon from Cyrene, who was on his way in from the country, and put the cross on him and made him carry it behind Jesus. [27] A large number of people followed him, including women who mourned and wailed for him. [28] Jesus turned and said to them, "Daughters of Jerusalem, do not weep for me; weep for yourselves and for your children. [29] For the time will come when you will say, 'Blessed are the childless women, the wombs that never bore and the breasts that never nursed!' [30] Then

" 'they will say to the mountains, "Fall on us!"
and to the hills, "Cover us!" ' [b]

[31] For if people do these things when the tree is green, what will happen when it is dry?"

[32] Two other men, both criminals, were also led out with him to be executed. [33] When they came to the place called the Skull, they crucified him there, along with the criminals—one on his right, the other on his left. [34] Jesus said, "Father, forgive

a 17 Some manuscripts include here words similar to Matt. 27:15 and Mark 15:6.   *b* 30 Hosea 10:8

them, for they do not know what they are doing."[a] And they divided up his clothes by casting lots.

[35] The people stood watching, and the rulers even sneered at him. They said, "He saved others; let him save himself if he is God's Messiah, the Chosen One."

[36] The soldiers also came up and mocked him. They offered him wine vinegar [37] and said, "If you are the king of the Jews, save yourself."

[38] There was a written notice above him, which read: THIS IS THE KING OF THE JEWS.

[39] One of the criminals who hung there hurled insults at him: "Aren't you the Messiah? Save yourself and us!"

[40] But the other criminal rebuked him. "Don't you fear God," he said, "since you are under the same sentence? [41] We are punished justly, for we are getting what our deeds deserve. But this man has done nothing wrong."

[42] Then he said, "Jesus, remember me when you come into your kingdom.[b]"

[43] Jesus answered him, "Truly I tell you, today you will be with me in paradise."

The Death of Jesus

[44] It was now about noon, and darkness came over the whole land until three in the afternoon, [45] for the sun stopped shining. And the curtain of the temple was torn in two. [46] Jesus called out with a loud voice, "Father, into your hands I commit my spirit."[c] When he had said this, he breathed his last.

[47] The centurion, seeing what had happened, praised God and said, "Surely this was a righteous man." [48] When all the people who had gathered to witness this sight saw what took place, they beat their breasts and went away. [49] But all those who knew him, including the women who had followed him from Galilee, stood at a distance, watching these things.

The Burial of Jesus

[50] Now there was a man named Joseph, a member of the Council, a good and upright man, [51] who had not consented to their decision and action. He came from the Jude-an town of Arimathea, and he himself was waiting for the kingdom of God. [52] Going to Pilate, he asked for Jesus' body. [53] Then he took it down, wrapped it in linen cloth and placed it in a tomb cut in the rock, one in which no one had yet been laid. [54] It was Preparation Day, and the Sabbath was about to begin.

[55] The women who had come with Jesus from Galilee followed Joseph and saw the tomb and how his body was laid in it. [56] Then they went home and prepared spices and perfumes. But they rested on the Sabbath in obedience to the commandment.

Jesus Has Risen

24 On the first day of the week, very early in the morning, the women took the spices they had prepared and went to the tomb. [2] They found the stone rolled away from the tomb, [3] but when they entered, they did not find the body of the Lord Jesus. [4] While they were wondering about this, suddenly two men in clothes that gleamed like lightning stood beside them. [5] In their fright the women bowed down with their faces to the ground, but the men said to them, "Why do you look for the living among the dead? [6] He is not here; he has risen! Remember how he told you, while he was still with you in Galilee: [7] 'The Son of Man must be delivered over to the hands of sinners, be crucified and on the third day be raised again.'" [8] Then they remembered his words.

[9] When they came back from the tomb, they told all these things to the Eleven and to all the others. [10] It was Mary Magdalene, Joanna, Mary the mother of James, and the others with them who told this to the apostles. [11] But they did not believe the women, because their words seemed to them like nonsense. [12] Peter, however, got up and ran to the tomb. Bending over, he saw the strips of linen lying by themselves, and he went away, wondering to himself what had happened.

On the Road to Emmaus

[13] Now that same day two of them were going to a village called Emmaus, about seven miles[d] from Jerusalem. [14] They were talking

---

[a] 34 Some early manuscripts do not have this sentence.   [b] 42 Some manuscripts *come with your kingly power*   [c] 46 Psalm 31:5   [d] 13 Or about 11 kilometers

FACING A SNEERING CROWD

READ: LUKE 23:39

As the hours ticked down to Jesus' crucifixion, he was surrounded by mockers. The soldiers who captured him ridiculed and beat him, wrapping his eyes in a blindfold and demanding he say who had hit him. They uttered "many other insulting things" (Luke 22:65), and that was just the start.

Jesus was taken to the Roman governor, Pilate, then to the king of Judea, Herod. When Jesus refused to answer Herod's questions, he and his soldiers decked him out in a royal robe (23:11).

As Jesus hung on the cross, rulers and everyday people continued to sneer. Then the two criminals being executed on either side of Jesus got mixed up in the fight. One of the criminals taunted Jesus, daring him to prove his identity as the Messiah by saving himself and them. But the other recognized an essential fact about Jesus. The other two guys were getting what they deserved, but Jesus had done nothing wrong.

BUILDING FAITH WISDOM STRENGTH

The Bible says that Jesus was like his human brothers and sisters in every way (Hebrews 2:17). That implies he had quirky habits or less-than-perfect physical traits just like the rest of us—points others would find easy to tease. But this mocking at the cross questioned his character, his truthfulness, even his sanity. When Jesus went to the cross for human sin, his pain wasn't just physical. He was ridiculed and rejected, all for your sake.

with each other about everything that had happened. ¹⁵As they talked and discussed these things with each other, Jesus himself came up and walked along with them; ¹⁶but they were kept from recognizing him.

¹⁷He asked them, "What are you discussing together as you walk along?"

They stood still, their faces downcast. ¹⁸One of them, named Cleopas, asked him, "Are you the only one visiting Jerusalem who does not know the things that have happened there in these days?"

¹⁹"What things?" he asked.

"About Jesus of Nazareth," they replied. "He was a prophet, powerful in word and deed before God and all the people. ²⁰The chief priests and our rulers handed him over to be sentenced to death, and they crucified him; ²¹but we had hoped that he was the one who was going to redeem Israel. And what is more, it is the third day since all this took place. ²²In addition, some of our women amazed us. They went to the tomb early this morning ²³but didn't find his body. They came and told us that they had seen a vision of angels, who said he was alive. ²⁴Then some of our companions went to the tomb and found it just as the women had said, but they did not see Jesus."

²⁵He said to them, "How foolish you are, and how slow to believe all that the prophets have spoken! ²⁶Did not the Messiah have to suffer these things and then enter his glory?" ²⁷And beginning with Moses and all the Prophets, he explained to them what was said in all the Scriptures concerning himself.

²⁸As they approached the village to which they were going, Jesus continued on as if he were going farther. ²⁹But they urged him strongly, "Stay with us, for it is nearly evening; the day is almost over." So he went in to stay with them.

³⁰When he was at the table with them, he took bread, gave thanks, broke it and began to give it to them. ³¹Then their eyes were opened and they recognized him, and he disappeared from their sight. ³²They asked each other, "Were not our hearts burning within us while he talked with us on the road and opened the Scriptures to us?"

³³They got up and returned at once to Jerusalem. There they found the Eleven and those with them, assembled together ³⁴and saying, "It is true! The Lord has risen and has appeared to Simon." ³⁵Then the two told what had happened on the way, and how Jesus was recognized by them when he broke the bread.

Jesus Appears to the Disciples

³⁶While they were still talking about this, Jesus himself stood among them and said to them, "Peace be with you."

³⁷They were startled and frightened, thinking they saw a ghost. ³⁸He said to them, "Why are you troubled, and why do doubts rise in your minds? ³⁹Look at my hands and my feet. It is I myself! Touch me and see; a ghost does not have flesh and bones, as you see I have."

⁴⁰When he had said this, he showed them his hands and feet. ⁴¹And while they still did not believe it because of joy and amazement, he asked them, "Do you have anything here to eat?" ⁴²They gave him a piece of broiled fish, ⁴³and he took it and ate it in their presence.

⁴⁴He said to them, "This is what I told you while I was still with you: Everything must be fulfilled that is written about me in the Law of Moses, the Prophets and the Psalms."

⁴⁵Then he opened their minds so they could understand the Scriptures. ⁴⁶He told them, "This is what is written: The Messiah will suffer and rise from the dead on the third day, ⁴⁷and repentance for the forgiveness of sins will be preached in his name to all nations, beginning at Jerusalem. ⁴⁸You are witnesses of these things. ⁴⁹I am going to send you what my Father has promised; but stay in the city until you have been clothed with power from on high."

The Ascension of Jesus

⁵⁰When he had led them out to the vicinity of Bethany, he lifted up his hands and blessed them. ⁵¹While he was blessing them, he left them and was taken up into heaven. ⁵²Then they worshiped him and returned to Jerusalem with great joy. ⁵³And they stayed continually at the temple, praising God.

JOHN

 ## WHEN DID THIS HAPPEN?

A.D. 1 to 36 in Palestine

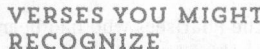 ## WHO IS IN THIS BOOK?

Jesus

John

Nicodemus

Samaritan woman

Philip

Thomas

Mary

Martha

Lazarus

Peter

VERSES YOU MIGHT RECOGNIZE

JOHN 3:16

"For God so loved the world that he gave his one and only Son, that whoever believes in him shall not perish but have eternal life."

JOHN 14:6

"Jesus answered, 'I am the way and the truth and the life. No one comes to the Father except through me.'"

WHAT'S IT ABOUT?

Differing from the other three gospel writers, John started his account at the beginning of time to establish that Jesus has always existed with God. John recorded miracles and teachings that show that Jesus is the Son of God and made a case for why people should believe in Jesus and be saved. His point is captured in John 20:31: "But these are written that you may believe that Jesus is the Messiah, the Son of God, and that by believing you may have life in his name."

This book contains seven signs, which include Jesus turning water into wine at a wedding and raising Lazarus from the dead. These signs show that Jesus possesses the power of God. John also included seven "I am" statements. Jesus said, "I am the living water," and "I am the resurrection and the life." These statements were Jesus' way of claiming that he is God, something that angered the religious leaders and ultimately led to his arrest and crucifixion.

John wrote this eyewitness account twenty years after the other gospels, near the end of his life. His words were designed to convince his readers that Jesus is the divine Savior who will set them free from their sins.

JOHN

The Word Became Flesh

1 In the beginning was the Word, and the Word was with God, and the Word was God. [2] He was with God in the beginning. [3] Through him all things were made; without him nothing was made that has been made. [4] In him was life, and that life was the light of all mankind. [5] The light shines in the darkness, and the darkness has not overcome[a] it.

[6] There was a man sent from God whose name was John. [7] He came as a witness to testify concerning that light, so that through him all might believe. [8] He himself was not the light; he came only as a witness to the light.

[9] The true light that gives light to everyone was coming into the world. [10] He was in the world, and though the world was made through him, the world did not recognize him. [11] He came to that which was his own, but his own did not receive him. [12] Yet to all who did receive him, to those who believed in his name, he gave the right to become children of God— [13] children born not of natural descent, nor of human decision or a husband's will, but born of God.

[14] The Word became flesh and made his dwelling among us. We have seen his glory, the glory of the one and only Son, who came from the Father, full of grace and truth.

[15] (John testified concerning him. He cried out, saying, "This is the one I spoke about when I said, 'He who comes after me has surpassed me because he was before me.'") [16] Out of his fullness we have all received grace in place of grace already given. [17] For the law was given through Moses; grace and truth came through Jesus Christ. [18] No one has ever seen God, but the one and only Son, who is himself God and[b] is in closest relationship with the Father, has made him known.

John the Baptist Denies Being the Messiah

[19] Now this was John's testimony when the Jewish leaders[c] in Jerusalem sent priests and Levites to ask him who he was. [20] He did not fail to confess, but confessed freely, "I am not the Messiah."

[21] They asked him, "Then who are you? Are you Elijah?"

He said, "I am not."

"Are you the Prophet?"

He answered, "No."

[22] Finally they said, "Who are you? Give us an answer to take back to those who sent us. What do you say about yourself?"

[23] John replied in the words of Isaiah the prophet, "I am the voice of one calling in the wilderness, 'Make straight the way for the Lord.'"[d]

[24] Now the Pharisees who had been sent [25] questioned him, "Why then do you baptize if you are not the Messiah, nor Elijah, nor the Prophet?"

[26] "I baptize with[e] water," John replied, "but among you stands one you do not know. [27] He is the one who comes after me, the straps of whose sandals I am not worthy to untie."

[28] This all happened at Bethany on the other side of the Jordan, where John was baptizing.

John Testifies About Jesus

[29] The next day John saw Jesus coming toward him and said, "Look, the Lamb of God, who takes away the sin of the world! [30] This is the one I meant when I said, 'A man who comes after me has surpassed me because he was before me.' [31] I myself did not know him, but the reason I came baptizing with water was that he might be revealed to Israel."

[32] Then John gave this testimony: "I saw

---

[a] 5 Or *understood*   [b] 18 Some manuscripts *but the only Son, who*   [c] 19 The Greek term traditionally translated *the Jews* (*hoi Ioudaioi*) refers here and elsewhere in John's Gospel to those Jewish leaders who opposed Jesus; also in 5:10, 15, 16; 7:1, 11, 13; 9:22; 18:14, 28, 36; 19:7, 12, 31, 38; 20:19.   [d] 23 Isaiah 40:3   [e] 26 Or *in*; also in verses 31 and 33 (twice)

the Spirit come down from heaven as a dove and remain on him. [33] And I myself did not know him, but the one who sent me to baptize with water told me, 'The man on whom you see the Spirit come down and remain is the one who will baptize with the Holy Spirit.' [34] I have seen and I testify that this is God's Chosen One."[a]

John's Disciples Follow Jesus

[35] The next day John was there again with two of his disciples. [36] When he saw Jesus passing by, he said, "Look, the Lamb of God!"

[37] When the two disciples heard him say this, they followed Jesus. [38] Turning around, Jesus saw them following and asked, "What do you want?"

They said, "Rabbi" (which means "Teacher"), "where are you staying?"

[39] "Come," he replied, "and you will see."

So they went and saw where he was staying, and they spent that day with him. It was about four in the afternoon.

[40] Andrew, Simon Peter's brother, was one of the two who heard what John had said and who had followed Jesus. [41] The first thing Andrew did was to find his brother Simon and tell him, "We have found the Messiah" (that is, the Christ). [42] And he brought him to Jesus.

Jesus looked at him and said, "You are Simon son of John. You will be called Cephas" (which, when translated, is Peter[b]).

Jesus Calls Philip and Nathanael

[43] The next day Jesus decided to leave for Galilee. Finding Philip, he said to him, "Follow me."

[44] Philip, like Andrew and Peter, was from the town of Bethsaida. [45] Philip found Nathanael and told him, "We have found the one Moses wrote about in the Law, and about whom the prophets also wrote — Jesus of Nazareth, the son of Joseph."

[46] "Nazareth! Can anything good come from there?" Nathanael asked.

"Come and see," said Philip.

[47] When Jesus saw Nathanael approaching, he said of him, "Here truly is an Israelite in whom there is no deceit."

[48] "How do you know me?" Nathanael asked.

Jesus answered, "I saw you while you were still under the fig tree before Philip called you."

[49] Then Nathanael declared, "Rabbi, you are the Son of God; you are the king of Israel."

[50] Jesus said, "You believe[c] because I told you I saw you under the fig tree. You will see greater things than that." [51] He then added, "Very truly I tell you,[d] you[d] will see 'heaven open, and the angels of God ascending and descending on'[e] the Son of Man."

Jesus Changes Water Into Wine

2 On the third day a wedding took place at Cana in Galilee. Jesus' mother was there, [2] and Jesus and his disciples had also been invited to the wedding. [3] When the wine was gone, Jesus' mother said to him, "They have no more wine."

[4] "Woman,[f] why do you involve me?" Jesus replied. "My hour has not yet come."

[5] His mother said to the servants, "Do whatever he tells you."

[6] Nearby stood six stone water jars, the kind used by the Jews for ceremonial washing, each holding from twenty to thirty gallons.[g]

[7] Jesus said to the servants, "Fill the jars with water"; so they filled them to the brim.

[8] Then he told them, "Now draw some out and take it to the master of the banquet."

They did so, [9] and the master of the banquet tasted the water that had been turned into wine. He did not realize where it had come from, though the servants who had drawn the water knew. Then he called the bridegroom aside [10] and said, "Everyone brings out the choice wine first and then the cheaper wine after the guests have had too much to drink; but you have saved the best till now."

[11] What Jesus did here in Cana of Galilee was the first of the signs through which he revealed his glory; and his disciples believed in him.

[12] After this he went down to Capernaum with his mother and brothers and his disciples. There they stayed for a few days.

---

[a] 34 See Isaiah 42:1; many manuscripts *is the Son of God.*   [b] 42 *Cephas* (Aramaic) and *Peter* (Greek) both mean *rock.*   [c] 50 Or *Do you believe . . . ?*   [d] 51 The Greek is plural.   [e] 51 Gen. 28:12   [f] 4 The Greek for *Woman* does not denote any disrespect.   [g] 6 Or *from about 75 to about 115 liters*

Jesus Clears the Temple Courts

¹³When it was almost time for the Jewish Passover, Jesus went up to Jerusalem. ¹⁴In the temple courts he found people selling cattle, sheep and doves, and others sitting at tables exchanging money. ¹⁵So he made a whip out of cords, and drove all from the temple courts, both sheep and cattle; he scattered the coins of the money changers and overturned their tables. ¹⁶To those who sold doves he said, "Get these out of here! Stop turning my Father's house into a market!" ¹⁷His disciples remembered that it is written: "Zeal for your house will consume me."ᵃ

¹⁸The Jews then responded to him, "What sign can you show us to prove your authority to do all this?"

¹⁹Jesus answered them, "Destroy this temple, and I will raise it again in three days."

²⁰They replied, "It has taken forty-six years to build this temple, and you are going to raise it in three days?" ²¹But the temple he had spoken of was his body. ²²After he was raised from the dead, his disciples recalled what he had said. Then they believed the scripture and the words that Jesus had spoken.

²³Now while he was in Jerusalem at the Passover Festival, many people saw the signs he was performing and believed in his name.ᵇ ²⁴But Jesus would not entrust himself to them, for he knew all people. ²⁵He did not need any testimony about mankind, for he knew what was in each person.

Jesus Teaches Nicodemus

3 Now there was a Pharisee, a man named Nicodemus who was a member of the Jewish ruling council. ²He came to Jesus at night and said, "Rabbi, we know that you are a teacher who has come from God. For no one could perform the signs you are doing if God were not with him."

³Jesus replied, "Very truly I tell you, no one can see the kingdom of God unless they are born again.ᶜ"

⁴"How can someone be born when they are old?" Nicodemus asked. "Surely they cannot enter a second time into their mother's womb to be born!"

⁵Jesus answered, "Very truly I tell you, no one can enter the kingdom of God unless they are born of water and the Spirit. ⁶Flesh gives birth to flesh, but the Spiritᵈ gives birth to spirit. ⁷You should not be surprised at my saying, 'Youᵉ must be born again.' ⁸The wind blows wherever it pleases. You hear its sound, but you cannot tell where it comes from or where it is going. So it is with everyone born of the Spirit."ᶠ

⁹"How can this be?" Nicodemus asked.

¹⁰"You are Israel's teacher," said Jesus, "and do you not understand these things? ¹¹Very truly I tell you, we speak of what we know, and we testify to what we have seen, but still you people do not accept our testimony. ¹²I have spoken to you of earthly things and you do not believe; how then will you believe if I speak of heavenly things? ¹³No one has ever gone into heaven except the one who came from heaven—the Son of Man.ᵍ ¹⁴Just as Moses lifted up the snake in the wilderness, so the Son of Man must be lifted up,ʰ ¹⁵that everyone who believes may have eternal life in him."ⁱ

¹⁶For God so loved the world that he gave his one and only Son, that whoever believes in him shall not perish but have eternal life. ¹⁷For God did not send his Son into the world to condemn the world, but to save the world through him. ¹⁸Whoever believes in him is not condemned, but whoever does not believe stands condemned already because they have not believed in the name of God's one and only Son. ¹⁹This is the verdict: Light has come into the world, but people loved darkness instead of light because their deeds were evil. ²⁰Everyone who does evil hates the light, and will not come into the light for fear that their deeds will be exposed. ²¹But whoever lives by the truth comes into the light, so that it may be seen plainly that what they have done has been done in the sight of God.

John Testifies Again About Jesus

²²After this, Jesus and his disciples went out into the Judean countryside, where he

---

ᵃ 17 Psalm 69:9   ᵇ 23 Or *in him*   ᶜ 3 The Greek for *again* also means *from above*; also in verse 7.   ᵈ 6 Or *but spirit*   ᵉ 7 The Greek is plural.   ᶠ 8 The Greek for *Spirit* is the same as that for *wind*.   ᵍ 13 Some manuscripts *Man, who is in heaven*   ʰ 14 The Greek for *lifted up* also means *exalted*.   ⁱ 15 Some interpreters end the quotation with verse 21.

THE INABILITY TO DO NOTHING

READ: JOHN 2:15

Joshua Chamberlain was awarded the Medal of Honor by President Grover Cleveland for "holding his position on the Little Round Top against repeated assaults, and carrying the advance position on the Great Round Top."

As Chamberlain got older, he would reflect back on that very day with these words: "I had deep within me the inability to do nothing. I knew I may die, but I also knew that I would not die with a bullet in my back."

The inability to do nothing!

Jesus set this very standard for us!

Without any troops, Jesus charged the money changers in the temple by turning their tables upside down and driving out their flocks. He confronted the Pharisees' hypocrisy. He exorcised a demon from a possessed man whom anyone else would be afraid to confront. And he stopped a funeral procession and raised a boy from the dead.

I would not call Jesus someone who was passive. He was the definition of passion. In fact, the last week of his life is referred to as "Passion Week."

We should possess the same kind of passion. Going all in means defying the "rules" of religion that the world has created to genuinely go after God.

When will we realize that indecision is a decision?

When will we come to terms with the fact that inaction is an action?

Two thousand years ago, Jesus gave us the command to charge. And he's never looked back.

BUILDING FAITH WISDOM STRENGTH

Taken from *All In Student Edition* by Mark Batterson and Parker Batterson, copyright © 2014 by Mark Batterson, published by Zondervan.

NICODEMUS

He came to Jesus at night and said, "Rabbi, we know that you are a teacher who has come from God. For no one could perform the signs you are doing if God were not with him." Jesus replied, "Very truly I tell you, no one can see the kingdom of God unless they are born again." JOHN 3:2–3

HIS NAME MEANS: "victor over the people"
READ HIS STORY: *John 3:1–21, 7:45–52, 19:38–42*

Nicodemus was a Pharisee. This means he worked hard to follow every single Jewish law carefully. Yet unlike many of the Pharisees who scoffed at Jesus and looked for ways to kill him, Nicodemus tried to discover who Jesus really was.

Jesus was a teacher sent from God; Nicodemus was sure of that. But was Jesus anything more? At first Nicodemus appears to be cautious and fearful of his peers. After all, if Jesus wasn't for real, Nicodemus was risking his reputation and his position—a big cost. He came to Jesus at night to ask questions in his search. But eventually, Nicodemus grew brave. One day he stood up for Jesus to his fellow members of the Jewish ruling council. And then on the day that Jesus was crucified and his followers fled for their lives, Nicodemus came to Golgotha, helped take the body of Jesus from the cross and put it in a nearby tomb.

When Nicodemus showed up at the foot of the cross in full view of the enemies of Jesus, Nicodemus showed by his actions he had chosen to believe the words Jesus said about being born again.

Like Nicodemus, you are faced with a choice. Will you risk your reputation, maybe even your position among your friends or family, to put your faith in Jesus alone?

spent some time with them, and baptized. [23] Now John also was baptizing at Aenon near Salim, because there was plenty of water, and people were coming and being baptized. [24] (This was before John was put in prison.) [25] An argument developed between some of John's disciples and a certain Jew over the matter of ceremonial washing. [26] They came to John and said to him, "Rabbi, that man who was with you on the other side of the Jordan — the one you testified about — look, he is baptizing, and everyone is going to him."

[27] To this John replied, "A person can receive only what is given them from heaven. [28] You yourselves can testify that I said, 'I am not the Messiah but am sent ahead of him.' [29] The bride belongs to the bridegroom. The friend who attends the bridegroom waits and listens for him, and is full of joy when he hears the bridegroom's voice. That joy is mine, and it is now complete. [30] He must become greater; I must become less."[a]

[31] The one who comes from above is above all; the one who is from the earth belongs to the earth, and speaks as one from the earth. The one who comes from heaven is above all. [32] He testifies to what he has seen and heard, but no one accepts his testimony. [33] Whoever has accepted it has certified that God is truthful. [34] For the one whom God has sent speaks the words of God, for God[b] gives the Spirit without limit. [35] The Father loves the Son and has placed everything in his hands. [36] Whoever believes in the Son has eternal life, but whoever rejects the Son will not see life, for God's wrath remains on them.

Jesus Talks With a Samaritan Woman

4 Now Jesus learned that the Pharisees had heard that he was gaining and baptizing more disciples than John — [2] although in fact it was not Jesus who baptized, but his disciples. [3] So he left Judea and went back once more to Galilee.

[4] Now he had to go through Samaria. [5] So he came to a town in Samaria called Sychar, near the plot of ground Jacob had given to his son Joseph. [6] Jacob's well was there, and Jesus, tired as he was from the journey, sat down by the well. It was about noon.

[7] When a Samaritan woman came to draw water, Jesus said to her, "Will you give me a drink?" [8] (His disciples had gone into the town to buy food.)

[9] The Samaritan woman said to him, "You are a Jew and I am a Samaritan woman. How can you ask me for a drink?" (For Jews do not associate with Samaritans.[c])

[10] Jesus answered her, "If you knew the gift of God and who it is that asks you for a drink, you would have asked him and he would have given you living water."

[11] "Sir," the woman said, "you have nothing to draw with and the well is deep. Where can you get this living water? [12] Are you greater than our father Jacob, who gave us the well and drank from it himself, as did also his sons and his livestock?"

[13] Jesus answered, "Everyone who drinks this water will be thirsty again, [14] but whoever drinks the water I give them will never thirst. Indeed, the water I give them will become in them a spring of water welling up to eternal life."

[15] The woman said to him, "Sir, give me this water so that I won't get thirsty and have to keep coming here to draw water."

[16] He told her, "Go, call your husband and come back."

[17] "I have no husband," she replied.

Jesus said to her, "You are right when you say you have no husband. [18] The fact is, you have had five husbands, and the man you now have is not your husband. What you have just said is quite true."

[19] "Sir," the woman said, "I can see that you are a prophet. [20] Our ancestors worshiped on this mountain, but you Jews claim that the place where we must worship is in Jerusalem."

[21] "Woman," Jesus replied, "believe me, a time is coming when you will worship the Father neither on this mountain nor in Jerusalem. [22] You Samaritans worship what you do not know; we worship what we do know, for salvation is from the Jews. [23] Yet a time is coming and has now come when the true worshipers will worship the Father in the Spirit and in truth, for they are the kind of worshipers the Father seeks. [24] God is spirit, and his worshipers must worship in the Spirit and in truth."

---

[a] 30 Some interpreters end the quotation with verse 36.   [b] 34 Greek he   [c] 9 Or do not use dishes Samaritans have used

²⁵The woman said, "I know that Messiah" (called Christ) "is coming. When he comes, he will explain everything to us."

²⁶Then Jesus declared, "I, the one speaking to you—I am he."

The Disciples Rejoin Jesus

²⁷Just then his disciples returned and were surprised to find him talking with a woman. But no one asked, "What do you want?" or "Why are you talking with her?"

²⁸Then, leaving her water jar, the woman went back to the town and said to the people, ²⁹"Come, see a man who told me everything I ever did. Could this be the Messiah?" ³⁰They came out of the town and made their way toward him.

³¹Meanwhile his disciples urged him, "Rabbi, eat something."

³²But he said to them, "I have food to eat that you know nothing about."

³³Then his disciples said to each other, "Could someone have brought him food?"

³⁴"My food," said Jesus, "is to do the will of him who sent me and to finish his work. ³⁵Don't you have a saying, 'It's still four months until harvest'? I tell you, open your eyes and look at the fields! They are ripe for harvest. ³⁶Even now the one who reaps draws a wage and harvests a crop for eternal life, so that the sower and the reaper may be glad together. ³⁷Thus the saying 'One sows and another reaps' is true. ³⁸I sent you to reap what you have not worked for. Others have done the hard work, and you have reaped the benefits of their labor."

Many Samaritans Believe

³⁹Many of the Samaritans from that town believed in him because of the woman's testimony, "He told me everything I ever did." ⁴⁰So when the Samaritans came to him, they urged him to stay with them, and he stayed two days. ⁴¹And because of his words many more became believers.

⁴²They said to the woman, "We no longer believe just because of what you said; now we have heard for ourselves, and we know that this man really is the Savior of the world."

Jesus Heals an Official's Son

⁴³After the two days he left for Galilee. ⁴⁴(Now Jesus himself had pointed out that a prophet has no honor in his own country.) ⁴⁵When he arrived in Galilee, the Galileans welcomed him. They had seen all that he had done in Jerusalem at the Passover Festival, for they also had been there.

⁴⁶Once more he visited Cana in Galilee, where he had turned the water into wine. And there was a certain royal official whose son lay sick at Capernaum. ⁴⁷When this man heard that Jesus had arrived in Galilee from Judea, he went to him and begged him to come and heal his son, who was close to death.

⁴⁸"Unless you people see signs and wonders," Jesus told him, "you will never believe."

⁴⁹The royal official said, "Sir, come down before my child dies."

⁵⁰"Go," Jesus replied, "your son will live."

The man took Jesus at his word and departed. ⁵¹While he was still on the way, his servants met him with the news that his boy was living. ⁵²When he inquired as to the time when his son got better, they said to him, "Yesterday, at one in the afternoon, the fever left him."

⁵³Then the father realized that this was the exact time at which Jesus had said to him, "Your son will live." So he and his whole household believed.

⁵⁴This was the second sign Jesus performed after coming from Judea to Galilee.

The Healing at the Pool

5 Some time later, Jesus went up to Jerusalem for one of the Jewish festivals. ²Now there is in Jerusalem near the Sheep Gate a pool, which in Aramaic is called Bethesda*ᵃ* and which is surrounded by five covered colonnades. ³Here a great number of disabled people used to lie—the blind, the lame, the paralyzed. [4]*ᵇ* ⁵One who was there had been an invalid for thirty-eight years. ⁶When Jesus saw him lying there and learned that he had been in this condition for a long time, he asked him, "Do you want to get well?"

ᵃ 2 Some manuscripts *Bethzatha*; other manuscripts *Bethsaida*   *ᵇ 3,4* Some manuscripts include here, wholly or in part, *paralyzed—and they waited for the moving of the waters. ⁴From time to time an angel of the Lord would come down and stir up the waters. The first one into the pool after each such disturbance would be cured of whatever disease they had.*

⁷"Sir," the invalid replied, "I have no one to help me into the pool when the water is stirred. While I am trying to get in, someone else goes down ahead of me."

⁸Then Jesus said to him, "Get up! Pick up your mat and walk." ⁹At once the man was cured; he picked up his mat and walked.

The day on which this took place was a Sabbath, ¹⁰and so the Jewish leaders said to the man who had been healed, "It is the Sabbath; the law forbids you to carry your mat."

¹¹But he replied, "The man who made me well said to me, 'Pick up your mat and walk.'"

¹²So they asked him, "Who is this fellow who told you to pick it up and walk?"

¹³The man who was healed had no idea who it was, for Jesus had slipped away into the crowd that was there.

¹⁴Later Jesus found him at the temple and said to him, "See, you are well again. Stop sinning or something worse may happen to you." ¹⁵The man went away and told the Jewish leaders that it was Jesus who had made him well.

The Authority of the Son

¹⁶So, because Jesus was doing these things on the Sabbath, the Jewish leaders began to persecute him. ¹⁷In his defense Jesus said to them, "My Father is always at his work to this very day, and I too am working." ¹⁸For this reason they tried all the more to kill him; not only was he breaking the Sabbath, but he was even calling God his own Father, making himself equal with God.

¹⁹Jesus gave them this answer: "Very truly I tell you, the Son can do nothing by himself; he can do only what he sees his Father doing, because whatever the Father does the Son also does. ²⁰For the Father loves the Son and shows him all he does. Yes, and he will show him even greater works than these, so that you will be amazed. ²¹For just as the Father raises the dead and gives them life, even so the Son gives life to whom he is pleased to give it. ²²Moreover, the Father judges no one, but has entrusted all judgment to the Son, ²³that all may honor the Son just as they honor the Father. Whoever does not honor the Son does not honor the Father, who sent him.

²⁴"Very truly I tell you, whoever hears my word and believes him who sent me has eternal life and will not be judged but has crossed over from death to life. ²⁵Very truly I tell you, a time is coming and has now come when the dead will hear the voice of the Son of God and those who hear will live. ²⁶For as the Father has life in himself, so he has granted the Son also to have life in himself. ²⁷And he has given him authority to judge because he is the Son of Man.

²⁸"Do not be amazed at this, for a time is coming when all who are in their graves will hear his voice ²⁹and come out—those who have done what is good will rise to live, and those who have done what is evil will rise to be condemned. ³⁰By myself I can do nothing; I judge only as I hear, and my judgment is just, for I seek not to please myself but him who sent me.

Testimonies About Jesus

³¹"If I testify about myself, my testimony is not true. ³²There is another who testifies in my favor, and I know that his testimony about me is true.

³³"You have sent to John and he has testified to the truth. ³⁴Not that I accept human testimony; but I mention it that you may be saved. ³⁵John was a lamp that burned and gave light, and you chose for a time to enjoy his light.

³⁶"I have testimony weightier than that of John. For the works that the Father has given me to finish—the very works that I am doing—testify that the Father has sent me. ³⁷And the Father who sent me has himself testified concerning me. You have never heard his voice nor seen his form, ³⁸nor does his word dwell in you, for you do not believe the one he sent. ³⁹You study*a* the Scriptures diligently because you think that in them you have eternal life. These are the very Scriptures that testify about me, ⁴⁰yet you refuse to come to me to have life.

⁴¹"I do not accept glory from human beings, ⁴²but I know you. I know that you do not have the love of God in your hearts. ⁴³I have come in my Father's name, and you do not accept me; but if someone else comes in his own name, you will accept him. ⁴⁴How can you believe since you accept glory from one

a 39 Or ³⁹*Study*

another but do not seek the glory that comes from the only God[a]?

⁴⁵"But do not think I will accuse you before the Father. Your accuser is Moses, on whom your hopes are set. ⁴⁶If you believed Moses, you would believe me, for he wrote about me. ⁴⁷But since you do not believe what he wrote, how are you going to believe what I say?"

Jesus Feeds the Five Thousand

6 Some time after this, Jesus crossed to the far shore of the Sea of Galilee (that is, the Sea of Tiberias), ²and a great crowd of people followed him because they saw the signs he had performed by healing the sick. ³Then Jesus went up on a mountainside and sat down with his disciples. ⁴The Jewish Passover Festival was near.

⁵When Jesus looked up and saw a great crowd coming toward him, he said to Philip, "Where shall we buy bread for these people to eat?" ⁶He asked this only to test him, for he already had in mind what he was going to do.

⁷Philip answered him, "It would take more than half a year's wages[b] to buy enough bread for each one to have a bite!"

⁸Another of his disciples, Andrew, Simon Peter's brother, spoke up, ⁹"Here is a boy with five small barley loaves and two small fish, but how far will they go among so many?"

¹⁰Jesus said, "Have the people sit down." There was plenty of grass in that place, and they sat down (about five thousand men were there). ¹¹Jesus then took the loaves, gave thanks, and distributed to those who were seated as much as they wanted. He did the same with the fish.

¹²When they had all had enough to eat, he said to his disciples, "Gather the pieces that are left over. Let nothing be wasted." ¹³So they gathered them and filled twelve baskets with the pieces of the five barley loaves left over by those who had eaten.

¹⁴After the people saw the sign Jesus performed, they began to say, "Surely this is the Prophet who is to come into the world." ¹⁵Jesus, knowing that they intended to come and make him king by force, withdrew again to a mountain by himself.

Jesus Walks on the Water

¹⁶When evening came, his disciples went down to the lake, ¹⁷where they got into a boat and set off across the lake for Capernaum. By now it was dark, and Jesus had not yet joined them. ¹⁸A strong wind was blowing and the waters grew rough. ¹⁹When they had rowed about three or four miles,[c] they saw Jesus approaching the boat, walking on the water; and they were frightened. ²⁰But he said to them, "It is I; don't be afraid." ²¹Then they were willing to take him into the boat, and immediately the boat reached the shore where they were heading.

²²The next day the crowd that had stayed on the opposite shore of the lake realized that only one boat had been there, and that Jesus had not entered it with his disciples, but that they had gone away alone. ²³Then some boats from Tiberias landed near the place where the people had eaten the bread after the Lord had given thanks. ²⁴Once the crowd realized that neither Jesus nor his disciples were there, they got into the boats and went to Capernaum in search of Jesus.

Jesus the Bread of Life

²⁵When they found him on the other side of the lake, they asked him, "Rabbi, when did you get here?"

²⁶Jesus answered, "Very truly I tell you, you are looking for me, not because you saw the signs I performed but because you ate the loaves and had your fill. ²⁷Do not work for food that spoils, but for food that endures to eternal life, which the Son of Man will give you. For on him God the Father has placed his seal of approval."

²⁸Then they asked him, "What must we do to do the works God requires?"

²⁹Jesus answered, "The work of God is this: to believe in the one he has sent."

³⁰So they asked him, "What sign then will you give that we may see it and believe you? What will you do? ³¹Our ancestors ate the manna in the wilderness; as it is written: 'He gave them bread from heaven to eat.'[d]"

³²Jesus said to them, "Very truly I tell you, it is not Moses who has given you the bread from heaven, but it is my Father who gives you the true bread from heaven. ³³For the

---

[a] 44 Some early manuscripts *the Only One*   [b] 7 Greek *take two hundred denarii*   [c] 19 Or about 5 or 6 kilometers   [d] 31 Exodus 16:4; Neh. 9:15; Psalm 78:24,25

bread of God is the bread that comes down from heaven and gives life to the world."

[34] "Sir," they said, "always give us this bread."

[35] Then Jesus declared, "I am the bread of life. Whoever comes to me will never go hungry, and whoever believes in me will never be thirsty. [36] But as I told you, you have seen me and still you do not believe. [37] All those the Father gives me will come to me, and whoever comes to me I will never drive away. [38] For I have come down from heaven not to do my will but to do the will of him who sent me. [39] And this is the will of him who sent me, that I shall lose none of all those he has given me, but raise them up at the last day. [40] For my Father's will is that everyone who looks to the Son and believes in him shall have eternal life, and I will raise them up at the last day."

[41] At this the Jews there began to grumble about him because he said, "I am the bread that came down from heaven." [42] They said, "Is this not Jesus, the son of Joseph, whose father and mother we know? How can he now say, 'I came down from heaven'?"

[43] "Stop grumbling among yourselves," Jesus answered. [44] "No one can come to me unless the Father who sent me draws them, and I will raise them up at the last day. [45] It is written in the Prophets: 'They will all be taught by God.'[a] Everyone who has heard the Father and learned from him comes to me. [46] No one has seen the Father except the one who is from God; only he has seen the Father. [47] Very truly I tell you, the one who believes has eternal life. [48] I am the bread of life. [49] Your ancestors ate the manna in the wilderness, yet they died. [50] But here is the bread that comes down from heaven, which anyone may eat and not die. [51] I am the living bread that came down from heaven. Whoever eats this bread will live forever. This bread is my flesh, which I will give for the life of the world."

[52] Then the Jews began to argue sharply among themselves, "How can this man give us his flesh to eat?"

[53] Jesus said to them, "Very truly I tell you, unless you eat the flesh of the Son of Man and drink his blood, you have no life in you. [54] Whoever eats my flesh and drinks my blood has eternal life, and I will raise them up at the last day. [55] For my flesh is real food and my blood is real drink. [56] Whoever eats my flesh and drinks my blood remains in me, and I in them. [57] Just as the living Father sent me and I live because of the Father, so the one who feeds on me will live because of me. [58] This is the bread that came down from heaven. Your ancestors ate manna and died, but whoever feeds on this bread will live forever." [59] He said this while teaching in the synagogue in Capernaum.

Many Disciples Desert Jesus

[60] On hearing it, many of his disciples said, "This is a hard teaching. Who can accept it?"

[61] Aware that his disciples were grumbling about this, Jesus said to them, "Does this offend you? [62] Then what if you see the Son of Man ascend to where he was before! [63] The Spirit gives life; the flesh counts for nothing. The words I have spoken to you — they are full of the Spirit[b] and life. [64] Yet there are some of you who do not believe." For Jesus had known from the beginning which of them did not believe and who would betray him. [65] He went on to say, "This is why I told you that no one can come to me unless the Father has enabled them."

[66] From this time many of his disciples turned back and no longer followed him.

[67] "You do not want to leave too, do you?" Jesus asked the Twelve.

[68] Simon Peter answered him, "Lord, to whom shall we go? You have the words of eternal life. [69] We have come to believe and to know that you are the Holy One of God."

[70] Then Jesus replied, "Have I not chosen you, the Twelve? Yet one of you is a devil!" [71] (He meant Judas, the son of Simon Iscariot, who, though one of the Twelve, was later to betray him.)

Jesus Goes to the Festival of Tabernacles

7 After this, Jesus went around in Galilee. He did not want[c] to go about in Judea because the Jewish leaders there were looking for a way to kill him. [2] But when the Jewish Festival of Tabernacles was near, [3] Jesus' brothers said to him, "Leave Galilee and go to Judea, so that your disciples there may see

---

[a] 45 Isaiah 54:13   [b] 63 Or *are Spirit*; or *are spirit*   [c] 1 Some manuscripts *not have authority*

ONE WAY

READ: JOHN 6:68-69

Put yourself in the scene in John 6:60-71 and replay in your mind the events of the last hours. Everything starts when the Lord turned a little boy's snack into a feast for thousands. Just when a mob is ready to sweep Jesus into power, he vanishes. Many hours and miles later, you catch up with Jesus and he begins one of his famous talks. But this time he dubs himself "the bread of life" (v. 35) and instructs you to eat his flesh and drink his blood (v. 53). What could that possibly mean? What should you do now?

Many hear those words and call them too hard to accept. They sound creepy to Jews forbidden to ever taste blood. Many turn around and go home.

BUILDING

FAITH

When Jesus calls himself the bread of life, he means he's the spiritual nourishment you require to meet your deepest needs. When he tells you to eat his flesh and drink his blood, he looks ahead to the cross and instructs you to feed on him to get life, counting on his death to make you right with God.

WISDOM

STRENGTH

You won't follow Jesus for long if you go home every time his teaching puzzles or challenges you. Peter expressed perfectly why this isn't the time to walk away. Jesus is the Son of God. He tells you how to get eternal life. There's nowhere else to go.

the works you do. [4]No one who wants to become a public figure acts in secret. Since you are doing these things, show yourself to the world." [5]For even his own brothers did not believe in him.

[6]Therefore Jesus told them, "My time is not yet here; for you any time will do. [7]The world cannot hate you, but it hates me because I testify that its works are evil. [8]You go to the festival. I am not[a] going up to this festival, because my time has not yet fully come." [9]After he had said this, he stayed in Galilee.

[10]However, after his brothers had left for the festival, he went also, not publicly, but in secret. [11]Now at the festival the Jewish leaders were watching for Jesus and asking, "Where is he?"

[12]Among the crowds there was widespread whispering about him. Some said, "He is a good man."

Others replied, "No, he deceives the people." [13]But no one would say anything publicly about him for fear of the leaders.

Jesus Teaches at the Festival

[14]Not until halfway through the festival did Jesus go up to the temple courts and begin to teach. [15]The Jews there were amazed and asked, "How did this man get such learning without having been taught?"

[16]Jesus answered, "My teaching is not my own. It comes from the one who sent me. [17]Anyone who chooses to do the will of God will find out whether my teaching comes from God or whether I speak on my own. [18]Whoever speaks on their own does so to gain personal glory, but he who seeks the glory of the one who sent him is a man of truth; there is nothing false about him. [19]Has not Moses given you the law? Yet not one of you keeps the law. Why are you trying to kill me?"

[20]"You are demon-possessed," the crowd answered. "Who is trying to kill you?"

[21]Jesus said to them, "I did one miracle, and you are all amazed. [22]Yet, because Moses gave you circumcision (though actually it did not come from Moses, but from the patriarchs), you circumcise a boy on the Sabbath. [23]Now if a boy can be circumcised on the Sabbath so that the law of Moses may not be broken, why are you angry with me for healing a man's whole body on the Sabbath? [24]Stop judging by mere appearances, but instead judge correctly."

Division Over Who Jesus Is

[25]At that point some of the people of Jerusalem began to ask, "Isn't this the man they are trying to kill? [26]Here he is, speaking publicly, and they are not saying a word to him. Have the authorities really concluded that he is the Messiah? [27]But we know where this man is from; when the Messiah comes, no one will know where he is from."

[28]Then Jesus, still teaching in the temple courts, cried out, "Yes, you know me, and you know where I am from. I am not here on my own authority, but he who sent me is true. You do not know him, [29]but I know him because I am from him and he sent me."

[30]At this they tried to seize him, but no one laid a hand on him, because his hour had not yet come. [31]Still, many in the crowd believed in him. They said, "When the Messiah comes, will he perform more signs than this man?"

[32]The Pharisees heard the crowd whispering such things about him. Then the chief priests and the Pharisees sent temple guards to arrest him.

[33]Jesus said, "I am with you for only a short time, and then I am going to the one who sent me. [34]You will look for me, but you will not find me; and where I am, you cannot come."

[35]The Jews said to one another, "Where does this man intend to go that we cannot find him? Will he go where our people live scattered among the Greeks, and teach the Greeks? [36]What did he mean when he said, 'You will look for me, but you will not find me,' and 'Where I am, you cannot come'?"

[37]On the last and greatest day of the festival, Jesus stood and said in a loud voice, "Let anyone who is thirsty come to me and drink. [38]Whoever believes in me, as Scripture has said, rivers of living water will flow from within them."[b] [39]By this he meant the Spirit, whom those who believed in him were later to receive. Up to that time the Spirit had

---

[a] 8 Some manuscripts *not yet*   [b] 37,38 Or *me. And let anyone drink* [38]*who believes in me." As Scripture has said, "Out of him* (or *them*) *will flow rivers of living water.*"

NO ROOM FOR STEREOTYPES

READ: JOHN 7:24

When we classify people into groups, it's easier to generalize and get away with it: "Well, people in the South are _____. Baptists are _____. Hispanics are _____. Californians are so stinking _____." If you're like me, you've filled in the blanks more times than you care to admit.

Our spiritual glasses narrow the focus to individual people. Your classmate. Your coach. The soldier at the airport. The man in line at Walmart. It's easier to speak in black and white and put the Jesus smackdown on a group of people. But when a person has a face and a name and a situation, you see things differently.

The reason we ask, "What would Jesus do?" is that he determined his actions according to what each and every individual he met needed at that time.

I'm not saying we change our view of God or our view of right and wrong based on each situation. I'm just saying we should love 'em like Jesus. There is black and white, right and wrong. But when we're talking about a group of people, it becomes easy to show an absence of mercy. When we get to specific people, we're much more likely to demonstrate concern.

But when I draw closer to my own Jesus, my vision sharpens. All of a sudden people aren't road cones to avoid anymore. They have a pulse, just like I do. They hurt, just like I do. They fear, just like I do. They long for that God-shaped void to be filled.

BUILDING

FAITH

WISDOM

STRENGTH

Taken from *Your Own Jesus Student Edition* by Mark Hall, copyright © 2009 by Mark Hall, published by Zondervan.

not been given, since Jesus had not yet been glorified.

[40] On hearing his words, some of the people said, "Surely this man is the Prophet."

[41] Others said, "He is the Messiah."

Still others asked, "How can the Messiah come from Galilee? [42] Does not Scripture say that the Messiah will come from David's descendants and from Bethlehem, the town where David lived?" [43] Thus the people were divided because of Jesus. [44] Some wanted to seize him, but no one laid a hand on him.

Unbelief of the Jewish Leaders

[45] Finally the temple guards went back to the chief priests and the Pharisees, who asked them, "Why didn't you bring him in?"

[46] "No one ever spoke the way this man does," the guards replied.

[47] "You mean he has deceived you also?" the Pharisees retorted. [48] "Have any of the rulers or of the Pharisees believed in him? [49] No! But this mob that knows nothing of the law — there is a curse on them."

[50] Nicodemus, who had gone to Jesus earlier and who was one of their own number, asked, [51] "Does our law condemn a man without first hearing him to find out what he has been doing?"

[52] They replied, "Are you from Galilee, too? Look into it, and you will find that a prophet does not come out of Galilee."

[The earliest manuscripts and many other ancient witnesses do not have John 7:53 — 8:11. A few manuscripts include these verses, wholly or in part, after John 7:36, John 21:25, Luke 21:38 or Luke 24:53.]

8 [53] Then they all went home, [1] but Jesus went to the Mount of Olives.

[2] At dawn he appeared again in the temple courts, where all the people gathered around him, and he sat down to teach them. [3] The teachers of the law and the Pharisees brought in a woman caught in adultery. They made her stand before the group [4] and said to Jesus, "Teacher, this woman was caught in the act of adultery. [5] In the Law Moses commanded us to stone such women. Now what do you say?" [6] They were using this question as a trap, in order to have a basis for accusing him.

But Jesus bent down and started to write on the ground with his finger. [7] When they kept on questioning him, he straightened up and said to them,

"Let any one of you who is without sin be the first to throw a stone at her." [8] Again he stooped down and wrote on the ground.

[9] At this, those who heard began to go away one at a time, the older ones first, until only Jesus was left, with the woman still standing there. [10] Jesus straightened up and asked her, "Woman, where are they? Has no one condemned you?"

[11] "No one, sir," she said.

"Then neither do I condemn you," Jesus declared. "Go now and leave your life of sin."

Dispute Over Jesus' Testimony

[12] When Jesus spoke again to the people, he said, "I am the light of the world. Whoever follows me will never walk in darkness, but will have the light of life."

[13] The Pharisees challenged him, "Here you are, appearing as your own witness; your testimony is not valid."

[14] Jesus answered, "Even if I testify on my own behalf, my testimony is valid, for I know where I came from and where I am going. But you have no idea where I come from or where I am going. [15] You judge by human standards; I pass judgment on no one. [16] But if I do judge, my decisions are true, because I am not alone. I stand with the Father, who sent me. [17] In your own Law it is written that the testimony of two witnesses is true. [18] I am one who testifies for myself; my other witness is the Father, who sent me."

[19] Then they asked him, "Where is your father?"

"You do not know me or my Father," Jesus replied. "If you knew me, you would know my Father also." [20] He spoke these words while teaching in the temple courts near the place where the offerings were put. Yet no one seized him, because his hour had not yet come.

Dispute Over Who Jesus Is

[21] Once more Jesus said to them, "I am going away, and you will look for me, and you will die in your sin. Where I go, you cannot come."

[22] This made the Jews ask, "Will he kill himself? Is that why he says, 'Where I go, you cannot come'?"

[23] But he continued, "You are from below; I am from above. You are of this world; I am not of this world. [24] I told you that you would

die in your sins; if you do not believe that I am he, you will indeed die in your sins."

²⁵ "Who are you?" they asked.

"Just what I have been telling you from the beginning," Jesus replied. ²⁶ "I have much to say in judgment of you. But he who sent me is trustworthy, and what I have heard from him I tell the world."

²⁷ They did not understand that he was telling them about his Father. ²⁸ So Jesus said, "When you have lifted up*a* the Son of Man, then you will know that I am he and that I do nothing on my own but speak just what the Father has taught me. ²⁹ The one who sent me is with me; he has not left me alone, for I always do what pleases him." ³⁰ Even as he spoke, many believed in him.

Dispute Over Whose Children Jesus' Opponents Are

³¹ To the Jews who had believed him, Jesus said, "If you hold to my teaching, you are really my disciples. ³² Then you will know the truth, and the truth will set you free."

³³ They answered him, "We are Abraham's descendants and have never been slaves of anyone. How can you say that we shall be set free?"

³⁴ Jesus replied, "Very truly I tell you, everyone who sins is a slave to sin. ³⁵ Now a slave has no permanent place in the family, but a son belongs to it forever. ³⁶ So if the Son sets you free, you will be free indeed. ³⁷ I know that you are Abraham's descendants. Yet you are looking for a way to kill me, because you have no room for my word. ³⁸ I am telling you what I have seen in the Father's presence, and you are doing what you have heard from your father.*b*"

³⁹ "Abraham is our father," they answered.

"If you were Abraham's children," said Jesus, "then you would*c* do what Abraham did. ⁴⁰ As it is, you are looking for a way to kill me, a man who has told you the truth that I heard from God. Abraham did not do such things. ⁴¹ You are doing the works of your own father."

"We are not illegitimate children," they protested. "The only Father we have is God himself."

⁴² Jesus said to them, "If God were your Father, you would love me, for I have come here from God. I have not come on my own; God sent me. ⁴³ Why is my language not clear to you? Because you are unable to hear what I say. ⁴⁴ You belong to your father, the devil, and you want to carry out your father's desires. He was a murderer from the beginning, not holding to the truth, for there is no truth in him. When he lies, he speaks his native language, for he is a liar and the father of lies. ⁴⁵ Yet because I tell the truth, you do not believe me! ⁴⁶ Can any of you prove me guilty of sin? If I am telling the truth, why don't you believe me? ⁴⁷ Whoever belongs to God hears what God says. The reason you do not hear is that you do not belong to God."

Jesus' Claims About Himself

⁴⁸ The Jews answered him, "Aren't we right in saying that you are a Samaritan and demon-possessed?"

⁴⁹ "I am not possessed by a demon," said Jesus, "but I honor my Father and you dishonor me. ⁵⁰ I am not seeking glory for myself; but there is one who seeks it, and he is the judge. ⁵¹ Very truly I tell you, whoever obeys my word will never see death."

⁵² At this they exclaimed, "Now we know that you are demon-possessed! Abraham died and so did the prophets, yet you say that whoever obeys your word will never taste death. ⁵³ Are you greater than our father Abraham? He died, and so did the prophets. Who do you think you are?"

⁵⁴ Jesus replied, "If I glorify myself, my glory means nothing. My Father, whom you claim as your God, is the one who glorifies me. ⁵⁵ Though you do not know him, I know him. If I said I did not, I would be a liar like you, but I do know him and obey his word. ⁵⁶ Your father Abraham rejoiced at the thought of seeing my day; he saw it and was glad."

⁵⁷ "You are not yet fifty years old," they said to him, "and you have seen Abraham!"

⁵⁸ "Very truly I tell you," Jesus answered, "before Abraham was born, I am!" ⁵⁹ At this, they picked up stones to stone him, but Jesus hid himself, slipping away from the temple grounds.

Jesus Heals a Man Born Blind

9 As he went along, he saw a man blind from birth. ² His disciples asked him,

---

a 28 The Greek for *lifted up* also means *exalted.*   *b* 38 Or *presence. Therefore do what you have heard from the Father.*   *c* 39 Some early manuscripts *"If you are Abraham's children," said Jesus, "then*

"Rabbi, who sinned, this man or his parents, that he was born blind?"

³"Neither this man nor his parents sinned," said Jesus, "but this happened so that the works of God might be displayed in him. ⁴As long as it is day, we must do the works of him who sent me. Night is coming, when no one can work. ⁵While I am in the world, I am the light of the world."

⁶After saying this, he spit on the ground, made some mud with the saliva, and put it on the man's eyes. ⁷"Go," he told him, "wash in the Pool of Siloam" (this word means "Sent"). So the man went and washed, and came home seeing.

⁸His neighbors and those who had formerly seen him begging asked, "Isn't this the same man who used to sit and beg?" ⁹Some claimed that he was.

Others said, "No, he only looks like him."

But he himself insisted, "I am the man."

¹⁰"How then were your eyes opened?" they asked.

¹¹He replied, "The man they call Jesus made some mud and put it on my eyes. He told me to go to Siloam and wash. So I went and washed, and then I could see."

¹²"Where is this man?" they asked him.

"I don't know," he said.

The Pharisees Investigate the Healing

¹³They brought to the Pharisees the man who had been blind. ¹⁴Now the day on which Jesus had made the mud and opened the man's eyes was a Sabbath. ¹⁵Therefore the Pharisees also asked him how he had received his sight. "He put mud on my eyes," the man replied, "and I washed, and now I see."

¹⁶Some of the Pharisees said, "This man is not from God, for he does not keep the Sabbath."

But others asked, "How can a sinner perform such signs?" So they were divided.

¹⁷Then they turned again to the blind man, "What have you to say about him? It was your eyes he opened."

The man replied, "He is a prophet."

¹⁸They still did not believe that he had been blind and had received his sight until they sent for the man's parents. ¹⁹"Is this your son?" they asked. "Is this the one you say was born blind? How is it that now he can see?"

²⁰"We know he is our son," the parents answered, "and we know he was born blind. ²¹But how he can see now, or who opened his eyes, we don't know. Ask him. He is of age; he will speak for himself." ²²His parents said this because they were afraid of the Jewish leaders, who already had decided that anyone who acknowledged that Jesus was the Messiah would be put out of the synagogue. ²³That was why his parents said, "He is of age; ask him."

²⁴A second time they summoned the man who had been blind. "Give glory to God by telling the truth," they said. "We know this man is a sinner."

²⁵He replied, "Whether he is a sinner or not, I don't know. One thing I do know. I was blind but now I see!"

²⁶Then they asked him, "What did he do to you? How did he open your eyes?"

²⁷He answered, "I have told you already and you did not listen. Why do you want to hear it again? Do you want to become his disciples too?"

²⁸Then they hurled insults at him and said, "You are this fellow's disciple! We are disciples of Moses! ²⁹We know that God spoke to Moses, but as for this fellow, we don't even know where he comes from."

³⁰The man answered, "Now that is remarkable! You don't know where he comes from, yet he opened my eyes. ³¹We know that God does not listen to sinners. He listens to the godly person who does his will. ³²Nobody has ever heard of opening the eyes of a man born blind. ³³If this man were not from God, he could do nothing."

³⁴To this they replied, "You were steeped in sin at birth; how dare you lecture us!" And they threw him out.

Spiritual Blindness

³⁵Jesus heard that they had thrown him out, and when he found him, he said, "Do you believe in the Son of Man?"

³⁶"Who is he, sir?" the man asked. "Tell me so that I may believe in him."

³⁷Jesus said, "You have now seen him; in fact, he is the one speaking with you."

³⁸Then the man said, "Lord, I believe," and he worshiped him.

³⁹Jesus said,ᵃ "For judgment I have come into this world, so that the blind will see and those who see will become blind."

ᵃ 38,39 Some early manuscripts do not have *Then the man said . . . ³⁹Jesus said.*

WELL, THAT'S DUMB

READ: JOHN 9:13-41

I often tell the story of one of our students who joined our youth group for a day at Islands of Adventure Theme Park at Universal Studios in Orlando, Florida. He sat right behind me as I accompanied several of our students on the Spiderman roller coaster. The ride requires 3-D glasses.

Shortly after the ride began, the kid started his critique. "This is dumb," he said. A few seconds later, he blurted out, "This is stupid." It took all the restraint I could muster not to turn around halfway through the ride and tell him to zip it.

As soon as we got off the roller coaster, I turned to give him a stern look of disapproval, but any inclination to chastise him faded when I realized why he had been so outspoken. He wasn't wearing his glasses.

The guy had endured the ride with a hazy, blurred focus that would've cleared if only he had worn his 3-D glasses. He couldn't enjoy all that the ride had for him because he didn't have the clarity that the makers of the ride had intended. In the same way, the condition of our heart determines what our eyes see. The more we follow God and obey him, the less we are conformed to this world and the more our minds are renewed. The more our minds are renewed, the more we are conformed to the image of Christ and see with his eyes.

BUILDING

FAITH

WISDOM

STRENGTH

Taken from *Thrive Student Edition* by Mark Hall with Tim Luke, copyright © 2014 by Mark Hall, published by Zondervan.

⁴⁰Some Pharisees who were with him heard him say this and asked, "What? Are we blind too?"

⁴¹Jesus said, "If you were blind, you would not be guilty of sin; but now that you claim you can see, your guilt remains.

The Good Shepherd and His Sheep

10 "Very truly I tell you Pharisees, anyone who does not enter the sheep pen by the gate, but climbs in by some other way, is a thief and a robber. ²The one who enters by the gate is the shepherd of the sheep. ³The gatekeeper opens the gate for him, and the sheep listen to his voice. He calls his own sheep by name and leads them out. ⁴When he has brought out all his own, he goes on ahead of them, and his sheep follow him because they know his voice. ⁵But they will never follow a stranger; in fact, they will run away from him because they do not recognize a stranger's voice." ⁶Jesus used this figure of speech, but the Pharisees did not understand what he was telling them.

⁷Therefore Jesus said again, "Very truly I tell you, I am the gate for the sheep. ⁸All who have come before me are thieves and robbers, but the sheep have not listened to them. ⁹I am the gate; whoever enters through me will be saved.ᵃ They will come in and go out, and find pasture. ¹⁰The thief comes only to steal and kill and destroy; I have come that they may have life, and have it to the full.

¹¹"I am the good shepherd. The good shepherd lays down his life for the sheep. ¹²The hired hand is not the shepherd and does not own the sheep. So when he sees the wolf coming, he abandons the sheep and runs away. Then the wolf attacks the flock and scatters it. ¹³The man runs away because he is a hired hand and cares nothing for the sheep.

¹⁴"I am the good shepherd; I know my sheep and my sheep know me— ¹⁵just as the Father knows me and I know the Father— and I lay down my life for the sheep. ¹⁶I have other sheep that are not of this sheep pen. I must bring them also. They too will listen to my voice, and there shall be one flock and one shepherd. ¹⁷The reason my Father loves me is that I lay down my life—only to take it up again. ¹⁸No one takes it from me, but I lay it down of my own accord. I have authority to lay it down and authority to take it up again. This command I received from my Father."

¹⁹The Jews who heard these words were again divided. ²⁰Many of them said, "He is demon-possessed and raving mad. Why listen to him?"

²¹But others said, "These are not the sayings of a man possessed by a demon. Can a demon open the eyes of the blind?"

Further Conflict Over Jesus' Claims

²²Then came the Festival of Dedicationᵇ at Jerusalem. It was winter, ²³and Jesus was in the temple courts walking in Solomon's Colonnade. ²⁴The Jews who were there gathered around him, saying, "How long will you keep us in suspense? If you are the Messiah, tell us plainly."

²⁵Jesus answered, "I did tell you, but you do not believe. The works I do in my Father's name testify about me, ²⁶but you do not believe because you are not my sheep. ²⁷My sheep listen to my voice; I know them, and they follow me. ²⁸I give them eternal life, and they shall never perish; no one will snatch them out of my hand. ²⁹My Father, who has given them to me, is greater than allᶜ; no one can snatch them out of my Father's hand. ³⁰I and the Father are one."

³¹Again his Jewish opponents picked up stones to stone him, ³²but Jesus said to them, "I have shown you many good works from the Father. For which of these do you stone me?"

³³"We are not stoning you for any good work," they replied, "but for blasphemy, because you, a mere man, claim to be God."

³⁴Jesus answered them, "Is it not written in your Law, 'I have said you are "gods"'ᵈ? ³⁵If he called them 'gods,' to whom the word of God came—and Scripture cannot be set aside— ³⁶what about the one whom the Father set apart as his very own and sent into the world? Why then do you accuse me of blasphemy because I said, 'I am God's Son'? ³⁷Do not believe me unless I do the works of my Father. ³⁸But if I do them, even though you do not believe me, believe the works,

---

ᵃ 9 Or *kept safe*   ᵇ 22 That is, Hanukkah   ᶜ 29 Many early manuscripts *What my Father has given me is greater than all*   ᵈ 34 Psalm 82:6

that you may know and understand that the Father is in me, and I in the Father." [39]Again they tried to seize him, but he escaped their grasp.

[40]Then Jesus went back across the Jordan to the place where John had been baptizing in the early days. There he stayed, [41]and many people came to him. They said, "Though John never performed a sign, all that John said about this man was true." [42]And in that place many believed in Jesus.

The Death of Lazarus

11 Now a man named Lazarus was sick. He was from Bethany, the village of Mary and her sister Martha. [2](This Mary, whose brother Lazarus now lay sick, was the same one who poured perfume on the Lord and wiped his feet with her hair.) [3]So the sisters sent word to Jesus, "Lord, the one you love is sick."

[4]When he heard this, Jesus said, "This sickness will not end in death. No, it is for God's glory so that God's Son may be glorified through it." [5]Now Jesus loved Martha and her sister and Lazarus. [6]So when he heard that Lazarus was sick, he stayed where he was two more days, [7]and then he said to his disciples, "Let us go back to Judea."

[8]"But Rabbi," they said, "a short while ago the Jews there tried to stone you, and yet you are going back?"

[9]Jesus answered, "Are there not twelve hours of daylight? Anyone who walks in the daytime will not stumble, for they see by this world's light. [10]It is when a person walks at night that they stumble, for they have no light."

[11]After he had said this, he went on to tell them, "Our friend Lazarus has fallen asleep; but I am going there to wake him up."

[12]His disciples replied, "Lord, if he sleeps, he will get better." [13]Jesus had been speaking of his death, but his disciples thought he meant natural sleep.

[14]So then he told them plainly, "Lazarus is dead, [15]and for your sake I am glad I was not there, so that you may believe. But let us go to him."

[16]Then Thomas (also known as Didymus[a]) said to the rest of the disciples, "Let us also go, that we may die with him."

Jesus Comforts the Sisters of Lazarus

[17]On his arrival, Jesus found that Lazarus had already been in the tomb for four days. [18]Now Bethany was less than two miles[b] from Jerusalem, [19]and many Jews had come to Martha and Mary to comfort them in the loss of their brother. [20]When Martha heard that Jesus was coming, she went out to meet him, but Mary stayed at home.

[21]"Lord," Martha said to Jesus, "if you had been here, my brother would not have died. [22]But I know that even now God will give you whatever you ask."

[23]Jesus said to her, "Your brother will rise again."

[24]Martha answered, "I know he will rise again in the resurrection at the last day."

[25]Jesus said to her, "I am the resurrection and the life. The one who believes in me will live, even though they die; [26]and whoever lives by believing in me will never die. Do you believe this?"

[27]"Yes, Lord," she replied, "I believe that you are the Messiah, the Son of God, who is to come into the world."

[28]After she had said this, she went back and called her sister Mary aside. "The Teacher is here," she said, "and is asking for you." [29]When Mary heard this, she got up quickly and went to him. [30]Now Jesus had not yet entered the village, but was still at the place where Martha had met him. [31]When the Jews who had been with Mary in the house, comforting her, noticed how quickly she got up and went out, they followed her, supposing she was going to the tomb to mourn there.

[32]When Mary reached the place where Jesus was and saw him, she fell at his feet and said, "Lord, if you had been here, my brother would not have died."

[33]When Jesus saw her weeping, and the Jews who had come along with her also weeping, he was deeply moved in spirit and troubled. [34]"Where have you laid him?" he asked.

"Come and see, Lord," they replied.

[35]Jesus wept.

[36]Then the Jews said, "See how he loved him!"

[37]But some of them said, "Could not he who opened the eyes of the blind man have kept this man from dying?"

---

[a] 16 *Thomas* (Aramaic) and *Didymus* (Greek) both mean *twin.*   [b] 18 Or about 3 kilometers

LAZARUS

After [Jesus] had said this, he went on to tell them, "Our friend Lazarus has fallen asleep; but I am going there to wake him up." JOHN 11:11

HIS NAME MEANS: "God has helped"
READ HIS STORY: *John 11:1–12:11*

Lazarus was a Jew who lived in the village of Bethany, about two miles from Jerusalem. His sisters, Mary and Martha, lived in Bethany also.

In Luke 10:38 we see that Martha "opened her home" to Jesus. Perhaps Mary and Lazarus lived in that home as well. In John 12:1-11, we see Jesus and Lazarus sharing a meal together with other people they knew. Over time, the two became close, so much so that Jesus cried at the news of Lazarus' death. When people saw Jesus weeping, they said, "See how he loved him!" (John 11:36).

Perhaps most significant in this friendship is the fact that when Lazarus died, Jesus brought him back to life. Many people witnessed the miracle. Lazarus became one of the greatest testimonies of Jesus' power. Because of this miracle, a large number of people came to believe Jesus was the Messiah—and the chief priests plotted to kill both Jesus and Lazarus.

Jesus treasured his relationship with Lazarus so much, he cried even though he knew he would see his friend alive again soon. Jesus longs to be your friend too. He loves you! Most of all, he wants to take the dark and dead places in your heart and bring you healing and new life—just as he did with his friend Lazarus.

BACK TO LIFE

READ: JOHN 11:25

The resurrection stands out in bold relief, framing Jesus as a one-of-a-kind religious founder. For us, the resurrection means more than heaven. The resurrection of Jesus is the core of our theology.

The resurrection shows that Jesus knew what he was talking about. He is an expert on both heaven and earth, the only spokesman we know who has literally lived on both sides of reality, the physical world and the spiritual world, and was able to tell us about it. He not only came from heaven to earth, but also after he died, he confirmed it, traveling into the spiritual world and undoing death unlike anyone else. Unlike reincarnation, Jesus returned as the same person, with the same voice, with his personal history intact.

BUILDING FAITH WISDOM STRENGTH

The resurrection validates human life. God isn't looking to give us an escape from planet earth, but to set things right. This earth belongs to the Lord and exists for us to relish the work of our hands. God plans to redeem every square inch of our planet that currently groans for renewal through the power of Jesus, who will cure injustice, hunger, painful tears; undo global pollution; and bring peace on the good earth.

Death frightens us, and understandably so, but we do not need to fear what existence will look like beyond the grave. C. S. Lewis said that when we look into the face of God, we will find ourselves recognizing all we have loved on this earth. He will be as familiar to us as our dearest friend.

Jesus Raises Lazarus From the Dead

38 Jesus, once more deeply moved, came to the tomb. It was a cave with a stone laid across the entrance. **39** "Take away the stone," he said.

"But, Lord," said Martha, the sister of the dead man, "by this time there is a bad odor, for he has been there four days."

40 Then Jesus said, "Did I not tell you that if you believe, you will see the glory of God?"

41 So they took away the stone. Then Jesus looked up and said, "Father, I thank you that you have heard me. **42** I knew that you always hear me, but I said this for the benefit of the people standing here, that they may believe that you sent me."

43 When he had said this, Jesus called in a loud voice, "Lazarus, come out!" **44** The dead man came out, his hands and feet wrapped with strips of linen, and a cloth around his face.

Jesus said to them, "Take off the grave clothes and let him go."

The Plot to Kill Jesus

45 Therefore many of the Jews who had come to visit Mary, and had seen what Jesus did, believed in him. **46** But some of them went to the Pharisees and told them what Jesus had done. **47** Then the chief priests and the Pharisees called a meeting of the Sanhedrin.

"What are we accomplishing?" they asked. "Here is this man performing many signs. **48** If we let him go on like this, everyone will believe in him, and then the Romans will come and take away both our temple and our nation."

49 Then one of them, named Caiaphas, who was high priest that year, spoke up, "You know nothing at all! **50** You do not realize that it is better for you that one man die for the people than that the whole nation perish."

51 He did not say this on his own, but as high priest that year he prophesied that Jesus would die for the Jewish nation, **52** and not only for that nation but also for the scattered children of God, to bring them together and make them one. **53** So from that day on they plotted to take his life.

54 Therefore Jesus no longer moved about publicly among the people of Judea. Instead he withdrew to a region near the wilderness, to a village called Ephraim, where he stayed with his disciples.

55 When it was almost time for the Jewish Passover, many went up from the country to Jerusalem for their ceremonial cleansing before the Passover. **56** They kept looking for Jesus, and as they stood in the temple courts they asked one another, "What do you think? Isn't he coming to the festival at all?" **57** But the chief priests and the Pharisees had given orders that anyone who found out where Jesus was should report it so that they might arrest him.

Jesus Anointed at Bethany

12 Six days before the Passover, Jesus came to Bethany, where Lazarus lived, whom Jesus had raised from the dead. **2** Here a dinner was given in Jesus' honor. Martha served, while Lazarus was among those reclining at the table with him. **3** Then Mary took about a pint*a* of pure nard, an expensive perfume; she poured it on Jesus' feet and wiped his feet with her hair. And the house was filled with the fragrance of the perfume.

4 But one of his disciples, Judas Iscariot, who was later to betray him, objected, **5** "Why wasn't this perfume sold and the money given to the poor? It was worth a year's wages.*b*" **6** He did not say this because he cared about the poor but because he was a thief; as keeper of the money bag, he used to help himself to what was put into it.

7 "Leave her alone," Jesus replied. "It was intended that she should save this perfume for the day of my burial. **8** You will always have the poor among you,*c* but you will not always have me."

9 Meanwhile a large crowd of Jews found out that Jesus was there and came, not only because of him but also to see Lazarus, whom he had raised from the dead. **10** So the chief priests made plans to kill Lazarus as well, **11** for on account of him many of the Jews were going over to Jesus and believing in him.

Jesus Comes to Jerusalem as King

12 The next day the great crowd that had come for the festival heard that Jesus was on his way to Jerusalem. **13** They took palm branches and went out to meet him, shouting,

---

a 3 Or about 0.5 liter   *b 5* Greek *three hundred denarii*   *c 8* See Deut. 15:11.

"Hosanna!*a*"

"Blessed is he who comes in the name
of the Lord!"*b*

"Blessed is the king of Israel!"

¹⁴Jesus found a young donkey and sat on it,
as it is written:

¹⁵ "Do not be afraid, Daughter Zion;
    see, your king is coming,
    seated on a donkey's colt."*c*

¹⁶At first his disciples did not understand all this. Only after Jesus was glorified did they realize that these things had been written about him and that these things had been done to him.

¹⁷Now the crowd that was with him when he called Lazarus from the tomb and raised him from the dead continued to spread the word. ¹⁸Many people, because they had heard that he had performed this sign, went out to meet him. ¹⁹So the Pharisees said to one another, "See, this is getting us nowhere. Look how the whole world has gone after him!"

Jesus Predicts His Death

²⁰Now there were some Greeks among those who went up to worship at the festival. ²¹They came to Philip, who was from Bethsaida in Galilee, with a request. "Sir," they said, "we would like to see Jesus." ²²Philip went to tell Andrew; Andrew and Philip in turn told Jesus.

²³Jesus replied, "The hour has come for the Son of Man to be glorified. ²⁴Very truly I tell you, unless a kernel of wheat falls to the ground and dies, it remains only a single seed. But if it dies, it produces many seeds. ²⁵Anyone who loves their life will lose it, while anyone who hates their life in this world will keep it for eternal life. ²⁶Whoever serves me must follow me; and where I am, my servant also will be. My Father will honor the one who serves me.

²⁷"Now my soul is troubled, and what shall I say? 'Father, save me from this hour'? No, it was for this very reason I came to this hour. ²⁸Father, glorify your name!"

Then a voice came from heaven, "I have glorified it, and will glorify it again." ²⁹The crowd that was there and heard it said it had thundered; others said an angel had spoken to him.

³⁰Jesus said, "This voice was for your benefit, not mine. ³¹Now is the time for judgment on this world; now the prince of this world will be driven out. ³²And I, when I am lifted up*d* from the earth, will draw all people to myself." ³³He said this to show the kind of death he was going to die.

³⁴The crowd spoke up, "We have heard from the Law that the Messiah will remain forever, so how can you say, 'The Son of Man must be lifted up'? Who is this 'Son of Man'?"

³⁵Then Jesus told them, "You are going to have the light just a little while longer. Walk while you have the light, before darkness overtakes you. Whoever walks in the dark does not know where they are going. ³⁶Believe in the light while you have the light, so that you may become children of light." When he had finished speaking, Jesus left and hid himself from them.

Belief and Unbelief Among the Jews

³⁷Even after Jesus had performed so many signs in their presence, they still would not believe in him. ³⁸This was to fulfill the word of Isaiah the prophet:

"Lord, who has believed our message
    and to whom has the arm of the Lord
        been revealed?"*e*

³⁹For this reason they could not believe, because, as Isaiah says elsewhere:

⁴⁰ "He has blinded their eyes
    and hardened their hearts,
so they can neither see with their eyes,
    nor understand with their hearts,
    nor turn — and I would heal them."*f*

⁴¹Isaiah said this because he saw Jesus' glory and spoke about him.

⁴²Yet at the same time many even among the leaders believed in him. But because of the Pharisees they would not openly acknowledge their faith for fear they would be put out of the synagogue; ⁴³for they loved human praise more than praise from God.

⁴⁴Then Jesus cried out, "Whoever believes

---

a 13 A Hebrew expression meaning "Save!" which became an exclamation of praise   *b 13* Psalm 118:25,26
c 15 Zech. 9:9   *d 32* The Greek for *lifted up* also means *exalted.*   *e 38* Isaiah 53:1   *f 40* Isaiah 6:10

in me does not believe in me only, but in the one who sent me. [45] The one who looks at me is seeing the one who sent me. [46] I have come into the world as a light, so that no one who believes in me should stay in darkness.

[47] "If anyone hears my words but does not keep them, I do not judge that person. For I did not come to judge the world, but to save the world. [48] There is a judge for the one who rejects me and does not accept my words; the very words I have spoken will condemn them at the last day. [49] For I did not speak on my own, but the Father who sent me commanded me to say all that I have spoken. [50] I know that his command leads to eternal life. So whatever I say is just what the Father has told me to say."

Jesus Washes His Disciples' Feet

13 It was just before the Passover Festival. Jesus knew that the hour had come for him to leave this world and go to the Father. Having loved his own who were in the world, he loved them to the end.

[2] The evening meal was in progress, and the devil had already prompted Judas, the son of Simon Iscariot, to betray Jesus. [3] Jesus knew that the Father had put all things under his power, and that he had come from God and was returning to God; [4] so he got up from the meal, took off his outer clothing, and wrapped a towel around his waist. [5] After that, he poured water into a basin and began to wash his disciples' feet, drying them with the towel that was wrapped around him.

[6] He came to Simon Peter, who said to him, "Lord, are you going to wash my feet?"

[7] Jesus replied, "You do not realize now what I am doing, but later you will understand."

[8] "No," said Peter, "you shall never wash my feet."

Jesus answered, "Unless I wash you, you have no part with me."

[9] "Then, Lord," Simon Peter replied, "not just my feet but my hands and my head as well!"

[10] Jesus answered, "Those who have had a bath need only to wash their feet; their whole body is clean. And you are clean, though not every one of you." [11] For he knew who was going to betray him, and that was why he said not every one was clean.

[12] When he had finished washing their feet, he put on his clothes and returned to his place. "Do you understand what I have done for you?" he asked them. [13] "You call me 'Teacher' and 'Lord,' and rightly so, for that is what I am. [14] Now that I, your Lord and Teacher, have washed your feet, you also should wash one another's feet. [15] I have set you an example that you should do as I have done for you. [16] Very truly I tell you, no servant is greater than his master, nor is a messenger greater than the one who sent him. [17] Now that you know these things, you will be blessed if you do them.

Jesus Predicts His Betrayal

[18] "I am not referring to all of you; I know those I have chosen. But this is to fulfill this passage of Scripture: 'He who shared my bread has turned[a] against me.'[b]

[19] "I am telling you now before it happens, so that when it does happen you will believe that I am who I am. [20] Very truly I tell you, whoever accepts anyone I send accepts me; and whoever accepts me accepts the one who sent me."

[21] After he had said this, Jesus was troubled in spirit and testified, "Very truly I tell you, one of you is going to betray me."

[22] His disciples stared at one another, at a loss to know which of them he meant. [23] One of them, the disciple whom Jesus loved, was reclining next to him. [24] Simon Peter motioned to this disciple and said, "Ask him which one he means."

[25] Leaning back against Jesus, he asked him, "Lord, who is it?"

[26] Jesus answered, "It is the one to whom I will give this piece of bread when I have dipped it in the dish." Then, dipping the piece of bread, he gave it to Judas, the son of Simon Iscariot. [27] As soon as Judas took the bread, Satan entered into him.

So Jesus told him, "What you are about to do, do quickly." [28] But no one at the meal understood why Jesus said this to him. [29] Since Judas had charge of the money, some thought Jesus was telling him to buy what was needed for the festival, or to give something to the poor. [30] As soon as Judas

---

[a] 18 Greek *has lifted up his heel*   [b] 18 Psalm 41:9

had taken the bread, he went out. And it was night.

Jesus Predicts Peter's Denial

[31] When he was gone, Jesus said, "Now the Son of Man is glorified and God is glorified in him. [32] If God is glorified in him,[a] God will glorify the Son in himself, and will glorify him at once.

[33] "My children, I will be with you only a little longer. You will look for me, and just as I told the Jews, so I tell you now: Where I am going, you cannot come.

[34] "A new command I give you: Love one another. As I have loved you, so you must love one another. [35] By this everyone will know that you are my disciples, if you love one another."

[36] Simon Peter asked him, "Lord, where are you going?"

Jesus replied, "Where I am going, you cannot follow now, but you will follow later."

[37] Peter asked, "Lord, why can't I follow you now? I will lay down my life for you."

[38] Then Jesus answered, "Will you really lay down your life for me? Very truly I tell you, before the rooster crows, you will disown me three times!

Jesus Comforts His Disciples

14 "Do not let your hearts be troubled. You believe in God[b]; believe also in me. [2] My Father's house has many rooms; if that were not so, would I have told you that I am going there to prepare a place for you? [3] And if I go and prepare a place for you, I will come back and take you to be with me that you also may be where I am. [4] You know the way to the place where I am going."

Jesus the Way to the Father

[5] Thomas said to him, "Lord, we don't know where you are going, so how can we know the way?"

[6] Jesus answered, "I am the way and the truth and the life. No one comes to the Father except through me. [7] If you really know me, you will know[c] my Father as well. From now on, you do know him and have seen him."

[8] Philip said, "Lord, show us the Father and that will be enough for us."

[9] Jesus answered: "Don't you know me, Philip, even after I have been among you such a long time? Anyone who has seen me has seen the Father. How can you say, 'Show us the Father'? [10] Don't you believe that I am in the Father, and that the Father is in me? The words I say to you I do not speak on my own authority. Rather, it is the Father, living in me, who is doing his work. [11] Believe me when I say that I am in the Father and the Father is in me; or at least believe on the evidence of the works themselves. [12] Very truly I tell you, whoever believes in me will do the works I have been doing, and they will do even greater things than these, because I am going to the Father. [13] And I will do whatever you ask in my name, so that the Father may be glorified in the Son. [14] You may ask me for anything in my name, and I will do it.

Jesus Promises the Holy Spirit

[15] "If you love me, keep my commands. [16] And I will ask the Father, and he will give you another advocate to help you and be with you forever— [17] the Spirit of truth. The world cannot accept him, because it neither sees him nor knows him. But you know him, for he lives with you and will be[d] in you. [18] I will not leave you as orphans; I will come to you. [19] Before long, the world will not see me anymore, but you will see me. Because I live, you also will live. [20] On that day you will realize that I am in my Father, and you are in me, and I am in you. [21] Whoever has my commands and keeps them is the one who loves me. The one who loves me will be loved by my Father, and I too will love them and show myself to them."

[22] Then Judas (not Judas Iscariot) said, "But, Lord, why do you intend to show yourself to us and not to the world?"

[23] Jesus replied, "Anyone who loves me will obey my teaching. My Father will love them, and we will come to them and make our home with them. [24] Anyone who does not love me will not obey my teaching. These words you hear are not my own; they belong to the Father who sent me.

[25] "All this I have spoken while still with you. [26] But the Advocate, the Holy Spirit, whom the Father will send in my name, will teach you all things and will remind you of

---

[a] 32 Many early manuscripts do not have *If God is glorified in him.*   [b] 1 Or *Believe in God*   [c] 7 Some manuscripts *If you really knew me, you would know*   [d] 17 Some early manuscripts *and is*

KNEES TO KNEES

READ: **JOHN 14:5-14**

Jesus walked in the flesh and, through patience and parables, boiled down the grandest truths so we could comprehend them. "No, let me explain that again. No, let me explain it again. Nope, not what I said. Let me explain it again. Nope, let me explain it a different way. Good grief. The seed story didn't work. Let's talk about children. Can we talk about kids?"

In humility, he chose to walk around and live life with these twelve guys. He ate with them, traveled with them, laughed with them, and cried with them. Then when he departed, he said, "Now do with others what I just did with you."

I always try to remember the humility of Christ when I go knees to knees with other believers.

New believers need you to do life with them and show them what a Christian looks like at school or on the field. When they see you extend grace and live out God's Word, it sticks.

And you need relational models who can lead you in discipleship, so you can then turn to your friend in love and make him a disciple. It's Christ's idea. Large classes and small groups have their purpose, and I'm a fan. If you had a hundred people in your youth or college group who decided to each disciple one person, it wouldn't just rock your group; it would rock your community.

BUILDING
FAITH
WISDOM
STRENGTH

Taken from *Thrive Student Edition* by Mark Hall with Tim Luke, copyright © 2014 by Mark Hall, published by Zondervan.

everything I have said to you. [27] Peace I leave with you; my peace I give you. I do not give to you as the world gives. Do not let your hearts be troubled and do not be afraid.

[28] "You heard me say, 'I am going away and I am coming back to you.' If you loved me, you would be glad that I am going to the Father, for the Father is greater than I. [29] I have told you now before it happens, so that when it does happen you will believe. [30] I will not say much more to you, for the prince of this world is coming. He has no hold over me, [31] but he comes so that the world may learn that I love the Father and do exactly what my Father has commanded me.

"Come now; let us leave.

The Vine and the Branches

15 "I am the true vine, and my Father is the gardener. [2] He cuts off every branch in me that bears no fruit, while every branch that does bear fruit he prunes[a] so that it will be even more fruitful. [3] You are already clean because of the word I have spoken to you. [4] Remain in me, as I also remain in you. No branch can bear fruit by itself; it must remain in the vine. Neither can you bear fruit unless you remain in me.

[5] "I am the vine; you are the branches. If you remain in me and I in you, you will bear much fruit; apart from me you can do nothing. [6] If you do not remain in me, you are like a branch that is thrown away and withers; such branches are picked up, thrown into the fire and burned. [7] If you remain in me and my words remain in you, ask whatever you wish, and it will be done for you. [8] This is to my Father's glory, that you bear much fruit, showing yourselves to be my disciples.

[9] "As the Father has loved me, so have I loved you. Now remain in my love. [10] If you keep my commands, you will remain in my love, just as I have kept my Father's commands and remain in his love. [11] I have told you this so that my joy may be in you and that your joy may be complete. [12] My command is this: Love each other as I have loved you. [13] Greater love has no one than this: to lay down one's life for one's friends. [14] You are my friends if you do what I command. [15] I no longer call you servants, because a servant does not know his master's business. Instead, I have called you friends, for everything that I learned from my Father I have made known to you. [16] You did not choose me, but I chose you and appointed you so that you might go and bear fruit—fruit that will last—and so that whatever you ask in my name the Father will give you. [17] This is my command: Love each other.

The World Hates the Disciples

[18] "If the world hates you, keep in mind that it hated me first. [19] If you belonged to the world, it would love you as its own. As it is, you do not belong to the world, but I have chosen you out of the world. That is why the world hates you. [20] Remember what I told you: 'A servant is not greater than his master.'[b] If they persecuted me, they will persecute you also. If they obeyed my teaching, they will obey yours also. [21] They will treat you this way because of my name, for they do not know the one who sent me. [22] If I had not come and spoken to them, they would not be guilty of sin; but now they have no excuse for their sin. [23] Whoever hates me hates my Father as well. [24] If I had not done among them the works no one else did, they would not be guilty of sin. As it is, they have seen, and yet they have hated both me and my Father. [25] But this is to fulfill what is written in their Law: 'They hated me without reason.'[c]

The Work of the Holy Spirit

[26] "When the Advocate comes, whom I will send to you from the Father—the Spirit of truth who goes out from the Father—he will testify about me. [27] And you also must testify, for you have been with me from the beginning.

16 "All this I have told you so that you will not fall away. [2] They will put you out of the synagogue; in fact, the time is coming when anyone who kills you will think they are offering a service to God. [3] They will do such things because they have not known the Father or me. [4] I have told you this, so that when their time comes you will remember that I warned you about them. I did not tell you this from the beginning because I was with you, [5] but now I am going to him who sent me. None of you asks me, 'Where are you going?' [6] Rather, you are filled with grief

---

[a] 2 The Greek for *he prunes* also means *he cleans.*   [b] 20 John 13:16   [c] 25 Psalms 35:19; 69:4

THE TENSION

READ: JOHN 15:18-19

Even if we keep our eyes on Christ, there's still the challenge of our relationship with the world that surrounds us. We struggle with this tension between the spirit and the flesh, between the godly and the worldly, between the desire to rock out in the world and the desire to worship in the presence of Jesus.

Jesus understood that we would have to live that tension. Consider these words from John 15:18-19. The same theme appears two chapters later, as Jesus prays for his followers (see John 17:14-18).

These words are the foundation for the well-known Christian call to be "in the world but not of the world." But why is this such a struggle? Why does our effort to live for God so quickly devolve into living in ways that are not true to who we are?

I think Jesus understood that we'd be torn between the desire to love him with our entire lives and a desire for what the world has to offer; that's normal. The truth is that there really isn't just one person inside each of us. There are two different people: The person attached to this world (our human person) and the person attached to the spiritual world (our soul person). We are both spirit and flesh, two beings packed in one form.

BUILDING
FAITH
WISDOM
STRENGTH

Taken from *Jesus Is for Liars: A Hypocrite's Guide to Authenticity* by Tim Baker, copyright © 2009 by Tim Baker, published by Zondervan.

because I have said these things. ⁷But very truly I tell you, it is for your good that I am going away. Unless I go away, the Advocate will not come to you; but if I go, I will send him to you. ⁸When he comes, he will prove the world to be in the wrong about sin and righteousness and judgment: ⁹about sin, because people do not believe in me; ¹⁰about righteousness, because I am going to the Father, where you can see me no longer; ¹¹and about judgment, because the prince of this world now stands condemned.

¹²"I have much more to say to you, more than you can now bear. ¹³But when he, the Spirit of truth, comes, he will guide you into all the truth. He will not speak on his own; he will speak only what he hears, and he will tell you what is yet to come. ¹⁴He will glorify me because it is from me that he will receive what he will make known to you. ¹⁵All that belongs to the Father is mine. That is why I said the Spirit will receive from me what he will make known to you."

The Disciples' Grief Will Turn to Joy

¹⁶Jesus went on to say, "In a little while you will see me no more, and then after a little while you will see me."

¹⁷At this, some of his disciples said to one another, "What does he mean by saying, 'In a little while you will see me no more, and then after a little while you will see me,' and 'Because I am going to the Father'?" ¹⁸They kept asking, "What does he mean by 'a little while'? We don't understand what he is saying."

¹⁹Jesus saw that they wanted to ask him about this, so he said to them, "Are you asking one another what I meant when I said, 'In a little while you will see me no more, and then after a little while you will see me'? ²⁰Very truly I tell you, you will weep and mourn while the world rejoices. You will grieve, but your grief will turn to joy. ²¹A woman giving birth to a child has pain because her time has come; but when her baby is born she forgets the anguish because of her joy that a child is born into the world. ²²So with you: Now is your time of grief, but I will see you again and you will rejoice, and no one will take away your joy. ²³In that day you will no longer ask me anything. Very truly I tell you, my Father will give you whatever you ask in my name. ²⁴Until now you have not asked for anything in my name. Ask and you will receive, and your joy will be complete.

²⁵"Though I have been speaking figuratively, a time is coming when I will no longer use this kind of language but will tell you plainly about my Father. ²⁶In that day you will ask in my name. I am not saying that I will ask the Father on your behalf. ²⁷No, the Father himself loves you because you have loved me and have believed that I came from God. ²⁸I came from the Father and entered the world; now I am leaving the world and going back to the Father."

²⁹Then Jesus' disciples said, "Now you are speaking clearly and without figures of speech. ³⁰Now we can see that you know all things and that you do not even need to have anyone ask you questions. This makes us believe that you came from God."

³¹"Do you now believe?" Jesus replied. ³²"A time is coming and in fact has come when you will be scattered, each to your own home. You will leave me all alone. Yet I am not alone, for my Father is with me.

³³"I have told you these things, so that in me you may have peace. In this world you will have trouble. But take heart! I have overcome the world."

Jesus Prays to Be Glorified

17 After Jesus said this, he looked toward heaven and prayed:

"Father, the hour has come. Glorify your Son, that your Son may glorify you. ²For you granted him authority over all people that he might give eternal life to all those you have given him. ³Now this is eternal life: that they know you, the only true God, and Jesus Christ, whom you have sent. ⁴I have brought you glory on earth by finishing the work you gave me to do. ⁵And now, Father, glorify me in your presence with the glory I had with you before the world began.

Jesus Prays for His Disciples

⁶"I have revealed you*ᵃ* to those whom you gave me out of the world. They were yours; you gave them to

---

ᵃ 6 Greek *your name*

me and they have obeyed your word. [7] Now they know that everything you have given me comes from you. [8] For I gave them the words you gave me and they accepted them. They knew with certainty that I came from you, and they believed that you sent me. [9] I pray for them. I am not praying for the world, but for those you have given me, for they are yours. [10] All I have is yours, and all you have is mine. And glory has come to me through them. [11] I will remain in the world no longer, but they are still in the world, and I am coming to you. Holy Father, protect them by the power of[a] your name, the name you gave me, so that they may be one as we are one. [12] While I was with them, I protected them and kept them safe by[b] that name you gave me. None has been lost except the one doomed to destruction so that Scripture would be fulfilled.

[13] "I am coming to you now, but I say these things while I am still in the world, so that they may have the full measure of my joy within them. [14] I have given them your word and the world has hated them, for they are not of the world any more than I am of the world. [15] My prayer is not that you take them out of the world but that you protect them from the evil one. [16] They are not of the world, even as I am not of it. [17] Sanctify them by[c] the truth; your word is truth. [18] As you sent me into the world, I have sent them into the world. [19] For them I sanctify myself, that they too may be truly sanctified.

Jesus Prays for All Believers

[20] "My prayer is not for them alone. I pray also for those who will believe in me through their message, [21] that all of them may be one, Father, just as you are in me and I am in you. May they also be in us so that the world may believe that you have sent me. [22] I have given them the glory that you gave me, that they may be one as we are one — [23] I in them and you in me — so that they may be brought to complete unity. Then

the world will know that you sent me and have loved them even as you have loved me.

[24] "Father, I want those you have given me to be with me where I am, and to see my glory, the glory you have given me because you loved me before the creation of the world.

[25] "Righteous Father, though the world does not know you, I know you, and they know that you have sent me. [26] I have made you[d] known to them, and will continue to make you known in order that the love you have for me may be in them and that I myself may be in them."

Jesus Arrested

18 When he had finished praying, Jesus left with his disciples and crossed the Kidron Valley. On the other side there was a garden, and he and his disciples went into it.

[2] Now Judas, who betrayed him, knew the place, because Jesus had often met there with his disciples. [3] So Judas came to the garden, guiding a detachment of soldiers and some officials from the chief priests and the Pharisees. They were carrying torches, lanterns and weapons.

[4] Jesus, knowing all that was going to happen to him, went out and asked them, "Who is it you want?"

[5] "Jesus of Nazareth," they replied.

"I am he," Jesus said. (And Judas the traitor was standing there with them.) [6] When Jesus said, "I am he," they drew back and fell to the ground.

[7] Again he asked them, "Who is it you want?"

"Jesus of Nazareth," they said.

[8] Jesus answered, "I told you that I am he. If you are looking for me, then let these men go." [9] This happened so that the words he had spoken would be fulfilled: "I have not lost one of those you gave me."[e]

[10] Then Simon Peter, who had a sword, drew it and struck the high priest's servant, cutting off his right ear. (The servant's name was Malchus.)

[11] Jesus commanded Peter, "Put your sword away! Shall I not drink the cup the Father has given me?"

---

[a] 11 Or *Father, keep them faithful to*   [b] 12 Or *kept them faithful to*   [c] 17 Or *them to live in accordance with*   [d] 26 Greek *your name*   [e] 9 John 6:39

¹²Then the detachment of soldiers with its commander and the Jewish officials arrested Jesus. They bound him ¹³and brought him first to Annas, who was the father-in-law of Caiaphas, the high priest that year. ¹⁴Caiaphas was the one who had advised the Jewish leaders that it would be good if one man died for the people.

Peter's First Denial

¹⁵Simon Peter and another disciple were following Jesus. Because this disciple was known to the high priest, he went with Jesus into the high priest's courtyard, ¹⁶but Peter had to wait outside at the door. The other disciple, who was known to the high priest, came back, spoke to the servant girl on duty there and brought Peter in.

¹⁷"You aren't one of this man's disciples too, are you?" she asked Peter.

He replied, "I am not."

¹⁸It was cold, and the servants and officials stood around a fire they had made to keep warm. Peter also was standing with them, warming himself.

The High Priest Questions Jesus

¹⁹Meanwhile, the high priest questioned Jesus about his disciples and his teaching.

²⁰"I have spoken openly to the world," Jesus replied. "I always taught in synagogues or at the temple, where all the Jews come together. I said nothing in secret. ²¹Why question me? Ask those who heard me. Surely they know what I said."

²²When Jesus said this, one of the officials nearby slapped him in the face. "Is this the way you answer the high priest?" he demanded.

²³"If I said something wrong," Jesus replied, "testify as to what is wrong. But if I spoke the truth, why did you strike me?" ²⁴Then Annas sent him bound to Caiaphas the high priest.

Peter's Second and Third Denials

²⁵Meanwhile, Simon Peter was still standing there warming himself. So they asked him, "You aren't one of his disciples too, are you?"

He denied it, saying, "I am not."

²⁶One of the high priest's servants, a relative of the man whose ear Peter had cut off, challenged him, "Didn't I see you with him in the garden?" ²⁷Again Peter denied it, and at that moment a rooster began to crow.

Jesus Before Pilate

²⁸Then the Jewish leaders took Jesus from Caiaphas to the palace of the Roman governor. By now it was early morning, and to avoid ceremonial uncleanness they did not enter the palace, because they wanted to be able to eat the Passover. ²⁹So Pilate came out to them and asked, "What charges are you bringing against this man?"

³⁰"If he were not a criminal," they replied, "we would not have handed him over to you."

³¹Pilate said, "Take him yourselves and judge him by your own law."

"But we have no right to execute anyone," they objected. ³²This took place to fulfill what Jesus had said about the kind of death he was going to die.

³³Pilate then went back inside the palace, summoned Jesus and asked him, "Are you the king of the Jews?"

³⁴"Is that your own idea," Jesus asked, "or did others talk to you about me?"

³⁵"Am I a Jew?" Pilate replied. "Your own people and chief priests handed you over to me. What is it you have done?"

³⁶Jesus said, "My kingdom is not of this world. If it were, my servants would fight to prevent my arrest by the Jewish leaders. But now my kingdom is from another place."

³⁷"You are a king, then!" said Pilate.

Jesus answered, "You say that I am a king. In fact, the reason I was born and came into the world is to testify to the truth. Everyone on the side of truth listens to me."

³⁸"What is truth?" retorted Pilate. With this he went out again to the Jews gathered there and said, "I find no basis for a charge against him. ³⁹But it is your custom for me to release to you one prisoner at the time of the Passover. Do you want me to release 'the king of the Jews'?"

⁴⁰They shouted back, "No, not him! Give us Barabbas!" Now Barabbas had taken part in an uprising.

Jesus Sentenced to Be Crucified

19 Then Pilate took Jesus and had him flogged. ²The soldiers twisted together a crown of thorns and put it on his head. They clothed him in a purple robe ³and went

up to him again and again, saying, "Hail, king of the Jews!" And they slapped him in the face.

[4]Once more Pilate came out and said to the Jews gathered there, "Look, I am bringing him out to you to let you know that I find no basis for a charge against him." [5]When Jesus came out wearing the crown of thorns and the purple robe, Pilate said to them, "Here is the man!"

[6]As soon as the chief priests and their officials saw him, they shouted, "Crucify! Crucify!"

But Pilate answered, "You take him and crucify him. As for me, I find no basis for a charge against him."

[7]The Jewish leaders insisted, "We have a law, and according to that law he must die, because he claimed to be the Son of God."

[8]When Pilate heard this, he was even more afraid, [9]and he went back inside the palace. "Where do you come from?" he asked Jesus, but Jesus gave him no answer. [10]"Do you refuse to speak to me?" Pilate said. "Don't you realize I have power either to free you or to crucify you?"

[11]Jesus answered, "You would have no power over me if it were not given to you from above. Therefore the one who handed me over to you is guilty of a greater sin."

[12]From then on, Pilate tried to set Jesus free, but the Jewish leaders kept shouting, "If you let this man go, you are no friend of Caesar. Anyone who claims to be a king opposes Caesar."

[13]When Pilate heard this, he brought Jesus out and sat down on the judge's seat at a place known as the Stone Pavement (which in Aramaic is Gabbatha). [14]It was the day of Preparation of the Passover; it was about noon.

"Here is your king," Pilate said to the Jews.

[15]But they shouted, "Take him away! Take him away! Crucify him!"

"Shall I crucify your king?" Pilate asked.

"We have no king but Caesar," the chief priests answered.

[16]Finally Pilate handed him over to them to be crucified.

The Crucifixion of Jesus

So the soldiers took charge of Jesus. [17]Carrying his own cross, he went out to the place of the Skull (which in Aramaic is called Golgotha). [18]There they crucified him, and with him two others — one on each side and Jesus in the middle.

[19]Pilate had a notice prepared and fastened to the cross. It read: JESUS OF NAZARETH, THE KING OF THE JEWS. [20]Many of the Jews read this sign, for the place where Jesus was crucified was near the city, and the sign was written in Aramaic, Latin and Greek. [21]The chief priests of the Jews protested to Pilate, "Do not write 'The King of the Jews,' but that this man claimed to be king of the Jews."

[22]Pilate answered, "What I have written, I have written."

[23]When the soldiers crucified Jesus, they took his clothes, dividing them into four shares, one for each of them, with the undergarment remaining. This garment was seamless, woven in one piece from top to bottom.

[24]"Let's not tear it," they said to one another. "Let's decide by lot who will get it."

This happened that the scripture might be fulfilled that said,

"They divided my clothes among them
    and cast lots for my garment."[a]

So this is what the soldiers did.

[25]Near the cross of Jesus stood his mother, his mother's sister, Mary the wife of Clopas, and Mary Magdalene. [26]When Jesus saw his mother there, and the disciple whom he loved standing nearby, he said to her, "Woman,[b] here is your son," [27]and to the disciple, "Here is your mother." From that time on, this disciple took her into his home.

The Death of Jesus

[28]Later, knowing that everything had now been finished, and so that Scripture would be fulfilled, Jesus said, "I am thirsty." [29]A jar of wine vinegar was there, so they soaked a sponge in it, put the sponge on a stalk of the hyssop plant, and lifted it to Jesus' lips. [30]When he had received the drink, Jesus said, "It is finished." With that, he bowed his head and gave up his spirit.

[31]Now it was the day of Preparation, and the next day was to be a special Sabbath. Because the Jewish leaders did not want the

---

[a] 24 Psalm 22:18   [b] 26 The Greek for *Woman* does not denote any disrespect.

SYMBOL OF DEATH

READ: JOHN 19:17-20

You've seen the most popular symbol in Christianity: the cross. It's not just a good-luck charm. And it's not a symbol to make us feel more spiritual. The cross is an ancient form of execution upon which Jesus died at the hands of wicked people. Jesus was tortured. He wore thorny brambles that penetrated his scalp. His hands and feet were pierced with large spikes. And he hung on cross-shaped beams, left to either suffocate or bleed to death, whichever came first.

As Jesus hung there, he looked down at those who were killing him and said, "Father, forgive them, for they do not know what they are doing" (Luke 23:34). What kind of love is this? What kind of Man is this who has a God's eye view of humans, yet he can look with pity upon those who are destroying his body and still speak of forgiveness? His last words were, "It is finished" (John 19:30).

BUILDING
FAITH
WISDOM
STRENGTH

What was finished? What does this all mean? It means Jesus took all of the evil of the world—including ours—upon his own shoulders. His spilled blood is like medicine for our corruption. He came to mend us of all the scars of brokenness and death.

And we know it worked because Jesus did something no other person in history has ever experienced. He came back to life again.

Taken from *Living with Questions* by Dale Fincher, copyright © 2007 by Charles Dale Fincher, published by Zondervan.

THOMAS

Then he said to Thomas, "Put your finger here; see my hands. Reach out your hand and put it into my side. Stop doubting and believe." JOHN 20:27

HIS NAME MEANS: "twin"

READ HIS STORY: *Matthew 10:1-8; Mark 3:13-19; John 11:1-16, 14:1-7, 20:19—21:14; Acts 1:12-14*

MEN OF THE BIBLE

Have you ever wrestled with doubts regarding your belief in Jesus Christ? Doubting is natural. And the most famous doubter in history was the disciple Thomas.

Thomas traveled with Jesus for three years. Thomas saw the Lord perform miracles. He heard Jesus' teaching. He knew that Jesus said he was the Messiah who would be killed in Jerusalem and raised from the dead on the third day (Matthew 16:20-21). But when Jesus first appeared to his disciples after his resurrection, Thomas wasn't there. He doubted their story, saying, "Unless I see the nail marks in his hands . . . and put my hand into his side, I will not believe" (John 20:25). A week went by before Jesus appeared again to his disciples. This time the Lord spoke directly to Thomas. Thomas immediately exclaimed, "My Lord and my God!"

When Thomas saw the risen Lord, all doubt went away. Thomas was with the other disciples, praying together before taking the good news of Jesus to the world (Acts 1:12-14). This is the last we hear of Thomas in the Bible, but according to tradition (not as reliable as the Scriptures, of course) he spread the gospel to India and was martyred there.

The doubter became a powerful evangelist. Theologians have noted a dramatic difference between doubt and unbelief. Doubt is open-minded. You're not sure. You need proof, and you're still looking for truth. With unbelief, your mind is made up. God can always work with an open mind, just like he did with Thomas.

bodies left on the crosses during the Sabbath, they asked Pilate to have the legs broken and the bodies taken down. [32] The soldiers therefore came and broke the legs of the first man who had been crucified with Jesus, and then those of the other. [33] But when they came to Jesus and found that he was already dead, they did not break his legs. [34] Instead, one of the soldiers pierced Jesus' side with a spear, bringing a sudden flow of blood and water. [35] The man who saw it has given testimony, and his testimony is true. He knows that he tells the truth, and he testifies so that you also may believe. [36] These things happened so that the scripture would be fulfilled: "Not one of his bones will be broken,"[a] [37] and, as another scripture says, "They will look on the one they have pierced."[b]

The Burial of Jesus

[38] Later, Joseph of Arimathea asked Pilate for the body of Jesus. Now Joseph was a disciple of Jesus, but secretly because he feared the Jewish leaders. With Pilate's permission, he came and took the body away. [39] He was accompanied by Nicodemus, the man who earlier had visited Jesus at night. Nicodemus brought a mixture of myrrh and aloes, about seventy-five pounds.[c] [40] Taking Jesus' body, the two of them wrapped it, with the spices, in strips of linen. This was in accordance with Jewish burial customs. [41] At the place where Jesus was crucified, there was a garden, and in the garden a new tomb, in which no one had ever been laid. [42] Because it was the Jewish day of Preparation and since the tomb was nearby, they laid Jesus there.

The Empty Tomb

20 Early on the first day of the week, while it was still dark, Mary Magdalene went to the tomb and saw that the stone had been removed from the entrance. [2] So she came running to Simon Peter and the other disciple, the one Jesus loved, and said, "They have taken the Lord out of the tomb, and we don't know where they have put him!"

[3] So Peter and the other disciple started for the tomb. [4] Both were running, but the other disciple outran Peter and reached the tomb first. [5] He bent over and looked in at the strips of linen lying there but did not go in. [6] Then Simon Peter came along behind him and went straight into the tomb. He saw the strips of linen lying there, [7] as well as the cloth that had been wrapped around Jesus' head. The cloth was still lying in its place, separate from the linen. [8] Finally the other disciple, who had reached the tomb first, also went inside. He saw and believed. [9] (They still did not understand from Scripture that Jesus had to rise from the dead.) [10] Then the disciples went back to where they were staying.

Jesus Appears to Mary Magdalene

[11] Now Mary stood outside the tomb crying. As she wept, she bent over to look into the tomb [12] and saw two angels in white, seated where Jesus' body had been, one at the head and the other at the foot.

[13] They asked her, "Woman, why are you crying?"

"They have taken my Lord away," she said, "and I don't know where they have put him." [14] At this, she turned around and saw Jesus standing there, but she did not realize that it was Jesus.

[15] He asked her, "Woman, why are you crying? Who is it you are looking for?"

Thinking he was the gardener, she said, "Sir, if you have carried him away, tell me where you have put him, and I will get him."

[16] Jesus said to her, "Mary."

She turned toward him and cried out in Aramaic, "Rabboni!" (which means "Teacher").

[17] Jesus said, "Do not hold on to me, for I have not yet ascended to the Father. Go instead to my brothers and tell them, 'I am ascending to my Father and your Father, to my God and your God.'"

[18] Mary Magdalene went to the disciples with the news: "I have seen the Lord!" And she told them that he had said these things to her.

Jesus Appears to His Disciples

[19] On the evening of that first day of the week, when the disciples were together, with the doors locked for fear of the Jewish leaders, Jesus came and stood among them and said, "Peace be with you!" [20] After he said

---

[a] 36 Exodus 12:46; Num. 9:12; Psalm 34:20   [b] 37 Zech. 12:10   [c] 39 Or about 34 kilograms

this, he showed them his hands and side. The disciples were overjoyed when they saw the Lord.

[21] Again Jesus said, "Peace be with you! As the Father has sent me, I am sending you." [22] And with that he breathed on them and said, "Receive the Holy Spirit. [23] If you forgive anyone's sins, their sins are forgiven; if you do not forgive them, they are not forgiven."

Jesus Appears to Thomas

[24] Now Thomas (also known as Didymus[a]), one of the Twelve, was not with the disciples when Jesus came. [25] So the other disciples told him, "We have seen the Lord!"

But he said to them, "Unless I see the nail marks in his hands and put my finger where the nails were, and put my hand into his side, I will not believe."

[26] A week later his disciples were in the house again, and Thomas was with them. Though the doors were locked, Jesus came and stood among them and said, "Peace be with you!" [27] Then he said to Thomas, "Put your finger here; see my hands. Reach out your hand and put it into my side. Stop doubting and believe."

[28] Thomas said to him, "My Lord and my God!"

[29] Then Jesus told him, "Because you have seen me, you have believed; blessed are those who have not seen and yet have believed."

The Purpose of John's Gospel

[30] Jesus performed many other signs in the presence of his disciples, which are not recorded in this book. [31] But these are written that you may believe[b] that Jesus is the Messiah, the Son of God, and that by believing you may have life in his name.

Jesus and the Miraculous Catch of Fish

21 Afterward Jesus appeared again to his disciples, by the Sea of Galilee.[c] It happened this way: [2] Simon Peter, Thomas (also known as Didymus[a]), Nathanael from Cana in Galilee, the sons of Zebedee, and two other disciples were together. [3] "I'm going out to fish," Simon Peter told them, and they said, "We'll go with you." So they went

out and got into the boat, but that night they caught nothing.

[4] Early in the morning, Jesus stood on the shore, but the disciples did not realize that it was Jesus.

[5] He called out to them, "Friends, haven't you any fish?"

"No," they answered.

[6] He said, "Throw your net on the right side of the boat and you will find some." When they did, they were unable to haul the net in because of the large number of fish.

[7] Then the disciple whom Jesus loved said to Peter, "It is the Lord!" As soon as Simon Peter heard him say, "It is the Lord," he wrapped his outer garment around him (for he had taken it off) and jumped into the water. [8] The other disciples followed in the boat, towing the net full of fish, for they were not far from shore, about a hundred yards.[d] [9] When they landed, they saw a fire of burning coals there with fish on it, and some bread.

[10] Jesus said to them, "Bring some of the fish you have just caught." [11] So Simon Peter climbed back into the boat and dragged the net ashore. It was full of large fish, 153, but even with so many the net was not torn. [12] Jesus said to them, "Come and have breakfast." None of the disciples dared ask him, "Who are you?" They knew it was the Lord. [13] Jesus came, took the bread and gave it to them, and did the same with the fish. [14] This was now the third time Jesus appeared to his disciples after he was raised from the dead.

Jesus Reinstates Peter

[15] When they had finished eating, Jesus said to Simon Peter, "Simon son of John, do you love me more than these?"

"Yes, Lord," he said, "you know that I love you."

Jesus said, "Feed my lambs."

[16] Again Jesus said, "Simon son of John, do you love me?"

He answered, "Yes, Lord, you know that I love you."

Jesus said, "Take care of my sheep."

[17] The third time he said to him, "Simon son of John, do you love me?"

---

[a] 24,2 *Thomas* (Aramaic) and *Didymus* (Greek) both mean *twin*.   [b] 31 Or *may continue to believe*
[c] 1 Greek *Tiberias*   [d] 8 Or *about 90 meters*

THE STRAIN

READ: JOHN 20:26-28

It's easy to assume that if Jesus ever stood before us in the flesh, we'd have the spiritual sensibility to recognize him for who he is and surrender to him. But I know myself. I'd act just like those who saw Jesus in person. And I have something the disciples never had—God's perfect and proven Word. Yet I still don't always recognize Jesus as Lord over my whole life.

It all comes down to the tension between the god we want and the God who is. The god we want fills our belly; the God *who is* fills us with the Holy Spirit. The god we want is happy in the middle; the God *who is* reigns from on high. The god we want looks a lot like us; the God *who is* wants us to be a reflection of him.

The god we want shows up in comfortable non-verses that we assume are in the Bible but really aren't. God helps those who help themselves. God blesses the rich so they can bless others. God won't give you anything you can't handle. What will the real God do? He'll put us out in the middle of a sea and tell us to walk on it. He'll place us before a giant with a rock and a sling. He'll allow a tornado or cancer or a breakup or an addiction or a rejection to come our way. He will give us more than we can handle just to show us that only he can handle things.

BUILDING

FAITH

WISDOM

STRENGTH

PETER

MEN OF THE BIBLE

When they had finished eating, Jesus said to Simon Peter, "Simon son of John, do you love me more than these?" "Yes, Lord," he said, "you know that I love you." Jesus said, "Feed my lambs." JOHN 21:15

HIS NAME MEANS: "rock"

READ HIS STORY: *Matthew 4:18-20, 8:14-15, 14:22-33, 16:13-19; Mark 8:27—9:9, 14:27-72; Luke 5:1-11, 22:31-62; John 13:1-17, 31-38, 21; Acts 2-5, 10:1—12:19, 15*

A fisherman by trade, Peter was one of the twelve disciples. He is mentioned frequently in the New Testament (sometimes as either Simon or Cephas) and was a prominent leader of the early Christian church after Jesus died and rose again.

Peter is known as the disciple who denied Jesus three times during the events leading up to Jesus' crucifixion. Another disciple, Judas, is known as the disciple who betrayed Jesus. The key difference between these two disciples, however, is that Judas ran away from Jesus after he felt remorse while Peter ran back to Jesus to receive forgiveness.

After the resurrection, Jesus appeared just to Peter before appearing to the other disciples (Luke 24:33-34; 1 Corinthians 15:5). Later, Peter and six other disciples went fishing in the Sea of Galilee. In the morning they saw a man standing on the shore. The disciple John exclaimed, "'It is the Lord!' As soon as Simon Peter heard him say, 'It is the Lord,' he wrapped his outer garment around him (for he had taken it off) and jumped into the water" (John 21:7). Peter was so eager to get to Jesus, he couldn't wait to row to shore with the others!

Sometimes, like Peter, we make mistakes. We turn our back on Jesus. We deny him. We forget him and get distracted by the things of the world. We sin.

When that happens, don't let guilt drag you down. Let true sorrow, like Peter's, send you back to Jesus instead. Come back to Jesus. Run to him as fast as you can! Tell him that you love him, and ask for his forgiveness. Jesus will accept you with open arms.

Peter was hurt because Jesus asked him the third time, "Do you love me?" He said, "Lord, you know all things; you know that I love you."

Jesus said, "Feed my sheep. [18]Very truly I tell you, when you were younger you dressed yourself and went where you wanted; but when you are old you will stretch out your hands, and someone else will dress you and lead you where you do not want to go." [19]Jesus said this to indicate the kind of death by which Peter would glorify God. Then he said to him, "Follow me!"

[20]Peter turned and saw that the disciple whom Jesus loved was following them. (This was the one who had leaned back against Jesus at the supper and had said, "Lord, who is going to betray you?") [21]When Peter saw him, he asked, "Lord, what about him?"

[22]Jesus answered, "If I want him to remain alive until I return, what is that to you? You must follow me." [23]Because of this, the rumor spread among the believers that this disciple would not die. But Jesus did not say that he would not die; he only said, "If I want him to remain alive until I return, what is that to you?"

[24]This is the disciple who testifies to these things and who wrote them down. We know that his testimony is true.

[25]Jesus did many other things as well. If every one of them were written down, I suppose that even the whole world would not have room for the books that would be written.

ACTS

WHEN DID THIS HAPPEN?

Between A.D. 36 and 63 in the Roman empire

WHO IS IN THIS BOOK?

Peter
John
Stephen
Paul
Philip
Cornelius
Barnabas
John Mark
Silas
Priscilla
Aquila
Ananias
Sapphira
Simon the Sorcerer

VERSES YOU MIGHT RECOGNIZE

ACTS 1:8

"But you will receive power when the Holy Spirit comes on you; and you will be my witnesses ... to the ends of the earth."

ACTS 16:31

"Believe in the Lord Jesus, and you will be saved—you and your household."

WHAT'S IT ABOUT?

Written by Luke, this book is the story of the spread of the gospel and the rise of the first-century church after Jesus ascended to heaven. It can be divided into two parts. The first twelve chapters follow Peter's ministry in Jerusalem and Samaria. Jesus chose Peter to be the foundation of the church (see Matthew 16:18). The remaining chapters of Acts follow the ministry of the apostle Paul and his missionary journeys through the Roman empire.

Acts shows how the gospel spread, beginning with Jews (with Peter) and then going out to Gentiles. We also get a better view of the third person of the Trinity—the Holy Spirit—and his role in the lives of believers. Acts, which comes from the Greek word "praxis"—meaning a belief put into action—recounts the great deeds of the apostles.

This book is packed with exciting stories about men and women who bravely took action to make sure that the good news about Jesus got out to the world. In only thirty years, the gospel spread from Jerusalem to the entire Roman empire. Only God could have accomplished such a feat.

ACTS

Jesus Taken Up Into Heaven

1 In my former book, Theophilus, I wrote about all that Jesus began to do and to teach [2] until the day he was taken up to heaven, after giving instructions through the Holy Spirit to the apostles he had chosen. [3] After his suffering, he presented himself to them and gave many convincing proofs that he was alive. He appeared to them over a period of forty days and spoke about the kingdom of God. [4] On one occasion, while he was eating with them, he gave them this command: "Do not leave Jerusalem, but wait for the gift my Father promised, which you have heard me speak about. [5] For John baptized with[a] water, but in a few days you will be baptized with[a] the Holy Spirit."

[6] Then they gathered around him and asked him, "Lord, are you at this time going to restore the kingdom to Israel?"

[7] He said to them: "It is not for you to know the times or dates the Father has set by his own authority. [8] But you will receive power when the Holy Spirit comes on you; and you will be my witnesses in Jerusalem, and in all Judea and Samaria, and to the ends of the earth."

[9] After he said this, he was taken up before their very eyes, and a cloud hid him from their sight.

[10] They were looking intently up into the sky as he was going, when suddenly two men dressed in white stood beside them. [11] "Men of Galilee," they said, "why do you stand here looking into the sky? This same Jesus, who has been taken from you into heaven, will come back in the same way you have seen him go into heaven."

Matthias Chosen to Replace Judas

[12] Then the apostles returned to Jerusalem from the hill called the Mount of Olives, a Sabbath day's walk[b] from the city. [13] When they arrived, they went upstairs to the room where they were staying. Those present were Peter, John, James and Andrew; Philip and Thomas, Bartholomew and Matthew; James son of Alphaeus and Simon the Zealot, and Judas son of James. [14] They all joined together constantly in prayer, along with the women and Mary the mother of Jesus, and with his brothers.

[15] In those days Peter stood up among the believers (a group numbering about a hundred and twenty) [16] and said, "Brothers and sisters,[c] the Scripture had to be fulfilled in which the Holy Spirit spoke long ago through David concerning Judas, who served as guide for those who arrested Jesus. [17] He was one of our number and shared in our ministry."

[18] (With the payment he received for his wickedness, Judas bought a field; there he fell headlong, his body burst open and all his intestines spilled out. [19] Everyone in Jerusalem heard about this, so they called that field in their language Akeldama, that is, Field of Blood.)

[20] "For," said Peter, "it is written in the Book of Psalms:

" 'May his place be deserted;
    let there be no one to dwell in it,'[d]

and,

" 'May another take his place of
    leadership.'[e]

[21] Therefore it is necessary to choose one of the men who have been with us the whole time the Lord Jesus was living among us, [22] beginning from John's baptism to the time when Jesus was taken up from us. For one of these must become a witness with us of his resurrection."

[23] So they nominated two men: Joseph called Barsabbas (also known as Justus)

---

[a] 5 Or in [b] 12 That is, about 5/8 mile or about 1 kilometer [c] 16 The Greek word for brothers and sisters (adelphoi) refers here to believers, both men and women, as part of God's family; also in 6:3; 11:29; 12:17; 16:40; 18:18, 27; 21:7, 17; 28:14, 15. [d] 20 Psalm 69:25 [e] 20 Psalm 109:8

YOU'RE GONNA NEED THIS

READ: ACTS 1:4-8

Jesus challenged people to define their relationship with him. For disciples this defining moment had to come when Jesus ascended into heaven leaving them here to advance his kingdom to the ends of the earth.

I'm sure this would have seemed overwhelming to his followers. It's one thing to follow Jesus when he's right there in the flesh leading the way. They could see him and talk to him. If they faced a storm, he was there to calm it. If they were hungry, he was there to provide food. If they were confused, he was there to help them understand. But as they watched him disappear into the clouds, they must have wondered how they could continue to follow him here on earth.

They were uneducated. They were under resourced. They had no strategic plan. They had no special power. How could they follow him if he wasn't there to lead? But Jesus said, "You will receive power when the Holy Spirit comes on you."

BUILDING
FAITH
WISDOM
STRENGTH

We're glad for the Holy Spirit, but we tend to think of him as being on the JV team of the Trinity. But that's not how Jesus portrayed the Holy Spirit to his followers. Jesus said it was better for him to leave, because when he goes the Holy Spirit will come.

When you become a Christian, you receive from God the gift of the Holy Spirit. So it's not a question of whether you have access to this power of the Holy Spirit; the question is, have you accessed it?

Taken from *Not a Fan Student Edition* by Kyle Idleman, copyright © 2012 by City on the Hill Studio, Inc., published by Zondervan.

and Matthias. [24]Then they prayed, "Lord, you know everyone's heart. Show us which of these two you have chosen [25]to take over this apostolic ministry, which Judas left to go where he belongs." [26]Then they cast lots, and the lot fell to Matthias; so he was added to the eleven apostles.

The Holy Spirit Comes at Pentecost

2 When the day of Pentecost came, they were all together in one place. [2]Suddenly a sound like the blowing of a violent wind came from heaven and filled the whole house where they were sitting. [3]They saw what seemed to be tongues of fire that separated and came to rest on each of them. [4]All of them were filled with the Holy Spirit and began to speak in other tongues[a] as the Spirit enabled them.

[5]Now there were staying in Jerusalem God-fearing Jews from every nation under heaven. [6]When they heard this sound, a crowd came together in bewilderment, because each one heard their own language being spoken. [7]Utterly amazed, they asked: "Aren't all these who are speaking Galileans? [8]Then how is it that each of us hears them in our native language? [9]Parthians, Medes and Elamites; residents of Mesopotamia, Judea and Cappadocia, Pontus and Asia,[b] [10]Phrygia and Pamphylia, Egypt and the parts of Libya near Cyrene; visitors from Rome [11](both Jews and converts to Judaism); Cretans and Arabs—we hear them declaring the wonders of God in our own tongues!" [12]Amazed and perplexed, they asked one another, "What does this mean?"

[13]Some, however, made fun of them and said, "They have had too much wine."

Peter Addresses the Crowd

[14]Then Peter stood up with the Eleven, raised his voice and addressed the crowd: "Fellow Jews and all of you who live in Jerusalem, let me explain this to you; listen carefully to what I say. [15]These people are not drunk, as you suppose. It's only nine in the morning! [16]No, this is what was spoken by the prophet Joel:

[17]"'In the last days, God says,
    I will pour out my Spirit on all people.

Your sons and daughters will prophesy,
    your young men will see visions,
    your old men will dream dreams.
[18]Even on my servants, both men and
        women,
    I will pour out my Spirit in those days,
    and they will prophesy.
[19]I will show wonders in the heavens above
    and signs on the earth below,
    blood and fire and billows of smoke.
[20]The sun will be turned to darkness
    and the moon to blood
    before the coming of the great and
        glorious day of the Lord.
[21]And everyone who calls
    on the name of the Lord will be saved.'[c]

[22]"Fellow Israelites, listen to this: Jesus of Nazareth was a man accredited by God to you by miracles, wonders and signs, which God did among you through him, as you yourselves know. [23]This man was handed over to you by God's deliberate plan and foreknowledge; and you, with the help of wicked men,[d] put him to death by nailing him to the cross. [24]But God raised him from the dead, freeing him from the agony of death, because it was impossible for death to keep its hold on him. [25]David said about him:

"'I saw the Lord always before me.
    Because he is at my right hand,
    I will not be shaken.
[26]Therefore my heart is glad and my
        tongue rejoices;
    my body also will rest in hope,
[27]because you will not abandon me to the
        realm of the dead,
    you will not let your holy one see
        decay.
[28]You have made known to me the paths
        of life;
    you will fill me with joy in your
        presence.'[e]

[29]"Fellow Israelites, I can tell you confidently that the patriarch David died and was buried, and his tomb is here to this day. [30]But he was a prophet and knew that God had promised him on oath that he would place one of his descendants on his throne. [31]Seeing what was to come, he spoke of the resurrection of the Messiah, that he was not

---

[a] 4 Or *languages*; also in verse 11   [b] 9 That is, the Roman province by that name   [c] 21 Joel 2:28-32
[d] 23 Or *of those not having the law* (that is, Gentiles)   [e] 28 Psalm 16:8-11 (see Septuagint)

NO MEMORY OF A COWARD

READ: **ACTS 2:14-15, 36-41**

What got into Peter? He was a coward at the crucifixion (John 18). A kind coward but a coward nonetheless. A question from a servant girl undid him. A soldier didn't bludgeon him. The Sanhedrin didn't browbeat him. Rome didn't threaten to export him to Siberia. No, a waitress from the downtown diner heard his accent and said he knew Jesus.

Peter panicked. He not only denied his Lord; he bleeped the very idea. But look at him on the day of Pentecost. Gutsy language. Lynch mobs feed on these accusations. The same crowd that shouted, "Crucify him!" could crucify him.

From wimp to warrior in fifty days. What happened? Oh, how we need to know. We admire the Pentecost Peter yet identify with the Passover one. We battle addictions we can't shake, pasts we can't escape, sorrow that won't fade.

What got into Peter? God's Spirit did. The Holy Spirit is not enthusiasm, compassion, or bravado. He might stimulate such emotions, but he himself is a person. He determines itineraries (Acts 16:6), distributes spiritual gifts (1 Corinthians 12:7-11), and selects church leaders (Acts 13:2). He teaches (John 14:26), guides (John 16:13), and comforts (John 16:7).

Occasional guest? No sir. The Holy Spirit is a year-round resident in the hearts of those who believe. As God's story becomes our story, his power becomes our power.

BUILDING FAITH WISDOM STRENGTH

Taken from *God's Story, Your Story: Youth Edition* by Max Lucado, copyright © 2011 by Max Lucado, published by Zondervan.

abandoned to the realm of the dead, nor did his body see decay. [32]God has raised this Jesus to life, and we are all witnesses of it. [33]Exalted to the right hand of God, he has received from the Father the promised Holy Spirit and has poured out what you now see and hear. [34]For David did not ascend to heaven, and yet he said,

> "'The Lord said to my Lord:
> "Sit at my right hand
> [35]until I make your enemies
> a footstool for your feet."'[a]

[36]"Therefore let all Israel be assured of this: God has made this Jesus, whom you crucified, both Lord and Messiah."

[37]When the people heard this, they were cut to the heart and said to Peter and the other apostles, "Brothers, what shall we do?"

[38]Peter replied, "Repent and be baptized, every one of you, in the name of Jesus Christ for the forgiveness of your sins. And you will receive the gift of the Holy Spirit. [39]The promise is for you and your children and for all who are far off — for all whom the Lord our God will call."

[40]With many other words he warned them; and he pleaded with them, "Save yourselves from this corrupt generation." [41]Those who accepted his message were baptized, and about three thousand were added to their number that day.

The Fellowship of the Believers

[42]They devoted themselves to the apostles' teaching and to fellowship, to the breaking of bread and to prayer. [43]Everyone was filled with awe at the many wonders and signs performed by the apostles. [44]All the believers were together and had everything in common. [45]They sold property and possessions to give to anyone who had need. [46]Every day they continued to meet together in the temple courts. They broke bread in their homes and ate together with glad and sincere hearts, [47]praising God and enjoying the favor of all the people. And the Lord added to their number daily those who were being saved.

Peter Heals a Lame Beggar

3 One day Peter and John were going up to the temple at the time of prayer — at three in the afternoon. [2]Now a man who was lame from birth was being carried to the temple gate called Beautiful, where he was put every day to beg from those going into the temple courts. [3]When he saw Peter and John about to enter, he asked them for money. [4]Peter looked straight at him, as did John. Then Peter said, "Look at us!" [5]So the man gave them his attention, expecting to get something from them.

[6]Then Peter said, "Silver or gold I do not have, but what I do have I give you. In the name of Jesus Christ of Nazareth, walk." [7]Taking him by the right hand, he helped him up, and instantly the man's feet and ankles became strong. [8]He jumped to his feet and began to walk. Then he went with them into the temple courts, walking and jumping, and praising God. [9]When all the people saw him walking and praising God, [10]they recognized him as the same man who used to sit begging at the temple gate called Beautiful, and they were filled with wonder and amazement at what had happened to him.

Peter Speaks to the Onlookers

[11]While the man held on to Peter and John, all the people were astonished and came running to them in the place called Solomon's Colonnade. [12]When Peter saw this, he said to them: "Fellow Israelites, why does this surprise you? Why do you stare at us as if by our own power or godliness we had made this man walk? [13]The God of Abraham, Isaac and Jacob, the God of our fathers, has glorified his servant Jesus. You handed him over to be killed, and you disowned him before Pilate, though he had decided to let him go. [14]You disowned the Holy and Righteous One and asked that a murderer be released to you. [15]You killed the author of life, but God raised him from the dead. We are witnesses of this. [16]By faith in the name of Jesus, this man whom you see and know was made strong. It is Jesus' name and the faith that comes through him that has completely healed him, as you can all see.

[17]"Now, fellow Israelites, I know that you acted in ignorance, as did your leaders. [18]But this is how God fulfilled what he had foretold through all the prophets, saying that his

[a] 35 Psalm 110:1

Messiah would suffer. [19]Repent, then, and turn to God, so that your sins may be wiped out, that times of refreshing may come from the Lord, [20]and that he may send the Messiah, who has been appointed for you — even Jesus. [21]Heaven must receive him until the time comes for God to restore everything, as he promised long ago through his holy prophets. [22]For Moses said, 'The Lord your God will raise up for you a prophet like me from among your own people; you must listen to everything he tells you. [23]Anyone who does not listen to him will be completely cut off from their people.'[a]

[24]"Indeed, beginning with Samuel, all the prophets who have spoken have foretold these days. [25]And you are heirs of the prophets and of the covenant God made with your fathers. He said to Abraham, 'Through your offspring all peoples on earth will be blessed.'[b] [26]When God raised up his servant, he sent him first to you to bless you by turning each of you from your wicked ways."

Peter and John Before the Sanhedrin

4 The priests and the captain of the temple guard and the Sadducees came up to Peter and John while they were speaking to the people. [2]They were greatly disturbed because the apostles were teaching the people, proclaiming in Jesus the resurrection of the dead. [3]They seized Peter and John and, because it was evening, they put them in jail until the next day. [4]But many who heard the message believed; so the number of men who believed grew to about five thousand.

[5]The next day the rulers, the elders and the teachers of the law met in Jerusalem. [6]Annas the high priest was there, and so were Caiaphas, John, Alexander and others of the high priest's family. [7]They had Peter and John brought before them and began to question them: "By what power or what name did you do this?"

[8]Then Peter, filled with the Holy Spirit, said to them: "Rulers and elders of the people! [9]If we are being called to account today for an act of kindness shown to a man who was lame and are being asked how he was healed, [10]then know this, you and all the people of Israel: It is by the name of Jesus Christ of Nazareth, whom you crucified but

whom God raised from the dead, that this man stands before you healed. [11]Jesus is

> "'the stone you builders rejected,
>   which has become the
>   cornerstone.'[c]

[12]Salvation is found in no one else, for there is no other name under heaven given to mankind by which we must be saved."

[13]When they saw the courage of Peter and John and realized that they were unschooled, ordinary men, they were astonished and they took note that these men had been with Jesus. [14]But since they could see the man who had been healed standing there with them, there was nothing they could say. [15]So they ordered them to withdraw from the Sanhedrin and then conferred together. [16]"What are we going to do with these men?" they asked. "Everyone living in Jerusalem knows they have performed a notable sign, and we cannot deny it. [17]But to stop this thing from spreading any further among the people, we must warn them to speak no longer to anyone in this name."

[18]Then they called them in again and commanded them not to speak or teach at all in the name of Jesus. [19]But Peter and John replied, "Which is right in God's eyes: to listen to you, or to him? You be the judges! [20]As for us, we cannot help speaking about what we have seen and heard."

[21]After further threats they let them go. They could not decide how to punish them, because all the people were praising God for what had happened. [22]For the man who was miraculously healed was over forty years old.

The Believers Pray

[23]On their release, Peter and John went back to their own people and reported all that the chief priests and the elders had said to them. [24]When they heard this, they raised their voices together in prayer to God. "Sovereign Lord," they said, "you made the heavens and the earth and the sea, and everything in them. [25]You spoke by the Holy Spirit through the mouth of your servant, our father David:

> "'Why do the nations rage
>   and the peoples plot in vain?

a 23 Deut. 18:15,18,19   *b 25* Gen. 22:18; 26:4   *c 11* Psalm 118:22

THERE'S ONLY ONE

READ: ACTS 4:12

People say you're safe to follow whatever religion you want, because they all say the same things and all point to the same God. Dedicated followers of almost every belief system disagree with that thought, and a couple thousand years ago the apostle Peter stood up and declared it isn't true.

Peter and John had been seized and put before the religious experts. They had heard reports of a man lame since birth leaping and jumping and praising God, and they wanted to know by what power the disciples had healed him (Acts 3:1–10). Peter had already told a crowd of astonished witnesses that the power wasn't their own. The real healer was Jesus (vv. 11–26).

When Peter continued his sermon in front of the religious leaders, he uttered a statement even more bold: Not only is Jesus the powerful healer, but he's the only one who can save us. Faith in him is the only way home to heaven. Those leaders were astonished by the disciples' courage, and the healing spoke for itself. But they forbade Peter and John to say anything more.

People might call you intolerant for claiming Jesus is the one real God and the only one who rescues humankind from sin. But you be the judge. Should you listen to people—or to God? He's the one who tells you to spread what you have seen and heard.

BUILDING
FAITH
WISDOM
STRENGTH

²⁶The kings of the earth rise up
  and the rulers band together
against the Lord
  and against his anointed one.*ᵃ'ᵇ*

²⁷Indeed Herod and Pontius Pilate met together with the Gentiles and the people of Israel in this city to conspire against your holy servant Jesus, whom you anointed. ²⁸They did what your power and will had decided beforehand should happen. ²⁹Now, Lord, consider their threats and enable your servants to speak your word with great boldness. ³⁰Stretch out your hand to heal and perform signs and wonders through the name of your holy servant Jesus."

³¹After they prayed, the place where they were meeting was shaken. And they were all filled with the Holy Spirit and spoke the word of God boldly.

The Believers Share Their Possessions

³²All the believers were one in heart and mind. No one claimed that any of their possessions was their own, but they shared everything they had. ³³With great power the apostles continued to testify to the resurrection of the Lord Jesus. And God's grace was so powerfully at work in them all ³⁴that there were no needy persons among them. For from time to time those who owned land or houses sold them, brought the money from the sales ³⁵and put it at the apostles' feet, and it was distributed to anyone who had need.

³⁶Joseph, a Levite from Cyprus, whom the apostles called Barnabas (which means "son of encouragement"), ³⁷sold a field he owned and brought the money and put it at the apostles' feet.

Ananias and Sapphira

5 Now a man named Ananias, together with his wife Sapphira, also sold a piece of property. ²With his wife's full knowledge he kept back part of the money for himself, but brought the rest and put it at the apostles' feet.

³Then Peter said, "Ananias, how is it that Satan has so filled your heart that you have lied to the Holy Spirit and have kept for yourself some of the money you received for the land? ⁴Didn't it belong to you before it was sold? And after it was sold, wasn't the mon-

ey at your disposal? What made you think of doing such a thing? You have not lied just to human beings but to God."

⁵When Ananias heard this, he fell down and died. And great fear seized all who heard what had happened. ⁶Then some young men came forward, wrapped up his body, and carried him out and buried him.

⁷About three hours later his wife came in, not knowing what had happened. ⁸Peter asked her, "Tell me, is this the price you and Ananias got for the land?"

"Yes," she said, "that is the price."

⁹Peter said to her, "How could you conspire to test the Spirit of the Lord? Listen! The feet of the men who buried your husband are at the door, and they will carry you out also."

¹⁰At that moment she fell down at his feet and died. Then the young men came in and, finding her dead, carried her out and buried her beside her husband. ¹¹Great fear seized the whole church and all who heard about these events.

The Apostles Heal Many

¹²The apostles performed many signs and wonders among the people. And all the believers used to meet together in Solomon's Colonnade. ¹³No one else dared join them, even though they were highly regarded by the people. ¹⁴Nevertheless, more and more men and women believed in the Lord and were added to their number. ¹⁵As a result, people brought the sick into the streets and laid them on beds and mats so that at least Peter's shadow might fall on some of them as he passed by. ¹⁶Crowds gathered also from the towns around Jerusalem, bringing their sick and those tormented by impure spirits, and all of them were healed.

The Apostles Persecuted

¹⁷Then the high priest and all his associates, who were members of the party of the Sadducees, were filled with jealousy. ¹⁸They arrested the apostles and put them in the public jail. ¹⁹But during the night an angel of the Lord opened the doors of the jail and brought them out. ²⁰"Go, stand in the temple courts," he said, "and tell the people all about this new life."

²¹At daybreak they entered the temple

ᵃ 26 That is, Messiah or Christ   *ᵇ 26* Psalm 2:1,2

GAMALIEL

But a Pharisee named Gamaliel, a teacher of the law, who was honored by all the people, stood up in the Sanhedrin and ordered that the men be put outside for a little while. ACTS 5:34

HIS NAME MEANS: "reward of God"
READ HIS STORY: *Acts 5:12–42, 22:3*

G amaliel was a well-educated and respected leader of the Jews. He was a very honored rabbi, a well-known teacher who trained Jewish boys in the ways and the heritage of their faith. When the apostle Paul was young, he was one of Gamaliel's students (Acts 22:3). Gamaliel was a member of the Pharisees, a group who followed the letter of the Jewish law down to the smallest detail. He was also an influential member of the Sanhedrin, the court of law that made important legal decisions for the Jewish people.

For all his education and influence, however, we do not know if Gamaliel ever believed in Jesus. He heard eyewitness reports of the death and resurrection of Jesus when the apostles said in Acts 5:32, "We are witnesses of these things, and so is the Holy Spirit, whom God has given to those who obey him." Gamaliel even recommended that the Sanhedrin let these men go in case they actually were from God.

But did he ever believe?

It's one thing to be highly educated and acquire book knowledge. It's another thing to take a leap of faith and believe Jesus is who he said he is. Knowledge can stand in the way of faith, but it doesn't have to. "Knowledge puffs up while love builds up" (1 Corinthians 8:1). Don't let your education or what you've learned make you miss the most important truth of all.

OF THE BIBLE

courts, as they had been told, and began to teach the people.

When the high priest and his associates arrived, they called together the Sanhedrin — the full assembly of the elders of Israel — and sent to the jail for the apostles. ²²But on arriving at the jail, the officers did not find them there. So they went back and reported, ²³"We found the jail securely locked, with the guards standing at the doors; but when we opened them, we found no one inside." ²⁴On hearing this report, the captain of the temple guard and the chief priests were at a loss, wondering what this might lead to.

²⁵Then someone came and said, "Look! The men you put in jail are standing in the temple courts teaching the people." ²⁶At that, the captain went with his officers and brought the apostles. They did not use force, because they feared that the people would stone them.

²⁷The apostles were brought in and made to appear before the Sanhedrin to be questioned by the high priest. ²⁸"We gave you strict orders not to teach in this name," he said. "Yet you have filled Jerusalem with your teaching and are determined to make us guilty of this man's blood."

²⁹Peter and the other apostles replied: "We must obey God rather than human beings! ³⁰The God of our ancestors raised Jesus from the dead — whom you killed by hanging him on a cross. ³¹God exalted him to his own right hand as Prince and Savior that he might bring Israel to repentance and forgive their sins. ³²We are witnesses of these things, and so is the Holy Spirit, whom God has given to those who obey him."

³³When they heard this, they were furious and wanted to put them to death. ³⁴But a Pharisee named Gamaliel, a teacher of the law, who was honored by all the people, stood up in the Sanhedrin and ordered that the men be put outside for a little while. ³⁵Then he addressed the Sanhedrin: "Men of Israel, consider carefully what you intend to do to these men. ³⁶Some time ago Theudas appeared, claiming to be somebody, and about four hundred men rallied to him. He was killed, all his followers were dispersed, and it all came to nothing. ³⁷After him, Judas the Galilean appeared in the days of the census and led a band of people in revolt. He too was killed, and all his followers were scattered. ³⁸Therefore, in the present case I advise you: Leave these men alone! Let them go! For if their purpose or activity is of human origin, it will fail. ³⁹But if it is from God, you will not be able to stop these men; you will only find yourselves fighting against God."

⁴⁰His speech persuaded them. They called the apostles in and had them flogged. Then they ordered them not to speak in the name of Jesus, and let them go.

⁴¹The apostles left the Sanhedrin, rejoicing because they had been counted worthy of suffering disgrace for the Name. ⁴²Day after day, in the temple courts and from house to house, they never stopped teaching and proclaiming the good news that Jesus is the Messiah.

The Choosing of the Seven

6 In those days when the number of disciples was increasing, the Hellenistic Jews^a among them complained against the Hebraic Jews because their widows were being overlooked in the daily distribution of food. ²So the Twelve gathered all the disciples together and said, "It would not be right for us to neglect the ministry of the word of God in order to wait on tables. ³Brothers and sisters, choose seven men from among you who are known to be full of the Spirit and wisdom. We will turn this responsibility over to them ⁴and will give our attention to prayer and the ministry of the word."

⁵This proposal pleased the whole group. They chose Stephen, a man full of faith and of the Holy Spirit; also Philip, Procorus, Nicanor, Timon, Parmenas, and Nicolas from Antioch, a convert to Judaism. ⁶They presented these men to the apostles, who prayed and laid their hands on them.

⁷So the word of God spread. The number of disciples in Jerusalem increased rapidly, and a large number of priests became obedient to the faith.

Stephen Seized

⁸Now Stephen, a man full of God's grace and power, performed great wonders and signs among the people. ⁹Opposition arose,

^a 1 That is, Jews who had adopted the Greek language and culture

DRAW THE LINE

READ: ACTS 6:8-14

Luke was hung by the neck from an olive tree in Greece. Doubting Thomas was stabbed with a pine spear, tortured with red-hot plates, and burned alive in India. Matthew was stabbed in the back in Ethiopia. Bartholomew was flogged to death in Armenia. And Peter was crucified upside down at his own request.

Our risks seem rather tame and most of our sacrifices seem pretty lame by comparison. Our normal is so subnormal that normal seems radical. To the first-century disciples, *normal* and *radical* were synonyms. We've turned them into antonyms.

Jesus threw down the gauntlet with his disciples. He wanted to see who was in and who was out. Or more accurately, who was all in. The disciples took that literally. We can at least take it figuratively. I'm not suggesting we will die physically for Christ, but we must die to ourselves. If Jesus hung on his cross, we can certainly carry ours! It's our highest privilege and greatest responsibility.

BUILDING FAITH WISDOM STRENGTH

Anything less than the complete surrender of our lives to the lordship of Jesus Christ is robbing God of the glory he demands and deserves. It's also cheating ourselves out of the eternal reward God has reserved for us. We won't come alive, in the truest and fullest sense, until we die to self. And we won't find ourselves until we lose ourselves in the cause of Christ.

however, from members of the Synagogue of the Freedmen (as it was called) — Jews of Cyrene and Alexandria as well as the provinces of Cilicia and Asia — who began to argue with Stephen. [10] But they could not stand up against the wisdom the Spirit gave him as he spoke.

[11] Then they secretly persuaded some men to say, "We have heard Stephen speak blasphemous words against Moses and against God."

[12] So they stirred up the people and the elders and the teachers of the law. They seized Stephen and brought him before the Sanhedrin. [13] They produced false witnesses, who testified, "This fellow never stops speaking against this holy place and against the law. [14] For we have heard him say that this Jesus of Nazareth will destroy this place and change the customs Moses handed down to us."

[15] All who were sitting in the Sanhedrin looked intently at Stephen, and they saw that his face was like the face of an angel.

Stephen's Speech to the Sanhedrin

7 Then the high priest asked Stephen, "Are these charges true?"

[2] To this he replied: "Brothers and fathers, listen to me! The God of glory appeared to our father Abraham while he was still in Mesopotamia, before he lived in Harran. [3] 'Leave your country and your people,' God said, 'and go to the land I will show you.'[a]

[4] So he left the land of the Chaldeans and settled in Harran. After the death of his father, God sent him to this land where you are now living. [5] He gave him no inheritance here, not even enough ground to set his foot on. But God promised him that he and his descendants after him would possess the land, even though at that time Abraham had no child. [6] God spoke to him in this way: 'For four hundred years your descendants will be strangers in a country not their own, and they will be enslaved and mistreated. [7] But I will punish the nation they serve as slaves,' God said, 'and afterward they will come out of that country and worship me in this place.'[b] [8] Then he gave Abraham the covenant of circumcision. And Abraham became the father of Isaac and circumcised

him eight days after his birth. Later Isaac became the father of Jacob, and Jacob became the father of the twelve patriarchs.

[9] "Because the patriarchs were jealous of Joseph, they sold him as a slave into Egypt. But God was with him [10] and rescued him from all his troubles. He gave Joseph wisdom and enabled him to gain the goodwill of Pharaoh king of Egypt. So Pharaoh made him ruler over Egypt and all his palace.

[11] "Then a famine struck all Egypt and Canaan, bringing great suffering, and our ancestors could not find food. [12] When Jacob heard that there was grain in Egypt, he sent our forefathers on their first visit. [13] On their second visit, Joseph told his brothers who he was, and Pharaoh learned about Joseph's family. [14] After this, Joseph sent for his father Jacob and his whole family, seventy-five in all. [15] Then Jacob went down to Egypt, where he and our ancestors died. [16] Their bodies were brought back to Shechem and placed in the tomb that Abraham had bought from the sons of Hamor at Shechem for a certain sum of money.

[17] "As the time drew near for God to fulfill his promise to Abraham, the number of our people in Egypt had greatly increased. [18] Then 'a new king, to whom Joseph meant nothing, came to power in Egypt.'[c] [19] He dealt treacherously with our people and oppressed our ancestors by forcing them to throw out their newborn babies so that they would die.

[20] "At that time Moses was born, and he was no ordinary child.[d] For three months he was cared for by his family. [21] When he was placed outside, Pharaoh's daughter took him and brought him up as her own son. [22] Moses was educated in all the wisdom of the Egyptians and was powerful in speech and action.

[23] "When Moses was forty years old, he decided to visit his own people, the Israelites. [24] He saw one of them being mistreated by an Egyptian, so he went to his defense and avenged him by killing the Egyptian. [25] Moses thought that his own people would realize that God was using him to rescue them, but they did not. [26] The next day Moses came upon two Israelites who were fighting. He tried to reconcile them by saying, 'Men, you

---

[a] 3 Gen. 12:1   [b] 7 Gen. 15:13,14   [c] 18 Exodus 1:8   [d] 20 Or *was fair in the sight of God*

are brothers; why do you want to hurt each other?'

²⁷"But the man who was mistreating the other pushed Moses aside and said, 'Who made you ruler and judge over us? ²⁸Are you thinking of killing me as you killed the Egyptian yesterday?'ᵃ ²⁹When Moses heard this, he fled to Midian, where he settled as a foreigner and had two sons.

³⁰"After forty years had passed, an angel appeared to Moses in the flames of a burning bush in the desert near Mount Sinai. ³¹When he saw this, he was amazed at the sight. As he went over to get a closer look, he heard the Lord say: ³²'I am the God of your fathers, the God of Abraham, Isaac and Jacob.'ᵇ Moses trembled with fear and did not dare to look.

³³"Then the Lord said to him, 'Take off your sandals, for the place where you are standing is holy ground. ³⁴I have indeed seen the oppression of my people in Egypt. I have heard their groaning and have come down to set them free. Now come, I will send you back to Egypt.'ᶜ

³⁵"This is the same Moses they had rejected with the words, 'Who made you ruler and judge?' He was sent to be their ruler and deliverer by God himself, through the angel who appeared to him in the bush. ³⁶He led them out of Egypt and performed wonders and signs in Egypt, at the Red Sea and for forty years in the wilderness.

³⁷"This is the Moses who told the Israelites, 'God will raise up for you a prophet like me from your own people.'ᵈ ³⁸He was in the assembly in the wilderness, with the angel who spoke to him on Mount Sinai, and with our ancestors; and he received living words to pass on to us.

³⁹"But our ancestors refused to obey him. Instead, they rejected him and in their hearts turned back to Egypt. ⁴⁰They told Aaron, 'Make us gods who will go before us. As for this fellow Moses who led us out of Egypt— we don't know what has happened to him!'ᵉ ⁴¹That was the time they made an idol in the form of a calf. They brought sacrifices to it and reveled in what their own hands had made. ⁴²But God turned away from them and gave them over to the worship of the sun, moon and stars. This agrees with what is written in the book of the prophets:

" 'Did you bring me sacrifices and
    offerings
forty years in the wilderness, people of
    Israel?
⁴³You have taken up the tabernacle of
    Molek
and the star of your god Rephan,
    the idols you made to worship.
Therefore I will send you into exile'ᶠ
    beyond Babylon.

⁴⁴"Our ancestors had the tabernacle of the covenant law with them in the wilderness. It had been made as God directed Moses, according to the pattern he had seen. ⁴⁵After receiving the tabernacle, our ancestors under Joshua brought it with them when they took the land from the nations God drove out before them. It remained in the land until the time of David, ⁴⁶who enjoyed God's favor and asked that he might provide a dwelling place for the God of Jacob.ᵍ ⁴⁷But it was Solomon who built a house for him.

⁴⁸"However, the Most High does not live in houses made by human hands. As the prophet says:

⁴⁹" 'Heaven is my throne,
    and the earth is my footstool.
What kind of house will you build for me?
                says the Lord.
    Or where will my resting place be?
⁵⁰Has not my hand made all these things?'ʰ

⁵¹"You stiff-necked people! Your hearts and ears are still uncircumcised. You are just like your ancestors: You always resist the Holy Spirit! ⁵²Was there ever a prophet your ancestors did not persecute? They even killed those who predicted the coming of the Righteous One. And now you have betrayed and murdered him— ⁵³you who have received the law that was given through angels but have not obeyed it."

The Stoning of Stephen

⁵⁴When the members of the Sanhedrin heard this, they were furious and gnashed their teeth at him. ⁵⁵But Stephen, full of the Holy Spirit, looked up to heaven and saw the

---

ᵃ 28 Exodus 2:14   ᵇ 32 Exodus 3:6   ᶜ 34 Exodus 3:5,7,8,10   ᵈ 37 Deut. 18:15   ᵉ 40 Exodus 32:1
ᶠ 43 Amos 5:25-27 (see Septuagint)   ᵍ 46 Some early manuscripts the house of Jacob
ʰ 50 Isaiah 66:1,2

PATRON SAINT OF SECOND CHANCES

READ: **ACTS 7:30-36**

You might feel passed by at some point in your life. Your dream seems like a lost cause. Reality just doesn't measure up. But the "crisis" presents us with a choice: throw in the towel once and for all or throw our hat back in the ring.

Too many people give up. They call it quits because they feel like it's too late. But Moses is the patron saint of second chances. And third. And tenth. And hundredth. No matter how many wrong turns we've taken and no matter how many detours we've been down, it's God's grace that gets us back into the party.

BUILDING
FAITH
WISDOM
STRENGTH

The irony of the Exodus story is that even though Moses thought he was unqualified, God used every past experience to prepare him for his date with destiny. No one knew the palace like the prince of Egypt. After all, he grew up in the thing! And after tending sheep for forty years, he knew the ways of the wilderness—the wildlife, the watering holes, the weather patterns. The sheep were practice for the Israelites, who were basically sheep.

Going all in for God isn't something you do once. You'll probably get it wrong more than once before you get it right. But it's just as important as success. Failure is the fertilizer that grows character—which means success won't backfire on you.

Taken from *All In Student Edition* by Mark Batterson and Parker Batterson, copyright © 2014 by Mark Batterson, published by Zondervan.

glory of God, and Jesus standing at the right hand of God. [56]"Look," he said, "I see heaven open and the Son of Man standing at the right hand of God."

[57]At this they covered their ears and, yelling at the top of their voices, they all rushed at him, [58]dragged him out of the city and began to stone him. Meanwhile, the witnesses laid their coats at the feet of a young man named Saul.

[59]While they were stoning him, Stephen prayed, "Lord Jesus, receive my spirit." [60]Then he fell on his knees and cried out, "Lord, do not hold this sin against them." When he had said this, he fell asleep.

8 And Saul approved of their killing him.

The Church Persecuted and Scattered

On that day a great persecution broke out against the church in Jerusalem, and all except the apostles were scattered throughout Judea and Samaria. [2]Godly men buried Stephen and mourned deeply for him. [3]But Saul began to destroy the church. Going from house to house, he dragged off both men and women and put them in prison.

Philip in Samaria

[4]Those who had been scattered preached the word wherever they went. [5]Philip went down to a city in Samaria and proclaimed the Messiah there. [6]When the crowds heard Philip and saw the signs he performed, they all paid close attention to what he said. [7]For with shrieks, impure spirits came out of many, and many who were paralyzed or lame were healed. [8]So there was great joy in that city.

Simon the Sorcerer

[9]Now for some time a man named Simon had practiced sorcery in the city and amazed all the people of Samaria. He boasted that he was someone great, [10]and all the people, both high and low, gave him their attention and exclaimed, "This man is rightly called the Great Power of God." [11]They followed him because he had amazed them for a long time with his sorcery. [12]But when they believed Philip as he proclaimed the good news of the kingdom of God and the name of Jesus Christ, they were baptized, both men

and women. [13]Simon himself believed and was baptized. And he followed Philip everywhere, astonished by the great signs and miracles he saw.

[14]When the apostles in Jerusalem heard that Samaria had accepted the word of God, they sent Peter and John to Samaria. [15]When they arrived, they prayed for the new believers there that they might receive the Holy Spirit, [16]because the Holy Spirit had not yet come on any of them; they had simply been baptized in the name of the Lord Jesus. [17]Then Peter and John placed their hands on them, and they received the Holy Spirit.

[18]When Simon saw that the Spirit was given at the laying on of the apostles' hands, he offered them money [19]and said, "Give me also this ability so that everyone on whom I lay my hands may receive the Holy Spirit."

[20]Peter answered: "May your money perish with you, because you thought you could buy the gift of God with money! [21]You have no part or share in this ministry, because your heart is not right before God. [22]Repent of this wickedness and pray to the Lord in the hope that he may forgive you for having such a thought in your heart. [23]For I see that you are full of bitterness and captive to sin."

[24]Then Simon answered, "Pray to the Lord for me so that nothing you have said may happen to me."

[25]After they had further proclaimed the word of the Lord and testified about Jesus, Peter and John returned to Jerusalem, preaching the gospel in many Samaritan villages.

Philip and the Ethiopian

[26]Now an angel of the Lord said to Philip, "Go south to the road — the desert road — that goes down from Jerusalem to Gaza." [27]So he started out, and on his way he met an Ethiopian[a] eunuch, an important official in charge of all the treasury of the Kandake (which means "queen of the Ethiopians"). This man had gone to Jerusalem to worship, [28]and on his way home was sitting in his chariot reading the Book of Isaiah the prophet. [29]The Spirit told Philip, "Go to that chariot and stay near it."

[30]Then Philip ran up to the chariot and heard the man reading Isaiah the prophet.

---

[a] 27 That is, from the southern Nile region

CASUAL CONVERSATION

READ: ACTS 8:26-39

How do you start the conversation when the opportunity comes to share the gospel? Two questions will help broach the subject. Usually, when you get the chance to share your faith, it's because your friend asks you something with a spiritual connotation. But maybe you sense the time is right. Maybe you feel God nudging you. Here it is: "In your opinion, what does it take for someone to go to heaven?"

You start by asking the other person's opinion. People like that. Now you have a conversation. There is no plan needed for this question. But our friend's answer will tell us where she is spiritually.

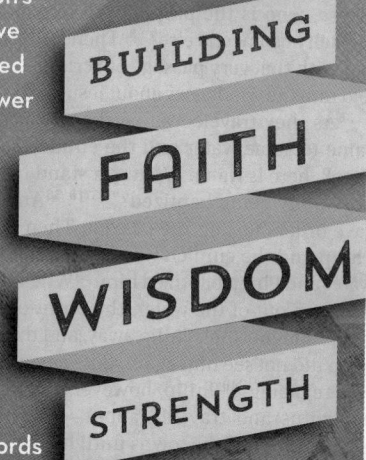

Second question: "Can I show you how the Bible answers that question?"

Now that may feel uncomfortable. What if the other person answers no? Uh-oh, what do you do?

Know Jesus.

Love your friend.

Keep listening.

Keep building a bridge with your words and your life.

What if the other person says, "I don't believe the Bible"?

Then try this: "OK, I understand. Let me show you what the Bible says so you can at least know what's in there. Then you can totally rule it out if you don't believe it."

Keep a Bible with you (a Bible app on your cell phone is helpful) and say, "Let me show you a few verses." Have your friend read the verses along with you. It helps to be able to show that what you're saying is in God's Word (Romans 3:23, 5:8, 6:23, 10:9, 2 Corinthians 5:20-21).

"Do you understand what you are reading?" Philip asked.

³¹ "How can I," he said, "unless someone explains it to me?" So he invited Philip to come up and sit with him.

³² This is the passage of Scripture the eunuch was reading:

> "He was led like a sheep to the slaughter,
>   and as a lamb before its shearer is
>   silent,
>   so he did not open his mouth.
> ³³ In his humiliation he was deprived of
>   justice.
>   Who can speak of his descendants?
>   For his life was taken from the earth."ᵃ

³⁴ The eunuch asked Philip, "Tell me, please, who is the prophet talking about, himself or someone else?" ³⁵ Then Philip began with that very passage of Scripture and told him the good news about Jesus.

³⁶ As they traveled along the road, they came to some water and the eunuch said, "Look, here is water. What can stand in the way of my being baptized?" [³⁷] ᵇ ³⁸ And he gave orders to stop the chariot. Then both Philip and the eunuch went down into the water and Philip baptized him. ³⁹ When they came up out of the water, the Spirit of the Lord suddenly took Philip away, and the eunuch did not see him again, but went on his way rejoicing. ⁴⁰ Philip, however, appeared at Azotus and traveled about, preaching the gospel in all the towns until he reached Caesarea.

Saul's Conversion

9 Meanwhile, Saul was still breathing out murderous threats against the Lord's disciples. He went to the high priest ² and asked him for letters to the synagogues in Damascus, so that if he found any there who belonged to the Way, whether men or women, he might take them as prisoners to Jerusalem. ³ As he neared Damascus on his journey, suddenly a light from heaven flashed around him. ⁴ He fell to the ground and heard a voice say to him, "Saul, Saul, why do you persecute me?"

⁵ "Who are you, Lord?" Saul asked.

"I am Jesus, whom you are persecuting," he replied. ⁶ "Now get up and go into the city, and you will be told what you must do."

⁷ The men traveling with Saul stood there speechless; they heard the sound but did not see anyone. ⁸ Saul got up from the ground, but when he opened his eyes he could see nothing. So they led him by the hand into Damascus. ⁹ For three days he was blind, and did not eat or drink anything.

¹⁰ In Damascus there was a disciple named Ananias. The Lord called to him in a vision, "Ananias!"

"Yes, Lord," he answered.

¹¹ The Lord told him, "Go to the house of Judas on Straight Street and ask for a man from Tarsus named Saul, for he is praying. ¹² In a vision he has seen a man named Ananias come and place his hands on him to restore his sight."

¹³ "Lord," Ananias answered, "I have heard many reports about this man and all the harm he has done to your holy people in Jerusalem. ¹⁴ And he has come here with authority from the chief priests to arrest all who call on your name."

¹⁵ But the Lord said to Ananias, "Go! This man is my chosen instrument to proclaim my name to the Gentiles and their kings and to the people of Israel. ¹⁶ I will show him how much he must suffer for my name."

¹⁷ Then Ananias went to the house and entered it. Placing his hands on Saul, he said, "Brother Saul, the Lord — Jesus, who appeared to you on the road as you were coming here — has sent me so that you may see again and be filled with the Holy Spirit." ¹⁸ Immediately, something like scales fell from Saul's eyes, and he could see again. He got up and was baptized, ¹⁹ and after taking some food, he regained his strength.

Saul in Damascus and Jerusalem

Saul spent several days with the disciples in Damascus. ²⁰ At once he began to preach in the synagogues that Jesus is the Son of God. ²¹ All those who heard him were astonished and asked, "Isn't he the man who raised havoc in Jerusalem among those who call on this name? And hasn't he come here to take them as prisoners to the chief priests?" ²² Yet Saul grew more and more

---

ᵃ 33 Isaiah 53:7,8 (see Septuagint)   ᵇ 37 Some manuscripts include here *Philip said, "If you believe with all your heart, you may." The eunuch answered, "I believe that Jesus Christ is the Son of God."*

powerful and baffled the Jews living in Damascus by proving that Jesus is the Messiah.

²³After many days had gone by, there was a conspiracy among the Jews to kill him, ²⁴but Saul learned of their plan. Day and night they kept close watch on the city gates in order to kill him. ²⁵But his followers took him by night and lowered him in a basket through an opening in the wall.

²⁶When he came to Jerusalem, he tried to join the disciples, but they were all afraid of him, not believing that he really was a disciple. ²⁷But Barnabas took him and brought him to the apostles. He told them how Saul on his journey had seen the Lord and that the Lord had spoken to him, and how in Damascus he had preached fearlessly in the name of Jesus. ²⁸So Saul stayed with them and moved about freely in Jerusalem, speaking boldly in the name of the Lord. ²⁹He talked and debated with the Hellenistic Jews,ᵃ but they tried to kill him. ³⁰When the believers learned of this, they took him down to Caesarea and sent him off to Tarsus.

³¹Then the church throughout Judea, Galilee and Samaria enjoyed a time of peace and was strengthened. Living in the fear of the Lord and encouraged by the Holy Spirit, it increased in numbers.

Aeneas and Dorcas

³²As Peter traveled about the country, he went to visit the Lord's people who lived in Lydda. ³³There he found a man named Aeneas, who was paralyzed and had been bedridden for eight years. ³⁴"Aeneas," Peter said to him, "Jesus Christ heals you. Get up and roll up your mat." Immediately Aeneas got up. ³⁵All those who lived in Lydda and Sharon saw him and turned to the Lord.

³⁶In Joppa there was a disciple named Tabitha (in Greek her name is Dorcas); she was always doing good and helping the poor. ³⁷About that time she became sick and died, and her body was washed and placed in an upstairs room. ³⁸Lydda was near Joppa; so when the disciples heard that Peter was in Lydda, they sent two men to him and urged him, "Please come at once!"

³⁹Peter went with them, and when he arrived he was taken upstairs to the room. All the widows stood around him, crying and showing him the robes and other clothing that Dorcas had made while she was still with them.

⁴⁰Peter sent them all out of the room; then he got down on his knees and prayed. Turning toward the dead woman, he said, "Tabitha, get up." She opened her eyes, and seeing Peter she sat up. ⁴¹He took her by the hand and helped her to her feet. Then he called for the believers, especially the widows, and presented her to them alive. ⁴²This became known all over Joppa, and many people believed in the Lord. ⁴³Peter stayed in Joppa for some time with a tanner named Simon.

Cornelius Calls for Peter

10 At Caesarea there was a man named Cornelius, a centurion in what was known as the Italian Regiment. ²He and all his family were devout and God-fearing; he gave generously to those in need and prayed to God regularly. ³One day at about three in the afternoon he had a vision. He distinctly saw an angel of God, who came to him and said, "Cornelius!"

⁴Cornelius stared at him in fear. "What is it, Lord?" he asked.

The angel answered, "Your prayers and gifts to the poor have come up as a memorial offering before God. ⁵Now send men to Joppa to bring back a man named Simon who is called Peter. ⁶He is staying with Simon the tanner, whose house is by the sea."

⁷When the angel who spoke to him had gone, Cornelius called two of his servants and a devout soldier who was one of his attendants. ⁸He told them everything that had happened and sent them to Joppa.

Peter's Vision

⁹About noon the following day as they were on their journey and approaching the city, Peter went up on the roof to pray. ¹⁰He became hungry and wanted something to eat, and while the meal was being prepared, he fell into a trance. ¹¹He saw heaven opened and something like a large sheet being let down to earth by its four corners. ¹²It contained all kinds of four-footed animals, as well as reptiles and birds. ¹³Then a voice told him, "Get up, Peter. Kill and eat."

ᵃ 29 That is, Jews who had adopted the Greek language and culture

¹⁴"Surely not, Lord!" Peter replied. "I have never eaten anything impure or unclean."

¹⁵The voice spoke to him a second time, "Do not call anything impure that God has made clean."

¹⁶This happened three times, and immediately the sheet was taken back to heaven.

¹⁷While Peter was wondering about the meaning of the vision, the men sent by Cornelius found out where Simon's house was and stopped at the gate. ¹⁸They called out, asking if Simon who was known as Peter was staying there.

¹⁹While Peter was still thinking about the vision, the Spirit said to him, "Simon, three*a* men are looking for you. ²⁰So get up and go downstairs. Do not hesitate to go with them, for I have sent them."

²¹Peter went down and said to the men, "I'm the one you're looking for. Why have you come?"

²²The men replied, "We have come from Cornelius the centurion. He is a righteous and God-fearing man, who is respected by all the Jewish people. A holy angel told him to ask you to come to his house so that he could hear what you have to say." ²³Then Peter invited the men into the house to be his guests.

Peter at Cornelius's House

The next day Peter started out with them, and some of the believers from Joppa went along. ²⁴The following day he arrived in Caesarea. Cornelius was expecting them and had called together his relatives and close friends. ²⁵As Peter entered the house, Cornelius met him and fell at his feet in reverence. ²⁶But Peter made him get up. "Stand up," he said, "I am only a man myself."

²⁷While talking with him, Peter went inside and found a large gathering of people. ²⁸He said to them: "You are well aware that it is against our law for a Jew to associate with or visit a Gentile. But God has shown me that I should not call anyone impure or unclean. ²⁹So when I was sent for, I came without raising any objection. May I ask why you sent for me?"

³⁰Cornelius answered: "Three days ago I was in my house praying at this hour, at three in the afternoon. Suddenly a man in shining clothes stood before me ³¹and said, 'Cornelius, God has heard your prayer and remembered your gifts to the poor. ³²Send to Joppa for Simon who is called Peter. He is a guest in the home of Simon the tanner, who lives by the sea.' ³³So I sent for you immediately, and it was good of you to come. Now we are all here in the presence of God to listen to everything the Lord has commanded you to tell us."

³⁴Then Peter began to speak: "I now realize how true it is that God does not show favoritism ³⁵but accepts from every nation the one who fears him and does what is right. ³⁶You know the message God sent to the people of Israel, announcing the good news of peace through Jesus Christ, who is Lord of all. ³⁷You know what has happened throughout the province of Judea, beginning in Galilee after the baptism that John preached—³⁸how God anointed Jesus of Nazareth with the Holy Spirit and power, and how he went around doing good and healing all who were under the power of the devil, because God was with him.

³⁹"We are witnesses of everything he did in the country of the Jews and in Jerusalem. They killed him by hanging him on a cross, ⁴⁰but God raised him from the dead on the third day and caused him to be seen. ⁴¹He was not seen by all the people, but by witnesses whom God had already chosen—by us who ate and drank with him after he rose from the dead. ⁴²He commanded us to preach to the people and to testify that he is the one whom God appointed as judge of the living and the dead. ⁴³All the prophets testify about him that everyone who believes in him receives forgiveness of sins through his name."

⁴⁴While Peter was still speaking these words, the Holy Spirit came on all who heard the message. ⁴⁵The circumcised believers who had come with Peter were astonished that the gift of the Holy Spirit had been poured out even on Gentiles. ⁴⁶For they heard them speaking in tongues*b* and praising God.

Then Peter said, ⁴⁷"Surely no one can stand in the way of their being baptized with water. They have received the Holy Spirit just as we have." ⁴⁸So he ordered that they be baptized in the name of Jesus Christ. Then

---

a 19 One early manuscript *two*; other manuscripts do not have the number.   *b* 46 Or *other languages*

I'LL TAKE THAT TOO

READ: ACTS 10:47-48

I was reading about a strange practice when the Knights of Templar would be baptized. When the church would baptize a knight, he would be baptized with his sword, but he wouldn't take his sword underwater with him. Instead he would hold his sword up out of the water. It was the knights' way of saying to Jesus, "You can have control of me but you can't have this. Jesus, I'm all yours, but who I am and what I do on the battlefield, how I use this sword, that's not part of the deal."

And if that was still the practice today, we might not hold up a sword, but many would hold up a wallet or a remote control. Others would hold up a laptop.

Jesus doesn't want followers who have a split allegiance. And so Jesus points to what you most value and are most concerned about, and says, "What about that?"

When you accept the invitation of Jesus to follow him, you are not just saying that he is a top priority in your life; you are making him the only priority in your life. He desperately wants you, but he won't share you. He wants you to invest in him more than your car or your clothes. He wants you to surrender to him more of your time than your friends get from of you. He wants you to expel more joy and energy in worshiping him than you do watching the big game. He will settle for nothing less.

BUILDING FAITH WISDOM STRENGTH

they asked Peter to stay with them for a few days.

Peter Explains His Actions

11 The apostles and the believers throughout Judea heard that the Gentiles also had received the word of God. ²So when Peter went up to Jerusalem, the circumcised believers criticized him ³and said, "You went into the house of uncircumcised men and ate with them."

⁴Starting from the beginning, Peter told them the whole story: ⁵"I was in the city of Joppa praying, and in a trance I saw a vision. I saw something like a large sheet being let down from heaven by its four corners, and it came down to where I was. ⁶I looked into it and saw four-footed animals of the earth, wild beasts, reptiles and birds. ⁷Then I heard a voice telling me, 'Get up, Peter. Kill and eat.'

⁸"I replied, 'Surely not, Lord! Nothing impure or unclean has ever entered my mouth.'

⁹"The voice spoke from heaven a second time, 'Do not call anything impure that God has made clean.' ¹⁰This happened three times, and then it was all pulled up to heaven again.

¹¹"Right then three men who had been sent to me from Caesarea stopped at the house where I was staying. ¹²The Spirit told me to have no hesitation about going with them. These six brothers also went with me, and we entered the man's house. ¹³He told us how he had seen an angel appear in his house and say, 'Send to Joppa for Simon who is called Peter. ¹⁴He will bring you a message through which you and all your household will be saved.'

¹⁵"As I began to speak, the Holy Spirit came on them as he had come on us at the beginning. ¹⁶Then I remembered what the Lord had said: 'John baptized with*ᵃ* water, but you will be baptized with*ᵃ* the Holy Spirit.' ¹⁷So if God gave them the same gift he gave us who believed in the Lord Jesus Christ, who was I to think that I could stand in God's way?"

¹⁸When they heard this, they had no further objections and praised God, saying, "So then, even to Gentiles God has granted repentance that leads to life."

The Church in Antioch

¹⁹Now those who had been scattered by the persecution that broke out when Stephen was killed traveled as far as Phoenicia, Cyprus and Antioch, spreading the word only among Jews. ²⁰Some of them, however, men from Cyprus and Cyrene, went to Antioch and began to speak to Greeks also, telling them the good news about the Lord Jesus. ²¹The Lord's hand was with them, and a great number of people believed and turned to the Lord.

²²News of this reached the church in Jerusalem, and they sent Barnabas to Antioch. ²³When he arrived and saw what the grace of God had done, he was glad and encouraged them all to remain true to the Lord with all their hearts. ²⁴He was a good man, full of the Holy Spirit and faith, and a great number of people were brought to the Lord.

²⁵Then Barnabas went to Tarsus to look for Saul, ²⁶and when he found him, he brought him to Antioch. So for a whole year Barnabas and Saul met with the church and taught great numbers of people. The disciples were called Christians first at Antioch.

²⁷During this time some prophets came down from Jerusalem to Antioch. ²⁸One of them, named Agabus, stood up and through the Spirit predicted that a severe famine would spread over the entire Roman world. (This happened during the reign of Claudius.) ²⁹The disciples, as each one was able, decided to provide help for the brothers and sisters living in Judea. ³⁰This they did, sending their gift to the elders by Barnabas and Saul.

Peter's Miraculous Escape From Prison

12 It was about this time that King Herod arrested some who belonged to the church, intending to persecute them. ²He had James, the brother of John, put to death with the sword. ³When he saw that this met with approval among the Jews, he proceeded to seize Peter also. This happened during the Festival of Unleavened Bread. ⁴After arresting him, he put him in prison, handing him over to be guarded by four squads of four soldiers each. Herod intended to bring him out for public trial after the Passover.

ᵃ 16 Or *in*

MEN

OF THE BIBLE

BARNABAS

When [Barnabas] arrived and saw what the grace of God had done, he was glad and encouraged them all to remain true to the Lord with all their hearts. He was a good man, full of the Holy Spirit and faith, and a great number of people were brought to the Lord. ACTS 11:23-24

HIS NAME MEANS: "son of encouragement"
READ HIS STORY: *Acts 4:36-37, 9:26-31, 11:19-30, 12:25—15:41*

The heart and ministry of Barnabas centered on encouraging other believers. When Paul arrived in Jerusalem after his conversion, the other Christians were afraid of him. It was Barnabas who accepted the new believer into their ranks and encouraged the others to believe Paul's testimony.

Sometime after that, Barnabas sought out Paul and brought him to Antioch. Then they set out on a missionary journey. Later, when Paul did not want to give Barnabas' younger cousin a second chance, Barnabas did. Barnabas took John Mark along with him on a second missionary journey even though his cousin hadn't done well on the first. Together, Barnabas and John Mark sailed to Cyprus and continued their missionary work. Barnabas helped John Mark grow stronger as a believer. Eventually, John Mark went on to continue in ministry with Paul and to write the Gospel of Mark.

Barnabas was an encourager and mentor of others. You can encourage and mentor others too. Do you know any new believers? Encourage them to be strong and grow in their faith. Do you know Christians who are younger than you, such as a younger sibling or a cousin? Invite them to serve alongside you. If they mess up, give them a second chance. Be a Barnabas.

[5]So Peter was kept in prison, but the church was earnestly praying to God for him.

[6]The night before Herod was to bring him to trial, Peter was sleeping between two soldiers, bound with two chains, and sentries stood guard at the entrance. [7]Suddenly an angel of the Lord appeared and a light shone in the cell. He struck Peter on the side and woke him up. "Quick, get up!" he said, and the chains fell off Peter's wrists.

[8]Then the angel said to him, "Put on your clothes and sandals." And Peter did so. "Wrap your cloak around you and follow me," the angel told him. [9]Peter followed him out of the prison, but he had no idea that what the angel was doing was really happening; he thought he was seeing a vision. [10]They passed the first and second guards and came to the iron gate leading to the city. It opened for them by itself, and they went through it. When they had walked the length of one street, suddenly the angel left him.

[11]Then Peter came to himself and said, "Now I know without a doubt that the Lord has sent his angel and rescued me from Herod's clutches and from everything the Jewish people were hoping would happen."

[12]When this had dawned on him, he went to the house of Mary the mother of John, also called Mark, where many people had gathered and were praying. [13]Peter knocked at the outer entrance, and a servant named Rhoda came to answer the door. [14]When she recognized Peter's voice, she was so overjoyed she ran back without opening it and exclaimed, "Peter is at the door!"

[15]"You're out of your mind," they told her. When she kept insisting that it was so, they said, "It must be his angel."

[16]But Peter kept on knocking, and when they opened the door and saw him, they were astonished. [17]Peter motioned with his hand for them to be quiet and described how the Lord had brought him out of prison. "Tell James and the other brothers and sisters about this," he said, and then he left for another place.

[18]In the morning, there was no small commotion among the soldiers as to what had become of Peter. [19]After Herod had a thorough search made for him and did not find him, he cross-examined the guards and ordered that they be executed.

Herod's Death

Then Herod went from Judea to Caesarea and stayed there. [20]He had been quarreling with the people of Tyre and Sidon; they now joined together and sought an audience with him. After securing the support of Blastus, a trusted personal servant of the king, they asked for peace, because they depended on the king's country for their food supply.

[21]On the appointed day Herod, wearing his royal robes, sat on his throne and delivered a public address to the people. [22]They shouted, "This is the voice of a god, not of a man." [23]Immediately, because Herod did not give praise to God, an angel of the Lord struck him down, and he was eaten by worms and died.

[24]But the word of God continued to spread and flourish.

Barnabas and Saul Sent Off

[25]When Barnabas and Saul had finished their mission, they returned from[a] Jerusalem, taking with them John, also called Mark. **13** [1]Now in the church at Antioch there were prophets and teachers: Barnabas, Simeon called Niger, Lucius of Cyrene, Manaen (who had been brought up with Herod the tetrarch) and Saul. [2]While they were worshiping the Lord and fasting, the Holy Spirit said, "Set apart for me Barnabas and Saul for the work to which I have called them." [3]So after they had fasted and prayed, they placed their hands on them and sent them off.

On Cyprus

[4]The two of them, sent on their way by the Holy Spirit, went down to Seleucia and sailed from there to Cyprus. [5]When they arrived at Salamis, they proclaimed the word of God in the Jewish synagogues. John was with them as their helper.

[6]They traveled through the whole island until they came to Paphos. There they met a Jewish sorcerer and false prophet named Bar-Jesus, [7]who was an attendant of the proconsul, Sergius Paulus. The proconsul, an intelligent man, sent for Barnabas and

_____
[a] 25 Some manuscripts *to*

EXPECTED SUFFERING

READ: ACTS 12:7

Christians felt the heat of persecution almost immediately after Jesus rose from the dead. His closest followers hid from their religious opponents (John 20:19). Peter and John were put on trial for teaching about the Lord (Acts 4:1–5:42). Stephen was killed for his faith (7:54–60). After his death, "a great persecution broke out against the church in Jerusalem," scattering believers everywhere (8:1–3). As time passed, there was little relief from the new believers' suffering. Soon one of the Lord's best friends, James, was beheaded, and another, Peter, was tossed in prison, sure to face the same doom.

Peter was shackled between two guards when an intense light filled his cell. He woke when an angel hit him, and as he got up his chains fell off. Until the reality of his escape sunk in, he thought it was all too good to be true. Peter's freedom was so shocking that when he arrived at a house where others were praying for him, a servant girl ran away happy and left him at the door.

Suffering for your faith should never surprise you, because the Bible shows it's an inescapable fact of following Jesus. Sometimes God pulls off surprising rescues that leave you and others gleefully bewildered. But even in the worst of circumstances, you can be sure the Lord watches over you.

BUILDING
FAITH
WISDOM
STRENGTH

Saul because he wanted to hear the word of God. [8] But Elymas the sorcerer (for that is what his name means) opposed them and tried to turn the proconsul from the faith. [9] Then Saul, who was also called Paul, filled with the Holy Spirit, looked straight at Elymas and said, [10] "You are a child of the devil and an enemy of everything that is right! You are full of all kinds of deceit and trickery. Will you never stop perverting the right ways of the Lord? [11] Now the hand of the Lord is against you. You are going to be blind for a time, not even able to see the light of the sun."

Immediately mist and darkness came over him, and he groped about, seeking someone to lead him by the hand. [12] When the proconsul saw what had happened, he believed, for he was amazed at the teaching about the Lord.

In Pisidian Antioch

[13] From Paphos, Paul and his companions sailed to Perga in Pamphylia, where John left them to return to Jerusalem. [14] From Perga they went on to Pisidian Antioch. On the Sabbath they entered the synagogue and sat down. [15] After the reading from the Law and the Prophets, the leaders of the synagogue sent word to them, saying, "Brothers, if you have a word of exhortation for the people, please speak."

[16] Standing up, Paul motioned with his hand and said: "Fellow Israelites and you Gentiles who worship God, listen to me! [17] The God of the people of Israel chose our ancestors; he made the people prosper during their stay in Egypt; with mighty power he led them out of that country; [18] for about forty years he endured their conduct[a] in the wilderness; [19] and he overthrew seven nations in Canaan, giving their land to his people as their inheritance. [20] All this took about 450 years.

"After this, God gave them judges until the time of Samuel the prophet. [21] Then the people asked for a king, and he gave them Saul son of Kish, of the tribe of Benjamin, who ruled forty years. [22] After removing Saul, he made David their king. God testified concerning him: 'I have found David son of Jesse, a man after my own heart; he will do everything I want him to do.'

[23] "From this man's descendants God has brought to Israel the Savior Jesus, as he promised. [24] Before the coming of Jesus, John preached repentance and baptism to all the people of Israel. [25] As John was completing his work, he said: 'Who do you suppose I am? I am not the one you are looking for. But there is one coming after me whose sandals I am not worthy to untie.'

[26] "Fellow children of Abraham and you God-fearing Gentiles, it is to us that this message of salvation has been sent. [27] The people of Jerusalem and their rulers did not recognize Jesus, yet in condemning him they fulfilled the words of the prophets that are read every Sabbath. [28] Though they found no proper ground for a death sentence, they asked Pilate to have him executed. [29] When they had carried out all that was written about him, they took him down from the cross and laid him in a tomb. [30] But God raised him from the dead, [31] and for many days he was seen by those who had traveled with him from Galilee to Jerusalem. They are now his witnesses to our people.

[32] "We tell you the good news: What God promised our ancestors [33] he has fulfilled for us, their children, by raising up Jesus. As it is written in the second Psalm:

> " 'You are my son;
>> today I have become your father.'[b]

[34] God raised him from the dead so that he will never be subject to decay. As God has said,

> " 'I will give you the holy and sure
>> blessings promised to David.'[c]

[35] So it is also stated elsewhere:

> " 'You will not let your holy one see
>> decay.'[d]

[36] "Now when David had served God's purpose in his own generation, he fell asleep; he was buried with his ancestors and his body decayed. [37] But the one whom God raised from the dead did not see decay.

[38] "Therefore, my friends, I want you to know that through Jesus the forgiveness of sins is proclaimed to you. [39] Through him everyone who believes is set free from every sin, a justification you were not able to

---

[a] 18 Some manuscripts *he cared for them*   [b] 33 Psalm 2:7   [c] 34 Isaiah 55:3   [d] 35 Psalm 16:10 (see Septuagint)

obtain under the law of Moses. ⁴⁰Take care that what the prophets have said does not happen to you:

⁴¹ " 'Look, you scoffers,
    wonder and perish,
for I am going to do something in
        your days
    that you would never believe,
    even if someone told you.'ᵃ"

⁴²As Paul and Barnabas were leaving the synagogue, the people invited them to speak further about these things on the next Sabbath. ⁴³When the congregation was dismissed, many of the Jews and devout converts to Judaism followed Paul and Barnabas, who talked with them and urged them to continue in the grace of God.

⁴⁴On the next Sabbath almost the whole city gathered to hear the word of the Lord. ⁴⁵When the Jews saw the crowds, they were filled with jealousy. They began to contradict what Paul was saying and heaped abuse on him.

⁴⁶Then Paul and Barnabas answered them boldly: "We had to speak the word of God to you first. Since you reject it and do not consider yourselves worthy of eternal life, we now turn to the Gentiles. ⁴⁷For this is what the Lord has commanded us:

" 'I have made youᵇ a light for the
        Gentiles,
    that youᵇ may bring salvation to the
        ends of the earth.'ᶜ"

⁴⁸When the Gentiles heard this, they were glad and honored the word of the Lord; and all who were appointed for eternal life believed.

⁴⁹The word of the Lord spread through the whole region. ⁵⁰But the Jewish leaders incited the God-fearing women of high standing and the leading men of the city. They stirred up persecution against Paul and Barnabas, and expelled them from their region. ⁵¹So they shook the dust off their feet as a warning to them and went to Iconium. ⁵²And the disciples were filled with joy and with the Holy Spirit.

In Iconium

14 At Iconium Paul and Barnabas went as usual into the Jewish synagogue. There they spoke so effectively that a great number of Jews and Greeks believed. ²But the Jews who refused to believe stirred up the other Gentiles and poisoned their minds against the brothers. ³So Paul and Barnabas spent considerable time there, speaking boldly for the Lord, who confirmed the message of his grace by enabling them to perform signs and wonders. ⁴The people of the city were divided; some sided with the Jews, others with the apostles. ⁵There was a plot afoot among both Gentiles and Jews, together with their leaders, to mistreat them and stone them. ⁶But they found out about it and fled to the Lycaonian cities of Lystra and Derbe and to the surrounding country, ⁷where they continued to preach the gospel.

In Lystra and Derbe

⁸In Lystra there sat a man who was lame. He had been that way from birth and had never walked. ⁹He listened to Paul as he was speaking. Paul looked directly at him, saw that he had faith to be healed ¹⁰and called out, "Stand up on your feet!" At that, the man jumped up and began to walk.

¹¹When the crowd saw what Paul had done, they shouted in the Lycaonian language, "The gods have come down to us in human form!" ¹²Barnabas they called Zeus, and Paul they called Hermes because he was the chief speaker. ¹³The priest of Zeus, whose temple was just outside the city, brought bulls and wreaths to the city gates because he and the crowd wanted to offer sacrifices to them.

¹⁴But when the apostles Barnabas and Paul heard of this, they tore their clothes and rushed out into the crowd, shouting: ¹⁵"Friends, why are you doing this? We too are only human, like you. We are bringing you good news, telling you to turn from these worthless things to the living God, who made the heavens and the earth and the sea and everything in them. ¹⁶In the past, he let all nations go their own way. ¹⁷Yet he has not left himself without testimony: He has shown kindness by giving you rain from heaven and crops in their seasons; he provides you with plenty of food and fills your hearts with joy." ¹⁸Even with these words, they had difficulty keeping the crowd from sacrificing to them.

ᵃ 41 Hab. 1:5   ᵇ 47 The Greek is singular.   ᶜ 47 Isaiah 49:6

[19] Then some Jews came from Antioch and Iconium and won the crowd over. They stoned Paul and dragged him outside the city, thinking he was dead. [20] But after the disciples had gathered around him, he got up and went back into the city. The next day he and Barnabas left for Derbe.

The Return to Antioch in Syria

[21] They preached the gospel in that city and won a large number of disciples. Then they returned to Lystra, Iconium and Antioch, [22] strengthening the disciples and encouraging them to remain true to the faith. "We must go through many hardships to enter the kingdom of God," they said. [23] Paul and Barnabas appointed elders[a] for them in each church and, with prayer and fasting, committed them to the Lord, in whom they had put their trust. [24] After going through Pisidia, they came into Pamphylia, [25] and when they had preached the word in Perga, they went down to Attalia.

[26] From Attalia they sailed back to Antioch, where they had been committed to the grace of God for the work they had now completed. [27] On arriving there, they gathered the church together and reported all that God had done through them and how he had opened a door of faith to the Gentiles. [28] And they stayed there a long time with the disciples.

The Council at Jerusalem

15 Certain people came down from Judea to Antioch and were teaching the believers: "Unless you are circumcised, according to the custom taught by Moses, you cannot be saved." [2] This brought Paul and Barnabas into sharp dispute and debate with them. So Paul and Barnabas were appointed, along with some other believers, to go up to Jerusalem to see the apostles and elders about this question. [3] The church sent them on their way, and as they traveled through Phoenicia and Samaria, they told how the Gentiles had been converted. This news made all the believers very glad. [4] When they came to Jerusalem, they were welcomed by the church and the apostles and elders, to whom they reported everything God had done through them.

[5] Then some of the believers who belonged to the party of the Pharisees stood up and said, "The Gentiles must be circumcised and required to keep the law of Moses."

[6] The apostles and elders met to consider this question. [7] After much discussion, Peter got up and addressed them: "Brothers, you know that some time ago God made a choice among you that the Gentiles might hear from my lips the message of the gospel and believe. [8] God, who knows the heart, showed that he accepted them by giving the Holy Spirit to them, just as he did to us. [9] He did not discriminate between us and them, for he purified their hearts by faith. [10] Now then, why do you try to test God by putting on the necks of Gentiles a yoke that neither we nor our ancestors have been able to bear? [11] No! We believe it is through the grace of our Lord Jesus that we are saved, just as they are."

[12] The whole assembly became silent as they listened to Barnabas and Paul telling about the signs and wonders God had done among the Gentiles through them. [13] When they finished, James spoke up. "Brothers," he said, "listen to me. [14] Simon[b] has described to us how God first intervened to choose a people for his name from the Gentiles. [15] The words of the prophets are in agreement with this, as it is written:

[16] "'After this I will return
    and rebuild David's fallen tent.
  Its ruins I will rebuild,
    and I will restore it,
[17] that the rest of mankind may seek
      the Lord,
    even all the Gentiles who bear
      my name,
    says the Lord, who does these things'[c] —
[18]   things known from long ago.[d]

[19] "It is my judgment, therefore, that we should not make it difficult for the Gentiles who are turning to God. [20] Instead we should write to them, telling them to abstain from food polluted by idols, from sexual immorality, from the meat of strangled animals and from blood. [21] For the law of Moses has been preached in every city from the earliest

---

[a] 23 Or *Barnabas ordained elders*; or *Barnabas had elders elected*   [b] 14 Greek *Simeon*, a variant of *Simon*; that is, Peter   [c] 17 Amos 9:11,12 (see Septuagint)   [d] 17,18 Some manuscripts *things'* — / [18]*the Lord's work is known to him from long ago*

HOW CLOSE ARE YOU?

READ: **ACTS 15:1, 5–11**

The Pharisees knew a lot about God. When someone wanted to play "Bible Trivial Pursuit," "God-opoly," or "Bible Baseball," they would dominate. They knew about God, but they really didn't know him.

Like the Pharisees, many fans have given their minds to the study of God, but they never surrendered their hearts. What separates fans from followers is often the difference between knowledge and intimacy. Fans have a tendency to confuse their knowledge for intimacy. They don't recognize the difference between knowing about Jesus and truly knowing Jesus.

In church we've often established systems of learning that result in knowledge, but not necessarily intimacy. Think about it: We love having Bible studies, many of which include some kind of *workbook*. We go through a Bible curriculum that often has *homework*. Messages are often accompanied by a *handout* that allows you to fill in the blanks and take notes.

BUILDING

FAITH

WISDOM

STRENGTH

Now don't get me wrong, studying and learning from God's Word is invaluable. Jesus referenced, read, and quoted all kinds of passages from the Old Testament. The problem isn't knowledge. The problem is that you can have knowledge without having intimacy.

In fact, knowledge can be a false indicator of intimacy. Clearly where there is intimacy there should be a growing knowledge, but too often there is knowledge without a growing intimacy. You can know a lot about a person, but that doesn't necessarily mean you are close.

Taken from *Not a Fan Student Edition* by Kyle Idleman, copyright © 2012 by City on the Hill Studio, Inc., published by Zondervan.

times and is read in the synagogues on every Sabbath."

The Council's Letter to Gentile Believers

²²Then the apostles and elders, with the whole church, decided to choose some of their own men and send them to Antioch with Paul and Barnabas. They chose Judas (called Barsabbas) and Silas, men who were leaders among the believers. ²³With them they sent the following letter:

The apostles and elders, your brothers,

To the Gentile believers in Antioch, Syria and Cilicia:

Greetings.

²⁴We have heard that some went out from us without our authorization and disturbed you, troubling your minds by what they said. ²⁵So we all agreed to choose some men and send them to you with our dear friends Barnabas and Paul— ²⁶men who have risked their lives for the name of our Lord Jesus Christ. ²⁷Therefore we are sending Judas and Silas to confirm by word of mouth what we are writing. ²⁸It seemed good to the Holy Spirit and to us not to burden you with anything beyond the following requirements: ²⁹You are to abstain from food sacrificed to idols, from blood, from the meat of strangled animals and from sexual immorality. You will do well to avoid these things.

Farewell.

³⁰So the men were sent off and went down to Antioch, where they gathered the church together and delivered the letter. ³¹The people read it and were glad for its encouraging message. ³²Judas and Silas, who themselves were prophets, said much to encourage and strengthen the believers. ³³After spending some time there, they were sent off by the believers with the blessing of peace to return to those who had sent them. [³⁴] ᵃ ³⁵But Paul and Barnabas remained in Antioch, where they and many others taught and preached the word of the Lord.

Disagreement Between Paul and Barnabas

³⁶Some time later Paul said to Barnabas, "Let us go back and visit the believers in all the towns where we preached the word of the Lord and see how they are doing." ³⁷Barnabas wanted to take John, also called Mark, with them, ³⁸but Paul did not think it wise to take him, because he had deserted them in Pamphylia and had not continued with them in the work. ³⁹They had such a sharp disagreement that they parted company. Barnabas took Mark and sailed for Cyprus, ⁴⁰but Paul chose Silas and left, commended by the believers to the grace of the Lord. ⁴¹He went through Syria and Cilicia, strengthening the churches.

Timothy Joins Paul and Silas

16 Paul came to Derbe and then to Lystra, where a disciple named Timothy lived, whose mother was Jewish and a believer but whose father was a Greek. ²The believers at Lystra and Iconium spoke well of him. ³Paul wanted to take him along on the journey, so he circumcised him because of the Jews who lived in that area, for they all knew that his father was a Greek. ⁴As they traveled from town to town, they delivered the decisions reached by the apostles and elders in Jerusalem for the people to obey. ⁵So the churches were strengthened in the faith and grew daily in numbers.

Paul's Vision of the Man of Macedonia

⁶Paul and his companions traveled throughout the region of Phrygia and Galatia, having been kept by the Holy Spirit from preaching the word in the province of Asia. ⁷When they came to the border of Mysia, they tried to enter Bithynia, but the Spirit of Jesus would not allow them to. ⁸So they passed by Mysia and went down to Troas. ⁹During the night Paul had a vision of a man of Macedonia standing and begging him, "Come over to Macedonia and help us." ¹⁰After Paul had seen the vision, we got ready at once to leave for Macedonia, concluding that God had called us to preach the gospel to them.

Lydia's Conversion in Philippi

¹¹From Troas we put out to sea and sailed straight for Samothrace, and the next day we

---

ᵃ 34 Some manuscripts include here *But Silas decided to remain there.*

TRY ANOTHER DOOR

READ: ACTS 16:6-7

Obstacles pack your path. Road, barricaded. Doorway, padlocked. You walk from one blocked door to another. Do you know the frustration of a blocked door? If so, you have a friend in the apostle Paul.

He, Silas, and Timothy were on their second missionary journey. On his first one Paul enjoyed success at every stop. God opened doors into Cyprus, Antioch, and Iconium. He opened the door of grace at the Jerusalem council and spurred spiritual growth in every city.

Paul set his sights on Asia. Yet no doors opened. So the three turned north into Bithynia but encountered more blocked doors. They jiggled the knobs and pressed against the entrances but no access. We aren't told how or why God blocked the doors. Just that he did. He still does.

Once God closes a door, no one can open it.

This is what Paul learned. God blocked his missionary team from going north, south, or east. Only west remained, so they ended up at Asia's westernmost point. They stood with their toes in the sand and looked out over the sea. As they slept, Paul had a vision of a man of Macedonia standing and begging him, "Come over to Macedonia and help us" (Acts 16:9).

The closed doors in Asia led to an open-armed invitation to Europe. God uses closed doors to advance his cause. And this is what God is trying to teach us. Your blocked door doesn't mean God doesn't love you. Quite the opposite. It's proof that he does.

BUILDING FAITH WISDOM STRENGTH

Taken from *God's Story, Your Story: Youth Edition* by Max Lucado, copyright © 2011 by Max Lucado, published by Zondervan.

went on to Neapolis. [12]From there we traveled to Philippi, a Roman colony and the leading city of that district[a] of Macedonia. And we stayed there several days.

[13]On the Sabbath we went outside the city gate to the river, where we expected to find a place of prayer. We sat down and began to speak to the women who had gathered there. [14]One of those listening was a woman from the city of Thyatira named Lydia, a dealer in purple cloth. She was a worshiper of God. The Lord opened her heart to respond to Paul's message. [15]When she and the members of her household were baptized, she invited us to her home. "If you consider me a believer in the Lord," she said, "come and stay at my house." And she persuaded us.

Paul and Silas in Prison

[16]Once when we were going to the place of prayer, we were met by a female slave who had a spirit by which she predicted the future. She earned a great deal of money for her owners by fortune-telling. [17]She followed Paul and the rest of us, shouting, "These men are servants of the Most High God, who are telling you the way to be saved." [18]She kept this up for many days. Finally Paul became so annoyed that he turned around and said to the spirit, "In the name of Jesus Christ I command you to come out of her!" At that moment the spirit left her.

[19]When her owners realized that their hope of making money was gone, they seized Paul and Silas and dragged them into the marketplace to face the authorities. [20]They brought them before the magistrates and said, "These men are Jews, and are throwing our city into an uproar [21]by advocating customs unlawful for us Romans to accept or practice."

[22]The crowd joined in the attack against Paul and Silas, and the magistrates ordered them to be stripped and beaten with rods. [23]After they had been severely flogged, they were thrown into prison, and the jailer was commanded to guard them carefully. [24]When he received these orders, he put them in the inner cell and fastened their feet in the stocks.

[25]About midnight Paul and Silas were praying and singing hymns to God, and the other prisoners were listening to them. [26]Suddenly there was such a violent earthquake that the foundations of the prison were shaken. At once all the prison doors flew open, and everyone's chains came loose. [27]The jailer woke up, and when he saw the prison doors open, he drew his sword and was about to kill himself because he thought the prisoners had escaped. [28]But Paul shouted, "Don't harm yourself! We are all here!"

[29]The jailer called for lights, rushed in and fell trembling before Paul and Silas. [30]He then brought them out and asked, "Sirs, what must I do to be saved?"

[31]They replied, "Believe in the Lord Jesus, and you will be saved—you and your household." [32]Then they spoke the word of the Lord to him and to all the others in his house. [33]At that hour of the night the jailer took them and washed their wounds; then immediately he and all his household were baptized. [34]The jailer brought them into his house and set a meal before them; he was filled with joy because he had come to believe in God—he and his whole household.

[35]When it was daylight, the magistrates sent their officers to the jailer with the order: "Release those men." [36]The jailer told Paul, "The magistrates have ordered that you and Silas be released. Now you can leave. Go in peace."

[37]But Paul said to the officers: "They beat us publicly without a trial, even though we are Roman citizens, and threw us into prison. And now do they want to get rid of us quietly? No! Let them come themselves and escort us out."

[38]The officers reported this to the magistrates, and when they heard that Paul and Silas were Roman citizens, they were alarmed. [39]They came to appease them and escorted them from the prison, requesting them to leave the city. [40]After Paul and Silas came out of the prison, they went to Lydia's house, where they met with the brothers and sisters and encouraged them. Then they left.

In Thessalonica

17 When Paul and his companions had passed through Amphipolis and Apollonia, they came to Thessalonica, where

---

[a] 12 The text and meaning of the Greek for *the leading city of that district* are uncertain.

LUKE

With this in mind, since I myself have carefully investigated everything from the beginning, I too decided to write an orderly account for you, most excellent Theophilus, so that you may know the certainty of the things you have been taught. LUKE 1:3–4

HIS NAME MEANS: "light"

READ HIS STORY: *Luke 1:1–4; Acts 1:1–11, 16:10–17, 20:5–21:18, 27–28; Colossians 4:14; 2 Timothy 4:11; Philemon 23–24*

A scholar and a well-educated man, Luke was a physician by profession. He was detailed and observant in his writings and his work. Affectionately referred to by Paul as "our dear friend Luke, the doctor" (Colossians 4:14), Luke converted to Christianity. Many scholars think that Luke was a Gentile who joined the followers of Jesus. Evidently, Luke became close friends with Paul and joined him on his second missionary journey. Later he joined Paul again on his third missionary journey, during which they eventually traveled back to Jerusalem, where Paul was arrested. Luke was once again with Paul when the apostle was transported by ship to prison in Rome. Many of the hardships that Paul faced, Luke faced right there with him.

As the author of the books of Luke and Acts, Luke wrote eyewitness reports of the life of Jesus and events in the early church as well as his own personal experiences. He was careful and exact in historical detail and serious about his responsibility to provide key details about the life of Jesus as well as the birth of the Christian church.

For all his support and role as Paul's travel companion, he never brought attention to himself. Luke had a heart for evangelism and shared the gospel wherever he went.

there was a Jewish synagogue. ²As was his custom, Paul went into the synagogue, and on three Sabbath days he reasoned with them from the Scriptures, ³explaining and proving that the Messiah had to suffer and rise from the dead. "This Jesus I am proclaiming to you is the Messiah," he said. ⁴Some of the Jews were persuaded and joined Paul and Silas, as did a large number of God-fearing Greeks and quite a few prominent women.

⁵But other Jews were jealous; so they rounded up some bad characters from the marketplace, formed a mob and started a riot in the city. They rushed to Jason's house in search of Paul and Silas in order to bring them out to the crowd.ᵃ ⁶But when they did not find them, they dragged Jason and some other believers before the city officials, shouting: "These men who have caused trouble all over the world have now come here, ⁷and Jason has welcomed them into his house. They are all defying Caesar's decrees, saying that there is another king, one called Jesus." ⁸When they heard this, the crowd and the city officials were thrown into turmoil. ⁹Then they made Jason and the others post bond and let them go.

In Berea

¹⁰As soon as it was night, the believers sent Paul and Silas away to Berea. On arriving there, they went to the Jewish synagogue. ¹¹Now the Berean Jews were of more noble character than those in Thessalonica, for they received the message with great eagerness and examined the Scriptures every day to see if what Paul said was true. ¹²As a result, many of them believed, as did also a number of prominent Greek women and many Greek men.

¹³But when the Jews in Thessalonica learned that Paul was preaching the word of God at Berea, some of them went there too, agitating the crowds and stirring them up. ¹⁴The believers immediately sent Paul to the coast, but Silas and Timothy stayed at Berea. ¹⁵Those who escorted Paul brought him to Athens and then left with instructions for Silas and Timothy to join him as soon as possible.

In Athens

¹⁶While Paul was waiting for them in Athens, he was greatly distressed to see that the city was full of idols. ¹⁷So he reasoned in the synagogue with both Jews and God-fearing Greeks, as well as in the marketplace day by day with those who happened to be there. ¹⁸A group of Epicurean and Stoic philosophers began to debate with him. Some of them asked, "What is this babbler trying to say?" Others remarked, "He seems to be advocating foreign gods." They said this because Paul was preaching the good news about Jesus and the resurrection. ¹⁹Then they took him and brought him to a meeting of the Areopagus, where they said to him, "May we know what this new teaching is that you are presenting? ²⁰You are bringing some strange ideas to our ears, and we would like to know what they mean." ²¹(All the Athenians and the foreigners who lived there spent their time doing nothing but talking about and listening to the latest ideas.)

²²Paul then stood up in the meeting of the Areopagus and said: "People of Athens! I see that in every way you are very religious. ²³For as I walked around and looked carefully at your objects of worship, I even found an altar with this inscription: TO AN UNKNOWN GOD. So you are ignorant of the very thing you worship—and this is what I am going to proclaim to you.

²⁴"The God who made the world and everything in it is the Lord of heaven and earth and does not live in temples built by human hands. ²⁵And he is not served by human hands, as if he needed anything. Rather, he himself gives everyone life and breath and everything else. ²⁶From one man he made all the nations, that they should inhabit the whole earth; and he marked out their appointed times in history and the boundaries of their lands. ²⁷God did this so that they would seek him and perhaps reach out for him and find him, though he is not far from any one of us. ²⁸'For in him we live and move and have our being.'ᵇ As some of your own poets have said, 'We are his offspring.'ᶜ

²⁹"Therefore since we are God's offspring, we should not think that the divine being is like gold or silver or stone—an image made by human design and skill. ³⁰In the past God overlooked such ignorance, but now he commands all people everywhere to repent. ³¹For he has set a day when he will judge the

---

ᵃ 5 Or *the assembly of the people*   ᵇ 28 From the Cretan philosopher Epimenides   ᶜ 28 From the Cilician Stoic philosopher Aratus

WORTH ADMIRING

READ: **ACTS 17:11**

f you're looking for Bible people to imitate, the Bereans are tough to beat. Scripture applauds their "noble character" (Acts 17:11), all because of a habit you can start building right now.

The apostle Paul was on the second of his four missionary trips, a three-year trek westward to spread the news about Jesus (15:36–18:22). Whenever he arrived in a city, he headed first for the Jewish synagogue. He used Scripture to reason with people, explaining that Jesus was the Messiah predicted in the Old Testament, the Savior who had to suffer and rise from the dead (17:1-4).

In Thessalonica, some of the Jews and Gentiles—both women and men—became convinced that Jesus was everything Paul said he was. Others violently objected, starting a riot aimed at Paul and Silas. But the people of Berea gave the truth about Jesus a friendly welcome. These Bereans "received the message with great eagerness." Their enthusiasm was good, and their next move was even better: they "examined the Scriptures every day to see if what Paul said was true" (v. 11).

You have a chance today and every day to search the Old and New Testament to understand the Bible's own reliability. And you can use the Bible to test the truthfulness of everything you hear and read. That's a solid habit you need right now and for the rest of your life.

BUILDING
FAITH
WISDOM
STRENGTH

world with justice by the man he has appointed. He has given proof of this to everyone by raising him from the dead."

[32] When they heard about the resurrection of the dead, some of them sneered, but others said, "We want to hear you again on this subject." [33] At that, Paul left the Council. [34] Some of the people became followers of Paul and believed. Among them was Dionysius, a member of the Areopagus, also a woman named Damaris, and a number of others.

In Corinth

18 After this, Paul left Athens and went to Corinth. [2] There he met a Jew named Aquila, a native of Pontus, who had recently come from Italy with his wife Priscilla, because Claudius had ordered all Jews to leave Rome. Paul went to see them, [3] and because he was a tentmaker as they were, he stayed and worked with them. [4] Every Sabbath he reasoned in the synagogue, trying to persuade Jews and Greeks.

[5] When Silas and Timothy came from Macedonia, Paul devoted himself exclusively to preaching, testifying to the Jews that Jesus was the Messiah. [6] But when they opposed Paul and became abusive, he shook out his clothes in protest and said to them, "Your blood be on your own heads! I am innocent of it. From now on I will go to the Gentiles."

[7] Then Paul left the synagogue and went next door to the house of Titius Justus, a worshiper of God. [8] Crispus, the synagogue leader, and his entire household believed in the Lord; and many of the Corinthians who heard Paul believed and were baptized.

[9] One night the Lord spoke to Paul in a vision: "Do not be afraid; keep on speaking, do not be silent. [10] For I am with you, and no one is going to attack and harm you, because I have many people in this city." [11] So Paul stayed in Corinth for a year and a half, teaching them the word of God.

[12] While Gallio was proconsul of Achaia, the Jews of Corinth made a united attack on Paul and brought him to the place of judgment. [13] "This man," they charged, "is persuading the people to worship God in ways contrary to the law."

[14] Just as Paul was about to speak, Gallio said to them, "If you Jews were making a complaint about some misdemeanor or serious crime, it would be reasonable for me to listen to you. [15] But since it involves questions about words and names and your own law—settle the matter yourselves. I will not be a judge of such things." [16] So he drove them off. [17] Then the crowd there turned on Sosthenes the synagogue leader and beat him in front of the proconsul; and Gallio showed no concern whatever.

Priscilla, Aquila and Apollos

[18] Paul stayed on in Corinth for some time. Then he left the brothers and sisters and sailed for Syria, accompanied by Priscilla and Aquila. Before he sailed, he had his hair cut off at Cenchreae because of a vow he had taken. [19] They arrived at Ephesus, where Paul left Priscilla and Aquila. He himself went into the synagogue and reasoned with the Jews. [20] When they asked him to spend more time with them, he declined. [21] But as he left, he promised, "I will come back if it is God's will." Then he set sail from Ephesus. [22] When he landed at Caesarea, he went up to Jerusalem and greeted the church and then went down to Antioch.

[23] After spending some time in Antioch, Paul set out from there and traveled from place to place throughout the region of Galatia and Phrygia, strengthening all the disciples.

[24] Meanwhile a Jew named Apollos, a native of Alexandria, came to Ephesus. He was a learned man, with a thorough knowledge of the Scriptures. [25] He had been instructed in the way of the Lord, and he spoke with great fervor[a] and taught about Jesus accurately, though he knew only the baptism of John. [26] He began to speak boldly in the synagogue. When Priscilla and Aquila heard him, they invited him to their home and explained to him the way of God more adequately.

[27] When Apollos wanted to go to Achaia, the brothers and sisters encouraged him and wrote to the disciples there to welcome him. When he arrived, he was a great help to those who by grace had believed. [28] For he vigorously refuted his Jewish opponents in

---

a 25 Or *with fervor in the Spirit*

public debate, proving from the Scriptures that Jesus was the Messiah.

Paul in Ephesus

19 While Apollos was at Corinth, Paul took the road through the interior and arrived at Ephesus. There he found some disciples ²and asked them, "Did you receive the Holy Spirit when*ᵃ* you believed?"

They answered, "No, we have not even heard that there is a Holy Spirit."

³So Paul asked, "Then what baptism did you receive?"

"John's baptism," they replied.

⁴Paul said, "John's baptism was a baptism of repentance. He told the people to believe in the one coming after him, that is, in Jesus." ⁵On hearing this, they were baptized in the name of the Lord Jesus. ⁶When Paul placed his hands on them, the Holy Spirit came on them, and they spoke in tongues*ᵇ* and prophesied. ⁷There were about twelve men in all.

⁸Paul entered the synagogue and spoke boldly there for three months, arguing persuasively about the kingdom of God. ⁹But some of them became obstinate; they refused to believe and publicly maligned the Way. So Paul left them. He took the disciples with him and had discussions daily in the lecture hall of Tyrannus. ¹⁰This went on for two years, so that all the Jews and Greeks who lived in the province of Asia heard the word of the Lord.

¹¹God did extraordinary miracles through Paul, ¹²so that even handkerchiefs and aprons that had touched him were taken to the sick, and their illnesses were cured and the evil spirits left them.

¹³Some Jews who went around driving out evil spirits tried to invoke the name of the Lord Jesus over those who were demon-possessed. They would say, "In the name of the Jesus whom Paul preaches, I command you to come out." ¹⁴Seven sons of Sceva, a Jewish chief priest, were doing this. ¹⁵One day the evil spirit answered them, "Jesus I know, and Paul I know about, but who are you?" ¹⁶Then the man who had the evil spirit jumped on them and overpowered them all. He gave them such a beating that they ran out of the house naked and bleeding.

¹⁷When this became known to the Jews and Greeks living in Ephesus, they were all seized with fear, and the name of the Lord Jesus was held in high honor. ¹⁸Many of those who believed now came and openly confessed what they had done. ¹⁹A number who had practiced sorcery brought their scrolls together and burned them publicly. When they calculated the value of the scrolls, the total came to fifty thousand drachmas.*ᶜ* ²⁰In this way the word of the Lord spread widely and grew in power.

²¹After all this had happened, Paul decided*ᵈ* to go to Jerusalem, passing through Macedonia and Achaia. "After I have been there," he said, "I must visit Rome also." ²²He sent two of his helpers, Timothy and Erastus, to Macedonia, while he stayed in the province of Asia a little longer.

The Riot in Ephesus

²³About that time there arose a great disturbance about the Way. ²⁴A silversmith named Demetrius, who made silver shrines of Artemis, brought in a lot of business for the craftsmen there. ²⁵He called them together, along with the workers in related trades, and said: "You know, my friends, that we receive a good income from this business. ²⁶And you see and hear how this fellow Paul has convinced and led astray large numbers of people here in Ephesus and in practically the whole province of Asia. He says that gods made by human hands are no gods at all. ²⁷There is danger not only that our trade will lose its good name, but also that the temple of the great goddess Artemis will be discredited; and the goddess herself, who is worshiped throughout the province of Asia and the world, will be robbed of her divine majesty."

²⁸When they heard this, they were furious and began shouting: "Great is Artemis of the Ephesians!" ²⁹Soon the whole city was in an uproar. The people seized Gaius and Aristarchus, Paul's traveling companions from Macedonia, and all of them rushed into the theater together. ³⁰Paul wanted to appear before the crowd, but the disciples would not let him. ³¹Even some of the officials of the province, friends of Paul, sent him a

---

ᵃ 2 Or *after*   *ᵇ* 6 Or *other languages*   *ᶜ* 19 A drachma was a silver coin worth about a day's wages.
ᵈ 21 Or *decided in the Spirit*

BIG BOOST

READ: ACTS 19:1-6

My wife and I and our four kids flew into the Atlanta airport from the island of Hispaniola where we had spent a month on a mission trip. After landing, we grabbed our bags and began a long hike through the airport. So I'm carrying about a half dozen bags through the airport. It's just a moving pile of bags with my head sticking out of the top.

We turn to go down a hallway that is about 100 yards long. My wife and kids all get on a moving sidewalk, but I'm carrying a wide load and it's impossible for me to navigate the turn and I miss the on ramp.

I wish you could have seen what it looked like from my perspective. They set the few bags they have on the moving sidewalk and just stand there watching me. I'm sweating like ... well, like a man carrying a half dozen suitcases through the airport. I'm trying to keep up with the pace. We end up arriving at the end of the sidewalk at about the same time. But there's a difference. I'm frustrated, exhausted, and annoyed, and they are ready to keep moving. That's what our lives look like when we try the self-empowered hike, instead of the Spirit-filled walkway.

Trying to follow without being filled with the power of the Holy Spirit leads to becoming overwhelmed by life's circumstances. Eventually something happens and you can't get through it on your own. It doesn't work without the power of the Spirit.

BUILDING
FAITH
WISDOM
STRENGTH

message begging him not to venture into the theater.

³²The assembly was in confusion: Some were shouting one thing, some another. Most of the people did not even know why they were there. ³³The Jews in the crowd pushed Alexander to the front, and they shouted instructions to him. He motioned for silence in order to make a defense before the people. ³⁴But when they realized he was a Jew, they all shouted in unison for about two hours: "Great is Artemis of the Ephesians!"

³⁵The city clerk quieted the crowd and said: "Fellow Ephesians, doesn't all the world know that the city of Ephesus is the guardian of the temple of the great Artemis and of her image, which fell from heaven? ³⁶Therefore, since these facts are undeniable, you ought to calm down and not do anything rash. ³⁷You have brought these men here, though they have neither robbed temples nor blasphemed our goddess. ³⁸If, then, Demetrius and his fellow craftsmen have a grievance against anybody, the courts are open and there are proconsuls. They can press charges. ³⁹If there is anything further you want to bring up, it must be settled in a legal assembly. ⁴⁰As it is, we are in danger of being charged with rioting because of what happened today. In that case we would not be able to account for this commotion, since there is no reason for it." ⁴¹After he had said this, he dismissed the assembly.

Through Macedonia and Greece

20 When the uproar had ended, Paul sent for the disciples and, after encouraging them, said goodbye and set out for Macedonia. ²He traveled through that area, speaking many words of encouragement to the people, and finally arrived in Greece, ³where he stayed three months. Because some Jews had plotted against him just as he was about to sail for Syria, he decided to go back through Macedonia. ⁴He was accompanied by Sopater son of Pyrrhus from Berea, Aristarchus and Secundus from Thessalonica, Gaius from Derbe, Timothy also, and Tychicus and Trophimus from the province of Asia. ⁵These men went on ahead and waited for us at Troas. ⁶But we sailed from Philippi after the Festival of Unleavened Bread, and five days later joined the others at Troas, where we stayed seven days.

Eutychus Raised From the Dead at Troas

⁷On the first day of the week we came together to break bread. Paul spoke to the people and, because he intended to leave the next day, kept on talking until midnight. ⁸There were many lamps in the upstairs room where we were meeting. ⁹Seated in a window was a young man named Eutychus, who was sinking into a deep sleep as Paul talked on and on. When he was sound asleep, he fell to the ground from the third story and was picked up dead. ¹⁰Paul went down, threw himself on the young man and put his arms around him. "Don't be alarmed," he said. "He's alive!" ¹¹Then he went upstairs again and broke bread and ate. After talking until daylight, he left. ¹²The people took the young man home alive and were greatly comforted.

Paul's Farewell to the Ephesian Elders

¹³We went on ahead to the ship and sailed for Assos, where we were going to take Paul aboard. He had made this arrangement because he was going there on foot. ¹⁴When he met us at Assos, we took him aboard and went on to Mitylene. ¹⁵The next day we set sail from there and arrived off Chios. The day after that we crossed over to Samos, and on the following day arrived at Miletus. ¹⁶Paul had decided to sail past Ephesus to avoid spending time in the province of Asia, for he was in a hurry to reach Jerusalem, if possible, by the day of Pentecost.

¹⁷From Miletus, Paul sent to Ephesus for the elders of the church. ¹⁸When they arrived, he said to them: "You know how I lived the whole time I was with you, from the first day I came into the province of Asia. ¹⁹I served the Lord with great humility and with tears and in the midst of severe testing by the plots of my Jewish opponents. ²⁰You know that I have not hesitated to preach anything that would be helpful to you but have taught you publicly and from house to house. ²¹I have declared to both Jews and Greeks that they must turn to God in repentance and have faith in our Lord Jesus.

²²"And now, compelled by the Spirit, I am going to Jerusalem, not knowing what will happen to me there. ²³I only know that in every city the Holy Spirit warns me that prison and hardships are facing me. ²⁴However,

I consider my life worth nothing to me; my only aim is to finish the race and complete the task the Lord Jesus has given me — the task of testifying to the good news of God's grace.

[25] "Now I know that none of you among whom I have gone about preaching the kingdom will ever see me again. [26] Therefore, I declare to you today that I am innocent of the blood of any of you. [27] For I have not hesitated to proclaim to you the whole will of God. [28] Keep watch over yourselves and all the flock of which the Holy Spirit has made you overseers. Be shepherds of the church of God,[a] which he bought with his own blood.[b] [29] I know that after I leave, savage wolves will come in among you and will not spare the flock. [30] Even from your own number men will arise and distort the truth in order to draw away disciples after them. [31] So be on your guard! Remember that for three years I never stopped warning each of you night and day with tears.

[32] "Now I commit you to God and to the word of his grace, which can build you up and give you an inheritance among all those who are sanctified. [33] I have not coveted anyone's silver or gold or clothing. [34] You yourselves know that these hands of mine have supplied my own needs and the needs of my companions. [35] In everything I did, I showed you that by this kind of hard work we must help the weak, remembering the words the Lord Jesus himself said: 'It is more blessed to give than to receive.'"

[36] When Paul had finished speaking, he knelt down with all of them and prayed. [37] They all wept as they embraced him and kissed him. [38] What grieved them most was his statement that they would never see his face again. Then they accompanied him to the ship.

On to Jerusalem

21 After we had torn ourselves away from them, we put out to sea and sailed straight to Kos. The next day we went to Rhodes and from there to Patara. [2] We found a ship crossing over to Phoenicia, went on board and set sail. [3] After sighting Cyprus and passing to the south of it, we sailed on to Syria. We landed at Tyre, where our ship was to unload its cargo. [4] We sought out the disciples there and stayed with them seven days. Through the Spirit they urged Paul not to go on to Jerusalem. [5] When it was time to leave, we left and continued on our way. All of them, including wives and children, accompanied us out of the city, and there on the beach we knelt to pray. [6] After saying goodbye to each other, we went aboard the ship, and they returned home.

[7] We continued our voyage from Tyre and landed at Ptolemais, where we greeted the brothers and sisters and stayed with them for a day. [8] Leaving the next day, we reached Caesarea and stayed at the house of Philip the evangelist, one of the Seven. [9] He had four unmarried daughters who prophesied.

[10] After we had been there a number of days, a prophet named Agabus came down from Judea. [11] Coming over to us, he took Paul's belt, tied his own hands and feet with it and said, "The Holy Spirit says, 'In this way the Jewish leaders in Jerusalem will bind the owner of this belt and will hand him over to the Gentiles.'"

[12] When we heard this, we and the people there pleaded with Paul not to go up to Jerusalem. [13] Then Paul answered, "Why are you weeping and breaking my heart? I am ready not only to be bound, but also to die in Jerusalem for the name of the Lord Jesus." [14] When he would not be dissuaded, we gave up and said, "The Lord's will be done."

[15] After this, we started on our way up to Jerusalem. [16] Some of the disciples from Caesarea accompanied us and brought us to the home of Mnason, where we were to stay. He was a man from Cyprus and one of the early disciples.

Paul's Arrival at Jerusalem

[17] When we arrived at Jerusalem, the brothers and sisters received us warmly. [18] The next day Paul and the rest of us went to see James, and all the elders were present. [19] Paul greeted them and reported in detail what God had done among the Gentiles through his ministry.

[20] When they heard this, they praised God. Then they said to Paul: "You see, brother, how many thousands of Jews have believed, and all of them are zealous for the

---

[a] 28 Many manuscripts *of the Lord*   [b] 28 Or *with the blood of his own Son.*

law. [21] They have been informed that you teach all the Jews who live among the Gentiles to turn away from Moses, telling them not to circumcise their children or live according to our customs. [22] What shall we do? They will certainly hear that you have come, [23] so do what we tell you. There are four men with us who have made a vow. [24] Take these men, join in their purification rites and pay their expenses, so that they can have their heads shaved. Then everyone will know there is no truth in these reports about you, but that you yourself are living in obedience to the law. [25] As for the Gentile believers, we have written to them our decision that they should abstain from food sacrificed to idols, from blood, from the meat of strangled animals and from sexual immorality."

[26] The next day Paul took the men and purified himself along with them. Then he went to the temple to give notice of the date when the days of purification would end and the offering would be made for each of them.

Paul Arrested

[27] When the seven days were nearly over, some Jews from the province of Asia saw Paul at the temple. They stirred up the whole crowd and seized him, [28] shouting, "Fellow Israelites, help us! This is the man who teaches everyone everywhere against our people and our law and this place. And besides, he has brought Greeks into the temple and defiled this holy place." [29] (They had previously seen Trophimus the Ephesian in the city with Paul and assumed that Paul had brought him into the temple.)

[30] The whole city was aroused, and the people came running from all directions. Seizing Paul, they dragged him from the temple, and immediately the gates were shut. [31] While they were trying to kill him, news reached the commander of the Roman troops that the whole city of Jerusalem was in an uproar. [32] He at once took some officers and soldiers and ran down to the crowd. When the rioters saw the commander and his soldiers, they stopped beating Paul.

[33] The commander came up and arrested him and ordered him to be bound with two chains. Then he asked who he was and what he had done. [34] Some in the crowd shouted one thing and some another, and since the commander could not get at the truth because of the uproar, he ordered that Paul be taken into the barracks. [35] When Paul reached the steps, the violence of the mob was so great he had to be carried by the soldiers. [36] The crowd that followed kept shouting, "Get rid of him!"

Paul Speaks to the Crowd

[37] As the soldiers were about to take Paul into the barracks, he asked the commander, "May I say something to you?"

"Do you speak Greek?" he replied. [38] "Aren't you the Egyptian who started a revolt and led four thousand terrorists out into the wilderness some time ago?"

[39] Paul answered, "I am a Jew, from Tarsus in Cilicia, a citizen of no ordinary city. Please let me speak to the people."

[40] After receiving the commander's permission, Paul stood on the steps and motioned to the crowd. When they were all silent, he said to them in Aramaic[a]: **22** [1] "Brothers and fathers, listen now to my defense."

[2] When they heard him speak to them in Aramaic, they became very quiet.

Then Paul said: [3] "I am a Jew, born in Tarsus of Cilicia, but brought up in this city. I studied under Gamaliel and was thoroughly trained in the law of our ancestors. I was just as zealous for God as any of you are today. [4] I persecuted the followers of this Way to their death, arresting both men and women and throwing them into prison, [5] as the high priest and all the Council can themselves testify. I even obtained letters from them to their associates in Damascus, and went there to bring these people as prisoners to Jerusalem to be punished.

[6] "About noon as I came near Damascus, suddenly a bright light from heaven flashed around me. [7] I fell to the ground and heard a voice say to me, 'Saul! Saul! Why do you persecute me?'

[8] " 'Who are you, Lord?' I asked.

" 'I am Jesus of Nazareth, whom you are persecuting,' he replied. [9] My companions saw the light, but they did not understand the voice of him who was speaking to me.

[10] " 'What shall I do, Lord?' I asked.

---

[a] 40 Or possibly *Hebrew*; also in 22:2

LIFTED UP

READ: **ACTS 21:27**

Countless friends had warned the apostle Paul not to go to Jerusalem, and their worst fears come true shortly after he reaches the city. Religious opponents whip up a crowd against Paul. They seize him and drag him from the temple. A Roman commander intervenes moments before the mob kills Paul, but the apostle still goes to prison. The last chapters of Acts tell the rest of his story.

Life doesn't always turn out the way you hope, and God doesn't always make bad situations instantly better. Parents fight, and some divorce. Someone close feels a strange pain, then receives a deadly diagnosis. Your schoolwork overwhelms you, and you fail a class. What are you supposed to do when awful things happen that you can't change?

As the crowd kept shouting "Get rid of him!" (Acts 21:36), Paul must have felt relieved to be bound and led to safety. He lets his captors know he isn't a terrorist, and he stands up for his rights as a Roman citizen (22:25–29). Then he presses on to accomplish what he came to do. He tells his enemies about Jesus.

When life beats you up, God still has a plan and a purpose for every minute of your day. He hasn't left you. He lifts you up if you let him. He helps you press on through life's hardest circumstances.

BUILDING FAITH WISDOM STRENGTH

" 'Get up,' the Lord said, 'and go into Damascus. There you will be told all that you have been assigned to do.' ¹¹ My companions led me by the hand into Damascus, because the brilliance of the light had blinded me.

¹² "A man named Ananias came to see me. He was a devout observer of the law and highly respected by all the Jews living there. ¹³ He stood beside me and said, 'Brother Saul, receive your sight!' And at that very moment I was able to see him.

¹⁴ "Then he said: 'The God of our ancestors has chosen you to know his will and to see the Righteous One and to hear words from his mouth. ¹⁵ You will be his witness to all people of what you have seen and heard. ¹⁶ And now what are you waiting for? Get up, be baptized and wash your sins away, calling on his name.'

¹⁷ "When I returned to Jerusalem and was praying at the temple, I fell into a trance ¹⁸ and saw the Lord speaking to me. 'Quick!' he said. 'Leave Jerusalem immediately, because the people here will not accept your testimony about me.'

¹⁹ " 'Lord,' I replied, 'these people know that I went from one synagogue to another to imprison and beat those who believe in you. ²⁰ And when the blood of your martyr[a] Stephen was shed, I stood there giving my approval and guarding the clothes of those who were killing him.'

²¹ "Then the Lord said to me, 'Go; I will send you far away to the Gentiles.' "

Paul the Roman Citizen

²² The crowd listened to Paul until he said this. Then they raised their voices and shouted, "Rid the earth of him! He's not fit to live!"

²³ As they were shouting and throwing off their cloaks and flinging dust into the air, ²⁴ the commander ordered that Paul be taken into the barracks. He directed that he be flogged and interrogated in order to find out why the people were shouting at him like this. ²⁵ As they stretched him out to flog him, Paul said to the centurion standing there, "Is it legal for you to flog a Roman citizen who hasn't even been found guilty?"

²⁶ When the centurion heard this, he went to the commander and reported it. "What are you going to do?" he asked. "This man is a Roman citizen."

²⁷ The commander went to Paul and asked, "Tell me, are you a Roman citizen?"

"Yes, I am," he answered.

²⁸ Then the commander said, "I had to pay a lot of money for my citizenship."

"But I was born a citizen," Paul replied.

²⁹ Those who were about to interrogate him withdrew immediately. The commander himself was alarmed when he realized that he had put Paul, a Roman citizen, in chains.

Paul Before the Sanhedrin

³⁰ The commander wanted to find out exactly why Paul was being accused by the Jews. So the next day he released him and ordered the chief priests and all the members of the Sanhedrin to assemble. Then he brought Paul and had him stand before them.

23 Paul looked straight at the Sanhedrin and said, "My brothers, I have fulfilled my duty to God in all good conscience to this day." ² At this the high priest Ananias ordered those standing near Paul to strike him on the mouth. ³ Then Paul said to him, "God will strike you, you whitewashed wall! You sit there to judge me according to the law, yet you yourself violate the law by commanding that I be struck!"

⁴ Those who were standing near Paul said, "How dare you insult God's high priest!"

⁵ Paul replied, "Brothers, I did not realize that he was the high priest; for it is written: 'Do not speak evil about the ruler of your people.'[b]"

⁶ Then Paul, knowing that some of them were Sadducees and the others Pharisees, called out in the Sanhedrin, "My brothers, I am a Pharisee, descended from Pharisees. I stand on trial because of the hope of the resurrection of the dead." ⁷ When he said this, a dispute broke out between the Pharisees and the Sadducees, and the assembly was divided. ⁸ (The Sadducees say that there is no resurrection, and that there are neither angels nor spirits, but the Pharisees believe all these things.)

⁹ There was a great uproar, and some of the teachers of the law who were Pharisees stood

NEITHER COUNTS

READ: ACTS 23:6-10

Within the Sanhedrin were the Sadducees and the Pharisees. These two groups did not get along. When interpreting Scripture, the Sadducees were very liberal, and the Pharisees were quite conservative. The Sadducees served the roles of chief priests and elders. If you were a Sadducee, it meant you were born into that position. There were, of course, other requirements, but it had to be part of your heritage. But to be a part of the Pharisees, your qualifications weren't based on the family you were born into; it was your hard work. Becoming a Pharisee required an incredible amount of study and training. And what I've noticed is that many fans of Jesus fit into one of these two camps.

BUILDING FAITH WISDOM STRENGTH

Some fans are like the Sadducees. Their faith was something they were born into. Maybe when you were born your parents handed you a mask, and you grew up acting like Christians act, talking how Christians talked, listening to the music Christians listened to; but you never fell in love with Jesus. Your faith has always been more about honoring your heritage than surrendering your heart.

On the other hand, some fans are like the Pharisees. They would measure their faith by their hard work at learning and following the law. Their intellectual knowledge and behavioral compliance was their target. But even though they were saying and doing the right things, it wasn't a reflection of who they really were.

You may say the right things and do the right things, but that's not enough for Jesus. He wants all of you.

Taken from *Not a Fan Student Edition* by Kyle Idleman, copyright © 2012 by City on the Hill Studio, Inc., published by Zondervan.

up and argued vigorously. "We find nothing wrong with this man," they said. "What if a spirit or an angel has spoken to him?" ¹⁰The dispute became so violent that the commander was afraid Paul would be torn to pieces by them. He ordered the troops to go down and take him away from them by force and bring him into the barracks.

¹¹The following night the Lord stood near Paul and said, "Take courage! As you have testified about me in Jerusalem, so you must also testify in Rome."

The Plot to Kill Paul

¹²The next morning some Jews formed a conspiracy and bound themselves with an oath not to eat or drink until they had killed Paul. ¹³More than forty men were involved in this plot. ¹⁴They went to the chief priests and the elders and said, "We have taken a solemn oath not to eat anything until we have killed Paul. ¹⁵Now then, you and the Sanhedrin petition the commander to bring him before you on the pretext of wanting more accurate information about his case. We are ready to kill him before he gets here."

¹⁶But when the son of Paul's sister heard of this plot, he went into the barracks and told Paul.

¹⁷Then Paul called one of the centurions and said, "Take this young man to the commander; he has something to tell him." ¹⁸So he took him to the commander.

The centurion said, "Paul, the prisoner, sent for me and asked me to bring this young man to you because he has something to tell you."

¹⁹The commander took the young man by the hand, drew him aside and asked, "What is it you want to tell me?"

²⁰He said: "Some Jews have agreed to ask you to bring Paul before the Sanhedrin tomorrow on the pretext of wanting more accurate information about him. ²¹Don't give in to them, because more than forty of them are waiting in ambush for him. They have taken an oath not to eat or drink until they have killed him. They are ready now, waiting for your consent to their request."

²²The commander dismissed the young man with this warning: "Don't tell anyone that you have reported this to me."

Paul Transferred to Caesarea

²³Then he called two of his centurions and ordered them, "Get ready a detachment of two hundred soldiers, seventy horsemen and two hundred spearmen*a* to go to Caesarea at nine tonight. ²⁴Provide horses for Paul so that he may be taken safely to Governor Felix."

²⁵He wrote a letter as follows:

²⁶Claudius Lysias,

To His Excellency, Governor Felix:

Greetings.

²⁷This man was seized by the Jews and they were about to kill him, but I came with my troops and rescued him, for I had learned that he is a Roman citizen. ²⁸I wanted to know why they were accusing him, so I brought him to their Sanhedrin. ²⁹I found that the accusation had to do with questions about their law, but there was no charge against him that deserved death or imprisonment. ³⁰When I was informed of a plot to be carried out against the man, I sent him to you at once. I also ordered his accusers to present to you their case against him.

³¹So the soldiers, carrying out their orders, took Paul with them during the night and brought him as far as Antipatris. ³²The next day they let the cavalry go on with him, while they returned to the barracks. ³³When the cavalry arrived in Caesarea, they delivered the letter to the governor and handed Paul over to him. ³⁴The governor read the letter and asked what province he was from. Learning that he was from Cilicia, ³⁵he said, "I will hear your case when your accusers get here." Then he ordered that Paul be kept under guard in Herod's palace.

Paul's Trial Before Felix

24 Five days later the high priest Ananias went down to Caesarea with some of the elders and a lawyer named Tertullus, and they brought their charges against Paul before the governor. ²When Paul was called in, Tertullus presented his case before Felix:

---

a 23 The meaning of the Greek for this word is uncertain.

STAY TRUE

READ: ACTS 24:25

As the apostle Paul stands before Felix, governor of Judah, he faces three charges. He's accused of igniting riots across the Roman empire, teaching people to disobey the law of Moses, and polluting the temple by bringing a Gentile into an area reserved for Jews (Acts 21:27-29).

Paul's opponents argue that these crimes deserve death, but Felix seems unconvinced and unconcerned. By the end of Acts 24, two years have passed. When Felix exits his post, he leaves Paul in prison.

In the meantime, Paul and Felix have intriguing conversations, at least one of which is attended by Felix's wife Drusilla, who is Jewish. Felix is already well acquainted with "the Way" (24:22), a common name for the early Christian faith, and he's eager to hear Paul talk about Jesus. But when Paul brings up purity, self-control, and a future judgment of sin, the governor sends the apostle back to his cell. Maybe Felix's Jewish wife starts feeling guilty for marrying a man who didn't worship God, because she doesn't come back for more conversations. The governor just hopes Paul's friends will pay a bribe to gain his release.

BUILDING FAITH WISDOM STRENGTH

Jesus wants you to tell people about him. When you do, you can't control how they react. Some run away. Others keep talking for all kinds of reasons. And a few truly want to meet your Lord. Whatever happens, your task is to keep speaking truth.

"We have enjoyed a long period of peace under you, and your foresight has brought about reforms in this nation. ³Everywhere and in every way, most excellent Felix, we acknowledge this with profound gratitude. ⁴But in order not to weary you further, I would request that you be kind enough to hear us briefly.

⁵"We have found this man to be a troublemaker, stirring up riots among the Jews all over the world. He is a ringleader of the Nazarene sect ⁶and even tried to desecrate the temple; so we seized him. [7]ᵃ ⁸By examining him yourself you will be able to learn the truth about all these charges we are bringing against him."

⁹The other Jews joined in the accusation, asserting that these things were true.

¹⁰When the governor motioned for him to speak, Paul replied: "I know that for a number of years you have been a judge over this nation; so I gladly make my defense. ¹¹You can easily verify that no more than twelve days ago I went up to Jerusalem to worship. ¹²My accusers did not find me arguing with anyone at the temple, or stirring up a crowd in the synagogues or anywhere else in the city. ¹³And they cannot prove to you the charges they are now making against me. ¹⁴However, I admit that I worship the God of our ancestors as a follower of the Way, which they call a sect. I believe everything that is in accordance with the Law and that is written in the Prophets, ¹⁵and I have the same hope in God as these men themselves have, that there will be a resurrection of both the righteous and the wicked. ¹⁶So I strive always to keep my conscience clear before God and man.

¹⁷"After an absence of several years, I came to Jerusalem to bring my people gifts for the poor and to present offerings. ¹⁸I was ceremonially clean when they found me in the temple courts doing this. There was no crowd with me, nor was I involved in any disturbance. ¹⁹But there are some Jews from the province of Asia, who ought to be here before you and bring charges if they have anything against me. ²⁰Or these who are here should state what crime they found in me when I stood before the Sanhedrin—

²¹unless it was this one thing I shouted as I stood in their presence: 'It is concerning the resurrection of the dead that I am on trial before you today.'"

²²Then Felix, who was well acquainted with the Way, adjourned the proceedings. "When Lysias the commander comes," he said, "I will decide your case." ²³He ordered the centurion to keep Paul under guard but to give him some freedom and permit his friends to take care of his needs.

²⁴Several days later Felix came with his wife Drusilla, who was Jewish. He sent for Paul and listened to him as he spoke about faith in Christ Jesus. ²⁵As Paul talked about righteousness, self-control and the judgment to come, Felix was afraid and said, "That's enough for now! You may leave. When I find it convenient, I will send for you." ²⁶At the same time he was hoping that Paul would offer him a bribe, so he sent for him frequently and talked with him.

²⁷When two years had passed, Felix was succeeded by Porcius Festus, but because Felix wanted to grant a favor to the Jews, he left Paul in prison.

Paul's Trial Before Festus

25 Three days after arriving in the province, Festus went up from Caesarea to Jerusalem, ²where the chief priests and the Jewish leaders appeared before him and presented the charges against Paul. ³They requested Festus, as a favor to them, to have Paul transferred to Jerusalem, for they were preparing an ambush to kill him along the way. ⁴Festus answered, "Paul is being held at Caesarea, and I myself am going there soon. ⁵Let some of your leaders come with me, and if the man has done anything wrong, they can press charges against him there."

⁶After spending eight or ten days with them, Festus went down to Caesarea. The next day he convened the court and ordered that Paul be brought before him. ⁷When Paul came in, the Jews who had come down from Jerusalem stood around him. They brought many serious charges against him, but they could not prove them.

ᵃ 6-8 Some manuscripts include here *him, and we would have judged him in accordance with our law.* ⁷*But the commander Lysias came and took him from us with much violence,* ⁸*ordering his accusers to come before you.*

[8] Then Paul made his defense: "I have done nothing wrong against the Jewish law or against the temple or against Caesar."

[9] Festus, wishing to do the Jews a favor, said to Paul, "Are you willing to go up to Jerusalem and stand trial before me there on these charges?"

[10] Paul answered: "I am now standing before Caesar's court, where I ought to be tried. I have not done any wrong to the Jews, as you yourself know very well. [11] If, however, I am guilty of doing anything deserving death, I do not refuse to die. But if the charges brought against me by these Jews are not true, no one has the right to hand me over to them. I appeal to Caesar!"

[12] After Festus had conferred with his council, he declared: "You have appealed to Caesar. To Caesar you will go!"

Festus Consults King Agrippa

[13] A few days later King Agrippa and Bernice arrived at Caesarea to pay their respects to Festus. [14] Since they were spending many days there, Festus discussed Paul's case with the king. He said: "There is a man here whom Felix left as a prisoner. [15] When I went to Jerusalem, the chief priests and the elders of the Jews brought charges against him and asked that he be condemned.

[16] "I told them that it is not the Roman custom to hand over anyone before they have faced their accusers and have had an opportunity to defend themselves against the charges. [17] When they came here with me, I did not delay the case, but convened the court the next day and ordered the man to be brought in. [18] When his accusers got up to speak, they did not charge him with any of the crimes I had expected. [19] Instead, they had some points of dispute with him about their own religion and about a dead man named Jesus who Paul claimed was alive. [20] I was at a loss how to investigate such matters; so I asked if he would be willing to go to Jerusalem and stand trial there on these charges. [21] But when Paul made his appeal to be held over for the Emperor's decision, I ordered him held until I could send him to Caesar."

[22] Then Agrippa said to Festus, "I would like to hear this man myself."

He replied, "Tomorrow you will hear him."

Paul Before Agrippa

[23] The next day Agrippa and Bernice came with great pomp and entered the audience room with the high-ranking military officers and the prominent men of the city. At the command of Festus, Paul was brought in. [24] Festus said: "King Agrippa, and all who are present with us, you see this man! The whole Jewish community has petitioned me about him in Jerusalem and here in Caesarea, shouting that he ought not to live any longer. [25] I found he had done nothing deserving of death, but because he made his appeal to the Emperor I decided to send him to Rome. [26] But I have nothing definite to write to His Majesty about him. Therefore I have brought him before all of you, and especially before you, King Agrippa, so that as a result of this investigation I may have something to write. [27] For I think it is unreasonable to send a prisoner on to Rome without specifying the charges against him."

26 Then Agrippa said to Paul, "You have permission to speak for yourself."

So Paul motioned with his hand and began his defense: [2] "King Agrippa, I consider myself fortunate to stand before you today as I make my defense against all the accusations of the Jews, [3] and especially so because you are well acquainted with all the Jewish customs and controversies. Therefore, I beg you to listen to me patiently.

[4] "The Jewish people all know the way I have lived ever since I was a child, from the beginning of my life in my own country, and also in Jerusalem. [5] They have known me for a long time and can testify, if they are willing, that I conformed to the strictest sect of our religion, living as a Pharisee. [6] And now it is because of my hope in what God has promised our ancestors that I am on trial today. [7] This is the promise our twelve tribes are hoping to see fulfilled as they earnestly serve God day and night. King Agrippa, it is because of this hope that these Jews are accusing me. [8] Why should any of you consider it incredible that God raises the dead?

[9] "I too was convinced that I ought to do all that was possible to oppose the name of Jesus of Nazareth. [10] And that is just what I did in Jerusalem. On the authority of the chief priests I put many of the Lord's people in prison, and when they were put to death, I cast my vote against them. [11] Many a time I went

LET GOD WORK IT OUT

READ: ACTS 26:1-31

Godly tolerance means we respect other's decisions. We refuse to withhold love from them because we dislike their views. There is no biblical precedent for forced conversion, whether by the sword or peer pressure or manipulation. Jesus gave people space to consider and follow him of their own free choice. He knew he was asking for their entire lives, and he didn't want hasty, fair-weather disciples. Even when people chose another path, Jesus let them go and grieved.

Paul invokes the differences in our consciences when he recommends to the believers in Rome to let each fellow believer consult their own conscience about eating meat sacrificed to idols. Even when Paul stands on trial before the empire, his life or death dependent on his ability to convince the governing authorities of the power and person of Jesus, Paul refuses to use trickery, coercion, or manipulation. He simply tells his story. Whether people follow Jesus or not, we can trust that Jesus is working. The Hound of Heaven pursues each of us, as evident in Jesus' words that he came to "seek and save what was lost." Lost things are wanted things. Though many resist being friends of God, we still love them, scorning the very idea that they must convert to earn our continued interest. This is how Jesus treated his friends—even the one he knew would betray him.

BUILDING
FAITH
WISDOM
STRENGTH

from one synagogue to another to have them punished, and I tried to force them to blaspheme. I was so obsessed with persecuting them that I even hunted them down in foreign cities.

[12] "On one of these journeys I was going to Damascus with the authority and commission of the chief priests. [13] About noon, King Agrippa, as I was on the road, I saw a light from heaven, brighter than the sun, blazing around me and my companions. [14] We all fell to the ground, and I heard a voice saying to me in Aramaic,[a] 'Saul, Saul, why do you persecute me? It is hard for you to kick against the goads.'

[15] "Then I asked, 'Who are you, Lord?'

" 'I am Jesus, whom you are persecuting,' the Lord replied. [16] 'Now get up and stand on your feet. I have appeared to you to appoint you as a servant and as a witness of what you have seen and will see of me. [17] I will rescue you from your own people and from the Gentiles. I am sending you to them [18] to open their eyes and turn them from darkness to light, and from the power of Satan to God, so that they may receive forgiveness of sins and a place among those who are sanctified by faith in me.'

[19] "So then, King Agrippa, I was not disobedient to the vision from heaven. [20] First to those in Damascus, then to those in Jerusalem and in all Judea, and then to the Gentiles, I preached that they should repent and turn to God and demonstrate their repentance by their deeds. [21] That is why some Jews seized me in the temple courts and tried to kill me. [22] But God has helped me to this very day; so I stand here and testify to small and great alike. I am saying nothing beyond what the prophets and Moses said would happen— [23] that the Messiah would suffer and, as the first to rise from the dead, would bring the message of light to his own people and to the Gentiles."

[24] At this point Festus interrupted Paul's defense. "You are out of your mind, Paul!" he shouted. "Your great learning is driving you insane."

[25] "I am not insane, most excellent Festus," Paul replied. "What I am saying is true and reasonable. [26] The king is familiar with these things, and I can speak freely to him.

I am convinced that none of this has escaped his notice, because it was not done in a corner. [27] King Agrippa, do you believe the prophets? I know you do."

[28] Then Agrippa said to Paul, "Do you think that in such a short time you can persuade me to be a Christian?"

[29] Paul replied, "Short time or long—I pray to God that not only you but all who are listening to me today may become what I am, except for these chains."

[30] The king rose, and with him the governor and Bernice and those sitting with them. [31] After they left the room, they began saying to one another, "This man is not doing anything that deserves death or imprisonment."

[32] Agrippa said to Festus, "This man could have been set free if he had not appealed to Caesar."

Paul Sails for Rome

27 When it was decided that we would sail for Italy, Paul and some other prisoners were handed over to a centurion named Julius, who belonged to the Imperial Regiment. [2] We boarded a ship from Adramyttium about to sail for ports along the coast of the province of Asia, and we put out to sea. Aristarchus, a Macedonian from Thessalonica, was with us.

[3] The next day we landed at Sidon; and Julius, in kindness to Paul, allowed him to go to his friends so they might provide for his needs. [4] From there we put out to sea again and passed to the lee of Cyprus because the winds were against us. [5] When we had sailed across the open sea off the coast of Cilicia and Pamphylia, we landed at Myra in Lycia. [6] There the centurion found an Alexandrian ship sailing for Italy and put us on board. [7] We made slow headway for many days and had difficulty arriving off Cnidus. When the wind did not allow us to hold our course, we sailed to the lee of Crete, opposite Salmone. [8] We moved along the coast with difficulty and came to a place called Fair Havens, near the town of Lasea.

[9] Much time had been lost, and sailing had already become dangerous because by now it was after the Day of Atonement.[b] So Paul warned them, [10] "Men, I can see that our

---

[a] 14 Or *Hebrew*   [b] 9 That is, Yom Kippur

voyage is going to be disastrous and bring great loss to ship and cargo, and to our own lives also." [11] But the centurion, instead of listening to what Paul said, followed the advice of the pilot and of the owner of the ship. [12] Since the harbor was unsuitable to winter in, the majority decided that we should sail on, hoping to reach Phoenix and winter there. This was a harbor in Crete, facing both southwest and northwest.

The Storm

[13] When a gentle south wind began to blow, they saw their opportunity; so they weighed anchor and sailed along the shore of Crete. [14] Before very long, a wind of hurricane force, called the Northeaster, swept down from the island. [15] The ship was caught by the storm and could not head into the wind; so we gave way to it and were driven along. [16] As we passed to the lee of a small island called Cauda, we were hardly able to make the lifeboat secure, [17] so the men hoisted it aboard. Then they passed ropes under the ship itself to hold it together. Because they were afraid they would run aground on the sandbars of Syrtis, they lowered the sea anchor[a] and let the ship be driven along. [18] We took such a violent battering from the storm that the next day they began to throw the cargo overboard. [19] On the third day, they threw the ship's tackle overboard with their own hands. [20] When neither sun nor stars appeared for many days and the storm continued raging, we finally gave up all hope of being saved.

[21] After they had gone a long time without food, Paul stood up before them and said: "Men, you should have taken my advice not to sail from Crete; then you would have spared yourselves this damage and loss. [22] But now I urge you to keep up your courage, because not one of you will be lost; only the ship will be destroyed. [23] Last night an angel of the God to whom I belong and whom I serve stood beside me [24] and said, 'Do not be afraid, Paul. You must stand trial before Caesar; and God has graciously given you the lives of all who sail with you.' [25] So keep up your courage, men, for I have faith in God that it will happen just as he told me.

[26] Nevertheless, we must run aground on some island."

The Shipwreck

[27] On the fourteenth night we were still being driven across the Adriatic[b] Sea, when about midnight the sailors sensed they were approaching land. [28] They took soundings and found that the water was a hundred and twenty feet[c] deep. A short time later they took soundings again and found it was ninety feet[d] deep. [29] Fearing that we would be dashed against the rocks, they dropped four anchors from the stern and prayed for daylight. [30] In an attempt to escape from the ship, the sailors let the lifeboat down into the sea, pretending they were going to lower some anchors from the bow. [31] Then Paul said to the centurion and the soldiers, "Unless these men stay with the ship, you cannot be saved." [32] So the soldiers cut the ropes that held the lifeboat and let it drift away.

[33] Just before dawn Paul urged them all to eat. "For the last fourteen days," he said, "you have been in constant suspense and have gone without food — you haven't eaten anything. [34] Now I urge you to take some food. You need it to survive. Not one of you will lose a single hair from his head." [35] After he said this, he took some bread and gave thanks to God in front of them all. Then he broke it and began to eat. [36] They were all encouraged and ate some food themselves. [37] Altogether there were 276 of us on board. [38] When they had eaten as much as they wanted, they lightened the ship by throwing the grain into the sea.

[39] When daylight came, they did not recognize the land, but they saw a bay with a sandy beach, where they decided to run the ship aground if they could. [40] Cutting loose the anchors, they left them in the sea and at the same time untied the ropes that held the rudders. Then they hoisted the foresail to the wind and made for the beach. [41] But the ship struck a sandbar and ran aground. The bow stuck fast and would not move, and the stern was broken to pieces by the pounding of the surf.

[42] The soldiers planned to kill the prisoners to prevent any of them from swimming away

---

[a] 17 Or *the sails*   [b] 27 In ancient times the name referred to an area extending well south of Italy.
[c] 28 Or about 37 meters   [d] 28 Or about 27 meters

and escaping. ⁴³But the centurion wanted to spare Paul's life and kept them from carrying out their plan. He ordered those who could swim to jump overboard first and get to land. ⁴⁴The rest were to get there on planks or on other pieces of the ship. In this way everyone reached land safely.

Paul Ashore on Malta

28 Once safely on shore, we found out that the island was called Malta. ²The islanders showed us unusual kindness. They built a fire and welcomed us all because it was raining and cold. ³Paul gathered a pile of brushwood and, as he put it on the fire, a viper, driven out by the heat, fastened itself on his hand. ⁴When the islanders saw the snake hanging from his hand, they said to each other, "This man must be a murderer; for though he escaped from the sea, the goddess Justice has not allowed him to live." ⁵But Paul shook the snake off into the fire and suffered no ill effects. ⁶The people expected him to swell up or suddenly fall dead; but after waiting a long time and seeing nothing unusual happen to him, they changed their minds and said he was a god.

⁷There was an estate nearby that belonged to Publius, the chief official of the island. He welcomed us to his home and showed us generous hospitality for three days. ⁸His father was sick in bed, suffering from fever and dysentery. Paul went in to see him and, after prayer, placed his hands on him and healed him. ⁹When this had happened, the rest of the sick on the island came and were cured. ¹⁰They honored us in many ways; and when we were ready to sail, they furnished us with the supplies we needed.

Paul's Arrival at Rome

¹¹After three months we put out to sea in a ship that had wintered in the island—it was an Alexandrian ship with the figurehead of the twin gods Castor and Pollux. ¹²We put in at Syracuse and stayed there three days. ¹³From there we set sail and arrived at Rhegium. The next day the south wind came up, and on the following day we reached Puteoli. ¹⁴There we found some brothers and sisters who invited us to spend a week with them. And so we came to Rome. ¹⁵The brothers and sisters there had heard that we were coming, and they traveled as far as the Forum of Appius and the Three Taverns to meet us. At the sight of these people Paul thanked God and was encouraged. ¹⁶When we got to Rome, Paul was allowed to live by himself, with a soldier to guard him.

Paul Preaches at Rome Under Guard

¹⁷Three days later he called together the local Jewish leaders. When they had assembled, Paul said to them: "My brothers, although I have done nothing against our people or against the customs of our ancestors, I was arrested in Jerusalem and handed over to the Romans. ¹⁸They examined me and wanted to release me, because I was not guilty of any crime deserving death. ¹⁹The Jews objected, so I was compelled to make an appeal to Caesar. I certainly did not intend to bring any charge against my own people. ²⁰For this reason I have asked to see you and talk with you. It is because of the hope of Israel that I am bound with this chain." ²¹They replied, "We have not received any letters from Judea concerning you, and none of our people who have come from there has reported or said anything bad about you. ²²But we want to hear what your views are, for we know that people everywhere are talking against this sect."

²³They arranged to meet Paul on a certain day, and came in even larger numbers to the place where he was staying. He witnessed to them from morning till evening, explaining about the kingdom of God, and from the Law of Moses and from the Prophets he tried to persuade them about Jesus. ²⁴Some were convinced by what he said, but others would not believe. ²⁵They disagreed among themselves and began to leave after Paul had made this final statement: "The Holy Spirit spoke the truth to your ancestors when he said through Isaiah the prophet:

²⁶ " 'Go to this people and say,
   "You will be ever hearing but never
        understanding;
     you will be ever seeing but never
        perceiving."
²⁷For this people's heart has become
        calloused;
     they hardly hear with their ears,
        and they have closed their eyes.
   Otherwise they might see with their eyes,
     hear with their ears,

SPREAD THE WORD

READ: ACTS 28:30-31

The book of Acts has a relatively happy ending. After multiple missionary journeys the apostle Paul travels back to Jerusalem, where he is promptly arrested (Acts 21:27-36). His imprisonment drags on, and he nearly dies in transit to Rome (27:1—28:10). But the last words of Acts show him freely preaching about Jesus while he awaits his trial before Caesar.

That's not the end of Paul's story. While in Rome he likely wrote his letters to the Colossians, Ephesians, Philippians, and Philemon, which all detail his ongoing work. Each Roman official who heard Paul up to this point had found him innocent, so there's good reason to think Caesar heard his case and set him free.

Ancient tradition reports that Paul went to Spain to preach Jesus in a place where the Lord was unknown, a wish he expressed in Romans 15:24. Tradition says that Paul was again arrested under a new, more hostile emperor, Nero, then condemned and beheaded for his faith in Jesus.

Paul's friend Luke likely finished the book of Acts where he did simply to avoid delay in sending this account to Theophilus (Acts 1:1). But the abrupt conclusion implies a bold truth. The spread of the good news about Jesus didn't end with Paul. Along with every Christian who ever lived, you too are part of the story of telling the world about him (v. 8).

BUILDING

FAITH

WISDOM

STRENGTH

understand with their hearts
and turn, and I would heal them.' *a*

28 "Therefore I want you to know that God's salvation has been sent to the Gentiles, and they will listen!" [29] *b*

30 For two whole years Paul stayed there in his own rented house and welcomed all who came to see him. 31 He proclaimed the kingdom of God and taught about the Lord Jesus Christ — with all boldness and without hindrance!

---

a 27 Isaiah 6:9,10 (see Septuagint)   *b* 29 Some manuscripts include here *After he said this, the Jews left, arguing vigorously among themselves.*

ROMANS

WHEN DID THIS HAPPEN?

Around A.D. 57 in Corinth

WHO IS IN THIS BOOK?

Paul

Abraham

Adam

VERSES YOU MIGHT RECOGNIZE

ROMANS 3:23

"All have sinned and fall short of the glory of God."

ROMANS 8:28

"And we know that in all things God works for the good of those who love him, who have been called according to his purpose."

WHAT'S IT ABOUT?

This book offers a complete picture of how people can be saved from their sins. Written by Paul, the book of Romans explains the basic truths of the Christian faith to the believers in Rome. Paul began by talking about the problem of sin, which came into the world through the first man, Adam. He explained that all people are separated from God because of their sin, but they can be justified—or forgiven of their debt—through faith in his Son. Jesus died on the cross and rose again to free people from sin. Redemption is only available through faith in Jesus Christ.

This book emphasizes that God's salvation is for all people, both Jews and Gentiles. People are not capable of righteousness on their own; it comes from God through Christ. Sanctification is the process of becoming more righteous by allowing God's Spirit to transform you, and this process continues throughout your life.

Though Paul was writing to Gentiles and Jews, he mentioned Adam and Abraham to prove that Jesus is the Messiah the Jews had been waiting for. While some of the Jews had been expecting an earthly ruler, Paul showed them that Jesus came for a much greater purpose—to restore the relationship between God and men.

ROMANS

1 Paul, a servant of Christ Jesus, called to be an apostle and set apart for the gospel of God— ²the gospel he promised beforehand through his prophets in the Holy Scriptures ³regarding his Son, who as to his earthly life[a] was a descendant of David, ⁴and who through the Spirit of holiness was appointed the Son of God in power[b] by his resurrection from the dead: Jesus Christ our Lord. ⁵Through him we received grace and apostleship to call all the Gentiles to the obedience that comes from[c] faith for his name's sake. ⁶And you also are among those Gentiles who are called to belong to Jesus Christ.

⁷To all in Rome who are loved by God and called to be his holy people:

Grace and peace to you from God our Father and from the Lord Jesus Christ.

Paul's Longing to Visit Rome

⁸First, I thank my God through Jesus Christ for all of you, because your faith is being reported all over the world. ⁹God, whom I serve in my spirit in preaching the gospel of his Son, is my witness how constantly I remember you ¹⁰in my prayers at all times; and I pray that now at last by God's will the way may be opened for me to come to you.

¹¹I long to see you so that I may impart to you some spiritual gift to make you strong— ¹²that is, that you and I may be mutually encouraged by each other's faith. ¹³I do not want you to be unaware, brothers and sisters,[d] that I planned many times to come to you (but have been prevented from doing so until now) in order that I might have a harvest among you, just as I have had among the other Gentiles.

¹⁴I am obligated both to Greeks and non-Greeks, both to the wise and the foolish.

¹⁵That is why I am so eager to preach the gospel also to you who are in Rome.

¹⁶For I am not ashamed of the gospel, because it is the power of God that brings salvation to everyone who believes: first to the Jew, then to the Gentile. ¹⁷For in the gospel the righteousness of God is revealed—a righteousness that is by faith from first to last,[e] just as it is written: "The righteous will live by faith."[f]

God's Wrath Against Sinful Humanity

¹⁸The wrath of God is being revealed from heaven against all the godlessness and wickedness of people, who suppress the truth by their wickedness, ¹⁹since what may be known about God is plain to them, because God has made it plain to them. ²⁰For since the creation of the world God's invisible qualities—his eternal power and divine nature—have been clearly seen, being understood from what has been made, so that people are without excuse.

²¹For although they knew God, they neither glorified him as God nor gave thanks to him, but their thinking became futile and their foolish hearts were darkened. ²²Although they claimed to be wise, they became fools ²³and exchanged the glory of the immortal God for images made to look like a mortal human being and birds and animals and reptiles.

²⁴Therefore God gave them over in the sinful desires of their hearts to sexual impurity for the degrading of their bodies with one another. ²⁵They exchanged the truth about God for a lie, and worshiped and served created things rather than the Creator—who is forever praised. Amen.

²⁶Because of this, God gave them over to shameful lusts. Even their women exchanged natural sexual relations for unnatural ones.

---

[a] 3 Or *who according to the flesh*   [b] 4 Or *was declared with power to be the Son of God*   [c] 5 Or *that is*
[d] 13 The Greek word for *brothers and sisters* (*adelphoi*) refers here to believers, both men and women, as part of God's family; also in 7:1, 4; 8:12, 29; 10:1; 11:25; 12:1; 15:14, 30; 16:14, 17.   [e] 17 Or *is from faith to faith*   [f] 17 Hab. 2:4

[27]In the same way the men also abandoned natural relations with women and were inflamed with lust for one another. Men committed shameful acts with other men, and received in themselves the due penalty for their error.

[28]Furthermore, just as they did not think it worthwhile to retain the knowledge of God, so God gave them over to a depraved mind, so that they do what ought not to be done. [29]They have become filled with every kind of wickedness, evil, greed and depravity. They are full of envy, murder, strife, deceit and malice. They are gossips, [30]slanderers, God-haters, insolent, arrogant and boastful; they invent ways of doing evil; they disobey their parents; [31]they have no understanding, no fidelity, no love, no mercy. [32]Although they know God's righteous decree that those who do such things deserve death, they not only continue to do these very things but also approve of those who practice them.

God's Righteous Judgment

2 You, therefore, have no excuse, you who pass judgment on someone else, for at whatever point you judge another, you are condemning yourself, because you who pass judgment do the same things. [2]Now we know that God's judgment against those who do such things is based on truth. [3]So when you, a mere human being, pass judgment on them and yet do the same things, do you think you will escape God's judgment? [4]Or do you show contempt for the riches of his kindness, forbearance and patience, not realizing that God's kindness is intended to lead you to repentance?

[5]But because of your stubbornness and your unrepentant heart, you are storing up wrath against yourself for the day of God's wrath, when his righteous judgment will be revealed. [6]God "will repay each person according to what they have done."[a] [7]To those who by persistence in doing good seek glory, honor and immortality, he will give eternal life. [8]But for those who are self-seeking and who reject the truth and follow evil, there will be wrath and anger. [9]There will be trouble and distress for every human being who does evil: first for the Jew, then for the Gentile; [10]but glory, honor and peace for every-one who does good: first for the Jew, then for the Gentile. [11]For God does not show favoritism.

[12]All who sin apart from the law will also perish apart from the law, and all who sin under the law will be judged by the law. [13]For it is not those who hear the law who are righteous in God's sight, but it is those who obey the law who will be declared righteous. [14](Indeed, when Gentiles, who do not have the law, do by nature things required by the law, they are a law for themselves, even though they do not have the law. [15]They show that the requirements of the law are written on their hearts, their consciences also bearing witness, and their thoughts sometimes accusing them and at other times even defending them.) [16]This will take place on the day when God judges people's secrets through Jesus Christ, as my gospel declares.

The Jews and the Law

[17]Now you, if you call yourself a Jew; if you rely on the law and boast in God; [18]if you know his will and approve of what is superior because you are instructed by the law; [19]if you are convinced that you are a guide for the blind, a light for those who are in the dark, [20]an instructor of the foolish, a teacher of little children, because you have in the law the embodiment of knowledge and truth — [21]you, then, who teach others, do you not teach yourself? You who preach against stealing, do you steal? [22]You who say that people should not commit adultery, do you commit adultery? You who abhor idols, do you rob temples? [23]You who boast in the law, do you dishonor God by breaking the law? [24]As it is written: "God's name is blasphemed among the Gentiles because of you."[b]

[25]Circumcision has value if you observe the law, but if you break the law, you have become as though you had not been circumcised. [26]So then, if those who are not circumcised keep the law's requirements, will they not be regarded as though they were circumcised? [27]The one who is not circumcised physically and yet obeys the law will condemn you who, even though you have the[c] written code and circumcision, are a lawbreaker.

[a] 6 Psalm 62:12; Prov. 24:12   [b] 24 Isaiah 52:5 (see Septuagint); Ezek. 36:20,22   [c] 27 Or *who, by means of a*

²⁸A person is not a Jew who is one only outwardly, nor is circumcision merely outward and physical. ²⁹No, a person is a Jew who is one inwardly; and circumcision is circumcision of the heart, by the Spirit, not by the written code. Such a person's praise is not from other people, but from God.

God's Faithfulness

3 What advantage, then, is there in being a Jew, or what value is there in circumcision? ²Much in every way! First of all, the Jews have been entrusted with the very words of God.

³What if some were unfaithful? Will their unfaithfulness nullify God's faithfulness? ⁴Not at all! Let God be true, and every human being a liar. As it is written:

"So that you may be proved right when
    you speak
and prevail when you judge."ᵃ

⁵But if our unrighteousness brings out God's righteousness more clearly, what shall we say? That God is unjust in bringing his wrath on us? (I am using a human argument.) ⁶Certainly not! If that were so, how could God judge the world? ⁷Someone might argue, "If my falsehood enhances God's truthfulness and so increases his glory, why am I still condemned as a sinner?" ⁸Why not say — as some slanderously claim that we say — "Let us do evil that good may result"? Their condemnation is just!

No One Is Righteous

⁹What shall we conclude then? Do we have any advantage? Not at all! For we have already made the charge that Jews and Gentiles alike are all under the power of sin. ¹⁰As it is written:

"There is no one righteous, not even one;
¹¹   there is no one who understands;
    there is no one who seeks God.
¹²All have turned away,
    they have together become worthless;
    there is no one who does good,
    not even one."ᵇ

¹³ "Their throats are open graves;
    their tongues practice deceit."ᶜ
"The poison of vipers is on their lips."ᵈ
¹⁴   "Their mouths are full of cursing
        and bitterness."ᵉ
¹⁵ "Their feet are swift to shed blood;
¹⁶   ruin and misery mark their ways,
¹⁷and the way of peace they do not
        know."ᶠ
¹⁸   "There is no fear of God before
        their eyes."ᵍ

¹⁹Now we know that whatever the law says, it says to those who are under the law, so that every mouth may be silenced and the whole world held accountable to God. ²⁰Therefore no one will be declared righteous in God's sight by the works of the law; rather, through the law we become conscious of our sin.

Righteousness Through Faith

²¹But now apart from the law the righteousness of God has been made known, to which the Law and the Prophets testify. ²²This righteousness is given through faith inʰ Jesus Christ to all who believe. There is no difference between Jew and Gentile, ²³for all have sinned and fall short of the glory of God, ²⁴and all are justified freely by his grace through the redemption that came by Christ Jesus. ²⁵God presented Christ as a sacrifice of atonement,ⁱ through the shedding of his blood — to be received by faith. He did this to demonstrate his righteousness, because in his forbearance he had left the sins committed beforehand unpunished — ²⁶he did it to demonstrate his righteousness at the present time, so as to be just and the one who justifies those who have faith in Jesus.

²⁷Where, then, is boasting? It is excluded. Because of what law? The law that requires works? No, because of the law that requires faith. ²⁸For we maintain that a person is justified by faith apart from the works of the law. ²⁹Or is God the God of Jews only? Is he not the God of Gentiles too? Yes, of Gentiles too, ³⁰since there is only one God, who will justify the circumcised by faith and the uncircumcised through that same faith. ³¹Do

ᵃ 4 Psalm 51:4   ᵇ 12 Psalms 14:1-3; 53:1-3; Eccles. 7:20   ᶜ 13 Psalm 5:9   ᵈ 13 Psalm 140:3
ᵉ 14 Psalm 10:7 (see Septuagint)   ᶠ 17 Isaiah 59:7,8   ᵍ 18 Psalm 36:1   ʰ 22 Or *through the*
faithfulness of   ⁱ 25 The Greek for *sacrifice of atonement* refers to the atonement cover on the ark of the covenant (see Lev. 16:15,16).

UNMISTAKEN IDENTITY

READ: ROMANS 3:20-22

Do you find your identity in who you are or whose you are? That subtle difference makes all the difference in the world.

You can base your identity on a thousand things—the degrees you'll get, the trophies you've won, the hobbies you have, the way you look, the way you dress, the school you go to, or the friends you have. But if you base your identity on any of those things, your identity is a literally a house of cards. That sucker's going to collapse sooner or later. There's one solid foundation, and that's Jesus Christ.

If you find security in what you've done in the past, you'll always fall short and you'll miss what God's doing now. The only one place to find your true identity and eternal security: what Christ has done for you.

BUILDING

FAITH

WISDOM

STRENGTH

Religion is spelled *do*.

The gospel is spelled *done*.

It's not 99 percent grace and 1 percent good works. Most of us still want 1 percent credit for the things we've done right, but there's no partial grace. You either let God forgive you or you spend the rest of your life trying to forgive yourself. You're not a part of the equation of salvation. Sorry. You cannot trust Jesus Christ 99 percent. Trust is a 100 percent proposition. It's addition by subtraction.

So the question is this: What is getting between you and God? Where do you find your security outside of Christ?

Taken from *All In Student Edition* by Mark Batterson and Parker Batterson, copyright © 2014 by Mark Batterson, published by Zondervan.

we, then, nullify the law by this faith? Not at all! Rather, we uphold the law.

Abraham Justified by Faith

4 What then shall we say that Abraham, our forefather according to the flesh, discovered in this matter? [2]If, in fact, Abraham was justified by works, he had something to boast about—but not before God. [3]What does Scripture say? "Abraham believed God, and it was credited to him as righteousness."[a]

[4]Now to the one who works, wages are not credited as a gift but as an obligation. [5]However, to the one who does not work but trusts God who justifies the ungodly, their faith is credited as righteousness. [6]David says the same thing when he speaks of the blessedness of the one to whom God credits righteousness apart from works:

[7]"Blessed are those
  whose transgressions are forgiven,
  whose sins are covered.
[8]Blessed is the one
  whose sin the Lord will never count
    against them."[b]

[9]Is this blessedness only for the circumcised, or also for the uncircumcised? We have been saying that Abraham's faith was credited to him as righteousness. [10]Under what circumstances was it credited? Was it after he was circumcised, or before? It was not after, but before! [11]And he received circumcision as a sign, a seal of the righteousness that he had by faith while he was still uncircumcised. So then, he is the father of all who believe but have not been circumcised, in order that righteousness might be credited to them. [12]And he is then also the father of the circumcised who not only are circumcised but who also follow in the footsteps of the faith that our father Abraham had before he was circumcised.

[13]It was not through the law that Abraham and his offspring received the promise that he would be heir of the world, but through the righteousness that comes by faith. [14]For if those who depend on the law are heirs, faith means nothing and the promise is worthless, [15]because the law brings wrath. And where there is no law there is no transgression.

[16]Therefore, the promise comes by faith, so that it may be by grace and may be guaranteed to all Abraham's offspring—not only to those who are of the law but also to those who have the faith of Abraham. He is the father of us all. [17]As it is written: "I have made you a father of many nations."[c] He is our father in the sight of God, in whom he believed—the God who gives life to the dead and calls into being things that were not.

[18]Against all hope, Abraham in hope believed and so became the father of many nations, just as it had been said to him, "So shall your offspring be."[d] [19]Without weakening in his faith, he faced the fact that his body was as good as dead—since he was about a hundred years old—and that Sarah's womb was also dead. [20]Yet he did not waver through unbelief regarding the promise of God, but was strengthened in his faith and gave glory to God, [21]being fully persuaded that God had power to do what he had promised. [22]This is why "it was credited to him as righteousness." [23]The words "it was credited to him" were written not for him alone, [24]but also for us, to whom God will credit righteousness—for us who believe in him who raised Jesus our Lord from the dead. [25]He was delivered over to death for our sins and was raised to life for our justification.

Peace and Hope

5 Therefore, since we have been justified through faith, we[e] have peace with God through our Lord Jesus Christ, [2]through whom we have gained access by faith into this grace in which we now stand. And we[f] boast in the hope of the glory of God. [3]Not only so, but we[f] also glory in our sufferings, because we know that suffering produces perseverance; [4]perseverance, character; and character, hope. [5]And hope does not put us to shame, because God's love has been poured out into our hearts through the Holy Spirit, who has been given to us.

[6]You see, at just the right time, when we were still powerless, Christ died for the ungodly. [7]Very rarely will anyone die for a righteous person, though for a good person someone might possibly dare to die. [8]But God demonstrates his own love for us in this: While we were still sinners, Christ died for us.

---

[a] 3 Gen. 15:6; also in verse 22   [b] 8 Psalm 32:1,2   [c] 17 Gen. 17:5   [d] 18 Gen. 15:5   [e] 1 Many manuscripts *let us*   [f] 2,3 Or *let us*

PROMISE KEEPER

READ: ROMANS 4:16

Unlike plenty of people you meet, the Lord doesn't think promises are meant to be broken. Numbers 23:19 assures you that "God is not human, that he should lie." So when the Lord says he makes you his friend because of what Jesus accomplished on the cross, it's a relief to know you can count on his words.

The apostle Paul wrote his letter to the Christians in Rome to tell them how to get right with God. He starts by detailing humankind's problem with sin. He explains that God "justifies" or "declares innocent" everyone who believes in Jesus. Then he keeps hammering the point that this "justification" happens through faith, not through doing good works. It's a gift that flows from the Lord's grace, the favor he gives you even when you don't deserve it. It's a sign God loves you even at your worst (Romans 5:8).

Some of God's words might seem too good to be true, but God guarantees his promises, giving you even more reason to trust. You can dare to be like Abraham, who "did not waver through unbelief regarding the promise of God, but was strengthened in his faith and gave glory to God," because he was "fully persuaded that God had power to do what he had promised" (4:20-21).

When God makes a promise to you, he keeps it. He has all the love and power he needs to make it come true.

BUILDING
FAITH
WISDOM
STRENGTH

⁹Since we have now been justified by his blood, how much more shall we be saved from God's wrath through him! ¹⁰For if, while we were God's enemies, we were reconciled to him through the death of his Son, how much more, having been reconciled, shall we be saved through his life! ¹¹Not only is this so, but we also boast in God through our Lord Jesus Christ, through whom we have now received reconciliation.

Death Through Adam, Life Through Christ

¹²Therefore, just as sin entered the world through one man, and death through sin, and in this way death came to all people, because all sinned —

¹³To be sure, sin was in the world before the law was given, but sin is not charged against anyone's account where there is no law. ¹⁴Nevertheless, death reigned from the time of Adam to the time of Moses, even over those who did not sin by breaking a command, as did Adam, who is a pattern of the one to come.

¹⁵But the gift is not like the trespass. For if the many died by the trespass of the one man, how much more did God's grace and the gift that came by the grace of the one man, Jesus Christ, overflow to the many! ¹⁶Nor can the gift of God be compared with the result of one man's sin: The judgment followed one sin and brought condemnation, but the gift followed many trespasses and brought justification. ¹⁷For if, by the trespass of the one man, death reigned through that one man, how much more will those who receive God's abundant provision of grace and of the gift of righteousness reign in life through the one man, Jesus Christ!

¹⁸Consequently, just as one trespass resulted in condemnation for all people, so also one righteous act resulted in justification and life for all people. ¹⁹For just as through the disobedience of the one man the many were made sinners, so also through the obedience of the one man the many will be made righteous.

²⁰The law was brought in so that the trespass might increase. But where sin increased, grace increased all the more, ²¹so that, just as sin reigned in death, so also grace might reign through righteousness to bring eternal life through Jesus Christ our Lord.

Dead to Sin, Alive in Christ

6 What shall we say, then? Shall we go on sinning so that grace may increase? ²By no means! We are those who have died to sin; how can we live in it any longer? ³Or don't you know that all of us who were baptized into Christ Jesus were baptized into his death? ⁴We were therefore buried with him through baptism into death in order that, just as Christ was raised from the dead through the glory of the Father, we too may live a new life.

⁵For if we have been united with him in a death like his, we will certainly also be united with him in a resurrection like his. ⁶For we know that our old self was crucified with him so that the body ruled by sin might be done away with,ᵃ that we should no longer be slaves to sin — ⁷because anyone who has died has been set free from sin.

⁸Now if we died with Christ, we believe that we will also live with him. ⁹For we know that since Christ was raised from the dead, he cannot die again; death no longer has mastery over him. ¹⁰The death he died, he died to sin once for all; but the life he lives, he lives to God.

¹¹In the same way, count yourselves dead to sin but alive to God in Christ Jesus. ¹²Therefore do not let sin reign in your mortal body so that you obey its evil desires. ¹³Do not offer any part of yourself to sin as an instrument of wickedness, but rather offer yourselves to God as those who have been brought from death to life; and offer every part of yourself to him as an instrument of righteousness. ¹⁴For sin shall no longer be your master, because you are not under the law, but under grace.

Slaves to Righteousness

¹⁵What then? Shall we sin because we are not under the law but under grace? By no means! ¹⁶Don't you know that when you offer yourselves to someone as obedient slaves, you are slaves of the one you obey — whether you are slaves to sin, which leads to death, or to obedience, which leads to righteousness? ¹⁷But thanks be to God that, though you used to be slaves to sin, you have come to

---

ᵃ 6 Or *be rendered powerless*

SICK OF MYSELF

READ: ROMANS 6:1-4

I had slotted my life into isolated compartments. School occupied one space. Church fit over here, music over there, and movies next to that. Parents here and friends there. All nice and tidy—and most of them closed off from Jesus. One moment I sang in church; the next I rocked out to profane music in my car. One moment I shared in Bible study class; the next I rented another R-rated horror movie. Some friends spoke truth to me, and I had to own up to it.

I felt I was at a crossroads. I remember the crisp air one night before a church service. I was going to be singing in ten minutes, and I was sick of myself.

BUILDING

FAITH

WISDOM

STRENGTH

"Lord, you don't have my life, do you? You just have pieces of me," I said. "But it's like I'm holding you in and keeping you from spilling over into all of these other areas."

My pasty tongue clung to the roof of my mouth, and my chest thumped. I knew I needed to change. "Father, I have to give you lordship here, and I have to lay down some things."

Part of me had to go away. I thought, *My Father, who loves me, who walks with me, who knows me and sees things in my life that are tearing me down, is now trying to free me from them.* It was a revelation. My blinders fell off, and I knew my relationship with God would follow his design instead of mine.

Taken from *Your Own Jesus Student Edition* by Mark Hall, copyright © 2009 by Mark Hall, published by Zondervan.

obey from your heart the pattern of teaching that has now claimed your allegiance. [18]You have been set free from sin and have become slaves to righteousness.

[19]I am using an example from everyday life because of your human limitations. Just as you used to offer yourselves as slaves to impurity and to ever-increasing wickedness, so now offer yourselves as slaves to righteousness leading to holiness. [20]When you were slaves to sin, you were free from the control of righteousness. [21]What benefit did you reap at that time from the things you are now ashamed of? Those things result in death! [22]But now that you have been set free from sin and have become slaves of God, the benefit you reap leads to holiness, and the result is eternal life. [23]For the wages of sin is death, but the gift of God is eternal life in[a] Christ Jesus our Lord.

Released From the Law, Bound to Christ

7 Do you not know, brothers and sisters — for I am speaking to those who know the law — that the law has authority over someone only as long as that person lives? [2]For example, by law a married woman is bound to her husband as long as he is alive, but if her husband dies, she is released from the law that binds her to him. [3]So then, if she has sexual relations with another man while her husband is still alive, she is called an adulteress. But if her husband dies, she is released from that law and is not an adulteress if she marries another man.

[4]So, my brothers and sisters, you also died to the law through the body of Christ, that you might belong to another, to him who was raised from the dead, in order that we might bear fruit for God. [5]For when we were in the realm of the flesh,[b] the sinful passions aroused by the law were at work in us, so that we bore fruit for death. [6]But now, by dying to what once bound us, we have been released from the law so that we serve in the new way of the Spirit, and not in the old way of the written code.

The Law and Sin

[7]What shall we say, then? Is the law sinful? Certainly not! Nevertheless, I would not have known what sin was had it not been for the law. For I would not have known what coveting really was if the law had not said, "You shall not covet."[c] [8]But sin, seizing the opportunity afforded by the commandment, produced in me every kind of coveting. For apart from the law, sin was dead. [9]Once I was alive apart from the law; but when the commandment came, sin sprang to life and I died. [10]I found that the very commandment that was intended to bring life actually brought death. [11]For sin, seizing the opportunity afforded by the commandment, deceived me, and through the commandment put me to death. [12]So then, the law is holy, and the commandment is holy, righteous and good.

[13]Did that which is good, then, become death to me? By no means! Nevertheless, in order that sin might be recognized as sin, it used what is good to bring about my death, so that through the commandment sin might become utterly sinful.

[14]We know that the law is spiritual; but I am unspiritual, sold as a slave to sin. [15]I do not understand what I do. For what I want to do I do not do, but what I hate I do. [16]And if I do what I do not want to do, I agree that the law is good. [17]As it is, it is no longer I myself who do it, but it is sin living in me. [18]For I know that good itself does not dwell in me, that is, in my sinful nature.[d] For I have the desire to do what is good, but I cannot carry it out. [19]For I do not do the good I want to do, but the evil I do not want to do — this I keep on doing. [20]Now if I do what I do not want to do, it is no longer I who do it, but it is sin living in me that does it.

[21]So I find this law at work: Although I want to do good, evil is right there with me. [22]For in my inner being I delight in God's law; [23]but I see another law at work in me, waging war against the law of my mind and making me a prisoner of the law of sin at work within me. [24]What a wretched man I am! Who will rescue me from this body that is subject to death? [25]Thanks be to God, who delivers me through Jesus Christ our Lord!

So then, I myself in my mind am a slave to God's law, but in my sinful nature[e] a slave to the law of sin.

---

[a] 23 Or *through*   [b] 5 In contexts like this, the Greek word for *flesh* (*sarx*) refers to the sinful state of human beings, often presented as a power in opposition to the Spirit.   [c] 7 Exodus 20:17; Deut. 5:21   [d] 18 Or *my flesh*   [e] 25 Or *in the flesh*

BETWEEN THE ALTAR AND THE DOOR

READ: ROMANS 7:15-18

When I see the difference between the person I'm called to be and the person I am, I can only fling up my hands and ask, "What's the deal?"

It's the difference between me at my desk with my Bible open and later in the day insisting on my way in a disagreement. It's me on my knees praying versus my traffic-jam utterances when I'm running late. It's me serving at an orphanage in Kenya and returning home to whine about the scuffed paint in my house.

BUILDING

I come to church and worship the Lord—and life is beautiful. I'm on the same page with my brothers and sisters and with God. I know where I'm headed. I'm full of purpose. Everything is black and white, and I know right from wrong. Sin reeks when I'm at the altar. I know what I need to lay down. I know what I need to pick up.

FAITH

WISDOM

STRENGTH

And then, somewhere between the altar and the door, everything falls apart. I slip out the door into the world, and it's as if everything I thought and felt and committed to sinks into a black hole.

The question frames our predicament. The place between the altar and the door is the place of follow-through—or lack thereof. It's a place of choice, where we either commit to follow what we know to be truth or we chase our own ideas.

Taken from *Your Own Jesus Student Edition* by Mark Hall, copyright © 2009 by Mark Hall, published by Zondervan.

Life Through the Spirit

8 Therefore, there is now no condemnation for those who are in Christ Jesus, [2] because through Christ Jesus the law of the Spirit who gives life has set you[a] free from the law of sin and death. [3] For what the law was powerless to do because it was weakened by the flesh,[b] God did by sending his own Son in the likeness of sinful flesh to be a sin offering.[c] And so he condemned sin in the flesh, [4] in order that the righteous requirement of the law might be fully met in us, who do not live according to the flesh but according to the Spirit.

[5] Those who live according to the flesh have their minds set on what the flesh desires; but those who live in accordance with the Spirit have their minds set on what the Spirit desires. [6] The mind governed by the flesh is death, but the mind governed by the Spirit is life and peace. [7] The mind governed by the flesh is hostile to God; it does not submit to God's law, nor can it do so. [8] Those who are in the realm of the flesh cannot please God.

[9] You, however, are not in the realm of the flesh but are in the realm of the Spirit, if indeed the Spirit of God lives in you. And if anyone does not have the Spirit of Christ, they do not belong to Christ. [10] But if Christ is in you, then even though your body is subject to death because of sin, the Spirit gives life[d] because of righteousness. [11] And if the Spirit of him who raised Jesus from the dead is living in you, he who raised Christ from the dead will also give life to your mortal bodies because of[e] his Spirit who lives in you.

[12] Therefore, brothers and sisters, we have an obligation — but it is not to the flesh, to live according to it. [13] For if you live according to the flesh, you will die; but if by the Spirit you put to death the misdeeds of the body, you will live.

[14] For those who are led by the Spirit of God are the children of God. [15] The Spirit you received does not make you slaves, so that you live in fear again; rather, the Spirit you received brought about your adoption to sonship.[f] And by him we cry, *"Abba,[g]* Father." [16] The Spirit himself testifies with our spirit that we are God's children. [17] Now if we are children, then we are heirs — heirs of God and co-heirs with Christ, if indeed we share in his sufferings in order that we may also share in his glory.

Present Suffering and Future Glory

[18] I consider that our present sufferings are not worth comparing with the glory that will be revealed in us. [19] For the creation waits in eager expectation for the children of God to be revealed. [20] For the creation was subjected to frustration, not by its own choice, but by the will of the one who subjected it, in hope [21] that[h] the creation itself will be liberated from its bondage to decay and brought into the freedom and glory of the children of God.

[22] We know that the whole creation has been groaning as in the pains of childbirth right up to the present time. [23] Not only so, but we ourselves, who have the firstfruits of the Spirit, groan inwardly as we wait eagerly for our adoption to sonship, the redemption of our bodies. [24] For in this hope we were saved. But hope that is seen is no hope at all. Who hopes for what they already have? [25] But if we hope for what we do not yet have, we wait for it patiently.

[26] In the same way, the Spirit helps us in our weakness. We do not know what we ought to pray for, but the Spirit himself intercedes for us through wordless groans. [27] And he who searches our hearts knows the mind of the Spirit, because the Spirit intercedes for God's people in accordance with the will of God.

[28] And we know that in all things God works for the good of those who love him, who[i] have been called according to his purpose. [29] For those God foreknew he also

---

[a] 2 The Greek is singular; some manuscripts me   *[b] 3 In contexts like this, the Greek word for* flesh (sarx) *refers to the sinful state of human beings, often presented as a power in opposition to the Spirit; also in verses 4-13.   [c] 3 Or* flesh, for sin   *[d] 10 Or* you, your body is dead because of sin, yet your spirit is alive   *[e] 11 Some manuscripts* bodies through   *[f] 15 The Greek word for* adoption to sonship *is a term referring to the full legal standing of an adopted male heir in Roman culture; also in verse 23.   [g] 15 Aramaic for* father   *[h] 20,21 Or* subjected it in hope. [21]For   *[i] 28 Or* that all things work together for good to those who love God, who; *or* that in all things God works together with those who love him to bring about what is good — with those who

A FEW ABSOLUTES

READ: ROMANS 8:26-30

We *know*... There are so many things we do not know. We do not know if the economy will dip or if our team will win. We do not know what our parents are thinking or what career we will pursue. But according to Paul, we can be absolutely certain about four things. We know...

1. God works. He is busy behind the scenes, above the fray, within the fury. He hasn't checked out or moved on. He is ceaseless and tireless. He never stops working.

2. God works for the good. Not for our comfort or pleasure or entertainment, but for our ultimate good. Since he is the ultimate good, would we expect anything less?

3. God works for the good of those who love him. Behold the benefit of loving God! Make his story your story, and your story takes on a happy ending. Guaranteed. Being the author of our salvation, he writes a salvation theme into our biography.

4. God works in all things. God works, not through a few things or through the good things, best things, or easy things. But in "all things" God works.

Puppet in the hands of fortune or fate? Not you. You are in the hands of a living, loving God. Random collection of disconnected short stories? Far from it. Your life is a crafted narrative written by a good God, who is working toward your supreme good.

BUILDING FAITH WISDOM STRENGTH

Taken from *God's Story, Your Story: Youth Edition* by Max Lucado, copyright © 2011 by Max Lucado, published by Zondervan.

predestined to be conformed to the image of his Son, that he might be the firstborn among many brothers and sisters. ³⁰And those he predestined, he also called; those he called, he also justified; those he justified, he also glorified.

More Than Conquerors

³¹What, then, shall we say in response to these things? If God is for us, who can be against us? ³²He who did not spare his own Son, but gave him up for us all—how will he not also, along with him, graciously give us all things? ³³Who will bring any charge against those whom God has chosen? It is God who justifies. ³⁴Who then is the one who condemns? No one. Christ Jesus who died—more than that, who was raised to life—is at the right hand of God and is also interceding for us. ³⁵Who shall separate us from the love of Christ? Shall trouble or hardship or persecution or famine or nakedness or danger or sword? ³⁶As it is written:

> "For your sake we face death all day long;
> we are considered as sheep to be
> slaughtered."ᵃ

³⁷No, in all these things we are more than conquerors through him who loved us. ³⁸For I am convinced that neither death nor life, neither angels nor demons,ᵇ neither the present nor the future, nor any powers, ³⁹neither height nor depth, nor anything else in all creation, will be able to separate us from the love of God that is in Christ Jesus our Lord.

Paul's Anguish Over Israel

9 I speak the truth in Christ—I am not lying, my conscience confirms it through the Holy Spirit— ²I have great sorrow and unceasing anguish in my heart. ³For I could wish that I myself were cursed and cut off from Christ for the sake of my people, those of my own race, ⁴the people of Israel. Theirs is the adoption to sonship; theirs the divine glory, the covenants, the receiving of the law, the temple worship and the promises. ⁵Theirs are the patriarchs, and from them is traced the human ancestry of the Messiah, who is God over all, forever praised!ᶜ Amen.

God's Sovereign Choice

⁶It is not as though God's word had failed. For not all who are descended from Israel are Israel. ⁷Nor because they are his descendants are they all Abraham's children. On the contrary, "It is through Isaac that your offspring will be reckoned."ᵈ ⁸In other words, it is not the children by physical descent who are God's children, but it is the children of the promise who are regarded as Abraham's offspring. ⁹For this was how the promise was stated: "At the appointed time I will return, and Sarah will have a son."ᵉ

¹⁰Not only that, but Rebekah's children were conceived at the same time by our father Isaac. ¹¹Yet, before the twins were born or had done anything good or bad—in order that God's purpose in election might stand: ¹²not by works but by him who calls—she was told, "The older will serve the younger."ᶠ ¹³Just as it is written: "Jacob I loved, but Esau I hated."ᵍ

¹⁴What then shall we say? Is God unjust? Not at all! ¹⁵For he says to Moses,

> "I will have mercy on whom I have mercy,
> and I will have compassion on whom I
> have compassion."ʰ

¹⁶It does not, therefore, depend on human desire or effort, but on God's mercy. ¹⁷For Scripture says to Pharaoh: "I raised you up for this very purpose, that I might display my power in you and that my name might be proclaimed in all the earth."ⁱ ¹⁸Therefore God has mercy on whom he wants to have mercy, and he hardens whom he wants to harden.

¹⁹One of you will say to me: "Then why does God still blame us? For who is able to resist his will?" ²⁰But who are you, a human being, to talk back to God? "Shall what is formed say to the one who formed it, 'Why did you make me like this?'"ʲ ²¹Does not the potter have the right to make out of the same lump of clay some pottery for special purposes and some for common use?

²²What if God, although choosing to show his wrath and make his power known, bore with great patience the objects of his wrath—prepared for destruction? ²³What

---

ᵃ 36 Psalm 44:22   ᵇ 38 Or *nor heavenly rulers*
Or *Messiah. God who is over all be forever praised!*   ᶜ 5 Or *Messiah, who is over all. God be forever praised!*
ᵍ 13 Mal. 1:2,3   ʰ 15 Exodus 33:19   ⁱ 17 Exodus 9:16   ᵈ 7 Gen. 21:12   ᵉ 9 Gen. 18:10,14   ᶠ 12 Gen. 25:23
ʲ 20 Isaiah 29:16; 45:9

if he did this to make the riches of his glory known to the objects of his mercy, whom he prepared in advance for glory— ²⁴even us, whom he also called, not only from the Jews but also from the Gentiles? ²⁵As he says in Hosea:

> "I will call them 'my people' who are not
>   my people;
> and I will call her 'my loved one' who is
>   not my loved one,"ᵃ

²⁶and,

> "In the very place where it was said to
>   them,
>   'You are not my people,'
> there they will be called 'children of
>   the living God.'"ᵇ

²⁷Isaiah cries out concerning Israel:

> "Though the number of the Israelites be
>   like the sand by the sea,
>   only the remnant will be saved.
> ²⁸For the Lord will carry out
>   his sentence on earth with speed and
>   finality."ᶜ

²⁹It is just as Isaiah said previously:

> "Unless the Lord Almighty
>   had left us descendants,
> we would have become like Sodom,
>   we would have been like Gomorrah."ᵈ

Israel's Unbelief

³⁰What then shall we say? That the Gentiles, who did not pursue righteousness, have obtained it, a righteousness that is by faith; ³¹but the people of Israel, who pursued the law as the way of righteousness, have not attained their goal. ³²Why not? Because they pursued it not by faith but as if it were by works. They stumbled over the stumbling stone. ³³As it is written:

> "See, I lay in Zion a stone that causes
>   people to stumble
>   and a rock that makes them fall,
> and the one who believes in him will
>   never be put to shame."ᵉ

10 Brothers and sisters, my heart's desire and prayer to God for the Isra-

elites is that they may be saved. ²For I can testify about them that they are zealous for God, but their zeal is not based on knowledge. ³Since they did not know the righteousness of God and sought to establish their own, they did not submit to God's righteousness. ⁴Christ is the culmination of the law so that there may be righteousness for everyone who believes.

⁵Moses writes this about the righteousness that is by the law: "The person who does these things will live by them."ᶠ ⁶But the righteousness that is by faith says: "Do not say in your heart, 'Who will ascend into heaven?'"ᵍ (that is, to bring Christ down) ⁷"or 'Who will descend into the deep?'"ʰ (that is, to bring Christ up from the dead). ⁸But what does it say? "The word is near you; it is in your mouth and in your heart,"ⁱ that is, the message concerning faith that we proclaim: ⁹If you declare with your mouth, "Jesus is Lord," and believe in your heart that God raised him from the dead, you will be saved. ¹⁰For it is with your heart that you believe and are justified, and it is with your mouth that you profess your faith and are saved. ¹¹As Scripture says, "Anyone who believes in him will never be put to shame."ʲ ¹²For there is no difference between Jew and Gentile—the same Lord is Lord of all and richly blesses all who call on him, ¹³for, "Everyone who calls on the name of the Lord will be saved."ᵏ

¹⁴How, then, can they call on the one they have not believed in? And how can they believe in the one of whom they have not heard? And how can they hear without someone preaching to them? ¹⁵And how can anyone preach unless they are sent? As it is written: "How beautiful are the feet of those who bring good news!"ˡ

¹⁶But not all the Israelites accepted the good news. For Isaiah says, "Lord, who has believed our message?"ᵐ ¹⁷Consequently, faith comes from hearing the message, and the message is heard through the word about Christ. ¹⁸But I ask: Did they not hear? Of course they did:

> "Their voice has gone out into all the
>   earth,
>   their words to the ends of the world."ⁿ

ᵃ 25 Hosea 2:23   ᵇ 26 Hosea 1:10   ᶜ 28 Isaiah 10:22,23 (see Septuagint)   ᵈ 29 Isaiah 1:9   ᵉ 33 Isaiah 8:14; 28:16   ᶠ 5 Lev. 18:5   ᵍ 6 Deut. 30:12   ʰ 7 Deut. 30:13   ⁱ 8 Deut. 30:14   ʲ 11 Isaiah 28:16 (see Septuagint)   ᵏ 13 Joel 2:32   ˡ 15 Isaiah 52:7   ᵐ 16 Isaiah 53:1   ⁿ 18 Psalm 19:4

BEEN THERE, DONE THAT?

READ: ROMANS 10:3,9

Whenever I share the gospel or talk to people about Jesus, one of the saddest and most frequent responses comes with a tone of resignation. "I tried that."

It's amazing what grammar and word choice reveal. "I tried Jesus. It didn't work." Jesus isn't an "it." He's a he. "It" didn't work, because "it" is religion.

I look at them and gently shake my head. "You cannot try Jesus. It's impossible," I say. " Jesus is not a sweater. He's not a diet. He's not a behavior system. If you're going to try Jesus, the closest you'll ever get is religion, and religion is the stuff of God without God in it. It's the shell."

It's as if people look for a quick fix and think, *I'm going to go hear about what Jesus people do and try that. I realize I've gone the wrong way, so after I learn what the Jesus people do, I'll try to get good and come back.*

We need to be prepared to tell them it's too late to get good. Once we sin, we cannot unbreak the chain in our own power.

Belonging to Jesus isn't going out and being better. It's not living a holy life so he'll love you. Being a believer is just that—believing. It means confessing with your mouth that Jesus is Lord and believing in your heart that God raised him from the dead (Romans 10:9).

BUILDING

FAITH

WISDOM

STRENGTH

¹⁹Again I ask: Did Israel not understand? First, Moses says,

"I will make you envious by those who
    are not a nation;
I will make you angry by a nation that
    has no understanding."^a

²⁰And Isaiah boldly says,

"I was found by those who did not seek me;
I revealed myself to those who did not
    ask for me."^b

²¹But concerning Israel he says,

"All day long I have held out my hands
    to a disobedient and obstinate people."^c

The Remnant of Israel

11 I ask then: Did God reject his people? By no means! I am an Israelite myself, a descendant of Abraham, from the tribe of Benjamin. ²God did not reject his people, whom he foreknew. Don't you know what Scripture says in the passage about Elijah — how he appealed to God against Israel: ³"Lord, they have killed your prophets and torn down your altars; I am the only one left, and they are trying to kill me"^d? ⁴And what was God's answer to him? "I have reserved for myself seven thousand who have not bowed the knee to Baal."^e ⁵So too, at the present time there is a remnant chosen by grace. ⁶And if by grace, then it cannot be based on works; if it were, grace would no longer be grace.

⁷What then? What the people of Israel sought so earnestly they did not obtain. The elect among them did, but the others were hardened, ⁸as it is written:

"God gave them a spirit of stupor,
    eyes that could not see
    and ears that could not hear,
to this very day."^f

⁹And David says:

"May their table become a snare and
        a trap,
    a stumbling block and a retribution
        for them.
¹⁰ May their eyes be darkened so they
        cannot see,
    and their backs be bent forever."^g

Ingrafted Branches

¹¹Again I ask: Did they stumble so as to fall beyond recovery? Not at all! Rather, because of their transgression, salvation has come to the Gentiles to make Israel envious. ¹²But if their transgression means riches for the world, and their loss means riches for the Gentiles, how much greater riches will their full inclusion bring!

¹³I am talking to you Gentiles. Inasmuch as I am the apostle to the Gentiles, I take pride in my ministry ¹⁴in the hope that I may somehow arouse my own people to envy and save some of them. ¹⁵For if their rejection brought reconciliation to the world, what will their acceptance be but life from the dead? ¹⁶If the part of the dough offered as firstfruits is holy, then the whole batch is holy; if the root is holy, so are the branches.

¹⁷If some of the branches have been broken off, and you, though a wild olive shoot, have been grafted in among the others and now share in the nourishing sap from the olive root, ¹⁸do not consider yourself to be superior to those other branches. If you do, consider this: You do not support the root, but the root supports you. ¹⁹You will say then, "Branches were broken off so that I could be grafted in." ²⁰Granted. But they were broken off because of unbelief, and you stand by faith. Do not be arrogant, but tremble. ²¹For if God did not spare the natural branches, he will not spare you either.

²²Consider therefore the kindness and sternness of God: sternness to those who fell, but kindness to you, provided that you continue in his kindness. Otherwise, you also will be cut off. ²³And if they do not persist in unbelief, they will be grafted in, for God is able to graft them in again. ²⁴After all, if you were cut out of an olive tree that is wild by nature, and contrary to nature were grafted into a cultivated olive tree, how much more readily will these, the natural branches, be grafted into their own olive tree!

All Israel Will Be Saved

²⁵I do not want you to be ignorant of this mystery, brothers and sisters, so that you may not be conceited: Israel has experienced a hardening in part until the full number of

---

^a 19 Deut. 32:21   ^b 20 Isaiah 65:1   ^c 21 Isaiah 65:2   ^d 3 1 Kings 19:10,14   ^e 4 1 Kings 19:18
^f 8 Deut. 29:4; Isaiah 29:10   ^g 10 Psalm 69:22,23

MISSING GRACE

READ: ROMANS 11:5-6

Christians sometimes act like cops, pulling people aside for breaking a biblical rule. Sin sniffing comes easily, especially in the moral areas we think we've mastered. We reveal our sin-sniffing noses when we internally rejoice when our enemy stumbles or when we say their sin is "what we expected all along."

Shaming and blaming works well to whip ourselves into shape, but it inaccurately teaches us that our worth is linked to our good behavior. Since we all long to feel worthy, we all try to behave. And we shame-and-blame ourselves and others we're trying to talk to about Jesus.

Sin sniffing spills out in our demeanor, in our perspectives, and in our conversations. If we see this tendency in ourselves, we can be sure others see it leaking from us too. Our friends will think of our God as a sin sniffer, as a blamer and shamer. Our guilt-ridden statements will end our spiritual conversations and skew what Jesus' life looks like in us. Yet Jesus shows us a way forward.

BUILDING FAITH WISDOM STRENGTH

Look again at Jesus kneeling down to help the paralytic or the prostitute. His gentle but authoritative power resounds like a symphony, "Your sins are forgiven!" He doesn't tell them to grovel or beat themselves up. He doesn't ask them to prove how sorry they are or to volunteer at the local synagogue. Often he doesn't even point out their sins. Instead, he asks them what they seek and invites them into new life.

the Gentiles has come in, [26]and in this way[a] all Israel will be saved. As it is written:

"The deliverer will come from Zion;
    he will turn godlessness away from
        Jacob.
[27]And this is[b] my covenant with them
    when I take away their sins."[c]

[28]As far as the gospel is concerned, they are enemies for your sake; but as far as election is concerned, they are loved on account of the patriarchs, [29]for God's gifts and his call are irrevocable. [30]Just as you who were at one time disobedient to God have now received mercy as a result of their disobedience, [31]so they too have now become disobedient in order that they too may now[d] receive mercy as a result of God's mercy to you. [32]For God has bound everyone over to disobedience so that he may have mercy on them all.

Doxology

[33]Oh, the depth of the riches of the wisdom
    and[e] knowledge of God!
    How unsearchable his judgments,
        and his paths beyond tracing out!
[34]"Who has known the mind of the Lord?
    Or who has been his counselor?"[f]
[35]"Who has ever given to God,
    that God should repay them?"[g]
[36]For from him and through him and for
    him are all things.
    To him be the glory forever! Amen.

A Living Sacrifice

12 Therefore, I urge you, brothers and sisters, in view of God's mercy, to offer your bodies as a living sacrifice, holy and pleasing to God — this is your true and proper worship. [2]Do not conform to the pattern of this world, but be transformed by the renewing of your mind. Then you will be able to test and approve what God's will is — his good, pleasing and perfect will.

Humble Service in the Body of Christ

[3]For by the grace given me I say to every one of you: Do not think of yourself more highly than you ought, but rather think of yourself with sober judgment, in accordance with the faith God has distributed to each of you. [4]For just as each of us has one body with many members, and these members do not all have the same function, [5]so in Christ we, though many, form one body, and each member belongs to all the others. [6]We have different gifts, according to the grace given to each of us. If your gift is prophesying, then prophesy in accordance with your[h] faith; [7]if it is serving, then serve; if it is teaching, then teach; [8]if it is to encourage, then give encouragement; if it is giving, then give generously; if it is to lead,[i] do it diligently; if it is to show mercy, do it cheerfully.

Love in Action

[9]Love must be sincere. Hate what is evil; cling to what is good. [10]Be devoted to one another in love. Honor one another above yourselves. [11]Never be lacking in zeal, but keep your spiritual fervor, serving the Lord. [12]Be joyful in hope, patient in affliction, faithful in prayer. [13]Share with the Lord's people who are in need. Practice hospitality.

[14]Bless those who persecute you; bless and do not curse. [15]Rejoice with those who rejoice; mourn with those who mourn. [16]Live in harmony with one another. Do not be proud, but be willing to associate with people of low position.[j] Do not be conceited.

[17]Do not repay anyone evil for evil. Be careful to do what is right in the eyes of everyone. [18]If it is possible, as far as it depends on you, live at peace with everyone. [19]Do not take revenge, my dear friends, but leave room for God's wrath, for it is written: "It is mine to avenge; I will repay,"[k] says the Lord. [20]On the contrary:

"If your enemy is hungry, feed him;
    if he is thirsty, give him something to
        drink.
In doing this, you will heap burning coals
    on his head."[l]

[21]Do not be overcome by evil, but overcome evil with good.

Submission to Governing Authorities

13 Let everyone be subject to the governing authorities, for there is no

---

[a] 26 Or *and so*   [b] 27 Or *will be*   [c] 27 Isaiah 59:20,21; 27:9 (see Septuagint); Jer. 31:33,34   [d] 31 Some manuscripts do not have *now*.   [e] 33 Or *riches and the wisdom and the*   [f] 34 Isaiah 40:13   [g] 35 Job 41:11   [h] 6 Or *the*   [i] 8 Or *to provide for others*   [j] 16 Or *willing to do menial work*   [k] 19 Deut. 32:35   [l] 20 Prov. 25:21,22

YEP, HE MEANS YOU

READ: ROMANS 12:1-2

Right at the start of chapter 12, Paul writes, "I urge you, brothers and sisters." So we know he's writing to fellow Christians. This means Paul told Christians to stop conforming to the pattern of this world. Guess what that means. It means Christians still conform to the world.

See, you thought you were the only hypocrite in the world. But Paul shows there were hypocrites way back then too. Even in the first century, with the church on fire and God shaking the world, believers blew it. They did just fine during a worship gathering, but as soon as the doors shut behind them, they faced an angry world. And they reacted like we react. They got stupid.

Paul told them to stop: "Don't let the world shape you. You're in the world, but you're not of it. Stop acting like you are." But Paul doesn't stay in the negative. He also gets proactive. He tells them to focus on the one thing that will change their behavior fastest. He tells them to renew their minds. This is a big deal. God's Word says I still need to be transformed after I've been transformed. My heart may be new, but my mind is still old. My thinking is still lost.

When we surrender to Christ, the spirit inside of us—the real person within the bag of bones we call a body—is renewed.

BUILDING FAITH WISDOM STRENGTH

Taken from *Thrive Student Edition* by Mark Hall with Tim Luke, copyright © 2014 by Mark Hall, published by Zondervan.

authority except that which God has established. The authorities that exist have been established by God. [2]Consequently, whoever rebels against the authority is rebelling against what God has instituted, and those who do so will bring judgment on themselves. [3]For rulers hold no terror for those who do right, but for those who do wrong. Do you want to be free from fear of the one in authority? Then do what is right and you will be commended. [4]For the one in authority is God's servant for your good. But if you do wrong, be afraid, for rulers do not bear the sword for no reason. They are God's servants, agents of wrath to bring punishment on the wrongdoer. [5]Therefore, it is necessary to submit to the authorities, not only because of possible punishment but also as a matter of conscience.

[6]This is also why you pay taxes, for the authorities are God's servants, who give their full time to governing. [7]Give to everyone what you owe them: If you owe taxes, pay taxes; if revenue, then revenue; if respect, then respect; if honor, then honor.

Love Fulfills the Law

[8]Let no debt remain outstanding, except the continuing debt to love one another, for whoever loves others has fulfilled the law. [9]The commandments, "You shall not commit adultery," "You shall not murder," "You shall not steal," "You shall not covet,"[a] and whatever other command there may be, are summed up in this one command: "Love your neighbor as yourself."[b] [10]Love does no harm to a neighbor. Therefore love is the fulfillment of the law.

The Day Is Near

[11]And do this, understanding the present time: The hour has already come for you to wake up from your slumber, because our salvation is nearer now than when we first believed. [12]The night is nearly over; the day is almost here. So let us put aside the deeds of darkness and put on the armor of light. [13]Let us behave decently, as in the daytime, not in carousing and drunkenness, not in sexual immorality and debauchery, not in dissension and jealousy. [14]Rather, clothe yourselves with the Lord Jesus Christ, and do not think about how to gratify the desires of the flesh.[c]

The Weak and the Strong

14 Accept the one whose faith is weak, without quarreling over disputable matters. [2]One person's faith allows them to eat anything, but another, whose faith is weak, eats only vegetables. [3]The one who eats everything must not treat with contempt the one who does not, and the one who does not eat everything must not judge the one who does, for God has accepted them. [4]Who are you to judge someone else's servant? To their own master, servants stand or fall. And they will stand, for the Lord is able to make them stand.

[5]One person considers one day more sacred than another; another considers every day alike. Each of them should be fully convinced in their own mind. [6]Whoever regards one day as special does so to the Lord. Whoever eats meat does so to the Lord, for they give thanks to God; and whoever abstains does so to the Lord and gives thanks to God. [7]For none of us lives for ourselves alone, and none of us dies for ourselves alone. [8]If we live, we live for the Lord; and if we die, we die for the Lord. So, whether we live or die, we belong to the Lord. [9]For this very reason, Christ died and returned to life so that he might be the Lord of both the dead and the living.

[10]You, then, why do you judge your brother or sister[d]? Or why do you treat them with contempt? For we will all stand before God's judgment seat. [11]It is written:

"'As surely as I live,' says the Lord,
'every knee will bow before me;
    every tongue will acknowledge God.'"[e]

[12]So then, each of us will give an account of ourselves to God.

[13]Therefore let us stop passing judgment on one another. Instead, make up your mind not to put any stumbling block or obstacle

---

[a] 9 Exodus 20:13-15,17; Deut. 5:17-19,21   [b] 9 Lev. 19:18   [c] 14 In contexts like this, the Greek word for *flesh* (*sarx*) refers to the sinful state of human beings, often presented as a power in opposition to the Spirit.   [d] 10 The Greek word for *brother or sister* (*adelphos*) refers here to a believer, whether man or woman, as part of God's family; also in verses 13, 15 and 21.   [e] 11 Isaiah 45:23

in the way of a brother or sister. [14] I am convinced, being fully persuaded in the Lord Jesus, that nothing is unclean in itself. But if anyone regards something as unclean, then for that person it is unclean. [15] If your brother or sister is distressed because of what you eat, you are no longer acting in love. Do not by your eating destroy someone for whom Christ died. [16] Therefore do not let what you know is good be spoken of as evil. [17] For the kingdom of God is not a matter of eating and drinking, but of righteousness, peace and joy in the Holy Spirit, [18] because anyone who serves Christ in this way is pleasing to God and receives human approval.

[19] Let us therefore make every effort to do what leads to peace and to mutual edification. [20] Do not destroy the work of God for the sake of food. All food is clean, but it is wrong for a person to eat anything that causes someone else to stumble. [21] It is better not to eat meat or drink wine or to do anything else that will cause your brother or sister to fall.

[22] So whatever you believe about these things keep between yourself and God. Blessed is the one who does not condemn himself by what he approves. [23] But whoever has doubts is condemned if they eat, because their eating is not from faith; and everything that does not come from faith is sin.[a]

15 We who are strong ought to bear with the failings of the weak and not to please ourselves. [2] Each of us should please our neighbors for their good, to build them up. [3] For even Christ did not please himself but, as it is written: "The insults of those who insult you have fallen on me."[b] [4] For everything that was written in the past was written to teach us, so that through the endurance taught in the Scriptures and the encouragement they provide we might have hope.

[5] May the God who gives endurance and encouragement give you the same attitude of mind toward each other that Christ Jesus had, [6] so that with one mind and one voice you may glorify the God and Father of our Lord Jesus Christ.

[7] Accept one another, then, just as Christ accepted you, in order to bring praise to God. [8] For I tell you that Christ has become a servant of the Jews[c] on behalf of God's truth, so that the promises made to the patriarchs might be confirmed [9] and, moreover, that the Gentiles might glorify God for his mercy. As it is written:

"Therefore I will praise you among the
    Gentiles;
  I will sing the praises of your name."[d]

[10] Again, it says,

"Rejoice, you Gentiles, with his people."[e]

[11] And again,

"Praise the Lord, all you Gentiles;
  let all the peoples extol him."[f]

[12] And again, Isaiah says,

"The Root of Jesse will spring up,
  one who will arise to rule over the
    nations;
  in him the Gentiles will hope."[g]

[13] May the God of hope fill you with all joy and peace as you trust in him, so that you may overflow with hope by the power of the Holy Spirit.

Paul the Minister to the Gentiles

[14] I myself am convinced, my brothers and sisters, that you yourselves are full of goodness, filled with knowledge and competent to instruct one another. [15] Yet I have written you quite boldly on some points to remind you of them again, because of the grace God gave me [16] to be a minister of Christ Jesus to the Gentiles. He gave me the priestly duty of proclaiming the gospel of God, so that the Gentiles might become an offering acceptable to God, sanctified by the Holy Spirit.

[17] Therefore I glory in Christ Jesus in my service to God. [18] I will not venture to speak of anything except what Christ has accomplished through me in leading the Gentiles to obey God by what I have said and done — [19] by the power of signs and wonders, through the power of the Spirit of God. So from Jerusalem all the way around to Illyricum, I have fully proclaimed the gospel of Christ. [20] It has always been my ambition

---

[a] 23 Some manuscripts place 16:25-27 here; others after 15:33.   [b] 3 Psalm 69:9   [c] 8 Greek circumcision   [d] 9 2 Samuel 22:50; Psalm 18:49   [e] 10 Deut. 32:43   [f] 11 Psalm 117:1
[g] 12 Isaiah 11:10 (see Septuagint)

DREAMER

God aims to give you ambitious dreams and concrete goals. Are you paying attention so he can show you what they might be?

The apostle Paul knows he is called to preach almost as soon as Jesus flashes a blinding light from heaven and drops the bad-tempered man to the ground. Paul immediately begins to tell the Jews that Jesus is God's Son (Acts 9:1–22). A while later he consciously chooses to take the message about Jesus to non-Jews (13:46). Somewhere along the way he develops a passion to preach Jesus in places the Lord was totally unknown.

BUILDING
FAITH
WISDOM
STRENGTH

The Bible presents countless people who are surprised by God's plan for their lives. Abraham hears a message from the Lord to pack up his family and journey to an unknown place (Genesis 12:1). Moses encounters God at a burning bush, where he's handed the task of leading an enormous multitude of slaves to freedom (Exodus 3:1–15). Ruth finds her destiny after her husband dies (Ruth 1:1–18). And Esther discovers her lifesaving mission after winning a beauty pageant to become queen of Persia (Esther 4:14). As you study the lives of these believers, you discover what drives their ambition.

They shift their focus off themselves to what the Lord wants them to do. They find their ultimate happiness in completing the tasks he gives them. They let God give them one-of-a-kind dreams. Even the most extreme stories here started when someone let God use them for his glory: God gave you gifts and a dream as well—keep your eyes open for where he wants to lead you.

to preach the gospel where Christ was not known, so that I would not be building on someone else's foundation. ²¹Rather, as it is written:

"Those who were not told about him
　　will see,
　and those who have not heard will
　　understand."ᵃ

²²This is why I have often been hindered from coming to you.

Paul's Plan to Visit Rome

²³But now that there is no more place for me to work in these regions, and since I have been longing for many years to visit you, ²⁴I plan to do so when I go to Spain. I hope to see you while passing through and to have you assist me on my journey there, after I have enjoyed your company for a while. ²⁵Now, however, I am on my way to Jerusalem in the service of the Lord's people there. ²⁶For Macedonia and Achaia were pleased to make a contribution for the poor among the Lord's people in Jerusalem. ²⁷They were pleased to do it, and indeed they owe it to them. For if the Gentiles have shared in the Jews' spiritual blessings, they owe it to the Jews to share with them their material blessings. ²⁸So after I have completed this task and have made sure that they have received this contribution, I will go to Spain and visit you on the way. ²⁹I know that when I come to you, I will come in the full measure of the blessing of Christ.

³⁰I urge you, brothers and sisters, by our Lord Jesus Christ and by the love of the Spirit, to join me in my struggle by praying to God for me. ³¹Pray that I may be kept safe from the unbelievers in Judea and that the contribution I take to Jerusalem may be favorably received by the Lord's people there, ³²so that I may come to you with joy, by God's will, and in your company be refreshed. ³³The God of peace be with you all. Amen.

Personal Greetings

16 I commend to you our sister Phoebe, a deaconᵇ,ᶜ of the church in Cenchreae. ²I ask you to receive her in the Lord in a way worthy of his people and to give her any help she may need from you, for she has been the benefactor of many people, including me.

³Greet Priscillaᵈ and Aquila, my co-workers in Christ Jesus. ⁴They risked their lives for me. Not only I but all the churches of the Gentiles are grateful to them.

⁵Greet also the church that meets at their house.

Greet my dear friend Epenetus, who was the first convert to Christ in the province of Asia.

⁶Greet Mary, who worked very hard for you.

⁷Greet Andronicus and Junia, my fellow Jews who have been in prison with me. They are outstanding amongᵉ the apostles, and they were in Christ before I was.

⁸Greet Ampliatus, my dear friend in the Lord.

⁹Greet Urbanus, our co-worker in Christ, and my dear friend Stachys.

¹⁰Greet Apelles, whose fidelity to Christ has stood the test.

Greet those who belong to the household of Aristobulus.

¹¹Greet Herodion, my fellow Jew.

Greet those in the household of Narcissus who are in the Lord.

¹²Greet Tryphena and Tryphosa, those women who work hard in the Lord.

Greet my dear friend Persis, another woman who has worked very hard in the Lord.

¹³Greet Rufus, chosen in the Lord, and his mother, who has been a mother to me, too.

¹⁴Greet Asyncritus, Phlegon, Hermes, Patrobas, Hermas and the other brothers and sisters with them.

¹⁵Greet Philologus, Julia, Nereus and his sister, and Olympas and all the Lord's people who are with them.

¹⁶Greet one another with a holy kiss.

All the churches of Christ send greetings.

¹⁷I urge you, brothers and sisters, to watch out for those who cause divisions and put obstacles in your way that are contrary to

---

ᵃ 21 Isaiah 52:15 (see Septuagint)　　ᵇ 1 Or *servant*　　ᶜ 1 The word *deacon* refers here to a Christian designated to serve with the overseers/elders of the church in a variety of ways; similarly in Phil. 1:1 and 1 Tim. 3:8,12.　　ᵈ 3 Greek *Prisca*, a variant of *Priscilla*　　ᵉ 7 Or *are esteemed by* the teaching you have learned. Keep away from them. [18]For such people are not serving our Lord Christ, but their own appetites. By smooth talk and flattery they deceive the minds of naive people. [19]Everyone has heard about your obedience, so I rejoice because of you; but I want you to be wise about what is good, and innocent about what is evil.

[20]The God of peace will soon crush Satan under your feet.

The grace of our Lord Jesus be with you.

[21]Timothy, my co-worker, sends his greetings to you, as do Lucius, Jason and Sosipater, my fellow Jews.

[22]I, Tertius, who wrote down this letter, greet you in the Lord.

[23]Gaius, whose hospitality I and the whole church here enjoy, sends you his greetings.

Erastus, who is the city's director of public works, and our brother Quartus send you their greetings. [24]a

[25]Now to him who is able to establish you in accordance with my gospel, the message I proclaim about Jesus Christ, in keeping with the revelation of the mystery hidden for long ages past, [26]but now revealed and made known through the prophetic writings by the command of the eternal God, so that all the Gentiles might come to the obedience that comes fromb faith— [27]to the only wise God be glory forever through Jesus Christ! Amen.

---

a 24 Some manuscripts include here *May the grace of our Lord Jesus Christ be with all of you. Amen.*
b 26 Or *that is*

1 CORINTHIANS

➡ WHEN DID THIS HAPPEN?
Around A.D. 55 in Ephesus

➡ WHO IS IN THIS BOOK?
Paul
Timothy

➡ VERSES YOU MIGHT RECOGNIZE

1 CORINTHIANS 10:31
"So whether you eat or drink or whatever you do, do it all for the glory of God."

1 CORINTHIANS 15:3–4
"For what I received I passed on to you as of first importance: that Christ died for our sins according to the Scriptures, that he was buried, that he was raised on the third day according to the Scriptures."

WHAT'S IT ABOUT?

This book can be seen as a kind of instruction manual for how a Christian should behave as part of the local church. It was written by Paul to address division and sin in the Corinthian church, a church he had founded. Because the church was still very new, the people needed instruction on how their lives as Christians should differ from the culture around them.

The people in Corinth were struggling with a variety of sins, including sexual immorality and quarreling. Paul called for absolute purity and reminded them that the gospel is the most important thing. The good news about Jesus should unite them. He also clarified some difficult teachings that were causing divisions among the believers, such as the Lord's Supper and the use of spiritual gifts.

The purpose of the church is to spread the good news about Jesus to the world. And it does that best when members of the body love each other well and live in ways that set them apart as followers of Jesus.

1 CORINTHIANS

1 Paul, called to be an apostle of Christ Jesus by the will of God, and our brother Sosthenes,

²To the church of God in Corinth, to those sanctified in Christ Jesus and called to be his holy people, together with all those everywhere who call on the name of our Lord Jesus Christ—their Lord and ours:

³Grace and peace to you from God our Father and the Lord Jesus Christ.

Thanksgiving

⁴I always thank my God for you because of his grace given you in Christ Jesus. ⁵For in him you have been enriched in every way—with all kinds of speech and with all knowledge— ⁶God thus confirming our testimony about Christ among you. ⁷Therefore you do not lack any spiritual gift as you eagerly wait for our Lord Jesus Christ to be revealed. ⁸He will also keep you firm to the end, so that you will be blameless on the day of our Lord Jesus Christ. ⁹God is faithful, who has called you into fellowship with his Son, Jesus Christ our Lord.

A Church Divided Over Leaders

¹⁰I appeal to you, brothers and sisters,ᵃ in the name of our Lord Jesus Christ, that all of you agree with one another in what you say and that there be no divisions among you, but that you be perfectly united in mind and thought. ¹¹My brothers and sisters, some from Chloe's household have informed me that there are quarrels among you. ¹²What I mean is this: One of you says, "I follow Paul"; another, "I follow Apollos"; another, "I follow Cephasᵇ"; still another, "I follow Christ."

¹³Is Christ divided? Was Paul crucified for you? Were you baptized in the name of Paul? ¹⁴I thank God that I did not baptize any of you except Crispus and Gaius, ¹⁵so no one

can say that you were baptized in my name. ¹⁶(Yes, I also baptized the household of Stephanas; beyond that, I don't remember if I baptized anyone else.) ¹⁷For Christ did not send me to baptize, but to preach the gospel—not with wisdom and eloquence, lest the cross of Christ be emptied of its power.

Christ Crucified Is God's Power and Wisdom

¹⁸For the message of the cross is foolishness to those who are perishing, but to us who are being saved it is the power of God. ¹⁹For it is written:

> "I will destroy the wisdom of the wise;
>   the intelligence of the intelligent I will
>   frustrate."ᶜ

²⁰Where is the wise person? Where is the teacher of the law? Where is the philosopher of this age? Has not God made foolish the wisdom of the world? ²¹For since in the wisdom of God the world through its wisdom did not know him, God was pleased through the foolishness of what was preached to save those who believe. ²²Jews demand signs and Greeks look for wisdom, ²³but we preach Christ crucified: a stumbling block to Jews and foolishness to Gentiles, ²⁴but to those whom God has called, both Jews and Greeks, Christ the power of God and the wisdom of God. ²⁵For the foolishness of God is wiser than human wisdom, and the weakness of God is stronger than human strength.

²⁶Brothers and sisters, think of what you were when you were called. Not many of you were wise by human standards; not many were influential; not many were of noble birth. ²⁷But God chose the foolish things of the world to shame the wise; God chose the weak things of the world to shame the strong. ²⁸God chose the lowly things of this world and the despised things—and the

---

ᵃ 10 The Greek word for *brothers and sisters* (*adelphoi*) refers here to believers, both men and women, as part of God's family; also in verses 11 and 26; and in 2:1; 3:1; 4:6; 6:8; 7:24, 29; 10:1; 11:33; 12:1; 14:6, 20, 26, 39; 15:1, 6, 50, 58; 16:15, 20.   ᵇ 12 That is, Peter   ᶜ 19 Isaiah 29:14

COOL FOOLS

READ: 1 CORINTHIANS 1:20-27

Faith is the willingness to look foolish. Noah looked a little dumb building a boat in the desert. Sarah looked foolish buying maternity clothes at ninety. Moses looked pretty stupid asking Pharaoh to let his slaves go. The Israelite army looked foolish marching around Jericho blowing horns. David probably seemed awfully dense coming at Goliath with a dinky slingshot. The Wise Men didn't seem so smart following a star to who knows where. Peter looked foolish stepping out of the boat in the middle of the lake in the middle of the night. And everyone thought Jesus was dead wrong when he died on the cross. But the results speak for themselves, don't they?

BUILDING FAITH WISDOM STRENGTH

Noah stayed afloat during the flood. Sarah gave birth to Isaac. Moses delivered Israel out of Egypt. The walls of Jericho came tumbling down. David defeated Goliath. The Wise Men found the Messiah. Peter walked on water. And Jesus rose from the dead. People are afraid to look stupid, and that's stupid! That's also why so many people have never built an ark, killed a giant, or walked on water.

I do know that faith is acting as if God has already answered. And acting as if God has answered means acting on our prayers.

Taken from *All In Student Edition* by Mark Batterson and Parker Batterson, copyright © 2014 by Mark Batterson, published by Zondervan.

things that are not — to nullify the things that are, [29]so that no one may boast before him. [30]It is because of him that you are in Christ Jesus, who has become for us wisdom from God — that is, our righteousness, holiness and redemption. [31]Therefore, as it is written: "Let the one who boasts boast in the Lord."[a]

2 And so it was with me, brothers and sisters. When I came to you, I did not come with eloquence or human wisdom as I proclaimed to you the testimony about God.[b] [2]For I resolved to know nothing while I was with you except Jesus Christ and him crucified. [3]I came to you in weakness with great fear and trembling. [4]My message and my preaching were not with wise and persuasive words, but with a demonstration of the Spirit's power, [5]so that your faith might not rest on human wisdom, but on God's power.

God's Wisdom Revealed by the Spirit

[6]We do, however, speak a message of wisdom among the mature, but not the wisdom of this age or of the rulers of this age, who are coming to nothing. [7]No, we declare God's wisdom, a mystery that has been hidden and that God destined for our glory before time began. [8]None of the rulers of this age understood it, for if they had, they would not have crucified the Lord of glory. [9]However, as it is written:

> "What no eye has seen,
>   what no ear has heard,
>   and what no human mind has
>   conceived"[c] —
>   the things God has prepared for those
>   who love him —

[10]these are the things God has revealed to us by his Spirit.

The Spirit searches all things, even the deep things of God. [11]For who knows a person's thoughts except their own spirit within them? In the same way no one knows the thoughts of God except the Spirit of God. [12]What we have received is not the spirit of the world, but the Spirit who is from God, so that we may understand what God has freely given us. [13]This is what we speak, not in words taught us by human wisdom but in words taught by the Spirit, explaining spiritual realities with Spirit-taught words.[d] [14]The person without the Spirit does not accept the things that come from the Spirit of God but considers them foolishness, and cannot understand them because they are discerned only through the Spirit. [15]The person with the Spirit makes judgments about all things, but such a person is not subject to merely human judgments, [16]for,

> "Who has known the mind of
>   the Lord
>   so as to instruct him?"[e]

But we have the mind of Christ.

The Church and Its Leaders

3 Brothers and sisters, I could not address you as people who live by the Spirit but as people who are still worldly — mere infants in Christ. [2]I gave you milk, not solid food, for you were not yet ready for it. Indeed, you are still not ready. [3]You are still worldly. For since there is jealousy and quarreling among you, are you not worldly? Are you not acting like mere humans? [4]For when one says, "I follow Paul," and another, "I follow Apollos," are you not mere human beings?

[5]What, after all, is Apollos? And what is Paul? Only servants, through whom you came to believe — as the Lord has assigned to each his task. [6]I planted the seed, Apollos watered it, but God has been making it grow. [7]So neither the one who plants nor the one who waters is anything, but only God, who makes things grow. [8]The one who plants and the one who waters have one purpose, and they will each be rewarded according to their own labor. [9]For we are co-workers in God's service; you are God's field, God's building.

[10]By the grace God has given me, I laid a foundation as a wise builder, and someone else is building on it. But each one should build with care. [11]For no one can lay any foundation other than the one already laid, which is Jesus Christ. [12]If anyone builds on this foundation using gold, silver, costly stones, wood, hay or straw, [13]their work will be shown for what it is, because the Day will bring it to light. It will be revealed with fire, and the fire will test the quality of each person's work. [14]If what has been built survives,

---

[a] 31 Jer. 9:24   [b] 1 Some manuscripts *proclaimed to you God's mystery*   [c] 9 Isaiah 64:4   [d] 13 Or *Spirit,*
interpreting spiritual truths to those who are spiritual   [e] 16 Isaiah 40:13

the builder will receive a reward. [15]If it is burned up, the builder will suffer loss but yet will be saved — even though only as one escaping through the flames.

[16]Don't you know that you yourselves are God's temple and that God's Spirit dwells in your midst? [17]If anyone destroys God's temple, God will destroy that person; for God's temple is sacred, and you together are that temple.

[18]Do not deceive yourselves. If any of you think you are wise by the standards of this age, you should become "fools" so that you may become wise. [19]For the wisdom of this world is foolishness in God's sight. As it is written: "He catches the wise in their craftiness"[a]; [20]and again, "The Lord knows that the thoughts of the wise are futile."[b] [21]So then, no more boasting about human leaders! All things are yours, [22]whether Paul or Apollos or Cephas[c] or the world or life or death or the present or the future — all are yours, [23]and you are of Christ, and Christ is of God.

The Nature of True Apostleship

4 This, then, is how you ought to regard us: as servants of Christ and as those entrusted with the mysteries God has revealed. [2]Now it is required that those who have been given a trust must prove faithful. [3]I care very little if I am judged by you or by any human court; indeed, I do not even judge myself. [4]My conscience is clear, but that does not make me innocent. It is the Lord who judges me. [5]Therefore judge nothing before the appointed time; wait until the Lord comes. He will bring to light what is hidden in darkness and will expose the motives of the heart. At that time each will receive their praise from God.

[6]Now, brothers and sisters, I have applied these things to myself and Apollos for your benefit, so that you may learn from us the meaning of the saying, "Do not go beyond what is written." Then you will not be puffed up in being a follower of one of us over against the other. [7]For who makes you different from anyone else? What do you have that you did not receive? And if you did receive it, why do you boast as though you did not?

[8]Already you have all you want! Already you have become rich! You have begun to reign — and that without us! How I wish that you really had begun to reign so that we also might reign with you! [9]For it seems to me that God has put us apostles on display at the end of the procession, like those condemned to die in the arena. We have been made a spectacle to the whole universe, to angels as well as to human beings. [10]We are fools for Christ, but you are so wise in Christ! We are weak, but you are strong! You are honored, we are dishonored! [11]To this very hour we go hungry and thirsty, we are in rags, we are brutally treated, we are homeless. [12]We work hard with our own hands. When we are cursed, we bless; when we are persecuted, we endure it; [13]when we are slandered, we answer kindly. We have become the scum of the earth, the garbage of the world — right up to this moment.

Paul's Appeal and Warning

[14]I am writing this not to shame you but to warn you as my dear children. [15]Even if you had ten thousand guardians in Christ, you do not have many fathers, for in Christ Jesus I became your father through the gospel. [16]Therefore I urge you to imitate me. [17]For this reason I have sent to you Timothy, my son whom I love, who is faithful in the Lord. He will remind you of my way of life in Christ Jesus, which agrees with what I teach everywhere in every church.

[18]Some of you have become arrogant, as if I were not coming to you. [19]But I will come to you very soon, if the Lord is willing, and then I will find out not only how these arrogant people are talking, but what power they have. [20]For the kingdom of God is not a matter of talk but of power. [21]What do you prefer? Shall I come to you with a rod of discipline, or shall I come in love and with a gentle spirit?

Dealing With a Case of Incest

5 It is actually reported that there is sexual immorality among you, and of a kind that even pagans do not tolerate: A man is sleeping with his father's wife. [2]And you are proud! Shouldn't you rather have gone into mourning and have put out of your fellowship the man who has been doing this? [3]For my part, even though I am not physically

---

[a] 19 Job 5:13   [b] 20 Psalm 94:11   [c] 22 That is, Peter

present, I am with you in spirit. As one who is present with you in this way, I have already passed judgment in the name of our Lord Jesus on the one who has been doing this. [4]So when you are assembled and I am with you in spirit, and the power of our Lord Jesus is present, [5]hand this man over to Satan for the destruction of the flesh,[a,b] so that his spirit may be saved on the day of the Lord.

[6]Your boasting is not good. Don't you know that a little yeast leavens the whole batch of dough? [7]Get rid of the old yeast, so that you may be a new unleavened batch — as you really are. For Christ, our Passover lamb, has been sacrificed. [8]Therefore let us keep the Festival, not with the old bread leavened with malice and wickedness, but with the unleavened bread of sincerity and truth.

[9]I wrote to you in my letter not to associate with sexually immoral people — [10]not at all meaning the people of this world who are immoral, or the greedy and swindlers, or idolaters. In that case you would have to leave this world. [11]But now I am writing to you that you must not associate with anyone who claims to be a brother or sister[c] but is sexually immoral or greedy, an idolater or slanderer, a drunkard or swindler. Do not even eat with such people.

[12]What business is it of mine to judge those outside the church? Are you not to judge those inside? [13]God will judge those outside. "Expel the wicked person from among you."[d]

Lawsuits Among Believers

6 If any of you has a dispute with another, do you dare to take it before the ungodly for judgment instead of before the Lord's people? [2]Or do you not know that the Lord's people will judge the world? And if you are to judge the world, are you not competent to judge trivial cases? [3]Do you not know that we will judge angels? How much more the things of this life! [4]Therefore, if you have disputes about such matters, do you ask for a ruling from those whose way of life is

scorned in the church? [5]I say this to shame you. Is it possible that there is nobody among you wise enough to judge a dispute between believers? [6]But instead, one brother takes another to court — and this in front of unbelievers!

[7]The very fact that you have lawsuits among you means you have been completely defeated already. Why not rather be wronged? Why not rather be cheated? [8]Instead, you yourselves cheat and do wrong, and you do this to your brothers and sisters. [9]Or do you not know that wrongdoers will not inherit the kingdom of God? Do not be deceived: Neither the sexually immoral nor idolaters nor adulterers nor men who have sex with men[e] [10]nor thieves nor the greedy nor drunkards nor slanderers nor swindlers will inherit the kingdom of God. [11]And that is what some of you were. But you were washed, you were sanctified, you were justified in the name of the Lord Jesus Christ and by the Spirit of our God.

Sexual Immorality

[12]"I have the right to do anything," you say — but not everything is beneficial. "I have the right to do anything" — but I will not be mastered by anything. [13]You say, "Food for the stomach and the stomach for food, and God will destroy them both." The body, however, is not meant for sexual immorality but for the Lord, and the Lord for the body. [14]By his power God raised the Lord from the dead, and he will raise us also. [15]Do you not know that your bodies are members of Christ himself? Shall I then take the members of Christ and unite them with a prostitute? Never! [16]Do you not know that he who unites himself with a prostitute is one with her in body? For it is said, "The two will become one flesh."[f] [17]But whoever is united with the Lord is one with him in spirit.[g]

[18]Flee from sexual immorality. All other sins a person commits are outside the body, but whoever sins sexually, sins against their own body. [19]Do you not know that your bodies are temples of the Holy Spirit, who is in

---

[a] 5 In contexts like this, the Greek word for *flesh* (*sarx*) refers to the sinful state of human beings, often presented as a power in opposition to the Spirit.   [b] 5 Or *of his body*   [c] 11 The Greek word for *brother or sister* (*adelphos*) refers here to a believer, whether man or woman, as part of God's family; also in 8:11, 13.   [d] 13 Deut. 13:5; 17:7; 19:19; 21:21; 22:21,24; 24:7   [e] 9 The words *men who have sex with men* translate two Greek words that refer to the passive and active participants in homosexual acts.   [f] 16 Gen. 2:24   [g] 17 Or *in the Spirit*

you, whom you have received from God? You are not your own; ²⁰you were bought at a price. Therefore honor God with your bodies.

Concerning Married Life

7 Now for the matters you wrote about: "It is good for a man not to have sexual relations with a woman." ²But since sexual immorality is occurring, each man should have sexual relations with his own wife, and each woman with her own husband. ³The husband should fulfill his marital duty to his wife, and likewise the wife to her husband. ⁴The wife does not have authority over her own body but yields it to her husband. In the same way, the husband does not have authority over his own body but yields it to his wife. ⁵Do not deprive each other except perhaps by mutual consent and for a time, so that you may devote yourselves to prayer. Then come together again so that Satan will not tempt you because of your lack of self-control. ⁶I say this as a concession, not as a command. ⁷I wish that all of you were as I am. But each of you has your own gift from God; one has this gift, another has that.

⁸Now to the unmarried[a] and the widows I say: It is good for them to stay unmarried, as I do. ⁹But if they cannot control themselves, they should marry, for it is better to marry than to burn with passion.

¹⁰To the married I give this command (not I, but the Lord): A wife must not separate from her husband. ¹¹But if she does, she must remain unmarried or else be reconciled to her husband. And a husband must not divorce his wife.

¹²To the rest I say this (I, not the Lord): If any brother has a wife who is not a believer and she is willing to live with him, he must not divorce her. ¹³And if a woman has a husband who is not a believer and he is willing to live with her, she must not divorce him. ¹⁴For the unbelieving husband has been sanctified through his wife, and the unbelieving wife has been sanctified through her believing husband. Otherwise your children would be unclean, but as it is, they are holy.

¹⁵But if the unbeliever leaves, let it be so. The brother or the sister is not bound in such circumstances; God has called us to live in peace. ¹⁶How do you know, wife, whether you will save your husband? Or, how do you know, husband, whether you will save your wife?

Concerning Change of Status

¹⁷Nevertheless, each person should live as a believer in whatever situation the Lord has assigned to them, just as God has called them. This is the rule I lay down in all the churches. ¹⁸Was a man already circumcised when he was called? He should not become uncircumcised. Was a man uncircumcised when he was called? He should not be circumcised. ¹⁹Circumcision is nothing and uncircumcision is nothing. Keeping God's commands is what counts. ²⁰Each person should remain in the situation they were in when God called them.

²¹Were you a slave when you were called? Don't let it trouble you—although if you can gain your freedom, do so. ²²For the one who was a slave when called to faith in the Lord is the Lord's freed person; similarly, the one who was free when called is Christ's slave. ²³You were bought at a price; do not become slaves of human beings. ²⁴Brothers and sisters, each person, as responsible to God, should remain in the situation they were in when God called them.

Concerning the Unmarried

²⁵Now about virgins: I have no command from the Lord, but I give a judgment as one who by the Lord's mercy is trustworthy. ²⁶Because of the present crisis, I think that it is good for a man to remain as he is. ²⁷Are you pledged to a woman? Do not seek to be released. Are you free from such a commitment? Do not look for a wife. ²⁸But if you do marry, you have not sinned; and if a virgin marries, she has not sinned. But those who marry will face many troubles in this life, and I want to spare you this.

²⁹What I mean, brothers and sisters, is that the time is short. From now on those who have wives should live as if they do not; ³⁰those who mourn, as if they did not; those who are happy, as if they were not; those who buy something, as if it were not theirs to keep; ³¹those who use the things of the

^a 8 Or *widowers*

world, as if not engrossed in them. For this world in its present form is passing away.

[32] I would like you to be free from concern. An unmarried man is concerned about the Lord's affairs—how he can please the Lord. [33] But a married man is concerned about the affairs of this world—how he can please his wife— [34] and his interests are divided. An unmarried woman or virgin is concerned about the Lord's affairs: Her aim is to be devoted to the Lord in both body and spirit. But a married woman is concerned about the affairs of this world—how she can please her husband. [35] I am saying this for your own good, not to restrict you, but that you may live in a right way in undivided devotion to the Lord.

[36] If anyone is worried that he might not be acting honorably toward the virgin he is engaged to, and if his passions are too strong[a] and he feels he ought to marry, he should do as he wants. He is not sinning. They should get married. [37] But the man who has settled the matter in his own mind, who is under no compulsion but has control over his own will, and who has made up his mind not to marry the virgin—this man also does the right thing. [38] So then, he who marries the virgin does right, but he who does not marry her does better.[b]

[39] A woman is bound to her husband as long as he lives. But if her husband dies, she is free to marry anyone she wishes, but he must belong to the Lord. [40] In my judgment, she is happier if she stays as she is—and I think that I too have the Spirit of God.

Concerning Food Sacrificed to Idols

8 Now about food sacrificed to idols: We know that "We all possess knowledge." But knowledge puffs up while love builds up. [2] Those who think they know something do not yet know as they ought to know. [3] But whoever loves God is known by God.[c]

[4] So then, about eating food sacrificed to idols: We know that "An idol is nothing at all

in the world" and that "There is no God but one." [5] For even if there are so-called gods, whether in heaven or on earth (as indeed there are many "gods" and many "lords"), [6] yet for us there is but one God, the Father, from whom all things came and for whom we live; and there is but one Lord, Jesus Christ, through whom all things came and through whom we live.

[7] But not everyone possesses this knowledge. Some people are still so accustomed to idols that when they eat sacrificial food they think of it as having been sacrificed to a god, and since their conscience is weak, it is defiled. [8] But food does not bring us near to God; we are no worse if we do not eat, and no better if we do.

[9] Be careful, however, that the exercise of your rights does not become a stumbling block to the weak. [10] For if someone with a weak conscience sees you, with all your knowledge, eating in an idol's temple, won't that person be emboldened to eat what is sacrificed to idols? [11] So this weak brother or sister, for whom Christ died, is destroyed by your knowledge. [12] When you sin against them in this way and wound their weak conscience, you sin against Christ. [13] Therefore, if what I eat causes my brother or sister to fall into sin, I will never eat meat again, so that I will not cause them to fall.

Paul's Rights as an Apostle

9 Am I not free? Am I not an apostle? Have I not seen Jesus our Lord? Are you not the result of my work in the Lord? [2] Even though I may not be an apostle to others, surely I am to you! For you are the seal of my apostleship in the Lord.

[3] This is my defense to those who sit in judgment on me. [4] Don't we have the right to food and drink? [5] Don't we have the right to take a believing wife along with us, as do the other apostles and the Lord's brothers and Cephas[d]? [6] Or is it only I and Barnabas who lack the right to not work for a living?

---

[a] 36 Or *if she is getting beyond the usual age for marriage*   [b] 36-38 Or [36]*If anyone thinks he is not treating his daughter properly, and if she is getting along in years* (or *if her passions are too strong*), *and he feels she ought to marry, he should do as he wants. He is not sinning. He should let her get married.* [37]*But the man who has settled the matter in his own mind, who is under no compulsion but has control over his own will, and who has made up his mind to keep the virgin unmarried—this man also does the right thing.* [38]*So then, he who gives his virgin in marriage does right, but he who does not give her in marriage does better.*
[c] 2,3 An early manuscript and another ancient witness *think they have knowledge do not yet know as they ought to know.* [3]*But whoever loves truly knows.*   [d] 5 That is, Peter

[7]Who serves as a soldier at his own expense? Who plants a vineyard and does not eat its grapes? Who tends a flock and does not drink the milk? [8]Do I say this merely on human authority? Doesn't the Law say the same thing? [9]For it is written in the Law of Moses: "Do not muzzle an ox while it is treading out the grain."[a] Is it about oxen that God is concerned? [10]Surely he says this for us, doesn't he? Yes, this was written for us, because whoever plows and threshes should be able to do so in the hope of sharing in the harvest. [11]If we have sown spiritual seed among you, is it too much if we reap a material harvest from you? [12]If others have this right of support from you, shouldn't we have it all the more?

But we did not use this right. On the contrary, we put up with anything rather than hinder the gospel of Christ.

[13]Don't you know that those who serve in the temple get their food from the temple, and that those who serve at the altar share in what is offered on the altar? [14]In the same way, the Lord has commanded that those who preach the gospel should receive their living from the gospel.

[15]But I have not used any of these rights. And I am not writing this in the hope that you will do such things for me, for I would rather die than allow anyone to deprive me of this boast. [16]For when I preach the gospel, I cannot boast, since I am compelled to preach. Woe to me if I do not preach the gospel! [17]If I preach voluntarily, I have a reward; if not voluntarily, I am simply discharging the trust committed to me. [18]What then is my reward? Just this: that in preaching the gospel I may offer it free of charge, and so not make full use of my rights as a preacher of the gospel.

Paul's Use of His Freedom

[19]Though I am free and belong to no one, I have made myself a slave to everyone, to win as many as possible. [20]To the Jews I became like a Jew, to win the Jews. To those under the law I became like one under the law (though I myself am not under the law), so as to win those under the law. [21]To those not having the law I became like one not having the law (though I am not free from God's law but am under Christ's law), so as to win those not having the law. [22]To the weak I became weak, to win the weak. I have become all things to all people so that by all possible means I might save some. [23]I do all this for the sake of the gospel, that I may share in its blessings.

The Need for Self-Discipline

[24]Do you not know that in a race all the runners run, but only one gets the prize? Run in such a way as to get the prize. [25]Everyone who competes in the games goes into strict training. They do it to get a crown that will not last, but we do it to get a crown that will last forever. [26]Therefore I do not run like someone running aimlessly; I do not fight like a boxer beating the air. [27]No, I strike a blow to my body and make it my slave so that after I have preached to others, I myself will not be disqualified for the prize.

Warnings From Israel's History

10 For I do not want you to be ignorant of the fact, brothers and sisters, that our ancestors were all under the cloud and that they all passed through the sea. [2]They were all baptized into Moses in the cloud and in the sea. [3]They all ate the same spiritual food [4]and drank the same spiritual drink; for they drank from the spiritual rock that accompanied them, and that rock was Christ. [5]Nevertheless, God was not pleased with most of them; their bodies were scattered in the wilderness.

[6]Now these things occurred as examples to keep us from setting our hearts on evil things as they did. [7]Do not be idolaters, as some of them were; as it is written: "The people sat down to eat and drink and got up to indulge in revelry."[b] [8]We should not commit sexual immorality, as some of them did—and in one day twenty-three thousand of them died. [9]We should not test Christ,[c] as some of them did—and were killed by snakes. [10]And do not grumble, as some of them did—and were killed by the destroying angel.

[11]These things happened to them as examples and were written down as warnings for us, on whom the culmination of the ages has come. [12]So, if you think you are standing

---

[a] 9 Deut. 25:4   [b] 7 Exodus 32:6   [c] 9 Some manuscripts *test the Lord*

DO SOMETHING ABOUT IT

READ: 1 CORINTHIANS 9:24-27

I decided that for a full calendar year I would drink no soft drinks and no sweet tea. Sweet tea is pretty much pancake syrup on ice, and down South we regard it as nectar from heaven. I made up my mind to forgo it for the first time in my life.

I got fired up. I went on Twitter and zinged it to my followers. I called it the HydroForce plan.

Several weeks into it, I had a sudden attack of allergies. I think my immune system recoiled. The first thing the nurse made me do was step on the scales. And the scales said I was fatter than ever.

I had one thought. *I'm walking out of this room. I'm going to Wendy's. I'm going to get a vat of Coke and a vat of sweet tea, and I'm going to hook them up in an IV tube to my arm for a week.*

I was so angry.

I went home and told my wife. She raised her eyebrows and cocked her head. "Well, you could exercise a little," she said.

BUILDING FAITH WISDOM STRENGTH

The truth that hit me was that sometimes we think we're going to get somewhere just by not doing stuff, by cutting things out of our lives. Sometimes we think we're Christians because of the things we *don't* do and where we *don't* go. We think, *I love Jesus, so I'm not going to do any of this stuff.* We cut it off, which is a good thing, but we don't add anything to ourselves. It's like a diet without exercise.

Taken from *Thrive Student Edition* by Mark Hall with Tim Luke, copyright © 2014 by Mark Hall, published by Zondervan.

firm, be careful that you don't fall! ¹³No temptation*a* has overtaken you except what is common to mankind. And God is faithful; he will not let you be tempted*a* beyond what you can bear. But when you are tempted,*a* he will also provide a way out so that you can endure it.

Idol Feasts and the Lord's Supper

¹⁴Therefore, my dear friends, flee from idolatry. ¹⁵I speak to sensible people; judge for yourselves what I say. ¹⁶Is not the cup of thanksgiving for which we give thanks a participation in the blood of Christ? And is not the bread that we break a participation in the body of Christ? ¹⁷Because there is one loaf, we, who are many, are one body, for we all share the one loaf.

¹⁸Consider the people of Israel: Do not those who eat the sacrifices participate in the altar? ¹⁹Do I mean then that food sacrificed to an idol is anything, or that an idol is anything? ²⁰No, but the sacrifices of pagans are offered to demons, not to God, and I do not want you to be participants with demons. ²¹You cannot drink the cup of the Lord and the cup of demons too; you cannot have a part in both the Lord's table and the table of demons. ²²Are we trying to arouse the Lord's jealousy? Are we stronger than he?

The Believer's Freedom

²³"I have the right to do anything," you say—but not everything is beneficial. "I have the right to do anything"—but not everything is constructive. ²⁴No one should seek their own good, but the good of others.

²⁵Eat anything sold in the meat market without raising questions of conscience, ²⁶for, "The earth is the Lord's, and everything in it."*b*

²⁷If an unbeliever invites you to a meal and you want to go, eat whatever is put before you without raising questions of conscience. ²⁸But if someone says to you, "This has been offered in sacrifice," then do not eat it, both for the sake of the one who told you and for the sake of conscience. ²⁹I am re-

ferring to the other person's conscience, not yours. For why is my freedom being judged by another's conscience? ³⁰If I take part in the meal with thankfulness, why am I denounced because of something I thank God for?

³¹So whether you eat or drink or whatever you do, do it all for the glory of God. ³²Do not cause anyone to stumble, whether Jews, Greeks or the church of God— ³³even as I try to please everyone in every way. For I am not seeking my own good but the good of many, so that they may be saved. ¹Follow my example, as I follow the example of Christ.

11

On Covering the Head in Worship

²I praise you for remembering me in everything and for holding to the traditions just as I passed them on to you. ³But I want you to realize that the head of every man is Christ, and the head of the woman is man,*c* and the head of Christ is God. ⁴Every man who prays or prophesies with his head covered dishonors his head. ⁵But every woman who prays or prophesies with her head uncovered dishonors her head—it is the same as having her head shaved. ⁶For if a woman does not cover her head, she might as well have her hair cut off; but if it is a disgrace for a woman to have her hair cut off or her head shaved, then she should cover her head.

⁷A man ought not to cover his head,*d* since he is the image and glory of God; but woman is the glory of man. ⁸For man did not come from woman, but woman from man; ⁹neither was man created for woman, but woman for man. ¹⁰It is for this reason that a woman ought to have authority over her own*e* head, because of the angels. ¹¹Nevertheless, in the Lord woman is not independent of man, nor is man independent of woman. ¹²For as woman came from man, so also man is born of woman. But everything comes from God.

¹³Judge for yourselves: Is it proper for a woman to pray to God with her head uncovered? ¹⁴Does not the very nature of things

---

a 13 The Greek for *temptation* and *tempted* can also mean *testing* and *tested*.   *b 26* Psalm 24:1
c 3 Or *of the wife is her husband*   *d 4-7* Or *⁴Every man who prays or prophesies with long hair dishonors his head. ⁵But every woman who prays or prophesies with no covering of hair dishonors her head—she is just like one of the "shorn women." ⁶If a woman has no covering, let her be for now with short hair; but since it is a disgrace for a woman to have her hair shorn or shaved, she should grow it again. ⁷A man ought not to have long hair*   *e 10* Or *have a sign of authority on her*

teach you that if a man has long hair, it is a disgrace to him, ¹⁵but that if a woman has long hair, it is her glory? For long hair is given to her as a covering. ¹⁶If anyone wants to be contentious about this, we have no other practice — nor do the churches of God.

Correcting an Abuse of the Lord's Supper

¹⁷In the following directives I have no praise for you, for your meetings do more harm than good. ¹⁸In the first place, I hear that when you come together as a church, there are divisions among you, and to some extent I believe it. ¹⁹No doubt there have to be differences among you to show which of you have God's approval. ²⁰So then, when you come together, it is not the Lord's Supper you eat, ²¹for when you are eating, some of you go ahead with your own private suppers. As a result, one person remains hungry and another gets drunk. ²²Don't you have homes to eat and drink in? Or do you despise the church of God by humiliating those who have nothing? What shall I say to you? Shall I praise you? Certainly not in this matter!

²³For I received from the Lord what I also passed on to you: The Lord Jesus, on the night he was betrayed, took bread, ²⁴and when he had given thanks, he broke it and said, "This is my body, which is for you; do this in remembrance of me." ²⁵In the same way, after supper he took the cup, saying, "This cup is the new covenant in my blood; do this, whenever you drink it, in remembrance of me." ²⁶For whenever you eat this bread and drink this cup, you proclaim the Lord's death until he comes.

²⁷So then, whoever eats the bread or drinks the cup of the Lord in an unworthy manner will be guilty of sinning against the body and blood of the Lord. ²⁸Everyone ought to examine themselves before they eat of the bread and drink from the cup. ²⁹For those who eat and drink without discerning the body of Christ eat and drink judgment on themselves. ³⁰That is why many among you are weak and sick, and a number of you have fallen asleep. ³¹But if we were more discerning with regard to ourselves, we would not come under such judgment. ³²Nevertheless, when we are judged in this way by the Lord,

we are being disciplined so that we will not be finally condemned with the world.

³³So then, my brothers and sisters, when you gather to eat, you should all eat together. ³⁴Anyone who is hungry should eat something at home, so that when you meet together it may not result in judgment.

And when I come I will give further directions.

Concerning Spiritual Gifts

12 Now about the gifts of the Spirit, brothers and sisters, I do not want you to be uninformed. ²You know that when you were pagans, somehow or other you were influenced and led astray to mute idols. ³Therefore I want you to know that no one who is speaking by the Spirit of God says, "Jesus be cursed," and no one can say, "Jesus is Lord," except by the Holy Spirit.

⁴There are different kinds of gifts, but the same Spirit distributes them. ⁵There are different kinds of service, but the same Lord. ⁶There are different kinds of working, but in all of them and in everyone it is the same God at work.

⁷Now to each one the manifestation of the Spirit is given for the common good. ⁸To one there is given through the Spirit a message of wisdom, to another a message of knowledge by means of the same Spirit, ⁹to another faith by the same Spirit, to another gifts of healing by that one Spirit, ¹⁰to another miraculous powers, to another prophecy, to another distinguishing between spirits, to another speaking in different kinds of tongues,ᵃ and to still another the interpretation of tongues.ᵃ ¹¹All these are the work of one and the same Spirit, and he distributes them to each one, just as he determines.

Unity and Diversity in the Body

¹²Just as a body, though one, has many parts, but all its many parts form one body, so it is with Christ. ¹³For we were all baptized byᵇ one Spirit so as to form one body — whether Jews or Gentiles, slave or free — and we were all given the one Spirit to drink. ¹⁴Even so the body is not made up of one part but of many.

¹⁵Now if the foot should say, "Because I am not a hand, I do not belong to the body," it would not for that reason stop being part

---

ᵃ 10 Or *languages*; also in verse 28   ᵇ 13 Or *with*; or *in*

EVERY ABILITY REQUIRED

READ: 1 CORINTHIANS 12:4,7

Y ou're awesomely gifted, and you might not even know it. Your God makes you and every other believer an unbreakable promise to endow you with special spiritual abilities.

Back at the start of this letter, the apostle Paul called out the bitter fights brewing between various groups in the church in Corinth. They made all kinds of excuses for their opinions and divisions (1 Corinthians 1:10–17, 3:1–4). Now Paul gives the believers a reason to pull together.

Paul starts off by saying he doesn't want the Corinthians to be ignorant about "the gifts of the Spirit" (12:1). These signs of God's working in and through people can look radically different, but they all flow from the same Holy Spirit. Some people might have unmatched wisdom. Others have abilities that look clearly supernatural, like the gift of prophecy. Still others have gifts that look a lot like everyday natural talents. Paul says more about these gifts in Romans 12:3–8 and Ephesians 4:7–16.

BUILDING
FAITH
WISDOM
STRENGTH

God gives you a crucial gift for the benefit of everyone around you inside the church and out. When you and other Christians each use the abilities God puts inside you, everyone grows up spiritually. But if anyone looks down on others or thinks their own gift is unimportant, everyone suffers. It's like a body missing a part. You can't survive without others, and they can't survive without you.

of the body. [16] And if the ear should say, "Because I am not an eye, I do not belong to the body," it would not for that reason stop being part of the body. [17] If the whole body were an eye, where would the sense of hearing be? If the whole body were an ear, where would the sense of smell be? [18] But in fact God has placed the parts in the body, every one of them, just as he wanted them to be. [19] If they were all one part, where would the body be? [20] As it is, there are many parts, but one body.

[21] The eye cannot say to the hand, "I don't need you!" And the head cannot say to the feet, "I don't need you!" [22] On the contrary, those parts of the body that seem to be weaker are indispensable, [23] and the parts that we think are less honorable we treat with special honor. And the parts that are unpresentable are treated with special modesty, [24] while our presentable parts need no special treatment. But God has put the body together, giving greater honor to the parts that lacked it, [25] so that there should be no division in the body, but that its parts should have equal concern for each other. [26] If one part suffers, every part suffers with it; if one part is honored, every part rejoices with it.

[27] Now you are the body of Christ, and each one of you is a part of it. [28] And God has placed in the church first of all apostles, second prophets, third teachers, then miracles, then gifts of healing, of helping, of guidance, and of different kinds of tongues. [29] Are all apostles? Are all prophets? Are all teachers? Do all work miracles? [30] Do all have gifts of healing? Do all speak in tongues[a]? Do all interpret? [31] Now eagerly desire the greater gifts.

Love Is Indispensable

And yet I will show you the most excellent way.

13 If I speak in the tongues[b] of men or of angels, but do not have love, I am only a resounding gong or a clanging cymbal. [2] If I have the gift of prophecy and can fathom all mysteries and all knowledge, and if I have a faith that can move mountains, but do not have love, I am nothing. [3] If I give

all I possess to the poor and give over my body to hardship that I may boast,[c] but do not have love, I gain nothing.

[4] Love is patient, love is kind. It does not envy, it does not boast, it is not proud. [5] It does not dishonor others, it is not self-seeking, it is not easily angered, it keeps no record of wrongs. [6] Love does not delight in evil but rejoices with the truth. [7] It always protects, always trusts, always hopes, always perseveres.

[8] Love never fails. But where there are prophecies, they will cease; where there are tongues, they will be stilled; where there is knowledge, it will pass away. [9] For we know in part and we prophesy in part, [10] but when completeness comes, what is in part disappears. [11] When I was a child, I talked like a child, I thought like a child, I reasoned like a child. When I became a man, I put the ways of childhood behind me. [12] For now we see only a reflection as in a mirror; then we shall see face to face. Now I know in part; then I shall know fully, even as I am fully known.

[13] And now these three remain: faith, hope and love. But the greatest of these is love.

Intelligibility in Worship

14 Follow the way of love and eagerly desire gifts of the Spirit, especially prophecy. [2] For anyone who speaks in a tongue[d] does not speak to people but to God. Indeed, no one understands them; they utter mysteries by the Spirit. [3] But the one who prophesies speaks to people for their strengthening, encouraging and comfort. [4] Anyone who speaks in a tongue edifies themselves, but the one who prophesies edifies the church. [5] I would like every one of you to speak in tongues,[e] but I would rather have you prophesy. The one who prophesies is greater than the one who speaks in tongues,[e] unless someone interprets, so that the church may be edified.

[6] Now, brothers and sisters, if I come to you and speak in tongues, what good will I be to you, unless I bring you some revelation or knowledge or prophecy or word of instruction? [7] Even in the case of lifeless things that make sounds, such as the pipe or harp,

---

[a] 30 Or *other languages*   [b] 1 Or *languages*   [c] 3 Some manuscripts *body to the flames*   [d] 2 Or *in another language*; also in verses 4, 13, 14, 19, 26 and 27   [e] 5 Or *in other languages*; also in verses 6, 18, 22, 23 and 39

STOP CLANGING!

READ: 1 CORINTHIANS 13:1-3

Differences in belief cannot make a human unworthy of our respect. Even if a person despises Christians, treat them with the highest value that Jesus offers, for every person bears the image of God.

We can test our level of respect for others by noticing how we talk about non-Christians when we are with other Christians. Do we mock them? Do we ascribe unverified motives to them because of their beliefs? For instance, do we find ourselves suspicious that a neighbor is godless or deceitful because she had an abortion? Do we snicker at a coworker who wears amulets and prays to the Goddess? Do we stereotype and denigrate gays with our lunchtime buddies?

If we are eager to talk about Jesus' sacrifice, we need to show them our own willingness to love them with sacrifice. We may find ourselves welcomed into someone else's life when we lay down our sword of ridicule. Mocking others, even behind their backs, destroys our capacity to respect them when we speak face to face.

If we don't listen out of respect, we can talk about Jesus all day long and make no more sense than a clanging cymbal. The good news ends up looking more like a weapon from an enemy forcing others into a narrow religion, rather than an open-hearted offer of a road map to a fellow traveler.

BUILDING FAITH WISDOM STRENGTH

how will anyone know what tune is being played unless there is a distinction in the notes? [8]Again, if the trumpet does not sound a clear call, who will get ready for battle? [9]So it is with you. Unless you speak intelligible words with your tongue, how will anyone know what you are saying? You will just be speaking into the air. [10]Undoubtedly there are all sorts of languages in the world, yet none of them is without meaning. [11]If then I do not grasp the meaning of what someone is saying, I am a foreigner to the speaker, and the speaker is a foreigner to me. [12]So it is with you. Since you are eager for gifts of the Spirit, try to excel in those that build up the church.

[13]For this reason the one who speaks in a tongue should pray that they may interpret what they say. [14]For if I pray in a tongue, my spirit prays, but my mind is unfruitful. [15]So what shall I do? I will pray with my spirit, but I will also pray with my understanding; I will sing with my spirit, but I will also sing with my understanding. [16]Otherwise when you are praising God in the Spirit, how can someone else, who is now put in the position of an inquirer,[a] say "Amen" to your thanksgiving, since they do not know what you are saying? [17]You are giving thanks well enough, but no one else is edified.

[18]I thank God that I speak in tongues more than all of you. [19]But in the church I would rather speak five intelligible words to instruct others than ten thousand words in a tongue.

[20]Brothers and sisters, stop thinking like children. In regard to evil be infants, but in your thinking be adults. [21]In the Law it is written:

> "With other tongues
> and through the lips of foreigners
> I will speak to this people,
> but even then they will not listen to me,
> says the Lord."[b]

[22]Tongues, then, are a sign, not for believers but for unbelievers; prophecy, however, is not for unbelievers but for believers. [23]So if the whole church comes together and everyone speaks in tongues, and inquirers or unbelievers come in, will they not say that you are out of your mind? [24]But if an unbeliever or an inquirer comes in while everyone is prophesying, they are convicted of sin and are brought under judgment by all, [25]as the secrets of their hearts are laid bare. So they will fall down and worship God, exclaiming, "God is really among you!"

Good Order in Worship

[26]What then shall we say, brothers and sisters? When you come together, each of you has a hymn, or a word of instruction, a revelation, a tongue or an interpretation. Everything must be done so that the church may be built up. [27]If anyone speaks in a tongue, two — or at the most three — should speak, one at a time, and someone must interpret. [28]If there is no interpreter, the speaker should keep quiet in the church and speak to himself and to God.

[29]Two or three prophets should speak, and the others should weigh carefully what is said. [30]And if a revelation comes to someone who is sitting down, the first speaker should stop. [31]For you can all prophesy in turn so that everyone may be instructed and encouraged. [32]The spirits of prophets are subject to the control of prophets. [33]For God is not a God of disorder but of peace — as in all the congregations of the Lord's people.

[34]Women[c] should remain silent in the churches. They are not allowed to speak, but must be in submission, as the law says. [35]If they want to inquire about something, they should ask their own husbands at home; for it is disgraceful for a woman to speak in the church.[d]

[36]Or did the word of God originate with you? Or are you the only people it has reached? [37]If anyone thinks they are a prophet or otherwise gifted by the Spirit, let them acknowledge that what I am writing to you is the Lord's command. [38]But if anyone ignores this, they will themselves be ignored.[e]

[39]Therefore, my brothers and sisters, be eager to prophesy, and do not forbid speaking in tongues. [40]But everything should be done in a fitting and orderly way.

---

[a] 16 The Greek word for *inquirer* is a technical term for someone not fully initiated into a religion; also in verses 23 and 24.   [b] 21 Isaiah 28:11,12   [c] 33,34 Or *peace. As in all the congregations of the Lord's people, [34]women*   [d] 34,35 In a few manuscripts these verses come after verse 40.   [e] 38 Some manuscripts *But anyone who is ignorant of this will be ignorant*

The Resurrection of Christ

15 Now, brothers and sisters, I want to remind you of the gospel I preached to you, which you received and on which you have taken your stand. ²By this gospel you are saved, if you hold firmly to the word I preached to you. Otherwise, you have believed in vain.

³For what I received I passed on to you as of first importance*ᵃ*: that Christ died for our sins according to the Scriptures, ⁴that he was buried, that he was raised on the third day according to the Scriptures, ⁵and that he appeared to Cephas,*ᵇ* and then to the Twelve. ⁶After that, he appeared to more than five hundred of the brothers and sisters at the same time, most of whom are still living, though some have fallen asleep. ⁷Then he appeared to James, then to all the apostles, ⁸and last of all he appeared to me also, as to one abnormally born.

⁹For I am the least of the apostles and do not even deserve to be called an apostle, because I persecuted the church of God. ¹⁰But by the grace of God I am what I am, and his grace to me was not without effect. No, I worked harder than all of them — yet not I, but the grace of God that was with me. ¹¹Whether, then, it is I or they, this is what we preach, and this is what you believed.

The Resurrection of the Dead

¹²But if it is preached that Christ has been raised from the dead, how can some of you say that there is no resurrection of the dead? ¹³If there is no resurrection of the dead, then not even Christ has been raised. ¹⁴And if Christ has not been raised, our preaching is useless and so is your faith. ¹⁵More than that, we are then found to be false witnesses about God, for we have testified about God that he raised Christ from the dead. But he did not raise him if in fact the dead are not raised. ¹⁶For if the dead are not raised, then Christ has not been raised either. ¹⁷And if Christ has not been raised, your faith is futile; you are still in your sins. ¹⁸Then those also who have fallen asleep in Christ are lost. ¹⁹If only for this life we have hope in Christ, we are of all people most to be pitied.

²⁰But Christ has indeed been raised from the dead, the firstfruits of those who have fallen asleep. ²¹For since death came through a man, the resurrection of the dead comes also through a man. ²²For as in Adam all die, so in Christ all will be made alive. ²³But each in turn: Christ, the firstfruits; then, when he comes, those who belong to him. ²⁴Then the end will come, when he hands over the kingdom to God the Father after he has destroyed all dominion, authority and power. ²⁵For he must reign until he has put all his enemies under his feet. ²⁶The last enemy to be destroyed is death. ²⁷For he "has put everything under his feet."*ᶜ* Now when it says that "everything" has been put under him, it is clear that this does not include God himself, who put everything under Christ. ²⁸When he has done this, then the Son himself will be made subject to him who put everything under him, so that God may be all in all.

²⁹Now if there is no resurrection, what will those do who are baptized for the dead? If the dead are not raised at all, why are people baptized for them? ³⁰And as for us, why do we endanger ourselves every hour? ³¹I face death every day — yes, just as surely as I boast about you in Christ Jesus our Lord. ³²If I fought wild beasts in Ephesus with no more than human hopes, what have I gained? If the dead are not raised,

"Let us eat and drink,
   for tomorrow we die."*ᵈ*

³³Do not be misled: "Bad company corrupts good character."*ᵉ* ³⁴Come back to your senses as you ought, and stop sinning; for there are some who are ignorant of God — I say this to your shame.

The Resurrection Body

³⁵But someone will ask, "How are the dead raised? With what kind of body will they come?" ³⁶How foolish! What you sow does not come to life unless it dies. ³⁷When you sow, you do not plant the body that will be, but just a seed, perhaps of wheat or of something else. ³⁸But God gives it a body as he has determined, and to each kind of seed he gives its own body. ³⁹Not all flesh is the same: People have one kind of flesh, animals

---

ᵃ 3 Or *you at the first*   *ᵇ 5* That is, Peter   *ᶜ 27* Psalm 8:6   *ᵈ 32* Isaiah 22:13   *ᵉ 33* From the Greek poet Menander

THERE'S PROOF

READ: 1 CORINTHIANS 15:3-4

I f you're looking for a tight way to remember what you believe as a Christian, this passage is it. The apostle Paul sums up the core truths of your faith.

Paul starts by declaring he didn't make up any of what he's about to say. He received this package of truths both from Old Testament prophets who foresaw Jesus' arrival and from New Testament eyewitnesses to the Lord's birth, life, death, and resurrection.

Then Paul unfurls facts you don't want to forget. Jesus died for your sins, which was predicted in passages like Isaiah 53:8–10. His death wasn't a prank or an illusion, and no one in those days argued that his lifeless body wasn't buried. After three days Jesus rose from the dead, as foretold in the Lord's own promise in Matthew 12:40.

Eyewitnesses guarantee that Jesus' resurrection was a real event. He appeared to Peter (Cephas), his closest followers, and his half-brother, James. Paul was the last person to see Jesus back from the dead (Acts 9:1–5). And the resurrected Jesus once appeared to a crowd of more than five hundred people. Paul mentions that most of these people were still living, so his readers could check the facts for themselves (1 Corinthians 15:6).

You don't have to wonder about what you believe. God lays out the basic facts for you and everyone else to examine.

BUILDING

FAITH

WISDOM

STRENGTH

have another, birds another and fish another. [40]There are also heavenly bodies and there are earthly bodies; but the splendor of the heavenly bodies is one kind, and the splendor of the earthly bodies is another. [41]The sun has one kind of splendor, the moon another and the stars another; and star differs from star in splendor.

[42]So will it be with the resurrection of the dead. The body that is sown is perishable, it is raised imperishable; [43]it is sown in dishonor, it is raised in glory; it is sown in weakness, it is raised in power; [44]it is sown a natural body, it is raised a spiritual body.

If there is a natural body, there is also a spiritual body. [45]So it is written: "The first man Adam became a living being"[a]; the last Adam, a life-giving spirit. [46]The spiritual did not come first, but the natural, and after that the spiritual. [47]The first man was of the dust of the earth; the second man is of heaven. [48]As was the earthly man, so are those who are of the earth; and as is the heavenly man, so also are those who are of heaven. [49]And just as we have borne the image of the earthly man, so shall we[b] bear the image of the heavenly man.

[50]I declare to you, brothers and sisters, that flesh and blood cannot inherit the kingdom of God, nor does the perishable inherit the imperishable. [51]Listen, I tell you a mystery: We will not all sleep, but we will all be changed— [52]in a flash, in the twinkling of an eye, at the last trumpet. For the trumpet will sound, the dead will be raised imperishable, and we will be changed. [53]For the perishable must clothe itself with the imperishable, and the mortal with immortality. [54]When the perishable has been clothed with the imperishable, and the mortal with immortality, then the saying that is written will come true: "Death has been swallowed up in victory."[c]

[55]"Where, O death, is your victory?
   Where, O death, is your sting?"[d]

[56]The sting of death is sin, and the power of sin is the law. [57]But thanks be to God! He gives us the victory through our Lord Jesus Christ.

[58]Therefore, my dear brothers and sisters, stand firm. Let nothing move you. Always give yourselves fully to the work of the Lord, because you know that your labor in the Lord is not in vain.

The Collection for the Lord's People

16 Now about the collection for the Lord's people: Do what I told the Galatian churches to do. [2]On the first day of every week, each one of you should set aside a sum of money in keeping with your income, saving it up, so that when I come no collections will have to be made. [3]Then, when I arrive, I will give letters of introduction to the men you approve and send them with your gift to Jerusalem. [4]If it seems advisable for me to go also, they will accompany me.

Personal Requests

[5]After I go through Macedonia, I will come to you—for I will be going through Macedonia. [6]Perhaps I will stay with you for a while, or even spend the winter, so that you can help me on my journey, wherever I go. [7]For I do not want to see you now and make only a passing visit; I hope to spend some time with you, if the Lord permits. [8]But I will stay on at Ephesus until Pentecost, [9]because a great door for effective work has opened to me, and there are many who oppose me.

[10]When Timothy comes, see to it that he has nothing to fear while he is with you, for he is carrying on the work of the Lord, just as I am. [11]No one, then, should treat him with contempt. Send him on his way in peace so that he may return to me. I am expecting him along with the brothers.

[12]Now about our brother Apollos: I strongly urged him to go to you with the brothers. He was quite unwilling to go now, but he will go when he has the opportunity.

[13]Be on your guard; stand firm in the faith; be courageous; be strong. [14]Do everything in love.

[15]You know that the household of Stephanas were the first converts in Achaia, and they have devoted themselves to the service of the Lord's people. I urge you, brothers and sisters, [16]to submit to such people and to everyone who joins in the work and labors at it. [17]I was glad when Stephanas, Fortunatus and Achaicus arrived, because they have

---

[a] 45 Gen. 2:7   [b] 49 Some early manuscripts *so let us*   [c] 54 Isaiah 25:8   [d] 55 Hosea 13:14

supplied what was lacking from you. [18] For they refreshed my spirit and yours also. Such men deserve recognition.

Final Greetings

[19] The churches in the province of Asia send you greetings. Aquila and Priscilla[a] greet you warmly in the Lord, and so does the church that meets at their house. [20] All the brothers and sisters here send you greetings. Greet one another with a holy kiss.

[21] I, Paul, write this greeting in my own hand.

[22] If anyone does not love the Lord, let that person be cursed! Come, Lord[b]!

[23] The grace of the Lord Jesus be with you.

[24] My love to all of you in Christ Jesus. Amen.[c]

---

[a] *19* Greek *Prisca*, a variant of *Priscilla*   [b] *22* The Greek for *Come, Lord* reproduces an Aramaic expression (*Marana tha*) used by early Christians.   [c] *24* Some manuscripts do not have *Amen*.

2 CORINTHIANS

→ WHEN DID THIS HAPPEN?

Around A.D. 55 in Macedonia

→ WHO IS IN THIS BOOK?

Paul

Titus

→ VERSES YOU MIGHT RECOGNIZE

2 CORINTHIANS 5:17

"Therefore, if anyone is in Christ, the new creation has come: The old has gone, the new is here!"

2 CORINTHIANS 9:7

"Each of you should give what you have decided in your heart to give, not reluctantly or under compulsion, for God loves a cheerful giver."

WHAT'S IT ABOUT?

This book is probably Paul's fourth letter to the Corinthians (as two of the letters were not preserved). Since writing 1 Corinthians, Paul had received a positive report about the Corinthians from Titus. But some false teachers were challenging Paul's authority. Using personal details about his sufferings for Christ, visions he had received and his knowledge of the Christian faith, Paul defended his ministry as an apostle of Jesus Christ. He also got real, talking about his thorn in the flesh—a mysterious affliction that kept him dependent on God.

Another major part of this book is Paul's admonition to the Corinthians on giving. He used the church of Macedonia as the example. Even in poverty, the people of this church gave to God's work generously, even beyond what they could afford. Paul urged the Corinthians to follow Macedonia's example and reminded them that giving was evidence of their faith.

This book ends with Paul's encouragement to the people to continue to live in peace and unity, encouraging each other. When they do, the God of love and peace will be with them (see 2 Corinthians 13:11).

2 CORINTHIANS

1 Paul, an apostle of Christ Jesus by the will of God, and Timothy our brother,

To the church of God in Corinth, together with all his holy people throughout Achaia:

[2] Grace and peace to you from God our Father and the Lord Jesus Christ.

Praise to the God of All Comfort

[3] Praise be to the God and Father of our Lord Jesus Christ, the Father of compassion and the God of all comfort, [4] who comforts us in all our troubles, so that we can comfort those in any trouble with the comfort we ourselves receive from God. [5] For just as we share abundantly in the sufferings of Christ, so also our comfort abounds through Christ. [6] If we are distressed, it is for your comfort and salvation; if we are comforted, it is for your comfort, which produces in you patient endurance of the same sufferings we suffer. [7] And our hope for you is firm, because we know that just as you share in our sufferings, so also you share in our comfort.

[8] We do not want you to be uninformed, brothers and sisters,[a] about the troubles we experienced in the province of Asia. We were under great pressure, far beyond our ability to endure, so that we despaired of life itself. [9] Indeed, we felt we had received the sentence of death. But this happened that we might not rely on ourselves but on God, who raises the dead. [10] He has delivered us from such a deadly peril, and he will deliver us again. On him we have set our hope that he will continue to deliver us, [11] as you help us by your prayers. Then many will give thanks on our behalf for the gracious favor granted us in answer to the prayers of many.

Paul's Change of Plans

[12] Now this is our boast: Our conscience testifies that we have conducted ourselves in the world, and especially in our relations with you, with integrity[b] and godly sincerity. We have done so, relying not on worldly wisdom but on God's grace. [13] For we do not write you anything you cannot read or understand. And I hope that, [14] as you have understood us in part, you will come to understand fully that you can boast of us just as we will boast of you in the day of the Lord Jesus.

[15] Because I was confident of this, I wanted to visit you first so that you might benefit twice. [16] I wanted to visit you on my way to Macedonia and to come back to you from Macedonia, and then to have you send me on my way to Judea. [17] Was I fickle when I intended to do this? Or do I make my plans in a worldly manner so that in the same breath I say both "Yes, yes" and "No, no"?

[18] But as surely as God is faithful, our message to you is not "Yes" and "No." [19] For the Son of God, Jesus Christ, who was preached among you by us — by me and Silas[c] and Timothy — was not "Yes" and "No," but in him it has always been "Yes." [20] For no matter how many promises God has made, they are "Yes" in Christ. And so through him the "Amen" is spoken by us to the glory of God. [21] Now it is God who makes both us and you stand firm in Christ. He anointed us, [22] set his seal of ownership on us, and put his Spirit in our hearts as a deposit, guaranteeing what is to come.

[23] I call God as my witness — and I stake my life on it — that it was in order to spare you that I did not return to Corinth. [24] Not that we lord it over your faith, but we work with you for your joy, because it is by faith 2 you stand firm. [1] So I made up my mind that I would not make another painful visit to you. [2] For if I grieve you, who is left to make me glad but you whom I have grieved? [3] I wrote as I did, so that when I came I would not be distressed by those who should have

---

[a] 8 The Greek word for *brothers and sisters* (*adelphoi*) refers here to believers, both men and women, as part of God's family; also in 8:1; 13:11.   [b] 12 Many manuscripts *holiness*   [c] 19 Greek *Silvanus*, a variant of *Silas*

THE POTATO CHIPS WON'T HELP

READ: 2 CORINTHIANS 1:3-4

Maybe the day brought its share of disappointments. Maybe you didn't receive the place on the team you were hoping for; maybe you had to endure another snarky post from a classmate; maybe school itself has become hard to face. Maybe it's family issues, and the thought of going home makes school seem like a day at the beach.

Instead of turning to God, how often do we turn to something else? We rant at a friend. Open up a quart of Blue Bell Pralines and Cream ice cream (just a random example). Or in some cases, sneak a drink from a parent's liquor bottle or go to a friend's house to get high. When the going gets tough, the tough get toking or drinking or chowing down. Drugs provide a quick and obvious shot of comfort. Alcohol and other drugs promise to make you feel better. The food lovingly prepared by a relative or poured from a crinkling bag promises to fill a hole. And they do—for a brief time.

BUILDING FAITH WISDOM STRENGTH

But no matter the method we choose, the god of the quick fix demands a high price once it's seated on the throne of your life.

Think about this: Comforter is one of the names God calls himself. He is the God of all comfort and he is ready to talk with you about your day. The Prince of Peace waits to give you his gifts and strengthen you. He wants to be your satisfaction and show you compassion.

made me rejoice. I had confidence in all of you, that you would all share my joy. ⁴For I wrote you out of great distress and anguish of heart and with many tears, not to grieve you but to let you know the depth of my love for you.

Forgiveness for the Offender

⁵If anyone has caused grief, he has not so much grieved me as he has grieved all of you to some extent — not to put it too severely. ⁶The punishment inflicted on him by the majority is sufficient. ⁷Now instead, you ought to forgive and comfort him, so that he will not be overwhelmed by excessive sorrow. ⁸I urge you, therefore, to reaffirm your love for him. ⁹Another reason I wrote you was to see if you would stand the test and be obedient in everything. ¹⁰Anyone you forgive, I also forgive. And what I have forgiven — if there was anything to forgive — I have forgiven in the sight of Christ for your sake, ¹¹in order that Satan might not outwit us. For we are not unaware of his schemes.

Ministers of the New Covenant

¹²Now when I went to Troas to preach the gospel of Christ and found that the Lord had opened a door for me, ¹³I still had no peace of mind, because I did not find my brother Titus there. So I said goodbye to them and went on to Macedonia.

¹⁴But thanks be to God, who always leads us as captives in Christ's triumphal procession and uses us to spread the aroma of the knowledge of him everywhere. ¹⁵For we are to God the pleasing aroma of Christ among those who are being saved and those who are perishing. ¹⁶To the one we are an aroma that brings death; to the other, an aroma that brings life. And who is equal to such a task? ¹⁷Unlike so many, we do not peddle the word of God for profit. On the contrary, in Christ we speak before God with sincerity, as those sent from God.

3 Are we beginning to commend ourselves again? Or do we need, like some people, letters of recommendation to you or from you? ²You yourselves are our letter, written on our hearts, known and read by everyone. ³You show that you are a letter from Christ, the result of our ministry, writ-

ten not with ink but with the Spirit of the living God, not on tablets of stone but on tablets of human hearts.

⁴Such confidence we have through Christ before God. ⁵Not that we are competent in ourselves to claim anything for ourselves, but our competence comes from God. ⁶He has made us competent as ministers of a new covenant — not of the letter but of the Spirit; for the letter kills, but the Spirit gives life.

The Greater Glory of the New Covenant

⁷Now if the ministry that brought death, which was engraved in letters on stone, came with glory, so that the Israelites could not look steadily at the face of Moses because of its glory, transitory though it was, ⁸will not the ministry of the Spirit be even more glorious? ⁹If the ministry that brought condemnation was glorious, how much more glorious is the ministry that brings righteousness! ¹⁰For what was glorious has no glory now in comparison with the surpassing glory. ¹¹And if what was transitory came with glory, how much greater is the glory of that which lasts!

¹²Therefore, since we have such a hope, we are very bold. ¹³We are not like Moses, who would put a veil over his face to prevent the Israelites from seeing the end of what was passing away. ¹⁴But their minds were made dull, for to this day the same veil remains when the old covenant is read. It has not been removed, because only in Christ is it taken away. ¹⁵Even to this day when Moses is read, a veil covers their hearts. ¹⁶But whenever anyone turns to the Lord, the veil is taken away. ¹⁷Now the Lord is the Spirit, and where the Spirit of the Lord is, there is freedom. ¹⁸And we all, who with unveiled faces contemplate[a] the Lord's glory, are being transformed into his image with ever-increasing glory, which comes from the Lord, who is the Spirit.

Present Weakness and Resurrection Life

4 Therefore, since through God's mercy we have this ministry, we do not lose heart. ²Rather, we have renounced secret and shameful ways; we do not use deception, nor do we distort the word of God. On the

---

[a] 18 Or *reflect*

FULL OF EMOTION

READ: 2 CORINTHIANS 3:18

If you want to identify your idols, you need to follow the trail of your tears or fears, your cheers or jeers. And if you do, you'll come face-to-face with the idols in your life.

What makes you mad or sad or glad? What ruins your day or makes your day? What triggers your strongest emotional reactions? How you show emotion isn't the issue.

Neither is when or where.

The real issue is why.

Does your heart break for the things that break the heart of God? That's the question.

The estimated number of unique human emotions ranges as high as 400, but no matter how many there are, we're called to love God with every single one of them. That's what it means to love God with all our heart.

BUILDING

FAITH

WISDOM

STRENGTH

The distance between your knees and the ground is only twenty-four inches, but it's the difference between you standing on your own and transformation. It's not enough to invite Jesus into your mind. You have to open the door to your heart. No door can stay locked. Even the door to your hidden room.

Nothing messes with emotions like sin. And if you sin long enough, it feels like a Gordian knot that seems impossible to untangle. But Jesus Christ went to the cross to undo what you've done. You can break the cycle!

Taken from *All In Student Edition* by Mark Batterson and Parker Batterson, copyright © 2014 by Mark Batterson, published by Zondervan.

contrary, by setting forth the truth plainly we commend ourselves to everyone's conscience in the sight of God. [3]And even if our gospel is veiled, it is veiled to those who are perishing. [4]The god of this age has blinded the minds of unbelievers, so that they cannot see the light of the gospel that displays the glory of Christ, who is the image of God. [5]For what we preach is not ourselves, but Jesus Christ as Lord, and ourselves as your servants for Jesus' sake. [6]For God, who said, "Let light shine out of darkness,"[a] made his light shine in our hearts to give us the light of the knowledge of God's glory displayed in the face of Christ.

[7]But we have this treasure in jars of clay to show that this all-surpassing power is from God and not from us. [8]We are hard pressed on every side, but not crushed; perplexed, but not in despair; [9]persecuted, but not abandoned; struck down, but not destroyed. [10]We always carry around in our body the death of Jesus, so that the life of Jesus may also be revealed in our body. [11]For we who are alive are always being given over to death for Jesus' sake, so that his life may also be revealed in our mortal body. [12]So then, death is at work in us, but life is at work in you.

[13]It is written: "I believed; therefore I have spoken."[b] Since we have that same spirit of[c] faith, we also believe and therefore speak, [14]because we know that the one who raised the Lord Jesus from the dead will also raise us with Jesus and present us with you to himself. [15]All this is for your benefit, so that the grace that is reaching more and more people may cause thanksgiving to overflow to the glory of God.

[16]Therefore we do not lose heart. Though outwardly we are wasting away, yet inwardly we are being renewed day by day. [17]For our light and momentary troubles are achieving for us an eternal glory that far outweighs them all. [18]So we fix our eyes not on what is seen, but on what is unseen, since what is seen is temporary, but what is unseen is eternal.

Awaiting the New Body

5 For we know that if the earthly tent we live in is destroyed, we have a building from God, an eternal house in heaven, not built by human hands. [2]Meanwhile we groan, longing to be clothed instead with our heavenly dwelling, [3]because when we are clothed, we will not be found naked. [4]For while we are in this tent, we groan and are burdened, because we do not wish to be unclothed but to be clothed instead with our heavenly dwelling, so that what is mortal may be swallowed up by life. [5]Now the one who has fashioned us for this very purpose is God, who has given us the Spirit as a deposit, guaranteeing what is to come.

[6]Therefore we are always confident and know that as long as we are at home in the body we are away from the Lord. [7]For we live by faith, not by sight. [8]We are confident, I say, and would prefer to be away from the body and at home with the Lord. [9]So we make it our goal to please him, whether we are at home in the body or away from it. [10]For we must all appear before the judgment seat of Christ, so that each of us may receive what is due us for the things done while in the body, whether good or bad.

The Ministry of Reconciliation

[11]Since, then, we know what it is to fear the Lord, we try to persuade others. What we are is plain to God, and I hope it is also plain to your conscience. [12]We are not trying to commend ourselves to you again, but are giving you an opportunity to take pride in us, so that you can answer those who take pride in what is seen rather than in what is in the heart. [13]If we are "out of our mind," as some say, it is for God; if we are in our right mind, it is for you. [14]For Christ's love compels us, because we are convinced that one died for all, and therefore all died. [15]And he died for all, that those who live should no longer live for themselves but for him who died for them and was raised again.

[16]So from now on we regard no one from a worldly point of view. Though we once regarded Christ in this way, we do so no longer. [17]Therefore, if anyone is in Christ, the new creation has come:[d] The old has gone, the new is here! [18]All this is from God, who reconciled us to himself through Christ and gave us the ministry of reconciliation: [19]that

---

[a] 6 Gen. 1:3   [b] 13 Psalm 116:10 (see Septuagint)   [c] 13 Or *Spirit-given*   [d] 17 Or *Christ, that person is a new creation.*

THE CHASE

READ: 2 CORINTHIANS 5:15

Homework will always be a chore until you decide you like to learn. Sports drills always get old if you don't fall in love with your game. In a similar way, living all-out for God won't ever happen freely and easily until something changes inside you.

As soon as you become a Christian, the Lord makes you a "new creation" (2 Corinthians 5:17). He forgives you and begins making you over. When that happens, his love begins to take over your heart. The more you experience that amazing love and grasp the awesome fact that Jesus died and rose for you, the more motivated you are to live for him.

That's what the apostle Paul means when he says, "Christ's love compels us" (v. 14). Christ's love inside you propels you from the inside out. You follow Jesus wholeheartedly because of what he's done for you. You obey because you want to, not because you have to.

BUILDING FAITH WISDOM STRENGTH

Living all-out for God isn't about you trying harder or needing someone to force you to be spiritual. Your head might be convinced that following Jesus is the best way to live, but there might be times you aren't so sure. Wanting to please Christians you respect might energize you for a while, but that wears off. Love from the heart will keep you chasing Jesus for the rest of your life.

God was reconciling the world to himself in Christ, not counting people's sins against them. And he has committed to us the message of reconciliation. [20]We are therefore Christ's ambassadors, as though God were making his appeal through us. We implore you on Christ's behalf: Be reconciled to God. [21]God made him who had no sin to be sin[a] for us, so that in him we might become the righteousness of God.

6 As God's co-workers we urge you not to receive God's grace in vain. [2]For he says,

> "In the time of my favor I
> heard you,
> and in the day of salvation
> I helped you."[b]

I tell you, now is the time of God's favor, now is the day of salvation.

Paul's Hardships

[3]We put no stumbling block in anyone's path, so that our ministry will not be discredited. [4]Rather, as servants of God we commend ourselves in every way: in great endurance; in troubles, hardships and distresses; [5]in beatings, imprisonments and riots; in hard work, sleepless nights and hunger; [6]in purity, understanding, patience and kindness; in the Holy Spirit and in sincere love; [7]in truthful speech and in the power of God; with weapons of righteousness in the right hand and in the left; [8]through glory and dishonor, bad report and good report; genuine, yet regarded as impostors; [9]known, yet regarded as unknown; dying, and yet we live on; beaten, and yet not killed; [10]sorrowful, yet always rejoicing; poor, yet making many rich; having nothing, and yet possessing everything.

[11]We have spoken freely to you, Corinthians, and opened wide our hearts to you. [12]We are not withholding our affection from you, but you are withholding yours from us. [13]As a fair exchange — I speak as to my children — open wide your hearts also.

Warning Against Idolatry

[14]Do not be yoked together with unbelievers. For what do righteousness and wickedness have in common? Or what fellowship can light have with darkness? [15]What harmony is there between Christ and Belial[c]? Or what does a believer have in common with an unbeliever? [16]What agreement is there between the temple of God and idols? For we are the temple of the living God. As God has said:

> "I will live with them
> and walk among them,
> and I will be their God,
> and they will be my people."[d]

[17]Therefore,

> "Come out from them
> and be separate,
> says the Lord.
> Touch no unclean thing,
> and I will receive you."[e]

[18]And,

> "I will be a Father to you,
> and you will be my sons and
> daughters,
> says the Lord Almighty."[f]

7 Therefore, since we have these promises, dear friends, let us purify ourselves from everything that contaminates body and spirit, perfecting holiness out of reverence for God.

Paul's Joy Over the Church's Repentance

[2]Make room for us in your hearts. We have wronged no one, we have corrupted no one, we have exploited no one. [3]I do not say this to condemn you; I have said before that you have such a place in our hearts that we would live or die with you. [4]I have spoken to you with great frankness; I take great pride in you. I am greatly encouraged; in all our troubles my joy knows no bounds.

[5]For when we came into Macedonia, we had no rest, but we were harassed at every turn — conflicts on the outside, fears within. [6]But God, who comforts the downcast, comforted us by the coming of Titus, [7]and not only by his coming but also by the comfort you had given him. He told us about your longing for me, your deep sorrow, your ardent concern for me, so that my joy was greater than ever.

[8]Even if I caused you sorrow by my letter, I do not regret it. Though I did regret it — I

---

[a] 21 Or *be a sin offering*   [b] 2 Isaiah 49:8   [c] 15 Greek *Beliar*, a variant of *Belial*   [d] 16 Lev. 26:12;
Jer. 32:38; Ezek. 37:27   [e] 17 Isaiah 52:11; Ezek. 20:34,41   [f] 18 2 Samuel 7:14; 7:8

THE TRANSFORMER

READ: 2 CORINTHIANS 5:16-21

You only get a relationship with God on his terms. It's not like we have any abilities (like making time stand still) that God needs. God is perfect and loving, so just take what he offers. The moment you bow your knee to the lordship of Jesus, all of your sin is transferred to Christ's account and erased from yours. He already paid for it. It was nailed to the cross 2,000 years ago! But that's only half the gospel. Mercy is not getting what you deserve—the wrath of God. Grace is getting what you don't deserve—the righteousness of Christ. Everything you've done wrong is forgiven and forgotten! And then God calls it even.

It's like God says, "I'll take the blame and shame for everything you did wrong and give you credit for everything I did right." It doesn't get any better than that, and that's why it's called the gospel. It's good news . . . the best news!

The gospel costs nothing. We can't buy it, and especially can't earn it. It can only be received as a free gift, through God's grace. It costs nothing, but it demands everything. And that's where most of us get stuck. We're too Christian to enjoy sin and too sinful to enjoy Christ. We've got just enough Jesus to be informed, but not enough to be transformed. And transformation is where it's at.

BUILDING
FAITH
WISDOM
STRENGTH

Taken from *All In Student Edition* by Mark Batterson and Parker Batterson, copyright © 2014 by Mark Batterson, published by Zondervan.

see that my letter hurt you, but only for a little while— [9]yet now I am happy, not because you were made sorry, but because your sorrow led you to repentance. For you became sorrowful as God intended and so were not harmed in any way by us. [10]Godly sorrow brings repentance that leads to salvation and leaves no regret, but worldly sorrow brings death. [11]See what this godly sorrow has produced in you: what earnestness, what eagerness to clear yourselves, what indignation, what alarm, what longing, what concern, what readiness to see justice done. At every point you have proved yourselves to be innocent in this matter. [12]So even though I wrote to you, it was neither on account of the one who did the wrong nor on account of the injured party, but rather that before God you could see for yourselves how devoted to us you are. [13]By all this we are encouraged.

In addition to our own encouragement, we were especially delighted to see how happy Titus was, because his spirit has been refreshed by all of you. [14]I had boasted to him about you, and you have not embarrassed me. But just as everything we said to you was true, so our boasting about you to Titus has proved to be true as well. [15]And his affection for you is all the greater when he remembers that you were all obedient, receiving him with fear and trembling. [16]I am glad I can have complete confidence in you.

The Collection for the Lord's People

8 And now, brothers and sisters, we want you to know about the grace that God has given the Macedonian churches. [2]In the midst of a very severe trial, their overflowing joy and their extreme poverty welled up in rich generosity. [3]For I testify that they gave as much as they were able, and even beyond their ability. Entirely on their own, [4]they urgently pleaded with us for the privilege of sharing in this service to the Lord's people. [5]And they exceeded our expectations: They gave themselves first of all to the Lord, and then by the will of God also to us. [6]So we urged Titus, just as he had earlier made a beginning, to bring also to completion this act of grace on your part. [7]But since you excel in everything—in faith, in speech, in knowledge, in complete earnestness and in

the love we have kindled in you[a]— see that you also excel in this grace of giving.

[8]I am not commanding you, but I want to test the sincerity of your love by comparing it with the earnestness of others. [9]For you know the grace of our Lord Jesus Christ, that though he was rich, yet for your sake he became poor, so that you through his poverty might become rich.

[10]And here is my judgment about what is best for you in this matter. Last year you were the first not only to give but also to have the desire to do so. [11]Now finish the work, so that your eager willingness to do it may be matched by your completion of it, according to your means. [12]For if the willingness is there, the gift is acceptable according to what one has, not according to what one does not have.

[13]Our desire is not that others might be relieved while you are hard pressed, but that there might be equality. [14]At the present time your plenty will supply what they need, so that in turn their plenty will supply what you need. The goal is equality, [15]as it is written: "The one who gathered much did not have too much, and the one who gathered little did not have too little."[b]

Titus Sent to Receive the Collection

[16]Thanks be to God, who put into the heart of Titus the same concern I have for you. [17]For Titus not only welcomed our appeal, but he is coming to you with much enthusiasm and on his own initiative. [18]And we are sending along with him the brother who is praised by all the churches for his service to the gospel. [19]What is more, he was chosen by the churches to accompany us as we carry the offering, which we administer in order to honor the Lord himself and to show our eagerness to help. [20]We want to avoid any criticism of the way we administer this liberal gift. [21]For we are taking pains to do what is right, not only in the eyes of the Lord but also in the eyes of man.

[22]In addition, we are sending with them our brother who has often proved to us in many ways that he is zealous, and now even more so because of his great confidence in you. [23]As for Titus, he is my partner and co-worker among you; as for our brothers, they

---

[a] 7 Some manuscripts *and in your love for us*   [b] 15 Exodus 16:18

are representatives of the churches and an honor to Christ. ²⁴Therefore show these men the proof of your love and the reason for our pride in you, so that the churches can see it.

9 There is no need for me to write to you about this service to the Lord's people. ²For I know your eagerness to help, and I have been boasting about it to the Macedonians, telling them that since last year you in Achaia were ready to give; and your enthusiasm has stirred most of them to action. ³But I am sending the brothers in order that our boasting about you in this matter should not prove hollow, but that you may be ready, as I said you would be. ⁴For if any Macedonians come with me and find you unprepared, we — not to say anything about you — would be ashamed of having been so confident. ⁵So I thought it necessary to urge the brothers to visit you in advance and finish the arrangements for the generous gift you had promised. Then it will be ready as a generous gift, not as one grudgingly given.

Generosity Encouraged

⁶Remember this: Whoever sows sparingly will also reap sparingly, and whoever sows generously will also reap generously. ⁷Each of you should give what you have decided in your heart to give, not reluctantly or under compulsion, for God loves a cheerful giver. ⁸And God is able to bless you abundantly, so that in all things at all times, having all that you need, you will abound in every good work. ⁹As it is written:

"They have freely scattered their gifts to the poor;
their righteousness endures forever."[a]

¹⁰Now he who supplies seed to the sower and bread for food will also supply and increase your store of seed and will enlarge the harvest of your righteousness. ¹¹You will be enriched in every way so that you can be generous on every occasion, and through us your generosity will result in thanksgiving to God.

¹²This service that you perform is not only supplying the needs of the Lord's people but is also overflowing in many expressions of thanks to God. ¹³Because of the service by which you have proved yourselves, others will praise God for the obedience that accompanies your confession of the gospel of Christ, and for your generosity in sharing with them and with everyone else. ¹⁴And in their prayers for you their hearts will go out to you, because of the surpassing grace God has given you. ¹⁵Thanks be to God for his indescribable gift!

Paul's Defense of His Ministry

10 By the humility and gentleness of Christ, I appeal to you — I, Paul, who am "timid" when face to face with you, but "bold" toward you when away! ²I beg you that when I come I may not have to be as bold as I expect to be toward some people who think that we live by the standards of this world. ³For though we live in the world, we do not wage war as the world does. ⁴The weapons we fight with are not the weapons of the world. On the contrary, they have divine power to demolish strongholds. ⁵We demolish arguments and every pretension that sets itself up against the knowledge of God, and we take captive every thought to make it obedient to Christ. ⁶And we will be ready to punish every act of disobedience, once your obedience is complete.

⁷You are judging by appearances.[b] If anyone is confident that they belong to Christ, they should consider again that we belong to Christ just as much as they do. ⁸So even if I boast somewhat freely about the authority the Lord gave us for building you up rather than tearing you down, I will not be ashamed of it. ⁹I do not want to seem to be trying to frighten you with my letters. ¹⁰For some say, "His letters are weighty and forceful, but in person he is unimpressive and his speaking amounts to nothing." ¹¹Such people should realize that what we are in our letters when we are absent, we will be in our actions when we are present.

¹²We do not dare to classify or compare ourselves with some who commend themselves. When they measure themselves by themselves and compare themselves with themselves, they are not wise. ¹³We, however, will not boast beyond proper limits, but will confine our boasting to the sphere of service God himself has assigned to us, a

---

[a] 9 Psalm 112:9   [b] 7 Or *Look at the obvious facts*

GENUINE GENEROSITY

READ: 2 CORINTHIANS 9:7

You buy cookie dough from the soccer team. You pledge dollars to a friend trekking to fight cancer. You purchase a car wash coupon from the choir, and you don't even own a car.

God applauds generosity, especially when you give to people who are facing genuine hardship. The Lord doesn't just want you to have warm feelings toward the poor. He challenges you to put your money where your mouth is. Like 1 John 3:17-18 says, "If anyone has material possessions and sees a brother or sister in need but has no pity on them, how can the love of God be in that person? Dear children, let us not love with words or speech but with actions and in truth." The New Testament gives details about a significant example of group generosity.

As the apostle Paul traveled the Mediterranean on his third mission trip, he requested money for impoverished believers in Jerusalem (Romans 15:25-28). He praises the people of northern Greece for their gifts (2 Corinthians 8:15), and urges the Corinthians to be just as generous (8:16—9:5).

Paul applies gentle pressure for the Corinthians to give, explaining why it's the right thing to do. But God doesn't squeeze you to give. He would rather have you grapple with real needs, make up your mind how much to give, then give from the heart.

BUILDING

FAITH

WISDOM

STRENGTH

sphere that also includes you. [14]We are not going too far in our boasting, as would be the case if we had not come to you, for we did get as far as you with the gospel of Christ. [15]Neither do we go beyond our limits by boasting of work done by others. Our hope is that, as your faith continues to grow, our sphere of activity among you will greatly expand, [16]so that we can preach the gospel in the regions beyond you. For we do not want to boast about work already done in someone else's territory. [17]But, "Let the one who boasts boast in the Lord."[a] [18]For it is not the one who commends himself who is approved, but the one whom the Lord commends.

Paul and the False Apostles

11 I hope you will put up with me in a little foolishness. Yes, please put up with me! [2]I am jealous for you with a godly jealousy. I promised you to one husband, to Christ, so that I might present you as a pure virgin to him. [3]But I am afraid that just as Eve was deceived by the serpent's cunning, your minds may somehow be led astray from your sincere and pure devotion to Christ. [4]For if someone comes to you and preaches a Jesus other than the Jesus we preached, or if you receive a different spirit from the Spirit you received, or a different gospel from the one you accepted, you put up with it easily enough.

[5]I do not think I am in the least inferior to those "super-apostles."[b] [6]I may indeed be untrained as a speaker, but I do have knowledge. We have made this perfectly clear to you in every way. [7]Was it a sin for me to lower myself in order to elevate you by preaching the gospel of God to you free of charge? [8]I robbed other churches by receiving support from them so as to serve you. [9]And when I was with you and needed something, I was not a burden to anyone, for the brothers who came from Macedonia supplied what I needed. I have kept myself from being a burden to you in any way, and will continue to do so. [10]As surely as the truth of Christ is in me, nobody in the regions of Achaia will stop this boasting of mine. [11]Why? Because I do not love you? God knows I do! [12]And I will keep on doing what I am doing in order to cut the ground from under

those who want an opportunity to be considered equal with us in the things they boast about. [13]For such people are false apostles, deceitful workers, masquerading as apostles of Christ. [14]And no wonder, for Satan himself masquerades as an angel of light. [15]It is not surprising, then, if his servants also masquerade as servants of righteousness. Their end will be what their actions deserve.

Paul Boasts About His Sufferings

[16]I repeat: Let no one take me for a fool. But if you do, then tolerate me just as you would a fool, so that I may do a little boasting. [17]In this self-confident boasting I am not talking as the Lord would, but as a fool. [18]Since many are boasting in the way the world does, I too will boast. [19]You gladly put up with fools since you are so wise! [20]In fact, you even put up with anyone who enslaves you or exploits you or takes advantage of you or puts on airs or slaps you in the face. [21]To my shame I admit that we were too weak for that!

Whatever anyone else dares to boast about—I am speaking as a fool—I also dare to boast about. [22]Are they Hebrews? So am I. Are they Israelites? So am I. Are they Abraham's descendants? So am I. [23]Are they servants of Christ? (I am out of my mind to talk like this.) I am more. I have worked much harder, been in prison more frequently, been flogged more severely, and been exposed to death again and again. [24]Five times I received from the Jews the forty lashes minus one. [25]Three times I was beaten with rods, once I was pelted with stones, three times I was shipwrecked, I spent a night and a day in the open sea, [26]I have been constantly on the move. I have been in danger from rivers, in danger from bandits, in danger from my fellow Jews, in danger from Gentiles; in danger in the city, in danger in the country, in danger at sea; and in danger from false believers. [27]I have labored and toiled and have often gone without sleep; I have known hunger and thirst and have often gone without food; I have been cold and naked. [28]Besides everything else, I face daily the pressure of my concern for all the churches. [29]Who is weak, and I do not feel weak? Who is led into sin, and I do not inwardly burn?

[30]If I must boast, I will boast of the things

---

[a] 17 Jer. 9:24   [b] 5 Or *to the most eminent apostles*

that show my weakness. [31] The God and Father of the Lord Jesus, who is to be praised forever, knows that I am not lying. [32] In Damascus the governor under King Aretas had the city of the Damascenes guarded in order to arrest me. [33] But I was lowered in a basket from a window in the wall and slipped through his hands.

Paul's Vision and His Thorn

12 I must go on boasting. Although there is nothing to be gained, I will go on to visions and revelations from the Lord. [2] I know a man in Christ who fourteen years ago was caught up to the third heaven. Whether it was in the body or out of the body I do not know—God knows. [3] And I know that this man—whether in the body or apart from the body I do not know, but God knows— [4] was caught up to paradise and heard inexpressible things, things that no one is permitted to tell. [5] I will boast about a man like that, but I will not boast about myself, except about my weaknesses. [6] Even if I should choose to boast, I would not be a fool, because I would be speaking the truth. But I refrain, so no one will think more of me than is warranted by what I do or say, [7] or because of these surpassingly great revelations. Therefore, in order to keep me from becoming conceited, I was given a thorn in my flesh, a messenger of Satan, to torment me. [8] Three times I pleaded with the Lord to take it away from me. [9] But he said to me, "My grace is sufficient for you, for my power is made perfect in weakness." Therefore I will boast all the more gladly about my weaknesses, so that Christ's power may rest on me. [10] That is why, for Christ's sake, I delight in weaknesses, in insults, in hardships, in persecutions, in difficulties. For when I am weak, then I am strong.

Paul's Concern for the Corinthians

[11] I have made a fool of myself, but you drove me to it. I ought to have been commended by you, for I am not in the least inferior to the "super-apostles,"[a] even though I am nothing. [12] I persevered in demonstrating among you the marks of a true apostle, including signs, wonders and miracles. [13] How were you inferior to the other churches, except that I was never a burden to you? Forgive me this wrong!

[14] Now I am ready to visit you for the third time, and I will not be a burden to you, because what I want is not your possessions but you. After all, children should not have to save up for their parents, but parents for their children. [15] So I will very gladly spend for you everything I have and expend myself as well. If I love you more, will you love me less? [16] Be that as it may, I have not been a burden to you. Yet, crafty fellow that I am, I caught you by trickery! [17] Did I exploit you through any of the men I sent to you? [18] I urged Titus to go to you and I sent our brother with him. Titus did not exploit you, did he? Did we not walk in the same footsteps by the same Spirit?

[19] Have you been thinking all along that we have been defending ourselves to you? We have been speaking in the sight of God as those in Christ; and everything we do, dear friends, is for your strengthening. [20] For I am afraid that when I come I may not find you as I want you to be, and you may not find me as you want me to be. I fear that there may be discord, jealousy, fits of rage, selfish ambition, slander, gossip, arrogance and disorder. [21] I am afraid that when I come again my God will humble me before you, and I will be grieved over many who have sinned earlier and have not repented of the impurity, sexual sin and debauchery in which they have indulged.

Final Warnings

13 This will be my third visit to you. "Every matter must be established by the testimony of two or three witnesses."[b] [2] I already gave you a warning when I was with you the second time. I now repeat it while absent: On my return I will not spare those who sinned earlier or any of the others, [3] since you are demanding proof that Christ is speaking through me. He is not weak in dealing with you, but is powerful among you. [4] For to be sure, he was crucified in weakness, yet he lives by God's power. Likewise, we are weak in him, yet by God's power we will live with him in our dealing with you.

[5] Examine yourselves to see whether you are in the faith; test yourselves. Do you not realize that Christ Jesus is in you—unless, of course, you fail the test? [6] And I trust that

---

[a] 11 Or *the most eminent apostles*   [b] 1 Deut. 19:15

you will discover that we have not failed the test. [7] Now we pray to God that you will not do anything wrong — not so that people will see that we have stood the test but so that you will do what is right even though we may seem to have failed. [8] For we cannot do anything against the truth, but only for the truth. [9] We are glad whenever we are weak but you are strong; and our prayer is that you may be fully restored. [10] This is why I write these things when I am absent, that when I come I may not have to be harsh in my use of authority — the authority the Lord gave me for building you up, not for tearing you down.

Final Greetings

[11] Finally, brothers and sisters, rejoice! Strive for full restoration, encourage one another, be of one mind, live in peace. And the God of love and peace will be with you.

[12] Greet one another with a holy kiss. [13] All God's people here send their greetings.

[14] May the grace of the Lord Jesus Christ, and the love of God, and the fellowship of the Holy Spirit be with you all.

GALATIANS

WHEN DID THIS HAPPEN?
Around A.D. 49 in Antioch

WHO IS IN THIS BOOK?
Paul
Barnabas
Titus
Peter
John

VERSE YOU MIGHT RECOGNIZE

GALATIANS 5:22–23
"But the fruit of the Spirit is love, joy, peace, forbearance, kindness, goodness, faithfulness, gentleness and self-control. Against such things there is no law."

WHAT'S IT ABOUT?

Paul wrote this letter to the church in Galatia because some people had begun to teach that Gentiles had to obey the Law of Moses to be saved. Paul made it clear that this was not the real gospel. They could never earn God's salvation by following the law; justification was a free gift that came through faith in Jesus. If people began depending on their works to save them, then Christ's death and resurrection would be meaningless!

Paul used a strong, sometimes angry tone to make sure the people understand the truth and are not led astray by a false gospel. Like using all caps to make a point, Paul even took the pen from his scribe and wrote the end of the letter himself in large letters (see Galatians 6:11).

Paul also mentioned some of the very first Jews, such as Abraham, Sarah and Isaac, to remind the people that no one has ever been saved by obeying the law. Instead, those people walked by faith, looking forward to a Savior—who was Jesus Christ. But just because Christ fulfilled the law didn't mean the people should live in sin. The Holy Spirit helps believers exhibit godly fruit as they live for him.

GALATIANS

1 Paul, an apostle — sent not from men nor by a man, but by Jesus Christ and God the Father, who raised him from the dead — ²and all the brothers and sisters[a] with me,

To the churches in Galatia:

³Grace and peace to you from God our Father and the Lord Jesus Christ, ⁴who gave himself for our sins to rescue us from the present evil age, according to the will of our God and Father, ⁵to whom be glory for ever and ever. Amen.

No Other Gospel

⁶I am astonished that you are so quickly deserting the one who called you to live in the grace of Christ and are turning to a different gospel — ⁷which is really no gospel at all. Evidently some people are throwing you into confusion and are trying to pervert the gospel of Christ. ⁸But even if we or an angel from heaven should preach a gospel other than the one we preached to you, let them be under God's curse! ⁹As we have already said, so now I say again: If anybody is preaching to you a gospel other than what you accepted, let them be under God's curse!

¹⁰Am I now trying to win the approval of human beings, or of God? Or am I trying to please people? If I were still trying to please people, I would not be a servant of Christ.

Paul Called by God

¹¹I want you to know, brothers and sisters, that the gospel I preached is not of human origin. ¹²I did not receive it from any man, nor was I taught it; rather, I received it by revelation from Jesus Christ.

¹³For you have heard of my previous way of life in Judaism, how intensely I persecuted the church of God and tried to destroy it. ¹⁴I was advancing in Judaism beyond many of my own age among my people and was extremely zealous for the traditions of my fathers. ¹⁵But when God, who set me apart from my mother's womb and called me by his grace, was pleased ¹⁶to reveal his Son in me so that I might preach him among the Gentiles, my immediate response was not to consult any human being. ¹⁷I did not go up to Jerusalem to see those who were apostles before I was, but I went into Arabia. Later I returned to Damascus.

¹⁸Then after three years, I went up to Jerusalem to get acquainted with Cephas[b] and stayed with him fifteen days. ¹⁹I saw none of the other apostles — only James, the Lord's brother. ²⁰I assure you before God that what I am writing you is no lie.

²¹Then I went to Syria and Cilicia. ²²I was personally unknown to the churches of Judea that are in Christ. ²³They only heard the report: "The man who formerly persecuted us is now preaching the faith he once tried to destroy." ²⁴And they praised God because of me.

Paul Accepted by the Apostles

2 Then after fourteen years, I went up again to Jerusalem, this time with Barnabas. I took Titus along also. ²I went in response to a revelation and, meeting privately with those esteemed as leaders, I presented to them the gospel that I preach among the Gentiles. I wanted to be sure I was not running and had not been running my race in vain. ³Yet not even Titus, who was with me, was compelled to be circumcised, even though he was a Greek. ⁴This matter arose because some false believers had infiltrated our ranks to spy on the freedom we have in Christ Jesus and to make us slaves. ⁵We did not give in to them for a moment, so that the truth of the gospel might be preserved for you.

⁶As for those who were held in high esteem — whatever they were makes no difference to me; God does not show favoritism —

---

[a] 2 The Greek word for *brothers and sisters* (*adelphoi*) refers here to believers, both men and women, as part of God's family; also in verse 11; and in 3:15; 4:12, 28, 31; 5:11, 13; 6:1, 18.   [b] 18 That is, Peter

THE SHAM

READ: GALATIANS 1:10

You know God should come first in your life. Yet almost anything can push him out of the top spot. Sometimes it's possessions, being owned by your stuff and always craving more. Or it might be activities, getting so busy that God gets bumped from your schedule. But often it's people who take God's place.

The book of Galatians is one of the apostle Paul's most potent letters. It's written to Christians living in a region that's now central Turkey. Just a few sentences into his note, Paul accuses the Galatians of abandoning Jesus for a different message, one that puts them at risk of going to hell. False teachers are defying the truth that God saves people because of his kindness when they believe in Jesus, not because they do good works (Ephesians 2:8-9). These frauds say Christians have to follow Old Testament rituals like circumcision to get right with the Lord.

BUILDING

FAITH

WISDOM

STRENGTH

Paul bluntly announces that he deserves God's curse if he ever preaches anything except the real facts about Jesus. And he reveals the secret of his willingness to stand up for truth: He doesn't care what anyone else thinks.

It's impossible to keep following Jesus if people's opinions matter to you more than what God wants. Sometimes you can make both God and people happy. But sometimes you can't. Then whose voice are you going to listen to?

PAUL

God, who set me apart from my mother's womb and called me by his grace, was pleased to reveal his Son in me so that I might preach him among the Gentiles.
GALATIANS 1:15-16

HIS NAME MEANS: "little" (His original name, Saul, means "asked for")

READ HIS STORY: *Acts 7:59—8:3, 9:1-31, 18, 21, 22, 25*

OF THE BIBLE

Meeting Jesus changes a person. Just look at Paul's life. The first time we read about Paul, then known as *Saul*, he was watching people stone and kill Stephen for his faith in Christ (Acts 7:58-60). Saul had devoted his life to stopping the spread of Christianity. But his aspirations did a U-turn when he met the risen Lord. As Saul traveled to Damascus, God knocked him down and blinded him with light. Saul heard Jesus ask, "Why do you persecute me?" Saul got up, went into the city and found some of Jesus' disciples. He realized how he'd proudly followed the law as a Pharisee and rejected God's grace. Now he saw the truth. After God restored his sight, Saul stopped persecuting Christians and became Jesus' greatest ambassador.

Paul (the name by which he is referred to beginning in Acts 13:9) traveled the world to tell previously unreached people about God's love and forgiveness. Instead of preaching obedience to the law, Paul preached grace. He knew good works and trying to obey God's laws don't save us (Ephesians 2:8-9). In his journeys through what is now Greece and Turkey, he set up churches and helped spread Christianity.

His travels weren't easy. He was often imprisoned and attacked. He avoided a mob set on killing him, only to be shipwrecked and bitten by a poisonous snake. Many scholars believe Paul was martyred during the reign of Emperor Nero. But his legacy didn't die in a Roman prison. Through his letters to churches and Christian leaders, Paul authored fourteen books in the New Testament.

they added nothing to my message. [7]On the contrary, they recognized that I had been entrusted with the task of preaching the gospel to the uncircumcised,[a] just as Peter had been to the circumcised.[b] [8]For God, who was at work in Peter as an apostle to the circumcised, was also at work in me as an apostle to the Gentiles. [9]James, Cephas[c] and John, those esteemed as pillars, gave me and Barnabas the right hand of fellowship when they recognized the grace given to me. They agreed that we should go to the Gentiles, and they to the circumcised. [10]All they asked was that we should continue to remember the poor, the very thing I had been eager to do all along.

Paul Opposes Cephas

[11]When Cephas came to Antioch, I opposed him to his face, because he stood condemned. [12]For before certain men came from James, he used to eat with the Gentiles. But when they arrived, he began to draw back and separate himself from the Gentiles because he was afraid of those who belonged to the circumcision group. [13]The other Jews joined him in his hypocrisy, so that by their hypocrisy even Barnabas was led astray.

[14]When I saw that they were not acting in line with the truth of the gospel, I said to Cephas in front of them all, "You are a Jew, yet you live like a Gentile and not like a Jew. How is it, then, that you force Gentiles to follow Jewish customs?

[15]"We who are Jews by birth and not sinful Gentiles [16]know that a person is not justified by the works of the law, but by faith in Jesus Christ. So we, too, have put our faith in Christ Jesus that we may be justified by faith in[d] Christ and not by the works of the law, because by the works of the law no one will be justified.

[17]"But if, in seeking to be justified in Christ, we Jews find ourselves also among the sinners, doesn't that mean that Christ promotes sin? Absolutely not! [18]If I rebuild what I destroyed, then I really would be a lawbreaker.

[19]"For through the law I died to the law so that I might live for God. [20]I have been crucified with Christ and I no longer live, but Christ lives in me. The life I now live in the body, I live by faith in the Son of God, who loved me and gave himself for me. [21]I do not set aside the grace of God, for if righteousness could be gained through the law, Christ died for nothing!"[e]

Faith or Works of the Law

3 You foolish Galatians! Who has bewitched you? Before your very eyes Jesus Christ was clearly portrayed as crucified. [2]I would like to learn just one thing from you: Did you receive the Spirit by the works of the law, or by believing what you heard? [3]Are you so foolish? After beginning by means of the Spirit, are you now trying to finish by means of the flesh?[f] [4]Have you experienced[g] so much in vain—if it really was in vain? [5]So again I ask, does God give you his Spirit and work miracles among you by the works of the law, or by your believing what you heard? [6]So also Abraham "believed God, and it was credited to him as righteousness."[h]

[7]Understand, then, that those who have faith are children of Abraham. [8]Scripture foresaw that God would justify the Gentiles by faith, and announced the gospel in advance to Abraham: "All nations will be blessed through you."[i] [9]So those who rely on faith are blessed along with Abraham, the man of faith.

[10]For all who rely on the works of the law are under a curse, as it is written: "Cursed is everyone who does not continue to do everything written in the Book of the Law."[j] [11]Clearly no one who relies on the law is justified before God, because "the righteous will live by faith."[k] [12]The law is not based on faith; on the contrary, it says, "The person who does these things will live by them."[l] [13]Christ redeemed us from the curse of the law by becoming a curse for us, for it is written: "Cursed is everyone who is hung on a pole."[m] [14]He redeemed us in order that the blessing given to Abraham might come to

---

[a] 7 That is, Gentiles   [b] 7 That is, Jews; also in verses 8 and 9   [c] 9 That is, Peter; also in verses 11 and 14   [d] 16 Or but through the faithfulness of . . . justified on the basis of the faithfulness of   [e] 21 Some interpreters end the quotation after verse 14.   [f] 3 In contexts like this, the Greek word for flesh (sarx) refers to the sinful state of human beings, often presented as a power in opposition to the Spirit.   [g] 4 Or suffered   [h] 6 Gen. 15:6   [i] 8 Gen. 12:3; 18:18; 22:18   [j] 10 Deut. 27:26   [k] 11 Hab. 2:4   [l] 12 Lev. 18:5   [m] 13 Deut. 21:23

GOTCHA!

READ: GALATIANS 3:1-5

Crafty and subtle, Satan takes the truth and tries to redefine it. For instance, in the most effective "gotcha" kind of way found in the best horror flicks, he's convinced a lot of believers that it's up to them to keep themselves saved and hold it all together. His approach works because such thinking is logical. It makes sense. We hold everything else in our lives together—or, at least on the surface, it looks like we do.

We keep our popularity by the way we perform on campus. We keep good grades through our homework and study. We keep ourselves on the team through hard work and diligence. The way we live can make or break a lot of friendships. In most areas of life, it makes sense to think we're the ones responsible for our success or failure.

Even though God's Word is the final authority on these matters, Satan somehow has convinced many people to believe they are responsible for earning their way to eternal life and heaven. Sadly, entire religions are based on works, and many of those folks who follow these religions will remain deceived until it's too late.

Let's aspire to let God have his Word back into our lives, so to speak. We need to let him—and only him—define what we are responsible for and what we do with our lives.

BUILDING

FAITH

WISDOM

STRENGTH

the Gentiles through Christ Jesus, so that by faith we might receive the promise of the Spirit.

The Law and the Promise

[15] Brothers and sisters, let me take an example from everyday life. Just as no one can set aside or add to a human covenant that has been duly established, so it is in this case. [16] The promises were spoken to Abraham and to his seed. Scripture does not say "and to seeds," meaning many people, but "and to your seed,"[a] meaning one person, who is Christ. [17] What I mean is this: The law, introduced 430 years later, does not set aside the covenant previously established by God and thus do away with the promise. [18] For if the inheritance depends on the law, then it no longer depends on the promise; but God in his grace gave it to Abraham through a promise.

[19] Why, then, was the law given at all? It was added because of transgressions until the Seed to whom the promise referred had come. The law was given through angels and entrusted to a mediator. [20] A mediator, however, implies more than one party; but God is one.

[21] Is the law, therefore, opposed to the promises of God? Absolutely not! For if a law had been given that could impart life, then righteousness would certainly have come by the law. [22] But Scripture has locked up everything under the control of sin, so that what was promised, being given through faith in Jesus Christ, might be given to those who believe.

Children of God

[23] Before the coming of this faith,[b] we were held in custody under the law, locked up until the faith that was to come would be revealed. [24] So the law was our guardian until Christ came that we might be justified by faith. [25] Now that this faith has come, we are no longer under a guardian.

[26] So in Christ Jesus you are all children of God through faith, [27] for all of you who were baptized into Christ have clothed yourselves with Christ. [28] There is neither Jew nor Gentile, neither slave nor free, nor is there male and female, for you are all one in Christ Jesus. [29] If you belong to Christ, then you are Abraham's seed, and heirs according to the promise.

4 What I am saying is that as long as an heir is underage, he is no different from a slave, although he owns the whole estate. [2] The heir is subject to guardians and trustees until the time set by his father. [3] So also, when we were underage, we were in slavery under the elemental spiritual forces[c] of the world. [4] But when the set time had fully come, God sent his Son, born of a woman, born under the law, [5] to redeem those under the law, that we might receive adoption to sonship.[d] [6] Because you are his sons, God sent the Spirit of his Son into our hearts, the Spirit who calls out, *"Abba,[e] Father."* [7] So you are no longer a slave, but God's child; and since you are his child, God has made you also an heir.

Paul's Concern for the Galatians

[8] Formerly, when you did not know God, you were slaves to those who by nature are not gods. [9] But now that you know God — or rather are known by God — how is it that you are turning back to those weak and miserable forces[f]? Do you wish to be enslaved by them all over again? [10] You are observing special days and months and seasons and years! [11] I fear for you, that somehow I have wasted my efforts on you.

[12] I plead with you, brothers and sisters, become like me, for I became like you. You did me no wrong. [13] As you know, it was because of an illness that I first preached the gospel to you, [14] and even though my illness was a trial to you, you did not treat me with contempt or scorn. Instead, you welcomed me as if I were an angel of God, as if I were Christ Jesus himself. [15] Where, then, is your blessing of me now? I can testify that, if you could have done so, you would have torn out your eyes and given them to me. [16] Have I now become your enemy by telling you the truth?

[17] Those people are zealous to win you over, but for no good. What they want is to

---

[a] 16 Gen. 12:7; 13:15; 24:7   [b] 22,23 Or *through the faithfulness of Jesus . . . [23] Before faith came*
[c] 3 Or *under the basic principles*   [d] 5 The Greek word for *adoption to sonship* is a legal term referring to the full legal standing of an adopted male heir in Roman culture.   [e] 6 Aramaic for *Father*
[f] 9 Or *principles*

TAKE A LOOK

READ: GALATIANS 4:8-10

Before Christ, the Jewish teachers took the Ten Commandments and transformed them into more than 600 laws. Galatians reveals a recurrence of this legalistic obsession in the early church. Judaizers had a knee-jerk reaction to the excessive liberties flaunted by some of the new grace-filled Christians.

Believers always should be wary of abusing freedom in Christ, but the Judaizers in Galatia mimicked their forefathers and weighted God's Word with their personal likes and dislikes.

When I look at the American church today, I see differences of opinion on nonessentials in Scripture. We need to be careful—and I'm holding up a mirror here—to communicate that the gospel is paramount; our issues and tastes are secondary. God is a God of mercy and truth. He is a God of balance. Too often I see fingers pointed behind harsh words.

I'm not more holy than you because I have a fish sticker on my car or because my hair is shorter than yours. At the same time, we shouldn't assume that wallowing in the slop somehow makes God appealing to the unbeliever we're trying to reach or endears us to God, as if the holiest of holies is impressed with our aptitude for all things human. God is not impressed with humanity. God is impressed with one person. Himself. There is nothing God wants glorified or seeks to spotlight more than himself.

And that's OK. He's God.

Since God made us in his image to glorify him, our job is to be a reflection of that spotlight.

BUILDING FAITH WISDOM STRENGTH

alienate you from us, so that you may have zeal for them. [18]It is fine to be zealous, provided the purpose is good, and to be so always, not just when I am with you. [19]My dear children, for whom I am again in the pains of childbirth until Christ is formed in you, [20]how I wish I could be with you now and change my tone, because I am perplexed about you!

Hagar and Sarah

[21]Tell me, you who want to be under the law, are you not aware of what the law says? [22]For it is written that Abraham had two sons, one by the slave woman and the other by the free woman. [23]His son by the slave woman was born according to the flesh, but his son by the free woman was born as the result of a divine promise.

[24]These things are being taken figuratively: The women represent two covenants. One covenant is from Mount Sinai and bears children who are to be slaves: This is Hagar. [25]Now Hagar stands for Mount Sinai in Arabia and corresponds to the present city of Jerusalem, because she is in slavery with her children. [26]But the Jerusalem that is above is free, and she is our mother. [27]For it is written:

"Be glad, barren woman,
   you who never bore a child;
shout for joy and cry aloud,
   you who were never in labor;
because more are the children of the
      desolate woman
   than of her who has a husband."[a]

[28]Now you, brothers and sisters, like Isaac, are children of promise. [29]At that time the son born according to the flesh persecuted the son born by the power of the Spirit. It is the same now. [30]But what does Scripture say? "Get rid of the slave woman and her son, for the slave woman's son will never share in the inheritance with the free woman's son."[b] [31]Therefore, brothers and sisters, we are not children of the slave woman, but of the free woman.

Freedom in Christ

5 It is for freedom that Christ has set us free. Stand firm, then, and do not let yourselves be burdened again by a yoke of slavery.

[2]Mark my words! I, Paul, tell you that if you let yourselves be circumcised, Christ will be of no value to you at all. [3]Again I declare to every man who lets himself be circumcised that he is obligated to obey the whole law. [4]You who are trying to be justified by the law have been alienated from Christ; you have fallen away from grace. [5]For through the Spirit we eagerly await by faith the righteousness for which we hope. [6]For in Christ Jesus neither circumcision nor uncircumcision has any value. The only thing that counts is faith expressing itself through love.

[7]You were running a good race. Who cut in on you to keep you from obeying the truth? [8]That kind of persuasion does not come from the one who calls you. [9]"A little yeast works through the whole batch of dough." [10]I am confident in the Lord that you will take no other view. The one who is throwing you into confusion, whoever that may be, will have to pay the penalty. [11]Brothers and sisters, if I am still preaching circumcision, why am I still being persecuted? In that case the offense of the cross has been abolished. [12]As for those agitators, I wish they would go the whole way and emasculate themselves!

Life by the Spirit

[13]You, my brothers and sisters, were called to be free. But do not use your freedom to indulge the flesh[c]; rather, serve one another humbly in love. [14]For the entire law is fulfilled in keeping this one command: "Love your neighbor as yourself."[d] [15]If you bite and devour each other, watch out or you will be destroyed by each other.

[16]So I say, walk by the Spirit, and you will not gratify the desires of the flesh. [17]For the flesh desires what is contrary to the Spirit, and the Spirit what is contrary to the flesh. They are in conflict with each other, so that you are not to do whatever[e] you want. [18]But if you are led by the Spirit, you are not under the law.

[19]The acts of the flesh are obvious: sexual immorality, impurity and debauchery; [20]idolatry and witchcraft; hatred, discord,

---

[a] 27 Isaiah 54:1   [b] 30 Gen. 21:10   [c] 13 In contexts like this, the Greek word for *flesh* (*sarx*) refers to the sinful state of human beings, often presented as a power in opposition to the Spirit; also in verses 16, 17, 19 and 24; and in 6:8.   [d] 14 Lev. 19:18   [e] 17 Or *you do not do what*

TAKE A BREATHER

READ: GALATIANS 5:16, 25

The teaching of Bill Bright helped me learn to become a follower who is filled with the Spirit. He teaches a spiritual exercise called "Spiritual Breathing." The basic idea is moment-by-moment awareness of the Spirit so walking in the Spirit becomes as natural—as habitual—as breathing.

Here's how it works: the moment you become aware of sin in your life you exhale. When you exhale, you breathe out and repent of your sin. Repentance becomes a natural response and clears out space in our hearts for the Spirit to fill us. So the moment you are prideful, jealous, lustful, harsh, selfish, dishonest, impatient, you exhale and repent of your sin.

The only way to be filled with the Spirit is to empty myself of me. When I empty me of me, it provides space for the Holy Spirit to fill me. You can't hold up your glass to be filled if it's already full. When the Holy Spirit moves in and takes up residence, then you should constantly be moving yourself out. And, slowly, you find that your pride, your impatience, your selfishness, your lust, and whatever else is bottled inside you is carried out the door. So exhale and breathe out the clutter and darkness of you to make room to be filled with the Spirit.

And then you inhale. Breathe in and pray to be filled with the Spirit and surrender control over to him. Exhale. Inhale.

BUILDING FAITH WISDOM STRENGTH

DITCH THE OLD

READ: GALATIANS 6:7-8

I f we keep planting things into our old life, what will come out of us? Old life. We have to dig deep into our new life, and when we read God's Word, we hear his voice.

I want to be so in tune with the Holy Spirit that I don't question whether I'm in step with Jesus. I know I am. Like a child who knows his mother is always near, I want to walk in the assurance of God's presence. I want temptation to stink in my nose. I want sin to sicken me rather than to woo me.

Galatians 6:7-8 is our GPS on how to get there.

Why do we feel closer to the Lord after we spend only one hour at church on Sunday? Because we took the time to pour into our new life. What if that was a lifestyle rather than a trip to a building every week (or every other week)? All we did was pour into our new life and starve our old life. We closed out the world and the distractions and opened up his Word, and in just one hour our perspective changed.

BUILDING FAITH WISDOM STRENGTH

This is an irrefutable principle: When I sow to the Spirit, God's Spirit begins to change my thinking, my tastes, my will, my emotions. This is how I learn to walk in the assurance of God's presence. When I pour into my new life, then new life will come out.

jealousy, fits of rage, selfish ambition, dissensions, factions [21] and envy; drunkenness, orgies, and the like. I warn you, as I did before, that those who live like this will not inherit the kingdom of God.

[22] But the fruit of the Spirit is love, joy, peace, forbearance, kindness, goodness, faithfulness, [23] gentleness and self-control. Against such things there is no law. [24] Those who belong to Christ Jesus have crucified the flesh with its passions and desires. [25] Since we live by the Spirit, let us keep in step with the Spirit. [26] Let us not become conceited, provoking and envying each other.

Doing Good to All

6 Brothers and sisters, if someone is caught in a sin, you who live by the Spirit should restore that person gently. But watch yourselves, or you also may be tempted. [2] Carry each other's burdens, and in this way you will fulfill the law of Christ. [3] If anyone thinks they are something when they are not, they deceive themselves. [4] Each one should test their own actions. Then they can take pride in themselves alone, without comparing themselves to someone else, [5] for each one should carry their own load. [6] Nevertheless, the one who receives instruction in the word should share all good things with their instructor.

[7] Do not be deceived: God cannot be mocked. A man reaps what he sows. [8] Whoever sows to please their flesh, from the flesh will reap destruction; whoever sows to please the Spirit, from the Spirit will reap eternal life. [9] Let us not become weary in doing good, for at the proper time we will reap a harvest if we do not give up. [10] Therefore, as we have opportunity, let us do good to all people, especially to those who belong to the family of believers.

Not Circumcision but the New Creation

[11] See what large letters I use as I write to you with my own hand!

[12] Those who want to impress people by means of the flesh are trying to compel you to be circumcised. The only reason they do this is to avoid being persecuted for the cross of Christ. [13] Not even those who are circumcised keep the law, yet they want you to be circumcised that they may boast about your circumcision in the flesh. [14] May I never boast except in the cross of our Lord Jesus Christ, through which[a] the world has been crucified to me, and I to the world. [15] Neither circumcision nor uncircumcision means anything; what counts is the new creation. [16] Peace and mercy to all who follow this rule—to[b] the Israel of God.

[17] From now on, let no one cause me trouble, for I bear on my body the marks of Jesus.

[18] The grace of our Lord Jesus Christ be with your spirit, brothers and sisters. Amen.

---

[a] 14 Or *whom*   [b] 16 Or *rule and to*

EPHESIANS

➡️ **WHEN DID THIS HAPPEN?**

Around A.D. 60 in Rome

➡️ **WHO IS IN THIS BOOK?**

Paul

Tychicus

➡️ **VERSES YOU MIGHT RECOGNIZE**

EPHESIANS 2:8–9

"For it is by grace you have been saved, through faith—and this is not from yourselves, it is the gift of God—not by works, so that no one can boast."

EPHESIANS 6:2

"'Honor your father and mother'—which is the first commandment with a promise."

WHAT'S IT ABOUT?

Paul's letter to the Ephesians was written during Paul's first imprisonment in Rome and is known as one of the four "prison epistles" (along with the books of Philippians, Colossians and Philemon). Unlike some of the other epistles, Paul did not write to address a particular problem in the church. In fact, he praised the Ephesians for their faith in Jesus and love for others. He wrote to help them understand who they were in Christ and how they should treat others based on that knowledge.

Paul began by talking about God's great purposes for his people—specifically through his church. Because of Jesus' death and resurrection, believers everywhere could come together as one body of Christ with many gifts. In this way, they demonstrate God's wisdom and glory to the world.

This book also focuses on how Christians are supposed to treat one another: husbands and wives, children and parents, slaves and masters. Finally, Paul reminded the Ephesians to put on the armor of God, which includes truth, righteousness and faith, as protection against the devil's schemes.

EPHESIANS

1 Paul, an apostle of Christ Jesus by the will of God,

To God's holy people in Ephesus,[a] the faithful in Christ Jesus:

[2]Grace and peace to you from God our Father and the Lord Jesus Christ.

Praise for Spiritual Blessings in Christ

[3]Praise be to the God and Father of our Lord Jesus Christ, who has blessed us in the heavenly realms with every spiritual blessing in Christ. [4]For he chose us in him before the creation of the world to be holy and blameless in his sight. In love [5]he[b] predestined us for adoption to sonship[c] through Jesus Christ, in accordance with his pleasure and will— [6]to the praise of his glorious grace, which he has freely given us in the One he loves. [7]In him we have redemption through his blood, the forgiveness of sins, in accordance with the riches of God's grace [8]that he lavished on us. With all wisdom and understanding, [9]he[d] made known to us the mystery of his will according to his good pleasure, which he purposed in Christ, [10]to be put into effect when the times reach their fulfillment—to bring unity to all things in heaven and on earth under Christ.

[11]In him we were also chosen,[e] having been predestined according to the plan of him who works out everything in conformity with the purpose of his will, [12]in order that we, who were the first to put our hope in Christ, might be for the praise of his glory. [13]And you also were included in Christ when you heard the message of truth, the gospel of your salvation. When you believed, you were marked in him with a seal, the promised Holy Spirit, [14]who is a deposit guaranteeing our inheritance until the redemption of those who are God's possession—to the praise of his glory.

Thanksgiving and Prayer

[15]For this reason, ever since I heard about your faith in the Lord Jesus and your love for all God's people, [16]I have not stopped giving thanks for you, remembering you in my prayers. [17]I keep asking that the God of our Lord Jesus Christ, the glorious Father, may give you the Spirit[f] of wisdom and revelation, so that you may know him better. [18]I pray that the eyes of your heart may be enlightened in order that you may know the hope to which he has called you, the riches of his glorious inheritance in his holy people, [19]and his incomparably great power for us who believe. That power is the same as the mighty strength [20]he exerted when he raised Christ from the dead and seated him at his right hand in the heavenly realms, [21]far above all rule and authority, power and dominion, and every name that is invoked, not only in the present age but also in the one to come. [22]And God placed all things under his feet and appointed him to be head over everything for the church, [23]which is his body, the fullness of him who fills everything in every way.

Made Alive in Christ

2 As for you, you were dead in your transgressions and sins, [2]in which you used to live when you followed the ways of this world and of the ruler of the kingdom of the air, the spirit who is now at work in those who are disobedient. [3]All of us also lived among them at one time, gratifying the cravings of our flesh[g] and following its desires and thoughts. Like the rest, we were by nature deserving of wrath. [4]But because of

---

[a] 1 Some early manuscripts do not have *in Ephesus.*   [b] 4,5 Or *sight in love.* [5]*He*   [c] 5 The Greek word for *adoption to sonship* is a legal term referring to the full legal standing of an adopted male heir in Roman culture.   [d] 8,9 Or *us with all wisdom and understanding.* [9]*And he*   [e] 11 Or *were made heirs*   [f] 17 Or *a spirit*   [g] 3 In contexts like this, the Greek word for *flesh* (*sarx*) refers to the sinful state of human beings, often presented as a power in opposition to the Spirit.

ALL GOD

READ: EPHESIANS 2:1-9

Now, what was our part in this? We were dead. We sinned. We blew it over and over. What was God's part? He did it all. He chose us, made us alive, lavished his grace on us, started us, and will complete what he started.

The next few verses go on to emphasize that at one time we were separated from Christ, without hope and without God. Now that God has saved us, we have been brought near to God by the blood of Christ, and he himself is our peace.

If you think you did something to start your relationship with God, it's only logical to think you could do something to end it. You can either rest in your picture of God or be haunted by it. This passage helps us determine whether we have painted a biblical picture of God and of ourselves.

You're going to attach your idea of God to what you know. If you don't know what he says about who he is, how are you going to get to know him? If you let God define himself for you and let him define you for you, now you're ready to start blooming.

BUILDING FAITH WISDOM STRENGTH

At the base of our roots must be the understanding that we did not figure this out; we did not turn over a new leaf; we did not decide one day that we were going to try this Jesus thing.

What God starts, he finishes.

The fun part comes in between.

his great love for us, God, who is rich in mercy, [5]made us alive with Christ even when we were dead in transgressions — it is by grace you have been saved. [6]And God raised us up with Christ and seated us with him in the heavenly realms in Christ Jesus, [7]in order that in the coming ages he might show the incomparable riches of his grace, expressed in his kindness to us in Christ Jesus. [8]For it is by grace you have been saved, through faith — and this is not from yourselves, it is the gift of God — [9]not by works, so that no one can boast. [10]For we are God's handiwork, created in Christ Jesus to do good works, which God prepared in advance for us to do.

Jew and Gentile Reconciled Through Christ

[11]Therefore, remember that formerly you who are Gentiles by birth and called "uncircumcised" by those who call themselves "the circumcision" (which is done in the body by human hands)— [12]remember that at that time you were separate from Christ, excluded from citizenship in Israel and foreigners to the covenants of the promise, without hope and without God in the world. [13]But now in Christ Jesus you who once were far away have been brought near by the blood of Christ.

[14]For he himself is our peace, who has made the two groups one and has destroyed the barrier, the dividing wall of hostility, [15]by setting aside in his flesh the law with its commands and regulations. His purpose was to create in himself one new humanity out of the two, thus making peace, [16]and in one body to reconcile both of them to God through the cross, by which he put to death their hostility. [17]He came and preached peace to you who were far away and peace to those who were near. [18]For through him we both have access to the Father by one Spirit.

[19]Consequently, you are no longer foreigners and strangers, but fellow citizens with God's people and also members of his household, [20]built on the foundation of the apostles and prophets, with Christ Jesus himself as the chief cornerstone. [21]In him the whole building is joined together and rises to become a holy temple in the Lord.

[22]And in him you too are being built together to become a dwelling in which God lives by his Spirit.

God's Marvelous Plan for the Gentiles

3 For this reason I, Paul, the prisoner of Christ Jesus for the sake of you Gentiles —

[2]Surely you have heard about the administration of God's grace that was given to me for you, [3]that is, the mystery made known to me by revelation, as I have already written briefly. [4]In reading this, then, you will be able to understand my insight into the mystery of Christ, [5]which was not made known to people in other generations as it has now been revealed by the Spirit to God's holy apostles and prophets. [6]This mystery is that through the gospel the Gentiles are heirs together with Israel, members together of one body, and sharers together in the promise in Christ Jesus.

[7]I became a servant of this gospel by the gift of God's grace given me through the working of his power. [8]Although I am less than the least of all the Lord's people, this grace was given me: to preach to the Gentiles the boundless riches of Christ, [9]and to make plain to everyone the administration of this mystery, which for ages past was kept hidden in God, who created all things. [10]His intent was that now, through the church, the manifold wisdom of God should be made known to the rulers and authorities in the heavenly realms, [11]according to his eternal purpose that he accomplished in Christ Jesus our Lord. [12]In him and through faith in him we may approach God with freedom and confidence. [13]I ask you, therefore, not to be discouraged because of my sufferings for you, which are your glory.

A Prayer for the Ephesians

[14]For this reason I kneel before the Father, [15]from whom every family[a] in heaven and on earth derives its name. [16]I pray that out of his glorious riches he may strengthen you with power through his Spirit in your inner being, [17]so that Christ may dwell in your hearts through faith. And I pray that you, being rooted and established in love, [18]may have power, together with all the Lord's holy

---

[a] 15 The Greek for *family* (*patria*) is derived from the Greek for *father* (*pater*).

PERFORMANCE ART

READ: EPHESIANS 3:16-18

For too many Christians our lives have been reduced to a bunch of dos and don'ts, a list of rules we are supposed to follow. These rules make us focus only on the surface, the stuff we can see in one another.

We get concerned about the stuff we see others do or say, and if they aren't living the way we think good Christians should, we form Frankenstein search parties to hunt them down. If people don't dress right, speak right, smell right, act right . . . if they don't read and watch what we watch and agree with "the rest of us," we chase them out of the Jesus Club.

Now it's natural that we should expect that following Jesus would make some difference in people's behavior. God's biblical guidance makes it clear what kind of people we are to become and how we are called to live. The God who loves us so much wants us to live in ways that clearly reflect that love. But when we lose sight of God's love as our motivation, when we trust human rules instead of God's guidelines, our lives become performance art. Our authentic struggle gets ruined when "living a life rooted in God's love" is replaced with "living a life that doesn't get other Christians talking about you."

That contrast and struggle of all this performing can leave us in a very lonely place.

BUILDING

FAITH

WISDOM

STRENGTH

people, to grasp how wide and long and high and deep is the love of Christ, [19]and to know this love that surpasses knowledge — that you may be filled to the measure of all the fullness of God.

[20]Now to him who is able to do immeasurably more than all we ask or imagine, according to his power that is at work within us, [21]to him be glory in the church and in Christ Jesus throughout all generations, for ever and ever! Amen.

Unity and Maturity in the Body of Christ

4 As a prisoner for the Lord, then, I urge you to live a life worthy of the calling you have received. [2]Be completely humble and gentle; be patient, bearing with one another in love. [3]Make every effort to keep the unity of the Spirit through the bond of peace. [4]There is one body and one Spirit, just as you were called to one hope when you were called; [5]one Lord, one faith, one baptism; [6]one God and Father of all, who is over all and through all and in all.

[7]But to each one of us grace has been given as Christ apportioned it. [8]This is why it[a] says:

"When he ascended on high,
  he took many captives
  and gave gifts to his people."[b]

[9](What does "he ascended" mean except that he also descended to the lower, earthly regions[c]? [10]He who descended is the very one who ascended higher than all the heavens, in order to fill the whole universe.) [11]So Christ himself gave the apostles, the prophets, the evangelists, the pastors and teachers, [12]to equip his people for works of service, so that the body of Christ may be built up [13]until we all reach unity in the faith and in the knowledge of the Son of God and become mature, attaining to the whole measure of the fullness of Christ.

[14]Then we will no longer be infants, tossed back and forth by the waves, and blown here and there by every wind of teaching and by the cunning and craftiness of people in their deceitful scheming. [15]Instead, speaking the truth in love, we will grow to become in every respect the mature body of him who is the head, that is, Christ. [16]From him the whole body, joined and held together by every supporting ligament, grows and builds itself up in love, as each part does its work.

Instructions for Christian Living

[17]So I tell you this, and insist on it in the Lord, that you must no longer live as the Gentiles do, in the futility of their thinking. [18]They are darkened in their understanding and separated from the life of God because of the ignorance that is in them due to the hardening of their hearts. [19]Having lost all sensitivity, they have given themselves over to sensuality so as to indulge in every kind of impurity, and they are full of greed.

[20]That, however, is not the way of life you learned [21]when you heard about Christ and were taught in him in accordance with the truth that is in Jesus. [22]You were taught, with regard to your former way of life, to put off your old self, which is being corrupted by its deceitful desires; [23]to be made new in the attitude of your minds; [24]and to put on the new self, created to be like God in true righteousness and holiness.

[25]Therefore each of you must put off falsehood and speak truthfully to your neighbor, for we are all members of one body. [26]"In your anger do not sin"[d]: Do not let the sun go down while you are still angry, [27]and do not give the devil a foothold. [28]Anyone who has been stealing must steal no longer, but must work, doing something useful with their own hands, that they may have something to share with those in need.

[29]Do not let any unwholesome talk come out of your mouths, but only what is helpful for building others up according to their needs, that it may benefit those who listen. [30]And do not grieve the Holy Spirit of God, with whom you were sealed for the day of redemption. [31]Get rid of all bitterness, rage and anger, brawling and slander, along with every form of malice. [32]Be kind and compassionate to one another, forgiving each other,

5 just as in Christ God forgave you. [1]Follow God's example, therefore, as dearly loved children [2]and walk in the way of love, just as Christ loved us and gave himself up for us as a fragrant offering and sacrifice to God.

[3]But among you there must not be even a

---

[a] 8 Or *God*   [b] 8 Psalm 68:18   [c] 9 Or *the depths of the earth*   [d] 26 Psalm 4:4 (see Septuagint)

THE BEST LIFE

READ: EPHESIANS 4:22

Forgiveness seems like a sweet excuse to do wrong. If God wipes away your sins as soon as you confess them, why not keep breaking his rules? The apostle Paul has nothing nice to say about that attitude. It's futile, darkened, ignorant, and insensitive (Ephesians 4:17-19). It's the way people think when they are cut off from God. It doesn't fit "the truth that is in Jesus" (v. 21). People who trust the Lord have caught a better outlook.

When you believe in Jesus, you get rid of old habits that come from evil desires, as if you're peeling off filthy clothes. God wants to refresh your mind, teaching you to think differently. He's begun a new life inside you, so you can build fresh habits. The Lord is remaking you to be just like him, full of his goodness and holiness.

BUILDING

FAITH

WISDOM

STRENGTH

That's the "way of life you learned when you heard about Christ" (vv. 20-21). If you want to know more of what that better life looks like, check out the rest of this book word by word. It gives details of practical ways the Lord plans to transform you.

God doesn't lay down rules for no reason. His commands aim to lead you to the best life ever. If you count on his death on the cross for your sins, then expect he has a new life in store for you.

hint of sexual immorality, or of any kind of impurity, or of greed, because these are improper for God's holy people. [4]Nor should there be obscenity, foolish talk or coarse joking, which are out of place, but rather thanksgiving. [5]For of this you can be sure: No immoral, impure or greedy person—such a person is an idolater—has any inheritance in the kingdom of Christ and of God.[a] [6]Let no one deceive you with empty words, for because of such things God's wrath comes on those who are disobedient. [7]Therefore do not be partners with them.

[8]For you were once darkness, but now you are light in the Lord. Live as children of light [9](for the fruit of the light consists in all goodness, righteousness and truth) [10]and find out what pleases the Lord. [11]Have nothing to do with the fruitless deeds of darkness, but rather expose them. [12]It is shameful even to mention what the disobedient do in secret. [13]But everything exposed by the light becomes visible—and everything that is illuminated becomes a light. [14]This is why it is said:

"Wake up, sleeper,
    rise from the dead,
    and Christ will shine on you."

[15]Be very careful, then, how you live—not as unwise but as wise, [16]making the most of every opportunity, because the days are evil. [17]Therefore do not be foolish, but understand what the Lord's will is. [18]Do not get drunk on wine, which leads to debauchery. Instead, be filled with the Spirit, [19]speaking to one another with psalms, hymns, and songs from the Spirit. Sing and make music from your heart to the Lord, [20]always giving thanks to God the Father for everything, in the name of our Lord Jesus Christ.

Instructions for Christian Households

[21]Submit to one another out of reverence for Christ.

[22]Wives, submit yourselves to your own husbands as you do to the Lord. [23]For the husband is the head of the wife as Christ is the head of the church, his body, of which he is the Savior. [24]Now as the church submits to Christ, so also wives should submit to their husbands in everything.

[25]Husbands, love your wives, just as Christ loved the church and gave himself up for her [26]to make her holy, cleansing[b] her by the washing with water through the word, [27]and to present her to himself as a radiant church, without stain or wrinkle or any other blemish, but holy and blameless. [28]In this same way, husbands ought to love their wives as their own bodies. He who loves his wife loves himself. [29]After all, no one ever hated their own body, but they feed and care for their body, just as Christ does the church— [30]for we are members of his body. [31]"For this reason a man will leave his father and mother and be united to his wife, and the two will become one flesh."[c] [32]This is a profound mystery—but I am talking about Christ and the church. [33]However, each one of you also must love his wife as he loves himself, and the wife must respect her husband.

6 Children, obey your parents in the Lord, for this is right. [2]"Honor your father and mother"—which is the first commandment with a promise— [3]"so that it may go well with you and that you may enjoy long life on the earth."[d]

[4]Fathers,[e] do not exasperate your children; instead, bring them up in the training and instruction of the Lord.

[5]Slaves, obey your earthly masters with respect and fear, and with sincerity of heart, just as you would obey Christ. [6]Obey them not only to win their favor when their eye is on you, but as slaves of Christ, doing the will of God from your heart. [7]Serve wholeheartedly, as if you were serving the Lord, not people, [8]because you know that the Lord will reward each one for whatever good they do, whether they are slave or free.

[9]And masters, treat your slaves in the same way. Do not threaten them, since you know that he who is both their Master and yours is in heaven, and there is no favoritism with him.

The Armor of God

[10]Finally, be strong in the Lord and in his mighty power. [11]Put on the full armor of God, so that you can take your stand against the devil's schemes. [12]For our struggle is not

---

[a] 5 Or *kingdom of the Messiah and God*   [b] 26 Or *having cleansed*   [c] 31 Gen. 2:24   [d] 3 Deut. 5:16
[e] 4 Or *Parents*

SPIRITUALLY DRUNK

READ: EPHESIANS 5:15-18

Debauchery is just a fancy way of saying bad or immoral behavior. Getting drunk or getting high leads to debauchery. You lose self-control. Your inhibitions go away, and you end up doing things and making decisions that you never would if you were sober. And many times these decisions lead to feelings of guilt, shame, and embarrassment once the buzz wears off.

Instead of getting drunk (and if he were writing today, he would probably add "high"), Paul gives us a better alternative. He tells us to be filled with the Spirit. Some people have even called it being drunk in the Spirit. Paul knows that by filling our lives with God's presence and following his will we'll be so joyful, content, and happy that we'll have no need for drugs or alcohol, or even a focus on food.

BUILDING
FAITH
WISDOM
STRENGTH

When it comes to most things in life, moderation is the key. We shouldn't eat too much, drink too much, exercise constantly, stare at a screen too much, or play video games for hours. But when it comes to our relationship with God, too much is never enough.

He doesn't want us to dip our toe in the pool. God wants us to cannonball into the deep end of our faith. He wants to surround our lives with his love and sit alone on the throne of our hearts.

Taken from *Gods at War Student Edition* by Kyle Idleman, copyright © 2014 by City on a Hill Studio, LLC, published by Zondervan.

LOVE AND PARENTS

READ: EPHESIANS 6:2-3

D o you really know your parents? Who are they? Is your mom someone whom other women call when they need advice? Is your dad the local handyman? Or do both of your parents hit the couch after dinner and stay there until bedtime?

Your parents' personalities are the fuel that runs your home. They set the emotional tone and decide if you live in a yelling house, a loving house, a laughing house, or a quiet house. They determine whether you live in a brand-new home with a messy lawn, a tiny apartment, or an old fixer-upper. They decide how you celebrate holidays, where you go on vacations, and most every other aspect of home life. And you'll likely carry a lot of that with you, in ways you won't even realize. You'll think about much of the world in the same way they do.

BUILDING FAITH WISDOM STRENGTH

How has God used that environment to make you who you are? What have you learned about who you are from your parents?

Love your parents. Yes. I said that. Love them. I know, you don't need another person telling you to respect and obey your parents. But think about the opportunity you have to influence and encourage your parents. They were your age once, and they struggle with things just like you do. They have souls that long for God just as you do. You have the opportunity to be someone in their life that encourages them.

Taken from *Leave a Footprint—Change the World* by Tim Baker, copyright © 2009 by Tim Baker, published by Zondervan.

against flesh and blood, but against the rulers, against the authorities, against the powers of this dark world and against the spiritual forces of evil in the heavenly realms. [13] Therefore put on the full armor of God, so that when the day of evil comes, you may be able to stand your ground, and after you have done everything, to stand. [14] Stand firm then, with the belt of truth buckled around your waist, with the breastplate of righteousness in place, [15] and with your feet fitted with the readiness that comes from the gospel of peace. [16] In addition to all this, take up the shield of faith, with which you can extinguish all the flaming arrows of the evil one. [17] Take the helmet of salvation and the sword of the Spirit, which is the word of God.

[18] And pray in the Spirit on all occasions with all kinds of prayers and requests. With this in mind, be alert and always keep on praying for all the Lord's people. [19] Pray also for me, that whenever I speak, words may be given me so that I will fearlessly make known the mystery of the gospel, [20] for which I am an ambassador in chains. Pray that I may declare it fearlessly, as I should.

Final Greetings

[21] Tychicus, the dear brother and faithful servant in the Lord, will tell you everything, so that you also may know how I am and what I am doing. [22] I am sending him to you for this very purpose, that you may know how we are, and that he may encourage you.

[23] Peace to the brothers and sisters,[a] and love with faith from God the Father and the Lord Jesus Christ. [24] Grace to all who love our Lord Jesus Christ with an undying love.[b]

---

[a] 23 The Greek word for *brothers and sisters* (*adelphoi*) refers here to believers, both men and women, as part of God's family.   [b] 24 Or *Grace and immortality to all who love our Lord Jesus Christ.*

PHILIPPIANS

WHEN DID THIS HAPPEN?
Around A.D. 61 in Rome

WHO IS IN THIS BOOK?
Paul
Timothy
Epaphroditus
Lydia

VERSES YOU MIGHT RECOGNIZE

PHILIPPIANS 2:3
"Do nothing out of selfish ambition or vain conceit. Rather, in humility value others above yourselves."

PHILIPPIANS 4:13
"I can do all this through him who gives me strength."

WHAT'S IT ABOUT?

Paul wrote this letter to the Philippians while he was imprisoned in Rome. It had been ten years since he had first visited Philippi (see Acts 16:12), but the people there were special to Paul. He wrote this letter to show his affection for them and to thank them for gifts they had sent.

He also gave instruction to the believers on living joyful lives in unity with one another. Paul used Jesus as the perfect example—a humble servant who, though he was God, was willing to die a humiliating death to bring us to the Father. Believers should have that same attitude of humility.

Paul encouraged the Philippians to make Jesus the center of their lives because "to live is Christ" (Philippians 1:21). He also reminded them that they don't have to follow the law to be saved. By living for Christ alone, they could experience true joy.

1

Paul and Timothy, servants of Christ Jesus,

To all God's holy people in Christ Jesus at Philippi, together with the overseers and deacons[a]:

[2] Grace and peace to you from God our Father and the Lord Jesus Christ.

Thanksgiving and Prayer

[3] I thank my God every time I remember you. [4] In all my prayers for all of you, I always pray with joy [5] because of your partnership in the gospel from the first day until now, [6] being confident of this, that he who began a good work in you will carry it on to completion until the day of Christ Jesus.

[7] It is right for me to feel this way about all of you, since I have you in my heart and, whether I am in chains or defending and confirming the gospel, all of you share in God's grace with me. [8] God can testify how I long for all of you with the affection of Christ Jesus.

[9] And this is my prayer: that your love may abound more and more in knowledge and depth of insight, [10] so that you may be able to discern what is best and may be pure and blameless for the day of Christ, [11] filled with the fruit of righteousness that comes through Jesus Christ — to the glory and praise of God.

Paul's Chains Advance the Gospel

[12] Now I want you to know, brothers and sisters,[b] that what has happened to me has actually served to advance the gospel. [13] As a result, it has become clear throughout the whole palace guard[c] and to everyone else that I am in chains for Christ. [14] And because of my chains, most of the brothers and sisters have become confident in the Lord and

dare all the more to proclaim the gospel without fear.

[15] It is true that some preach Christ out of envy and rivalry, but others out of goodwill. [16] The latter do so out of love, knowing that I am put here for the defense of the gospel. [17] The former preach Christ out of selfish ambition, not sincerely, supposing that they can stir up trouble for me while I am in chains. [18] But what does it matter? The important thing is that in every way, whether from false motives or true, Christ is preached. And because of this I rejoice.

Yes, and I will continue to rejoice, [19] for I know that through your prayers and God's provision of the Spirit of Jesus Christ what has happened to me will turn out for my deliverance.[d] [20] I eagerly expect and hope that I will in no way be ashamed, but will have sufficient courage so that now as always Christ will be exalted in my body, whether by life or by death. [21] For to me, to live is Christ and to die is gain. [22] If I am to go on living in the body, this will mean fruitful labor for me. Yet what shall I choose? I do not know! [23] I am torn between the two: I desire to depart and be with Christ, which is better by far; [24] but it is more necessary for you that I remain in the body. [25] Convinced of this, I know that I will remain, and I will continue with all of you for your progress and joy in the faith, [26] so that through my being with you again your boasting in Christ Jesus will abound on account of me.

Life Worthy of the Gospel

[27] Whatever happens, conduct yourselves in a manner worthy of the gospel of Christ. Then, whether I come and see you or only hear about you in my absence, I will know that you stand firm in the one Spirit,[e] striving together as one for the faith of the gospel

---

[a] 1 The word *deacons* refers here to Christians designated to serve with the overseers/elders of the church in a variety of ways; similarly in Romans 16:1 and 1 Tim. 3:8,12. [b] 12 The Greek word for *brothers and sisters* (*adelphoi*) refers here to believers, both men and women, as part of God's family; also in verse 14; and in 3:1, 13, 17; 4:1, 8, 21. [c] 13 Or *whole palace* [d] 19 Or *vindication; or salvation* [e] 27 Or *in one spirit*

28without being frightened in any way by those who oppose you. This is a sign to them that they will be destroyed, but that you will be saved — and that by God. 29For it has been granted to you on behalf of Christ not only to believe in him, but also to suffer for him, 30since you are going through the same struggle you saw I had, and now hear that I still have.

Imitating Christ's Humility

2 Therefore if you have any encouragement from being united with Christ, if any comfort from his love, if any common sharing in the Spirit, if any tenderness and compassion, 2then make my joy complete by being like-minded, having the same love, being one in spirit and of one mind. 3Do nothing out of selfish ambition or vain conceit. Rather, in humility value others above yourselves, 4not looking to your own interests but each of you to the interests of the others.

5In your relationships with one another, have the same mindset as Christ Jesus:

6Who, being in very nature*a* God,
  did not consider equality with God
    something to be used to his own
    advantage;
7rather, he made himself nothing
  by taking the very nature*b* of a servant,
    being made in human likeness.
8And being found in appearance as a man,
  he humbled himself
  by becoming obedient to death —
    even death on a cross!

9Therefore God exalted him to the highest
    place
  and gave him the name that is above
    every name,
10that at the name of Jesus every knee
    should bow,
  in heaven and on earth and under
    the earth,
11and every tongue acknowledge that Jesus
    Christ is Lord,
  to the glory of God the Father.

Do Everything Without Grumbling

12Therefore, my dear friends, as you have always obeyed — not only in my presence, but now much more in my absence — continue to work out your salvation with fear and trembling, 13for it is God who works in you to will and to act in order to fulfill his good purpose.

14Do everything without grumbling or arguing, 15so that you may become blameless and pure, "children of God without fault in a warped and crooked generation."*c* Then you will shine among them like stars in the sky 16as you hold firmly to the word of life. And then I will be able to boast on the day of Christ that I did not run or labor in vain. 17But even if I am being poured out like a drink offering on the sacrifice and service coming from your faith, I am glad and rejoice with all of you. 18So you too should be glad and rejoice with me.

Timothy and Epaphroditus

19I hope in the Lord Jesus to send Timothy to you soon, that I also may be cheered when I receive news about you. 20I have no one else like him, who will show genuine concern for your welfare. 21For everyone looks out for their own interests, not those of Jesus Christ. 22But you know that Timothy has proved himself, because as a son with his father he has served with me in the work of the gospel. 23I hope, therefore, to send him as soon as I see how things go with me. 24And I am confident in the Lord that I myself will come soon.

25But I think it is necessary to send back to you Epaphroditus, my brother, co-worker and fellow soldier, who is also your messenger, whom you sent to take care of my needs. 26For he longs for all of you and is distressed because you heard he was ill. 27Indeed he was ill, and almost died. But God had mercy on him, and not on him only but also on me, to spare me sorrow upon sorrow. 28Therefore I am all the more eager to send him, so that when you see him again you may be glad and I may have less anxiety. 29So then, welcome him in the Lord with great joy, and honor people like him, 30because he almost died for the work of Christ. He risked his life to make up for the help you yourselves could not give me.

No Confidence in the Flesh

3 Further, my brothers and sisters, rejoice in the Lord! It is no trouble for me

---

a 6 Or *in the form of*   *b* 7 Or *the form*   *c* 15 Deut. 32:5

PRESS ON

READ: PHILIPPIANS 3:13-14

A t some point, most of us stop living out of imagination and start living out of memory. That's the day we stop living and start dying. To be fully alive is to be fully present. And to do that, you've got to leave the past in the past. Paul says it best in Philippians 3:13-14.

Press on indeed. That's gold! Whenever I hear it, I have flashbacks to my college basketball days. There are two ways of playing defense. You can sit back in a half-court defense and let the other team come to you. It's a defensive way of playing the game. It's protecting the lead. It's playing not to lose. In football, it's called a prevent defense. But there is an offensive form of defense—the full-court press. You don't let the game come to you. You take it to them.

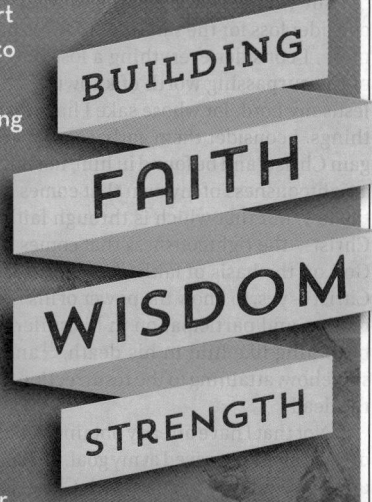

BUILDING

FAITH

WISDOM

STRENGTH

I'm afraid the church is content with a prevent defense while God is calling for a full-court press.

Are you relating reactively or proactively with your friends? Who's influencing whom? Are you working for a paycheck or stewarding your God-given gifts pursuing a God-ordained dream? Are you trying to break even spiritually by avoiding sin? Or are you going for broke?

Too many of us get comfortable with comfort. We follow Christ to the edge of inconvenience but no farther. I'll challenge you to go for broke. Carry the light with you everywhere!

Taken from *All In Student Edition* by Mark Batterson and Parker Batterson, copyright © 2014 by Mark Batterson, published by Zondervan.

to write the same things to you again, and it is a safeguard for you. [2]Watch out for those dogs, those evildoers, those mutilators of the flesh. [3]For it is we who are the circumcision, we who serve God by his Spirit, who boast in Christ Jesus, and who put no confidence in the flesh — [4]though I myself have reasons for such confidence.

If someone else thinks they have reasons to put confidence in the flesh, I have more: [5]circumcised on the eighth day, of the people of Israel, of the tribe of Benjamin, a Hebrew of Hebrews; in regard to the law, a Pharisee; [6]as for zeal, persecuting the church; as for righteousness based on the law, faultless.

[7]But whatever were gains to me I now consider loss for the sake of Christ. [8]What is more, I consider everything a loss because of the surpassing worth of knowing Christ Jesus my Lord, for whose sake I have lost all things. I consider them garbage, that I may gain Christ [9]and be found in him, not having a righteousness of my own that comes from the law, but that which is through faith in[a] Christ — the righteousness that comes from God on the basis of faith. [10]I want to know Christ — yes, to know the power of his resurrection and participation in his sufferings, becoming like him in his death, [11]and so, somehow, attaining to the resurrection from the dead.

[12]Not that I have already obtained all this, or have already arrived at my goal, but I press on to take hold of that for which Christ Jesus took hold of me. [13]Brothers and sisters, I do not consider myself yet to have taken hold of it. But one thing I do: Forgetting what is behind and straining toward what is ahead, [14]I press on toward the goal to win the prize for which God has called me heavenward in Christ Jesus.

Following Paul's Example

[15]All of us, then, who are mature should take such a view of things. And if on some point you think differently, that too God will make clear to you. [16]Only let us live up to what we have already attained.

[17]Join together in following my example, brothers and sisters, and just as you have us as a model, keep your eyes on those who live as we do. [18]For, as I have often told you before and now tell you again even with tears, many live as enemies of the cross of Christ. [19]Their destiny is destruction, their god is their stomach, and their glory is in their shame. Their mind is set on earthly things. [20]But our citizenship is in heaven. And we eagerly await a Savior from there, the Lord Jesus Christ, [21]who, by the power that enables him to bring everything under his control, will transform our lowly bodies so that they will be like his glorious body.

Closing Appeal for Steadfastness and Unity

4 Therefore, my brothers and sisters, you whom I love and long for, my joy and crown, stand firm in the Lord in this way, dear friends!

[2]I plead with Euodia and I plead with Syntyche to be of the same mind in the Lord. [3]Yes, and I ask you, my true companion, help these women since they have contended at my side in the cause of the gospel, along with Clement and the rest of my co-workers, whose names are in the book of life.

Final Exhortations

[4]Rejoice in the Lord always. I will say it again: Rejoice! [5]Let your gentleness be evident to all. The Lord is near. [6]Do not be anxious about anything, but in every situation, by prayer and petition, with thanksgiving, present your requests to God. [7]And the peace of God, which transcends all understanding, will guard your hearts and your minds in Christ Jesus.

[8]Finally, brothers and sisters, whatever is true, whatever is noble, whatever is right, whatever is pure, whatever is lovely, whatever is admirable — if anything is excellent or praiseworthy — think about such things. [9]Whatever you have learned or received or heard from me, or seen in me — put it into practice. And the God of peace will be with you.

Thanks for Their Gifts

[10]I rejoiced greatly in the Lord that at last you renewed your concern for me. Indeed, you were concerned, but you had no opportunity to show it. [11]I am not saying this

---

[a] 9 Or *through the faithfulness of*

FINDING A FILTER

READ: PHILIPPIANS 4:8-9

Could it be as simple as Paul makes it sound here? The stuff on Paul's list is the stuff our souls should migrate toward, the stuff we should let fill us. Instead of a list of things we should never do, Paul creates a list of things we are invited to pursue.

There's no hint here that Paul wants us to live from within some protective bubble of irrelevant churchianity. Paul encourages us to go out into the world that Christ loved and seek out those praiseworthy things in the same way a bird searches for a piece of bread. His list encourages us to be people who are always on the lookout for the lovely, not on a search party to find people who aren't obeying our human-created standards.

BUILDING

FAITH

WISDOM

STRENGTH

Paul's words leave us with authentic questions to ask ourselves as we live each day. Does the music we listen to agree with this passage? Do the movies we watch fill our minds with true and noble thoughts? Do the books we read help fill our minds with praiseworthy thoughts? Truly, such a life moves way beyond performance art and steps squarely into the world of our relationship with Jesus. What we do in Christ cannot be for others; our lives have to be lived for him.

And, to that end, what are we doing to enhance that? Are we living in ways that take in the pure and lovely?

Taken from *Jesus Is for Liars: A Hypocrite's Guide to Authenticity* by Tim Baker, copyright © 2009 by Tim Baker, published by Zondervan.

because I am in need, for I have learned to be content whatever the circumstances. [12] I know what it is to be in need, and I know what it is to have plenty. I have learned the secret of being content in any and every situation, whether well fed or hungry, whether living in plenty or in want. [13] I can do all this through him who gives me strength.

[14] Yet it was good of you to share in my troubles. [15] Moreover, as you Philippians know, in the early days of your acquaintance with the gospel, when I set out from Macedonia, not one church shared with me in the matter of giving and receiving, except you only; [16] for even when I was in Thessalonica, you sent me aid more than once when I was in need. [17] Not that I desire your gifts; what I desire is that more be credited to your account. [18] I have received full payment and have more than enough. I am amply supplied, now that I have received from Epaphroditus the gifts you sent. They are a fragrant offering, an acceptable sacrifice, pleasing to God. [19] And my God will meet all your needs according to the riches of his glory in Christ Jesus.

[20] To our God and Father be glory for ever and ever. Amen.

Final Greetings

[21] Greet all God's people in Christ Jesus. The brothers and sisters who are with me send greetings. [22] All God's people here send you greetings, especially those who belong to Caesar's household.

[23] The grace of the Lord Jesus Christ be with your spirit. Amen.[a]

---

[a] 23 Some manuscripts do not have *Amen*.

COLOSSIANS

WHAT'S IT ABOUT?

Even though Paul had never visited the church in Colossae, he wrote to correct an error in their beliefs about Christ. Some false teachers were preaching that Jesus was not God. They were even adding extra practices to the Christian faith, such as angel worship, special ceremonies and rules about what people could eat or drink. Paul explained that Jesus is supreme and totally sufficient for salvation.

Paul presented Jesus as the Creator, the image of the invisible God, the head of the church, and the only one who can forgive people's sins and reconcile them to God. He then instructed them how they ought to live in light of this truth. They should rid themselves of sin, such as sexual immorality, evil desires and greed, and put on compassion, kindness and humility—qualities that come from being made alive in Christ. Not only does Jesus have the power to save us, he also has the power to make our lives into something beautiful.

COLOSSIANS

1 Paul, an apostle of Christ Jesus by the will of God, and Timothy our brother,

[2] To God's holy people in Colossae, the faithful brothers and sisters[a] in Christ:

Grace and peace to you from God our Father.[b]

Thanksgiving and Prayer

[3] We always thank God, the Father of our Lord Jesus Christ, when we pray for you, [4] because we have heard of your faith in Christ Jesus and of the love you have for all God's people — [5] the faith and love that spring from the hope stored up for you in heaven and about which you have already heard in the true message of the gospel [6] that has come to you. In the same way, the gospel is bearing fruit and growing throughout the whole world — just as it has been doing among you since the day you heard it and truly understood God's grace. [7] You learned it from Epaphras, our dear fellow servant,[c] who is a faithful minister of Christ on our[d] behalf, [8] and who also told us of your love in the Spirit.

[9] For this reason, since the day we heard about you, we have not stopped praying for you. We continually ask God to fill you with the knowledge of his will through all the wisdom and understanding that the Spirit gives,[e] [10] so that you may live a life worthy of the Lord and please him in every way: bearing fruit in every good work, growing in the knowledge of God, [11] being strengthened with all power according to his glorious might so that you may have great endurance and patience, [12] and giving joyful thanks to the Father, who has qualified you[f] to share in the inheritance of his holy people in the kingdom of light. [13] For he has rescued us from the dominion of darkness and brought us into the kingdom of the Son he loves, [14] in whom we have redemption, the forgiveness of sins.

The Supremacy of the Son of God

[15] The Son is the image of the invisible God, the firstborn over all creation. [16] For in him all things were created: things in heaven and on earth, visible and invisible, whether thrones or powers or rulers or authorities; all things have been created through him and for him. [17] He is before all things, and in him all things hold together. [18] And he is the head of the body, the church; he is the beginning and the firstborn from among the dead, so that in everything he might have the supremacy. [19] For God was pleased to have all his fullness dwell in him, [20] and through him to reconcile to himself all things, whether things on earth or things in heaven, by making peace through his blood, shed on the cross.

[21] Once you were alienated from God and were enemies in your minds because of[g] your evil behavior. [22] But now he has reconciled you by Christ's physical body through death to present you holy in his sight, without blemish and free from accusation — [23] if you continue in your faith, established and firm, and do not move from the hope held out in the gospel. This is the gospel that you heard and that has been proclaimed to every creature under heaven, and of which I, Paul, have become a servant.

Paul's Labor for the Church

[24] Now I rejoice in what I am suffering for you, and I fill up in my flesh what is still lacking in regard to Christ's afflictions, for the sake of his body, which is the church. [25] I have become its servant by the commission God gave me to present to you the word of

---

[a] 2 The Greek word for *brothers and sisters* (*adelphoi*) refers here to believers, both men and women, as part of God's family; also in 4:15.   [b] 2 Some manuscripts *Father and the Lord Jesus Christ*   [c] 7 Or *slave*
[d] 7 Some manuscripts *your*   [e] 9 Or *all spiritual wisdom and understanding*   [f] 12 Some manuscripts *us*
[g] 21 Or *minds, as shown by*

YOU'RE WISE TO ASK

READ: COLOSSIANS 1:9

Figuring out what the Lord has in store for you can sound baffling. But the Lord promises to let you in on his plans.

The apostle Paul starts his letter to the Colossians thanking God for their solid faith in Jesus and love for the Lord's people. These believers know heaven awaits them because they trust God's good news. They live in God's grace, his kindness they can't do anything to earn.

Now Paul prays that God will fill their minds with a thorough knowledge of his "will," an understanding of how he wants them to live. Paul doesn't offer these Christians easy steps to follow. He instead hints they need to stay close to the Holy Spirit, counting on him for wisdom and insight.

BUILDING

FAITH

WISDOM

STRENGTH

Most of what the Lord has planned for you becomes clear in the commands of Scripture. He wants you to show love, to respect your parents, to live with honesty and purity, and much more. As you do these obvious things, his Spirit fills in the details so you can honor God and please him in every way. You will do good, know the Lord better, and live in his might.

You can't live for God if you don't know what he wants. So invite him to teach you. Whenever you lack wisdom, just ask (James 1:5). He's glad to show you your next steps.

God in its fullness — [26]the mystery that has been kept hidden for ages and generations, but is now disclosed to the Lord's people. [27]To them God has chosen to make known among the Gentiles the glorious riches of this mystery, which is Christ in you, the hope of glory.

[28]He is the one we proclaim, admonishing and teaching everyone with all wisdom, so that we may present everyone fully mature in Christ. [29]To this end I strenuously contend with all the energy Christ so powerfully works in me.

2 I want you to know how hard I am contending for you and for those at Laodicea, and for all who have not met me personally. [2]My goal is that they may be encouraged in heart and united in love, so that they may have the full riches of complete understanding, in order that they may know the mystery of God, namely, Christ, [3]in whom are hidden all the treasures of wisdom and knowledge. [4]I tell you this so that no one may deceive you by fine-sounding arguments. [5]For though I am absent from you in body, I am present with you in spirit and delight to see how disciplined you are and how firm your faith in Christ is.

Spiritual Fullness in Christ

[6]So then, just as you received Christ Jesus as Lord, continue to live your lives in him, [7]rooted and built up in him, strengthened in the faith as you were taught, and overflowing with thankfulness.

[8]See to it that no one takes you captive through hollow and deceptive philosophy, which depends on human tradition and the elemental spiritual forces[a] of this world rather than on Christ.

[9]For in Christ all the fullness of the Deity lives in bodily form, [10]and in Christ you have been brought to fullness. He is the head over every power and authority. [11]In him you were also circumcised with a circumcision not performed by human hands. Your whole self ruled by the flesh[b] was put off when you were circumcised by[c] Christ, [12]having been buried with him in baptism, in which you were also raised with him through your faith in the working of God, who raised him from the dead.

[13]When you were dead in your sins and in the uncircumcision of your flesh, God made you[d] alive with Christ. He forgave us all our sins, [14]having canceled the charge of our legal indebtedness, which stood against us and condemned us; he has taken it away, nailing it to the cross. [15]And having disarmed the powers and authorities, he made a public spectacle of them, triumphing over them by the cross.[e]

Freedom From Human Rules

[16]Therefore do not let anyone judge you by what you eat or drink, or with regard to a religious festival, a New Moon celebration or a Sabbath day. [17]These are a shadow of the things that were to come; the reality, however, is found in Christ. [18]Do not let anyone who delights in false humility and the worship of angels disqualify you. Such a person also goes into great detail about what they have seen; they are puffed up with idle notions by their unspiritual mind. [19]They have lost connection with the head, from whom the whole body, supported and held together by its ligaments and sinews, grows as God causes it to grow.

[20]Since you died with Christ to the elemental spiritual forces of this world, why, as though you still belonged to the world, do you submit to its rules: [21]"Do not handle! Do not taste! Do not touch!"? [22]These rules, which have to do with things that are all destined to perish with use, are based on merely human commands and teachings. [23]Such regulations indeed have an appearance of wisdom, with their self-imposed worship, their false humility and their harsh treatment of the body, but they lack any value in restraining sensual indulgence.

Living as Those Made Alive in Christ

3 Since, then, you have been raised with Christ, set your hearts on things above, where Christ is, seated at the right hand of God. [2]Set your minds on things above, not on earthly things. [3]For you died, and your life is now hidden with Christ in God. [4]When

---

[a] 8 Or *the basic principles*; also in verse 20   [b] 11 In contexts like this, the Greek word for *flesh* (*sarx*) refers to the sinful state of human beings, often presented as a power in opposition to the Spirit; also in verse 13.   [c] 11 Or *put off in the circumcision of*   [d] 13 Some manuscripts *us*   [e] 15 Or *them in him*

MISSING WHAT REALLY MATTERS

READ: COLOSSIANS 2:16-17

I was speaking in Houston, Texas, and a good-sized man, with a good-sized belt buckle, came up to me with tears in his eyes. He began to tell me the story of his prodigal daughter, how she went to college and totally turned her back on the faith. As soon as he started the story, I knew how it would go. I've heard it so many times that even the details seem predictable. But when he finished, he wasn't looking for an explanation. Instead, with one sentence he put his finger on what he thought happened.

"We raised her in Church, but we didn't raise her in Christ." Like some of you, she had been taught to keep all the rules and say the right prayers, but somehow missed that those things come from a personal and genuine relationship with Jesus. She was made to feel guilty for what she did wrong, but didn't realize God's amazing grace available through Christ.

Maybe you grew up in a home where you were taught all about Jesus. You learned to keep as many of the rules as possible, hoping it would be enough to keep you out of hell. Instead of becoming a follower of Christ, you became a follower of religion.

Jesus came to free you from religion. To those who have been hauling around a long list of rules, to those who are weighed down with the fear and guilt of religion, Jesus invites you to follow him.

BUILDING

FAITH

WISDOM

STRENGTH

Taken from *Not a Fan Student Edition* by Kyle Idleman, copyright © 2012 by City on the Hill Studio, Inc., published by Zondervan.

HOW DEAD PEOPLE ACT

READ: COLOSSIANS 3:3

A friend was telling me about how someone came up to him and said, "If you died tonight, do you know where you would go?" My friend was a little unnerved by the question, and by the end of the night my friend accepted Jesus as his Savior.

My friend said to me, "The problem is I didn't die that night." I didn't quite understand what he meant. My friend explained to me that when he accepted Christ he knew that when he died he would receive eternal life, but no one told him that when he accepted Christ he was making a decision to die right then. He got the message that when he died he would go to heaven to be with God, but it was ten years later before he understood that death starts now.

I've been around my share of dead people. I've been in the room before the coroner comes in. I have stood next to many open caskets. And I don't mean to be uncouth, but I've noticed something about dead people.

BUILDING

FAITH

WISDOM

STRENGTH

People who are dead don't seem to care very much what other people think of them. Dead people aren't concerned with how nice their clothes are. Dead people aren't caught up in how much money is in their account. Dead people aren't at all thinking about getting the Ivy League scholarship. The point is that death is the ultimate surrender of yourself and all that you have. When you're dead, you're no longer concerned with your life.

Taken from *Not a Fan Student Edition* by Kyle Idleman, copyright © 2012 by City on the Hill Studio, Inc., published by Zondervan.

Christ, who is your *a* life, appears, then you also will appear with him in glory.

⁵Put to death, therefore, whatever belongs to your earthly nature: sexual immorality, impurity, lust, evil desires and greed, which is idolatry. ⁶Because of these, the wrath of God is coming.*b* ⁷You used to walk in these ways, in the life you once lived. ⁸But now you must also rid yourselves of all such things as these: anger, rage, malice, slander, and filthy language from your lips. ⁹Do not lie to each other, since you have taken off your old self with its practices ¹⁰and have put on the new self, which is being renewed in knowledge in the image of its Creator. ¹¹Here there is no Gentile or Jew, circumcised or uncircumcised, barbarian, Scythian, slave or free, but Christ is all, and is in all.

¹²Therefore, as God's chosen people, holy and dearly loved, clothe yourselves with compassion, kindness, humility, gentleness and patience. ¹³Bear with each other and forgive one another if any of you has a grievance against someone. Forgive as the Lord forgave you. ¹⁴And over all these virtues put on love, which binds them all together in perfect unity.

¹⁵Let the peace of Christ rule in your hearts, since as members of one body you were called to peace. And be thankful. ¹⁶Let the message of Christ dwell among you richly as you teach and admonish one another with all wisdom through psalms, hymns, and songs from the Spirit, singing to God with gratitude in your hearts. ¹⁷And whatever you do, whether in word or deed, do it all in the name of the Lord Jesus, giving thanks to God the Father through him.

Instructions for Christian Households

¹⁸Wives, submit yourselves to your husbands, as is fitting in the Lord.

¹⁹Husbands, love your wives and do not be harsh with them.

²⁰Children, obey your parents in everything, for this pleases the Lord.

²¹Fathers,*c* do not embitter your children, or they will become discouraged.

²²Slaves, obey your earthly masters in everything; and do it, not only when their eye is on you and to curry their favor, but with sincerity of heart and reverence for the Lord. ²³Whatever you do, work at it with all your heart, as working for the Lord, not for human masters, ²⁴since you know that you will receive an inheritance from the Lord as a reward. It is the Lord Christ you are serving. ²⁵Anyone who does wrong will be repaid for their wrongs, and there is no favoritism.

4 Masters, provide your slaves with what is right and fair, because you know that you also have a Master in heaven.

Further Instructions

²Devote yourselves to prayer, being watchful and thankful. ³And pray for us, too, that God may open a door for our message, so that we may proclaim the mystery of Christ, for which I am in chains. ⁴Pray that I may proclaim it clearly, as I should. ⁵Be wise in the way you act toward outsiders; make the most of every opportunity. ⁶Let your conversation be always full of grace, seasoned with salt, so that you may know how to answer everyone.

Final Greetings

⁷Tychicus will tell you all the news about me. He is a dear brother, a faithful minister and fellow servant*d* in the Lord. ⁸I am sending him to you for the express purpose that you may know about our*e* circumstances and that he may encourage your hearts. ⁹He is coming with Onesimus, our faithful and dear brother, who is one of you. They will tell you everything that is happening here.

¹⁰My fellow prisoner Aristarchus sends you his greetings, as does Mark, the cousin of Barnabas. (You have received instructions about him; if he comes to you, welcome him.) ¹¹Jesus, who is called Justus, also sends greetings. These are the only Jews*f* among my co-workers for the kingdom of God, and they have proved a comfort to me. ¹²Epaphras, who is one of you and a servant of Christ Jesus, sends greetings. He is always wrestling in prayer for you, that you may stand firm in all the will of God, mature and fully assured. ¹³I vouch for him that he

---

a 4 Some manuscripts *our*   *b 6* Some early manuscripts *coming on those who are disobedient*
c 21 Or *Parents*   *d 7* Or *slave*; also in verse 12   *e 8* Some manuscripts *that he may know about your*
f 11 Greek *only ones of the circumcision group*

THE BEST CONVERSATIONS

READ: COLOSSIANS 4:5-6

"You know what's really unattractive about Christians?" our artist friend Jeff once said to us. "They're always on a mission. Too many Christians think they have nothing to gain from others except to get them saved. I don't like it when anyone has an agenda and is not visiting with me straight up. Why can't they stop, pay attention, and listen?"

In his letter to the church in Colossae, Paul taught to be wise in the way we act toward those who believe differently from us, to make the most of every opportunity by conversing in ways full of grace.

For several years, we've been growing into a new way of conversing that is helping us listen. Every person, we believe, has something to teach us about life. While we believe Jesus distinguishes himself as the Savior and King of us all, while we obey his teachings because we believe they give us the best road map for life, we also believe the biblical idea that all humans—be they Christians, Buddhists, Mormons, atheists—are made in God's image.

BUILDING FAITH WISDOM STRENGTH

All humans reflect God in varying degrees of clarity. Therefore, we approach every conversation as fellow learners rather than as experts. We can gather data and truth even from those who do not follow Jesus, growing in wisdom and love, and giving others dignity by assuming they are doing the same. If we want our conversations to always be full of grace, then humility, not deft arguments or clever words, must become our first concern. Jesus struck up conversations with humility.

Taken from *Coffee Shop Conversations* by Dale Fincher and Jonalyn Fincher, copyright © 2010 by Charles Dale Fincher and Jonalyn Grace Fincher, published by Zondervan.

is working hard for you and for those at Laodicea and Hierapolis. [14]Our dear friend Luke, the doctor, and Demas send greetings. [15]Give my greetings to the brothers and sisters at Laodicea, and to Nympha and the church in her house.

[16]After this letter has been read to you, see that it is also read in the church of the Laod-iceans and that you in turn read the letter from Laodicea.

[17]Tell Archippus: "See to it that you complete the ministry you have received in the Lord."

[18]I, Paul, write this greeting in my own hand. Remember my chains. Grace be with you.

1 THESSALONIANS

WHEN DID THIS HAPPEN?

Around A.D. 51 in Corinth

WHO IS IN THIS BOOK?

Paul

Timothy

VERSES YOU MIGHT RECOGNIZE

1 THESSALONIANS 3:13

"May he strengthen your hearts so that you will be blameless and holy in the presence of our God and Father when our Lord Jesus comes with all his holy ones."

1 THESSALONIANS 5:24

"The one who calls you is faithful, and he will do it."

WHAT'S IT ABOUT?

Nothing is more comforting than knowing what will happen in the future. The Thessalonians were being persecuted, and Paul wrote this book to encourage them with information about Christ's return. He told them that when that day comes, the dead will rise first, followed closely by the living believers. All of them would meet Christ in the air and spend eternity with him in heaven (see 1 Thessalonians 4:16–18). Believers in Jesus did not have to fear death or wonder what would happen when they died.

Paul encouraged the people to stay alert so they would be ready for the day Christ returns. He even built on some of the teachings of Jesus on this subject (see Matthew 24:43–44), reminding people of Christ's promise to come again. Their hope in his return should motivate them to grow in godliness. No matter what they were going through now, Jesus would come back and they would be with him someday!

1 THESSALONIANS

1 Paul, Silas[a] and Timothy,

To the church of the Thessalonians in God the Father and the Lord Jesus Christ:

Grace and peace to you.

Thanksgiving for the Thessalonians' Faith

[2] We always thank God for all of you and continually mention you in our prayers. [3] We remember before our God and Father your work produced by faith, your labor prompted by love, and your endurance inspired by hope in our Lord Jesus Christ.

[4] For we know, brothers and sisters[b] loved by God, that he has chosen you, [5] because our gospel came to you not simply with words but also with power, with the Holy Spirit and deep conviction. You know how we lived among you for your sake. [6] You became imitators of us and of the Lord, for you welcomed the message in the midst of severe suffering with the joy given by the Holy Spirit. [7] And so you became a model to all the believers in Macedonia and Achaia. [8] The Lord's message rang out from you not only in Macedonia and Achaia — your faith in God has become known everywhere. Therefore we do not need to say anything about it, [9] for they themselves report what kind of reception you gave us. They tell how you turned to God from idols to serve the living and true God, [10] and to wait for his Son from heaven, whom he raised from the dead — Jesus, who rescues us from the coming wrath.

Paul's Ministry in Thessalonica

2 You know, brothers and sisters, that our visit to you was not without results. [2] We had previously suffered and been treated outrageously in Philippi, as you know, but with the help of our God we dared to tell you his gospel in the face of strong opposition. [3] For the appeal we make does not spring from error or impure motives, nor are we trying to trick you. [4] On the contrary, we speak as those approved by God to be entrusted with the gospel. We are not trying to please people but God, who tests our hearts. [5] You know we never used flattery, nor did we put on a mask to cover up greed — God is our witness. [6] We were not looking for praise from people, not from you or anyone else, even though as apostles of Christ we could have asserted our authority. [7] Instead, we were like young children[c] among you.

Just as a nursing mother cares for her children, [8] so we cared for you. Because we loved you so much, we were delighted to share with you not only the gospel of God but our lives as well. [9] Surely you remember, brothers and sisters, our toil and hardship; we worked night and day in order not to be a burden to anyone while we preached the gospel of God to you. [10] You are witnesses, and so is God, of how holy, righteous and blameless we were among you who believed. [11] For you know that we dealt with each of you as a father deals with his own children, [12] encouraging, comforting and urging you to live lives worthy of God, who calls you into his kingdom and glory.

[13] And we also thank God continually because, when you received the word of God, which you heard from us, you accepted it not as a human word, but as it actually is, the word of God, which is indeed at work in you who believe. [14] For you, brothers and sisters, became imitators of God's churches in Judea, which are in Christ Jesus: You suffered from your own people the same things those churches suffered from the Jews [15] who killed the Lord Jesus and the prophets and also drove us out. They displease God and are hostile to everyone [16] in their

---

[a] 1 Greek *Silvanus*, a variant of *Silas*   [b] 4 The Greek word for *brothers and sisters* (*adelphoi*) refers here to believers, both men and women, as part of God's family; also in 2:1, 9, 14, 17; 3:7; 4:1, 10, 13; 5:1, 4, 12, 14, 25, 27.   [c] 7 Some manuscripts *were gentle*

FOLLOW THE PACK

READ: 1 THESSALONIANS 1:5

I t's easy to assume you're the fastest runner in the race until you meet someone who blows past you. So if you think you have a sweet relationship with God that couldn't get any better, challenge yourself with the example of the Thessalonian believers.

The apostle Paul started the church in Thessalonica, spending three weeks reasoning with them, proving that Jesus had to suffer and rise from the dead (Acts 17:1–9). He saw immediate evidence of their authentic faith. They experienced the Holy Spirit's power and became completely convinced of the facts about Jesus. They strove to imitate both Paul and the Lord, and they joyfully endured fierce persecution for their faith from their non-Christian neighbors (1 Thessalonians 1:6, 2:14). The account of their faith spread throughout their nation as they became a model of how to turn from idols "to serve the living and true God" (1:9).

BUILDING

FAITH

WISDOM

STRENGTH

Being a Christian isn't a competition. But it never hurts to study other followers of Jesus so you get a picture what real maturity can look like. God wants to make astounding changes in your life, but that only happens when you let him take over your whole life and remake your every thought, word, and action.

The Thessalonians ran hard and fast after Jesus. If that's your goal, study their example. Let them set the pace.

effort to keep us from speaking to the Gentiles so that they may be saved. In this way they always heap up their sins to the limit. The wrath of God has come upon them at last.[a]

Paul's Longing to See the Thessalonians

[17]But, brothers and sisters, when we were orphaned by being separated from you for a short time (in person, not in thought), out of our intense longing we made every effort to see you. [18]For we wanted to come to you—certainly I, Paul, did, again and again—but Satan blocked our way. [19]For what is our hope, our joy, or the crown in which we will glory in the presence of our Lord Jesus when he comes? Is it not you? [20]Indeed, you are our glory and joy.

3 So when we could stand it no longer, we thought it best to be left by ourselves in Athens. [2]We sent Timothy, who is our brother and co-worker in God's service in spreading the gospel of Christ, to strengthen and encourage you in your faith, [3]so that no one would be unsettled by these trials. For you know quite well that we are destined for them. [4]In fact, when we were with you, we kept telling you that we would be persecuted. And it turned out that way, as you well know. [5]For this reason, when I could stand it no longer, I sent to find out about your faith. I was afraid that in some way the tempter had tempted you and that our labors might have been in vain.

Timothy's Encouraging Report

[6]But Timothy has just now come to us from you and has brought good news about your faith and love. He has told us that you always have pleasant memories of us and that you long to see us, just as we also long to see you. [7]Therefore, brothers and sisters, in all our distress and persecution we were encouraged about you because of your faith. [8]For now we really live, since you are standing firm in the Lord. [9]How can we thank God enough for you in return for all the joy we have in the presence of our God because of you? [10]Night and day we pray most earnestly that we may see you again and supply what is lacking in your faith.

[11]Now may our God and Father himself and our Lord Jesus clear the way for us to come to you. [12]May the Lord make your love increase and overflow for each other and for everyone else, just as ours does for you. [13]May he strengthen your hearts so that you will be blameless and holy in the presence of our God and Father when our Lord Jesus comes with all his holy ones.

Living to Please God

4 As for other matters, brothers and sisters, we instructed you how to live in order to please God, as in fact you are living. Now we ask you and urge you in the Lord Jesus to do this more and more. [2]For you know what instructions we gave you by the authority of the Lord Jesus.

[3]It is God's will that you should be sanctified: that you should avoid sexual immorality; [4]that each of you should learn to control your own body[b] in a way that is holy and honorable, [5]not in passionate lust like the pagans, who do not know God; [6]and that in this matter no one should wrong or take advantage of a brother or sister.[c] The Lord will punish all those who commit such sins, as we told you and warned you before. [7]For God did not call us to be impure, but to live a holy life. [8]Therefore, anyone who rejects this instruction does not reject a human being but God, the very God who gives you his Holy Spirit.

[9]Now about your love for one another we do not need to write to you, for you yourselves have been taught by God to love each other. [10]And in fact, you do love all of God's family throughout Macedonia. Yet we urge you, brothers and sisters, to do so more and more, [11]and to make it your ambition to lead a quiet life: You should mind your own business and work with your hands, just as we told you, [12]so that your daily life may win the respect of outsiders and so that you will not be dependent on anybody.

Believers Who Have Died

[13]Brothers and sisters, we do not want you to be uninformed about those who sleep in death, so that you do not grieve like the rest of mankind, who have no hope. [14]For we

---

[a] 16 Or *them fully*   [b] 4 Or *learn to live with your own wife*; or *learn to acquire a wife*   [c] 6 The Greek word for *brother or sister* (*adelphos*) refers here to a believer, whether man or woman, as part of God's family.

THE MERCY OF DEATH

READ: 1 THESSALONIANS 4:14

Resurrection means to rise from the dead, not zombie-like, but full and whole. When Jesus rose, he wasn't a spirit floating around and haunting Jerusalem. He was flesh and bone. The disciples touched him. Thomas put his fingers into the scarred holes in Jesus' hands. The disciples met Jesus on the seashore, and they even ate food with him. His was a new body—the first time a new body had ever been given to a human being after the old body had died.

Three months before my mother died, she visited us in California. Mom had undergone almost a dozen major chemotherapies throughout her nine-year battle with cancer. Each of them wore her down, no matter how hard she fought.

As she weakened, the doctors couldn't give her the higher doses of chemo that were available because her body couldn't handle the poison. She was running out of options. I said to her, "So, Mom, with all of these doctors and medicines, where is the hope?"

BUILDING FAITH WISDOM STRENGTH

I expected her to say that new breakthroughs are offering her some new drugs to fight the cancer. I expected her to shed light on her medical situation. But she didn't say these things. "The hope?" she said in her matter-of-fact way. "Son, the hope is in the resurrection." That is the most profound answer.

My mother was right. If our bodies are to be remade, then they have to be resurrected. We need the severe mercy of death so we can be remade.

believe that Jesus died and rose again, and so we believe that God will bring with Jesus those who have fallen asleep in him. ¹⁵According to the Lord's word, we tell you that we who are still alive, who are left until the coming of the Lord, will certainly not precede those who have fallen asleep. ¹⁶For the Lord himself will come down from heaven, with a loud command, with the voice of the archangel and with the trumpet call of God, and the dead in Christ will rise first. ¹⁷After that, we who are still alive and are left will be caught up together with them in the clouds to meet the Lord in the air. And so we will be with the Lord forever. ¹⁸Therefore encourage one another with these words.

The Day of the Lord

5 Now, brothers and sisters, about times and dates we do not need to write to you, ²for you know very well that the day of the Lord will come like a thief in the night. ³While people are saying, "Peace and safety," destruction will come on them suddenly, as labor pains on a pregnant woman, and they will not escape.

⁴But you, brothers and sisters, are not in darkness so that this day should surprise you like a thief. ⁵You are all children of the light and children of the day. We do not belong to the night or to the darkness. ⁶So then, let us not be like others, who are asleep, but let us be awake and sober. ⁷For those who sleep, sleep at night, and those who get drunk, get drunk at night. ⁸But since we belong to the day, let us be sober, putting on faith and love as a breastplate, and the hope of salvation as a helmet. ⁹For God did not appoint us to suffer wrath but to receive salvation through our Lord Jesus Christ. ¹⁰He died for us so that, whether we are awake or asleep, we may live together with him. ¹¹Therefore encourage one another and build each other up, just as in fact you are doing.

Final Instructions

¹²Now we ask you, brothers and sisters, to acknowledge those who work hard among you, who care for you in the Lord and who admonish you. ¹³Hold them in the highest regard in love because of their work. Live in peace with each other. ¹⁴And we urge you, brothers and sisters, warn those who are idle and disruptive, encourage the disheartened, help the weak, be patient with everyone. ¹⁵Make sure that nobody pays back wrong for wrong, but always strive to do what is good for each other and for everyone else.

¹⁶Rejoice always, ¹⁷pray continually, ¹⁸give thanks in all circumstances; for this is God's will for you in Christ Jesus.

¹⁹Do not quench the Spirit. ²⁰Do not treat prophecies with contempt ²¹but test them all; hold on to what is good, ²²reject every kind of evil.

²³May God himself, the God of peace, sanctify you through and through. May your whole spirit, soul and body be kept blameless at the coming of our Lord Jesus Christ. ²⁴The one who calls you is faithful, and he will do it.

²⁵Brothers and sisters, pray for us. ²⁶Greet all God's people with a holy kiss. ²⁷I charge you before the Lord to have this letter read to all the brothers and sisters.

²⁸The grace of our Lord Jesus Christ be with you.

2 THESSALONIANS

 WHEN DID THIS HAPPEN?
Around A.D. 52 in Corinth

 WHO IS IN THIS BOOK?
Paul
Silas
Timothy
man of lawlessness

 VERSE YOU MIGHT RECOGNIZE

2 THESSALONIANS 2:15
"So then, brothers and sisters, stand firm and hold fast to the teachings we passed on to you."

WHAT'S IT ABOUT?

Similar to 1 Thessalonians, this book contains detailed teaching on the end times. Led astray by false teachers, the Christians in Thessalonica thought that Christ would return at any moment—rescuing them from persecution. Some false teachers were even claiming that the "day of the Lord" had already happened. Because of this, many had quit living fruitful lives and become unproductive in the Lord's work. Paul corrected their error and told them to work hard until Jesus returns.

Paul told the people about three events that would help them recognize the real day of the Lord. First, a rebellion would occur (see 2 Thessalonians 2:3). Then the one who was holding back evil (likely the Holy Spirit) would be removed from the earth (see 2:6-7). And finally, a person controlled by Satan, the "man of lawlessness," would rise up against God (see chapter 2). Until that happened, Christians should work hard and live holy lives motivated by the sure hope that Christ will return.

2 THESSALONIANS

1 Paul, Silas[a] and Timothy,

To the church of the Thessalonians in God our Father and the Lord Jesus Christ:

[2] Grace and peace to you from God the Father and the Lord Jesus Christ.

Thanksgiving and Prayer

[3] We ought always to thank God for you, brothers and sisters,[b] and rightly so, because your faith is growing more and more, and the love all of you have for one another is increasing. [4] Therefore, among God's churches we boast about your perseverance and faith in all the persecutions and trials you are enduring.

[5] All this is evidence that God's judgment is right, and as a result you will be counted worthy of the kingdom of God, for which you are suffering. [6] God is just: He will pay back trouble to those who trouble you [7] and give relief to you who are troubled, and to us as well. This will happen when the Lord Jesus is revealed from heaven in blazing fire with his powerful angels. [8] He will punish those who do not know God and do not obey the gospel of our Lord Jesus. [9] They will be punished with everlasting destruction and shut out from the presence of the Lord and from the glory of his might [10] on the day he comes to be glorified in his holy people and to be marveled at among all those who have believed. This includes you, because you believed our testimony to you.

[11] With this in mind, we constantly pray for you, that our God may make you worthy of his calling, and that by his power he may bring to fruition your every desire for goodness and your every deed prompted by faith. [12] We pray this so that the name of our Lord Jesus may be glorified in you, and you in him, according to the grace of our God and the Lord Jesus Christ.[c]

The Man of Lawlessness

2 Concerning the coming of our Lord Jesus Christ and our being gathered to him, we ask you, brothers and sisters, [2] not to become easily unsettled or alarmed by the teaching allegedly from us — whether by a prophecy or by word of mouth or by letter — asserting that the day of the Lord has already come. [3] Don't let anyone deceive you in any way, for that day will not come until the rebellion occurs and the man of lawlessness[d] is revealed, the man doomed to destruction. [4] He will oppose and will exalt himself over everything that is called God or is worshiped, so that he sets himself up in God's temple, proclaiming himself to be God.

[5] Don't you remember that when I was with you I used to tell you these things? [6] And now you know what is holding him back, so that he may be revealed at the proper time. [7] For the secret power of lawlessness is already at work; but the one who now holds it back will continue to do so till he is taken out of the way. [8] And then the lawless one will be revealed, whom the Lord Jesus will overthrow with the breath of his mouth and destroy by the splendor of his coming. [9] The coming of the lawless one will be in accordance with how Satan works. He will use all sorts of displays of power through signs and wonders that serve the lie, [10] and all the ways that wickedness deceives those who are perishing. They perish because they refused to love the truth and so be saved. [11] For this reason God sends them a powerful delusion so that they will believe the lie [12] and so that all will be condemned who have not believed the truth but have delighted in wickedness.

Stand Firm

[13] But we ought always to thank God for you, brothers and sisters loved by the Lord,

---

[a] 1 Greek *Silvanus*, a variant of *Silas*   [b] 3 The Greek word for *brothers and sisters* (*adelphoi*) refers here to believers, both men and women, as part of God's family; also in 2:1, 13, 15; 3:1, 6, 13.   [c] 12 Or *God and Lord, Jesus Christ*   [d] 3 Some manuscripts *sin*

KEEP IT UP

READ: 2 THESSALONIANS 1:3

Those Thessalonian Christians were models of faith, pacesetters in the long run to heaven. The apostle Paul wrote them not long after he founded their church (Acts 17:1–9). His first letter applauded their solid first steps in following Jesus. His second note tells them how to stay on track.

By the end of 1 Thessalonians Paul was already reminding his friends to keep doing what he had previously taught them. He says they know "how to live in order to please God, as in fact you are living," then he urges them to "do this more and more" (1 Thessalonians 4:1). Now in 2 Thessalonians he says their faith is growing "more and more" and their love for each other is steadily increasing (2 Thessalonians 1:3). It all sounds so basic.

You might wonder if the Thessalonians got tired of hearing the same old commands, as if a track coach were telling them over and over to keep putting one foot in front of the other. But they must have welcomed these reminders from Paul, who praised their perseverance even through violent persecution. Their step-by-step obedience signaled their faith was authentic and enduring.

Opening your Bible every day might not always wow you with surprises. A sermon or study might not communicate startling new information. But the Lord loves when you keep hearing and acting on his simplest reminders.

BUILDING
FAITH
WISDOM
STRENGTH

because God chose you as firstfruits[a] to be saved through the sanctifying work of the Spirit and through belief in the truth. [14]He called you to this through our gospel, that you might share in the glory of our Lord Jesus Christ.

[15]So then, brothers and sisters, stand firm and hold fast to the teachings[b] we passed on to you, whether by word of mouth or by letter.

[16]May our Lord Jesus Christ himself and God our Father, who loved us and by his grace gave us eternal encouragement and good hope, [17]encourage your hearts and strengthen you in every good deed and word.

Request for Prayer

3 As for other matters, brothers and sisters, pray for us that the message of the Lord may spread rapidly and be honored, just as it was with you. [2]And pray that we may be delivered from wicked and evil people, for not everyone has faith. [3]But the Lord is faithful, and he will strengthen you and protect you from the evil one. [4]We have confidence in the Lord that you are doing and will continue to do the things we command. [5]May the Lord direct your hearts into God's love and Christ's perseverance.

Warning Against Idleness

[6]In the name of the Lord Jesus Christ, we command you, brothers and sisters, to keep away from every believer who is idle and disruptive and does not live according to the teaching[c] you received from us. [7]For you yourselves know how you ought to follow our example. We were not idle when we were with you, [8]nor did we eat anyone's food without paying for it. On the contrary, we worked night and day, laboring and toiling so that we would not be a burden to any of you. [9]We did this, not because we do not have the right to such help, but in order to offer ourselves as a model for you to imitate. [10]For even when we were with you, we gave you this rule: "The one who is unwilling to work shall not eat."

[11]We hear that some among you are idle and disruptive. They are not busy; they are busybodies. [12]Such people we command and urge in the Lord Jesus Christ to settle down and earn the food they eat. [13]And as for you, brothers and sisters, never tire of doing what is good.

[14]Take special note of anyone who does not obey our instruction in this letter. Do not associate with them, in order that they may feel ashamed. [15]Yet do not regard them as an enemy, but warn them as you would a fellow believer.

Final Greetings

[16]Now may the Lord of peace himself give you peace at all times and in every way. The Lord be with all of you.

[17]I, Paul, write this greeting in my own hand, which is the distinguishing mark in all my letters. This is how I write.

[18]The grace of our Lord Jesus Christ be with you all.

---

[a] 13 Some manuscripts *because from the beginning God chose you*   [b] 15 Or *traditions*   [c] 6 Or *tradition*

1 TIMOTHY

WHEN DID THIS HAPPEN?
Around A.D. 65 in Rome

WHO IS IN THIS BOOK?
Paul
Timothy
Hymenaeus
Alexander

VERSES YOU MIGHT RECOGNIZE

1 TIMOTHY 4:12
"Don't let anyone look down on you because you are young, but set an example for the believers in speech, in conduct, in love, in faith and in purity."

1 TIMOTHY 6:12
"Fight the good fight of the faith. Take hold of the eternal life to which you were called when you made your good confession in the presence of many witnesses."

WHAT'S IT ABOUT?

Paul wrote to Timothy to instruct him on leading the church in Ephesus. This book along with 2 Timothy and Titus are referred to as the "pastoral epistles." First Timothy contains some of the most detailed instructions in the whole Bible for church worship, qualifications of church leaders and guidelines for church discipline. Paul also instructed Timothy on how to live as a leader.

Timothy was like a son to Paul. They had known each other for ten years when this letter was written, and they had traveled together on Paul's second missionary journey (see Acts 16:1–3). Timothy stayed with Paul after that—even when he was imprisoned in Rome.

As a young pastor, Timothy may have faced some challenges with older believers looking down on him and assuming he didn't have the knowledge or experience to do the job. But Paul encouraged him to "set an example for the believers" (1 Timothy 4:12) and "fight the good fight" (6:12) as he ministered to the church.

1 Paul, an apostle of Christ Jesus by the command of God our Savior and of Christ Jesus our hope,

[2] To Timothy my true son in the faith:

Grace, mercy and peace from God the Father and Christ Jesus our Lord.

Timothy Charged to Oppose False Teachers

[3] As I urged you when I went into Macedonia, stay there in Ephesus so that you may command certain people not to teach false doctrines any longer [4] or to devote themselves to myths and endless genealogies. Such things promote controversial speculations rather than advancing God's work — which is by faith. [5] The goal of this command is love, which comes from a pure heart and a good conscience and a sincere faith. [6] Some have departed from these and have turned to meaningless talk. [7] They want to be teachers of the law, but they do not know what they are talking about or what they so confidently affirm.

[8] We know that the law is good if one uses it properly. [9] We also know that the law is made not for the righteous but for lawbreakers and rebels, the ungodly and sinful, the unholy and irreligious, for those who kill their fathers or mothers, for murderers, [10] for the sexually immoral, for those practicing homosexuality, for slave traders and liars and perjurers — and for whatever else is contrary to the sound doctrine [11] that conforms to the gospel concerning the glory of the blessed God, which he entrusted to me.

The Lord's Grace to Paul

[12] I thank Christ Jesus our Lord, who has given me strength, that he considered me trustworthy, appointing me to his service. [13] Even though I was once a blasphemer and a persecutor and a violent man, I was shown mercy because I acted in ignorance and unbelief. [14] The grace of our Lord was poured out on me abundantly, along with the faith and love that are in Christ Jesus.

[15] Here is a trustworthy saying that deserves full acceptance: Christ Jesus came into the world to save sinners — of whom I am the worst. [16] But for that very reason I was shown mercy so that in me, the worst of sinners, Christ Jesus might display his immense patience as an example for those who would believe in him and receive eternal life. [17] Now to the King eternal, immortal, invisible, the only God, be honor and glory for ever and ever. Amen.

The Charge to Timothy Renewed

[18] Timothy, my son, I am giving you this command in keeping with the prophecies once made about you, so that by recalling them you may fight the battle well, [19] holding on to faith and a good conscience, which some have rejected and so have suffered shipwreck with regard to the faith. [20] Among them are Hymenaeus and Alexander, whom I have handed over to Satan to be taught not to blaspheme.

Instructions on Worship

2 I urge, then, first of all, that petitions, prayers, intercession and thanksgiving be made for all people — [2] for kings and all those in authority, that we may live peaceful and quiet lives in all godliness and holiness. [3] This is good, and pleases God our Savior, [4] who wants all people to be saved and to come to a knowledge of the truth. [5] For there is one God and one mediator between God and mankind, the man Christ Jesus, [6] who gave himself as a ransom for all people. This has now been witnessed to at the proper time. [7] And for this purpose I was appointed a herald and an apostle — I am telling the truth, I am not lying — and a true and faithful teacher of the Gentiles.

[8] Therefore I want the men everywhere to pray, lifting up holy hands without anger or disputing. [9] I also want the women to

WORST OF ALL

READ: 1 TIMOTHY 1:12-16

I'm thankful that much of the New Testament was written by the biggest sinner the world has ever known. At least that's what the apostle Paul considered himself to be.

Paul claims he's the worst sinner who ever lived. While it is an example of his humility, I love how he put a special emphasis on his claim. One of the only times in his letters when Paul gets in our grill and says "you really need to hear what I'm saying" is to tell us he's a loser.

It's pretty awesome that a guy who was elevated so highly in spiritual matters was still keeping his humble place at the feet of Jesus.

Why did Paul see himself in such a radical way? Because Christ had changed him, and he was able to look at where he came from and where he was going through the lens of the gospel. Paul had been one of the religious elite, among the most highly regarded people in society. Yet through surrender and obedience to Christ, Paul's vision had changed to the point that he considered everything outside of knowing Jesus to be rubbish (Philippians 3:8). To see with Christ's eyes is to have an eternal perspective, which is essential for us in our reaching out. If we are to know God and make him known, it matters how we see God and how we see ourselves.

BUILDING FAITH WISDOM STRENGTH

Taken from *Thrive Student Edition* by Mark Hall with Tim Luke, copyright © 2014 by Mark Hall, published by Zondervan.

dress modestly, with decency and propriety, adorning themselves, not with elaborate hairstyles or gold or pearls or expensive clothes, [10]but with good deeds, appropriate for women who profess to worship God.

[11]A woman[a] should learn in quietness and full submission. [12]I do not permit a woman to teach or to assume authority over a man;[b] she must be quiet. [13]For Adam was formed first, then Eve. [14]And Adam was not the one deceived; it was the woman who was deceived and became a sinner. [15]But women[c] will be saved through childbearing—if they continue in faith, love and holiness with propriety.

Qualifications for Overseers and Deacons

3 Here is a trustworthy saying: Whoever aspires to be an overseer desires a noble task. [2]Now the overseer is to be above reproach, faithful to his wife, temperate, self-controlled, respectable, hospitable, able to teach, [3]not given to drunkenness, not violent but gentle, not quarrelsome, not a lover of money. [4]He must manage his own family well and see that his children obey him, and he must do so in a manner worthy of full[d] respect. [5](If anyone does not know how to manage his own family, how can he take care of God's church?) [6]He must not be a recent convert, or he may become conceited and fall under the same judgment as the devil. [7]He must also have a good reputation with outsiders, so that he will not fall into disgrace and into the devil's trap.

[8]In the same way, deacons[e] are to be worthy of respect, sincere, not indulging in much wine, and not pursuing dishonest gain. [9]They must keep hold of the deep truths of the faith with a clear conscience. [10]They must first be tested; and then if there is nothing against them, let them serve as deacons.

[11]In the same way, the women[f] are to be worthy of respect, not malicious talkers but temperate and trustworthy in everything.

[12]A deacon must be faithful to his wife and must manage his children and his household well. [13]Those who have served well gain an excellent standing and great assurance in their faith in Christ Jesus.

Reasons for Paul's Instructions

[14]Although I hope to come to you soon, I am writing you these instructions so that, [15]if I am delayed, you will know how people ought to conduct themselves in God's household, which is the church of the living God, the pillar and foundation of the truth. [16]Beyond all question, the mystery from which true godliness springs is great:

He appeared in the flesh,
    was vindicated by the Spirit,[g]
was seen by angels,
    was preached among the nations,
was believed on in the world,
    was taken up in glory.

4 The Spirit clearly says that in later times some will abandon the faith and follow deceiving spirits and things taught by demons. [2]Such teachings come through hypocritical liars, whose consciences have been seared as with a hot iron. [3]They forbid people to marry and order them to abstain from certain foods, which God created to be received with thanksgiving by those who believe and who know the truth. [4]For everything God created is good, and nothing is to be rejected if it is received with thanksgiving, [5]because it is consecrated by the word of God and prayer.

[6]If you point these things out to the brothers and sisters,[h] you will be a good minister of Christ Jesus, nourished on the truths of the faith and of the good teaching that you have followed. [7]Have nothing to do with godless myths and old wives' tales; rather, train yourself to be godly. [8]For physical training is of some value, but godliness has value for all things, holding promise for both the present life and the life to come. [9]This is a trustworthy saying that deserves full acceptance. [10]That is why we labor and strive, because we have put our hope in the living God, who is the Savior of all people, and especially of those who believe.

---

[a] 11 Or *wife*; also in verse 12   [b] 12 Or *over her husband*   [c] 15 Greek *she*   [d] 4 Or *him with proper*
[e] 8 The word *deacons* refers here to Christians designated to serve with the overseers/elders of the church in a variety of ways; similarly in verse 12; and in Romans 16:1 and Phil. 1:1.   [f] 11 Possibly deacons' wives or women who are deacons   [g] 16 Or *vindicated in spirit*   [h] 6 The Greek word for *brothers and sisters* (*adelphoi*) refers here to believers, both men and women, as part of God's family.

WHO CARES HOW YOU LOOK?

READ: 1 TIMOTHY 4:8

The god of appearance is attractive, compelling, charismatic. He walks into your everyday world and shows you what life could be if you looked just a little bit better. He offers us the popularity and envy that makes life sweet.

He plays on the most basic problem of humanity—that pull toward doing it our way, aka pride. What if your biceps were a little bigger? How would you feel if your legs were a little bit stronger?

The gods of appearance give us very convenient ways to keep score: how we look in the mirror, the size of our clothes, the awards we win, the number of people who know our name. The gods of appearance encourage you to find your worth inside of yourself instead of depending on Jesus to fill you up.

The Bible addresses our appearance in numerous passages.

And while many Scriptures about appearance are aimed at women, guys don't get off the hook. The Lord knows that the god of appearance often plays to male pride. The apostle Paul wrote a lot about sports and training in the New Testament.

BUILDING FAITH WISDOM STRENGTH

Look at your life. Do you spend as much time training spiritually as you do building up your physical body? This isn't meant to be a guilt trip. Paul doesn't say physical training is a bad thing. In other places in the Bible, he even encourages us to train in such a way to win the prize. But earthly honors aren't Paul's aim, and they shouldn't be ours either.

Taken from *Gods at War Student Edition* by Kyle Idleman, copyright © 2014 by City on a Hill Studio, LLC, published by Zondervan.

[11] Command and teach these things. [12] Don't let anyone look down on you because you are young, but set an example for the believers in speech, in conduct, in love, in faith and in purity. [13] Until I come, devote yourself to the public reading of Scripture, to preaching and to teaching. [14] Do not neglect your gift, which was given you through prophecy when the body of elders laid their hands on you.

[15] Be diligent in these matters; give yourself wholly to them, so that everyone may see your progress. [16] Watch your life and doctrine closely. Persevere in them, because if you do, you will save both yourself and your hearers.

Widows, Elders and Slaves

5 Do not rebuke an older man harshly, but exhort him as if he were your father. Treat younger men as brothers, [2] older women as mothers, and younger women as sisters, with absolute purity.

[3] Give proper recognition to those widows who are really in need. [4] But if a widow has children or grandchildren, these should learn first of all to put their religion into practice by caring for their own family and so repaying their parents and grandparents, for this is pleasing to God. [5] The widow who is really in need and left all alone puts her hope in God and continues night and day to pray and to ask God for help. [6] But the widow who lives for pleasure is dead even while she lives. [7] Give the people these instructions, so that no one may be open to blame. [8] Anyone who does not provide for their relatives, and especially for their own household, has denied the faith and is worse than an unbeliever.

[9] No widow may be put on the list of widows unless she is over sixty, has been faithful to her husband, [10] and is well known for her good deeds, such as bringing up children, showing hospitality, washing the feet of the Lord's people, helping those in trouble and devoting herself to all kinds of good deeds.

[11] As for younger widows, do not put them on such a list. For when their sensual desires overcome their dedication to Christ, they want to marry. [12] Thus they bring judgment on themselves, because they have broken their first pledge. [13] Besides, they get into the habit of being idle and going about from house to house. And not only do they become idlers, but also busybodies who talk nonsense, saying things they ought not to. [14] So I counsel younger widows to marry, to have children, to manage their homes and to give the enemy no opportunity for slander. [15] Some have in fact already turned away to follow Satan.

[16] If any woman who is a believer has widows in her care, she should continue to help them and not let the church be burdened with them, so that the church can help those widows who are really in need.

[17] The elders who direct the affairs of the church well are worthy of double honor, especially those whose work is preaching and teaching. [18] For Scripture says, "Do not muzzle an ox while it is treading out the grain,"[a] and "The worker deserves his wages."[b] [19] Do not entertain an accusation against an elder unless it is brought by two or three witnesses. [20] But those elders who are sinning you are to reprove before everyone, so that the others may take warning. [21] I charge you, in the sight of God and Christ Jesus and the elect angels, to keep these instructions without partiality, and to do nothing out of favoritism.

[22] Do not be hasty in the laying on of hands, and do not share in the sins of others. Keep yourself pure.

[23] Stop drinking only water, and use a little wine because of your stomach and your frequent illnesses.

[24] The sins of some are obvious, reaching the place of judgment ahead of them; the sins of others trail behind them. [25] In the same way, good deeds are obvious, and even those that are not obvious cannot remain hidden forever.

6 All who are under the yoke of slavery should consider their masters worthy of full respect, so that God's name and our teaching may not be slandered. [2] Those who have believing masters should not show them disrespect just because they are fellow believers. Instead, they should serve them even better because their masters are dear to them as fellow believers and are devoted to the welfare[c] of their slaves.

---

[a] 18 Deut. 25:4 [b] 18 Luke 10:7 [c] 2 Or *and benefit from the service*

YOUNG AND HUNGRY

READ: 1 TIMOTHY 4:12

Some sales people stare you down like you're plotting to steal the store. Some teachers severely underestimate your abilities and aspirations. Some people don't bother to understand the marvelous things happening in your adolescent brain. But the Lord has a staggeringly high view of you. He never puts you down because of your age. He even gives you a way to silence people who glance at you sideways because you're not yet an adult.

Timothy was a young disciple when he met the apostle Paul, a man who would serve as his mentor and ministry partner as long as the apostle lived (Acts 16:1). Timothy joined Paul on his mission trips across the Mediterranean (v. 4). By the time Paul wrote him this letter, he was no longer a kid. In those days "young" (1 Timothy 4:12) was a word used to describe men as old as forty. Timothy still has to prove himself to people who look down on him because of his age. So Paul tells his youngish friend to make his life a model for everyone to follow. He should set an example in his words and actions. He should display maturity in "love," his sacrifices for others; in "faith," his trust in God; and in "purity," his obedience to God's sexual standards in both actions and thoughts.

You can't control the fact that some adults look at you harshly. But you can challenge and change what they see.

BUILDING FAITH WISDOM STRENGTH

False Teachers and the Love of Money

These are the things you are to teach and insist on. [3] If anyone teaches otherwise and does not agree to the sound instruction of our Lord Jesus Christ and to godly teaching, [4] they are conceited and understand nothing. They have an unhealthy interest in controversies and quarrels about words that result in envy, strife, malicious talk, evil suspicions [5] and constant friction between people of corrupt mind, who have been robbed of the truth and who think that godliness is a means to financial gain.

[6] But godliness with contentment is great gain. [7] For we brought nothing into the world, and we can take nothing out of it. [8] But if we have food and clothing, we will be content with that. [9] Those who want to get rich fall into temptation and a trap and into many foolish and harmful desires that plunge people into ruin and destruction. [10] For the love of money is a root of all kinds of evil. Some people, eager for money, have wandered from the faith and pierced themselves with many griefs.

Final Charge to Timothy

[11] But you, man of God, flee from all this, and pursue righteousness, godliness, faith, love, endurance and gentleness. [12] Fight the good fight of the faith. Take hold of the eternal life to which you were called when you made your good confession in the presence of many witnesses. [13] In the sight of God, who gives life to everything, and of Christ Jesus, who while testifying before Pontius Pilate made the good confession, I charge you [14] to keep this command without spot or blame until the appearing of our Lord Jesus Christ, [15] which God will bring about in his own time — God, the blessed and only Ruler, the King of kings and Lord of lords, [16] who alone is immortal and who lives in unapproachable light, whom no one has seen or can see. To him be honor and might forever. Amen.

[17] Command those who are rich in this present world not to be arrogant nor to put their hope in wealth, which is so uncertain, but to put their hope in God, who richly provides us with everything for our enjoyment. [18] Command them to do good, to be rich in good deeds, and to be generous and willing to share. [19] In this way they will lay up treasure for themselves as a firm foundation for the coming age, so that they may take hold of the life that is truly life.

[20] Timothy, guard what has been entrusted to your care. Turn away from godless chatter and the opposing ideas of what is falsely called knowledge, [21] which some have professed and in so doing have departed from the faith.

Grace be with you all.

2 TIMOTHY

WHEN DID THIS HAPPEN?

Around A.D. 67 in Rome

WHO IS IN THIS BOOK?

Paul

Timothy

Lois

Eunice

Onesiphorus

Phygelus

Alexander

VERSES YOU MIGHT RECOGNIZE

2 TIMOTHY 3:16

"All Scripture is God-breathed and is useful for teaching, rebuking, correcting and training in righteousness."

2 TIMOTHY 4:7

"I have fought the good fight, I have finished the race, I have kept the faith."

WHAT'S IT ABOUT?

About four years after Timothy began ministering to the church in Ephesus, Paul sent him a second letter. This time, Paul was writing from a prison in Rome where he would soon be killed for his faith. He instructed Timothy in how to carry on by protecting sound doctrine, encouraging believers to live for Christ and continuing to spread the gospel. Paul even provided a list of some of the people who had been helpful to him and others who had caused trouble.

Though hard times would come for Timothy, Paul urged him to continue in the faith he had been taught, not only by Paul, but also by his mother and grandmother. Timothy could draw upon this spiritual heritage to strengthen and encourage others.

Paul repeated the phrase "fight the good fight" from 1 Timothy 6:12, but this time he turned it on himself: "I have fought the good fight, I have finished the race, I have kept the faith" (2 Timothy 4:7). The older man also reaffirmed the authority of Scripture. Because of Paul's example, Timothy knew it was possible to stay strong in your faith throughout your whole life.

1 Paul, an apostle of Christ Jesus by the will of God, in keeping with the promise of life that is in Christ Jesus,

²To Timothy, my dear son:

Grace, mercy and peace from God the Father and Christ Jesus our Lord.

Thanksgiving

³I thank God, whom I serve, as my ancestors did, with a clear conscience, as night and day I constantly remember you in my prayers. ⁴Recalling your tears, I long to see you, so that I may be filled with joy. ⁵I am reminded of your sincere faith, which first lived in your grandmother Lois and in your mother Eunice and, I am persuaded, now lives in you also.

Appeal for Loyalty to Paul and the Gospel

⁶For this reason I remind you to fan into flame the gift of God, which is in you through the laying on of my hands. ⁷For the Spirit God gave us does not make us timid, but gives us power, love and self-discipline. ⁸So do not be ashamed of the testimony about our Lord or of me his prisoner. Rather, join with me in suffering for the gospel, by the power of God. ⁹He has saved us and called us to a holy life — not because of anything we have done but because of his own purpose and grace. This grace was given us in Christ Jesus before the beginning of time, ¹⁰but it has now been revealed through the appearing of our Savior, Christ Jesus, who has destroyed death and has brought life and immortality to light through the gospel. ¹¹And of this gospel I was appointed a herald and an apostle and a teacher. ¹²That is why I am suffering as I am. Yet this is no cause for shame, because I know whom I have believed, and am convinced that he is able to guard what I have entrusted to him until that day.

¹³What you heard from me, keep as the pattern of sound teaching, with faith and love in Christ Jesus. ¹⁴Guard the good deposit that was entrusted to you — guard it with the help of the Holy Spirit who lives in us.

Examples of Disloyalty and Loyalty

¹⁵You know that everyone in the province of Asia has deserted me, including Phygelus and Hermogenes.

¹⁶May the Lord show mercy to the household of Onesiphorus, because he often refreshed me and was not ashamed of my chains. ¹⁷On the contrary, when he was in Rome, he searched hard for me until he found me. ¹⁸May the Lord grant that he will find mercy from the Lord on that day! You know very well in how many ways he helped me in Ephesus.

The Appeal Renewed

2 You then, my son, be strong in the grace that is in Christ Jesus. ²And the things you have heard me say in the presence of many witnesses entrust to reliable people who will also be qualified to teach others. ³Join with me in suffering, like a good soldier of Christ Jesus. ⁴No one serving as a soldier gets entangled in civilian affairs, but rather tries to please his commanding officer. ⁵Similarly, anyone who competes as an athlete does not receive the victor's crown except by competing according to the rules. ⁶The hardworking farmer should be the first to receive a share of the crops. ⁷Reflect on what I am saying, for the Lord will give you insight into all this.

⁸Remember Jesus Christ, raised from the dead, descended from David. This is my gospel, ⁹for which I am suffering even to the point of being chained like a criminal. But God's word is not chained. ¹⁰Therefore I endure everything for the sake of the elect, that they too may obtain the salvation that is in Christ Jesus, with eternal glory.

¹¹Here is a trustworthy saying:

TIMOTHY

I am reminded of your sincere faith, which first lived in your grandmother Lois and in your mother Eunice and, I am persuaded, now lives in you also. 2 TIMOTHY 1:5

HIS NAME MEANS: "honoring God"

READ HIS STORY: *Acts 16:1–5, 18:5–6, 20:1–6; 1 Timothy 1:1–7; 2 Timothy 1:1–8, 3:10–17*

OF THE BIBLE

Paul wrote two letters to Timothy that became part of the Bible. Timothy was probably a teenager when he met Paul, most likely when the evangelist was nearly killed in Lystra (Acts 14:8–23). Timothy's family stood out for its faith. Paul knew Timothy had studied the Scriptures as a child (2 Timothy 3:15). He helped Timothy understand that Jesus was the promised Messiah, who came to forgive the sins of those who believed. Timothy accepted the truth. At the beginning of Paul's second missionary journey, he went back to Lystra and invited Timothy to travel with him to tell people the good news about Jesus Christ (Acts 16:1–5).

The duo worked well together. Early in their ministry, they saw churches grow and people strengthened in their faith. Together, they set up churches in Philippi, Thessalonica and Berea. But stepping out didn't come without persecution. Just like Paul, Timothy was abused for talking about Jesus.

Despite hardships, including helping Paul while he was in prison in Rome for two years, Timothy stayed committed to the cause of communicating Christian truth. Paul often gave Timothy difficult assignments, such as building up a backsliding church or comforting Christians who were being persecuted. Throughout Timothy's life, he lived up to Paul's encouragement to set an example—regardless of his age.

OLDER AND YOUNGER

READ: 2 TIMOTHY 1:5

God talks to us all the time. He is called Wonderful Counselor for a reason. He doesn't just speak through hundred-year-old theology books. He'll also speak to you through other kids who will hit you between the eyes. Through the body, through community and being around Pauls and Timothys, you dig deep into your spiritual roots. Timothy devoted his life to Jesus Christ through the ministry of the apostle Paul. The New Testament outlines how Paul discipled Timothy and continued to encourage and instruct him even after Timothy became the pastor of the church at Ephesus.

BUILDING

FAITH

WISDOM

STRENGTH

We all need some Pauls in our lives. Pauls are people who challenge us and earn the right with their lives to talk to us. They're further along spiritually than we are and have deeper roots than we do. Who are your Pauls?

We all need Timothys too. We need to pour into others. You'll be amazed what you learn from your Timothys. They bring a fresh perspective. They often regurgitate uncomfortable reminders like, "You said God can do anything, right?"

Just as God will use you as a Paul in someone's life, he'll also use your Timothys to help keep you focused on him and vibrant in ministry. One feeds off the other. One helps the other. Both love each other. All of it glorifies Jesus.

It honors God when we do something bigger than ourselves and need each other to do it.

Taken from *Thrive Student Edition* by Mark Hall with Tim Luke, copyright © 2014 by Mark Hall, published by Zondervan.

If we died with him,
  we will also live with him;
[12] if we endure,
  we will also reign with him.
If we disown him,
  he will also disown us;
[13] if we are faithless,
  he remains faithful,
  for he cannot disown himself.

Dealing With False Teachers

[14] Keep reminding God's people of these things. Warn them before God against quarreling about words; it is of no value, and only ruins those who listen. [15] Do your best to present yourself to God as one approved, a worker who does not need to be ashamed and who correctly handles the word of truth. [16] Avoid godless chatter, because those who indulge in it will become more and more ungodly. [17] Their teaching will spread like gangrene. Among them are Hymenaeus and Philetus, [18] who have departed from the truth. They say that the resurrection has already taken place, and they destroy the faith of some. [19] Nevertheless, God's solid foundation stands firm, sealed with this inscription: "The Lord knows those who are his," and, "Everyone who confesses the name of the Lord must turn away from wickedness."

[20] In a large house there are articles not only of gold and silver, but also of wood and clay; some are for special purposes and some for common use. [21] Those who cleanse themselves from the latter will be instruments for special purposes, made holy, useful to the Master and prepared to do any good work.

[22] Flee the evil desires of youth and pursue righteousness, faith, love and peace, along with those who call on the Lord out of a pure heart. [23] Don't have anything to do with foolish and stupid arguments, because you know they produce quarrels. [24] And the Lord's servant must not be quarrelsome but must be kind to everyone, able to teach, not resentful. [25] Opponents must be gently instructed, in the hope that God will grant them repentance leading them to a knowledge of the truth, [26] and that they will come to their senses and escape from the trap of the devil, who has taken them captive to do his will.

3 But mark this: There will be terrible times in the last days. [2] People will be lovers of themselves, lovers of money, boastful, proud, abusive, disobedient to their parents, ungrateful, unholy, [3] without love, unforgiving, slanderous, without self-control, brutal, not lovers of the good, [4] treacherous, rash, conceited, lovers of pleasure rather than lovers of God— [5] having a form of godliness but denying its power. Have nothing to do with such people.

[6] They are the kind who worm their way into homes and gain control over gullible women, who are loaded down with sins and are swayed by all kinds of evil desires, [7] always learning but never able to come to a knowledge of the truth. [8] Just as Jannes and Jambres opposed Moses, so also these teachers oppose the truth. They are men of depraved minds, who, as far as the faith is concerned, are rejected. [9] But they will not get very far because, as in the case of those men, their folly will be clear to everyone.

A Final Charge to Timothy

[10] You, however, know all about my teaching, my way of life, my purpose, faith, patience, love, endurance, [11] persecutions, sufferings—what kinds of things happened to me in Antioch, Iconium and Lystra, the persecutions I endured. Yet the Lord rescued me from all of them. [12] In fact, everyone who wants to live a godly life in Christ Jesus will be persecuted, [13] while evildoers and impostors will go from bad to worse, deceiving and being deceived. [14] But as for you, continue in what you have learned and have become convinced of, because you know those from whom you learned it, [15] and how from infancy you have known the Holy Scriptures, which are able to make you wise for salvation through faith in Christ Jesus. [16] All Scripture is God-breathed and is useful for teaching, rebuking, correcting and training in righteousness, [17] so that the servant of God[a] may be thoroughly equipped for every good work.

4 In the presence of God and of Christ Jesus, who will judge the living and the dead, and in view of his appearing and his kingdom, I give you this charge: [2] Preach the word; be prepared in season and out of

---

[a] 17 Or *that you, a man of God,*

STRANGE SYMBOL

READ: 2 TIMOTHY 3:12

Before crucifying a criminal, it was common for the Romans to beat them the way they did Jesus. For this scourging, the man was stripped of his clothing, and his hands were tied most often to an upright post. The person would have their hands tied around a post so that the flesh on their body would be stretched out tightly in preparation for the scourging. The number of lashes wasn't what the Romans paid attention to; they were experts in beating a person just to the edge of death.

After beating a criminal beyond recognition, the Roman soldiers put the horizontal beam of the cross on the man's back. Perhaps some of the vertebrae were exposed from the flogging. This 125-pound beam was placed on his open wounds. It's no wonder Jesus had a difficult time carrying the cross as he stumbled down the narrow roads of the Via Dolarosa (or the Way of Suffering).

Taking up your cross and following Jesus can and will bring pain and suffering. You can't carry a cross without suffering. There is no comfortable way to carry a cross; I don't care how you position it.

I often talk to people who are convinced that some suffering or pain in their lives is an indication that they must not be following Jesus. The biblical reality is that when people say yes to following Jesus, they are agreeing to carry a cross, and that will be painful at times.

BUILDING FAITH WISDOM STRENGTH

Taken from *Not a Fan Student Edition* by Kyle Idleman, copyright © 2012 by City on the Hill Studio, Inc., published by Zondervan.

season; correct, rebuke and encourage — with great patience and careful instruction. [3] For the time will come when people will not put up with sound doctrine. Instead, to suit their own desires, they will gather around them a great number of teachers to say what their itching ears want to hear. [4] They will turn their ears away from the truth and turn aside to myths. [5] But you, keep your head in all situations, endure hardship, do the work of an evangelist, discharge all the duties of your ministry.

[6] For I am already being poured out like a drink offering, and the time for my departure is near. [7] I have fought the good fight, I have finished the race, I have kept the faith. [8] Now there is in store for me the crown of righteousness, which the Lord, the righteous Judge, will award to me on that day — and not only to me, but also to all who have longed for his appearing.

Personal Remarks

[9] Do your best to come to me quickly, [10] for Demas, because he loved this world, has deserted me and has gone to Thessalonica. Crescens has gone to Galatia, and Titus to Dalmatia. [11] Only Luke is with me. Get Mark and bring him with you, because he is helpful to me in my ministry. [12] I sent Tychicus to Ephesus. [13] When you come, bring the cloak that I left with Carpus at Troas, and my scrolls, especially the parchments.

[14] Alexander the metalworker did me a great deal of harm. The Lord will repay him for what he has done. [15] You too should be on your guard against him, because he strongly opposed our message.

[16] At my first defense, no one came to my support, but everyone deserted me. May it not be held against them. [17] But the Lord stood at my side and gave me strength, so that through me the message might be fully proclaimed and all the Gentiles might hear it. And I was delivered from the lion's mouth. [18] The Lord will rescue me from every evil attack and will bring me safely to his heavenly kingdom. To him be glory for ever and ever. Amen.

Final Greetings

[19] Greet Priscilla[a] and Aquila and the household of Onesiphorus. [20] Erastus stayed in Corinth, and I left Trophimus sick in Miletus. [21] Do your best to get here before winter. Eubulus greets you, and so do Pudens, Linus, Claudia and all the brothers and sisters.[b]

[22] The Lord be with your spirit. Grace be with you all.

---

[a] 19 Greek *Prisca*, a variant of *Priscilla*   [b] 21 The Greek word for *brothers and sisters* (*adelphoi*) refers here to believers, both men and women, as part of God's family.

TITUS

WHEN DID THIS HAPPEN?

Around A.D. 64 in Ephesus

WHO IS IN THIS BOOK?

Paul

Titus

VERSES YOU MIGHT RECOGNIZE

TITUS 2:11

"For the grace of God has appeared that offers salvation to all people."

TITUS 3:5

"He saved us, not because of righteous things we had done, but because of his mercy. He saved us through the washing of rebirth and renewal by the Holy Spirit."

WHAT'S IT ABOUT?

After Paul commissioned Titus to lead the churches on the island of Crete, he wrote him a letter instructing him on how to be a leader. Paul tells him that his top priority should be teaching sound doctrine. He focuses specifically on the doctrine of the incarnation of Jesus Christ—God becoming human to offer salvation to all people—and how that should cause believers to live "upright and godly lives." Paul makes it clear that God's grace must be the motivation for good deeds.

Paul also tells Titus how to teach different groups of people, such as older men, younger men, older women, younger women and slaves. Titus had known Paul for fifteen years and had probably accompanied him on his third missionary journey. As Paul was nearing the end of his life, he began training younger men, such as Titus and Timothy, to carry on the ministry of the gospel after he was gone.

TITUS

1 Paul, a servant of God and an apostle of Jesus Christ to further the faith of God's elect and their knowledge of the truth that leads to godliness— [2]in the hope of eternal life, which God, who does not lie, promised before the beginning of time, [3]and which now at his appointed season he has brought to light through the preaching entrusted to me by the command of God our Savior,

[4]To Titus, my true son in our common faith:

Grace and peace from God the Father and Christ Jesus our Savior.

Appointing Elders Who Love What Is Good

[5]The reason I left you in Crete was that you might put in order what was left unfinished and appoint[a] elders in every town, as I directed you. [6]An elder must be blameless, faithful to his wife, a man whose children believe[b] and are not open to the charge of being wild and disobedient. [7]Since an overseer manages God's household, he must be blameless—not overbearing, not quick-tempered, not given to drunkenness, not violent, not pursuing dishonest gain. [8]Rather, he must be hospitable, one who loves what is good, who is self-controlled, upright, holy and disciplined. [9]He must hold firmly to the trustworthy message as it has been taught, so that he can encourage others by sound doctrine and refute those who oppose it.

Rebuking Those Who Fail to Do Good

[10]For there are many rebellious people, full of meaningless talk and deception, especially those of the circumcision group. [11]They must be silenced, because they are disrupting whole households by teaching things they ought not to teach—and that for the sake of dishonest gain. [12]One of Crete's own prophets has said it: "Cretans are always liars, evil brutes, lazy gluttons."[c] [13]This saying is true. Therefore rebuke them sharply, so that they will be sound in the faith [14]and will pay no attention to Jewish myths or to the merely human commands of those who reject the truth. [15]To the pure, all things are pure, but to those who are corrupted and do not believe, nothing is pure. In fact, both their minds and consciences are corrupted. [16]They claim to know God, but by their actions they deny him. They are detestable, disobedient and unfit for doing anything good.

Doing Good for the Sake of the Gospel

2 You, however, must teach what is appropriate to sound doctrine. [2]Teach the older men to be temperate, worthy of respect, self-controlled, and sound in faith, in love and in endurance.

[3]Likewise, teach the older women to be reverent in the way they live, not to be slanderers or addicted to much wine, but to teach what is good. [4]Then they can urge the younger women to love their husbands and children, [5]to be self-controlled and pure, to be busy at home, to be kind, and to be subject to their husbands, so that no one will malign the word of God.

[6]Similarly, encourage the young men to be self-controlled. [7]In everything set them an example by doing what is good. In your teaching show integrity, seriousness [8]and soundness of speech that cannot be condemned, so that those who oppose you may be ashamed because they have nothing bad to say about us.

[9]Teach slaves to be subject to their masters in everything, to try to please them, not to talk back to them, [10]and not to steal from them, but to show that they can be fully trusted, so that in every way they will make the teaching about God our Savior attractive.

[11]For the grace of God has appeared that offers salvation to all people. [12]It teaches us

---

[a] 5 Or ordain   [b] 6 Or children are trustworthy   [c] 12 From the Cretan philosopher Epimenides

CASTAWAY

READ: TITUS 2:11-12

Titus must have thought he was on the wrong end of a prank. The apostle Paul left this guy behind on the island of Crete, instructing him to put everything in order by organizing and pastoring a church eager to follow Jesus. But the people of the island were famous across the Mediterranean for their violent crudeness. The Cretan poet Epimenides even said his fellow islanders were "always liars, evil brutes, lazy gluttons" (Titus 1:12).

Against those odds, God has a plan to remake this island of pirates and thugs. Titus is to start by picking leaders who live up to Jesus' teaching. He should silence false teachers who are spreading lies. And he must deliver hard-hitting practical teaching to every kind of person in his church.

BUILDING FAITH WISDOM STRENGTH

The Lord has reason to be confident the Cretans can be transformed. Out of his limitless kindness he offers to save anyone who believes, giving them a forever home in heaven. But his grace also teaches them to say no to cravings of people set against God. It changes them inwardly, so they have self-control; outwardly, so they act uprightly toward others; and upwardly, so their godly lives are totally committed to him. God knows how to change even the most stubborn people. He rescues you from the ugliest bad habits and makes you eager to do what's good.

to say "No" to ungodliness and worldly passions, and to live self-controlled, upright and godly lives in this present age, [13]while we wait for the blessed hope — the appearing of the glory of our great God and Savior, Jesus Christ, [14]who gave himself for us to redeem us from all wickedness and to purify for himself a people that are his very own, eager to do what is good.

[15]These, then, are the things you should teach. Encourage and rebuke with all authority. Do not let anyone despise you.

Saved in Order to Do Good

3 Remind the people to be subject to rulers and authorities, to be obedient, to be ready to do whatever is good, [2]to slander no one, to be peaceable and considerate, and always to be gentle toward everyone.

[3]At one time we too were foolish, disobedient, deceived and enslaved by all kinds of passions and pleasures. We lived in malice and envy, being hated and hating one another. [4]But when the kindness and love of God our Savior appeared, [5]he saved us, not because of righteous things we had done, but because of his mercy. He saved us through the washing of rebirth and renewal by the Holy Spirit, [6]whom he poured out on us generously through Jesus Christ our Savior, [7]so that, having been justified by his grace, we might become heirs having the hope of eternal life. [8]This is a trustworthy saying. And I want you to stress these things, so that those who have trusted in God may be careful to devote themselves to doing what is good. These things are excellent and profitable for everyone.

[9]But avoid foolish controversies and genealogies and arguments and quarrels about the law, because these are unprofitable and useless. [10]Warn a divisive person once, and then warn them a second time. After that, have nothing to do with them. [11]You may be sure that such people are warped and sinful; they are self-condemned.

Final Remarks

[12]As soon as I send Artemas or Tychicus to you, do your best to come to me at Nicopolis, because I have decided to winter there. [13]Do everything you can to help Zenas the lawyer and Apollos on their way and see that they have everything they need. [14]Our people must learn to devote themselves to doing what is good, in order to provide for urgent needs and not live unproductive lives.

[15]Everyone with me sends you greetings. Greet those who love us in the faith.

Grace be with you all.

PHILEMON

 WHEN DID THIS HAPPEN?

Around A.D. 60 in Rome

 WHO IS IN THIS BOOK?

Paul

Onesimus

Philemon

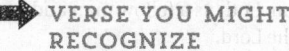 **VERSE YOU MIGHT RECOGNIZE**

PHILEMON 1:6

"I pray that your partnership with us in the faith may be effective in deepening your understanding of every good thing we share for the sake of Christ."

WHAT'S IT ABOUT?

Paul wrote this letter to Philemon, the owner of a runaway slave named Onesimus. Philemon lived in Colossae and had come to know the Lord through Paul. After Onesimus ran away from his master to Rome, he also became a Christian with Paul's guidance and had to return to his master to make things right. Paul sent him with a letter, asking Philemon to forgive Onesimus and accept him as a brother in Christ.

Philemon, which was written at the same time as Ephesians and Colossians, shows that God takes a personal interest in the details of our lives, including relationships with others. The gospel is practical for whatever we face.

Paul presented a powerful picture of the meaning of forgiveness and Christian brotherhood as he urged Philemon to embrace Onesimus as a fellow believer. Paul asked Philemon to show his runaway slave the same love he himself experienced from Christ.

PHILEMON

¹Paul, a prisoner of Christ Jesus, and Timothy our brother,

To Philemon our dear friend and fellow worker— ²also to Apphia our sister and Archippus our fellow soldier—and to the church that meets in your home:

³Grace and peace to you*ᵃ* from God our Father and the Lord Jesus Christ.

Thanksgiving and Prayer

⁴I always thank my God as I remember you in my prayers, ⁵because I hear about your love for all his holy people and your faith in the Lord Jesus. ⁶I pray that your partnership with us in the faith may be effective in deepening your understanding of every good thing we share for the sake of Christ. ⁷Your love has given me great joy and encouragement, because you, brother, have refreshed the hearts of the Lord's people.

Paul's Plea for Onesimus

⁸Therefore, although in Christ I could be bold and order you to do what you ought to do, ⁹yet I prefer to appeal to you on the basis of love. It is as none other than Paul—an old man and now also a prisoner of Christ Jesus— ¹⁰that I appeal to you for my son Onesimus,*ᵇ* who became my son while I was in chains. ¹¹Formerly he was useless to you, but now he has become useful both to you and to me.

¹²I am sending him—who is my very heart—back to you. ¹³I would have liked to keep him with me so that he could take your place in helping me while I am in chains for the gospel. ¹⁴But I did not want to do anything without your consent, so that any favor you do would not seem forced but would be voluntary. ¹⁵Perhaps the reason he was separated from you for a little while was that you might have him back forever— ¹⁶no longer as a slave, but better than a slave, as a dear brother. He is very dear to me but even dearer to you, both as a fellow man and as a brother in the Lord.

¹⁷So if you consider me a partner, welcome him as you would welcome me. ¹⁸If he has done you any wrong or owes you anything, charge it to me. ¹⁹I, Paul, am writing this with my own hand. I will pay it back— not to mention that you owe me your very self. ²⁰I do wish, brother, that I may have some benefit from you in the Lord; refresh my heart in Christ. ²¹Confident of your obedience, I write to you, knowing that you will do even more than I ask.

²²And one thing more: Prepare a guest room for me, because I hope to be restored to you in answer to your prayers.

²³Epaphras, my fellow prisoner in Christ Jesus, sends you greetings. ²⁴And so do Mark, Aristarchus, Demas and Luke, my fellow workers.

²⁵The grace of the Lord Jesus Christ be with your spirit.

ᵃ 3 The Greek is plural; also in verses 22 and 25; elsewhere in this letter "you" is singular.
ᵇ 10 Onesimus means *useful.*

PHILEMON AND ONESIMUS

I always thank my God as I remember you in my prayers, because I hear about your love for all his holy people and your faith in the Lord Jesus. PHILEMON 4-5

THEIR NAMES MEAN: Philemon—"loving," Onesimus—"useful"

READ THEIR STORY: *Philemon*

Philemon and Onesimus will forever be linked through the apostle Paul's letter, written from prison in Rome. Philemon was a rich, influential man who lived in Colossae. Onesimus was his runaway slave.

At some time and place in the past, Paul evidently led Philemon to believe in Jesus, and understand the forgiveness found in Christ. Philemon had then become a leader in the church, hosting meetings in his home. He was generous with his wealth, welcoming in fellow believers. Although Paul had never been to Colossae, he heard about Philemon's kindness and service to God's people.

Onesimus had made his way to Rome, where he met Paul and believed in Jesus as his Savior. He helped Paul in prison. Now Paul was sending Onesimus back to Philemon—not as a slave, but as a brother in Christ.

We don't know the conversation that took place between Philemon and Onesimus when he showed up with Paul's letter. At first, Philemon probably wasn't too happy to see him. Slaves were considered property and running away wasn't tolerated. Philemon could have had Onesimus whipped or even killed. Instead, Philemon surely forgave Onesimus. One church history tradition says that Onesimus was freed as a slave, becoming a great ambassador for Christ and a church leader . . . all because Philemon chose to forgive, just as Christ had forgiven him.

HEBREWS

WHEN DID THIS HAPPEN?

Around A.D. 68 in Rome

WHO IS IN THIS BOOK?

Jesus

Moses

Melchizedek

Abraham

VERSES YOU MIGHT RECOGNIZE

HEBREWS 11:1

"Now faith is confidence in what we hope for and assurance about what we do not see."

HEBREWS 12:1

"Therefore, since we are surrounded by such a great cloud of witnesses, let us throw off everything that hinders and the sin that so easily entangles. And let us run with perseverance the race marked out for us."

WHAT'S IT ABOUT?

This book was written for Jewish Christians who were wondering if they should give up their new faith in Christ and return to their old Jewish practices. The author, who is unknown, shows that Jesus is superior to anything found in the old covenant. As High Priest, he perfectly fulfilled the Law of Moses. He is superior to angels, a better sacrifice than bulls and lambs, and he offers a better hope and inheritance. Hebrews tells us that Jesus' sacrifice is perfect and once for all.

At this time in history, some Christians were facing persecution under the cruel emperor Nero. This was causing them to question their faith. The author of Hebrews provided a list of great men and women of the Old Testament who stood strong in their faith, including Noah, Abraham, Sarah, Moses, and even Rahab. This list reminded its readers that they were in good company and that their faith should be based on their hope in Christ—the perfect Messiah—rather than on what they could see.

God's Final Word: His Son

1 In the past God spoke to our ancestors through the prophets at many times and in various ways, ²but in these last days he has spoken to us by his Son, whom he appointed heir of all things, and through whom also he made the universe. ³The Son is the radiance of God's glory and the exact representation of his being, sustaining all things by his powerful word. After he had provided purification for sins, he sat down at the right hand of the Majesty in heaven. ⁴So he became as much superior to the angels as the name he has inherited is superior to theirs.

The Son Superior to Angels

⁵For to which of the angels did God ever say,

"You are my Son;
today I have become your Father"[a]?

Or again,

"I will be his Father,
and he will be my Son"[b]?

⁶And again, when God brings his firstborn into the world, he says,

"Let all God's angels worship him."[c]

⁷In speaking of the angels he says,

"He makes his angels spirits,
and his servants flames of fire."[d]

⁸But about the Son he says,

"Your throne, O God, will last for ever
and ever;
a scepter of justice will be the scepter
of your kingdom.
⁹You have loved righteousness and hated
wickedness;
therefore God, your God, has set you
above your companions
by anointing you with the oil of joy."[e]

¹⁰He also says,

"In the beginning, Lord, you laid the
foundations of the earth,
and the heavens are the work of your
hands.
¹¹They will perish, but you remain;
they will all wear out like a garment.
¹²You will roll them up like a robe;
like a garment they will be changed.
But you remain the same,
and your years will never end."[f]

¹³To which of the angels did God ever say,

"Sit at my right hand
until I make your enemies
a footstool for your feet"[g]?

¹⁴Are not all angels ministering spirits sent to serve those who will inherit salvation?

Warning to Pay Attention

2 We must pay the most careful attention, therefore, to what we have heard, so that we do not drift away. ²For since the message spoken through angels was binding, and every violation and disobedience received its just punishment, ³how shall we escape if we ignore so great a salvation? This salvation, which was first announced by the Lord, was confirmed to us by those who heard him. ⁴God also testified to it by signs, wonders and various miracles, and by gifts of the Holy Spirit distributed according to his will.

Jesus Made Fully Human

⁵It is not to angels that he has subjected the world to come, about which we are speaking. ⁶But there is a place where someone has testified:

"What is mankind that you are mindful
of them,
a son of man that you care for him?

---

[a] 5 Psalm 2:7   [b] 5 2 Samuel 7:14; 1 Chron. 17:13   [c] 6 Deut. 32:43 (see Dead Sea Scrolls and Septuagint)
[d] 7 Psalm 104:4   [e] 9 Psalm 45:6,7   [f] 12 Psalm 102:25-27   [g] 13 Psalm 110:1

MAKING CONNECTIONS

READ: HEBREWS 1:1-2

If you struggle to see the connection between the Old Testament and the New Testament, Hebrews is your book. While you might occasionally get turned around as you wander its pages, this is the most detailed information ever for making sense of how Jesus perfectly fulfills everything you read in the front part of your Bible.

No one knows who wrote Hebrews, though for centuries scholars have suggested possible authors including Apollos (Acts 18:24), Priscilla (v. 2), and Barnabas (4:36). Although the book is anonymous, it's obvious the author doesn't want you to miss the fact that Jesus reveals the one real God.

The author begins with the news that the Lord spoke throughout history through the prophets "at many times and in various ways," but now "he has spoken to us by his Son" (Hebrews 1:1-2). The universe was made through Jesus, and he is "the radiance of God's glory and the exact representation of his being" (v. 3). His throne "will last for ever and ever" (v. 8).

BUILDING

FAITH

WISDOM

STRENGTH

That's just the start of this book's portrait of who Jesus is and what he accomplished. He's the one who "provided purification for sins" and "sat down at the right hand of the Majesty in heaven" (v. 3). If you want to learn more about the Jesus you strive to know and follow, press on into these pages.

[7] You made them a little[a] lower than
the angels;
you crowned them with glory and
honor
[8] and put everything under their feet."[b,c]

In putting everything under them,[d] God left
nothing that is not subject to them.[d] Yet at
present we do not see everything subject to
them.[d] [9] But we do see Jesus, who was made
lower than the angels for a little while, now
crowned with glory and honor because he
suffered death, so that by the grace of God
he might taste death for everyone.

[10] In bringing many sons and daughters to
glory, it was fitting that God, for whom and
through whom everything exists, should
make the pioneer of their salvation perfect
through what he suffered. [11] Both the one
who makes people holy and those who are
made holy are of the same family. So Jesus is
not ashamed to call them brothers and sisters.[e] [12] He says,

"I will declare your name to my brothers
and sisters;
in the assembly I will sing your
praises."[f]

[13] And again,

"I will put my trust in him."[g]

And again he says,

"Here am I, and the children God has
given me."[h]

[14] Since the children have flesh and blood,
he too shared in their humanity so that by
his death he might break the power of him
who holds the power of death — that is, the
devil — [15] and free those who all their lives
were held in slavery by their fear of death.
[16] For surely it is not angels he helps, but
Abraham's descendants. [17] For this reason
he had to be made like them,[i] fully human in
every way, in order that he might become a
merciful and faithful high priest in service to
God, and that he might make atonement for
the sins of the people. [18] Because he himself
suffered when he was tempted, he is able to
help those who are being tempted.

Jesus Greater Than Moses

3 Therefore, holy brothers and sisters,
who share in the heavenly calling, fix
your thoughts on Jesus, whom we acknowledge as our apostle and high priest. [2] He was
faithful to the one who appointed him, just
as Moses was faithful in all God's house.
[3] Jesus has been found worthy of greater honor than Moses, just as the builder of a house
has greater honor than the house itself. [4] For
every house is built by someone, but God is
the builder of everything. [5] "Moses was faithful as a servant in all God's house,"[j] bearing
witness to what would be spoken by God in
the future. [6] But Christ is faithful as the Son
over God's house. And we are his house, if indeed we hold firmly to our confidence and
the hope in which we glory.

Warning Against Unbelief

[7] So, as the Holy Spirit says:

"Today, if you hear his voice,
[8] do not harden your hearts
as you did in the rebellion,
during the time of testing in the
wilderness,
[9] where your ancestors tested and
tried me,
though for forty years they saw what
I did.
[10] That is why I was angry with that
generation;
I said, 'Their hearts are always going
astray,
and they have not known
my ways.'
[11] So I declared on oath in my anger,
'They shall never enter my rest.'"[k]

[12] See to it, brothers and sisters, that none
of you has a sinful, unbelieving heart that
turns away from the living God. [13] But encourage one another daily, as long as it is
called "Today," so that none of you may be
hardened by sin's deceitfulness. [14] We have
come to share in Christ, if indeed we hold
our original conviction firmly to the very
end. [15] As has just been said:

---

[a] 7 Or *them for a little while*   [b] 6-8 Psalm 8:4-6   [c] 7,8 Or *7You made him a little lower than the angels;/
you crowned him with glory and honor/ 8and put everything under his feet."*   [d] 8 Or *him*   [e] 11 The
Greek word for *brothers and sisters* (*adelphoi*) refers here to believers, both men and women, as part of
God's family; also in verse 12; and in 3:1, 12; 10:19; 13:22.   [f] 12 Psalm 22:22   [g] 13 Isaiah 8:17
[h] 13 Isaiah 8:18   [i] 17 Or *like his brothers*   [j] 5 Num. 12:7   [k] 11 Psalm 95:7-11

"Today, if you hear his voice,
  do not harden your hearts
    as you did in the rebellion."[a]

[16]Who were they who heard and rebelled? Were they not all those Moses led out of Egypt? [17]And with whom was he angry for forty years? Was it not with those who sinned, whose bodies perished in the wilderness? [18]And to whom did God swear that they would never enter his rest if not to those who disobeyed? [19]So we see that they were not able to enter, because of their unbelief.

A Sabbath-Rest for the People of God

4 Therefore, since the promise of entering his rest still stands, let us be careful that none of you be found to have fallen short of it. [2]For we also have had the good news proclaimed to us, just as they did; but the message they heard was of no value to them, because they did not share the faith of those who obeyed.[b] [3]Now we who have believed enter that rest, just as God has said,

"So I declared on oath in my anger,
  'They shall never enter my rest.'"[c]

And yet his works have been finished since the creation of the world. [4]For somewhere he has spoken about the seventh day in these words: "On the seventh day God rested from all his works."[d] [5]And again in the passage above he says, "They shall never enter my rest."

[6]Therefore since it still remains for some to enter that rest, and since those who formerly had the good news proclaimed to them did not go in because of their disobedience, [7]God again set a certain day, calling it "Today." This he did when a long time later he spoke through David, as in the passage already quoted:

"Today, if you hear his voice,
  do not harden your hearts."[a]

[8]For if Joshua had given them rest, God would not have spoken later about another day. [9]There remains, then, a Sabbath-rest for the people of God; [10]for anyone who enters God's rest also rests from their works,[e] just as

God did from his. [11]Let us, therefore, make every effort to enter that rest, so that no one will perish by following their example of disobedience.

[12]For the word of God is alive and active. Sharper than any double-edged sword, it penetrates even to dividing soul and spirit, joints and marrow; it judges the thoughts and attitudes of the heart. [13]Nothing in all creation is hidden from God's sight. Everything is uncovered and laid bare before the eyes of him to whom we must give account.

Jesus the Great High Priest

[14]Therefore, since we have a great high priest who has ascended into heaven,[f] Jesus the Son of God, let us hold firmly to the faith we profess. [15]For we do not have a high priest who is unable to empathize with our weaknesses, but we have one who has been tempted in every way, just as we are — yet he did not sin. [16]Let us then approach God's throne of grace with confidence, so that we may receive mercy and find grace to help us in our time of need.

5 Every high priest is selected from among the people and is appointed to represent the people in matters related to God, to offer gifts and sacrifices for sins. [2]He is able to deal gently with those who are ignorant and are going astray, since he himself is subject to weakness. [3]This is why he has to offer sacrifices for his own sins, as well as for the sins of the people. [4]And no one takes this honor on himself, but he receives it when called by God, just as Aaron was.

[5]In the same way, Christ did not take on himself the glory of becoming a high priest. But God said to him,

"You are my Son;
  today I have become your Father."[g]

[6]And he says in another place,

"You are a priest forever,
  in the order of Melchizedek."[h]

[7]During the days of Jesus' life on earth, he offered up prayers and petitions with fervent cries and tears to the one who could save him from death, and he was heard because of his reverent submission. [8]Son

---

a 15,7 Psalm 95:7,8   b 2 Some manuscripts *because those who heard did not combine it with faith*
c 3 Psalm 95:11; also in verse 5   d 4 Gen. 2:2   e 10 Or *labor*   f 14 Greek *has gone through the heavens*
g 5 Psalm 2:7   h 6 Psalm 110:4

though he was, he learned obedience from what he suffered [9]and, once made perfect, he became the source of eternal salvation for all who obey him [10]and was designated by God to be high priest in the order of Melchizedek.

Warning Against Falling Away

[11]We have much to say about this, but it is hard to make it clear to you because you no longer try to understand. [12]In fact, though by this time you ought to be teachers, you need someone to teach you the elementary truths of God's word all over again. You need milk, not solid food! [13]Anyone who lives on milk, being still an infant, is not acquainted with the teaching about righteousness. [14]But solid food is for the mature, who by constant use have trained themselves to distinguish good from evil.

6 Therefore let us move beyond the elementary teachings about Christ and be taken forward to maturity, not laying again the foundation of repentance from acts that lead to death,[a] and of faith in God, [2]instruction about cleansing rites,[b] the laying on of hands, the resurrection of the dead, and eternal judgment. [3]And God permitting, we will do so.

[4]It is impossible for those who have once been enlightened, who have tasted the heavenly gift, who have shared in the Holy Spirit, [5]who have tasted the goodness of the word of God and the powers of the coming age [6]and who have fallen[c] away, to be brought back to repentance. To their loss they are crucifying the Son of God all over again and subjecting him to public disgrace. [7]Land that drinks in the rain often falling on it and that produces a crop useful to those for whom it is farmed receives the blessing of God. [8]But land that produces thorns and thistles is worthless and is in danger of being cursed. In the end it will be burned.

[9]Even though we speak like this, dear friends, we are convinced of better things in your case—the things that have to do with salvation. [10]God is not unjust; he will not forget your work and the love you have shown him as you have helped his people and continue to help them. [11]We want each of you to show this same diligence to the

very end, so that what you hope for may be fully realized. [12]We do not want you to become lazy, but to imitate those who through faith and patience inherit what has been promised.

The Certainty of God's Promise

[13]When God made his promise to Abraham, since there was no one greater for him to swear by, he swore by himself, [14]saying, "I will surely bless you and give you many descendants."[d] [15]And so after waiting patiently, Abraham received what was promised.

[16]People swear by someone greater than themselves, and the oath confirms what is said and puts an end to all argument. [17]Because God wanted to make the unchanging nature of his purpose very clear to the heirs of what was promised, he confirmed it with an oath. [18]God did this so that, by two unchangeable things in which it is impossible for God to lie, we who have fled to take hold of the hope set before us may be greatly encouraged. [19]We have this hope as an anchor for the soul, firm and secure. It enters the inner sanctuary behind the curtain, [20]where our forerunner, Jesus, has entered on our behalf. He has become a high priest forever, in the order of Melchizedek.

Melchizedek the Priest

7 This Melchizedek was king of Salem and priest of God Most High. He met Abraham returning from the defeat of the kings and blessed him, [2]and Abraham gave him a tenth of everything. First, the name Melchizedek means "king of righteousness"; then also, "king of Salem" means "king of peace." [3]Without father or mother, without genealogy, without beginning of days or end of life, resembling the Son of God, he remains a priest forever.

[4]Just think how great he was: Even the patriarch Abraham gave him a tenth of the plunder! [5]Now the law requires the descendants of Levi who become priests to collect a tenth from the people—that is, from their fellow Israelites—even though they also are descended from Abraham. [6]This man, however, did not trace his descent from Levi, yet he collected a tenth from Abraham and blessed him who had the promises. [7]And

---

[a] 1 Or *from useless rituals*   [b] 2 Or *about baptisms*   [c] 6 Or *age,* [6]*if they fall*   [d] 14 Gen. 22:17

GROW UP!

READ: HEBREWS 5:14

When you were a baby, you did nothing but eat, sleep, mess your diaper—and look exceedingly cute. But you're not so adorable if you reach adolescence and still act like a baby. That's true of your spiritual life too. The author of Hebrews aims to help you grow up.

Hebrews teaches monumental ideas about the Lord. But they all make a practical point. The author begs you to pay attention so you don't drift from God (Hebrews 2:1). He urges you to believe God's truth so you don't end up hard-hearted (3:12-13). He tells you to run to Jesus so you get all the help you need (4:14-16).

BUILDING

FAITH

Merely hearing those words doesn't make you mature. In fact, at the end of Hebrews 5 you catch some of the author's frustration. He has far more to teach, but his readers have given up trying to understand. They should be teachers, but they need to go back to school. They should eat meat, but they still sip milk.

WISDOM

STRENGTH

It stings when someone you respect tells you to "Grow up!" But it supplies you with a reason to look at yourself and ask if you're making the most of all the opportunities God gives you to mature in the faith, like studying his Word, acting on what you know, and teaming with others to do big things. You're ready for grown-up food. Don't settle for baby mush.

without doubt the lesser is blessed by the greater. [8]In the one case, the tenth is collected by people who die; but in the other case, by him who is declared to be living. [9]One might even say that Levi, who collects the tenth, paid the tenth through Abraham, [10]because when Melchizedek met Abraham, Levi was still in the body of his ancestor.

Jesus Like Melchizedek

[11]If perfection could have been attained through the Levitical priesthood — and indeed the law given to the people established that priesthood — why was there still need for another priest to come, one in the order of Melchizedek, not in the order of Aaron? [12]For when the priesthood is changed, the law must be changed also. [13]He of whom these things are said belonged to a different tribe, and no one from that tribe has ever served at the altar. [14]For it is clear that our Lord descended from Judah, and in regard to that tribe Moses said nothing about priests. [15]And what we have said is even more clear if another priest like Melchizedek appears, [16]one who has become a priest not on the basis of a regulation as to his ancestry but on the basis of the power of an indestructible life. [17]For it is declared:

"You are a priest forever,
    in the order of Melchizedek."[a]

[18]The former regulation is set aside because it was weak and useless [19](for the law made nothing perfect), and a better hope is introduced, by which we draw near to God.

[20]And it was not without an oath! Others became priests without any oath, [21]but he became a priest with an oath when God said to him:

"The Lord has sworn
    and will not change his mind:
    'You are a priest forever.'"[a]

[22]Because of this oath, Jesus has become the guarantor of a better covenant.

[23]Now there have been many of those priests, since death prevented them from continuing in office; [24]but because Jesus lives forever, he has a permanent priesthood. [25]Therefore he is able to save completely[b] those who come to God through him, because he always lives to intercede for them.

[26]Such a high priest truly meets our need — one who is holy, blameless, pure, set apart from sinners, exalted above the heavens. [27]Unlike the other high priests, he does not need to offer sacrifices day after day, first for his own sins, and then for the sins of the people. He sacrificed for their sins once for all when he offered himself. [28]For the law appoints as high priests men in all their weakness; but the oath, which came after the law, appointed the Son, who has been made perfect forever.

The High Priest of a New Covenant

8 Now the main point of what we are saying is this: We do have such a high priest, who sat down at the right hand of the throne of the Majesty in heaven, [2]and who serves in the sanctuary, the true tabernacle set up by the Lord, not by a mere human being.

[3]Every high priest is appointed to offer both gifts and sacrifices, and so it was necessary for this one also to have something to offer. [4]If he were on earth, he would not be a priest, for there are already priests who offer the gifts prescribed by the law. [5]They serve at a sanctuary that is a copy and shadow of what is in heaven. This is why Moses was warned when he was about to build the tabernacle: "See to it that you make everything according to the pattern shown you on the mountain."[c] [6]But in fact the ministry Jesus has received is as superior to theirs as the covenant of which he is mediator is superior to the old one, since the new covenant is established on better promises.

[7]For if there had been nothing wrong with that first covenant, no place would have been sought for another. [8]But God found fault with the people and said[d]:

"The days are coming, declares the Lord,
    when I will make a new covenant
with the people of Israel
    and with the people of Judah.
[9]It will not be like the covenant
    I made with their ancestors
when I took them by the hand
    to lead them out of Egypt,

---

[a] 17,21 Psalm 110:4   [b] 25 Or *forever*   [c] 5 Exodus 25:40   [d] 8 Some manuscripts may be translated *fault and said to the people.*

because they did not remain faithful to
my covenant,
and I turned away from them,
declares the Lord.
[10] This is the covenant I will establish with
the people of Israel
after that time, declares the Lord.
I will put my laws in their minds
and write them on their hearts.
I will be their God,
and they will be my people.
[11] No longer will they teach their
neighbor,
or say to one another, 'Know
the Lord,'
because they will all know me,
from the least of them to the
greatest.
[12] For I will forgive their wickedness
and will remember their sins
no more."[a]

[13] By calling this covenant "new," he has
made the first one obsolete; and what is obsolete and outdated will soon disappear.

Worship in the Earthly Tabernacle

9 Now the first covenant had regulations
for worship and also an earthly sanctuary. [2] A tabernacle was set up. In its first
room were the lampstand and the table with
its consecrated bread; this was called the
Holy Place. [3] Behind the second curtain was
a room called the Most Holy Place, [4] which
had the golden altar of incense and the gold-
covered ark of the covenant. This ark contained the gold jar of manna, Aaron's staff
that had budded, and the stone tablets of the
covenant. [5] Above the ark were the cherubim
of the Glory, overshadowing the atonement
cover. But we cannot discuss these things in
detail now.

[6] When everything had been arranged like
this, the priests entered regularly into the
outer room to carry on their ministry. [7] But
only the high priest entered the inner room,
and that only once a year, and never without
blood, which he offered for himself and for
the sins the people had committed in ignorance. [8] The Holy Spirit was showing by this
that the way into the Most Holy Place had not
yet been disclosed as long as the first taber-

nacle was still functioning. [9] This is an illustration for the present time, indicating that
the gifts and sacrifices being offered were
not able to clear the conscience of the worshiper. [10] They are only a matter of food and
drink and various ceremonial washings—
external regulations applying until the time
of the new order.

The Blood of Christ

[11] But when Christ came as high priest of
the good things that are now already here,[b]
he went through the greater and more perfect tabernacle that is not made with human
hands, that is to say, is not a part of this creation. [12] He did not enter by means of the
blood of goats and calves; but he entered
the Most Holy Place once for all by his own
blood, thus obtaining[c] eternal redemption.
[13] The blood of goats and bulls and the ashes
of a heifer sprinkled on those who are ceremonially unclean sanctify them so that they
are outwardly clean. [14] How much more,
then, will the blood of Christ, who through
the eternal Spirit offered himself unblem-
ished to God, cleanse our consciences from
acts that lead to death,[d] so that we may serve
the living God!

[15] For this reason Christ is the mediator of
a new covenant, that those who are called
may receive the promised eternal inheritance—now that he has died as a ransom to
set them free from the sins committed under
the first covenant.

[16] In the case of a will,[e] it is necessary to
prove the death of the one who made it, [17] because a will is in force only when somebody
has died; it never takes effect while the one
who made it is living. [18] This is why even the
first covenant was not put into effect without blood. [19] When Moses had proclaimed
every command of the law to all the people,
he took the blood of calves, together with
water, scarlet wool and branches of hyssop,
and sprinkled the scroll and all the people.
[20] He said, "This is the blood of the covenant,
which God has commanded you to keep."[f]
[21] In the same way, he sprinkled with the
blood both the tabernacle and everything
used in its ceremonies. [22] In fact, the law requires that nearly everything be cleansed

---

[a] 12 Jer. 31:31-34   [b] 11 Some early manuscripts *are to come*   [c] 12 Or *blood, having obtained*
[d] 14 Or *from useless rituals*   [e] 16 Same Greek word as *covenant*; also in verse 17   [f] 20 Exodus 24:8

with blood, and without the shedding of blood there is no forgiveness.

²³It was necessary, then, for the copies of the heavenly things to be purified with these sacrifices, but the heavenly things themselves with better sacrifices than these. ²⁴For Christ did not enter a sanctuary made with human hands that was only a copy of the true one; he entered heaven itself, now to appear for us in God's presence. ²⁵Nor did he enter heaven to offer himself again and again, the way the high priest enters the Most Holy Place every year with blood that is not his own. ²⁶Otherwise Christ would have had to suffer many times since the creation of the world. But he has appeared once for all at the culmination of the ages to do away with sin by the sacrifice of himself. ²⁷Just as people are destined to die once, and after that to face judgment, ²⁸so Christ was sacrificed once to take away the sins of many; and he will appear a second time, not to bear sin, but to bring salvation to those who are waiting for him.

Christ's Sacrifice Once for All

10 The law is only a shadow of the good things that are coming — not the realities themselves. For this reason it can never, by the same sacrifices repeated endlessly year after year, make perfect those who draw near to worship. ²Otherwise, would they not have stopped being offered? For the worshipers would have been cleansed once for all, and would no longer have felt guilty for their sins. ³But those sacrifices are an annual reminder of sins. ⁴It is impossible for the blood of bulls and goats to take away sins.

⁵Therefore, when Christ came into the world, he said:

"Sacrifice and offering you did not desire,
    but a body you prepared for me;
⁶with burnt offerings and sin offerings
    you were not pleased.
⁷Then I said, 'Here I am — it is written
    about me in the scroll —
I have come to do your will, my God.' "^a

⁸First he said, "Sacrifices and offerings, burnt offerings and sin offerings you did not desire, nor were you pleased with them" — though they were offered in accordance with

the law. ⁹Then he said, "Here I am, I have come to do your will." He sets aside the first to establish the second. ¹⁰And by that will, we have been made holy through the sacrifice of the body of Jesus Christ once for all.

¹¹Day after day every priest stands and performs his religious duties; again and again he offers the same sacrifices, which can never take away sins. ¹²But when this priest had offered for all time one sacrifice for sins, he sat down at the right hand of God, ¹³and since that time he waits for his enemies to be made his footstool. ¹⁴For by one sacrifice he has made perfect forever those who are being made holy.

¹⁵The Holy Spirit also testifies to us about this. First he says:

¹⁶"This is the covenant I will make with
    them
    after that time, says the Lord.
I will put my laws in their hearts,
    and I will write them on their minds."^b

¹⁷Then he adds:

"Their sins and lawless acts
    I will remember no more."^c

¹⁸And where these have been forgiven, sacrifice for sin is no longer necessary.

A Call to Persevere in Faith

¹⁹Therefore, brothers and sisters, since we have confidence to enter the Most Holy Place by the blood of Jesus, ²⁰by a new and living way opened for us through the curtain, that is, his body, ²¹and since we have a great priest over the house of God, ²²let us draw near to God with a sincere heart and with the full assurance that faith brings, having our hearts sprinkled to cleanse us from a guilty conscience and having our bodies washed with pure water. ²³Let us hold unswervingly to the hope we profess, for he who promised is faithful. ²⁴And let us consider how we may spur one another on toward love and good deeds, ²⁵not giving up meeting together, as some are in the habit of doing, but encouraging one another — and all the more as you see the Day approaching.

²⁶If we deliberately keep on sinning after we have received the knowledge of the truth, no sacrifice for sins is left, ²⁷but only a fearful

^a 7 Psalm 40:6-8 (see Septuagint)   ^b 16 Jer. 31:33   ^c 17 Jer. 31:34

LEAN ON ME

READ: HEBREWS 10:24-25

We either believe we are a small but essential part of the body of Christ or we don't. We either believe Jesus meant it when he called us to community or we don't. Every time somebody tells you to go to church, they spit out some version of Hebrews 10:25, which says to not forsake the assembling of yourselves together. That's a good verse, but I hope we don't need a directive. If God calls his church the body of Christ, what other encouragement do we need to get together and stay together?

Jesus is God himself, and during his time on earth he didn't do ministry alone. He started the church by discipling a group of men. Similarly, we forfeit a significant part of our growth when we do not join with other believers.

Why is community so important? Because one of the primary ways God ministers to us is through other believers. When Jesus was crucified, the disciples huddled in fear of the authorities. On the surface, it's easy to judge them in their weakness, even though every one of us would have trembled right there with them. But what is apparent in this picture is beautiful fellowship and community because of the trial they were enduring as a body. Fellowship is not pizza and Coke after church; it's the certainty that we're in something together and that our common faith will keep us going.

BUILDING FAITH WISDOM STRENGTH

Taken from *Thrive Student Edition* by Mark Hall with Tim Luke, copyright © 2014 by Mark Hall, published by Zondervan.

expectation of judgment and of raging fire that will consume the enemies of God. ²⁸Anyone who rejected the law of Moses died without mercy on the testimony of two or three witnesses. ²⁹How much more severely do you think someone deserves to be punished who has trampled the Son of God underfoot, who has treated as an unholy thing the blood of the covenant that sanctified them, and who has insulted the Spirit of grace? ³⁰For we know him who said, "It is mine to avenge; I will repay," *a* and again, "The Lord will judge his people." *b* ³¹It is a dreadful thing to fall into the hands of the living God.

³²Remember those earlier days after you had received the light, when you endured in a great conflict full of suffering. ³³Sometimes you were publicly exposed to insult and persecution; at other times you stood side by side with those who were so treated. ³⁴You suffered along with those in prison and joyfully accepted the confiscation of your property, because you knew that you yourselves had better and lasting possessions. ³⁵So do not throw away your confidence; it will be richly rewarded.

³⁶You need to persevere so that when you have done the will of God, you will receive what he has promised. ³⁷For,

> "In just a little while,
> he who is coming will come
> and will not delay." *c*

³⁸And,

> "But my righteous *d* one will live by faith.
> And I take no pleasure
> in the one who shrinks back." *e*

³⁹But we do not belong to those who shrink back and are destroyed, but to those who have faith and are saved.

Faith in Action

11 Now faith is confidence in what we hope for and assurance about what we do not see. ²This is what the ancients were commended for.

³By faith we understand that the universe was formed at God's command, so that what is seen was not made out of what was visible.

⁴By faith Abel brought God a better offering than Cain did. By faith he was commended as righteous, when God spoke well of his offerings. And by faith Abel still speaks, even though he is dead.

⁵By faith Enoch was taken from this life, so that he did not experience death: "He could not be found, because God had taken him away." *f* For before he was taken, he was commended as one who pleased God. ⁶And without faith it is impossible to please God, because anyone who comes to him must believe that he exists and that he rewards those who earnestly seek him.

⁷By faith Noah, when warned about things not yet seen, in holy fear built an ark to save his family. By his faith he condemned the world and became heir of the righteousness that is in keeping with faith.

⁸By faith Abraham, when called to go to a place he would later receive as his inheritance, obeyed and went, even though he did not know where he was going. ⁹By faith he made his home in the promised land like a stranger in a foreign country; he lived in tents, as did Isaac and Jacob, who were heirs with him of the same promise. ¹⁰For he was looking forward to the city with foundations, whose architect and builder is God. ¹¹And by faith even Sarah, who was past childbearing age, was enabled to bear children because she *g* considered him faithful who had made the promise. ¹²And so from this one man, and he as good as dead, came descendants as numerous as the stars in the sky and as countless as the sand on the seashore.

¹³All these people were still living by faith when they died. They did not receive the things promised; they only saw them and welcomed them from a distance, admitting that they were foreigners and strangers on earth. ¹⁴People who say such things show that they are looking for a country of their own. ¹⁵If they had been thinking of the country they had left, they would have had opportunity to return. ¹⁶Instead, they were longing for a better country — a heavenly one. Therefore God is not ashamed to be called their God, for he has prepared a city for them.

---

a 30 Deut. 32:35   *b 30* Deut. 32:36; Psalm 135:14   *c 37* Isaiah 26:20; Hab. 2:3   *d 38* Some early manuscripts *But the righteous*   *e 38* Hab. 2:4 (see Septuagint)   *f 5* Gen. 5:24   *g 11* Or *By faith Abraham, even though he was too old to have children — and Sarah herself was not able to conceive — was enabled to become a father because he*

[17]By faith Abraham, when God tested him, offered Isaac as a sacrifice. He who had embraced the promises was about to sacrifice his one and only son, [18]even though God had said to him, "It is through Isaac that your offspring will be reckoned."[a] [19]Abraham reasoned that God could even raise the dead, and so in a manner of speaking he did receive Isaac back from death.

[20]By faith Isaac blessed Jacob and Esau in regard to their future.

[21]By faith Jacob, when he was dying, blessed each of Joseph's sons, and worshiped as he leaned on the top of his staff.

[22]By faith Joseph, when his end was near, spoke about the exodus of the Israelites from Egypt and gave instructions concerning the burial of his bones.

[23]By faith Moses' parents hid him for three months after he was born, because they saw he was no ordinary child, and they were not afraid of the king's edict.

[24]By faith Moses, when he had grown up, refused to be known as the son of Pharaoh's daughter. [25]He chose to be mistreated along with the people of God rather than to enjoy the fleeting pleasures of sin. [26]He regarded disgrace for the sake of Christ as of greater value than the treasures of Egypt, because he was looking ahead to his reward. [27]By faith he left Egypt, not fearing the king's anger; he persevered because he saw him who is invisible. [28]By faith he kept the Passover and the application of blood, so that the destroyer of the firstborn would not touch the firstborn of Israel.

[29]By faith the people passed through the Red Sea as on dry land; but when the Egyptians tried to do so, they were drowned.

[30]By faith the walls of Jericho fell, after the army had marched around them for seven days.

[31]By faith the prostitute Rahab, because she welcomed the spies, was not killed with those who were disobedient.[b]

[32]And what more shall I say? I do not have time to tell about Gideon, Barak, Samson and Jephthah, about David and Samuel and the prophets, [33]who through faith conquered kingdoms, administered justice, and gained what was promised; who shut the mouths of lions, [34]quenched the fury of the flames, and escaped the edge of the sword; whose weakness was turned to strength; and who became powerful in battle and routed foreign armies. [35]Women received back their dead, raised to life again. There were others who were tortured, refusing to be released so that they might gain an even better resurrection. [36]Some faced jeers and flogging, and even chains and imprisonment. [37]They were put to death by stoning;[c] they were sawed in two; they were killed by the sword. They went about in sheepskins and goatskins, destitute, persecuted and mistreated— [38]the world was not worthy of them. They wandered in deserts and mountains, living in caves and in holes in the ground.

[39]These were all commended for their faith, yet none of them received what had been promised, [40]since God had planned something better for us so that only together with us would they be made perfect.

12 Therefore, since we are surrounded by such a great cloud of witnesses, let us throw off everything that hinders and the sin that so easily entangles. And let us run with perseverance the race marked out for us, [2]fixing our eyes on Jesus, the pioneer and perfecter of faith. For the joy set before him he endured the cross, scorning its shame, and sat down at the right hand of the throne of God. [3]Consider him who endured such opposition from sinners, so that you will not grow weary and lose heart.

God Disciplines His Children

[4]In your struggle against sin, you have not yet resisted to the point of shedding your blood. [5]And have you completely forgotten this word of encouragement that addresses you as a father addresses his son? It says,

"My son, do not make light of the Lord's discipline,
    and do not lose heart when he rebukes you,
[6]because the Lord disciplines the one he loves,
    and he chastens everyone he accepts as his son."[d]

[7]Endure hardship as discipline; God is treating you as his children. For what children

---

BROWSING THE NOTABLES

READ: HEBREWS 11:24-25

Hebrews 11 presents the Bible's grand "Hall of Faith." It's a unique account of famous Old Testament believers and their bold trust in God.

This famous chapter starts by making sure you know exactly what faith is and how it works. Faith is a firm belief in the existence of things you can't see. As Hebrews 11:1 says, it's "confidence in what we hope for and assurance about what we do not see." You can't please the Lord without this certainty in his existence and promises. Hebrews 11:6 declares that "without faith it is impossible to please God, because anyone who comes to him must believe that he exists and that he rewards those who earnestly seek him."

The ancient saints who fill this chapter excelled at trusting God. By faith Noah built an ark long before floods rose. Abraham left his home for a new land he couldn't pinpoint on a map. Joseph foresaw that his family would one day head back home. Moses left Pharaoh's palace to lead the Israelites to freedom. Rahab welcomed spies. By faith some experienced victory and success. Others were mistreated, imprisoned, beaten, stoned, and sawed in half.

All of these people were "commended for their faith" (v. 39). They were applauded by the Lord for their trust in him. They're all models of how you can live for God.

BUILDING FAITH WISDOM STRENGTH

I'D DIE FOR YOU

READ: HEBREWS 12:2

Once upon a time, our family vacationed at a friend's cabin. Late one night, I decided to get into the hot tub with my two kids. It was cold and snowy, so steam was rising. The trees blocked the moonlight, so it was pitch black. And all we could hear were the sounds of the deep woods.

In an overly dramatic voice, I made a fatherly declaration to my children: "If a bear came out of these woods and attacked us, I want you to know that I would die for you." My kids were six and eight at the time. They ran into the house screaming, and it's a miracle they aren't scarred to this day!

I maybe could've delivered that a little differently, but I'll never forget what I felt. I meant what I said. I would die for my children without a moment's hesitation.

That right there is the heavenly Father's deepest impulse toward us. Anyone who messes with you messes with him. His protective instincts are pretty obvious at the cross. That's where the Creator stepped between every sinner (that's you and me) and Satan. That's where the Advocate took on the Accuser of the brethren.

BUILDING FAITH WISDOM STRENGTH

The Sinless Son of God took the fall for us! The cross is God's way of saying, "You're totally a hundred percent worth dying for." When that life-giving truth penetrates into the deepest place in your heart, it transforms how you think, feel, and live.

Taken from *All In Student Edition* by Mark Batterson and Parker Batterson, copyright © 2014 by Mark Batterson, published by Zondervan.

are not disciplined by their father? [8]If you are not disciplined—and everyone undergoes discipline—then you are not legitimate, not true sons and daughters at all. [9]Moreover, we have all had human fathers who disciplined us and we respected them for it. How much more should we submit to the Father of spirits and live! [10]They disciplined us for a little while as they thought best; but God disciplines us for our good, in order that we may share in his holiness. [11]No discipline seems pleasant at the time, but painful. Later on, however, it produces a harvest of righteousness and peace for those who have been trained by it.

[12]Therefore, strengthen your feeble arms and weak knees. [13]"Make level paths for your feet,"[a] so that the lame may not be disabled, but rather healed.

Warning and Encouragement

[14]Make every effort to live in peace with everyone and to be holy; without holiness no one will see the Lord. [15]See to it that no one falls short of the grace of God and that no bitter root grows up to cause trouble and defile many. [16]See that no one is sexually immoral, or is godless like Esau, who for a single meal sold his inheritance rights as the oldest son. [17]Afterward, as you know, when he wanted to inherit this blessing, he was rejected. Even though he sought the blessing with tears, he could not change what he had done.

The Mountain of Fear and the Mountain of Joy

[18]You have not come to a mountain that can be touched and that is burning with fire; to darkness, gloom and storm; [19]to a trumpet blast or to such a voice speaking words that those who heard it begged that no further word be spoken to them, [20]because they could not bear what was commanded: "If even an animal touches the mountain, it must be stoned to death."[b] [21]The sight was so terrifying that Moses said, "I am trembling with fear."[c]

[22]But you have come to Mount Zion, to the city of the living God, the heavenly Jerusalem. You have come to thousands upon thousands of angels in joyful assembly, [23]to the church of the firstborn, whose names are written in heaven. You have come to God,

the Judge of all, to the spirits of the righteous made perfect, [24]to Jesus the mediator of a new covenant, and to the sprinkled blood that speaks a better word than the blood of Abel.

[25]See to it that you do not refuse him who speaks. If they did not escape when they refused him who warned them on earth, how much less will we, if we turn away from him who warns us from heaven? [26]At that time his voice shook the earth, but now he has promised, "Once more I will shake not only the earth but also the heavens."[d] [27]The words "once more" indicate the removing of what can be shaken—that is, created things—so that what cannot be shaken may remain.

[28]Therefore, since we are receiving a kingdom that cannot be shaken, let us be thankful, and so worship God acceptably with reverence and awe, [29]for our "God is a consuming fire."[e]

Concluding Exhortations

13 Keep on loving one another as brothers and sisters. [2]Do not forget to show hospitality to strangers, for by so doing some people have shown hospitality to angels without knowing it. [3]Continue to remember those in prison as if you were together with them in prison, and those who are mistreated as if you yourselves were suffering.

[4]Marriage should be honored by all, and the marriage bed kept pure, for God will judge the adulterer and all the sexually immoral. [5]Keep your lives free from the love of money and be content with what you have, because God has said,

"Never will I leave you;
    never will I forsake you."[f]

[6]So we say with confidence,

"The Lord is my helper; I will not be afraid.
    What can mere mortals do to me?"[g]

[7]Remember your leaders, who spoke the word of God to you. Consider the outcome of their way of life and imitate their faith. [8]Jesus Christ is the same yesterday and today and forever.

---

[a] 13 Prov. 4:26   [b] 20 Exodus 19:12,13   [c] 21 See Deut. 9:19.   [d] 26 Haggai 2:6   [e] 29 Deut. 4:24
[f] 5 Deut. 31:6   [g] 6 Psalm 118:6,7

[9] Do not be carried away by all kinds of strange teachings. It is good for our hearts to be strengthened by grace, not by eating ceremonial foods, which is of no benefit to those who do so. [10] We have an altar from which those who minister at the tabernacle have no right to eat.

[11] The high priest carries the blood of animals into the Most Holy Place as a sin offering, but the bodies are burned outside the camp. [12] And so Jesus also suffered outside the city gate to make the people holy through his own blood. [13] Let us, then, go to him outside the camp, bearing the disgrace he bore. [14] For here we do not have an enduring city, but we are looking for the city that is to come.

[15] Through Jesus, therefore, let us continually offer to God a sacrifice of praise — the fruit of lips that openly profess his name. [16] And do not forget to do good and to share with others, for with such sacrifices God is pleased.

[17] Have confidence in your leaders and submit to their authority, because they keep watch over you as those who must give an account. Do this so that their work will be a joy, not a burden, for that would be of no benefit to you.

[18] Pray for us. We are sure that we have a clear conscience and desire to live honorably in every way. [19] I particularly urge you to pray so that I may be restored to you soon.

Benediction and Final Greetings

[20] Now may the God of peace, who through the blood of the eternal covenant brought back from the dead our Lord Jesus, that great Shepherd of the sheep, [21] equip you with everything good for doing his will, and may he work in us what is pleasing to him, through Jesus Christ, to whom be glory for ever and ever. Amen.

[22] Brothers and sisters, I urge you to bear with my word of exhortation, for in fact I have written to you quite briefly.

[23] I want you to know that our brother Timothy has been released. If he arrives soon, I will come with him to see you.

[24] Greet all your leaders and all the Lord's people. Those from Italy send you their greetings.

[25] Grace be with you all.

JAMES

 **WHEN DID THIS
HAPPEN?**
Around A.D. 45 in Jerusalem

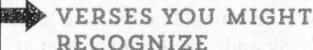 **WHO IS IN THIS
BOOK?**
James
Jesus

**VERSES YOU MIGHT
RECOGNIZE**

JAMES 1:22
*"Do not merely listen to
the word, and so deceive
yourselves. Do what it says."*

JAMES 2:17
*"In the same way, faith by
itself, if it is not accompanied
by action, is dead."*

WHAT'S IT ABOUT?

Like Proverbs in the Old Testament, this book provides a practical guide for how believers should live. Written by James, the half brother of Jesus, who became a leader in the early church, this book was likely the first of the New Testament books to be completed. James' message was clear: Faith produces action. He went so far as to say that faith without action is dead (see James 2:17). While the good things believers do won't save them, these actions do please God and show that a person believes in Jesus.

James wrote about things Christians should do, such as putting God's Word into practice and caring for widows and orphans. He also set down things believers need to avoid, such as showing favoritism and failing to control their tongues. And because he was writing to former Jews, he used Old Testament characters, such as Abraham, Job and Elijah, to show them how people of faith should act.

JAMES

1 James, a servant of God and of the Lord Jesus Christ,

To the twelve tribes scattered among the nations:

Greetings.

Trials and Temptations

² Consider it pure joy, my brothers and sisters,*ᵃ* whenever you face trials of many kinds, ³ because you know that the testing of your faith produces perseverance. ⁴ Let perseverance finish its work so that you may be mature and complete, not lacking anything. ⁵ If any of you lacks wisdom, you should ask God, who gives generously to all without finding fault, and it will be given to you. ⁶ But when you ask, you must believe and not doubt, because the one who doubts is like a wave of the sea, blown and tossed by the wind. ⁷ That person should not expect to receive anything from the Lord. ⁸ Such a person is double-minded and unstable in all they do.

⁹ Believers in humble circumstances ought to take pride in their high position. ¹⁰ But the rich should take pride in their humiliation — since they will pass away like a wild flower. ¹¹ For the sun rises with scorching heat and withers the plant; its blossom falls and its beauty is destroyed. In the same way, the rich will fade away even while they go about their business.

¹² Blessed is the one who perseveres under trial because, having stood the test, that person will receive the crown of life that the Lord has promised to those who love him.

¹³ When tempted, no one should say, "God is tempting me." For God cannot be tempted by evil, nor does he tempt anyone; ¹⁴ but each person is tempted when they are dragged away by their own evil desire and enticed. ¹⁵ Then, after desire has conceived, it gives birth to sin; and sin, when it is full-grown, gives birth to death.

¹⁶ Don't be deceived, my dear brothers and sisters. ¹⁷ Every good and perfect gift is from above, coming down from the Father of the heavenly lights, who does not change like shifting shadows. ¹⁸ He chose to give us birth through the word of truth, that we might be a kind of firstfruits of all he created.

Listening and Doing

¹⁹ My dear brothers and sisters, take note of this: Everyone should be quick to listen, slow to speak and slow to become angry, ²⁰ because human anger does not produce the righteousness that God desires. ²¹ Therefore, get rid of all moral filth and the evil that is so prevalent and humbly accept the word planted in you, which can save you.

²² Do not merely listen to the word, and so deceive yourselves. Do what it says. ²³ Anyone who listens to the word but does not do what it says is like someone who looks at his face in a mirror ²⁴ and, after looking at himself, goes away and immediately forgets what he looks like. ²⁵ But whoever looks intently into the perfect law that gives freedom, and continues in it — not forgetting what they have heard, but doing it — they will be blessed in what they do.

²⁶ Those who consider themselves religious and yet do not keep a tight rein on their tongues deceive themselves, and their religion is worthless. ²⁷ Religion that God our Father accepts as pure and faultless is this: to look after orphans and widows in their distress and to keep oneself from being polluted by the world.

Favoritism Forbidden

2 My brothers and sisters, believers in our glorious Lord Jesus Christ must not show favoritism. ² Suppose a man comes into your meeting wearing a gold ring and fine clothes, and a poor man in filthy old clothes also comes in. ³ If you show special

---

ᵃ 2 The Greek word for *brothers and sisters* (*adelphoi*) refers here to believers, both men and women, as part of God's family; also in verses 16 and 19; and in 2:1, 5, 14; 3:10, 12; 4:11; 5:7, 9, 10, 12, 19.

attention to the man wearing fine clothes and say, "Here's a good seat for you," but say to the poor man, "You stand there" or "Sit on the floor by my feet," [4]have you not discriminated among yourselves and become judges with evil thoughts?

[5]Listen, my dear brothers and sisters: Has not God chosen those who are poor in the eyes of the world to be rich in faith and to inherit the kingdom he promised those who love him? [6]But you have dishonored the poor. Is it not the rich who are exploiting you? Are they not the ones who are dragging you into court? [7]Are they not the ones who are blaspheming the noble name of him to whom you belong?

[8]If you really keep the royal law found in Scripture, "Love your neighbor as yourself,"[a] you are doing right. [9]But if you show favoritism, you sin and are convicted by the law as lawbreakers. [10]For whoever keeps the whole law and yet stumbles at just one point is guilty of breaking all of it. [11]For he who said, "You shall not commit adultery,"[b] also said, "You shall not murder."[c] If you do not commit adultery but do commit murder, you have become a lawbreaker.

[12]Speak and act as those who are going to be judged by the law that gives freedom, [13]because judgment without mercy will be shown to anyone who has not been merciful. Mercy triumphs over judgment.

Faith and Deeds

[14]What good is it, my brothers and sisters, if someone claims to have faith but has no deeds? Can such faith save them? [15]Suppose a brother or a sister is without clothes and daily food. [16]If one of you says to them, "Go in peace; keep warm and well fed," but does nothing about their physical needs, what good is it? [17]In the same way, faith by itself, if it is not accompanied by action, is dead.

[18]But someone will say, "You have faith; I have deeds."

Show me your faith without deeds, and I will show you my faith by my deeds. [19]You believe that there is one God. Good! Even the demons believe that—and shudder.

[20]You foolish person, do you want evidence that faith without deeds is useless[d]?

[21]Was not our father Abraham considered righteous for what he did when he offered his son Isaac on the altar? [22]You see that his faith and his actions were working together, and his faith was made complete by what he did. [23]And the scripture was fulfilled that says, "Abraham believed God, and it was credited to him as righteousness,"[e] and he was called God's friend. [24]You see that a person is considered righteous by what they do and not by faith alone.

[25]In the same way, was not even Rahab the prostitute considered righteous for what she did when she gave lodging to the spies and sent them off in a different direction? [26]As the body without the spirit is dead, so faith without deeds is dead.

Taming the Tongue

3 Not many of you should become teachers, my fellow believers, because you know that we who teach will be judged more strictly. [2]We all stumble in many ways. Anyone who is never at fault in what they say is perfect, able to keep their whole body in check.

[3]When we put bits into the mouths of horses to make them obey us, we can turn the whole animal. [4]Or take ships as an example. Although they are so large and are driven by strong winds, they are steered by a very small rudder wherever the pilot wants to go. [5]Likewise, the tongue is a small part of the body, but it makes great boasts. Consider what a great forest is set on fire by a small spark. [6]The tongue also is a fire, a world of evil among the parts of the body. It corrupts the whole body, sets the whole course of one's life on fire, and is itself set on fire by hell.

[7]All kinds of animals, birds, reptiles and sea creatures are being tamed and have been tamed by mankind, [8]but no human being can tame the tongue. It is a restless evil, full of deadly poison.

[9]With the tongue we praise our Lord and Father, and with it we curse human beings, who have been made in God's likeness. [10]Out of the same mouth come praise and cursing. My brothers and sisters, this should not be. [11]Can both fresh water and salt water flow

---

[a] 8 Lev. 19:18   [b] 11 Exodus 20:14; Deut. 5:18   [c] 11 Exodus 20:13; Deut. 5:17   [d] 20 Some early manuscripts *dead*   [e] 23 Gen. 15:6

WORTH IT?

READ: JAMES 2:26

There is something within us that loves to git-r-done. Think about our experience as children: Cub Scouts or Boy Scouts. You perform a task, and you win a merit badge. Go on a hike and fulfill the given requirements, and you receive that colorful "camping" patch. Do you remember how great it feels when the scoutmaster pins that patch to your uniform?

That's the same feeling we get when we add pins or patches to a letterman jacket. Or maybe you're a high-achiever type who finds their identity in good grades and making the honor roll and earning a spot with National Honor Society. Others love the spotlight of landing the lead role in the musical or getting the solo in the choir. And many of us have long-term goals of what we could achieve by making it into the right college and building the right career. Who knows what we could achieve one day? And so the vest wrapped with badges, the jacket covered in patches, the trophies on the shelf, the ribbons, the medals, the report cards, the diplomas, and one day the degrees, the promotions, the paychecks represent what we have accomplished through our hard work and dedication.

BUILDING FAITH WISDOM STRENGTH

Obviously there is nothing wrong with any of these achievements. In fact, these achievements can be acts of worship that glorify God. But when our lives are all about getting things done, we can find that there is not much room for God.

Taken from *Gods at War Student Edition* by Kyle Idleman, copyright © 2014 by City on a Hill Studio, LLC, published by Zondervan.

from the same spring? ¹²My brothers and sisters, can a fig tree bear olives, or a grapevine bear figs? Neither can a salt spring produce fresh water.

Two Kinds of Wisdom

¹³Who is wise and understanding among you? Let them show it by their good life, by deeds done in the humility that comes from wisdom. ¹⁴But if you harbor bitter envy and selfish ambition in your hearts, do not boast about it or deny the truth. ¹⁵Such "wisdom" does not come down from heaven but is earthly, unspiritual, demonic. ¹⁶For where you have envy and selfish ambition, there you find disorder and every evil practice.

¹⁷But the wisdom that comes from heaven is first of all pure; then peace-loving, considerate, submissive, full of mercy and good fruit, impartial and sincere. ¹⁸Peacemakers who sow in peace reap a harvest of righteousness.

Submit Yourselves to God

4 What causes fights and quarrels among you? Don't they come from your desires that battle within you? ²You desire but do not have, so you kill. You covet but you cannot get what you want, so you quarrel and fight. You do not have because you do not ask God. ³When you ask, you do not receive, because you ask with wrong motives, that you may spend what you get on your pleasures.

⁴You adulterous people,[a] don't you know that friendship with the world means enmity against God? Therefore, anyone who chooses to be a friend of the world becomes an enemy of God. ⁵Or do you think Scripture says without reason that he jealously longs for the spirit he has caused to dwell in us[b]? ⁶But he gives us more grace. That is why Scripture says:

> "God opposes the proud
>   but shows favor to the humble."[c]

⁷Submit yourselves, then, to God. Resist the devil, and he will flee from you. ⁸Come near to God and he will come near to you. Wash your hands, you sinners, and purify your hearts, you double-minded. ⁹Grieve, mourn and wail. Change your laughter to mourning and your joy to gloom. ¹⁰Humble yourselves before the Lord, and he will lift you up.

¹¹Brothers and sisters, do not slander one another. Anyone who speaks against a brother or sister[d] or judges them speaks against the law and judges it. When you judge the law, you are not keeping it, but sitting in judgment on it. ¹²There is only one Lawgiver and Judge, the one who is able to save and destroy. But you—who are you to judge your neighbor?

Boasting About Tomorrow

¹³Now listen, you who say, "Today or tomorrow we will go to this or that city, spend a year there, carry on business and make money." ¹⁴Why, you do not even know what will happen tomorrow. What is your life? You are a mist that appears for a little while and then vanishes. ¹⁵Instead, you ought to say, "If it is the Lord's will, we will live and do this or that." ¹⁶As it is, you boast in your arrogant schemes. All such boasting is evil. ¹⁷If anyone, then, knows the good they ought to do and doesn't do it, it is sin for them.

Warning to Rich Oppressors

5 Now listen, you rich people, weep and wail because of the misery that is coming on you. ²Your wealth has rotted, and moths have eaten your clothes. ³Your gold and silver are corroded. Their corrosion will testify against you and eat your flesh like fire. You have hoarded wealth in the last days. ⁴Look! The wages you failed to pay the workers who mowed your fields are crying out against you. The cries of the harvesters have reached the ears of the Lord Almighty. ⁵You have lived on earth in luxury and self-indulgence. You have fattened yourselves in the day of slaughter.[e] ⁶You have condemned and murdered the innocent one, who was not opposing you.

Patience in Suffering

⁷Be patient, then, brothers and sisters, until the Lord's coming. See how the farmer waits for the land to yield its valuable crop, patiently waiting for the autumn and spring

---

[a] 4 An allusion to covenant unfaithfulness; see Hosea 3:1.   [b] 5 Or *that the spirit he caused to dwell in us envies intensely;* or *that the Spirit he caused to dwell in us longs jealously*   [c] 6 Prov. 3:34   [d] 11 The Greek word for *brother or sister (adelphos)* refers here to a believer, whether man or woman, as part of God's family.   [e] 5 Or *yourselves as in a day of feasting*

ME FIRST!

READ: JAMES 4:1

God knows why you get into spats and fights. As tempting as it might be to blame others for your arguments and tiffs, the Lord puts his finger on something going on inside you.

The apostle James has just finished warning his readers that the world has two kinds of wisdom (James 3:13-18). There's a wisdom that comes straight from God in heaven. It shows up in qualities like peacefulness, mercy, submission, and consideration for others. There's another kind of wisdom that flows from a far different place. James calls this pattern of thinking "earthly, unspiritual, demonic" (v. 15). It shows up in disorder and all kinds of evil. It's driven by envy and selfish ambition.

That me-first attitude is what fuels conflict. James points out that all human beings have desires raging within. Those longings aren't just ordinary wants and needs; they're urges to get as much pleasure and personal happiness as possible. If you let those cravings run your life, you will try to destroy anything that stands in your way. You "covet," wanting what others have. You "quarrel," demanding you get your way. You "fight," even to the point of physical battles (4:2).

There's a solution to this inner war. Ask the Lord for what you want. But don't bother praying that prayer if you plan to keep his gifts all to yourself. He doesn't answer selfish requests.

BUILDING

FAITH

WISDOM

STRENGTH

rains. [8]You too, be patient and stand firm, because the Lord's coming is near. [9]Don't grumble against one another, brothers and sisters, or you will be judged. The Judge is standing at the door!

[10]Brothers and sisters, as an example of patience in the face of suffering, take the prophets who spoke in the name of the Lord. [11]As you know, we count as blessed those who have persevered. You have heard of Job's perseverance and have seen what the Lord finally brought about. The Lord is full of compassion and mercy.

[12]Above all, my brothers and sisters, do not swear — not by heaven or by earth or by anything else. All you need to say is a simple "Yes" or "No." Otherwise you will be condemned.

The Prayer of Faith

[13]Is anyone among you in trouble? Let them pray. Is anyone happy? Let them sing songs of praise. [14]Is anyone among you sick? Let them call the elders of the church to pray over them and anoint them with oil in the name of the Lord. [15]And the prayer offered in faith will make the sick person well; the Lord will raise them up. If they have sinned, they will be forgiven. [16]Therefore confess your sins to each other and pray for each other so that you may be healed. The prayer of a righteous person is powerful and effective.

[17]Elijah was a human being, even as we are. He prayed earnestly that it would not rain, and it did not rain on the land for three and a half years. [18]Again he prayed, and the heavens gave rain, and the earth produced its crops.

[19]My brothers and sisters, if one of you should wander from the truth and someone should bring that person back, [20]remember this: Whoever turns a sinner from the error of their way will save them from death and cover over a multitude of sins.

1 PETER

➡ **WHEN DID THIS HAPPEN?**

Around A.D. 62 to 64 in Rome

➡ **WHO IS IN THIS BOOK?**

Peter

Silas

Mark

➡ **VERSES YOU MIGHT RECOGNIZE**

1 PETER 4:8

"Above all, love each other deeply, because love covers over a multitude of sins."

1 PETER 5:7

"Cast all your anxiety on him because he cares for you."

WHAT'S IT ABOUT?

Peter wrote at a time when the Christians were facing extreme persecution.

They were being tortured and killed by Emperor Nero. As one of Jesus' disciples and a leader of the church, Peter knew something about following God during hard times. Peter told the Christians in Jerusalem how they could live godly lives during trials and suffering by making Christ their top priority.

Peter told the Christians to live holy lives. He reminded them that they were foreigners to this life and should live in a different way than those who did not believe. Peter told them to submit to authority—even the corrupt government—to demonstrate their allegiance to God.

Christians should appear differently than the rest of the world because their minds are set on Christ. Peter tells us that persecution should not be a surprise because we have an enemy, Satan, who is trying to destroy us. But even in times of great suffering, God cares for us, and we can trust him with our worries.

1 PETER

1 Peter, an apostle of Jesus Christ,

To God's elect, exiles scattered throughout the provinces of Pontus, Galatia, Cappadocia, Asia and Bithynia, **²**who have been chosen according to the foreknowledge of God the Father, through the sanctifying work of the Spirit, to be obedient to Jesus Christ and sprinkled with his blood:

Grace and peace be yours in abundance.

Praise to God for a Living Hope

³Praise be to the God and Father of our Lord Jesus Christ! In his great mercy he has given us new birth into a living hope through the resurrection of Jesus Christ from the dead, **⁴**and into an inheritance that can never perish, spoil or fade. This inheritance is kept in heaven for you, **⁵**who through faith are shielded by God's power until the coming of the salvation that is ready to be revealed in the last time. **⁶**In all this you greatly rejoice, though now for a little while you may have had to suffer grief in all kinds of trials. **⁷**These have come so that the proven genuineness of your faith — of greater worth than gold, which perishes even though refined by fire — may result in praise, glory and honor when Jesus Christ is revealed. **⁸**Though you have not seen him, you love him; and even though you do not see him now, you believe in him and are filled with an inexpressible and glorious joy, **⁹**for you are receiving the end result of your faith, the salvation of your souls.

¹⁰Concerning this salvation, the prophets, who spoke of the grace that was to come to you, searched intently and with the greatest care, **¹¹**trying to find out the time and circumstances to which the Spirit of Christ in them was pointing when he predicted the sufferings of the Messiah and the glories that would follow. **¹²**It was revealed to them that they were not serving themselves but you, when they spoke of the things that have now been told you by those who have preached the gospel to you by the Holy Spirit sent from heaven. Even angels long to look into these things.

Be Holy

¹³Therefore, with minds that are alert and fully sober, set your hope on the grace to be brought to you when Jesus Christ is revealed at his coming. **¹⁴**As obedient children, do not conform to the evil desires you had when you lived in ignorance. **¹⁵**But just as he who called you is holy, so be holy in all you do; **¹⁶**for it is written: "Be holy, because I am holy."*ᵃ*

¹⁷Since you call on a Father who judges each person's work impartially, live out your time as foreigners here in reverent fear. **¹⁸**For you know that it was not with perishable things such as silver or gold that you were redeemed from the empty way of life handed down to you from your ancestors, **¹⁹**but with the precious blood of Christ, a lamb without blemish or defect. **²⁰**He was chosen before the creation of the world, but was revealed in these last times for your sake. **²¹**Through him you believe in God, who raised him from the dead and glorified him, and so your faith and hope are in God.

²²Now that you have purified yourselves by obeying the truth so that you have sincere love for each other, love one another deeply, from the heart.*ᵇ* **²³**For you have been born again, not of perishable seed, but of imperishable, through the living and enduring word of God. **²⁴**For,

"All people are like grass,
    and all their glory is like the flowers of
        the field;
the grass withers and the flowers fall,
25   but the word of the Lord endures
        forever."*ᶜ*

ᵃ 16 Lev. 11:44,45; 19:2   *ᵇ 22* Some early manuscripts *from a pure heart*   *ᶜ 25* Isaiah 40:6-8 (see Septuagint)

And this is the word that was preached to you.

2 Therefore, rid yourselves of all malice and all deceit, hypocrisy, envy, and slander of every kind. [2] Like newborn babies, crave pure spiritual milk, so that by it you may grow up in your salvation, [3] now that you have tasted that the Lord is good.

The Living Stone and a Chosen People

[4] As you come to him, the living Stone — rejected by humans but chosen by God and precious to him — [5] you also, like living stones, are being built into a spiritual house[a] to be a holy priesthood, offering spiritual sacrifices acceptable to God through Jesus Christ. [6] For in Scripture it says:

"See, I lay a stone in Zion,
a chosen and precious cornerstone,
and the one who trusts in him
will never be put to shame."[b]

[7] Now to you who believe, this stone is precious. But to those who do not believe,

"The stone the builders rejected
has become the cornerstone,"[c]

[8] and,

"A stone that causes people to stumble
and a rock that makes them fall."[d]

They stumble because they disobey the message — which is also what they were destined for.

[9] But you are a chosen people, a royal priesthood, a holy nation, God's special possession, that you may declare the praises of him who called you out of darkness into his wonderful light. [10] Once you were not a people, but now you are the people of God; once you had not received mercy, but now you have received mercy.

Living Godly Lives in a Pagan Society

[11] Dear friends, I urge you, as foreigners and exiles, to abstain from sinful desires, which wage war against your soul. [12] Live such good lives among the pagans that, though they accuse you of doing wrong, they may see your good deeds and glorify God on the day he visits us.

[13] Submit yourselves for the Lord's sake to every human authority: whether to the emperor, as the supreme authority, [14] or to governors, who are sent by him to punish those who do wrong and to commend those who do right. [15] For it is God's will that by doing good you should silence the ignorant talk of foolish people. [16] Live as free people, but do not use your freedom as a cover-up for evil; live as God's slaves. [17] Show proper respect to everyone, love the family of believers, fear God, honor the emperor.

[18] Slaves, in reverent fear of God submit yourselves to your masters, not only to those who are good and considerate, but also to those who are harsh. [19] For it is commendable if someone bears up under the pain of unjust suffering because they are conscious of God. [20] But how is it to your credit if you receive a beating for doing wrong and endure it? But if you suffer for doing good and you endure it, this is commendable before God. [21] To this you were called, because Christ suffered for you, leaving you an example, that you should follow in his steps.

[22] "He committed no sin,
and no deceit was found in his
mouth."[e]

[23] When they hurled their insults at him, he did not retaliate; when he suffered, he made no threats. Instead, he entrusted himself to him who judges justly. [24] "He himself bore our sins" in his body on the cross, so that we might die to sins and live for righteousness; "by his wounds you have been healed." [25] For "you were like sheep going astray,"[f] but now you have returned to the Shepherd and Overseer of your souls.

3 Wives, in the same way submit yourselves to your own husbands so that, if any of them do not believe the word, they may be won over without words by the behavior of their wives, [2] when they see the purity and reverence of your lives. [3] Your beauty should not come from outward adornment, such as elaborate hairstyles and the wearing of gold jewelry or fine clothes. [4] Rather, it should be that of your inner self, the unfading beauty of a gentle and quiet spirit, which is of great worth in God's sight. [5] For this is the way the holy women of the past who put their hope in God used to adorn themselves.

[a] 5 Or *into a temple of the Spirit*   [b] 6 Isaiah 28:16   [c] 7 Psalm 118:22   [d] 8 Isaiah 8:14
[e] 22 Isaiah 53:9   [f] 24,25 Isaiah 53:4,5,6 (see Septuagint)

BRING ON THE GLORY

READ: 1 PETER 2:12

Biblical glory means a weighty presence or reputation, which may not involve bright lights. Try replacing *glory* with *reputation*. When we talk about the glory of a person, we're talking about the "weight" of their presence, who they are, what they care about, how they fill a room. The glory of Billy Graham is not the same as the glory of Big Bird. When angels sang about God's glory at the birth of Jesus, they were showing the world the profoundly heavy reputation of God. Giving God glory means we show others God's weighty reputation; it means we show the world what God is like.

We are made to reveal what God is like. Every aspect of our lives gives us a chance to reflect God. In the words of Paul, whether we eat or drink or whatever we do, we do it all for the glory of God (1 Corinthians 10:31). Even the smallest of daily human experiences—eating, drinking, driving our car, getting dressed—are all ways we get to show the world what God is like. Paul shockingly tells us that every act can be an act of worship; every act a radiance of glory. Every day, in every conversation, we can give God glory by letting people see God's attributes in us. If we're glorifying God, we're telling others this is what God looks like.

BUILDING

FAITH

WISDOM

STRENGTH

Taken from *Coffee Shop Conversations* by Dale Fincher and Jonalyn Fincher, copyright © 2010 by Charles Dale Fincher and Jonalyn Grace Fincher, published by Zondervan.

They submitted themselves to their own husbands, [6]like Sarah, who obeyed Abraham and called him her lord. You are her daughters if you do what is right and do not give way to fear.

[7]Husbands, in the same way be considerate as you live with your wives, and treat them with respect as the weaker partner and as heirs with you of the gracious gift of life, so that nothing will hinder your prayers.

Suffering for Doing Good

[8]Finally, all of you, be like-minded, be sympathetic, love one another, be compassionate and humble. [9]Do not repay evil with evil or insult with insult. On the contrary, repay evil with blessing, because to this you were called so that you may inherit a blessing. [10]For,

"Whoever would love life
    and see good days
must keep their tongue from evil
    and their lips from deceitful speech.
[11]They must turn from evil and do good;
    they must seek peace and pursue it.
[12]For the eyes of the Lord are on the
        righteous
    and his ears are attentive to their
        prayer,
but the face of the Lord is against those
    who do evil."[a]

[13]Who is going to harm you if you are eager to do good? [14]But even if you should suffer for what is right, you are blessed. "Do not fear their threats[b]; do not be frightened."[c] [15]But in your hearts revere Christ as Lord. Always be prepared to give an answer to everyone who asks you to give the reason for the hope that you have. But do this with gentleness and respect, [16]keeping a clear conscience, so that those who speak maliciously against your good behavior in Christ may be ashamed of their slander. [17]For it is better, if it is God's will, to suffer for doing good than for doing evil. [18]For Christ also suffered once for sins, the righteous for the unrighteous, to bring you to God. He was put to death in the body but made alive in the Spirit. [19]After being made alive,[d] he went and made proclamation to the imprisoned spirits— [20]to those who were disobedient long ago when God waited patiently in the days of Noah while the ark was being built. In it only a few people, eight in all, were saved through water, [21]and this water symbolizes baptism that now saves you also—not the removal of dirt from the body but the pledge of a clear conscience toward God.[e] It saves you by the resurrection of Jesus Christ, [22]who has gone into heaven and is at God's right hand—with angels, authorities and powers in submission to him.

Living for God

4 Therefore, since Christ suffered in his body, arm yourselves also with the same attitude, because whoever suffers in the body is done with sin. [2]As a result, they do not live the rest of their earthly lives for evil human desires, but rather for the will of God. [3]For you have spent enough time in the past doing what pagans choose to do—living in debauchery, lust, drunkenness, orgies, carousing and detestable idolatry. [4]They are surprised that you do not join them in their reckless, wild living, and they heap abuse on you. [5]But they will have to give account to him who is ready to judge the living and the dead. [6]For this is the reason the gospel was preached even to those who are now dead, so that they might be judged according to human standards in regard to the body, but live according to God in regard to the spirit.

[7]The end of all things is near. Therefore be alert and of sober mind so that you may pray. [8]Above all, love each other deeply, because love covers over a multitude of sins. [9]Offer hospitality to one another without grumbling. [10]Each of you should use whatever gift you have received to serve others, as faithful stewards of God's grace in its various forms. [11]If anyone speaks, they should do so as one who speaks the very words of God. If anyone serves, they should do so with the strength God provides, so that in all things God may be praised through Jesus Christ. To him be the glory and the power for ever and ever. Amen.

Suffering for Being a Christian

[12]Dear friends, do not be surprised at the fiery ordeal that has come on you to test you,

---

[a] 12 Psalm 34:12-16   [b] 14 Or *fear what they fear*   [c] 14 Isaiah 8:12   [d] 18,19 Or *but made alive in the spirit,* [19]*in which also*   [e] 21 Or *but an appeal to God for a clear conscience*

MORTAL ENEMY

READ: 1 PETER 5:8

Long before the race of humans came into the world, there was a mighty angel—great in both rank and honor—serving in the high court of God. Though we know few details, we do know this angel wanted a station higher than the one he was created to possess. He wanted God's place, God's throne, God's power. And with that, God struck him down. The angel wasn't built to be God; if he wouldn't choose what he was created to be, then he'd become far less.

His angelic name was Lucifer, the light bringer. Today, he's known as Satan, and he's no storybook creature with horns and a pitchfork. Even depictions of him in movies hardly match his twistedness.

Satan has more power than the world's empires combined, yet he can subtly influence the hearts of men and women with prettiness, pleasure, and half-truths.

Why doesn't God just crush this horrible creature? Well, God could, and God will—one day. But not yet. The battle is not between God and Satan. The battle is over what we will do with our ideas about God.

There is a battle between heaven and hell over whether God is good. And the battle is for the human heart. God is more concerned about us. Will we see God as good? Will we choose to be God's friend? Or will we pretend we are God? Will we tell God to buzz off? Satan may influence us in many directions, but we still have the freedom to pursue God—or not.

BUILDING FAITH WISDOM STRENGTH

Taken from *Living with Questions* by Dale Fincher, copyright © 2007 by Charles Dale Fincher, published by Zondervan.

as though something strange were happening to you. [13] But rejoice inasmuch as you participate in the sufferings of Christ, so that you may be overjoyed when his glory is revealed. [14] If you are insulted because of the name of Christ, you are blessed, for the Spirit of glory and of God rests on you. [15] If you suffer, it should not be as a murderer or thief or any other kind of criminal, or even as a meddler. [16] However, if you suffer as a Christian, do not be ashamed, but praise God that you bear that name. [17] For it is time for judgment to begin with God's household; and if it begins with us, what will the outcome be for those who do not obey the gospel of God? [18] And,

> "If it is hard for the righteous to be saved,
>   what will become of the ungodly and
>   the sinner?"[a]

[19] So then, those who suffer according to God's will should commit themselves to their faithful Creator and continue to do good.

To the Elders and the Flock

5 To the elders among you, I appeal as a fellow elder and a witness of Christ's sufferings who also will share in the glory to be revealed: [2] Be shepherds of God's flock that is under your care, watching over them — not because you must, but because you are willing, as God wants you to be; not pursuing dishonest gain, but eager to serve; [3] not lording it over those entrusted to you, but being examples to the flock. [4] And when the Chief Shepherd appears, you will receive the crown of glory that will never fade away.

[5] In the same way, you who are younger, submit yourselves to your elders. All of you, clothe yourselves with humility toward one another, because,

> "God opposes the proud
>   but shows favor to the humble."[b]

[6] Humble yourselves, therefore, under God's mighty hand, that he may lift you up in due time. [7] Cast all your anxiety on him because he cares for you.

[8] Be alert and of sober mind. Your enemy the devil prowls around like a roaring lion looking for someone to devour. [9] Resist him, standing firm in the faith, because you know that the family of believers throughout the world is undergoing the same kind of sufferings.

[10] And the God of all grace, who called you to his eternal glory in Christ, after you have suffered a little while, will himself restore you and make you strong, firm and steadfast. [11] To him be the power for ever and ever. Amen.

Final Greetings

[12] With the help of Silas,[c] whom I regard as a faithful brother, I have written to you briefly, encouraging you and testifying that this is the true grace of God. Stand fast in it.

[13] She who is in Babylon, chosen together with you, sends you her greetings, and so does my son Mark. [14] Greet one another with a kiss of love.

Peace to all of you who are in Christ.

---

[a] 18 Prov. 11:31 (see Septuagint)   [b] 5 Prov. 3:34   [c] 12 Greek *Silvanus*, a variant of *Silas*

2 PETER

WHEN DID THIS HAPPEN?

Around A.D. 67 in Rome

WHO IS IN THIS BOOK?

Peter

Paul

VERSES YOU MIGHT RECOGNIZE

2 PETER 1:3

"His divine power has given us everything we need for a godly life through our knowledge of him who called us by his own glory and goodness."

2 PETER 3:14

"So then, dear friends ... make every effort to be found spotless, blameless and at peace with him."

WHAT'S IT ABOUT?

Peter wrote to the same group of believers who received his first letter, to encourage them to stay firmly rooted in their belief in Jesus Christ and not be misled by false teachers. He reminded them that they were eyewitnesses to the events of Jesus' life and told them to stay rooted in the knowledge of God. One source of this knowledge is Scripture, which comes from God, not humans (see 2 Peter 1:21).

Peter warned the people about false teachers. These people, whom he described as "springs without water," would receive strict punishment for denying Jesus and leading others astray. Peter also said scoffers would say that Jesus isn't really coming back. Believers should not listen to these false teachers because they will be severely punished.

Peter ended by telling the believers to fill their minds with the knowledge of God, be on guard against false teaching, and grow in spiritual maturity and holiness.

2 PETER

1 Simon Peter, a servant and apostle of Jesus Christ,

To those who through the righteousness of our God and Savior Jesus Christ have received a faith as precious as ours:

[2] Grace and peace be yours in abundance through the knowledge of God and of Jesus our Lord.

Confirming One's Calling and Election

[3] His divine power has given us everything we need for a godly life through our knowledge of him who called us by his own glory and goodness. [4] Through these he has given us his very great and precious promises, so that through them you may participate in the divine nature, having escaped the corruption in the world caused by evil desires.

[5] For this very reason, make every effort to add to your faith goodness; and to goodness, knowledge; [6] and to knowledge, self-control; and to self-control, perseverance; and to perseverance, godliness; [7] and to godliness, mutual affection; and to mutual affection, love. [8] For if you possess these qualities in increasing measure, they will keep you from being ineffective and unproductive in your knowledge of our Lord Jesus Christ. [9] But whoever does not have them is nearsighted and blind, forgetting that they have been cleansed from their past sins.

[10] Therefore, my brothers and sisters,[a] make every effort to confirm your calling and election. For if you do these things, you will never stumble, [11] and you will receive a rich welcome into the eternal kingdom of our Lord and Savior Jesus Christ.

Prophecy of Scripture

[12] So I will always remind you of these things, even though you know them and are firmly established in the truth you now have. [13] I think it is right to refresh your memory as long as I live in the tent of this body, [14] because I know that I will soon put it aside, as our Lord Jesus Christ has made clear to me. [15] And I will make every effort to see that after my departure you will always be able to remember these things.

[16] For we did not follow cleverly devised stories when we told you about the coming of our Lord Jesus Christ in power, but we were eyewitnesses of his majesty. [17] He received honor and glory from God the Father when the voice came to him from the Majestic Glory, saying, "This is my Son, whom I love; with him I am well pleased."[b] [18] We ourselves heard this voice that came from heaven when we were with him on the sacred mountain.

[19] We also have the prophetic message as something completely reliable, and you will do well to pay attention to it, as to a light shining in a dark place, until the day dawns and the morning star rises in your hearts. [20] Above all, you must understand that no prophecy of Scripture came about by the prophet's own interpretation of things. [21] For prophecy never had its origin in the human will, but prophets, though human, spoke from God as they were carried along by the Holy Spirit.

False Teachers and Their Destruction

2 But there were also false prophets among the people, just as there will be false teachers among you. They will secretly introduce destructive heresies, even denying the sovereign Lord who bought them — bringing swift destruction on themselves. [2] Many will follow their depraved conduct and will bring the way of truth into disrepute. [3] In their greed these teachers will exploit you with fabricated stories. Their condemnation has long been hanging over them, and their destruction has not been sleeping.

---

[a] 10 The Greek word for *brothers and sisters* (*adelphoi*) refers here to believers, both men and women, as part of God's family.   [b] 17 Matt. 17:5; Mark 9:7; Luke 9:35

[4] For if God did not spare angels when they sinned, but sent them to hell,[a] putting them in chains of darkness[b] to be held for judgment; [5] if he did not spare the ancient world when he brought the flood on its ungodly people, but protected Noah, a preacher of righteousness, and seven others; [6] if he condemned the cities of Sodom and Gomorrah by burning them to ashes, and made them an example of what is going to happen to the ungodly; [7] and if he rescued Lot, a righteous man, who was distressed by the depraved conduct of the lawless [8] (for that righteous man, living among them day after day, was tormented in his righteous soul by the lawless deeds he saw and heard)— [9] if this is so, then the Lord knows how to rescue the godly from trials and to hold the unrighteous for punishment on the day of judgment. [10] This is especially true of those who follow the corrupt desire of the flesh[c] and despise authority.

Bold and arrogant, they are not afraid to heap abuse on celestial beings; [11] yet even angels, although they are stronger and more powerful, do not heap abuse on such beings when bringing judgment on them from[d] the Lord. [12] But these people blaspheme in matters they do not understand. They are like unreasoning animals, creatures of instinct, born only to be caught and destroyed, and like animals they too will perish.

[13] They will be paid back with harm for the harm they have done. Their idea of pleasure is to carouse in broad daylight. They are blots and blemishes, reveling in their pleasures while they feast with you.[e] [14] With eyes full of adultery, they never stop sinning; they seduce the unstable; they are experts in greed—an accursed brood! [15] They have left the straight way and wandered off to follow the way of Balaam son of Bezer,[f] who loved the wages of wickedness. [16] But he was rebuked for his wrongdoing by a donkey—an animal without speech—who spoke with a human voice and restrained the prophet's madness.

[17] These people are springs without water and mists driven by a storm. Blackest darkness is reserved for them. [18] For they mouth empty, boastful words and, by appealing to the lustful desires of the flesh, they entice people who are just escaping from those who live in error. [19] They promise them freedom, while they themselves are slaves of depravity—for "people are slaves to whatever has mastered them." [20] If they have escaped the corruption of the world by knowing our Lord and Savior Jesus Christ and are again entangled in it and are overcome, they are worse off at the end than they were at the beginning. [21] It would have been better for them not to have known the way of righteousness, than to have known it and then to turn their backs on the sacred command that was passed on to them. [22] Of them the proverbs are true: "A dog returns to its vomit,"[g] and, "A sow that is washed returns to her wallowing in the mud."

The Day of the Lord

3 Dear friends, this is now my second letter to you. I have written both of them as reminders to stimulate you to wholesome thinking. [2] I want you to recall the words spoken in the past by the holy prophets and the command given by our Lord and Savior through your apostles.

[3] Above all, you must understand that in the last days scoffers will come, scoffing and following their own evil desires. [4] They will say, "Where is this 'coming' he promised? Ever since our ancestors died, everything goes on as it has since the beginning of creation." [5] But they deliberately forget that long ago by God's word the heavens came into being and the earth was formed out of water and by water. [6] By these waters also the world of that time was deluged and destroyed. [7] By the same word the present heavens and earth are reserved for fire, being kept for the day of judgment and destruction of the ungodly.

[8] But do not forget this one thing, dear friends: With the Lord a day is like a thousand years, and a thousand years are like a day. [9] The Lord is not slow in keeping his promise, as some understand slowness. Instead he is patient with you, not wanting anyone to perish, but everyone to come to repentance.

---

[a] 4 Greek *Tartarus*   [b] 4 Some manuscripts *in gloomy dungeons*   [c] 10 In contexts like this, the Greek word for *flesh* (*sarx*) refers to the sinful state of human beings, often presented as a power in opposition to the Spirit; also in verse 18.   [d] 11 Many manuscripts *beings in the presence of*   [e] 13 Some manuscripts *in their love feasts*   [f] 15 Greek *Bosor*   [g] 22 Prov. 26:11

HE'S GIVING SECOND CHANCES

READ: 2 PETER 3:9

People in Peter's day were laughing out loud. After all, the Old Testament predicted a "day of the Lord" when God would strike earth and put an end to evil (Amos 5:18-20). So where was he? And Jesus vowed to return to earth riding the clouds in phenomenal power and glory to judge the world (Matthew 24:30). Why wasn't he here?

The apostle Peter says the Lord has a good reason for what humans perceive as a delay. First, the Lord doesn't count time the way humans do. "With the Lord a day is like a thousand years," he wrote, "and a thousand years are like a day" (2 Peter 3:8). Second, God is slow to show up because he doesn't want anyone to die. He's giving everyone time to repent—to quit sinning and turn to him. That doesn't mean Jesus will never come back. The day of the Lord will surprise the world like a thief, yet no one will miss when the sky and earth melt with fire.

BUILDING

FAITH

WISDOM

STRENGTH

Then Peter asks a crucial question. "Since everything will be destroyed in this way, what kind of people ought you to be?" (2 Peter 3:11). There's a clear answer. You look forward and strive to be holy, committing yourself completely to the Lord as you anticipate his stupendous arrival.

Jesus said you can't predict when he will come back (Matthew 24:36). But whenever he shows up, you can be ready.

[10] But the day of the Lord will come like a thief. The heavens will disappear with a roar; the elements will be destroyed by fire, and the earth and everything done in it will be laid bare.[a]

[11] Since everything will be destroyed in this way, what kind of people ought you to be? You ought to live holy and godly lives [12] as you look forward to the day of God and speed its coming.[b] That day will bring about the destruction of the heavens by fire, and the elements will melt in the heat. [13] But in keeping with his promise we are looking forward to a new heaven and a new earth, where righteousness dwells.

[14] So then, dear friends, since you are looking forward to this, make every effort to be found spotless, blameless and at peace with him. [15] Bear in mind that our Lord's patience means salvation, just as our dear brother Paul also wrote you with the wisdom that God gave him. [16] He writes the same way in all his letters, speaking in them of these matters. His letters contain some things that are hard to understand, which ignorant and unstable people distort, as they do the other Scriptures, to their own destruction.

[17] Therefore, dear friends, since you have been forewarned, be on your guard so that you may not be carried away by the error of the lawless and fall from your secure position. [18] But grow in the grace and knowledge of our Lord and Savior Jesus Christ. To him be glory both now and forever! Amen.

---

[a] 10 Some manuscripts *be burned up*   [b] 12 Or *as you wait eagerly for the day of God to come*

1 JOHN

WHEN DID THIS HAPPEN?

Between A.D. 85 and 90 in the churches of Asia

WHO IS IN THIS BOOK?

John

VERSES YOU MIGHT RECOGNIZE

1 JOHN 1:9

"If we confess our sins, he is faithful and just and will forgive us our sins and purify us from all unrighteousness."

1 JOHN 4:7

"Dear friends, let us love one another, for love comes from God. Everyone who loves has been born of God and knows God."

WHAT'S IT ABOUT?

Written by John the disciple, who also wrote the Gospel of John, this book tells its readers how they can know that they are Christians and how they can have fellowship with God and other believers. John used comparisons—such as darkness and light, righteousness and sin, and love of the Father and love of the world—to show what it means to be a Christian. False teachers had been creeping in, so John provides these tests to help believers see what true faith in Jesus looks like.

John wrote this book near the end of his life, and it was circulated around the churches. Some people in the churches were discouraged because Jesus had been gone for so long. John encouraged them to keep going and reminded them of the great love the Father has for them and that they belong to him (see 1 John 3:1).

When he wrote his gospel, John told people how to believe in Jesus; in *this* book he told them how to know for sure that they *do* believe. He wrote so that the people will know that they have eternal life. Being reminded of what Jesus had done for them and that they were children of God must have brought comfort to the believers who read John's letter.

The Incarnation of the Word of Life

1 That which was from the beginning, which we have heard, which we have seen with our eyes, which we have looked at and our hands have touched — this we proclaim concerning the Word of life. [2] The life appeared; we have seen it and testify to it, and we proclaim to you the eternal life, which was with the Father and has appeared to us. [3] We proclaim to you what we have seen and heard, so that you also may have fellowship with us. And our fellowship is with the Father and with his Son, Jesus Christ. [4] We write this to make our[a] joy complete.

Light and Darkness, Sin and Forgiveness

[5] This is the message we have heard from him and declare to you: God is light; in him there is no darkness at all. [6] If we claim to have fellowship with him and yet walk in the darkness, we lie and do not live out the truth. [7] But if we walk in the light, as he is in the light, we have fellowship with one another, and the blood of Jesus, his Son, purifies us from all[b] sin.

[8] If we claim to be without sin, we deceive ourselves and the truth is not in us. [9] If we confess our sins, he is faithful and just and will forgive us our sins and purify us from all unrighteousness. [10] If we claim we have not sinned, we make him out to be a liar and his word is not in us.

2 My dear children, I write this to you so that you will not sin. But if anybody does sin, we have an advocate with the Father — Jesus Christ, the Righteous One. [2] He is the atoning sacrifice for our sins, and not only for ours but also for the sins of the whole world.

Love and Hatred for Fellow Believers

[3] We know that we have come to know him if we keep his commands. [4] Whoever says, "I know him," but does not do what he commands is a liar, and the truth is not in that person. [5] But if anyone obeys his word, love for God[c] is truly made complete in them. This is how we know we are in him: [6] Whoever claims to live in him must live as Jesus did.

[7] Dear friends, I am not writing you a new command but an old one, which you have had since the beginning. This old command is the message you have heard. [8] Yet I am writing you a new command; its truth is seen in him and in you, because the darkness is passing and the true light is already shining.

[9] Anyone who claims to be in the light but hates a brother or sister[d] is still in the darkness. [10] Anyone who loves their brother and sister[e] lives in the light, and there is nothing in them to make them stumble. [11] But anyone who hates a brother or sister is in the darkness and walks around in the darkness. They do not know where they are going, because the darkness has blinded them.

Reasons for Writing

[12] I am writing to you, dear children,
  because your sins have been forgiven
    on account of his name.
[13] I am writing to you, fathers,
  because you know him who is from the
    beginning.
I am writing to you, young men,
  because you have overcome the
    evil one.

[14] I write to you, dear children,
  because you know the Father.
I write to you, fathers,
  because you know him who is from
    the beginning.
I write to you, young men,
  because you are strong,
  and the word of God lives in you,
  and you have overcome the evil one.

---

[a] 4 Some manuscripts *your*   [b] 7 Or *every*   [c] 5 Or *word, God's love*   [d] 9 The Greek word for *brother or sister* (*adelphos*) refers here to a believer, whether man or woman, as part of God's family; also in verse 11; and in 3:15, 17; 4:20; 5:16.   [e] 10 The Greek word for *brother and sister* (*adelphos*) refers here to a believer, whether man or woman, as part of God's family; also in 3:10; 4:20, 21.

PICKED BACK UP

READ: 1 JOHN 1:9

You're fooling yourself if you think you never mess up. It's tough to dig into the commands of the Bible—all the dos and don'ts—and miss the point that you fall short of God's expectations. In case you're persuaded that you're perfect, 1 John 1:8 sets you straight. It says, "If we claim to be without sin, we deceive ourselves and the truth is not in us."

That's difficult to hear, until you get to the next verse, 1 John 1:9. It teaches, "If we confess our sins, he is faithful and just and will forgive us our sins and purify us from all unrighteousness." If you roll those two verses together, you get one of the Bible's most crucial messages. We all fall down. But God picks us back up. The literal meaning of the verb "to sin" is "to miss the mark," like shooting an arrow and failing to hit the bull's-eye. It doesn't matter whether you miss by a little or a lot. It's still sin. But you're a truly bad shot if you claim you hit the target when you don't.

BUILDING

FAITH

WISDOM

STRENGTH

God has a simple requirement. He wants you to "confess" or "acknowledge" your sins to him, agreeing with him about what you did wrong. When you admit your failings, God has an equally simple reaction. He forgives you and cleanses you from every wrong.

On Not Loving the World

¹⁵Do not love the world or anything in the world. If anyone loves the world, love for the Father*ᵃ* is not in them. ¹⁶For everything in the world — the lust of the flesh, the lust of the eyes, and the pride of life — comes not from the Father but from the world. ¹⁷The world and its desires pass away, but whoever does the will of God lives forever.

Warnings Against Denying the Son

¹⁸Dear children, this is the last hour; and as you have heard that the antichrist is coming, even now many antichrists have come. This is how we know it is the last hour. ¹⁹They went out from us, but they did not really belong to us. For if they had belonged to us, they would have remained with us; but their going showed that none of them belonged to us.

²⁰But you have an anointing from the Holy One, and all of you know the truth.*ᵇ* ²¹I do not write to you because you do not know the truth, but because you do know it and because no lie comes from the truth. ²²Who is the liar? It is whoever denies that Jesus is the Christ. Such a person is the antichrist — denying the Father and the Son. ²³No one who denies the Son has the Father; whoever acknowledges the Son has the Father also.

²⁴As for you, see that what you have heard from the beginning remains in you. If it does, you also will remain in the Son and in the Father. ²⁵And this is what he promised us — eternal life.

²⁶I am writing these things to you about those who are trying to lead you astray. ²⁷As for you, the anointing you received from him remains in you, and you do not need anyone to teach you. But as his anointing teaches you about all things and as that anointing is real, not counterfeit — just as it has taught you, remain in him.

God's Children and Sin

²⁸And now, dear children, continue in him, so that when he appears we may be confident and unashamed before him at his coming.

²⁹If you know that he is righteous, you know that everyone who does what is right has been born of him.

3 See what great love the Father has lavished on us, that we should be called children of God! And that is what we are! The reason the world does not know us is that it did not know him. ²Dear friends, now we are children of God, and what we will be has not yet been made known. But we know that when Christ appears,*ᶜ* we shall be like him, for we shall see him as he is. ³All who have this hope in him purify themselves, just as he is pure.

⁴Everyone who sins breaks the law; in fact, sin is lawlessness. ⁵But you know that he appeared so that he might take away our sins. And in him is no sin. ⁶No one who lives in him keeps on sinning. No one who continues to sin has either seen him or known him.

⁷Dear children, do not let anyone lead you astray. The one who does what is right is righteous, just as he is righteous. ⁸The one who does what is sinful is of the devil, because the devil has been sinning from the beginning. The reason the Son of God appeared was to destroy the devil's work. ⁹No one who is born of God will continue to sin, because God's seed remains in them; they cannot go on sinning, because they have been born of God. ¹⁰This is how we know who the children of God are and who the children of the devil are: Anyone who does not do what is right is not God's child, nor is anyone who does not love their brother and sister.

More on Love and Hatred

¹¹For this is the message you heard from the beginning: We should love one another. ¹²Do not be like Cain, who belonged to the evil one and murdered his brother. And why did he murder him? Because his own actions were evil and his brother's were righteous. ¹³Do not be surprised, my brothers and sisters,*ᵈ* if the world hates you. ¹⁴We know that we have passed from death to life, because we love each other. Anyone who does not love remains in death. ¹⁵Anyone who hates a brother or sister is a murderer,

---

ᵃ 15 Or *world, the Father's love*   *ᵇ 20* Some manuscripts *and you know all things*   *ᶜ 2* Or *when it is made known*   *ᵈ 13* The Greek word for *brothers and sisters* (*adelphoi*) refers here to believers, both men and women, as part of God's family; also in verse 16.

NO HOLDING OUT

READ: 1 JOHN 3:12

Original sin is the sin Adam and Eve committed when they bought the Enemy's lie that God was holding out on them. If you believe that God is holding out on you, you won't go all in with God. So the second sin recorded in Scripture (the first outside Eden) is a stepchild of the original sin. Cain held back—just like his parents.

Abel was all in. He brought God the best of the best—his choice lambs. But Cain held out. He gave God leftovers—the throwaway part of his harvest.

Nothing has changed. The choice is still ours to make—hold out on God or go all in. Isn't that the lesson to be learned from Ananias and Sapphira (Acts 5)? They gave the proceeds from a property sale to the church, but God struck them dead. What!? Why? Because they bald-faced lied about being all in. They claimed they had given up everything, but they kept a little pocket change.

BUILDING
FAITH
WISDOM
STRENGTH

The true value of an offering isn't measured by how much we give. It's measured by how much we keep. Look at the widow. She gave two copper coins—less than anybody else, but she kept nothing for herself (Mark 12:41-44). That's why Jesus honored the little boy who gave five loaves and two fish (John 6). It wasn't much, but it was everything he had.

Taken from *All In Student Edition* by Mark Batterson and Parker Batterson, copyright © 2014 by Mark Batterson, published by Zondervan.

and you know that no murderer has eternal life residing in him.

[16]This is how we know what love is: Jesus Christ laid down his life for us. And we ought to lay down our lives for our brothers and sisters. [17]If anyone has material possessions and sees a brother or sister in need but has no pity on them, how can the love of God be in that person? [18]Dear children, let us not love with words or speech but with actions and in truth.

[19]This is how we know that we belong to the truth and how we set our hearts at rest in his presence: [20]If our hearts condemn us, we know that God is greater than our hearts, and he knows everything. [21]Dear friends, if our hearts do not condemn us, we have confidence before God [22]and receive from him anything we ask, because we keep his commands and do what pleases him. [23]And this is his command: to believe in the name of his Son, Jesus Christ, and to love one another as he commanded us. [24]The one who keeps God's commands lives in him, and he in them. And this is how we know that he lives in us: We know it by the Spirit he gave us.

On Denying the Incarnation

4 Dear friends, do not believe every spirit, but test the spirits to see whether they are from God, because many false prophets have gone out into the world. [2]This is how you can recognize the Spirit of God: Every spirit that acknowledges that Jesus Christ has come in the flesh is from God, [3]but every spirit that does not acknowledge Jesus is not from God. This is the spirit of the antichrist, which you have heard is coming and even now is already in the world.

[4]You, dear children, are from God and have overcome them, because the one who is in you is greater than the one who is in the world. [5]They are from the world and therefore speak from the viewpoint of the world, and the world listens to them. [6]We are from God, and whoever knows God listens to us; but whoever is not from God does not listen to us. This is how we recognize the Spirit[a] of truth and the spirit of falsehood.

God's Love and Ours

[7]Dear friends, let us love one another, for love comes from God. Everyone who loves

has been born of God and knows God. [8]Whoever does not love does not know God, because God is love. [9]This is how God showed his love among us: He sent his one and only Son into the world that we might live through him. [10]This is love: not that we loved God, but that he loved us and sent his Son as an atoning sacrifice for our sins. [11]Dear friends, since God so loved us, we also ought to love one another. [12]No one has ever seen God; but if we love one another, God lives in us and his love is made complete in us.

[13]This is how we know that we live in him and he in us: He has given us of his Spirit. [14]And we have seen and testify that the Father has sent his Son to be the Savior of the world. [15]If anyone acknowledges that Jesus is the Son of God, God lives in them and they in God. [16]And so we know and rely on the love God has for us.

God is love. Whoever lives in love lives in God, and God in them. [17]This is how love is made complete among us so that we will have confidence on the day of judgment: In this world we are like Jesus. [18]There is no fear in love. But perfect love drives out fear, because fear has to do with punishment. The one who fears is not made perfect in love.

[19]We love because he first loved us. [20]Whoever claims to love God yet hates a brother or sister is a liar. For whoever does not love their brother and sister, whom they have seen, cannot love God, whom they have not seen. [21]And he has given us this command: Anyone who loves God must also love their brother and sister.

Faith in the Incarnate Son of God

5 Everyone who believes that Jesus is the Christ is born of God, and everyone who loves the father loves his child as well. [2]This is how we know that we love the children of God: by loving God and carrying out his commands. [3]In fact, this is love for God: to keep his commands. And his commands are not burdensome, [4]for everyone born of God overcomes the world. This is the victory that has overcome the world, even our faith. [5]Who is it that overcomes the world? Only the one who believes that Jesus is the Son of God.

[a] 6 Or *spirit*

JOHN THE DISCIPLE

Dear friends, let us love one another, for love comes from God. Everyone who loves has been born of God and knows God. 1 JOHN 4:7

HIS NAME MEANS: "the LORD is gracious"

READ HIS STORY: *Mark 1:19-20, 3:13-19, 10:35-45; Luke 9:28-36; John 13:22-25, 19:25-27, 20:1-10, 21:18-25; Acts 3:1-4:22; 1 John 4:7-21*

How would you like to be known as "the disciple whom Jesus loved"? What if you referred to *yourself* as "the one Jesus loved"? That might seem boastful. John used that term in his gospel, but he wasn't boasting. He was stating a fact.

Jesus had twelve disciples, but he was closest to three of them: John, James and Peter. They were among the first people called by Jesus (Mark 1:16-20). James and John were brothers and fishermen, just like Peter and his brother Andrew. While all the disciples traveled together, John, James and Peter were invited to see things the others didn't. The Gospels describe how those three climbed a mountain with Jesus when he met with God and was transfigured before them.

The Lord had a specific role for each disciple. During the Last Supper, John had a place of honor, sitting next to Jesus (John 13:23). Because he lived so long, many believe John was the youngest disciple. Yet when Jesus died on the cross, he asked John to take care of his mother (John 19:25-27). Jesus loved all the disciples equally, just like he loves all of us unconditionally. He didn't love John more, but John may have understood God's love the most.

After Jesus' death, the disciple Jesus loved showed his love for Christ. He became a leader in the church in Jerusalem. He served in Ephesus. He also wrote several biblical texts (the books of John, 1 John, 2 John, 3 John and Revelation). His writings explain God's love in sending his Son to die, rise again and return triumphantly.

TOTALLY, COMPLETELY

READ: 1 JOHN 4:18

G rowing up in church, I often heard we don't deserve God's love, that we're worthless like worms. And it puzzled me why God would love me if I were really worthless.

But I'm not a worm, and I'm not worthless. God made me valuable, even when I'm not living up to my potential all the time. God loved me enough to make me valuable, even before I was alive enough to know it.

And what does it mean to be loved by God? It means God draws near to you, has his eye on you, is pleased in you, and wants you to be his.

I have a friend from the Czech Republic who is often caught walking around his apartment in the morning saying, "There is nothing I can do today to make God love me less." Now that may be old to some, but it's new to others. And it's true. God does not love us because we act lovable all the time. God loves us because God wants to love us (1 John 4:16). And God's love made us valuable in our very being, regardless of our merit. Period.

BUILDING

FAITH

WISDOM

STRENGTH

There is absolutely nothing bad that you can do to make God love you less. God loves you because he made you. Add up all your bad things together, multiply them by a million, and God still loves you the same with his infinite love. Then my Czech friend will say, "There is nothing I can do to make God love me more." God is love. Period.

⁶This is the one who came by water and blood—Jesus Christ. He did not come by water only, but by water and blood. And it is the Spirit who testifies, because the Spirit is the truth. ⁷For there are three that testify: ⁸the*a* Spirit, the water and the blood; and the three are in agreement. ⁹We accept human testimony, but God's testimony is greater because it is the testimony of God, which he has given about his Son. ¹⁰Whoever believes in the Son of God accepts this testimony. Whoever does not believe God has made him out to be a liar, because they have not believed the testimony God has given about his Son. ¹¹And this is the testimony: God has given us eternal life, and this life is in his Son. ¹²Whoever has the Son has life; whoever does not have the Son of God does not have life.

Concluding Affirmations

¹³I write these things to you who believe in the name of the Son of God so that you may know that you have eternal life. ¹⁴This is the confidence we have in approaching God: that if we ask anything according to his will, he hears us. ¹⁵And if we know that he hears us—whatever we ask—we know that we have what we asked of him.

¹⁶If you see any brother or sister commit a sin that does not lead to death, you should pray and God will give them life. I refer to those whose sin does not lead to death. There is a sin that leads to death. I am not saying that you should pray about that. ¹⁷All wrongdoing is sin, and there is sin that does not lead to death.

¹⁸We know that anyone born of God does not continue to sin; the One who was born of God keeps them safe, and the evil one cannot harm them. ¹⁹We know that we are children of God, and that the whole world is under the control of the evil one. ²⁰We know also that the Son of God has come and has given us understanding, so that we may know him who is true. And we are in him who is true by being in his Son Jesus Christ. He is the true God and eternal life.

²¹Dear children, keep yourselves from idols.

---

a 7,8 Late manuscripts of the Vulgate *testify in heaven: the Father, the Word and the Holy Spirit, and these three are one.* *ᵍAnd there are three that testify on earth: the* (not found in any Greek manuscript before the fourteenth century)

2 JOHN

WHEN DID THIS HAPPEN?

Around A.D. 90 in the churches of Asia

WHO IS IN THIS BOOK?

John

VERSE YOU MIGHT RECOGNIZE

2 JOHN 5

"I am not writing you a new command but one we have had from the beginning. I ask that we love one another."

WHAT'S IT ABOUT?

John begins this letter, "To the lady chosen by God and to her children." No one knows for sure if John was writing to a particular woman and her children, or if he was talking about the church and its members.

The readers of this letter were dealing with false teachers who had come into the church. These deceivers were saying that Jesus had not really come in human form. John corrected this error and told his readers to be alert so they would not be led astray. He even warned them not to associate with these false teachers or welcome them into their homes. Instead, they should have nothing to do with them.

John urged his readers to love one another, a command that had been with them since Moses. Love is the trademark of those who walk in the truth. And without Jesus, no one can reach God.

2 JOHN

¹The elder,

To the lady chosen by God and to her children, whom I love in the truth — and not I only, but also all who know the truth — ²because of the truth, which lives in us and will be with us forever:

³Grace, mercy and peace from God the Father and from Jesus Christ, the Father's Son, will be with us in truth and love.

⁴It has given me great joy to find some of your children walking in the truth, just as the Father commanded us. ⁵And now, dear lady, I am not writing you a new command but one we have had from the beginning. I ask that we love one another. ⁶And this is love: that we walk in obedience to his commands. As you have heard from the beginning, his command is that you walk in love.

⁷I say this because many deceivers, who do not acknowledge Jesus Christ as coming in the flesh, have gone out into the world. Any such person is the deceiver and the antichrist. ⁸Watch out that you do not lose what we*a* have worked for, but that you may be rewarded fully. ⁹Anyone who runs ahead and does not continue in the teaching of Christ does not have God; whoever continues in the teaching has both the Father and the Son. ¹⁰If anyone comes to you and does not bring this teaching, do not take them into your house or welcome them. ¹¹Anyone who welcomes them shares in their wicked work.

¹²I have much to write to you, but I do not want to use paper and ink. Instead, I hope to visit you and talk with you face to face, so that our joy may be complete.

¹³The children of your sister, who is chosen by God, send their greetings.

---

a 8 Some manuscripts *you*

WHY ARE WE SO ANGRY?

READ: 2 JOHN 2-6

We're saved and we're a bunch of train wrecks, but we're mad at the world for doing lost stuff. At least that's the message they're hearing. We're angry at lost people for sinning.

We somehow have to connect with the folks who have the wrong image of God's people and God's love. It's apparent some truth made it out to the world, but love didn't always go with it.

Love earns the right to speak truth. And truth proves that we really love. That's why we have to speak truth in love. If all you are is truth, you're hammering rules and standards and unreachable goals. If all you are is love, you're giving everything a pass; love wins and everybody is going to be fine. We honor God when we strike a balance between the two.

BUILDING FAITH WISDOM STRENGTH

We all see the sinners, and we all judge them. This girl over here is living a reckless lifestyle and going from guy to guy because she never had a loving dad.

This guy buys the nicest clothes and latest tech gadgets and never has a hair out of place because he pursues an acceptance he never found at home.

These examples are generalizations that have one thing in common. They're people who long for intimate relationships and acceptance because they've never had it and have never met Jesus. We gravitate to where we are accepted. It's a sad day when the reason so many people remain entrenched in sinful lifestyles is because some of us Jesus people decided, Jesus wasn't a friend of sinners, and neither am I.

Taken from *Thrive Student Edition* by Mark Hall with Tim Luke, copyright © 2014 by Mark Hall, published by Zondervan.

TRUSTWORTHY TRIO

READ: 2 JOHN 5

This letter isn't any longer than a short bit of homework, yet it offers a glimpse into the real struggles of early Christians. Make sure you read 2 John alongside 3 John, because each note tackles the same problem from a different angle.

John wrote in his first letter about the Lord's command to love each other (1 John 3:23). This time around he doesn't apologize for repeating the same instruction (2 John v. 5). But it sounds like his readers have taken love in the wrong direction. John needs to warn them that the world is full of deceivers who teach that Jesus didn't have a real body. They make the Lord nothing more than a spirit, and a Savior without a physical body can't pay the price for human sin.

John tells his readers to shut out these false teachers. Welcoming them into their homes is sharing in their sin (2 John v. 11). John's third letter shows his readers have taken that warning to heart, but now they're slamming the door on genuine preachers. John tells his readers they should welcome these messengers of truth (3 John v. 8).

This trio of letters points out that the right way to love isn't always obvious. The Bible is your first and greatest source of wisdom. But don't be afraid to get input from experienced, trustworthy leaders. Whatever your situation, they can help you figure out the right way to act.

BUILDING

FAITH

WISDOM

STRENGTH

3 JOHN

➡ WHEN DID THIS HAPPEN?

Around A.D. 90 in the
churches of Asia

➡ WHO IS IN THIS BOOK?

John
Gaius
Demetrius
Diotrephes

➡ VERSE YOU MIGHT RECOGNIZE

3 JOHN 11

*"Dear friend, do not imitate
what is evil but what is good.
Anyone who does what is
good is from God. Anyone
who does what is evil has not
seen God."*

WHAT'S IT ABOUT?

At the time John wrote this letter,
church leaders traveled from town
to town, preaching the gospel. The
believers at a particular church would take
these missionaries into their homes. John wrote
to Gaius, a church member who was doing a
good job of showing hospitality, and praised
him for his faithfulness. He called attention
to another church member, Diotrephes, who
was causing trouble. Motivated by a need to
be first, Diotrephes was spreading rumors and
refusing to welcome these missionaries into the
church.

John wanted to make sure that those who
traveled around preaching the gospel would
receive a warm welcome from the churches
they visited. He once again emphasized that
believers need to love one another. This
love is put into action through encouraging
one another and showing hospitality, so that
believers can "work together for the truth" (see
3 John 1:8). John reminded the believers that
they had a common goal: spreading the good
news of Jesus. When they help each other, they
can accomplish more.

3 JOHN

¹The elder,

To my dear friend Gaius, whom I love in the truth.

²Dear friend, I pray that you may enjoy good health and that all may go well with you, even as your soul is getting along well. ³It gave me great joy when some believers came and testified about your faithfulness to the truth, telling how you continue to walk in it. ⁴I have no greater joy than to hear that my children are walking in the truth.

⁵Dear friend, you are faithful in what you are doing for the brothers and sisters,ᵃ even though they are strangers to you. ⁶They have told the church about your love. Please send them on their way in a manner that honors God. ⁷It was for the sake of the Name that they went out, receiving no help from the pagans. ⁸We ought therefore to show hospitality to such people so that we may work together for the truth.

⁹I wrote to the church, but Diotrephes, who loves to be first, will not welcome us. ¹⁰So when I come, I will call attention to what he is doing, spreading malicious nonsense about us. Not satisfied with that, he even refuses to welcome other believers. He also stops those who want to do so and puts them out of the church.

¹¹Dear friend, do not imitate what is evil but what is good. Anyone who does what is good is from God. Anyone who does what is evil has not seen God. ¹²Demetrius is well spoken of by everyone — and even by the truth itself. We also speak well of him, and you know that our testimony is true.

¹³I have much to write you, but I do not want to do so with pen and ink. ¹⁴I hope to see you soon, and we will talk face to face.

Peace to you. The friends here send their greetings. Greet the friends there by name.

JUDE

 WHEN DID THIS HAPPEN?

Around A.D. 65 in Palestine

 WHO IS IN THIS BOOK?

Jude
James
Enoch
Cain
Balaam

 VERSE YOU MIGHT RECOGNIZE

JUDE 20–21

"But you, dear friends, by building yourselves up in your most holy faith and praying in the Holy Spirit, keep yourselves in God's love."

WHAT'S IT ABOUT?

Some things are worth fighting for, and pure faith in Christ is one of them. Jude, the brother of James and Jesus, wrote this book. He began by telling his readers that he wanted to write about their shared salvation, but he went on to write a warning instead. False teachers had slipped into the church, and Jude told the believers not to associate with them. These false teachers did not honor Christ as Lord and were saying that sinful, pleasure-seeking behavior was okay.

Using Old Testament examples of the ungodly and rebellious, such as Cain, Balaam and Korah, Jude pointed out how serious it is when someone turns away from God. Jude had a similar message as 2 Peter, and it's possible that he was inspired to write his letter after reading Peter's. But Jude focused more deeply on false teaching.

Jude said believers can avoid unbelief by remembering the teaching of the apostles, building each other up in the faith and keeping themselves in the love of God. He ended with a powerful benediction affirming that God is able to help them stand firm and not stumble.

JUDE

[1]Jude, a servant of Jesus Christ and a brother of James,

To those who have been called, who are loved in God the Father and kept for[a] Jesus Christ:

[2]Mercy, peace and love be yours in abundance.

The Sin and Doom of Ungodly People

[3]Dear friends, although I was very eager to write to you about the salvation we share, I felt compelled to write and urge you to contend for the faith that was once for all entrusted to God's holy people. [4]For certain individuals whose condemnation was written about[b] long ago have secretly slipped in among you. They are ungodly people, who pervert the grace of our God into a license for immorality and deny Jesus Christ our only Sovereign and Lord.

[5]Though you already know all this, I want to remind you that the Lord[c] at one time delivered his people out of Egypt, but later destroyed those who did not believe. [6]And the angels who did not keep their positions of authority but abandoned their proper dwelling — these he has kept in darkness, bound with everlasting chains for judgment on the great Day. [7]In a similar way, Sodom and Gomorrah and the surrounding towns gave themselves up to sexual immorality and perversion. They serve as an example of those who suffer the punishment of eternal fire.

[8]In the very same way, on the strength of their dreams these ungodly people pollute their own bodies, reject authority and heap abuse on celestial beings. [9]But even the archangel Michael, when he was disputing with the devil about the body of Moses, did not himself dare to condemn him for slander but said, "The Lord rebuke you!"[d] [10]Yet these people slander whatever they do not understand, and the very things they do understand by instinct — as irrational animals do — will destroy them.

[11]Woe to them! They have taken the way of Cain; they have rushed for profit into Balaam's error; they have been destroyed in Korah's rebellion.

[12]These people are blemishes at your love feasts, eating with you without the slightest qualm — shepherds who feed only themselves. They are clouds without rain, blown along by the wind; autumn trees, without fruit and uprooted — twice dead. [13]They are wild waves of the sea, foaming up their shame; wandering stars, for whom blackest darkness has been reserved forever.

[14]Enoch, the seventh from Adam, prophesied about them: "See, the Lord is coming with thousands upon thousands of his holy ones [15]to judge everyone, and to convict all of them of all the ungodly acts they have committed in their ungodliness, and of all the defiant words ungodly sinners have spoken against him."[e] [16]These people are grumblers and faultfinders; they follow their own evil desires; they boast about themselves and flatter others for their own advantage.

A Call to Persevere

[17]But, dear friends, remember what the apostles of our Lord Jesus Christ foretold. [18]They said to you, "In the last times there will be scoffers who will follow their own ungodly desires." [19]These are the people who divide you, who follow mere natural instincts and do not have the Spirit.

[20]But you, dear friends, by building yourselves up in your most holy faith and praying

---

a 1 Or *by; or in*   *b 4* Or *individuals who were marked out for condemnation*   *c 5* Some early manuscripts *Jesus*   *d 9* Jude is alluding to the Jewish *Testament of Moses* (approximately the first century A.D.).   *e 14,15* From the Jewish *First Book of Enoch* (approximately the first century B.C.).

LIVING WITH QUESTIONS

READ: JUDE 22

Some people struggle with doubt. They question things in life, feel guilty about asking, and then suppress any further questions because they're told "doubting is wrong."

Let me just say it now: Doubt is not immoral, nor is it wrong. It's struggling to find out what is true. Doubt is a fire alarm that says something doesn't make sense. Doubt pushes us into our quest—even when ignoring our doubts sounds more comfortable at the moment. Doubt is what gives us the motivation to face our fears and see if we have the courage to venture into dark places. Doubt is often a friend who says, "Everything is not okay, so let's find a place that is."

Besides, everyone lives with doubt to some degree, even under very ordinary circumstances in their daily lives. People wonder, *Did I recharge my phone? Did I write down the correct answer on today's quiz? Did he really mean he liked that movie?*

Doubt happens, and we all do it. So let's not fret over it. After all, there's something far more tragic than doubting—refusing to deal with the truth when you know it's staring you in the face. We've all heard of immoral behavior. Well, refusing to deal with truth is immoral intellectual behavior. Doubt is a bundle of questions about the map and the journey; stubbornness dishonestly tears up the treasure map altogether.

BUILDING
FAITH
WISDOM
STRENGTH

Taken from *Living with Questions* by Dale Fincher, copyright © 2007 by Charles Dale Fincher, published by Zondervan.

in the Holy Spirit, ²¹ keep yourselves in God's love as you wait for the mercy of our Lord Jesus Christ to bring you to eternal life.

²² Be merciful to those who doubt; ²³ save others by snatching them from the fire; to others show mercy, mixed with fear — hating even the clothing stained by corrupted flesh.^a

Doxology

²⁴ To him who is able to keep you from stumbling and to present you before his glorious presence without fault and with great joy — ²⁵ to the only God our Savior be glory, majesty, power and authority, through Jesus Christ our Lord, before all ages, now and forevermore! Amen.

---

^a 22,23 The Greek manuscripts of these verses vary at several points.

REVELATION

WHEN DID THIS HAPPEN?

Written around A.D. 90 on the island of Patmos

WHO IS IN THIS BOOK?

John

Jesus

the Lamb

the rider on the white horse

the false prophet

the beast

Satan

VERSES YOU MIGHT RECOGNIZE

REVELATION 3:20

"Here I am! I stand at the door and knock. If anyone hears my voice and opens the door, I will come in and eat with that person, and they with me."

REVELATION 21:4

"There will be no more death or mourning or crying or pain, for the old order of things has passed away."

WHAT'S IT ABOUT?

John the disciple wrote this book near the end of his life, while he was banished to the island of Patmos for preaching the gospel in Asia. While he was there, John received a vision of what would take place in the future at the end of the world. John saw that a time would come, called the tribulation, where those who don't believe will be judged for their sins. Jesus, the Lamb, will return to conquer evil and create a new earth for those he has redeemed.

Since the very first man and woman sinned, the earth and the people in it have been experiencing the consequences of sin—evil, pain, sickness and death. The first time he came, Jesus died on the cross to save people from sin and bring them to God. When he returns, he will come as a mighty conqueror to end sin and Satan once and for all.

Like an action-packed dream, Revelation can be hard to understand and contains frightening characters such as the false prophet, the beast and the dragon. But John wrote Revelation as an encouragement to believers and said, "Blessed are those who hear it and take to heart what is written in it" (Revelation 1:3). One day, Jesus will return in justice and power to right everything that is wrong. Those who know him have nothing to fear.

REVELATION

Prologue

1 The revelation from Jesus Christ, which God gave him to show his servants what must soon take place. He made it known by sending his angel to his servant John, ²who testifies to everything he saw—that is, the word of God and the testimony of Jesus Christ. ³Blessed is the one who reads aloud the words of this prophecy, and blessed are those who hear it and take to heart what is written in it, because the time is near.

Greetings and Doxology

⁴John,

To the seven churches in the province of Asia:

Grace and peace to you from him who is, and who was, and who is to come, and from the seven spirits*ᵃ* before his throne, ⁵and from Jesus Christ, who is the faithful witness, the firstborn from the dead, and the ruler of the kings of the earth.

To him who loves us and has freed us from our sins by his blood, ⁶and has made us to be a kingdom and priests to serve his God and Father—to him be glory and power for ever and ever! Amen.

⁷"Look, he is coming with the clouds,"*ᵇ*
    and "every eye will see him,
    even those who pierced him";
    and all peoples on earth "will mourn
        because of him."*ᶜ*
                So shall it be! Amen.

⁸"I am the Alpha and the Omega," says the Lord God, "who is, and who was, and who is to come, the Almighty."

John's Vision of Christ

⁹I, John, your brother and companion in the suffering and kingdom and patient endurance that are ours in Jesus, was on the island of Patmos because of the word of God and the testimony of Jesus. ¹⁰On the Lord's Day I was in the Spirit, and I heard behind me a loud voice like a trumpet, ¹¹which said: "Write on a scroll what you see and send it to the seven churches: to Ephesus, Smyrna, Pergamum, Thyatira, Sardis, Philadelphia and Laodicea."

¹²I turned around to see the voice that was speaking to me. And when I turned I saw seven golden lampstands, ¹³and among the lampstands was someone like a son of man,*ᵈ* dressed in a robe reaching down to his feet and with a golden sash around his chest. ¹⁴The hair on his head was white like wool, as white as snow, and his eyes were like blazing fire. ¹⁵His feet were like bronze glowing in a furnace, and his voice was like the sound of rushing waters. ¹⁶In his right hand he held seven stars, and coming out of his mouth was a sharp, double-edged sword. His face was like the sun shining in all its brilliance.

¹⁷When I saw him, I fell at his feet as though dead. Then he placed his right hand on me and said: "Do not be afraid. I am the First and the Last. ¹⁸I am the Living One; I was dead, and now look, I am alive for ever and ever! And I hold the keys of death and Hades.

¹⁹"Write, therefore, what you have seen, what is now and what will take place later. ²⁰The mystery of the seven stars that you saw in my right hand and of the seven golden lampstands is this: The seven stars are the angels*ᵉ* of the seven churches, and the seven lampstands are the seven churches.

To the Church in Ephesus

2 "To the angel*ᶠ* of the church in Ephesus write:

These are the words of him who holds the seven stars in his right hand

---

ᵃ 4 That is, the sevenfold Spirit   *ᵇ 7* Daniel 7:13   *ᶜ 7* Zech. 12:10   *ᵈ 13* See Daniel 7:13.
ᵉ 20 Or *messengers*   *ᶠ 1* Or *messenger*; also in verses 8, 12 and 18

and walks among the seven golden lampstands. [2]I know your deeds, your hard work and your perseverance. I know that you cannot tolerate wicked people, that you have tested those who claim to be apostles but are not, and have found them false. [3]You have persevered and have endured hardships for my name, and have not grown weary.

[4]Yet I hold this against you: You have forsaken the love you had at first. [5]Consider how far you have fallen! Repent and do the things you did at first. If you do not repent, I will come to you and remove your lampstand from its place. [6]But you have this in your favor: You hate the practices of the Nicolaitans, which I also hate.

[7]Whoever has ears, let them hear what the Spirit says to the churches. To the one who is victorious, I will give the right to eat from the tree of life, which is in the paradise of God.

To the Church in Smyrna

[8]"To the angel of the church in Smyrna write:

These are the words of him who is the First and the Last, who died and came to life again. [9]I know your afflictions and your poverty — yet you are rich! I know about the slander of those who say they are Jews and are not, but are a synagogue of Satan. [10]Do not be afraid of what you are about to suffer. I tell you, the devil will put some of you in prison to test you, and you will suffer persecution for ten days. Be faithful, even to the point of death, and I will give you life as your victor's crown.

[11]Whoever has ears, let them hear what the Spirit says to the churches. The one who is victorious will not be hurt at all by the second death.

To the Church in Pergamum

[12]"To the angel of the church in Pergamum write:

These are the words of him who has the sharp, double-edged sword. [13]I know where you live — where Satan has his throne. Yet you remain true to my name. You did not renounce your faith in me, not even in the days of An-tipas, my faithful witness, who was put to death in your city — where Satan lives.

[14]Nevertheless, I have a few things against you: There are some among you who hold to the teaching of Balaam, who taught Balak to entice the Israelites to sin so that they ate food sacrificed to idols and committed sexual immorality. [15]Likewise, you also have those who hold to the teaching of the Nicolaitans. [16]Repent therefore! Otherwise, I will soon come to you and will fight against them with the sword of my mouth.

[17]Whoever has ears, let them hear what the Spirit says to the churches. To the one who is victorious, I will give some of the hidden manna. I will also give that person a white stone with a new name written on it, known only to the one who receives it.

To the Church in Thyatira

[18]"To the angel of the church in Thyatira write:

These are the words of the Son of God, whose eyes are like blazing fire and whose feet are like burnished bronze. [19]I know your deeds, your love and faith, your service and perseverance, and that you are now doing more than you did at first.

[20]Nevertheless, I have this against you: You tolerate that woman Jezebel, who calls herself a prophet. By her teaching she misleads my servants into sexual immorality and the eating of food sacrificed to idols. [21]I have given her time to repent of her immorality, but she is unwilling. [22]So I will cast her on a bed of suffering, and I will make those who commit adultery with her suffer intensely, unless they repent of her ways. [23]I will strike her children dead. Then all the churches will know that I am he who searches hearts and minds, and I will repay each of you according to your deeds.

[24]Now I say to the rest of you in Thyatira, to you who do not hold to her teaching and have not learned Satan's so-called deep secrets, 'I will not impose any other burden on you,

²⁵except to hold on to what you have until I come.'

²⁶To the one who is victorious and does my will to the end, I will give authority over the nations — ²⁷that one

'will rule them with an iron scepter
and will dash them to pieces like pottery'[a] — just as I have received authority from my Father. ²⁸I will also give that one the morning star. ²⁹Whoever has ears, let them hear what the Spirit says to the churches.

To the Church in Sardis

3 "To the angel[b] of the church in Sardis write:

These are the words of him who holds the seven spirits[c] of God and the seven stars. I know your deeds; you have a reputation of being alive, but you are dead. ²Wake up! Strengthen what remains and is about to die, for I have found your deeds unfinished in the sight of my God. ³Remember, therefore, what you have received and heard; hold it fast, and repent. But if you do not wake up, I will come like a thief, and you will not know at what time I will come to you.

⁴Yet you have a few people in Sardis who have not soiled their clothes. They will walk with me, dressed in white, for they are worthy. ⁵The one who is victorious will, like them, be dressed in white. I will never blot out the name of that person from the book of life, but will acknowledge that name before my Father and his angels. ⁶Whoever has ears, let them hear what the Spirit says to the churches.

To the Church in Philadelphia

⁷"To the angel of the church in Philadelphia write:

These are the words of him who is holy and true, who holds the key of David. What he opens no one can shut, and what he shuts no one can open. ⁸I know your deeds. See, I have placed before you an open door that no one can shut. I know that you have little strength, yet you have kept my word and have not denied my name. ⁹I will make those who are of the synagogue of Satan, who claim to be Jews though they are not, but are liars — I will make them come and fall down at your feet and acknowledge that I have loved you. ¹⁰Since you have kept my command to endure patiently, I will also keep you from the hour of trial that is going to come on the whole world to test the inhabitants of the earth.

¹¹I am coming soon. Hold on to what you have, so that no one will take your crown. ¹²The one who is victorious I will make a pillar in the temple of my God. Never again will they leave it. I will write on them the name of my God and the name of the city of my God, the new Jerusalem, which is coming down out of heaven from my God; and I will also write on them my new name. ¹³Whoever has ears, let them hear what the Spirit says to the churches.

To the Church in Laodicea

¹⁴"To the angel of the church in Laodicea write:

These are the words of the Amen, the faithful and true witness, the ruler of God's creation. ¹⁵I know your deeds, that you are neither cold nor hot. I wish you were either one or the other! ¹⁶So, because you are lukewarm — neither hot nor cold — I am about to spit you out of my mouth. ¹⁷You say, 'I am rich; I have acquired wealth and do not need a thing.' But you do not realize that you are wretched, pitiful, poor, blind and naked. ¹⁸I counsel you to buy from me gold refined in the fire, so you can become rich; and white clothes to wear, so you can cover your shameful nakedness; and salve to put on your eyes, so you can see.

¹⁹Those whom I love I rebuke and discipline. So be earnest and repent. ²⁰Here I am! I stand at the door and knock. If anyone hears my voice and opens the door, I will come in and eat with that person, and they with me.

²¹To the one who is victorious, I

---

a 27 Psalm 2:9   *b* 1 Or *messenger*; also in verses 7 and 14   *c* 1 That is, the sevenfold Spirit

FENCE SITTERS

READ: REVELATION 3:15-19

I remember some of the water fountains at my elementary school. I'd come in from recess, sweat streaking my face and matting my hair, dying for a long drink of cold water—only to find that a broken compressor had left the water without that refreshing chill. Few experiences are more unsatisfying than slurping from a lukewarm water supply.

Jesus uses this vivid word picture to describe the lack of passion and effectiveness of saints who are fence sitters. The church in Laodicea wanted both Jesus and the world—but it doesn't work like that. "Quit pretending," Jesus says. "This gap between what you say and how you live makes me want to spit you out."

Nobody walks out of church wanting to fail. Nobody wants to compromise. We trip and fall because life is hard. The world confronting us is fallen, broken, and decimated by sin. It is controlled by the prince of the power of the air, Satan himself.

BUILDING

FAITH

WISDOM

STRENGTH

There's no way we can make it without Jesus. The believer without a meaningful and practiced walk with Jesus and without a deep-rooted support system is a believer susceptible to the world's sway. The slow fade takes that believer far away from his anchor and leaves him somewhere in the middle, somewhere between the altar of his faith and the door of living out that faith.

ALL OR NOTHING

READ: REVELATION 3:15-16

Within a few months of coming to church, Jesus brought a radical change to a young single guy's life. It was easy to see the joy that he found in Christ.

Not long ago he asked if I would have coffee with him and his mom. When the three of us sat down, I thought I knew what she wanted to talk to me about. I was aware that she went to church, and I assumed that she wanted to say thank you for what was happening in her son's life. But that wasn't the case.

She was upset. "My son has taken all of this too far." She was not pleased with how much time he was spending at the church. Some of their relatives were bothered by his desire to always want to pray before the family meals. He wouldn't be quiet about the sermons ... And he had been talking about going on a mission trip. With frustration she asked me, "Can you please tell him that the Bible teaches 'everything in moderation'? Tell him that it doesn't have to be all or nothing?"

BUILDING FAITH WISDOM STRENGTH

I tried to keep a pleasant smile, but my teeth were clenched. So I did what I always do when I get angry; I started quoting Scripture from Revelation. I said to this lady who had been in church most of her life, "Jesus doesn't say, 'Everything in moderation'; he says you can't be my follower if you don't give up everything. His invitation is an all or nothing invitation."

Taken from *Not a Fan Student Edition* by Kyle Idleman, copyright © 2012 by City on the Hill Studio, Inc., published by Zondervan.

will give the right to sit with me on my throne, just as I was victorious and sat down with my Father on his throne. [22]Whoever has ears, let them hear what the Spirit says to the churches."

The Throne in Heaven

4 After this I looked, and there before me was a door standing open in heaven. And the voice I had first heard speaking to me like a trumpet said, "Come up here, and I will show you what must take place after this." [2]At once I was in the Spirit, and there before me was a throne in heaven with someone sitting on it. [3]And the one who sat there had the appearance of jasper and ruby. A rainbow that shone like an emerald encircled the throne. [4]Surrounding the throne were twenty-four other thrones, and seated on them were twenty-four elders. They were dressed in white and had crowns of gold on their heads. [5]From the throne came flashes of lightning, rumblings and peals of thunder. In front of the throne, seven lamps were blazing. These are the seven spirits[a] of God. [6]Also in front of the throne there was what looked like a sea of glass, clear as crystal.

In the center, around the throne, were four living creatures, and they were covered with eyes, in front and in back. [7]The first living creature was like a lion, the second was like an ox, the third had a face like a man, the fourth was like a flying eagle. [8]Each of the four living creatures had six wings and was covered with eyes all around, even under its wings. Day and night they never stop saying:

" 'Holy, holy, holy
is the Lord God Almighty,'[b]
who was, and is, and is to come."

[9]Whenever the living creatures give glory, honor and thanks to him who sits on the throne and who lives for ever and ever, [10]the twenty-four elders fall down before him who sits on the throne and worship him who lives for ever and ever. They lay their crowns before the throne and say:

[11] "You are worthy, our Lord and God,
to receive glory and honor and power,
for you created all things,

and by your will they were
created
and have their being."

The Scroll and the Lamb

5 Then I saw in the right hand of him who sat on the throne a scroll with writing on both sides and sealed with seven seals. [2]And I saw a mighty angel proclaiming in a loud voice, "Who is worthy to break the seals and open the scroll?" [3]But no one in heaven or on earth or under the earth could open the scroll or even look inside it. [4]I wept and wept because no one was found who was worthy to open the scroll or look inside. [5]Then one of the elders said to me, "Do not weep! See, the Lion of the tribe of Judah, the Root of David, has triumphed. He is able to open the scroll and its seven seals."

[6]Then I saw a Lamb, looking as if it had been slain, standing at the center of the throne, encircled by the four living creatures and the elders. The Lamb had seven horns and seven eyes, which are the seven spirits[a] of God sent out into all the earth. [7]He went and took the scroll from the right hand of him who sat on the throne. [8]And when he had taken it, the four living creatures and the twenty-four elders fell down before the Lamb. Each one had a harp and they were holding golden bowls full of incense, which are the prayers of God's people. [9]And they sang a new song, saying:

"You are worthy to take the scroll
and to open its seals,
because you were slain,
and with your blood you purchased
for God
persons from every tribe and language
and people and nation.
[10]You have made them to be a kingdom and
priests to serve our God,
and they will reign[c] on the earth."

[11]Then I looked and heard the voice of many angels, numbering thousands upon thousands, and ten thousand times ten thousand. They encircled the throne and the living creatures and the elders. [12]In a loud voice they were saying:

"Worthy is the Lamb, who was
slain,

---

[a] 5,6 That is, the sevenfold Spirit   [b] 8 Isaiah 6:3   [c] 10 Some manuscripts *they reign*

> to receive power and wealth and
> wisdom and strength
> and honor and glory and praise!"

¹³Then I heard every creature in heaven and on earth and under the earth and on the sea, and all that is in them, saying:

> "To him who sits on the throne and to
> the Lamb
> be praise and honor and glory and
> power,
> for ever and ever!"

¹⁴The four living creatures said, "Amen," and the elders fell down and worshiped.

The Seals

6 I watched as the Lamb opened the first of the seven seals. Then I heard one of the four living creatures say in a voice like thunder, "Come!" ²I looked, and there before me was a white horse! Its rider held a bow, and he was given a crown, and he rode out as a conqueror bent on conquest.

³When the Lamb opened the second seal, I heard the second living creature say, "Come!" ⁴Then another horse came out, a fiery red one. Its rider was given power to take peace from the earth and to make people kill each other. To him was given a large sword.

⁵When the Lamb opened the third seal, I heard the third living creature say, "Come!" I looked, and there before me was a black horse! Its rider was holding a pair of scales in his hand. ⁶Then I heard what sounded like a voice among the four living creatures, saying, "Two pounds*ᵃ* of wheat for a day's wages,*ᵇ* and six pounds*ᶜ* of barley for a day's wages,*ᵇ* and do not damage the oil and the wine!"

⁷When the Lamb opened the fourth seal, I heard the voice of the fourth living creature say, "Come!" ⁸I looked, and there before me was a pale horse! Its rider was named Death, and Hades was following close behind him. They were given power over a fourth of the earth to kill by sword, famine and plague, and by the wild beasts of the earth.

⁹When he opened the fifth seal, I saw under the altar the souls of those who had been slain because of the word of God and the testimony they had maintained. ¹⁰They called out in a loud voice, "How long, Sovereign Lord, holy and true, until you judge the inhabitants of the earth and avenge our blood?" ¹¹Then each of them was given a white robe, and they were told to wait a little longer, until the full number of their fellow servants, their brothers and sisters,*ᵈ* were killed just as they had been.

¹²I watched as he opened the sixth seal. There was a great earthquake. The sun turned black like sackcloth made of goat hair, the whole moon turned blood red, ¹³and the stars in the sky fell to earth, as figs drop from a fig tree when shaken by a strong wind. ¹⁴The heavens receded like a scroll being rolled up, and every mountain and island was removed from its place.

¹⁵Then the kings of the earth, the princes, the generals, the rich, the mighty, and everyone else, both slave and free, hid in caves and among the rocks of the mountains. ¹⁶They called to the mountains and the rocks, "Fall on us and hide us*ᵉ* from the face of him who sits on the throne and from the wrath of the Lamb! ¹⁷For the great day of their*ᶠ* wrath has come, and who can withstand it?"

144,000 Sealed

7 After this I saw four angels standing at the four corners of the earth, holding back the four winds of the earth to prevent any wind from blowing on the land or on the sea or on any tree. ²Then I saw another angel coming up from the east, having the seal of the living God. He called out in a loud voice to the four angels who had been given power to harm the land and the sea: ³"Do not harm the land or the sea or the trees until we put a seal on the foreheads of the servants of our God." ⁴Then I heard the number of those who were sealed: 144,000 from all the tribes of Israel.

> ⁵From the tribe of Judah 12,000 were
> sealed,
> from the tribe of Reuben 12,000,
> from the tribe of Gad 12,000,
> ⁶from the tribe of Asher 12,000,
> from the tribe of Naphtali 12,000,
> from the tribe of Manasseh 12,000,

ᵃ 6 Or about 1 kilogram   *ᵇ 6* Greek *a denarius*   *ᶜ 6* Or about 3 kilograms   *ᵈ 11* The Greek word for *brothers and sisters* (*adelphoi*) refers here to believers, both men and women, as part of God's family; also in 12:10; 19:10.   *ᵉ 16* See Hosea 10:8.   *ᶠ 17* Some manuscripts *his*

AND GOD SANG

READ: REVELATION 5:13

A ll things were created by God and for God. Every note of music. Every color on the palette. Every flavor of Skittles. Arnold Summerfield, the German physicist and pianist, noticed that a single hydrogen atom, which lets off 100 frequencies, is more musical than a grand piano, which only lets off eighty-eight frequencies.

Every single atom is a unique expression of God's creative genius. And God can create better music with an atom you can't see than with a giant grand piano. Every atom is a unique expression of worship. That's cool.

Composer Leonard Bernstein believed that the best translation of Genesis 1:3 isn't "and God said." He believed a more accurate translation would have been "and God sang." The Almighty sang every atom into existence, and every atom echoes that original melody sung in three-part harmony by the Father, Son, and Holy Spirit.

BUILDING
FAITH
WISDOM
STRENGTH

Whale songs can travel thousands of miles underwater. Meadowlarks have a range of 300 notes. Stars emit sounds too! Research in "bioacoustics" has revealed that we're surrounded by millions of ultrasonic songs. Supersensitive sound instruments have discovered that even earthworms make faint sounds.

The songs we can hear audibly are only one instrument in the symphony orchestra that is creation. Someday, heavenly eardrums will reveal millions of songs we could never hear with the human ear.

7 from the tribe of Simeon 12,000,
from the tribe of Levi 12,000,
from the tribe of Issachar 12,000,
8 from the tribe of Zebulun 12,000,
from the tribe of Joseph 12,000,
from the tribe of Benjamin 12,000.

The Great Multitude in White Robes

9 After this I looked, and there before me was a great multitude that no one could count, from every nation, tribe, people and language, standing before the throne and before the Lamb. They were wearing white robes and were holding palm branches in their hands. 10 And they cried out in a loud voice:

"Salvation belongs to our God,
who sits on the throne,
and to the Lamb."

11 All the angels were standing around the throne and around the elders and the four living creatures. They fell down on their faces before the throne and worshiped God, 12 saying:

"Amen!
Praise and glory
and wisdom and thanks and honor
and power and strength
be to our God for ever and ever.
Amen!"

13 Then one of the elders asked me, "These in white robes — who are they, and where did they come from?"

14 I answered, "Sir, you know."

And he said, "These are they who have come out of the great tribulation; they have washed their robes and made them white in the blood of the Lamb. 15 Therefore,

"they are before the throne of God
and serve him day and night in his
temple;
and he who sits on the throne
will shelter them with his
presence.
16 'Never again will they hunger;
never again will they thirst.
The sun will not beat down on them,'[a]
nor any scorching heat.
17 For the Lamb at the center of the throne
will be their shepherd;

'he will lead them to springs of living
water.'[a]
'And God will wipe away every tear
from their eyes.'[b]"

The Seventh Seal and the Golden Censer

8 When he opened the seventh seal, there was silence in heaven for about half an hour.

2 And I saw the seven angels who stand before God, and seven trumpets were given to them.

3 Another angel, who had a golden censer, came and stood at the altar. He was given much incense to offer, with the prayers of all God's people, on the golden altar in front of the throne. 4 The smoke of the incense, together with the prayers of God's people, went up before God from the angel's hand. 5 Then the angel took the censer, filled it with fire from the altar, and hurled it on the earth; and there came peals of thunder, rumblings, flashes of lightning and an earthquake.

The Trumpets

6 Then the seven angels who had the seven trumpets prepared to sound them.

7 The first angel sounded his trumpet, and there came hail and fire mixed with blood, and it was hurled down on the earth. A third of the earth was burned up, a third of the trees were burned up, and all the green grass was burned up.

8 The second angel sounded his trumpet, and something like a huge mountain, all ablaze, was thrown into the sea. A third of the sea turned into blood, 9 a third of the living creatures in the sea died, and a third of the ships were destroyed.

10 The third angel sounded his trumpet, and a great star, blazing like a torch, fell from the sky on a third of the rivers and on the springs of water — 11 the name of the star is Wormwood.[c] A third of the waters turned bitter, and many people died from the waters that had become bitter.

12 The fourth angel sounded his trumpet, and a third of the sun was struck, a third of the moon, and a third of the stars, so that a third of them turned dark. A third of the day was without light, and also a third of the night.

---

[a] 16,17 Isaiah 49:10   [b] 17 Isaiah 25:8   [c] 11 Wormwood is a bitter substance.

13 As I watched, I heard an eagle that was flying in midair call out in a loud voice: "Woe! Woe! Woe to the inhabitants of the earth, because of the trumpet blasts about to be sounded by the other three angels!"

9 The fifth angel sounded his trumpet, and I saw a star that had fallen from the sky to the earth. The star was given the key to the shaft of the Abyss. 2 When he opened the Abyss, smoke rose from it like the smoke from a gigantic furnace. The sun and sky were darkened by the smoke from the Abyss. 3 And out of the smoke locusts came down on the earth and were given power like that of scorpions of the earth. 4 They were told not to harm the grass of the earth or any plant or tree, but only those people who did not have the seal of God on their foreheads. 5 They were not allowed to kill them but only to torture them for five months. And the agony they suffered was like that of the sting of a scorpion when it strikes. 6 During those days people will seek death but will not find it; they will long to die, but death will elude them.

7 The locusts looked like horses prepared for battle. On their heads they wore something like crowns of gold, and their faces resembled human faces. 8 Their hair was like women's hair, and their teeth were like lions' teeth. 9 They had breastplates like breastplates of iron, and the sound of their wings was like the thundering of many horses and chariots rushing into battle. 10 They had tails with stingers, like scorpions, and in their tails they had power to torment people for five months. 11 They had as king over them the angel of the Abyss, whose name in Hebrew is Abaddon and in Greek is Apollyon (that is, Destroyer).

12 The first woe is past; two other woes are yet to come.

13 The sixth angel sounded his trumpet, and I heard a voice coming from the four horns of the golden altar that is before God. 14 It said to the sixth angel who had the trumpet, "Release the four angels who are bound at the great river Euphrates." 15 And the four angels who had been kept ready for this very hour and day and month and year were released to kill a third of mankind. 16 The number of the mounted troops was twice ten thousand times ten thousand. I heard their number.

17 The horses and riders I saw in my vision looked like this: Their breastplates were fiery red, dark blue, and yellow as sulfur. The heads of the horses resembled the heads of lions, and out of their mouths came fire, smoke and sulfur. 18 A third of mankind was killed by the three plagues of fire, smoke and sulfur that came out of their mouths. 19 The power of the horses was in their mouths and in their tails; for their tails were like snakes, having heads with which they inflict injury.

20 The rest of mankind who were not killed by these plagues still did not repent of the work of their hands; they did not stop worshiping demons, and idols of gold, silver, bronze, stone and wood—idols that cannot see or hear or walk. 21 Nor did they repent of their murders, their magic arts, their sexual immorality or their thefts.

The Angel and the Little Scroll

10 Then I saw another mighty angel coming down from heaven. He was robed in a cloud, with a rainbow above his head; his face was like the sun, and his legs were like fiery pillars. 2 He was holding a little scroll, which lay open in his hand. He planted his right foot on the sea and his left foot on the land, 3 and he gave a loud shout like the roar of a lion. When he shouted, the voices of the seven thunders spoke. 4 And when the seven thunders spoke, I was about to write; but I heard a voice from heaven say, "Seal up what the seven thunders have said and do not write it down."

5 Then the angel I had seen standing on the sea and on the land raised his right hand to heaven. 6 And he swore by him who lives for ever and ever, who created the heavens and all that is in them, the earth and all that is in it, and the sea and all that is in it, and said, "There will be no more delay! 7 But in the days when the seventh angel is about to sound his trumpet, the mystery of God will be accomplished, just as he announced to his servants the prophets."

8 Then the voice that I had heard from heaven spoke to me once more: "Go, take the scroll that lies open in the hand of the angel who is standing on the sea and on the land."

9 So I went to the angel and asked him to give me the little scroll. He said to me, "Take it and eat it. It will turn your stomach sour, but 'in your mouth it will be as sweet as

EVIL IMITATORS

READ: REVELATION 9:20

R evelation shows off ultimate human stubbornness. From the instant the Lamb opens the first of seven seals on a heavenly scroll (Revelation 6:1), God starts to pour judgment on the earth. Yet some humans refuse to quit sinning.

Revelation paints vivid pictures of destruction ranging from war to famine to plagues. Earthquakes rock the earth. The sun turns black, and the moon goes red. Stars drop from the sky, and the heavens roll up like a scroll. Everyone from rulers to regular people scurry to hide from the Lord's anger. "For the great day of their wrath has come," they say, "and who can withstand it?" (v. 17).

This last book of the Bible shows slain believers patiently waiting for their deaths to be avenged (vv. 9–11) and others killed during the great tribulation (7:14). Then seven trumpets signal more destruction. Humans die in vast numbers. Some people survive these plagues. Despite having seen evil punished on an immense scale, they refuse to repent—to quit sinning and turn to God. They continue worshiping idols, practicing dark arts, and committing sexual sin.

BUILDING FAITH WISDOM STRENGTH

It's tough to imagine how these people living at the end of time can see the harsh consequences of sin and continue doing evil. Yet refusing to follow the Lord here and now is like imitating their stubbornness. And no matter when or where you live, that's not a smart move.

honey.'^{a}" ^{10}I took the little scroll from the angel's hand and ate it. It tasted as sweet as honey in my mouth, but when I had eaten it, my stomach turned sour. ^{11}Then I was told, "You must prophesy again about many peoples, nations, languages and kings."

The Two Witnesses

11 I was given a reed like a measuring rod and was told, "Go and measure the temple of God and the altar, with its worshipers. ^{2}But exclude the outer court; do not measure it, because it has been given to the Gentiles. They will trample on the holy city for 42 months. ^{3}And I will appoint my two witnesses, and they will prophesy for 1,260 days, clothed in sackcloth." ^{4}They are "the two olive trees" and the two lampstands, and "they stand before the Lord of the earth."^{b} ^{5}If anyone tries to harm them, fire comes from their mouths and devours their enemies. This is how anyone who wants to harm them must die. ^{6}They have power to shut up the heavens so that it will not rain during the time they are prophesying; and they have power to turn the waters into blood and to strike the earth with every kind of plague as often as they want.

^{7}Now when they have finished their testimony, the beast that comes up from the Abyss will attack them, and overpower and kill them. ^{8}Their bodies will lie in the public square of the great city—which is figuratively called Sodom and Egypt—where also their Lord was crucified. ^{9}For three and a half days some from every people, tribe, language and nation will gaze on their bodies and refuse them burial. ^{10}The inhabitants of the earth will gloat over them and will celebrate by sending each other gifts, because these two prophets had tormented those who live on the earth.

^{11}But after the three and a half days the breath^{c} of life from God entered them, and they stood on their feet, and terror struck those who saw them. ^{12}Then they heard a loud voice from heaven saying to them, "Come up here." And they went up to heaven in a cloud, while their enemies looked on.

^{13}At that very hour there was a severe earthquake and a tenth of the city collapsed. Seven thousand people were killed in the earthquake, and the survivors were terrified and gave glory to the God of heaven.

^{14}The second woe has passed; the third woe is coming soon.

The Seventh Trumpet

^{15}The seventh angel sounded his trumpet, and there were loud voices in heaven, which said:

"The kingdom of the world has become
  the kingdom of our Lord and of his
    Messiah,
  and he will reign for ever and ever."

^{16}And the twenty-four elders, who were seated on their thrones before God, fell on their faces and worshiped God, ^{17}saying:

"We give thanks to you, Lord God
    Almighty,
  the One who is and who was,
because you have taken your great
      power
  and have begun to reign.
^{18}The nations were angry,
  and your wrath has come.
The time has come for judging the dead,
  and for rewarding your servants the
    prophets
and your people who revere your name,
  both great and small—
and for destroying those who destroy
    the earth."

^{19}Then God's temple in heaven was opened, and within his temple was seen the ark of his covenant. And there came flashes of lightning, rumblings, peals of thunder, an earthquake and a severe hailstorm.

The Woman and the Dragon

12 A great sign appeared in heaven: a woman clothed with the sun, with the moon under her feet and a crown of twelve stars on her head. ^{2}She was pregnant and cried out in pain as she was about to give birth. ^{3}Then another sign appeared in heaven: an enormous red dragon with seven heads and ten horns and seven crowns on its heads. ^{4}Its tail swept a third of the stars out of the sky and flung them to the earth. The dragon stood in front of the woman who was about to give birth, so that it might devour

^{a} 9 Ezek. 3:3 ^{b} 4 See Zech. 4:3,11,14. ^{c} 11 Or *Spirit* (see Ezek. 37:5,14)

her child the moment he was born. [5]She gave birth to a son, a male child, who "will rule all the nations with an iron scepter."[a] And her child was snatched up to God and to his throne. [6]The woman fled into the wilderness to a place prepared for her by God, where she might be taken care of for 1,260 days.

[7]Then war broke out in heaven. Michael and his angels fought against the dragon, and the dragon and his angels fought back. [8]But he was not strong enough, and they lost their place in heaven. [9]The great dragon was hurled down — that ancient serpent called the devil, or Satan, who leads the whole world astray. He was hurled to the earth, and his angels with him.

[10]Then I heard a loud voice in heaven say:

"Now have come the salvation and the
power
and the kingdom of our God,
and the authority of his Messiah.
For the accuser of our brothers and
sisters,
who accuses them before our God
day and night,
has been hurled down.
[11]They triumphed over him
by the blood of the Lamb
and by the word of their testimony;
they did not love their lives so much
as to shrink from death.
[12]Therefore rejoice, you heavens
and you who dwell in them!
But woe to the earth and the sea,
because the devil has gone down
to you!
He is filled with fury,
because he knows that his time
is short."

[13]When the dragon saw that he had been hurled to the earth, he pursued the woman who had given birth to the male child. [14]The woman was given the two wings of a great eagle, so that she might fly to the place prepared for her in the wilderness, where she would be taken care of for a time, times and half a time, out of the serpent's reach. [15]Then from his mouth the serpent spewed water like a river, to overtake the woman and sweep her away with the torrent. [16]But the earth helped the woman by opening its mouth and swallowing the river that the dragon had spewed out of his mouth. [17]Then the dragon was enraged at the woman and went off to wage war against the rest of her offspring — those who keep God's commands and hold fast their testimony about Jesus.

The Beast out of the Sea

13 The dragon[b] stood on the shore of the sea. And I saw a beast coming out of the sea. It had ten horns and seven heads, with ten crowns on its horns, and on each head a blasphemous name. [2]The beast I saw resembled a leopard, but had feet like those of a bear and a mouth like that of a lion. The dragon gave the beast his power and his throne and great authority. [3]One of the heads of the beast seemed to have had a fatal wound, but the fatal wound had been healed. The whole world was filled with wonder and followed the beast. [4]People worshiped the dragon because he had given authority to the beast, and they also worshiped the beast and asked, "Who is like the beast? Who can wage war against it?"

[5]The beast was given a mouth to utter proud words and blasphemies and to exercise its authority for forty-two months. [6]It opened its mouth to blaspheme God, and to slander his name and his dwelling place and those who live in heaven. [7]It was given power to wage war against God's holy people and to conquer them. And it was given authority over every tribe, people, language and nation. [8]All inhabitants of the earth will worship the beast — all whose names have not been written in the Lamb's book of life, the Lamb who was slain from the creation of the world.[c]

[9]Whoever has ears, let them hear.

[10]"If anyone is to go into captivity,
into captivity they will go.
If anyone is to be killed[d] with the sword,
with the sword they will be killed."[e]

This calls for patient endurance and faithfulness on the part of God's people.

The Beast out of the Earth

[11]Then I saw a second beast, coming out of the earth. It had two horns like a lamb,

---

[a] 5 Psalm 2:9   [b] 1 Some manuscripts *And I*   [c] 8 Or *written from the creation of the world in the book of* life *belonging to the Lamb who was slain*   [d] 10 Some manuscripts *anyone kills*   [e] 10 Jer. 15:2

WREAKING HAVOC

READ: **REVELATION 12:7–12**

How do we explain our badness? Our stubborn hearts and hurtful hands and conniving ways? How do we explain Auschwitz, human trafficking, abuse? Trace malevolence upriver to its beginning, where will the river take us? What will we see?

If I were the devil, I'd blame evil on a broken political system. A crippled economy. The roll of the dice. The Wicked Witch of the West. I'd want you to feel attacked by an indefinable, nebulous force. After all, if you can't diagnose the source of your ills, how can you treat them? If I were the devil, I'd keep my name out of it.

But God doesn't let the devil get away with this and tells us his name. The Greek word for devil is *diabolos*, which shares a root with the verb *diaballein*, which means *to split*. The devil is a splitter, a divider, a wedge driver. He divided Adam and Eve from God in the garden, and has every intent of doing the same to you. Blame all unrest on him. Don't fault the plunging economy or a society that doesn't "get" teenagers for your anxiety.

BUILDING FAITH WISDOM STRENGTH

We can't understand God's narrative without understanding Satan's strategy. Nothing thrills Satan more than the current skepticism with which he is viewed. When people deny his existence or chalk up his works to the ills of society, he rubs his hands with glee. The more we doubt his very existence, the more he can work without hindrance.

Taken from *God's Story, Your Story: Youth Edition* by Max Lucado, copyright © 2011 by Max Lucado, published by Zondervan.

but it spoke like a dragon. [12]It exercised all the authority of the first beast on its behalf, and made the earth and its inhabitants worship the first beast, whose fatal wound had been healed. [13]And it performed great signs, even causing fire to come down from heaven to the earth in full view of the people. [14]Because of the signs it was given power to perform on behalf of the first beast, it deceived the inhabitants of the earth. It ordered them to set up an image in honor of the beast who was wounded by the sword and yet lived. [15]The second beast was given power to give breath to the image of the first beast, so that the image could speak and cause all who refused to worship the image to be killed. [16]It also forced all people, great and small, rich and poor, free and slave, to receive a mark on their right hands or on their foreheads, [17]so that they could not buy or sell unless they had the mark, which is the name of the beast or the number of its name.

[18]This calls for wisdom. Let the person who has insight calculate the number of the beast, for it is the number of a man.[a] That number is 666.

The Lamb and the 144,000

14 Then I looked, and there before me was the Lamb, standing on Mount Zion, and with him 144,000 who had his name and his Father's name written on their foreheads. [2]And I heard a sound from heaven like the roar of rushing waters and like a loud peal of thunder. The sound I heard was like that of harpists playing their harps. [3]And they sang a new song before the throne and before the four living creatures and the elders. No one could learn the song except the 144,000 who had been redeemed from the earth. [4]These are those who did not defile themselves with women, for they remained virgins. They follow the Lamb wherever he goes. They were purchased from among mankind and offered as firstfruits to God and the Lamb. [5]No lie was found in their mouths; they are blameless.

The Three Angels

[6]Then I saw another angel flying in midair, and he had the eternal gospel to proclaim to those who live on the earth — to every nation, tribe, language and people. [7]He said in a loud voice, "Fear God and give him glory, because the hour of his judgment has come. Worship him who made the heavens, the earth, the sea and the springs of water."

[8]A second angel followed and said, " 'Fallen! Fallen is Babylon the Great,'[b] which made all the nations drink the maddening wine of her adulteries."

[9]A third angel followed them and said in a loud voice: "If anyone worships the beast and its image and receives its mark on their forehead or on their hand, [10]they, too, will drink the wine of God's fury, which has been poured full strength into the cup of his wrath. They will be tormented with burning sulfur in the presence of the holy angels and of the Lamb. [11]And the smoke of their torment will rise for ever and ever. There will be no rest day or night for those who worship the beast and its image, or for anyone who receives the mark of its name." [12]This calls for patient endurance on the part of the people of God who keep his commands and remain faithful to Jesus.

[13]Then I heard a voice from heaven say, "Write this: Blessed are the dead who die in the Lord from now on."

"Yes," says the Spirit, "they will rest from their labor, for their deeds will follow them."

Harvesting the Earth and Trampling the Winepress

[14]I looked, and there before me was a white cloud, and seated on the cloud was one like a son of man[c] with a crown of gold on his head and a sharp sickle in his hand. [15]Then another angel came out of the temple and called in a loud voice to him who was sitting on the cloud, "Take your sickle and reap, because the time to reap has come, for the harvest of the earth is ripe." [16]So he who was seated on the cloud swung his sickle over the earth, and the earth was harvested.

[17]Another angel came out of the temple in heaven, and he too had a sharp sickle. [18]Still another angel, who had charge of the fire, came from the altar and called in a loud voice to him who had the sharp sickle, "Take your sharp sickle and gather the clusters of grapes from the earth's vine, because its grapes are ripe." [19]The angel swung his

---

a 18 Or *is humanity's number*   *b 8* Isaiah 21:9   *c 14* See Daniel 7:13.

FAITHFUL ENDURANCE

READ: REVELATION 14:9-10

You met the beast back in Revelation 13, where he emerges from the sea to fill everyone with awe and wage war against God's people. He ultimately gains control of anyone who hasn't trusted in Jesus and had their names inscribed in the Lamb's book of life (Revelation 13:7–8).

A second beast emerges from the sea to promote the first beast. This deceiver forces everyone on earth to receive a mark on their right hand or forehead necessary to buy or sell anything. The "number" or "name" of the first beast is 666. That name identifies him as the most dominant man ever, a ruler John calls "the antichrist" (1 John 2:18).

Revelation 14 shows a crowd of people with a different mark. These 144,000 wear the names of the Lamb and his Father on their foreheads, and they sing a fresh song. After that pause three angels take wing to proclaim the gospel to the world and warn that anyone who worships the beast and receives his mark will face God's fury.

BUILDING
FAITH
WISDOM
STRENGTH

All of these details are baffling. But the Bible tells you how you should respond to these things now and forever. It says, "This calls for patient endurance on the part of the people of God who keep his commands and remain faithful to Jesus" (Revelation 14:12). Keep obeying God, count on his love, and let him take care of your future.

sickle on the earth, gathered its grapes and threw them into the great winepress of God's wrath. [20] They were trampled in the winepress outside the city, and blood flowed out of the press, rising as high as the horses' bridles for a distance of 1,600 stadia.[a]

Seven Angels With Seven Plagues

15 I saw in heaven another great and marvelous sign: seven angels with the seven last plagues—last, because with them God's wrath is completed. [2] And I saw what looked like a sea of glass glowing with fire and, standing beside the sea, those who had been victorious over the beast and its image and over the number of its name. They held harps given them by God [3] and sang the song of God's servant Moses and of the Lamb:

"Great and marvelous are your deeds,
Lord God Almighty.
Just and true are your ways,
King of the nations.[b]
[4] Who will not fear you, Lord,
and bring glory to your name?
For you alone are holy.
All nations will come
and worship before you,
for your righteous acts have been
revealed."[c]

[5] After this I looked, and I saw in heaven the temple—that is, the tabernacle of the covenant law—and it was opened. [6] Out of the temple came the seven angels with the seven plagues. They were dressed in clean, shining linen and wore golden sashes around their chests. [7] Then one of the four living creatures gave to the seven angels seven golden bowls filled with the wrath of God, who lives for ever and ever. [8] And the temple was filled with smoke from the glory of God and from his power, and no one could enter the temple until the seven plagues of the seven angels were completed.

The Seven Bowls of God's Wrath

16 Then I heard a loud voice from the temple saying to the seven angels, "Go, pour out the seven bowls of God's wrath on the earth."

[2] The first angel went and poured out his bowl on the land, and ugly, festering sores broke out on the people who had the mark of the beast and worshiped its image.

[3] The second angel poured out his bowl on the sea, and it turned into blood like that of a dead person, and every living thing in the sea died.

[4] The third angel poured out his bowl on the rivers and springs of water, and they became blood. [5] Then I heard the angel in charge of the waters say:

"You are just in these judgments,
O Holy One,
you who are and who were;
[6] for they have shed the blood of your holy
people and your prophets,
and you have given them blood to
drink as they deserve."

[7] And I heard the altar respond:

"Yes, Lord God Almighty,
true and just are your judgments."

[8] The fourth angel poured out his bowl on the sun, and the sun was allowed to scorch people with fire. [9] They were seared by the intense heat and they cursed the name of God, who had control over these plagues, but they refused to repent and glorify him.

[10] The fifth angel poured out his bowl on the throne of the beast, and its kingdom was plunged into darkness. People gnawed their tongues in agony [11] and cursed the God of heaven because of their pains and their sores, but they refused to repent of what they had done.

[12] The sixth angel poured out his bowl on the great river Euphrates, and its water was dried up to prepare the way for the kings from the East. [13] Then I saw three impure spirits that looked like frogs; they came out of the mouth of the dragon, out of the mouth of the beast and out of the mouth of the false prophet. [14] They are demonic spirits that perform signs, and they go out to the kings of the whole world, to gather them for the battle on the great day of God Almighty.

[15] "Look, I come like a thief! Blessed is the one who stays awake and remains clothed, so as not to go naked and be shamefully exposed."

---

[a] 20 That is, about 180 miles or about 300 kilometers; this song are drawn from Psalm 111:2,3; Deut. 32:4; Jer. 10:7; Psalms 86:9; 98:2.   [b] 3 Some manuscripts *ages*   [c] 3,4 Phrases in

¹⁶Then they gathered the kings together to the place that in Hebrew is called Armageddon.

¹⁷The seventh angel poured out his bowl into the air, and out of the temple came a loud voice from the throne, saying, "It is done!" ¹⁸Then there came flashes of lightning, rumblings, peals of thunder and a severe earthquake. No earthquake like it has ever occurred since mankind has been on earth, so tremendous was the quake. ¹⁹The great city split into three parts, and the cities of the nations collapsed. God remembered Babylon the Great and gave her the cup filled with the wine of the fury of his wrath. ²⁰Every island fled away and the mountains could not be found. ²¹From the sky huge hailstones, each weighing about a hundred pounds,^a fell on people. And they cursed God on account of the plague of hail, because the plague was so terrible.

Babylon, the Prostitute on the Beast

17 One of the seven angels who had the seven bowls came and said to me, "Come, I will show you the punishment of the great prostitute, who sits by many waters. ²With her the kings of the earth committed adultery, and the inhabitants of the earth were intoxicated with the wine of her adulteries."

³Then the angel carried me away in the Spirit into a wilderness. There I saw a woman sitting on a scarlet beast that was covered with blasphemous names and had seven heads and ten horns. ⁴The woman was dressed in purple and scarlet, and was glittering with gold, precious stones and pearls. She held a golden cup in her hand, filled with abominable things and the filth of her adulteries. ⁵The name written on her forehead was a mystery:

BABYLON THE GREAT
THE MOTHER OF PROSTITUTES
AND OF THE ABOMINATIONS
OF THE EARTH.

⁶I saw that the woman was drunk with the blood of God's holy people, the blood of those who bore testimony to Jesus.

When I saw her, I was greatly astonished. ⁷Then the angel said to me: "Why are you astonished? I will explain to you the mystery of the woman and of the beast she rides, which has the seven heads and ten horns. ⁸The beast, which you saw, once was, now is not, and yet will come up out of the Abyss and go to its destruction. The inhabitants of the earth whose names have not been written in the book of life from the creation of the world will be astonished when they see the beast, because it once was, now is not, and yet will come.

⁹"This calls for a mind with wisdom. The seven heads are seven hills on which the woman sits. ¹⁰They are also seven kings. Five have fallen, one is, the other has not yet come; but when he does come, he must remain for only a little while. ¹¹The beast who once was, and now is not, is an eighth king. He belongs to the seven and is going to his destruction.

¹²"The ten horns you saw are ten kings who have not yet received a kingdom, but who for one hour will receive authority as kings along with the beast. ¹³They have one purpose and will give their power and authority to the beast. ¹⁴They will wage war against the Lamb, but the Lamb will triumph over them because he is Lord of lords and King of kings — and with him will be his called, chosen and faithful followers."

¹⁵Then the angel said to me, "The waters you saw, where the prostitute sits, are peoples, multitudes, nations and languages. ¹⁶The beast and the ten horns you saw will hate the prostitute. They will bring her to ruin and leave her naked; they will eat her flesh and burn her with fire. ¹⁷For God has put it into their hearts to accomplish his purpose by agreeing to hand over to the beast their royal authority, until God's words are fulfilled. ¹⁸The woman you saw is the great city that rules over the kings of the earth."

Lament Over Fallen Babylon

18 After this I saw another angel coming down from heaven. He had great authority, and the earth was illuminated by his splendor. ²With a mighty voice he shouted:

"'Fallen! Fallen is Babylon the Great!'^b
    She has become a dwelling for demons
and a haunt for every impure spirit,
    a haunt for every unclean bird,

---

^a 21 Or about 45 kilograms   ^b 2 Isaiah 21:9

a haunt for every unclean and
detestable animal.
³ For all the nations have drunk
the maddening wine of her adulteries.
The kings of the earth committed
adultery with her,
and the merchants of the earth grew
rich from her excessive luxuries."

Warning to Escape Babylon's Judgment

⁴ Then I heard another voice from heaven
say:

" 'Come out of her, my people,'ᵃ
so that you will not share in her sins,
so that you will not receive any of her
plagues;
⁵ for her sins are piled up to heaven,
and God has remembered
her crimes.
⁶ Give back to her as she has given;
pay her back double for what she has
done.
Pour her a double portion from her
own cup.
⁷ Give her as much torment and grief
as the glory and luxury she gave
herself.
In her heart she boasts,
'I sit enthroned as queen.
I am not a widow;ᵇ
I will never mourn.'
⁸ Therefore in one day her plagues will
overtake her:
death, mourning and famine.
She will be consumed by fire,
for mighty is the Lord God who
judges her.

Threefold Woe Over Babylon's Fall

⁹ "When the kings of the earth who committed adultery with her and shared her luxury see the smoke of her burning, they will
weep and mourn over her. ¹⁰ Terrified at her
torment, they will stand far off and cry:

" 'Woe! Woe to you, great city,
you mighty city of Babylon!
In one hour your doom has come!'

¹¹ "The merchants of the earth will weep
and mourn over her because no one buys
their cargoes anymore — ¹² cargoes of gold,
silver, precious stones and pearls; fine linen,

purple, silk and scarlet cloth; every sort of
citron wood, and articles of every kind made
of ivory, costly wood, bronze, iron and marble; ¹³ cargoes of cinnamon and spice, of incense, myrrh and frankincense, of wine and
olive oil, of fine flour and wheat; cattle and
sheep; horses and carriages; and human beings sold as slaves.

¹⁴ "They will say, 'The fruit you longed for
is gone from you. All your luxury and splendor have vanished, never to be recovered.'
¹⁵ The merchants who sold these things and
gained their wealth from her will stand far
off, terrified at her torment. They will weep
and mourn ¹⁶ and cry out:

" 'Woe! Woe to you, great city,
dressed in fine linen, purple
and scarlet,
and glittering with gold, precious
stones and pearls!
¹⁷ In one hour such great wealth has been
brought to ruin!'

"Every sea captain, and all who travel by
ship, the sailors, and all who earn their living from the sea, will stand far off. ¹⁸ When
they see the smoke of her burning, they will
exclaim, 'Was there ever a city like this great
city?' ¹⁹ They will throw dust on their heads,
and with weeping and mourning cry out:

" 'Woe! Woe to you, great city,
where all who had ships on
the sea
became rich through her wealth!
In one hour she has been brought
to ruin!'

²⁰ "Rejoice over her, you heavens!
Rejoice, you people of God!
Rejoice, apostles and prophets!
For God has judged her
with the judgment she imposed
on you."

The Finality of Babylon's Doom

²¹ Then a mighty angel picked up a boul-
der the size of a large millstone and threw it
into the sea, and said:

"With such violence
the great city of Babylon will be
thrown down,
never to be found again.

ᵃ 4 Jer. 51:45   ᵇ 7 See Isaiah 47:7,8.

²²The music of harpists and musicians,
> pipers and trumpeters,
>   will never be heard in you again.
No worker of any trade
>   will ever be found in you again.
The sound of a millstone
>   will never be heard in you again.
²³The light of a lamp
>   will never shine in you again.
The voice of bridegroom and bride
>   will never be heard in you again.
Your merchants were the world's
>   important people.
> By your magic spell all the nations
>   were led astray.
²⁴In her was found the blood of prophets
>   and of God's holy people,
> of all who have been slaughtered on
>   the earth."

Threefold Hallelujah Over Babylon's Fall

19 After this I heard what sounded like the roar of a great multitude in heaven shouting:

> "Hallelujah!
> Salvation and glory and power belong
>   to our God,
² for true and just are his judgments.
> He has condemned the great
>   prostitute
>   who corrupted the earth by her
>   adulteries.
> He has avenged on her the blood of his
>   servants."

³And again they shouted:

> "Hallelujah!
> The smoke from her goes up for ever
>   and ever."

⁴The twenty-four elders and the four living creatures fell down and worshiped God, who was seated on the throne. And they cried:

> "Amen, Hallelujah!"

⁵Then a voice came from the throne, saying:

> "Praise our God,
>   all you his servants,
> you who fear him,
>   both great and small!"

⁶Then I heard what sounded like a great multitude, like the roar of rushing waters and like loud peals of thunder, shouting:

> "Hallelujah!
>   For our Lord God Almighty reigns.
⁷Let us rejoice and be glad
>   and give him glory!
> For the wedding of the Lamb has come,
>   and his bride has made herself
>   ready.
⁸Fine linen, bright and clean,
>   was given her to wear."

(Fine linen stands for the righteous acts of God's holy people.)

⁹Then the angel said to me, "Write this: Blessed are those who are invited to the wedding supper of the Lamb!" And he added, "These are the true words of God."

¹⁰At this I fell at his feet to worship him. But he said to me, "Don't do that! I am a fellow servant with you and with your brothers and sisters who hold to the testimony of Jesus. Worship God! For it is the Spirit of prophecy who bears testimony to Jesus."

The Heavenly Warrior Defeats the Beast

¹¹I saw heaven standing open and there before me was a white horse, whose rider is called Faithful and True. With justice he judges and wages war. ¹²His eyes are like blazing fire, and on his head are many crowns. He has a name written on him that no one knows but he himself. ¹³He is dressed in a robe dipped in blood, and his name is the Word of God. ¹⁴The armies of heaven were following him, riding on white horses and dressed in fine linen, white and clean. ¹⁵Coming out of his mouth is a sharp sword with which to strike down the nations. "He will rule them with an iron scepter."ᵃ He treads the winepress of the fury of the wrath of God Almighty. ¹⁶On his robe and on his thigh he has this name written:

KING OF KINGS AND
LORD OF LORDS.

¹⁷And I saw an angel standing in the sun, who cried in a loud voice to all the birds flying in midair, "Come, gather together for the great supper of God, ¹⁸so that you may eat the flesh of kings, generals, and the mighty,

ᵃ 15 Psalm 2:9

BOW DOWN NOW

READ: REVELATION 19:16

Sometimes it doesn't look like Jesus is boss of your world. Evil runs rampant. Violent people get away with murder and more. Politicians lie, businesses cheat, and peers do wrong without ever getting in trouble. How can anyone think the Lord controls the world? God made the world, so he owns it (Psalm 24:1–2). Yet his creation has lived in all-out rebellion since Adam and Eve disobeyed the Lord (Genesis 3:1–24). The world doesn't submit to Jesus now, but one day it will. The Bible declares that one day every human being will admit that Jesus Christ is Lord (Philippians 2:10–11).

The book of Revelation alerts you to facts about the future, but sometimes it also flashes back to the past. And there was a monumental moment in Revelation 11. Heaven shouted because at that moment "the kingdom of the world" became "the kingdom of our Lord and of his Messiah" and "he will reign for ever and ever" (Revelation 11:15). Jesus took his enormous power and began to rule (v. 17).

BUILDING

FAITH

WISDOM

STRENGTH

The arrival of that kingdom commenced when Jesus came to earth to live, die, and rise. But his reign won't be complete until he comes back as King of Kings and Lord of Lords. So you can bow to him now and live for him. If you don't, you will still bow to him later.

of horses and their riders, and the flesh of all people, free and slave, great and small."

¹⁹Then I saw the beast and the kings of the earth and their armies gathered together to wage war against the rider on the horse and his army. ²⁰But the beast was captured, and with it the false prophet who had performed the signs on its behalf. With these signs he had deluded those who had received the mark of the beast and worshiped its image. The two of them were thrown alive into the fiery lake of burning sulfur. ²¹The rest were killed with the sword coming out of the mouth of the rider on the horse, and all the birds gorged themselves on their flesh.

The Thousand Years

20 And I saw an angel coming down out of heaven, having the key to the Abyss and holding in his hand a great chain. ²He seized the dragon, that ancient serpent, who is the devil, or Satan, and bound him for a thousand years. ³He threw him into the Abyss, and locked and sealed it over him, to keep him from deceiving the nations anymore until the thousand years were ended. After that, he must be set free for a short time.

⁴I saw thrones on which were seated those who had been given authority to judge. And I saw the souls of those who had been beheaded because of their testimony about Jesus and because of the word of God. They[a] had not worshiped the beast or its image and had not received its mark on their foreheads or their hands. They came to life and reigned with Christ a thousand years. ⁵(The rest of the dead did not come to life until the thousand years were ended.) This is the first resurrection. ⁶Blessed and holy are those who share in the first resurrection. The second death has no power over them, but they will be priests of God and of Christ and will reign with him for a thousand years.

The Judgment of Satan

⁷When the thousand years are over, Satan will be released from his prison ⁸and will go out to deceive the nations in the four corners of the earth—Gog and Magog—and to gather them for battle. In number they are like the sand on the seashore. ⁹They marched across the breadth of the earth and surrounded the camp of God's people, the city he loves. But fire came down from heaven and devoured them. ¹⁰And the devil, who deceived them, was thrown into the lake of burning sulfur, where the beast and the false prophet had been thrown. They will be tormented day and night for ever and ever.

The Judgment of the Dead

¹¹Then I saw a great white throne and him who was seated on it. The earth and the heavens fled from his presence, and there was no place for them. ¹²And I saw the dead, great and small, standing before the throne, and books were opened. Another book was opened, which is the book of life. The dead were judged according to what they had done as recorded in the books. ¹³The sea gave up the dead that were in it, and death and Hades gave up the dead that were in them, and each person was judged according to what they had done. ¹⁴Then death and Hades were thrown into the lake of fire. The lake of fire is the second death. ¹⁵Anyone whose name was not found written in the book of life was thrown into the lake of fire.

A New Heaven and a New Earth

21 Then I saw "a new heaven and a new earth,"[b] for the first heaven and the first earth had passed away, and there was no longer any sea. ²I saw the Holy City, the new Jerusalem, coming down out of heaven from God, prepared as a bride beautifully dressed for her husband. ³And I heard a loud voice from the throne saying, "Look! God's dwelling place is now among the people, and he will dwell with them. They will be his people, and God himself will be with them and be their God. ⁴'He will wipe every tear from their eyes. There will be no more death'[c] or mourning or crying or pain, for the old order of things has passed away."

⁵He who was seated on the throne said, "I am making everything new!" Then he said, "Write this down, for these words are trustworthy and true."

⁶He said to me: "It is done. I am the Alpha and the Omega, the Beginning and the End. To the thirsty I will give water without cost from the spring of the water of life. ⁷Those

---

a 4 Or *God; I also saw those who* b 1 Isaiah 65:17 c 4 Isaiah 25:8

WAITING TO GO HOME

READ: REVELATION 21:1-5

In a way, every story is about getting home, finding a home, or fixing something to make it the way it should be at home. Home is the place where you hope to find truth and justice and happiness and family. And love, of course.

Heroes are often driven to make things right (or escape what's wrong). Good stories show heroes trying to make the world they live in better homes for themselves or others.

Your part in God's story is a lot like that too. None of us are home yet. And we'll never find the home we dream of in this life. Our only hope for the perfect home, the perfect family, the perfect love is in the life to come when we'll finally be reunited with our Father.

You were born with a hunger for your heavenly home. Need proof?

Consider your questions. Questions about death and time, significance and relevance. Animals don't seem to ask the questions we do. Dogs howl at the moon, but we stare at it. How did we get here? What are we here for?

Are we someone's idea or something's accident? Why on earth are we on this earth? We ask questions about pain. And war. Can't conflict go the way of phonograph records and telegrams? And the grave. Why is the dash between the dates on a tombstone so small? Something tells us this isn't right, good, fair. This isn't home. Because according to Jesus we aren't home yet.

BUILDING
FAITH
WISDOM
STRENGTH

who are victorious will inherit all this, and I will be their God and they will be my children. [8]But the cowardly, the unbelieving, the vile, the murderers, the sexually immoral, those who practice magic arts, the idolaters and all liars — they will be consigned to the fiery lake of burning sulfur. This is the second death."

The New Jerusalem, the Bride of the Lamb

[9]One of the seven angels who had the seven bowls full of the seven last plagues came and said to me, "Come, I will show you the bride, the wife of the Lamb." [10]And he carried me away in the Spirit to a mountain great and high, and showed me the Holy City, Jerusalem, coming down out of heaven from God. [11]It shone with the glory of God, and its brilliance was like that of a very precious jewel, like a jasper, clear as crystal. [12]It had a great, high wall with twelve gates, and with twelve angels at the gates. On the gates were written the names of the twelve tribes of Israel. [13]There were three gates on the east, three on the north, three on the south and three on the west. [14]The wall of the city had twelve foundations, and on them were the names of the twelve apostles of the Lamb.

[15]The angel who talked with me had a measuring rod of gold to measure the city, its gates and its walls. [16]The city was laid out like a square, as long as it was wide. He measured the city with the rod and found it to be 12,000 stadia[a] in length, and as wide and high as it is long. [17]The angel measured the wall using human measurement, and it was 144 cubits[b] thick.[c] [18]The wall was made of jasper, and the city of pure gold, as pure as glass. [19]The foundations of the city walls were decorated with every kind of precious stone. The first foundation was jasper, the second sapphire, the third agate, the fourth emerald, [20]the fifth onyx, the sixth ruby, the seventh chrysolite, the eighth beryl, the ninth topaz, the tenth turquoise, the eleventh jacinth, and the twelfth amethyst.[d] [21]The twelve gates were twelve pearls, each gate made of a single pearl. The great street of the city was of gold, as pure as transparent glass.

[22]I did not see a temple in the city, because the Lord God Almighty and the Lamb are its temple. [23]The city does not need the sun or the moon to shine on it, for the glory of God gives it light, and the Lamb is its lamp. [24]The nations will walk by its light, and the kings of the earth will bring their splendor into it. [25]On no day will its gates ever be shut, for there will be no night there. [26]The glory and honor of the nations will be brought into it. [27]Nothing impure will ever enter it, nor will anyone who does what is shameful or deceitful, but only those whose names are written in the Lamb's book of life.

Eden Restored

22 Then the angel showed me the river of the water of life, as clear as crystal, flowing from the throne of God and of the Lamb [2]down the middle of the great street of the city. On each side of the river stood the tree of life, bearing twelve crops of fruit, yielding its fruit every month. And the leaves of the tree are for the healing of the nations. [3]No longer will there be any curse. The throne of God and of the Lamb will be in the city, and his servants will serve him. [4]They will see his face, and his name will be on their foreheads. [5]There will be no more night. They will not need the light of a lamp or the light of the sun, for the Lord God will give them light. And they will reign for ever and ever.

John and the Angel

[6]The angel said to me, "These words are trustworthy and true. The Lord, the God who inspires the prophets, sent his angel to show his servants the things that must soon take place."

[7]"Look, I am coming soon! Blessed is the one who keeps the words of the prophecy written in this scroll."

[8]I, John, am the one who heard and saw these things. And when I had heard and seen them, I fell down to worship at the feet of the angel who had been showing them to me. [9]But he said to me, "Don't do that! I am a fellow servant with you and with your fellow prophets and with all who keep the words of this scroll. Worship God!"

---

[a] 16 That is, about 1,400 miles or about 2,200 kilometers   [b] 17 That is, about 200 feet or about 65 meters
[c] 17 Or high   [d] 20 The precise identification of some of these precious stones is uncertain.

PERSONAL INVITATION

READ: **REVELATION 22:3-4**

The Bible is a rare book where it's okay to peek at the final pages to see how it ends. The Lord wants you to be sure not only about the future of your planet and everything you call home but also about your own eternal destiny.

After all the seals and trumpets and bowls of Revelation, the book describes God's new city descending from heaven. It shines with God's glory, a crystal-clear brilliance. The city is constructed of pure gold, built on foundations bedazzled with every kind of precious stone. Each of the city's twelve gates is carved from a gigantic pearl (Revelation 21:9-21).

But the stunning appearance of this fresh construction isn't what matters most. The best part of heaven is God himself. He now lives with believers forever and ever. The Bible declares that "they will be his people, and God himself will be with them and be their God" (v. 3). And the Lord will "wipe every tear from their eyes. There will be no more death or mourning or crying or pain, for the old order of things has passed away" (v. 4).

This book—and the Bible—wrap up with the truth that Jesus is coming soon (22:20). He invites you to come and drink of his free water of eternal life (v. 17). The Lord himself is the only thing that can quench your thirst now and forever.

BUILDING
FAITH
WISDOM
STRENGTH

¹⁰Then he told me, "Do not seal up the words of the prophecy of this scroll, because the time is near. ¹¹Let the one who does wrong continue to do wrong; let the vile person continue to be vile; let the one who does right continue to do right; and let the holy person continue to be holy."

Epilogue: Invitation and Warning

¹²"Look, I am coming soon! My reward is with me, and I will give to each person according to what they have done. ¹³I am the Alpha and the Omega, the First and the Last, the Beginning and the End.

¹⁴"Blessed are those who wash their robes, that they may have the right to the tree of life and may go through the gates into the city. ¹⁵Outside are the dogs, those who practice magic arts, the sexually immoral, the murderers, the idolaters and everyone who loves and practices falsehood.

¹⁶"I, Jesus, have sent my angel to give you*ᵃ* this testimony for the churches. I am the Root and the Offspring of David, and the bright Morning Star."

¹⁷The Spirit and the bride say, "Come!" And let the one who hears say, "Come!" Let the one who is thirsty come; and let the one who wishes take the free gift of the water of life.

¹⁸I warn everyone who hears the words of the prophecy of this scroll: If anyone adds anything to them, God will add to that person the plagues described in this scroll. ¹⁹And if anyone takes words away from this scroll of prophecy, God will take away from that person any share in the tree of life and in the Holy City, which are described in this scroll.

²⁰He who testifies to these things says, "Yes, I am coming soon."

Amen. Come, Lord Jesus.

²¹The grace of the Lord Jesus be with God's people. Amen.

ᵃ 16 The Greek is plural.

TABLE OF WEIGHTS
AND MEASURES

	Biblical Unit	Approximate American Equivalent	Approximate Metric Equivalent
WEIGHTS	talent (60 minas)	75 pounds	34 kilograms
	mina (50 shekels)	1 1/4 pounds	560 grams
	shekel (2 bekas)	2/5 ounce	11.5 grams
	pim (2/3 shekel)	1/4 ounce	7.8 grams
	beka (10 gerahs)	1/5 ounce	5.7 grams
	gerah	1/50 ounce	0.6 gram
	daric	1/3 ounce	8.4 grams
LENGTH	cubit	18 inches	45 centimeters
	span	9 inches	23 centimeters
	handbreadth	3 inches	7.5 centimeters
	stadion (pl. stadia)	600 feet	183 meters
CAPACITY			
Dry Measure	cor [homer] (10 ephahs)	6 bushels	220 liters
	lethek (5 ephahs)	3 bushels	110 liters
	ephah (10 omers)	3/5 bushel	22 liters
	seah (1/3 ephah)	7 quarts	7.5 liters
	omer (1/10 ephah)	2 quarts	2 liters
	cab (1/18 ephah)	1 quart	1 liter
Liquid Measure	bath (1 ephah)	6 gallons	22 liters
	hin (1/6 bath)	1 gallon	3.8 liters
	log (1/72 bath)	1/3 quart	0.3 liter

The figures of the table are calculated on the basis of a shekel equaling 11.5 grams, a cubit equaling 18 inches and an ephah equaling 22 liters. The quart referred to is either a dry quart (slightly larger than a liter) or a liquid quart (slightly smaller than a liter), whichever is applicable. The ton referred to in the footnotes is the American ton of 2,000 pounds. These weights are calculated relative to the particular commodity involved. Accordingly, the same measure of capacity in the text may be converted into different weights in the footnotes.

This table is based upon the best available information, but it is not intended to be mathematically precise; like the measurement equivalents in the footnotes, it merely gives approximate amounts and distances. Weights and measures differed somewhat at various times and places in the ancient world. There is uncertainty particularly about the ephah and the bath; further discoveries may shed more light on these units of capacity.

TOPICAL INDEX

MEN OF THE BIBLE
INDEX

INDEX OF DEVOTIONS FOR BUILDING FAITH, WISDOM AND STRENGTH

CONCORDANCE

The NIV Concordance, created by John R. Kohlenberger III, has been developed specifically for use with the New International Version (NIV). Like all concordances, it is a special index that contains an alphabetical listing of words used in the Bible text.

This concordance contains 2,474 word entries, with more than 10,000 Scripture references. Each word entry is followed by significant Scripture references in which that particular word is found, as well as by a brief excerpt from the surrounding context. In the context, the entry word is abbreviated by its first letter in bold print. Other forms of the entry word and related words indexed in this concordance are in parentheses.

This concordance also contains 155 biographical entries for significant people in the Bible. The descriptive phrases replace the brief context surrounding each occurrence of the name. In those instances where more than one Bible character has the same name, that name is placed under one block entry, and each person is given a number (1), (2), etc.

Two entries are marked with an asterisk (*). LORD* and LORD'S* list occurrences of the proper name of God, *Yahweh*, spelled "LORD" and "LORD's" in the NIV. These entries are distinguished from LORD and LORD's, which list occurrences of the title "Lord" and "Lord's."

This concordance is a valuable tool for Bible study. While one of its key purposes is to help the reader find forgotten references to familiar verses, it can also be used to do word studies and to locate and trace biblical themes. Whenever you find a significant context, be sure to read at least the whole verse in the NIV to discover its fuller meaning in its larger context.

AARON
Priesthood of (Ex 28:1; Nu 17; Heb 5:1–4; 7), garments (Ex 28; 39), consecration (Ex 29), ordination (Lev 8).
Spokesman for Moses (Ex 4:14–16, 27–31; 7:1–2). Supported Moses' hands in battle (Ex 17:8–13). Built golden calf (Ex 32; Dt 9:20). Talked against Moses (Nu 12). Priesthood opposed (Nu 16); staff budded (Nu 17). Forbidden to enter land (Nu 20:1–12). Death (Nu 20:22–29; 33:38–39).

ABANDON
Dt	4: 31	he will not a or destroy you
1Ti	4: 1	in later times some will a the faith

ABBA
Ro	8: 15	And by him we cry, "A, Father."
Gal	4: 6	the Spirit who calls out, "A,

ABEL
Second son of Adam (Ge 4:2). Offered proper sacrifice (Ge 4:4; Heb 11:4). Murdered by Cain (Ge 4:8; Mt 23:35; Lk 11:51; 1Jn 3:12).

ABIGAIL
Wife of Nabal (1Sa 25:30); pled for his life with David (1Sa 25:14–35). Became David's wife (1Sa 25:36–42).

ABIJAH
Son of Rehoboam; king of Judah (1Ki 14:31—15:8; 2Ch 12:16—14:1).

ABILITY (ABLE)
Ezr	2: 69	According to their a they gave
2Co	1: 8	far beyond our a to endure,
	8: 3	were able, and even beyond their a.

ABIMELEK
1. King of Gerar who took Abraham's wife Sarah, believing her to be his sister (Ge 20). Later made a covenant with Abraham (Ge 21:22–33).
2. King of Gerar who took Isaac's wife Rebekah, believing her to be his sister (Ge 26:1–11). Later made a covenant with Isaac (Ge 26:12–31).

ABLE (ABILITY ENABLE ENABLED ENABLES)
Eze	7: 19	gold will not be a to deliver them
Da	3: 17	the God we serve is a to deliver us
Ro	8: 39	will be a to separate us
	14: 4	the Lord is a to make them stand.
	16: 25	to him who is a to establish you
2Co	9: 8	God is a to bless you abundantly,
Eph	3: 20	him who is a to do immeasurably
2Ti	1: 12	that he is a to guard what I have
	3: 15	which are a to make you wise
Heb	7: 25	he is a to save completely

Jude	: 24	To him who is a to keep you
Rev	5: 5	He is a to open the scroll and its

ABOLISH
Mt	5: 17	think that I have come to a the Law

ABOMINATION
Da	11: 31	set up the a that causes desolation.

ABOUND (ABOUNDING ABOUNDS)
2Co	9: 8	you will a in every good work.
Php	1: 9	your love may a more and more

ABOUNDING (ABOUND)
Ex	34: 6	to anger, a in love and faithfulness,
Ps	86: 5	a in love to all who call to you.

ABOUNDS (ABOUND)
2Co	1: 5	also our comfort a through Christ.

ABRAHAM
Covenant relation with the LORD (Ge 12:1–3; 13:14–17; 15; 17; 22:15–18; Ex 2:24; Ne 9:8; Ps 105; Mic 7:20; Lk 1:68–75; Ro 4; Heb 6:13–15).
Called from Ur, via Harran, to Canaan (Ge 12:1; Ac 7:2–4; Heb 11:8–10). Moved to Egypt, nearly lost Sarah to Pharoah (Ge 12:10–20). Divided the land with Lot (Ge 13). Saved Lot from four kings (Ge 14:1–16); blessed by Melchizedek (Ge 14:17–20; Heb 7:1–20). Declared righteous by faith (Ge 15:6; Ro 4:3; Gal 3:6–9). Fathered Ishmael by Hagar (Ge 16).
Name changed from Abram (Ge 17:5; Ne 9:7). Circumcised (Ge 17; Ro 4:9–12). Entertained three visitors (Ge 18); promised a son by Sarah (Ge 18:9–15; 17:16). Moved to Gerar; nearly lost Sarah to Abimelek (Ge 20). Fathered Isaac by Sarah (Ge 21:1–7; Ac 7:8; Heb 11:11–12); sent away Hagar and Ishmael (Ge 21:8–21; Gal 4:22–30). Tested by offering Isaac (Ge 22; Heb 11:17–19; Jas 2:21–24). Sarah died; bought field of Ephron for burial (Ge 23). Secured wife for Isaac (Ge 24). Death (Ge 25:7–11).

ABSALOM
Son of David by Maakah (2Sa 3:3; 1Ch 3:2). Killed Amnon for rape of his sister Tamar; banished by David (2Sa 13). Returned to Jerusalem; received by David (2Sa 14). Rebelled against David; seized kingdom (2Sa 15–17). Killed (2Sa 18).

ABSTAIN (ABSTAINS)
1Pe	2: 11	and exiles, to a from sinful desires,

ABSTAINS (ABSTAIN)
Ro	14: 6	and whoever a does so to the Lord

ABUNDANCE (ABUNDANT)
Lk	12: 15	not consist in an a of possessions."
Jude	: 2	peace and love be yours in a.

ABUNDANT (ABUNDANCE)
Dt 28: 11 will grant you **a** prosperity—
Ps 145: 7 They celebrate your **a** goodness
Pr 28: 19 work their land will have a food,
Ro 5: 17 who receive God's **a** provision

ABUSE
2Pe 2: 11 do not heap **a** on such beings

ACCEPT (ACCEPTED ACCEPTS)
Ex 23: 8 "Do not **a** a bribe, for a bribe
Pr 10: 8 The wise in heart **a** commands,
19: 20 Listen to advice and **a** discipline,
Ro 15: 7 **A** one another, then, just as Christ
Jas 1: 21 humbly **a** the word planted in you,

ACCEPTED (ACCEPT)
Lk 4: 24 "no prophet is **a** in his hometown.

ACCEPTS (ACCEPT)
Ps 6: 9 the LORD **a** my prayer.
Jn 13: 20 whoever **a** anyone I send **a** me;

ACCOMPANY
Mk 16: 17 *these signs will* **a** *those who believe:*

ACCOMPLISH
Isa 55: 11 but will **a** what I desire and achieve

ACCORD
Nu 24: 13 not do anything of my own **a**,
Jn 10: 18 me, but I lay it down of my own **a**.

ACCOUNT (ACCOUNTABLE)
Mt 12: 36 will have to give **a** on the day
Ro 14: 12 of us will give an **a** of ourselves
Heb 4: 13 of him to whom we must give **a**.

ACCOUNTABLE (ACCOUNT)
Eze 33: 6 I will hold the watchman **a** for
Ro 3: 19 and the whole world held **a** to God.

ACCUSATION (ACCUSE)
1Ti 5: 19 not entertain an **a** against an elder

ACCUSE (ACCUSATION)
Pr 3: 30 Do not **a** anyone for no reason—
Lk 3: 14 money and don't **a** people falsely—

ACHAN
Sin at Jericho caused defeat at Ai; stoned (Jos 7; 22:20; 1Ch 2:7).

ACHE
Pr 14: 13 Even in laughter the heart may **a**,

ACKNOWLEDGE
Mt 10: 32 also **a** before my Father in heaven.
1Th 5: 12 **a** those who work hard among you,
Php 2: 11 every tongue **a** that Jesus Christ is
1Jn 4: 3 spirit that does not **a** Jesus is not

ACQUIT
Ex 23: 7 to death, for I will not **a** the guilty.

ACTION (ACTIONS ACTIVE ACTS)
Jas 2: 17 if it is not accompanied by **a**,

ACTIONS (ACTION)
Gal 6: 4 Each one should test their own **a**.
Titus 1: 16 God, but by their **a** they deny him.

ACTIVE (ACTION)
Heb 4: 12 For the word of God is alive and **a**.

ACTS (ACTION)
Ps 145: 12 people may know of your mighty **a**
150: 2 Praise him for his **a** of power;
Isa 64: 6 all our righteous **a** are like filthy

ADAM
First man (Ge 1:26—2:25; Ro 5:14; 1Ti 2:13). Sin of (Ge 3; Hos 6:7; Ro 5:12–21). Children of (Ge 4:1—5:5). Death of (Ge 5:5; Ro 5:12–21; 1Co 15:22).

ADD
Dt 12: 32 do not **a** to it or take away from it.
Pr 30: 6 Do not **a** to his words, or he will
Lk 12: 25 by worrying can **a** a single hour
Rev 22: 18 them, God will **a** to that person

ADMIRABLE
Php 4: 8 whatever is lovely, whatever is **a**—

ADMONISH
Col 3: 16 and **a** one another with all wisdom

ADOPTION
Ro 8: 23 wait eagerly for our **a** to sonship,
Eph 1: 5 he predestined us for **a** to sonship

ADORE
SS 1: 4 How right they are to **a** you!

ADORNMENT (ADORNS)
1Pe 3: 3 should not come from outward **a**,

ADORNS (ADORNMENT)
Ps 93: 5 holiness **a** your house for endless

ADULTERY
Ex 20: 14 "You shall not commit **a**.
Mt 5: 27 was said, 'You shall not commit **a**.'
5: 28 lustfully has already committed **a**.
5: 32 a divorced woman commits **a**.
15: 19 murder, **a**, sexual immorality, theft,

ADULTS
1Co 14: 20 but in your thinking be **a**.

ADVANCED
Job 32: 7 **a** years should teach wisdom.'

ADVANTAGE
Ex 22: 22 "Do not take **a** of the widow
Dt 24: 14 Do not take **a** of a hired worker
1Th 4: 6 should wrong or take **a** of a brother

ADVERSITY
Pr 17: 17 a brother is born for a time of **a**.

ADVICE
1Ki 12: 8 Rehoboam rejected the **a** the elders
12: 14 he followed the **a** of the young men
Pr 12: 5 but the **a** of the wicked is deceitful.
12: 15 to them, but the wise listen to **a**.
19: 20 Listen to **a** and accept discipline,
20: 18 Plans are established by seeking **a**;

ADVOCATE
Jn 14: 16 he will give you another **a** to help
14: 26 But the **A**, the Holy Spirit,
1Jn 2: 1 sin, we have an **a** with the Father—

AFFECTION
2Pe 1: 7 and to godliness, mutual **a**; and to mutual **a**, love.

AFFLICTION
Ro 12: 12 patient in **a**, faithful in prayer.

AFRAID (FEAR)
Ge 26: 24 Do not be **a**, for I am with you;
Ex 3: 6 because he was **a** to look at God.
Ps 27: 1 of my life—of whom shall I be **a**?
56: 3 When I am **a**, I put my trust in
Pr 3: 24 you lie down, you will not be **a**;
Jer 1: 8 Do not be **a** of them, for I am
Mt 8: 26 of little faith, why are you so **a**?"
10: 28 Do not be **a** of those who kill
10: 31 So don't be **a**; you are worth more
Mk 5: 36 said, Jesus told him, "Don't be **a**;
Jn 14: 27 hearts be troubled and do not be **a**.
Heb 13: 6 Lord is my helper; I will not be **a**.

AGED
Job 12: 12 Is not wisdom found among the **a**?
Pr 17: 6 children are a crown to the **a**,

AGREE
Mt 18: 19 earth **a** about anything they ask for,
Ro 7: 16 want to do, I **a** that the law is good.

AHAB
Son of Omri; king of Israel (1Ki 16:28—22:40), husband of Jezebel (1Ki 16:31). Promoted Baal worship (1Ki 16:31–33); opposed by Elijah (1Ki 17:1; 18; 21), a prophet (1Ki 20:35–43), Micaiah (1Ki 22:1–28). Defeated Ben-Hadad (1Ki 20). Killed for failing to kill Ben-Hadad and for murder of Naboth (1Ki 20:35—21:40).

AHAZ
Son of Jotham; king of Judah, (2Ki 16; 2Ch 28; Isa 7).

AHAZIAH
1. Son of Ahab; king of Israel (1Ki 22:51–2Ki 1:18; 2Ch 20:35–37).
2. Son of Jehoram; king of Judah (2Ki 8:25–29; 9:14–29), also called Jehoahaz (2Ch 21:17—22:9; 25:23).

AIM
1Co 7: 34 Her **a** is to be devoted to the Lord

AIR
1Co 9: 26 not fight like a boxer beating the **a**.
Eph 2: 2 the ruler of the kingdom of the **a**,
1Th 4: 17 clouds to meet the Lord in the **a**.

ALABASTER
Mt 26: 7 him with an **a** jar of very expensive

ALERT
Jos 8: 4 far from it. All of you be on the **a**.
Mk 13: 33 Be **a**! You do not know
Eph 6: 18 be **a** and always keep on praying
1Pe 1: 13 with minds that are **a** and fully

ALIENATED
Gal 5: 4 the law have been **a** from Christ;

ALIVE (LIVE)
Ac 1: 3 convincing proofs that he was **a**.
Ro 6: 11 to sin but **a** to God in Christ Jesus.

1Co 15: 22 die, so in Christ all will be made **a**.
Heb 4: 12 the word of God is **a** and active.
ALMIGHTY (MIGHT)
Ge 17: 1 to him and said, "I am God **A**;
Job 11: 7 Can you probe the limits of the **A**?
33: 4 the breath of the **A** gives me life.
Ps 91: 1 will rest in the shadow of the **A**.
Isa 6: 3 "Holy, holy, holy is the LORD **A**;
ALTAR
Ge 22: 9 Abraham built an **a** there
Ex 27: 1 "Build an **a** of acacia wood,
1Ki 18: 30 he repaired the **a** of the LORD,
2Ch 4: 1 a bronze **a** twenty cubits long,
4: 19 the golden **a**; the tables
ALWAYS
Ps 16: 8 I keep my eyes **a** on the LORD.
26: 3 for I have **a** been mindful of your
51: 3 and my sin is **a** before me.
Mt 26: 11 The poor you will **a** have with you,
28: 20 And surely I am with you **a**,
1Co 13: 7 It **a** protects, **a** trusts, **a** hopes,
Php 4: 4 Rejoice in the Lord **a**. I will say it
1Pe 3: 15 **A** be prepared to give an answer
AMAZIAH
Son of Joash; king of Judah (2Ki 14; 2Ch 25).
AMBASSADORS
2Co 5: 20 We are therefore Christ's **a**,
AMBITION
Ro 15: 20 It has always been my **a** to preach
1Th 4: 11 make it your **a** to lead a quiet life:
AMON
Son of Manasseh; king of Judah (2Ki 21:18–26; 1Ch 3:14; 2Ch 33:21–25).
ANANIAS
1. Husband of Sapphira; died for lying to God (Ac 5:1–11).
2. Disciple who baptized Saul (Ac 9:10–19).
3. High priest at Paul's arrest (Ac 22:30—24:1).
ANCESTORS
Heb 1: 1 spoke to our **a** through the prophets
ANCHOR
Heb 6: 19 We have this hope as an **a**
ANCIENT
Da 7: 9 and the **A** of Days took his seat.
ANDREW
Apostle; brother of Simon Peter (Mt 4:18; 10:2; Mk 1:16–18, 29; 3:18; 13:3; Lk 6:14; Jn 1:35–44; 6:8–9; 12:22; Ac 1:13).
ANGEL (ANGELS ARCHANGEL)
Ps 34: 7 The **a** of the LORD encamps
Ac 6: 15 his face was like the face of an **a**.
2Co 11: 14 Satan himself masquerades as an **a**
Gal 1: 8 or an **a** from heaven should preach
ANGELS (ANGEL)
Ps 8: 5 a little lower than the **a**
91: 11 command his **a** concerning you
Mt 18: 10 that their **a** in heaven always see
25: 41 fire prepared for the devil and his **a**.
Lk 20: 36 for they are like the **a**.
1Co 6: 3 you not know that we will judge **a**?
Heb 1: 4 the **a** as the name he has inherited
1: 14 Are not all **a** ministering spirits
2: 7 them a little lower than the **a**;
13: 2 hospitality to **a** without knowing it.
1Pe 1: 12 Even **a** long to look into these
2Pe 2: 4 if God did not spare **a** when they
ANGER (ANGERED ANGRY)
Ex 32: 10 that my **a** may burn against them
34: 6 slow to **a**, abounding in love
Dt 29: 28 In furious **a** and in great wrath
2Ki 22: 13 Great is the LORD's **a** that burns
Ps 30: 5 For his **a** lasts only a moment,
Pr 15: 1 wrath, but a harsh word stirs up **a**.
ANGERED (ANGER)
Pr 22: 24 do not associate with one easily **a**,
1Co 13: 5 it is not easily **a**, it keeps no record
ANGRY (ANGER)
Ps 2: 12 he will be **a** and your way will lead
Pr 29: 22 An **a** person stirs up conflict,
Jas 1: 19 to speak and slow to become **a**,
ANOINT
Ps 23: 5 You **a** my head with oil;
Jas 5: 14 **a** them with oil in the name

ANOTHER
1Pe 3: 8 love one **a**, be compassionate
ANT
Pr 6: 6 Go to the **a**, you sluggard;
ANTICHRIST
1Jn 2: 18 have heard that the **a** is coming,
2Jn : 7 person is the deceiver and the **a**.
ANTIOCH
Ac 11: 26 were called Christians first at **A**.
ANXIETY (ANXIOUS)
Pr 12: 25 **A** weighs down the heart,
1Pe 5: 7 Cast all your **a** on him because he
ANXIOUS (ANXIETY)
Php 4: 6 Do not be **a** about anything,
APOLLOS
Christian from Alexandria, learned in the Scriptures; instructed by Aquila and Priscilla (Ac 18:24–28). Ministered at Corinth (Ac 19:1; 1Co 1:12; 3; Titus 3:13).
APOSTLES
See also Andrew, Bartholomew, James, John, Judas, Matthew, Nathanael, Paul, Peter, Philip, Simon, Thaddaeus, Thomas.
Ac 1: 26 so he was added to the eleven **a**.
2: 43 and signs performed by the **a**.
1Co 12: 28 placed in the church first of all **a**,
15: 9 For I am the least of the **a** and do
2Co 11: 13 For such people are false **a**,
Eph 2: 20 built on the foundation of the **a**
APPEAR (APPEARANCE APPEARING)
Mk 13: 22 false prophets will **a** and perform
2Co 5: 10 we must all **a** before the judgment
Col 3: 4 you also will **a** with him in glory.
Heb 9: 24 now to **a** for us in God's presence.
9: 28 and he will **a** a second time,
APPEARANCE (APPEAR)
1Sa 16: 7 People look at the outward **a**,
APPEARING (APPEAR)
2Ti 4: 8 to all who have longed for his **a**.
Titus 2: 13 the **a** of the glory of our great God
APPLY
Pr 22: 17 **a** your heart to what I teach,
23: 12 **A** your heart to instruction and
APPROACH
Eph 3: 12 we may **a** God with freedom
Heb 4: 16 then **a** God's throne of grace
APPROVED
2Ti 2: 15 to present yourself to God as one **a**,
AQUILA
Husband of Priscilla; co-worker with Paul, instructor of Apollos (Ac 18; Ro 16:3; 1Co 16:19; 2Ti 4:19).
ARARAT
Ge 8: 4 to rest on the mountains of **A**.
ARCHANGEL (ANGEL)
1Th 4: 16 with the voice of the **a**
Jude : 9 But even the **a** Michael, when he
ARCHITECT
Heb 11: 10 whose **a** and builder is God.
ARGUING
Php 2: 14 everything without grumbling or **a**,
ARK
Ge 6: 14 So make yourself an **a** of cypress
Dt 10: 5 put the tablets in the **a** I had made,
2Ch 35: 3 "Put the sacred **a** in the temple
Heb 9: 4 This **a** contained the gold jar
ARM (ARMY)
Nu 11: 23 "Is the LORD's **a** too short?
1Pe 4: 1 **a** yourselves also with the same
ARMAGEDDON
Rev 16: 16 place that in Hebrew is called **A**.
ARMOR (ARMY)
1Ki 20: 11 his **a** should not boast like one who
Eph 6: 11 Put on the full **a** of God, so that
6: 13 Therefore put on the full **a** of God,
ARMS (ARMY)
Dt 33: 27 underneath are the everlasting **a**.
Ps 18: 32 It is God who **a** me with strength
Pr 31: 20 She opens her **a** to the poor
Isa 40: 11 He gathers the lambs in his **a**
Mk 10: 16 And he took the children in his **a**,
ARMY (ARM ARMOR ARMS)
Ps 33: 16 king is saved by the size of his **a**;
Rev 19: 19 the rider on the horse and his **a**.

AROMA
2Co 2: 15 the pleasing **a** of Christ among
      2: 16 one we are an **a** that brings death;
      2: 16 to the other, an **a** that brings life.
ARRAYED
Ps 110: 3 **A** in holy splendor, your young
Isa 61: 10 **a** me in a robe of his righteousness,
ARROGANT
Ro 11: 20 Do not be **a**, but tremble.
ARROWS
Eph 6: 16 can extinguish all the flaming **a**
ASA
      King of Judah (1Ki 15:8–24; 1Ch 3:10; 2Ch 14–16).
ASCENDED
Eph 4: 8 "When he **a** on high, he took many
ASCRIBE
1Ch 16: 28 **A** to the LORD, all you families
     16: 28 **a** to the LORD glory and strength.
Job 36: 3 I will **a** justice to my Maker.
Ps 29: 2 **A** to the LORD the glory due his
ASHAMED (SHAME)
Lk   9: 26 Whoever is **a** of me and my words, the Son of Man
              will be **a** of them
Ro   1: 16 For I am not **a** of the gospel,
2Ti 1: 8 So do not be **a** of the testimony
      2: 15 worker who does not need to be **a**
ASSIGNED
Mk 13: 34 each with their **a** task, and tells
1Co 3: 5 as the Lord has **a** to each his task.
      7: 17 whatever situation the Lord has **a**
ASSOCIATE
Pr 22: 24 do not **a** with one easily angered,
Ro 12: 16 be willing to **a** with people of low
1Co 5: 11 you must not **a** with anyone who
2Th 3: 14 Do not **a** with them, in order
ASSURANCE
Heb 10: 22 and with the full **a** that faith brings,
ASTRAY
Pr 10: 17 ignores correction leads others **a**.
Isa 53: 6 have gone **a**, each of us has turned
Jer 50: 6 their shepherds have led them **a**
1Pe 2: 25 For "you were like sheep going **a**,"
1Jn 3: 7 do not let anyone lead you **a**.
ATHALIAH
      Evil queen of Judah (2Ki 11; 2Ch 23).
ATHLETE
2Ti 2: 5 competes as an **a** does not receive
ATONEMENT
Ex 25: 17 "Make an **a** cover of pure gold—
     30: 10 Once a year Aaron shall make **a**
Lev 17: 11 blood that makes **a** for one's life.
     23: 27 this seventh month is the Day of **A**.
Nu 25: 13 God and made **a** for the Israelites."
Ro   3: 25 presented Christ as a sacrifice of **a**,
Heb 2: 17 that he might make **a** for the sins
ATTENTION
Pr   4: 1 pay **a** and gain understanding.
      5: 1 My son, pay **a** to my wisdom,
     22: 17 Pay **a** and turn your ear
Titus 1: 14 and will pay no **a** to Jewish myths
ATTITUDE (ATTITUDES)
Eph 4: 23 made new in the **a** of your minds;
1Pe 4: 1 yourselves also with the same **a**,
ATTITUDES (ATTITUDE)
Heb 4: 12 the thoughts and **a** of the heart.
ATTRACTIVE
Titus 2: 10 teaching about God our Savior **a**.
AUTHORITIES (AUTHORITY)
Ro 13: 5 it is necessary to submit to the **a**,
     13: 6 for the **a** are God's servants,
Titus 3: 1 to be subject to rulers and **a**,
1Pe 3: 22 **a** and powers in submission to him.
AUTHORITY (AUTHORITIES)
Mt   7: 29 he taught as one who had **a**,
      9: 6 the Son of Man has **a** on earth
     28: 18 "All **a** in heaven and on earth has
Ro   1: 1 for there is no **a** except
     13: 2 rebels against the **a** is rebelling
1Co 11: 10 ought to have **a** over her own head,
1Ti 2: 2 for kings and all those in **a**, that we
      2: 12 to teach or to assume **a** over a man;
Heb 13: 17 your leaders and submit to their **a**,

AVENGE (VENGEANCE)
Dt 32: 35 It is mine to **a**; I will repay.
AVOID
Pr 20: 3 It is to one's honor to **a** strife,
     20: 19 so **a** anyone who talks too much.
1Th 4: 3 you should **a** sexual immorality;
2Ti 2: 16 **A** godless chatter, because those
Titus 3: 9 But **a** foolish controversies
AWAKE
Ps 17: 15 when I **a**, I will be satisfied
1Th 5: 6 asleep, but let us be **a** and sober.
AWE (AWESOME)
Job 25: 2 "Dominion and **a** belong to God;
Ps 119:120 of you; I stand in **a** of your laws.
Isa 29: 23 will stand in **a** of the God of Israel.
Jer 33: 9 they will be in **a** and will tremble
Hab 3: 2 I stand in **a** of your deeds, LORD.
Mal 2: 5 me and stood in **a** of my name.
Mt   9: 8 saw this, they were filled with **a**;
Lk   7: 16 They were all filled with **a**
Ac   2: 43 Everyone was filled with **a**
Heb 12: 28 acceptably with reverence and **a**,
AWESOME (AWE)
Ge 28: 17 and said, "How **a** is this place!
Ex 15: 11 majestic in holiness, **a** in glory,
Dt   7: 21 is among you, is a great and **a** God.
     10: 17 God, mighty and **a**, who shows no
     28: 58 revere this glorious and **a** name—
Jdg 13: 6 looked like an angel of God, very **a**.
Ne   1: 5 the great and **a** God, who keeps his
      9: 32 God, mighty and **a**, who keeps his
Job 10: 16 again display your **a** power against
     37: 22 God comes in **a** majesty.
Ps 45: 4 your right hand achieve **a** deeds.
     47: 2 For the LORD Most High is **a**,
     66: 5 has done, his **a** deeds for mankind!
     68: 35 You, God, are **a** in your sanctuary;
     89: 7 he is more **a** than all who surround
     99: 3 praise your great and **a** name—
    111: 9 holy and **a** is his name.
    145: 6 tell of the power of your **a** works—
Da   9: 4 the great and **a** God, who keeps his
BAAL
1Ki 18: 25 Elijah said to the prophets of **B**,
BAASHA
      King of Israel (1Ki 15:16—16:7; 2Ch 16:1–6).
BABIES (BABY)
Lk 18: 15 bringing **b** to Jesus for him to place
1Pe 2: 2 Like newborn **b**, crave pure
BABY (BABIES)
Isa 49: 15 "Can a mother forget the **b** at her
Lk   1: 44 the **b** in my womb leaped for joy.
      2: 12 You will find a **b** wrapped in cloths
Jn 16: 21 **b** is born she forgets the anguish
BABYLON
Ps 137: 1 By the rivers of **B** we sat and wept
BACKSLIDING
Jer 3: 22 I will cure you of **b**."
Eze 37: 23 save them from all their sinful **b**,
BAGS
Mt 25: 15 To one he gave five **b** of gold, to another two **b**, and
              to another one
BALAAM
      Prophet who attempted to curse Israel (Nu 22–24; Dt
      23:4–5; 2Pe 2:15; Jude 11). Killed (Nu 31:8; Jos 13:22).
BALM
Jer 8: 22 Is there no **b** in Gilead? Is there no
BANISH
Jer 25: 10 will **b** from them the sounds of joy
BANQUET
SS   2: 4 Let him lead me to the **b** hall,
Lk 14: 13 But when you give a **b**,
BAPTIZE (BAPTIZED)
Mt   3: 11 "I **b** you with water for repentance.
      3: 11 He will **b** you with the Holy Spirit
Mk   1: 8 I **b** you with water, but he will **b**
1Co 1: 17 For Christ did not send me to **b**,
BAPTIZED (BAPTIZE)
Mt   3: 6 they were **b** by him in the Jordan
Mk   1: 9 and was **b** by John in the Jordan.
     10: 38 be **b** with the baptism I am **b** with?"
     16: 16 *believes and is **b** will be saved,*

Jn 4: 2 in fact it was not Jesus who **b**,
Ac 1: 5 For John **b** with water, but in a few
BARABBAS
Mt 27: 17 release to you: Jesus **B**, or Jesus
BARBS
Nu 33: 55 remain will become **b** in your eyes
BARE
Heb 4: 13 and laid **b** before the eyes of him
BARNABAS
    Disciple, originally Joseph (Ac 4:36), prophet (Ac 13:1), apostle (Ac 14:14). Brought Paul to apostles (Ac 9:27), Antioch (Ac 11:22–29; Gal 2:1–13), on the first missionary journey (Ac 13–14). Together at Jerusalem Council, they separated over John Mark (Ac 15). Later co-workers (1Co 9:6; Col 4:10).
BARTHOLOMEW
    Apostle (Mt 10:3; Mk 3:18; Lk 6:14; Ac 1:13). Possibly also known as Nathanael (Jn 1:45–49; 21:2).
BATH
Jn 13: 10 who have had a **b** need only
BATHSHEBA
    Wife of Uriah who committed adultery with and became wife of David (2Sa 11), mother of Solomon (2Sa 12:24; 1Ki 1–2; 1Ch 3:5).
BATTLE
2Ch 20: 15 For the **b** is not yours, but God's.
Ps 24: 8 mighty, the LORD mighty in **b**.
Ecc 9: 11 to the swift or the **b** to the strong,
BEAR (BEARING BIRTH BIRTHRIGHT BORE BORN
    FIRSTBORN NEWBORN)
Ge 4: 13 punishment is more than I can **b**.
Ps 38: 4 me like a burden too heavy to **b**.
Isa 53: 11 many, and he will **b** their iniquities.
Da 7: 1 beast, which looked like a **b**.
Mt 7: 18 A good tree cannot **b** bad fruit,
Jn 15: 2 branch that does **b** fruit he prunes
15: 16 so that you might go and **b** fruit—
Ro 15: 1 We who are strong ought to **b**
1Co 10: 13 tempted beyond what you can **b**.
Col 3: 13 **B** with each other and forgive one
BEARING (BEAR)
Eph 4: 2 patient, **b** with one another in love.
Col 1: 10 **b** fruit in every good work,
BEAST
Rev 13: 18 calculate the number of the **b**, for it
BEAT (BEATING)
Isa 2: 4 They will **b** their swords
Joel 3: 10 **B** your plowshares into swords
BEATING (BEAT)
1Co 9: 26 I do not fight like a boxer **b** the air.
1Pe 2: 20 if you receive a **b** for doing wrong
BEAUTIFUL (BEAUTY)
Ge 6: 2 the daughters of humans were **b**,
12: 11 "I know what a **b** woman you are.
12: 14 saw that Sarai was a very **b** woman.
24: 16 The woman was very **b**, a virgin;
26: 7 of Rebekah, because she is **b**."
29: 17 had a lovely figure and was **b**.
Pr 11: 22 snout is a **b** woman who shows no
Ecc 3: 11 He has made everything **b** in its
Isa 4: 2 the Branch of the LORD will be **b**
52: 7 How **b** on the mountains are the
Eze 20: 6 the most **b** of all lands.
Zec 9: 17 How attractive and **b** they will be!
Mt 23: 27 which look **b** on the outside
26: 10 She has done a **b** thing to me.
Ro 10: 15 "How **b** are the feet of those who
BEAUTY (BEAUTIFUL)
Ps 27: 4 to gaze on the **b** of the LORD
45: 11 the king be enthralled by your **b**;
Pr 31: 30 is deceptive, and **b** is fleeting;
Isa 33: 17 Your eyes will see the king in his **b**
53: 2 He had no **b** or majesty to attract
61: 3 them a crown of **b** instead of ashes,
Eze 28: 12 full of wisdom and perfect in **b**.
1Pe 3: 4 unfading **b** of a gentle and quiet
BED
Heb 13: 4 and the marriage **b** kept pure,
BEELZEBUL
Lk 11: 15 said, "By **B**, the prince of demons,
BEER
Pr 20: 1 Wine is a mocker and **b** a brawler;

BEERSHEBA
Jdg 20: 1 all Israel from Dan to **B**
BEGINNING
Ge 1: 1 In the **b** God created the heavens
Ps 102: 25 In the **b** you laid the foundations
111: 10 of the LORD is the **b** of wisdom;
Pr 1: 7 the LORD is the **b** of knowledge,
4: 7 The **b** of wisdom is this:
Jn 1: 1 In the **b** was the Word,
1Jn 1: 1 That which was from the **b**,
Rev 21: 6 and the Omega, the **B** and the End.
BEHAVE (BEHAVIOR)
Ro 13: 13 us **b** decently, as in the daytime,
BEHAVIOR (BEHAVE)
Pr 1: 3 receiving instruction in prudent **b**,
BELIEVE (BELIEVED BELIEVER BELIEVERS BELIEVES
    BELIEVING)
Pr 14: 15 The simple **b** anything,
Mt 18: 6 those who **b** in me—
21: 22 If you **b**, you will receive whatever
Mk 1: 15 Repent and **b** the good news!"
9: 24 the boy's father exclaimed, "I do **b**;
16: 17 *accompany those who **b**:*
Lk 8: 50 just **b**, and she will be healed."
24: 25 how slow to **b** all that the prophets
Jn 1: 7 so that through him all might **b**.
3: 18 does not **b** stands condemned
6: 29 to **b** in the one he has sent."
10: 38 even though you do not **b** me,
11: 27 "**I b** that you are the Messiah,
14: 1 You **b** in God; **b** also in me.
14: 11 **B** me when I say that I am
16: 30 This makes us **b** that you came
16: 31 "Do you now **b**?" Jesus replied.
17: 21 the world may **b** that you have sent
20: 27 into my side. Stop doubting and **b**."
20: 31 may **b** that Jesus is the Messiah,
Ac 16: 31 They replied, "**B** in the Lord Jesus,
24: 14 **I b** everything that is in accordance
Ro 3: 22 faith in Jesus Christ to all who **b**.
4: 11 he is the father of all who **b**
10: 9 **b** in your heart that God raised
10: 14 how can they **b** in the one of whom
1Th 4: 14 For we **b** that Jesus died and rose
2Th 2: 11 delusion so that they will **b** the lie
1Ti 4: 10 and especially of those who **b**.
Titus 1: 6 a man whose children **b** and are
Heb 11: 6 comes to him must **b** that he exists
Jas 2: 19 You **b** that there is one God. Good! Even the demons **b** that—
1Jn 4: 1 Dear friends, do not **b** every spirit,
BELIEVED (BELIEVE)
Ge 15: 6 Abram **b** the LORD, and he
Jnh 3: 5 The Ninevites **b** God. A fast was
Jn 1: 12 to those who **b** in his name,
2: 22 Then they **b** the scripture
3: 18 already because they have not **b**
20: 8 also went inside. He saw and **b**.
20: 29 who have not seen and yet have **b**."
Ac 13: 48 were appointed for eternal life **b**.
Ro 4: 3 "Abraham **b** God, and it was
10: 14 call on the one they have not **b** in?
1Co 15: 2 Otherwise, you have **b** in vain.
Gal 3: 6 So also Abraham **b** God, and it
2Ti 1: 12 because I know whom I have **b**,
Jas 2: 23 that says, "Abraham **b** God, and it
BELIEVER (BELIEVE)
1Co 7: 12 brother has a wife who is not a **b**
2Co 6: 15 what does a **b** have in common
BELIEVERS (BELIEVE)
Ac 4: 32 All the **b** were one in heart
5: 12 all the **b** used to meet together
1Co 6: 5 to judge a dispute between **b**?
1Ti 4: 12 set an example for the **b** in speech,
1Pe 2: 17 love the family of **b**, fear God,
BELIEVES (BELIEVE)
Mk 9: 23 is possible for one who **b**."
11: 23 **b** that what they say will happen,
16: 16 *Whoever **b** and is baptized*
Jn 3: 16 whoever **b** in him shall not perish
3: 36 Whoever **b** in the Son has eternal
5: 24 **b** him who sent me has eternal life
6: 35 and whoever **b** in me will never be

Jn 6: 40 and **b** in him shall have eternal life,
6: 47 you, the one who **b** has eternal life.
7: 38 Whoever **b** in me, as Scripture has
Ro 1: 16 salvation to everyone who **b**:
9: 33 the one who **b** in him will never be
10: 4 righteousness for everyone who **b**.
1Jn 5: 1 Everyone who **b** that Jesus is
5: 5 Only the one who **b** that Jesus is

BELIEVING (BELIEVE)
Jn 11: 26 whoever lives by **b** in me will never
20: 31 by **b** you may have life in his name.

BELONG (BELONGS)
Dt 29: 29 The secret things **b** to the LORD
Job 25: 2 "Dominion and awe **b** to God;
Ps 47: 9 for the kings of the earth **b** to God;
95: 4 and the mountain peaks **b** to him.
Jn 8: 44 You **b** to your father, the devil,
15: 19 As it is, you do not **b** to the world,
Ro 1: 6 those Gentiles who are called to **b**
7: 4 that you might **b** to another, to him
14: 8 we live or die, we **b** to the Lord.
Gal 5: 24 Those who **b** to Christ Jesus have
1Th 5: 8 But since we **b** to the day, let us be

BELONGS (BELONG)
Job 41: 11 Everything under heaven **b** to me.
Ps 111: 10 To him **b** eternal praise.
Eze 18: 4 For everyone **b** to me, the parent as
Jn 8: 47 Whoever **b** to God hears what God
Ro 12: 5 each member **b** to all the others.

BELOVED (LOVE)
Dt 33: 12 "Let the **b** of the LORD rest
SS 2: 16 My **b** is mine and I am his;
7: 10 I belong to my **b**, and his desire is

BELT
Isa 11: 5 Righteousness will be his **b**
Eph 6: 14 the **b** of truth buckled around your

BENEFICIAL (BENEFIT)
1Co 10: 23 but not everything is **b**.

BENEFIT (BENEFICIAL BENEFITS)
Ro 6: 22 the **b** you reap leads to holiness,
2Co 4: 15 All this is for your **b**,

BENEFITS (BENEFIT)
Ps 103: 2 my soul, and forget not all his **b**—
Jn 4: 38 and you have reaped the **b** of their

BENJAMIN
Twelfth son of Jacob by Rachel (Ge 35:16–24; 46:19–21;
1Ch 2:2). Jacob refused to send him to Egypt, but relented
(Ge 42–45).

BEREAN
Ac 17: 11 the **B** Jews were of more noble

BESTOWS
Ps 84: 11 the LORD **b** favor and honor;

BETHLEHEM
Mt 2: 1 After Jesus was born in **B** in Judea,

BETRAY
Pr 25: 9 do not **b** another's confidence,

BIND (BINDS)
Dt 6: 8 and **b** them on your foreheads.
Pr 6: 21 **B** them always on your heart;
Isa 61: 1 He has sent me to **b**
Mt 16: 19 whatever you **b** on earth will be

BINDS (BIND)
Ps 147: 3 and **b** up their wounds.
Isa 30: 26 when the LORD **b** up the bruises

BIRDS
Mt 8: 20 "Foxes have dens and **b** have nests,

BIRTH (BEAR)
Ps 58: 3 Even from the wicked go astray;
Mt 1: 18 This is how the **b** of Jesus
1Pe 1: 3 great mercy he has given us new **b**

BIRTHRIGHT (BEAR)
Ge 25: 34 up and left. So Esau despised his **b**.

BLAMELESS
Ge 17: 1 walk before me faithfully and be **b**.
Job 1: 1 This man was **b** and upright;
Ps 84: 11 from those whose walk is **b**.
119: 1 are those whose ways are **b**,
Pr 19: 1 poor whose walk is **b** than a fool
1Co 1: 8 so that you will be **b** on the day
Eph 5: 27 any other blemish, but holy and **b**.
Php 2: 15 that you may become **b** and pure,
1Th 3: 13 your hearts so that you will be **b**

1Th 5: 23 body be kept **b** at the coming of
Titus 1: 6 An elder must be **b**, faithful to his
Heb 7: 26 one who is holy, **b**, pure, set apart
2Pe 3: 14 spotless, **b** and at peace with him.

BLASPHEMES
Mk 3: 29 whoever **b** against the Holy Spirit

BLEMISH
1Pe 1: 19 Christ, a lamb without **b** or defect.

BLESS (BLESSED BLESSING BLESSINGS)
Ge 12: 3 I will **b** those who **b** you,
Ro 12: 14 **B** those who persecute you;

BLESSED (BLESS)
Ge 1: 22 God **b** them and said, "Be fruitful
2: 3 Then God **b** the seventh day
22: 18 all nations on earth will be **b**,
Ps 1: 1 **B** is the one who does not walk
2: 12 **B** are all who take refuge in him.
33: 12 **B** is the nation whose God is
41: 1 **B** are those who have regard
84: 5 **B** are those whose strength is
106: 3 **B** are those who act justly,
112: 1 **B** are those who fear the LORD,
118: 26 **B** is he who comes in the name
Pr 29: 18 **b** is the one who heeds wisdom's
31: 28 Her children arise and call her **b**;
Mt 5: 3 "**B** are the poor in spirit, for theirs
5: 4 **B** are those who mourn, for they
5: 5 **B** are the meek, for they will
5: 6 **B** are those who hunger and thirst
5: 7 **B** are the merciful, for they will
5: 8 **B** are the pure in heart, for they
5: 9 **B** are the peacemakers, for they
5: 10 **B** are those who are persecuted
5: 11 "**B** are you when people insult you,
Lk 1: 48 on all generations will call me **b**,
Jn 12: 13 "**B** is he who comes in the name
Ac 20: 35 'It is more **b** to give than
Titus 2: 13 while we wait for the **b** hope—
Jas 1: 12 **B** is the one who perseveres under
Rev 1: 3 **B** is the one who reads aloud
22: 14 "**B** are those who wash their robes,

BLESSING (BLESS)
Eze 34: 26 there will be showers of **b**.

BLESSINGS (BLESS)
Pr 10: 6 **B** crown the head of the righteous,

BLIND
Mt 15: 14 If the **b** lead the **b**, both will fall
23: 16 "Woe to you, **b** guides! You say,
Jn 9: 25 I do know. I was **b** but now I see!"

BLOOD
Ge 9: 6 "Whoever sheds human **b**, by humans shall their **b**
be shed;
Ex 12: 13 The **b** will be a sign for you
24: 8 "This is the **b** of the covenant,
Lev 17: 11 For the life of a creature is in the **b**,
17: 11 it is the **b** that makes atonement
Ps 72: 14 for precious is their **b** in his sight.
Pr 6: 17 hands that shed innocent **b**,
Mt 26: 28 This is my **b** of the covenant,
Ro 3: 25 through the shedding of his **b**—
5: 9 have now been justified by his **b**,
1Co 11: 25 cup is the new covenant in my **b**;
Eph 1: 7 we have redemption through his **b**,
2: 13 brought near by the **b** of Christ.
Col 1: 20 by making peace through his **b**,
Heb 9: 12 once for all by his own **b**,
9: 22 everything be cleansed with **b**,
1Pe 1: 19 but with the precious **b** of Christ,
1Jn 1: 7 and the **b** of Jesus, his Son,
Rev 1: 5 has freed us from our sins by his **b**,
5: 9 with your **b** you purchased for God
7: 14 them white in the **b** of the Lamb.
12: 11 over him by the **b** of the Lamb

BLOT (BLOTS)
Ex 32: 32 **b** me out of the book you have
Ps 51: 1 to your great compassion **b** out my
Rev 3: 5 I will never **b** out the name

BLOTS (BLOT)
Isa 43: 25 "I, even I, am he who **b** out your

BLOWN
Eph 4: 14 and **b** here and there by every wind
Jas 1: 6 the sea, **b** and tossed by the wind.

BOAST
1Ki	20: 11	his armor should not **b** like one
Ps	44: 8	In God we make our **b** all day long,
Pr	27: 1	Do not **b** about tomorrow, for you
1Co	1: 31	"Let the one who boasts **b**
Gal	6: 14	May I never **b** except in the cross
Eph	2: 9	not by works, so that no one can **b**.

BOAZ
Wealthy Bethlehemite who showed favor to Ruth (Ru 2), married her (Ru 4). Ancestor of David (Ru 4:18–22; 1Ch 2:12–15), Jesus (Mt 1:5–16; Lk 3:23–32).

BODIES (BODY)
Ro	12: 1	to offer your **b** as a living sacrifice,
1Co	6: 15	not know that your **b** are members
	6: 19	not know that your **b** are temples
Eph	5: 28	to love their wives as their own **b**.

BODY (BODIES)
Zec	13: 6	are these wounds on your **b**?'
Mt	10: 28	can destroy both soul and **b** in hell.
	10: 28	be afraid of those who kill the **b**
	26: 26	"Take and eat; this is my **b**."
Jn	13: 10	their whole **b** is clean.
1Co	11: 24	"This is my **b**, which is for you;
	12: 12	Just as a **b**, though one, has many
Eph	5: 30	for we are members of his **b**.

BOLD (BOLDNESS)
Pr	21: 29	The wicked put up a **b** front,
	28: 1	but the righteous are as **b** as a lion.

BOLDNESS (BOLD)
Ac	4: 29	to speak your word with great **b**.

BONDAGE
Ezr	9: 9	God has not forsaken us in our **b**.

BOOK (BOOKS)
Jos	1: 8	Keep this **B** of the Law always
Ne	8: 8	They read from the **B** of the Law
Jn	20: 30	which are not recorded in this **b**.
Php	4: 3	whose names are in the **b** of life.
Rev	21: 27	are written in the Lamb's **b** of life.

BOOKS (BOOK)
Ecc	12: 12	Of making many **b** there is no end,

BORE (BEAR)
Isa	53: 4	up our pain and **b** our suffering,

BORN (BEAR)
Isa	9: 6	For to us a child is **b**, to us a son is
Jn	3: 7	my saying, 'You must be **b** again.'
1Pe	1: 23	For you have been **b** again,
1Jn	4: 7	Everyone who loves has been **b**
	5: 1	that Jesus is the Christ is **b** of God,

BORROWER
Pr	22: 7	and the **b** is slave to the lender.

BOUGHT
Ac	20: 28	which he **b** with his own blood.
1Co	6: 20	you were **b** at a price.
	7: 23	You were **b** at a price;
2Pe	2: 1	the sovereign Lord who **b** them—

BOUNDLESS
Eph	3: 8	the Gentiles the **b** riches of Christ,

BOW
Ps	95: 6	Come, let us **b** down in worship,
Isa	45: 23	Before me every knee will **b**;
Ro	14: 11	Lord, 'every knee will **b** before me;
Php	2: 10	name of Jesus every knee should **b**,

BRANCH (BRANCHES)
Isa	4: 2	that day the **B** of the LORD will be
Jer	33: 15	I will make a righteous **B** sprout

BRANCHES (BRANCH)
Jn	15: 5	"I am the vine; you are the **b**.

BRAVE
2Sa	2: 7	then, be strong and **b**, for Saul your

BREAD
Dt	8: 3	that man does not live on **b** alone
Pr	30: 8	riches, but give me only my daily **b**.
Isa	55: 2	spend money on what is not **b**,
Mt	4: 4	'Man shall not live on **b** alone,
	6: 11	Give us today our daily **b**.
Jn	6: 35	Jesus declared, "I am the **b** of life.
	21: 13	took the **b** and gave it to them,
1Co	11: 23	the night he was betrayed, took **b**,

BREAK (BREAKING BROKEN)
Nu	30: 2	he must not **b** his word but must
Jdg	2: 1	'I will never **b** my covenant
Ps	2: 9	You will **b** them with a rod of iron;

Isa	42: 3	A bruised reed he will not **b**,
Mt	12: 20	A bruised reed he will not **b**,

BREAKING (BREAK)
Jas	2: 10	just one point is guilty of **b** all of it.

BREASTPIECE (BREASTPLATE)
Ex	28: 15	"Fashion a **b** for making decisions

BREASTPLATE (BREASTPIECE)
Isa	59: 17	He put on righteousness as his **b**,
Eph	6: 14	the **b** of righteousness in place,
1Th	5: 8	putting on faith and love as a **b**,

BREATHED (GOD-BREATHED)
Ge	2: 7	**b** into his nostrils the breath of life,
Jn	20: 22	with that he **b** on them and said,

BRIBE
Ex	23: 8	"Do not accept a **b**, for a **b** blinds
Pr	6: 35	he will refuse a **b**, however great it

BRIDE
Rev	19: 7	and his **b** has made herself ready.

BRIGHTER (BRIGHTNESS)
Pr	4: 18	shining ever **b** till the full light

BRIGHTNESS (BRIGHTER)
2Sa	22: 13	Out of the **b** of his presence bolts
Da	12: 3	who are wise will shine like the **b**

BROAD
Mt	7: 13	gate and **b** is the road that leads

BROKEN (BREAK)
Ps	51: 17	My sacrifice, O God, is a **b** spirit;
Ecc	4: 12	of three strands is not quickly **b**.

BROKENHEARTED (HEART)
Ps	34: 18	The LORD is close to the **b**
	109: 16	the poor and the needy and the **b**.
	147: 3	He heals the **b** and binds up their
Isa	61: 1	He has sent me to bind up the **b**,

BROTHER (BROTHER'S BROTHERS)
Pr	17: 17	a **b** is born for a time of adversity.
	18: 24	a friend who sticks closer than a **b**.
Mt	18: 15	"If your **b** or sister sins,
Mk	3: 35	Whoever does God's will is my **b**
Lk	17: 3	"If your **b** or sister sins against you,
1Co	8: 13	if what I eat causes my **b** or sister
1Jn	2: 10	who loves their **b** and sister

BROTHER'S (BROTHER)
Ge	4: 9	"Am I my **b** keeper?"

BROTHERS (BROTHER)
Mt	25: 40	did for one of the least of these **b**
Mk	10: 29	"no one who has left home or **b**
Heb	13: 1	Keep on loving one another as **b**

BUILD (BUILDING BUILDS BUILT)
Mt	16: 18	on this rock I will **b** my church,
Ac	20: 32	which can **b** you up and give you
1Co	3: 10	But each one should **b** with care.
	14: 12	excel in those that **b** up the church.
1Th	5: 11	one another and **b** each other up,

BUILDING (BUILD)
1Co	3: 9	you are God's field, God's **b**.
2Co	10: 8	authority the Lord gave us for **b**
Eph	4: 29	only what is helpful for **b** others

BUILDS (BUILD)
Ps	127: 1	Unless the LORD **b** the house,
1Co	8: 1	puffs up while love **b** up.

BUILT (BUILD)
Mt	7: 24	is like a wise man who **b** his house
1Co	14: 26	so that the church may be **b** up.
Eph	2: 20	**b** on the foundation of the apostles
	4: 12	that the body of Christ may be **b**

BURDEN (BURDENED BURDENS)
Ps	38: 4	overwhelmed me like a **b** too heavy
Mt	11: 30	my yoke is easy and my **b** is light."

BURDENED (BURDEN)
Gal	5: 1	do not let yourselves be **b** again

BURDENS (BURDEN)
Ps	68: 19	our Savior, who daily bears our **b**.
Gal	6: 2	Carry each other's **b**, and in this

BURIED
Ro	6: 4	We were therefore **b** with him
1Co	15: 4	that he was **b**, that he was raised

BURNING
Lev	6: 9	the fire must be kept **b** on the altar.
Ro	12: 20	you will heap **b** coals on his head."

BUSINESS
Da	8: 27	got up and went about the king's **b**.
1Th	4: 11	You should mind your own **b**

BUSY
1Ki 20: 40 While your servant was **b** here
2Th 3: 11 are not **b**; they are busybodies.
Titus 2: 5 pure, to be **b** at home, to be kind,
CAESAR
Mt 22: 21 give back to **C** what is Caesar's,
CAIN
Firstborn of Adam (Ge 4:1), murdered brother Abel (Ge 4:1–16; 1Jn 3:12).
CALEB
Judahite who spied out Canaan (Nu 13:6); allowed to enter land because of faith (Nu 13:30—14:38; Dt 1:36). Possessed Hebron (Jos 14:6—15:19).
CALF
Ex 32: 4 into an idol cast in the shape of a **c**,
Lk 15: 23 Bring the fattened **c** and kill it.
CALL (CALLED CALLING CALLS)
Ps 145: 18 LORD is near to all who **c** on him,
Pr 31: 28 children arise and **c** her blessed;
Isa 5: 20 Woe to those who **c** evil good
55: 6 **c** on him while he is near.
65: 24 Before they **c** I will answer;
Jer 33: 3 '**C** to me and I will answer you
Mt 9: 13 I have not come to **c** the righteous,
Ro 10: 12 richly blesses all who **c** on him,
11: 29 gifts and his **c** are irrevocable,
1Th 4: 7 For God did not **c** us to be impure,
CALLED (CALL)
1Sa 3: 5 and said, "Here I am; you **c** me."
2Ch 7: 14 my people, who are **c** by my name,
Ps 34: 6 This poor man **c**, and the LORD
Mt 21: 13 " 'My house will be **c** a house
Ro 8: 30 And those he predestined, he also **c**; those he **c**, he also justified;
1Co 7: 15 God has **c** us to live in peace.
Gal 5: 13 and sisters, were **c** to be free.
1Pe 2: 9 the praises of him who **c** you
CALLING (CALL)
Jn 1: 23 voice of one **c** in the wilderness,
Ac 22: 16 your sins away, **c** on his name.'
Eph 4: 1 worthy of the **c** you have received.
2Pe 1: 10 every effort to confirm your **c**
CALLS (CALL)
Joel 2: 32 everyone who **c** on the name
Jn 10: 3 He **c** his own sheep by name
Ro 10: 13 "Everyone who **c** on the name
CALM
Pr 29: 11 but the wise bring **c** in the end.
CAMEL
Mt 19: 24 easier for a **c** to go through the eye
23: 24 strain out a gnat but swallow a **c**.
CANAAN
1Ch 16: 18 **C** as the portion you will inherit."
CANCELED
Col 2: 14 having **c** the charge of our legal
CAPITAL
Dt 21: 22 someone guilty of a **c** offense is put
CARE (CAREFUL CAREFULLY CARES CARING)
Ps 8: 4 human beings that you **c** for them?
Pr 29: 7 The righteous **c** about justice
Lk 10: 34 him to an inn and took **c** of him.
Jn 21: 16 Jesus said, "Take **c** of my sheep."
1Co 3: 10 But each one should build with **c**.
Eph 5: 29 but they feed and **c** for their body,
Heb 2: 6 a son of man that you **c** for him?
1Pe 5: 2 of God's flock that is under your **c**,
CAREFUL (CARE)
Ex 23: 13 "Be **c** to do everything I have said
Dt 6: 3 be **c** to obey so that it may go well
Jos 23: 6 be **c** to obey all that is written
23: 11 So be very **c** to love the LORD
Pr 13: 24 one who hates their children is **c**
Mt 6: 1 "Be **c** not to practice your
Ro 12: 17 Be **c** to do what is right in the eyes
1Co 8: 9 Be **c**, however, that the exercise of
Eph 5: 15 Be very **c**, then, how you live—
CAREFULLY (CARE)
Pr 12: 26 righteous choose their friends **c**,
CARES (CARE)
Ps 55: 22 Cast your **c** on the LORD and he
Na 1: 7 He **c** for those who trust in him,
1Th 2: 7 Just as a nursing mother **c** for her
1Pe 5: 7 on him because he **c** for you.

CARING (CARE)
1Ti 5: 4 practice by **c** for their own family
CARRIED (CARRY)
Ex 19: 4 and how I **c** you on eagles' wings
Heb 13: 9 Do not be **c** away by all kinds
2Pe 1: 21 God as they were **c** along
CARRIES (CARRY)
Dt 32: 11 to catch them and **c** them aloft.
Isa 40: 11 arms and **c** them close to his heart;
CARRY (CARRIED CARRIES)
Lk 14: 27 whoever does not **c** their cross
Gal 6: 2 **C** each other's burdens, and in this
6: 5 each one should **c** their own load.
CAST
Ps 22: 18 them and **c** lots for my garment.
55: 22 **C** your cares on the LORD and he
Jn 19: 24 them and **c** lots for my garment."
1Pe 5: 7 **C** all your anxiety on him because
CATTLE
Ps 50: 10 and the **c** on a thousand hills.
CAUGHT
1Th 4: 17 are left will be **c** up together
CAUSE (CAUSES)
Pr 24: 28 against your neighbor without **c**—
Ecc 3: 2 Do not stand up for a bad **c**, for he
Mt 18: 7 the things that **c** people to stumble!
Ro 21: 14 that will **c** your brother or sister
1Co 10: 32 Do not **c** anyone to stumble,
CAUSES (CAUSE)
Isa 8: 14 he will be a stone that **c** people
Mt 18: 6 "If anyone **c** one of these little
CEASE
Ps 46: 9 He makes wars **c** to the ends
CELEBRATE
Ps 2: 11 fear and **c** his rule with trembling.
CENSER
Lev 16: 12 is to take a **c** full of burning coals
CENTURION
Mt 8: 5 Capernaum, a **c** came to him,
CERTAINTY
Lk 1: 4 you may know the **c** of the things
Jn 17: 8 They knew with **c** that I came
CHAFF
Ps 1: 4 They are like **c** that the wind blows
CHAINED
2Ti 2: 9 But God's word is not **c**.
CHAMPION
Ps 19: 5 like a **c** rejoicing to run his course.
CHANGE (CHANGED)
1Sa 15: 29 does not lie or **c** his mind;
Ps 110: 4 has sworn and will not **c** his mind:
Jer 7: 5 If you really **c** your ways and your
Mal 3: 6 "I the LORD do not **c**. So you,
Mt 18: 3 unless you **c** and become like little
Heb 7: 21 has sworn and will not **c** his mind:
Jas 1: 17 lights, who does not **c** like shifting
CHANGED (CHANGE)
1Co 15: 51 not all sleep, but we will all be **c**—
CHARACTER
Ru 3: 11 that you are a woman of noble **c**.
Pr 31: 10 A wife of noble **c** who can find?
Ro 5: 4 perseverance, **c**; and **c**, hope.
1Co 15: 33 "Bad company corrupts good **c**."
CHARGE
Ro 8: 33 will bring any **c** against those
2Co 11: 7 the gospel of God to you free of **c**?
2Ti 4: 1 and his kingdom, I give you this **c**:
CHARIOTS
2Ki 6: 17 and **c** of fire all around Elisha.
Ps 20: 7 Some trust in **c** and some in horses
CHARM
Pr 31: 30 **C** is deceptive, and beauty is
CHASE
Pr 12: 11 who **c** fantasies have no sense.
CHATTER (CHATTERING)
1Ti 6: 20 Turn away from godless **c**
2Ti 2: 16 Avoid godless **c**, because those who
CHATTERING (CHATTER)
Pr 10: 8 but a **c** fool comes to ruin.
10: 10 grief, and a **c** fool comes to ruin.
CHEAT (CHEATED)
Mal 1: 14 "Cursed is the **c** who has
1Co 6: 8 you yourselves **c** and do wrong,

CHEATED (CHEAT)
Lk 19: 8 if I have **c** anybody out of anything,
1Co 6: 7 Why not rather be **c**?

CHEEK
Mt 5: 39 turn to them the other **c** also.

CHEERFUL (CHEERS)
Pr 15: 13 A happy heart makes the face **c**,
15: 15 the **c** heart has a continual feast.
17: 22 A **c** heart is good medicine,
2Co 9: 7 for God loves a **c** giver.

CHEERS (CHEERFUL)
Pr 12: 25 the heart, but a kind word **c** it up.

CHILD (CHILDHOOD CHILDLESS CHILDREN)
Pr 22: 15 Folly is bound up in the heart of a **c**,
23: 13 not withhold discipline from a **c**;
29: 15 but a **c** left undisciplined disgraces
Isa 9: 6 For to us a **c** is born, to us a son is
11: 6 and a little **c** will lead them.
66: 13 As a mother comforts her **c**, so will
Mt 18: 2 He called a little **c** to him,
Lk 1: 42 and blessed is the **c** you will bear!
1: 80 And the **c** grew and became strong
1Co 13: 11 When I was a **c**, I talked like a **c**,
1Jn 5: 1 loves the father loves his **c** as well.

CHILDHOOD (CHILD)
1Co 13: 11 I put the ways of **c** behind me.

CHILDLESS (CHILD)
Ps 113: 9 settles the **c** woman in her home

CHILDREN (CHILD)
Dt 4: 9 Teach them to your **c** and to their **c**
11: 19 Teach them to your **c**,
Ps 8: 2 Through the praise of **c** and infants
Pr 13: 24 spares the rod hates their **c**,
17: 6 parents are the pride of their **c**,
20: 11 Even small **c** are known by their
22: 6 Start **c** off on the way they should
29: 17 Discipline your **c**, and they will
31: 28 Her **c** arise and call her blessed;
Mt 7: 11 how to give good gifts to your **c**,
11: 25 and revealed them to little **c**.
18: 3 change and become like little **c**,
19: 14 said, "Let the little **c** come to me,
21: 16 " 'From the lips of **c** and infants
Mk 9: 37 these little **c** in my name welcomes
10: 14 them, "Let the little **c** come to me,
10: 16 And he took the **c** in his arms,
13: 12 **c** will rebel against their parents
Lk 10: 21 and revealed them to little **c**.
18: 16 said, "Let the little **c** come to me,
Jn 12: 36 so that you may become **c** of light."
Ro 8: 16 with our spirit that we are God's **c**.
2Co 12: 14 **c** should not have to save for
Eph 6: 1 **c**, obey your parents in the Lord,
6: 4 Fathers, do not exasperate your **c**;
Col 3: 20 **c**, obey your parents in everything,
3: 21 do not embitter your **c**, or they will
1Ti 3: 4 well and see that his **c** obey him,
3: 12 and must manage his **c** and his
5: 10 such as bringing up **c**,
Heb 12: 7 God is treating you as his **c**.
1Jn 3: 1 that we should be called **c** of God!

CHOOSE (CHOOSES CHOSE CHOSEN)
Dt 30: 19 Now **c** life, so that you and your
Jos 24: 15 **c** for yourselves this day whom you
Pr 8: 10 **C** my instruction instead of silver,
Jn 15: 16 You did not **c** me, but I chose you
Ac 15: 14 God first intervened to **c** a people

CHOOSES (CHOOSE)
Jn 7: 17 who **c** to do the will of God

CHOSE (CHOOSE)
Ge 13: 11 Lot **c** for himself the whole plain
Ps 33: 12 the people he **c** for his inheritance.
Jn 15: 16 but I **c** you and appointed you so
1Co 1: 27 But God **c** the foolish things
Eph 1: 4 For he **c** us in him before
2Th 2: 13 because God **c** you as firstfruits

CHOSEN (CHOOSE)
Isa 41: 8 whom I have **c**, you descendants
Mt 22: 14 many are invited, but few are **c**."
Lk 10: 42 Mary has **c** what is better, and it
23: 35 if he is God's Messiah, the **C** One."
Jn 15: 19 but I have **c** you out of the world.

1Pe 1: 20 He was **c** before the creation
2: 9 But you are a **c** people, a royal

CHRIST (CHRIST'S CHRISTIAN MESSIAH)
Jn 1: 41 found the Messiah" (that is, the **C**).
Ro 3: 22 faith in Jesus **C** to all who believe.
5: 6 powerless, **C** died for the ungodly.
5: 8 we were still sinners, **C** died for us.
5: 17 life through the one man, Jesus **C**!
6: 4 just as **C** was raised from the dead
8: 1 for those who are in **C** Jesus,
8: 9 does not have the Spirit of **C**, they do not belong to **C**.
8: 35 separate us from the love of **C**?
10: 4 **C** is the culmination of the law so
14: 9 **C** died and returned to life so that
15: 3 even **C** did not please himself but,
1Co 1: 23 but we preach **C** crucified:
2: 2 while I was with you except Jesus **C**
3: 11 one already laid, which is Jesus **C**.
5: 7 For **C**, our Passover lamb, has been
8: 6 Jesus **C**, through whom all things
10: 4 them, and that rock was **C**.
10: 9 We should not test **C**, as some
11: 1 as I follow the example of **C**.
11: 3 that the head of every man is **C**,
11: 3 and the head of **C** is God.
12: 27 Now you are the body of **C**,
15: 3 **C** died for our sins according
15: 14 And if **C** has not been raised,
15: 22 die, so in **C** all will be made alive.
15: 57 victory through our Lord Jesus **C**.
2Co 3: 3 show that you are a letter from **C**,
4: 5 but Jesus **C** as Lord, and ourselves
5: 10 before the judgment seat of **C**,
5: 17 if anyone is in **C**, the new creation
11: 2 to **C**, so that I might present you as
Gal 2: 20 I have been crucified with **C**
3: 13 **C** redeemed us from the curse
6: 14 in the cross of our Lord Jesus **C**,
Eph 1: 3 and Father of our Lord Jesus **C**,
3: 8 Gentiles the boundless riches of **C**.
4: 13 whole measure of the fullness of **C**.
5: 2 just as **C** loved us and gave himself
5: 23 head of the wife as **C** is the head
5: 25 just as **C** loved the church and gave
Php 1: 21 to live is **C** and to die is gain.
1: 27 manner worthy of the gospel of **C**.
4: 19 to the riches of his glory in **C** Jesus.
Col 1: 27 which is **C** in you, the hope
1: 28 present everyone fully mature in **C**.
2: 6 as you received **C** Jesus as Lord,
2: 17 the reality, however, is found in **C**.
3: 15 Let the peace of **C** rule in your
2Th 2: 1 the coming of our Lord Jesus **C**
1Ti 1: 15 **C** Jesus came into the world to save
2: 5 and mankind, the man **C** Jesus,
2Ti 2: 3 like a good soldier of **C** Jesus.
3: 15 salvation through faith in **C** Jesus.
Titus 2: 13 our great God and Savior, Jesus **C**,
Heb 3: 14 We have come to share in **C**,
9: 14 will the blood of **C**, who through
9: 15 For this reason **C** is the mediator
9: 28 so **C** was sacrificed once to take
10: 10 of the body of Jesus **C** once for all.
13: 8 Jesus **C** is the same yesterday
1Pe 1: 19 but with the precious blood of **C**,
2: 21 called, because **C** suffered for you,
3: 18 For **C** also suffered once for sins,
4: 14 insulted because of the name of **C**,
1Jn 2: 22 whoever denies that Jesus is the **C**.
3: 16 Jesus **C** laid down his life for us.
5: 1 who believes that Jesus is the **C**
Rev 20: 4 reigned with **C** a thousand years.

CHRISTIAN (CHRIST)
1Pe 4: 16 If you suffer as a **C**, do not be

CHRIST'S (CHRIST)
2Co 5: 14 For **C** love compels us, because we
5: 20 We are therefore **C** ambassadors,
12: 9 so that **C** power may rest on me.

CHURCH
Mt 16: 18 and on this rock I will build my **c**,
18: 17 if they refuse to listen even to the **c**,
Ac 20: 28 Be shepherds of the **c** of God,

1Co 5: 12 mine to judge those outside the **c**?
14: 4 one who prophesies edifies the **c**.
14: 12 excel in those that build up the **c**.
14: 26 done so that the **c** may be built up.
Eph 5: 23 wife as Christ is the head of the **c**,
Col 1: 24 the sake of his body, which is the **c**.

CIRCUMCISED
Ge 17: 10 Every male among you shall be **c**.
Gal 2: 8 in Peter as an apostle to the **c**,

CIRCUMSTANCES
Php 4: 11 to be content whatever the **c**.
1Th 5: 18 give thanks in all **c**; for this is God's

CITIZENS (CITIZENSHIP)
Eph 2: 19 but fellow **c** with God's people

CITIZENSHIP (CITIZENS)
Php 3: 20 But our **c** is in heaven.

CITY
Heb 13: 14 here we do not have an enduring **c**,

CIVILIAN
2Ti 2: 4 a soldier gets entangled in **c** affairs,

CLAIM (CLAIMS)
Pr 25: 6 do not **c** a place among his great
1Jn 1: 6 If we **c** to have fellowship with him
1: 8 If we **c** to be without sin,
1: 10 If we **c** we have not sinned,

CLAIMS (CLAIM)
Jas 2: 14 if someone **c** to have faith but has
1Jn 2: 6 Whoever **c** to live in him must live
2: 9 Anyone who **c** to be in the light

CLAP
Ps 47: 1 **C** your hands, all you nations;
Isa 55: 12 trees of the field will **c** their hands.

CLAY
Isa 45: 9 Does the **c** say to the potter,
64: 8 We are the **c**, you are the potter;
Jer 18: 6 "Like **c** in the hand of the potter,
La 4: 2 are now considered as pots of **c**,
Da 2: 33 of iron and partly of baked **c**.
Ro 9: 21 the same lump of **c** some pottery
2Co 4: 7 this treasure in jars of **c** to show
2Ti 2: 20 and silver, but also of wood and **c**;

CLEAN
Lev 16: 30 you will be **c** from all your sins.
Ps 24: 4 one who has **c** hands and a pure
Mt 12: 44 swept **c** and put in order.
23: 25 You **c** the outside of the cup
Mk 7: 19 this, Jesus declared all foods **c**.)
Jn 13: 10 you are **c**, though not every one
15: 3 You are already **c** because
Ac 10: 15 impure that God has made **c**."
Ro 14: 20 All food is **c**, but it is wrong

CLING
Ps 63: 8 I **c** to you; your right hand upholds
Ro 12: 9 Hate what is evil; **c** to what is good.

CLOAK
2Ki 4: 29 "Tuck your **c** into your belt,

CLOSE (CLOSER)
Ps 34: 18 The Lord is **c**
Isa 40: 11 and carries them **c** to his heart;
Jer 30: 21 near and he will come **c** to me—

CLOSER (CLOSE)
Ex 3: 5 "Do not come any **c**," God said.
Pr 18: 24 friend who sticks **c** than a brother.

CLOTHE (CLOTHED CLOTHES CLOTHING)
Ps 45: 3 **c** yourself with splendor
Isa 52: 1 Zion, **c** yourself with strength!
Ro 13: 14 **c** yourselves with the Lord Jesus
Col 3: 12 **c** yourselves with compassion,
1Pe 5: 5 **c** yourselves with humility toward

CLOTHED (CLOTHE)
Ps 30: 11 my sackcloth and **c** me with joy,
Pr 31: 25 She is **c** with strength and dignity;
Lk 24: 49 the city until you have been **c**

CLOTHES (CLOTHE)
Mt 6: 25 food, and the body more than **c**?
6: 28 "And why do you worry about **c**?
Jn 11: 44 "Take off the grave **c** and let him

CLOTHING (CLOTHE)
Dt 22: 5 nor a man wear women's **c**,
Mt 7: 15 They come to you in sheep's **c**,

CLOUD (CLOUDS)
Ex 13: 21 them in a pillar of **c** to guide them
Isa 19: 1 the Lord rides on a swift **c** and is

Lk 21: 27 of Man coming in a **c** with power
Heb 12: 1 by such a great **c** of witnesses,

CLOUDS (CLOUD)
Ps 104: 3 He makes the **c** his chariot and
Da 7: 13 man, coming with the **c** of heaven.
Mk 13: 26 Man coming in **c** with great power
1Th 4: 17 them in the **c** to meet the Lord

CO-HEIRS (INHERIT)
Ro 8: 17 heirs of God and **c** with Christ,

COALS
Pr 25: 22 will heap burning **c** on his head,
Ro 12: 20 this, you will heap burning **c** on his

COAT
Lk 6: 29 If someone takes your **c**, do not

COLD
Pr 25: 25 Like **c** water to a weary soul is
Mt 10: 42 anyone gives even a cup of **c** water
24: 12 the love of most will grow **c**,

COMFORT (COMFORTED COMFORTS)
Ps 23: 4 your rod and your staff, they **c** me.
119: 52 ancient laws, and I find **c** in them.
119: 76 May your unfailing love be my **c**,
Zec 1: 17 the Lord will again **c** Zion
1Co 14: 3 strengthening, encouraging and **c**.
2Co 1: 4 that we can **c** those in any trouble
2: 7 you ought to forgive and **c** him,

COMFORTED (COMFORT)
Mt 5: 4 who mourn, for they will be **c**.

COMFORTS (COMFORT)
Job 29: 25 I was like one who **c** mourners.
Isa 49: 13 For the Lord **c** his people
51: 12 "I, even I, am he who **c** you.
66: 13 As a mother **c** her child, so will I
2Co 1: 4 who **c** us in all our troubles,
7: 6 But God, who **c** the downcast,

COMMAND (COMMANDED COMMANDING COMMANDMENT COMMANDMENTS COMMANDS)
Ex 7: 2 You are to say everything I **c** you,
Nu 24: 13 to go beyond the **c** of the Lord—
Dt 4: 2 Do not add to what I **c** you and do
30: 16 For I **c** you today to love
32: 46 so that you may **c** your children
Ps 91: 11 he will **c** his angels concerning you
148: 5 for at his **c** they were created,
Pr 6: 23 For this **c** is a lamp, this teaching is
13: 13 whoever respects a **c** is rewarded.
Ecc 8: 2 Obey the king's **c**, I say,
Joel 2: 11 mighty is the army that obeys his **c**.
Jn 13: 34 "A new **c** I give you:
15: 12 My **c** is this: Love each other as I
1Co 14: 37 I am writing to you is the Lord's **c**.
Gal 5: 14 is fulfilled in keeping this one **c**:
1Ti 1: 5 The goal of this **c** is love,
Heb 11: 3 the universe was formed at God's **c**,
1Jn 3: 23 And this is his **c**: to believe
2Jn : 6 his **c** is that you walk in love.

COMMANDED (COMMAND)
Ps 33: 9 came to be; he **c**, and it stood firm.
Mt 28: 20 to obey everything I have **c** you.
1Co 9: 14 way, the Lord has **c** that those who
1Jn 3: 23 and to love one another as he **c** us.

COMMANDING (COMMAND)
2Ti 2: 4 rather tries to please his **c** officer.

COMMANDMENT (COMMAND)
Jos 22: 5 be very careful to keep the **c**
Mt 22: 38 This is the first and greatest **c**.
Ro 7: 12 and the **c** is holy,
Eph 6: 2 is the first **c** with a promise—

COMMANDMENTS (COMMAND)
Ex 20: 6 those who love me and keep my **c**.
34: 28 words of the covenant—the Ten **C**.
Dt 7: 9 those who love him and keep his **c**.
Ecc 12: 13 Fear God and keep his **c**, for this is
Da 9: 4 those who love him and keep his **c**,
Mt 22: 40 the Prophets hang on these two **c**."

COMMANDS (COMMAND)
Dt 11: 27 you obey the **c** of the Lord your
Ps 112: 1 who find great delight in his **c**.
119: 47 in your **c** because I love them.
119: 86 All your **c** are trustworthy;
119: 98 Your **c** are always with me
119: 127 I love your **c** more than gold,

Ps 119:143 me, but your **c** give me delight.
119:172 word, for all your **c** are righteous.
Pr 3: 1 but keep my **c** in your heart,
10: 8 The wise in heart accept **c**,
Mt 5: 19 teaches these **c** will be called great
Jn 14: 15 "If you love me, keep my **c**.
14: 21 Whoever has my **c** and keeps them
Ac 17: 30 now he **c** all people everywhere
1Co 7: 19 Keeping God's **c** is what counts.
1Jn 5: 3 this is love for God: to keep his **c**. And his **c** are not burdensome,

COMMEND (COMMENDED COMMENDS)
Ecc 8: 15 So I **c** the enjoyment of life,
1Pe 2: 14 wrong and to **c** those who do right.

COMMENDED (COMMEND)
Ro 13: 3 do what is right and you will be **c**.
Heb 11: 39 These were all **c** for their faith,

COMMENDS (COMMEND)
2Co 10: 18 but the one whom the Lord **c**.

COMMIT (COMMITS COMMITTED)
Ex 20: 14 "You shall not **c** adultery.
Ps 37: 5 **C** your way to the LORD;
Mt 5: 27 was said, 'You shall not **c** adultery.'
Lk 23: 46 into your hands I **c** my spirit."
Ac 20: 32 "Now I **c** you to God
1Co 10: 8 We should not **c** sexual immorality,
1Pe 4: 19 to God's will should **c** themselves

COMMITS (COMMIT)
Pr 6: 32 a man who **c** adultery has no sense;
29: 22 hot-tempered person **c** many sins.
Mt 19: 9 marries another woman **c** adultery."

COMMITTED (COMMIT)
Nu 5: 7 must confess the sin they have **c**.
1Ki 8: 61 may your hearts be fully **c**
2Ch 16: 9 those whose hearts are fully **c**
Mt 5: 28 lustfully has already **c** adultery
2Co 5: 19 And he has **c** to us the message
1Pe 2: 22 "He **c** no sin, and no deceit was

COMMON
Pr 22: 2 Rich and poor have this in **c**:
1Co 10: 13 has overtaken you except what is **c**
2Co 6: 14 and wickedness have in **c**?

COMPANION
Pr 13: 20 for a **c** of fools suffers harm.
28: 7 a **c** of gluttons disgraces his father.
29: 3 but a **c** of prostitutes squanders his

COMPANY
Pr 24: 1 the wicked, do not desire their **c**;
Jer 15: 17 I never sat in the **c** of revelers,
1Co 15: 33 "Bad **c** corrupts good character."

COMPARED (COMPARING)
Eze 31: 2 "'Who can be **c** with you

COMPARING (COMPARED)
Ro 8: 18 present sufferings are not worth **c**
2Co 8: 8 of your love by **c** it
Gal 6: 4 without **c** themselves to someone

COMPASSION (COMPASSIONATE COMPASSIONS)
Ex 33: 19 I will have **c** on whom I will have **c**.
Ne 9: 19 your great **c** you did not abandon
9: 28 in your **c** you delivered them time
Ps 51: 1 to your great **c** blot out my
103: 4 pit and crowns you with love and **c**,
103: 13 As a father has **c** on his children,
145: 9 he has **c** on all he has made.
Isa 49: 13 will have **c** on his afflicted ones.
49: 15 and have no **c** on the child she has
Hos 2: 19 and justice, in love and **c**.
11: 8 all my **c** is aroused.
Jnh 3: 9 with **c** turn from his fierce anger so
Mt 9: 36 saw the crowds, he had **c** on them,
Mk 1: 2 "I have **c** for these people;
Ro 9: 15 I will have **c** on whom I have **c**."
Col 3: 12 clothe yourselves with **c**, kindness,
Jas 5: 11 The Lord is full of **c** and mercy.

COMPASSIONATE (COMPASSION)
Ne 9: 17 gracious and **c**, slow to anger
Ps 103: 8 The LORD is **c** and gracious,
112: 4 for those who are gracious and **c**
Eph 4: 32 Be kind and **c** to one another,
1Pe 3: 8 love one another, be **c** and humble.

COMPASSIONS (COMPASSION)
La 3: 22 not consumed, for his **c** never fail.

COMPEL (COMPELLED COMPELS)
Lk 14: 23 lanes and **c** them to come in,

COMPELLED (COMPEL)
Ac 20: 22 "And now, **c** by the Spirit, I am
1Co 9: 16 boast, since I am **c** to preach.

COMPELS (COMPEL)
2Co 5: 14 For Christ's love **c** us, because we

COMPETENCE (COMPETENT)
2Co 3: 5 but our **c** comes from God.

COMPETENT (COMPETENCE)
Ro 15: 14 and **c** to instruct one another.
1Co 6: 2 are you not **c** to judge trivial cases?
2Co 3: 5 Not that we are **c** in ourselves
3: 6 He has made us **c** as ministers

COMPETES
1Co 9: 25 Everyone who **c** in the games goes
2Ti 2: 5 anyone who **c** as an athlete does

COMPLACENT
Am 6: 1 Woe to you who are **c** in Zion,

COMPLETE
Jn 15: 11 in you and that your joy may be **c**.
16: 24 will receive, and your joy will be **c**.
17: 23 they may be brought to **c** unity.
Ac 20: 24 **c** the task the Lord Jesus has given
Php 2: 2 then make my joy **c** by being
Col 4: 17 it that you **c** the ministry you have
Jas 1: 4 so that you may be mature and **c**,
2: 22 faith was made **c** by what he did.

CONCEAL (CONCEALED CONCEALS)
Ps 40: 10 I do not **c** your love and your
Pr 25: 2 It is the glory of God to **c** a matter;

CONCEALED (CONCEAL)
Jer 16: 17 me, nor is their sin **c** from my eyes.
Mt 10: 26 for there is nothing **c** that will not
Mk 4: 22 whatever is **c** is meant to be

CONCEALS (CONCEAL)
Pr 28: 13 Whoever **c** their sins does not

CONCEITED
Gal 5: 26 Let us not become **c**,
1Ti 6: 4 they are **c** and understand nothing.

CONCEIVE (CONCEIVED)
Isa 7: 14 The virgin will **c** and give birth
Mt 1: 23 "The virgin will **c** and give birth

CONCEIVED (CONCEIVE)
Mt 1: 20 because what is **c** in her is
1Co 2: 9 and what no human mind has **c**"—

CONCERN (CONCERNED)
Eze 36: 21 I had **c** for my holy name,
1Co 7: 32 would like you to be free from **c**.
12: 25 that its parts should have equal **c**
2Co 11: 28 of my **c** for all the churches.

CONCERNED (CONCERN)
Jnh 4: 10 "You have been **c** about this plant,
1Co 7: 32 An unmarried man is **c**

CONDEMN (CONDEMNATION CONDEMNED CONDEMNING CONDEMNS)
Job 40: 8 you **c** me to justify yourself?
Isa 50: 9 Who will **c** me? They will all wear
Lk 6: 37 Do not **c**, and you will not be
Jn 3: 17 Son into the world to **c** the world,
12: 48 words I have spoken will **c** them
Ro 2: 27 yet obeys the law will **c** you who,
1Jn 3: 20 If our hearts **c** us, we know that

CONDEMNATION (CONDEMN)
Ro 5: 18 just as one trespass resulted in **c**
8: 1 there is now no **c** for those who are
2Co 3: 9 that brought **c** was glorious,

CONDEMNED (CONDEMN)
Ps 34: 22 who takes refuge in him will be **c**.
Mt 12: 37 and by your words you will be **c**."
23: 33 How will you escape being **c**
Jn 3: 18 Whoever believes in him is not **c**,
16: 11 prince of this world now stands **c**.
Ro 14: 23 whoever has doubts is **c** if they eat,
1Co 11: 32 that we will not be finally **c**
Heb 11: 7 By his faith he **c** the world

CONDEMNING (CONDEMN)
Pr 17: 15 the guilty and **c** the innocent—
Ro 2: 1 you are **c** yourself, because you

CONDEMNS (CONDEMN)
Pr 14: 34 exalts a nation, but sin **c** any people
Ro 8: 34 Who then is the one who **c**?

CORNELIUS
Roman to whom Peter preached; first Gentile Christian (Ac 10).

CORNERSTONE (STONE)
Ps 118: 22 builders rejected has become the **c**;
Isa 28: 16 a precious **c** for a sure foundation;
Eph 2: 20 Christ Jesus himself as the chief **c**.
1Pe 2: 6 a chosen and precious **c**,
2: 7 rejected has become the **c**,"

CORRECT (CORRECTING CORRECTION CORRECTS)
2Ti 4: 2 **c**, rebuke and encourage—

CORRECTING (CORRECT)
2Ti 3: 16 **c** and training in righteousness,

CORRECTION (CORRECT)
Pr 10: 17 but whoever ignores **c** leads others
12: 1 but whoever hates **c** is stupid.
15: 5 whoever heeds **c** shows prudence.
15: 10 the one who hates **c** will die.

CORRECTS (CORRECT)
Job 5: 17 "Blessed is the one whom God **c**;
Pr 9: 7 Whoever **c** a mocker invites insults

CORRUPT (CORRUPTS)
Ge 6: 11 Now the earth was **c** in God's sight

CORRUPTS (CORRUPT)
Ecc 7: 7 into a fool, and a bribe **c** the heart.
1Co 15: 33 "Bad company **c** good character."
Jas 3: 6 It **c** the whole body, sets the whole

COST
Pr 4: 7 Though it **c** all you have,
Isa 55: 1 milk without money and without **c**.
Rev 21: 6 thirsty I will give water without **c**

COUNSEL (COUNSELOR)
1Ki 22: 5 "First seek the **c** of the Lord."
Pr 15: 22 Plans fail for lack of **c**,
Rev 3: 18 I **c** you to buy from me gold

COUNSELOR (COUNSEL)
Isa 9: 6 And he will be called Wonderful **C**,

COUNT (COUNTING COUNTS)
Ro 4: 8 Lord will never **c** against them."
6: 11 **c** yourselves dead to sin but alive

COUNTING (COUNT)
2Co 5: 19 not **c** people's sins against them.

COUNTRY
Jn 4: 44 prophet has no honor in his own **c**.

COUNTS (COUNT)
Jn 6: 63 the flesh **c** for nothing.
1Co 7: 19 God's commands is what **c**.
Gal 5: 6 **c** is faith expressing itself through

COURAGE (COURAGEOUS)
Ac 23: 11 stood near Paul and said, "Take **c**!

COURAGEOUS (COURAGE)
Dt 31: 6 Be strong and **c**. Do not be afraid
Jos 1: 6 Be strong and **c**, because you will
1Co 16: 13 firm in the faith; be **c**; be strong.

COURSE
Ps 19: 5 a champion rejoicing to run his **c**.
Pr 15: 21 understanding keeps a straight **c**.

COURTS
Ps 84: 10 your **c** than a thousand elsewhere;
100: 4 thanksgiving and his **c** with praise;

COVENANT (COVENANTS)
Ge 9: 9 "I now establish my **c** with you
Ex 19: 5 if you obey me fully and keep my **c**,
1Ch 16: 15 He remembers his **c** forever,
Job 31: 1 "I made a **c** with my eyes not
Jer 31: 31 I will make a new **c** with the people
1Co 11: 25 "This cup is the new **c** in my blood;
Gal 4: 24 One **c** is from Mount Sinai
Heb 9: 15 Christ is the mediator of a new **c**,

COVENANTS (COVENANT)
Ro 9: 4 the **c**, the receiving of the law,
Gal 4: 24 The women represent two **c**.

COVER (COVER-UP COVERED COVERS)
Ps 91: 4 He will **c** you with his feathers,
Jas 5: 20 and **c** over a multitude of sins.

COVERED (COVER)
Ps 32: 1 are forgiven, whose sins are **c**.
Isa 6: 2 With two wings they **c** their faces,
Ro 4: 7 are forgiven, whose sins are **c**.
1Co 11: 4 with his head **c** dishonors his head.

COVERS (COVER)
Pr 10: 12 conflict, but love **c** over all wrongs.
1Pe 4: 8 because love **c** over a multitude

COVER-UP (COVER)
1Pe 2: 16 do not use your freedom as a **c**

COVET
Ex 20: 17 "You shall not **c** your neighbor's
Ro 13: 9 "You shall not **c**," and whatever

COWARDLY
Rev 21: 8 But the **c**, the unbelieving, the vile,

CRAFTINESS (CRAFTY)
1Co 3: 19 "He catches the wise in their **c**";

CRAFTY (CRAFTINESS)
Ge 3: 1 the serpent was more **c** than any
2Co 12: 16 Yet, **c** fellow that I am, I caught you

CRAVE
Pr 23: 3 Do not **c** his delicacies, for that
1Pe 2: 2 babies, **c** pure spiritual milk,

CREATE (CREATED CREATION CREATOR)
Ps 51: 10 **C** in me a pure heart, O God,
Isa 45: 18 he did not **c** it to be empty,

CREATED (CREATE)
Ge 1: 1 In the beginning God **c** the heavens
1: 21 So God **c** the great creatures
1: 27 So God **c** mankind in his own
1: 27 male and female he **c** them.
Ps 148: 5 for at his command they were **c**,
Ro 1: 25 and served **c** things rather than
1Co 11: 9 neither was man **c** for woman,
Col 1: 16 For in him all things were **c**:
1Ti 4: 4 For everything God **c** is good,
Rev 10: 6 who **c** the heavens and all that is

CREATION (CREATE)
Mk 16: 15 preach the gospel to all **c**.
Jn 17: 24 because you loved me before the **c**
Ro 8: 19 For the **c** waits in eager expectation
8: 39 nor anything else in all **c**, will be
2Co 5: 17 is in Christ, the new **c** has come:
Col 1: 15 God, the firstborn over all **c**.
1Pe 1: 20 He was chosen before the **c**
Rev 13: 8 was slain from the **c** of the world.

CREATOR (CREATE)
Ge 14: 22 Most High, **C** of heaven and earth,
Isa 42: 5 Lord says—the **C** of the heavens,
Ro 1: 25 created things rather than the **C**—

CREATURE (CREATURES)
Lev 17: 11 For the life of a **c** is in the blood,

CREATURES (CREATURE)
Ge 6: 19 into the ark two of all living **c**,
Ps 104: 24 the earth is full of your **c**.

CREDIT (CREDITED)
Ro 4: 24 whom God will **c** righteousness—
1Pe 2: 20 it to your **c** if you receive a beating

CREDITED (CREDIT)
Ge 15: 6 and he **c** it to him as righteousness.
Ro 4: 5 their faith is **c** as righteousness.
Gal 3: 6 it was **c** to him as righteousness."
Jas 2: 23 it was **c** to him as righteousness,"

CRIED (CRY)
Ps 18: 6 I **c** to my God for help.

CRIMSON
Isa 1: 18 though they are red as **c**, they shall

CRIPPLED
Mk 9: 45 to enter life **c** than to have two feet

CRITICISM
2Co 8: 20 want to avoid any **c** of the way we

CROOKED
Pr 10: 9 whoever takes **c** paths will be
Php 2: 15 fault in a warped and **c** generation."

CROSS
Mt 10: 38 Whoever does not take up their **c**
Lk 9: 23 take up their **c** daily and follow me.
Ac 2: 23 to death by nailing him to the **c**.
1Co 1: 17 lest the **c** of Christ be emptied of
Gal 6: 14 in the **c** of our Lord Jesus Christ,
Php 2: 8 even death on a **c**!
Col 1: 20 through his blood, shed on the **c**.
2: 14 taken it away, nailing it to the **c**.
2: 15 triumphing over them by the **c**.
Heb 12: 2 joy set before him he endured the **c**,

CROWD
Ex 23: 2 pervert justice by siding with the **c**,

CROWN (CROWNED CROWNS)
Pr 4: 9 and present you with a glorious **c**."
10: 6 Blessings **c** the head

Pr 12: 4 noble character is her husband's **c**,
17: 6 Children's children are a **c**
Isa 61: 3 on them a **c** of beauty instead
Zec 9: 16 in his land like jewels in a **c**.
Mt 27: 29 then twisted together a **c** of thorns
1Co 9: 25 to get a **c** that will last forever.
2Ti 4: 8 store for me the **c** of righteousness,
Rev 2: 10 will give you life as your victor's **c**.

CROWNED (CROWN)
Ps 8: 5 the angels and **c** them with glory
Pr 14: 18 the prudent are **c** with knowledge.
Heb 2: 7 you **c** them with glory and honor

CROWNS (CROWN)
Rev 4: 10 They lay their **c** before the throne
19: 12 fire, and on his head are many **c**.

CRUCIFIED (CRUCIFY)
Mt 20: 19 to be mocked and flogged and **c**.
27: 38 Two rebels were **c** with him,
Lk 24: 7 be **c** and on the third day be raised
Jn 19: 18 they **c** him, and with him two
Ac 2: 36 Jesus, whom you **c**, both Lord
Ro 6: 6 that our old self was **c** with him so
1Co 1: 23 but we preach Christ **c**:
2: 2 you except Jesus Christ and him **c**.
Gal 2: 20 I have been **c** with Christ and I no
5: 24 Christ Jesus have **c** the flesh with

CRUCIFY (CRUCIFIED CRUCIFYING)
Mt 27: 22 They all answered, "**C** him!"
27: 31 Then they led him away to **c** him.

CRUCIFYING (CRUCIFY)
Heb 6: 6 their loss they are **c** the Son of God

CRUSH (CRUSHED)
Ge 3: 15 he will **c** your head, and you will
Isa 53: 10 it was the Lord's will to **c** him
Ro 16: 20 peace will soon **c** Satan under your

CRUSHED (CRUSH)
Ps 34: 18 and saves those who are **c** in spirit.
Isa 53: 5 he was **c** for our iniquities;
2Co 4: 8 pressed on every side, but not **c**;

CRY (CRIED)
Ps 34: 15 and his ears are attentive to their **c**,
40: 1 he turned to me and heard my **c**.
130: 1 Out of the depths I **c** to you,

CULMINATION
Ro 10: 4 Christ is the **c** of the law so

CUP
Ps 23: 5 my head with oil; my **c** overflows.
Mt 10: 42 anyone gives even a **c** of cold water
23: 25 You clean the outside of the **c**
26: 39 may this **c** be taken from me.
1Co 11: 25 "This **c** is the new covenant in my

CURSE (CURSED)
Dt 11: 26 you today a blessing and a **c**—
21: 23 is hung on a pole is under God's **c**.
Lk 6: 28 bless those who **c** you,
Gal 1: 8 to you, let them be under God's **c**!
3: 13 redeemed us from the **c** of the law by becoming a **c** for us,
Rev 22: 3 No longer will there be any **c**.

CURSED (CURSE)
Ge 3: 17 "**C** is the ground because of you;
Dt 27: 15 "**C** is anyone who makes an idol—
27: 16 "**C** is anyone who dishonors their
27: 17 "**C** is anyone who moves their
27: 18 "**C** is anyone who leads the blind
27: 19 "**C** is anyone who withholds justice
27: 20 "**C** is anyone who sleeps with his
27: 21 "**C** is anyone who has sexual
27: 22 "**C** is anyone who sleeps with his
27: 23 "**C** is anyone who sleeps with his
27: 24 "**C** is anyone who kills their
27: 25 "**C** is anyone who accepts a bribe
27: 26 "**C** is anyone who does not uphold
Ro 9: 3 I could wish that I myself were **c**
Gal 3: 10 "**C** is everyone who does not

CURTAIN
Ex 26: 33 Hang the **c** from the clasps
26: 33 The **c** will separate the Holy Place
Lk 23: 45 the **c** of the temple was torn in two.
Heb 10: 20 way opened for us through the **c**,

CYMBAL
1Co 13: 1 a resounding gong or a clanging **c**.

DANCE (DANCING)
Ecc 3: 4 a time to mourn and a time to **d**,
Mt 11: 17 the pipe for you, and you did not **d**;

DANCING (DANCE)
Ps 30: 11 You turned my wailing into **d**;
149: 3 Let them praise his name with **d**

DANGER
Pr 27: 12 The prudent see **d** and take refuge,
Ro 8: 35 or nakedness or **d** or sword?

DANIEL
Hebrew exile to Babylon, name changed to Belteshazzar (Da 1:6–7). Refused to eat unclean food (Da 1:8–21). Interpreted Nebuchadnezzar's dreams (Da 2; 4), writing on the wall (Da 5). Thrown into lions' den (Da 6). Visions of (Da 7–12).

DARK (DARKEST DARKNESS)
Ro 1: 9 a light for those who are in the **d**,
2Pe 1: 19 it, as to a light shining in a **d** place,

DARKEST (DARK)
Ps 23: 4 though I walk through the **d** valley,

DARKNESS (DARK)
Ge 1: 4 he separated the light from the **d**.
2Sa 22: 29 the Lord turns my **d** into light.
Job 34: 22 utter **d**, where evildoers can hide.
Jn 3: 19 but people loved **d** instead of light
2Co 6: 14 fellowship can light have with **d**?
Eph 5: 8 For you were once **d**, but now you
1Pe 2: 9 out of **d** into his wonderful light.
1Jn 1: 5 in him there is no **d** at all.
2: 9 a brother or sister is still in the **d**.

DAUGHTERS
Joel 2: 28 Your sons and **d** will prophesy,

DAVID
Son of Jesse (Ru 4:17–22; 1Ch 2:13–15), ancestor of Jesus (Mt 1:1–17; Lk 3:31).
Anointed king by Samuel (1Sa 16:1–13). Musician to Saul (1Sa 16:14–23; 18:10). Killed Goliath (1Sa 17). Relation with Jonathan (1Sa 18:1–4; 19–20; 23:16–18; 2Sa 1). Disfavor of Saul (1Sa 18:6—23:29). Spared Saul's life (1Sa 24; 26). Among Philistines (1Sa 21:10–14; 27–30). Lament for Saul and Jonathan (2Sa 1).
Anointed king of Judah (2Sa 2:1–11); of Israel (2Sa 5:1–4; 1Ch 11:1–3). Promised eternal dynasty (2Sa 7; 1Ch 17; Ps 132). Adultery with Bathsheba (2Sa 11–12). Absalom's revolt (2Sa 14–18). Last words (2Sa 23:1–7). Death (1Ki 2:10–12; 1Ch 29:28).

DAWN
Ps 37: 6 righteous reward shine like the **d**,

DAY (DAYS)
Ge 1: 5 God called the light "**d**,"
Ex 20: 8 "Remember the Sabbath **d**
Lev 23: 28 because it is the **D** of Atonement,
Nu 14: 14 them in a pillar of cloud by **d**
Jos 1: 8 meditate on it **d** and night,
Ps 84: 10 Better is one **d** in your courts than
96: 2 proclaim his salvation **d** after **d**.
118: 24 The Lord has done it this very **d**;
Pr 27: 1 do not know what a **d** may bring.
Joel 2: 31 great and dreadful **d** of the Lord.
Ob : 15 "The **d** of the Lord is near for all
Lk 11: 3 Give us each **d** our daily bread.
Ac 17: 11 examined the Scriptures every **d**
2Co 4: 16 we are being renewed **d** by **d**.
1Th 5: 2 the **d** of the Lord will come like
2Pe 3: 8 With the Lord a **d** is like a thousand

DAYS (DAY)
Dt 17: 19 he is to read it all the **d** of his life so
Ps 23: 6 love will follow me all the **d** of my
90: 10 Our **d** may come to seventy years,
Ecc 12: 1 Creator in the **d** of your youth,
Joel 2: 29 I will pour out my Spirit in those **d**.
Mic 4: 1 In the last **d** the mountain
Heb 1: 2 in these last **d** he has spoken to us
2Pe 3: 3 that in the last **d** scoffers will come,

DEACONS
1Ti 3: 8 way, **d** are to be worthy of respect,

DEAD (DIE)
Dt 18: 11 or spiritist or who consults the **d**.
Mt 28: 7 'He has risen from the **d** and is
Ro 6: 11 count yourselves **d** to sin but alive
Eph 2: 1 you were **d** in your transgressions
1Th 4: 16 and the **d** in Christ will rise first.

Jas 2: 17 is not accompanied by action, is **d**.
2: 26 so faith without deeds is **d**.
DEATH (DIE)
Nu 35: 16 the murderer is to be put to **d**.
Ps 116: 15 of the LORD is the **d** of his faithful
Pr 8: 36 all who hate me love **d**."
14: 12 right, but in the end it leads to **d**.
Ecc 7: 2 for **d** is the destiny of everyone;
Isa 25: 8 he will swallow up **d** forever.
53: 12 he poured out his life unto **d**,
Jn 5: 24 but has crossed over from **d** to life.
Ro 5: 12 **d** through sin, and in this way **d**
6: 23 For the wages of sin is **d**,
8: 13 Spirit you put to **d** the misdeeds
1Co 15: 21 For since **d** came through a man,
15: 31 I face **d** every day—yes, just as
15: 55 "Where, O **d**, is your victory?
1Pe 3: 18 He was put to **d** in the body
Rev 1: 18 I hold the keys of **d** and Hades.
20: 6 The second **d** has no power over
20: 14 The lake of fire is the second **d**.
21: 4 There will be no more **d**'
DEBAUCHERY
Ro 13: 13 not in sexual immorality and **d**,
Eph 5: 18 drunk on wine, which leads to **d**.
DEBORAH
Prophetess who led Israel to victory over Canaanites (Jdg 4–5).
DEBT (DEBTORS DEBTS)
Ro 13: 8 except the continuing **d** to love
DEBTORS (DEBT)
Mt 6: 12 as we also have forgiven our **d**.
DEBTS (DEBT)
Dt 15: 1 seven years you must cancel **d**.
Mt 6: 12 And forgive us our **d**, as we
DECAY
Ps 16: 10 will you let your faithful one see **d**.
Ac 2: 27 will not let your holy one see **d**.
DECEIT (DECEIVE)
Mk 7: 22 greed, malice, **d**, lewdness, envy,
1Pe 2: 1 yourselves of all malice and all **d**,
2: 22 and no **d** was found in his mouth."
DECEITFUL (DECEIVE)
Jer 17: 9 The heart is **d** above all things
2Co 11: 13 are false apostles, **d** workers,
DECEITFULNESS (DECEIVE)
Mk 4: 19 the **d** of wealth and the desires
Heb 3: 13 of you may be hardened by sin's **d**.
DECEIVE (DECEIT DECEITFUL DECEITFULNESS DECEIVED DECEPTIVE)
Lev 19: 11 "'Do not **d** one another.
Pr 14: 5 An honest witness does not **d**,
Mt 24: 5 am the Messiah,' and will **d** many.
Ro 16: 18 flattery they **d** the minds of naive
1Co 3: 18 Do not **d** yourselves. If any of you
Gal 6: 3 they are not, they **d** themselves.
Eph 5: 6 no one **d** you with empty words,
Jas 1: 22 to the word, and so **d** yourselves.
Jas 1: 26 rein on their tongues **d** themselves,
1Jn 1: 8 we **d** ourselves and the truth is not
DECEIVED (DECEIVE)
Ge 3: 13 said, "The serpent **d** me, and I ate."
Gal 6: 7 Do not be **d**: God cannot be
1Ti 2: 14 And Adam was not the one **d**; it was the woman who was **d**
2Ti 3: 13 to worse, deceiving and being **d**.
Jas 1: 16 Don't be **d**, my dear brothers
DECENCY
1Ti 2: 9 modestly, with **d** and propriety,
DECEPTIVE (DECEIVE)
Pr 31: 30 Charm is **d**, and beauty is fleeting;
Col 2: 8 through hollow and **d** philosophy,
DECLARE (DECLARED DECLARING)
1Ch 16: 24 **D** his glory among the nations,
Ps 19: 1 The heavens **d** the glory of God;
96: 3 **D** his glory among the nations,
Isa 42: 9 taken place, and new things I **d**;
Ro 10: 9 If you **d** with your mouth, "Jesus is
DECLARED (DECLARE)
Mk 7: 19 saying this, Jesus **d** all foods clean.)
Ro 2: 13 the law who will be **d** righteous.
3: 20 no one will be **d** righteous

DECLARING (DECLARE)
Ps 71: 8 **d** your splendor all day long.
Ac 2: 11 hear them **d** the wonders of God
DECREED (DECREES)
La 3: 37 it happen if the Lord has not **d** it?
Lk 22: 22 Son of Man will go as it has been **d**.
DECREES (DECREED)
Lev 10: 11 Israelites all the **d** the LORD has
Ps 119: 112 on keeping your **d** to the very end.
DEDICATE (DEDICATION)
Pr 20: 25 It is a trap to **d** something rashly
DEDICATION (DEDICATE)
1Ti 5: 11 sensual desires overcome their **d**
DEED (DEEDS)
Col 3: 17 whether in word or **d**, do it all
DEEDS (DEED)
1Sa 2: 3 knows, and by him **d** are weighed.
Ps 65: 5 us with awesome and righteous **d**,
66: 3 to God, "How awesome are your **d**!
78: 4 next generation the praiseworthy
86: 10 you are great and do marvelous **d**;
92: 4 For you make me glad by your **d**,
111: 3 Glorious and majestic are his **d**,
Hab 3: 2 I stand in awe of your **d**, LORD.
Mt 5: 16 that they may see your good **d**
11: 19 wisdom is proved right by her **d**."
Ac 26: 20 their repentance by their **d**.
Jas 2: 14 claims to have faith but has no **d**?
2: 20 that faith without **d** is useless?
1Pe 2: 12 they may see your good **d**
DEEP (DEPTH)
1Co 2: 10 things, even the **d** things of God.
1Ti 3: 9 must keep hold of the **d** truths
DEER
Ps 42: 1 As the **d** pants for streams of water,
DEFEND (DEFENSE)
Ps 74: 22 Rise up, O God, and **d** your cause;
Pr 31: 9 **d** the rights of the poor and needy.
Jer 50: 34 He will vigorously **d** their cause so
DEFENSE (DEFEND)
Ps 35: 23 Awake, and rise to my **d**!
Php 1: 16 put here for the **d** of the gospel.
DEFERRED
Pr 13: 12 Hope **d** makes the heart sick,
DEFILE (DEFILED)
Da 1: 8 Daniel resolved not to **d** himself
DEFILED (DEFILE)
Isa 24: 5 The earth is **d** by its people;
DEFRAUD
Lev 19: 13 "'Do not **d** or rob your neighbor.
DEITY
Col 2: 9 Christ all the fullness of the **D** lives
DELIGHT (DELIGHTS)
1Sa 15: 22 "Does the LORD **d** in burnt
Ps 1: 2 but whose **d** is in the law
16: 3 noble ones in whom is all my **d**."
35: 9 the LORD and **d** in his salvation.
37: 4 Take **d** in the LORD, and he will
43: 4 of God, to God, my joy and my **d**.
51: 16 You do not **d** in sacrifice,
119: 77 I may live, for your law is my **d**.
Isa 42: 1 my chosen one in whom I **d**;
55: 2 you will **d** in the richest of fare.
61: 10 I **d** greatly in the LORD;
Jer 9: 24 earth, for in these I **d**,"
15: 16 they were my joy and my heart's **d**,
Mic 7: 18 angry forever but **d** to show mercy.
Zep 3: 17 He will take great **d** in you;
Mt 12: 18 the one I love, in whom I **d**;
1Co 13: 6 Love does not **d** in evil but rejoices
2Co 12: 10 for Christ's sake, I **d** in weaknesses,
DELIGHTS (DELIGHT)
Ps 22: 8 deliver him, since he **d** in him."
35: 27 who **d** in the well-being of his
36: 8 them drink from your river of **d**.
Pr 3: 12 he loves, as a father the son he **d** in.
12: 22 **d** in people who are trustworthy.
29: 17 will bring you the **d** you desire.
DELILAH
Woman who betrayed Samson (Jdg 16:4–22).
DELIVER (DELIVERANCE DELIVERED DELIVERER DELIVERS)
Ps 72: 12 he will **d** the needy who cry out,

Ps 79: 9 **d** us and forgive our sins for your
Da 3: 17 the God we serve is able to **d** us
Mt 6: 13 but **d** us from the evil one.'
2Co 1: 10 that he will continue to **d** us,
DELIVERANCE (DELIVER)
Ps 3: 8 From the LORD comes **d**.
32: 7 and surround me with songs of **d**.
33: 17 A horse is a vain hope for **d**;
DELIVERED (DELIVER)
Ps 34: 4 he **d** me from all my fears.
Ro 4: 25 He was **d** over to death for our sins
DELIVERER (DELIVER)
Ps 18: 2 is my rock, my fortress and my **d**;
40: 17 You are my help and my **d**;
140: 7 my strong **d**, you shield my head
144: 2 stronghold and my **d**, my shield,
DELIVERS (DELIVER)
Ps 34: 17 he **d** them from all their troubles.
34: 19 The LORD **d** him from them all;
37: 40 The LORD helps them and **d** them;
DEMANDED
Lk 12: 20 This very night your life will be **d**
12: 48 been given much, much will be **d**;
DEMONS
Mt 12: 27 And if I drive out **d** by Beelzebul,
Mk 5: 15 been possessed by the legion of **d**,
Ro 8: 38 life, neither angels nor **d**,
Jas 2: 19 Good! Even the **d** believe that—
DEMONSTRATE (DEMONSTRATES)
Ac 26: 20 their repentance by their deeds.
Ro 3: 26 he did it to **d** his righteousness
DEMONSTRATES (DEMONSTRATE)
Ro 5: 8 God **d** his own love for us in this:
DEN
Da 6: 16 and threw him into the lions' **d**.
Mt 21: 13 but you are making it 'a **d**
DENARIUS
Mk 12: 15 "Bring me a **d** and let me look
DENIED (DENY)
1Ti 5: 8 has **d** the faith and is worse than
DENIES (DENY)
1Jn 2: 23 No one who **d** the Son has
DENY (DENIED DENIES DENYING)
Ex 23: 6 "Do not **d** justice to your poor
Job 27: 5 till I die, I will not **d** my integrity.
La 3: 35 **d** people their rights before the
Lk 9: 23 be my disciple must **d** themselves
Titus 1: 16 but by their actions they **d** him.
DENYING (DENY)
Eze 22: 29 the foreigner, **d** them justice.
2Ti 3: 5 a form of godliness but **d** its power.
2Pe 2: 1 even **d** the sovereign Lord who
DEPART (DEPARTED)
Ge 49: 10 The scepter will not **d** from Judah,
Job 1: 21 mother's womb, and naked I will **d**.
Mt 25: 41 to those on his left, '**D** from me,
Php 1: 23 I desire to **d** and be with Christ,
DEPARTED (DEPART)
1Sa 4: 21 "The Glory has **d** from Israel"—
Ps 119:102 I have not **d** from your laws,
DEPOSIT
2Co 1: 22 put his Spirit in our hearts as a **d**,
5: 5 who has given us the Spirit as a **d**,
Eph 1: 14 who is a **d** guaranteeing our
2Ti 1: 14 Guard the good **d** that was entrusted
DEPRAVED (DEPRAVITY)
Ro 1: 28 God gave them over to a **d** mind,
2Pe 2: 7 was distressed by the **d** conduct
DEPRAVITY (DEPRAVED)
Ro 1: 29 of wickedness, evil, greed and **d**.
DEPRIVE
Dt 24: 17 Do not **d** the foreigner
Pr 18: 5 and so **d** the innocent of justice.
Isa 10: 2 to **d** the poor of their rights
29: 21 with false testimony **d** the innocent
1Co 7: 5 Do not **d** each other except
DEPTH (DEEP)
Ro 8: 39 neither height nor **d**, nor anything
11: 33 the **d** of the riches of the wisdom
DESERTED (DESERTS)
Mt 26: 56 all the disciples **d** him and fled.
2Ti 1: 15 in the province of Asia has **d** me,

DESERTING (DESERTS)
Gal 1: 6 you are so quickly **d** the one who
DESERTS (DESERTED DESERTING)
Zec 11: 17 shepherd, who **d** the flock!
DESERVE (DESERVES)
Ps 103: 10 he does not treat us as our sins **d**
Jer 21: 14 I will punish you as your deeds **d**,
Mt 22: 8 those I invited did not **d** to come.
Ro 1: 32 those who do such things **d** death,
DESERVES (DESERVE)
Lk 10: 7 for the worker **d** his wages.
1Ti 5: 18 and "The worker **d** his wages."
DESIRABLE (DESIRE)
Pr 22: 1 name is more **d** than great riches;
DESIRE (DESIRABLE DESIRES)
Ge 3: 16 Your **d** will be for your husband,
Dt 5: 21 You shall not set your **d** on your
Ps 40: 6 and offering you did not **d**—
40: 8 I **d** to do your will, my God;
73: 25 earth has nothing I **d** besides you.
Pr 3: 15 nothing you **d** can compare
10: 24 what the righteous **d** will be
11: 23 The **d** of the righteous ends only
19: 2 **D** without knowledge is not good
Isa 26: 8 and renown are the **d** of our hearts.
53: 2 appearance that we should **d** him.
55: 11 but will accomplish what I **d**
Hos 6: 6 For I **d** mercy, not sacrifice,
Mt 9: 13 'I **d** mercy, not sacrifice.'
Ro 7: 18 For I have the **d** to do what is good,
1Co 12: 31 Now eagerly **d** the greater gifts.
14: 1 and eagerly **d** gifts of the Spirit,
Php 1: 23 I **d** to depart and be with Christ,
Heb 13: 18 **d** to live honorably in every way.
Jas 1: 15 after **d** has conceived, it gives birth
DESIRES (DESIRE)
Ge 4: 7 it **d** to have you, but you must rule
1Ch 29: 18 keep these **d** and thoughts
Ps 34: 12 life and **d** to see many good days,
37: 4 will give you the **d** of your heart.
103: 5 who satisfies your **d** with good
145: 19 He fulfills the **d** of those who fear
Pr 11: 6 the unfaithful are trapped by evil **d**.
19: 22 What a person **d** is unfailing love;
Mk 4: 19 and the **d** for other things come
Ro 8: 5 minds set on what the Spirit **d**.
13: 14 how to gratify the **d** of the flesh.
Gal 5: 16 and you will not gratify the **d**
5: 17 For the flesh **d** what is contrary
1Ti 3: 1 to be an overseer **d** a noble task.
6: 9 harmful **d** that plunge people
2Ti 2: 22 Flee the evil **d** of youth and pursue
Jas 1: 20 the righteousness that God **d**.
4: 1 from your **d** that battle within you?
1Pe 2: 11 to abstain from sinful **d**,
1Jn 2: 17 The world and its **d** pass away,
DESOLATE
Isa 54: 1 the children of the **d** woman than
DESPAIR
Isa 61: 3 of praise instead of a spirit of **d**.
2Co 4: 8 perplexed, but not in **d**;
DESPISE (DESPISED DESPISES)
Job 42: 6 Therefore I **d** myself and repent
Pr 1: 7 fools **d** wisdom and instruction.
3: 11 do not **d** the LORD's discipline,
14: 21 It is a sin to **d** one's neighbor,
15: 32 disregard discipline **d** themselves,
23: 22 do not **d** your mother when she is
Zec 4: 10 "Who dares **d** the day of small
Lk 16: 13 devoted to the one and **d** the other.
Titus 2: 15 Do not let anyone **d** you.
DESPISED (DESPISE)
Ge 25: 34 and left. So Esau **d** his birthright.
Isa 53: 3 He was **d** and rejected by mankind,
1Co 1: 28 of this world and the **d** things—
DESPISES (DESPISE)
Pr 15: 20 but a foolish man **d** his mother.
DESTINED (DESTINY)
Lk 2: 34 "This child is **d** to cause the falling
DESTINY (DESTINED PREDESTINED)
Ps 73: 17 then I understood their final **d**.
Ecc 7: 2 for death is the **d** of everyone;

DESTITUTE
Pr 31: 8 for the rights of all who are **d**.
Heb 11: 37 in sheepskins and goatskins, **d**,
DESTROY (DESTROYED DESTROYS DESTRUCTION)
Pr 1: 32 complacency of fools will **d** them;
11: 9 the godless **d** their neighbors,
Mt 10: 28 of the One who can **d** both soul
DESTROYED (DESTROY)
Job 19: 26 And after my skin has been **d**,
1Co 8: 11 is **d** by your knowledge.
15: 26 The last enemy to be **d** is death.
2Co 5: 1 if the earthly tent we live in is **d**,
Heb 10: 39 those who shrink back and are **d**,
2Pe 3: 10 the elements will be **d** by fire,
DESTROYS (DESTROY)
Pr 6: 32 whoever does so **d** himself.
18: 9 his work is brother to one who **d**.
28: 24 wrong," is partner to one who **d**.
Ecc 9: 18 but one sinner **d** much good.
1Co 3: 17 If anyone **d** God's temple, God will
DESTRUCTION (DESTROY)
Ps 1: 6 the way of the wicked leads to **d**.
Pr 16: 18 Pride goes before **d**, a haughty
Hos 13: 14 Where, O grave, is your **d**?
Mt 7: 13 broad is the road that leads to **d**,
Gal 6: 8 flesh, from the flesh will reap **d**;
2Th 1: 9 will be punished with everlasting **d**
1Ti 6: 9 that plunge people into ruin and **d**.
2Pe 2: 1 bringing swift **d** on themselves.
3: 16 other Scriptures, to their own **d**.
DETERMINED (DETERMINES)
Job 14: 5 A person's days are **d**;
Isa 14: 26 This is the plan **d** for the whole
Da 11: 36 what has been **d** must take place.
DETERMINES (DETERMINED)
Ps 147: 4 He **d** the number of the stars
1Co 12: 11 them to each one, just as he **d**.
DETESTABLE (DETESTS)
Pr 21: 27 The sacrifice of the wicked is **d**—
28: 9 even their prayers are **d**.
Isa 1: 13 Your incense is **d** to me.
Lk 16: 15 What people value highly is **d**
Titus 1: 16 They are **d**, disobedient and unfit
DETESTS (DETESTABLE)
Dt 22: 5 the LORD your God **d** anyone who
23: 18 the LORD your God **d** them both.
25: 16 the LORD your God **d** anyone who
Pr 11: 1 The LORD **d** dishonest scales,
12: 22 The LORD **d** lying lips, but he
15: 8 The LORD **d** the sacrifice
15: 9 The LORD **d** the way
15: 26 The LORD **d** the thoughts
16: 5 The LORD **d** all the proud
17: 15 The LORD **d** them both.
20: 23 The LORD **d** differing weights,
DEVIL (DEVIL'S)
Mt 13: 39 the enemy who sows them is the **d**.
25: 41 the eternal fire prepared for the **d**
Lk 4: 2 forty days he was tempted by the **d**.
8: 12 then the **d** comes and takes away
Eph 4: 27 and do not give the **d** a foothold.
2Ti 2: 26 and escape from the trap of the **d**,
Jas 4: 7 Resist the **d**, and he will flee
1Pe 5: 8 Your enemy the **d** prowls around
1Jn 3: 8 who does what is sinful is of the **d**,
Rev 12: 9 that ancient serpent called the **d**,
DEVIL'S (DEVIL)
Eph 6: 11 your stand against the **d** schemes.
1Ti 3: 7 into disgrace and into the **d** trap.
1Jn 3: 8 was to destroy the **d** work.
DEVISED
2Pe 1: 16 we did not follow cleverly **d** stories
DEVOTE (DEVOTED DEVOTING DEVOTION DEVOUT)
Job 11: 13 "Yet if you **d** your heart to him
Jer 30: 21 who is he who will **d** himself to be
Col 4: 2 **D** yourselves to prayer,
1Ti 4: 13 **d** yourself to the public reading
Titus 3: 8 may be careful to **d** themselves
DEVOTED (DEVOTE)
Ezr 7: 10 For Ezra had **d** himself to the study
Ac 2: 42 They **d** themselves to the apostles'
Ro 12: 10 Be **d** to one another in love.
1Co 7: 34 Her aim is to be **d** to the Lord

DEVOTING (DEVOTE)
1Ti 5: 10 **d** herself to all kinds of good deeds.
DEVOTION (DEVOTE)
1Ch 28: 9 serve him with wholehearted **d**
1Co 7: 35 way in undivided **d** to the Lord.
2Co 11: 3 your sincere and pure **d** to Christ.
DEVOUR
2Sa 2: 26 to Joab, "Must the sword **d** forever?
Mk 12: 40 They **d** widows' houses
1Pe 5: 8 lion looking for someone to **d**.
DEVOUT (DEVOTE)
Lk 2: 25 Simeon, who was righteous and **d**.
DIE (DEAD DEATH DIED DIES)
Ge 2: 17 eat from it you will certainly **d**."
Ex 11: 5 Every firstborn son in Egypt will **d**,
Ru 1: 17 Where you **d** I will **d**, and there I
2Ki 14: 6 each will **d** for their own sin."
Pr 5: 23 For lack of discipline they will **d**,
10: 21 many, but fools **d** for lack of sense.
11: 7 placed in mortals **d** with them;
15: 10 one who hates correction will **d**
23: 13 them with the rod, they will not **d**.
Ecc 3: 2 a time to be born and a time to **d**,
Isa 66: 24 the worms that eat them will not **d**,
Eze 3: 18 wicked person will **d** for their sin,
18: 4 one who sins is the one who will **d**.
33: 8 wicked person will **d** for their sin,
Mt 26: 52 all who draw the sword will **d**
Jn 11: 25 in me will live, even though they **d**;
11: 26 by believing in me will never **d**.
Ro 5: 7 Very rarely will anyone **d**
14: 8 and if we **d**, we **d** for the Lord.
1Co 15: 22 For as in Adam all **d**, so in Christ
Php 1: 21 to live is Christ and to **d** is gain.
Heb 9: 27 as people are destined to **d** once,
Rev 14: 13 Blessed are the dead who **d**
DIED (DIE)
Ro 5: 6 Christ **d** for the ungodly.
6: 2 We are those who have **d** to sin;
6: 8 Now if we **d** with Christ, we believe
14: 15 someone for whom Christ **d**.
1Co 8: 11 for whom Christ **d**, is destroyed
15: 3 that Christ **d** for our sins according
2Co 5: 14 one **d** for all, and therefore all **d**.
Col 3: 3 For you **d**, and your life is now
1Th 5: 10 He **d** for us so that, whether we are
2Ti 2: 11 If we **d** with him, we will also live
Heb 9: 15 that he has **d** as a ransom to set
Rev 2: 8 Last, who **d** and came to life again.
DIES (DIE)
Job 14: 14 If someone **d**, will they live again?
1Co 15: 36 does not come to life unless it **d**.
DIFFERENCE (DIFFERENT)
Ro 10: 12 For there is no **d** between Jew
DIFFERENT (DIFFERENCE)
1Co 12: 4 There are **d** kinds of gifts,
2Co 11: 4 or a **d** gospel from the one you
DIGNITY
Pr 31: 25 She is clothed with strength and **d**;
DIGS
Pr 26: 27 Whoever **d** a pit will fall into it;
DILIGENCE (DILIGENT)
Heb 6: 11 show this same **d** to the very end,
DILIGENT (DILIGENCE)
Pr 21: 5 The plans of the **d** lead to profit as
1Ti 4: 15 Be **d** in these matters;
DIRECT (DIRECTS)
Ps 119: 35 **D** me in the path of your
119:133 **D** my footsteps according to your
Jer 10: 23 it is not for them to **d** their steps.
2Th 3: 5 May the Lord **d** your hearts
DIRECTS (DIRECT)
Ps 42: 8 By day the LORD **d** his love,
Isa 48: 17 who **d** you in the way you should
DIRGE
Mt 11: 17 we sang a **d**, and you did not
DISAPPEAR
Mt 5: 18 until heaven and earth **d**,
Lk 16: 17 earth to **d** than for the least stroke
DISASTER
Ps 57: 1 your wings until the **d** has passed.
Pr 3: 25 Have no fear of sudden **d**

Pr 17: 5 whoever gloats over **d** will not go
Isa 45: 7 I bring prosperity and create **d**;
Eze 7: 5 Unheard-of **d**! See, it comes!
DISCERN (DISCERNING)
Ps 19: 12 But who can **d** their own errors?
139: 3 You **d** my going out and my lying
Php 1: 10 you may be able to **d** what is best
DISCERNING (DISCERN)
Pr 14: 6 knowledge comes easily to the **d**.
15: 14 The **d** heart seeks knowledge,
17: 10 A rebuke impresses a **d** person
17: 24 A **d** person keeps wisdom in view,
17: 28 and **d** if they hold their tongues.
19: 25 rebuke the **d**, and they will gain
28: 11 and **d** sees how deluded they are.
DISCIPLE (DISCIPLES)
Mt 10: 42 of these little ones who is my **d**,
Lk 14: 27 and follow me cannot be my **d**.
DISCIPLES (DISCIPLE)
Mt 28: 19 go and make **d** of all nations,
Jn 8: 31 my teaching, you are really my **d**.
13: 35 will know that you are my **d**, if you
Ac 11: 26 The **d** were called Christians first
DISCIPLINE (DISCIPLINED DISCIPLINES)
Ps 38: 1 your anger or **d** me in your wrath.
39: 11 rebuke and **d** anyone for their sin,
94: 12 Blessed is the one you **d**, LORD,
Pr 3: 11 do not despise the LORD's **d**,
5: 12 You will say, "How I hated **d**!
5: 23 For lack of **d** they will die,
10: 17 Whoever heeds **d** shows the way
12: 1 Whoever loves **d** loves knowledge,
13: 18 Whoever disregards **d** comes
13: 24 their children is careful to **d** them.
15: 5 A fool spurns a parent's **d**,
15: 32 disregard themselves,
19: 18 **D** your children, for in that there is
19: 20 Listen to advice and accept **d**,
22: 15 the rod of **d** will drive it far away.
23: 13 Do not withhold **d** from a child;
29: 17 **D** your children, and they will give
Heb 12: 5 do not make light of the Lord's **d**,
12: 7 Endure hardship as **d**;
12: 11 No **d** seems pleasant at the time,
Rev 3: 19 Those whom I love I rebuke and **d**.
DISCIPLINED (DISCIPLINE)
Jer 31: 18 'You **d** me like an unruly calf,
1Co 11: 32 we are being **d** so that we will not
Col 2: 5 delight to see how **d** you are
Titus 1: 8 upright, holy and **d**.
Heb 12: 7 For what children are not **d** by
DISCIPLINES (DISCIPLINE)
Dt 8: 5 so the LORD your God **d** you.
Pr 3: 12 because the LORD **d** those he
Heb 12: 6 the Lord the one he loves,
12: 10 but God **d** us for our good,
DISCLOSED
Lk 8: 17 nothing hidden that will not be **d**,
DISCOURAGED
Jos 1: 9 do not be **d**, for the LORD your
10: 25 "Do not be afraid; do not be **d**.
1Ch 28: 20 Do not be afraid or **d**,
Isa 42: 4 or be **d** till he establishes justice
Col 3: 21 children, or they will become **d**.
DISCREDITED
2Co 6: 3 so that our ministry will not be **d**.
DISCRETION
1Ch 22: 12 May the LORD give you **d**
Pr 1: 4 knowledge and **d** to the young—
2: 11 **D** will protect you,
5: 2 that you may maintain **d** and your
8: 12 I possess knowledge and **d**.
11: 22 beautiful woman who shows no **d**.
DISCRIMINATED
Jas 2: 4 have you not **d** among yourselves
DISFIGURED
Isa 52: 14 his appearance was so **d** beyond
DISGRACE (DISGRACEFUL DISGRACES)
Pr 11: 2 then comes **d**, but with humility
19: 26 is a child who brings shame and **d**.
Ac 5: 41 worthy of suffering **d** for the Name.
Heb 13: 13 the camp, bearing the **d** he bore.

DISGRACEFUL (DISGRACE)
Pr 10: 5 sleeps during harvest is a **d** son.
17: 2 servant will rule over a **d** son
DISGRACES (DISGRACE)
Pr 28: 7 companion of gluttons **d** his father.
29: 15 left undisciplined **d** its mother.
DISGUISE
Pr 26: 24 Enemies **d** themselves with their
DISHONEST
Pr 11: 1 The LORD detests **d** scales,
29: 27 The righteous detest the **d**;
Lk 16: 10 whoever is **d** with very little will
1Ti 3: 8 wine, and not pursuing **d** gain.
DISHONOR (DISHONORS)
Lev 18: 7 "'Do not **d** your father by having
Pr 30: 9 and so **d** the name of my God.
1Co 15: 3 It does not **d** others, it is not
15: 43 it is sown in **d**, it is raised in glory;
DISHONORS (DISHONOR)
Dt 27: 16 is anyone who **d** their father
DISMAYED
Isa 41: 10 do not be **d**, for I am your God.
DISOBEDIENCE (DISOBEY)
Ro 5: 19 as through the **d** of the one man
11: 32 has bound everyone over to **d** so
Heb 2: 2 and **d** received its just punishment,
4: 6 did not go in because of their **d**,
4: 11 by following their example of **d**.
DISOBEDIENT (DISOBEY)
2Ti 3: 2 proud, abusive, **d** to their parents,
Titus 1: 6 to the charge of being wild and **d**.
1: 16 **d** and unfit for doing anything
DISOBEY (DISOBEDIENCE DISOBEDIENT)
Dt 11: 28 the curse if you **d** the commands
2Ch 24: 20 'Why do you **d** the LORD's
Ro 1: 30 of doing evil; they **d** their parents;
DISORDER
1Co 14: 33 For God is not a God of **d**
2Co 12: 20 slander, gossip, arrogance and **d**.
Jas 3: 16 there you find **d** and every evil
DISOWN
Pr 30: 9 I may have too much and **d** you
Mt 10: 33 will **d** before my Father in heaven.
26: 35 to die with you, I will never **d** you."
2Ti 2: 12 If we **d** him, he will also **d** us;
DISPLAY (DISPLAYS)
Eze 39: 21 "I will **d** my glory among
1Ti 1: 16 Christ Jesus might **d** his immense
DISPLAYS (DISPLAY)
Isa 44: 23 Jacob, he **d** his glory in Israel.
DISPUTE (DISPUTES)
Pr 17: 14 the matter before a **d** breaks out.
1Co 6: 1 If any of you has a **d** with another,
DISPUTES (DISPUTE)
Pr 18: 18 Casting the lot settles **d** and keeps
DISQUALIFIED
1Co 9: 27 I myself will not be **d** for the prize.
DISREGARD
Pr 15: 32 Those who **d** discipline despise
DISREPUTE
2Pe 2: 2 will bring the way of truth into **d**.
DISSENSION
Ro 13: 13 debauchery, not in **d** and jealousy.
DISTINGUISH
1Ki 3: 9 and to **d** between right and wrong.
Heb 5: 14 have trained themselves to **d** good
DISTORT
2Co 4: 2 nor do we **d** the word of God.
2Pe 3: 16 ignorant and unstable people **d**,
DISTRESS (DISTRESSED)
Ps 18: 6 In my **d** I called to the LORD;
Jnh 2: 2 "In my **d** I called to the LORD,
Jas 1: 27 and widows in their **d** and to keep
DISTRESSED (DISTRESS)
Ro 14: 15 sister is **d** because of what you eat,
DIVIDED (DIVISION)
Mt 12: 25 "Every kingdom **d** against itself
Lk 3: 34 up his clothes by casting lots.
1Co 1: 13 Is Christ **d**? Was Paul crucified
DIVINATION
Lev 19: 26 "'Do not practice **d** or seek

DIVINE
Ro   1: 20   his eternal power and **d** nature—
2Co 10: 4   they have **d** power to demolish
2Pe 1: 4   may participate in the **d** nature,
DIVISION (DIVIDED DIVISIONS DIVISIVE)
Lk 12: 51   peace on earth? No, I tell you, but **d**.
1Co 12: 25   there should be no **d** in the body,
DIVISIONS (DIVISION)
Ro 16: 17   to watch out for those who cause **d**
1Co 1: 10   and that there be no **d** among you,
      11: 18   as a church, there are **d** among you,
DIVISIVE (DIVISION)
Titus 3: 10   Warn a **d** person once,
DIVORCE (DIVORCES)
Mt 19: 3   for a man to **d** his wife for any
1Co 7: 11   a husband must not **d** his wife.
DIVORCES (DIVORCE)
Mal 2: 16   man who hates and **d** his wife,"
DOCTOR
Mt   9: 12   "It is not the healthy who need a **d**,
DOCTRINE
1Ti 4: 16   Watch your life and **d** closely.
Titus 2: 1   what is appropriate to sound **d**.
DOMINION
Ps 22: 28   for **d** belongs to the LORD and he
DOOR
Ps 141: 3   keep watch over the **d** of my lips.
Mt   6: 6   close the **d** and pray to your Father,
      7: 7   and the **d** will be opened to you.
Rev 3: 20   I stand at the **d** and knock.
DOORKEEPER
Ps 84: 10   I would rather be a **d** in the house
DOUBLE-EDGED
Heb 4: 12   Sharper than any **d** sword,
Rev 1: 16   of his mouth was a sharp, **d** sword.
      2: 16   of him who has the sharp, **d** sword.
DOUBLE-MINDED (MIND)
Ps 119: 113   I hate **d** people, but I love your law.
Jas 1: 8   Such a person is **d** and unstable
DOUBT
Mt 14: 31   faith," he said, "why did you **d**?"
      21: 21   if you have faith and do not **d**,
Mk 11: 23   and does not **d** in their heart
Jas 1: 6   you must believe and not **d**,
Jude   : 22   Be merciful to those who **d**;
DOWNCAST
Ps 42: 5   Why, my soul, are you **d**?
2Co 7: 6   who comforts the **d**, comforted us
DRAW (DRAWING DRAWS)
Mt 26: 52   "for all who **d** the sword will die
Jn 12: 32   earth, will **d** all people to myself."
Heb 10: 22   let us **d** near to God with a sincere
DRAWING (DRAW)
Lk 21: 28   your redemption is **d** near."
DRAWS (DRAW)
Jn   6: 44   the Father who sent me **d** them,
DREADFUL
Heb 10: 31   It is a **d** thing to fall into the hands
DRESS
1Ti 2: 9   want the women to **d** modestly,
DRINK (DRUNK DRUNKARDS DRUNKENNESS)
Pr   5: 15   **D** water from your own cistern,
Lk 12: 19   eat, **d** and be merry."'
Jn   7: 37   who is thirsty come to me and **d**.
1Co 12: 13   were all given the one Spirit to **d**.
DRIVES
1Jn 4: 18   But perfect love **d** out fear,
DROP
Pr 17: 14   so **d** the matter before a dispute
Isa 40: 15   Surely the nations are like a **d**
DRUNK (DRINK)
Eph 5: 18   Do not get **d** on wine, which leads
DRUNKARDS (DRINK)
Pr 23: 21   for **d** and gluttons become poor,
1Co 6: 10   the greedy nor **d** nor slanderers
DRUNKENNESS (DRINK)
Lk 21: 34   **d** and the anxieties of life,
Ro 13: 13   not in carousing and **d**,
Gal 5: 21   and envy; **d**, orgies, and the like.
1Pe 4: 3   living in debauchery, lust, **d**, orgies,
DRY
Isa 53: 2   and like a root out of **d** ground.
Eze 37: 4   bones and say to them, '**D** bones,

DUST
Ge   2: 7   a man from the **d** of the ground
Ps 103: 14   he remembers that we are **d**.
Ecc 3: 20   come from **d**, and to **d** all return.
DUTY
Ecc 12: 13   for this is the **d** of all mankind.
Ac 23: 1   I have fulfilled my **d** to God in all
1Co 7: 3   husband should fulfill his marital **d**
DWELL (DWELLING DWELLS)
1Ki 8: 27   "But will God really **d** on earth?
Ps 23: 6   I will **d** in the house of the LORD
Isa 43: 18   do not **d** on the past.
Eph 3: 17   Christ may **d** in your hearts
Col 1: 19   to have all his fullness **d** in him,
      3: 16   of Christ **d** among you richly
DWELLING (DWELL)
Eph 2: 22   built together to become a **d**
DWELLS (DWELL)
1Co 3: 16   that God's Spirit **d** in your midst?
EAGER
Pr 31: 13   and flax and works with **e** hands.
1Pe 5: 2   dishonest gain, but **e** to serve;
EAGLE'S (EAGLES)
Ps 103: 5   your youth is renewed like the **e**.
EAGLES (EAGLE'S)
Isa 40: 31   They will soar on wings like **e**;
EAR (EARS)
1Co 2: 9   eye has seen, what no **e** has heard,
      12: 16   And if the **e** should say, "Because I
EARS (EAR)
Job 42: 5   My **e** had heard of you but now my
Ps 34: 15   and his **e** are attentive to their cry;
Pr 21: 13   Whoever shuts their **e** to the cry
2Ti 4: 3   to say what their itching **e** want
EARTH (EARTHLY)
Ge   1: 1   God created the heavens and the **e**.
Ps 24: 1   The **e** is the LORD's,
     108: 5   let your glory be over all the **e**.
Isa   6: 3   the whole **e** is full of his glory."
      51: 6   the **e** will wear out like a garment
      55: 9   the heavens are higher than the **e**,
      66: 1   throne, and the **e** is my footstool.
Jer 23: 24   "Do not I fill heaven and **e**?"
Hab 2: 20   let all the **e** be silent before him.
Mt   6: 10   will be done, on **e** as it is in heaven.
      16: 19   you bind on **e** will be bound
      24: 35   Heaven and **e** will pass away,
      28: 18   and on **e** has been given to me.
Lk   2: 14   on **e** peace to those on whom his
1Co 10: 26   for, "The **e** is the Lord's,
Php 2: 10   heaven and on **e** and under the **e**,
2Pe 3: 13   to a new heaven and a new **e**,
EARTHLY (EARTH)
Php 3: 19   Their mind is set on **e** things.
Col 3: 2   on things above, not on **e** things.
EAST
Ps 103: 12   as far as the **e** is from the west,
EASY
Mt 11: 30   For my yoke is **e** and my burden is
EAT (EATING)
Ge   2: 17   you must not **e** from the tree
Isa 55: 1   have no money, come, buy and **e**!
      65: 25   the lion will **e** straw like the ox,
Mt 26: 26   his disciples, saying, "Take and **e**;
Ro 14: 2   faith allows them to **e** anything,
1Co 8: 13   if what I **e** causes my brother
      10: 31   So whether you **e** or drink
2Th 3: 10   is unwilling to work shall not **e**."
EATING (EAT)
Ro 14: 17   kingdom of God is not a matter of **e**
EDICT
Heb 11: 23   they were not afraid of the king's **e**.
EDIFIES
1Co 14: 4   speaks in a tongue **e** themselves,
EFFECT
Isa 32: 17   its **e** will be quietness
Heb 9: 18   was not put into **e** without blood.
EFFORT
Lk 13: 24   "Make every **e** to enter through
Ro   9: 16   depend on human desire or **e**,
      14: 19   Let us therefore make every **e** to do
Eph 4: 3   Make every **e** to keep the unity

Heb 4: 11 make every **e** to enter that rest,
     12: 14 Make every **e** to live in peace
2Pe 1: 5 make every **e** to add to your faith
      3: 14 make every **e** to be found spotless,

ELAH
Son of Baasha; king of Israel (1Ki 16:6–14).

ELDERLY (ELDERS)
Lev 19: 32 show respect for the **e** and revere

ELDERS (ELDERLY)
1Ti 5: 17 The **e** who direct the affairs

ELECTION
Ro   9: 11 God's purpose in **e** might stand:
2Pe 1: 10 to confirm your calling and **e.**

ELI
High priest in youth of Samuel (1Sa 1–4). Blessed Hannah (1Sa 1:12–18); raised Samuel (1Sa 2:11–26).

ELIJAH
Prophet; predicted famine in Israel (1Ki 17:1; Jas 5:17). Fed by ravens (1Ki 17:2–6). Raised Sidonian widow's son (1Ki 17:7–24). Defeated prophets of Baal at Carmel (1Ki 18:16–46). Ran from Jezebel (1Ki 19:1–9). Prophesied death of Azariah (2Ki 1). Succeeded by Elisha (1Ki 19:19–21; 2Ki 2:1–18). Taken to heaven in whirlwind (2Ki 2:11–12).
Return prophesied (Mal 4:5–6); equated with John the Baptist (Mt 17:9–13; Mk 9:9–13; Lk 1:17). Appeared with Moses in transfiguration of Jesus (Mt 17:1–8; Mk 9:1–8).

ELISHA
Prophet; successor of Elijah (1Ki 19:16–21); inherited his cloak (2Ki 2:1–18). Miracles of (2Ki 2–6).

ELIZABETH
Mother of John the Baptist, relative of Mary (Lk 1:5–58).

EMBITTER
Col 3: 21 Fathers, do not **e** your children,

EMPEROR
1Pe 2: 17 of believers, fear God, honor the **e.**

EMPTY
Mt 12: 36 for every **e** word they have spoken.
Eph 5: 6 no one deceive you with **e** words,
1Pe 1: 18 you were redeemed from the **e** way

ENABLE (ABLE)
Lk   1: 74 to **e** us to serve him without fear
Ac   4: 29 **e** your servants to speak your word

ENABLED (ABLE)
Lev 26: 13 **e** you to walk with heads held high.
Jn   6: 65 me unless the Father has **e** them."

ENABLES (ABLE)
Php 3: 21 by the power that **e** him to bring

ENCAMPS
Ps 34: 7 the Lᴏʀᴅ **e** around those who fear

ENCOURAGE (ENCOURAGEMENT ENCOURAGING)
Ps 10: 17 you **e** them, and you listen to their
Ac 15: 32 said much to **e** and strengthen
Ro 12: 8 if it is to **e**, then give
1Th 4: 18 Therefore **e** one another with these
2Ti 4: 2 correct, rebuke and **e**—
Titus 2: 6 Similarly, **e** the young men to be
Heb 3: 13 But **e** one another daily, as long as

ENCOURAGEMENT (ENCOURAGE)
Ac   4: 36 (which means "son of **e**"),
Ro 15: 4 the **e** they provide we might have
     15: 5 **e** give you the same attitude of
Heb 12: 5 completely forgotten this word of **e**

ENCOURAGING (ENCOURAGE)
1Co 14: 3 their strengthening, **e** and comfort.
Heb 10: 25 habit of doing, but **e** one another—

END
Ps 119: 33 that I may follow it to the **e.**
Pr 14: 12 right, but in the **e** it leads to death.
     19: 20 the **e** you will be counted among
     23: 32 In the **e** it bites like a snake
Ecc 12: 12 making many books there is no **e**,
Mt 10: 22 stands firm to the **e** will be saved."
Lk 21: 9 but the **e** will not come right away."
1Co 15: 24 Then the **e** will come, when he

ENDURANCE (ENDURE)
Ro 15: 4 so that through the **e** taught
     15: 5 May the God who gives **e**
2Co 1: 6 you patient of the same sufferings
Col 1: 11 might so that you may have great **e**
1Ti 6: 11 faith, love, **e** and gentleness.
Titus 2: 2 and sound in faith, in love and in **e.**

ENDURE (ENDURANCE ENDURES)
Ps 72: 17 May his name **e** forever;
Pr 12: 19 Truthful lips **e** forever, but a lying
     27: 24 for riches do not **e** forever,
Ecc 3: 14 everything God does will **e** forever;
Mal 3: 2 who can **e** the day of his coming?
2Ti 2: 12 if we **e**, we will also reign with him.
Heb 12: 7 **E** hardship as discipline;
Rev 3: 10 kept my command to **e** patiently,

ENDURES (ENDURE)
Ps 112: 9 poor, their righteousness **e** forever;
    136: 1 His love **e** forever.
Da   9: 15 yourself a name that **e** to this day,
1Pe 1: 25 but the word of the Lord **e** forever."

ENEMIES (ENEMY)
Ps 23: 5 before me in the presence of my **e.**
Mic 7: 6 a man's **e** are the members of his
Mt   5: 44 love your **e** and pray for those who
Lk 20: 43 until I make your **e** a footstool

ENEMY (ENEMIES ENMITY)
Pr 24: 17 Do not gloat when your **e** falls;
     25: 21 If your **e** is hungry, give him food
     27: 6 trusted, but an **e** multiplies kisses.
1Co 15: 26 The last **e** to be destroyed is death.
1Ti 5: 14 and to give the **e** no opportunity
Jas 4: 4 of the world becomes an **e** of God.

ENJOY (JOY)
Dt   6: 2 and so that you may **e** long life.
Eph 6: 3 and that you may **e** long life
Heb 11: 25 than to **e** the fleeting pleasures

ENJOYMENT (JOY)
Ecc 4: 8 why am I depriving myself of **e**?"
1Ti 6: 17 us with everything for our **e.**

ENLIGHTENED (LIGHT)
Eph 1: 18 eyes of your heart may be **e** in
Heb 6: 4 for those who have once been **e**,

ENMITY (ENEMY)
Ge   3: 15 I will put **e** between you

ENOCH
Walked with God and taken by him (Ge 5:18–24; Heb 11:5). Prophet (Jude 14).

ENTANGLED (ENTANGLES)
2Ti 2: 4 soldier gets **e** in civilian affairs,
2Pe 2: 20 Jesus Christ and are again **e** in it

ENTANGLES (ENTANGLED)
Heb 12: 1 hinders and the sin that so easily **e.**

ENTER (ENTERED ENTERS)
Ps 100: 4 **E** his gates with thanksgiving
Mt   5: 20 will certainly not **e** the kingdom
      7: 13 "**E** through the narrow gate.
     18: 8 It is better for you to **e** life maimed
Mk 10: 15 like a little child will never **e** it."
     10: 23 the rich to **e** the kingdom of God!"

ENTERED (ENTER)
Ro   5: 12 just as sin **e** the world through one
Heb 9: 12 he **e** the Most Holy Place once

ENTERS (ENTER)
Mk   7: 18 that nothing that **e** a person
Jn 10: 2 The one who **e** by the gate is

ENTERTAIN
1Ti 5: 19 Do not **e** an accusation against

ENTHRALLED
Ps 45: 11 Let the king be **e** by your beauty.

ENTHRONED (THRONE)
1Sa 4: 4 who is **e** between the cherubim.
Ps   2: 4 The One who **e** in heaven laughs;
    102: 12 But you, Lᴏʀᴅ, sit **e** forever;
Isa 40: 22 He sits **e** above the circle

ENTICE
Pr   1: 10 if sinful men **e** you, do not give
2Pe 2: 18 they **e** people who are just escaping

ENTIRE
Gal 5: 14 For the **e** law is fulfilled in keeping

ENTRUSTED (TRUST)
1Ti 6: 20 guard what has been **e** to your care.
2Ti 1: 12 to guard what I have **e** to him until
      1: 14 good deposit that was **e** to you—
Jude : 3 once for all **e** to God's holy people.

ENVY
Pr   3: 31 Do not **e** the violent or choose any
     14: 30 to the body, but **e** rots the bones.
1Co 13: 4 It does not **e**, it does not boast,

EPHRAIM
1. Second son of Joseph (Ge 41:52; 46:20). Blessed as first-born by Jacob (Ge 48).
2. Synonymous with Northern Kingdom (Isa 7:17; Hos 5).

EQUAL
Isa	40: 25	Or who is my **e**?" says the Holy
Jn	5: 18	Father, making himself **e** with God.
1Co	12: 25	its parts should have **e** concern

EQUIP (EQUIPPED)
Eph	4: 12	to **e** his people for works of service,
Heb	13: 21	**e** you with everything good

EQUIPPED (EQUIP)
2Ti	3: 17	God may be thoroughly **e** for every

ERROR
Jas	5: 20	the **e** of their way will save them

ESAU
Firstborn of Isaac, twin of Jacob (Ge 25:21–26). Also called Edom (Ge 25:30). Sold Jacob his birthright (Ge 25:29–34); lost blessing (Ge 27). Reconciled to Jacob (Gen 33).

ESCAPE (ESCAPING)
Ro	2: 3	think you will **e** God's judgment?
Heb	2: 3	how shall we **e** if we ignore so great

ESCAPING (ESCAPE)
1Co	3: 15	only as one **e** through the flames.

ESTABLISH (ESTABLISHED ESTABLISHES)
Ge	6: 18	But I will **e** my covenant with you,
1Ch	28: 7	I will **e** his kingdom forever if he is
Ro	10: 3	of God and sought to **e** their own,

ESTABLISHED (ESTABLISH)
Ps	8: 2	infants you have **e** a stronghold

ESTABLISHES (ESTABLISH)
Pr	16: 9	course, but the LORD **e** their steps.

ESTEEM (ESTEEMED)
Isa	53: 3	and we held him in low **e**.

ESTEEMED (ESTEEM)
Pr	22: 1	to be **e** is better than silver or gold.

ESTHER
Jewess who lived in Persia; cousin of Mordecai (Est 2:7). Chosen queen of Xerxes (Est 2:8–18). Foiled Haman's plan to exterminate the Jews (Est 3–4; 7–9).

ETERNAL (ETERNITY)
Ps	16: 11	with **e** pleasures at your right hand.
	111: 10	To him belongs **e** praise.
	119: 89	Your word, LORD, is **e**;
Isa	26: 4	the LORD himself, is the Rock **e**.
Mt	19: 16	good thing must I do to get **e** life?"
	25: 41	the **e** fire prepared for the devil
	25: 46	but the righteous to **e** life."
Jn	3: 15	who believes may have **e** life
	3: 16	him shall not perish but have **e** life.
	3: 36	believes in the Son has **e** life,
	4: 14	of water welling up to **e** life."
	5: 24	believes him who sent me has **e** life
	6: 47	the one who believes has **e** life.
	6: 68	You have the words of **e** life.
	10: 28	I give them **e** life, and they shall
	17: 3	Now this is **e** life: that they know
Ro	1: 20	his **e** power and divine nature—
	6: 23	of God is **e** life in Christ Jesus our
2Co	4: 17	for us an **e** glory that far outweighs
	4: 18	temporary, but what is unseen is **e**.
1Ti	1: 16	believe in him and receive **e** life.
	1: 17	Now to the King **e**, immortal,
Heb	9: 12	thus obtaining **e** redemption.
1Jn	5: 11	God has given us **e** life, and this life
	5: 13	you may know that you have **e** life.

ETERNITY (ETERNAL)
Ps	93: 2	you are from all **e**.
Ecc	3: 11	has also set **e** in the human heart;

ETHIOPIAN
Jer	13: 23	Can an **E** change his skin

EUNUCHS
Mt	19: 12	choose to live like **e** for the sake

EVANGELIST (EVANGELISTS)
2Ti	4: 5	do the work of an **e**, discharge all

EVANGELISTS (EVANGELIST)
Eph	4: 11	the **e**, the pastors and teachers,

EVE
2Co	11: 3	afraid that just as **E** was deceived
1Ti	2: 13	For Adam was formed first, then **E**.

EVEN-TEMPERED
Pr	17: 27	whoever has understanding is **e**.

EVER (EVERLASTING FOREVER)
Ex	15: 18	"The LORD reigns for **e** and **e**."
Dt	8: 19	you **e** forget the LORD your God
Ps	5: 11	you be glad; let them **e** sing for joy.
	10: 16	The LORD is King for **e** and **e**;
	25: 3	one who hopes in you will **e** be put
	45: 6	throne, O God, will last for **e** and **e**;
	52: 8	I trust in God's unfailing love for **e**
	89: 33	nor will I **e** betray my faithfulness.
	145: 1	I will praise your name for **e** and **e**.
Pr	4: 18	shining **e** brighter till the full light
	5: 19	may you **e** be intoxicated with her
Isa	66: 8	Who has **e** heard of such things?
Jer	31: 36	"will Israel **e** cease being a nation
Da	7: 18	possess it forever—yes, for **e** and **e**.'
	12: 3	like the stars for **e** and **e**.
Mk	4: 12	" 'they may be **e** seeing but never
Jn	1: 18	No one has **e** seen God, but
Rev	1: 18	now look, I am alive for **e** and **e**!
	22: 5	And they will reign for **e** and **e**.

EVER-INCREASING (INCREASE)
Ro	6: 19	to impurity and to **e** wickedness,
2Co	3: 18	into his image with **e** glory,

EVERLASTING (EVER)
Dt	33: 27	and underneath are the **e** arms.
Ne	9: 5	your God, who is from **e** to **e**."
Ps	90: 2	world, from **e** to **e** you are God.
	139: 24	in me, and lead me in the way **e**.
Isa	9: 6	Mighty God, **E** Father,
	33: 14	of us can dwell with **e** burning?"
	35: 10	**e** joy will crown their heads.
	45: 17	by the LORD with an **e** salvation;
	54: 8	**e** kindness I will have compassion
	55: 3	I will make an **e** covenant with you,
	63: 12	them, to gain for himself **e** renown,
Jer	31: 3	"I have loved you with an **e** love;
Da	9: 24	to bring in **e** righteousness, to seal
	12: 2	some to **e** life, others to shame and **e** contempt.
2Th	1: 9	will be punished with **e** destruction
Jude	: 6	bound with **e** chains for judgment

EVER-PRESENT
Ps	46: 1	and strength, an **e** help in trouble.

EVIDENCE (EVIDENT)
Jn	14: 11	on the **e** of the works themselves.

EVIDENT (EVIDENCE)
Php	4: 5	Let your gentleness be **e** to all.

EVIL (EVILDOER EVILDOERS)
Ge	2: 9	of the knowledge of good and **e**.
Job	1: 1	he feared God and shunned **e**.
	1: 8	a man who fears God and shuns **e**."
	34: 10	Far be it from God to do **e**,
Ps	23: 4	will fear no **e**, for you are with me;
	34: 14	Turn from **e** and do good;
	51: 4	and done what is **e** in your sight;
	97: 10	those who love the LORD hate **e**,
	101: 4	have nothing to do with what is **e**.
Pr	8: 13	To fear the LORD is to hate **e**;
	11: 27	**e** comes to one who searches for it.
Isa	5: 20	who call **e** good and good **e**,
	13: 11	I will punish the world for its **e**,
Hab	1: 13	Your eyes are too pure to look on **e**;
Mt	5: 45	He causes his sun to rise on the **e**
	6: 13	but deliver us from the **e** one.'
	7: 11	you are **e**, know how to give
	12: 35	an **e** man brings **e** things out of the **e**
Jn	17: 15	you protect them from the **e** one.
Ro	2: 9	for every human being who does **e**:
	12: 9	Hate what is **e**; cling to what is
	12: 17	Do not repay anyone **e** for **e**.
	16: 19	and innocent about what is **e**.
1Co	13: 6	Love does not delight in **e**
	14: 20	In regard to **e** be infants, but in
Eph	6: 16	all the flaming arrows of the **e** one.
1Th	5: 22	reject every kind of **e**.
1Ti	6: 10	of money is a root of all kinds of **e**.
2Ti	2: 22	Flee the **e** desires of youth
Jas	1: 13	For God cannot be tempted by **e**,
1Pe	2: 16	your freedom as a cover-up for **e**;
	3: 9	Do not repay **e** with **e** or insult
	3: 9	the contrary, repay **e** with blessing,

EVILDOER (EVIL)
Pr	24: 20	for the **e** has no future hope,

EVILDOERS (EVIL)
Pr 24: 19 Do not fret because of **e** or be
EXACT
Heb 1: 3 the **e** representation of his being,
EXALT (EXALTED EXALTS)
Ps 30: 1 I will **e** you, Lord, for you lifted
34: 3 let us **e** his name together.
118: 28 you are my God, and I will **e** you.
Isa 24: 15 **e** the name of the Lord, the God
Mt 23: 12 For those who **e** themselves will be
EXALTED (EXALT)
2Sa 22: 47 **E** be my God, the Rock, my Savior!
1Ch 29: 11 you are **e** as head over all.
Ne 9: 5 and may it be **e** above all blessing
Ps 21: 13 Be **e** in your strength, Lord;
46: 10 I will be **e** among the nations,
57: 5 Be **e**, O God, above the heavens;
97: 9 you are **e** far above all gods.
99: 2 he is **e** over all the nations.
108: 5 Be **e**, O God, above the heavens;
148: 13 the Lord, for his name alone is **e**;
Isa 6: 1 high and **e**, seated on a throne;
12: 4 and proclaim that his name is **e**.
33: 5 The Lord is **e**, for he dwells
Eze 21: 26 The lowly will be **e** and the **e** will
Mt 23: 12 who humble themselves will be **e**.
Php 1: 20 now as always Christ will be **e**
2: 9 Therefore God **e** him to the highest
EXALTS (EXALT)
Ps 75: 7 He brings one down, he **e** another.
Pr 14: 34 Righteousness **e** a nation, but sin
EXAMINE (EXAMINED)
Ps 26: 2 try me, **e** my heart and my mind;
Jer 17: 10 search the heart and **e** the mind,
La 3: 40 Let us **e** our ways and test them,
1Co 11: 28 to **e** themselves before they eat
2Co 13: 5 **E** yourselves to see whether you
EXAMINED (EXAMINE)
Ac 17: 11 **e** the Scriptures every day to see
EXAMPLE (EXAMPLES)
Jn 13: 15 I have set you an **e** that you should
1Co 11: 1 Follow my **e**, as I follow the **e**
1Ti 4: 12 set an **e** for the believers in speech,
Titus 2: 7 everything set them an **e** by doing
1Pe 2: 21 leaving you an **e**, that you should
EXAMPLES (EXAMPLE)
1Co 10: 6 Now these things occurred as **e**
10: 11 things happened to them as **e**
1Pe 5: 3 to you, but being **e** to the flock.
EXASPERATE
Eph 6: 4 Fathers, do not **e** your children;
EXCEL (EXCELLENT)
1Co 14: 12 try to **e** in those that build
2Co 8: 7 you also **e** in this grace of giving.
EXCELLENT (EXCEL)
1Co 12: 31 yet I will show you the most **e** way.
Php 4: 8 if anything is **e** or praiseworthy—
1Ti 3: 13 have served well gain an **e** standing
Titus 3: 8 These things are **e** and profitable
EXCHANGED
Ro 1: 23 **e** the glory of the immortal God
1: 25 **e** the truth about God for a lie,
EXCUSE (EXCUSES)
Jn 15: 22 now they have no **e** for their sin.
Ro 1: 20 made, so that people are without **e**.
EXCUSES (EXCUSE)
Lk 14: 18 "But they all alike began to make **e**.
EXISTS
Heb 2: 10 and through whom everything **e**,
11: 6 to him must believe that he **e**
EXPECT (EXPECTATION)
Mt 24: 44 at an hour when you do not **e** him.
EXPECTATION (EXPECT)
Ro 8: 19 waits in eager **e** for the children
Heb 10: 27 but only a fearful **e** of judgment
EXPEL
1Co 5: 13 "**E** the wicked person from among
EXPENSIVE
1Ti 2: 9 or gold or pearls or **e** clothes,
EXPLOIT
Pr 22: 22 Do not **e** the poor because they are
2Co 12: 17 I **e** you through any of the men

EXPOSE
1Co 4: 5 and will **e** the motives of the heart.
Eph 5: 11 of darkness, but rather **e** them.
EXTENDS
Pr 31: 20 poor and **e** her hands to the needy.
Lk 1: 50 His mercy **e** to those who fear him,
EXTINGUISHED
2Sa 21: 17 the lamp of Israel will not be **e**."
EXTOL
Job 36: 24 Remember to **e** his work,
Ps 34: 1 I will **e** the Lord at all times;
68: 4 **e** him who rides on the clouds;
95: 2 thanksgiving and **e** him with music
109: 30 mouth I will greatly **e** the Lord;
111: 1 I will **e** the Lord with all my
115: 18 it is we who **e** the Lord,
117: 1 **e** him, all you peoples.
145: 2 and **e** your name for ever
145: 10 your faithful people **e** you.
147: 12 **E** the Lord, Jerusalem;
EXTORT
Lk 3: 14 "Don't **e** money and don't accuse
EYE (EYES)
Ex 21: 24 **e** for **e**, tooth for tooth,
Ps 94: 9 Does he who formed the **e** not see?
Mt 5: 29 If your right **e** causes you
5: 38 have heard that it was said, '**E** for **e**,
7: 3 speck of sawdust in your brother's **e**
1Co 2: 9 "What no **e** has seen, what no ear
Col 3: 22 not only when their **e** is on you
Rev 1: 7 and "every **e** will see him,
EYES (EYE)
Nu 33: 55 remain will become barbs in your **e**
Jos 23: 13 your backs and thorns in your **e**,
2Ch 16: 9 For the **e** of the Lord range
Job 31: 1 "I made a covenant with my **e** not
36: 7 not take his **e** off the righteous;
Ps 119: 18 Open my **e** that I may see
121: 1 I lift up my **e** to the mountains—
141: 8 But my **e** are fixed on you,
Pr 3: 7 Do not be wise in your own **e**;
4: 25 Let your **e** look straight ahead;
15: 3 The **e** of the Lord are
Isa 6: 5 and my **e** have seen the King,
Hab 1: 13 Your **e** are too pure to look on evil;
Jn 4: 35 open your **e** and look at the fields!
2Co 4: 18 So we fix our **e** not on what is seen,
Heb 12: 2 fixing our **e** on Jesus, the pioneer
Jas 2: 5 who are poor in the **e** of the world
1Pe 3: 12 For the **e** of the Lord are
Rev 7: 17 away every tear from their **e**.'"
21: 4 will wipe every tear from their **e**.
EZEKIEL
Priest called to be prophet to the exiles (Eze 1–3).
EZRA
Priest and teacher of the Law who led a return of exiles to Israel to reestablish temple and worship (Ezr 7–8). Corrected intermarriage of priests (Ezr 9–10). Read Law at celebration of Feast of Tabernacles (Neh 8).
FACE (FACES)
Ge 32: 30 "It is because I saw God **f** to **f**,
Ex 34: 29 that his **f** was radiant because he
Nu 6: 25 the Lord make his **f** shine on you
1Ch 16: 11 and his strength; seek his **f** always.
2Ch 7: 14 and seek my **f** and turn from their
Ps 4: 6 Let the light of your **f** shine on us.
27: 8 My heart says of you, "Seek his **f**!"
31: 16 Let your **f** shine on your servant;
105: 4 and his strength; seek his **f** always.
119:135 Make your **f** shine on your servant
Isa 50: 7 Therefore have I set my **f** like flint,
Mt 17: 2 His **f** shone like the sun, and his
1Co 13: 12 in a mirror; then we shall see **f** to **f**.
2Co 4: 6 glory displayed in the **f** of Christ.
1Pe 3: 12 the **f** of the Lord is against those
Rev 1: 16 His **f** was like the sun shining in all
FACES (FACE)
2Co 3: 18 unveiled **f** contemplate the Lord's
FACTIONS
Gal 5: 20 rage, selfish ambition, dissensions,
FADE
1Pe 5: 4 of glory that will never **f** away.

FAIL (FAILING FAILINGS FAILS)
1Ch 28: 20 He will not **f** you or forsake you
2Ch 34: 33 they did not **f** to follow the LORD,
Ps 89: 28 my covenant with him will never **f**.
Pr 15: 22 Plans **f** for lack of counsel,
Isa 51: 6 my righteousness will never **f**.
La 3: 22 for his compassions never **f**.
2Co 13: 5 unless, of course, you **f** the test?
FAILING (FAIL)
1Sa 12: 23 I should sin against the LORD by **f**
FAILINGS (FAIL)
Ro 15: 1 to bear with the **f** of the weak
FAILS (FAIL)
1Co 13: 8 Love never **f**. But where there are
FAINT
Isa 40: 31 weary, they will walk and not be **f**.
FAIR
Pr 1: 3 doing what is right and just and **f**;
Col 4: 1 your slaves with what is right and **f**,
FAITH (FAITHFUL FAITHFULLY FAITHFULNESS
FAITHLESS)
2Ch 20: 20 Have **f** in the LORD your God
20: 20 have **f** in his prophets
Mt 9: 29 "According to your **f** let it be done
17: 20 if you have **f** as small as a mustard
24: 10 many will turn away from the **f**
Mk 11: 22 "Have **f** in God," Jesus answered.
Lk 7: 9 I have not found such great **f** even
12: 28 will he clothe you—you of little **f**!
17: 5 said to the Lord, "Increase our **f**!"
18: 8 comes, will he find **f** on the earth?"
Ac 14: 9 him, saw that he had **f** to be healed
14: 27 how he had opened a door of **f**
Ro 1: 12 encouraged by each other's **f**.
1: 17 "The righteous will live by **f**."
1: 17 righteousness is by **f** from first
3: 22 righteousness is given through **f**
3: 25 of his blood—to be received by **f**.
4: 5 their **f** is credited as righteousness.
5: 1 we have been justified through **f**,
10: 17 **f** comes from hearing the message,
14: 1 Accept the one whose **f** is weak,
14: 23 that does not come from **f** is sin.
16: 26 the obedience that comes from **f**—
1Co 13: 2 have a **f** that can move mountains,
13: 13 three remain: **f**, hope and love.
16: 13 stand firm in the **f**; be courageous;
2Co 5: 7 For we live by **f**, not by sight.
13: 5 to see whether you are in the **f**;
Gal 2: 16 we may be justified by **f** in Christ
2: 20 body, I live by **f** in the Son of God,
3: 11 "the righteous will live by **f**."
3: 24 that we might be justified by **f**.
Eph 2: 8 you have been saved, through **f**—
4: 5 one Lord, one **f**, one baptism;
6: 16 take up the shield of **f**,
Col 1: 23 if you continue in your **f**,
1Th 5: 8 be sober, putting on **f** and love as
1Ti 2: 15 if they continue in **f**,
4: 1 later times some will abandon the **f**
5: 8 has denied the **f** and is worse than
6: 12 Fight the good fight of the **f**.
2Ti 3: 15 salvation through in Christ Jesus.
4: 7 finished the race, I have kept the **f**.
Phm : 6 with us in the **f** may be effective
Heb 10: 38 my righteous one will live by **f**.
11: 1 Now **f** is confidence in what we
11: 3 By **f** we understand that the
11: 5 By **f** Enoch was taken from this
11: 6 without **f** it is impossible to please
11: 7 By **f** Noah, when warned
11: 7 By his **f** he condemned the world
11: 8 By **f** Abraham, when called to go
11: 17 By **f** Abraham, when God tested
11: 20 By **f** Isaac blessed Jacob and Esau
11: 21 By **f** Jacob, when he was dying,
11: 22 By **f** Joseph, when his end was
11: 24 By **f** Moses, when he had grown
11: 31 By **f** the prostitute Rahab,
12: 2 Jesus, the pioneer and perfecter of **f**.
Jas 2: 14 Can such **f** save them?
2: 17 In the same way, **f** by itself, if it is

Jas 2: 26 is dead, so **f** without deeds is dead.
2Pe 1: 5 effort to add to your **f** goodness;
1Jn 5: 4 overcome the world, even our **f**.
Jude : 3 contend for the **f** that was once
FAITHFUL (FAITH)
Nu 12: 7 he is **f** in all my house.
Dt 7: 9 he is the **f** God, keeping his
32: 4 A **f** God who does no wrong,
2Sa 22: 26 "To the **f** you show yourself **f**,
Ps 16: 10 will you let your **f** one see decay.
25: 10 and **f** toward those who keep
31: 23 Love the LORD, all his **f** people!
33: 4 right and true; he is **f** in all he does.
37: 28 just and will not forsake his **f** ones.
97: 10 for he guards the lives of his **f** ones
116: 15 is the death of his **f** servants.
145: 13 all he promises and **f** in all he does.
145: 17 in all his ways and **f** in all he does.
146: 6 he remains **f** forever.
Pr 31: 26 and instruction is on her tongue.
Mt 25: 21 'Well done, good and **f** servant!
25: 21 You have been **f** with a few things;
Ro 12: 12 patient in affliction, **f** in prayer.
1Co 4: 2 been given a trust must prove **f**.
10: 13 And God is **f**; he will not let you be
1Th 5: 24 The one who calls you is **f**, and he
1Ti 3: 2 to be above reproach, **f** to his wife,
2Ti 2: 13 he remains **f**, for he cannot disown
Heb 3: 6 Christ is **f** as the Son over God's
10: 23 profess, for he who promised is **f**.
1Pe 4: 10 as **f** stewards of God's grace in its
4: 19 themselves to their **f** Creator
1Jn 1: 9 he is **f** and just and will forgive us
Rev 1: 5 who is the **f** witness, the firstborn
2: 10 Be **f**, even to the point of death,
19: 11 whose rider is called **F** and True.
FAITHFULLY (FAITH)
Dt 11: 13 So if you **f** obey the commands
1Sa 12: 24 and serve him **f** with all your heart;
1Ki 2: 4 if they walk **f** before me with all
FAITHFULNESS (FAITH)
Ps 51: 6 you desired **f** even in the womb;
57: 10 your **f** reaches to the skies.
85: 10 Love and **f** meet together;
86: 15 to anger, abounding in love and **f**.
89: 1 make your **f** known through all
89: 14 love and **f** go before you.
91: 4 his **f** will be your shield
117: 2 the **f** of the LORD endures forever.
119: 75 and that in **f** you have afflicted me.
Pr 3: 3 Let love and **f** never leave you;
Isa 11: 5 and **f** the sash around his waist.
La 3: 23 new every morning; great is your **f**.
Hab 2: 4 righteous person will live by his **f**—
Ro 3: 3 their unfaithfulness nullify God's **f**?
Gal 5: 22 forbearance, kindness, goodness, **f**,
FAITHLESS (FAITH)
Ps 119:158 I look on the **f** with loathing,
Jer 3: 22 "Return, **f** people; I will cure you
2Ti 2: 13 if we are **f**, he remains faithful,
FALL (FALLEN FALLS)
Ps 37: 24 he will not **f**, for the LORD
69: 9 of those who insult you **f** on me.
Pr 11: 28 who trust in their riches will **f**,
Lk 11: 17 a house divided against itself will **f**.
Jn 16: 1 you so that you will not **f** away.
Ro 3: 23 and **f** short of the glory of God,
14: 4 own master, servants stand or **f**.
FALLEN (FALL)
2Sa 1: 19 How the mighty have **f**!
Isa 14: 12 How you have **f** from heaven,
1Co 15: 20 of those who have **f** asleep,
Gal 5: 4 you have **f** away from grace.
1Th 4: 15 precede those who have **f** asleep.
Heb 6: 6 and who have **f** away, to be brought
FALLS (FALL)
Pr 24: 17 Do not gloat when your enemy **f**;
Jn 12: 24 a kernel of wheat **f** to the ground
FALSE (FALSEHOOD FALSELY)
Ex 20: 16 shall not give **f** testimony against
23: 1 "Do not spread **f** reports.
Pr 13: 5 The righteous hate what is **f**,

Pr 19: 5 A **f** witness will not go unpunished,
Mt 7: 15 "Watch out for **f** prophets.
    19: 18 steal, you shall not give **f** testimony,
    24: 11 and many **f** prophets will appear
Php 1: 18 whether from **f** motives or true,
1Ti 1: 3 not to teach **f** doctrines any longer
2Pe 2: 1 there will be **f** teachers among you.
FALSEHOOD (FALSE)
Ps 119:163 and detest **f** but I love your law.
Pr 30: 8 Keep **f** and lies far from me;
Eph 4: 25 each of you must put off **f**
FALSELY (FALSE)
Lev 19: 12 " 'Do not swear **f** by my name
Lk 3: 14 money and don't accuse people **f**—
1Ti 6: 20 ideas of what is **f** called knowledge,
FALTER
Pr 24: 10 If you **f** in a time of trouble,
Isa 42: 4 he will not **f** or be discouraged till
FAMILIES (FAMILY)
Ps 68: 6 God sets the lonely in **f**, he leads
FAMILY (FAMILIES)
Pr 31: 15 she provides food for her **f**
Lk 9: 61 go back and say goodbye to my **f**."
    12: 52 in one **f** divided against each other,
1Ti 3: 4 He must manage his own **f** well
    3: 5 know how to manage his own **f**,
    5: 4 practice by caring for their own **f**
FAMINE
Ge 41: 30 seven years of **f** will follow them.
Am 8: 11 I will send a **f** through the land—
Ro 8: 35 or persecution or **f** or nakedness
FAN
2Ti 1: 6 this reason I remind you to **f**
FAST
Dt 13: 4 serve him and hold **f** to him.
Jos 22: 5 to hold **f** to him and to serve him
    23: 8 to hold **f** to the LORD your God,
Ps 119: 31 I hold **f** to your statutes, LORD;
    139: 10 me, your right hand will hold me **f**.
Mt 6: 16 "When you **f**, do not look somber
1Pe 5: 12 the true grace of God. Stand **f** in it.
FATHER (FATHER'S FATHERLESS FATHERS)
Ge 2: 24 That is why a man leaves his **f**
    17: 4 You will be the **f** of many nations.
Ex 20: 12 "Honor your **f** and your mother,
    21: 15 "Anyone who attacks their **f**
    21: 17 "Anyone who curses their **f**
Lev 18: 7 " 'Do not dishonor your **f**
    19: 3 must respect your mother and **f**,
Dt 5: 16 "Honor your **f** and your mother,
    21: 18 son who does not obey his **f**
Ps 27: 10 Though my **f** and mother forsake
    68: 5 A **f** to the fatherless, a defender
Pr 10: 1 A wise son brings joy to his **f**,
    23: 22 Listen to your **f**, who gave you life,
    23: 24 The **f** of a righteous child has great
    28: 7 of gluttons disgraces his **f**.
    29: 3 loves wisdom brings joy to his **f**,
Isa 9: 6 Everlasting **F**, Prince of Peace.
Mt 6: 9 " 'Our **F** in heaven, hallowed be
    10: 37 "Anyone who loves their **f**
    15: 4 said, 'Honor your **f** and mother'
    19: 5 this reason a man will leave his **f**
Lk 12: 53 **f** against son and son against **f**,
    23: 34 Jesus said, "**F**, forgive them,
Jn 6: 44 unless the **F** who sent me draws
    6: 46 from God; only he has seen the **F**.
    8: 44 You belong to your **f**, the devil,
    10: 30 I and the **F** are one."
    14: 6 comes to the **F** except through me.
    14: 9 who has seen me has seen the **F**.
Ro 4: 11 he is the **f** of all who believe
2Co 6: 18 And, "I will be a **F** to you, and you
Eph 6: 2 "Honor your **f** and mother"—
Heb 12: 7 are not disciplined by their **f**?
FATHER'S (FATHER)
Pr 13: 1 wise son heeds his **f** instruction,
    19: 13 A foolish child is a **f** ruin,
Lk 2: 49 know I had to be in my **F** house?"
Jn 2: 16 Stop turning my **F** house
    10: 29 can snatch them out of my **F** hand.
    14: 2 My **F** house has many rooms;

FATHERLESS (FATHER)
Dt 10: 18 He defends the cause of the **f**
    24: 17 the foreigner or the **f** of justice,
    24: 19 the foreigner, the **f** and the widow,
Ps 68: 5 A father to the **f**, a defender
Pr 23: 10 or encroach on the fields of the **f**,
FATHERS (FATHER)
Lk 11: 11 "Which of you **f**, if your son asks
Eph 6: 4 **F**, do not exasperate your children;
Col 3: 21 **F**, do not embitter your children,
FATHOM
Job 11: 7 "Can you **f** the mysteries of God?
Ps 145: 3 his greatness no one can **f**.
Ecc 3: 11 no one can **f** what God has done
Isa 40: 28 his understanding no one can **f**.
1Co 13: 2 of prophecy and can **f** all mysteries
FAULT (FAULTS)
Mt 18: 15 sins, go and point out their **f**,
Php 2: 15 of God without **f** in a warped
Jas 1: 5 generously to all without finding **f**,
Jude : 24 his glorious presence without **f**
FAULTFINDERS
Jude : 16 These people are grumblers and **f**;
FAULTS (FAULT)
Ps 19: 12 Forgive my hidden **f**.
FAVORITISM
Ex 23: 3 do not show **f** to a poor person
Lev 19: 15 to the poor or **f** to the great,
Ac 10: 34 true it is that God does not show **f**
Ro 2: 11 For God does not show **f**.
Gal 2: 6 God does not show **f**—
Eph 6: 9 heaven, and there is no **f** with him.
Col 3: 25 for their wrongs, and there is no **f**.
1Ti 5: 21 and to do nothing out of **f**.
Jas 2: 1 Lord Jesus Christ must not show **f**.
    2: 9 But if you show **f**, you sin and are
FEAR (AFRAID FEARS)
Dt 6: 13 **F** the LORD your God, serve him
    10: 12 you but to **f** the LORD your God,
    31: 12 learn to **f** the LORD your God
Ps 19: 9 The **f** of the LORD is pure,
    23: 4 the darkest valley, I will **f** no evil,
    27: 1 and my salvation—whom shall I **f**?
    91: 5 not **f** the terror of night,
    111: 10 The **f** of the LORD is
Pr 8: 13 To **f** the LORD is to hate evil;
    9: 10 The **f** of the LORD is
    10: 27 The **f** of the LORD adds length
    14: 27 The **f** of the LORD is a fountain
    15: 33 instruction is to **f** the LORD,
    16: 6 through the **f** of the LORD evil is
    19: 23 The **f** of the LORD leads to life;
    29: 25 **F** of man will prove to be a snare,
Ecc 5: 7 Therefore **f** God.
Isa 11: 3 will delight in the **f** of the LORD.
    41: 10 So do not **f**, for I am with you;
Lk 12: 5 will show you whom you should **f**:
Php 2: 12 to work out your salvation with **f**
1Jn 4: 18 There is no **f** in love. But perfect love drives out **f**,
FEARS (FEAR)
Job 1: 8 a man who **f** God and shuns evil."
Ps 34: 4 he delivered me from all my **f**.
Pr 31: 30 a woman who **f** the LORD is to be
1Jn 4: 18 The one who **f** is not made perfect
FEED
Jn 21: 15 Jesus said, "**F** my lambs."
    21: 17 Jesus said, "**F** my sheep.
Ro 12: 20 "If your enemy is hungry, **f** him;
Jude : 12 shepherds who **f** only themselves.
FEET (FOOT)
Ps 8: 6 you put everything under their **f**:
    22: 16 they pierce my hands and my **f**.
    40: 2 he set my **f** on a rock and gave me
    110: 1 enemies a footstool for your **f**."
    119:105 Your word is a lamp to my **f**
Ro 10: 15 "How beautiful are the **f** of those
1Co 12: 21 And the head cannot say to the **f**,
    15: 25 has put all his enemies under his **f**.
Heb 12: 13 "Make level paths for your **f**,"
FELLOWSHIP
2Co 6: 14 **f** can light have with darkness?
    13: 14 the **f** of the Holy Spirit be with you

1Jn 1: 6 If we claim to have **f** with him
　　 1: 7 light, we have **f** with one another,
FEMALE
Ge 1: 27 male and **f** he created them.
Gal 3: 28 nor is there male and **f**, for you are
FERVOR
Ro 12: 11 but keep your spiritual **f**,
FIDELITY
Ro 1: 31 no understanding, no **f**, no love,
FIELD (FIELDS)
Mt 6: 28 See how the flowers of the **f** grow.
　　 13: 38 The **f** is the world, and the good
1Co 3: 9 you are God's **f**, God's building.
FIELDS (FIELD)
Lk 2: 8 shepherds living out in the **f**
Jn 4: 35 open your eyes and look at the **f**!
FIERY (FIRE)
1Pe 4: 12 do not be surprised at the **f** ordeal
FIG (FIGS)
Ge 3: 7 so they sewed **f** leaves together
FIGHT (FOUGHT)
Ex 14: 14 The Lord will **f** for you;
Dt 1: 30 is going before you, will **f** for you,
　　 3: 22 the Lord your God himself will **f**
Ne 4: 20 Our God will **f** for us!"
Ps 35: 1 **f** against those who **f** against me.
Jn 18: 36 my servants would **f** to prevent my
1Co 9: 26 I do not **f** like a boxer beating
2Co 10: 4 The weapons we **f** with are not
1Ti 1: 18 you may the battle well,
　　 6: 12 **F** the good **f** of the faith.
2Ti 4: 7 I have fought the good **f**, I have
FIGS (FIG)
Lk 6: 44 People do not pick **f**
FILL (FILLED FILLS FULL FULLNESS FULLY)
Ge 1: 28 **f** the earth and subdue it.
Ps 16: 11 you will **f** me with joy in your
　　 81: 10 wide your mouth and I will **f** it.
Pr 28: 19 chase fantasies will have their **f**
Hag 2: 7 and I will **f** this house with glory,'
Jn 6: 26 you ate the loaves and had your **f**.
Ac 2: 28 you will **f** me with joy in your
Ro 15: 13 May the God of hope **f** you with all
FILLED (FILL)
Ps 72: 19 may the whole earth be **f** with his
　　 119: 64 The earth is **f** with your love,
Isa 11: 9 for the earth will be **f**
Eze 43: 5 glory of the Lord **f** the temple.
Hab 2: 14 For the earth will be **f**
Lk 1: 15 he will be **f** with the Holy Spirit
　　 1: 41 Elizabeth was **f** with the Holy Spirit.
Jn 12: 3 the house was **f** with the fragrance
Ac 2: 4 of them were **f** with the Holy Spirit
　　 4: 8 Then Peter, **f** with the Holy Spirit,
　　 9: 17 and be **f** with the Holy Spirit."
　　 13: 9 called Paul, **f** with the Holy Spirit,
Eph 5: 18 Instead, be **f** with the Spirit,
Php 1: 11 **f** with the fruit of righteousness
FILLS (FILL)
Nu 14: 21 of the Lord **f** the whole earth,
Ps 107: 9 and **f** the hungry with good things.
Eph 1: 23 him who **f** everything in every way.
FILTHY
Isa 64: 6 all our righteous acts are like **f** rags;
Col 3: 8 and **f** language from your lips.
FIND (FINDS FOUND)
Nu 32: 23 be sure that your sin will **f** you out.
Dt 4: 29 you will **f** him if you seek him
1Sa 23: 16 and helped him **f** strength in God.
Ps 91: 4 under his wings you will **f** refuge;
　　 112: 1 Lord, who **f** great delight in his
Pr 14: 22 those who plan what is good **f** love
　　 31: 10 wife of noble character who can **f**?
Jer 6: 16 and you will **f** rest for your souls.
Mt 7: 7 seek and you will **f**;
　　 11: 29 and you will **f** rest for your souls.
　　 16: 25 loses their life for me will **f** it.
Lk 18: 8 will he **f** faith on the earth?"
Jn 10: 9 come in and go out, and **f** pasture.
FINDS (FIND)
Ps 62: 1 Truly my soul **f** rest in God;
　　 119:162 promise like one who **f** great spoil.

Pr 18: 22 He who **f** a wife **f** what is good
Mt 7: 8 the one who seeks **f**; and to the one
　　 10: 39 Whoever **f** their life will lose it,
Lk 12: 37 whose master **f** them watching
　　 15: 4 go after the lost sheep until he **f** it?
FINISH (FINISHED)
Jn 4: 34 him who sent me and to **f** his work.
　　 5: 36 that the Father has given me to **f**—
Ac 20: 24 my only aim is to **f** the race
2Co 8: 11 Now **f** the work, so that your eager
Gal 3: 3 are you now trying to **f** by means
Jas 1: 4 Let perseverance **f** its work so
FINISHED (FINISH)
Ge 2: 2 seventh day God had **f** the work he
Jn 19: 30 the drink, Jesus said, "It is **f**."
2Ti 4: 7 the good fight, I have **f** the race,
FIRE (FIERY)
Ex 13: 21 in a pillar of **f** to give them light,
Lev 6: 12 The **f** on the altar must be kept
Isa 30: 27 and his tongue is a consuming **f**.
Jer 23: 29 "Is not my word like **f**,"
Mt 3: 11 you with the Holy Spirit and **f**.
　　 5: 22 will be in danger of the **f** of hell.
　　 25: 41 the eternal **f** prepared for the devil
Mk 9: 43 hell, where the **f** never goes out.
Ac 2: 3 to be tongues of **f** that separated
1Co 3: 13 It will be revealed with **f**, and the **f**
Heb 12: 29 for our "God is a consuming **f**."
Jas 3: 5 what a great forest is set on **f**
2Pe 3: 10 the elements will be destroyed by **f**,
Jude : 23 by snatching them from the **f**;
Rev 20: 14 **f**. The lake of **f** is the second death.
FIRM
Ex 14: 13 Stand **f** and you will see
2Ch 20: 17 stand **f** and see the deliverance
Ps 33: 11 plans of the Lord stand **f** forever,
　　 37: 23 The Lord makes **f** the steps
　　 40: 2 and gave me a **f** place to stand.
　　 89: 2 that your love stands **f** forever,
　　 119: 89 it stands **f** in the heavens.
Zec 8: 23 nations will take **f** hold of one Jew
Mk 13: 13 the one who stands **f** to the end
1Co 16: 13 on your guard; stand **f** in the faith;
2Co 1: 24 because it is by faith you stand **f**.
Eph 6: 14 Stand **f** then, with the belt of truth
Col 4: 12 that you may stand **f** in all the will
2Th 2: 15 stand **f** and hold fast to the teachings
2Ti 2: 19 God's solid foundation stands **f**,
Heb 6: 19 anchor for the soul, **f** and secure.
1Pe 5: 9 Resist him, standing **f** in the faith,
FIRST
Isa 44: 6 I am the **f** and I am the last;
　　 48: 12 I am the **f** and I am the last.
Mt 5: 24 **F** go and be reconciled to them;
　　 6: 33 But seek **f** his kingdom and his
　　 7: 5 **f** take the plank out of your own
　　 20: 27 wants to be **f** must be your slave—
　　 22: 38 This is the **f** and greatest
　　 23: 26 **F** clean the inside of the cup
Mk 10: 44 the gospel must **f** be preached to all
Ac 11: 26 disciples were called Christians **f**
Ro 1: 16 **f** to the Jew, then to the Gentile.
1Co 12: 28 in the church **f** of all apostles,
2Co 8: 5 They gave themselves **f** of all
1Ti 2: 13 For Adam was formed **f**, then Eve.
Jas 3: 17 comes from heaven is **f** of all pure;
1Jn 4: 19 We love because he **f** loved us.
3Jn : 9 who loves to be **f**, will not welcome
Rev 1: 17 I am the **F** and the Last.
　　 2: 4 have forsaken the love you had at **f**.
FIRSTBORN (BEAR)
Ex 11: 5 Every **f** son in Egypt will die,
FIRSTFRUITS
Ex 23: 19 "Bring the best of the **f** of your soil
FISH
Mk 1: 17 I will send you out to **f** for people."
Lk 5: 10 from now on you will **f** for people."
FITTING
Ps 33: 1 it is **f** for the upright to praise him.
　　 147: 1 how pleasant and **f** to praise him!
Pr 19: 10 It is not **f** for a fool to live
　　 26: 1 in harvest, honor is not **f** for a fool.

1Co 14: 40 everything should be done in a **f**
Col 3: 18 your husbands, as is **f** in the Lord.
Heb 2: 10 to glory, it was **f** that God,
FIX (FIXING)
Dt 11: 18 **F** these words of mine in your
Pr 4: 25 **f** your gaze directly before you.
2Co 4: 18 So we **f** our eyes not on what is
Heb 3: 1 calling, **f** your thoughts on Jesus,
FIXING (FIX)
Heb 12: 2 **f** our eyes on Jesus, the pioneer
FLAME (FLAMES FLAMING)
2Ti 1: 6 you to fan into **f** the gift of God,
FLAMES (FLAME)
1Co 3: 15 only as one escaping through the **f**.
FLAMING (FLAME)
Eph 6: 16 you can extinguish all the **f** arrows
FLASH
1Co 15: 52 in a **f**, in the twinkling of an eye,
FLATTER (FLATTERING FLATTERY)
Ps 12: 2 they **f** with their lips but harbor
Job 32: 21 no partiality, nor will I **f** anyone;
Jude : 16 **f** others for their own advantage.
FLATTERING (FLATTER)
Ps 12: 3 May the LORD silence all **f** lips
Pr 26: 28 it hurts, and a **f** mouth works ruin.
FLATTERY (FLATTER)
Ro 16: 18 **f** they deceive the minds of naive
1Th 2: 5 You know we never used **f**, nor did
FLAWLESS
2Sa 22: 31 The LORD's word is **f**;
Job 11: 4 'My beliefs are **f** and I am pure
Ps 12: 6 And the words of the LORD are **f**,
18: 30 The LORD's word is **f**;
Pr 30: 5 "Every word of God is **f**; he is
SS 5: 2 my darling, my dove, my **f** one.
FLEE
Ps 139: 7 Where can I **f** from your presence?
1Co 6: 18 **F** from sexual immorality.
10: 14 my dear friends, **f** from idolatry.
1Ti 6: 11 man of God, **f** from all this,
2Ti 2: 22 **F** the evil desires of youth
Jas 4: 7 the devil, and he will **f** from you.
FLEETING
Ps 89: 47 Remember how **f** is my life.
Pr 31: 30 is deceptive, and beauty is **f**;
FLESH
Ge 2: 23 bone of my bones and **f** of my **f**;
2: 24 to his wife, and they become one **f**.
Job 19: 26 yet in my **f** I will see God;
Eze 11: 19 of stone and give them a heart of **f**.
36: 26 of stone and give you a heart of **f**.
Mt 26: 41 spirit is willing, but the **f** is weak."
Mk 10: 8 and the two will become one **f**.'
Jn 1: 14 The Word became **f** and made his
6: 51 bread is my **f**, which I will give
Ro 8: 4 do not live according to the **f** but
8: 8 realm of the **f** cannot please God.
1Co 6: 16 said, "The two will become one **f**."
Gal 3: 3 trying to finish by means of the **f**?
5: 19 The acts of the **f** are obvious:
5: 24 crucified the **f** with its passions
Eph 5: 31 and the two will become one **f**."
6: 12 For our struggle is not against **f**
FLOCK (FLOCKS)
Isa 40: 11 He tends his **f** like a shepherd:
Eze 34: 2 not shepherds take care of the **f**?
Zec 11: 17 shepherd, who deserts the **f**!
Mt 26: 31 the sheep of the **f** will be scattered.'
Ac 20: 28 all the **f** of which the Holy Spirit
1Pe 5: 2 of God's **f** that is under your care,
FLOCKS (FLOCK)
Lk 2: 8 keeping watch over their **f** at night.
FLOG
Ac 22: 25 **f** a Roman citizen who hasn't even
FLOODGATES
Mal 3: 10 will not throw open the **f** of heaven
FLOURISHING
Ps 52: 8 am like an olive tree **f** in the house
FLOW (FLOWING)
Nu 13: 27 and it does **f** with milk and honey!
Jn 7: 38 of living water will **f** from within

FLOWERS
Isa 40: 7 The grass withers and the **f** fall,
Lk 12: 27 "Consider how the wild **f** grow.
FLOWING (FLOW)
Ex 3: 8 a land **f** with milk and honey—
FOLDING
Pr 6: 10 a little **f** of the hands to rest—
FOLLOW (FOLLOWS)
Ex 23: 2 "Do not **f** the crowd in doing
Lev 18: 4 laws and be careful to **f** my decrees.
Dt 5: 1 Learn them and be sure to **f** them.
Ps 23: 6 love will **f** me all the days of my
Mt 16: 24 and take up their cross and **f** me.
Jn 10: 4 his sheep **f** him because they know
1Co 14: 1 **F** the way of love and eagerly desire
Eph 5: 1 **F** God's example, therefore,
Rev 14: 4 They **f** the Lamb wherever he goes.
FOLLOWS (FOLLOW)
Jn 8: 12 Whoever **f** me will never walk
FOOD (FOODS)
Pr 20: 13 awake and you will have **f** to spare.
22: 9 for they share their **f** with the poor.
25: 21 enemy is hungry, give him **f** to eat;
31: 15 she provides **f** for her family
Da 1: 8 to defile himself with the royal **f**
Jn 6: 27 Do not work for **f** that spoils, but for **f** that endures to eternal life,
1Co 8: 8 **f** does not bring us near to God;
1Ti 6: 8 But if we have **f** and clothing,
Jas 2: 15 sister is without clothes and daily **f**.
FOODS (FOOD)
Mk 7: 19 this, Jesus declared all **f** clean.)
FOOL (FOOLISH FOOLISHNESS FOOLS)
Ps 14: 1 The **f** says in his heart, "There
Pr 15: 5 A **f** spurns a parent's discipline,
26: 5 Answer a **f** according to his folly,
Mt 5: 22 And anyone who says, 'You **f**!'
FOOLISH (FOOL)
Pr 10: 1 a **f** son brings grief to his mother.
17: 25 A **f** son brings grief to his father
Mt 7: 26 practice is like a **f** man who built
25: 2 Five of them were **f** and five were
1Co 1: 27 God chose the **f** things of the world
FOOLISHNESS (FOOL)
1Co 1: 18 of the cross is **f** to those who are
1: 25 the **f** of God is wiser than human
2: 14 Spirit of God but considers them **f**,
3: 19 of this world is **f** in God's sight.
FOOLS (FOOL)
Pr 14: 9 **F** mock at making amends for sin,
17: 28 Even **f** are thought wise if they
18: 2 **F** find no pleasure in understanding
28: 26 who trust in themselves are **f**,
1Co 4: 10 We are **f** for Christ, but you are so
FOOT (FEET FOOTHOLD)
Jos 1: 3 every place where you set your **f**,
Isa 1: 6 the sole of your **f** to the top of your
1Co 12: 15 Now if the **f** should say, "Because I
FOOTHOLD (FOOT)
Eph 4: 27 and do not give the devil a **f**.
FORBEARANCE
Ro 3: 25 his **f** he had left the sins committed
Gal 5: 22 love, joy, peace, **f**, kindness,
FORBID
1Co 14: 39 and do not **f** speaking in tongues.
FOREIGNER (FOREIGNERS)
Ex 22: 21 "Do not mistreat or oppress a **f**,
FOREIGNERS (FOREIGNER)
1Pe 2: 11 urge you, as **f** and exiles, to abstain
FOREKNEW (KNOW)
Ro 8: 29 those God he also predestined
11: 2 not reject his people, whom he **f**.
FOREVER (EVER)
1Ch 16: 15 He remembers his covenant **f**,
16: 34 for he is good; his love endures **f**.
Ps 9: 7 The LORD reigns **f**;
23: 6 dwell in the house of the LORD **f**.
33: 11 plans of the LORD stand firm **f**,
86: 12 I will glorify your name **f**.
92: 8 But you, LORD, are **f** exalted.
110: 4 "You are a priest **f**, in the order
119: 111 Your statutes are my heritage **f**;

Jn   6: 51 Whoever eats this bread will live **f**.
      14: 16 to help you and be with you **f**—
1Co   9: 25 do it to get a crown that will last **f**.
1Th   4: 17 And so we will be with the Lord **f**.
Heb 13:   8 the same yesterday and today and **f**.
1Pe   1: 25 the word of the Lord endures **f**."
1Jn   2: 17 does the will of God lives **f**.

FORFEIT
Lk   9: 25 and yet lose or **f** their very self?

FORGAVE (FORGIVE)
Ps   32:   5 And you **f** the guilt of my sin.
Lk   7: 42 him back, so he **f** the debts of both.
Eph   4: 32 other, just as in Christ God **f** you.
Col   2: 13 He **f** us all our sins,
      3: 13 Forgive as the Lord **f** you.

FORGET (FORGETS FORGETTING)
Dt   6: 12 that you do not **f** the LORD,
Ps 103:   2 my soul, and **f** not all his benefits—
     137:       If I **f** you, Jerusalem, may my right
Isa 49: 15 Though she may **f**, I will not **f** you!
Heb   6: 10 will not **f** your work and the love

FORGETS (FORGET)
Jn   16: 21 is born she **f** the anguish because
Jas   1: 24 immediately **f** what he looks like.

FORGETTING (FORGET)
Php   3: 13 **F** what is behind and straining

FORGIVE (FORGAVE FORGIVENESS FORGIVING)
2Ch   7: 14 and I will **f** their sin and will heal
Ps   19: 12 **F** my hidden faults.
Mt   6: 12 And **f** us our debts, as we also have
      6: 14 if you **f** other people when they sin
     18: 21 many times shall I **f** my brother
Mk   11: 25 anything against anyone, **f** them,
Lk   11:   4 **F** us our sins, for we also **f** everyone
     23: 34 "Father, **f** them, for they do not
Col   3: 13 **F** as the Lord forgave you.
1Jn   1:   9 and will **f** us our sins and purify

FORGIVENESS (FORGIVE)
Ps 130:   4 But with you there is **f**, so that we
Ac   10: 43 in him receives **f** of sins through
Eph   1:   7 through his blood, the **f** of sins,
Col   1: 14 we have redemption, the **f** of sins.
Heb   9: 22 the shedding of blood there is no **f**.

FORGIVING (FORGIVE)
Ne   9: 17 But you are a **f** God,
Eph   4: 32 to one another, **f** each other, just as

FORMED
Ge   2:   7 the LORD God **f** a man
Ps 103: 14 for he knows how we are **f**,
Isa 45: 18 be empty, but **f** it to be inhabited—
Ro   9: 20 what is **f** say to the one who **f** it,
1Ti   2: 13 For Adam was **f** first, then Eve.
Heb 11:   3 that the universe was **f** at God's

FORSAKE (FORSAKEN)
Jos   1:   5 I will never leave you nor **f** you.
     24: 16 us to **f** the LORD to serve other
2Ch 15:   2 you, but if you **f** him, he will **f** you.
Ps   27: 10 Though my father and mother **f** me,
Isa 55:   7 Let the wicked **f** their ways
Heb 13:   5 will I leave you; never will I **f** you."

FORSAKEN (FORSAKE)
Ezr   9:   9 God has not **f** us in our bondage.
Ps   22:   1 God, my God, why have you **f** me?
     37: 25 I have never seen the righteous **f**
Mt   27: 46 my God, why have you **f** me?").
Rev   2:   4 You have **f** the love you had at first.

FORTIFIED
Pr   18: 10 name of the LORD is a **f** tower;

FORTRESS
Ps   18:   2 is my rock, my **f** and my deliverer;
     71:   3 me, for you are my rock and my **f**.

FOUGHT (FIGHT)
2Ti   4:   7 I have **f** the good fight, I have

FOUND (FIND)
1Ch 28:   9 If you seek him, he will be **f** by you;
Isa 55:   6 Seek the LORD while he may be **f**;
Da   5: 27 on the scales and **f** wanting.
Lk   15:   6 I have **f** my lost sheep.'
     15:   9 I have **f** my lost coin.'
Ac   4: 12 Salvation is **f** in no one else,

FOUNDATION
Isa 28: 16 a precious cornerstone for a sure **f**;

1Co   3: 11 can lay any **f** other than the one
Eph   2: 20 built on the **f** of the apostles
2Ti   2: 19 God's solid **f** stands firm,

FOXES
Mt   8: 20 "**F** have dens and birds have nests,

FRANKINCENSE
Mt   2: 11 him with gifts of gold, **f** and myrrh.

FREE (FREED FREEDOM FREELY)
Ps 146:   7 The LORD sets prisoners **f**,
Jn   8: 32 truth, and the truth will set you **f**."
Ro   6: 18 You have been set **f** from sin
Gal   3: 28 neither slave nor **f**, nor is there
1Pe   2: 16 Live as **f** people, but do not use

FREED (FREE)
Rev   1:   5 has **f** us from our sins by his blood,

FREEDOM (FREE)
Ro   8: 21 brought into the **f** and glory
2Co   3: 17 the Spirit of the Lord is, there is **f**.
Gal   5: 13 But do not use your **f** to indulge
1Pe   2: 16 do not use your **f** as

FREELY (FREE)
Isa 55:   7 to our God, for he will **f** pardon.
Mt   10:   8 **F** you have received; **f** give.
Ro   3: 24 and all are justified **f** by his grace
Eph   1:   6 which he has **f** given us in the One

FRIEND (FRIENDS)
Ex   33: 11 face to face, as one speaks to a **f**
Pr   17: 17 A **f** loves at all times, and a brother
     18: 24 there is a **f** who sticks closer than
     27:   6 Wounds from a **f** can be trusted,
     27: 10 Do not forsake your **f** or a **f** of your
Jas   4:   4 to be a **f** of the world becomes

FRIENDS (FRIEND)
Pr   16: 28 and a gossip separates close **f**.
     18: 24 who has unreliable **f** soon comes
Zec 13:   6 I was given at the house of my **f**.'
Jn   15: 13 to lay down one's life for one's **f**.

FRUIT (FRUITFUL)
Ps   1:   3 which yields its **f** in season
Pr   11: 30 The **f** of the righteous is a tree
Mt   7: 16 By their **f** you will recognize them.
Jn   15:   2 branch that does bear **f** he prunes
Gal   5: 22 But the **f** of the Spirit is love, joy,
Rev 22:   2 bearing twelve crops of **f**, yielding its **f** every month.

FRUITFUL (FRUIT)
Ge   1: 22 "Be **f** and increase in number
Ps 128:   3 wife will be like a **f** vine within
Jn   15:   2 so that it will be even more **f**.

FULFILL (FULFILLED FULFILLMENT)
Ps 116: 14 I will **f** my vows to the LORD
Mt   5: 17 to abolish them but to **f** them.
1Co   7:   3 The husband should **f** his marital

FULFILLED (FULFILL)
Pr   13: 19 A longing **f** is sweet to the soul,
Mk   14: 49 But the Scriptures must be **f**."
Ro   13:   8 whoever loves others has **f** the law.

FULFILLMENT (FULFILL)
Ro   13: 10 Therefore love is the **f** of the law.

FULL (FILL)
Ps 127:   5 Blessed is the man whose quiver is **f**
Pr   31: 11 Her husband has **f** confidence in her
Isa   6:   3 the whole earth is **f** of his glory."
Lk   6: 45 speaks what the heart is **f** of.
Jn   10: 10 may have life, and have it to the **f**.
Ac   6:   3 who are known to be **f** of the Spirit

FULLNESS (FILL)
Col   1: 19 to have all his **f** dwell in him,
      2:   9 in Christ all the **f** of the Deity lives

FULLY (FILL)
1Ki   8: 61 may your hearts be **f** committed
2Ch 16:   9 whose hearts are **f** committed
Ps 119:   4 precepts that are to be **f** obeyed.
     119:138 righteous; they are **f** trustworthy.
1Co 15: 58 Always give yourselves **f**

FUTURE
Ps   37: 37 a **f** awaits those who seek peace.
Pr   23: 18 There is surely a **f** hope for you,
Ro   8: 38 neither the present nor the **f**,

GABRIEL
    Angel who interpreted Daniel's visions (Da 8:16–26; 9:20–27); announced births of John (Lk 1:11–20), Jesus (Lk 1:26–38).

GAIN (GAINED)
Ps 60: 12 With God we will **g** the victory,
Mk 8: 36 for someone to **g** the whole world,
1Co 13: 3 but do not have love, I **g** nothing.
Php 1: 21 me, to live is Christ and to die is **g**.
3: 8 them garbage, that I may **g** Christ
1Ti 6: 6 with contentment is great **g**.
1Pe 5: 2 not pursuing dishonest **g**, but eager

GAINED (GAIN)
Ro 5: 2 through whom we have **g** access

GALILEE
Isa 9: 1 in the future he will honor **G**

GALL
Mt 27: 34 Jesus wine to drink, mixed with **g**;

GAP
Eze 22: 30 stand before me in the **g** on behalf

GARBAGE
Php 3: 8 I consider them **g**, that I may gain

GARDENER
Jn 15: 1 true vine, and my Father is the **g**.

GARMENT (GARMENTS)
Ps 102: 26 they will all wear out like a **g**.
Mt 9: 16 the patch will pull away from the **g**,
Jn 19: 23 This **g** was seamless, woven in one
19: 24 them and cast lots for my **g**."

GARMENTS (GARMENT)
Ge 3: 21 The LORD God made **g** of skin
Isa 61: 10 For he has clothed me with **g**
63: 1 with his **g** stained crimson?

GATE (GATES)
Mt 7: 13 "Enter through the narrow **g**.
Jn 10: 9 I am the **g**; whoever enters through

GATES (GATE)
Ps 100: 4 Enter his **g** with thanksgiving
Mt 16: 18 the **g** of Hades will not overcome

GATHER (GATHERS)
Zec 14: 2 I will **g** all the nations to Jerusalem
Mt 12: 30 and whoever does not **g** with me
23: 37 longed to **g** your children together,

GATHERS (GATHER)
Isa 40: 11 He **g** the lambs in his arms
Mt 23: 37 as a hen **g** her chicks under her

GAVE (GIVE)
Ezr 2: 69 their ability they **g** to the treasury
Job 1: 21 The LORD **g** and the LORD has
Jn 3: 16 so loved the world that he **g** his
2Co 8: 5 They **g** themselves first of all
Gal 2: 20 loved me and **g** himself for me.
1Ti 2: 6 who **g** himself as a ransom for all

GAZE
Ps 27: 4 to **g** on the beauty of the LORD
Pr 4: 25 fix your **g** directly before you.

GENEALOGIES
1Ti 1: 4 themselves to myths and endless **g**.

GENERATIONS
Ps 22: 30 **g** will be told about the Lord.
102: 12 renown endures through all **g**.
145: 13 dominion endures through all **g**.
Lk 1: 48 now on all **g** will call me blessed,
Eph 3: 5 other **g** as it has now been revealed

GENEROUS
Ps 112: 5 Good will come to those who are **g**
Pr 11: 25 The **g** will themselves be blessed,
2Co 9: 5 Then it will be ready as a **g** gift,
1Ti 6: 18 and to be **g** and willing to share.

GENTILE (GENTILES)
Ro 1: 16 first to the Jew, then to the **G**.
10: 12 no difference between Jew and **G**—

GENTILES (GENTILE)
Isa 42: 6 for the people and a light for the **G**,
Ro 3: 7 **G** alike are all under the power
11: 13 as I am the apostle to the **G**, I take
1Co 1: 23 block to Jews and foolishness to **G**,

GENTLE (GENTLENESS)
Pr 15: 1 A **g** answer turns away wrath,
Mt 11: 29 for I am **g** and humble in heart,
21: 5 to you, **g** and riding on a donkey,
1Co 4: 21 I come in love and with a **g** spirit?
1Pe 3: 4 unfading beauty of a **g** and quiet

GENTLENESS (GENTLE)
2Co 10: 1 By the humility and **g** of Christ,
Gal 5: 23 **g** and self-control.

Php 4: 5 Let your **g** be evident to all.
Col 3: 12 kindness, humility, **g** and patience.
1Ti 6: 11 faith, love, endurance and **g**.
1Pe 3: 15 But do this with **g** and respect,

GETHSEMANE
Mt 26: 36 his disciples to a place called **G**,

GIDEON
Judge, also called Jerub-Baal; freed Israel from Midianites (Jdg 6–8; Heb 11:32). Given sign of fleece (Jdg 6:36–40).

GIFT (GIFTS)
Pr 21: 14 A **g** given in secret soothes anger,
Mt 5: 23 you are offering your **g** at the altar
Ac 2: 38 you will receive the **g** of the Holy
Ro 6: 23 the **g** of God is eternal life in Christ
1Co 7: 7 of you has your own **g** from God;
2Co 8: 12 the **g** is acceptable according
9: 15 be to God for his indescribable **g**!
Eph 2: 8 yourselves, it is the **g** of God—
1Ti 4: 14 Do not neglect your **g**, which was
2Ti 1: 6 you to fan into flame the **g** of God,
Jas 1: 17 good and perfect **g** is from above,
1Pe 4: 10 should use whatever **g** you have

GIFTS (GIFT)
Ro 11: 29 for God's **g** and his call are
12: 6 We have different **g**,
1Co 12: 4 There are different kinds of **g**,
12: 31 Now eagerly desire the greater **g**.
14: 1 and eagerly desire of the Spirit,
14: 12 Since you are eager for **g**

GILEAD
Jer 8: 22 Is there no balm in **G**? Is there no

GIVE (GAVE GIVEN GIVER GIVES GIVING)
Nu 6: 26 toward you and **g** you peace." '
1Sa 1: 11 forget your servant but **g** her a son,
1: 11 I will **g** him to the LORD for all
2Ch 15: 7 be strong and do not **g** up, for your
Pr 21: 26 the righteous **g** without sparing.
23: 26 **g** me your heart and let your eyes
28: 27 Those who **g** to the poor will lack
30: 8 but **g** me only my daily bread.
Eze 36: 26 I will **g** you a new heart and put
Mt 6: 11 **G** us today our daily bread.
10: 8 Freely you have received; freely **g**.
22: 21 them, "So **g** back to Caesar what is
Mk 8: 37 what can anyone **g** in exchange
Lk 6: 38 **G**, and it will be given to you.
11: 13 Father in heaven **g** the Holy Spirit
Jn 10: 28 I **g** them eternal life, and they shall
13: 34 "A new command I **g** you:
Ac 20: 35 'It is more blessed to **g** than
Ro 12: 8 encourage, then **g** encouragement;
12: 8 if it is giving, then **g** generously;
13: 7 **G** to everyone what you owe them:
14: 12 then, each of us will **g** an account
2Co 9: 7 should **g** what you have decided
Rev 14: 7 voice, "Fear God and **g** him glory,

GIVEN (GIVE)
Nu 8: 16 Israelites who are to be **g** wholly
Ps 115: 16 but the earth he has **g** to mankind.
Isa 9: 6 a son is **g**, and the government
Mt 6: 33 all these things will be **g** to you as
7: 7 "Ask and it will be **g** to you;
Lk 22: 19 saying, "This is my body **g** for you;
Jn 3: 27 can receive only what is **g** them
Ro 5: 5 Holy Spirit, who has been **g** to us.
1Co 4: 2 those who have been **g** a trust must
12: 13 and we were all **g** the one Spirit
Eph 4: 7 of us grace has been **g** as Christ

GIVER (GIVE)
Pr 18: 16 ushers the **g** into the presence
2Co 9: 7 for God loves a cheerful **g**.

GIVES (GIVE)
Ps 119:130 unfolding of your words **g** light;
Pr 14: 30 A heart at peace **g** life to the body,
15: 30 good news **g** health to the bones.
Isa 40: 29 He **g** strength to the weary
Mt 10: 42 anyone **g** even a cup of cold water
Jn 6: 63 The Spirit **g** life; the flesh counts
1Co 15: 57 He **g** us the victory through our
2Co 3: 6 the letter kills, but the Spirit **g** life.

GIVING (GIVE)
Ne 8: 8 **g** the meaning so that the people

Ps 19: 8 LORD are right, **g** joy to the heart.
Mt 6: 4 so that your **g** may be in secret.
2Co 8: 7 you also excel in this grace of **g**.
GLAD (GLADNESS)
Ps 31: 7 I will be **g** and rejoice in your love,
46: 4 whose streams make **g** the city
97: 1 LORD reigns, let the earth be **g**;
118: 24 let us rejoice today and be **g**.
Zec 2: 10 "Shout and be **g**, Daughter Zion.
Mt 5: 12 Rejoice and be **g**, because great is
GLADNESS (GLAD)
Ps 45: 15 Led in with joy and **g**, they enter
51: 8 Let me hear joy and **g**;
100: 2 Worship the LORD with **g**;
Jer 31: 13 I will turn their mourning into **g**;
GLORIFIED (GLORY)
Jn 13: 31 "Now the Son of Man is **g** and God is **g** in him.
Ro 8: 30 those he justified, he also **g**.
2Th 1: 10 he comes to be **g** in his holy people
GLORIFY (GLORY)
Ps 34: 3 **G** the LORD with me; let us exalt
86: 12 I will **g** your name forever.
Mt 5: 16 deeds and **g** your Father in heaven.
Jn 13: 32 God will **g** the Son in himself,
17: 1 **G** your Son, that your Son may **g**
GLORIOUS (GLORY)
Ps 45: 13 All **g** is the princess within her
111: 3 **G** and majestic are his deeds,
145: 5 They speak of the **g** splendor
Isa 4: 2 the LORD will be beautiful and **g**,
12: 5 LORD, for he has done **g** things;
42: 21 to make his law great and **g**.
63: 15 from your lofty throne, holy and **g**.
Mt 19: 28 Son of Man sits on his **g** throne,
Lk 9: 30 and Elijah, appeared in **g** splendor,
Ac 2: 20 of the great and **g** day of the Lord.
2Co 3: 8 of the Spirit be even more **g**?
Php 3: 21 so that they will be like his **g** body.
Jude : 24 you before his **g** presence without
GLORY (GLORIFIED GLORIFY GLORIOUS)
Ex 15: 11 awesome in **g**, working wonders?
33: 18 said, "Now show me your **g**."
1Sa 4: 21 "The **G** has departed from Israel"
1Ch 16: 24 Declare his **g** among the nations,
16: 28 ascribe to the LORD **g**
29: 11 power and the **g** and the majesty
Ps 8: 5 crowned them with **g** and honor.
19: 1 The heavens declare the **g** of God;
24: 7 that the King of **g** may come in.
29: 1 beings, ascribe to the LORD **g**
34: 2 I will **g** in the LORD;
72: 19 the whole earth be filled with his **g**.
96: 3 Declare his **g** among the nations,
Pr 19: 11 is to one's **g** to overlook an offense.
25: 2 It is the **g** of God to conceal
25: 2 a matter is the **g** of kings.
Isa 6: 3 the whole earth is full of his **g**."
42: 8 I will not yield my **g** to another
48: 11 I will not yield my **g** to another.
Eze 43: 2 and I saw the **g** of the God of Israel
Mt 24: 30 of heaven, with power and great **g**.
25: 31 the Son of Man comes in his **g**,
Mk 8: 38 in his Father's **g** with the holy
13: 26 in clouds with great power and **g**.
Lk 2: 9 and the **g** of the Lord shone around
2: 14 "**G** to God in the highest heaven,
Jn 1: 14 have seen his **g**, the **g** of the one
17: 5 your presence with the **g** I had
17: 24 and to see my **g**, the **g** you have
Ac 7: 2 God of **g** appeared to our father
Ro 1: 23 exchanged the **g** of the immortal
3: 23 and fall short of the **g** of God,
8: 18 with the **g** that will be revealed
9: 4 theirs the divine **g**, the covenants,
1Co 10: 31 you do, do it all for the **g** of God.
11: 7 since he is the image and **g** of God;
11: 7 but woman is the **g** of man.
15: 43 sown in dishonor, it is raised in **g**;
2Co 3: 10 what was glorious has no **g** now
3: 18 faces contemplate the Lord's **g**,
4: 17 us an eternal **g** that far outweighs
Php 4: 19 the riches of his **g** in Christ Jesus.

Col 1: 27 is Christ in you, the hope of **g**.
3: 4 you also will appear with him in **g**.
1Ti 3: 16 on in the world, was taken up in **g**.
Titus 2: 13 appearing of the **g** of our great God
Heb 1: 3 The Son is the radiance of God's **g**
2: 7 crowned them with **g** and honor.
1Pe 1: 24 all their **g** is like the flowers
Rev 4: 11 to receive **g** and honor and power,
21: 23 for the **g** of God gives it light,
GLUTTONS
Titus 1: 12 always liars, evil brutes, lazy **g**."
GNASHING
Mt 8: 12 will be weeping and **g** of teeth."
GNAT
Mt 23: 24 You strain out a **g** but swallow
GOAL
2Co 5: 9 So we make it our **g** to please him,
Php 3: 14 on toward the **g** to win the prize
GOAT (GOATS SCAPEGOAT)
Isa 11: 6 leopard will lie down with the **g**,
GOATS (GOAT)
Nu 7: 17 five male **g** and five male lambs
GOD (GOD'S GODLINESS GODLY GODS)
Ge 1: 1 beginning **G** created the heavens
1: 2 of **G** was hovering over the waters.
1: 26 Then **G** said, "Let us make
1: 27 So **G** created mankind in his own
1: 31 **G** saw all that he had made, and it
2: 3 Then **G** blessed the seventh day
2: 22 the LORD **G** made a woman
3: 21 The LORD **G** made garments
3: 23 So the LORD **G** banished him
5: 22 walked faithfully with **G** 300 years
6: 2 sons of **G** saw that the daughters
9: 16 everlasting covenant between **G**
17: 1 to him and said, "I am **G** Almighty;
21: 33 name of the LORD, the Eternal **G**.
22: 8 "**G** himself will provide the lamb
28: 12 the angels of **G** were ascending
32: 28 because you have struggled with **G**
32: 30 "It is because I saw **G** face to face,
35: 10 said to him, "Your name is
41: 51 said, "It is because **G** has made me
50: 20 me, but **G** intended it for good
Ex 2: 24 **G** heard their groaning and he
3: 6 he said, "I am the **G** of your father,
3: 6 because he was afraid to look at **G**.
6: 7 know that I am the LORD your **G**,
8: 10 is no one like the LORD our **G**.
13: 18 So **G** led the people around
15: 2 He is my **G**, and I will praise him,
17: 9 with the staff of **G** in my hands."
19: 3 Then Moses went up to **G**,
20: 2 "I am the LORD your **G**,
20: 5 the LORD your **G**, am a jealous **G**,
20: 19 But do not have **G** speak to us
22: 28 "Do not blaspheme **G** or curse
31: 18 stone inscribed by the finger of **G**.
34: 6 the compassionate and gracious **G**,
34: 14 name is Jealous, is a jealous **G**.
Lev 18: 21 not profane the name of your **G**.
19: 2 I, the LORD your **G**, am holy.
26: 12 walk among you and be your **G**,
Nu 22: 38 I must speak only what **G** puts
23: 19 **G** is not human, that he should lie,
Dt 1: 17 anyone, for judgment belongs to **G**.
3: 22 the LORD your **G** himself will
3: 24 For what **g** is there in heaven
4: 24 **G** is a consuming fire, a jealous **G**.
4: 31 the LORD your **G** is a merciful **G**;
4: 39 day that the LORD is **G** in heaven
5: 11 the name of the LORD your **G**,
5: 14 is a sabbath to the LORD your **G**.
5: 26 voice of the living **G** speaking
6: 4 The LORD our **G**, the LORD is
6: 5 Love the LORD your **G** with all
6: 13 Fear the LORD your **G**, serve him
6: 16 Do not put the LORD your **G**
7: 9 is **G**; he is the faithful **G**,
7: 12 the LORD your **G** will keep his
7: 21 is a great and awesome **G**.
8: 5 the LORD your **G** disciplines you.

Dt	10: 12	what does the LORD your **G** ask you but to fear the LORD your **G**,
	10: 14	To the LORD your **G** belong
	10: 17	For the LORD your **G** is **G** of gods
	11: 13	to love the LORD your **G**
	13: 3	The LORD your **G** is testing you
	13: 4	It is the LORD your **G** you must
	15: 6	the LORD your **G** will bless you
	19: 9	to love the LORD your **G**
	25: 16	the LORD your **G** detests anyone
	29: 29	things belong to the LORD our **G**,
	30: 2	return to the LORD your **G**
	30: 16	today to love the LORD your **G**,
	30: 20	you may love the LORD your **G**,
	31: 6	the LORD your **G** goes with you;
	32: 3	Oh, praise the greatness of our **G**!
	32: 4	A faithful **G** who does no wrong,
	33: 27	The eternal **G** is your refuge,
Jos	1: 9	the LORD your **G** will be with you
	14: 8	the LORD my **G** wholeheartedly.
	22: 5	to love the LORD your **G**, to walk
	22: 34	that the LORD is **G**.
	23: 11	careful to love the LORD your **G**.
	23: 14	the LORD your **G** gave you has
Jdg	16: 28	Please, LORD, strengthen me just once
Ru	1: 16	be my people and your **G** my **G**.
1Sa	2: 2	there is no Rock like our **G**.
	2: 3	for the LORD is a **G** who knows,
	2: 25	**G** may mediate for the offender;
	10: 26	men whose hearts **G** had touched.
	12: 12	the LORD your **G** was your king.
	17: 26	defy the armies of the living **G**?"
	17: 46	know that there is a **G** in Israel.
	30: 6	found strength in the LORD his **G**.
2Sa	14: 14	But that is not what **G** desires;
	22: 3	my **G** is my rock, in whom I take
	22: 31	"As for **G**, his way is perfect:
1Ki	4: 29	**G** gave Solomon wisdom and very
	8: 23	there is no **G** like you in heaven
	8: 27	"But will **G** really dwell on earth?
	8: 61	committed to the LORD our **G**,
	18: 21	If the LORD is **G**, follow him;
	18: 37	are **G**, and that you are turning
	20: 28	think the LORD is a **g** the hills
2Ki	19: 15	you alone are **G** over all
1Ch	16: 35	Cry out, "Save us, **G** our Savior,
	28: 2	for the footstool of our **G**, and I
	28: 9	acknowledge the **G** of your father,
	29: 10	LORD, the **G** of our father Israel,
	29: 17	my **G**, that you test the heart and
2Ch	2: 4	for the Name of the LORD my **G**
	5: 14	the LORD filled the temple of **G**.
	6: 18	will **G** really dwell on earth
	18: 13	can tell him only what my **G** says."
	20: 6	you not the **G** who is in heaven?
	25: 8	for **G** has the power to help
	30: 9	for the LORD your **G** is gracious
	33: 12	the favor of the LORD his **G**
Ezr	8: 22	"The gracious hand of our **G** is
	9: 6	my **G**, to lift up my face to you,
	9: 13	our **G**, you have punished us less
Ne	1: 5	the great and awesome **G**,
	8: 8	from the Book of the Law of **G**,
	9: 17	But you are a forgiving **G**,
	9: 32	"Now therefore, our **G**, the great **G**,
Job	1: 1	he feared **G** and shunned evil.
	2: 10	Shall we accept good from **G**,
	4: 17	mortal be more righteous than **G**?
	5: 17	is the one whom **G** corrects;
	11: 7	you fathom the mysteries of **G**?
	19: 26	yet in my flesh I will see **G**;
	22: 13	Yet you say, 'What does **G** know?
	25: 4	a mortal be righteous before **G**?
	33: 14	For **G** does speak—now one way,
	34: 12	unthinkable that **G** would do wrong,
	36: 26	How great is **G**—
	37: 22	**G** comes in awesome majesty.
Ps	18: 2	my **G** is my rock, in whom I take
	18: 28	my **G** turns my darkness into light.
	19: 1	The heavens declare the glory of **G**;
	22: 1	My **G**, my **G**, why have you
	29: 3	the **G** of glory thunders, the LORD
	31: 14	I say, "You are my **G**."

Ps	40: 3	mouth, a hymn of praise to our **G**.
	40: 8	I desire to do your will, my **G**;
	42: 2	My soul thirsts for **G**, for the living
	42: 2	When can I go and meet with **G**?
	42: 11	Put your hope in **G**, for I will yet
	45: 6	O **G**, will last for ever and ever;
	46: 1	**G** is our refuge and strength,
	46: 10	"Be still, and know that I am **G**;
	47: 7	For **G** is the King of all the earth;
	50: 3	Our **G** comes and will not be silent
	51: 1	O **G**, according to your unfailing
	51: 10	O **G**, and renew a steadfast spirit
	51: 17	sacrifice, O **G**, is a broken spirit;
	62: 7	and my honor depend on **G**;
	65: 5	and righteous deeds, **G** our Savior,
	66: 1	Shout for joy to **G**, all the earth!
	66: 16	Come and hear, all you who fear **G**;
	68: 6	**G** sets the lonely in families,
	71: 17	my youth, **G**, you have taught
	71: 19	Who is like you, **G**?
	71: 22	harp for your faithfulness, my **G**;
	73: 26	but **G** is the strength of my heart
	77: 13	What **g** is as great as our **G**?
	78: 19	They spoke against **G**;
	81: 1	Sing for joy to **G** our strength;
	84: 2	my flesh cry out for the living **G**.
	84: 10	the house of my **G** than dwell
	86: 12	you, Lord my **G**, with all my heart;
	89: 7	of the holy ones **G** is greatly feared;
	90: 2	to everlasting you are **G**.
	91: 2	fortress, my **G**, in whom I trust."
	95: 7	for he is our **G** and we are
	100: 3	Know that the LORD is **G**. It is he
	108: 1	My heart, O **G**, is steadfast;
	113: 5	Who is like the LORD our **G**,
	139: 23	Search me, **G**, and know my heart;
Pr	3: 4	a good name in the sight of **G**
	25: 2	It is the glory of **G** to conceal
	30: 5	"Every word of **G** is flawless;
Ecc	3: 11	can fathom what **G** has done
	11: 5	cannot understand the work of **G**,
	12: 13	of the matter: Fear **G** and keep his
Isa	9: 6	Mighty **G**, Everlasting Father,
	37: 16	you alone are **G** over all
	40: 3	in the desert a highway for our **G**.
	40: 8	the word of our **G** endures forever."
	40: 28	The LORD is the everlasting **G**,
	41: 10	not be dismayed, for I am your **G**.
	44: 6	apart from me there is no **G**.
	52: 7	who say to Zion, "Your **G** reigns!"
	55: 7	and to our **G**, for he will freely
	57: 21	says my **G**, "for the wicked."
	59: 2	have separated you from your **G**;
	61: 10	my soul rejoices in my **G**.
	62: 5	so will your **G** rejoice over you.
Jer	23: 23	"Am I only a **G** nearby,"
	31: 33	I will be their **G**, and they will be
	32: 27	the LORD, the **G** of all mankind.
Eze	28: 13	You were in Eden, the garden of **G**;
Da	3: 17	the **G** we serve is able to deliver us
	9: 4	the great and awesome **G**,
Hos	12: 6	But you must return to your **G**;
Joel	2: 13	Return to the LORD your **G**, for he
Am	4: 12	Israel, prepare to meet your **G**."
Mic	6: 8	and to walk humbly with your **G**.
Na	1: 2	is a jealous and avenging **G**;
Zec	14: 5	Then the LORD my **G** will come,
Mal	3: 8	"Will a mere mortal rob **G**?
Mt	1: 23	(which means "**G** with us").
	5: 8	pure in heart, for they will see **G**.
	6: 24	You cannot serve both **G**
	19: 6	Therefore what **G** has joined
	19: 26	but with **G** all things are possible."
	22: 21	Caesar's, and to **G** what is God's."
	22: 37	"'Love the Lord your **G** with all
	27: 46	(which means "My **G**, my **G**,
Mk	12: 29	The Lord our **G**, the Lord is one.
	16: 19	at the right hand of **G**.
Lk	1: 37	For no word from **G** will ever fail."
	1: 47	my spirit rejoices in **G** my Savior,
	10: 9	'The kingdom of **G** has come near
	10: 27	"'Love the Lord your **G** with all
	18: 19	"No one is good—except **G** alone.

Jn 1: 1 and the Word was with **G**, and the Word was **G**.
1: 18 No one has ever seen **G**, but
1: 18 who is himself **G** and is in closest
3: 16 For **G** so loved the world that he
4: 24 **G** is spirit, and his worshipers must
7: 17 to do the will of **G** will find
14: 1 You believe in **G**;
20: 28 said to him, "My Lord and my **G**!"
Ac 2: 24 But **G** raised him from the dead,
5: 4 lied just to human beings but to **G**."
5: 29 "We must obey **G** rather than
7: 55 to heaven and saw the glory of **G**,
17: 23 inscription: TO AN UNKNOWN **G**.
20: 27 to you the whole will of **G**.
20: 32 "Now I commit you to **G**
Ro 1: 17 righteousness of **G** is revealed—
2: 11 For **G** does not show favoritism.
3: 4 Let **G** be true, and every human
3: 23 and fall short of the glory of **G**,
4: 24 **G** will credit righteousness—
5: 8 **G** demonstrates his own love for us
6: 23 the gift of **G** is eternal life in Christ
8: 28 in all things **G** works for the good
11: 22 the kindness and sternness of **G**:
14: 12 give an account of ourselves to **G**.
1Co 1: 20 not **G** made foolish the wisdom
2: 9 the things **G** has prepared for those
3: 6 it, but **G** has been making it grow.
6: 20 Therefore honor **G** with your
7: 24 they were in when **G** called them.
8: 8 food does not bring us near to **G**;
10: 13 **G** is faithful; he will not let you
10: 31 you do, do it all for the glory of **G**.
14: 33 For **G** is not a **G** of disorder
15: 28 him, so that **G** may be all in all.
2Co 1: 9 not rely on ourselves but on **G**,
2: 14 But thanks be to **G**, who always
3: 5 our competence comes from **G**.
4: 7 this all-surpassing power is from **G**
5: 19 that **G** was reconciling the world
5: 21 become the righteousness of **G**.
6: 16 we are the temple of the living **G**.
9: 7 for **G** loves a cheerful giver.
9: 8 **G** is able to bless you abundantly,
Gal 2: 6 **G** does not show favoritism—
6: 7 **G** cannot be mocked.
Eph 2: 10 **G** prepared in advance for us
4: 6 one **G** and Father of all, who is
Php 2: 6 being in very nature **G**, did not consider equality
with **G**
4: 19 And my **G** will meet all your needs
1Th 2: 4 not trying to please people but **G**,
4: 7 For **G** did not call us to be impure,
4: 9 yourselves have been taught by **G**
5: 9 For **G** did not appoint us to suffer
1Ti 2: 5 there is one **G** and one mediator
4: 4 For everything **G** created is good,
5: 4 for this is pleasing to **G**.
Titus 2: 13 of the glory of our great **G**
Heb 1: 1 the past **G** spoke to our ancestors
4: 12 For the word of **G** is alive
6: 10 **G** is not unjust; he will not forget
10: 31 fall into the hands of the living **G**.
11: 6 faith it is impossible to please **G**,
12: 10 but **G** disciplines us for our good,
12: 29 for our "**G** is a consuming fire."
13: 15 us continually offer to **G** a sacrifice
Jas 1: 13 For **G** cannot be tempted by evil,
2: 19 You believe that there is one **G**.
2: 23 "Abraham believed **G**, and it was
4: 4 the world becomes an enemy of **G**.
4: 8 Come near to **G** and he will come
1Pe 4: 11 who speaks the very words of **G**.
2Pe 1: 21 from **G** as they were carried along
1Jn 1: 5 him and declare to you: **G** is light;
2: 5 love for **G** is truly made complete
3: 20 that **G** is greater than our hearts,
4: 7 another, for love comes from **G**.
4: 7 has been born of **G** and knows **G**.
4: 9 This is how **G** showed his love
4: 11 Dear friends, since **G** so loved us,
4: 12 No one has ever seen **G**; but if we
4: 16 Whoever lives in love lives in **G**,

Rev 4: 8 holy is the Lord **G** Almighty,'
7: 17 **G** will wipe away every tear
19: 6 For our Lord **G** Almighty reigns.
GOD-BREATHED (BREATHED)
2Ti 3: 16 All Scripture is **G** and is useful
GODLINESS (GOD)
1Ti 2: 2 quiet lives in all **g** and holiness.
4: 8 value, but **g** has value for all things,
6: 6 **g** with contentment is great gain.
6: 11 and pursue righteousness, **g**, faith,
GODLY (GOD)
2Co 7: 10 **G** sorrow brings repentance
11: 2 jealous for you with a **g** jealousy.
2Ti 3: 12 live a **g** life in Christ Jesus will be
2Pe 3: 11 You ought to live holy and **g** lives
GOD'S (GOD)
2Ch 20: 15 For the battle is not yours, but **G**.
Job 37: 14 stop and consider **G** wonders.
Ps 52: 8 I trust in **G** unfailing love for ever
69: 30 I will praise **G** name in song
Mk 3: 35 Whoever does **G** will is my brother
Jn 10: 36 because I said, 'I am **G** Son'?
Ro 2: 3 think you will escape **G** judgment?
2: 4 that **G** kindness is intended
3: 3 nullify **G** faithfulness?
7: 22 my inner being I delight in **G** law;
9: 16 desire or effort, but on **G** mercy.
11: 29 for **G** gifts and his call are
12: 2 test and approve what **G** will is—
13: 6 for the authorities are **G** servants,
1Co 7: 19 Keeping **G** commands is what
2Co 6: 2 now is the time of **G** favor, now is
Eph 1: 7 with the riches of **G** grace
5: 1 Follow **G** example, therefore,
1Th 4: 3 It is **G** will that you should be
5: 18 for this is **G** will for you in Christ
1Ti 6: 1 so that **G** name and our teaching
2Ti 2: 19 **G** solid foundation stands firm,
Titus 1: 7 an overseer manages **G** household,
Heb 1: 3 The Son is the radiance of **G** glory
9: 24 to appear for us in **G** presence.
11: 3 was formed at **G** command,
1Pe 2: 15 For it is **G** will that by doing good
3: 4 which is of great worth in **G** sight.
GODS (GOD)
Ex 20: 3 shall have no other **g** before me.
Ac 19: 26 by human hands are no **g** at all.
GOLD
Job 23: 10 tested me, I will come forth as **g**.
Ps 19: 10 precious than **g**, than much pure **g**;
119:127 love your commands more than **g**,
Pr 22: 1 esteemed is better than silver or **g**.
GOLGOTHA
Jn 19: 17 (which in Aramaic is called **G**).
GOLIATH
Philistine giant killed by David (1Sa 17; 21:9).
GOOD
Ge 1: 4 God saw that the light was **g**,
1: 31 he had made, and it was very **g**.
2: 18 "It is not **g** for the man to be alone.
50: 20 God intended it for **g**
Job 2: 10 Shall we accept **g** from God,
Ps 14: 1 there is no one who does **g**.
34: 8 Taste and see that the LORD is **g**;
37: 3 Trust in the LORD and do **g**;
84: 11 no **g** thing does he withhold
86: 5 are forgiving and **g**,
103: 5 your desires with **g** things so
119: 68 You are **g**, and what you do is **g**;
133: 1 How **g** and pleasant it is
147: 1 How **g** it is to sing praises to our
Pr 3: 4 and a **g** name in the sight of God
11: 27 Whoever seeks **g** finds favor,
13: 21 are rewarded with **g** things.
17: 22 A cheerful heart is **g** medicine,
18: 22 He who finds a wife finds what is **g**
22: 1 A **g** name is more desirable than
31: 12 She brings him **g**, not harm,
Isa 5: 20 Woe to those who call evil **g** and **g**
52: 7 the feet of those who bring **g** news,
Jer 6: 16 ask where the **g** way is, and walk
Mic 6: 8 shown you, O mortal, what is **g**.

Mt   5: 45 sun to rise on the evil and the **g**,
       7: 17 Likewise, every **g** tree bears **g** fruit,
      12: 35 A **g** man brings **g** things out of the **g**
      19: 17 "There is only One who is **g**.
      25: 21 'Well done, **g** and faithful servant!
Mk   3:   4 to do **g** or to do evil, to save life
       8: 36 What **g** is it for someone to gain
Lk   6: 27 do **g** to those who hate you,
Jn   10: 11 "I am the **g** shepherd. The **g**
Ro   8: 28 for the **g** of those who love him,
      10: 15 feet of those who bring **g** news!"
      12:   9 Hate what is evil; cling to what is **g**.
1Co   10: 24 their own, but the **g** of others.
      15: 33 company corrupts **g** character."
2Co   9:   8 you will abound in every **g** work.
Gal   6:   9 us not become weary in doing **g**,
       6: 10 let us do **g** to all people,
Eph   2: 10 in Christ Jesus to do **g** works,
Php   1:   6 he who began a **g** work in you will
1Th   5: 21 test them all; hold on to what is **g**,
2Th   3: 13 never tire of doing what is **g**.
1Ti   3:   7 have a **g** reputation with outsiders,
       4:   4 For everything God created is **g**,
       6: 12 Fight the **g** fight of the faith.
       6: 18 do **g**, to be rich in **g** deeds,
2Ti   3: 17 equipped for every **g** work.
       4:   7 I have fought the **g** fight, I have
Heb   12: 10 but God disciplines us for our **g**,
1Pe   2:   3 you have tasted that the Lord is **g**.
       2: 12 Live such **g** lives among the pagans
GOSPEL
Ro   1: 16 For I am not ashamed of the **g**,
      15: 16 duty of proclaiming the **g** of God,
1Co   1: 17 to baptize, but to preach the **g**—
       9: 16 Woe to me if I do not preach the **g**!
      15:   1 to remind you of the **g** I preached
Gal   1:   7 trying to pervert the **g** of Christ.
Php   1: 27 a manner worthy of the **g** of Christ.
       1: 27 as one for the faith of the **g**
GOSSIP
Pr   11: 13 A **g** betrays a confidence,
      16: 28 and a **g** separates close friends.
      18:   8 of a **g** are like choice morsels;
      26: 20 without a **g** a quarrel dies down.
2Co   12: 20 slander, **g**, arrogance and disorder.
GOVERNED
Ro   8:   6 the mind **g** by the Spirit is life
GRACE (GRACIOUS)
Ps   45:   2 lips have been anointed with **g**,
Jn   1: 17 **g** and truth came through Jesus
Ac   20: 32 to God and to the word of his **g**,
Ro   3: 24 by his **g** through the redemption
       5: 15 that came by the **g** of the one man,
       5: 17 God's abundant provision of **g**
       5: 20 increased, **g** increased all the more,
       6: 14 are not under the law, but under **g**.
      11:   6 if it were, **g** would no longer be **g**.
2Co   6:   1 you not to receive God's **g** in vain.
       8:   9 you know the **g** of our Lord Jesus
      12:   9 to me, "My **g** is sufficient for you,
Gal   2: 21 I do not set aside the **g** of God,
       5:   4 you have fallen away from **g**.
Eph   1:   7 with the riches of God's **g**
       2:   5 it is by **g** you have been saved.
       2:   7 the incomparable riches of his **g**,
       2:   8 For it is by **g** you have been saved,
Php   1:   7 all of you share in God's **g** with me.
Col   4:   6 conversation be always full of **g**,
2Th   2: 16 **g** gave us eternal encouragement
2Ti   2:   1 be strong in the **g** that is in Christ
Titus 2: 11 For the **g** of God has appeared
       3:   7 having been justified by his **g**,
Heb   2:   9 the **g** of God he might taste death
       4: 16 approach God's throne of **g**
       4: 16 **g** to help us in our time of need.
Jas   4:   6 But he gives us more **g**. That is why
2Pe   3: 18 grow in the **g** and knowledge of
GRACIOUS (GRACE)
Nu   6: 25 face shine on you and be **g** to you;
Isa   30: 18 the Lᴏʀᴅ longs to be **g** to you;
GRAIN
Ecc   11:   1 Ship your **g** across the sea;
1Co   9:   9 an ox while it is treading out the **g**."

GRANTED
Php   1: 29 For it has been **g** to you on behalf
GRASS
Ps   103: 15 The life of mortals is like **g**,
1Pe   1: 24 the **g** withers and the flowers fall,
GRAVE (GRAVES)
Pr   7: 27 Her house is a highway to the **g**,
Hos   13: 14 Where, O **g**, is your destruction?
GRAVES (GRAVE)
Jn   5: 28 are in their **g** will hear his voice
Ro   3: 13 "Their throats are open **g**;
GREAT (GREATER GREATEST GREATNESS)
Ge   12:   2 "I will make you into a **g** nation,
Dt   10: 17 gods and Lord of lords, the **g** God,
2Sa   22: 36 your help has made me **g**.
Ps   19: 11 in keeping them there is a **g** reward.
      89:   1 sing of the Lᴏʀᴅ's **g** love forever;
     103: 11 so **g** is his love for those who fear
     108:   4 For **g** is your love, higher than
     119:165 **G** peace have those who love your
     145:   3 **G** is the Lᴏʀᴅ and most worthy
Pr   23: 24 father of a righteous child has **g** joy
Isa   42: 21 his righteousness to make his law **g**
La   3: 23 **g** is your faithfulness.
Mk   10: 43 become **g** among you must be your
Lk   21: 27 in a cloud with power and **g** glory.
1Ti   6:   6 with contentment is **g** gain.
Titus 2: 13 appearing the glory of our **g** God
Heb   2:   3 if we ignore so **g** a salvation?
1Jn   3:   1 See what **g** love the Father has
GREATER (GREAT)
Mk   12: 31 is no commandment **g** than these."
Jn   1: 50 You will see **g** things than that."
      15: 13 **G** love has no one than this:
1Co   12: 31 Now eagerly desire the **g** gifts.
Heb   11: 26 as of **g** value than the treasures
1Jn   3: 20 that God is **g** than our hearts,
       4:   4 is in you is **g** than the one who is
GREATEST (GREAT)
Mt   22: 38 is the first and **g** commandment.
Lk   9: 48 least among you all who is the **g**."
1Co   13: 13 But the **g** of these is love.
GREATNESS (GREAT)
Ps   145:   3 his **g** no one can fathom.
     150:   2 praise him for his surpassing **g**.
Isa   9:   7 the **g** of his government and peace
      63:   1 forward in the **g** of his strength?
GREED (GREEDY)
Lk   12: 15 guard against all kinds of **g**;
Ro   1: 29 wickedness, evil, **g** and depravity.
Eph   5:   3 or of **g**, because these are improper
Col   3:   5 desires and **g**, which is idolatry.
2Pe   2: 14 they are experts in **g**—
GREEDY (GREED)
Pr   15: 27 The **g** bring ruin to their
1Co   6: 10 thieves nor the **g** nor drunkards
Eph   5:   5 No immoral, impure or **g** person—
GREEN
Ps   23:   2 makes me lie down in **g** pastures,
GREW (GROW)
Lk   2: 52 And Jesus **g** in wisdom and stature,
Ac   16:   5 in the faith and **g** daily in numbers.
GRIEF (GRIEVE)
Ps   10: 14 you consider their **g** and take it
Pr   14: 13 ache, and rejoicing may end in **g**.
La   3: 32 Though he brings **g**, he will show
Jn   16: 20 grieve, but your **g** will turn to joy.
1Pe   1:   6 have had to suffer **g** in all kinds
GRIEVE (GRIEF)
Eph   4: 30 do not **g** the Holy Spirit of God,
1Th   4: 13 so that you do not **g** like the rest
GROUND
Ge   3: 17 it,' "Cursed is the **g** because of you;
Ex   3:   5 where you are standing is holy **g**."
Eph   6: 13 you may be able to stand your **g**,
GROW (GREW)
Pr   13: 11 money little by little makes it **g**.
1Co   3:   6 it, but God has been making it **g**.
2Pe   3: 18 But **g** in the grace and knowledge
GRUMBLE (GRUMBLING)
1Co   10: 10 do not **g**, as some of them did—
Jas   5:   9 Don't **g** against one another,

GRUMBLING (GRUMBLE)
Jn   6: 43   "Stop **g** among yourselves,"
1Pe   4:   9   hospitality to one another without **g**.
GUARANTEEING (GUARANTOR)
2Co   1: 22   as a deposit, **g** what is to come.
Eph   1: 14   is a deposit **g** our inheritance until
GUARANTOR (GUARANTEEING)
Heb   7: 22   Jesus has become the **g** of a better
GUARD (GUARDIAN, GUARDIAN-REDEEMER)
Ps 141:   3   Set a **g** over my mouth, LORD;
Pr   4: 23   Above all else, **g** your heart,
         13:   3   Those who **g** their lips preserve
         21: 23   Those who **g** their mouths and
Isa   52: 12   God of Israel will be your rear **g**.
Mk   13: 33   Be on **g**! Be alert! You do not know
1Co 16: 13   Be on your **g**; stand firm
Php   4:   7   will **g** your hearts and your minds
1Ti   6: 20   **g** what has been entrusted to your
GUARDIAN (GUARD)
Gal   3: 25   come, we are no longer under a **g**.
GUARDIAN-REDEEMER (GUARD)
Ru   3:   9   since you are a **g** of our family."
GUIDE
Ex   13: 21   of cloud to **g** them on their way
         15: 13   In your strength you will **g** them
Ne   9: 19   cloud did not fail to **g** them on
Ps   25:   5   **G** me in your truth and teach me,
         48: 14   he will be our **g** even to the end.
         67:   4   and **g** the nations of the earth.
         73: 24   You **g** me with your counsel,
       139: 10   even there your hand will **g** me,
Pr   6: 22   When you walk, they will **g** you;
Isa   58: 11   The LORD will **g** you always;
Jn   16: 13   he will **g** you into all the truth.
GUILTY
Ex   34:   7   does not leave the **g** unpunished;
Jn   8: 46   Can any of you prove me **g** of sin?
Heb 10: 22   to cleanse us from a **g** conscience
Jas   2: 10   at just one point is **g** of breaking all
HADES
Mt   16: 18   the gates of **H** will not overcome it.
Lk   16: 23   In **H**, where he was in torment,
HAGAR
Servant of Sarah, wife of Abraham, mother of Ishmael (Ge 16:1–6; 25:12). Driven away by Sarah while pregnant (Ge 16:5–16); after birth of Isaac (Ge 21:9–21; Gal 4:21–31).
HAGGAI
Post-exilic prophet who encouraged rebuilding of the temple (Ezr 5:1; 6:14; Hag 1–2).
HAIR (HAIRS)
Lk   21: 18   not a **h** of your head will perish.
1Co 11:   6   for a woman to have her **h** cut off
HAIRS (HAIR)
Mt   10: 30   even the very **h** of your head are all
HALLELUJAH
Rev 19:   1, multitude in heaven shouting: "**H**!
HALLOWED (HOLY)
Mt   6:   9   Father in heaven, **h** be your name,
HAND (HANDIWORK HANDS)
Ps   16:   8   With him at my right **h**, I will not
         37: 24   the LORD upholds him with his **h**.
       139: 10   even there your **h** will guide me,
Ecc   9: 10   Whatever your **h** finds to do, do it
Mt   6:   3   not let your left **h** know what your right **h** is doing,
Jn   10: 28   one will snatch them out of my **h**.
1Co 12: 15   say, "Because I am not a **h**, I do not
HANDIWORK (HAND WORK)
Eph   2: 10   For we are God's **h**,
HANDS (HAND)
Ps   22: 16   they pierce my **h** and my feet.
         24:   4   one who has clean **h** and a pure
         31:   5   Into your **h** I commit my spirit;
         31: 15   My times are in your **h**;
Pr   10:   4   but diligent **h** bring wealth.
         31: 20   and extends her **h** to the needy.
Isa   55: 12   trees of the field will clap their **h**.
         65:   2   out my **h** to an obstinate people,
Lk   23: 46   into your **h** I commit my spirit."
1Th   4: 11   business and work with your **h**,
1Ti   2:   8   lifting up holy **h** without anger
         5: 22   not be hasty in the laying on of **h**,

HANNAH
Wife of Elkanah, mother of Samuel (1Sa 1). Prayer at dedication of Samuel (1Sa 2:1–10). Blessed (1Sa 2:18–21).
HAPPY
Ps   68:   3   may they be **h** and joyful.
Pr   15: 13   A **h** heart makes the face cheerful,
Ecc   3: 12   better for people than to be **h**
Jas   5: 13   Is anyone **h**? Let them sing songs
HARD (HARDEN HARDSHIP)
Ge   18: 14   Is anything too **h** for the LORD?
Ps 118:   5   When **h** pressed, I cried
Mt   19: 23   it is **h** for someone who is rich
1Co   4: 12   We work **h** with our own hands.
1Th   5: 12   those who work **h** among you,
HARDEN (HARD)
Ro   9: 18   he hardens whom he wants to **h**.
Heb   3:   8   do not **h** your hearts as you did
HARDHEARTED (HEART)
Dt   15:   7   do not be **h** or tightfisted toward
HARDSHIP (HARD)
Ro   8: 35   Shall trouble or **h** or persecution
2Ti   4:   5   endure **h**, do the work
Heb 12:   7   Endure **h** as discipline;
HARM
Ps 121:   6   the sun will not **h** you by day,
Pr   3: 29   not plot **h** against your neighbor,
         31: 12   good, not **h**, all the days of her life.
Ro   13: 10   Love does no **h** to a neighbor.
1Jn   5: 18   and the evil one cannot **h** them.
HARMONY
Ro   12: 16   Live in **h** with one another.
2Co   6: 15   What **h** is there between Christ
HARVEST
Mt   9: 37   "The **h** is plentiful but the workers
Jn   4: 35   at the fields! They are ripe for **h**.
Gal   6:   9   at the proper time we will reap a **h**
Heb 12: 11   it produces a **h** of righteousness
HASTE (HASTY)
Pr   21:   5   lead to profit as surely as **h** leads
         29: 20   you see someone who speaks in **h**?
HASTY (HASTE)
Pr   19:   2   how much more will **h** feet miss
Ecc   5:   2   do not be **h** in your heart to utter
1Ti   5: 22   Do not be **h** in the laying
HATE (HATED HATES HATRED)
Lev 19: 17   " 'Do not **h** a fellow Israelite
Ps   5:   5   You **h** all who do wrong;
         45:   7   righteousness and **h** wickedness;
         97: 10   those who love the LORD **h** evil,
       139: 21   Do I not **h** those who **h** you,
Pr   8: 13   To fear the LORD is to **h** evil; I **h**
Am   5: 15   **H** evil, love good;
Mt   5: 43   your neighbor and **h** your enemy.'
Lk   6: 27   do good to those who **h** you,
Ro   12:   9   **H** what is evil; cling to what is
HATED (HATE)
Mt   10: 22   be **h** by everyone because of me,
Ro   9: 13   "Jacob I loved, but Esau I **h**."
Eph   5: 29   all, no one ever **h** their own body,
Heb   1:   9   righteousness and **h** wickedness;
HATES (HATE)
Pr   6: 16   There are six things the LORD **h**,
         13: 24   spares the rod **h** their children,
Mal   2: 16   "The man who **h** and divorces his
Jn   3: 20   Everyone who does evil **h** the light,
1Jn   2:   9   to be in the light but **h** a brother
HATRED (HATE)
Pr   10: 12   **H** stirs up conflict, but love covers
HAUGHTY
Pr   16: 18   destruction, a **h** spirit before a fall.
HAY
1Co   3: 12   costly stones, wood, **h** or straw,
HEAD (HEADS HOTHEADED)
Ge   3: 15   he will crush your **h**, and you will
Ps   23:   5   You anoint my **h** with oil;
Pr   25: 22   will heap burning coals on his **h**,
Isa   59: 17   the helmet of salvation on his **h**;
Mt   8: 20   of Man has no place to lay his **h**."
Ro   12: 20   will heap burning coals on his **h**."
1Co 11:   3   the **h** of every man is Christ, and the **h** of the woman is man, and the **h** of Christ is God.
         12: 21   And the **h** cannot say to the feet,

Eph 5: 23 the husband is the **h** of the wife as Christ is the **h**
2Ti 4: 5 keep your **h** in all situations,
Rev 19: 12 fire, and on his **h** are many crowns.

HEADS (HEAD)
Lev 26: 13 you to walk with **h** held high.
Isa 35: 10 everlasting joy will crown their **h**.

HEAL (HEALED HEALING HEALS)
2Ch 7: 14 their sin and will **h** their land.
Ps 41: 4 **h** me, for I have sinned against
Mt 10: 8 **H** the sick, raise the dead,
Lk   4: 23 'Physician, **h** yourself!'
     5: 17 Lord was with Jesus to **h** the sick.

HEALED (HEAL)
Isa 53: 5 him, and by his wounds we are **h**.
Mt   9: 22 he said, "your faith has **h** you."
    14: 36 and all who touched it were **h**.
Ac   4: 10 that this man stands before you **h**.
    14: 9 saw that he had faith to be **h**
Jas 5: 16 each other so that you may be **h**.
1Pe 2: 24 "by his wounds you have been **h**."

HEALING (HEAL)
Eze 47: 12 for food and their leaves for **h**."
Mal 4: 2 righteousness will rise with **h** in its
1Co 12: 9 to another gifts of **h** by that one
    12: 30 Do all have gifts of **h**? Do all speak
Rev 22: 2 the tree are for the **h** of the nations.

HEALS (HEAL)
Ex 15: 26 for I am the LORD, who **h** you."
Ps 103: 3 your sins and **h** all your diseases,
   147: 3 He **h** the brokenhearted and binds

HEALTH (HEALTHY)
Pr   3: 8 This will bring **h** to your body
    15: 30 good news gives **h** to the bones.

HEALTHY (HEALTH)
Mk   2: 17 "It is not the **h** who need a doctor,

HEAR (HEARD HEARING HEARS)
Dt   6: 4 **H**, O Israel: The LORD our God,
    31: 13 law, must **h** it and learn to fear
2Ch 7: 14 then I will **h** from heaven,
Ps 94: 9 he who fashioned the ear not **h**?
Isa 29: 18 day the deaf will **h** the words
    65: 24 they are still speaking I will **h**.
Mt 11: 15 Whoever has ears, let them **h**.
Jn   8: 47 The reason you do not **h** is that
2Ti 4: 3 what their itching ears want to **h**.

HEARD (HEAR)
Job 42: 5 My ears had **h** of you but now my
Isa 66: 8 Who has ever **h** of such things?
Mt   5: 21 "You have **h** that it was said
     5: 27 "You have **h** that it was said,
     5: 33 you have **h** that it was said
     5: 38 "You have **h** that it was said,
     5: 43 "You have **h** that it was said,
1Co 2: 9 what no ear has **h**, and what no
1Th 2: 13 which you **h** from us, you accepted
2Ti 1: 13 What you **h** from me, keep as
Jas 1: 25 not forgetting what they have **h**,

HEARING (HEAR)
Ro 10: 17 faith comes from **h** the message,

HEARS (HEAR)
Jn   5: 24 whoever **h** my word and believes
1Jn 5: 14 according to his will, he **h** us.
Rev 3: 20 If anyone **h** my voice and opens

HEART (BROKENHEARTED HARDHEARTED HEARTS
        WHOLEHEARTEDLY)
Ex 25: 2 everyone whose **h** prompts them
Lev 19: 17 not hate a fellow Israelite in your **h**.
Dt   4: 29 him if you seek him with all your **h**
     6: 5 LORD your God with all your **h**
    10: 12 LORD your God with all your **h**
    15: 10 and do so without a grudging **h**;
    30: 6 you may love him with all your **h**
    30: 10 LORD your God with all your **h**
Jos 22: 5 and to serve him with all your **h**
1Sa 13: 14 sought out a man after his own **h**
    16: 7 but the LORD looks at the **h**."
2Ki 23: 3 and decrees with all his **h** and
1Ch 28: 9 for the LORD searches every **h**
2Ch 7: 16 eyes and my **h** will always be there.
Job 22: 22 and lay up his words in your **h**.
    37: 1 "At this my **h** pounds and leaps
Ps 14: 1 says in his **h**, "There is no God."

Ps 19: 14 this meditation of my **h** be pleasing
    37: 4 will give you the desires of your **h**.
    45: 1 My **h** is stirred by a noble theme as
    51: 10 Create in me a pure **h**, O God,
    51: 17 a broken and contrite **h** you, God,
    66: 18 If I had cherished sin in my **h**,
    86: 11 give me an undivided **h**, that I may
   119: 11 in my **h** that I might not sin against
   139: 23 Search me, God, and know my **h**;
Pr   3: 5 Trust in the LORD with all your **h**
     4: 21 sight, keep them within your **h**;
     4: 23 guard your **h**, for everything you
     7: 3 write them on the tablet of your **h**.
    13: 12 Hope deferred makes the **h** sick,
    14: 13 Even in laughter the **h** may ache,
    15: 30 eyes brings joy to the **h**, and good
    17: 22 A cheerful **h** is good medicine,
    24: 17 stumble, do not let your **h** rejoice,
    27: 19 the face, so one's life reflects the **h**.
Ecc 3: 11 also set eternity in the human **h**;
     8: 5 the wise **h** will know the proper
SS   4: 9 You have stolen my **h**, my sister,
Isa 40: 11 and carries them close to his **h**;
    57: 15 and to revive the **h** of the contrite.
Jer 17: 9 The **h** is deceitful above all things
    29: 13 when you seek me with all your **h**.
Eze 36: 26 I will give you a new **h** and put
Mt   5: 8 Blessed are the pure in **h**, for they
     6: 21 treasure is, there your **h** will be
    12: 34 mouth speaks what the **h** is full of.
    22: 37 the Lord your God with all your **h**
Lk   6: 45 mouth speaks what the **h** is full of.
Ro   2: 29 is circumcision of the **h**,
    10: 10 it is with your **h** that you believe
Eph 5: 19 music from your **h** to the Lord,
     6: 6 doing the will of God from your **h**.
Col 3: 23 you do, work at it with all your **h**,
1Pe 1: 22 one another deeply, from the **h**.

HEARTS (HEART)
Dt 11: 18 These words of mine in your **h**
1Ki 8: 39 do, since you know their **h** (for you
     8: 61 may your **h** be fully committed
Ps 62: 8 pour out your **h** to him, for God is
Jer 31: 33 their minds and write it on their **h**.
Lk 16: 15 of others, but God knows your **h**.
    24: 32 "Were not our **h** burning within us
Jn 14: 1 "Do not let your **h** be troubled.
Ac 15: 9 for he purified their **h** by faith.
Ro   2: 15 of the law are written on their **h**,
1Co 14: 25 the secrets of their **h** are laid bare.
2Co 3: 2 written on our **h**, known and read
     3: 3 of stone but on tablets of human **h**.
     4: 6 shine in our **h** to give us the light
Eph 3: 17 may dwell in your **h** through faith.
Col 3: 1 Christ, set your **h** on things above,
Heb 3: 8 do not harden your **h** as you did
    10: 16 I will put my laws in their **h**, and I
1Jn 3: 20 that God is greater than our **h**,

HEAT
2Pe 3: 12 and the elements will melt in the **h**.

HEAVEN (HEAVENLY HEAVENS)
Ge 14: 19 Most High, Creator of **h** and earth.
1Ki 8: 27 even the highest **h**, cannot contain
2Ki 2: 1 take Elijah up to **h** in a whirlwind,
2Ch 7: 14 then I will hear from **h**, and I will
Isa 14: 12 How you have fallen from **h**,
    66: 1 "**H** is my throne, and the earth is
Da   7: 13 man, coming with the clouds of **h**.
Mt   6: 9 "'Our Father in **h**, hallowed be
     6: 20 up for yourselves treasures in **h**,
    16: 19 you the keys of the kingdom of **h**;
    16: 19 bind on earth will be bound in **h**,
    19: 23 is rich to enter the kingdom of **h**.
    24: 35 **H** and earth will pass away, but my
    26: 64 and coming on the clouds of **h**.
    28: 18 "All authority in **h** and on earth has
Mk 16: 19 *was taken up into* **h**
Lk 15: 7 **h** over one sinner who repents
    18: 22 and you will have treasure in **h**.
Ro 10: 6 heart, 'Who will ascend into **h**?'"
2Co 5: 1 an eternal house in **h**, not built
    12: 2 ago was caught up to the third **h**.
Php 2: 10 in **h** and on earth and under

Php 3: 20 But our citizenship is in **h**.
1Th 1: 10 and to wait for his Son from **h**,
Heb 8: 5 a copy and shadow of what is in **h**.
9: 24 he entered **h** itself, now to appear
2Pe 3: 13 we are looking forward to a new **h**
Rev 21: 1 I saw "a new **h** and a new earth,"

HEAVENLY (HEAVEN)
2Co 5: 2 clothed instead with our **h** dwelling,
Eph 1: 3 who has blessed us in the **h** realms
1: 20 at his right hand in the **h** realms,
2Ti 4: 18 bring me safely to his **h** kingdom.
Heb 12: 22 of the living God, the **h** Jerusalem.

HEAVENS (HEAVEN)
Ge 1: 1 In the beginning God created the **h**
1Ki 8: 27 The **h**, even the highest heaven,
2Ch 2: 6 since the **h**, even the highest **h**,
Ps 8: 3 When I consider your **h**, the work
19: 1 The **h** declare the glory of God;
102: 25 the **h** are the work of your hands.
108: 4 is your love, higher than the **h**;
119: 89 it stands firm in the **h**.
139: 8 If I go up to the **h**, you are there;
Isa 51: 6 the **h** will vanish like smoke,
55: 9 "As the **h** are higher than the earth,
65: 17 will create new **h** and a new earth.
Joel 2: 30 I will show wonders in the **h**
Eph 4: 10 ascended higher than all the **h**,
2Pe 3: 10 The **h** will disappear with a roar;

HEBREW
Ge 14: 13 and reported this to Abram the **H**.

HEEDS
Pr 13: 1 A wise son **h** his father's
13: 18 whoever **h** correction is honored.
15: 5 but whoever **h** correction shows
15: 32 but the one who **h** correction gains

HEEL
Ge 3: 15 head, and you will strike his **h**."

HEIRS (INHERIT)
Ro 8: 17 **h** of God and co-heirs with Christ,
Gal 3: 29 and **h** according to the promise.
Eph 3: 6 gospel the Gentiles are **h** together
1Pe 3: 7 as **h** with you of the gracious gift

HELL
Mt 5: 22 will be in danger of the fire of **h**.
2Pe 2: 4 but sent them to **h**, putting them

HELMET
Isa 59: 17 and the **h** of salvation on his head;
Eph 6: 17 Take the **h** of salvation
1Th 5: 8 and the hope of salvation as a **h**.

HELP (HELPED HELPER HELPING HELPS)
2Sa 22: 36 You make your saving **h** my shield;
Ps 18: 6 I cried to my God for **h**.
30: 2 called to you for **h**, and you healed
46: 1 an ever-present **h** in trouble.
70: 4 long for your saving **h** always say,
79: 9 **H** us, God our Savior, for the glory
121: 1 where does my **h** come from?
Isa 41: 10 I will strengthen you and **h** you;
Jnh 2: 2 the realm of the dead I called for **h**,
Mk 9: 24 **h** me overcome my unbelief!"
Ac 16: 9 over to Macedonia and **h** us."

HELPED (HELP)
1Sa 7: 12 "Thus far the LORD has **h** us."

HELPER (HELP)
Ge 2: 18 I will make a **h** suitable for him."
Ps 10: 14 you are the **h** of the fatherless.
Heb 13: 6 confidence, "The Lord is my **h**;

HELPING (HELP)
Ac 9: 36 always doing good and **h** the poor.
1Co 12: 28 gifts of healing, of **h**, of guidance,
1Ti 5: 10 **h** those in trouble and devoting

HELPS (HELP)
Ro 8: 26 the Spirit **h** us in our weakness.

HEN
Mt 23: 37 as a **h** gathers her chicks under her

HERITAGE (INHERIT)
Ps 127: 3 Children are a **h** from the LORD,

HEROD
1. King of Judea who tried to kill Jesus (Mt 2; Lk 1:5).
2. Son of 1. Tetrarch of Galilee who arrested and beheaded John the Baptist (Mt 14:1–12; Mk 6:14–29; Lk 3:1, 19–20; 9:7–9); tried Jesus (Lk 23:6–15).

3. Grandson of 1. King of Judea who killed James (Ac 12:2); arrested Peter (Ac 12:3–19). Death (Ac 12:19–23).

HERODIAS
Wife of Herod the Tetrarch who persuaded her daughter to ask for John the Baptist's head (Mt 14:1–12; Mk 6:14–29).

HEZEKIAH
King of Judah. Restored the temple and worship (2Ch 29–31). Sought the LORD for help against Assyria (2Ki 18–19; 2Ch 32:1–23; Isa 36–37). Illness healed (2Ki 20:1–11; 2Ch 32:24–26; Isa 38). Judged for showing Babylonians his treasures (2Ki 20:12–21; 2Ch 32:31; Isa 39).

HID (HIDE)
Ge 3: 8 they **h** from the LORD God among
Ex 2: 2 child, she **h** him for three months.
Jos 6: 17 because she **h** the spies we sent.
Heb 11: 23 faith Moses' parents **h** him for

HIDDEN (HIDE)
Ps 19: 12 Forgive my **h** faults.
119: 11 I have **h** your word in my heart
Pr 2: 4 and search for it as for **h** treasure,
Isa 59: 2 your sins have **h** his face from you,
Mt 5: 14 A town built on a hill cannot be **h**.
13: 44 heaven is like treasure **h** in a field.
Col 1: 26 that has been kept **h** for ages
2: 3 in whom are **h** all the treasures
3: 3 and your life is now **h** with Christ

HIDE (HID HIDDEN)
Ps 17: 8 **h** me in the shadow of your wings
143: 9 LORD, for I **h** myself in you.

HIGH
Isa 57: 15 "I live in a **h** and holy place,

HILL (HILLS)
Mt 5: 14 town built on a **h** cannot be hidden.

HILLS (HILL)
Ps 50: 10 and the cattle on a thousand **h**.

HINDER (HINDERS)
1Sa 14: 6 Nothing can **h** the LORD
Mt 19: 14 do not **h** them, for the kingdom
1Co 9: 12 anything rather than **h** the gospel
1Pe 3: 7 so that nothing will **h** your prayers.

HINDERS (HINDER)
Heb 12: 1 let us throw off everything that **h**

HINT
Eph 5: 3 you there must not be even a **h**

HOLD
Ex 20: 7 LORD will not **h** anyone guiltless
Lev 19: 13 "'Do not **h** back the wages
Jos 22: 5 to **h** fast to him and to serve him
Ps 73: 23 you **h** me by my right hand.
Pr 4: 4 "Take **h** of my words with all your
Isa 54: 2 tent curtains wide, do not **h** back;
Mk 11: 25 if you **h** anything against anyone,
Php 2: 16 as you **h** firmly to the word of life.
3: 12 which Christ Jesus took **h** of me.
Col 1: 17 and in him all things **h** together.
1Th 5: 21 test them all; **h** on to what is good,
1Ti 6: 12 Take **h** of the eternal life
Heb 10: 23 Let us **h** unswervingly to the hope

HOLINESS (HOLY)
Ex 15: 11 majestic in **h**, awesome in glory,
Ps 29: 2 the LORD in the splendor of his **h**.
96: 9 the LORD in the splendor of his **h**;
Ro 6: 19 to righteousness leading to **h**.
2Co 7: 1 perfecting **h** out of reverence
Eph 4: 24 God in true righteousness and **h**.
Heb 12: 10 in order that we may share in his **h**.
12: 14 without **h** no one will see the Lord.

HOLY (HALLOWED HOLINESS)
Ex 19: 6 kingdom of priests and a **h** nation.'
20: 8 the Sabbath day by keeping it **h**.
Lev 11: 44 and be **h**, because I am **h**.
20: 7 yourselves and be **h**, because I am
20: 26 You are to be **h** to me because I,
21: 8 LORD am **h**—I who make you **h**.
22: 32 Do not profane my **h** name,
Ps 24: 3 Who may stand in his **h** place?
77: 13 Your ways, God, are **h**. What god is
99: 3 great and awesome name—he is **h**.
99: 5 worship at his footstool; he is **h**.
99: 9 for the LORD our God is **h**.
111: 9 **h** and awesome is his name.
Isa 5: 16 the **h** God will be proved **h** by his

Isa   6:   3 "**H, h, h** is the Lᴏʀᴅ Almighty;
   40: 25 who is my equal?" says the **H** One.
   57: 15 who lives forever, whose name is **h**:
Eze 28: 5 I will be proved **h** through them
Da   9: 24 and to anoint the Most **H** Place.
Hab 2: 20 The Lᴏʀᴅ is in his **h** temple;
Ac   2: 27 will not let your **h** one see decay.
Ro   7: 12 the law is **h**, and the commandment is **h**,
   12: 1 sacrifice, **h** and pleasing to God—
2Th 1: 10 to be glorified in his **h** people
2Ti 1: 9 saved us and called us to a **h** life—
   3: 15 you have known the **H** Scriptures,
Titus 1: 8 upright, **h** and disciplined.
1Pe 1: 15 is **h**, so be **h** in all you do;
   1: 16 "Be **h**, because I am **h**."
   2: 9 a royal priesthood, a **h** nation,
2Pe 3: 11 You ought to live **h** and godly lives
Rev 4: 8 "'**H, h, h** is the Lord God

HOME (HOMES)
Dt   6: 7 Talk about them when you sit at **h**
Ps 84: 3 Even the sparrow has found a **h**,
Pr 3: 33 he blesses the **h** of the righteous.
Mk 10: 29 "no one who has left **h** or brothers
Jn 14: 23 and make our **h** with them.
Titus 2: 5 pure, to be busy at **h**, to be kind,

HOMES (HOME)
Ne   4: 14 daughters, your wives and your **h**."
1Ti 5: 14 to manage their **h** and to give

HOMOSEXUALITY
1Ti 1: 10 for those practicing **h**, for slave

HONEST
Lev 19: 36 **h** weights, an **h** ephah and an **h** hin.
Dt 25: 15 must have accurate and **h** weights
Job 31: 6 let God weigh me in **h** scales and
Pr 12: 17 An **h** witness tells the truth,

HONEY
Ex 3: 8 a land flowing with milk and **h**—
Ps 19: 10 they are sweeter than **h**, than **h**
 119:103 taste, sweeter than **h** to my mouth!

HONOR (HONORABLE HONORABLY HONORED
     HONORS)
Ex 20: 12 "**H** your father and your mother,
Nu 25: 13 he was zealous for the **h** of his God
Dt   5: 16 "**H** your father and your mother,
1Sa 2: 30 Those who **h** me I will **h**, but those
Ps   8: 5 crowned them with glory and **h**.
Pr 3: 9 **H** the Lᴏʀᴅ with your wealth,
   11: 16 A kindhearted woman gains **h**,
   15: 33 and humility comes before **h**.
   20: 3 It is to one's **h** to avoid strife,
   31: 31 **H** her for all that her hands have
Mt 15: 4 '**H** your father and mother'
Ro 12: 10 **H** one another above yourselves.
1Co 6: 20 Therefore **h** God with your bodies.
Eph 6: 2 "**H** your father and mother"—
1Ti 5: 17 church well are worthy of double **h**,
Heb 2: 7 crowned them with glory and **h**
Rev 4: 9 **h** and thanks to him who sits

HONORABLE (HONOR)
1Th 4: 4 body in a way that is holy and **h**,

HONORABLY (HONOR)
Heb 13: 18 and desire to live **h** in every way.

HONORED (HONOR)
Ps 12: 8 what is vile is **h** by the human race.
Pr 13: 18 but whoever heeds correction is **h**.
1Co 12: 26 if one part is **h**, every part rejoices
Heb 13: 4 Marriage should be **h** by all,

HONORS (HONOR)
Ps 15: 4 but **h** those who fear the Lᴏʀᴅ;
Pr 14: 31 is kind to the needy **h** God.
3Jn   : 6 their way in a manner that **h** God.

HOOKS
Isa 2: 4 and their spears into pruning **h**.
Joel 3: 10 and your pruning **h** into spears.

HOPE (HOPES)
Job 13: 15 he slay me, yet will I **h** in him;
Ps 42: 5 Put your **h** in God, for I will yet
  62: 5 rest in God; my **h** comes from him.
 119: 74 for I have put my **h** in your word.
 130: 7 Israel, put your **h** in the Lᴏʀᴅ,
 147: 11 put their **h** in his unfailing love.
Pr 13: 12 **H** deferred makes the heart sick,

Isa 40: 31 but those who **h** in the Lᴏʀᴅ will
Ro   5: 4 and character, **h**.
   8: 24 But **h** that is seen is no **h** at all.
   12: 12 Be joyful in **h**, patient in affliction,
   15: 4 they provide we might have **h**.
1Co 13: 13 three remain: faith, **h** and love.
   15: 19 for this life we have **h** in Christ,
Col 1: 27 is Christ in you, the **h** of glory.
1Th 5: 8 and the **h** of salvation as a helmet.
1Ti 6: 17 to put their **h** in God, who richly
Titus 2: 13 while we wait for the blessed **h**—
Heb 6: 19 We have this **h** as an anchor
   11: 1 faith is confidence in what we **h**
1Jn 3: 3 All who have this **h** in him purify

HOPES (HOPE)
1Co 13: 7 trusts, always **h**, always perseveres.

HORSE
Ps 147: 10 is not in the strength of the **h**,
Pr 26: 3 A whip for the **h**, a bridle
Zec 1: 8 me was a man mounted on a red **h**.
Rev 6: 2 and there before me was a white **h**!
   6: 4 Then another **h** came out, a fiery
   6: 5 and there before me was a black **h**!
   6: 8 and there before me was a pale **h**!
   19: 11 and there before me was a white **h**,

HOSANNA
Mt 21: 9 shouted, "**H** to the Son of David!"

HOSHEA
   Last king of Israel (2Ki 15:30; 17:1–6).

HOSPITABLE (HOSPITALITY)
1Ti 3: 2 respectable, **h**, able to teach,
Titus 1: 8 he must be **h**, one who loves what

HOSPITALITY (HOSPITABLE)
Ro 12: 13 people who are in need. Practice **h**.
1Ti 5: 10 showing **h**, washing the feet
Heb 13: 2 shown **h** to angels without knowing
1Pe 4: 9 Offer **h** to one another without

HOSTILE
Ro 8: 7 governed by the flesh is **h** to God;

HOT
1Ti 4: 2 have been seared as with a **h** iron.
Rev 3: 15 that you are neither cold nor **h**.

HOT-TEMPERED
Pr 15: 18 A **h** person stirs up conflict,
   19: 19 A **h** person must pay the penalty;
   22: 24 not make friends with a **h** person,
   29: 22 and a **h** person commits many sins.

HOTHEADED (HEAD)
Pr 14: 16 but a fool is **h** and yet feels secure.

HOUR
Ecc 9: 12 one knows when their **h** will come:
Mt 6: 27 worrying add a single **h** to your life?
Lk 12: 40 an **h** when you do not expect him."
Jn 12: 23 "The **h** has come for the Son
   12: 27 this very reason I came to this **h**.

HOUSE (HOUSEHOLD HOUSEHOLDS STOREHOUSE)
Ex 20: 17 shall not covet your neighbor's **h**.
Ps 23: 6 in the **h** of the Lᴏʀᴅ forever.
  84: 10 in the **h** of my God than dwell
 122: 1 "Let us go to the **h** of the Lᴏʀᴅ."
 127: 1 Unless the Lᴏʀᴅ builds the **h**,
Pr 7: 27 Her **h** is a highway to the grave,
   21: 9 of the roof than share a **h**
Isa 56: 7 my **h** will be called a **h** of prayer
Zec 13: 6 I was given at the **h** of my friends.'
Mt 7: 24 is like a wise man who built his **h**
   12: 29 can anyone enter a strong man's **h**
   21: 13 "'My **h** will be called a **h**
Mk 3: 25 If a **h** is divided against itself, that **h**
Lk 11: 17 a **h** divided against itself will fall.
Jn 2: 16 Stop turning my Father's **h**
   12: 3 the **h** was filled with the fragrance
   14: 2 My Father's **h** has many rooms;
Heb 3: 3 of a **h** has greater honor than the **h**

HOUSEHOLD (HOUSE)
Jos 24: 15 But as for me and my **h**, we will
Mic 7: 6 are the members of his own **h**.
Mt 10: 36 will be the members of his own **h**.'
   12: 25 or **h** divided against itself will not
1Ti 3: 4 manage his children and his **h** well.
   3: 15 to conduct themselves in God's **h**,

HOUSEHOLDS (HOUSE)
Pr 15: 27 The greedy bring ruin to their **h**,

HUMAN (HUMANITY)
Ge 9: 6 "Whoever sheds **h** blood,
1Sa 15: 29 for he is not a **h** being, that he
Ac   5: 29 obey God rather than **h** beings!
2Pe 1: 21 never had its origin in the **h** will,
HUMANITY (HUMAN)
Heb 2: 14 he too shared in their **h** so
HUMBLE (HUMBLED HUMILIATE HUMILIATING
      HUMILITY)
2Ch 7: 14 will **h** themselves and pray and
Ps 25: 9 He guides the **h** in what is right
Pr   3: 34 favor to the **h** and oppressed.
Isa 66: 2 those who are **h** and contrite
Mt 11: 29 for I am gentle and **h** in heart,
Eph 4: 2 Be completely **h** and gentle;
Jas 4: 10 **H** yourselves before the Lord,
1Pe 5: 6 **H** yourselves, therefore,
HUMBLED (HUMBLE)
Mt 23: 12 who exalt themselves will be **h**,
Php 2: 8 he **h** himself by becoming obedient
HUMILIATE (HUMBLE)
Pr 25: 7 for him to **h** you before his nobles.
HUMILIATING (HUMBLE)
1Co 11: 22 God by **h** those who have nothing?
HUMILITY (HUMBLE)
Pr 11: 2 but with **h** comes wisdom.
     15: 33 LORD, and **h** comes before honor.
2Co 10: 1 the **h** and gentleness of Christ,
Php 2: 3 in **h** value others above yourselves,
1Pe 5: 5 with **h** toward one another,
HUNGRY
Ps 107: 9 and fills the **h** with good things.
     146: 7 oppressed and gives food to the **h**.
Pr 25: 21 If your enemy is **h**, give him food
Eze 18: 7 his food to the **h** and provides
Mt 25: 35 For I was **h** and you gave me
Lk   1: 53 has filled the **h** with good things
Jn   6: 35 comes to me will never go **h**,
Ro 12: 20 "If your enemy is **h**, feed him;
HURT (HURTS)
Ecc 8: 9 lords it over others to his own **h**.
Mk 16: 18 *it will not* **h** *them*
Rev 2: 11 one who is victorious will not be **h**
HURTS (HURT)
Ps 15: 4 who keeps an oath even when it **h**,
Pr 26: 28 A lying tongue hates those it **h**,
HUSBAND (HUSBAND'S HUSBANDS)
1Co 7: 3 The **h** should fulfill his marital
      7: 3 and likewise the wife to her **h**.
      7: 4 her own body but yields it to her **h**.
      7: 4 the **h** does not have authority over
      7: 10 wife must not separate from her **h**.
      7: 11 And a **h** must not divorce his wife.
      7: 13 And if a woman has a **h** who is not
      7: 39 But if her **h** dies, she is free
2Co 11: 2 I promised you to one **h**, to Christ,
Eph 5: 23 For the **h** is the head of the wife as
      5: 33 and the wife must respect her **h**.
HUSBAND'S (HUSBAND)
Pr 12: 4 of noble character is her **h** crown,
HUSBANDS (HUSBAND)
Eph 5: 22 yourselves to your own **h** as you do
      5: 25 **H**, love your wives, just as Christ
Titus 2: 4 the younger women to love their **h**
1Pe 3: 1 yourselves to your own **h** so that,
      3: 7 **H**, in the same way be considerate
HYMN
1Co 14: 26 each of you has a **h**, or a word
HYPOCRISY (HYPOCRITE HYPOCRITES)
Mt 23: 28 on the inside you are full of **h**
1Pe 2: 1 of all malice and deceit, **h**, envy,
HYPOCRITE (HYPOCRISY)
Mt   7: 5 You **h**, first take the plank
HYPOCRITES (HYPOCRISY)
Ps 26: 4 deceitful, nor do I associate with **h**.
Mt   6: 5 do not be like the **h**, for they love
HYSSOP
Ps 51: 7 Cleanse me with **h**, and I will be
IDLE (IDLENESS)
1Th 5: 14 those who are **i** and disruptive,
2Th 3: 6 away from every believer who is **i**
1Ti 5: 13 they get into the habit of being **i**

IDLENESS (IDLE)
Pr 31: 27 and does not eat the bread of **i**.
IDOL (IDOLATRY IDOLS)
Isa 44: 17 From the rest he makes a god, his **i**;
1Co 8: 4 We know that "An **i** is nothing
IDOLATRY (IDOL)
Col 3: 5 evil desires and greed, which is **i**.
IDOLS (IDOL)
1Co 8: 1 Now about food sacrificed to **i**:
IGNORANT (IGNORE)
1Co 15: 34 there are some who are **i** of God—
Heb 5: 2 to deal gently with those who are **i**
1Pe 2: 15 good you should silence the **i** talk
2Pe 3: 16 **i** and unstable people distort,
IGNORE (IGNORANT IGNORES)
Dt 22: 1 not **i** it but be sure to take it back
Ps   9: 12 he does not **i** the cries
Heb 2: 3 escape if we **i** so great a salvation?
IGNORES (IGNORE)
Pr 10: 17 whoever **i** correction leads others
ILLUMINATED
Rev 18: 1 and the earth was **i** by his splendor.
IMAGE
Ge   1: 26 "Let us make mankind in our **i**,
      1: 27 God created mankind in his own **i**, in the **i** of God he
                   created them;
Ro   8: 29 to be conformed to the **i** of his Son,
1Co 15: 7 since he is the **i** and glory of God;
2Co 3: 18 into his **i** with ever-increasing glory,
Col 1: 15 The Son is the **i** of the invisible
      3: 10 in knowledge in the **i** of its Creator.
IMAGINE
Eph 3: 20 more than all we ask or **i**,
IMITATE (IMITATORS)
1Co 4: 16 Therefore I urge you to **i** me.
Heb 6: 12 but to **i** those who through faith
     13: 7 of their way of life and **i** their faith.
3Jn   : 11 do not **i** what is evil but what is
IMITATORS (IMITATE)
1Th 1: 6 You became **i** of us and of the Lord,
      2: 14 became **i** of God's churches
IMMANUEL
Isa 7: 14 birth to a son, and will call him **I**.
Mt   1: 23 they will call him **I**" (which means
IMMORAL (IMMORALITY)
1Co 5: 9 to associate with sexually **i** people
      5: 10 the people of this world who are **i**,
      5: 11 or sister but is sexually **i** or greedy,
      6: 9 Neither the sexually **i** nor idolaters
Eph 5: 5 No **i**, impure or greedy person—
Heb 12: 16 See that no one is sexually **i**, or is
     13: 4 the adulterer and all the sexually **i**.
Rev 21: 8 the sexually **i**, those who practice
     22: 15 arts, the sexually **i**, the murderers,
IMMORALITY (IMMORAL)
Mt   5: 32 except for sexual **i**, makes her
     19: 9 except for sexual **i**, and marries
1Co 6: 13 is not meant for sexual **i**
      6: 18 Flee from sexual **i**. All other sins
     10: 8 We should not commit sexual **i**,
Gal 5: 19 sexual **i**, impurity and debauchery;
Eph 5: 3 must not be even a hint of sexual **i**,
1Th 4: 3 that you should avoid sexual **i**;
Jude   4 grace of our God into a license for **i**
IMMORTAL (IMMORTALITY)
Ro   1: 23 exchanged the glory of the **i** God
1Ti 1: 17 Now to the King eternal, **i**,
      6: 16 who alone is **i** and who lives
IMMORTALITY (IMMORTAL)
Ro   2: 7 and **i**, he will give eternal life.
1Co 15: 53 and the mortal with **i**.
2Ti 1: 10 and **i** to light through the gospel.
IMPERISHABLE
1Pe 1: 23 seed, but of **i**, through the living
IMPORTANCE (IMPORTANT)
1Co 15: 3 I passed on to you as of first **i**:
IMPORTANT (IMPORTANCE)
Mt 23: 23 have neglected the more **i** matters
Mk 12: 29 "The most **i** one," answered Jesus,
     12: 33 as yourself is more **i** than all burnt
Php 1: 18 The **i** thing is that in every way,

IMPOSSIBLE
Mt 17: 20 Nothing will be **i** for you."
Lk 18: 27 "What is **i** with man is possible
Heb 6: 18 in which it is **i** for God to lie,
    11: 6 without faith it is **i** to please God,
IMPROPER
Eph 5: 3 because these are **i** for God's holy
IMPURE (IMPURITY)
Ac 10: 15 "Do not call anything **i** that God
Eph 5: 5 No immoral, **i** or greedy person—
1Th 4: 7 For God did not call us to be **i**,
Rev 21: 27 Nothing **i** will ever enter it,
IMPURITY (IMPURE)
Ro 1: 24 hearts to sexual **i** for the degrading
Eph 5: 3 or of any kind of **i**, or of greed,
INCENSE
Ex 40: 5 Place the gold altar of **i** in front
Ps 141: 2 my prayer be set before you like **i**;
INCOME
Ecc 5: 10 is never satisfied with their **i**.
1Co 16: 2 of money in keeping with your **i**,
INCOMPARABLE
Eph 2: 7 ages he might show the **i** riches
INCREASE (EVER-INCREASING INCREASED INCREASING)
Ge 1: 22 "Be fruitful and **i** in number and
Ps 62: 10 though your riches **i**, do not set
Lk 17: 5 said to the Lord, "**I** our faith!"
1Th 3: 12 May the Lord make your love **i**
INCREASED (INCREASE)
Ac 6: 7 of disciples in Jerusalem **i** rapidly,
Ro 5: 20 where sin **i**, grace **i** all the more,
INCREASING (INCREASE)
Ac 6: 1 the number of disciples was **i**,
2Th 1: 3 all of you have for one another is **i**.
2Pe 1: 8 these qualities in **i** measure,
INDEPENDENT
1Co 11: 11 in the Lord woman is not **i** of man, nor is man **i** of woman.
INDESCRIBABLE
2Co 9: 15 Thanks be to God for his **i** gift!
INDISPENSABLE
1Co 12: 22 body that seem to be weaker are **i**,
INEFFECTIVE
2Pe 1: 8 they will keep you from being **i**
INEXPRESSIBLE
2Co 12: 4 up to paradise and heard **i** things,
1Pe 1: 8 are filled with an **i** and glorious joy,
INFANTS
Mt 21: 16 the lips of children and **i** you, Lord,
1Co 14: 20 In regard to evil be **i**, but in your
INHERIT (CO-HEIRS HEIRS HERITAGE INHERITANCE)
Ps 37: 11 the meek will **i** the land and enjoy
    37: 29 The righteous will **i** the land
Mt 5: 5 the meek, for they will **i** the earth.
Mk 10: 17 "what must I do to **i** eternal life?"
1Co 15: 50 cannot **i** the kingdom of God,
INHERITANCE (INHERIT)
Dt 4: 20 to be the people of his **i**, as you
Pr 13: 22 A good person leaves an **i** for their
Eph 1: 14 deposit guaranteeing our **i** until
    5: 5 has any **i** in the kingdom of Christ
Heb 9: 15 receive the promised eternal **i**—
1Pe 1: 4 This **i** is kept in heaven for you,
INIQUITIES (INIQUITY)
Ps 78: 38 he forgave their **i** and did not
    103: 10 or repay us according to our **i**.
Isa 59: 2 your **i** have separated you from
Mic 7: 19 hurl all our **i** into the depths
INIQUITY (INIQUITIES)
Ps 51: 2 Wash away all my **i** and cleanse me
Isa 53: 6 has laid on him the **i** of us all.
INJUSTICE
2Ch 19: 7 the LORD our God there is no **i**
INNOCENT
Pr 17: 26 a fine on the **i** is not good,
Mt 10: 16 shrewd as snakes and as **i** as doves.
    27: 4 said, "for I have betrayed **i** blood."
1Co 4: 4 clear, but that does not make me **i**.
INSCRIPTION
Mt 22: 20 image is this? And whose **i**?"
INSOLENT
Ro 1: 30 **i**, arrogant and boastful;

INSTITUTED
Ro 13: 2 is rebelling against what God has **i**,
INSTRUCT (INSTRUCTED INSTRUCTION)
Ps 32: 8 I will **i** you and teach you
Pr 9: 9 **I** the wise and they will be wiser
Ro 15: 14 and competent to **i** one another.
INSTRUCTED (INSTRUCT)
2Ti 2: 25 Opponents must be gently **i**,
INSTRUCTION (INSTRUCT)
Pr 1: 3 for receiving **i** in prudent behavior,
    1: 7 but fools despise wisdom and **i**.
    1: 8 your father's **i** and do not forsake
    4: 1 Listen, my sons, to a father's **i**;
    4: 13 Hold on to **i**, do not let it go;
    6: 23 correction and **i** are the way to life,
    8: 10 Choose my **i** instead of silver,
    8: 33 Listen to my **i** and be wise;
    13: 1 A wise son heeds his father's **i**,
    13: 13 Whoever scorns **i** will pay for it,
    16: 20 Whoever gives heed to **i** prospers,
    16: 21 and gracious words promote **i**.
    23: 12 Apply your heart to **i** and your ears
    23: 23 wisdom, **i** and insight as well.
Isa 8: 20 Consult God's **i** and the testimony
1Co 14: 6 or prophecy or word of **i**?
    14: 26 hymn, or a word of **i**, a revelation,
Eph 6: 4 in the training and **i** of the Lord.
1Th 4: 8 who rejects this **i** does not reject
2Th 3: 14 anyone who does not obey our **i**
1Ti 6: 3 sound **i** of our Lord Jesus Christ
2Ti 4: 2 with great patience and careful **i**.
INSULT (INSULTS)
Pr 12: 16 but the prudent overlook an **i**.
Mt 5: 11 are you when people **i** you,
Lk 6: 22 when they exclude you and **i** you
1Pe 3: 9 not repay evil with evil or **i** with **i**.
INSULTS (INSULT)
Pr 9: 7 corrects a mocker invites **i**;
INTEGRITY
1Ki 9: 4 walk before me faithfully with **i**
Job 2: 3 And he still maintains his **i**,
    27: 5 till I die, I will not deny my **i**.
Pr 10: 9 Whoever walks in **i** walks securely,
    11: 3 The **i** of the upright guides them,
    29: 10 the bloodthirsty hate a person of **i**
Titus 2: 7 In your teaching show **i**,
INTELLIGENCE
Isa 29: 14 the **i** of the intelligent will vanish."
1Co 1: 19 the **i** of the intelligent I will
INTELLIGIBLE
1Co 14: 19 I would rather speak five **i** words
INTERCEDE (INTERCEDES INTERCESSION)
Heb 7: 25 him, because he always lives to **i**
INTERCEDES (INTERCEDE)
Ro 8: 26 the Spirit himself **i** for us through
INTERCESSION (INTERCEDE)
Isa 53: 12 and made **i** for the transgressors.
1Ti 2: 1 **i** and thanksgiving be made for all
INTEREST
Ne 5: 10 But let us stop charging **i**!
INTERESTS
1Co 7: 34 and his **i** are divided.
Php 2: 4 not looking to your own **i** but each of you to the **i** of the others.
    2: 21 everyone looks out for their own **i**,
INTERMARRY (MARRY)
Dt 7: 3 Do not **i** with them. Do not give
INVESTIGATED
Lk 1: 3 I myself have carefully **i** everything
INVISIBLE
Ro 1: 20 of the world God's **i** qualities—
Col 1: 15 The Son is the image of the **i** God,
1Ti 1: 17 eternal, immortal, **i**, the only God,
INVITE (INVITED INVITES)
Lk 14: 13 you give a banquet, **i** the poor,
INVITED (INVITE)
Mt 22: 14 "For many are **i**, but few are
    25: 35 I was a stranger and you **i** me in,
INVITES (INVITE)
1Co 10: 27 If an unbeliever **i** you to a meal
IRON
1Ti 4: 2 have been seared as with a hot **i**.
Rev 2: 27 'will rule them with an **i** scepter

IRREVOCABLE
Ro 11: 29 for God's gifts and his call are **i**.

ISAAC
Son of Abraham by Sarah (Ge 17:19; 21:1–7; 1Ch 1:28). Offered up by Abraham (Ge 22; Heb 11:17–19). Rebekah taken as wife (Ge 24). Fathered Esau and Jacob (Ge 25:19–26; 1Ch 1:34). Tricked into blessing Jacob (Ge 27). Father of Israel (Ex 3:6; Dt 29:13; Ro 9:10).

ISAIAH
Prophet to Judah (Isa 1:1). Called by the LORD (Isa 6).

ISHMAEL
Son of Abraham by Hagar (Ge 16; 1Ch 1:28). Blessed, but not son of covenant (Ge 17:18–21; Gal 4:21–31). Sent away by Sarah (Ge 21:8–21).

ISRAEL (ISRAELITES)
1. Name given to Jacob (see JACOB).
2. Corporate name of Jacob's descendants; often specifically Northern Kingdom.

Dt 6: 4 Hear, O I: The LORD our God,
1Sa 4: 21 "The Glory has departed from I"—
Isa 27: 6 I will bud and blossom and fill all
Jer 31: 10 'He who scattered I will gather
Eze 39: 23 that the people of I went into exile
Mk 12: 29 'Hear, O I: The Lord our God,
Lk 22: 30 judging the twelve tribes of I.
Ro 9: 6 all who are descended from I are I.
     11: 26 and in this way all I will be saved.
Eph 3: 6 Gentiles are heirs together with I,

ISRAELITES (ISRAEL)
Ex 14: 12 for I went through the sea on dry
     16: 35 The I ate manna forty years,
Hos 1: 10 "Yet the I will be like the sand
Ro 9: 27 number of the I be like the sand

ITCHING
2Ti 4: 3 say what their i ears want to hear.

JACOB
Second son of Isaac, twin of Esau (Ge 25:21–26; 1Ch 1:34). Bought Esau's birthright (Ge 25:29–34); tricked Isaac into blessing him (Ge 27:1–37). Abrahamic covenant perpetuated through (Ge 28:13–15; Mal 1:2). Vision at Bethel (Ge 28:10–22). Wives and children (Ge 29:1—30:24; 35:16–26; 1Ch 2–9). Wrestled with God; name changed to Israel (Ge 32:22–32). Sent sons to Egypt during famine (Ge 42–43). Settled in Egypt (Ge 46). Blessed Ephraim and Manasseh (Ge 48). Blessed sons (Ge 49:1–28; Heb 11:21). Death (Ge 49:29–33). Burial (Ge 50:1–14).

JAMES
1. Apostle; brother of John (Mt 4:21–22; 10:2; Mk 3:17; Lk 5:1–10). At transfiguration (Mt 17:1–13; Mk 9:1–13; Lk 9:28–36). Killed by Herod (Ac 12:2).
2. Apostle; son of Alphaeus (Mt 10:3; Mk 3:18; Lk 6:15).
3. Brother of Jesus (Mt 13:55; Mk 6:3; Lk 24:10; Gal 1:19) and Judas (Jude 1). With believers before Pentecost (Ac 1:13). Leader of church at Jerusalem (Ac 12:17; 15; 21:18; Gal 2:9, 12). Author of epistle (Jas 1:1).

JAPHETH
Son of Noah (Ge 5:32; 1Ch 1:4–5). Blessed (Ge 9:18–28).

JARS
2Co 4: 7 we have this treasure in j of clay

JEALOUS (JEALOUSY)
Ex 20: 5 am a j God, punishing the children
     34: 14 whose name is J, is a j God.
Dt 4: 24 God is a consuming fire, a j God.
Joel 2: 18 Then the LORD was j for his land
Zec 1: 14 I am very j for Jerusalem and Zion,
2Co 11: 2 am j for you with a godly jealousy.

JEALOUSY (JEALOUS)
1Co 3: 3 For since there is j and quarreling
2Co 11: 2 I am jealous for you with a godly j.
Gal 5: 20 hatred, discord, j, fits of rage,

JEHOAHAZ
1. Son of Jehu; king of Israel (2Ki 13:1–9).
2. Son of Josiah; king of Judah (2Ki 23:31–34; 2Ch 36:1–4).

JEHOASH
Son of Jehoahaz; king of Israel (2Ki 13–14; 2Ch 25).

JEHOIACHIN
Son of Jehoiakim; king of Judah exiled by Nebuchadnezzar (2Ki 24:8–17; 2Ch 36:8–10; Jer 22:24–30; 24:1). Raised from prisoner status (2Ki 25:27–30; Jer 52:31–34).

JEHOIAKIM
Son of Josiah; king of Judah (2Ki 23:34—24:6; 2Ch 36:4–8; Jer 22:18–23; 36).

JEHORAM
Son of Jehoshaphat; king of Judah (2Ki 8:16–24).

JEHOSHAPHAT
Son of Asa; king of Judah (1Ki 22:41–50; 2Ki 3; 2Ch 17–20).

JEHU
King of Israel (1Ki 19:16–19; 2Ki 9–10).

JEPHTHAH
Judge from Gilead who delivered Israel from Ammon (Jdg 10:6—12:7). Made rash vow concerning his daughter (Jdg 11:30–40).

JEREMIAH
Prophet to Judah (Jer 1:1–3). Called by the LORD (Jer 1). Put in stocks (Jer 20:1–3). Threatened for prophesying (Jer 11:18–23; 26). Opposed by Hananiah (Jer 28). Scroll burned (Jer 36). Imprisoned (Jer 37). Thrown into cistern (Jer 38). Forced to Egypt with those fleeing Babylonians (Jer 43).

JEROBOAM
1. Official of Solomon; rebelled to become first king of Israel (1Ki 11:26–40; 12:1–20; 2Ch 10). Idolatry (1Ki 12:25–33); judgment for (1Ki 13–14; 2Ch 13).
2. Son of Jehoash; king of Israel (1Ki 14:23–29).

JERUSALEM
2Ki 23: 27 and I will reject J, the city I chose,
2Ch 6: 6 now I have chosen J for my Name
Ne 2: 17 let us rebuild the wall of J,
Ps 122: 6 Pray for the peace of J:
     125: 2 As the mountains surround J,
     137: 5 If I forget you, J, may my right
Isa 40: 9 You who bring good news to J,
     65: 18 for I will create J to be a delight
Joel 3: 17 J will be holy; never again will
Zep 3: 16 On that day they will say to J,
Zec 2: 4 "man, 'J will be a city without walls
     8: 8 I will bring them back to live in J;
     14: 8 living water will flow out from J,
Mt 23: 37 "J, J, you who kill the prophets
Lk 13: 34 "J, J, you who kill the prophets
     21: 24 J will be trampled
Jn 4: 20 where we must worship is in J."
Ac 1: 8 and you will be my witnesses in J,
Gal 4: 25 to the present city of J,
Rev 21: 2 the new J, coming down

JESUS
LIFE: Genealogy (Mt 1:1–17; Lk 3:21–37). Birth announced (Mt 1:18–25; Lk 1:26–45). Birth (Mt 2:1–12; Lk 2:1–40). Escape to Egypt (Mt 2:13–23). As a boy in the temple (Lk 2:41–52). Baptism (Mt 3:13–17; Mk 1:9–11; Lk 3:21–22; Jn 1:32–34). Temptation (Mt 4:1–11; Mk 1:12–13; Lk 4:1–13). Ministry in Galilee (Mt 4:12—18:35; Mk 1:14—9:50; Lk 4:14—13:9; Jn 1:35—2:11; 4; 6). Transfiguration (Mt 17:1–8; Mk 9:2–8; Lk 9:28–36), on the way to Jerusalem (Mt 19–20; Mk 10; Lk 13:10—19:27), in Jerusalem (Mt 21–25; Mk 11–13; Lk 19:28—21:38; Jn 2:12—3:36; 5; 7–12). Last supper (Mt 26:17–35; Mk 14:12–31; Lk 22:1–38; Jn 13–17). Arrest and trial (Mt 26:36—27:31; Mk 14:43—15:20; Lk 22:39—23:25; Jn 18:1—19:16). Crucifixion (Mt 27:32–66; Mk 15:21–47; Lk 23:26–55; Jn 19:28–42). Resurrection and appearances (Mt 28; Mk 16; Lk 24; Jn 20–21; Ac 1:1–11; 7:56; 9:3–6; 1Co 15:1–8; Rev 1:1–20).

MIRACLES. Healings: official's son (Jn 4:43–54), demoniac in Capernaum (Mk 1:23–26; Lk 4:33–35), Peter's mother-in-law (Mt 8:14–17; Mk 1:29–31; Lk 4:38–39), leper (Mt 8:2–4; Mk 1:40–45; Lk 5:12–16), paralytic (Mt 9:1–8; Mk 2:1–12; Lk 5:17–26), cripple (Jn 5:1–9), shriveled hand (Mt 12:10–13; Mk 3:1–5; Lk 6:6–11), centurion's servant (Mt 8:5–13; Lk 7:1–10), widow's son raised (Lk 7:11–17), demoniac (Mt 12:22–23; Lk 11:14), Gadarene demoniacs (Mt 8:28–34; Mk 5:1–20; Lk 8:26–39), woman's bleeding and Jairus' daughter (Mt 9:18–26; Mk 5:21–43; Lk 8:40–56), blind man (Mt 9:27–31), mute man (Mt 9:32–33), Canaanite woman's daughter (Mt 15:21–28; Mk 7:24–30), deaf man (Mk 7:31–37), blind man (Mk 8:22–26), demoniac boy (Mt 17:14–18; Mk 9:14–29; Lk 9:37–43), ten lepers (Lk 17:11–19), man born blind (Jn 9:1–7), Lazarus raised (Jn 11), crippled woman (Lk 13:11–17), man with dropsy (Lk 14:1–6), two blind men (Mt 20:29–34; Mk 10:46–52; Lk 18:35–43), Malchus' ear (Lk 22:50–51). Other Miracles: water to wine (Jn 2:1–11), catch of fish (Lk 5:1–11), storm stilled (Mt 8:23–27; Mk 4:37–41; Lk 8:22–25), 5,000 fed (Mt 14:15–21; Mk 6:35–44; Lk 9:10–17; Jn 6:1–14), walking on water (Mt 14:25–33; Mk 6:48–52; Jn 6:15–21), 4,000 fed (Mt 15:32–39; Mk 8:1–9), money from fish (Mt 17:24–27), fig tree cursed (Mt 21:18–22; Mk 11:12–14), catch of fish (Jn 21:1–14).

MAJOR TEACHING: Sermon on the Mount (Mt 5–7;

Lk 6:17–49), to Nicodemus (Jn 3), to Samaritan woman (Jn 4), Bread of Life (Jn 6:22–59), at Feast of Tabernacles (Jn 7–8), woes to Pharisees (Mt 23; Lk 11:37–54), Good Shepherd (Jn 10:1–18), Olivet Discourse (Mt 24–25; Mk 13; Lk 21:5–36), Upper Room Discourse (Jn 13–16).

PARABLES: Sower (Mt 13:3–23; Mk 4:3–25; Lk 8:5–18), seed's growth (Mk 4:26–29), wheat and weeds (Mt 13:24–30, 36–43), mustard seed (Mt 13:31–32; Mk 4:30–32), yeast (Mt 13:33; Lk 13:20–21), hidden treasure (Mt 13:44), valuable pearl (Mt 13:45–46), net (Mt 13:47–51), house owner (Mt 13:52), good Samaritan (Lk 10:25–37), unmerciful servant (Mt 18:15–35), lost sheep (Mt 18:10–14; Lk 15:4–7), lost coin (Lk 15:8–10), prodigal son (Lk 15:11–32), dishonest manager (Lk 16:1–13), rich man and Lazarus (Lk 16:19–31), persistent widow (Lk 18:1–8), Pharisee and tax collector (Lk 18:9–14), payment of workers (Mt 20:1–16), tenants and the vineyard (Mt 21:28–46; Mk 12:1–12; Lk 20:9–19), wedding banquet (Mt 22:1–14), faithful servant (Mt 24:45–51), ten virgins (Mt 25:1–13), talents (Mt 25:1–30; Lk 19:12–27).

DISCIPLES see APOSTLES. Call of (Jn 1:35–51; Mt 4:18–22; 9:9; Mk 1:16–20; 2:13–14; Lk 5:1–11, 27–28). Named Apostles (Mk 3:13–19; Lk 6:12–16). Seventy sent out (Lk 10:1–24). Defection of (Jn 6:60–71; Mt 26:56; Mk 14:50–52). Final commission (Mt 28:16–20; Jn 21:15–23; Ac 1:3–8).

Ac	2: 32	God has raised this J to life, and we
	9: 5	Saul asked. "I am J, whom you are
	15: 11	of our Lord J that we are saved,
	16: 31	"Believe in the Lord J, and you will
Ro	3: 24	redemption that came by Christ J.
	5: 17	life through the one man, J Christ!
	8: 1	for those who are in Christ J,
1Co	2: 2	I was with you except J Christ
	8: 6	and there is but one Lord, J Christ,
	12: 3	and no one can say, "J is Lord,"
2Co	4: 5	but J Christ as Lord, and ourselves
Gal	2: 16	of the law, but by faith in J Christ.
	3: 28	for you are all one in Christ J.
	5: 6	in Christ J neither circumcision
Eph	2: 10	in Christ J to do good works,
	2: 20	with Christ J himself as the chief
Php	1: 6	until the day of Christ J.
	2: 5	have the same mindset as Christ J:
	2: 10	name of J every knee should bow,
Col	3: 17	do it all in the name of the Lord J,
2Th	2: 1	the coming of our Lord J Christ
1Ti	1: 15	J came into the world to save
2Ti	3: 12	life in Christ J will be persecuted,
Titus	2: 13	our great God and Savior, J Christ,
Heb	2: 9	But we do see J, who was made
	3: 1	fix your thoughts on J, whom we
	4: 14	into heaven, J the Son of God,
	7: 22	J has become the guarantor
	7: 24	but because J lives forever, he has
	12: 2	fixing our eyes on J, the pioneer
2Pe	1: 16	of our Lord J Christ in power,
1Jn	1: 7	and the blood of J, his Son,
	2: 1	J Christ, the Righteous One.
	2: 6	to live in him must live as J did.
	4: 15	acknowledges that J is the Son
Rev	22: 20	Amen. Come, Lord J.

JEW (JEWS JUDAISM)

Zec	8: 23	take firm hold of one J by the hem
Ro	1: 16	first to the J, then to the Gentile.
	10: 12	there is no difference between J
1Co	9: 20	To the Jews I became like a J,
Gal	3: 28	There is neither J nor Gentile,

JEWELRY (JEWELS)

1Pe	3: 3	wearing of gold j or fine clothes.

JEWELS (JEWELRY)

Isa	61: 10	as a bride adorns herself with her j.
Zec	9: 16	in his land like j in a crown.

JEWS (JEW)

Mt	2: 2	who has been born king of the J?
	27: 11	him, "Are you the king of the J?"
Jn	4: 22	know, for salvation is from the J.
Ro	3: 29	Or is God the God of J only?
1Co	1: 22	J demand signs and Greeks look
	9: 20	To the J I became like a Jew, to win
	12: 13	whether J or Gentiles,
Rev	3: 9	claim to be J though they are not,

JEZEBEL

Sidonian wife of Ahab (1Ki 16:31). Promoted Baal worship (1Ki 16:32–33). Killed prophets of the LORD (1Ki 18:4, 13). Opposed Elijah (1Ki 19:1–2). Had Naboth killed (1Ki 21). Death prophesied (1Ki 21:17–24). Killed by Jehu (2Ki 9:30–37).

JOASH

Son of Ahaziah; king of Judah. Sheltered from Athaliah by Jehoiada (2Ki 11; 2Ch 22:10—23:21). Repaired temple (2Ki 12; 2Ch 24).

JOB

Wealthy man from Uz; feared God (Job 1:1–5). Righteousness tested by disaster (Job 1:6–22), personal affliction (Job 2). Maintained innocence in debate with three friends (Job 3–31), Elihu (Job 32–37). Rebuked by the LORD (Job 38–41). Vindicated and restored to greater stature by the LORD (Job 42). Example of righteousness (Eze 14:14, 20).

JOHN

1. Son of Zechariah and Elizabeth (Lk 1). Called the Baptist (Mt 3:1–12; Mk 1:2–8). Witness to Jesus (Mt 3:11–12; Mk 1:7–8; Lk 3:15–18; Jn 1:6–35; 3:27–30; 5:33–36). Doubts about Jesus (Mt 11:2–6; Lk 7:18–23). Arrest (Mt 4:12; Mk 1:14). Execution (Mt 14:1–12; Mk 6:14–29; Lk 9:7–9). Ministry compared to Elijah (Mt 11:7–19; Mk 9:11–13; Lk 7:24–35).

2. Apostle; brother of James (Mt 4:21–22; 10:2; Mk 3:17; Lk 5:1–10). At transfiguration (Mt 17:1–13; Mk 9:1–13; Lk 9:28–36). Desire to be greatest (Mk 10:35–45). Leader of church at Jerusalem (Ac 4:1–3; Gal 2:9). Elder who wrote epistles (2Jn 1; 3Jn 1). Prophet who wrote Revelation (Rev 1:1; 22:8).

3. Cousin of Barnabas, co-worker with Paul, (Ac 12:12—13:13; 15:37), see MARK.

JOIN (JOINED)

Pr	23: 20	not j those who drink too much
	24: 21	do not j with rebellious officials,
Ro	15: 30	to j me in my struggle by praying
2Ti	1: 8	j with me in suffering
2Ti	2: 3	J with me in suffering, like a good

JOINED (JOIN)

Mt	19: 6	Therefore what God has j together,
Mk	10: 9	Therefore what God has j together,
Eph	2: 21	the whole building is j together
	4: 16	body, j and held together by every

JOINTS

Heb	4: 12	soul and spirit, j and marrow;

JOKING

Eph	5: 4	foolish talk or coarse j, which are

JONAH

Prophet in days of Jeroboam II (2Ki 14:25). Called to Nineveh; fled to Tarshish (Jnh 1:1–3). Cause of storm; thrown into sea (Jnh 1:4–16). Swallowed by fish (Jnh 1:17). Prayer (Jnh 2). Preached to Nineveh (Jnh 3). Attitude reproved by the LORD (Jnh 4). Sign of (Mt 12:39–41; Lk 11:29–32).

JONATHAN

Son of Saul (1Sa 13:16; 1Ch 8:33). Valiant warrior (1Sa 13–14). Relation to David (1Sa 18:1–4; 19–20; 23:16–18). Killed at Gilboa (1Sa 31). Mourned by David (2Sa 1).

JORAM

Son of Ahab; king of Israel (2Ki 3; 8–9; 2Ch 22).

JORDAN

Nu	34: 12	boundary will go down along the J
Jos	4: 22	'Israel crossed the J on dry ground.'
Mt	3: 6	baptized by him in the J River.

JOSEPH

1. Son of Jacob by Rachel (Ge 30:24; 1Ch 2:2). Favored by Jacob, hated by brothers (Ge 37:3–4). Dreams (Ge 37:5–11). Sold by brothers (Ge 37:12–36). Served Potiphar; imprisoned by false accusation (Ge 39). Interpreted dreams of Pharaoh's servants (Ge 40), of Pharaoh (Ge 41:4–40). Made greatest in Egypt (Ge 41:41–57). Sold grain to brothers (Ge 42–45). Brought Jacob and sons to Egypt (Ge 46–47). Sons Ephraim and Manasseh blessed (Ge 48). Blessed (Ge 49:22–26; Dt 33:13–17). Death (Ge 50:22–26; Ex 13:19; Heb 11:22). 12,000 from (Rev 7:8).

2. Husband of Mary, mother of Jesus (Mt 1:16–24; 2:13–19; Lk 1:27; 2; Jn 1:45).

3. Disciple from Arimathea, who gave his tomb for Jesus' burial (Mt 27:57–61; Mk 15:43–47; Lk 23:50–53).

4. Original name of Barnabas (Ac 4:36).

JOSHUA

1. Son of Nun; name changed from Hoshea (Nu 13:8, 16; 1Ch 7:27). Fought Amalekites under Moses (Ex 17:9–14). Servant of Moses on Sinai (Ex 24:13; 32:17). Spied Canaan (Nu 13). With Caleb, allowed to enter land (Nu 14:6, 30). Succeeded Moses (Dt 1:38; 31:1–8; 34:9).

Charged Israel to conquer Canaan (Jos 1). Crossed Jordan (Jos 3–4). Circumcised sons of wilderness wanderings (Jos 5). Conquered Jericho (Jos 6), Ai (Jos 7–8), five kings at Gibeon (Jos 10:1–28), southern Canaan (Jos 10:29–43), northern Canaan (Jos 11–12). Defeated at Ai (Jos 7). Deceived by Gibeonites (Jos 9). Renewed covenant (Jos 8:30–35; 24:1–27). Divided land among tribes (Jos 13–22). Last words (Jos 23). Death (Jos 24:28–31).

2. High priest during rebuilding of temple (Hag 1–2; Zec 3:1–9; 6:11).

JOSIAH
Son of Amon; king of Judah (2Ki 22–23; 2Ch 34–35).

JOTHAM
Son of Azariah (Uzziah); king of Judah (2Ki 15:32–38; 2Ch 26:21—27:9).

JOY (ENJOY ENJOYMENT JOYFUL OVERJOYED REJOICE REJOICES REJOICING)
Dt	16: 15	hands, and your **j** will be complete.
1Ch	16: 27	and **j** are in his dwelling place.
Ne	8: 10	for the **j** of the LORD is your
Est	9: 22	their sorrow was turned into **j**
Job	38: 7	and all the angels shouted for **j**?
Ps	4: 7	Fill my heart with **j** when their
	21: 6	glad with the **j** of your presence.
	30: 11	sackcloth and clothed me with **j**,
	43: 4	God, to God, my **j** and my delight.
	51: 12	to me the **j** of your salvation
	66: 1	Shout for **j** to God, all the earth!
	96: 12	all the trees of the forest sing for **j**.
	107: 22	tell of his works with songs of **j**.
	119: 111	forever; they are the **j** of my heart.
Pr	10: 1	A wise son brings **j** to his father,
	10: 28	The prospect of the righteous is **j**,
	12: 20	those who promote peace have **j**.
	15: 30	in a messenger's eyes brings **j**
Isa	35: 10	everlasting **j** will crown their heads
	51: 11	Gladness and **j** will overtake them,
	55: 12	You will go out in **j** and be led
Lk	1: 44	the baby in my womb leaped for **j**.
	2: 10	will cause great **j** for all the people.
Jn	15: 11	and that your **j** may be complete.
	16: 20	grieve, but your grief will turn to **j**.
2Co	8: 2	trial, their overflowing **j** and their
Php	2: 2	then make my **j** complete by being
	4: 1	love and long for, my **j** and crown,
1Th	2: 19	our **j**, or the crown in which we
Phm	: 7	Your love has given me great **j**
Heb	12: 2	the **j** set before him he endured
Jas	1: 2	Consider it pure **j**, my brothers
1Pe	1: 8	an inexpressible and glorious **j**,
2Jn	: 4	It has given me great **j** to find some
3Jn	: 4	I have no greater **j** than to hear

JOYFUL (JOY)
Ps	100: 2	come before him with **j** songs.
Pr	23: 25	may she who gave you birth be **j**!
Hab	3: 18	I will be **j** in God my Savior.

JUDAH
1. Son of Jacob by Leah (Ge 29:35; 35:23; 1Ch 2:1). Tribe of blessed as ruling tribe (Ge 49:8–12; Dt 33:7).
2. Name used for people and land of Southern Kingdom.
Jer	13: 19	All **J** will be carried into exile,
Zec	10: 4	From **J** will come the cornerstone,
Heb	7: 14	that our Lord descended from **J**,

JUDAISM (JEW)
Gal	1: 13	of my previous way of life in **J**,

JUDAS
1. Apostle (Lk 6:16; Jn 14:22; Ac 1:13). Probably also called Thaddaeus (Mt 10:3; Mk 3:18).
2. Brother of James and Jesus (Mt 13:55; Mk 6:3), also called Jude (Jude 1).
3. Apostle, also called Iscariot, who betrayed Jesus (Mt 10:4; 26:14–56; Mk 3:19; 14:10–50; Lk 6:16; 22:3–53; Jn 6:71; 12:4; 13:2–30; 18:2–11). Suicide of (Mt 27:3–5; Ac 1:16–25).

JUDGE (JUDGED JUDGES JUDGING JUDGMENT)
Ge	18: 25	Will not the **J** of all the earth do
1Ch	16: 33	LORD, for he comes to **j** the earth.
Joel	3: 12	there I will sit to **j** all the nations
Mt	7: 1	"Do not **j**, or you too will be
Jn	7: 24	but instead **j** correctly."
	12: 47	For I did not come to **j** the world,
Ac	17: 31	set a day when he will **j** the world
1Co	4: 3	indeed, I do not even **j** myself.

1Co	6: 2	the Lord's people will **j** the world?
2Ti	4: 1	who will **j** the living and the dead,
	4: 8	the righteous **J**, will award to me
Jas	4: 12	who are you to **j** your neighbor?
Rev	20: 4	who had been given authority to **j**.

JUDGED (JUDGE)
Mt	7: 1	"Do not judge, or you too will be **j**.
Jn	5: 24	will not be **j** but has crossed over
Jas	3: 1	who teach will be **j** more strictly.
Rev	20: 12	The dead were **j** according to what

JUDGES (JUDGE)
Jdg	2: 16	Then the LORD raised up **j**,
Ps	9: 8	and **j** the peoples with equity.
	58: 11	there is a God who **j** the earth."
Ro	2: 16	God **j** people's secrets through Jesus
Heb	4: 12	it **j** the thoughts and attitudes
Rev	19: 11	With justice he **j** and wages war.

JUDGING (JUDGE)
Mt	19: 28	**j** the twelve tribes of Israel.
Jn	7: 24	Stop **j** by mere appearances,
2Co	10: 7	You are **j** by appearances.

JUDGMENT (JUDGE)
Dt	1: 17	of anyone, for **j** belongs to God.
Ps	1: 5	the wicked will not stand in the **j**,
	119: 66	Teach me knowledge and good **j**,
Ecc	12: 14	God will bring every deed into **j**,
Isa	66: 16	his sword the LORD will execute **j**
Mt	5: 21	who murders will be subject to **j**.'
	10: 15	Gomorrah on the day of **j** than
	12: 36	the day of **j** for every empty word
Jn	5: 22	but has entrusted all **j** to the Son,
	16: 8	about sin and righteousness and **j**:
Ro	14: 10	will all stand before God's **j** seat.
	14: 13	Therefore let us stop passing **j**
1Co	11: 29	eat and drink **j** on themselves.
	11: 31	we would not come under such **j**.
2Co	5: 10	we must all appear before the **j** seat
Heb	9: 27	to die once, and after that to face **j**,
	10: 27	only a fearful expectation of **j**
1Pe	4: 17	For it is time for **j** to begin
Jude	: 6	everlasting chains for **j** on the great

JUST (JUSTICE JUSTIFICATION JUSTIFIED JUSTIFY JUSTLY)
Dt	32: 4	are perfect, and all his ways are **j**.
Ps	37: 28	For the LORD loves the **j** and will
	111: 7	of his hands are faithful and **j**;
Pr	1: 3	doing what is right and **j** and fair;
	2: 8	for he guards the course of the **j**
Da	4: 37	does is right and all his ways are **j**.
Ro	3: 26	time, so as to be **j** and the one who
Heb	2: 2	received its **j** punishment,
1Jn	1: 9	he is faithful and **j** and will forgive
Rev	16: 7	true and **j** are your judgments."

JUSTICE (JUST)
Ex	23: 2	do not pervert **j** by siding
	23: 6	"Do not deny **j** to your poor people
Job	37: 23	in his **j** and great righteousness,
Ps	9: 16	LORD is known by his acts of **j**;
	11: 7	the LORD is righteous, he loves **j**;
	45: 6	a scepter of **j** will be the scepter
	101: 1	I will sing of your love and **j**;
Pr	21: 15	When **j** is done, it brings joy
	29: 4	By a king gives a country stability,
	29: 26	is from the LORD that one gets **j**.
Isa	9: 7	and upholding it with **j**
	28: 17	I will make **j** the measuring line
	30: 18	For the LORD is a God of **j**.
	42: 1	and he will bring **j** to the nations.
	42: 4	be discouraged till he establishes **j**
	56: 1	"Maintain **j** and do what is right,
	61: 8	"For I, the LORD, love **j**;
Eze	34: 16	I will shepherd the flock with **j**.
Am	5: 15	maintain **j** in the courts.
	5: 24	But let **j** roll on like a river,
Zec	7: 9	'Administer true **j**; show mercy
Lk	11: 42	you neglect **j** and the love of God.

JUSTIFICATION (JUST)
Ac	13: 39	sin, a **j** you were not able to obtain
Ro	4: 25	sins and was raised to life for our **j**.
	5: 18	one righteous act resulted in **j**

JUSTIFIED (JUST)
Ro	3: 24	all are **j** freely by his grace through

Ro 3: 28 that a person is **j** by faith apart
    5: 1 since we have been **j** through faith,
    5: 9 Since we have now been **j** by his
    8: 30 he called, he also **j**; those he **j**,
1Co 6: 11 you were **j** in the name of the Lord
Gal 2: 16 that a person is not **j** by the works
    3: 11 relies on the law is **j** before God,
    3: 24 came that we might be **j** by faith.

JUSTIFY (JUST)
Gal 3: 8 that God would **j** the Gentiles

JUSTLY (JUST)
Ps 106: 3 Blessed are those who act **j**,
Mic 6: 8 To act **j** and to love mercy

KEEP (KEEPER KEEPING KEEPS KEPT)
Ge 31: 49 "May the Lord **k** watch between
Ex 20: 6 love me and **k** my commandments.
Nu   6: 24 Lord bless you and **k** you;
Ps 18: 28 You, Lord, **k** my lamp burning;
    19: 13 **K** your servant also from willful
   121: 7 The Lord will **k** you from all
   141: 3 **k** watch over the door of my lips.
Pr   4: 24 **K** your mouth free of perversity;
    17: 28 are thought wise if they **k** silent,
Isa 26: 3 You will **k** in perfect peace those
Am   5: 13 Therefore the prudent **k** quiet
Mt 10: 10 staff, for the worker is worth his **k**.
Lk 12: 35 service and **k** your lamps burning,
Gal 5: 25 let us **k** in step with the Spirit.
Eph 4: 3 Make every effort to **k** the unity
1Ti 5: 22 the sins of others. **K** yourself pure.
2Ti 4: 5 you, **k** your head in all situations,
Heb 13: 5 **K** your lives free from the love
Jas 1: 26 and yet do not **k** a tight rein on
    2: 8 If you really **k** the royal law found
1Jn 5: 3 love for God: to **k** his commands.
Jude : 24 To him who is able to **k** you

KEEPER (KEEP)
Ge   4: 9 "Am I my brother's **k**?"

KEEPING (KEEP)
Ex 20: 8 the Sabbath day by **k** it holy.
Ps 19: 11 in **k** them there is great reward.
Mt   3: 8 Produce fruit in **k** with repentance.
Lk   2: 8 **k** watch over their flocks at night.
1Co 7: 19 **K** God's commands is what counts.
2Pe 3: 9 Lord is not slow in **k** his promise,

KEEPS (KEEP)
1Co 13: 5 angered, it **k** no record of wrongs.
Jas 2: 10 For whoever **k** the whole law

KEPT (KEEP)
Ps 130: 3 Lord, **k** a record of sins, Lord,
2Ti 4: 7 finished the race, I have **k** the faith.
1Pe 1: 4 This inheritance is **k** in heaven

KEYS
Mt 16: 19 will give you the **k** of the kingdom

KILL (KILLS)
Mt 17: 23 will **k** him, and on the third day

KILLS (KILL)
Lev 24: 21 whoever **k** a human being is to be
2Co 3: 6 for the letter **k**, but the Spirit gives

KIND (KINDNESS KINDS)
Ge   1: 24 animals, each according to its **k**."
2Ch 10: 7 "If you will be **k** to these people
Pr 11: 17 Those who are **k** benefit themselves,
    12: 25 the heart, but a **k** word cheers it up.
    14: 21 blessed is the one who is **k**
    14: 31 whoever is **k** to the needy honors
    19: 17 Whoever is **k** to the poor lends
Da   4: 27 by being **k** to the oppressed.
Lk   6: 35 because he is **k** to the ungrateful
1Co 13: 4 Love is patient, love is **k**.
    15: 35 what **k** of body will they come?"
Eph 4: 32 Be **k** and compassionate to one
2Ti 2: 24 but must be **k** to everyone,
Titus 2: 5 to be **k**, and to be subject to their

KINDNESS (KIND)
Ac 14: 17 He has shown **k** by giving you rain
Ro 11: 22 but **k** to you, provided that you continue in his **k**.
Gal 5: 22 peace, forbearance, **k**, goodness,
Eph 2: 7 expressed in his **k** to us in Christ

KINDS (KIND)
1Co 12: 4 There are different **k** of gifts,
1Ti 6: 10 of money is a root of all **k** of evil.

KING (KINGDOM KINGS)
1. Kings of Judah and Israel: see Saul, David, Solomon.
2. Kings of Judah: see Rehoboam, Abijah, Asa, Jehoshaphat, Jehoram, Ahaziah, Athaliah (Queen), Joash, Amaziah, Uzziah, Jotham, Ahaz, Hezekiah, Manasseh, Amon, Josiah, Jehoahaz, Jehoiakim, Jehoiachin, Zedekiah.
3. Kings of Israel: see Jeroboam I, Nadab, Baasha, Elah, Zimri, Tibni, Omri, Ahab, Ahaziah, Joram, Jehu, Jehoahaz, Jehoash, Jeroboam II, Zechariah, Shallum, Menahem, Pekah, Pekahiah, Hoshea.

Jdg 17: 6 In those days Israel had no **k**;
1Sa 12: 12 'No, we want a **k** to rule over us'—
    12: 12 the Lord your God was your **k**.
Ps 24: 7 that the **K** of glory may come in.
Isa 32: 1 a **k** will reign in righteousness
Zec 9: 9 See, your **k** comes to you,
1Ti 6: 15 the **K** of kings and Lord of lords,
Rev 19: 16 thigh he has this name written: **K**

KINGDOM (KING)
Ex 19: 6 you will be for me a **k** of priests
1Ch 29: 11 Yours, Lord, is the **k**;
Ps 45: 6 justice will be the scepter of your **k**.
Da   4: 3 His **k** is an eternal **k**;
Mt   3: 2 for the **k** of heaven has come near."
    5: 3 spirit, for theirs is the **k** of heaven.
    6: 10 your **k** come, your will be done,
    6: 33 But seek first his **k** and his
    7: 21 Lord,' will enter the **k** of heaven,
    11: 11 **k** of heaven is greater than he.
    13: 24 "The **k** of heaven is like a man who
    13: 31 "The **k** of heaven is like a mustard
    13: 33 "The **k** of heaven is like yeast
    13: 44 "The **k** of heaven is like treasure
    13: 45 the **k** of heaven is like a merchant
    13: 47 the **k** of heaven is like a net that
    16: 19 you the keys of the **k** of heaven;
    18: 23 the **k** of heaven is like a king who
    19: 24 who is rich to enter the **k** of God."
    24: 7 rise against nation, and **k** against **k**.
    24: 14 gospel of the **k** will be preached
    25: 34 the **k** prepared for you since
Mk   9: 47 you to enter the **k** of God with one
    10: 14 for the **k** of God belongs to such as
    10: 23 for the rich to enter the **k** of God!"
Lk 10: 9 'The **k** of God has come near
    12: 31 But seek his **k**, and these things
    17: 21 is,' because the **k** of God is in your
Jn   3: 5 one can enter the **k** of God unless
    18: 36 said, "My **k** is not of this world.
1Co 6: 9 wrongdoers will not inherit the **k**
    15: 24 when he hands over the **k** to God
Rev 1: 6 has made us to be a **k** and priests
    11: 15 "The **k** of the world has become

KINGS (KING)
Ps   2: 2 The **k** of the earth rise
    72: 11 May all **k** bow down to him and all
Da   7: 24 ten horns are ten **k** who will come
1Ti 2: 2 for **k** and all those in authority,
Rev 1: 5 and the ruler of the **k** of the earth.

KISS
Ps   2: 12 **K** his son, or he will be angry
Pr 24: 26 An honest answer is like a **k**
Lk 22: 48 the Son of Man with a **k**?"

KNEE (KNEES)
Isa 45: 23 Before me every **k** will bow;
Ro 14: 11 Lord, 'every **k** will bow before me;
Php 2: 10 name of Jesus every **k** should bow,

KNEES (KNEE)
Isa 35: 3 hands, steady the **k** that give way;
Heb 12: 12 your feeble arms and weak **k**.

KNEW (KNOW)
Job 23: 3 If only I **k** where to find him;
Jnh 4: 2 I **k** that you are a gracious
Mt   7: 23 tell them plainly, 'I never **k** you.

KNOCK
Mt   7: 7 **k** and the door will be opened
Rev 3: 20 I stand at the door and **k**.

KNOW (FOREKNEW KNEW KNOWING KNOWLEDGE KNOWN KNOWS)
Dt 18: 21 "How can we **k** when a message
Job 19: 25 I **k** that my redeemer lives,
    42: 3 things too wonderful for me to **k**.

Ps 46: 10 says, "Be still, and **k** that I am God;
73: 11 Does the Most High **k** anything?"
139: 1 LORD, and you **k** me.
139: 23 Search me, God, and **k** my heart;
Pr 27: 1 you do not **k** what a day may bring.
Jer 24: 7 I will give them a heart to **k** me,
31: 34 because they will all **k** me,
Mt 6: 3 let your left hand **k** what your right
24: 42 because you do not **k** on what day
Lk 1: 4 so that you may **k** the certainty
Jn 3: 11 you, we speak of what we **k**, and we
4: 22 worship what you do not **k**;
9: 25 One thing I do **k**. I was blind
10: 14 I **k** my sheep and my sheep **k** me—
17: 3 that they **k** you, the only true God,
21: 24 We **k** that his testimony is true.
Ac 1: 7 "It is not for you to **k** the times
Ro 6: 6 we **k** that our old self was crucified
7: 18 I **k** that good itself does not dwell
8: 28 we **k** that in all things God works
1Co 2: 2 I resolved to **k** nothing while I was
6: 15 Do you not **k** that your bodies are
6: 19 Do you not **k** that your bodies are
8: 2 do not yet **k** as they ought to **k**.
13: 12 Now I **k** in part; then I shall **k** fully,
15: 58 because you **k** that your labor
Php 1: 23 I want to **k** Christ—yes, to **k**
2Ti 1: 12 because I **k** whom I have believed,
Jas 4: 14 do not even **k** what will happen
1Jn 2: 4 Whoever says, "I **k** him," but does
3: 14 We **k** that we have passed
3: 16 This is how we **k** what love is:
5: 2 This is how we **k** that we love
5: 13 may **k** that you have eternal life.
KNOWING (KNOW)
Ge 3: 5 will be like God, **k** good and evil."
Php 3: 8 worth of **k** Christ Jesus my Lord,
KNOWLEDGE (KNOW)
Ge 2: 9 the tree of the **k** of good and evil.
Job 42: 3 that obscures my plans without **k**?'
Ps 19: 2 night after night they reveal **k**.
139: 6 Such **k** is too wonderful for me,
Pr 1: 7 of the LORD is the beginning of **k**,
10: 14 The wise store up **k**, but the mouth
12: 1 Whoever loves discipline loves **k**,
13: 16 All who are prudent act with **k**,
19: 2 Desire without **k** is not good—
Isa 11: 9 the **k** of the LORD as the waters
Hab 2: 14 will be filled with the **k** of the glory
Ro 11: 33 riches of the wisdom and **k** of God!
1Co 8: 1 But **k** puffs up while love builds up.
8: 11 Christ died, is destroyed by your **k**.
13: 2 can fathom all mysteries and all **k**,
2Co 2: 14 aroma of the **k** of him everywhere.
4: 6 of the **k** of God's glory displayed
Eph 3: 19 know this love that surpasses **k**—
Col 2: 3 all the treasures of wisdom and **k**.
1Ti 6: 20 ideas of what is falsely called **k**,
2Pe 3: 18 grow in the grace and **k** of our Lord
KNOWN (KNOW)
Ps 16: 11 You make **k** to me the path of life;
105: 1 make **k** among the nations what he
Isa 46: 10 I make **k** the end
Mt 10: 26 or hidden that will not be made **k**.
Ro 1: 19 since what may be **k** about God is
11: 34 "Who has **k** the mind of the Lord?
15: 20 the gospel where Christ was not **k**,
2Co 3: 2 our hearts, and read by everyone.
2Pe 2: 21 than to have **k** it and then to turn
KNOWS (KNOW)
1Sa 2: 3 for the LORD is a God who **k**,
Job 23: 10 But he **k** the way that I take;
Ps 44: 21 since he **k** the secrets of the heart?
94: 11 The LORD **k** all human plans; he **k**
Ecc 8: 7 Since no one **k** the future, who can
Mt 6: 8 your Father **k** what you need
24: 36 about that day or hour no one **k**,
Ro 8: 27 searches our hearts **k** the mind
2Ti 2: 19 "The Lord **k** those who are his,"
LABAN
Brother of Rebekah (Ge 24:29–51), father of Rachel and Leah (Ge 29–31).

LABOR
Ex 20: 9 Six days you shall **l** and do all your
Isa 55: 2 your **l** on what does not satisfy?
Mt 6: 28 They do not **l** or spin.
1Co 3: 8 rewarded according to their own **l**.
15: 58 know that your **l** in the Lord is not
LACK (LACKING LACKS)
Pr 15: 22 Plans fail for **l** of counsel,
Col 2: 23 but they **l** any value in restraining
LACKING (LACK)
Ro 12: 11 Never be **l** in zeal, but keep your
Jas 1: 4 and complete, not **l** anything.
LACKS (LACK)
Jas 1: 5 If any of you **l** wisdom, you should
LAID (LAY)
Isa 53: 6 and the LORD has **l** on him
1Co 3: 11 other than the one already **l**,
1Jn 3: 16 Jesus Christ **l** down his life for us.
LAKE
Rev 19: 20 into the fiery **l** of burning sulfur.
20: 14 The **l** of fire is the second death.
LAMB (LAMB'S LAMBS)
Ge 22: 8 "God himself will provide the **l**
Ex 12: 21 and slaughter the Passover **l**.
Isa 11: 6 The wolf will live with the **l**,
53: 7 he was led like a **l** to the slaughter,
Jn 1: 29 "Look, the **L** of God, who takes
1Co 5: 7 our Passover **l**, has been sacrificed.
1Pe 1: 19 a **l** without blemish or defect.
Rev 5: 6 Then I saw a **L**, looking as if it had
5: 12 "Worthy is the **L**, who was slain,
14: 4 as firstfruits to God and the **L**.
LAMB'S (LAMB)
Rev 21: 27 names are written in the **L** book
LAMBS (LAMB)
Lk 10: 3 you out like **l** among wolves.
Jn 21: 15 Jesus said, "Feed my **l**."
LAMENT
2Sa 1: 17 took up this **l** concerning Saul
LAMP (LAMPS)
2Sa 22: 29 You, LORD, are my **l**;
Ps 18: 28 You, LORD, keep my **l** burning;
119:105 Your word is a **l** to my feet
Pr 31: 18 and her **l** does not go out at night.
Lk 8: 16 "No one lights a **l** and hides it
Rev 21: 23 gives it light, and the Lamb is its **l**.
LAMPS (LAMP)
Mt 25: 1 be like ten virgins who took their **l**
Lk 12: 35 service and keep your **l** burning,
LAND
Ge 1: 10 God called the dry ground "**l**,"
1: 11 said, "Let the **l** produce vegetation:
12: 7 your offspring I will give this **l**."
Ex 3: 8 a **l** flowing with milk and honey—
Nu 35: 33 Bloodshed pollutes the **l**,
Dt 34: 1 LORD showed him the whole **l**—
Jos 13: 2 "This is the **l** that remains:
14: 4 Levites received no share of the **l**
2Ch 7: 14 their sin and will heal their **l**.
7: 20 then I will uproot Israel from my **l**,
Eze 36: 24 bring you back into your own **l**.
LANGUAGE
Ge 11: 1 Now the whole world had one **l**
Jn 8: 44 speaks his native **l**, for he is a liar
Ac 2: 6 heard their own **l** being spoken.
Col 3: 8 slander, and filthy **l** from your lips.
Rev 5: 9 God persons from every tribe and **l**
LAST (LASTING LASTS LATTER)
2Sa 23: 1 These are the **l** words of David:
Isa 44: 6 I am the first and I am the **l**;
Mt 19: 30 But many who are first will be **l**,
Mk 10: 31 will be **l**, and the **l** first."
Jn 15: 16 fruit that will **l**—and so
Ro 1: 17 that is by faith from first to **l**,
2Ti 3: 1 will be terrible times in the **l** days.
2Pe 3: 3 in the **l** days scoffers will come,
Rev 1: 17 I am the First and the **L**.
22: 13 the First and the **L**, the Beginning
LASTING (LAST)
Ex 12: 14 to the LORD—a **l** ordinance.
Lev 24: 8 of the Israelites, as a **l** covenant.
Nu 25: 13 have a covenant of a **l** priesthood,
Heb 10: 34 had better and **l** possessions.

LASTS (LAST)
Ps 30: 5 For his anger I only a moment,
2Co 3: 11 greater is the glory of that which I!
LATTER (LAST)
Job 42: 12 The LORD blessed the I part
LAUGH (LAUGHS)
Ecc 3: 4 a time to weep and a time to I,
LAUGHS (LAUGH)
Ps 2: 4 The One enthroned in heaven I;
37: 13 but the Lord I at the wicked, for he
LAVISHED
Eph 1: 8 that he I on us. With all wisdom
1Jn 3: 1 See what great love the Father has I
LAW (LAWS)
Dt 31: 11 you shall read this I before them
31: 26 "Take this Book of the L and place
Jos 1: 8 Keep this Book of the L always
Ne 8: 8 from the Book of the L of God,
Ps 1: 2 delight is in the I of the LORD,
19: 7 The I of the LORD is perfect,
119: 18 may see wonderful things in your I.
119: 72 The I from your mouth is more
119: 97 Oh, how I love your I! I meditate
119:165 peace have those who love your I,
Jer 31: 33 "I will put my I in their minds
Mt 5: 17 that I have come to abolish the L
7: 12 you, for this sums up the L
22: 40 All the L and the Prophets hang
Lk 16: 17 stroke of a pen to drop out of the L.
Jn 1: 17 For the I was given through Moses;
Ro 2: 12 All who sin apart from the I will
2: 15 requirements of the I are written
5: 13 account where there is no I.
5: 20 The I was brought in so
6: 14 because you are not under the I,
7: 6 we have been released from the I so
7: 12 So then, the I is holy,
8: 3 For what the I was powerless to do
10: 4 Christ is the culmination of the I
13: 10 love is the fulfillment of the I.
Gal 3: 13 curse of the I by becoming a curse
3: 24 So the I was our guardian until
5: 3 he is obligated to obey the whole I.
5: 4 by the I have been alienated
5: 14 For the entire I is fulfilled
Heb 7: 19 (for the I made nothing perfect),
10: 1 The I is only a shadow of the good
Jas 1: 25 the perfect I that gives freedom,
2: 10 For whoever keeps the whole I
LAWLESSNESS
2Th 2: 3 occurs and the man of I is revealed,
2: 7 the secret power of I is already
1Jn 3: 4 sins breaks the law; in fact, sin is I.
LAWS (LAW)
Lev 25: 18 and be careful to obey my I,
Ps 119: 30 I have set my heart on your I.
119:120 fear of you; I stand in awe of your I.
Heb 8: 10 I will put my I in their minds
10: 16 I will put my I in their hearts, and I
LAY (LAID LAYING)
Job 22: 22 and I up his words in your heart.
Isa 28: 16 "See, I I a stone in Zion, a tested
Mt 8: 20 of Man has no place to I his head."
Jn 10: 15 and I I down my life for the sheep.
15: 13 to I down one's life for one's
1Co 3: 11 no one can I any foundation other
1Jn 3: 16 we ought to I down our lives for
Rev 4: 10 They I their crowns before
LAYING (LAY)
1Ti 5: 22 not be hasty in the I on of hands,
Heb 6: 1 not I again the foundation
LAZARUS
   1. Poor man in Jesus' parable (Lk 16:19–31).
   2. Brother of Mary and Martha whom Jesus raised from the dead (Jn 11:1—12:19).
LAZY
Pr 10: 4 L hands make for poverty,
Heb 6: 12 We do not want you to become I,
LEAD (LEADERS LEADS LED)
Ex 15: 13 love you will I the people you have
Ps 27: 11 I me in a straight path because
61: 2 I me to the rock that is higher than I.

Ps 139: 24 and I me in the way everlasting.
143: 10 may your good Spirit I me on level
Ecc 5: 6 Do not let your mouth I you
Isa 11: 6 and a little child will I them.
Da 12: 3 those who I many to righteousness,
Mt 6: 13 And I us not into temptation,
1Jn 3: 7 do not let anyone I you astray.
LEADERS (LEAD)
Heb 13: 7 Remember your I, who spoke
13: 17 Have confidence in your I
LEADS (LEAD)
Ps 23: 2 he I me beside quiet waters,
Pr 19: 23 The fear of the LORD I to life;
Isa 40: 11 he gently I those that have young.
Mt 7: 13 gate and broad is the road that I
Jn 10: 3 sheep by name and I them out.
Ro 14: 19 every effort to do what I to peace
2Co 2: 14 God, who always I us as captives
LEAH
   Wife of Jacob (Ge 29:16–30); bore six sons and one daughter (Ge 29:31—30:21; 34:1; 35:23).
LEAN
Pr 3: 5 I not on your own understanding;
LEARN (LEARNED LEARNING)
Isa 1: 17 L to do right; seek justice.
Mt 11: 29 my yoke upon you and I from me,
LEARNED (LEARN)
Php 4: 11 I have I to be content whatever
2Ti 3: 14 know those from whom you I it,
LEARNING (LEARN)
Pr 1: 5 the wise listen and add to their I,
2Ti 3: 7 always I but never able to come
LED (LEAD)
Isa 53: 7 he was I like a lamb
Am 2: 10 I you forty years in the wilderness
Ro 8: 14 For those who are I by the Spirit
LEFT
Jos 1: 7 turn from it to the right or to the I,
Pr 4: 27 Do not turn to the right or the I;
Mt 6: 3 do not let your I hand know what
25: 33 on his right and the goats on his I.
LEGION
Mk 5: 9 "My name is L," he replied,
LEND (LENDS)
Dt 15: 8 freely I them whatever they need.
Ps 37: 26 are always generous and I freely;
Lk 6: 34 Even sinners I to sinners,
LENDS (LEND)
Pr 19: 17 kind to the poor I to the LORD,
LENGTH (LONG)
Pr 10: 27 fear of the LORD adds I to life,
LEPROSY
2Ki 7: 3 Now there were four men with I
LETTER (LETTERS)
Mt 5: 18 not the smallest I, not the least
2Co 3: 2 You yourselves are our I,
3: 6 not of the I but of the Spirit; for the I kills,
2Th 3: 14 not obey our instruction in this I.
LETTERS (LETTER)
2Co 3: 7 which was engraved in I on stone,
10: 10 "His I are weighty and forceful,
2Pe 3: 16 He writes the same way in all his I,
LEVEL
Ps 143: 10 good Spirit lead me on I ground.
Isa 26: 7 The path of the righteous is I;
Heb 12: 13 "Make I paths for your feet,"
LEVI (LEVITES)
   1. Son of Jacob by Leah (Ge 29:34; 46:11; 1Ch 2:1). Tribe of blessed (Ge 49:5–7; Dt 33:8–11), chosen as priests (Nu 3–4), numbered (Nu 3:39; 26:62), allotted cities, but not land (Nu 18; 35; Dt 10:9; Jos 13:14; 21), land (Eze 48:8–22), 12,000 from (Rev 7:7).
   2. See MATTHEW.
LEVITES (LEVI)
Nu 1: 53 The L are to be responsible
8: 6 "Take the L from among all
18: 21 "I give to the L all the tithes
LEWDNESS
Mk 7: 22 malice, deceit, I, envy, slander,
LIAR (LIE)
Pr 19: 22 better to be poor than a I.
Jn 8: 44 for he is a I and the father of lies.
Ro 3: 4 be true, and every human being a I.

LIBERATED
Ro   8: 21   the creation itself will be **l** from its
LIE (LIAR LIED LIES LYING)
Lev 19: 11   "'Do not **l**. "'Do not deceive
Nu 23: 19   that he should **l**, not a human
Dt   6: 7   when you **l** down and when you
Ps 23: 2   He makes me **l** down in green
Isa 11: 6   the leopard will **l** down
Eze 34: 14   There they will **l** down in good
Ro   1: 25   the truth about God for a **l**,
Col   3: 9   Do not **l** to each other, since you
Heb 6: 18   which it is impossible for God to **l**,
LIED (LIE)
Ac   5: 4   You have not **l** just to human
LIES (LIE)
Ps 34: 13   evil and your lips from telling **l**.
Jn   8: 44   for he is a liar and the father of **l**.
LIFE (LIVE)
Ge   2: 7   into his nostrils the breath of **l**,
       2: 9   of the garden were the tree of **l**
       9: 11   Never again will all **l** be destroyed
Ex 21: 23   injury, you are to take **l** for **l**,
Lev 17: 14   because the **l** of every creature is its
    24: 18   must make restitution—**l** for **l**.
Dt 30: 19   Now choose **l**, so that you and your
Ps 16: 11   make known to me the path of **l**;
    23: 6   will follow me all the days of my **l**,
    34: 12   Whoever of you loves **l** and desires
    39: 4   let me know how fleeting my **l** is.
    49: 7   one can redeem the **l** of another
  104: 33   I will sing to the LORD all my **l**;
Pr   6: 23   and instruction are the way to **l**,
     7: 23   little knowing it will cost him his **l**.
     8: 35   For those who find me find **l**
   11: 30   fruit of the righteous is a tree of **l**,
   21: 21   righteousness and love finds **l**,
Eze 37: 5   enter you, and you will come to **l**.
Da 12: 2   some to everlasting **l**,
Mt   6: 25   do not worry about your **l**,
     7: 14   and narrow the road that leads to **l**,
   10: 39   whoever loses their **l** for my sake
   16: 25   wants to save their **l** will lose it,
   20: 28   to give his **l** as a ransom for many."
Mk 10: 45   to give his **l** as a ransom for many."
Lk 12: 15   **l** does not consist in an abundance
   12: 22   do not worry about your **l**,
   14: 26   yes, even their own **l**—
Jn   1: 4   In him was **l**, and that **l** was the light
    3: 15   who believes may have eternal **l**
    3: 36   believes in the Son has eternal **l**,
    4: 14   of water welling up to eternal **l**."
    5: 24   has crossed over from death to **l**.
    6: 35   Jesus declared, "I am the bread of **l**.
    6: 47   the one who believes has eternal **l**.
    6: 68   You have the words of eternal **l**.
   10: 10   I have come that they may have **l**,
   10: 15   and I lay down my **l** for the sheep.
   10: 28   I give them eternal **l**, and they shall
   11: 25   "I am the resurrection and the **l**.
   14: 6   am the way and the truth and the **l**.
   15: 13   lay down one's **l** for one's friends.
   20: 31   by believing you may have **l** in his
Ac 13: 48   appointed for eternal **l** believed.
Ro   4: 25   was raised to **l** for our justification.
    6: 13   have been brought from death to **l**;
    6: 23   God is eternal **l** in Christ Jesus our
    8: 38   convinced that neither death nor **l**,
1Co 15: 19   If only for this **l** we have hope
2Co 3: 6   the letter kills, but the Spirit gives **l**.
Gal 2: 20   The **l** I now live in the body, I live
Eph 4: 1   to live a **l** worthy of the calling you
Php 2: 16   as you hold firmly to the word of **l**.
Col   1: 10   you may live a **l** worthy of the Lord
1Th 4: 12   your daily **l** may win the respect
1Ti   4: 8   the present **l** and the **l** to come.
    4: 16   Watch your **l** and doctrine closely.
    6: 19   take hold of the **l** that is truly **l**.
2Ti   3: 12   live a godly **l** in Christ Jesus will be
Jas   1: 12   person will receive the crown of **l**
    3: 13   Let them show it by their good **l**,
1Pe 3: 10   "Whoever would love **l** and see
2Pe 1: 3   a godly **l** through our knowledge
1Jn 3: 14   we have passed from death to **l**,

1Jn 5: 11   God has given us eternal **l**, and this **l**
Rev 13: 8   written in the Lamb's book of **l**,
   20: 12   was opened, which is the book of **l**.
   21: 27   are written in the Lamb's book of **l**.
   22: 2   side of the river stood the tree of **l**,
LIFT (LIFTED LIFTING)
Ps 121: 1   I **l** up my eyes to the mountains—
  134: 2   **L** up your hands in the sanctuary
La   3: 41   Let us **l** up our hearts and our hands
LIFTED (LIFT)
Ps 40: 2   He **l** me out of the slimy pit,
Jn   3: 14   so the Son of Man must be **l** up,
   12: 32   I, when I am **l** up from the earth,
LIFTING (LIFT)
1Ti 2: 8   **l** up holy hands without anger
LIGHT (ENLIGHTENED)
Ge   1: 3   "Let there be **l**," and there was **l**.
2Sa 22: 29   LORD turns my darkness into **l**.
Job 38: 19   "What is the way to the abode of **l**?
Ps   4: 6   Let the **l** of your face shine on us.
   19: 8   are radiant, giving **l** to the eyes.
   27: 1   The LORD is my **l** and my
   56: 13   walk before God in the **l** of life.
   76: 4   You are radiant with **l**,
  104: 2   The LORD wraps himself in **l** as
 119:105   lamp to my feet and a **l** for my path.
 119:130   unfolding of your words gives **l**;
Isa   2: 5   let us walk in the **l** of the LORD.
    9: 2   in darkness have seen a great **l**;
   49: 6   also make you a **l** for the Gentiles,
Mt   4: 16   shadow of death a **l** has dawned."
    5: 16   way, let your **l** shine before others,
   11: 30   yoke is easy and my burden is **l**."
Jn   3: 19   **L** has come into the world,
    8: 12   he said, "I am the **l** of the world.
2Co 4: 6   made his **l** shine in our hearts
    6: 14   Or what fellowship can **l** have
   11: 14   masquerades as an angel of **l**.
1Ti 6: 16   and who lives in unapproachable **l**,
1Pe 2: 9   of darkness into his wonderful **l**.
1Jn 1: 5   God is **l**; in him there is no darkness
    1: 7   But if we walk in the **l**, as he is
Rev 21: 23   for the glory of God gives it **l**,
LIGHTNING
Da 10: 6   his face like **l**, his eyes like flaming
Mt 24: 27   For as **l** that comes from the east is
   28: 3   His appearance was like **l**, and his
LIKENESS
Ge   1: 26   in our **l**, so that they may rule over
Ps 17: 15   will be satisfied with seeing your **l**.
Isa 52: 14   his form marred beyond human **l**
Ro   8: 3   his own Son in the **l** of sinful flesh
Php 2: 7   a servant, being made in human **l**.
Jas 3: 9   who have been made in God's **l**.
LION
Isa 11: 7   and the **l** will eat straw like the ox.
1Pe 5: 8   around like a roaring **l** looking
Rev 5: 5   See, the **L** of the tribe of Judah,
LIPS
Ps 34: 1   his praise will always be on my **l**.
 119:171   May my **l** overflow with praise,
Pr 13: 3   who guard their **l** preserve their
   27: 2   an outsider, and not your own **l**.
Isa   6: 5   For I am a man of unclean **l**, and I
Mt 21: 16   read, "'From the **l** of children
Col   3: 8   and filthy language from your **l**.
LISTEN (LISTENING)
Dt 30: 20   LORD your God, **l** to his voice,
Pr   1: 5   let the wise **l** and add to their
   12: 15   to them, but the wise **l** to advice.
Jn 10: 27   My sheep **l** to my voice;
Jas 1: 19   Everyone should be quick to **l**,
   1: 22   Do not merely **l** to the word,
LISTENING (LISTEN)
1Sa 3: 9   LORD, for your servant is **l**.'"
Pr 18: 13   To answer before **l**—that is folly
LIVE (ALIVE LIFE LIVES LIVING)
Ex 20: 12   that you may **l** long in the land
   33: 20   face, for no one may see me and **l**."
Dt   8: 3   that man does not **l** on bread alone
Job 14: 14   If someone dies, will they **l** again?
Ps 119:175   Let me **l** that I may praise you,

Isa 55: 3 come to me; listen, that you may **l**.
Eze 37: 3 "Son of man, can these bones **l**?"
Hab 2: 4 the righteous person will **l** by his
Mt 4: 4 'Man shall not **l** on bread alone,
Ac 17: 24 not **l** in temples built by human
17: 28 'For in him we **l** and move and
Ro 1: 17 "The righteous will **l** by faith."
2Co 5: 7 For we **l** by faith, not by sight.
Gal 2: 20 The life I now **l** in the body,
5: 25 Since we **l** by the Spirit, let us keep
Php 1: 21 me, to **l** is Christ and to die is gain.
1Th 5: 13 **l** in peace with each other.
2Ti 3: 12 who wants to **l** a godly life
Heb 12: 14 Make every effort to **l** in peace
1Pe 1: 17 **l** out your time as foreigners here
LIVES (LIVE)
Job 19: 25 I know that my redeemer **l**,
Pr 11: 30 and the one who is wise saves **l**.
Isa 57: 15 he who **l** forever, whose name is
Da 3: 28 to give up their **l** rather than serve
Jn 14: 17 he **l** with you and will be in you.
Gal 2: 20 I no longer live, but Christ **l** in me.
Heb 13: 5 Keep your **l** free from the love
2Pe 3: 11 You ought to live holy and godly **l**
1Jn 3: 16 to lay down our **l** for our brothers
4: 16 Whoever **l** in love **l** in God,
LIVING (LIVE)
Ge 2: 7 life, and the man became a **l** being.
Jer 2: 13 the spring of **l** water, and have dug
Mt 22: 32 the God of the dead but of the **l**."
Jn 7: 38 said, rivers of **l** water will flow
Ro 12: 1 to offer your bodies as a **l** sacrifice,
Heb 10: 31 to fall into the hands of the **l** God.
Rev 1: 18 I am the **L** One; I was dead,
LOAD
Gal 6: 5 each one should carry their own **l**.
LOCUSTS
Mt 3: 4 His food was **l** and wild honey.
LOFTY
Ps 139: 6 for me, too **l** for me to attain.
LONELY
Ps 68: 6 God sets the **l** in families, he leads
LONG (LENGTH LONGED LONGING LONGS)
1Ki 18: 21 "How **l** will you waver between
Jn 9: 4 As **l** as it is day, we must do
Eph 3: 18 to grasp how wide and **l** and high
1Pe 1: 12 Even angels **l** to look into these
LONGED (LONG)
Mt 13: 17 righteous people **l** to see what you
23: 37 how often I have **l** to gather your
2Ti 4: 8 to all who have **l** for his appearing.
LONGING (LONG)
Pr 13: 19 A **l** fulfilled is sweet to the soul,
2Co 5: 2 **l** to be clothed instead with our
LONGS (LONG)
Isa 30: 18 Yet the Lᴏʀᴅ **l** to be gracious
LOOK (LOOKING LOOKS)
Job 31: 1 my eyes not to **l** lustfully at a young
Ps 34: 5 Those who **l** to him are radiant;
Pr 4: 25 Let your eyes **l** straight ahead;
Isa 60: 5 Then you will **l** and be radiant,
Hab 1: 13 Your eyes are too pure to **l** on evil;
Zec 12: 10 They will **l** on me, the one they
Mk 13: 21 is the Messiah!' or, '**L**, there he is!'
Lk 24: 39 **L** at my hands and my feet. It is I
Jn 1: 36 by, he said, "**L**, the Lamb of God!"
4: 35 open your eyes and **l** at the fields!
19: 37 "They will **l** on the one they have
Jas 1: 27 to **l** after orphans and widows
1Pe 1: 12 Even angels long to **l** into these
LOOKING (LOOK)
Rev 5: 6 a Lamb, **l** as if it had been slain,
LOOKS (LOOK)
1Sa 16: 7 but the Lᴏʀᴅ **l** at the heart."
Lk 9: 62 puts a hand to the plow and **l** back
Php 2: 21 everyone **l** out for their own interests,
LORD (LORD'S LORDING)
Ne 4: 14 Remember the **L**, who is great
Job 28: 28 human race, "The fear of the **L**—
Ps 54: 4 the **L** is the one who sustains me.
62: 12 and with you, **L**, is unfailing love";
86: 5 You, **L**, are forgiving and good,

Ps 110: 1 The Lᴏʀᴅ says to my **l**:
147: 5 Great is our **L** and mighty in power
Isa 6: 1 died, I saw the **L**, high and exalted,
Da 9: 4 "**L**, the great and awesome God,
Mt 3: 3 'Prepare the way for the **L**,
4: 7 'Do not put the **L** your God
7: 21 "Not everyone who says to me, '**L**,
22: 37 " 'Love the **L** your God with all
22: 44 " 'The **L** said to my **L**: "Sit at my
Mk 12: 11 the **L** has done this, and it is
12: 29 "The **L** our God, the **L** is one.
Lk 2: 9 An angel of the **L** appeared to
6: 46 "Why do you call me, '**L**, **L**,'
10: 27 " 'Love the **L** your God with all
Ac 2: 21 on the name of the **L** will be saved.'
16: 31 "Believe in the **L** Jesus, and you
Ro 10: 9 "Jesus is **L**," and believe in your
10: 13 the name of the **L** will be saved."
12: 11 your spiritual fervor, serving the **L**.
14: 8 we live or die, we belong to the **L**.
1Co 1: 31 the one who boasts boast in the **L**."
3: 5 as the **L** has assigned to each his
7: 34 to be devoted to the **L** in both body
11: 23 The **L** Jesus, on the night he was
12: 3 "Jesus is **L**," except by the Holy
15: 57 victory through our **L** Jesus Christ.
16: 22 let that person be cursed! Come, **L**!
2Co 3: 17 Now the **L** is the Spirit, and where
8: 5 gave themselves first of all to the **L**,
10: 17 the one who boasts boast in the **L**.
Gal 6: 14 in the cross of our **L** Jesus Christ,
Eph 4: 5 one **L**, one faith, one baptism;
5: 10 and find out what pleases the **L**.
5: 19 music from your heart to the **L**,
Php 2: 11 acknowledge that Jesus Christ is **L**,
3: 1 and sisters, rejoice in the **L**!
4: 4 Rejoice in the **L** always. I will say it
Col 2: 6 as you received Christ Jesus as **L**,
3: 17 do it all in the name of the **L** Jesus,
3: 23 working for the **L**, not for human
4: 17 you have received in the **L**."
1Th 3: 12 May the **L** make your love increase
5: 2 day of the **L** will come like a thief
5: 23 at the coming of our **L** Jesus Christ.
2Th 2: 1 the coming of our **L** Jesus Christ
2Ti 2: 19 "The **L** knows those who are his,"
Heb 12: 14 holiness no one will see the **L**.
13: 6 confidence, "The **L** is my helper;
Jas 4: 10 Humble yourselves before the **L**,
1Pe 1: 25 the word of the **L** endures forever."
2: 3 you have tasted that the **L** is good.
3: 15 in your hearts revere Christ as **L**.
2Pe 1: 16 the coming of our **L** Jesus Christ
2: 1 sovereign **L** who bought them—
3: 9 The **L** is not slow in keeping his
Jude : 14 the **L** is coming with thousands
Rev 4: 8 holy is the **L** God Almighty,'
4: 11 "You are worthy, our **L** and God,
17: 14 triumph over them because he is **L**
22: 20 Amen. Come, **L** Jesus.
LORD'S (LORD)
Ac 21: 14 up and said, "The **L** will be done."
1Co 10: 26 "The earth is the **L**, and everything
11: 26 you proclaim the **L** death until he
2Co 3: 18 faces contemplate the **L** glory,
2Ti 2: 24 And the **L** servant must not be
Jas 4: 15 "If it is the **L** will, we will live
LORDING (LORD)
1Pe 5: 3 not **l** it over those entrusted to you,
LORD* (LORD'S*; this is the proper name of God, *Yahweh*, spelled "Lᴏʀᴅ" in the NIV)
Ge 2: 4 when the **L** God made the earth
2: 7 the **L** God formed a man
3: 21 the **L** God made garments of skin
7: 16 Then the **L** shut him in.
15: 6 Abram believed the **L**, and he
18: 14 Is anything too hard for the **L**?
31: 49 "May the **L** keep watch between
Ex 3: 2 There the angel of the **L** appeared
9: 12 But the **L** hardened Pharaoh's heart
14: 30 That day the **L** saved Israel
20: 2 "I am the **L** your God, who
33: 11 The **L** would speak to Moses face

Ex	40: 34	glory of the **L** filled the tabernacle.
Lev	19: 2	'Be holy because I, the **L** your God,
Nu	8: 5	The **L** said to Moses:
	14: 21	glory of the **L** fills the whole earth,
Dt	2: 7	The **L** your God has blessed you
	5: 9	for I, the **L** your God, am a jealous
	6: 4	The **L** our God, the **L** is one.
	6: 5	Love the **L** your God with all your
	6: 16	Do not put the **L** your God
	10: 14	**L** your God belong the heavens,
	10: 17	For the **L** your God is God of gods
	11: 1	Love the **L** your God and keep his
	28: 1	If you fully obey the **L** your God
	30: 16	you today to love the **L** your God,
	30: 20	For the **L** is your life, and he will
	31: 6	for the **L** your God goes with you;
Jos	22: 5	to love the **L** your God, to walk
	24: 15	household, we will serve the **L**."
1Sa	1: 28	So now I give him to the **L**.
	2: 2	"There is no one holy like the **L**;
	7: 12	"Thus far the **L** has helped us."
	12: 22	his great name the **L** will not reject
	15: 22	as much as in obeying the **L**?
2Sa	22: 2	"The **L** is my rock, my fortress
1Ki	2: 3	and observe what the **L** your God
	8: 11	the glory of the **L** filled his temple.
	8: 61	fully committed to the **L** our God,
	18: 21	If the **L** is God, follow him;
2Ki	13: 23	But the **L** was gracious to them
1Ch	16: 8	Give praise to the **L**, proclaim his
	16: 23	Sing to the **L**, all the earth;
	28: 9	for the **L** searches every heart
	29: 11	Yours, **L**, is the kingdom;
2Ch	5: 14	the glory of the **L** filled the temple
	16: 9	the **L** range throughout the earth
	19: 6	for mere mortals but for the **L**,
	30: 9	for the **L** your God is gracious
Ne	1: 5	"**L**, the God of heaven, the great
Job	1: 21	The **L** gave and the **L** has taken
	38: 1	the **L** spoke to Job out of the storm.
	42: 9	did what the **L** told them;
Ps	1: 2	whose delight is in the law of the **L**,
	9: 9	The **L** is a refuge for the oppressed,
	12: 6	the words of the **L** are flawless,
	16: 8	I keep my eyes always on the **L**.
	19: 7	The law of the **L** is perfect,
	19: 14	heart be pleasing in your sight, **L**,
	23: 1	The **L** is my shepherd, I lack
	23: 6	dwell in the house of the **L** forever.
	27: 1	The **L** is the stronghold of my life
	27: 4	to gaze on the beauty of the **L**
	29: 1	ascribe to the **L** glory and strength.
	32: 2	one whose sin the **L** does not count
	33: 12	is the nation whose God is the **L**,
	33: 18	the eyes of the **L** are on those who
	34: 3	Glorify the **L** with me; let us exalt
	34: 7	of the **L** encamps around those
	34: 8	Taste and see that the **L** is good;
	34: 18	The **L** is close to the brokenhearted
	37: 4	Take delight in the **L**, and he will
	40: 1	I waited patiently for the **L**;
	47: 2	For the **L** Most High is awesome,
	48: 1	Great is the **L**, and most worthy
	55: 22	Cast your cares on the **L** and he
	75: 8	In the hand of the **L** is a cup full
	84: 11	For the **L** God is a sun and shield;
	86: 11	Teach me your way, **L**, that I may
	89: 5	heavens praise your wonders, **L**,
	95: 1	Come, let us sing for joy to the **L**;
	96: 1	Sing to the **L** a new song;
	98: 4	Shout for joy to the **L**, all the earth,
	100: 1	Shout for joy to the **L**, all the earth.
	103: 1	Praise the **L**, my soul; all my
	103: 8	The **L** is compassionate
	104: 1	Praise the **L**, my soul. My God,
	107: 8	to the **L** for his unfailing love
	110: 1	The **L** says to my lord: "Sit at my
	113: 4	The **L** is exalted over all the nations
	115: 1	Not to us, **L**, not to us but to your
	116: 15	the sight of the **L** is the death of his
	118: 1	Give thanks to the **L**, for he is good;
	118: 24	The **L** has done it this very day;
	121: 2	My help comes from the **L**,

Ps	121: 5	The **L** watches over you—the **L** is
	125: 2	so the **L** surrounds his people both
	127: 1	Unless the **L** builds the house,
	127: 3	Children are a heritage from the **L**,
	130: 3	If you, **L**, kept a record of sins,
	135: 6	The **L** does whatever pleases him,
	136: 1	Give thanks to the **L**, for he is good.
	139: 1	You have searched me, **L**, and you
	144: 3	**L**, what are human beings that you
	145: 3	Great is the **L** and most worthy
	145: 18	The **L** is near to all who call on him,
Pr	1: 7	The fear of the **L** is the beginning
	3: 5	Trust in the **L** with all your heart
	3: 9	Honor the **L** with your wealth,
	3: 12	because the **L** disciplines those he
	3: 19	By wisdom the **L** laid the earth's
	5: 21	your ways are in full view of the **L**,
	6: 16	There are six things the **L** hates,
	10: 27	The fear of the **L** adds length to life,
	11: 1	The **L** detests dishonest scales,
	12: 22	The **L** detests lying lips, but he
	14: 26	Whoever fears the **L** has a secure
	15: 3	The eyes of the **L** are everywhere,
	16: 2	but motives are weighed by the **L**.
	16: 4	The **L** works out everything to its
	16: 9	but the **L** establishes their steps.
	16: 33	but its every decision is from the **L**.
	18: 10	name of the **L** is a fortified tower;
	18: 22	and receives favor from the **L**.
	19: 14	but a prudent wife is from the **L**.
	19: 17	is kind to the poor lends to the **L**,
	21: 3	acceptable to the **L** than sacrifice.
	21: 30	plan that can succeed against the **L**.
	21: 31	battle, but victory rests with the **L**.
	22: 2	The **L** is the Maker of them all.
	24: 18	or the **L** will see and disapprove
	31: 30	a woman who fears the **L** is to be
Isa	6: 3	holy, holy is the **L** Almighty;
	11: 2	The Spirit of the **L** will rest on him
	11: 9	of the **L** as the waters cover the sea.
	12: 2	The **L**, the **L** himself, is my strength
	24: 1	the **L** is going to lay waste the earth
	25: 8	The Sovereign **L** will wipe away
	29: 15	to hide their plans from the **L**,
	33: 6	the fear of the **L** is the key to this
	35: 10	those the **L** has rescued will return.
	40: 5	For the mouth of the **L** has spoken.
	40: 7	because the breath of the **L** blows
	40: 10	the Sovereign **L** comes with power,
	40: 28	The **L** is the everlasting God,
	40: 31	in the **L** will renew their strength.
	42: 8	"I am the **L**; that is my name!
	43: 11	I am the **L**, and apart from me
	44: 24	I am the **L**, the Maker of all things,
	45: 5	I am the **L**, and there is no other;
	45: 21	Was it not I, the **L**? And there is no
	51: 11	Those the **L** has rescued will return
	53: 6	the **L** has laid on him the iniquity
	53: 10	the will of the **L** will prosper in his
	55: 6	Seek the **L** while he may be found;
	58: 8	of the **L** will be your rear guard.
	58: 11	The **L** will guide you always;
	59: 1	the arm of the **L** is not too short
	61: 3	a planting of the **L** for the display
	61: 10	I delight greatly in the **L**;
Jer	1: 9	Then the **L** reached out his hand
	9: 24	in these I delight," declares the **L**.
	16: 19	**L**, my strength and my fortress,
	17: 7	is the one who trusts in the **L**,
La	3: 40	and let us return to the **L**.
Eze	1: 28	of the likeness of the glory of the **L**.
Hos	1: 7	but I, the **L** their God, will save
	3: 5	return and seek the **L** their God
	6: 1	"Come, let us return to the **L**.
Joel	2: 1	for the day of the **L** is coming.
	2: 11	The day of the **L** is great;
	3: 14	day of the **L** is near in the valley
Am	5: 18	you who long for the day of the **L**!
Jnh	1: 3	But Jonah ran away from the **L**
Mic	4: 2	the word of the **L** from Jerusalem.
	6: 8	what does the **L** require of you?
Na	1: 2	The **L** is a jealous and avenging
	1: 3	The **L** is slow to anger but great

Hab	2: 14	of the **L** as the waters cover the sea.
	2: 20	The **L** is in his holy temple;
Zep	3: 17	The **L** your God is with you,
Zec	1: 17	and the **L** will again comfort Zion
	9: 16	The **L** their God will save his people
	14: 5	Then the **L** my God will come,
	14: 9	On that day there will be one **L**,
Mal	4: 5	and dreadful day of the **L** comes.

LORD'S* (LORD*); this is the proper name of God, *Yahweh*, spelled "LORD'S" in the NIV)

Ex	34: 34	he entered the **L** presence to speak
Nu	14: 41	you disobeying the **L** command?
Dt	6: 18	is right and good in the **L** sight,
	32: 9	For the **L** portion is his people,
Jos	21: 45	all the **L** good promises to Israel
Ps	24: 1	The earth is the **L**,
	32: 10	the **L** unfailing love surrounds
	89: 1	I will sing of the **L** great love
	103: 17	the **L** love is with those who fear
Pr	3: 11	do not despise the **L** discipline,
Isa	24: 14	west they acclaim the **L** majesty.
	62: 3	a crown of splendor in the **L** hand,
Jer	48: 10	who is lax in doing the **L** work!
La	3: 22	Because of the **L** great love we are
Mic	4: 1	the mountain of the **L** temple will

LOSE (LOSES LOSS LOST)

1Sa	17: 32	"Let no one **l** heart on account
Mt	10: 39	Whoever finds their life will **l** it,
Lk	9: 25	and yet **l** or forfeit their very self?
Jn	6: 39	that I shall **l** none of all those
Heb	12: 3	will not grow weary and **l** heart.
	12: 5	not **l** heart when he rebukes you,

LOSES (LOSE)

Mt	5: 13	But if the salt **l** its saltiness,
Lk	15: 4	a hundred sheep and **l** one of them.
	15: 8	has ten silver coins and **l** one.

LOSS (LOSE)

Ro	11: 12	their **l** means riches for the Gentiles,
1Co	3: 15	the builder will suffer **l** but yet will
Php	3: 8	I consider everything a **l** because

LOST (LOSE)

Ps	73: 2	I had nearly **l** my foothold.
Jer	50: 6	"My people have been **l** sheep;
Eze	34: 4	the strays or searched for the **l**.
	34: 16	I will search for the **l** and bring
Lk	15: 4	go after the **l** sheep until he finds
	15: 6	I have found my **l** sheep.'
	15: 9	I have found my **l** coin.'
	15: 24	he was **l** and is found.'
	19: 10	came to seek and to save the **l**."
Php	3: 8	for whose sake I have **l** all things.

LOT (LOTS)

Nephew of Abraham (Ge 11:27; 12:5). Chose to live in Sodom (Ge 13). Rescued from four kings (Ge 14). Rescued from Sodom (Ge 19:1–29; 2Pe 2:7). Fathered Moab and Ammon by his daughters (Ge 19:30–38).

Est	3: 7	the **l** was cast in the presence
	9: 24	the **l**) for their ruin and destruction.
Pr	16: 33	The **l** is cast into the lap, but its
	18: 18	Casting the **l** settles disputes
Ecc	3: 22	their work, because that is their **l**.
Ac	1: 26	cast lots, and the **l** fell to Matthias;

LOTS (LOT)

Ps	22: 18	them and cast **l** for my garment.
Mt	27: 35	divided up his clothes by casting **l**.

LOVE (BELOVED LOVED LOVELY LOVER LOVERS LOVES LOVING)

Ge	22: 2	son, your only son, whom you **l**—
Ex	15: 13	In your unfailing **l** you will lead
	20: 6	showing **l** to a thousand generations
	34: 6	abounding in **l** and faithfulness,
Lev	19: 18	but **l** your neighbor as yourself.
	19: 34	**L** them as yourself, for you were
Nu	14: 18	abounding in **l** and forgiving sin
Dt	5: 10	showing **l** to a thousand generations
	6: 5	**L** the LORD your God with all
	7: 13	He will **l** you and bless you
	10: 12	to **l** him, to serve the LORD your
	11: 13	to **l** the LORD your God
	13: 6	or the wife you **l**, or your closest
	30: 6	you may **l** him with all your heart
Jos	22: 5	to **l** the LORD your God, to walk

1Ki	3: 3	Solomon showed his **l**
	8: 23	you who keep your covenant of **l**
2Ch	5: 13	his **l** endures forever."
Ne	1: 5	covenant of **l** with those who **l** him
Ps	18: 1	I **l** you, LORD, my strength.
	23: 6	I will follow me all the days of my
	25: 6	your great mercy and **l**, for they are
	31: 16	save me in your unfailing **l**.
	32: 10	LORD's unfailing **l** surrounds
	33: 5	the earth is full of his unfailing **l**.
	33: 18	whose hope is in his unfailing **l**,
	36: 5	Your **l**, LORD,
	36: 7	How priceless is your unfailing **l**,
	45: 7	You **l** righteousness and hate
	51: 1	God, according to your unfailing **l**;
	57: 10	For great is your **l**,
	63: 3	Because your **l** is better than life,
	66: 20	prayer or withheld his **l** from me!
	77: 8	his unfailing **l** vanished forever?
	85: 7	Show us your unfailing **l**, LORD,
	85: 10	**L** and faithfulness meet together;
	86: 13	For great is your **l** toward me;
	89: 1	sing of the LORD's great **l** forever;
	89: 33	but I will not take my **l** from him,
	92: 2	proclaiming your **l** in the morning
	94: 18	slipping," your unfailing **l**, LORD,
	100: 5	is good and his **l** endures forever;
	101: 1	I will sing of your **l** and justice;
	103: 4	crowns you with **l** and compassion,
	103: 8	slow to anger, abounding in **l**.
	103: 11	so great is his **l** for those who fear
	107: 8	to the LORD for his unfailing **l**
	108: 4	For great is your **l**, higher than
	116: 1	I **l** the LORD, for he heard my
	118: 1	he is good; his **l** endures forever.
	119: 47	your commands because I **l** them.
	119: 64	The earth is filled with your **l**,
	119: 76	May your unfailing **l** be my
	119: 97	Oh, how I **l** your law! I meditate
	119: 119	dross; therefore I **l** your statutes.
	119: 124	your servant according to your **l**
	119: 132	do to those who **l** your name.
	119: 159	See how I **l** your precepts;
	119: 163	detest falsehood but I **l** your law.
	119: 165	peace have those who **l** your law,
	122: 6	"May those who **l** you be secure.
	130: 7	for with the LORD is unfailing **l**
	136: 1	*His **l** endures forever.*
	143: 8	bring me word of your unfailing **l**,
	145: 8	slow to anger and rich in **l**.
	145: 20	LORD watches over all who **l** him,
	147: 11	put their hope in his unfailing **l**.
Pr	3: 3	Let **l** and faithfulness never leave
	4: 6	**l** her, and she will watch over you.
	5: 19	you ever be intoxicated with her **l**.
	8: 17	I **l** those who **l** me, and those who
	9: 8	rebuke the wise and they will **l** you.
	10: 12	but **l** covers over all wrongs.
	14: 22	those who plan what is good find **l**
	15: 17	with **l** than a fattened calf
	17: 9	Whoever would foster **l** covers
	19: 22	a person desires is unfailing **l**;
	20: 6	Many claim to have unfailing **l**,
	20: 13	Do not **l** sleep or you will grow
	20: 28	**L** and faithfulness keep a king safe;
	21: 21	righteousness and **l** finds life,
	27: 5	is open rebuke than hidden **l**.
Ecc	9: 6	Their **l**, their hate and their
	9: 9	whom you **l**, all the days of this
SS	2: 4	and let his banner over me be **l**.
	8: 6	for **l** is as strong as death,
	8: 7	Many waters cannot quench **l**;
Isa	5: 1	sing for the one I **l** a song about his
	16: 5	In **l** a throne will be established;
	38: 17	In your **l** you kept me from the pit
	54: 10	yet my unfailing **l** for you will not
	55: 3	my faithful **l** promised to David.
	61: 8	"For I, the LORD, **l** justice;
	63: 9	In his **l** and mercy he redeemed
Jer	5: 31	and my people **l** it this way.
	31: 3	loved you with an everlasting **l**;
	32: 18	You show **l** to thousands but bring
	33: 11	his **l** endures forever."

La	3: 22	of the LORD's great l we are not
	3: 32	so great is his unfailing l.
Eze	33: 32	more than one who sings l songs
Da	9: 4	covenant of l with those who l him
Hos	2: 19	and justice, in l and compassion.
	3: 1	L her as the LORD loves
	11: 4	of human kindness, with ties of l.
	12: 6	maintain l and justice, and wait
Joel	2: 13	slow to anger and abounding in l,
Am	5: 15	Hate evil, l good; maintain justice
Mic	3: 2	you who hate good and l evil;
	6: 8	to l mercy and to walk humbly
Zep	3: 17	his l he will no longer rebuke you,
Zec	8: 19	Therefore l truth and peace."
Mt	3: 17	said, "This is my Son, whom I l;
	5: 44	l your enemies and pray for those
	6: 24	will hate the one and l the other,
	17: 5	said, "This is my Son, whom I l;
	19: 19	'l your neighbor as yourself.' "
	22: 37	" 'L the Lord your God with all
Lk	6: 32	"If you l those who l you,
	7: 42	which of them will l him more?"
	20: 13	I will send my son, whom I l;
Jn	13: 34	command I give you: L one another.
	13: 35	my disciples, if you l one another."
	14: 15	"If you l me, keep my commands.
	15: 13	Greater l has no one than this:
	15: 17	This is my command: L each other.
	21: 15	do you l me more than these?"
Ro	5: 5	because God's l has been poured
	5: 8	God demonstrates his own l for us
	8: 28	for the good of those who l him,
	8: 35	separate us from the l of Christ?
	8: 39	separate us from the l of God that
	12: 9	L must be sincere. Hate what is
	12: 10	Be devoted to one another in l.
	13: 8	continuing debt to l one another,
	13: 9	"L your neighbor as yourself."
	13: 10	Therefore l is the fulfillment
1Co	2: 9	prepared for those who l him—
	8: 1	puffs up while l builds up.
	13: 1	but do not have l, I am only
	13: 2	but do not have l, I am nothing.
	13: 3	but do not have l, I gain nothing.
	13: 4	L is patient, l is kind. It does not
	13: 6	L does not delight in evil
	13: 8	L never fails. But where there are
	13: 13	these three remain: faith, hope and l. But the greatest of these is l.
	14: 1	Follow the way of l and eagerly
	16: 14	Do everything in l.
2Co	5: 14	For Christ's l compels us,
	8: 8	sincerity of your l by comparing it
	8: 24	show these men the proof of your l
Gal	5: 6	is faith expressing itself through l.
	5: 13	serve one another humbly in l.
	5: 22	But the fruit of the Spirit is l, joy,
Eph	1: 4	holy and blameless in his sight. In l
	2: 4	But because of his great l for us,
	3: 17	being rooted and established in l,
	3: 18	high and deep is the l of Christ,
	3: 19	and to know this l that surpasses
	4: 2	bearing with one another in l.
	4: 15	speaking the truth in l,
	5: 2	and walk in the way of l, just as
	5: 25	Husbands, l your wives, just as
	5: 28	to l their wives as their own bodies.
	5: 33	must l his wife as he loves himself,
Php	1: 9	that your l may abound more
	2: 2	having the same l, being one
Col	1: 5	l that spring from the hope stored
	2: 2	in heart and united in l,
	3: 14	And over all these virtues put on l,
	3: 19	l your wives and do not be harsh
1Th	1: 3	your labor prompted by l, and your
	4: 9	been taught by God to l each other.
	5: 8	on faith and l as a breastplate,
2Th	3: 5	Lord direct your hearts into God's l
1Ti	1: 5	The goal of this command is l,
	2: 15	faith, l and holiness with propriety.
	4: 12	conduct, in l, in faith and in purity.
	6: 10	For the l of money is a root of all
	6: 11	faith, l, endurance and gentleness.

2Ti	1: 7	us power, l and self-discipline.
	2: 22	faith, l and peace, along with those
	3: 10	faith, patience, l, endurance,
Titus	2: 4	women to l their husbands
Phm	: 9	to appeal to you on the basis of l.
Heb	6: 10	the l you have shown him as you
	10: 24	may spur one another on toward l
	13: 5	your lives free from the l of money
Jas	1: 12	has promised to those who l him.
	2: 5	he promised those who l him?
	2: 8	"L your neighbor as yourself,"
1Pe	1: 22	you have sincere l for each other,
	2: 17	everyone, l the family of believers,
	3: 8	be sympathetic, l one another,
	3: 10	For, "Whoever would l life and see
	4: 8	Above all, l each other deeply,
	4: 8	because l covers over a multitude
	5: 14	Greet one another with a kiss of l.
2Pe	1: 7	and to mutual affection, l.
	1: 17	saying, "This is my Son, whom I l;
1Jn	2: 5	l for God is truly made complete
	2: 15	Do not l the world or anything
	3: 1	See what great l the Father has
	3: 10	who does not l their brother
	3: 11	We should l one another.
	3: 14	to life, because we l each other.
	3: 16	This is how we know what l is:
	3: 18	let us not l with words or speech
	3: 23	l one another as he commanded
	4: 7	one another, for l comes from God.
	4: 8	not know God, because God is l.
	4: 9	is how God showed his l among us:
	4: 10	This is l: not that we loved God,
	4: 11	us, we also ought to l one another.
	4: 12	but if we l one another, God lives
	4: 16	God is l. Whoever lives in l lives
	4: 17	This is how l is made complete
	4: 18	There is no fear in l. But perfect l
	4: 19	We l because he first loved us.
	4: 20	whoever does not l their brother
	4: 21	loves God must also l their brother
	5: 2	we know that we l the children
	5: 3	In fact, this is l for God: to keep his
2Jn	: 5	I ask that we l one another.
	: 6	his command is that you walk in l.
Jude	: 12	are blemishes at your l feasts,
	: 21	yourselves in God's l as you wait
Rev	2: 4	You have forsaken the l you had
	3: 19	Those whom I l I rebuke
	12: 11	they did not l their lives so much

LOVED (LOVE)

Ge	24: 67	she became his wife, and he l her;
	37: 3	Now Israel l Joseph more than any
Dt	7: 8	it was because the LORD l you
1Sa	1: 5	a double portion because he l her,
	20: 17	because he l him as he l himself.
Ps	44: 3	light of your face, for you l them.
Jer	2: 2	youth, how as a bride you l me
	31: 3	"I have l you with an everlasting
Hos	2: 23	to the one I called 'Not my l one.'
	3: 1	though she is l by another man
	9: 10	became as vile as the thing they l.
	11: 1	"When Israel was a child, I l him,
Mal	1: 2	"I have l you," says the LORD.
Mk	12: 6	one left to send, a son, whom he l.
Jn	3: 16	For God so l the world that he gave
	3: 19	people l darkness instead of light
	11: 5	Now Jesus l Martha and her sister
	12: 43	for they l human praise more than
	13: 1	in the world, he l them to the end.
	13: 23	the disciple whom Jesus l,
	13: 34	As I have l you, so you must love
	14: 21	The one who loves me will be l
	15: 9	"As the Father has l me, so have I l
	15: 12	Love each other as I have l you.
	19: 26	disciple whom he l standing
Ro	8: 37	conquerors through him who l us.
	9: 13	"Jacob I l, but Esau I hated."
	9: 25	'my l one' who is not my l one,"
	11: 28	they are l on account
Gal	2: 20	who l me and gave himself for me.
Eph	5: 2	just as Christ l us and gave himself
	5: 25	just as Christ l the church and gave

2Th 2: 16 who **l** us and by his grace gave us
2Ti 4: 10 for Demas, because he **l** this world,
Heb 1: 9 You have **l** righteousness and hated
1Jn 4: 10 not that we **l** God, but that he **l** us
4: 11 since God so **l** us, we also ought
4: 19 We love because he first **l** us.

LOVELY (LOVE)
Ps 84: 1 How **l** is your dwelling place,
SS 2: 14 voice is sweet, and your face is **l**.
5: 16 sweetness itself; he is altogether **l**.
Php 4: 8 is pure, whatever is **l**, whatever is

LOVER (LOVE)
1Ti 3: 3 not quarrelsome, not a **l** of money.

LOVERS (LOVE)
2Ti 3: 2 People will be **l** of themselves,
3: 3 brutal, not **l** of the good,
3: 4 **l** of pleasure rather than **l** of God—

LOVES (LOVE)
Ps 11: 7 LORD is righteous, he **l** justice;
33: 5 The LORD **l** righteousness
34: 12 Whoever of you **l** life and desires
127: 2 for he grants sleep to those he **l**.
Pr 3: 12 the LORD disciplines those he **l**,
12: 1 Whoever **l** discipline **l** knowledge,
17: 17 A friend **l** at all times, and
17: 19 Whoever **l** a quarrel **l** sin;
22: 11 One who **l** a pure heart and who
Mt 10: 37 "Anyone who **l** their father
Lk 7: 47 has been forgiven little **l** little."
Jn 3: 35 The Father **l** the Son and has
10: 17 The reason my Father **l** me is that I
14: 21 The one who **l** me will be loved
14: 23 "Anyone who **l** me will obey my
Ro 13: 8 for whoever **l** others has fulfilled
2Co 9: 7 for God **l** a cheerful giver.
Eph 5: 28 He who **l** his wife **l** himself.
5: 33 must love his wife as he **l** himself,
Heb 12: 6 the Lord disciplines the one he **l**,
1Jn 4: 7 Everyone who **l** has been born
5: 1 who **l** the father **l** his child
3Jn : 9 but Diotrephes, who **l** to be first,
Rev 1: 5 To him who **l** us and has freed us

LOVING (LOVE)
Ps 25: 10 All the ways of the LORD are **l**
Heb 13: 1 Keep on **l** one another as brothers
1Jn 5: 2 by **l** God and carrying out his

LOWLY
Job 5: 11 The **l** he sets on high, and those
Pr 29: 23 low, but the **l** in spirit gain honor.
Isa 57: 15 to revive the spirit of the **l**
Eze 21: 26 The **l** will be exalted and
Mt 18: 4 whoever takes the **l** position
1Co 1: 28 God chose the **l** things of this

LUKE
Co-worker with Paul (Col 4:14; 2Ti 4:11; Phm 24).

LUKEWARM
Rev 3: 16 So, because you are **l**—

LUST
Pr 6: 25 Do not **l** in your heart after her
Col 3: 5 impurity, **l**, evil desires and greed,
1Th 4: 5 not in passionate **l** like the pagans,
1Jn 2: 16 the **l** of the flesh, the **l** of the eyes,

LYING (LIE)
Pr 6: 17 haughty eyes, a **l** tongue,
26: 28 A **l** tongue hates those it hurts,

MACEDONIA
Ac 16: 9 a vision of a man of **M** standing

MADE (MAKE)
Ge 1: 16 God **m** two great lights—
1: 25 God **m** the wild animals according
2: 22 the LORD God **m** a woman
2Ki 19: 15 You have **m** heaven and earth.
Ps 95: 5 for he **m** it, and his hands formed
100: 3 It is he who **m** us, and we are his;
139: 14 I am fearfully and wonderfully **m**;
Ecc 3: 11 He has **m** everything beautiful in
Mk 2: 27 "The Sabbath was **m** for man,
Jn 1: 3 Through him all things were **m**;
Ac 17: 24 "The God who **m** the world
Heb 1: 2 whom also he **m** the universe.
Rev 14: 7 Worship him who **m** the heavens,

MAGI
Mt 2: 1 **M** from the east came to Jerusalem

MAGOG
Eze 38: 2 of the land of **M**, the chief prince
39: 6 I will send fire on **M** and on those
Rev 20: 8 Gog and **M**—and to gather them

MAIMED
Mt 18: 8 It is better for you to enter life **m**

MAJESTIC (MAJESTY)
Ex 15: 6 hand, LORD, was **m** in power.
15: 11 **m** in holiness, awesome in glory,
Ps 8: 1 **m** is your name in all the earth!
29: 4 the voice of the LORD is **m**.
111: 3 Glorious and **m** are his deeds,
SS 6: 10 sun, **m** as the stars in procession?
2Pe 1: 17 came to him from the **M** Glory,

MAJESTY (MAJESTIC)
Ex 15: 7 your **m** you threw down those who
Dt 33: 26 and on the clouds in his **m**.
1Ch 16: 27 Splendor and **m** are before him;
Est 1: 4 the splendor and glory of his **m**.
Job 37: 22 God comes in awesome **m**.
40: 10 clothe yourself in honor and **m**.
Ps 45: 4 In your **m** ride forth victoriously
93: 1 LORD reigns, he is robed in **m**;
145: 5 the glorious splendor of your **m**—
Isa 53: 2 beauty or **m** to attract us to him,
Eze 31: 2 can be compared with you in **m**?
2Pe 1: 16 but we were eyewitnesses of his **m**.
Jude : 25 only God our Savior be glory, **m**,

MAKE (MADE MAKER MAKES MAKING)
Ge 1: 26 "Let us **m** mankind in our image,
2: 18 I will **m** a helper suitable for him."
12: 2 "I will **m** you into a great nation,
Ex 22: 3 steals must certainly **m** restitution,
Nu 6: 25 the LORD **m** his face shine on you
Ps 108: 1 sing and **m** music with all my soul.
Isa 14: 14 I will **m** myself like the Most
29: 16 formed it, "You did not **m** me"?
Jer 31: 31 "when I will **m** a new covenant
Mt 3: 3 Lord, **m** straight paths for him.'"
28: 19 go and **m** disciples of all nations,
Lk 13: 24 "**M** every effort to enter through
Ro 14: 19 Let us therefore **m** every effort to
2Co 5: 9 So we **m** it our goal to please him,
Eph 4: 3 **M** every effort to keep the unity
Col 4: 5 **m** the most of every opportunity,
1Th 4: 11 **m** it your ambition to lead a quiet
Heb 4: 11 **m** every effort to enter that rest,
12: 14 **M** every effort to live in peace
2Pe 1: 5 **m** every effort to add to your faith
3: 14 **m** every effort to be found spotless,

MAKER (MAKE)
Job 4: 17 man be more pure than his **M**?
36: 3 I will ascribe justice to my **M**.
Ps 95: 6 us kneel before the LORD our **M**;
Pr 22: 2 The LORD is the **M** of them all.
Isa 45: 9 to those who quarrel with their **M**,
54: 5 For your **M** is your husband—
Jer 10: 16 these, for he is the **M** of all things,

MAKES (MAKE)
1Co 3: 7 but only God, who **m** things grow.

MAKING (MAKE)
Ps 19: 7 are trustworthy, **m** wise the simple.
Ecc 12: 12 Of many books there is no end,
Jn 5: 18 Father, **m** himself equal with God.
Eph 5: 16 **m** the most of every opportunity,

MALE
Ge 1: 27 **m** and female he created them.
Gal 3: 28 nor free, nor is there **m** and female,

MALICE (MALICIOUS)
Ro 1: 29 envy, murder, strife, deceit and **m**.
Col 3: 8 anger, rage, **m**, slander, and filthy
1Pe 2: 1 rid yourselves of all **m** and all

MALICIOUS (MALICE)
1Ti 3: 11 not **m** talkers but temperate
6: 4 envy, strife, **m** talk, evil suspicions

MAN (MANKIND MEN WOMAN WOMEN)
Ge 2: 7 the LORD God formed a **m**
2: 18 not good for the **m** to be alone.
2: 23 for she was taken out of **m**."
Dt 8: 3 **m** does not live on bread alone
1Sa 13: 14 sought out a **m** after his own heart
Ps 127: 5 Blessed is the **m** whose quiver is

Pr   30: 19   way of a **m** with a young woman.
Isa 53: 3   by mankind, a **m** of suffering,
Mt   19: 5   this reason a **m** will leave his father
Lk   4: 4   '**M** shall not live on bread alone.' "
Ro   5: 12   entered the world through one **m**,
1Co   7: 2   **m** should have sexual relations
     11: 3   that the head of every **m** is Christ,
     11: 3   and the head of the woman is **m**,
     13: 11   When I became a **m**, I put the ways
Php   2: 8   being found in appearance as a **m**,
1Ti   2: 5   and mankind, the **m** Christ Jesus,
      2: 12   or to assume authority over a **m**;

MANAGE
Jer 12: 5   how will you **m** in the thickets
1Ti   3: 4   He must **m** his own family well
      3: 12   to his wife and must **m** his children
      5: 14   to **m** their homes and to give

MANASSEH
   1. Firstborn of Joseph (Ge 41:51; 46:20). Blessed (Ge 48).
   2. Son of Hezekiah; king of Judah (2Ki 21:1–18; 2Ch 33:1–20).

MANGER
Lk   2: 12   in cloths and lying in a **m**."

MANKIND (MAN)
Ge   1: 26   "Let us make **m** in our image,

MANNA
Ex   16: 31   people of Israel called the bread **m**.
Dt   8: 16   He gave you **m** to eat
Jn   6: 49   Your ancestors ate the **m**
Rev   2: 17   I will give some of the hidden **m**.

MANNER
1Co 11: 27   in an unworthy **m** will be guilty
Php   1: 27   conduct yourselves in a **m** worthy

MARITAL (MARRY)
Ex   21: 10   of her food, clothing and **m** rights.
1Co   7: 3   husband should fulfill his **m** duty

MARK (MARKS)
   Cousin of Barnabas (Col 4:10; 2Ti 4:11; Phm 24; 1Pe 5:13), see JOHN.

Ge   4: 15   the LORD put a **m** on Cain so
Rev 13: 16   to receive a **m** on their right hands

MARKS (MARK)
Jn   20: 25   "Unless I see the nail **m** in his
Gal   6: 17   I bear on my body the **m** of Jesus.

MARRED
Isa 52: 14   and his form **m** beyond human

MARRIAGE (MARRY)
Mt   22: 30   neither marry nor be given in **m**;
     24: 38   marrying and giving in **m**,
Heb 13: 4   **M** should be honored by all,

MARRIED (MARRY)
Ro   7: 2   by law a **m** woman is bound to her
1Co   7: 33   But a **m** man is concerned
      7: 36   is not sinning. They should get **m**.

MARRIES (MARRY)
Mt   5: 32   anyone who **m** a divorced woman
     19: 9   and **m** another woman commits
Lk   16: 18   the man who **m** a divorced woman

MARRY (INTERMARRY MARITAL MARRIAGE MARRIED MARRIES)
Mt   22: 30   people will neither **m** nor be given
1Co   7: 9   they should **m**, for it is better to **m**
1Ti   5: 14   So I counsel younger widows to **m**,

MARTHA
   Sister of Mary and Lazarus (Lk 10:38–42; Jn 11; 12:2).

MARVELED
Lk   2: 33   mother **m** at what was said

MARY
   1. Mother of Jesus (Mt 1:16–25; Lk 1:27–56; 2:1–40). With Jesus at temple (Lk 2:41–52), at the wedding in Cana (Jn 2:1–5), questioning his sanity (Mk 3:21), at the cross (Jn 19:25–27). Among disciples after Ascension (Ac 1:14).
   2. Magdalene; former demoniac (Lk 8:2). Helped support Jesus' ministry (Lk 8:1–3). At the cross (Mt 27:56; Mk 15:40; Jn 19:25), burial (Mt 27:61; Mk 15:47). Saw angel after resurrection (Mt 28:1–10; Mk 16:1–9; Lk 24:1–12); also Jesus (Jn 20:1–18).
   3. Sister of Martha and Lazarus (Jn 11). Washed Jesus' feet (Jn 12:1–8).

MASQUERADES
2Co 11: 14   for Satan himself **m** as an angel

MASTER (MASTERED MASTERS)
Mt   10: 24   teacher, nor a servant above his **m**.
     24: 46   servant whose **m** finds him doing
     25: 21   "His **m** replied, 'Well done,
Ro   6: 14   For sin shall no longer be your **m**,
      6: 14   To their own **m**, servants stand
2Ti   2: 21   useful to the **M** and prepared to do

MASTERED (MASTER)
1Co   6: 12   but I will not be **m** by anything.
2Pe   2: 19   are slaves to whatever has **m** them."

MASTERS (MASTER)
Mt   6: 24   "No one can serve two **m**.
Eph   6: 5   obey your earthly **m** with respect
      6: 9   **m**, treat your slaves in the same
Titus 2: 9   be subject to their **m** in everything,

MATTHEW
   Apostle; former tax collector (Mt 9:9–13; 10:3; Mk 3:18; Lk 6:15; Ac 1:13). Also called Levi (Mk 2:14–17; Lk 5:27–32).

MATURE (MATURITY)
Eph   4: 13   of the Son of God and become **m**,
Php   3: 15   who are **m** should take such a view
Heb   5: 14   But solid food is for the **m**,
Jas   1: 4   its work so that you may be **m**

MATURITY (MATURE)
Heb   6: 1   Christ and be taken forward to **m**,

MEAL
1Co 10: 27   If an unbeliever invites you to a **m**
Heb 12: 16   single **m** sold his inheritance rights

MEANING
Ne   8: 8   and giving the **m** so that the people

MEANS
1Co   9: 22   by all possible **m** I might save some.

MEAT
Ro   14: 6   eats **m** does so to the Lord,
     14: 21   It is better not to eat **m** or drink

MEDIATOR
1Ti   2: 5   one God and one **m** between God
Heb   8: 6   which he is **m** is superior to the old
      9: 15   this reason Christ is the **m** of a new
     12: 24   to Jesus the **m** of a new covenant,

MEDICINE
Pr   17: 22   A cheerful heart is good **m**,

MEDITATE (MEDITATES MEDITATION)
Jos   1: 8   **m** on it day and night, so that you
Ps 119: 15   I **m** on your precepts and consider
    119: 78   but I will **m** on your precepts.
    119: 97   I **m** on it all day long.
    145: 5   I will **m** on your wonderful works.

MEDITATES (MEDITATE)
Ps   1: 2   who **m** on his law day and night.

MEDITATION (MEDITATE)
Ps   19: 14   this **m** of my heart be pleasing
    104: 34   May my **m** be pleasing to him, as I

MEDIUM
Lev 20: 27   or woman who is a **m** or spiritist

MEEK
Ps   37: 11   But the **m** will inherit the land
Mt   5: 5   Blessed are the **m**, for they will

MEET (MEETING)
Ps   85: 10   Love and faithfulness **m** together;
Am   4: 12   Israel, prepare to **m** your God."
1Th   4: 17   the clouds to **m** the Lord in the air.

MEETING (MEET)
Heb 10: 25   not giving up **m** together, as some

MELCHIZEDEK
Ge   14: 18   **M** king of Salem brought out bread
Ps 110: 4   a priest forever, in the order of **M**."
Heb   7: 11   one in the order of **M**,

MELT
2Pe   3: 12   the elements will **m** in the heat.

MEMBERS
Mic   7: 6   a man's enemies are the **m** of his
Ro   12: 4   of us has one body with many **m**,
1Co   6: 15   your bodies are **m** of Christ
Eph   4: 25   for we are all **m** of one body.
Col   3: 15   since as **m** of one body you were

MEN (MAN)
Ro   1: 27   **M** committed shameful acts with other **m**,
1Ti   2: 8   Therefore I want the **m** everywhere

MENAHEM
   King of Israel (2Ki 15:17–22).

MERCIFUL (MERCY)
Dt   4: 31 the Lord your God is a **m** God;
Ne   9: 31 for you are a gracious and **m** God.
Mt   5:   7 Blessed are the **m**, for they will be
Lk   6: 36 Be **m**, just as your Father is **m**.
Heb 2: 17 in order that he might become a **m**
Jude   : 22 Be **m** to those who doubt;

MERCY (MERCIFUL)
Ex 33: 19 have **m** on whom I will have **m**,
Ps 25:   6 Lord, your great **m** and love,
Isa 63:   9 his love and **m** he redeemed them;
Hos 6:   6 For I desire **m**, not sacrifice,
Mic 6:   8 to love **m** and to walk humbly
Hab 3:   2 in wrath remember **m**.
Mt 12:   7 mean, 'I desire **m**, not sacrifice,'
     23: 23 justice, **m** and faithfulness.
Ro   9: 15 "I will have **m** on whom I have **m**,
Eph 2:   4 love for us, God, who is rich in **m**,
Jas 2: 13 **M** triumphs over judgment.
1Pe 1:   3 In his great **m** he has given us new

MESSAGE
Isa 53:   1 Who has believed our **m**
Jn 12: 38 who has believed our **m**
Ro 10: 17 faith comes from hearing the **m**,
1Co 1: 18 the **m** of the cross is foolishness
2Co 5: 19 to us the **m** of reconciliation.

MESSIAH (CHRIST MESSIAHS)
Mt   1: 16 of Jesus who is called the **M**.
     16: 16 "You are the **M**, the Son
     22: 42 "What do you think about the **M**?
Jn   1: 41 "We have found the **M**" (that is,
      4: 25 that **M**" (called Christ) "is coming.
     20: 31 may believe that Jesus is the **M**,
Ac   2: 36 you crucified, both Lord and **M**."
      5: 42 the good news that Jesus is the **M**.
      9: 22 by proving that Jesus is the **M**.
     17:   3 proving that the **M** had to suffer
     18: 28 the Scriptures that Jesus was the **M**.
     26: 23 that the **M** would suffer and,

MESSIAHS (MESSIAH)
Mt 24: 24 For false **m** and false prophets will

METHUSELAH
Ge   5: 27 **M** lived a total of 969 years,

MICHAEL
Archangel (Jude 9); warrior in angelic realm, protector of Israel (Da 10:13, 21; 12:1; Rev 12:7).

MIDWIVES
Ex   1: 17 The **m**, however, feared God

MIGHT (ALMIGHTY MIGHTY)
Jdg 16: 30 Then he pushed with all his **m**,
2Sa 6: 14 before the Lord with all his **m**,
Ps 21: 13 we will sing and praise your **m**.
Zec 4:   6 'Not by **m** nor by power, but by my
1Ti 6: 16 To him be honor and **m** forever.

MIGHTY (MIGHT)
Ex   6:   1 of my **m** hand he will let them go;
Dt   7:   8 he brought you out with a **m** hand
2Sa 1: 19 How the **m** have fallen!
     23:   8 the names of David's **m** warriors:
Ps 24:   8 and **m**, the Lord **m** in battle.
     50:   1 The **M** One, God, the Lord,
     89:   8 are **m**, and your faithfulness
   136: 12 a **m** hand and outstretched arm;
   147:   5 Great is our Lord and **m** in power;
Isa 9:   6 Wonderful Counselor, **M** God,
Zep 3: 17 you, the **M** Warrior who saves.
Eph 6: 10 in the Lord and in his **m** power.

MILE
Mt   5: 41 If anyone forces you to go one **m**,

MILK
Ex   3:   8 a land flowing with **m** and honey—
Isa 55:   1 buy wine and **m** without money
1Co 3:   2 I gave you **m**, not solid food,
Heb 5: 12 You need **m**, not solid food!
1Pe 2:   2 crave pure spiritual **m**, so that by it

MILLSTONE (STONE)
Lk 17:   2 with a **m** tied around their neck

MIND (DOUBLE-MINDED MINDFUL MINDS MINDSET)
1Sa 15: 29 does not lie or change his **m**;
1Ch 28:   9 devotion and with a willing **m**,
Ps 26:   2 me, examine my heart and my **m**;
Mt 22: 37 all your soul and with all your **m**.'

MERCIFUL (MERCY) — column 2
Ac   4: 32 believers were one in heart and **m**.
Ro   7: 25 then, I myself in my **m** am a slave
      8:   7 The **m** governed by the flesh is
     12:   2 by the renewing of your **m**.
1Co 2:   9 what no human **m** has conceived"
     14: 14 spirit prays, but my **m** is unfruitful.
2Co 13: 11 another, be of one **m**, live in peace.
Php 3: 19 Their **m** is set on earthly things.
1Th 4: 11 You should **m** your own business
Heb 7: 21 sworn and will not change his **m**:

MINDFUL (MIND)
Ps   8:   4 is mankind that you are **m** of them,
Lk   1: 48 he has been **m** of the humble state
Heb 2:   6 is mankind that you are **m** of them,

MINDS (MIND)
Ps   7:   9 the righteous God who probes **m**
Isa 26:   3 peace those whose **m** are steadfast,
Jer 31: 33 "I will put my law in their **m**
Eph 4: 23 new in the attitude of your **m**;
Col   3:   2 Set your **m** on things above,
Heb 8: 10 I will put my laws in their **m**
Rev 2: 23 he who searches hearts and **m**,

MINDSET (MIND)
Php 2:   5 have the same **m** as Christ Jesus:

MINISTERING (MINISTRY)
Heb 1: 14 Are not all angels **m** spirits sent

MINISTRY (MINISTERING)
Ac   6:   4 to prayer and the **m** of the word."
2Co 5: 18 gave us the **m** of reconciliation.
2Ti 4:   5 discharge all the duties of your **m**.

MIRACLES
1Ch 16: 12 done, his **m**, and the judgments he
Ps 77: 14 You are the God who performs **m**;
Mt 11: 20 most of his **m** had been performed,
     11: 21 the **m** that were performed in you
Mk 6:   2 What are these remarkable **m** he is
Ac   2: 22 accredited by God to you by **m**,
     19: 11 did extraordinary **m** through Paul,
1Co 12: 10 then **m**, then gifts of healing,
Heb 2:   4 wonders and various **m**, and by

MIRE
Ps 40:   2 slimy pit, out of the mud and **m**;
Isa 57: 20 whose waves cast up **m** and mud.

MIRIAM
Sister of Moses and Aaron (Nu 26:59). Led dancing at Red Sea (Ex 15:20–21). Struck with leprosy for criticizing Moses (Nu 12). Death (Nu 20:1).

MIRROR
Jas 1: 23 who looks at his face in a **m**

MISERY
Ex   3:   7 "I have indeed seen the **m** of my
Jdg 10: 16 he could bear Israel's **m** no longer.
Hos 5: 15 in their **m** they will earnestly seek
Ro   3: 16 ruin and **m** mark their ways,
Jas 5:   1 because of the **m** that is coming

MISLED
1Co 15: 33 Do not be **m**:

MISS
Pr 19:   2 more will hasty feet **m** the way!

MIST
Hos 6:   4 Your love is like the morning **m**,
Jas 4: 14 You are a **m** that appears for a little

MISUSE
Ex 20:   7 "You shall not **m** the name
Dt   5: 11 "You shall not **m** the name
Ps 139: 20 your adversaries **m** your name.

MOCK (MOCKED MOCKER MOCKERS MOCKING)
Ps 22:   7 All who see me **m** me;
Pr 14:   9 Fools **m** at making amends for sin,
Mk 10: 34 who will **m** him and spit on him,

MOCKED (MOCK)
Mt 27: 29 knelt in front of him and **m** him.
     27: 41 of the law and the elders **m** him.
Gal 6:   7 not be deceived: God cannot be **m**.

MOCKER (MOCK)
Pr 9:   7 corrects a **m** invites insults;
     9: 12 you are a **m**, you alone will suffer.
     20:   1 Wine is a **m** and beer a brawler;
     22: 10 Drive out the **m**, and out goes

MOCKERS (MOCK)
Ps   1:   1 take or sit in the company of **m**,

MOCKING (MOCK)
Isa 50: 6 I did not hide my face from **m**

MODEL
1Th 1: 7 And so you became a **m** to all
2Th 3: 9 to offer ourselves as a **m** for you

MOMENT
Job 20: 5 the joy of the godless lasts but a **m**.
Ps 30: 5 For his anger lasts only a **m**, but his
Isa 66: 8 a nation be brought forth in a **m**?
Gal 2: 5 We did not give in to them for a **m**,

MONEY
Ecc 5: 10 loves **m** never has enough;
Isa 55: 1 and you who have no **m**, come,
Mt 6: 24 You cannot serve both God and **m**.
Lk 9: 3 bag, no bread, no **m**, no extra shirt.
1Co 16: 2 you should set aside a sum of **m**
1Ti 3: 3 not quarrelsome, not a lover of **m**.
6: 10 the love of **m** is a root of all kinds
2Ti 3: 2 themselves, lovers of **m**, boastful,
Heb 13: 5 your lives free from the love of **m**

MOON
Ps 121: 6 you by day, nor the **m** by night.
Joel 2: 31 the **m** to blood before the coming
1Co 15: 41 the **m** another and the stars

MORNING
Ge 1: 5 was evening, and there was **m**—
Dt 28: 67 In the **m** you will say, "If only it
Ps 5: 3 In the **m**, LORD, you hear my
2Pe 1: 19 and the **m** star rises in your hearts.
Rev 22: 16 of David, and the bright **M** Star."

MORTAL
1Co 15: 53 and the **m** with immortality.

MOSES
Levite; brother of Aaron (Ex 6:20; 1Ch 6:3). Put in basket into Nile; discovered and raised by Pharaoh's daughter (Ex 2:1–10). Fled to Midian after killing Egyptian (Ex 2:11–15). Married to Zipporah, fathered Gershom (Ex 2:16–22).

Called by the LORD to deliver Israel (Ex 3–4). Pharaoh's resistance (Ex 5). Ten plagues (Ex 7–11). Passover and Exodus (Ex 12–13). Led Israel through Red Sea (Ex 14). Song of deliverance (Ex 15:1–21). Brought water from rock (Ex 17:1–7). Raised hands to defeat Amalekites (Ex 17:8–16). Delegated judges (Ex 18; Dt 1:9–18).

Received Law at Sinai (Ex 19–23; 25–31; Jn 1:17). Announced Law to Israel (Ex 19:7–8; 24; 35). Broke tablets because of golden calf (Ex 32; Dt 9). Saw glory of the LORD (Ex 33–34). Supervised building of tabernacle (Ex 36–40). Set apart Aaron and priests (Lev 8–9). Numbered tribes (Nu 1–4; 26). Opposed by Aaron and Miriam (Nu 12). Sent spies into Canaan (Nu 13). Announced forty years of wandering for failure to enter land (Nu 14). Opposed by Korah (Nu 16). Forbidden to enter land for striking rock (Nu 20:1–13; Dt 1:37). Lifted bronze snake for healing (Nu 21:4–9; Jn 3:14). Final address to Israel (Dt 1–33). Succeeded by Joshua (Nu 27:12–23; Dt 34). Death (Dt 34:5–12).

"Law of Moses" (1Ki 2:3; Ezr 3:2; Mk 12:26; Lk 24:44). "Book of Moses" (2Ch 25:12; Ne 13:1). "Song of Moses" (Ex 15:1–21; Rev 15:3). "Prayer of Moses" (Ps 90).

MOTHER (MOTHER'S)
Ge 2: 24 why a man leaves his father and **m**
3: 20 because she would become the **m**
Ex 20: 12 "Honor your father and your **m**,
Lev 20: 9 they have cursed their father or **m**,
Dt 5: 16 "Honor your father and your **m**,
21: 18 does not obey his father and **m**
27: 16 who dishonors their father or **m**."
1Sa 2: 19 Each year his **m** made him a little
Ps 113: 9 her home as a happy **m** of children.
Pr 23: 25 May your father and **m** rejoice;
29: 15 left undisciplined disgraces its **m**.
31: 1 utterance his **m** taught him.
Isa 49: 15 "Can a **m** forget the baby at her
66: 13 As a **m** comforts her child, so will I
Mt 10: 37 or **m** more than me is not worthy
15: 4 said, 'Honor your father and **m**'
19: 5 a man will leave his father and **m**
Mk 7: 10 'Honor your father and **m**,' and,
10: 19 honor your father and **m**.'"
Jn 19: 27 to the disciple, "Here is your **m**."

MOTHER'S (MOTHER)
Job 1: 21 "Naked I came from my **m** womb,
Pr 1: 8 do not forsake your **m** teaching.

MOTHS
Mt 6: 19 where **m** and vermin destroy,

MOTIVES
Pr 16: 2 but **m** are weighed by the LORD.
1Co 4: 5 and will expose the **m** of the heart.
Php 1: 18 way, whether from false **m** or true,
1Th 2: 3 not spring from error or impure **m**,
Jas 4: 3 because you ask with wrong **m**,

MOUNTAIN (MOUNTAINS)
Mic 4: 2 let us go up to the **m** of the LORD,
Mt 17: 20 you can say to this **m**,

MOUNTAINS (MOUNTAIN)
Isa 52: 7 beautiful on the **m** are the feet
55: 12 and hills will burst into song
1Co 13: 2 if I have a faith that can move **m**,

MOURN (MOURNING)
Ecc 3: 4 a time to **m** and a time to dance,
Isa 61: 2 of our God, to comfort all who **m**,
Mt 5: 4 Blessed are those who **m**, for they
Ro 12: 15 **m** with those who **m**.

MOURNING (MOURN)
Jer 31: 13 I will turn their **m** into gladness;
Rev 21: 4 There will be no more death' or **m**

MOUTH
Ps 19: 14 May these words of my **m** and this
40: 3 He put a new song in my **m**,
119:103 taste, sweeter than honey to my **m**!
Pr 27: 2 praise you, and not your own **m**;
Isa 51: 16 I have put my words in your **m**
Mt 12: 34 the **m** speaks what the heart is full
15: 11 but what comes out of their **m**,
Ro 10: 9 If you declare with your **m**,

MUD
Ps 40: 2 slimy pit, out of the **m** and mire;
Isa 57: 20 whose waves cast up mire and **m**.
2Pe 2: 22 returns to their wallowing in the **m**."

MULTITUDE (MULTITUDES)
Isa 31: 1 who trust in the **m** of their chariots
1Pe 4: 8 because love covers over a **m**
Rev 7: 9 there before me was a great **m**

MULTITUDES (MULTITUDE)
Joel 3: 14 **M, m** in the valley of decision!

MURDER (MURDERER MURDERERS)
Ex 20: 13 "You shall not **m**.
Mt 15: 19 **m**, adultery, sexual immorality,
Ro 13: 9 "You shall not **m**," "You shall not
Jas 2: 11 commit adultery but do commit **m**,

MURDERER (MURDER)
Nu 35: 16 a **m**; the **m** is to be put to death.
Jn 8: 44 He was a **m** from the beginning,
1Jn 3: 15 hates a brother or sister is a **m**,

MURDERERS (MURDER)
1Ti 1: 9 kill their fathers or mothers, for **m**,
Rev 21: 8 vile, the **m**, the sexually immoral,

MUSIC
Ps 27: 6 sing and make **m** to the LORD.
95: 2 and extol him with **m** and song.
98: 4 burst into jubilant song with **m**;
108: 1 sing and make **m** with all my soul.
Eph 5: 19 make **m** from your heart to the Lord,

MUSTARD
Mt 13: 31 kingdom of heaven is like a **m** seed,
17: 20 you have faith as small as a **m** seed,

MUZZLE
Dt 25: 4 Do not **m** an ox while it is treading
Ps 39: 1 I will put a **m** on my mouth while
1Co 9: 9 Do not **m** an ox while it is treading

MYRRH
Mt 2: 11 gifts of gold, frankincense and **m**.
Mk 15: 23 offered him wine mixed with **m**,

MYSTERY
Ro 16: 25 the revelation of the **m** hidden
1Co 15: 51 Listen, I tell you a **m**: We will not
Eph 5: 32 This is a profound **m**—but I am
Col 1: 26 the **m** that has been kept hidden
1Ti 3: 16 the **m** from which true godliness

MYTHS
1Ti 4: 7 Have nothing to do with godless **m**

NADAB
Son of Jeroboam I; king of Israel (1Ki 15:25–32).

NAIL (NAILING)
Jn 20: 25 "Unless I see the **n** marks in his

NAILING (NAIL)
Ac   2: 23   him to death by **n** him to the cross.
Col 2: 14   has taken it away, **n** it to the cross.
NAKED
Ge   2: 25   Adam and his wife were both **n**,
Job 1: 21   womb, and **n** I will depart.
Isa 58: 7   you see the **n**, to clothe them,
2Co 5: 3   are clothed, we will not be found **n**.
NAME
Ex   3: 15   "This is my **n** forever, the **n** you
      20: 7   "You shall not misuse the **n**
Dt   5: 11   "You shall not misuse the **n**
     28: 58   this glorious and awesome **n**—
1Ki 5: 5   will build the temple for my **N**.'
2Ch 7: 14   people, who are called by my **n**,
Ps 34: 3   let us exalt his **n** together.
   103: 1   my inmost being, praise his holy **n**.
   147: 4   the stars and calls them each by **n**.
Pr 22: 1   A good **n** is more desirable than
     30: 4   What is his **n**, and what is the **n**
Isa 40: 26   and calls forth each of them by **n**.
     57: 15   who lives forever, whose **n** is holy:
Jer 14: 7   Lᴏʀᴅ, for the sake of your **n**.
Da 12: 1   everyone whose **n** is found written
Joel 2: 32   the **n** of the Lᴏʀᴅ will be saved;
Zec 14: 9   one Lᴏʀᴅ, and his **n** the only n.
Mt   1: 21   you are to give him the **n** Jesus,
      6: 9   in heaven, hallowed be your **n**,
    18: 20   where two or three gather in my **n**,
Jn 10: 3   He calls his own sheep by **n**
    16: 24   not asked for anything in my **n**.
Ac   4: 12   is no other **n** under heaven given
Ro 10: 13   on the **n** of the Lord will be saved."
Php 2: 9   the **n** that is above every **n**,
Col 3: 17   do it all in the **n** of the Lord Jesus,
Heb 1: 4   the angels as the **n** he has inherited
Rev 20: 15   whose **n** was not found written
NAOMI
    Mother-in-law of Ruth (Ru 1). Advised Ruth to seek marriage with Boaz (Ru 2–4).
NARROW
Mt   7: 13   "Enter through the **n** gate.
NATHANAEL
    Apostle (Jn 1:45–49; 21:2). Probably also called Bartholomew (Mt 10:3).
NATION (NATIONS)
Ge 12: 2   "I will make you into a great **n**,
Ps 33: 12   Blessed is the **n** whose God is
Pr 14: 34   Righteousness exalts a **n**, but sin
Isa 65: 1   a **n** that did not call on my name,
1Pe 2: 9   a holy **n**, God's special possession,
Rev 7: 9   could count, from every **n**, tribe,
NATIONS (NATION)
Ge 17: 4   You will be the father of many **n**.
    18: 18   and all **n** on earth will be blessed
Ex 19: 5   of all **n** you will be my treasured
Ne   1: 8   I will scatter you among the **n**,
Ps 96: 3   Declare his glory among the **n**,
Isa 40: 15   Surely the **n** are like a drop
Eze 36: 23   has been profaned among the **n**,
Hag 2: 7   what is desired by all **n** will come,
Zec 8: 23   **n** will take firm hold of one Jew
    14: 2   I will gather all the **n** to Jerusalem
Mt 28: 19   go and make disciples of all **n**,
Rev 21: 24   The **n** will walk by its light,
NATURAL (NATURE)
1Co 15: 44   it is sown a **n** body, it is raised
NATURE (NATURAL)
Php 2: 6   Who, being in very **n** God, did not
NAZARENE
Mt   2: 23   that he would be called a **N**.
NAZIRITE
Jdg 13: 7   because the boy will be a **N** of God
NECESSARY
Ro 13: 5   it is **n** to submit to the authorities,
NEED (NEEDS NEEDY)
Mt   6: 8   knows what you **n** before you ask
Ro 12: 13   the Lord's people who are in **n**.
1Co 12: 21   say to the hand, "I don't **n** you!"
1Jn 3: 17   sister in **n** but has no pity on them,
NEEDLE
Mt 19: 24   to go through the eye of a **n** than

NEEDS (NEED)
Isa 58: 11   he will satisfy your **n**
Php 4: 19   God will meet all your **n** according
NEEDY (NEED)
Pr 14: 21   is the one who is kind to the **n**.
    14: 31   is kind to the **n** honors God.
    31: 20   and extends her hands to the **n**.
Mt   6: 2   "So when you give to the **n**, do not
NEGLECT (NEGLECTED)
Ne 10: 39   "We will not **n** the house of our
Ps 119: 16   I will not **n** your word.
Ac   6: 2   for us to **n** the ministry of the word
1Ti 4: 14   not **n** your gift, which was given
NEGLECTED (NEGLECT)
Mt 23: 23   But you have **n** the more important
NEHEMIAH
    Cupbearer of Artaxerxes (Ne 2:1); governor of Israel (Ne 8:9). Returned to Jerusalem to rebuild walls (Ne 2–6). With Ezra, reestablished worship (Ne 8). Prayer confessing nation's sin (Ne 9). Dedicated wall (Ne 12).
NEIGHBOR (NEIGHBOR'S)
Ex 20: 16   give false testimony against your **n**.
Lev 19: 18   people, but love your **n** as yourself.
Pr 27: 10   better a **n** nearby than a relative far
Mt 19: 19   and 'love your **n** as yourself.' "
Lk 10: 29   asked Jesus, "And who is my **n**?"
Ro 13: 10   Love does no harm to a **n**.
NEIGHBOR'S (NEIGHBOR)
Ex 20: 17   "You shall not covet your **n** house.
Dt   5: 21   "You shall not covet your **n** wife.
    19: 14   not move your **n** boundary stone
Pr 25: 17   Seldom set foot in your **n** house—
NEW
Ps 40: 3   He put a **n** song in my mouth,
Ecc 1: 9   there is nothing **n** under the sun.
Isa 65: 17   I will create **n** heavens and a **n**
Jer 31: 31   I will make a **n** covenant
Eze 36: 26   I will give you a **n** heart and put a **n** spirit in you;
Mt   9: 17   they pour **n** wine into **n** wineskins,
Lk 22: 20   "This cup is the **n** covenant in my
2Co 5: 17   in Christ, the **n** creation has come:
Eph 4: 24   and to put on the **n** self,
2Pe 3: 13   to a **n** heaven and a **n** earth,
1Jn 2: 8   Yet I am writing you a **n** command;
NEWBORN (BEAR)
1Pe 2: 2   Like **n** babies, crave pure spiritual
NEWS
Isa 52: 7   the feet of those who bring good **n**,
Mk   1: 15   Repent and believe the good **n**!"
Lk   2: 10   I bring you good **n** that will cause
Ac   5: 42   proclaiming the good **n** that Jesus
    17: 18   Paul was preaching the good **n**
Ro 10: 15   feet of those who bring good **n**!"
NICODEMUS
    Pharisee who visited Jesus at night (Jn 3). Argued fair treatment of Jesus (Jn 7:50–52). With Joseph, prepared Jesus for burial (Jn 19:38–42).
NIGHT
Job 35: 10   Maker, who gives songs in the **n**,
Ps   1: 2   meditates on his law day and **n**.
    91: 5   You will not fear the terror of **n**,
Jn   3: 2   He came to Jesus at **n** and said,
1Th 5: 2   Lord will come like a thief in the **n**.
     5: 5   We do not belong to the **n**
Rev 21: 25   shut, for there will be no **n** there.
NOAH
    Righteous man (Eze 14:14, 20) called to build ark (Ge 6–8; Heb 11:7; 1Pe 3:20; 2Pe 2:5). God's covenant with (Ge 9:1–17). Drunkenness of (Ge 9:18–23). Blessed sons, cursed Canaan (Ge 9:24–27).
NOBLE
Ru   3: 11   you are a woman of **n** character.
Ps 45: 1   by a **n** theme as I recite my verses
Pr 12: 4   **n** character is her husband's crown,
    31: 10   wife of **n** character who can find?
    31: 29   "Many women do **n** things, but
Isa 32: 8   But the **n** make **n** plans, and by **n**
Lk   8: 15   good soil stands for those with a **n**
Php 4: 8   whatever is **n**, whatever is right,
NOTHING
Ne   9: 21   they lacked **n**, their clothes did not
Jer 32: 17   **N** is too hard for you.
Jn 15: 5   apart from me you can do **n**.

NULLIFY
Ro   3: 31 we, then, **n** the law by this faith?
OATH
Dt   7: 8 and kept the **o** he swore to your
OBEDIENCE (OBEY)
2Ch 31: 21 of God's temple and in **o** to the law
Ro   1: 5 all the Gentiles to the **o** that comes
     6: 16 to death, or to **o**, which leads
2Jn   : 6 that we walk in **o** to his commands.
OBEDIENT (OBEY)
Lk   2: 51 with them and was **o** to them.
Php 2: 8 himself by becoming **o** to death—
1Pe 1: 14 As **o** children, do not conform
OBEY (OBEDIENCE OBEDIENT OBEYED)
Ex 12: 24 "**O** these instructions as a lasting
Dt   6: 3 be careful to **o** so that it may go
    13: 4 Keep his commands and **o** him;
    21: 18 son who does not **o** his father
    30: 2 God and **o** him with all your heart
    32: 46 to **o** carefully all the words
1Sa 15: 22 To **o** is better than sacrifice,
Ps 119: 34 your law and **o** it with all my heart.
Mt 28: 20 to **o** everything I have commanded
Jn 14: 23 who loves me will **o** my teaching.
Ac   5: 29 must **o** God rather than human
Ro   6: 16 you are slaves of the one you **o**—
Gal 5: 3 he is obligated to **o** the whole law.
Eph 6: 1 **o** your parents in the Lord, for this
     6: 5 heart, just as you would **o** Christ.
Col 3: 20 **o** your parents in everything,
1Ti 3: 4 and see that his children **o** him,
OBEYED (OBEY)
Ps 119: 4 precepts that are to be fully **o**.
Jnh 3: 3 Jonah **o** the word of the LORD
Jn 17: 6 to me and they have **o** your word.
Heb 11: 8 as his inheritance, **o** and went,
1Pe 3: 6 who **o** Abraham and called him
OBLIGATED
Ro   1: 14 I am **o** both to Greeks
Gal 5: 3 that he is **o** to obey the whole law.
OBSCENITY
Eph 5: 4 Nor should there be **o**, foolish talk
OBSOLETE
Heb 8: 13 "new," he has made the first one **o**;
OBTAINED
Ro   9: 30 not pursue righteousness, have **o** it,
Php 3: 12 Not that I have already **o** all this,
OFFENSE (OFFENSIVE)
Pr 17: 9 would foster love covers over an **o**,
    19: 11 it is to one's glory to overlook an **o**.
OFFENSIVE (OFFENSE)
Ps 139: 24 See if there is any **o** way in me,
OFFER (OFFERED OFFERING OFFERINGS)
Ro 12: 1 **o** your bodies as a living sacrifice,
Heb 13: 15 let us continually **o** to God
OFFERED (OFFER)
Heb 7: 27 sins once for all when he **o** himself.
OFFERING (OFFER)
Ge 22: 8 provide the lamb for the burnt **o**,
Ps 40: 6 Sacrifice and **o** you did not desire
Isa 53: 10 the LORD makes his life an **o**
Mt   5: 23 if you are **o** your gift at the altar
Eph 5: 2 himself up for us as a fragrant **o**
Heb 10: 5 "Sacrifice and **o** you did not desire,
OFFERINGS (OFFER)
Mal 3: 8 we robbing you?' "In tithes and **o**.
Mk 12: 33 is more important than all burnt **o**
OFFICER
2Ti 2: 4 tries to please his commanding **o**.
OFFSPRING
Ge   3: 15 and between your **o** and hers;
    12: 7 "To your **o** I will give this land."
OIL
Ps 23: 5 You anoint my head with **o**;
Isa 61: 3 the **o** of joy instead of mourning,
Heb 1: 9 by anointing you with the **o** of joy."
OLIVE (OLIVES)
Zec 4: 3 Also there are two **o** trees by it,
Ro 11: 17 though a wild **o** shoot, have been
Rev 11: 4 They are "the two **o** trees"
OLIVES (OLIVE)
Jas 3: 12 can a fig tree bear **o**, or a grapevine

OMEGA
Rev 1: 8 "I am the Alpha and the **O**,"
OMRI
     King of Israel (1Ki 16:21–26).
OPINIONS
1Ki 18: 21 will you waver between two **o**?
Pr 18: 2 but delight in airing their own **o**.
OPPORTUNITY
Ro   7: 11 sin, seizing the **o** afforded
Gal 6: 10 as we have **o**, let us do good to all
Eph 5: 16 making the most of every **o**,
Col 4: 5 make the most of every **o**.
1Ti 5: 14 to give the enemy no **o** for slander.
OPPOSES
Jas 4: 6 "God **o** the proud but shows favor
1Pe 5: 5 "God **o** the proud but shows favor
OPPRESS (OPPRESSED)
Ex 22: 21 "Do not mistreat or **o** a foreigner,
Zec 7: 10 Do not **o** the widow
OPPRESSED (OPPRESS)
Ps   9: 9 The LORD is a refuge for the **o**,
Isa 53: 7 He was **o** and afflicted, yet he did
Zec 10: 2 the people wander like sheep **o**
ORDERLY
1Co 14: 40 be done in a fitting and **o** way.
ORGIES
Gal 5: 21 drunkenness, **o**, and the like.
1Pe 4: 3 lust, drunkenness, **o**,
ORIGIN
2Pe 1: 21 For prophecy never had its **o**
ORPHANS
Jn 14: 18 I will not leave you as **o**;
Jas 1: 27 to look after **o** and widows in their
OUTCOME
Heb 13: 7 Consider the **o** of their way of life
1Pe 4: 17 what will the **o** be for those who do
OUTSIDERS
Col 4: 5 wise in the way you act toward **o**;
1Th 4: 12 daily life may win the respect of **o**
1Ti 3: 7 also have a good reputation with **o**,
OUTSTANDING
SS   5: 10 and ruddy, **o** among ten thousand.
Ro 13: 8 Let no debt remain **o**,
OUTSTRETCHED
Ex   6: 6 I will redeem you with an **o** arm
Jer 27: 5 power and **o** arm I made the earth
Eze 20: 33 with a mighty hand and an **o** arm
OUTWEIGHS
2Co 4: 17 an eternal glory that far **o** them all.
OVERCOME (OVERCOMES)
Mt 16: 18 and the gates of Hades will not **o** it.
Mk   9: 24 help me **o** my unbelief!"
Jn 16: 33 But take heart! I have **o** the world."
Ro 12: 21 Do not be **o** by evil, but **o** evil
1Jn 5: 4 is the victory that has **o** the world,
OVERCOMES (OVERCOME)
1Jn 5: 4 everyone born of God **o** the world.
     5: 5 Who is it that **o** the world?
OVERFLOW (OVERFLOWS)
Ps 119:171 May my lips **o** with praise, for you
Ro 15: 13 so that you may **o** with hope
2Co 4: 15 may cause thanksgiving to **o**
1Th 3: 12 love increase and **o** for each other
OVERFLOWS (OVERFLOW)
Ps 23: 5 anoint my head with oil; my cup **o**.
OVERJOYED (JOY)
Da   6: 23 The king was **o** and gave orders
Mt   2: 10 they saw the star, they were **o**.
Jn 20: 20 disciples were **o** when they saw
Ac 12: 14 she was so **o** she ran back without
1Pe 4: 13 that you may be **o** when his glory
OVERSEER (OVERSEERS)
1Ti 3: 1 to be an **o** desires a noble task.
     3: 2 Now the **o** is to be above reproach,
Titus 1: 7 Since an **o** manages God's
OVERSEERS (OVERSEER)
Ac 20: 28 the Holy Spirit has made you **o**.
Php 1: 1 together with the **o** and deacons:
OVERWHELMED
Ps 38: 4 My guilt has **o** me like a burden
    65: 3 When we were **o** by sins,
Mt 26: 38 "My soul is **o** with sorrow
Mk   7: 37 People were **o** with amazement.

OWE
Ro 13: 7 Give to everyone what you **o** them:
Phm : 19 that you **o** me your very self.

OX
Dt 25: 4 Do not muzzle an **o** while it is
Isa 11: 7 the lion will eat straw like the **o**.
1Co 9: 9 "Do not muzzle an **o** while it is

PAGANS
Mt 5: 47 Do not even **p** do that?
1Pe 2: 12 such good lives among the **p** that,

PAIN (PAINFUL PAINS)
Job 33: 19 on a bed of **p** with constant distress
Jn 16: 21 to a child has **p** because her time

PAINFUL (PAIN)
Ge 3: 17 through **p** toil you will eat food
Heb 12: 11 seems pleasant at the time, but **p**.

PAINS (PAIN)
Ge 3: 16 "I will make your **p** in childbearing

PALMS
Isa 49: 16 engraved you on the **p** of my hands

PANTS
Ps 42: 1 As the deer **p** for streams of water, so my
soul **p** for you,

PARADISE
Lk 23: 43 today you will be with me in **p**."
2Co 12: 4 was caught up to **p** and heard
Rev 2: 7 tree of life, which is in the **p** of God.

PARALYZED
Mk 2: 3 bringing to him a **p** man,

PARDON (PARDONS)
Isa 55: 7 and to our God, for he will freely **p**.

PARDONS (PARDON)
Mic 7: 18 like you, who **p** sin and forgives

PARENT (PARENT'S PARENTS)
Pr 17: 21 is no joy for the **p** of a godless fool.

PARENT'S (PARENT)
15: 5 A fool spurns a **p** discipline,

PARENTS (PARENT)
Ex 20: 5 for the sin of the **p** to the third
Pr 17: 6 **p** are the pride of their children.
Lk 18: 29 sisters or **p** or children for the sake
21: 16 You will be betrayed even by **p**,
Ro 1: 30 of doing evil; they disobey their **p**;
2Co 12: 14 not have to save up for their **p**,
Eph 6: 1 Children, obey your **p** in the Lord,
Col 3: 20 obey your **p** in everything,
2Ti 3: 2 disobedient to their **p**, ungrateful,

PARTIALITY
Dt 10: 17 who shows no **p** and accepts no
2Ch 19: 7 our God shows no injustice or **p**
Lk 20: 21 that you do not show **p** but teach

PARTICIPATION
1Co 10: 16 bread that we break a **p** in the body

PASS
Ex 12: 13 I see the blood, I will **p** over you.
La 1: 12 nothing to you, all you who **p** by?
Lk 21: 33 but my words will never **p** away.
1Co 13: 8 there is knowledge, it will **p** away.

PASSION (PASSIONS)
1Co 7: 9 to marry than to burn with **p**.

PASSIONS (PASSION)
Gal 5: 24 have crucified the flesh with its **p**
Titus 2: 12 to ungodliness and worldly **p**,

PASSOVER
Ex 12: 11 Eat it in haste; it is the LORD's **P**.
Dt 16: 1 celebrate the **P** of the LORD your
1Co 5: 7 For Christ, our **P** lamb, has been

PAST
Isa 43: 18 do not dwell on the **p**.
Ro 15: 4 was written in the **p** was written
Heb 1: 1 the **p** God spoke to our ancestors

PASTORS
Eph 4: 11 the evangelists, the **p** and teachers,

PASTURE (PASTURES)
Ps 37: 3 dwell in the land and enjoy safe **p**.
100: 3 are his people, the sheep of his **p**.
Jer 50: 7 their verdant **p**, the LORD,
Eze 34: 13 I will **p** them on the mountains
Jn 10: 9 come in and go out, and find **p**.

PASTURES (PASTURE)
Ps 23: 2 He makes me lie down in green **p**,

PATCH
Mt 9: 16 No one sews a **p** of unshrunk cloth

PATH (PATHS)
Ps 27: 11 me in a straight **p** because of my
119: 9 person stay on the **p** of purity?
119:105 to my feet and a light for my **p**.
Pr 15: 19 the **p** of the upright is a highway.
15: 24 The **p** of life leads upward
Isa 26: 7 The **p** of the righteous is level;
Lk 1: 79 guide our feet into the **p** of peace."
2Co 6: 3 no stumbling block in anyone's **p**,

PATHS (PATH)
Ps 23: 3 He guides me along the right **p**
25: 4 ways, LORD, teach me your **p**.
Pr 3: 6 and he will make your **p** straight.
Ro 11: 33 and his **p** beyond tracing out!
Heb 12: 13 "Make level **p** for your feet,"

PATIENCE (PATIENT)
Pr 19: 11 A person's wisdom yields **p**; it is
2Co 6: 6 understanding, **p** and kindness;
Col 1: 11 may have great endurance and **p**,
3: 12 humility, gentleness and **p**.

PATIENT (PATIENCE PATIENTLY)
Pr 15: 18 the one who is **p** calms a quarrel.
Ro 12: 12 Be joyful in hope, **p** in affliction.
1Co 13: 4 Love is **p**, love is kind. It does not
Eph 4: 2 be **p**, bearing with one another
1Th 5: 14 help the weak, be **p** with everyone.

PATIENTLY (PATIENT)
Ps 40: 1 I waited **p** for the LORD;
Ro 8: 25 we do not yet have, we wait for it **p**.

PATTERN
Ro 5: 14 who is a **p** of the one to come.
12: 2 not conform to the **p** of this world,
2Ti 1: 13 keep as the **p** of sound teaching,

PAUL
Also called Saul (Ac 13:9). Pharisee from Tarsus (Ac 9:11; Php 3:5). Apostle (Ac 1). At stoning of Stephen (Ac 8:1). Persecuted Church (Ac 9:1–2; Gal 1:13). Vision of Jesus on road to Damascus (Ac 9:4–9; 26:12–18). In Arabia (Gal 1:17). Preached in Damascus; escaped death through the wall in a basket (Ac 9:19–25). In Jerusalem; sent back to Tarsus (Ac 9:26–30).

Brought to Antioch by Barnabas (Ac 11:22–26). First missionary journey to Cyprus and Galatia (Ac 13–14). Stoned at Lystra (Ac 14:19–20). At Jerusalem council (Ac 15). Split with Barnabas over Mark (Ac 15:36–41).

Second missionary journey with Silas (Ac 16–20). Called to Macedonia (Ac 16:6–10). Freed from prison in Philippi (Ac 16:16–40). In Thessalonica (Ac 17:1–9). Speech in Athens (Ac 17:16–33). In Corinth (Ac 18). In Ephesus (Ac 19). Return to Jerusalem (Ac 20:13–38). Farewell to Ephesian elders (Ac 20:13–38). Arrival in Jerusalem (Ac 21:1–26). Arrested (Ac 21:27–36). Addressed crowds (Ac 22), Sanhedrin (Ac 23:1–11). Transferred to Caesarea (Ac 23:12–35). Trial before Felix (Ac 24), Festus (Ac 25:1–12). Before Agrippa (Ac 25:13—26:32). Voyage to Rome; shipwreck (Ac 27). Arrival in Rome (Ac 28).

PAY (REPAID REPAY)
Lev 26: 43 They will **p** for their sins because
Pr 22: 17 **P** attention and turn your ear
Mt 22: 17 Is it right to **p** the imperial tax
Ro 13: 5 This is also why you **p** taxes,
2Pe 1: 19 you will do well to **p** attention to it,

PEACE (PEACEMAKERS)
Nu 6: 26 toward you and give you **p**." '
Ps 34: 14 and do good; seek **p** and pursue it.
85: 10 righteousness and **p** kiss each
119:165 Great **p** have those who love your
122: 6 Pray for the **p** of Jerusalem:
Pr 14: 30 A heart at **p** gives life to the body,
17: 1 Better a dry crust with **p** and quiet
Isa 9: 6 Everlasting Father, Prince of **P**.
26: 3 in perfect **p** those whose minds are
48: 22 "There is no **p**," says the LORD,
Zec 9: 10 He will proclaim **p** to the nations.
Mt 10: 34 I did not come to bring **p**,
Lk 2: 14 and on earth **p** to those on whom
Jn 14: 27 **P** I leave with you; my **p** I give you.
16: 33 so that in me you may have **p**.
Ro 5: 1 we have **p** with God through our
1Co 7: 15 God has called us to live in **p**.
14: 33 is not a God of disorder but of **p**—

Gal 5: 22 Spirit is love, joy, **p**, forbearance,
Eph 2: 14 For he himself is our **p**, who has
Php 4: 7 the **p** of God, which transcends
Col 1: 20 by making **p** through his blood,
 3: 15 Let the **p** of Christ rule in your
1Th 5: 3 people are saying, "**P** and safety,"
2Th 3: 16 the Lord of **p** himself give you **p**
2Ti 2: 22 love and **p**, along with those who
1Pe 3: 11 they must seek **p** and pursue it.
Rev 6: 4 power to take **p** from the earth
PEACEMAKERS (PEACE)
Mt 5: 9 Blessed are the **p**, for they will be
Jas 3: 18 **P** who sow in peace reap a harvest
PEARL (PEARLS)
Rev 21: 21 each gate made of a single **p**.
PEARLS (PEARL)
Mt 7: 6 do not throw your **p** to pigs.
 13: 45 like a merchant looking for fine **p**.
1Ti 2: 9 or gold or **p** or expensive clothes,
Rev 21: 21 The twelve gates were twelve **p**,
PEKAH
 King of Israel (2Ki 15:25–31; Isa 7:1).
PEKAHIAH
 Son of Menahem; king of Israel (2Ki 15:22–26).
PEN
Mt 5: 18 not the least stroke of a **p**,
PENTECOST
Ac 2: 1 When the day of **P** came, they were
PEOPLE (PEOPLES)
Dt 32: 9 For the Lord's portion is his **p**,
Ru 1: 16 Your **p** will be my **p** and your God
2Ch 7: 14 if my **p**, who are called by my
Ps 133: 1 it is when God's **p** live together
Jer 24: 7 They will be my **p**, and I will be
Zec 2: 11 in that day and will become my **p**.
Mt 4: 19 I will send you out to fish for **p**."
Lk 2: 10 will cause great joy for all the **p**.
Jn 12: 32 earth, will draw all **p** to myself."
Ac 15: 14 to choose a **p** for his name
Ro 5: 12 and in this way death came to all **p**,
 8: 27 for God's **p** in accordance
1Co 9: 22 I have become all things to all **p** so
2Co 6: 16 their God, and they will be my **p**."
Eph 1: 18 glorious inheritance in his holy **p**,
 6: 18 keep on praying for all the Lord's **p**.
1Ti 2: 4 who wants all **p** to be saved
2Ti 2: 2 entrust to reliable **p** who will also
Titus 2: 14 himself a **p** that are very own,
Heb 9: 27 Just as **p** are destined to die once,
1Pe 2: 9 But you are a chosen **p**, a royal
Rev 5: 8 which are the prayers of God's **p**,
 19: 8 the righteous acts of God's holy **p**.)
 21: 3 They will be his **p**, and God
PEOPLES (PEOPLE)
Da 7: 14 **p** of every language worshiped him
Mic 4: 1 the hills, and **p** will stream to it.
PERCEIVING
Isa 6: 9 be ever seeing, but never **p**.'
PERFECT (PERFECTER PERFECTION)
SS 6: 9 but my dove, my **p** one, is unique,
Isa 26: 3 in **p** peace those whose minds are
Mt 5: 48 Be **p**, therefore, as your heavenly Father is **p**.
Ro 12: 2 his good, pleasing and **p** will.
2Co 12: 9 my power is made **p** in weakness."
Col 3: 14 binds them all together in **p** unity.
Heb 9: 11 more **p** tabernacle that is not made
 10: 14 he has made **p** forever those who
Jas 1: 17 good and **p** gift is from above,
 1: 25 looks intently into the **p** law
 3: 2 never at fault in what they say is **p**,
1Jn 4: 18 But **p** love drives out fear,
PERFECTER (PERFECT)
Heb 12: 2 on Jesus, the pioneer and **p** of faith.
PERFECTION (PERFECT)
Ps 119: 96 To all **p** I see a limit, but your
Heb 7: 11 If **p** could have been attained
PERFORMS
Ps 77: 14 You are the God who **p** miracles;
PERISH (PERISHABLE)
Ps 102: 26 They will **p**, but you remain;
Lk 13: 3 you repent, you too will all **p**.
Jn 10: 28 eternal life, and they shall never **p**;

Col 2: 22 that are all destined to **p** with use,
Heb 1: 11 They will **p**, but you remain;
2Pe 3: 9 you, not wanting anyone to **p**,
PERISHABLE (PERISH)
1Co 15: 42 The body that is sown is **p**, it is
PERJURERS
1Ti 1: 10 for slave traders and liars and **p**—
PERMIT
1Ti 2: 12 I do not **p** a woman to teach
PERSECUTE (PERSECUTED PERSECUTION)
Mt 5: 11 **p** you and falsely say all kinds
Jn 15: 20 persecuted me, they will **p** you
Ac 9: 4 "Saul, Saul, why do you **p** me?"
Ro 12: 14 Bless those who **p** you; bless and
PERSECUTED (PERSECUTE)
1Co 4: 12 when we are **p**, we endure it;
2Ti 3: 12 godly life in Christ Jesus will be **p**,
PERSECUTION (PERSECUTE)
Ro 8: 35 trouble or hardship or **p** or famine
PERSEVERANCE (PERSEVERE)
Ro 5: 3 we know that suffering produces **p**;
 5: 4 **p**, character; and character, hope.
Heb 12: 1 let us run with **p** the race marked
Jas 1: 3 testing of your faith produces **p**.
2Pe 1: 6 and to self-control, **p**; and to **p**,
PERSEVERE (PERSEVERANCE PERSEVERED PERSEVERES)
1Ti 4: 16 **P** in them, because if you do,
Heb 10: 36 You need to **p** so that when you
PERSEVERED (PERSEVERE)
Heb 11: 27 he **p** because he saw him who is
Jas 5: 11 count as blessed those who have **p**.
Rev 2: 3 You have **p** and have endured
PERSEVERES (PERSEVERE)
1Co 13: 7 trusts, always hopes, always **p**.
Jas 1: 12 one who **p** under trial because,
PERSUADE
2Co 5: 11 to fear the Lord, we try to **p** others.
PERVERSION (PERVERT)
Lev 18: 23 sexual relations with it; that is a **p**.
Jude : 7 up to sexual immorality and **p**.
PERVERT (PERVERSION)
Gal 1: 7 are trying to **p** the gospel of Christ.
PESTILENCE
Ps 91: 6 the **p** that stalks in the darkness,
PETER
 Apostle, brother of Andrew, also called Simon (Mt 10:2; Mk 3:16; Lk 6:14; Ac 1:13), and Cephas (Jn 1:42). Confession of Christ (Mt 16:13–20; Mk 8:27–30; Lk 9:18–27). At transfiguration (Mt 17:1–8; Mk 9:2–8; Lk 9:28–36; 2Pe 1:16–18). Caught fish with coin (Mt 17:24–27). Denial of Jesus predicted (Mt 26:31–35; Mk 14:27–31; Lk 22:31–34; Jn 13:31–38). Denied Jesus (Mt 26:69–75; Mk 14:66–72; Lk 22:54–62; Jn 18:15–27). Commissioned by Jesus to shepherd his flock (Jn 21:15–23).
 Speech at Pentecost (Ac 2). Healed beggar (Ac 3:1–10). Speech at temple (Ac 3:11–26), before Sanhedrin (Ac 4:1–22). In Samaria (Ac 8:14–25). Sent by vision to Cornelius (Ac 10). Announced salvation of Gentiles in Jerusalem (Ac 11; 15). Freed from prison (Ac 12). Inconsistency at Antioch (Gal 2:11–21). At Jerusalem Council (Ac 15).
PHARISEES
Mt 5: 20 surpasses that of the **P**
PHILIP
 1. Apostle (Mt 10:3; Mk 3:18; Lk 6:14; Jn 1:43–48; 14:8; Ac 1:13).
 2. Deacon (Ac 6:1–7); evangelist in Samaria (Ac 8:4–25), to Ethiopian (Ac 8:26–40).
PHILOSOPHY
Col 2: 8 through hollow and deceptive **p**,
PHYLACTERIES
Mt 23: 5 They make their **p** wide
PHYSICAL
1Ti 4: 8 For **p** training is of some value,
Jas 2: 16 does nothing about their **p** needs,
PIECES
Ge 15: 17 and passed between the **p**.
Jer 34: 18 two and then walked between its **p**.
PIERCE (PIERCED)
Ps 22: 16 they **p** my hands and my feet.
PIERCED (PIERCE)
Isa 53: 5 he was **p** for our transgressions,
Zec 12: 10 the one they have **p**, and they will
Jn 19: 37 will look on the one they have **p**."

PIGS
Mt 7: 6 do not throw your pearls to **p**.
PILATE
    Governor of Judea. Questioned Jesus (Mt 27:1–26; Mk 15:15; Lk 22:66—23:25; Jn 18:28—19:16); sent him to Herod (Lk 23:6–12); consented to his crucifixion when crowds chose Barabbas (Mt 27:15–26; Mk 15:6–15; Lk 23:13–25; Jn 19:1–10).
PILLAR
Ge 19: 26 back, and she became a **p** of salt.
Ex 13: 21 by night in a **p** of fire to give them
1Ti 3: 15 the **p** and foundation of the truth.
PIT
Ps 40: 2 He lifted me out of the slimy **p**,
    103: 4 who redeems your life from the **p**
Mt 15: 14 the blind, both will fall into a **p**."
PITIED
1Co 15: 19 we are of all people most to be **p**.
PLAGUE
2Ch 6: 28 famine or **p** comes to the land,
PLAIN
Ro 1: 19 God has made it **p** to them.
PLAN (PLANNED PLANS)
Pr 14: 22 those who **p** what is good find love
Eph 1: 11 to the **p** of him who works
PLANK
Mt 7: 3 attention to the **p** in your own eye?
Lk 6: 41 attention to the **p** in your own eye?
PLANNED (PLAN)
Ps 40: 5 have done, the things you **p** for us.
Isa 46: 11 what I have **p**, that I will do.
Heb 11: 40 since God had **p** something better
PLANS (PLAN)
Ps 20: 4 heart and make all your **p** succeed.
    33: 11 But the **p** of the LORD stand firm
Pr 20: 18 **P** are established by seeking advice;
Isa 32: 8 But the noble make noble **p**,
PLANTED (PLANTS)
Ps 1: 3 person is like a tree **p** by streams
Mt 15: 13 Father has not **p** will be pulled
1Co 3: 6 I **p** the seed, Apollos watered it,
PLANTS (PLANTED)
1Co 3: 7 neither the one who **p** nor the one
    9: 7 Who **p** a vineyard and does not eat
PLATTER
Mk 6: 25 head of John the Baptist on a **p**."
PLAYED
Lk 7: 32 "'We **p** the pipe for you, and you
1Co 14: 7 what tune is being **p** unless there is
PLEADED
2Co 12: 8 Three times I **p** with the Lord
PLEASANT (PLEASE)
Ps 16: 6 lines have fallen for me in **p** places;
    133: 1 and **p** it is when God's people live
    147: 1 how **p** and fitting to praise him!
Heb 12: 11 No discipline seems **p** at the time,
PLEASE (PLEASANT PLEASED PLEASES PLEASING PLEASURE PLEASURES)
Pr 20: 23 and dishonest scales do not **p** him.
Jer 6: 20 your sacrifices do not **p** me."
Jn 5: 30 for I seek not to **p** myself but him
Ro 8: 8 realm of the flesh cannot **p** God.
    15: 2 Each of us should **p** our neighbors
1Co 7: 32 how he can **p** the Lord.
    10: 33 even as I try to **p** everyone in every
2Co 5: 9 So we make it our goal to **p** him,
Gal 1: 10 If I were still trying to **p** people,
1Th 4: 1 you how to live in order to **p** God,
2Ti 2: 4 tries to **p** his commanding officer.
Heb 11: 6 faith it is impossible to **p** God,
PLEASED (PLEASE)
Mt 3: 17 with him I am well **p**."
1Co 1: 21 God was **p** through the foolishness
Col 1: 19 God was **p** to have all his fullness
Heb 11: 5 commended as one who **p** God.
2Pe 1: 17 with him I am well **p**."
PLEASES (PLEASE)
Ps 135: 6 The LORD does whatever **p** him,
Pr 15: 8 the prayer of the upright **p** him.
Jn 3: 8 The wind blows wherever it **p**.
    8: 29 alone, for I always do what **p** him."
Col 3: 20 in everything, for this **p** the Lord.

1Ti 2: 3 is good, and **p** God our Savior,
1Jn 3: 22 his commands and do what **p** him.
PLEASING (PLEASE)
Ps 104: 34 May my meditation be **p** to him,
Ro 12: 1 living sacrifice, holy and **p** to God
Php 4: 18 an acceptable sacrifice, **p** to God.
Heb 13: 21 he work in us what is **p** to him,
PLEASURE (PLEASE)
Ps 147: 10 His **p** is not in the strength
Pr 21: 17 loves **p** will become poor;
Eze 18: 32 For I take no **p** in the death
Eph 1: 5 in accordance with his **p** and will—
    1: 9 of his will according to his good **p**,
2Ti 3: 4 lovers of **p** rather than lovers
PLEASURES (PLEASE)
Ps 16: 11 with eternal **p** at your right hand.
Heb 11: 25 than to enjoy the fleeting **p** of sin.
2Pe 2: 13 reveling in their **p** while they feast
PLENTIFUL
Mt 9: 37 "The harvest is **p** but the workers
PLOW (PLOWSHARES)
Lk 9: 62 "No one who puts a hand to the **p**
PLOWSHARES (PLOW)
Isa 2: 4 They will beat their swords into **p**
Joel 3: 10 Beat your **p** into swords and your
PLUNDER
Ex 3: 22 And so you will **p** the Egyptians."
POINT
Jas 2: 10 yet stumbles at just one **p** is guilty
POISON
Mk 16: 18 *and when they drink deadly **p**,*
Jas 3: 8 It is a restless evil, full of deadly **p**.
POLLUTE (POLLUTED)
Nu 35: 33 "'Do not **p** the land where you
Jude : 8 these ungodly people **p** their own
POLLUTED (POLLUTE)
Ezr 9: 11 is a land of the corruption
Pr 25: 26 a **p** well are the righteous who give
Ac 15: 20 to abstain from food **p** by idols,
Jas 1: 27 oneself from being **p** by the world.
PONDER
Ps 64: 9 of God and **p** what he has done.
    119: 95 me, but I will **p** your statutes.
POOR (POVERTY)
Dt 15: 4 need be no **p** people among you,
    15: 11 There will always be **p** people
Ps 34: 6 This **p** man called, and the LORD
    82: 3 uphold the cause of the **p**
    112: 9 freely scattered their gifts to the **p**,
Pr 13: 7 another pretends to be **p**, yet has
    14: 31 oppresses the **p** shows contempt
    19: 1 Better the **p** whose walk is
    19: 17 Whoever is kind to the **p** lends
    22: 2 Rich and **p** have this in common:
    22: 9 they share their food with the **p**.
    28: 6 Better the **p** whose walk is
    31: 20 She opens her arms to the **p**
Isa 61: 1 to proclaim good news to the **p**.
Mt 5: 3 "Blessed are the **p** in spirit,
    11: 5 good news is proclaimed to the **p**.
    19: 21 your possessions and give to the **p**,
    26: 11 The **p** you will always have
Mk 12: 42 a **p** widow came and put in two
Ac 10: 4 and gifts to the **p** have come up as
1Co 13: 3 If I give all I possess to the **p**
2Co 8: 9 yet for your sake he became **p**,
Jas 2: 2 and a **p** man in filthy old clothes
PORTION
Dt 32: 9 For the LORD's **p** is his people,
2Ki 2: 9 "Let me inherit a double **p** of your
La 3: 24 to myself, "The LORD is my **p**;
POSSESS (POSSESSING POSSESSION POSSESSIONS)
Nu 33: 53 for I have given you the land to **p**.
POSSESSING (POSSESS)
2Co 6: 10 nothing, and yet **p** everything.
POSSESSION (POSSESS)
Ge 15: 7 give you this land to take **p** of it."
Nu 13: 30 go up and take **p** of the land,
Eph 1: 14 of those who are God's **p**—
POSSESSIONS (POSSESS)
Lk 12: 15 not consist in an abundance of **p**."
2Co 12: 14 because what I want is not your **p**
1Jn 3: 17 If anyone has material **p** and sees

POSSIBLE
Mt 19: 26 but with God all things are **p**.”
Mk 9: 23 “Everything is **p** for one who
10: 27 all things are **p** with God.”
Ro 12: 18 If it is **p**, as far as it depends on you
1Co 9: 22 by all **p** means I might save some.

POT (POTSHERDS POTTER POTTERY)
2Ki 4: 40 of God, there is death in the **p**!”
Jer 18: 4 the potter formed it into another **p**,

POTSHERDS (POT)
Isa 45: 9 but **p** among the **p** on the ground.

POTTER (POT)
Isa 29: 16 Can the pot say to the **p**,
45: 9 Does the clay say to the **p**,
64: 8 We are the clay, you are the **p**;
Jer 18: 6 do with you, Israel, as this **p** does?”
Ro 9: 21 Does not the **p** have the right

POTTERY (POT)
Ro 9: 21 of clay some **p** for special purposes

POUR (POURED)
Ps 62: 8 **p** out your hearts to him, for God
Joel 2: 28 I will **p** out my Spirit on all people.
Mal 3: 10 **p** out so much blessing that there
Ac 2: 17 I will **p** out my Spirit on all people.

POURED (POUR)
Ac 10: 45 the Holy Spirit had been **p** out
Ro 5: 5 because God's love has been **p**

POVERTY (POOR)
Pr 14: 23 but mere talk leads only to **p**.
21: 5 profit as surely as haste leads to **p**.
30: 8 give me neither **p** nor riches,
Mk 12: 44 she, out of her **p**, put in everything
2Co 8: 2 their extreme **p** welled up in rich
8: 9 you through his **p** might become

POWER (POWERFUL POWERS)
1Ch 29: 11 greatness and the **p** and the glory
2Ch 32: 7 for there is a greater **p** with us than
Job 36: 22 “God is exalted in his **p**. Who is
Ps 63: 2 and beheld your **p** and your glory.
68: 34 Proclaim the **p** of God,
147: 5 Great is our Lord and mighty in **p**;
Pr 24: 5 The wise prevail through great **p**,
Isa 40: 10 Sovereign Lord comes with **p**,
Zec 4: 6 'Not by might nor by **p**, but by my
Mt 22: 29 the Scriptures or the **p** of God.
24: 30 of heaven, with **p** and great glory.
Ac 1: 8 you will receive **p** when the Holy
4: 33 With great **p** the apostles
10: 38 with the Holy Spirit and **p**,
Ro 1: 16 because it is the **p** of God
1Co 1: 18 us who are being saved it is the **p**
15: 56 is sin, and the **p** of sin is the law.
2Co 12: 9 so that Christ's **p** may rest on me.
Eph 1: 19 his incomparably great **p** for us
Php 3: 10 to know the **p** of his resurrection
Col 1: 11 strengthened with all **p** according
2Ti 1: 7 us timid, but gives us **p**,
Heb 7: 16 of the **p** of an indestructible life.
Rev 4: 11 to receive glory and honor and **p**,
19: 1 glory and **p** belong to our God,
20: 6 second death has no **p** over them,

POWERFUL (POWER)
Ps 29: 4 The voice of the Lord is **p**;
Lk 24: 19 **p** in word and deed before God
2Th 1: 7 in blazing fire with his **p** angels.
Heb 1: 3 sustaining all things by his **p** word.
Jas 5: 16 prayer of a righteous person is **p**

POWERLESS
Ro 5: 6 when we were still **p**, Christ died
8: 3 what the law was **p** to do because it

POWERS (POWER)
Ro 8: 38 present nor the future, nor any **p**,
1Co 12: 10 to another miraculous **p**,
Col 1: 16 whether thrones or **p** or rulers
2: 15 And having disarmed the **p**

PRACTICE
Lev 19: 26 “'Do not **p** divination or seek
Mt 23: 3 for they do not **p** what they preach.
Lk 8: 21 hear God's word and put it into **p**.”
Ro 12: 13 who are in need. **P** hospitality.
1Ti 5: 4 put their religion into **p** by caring

PRAISE (PRAISED PRAISES PRAISING)
Ex 15: 2 and I will **p** him, my father's God,
Dt 32: 3 Oh, **p** the greatness of our God!
Ru 4: 14 “**P** be to the Lord, who this day
2Sa 22: 47 **P** be to my Rock!
1Ch 16: 25 the Lord and most worthy of **p**;
2Ch 20: 21 to **p** him for the splendor of his
Ps 8: 2 Through the **p** of children
33: 1 it is fitting for the upright to **p** him.
34: 1 his **p** will always be on my lips.
40: 3 mouth, a hymn of **p** to our God.
48: 1 and most worthy of **p**, in the city
68: 19 **P** be to the Lord, to God our Savior,
89: 5 The heavens **p** your wonders,
100: 4 give thanks to him and **p** his name.
105: 2 Sing to him, sing **p** to him;
106: 1 **P** the Lord. Give thanks
119:175 Let me live that I may **p** you,
139: 14 I **p** you because I am fearfully
145: 21 Let every creature **p** his holy name
146: 1 **P** the Lord. **P** the Lord, my soul.
150: 2 **p** him for his surpassing greatness.
150: 6 Let everything that has breath **p** the Lord. **P** the Lord.
Pr 27: 2 Let someone else **p** you, and not
27: 21 but people are tested by their **p**.
31: 31 let her works bring her **p** at the city
Mt 21: 16 Lord, have called forth your **p**'?”
Jn 12: 43 they loved human **p** more than **p** from God.
Eph 1: 6 to the **p** of his glorious grace,
1: 12 might be for the **p** of his glory.
1: 14 to the **p** of his glory.
Heb 13: 15 offer to God a sacrifice of **p**—
Jas 5: 13 Let them sing songs of **p**.

PRAISED (PRAISE)
1Ch 29: 10 David **p** the Lord in the presence
Ne 8: 6 Ezra **p** the Lord, the great God;
Da 2: 19 Then Daniel **p** the God of heaven
Ro 9: 5 who is God over all, forever **p**!
1Pe 4: 11 God may be **p** through Jesus Christ

PRAISES (PRAISE)
2Sa 22: 50 I will sing the **p** of your name.
Ps 47: 6 Sing **p** to God, sing **p**; sing **p**
147: 1 good it is to sing **p** to our God,
Pr 31: 28 her husband also, and he **p** her:

PRAISING (PRAISE)
Ac 10: 46 speaking in tongues and **p** God.
1Co 14: 16 when you are **p** God in the Spirit,

PRAY (PRAYED PRAYERS PRAYING)
Dt 4: 7 our God is near us whenever we **p**
1Sa 12: 23 the Lord by failing to **p** for you.
2Ch 7: 14 will humble themselves and **p**
Job 42: 8 My servant Job will **p** for you,
Ps 122: 6 **P** for the peace of Jerusalem:
Mt 5: 44 and **p** for those who persecute you,
6: 5 for they love to **p** standing
6: 9 “This, then, is how you should **p**:
26: 36 here while I go over there and **p**.”
Lk 6: 28 you, **p** for those who mistreat you.
18: 1 them that they should always **p**
22: 40 them, “**P** that you will not fall
Ro 8: 26 not know what we ought to **p** for,
1Co 14: 13 in a tongue should **p** that they may
1Th 5: 17 **p** continually,
Jas 5: 13 Let them **p**. Is anyone happy?
5: 16 **p** for each other so that you may be

PRAYED (PRAY)
1Sa 1: 27 I **p** for this child, and the Lord
Jnh 2: 1 From inside the fish Jonah **p**
Mk 14: 35 and **p** that if possible the hour

PRAYER (PRAY)
2Ch 30: 27 for their **p** reached heaven, his holy
Ezr 8: 23 about this, and he answered our **p**.
Ps 6: 9 the Lord accepts my **p**.
86: 6 Hear my **p**, Lord; listen to my
Pr 15: 8 the **p** of the upright pleases him.
Isa 56: 7 house will be called a house of **p**
Mt 21: 13 house will be called a house of **p**,'
Mk 11: 24 whatever you ask for in **p**,
Jn 17: 15 My **p** is not that you take them
Ac 6: 4 will give our attention to **p**
Php 4: 6 every situation, by **p** and petition,

Jas 5: 15 the **p** offered in faith will make
1Pe 3: 12 and his ears are attentive to their **p**,
PRAYERS (PRAY)
1Ch 5: 20 He answered their **p**, because they
Mk 12: 40 and for a show make lengthy **p**.
1Pe 3: 7 so that nothing will hinder your **p**.
Rev 5: 8 which are the **p** of God's people.
PRAYING (PRAY)
Mk 11: 25 And when you stand **p**, if you hold
Jn 17: 9 I am not **p** for the world,
Ac 16: 25 Silas were **p** and singing hymns
Eph 6: 18 always keep on **p** for all the Lord's
PREACH (PREACHED PREACHING)
Mt 23: 3 they do not practice what they **p**.
Mk 16: 15 *and **p** the gospel to all creation.*
Ac 9: 20 At once he began to **p**
Ro 10: 15 how can anyone **p** unless they are
15: 20 to **p** the gospel where Christ was
1Co 1: 17 to baptize, but to **p** the gospel—
1: 23 but we **p** Christ crucified:
9: 14 that those who **p** the gospel should
9: 16 Woe to me if I do not **p** the gospel!
2Co 10: 16 so that we can **p** the gospel
Gal 1: 8 heaven should **p** a gospel other
2Ti 4: 2 **P** the word; be prepared in season
PREACHED (PREACH)
Mk 13: 10 the gospel must first be **p** to all
Ac 8: 4 who had been scattered **p** the word
1Co 9: 27 so that after I have **p** to others,
15: 1 remind you of the gospel I **p** to you
2Co 11: 4 a Jesus other than the Jesus we **p**,
Gal 1: 8 a gospel other than the one we **p**
Php 1: 18 false motives or true, Christ is **p**.
1Ti 3: 16 angels, was **p** among the nations,
PREACHING (PREACH)
Ro 10: 14 can they hear without someone **p**
1Co 9: 18 in **p** the gospel I may offer it free
1Ti 4: 13 of Scripture, to **p** and to teaching.
5: 17 especially those whose work is **p**
PRECEPTS
Ps 19: 8 The **p** of the LORD are right,
111: 7 all his **p** are trustworthy.
111: 10 all who follow his **p** have good
119: 40 How I long for your **p**!
119: 69 I keep your **p** with all my heart.
119:104 I gain understanding from your **p**;
119:159 See how I love your **p**; preserve my
PRECIOUS
Ps 19: 10 They are more **p** than gold,
116: 15 **P** in the sight of the LORD is
Pr 8: 11 for wisdom is more **p** than rubies,
Isa 28: 16 stone, a **p** cornerstone for a sure
1Pe 1: 19 but with the **p** blood of Christ,
2: 6 a chosen and **p** cornerstone,
2Pe 1: 4 us his very great and **p** promises,
PREDESTINED (DESTINY)
Ro 8: 29 **p** to be conformed to the image
8: 30 And those he **p**, he also called;
Eph 1: 5 he **p** us for adoption to sonship
1: 11 been **p** according to the plan
PREDICTION
Jer 28: 9 LORD only if his **p** comes true."
PREPARE (PREPARED)
Ps 23: 5 You **p** a table before me
Am 4: 12 to you, Israel, **p** to meet your God."
Jn 14: 2 that I am going there to **p** a place
PREPARED (PREPARE)
Mt 25: 34 the kingdom **p** for you since
1Co 2: 9 the things God has **p** for those who
Eph 2: 10 which God **p** in advance for us
2Ti 4: 2 be **p** in season and out of season;
1Pe 3: 15 Always be **p** to give an answer
PRESENCE (PRESENT)
Ex 25: 30 Put the bread of the **P** on this table
Ezr 9: 15 not one of us can stand in your **p**."
Ps 31: 20 the shelter of your **p** you hide them
89: 15 who walk in the light of your **p**,
90: 8 secret sins in the light of your **p**.
139: 7 Where can I flee from your **p**?
Jer 5: 22 "Should you not tremble in my **p**?
Heb 9: 24 now to appear for us in God's **p**.
Jude : 24 before his glorious **p** without fault

PRESENT (PRESENCE)
2Co 11: 2 that I might **p** you as a pure virgin
Eph 5: 27 and to **p** her to himself as a radiant
2Ti 2: 15 Do your best to **p** yourself to God
PRESERVES
Ps 119: 50 Your promise **p** my life.
PRESS (PRESSED PRESSURE)
Php 3: 14 I **p** on toward the goal to win
PRESSED (PRESS)
Lk 6: 38 A good measure, **p** down,
PRESSURE (PRESS)
2Co 1: 8 We were under great **p**, far beyond
11: 28 I face daily the **p** of my concern
PREVAILS
1Sa 2: 9 "It is not by strength that one **p**;
PRICE
Job 28: 18 the **p** of wisdom is beyond rubies.
1Co 6: 20 you were bought at a **p**.
7: 23 You were bought at a **p**;
PRIDE (PROUD)
Pr 8: 13 I hate **p** and arrogance,
16: 18 **P** goes before destruction,
Da 4: 37 those who walk in **p** he is able
Gal 6: 4 can take **p** in themselves alone,
Jas 1: 9 to take **p** in their high position.
PRIEST (PRIESTHOOD PRIESTS)
Heb 4: 14 a great high **p** who has ascended
4: 15 do not have a high **p** who is unable
7: 26 Such a high **p** truly meets our need
8: 1 We do have such a high **p**, who sat
PRIESTHOOD (PRIEST)
Heb 7: 24 lives forever, he has a permanent **p**.
1Pe 2: 5 a spiritual house to be a holy **p**,
2: 9 people, a royal **p**, a holy nation,
PRIESTS (PRIEST)
Ex 19: 6 you will be for me a kingdom of **p**
Rev 5: 10 a kingdom and **p** to serve our God,
PRINCE
Isa 9: 6 Everlasting Father, **P** of Peace.
Jn 12: 31 now the **p** of this world will be
Ac 5: 31 him to his own right hand as **P**
PRISON (PRISONER)
Isa 42: 7 blind, to free captives from **p**
Mt 25: 36 I was in **p** and you came to visit
Rev 20: 7 Satan will be released from his **p**
PRISONER (PRISON)
Ro 7: 23 making me a **p** of the law of sin
Eph 3: 1 the **p** of Christ Jesus for the sake
PRIVILEGE
2Co 8: 4 for the **p** of sharing in this service
PRIZE
1Co 9: 24 Run in such a way as to get the **p**.
Php 3: 14 on toward the goal to win the **p**
PROCLAIM (PROCLAIMED)
1Ch 16: 23 **p** his salvation day after day.
Ps 19: 1 the skies **p** the work of his hands.
50: 6 the heavens **p** his righteousness,
68: 34 **P** the power of God, whose majesty
118: 17 will **p** what the LORD has done.
Zec 9: 10 He will **p** peace to the nations.
Ac 20: 27 I have not hesitated to **p** to you
Ro 10: 8 concerning faith that we **p**:
1Co 11: 26 cup, you **p** the Lord's death until
PROCLAIMED (PROCLAIM)
Ro 15: 19 I have fully **p** the gospel of Christ.
Col 1: 23 has been **p** to every creature under
PRODUCE (PRODUCES)
Mt 3: 8 **P** fruit in keeping with repentance.
3: 10 does not **p** good fruit will be cut
PRODUCES (PRODUCE)
Pr 30: 33 so stirring up anger **p** strife."
Ro 5: 3 that suffering **p** perseverance;
Heb 12: 11 it **p** a harvest of righteousness
PROFANE
Lev 22: 32 Do not **p** my holy name, for I must
PROFESS
1Ti 2: 10 for women who **p** to worship God.
Heb 4: 14 let us hold firmly to the faith we **p**.
10: 23 unswervingly to the hope we **p**,
PROMISE (PROMISED PROMISES)
1Ki 8: 20 LORD has kept the **p** he made:
Ac 2: 39 The **p** is for you and your children

Gal 3: 14 faith we might receive the **p**
1Ti 4: 8 holding **p** for both the present life
2Pe 3: 9 Lord is not slow in keeping his **p**,
PROMISED (PROMISE)
Ex 3: 17 I have **p** to bring you up out of
Dt 26: 18 his treasured possession as he **p**,
Ps 119: 57 I have **p** to obey your words.
Ro 4: 21 had power to do what he had **p**.
Heb 10: 23 we profess, for he who **p** is faithful.
2Pe 3: 4 say, "Where is this 'coming' he **p**?
PROMISES (PROMISE)
Jos 21: 45 of all the LORD's good **p** to Israel
Ro 9: 4 law, the temple worship and the **p**.
2Pe 1: 4 us his very great and precious **p**,
PROMPTED
1Th 1: 3 by faith, your labor **p** by love,
2Th 1: 11 and your every deed **p** by faith.
PROPHECIES (PROPHESY)
1Co 13: 8 But where there are **p**, they will
1Th 5: 20 Do not treat **p** with contempt
PROPHECY (PROPHESY)
1Co 14: 1 gifts of the Spirit, especially **p**.
2Pe 1: 20 that no **p** of Scripture came
PROPHESY (PROPHECIES PROPHECY PROPHESYING PROPHET PROPHETS)
Joel 2: 28 Your sons and daughters will **p**,
Mt 7: 22 did we not **p** in your name
1Co 14: 39 be eager to **p**, and do not forbid
PROPHESYING (PROPHESY)
Ro 12: 6 If your gift is **p**, then prophesy
PROPHET (PROPHESY)
Dt 18: 18 for them a **p** like you from among
Am 7: 14 neither a **p** nor the son of a **p**,
Mt 10: 41 Whoever welcomes a **p** as a **p** will
Lk 4: 24 "no **p** is accepted in his hometown.
PROPHETS (PROPHESY)
Ps 105: 15 do my **p** no harm."
Mt 5: 17 come to abolish the Law or the **P**;
7: 12 for this sums up the Law and the **P**.
24: 24 messiahs and false **p** will appear
Lk 24: 25 believe all that the **p** have spoken!
Ac 10: 43 All the **p** testify about him
1Co 12: 28 apostles, second **p**, third teachers,
14: 32 The spirits of **p** are subject
Eph 2: 20 foundation of the apostles and **p**,
Heb 1: 1 ancestors through the **p** at many
1Pe 1: 10 the **p**, who spoke of the grace
PROSPER (PROSPERITY PROSPERS)
Pr 28: 25 who trust in the LORD will **p**.
PROSPERITY (PROSPER)
Ps 73: 3 when I saw the **p** of the wicked.
PROSPERS (PROSPER)
Ps 1: 3 whatever they do **p**.
PROSTITUTE (PROSTITUTES)
1Co 6: 15 of Christ and unite them with a **p**?
PROSTITUTES (PROSTITUTE)
Mt 21: 31 **p** are entering the kingdom of God
Lk 15: 30 your property with **p** comes home,
PROSTRATE
Dt 9: 18 again I fell **p** before the LORD
PROTECT (PROTECTS)
Ps 32: 7 you will **p** me from trouble
Pr 2: 11 Discretion will **p** you,
Jn 17: 11 **p** them by the power of your name,
PROTECTS (PROTECT)
1Co 13: 7 It always **p**, always trusts,
PROUD (PRIDE)
Pr 16: 5 The LORD detests all the **p**
Ro 12: 16 Do not be **p**, but be willing
1Co 13: 4 envy, it does not boast, it is not **p**.
PROVE
1Co 4: 2 been given a trust must **p** faithful.
PROVIDE (PROVIDED PROVIDES)
Ge 22: 8 "God himself will **p** the lamb
Isa 43: 20 because I **p** water in the wilderness
1Ti 5: 8 Anyone who does not **p** for their
PROVIDED (PROVIDE)
Jnh 1: 17 Now the LORD **p** a huge fish
4: 6 the LORD God **p** a leafy plant
4: 7 dawn the next day God **p** a worm,
4: 8 rose, God **p** a scorching east wind,

PROVIDES (PROVIDE)
1Ti 6: 17 who richly **p** us with everything
1Pe 4: 11 do so with the strength God **p**,
PROVOKED
Ecc 7: 9 Do not be quickly **p** in your spirit,
PRUDENT
Pr 14: 15 the **p** give thought to their steps.
19: 14 but a **p** wife is from the LORD.
Am 5: 13 Therefore the **p** keep quiet in such
PRUNING
Isa 2: 4 and their spears into **p** hooks.
Joel 3: 10 and your **p** hooks into spears.
PSALMS
Eph 5: 19 speaking to one another with **p**,
Col 3: 16 with all wisdom through **p**,
PUBLICLY
Ac 20: 20 have taught you **p** and from house
PUFFS
1Co 8: 1 knowledge **p** up while love builds
PUNISH (PUNISHED)
Ex 32: 34 to **p**, I will **p** them for their sin."
Pr 23: 13 if you **p** them with the rod,
Isa 13: 11 I will **p** the world for its evil,
1Pe 2: 14 by him to **p** those who do wrong
PUNISHED (PUNISH)
La 3: 39 should the living complain when **p**
2Th 1: 9 They will be **p** with everlasting
Heb 10: 29 to be **p** who has trampled the Son
PURE (PURIFIES PURIFY PURITY)
2Sa 22: 27 to the **p** you show yourself **p**,
Ps 24: 4 who has clean hands and a **p** heart,
51: 10 Create in me a **p** heart, O God,
Pr 20: 9 can say, "I have kept my heart **p**;
Isa 52: 11 Come out from it and be **p**,
Hab 1: 13 Your eyes are too **p** to look on evil;
Mt 5: 8 Blessed are the **p** in heart, for they
2Co 11: 2 I might present you as a **p** virgin
Php 4: 8 whatever is **p**, whatever is lovely,
1Ti 5: 22 the sins of others. Keep yourself **p**.
Titus 1: 15 To the **p**, all things are **p**,
2: 5 to be self-controlled and **p**, to be
Heb 13: 4 all, and the marriage bed kept **p**,
1Jn 3: 3 purify themselves, just as he is **p**.
PURGE
Pr 20: 30 and beatings **p** the inmost being.
PURIFIES (PURE)
1Jn 1: 7 of Jesus, his Son, **p** us from all sin.
PURIFY (PURE)
Titus 2: 14 to **p** for himself a people that are
1Jn 1: 9 and **p** us from all unrighteousness.
3: 3 this hope in him **p** themselves,
PURITY (PURE)
Ps 119: 9 person stay on the path of **p**?
2Co 6: 6 in **p**, understanding,
1Ti 4: 12 conduct, in love, in faith and in **p**.
PURPOSE
Pr 19: 21 it is the LORD's **p** that prevails.
Isa 55: 11 achieve the **p** for which I sent it.
Ro 8: 28 been called according to his **p**.
PURSES
Lk 12: 33 Provide **p** for yourselves that will
PURSUE
Ps 34: 14 and do good; seek peace and **p** it.
2Ti 2: 22 of youth and **p** righteousness, faith,
1Pe 3: 11 they must seek peace and **p** it.
QUALITIES (QUALITY)
2Pe 1: 8 if you possess these **q** in increasing
QUALITY (QUALITIES)
1Co 3: 13 and the fire will test the **q** of each
QUARREL (QUARRELSOME)
Pr 15: 18 the one who is patient calms a **q**.
17: 14 Starting a **q** is like breaching a dam
17: 19 Whoever loves a **q** loves sin;
QUARRELSOME (QUARREL)
Pr 19: 13 **q** wife is like the constant dripping
1Ti 3: 3 gentle, not **q**, not a lover of money.
2Ti 2: 24 the Lord's servant must not be **q**
QUENCH
1Th 5: 19 Do not **q** the Spirit.
QUICK-TEMPERED
Titus 1: 7 not **q**, not given to drunkenness,

QUIET (QUIETNESS)
Ps   23:   2   he leads me beside **q** waters,
Lk   19: 40   "if they keep **q**, the stones will cry
1Ti   2:   2   peaceful and **q** lives in all godliness
1Pe   3:   4   beauty of a gentle and **q** spirit,
QUIETNESS (QUIET)
Isa 30: 15   in **q** and trust is your strength,
       32: 17   its effect will be **q** and confidence
1Ti   2: 11   woman should learn in **q** and full
QUIVER
Ps 127:   5   Blessed is the man whose **q** is full
RACE
Ecc   9: 11   The **r** is not to the swift or
1Co   9: 24   that in a **r** all the runners run,
2Ti   4:   7   I have finished the **r**, I have kept
Heb 12:   1   with perseverance the **r** marked
RACHEL
       Daughter of Laban (Ge 29:16); wife of Jacob (Ge 29:28); bore two sons (Ge 30:22–24; 35:16–24; 46:19).
RADIANCE (RADIANT)
Heb   1:   3   The Son is the **r** of God's glory
RADIANT (RADIANCE)
Ex   34: 29   that his face was **r** because he had
Ps   34:   5   Those who look to him are **r**;
SS   5: 10   My beloved is **r** and ruddy,
Isa 60:   5   Then you will look and be **r**,
Eph   5: 27   her to himself as a **r** church,
RAIN (RAINBOW)
Mt   5: 45   and sends **r** on the righteous
RAINBOW (RAIN)
Ge   9: 13   I have set my **r** in the clouds, and it
RAISED (RISE)
Ro   4: 25   was **r** to life for our justification.
       10:   9   your heart that God **r** him
1Co 15:   4   he was **r** on the third day according
RAN (RUN)
Jnh   1:   3   But Jonah **r** away from the LORD
RANSOM
Mt   20: 28   to give his life as a **r** for many."
Heb   9: 15   he has died as a **r** to set them free
RAVENS
1Ki 17:   6   The **r** brought him bread and meat
Lk   12: 24   Consider the **r**: They do not sow
READ (READS)
Jos   8: 34   Joshua **r** all the words of the law—
Ne   8:   8   understood what was being **r**.
2Co   3:   2   hearts, known and **r** by everyone.
READS (READ)
Rev   1:   3   is the one who **r** aloud the words
REAL (REALITY)
Jn   6: 55   For my flesh is **r** food and my blood is **r** drink.
REALITY (REAL)
Col   2: 17   the **r**, however, is found in Christ.
REAP (REAPS)
Job   4:   8   evil and those who sow trouble **r** it.
2Co   9:   6   generously will also **r** generously.
REAPS (REAP)
Gal   6:   7   A man **r** what he sows.
REASON
1Pe   3: 15   asks you to give the **r** for the hope
REBEKAH
       Sister of Laban, secured as bride for Isaac (Ge 24). Mother of Esau and Jacob (Ge 25:19–26). Taken by Abimelek as sister of Isaac; returned (Ge 26:1–11). Encouraged Jacob to trick Isaac out of blessing (Ge 27:1–17).
REBEL
Mt   10: 21   children will **r** against their parents
REBUKE (REBUKING)
Pr   9:   8   **r** the wise and they will love you.
       27:   5   Better is open **r** than hidden love.
Lk   17:   3   or sister sins against you, **r** them;
2Ti   4:   2   correct, **r** and encourage—
Rev   3: 19   Those whom I love I **r**
REBUKING (REBUKE)
2Ti   3: 16   and is useful for teaching, **r**,
RECEIVE (RECEIVED RECEIVES)
Ac   1:   8   you will **r** power when the Holy
       20: 35   more blessed to give than to **r**.' "
2Co   6: 17   no unclean thing, and I will **r** you."
Rev   4: 11   to **r** glory and honor and power,
RECEIVED (RECEIVE)
Mt   6:   2   they have **r** their reward in full.

Mt   10:   8   Freely you have **r**; freely give.
1Co 11: 23   For I **r** from the Lord what I
Col   2:   6   just as you **r** Christ Jesus as Lord,
1Pe   4: 10   should use whatever gift you have **r**
RECEIVES (RECEIVE)
Mt   7:   8   For everyone who asks **r**;
Ac   10: 43   who believes in him **r** forgiveness
RECKONING
Isa 10:   3   What will you do on the day of **r**,
RECOGNIZE (RECOGNIZED)
Mt   7: 16   By their fruit you will **r** them.
RECOGNIZED (RECOGNIZE)
Mt   12: 33   be bad, for a tree is **r** by its fruit.
Ro   7: 13   in order that sin might be **r** as sin,
RECOMPENSE
Isa 40: 10   him, and his **r** accompanies him.
RECONCILE (RECONCILED RECONCILIATION)
Eph   2: 16   and in one body to **r** both of them
RECONCILED (RECONCILE)
Mt   5: 24   First go and be **r** to them;
Ro   5: 10   were **r** to him through the death
2Co   5: 18   who **r** us to himself through Christ
RECONCILIATION (RECONCILE)
Ro   5: 11   whom we have now received **r**.
       11: 15   For if their rejection brought **r**
2Co   5: 18   and gave us the ministry of **r**:
       5: 19   committed to us the message of **r**.
RECORD
Ps 130:   3   you, LORD, kept a **r** of sins, Lord,
RED
Isa   though they are **r** as crimson,
REDEEM (REDEEMED REDEEMER REDEMPTION)
2Sa   7: 23   out to **r** as a people for himself,
Ps   49:   7   No one can **r** the life of another
Gal   4:   5   to **r** those under the law, that we
REDEEMED (REDEEM)
Gal   3: 13   Christ **r** us from the curse of the law
1Pe   1: 18   you were **r** from the empty way
REDEEMER (REDEEM)
Job 19: 25   I know that my **r** lives,
REDEMPTION (REDEEM)
Ps 130:   7   love and with him is full **r**.
Lk   21: 28   because your **r** is drawing near."
Ro   8: 23   to sonship, the **r** of our bodies.
Eph   1:   7   we have **r** through his blood,
Col   1: 14   in whom we have **r**, the forgiveness
Heb   9: 12   blood, thus obtaining eternal **r**.
REFUGE
Nu   35: 11   some towns to be your cities of **r**,
Dt   33: 27   The eternal God is your **r**,
Ru   2: 12   wings you have come to take **r**."
Ps   46:   1   God is our **r** and strength,
       91:   2   "He is my **r** and my fortress,
REHOBOAM
       Son of Solomon (1Ki 11:43; 1Ch 3:10). Harsh treatment of subjects caused divided kingdom (1Ki 12:1–24; 14:21–31; 2Ch 10–12).
REIGN (REIGNS)
Ro   6: 12   not let sin **r** in your mortal body
1Co 15: 25   he must **r** until he has put all his
2Ti   2: 12   if we endure, we will also **r** with
Rev 20:   6   **r** with him for a thousand years.
REIGNS (REIGN)
Ex   15: 18   "The LORD **r** for ever and ever."
REJECTED (REJECTS)
Ps 118: 22   stone the builders **r** has become
Isa 53:   3   was despised and **r** by mankind,
1Ti   4:   4   nothing is to be **r** if it is received
1Pe   2:   4   **r** by humans but chosen by God
       2:   7   stone the builders **r** has become
REJECTS (REJECTED)
Lk   10: 16   whoever **r** me **r** him who sent me."
Jn   3: 36   whoever **r** the Son will not see life,
REJOICE (JOY)
Ps   66:   6   come, let us **r** in him.
     118: 24   let us **r** today and be glad.
Pr   5: 18   you **r** in the wife of your youth.
Lk   10: 20   but **r** that your names are written
       15:   6   together and says, '**R** with me;
Ro   12: 15   **R** with those who **r**;
Php   4:   4   **R** in the Lord always. I will say it again: **R**!

REJOICES (JOY)
Isa 61: 10 my soul **r** in my God.
Lk   1: 47 and my spirit **r** in God my Savior,
1Co 12: 26 is honored, every part **r** with it.
     13: 6 delight in evil but **r** with the truth.
REJOICING (JOY)
Ps 30: 5 night, but **r** comes in the morning.
Lk 15: 7 the same way there will be more **r**
Ac   5: 41 **r** because they had been counted
RELIABLE
2Ti 2: 2 entrust to **r** people who will also be
RELIGION
1Ti 5: 4 of all to put their **r** into practice
Jas 1: 27 **R** that God our Father accepts as
REMAIN (REMAINS)
Nu 33: 55 you allow to **r** will become barbs
Jn 15: 7 If you **r** in me and my words **r**
Ro 13: 8 Let no debt **r** outstanding,
1Co 13: 13 And now these three **r**:
REMAINS (REMAIN)
Ps 146: 6 he **r** faithful forever.
2Ti 2: 13 if we are faithless, he **r** faithful,
Heb 7: 3 Son of God, he **r** a priest forever.
REMEMBER (REMEMBERS REMEMBRANCE)
Ex 20: 8 "**R** the Sabbath day by keeping it
1Ch 16: 12 **R** the wonders he has done,
Ecc 12: 1 **R** your Creator in the days of your
Jer 31: 34 and will **r** their sins no more."
Gal 2: 10 we should continue to **r** the poor,
Php 1: 3 I thank my God every time I **r** you.
Heb 8: 12 and will **r** their sins no more."
REMEMBERS (REMEMBER)
Ps 103: 14 are formed, he **r** that we are dust.
    111: 5 he **r** his covenant forever.
Isa 43: 25 own sake, and **r** your sins no more.
REMEMBRANCE (REMEMBER)
1Co 11: 24 is for you; do this in **r** of me."
REMIND
Jn 14: 26 will **r** you of everything I have said
REMOVED
Ps 30: 11 you **r** my sackcloth and clothed me
    103: 12 so far has he **r** our transgressions
Jn 20: 1 that the stone had been **r**
RENEW (RENEWED RENEWING)
Ps 51: 10 and **r** a steadfast spirit within me.
Isa 40: 31 in the LORD will **r** their strength.
RENEWED (RENEW)
Ps 103: 5 that your youth is **r** like the eagle's.
2Co 4: 16 yet inwardly we are being **r** day
RENEWING (RENEW)
Ro 12: 2 transformed by the **r** of your mind.
RENOUNCE (RENOUNCES)
Da   4: 27 **R** your sins by doing what is right,
RENOUNCES (RENOUNCE)
Pr 28: 13 confesses and **r** them finds mercy.
RENOWN
Isa 63: 12 to gain for himself everlasting **r**,
Jer 32: 20 have gained the **r** that is still yours.
REPAID (PAY)
Lk 14: 14 you will be **r** at the resurrection
Col 3: 25 Anyone who does wrong will be **r**
REPAY (PAY)
Dt 32: 35 It is mine to avenge; I will **r**.
Ru   2: 12 May the LORD **r** you for what you
Ro 12: 19 I will **r**," says the Lord.
1Pe 3: 9 the contrary, **r** evil with blessing,
REPENT (REPENTANCE REPENTS)
Job 42: 6 I despise myself and **r** in dust
Jer 15: 19 "If you **r**, I will restore you that you
Mt   4: 17 time on Jesus began to preach, "**R**,
Lk 13: 3 But unless you **r**, you too will all
     17: 3 and if they **r**, forgive them.
Ac   2: 38 Peter replied, "**R** and be baptized,
     17: 30 all people everywhere to **r**.
REPENTANCE (REPENT)
Lk   3: 8 Produce fruit in keeping with **r**.
     5: 32 call the righteous, but sinners to **r**."
Ac 26: 20 demonstrate their **r** by their deeds.
2Co 7: 10 Godly sorrow brings **r** that leads
REPENTS (REPENT)
Lk 15: 10 of God over one sinner who **r**."

REPROACH
1Ti 3: 2 Now the overseer is to be above **r**,
REPUTATION
1Ti 3: 7 also have a good **r** with outsiders,
REQUESTS
Ps 20: 5 May the LORD grant all your **r**.
Php 4: 6 present your **r** to God.
REQUIRE
Mic 6: 8 what does the LORD **r** of you?
RESCUE (RESCUES)
Da   6: 20 been able to **r** you from the lions?"
2Pe 2: 9 the Lord knows how to **r** the godly
RESCUES (RESCUE)
1Th 1: 10 who **r** us from the coming wrath.
RESIST
Jas 4: 7 **R** the devil, and he will flee
1Pe 5: 9 **R** him, standing firm in the faith,
RESOLVED
Da   1: 8 Daniel **r** not to defile himself
1Co 2: 2 For I **r** to know nothing while I
RESPECT (RESPECTABLE)
Lev 19: 3 of you must **r** your mother
     19: 32 show **r** for the elderly and revere
Mal 1: 6 a master, where is the **r** due me?"
1Th 4: 12 that your daily life may win the **r**
1Ti 3: 4 do so in a manner worthy of full **r**.
1Pe 2: 17 Show proper **r** to everyone,
     3: 7 them with **r** as the weaker partner
RESPECTABLE (RESPECT)
1Ti 3: 2 self-controlled, **r**, hospitable,
REST
Ex 31: 15 seventh day is a day of sabbath **r**,
Ps 91: 1 the Most High will **r** in the shadow
Jer 6: 16 and you will find **r** for your souls.
Mt 11: 28 burdened, and I will give you **r**.
RESTITUTION
Ex 22: 3 who steals must certainly make **r**,
Lev 6: 5 must make **r** in full, add a fifth
RESTORE
Ps 51: 12 **R** to me the joy of your salvation
Gal 6: 1 by the Spirit should **r** that person
RESURRECTION
Mt 22: 30 the **r** people will neither marry nor
Lk 14: 14 be repaid at the **r** of the righteous."
Jn 11: 25 said to her, "I am the **r** and the life.
Ro   1: 4 in power by his **r** from the dead:
1Co 15: 12 say that there is no **r** of the dead?
Php 3: 10 yes, to know the power of his **r**
Rev 20: 5 This is the first **r**.
RETRIBUTION
Jer 51: 56 For the LORD is a God of **r**;
RETURN
2Ch 30: 9 If you **r** to the LORD, then your
Ne   1: 9 but if you **r** to me and obey my
Isa 55: 11 It will not **r** to me empty, but will
Hos 6: 1 "Come, let us **r** to the LORD.
Joel 2: 12 "**r** to me with all your heart,
REVEALED (REVELATION)
Dt 29: 29 but the things **r** belong to us
Isa 40: 5 the glory of the LORD will be **r**,
Mt 11: 25 and **r** them to little children.
Ro   1: 17 the righteousness of God is **r**—
     8: 18 with the glory that will be **r** in us.
REVELATION (REVEALED)
Gal 1: 12 I received it by **r** from Jesus Christ.
Rev 1: 1 The **r** from Jesus Christ,
REVENGE (VENGEANCE)
Lev 19: 18 " 'Do not seek **r** or bear a grudge
Ro 12: 19 Do not take **r**, my dear friends,
REVERE (REVERENCE)
Ps 33: 8 all the people of the world **r** him.
REVERENCE (REVERE)
Lev 19: 30 and have **r** for my sanctuary.
Ps   5: 7 in **r** I bow down toward your holy
Col 3: 22 of heart and **r** for the Lord.
1Pe 3: 2 see the purity and **r** of your lives.
REVIVE
Ps 85: 6 Will you not **r** us again, that your
Isa 57: 15 to the spirit of the lowly and to **r**
REWARD (REWARDED)
Ps 19: 11 in keeping them there is great **r**.
    127: 3 the LORD, offspring a **r** from him.

Pr	19: 17	he will **r** them for what they have
	25: 22	head, and the Lord will **r** you.
Jer	17: 10	to **r** each person according to their
Mt	5: 12	because great is your **r** in heaven,
	6: 5	they have received their **r** in full.
	16: 27	he will **r** each person according
1Co	3: 14	the builder will receive a **r**.
Rev	22: 12	My **r** is with me, and I will give

REWARDED (REWARD)

Ru	2: 12	May you be richly **r** by the Lord,
Ps	18: 24	The Lord has **r** me according
Pr	14: 14	and the good **r** for theirs.
1Co	3: 8	and they will each be **r** according

RICH (RICHES)

Pr	23: 4	Do not wear yourself out to get **r**;
Jer	9: 23	or the **r** boast of their riches,
Mt	19: 23	for someone who is **r** to enter
2Co	6: 10	poor, yet making many **r**;
	8: 9	his poverty might become **r**.
1Ti	6: 17	Command those who are **r** in this

RICHES (RICH)

Ps	119: 14	statutes as one rejoices in great **r**.
Pr	30: 8	give me neither poverty nor **r**,
Isa	10: 3	Where will you leave your **r**?
Ro	9: 23	to make the **r** of his glory known
	11: 33	the depth of the **r** of the wisdom
Eph	2: 7	he might show the incomparable **r**
	3: 8	to the Gentiles the boundless **r**
Col	1: 27	among the Gentiles the glorious **r**

RID

Ge	21: 10	"Get **r** of that slave woman and her
1Co	5: 7	Get **r** of the old yeast, so that you
Gal	4: 30	"Get **r** of the slave woman and her

RIGHT (RIGHTS)

Ge	18: 25	not the Judge of all the earth do **r**?"
Ex	15: 26	God and do what is **r** in his eyes,
Dt	5: 32	do not turn aside to the **r**
Ps	16: 8	With him at my **r** hand, I will not
	19: 8	The precepts of the Lord are **r**,
	63: 8	your **r** hand upholds me.
	110: 1	"Sit at my **r** hand until I make your
Pr	4: 27	Do not turn to the **r** or the left;
	14: 12	There is a way that appears to be **r**,
Isa	1: 17	Learn to do **r**; seek justice.
Jer	23: 5	do what is just and **r** in the land.
Hos	14: 9	The ways of the Lord are **r**;
Mt	6: 3	know what your **r** hand is doing,
Jn	1: 12	he gave the **r** to become children
Ro	9: 21	Does not the potter have the **r**
	12: 17	careful to do what is **r** in the eyes
Eph	1: 20	and seated him at his **r** hand
Php	4: 8	whatever is **r**, whatever is pure,

RIGHTEOUS (RIGHTEOUSNESS)

Ps	34: 15	eyes of the Lord are on the **r**,
	37: 25	yet I have never seen the **r** forsaken
	119:137	You are **r**, Lord, and your laws
	143: 2	no one living is **r** before you.
Pr	3: 33	but he blesses the home of the **r**.
	11: 30	The fruit of the **r** is a tree of life,
	18: 10	the **r** run to it and are safe.
Isa	64: 6	all our **r** acts are like filthy rags;
Hab	2: 4	but the **r** person will live by his
Mt	5: 45	and sends rain on the **r**
	9: 13	For I have not come to call the **r**,
	13: 49	and separate the wicked from the **r**
	25: 46	but the **r** to eternal life."
Ro	1: 17	"The **r** will live by faith."
	3: 10	"There is no one **r**, not even one;
1Ti	1: 9	that the law is made not for the **r**
Jas	2: 24	is considered **r** by what they do
1Pe	3: 18	for sins, the **r** for the unrighteous,
1Jn	3: 7	is right is **r**, just as he is **r**.
Rev	19: 8	(Fine linen stands for the **r** acts

RIGHTEOUSNESS (RIGHTEOUS)

Ge	15: 6	and he credited it to him as **r**.
1Sa	26: 23	rewards everyone for their **r**
Ps	9: 8	He rules the world in **r** and judges
	45: 7	You love **r** and hate wickedness;
	85: 10	**r** and peace kiss each other.
	89: 14	**R** and justice are the foundation
	111: 3	deeds, and his **r** endures forever.
Pr	14: 34	**R** exalts a nation, but sin

Pr	21: 21	Whoever pursues **r** and love finds
Isa	59: 17	He put on **r** as his breastplate,
Eze	18: 20	The **r** of the righteous will be
Da	9: 24	to bring in everlasting **r**, to seal
	12: 3	and those who lead many to **r**,
Mal	4: 2	the sun of **r** will rise with healing
Mt	5: 6	those who hunger and thirst for **r**,
	5: 20	you that unless your **r** surpasses
	6: 1	practice your **r** in front of others
	6: 33	seek first his kingdom and his **r**,
Ro	3: 25	He did this to demonstrate his **r**,
	4: 3	and it was credited to him as **r**."
	4: 9	faith was credited to him as **r**.
	6: 13	to him as an instrument of **r**.
2Co	5: 21	we might become the **r** of God.
Gal	2: 21	**r** could be gained through the law,
	3: 6	and it was credited to him as **r**."
Eph	6: 14	with the breastplate of **r** in place,
Php	3: 9	not having a **r** of my own
2Ti	3: 16	correcting and training in **r**,
	4: 8	is in store for me the crown of **r**,
Heb	11: 7	and became heir of the **r** that is
2Pe	2: 21	not to have known the way of **r**,

RIGHTS (RIGHT)

La	3: 35	deny people their **r** before the Most

RISE (RAISED)

Isa	26: 19	their bodies will **r**—let those who
Mt	27: 63	'After three days I will **r** again.'
Jn	5: 29	who have done what is good will **r**
1Th	4: 16	and the dead in Christ will **r** first.

ROAD

Mt	7: 13	gate and broad is the **r** that leads

ROBBERS

Jer	7: 11	Name, become a den of **r** to you?
Lk	19: 46	you have made it 'a den of **r**.'"
Jn	10: 8	come before me are thieves and **r**,

ROCK

Ps	18: 2	The Lord is my **r**, my fortress
	40: 2	he set my feet on a **r** and gave me
Mt	7: 24	man who built his house on the **r**.
	16: 18	on this **r** I will build my church,
Ro	9: 33	and a **r** that makes them fall,
1Co	10: 4	them, and that **r** was Christ.

ROD

Ps	23: 4	your **r** and your staff, they comfort
Pr	13: 24	Whoever spares the **r** hates their
	23: 13	if you punish them with the **r**,

ROOM (ROOMS)

Mt	6: 6	go into your **r**, close the door
Lk	2: 7	there was no guest **r** available
Jn	21: 25	the whole world would not have **r**

ROOMS (ROOM)

Jn	14: 2	My Father's house has many **r**;

ROOT

Isa	53: 2	and like a **r** out of dry ground.
1Ti	6: 10	the love of money is a **r** of all kinds

ROYAL

Jas	2: 8	If you really keep the **r** law found
1Pe	2: 9	are a chosen people, a **r** priesthood,

RUIN (RUINS)

Pr	18: 24	unreliable friends soon comes to **r**,
	19: 3	person's own folly leads to their **r**,
1Ti	6: 9	desires that plunge people into **r**

RUINS (RUIN)

2Ti	2: 14	value, and only **r** those who listen.

RULE (RULER RULERS RULES)

1Sa	12: 12	'No, we want a king to **r** over us'—
Ps	119:133	to your word; let no sin **r** over me.
Zec	9: 10	His **r** will extend from sea to sea
Col	3: 15	peace of Christ **r** in your hearts,
Rev	2: 27	that one 'will **r** them with an iron

RULER (RULE)

Eph	2: 2	of the **r** of the kingdom of the air,
1Ti	1: 15	the blessed and only **R**, the King

RULERS (RULE)

Ps	2: 2	and the **r** band together against
	8: 6	You made them **r** over the works
Col	1: 16	or powers or **r** or authorities;

RULES (RULE)

Ps	103: 19	heaven, and his kingdom **r** over all.
Lk	22: 26	and the one who **r** like the one who
2Ti	2: 5	by competing according to the **r**.

RUMORS
Mt 24: 6 You will hear of wars and **r** of wars,
RUN (RAN)
Isa 40: 31 they will **r** and not grow weary,
1Co 9: 24 **R** in such a way as to get the prize.
Heb 12: 1 let us **r** with perseverance the race
RUTH
Moabitess; widow who went to Bethlehem with mother-in-law Naomi (Ru 1). Gleaned in field of Boaz; shown favor (Ru 2). Proposed marriage to Boaz (Ru 3). Married (Ru 4:1–12); bore Obed, ancestor of David (Ru 4:13–22), Jesus (Mt 1:5).
SABBATH
Ex 20: 8 "Remember the **S** day by keeping it
Dt 5: 12 "Observe the **S** day by keeping it
Col 2: 16 New Moon celebration or a **S** day.
SACKCLOTH
Mt 11: 21 would have repented long ago in **s**
SACRED
Mt 7: 6 "Do not give dogs what is **s**;
1Co 3: 17 for God's temple is **s**, and you
SACRIFICE (SACRIFICED)
Ge 22: 2 **S** him there as a burnt offering
Ex 12: 27 'It is the Passover **s** to the Lord,
1Sa 15: 22 To obey is better than **s**,
Ps 51: 17 My **s**, O God, is a broken spirit;
Hos 6: 6 not **s**, and acknowledgment of God
Mt 9: 13 'I desire mercy, not **s**.'
Ro 12: 1 to offer your bodies as a living **s**,
Heb 9: 26 away with sin by the **s** of himself.
13: 15 offer to God a **s** of praise—
1Jn 2: 2 He is the atoning **s** for our sins,
SACRIFICED (SACRIFICE)
1Co 5: 7 our Passover lamb, has been **s**.
8: 1 Now about food **s** to idols:
Heb 9: 28 so Christ was **s** once to take away
SADDUCEES
Mk 12: 18 Then the **S**, who say there is no
SAFE (SAVE)
Ps 37: 3 in the land and enjoy **s** pasture.
Pr 18: 10 the righteous run to it and are **s**.
SAFETY (SAVE)
Ps 4: 8 alone, Lord, make me dwell in **s**.
1Th 5: 3 "Peace and **s**," destruction will
SAINTS See FAITHFUL, [GOD'S] PEOPLE
SAKE
Ps 44: 22 your **s** we face death all day long;
Php 3: 7 consider loss for the **s** of Christ.
Heb 11: 26 disgrace for the **s** of Christ as
SALT
Ge 19: 26 back, and she became a pillar of **s**.
Mt 5: 13 "You are the **s** of the earth.
SALVATION (SAVE)
Ex 15: 2 he has become my **s**.
1Ch 16: 23 proclaim his **s** day after day.
Ps 27: 1 The Lord is my light and my **s**—
51: 12 Restore to me the joy of your **s**
62: 2 he is my rock and my **s**;
85: 9 Surely his **s** is near those who fear
96: 2 proclaim his **s** day after day.
Isa 25: 9 let us rejoice and be glad in his **s**."
45: 17 the Lord with an everlasting **s**;
51: 6 But my **s** will last forever,
59: 17 and the helmet of **s** on his head;
61: 10 has clothed me with garments of **s**
Jnh 2: 9 '**S** comes from the Lord.'"
Lk 2: 30 For my eyes have seen your **s**,
Jn 4: 22 we do know, for **s** is from the Jews.
Ac 4: 12 **S** is found in no one else, for there
13: 47 that you may bring **s** to the ends
Ro 11: 11 **s** has come to the Gentiles to make
2Co 7: 10 brings repentance that leads to **s**
Eph 6: 17 Take the helmet of **s** and the sword
Php 2: 12 to work out your **s** with fear
1Th 5: 8 and the hope of **s** as a helmet.
2Ti 3: 15 make you wise for **s** through faith
Heb 2: 3 we escape if we ignore so great a **s**?
6: 9 the things that have to do with **s**.
1Pe 1: 10 Concerning this **s**, the prophets,
2: 2 by it you may grow up in your **s**,
SAMARITAN
Lk 10: 33 But a **S**, as he traveled, came where

SAMSON
Danite judge. Birth promised (Jdg 13). Married to Philistine (Jdg 14). Vengeance on Philistines (Jdg 15). Betrayed by Delilah (Jdg 16:1–22). Death (Jdg 16:23–31). Feats of strength: killed lion (Jdg 14:6), 30 Philistines (Jdg 14:19), 1,000 Philistines with jawbone (Jdg 15:13–17), carried off gates of Gaza (Jdg 16:3), pushed down temple of Dagon (Jdg 16:25–30).
SAMUEL
Ephraimite judge and prophet (Heb 11:32). Birth prayed for (1Sa 1:10–18). Dedicated to temple by Hannah (1Sa 1:21–28). Raised by Eli (1Sa 2:11, 18–26). Called as prophet (1Sa 3). Led Israel to victory over Philistines (1Sa 7). Asked by Israel for a king (1Sa 8). Anointed Saul as king (1Sa 9–10). Farewell speech (1Sa 12). Rebuked Saul for sacrifice (1Sa 13). Announced rejection of Saul (1Sa 15). Anointed David as king (1Sa 16). Protected David from Saul (1Sa 19:18–24). Death (1Sa 25:1). Returned from dead to condemn Saul (1Sa 28).
SANCTIFIED (SANCTIFY)
Ac 20: 32 among all those who are **s**.
Ro 15: 16 to God, **s** by the Holy Spirit.
1Co 6: 11 you were **s**, you were justified
7: 14 husband has been **s** through his
Heb 10: 29 blood of the covenant that **s** them,
SANCTIFY (SANCTIFIED SANCTIFYING)
1Th 5: 23 peace, **s** you through and through.
SANCTIFYING (SANCTIFY)
2Th 2: 13 be saved through the **s** work
SANCTUARY
Ex 25: 8 "Then have them make a **s** for me,
SAND
Ge 22: 17 sky and as the **s** on the seashore.
Mt 7: 26 man who built his house on **s**.
SANDALS
Ex 3: 5 "Take off your **s**, for the place
Jos 5: 15 "Take off your **s**, for the place
SANG (SING)
Job 38: 7 while the morning stars **s** together
Rev 5: 9 And they **s** a new song, saying:
SARAH
Wife of Abraham, originally named Sarai; barren (Ge 11:29–31; 1Pe 3:6). Taken by Pharaoh as Abraham's sister; returned (Ge 12:10–20). Gave Hagar to Abraham; sent her away in pregnancy (Ge 16). Name changed; Isaac promised (Ge 17:15–21; 18:10–15; Heb 11:11). Taken by Abimelek as Abraham's sister; returned (Ge 20). Isaac born; Hagar and Ishmael sent away (Ge 21:1–21; Gal 4:21–31). Death (Ge 23).
SATAN
Job 1: 6 and **S** also came with them.
Zec 3: 2 to **S**, "The Lord rebuke you, **S**!
Mk 4: 15 **S** comes and takes away the word
2Co 11: 14 **S** himself masquerades as an angel
12: 7 a messenger of **S**, to torment me.
Rev 12: 9 or **S**, who leads the whole world
20: 2 **S**, and bound him for a thousand
20: 7 **S** will be released from his prison
SATISFIED (SATISFY)
Isa 53: 11 he will see the light of life and be **s**;
SATISFIES (SATISFY)
Ps 103: 5 **s** your desires with good things
SATISFY (SATISFIED SATISFIES)
Isa 55: 2 and your labor on what does not **s**?
SAUL
1. Benjamite; anointed by Samuel as first king of Israel (1Sa 9–10). Defeated Ammonites (1Sa 11). Rebuked for offering sacrifice (1Sa 13:1–15). Defeated Philistines (1Sa 14). Rejected as king for failing to annihilate Amalekites (1Sa 15). Soothed from evil spirit by David (1Sa 16:14–23). Sent David against Goliath (1Sa 17). Jealousy and attempted murder of David (1Sa 18:1–11). Gave David Michal as wife (1Sa 18:12–30). Second attempt to kill David (1Sa 19). Anger at Jonathan (1Sa 20:26–34). Pursued David: killed priests at Nob (1Sa 22), went to Keilah and Ziph (1Sa 23), life spared by David at En Gedi (1Sa 24) and in his tent (1Sa 26). Rebuked by Samuel's spirit for consulting witch at Endor (1Sa 28). Wounded by Philistines; took his own life (1Sa 31; 1Ch 10).
2. See PAUL
SAVE (SAFE SAFETY SALVATION SAVED SAVIOR)
Isa 63: 1 proclaiming victory, mighty to **s**."
Mt 1: 21 because he will **s** his people
16: 25 wants to **s** their life will lose it,
Lk 19: 10 came to seek and to **s** the lost."

Jn   3: 17 but to **s** the world through him.
1Ti   1: 15 came into the world to **s** sinners—
Jas   5: 20 of their way will **s** them from death
SAVED (SAVE)
Ps   34:   6 he **s** him out of all his troubles.
Isa 45: 22 "Turn to me and be **s**, all you ends
Joel 2: 32 the name of the LORD will be **s**;
Mk   13: 13 stands firm to the end will be **s**.
     16: 16 believes and is baptized will be **s**,
Jn   10:   9 enters through me will be **s**.
Ac   4: 12 mankind by which we must be **s**."
     16: 30 "Sirs, what must I do to be **s**?"
Ro   9: 27 the sea, only the remnant will be **s**.
     10:   9 him from the dead, you will be **s**.
1Co   3: 15 will suffer loss but yet will be **s**—
     15:   2 By this gospel you are **s**, if you hold
Eph   2:   5 it is by grace you have been **s**.
      2:   8 For it is by grace you have been **s**,
1Ti   2:   4 who wants all people to be **s**
SAVIOR (SAVE)
Ps   89: 26 Father, my God, the Rock my **S**.'
Isa 43: 11 and apart from me there is no **s**.
Hos 13:   4 no God but me, no **S** except me.
Lk   1: 47 and my spirit rejoices in God my **S**,
      2: 11 town of David a **S** has been born
Jn   4: 42 that this man really is the **S**
Eph   5: 23 his body, of which he is the **S**.
1Ti   4: 10 God, who is the **S** of all people,
Titus 2: 10 about God our **S** attractive.
      2: 13 the glory of our great God and **S**,
      3:   4 and love of God our **S** appeared,
1Jn   4: 14 his Son to be the **S** of the world.
Jude : 25 to the only God our **S** be glory,
SCALES
Lev 19: 36 Use honest **s** and honest weights,
Da   5: 27 You have been weighed on the **s**
SCAPEGOAT (GOAT)
Lev 16: 10 it into the wilderness as a **s**.
SCARLET
Isa   1: 18 "Though your sins are like **s**,
SCATTERED
Jer 31: 10 'He who **s** Israel will gather them
Ac   4:   4 who had been **s** preached the word
SCEPTER
Rev 19: 15 "He will rule them with an iron **s**."
SCHEMES
2Co   2: 11 For we are not unaware of his **s**.
Eph   6: 11 your stand against the devil's **s**.
SCOFFERS
2Pe   3:   3 that in the last days **s** will come,
SCORPION
Rev   9:   5 of the sting of a **s** when it strikes.
SCRIPTURE (SCRIPTURES)
Jn   10: 35 and **S** cannot be set aside—
1Ti   4: 13 yourself to the public reading of **S**,
2Ti   3: 16 All **S** is God-breathed and is useful
2Pe   1: 20 that no prophecy of **S** came
SCRIPTURES (SCRIPTURE)
Lk   24: 27 in all the **S** concerning himself.
Jn   5: 39 You study the **S** diligently because
Ac   17: 11 examined the **S** every day to see
SCROLL
Eze   3:   1 eat what is before you, eat this **s**;
SEA
Ex   14: 16 the Israelites can go through the **s**
Isa 57: 20 the wicked are like the tossing **s**,
Mic   7: 19 iniquities into the depths of the **s**.
Jas   1:   6 who doubts is like a wave of the **s**,
Rev 13:   1 I saw a beast coming out of the **s**.
SEAL (SEALS)
Jn   6: 27 God the Father has placed his **s**
2Co   1: 22 set his **s** of ownership on us,
Eph   1: 13 you were marked in him with a **s**,
SEALS (SEAL)
Rev   5:   2 "Who is worthy to break the **s**
      6:   1 opened the first of the seven **s**.
SEARCH (SEARCHED SEARCHES SEARCHING)
Ps   4:   4 beds, **s** your hearts and be silent.
    139: 23 **S** me, God, and know my heart;
Pr   2:   4 and **s** for it as for hidden treasure,
Jer 17: 10 "I the LORD **s** the heart
Eze 34: 16 I will **s** for the lost and bring back
Lk   15:   8 and **s** carefully until she finds it?

SEARCHED (SEARCH)
Ps 139:   1 You have **s** me, LORD, and you
SEARCHES (SEARCH)
Ro   8: 27 who **s** our hearts knows the mind
1Co   2: 10 The Spirit **s** all things, even the
SEARCHING (SEARCH)
Am   8: 12 east, **s** for the word of the LORD,
SEARED
1Ti   4:   2 whose consciences have been **s** as
SEASON
2Ti   4:   2 be prepared in **s** and out of **s**;
SEAT (SEATED SEATS)
Da   7:   9 and the Ancient of Days took his **s**.
2Co   5: 10 all appear before the judgment **s**
SEATED (SEAT)
Ps   47:   8 God is **s** on his holy throne.
Isa   6:   1 high and exalted, **s** on a throne;
Col   3:   1 Christ is, **s** at the right hand of God.
SEATS (SEAT)
Lk   11: 43 you love the most important **s**
SECRET (SECRETS)
Dt   29: 29 The **s** things belong to the LORD
Jdg 16:   6 "Tell me the **s** of your great
Ps   90:   8 you, our **s** sins in the light of your
Pr   11: 13 but a trustworthy person keeps a **s**.
Mt   6:   4 so that your giving may be in **s**.
2Co   4:   2 we have renounced **s** and shameful
Php   4: 12 have learned the **s** of being content
SECRETS (SECRET)
Ps   44: 21 since he knows the **s** of the heart?
Lk   14: 25 as the **s** of their hearts are laid bare.
SECURE (SECURITY)
Ps 112:   8 Their hearts are **s**, they will have
Heb   6: 19 an anchor for the soul, firm and **s**.
SECURITY (SECURE)
Job 31: 24 or said to pure gold, 'You are my **s**,'
SEED (SEEDS)
Lk   8: 11 The **s** is the word of God.
1Co   3:   6 I planted the **s**, Apollos watered it,
2Co   9: 10 he who supplies **s** to the sower
Gal   3: 29 you are Abraham's **s**, and heirs
1Pe   1: 23 again, not of perishable **s**,
SEEDS (SEED)
Jn   12: 24 But if it dies, it produces many **s**.
Gal   3: 16 Scripture does not say "and to **s**,"
SEEK (SEEKS SELF-SEEKING)
Dt   4: 29 you will find him if you **s** him
1Ch 28:   9 If you **s** him, he will be found
2Ch   7: 14 pray and **s** my face and turn
Ps 119: 10 I **s** you with all my heart; do not let
Isa 55:   6 **S** the LORD while he may be
     65:   1 found by those who did not **s** me.
Mt   6: 33 But **s** first his kingdom and his
Lk   19: 10 For the Son of Man came to **s**
Ro   10: 20 found by those who did not **s** me;
1Co   7: 27 Do not **s** to be released.
SEEKS (SEEK)
Jn   4: 23 the kind of worshipers the Father **s**.
SEER
1Sa   9:   9 of today used to be called a **s**.)
SELF-CONTROL (CONTROL)
1Co   7:   5 tempt you because of your lack of **s**.
Gal   5: 23 gentleness and **s**.
2Pe   1:   6 and to knowledge, **s**; and to **s**,
SELF-CONTROLLED (CONTROL)
1Ti   3:   2 his wife, temperate, **s**, respectable,
Titus 1:   8 what is good, who is **s**, upright,
      2:   2 worthy of respect, **s**, and sound
      2:   5 to be **s** and pure, to be busy
      2:   6 encourage the young men to be **s**.
      2: 12 to live **s**, upright and godly lives
SELF-INDULGENCE
Mt   23: 25 inside they are full of greed and **s**.
SELFISH
Ps 119: 36 statutes and not toward **s** gain.
Pr   18:   1 unfriendly person pursues **s** ends
Gal   5: 20 fits of rage, **s** ambition, dissensions,
Php   1: 17 preach Christ out of **s** ambition,
      2:   3 Do nothing out of **s** ambition
Jas   3: 14 envy and **s** ambition in your hearts,
      3: 16 you have envy and **s** ambition,

SELF-SEEKING (SEEK)
1Co 13: 5 it is not **s**, it is not easily angered,
SEND (SENDING SENT)
Isa 6: 8 And I said, "Here am I. **S** me!"
Mt 9: 38 to **s** out workers into his harvest
Jn 16: 7 but if I go, I will **s** him to you.
SENDING (SEND)
Jn 20: 21 the Father has sent me, I am **s** you."
SENSES
Lk 15: 17 "When he came to his **s**, he said,
1Co 15: 34 Come back to your **s** as you ought,
2Ti 2: 26 that they will come to their **s**
SENSUAL
Col 2: 23 value in restraining **s** indulgence.
SENT (SEND)
Isa 55: 11 achieve the purpose for which I **s** it.
Mt 10: 40 me welcomes the one who **s** me.
Jn 4: 34 "is to do the will of him who **s** me
Ro 10: 15 anyone preach unless they are **s**?
1Jn 4: 10 **s** his Son as an atoning sacrifice
SEPARATE (SEPARATED SEPARATES)
Mt 19: 6 has joined together, let no one **s**."
Ro 8: 35 Who shall **s** us from the love
1Co 7: 10 A wife must not **s** from her
2Co 6: 17 "Come out from them and be **s**,
SEPARATED (SEPARATE)
Isa 59: 2 your iniquities have **s** you from
SEPARATES (SEPARATE)
Pr 16: 28 and a gossip **s** close friends.
SERPENT
Ge 3: 1 Now the **s** was more crafty than
Rev 12: 9 that ancient **s** called the devil,
SERVANT (SERVANTS)
1Sa 3: 10 "Speak, for your **s** is listening."
Mt 20: 26 great among you must be your **s**,
    25: 21 'Well done, good and faithful **s**!
Php 2: 7 by taking the very nature of a **s**,
2Ti 2: 24 And the Lord's **s** must not be
SERVANTS (SERVANT)
Lk 17: 10 do, should say, 'We are unworthy **s**;
Jn 15: 15 I no longer call you **s**,
SERVE (SERVICE SERVING)
Dt 10: 12 to **s** the LORD your God with all
Jos 22: 5 and to **s** him with all your heart
    24: 15 household, we will **s** the LORD."
Mt 4: 10 Lord your God, and **s** him only.' "
     6: 24 "No one can **s** two masters.
     6: 24 You cannot **s** both God and money.
    20: 28 but to **s**, and to give his life as
Eph 6: 7 **S** wholeheartedly, as if you were
SERVICE (SERVE)
1Co 12: 5 There are different kinds of **s**,
Eph 4: 12 to equip his people for works of **s**,
SERVING (SERVE)
Ro 12: 11 your spiritual fervor, **s** the Lord.
Eph 6: 7 as if you were **s** the Lord,
Col 3: 24 It is the Lord Christ you are **s**.
2Ti 2: 4 No one **s** as a soldier gets entangled
SEVEN (SEVENTH)
Ge 7: 2 Take with you **s** pairs of every kind
Jos 6: 4 march around the city **s** times,
1Ki 19: 18 Yet I reserve **s** thousand in Israel—
Pr 6: 16 hates, **s** that are detestable to him:
    24: 16 though the righteous fall **s** times,
Isa 4: 1 that day **s** women will take hold
Da 9: 25 comes, there will be **s** 'sevens,'
Mt 18: 21 sins against me? Up to **s** times?
Lk 11: 26 takes **s** other spirits more wicked
Ro 11: 4 myself **s** thousand who have not
Rev 1: 4 To the **s** churches in the province
     1: 4 from the **s** spirits before his throne,
     6: 1 Lamb opened the first of the **s** seals.
     8: 2 I saw the **s** angels who stand before
     8: 2 and **s** trumpets were given to them.
    10: 4 And when the **s** thunders spoke,
    15: 7 to the **s** angels **s** golden bowls filled
SEVENTH (SEVEN)
Ge 2: 2 so on the **s** day he rested from all
Ex 23: 12 but on the **s** day do not work,
SEX (SEXUAL SEXUALLY)
1Co 6: 9 nor men who have **s** with men

SEXUAL (SEX)
Mt 5: 32 except for **s** immorality, makes her
    19: 9 except for **s** immorality,
1Co 6: 13 is not meant for **s** immorality
     6: 18 Flee from **s** immorality.
     7: 1 a man not to have **s** relations
    10: 8 should not commit **s** immorality,
Eph 5: 3 not be even a hint of **s** immorality,
1Th 4: 3 you should avoid **s** immorality;
SEXUALLY (SEX)
1Co 5: 9 associate with **s** immoral people—
     6: 18 but whoever sins **s**, sins against
SHADOW
Ps 36: 7 take refuge in the **s** of your wings.
Heb 10: 1 The law is only a **s** of the good
SHALLUM
    King of Israel (2Ki 15:10–16).
SHAME (ASHAMED)
Ps 22: 5 they trusted and were not put to **s**.
    34: 5 faces are never covered with **s**.
Pr 13: 18 discipline comes to poverty and **s**,
Heb 12: 2 scorning its **s**, and sat down
SHARE (SHARED)
Ge 21: 10 that woman's son will never **s**
Lk 3: 11 who has two shirts should **s**
Gal 4: 30 the slave woman's son will never **s**
     6: 6 the word should **s** all good things
Eph 4: 28 they may have something to **s**
1Ti 6: 18 to be generous and willing to **s**.
Heb 12: 10 order that we may **s** in his holiness.
    13: 16 to do good and to **s** with others,
SHARED (SHARE)
Heb 2: 14 he too **s** in their humanity so
SHARON
SS 2: 1 I am a rose of **S**, a lily
SHARPER
Heb 4: 12 **S** than any double-edged sword,
SHED (SHEDDING)
Ge 9: 6 by humans shall their blood be **s**;
Col 1: 20 through his blood, **s** on the cross.
SHEDDING (SHED)
Heb 9: 22 without the **s** of blood there is no
SHEEP
Ps 100: 3 are his people, the **s** of his pasture.
   119:176 I have strayed like a lost **s**.
Isa 53: 6 We all, like **s**, have gone astray,
Jer 50: 6 "My people have been lost **s**;
Eze 34: 11 I myself will search for my **s**
Mt 9: 36 helpless, like **s** without a shepherd.
Jn 10: 3 He calls his own **s** by name
    10: 15 and I lay down my life for the **s**.
    10: 27 My **s** listen to my voice;
    21: 17 Jesus said, "Feed my **s**.
1Pe 2: 25 For "you were like **s** going astray,"
SHELTER
Ps 61: 4 take refuge in the **s** of your wings.
    91: 1 in the **s** of the Most High will rest
SHEM
    Son of Noah (Ge 5:32; 6:10). Blessed (Ge 9:26). Descendants (Ge 10:21–31; 11:10–32).
SHEPHERD (SHEPHERDS)
Ps 23: 1 The LORD is my **s**, I lack nothing.
Isa 40: 11 He tends his flock like a **s**:
Jer 31: 10 will watch over his flock like a **s**.'
Eze 34: 12 a **s** looks after his scattered flock
Zec 11: 17 "Woe to the worthless **s**,
Mt 9: 36 and helpless, like sheep without a **s**.
Jn 10: 11 "I am the good **s**. The good **s** lays
    10: 16 there shall be one flock and one **s**.
1Pe 5: 4 And when the Chief **S** appears,
SHEPHERDS (SHEPHERD)
Jer 23: 1 "Woe to the **s** who are destroying
Lk 2: 8 there were **s** living out in the fields
Ac 20: 28 Be **s** of the church of God,
1Pe 5: 2 Be **s** of God's flock that is under
SHIELD
Ps 28: 7 LORD is my strength and my **s**;
Eph 6: 16 take up the **s** of faith,
SHINE (SHONE)
Ps 4: 6 Let the light of your face **s** on us.
    80: 1 between the cherubim, **s** forth
Isa 60: 1 "Arise, **s**, for your light has come,

Da 12: 3 are wise will **s** like the brightness
Mt 5: 16 let your light **s** before others,
13: 43 the righteous will **s** like the sun
2Co 4: 6 made his light **s** in our hearts
Eph 5: 14 the dead, and Christ will **s** on you."

SHIPWRECK (SHIPWRECKED)
1Ti 1: 19 so have suffered **s** with regard
SHIPWRECKED (SHIPWRECK)
2Co 11: 25 three times I was **s**, I spent a night
SHONE (SHINE)
Mt 17: 2 His face **s** like the sun, and his
Lk 2: 9 glory of the Lord **s** around them,
Rev 21: 11 It **s** with the glory of God, and its
SHORT
Isa 59: 1 of the Lord is not too **s** to save,
Ro 3: 23 and fall **s** of the glory of God,
SHOULDERS
Isa 9: 6 the government will be on his **s**.
Lk 15: 5 finds it, he joyfully puts it on his **s**
SHOWED
1Jn 4: 9 This is how God **s** his love among
SHREWD
Mt 10: 16 Therefore be as **s** as snakes and as
SHUN
Job 28: 28 and to **s** evil is understanding."
Pr 3: 7 fear the Lord and **s** evil.
SICK
Pr 13: 12 Hope deferred makes the heart **s**,
Mt 9: 12 who need a doctor, but the **s**.
25: 36 I was **s** and you looked after me,
Jas 5: 14 Is anyone among you **s**?
SICKLE
Joel 3: 13 Swing the **s**, for the harvest is ripe.
SIDE
Ps 91: 7 A thousand may fall at your **s**,
124: 1 the Lord had not been on our **s**—
2Ti 4: 17 Lord stood at my **s** and gave me
SIGHT
Ps 90: 4 years in your **s** are like a day
116: 15 in the **s** of the Lord is the death
2Co 5: 7 For we live by faith, not by **s**.
1Pe 3: 4 which is of great worth in God's **s**.
SIGN (SIGNS)
Isa 7: 14 the Lord himself will give you a **s**:
SIGNS (SIGN)
Mt 24: 24 and perform great **s** and wonders
Mk 16: 17 *these* **s** *will accompany those who*
Jn 3: 2 could perform the **s** you are doing
9: 16 can a sinner perform such **s**?
20: 30 Jesus performed many other **s**
1Co 1: 22 Jews demand **s** and Greeks look
SILENT
Pr 17: 28 are thought wise if they keep **s**,
Isa 53: 7 as a sheep before its shearers is **s**,
Hab 2: 20 let all the earth be **s** before him.
1Co 14: 34 Women should remain **s**
SILVER
Pr 25: 11 of **s** is a ruling rightly given.
Hag 2: 8 'The **s** is mine and the gold is
1Co 3: 12 on this foundation using gold, **s**,
SIMON
1. See PETER.
2. Apostle, called the Zealot (Mt 10:4; Mk 3:18; Lk 6:15; Ac 1:13).
3. Samaritan sorcerer (Ac 8:9–24).
SIN (SINFUL SINNED SINNER SINNERS SINNING SINS)
Nu 5: 7 and must confess the **s** they have
32: 23 sure that your **s** will find you out.
Dt 24: 16 each will die for their own **s**.
1Ki 8: 46 there is no one who does not **s**—
2Ch 7: 14 I will forgive their **s** and will heal
Ps 4: 4 Tremble and do not **s**; when you
32: 2 is the one whose **s** the Lord does
32: 5 And you forgave the guilt of my **s**.
51: 2 iniquity and cleanse me from my **s**.
66: 18 If I had cherished **s** in my heart,
119: 11 that I might not **s** against you.
119: 133 to your word; let no **s** rule over me.
Isa 6: 7 taken away and your **s** atoned for."
Mic 7: 18 you, who pardons **s** and forgives
Jn 1: 29 who takes away the **s** of the world!
8: 34 everyone who sins is a slave to **s**.

Ro 5: 12 just as **s** entered the world through
5: 20 But where **s** increased,
6: 11 count yourselves dead to **s** but alive
6: 23 For the wages of **s** is death,
14: 23 that does not come from faith is **s**.
2Co 5: 21 God made him who had no **s** to be **s**
Gal 6: 1 if someone is caught in a **s**,
Heb 9: 26 to do away with **s** by the sacrifice
11: 25 to enjoy the fleeting pleasures of **s**.
12: 1 and the **s** that so easily entangles.
1Pe 2: 22 "He committed no **s**, and no deceit
1Jn 1: 8 If we claim to be without **s**,
3: 4 in fact, **s** is lawlessness.
3: 5 away our sins. And in him is no **s**.
3: 9 is born of God will continue to **s**,
5: 18 born of God does not continue to **s**;
SINCERE
Ro 12: 9 Love must be **s**. Hate what is evil;
Heb 10: 22 us draw near to God with a **s** heart
SINFUL (SIN)
Ps 51: 5 Surely I was **s** at birth,
Ro 7: 5 the **s** passions aroused by the law
1Pe 2: 11 to abstain from **s** desires,
SINFUL NATURE See FLESH
SING (SANG SINGING SONG SONGS)
Ps 30: 4 **S** the praises of the Lord, you his
47: 6 **S** praises to God, **s** praises; **s** praises
59: 16 in the morning I will **s** of your love
89: 1 I will **s** of the Lord's great love
101: 1 I will **s** of your love and justice;
Eph 5: 19 **S** and make music from your heart
SINGING (SING)
Ps 63: 5 **s** lips my mouth will praise you.
Ac 16: 25 were praying and **s** hymns to God,
SINNED (SIN)
2Sa 12: 13 "I have **s** against the Lord."
Job 1: 5 "Perhaps my children have **s**
Ps 51: 4 have I **s** and done what is evil
Da 9: 5 we have **s** and done wrong.
Mic 7: 9 Because I have **s** against him, I will
Lk 15: 18 I have **s** against heaven and against
Ro 3: 23 for all have **s** and fall short
1Jn 1: 10 If we claim we have not **s**, we make
SINNER (SIN)
Ecc 9: 18 war, but one **s** destroys much good.
Lk 15: 7 heaven over one **s** who repents
18: 13 said, 'God, have mercy on me, a **s**.'
Jas 5: 20 Whoever turns a **s** from the error
1Pe 4: 18 become of the ungodly and the **s**?"
SINNERS (SIN)
Ps 1: 1 stand in the way that **s** take or sit
Pr 23: 17 Do not let your heart envy **s**,
Mt 9: 13 come to call the righteous, but **s**."
Ro 5: 8 While we were still **s**, Christ died
1Ti 1: 15 came into the world to save **s**—
SINNING (SIN)
Ex 20: 20 be with you to keep you from **s**."
1Co 15: 34 senses as you ought, and stop **s**;
Heb 10: 26 If we deliberately keep on **s** after
1Jn 3: 6 one who lives in him keeps on **s**.
3: 9 they cannot go on **s**, because they
SINS (SIN)
Ezr 9: 6 because our **s** are higher than our
Ps 19: 13 your servant also from willful **s**;
32: 1 are forgiven, whose **s** are covered.
103: 3 who forgives all your **s** and heals
130: 3 Lord, kept a record of **s**, Lord,
Pr 28: 13 Whoever conceals their **s** does not
Isa 1: 18 "Though your **s** are like scarlet,
43: 25 and remembers your **s** no more.
59: 2 your **s** have hidden his face
Eze 18: 4 The one who **s** is the one who will
Mt 1: 21 will save his people from their **s**."
18: 15 "If your brother or sister **s**,
Lk 11: 4 Forgive us our **s**, for we also forgive everyone who **s** against us.
17: 3 your brother or sister **s** against you,
Ac 22: 16 be baptized and wash your **s** away,
1Co 15: 3 Christ died for our **s** according
Eph 2: 1 dead in your transgressions and **s**,
Col 2: 13 He forgave us all our **s**,
Heb 1: 3 he had provided purification for **s**,
7: 27 He sacrificed for their **s** once for all

Heb 8: 12 will remember their **s** no more."
　 10: 12 for all time one sacrifice for **s**,
Jas 5: 16 Therefore confess your **s** to each
　 5: 20 and cover over a multitude of **s**.
1Pe 2: 24 so that we might die to **s** and live
　 3: 18 For Christ also suffered once for **s**,
1Jn 1: 9 If we confess our **s**, he is faithful
　 1: 9 will forgive us our **s** and purify us
Rev 1: 5 freed us from our **s** by his blood,

SITS
Ps 99: 1 he **s** enthroned between
Isa 40: 22 He **s** enthroned above the circle
Mt 19: 28 Son of Man **s** on his glorious throne,
Rev 4: 9 thanks to him who **s** on the throne

SKIN
Job 19: 20 escaped only by the **s** of my teeth.
　 19: 26 And after my **s** has been destroyed,
Jer 13: 23 Can an Ethiopian change his **s**

SLAIN (SLAY)
Rev 5: 12 who was **s**, to receive power

SLANDER (SLANDERED SLANDERERS)
Lev 19: 16 spreading **s** among your people.
1Ti 5: 14 the enemy no opportunity for **s**.
Titus 3: 2 to **s** no one, to be peaceable

SLANDERED (SLANDER)
1Co 4: 13 when we are **s**, we answer kindly.

SLANDERERS (SLANDER)
Ro 1: 30 **s**, God-haters, insolent,
1Co 6: 10 nor drunkards nor **s** nor swindlers
Titus 2: 3 not to be **s** or addicted to much

SLAUGHTER
Isa 53: 7 he was led like a lamb to the **s**,

SLAVE (SLAVERY SLAVES)
Ge 21: 10 "Get rid of that **s** woman and her
Mt 20: 27 wants to be first must be your **s**—
Jn 8: 34 everyone who sins is a **s** to sin.
1Co 12: 13 whether Jews or Gentiles, **s** or free
Gal 3: 28 Jew nor Gentile, neither **s** nor free,
　 4: 30 the **s** woman's son will never share

SLAVERY (SLAVE)
Gal 4: 3 in **s** under the elemental spiritual

SLAVES (SLAVE)
Ro 6: 6 we should no longer be **s** to sin—
　 6: 22 and have become **s** of God,
2Pe 2: 19 for "people are **s** to whatever has

SLAY (SLAIN)
Job 13: 15 Though he **s** me, yet will I hope

SLEEP (SLEEPING)
Ps 121: 4 Israel will neither slumber nor **s**.
1Co 15: 51 We will not all **s**, but we will all be

SLEEPING (SLEEP)
Mk 13: 36 do not let him find you **s**.

SLOW
Ex 34: 6 and gracious God, **s** to anger,
Jas 1: 19 **s** to speak and **s** to become angry,
2Pe 3: 9 The Lord is not **s** in keeping his

SLUGGARD (SLUGGARDS)
Pr 6: 6 Go to the ant, you **s**;

SLUGGARDS (SLUGGARD)
Pr 20: 4 **S** do not plow in season;

SLUMBER
Ps 121: 3 he who watches over you will not **s**;
Pr 6: 10 little **s**, a little folding of the hands
Ro 13: 11 for you to wake up from your **s**,

SNAKE (SNAKES)
Nu 21: 8 "Make a **s** and put it up on a pole;
Pr 23: 32 In the end it bites like a **s**
Jn 3: 14 lifted up the **s** in the wilderness,

SNAKES (SNAKE)
Mt 10: 16 Therefore be as shrewd as **s** and as
Mk 16: 18 *they will pick up* **s**

SNATCH (SNATCHING)
Jn 10: 28 no one will **s** them out of my hand.

SNATCHING (SNATCH)
Jude 23 save others by **s** them from the fire;

SNOW
Ps 51: 7 me, and I will be whiter than **s**.

SOAR
Isa 40: 31 They will **s** on wings like eagles;

SODOM
Ge 19: 24 rained down burning sulfur on **S**
Ro 9: 29 we would have become like **S**,

SOIL
Ge 4: 2 kept flocks, and Cain worked the **s**.
Mt 13: 23 the seed falling on good **s** refers

SOLDIER
1Co 9: 7 Who serves as a **s** at his own
2Ti 2: 3 like a good **s** of Christ Jesus.

SOLE
Dt 28: 65 resting place for the **s** of your foot.
Isa 1: 6 From the **s** of your foot to the top

SOLID
2Ti 2: 19 God's **s** foundation stands firm,
Heb 5: 12 You need milk, not **s** food!

SOLOMON
　 Son of David by Bathsheba; king of Judah (2Sa 12:24; 1Ch 3:5, 10). Appointed king by David (1Ki 1); adversaries Adonijah, Joab, Shimei killed by Benaiah (1Ki 2). Asked for wisdom (1Ki 3; 2Ch 1). Judged between two prostitutes (1Ki 3:16–28). Built temple (1Ki 5–7; 2Ch 2–5); prayer of dedication (1Ki 8; 2Ch 6). Visited by Queen of Sheba (1Ki 10; 2Ch 9). Wives turned his heart from God (1Ki 11:1–13). Jeroboam rebelled against (1Ki 11:26–40). Death (1Ki 11:41–43; 2Ch 9:29–31).
　 Proverbs of (1Ki 4:32; Pr 1:1; 10:1; 25:1); psalms of (Ps 72; 127); song of (SS 1:1).

SON (SONS)
Ge 22: 2 said, "Take your **s**, your only **s**,
Ex 11: 5 Every firstborn **s** in Egypt will die,
Dt 21: 18 rebellious **s** who does not obey his
Ps 2: 7 He said to me, "You are my **s**;
　 2: 12 Kiss his **s**, or he will be angry
Pr 10: 1 A wise **s** brings joy to his father,
Isa 7: 14 will conceive and give birth to a **s**,
Hos 11: 1 and out of Egypt I called my **s**.
Mt 2: 15 "Out of Egypt I called my **s**."
　 3: 17 said, "This is my **S**, whom I love;
　 11: 27 knows the **S** except the Father,
　 11: 27 knows the Father except the **S**
　 16: 16 Messiah, the **S** of the living God."
　 17: 5 said, "This is my **S**, whom I love;
　 20: 18 the **S** of Man will be delivered over
　 24: 30 appear the sign of the **S** of Man
　 24: 44 because the **S** of Man will come
　 27: 54 "Surely he was the **S** of God!"
　 28: 19 and of the **S** and of the Holy Spirit,
Mk 10: 45 even the **S** of Man did not come
　 14: 62 you will see the **S** of Man sitting
Lk 9: 58 the **S** of Man has no place to lay his
　 18: 8 when the **S** of Man comes, will he
　 19: 10 For the **S** of Man came to seek
Jn 3: 14 so the **S** of Man must be lifted up,
　 3: 16 that he gave his one and only **S**,
　 17: 1 Glorify your **S**, that your **S** may
Ro 8: 29 conformed to the image of his **S**,
　 8: 32 He who did not spare his own **S**,
1Co 15: 28 the **S** himself will be made subject
Gal 4: 30 for the slave woman's **s** will never
1Th 1: 10 and to wait for his **S** from heaven,
Heb 1: 2 days he has spoken to us by his **S**,
　 10: 29 punished who has trampled the **S**
1Jn 1: 7 Jesus, his **S**, purifies us from all sin.
　 4: 9 only **S** into the world that we might
　 5: 5 believes that Jesus is the **S** of God.
　 5: 11 eternal life, and this life is in his **S**.

SONG (SING)
Ps 40: 3 He put a new **s** in my mouth,
　 96: 1 Sing to the Lord a new **s**;
　 149: 1 Sing to the Lord a new **s**,
Isa 49: 13 burst into **s**, you mountains!
　 55: 12 hills will burst into **s** before you,
Rev 5: 9 And they sang a new **s**, saying:
　 15: 3 sang the **s** of God's servant Moses

SONGS (SING)
Job 35: 10 Maker, who gives **s** in the night,
Ps 100: 2 come before him with joyful **s**.
Eph 5: 19 hymns, and **s** from the Spirit.
Jas 5: 13 Let them sing **s** of praise.

SONS (SON)
Joel 2: 28 **s** and daughters will prophesy,
2Co 6: 18 you will be my **s** and daughters,

SORROW
Jer 31: 12 garden, and they will **s** no more.
Ro 9: 2 I have great **s** and unceasing
2Co 7: 10 Godly **s** brings repentance that

SOUL (SOULS)
Dt	6: 5	and with all your **s** and with all
	10: 12	all your heart and with all your **s**,
Jos 22:	5	all your heart and with all your **s**."
Ps	23: 3	he refreshes my **s**. He guides me
	42: 1	of water, so my **s** pants for you,
	42: 11	Why, my **s**, are you downcast?
	103: 1	Praise the LORD, my **s**;
Pr	13: 19	A longing fulfilled is sweet to the **s**,
Mt	10: 28	of the One who can destroy both **s**
	16: 26	the whole world, yet forfeit their **s**?
	22: 37	with all your **s** and with all your
Heb	4: 12	it penetrates even to dividing **s**

SOULS (SOUL)
Jer	6: 16	and you will find rest for your **s**.
Mt	11: 29	and you will find rest for your **s**.

SOUND
1Co 14:	8	the trumpet does not **s** a clear call,
	15: 52	the trumpet will **s**, the dead will
2Ti	4: 3	will not put up with **s** doctrine.

SOVEREIGN
Da	4: 25	Most High is **s** over all kingdoms

SOW (SOWS)
Job	4: 8	and those who **s** trouble reap it.
Mt	6: 26	they do not **s** or reap or store away
2Pe	2: 22	"A **s** that is washed returns to her

SOWS (SOW)
2Co	9: 6	and whoever **s** generously will

SPARE (SPARES)
Ro	8: 32	He who did not **s** his own Son,
	11: 21	God did not **s** the natural branches,

SPARES (SPARE)
Pr	13: 24	Whoever **s** the rod hates their

SPEARS
Isa	2: 4	and their **s** into pruning hooks.
Joel	3: 10	and your pruning hooks into **s**.
Mic	4: 3	and their **s** into pruning hooks.

SPECTACLE
1Co	4: 9	have been made a **s** to the whole
Col	2: 15	he made a public **s** of them,

SPIN
Mt	6: 28	They do not labor or **s**.

SPIRIT (SPIRITS SPIRITUAL)
Ge	1: 2	the **S** of God was hovering over
	6: 3	said, "My **S** will not contend
2Ki	2: 9	inherit a double portion of your **s**,"
Job 33:	4	The **S** of God has made me;
Ps	31: 5	Into your hands I commit my **s**;
	51: 10	and renew a steadfast **s** within me.
	51: 11	or take your Holy **S** from me.
	51: 17	My sacrifice, O God, is a broken **s**;
	139: 7	Where can I go from your **S**?
Isa	57: 15	to revive the **s** of the lowly
	63: 10	rebelled and grieved his Holy **S**.
Eze	11: 19	heart and put a new **s** in them;
	36: 26	a new heart and put a new **s** in you;
Joel	2: 28	I will pour out my **S** on all people.
Zec	4: 6	but by my **S**,' says the LORD
Mt	1: 18	to be pregnant through the Holy **S**.
	3: 11	He will baptize you with the Holy **S**
	3: 16	he saw the **S** of God descending
	4: 1	led by the **S** into the wilderness
	5: 3	"Blessed are the poor in **s**, for
	26: 41	The **s** is willing, but the flesh is
	28: 19	and of the Son and of the Holy **S**,
Lk	1: 80	child grew and became strong in **s**;
	11: 13	in heaven give the Holy **S** to those
Jn	4: 24	God is **s**, and his worshipers must worship in the **S**
	7: 39	that time the **S** had not been given,
	14: 26	the Holy **S**, whom the Father will
	16: 13	But when he, the **S** of truth, comes,
	20: 22	and said, "Receive the Holy **S**.
Ac	2: 4	will be baptized with the Holy **S**."
	2: 4	tongues as the **S** enabled them.
	2: 38	will receive the gift of the Holy **S**.
	6: 3	who are known to be full of the **S**
	19: 2	"Did you receive the Holy **S**
Ro	8: 9	if indeed the **S** of God lives in you.
	8: 26	the **S** helps us in our weakness.
1Co	2: 10	God has revealed to us by his **S**.
	2: 10	The **S** searches all things,
	2: 14	without the **S** does not accept

1Co
1Co	3: 1	as people who live by the **S** but as
	6: 19	bodies are temples of the Holy **S**,
	12: 1	Now about the gifts of the **S**,
	12: 13	we were all baptized by one **S**
	12: 13	and we were all given the one **S**
	14: 1	and eagerly desire gifts of the **S**,
2Co	3: 6	the letter kills, but the **S** gives life.
	5: 5	who has given us the **S** as a deposit,
Gal	5: 16	say, walk by the **S**, and you will not
	5: 22	But the fruit of the **S** is love, joy,
	5: 25	Since we live by the **S**, let us keep
Gal	6: 1	who live by the **S** should restore
Eph	1: 13	with a seal, the promised Holy **S**,
	4: 30	do not grieve the Holy **S** of God,
	5: 18	Instead, be filled with the **S**,
	5: 19	hymns, and songs from the **S**.
	6: 17	of salvation and the sword of the **S**,
1Th	5: 19	Do not quench the **S**.
2Th	2: 13	the sanctifying work of the **S**
Heb	4: 12	even to dividing soul and **s**,
1Pe	3: 4	beauty of a gentle and quiet **s**,
2Pe	1: 21	were carried along by the Holy **S**.
1Jn	4: 1	do not believe every **s**, but test

SPIRITS (SPIRIT)
1Co 12:	10	another distinguishing between **s**,
	14: 32	The **s** of prophets are subject
1Jn	4: 1	but test the **s** to see whether they

SPIRITUAL (SPIRIT)
Ro	12: 11	but keep your **s** fervor,
1Co	2: 13	the Spirit, explaining **s** realities
	15: 44	a natural body, it is raised a **s** body.
Eph	1: 3	realms with every **s** blessing
	6: 12	against the **s** forces of evil
1Pe	2: 2	crave pure **s** milk, so that by it you
	2: 5	offering **s** sacrifices acceptable

SPLENDOR
1Ch 16:	29	the LORD in the **s** of his holiness.
	29: 11	glory and the majesty and the **s**,
Job 37:	22	of the north he comes in golden **s**;
Ps	29: 2	the LORD in the **s** of his holiness.
	45: 3	clothe yourself with **s** and majesty.
	96: 6	**S** and majesty are before him;
	96: 9	the LORD in the **s** of his holiness;
	104: 1	you are clothed with **s** and majesty.
	145: 5	of the glorious **s** of your majesty—
Isa	61: 3	the LORD for the display of his **s**.
	63: 1	robed in **s**, striding forward
Lk	9: 30	Elijah, appeared in glorious **s**,
2Th	2: 8	and destroy by the **s** of his coming.

SPOIL
Ps 119:162		promise like one who finds great **s**.

SPOTLESS
2Pe	3: 14	make every effort to be found **s**,

SPREAD (SPREADING)
Ac	12: 24	the word of God continued to **s**
	19: 20	way the word of the Lord **s** widely

SPREADING (SPREAD)
1Th	3: 2	in God's service in **s** the gospel

SPRING
Jer	2: 13	forsaken me, the **s** of living water,
Jn	4: 14	in them a **s** of water welling
Jas	3: 12	can a salt **s** produce fresh water.

SPUR
Heb 10:	24	how we may **s** one another

SPURNS
Pr	15: 5	A fool **s** a parent's discipline,

STAFF
Ps	23: 4	your rod and your **s**, they comfort

STAKES
Isa	54: 2	your cords, strengthen your **s**.

STAND (STANDING STANDS)
Ex	14: 13	**S** firm and you will see
2Ch 20:	17	**s** firm and see the deliverance
Ps	1: 5	Therefore the wicked will not **s**
	40: 2	rock and gave me a firm place to **s**.
	119:120	fear of you; I **s** in awe of your laws.
Eze 22:	30	**s** before me in the gap on behalf
Zec 14:	4	day his feet will **s** on the Mount
Mt	12: 25	divided against itself will not **s**.
Ro	14: 10	we will all **s** before God's judgment
1Co 15:	58	dear brothers and sisters, **s** firm.
Eph	6: 14	**S** firm then, with the belt of truth

2Th 2: 15 firm and hold fast to the teachings
Jas 5: 8 be patient and **s** firm,
Rev 3: 20 I **s** at the door and knock.
STANDING (STAND)
Ex 3: 5 where you are **s** is holy ground."
Jos 5: 15 the place where you are **s** is holy."
1Pe 5: 9 Resist him, **s** firm in the faith,
STANDS (STAND)
Ps 89: 2 that your love **s** firm forever,
119: 89 it **s** firm in the heavens.
2Ti 2: 19 God's solid foundation **s** firm,
STAR (STARS)
Nu 24: 17 A **s** will come out of Jacob;
Rev 22: 16 David, and the bright Morning **S.**"
STARS (STAR)
Da 12: 3 like the **s** for ever and ever.
Php 2: 15 you will shine among them like **s**
STEADFAST
Ps 51: 10 and renew a **s** spirit within me.
Isa 26: 3 peace those whose minds are **s**,
1Pe 5: 10 and make you strong, firm and **s.**
STEAL
Ex 20: 15 "You shall not **s.**
Mt 19: 18 you shall not **s**, you shall not give
Eph 4: 28 has been stealing must **s** no longer,
STEP (STEPS)
Gal 5: 25 let us keep in **s** with the Spirit.
STEPS (STEP)
Pr 16: 9 but the LORD establishes their **s.**
Jer 10: 23 it is not for them to direct their **s.**
1Pe 2: 21 that you should follow in his **s.**
STICKS
Pr 18: 24 there is a friend who **s** closer than
STIFF-NECKED
Ex 34: 9 Although this is a **s** people,
STILL
Ps 46: 10 "Be **s**, and know that I am God;
Zec 2: 13 Be **s** before the LORD,
STIRS
Pr 6: 19 a person who **s** up conflict
10: 12 Hatred **s** up conflict, but love
15: 1 wrath, but a harsh word **s** up anger.
29: 22 An angry person **s** up conflict,
STONE (CORNERSTONE MILLSTONE)
1Sa 17: 50 the Philistine with a sling and a **s**;
Isa 8: 14 and Judah he will be a **s** that causes
Eze 11: 19 remove from them their heart of **s**
Mk 16: 3 "Who will roll the **s** away
Lk 4: 3 God, tell this **s** to become bread."
Jn 8: 7 *the first to throw a **s** at her.*"
2Co 3: 3 not on tablets of **s** but on tablets
STORE
Pr 10: 14 The wise **s** up knowledge,
Mt 6: 19 "Do not **s** up for yourselves
STOREHOUSE (HOUSE)
Mal 3: 10 Bring the whole tithe into the **s**,
STRAIGHT
Pr 3: 6 and he will make your paths **s.**
4: 25 Let your eyes look **s** ahead;
15: 21 understanding keeps a **s** course.
Jn 1: 23 'Make **s** the way for the Lord.'"
STRAIN
Mt 23: 24 You **s** out a gnat but swallow
STRANGER
Mt 25: 35 I was a **s** and you invited me in,
Jn 10: 5 But they will never follow a **s**;
STRAPS
Mk 1: 7 **s** of whose sandals I am not worthy
STREAMS
Ps 1: 3 person is like a tree planted by **s**
46: 4 a river whose **s** make glad the city
Ecc 1: 7 All **s** flow into the sea, yet the sea is
STRENGTH (STRONG)
Ex 15: 2 "The LORD is my **s** and my
Dt 6: 5 all your soul and with all your **s.**
2Sa 22: 33 It is God who arms me with **s**
Ne 8: 10 the joy of the LORD is your **s.**"
Ps 28: 7 The LORD is my **s** and my shield;
46: 1 God is our refuge and a **s**,
96: 7 ascribe to the LORD glory and **s.**
118: 14 The LORD is my **s** and my
147: 10 pleasure is not in the **s** of the horse,

Isa 40: 31 in the LORD will renew their **s.**
Mk 12: 30 all your mind and with all your **s.**'
1Co 1: 25 of God is stronger than human **s.**
Php 4: 13 this through him who gives me **s.**
1Pe 4: 11 do so with the **s** God provides,
STRENGTHEN (STRONG)
2Ch 16: 9 to **s** those whose hearts are fully
Ps 119: 28 **s** me according to your word.
Isa 35: 3 **S** the feeble hands, steady the
41: 10 I will **s** you and help you;
Eph 3: 16 of his glorious riches he may **s** you
2Th 2: 17 and **s** you in every good deed
Heb 12: 12 **s** your feeble arms and weak knees.
STRIFE
Pr 20: 3 It is to one's honor to avoid **s**,
22: 10 out the mocker, and out goes **s**;
STRIKE
Ge 3: 15 your head, and you will **s** his heel."
Zec 13: 7 "**S** the shepherd, and the sheep will
Mt 26: 31 "'I will **s** the shepherd,
STRONG (STRENGTH STRENGTHEN)
Dt 31: 6 Be **s** and courageous. Do not be
1Ki 2: 2 "So be **s**, act like a man,
Pr 31: 17 her arms are **s** for her tasks.
SS 8: 6 for love is as **s** as death, its jealousy
Lk 2: 40 And the child grew and became **s**;
Ro 15: 1 We who are **s** ought to bear
1Co 1: 27 things of the world to shame the **s.**
16: 13 in the faith; be courageous; be **s.**
2Co 12: 10 For when I am weak, then I am **s.**
Eph 6: 10 be **s** in the Lord and in his mighty
STRUGGLE
Ro 15: 30 join me in my **s** by praying to God
Eph 6: 12 For our **s** is not against flesh
Heb 12: 4 In your **s** against sin, you have not
STUDY
Ezr 7: 10 Ezra had devoted himself to the **s**
Ecc 12: 12 end, and much **s** wearies the body.
Jn 5: 39 You **s** the Scriptures diligently
STUMBLE (STUMBLING)
Ps 37: 24 though he may **s**, he will not fall,
119:165 law, and nothing can make them **s.**
Isa 8: 14 be a stone that causes people to **s**
Jer 31: 9 a level path where they will not **s**,
Eze 7: 19 for it has caused them to **s** into sin.
1Co 10: 32 Do not cause anyone to **s**,
1Pe 2: 8 "A stone that causes people to **s**
STUMBLING (STUMBLE)
Ro 14: 13 your mind not to put any **s** block
1Co 8: 9 rights does not become a **s** block
2Co 6: 3 We put no **s** block in anyone's path,
SUBDUE
Ge 1: 28 fill the earth and **s** it.
SUBJECT (SUBJECTED)
1Co 14: 32 of prophets are **s** to the control
15: 28 the Son himself will be made **s**
Titus 2: 5 and to be **s** to their husbands,
2: 9 slaves to be **s** to their masters
3: 1 Remind the people to be **s** to rulers
SUBJECTED (SUBJECT)
Ro 8: 20 the creation was **s** to frustration,
SUBMISSION (SUBMIT)
1Co 14: 34 but must be in **s**, as the law says.
1Ti 2: 11 learn in quietness and full **s.**
SUBMISSIVE (SUBMIT)
Jas 3: 17 considerate, **s**, full of mercy
SUBMIT (SUBMISSION SUBMISSIVE SUBMITS)
Ro 13: 5 necessary to **s** to the authorities,
1Co 16: 16 to **s** to such people and to everyone
Eph 5: 21 **S** to one another out of reverence
Col 3: 18 **s** yourselves to your husbands, as is
Heb 12: 9 How much more should we **s**
13: 17 leaders and **s** to their authority,
Jas 4: 7 **S** yourselves, then, to God.
1Pe 2: 18 reverent fear of God **s** yourselves
SUBMITS (SUBMIT)
Eph 5: 24 Now as the church **s** to Christ,
SUCCESSFUL
Jos 1: 7 that you may be **s** wherever you go.
2Ki 18: 7 he was **s** in whatever he undertook.
2Ch 20: 20 in his prophets and you will be **s.**"

SUFFER (SUFFERED SUFFERING SUFFERINGS SUFFERS)
Isa 53: 10 to crush him and cause him to **s**,
Mk 8: 31 Son of Man must **s** many things
Lk 24: 26 the Messiah have to **s** these things
     24: 46 The Messiah will **s** and rise
Php 1: 29 believe in him, but also to **s** for him,
1Pe 4: 16 if you **s** as a Christian, do not be
SUFFERED (SUFFER)
Heb 2: 9 and honor because he **s** death,
      2: 18 Because he himself **s** when he was
1Pe 2: 21 called, because Christ **s** for you,
SUFFERING (SUFFER)
Isa 53: 3 a man of **s**, and familiar with pain.
Ac 5: 41 been counted worthy of **s** disgrace
2Ti 1: 8 join with me in **s** for the gospel,
SUFFERINGS (SUFFER)
Ro 8: 17 if indeed we share in his **s** in order
     8: 18 that our present **s** are not worth
2Co 1: 5 share abundantly in the **s** of Christ,
Php 3: 10 and participation in his **s**,
SUFFERS (SUFFER)
Pr 13: 20 for a companion of fools **s** harm.
1Co 12: 26 If one part **s**, every part **s** with it;
SUFFICIENT
2Co 12: 9 said to me, "My grace is **s** for you,
SUITABLE
Ge 2: 18 I will make a helper **s** for him."
SUN
Ecc 1: 9 there is nothing new under the **s**.
Mal 4: 2 the **s** of righteousness will rise
Mt 5: 45 He causes his **s** to rise on the evil
        17: 2 His face shone like the **s**, and his
Rev 1: 16 His face was like the **s** shining in
    21: 23 The city does not need the **s**
SUPERIOR
Heb 1: 4 as the name he has inherited is **s**
      8: 6 he is mediator is **s** to the old one,
SUPREMACY
Col 1: 18 in everything he might have the **s**.
SURE
Nu 32: 23 you may be **s** that your sin will find
Dt 6: 17 Be **s** to keep the commands
    14: 22 Be **s** to set aside a tenth of all
Isa 28: 16 cornerstone for a **s** foundation;
SURPASS (SURPASSES SURPASSING)
Pr 31: 29 noble things, but you **s** them all."
SURPASSES (SURPASS)
Mt 5: 20 that unless your righteousness **s**
Eph 3: 19 to know this love that **s** knowledge
SURPASSING (SURPASS)
Ps 150: 2 praise him for his **s** greatness.
2Co 3: 10 in comparison with the **s** glory.
      9: 14 of the **s** grace God has given you.
Php 3: 8 a loss because of the **s** worth
SURROUNDED
Heb 12: 1 since we are **s** by such a great cloud
SUSPENDS
Job 26: 7 he **s** the earth over nothing.
SUSTAINING (SUSTAINS)
Heb 1: 3 **s** all things by his powerful word.
SUSTAINS (SUSTAINING)
Ps 18: 35 shield, and your right hand **s** me;
  146: 9 the foreigner and **s** the fatherless
  147: 6 The LORD **s** the humble but casts
Isa 50: 4 to know the word that **s** the weary.
SWALLOWED
1Co 15: 54 "Death has been **s** up in victory."
2Co 5: 4 so that what is mortal may be **s**
SWEAR
Mt 5: 34 I tell you, do not **s** an oath at all:
SWORD (SWORDS)
Ps 45: 3 Gird your **s** on your side,
Mt 10: 34 not come to bring peace, but a **s**.
  26: 52 all who draw the **s** will die by the **s**.
Lk 2: 35 a **s** will pierce your own soul too."
Ro 13: 4 for rulers do not bear the **s** for no
Eph 6: 17 of salvation and the **s** of the Spirit,
Heb 4: 12 Sharper than any double-edged **s**,
Rev 1: 16 was a sharp, double-edged **s**.
SWORDS (SWORD)
Pr 12: 18 words of the reckless pierce like **s**,
Isa 2: 4 They will beat their **s**
Joel 3: 10 Beat your plowshares into **s**

SYMPATHETIC
1Pe 3: 8 be **s**, love one another,
SYNAGOGUE
Lk 4: 16 the Sabbath day he went into the **s**,
Ac 17: 2 Paul went into the **s**, and on three
TABERNACLE
Ex 40: 34 the glory of the LORD filled the **t**.
TABLE (TABLES)
Ps 23: 5 You prepare a **t** before me
TABLES (TABLE)
Ac 6: 2 word of God in order to wait on **t**.
TABLET (TABLETS)
Pr 3: 3 write them on the **t** of your heart.
     7: 3 write them on the **t** of your heart.
TABLETS (TABLET)
Ex 31: 18 Sinai, he gave him the two **t**
Dt 10: 5 put the **t** in the ark I had made,
2Co 3: 3 not on **t** of stone but on **t** of human
TAKE (TAKEN TAKES TAKING TOOK)
Dt 12: 32 do not add to it or **t** away from it.
    31: 26 "**T** this Book of the Law and place
Job 23: 10 But he knows the way that I **t**;
Ps 49: 17 for they will **t** nothing with them
    51: 11 or **t** your Holy Spirit from me.
Mt 10: 38 Whoever does not **t** up their cross
    11: 29 **T** my yoke upon you and learn
    16: 24 deny themselves and **t** up their cross
TAKEN (TAKE)
Lev 6: 4 they have stolen or **t** by extortion,
Isa 6: 7 your guilt is **t** away and your sin
Mt 24: 40 one will be **t** and the other left.
Mk 16: 19 *them, he was* **t** *up into heaven*
1Ti 3: 16 on in the world, was **t** up in glory.
TAKES (TAKE)
1Ki 20: 11 not boast like one who **t** it off.'"
Jn 1: 29 who **t** away the sin of the world!
Rev 22: 19 if anyone **t** words away from this
TAKING (TAKE)
Php 2: 7 nothing by **t** the very nature
TALENT See BAGS
TAME
Jas 3: 8 no human being can **t** the tongue.
TASK
Mk 13: 34 each with their assigned **t**, and tells
Ac 20: 24 complete the **t** the Lord Jesus has
1Co 3: 5 the Lord has assigned to each his **t**.
2Co 2: 16 And who is equal to such a **t**?
TASTE (TASTED)
Ps 34: 8 **T** and see that the LORD is good;
Col 2: 21 Do not **t**! Do not touch!"?
Heb 2: 9 God he might **t** death for everyone.
TASTED (TASTE)
1Pe 2: 3 you have **t** that the Lord is good.
TAUGHT (TEACH)
Mt 7: 29 because he **t** as one who had
1Co 2: 13 but in words **t** by the Spirit,
Gal 1: 12 it from any man, nor was I **t** it;
TAX (TAXES)
Mt 22: 17 to pay the imperial **t** to Caesar
TAXES (TAX)
Ro 13: 7 you owe them: If you owe **t**, pay **t**;
TEACH (TAUGHT TEACHER TEACHERS TEACHES TEACHING)
Ex 33: 13 **t** me your ways so I may know you
Dt 4: 9 **T** them to your children and to
     8: 3 to **t** you that man does not live
    11: 19 **T** them to your children,
1Sa 12: 23 I will **t** you the way that is good
Ps 32: 8 **t** you in the way you should go;
    51: 13 I will **t** transgressors your ways,
    90: 12 **T** us to number our days, that we
  143: 10 **T** me to do your will, for you are
Jer 31: 34 longer will they **t** their neighbor,
Lk 11: 1 "Lord, **t** us to pray, just as John
Jn 14: 26 will **t** you all things and will
1Ti 2: 12 I do not permit a woman to **t**
     3: 2 respectable, hospitable, able to **t**,
Titus 1: 1 what is appropriate to sound
Heb 8: 11 longer will they **t** their neighbor,
Jas 3: 1 that we who **t** will be judged more
1Jn 2: 27 you do not need anyone to **t** you.

TEACHER (TEACH)
Mt 10: 24 "The student is not above the **t**,
      23: 8 for you have one **T**, and you are
Jn 13: 14 your Lord and **T**, have washed
TEACHERS (TEACH)
1Co 12: 28 prophets, third **t**, then miracles,
Eph 4: 11 the evangelists, the pastors and **t**,
Heb 5: 12 by this time you ought to be **t**,
TEACHES (TEACH)
1Ti 6: 3 If anyone **t** otherwise and does not
TEACHING (TEACH)
Pr   1: 8 and do not forsake your mother's **t**.
Mt 28: 20 **t** them to obey everything I have
Jn   7: 17 out whether my **t** comes from God
      14: 23 who loves me will obey my **t**.
1Ti 4: 13 of Scripture, to preaching and to **t**.
2Ti 3: 16 is God-breathed and is useful for **t**,
Titus 2: 7 In your **t** show integrity,
TEAR (TEARS)
Rev 7: 17 God will wipe away every **t**
TEARS (TEAR)
Ps 126: 5 Those who sow with **t** will reap
Php 3: 18 and now tell you again even with **t**,
TEETH (TOOTH)
Mt   8: 12 will be weeping and gnashing of **t**."
TEMPERATE
1Ti 3: 2 reproach, faithful to his wife, **t**,
      3: 11 not malicious talkers but **t**
Titus 2: 2 Teach the older men to be **t**,
TEMPEST
Ps 55: 8 shelter, far from the **t** and storm."
TEMPLE (TEMPLES)
1Ki 8: 27 How much less this **t** I have built!
Hab 2: 20 The Lord is in his holy **t**;
1Co 3: 16 that you yourselves are God's **t**
2Co 6: 16 For we are the **t** of the living God.
TEMPLES (TEMPLE)
Ac 17: 24 does not live in **t** built by human
1Co 6: 19 your bodies are **t** of the Holy Spirit,
TEMPT (TEMPTATION TEMPTED)
1Co 7: 5 Satan will not **t** you because of
TEMPTATION (TEMPT)
Mt   6: 13 lead us not into **t**, but deliver us
      26: 41 pray so that you will not fall into **t**.
1Co 10: 13 No **t** has overtaken you except
TEMPTED (TEMPT)
Mt   4: 1 the wilderness to be **t** by the devil.
1Co 10: 13 not let you be **t** beyond what you
Heb 2: 18 he himself suffered when he was **t**,
      2: 18 able to help those who are being **t**.
      4: 15 but we have one who has been **t**
Jas 1: 13 For God cannot be **t** by evil,
TEN (TENTH TITHE TITHES)
Ex 34: 28 the **T** Commandments.
Ps 91: 7 side, **t** thousand at your right hand,
Mt 25: 28 give it to the one who has **t** bags.
Lk 15: 8 suppose a woman has **t** silver coins
TENTH (TEN)
Dt 14: 22 Be sure to set aside a **t** of all
TERRIBLE (TERROR)
2Ti 3: 1 There will be **t** times in the last
TERROR (TERRIBLE)
Ps 91: 5 You will not fear the **t** of night,
Lk 21: 26 People will faint from **t**,
Ro 13: 3 rulers hold no **t** for those who do
TEST (TESTED TESTS)
Dt   6: 16 your God to the **t** as you did
Ps 139: 23 **t** me and know my anxious
Ro 12: 2 you will be able to **t** and approve
1Co 3: 13 the fire will **t** the quality of each
1Jn 4: 1 **t** the spirits to see whether they are
TESTED (TEST)
Ge 22: 1 Some time later God **t** Abraham.
Job 23: 10 when he has **t** me, I will come forth
Pr 27: 21 but people are **t** by their praise.
1Ti 3: 10 They must first be **t**;
TESTIFY (TESTIMONY)
Jn   5: 39 These are the very Scriptures that **t**
TESTIMONY (TESTIFY)
Isa 8: 20 instruction and the **t** of warning.
Lk 18: 20 you shall not give false **t**,
2Ti 1: 8 be ashamed of the **t** about our Lord

TESTS (TEST)
Pr 17: 3 for gold, but the Lord **t** the heart.
1Th 2: 4 people but God, who **t** our hearts.
THADDAEUS
   Apostle (Mt 10:3; Mk 3:18); probably also known as Judas son of James (Lk 6:16; Ac 1:13).
THANKFUL (THANKS)
Heb 12: 28 let us be **t**, and so worship God
THANKS (THANKFUL THANKSGIVING)
Ne 12: 31 assigned two large choirs to give **t**.
Ps 100: 4 give **t** to him and praise his name.
1Co 15: 57 But **t** be to God! He gives us
2Co 2: 14 But **t** be to God, who always leads
      9: 15 **T** be to God for his indescribable
1Th 5: 18 give **t** in all circumstances;
THANKSGIVING (THANKS)
Ps 95: 2 Let us come before him with **t**
     100: 4 Enter his gates with **t** and his
Php 4: 6 **t**, present your requests to God.
1Ti 4: 3 to be received with **t** by those who
THIEF (THIEVES)
1Th 5: 2 of the Lord will come like a **t**
Rev 16: 15 "Look, I come like a **t**!
THIEVES (THIEF)
1Co 6: 10 nor **t** nor the greedy nor drunkards
THINK (THOUGHT THOUGHTS)
Ro 12: 3 Do not **t** of yourself more highly
Php 4: 8 **t** about such things.
THIRST (THIRSTY)
Ps 69: 21 food and gave me vinegar for my **t**.
Mt   5: 6 hunger and **t** for righteousness,
Jn   4: 14 the water I give them will never **t**.
THIRSTY (THIRST)
Isa 55: 1 all you who are **t**,
Jn   7: 37 "Let anyone who is **t** come to me
Rev 22: 17 Let the one who is **t** come;
THOMAS
   Apostle (Mt 10:3; Mk 3:18; Lk 6:15; Jn 11:16; 14:5; 21:2; Ac 1:13). Doubted resurrection (Jn 20:24–28).
THORN (THORNS)
2Co 12: 7 I was given a **t** in my flesh,
THORNS (THORN)
Nu 33: 55 in your eyes and **t** in your sides.
Mt 27: 29 twisted together a crown of **t** and
Heb 6: 8 land that produces **t** and thistles is
THOUGHT (THINK)
Pr 14: 15 the prudent give **t** to their steps.
1Co 13: 11 I talked like a child, I **t** like a child,
THOUGHTS (THINK)
Ps 139: 23 test me and know my anxious **t**.
Isa 55: 8 "For my **t** are not your **t**, neither
Heb 4: 12 it judges the **t** and attitudes
THREE
Ecc 4: 12 of **t** strands is not quickly broken.
Mt 12: 40 the Son of Man will be **t** days and **t** nights in the heart of the earth.
      18: 20 where two or **t** gather in my name,
      27: 63 said, 'After **t** days I will rise again.'
1Co 13: 13 And now these **t** remain:
      14: 27 or at the most **t**—should speak,
2Co 13: 1 testimony of two or **t** witnesses."
THRESHING
2Sa 24: 18 altar to the Lord on the **t** floor
THRONE (ENTHRONED)
2Sa 7: 16 your **t** will be established
Ps 45: 6 Your **t**, O God, will last for ever
      47: 8 God is seated on his holy **t**.
Isa 6: 1 high and exalted, seated on a **t**;
      66: 1 "Heaven is my **t**, and the earth is
Heb 4: 16 then approach God's **t** of grace
      12: 2 at the right hand of the **t** of God.
Rev 4: 10 They lay their crowns before the **t**
      20: 11 I saw a great white **t** and him who
      22: 3 The **t** of God and of the Lamb will
THROW
Jn   8: 7 *the first to t a stone at her."*
Heb 10: 35 So do not **t** away your confidence;
      12: 1 let us **t** off everything that hinders
THWART
Isa 14: 27 has purposed, and who can **t** him?
TIBNI
   King of Israel (1Ki 16:21–22).

TIME (TIMES)
Est 4: 14 royal position for such a **t** as this?"
Da 7: 25 be delivered into his hands for a **t**, times and half a **t**.
Hos 10: 12 for it is **t** to seek the Lord,
Ro 9:   9 "At the appointed **t** I will return,
Heb 9: 28 and he will appear a second **t**,
      10: 12 had offered for all **t** one sacrifice
1Pe 4: 17 For it is **t** for judgment to begin

TIMES (TIME)
Ps 9:   9 a stronghold in **t** of trouble.
     31: 15 My **t** are in your hands;
     62:   8 Trust in him at all **t**, you people;
Pr 17: 17 A friend loves at all **t**,
Am 5: 13 in such **t**, for the **t** are evil.
Mt 18: 21 sins against me? Up to seven **t**?"
Ac 1:   7 "It is not for you to know the **t**
Rev 12: 14 care of for a time, **t** and half a time,

TIMID
2Ti 1:   7 God gave us does not make us **t**,

TIMOTHY
Believer from Lystra (Ac 16:1). Joined Paul on second missionary journey (Ac 16–20). Sent to settle problems at Corinth (1Co 4:17; 16:10). Led church at Ephesus (1Ti 1:3). Co-writer with Paul (1Th 1:1; 2Ti 1:1; Phm 1).

TIRE (TIRED)
2Th 3: 13 never **t** of doing what is good.

TIRED (TIRE)
Ex 17: 12 When Moses' hands grew **t**,
Isa 40: 28 He will not grow **t** or weary,

TITHE (TEN)
Lev 27: 30 "A **t** of everything
Dt 12: 17 your own towns the **t** of your grain
Mal 3: 10 Bring the whole **t**

TITHES (TEN)
Mal 3:   8 "In **t** and offerings.

TITUS
Gentile co-worker of Paul (Gal 2:1–3; 2Ti 4:10); sent to Corinth (2Co 2:13; 7–8; 12:18), Crete (Titus 1:4–5).

TODAY
Mt 6: 11 Give us **t** our daily bread.
Lk 23: 43 **t** you will be with me in paradise."
Heb 3: 13 as long as it is called "**T**,"
     13:   8 Christ is the same yesterday and **t**

TOIL
Ge 3: 17 through painful **t** you will eat food

TOLERATE
Hab 1: 13 then do you **t** the treacherous?
Rev 2:   2 that you cannot **t** wicked people,

TOMB
Mt 27: 65 make the **t** as secure as you know
Lk 24:   2 the stone rolled away from the **t**,

TOMORROW
Pr 27:   1 not boast about **t**, for you do not
Isa 22: 13 drink," you say, "for **t** we die!"
Mt 6: 34 do not worry about **t**, for **t**
Jas 4: 13 "Today or **t** we will go to this

TONGUE (TONGUES)
Ps 39:   1 my ways and keep my **t** from sin;
Pr 12: 18 but the **t** of the wise brings healing.
1Co 14:   2 who speaks in a **t** does not speak
     14:   4 speaks in a **t** edifies themselves,
     14: 13 one who speaks in a **t** should pray
     14: 19 than ten thousand words in a **t**.
Php 2: 11 and every **t** acknowledge that Jesus
Jas 3:   8 no human being can tame the **t**.

TONGUES (TONGUE)
Isa 28: 11 strange **t** God will speak to this
Mk 16: 17 *they will speak in new* **t**;
Ac 2:   4 other **t** as the Spirit enabled them.
     10: 46 For they heard them speaking in **t**
     19:   6 they spoke in **t** and prophesied.
1Co 12: 30 Do all speak in **t**? Do all interpret?
     14: 18 I speak in **t** more than all of you.
     14: 39 and do not forbid speaking in **t**.
Jas 1: 26 rein on their **t** deceive themselves,

TOOK (TAKE)
1Co 11: 23 the night he was betrayed, **t** bread,
Php 3: 12 which Christ Jesus **t** hold of me.

TOOTH (TEETH)
Ex 21: 24 eye for eye, **t** for **t**, hand for hand,
Mt 5: 38 was said, 'Eye for eye, and **t** for **t**.'

TORMENTED
Rev 20: 10 They will be **t** day and night

TORN
Gal 4: 15 you would have **t** out your eyes
Php 1: 23 I am **t** between the two: I desire

TOUCH (TOUCHED)
Ps 105: 15 "Do not **t** my anointed ones;
Lk 24: 39 **T** me and see; a ghost does not
2Co 6: 17 **T** no unclean thing, and I will
Col 2: 21 Do not taste! Do not **t**!"?

TOUCHED (TOUCH)
1Sa 10: 26 men whose hearts God had **t**.
Mt 14: 36 cloak, and all who **t** it were healed.

TOWER
Ge 11:   4 a **t** that reaches to the heavens,
Pr 18: 10 name of the Lord is a fortified **t**;

TOWN (TOWNS)
Mt 5: 14 **t** built on a hill cannot be hidden.

TOWNS (TOWN)
Nu 35:   2 to give the Levites **t** to live
     35: 15 These six **t** will be a place of refuge

TRACING
Ro 11: 33 and his paths beyond **t** out!

TRADITION
Mt 15:   6 word of God for the sake of your **t**.
Col 2:   8 which depends on human **t**

TRAINING
1Co 9: 25 in the games goes into strict **t**.
2Ti 3: 16 correcting and **t** in righteousness,

TRAMPLED
Lk 21: 24 Jerusalem will be **t**
Heb 10: 29 to be punished who has **t** the Son

TRANCE
Ac 10: 10 was being prepared, he fell into a **t**.

TRANSCENDS
Php 4:   7 God, which **t** all understanding,

TRANSFIGURED
Mt 17:   2 There he was **t** before them.

TRANSFORM (TRANSFORMED)
Php 3: 21 will **t** our lowly bodies so that they

TRANSFORMED (TRANSFORM)
Ro 12:   2 be **t** by the renewing of your mind.
2Co 3: 18 are being **t** into his image

TRANSGRESSION (TRANSGRESSIONS TRANSGRESSORS)
Isa 53:   8 **t** of my people he was punished.
Ro 4: 15 where there is no law there is no **t**.

TRANSGRESSIONS (TRANSGRESSION)
Ps 32:   1 is the one whose **t** are forgiven,
     51:   1 great compassion blot out my **t**.
   103: 12 so far has he removed our **t** from
Isa 53:   5 But he was pierced for our **t**,
Eph 2:   1 you were dead in your **t** and sins,

TRANSGRESSORS (TRANSGRESSION)
Ps 51: 13 Then I will teach **t** your ways,
Isa 53: 12 and was numbered with the **t**,
     53: 12 and made intercession for the **t**.

TREADING
Dt 25:   4 Do not muzzle an ox while it is **t**
1Co 9:   9 "Do not muzzle an ox while it is **t**

TREASURE (TREASURED TREASURES)
Isa 33:   6 of the Lord is the key to this **t**.
Mt 6: 21 where your **t** is, there your heart
2Co 4:   7 But we have this **t** in jars of clay

TREASURED (TREASURE)
Dt 7:   6 to be his people, his **t** possession.
Lk 2: 19 But Mary **t** up all these things

TREASURES (TREASURE)
Mt 6: 19 store up for yourselves **t** on earth,
Col 2:   3 in whom are hidden all the **t**
Heb 11: 26 of greater value than the **t** of Egypt,

TREAT
Lev 22:   2 sons to **t** with respect the sacred
1Ti 5:   1 **T** younger men as brothers,
1Pe 3:   7 **t** them with respect as the weaker

TREATY
Dt 7:   2 Make no **t** with them, and show

TREE
Ge 2:   9 of the garden were the **t** of life
     2:   9 and the **t** of the knowledge of good
Ps 1:   3 is like a **t** planted by streams
Mt 3: 10 every **t** that does not produce good
     12: 33 for a **t** is recognized by its fruit.
Rev 22: 14 may have the right to the **t** of life

TREMBLE (TREMBLING)
1Ch 16: 30 **T** before him, all the earth!
Ps 114: 7 **T**, earth, at the presence of the Lord,
TREMBLING (TREMBLE)
Ps   2: 11 fear and celebrate his rule with **t**.
Php 2: 12 out your salvation with fear and **t**,
TRESPASS
Ro   5: 17 if, by the **t** of the one man,
TRIALS
1Th 3: 3 one would be unsettled by these **t**.
Jas   1: 2 whenever you face **t** of many kinds,
2Pe 2: 9 how to rescue the godly from **t**
TRIBES
Ge 49: 28 All these are the twelve **t** of Israel,
Mt 19: 28 judging the twelve **t** of Israel.
TRIBULATION
Rev 7: 14 who have come out of the great **t**;
TRIUMPHAL (TRIUMPHING)
Isa 60: 11 their kings led in **t** procession.
2Co 2: 14 as captives in Christ's **t** procession
TRIUMPHING (TRIUMPHAL)
Col   2: 15 of them, **t** over them by the cross.
TROUBLE (TROUBLED TROUBLES)
Job 14: 1 are of few days and full of **t**.
Ps 46: 1 strength, an ever-present help in **t**.
    107: 13 they cried to the LORD in their **t**,
Pr 24: 10 If you falter in a time of **t**,
Mt   6: 34 Each day has enough **t** of its own.
Jn 16: 33 In this world you will have **t**.
Ro   8: 35 Shall **t** or hardship or persecution
TROUBLED (TROUBLE)
Jn 14: 1 "Do not let your hearts be **t**.
    14: 27 Do not let your hearts be **t** and do
TROUBLES (TROUBLE)
1Co 7: 28 those who marry will face many **t**
2Co 1: 4 who comforts us in all our **t**,
    4: 17 momentary **t** are achieving for us
TRUE (TRUTH)
Dt 18: 22 does not take place or come **t**,
1Sa 9: 6 and everything he says comes **t**.
Ps 119:160 All your words are **t**; all your
Jn 17: 3 the only **t** God, and Jesus Christ,
Ro   3: 4 Let God be **t**, and every human
Php 4: 8 whatever is **t**, whatever is noble,
Rev 22: 6 These words are trustworthy and **t**.
TRUMPET
1Co 14: 8 if the **t** does not sound a clear call,
    15: 52 twinkling of an eye, at the last **t**.
TRUST (ENTRUSTED TRUSTED TRUSTWORTHY)
Ps 20: 7 we **t** in the name of the LORD our
    37: 3 **T** in the LORD and do good;
    56: 4 in God I **t** and am not afraid.
    119: 42 taunts me, for I **t** in your word.
Pr   3: 5 **T** in the LORD with all your heart
Isa 30: 15 in quietness and **t** is your strength,
1Co 4: 2 been given a **t** must prove faithful.
TRUSTED (TRUST)
Ps 26: 1 I have **t** in the LORD and have not
Isa 25: 9 we **t** in him, and he saved us.
Da   3: 28 They **t** in him and defied the king's
Lk 16: 10 "Whoever can be **t** with very little
TRUSTWORTHY (TRUST)
Ps 119:138 are righteous; they are fully **t**.
Pr 11: 13 but a **t** person keeps a secret.
Rev 22: 6 to me, "These words are **t** and true.
TRUTH (TRUE TRUTHFUL TRUTHS)
Isa 45: 19 I, the LORD, speak the **t**;
Zec 8: 16 Speak the **t** to each other,
Jn   4: 23 the Father in the Spirit and in **t**,
    8: 32 Then you will know the **t**, and the **t**
    14: 6 "I am the way and the **t** and the life.
    16: 13 he will guide you into all the **t**.
    18: 38 "What is **t**?" retorted Pilate.
Ro   1: 25 They exchanged the **t** about God
1Co 13: 6 in evil but rejoices with the **t**.
2Co 13: 8 against the **t**, but only for the **t**.
Eph 4: 15 Instead, speaking the **t** in love,
    6: 14 belt of **t** buckled around your waist,
2Th 2: 10 because they refused to love the **t**
1Ti 2: 4 to come to a knowledge of the **t**.
    3: 15 the pillar and foundation of the **t**.
2Ti 2: 15 correctly handles the word of **t**.
    3: 7 to come to a knowledge of the **t**.

Heb 10: 26 received the knowledge of the **t**,
1Pe 1: 22 by obeying the **t** so that you have
2Pe 2: 2 and will bring the way of **t**
1Jn 1: 6 we lie and do not live out the **t**.
    1: 8 ourselves and the **t** is not in us.
TRUTHFUL (TRUTH)
Jn   3: 33 it has certified that God is **t**.
TRUTHS (TRUTH)
1Ti 3: 9 keep hold of the deep **t** of the faith
Heb 5: 12 teach you the elementary **t** of God's
TRY (TRYING)
Ps 26: 2 and **t** me, examine my heart and
Isa 7: 13 Will you **t** the patience of my God
1Co 14: 12 **t** to excel in those that build
2Co 5: 11 the Lord, we **t** to persuade others.
TRYING (TRY)
2Co 5: 12 We are not **t** to commend ourselves
1Th 2: 4 We are not **t** to please people
TURN (TURNED TURNS)
Ex 32: 12 **T** from your fierce anger;
Dt   5: 32 do not **t** aside to the right
    28: 14 Do not **t** aside from any
Jos 1: 7 do not **t** from it to the right
2Ch 7: 14 face and **t** from their wicked ways,
    30: 9 He will not **t** his face from you
Ps 78: 6 they in **t** would tell their children.
Pr 22: 6 they are old they will not **t** from it.
Isa 29: 16 You **t** things upside down,
    30: 21 Whether you **t** to the right
    45: 22 "**T** to me and be saved, all you ends
    55: 7 Let them **t** to the LORD, and he
Eze 33: 11 they **t** from their ways and live.
Mal 4: 6 He will **t** the hearts of the parents
Mt   5: 39 **t** to them the other cheek also.
    10: 35 to **t** " 'a man against his father,
Jn 12: 40 understand with their hearts, nor **t**
Ac   3: 19 and **t** to God, so that your sins may
    26: 18 and **t** them from darkness to light,
1Ti 6: 20 **T** away from godless chatter
1Pe 3: 11 must **t** from evil and do good;
TURNED (TURN)
Ps 30: 11 You **t** my wailing into dancing;
    40: 1 he **t** to me and heard my cry.
Isa 53: 6 each of us has **t** to our own way;
Hos 7: 8 Ephraim is a flat loaf not **t** over.
Joel 2: 31 The sun will be **t** to darkness
Ro   3: 12 All have **t** away, they have together
TURNS (TURN)
2Sa 22: 29 the LORD **t** my darkness
Pr 15: 1 A gentle answer **t** away wrath,
Isa 44: 25 of the wise and **t** it into nonsense,
Jas 5: 20 Whoever **t** a sinner from the error
TWELVE
Ge 49: 28 All these are the **t** tribes of Israel,
Mt 10: 1 Jesus called his **t** disciples to him
TWINKLING
1Co 15: 52 a flash, in the **t** of an eye, at the last
UNAPPROACHABLE
1Ti 6: 16 immortal and who lives in **u** light,
UNBELIEF (UNBELIEVER UNBELIEVERS UNBELIEVING)
Mk   9: 24 help me overcome my **u**!"
Ro 11: 20 they were broken off because of **u**,
Heb 3: 19 able to enter, because of their **u**.
UNBELIEVER (UNBELIEF)
1Co 7: 15 But if the **u** leaves, let it be so.
    10: 27 If an **u** invites you to a meal
    14: 24 if an **u** or an inquirer comes in
2Co 6: 15 have in common with an **u**?
1Ti 5: 8 the faith and is worse than an **u**.
UNBELIEVERS (UNBELIEF)
1Co 6: 6 and this in front of **u**!
2Co 6: 14 Do not be yoked together with **u**.
UNBELIEVING (UNBELIEF)
1Co 7: 14 the **u** husband has been sanctified
    7: 14 and the **u** wife has been sanctified
Rev 21: 8 But the cowardly, the **u**, the vile,
UNCERTAIN
1Ti 6: 17 which is so **u**, but to put their hope
UNCHANGEABLE
Heb 6: 18 that, by two **u** things in which it is
UNCIRCUMCISED
1Sa 17: 26 Who is this **u** Philistine that he
Col   3: 11 or Jew, circumcised or **u**,

UNCIRCUMCISION
1Co 7: 19 is nothing and **u** is nothing.
Gal 5: 6 neither circumcision nor **u** has any

UNCLEAN
Isa 6: 5 For I am a man of **u** lips, and I live
Ro 14: 14 Jesus, that nothing is **u** in itself.
2Co 6: 17 Touch no **u** thing, and I will

UNCONCERNED
Eze 16: 49 were arrogant, overfed and **u**;

UNCOVERED
Heb 4: 13 Everything is **u** and laid bare

UNDERSTAND (UNDERSTANDING UNDERSTANDS)
Job 42: 3 Surely I spoke of things I did not **u**,
Ps 73: 16 When I tried to **u** all this,
119:125 that I may **u** your statutes.
Lk 24: 45 so they could **u** the Scriptures.
Ac 8: 30 "Do you **u** what you are reading?"
Ro 7: 15 I do not **u** what I do. For what I
1Co 2: 14 and cannot **u** them because they
Eph 5: 17 but **u** what the Lord's will is.
2Pe 3: 16 some things that are hard to **u**,

UNDERSTANDING (UNDERSTAND)
Ps 119: 32 for you have broadened my **u**.
119:104 I gain **u** from your precepts;
147: 5 in power; his **u** has no limit.
Pr 3: 5 heart and lean not on your own **u**;
4: 7 Though it cost all you have, get **u**.
10: 23 a person of **u** delights in wisdom.
11: 12 one who has **u** holds their tongue.
15: 21 but whoever has **u** keeps a straight
15: 32 one who heeds correction gains **u**.
Isa 40: 28 and his **u** no one can fathom.
Da 5: 12 a keen mind and knowledge and **u**,
Mk 4: 12 and ever hearing but never **u**;
12: 33 with all your **u** and with all your
Php 4: 7 which transcends all **u**, will guard

UNDERSTANDS (UNDERSTAND)
1Ch 28: 9 every heart and **u** every desire

UNDIVIDED
1Ch 12: 33 to help David with **u** loyalty—
Ps 86: 11 give me an **u** heart, that I may fear
Eze 11: 19 I will give them an **u** heart and put
1Co 7: 35 in a right way in **u** devotion

UNDOING
Pr 18: 7 The mouths of fools are their **u**,

UNDYING
Eph 6: 24 Lord Jesus Christ with an **u** love.

UNFADING
1Pe 3: 4 the **u** beauty of a gentle and quiet

UNFAILING
Ps 33: 5 the earth is full of his **u** love.
119: 76 May your **u** love be my comfort,
143: 8 bring me word of your **u** love, for I
Pr 19: 22 What a person desires is **u** love;
La 3: 32 compassion, so great is his **u** love.

UNFAITHFUL
Lev 6: 2 is **u** to the LORD by deceiving
1Ch 10: 13 Saul died because he was **u**
Pr 13: 15 but the way of the **u** leads to their

UNFOLDING
Ps 119:130 The **u** of your words gives light;

UNGODLINESS
Titus 2: 12 It teaches us to say "No" to **u**

UNITED (UNITY)
Ro 6: 5 For if we have been **u** with him
Php 2: 1 from being **u** with Christ, if any
Col 2: 2 encouraged in heart and **u** in love,

UNITY (UNITED)
Ps 133: 1 God's people live together in **u**!
Eph 4: 3 keep the **u** of the Spirit through
4: 13 until we all reach **u** in the faith
Col 3: 14 them all together in perfect **u**.

UNIVERSE
Heb 1: 2 through whom also he made the **u**.

UNKNOWN
Ac 17: 23 with this inscription: TO AN **U** GOD.

UNLEAVENED
Ex 12: 17 "Celebrate the Festival of **U** Bread,

UNPROFITABLE
Titus 3: 9 because these are **u** and useless.

UNPUNISHED
Ex 34: 7 Yet he does not leave the guilty **u**;
Pr 19: 5 A false witness will not go **u**,

UNREPENTANT
Ro 2: 5 stubbornness and your **u** heart,

UNRIGHTEOUS
Zep 3: 5 not fail, yet the **u** know no shame.
Mt 5: 45 rain on the righteous and the **u**.
1Pe 3: 18 the righteous for the **u**, to bring
2Pe 2: 9 to hold the **u** for punishment

UNSEARCHABLE
Ro 11: 33 How **u** his judgments, and his

UNSEEN
2Co 4: 18 temporary, but what is **u** is eternal.

UNSTABLE
Jas 1: 8 double-minded and **u** in all they
2Pe 2: 14 they seduce the **u**; they are experts
3: 16 ignorant and **u** people distort,

UNTHINKABLE
Job 34: 12 It is **u** that God would do wrong,

UNVEILED
2Co 3: 18 with **u** faces contemplate the Lord's

UNWORTHY
Job 40: 4 "I am **u**—how can I reply to you?
Lk 17: 10 do, should say, 'We are **u** servants;

UPRIGHT
Job 1: 1 This man was blameless and **u**;
Pr 2: 7 He holds success in store for the **u**,
15: 8 but the prayer of the **u** pleases him.
Titus 1: 8 who is self-controlled, **u**,
2: 12 **u** and godly lives in this present

UPROOTED
Jude : 12 autumn trees, without fruit and **u**

USEFUL
2Ti 2: 21 **u** to the Master and prepared to do
3: 16 God-breathed and is **u** for teaching

USELESS
1Co 15: 14 our preaching is **u** and so is your
Jas 2: 20 that faith without deeds is **u**?

UZZIAH
Son of Amaziah; king of Judah also known as Azariah (2Ki 15:1–7; 1Ch 6:24; 2Ch 26).

VAIN
Ps 33: 17 A horse is a **v** hope for deliverance;
Isa 65: 23 They will not labor in **v**, nor will
1Co 15: 2 Otherwise, you have believed in **v**.
15: 58 your labor in the Lord is not in **v**.
2Co 6: 1 you not to receive God's grace in **v**.

VALLEY
Ps 23: 4 I walk through the darkest **v**,
Isa 40: 4 Every **v** shall be raised up,
Joel 3: 14 LORD is near in the **v** of decision.

VALUABLE (VALUE)
Lk 12: 24 how much more **v** you are than

VALUE (VALUABLE)
Mt 13: 46 When he found one of great **v**,
1Ti 4: 8 For physical training is of some **v**, but godliness has **v** for all things,
Heb 11: 26 as of greater **v** than the treasures

VEIL
Ex 34: 33 to them, he put a **v** over his face.
2Co 3: 14 to this day the same **v** remains

VENGEANCE (AVENGE REVENGE)
Isa 34: 8 For the LORD has a day of **v**,

VICTORIES (VICTORY)
Ps 18: 50 He gives his king great **v**;
21: 1 great is his joy in the **v** you give!

VICTORIOUS (VICTORY)
Zec 9: 9 king comes to you, righteous and **v**,
Rev 2: 7 To the one who is **v**, I will give
2: 11 The one who is **v** will not be hurt
2: 17 To the one who is **v**, I will give
2: 26 To the one who is **v** and does my
3: 5 The one who is **v** will, like them,
3: 12 The one who is **v** I will make
3: 21 To the one who is **v**, I will give
21: 7 Those who are **v** will inherit all

VICTORIOUSLY (VICTORY)
Ps 45: 4 In your majesty ride forth **v**

VICTORY (VICTORIES VICTORIOUS VICTORIOUSLY)
Ps 60: 12 With God we will gain the **v**,
1Co 15: 54 has been swallowed up in **v**."
15: 57 He gives us the **v** through our Lord
1Jn 5: 4 This is the **v** that has overcome

VINDICATED
1Ti 3: 16 in the flesh, was **v** by the Spirit,
VINE
Jn 15: 1 "I am the true **v**, and my Father is
VINEGAR
Mk 15: 36 filled a sponge with wine **v**, put it
VIOLATION
Heb 2: 2 every **v** and disobedience received
VIOLENCE
Isa 60: 18 No longer will **v** be heard in your
Eze 45: 9 Give up your **v** and oppression
VIPERS
Ro 3: 13 "The poison of **v** is on their lips."
VIRGIN
Isa 7: 14 The **v** will conceive and give birth
Mt 1: 23 "The **v** will conceive and give birth
2Co 11: 2 I might present you as a pure **v**
VIRTUES
Col 3: 14 And over all these **v** put on love,
VISION
Ac 26: 19 disobedient to the **v** from heaven.
VOICE
Ps 95: 7 if only you would hear his **v**,
Isa 30: 21 your ears will hear a **v** behind you,
Jn 5: 28 are in their graves will hear his **v**
10: 3 him, and the sheep listen to his **v**.
Heb 3: 7 "Today, if you hear his **v**,
Rev 3: 20 If anyone hears my **v** and opens
VOMIT
Pr 26: 11 As a dog returns to its **v**, so fools
2Pe 2: 22 "A dog returns to its **v**," and,
VOW
Nu 30: 2 a man makes a **v** to the LORD
WAGES
Lk 10: 7 you, for the worker deserves his **w**.
Ro 4: 4 **w** are not credited as a gift but as
6: 23 the **w** of sin is death, but the gift
WAILING
Ps 30: 11 You turned my **w** into dancing;
WAIST
2Ki 1: 8 had a leather belt around his **w**."
Mt 3: 4 he had a leather belt around his **w**.
WAIT (WAITED WAITS)
Ps 27: 14 **w** for the LORD; be strong
130: 5 I **w** for the LORD, my whole being
Isa 30: 18 Blessed are all who **w** for him!
Ac 1: 4 **w** for the gift my Father promised,
Ro 8: 23 groan inwardly as we **w** eagerly
1Th 1: 10 and to **w** for his Son from heaven,
Titus 2: 13 while we **w** for the blessed hope—
WAITED (WAIT)
Ps 40: 1 I **w** patiently for the LORD;
WAITS (WAIT)
Ro 8: 19 the creation **w** in eager expectation
WALK (WALKED)
Dt 11: 19 and when you **w** along the road,
Ps 1: 1 Blessed is the one who does not **w**
23: 4 though I **w** through the darkest
89: 15 **w** in the light of your presence,
Isa 2: 5 let us **w** in the light of the LORD.
30: 21 saying, "This is the way; **w** in it."
40: 31 weary, they will **w** and not be faint.
Jer 6: 16 and **w** in it, and you will find rest
Da 4: 37 those who **w** in pride he is able
Am 3: 3 Do two **w** together unless they
Mic 6: 8 and to **w** humbly with your God.
Mk 2: 9 say, 'Get up, take your mat and **w**'?
Jn 8: 12 Whoever follows me will never **w**
1Jn 1: 7 But if we **w** in the light, as he is
2Jn : 6 his command is that you **w** in love.
WALKED (WALK)
Ge 5: 24 Enoch **w** faithfully with God;
Jos 14: 9 which your feet have **w** will be
Mt 14: 29 **w** on the water and came toward
WALL
Jos 6: 20 gave a loud shout, the **w** collapsed;
Ne 2: 17 let us rebuild the **w** of Jerusalem.
Rev 21: 12 a great, high **w** with twelve gates,
WALLOWING
2Pe 2: 22 returns to her **w** in the mud."
WANT (WANTED WANTING WANTS)
1Sa 8: 19 they said. "We **w** a king over us.

Lk 19: 14 say, 'We don't **w** this man to be our
Ro 7: 15 For what I **w** to do I do not do,
Php 3: 10 I **w** to know Christ—yes, to know
WANTED (WANT)
1Co 12: 18 of them, just as he **w** them to be.
WANTING (WANT)
Da 5: 27 weighed on the scales and found **w**.
2Pe 3: 9 with you, not **w** anyone to perish,
WANTS (WANT)
Mt 20: 26 whoever **w** to become great among
Mk 8: 35 For whoever **w** to save their life
Ro 9: 18 on whom he **w** to have mercy,
9: 18 he hardens whom he **w** to harden.
1Ti 2: 4 who **w** all people to be saved
WAR (WARS)
Isa 2: 4 nor will they train for **w** anymore.
Da 9: 26 **W** will continue until the end,
2Co 10: 3 we do not wage **w** as the world
Rev 19: 11 justice he judges and wages **w**.
WARN (WARNED WARNINGS)
Eze 3: 19 if you do **w** the wicked person
33: 9 if you do **w** the wicked person
WARNED (WARN)
Ps 19: 11 By them your servant is **w**;
WARNINGS (WARN)
1Co 10: 11 and were written down as **w** for us,
WARS (WAR)
Ps 46: 9 He makes **w** cease to the ends
Mt 24: 6 will hear of **w** and rumors of **w**,
WASH (WASHED WASHING)
Ps 51: 7 **w** me, and I will be whiter than
Jn 13: 5 and began to **w** his disciples' feet,
Ac 22: 16 be baptized and **w** your sins away,
Rev 22: 14 are those who **w** their robes,
WASHED (WASH)
1Co 6: 11 But you were **w**, you were
Rev 7: 14 they have **w** their robes and made
WASHING (WASH)
Eph 5: 26 the **w** with water through the word,
Titus 3: 5 saved us through the **w** of rebirth
WATCH (WATCHES WATCHING WATCHMAN)
Ge 31: 49 the LORD keep **w** between you
Jer 31: 10 them and will **w** over his flock like
Mt 24: 42 "Therefore keep **w**, because you do
26: 41 "**W** and pray so that you will not
Lk 2: 8 keeping **w** over their flocks at night
1Ti 4: 16 **W** your life and doctrine closely.
WATCHES (WATCH)
Ps 1: 6 For the LORD **w** over the way
121: 3 he who **w** over you will not
WATCHING (WATCH)
Lk 12: 37 servants whose master finds them **w**
WATCHMAN (WATCH)
Eze 3: 17 I have made you a **w** for the people
WATER (WATERED WATERS)
Ps 1: 3 like a tree planted by streams of **w**,
22: 14 I am poured out like **w**, and all my
Pr 25: 21 if he is thirsty, give him **w** to drink.
Isa 49: 10 and lead them beside springs of **w**.
Jer 2: 13 broken cisterns that cannot hold **w**
Zec 14: 8 On that day living **w** will flow
Mk 9: 41 anyone who gives you a cup of **w**
Jn 4: 10 he would have given you living **w**."
7: 38 rivers of living **w** will flow
Eph 5: 26 washing with **w** through the word,
1Pe 3: 21 this **w** symbolizes baptism that
Rev 21: 6 thirsty I will give **w** without cost
WATERED (WATER)
1Co 3: 6 I planted the seed, Apollos **w** it,
WATERS (WATER)
Ps 23: 2 he leads me beside quiet **w**,
Isa 58: 11 like a spring whose **w** never fail.
1Co 3: 7 nor the one who **w** is anything,
WAVE (WAVES)
Jas 1: 6 the one who doubts is like a **w**
WAVES (WAVE)
Isa 57: 20 whose **w** cast up mire and mud.
Mt 8: 27 the winds and the **w** obey him!"
Eph 4: 14 tossed back and forth by the **w**,
WAY (WAYS)
Dt 1: 33 to show you the **w** you should go.
2Sa 22: 31 "As for God, his **w** is perfect:

Job 23: 10 But he knows the **w** that I take;
Ps   1:   1 stand in the **w** that sinners take
      37:   5 Commit your **w** to the LORD;
     139: 24 and lead me in the **w** everlasting.
Pr   14: 12 is a **w** that appears to be right,
      22:   6 off on the **w** they should go,
Isa 30: 21 behind you, saying, "This is the **w**;
      53:   6 of us has turned to our own **w**;
Mt   3:   3 'Prepare the **w** for the Lord,
Jn   14:   6 "I am the **w** and the truth
1Co 10: 13 provide a **w** out so that you can
      12: 31 will show you the most excellent **w**.
Heb   4: 15 who has been tempted in every **w**,
       9:   8 the **w** into the Most Holy Place had
      10: 20 living **w** opened for us through

WAYS (WAY)

Ex   33: 13 teach me your **w** so I may know
Ps   25: 10 All the **w** of the LORD are loving
      51: 13 I will teach transgressors your **w**,
Pr   3:   6 in all your **w** submit to him, and he
      16: 17 who guard their **w** preserve their
Isa 55:   7 Let the wicked forsake their **w**
      55:   8 neither are your **w** my **w**,"
Jas   3:   2 We all stumble in many **w**.

WEAK (WEAKER WEAKNESS)

Mt   26: 41 spirit is willing, but the flesh is **w**."
Ro   14:   1 Accept the one whose faith is **w**,
1Co   1: 27 chose the **w** things of the world
       8:   9 a stumbling block to the **w**.
       9: 22 To the **w** I became **w**, to win the **w**.
2Co 12: 10 For when I am **w**, then I am strong.
Heb 12: 12 your feeble arms and **w** knees.

WEAKER (WEAK)

1Co 12: 22 seem to be **w** are indispensable,
1Pe   3:   7 them with respect as the **w** partner

WEAKNESS (WEAK)

Ro   8: 26 way, the Spirit helps us in our **w**.
1Co   1: 25 **w** of God is stronger than human
2Co 12:   9 my power is made perfect in **w**."
Heb   5:   2 since he himself is subject to **w**.

WEALTH

Pr   3:   9 Honor the LORD with your **w**,
Mk   10: 22 away sad, because he had great **w**.
Lk   15: 13 and there squandered his **w** in wild

WEAPONS

2Co 10:   4 The **w** we fight with are not the **w**

WEARIES (WEARY)

Ecc 12: 12 and much study **w** the body.

WEARY (WEARIES)

Isa 40: 31 they will run and not grow **w**,
Mt   11: 28 all you who are **w** and burdened,
Gal   6:   9 not become **w** in doing good,

WEDDING

Mt   22: 11 who was not wearing **w** clothes.
Rev 19:   7 For the **w** of the Lamb has come,

WEEP (WEEPING WEPT)

Ecc   3:   4 a time to **w** and a time to laugh,
Lk   6: 21 Blessed are you who **w** now, for

WEEPING (WEEP)

Ps   30:   5 **w** may stay for the night,
     126:   6 Those who go out **w**, carrying seed
Mt   8: 12 where there will be **w** and gnashing

WELCOMES

Mt   18:   5 **w** one such child in my name **w** me.
2Jn   : 11 Anyone who **w** them shares in

WELL

Lk   17: 19 your faith has made you **w**."
Jas   5: 15 faith will make the sick person **w**;

WEPT (WEEP)

Ps 137:   1 and **w** when we remembered Zion.
Jn   11: 35 Jesus **w**.

WEST

Ps 103: 12 as far as the east is from the **w**,

WHIRLWIND (WIND)

2Ki   2:   1 to take Elijah up to heaven in a **w**,
Hos   8:   7 They sow the wind and reap the **w**.
Na   1:   3 His way is in the **w** and the storm,

WHITE (WHITER)

Isa   1: 18 scarlet, they shall be as **w** as snow;
Da   7:   9 His clothing was as **w** as snow;
Rev   1: 14 hair on his head was **w** like wool,
       3:   4 dressed in **w**, for they are worthy.
      20: 11 I saw a great **w** throne and him

WHITER (WHITE)

Ps   51:   7 wash me, and I will be **w** than snow.

WHOLE

Mt   16: 26 for someone to gain the **w** world,
      24: 14 in the **w** world as a testimony to all
Jn   13: 10 their **w** body is clean.
      21: 25 even the **w** world would not have
Ac   20: 27 proclaim to you the **w** will of God.
Ro   3: 19 and the **w** world held accountable
       8: 22 the **w** creation has been groaning
Gal   5:   3 he is obligated to obey the **w** law.
Eph   4: 13 attaining to the **w** measure
Jas   2: 10 For whoever keeps the **w** law
1Jn   2:   2 but also for the sins of the **w** world.

WHOLEHEARTEDLY (HEART)

Dt   1: 36 he followed the LORD **w**."
Eph   6:   7 Serve **w**, as if you were serving

WICKED (WICKEDNESS)

Ps   1:   1 does not walk in step with the **w**
       1:   5 Therefore the **w** will not stand
      73:   3 when I saw the prosperity of the **w**.
Pr   10: 20 the heart of the **w** is of little value.
      11: 21 The **w** will not go unpunished,
Isa 53:   9 was assigned a grave with the **w**,
      55:   7 Let the **w** forsake their ways
      57: 20 But the **w** are like the tossing sea,
Eze   3: 18 that **w** person will die for their sin,
      18: 23 any pleasure in the death of the **w**?
      33: 14 And if I say to a **w** person,

WICKEDNESS (WICKED)

Eze 28: 15 you were created till **w** was found

WIDE

Isa 54:   2 stretch your tent curtains **w**, do not
Mt   7: 13 For **w** is the gate and broad is
Eph   3: 18 to grasp how **w** and long and high

WIDOW (WIDOWS)

Dt   10: 18 cause of the fatherless and the **w**,
Lk   21:   2 saw a poor **w** put in two very small

WIDOWS (WIDOW)

Jas   1: 27 orphans and **w** in their distress

WIFE (WIVES)

Ge   2: 24 and mother and is united to his **w**,
      24: 67 So she became his **w**, and he loved
Ex   20: 17 shall not covet your neighbor's **w**.
Dt   5: 21 shall not covet your neighbor's **w**.
Pr   5: 18 you rejoice in the **w** of your youth.
      12:   4 A **w** of noble character is her
      18: 22 who finds a **w** finds what is good
      19: 13 quarrelsome **w** is like the constant
      31: 10 A **w** of noble character who can
Mt   19:   3 for a man to divorce his **w** for any
1Co   7:   2 sexual relations with his own **w**,
       7: 33 how he can please his **w**—
Eph   5: 23 head of the **w** as Christ is the head
       5: 33 must love his **w** as he loves himself,
       5: 33 the **w** must respect her husband.
1Ti   3:   2 faithful to his **w**, temperate,
Rev 21:   9 you the bride, the **w** of the Lamb."

WILD

Lk   15: 13 squandered his wealth in **w** living.
Ro   11: 17 and you, though a **w** olive shoot,

WILL (WILLING WILLINGNESS)

Ps   40:   8 I desire to do your **w**, my God;
     143: 10 Teach me to do your **w**, for you are
Isa 53: 10 Yet it was the LORD's **w** to crush
Mt   6: 10 kingdom come, your **w** be done,
      26: 39 Yet not as I **w**, but as you **w**."
Jn   7: 17 chooses to do the **w** of God **w** find
Ac   20: 27 to you the whole **w** of God.
Ro   12:   2 test and approve what God's **w** is—
1Co   7: 37 but has control over his own **w**,
Eph   5: 17 understand what the Lord's **w** is.
Php   2: 13 for it is God who works in you to **w**
1Th   4:   3 It is God's **w** that you should be
       5: 18 for this is God's **w** for you in Christ
Heb   9: 16 In the case of a **w**, it is necessary
      10:   7 I have come to do your **w**,
Jas   4: 15 "If it is the Lord's **w**, we **w** live
1Jn   5: 14 ask anything according to his **w**,
Rev   4: 11 by your **w** they were created

WILLING (WILL)

Ps   51: 12 salvation and grant me a **w** spirit,

Da	3: 28	were **w** to give up their lives rather
Mt	18: 14	Father in heaven is not **w** that any
	23: 37	her wings, and you were not **w**.
	26: 41	The spirit is **w**, but the flesh is

WILLINGNESS (WILL)

| 2Co | 8: 12 | For if the **w** is there, the gift is |

WIN

| Php | 3: 14 | on toward the goal to **w** the prize |
| 1Th | 4: 12 | your daily life may **w** the respect |

WIND (WHIRLWIND)

| Jas | 1: 6 | the sea, blown and tossed by the **w**. |

WINE

Pr	20: 1	**W** is a mocker and beer a brawler;
Isa	55: 1	buy **w** and milk without money
Mt	9: 17	Neither do people pour new **w**
Lk	23: 36	They offered him **w** vinegar
Ro	14: 21	drink **w** or to do anything else
Eph	5: 18	Do not get drunk on **w**, which

WINESKINS

| Mt | 9: 17 | people pour new wine into old **w**. |

WINGS

Ru	2: 12	under whose **w** you have come
Ps	17: 8	hide me in the shadow of your **w**
Isa	40: 31	They will soar on **w** like eagles;
Lk	13: 34	gathers her chicks under her **w**,

WIPE

| Rev | 7: 17 | God will **w** away every tear |

WISDOM (WISE)

1Ki	4: 29	God gave Solomon **w** and very
Ps	111: 10	the LORD is the beginning of **w**;
Pr	31: 26	She speaks with **w**, and faithful
Jer	10: 12	he founded the world by his **w**
Mt	11: 19	**w** is proved right by her deeds."
Lk	2: 52	And Jesus grew in **w** and stature,
Ro	11: 33	the depth of the riches of the **w**
Col	2: 3	are hidden all the treasures of **w**
Jas	1: 5	If any of you lacks **w**, you should

WISE (WISDOM WISER)

1Ki	3: 12	I will give you a **w** and discerning
Job	5: 13	He catches the **w** in their craftiness,
Ps	19: 7	trustworthy, making the simple.
Pr	3: 7	Do not be **w** in your own eyes;
	9: 8	rebuke the **w** and they will love
	10: 1	A **w** son brings joy to his father,
	11: 30	and the one who is **w** saves lives.
	13: 20	Walk with the **w** and become **w**,
	17: 28	Even fools are thought **w** if they
Da	12: 3	Those who are **w** will shine like
Mt	11: 25	hidden these things from the **w**
1Co	1: 27	things of the world to shame the **w**;
2Ti	3: 15	make you **w** for salvation through

WISER (WISE)

| 1Co | 1: 25 | of God is **w** than human wisdom, |

WITHER (WITHERS)

| Ps | 1: 3 | and whose leaf does not **w**— |

WITHERS (WITHER)

| Isa | 40: 7 | The grass **w** and the flowers fall, |
| 1Pe | 1: 24 | the grass **w** and the flowers fall, |

WITHHOLD

| Ps | 84: 11 | no good thing does he **w** from |
| Pr | 23: 13 | Do not **w** discipline from a child; |

WITNESS (WITNESSES)

| Jn | 1: 8 | he came only as a **w** to the light. |

WITNESSES (WITNESS)

| Dt | 19: 15 | by the testimony of two or three **w**. |
| Ac | 1: 8 | and you will be my **w** in Jerusalem, |

WIVES (WIFE)

Eph	5: 22	**W**, submit yourselves to your own
	5: 25	love your **w**, just as Christ loved
1Pe	3: 1	**W**, in the same way submit

WOE

| Isa | 6: 5 | "**W** to me!" I cried. "I am ruined! |

WOLF

| Isa | 65: 25 | The **w** and the lamb will feed |

WOMAN (MAN)

Ge	2: 22	the LORD God made a **w**
	3: 15	put enmity between you and the **w**,
Lev	20: 13	with a man as one does with a **w**,
Dt	22: 5	A **w** must not wear men's clothing,
Ru	3: 11	that you are a **w** of noble character.
Pr	31: 30	a **w** who fears the LORD is to be
Mt	5: 28	a **w** lustfully has already committed

Jn	8: 3	brought in a **w** caught
Ro	7: 2	by law a married **w** is bound to her
1Co	11: 3	and the head of the **w** is man,
	11: 13	Is it proper for a **w** to pray to God
1Ti	2: 11	A **w** should learn in quietness

WOMB

Job	1: 21	I came from my mother's **w**,
Jer	1: 5	I formed you in the **w** I knew you,
Lk	1: 44	the baby in my **w** leaped for joy.

WOMEN (MAN)

Lk	1: 42	"Blessed are you among **w**,
1Co	14: 34	**W** should remain silent
1Ti	2: 9	I also want the **w** to dress modestly,
Titus	2: 3	teach the older **w** to be reverent
1Pe	3: 5	the way the holy **w** of the past

WONDERFUL (WONDERS)

Job	42: 3	things too **w** for me to know.
Ps	119: 18	that I may see **w** things in your law.
	119: 27	I may meditate on your **w** deeds.
	119:129	statutes are **w**; therefore I obey
	139: 6	Such knowledge is too **w** for me,
Isa	9: 6	he will be called **W** Counselor,
1Pe	2: 9	out of darkness into his **w** light.

WONDERS (WONDERFUL)

Job	37: 14	stop and consider God's **w**.
Ps	17: 7	Show me the **w** of your great love,
	31: 21	for he showed me the **w** of his love
Joel	2: 30	I will show **w** in the heavens
Ac	2: 19	I will show **w** in the heavens

WOOD

| Isa | 44: 19 | Shall I bow down to a block of **w**?" |
| 1Co | 3: 12 | costly stones, **w**, hay or straw, |

WORD (WORDS)

Dt	8: 3	but on every **w** that comes
2Sa	22: 31	The LORD's **w** is flawless;
Ps	119: 9	By living according to your **w**.
	119: 11	I have hidden your **w** in my heart
	119:105	Your **w** is a lamp to my feet
Pr	12: 25	the heart, but a kind **w** cheers it up.
	30: 5	"Every **w** of God is flawless; he is
Isa	55: 11	so is my **w** that goes out from my
Jn	1: 1	In the beginning was the **W**, and the **W** was with God, and the **W** was God.
	1: 14	The **W** became flesh and made his
2Co	2: 17	we do not peddle the **w** of God
	2: 17	nor do we distort the **w** of God.
Eph	6: 17	of the Spirit, which is the **w** of God.
Php	2: 16	as you hold firmly to the **w** of life.
2Ti	2: 15	and who correctly handles the **w**
Heb	4: 12	the **w** of God is alive and active.
Jas	1: 22	Do not merely listen to the **w**,

WORDS (WORD)

Dt	11: 18	Fix these **w** of mine in your hearts
Ps	119:103	How sweet are your **w** to my taste,
	119:130	unfolding of your **w** gives light;
	119:160	All your **w** are true; all your
Pr	30: 6	Do not add to his **w**, or he will
Jer	15: 16	When your **w** came, I ate them;
Mt	24: 35	but my **w** will never pass away.
Jn	6: 68	You have the **w** of eternal life.
	15: 7	in me and my **w** remain in you,
1Co	14: 19	rather speak five intelligible **w**
Rev	22: 19	if anyone takes **w** away from this

WORK (HANDIWORK WORKER WORKERS WORKING WORKS)

Ex	23: 12	but on the seventh day do not **w**,
Nu	8: 11	be ready to do the **w** of the LORD.
Dt	5: 14	On it you shall not do any **w**,
Jer	48: 10	who is lax in doing the LORD's **w**!
Jn	6: 27	Do not **w** for food that spoils,
	9: 4	is coming, when no one can **w**.
1Co	3: 13	test the quality of each person's **w**.
Php	1: 6	he who began a good **w** in you will
	2: 12	continue to **w** out your salvation
Col	3: 23	you do, **w** at it with all your heart,
1Th	5: 12	those who **w** hard among you,
2Th	3: 10	is unwilling to **w** shall not eat."
2Ti	3: 17	equipped for every good **w**
Heb	6: 10	he will not forget your **w**

WORKER (WORKERS)

Lk	10: 7	for the **w** deserves his wages.
1Ti	5: 18	and "The **w** deserves his wages."
2Ti	2: 15	a **w** who does not need to

WORKERS (WORK)
Mt 9: 37 is plentiful but the **w** are few.
1Co 3: 9 For we are **c** in God's service;
WORKING (WORK)
Col 3: 23 all your heart, as **w** for the Lord,
WORKS (WORK)
Pr 31: 31 her **w** bring her praise at the city
Ro 8: 28 in all things God **w** for the good
Eph 2: 9 not by **w**, so that no one can boast.
4: 12 to equip his people for **w** of service,
WORLD (WORLDLY)
Ps 50: 12 for the **w** is mine, and all that is
Isa 13: 11 I will punish the **w** for its evil,
Mt 5: 14 "You are the light of the **w**.
16: 26 for someone to gain the whole **w**,
Mk 16: 15 "Go into all the **w** and preach
Jn 1: 29 who takes away the sin of the **w**!
3: 16 God so loved the **w** that he gave his
8: 12 he said, "I am the light of the **w**.
15: 19 but I have chosen you out of the **w**. That is why
the **w** hates you.
16: 33 I have overcome the **w**."
18: 36 said, "My kingdom is not of this **w**.
Ro 3: 19 and the whole **w** held accountable
1Co 3: 19 the wisdom of this **w** is foolishness
2Co 5: 19 that God was reconciling the **w**
10: 3 For though we live in the **w**, we do
1Ti 6: 7 For we brought nothing into the **w**,
1Jn 2: 2 but also for the sins of the whole **w**.
2: 15 not love the **w** or anything in the **w**.
Rev 13: 8 slain from the creation of the **w**.
WORLDLY (WORLD)
Titus 2: 12 to ungodliness and **w** passions,
WORMS
Mk 9: 48 where "'the **w** that eat them do
WORRY (WORRYING)
Mt 6: 25 I tell you, do not **w** about your life,
10: 19 do not **w** about what to say or how
WORRYING (WORRY)
Mt 6: 27 you by **w** add a single hour to your
WORSHIP
1Ch 16: 29 **W** the LORD in the splendor of his
Ps 95: 6 let us bow down in **w**, let us kneel
Mt 2: 2 it rose and have come to **w** him."
Jn 4: 24 his worshipers must **w** in the Spirit
Ro 12: 1 this is your true and proper **w**.
WORTH (WORTHY)
Job 28: 13 No mortal comprehends its **w**;
Pr 31: 10 She is **w** far more than rubies.
Mt 10: 31 you are **w** more than many
Ro 8: 18 sufferings are not **w** comparing
1Pe 1: 7 of greater **w** than gold,
3: 4 which is of great **w** in God's sight.
WORTHLESS
Pr 11: 4 Wealth is **w** in the day of wrath,
Jas 1: 26 themselves, and their religion is **w**.
WORTHY (WORTH)
1Ch 16: 25 is the LORD and most **w** of praise;
Eph 4: 1 live a life **w** of the calling you have
Php 1: 27 in a manner **w** of the gospel
Rev 5: 2 "Who is **w** to break the seals
WOUNDS
Pr 27: 6 **W** from a friend can be trusted,
Isa 53: 5 and by his **w** we are healed.
Zec 13: 6 'What are these **w** on your body?'
1Pe 2: 24 "by his **w** you have been healed."
WRATH
2Ch 36: 16 at his prophets until the **w**
Ps 2: 5 anger and terrifies them in his **w**,
76: 10 Surely your **w** against mankind
Pr 15: 1 A gentle answer turns away **w**,
Jer 25: 15 cup filled with the wine of my **w**

Ro 1: 18 The **w** of God is being revealed
5: 9 saved from God's **w** through him!
1Th 5: 9 God did not appoint us to suffer **w**
Rev 6: 16 and from the **w** of the Lamb!
WRESTLED
Ge 32: 24 a man **w** with him till daybreak.
WRITE (WRITING WRITTEN)
Dt 6: 9 **W** them on the doorframes of your
Pr 7: 3 **w** them on the tablet of your heart.
Heb 8: 10 minds and **w** them on their hearts.
WRITING (WRITE)
1Co 14: 37 what I am **w** to you is the Lord's
WRITTEN (WRITE)
Jos 1: 8 be careful to do everything **w** in it.
Da 12: 1 everyone whose name is found **w**
Lk 10: 20 that your names are **w** in heaven."
Jn 20: 31 these are **w** that you may believe
1Co 4: 6 "Do not go beyond what is **w**."
2Co 3: 3 **w** not with ink but with the Spirit
Heb 12: 23 whose names are **w** in heaven.
WRONG (WRONGDOING WRONGED WRONGS)
Ex 23: 2 not follow the crowd in doing **w**.
Nu 5: 7 restitution for the **w** they have
Job 34: 12 unthinkable that God would do **w**,
1Th 5: 15 that nobody pays back **w** for **w**,
WRONGDOING (WRONG)
Job 1: 22 not sin by charging God with **w**.
WRONGED (WRONG)
1Co 6: 7 Why not rather be **w**?
WRONGS (WRONG)
Pr 10: 12 conflict, but love covers over all **w**.
1Co 13: 5 angered, it keeps no record of **w**.
YEARS
Ps 90: 4 A thousand **y** in your sight are like
90: 10 Our days may come to seventy **y**,
2Pe 3: 8 the Lord a day is like a thousand **y**,
Rev 20: 2 and bound him for a thousand **y**.
YESTERDAY
Heb 13: 8 Jesus Christ is the same **y** and today
YOKE (YOKED)
Mt 11: 29 Take my **y** upon you and learn
YOKED (YOKE)
2Co 6: 14 Do not be **y** together
YOUNG (YOUTH)
Ps 119: 9 can a **y** person stay on the path
1Ti 4: 12 down on you because you are **y**,
YOUTH (YOUNG)
Ps 103: 5 your **y** is renewed like the eagle's.
Ecc 12: 1 your Creator in the days of your **y**,
2Ti 2: 22 Flee the evil desires of **y** and
ZEAL
Jn 2: 17 **Z** for your house will consume me.
Ro 12: 11 Never be lacking in **z**, but keep
ZECHARIAH
1. Son of Jeroboam II; king of Israel (2Ki 15:8–12).
2. Post-exilic prophet who encouraged rebuilding of temple (Ezr 5:1; 6:14; Zec 1:1).
3. Father of John the Baptist (Lk 1:13; 3:2).
ZEDEKIAH
Mattaniah, son of Josiah (1Ch 3:15), made king of Judah by Nebuchadnezzar (2Ki 24:17—25:7; 2Ch 36:10–14; Jer 37–39; 52:1–11).
ZERUBBABEL
Descendant of David (1Ch 3:19; Mt 1:3). Led return from exile (Ezr 2–3; Ne 7:7; Hag 1–2; Zec 4).
ZIMRI
King of Israel (1Ki 16:9–20).
ZION
Ps 137: 3 "Sing us one of the songs of **Z**!"
Jer 50: 5 They will ask the way to **Z** and
Ro 9: 33 I lay in **Z** a stone that causes people
11: 26 "The deliverer will come from **Z**;